LORE OLYMPUS

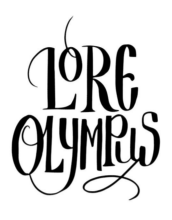

VOLUME THREE

VOLUME THREE

RACHEL SMYTHE

NEW YORK

Lore Olympus: Volume Three is a work of fiction.
Names, places, characters, and incidents either are
the product of the author's imagination or are used fictitiously.
Any resemblance to actual persons, living or dead, events,
or locales is entirely coincidental.

Published in the United States by Del Rey,
an imprint of Random House, a division of
Penguin Random House LLC, New York.

DEL REY and the HOUSE colophon are registered trademarks of Penguin Random House LLC.

Portions of this work originally appeared on Webtoons.com.

Hardcover ISBN 978-0-593-16031-2
Trade Paperback ISBN 978-0-593-35609-8

Printed in China

With thanks to:
Johana R. Ahumada, Yulia Garibova (Hita), Jaki Haboon, Amy Kim,
Kristina Ness, Karen Pavon, M. Rawlings, and Court Rogers

Penguin Random House team:
Ted Allen, Erin Korenko, Sarah Peed, and Elizabeth Schaefer

randomhousebooks.com

2 4 6 8 9 7 5 3 1

First Edition

Book design by Edwin Vazquez

To Jem Yoshioka

An excellent friendship to share a lifetime of stories.

CONTENT WARNING
FROM RACHEL SMYTHE

Lore Olympus regularly deals with themes of physical and mental abuse, sexual trauma, and toxic relationships.

Some of the interactions in this volume may be distressing for some readers. Please exercise discretion, and seek out the support of others if you require it.

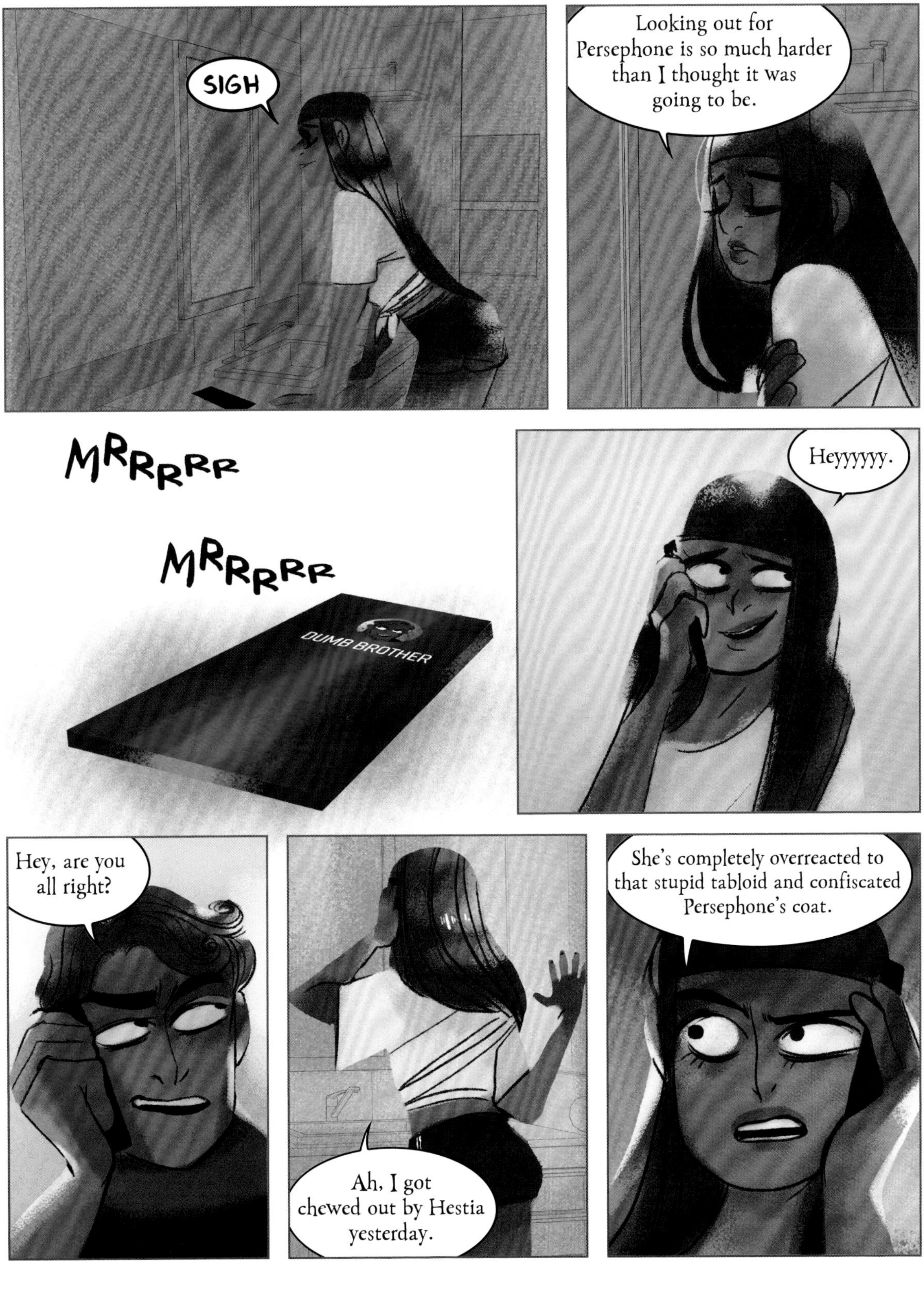
SIGH
Looking out for Persephone is so much harder than I thought it was going to be.
MRRRRR
MRRRRR
DUMB BROTHER
Heyyyyyy.
Hey, are you all right?
Ah, I got chewed out by Hestia yesterday.
She's completely overreacted to that stupid tabloid and confiscated Persephone's coat.

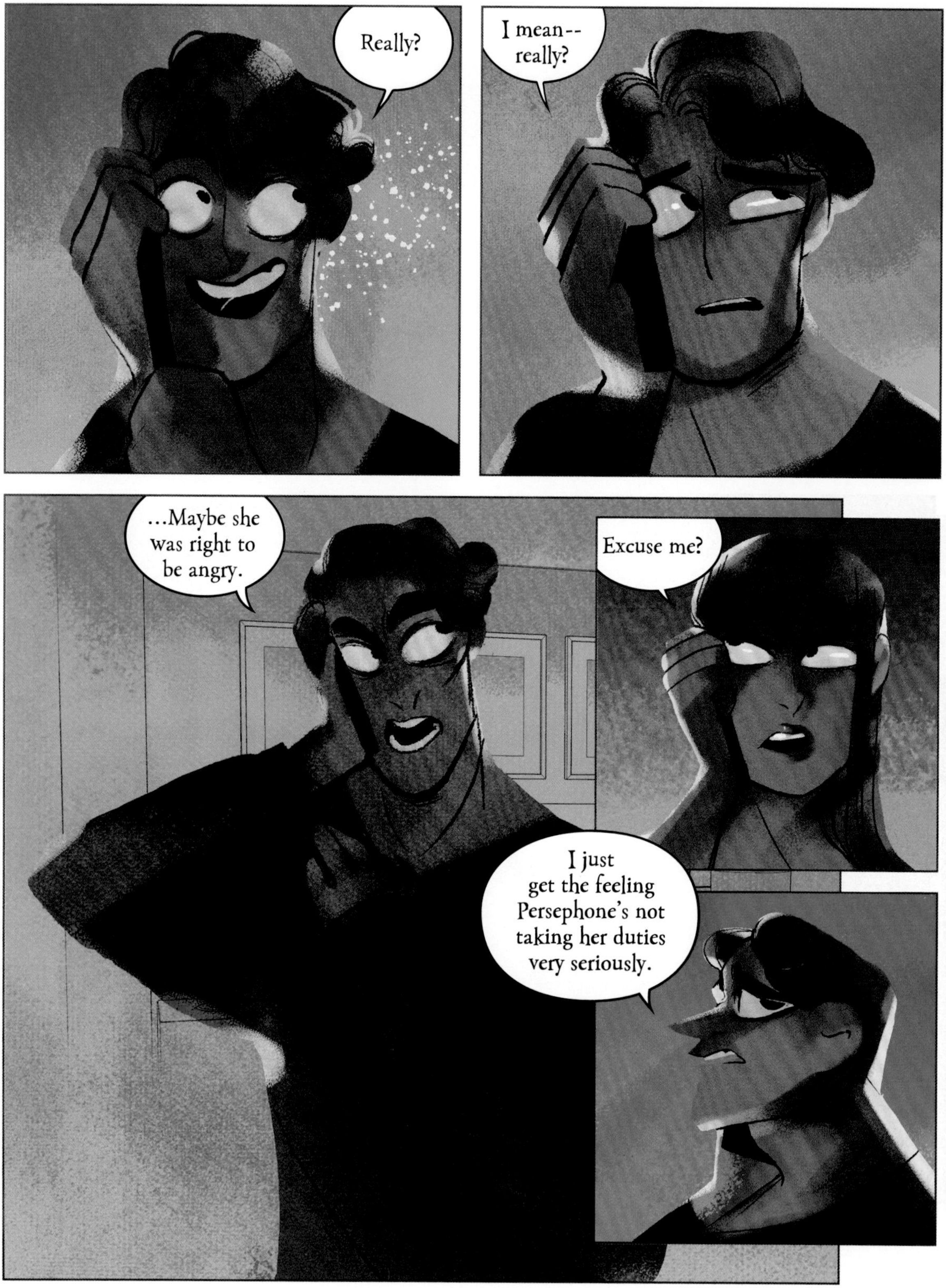
Really?
I mean-- really?
...Maybe she was right to be angry.
Excuse me?
I just get the feeling Persephone's not taking her duties very seriously.

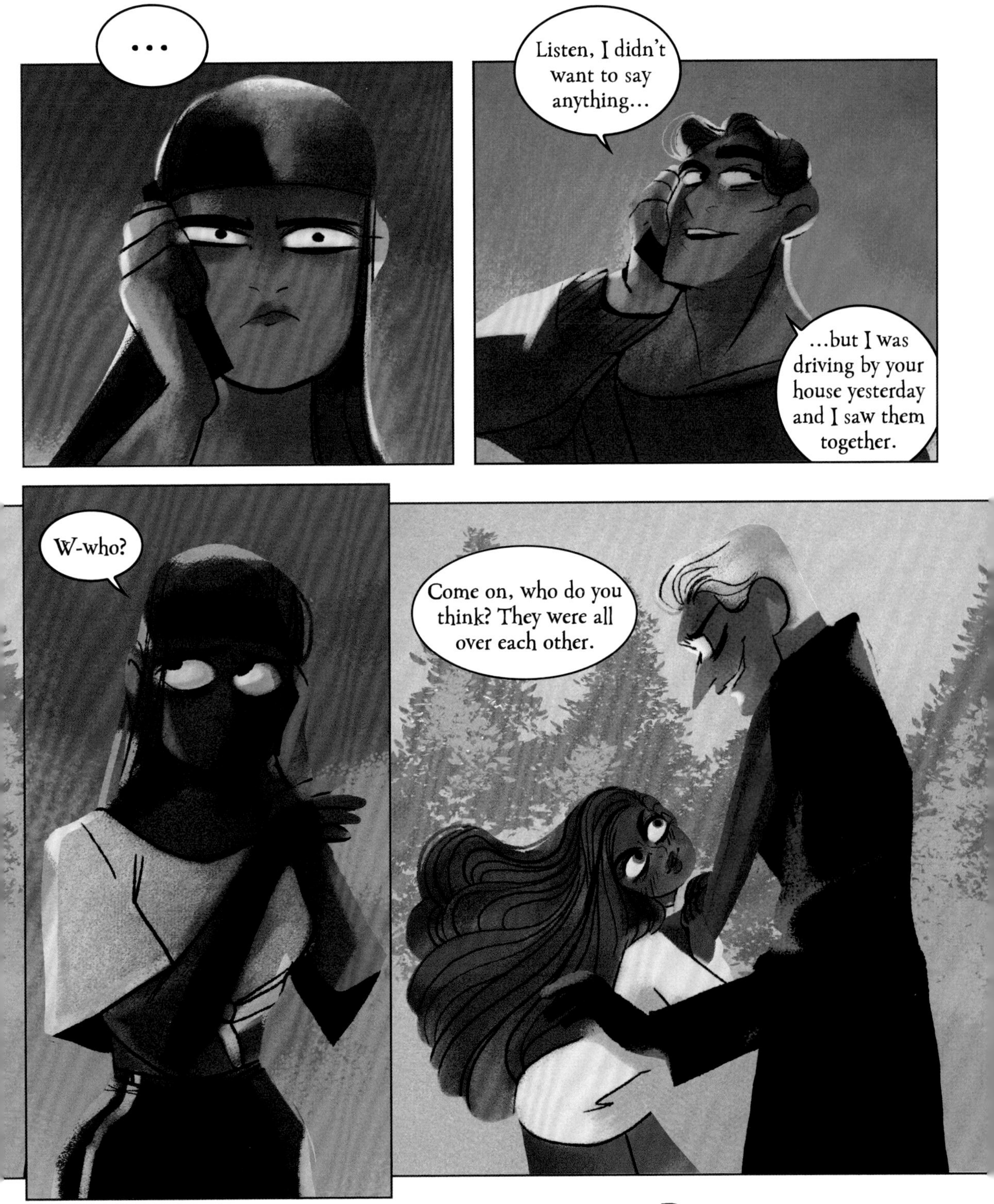
...
Listen, I didn't want to say anything...
...but I was driving by your house yesterday and I saw them together.
W-who?
Come on, who do you think? They were all over each other.
Dramatic Reenactment

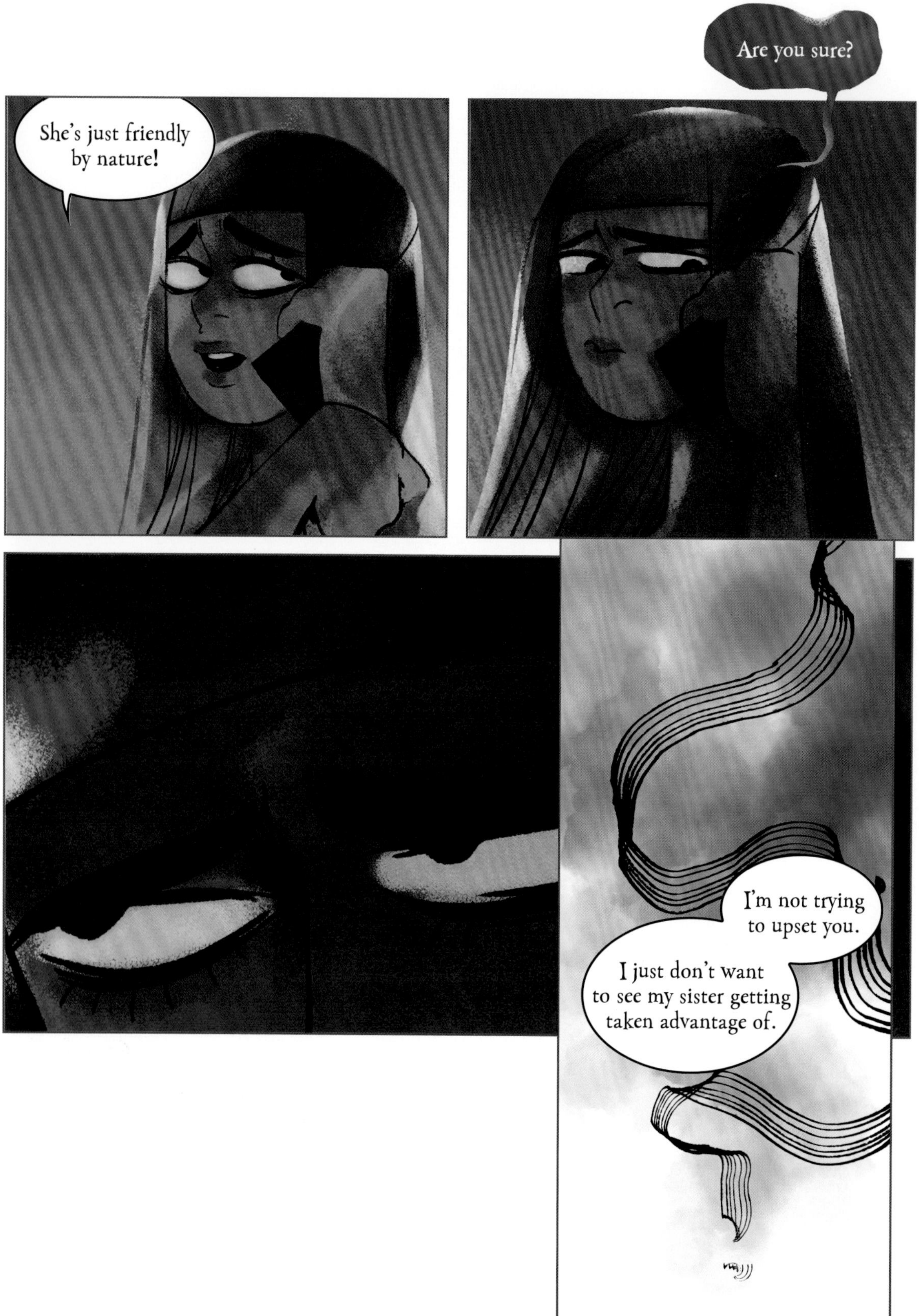
She's just friendly by nature!
Are you sure?
I'm not trying to upset you.
I just don't want to see my sister getting taken advantage of.

EPISODE 50: NARK

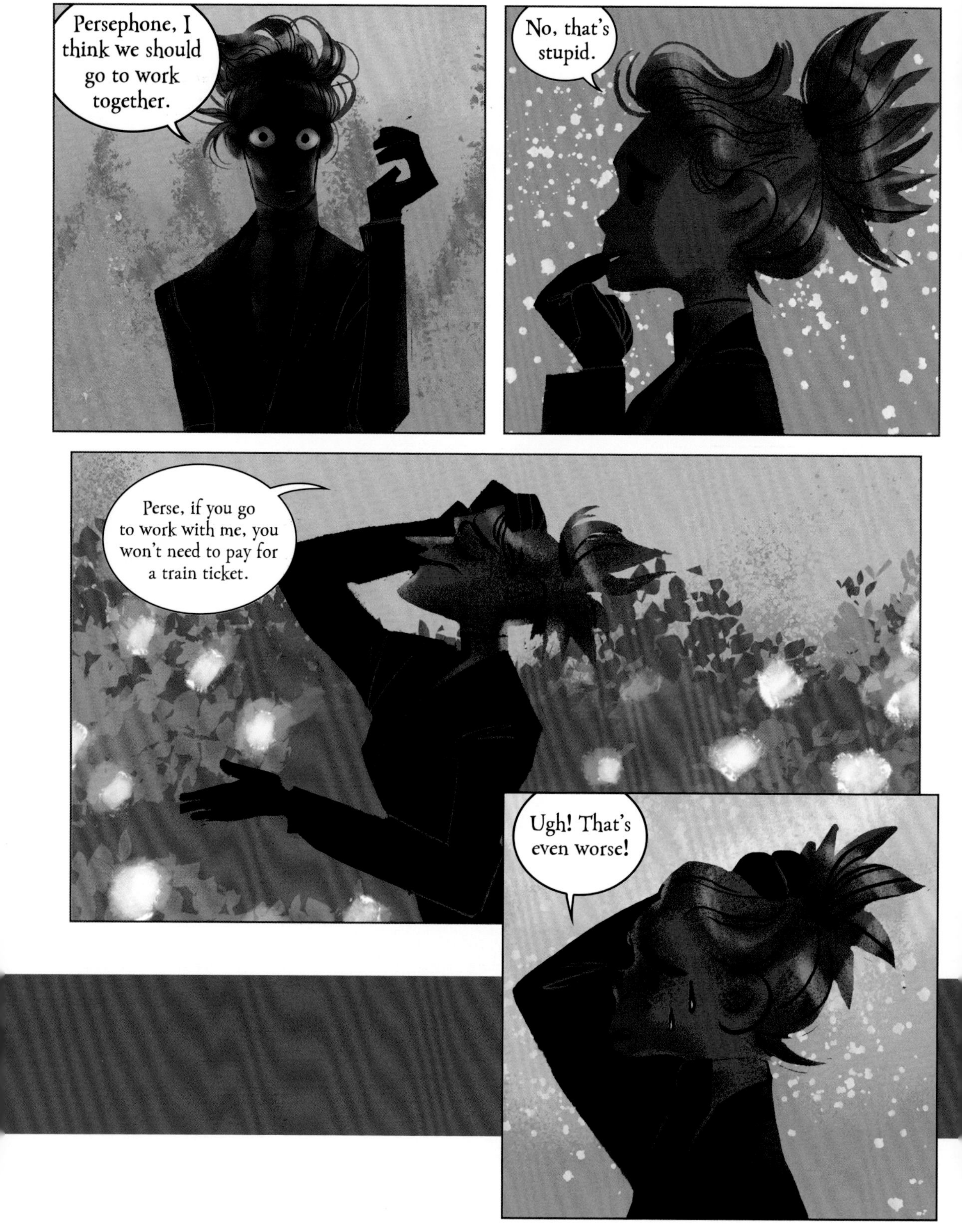

Persephone, I think we should go to work together.
No, that's stupid.
Perse, if you go to work with me, you won't need to pay for a train ticket.
Ugh! That's even worse!

Okay, okay. Fuck it.
KNOCK. KNOCK. KNOCK. KNOCK. KNOCK. KNOCK. KNOCK. KNOCK. KNOCK. KNOCK.

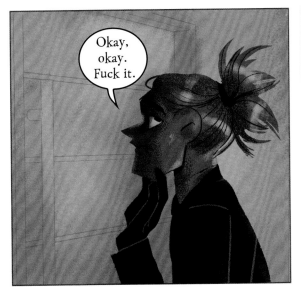

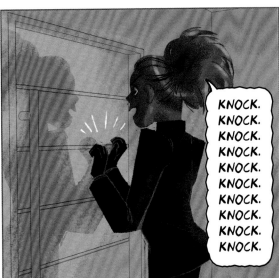

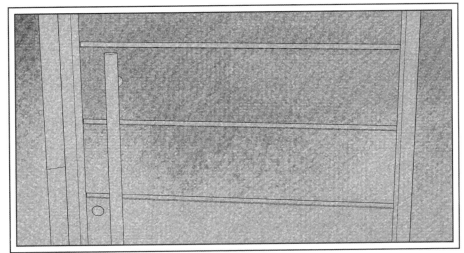

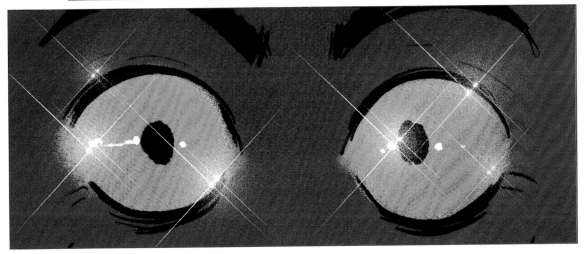

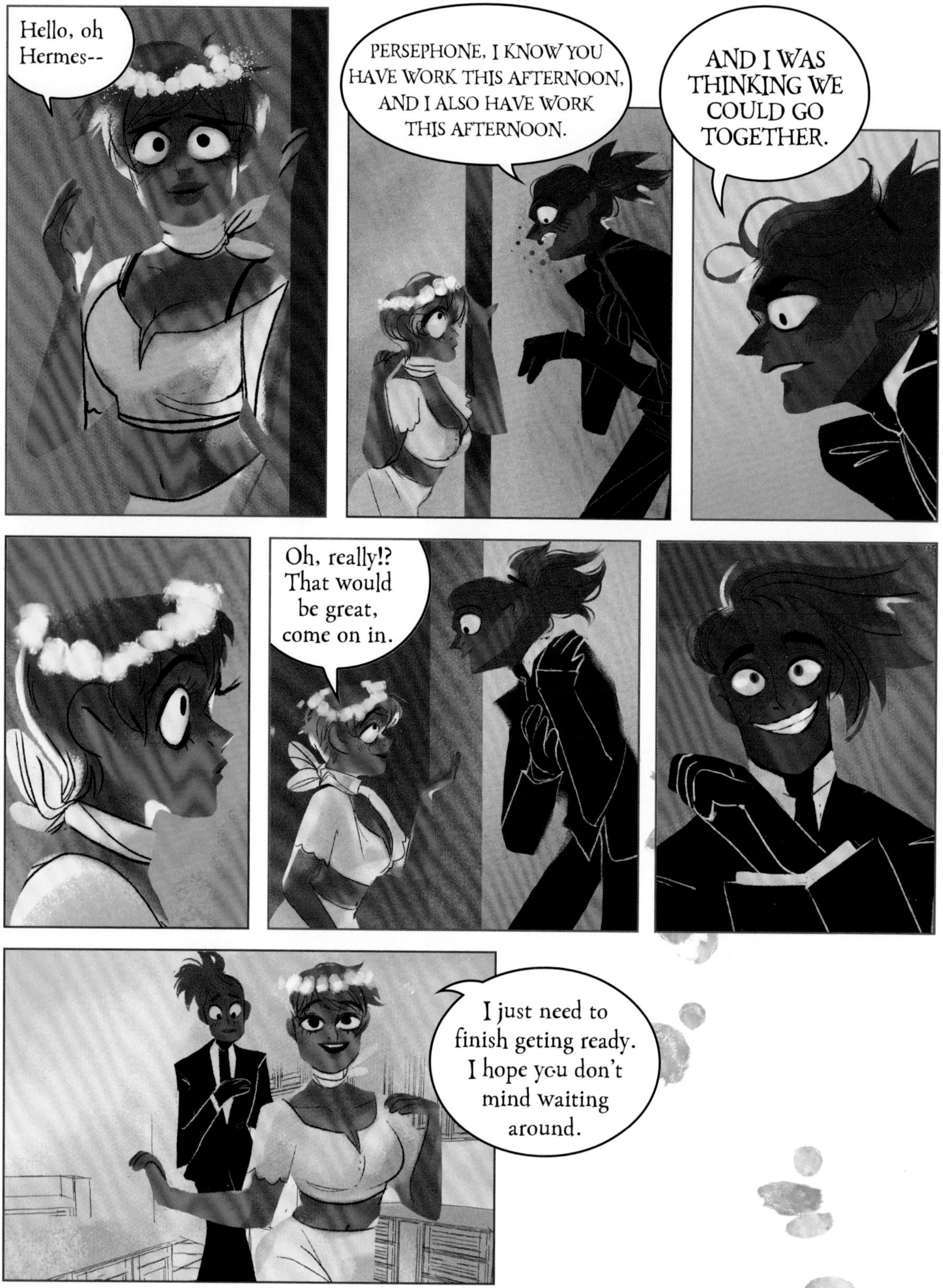
Hello, oh Hermes--
PERSEPHONE, I KNOW YOU HAVE WORK THIS AFTERNOON, AND I ALSO HAVE WORK THIS AFTERNOON.
AND I WAS THINKING WE COULD GO TOGETHER.
Oh, really!? That would be great, come on in.
I just need to finish geting ready. I hope you don't mind waiting around.

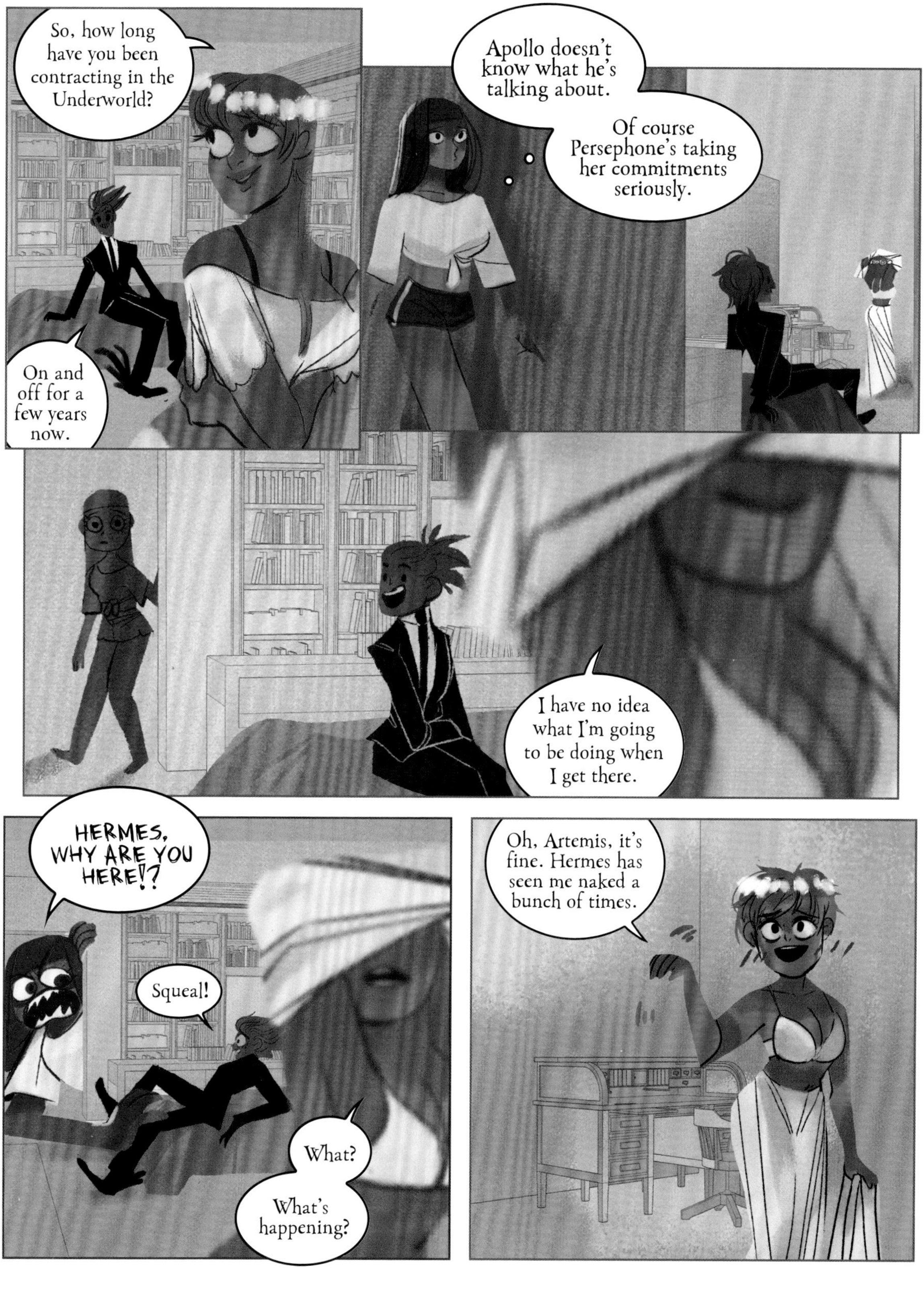
So, how long have you been contracting in the Underworld?
On and off for a few years now.
Apollo doesn't know what he's talking about.
Of course Persephone's taking her commitments seriously.
I have no idea what I'm going to be doing when I get there.
HERMES, WHY ARE YOU HERE!?
Squeal!
What?
What's happening?
Oh, Artemis, it's fine. Hermes has seen me naked a bunch of times.

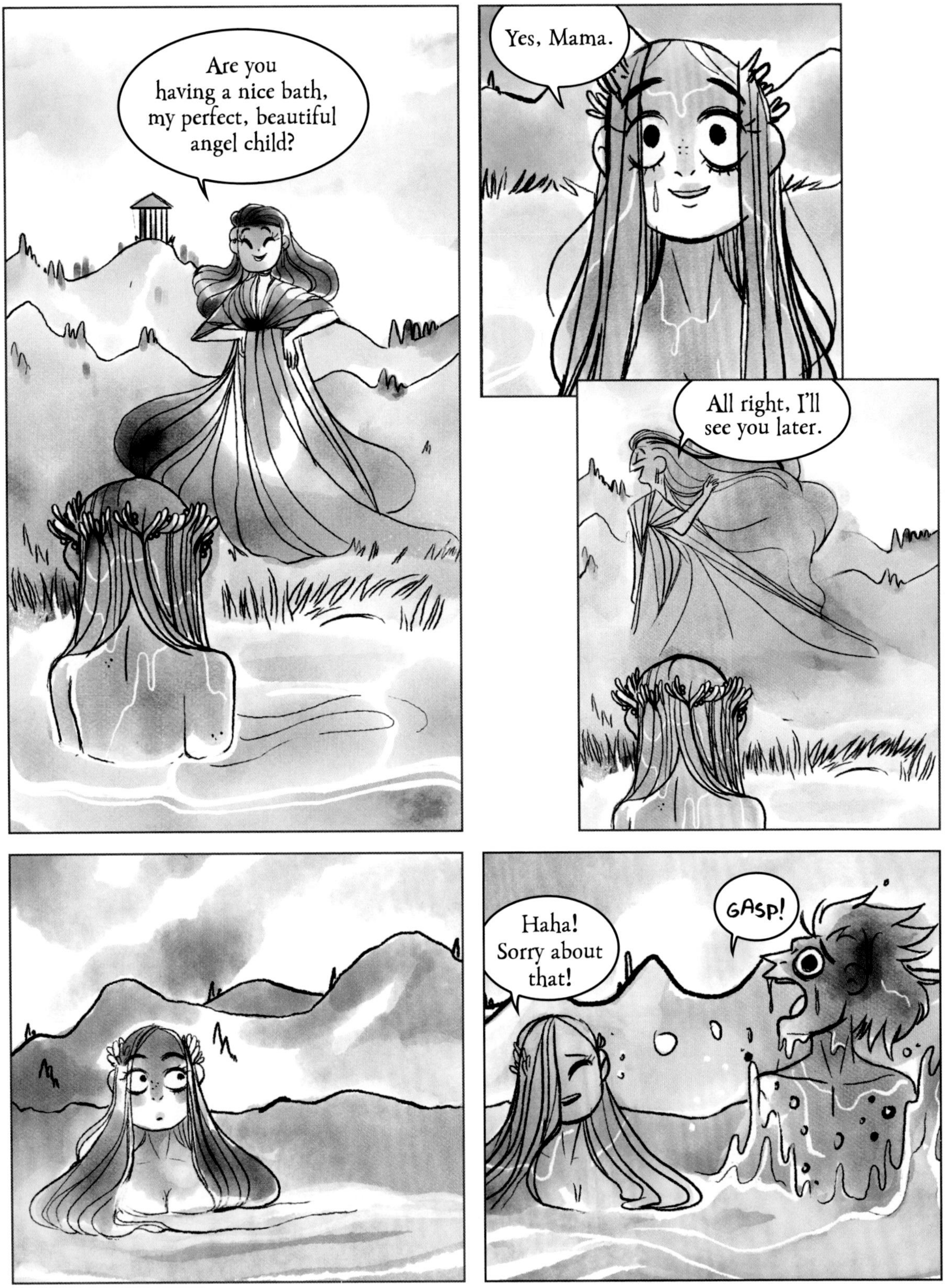
Are you having a nice bath, my perfect, beautiful angel child?
Yes, Mama.
All right, I'll see you later.
Haha! Sorry about that!
GASP!

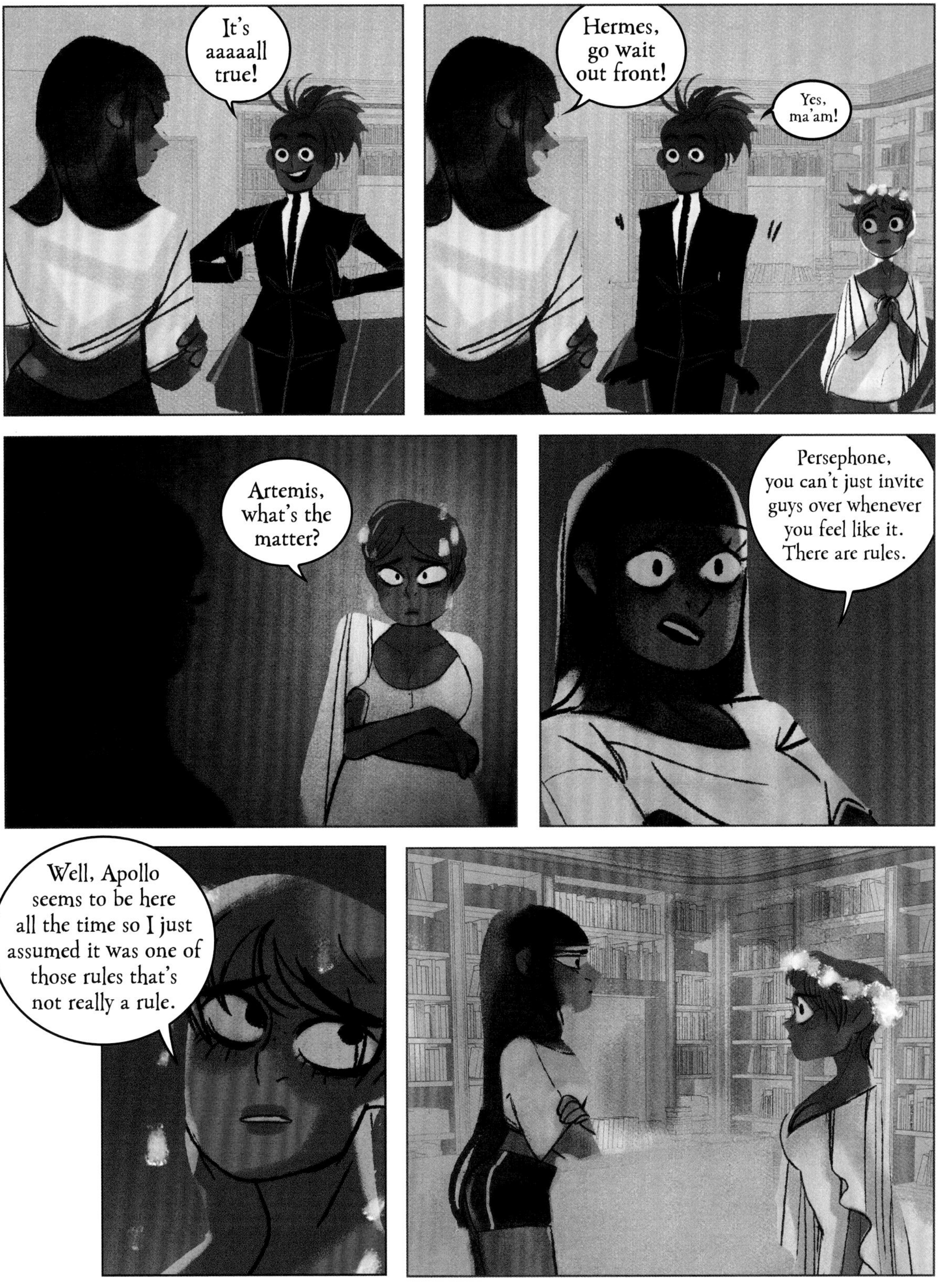
It's aaaaall true!
Hermes, go wait out front!
Yes, ma'am!
Artemis, what's the matter?
Persephone, you can't just invite guys over whenever you feel like it. There are rules.
Well, Apollo seems to be here all the time so I just assumed it was one of those rules that's not really a rule.

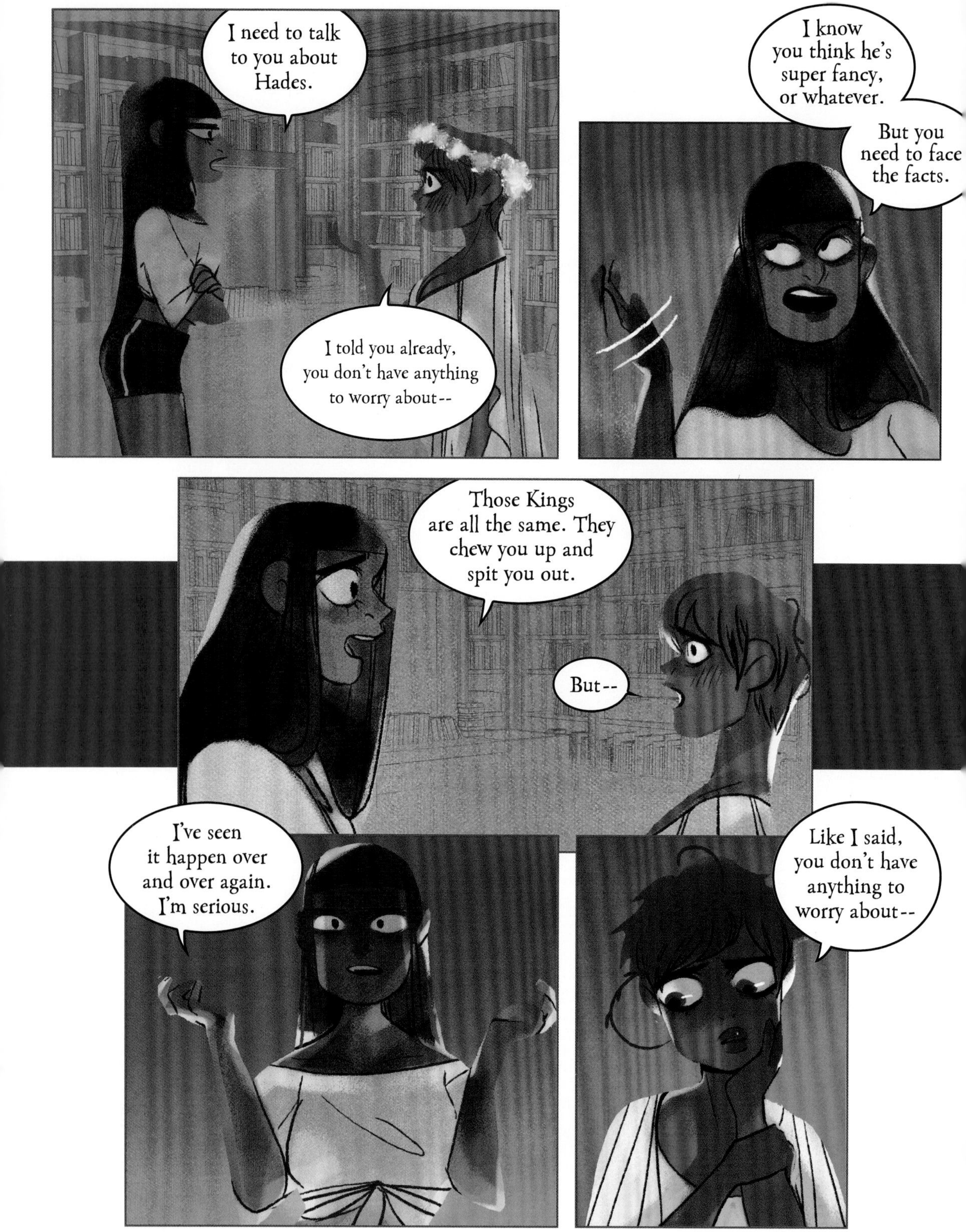
I need to talk to you about Hades.
I told you already, you don't have anything to worry about--
I know you think he's super fancy, or whatever.
But you need to face the facts.
Those Kings are all the same. They chew you up and spit you out.
But--
I've seen it happen over and over again. I'm serious.
Like I said, you don't have anything to worry about--

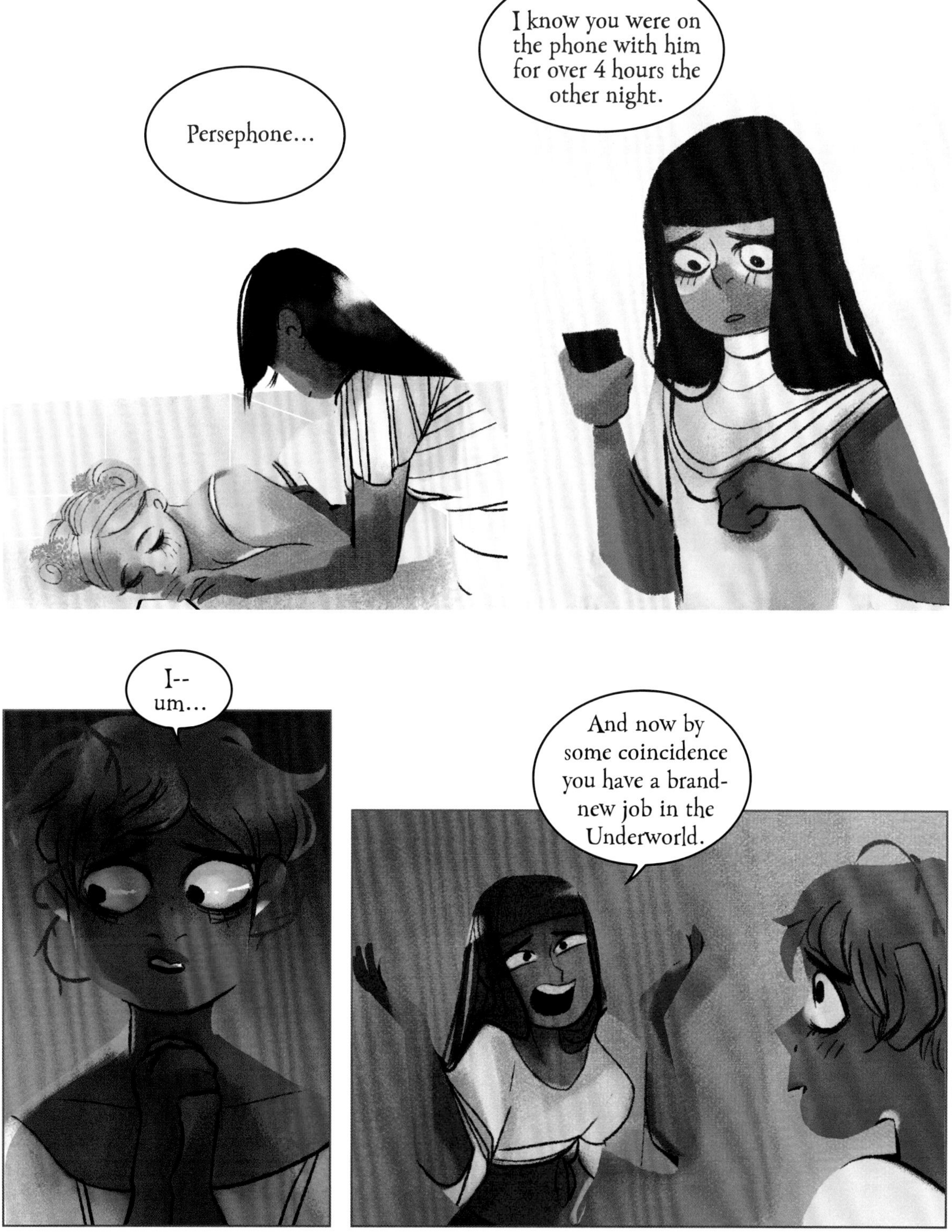
Persephone...
I know you were on the phone with him for over 4 hours the other night.
I-- um...
And now by some coincidence you have a brand-new job in the Underworld.

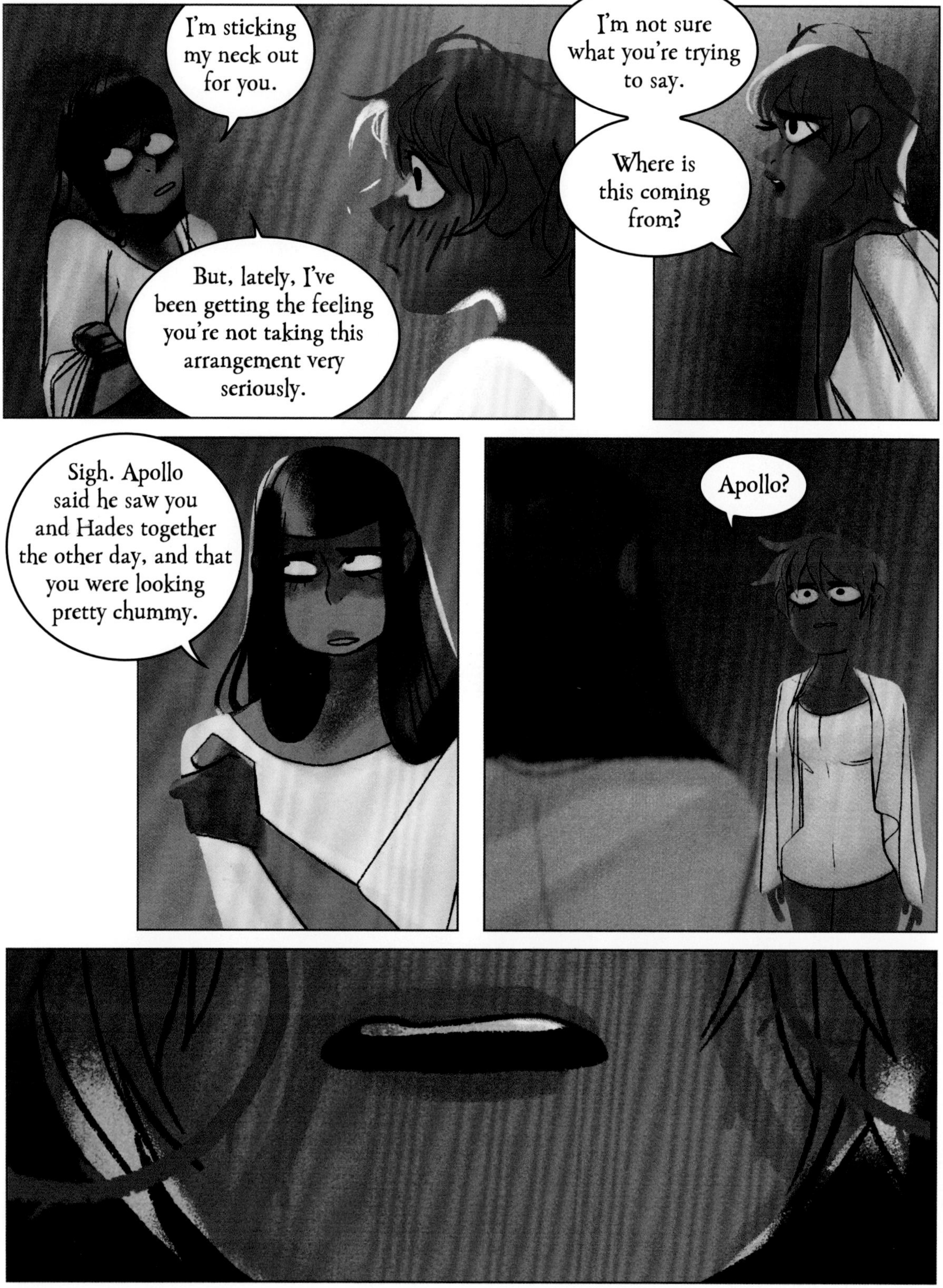
I'm sticking my neck out for you.
But, lately, I've been getting the feeling you're not taking this arrangement very seriously.
I'm not sure what you're trying to say.
Where is this coming from?
Sigh. Apollo said he saw you and Hades together the other day, and that you were looking pretty chummy.
Apollo?

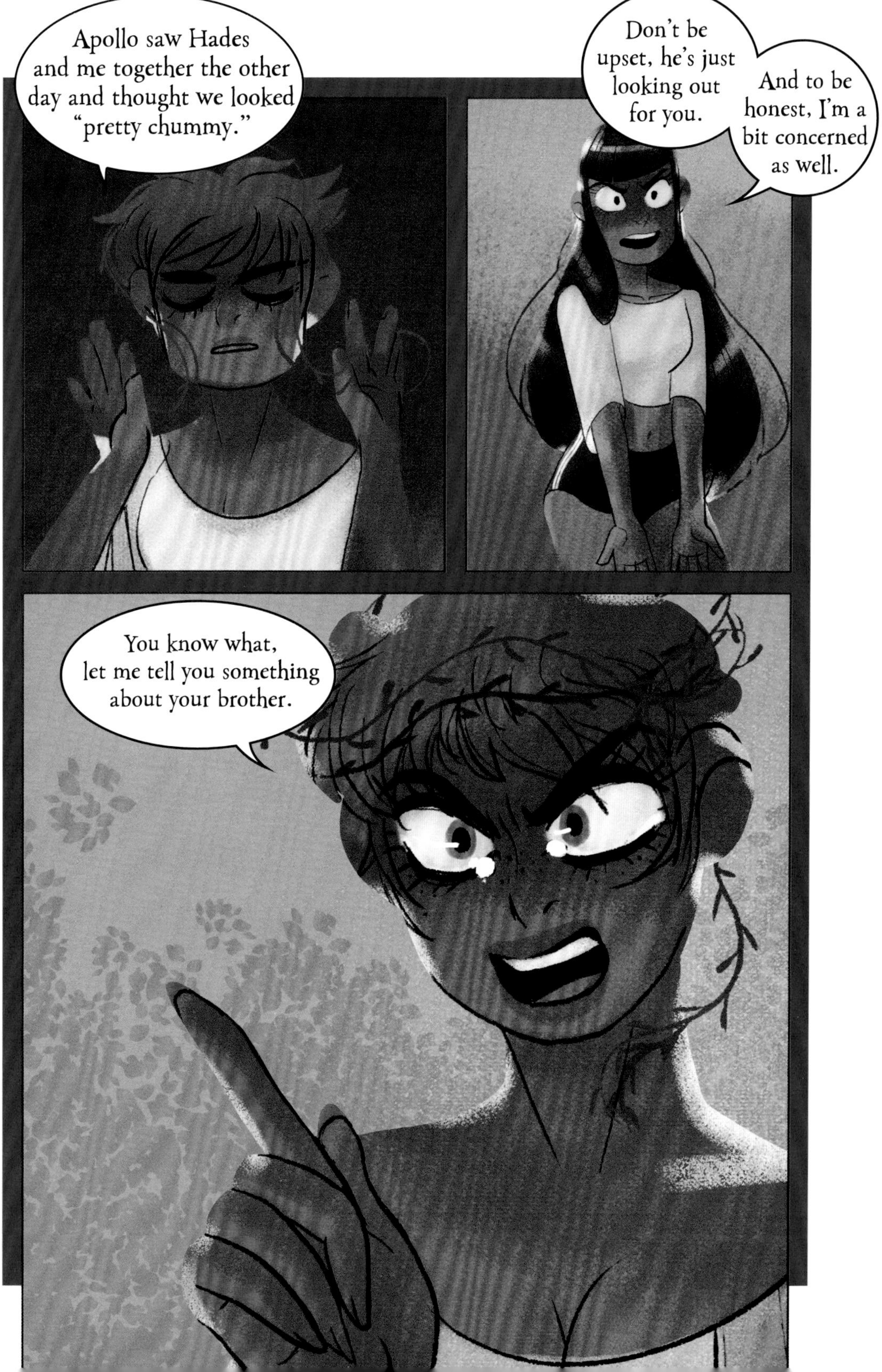

Apollo saw Hades and me together the other day and thought we looked "pretty chummy."
Don't be upset, he's just looking out for you.
And to be honest, I'm a bit concerned as well.
You know what, let me tell you something about your brother.

You know what,

let me tell you something about your brother.

W-what about my brother?

What am I supposed to tell her?

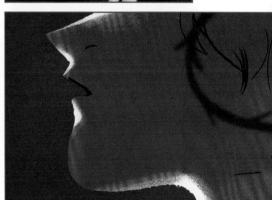

I don't even know what to tell myself...

I don't want to hurt her.

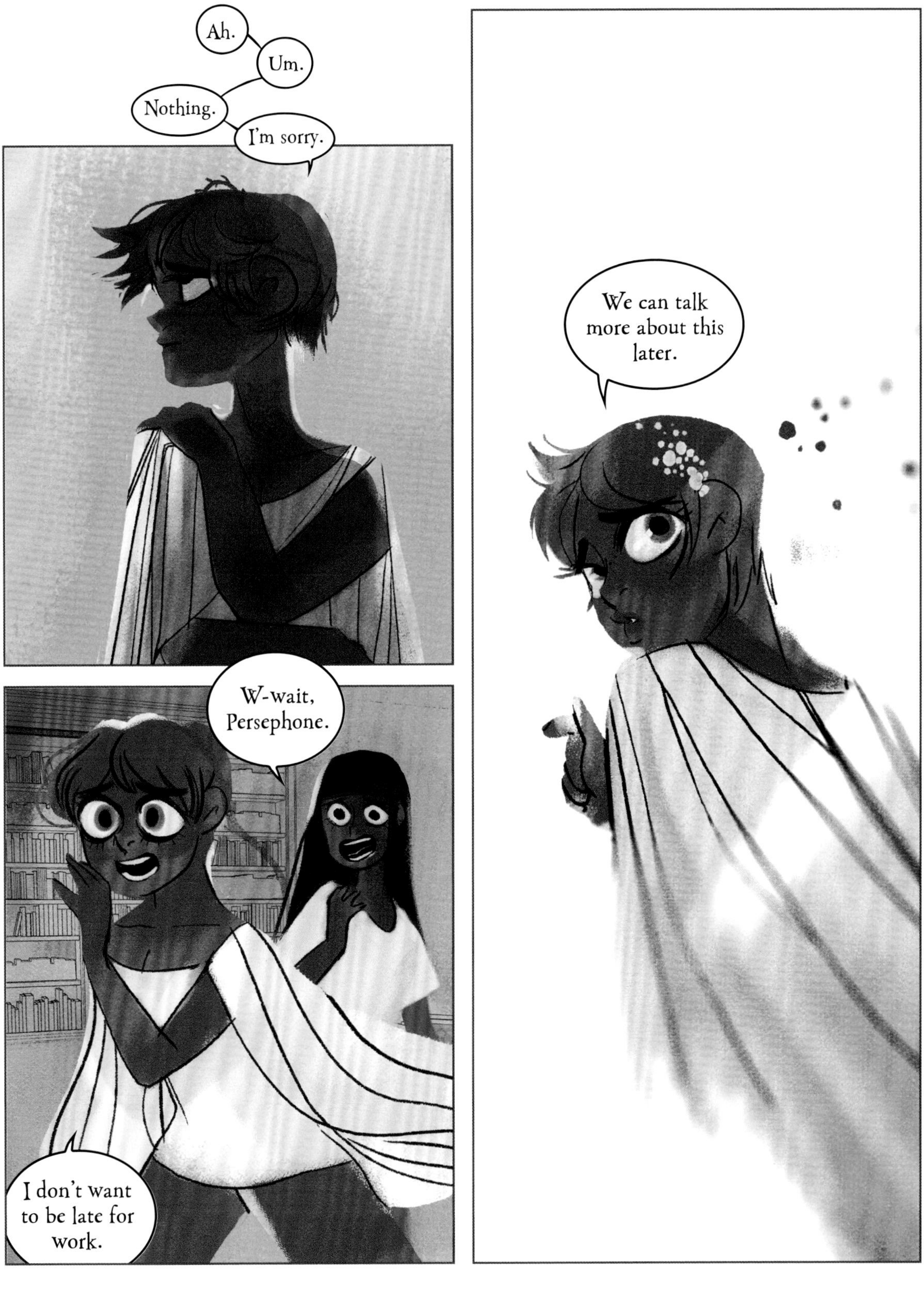
Ah.
Um.
Nothing.
I'm sorry.
W-wait, Persephone.
I don't want to be late for work.
We can talk more about this later.

EPISODE 51: DISTANCE

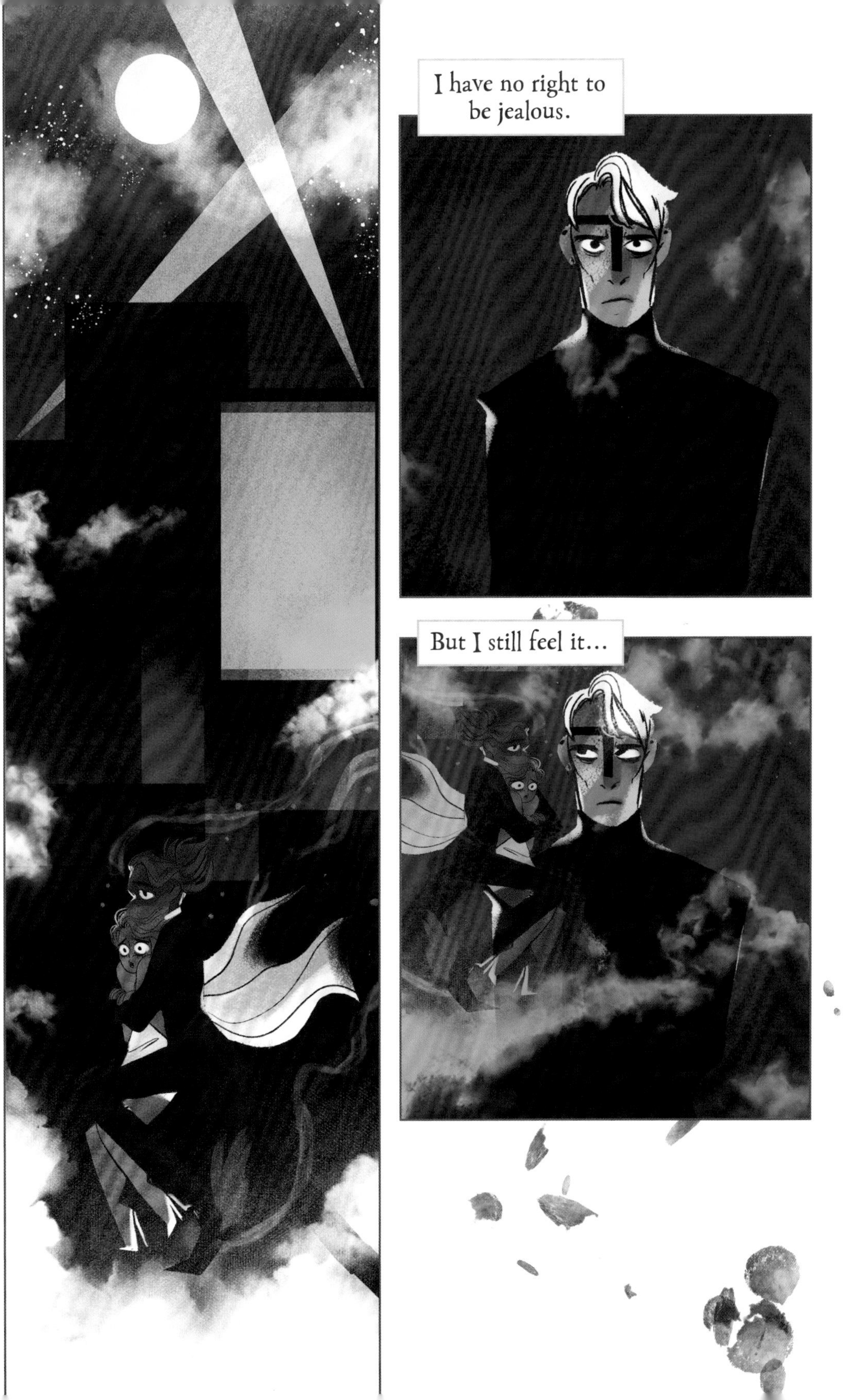
I have no right to be jealous.
But I still feel it...

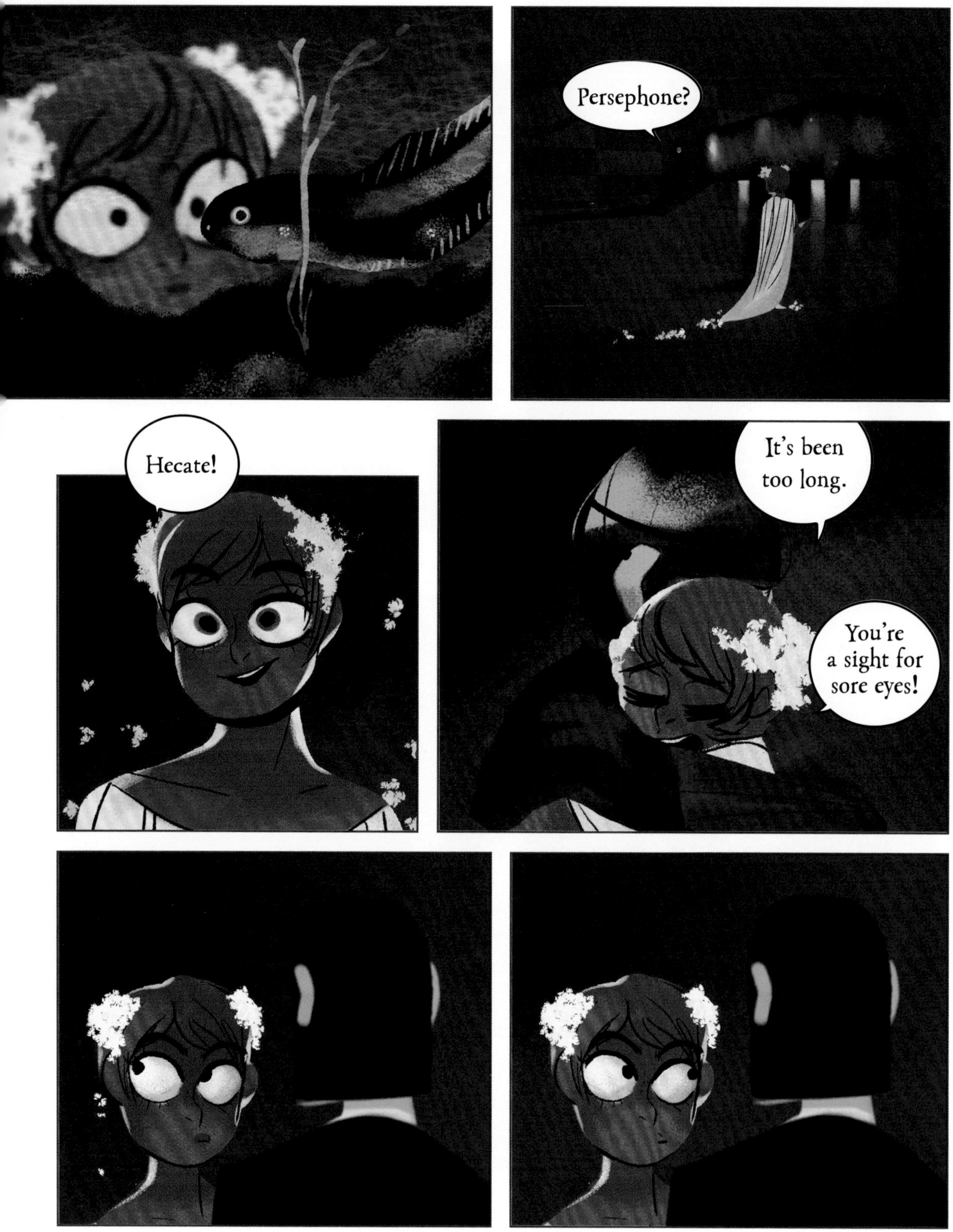
Persephone?
Hecate!
It's been too long.
You're a sight for sore eyes!

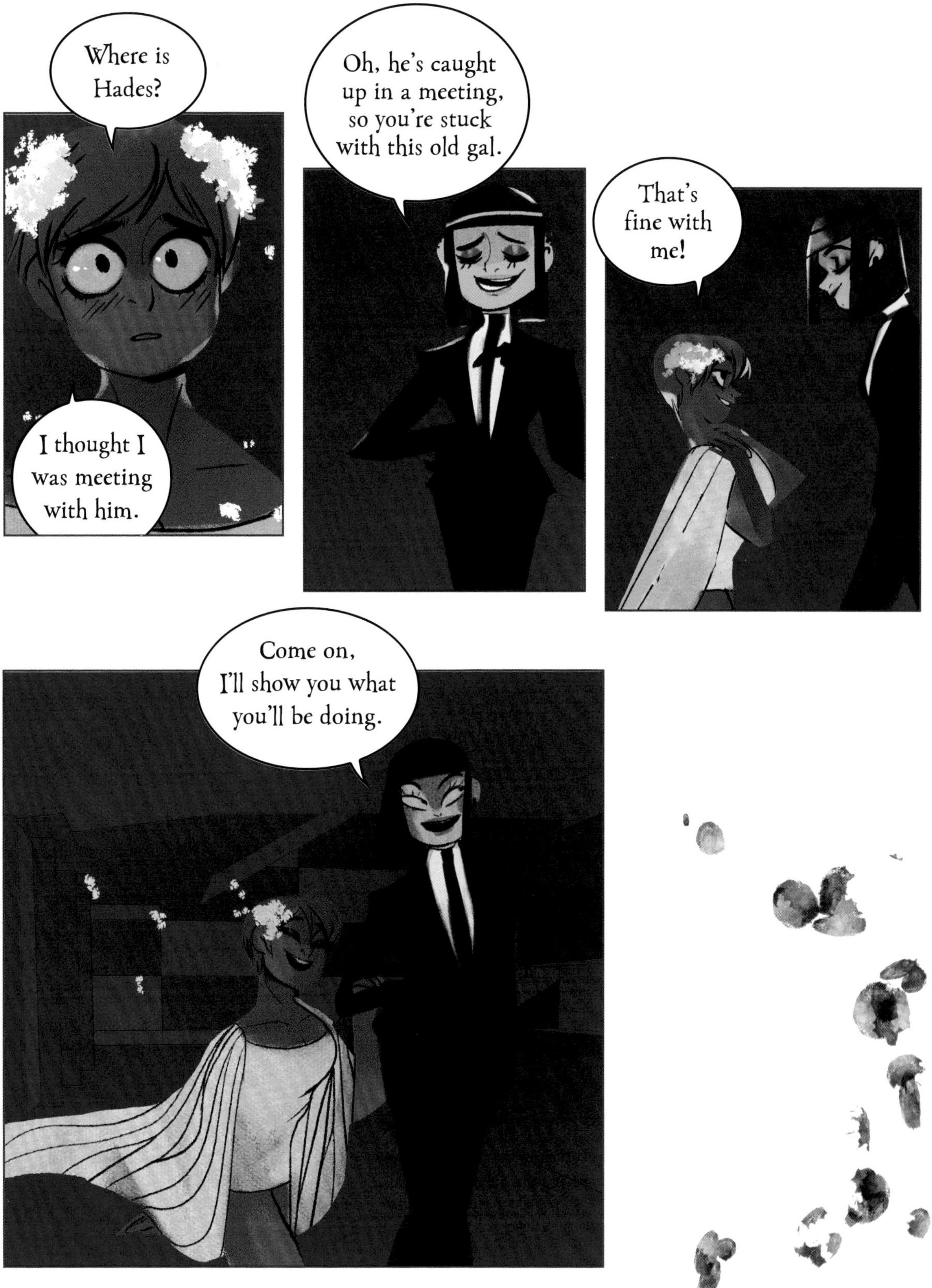
Where is Hades?
I thought I was meeting with him.
Oh, he's caught up in a meeting, so you're stuck with this old gal.
That's fine with me!
Come on, I'll show you what you'll be doing.

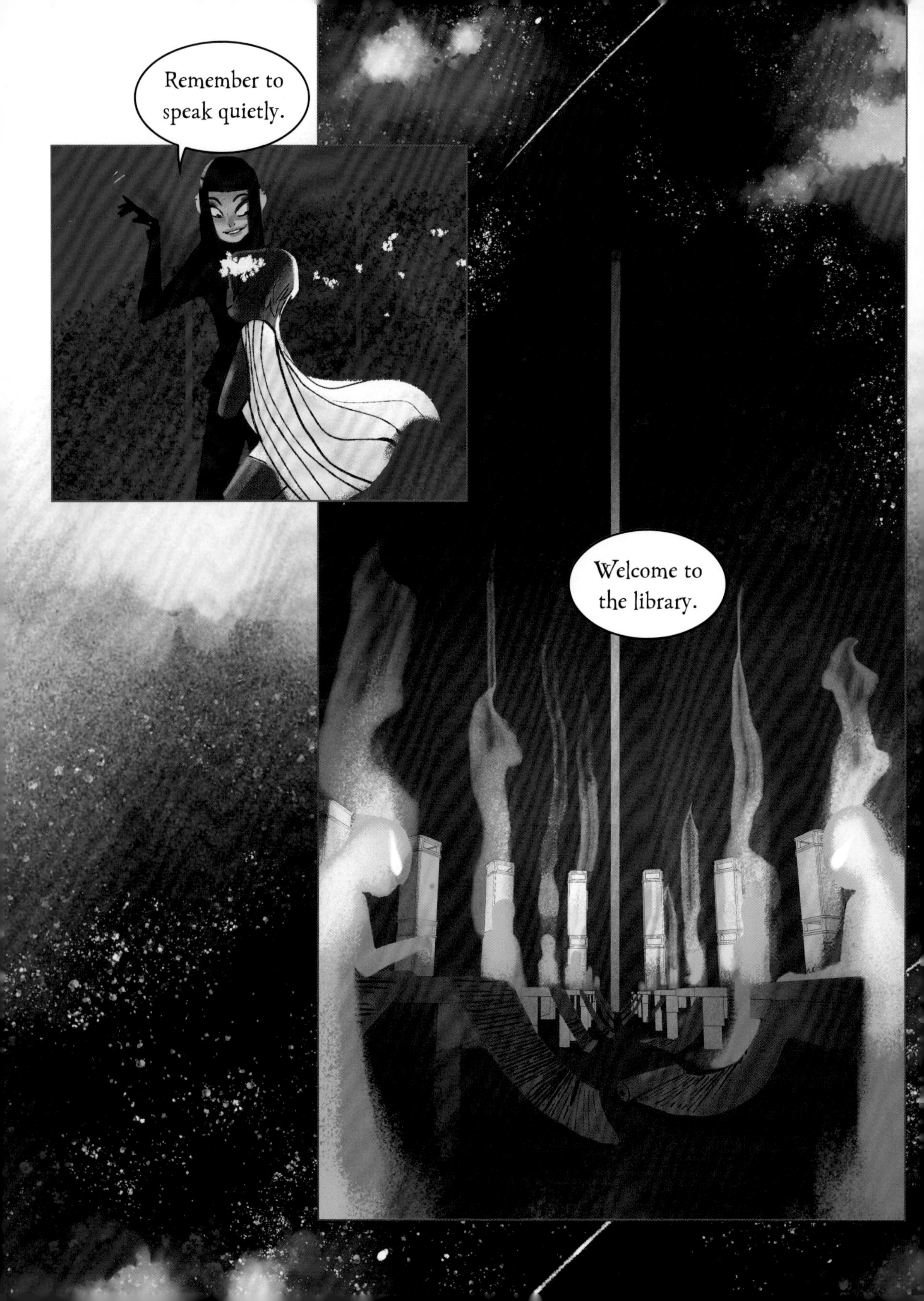
Remember to speak quietly.
Welcome to the library.

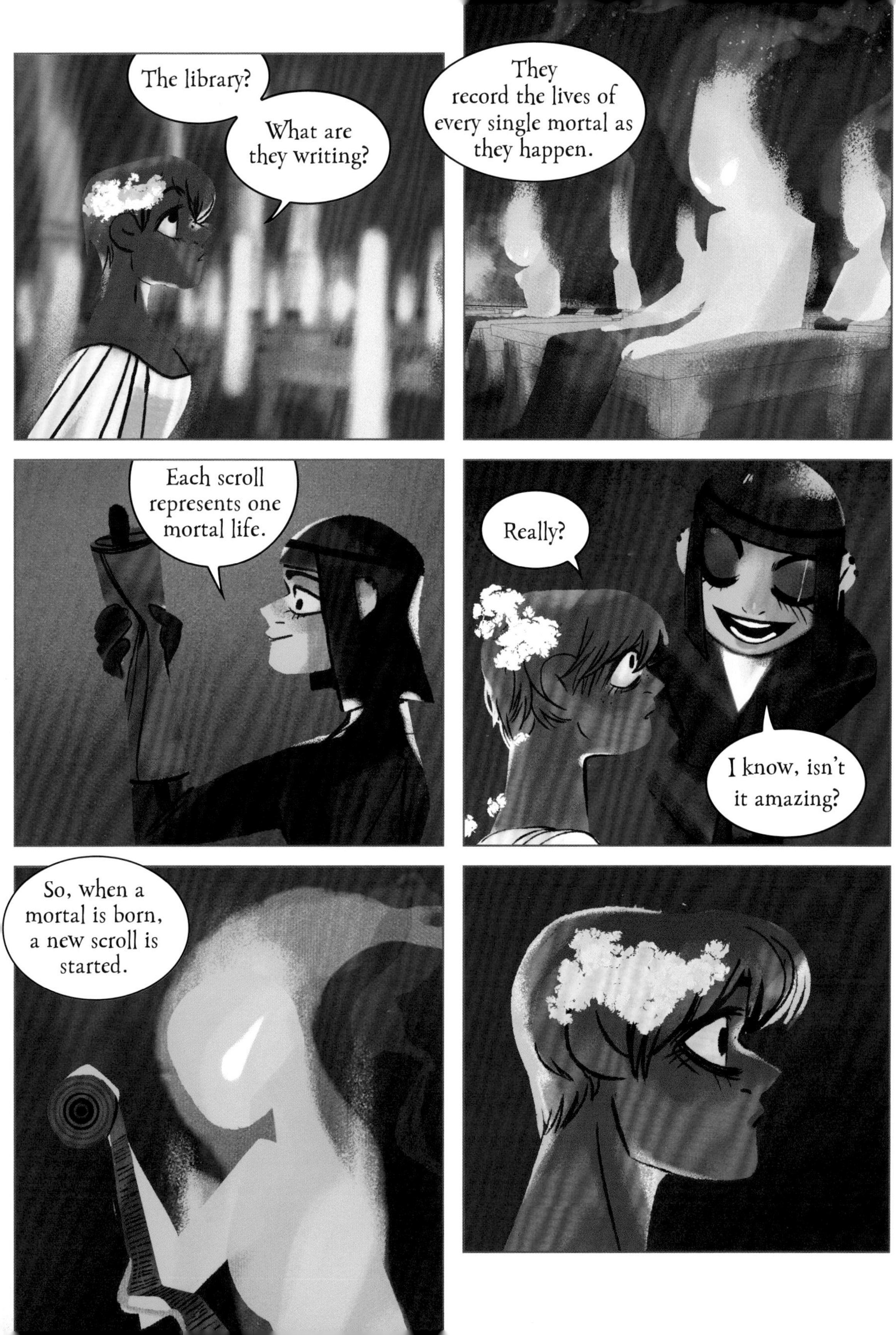
The library?
What are they writing?
They record the lives of every single mortal as they happen.
Each scroll represents one mortal life.
Really?
I know, isn't it amazing?
So, when a mortal is born, a new scroll is started.

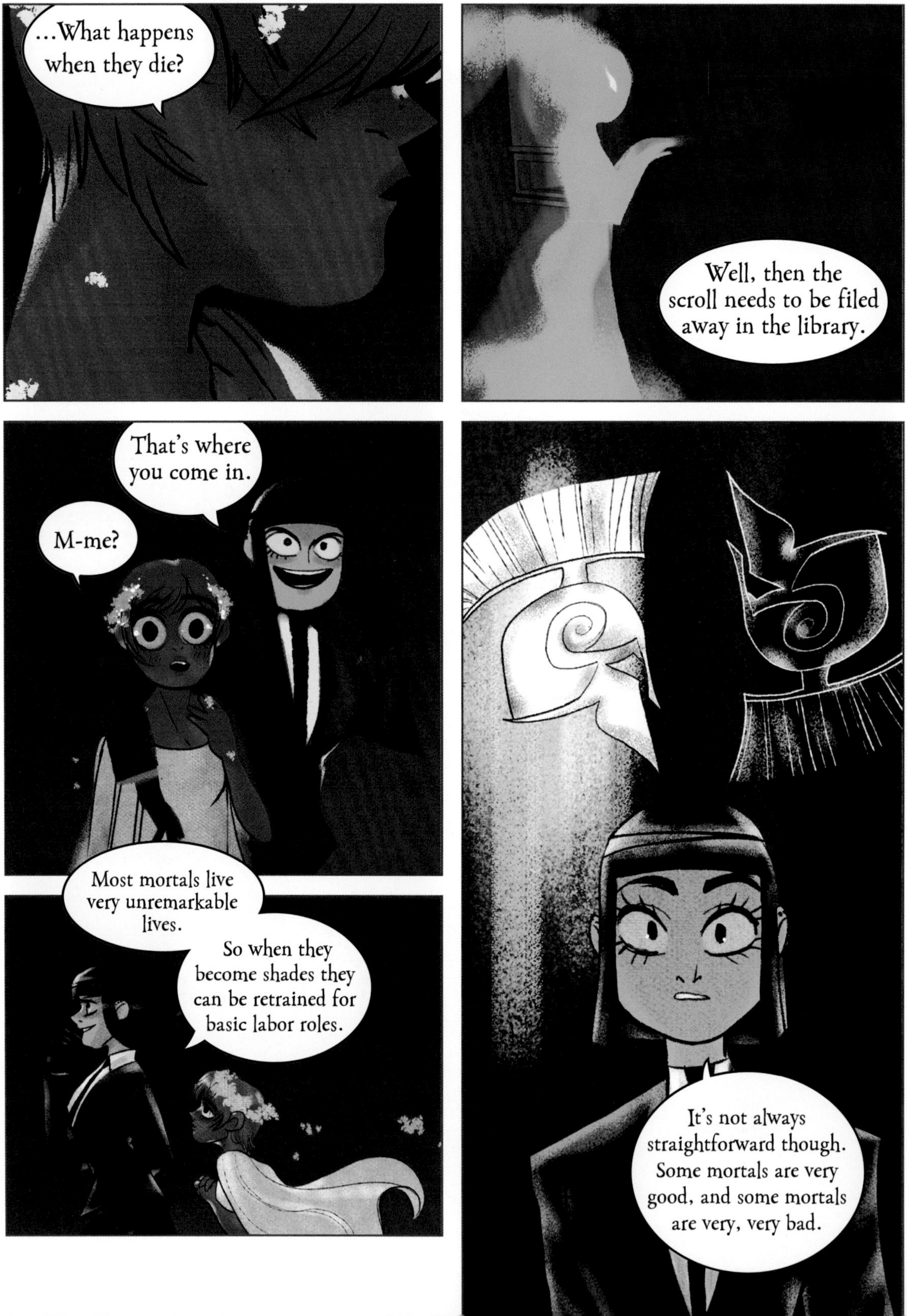
...What happens when they die?
Well, then the scroll needs to be filed away in the library.
That's where you come in.
M-me?
Most mortals live very unremarkable lives.
So when they become shades they can be retrained for basic labor roles.
It's not always straightforward though. Some mortals are very good, and some mortals are very, very bad.

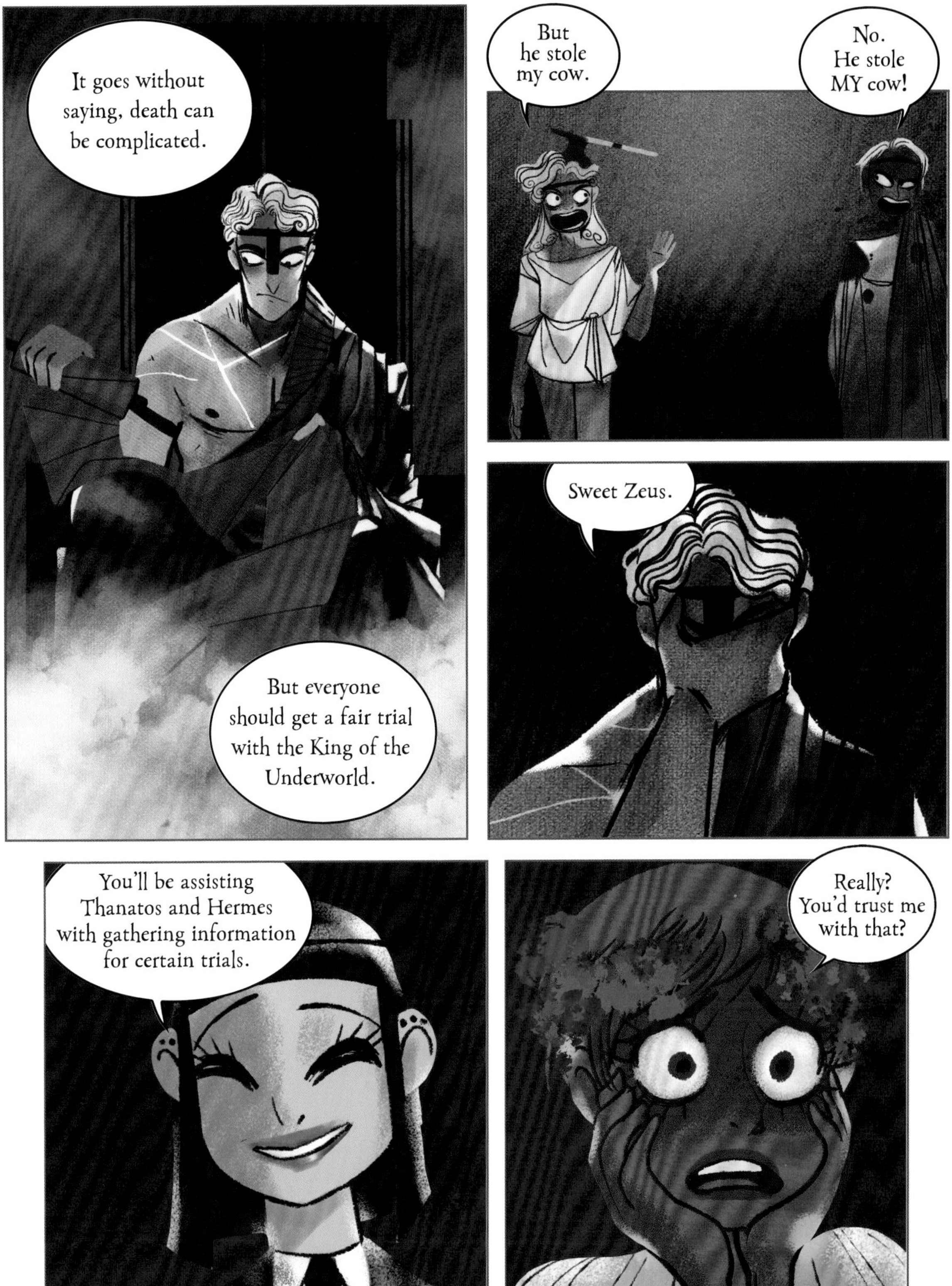
It goes without saying, death can be complicated.
But everyone should get a fair trial with the King of the Underworld.
But he stole my cow.
No. He stole MY cow!
Sweet Zeus.
You'll be assisting Thanatos and Hermes with gathering information for certain trials.
Really? You'd trust me with that?

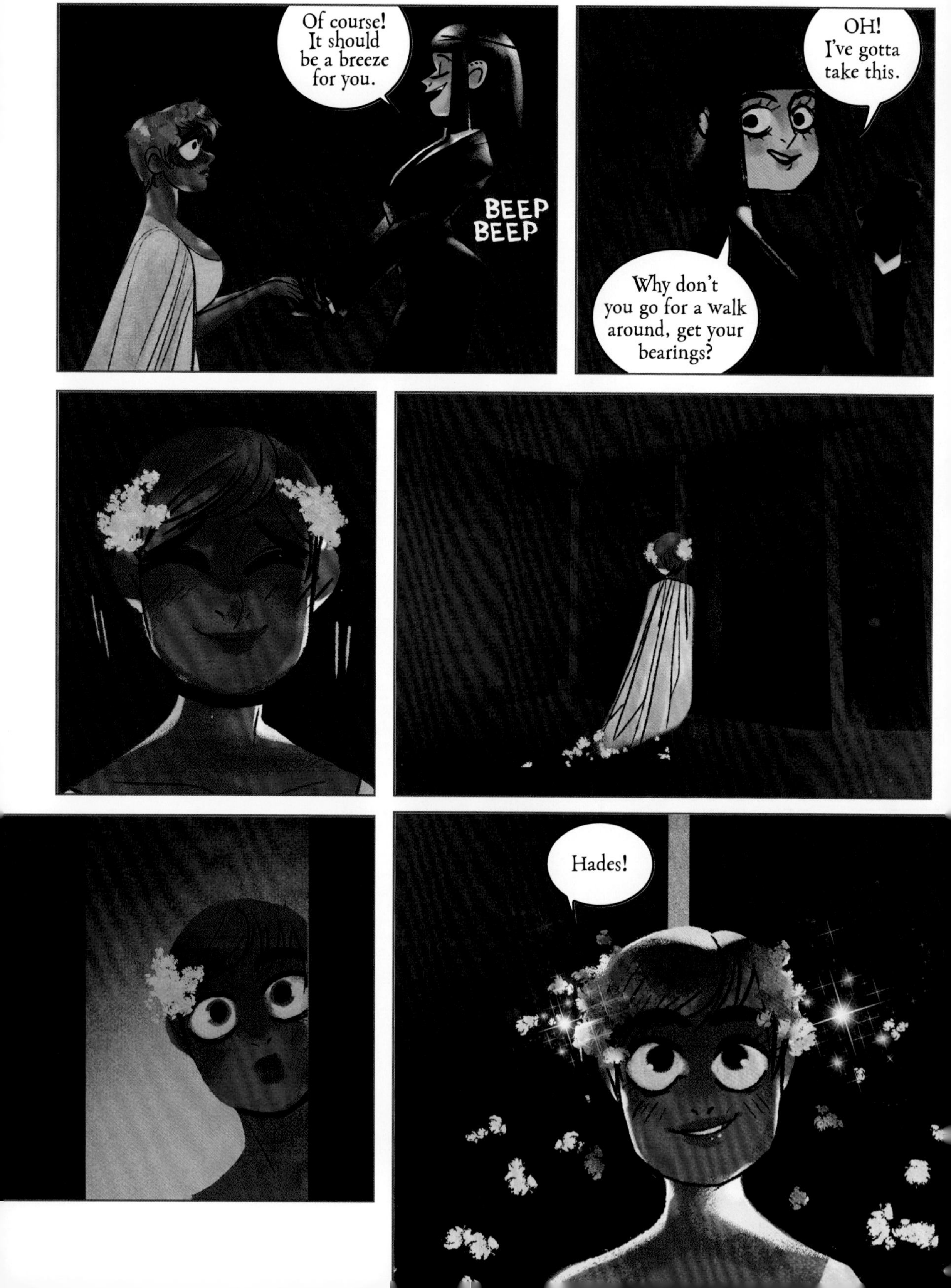
Of course! It should be a breeze for you.
BEEP BEEP
OH! I've gotta take this.
Why don't you go for a walk around, get your bearings?
Hades!

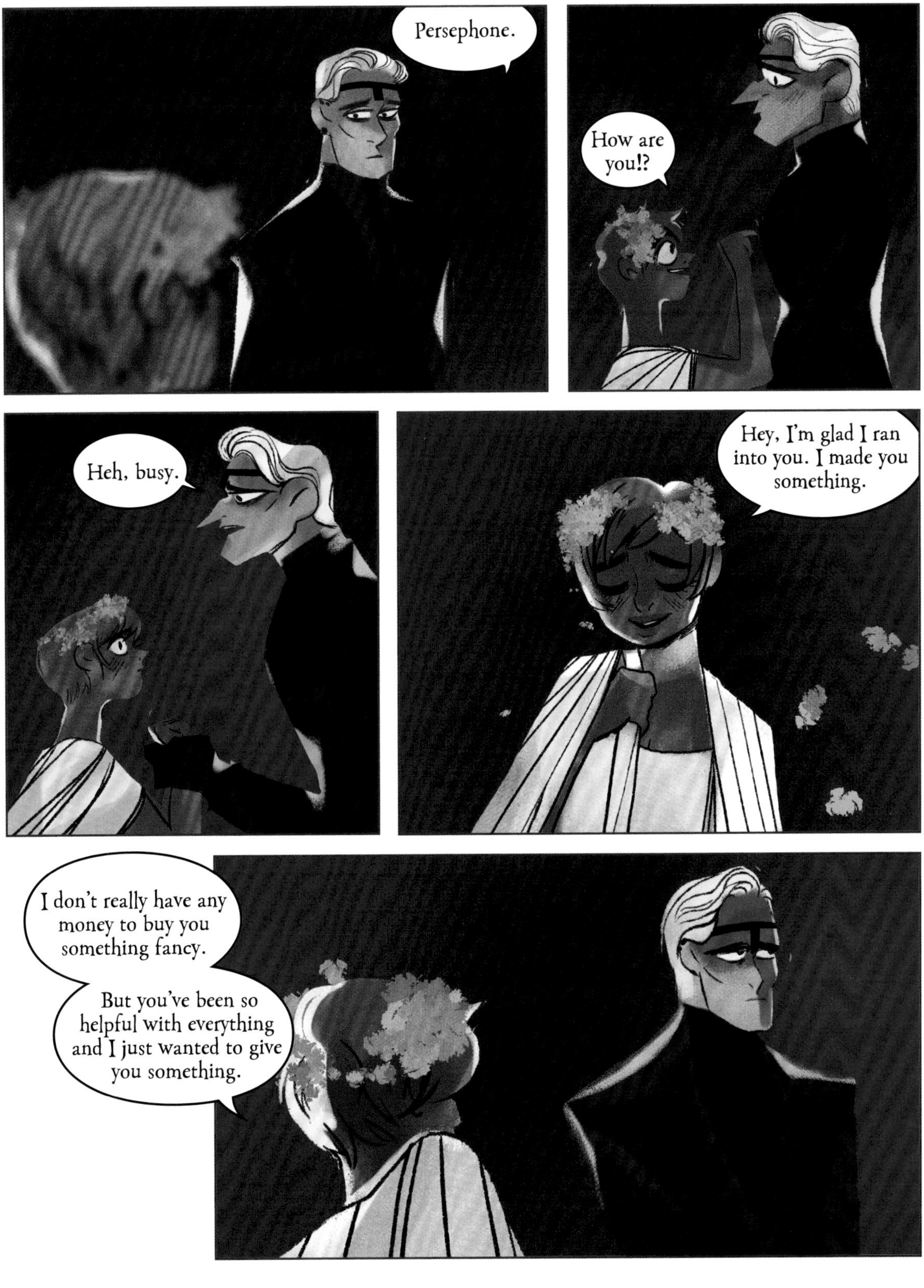
Persephone.
How are you!?
Heh, busy.
Hey, I'm glad I ran into you. I made you something.
I don't really have any money to buy you something fancy.
But you've been so helpful with everything and I just wanted to give you something.

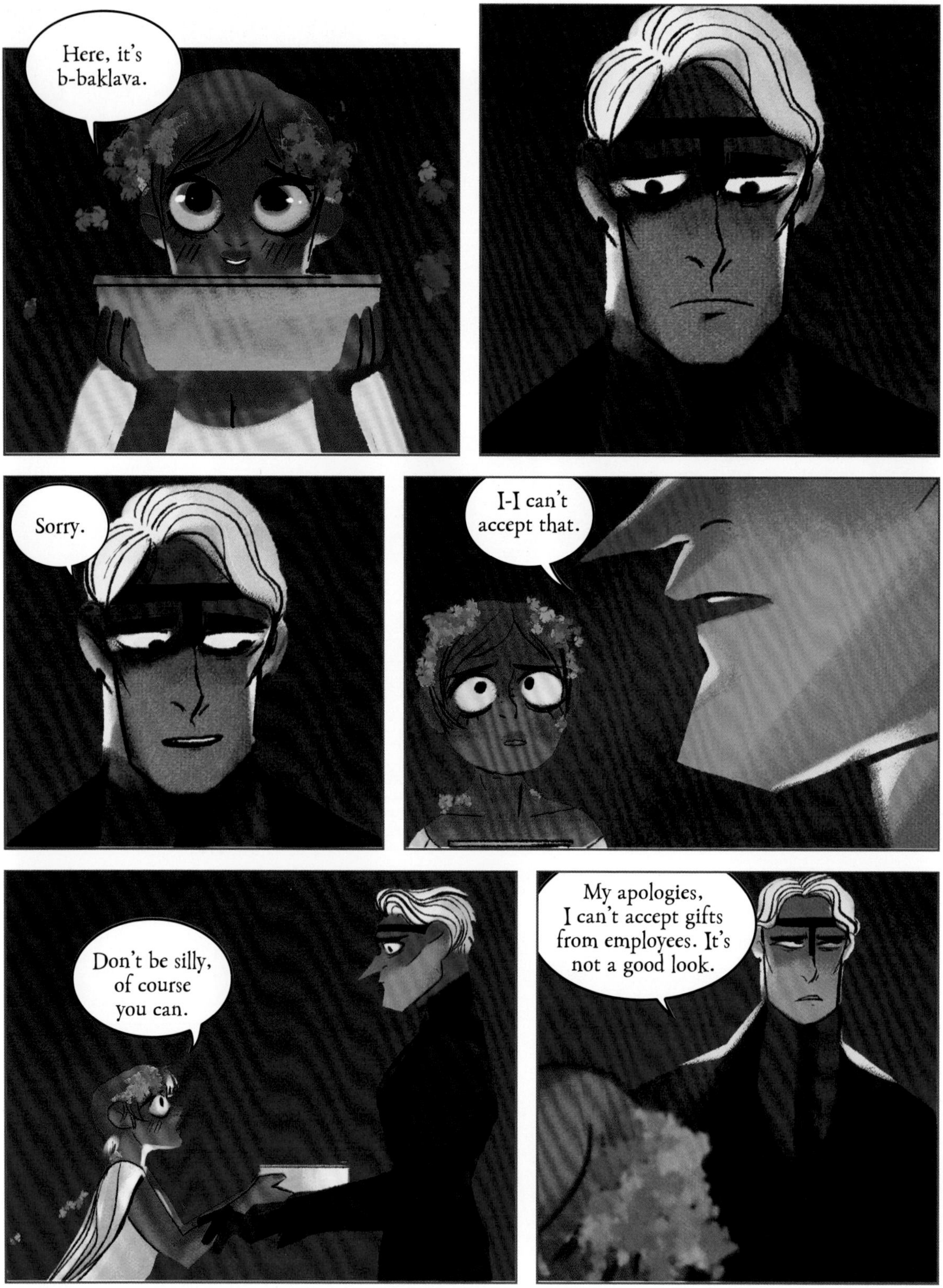
Here, it's b-baklava.
Sorry.
I-I can't accept that.
Don't be silly, of course you can.
My apologies, I can't accept gifts from employees. It's not a good look.

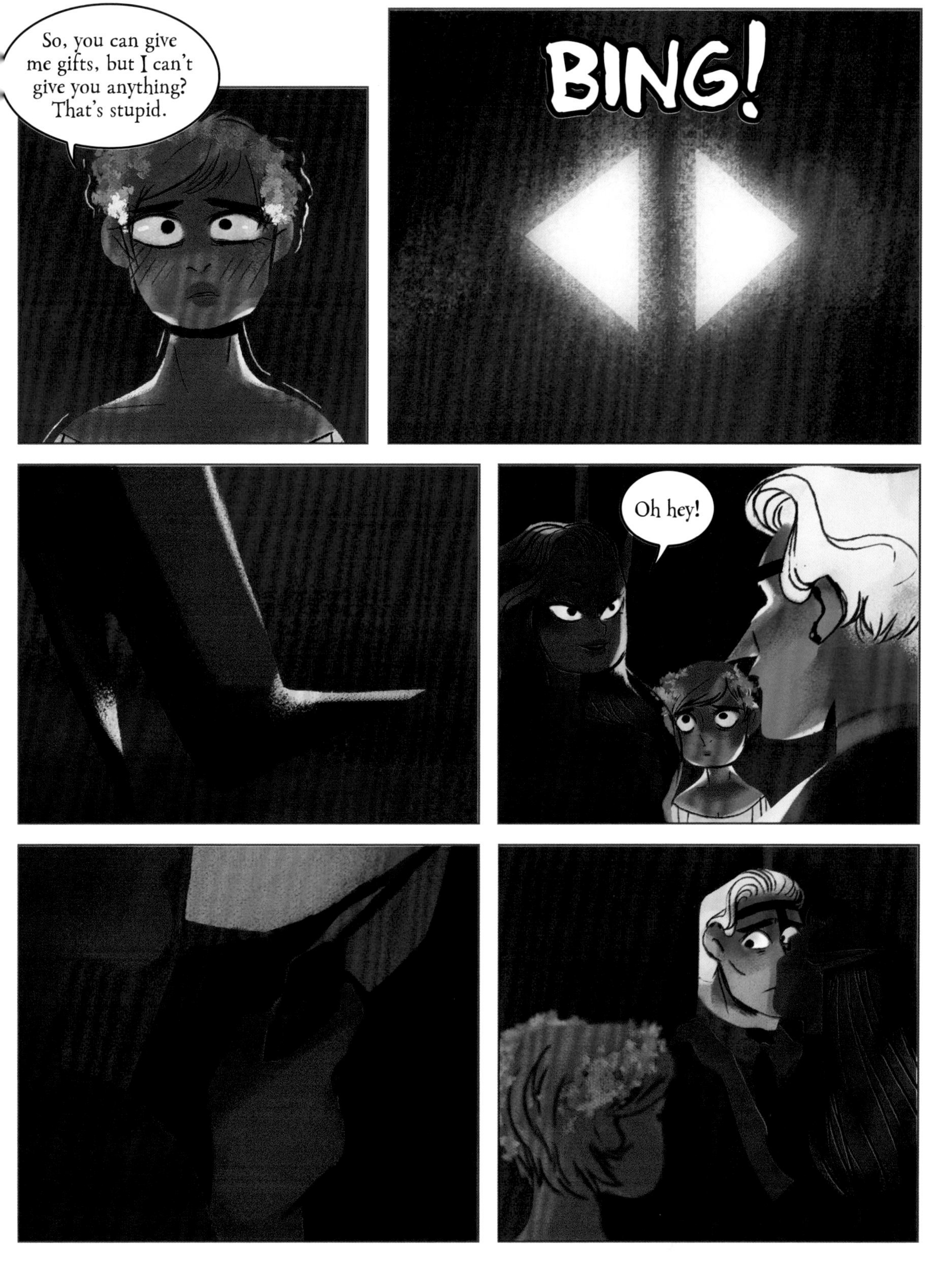
So, you can give me gifts, but I can't give you anything? That's stupid.
BING!
Oh hey!

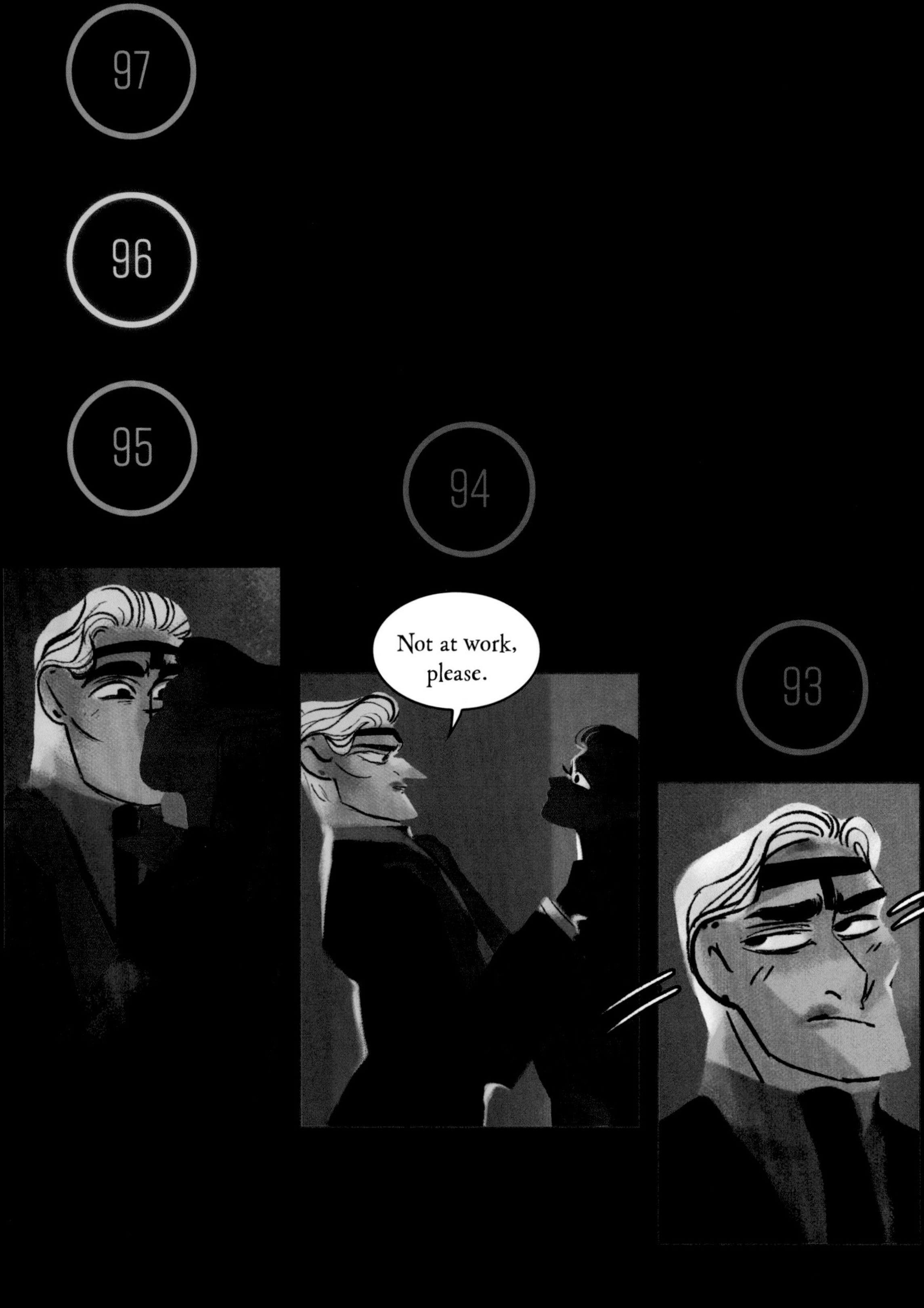
97
96
95
94
Not at work, please.
93

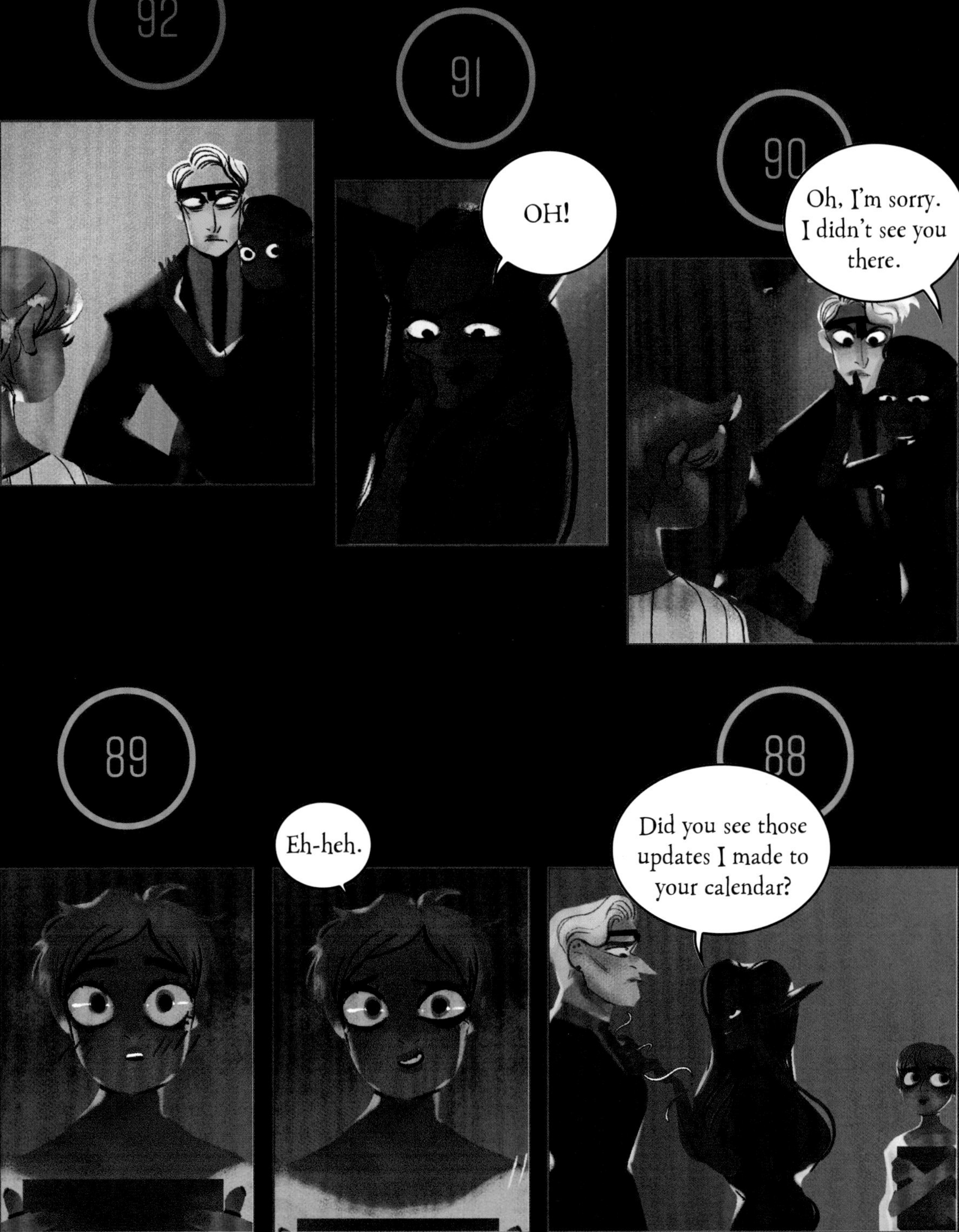
92
91
90
OH!
Oh, I'm sorry. I didn't see you there.
89
88
Eh-heh.
Did you see those updates I made to your calendar?

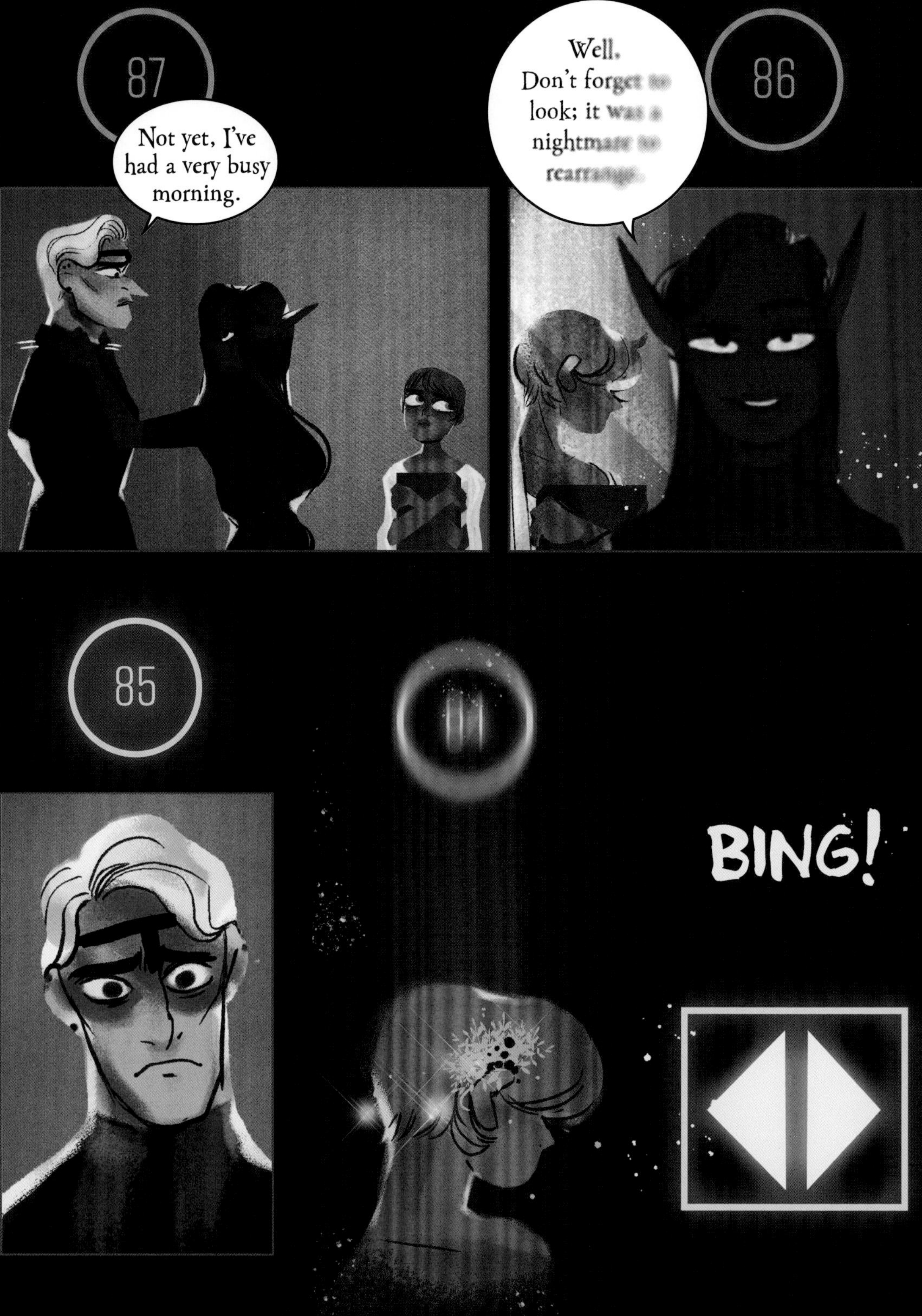
87
Not yet, I've had a very busy morning.
Well. Don't forget to look; it was a nightmare to rearrange.
86
85
BING!

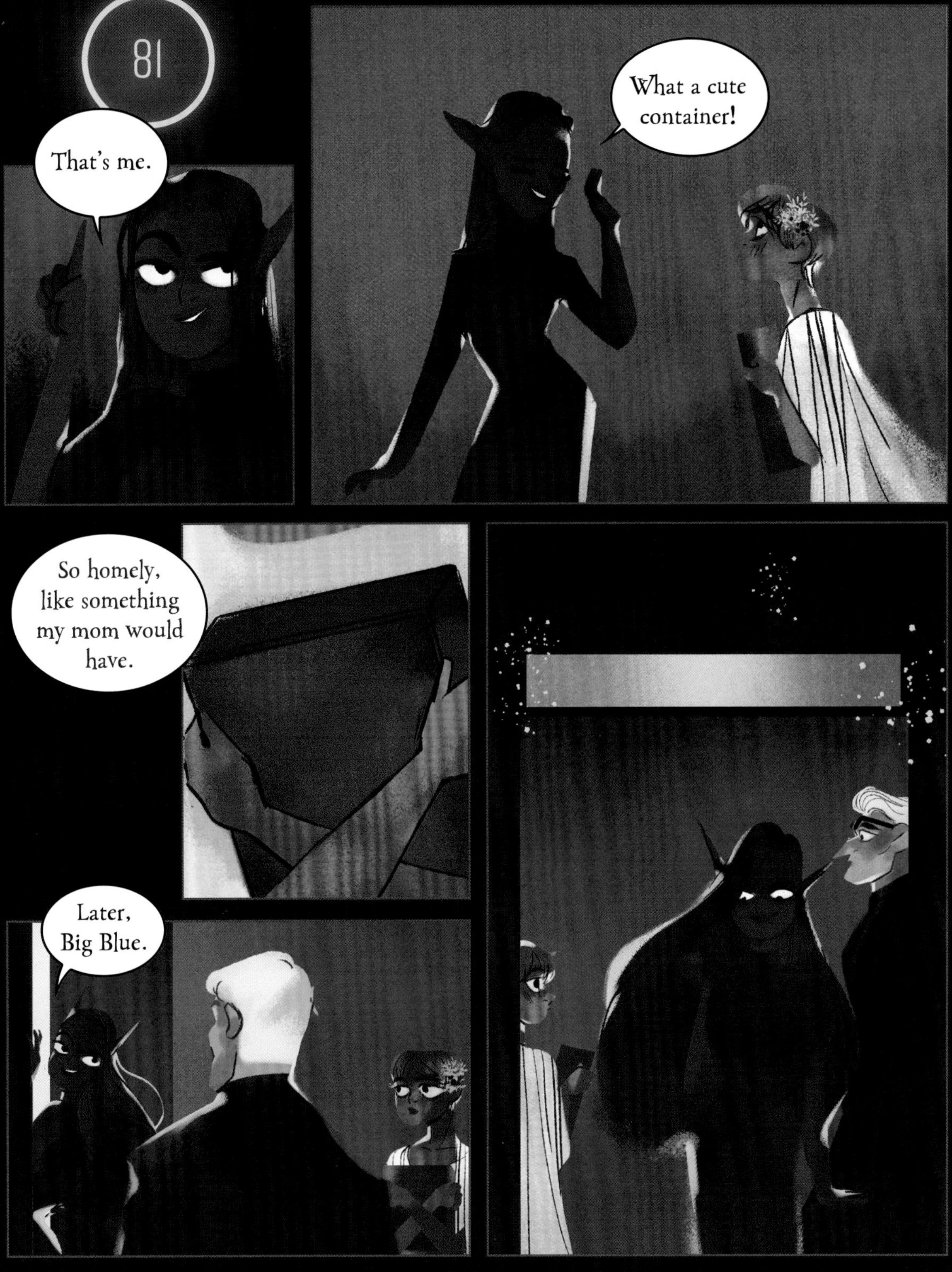
81
That's me.
What a cute container!
So homely, like something my mom would have.
Later, Big Blue.

EPISODE 52: GOING DOWN

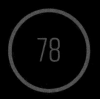

Of course, he was just humoring me before.

He doesn't want your stupid food.

Dumb village girl.

You make a beautiful couple. You must be happy.

I--

BING!

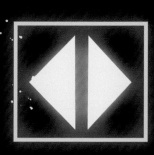

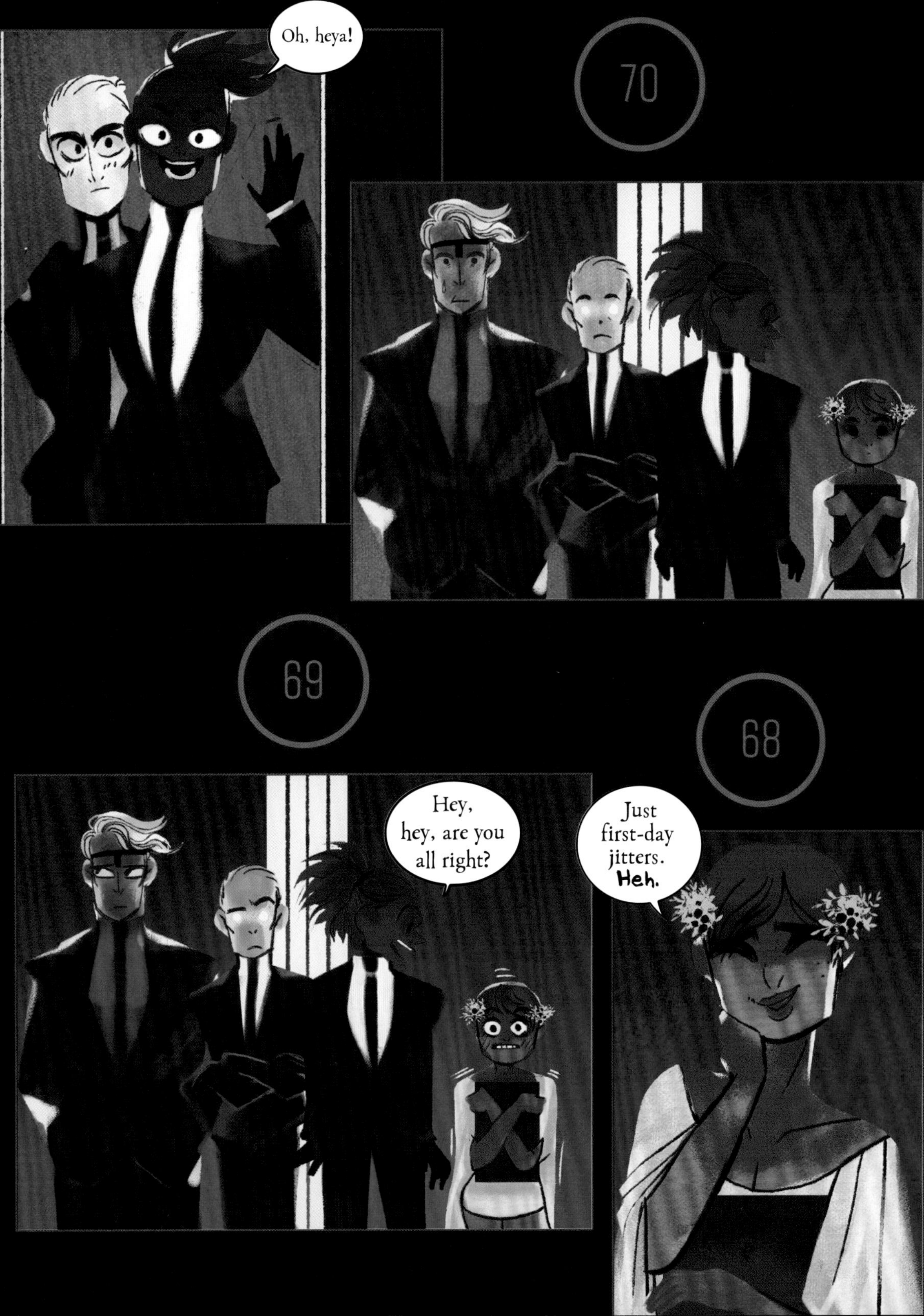
Oh, heya!
70
69
68
Hey, hey, are you all right?
Just first-day jitters. Heh.

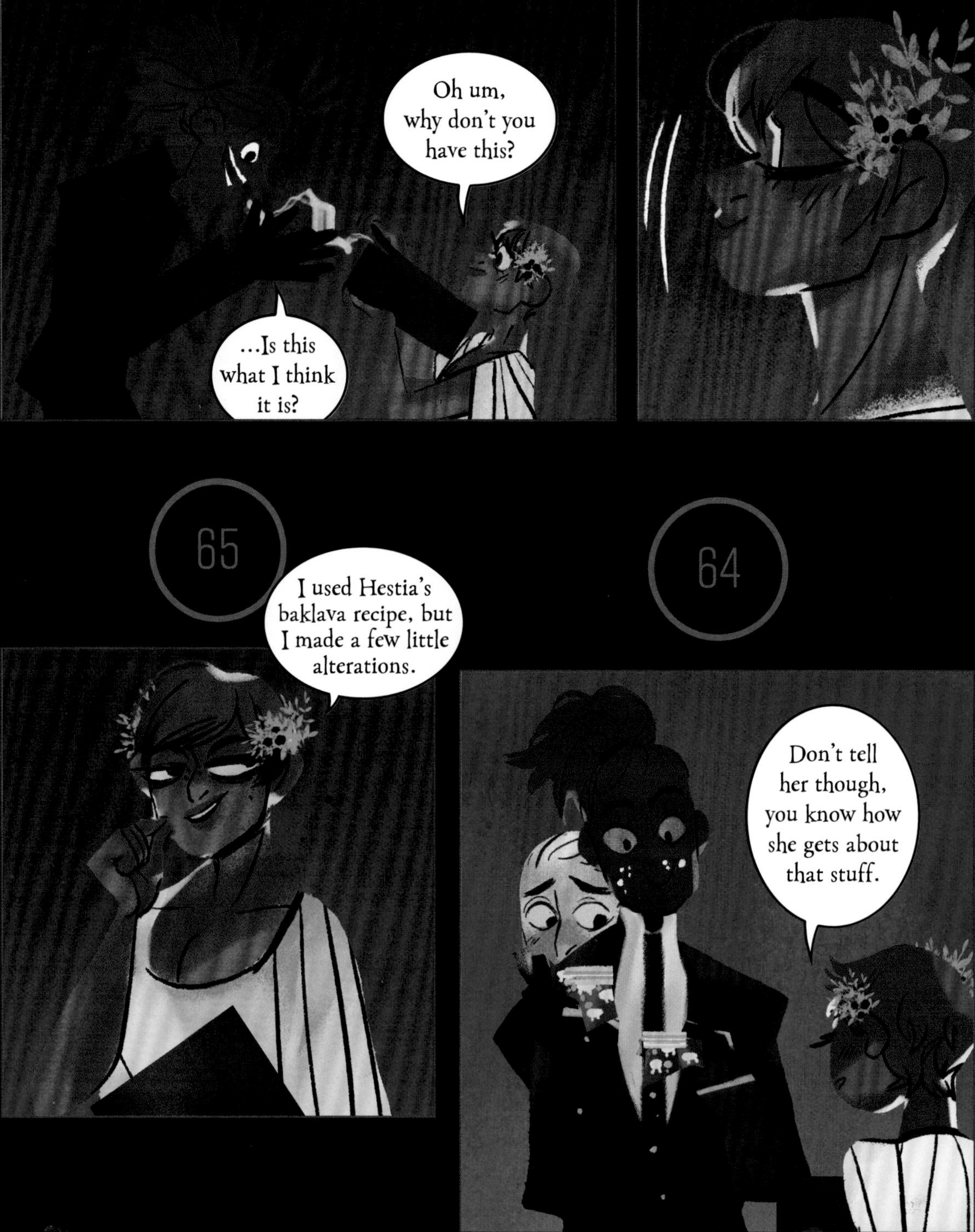
Oh um, why don't you have this?
...Is this what I think it is?
I used Hestia's baklava recipe, but I made a few little alterations.
Don't tell her though, you know how she gets about that stuff.

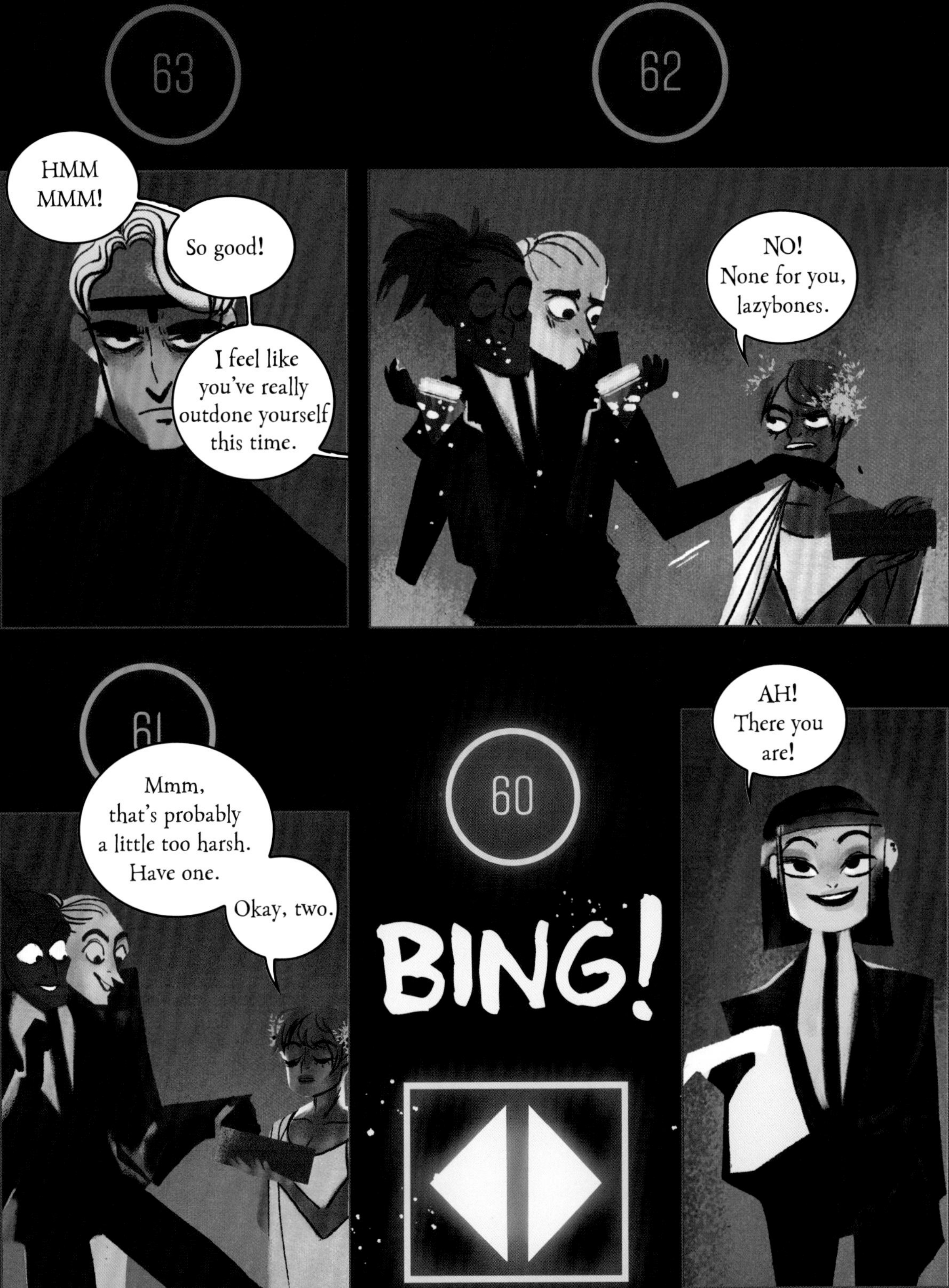
63
62
HMM MMM!
So good!
I feel like you've really outdone yourself this time.
NO! None for you, lazybones.
61
Mmm, that's probably a little too harsh. Have one.
Okay, two.
60
BING!
AH! There you are!

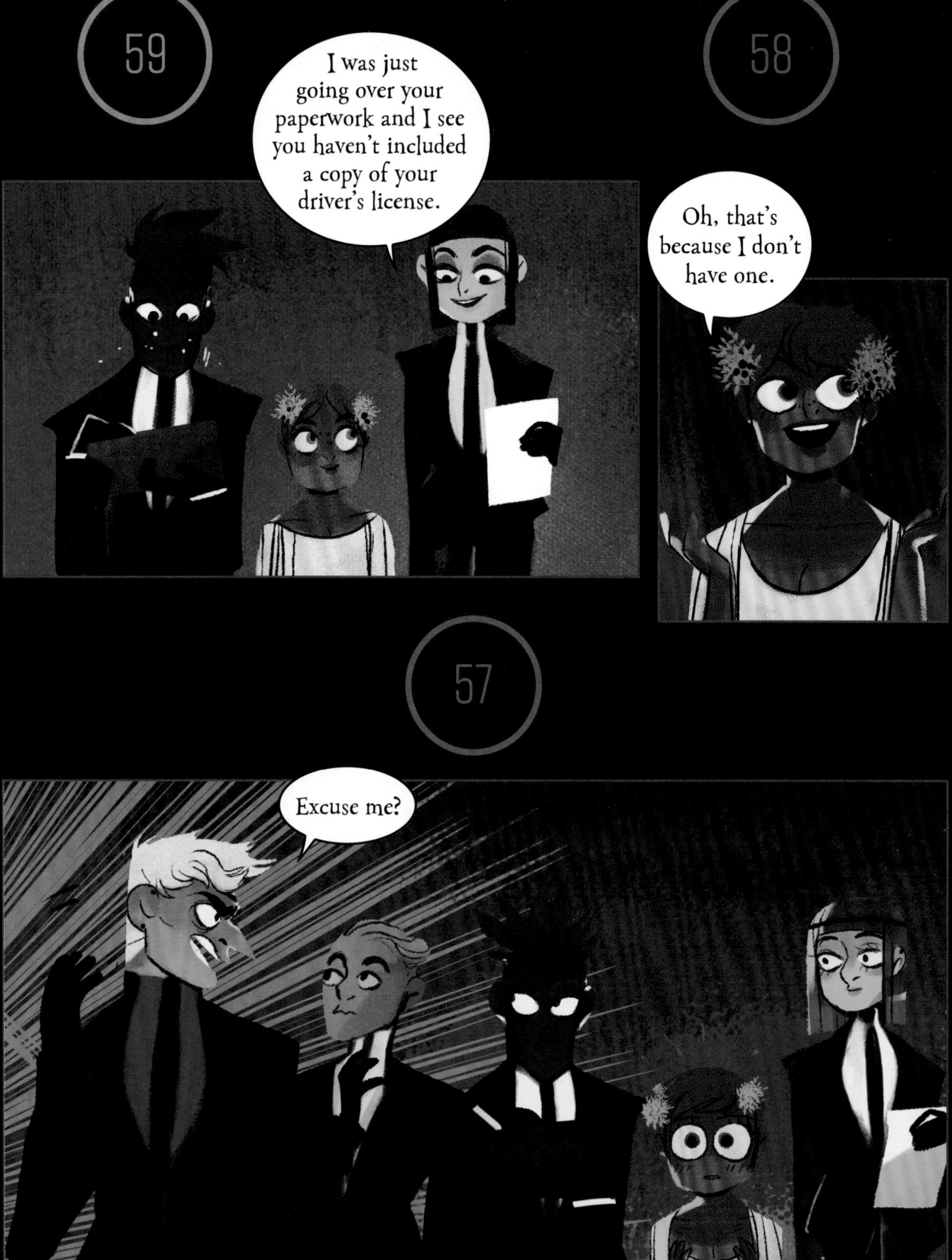
59
I was just going over your paperwork and I see you haven't included a copy of your driver's license.
58
Oh, that's because I don't have one.
57
Excuse me?

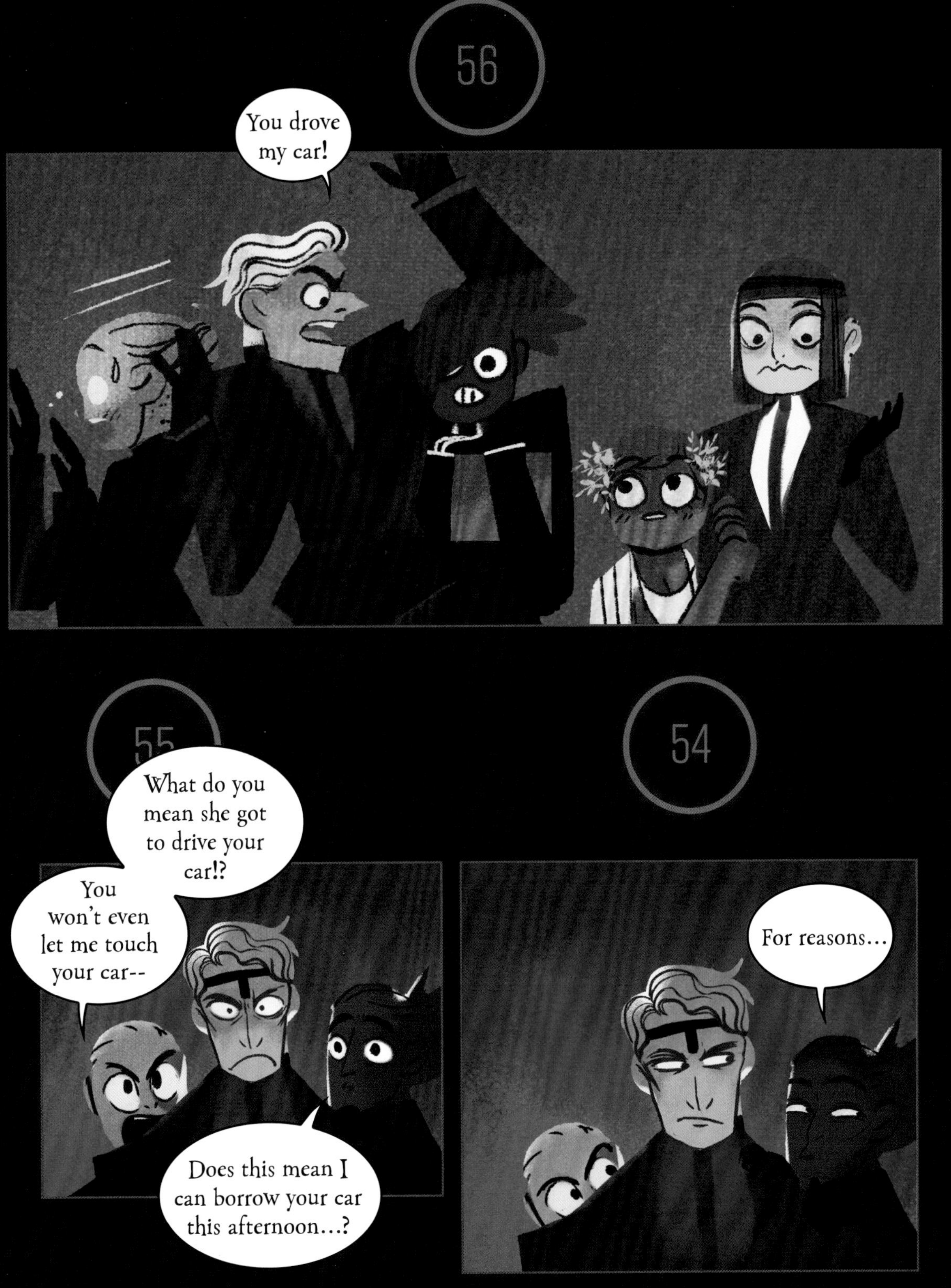
56
You drove my car!
55
What do you mean she got to drive your car!?
You won't even let me touch your car--
Does this mean I can borrow your car this afternoon...?
54
For reasons...

53

Explain.

52

I-I know how to drive.

...I just don't have a license.

51

50

You can't drive without a license!

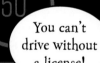

49

How could I possibly get into trouble with the King of the Underworld as my escort?

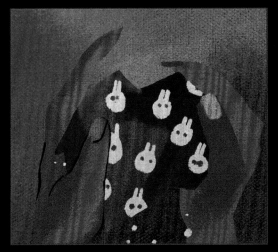

PAT
PAT

Here, when you're done being snippy, you can eat that.

You told me you were an excellent driver!

You can't just smooth over your blatant disregard of bureaucracy w-with baked goods!

It's not a big deal, I read about it in a book once and it wasn't that hard!

AWKWARD

...I may have fudged the truth a little.

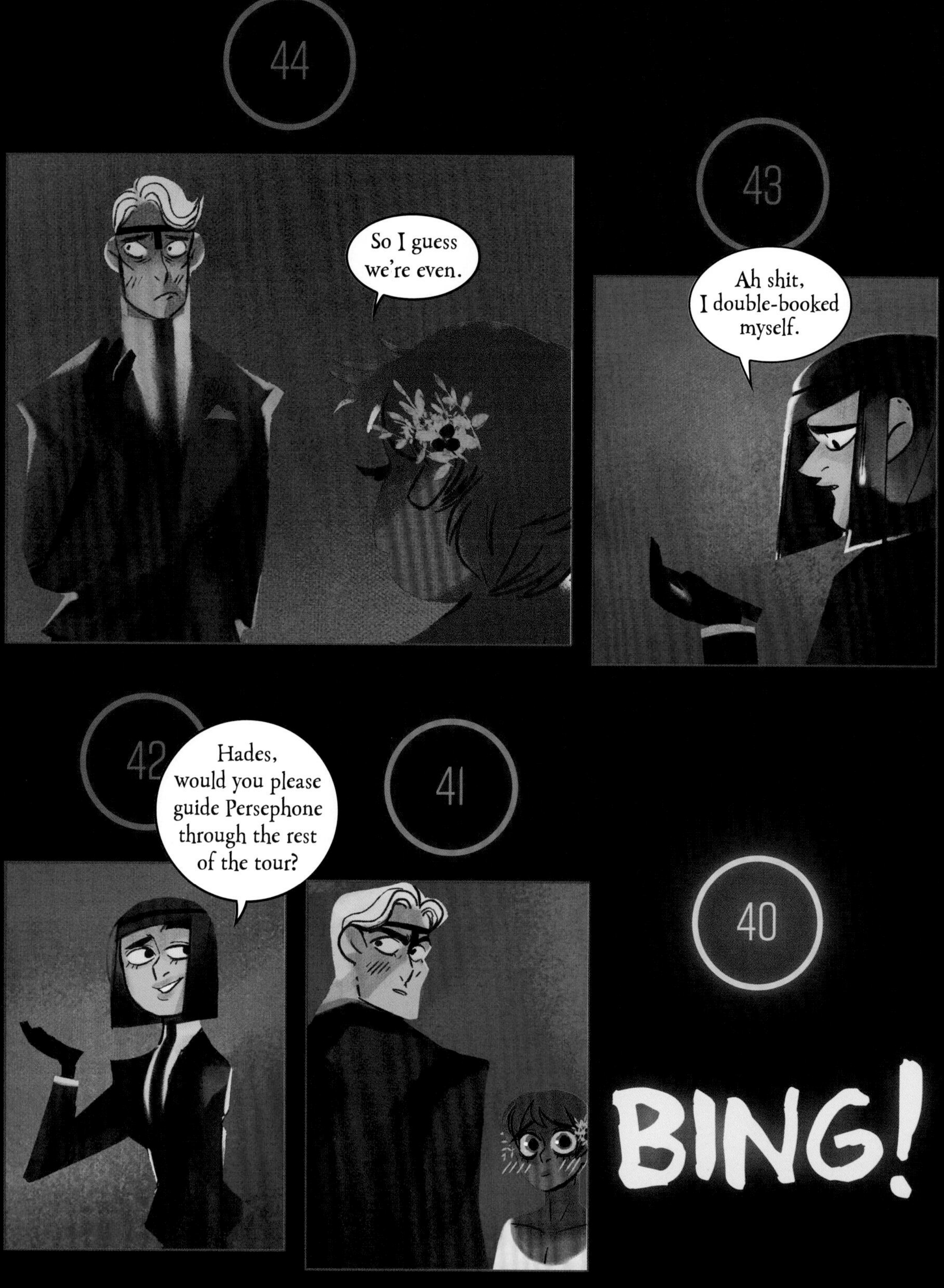
44
So I guess we're even.
43
Ah shit, I double-booked myself.
42
Hades, would you please guide Persephone through the rest of the tour?
41
40
BING!

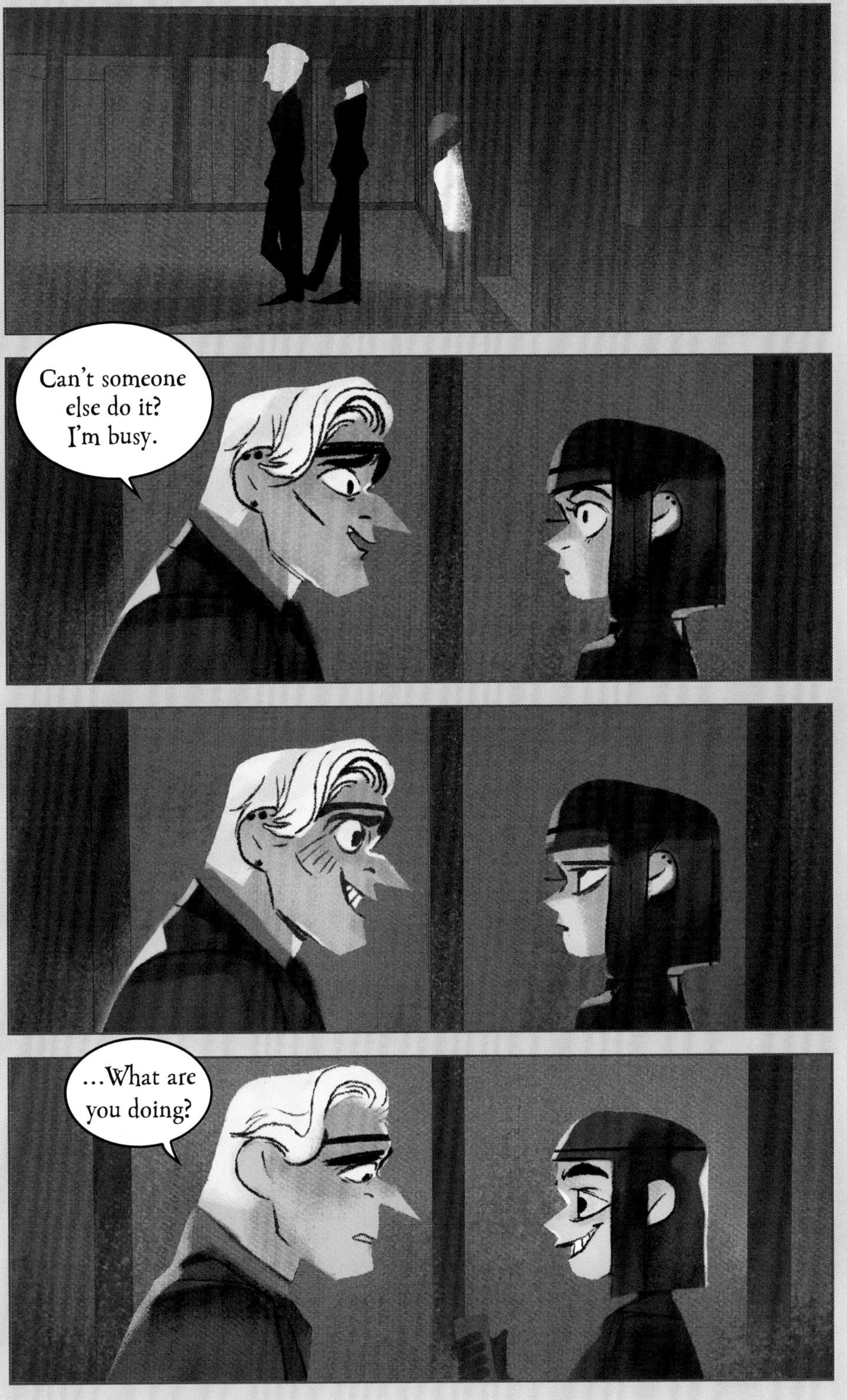
Can't someone else do it? I'm busy.
...What are you doing?

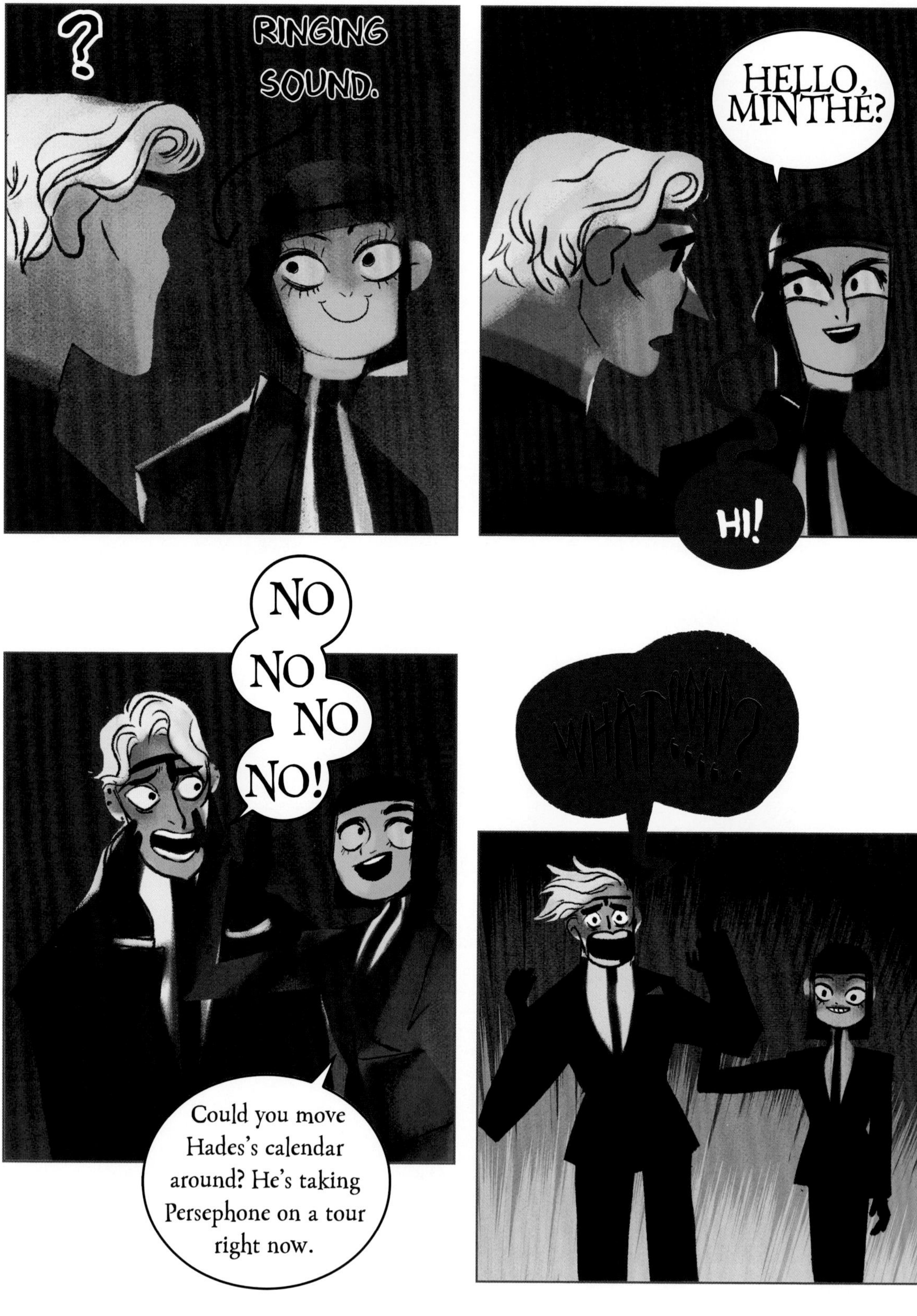
?
RINGING SOUND.
HELLO, MINTHE?
HI!
NO NO NO NO!
Could you move Hades's calendar around? He's taking Persephone on a tour right now.
WHAT!!!!?

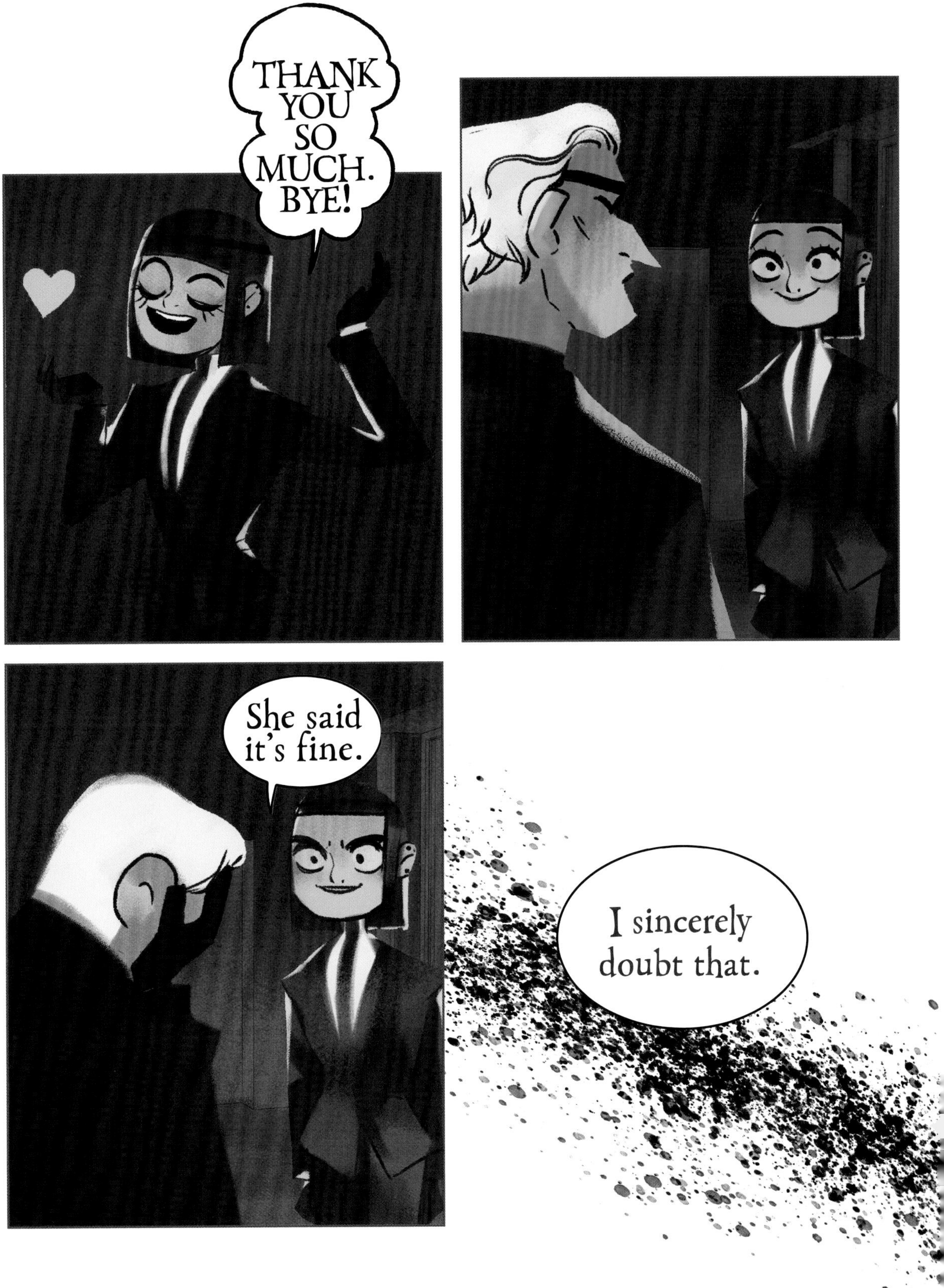
THANK YOU SO MUCH. BYE!
She said it's fine.
I sincerely doubt that.

EPISODE 53: THE TOUR (PART I)

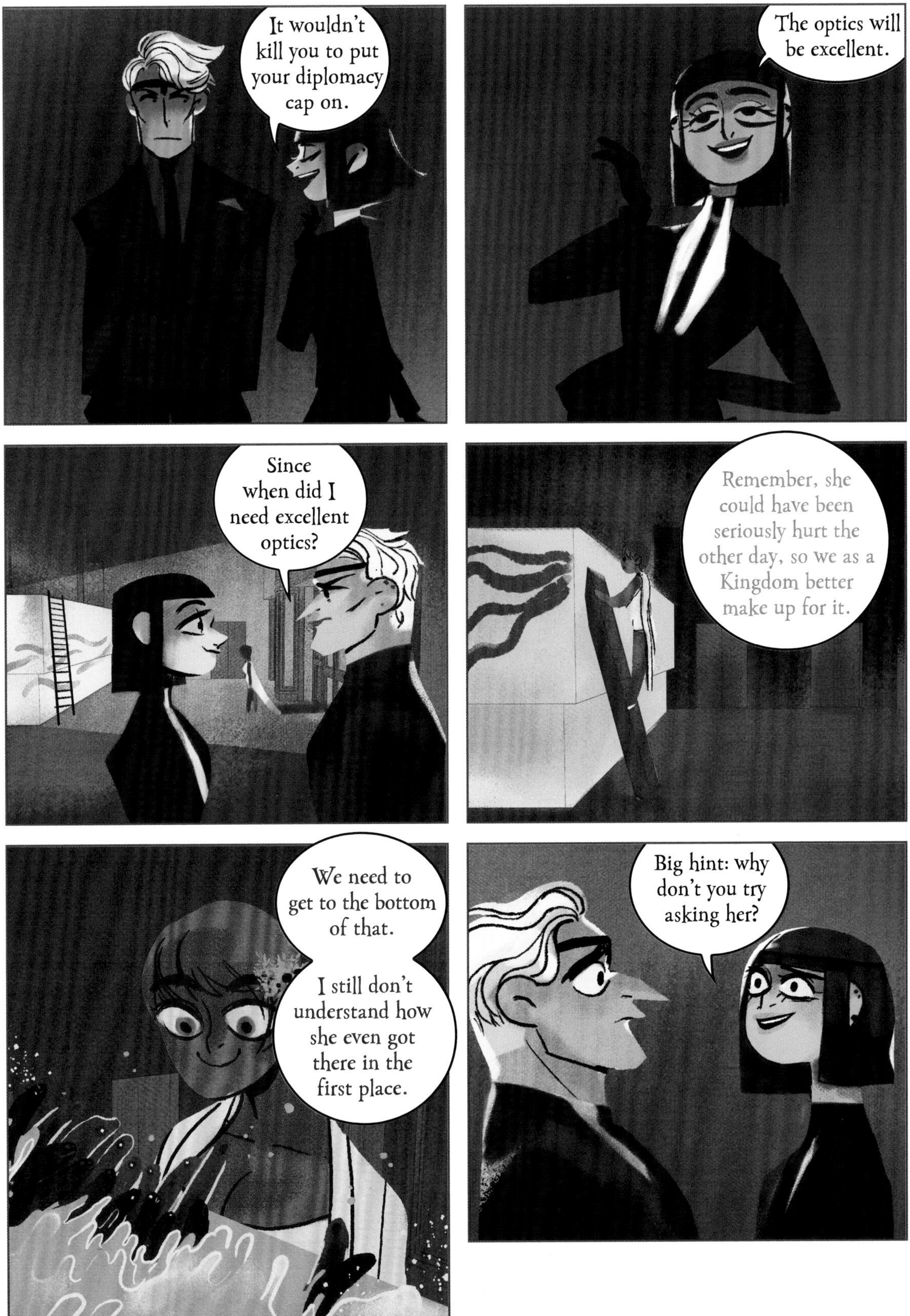
It wouldn't kill you to put your diplomacy cap on.
The optics will be excellent.
Since when did I need excellent optics?
Remember, she could have been seriously hurt the other day, so we as a Kingdom better make up for it.
We need to get to the bottom of that.
I still don't understand how she even got there in the first place.
Big hint: why don't you try asking her?

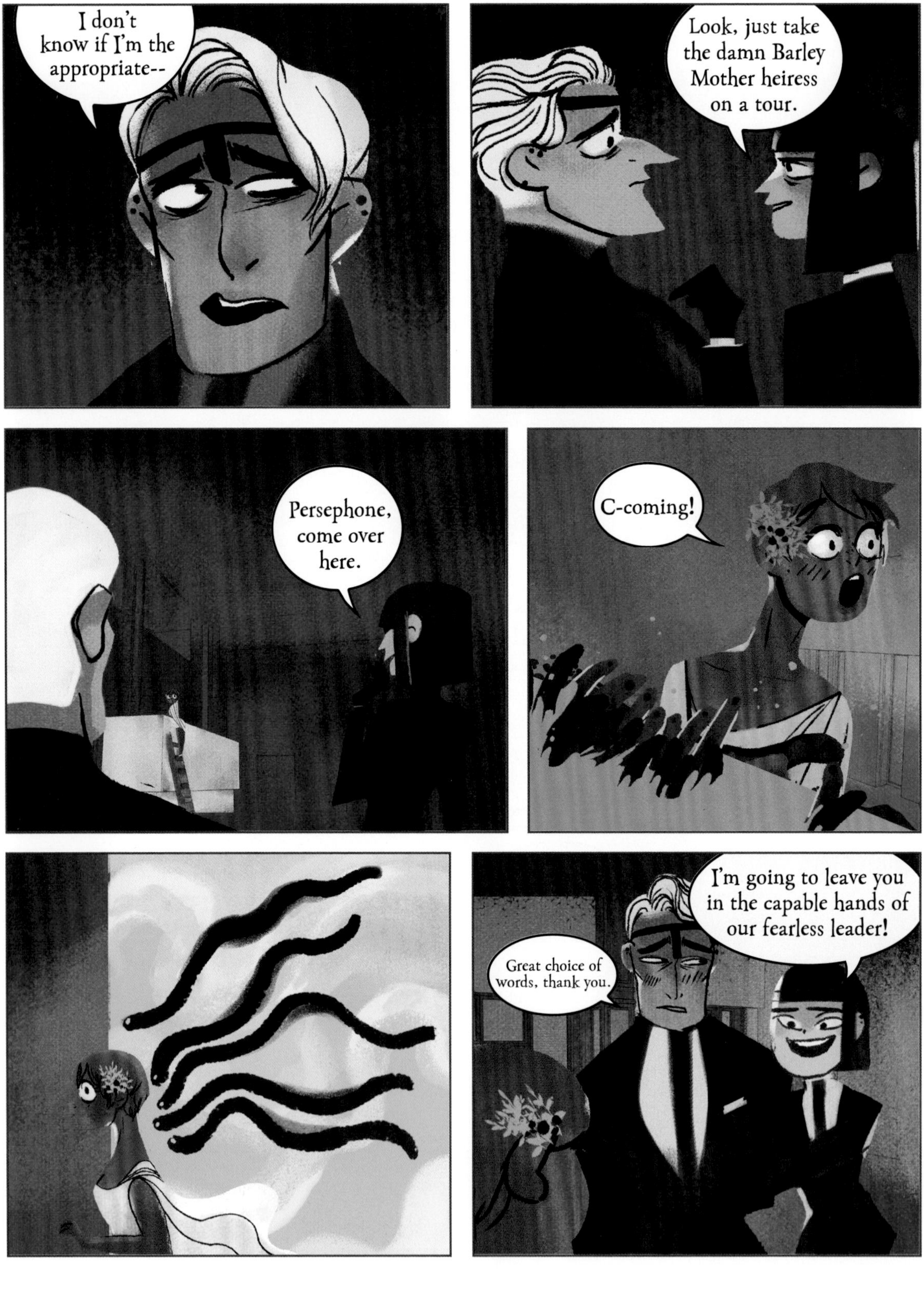
I don't know if I'm the appropriate--
Look, just take the damn Barley Mother heiress on a tour.
Persephone, come over here.
C-coming!
I'm going to leave you in the capable hands of our fearless leader!
Great choice of words, thank you.

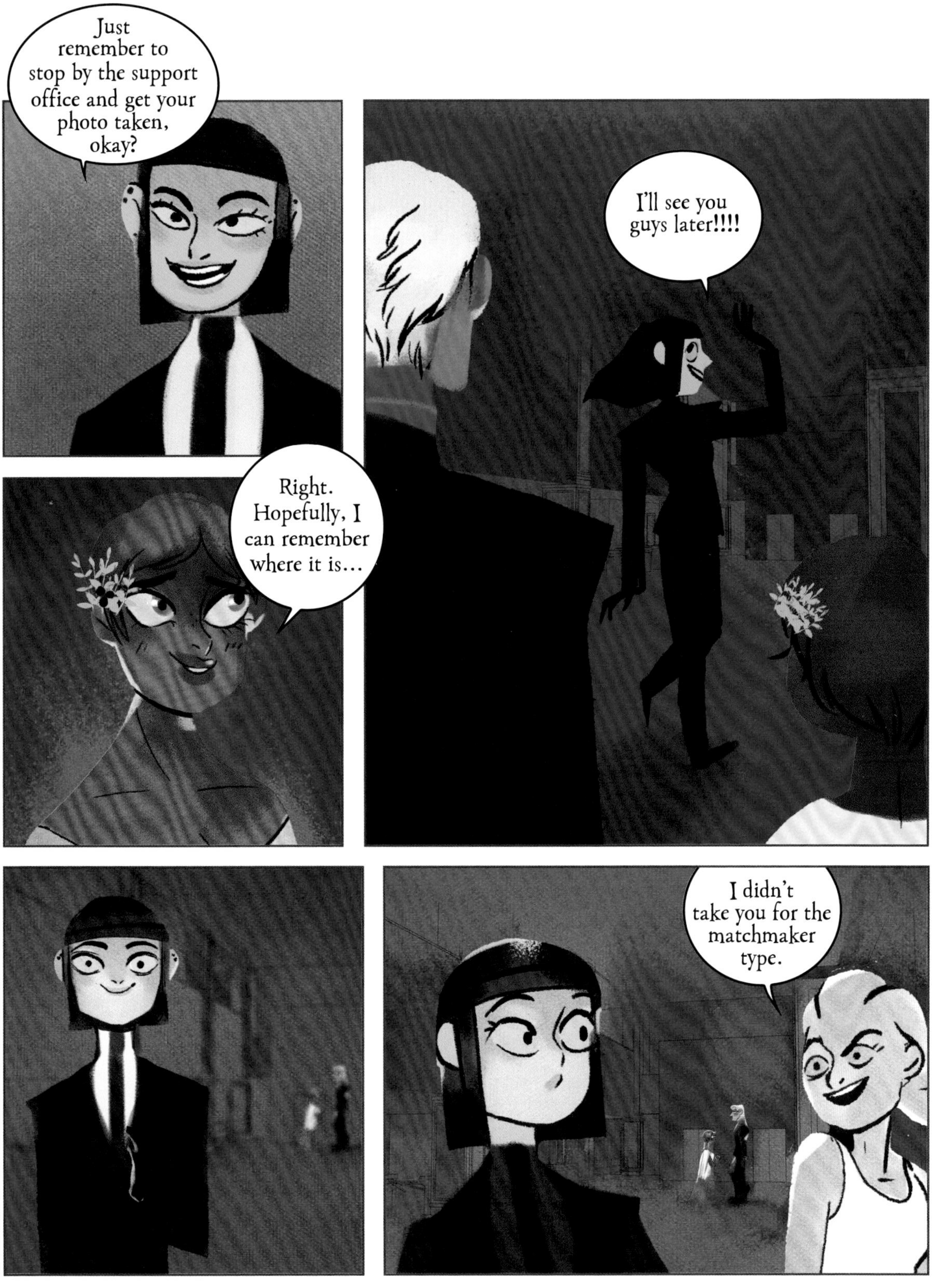
Just remember to stop by the support office and get your photo taken, okay?
I'll see you guys later!!!!
Right. Hopefully, I can remember where it is...
I didn't take you for the matchmaker type.

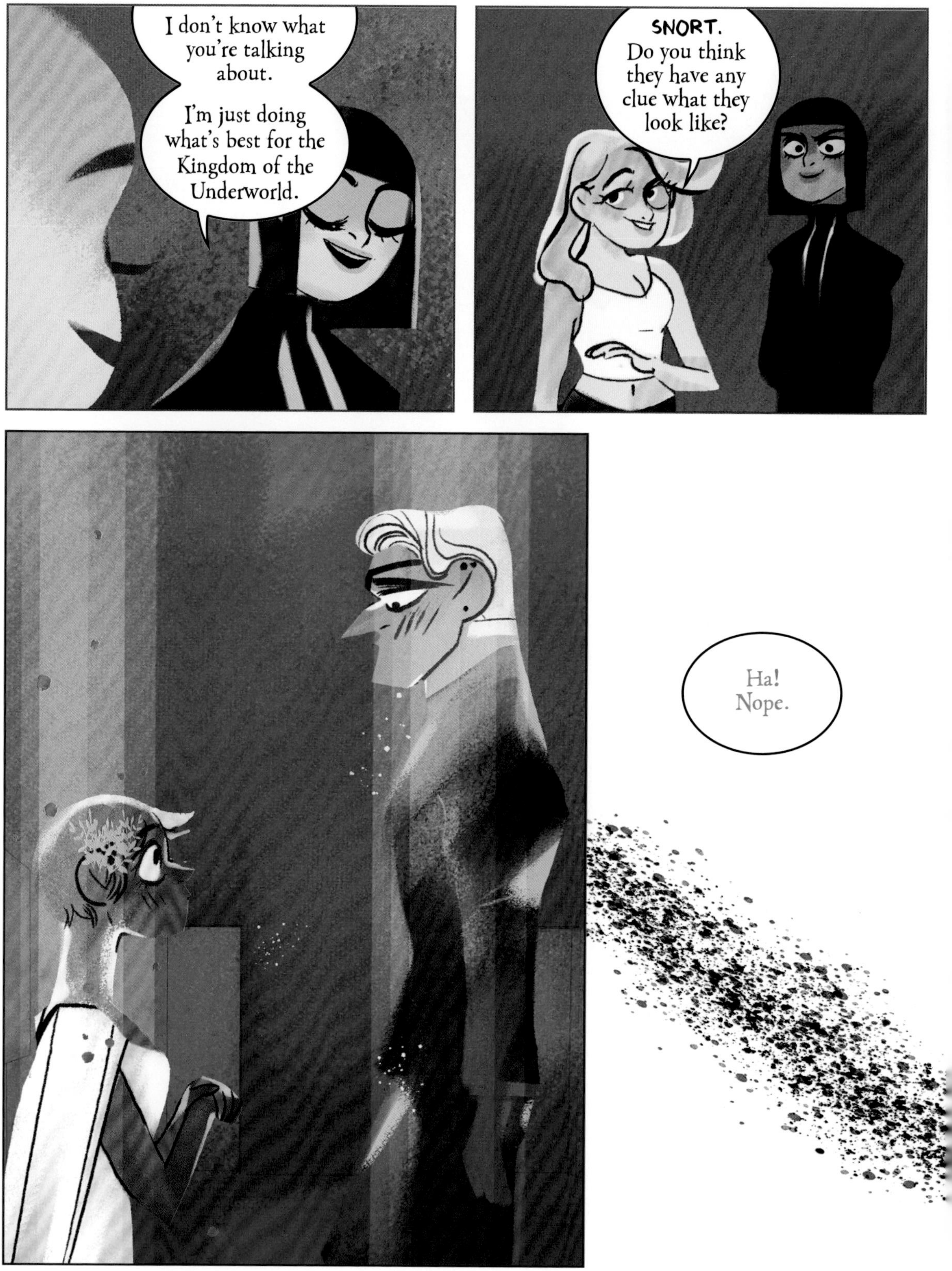
I don't know what you're talking about.
I'm just doing what's best for the Kingdom of the Underworld.
SNORT.
Do you think they have any clue what they look like?
Ha! Nope.

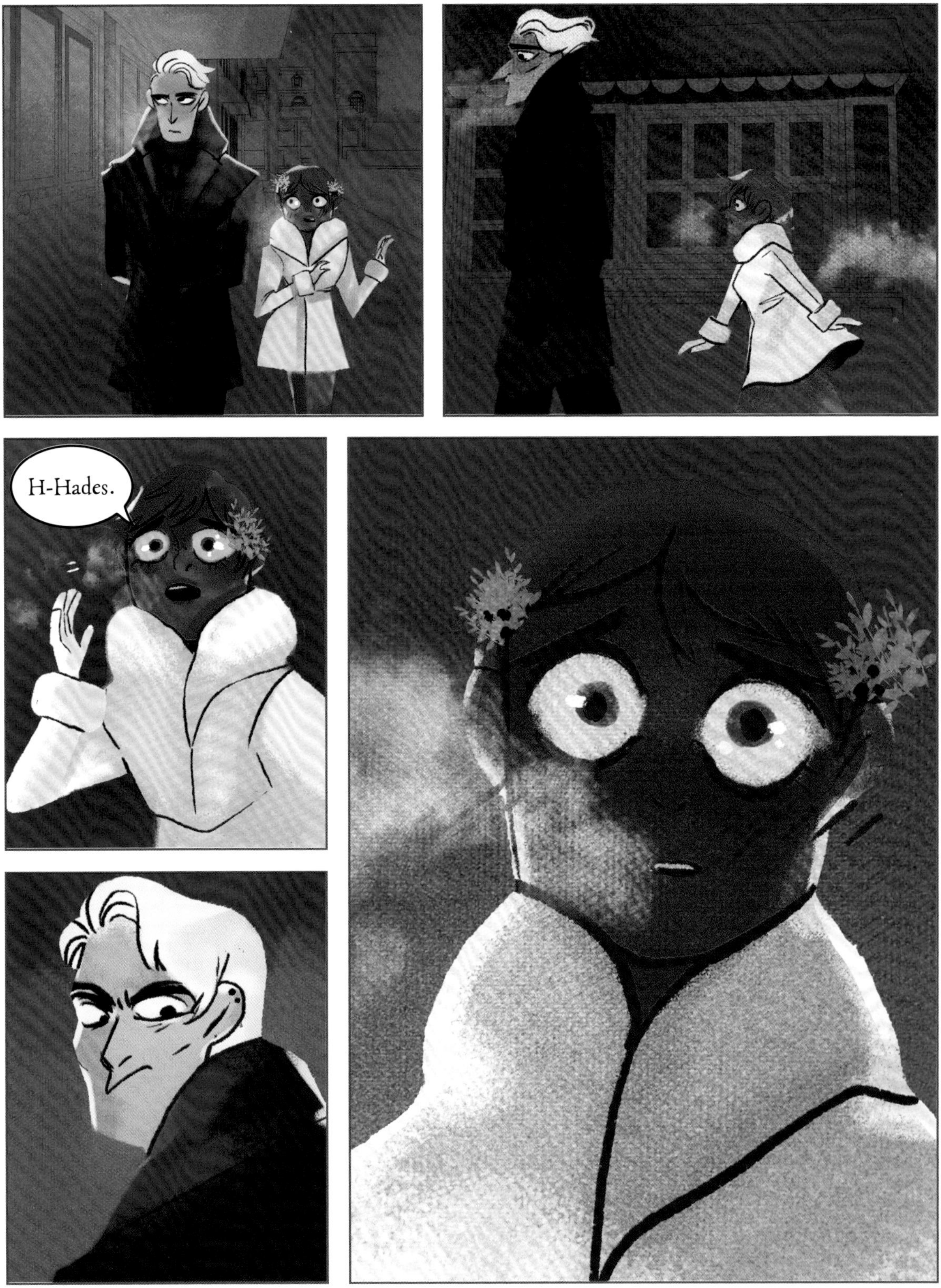
H-Hades.

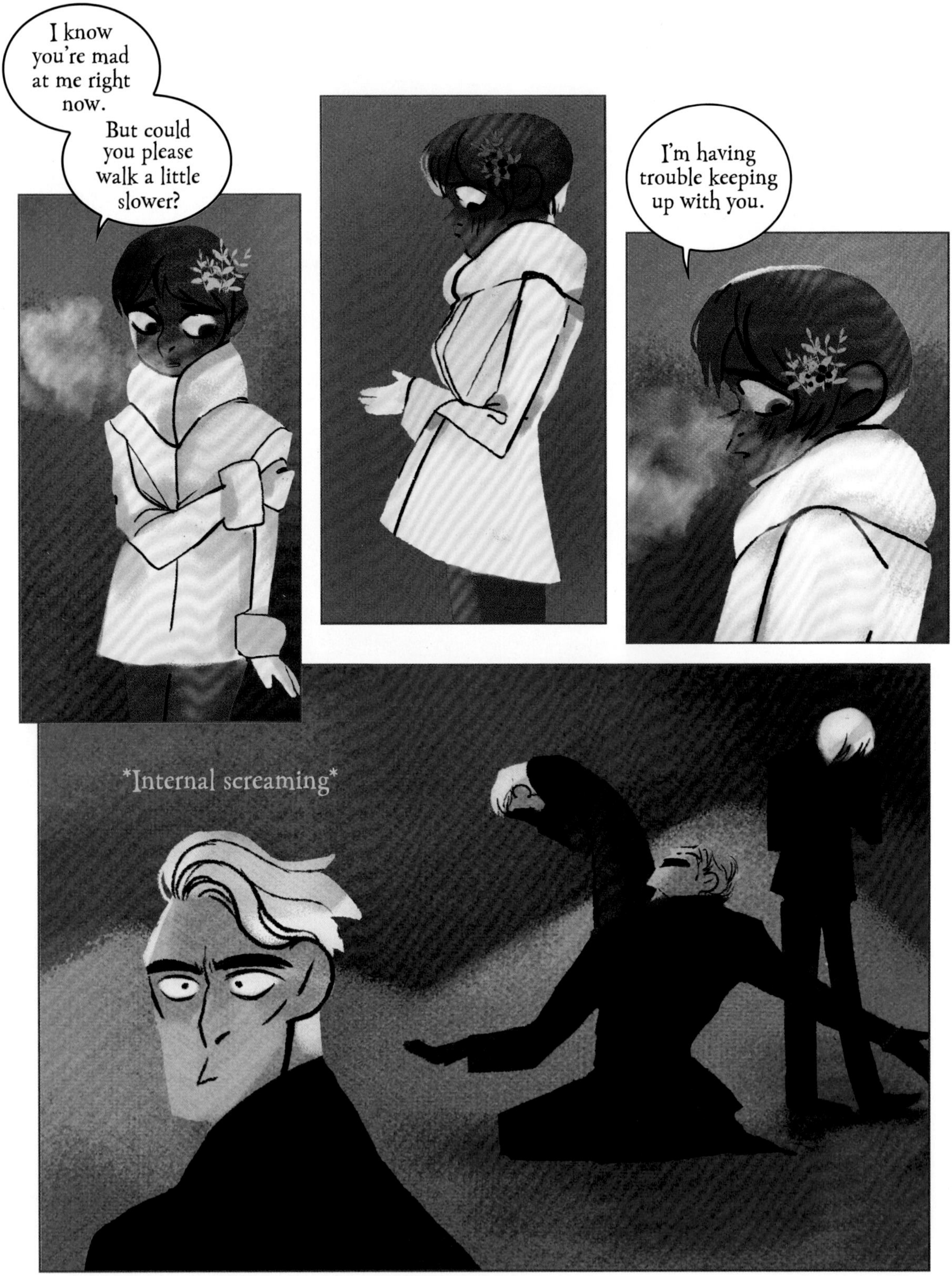
I know you're mad at me right now.
But could you please walk a little slower?
I'm having trouble keeping up with you.
Internal screaming

S-sorry about the car.

It's just been a while since I've had fun.

I know that's not an excuse. I get it if you want me to leave.

TWIST

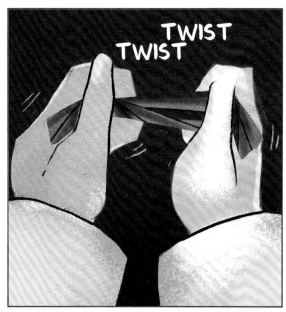

TWIST TWIST

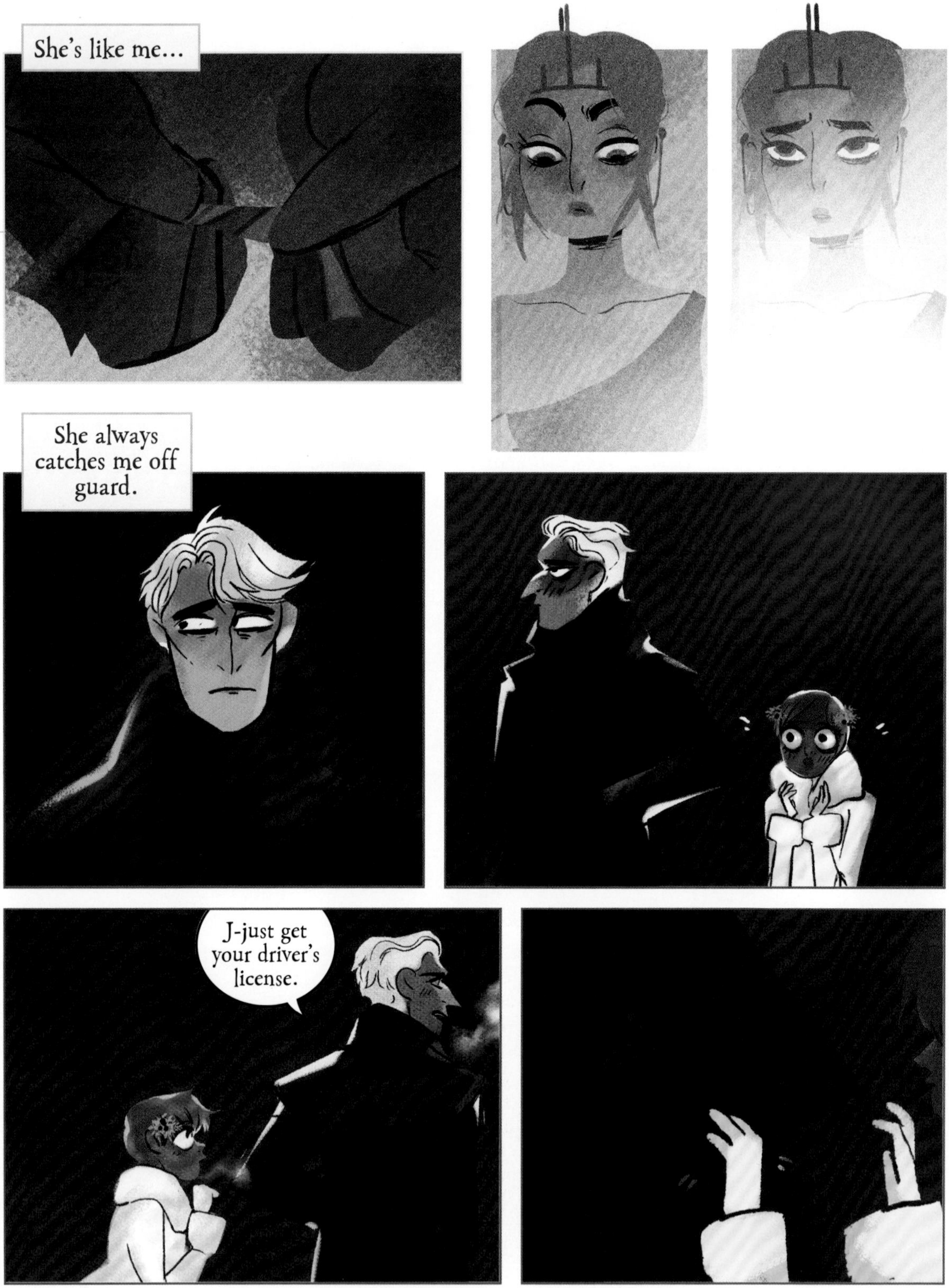
She's like me...
She always catches me off guard.
J-just get your driver's license.

I'm sorry...

...f-for walking too fast.

...That's okay.

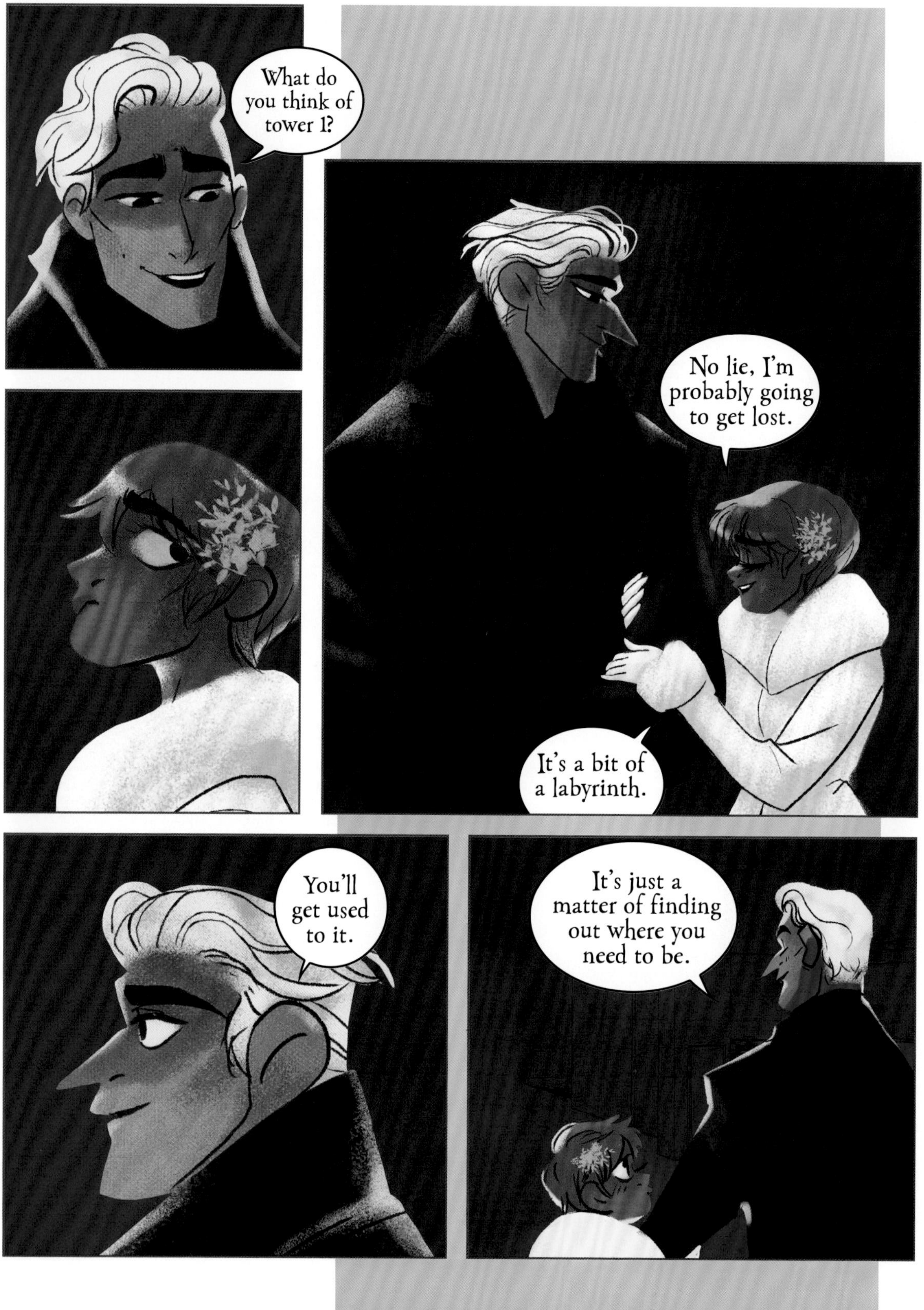
What do you think of tower 1?
No lie, I'm probably going to get lost.
It's a bit of a labyrinth.
You'll get used to it.
It's just a matter of finding out where you need to be.

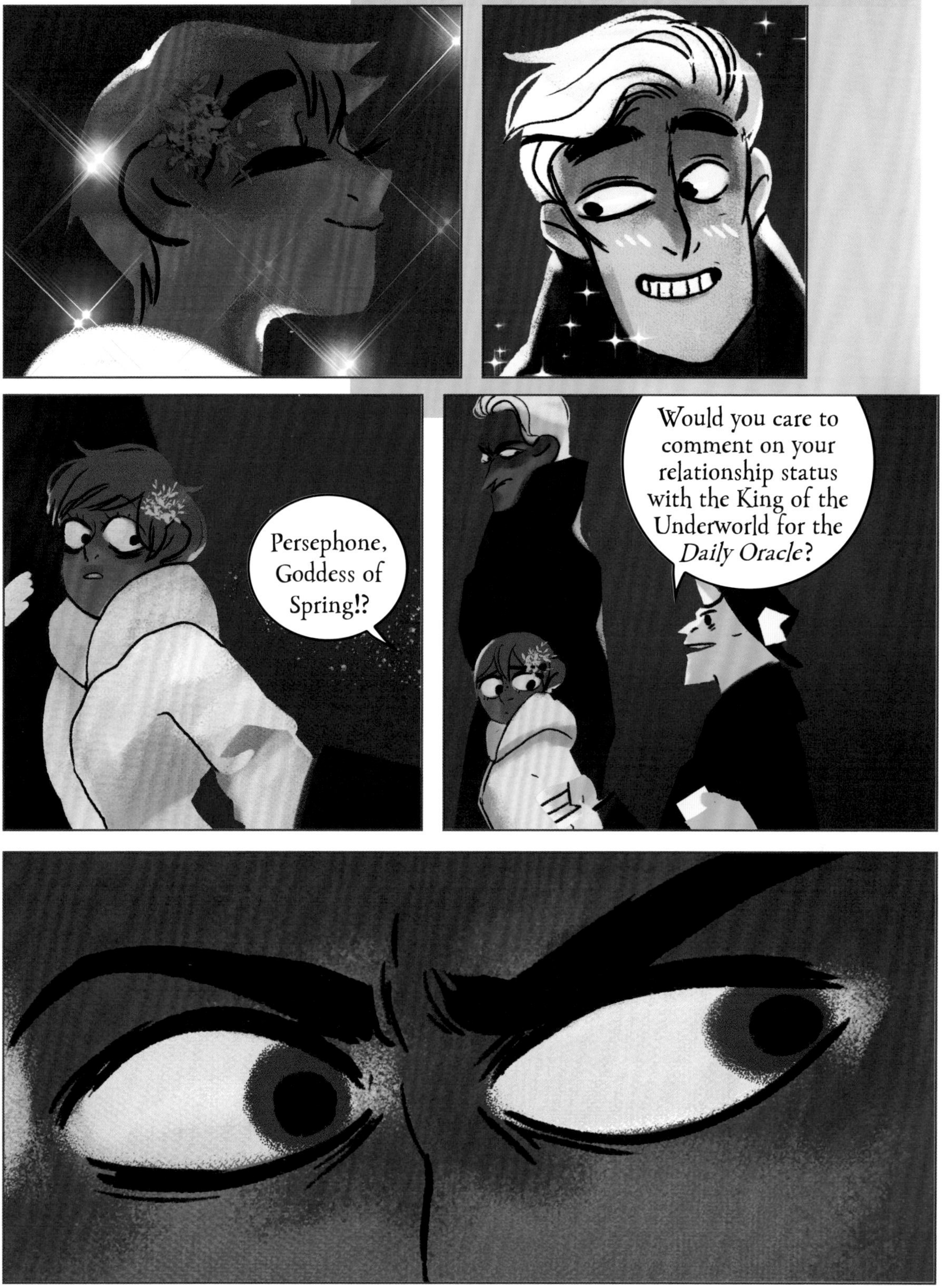
Persephone, Goddess of Spring!?
Would you care to comment on your relationship status with the King of the Underworld for the *Daily Oracle*?

EPISODE 54: THE TOUR (PART 2)

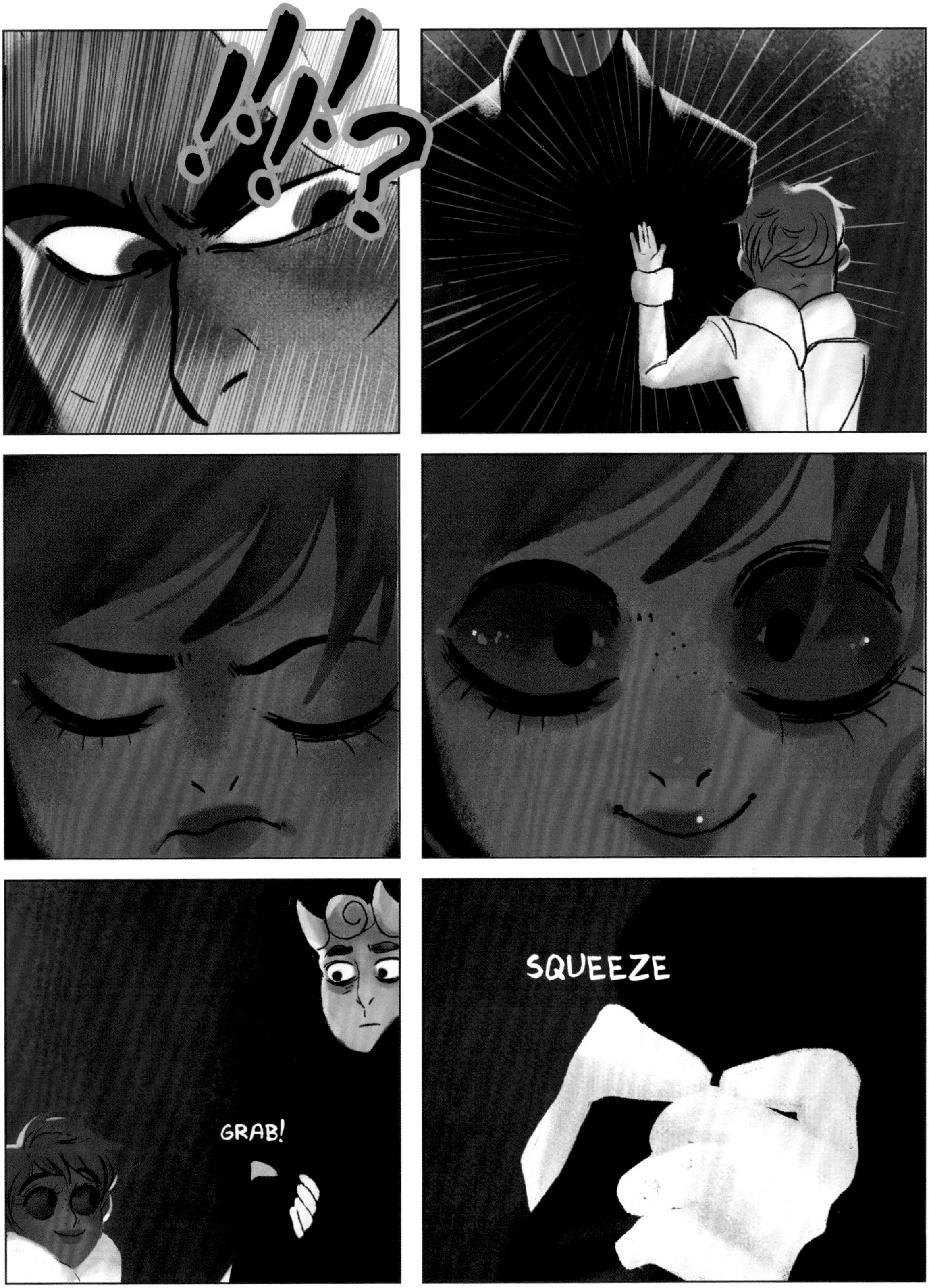
!!?
GRAB!
SQUEEZE

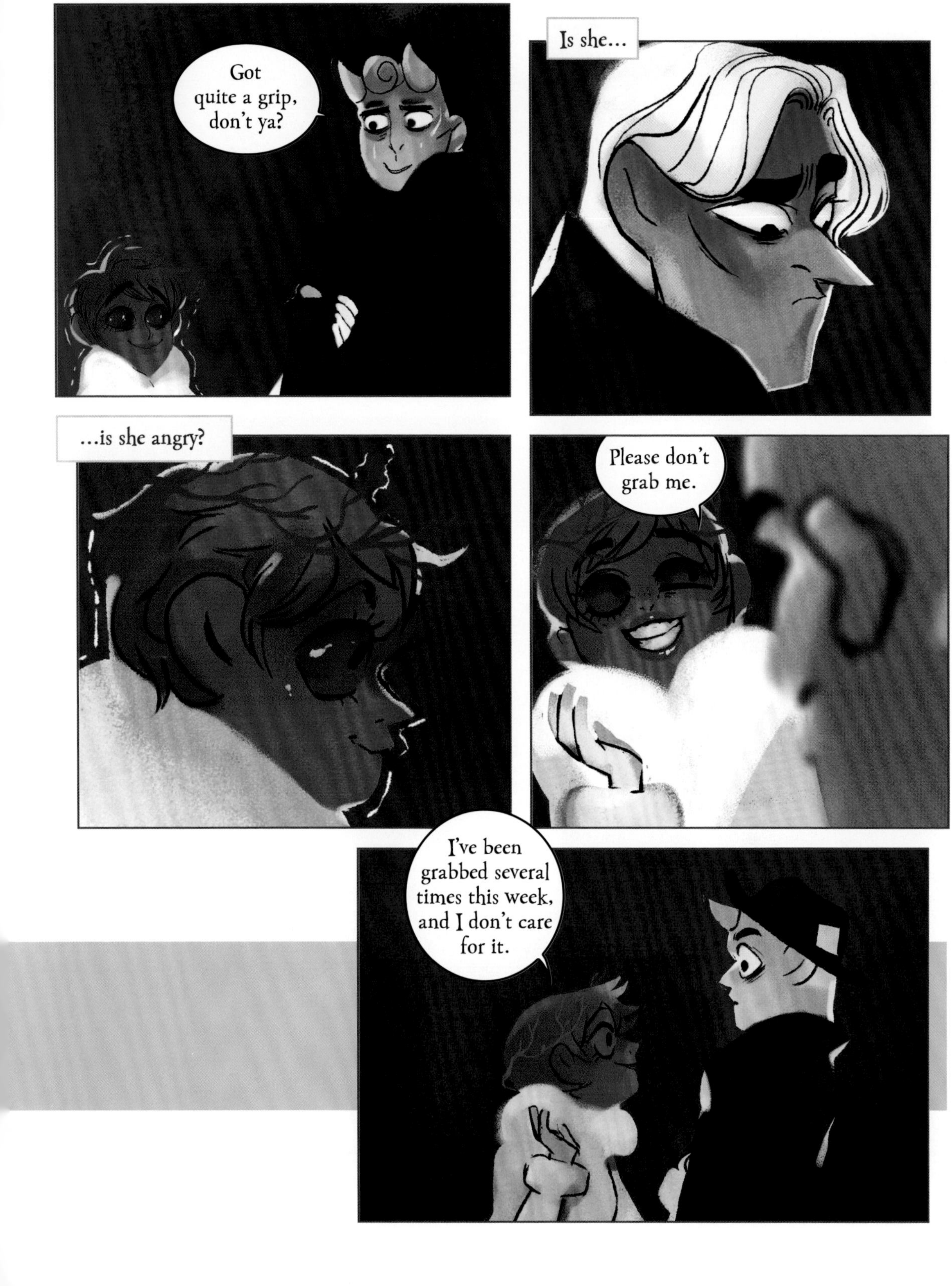

Got quite a grip, don't ya?
Is she...
...is she angry?
Please don't grab me.
I've been grabbed several times this week, and I don't care for it.

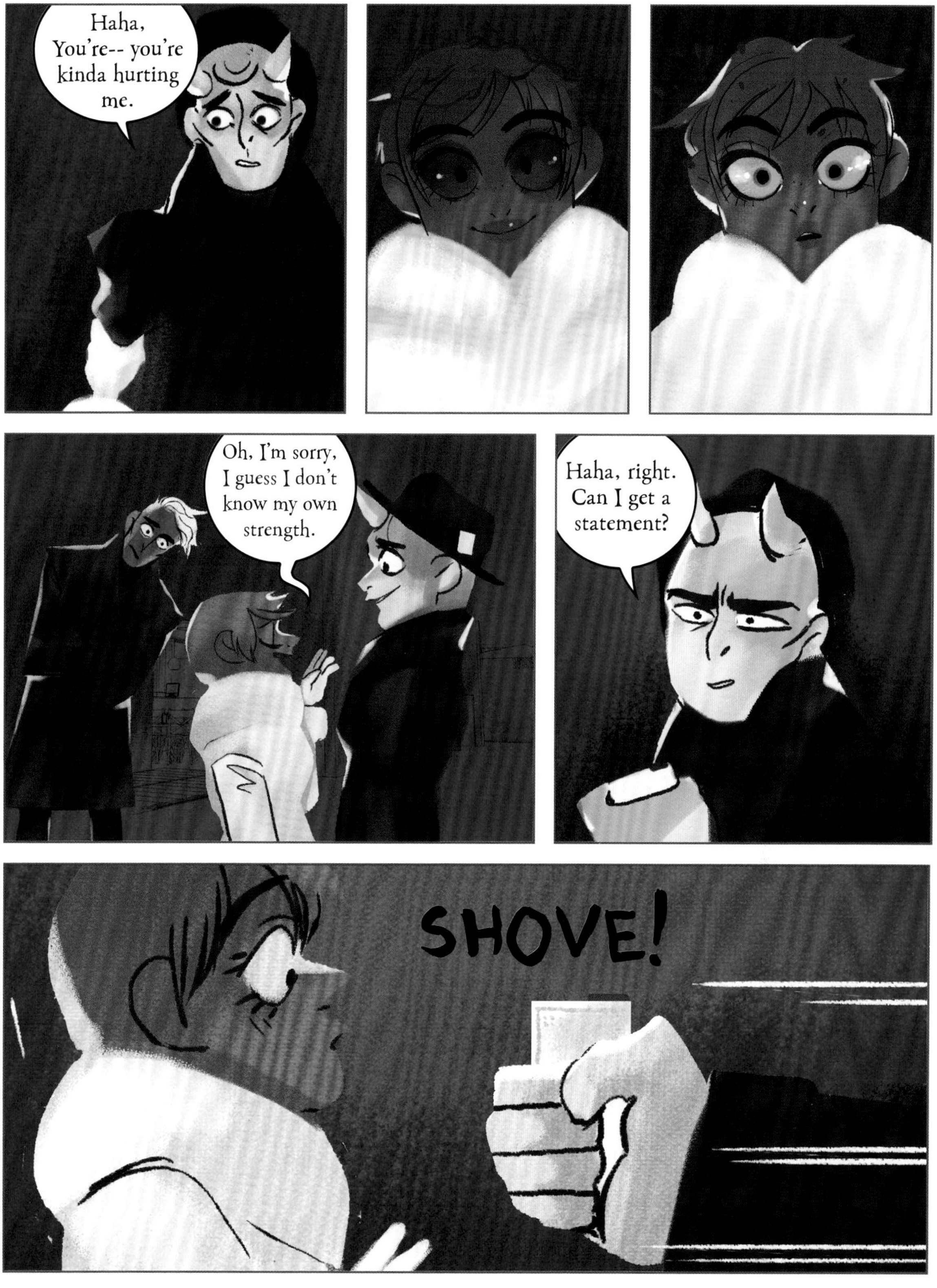
Haha, You're-- you're kinda hurting me.
Oh, I'm sorry, I guess I don't know my own strength.
Haha, right. Can I get a statement?
SHOVE!

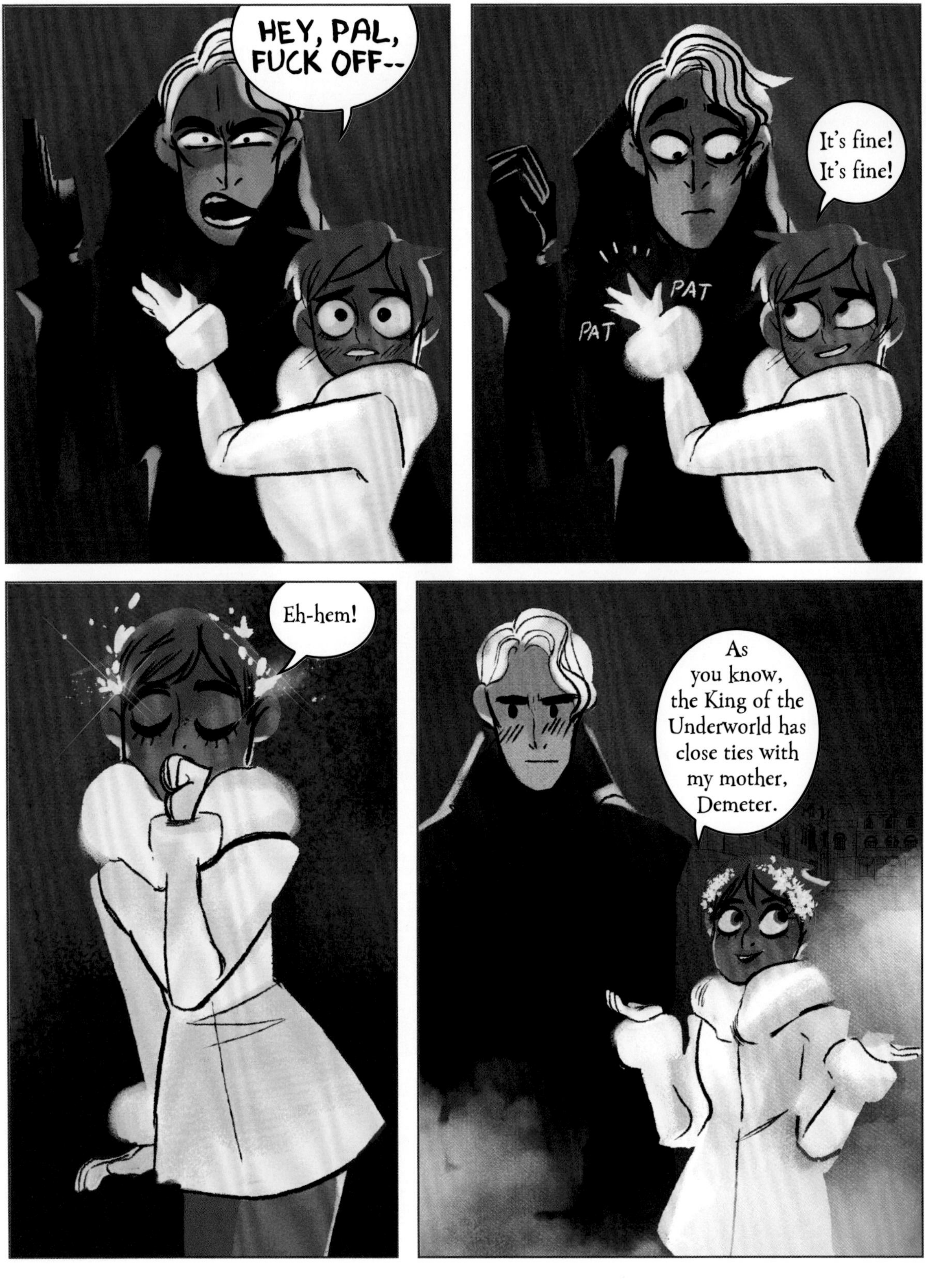
HEY, PAL, FUCK OFF--
It's fine! It's fine!
PAT
PAT
Eh-hem!
As you know, the King of the Underworld has close ties with my mother, Demeter.

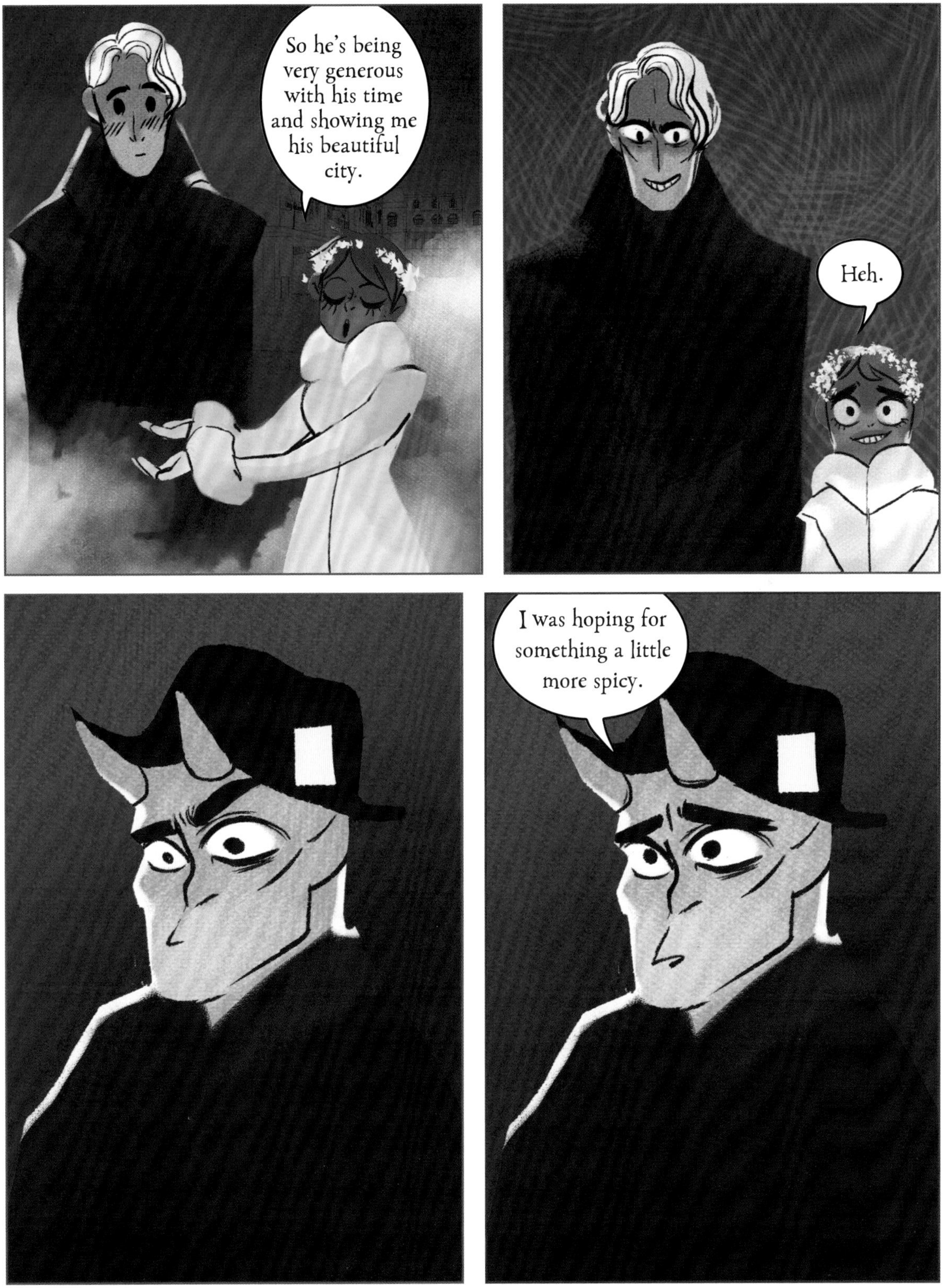
So he's being very generous with his time and showing me his beautiful city.
Heh.
I was hoping for something a little more spicy.

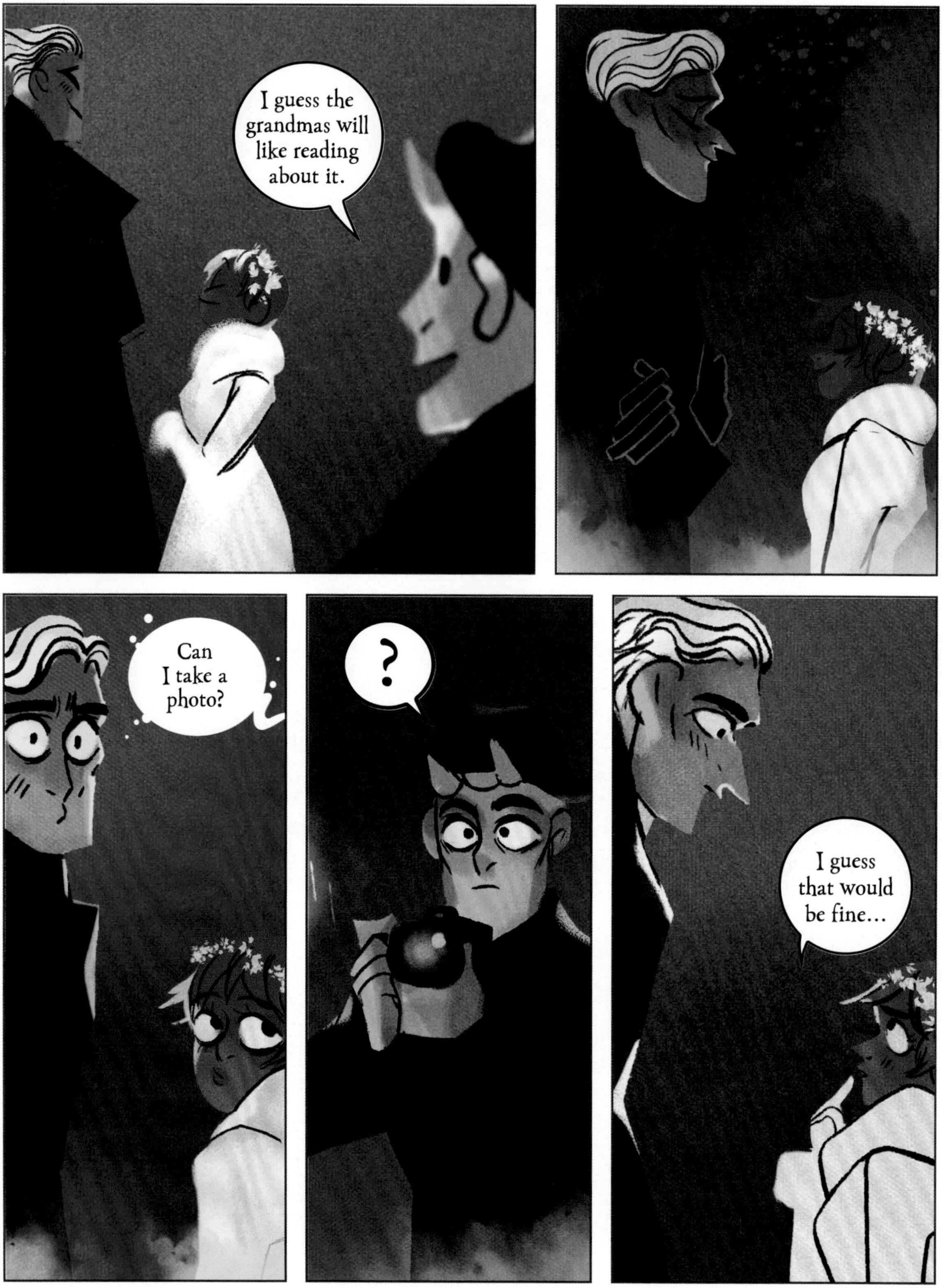
I guess the grandmas will like reading about it.
Can I take a photo?
?
I guess that would be fine...

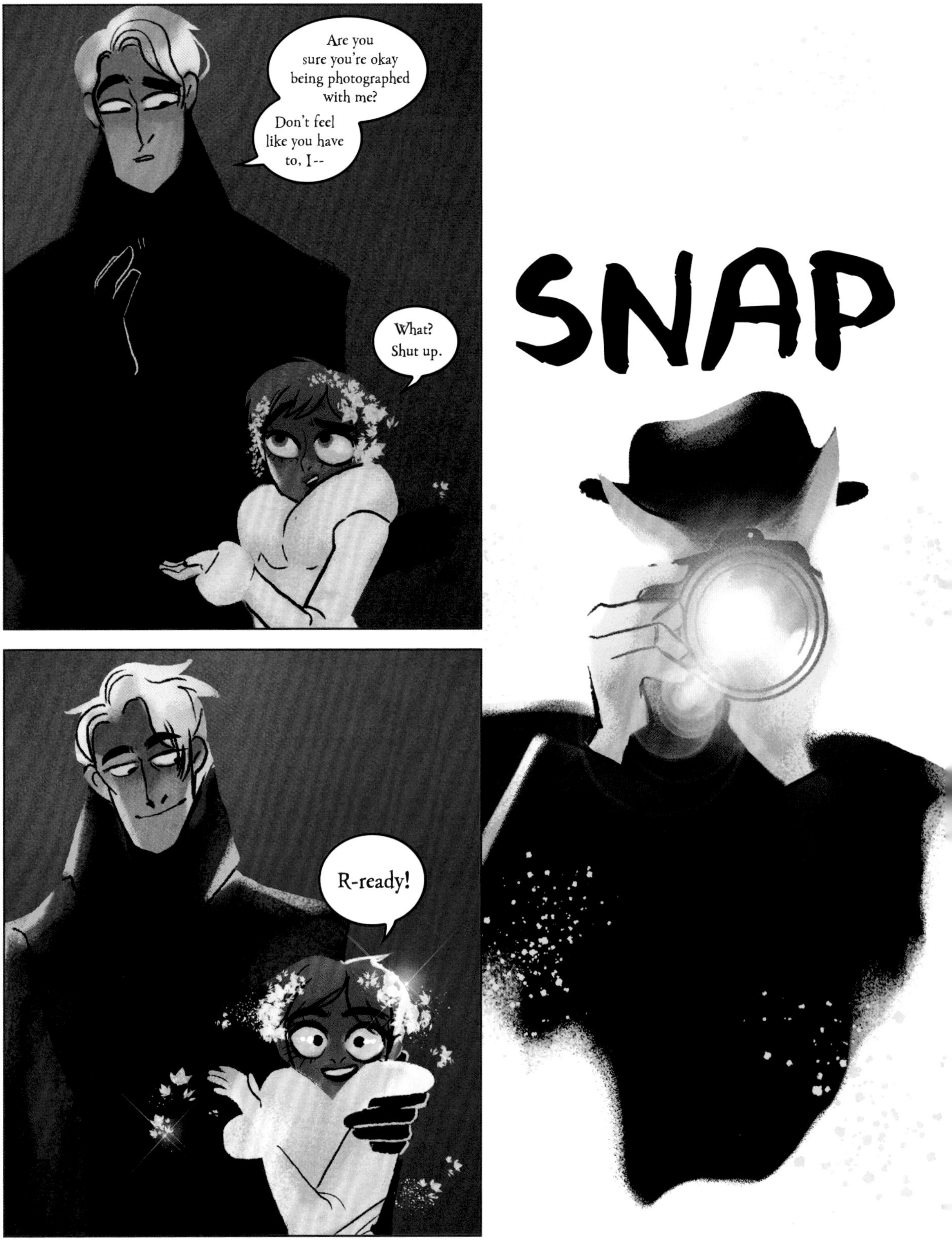
Are you sure you're okay being photographed with me?
Don't feel like you have to, I--
What? Shut up.
R-ready!
SNAP

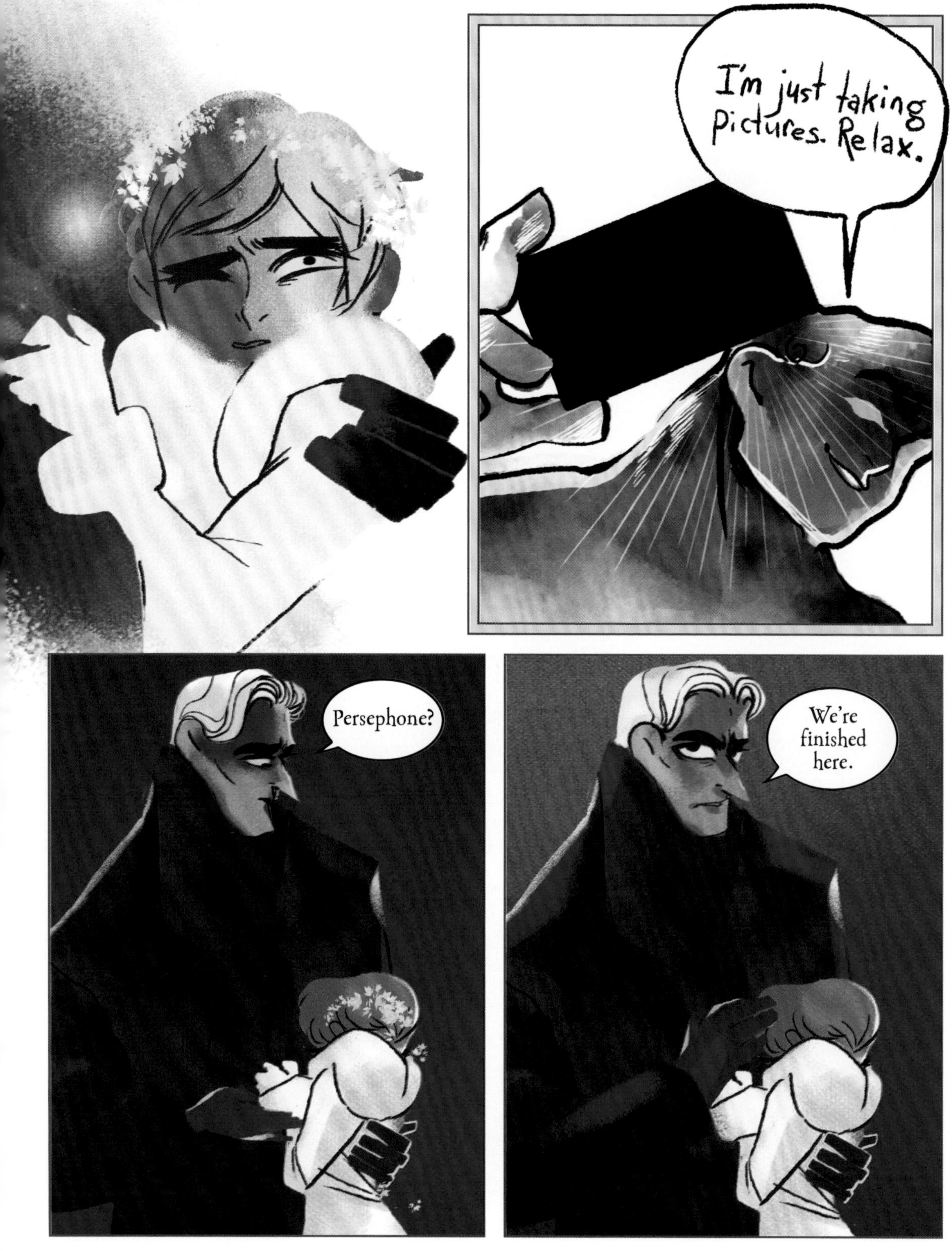
I'm just taking pictures. Relax.
Persephone?
We're finished here.

GONE

Weird.

S-sorry! The flash just made me dizzy.

Dizzy? Do you want to go home?

I'm fine. Just embarrassed. Really.

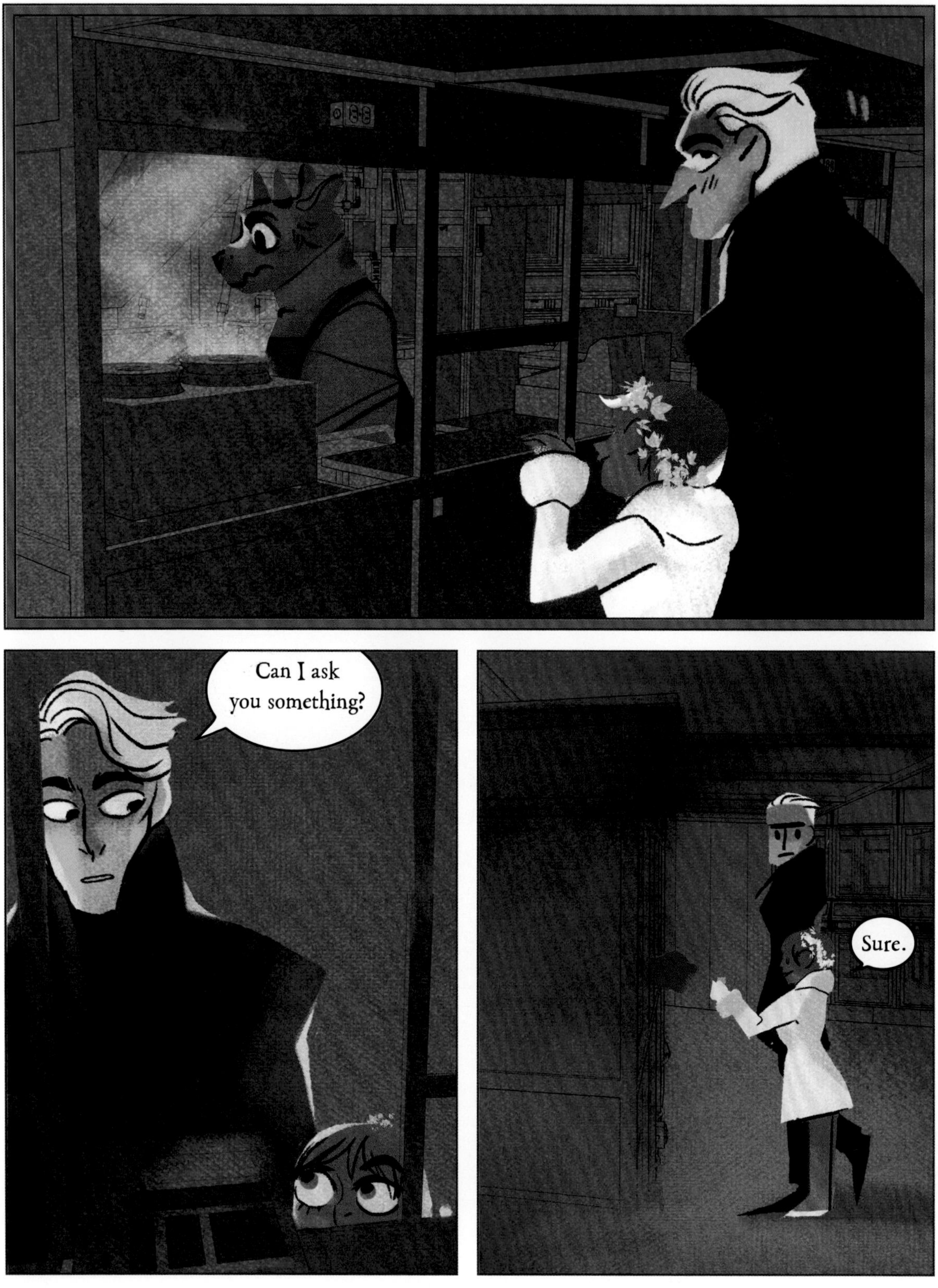
Can I ask you something?
Sure.

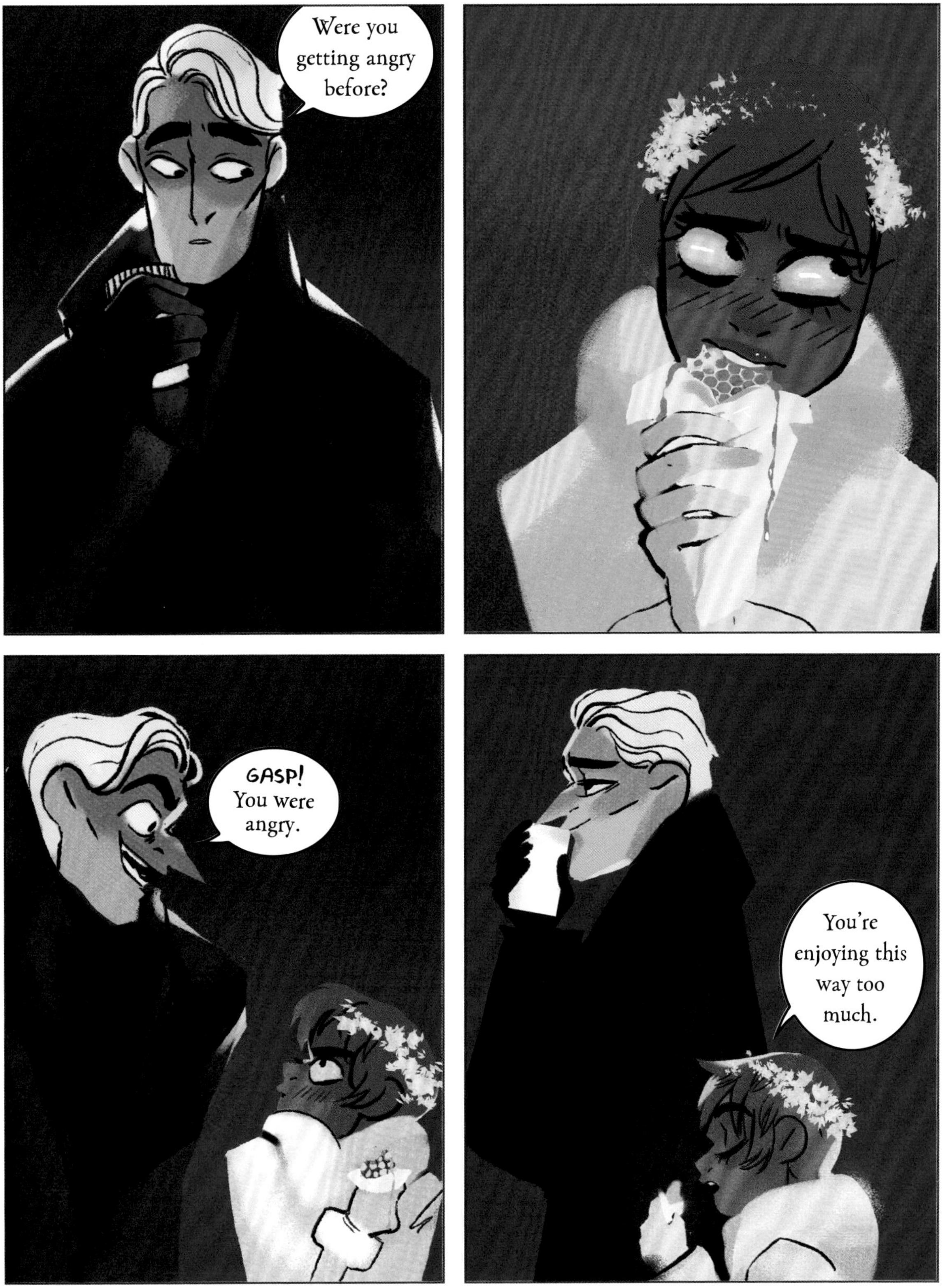
Were you getting angry before?
GASP! You were angry.
You're enjoying this way too much.

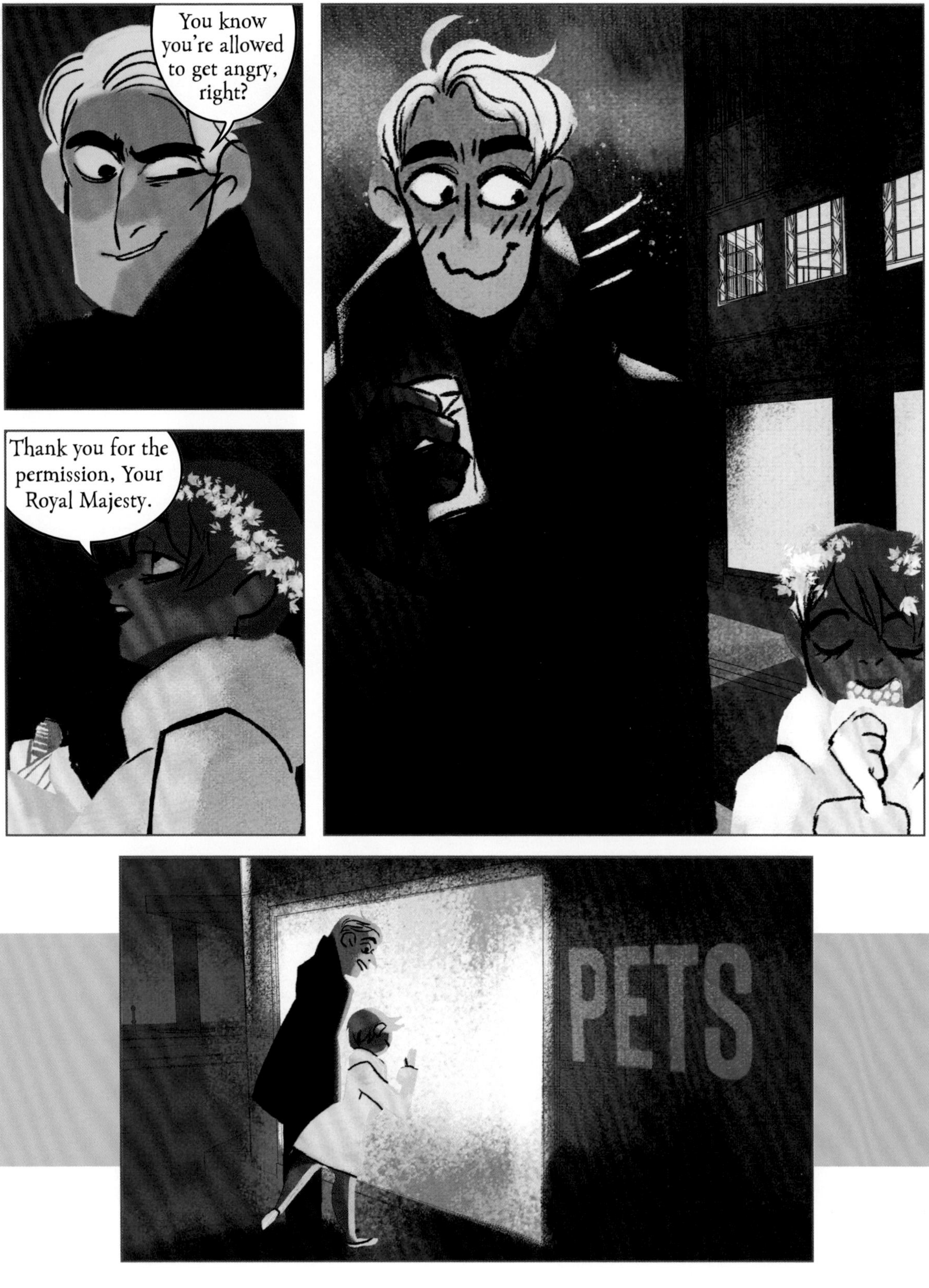
You know you're allowed to get angry, right?
Thank you for the permission, Your Royal Majesty.
PETS

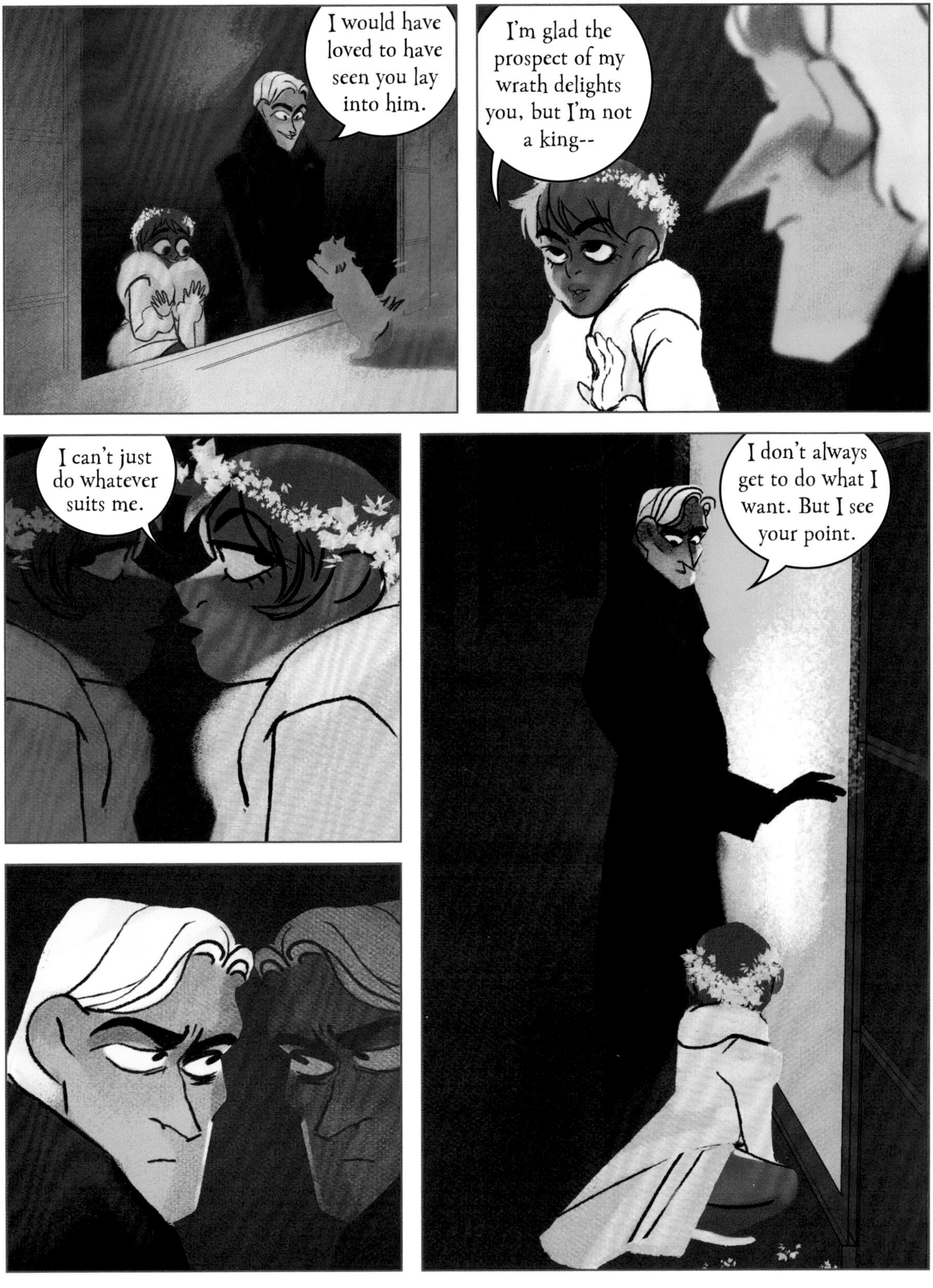
I would have loved to have seen you lay into him.
I'm glad the prospect of my wrath delights you, but I'm not a king--
I can't just do whatever suits me.
I don't always get to do what I want. But I see your point.

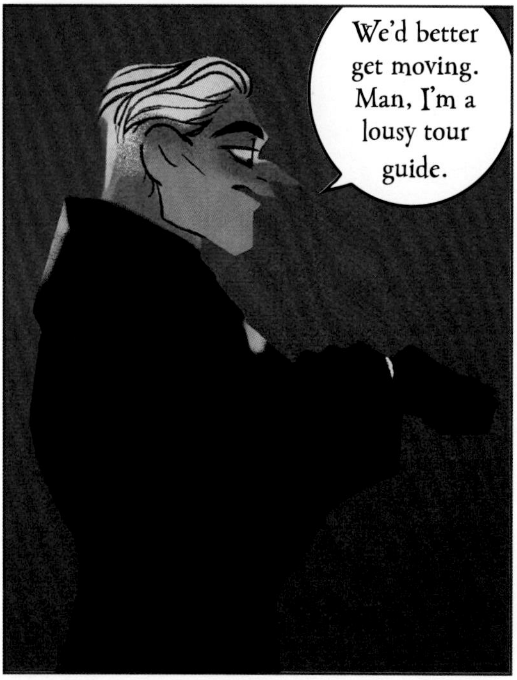
We'd better get moving. Man, I'm a lousy tour guide.

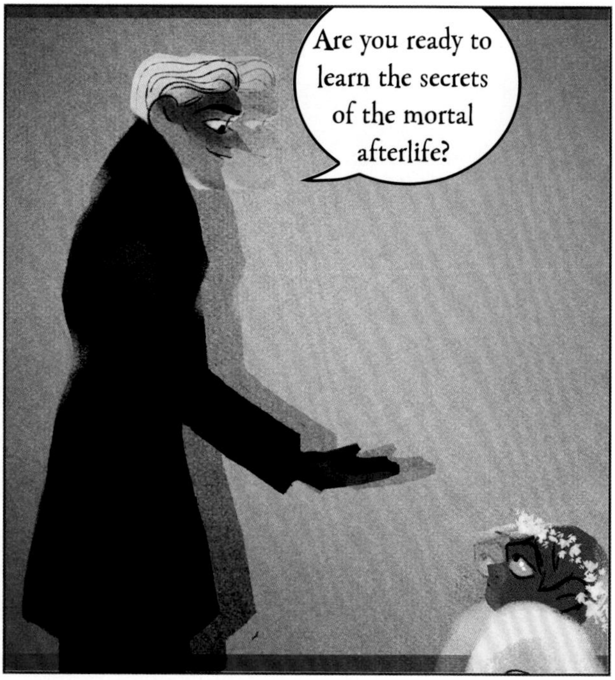
Are you ready to learn the secrets of the mortal afterlife?

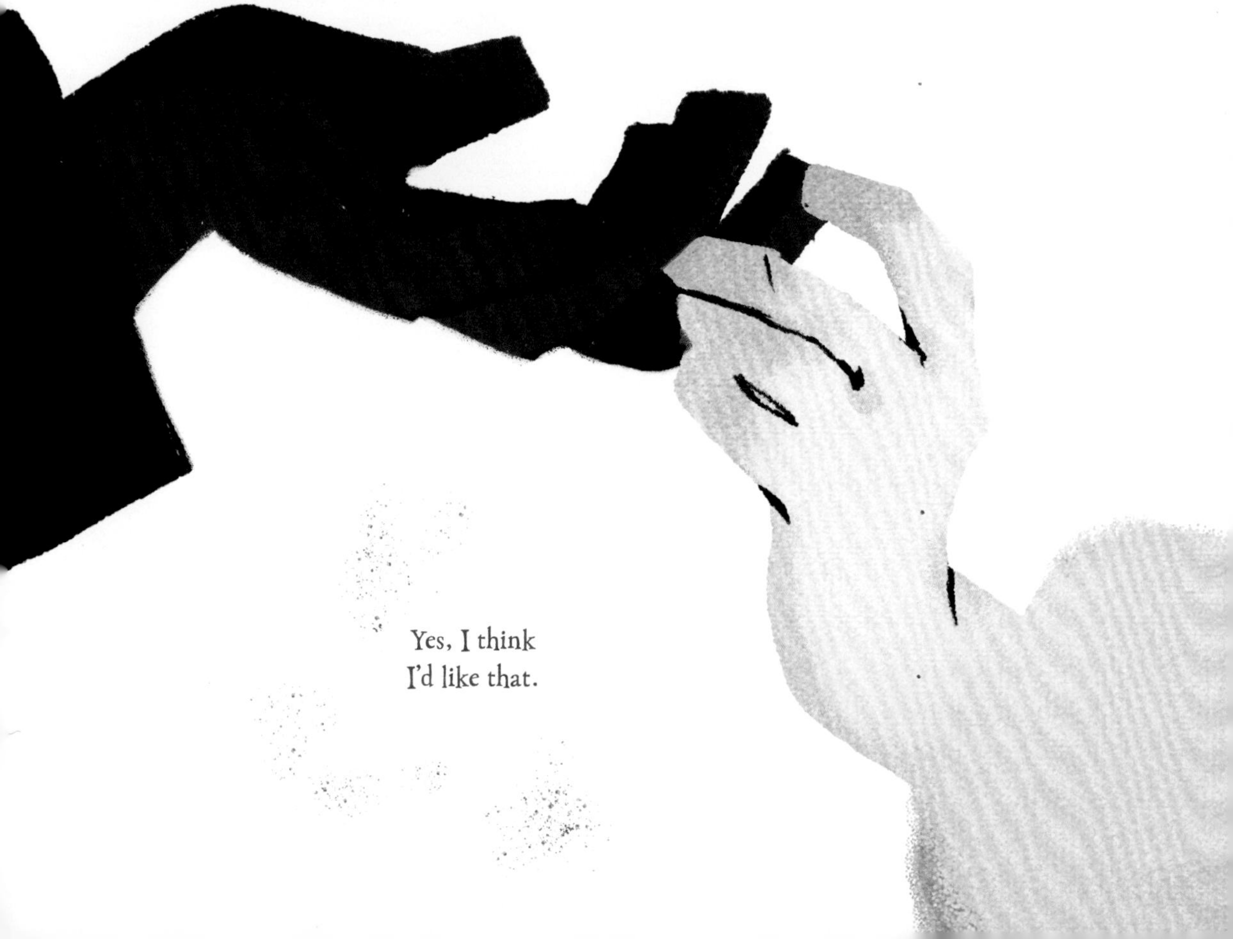
Yes, I think I'd like that.

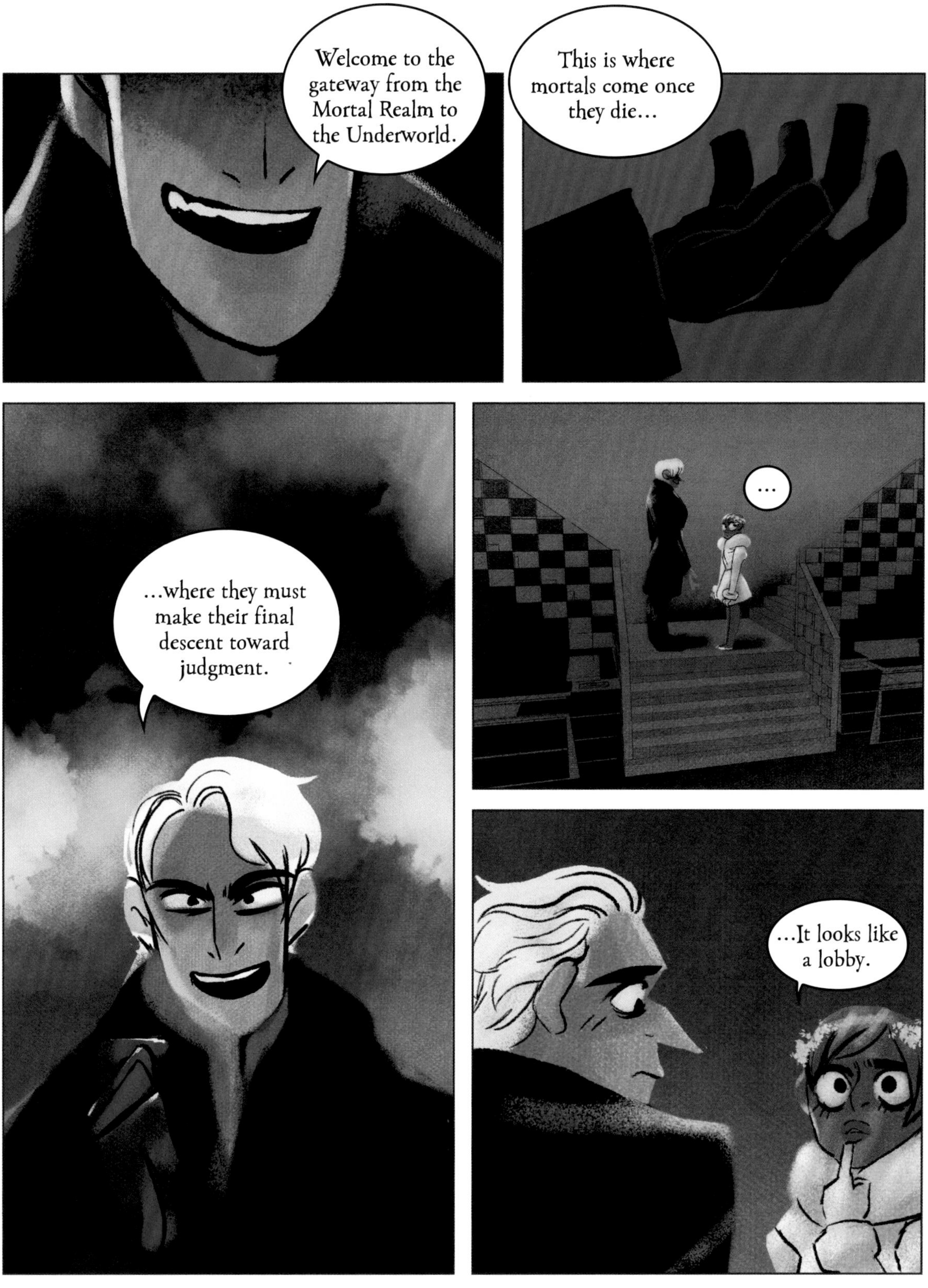
Welcome to the gateway from the Mortal Realm to the Underworld.
This is where mortals come once they die...
...where they must make their final descent toward judgment.
...
...It looks like a lobby.

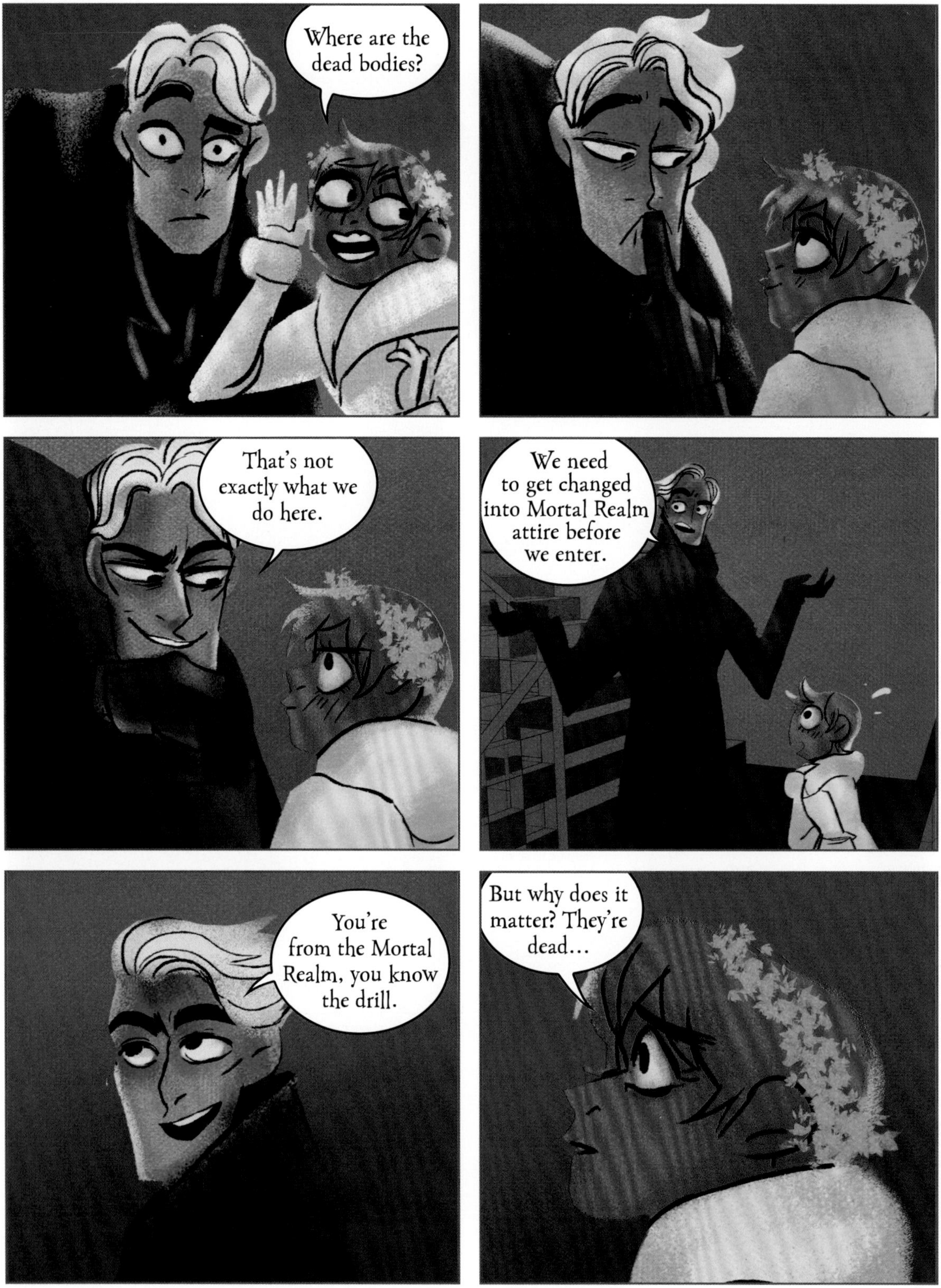
Where are the dead bodies?
That's not exactly what we do here.
We need to get changed into Mortal Realm attire before we enter.
You're from the Mortal Realm, you know the drill.
But why does it matter? They're dead...

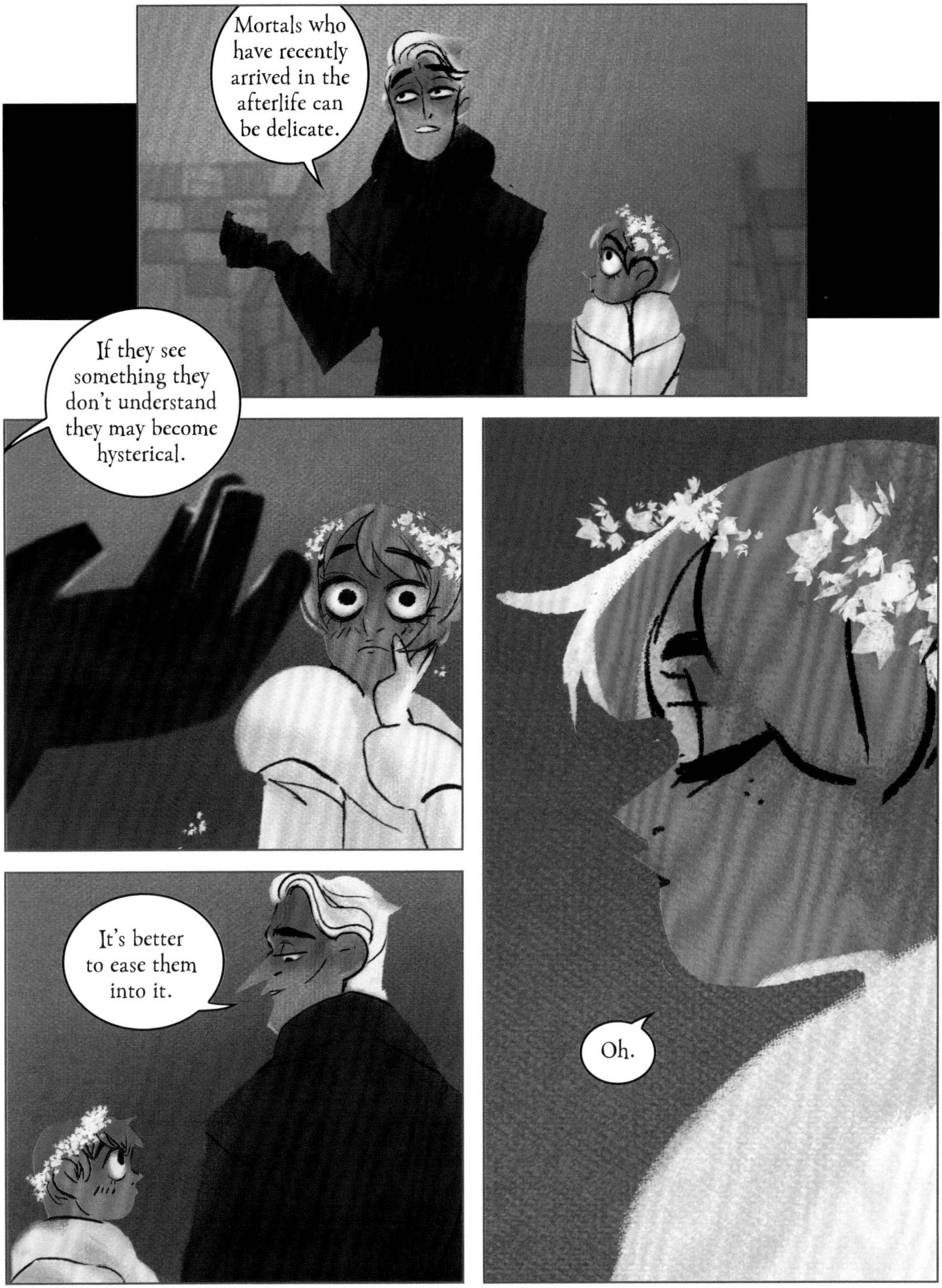
Mortals who have recently arrived in the afterlife can be delicate.
If they see something they don't understand they may become hysterical.
It's better to ease them into it.
Oh.

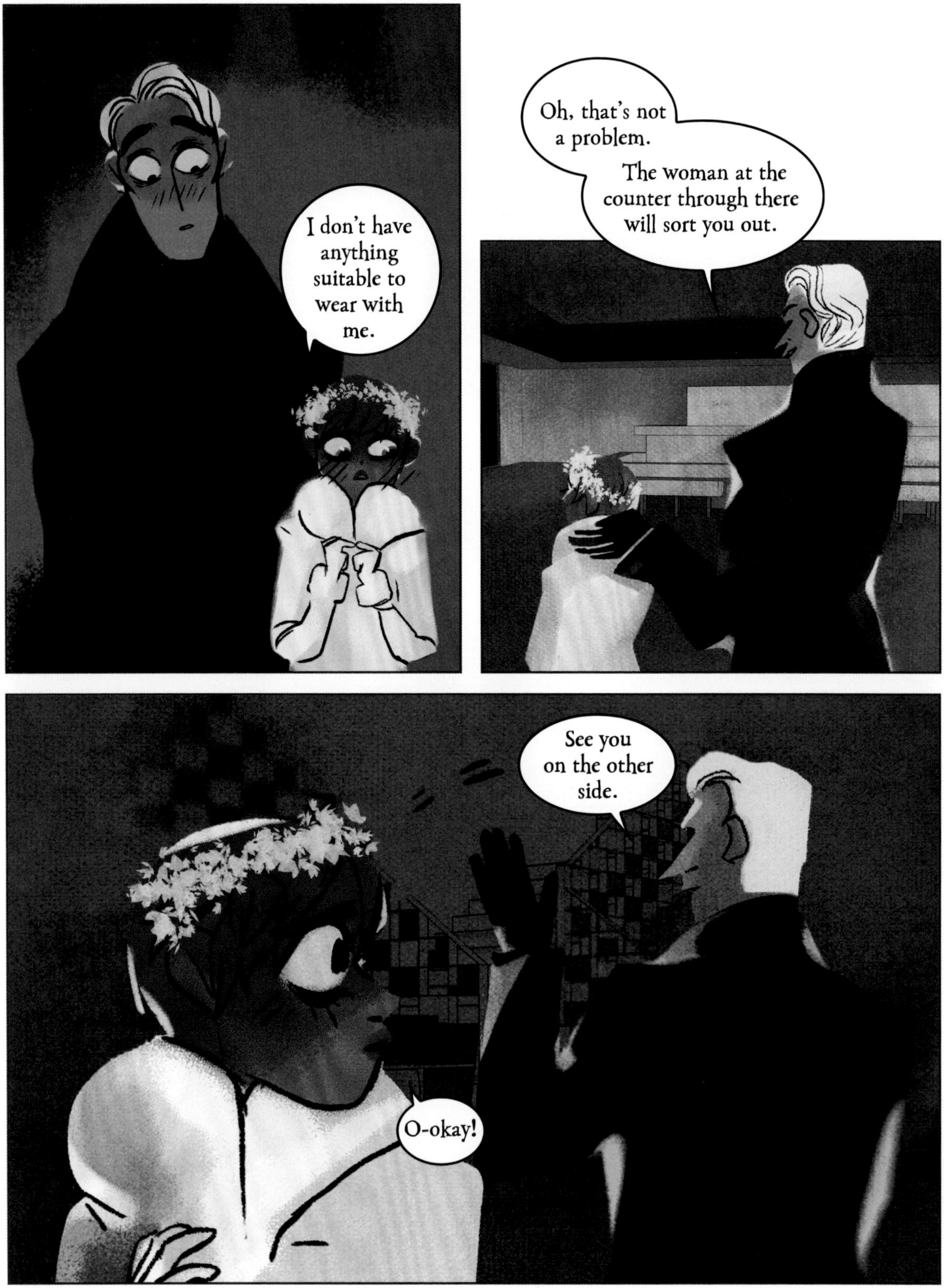
I don't have anything suitable to wear with me.
Oh, that's not a problem.
The woman at the counter through there will sort you out.
See you on the other side.
O-okay!

EPISODE 55: THE TOUR (PART 3)

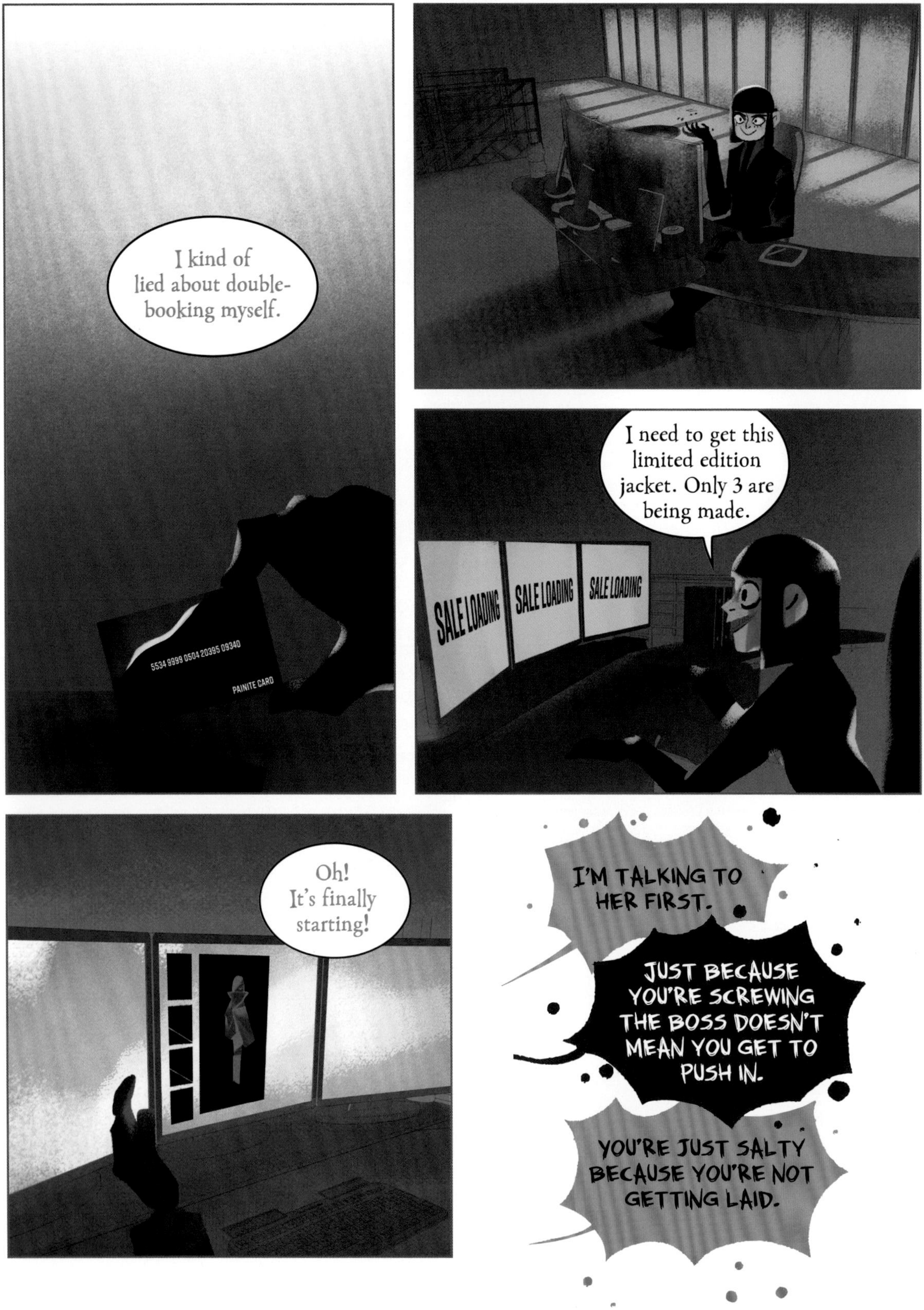

I kind of lied about double-booking myself.
5534 9999 0504 20395 09340
PAINITE CARD
I need to get this limited edition jacket. Only 3 are being made.
SALE LOADING
SALE LOADING
SALE LOADING
Oh! It's finally starting!
I'M TALKING TO HER FIRST.
JUST BECAUSE YOU'RE SCREWING THE BOSS DOESN'T MEAN YOU GET TO PUSH IN.
YOU'RE JUST SALTY BECAUSE YOU'RE NOT GETTING LAID.

Please, Gaia, not the brats.

CAN YOU PLEASE EXPLAIN TO ME WHY THAT LITTLE PINK BIMBO IS NOW EMPLOYED HERE!?

And why does Hades have to show her around?

EM OUT OF STOCK   ITEM OUT OF STOCK   ITEM O OF STO

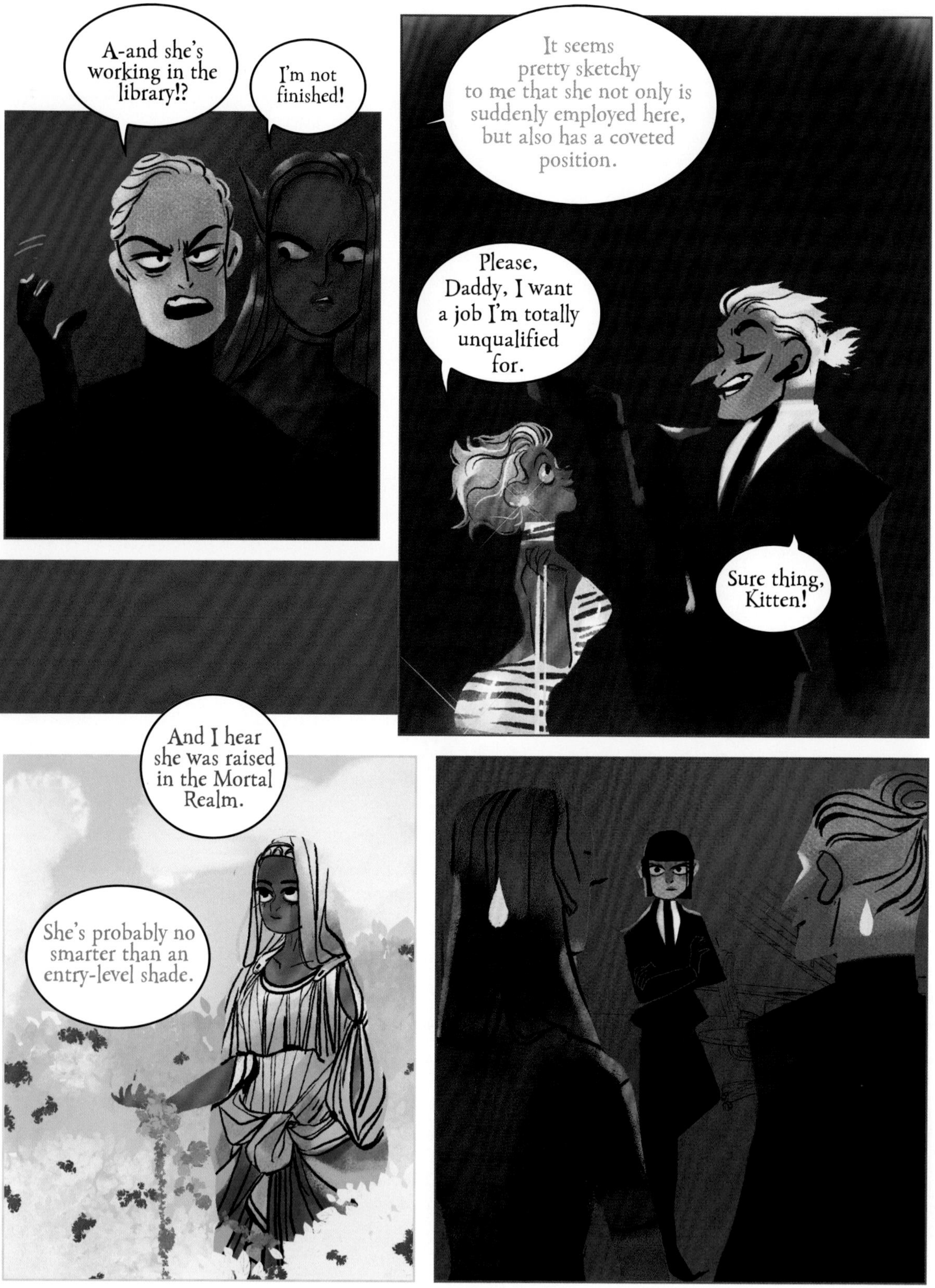
A-and she's working in the library!?
I'm not finished!
It seems pretty sketchy to me that she not only is suddenly employed here, but also has a coveted position.
Please, Daddy, I want a job I'm totally unqualified for.
Sure thing, Kitten!
And I hear she was raised in the Mortal Realm.
She's probably no smarter than an entry-level shade.

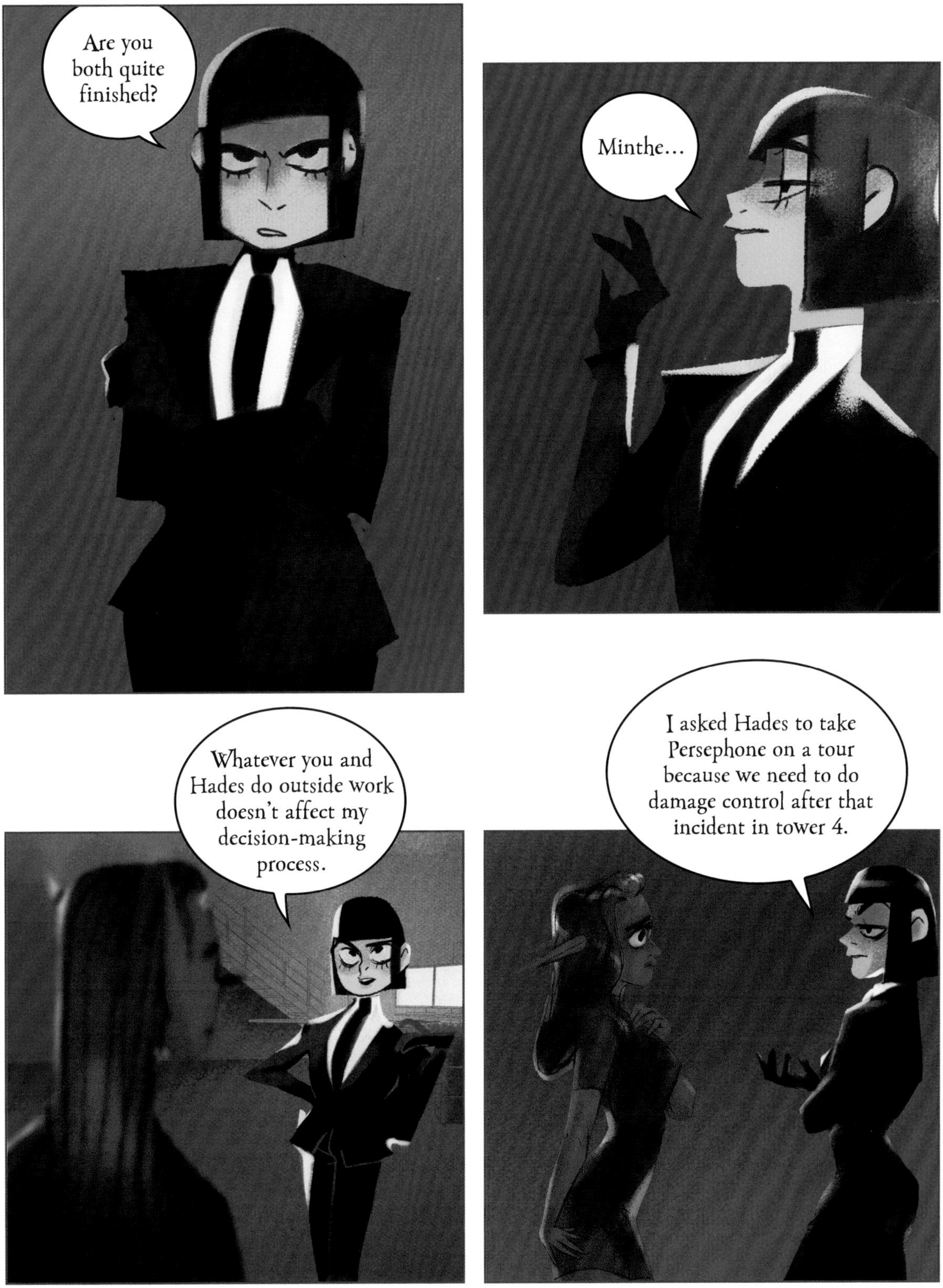
Are you both quite finished?
Minthe...
Whatever you and Hades do outside work doesn't affect my decision-making process.
I asked Hades to take Persephone on a tour because we need to do damage control after that incident in tower 4.

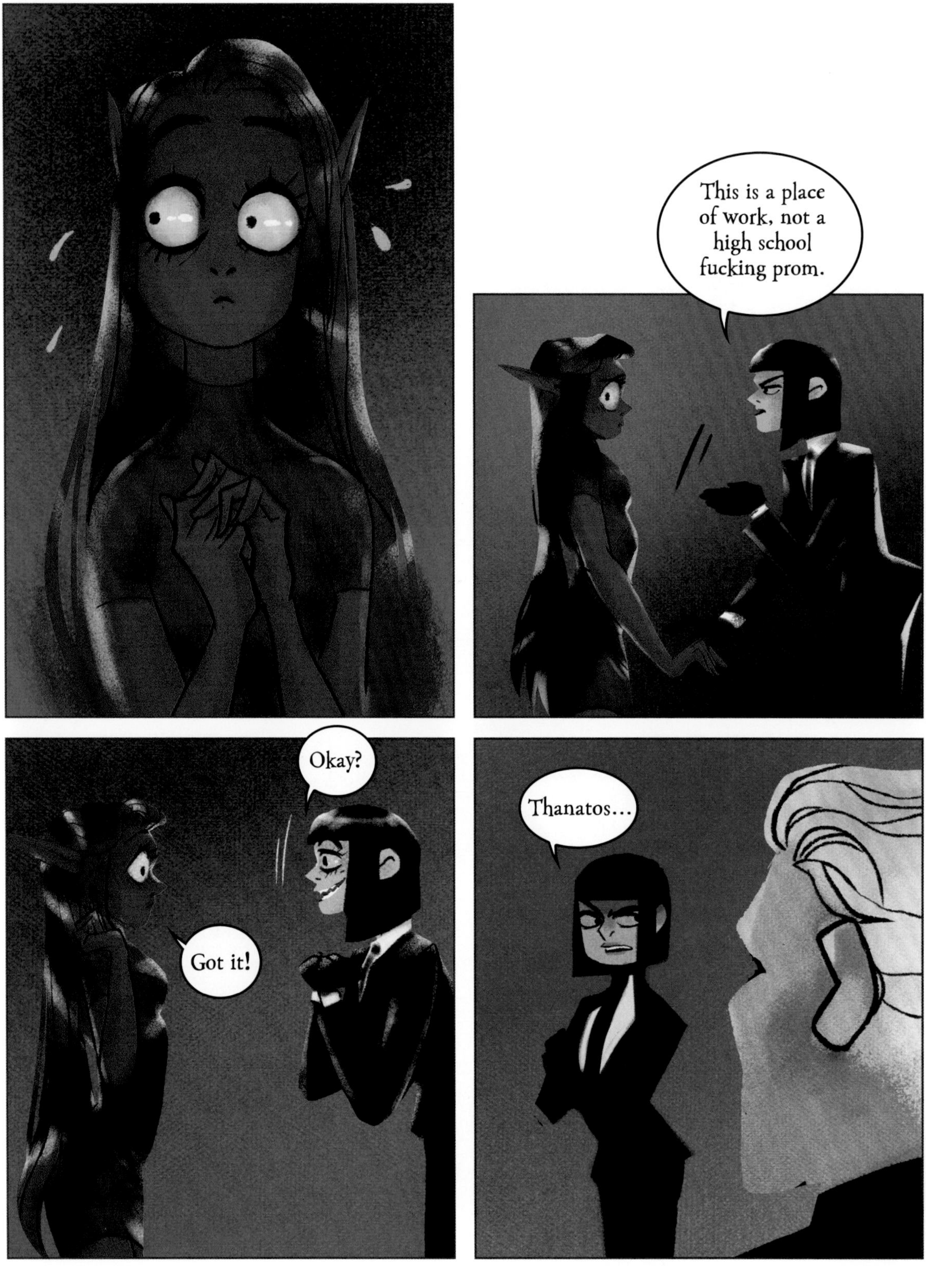
This is a place of work, not a high school fucking prom.
Okay?
Got it!
Thanatos...

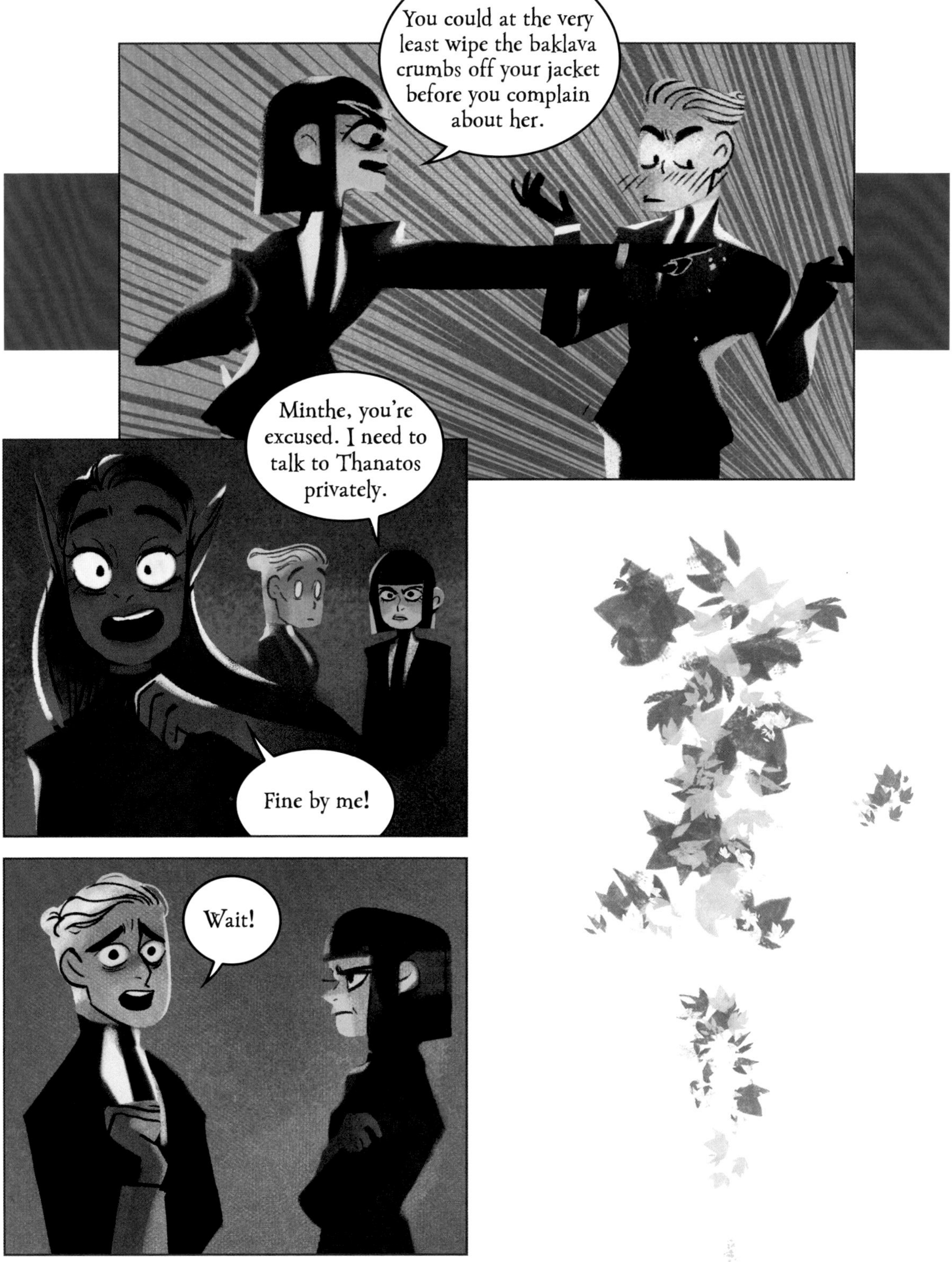
You could at the very least wipe the baklava crumbs off your jacket before you complain about her.
Minthe, you're excused. I need to talk to Thanatos privately.
Fine by me!
Wait!

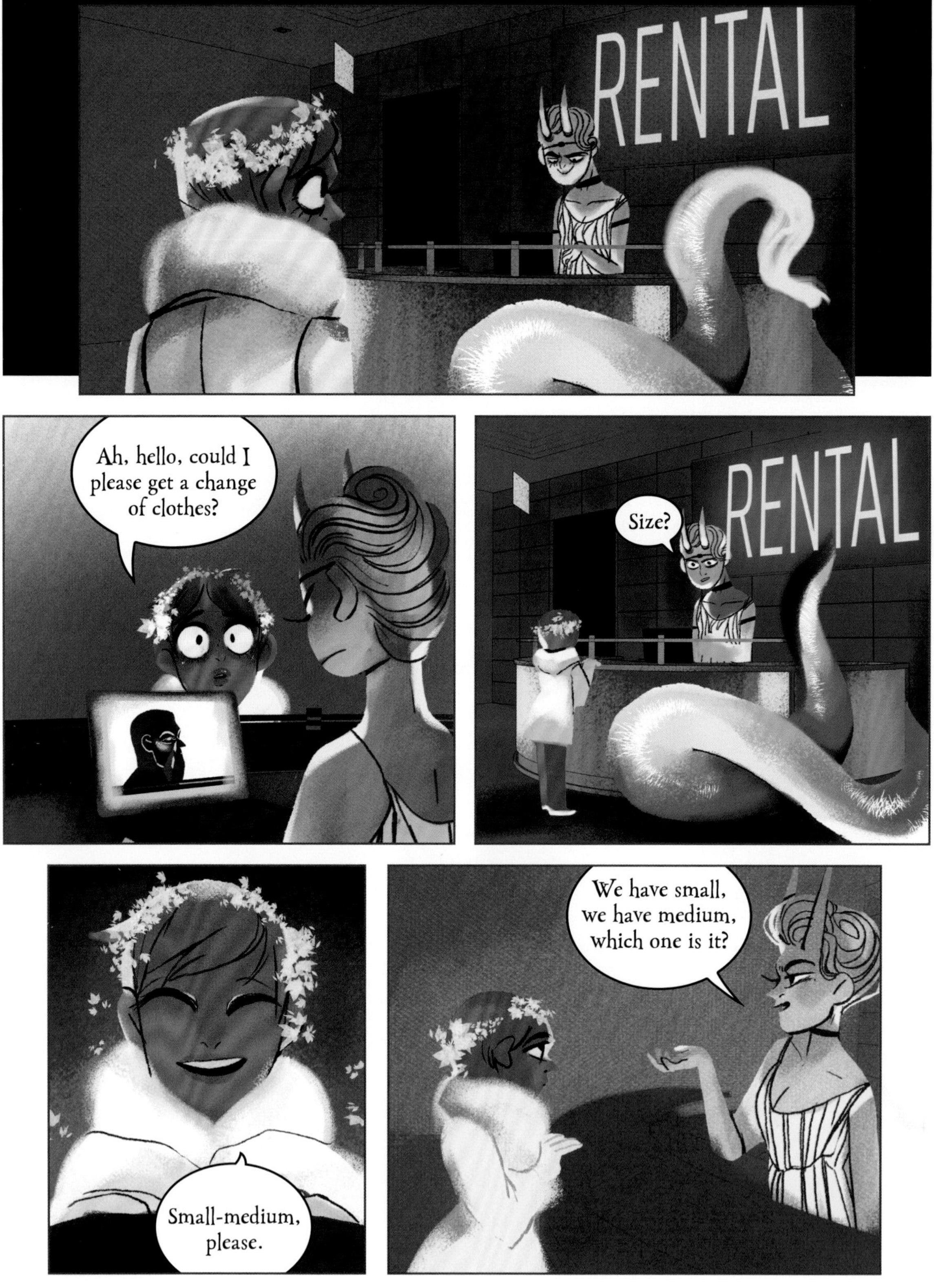
RENTAL
Ah, hello, could I please get a change of clothes?
RENTAL
Size?
Small-medium, please.
We have small, we have medium, which one is it?

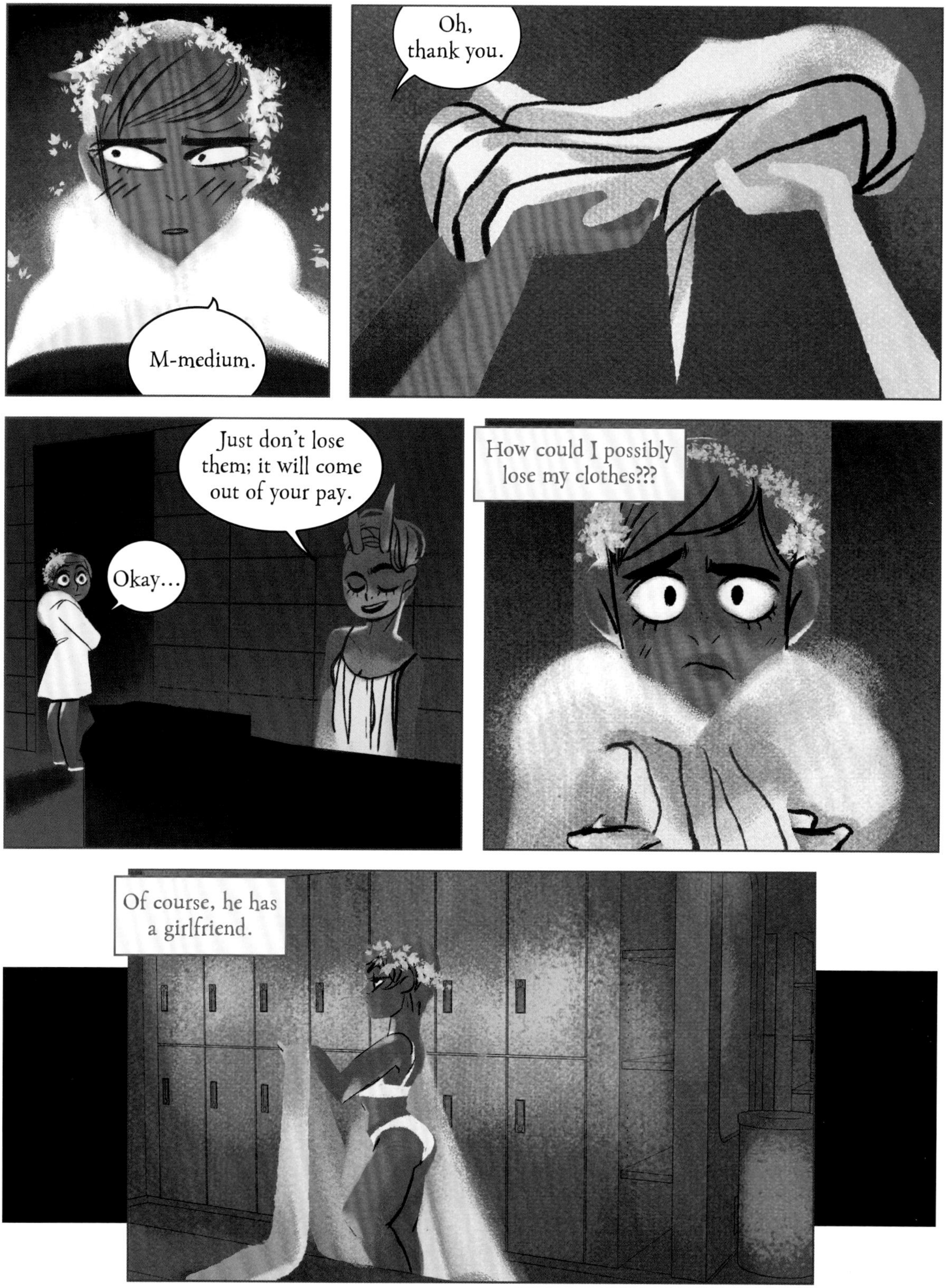
M-medium.
Oh, thank you.
Just don't lose them; it will come out of your pay.
Okay...
How could I possibly lose my clothes???
Of course, he has a girlfriend.

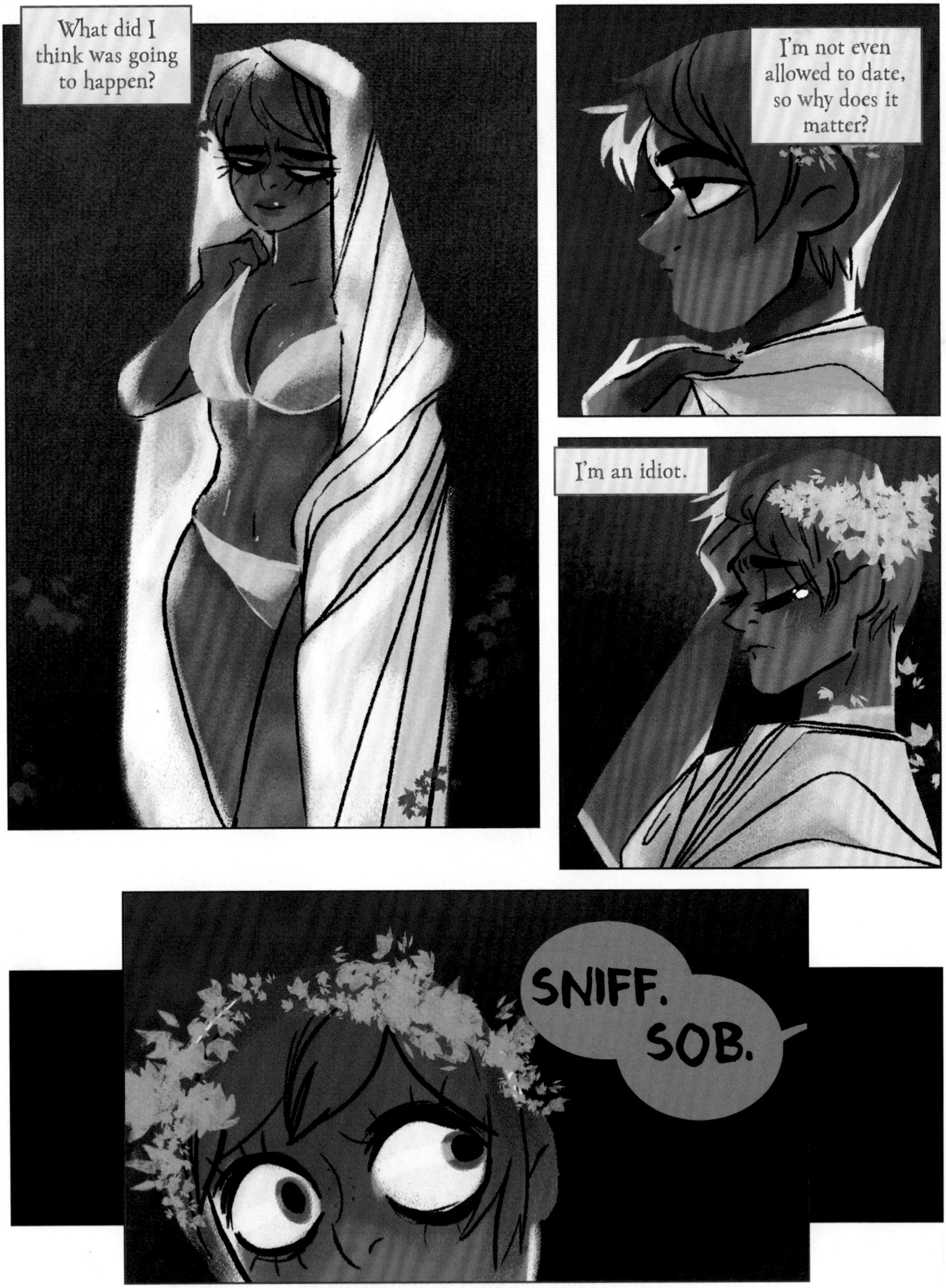
What did I think was going to happen?
I'm not even allowed to date, so why does it matter?
I'm an idiot.
SNIFF.
SOB.

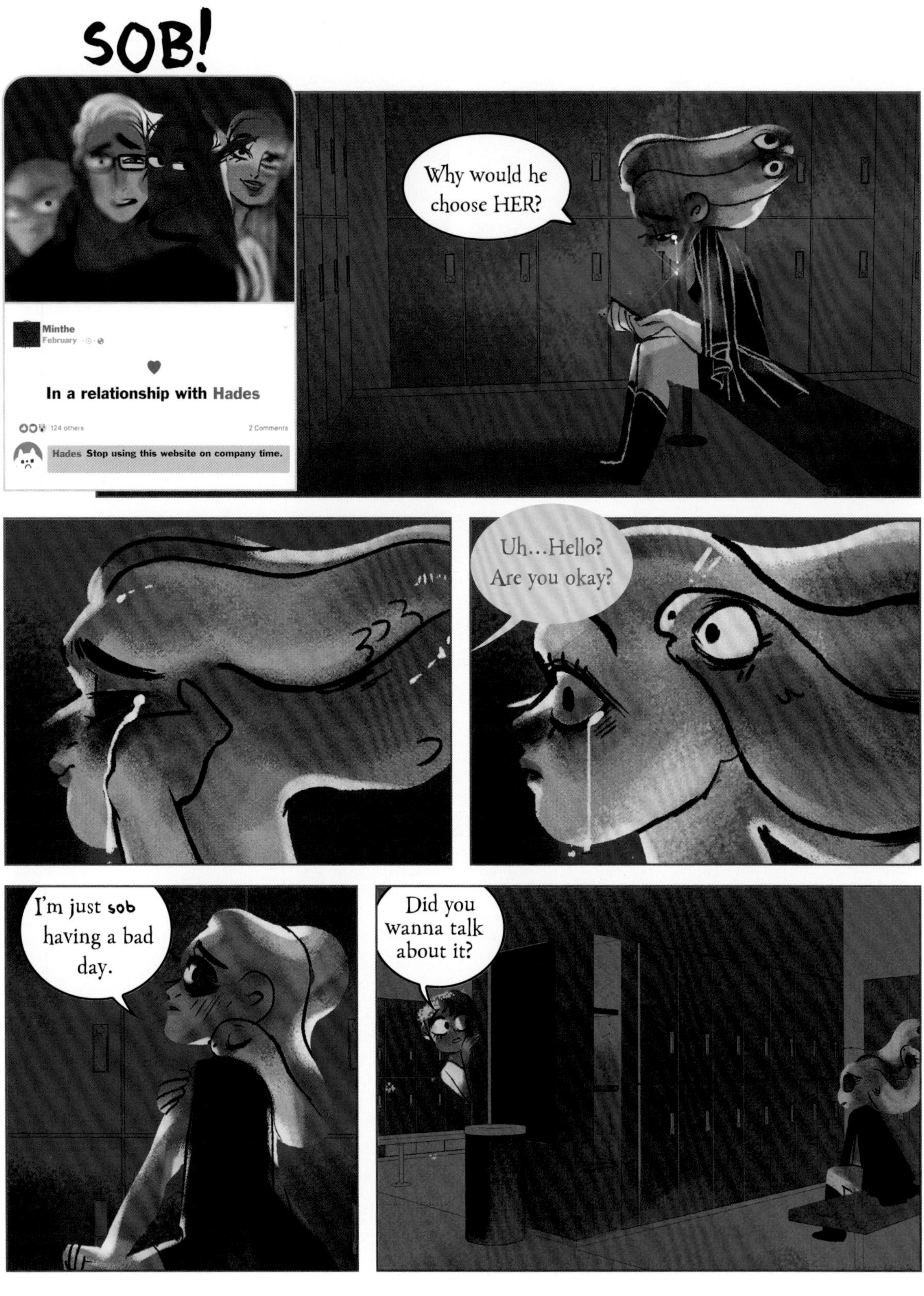
SOB!
Minthe
February
In a relationship with Hades
124 others
2 Comments
Hades Stop using this website on company time.
Why would he choose HER?
Uh...Hello? Are you okay?
I'm just sob having a bad day.
Did you wanna talk about it?

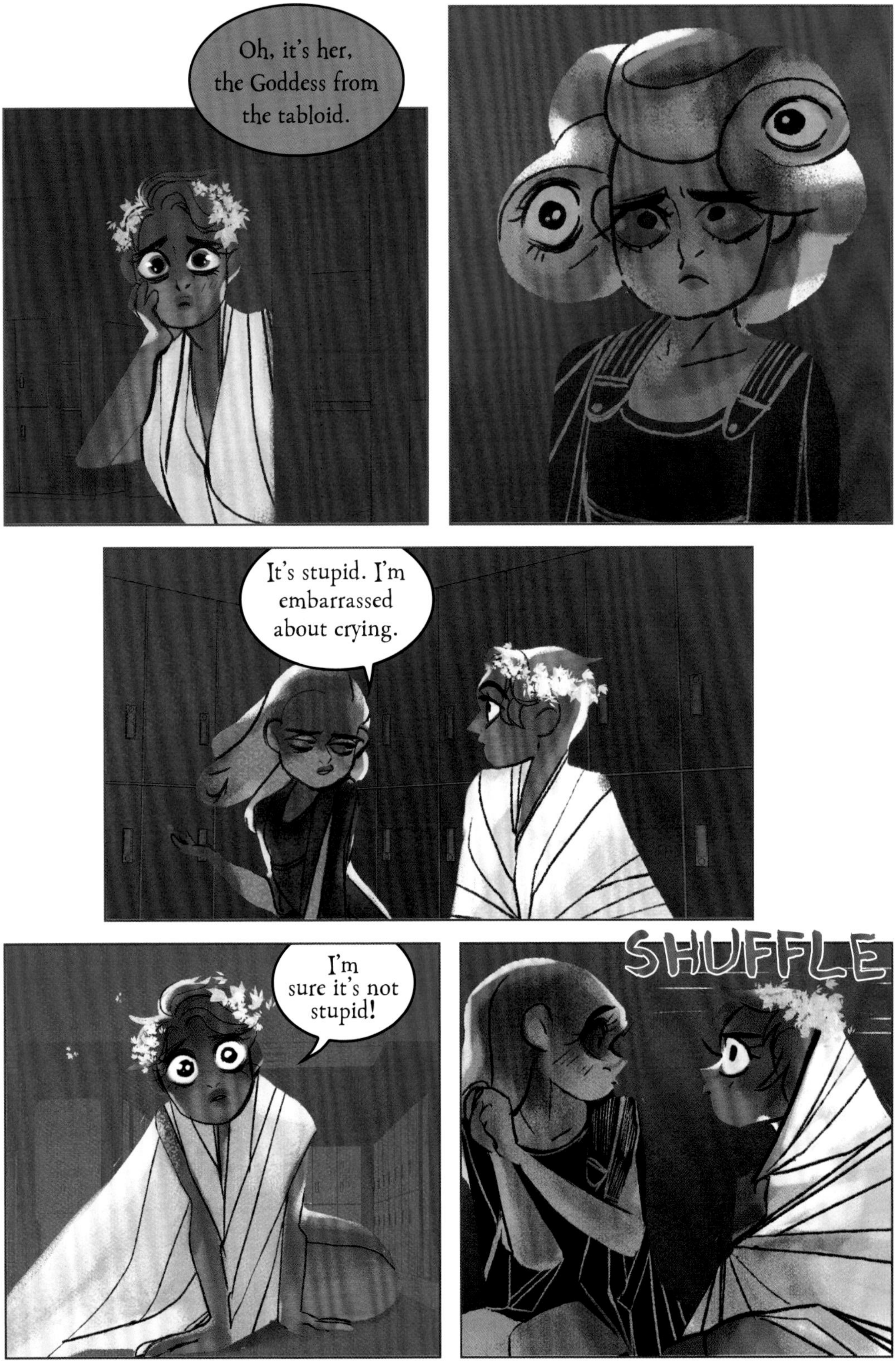
Oh, it's her, the Goddess from the tabloid.
It's stupid. I'm embarrassed about crying.
I'm sure it's not stupid!
SHUFFLE

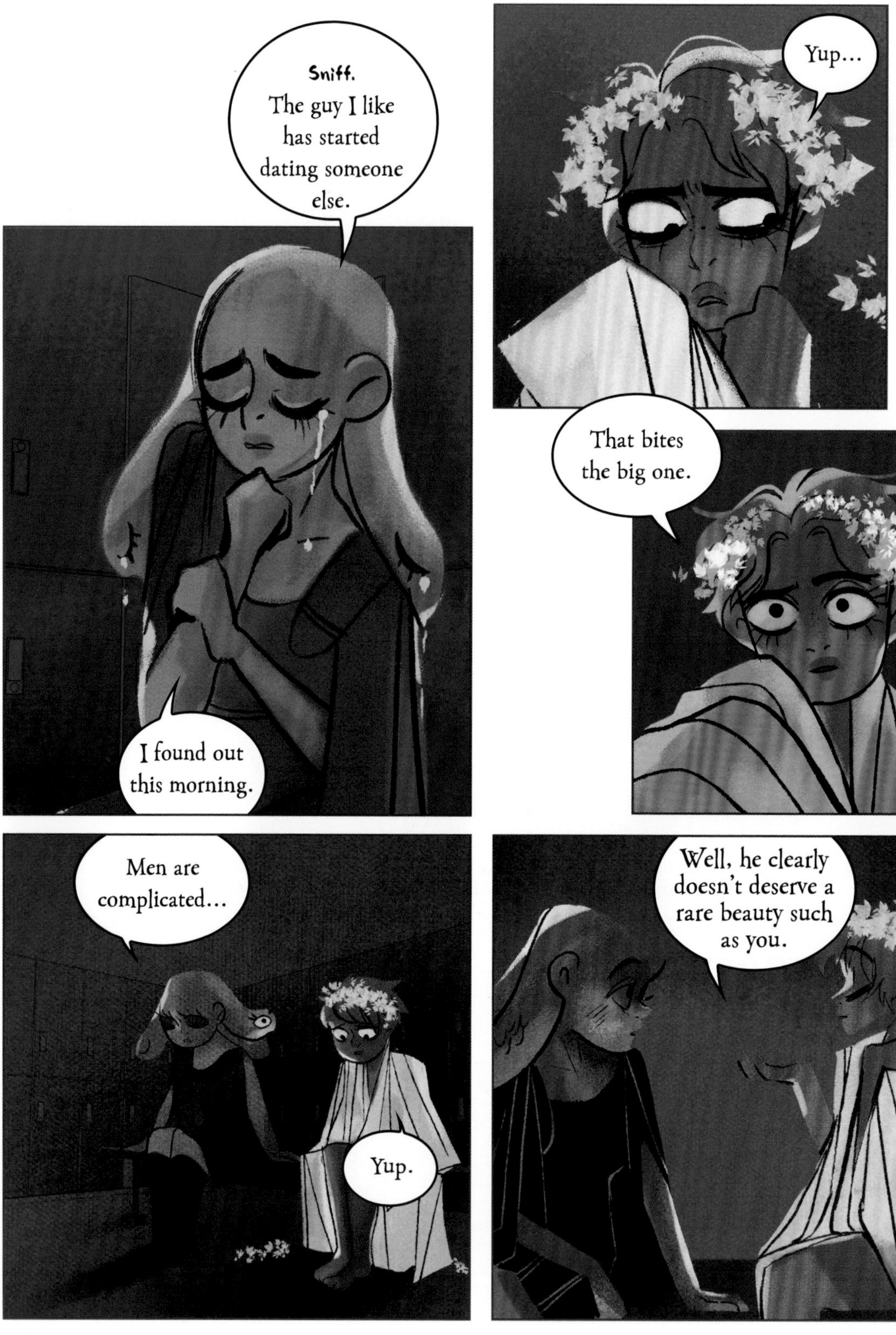
Sniff.
The guy I like has started dating someone else.
I found out this morning.
Yup...
That bites the big one.
Men are complicated...
Yup.
Well, he clearly doesn't deserve a rare beauty such as you.

Is that a rental?

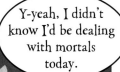

Y-yeah, I didn't know I'd be dealing with mortals today.

We're kind of the same size. You can borrow something from me if you want.

EPISODE 56: A NEW POINT OF VIEW

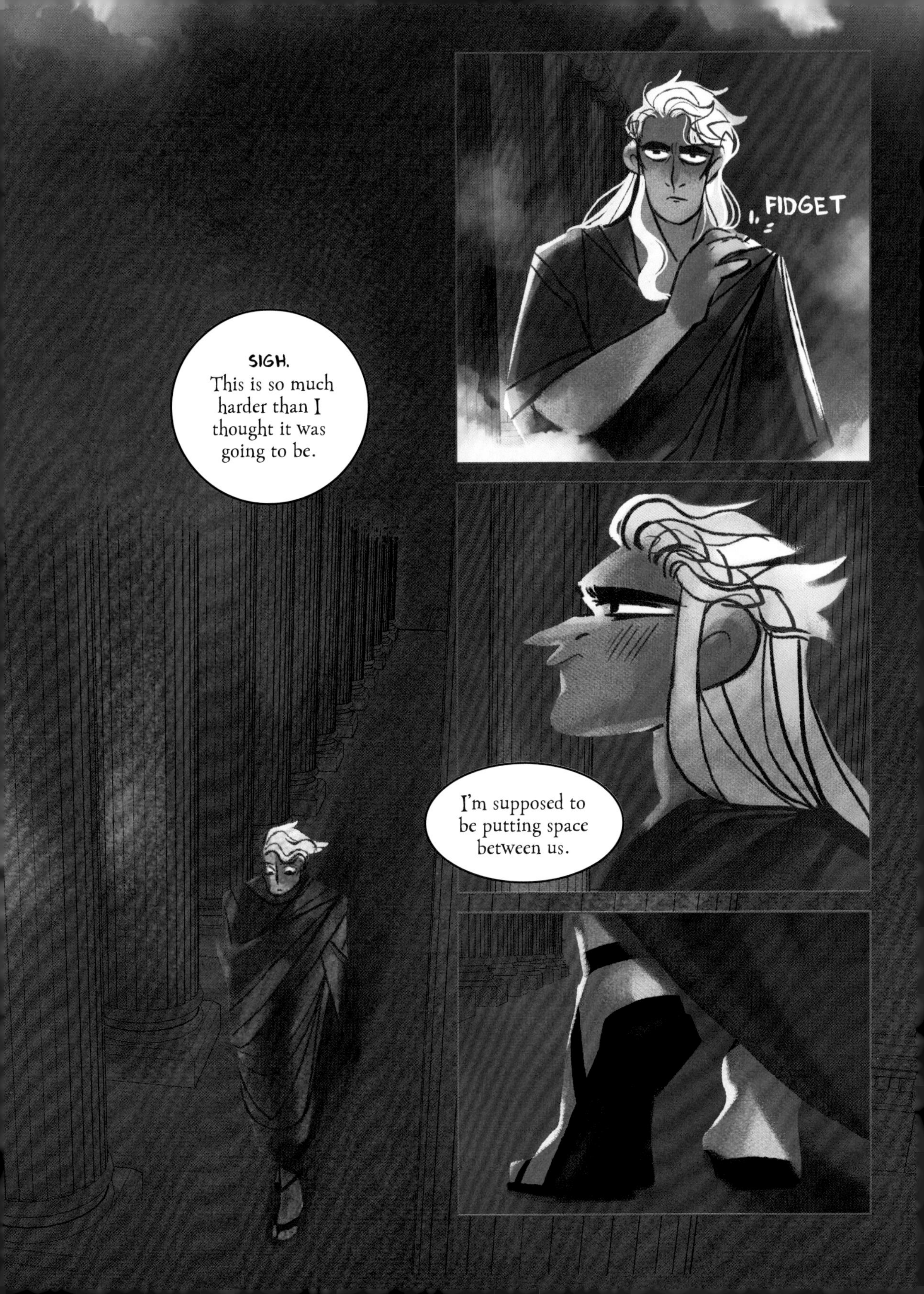
FIDGET
SIGH.
This is so much harder than I thought it was going to be.
I'm supposed to be putting space between us.

She makes everything so easy though...

No!

Self-control.

I have self-control.

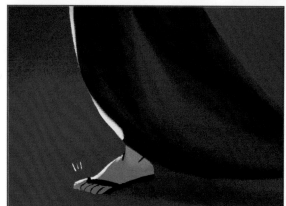

I'm an all-powerful God...

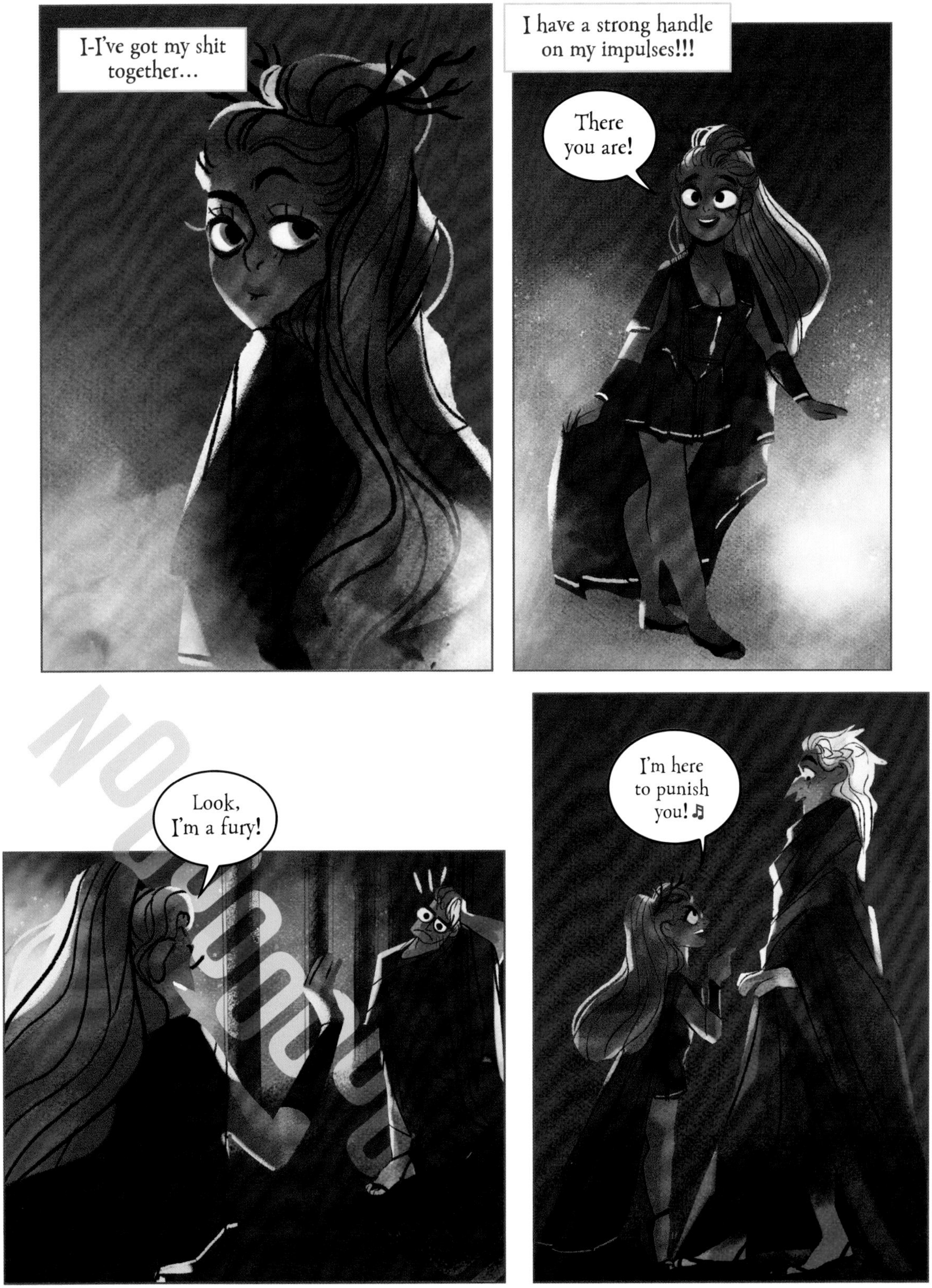
I-I've got my shit together...
I have a strong handle on my impulses!!!
There you are!
Look, I'm a fury!
I'm here to punish you! ♬

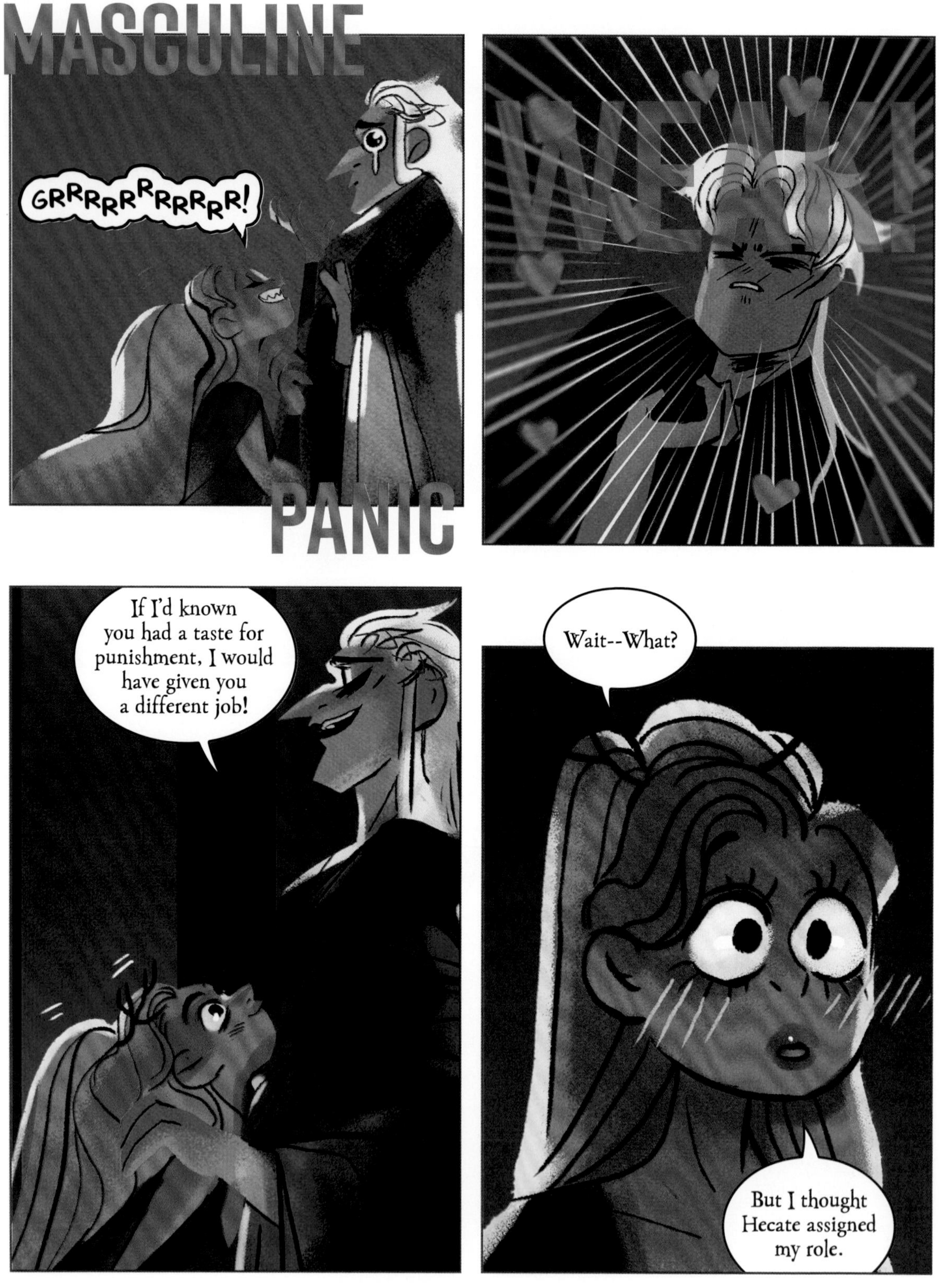
MASCULINE
GRRRRRRRRRRRR!
PANIC
If I'd known you had a taste for punishment, I would have given you a different job!
Wait--What?
But I thought Hecate assigned my role.

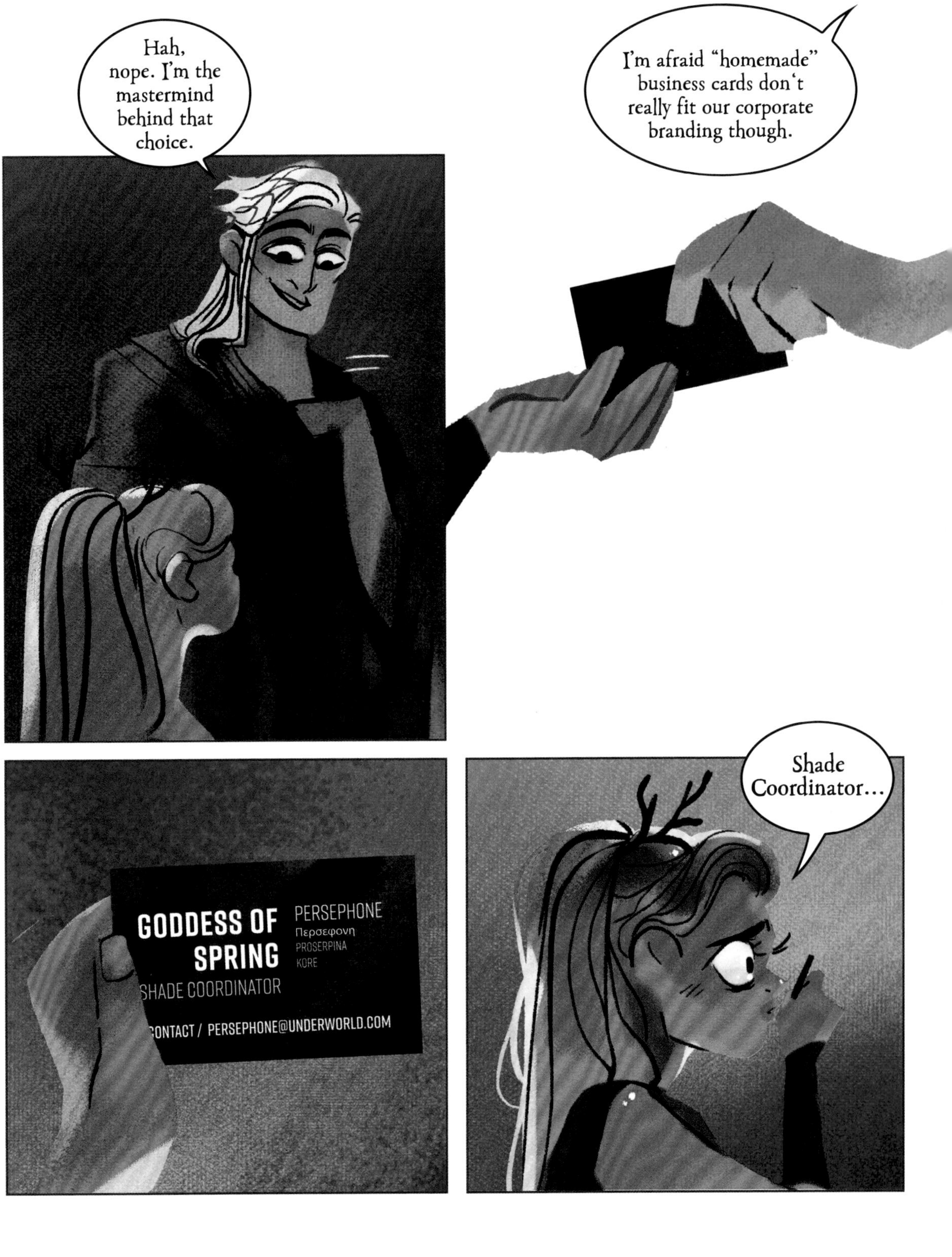
Hah, nope. I'm the mastermind behind that choice.
I'm afraid "homemade" business cards don't really fit our corporate branding though.
GODDESS OF SPRING
SHADE COORDINATOR
PERSEPHONE
Περσεφονη
PROSERPINA
KORE
CONTACT / PERSEPHONE@UNDERWORLD.COM
Shade Coordinator...

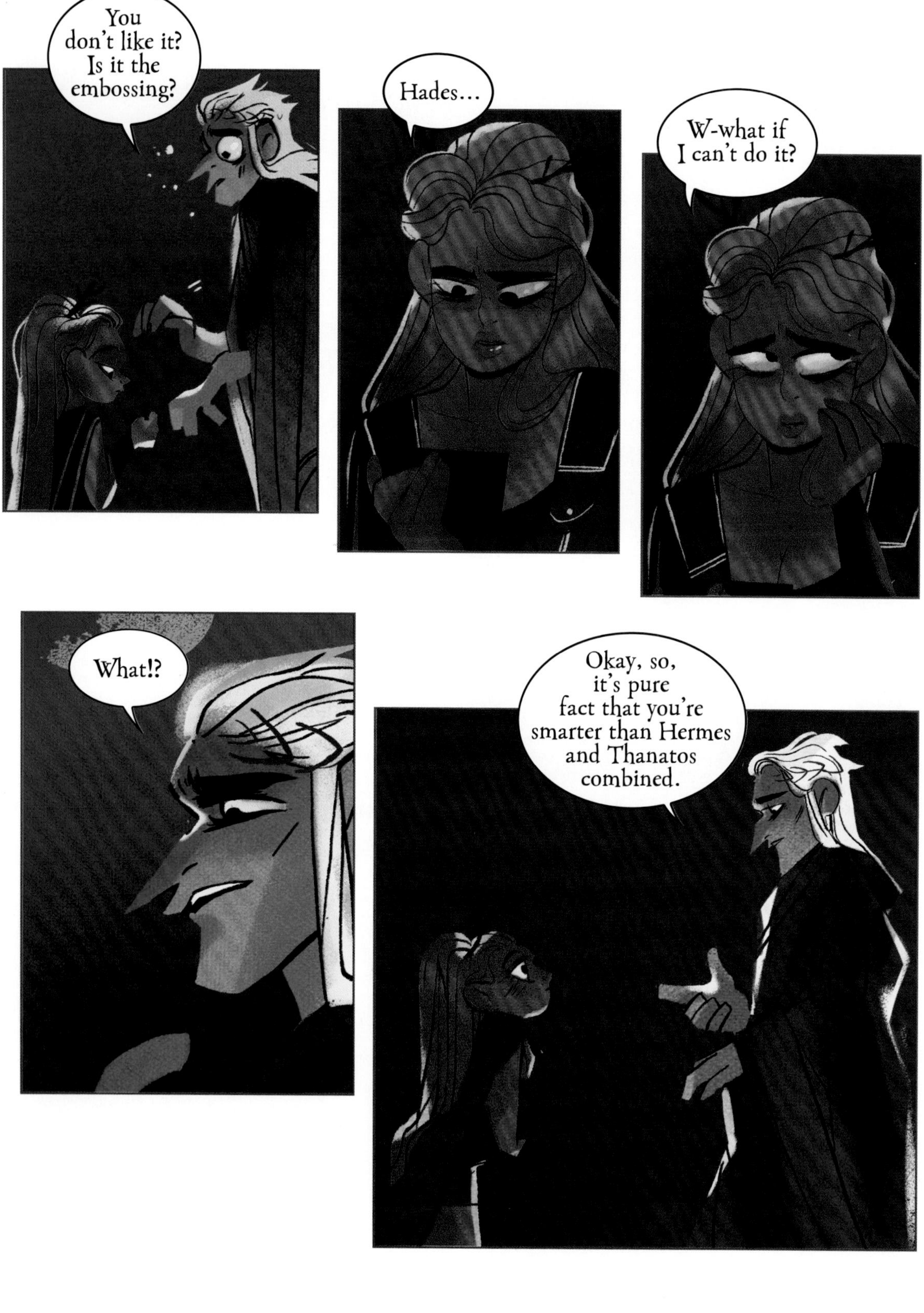
You don't like it? Is it the embossing?
Hades...
W-what if I can't do it?
What!?
Okay, so, it's pure fact that you're smarter than Hermes and Thanatos combined.

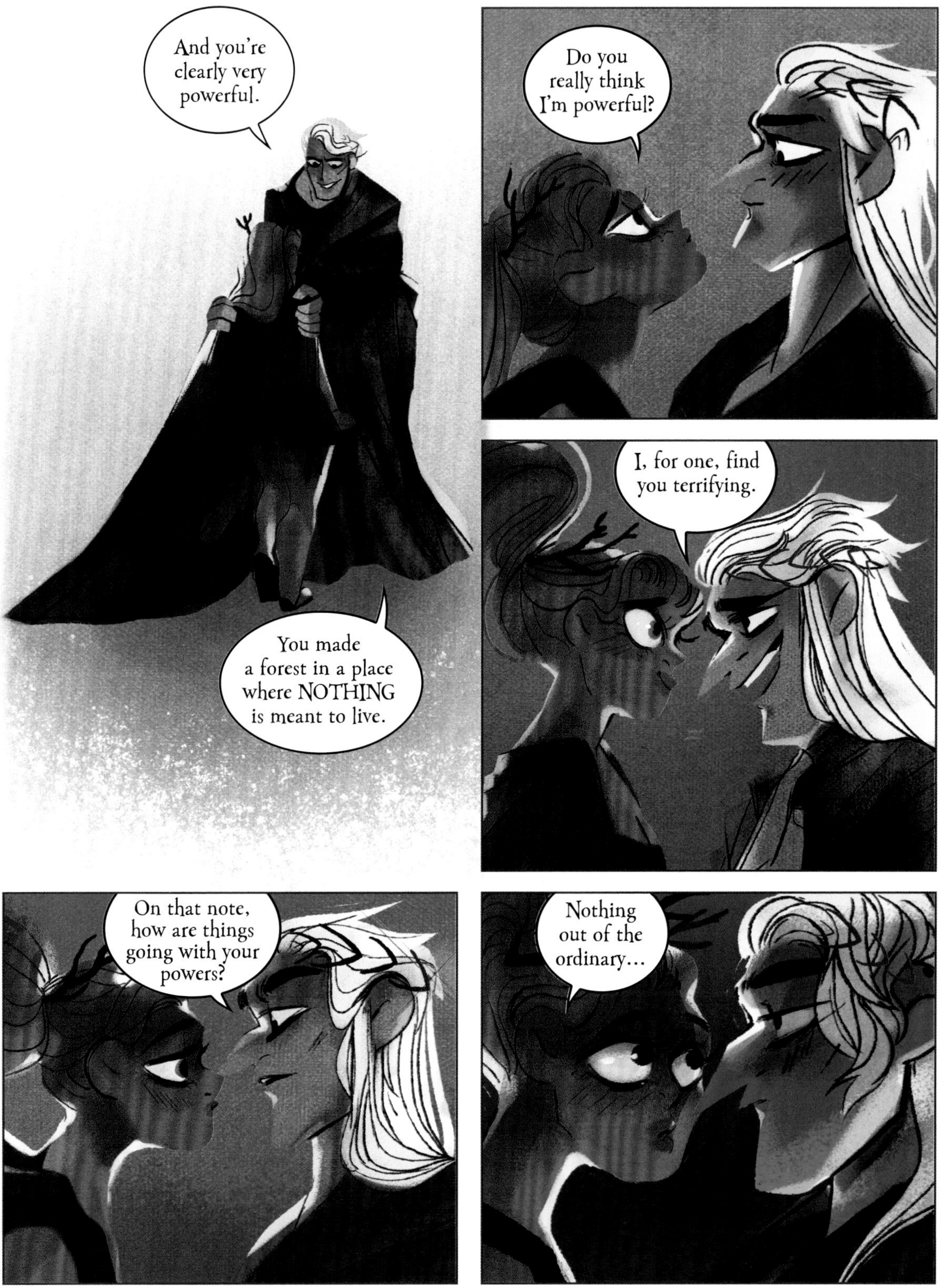
And you're clearly very powerful.
You made a forest in a place where NOTHING is meant to live.
Do you really think I'm powerful?
I, for one, find you terrifying.
On that note, how are things going with your powers?
Nothing out of the ordinary...

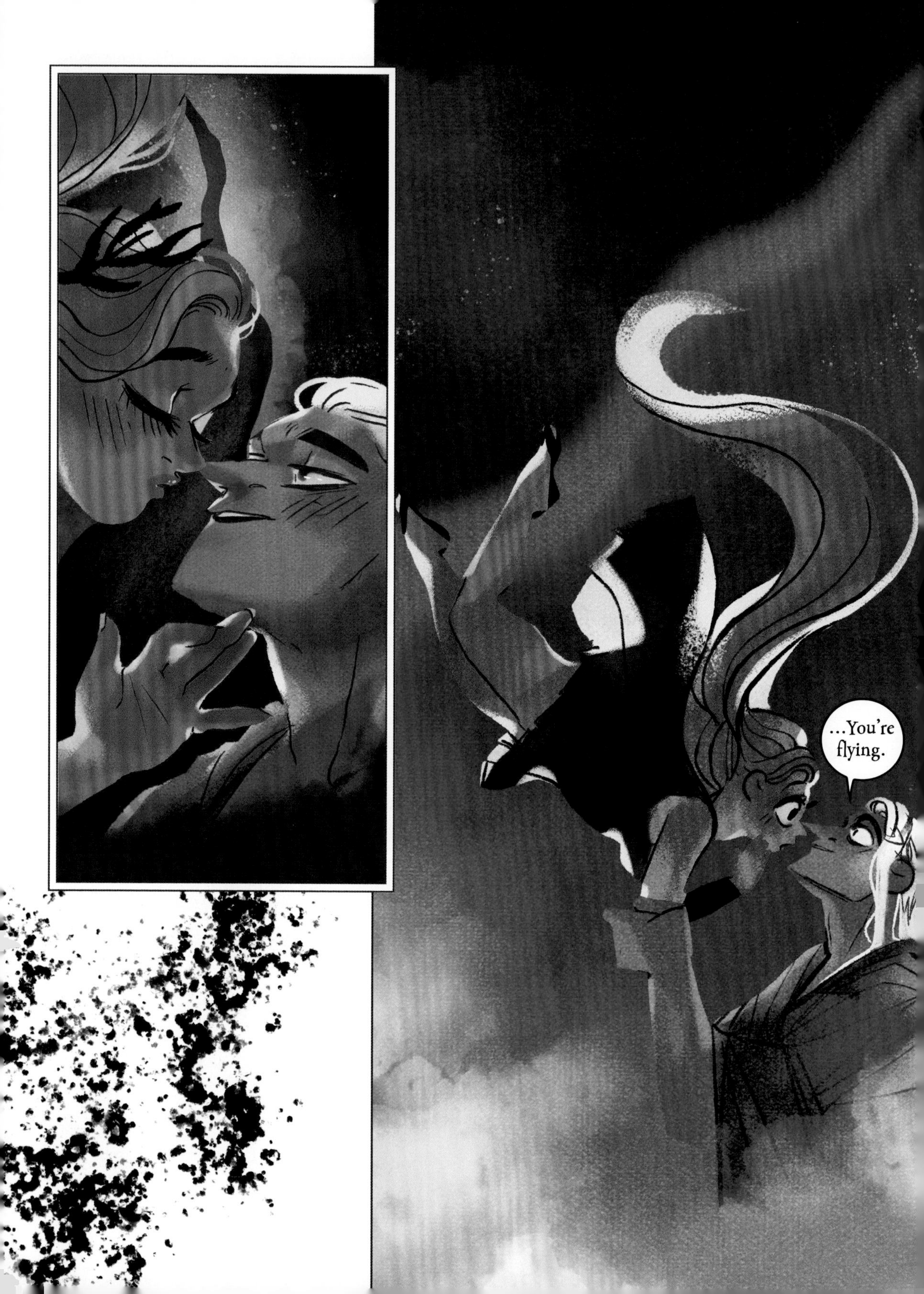
…You're flying.

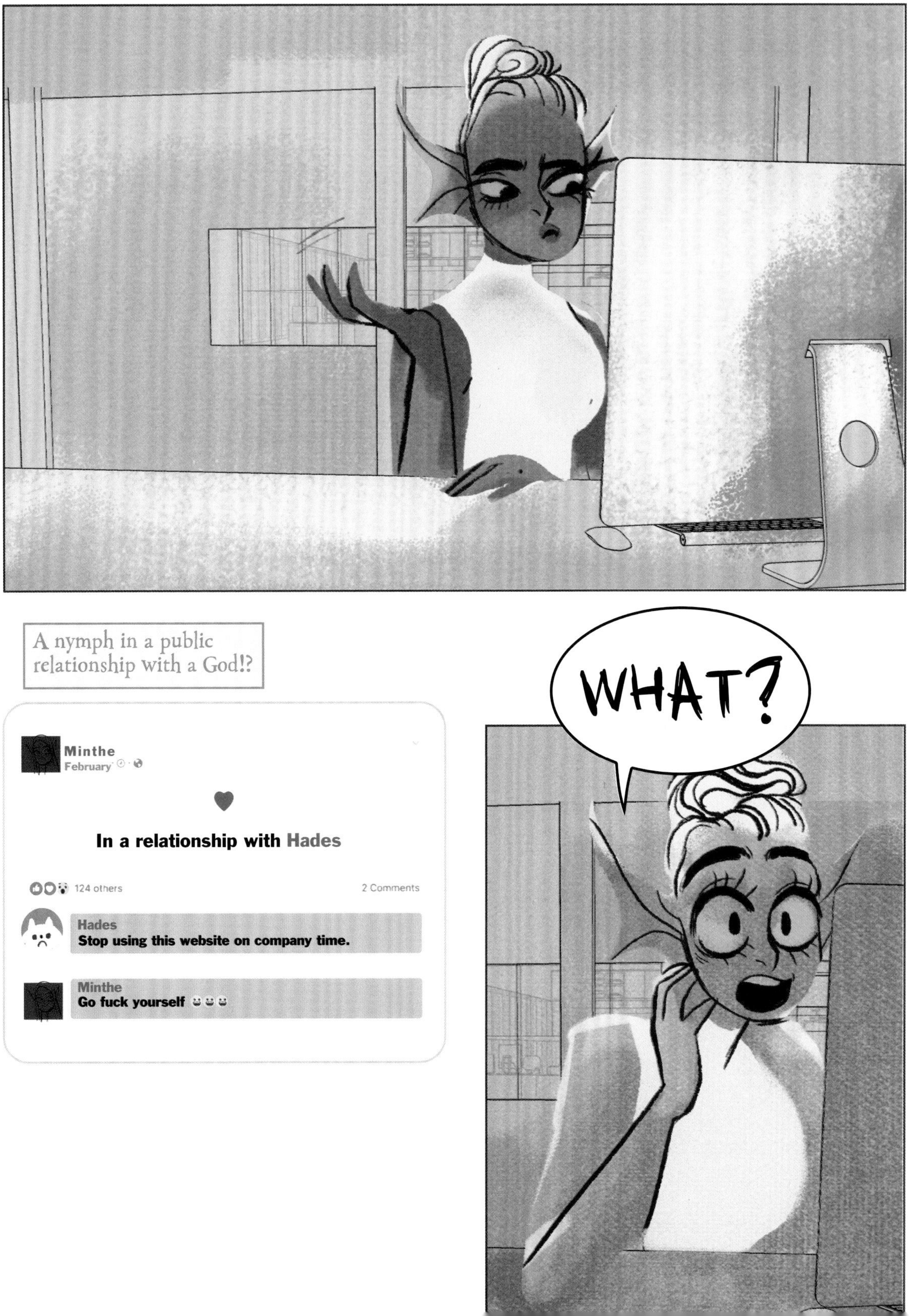
A nymph in a public relationship with a God!?
Minthe
February
In a relationship with Hades
124 others
2 Comments
Hades
Stop using this website on company time.
Minthe
Go fuck yourself
WHAT?

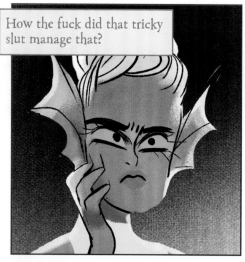

How the fuck did that tricky slut manage that?

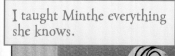

I taught Minthe everything she knows.

How can she be doing better than me!?

I-I need to step up my game.

Crap!

I forgot his family was coming in today.

What a perfect family.

I'll have to fix that.

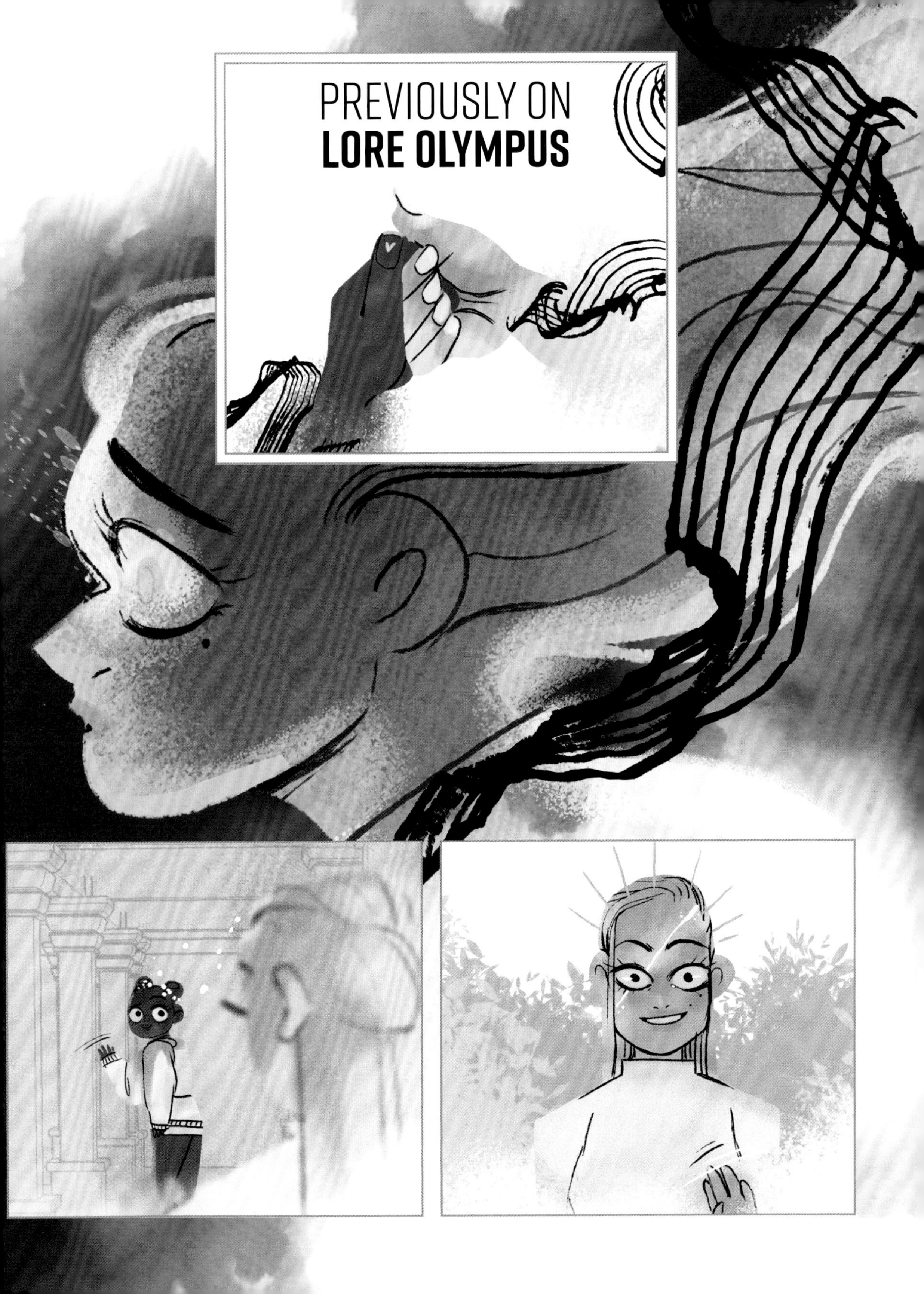
PREVIOUSLY ON
LORE OLYMPUS

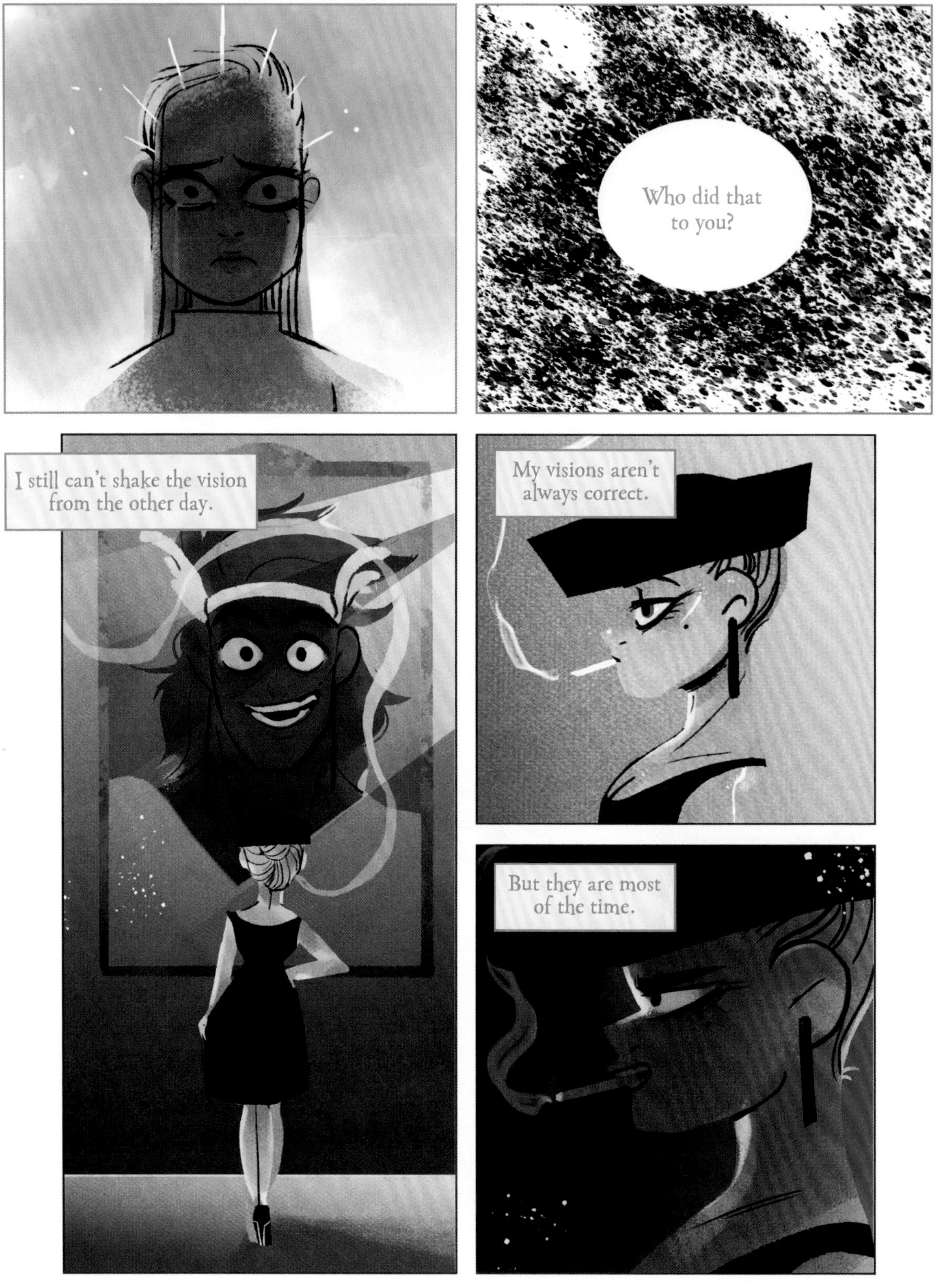
Who did that to you?
I still can't shake the vision from the other day.
My visions aren't always correct.
But they are most of the time.

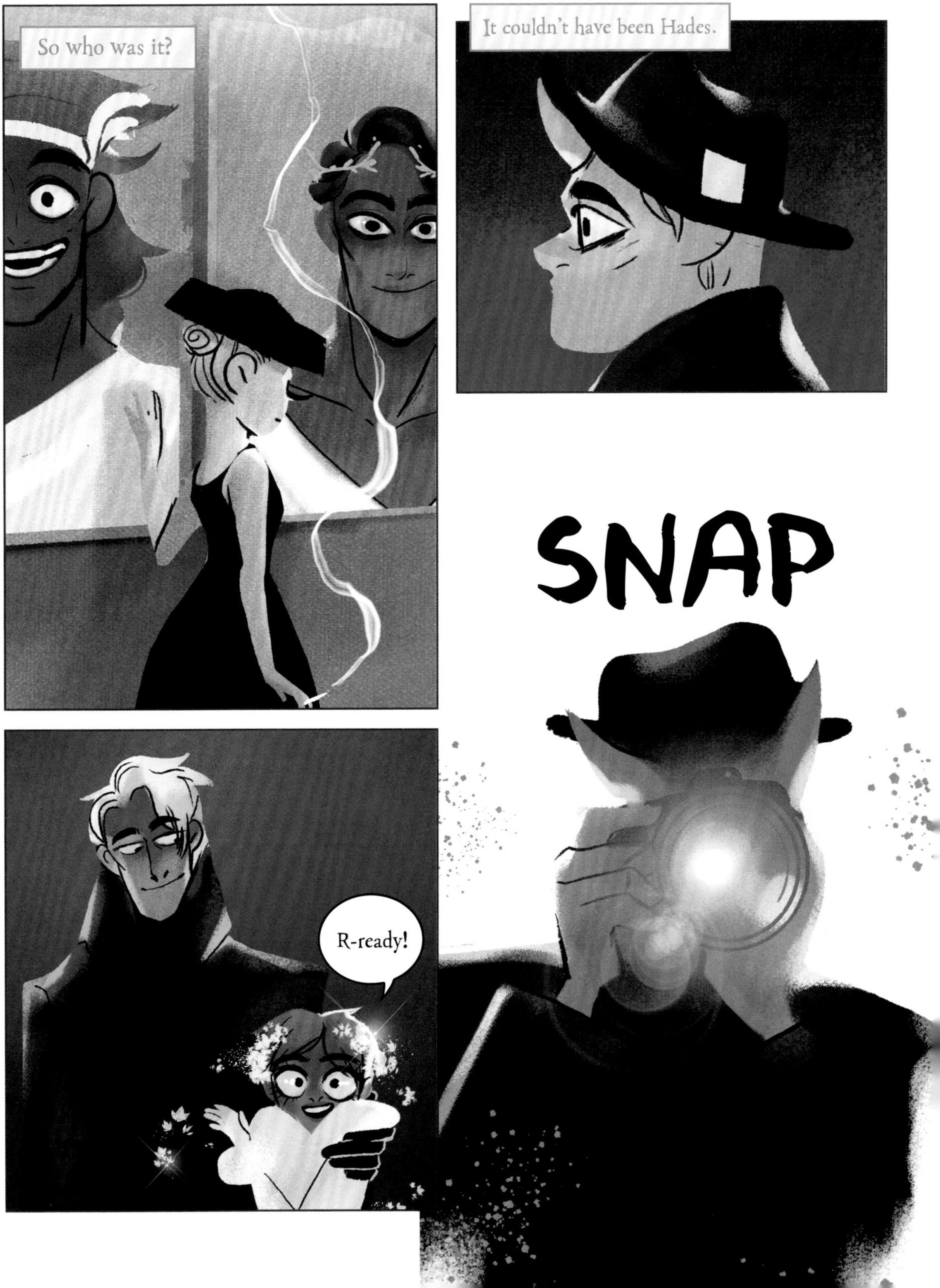

So who was it?
It couldn't have been Hades.
R-ready!
SNAP

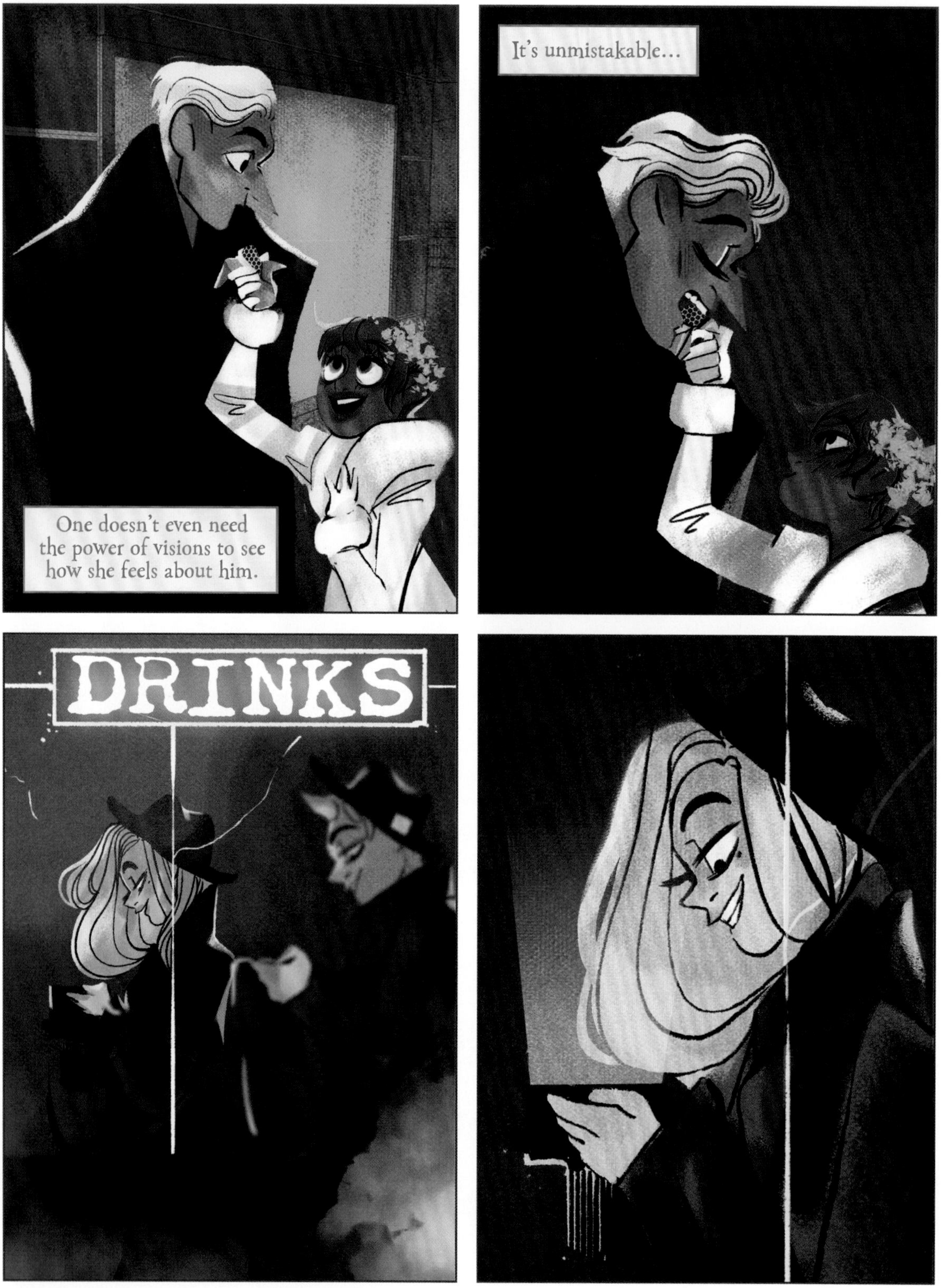
One doesn't even need the power of visions to see how she feels about him.
It's unmistakable...
DRINKS

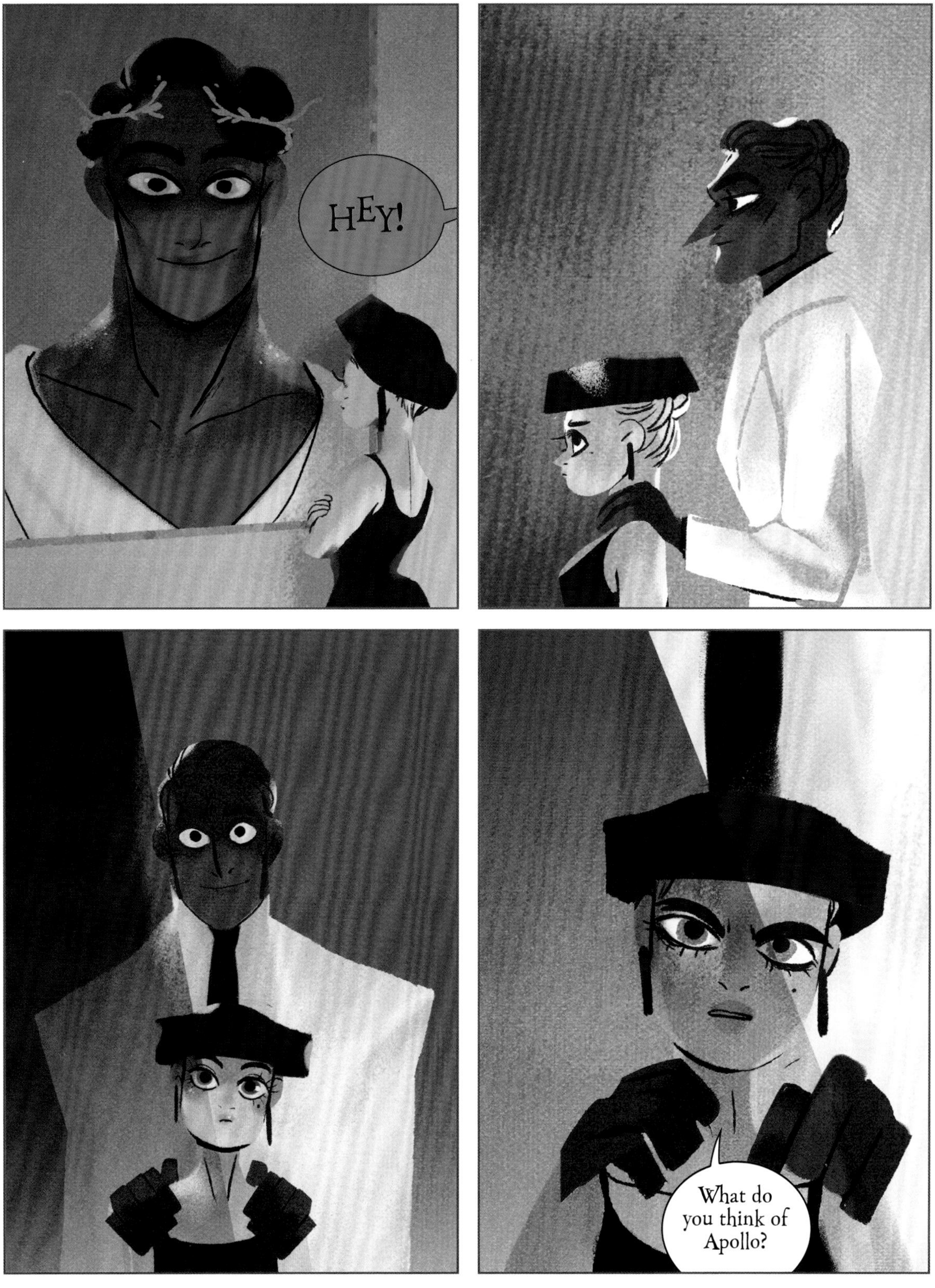
HEY!
What do you think of Apollo?

EPISODE 57: THE BEACH

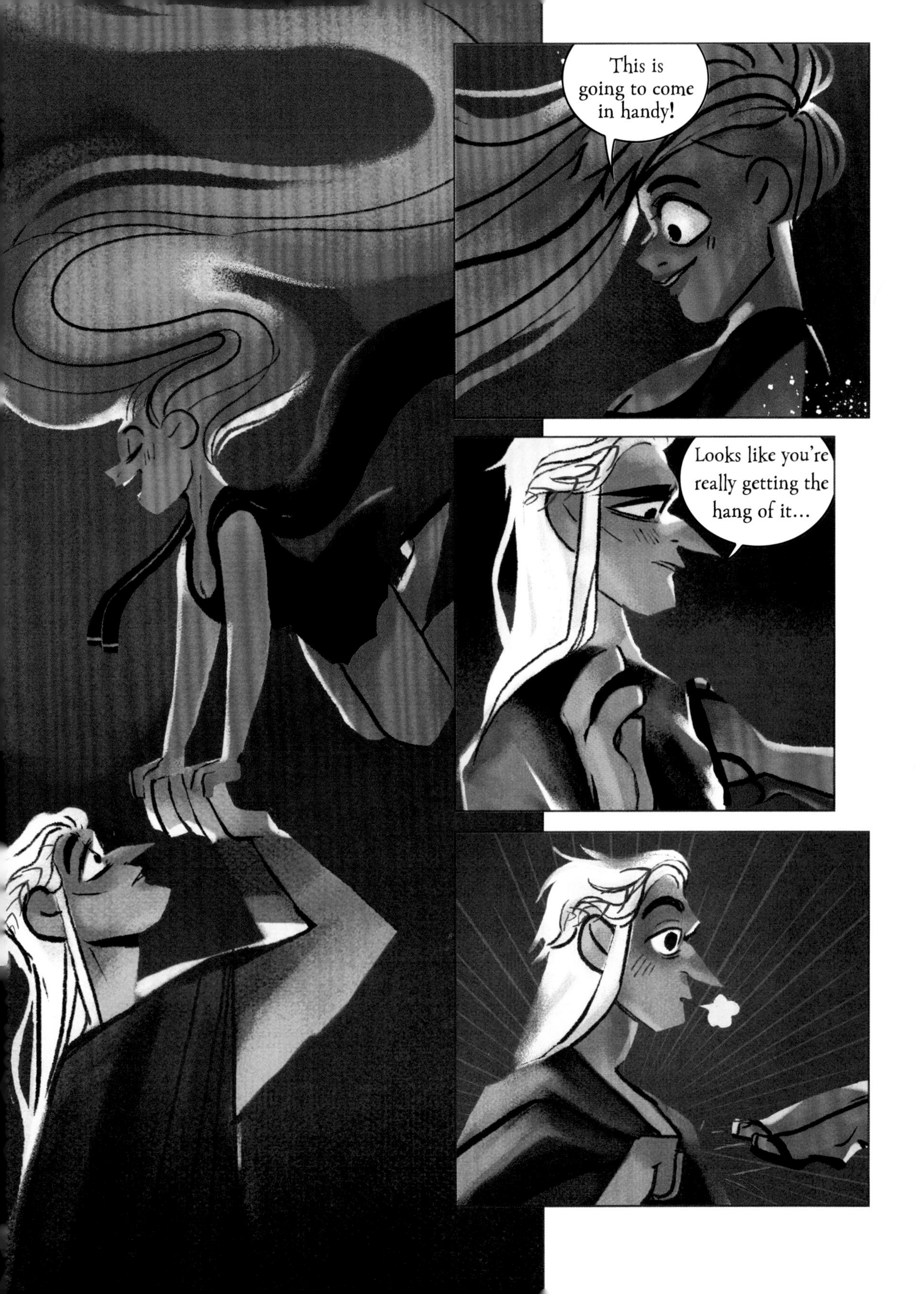
This is going to come in handy!
Looks like you're really getting the hang of it...

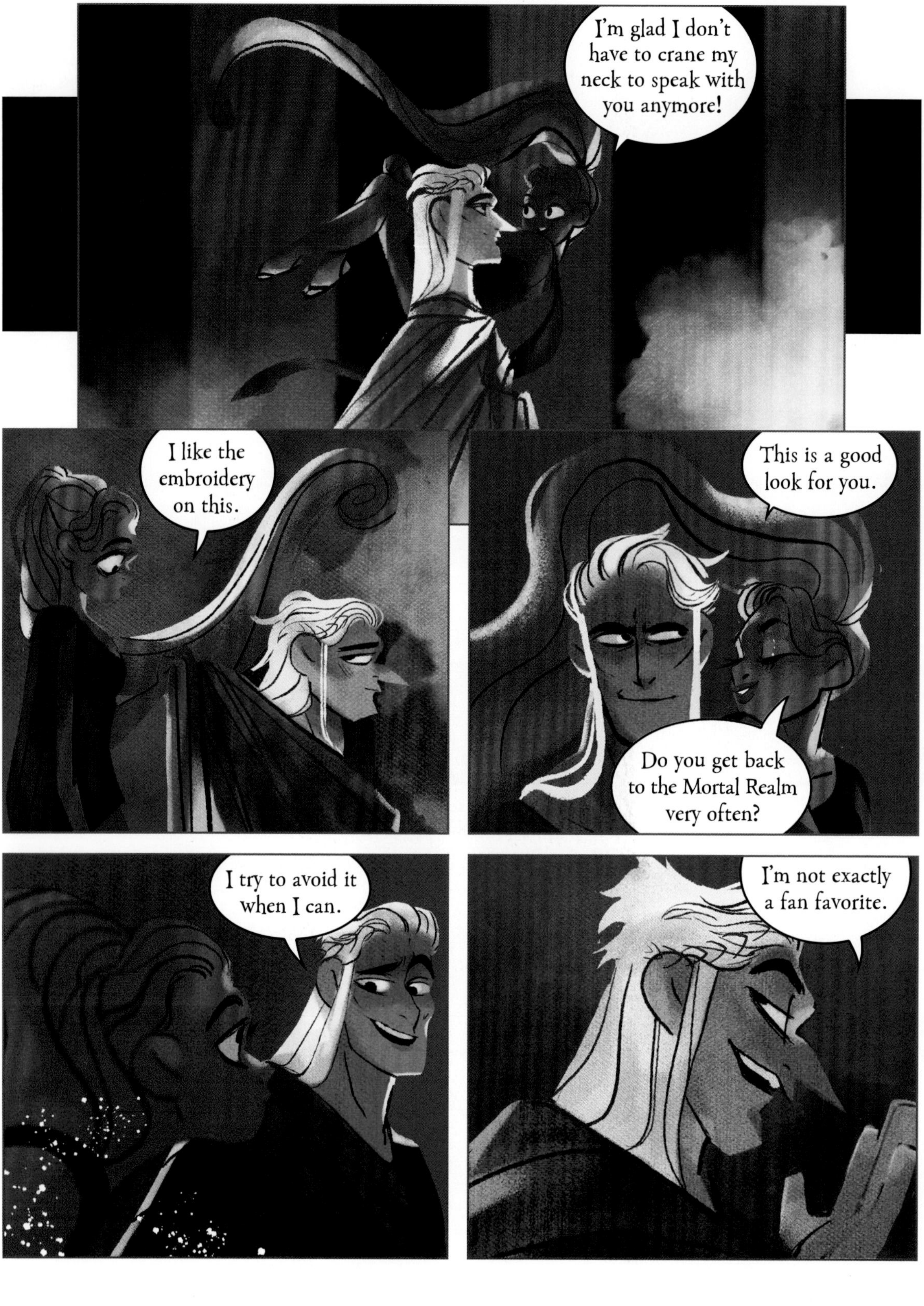
I'm glad I don't have to crane my neck to speak with you anymore!
I like the embroidery on this.
This is a good look for you.
Do you get back to the Mortal Realm very often?
I try to avoid it when I can.
I'm not exactly a fan favorite.

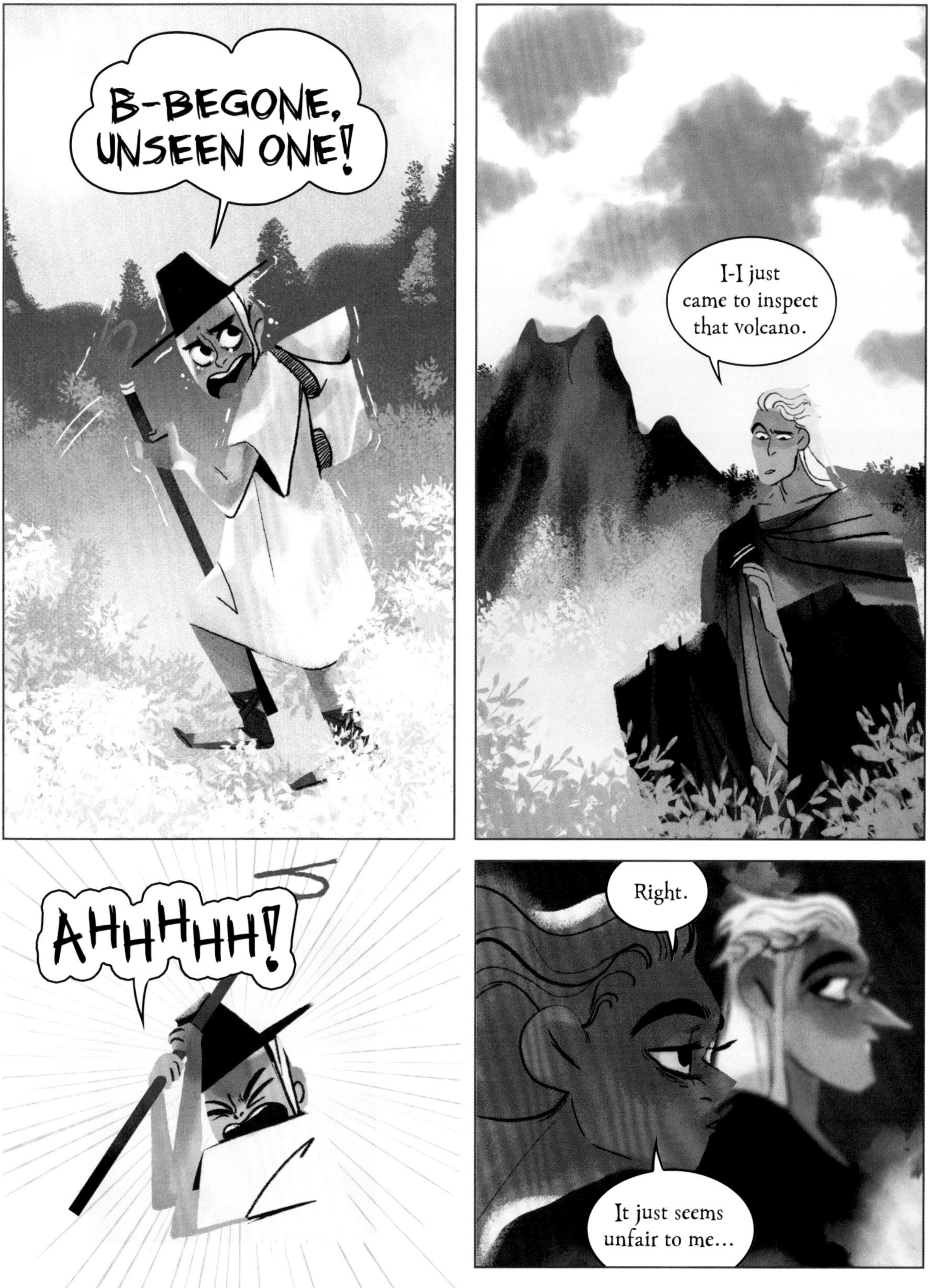
B-BEGONE, UNSEEN ONE!
I-I just came to inspect that volcano.
AHHHHH!
Right.
It just seems unfair to me...

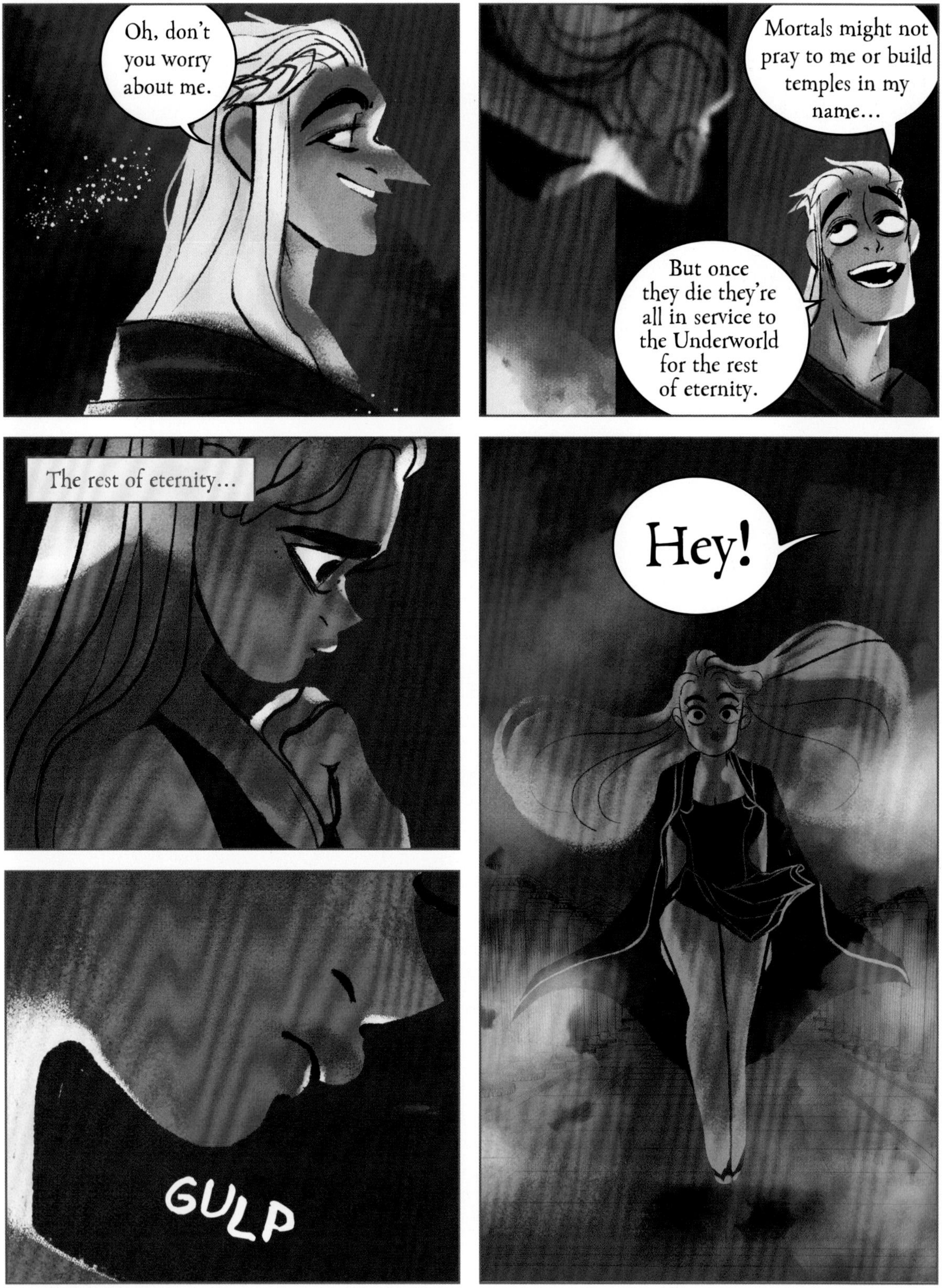
Oh, don't you worry about me.
Mortals might not pray to me or build temples in my name...
But once they die they're all in service to the Underworld for the rest of eternity.
The rest of eternity...
GULP
Hey!

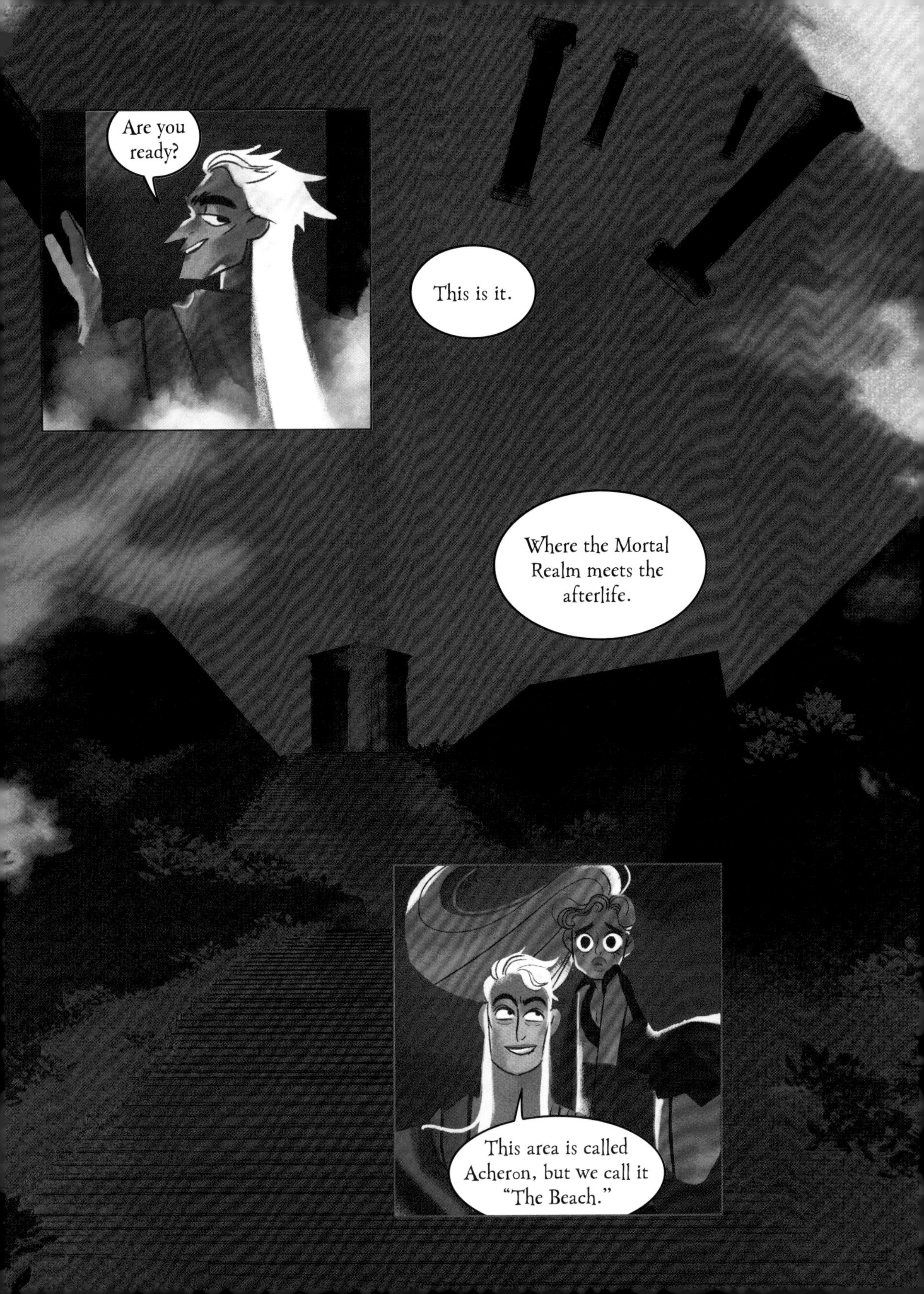

Are you ready?
This is it.
Where the Mortal Realm meets the afterlife.
This area is called Acheron, but we call it "The Beach."

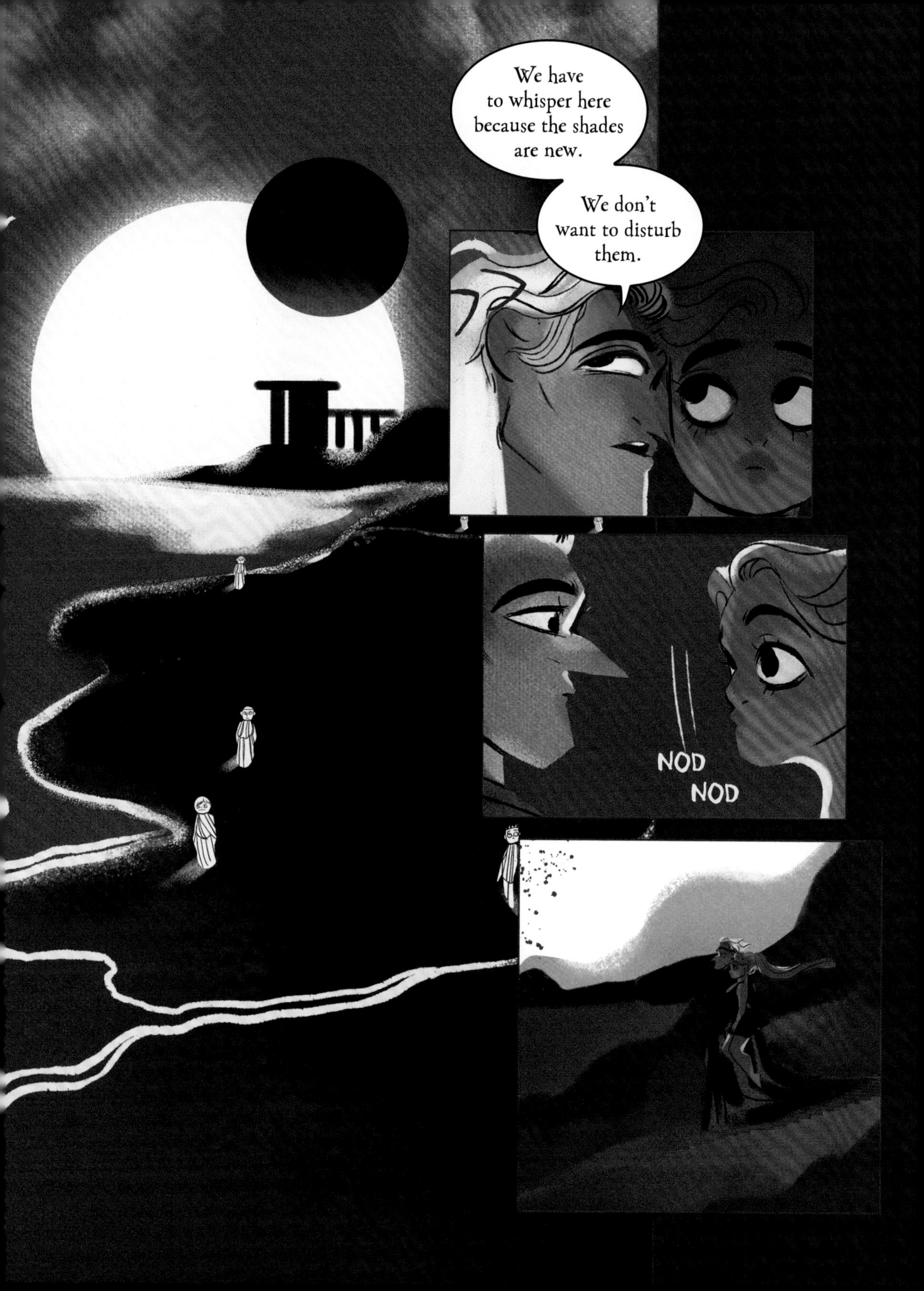
We have to whisper here because the shades are new.
We don't want to disturb them.
NOD
NOD

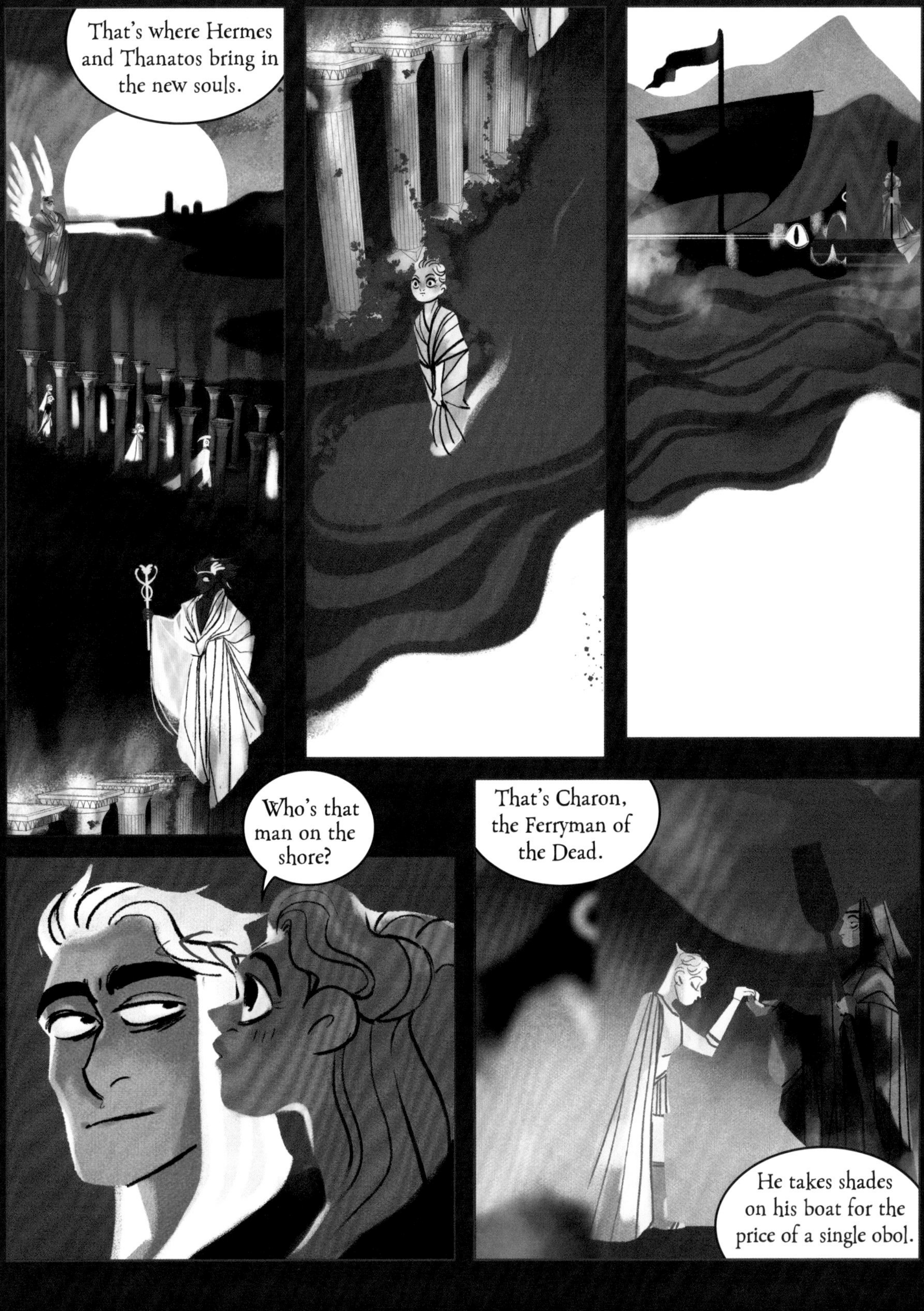
That's where Hermes and Thanatos bring in the new souls.
Who's that man on the shore?
That's Charon, the Ferryman of the Dead.
He takes shades on his boat for the price of a single obol.

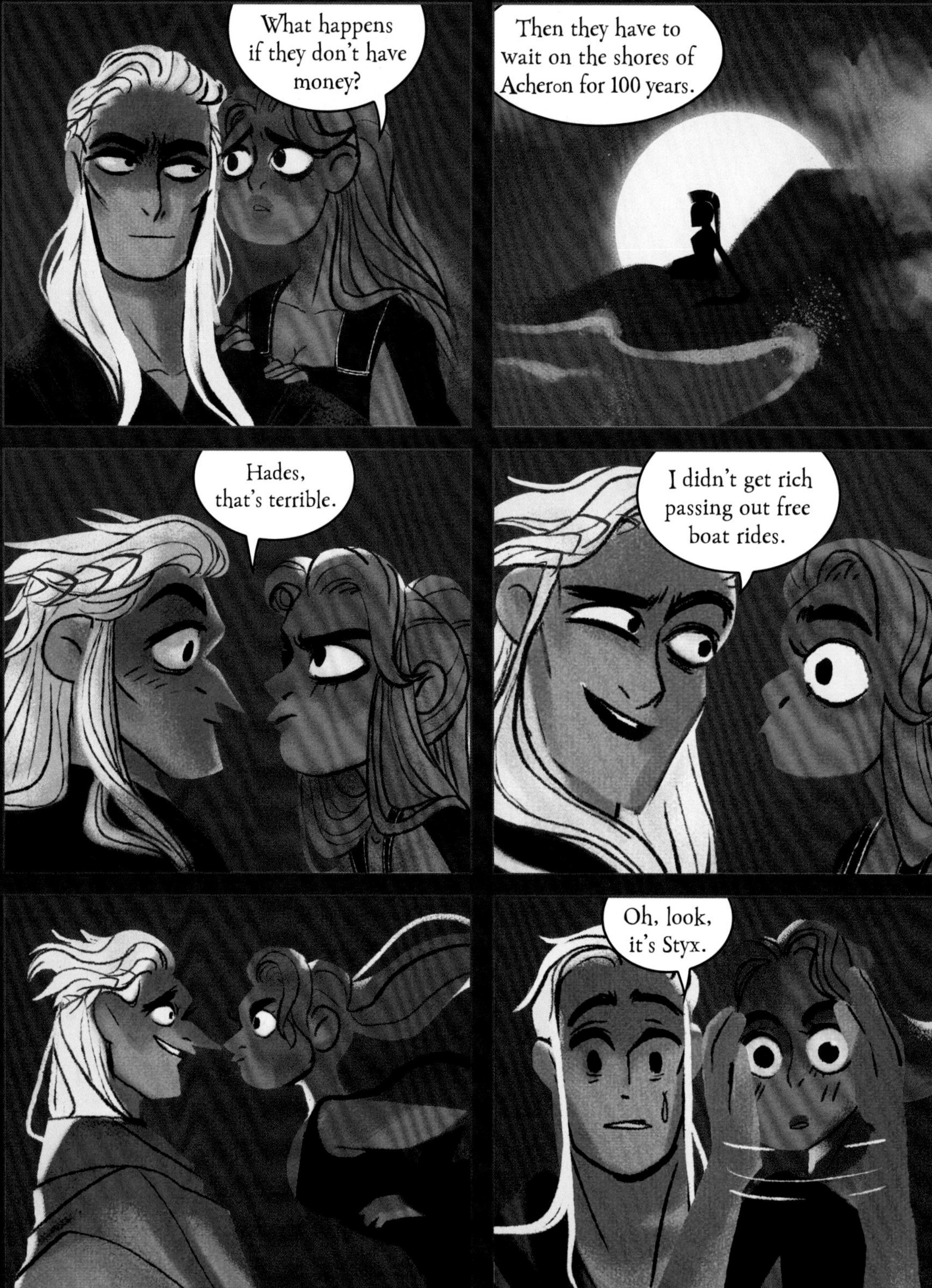
What happens if they don't have money?
Then they have to wait on the shores of Acheron for 100 years.
Hades, that's terrible.
I didn't get rich passing out free boat rides.
Oh, look, it's Styx.

She's the Underworld's most powerful river.
She carries all the boats farther into the Underworld for judgment.
That's where I come in.

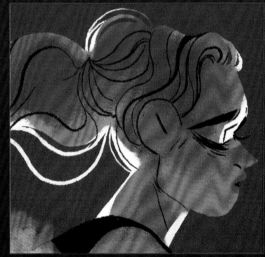

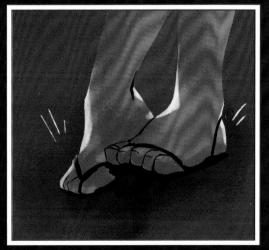

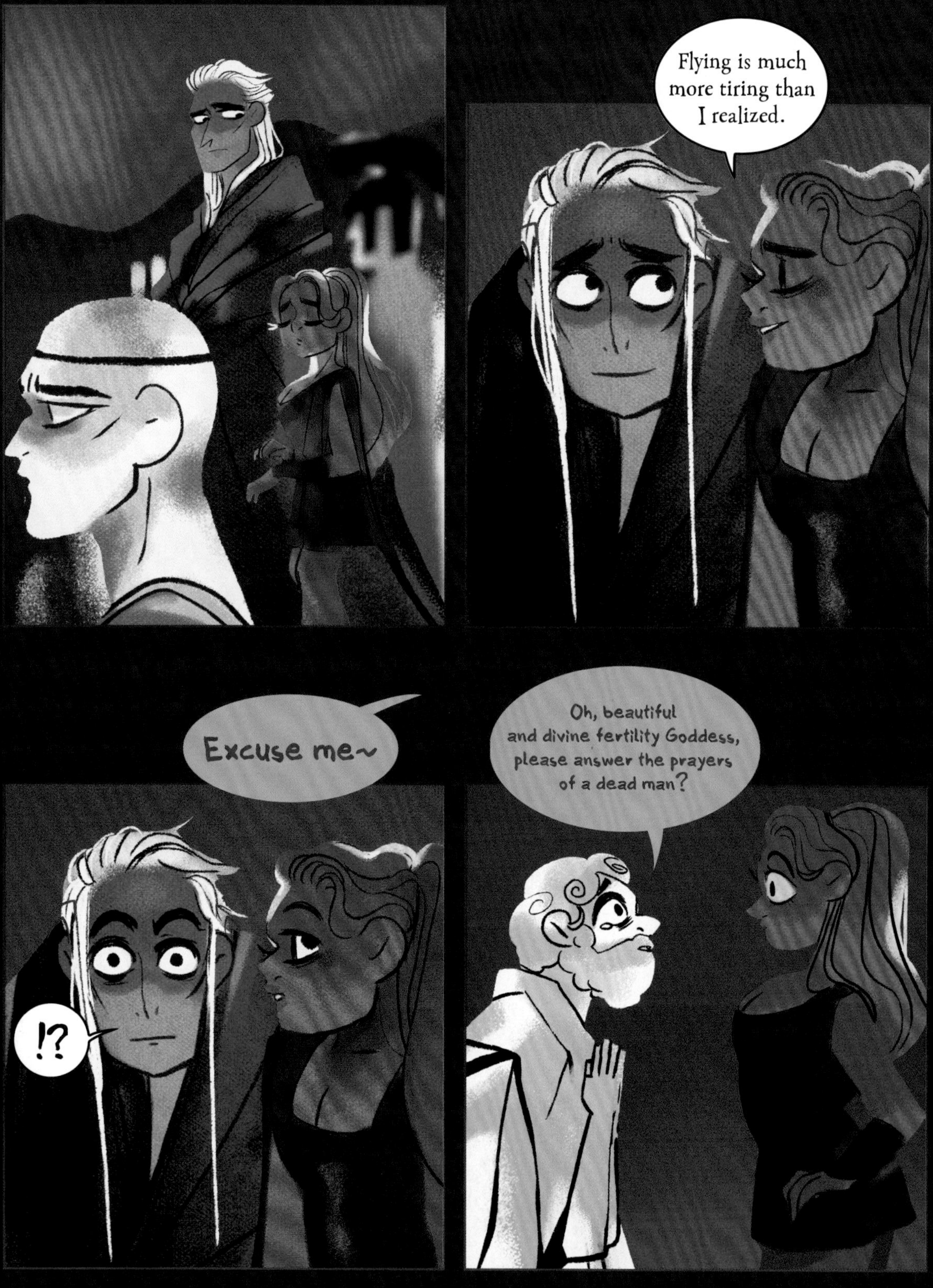
Flying is much more tiring than I realized.
Excuse me~
!?
Oh, beautiful and divine fertility Goddess, please answer the prayers of a dead man?

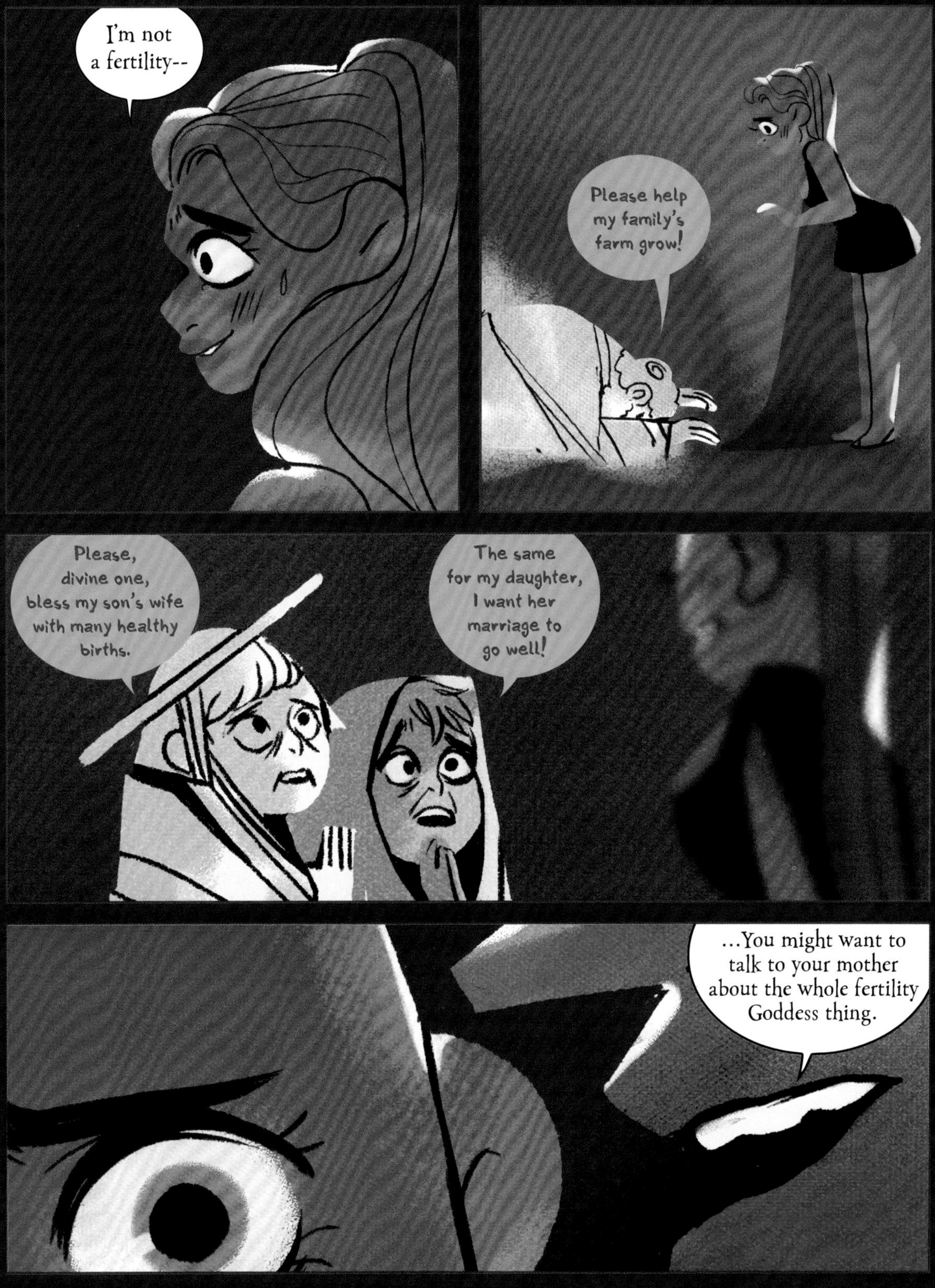
I'm not a fertility--
Please help my family's farm grow!
Please, divine one, bless my son's wife with many healthy births.
The same for my daughter, I want her marriage to go well!
...You might want to talk to your mother about the whole fertility Goddess thing.

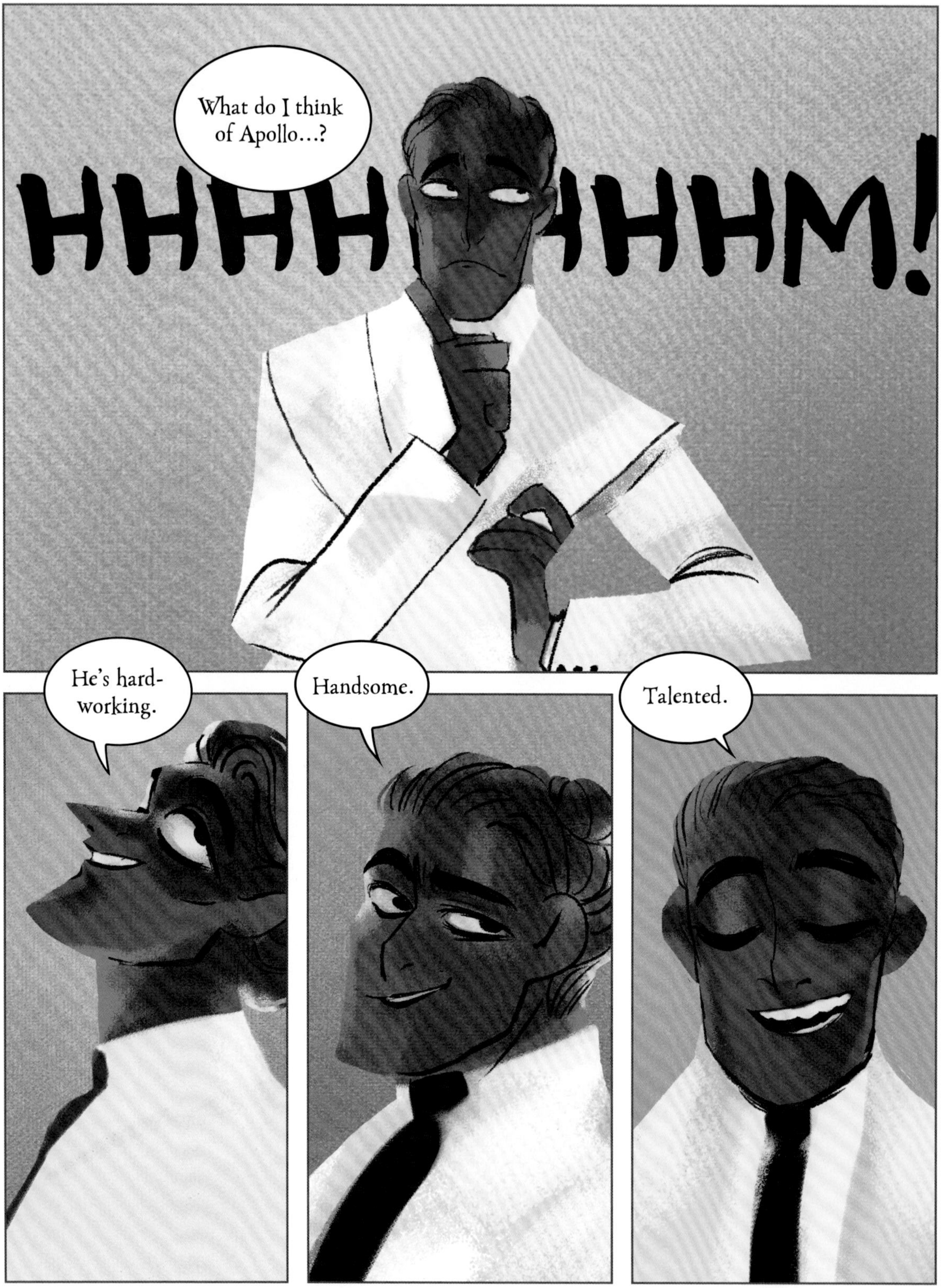
What do I think of Apollo...?
HHHHHHHHHM!
He's hard-working.
Handsome.
Talented.

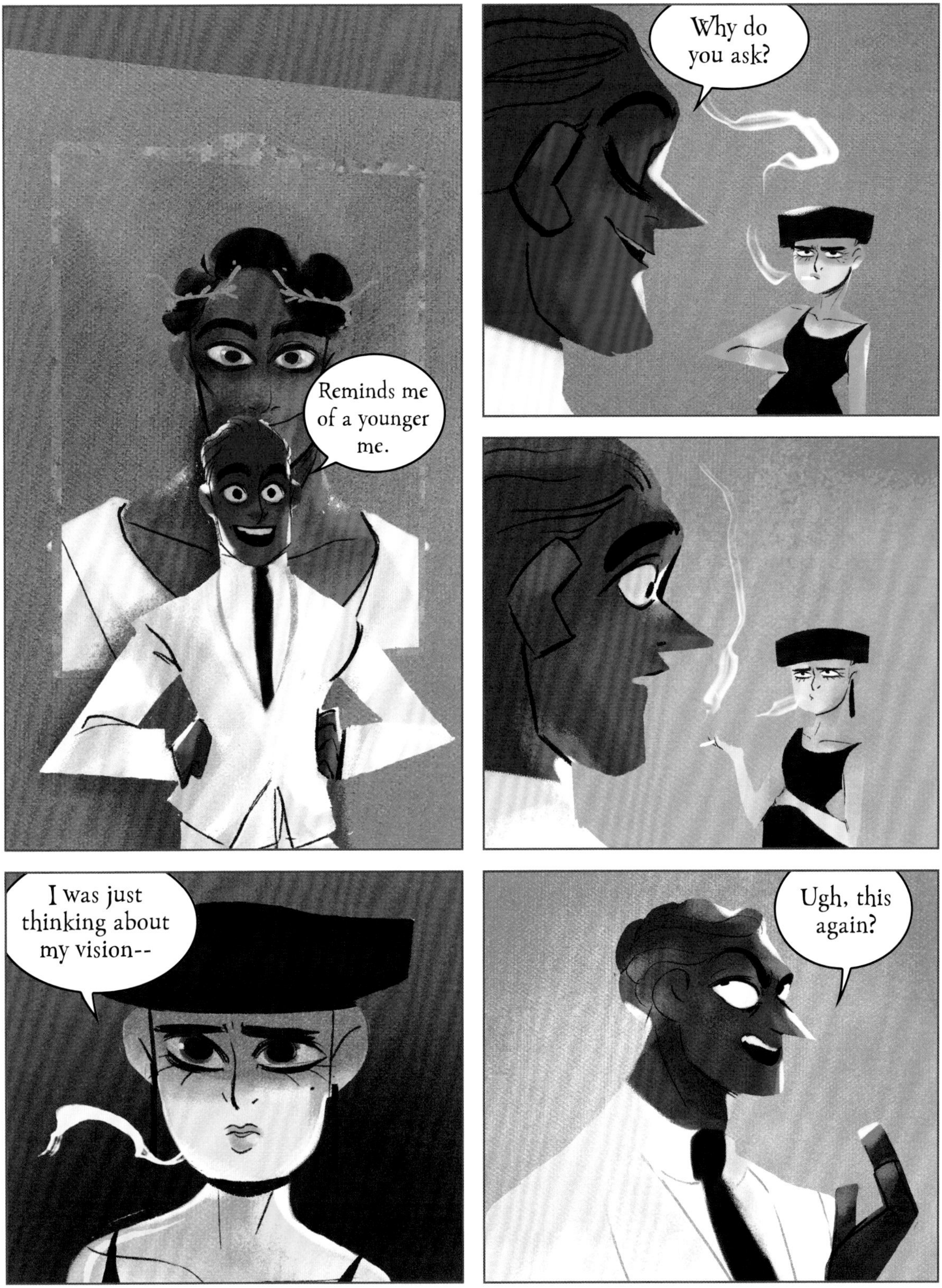
Reminds me of a younger me.
Why do you ask?
I was just thinking about my vision--
Ugh, this again?

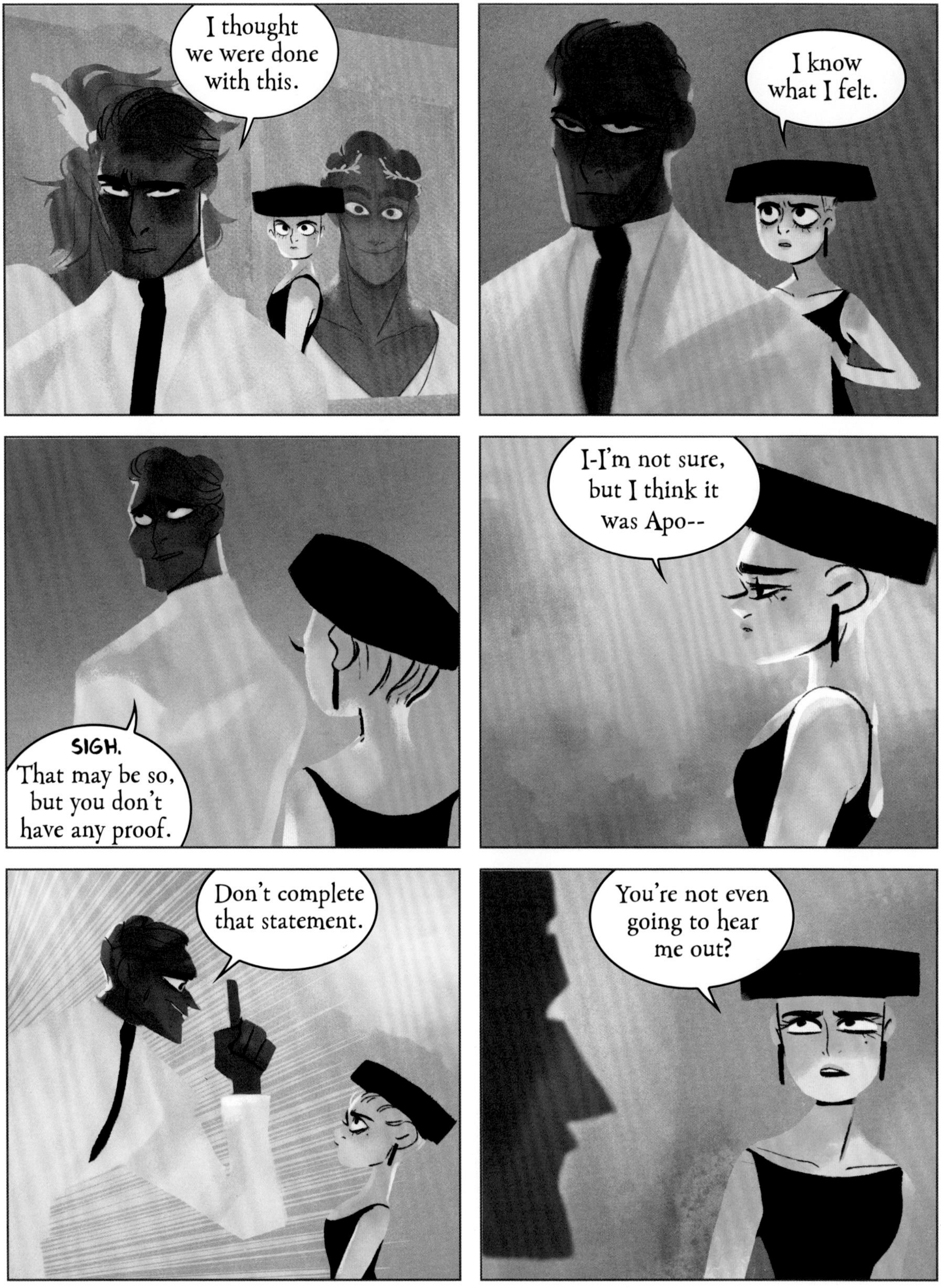
I thought we were done with this.
I know what I felt.
SIGH.
That may be so, but you don't have any proof.
I-I'm not sure, but I think it was Apo--
Don't complete that statement.
You're not even going to hear me out?

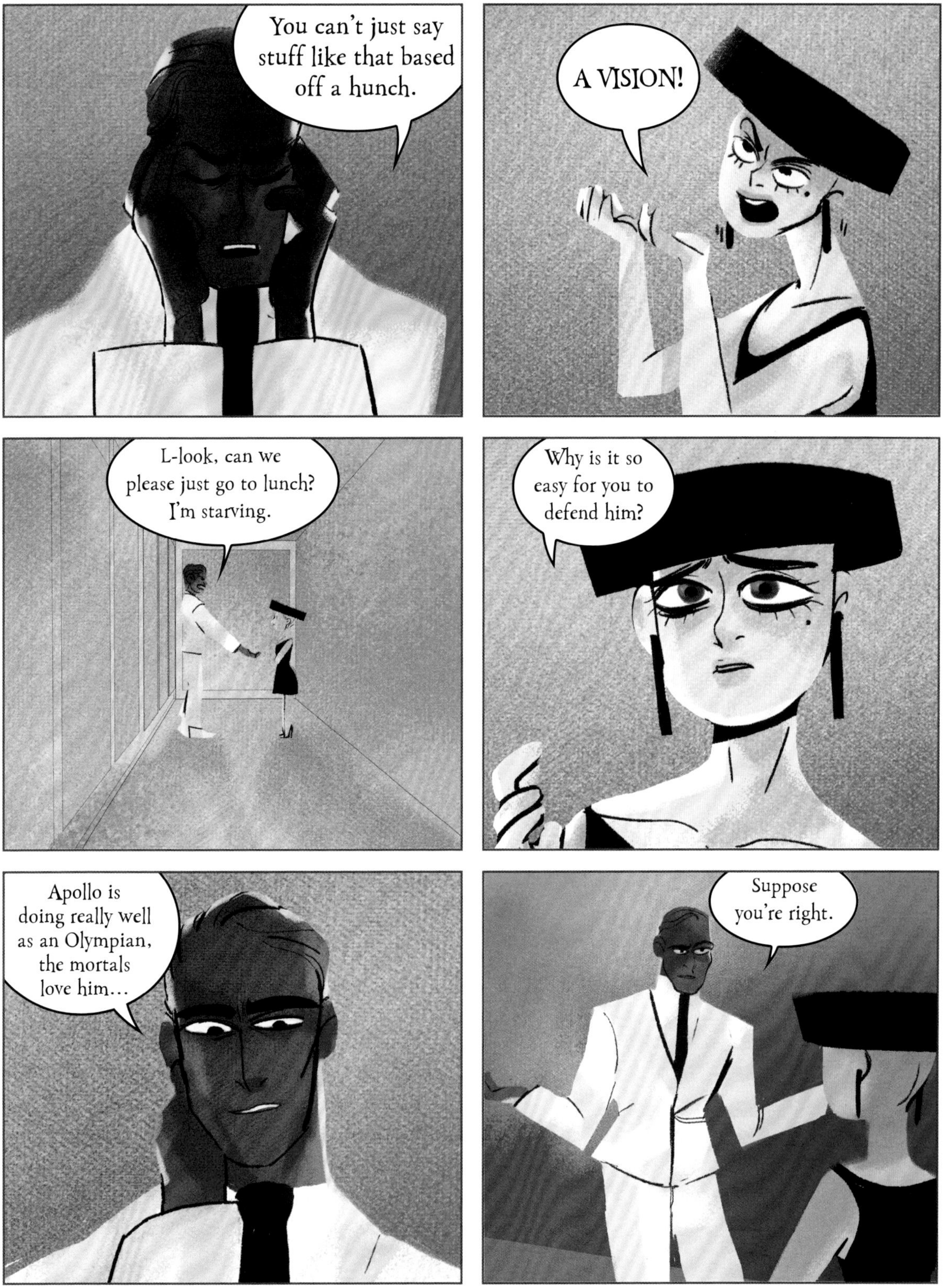
You can't just say stuff like that based off a hunch.
A VISION!
L-look, can we please just go to lunch? I'm starving.
Why is it so easy for you to defend him?
Apollo is doing really well as an Olympian, the mortals love him...
Suppose you're right.

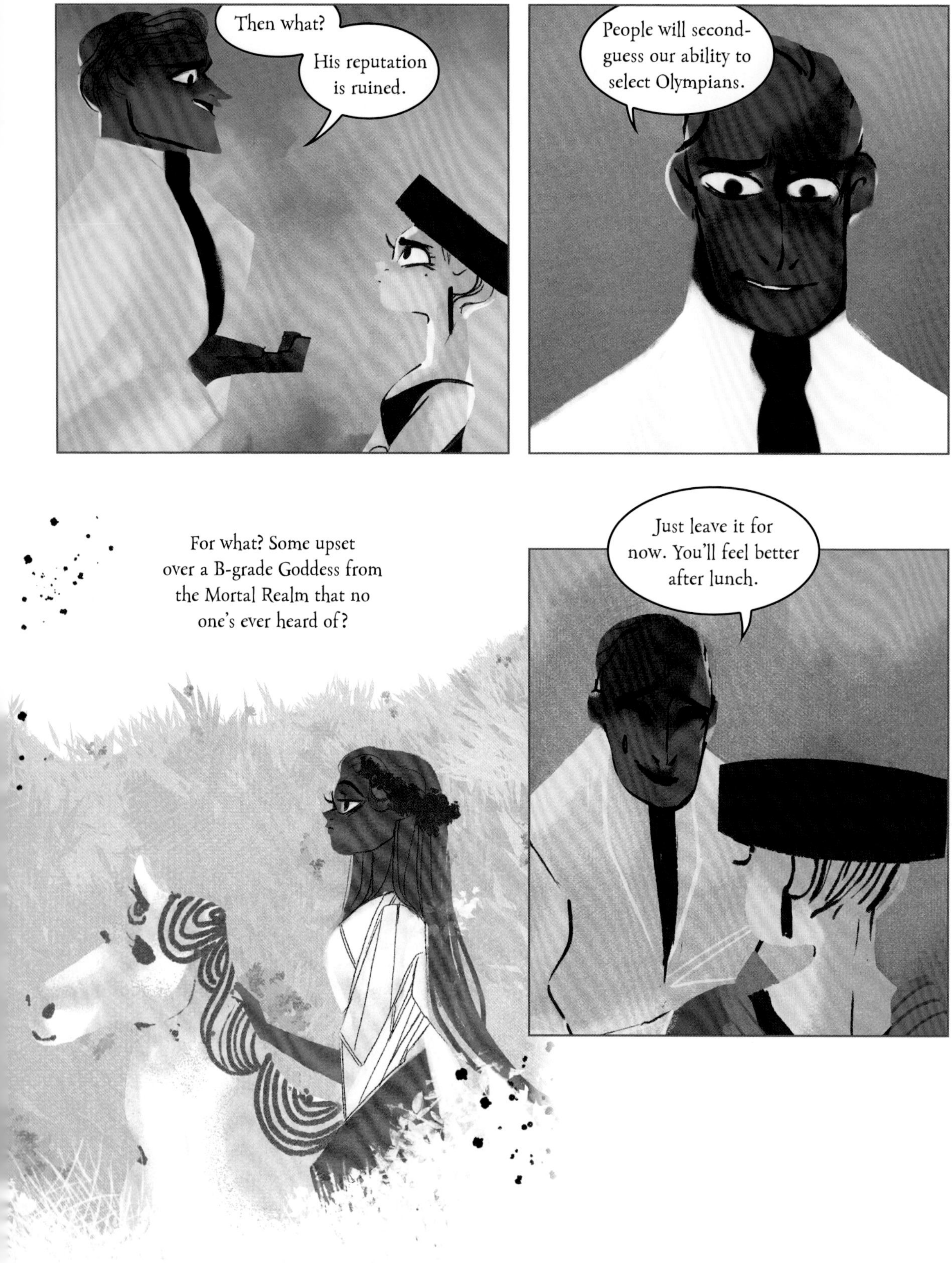
Then what?
His reputation is ruined.
People will second-guess our ability to select Olympians.
For what? Some upset over a B-grade Goddess from the Mortal Realm that no one's ever heard of?
Just leave it for now. You'll feel better after lunch.

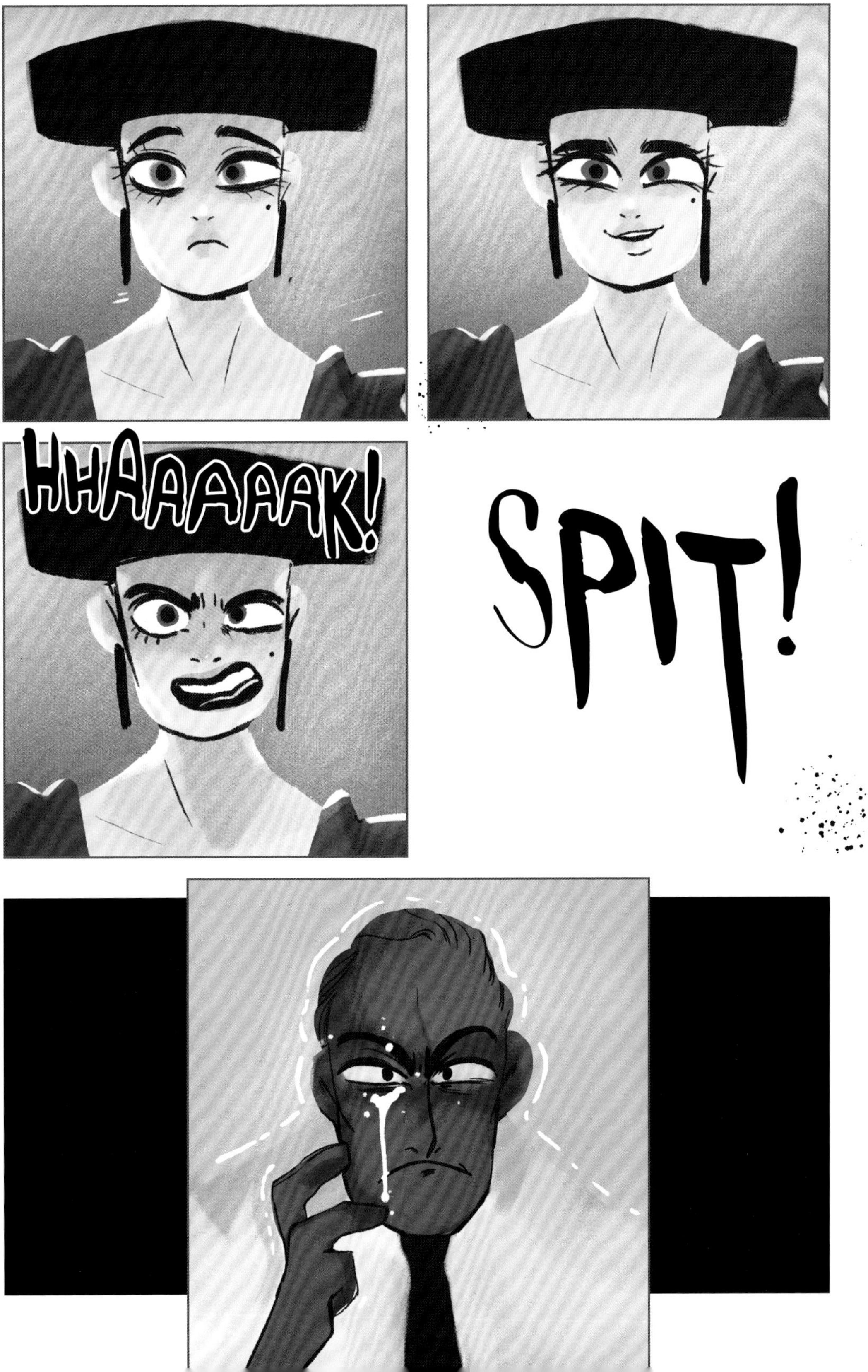
HHAAAAAK!
SPIT!

EPISODE 58: THE OFFER

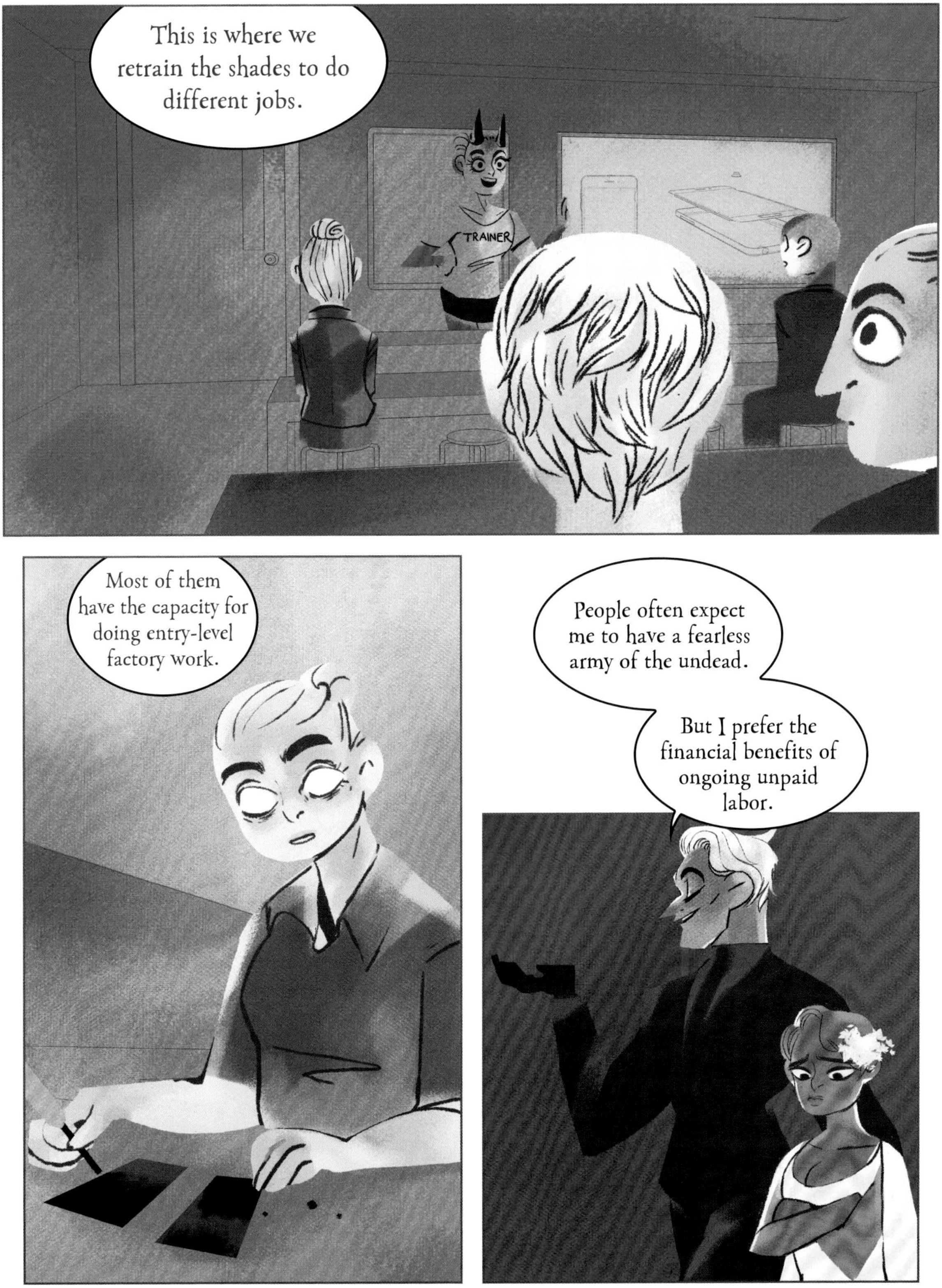
This is where we retrain the shades to do different jobs.
TRAINER
Most of them have the capacity for doing entry-level factory work.
People often expect me to have a fearless army of the undead.
But I prefer the financial benefits of ongoing unpaid labor.

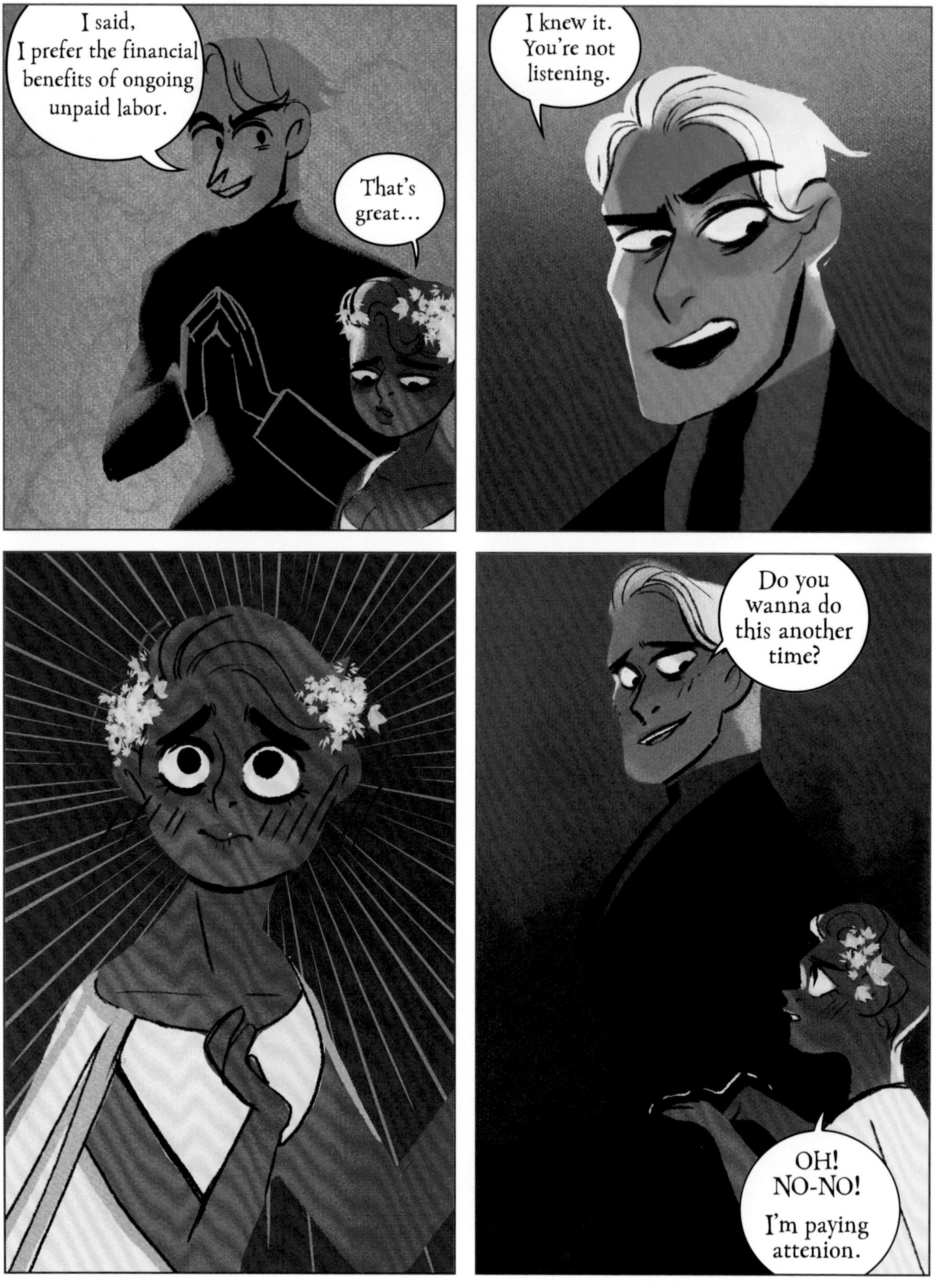
I said, I prefer the financial benefits of ongoing unpaid labor.
That's great...
I knew it. You're not listening.
Do you wanna do this another time?
OH! NO-NO!
I'm paying attenion.

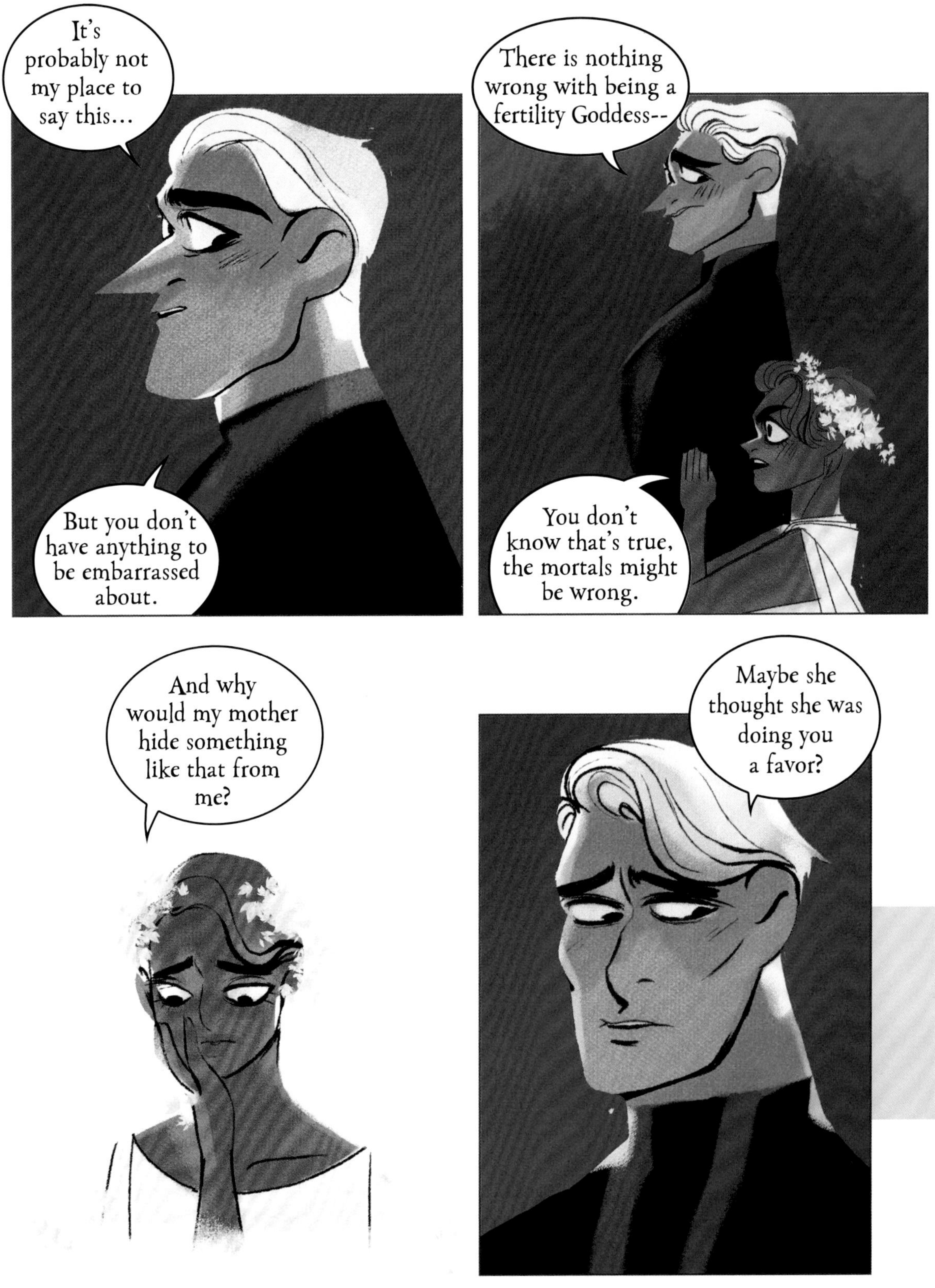

It's probably not my place to say this...
But you don't have anything to be embarrassed about.
There is nothing wrong with being a fertility Goddess--
You don't know that's true, the mortals might be wrong.
And why would my mother hide something like that from me?
Maybe she thought she was doing you a favor?

Well... aren't you one of The Goddesses of Eternal Maidenhood?

It's a little contradictory for a fertility Goddess to be a virgin for all eternity--

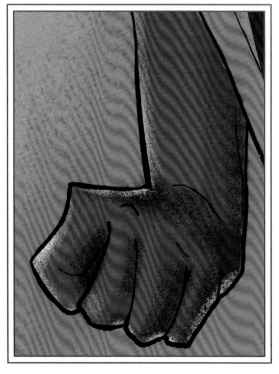

So you know about that, huh?

Sorry! It's in your transcript.

Ah, my scholarship.

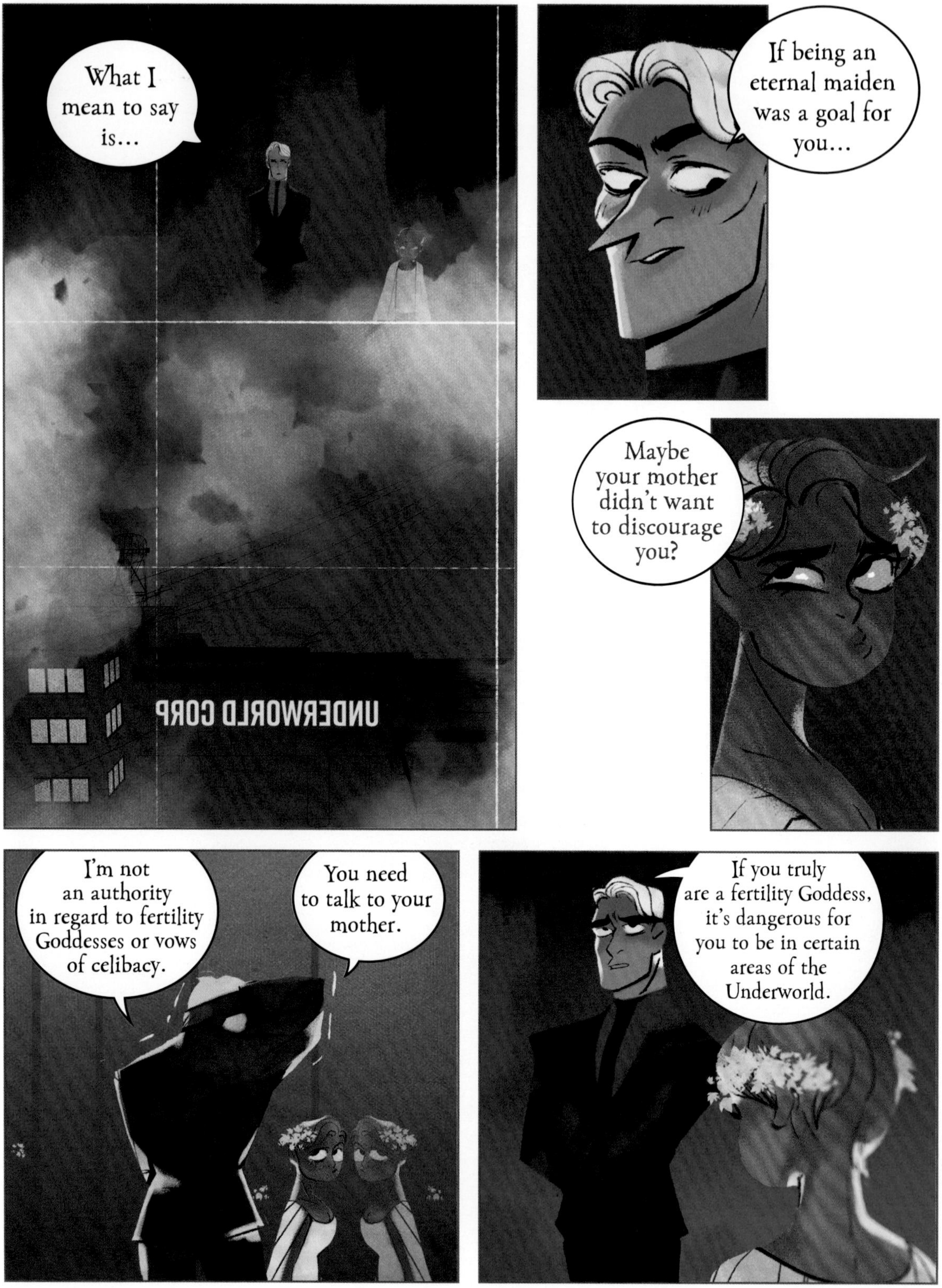
What I mean to say is…
UNDERWORLD CORP
If being an eternal maiden was a goal for you…
Maybe your mother didn't want to discourage you?
I'm not an authority in regard to fertility Goddesses or vows of celibacy.
You need to talk to your mother.
If you truly are a fertility Goddess, it's dangerous for you to be in certain areas of the Underworld.

R-really!?

O-oh, do-don't worry.

Just stay away from tower 4 until we get to the bottom of this.

I'm not sure how to put this...

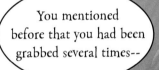

You mentioned before that you had been grabbed several times--

...

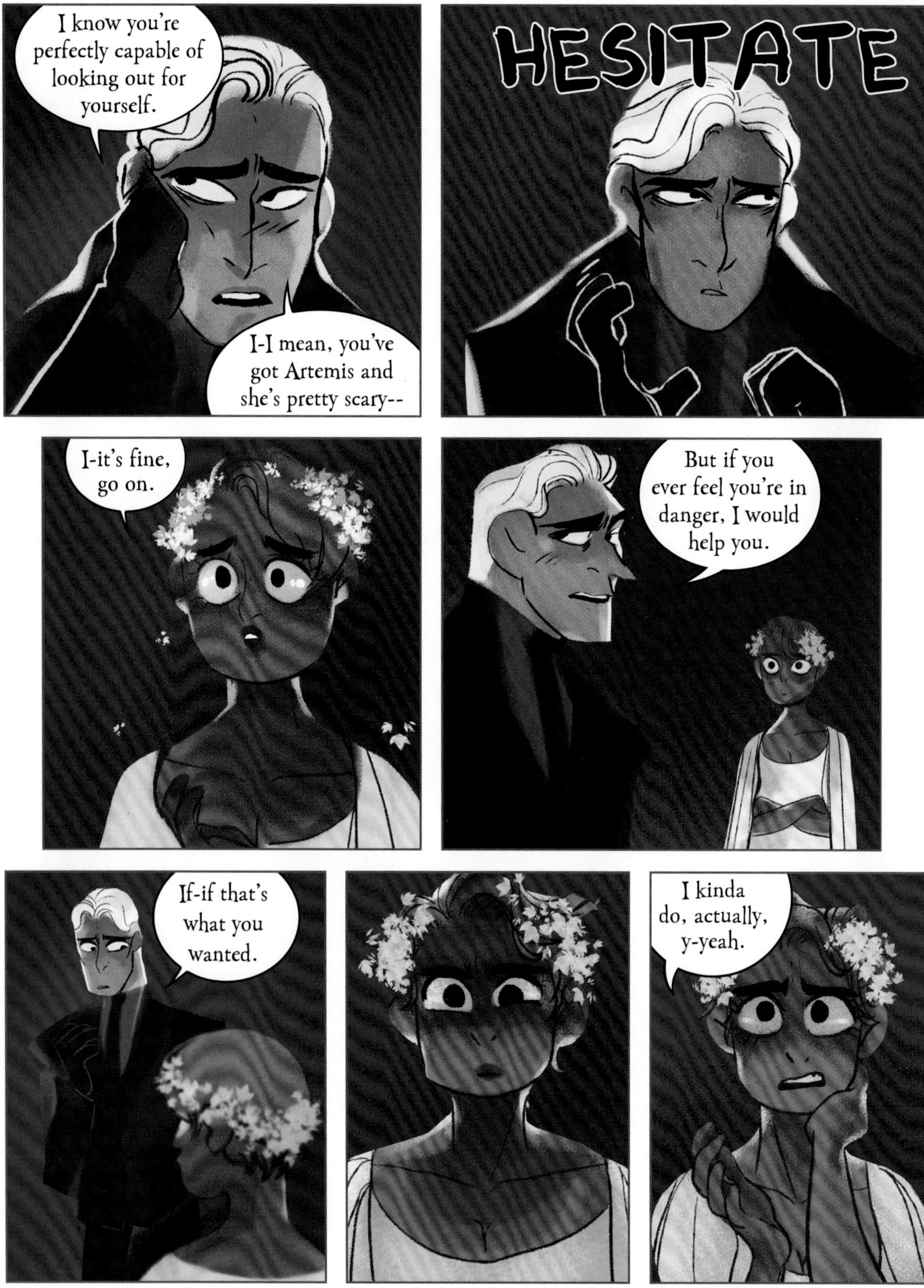
I know you're perfectly capable of looking out for yourself.
I-I mean, you've got Artemis and she's pretty scary--
HESITATE
I-it's fine, go on.
But if you ever feel you're in danger, I would help you.
If-if that's what you wanted.
I kinda do, actually, y-yeah.

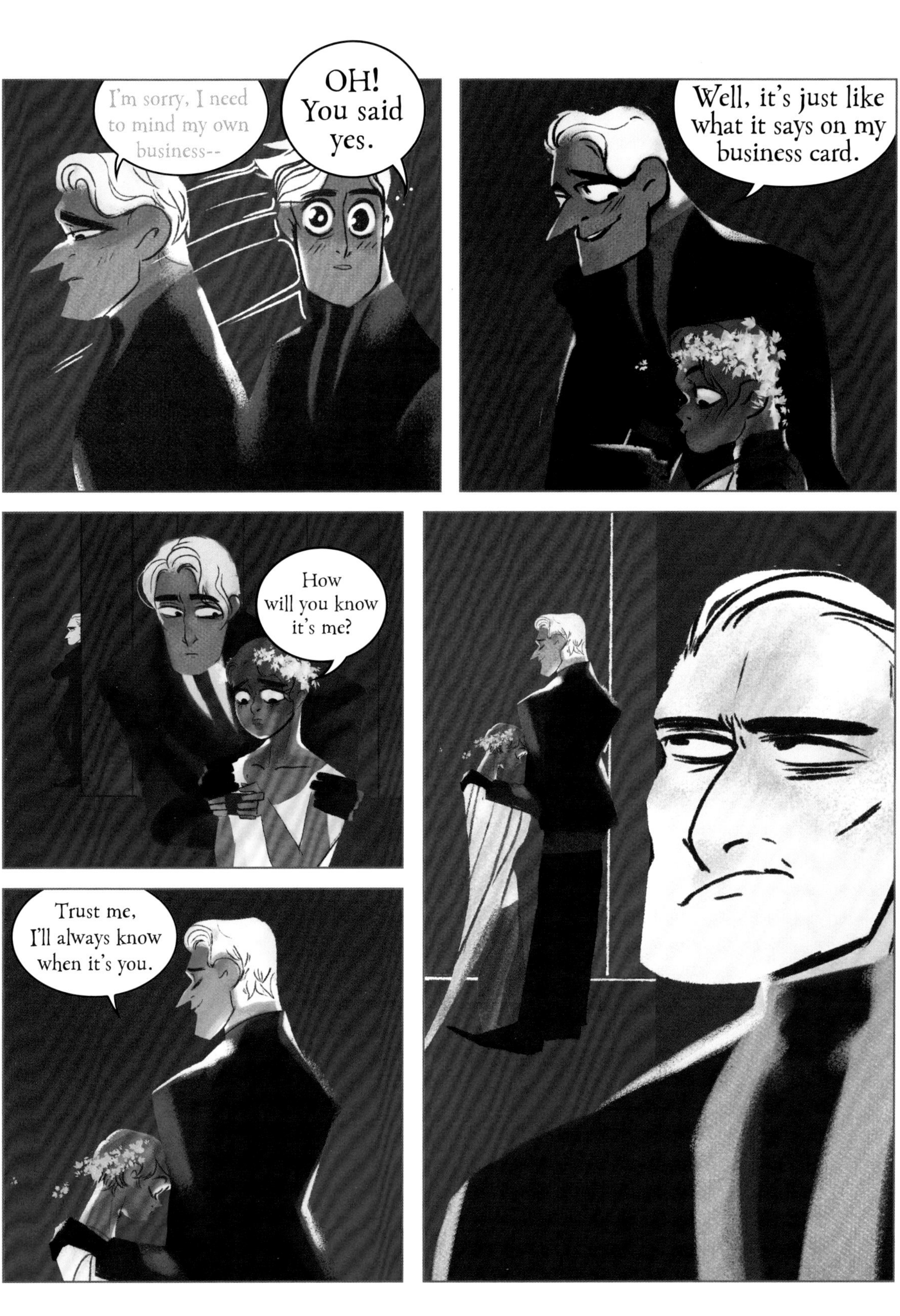
I'm sorry, I need to mind my own business--
OH! You said yes.
Well, it's just like what it says on my business card.
How will you know it's me?
Trust me, I'll always know when it's you.

EPISODE 59: WHIPLASH

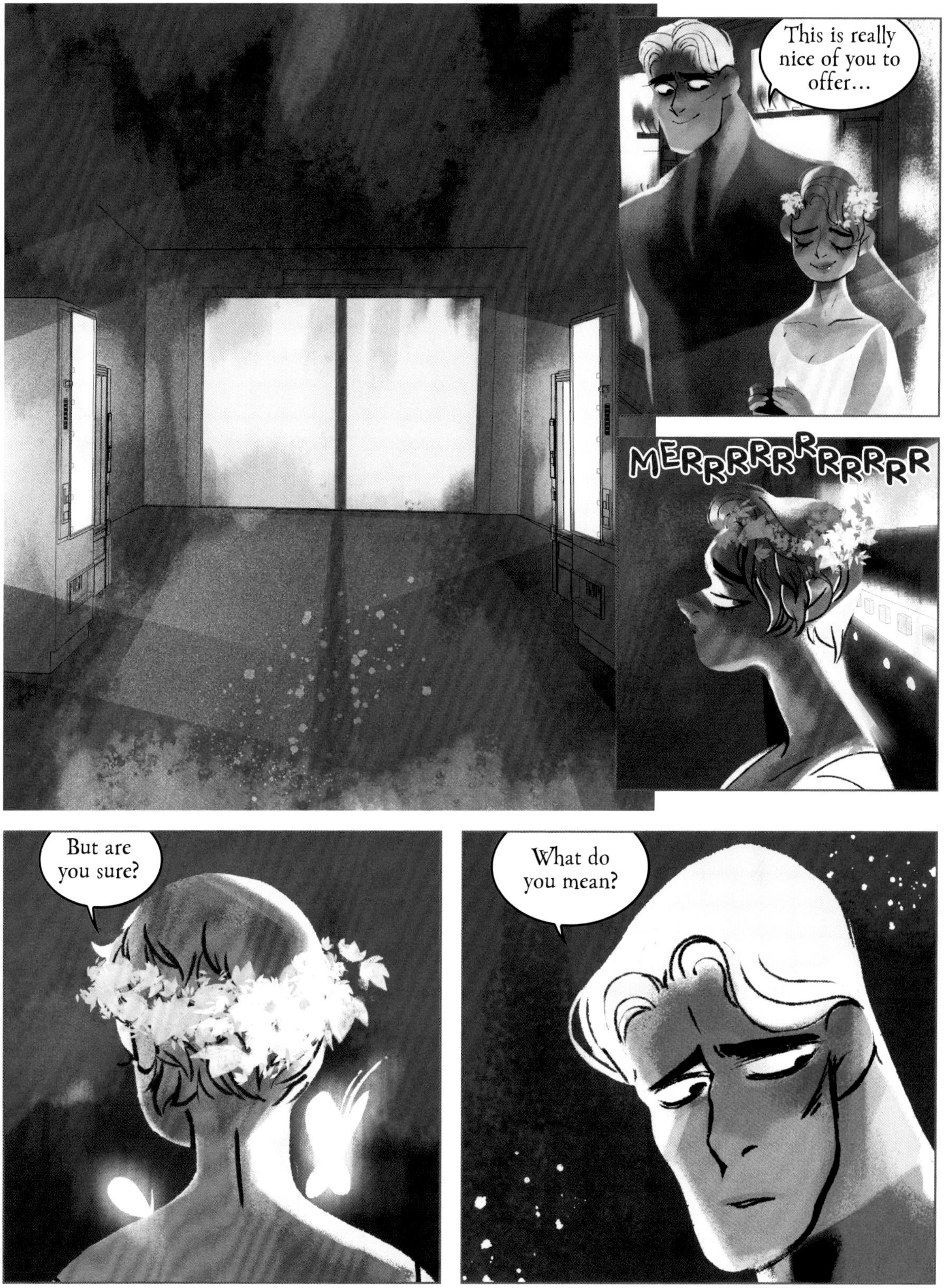
This is really nice of you to offer…
MERRRRRRRRRRR
But are you sure?
What do you mean?

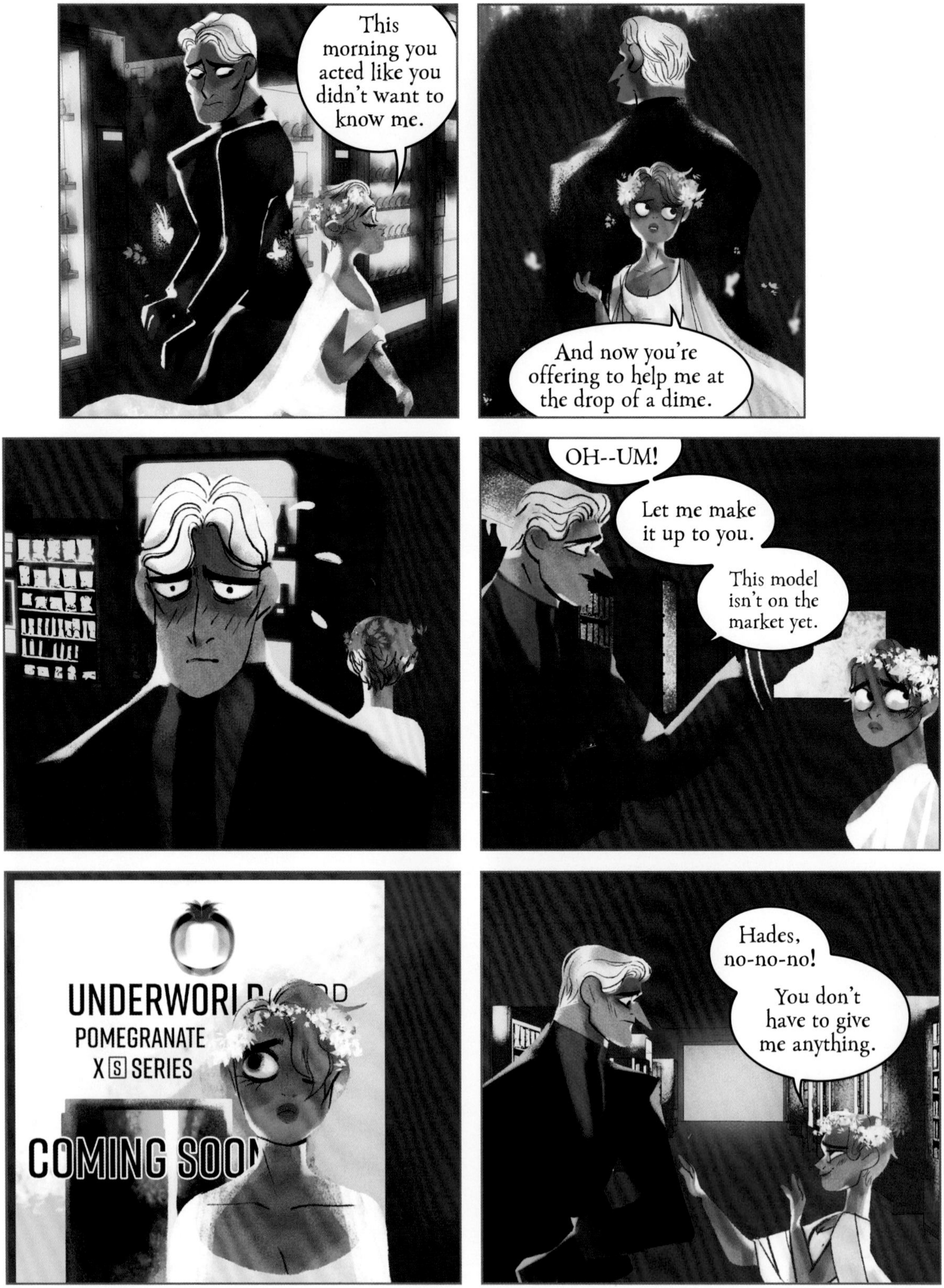
This morning you acted like you didn't want to know me.
And now you're offering to help me at the drop of a dime.
OH--UM!
Let me make it up to you.
This model isn't on the market yet.
UNDERWORLD
POMEGRANATE
X S SERIES
COMING SOO
Hades, no-no-no!
You don't have to give me anything.

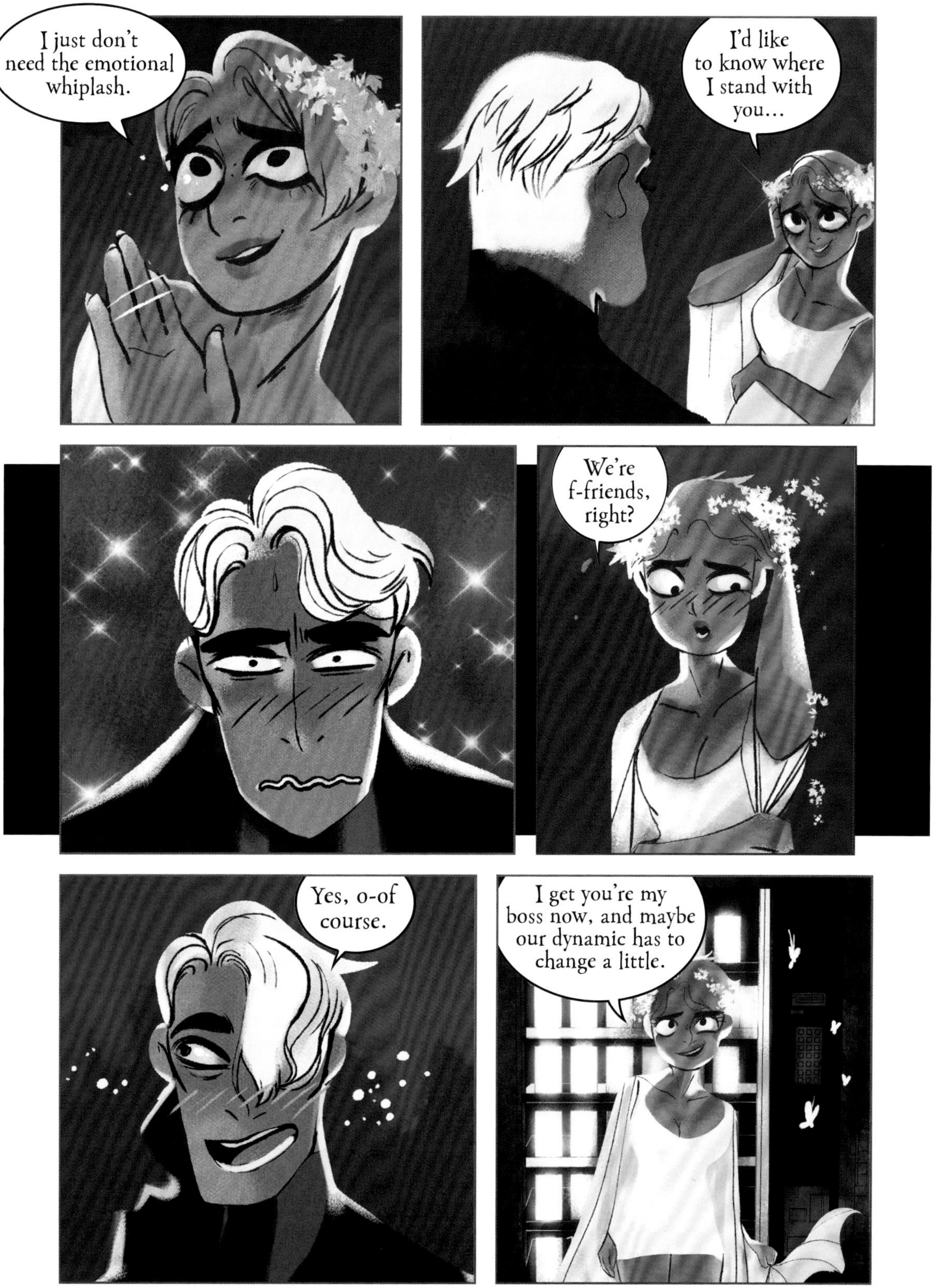
I just don't need the emotional whiplash.
I'd like to know where I stand with you...
We're f-friends, right?
Yes, o-of course.
I get you're my boss now, and maybe our dynamic has to change a little.

Just let me know what your boundaries are.
I know sometimes I can be a little too friendly...
It's just weird going out into the world and not having a hand to hold.

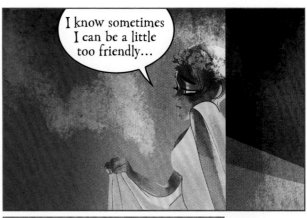

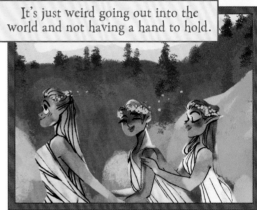

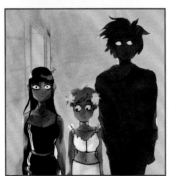

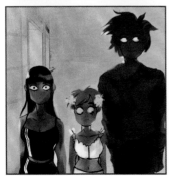

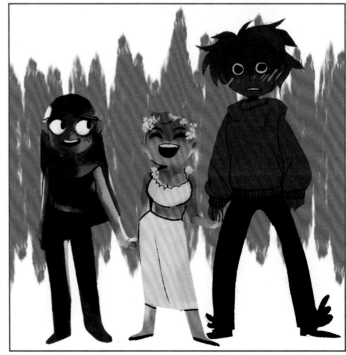

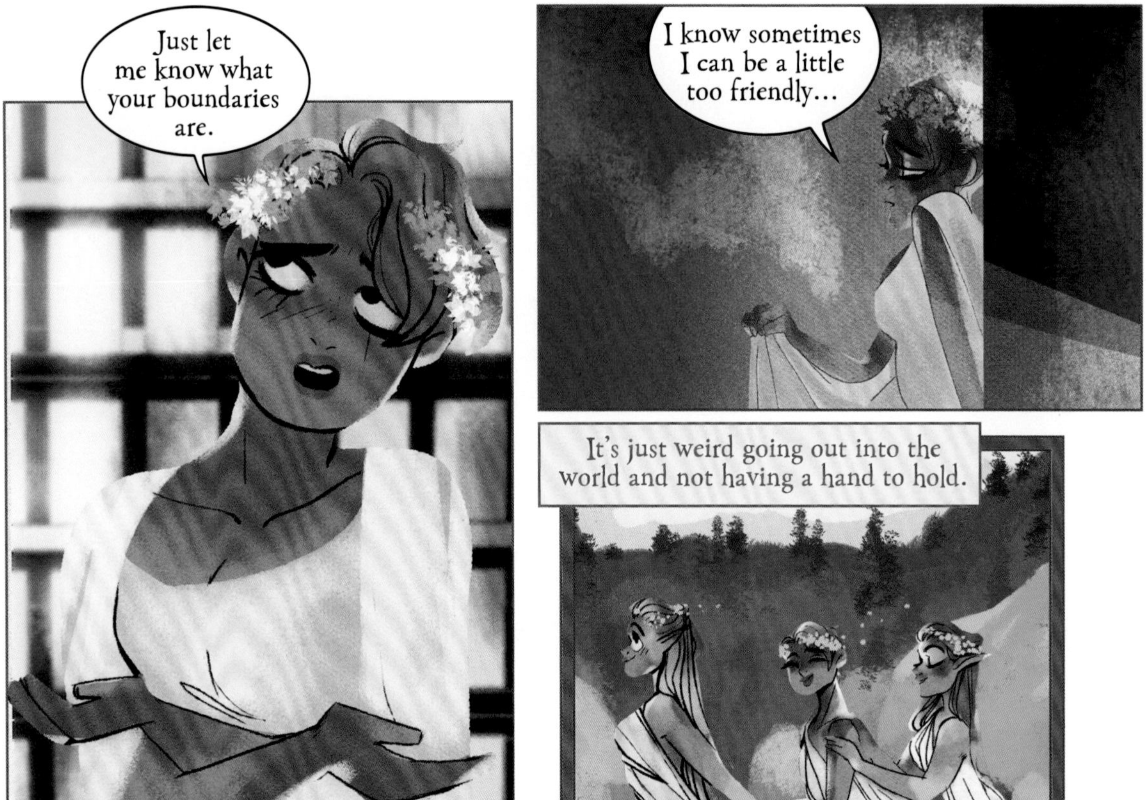

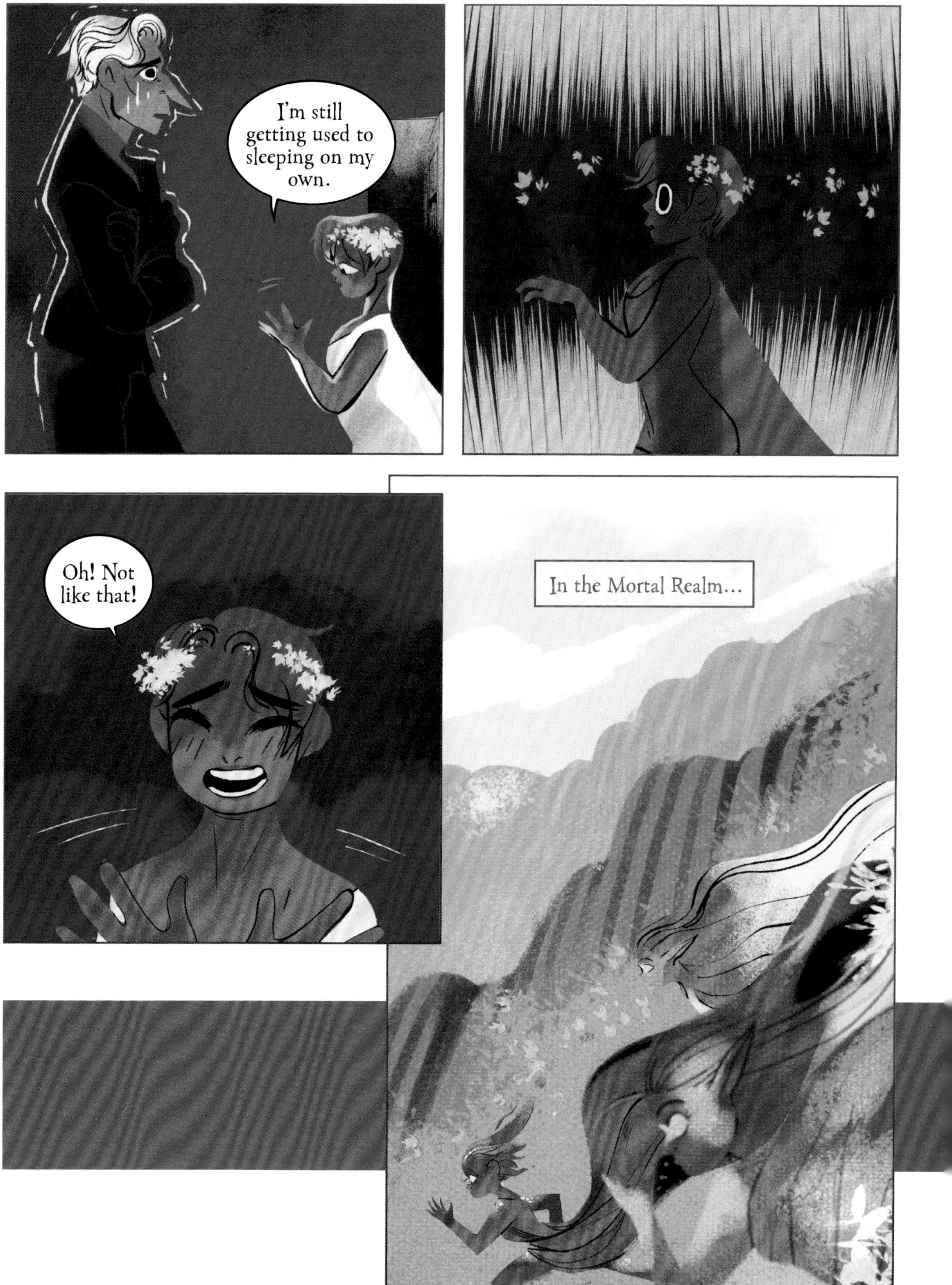
I'm still getting used to sleeping on my own.
Oh! Not like that!
In the Mortal Realm...

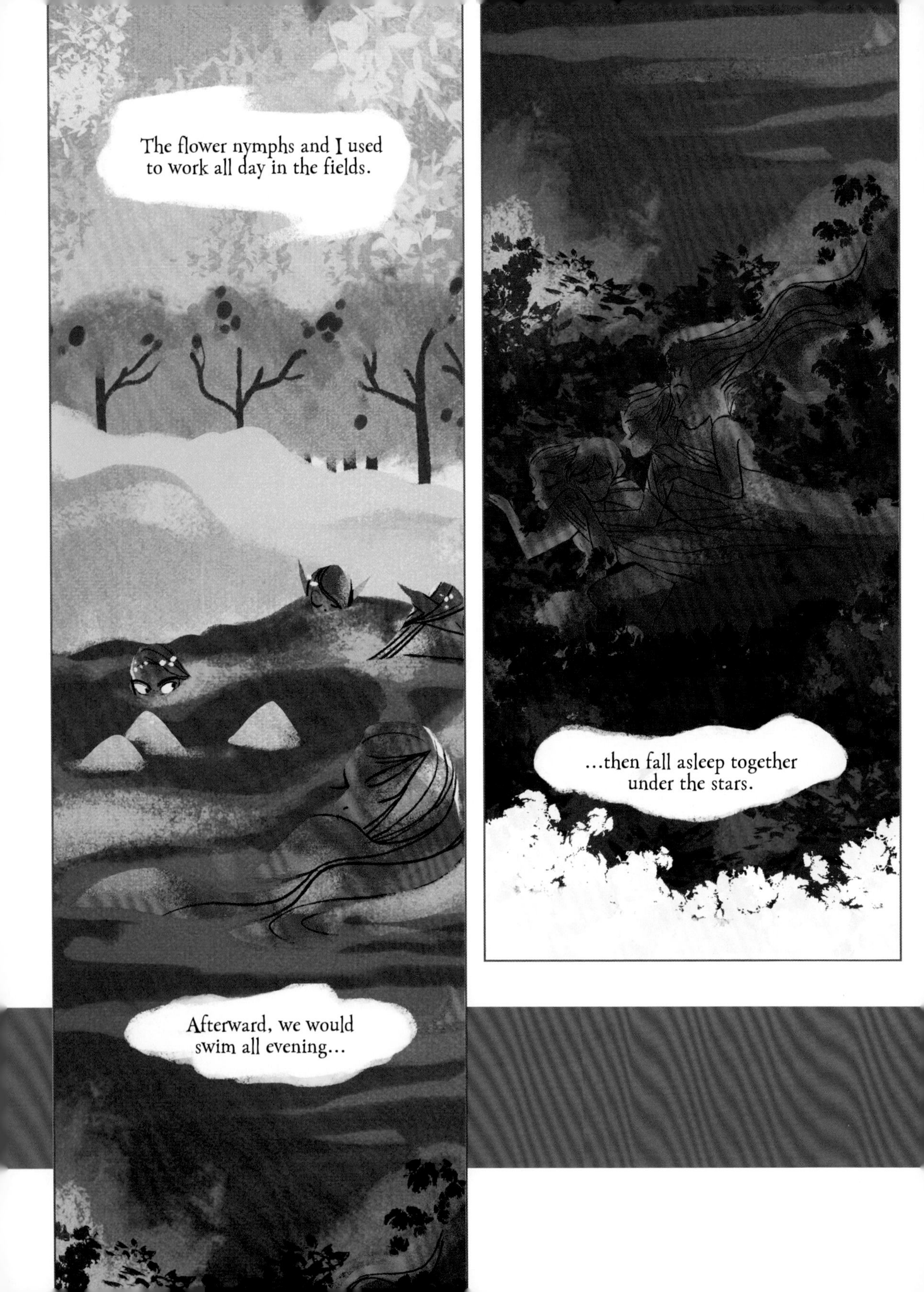
The flower nymphs and I used to work all day in the fields.
Afterward, we would swim all evening...
...then fall asleep together under the stars.

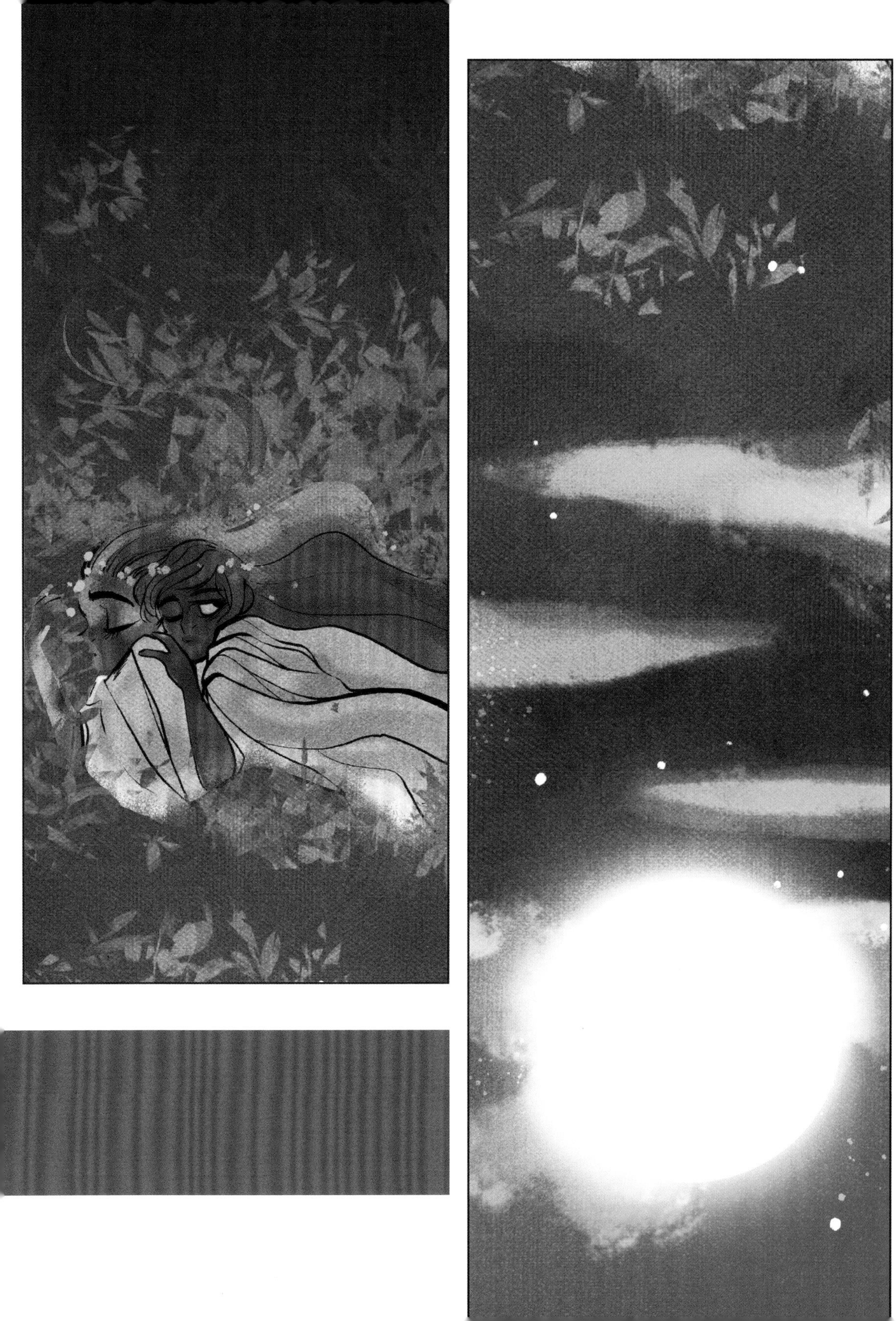

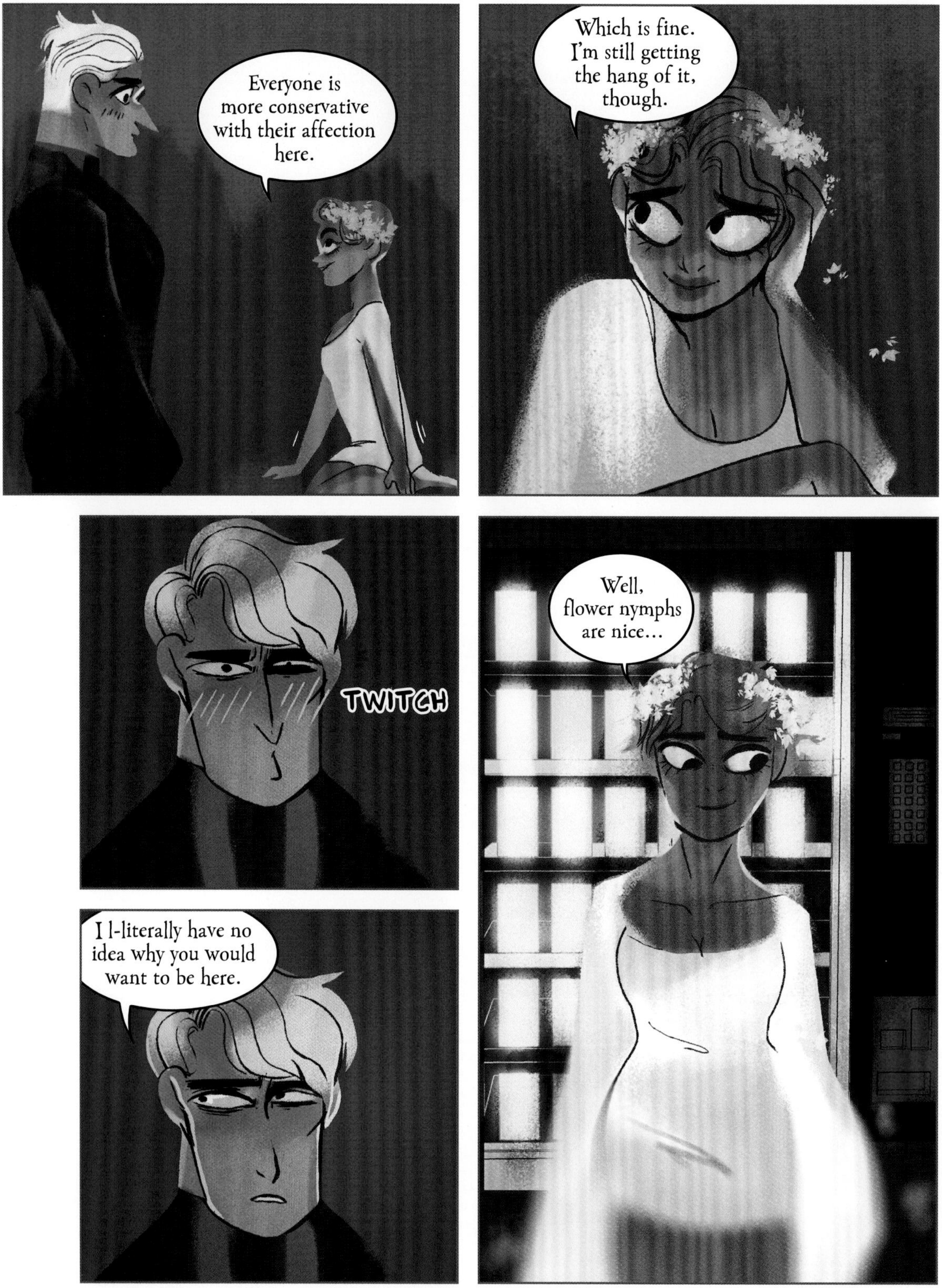
Everyone is more conservative with their affection here.
Which is fine. I'm still getting the hang of it, though.
TWITCH
I l-literally have no idea why you would want to be here.
Well, flower nymphs are nice...

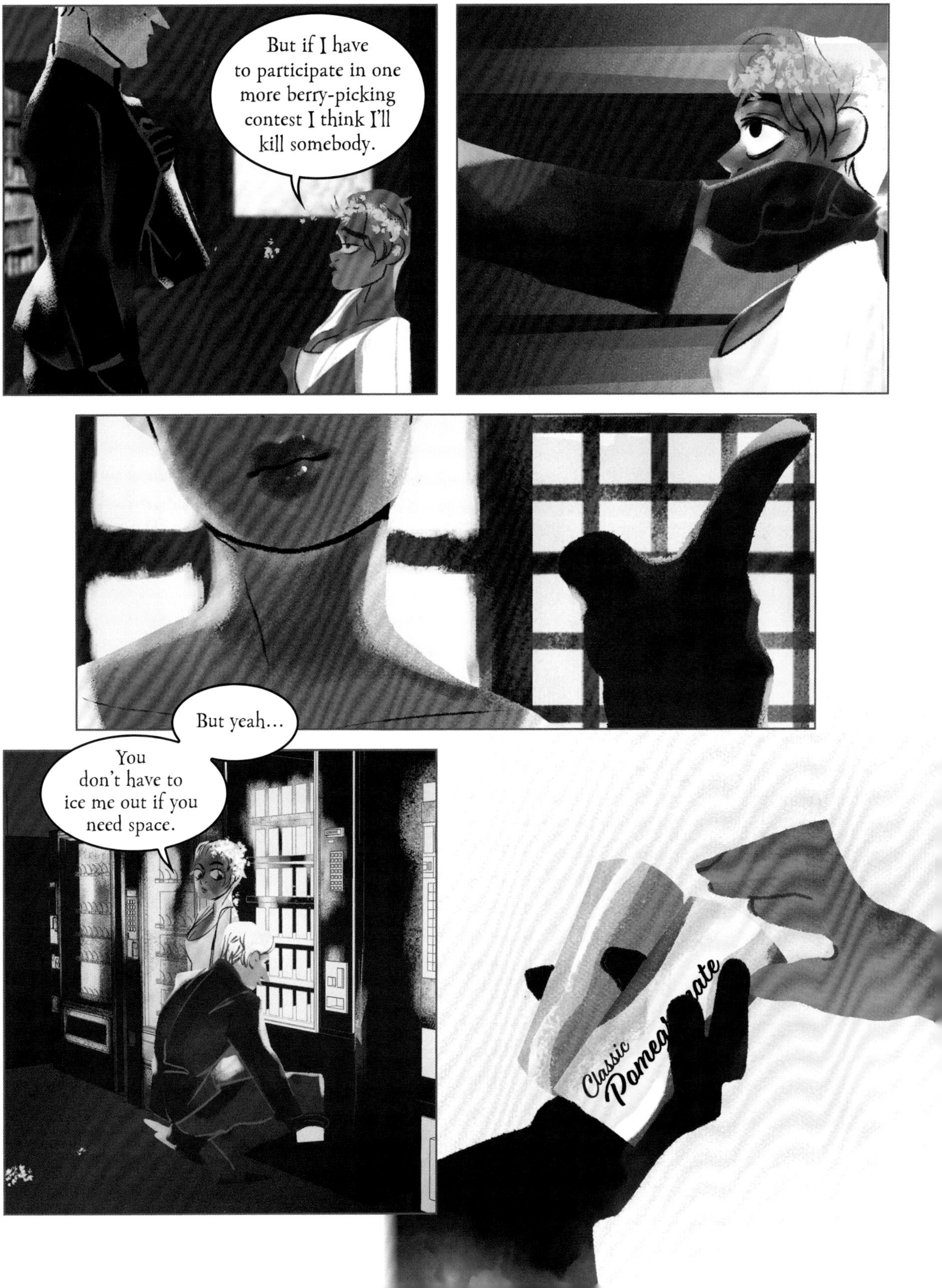
But if I have to participate in one more berry-picking contest I think I'll kill somebody.
But yeah...
You don't have to ice me out if you need space.
Classic

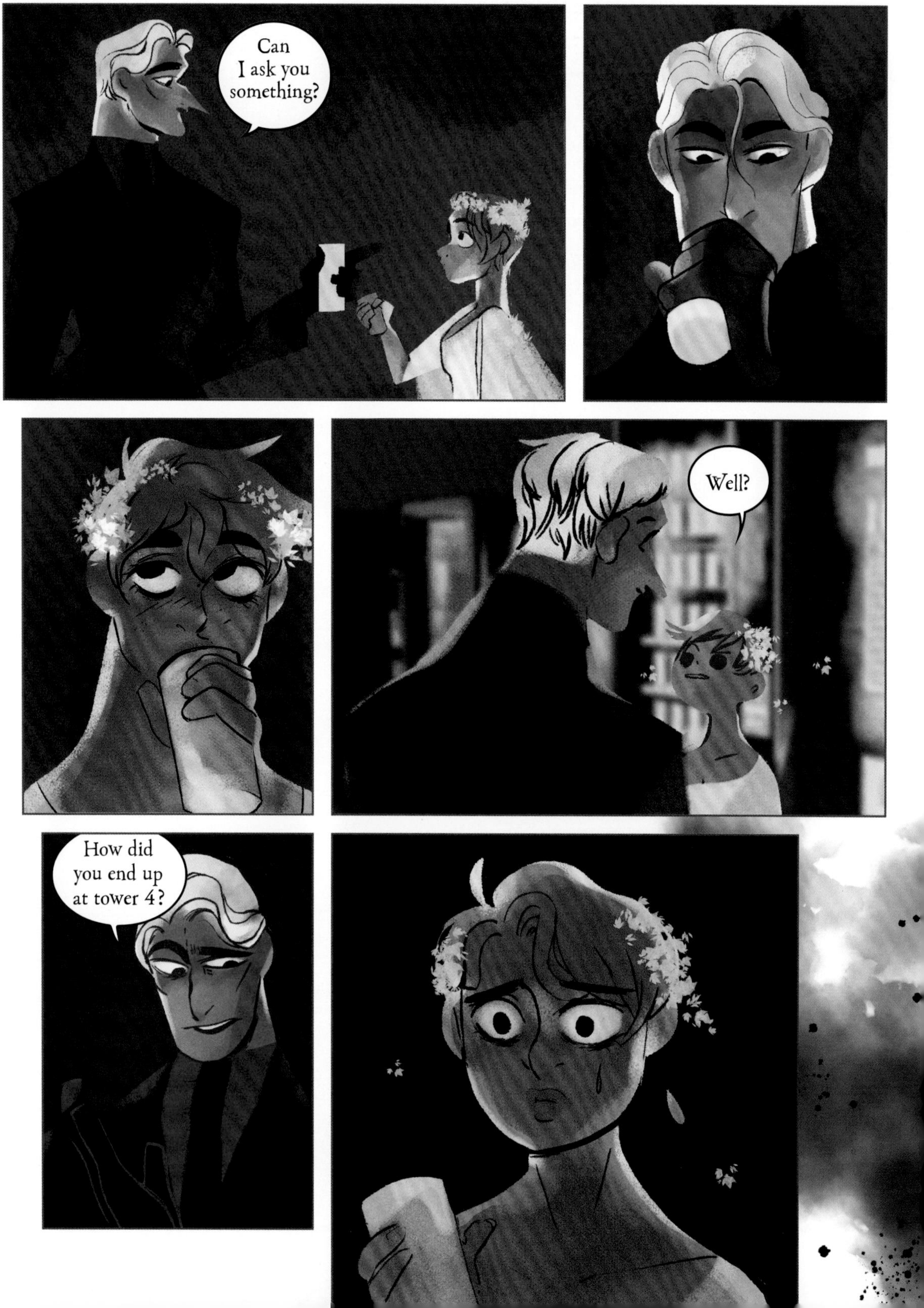
Can I ask you something?
Well?
How did you end up at tower 4?

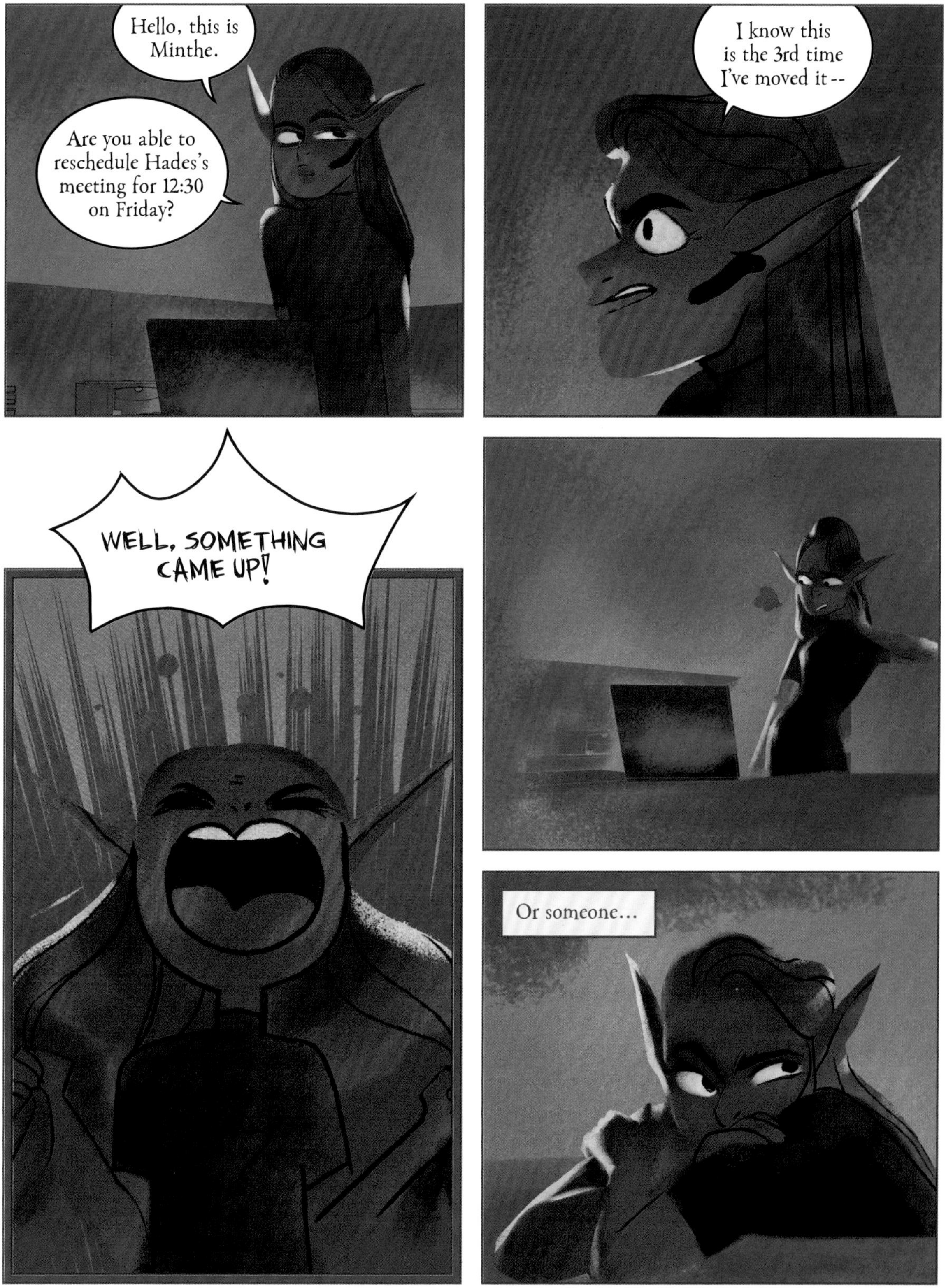
Hello, this is Minthe.
Are you able to reschedule Hades's meeting for 12:30 on Friday?
I know this is the 3rd time I've moved it --
WELL, SOMETHING CAME UP!
Or someone...

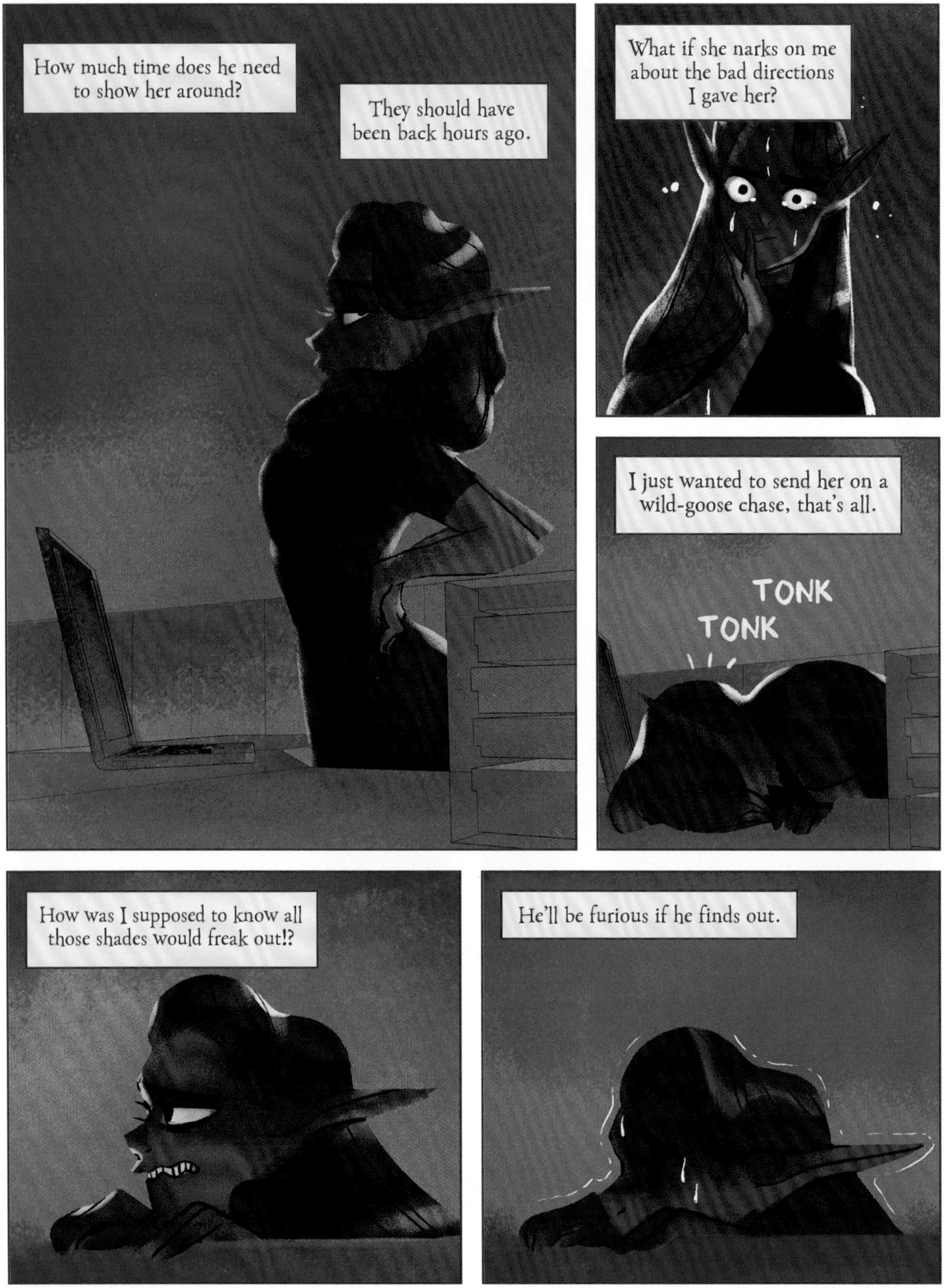
How much time does he need to show her around?
They should have been back hours ago.
What if she narks on me about the bad directions I gave her?
I just wanted to send her on a wild-goose chase, that's all.
TONK
TONK
How was I supposed to know all those shades would freak out!?
He'll be furious if he finds out.

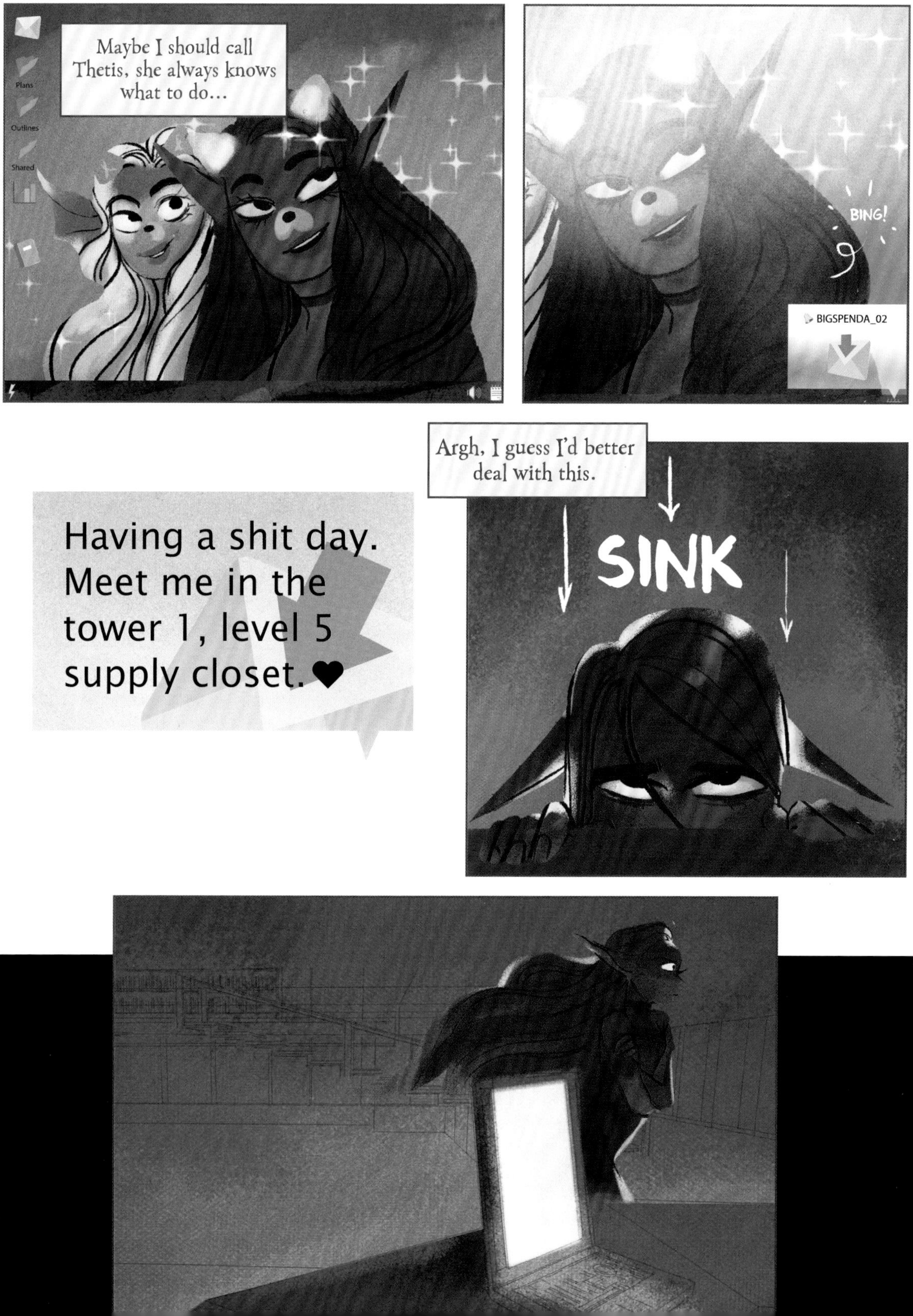
Maybe I should call Thetis, she always knows what to do...
Plans
Outlines
Shared
BING!
BIGSPENDA_02
Having a shit day. Meet me in the tower 1, level 5 supply closet. ♥
Argh, I guess I'd better deal with this.
SINK

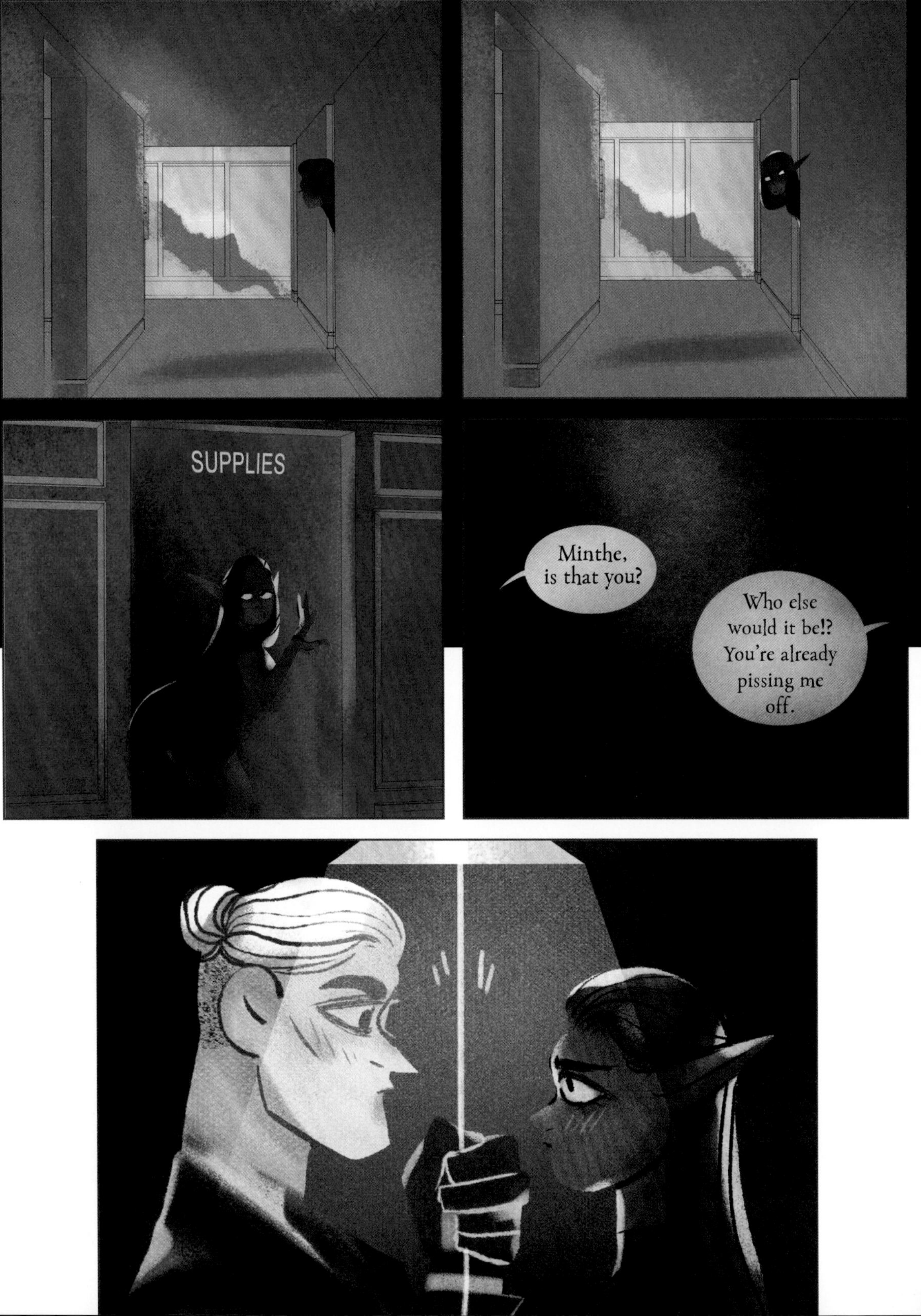
SUPPLIES
Minthe, is that you?
Who else would it be!? You're already pissing me off.

How did
you end up
at tower 4?

That nymph...

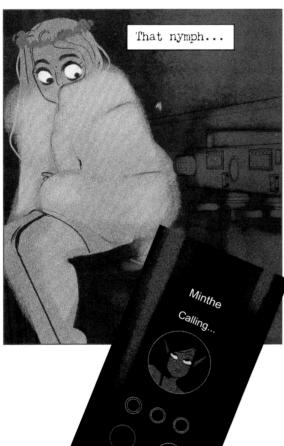

Minthe

Calling...

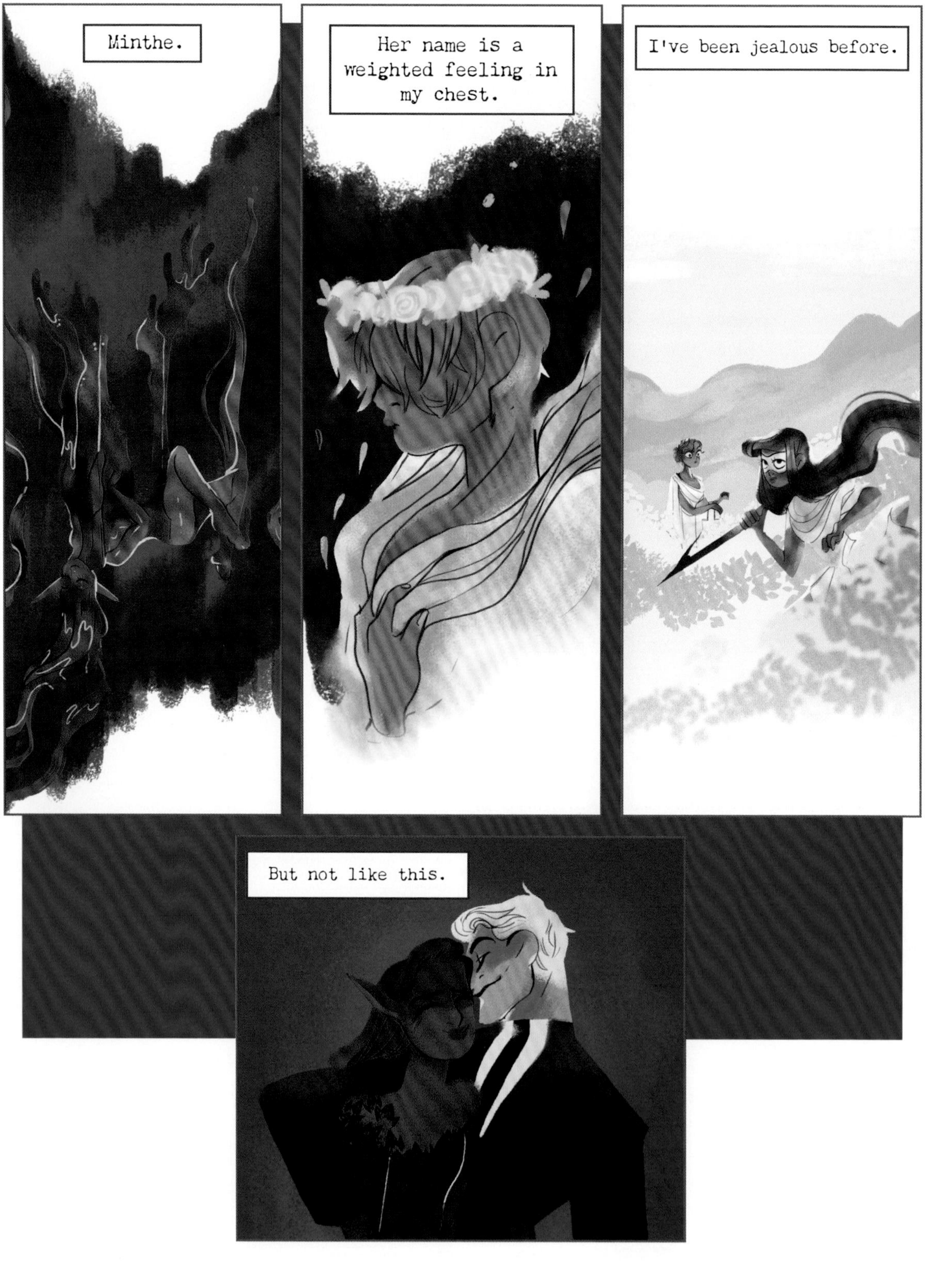
Minthe.
Her name is a weighted feeling in my chest.
I've been jealous before.
But not like this.

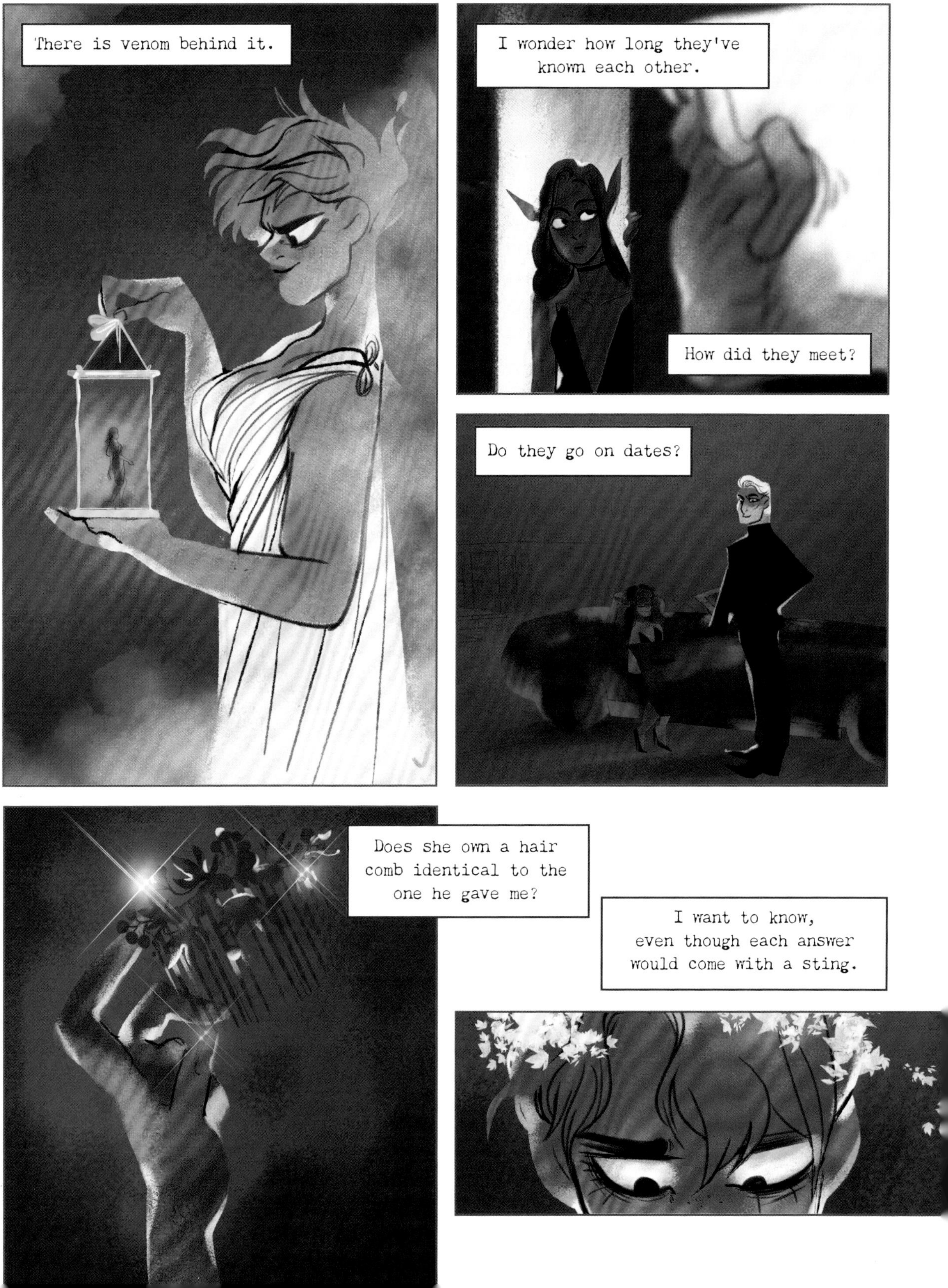
There is venom behind it.
I wonder how long they've known each other.
How did they meet?
Do they go on dates?
Does she own a hair comb identical to the one he gave me?
I want to know, even though each answer would come with a sting.

I could tell him the truth.

Get her in trouble.

Maybe she would even get fired.

...Would they break up?

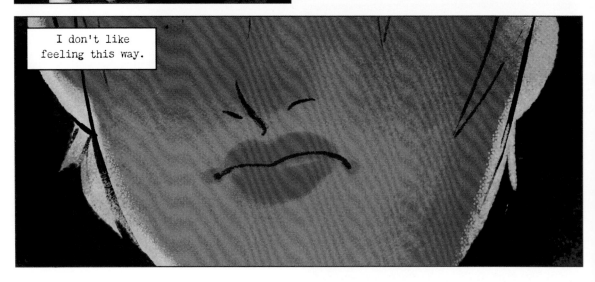

I don't like feeling this way.

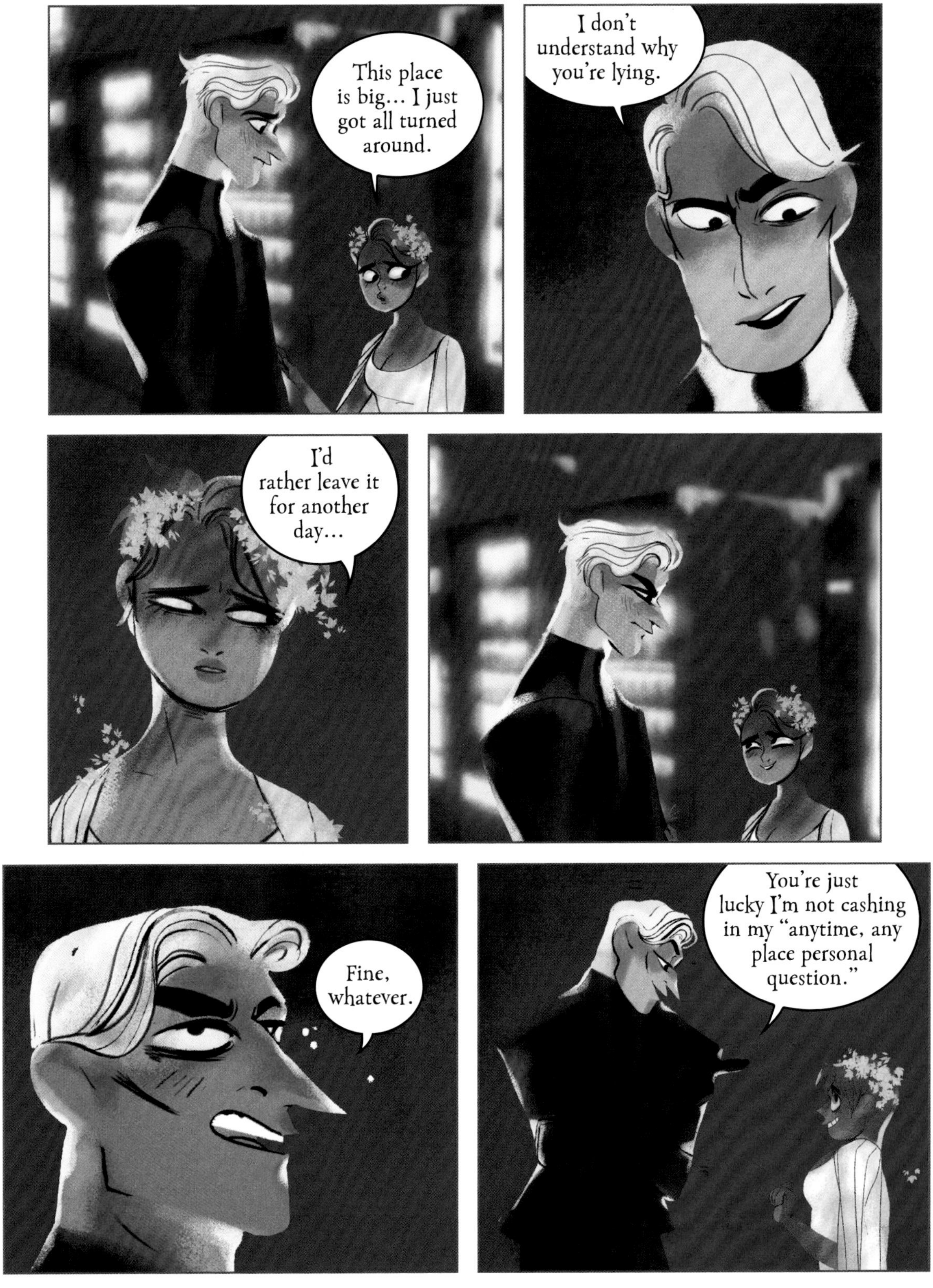
This place is big... I just got all turned around.
I don't understand why you're lying.
I'd rather leave it for another day...
Fine, whatever.
You're just lucky I'm not cashing in my "anytime, any place personal question."

Thanks.

EPISODE 60: THAT NYMPH OVER THERE

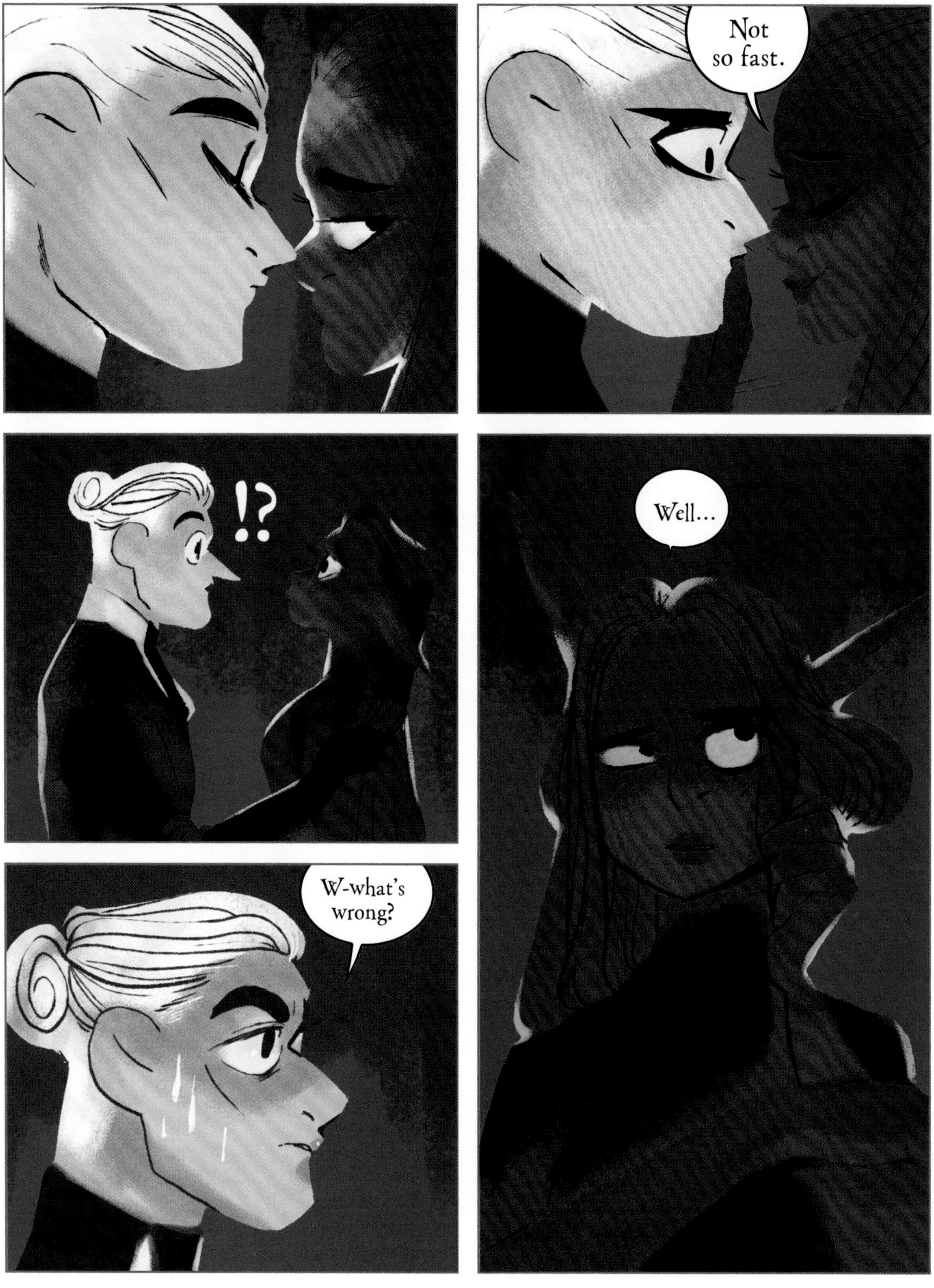
Not so fast.
!?
W-what's wrong?
Well...

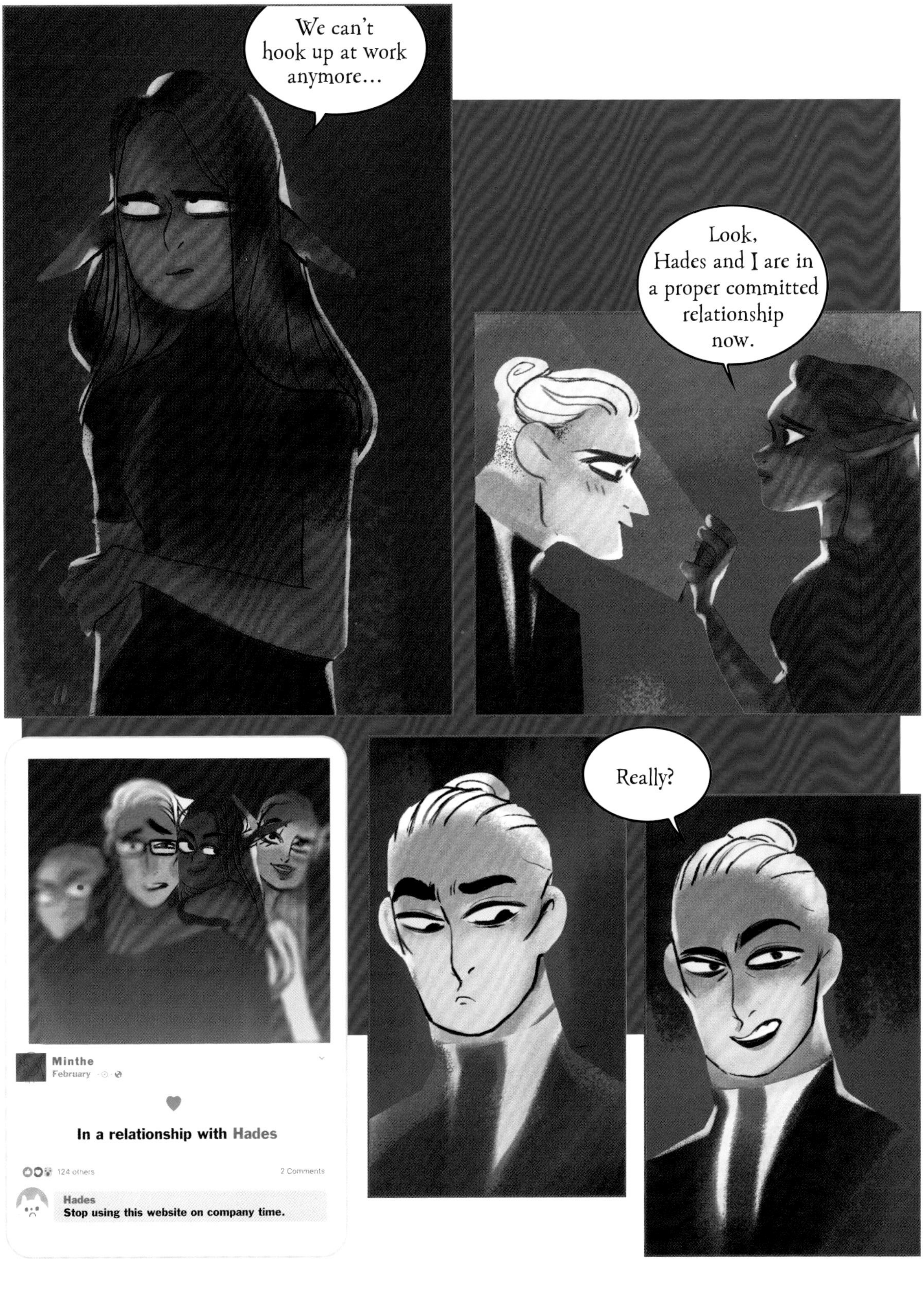
We can't hook up at work anymore...
Look, Hades and I are in a proper committed relationship now.
Minthe
February
In a relationship with Hades
124 others
2 Comments
Hades
Stop using this website on company time.
Really?

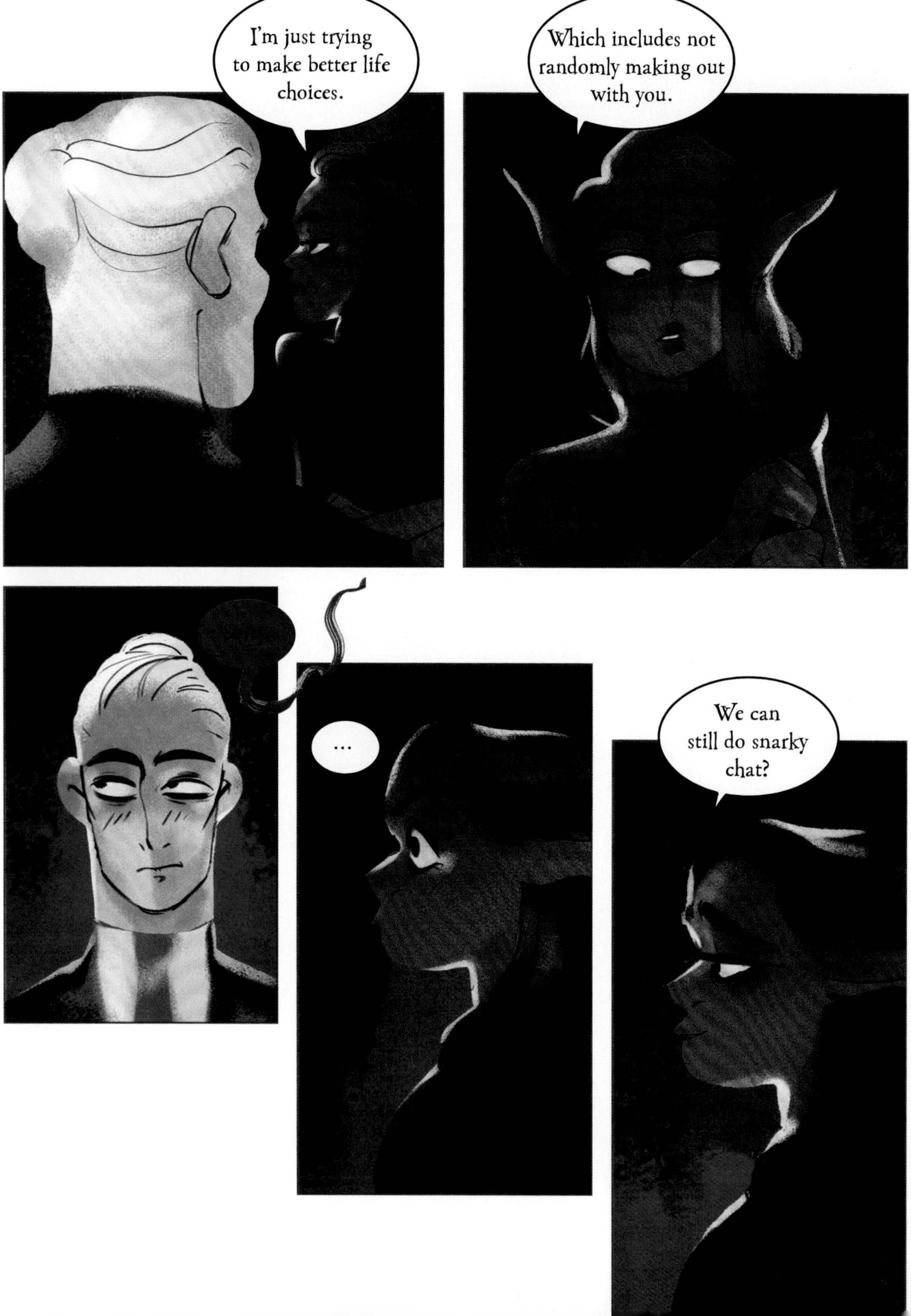
I'm just trying to make better life choices.
Which includes not randomly making out with you.
...
We can still do snarky chat?

[WHAT IS SNARKY CHAT?]

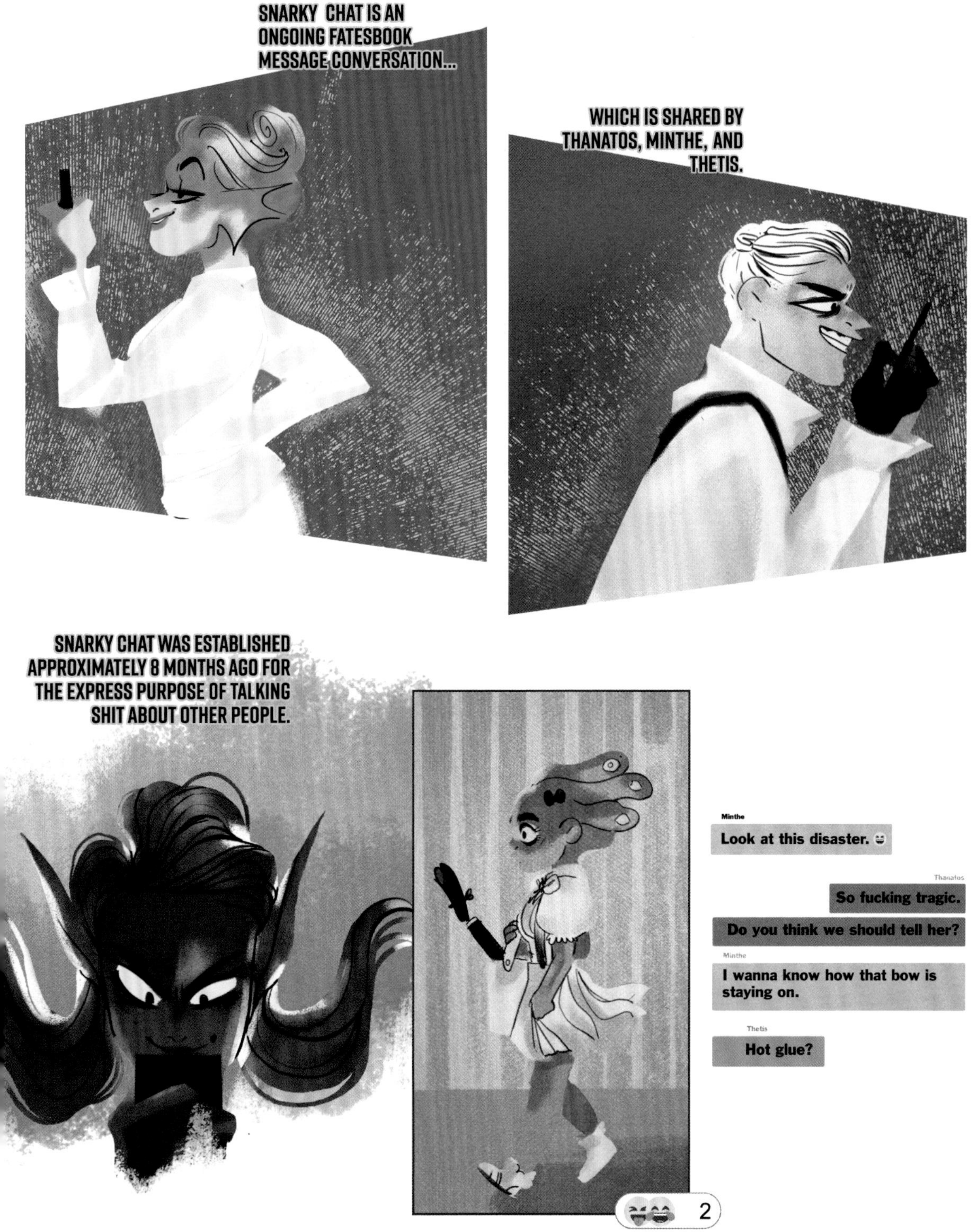
SNARKY CHAT IS AN ONGOING FATESBOOK MESSAGE CONVERSATION...
WHICH IS SHARED BY THANATOS, MINTHE, AND THETIS.
SNARKY CHAT WAS ESTABLISHED APPROXIMATELY 8 MONTHS AGO FOR THE EXPRESS PURPOSE OF TALKING SHIT ABOUT OTHER PEOPLE.
Minthe
Look at this disaster.
Thanatos
So fucking tragic.
Do you think we should tell her?
Minthe
I wanna know how that bow is staying on.
Thetis
Hot glue?
2

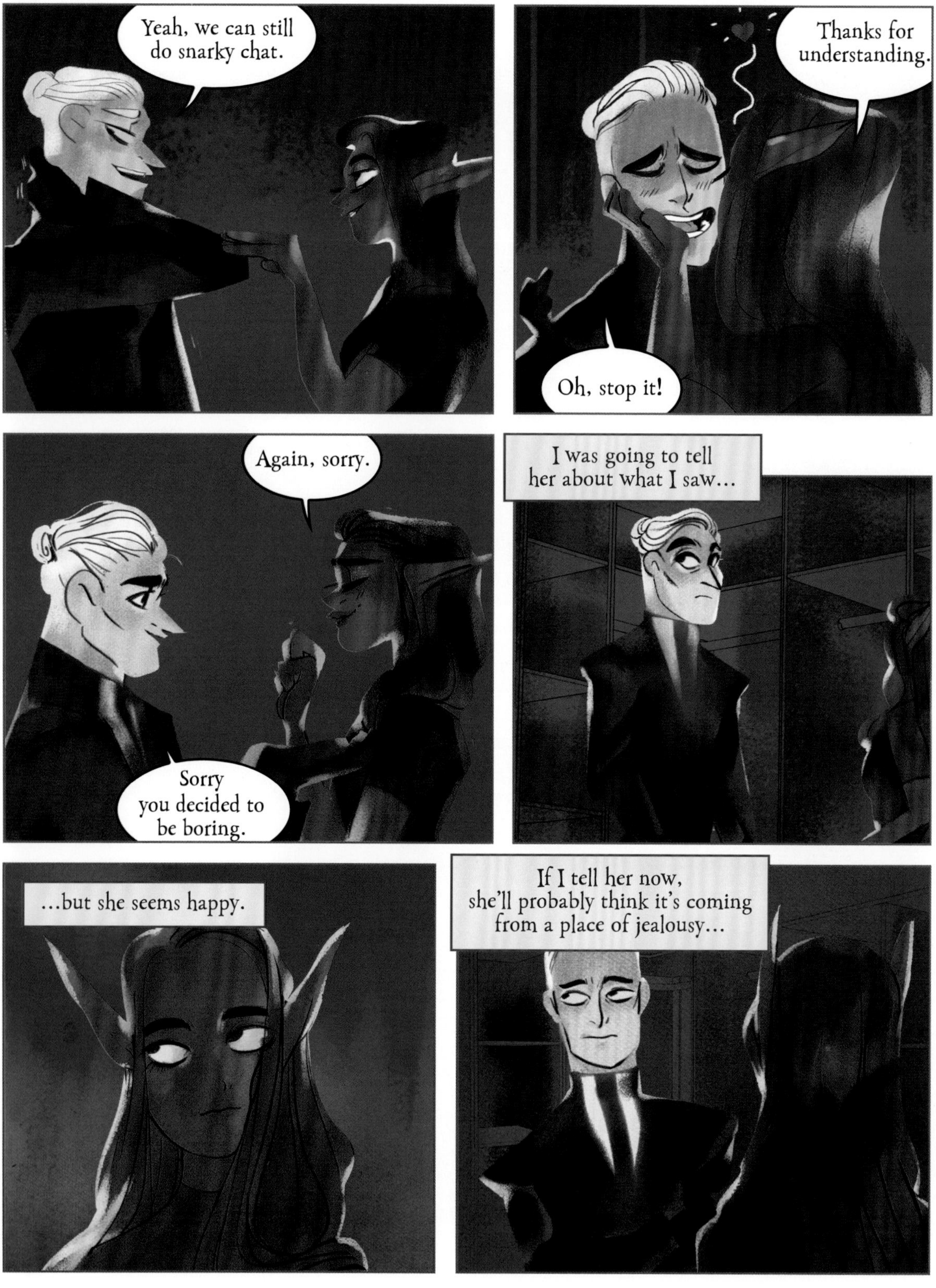
Yeah, we can still do snarky chat.
Thanks for understanding.
Oh, stop it!
Again, sorry.
Sorry you decided to be boring.
I was going to tell her about what I saw...
...but she seems happy.
If I tell her now, she'll probably think it's coming from a place of jealousy...

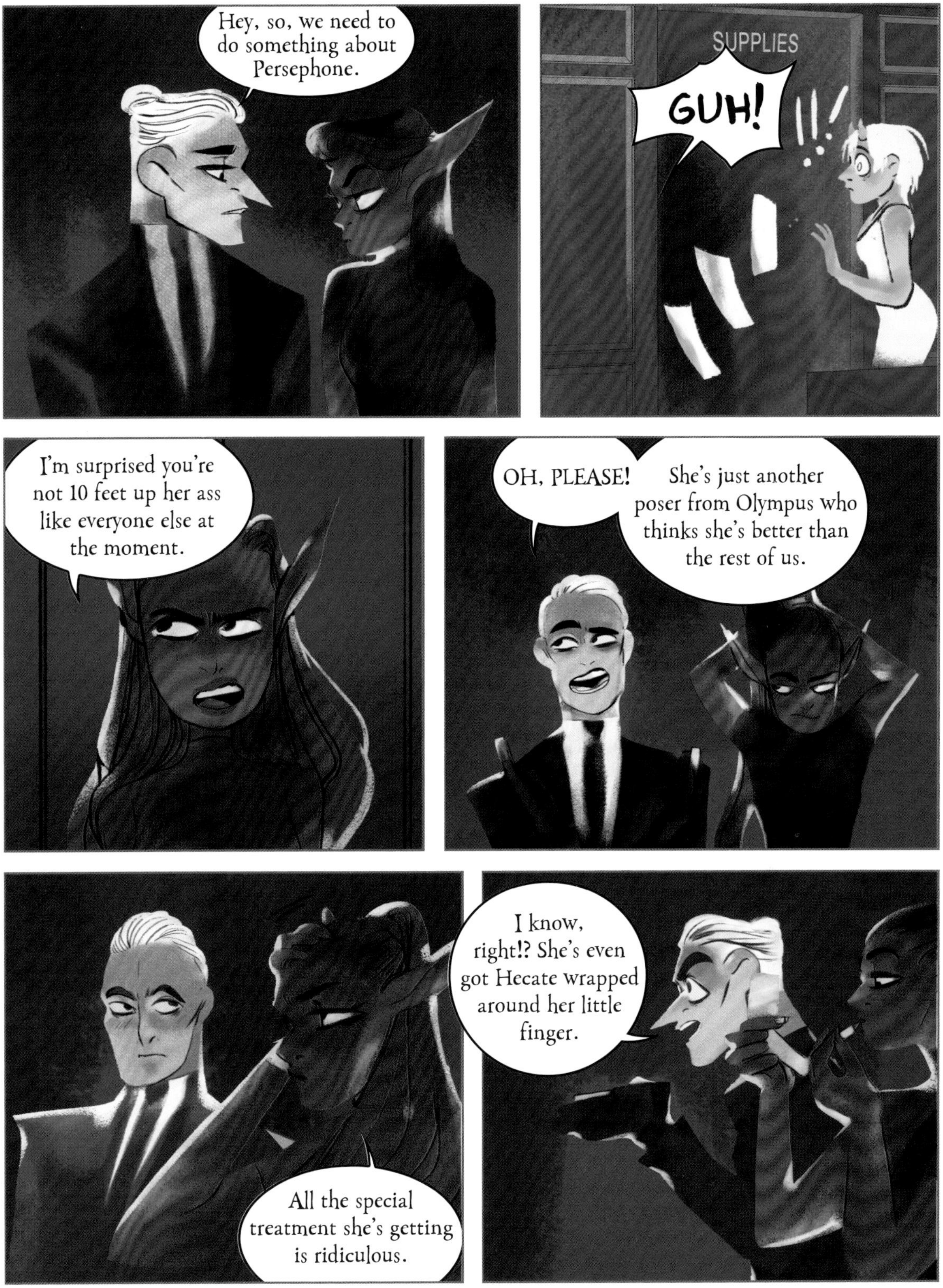
Hey, so, we need to do something about Persephone.
SUPPLIES
GUH!
!!!
I'm surprised you're not 10 feet up her ass like everyone else at the moment.
OH, PLEASE!
She's just another poser from Olympus who thinks she's better than the rest of us.
All the special treatment she's getting is ridiculous.
I know, right!? She's even got Hecate wrapped around her little finger.

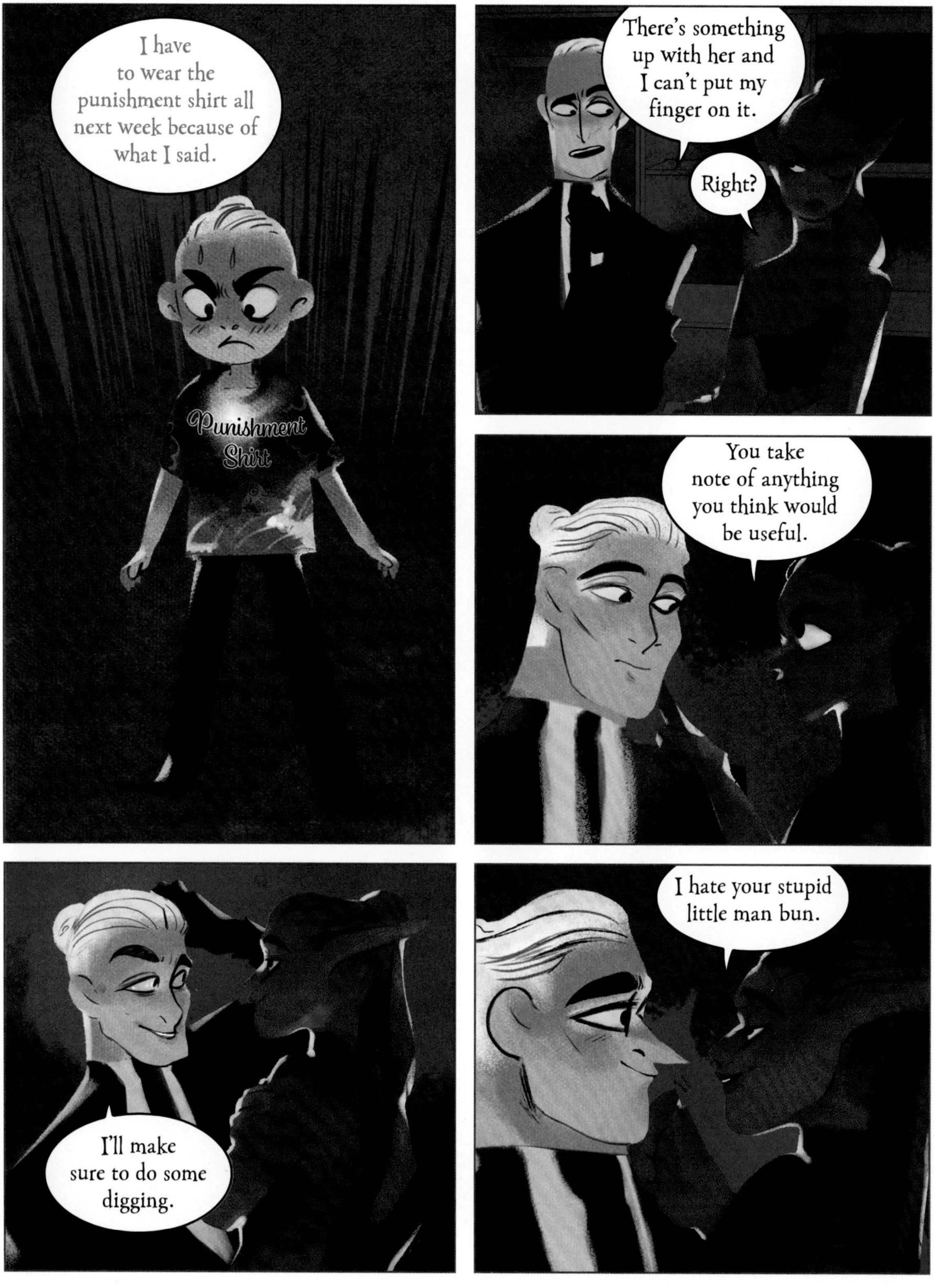
I have to wear the punishment shirt all next week because of what I said.
Punishment Shirt
There's something up with her and I can't put my finger on it.
Right?
You take note of anything you think would be useful.
I'll make sure to do some digging.
I hate your stupid little man bun.

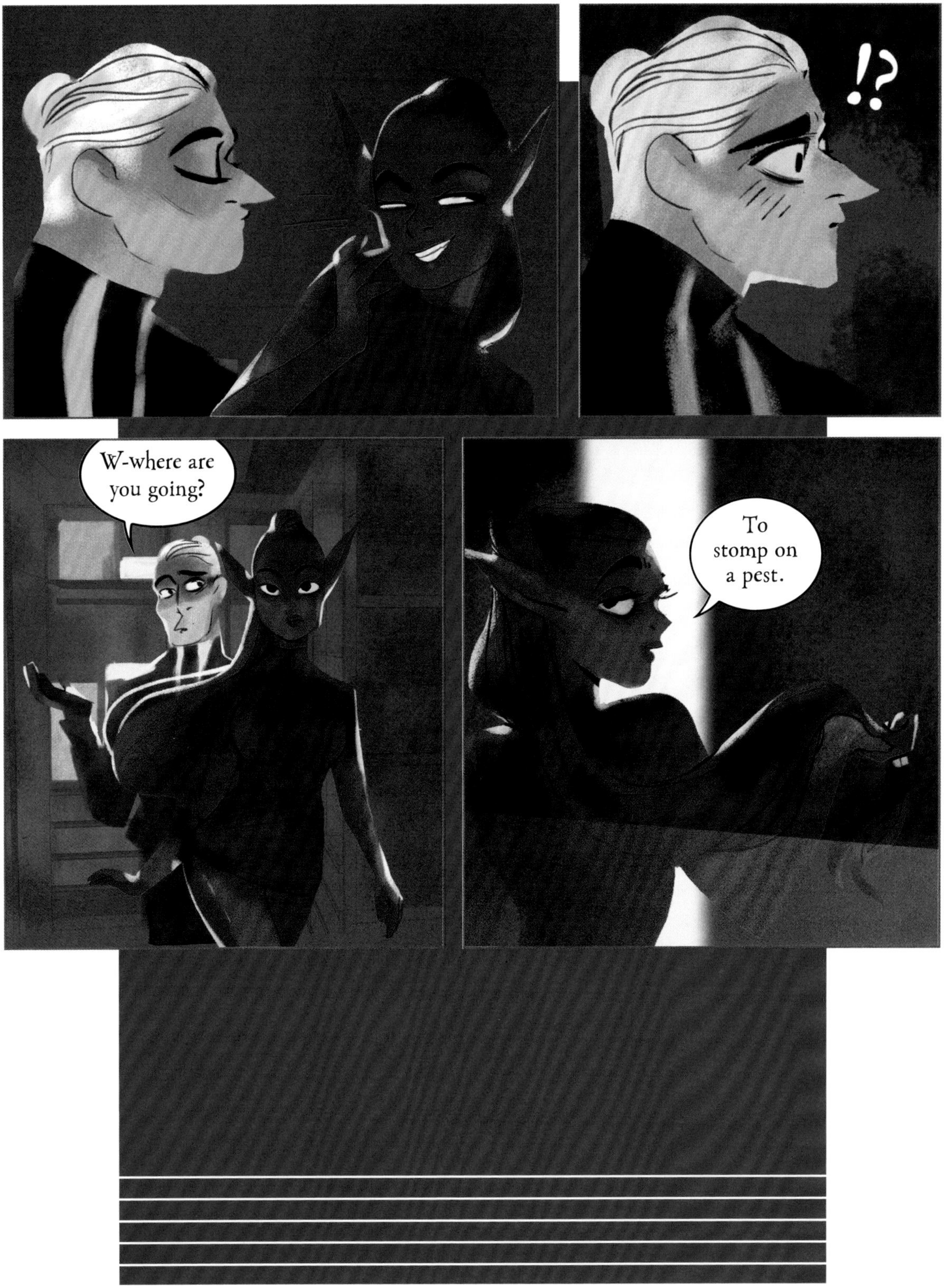
!?
W-where are you going?
To stomp on a pest.

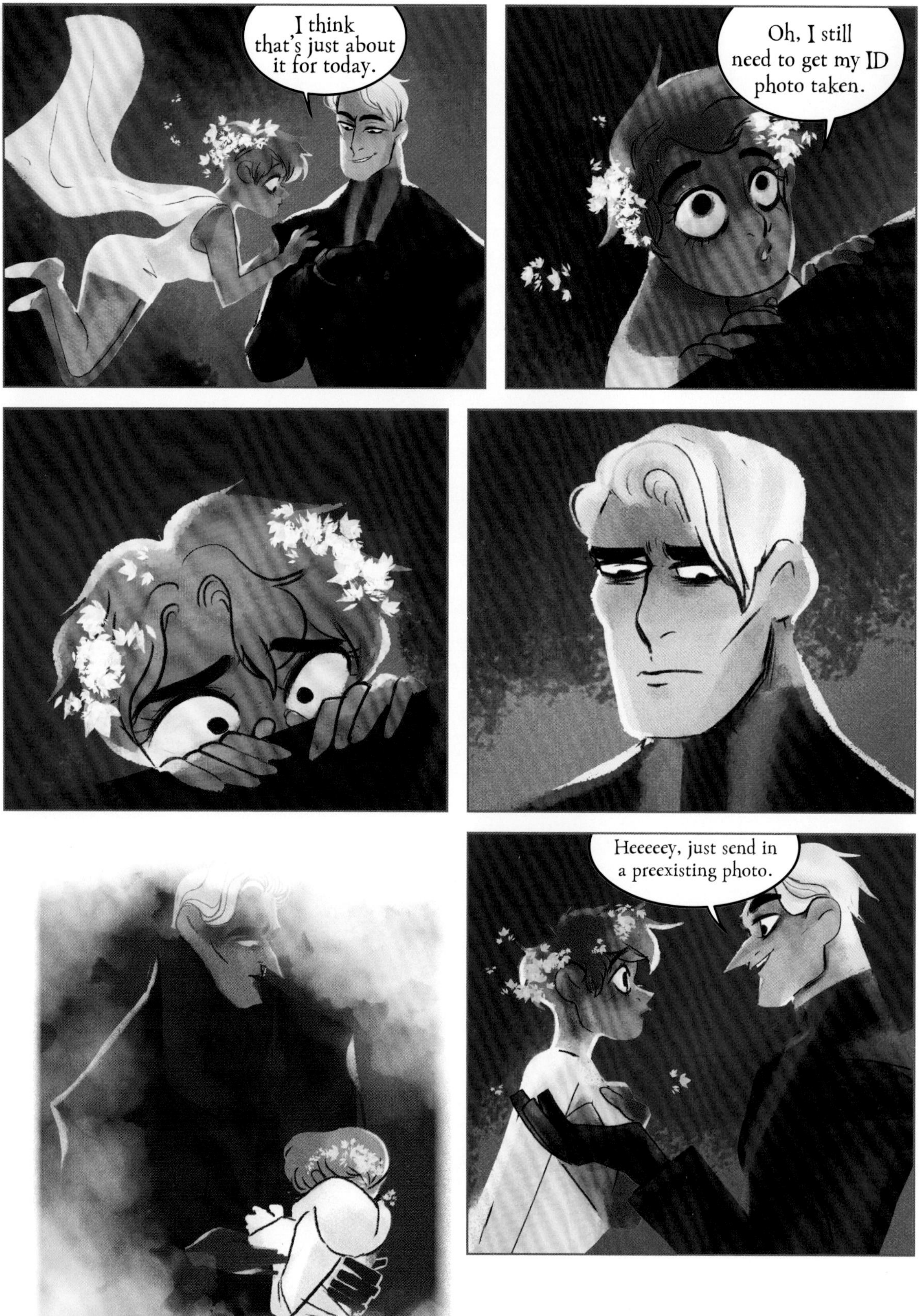
I think that's just about it for today.
Oh, I still need to get my ID photo taken.
Heeeeey, just send in a preexisting photo.

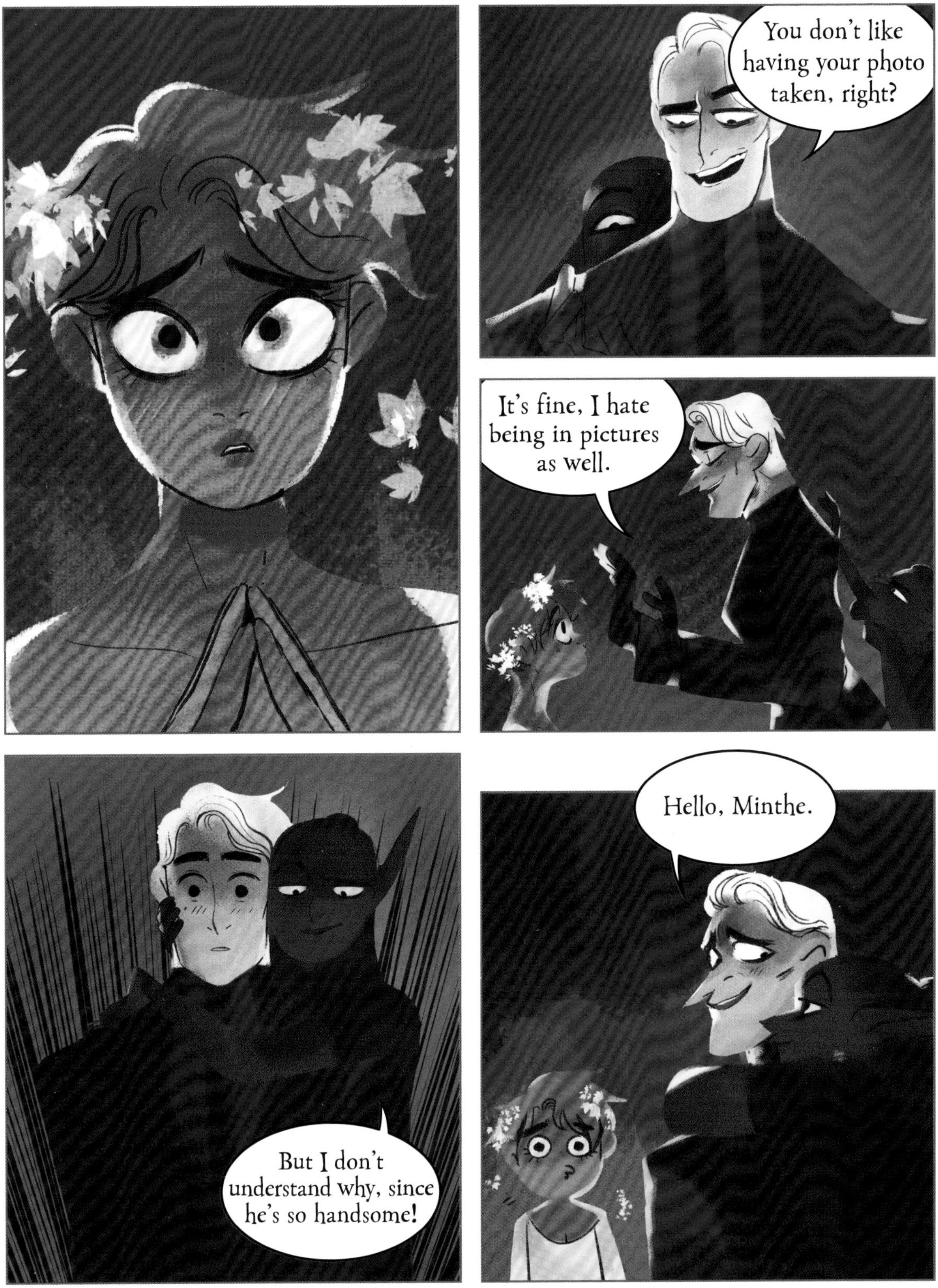
You don't like having your photo taken, right?
It's fine, I hate being in pictures as well.
But I don't understand why, since he's so handsome!
Hello, Minthe.

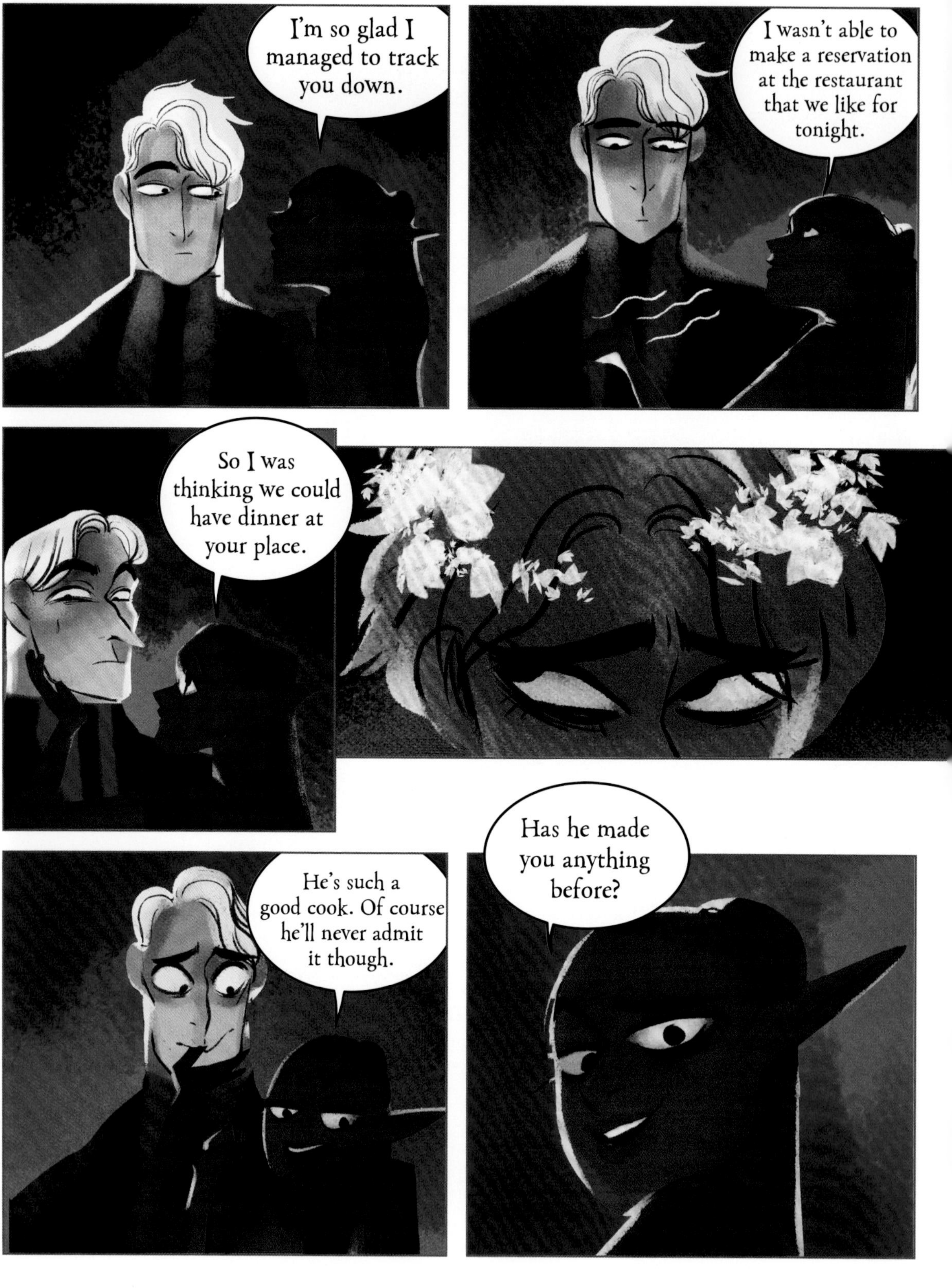
I'm so glad I managed to track you down.
I wasn't able to make a reservation at the restaurant that we like for tonight.
So I was thinking we could have dinner at your place.
He's such a good cook. Of course he'll never admit it though.
Has he made you anything before?

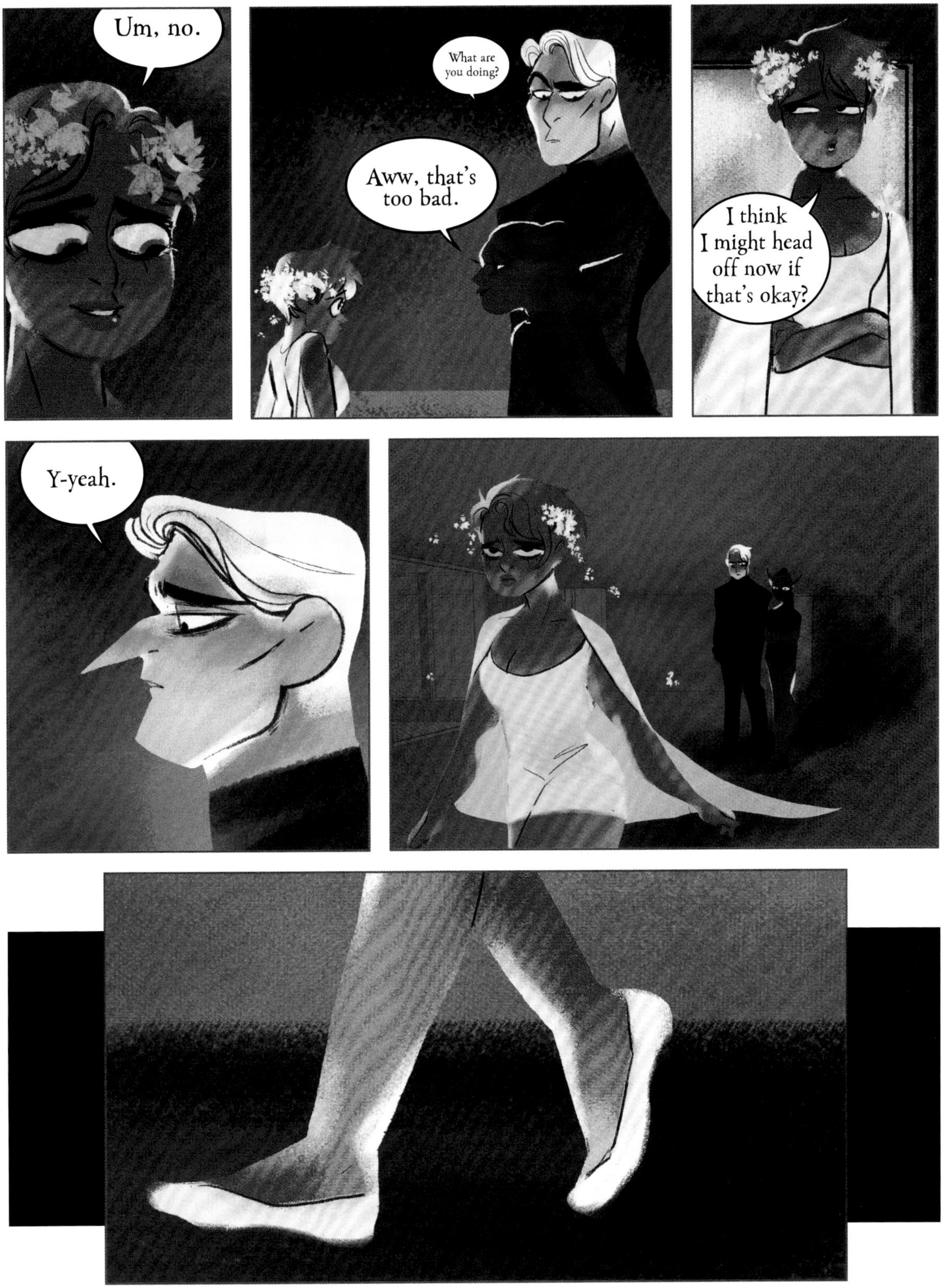
Um, no.
What are you doing?
Aww, that's too bad.
I think I might head off now if that's okay?
Y-yeah.

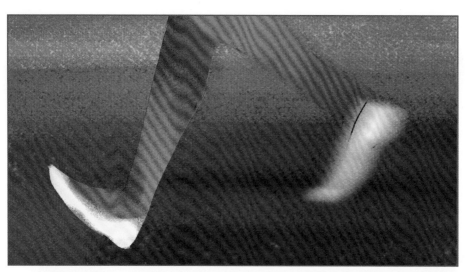

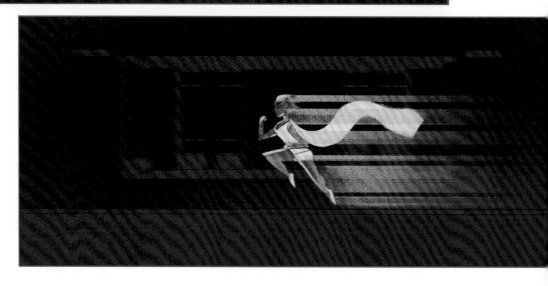

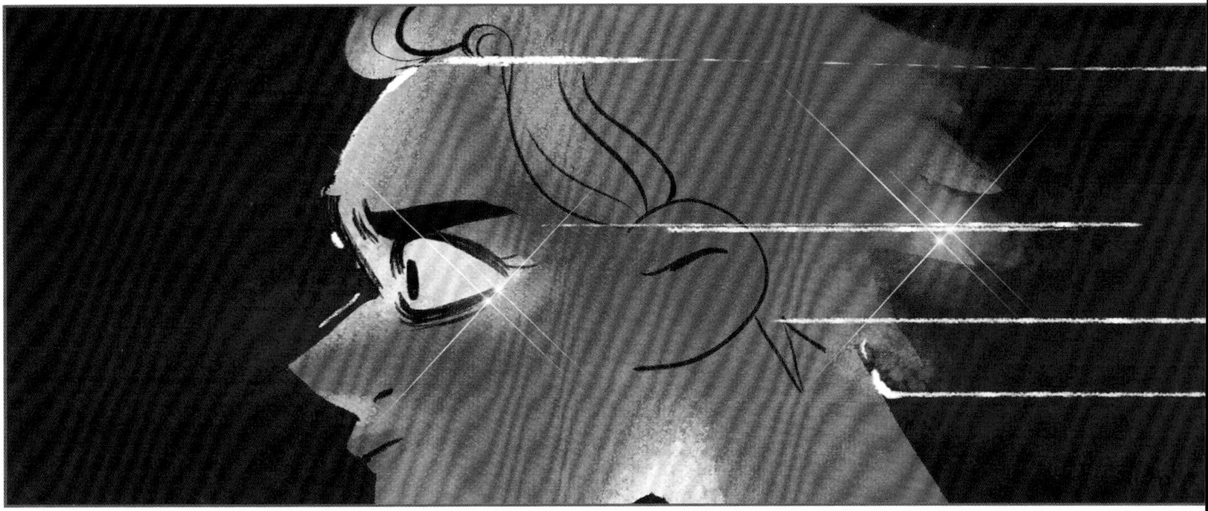

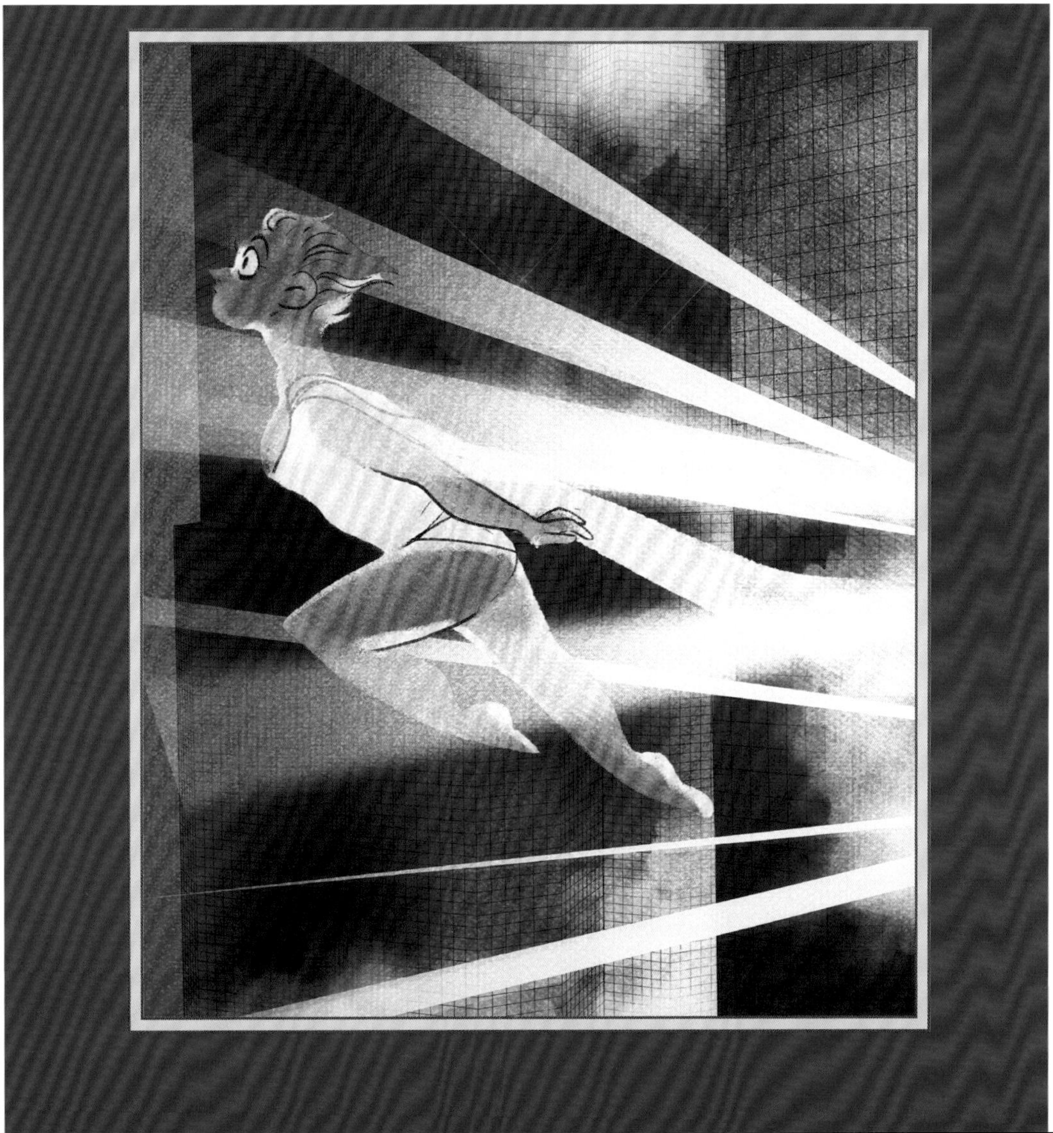

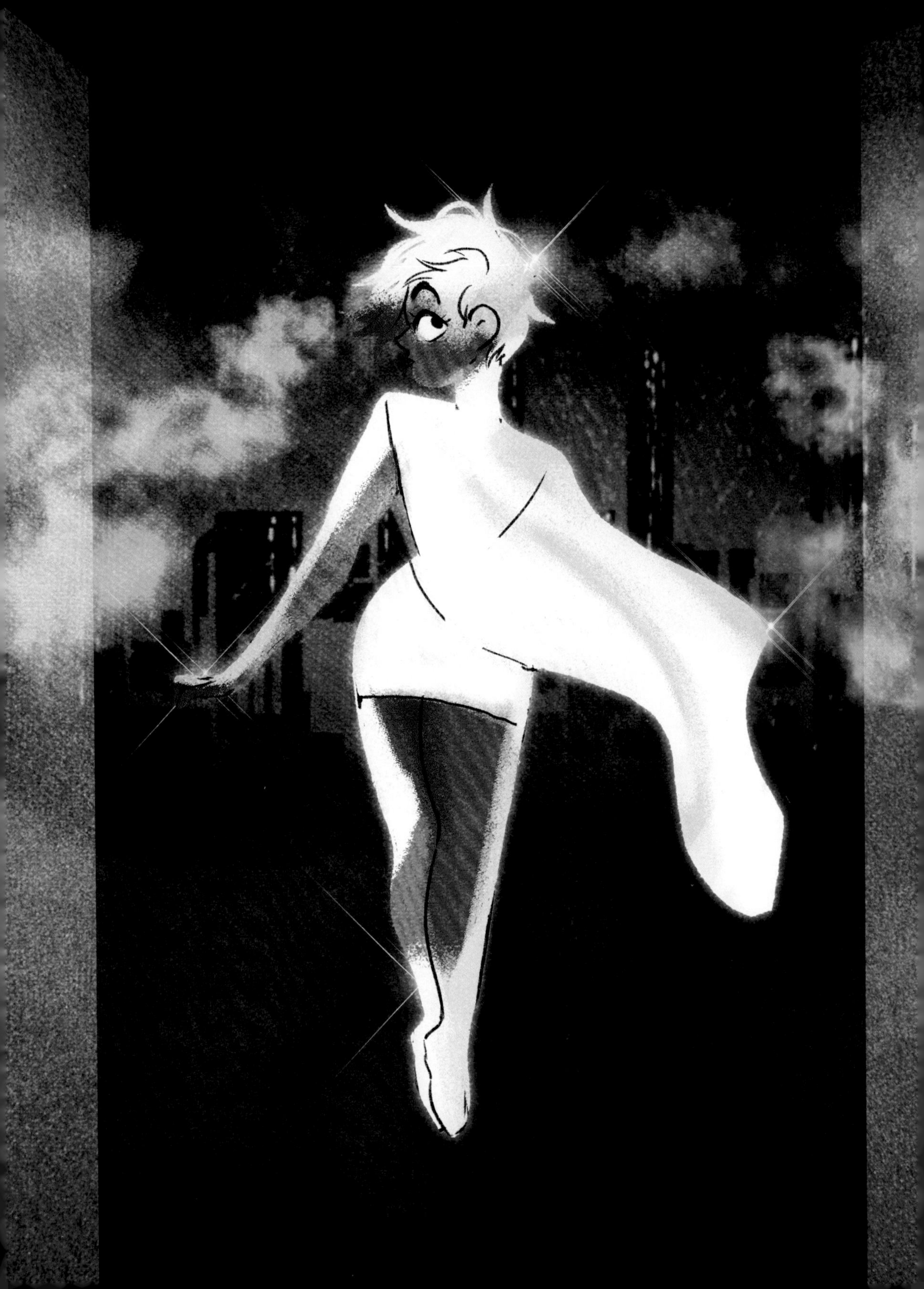

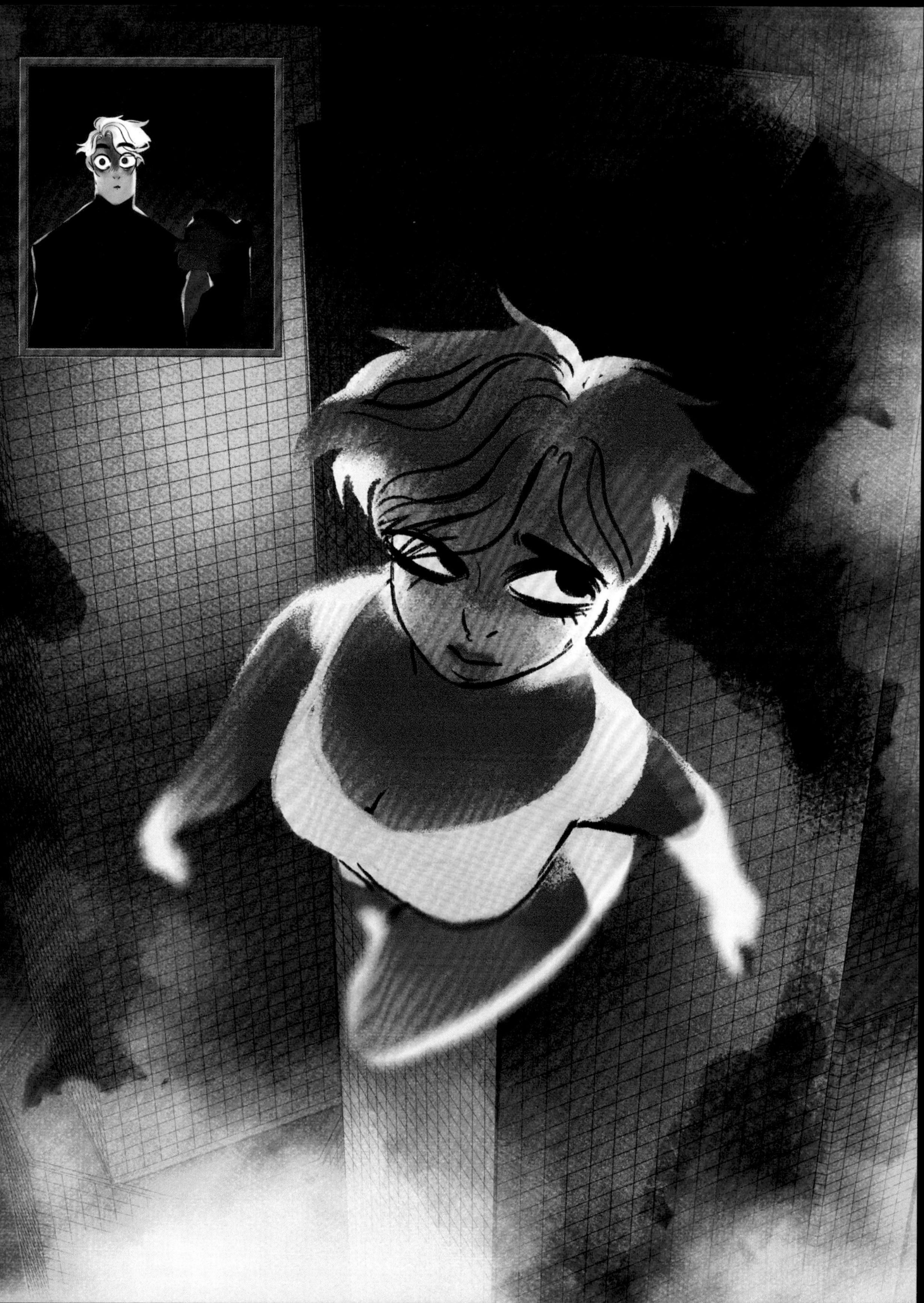

EPISODE 61: ITTY

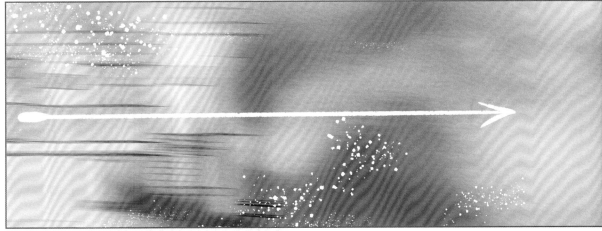

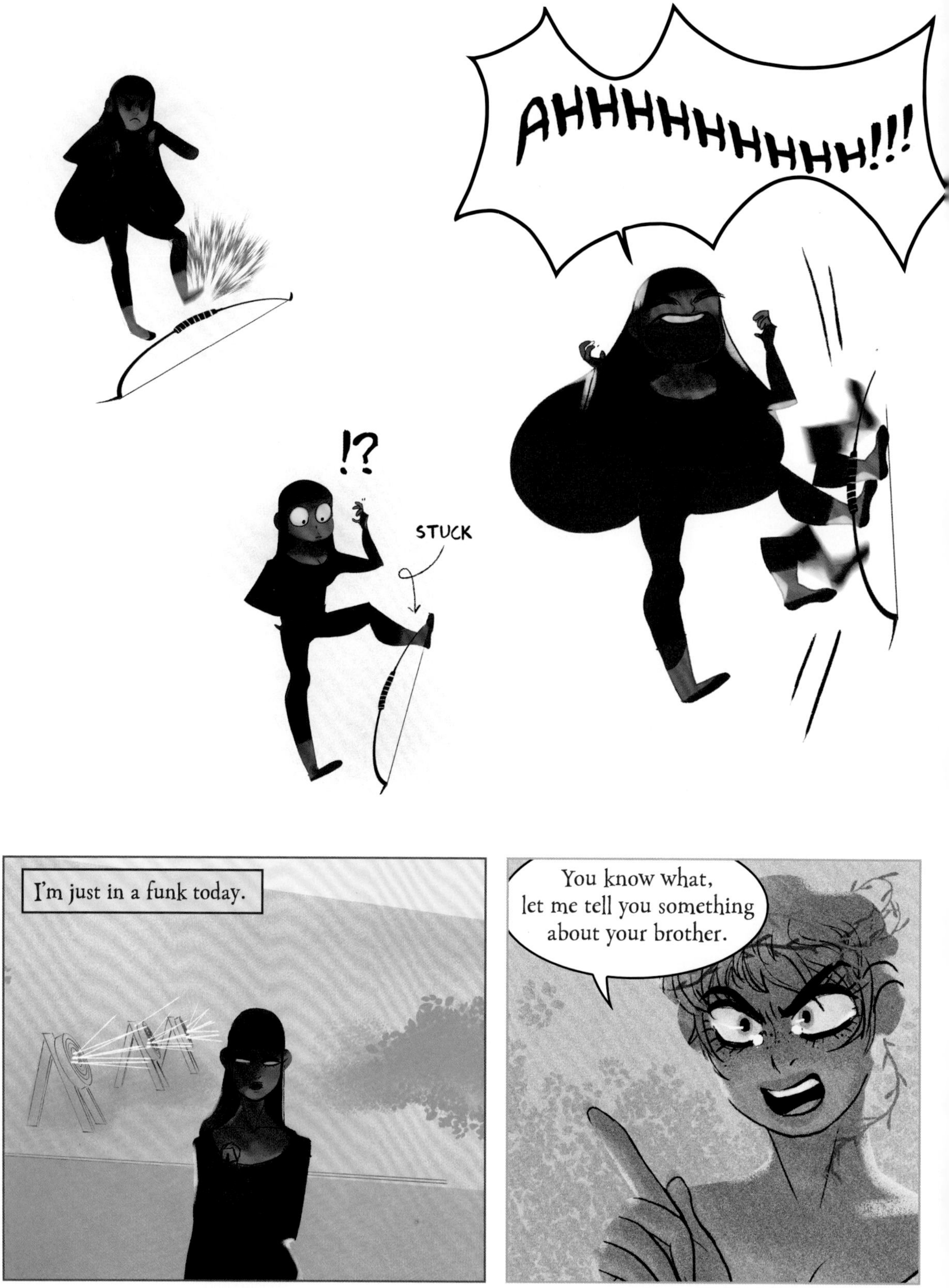
!?
STUCK
AHHHHHHHHHH!!!
I'm just in a funk today.
You know what, let me tell you something about your brother.

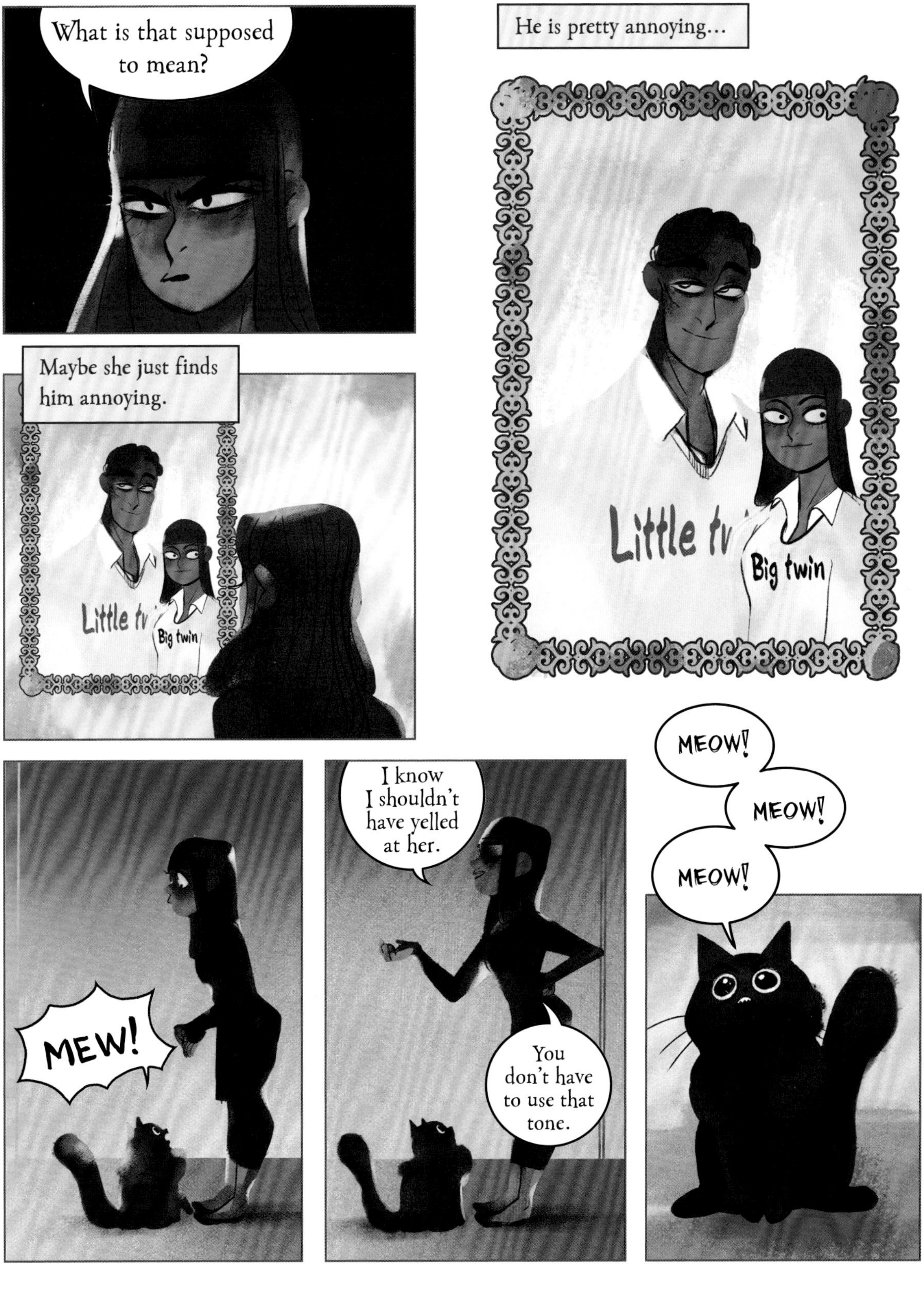
What is that supposed to mean?
He is pretty annoying...
Maybe she just finds him annoying.
Little tw
Big twin
Little tw
Big twin
MEW!
I know I shouldn't have yelled at her.
You don't have to use that tone.
MEOW!
MEOW!
MEOW!

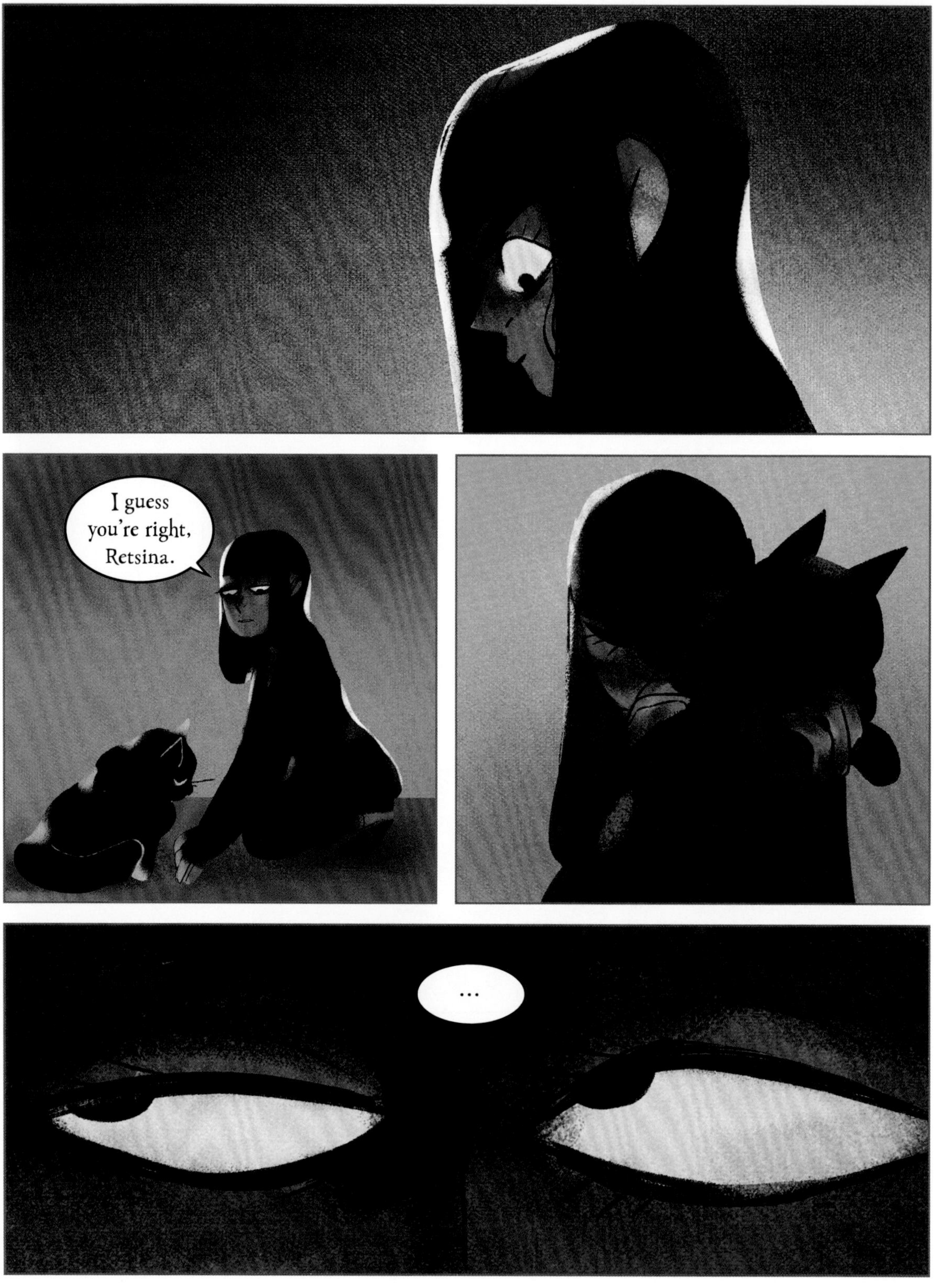
I guess you're right, Retsina.
...

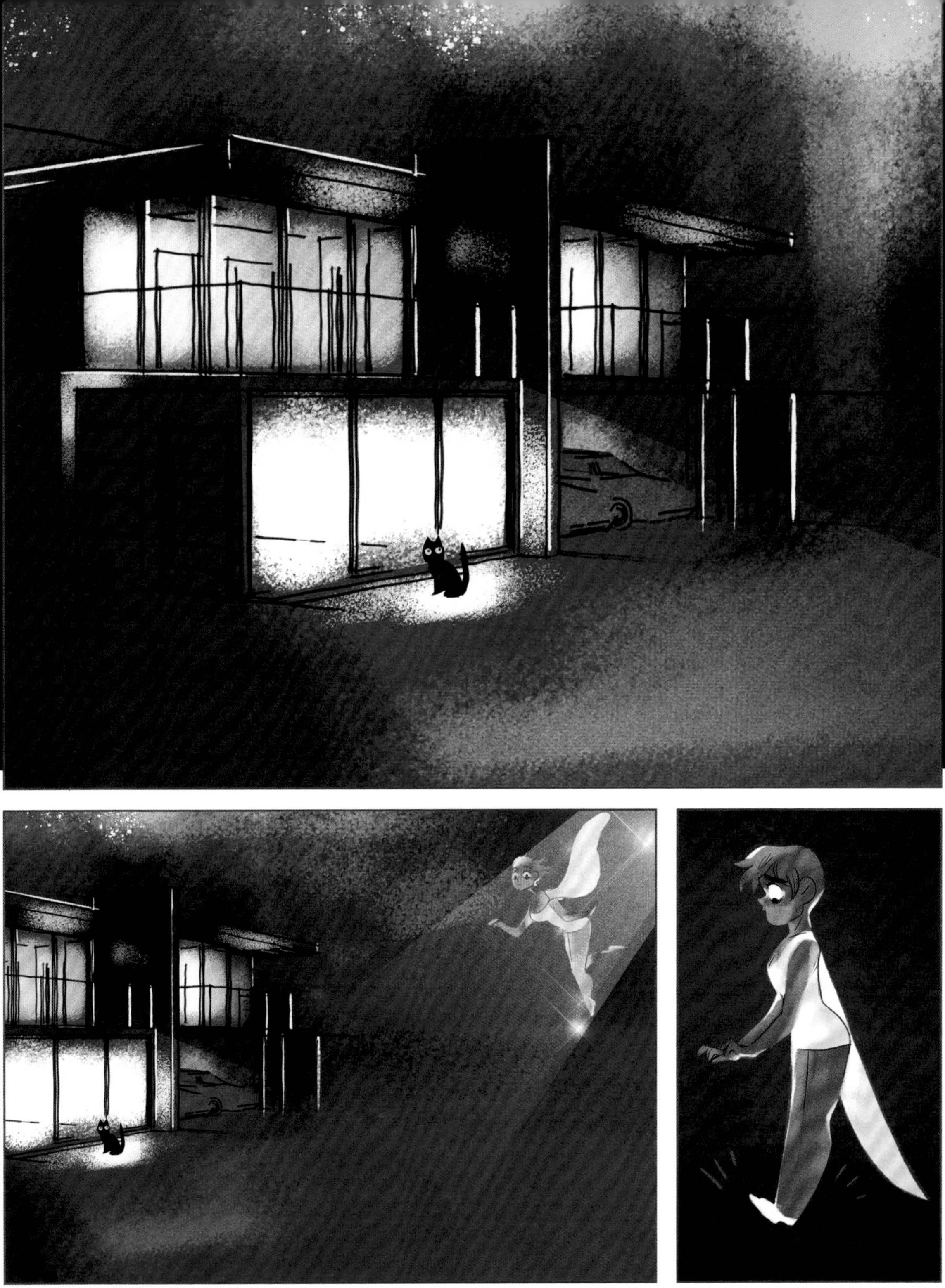

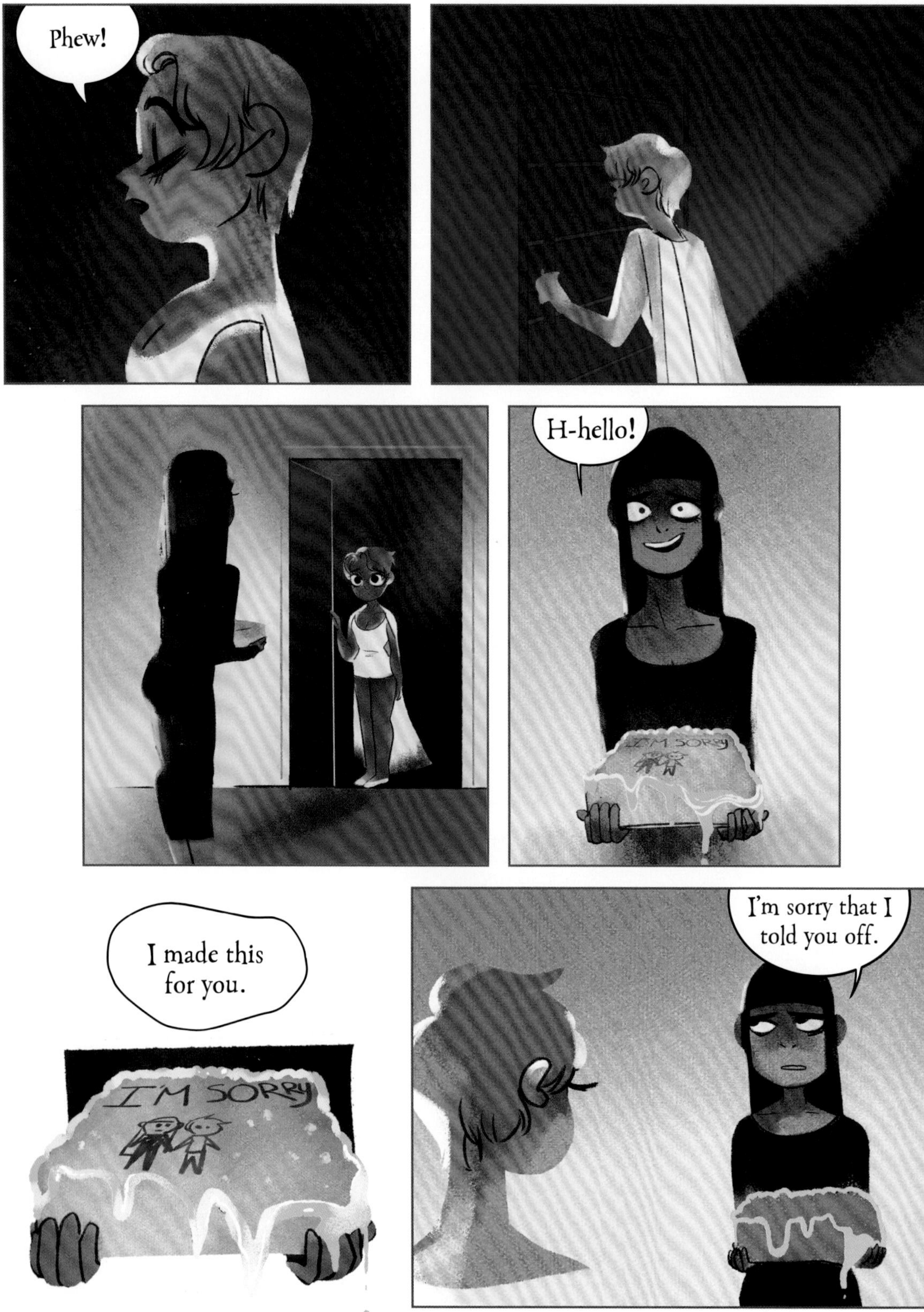
Phew!
H-hello!
I made this for you.
I'M SORRY
I'm sorry that I told you off.

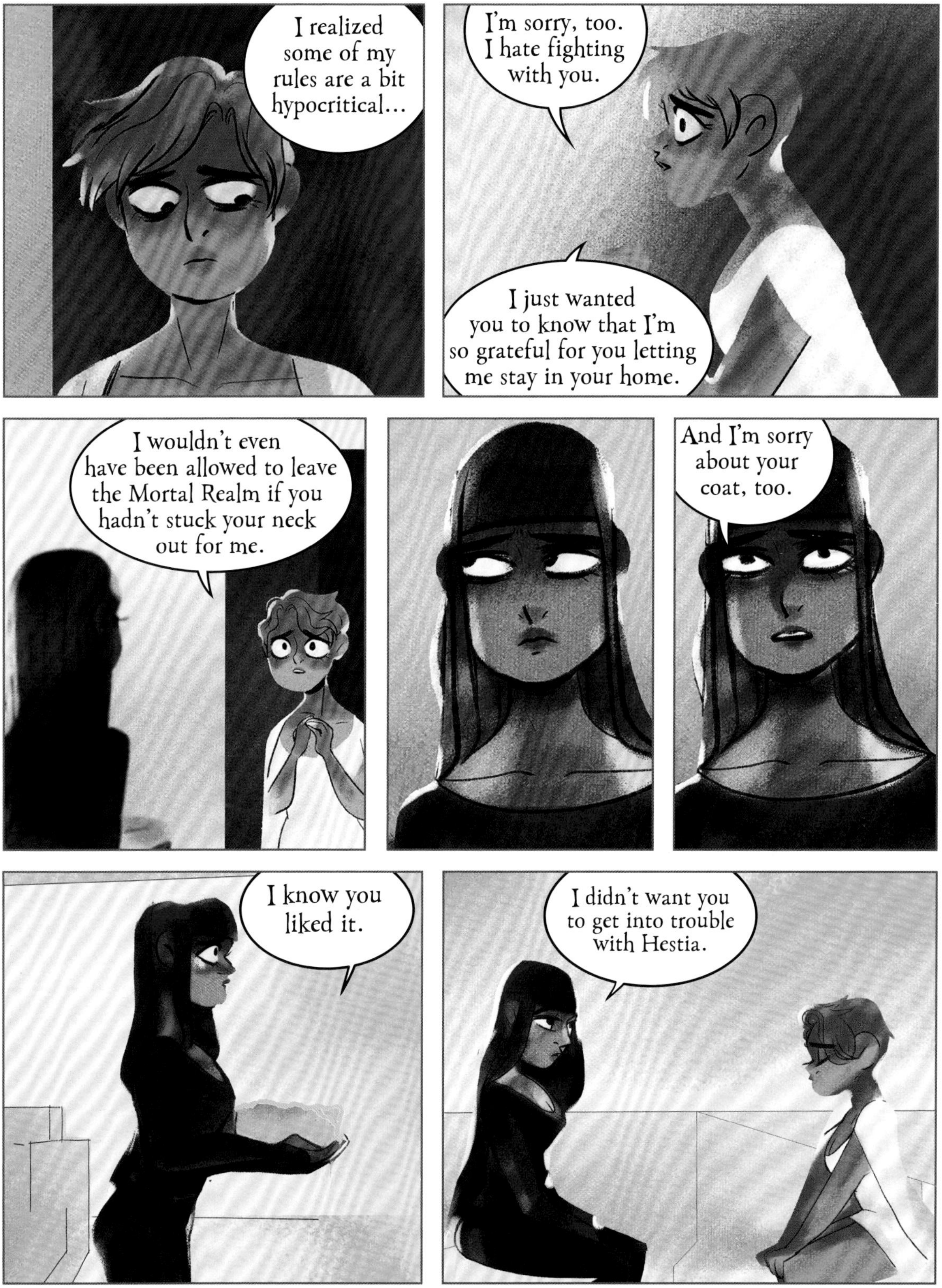
I realized some of my rules are a bit hypocritical...
I'm sorry, too. I hate fighting with you.
I just wanted you to know that I'm so grateful for you letting me stay in your home.
I wouldn't even have been allowed to leave the Mortal Realm if you hadn't stuck your neck out for me.
And I'm sorry about your coat, too.
I know you liked it.
I didn't want you to get into trouble with Hestia.

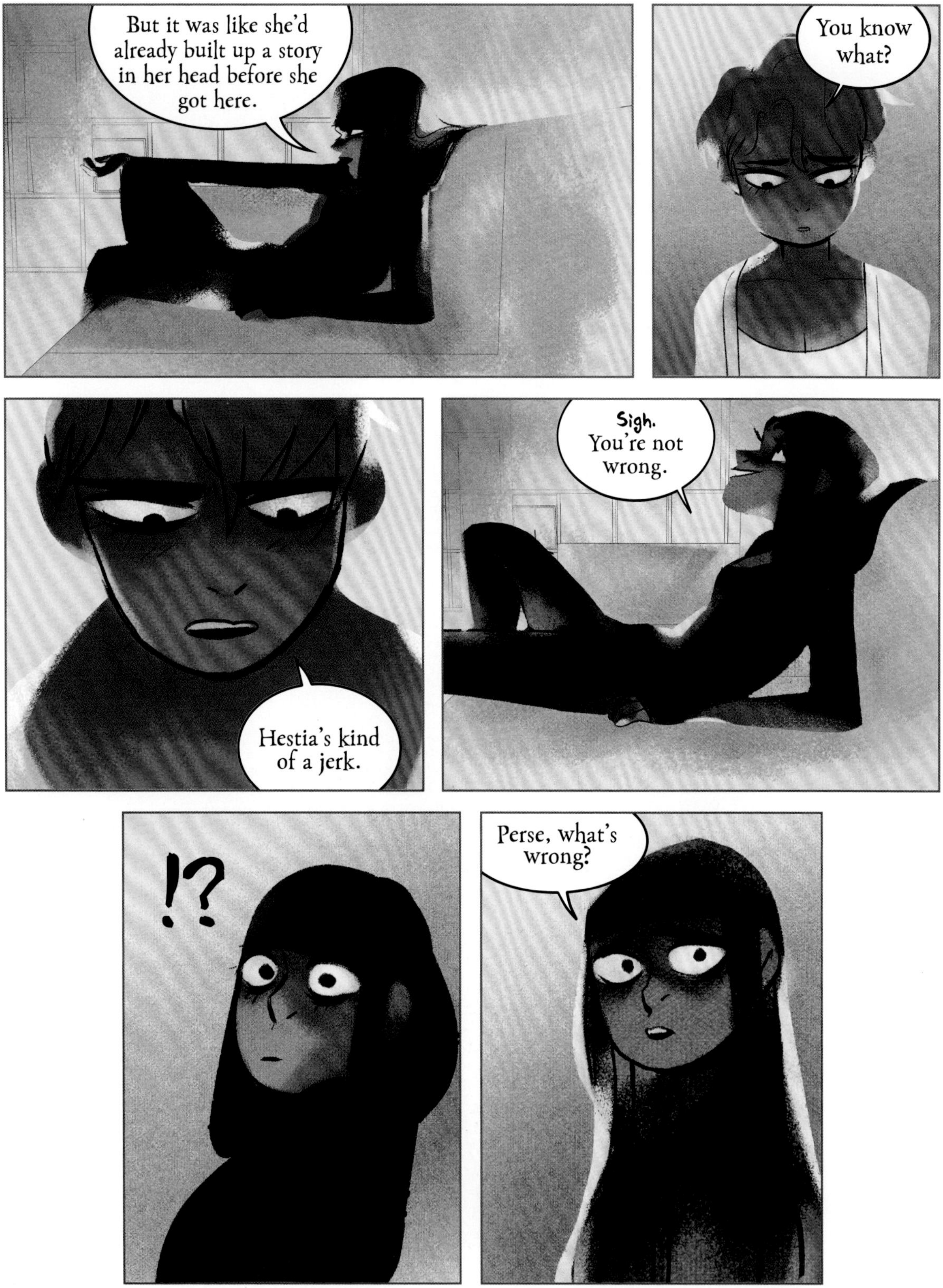
But it was like she'd already built up a story in her head before she got here.
You know what?
Hestia's kind of a jerk.
Sigh.
You're not wrong.
!?
Perse, what's wrong?

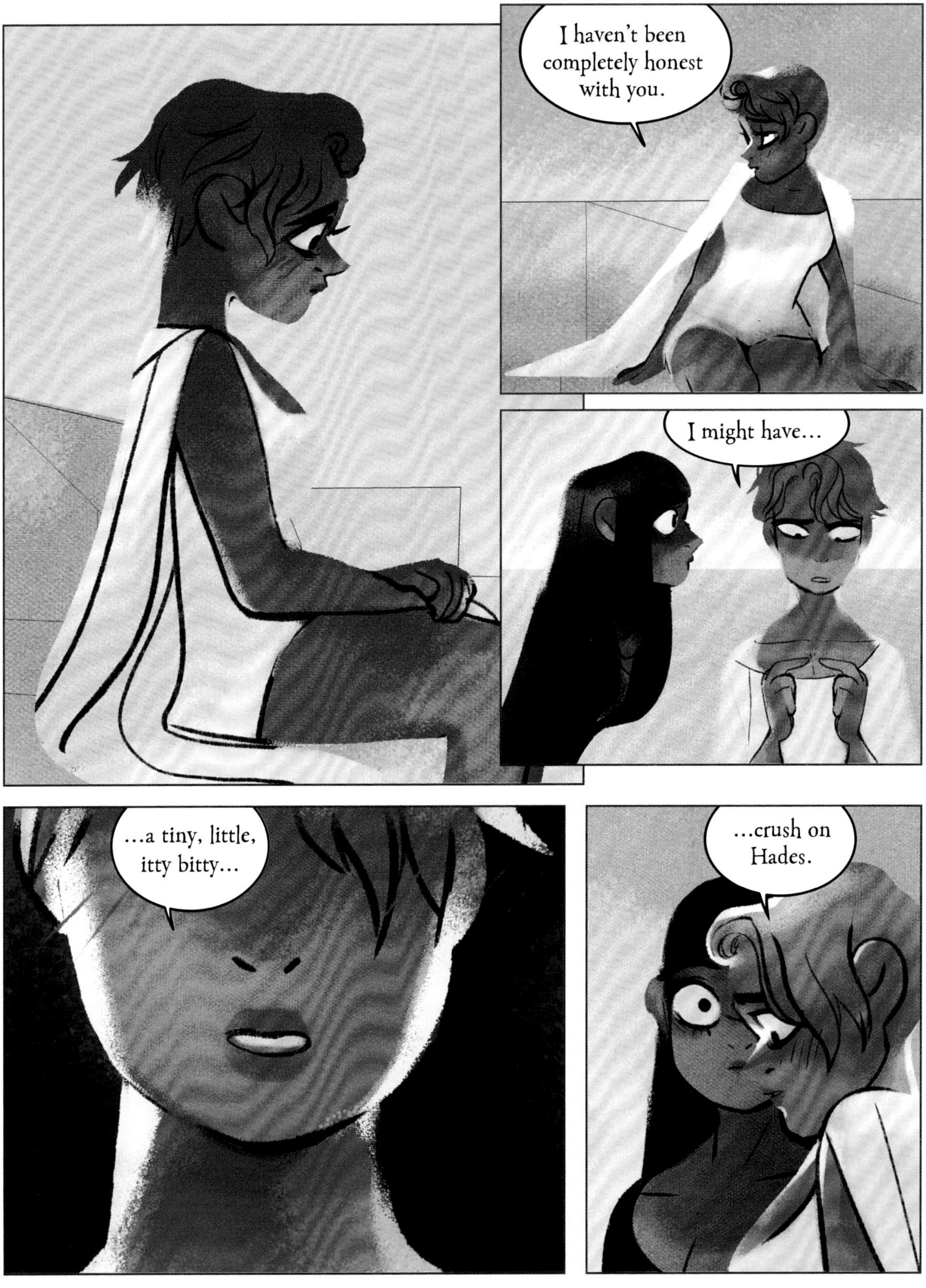
I haven't been completely honest with you.
I might have...
...a tiny, little, itty bitty...
...crush on Hades.

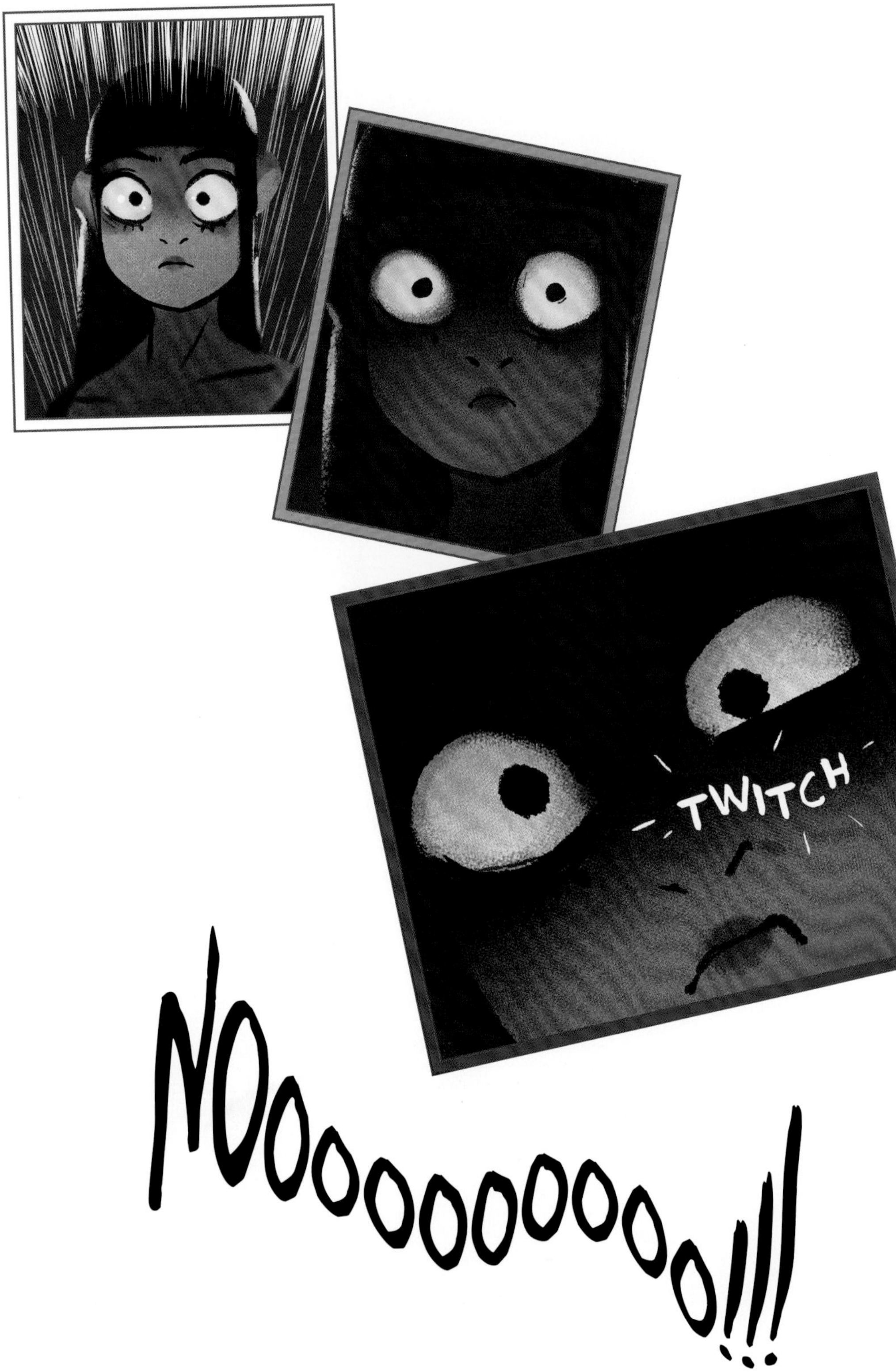
TWITCH
NOOOOOOOOOOO!!!

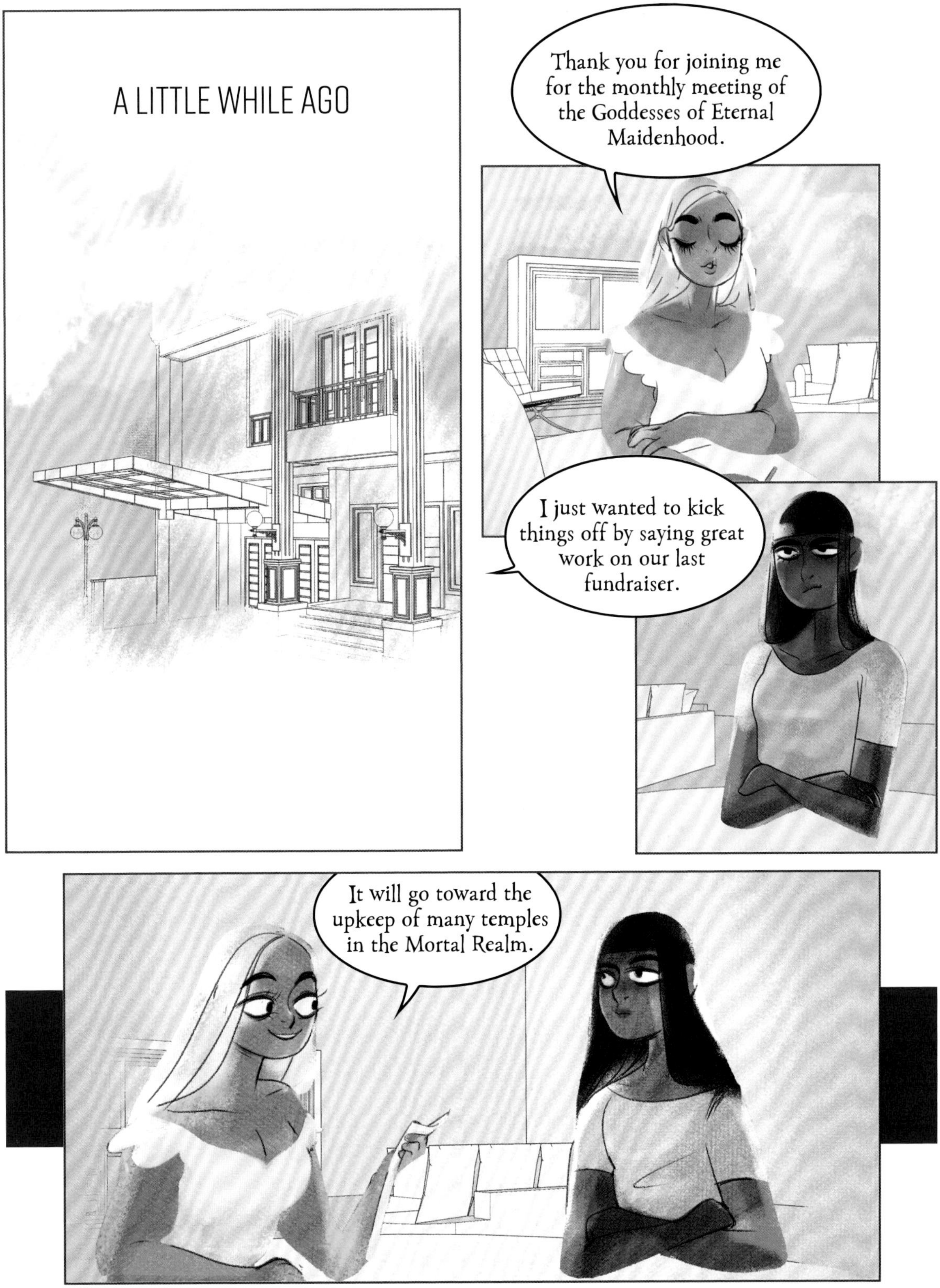
A LITTLE WHILE AGO
Thank you for joining me for the monthly meeting of the Goddesses of Eternal Maidenhood.
I just wanted to kick things off by saying great work on our last fundraiser.
It will go toward the upkeep of many temples in the Mortal Realm.

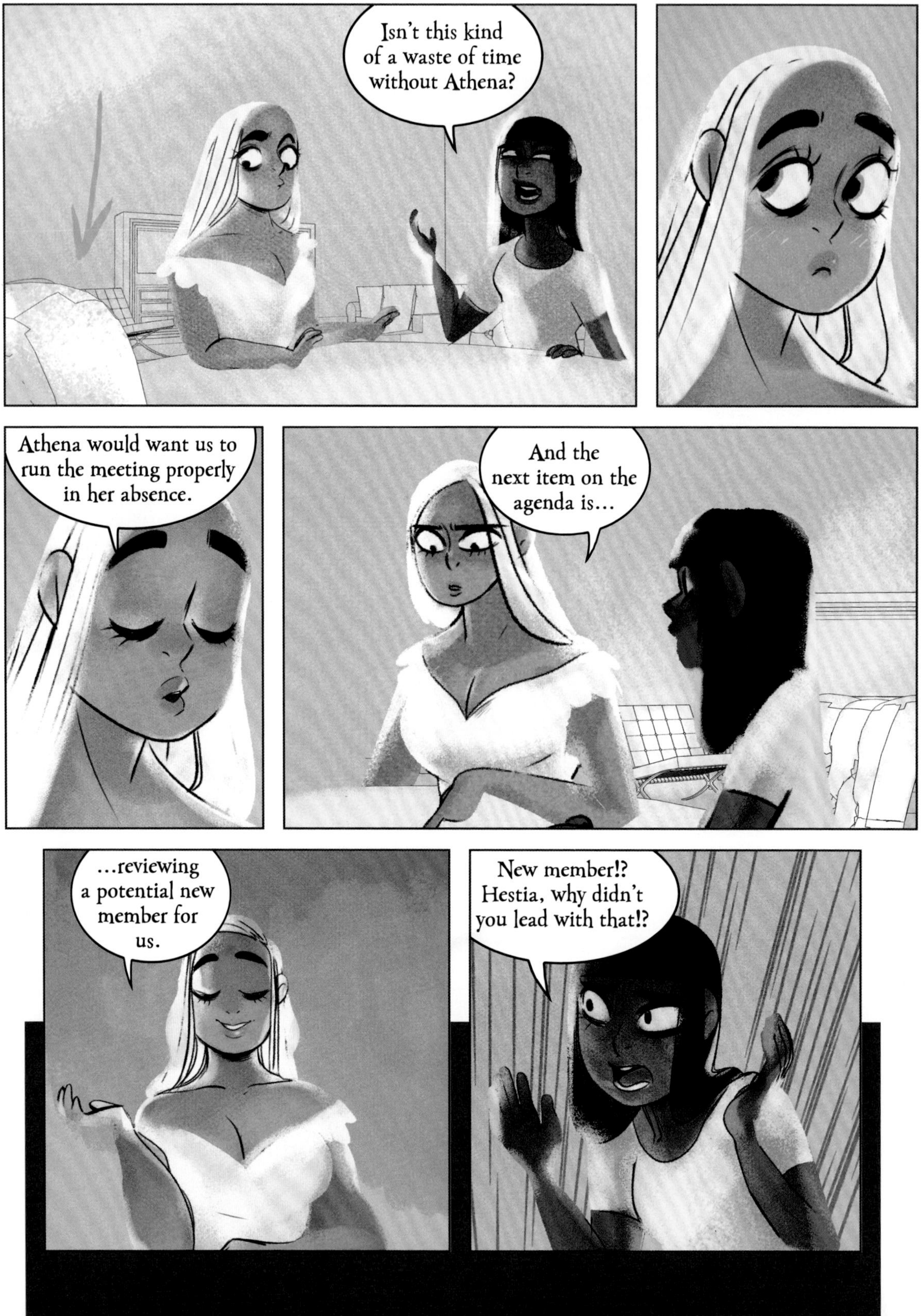
Isn't this kind of a waste of time without Athena?
Athena would want us to run the meeting properly in her absence.
And the next item on the agenda is...
...reviewing a potential new member for us.
New member!? Hestia, why didn't you lead with that!?

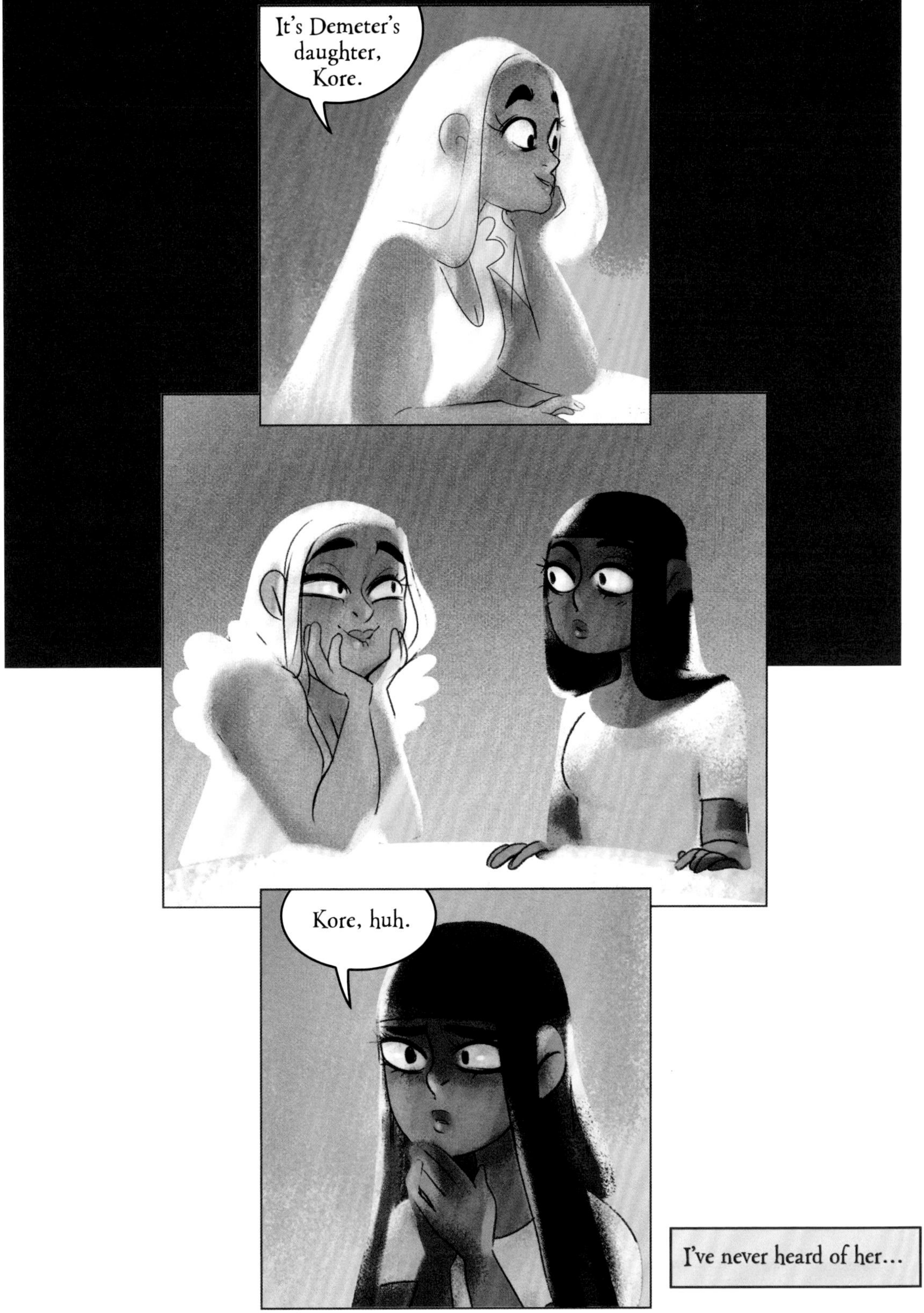

It's Demeter's daughter, Kore.
Kore, huh.
I've never heard of her...

EPISODE 62: DOE

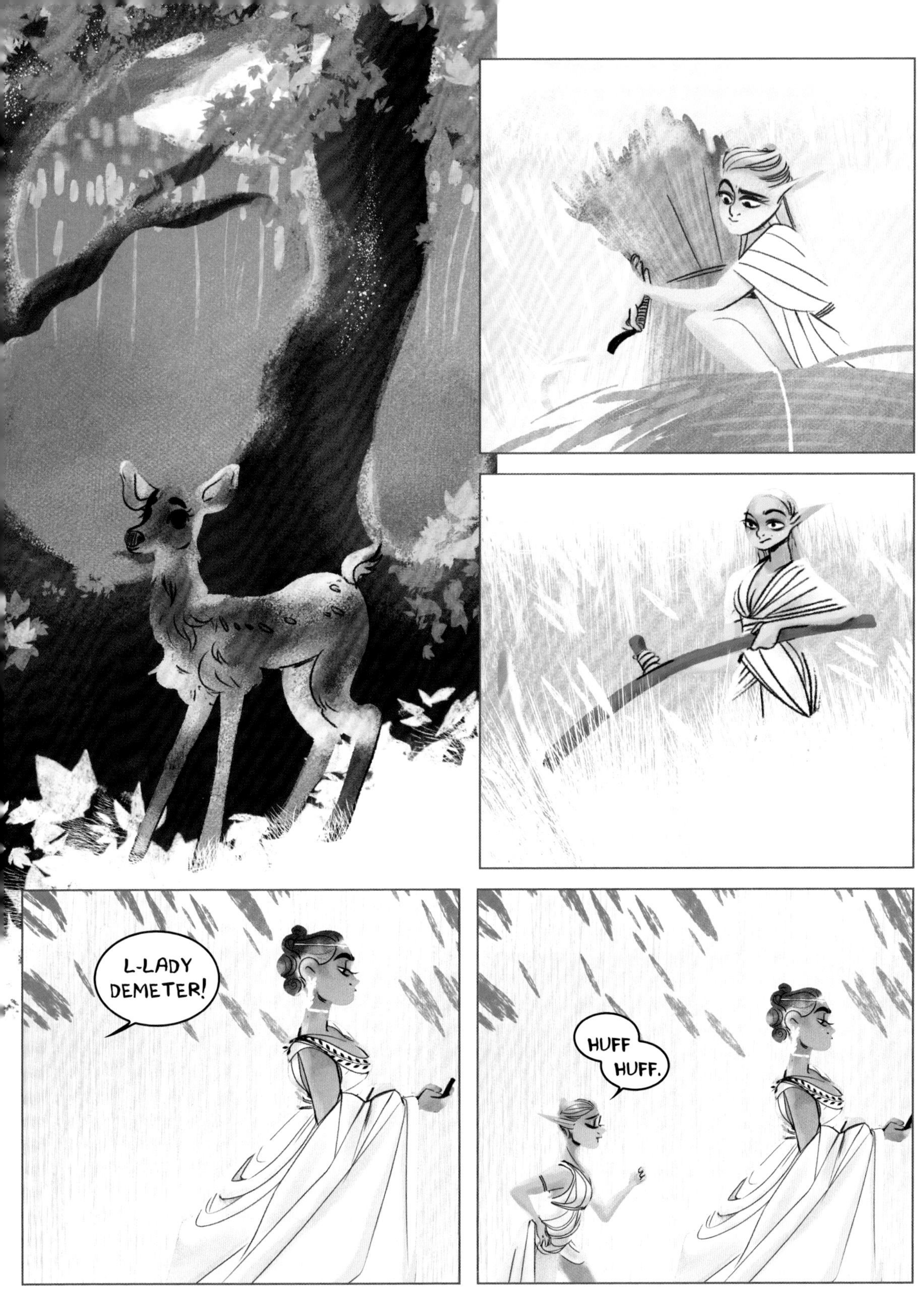
L-LADY DEMETER!
HUFF HUFF.

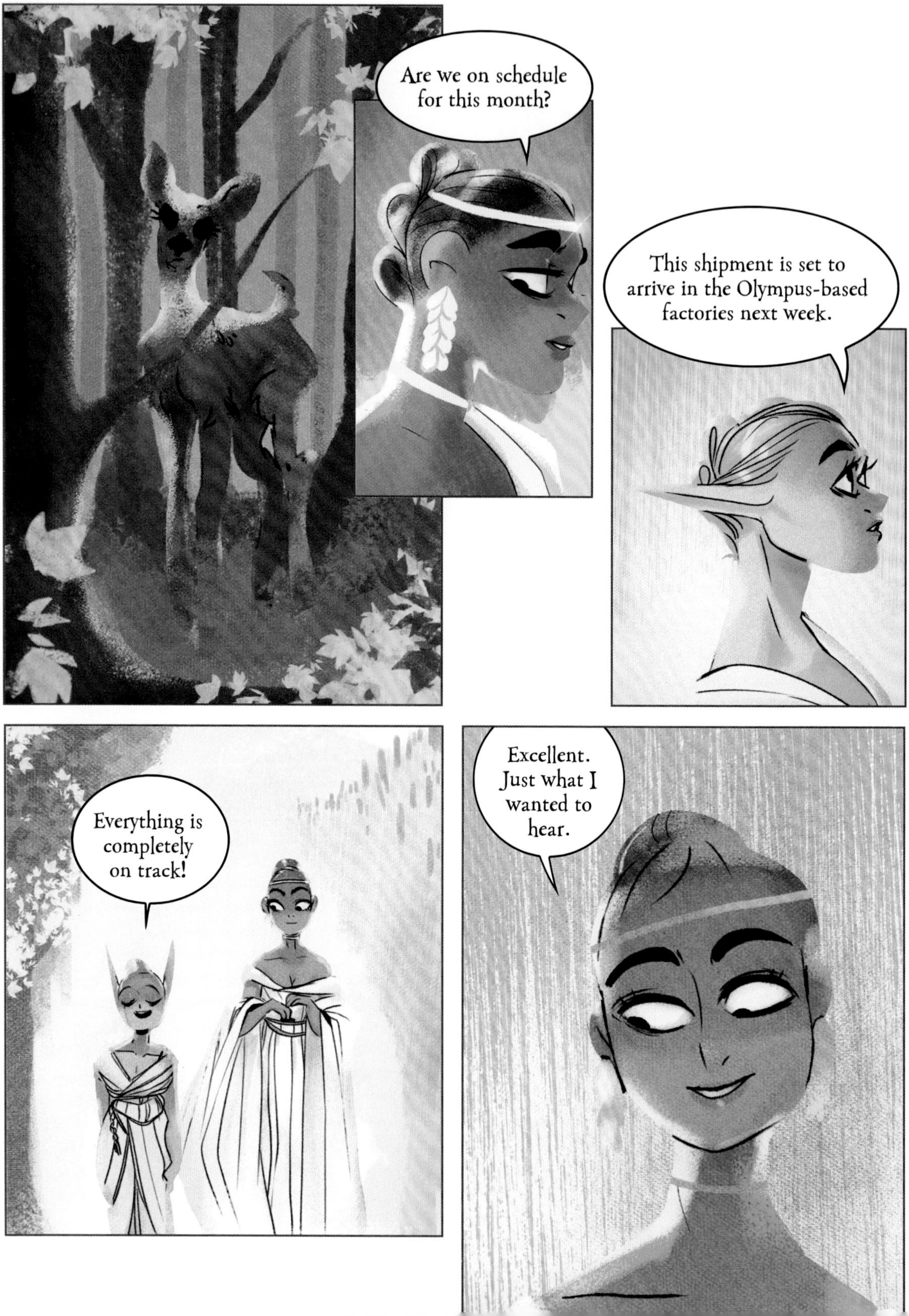
Are we on schedule for this month?
This shipment is set to arrive in the Olympus-based factories next week.
Everything is completely on track!
Excellent. Just what I wanted to hear.

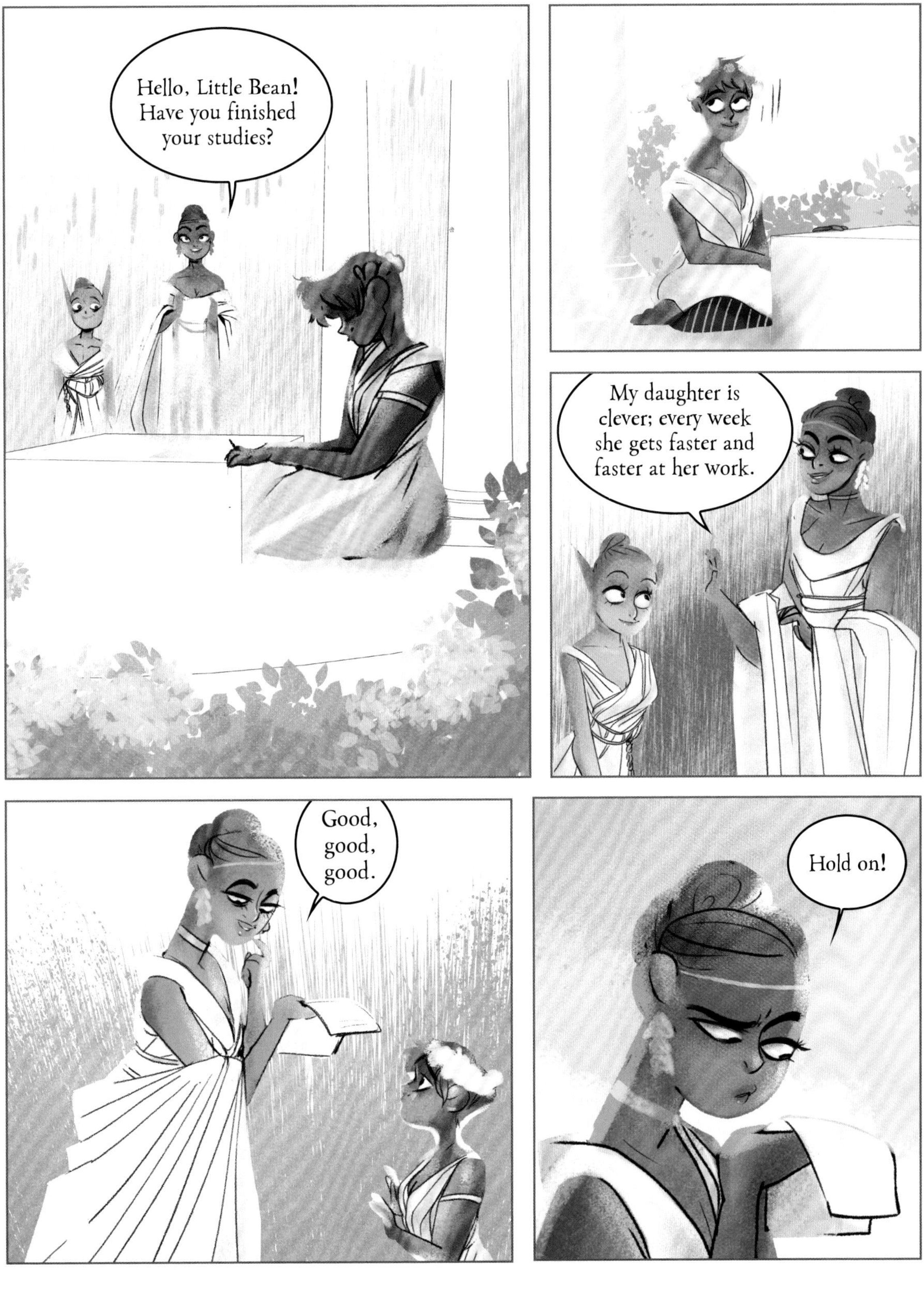
Hello, Little Bean! Have you finished your studies?
My daughter is clever; every week she gets faster and faster at her work.
Good, good, good.
Hold on!

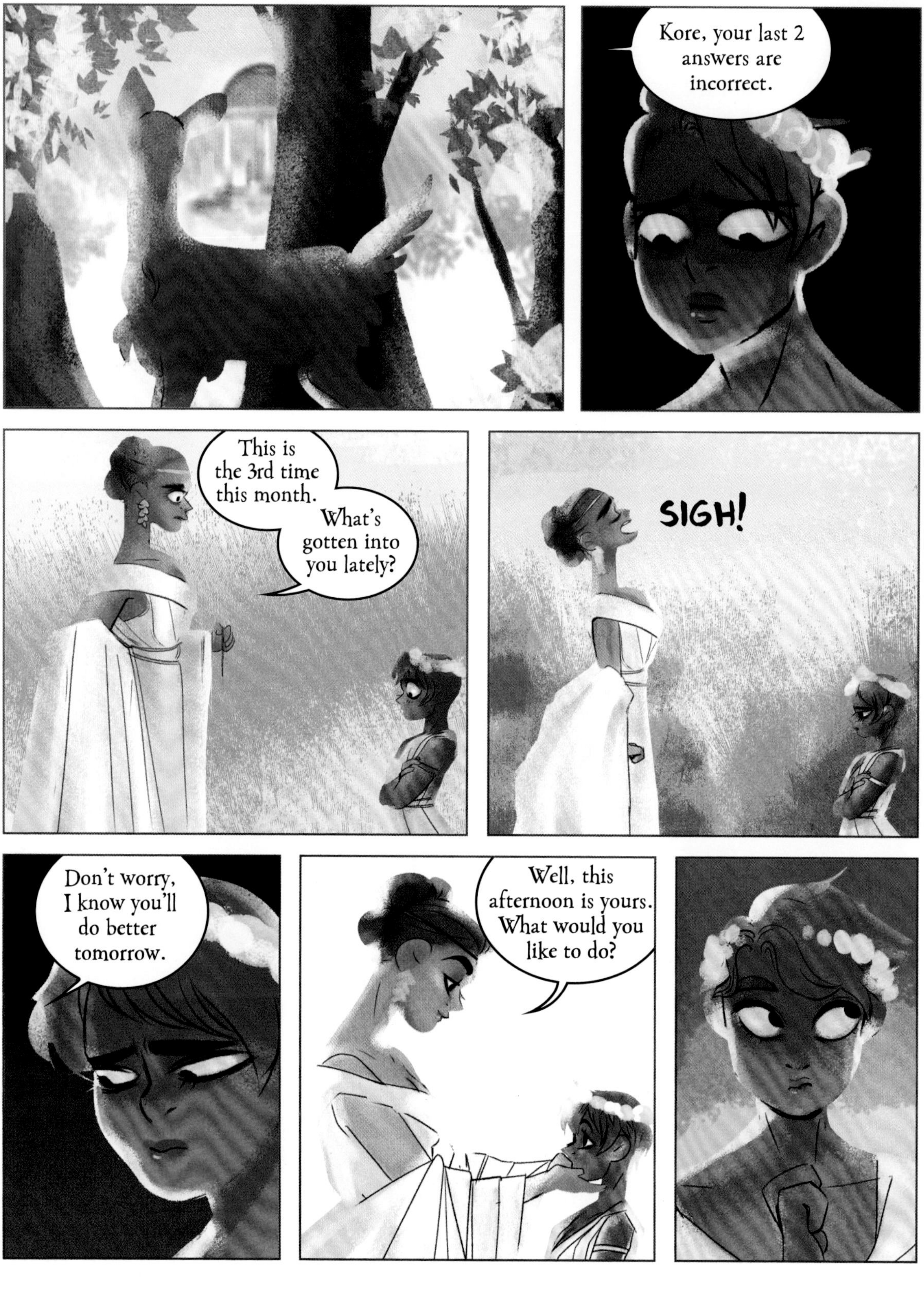
Kore, your last 2 answers are incorrect.
This is the 3rd time this month.
What's gotten into you lately?
SIGH!
Don't worry, I know you'll do better tomorrow.
Well, this afternoon is yours. What would you like to do?

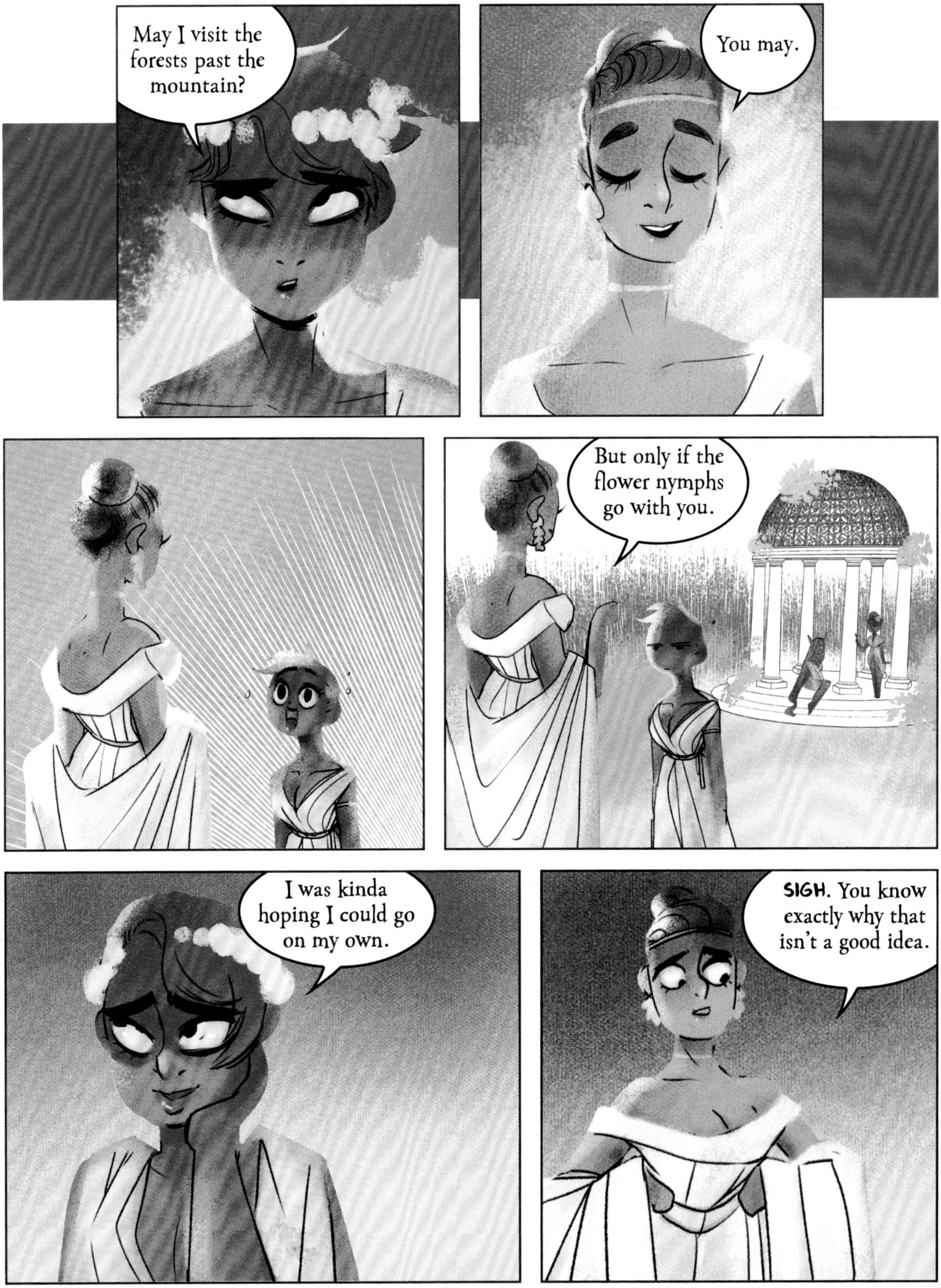
May I visit the forests past the mountain?
You may.
But only if the flower nymphs go with you.
I was kinda hoping I could go on my own.
SIGH. You know exactly why that isn't a good idea.

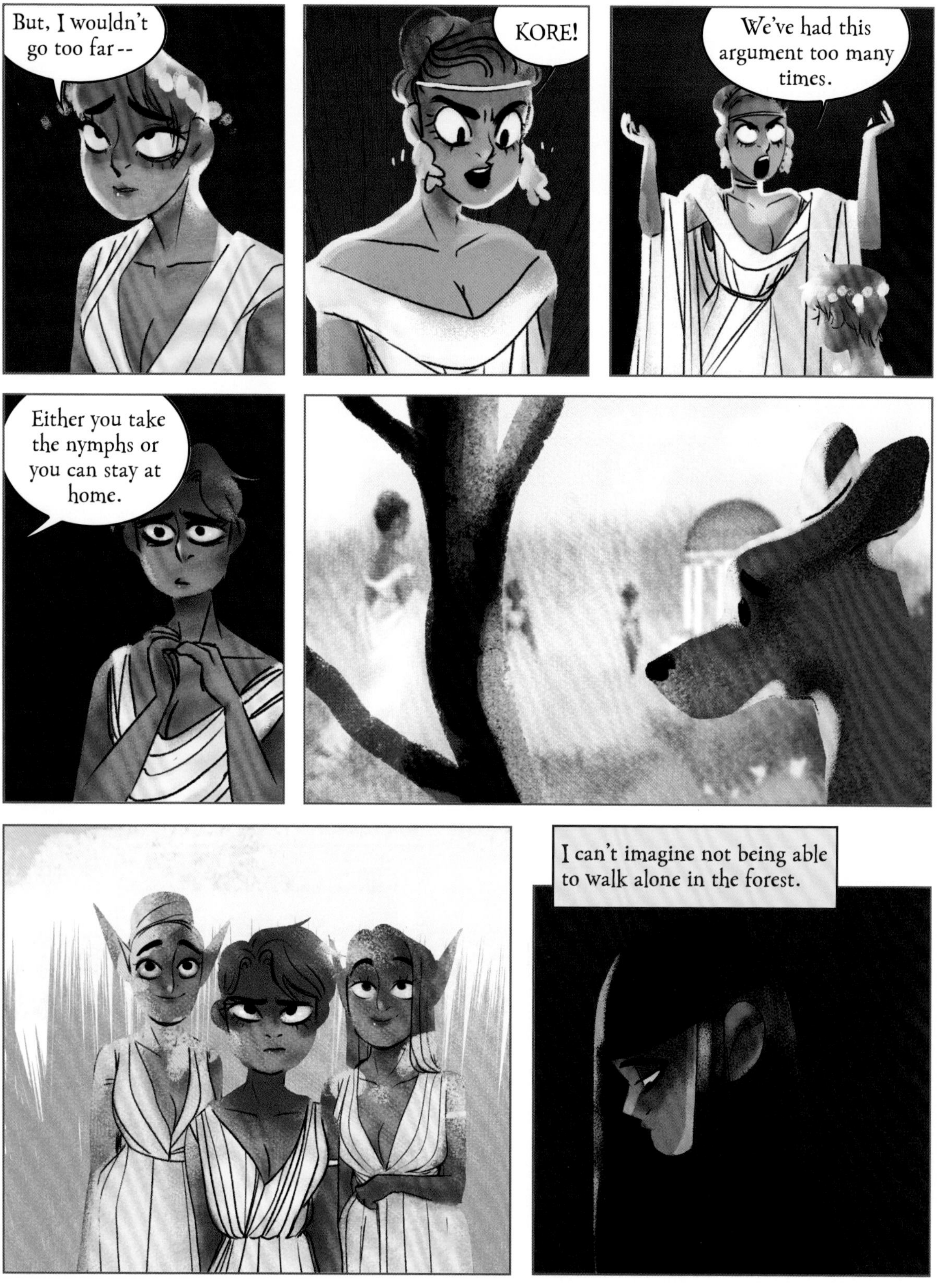
But, I wouldn't go too far--
KORE!
We've had this argument too many times.
Either you take the nymphs or you can stay at home.
I can't imagine not being able to walk alone in the forest.

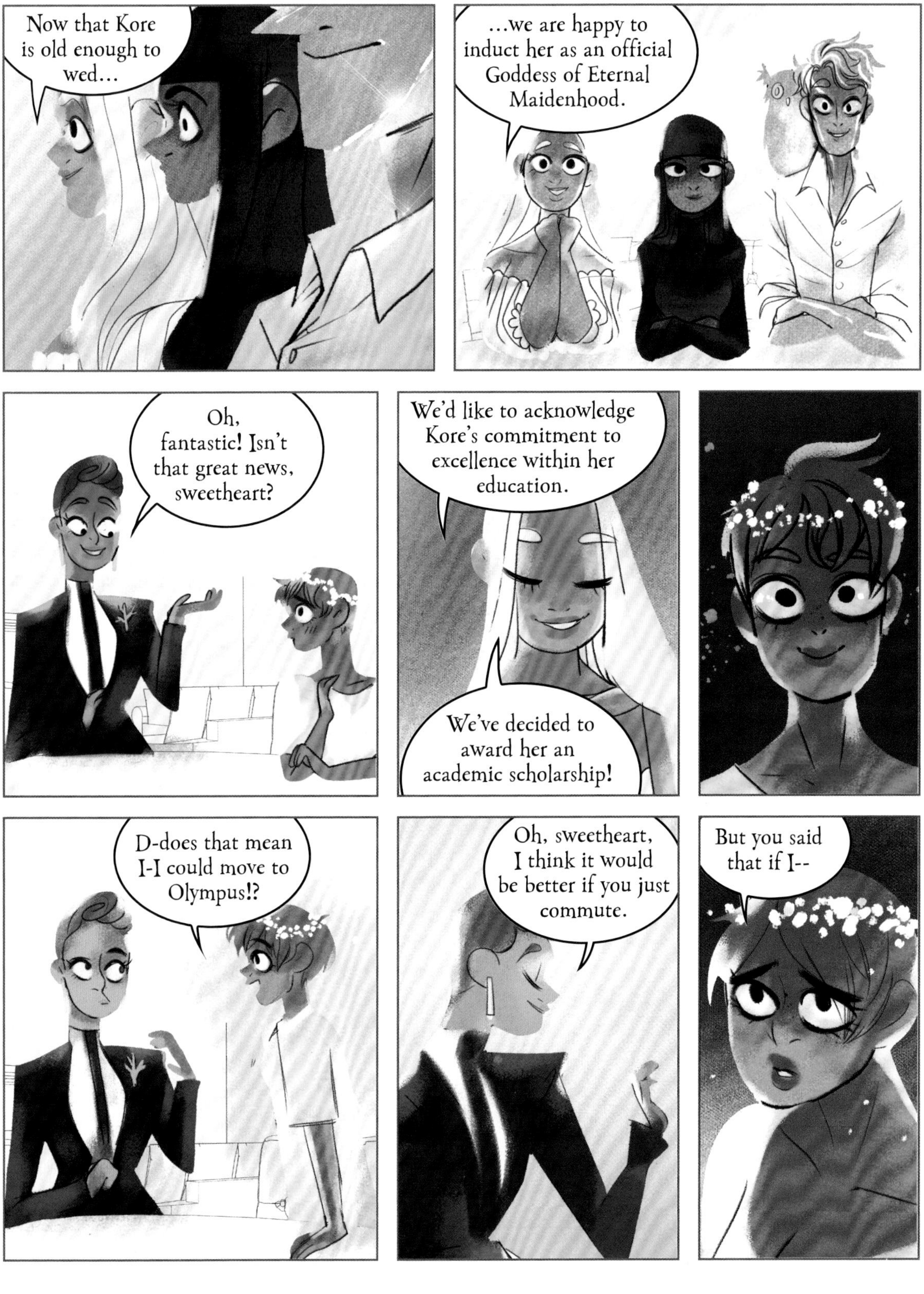

Now that Kore is old enough to wed...
...we are happy to induct her as an official Goddess of Eternal Maidenhood.
Oh, fantastic! Isn't that great news, sweetheart?
We'd like to acknowledge Kore's commitment to excellence within her education.
We've decided to award her an academic scholarship!
D-does that mean I-I could move to Olympus!?
Oh, sweetheart, I think it would be better if you just commute.
But you said that if I--

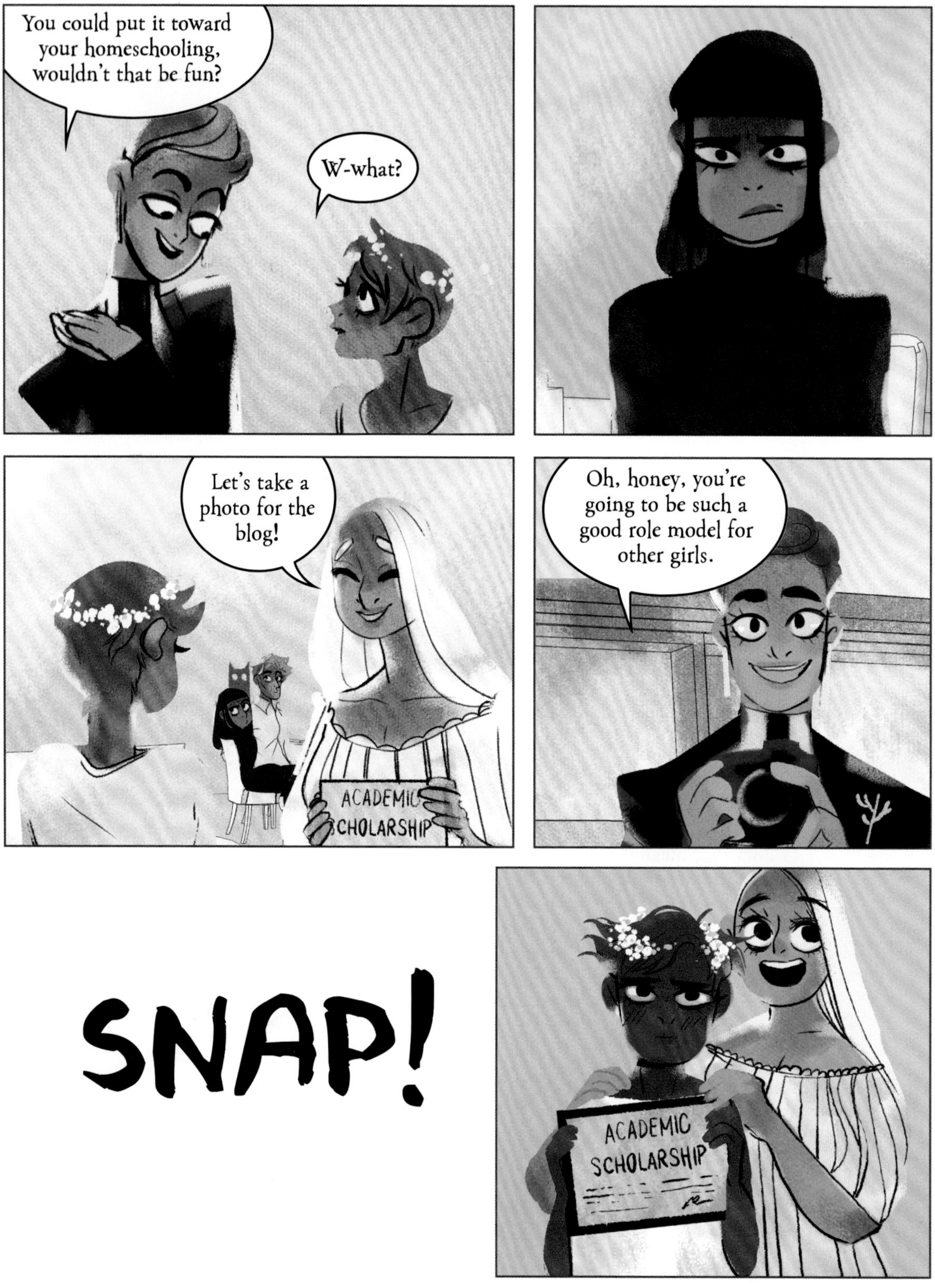
You could put it toward your homeschooling, wouldn't that be fun?
W-what?
Let's take a photo for the blog!
ACADEMIC SCHOLARSHIP
Oh, honey, you're going to be such a good role model for other girls.
SNAP!
ACADEMIC SCHOLARSHIP

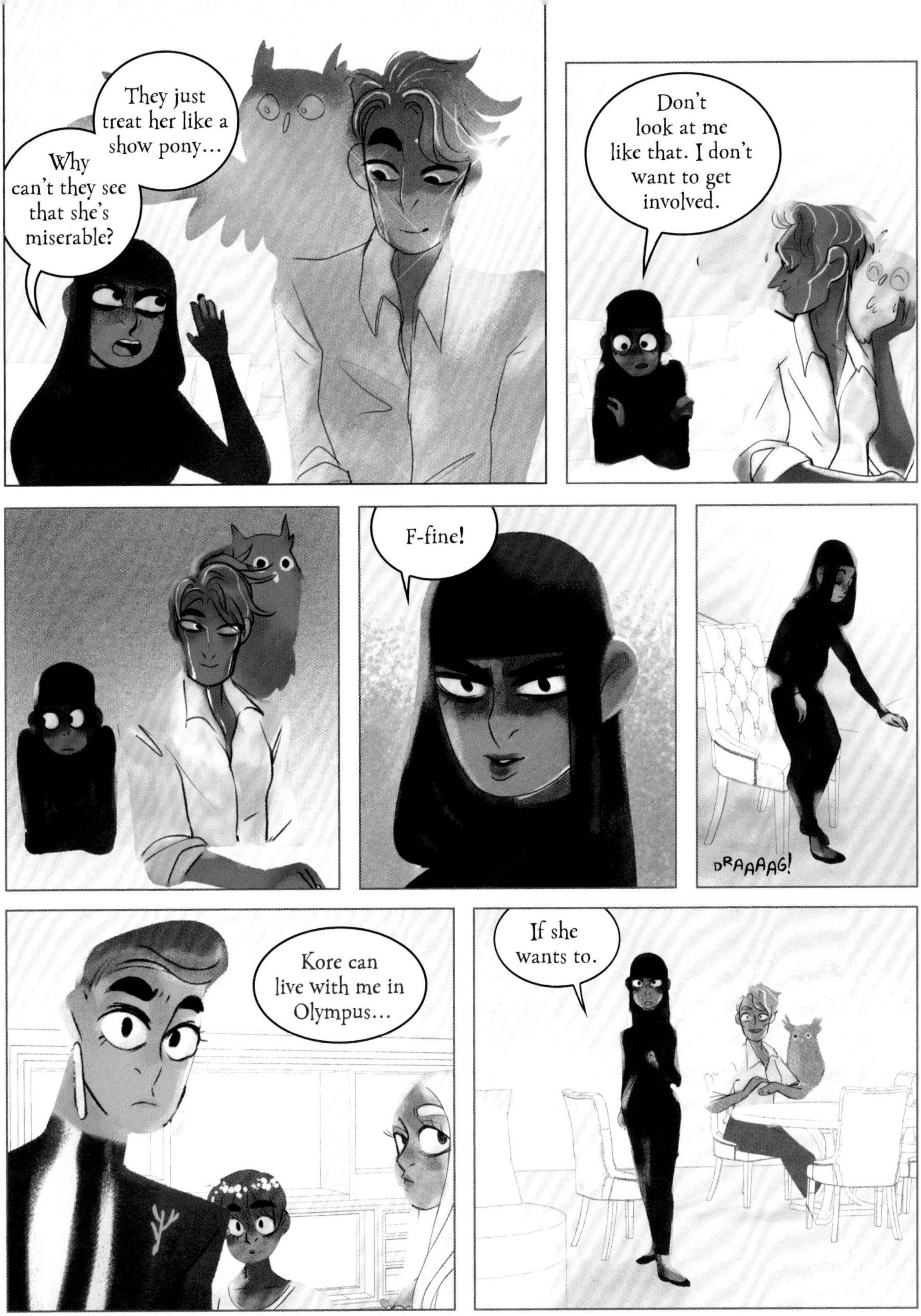
Why can't they see that she's miserable?
They just treat her like a show pony...
Don't look at me like that. I don't want to get involved.
F-fine!
DRAAAAG!
Kore can live with me in Olympus...
If she wants to.

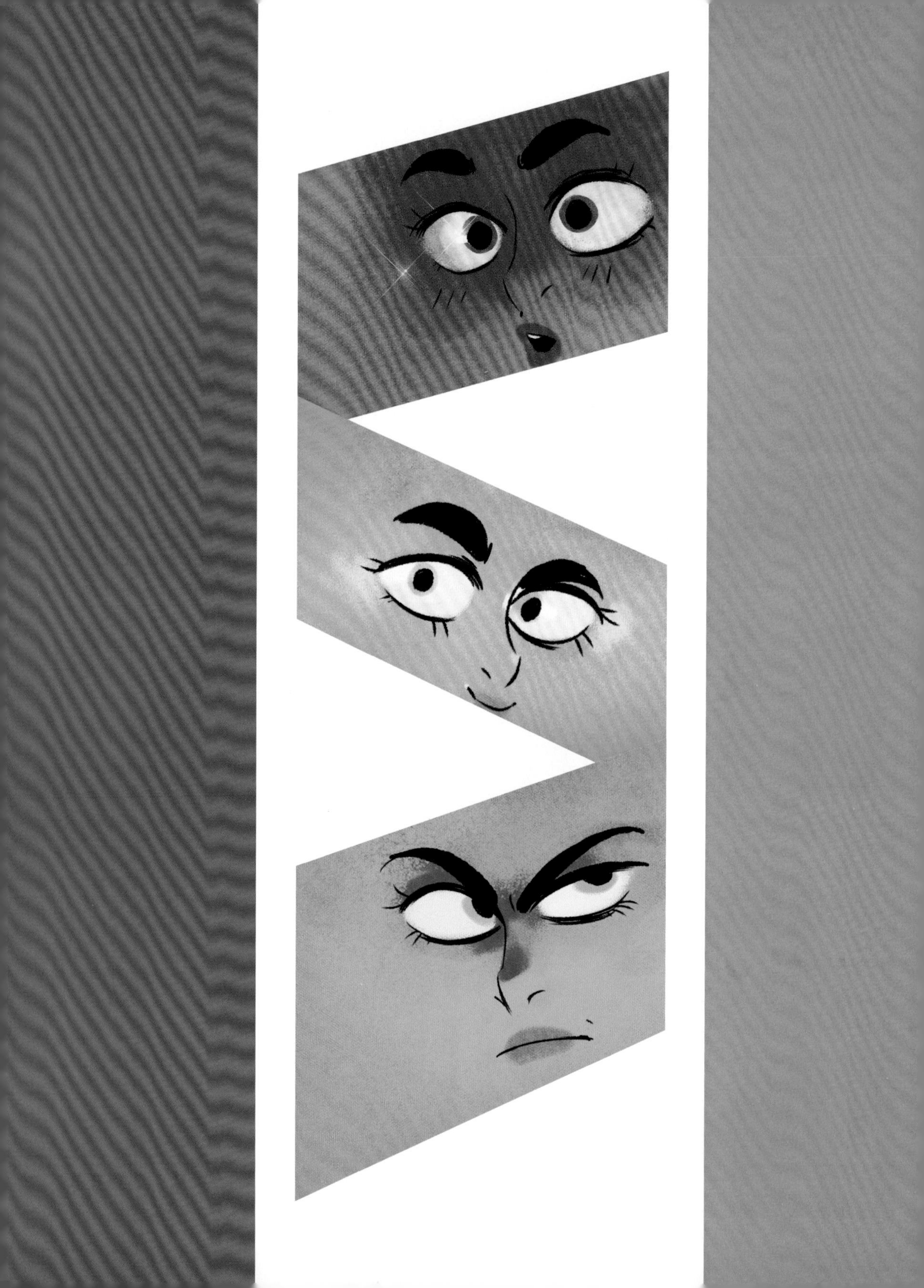

EPISODE 63: HUSH HUSH

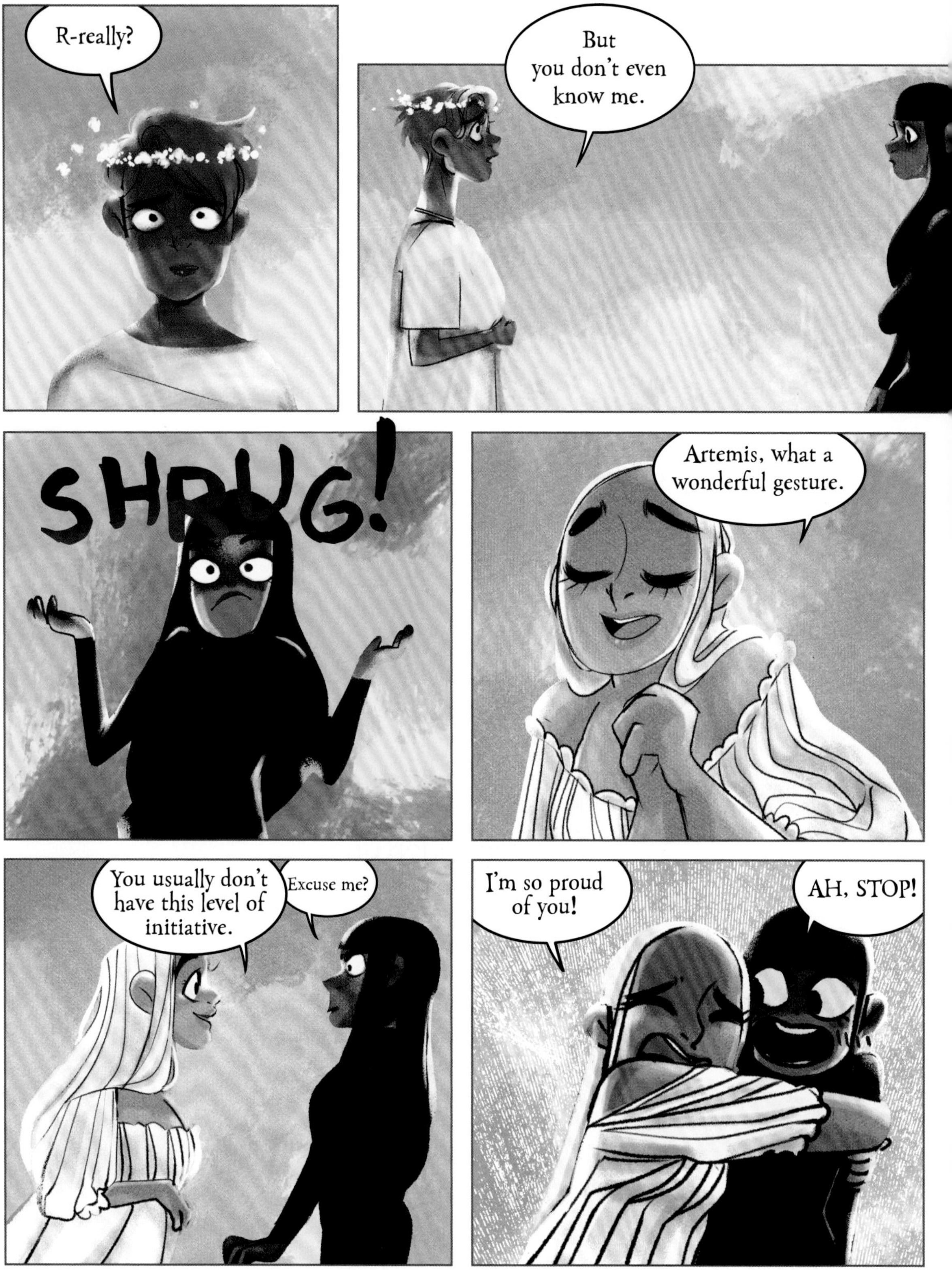

R-really?
But you don't even know me.
SHRUG!
Artemis, what a wonderful gesture.
You usually don't have this level of initiative.
Excuse me?
I'm so proud of you!
AH, STOP!

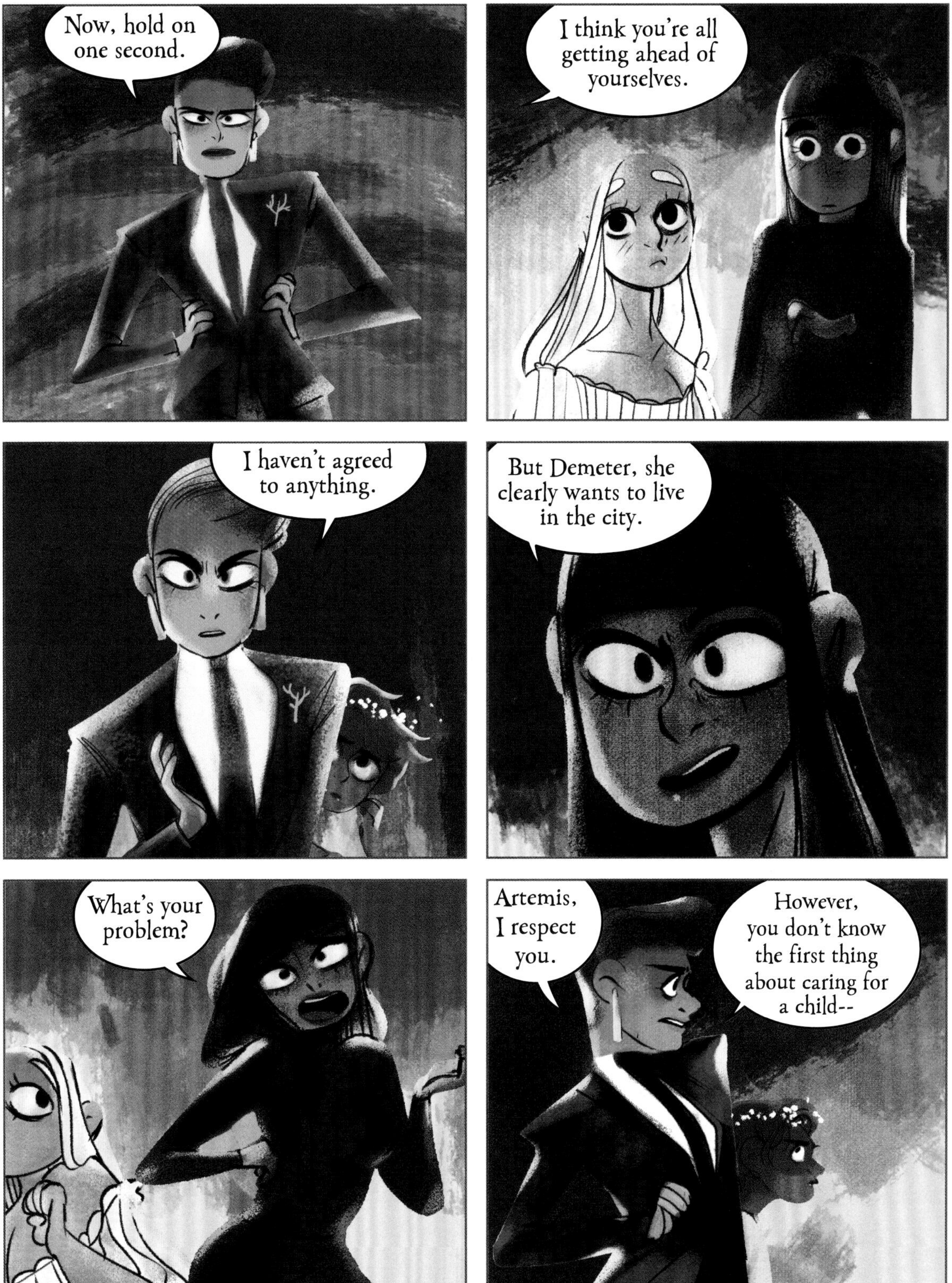
Now, hold on one second.
I think you're all getting ahead of yourselves.
I haven't agreed to anything.
But Demeter, she clearly wants to live in the city.
What's your problem?
Artemis, I respect you.
However, you don't know the first thing about caring for a child--

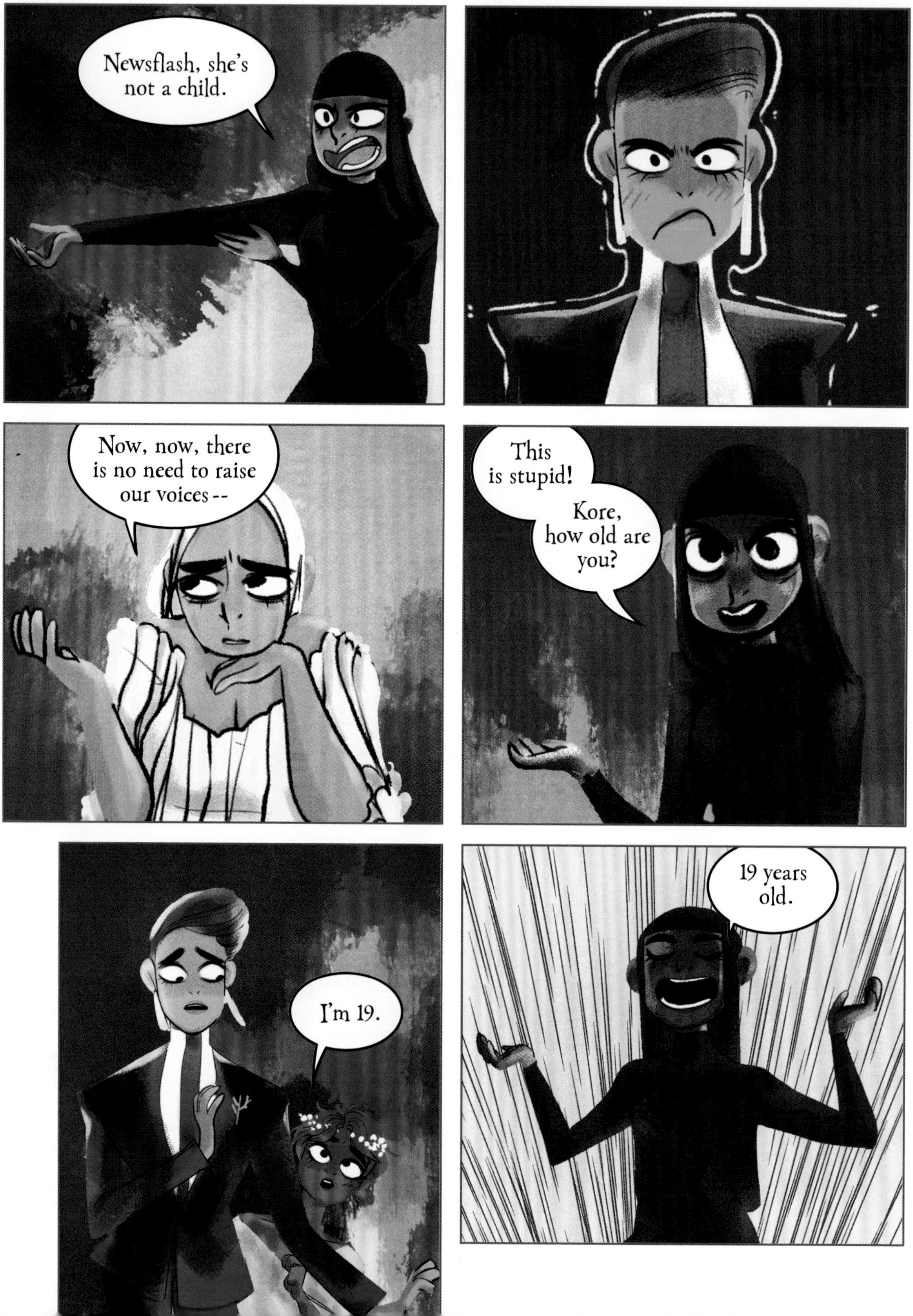
Newsflash, she's not a child.
Now, now, there is no need to raise our voices --
This is stupid!
Kore, how old are you?
I'm 19.
19 years old.

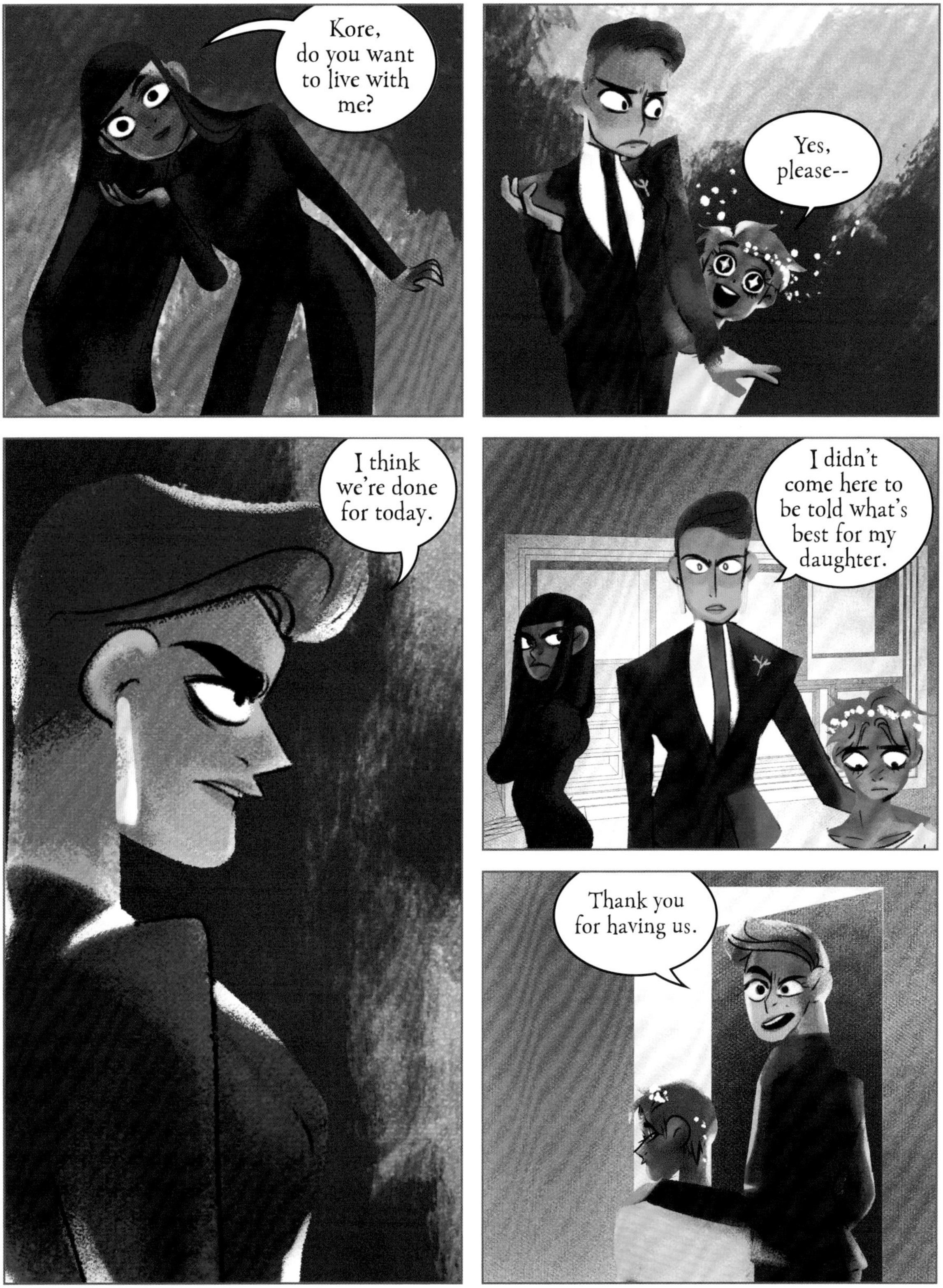

Kore, do you want to live with me?
Yes, please--
I think we're done for today.
I didn't come here to be told what's best for my daughter.
Thank you for having us.

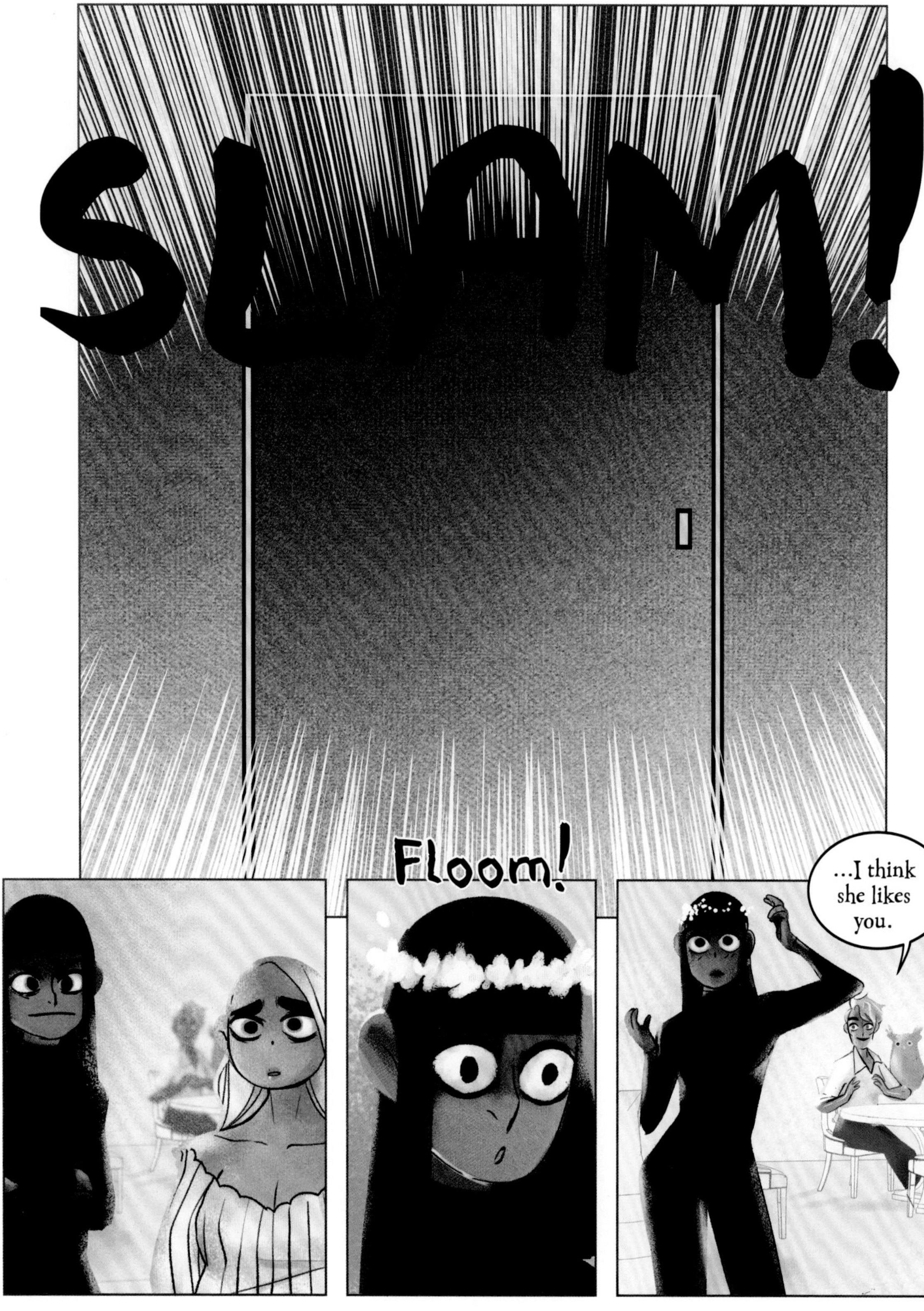
SLAM!
Floom!
...I think she likes you.

A FEW WEEKS LATER

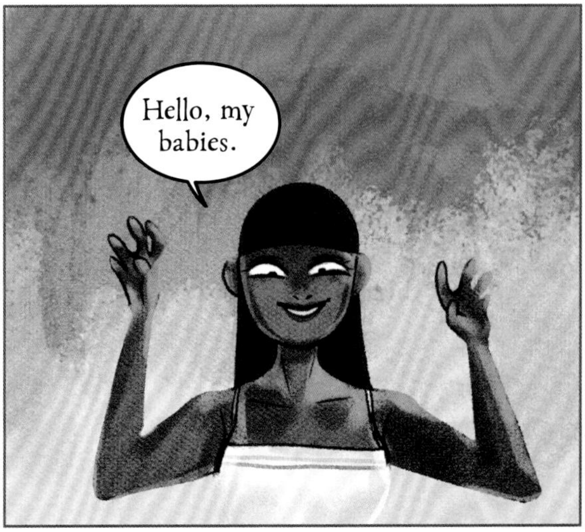
Hello, my babies.

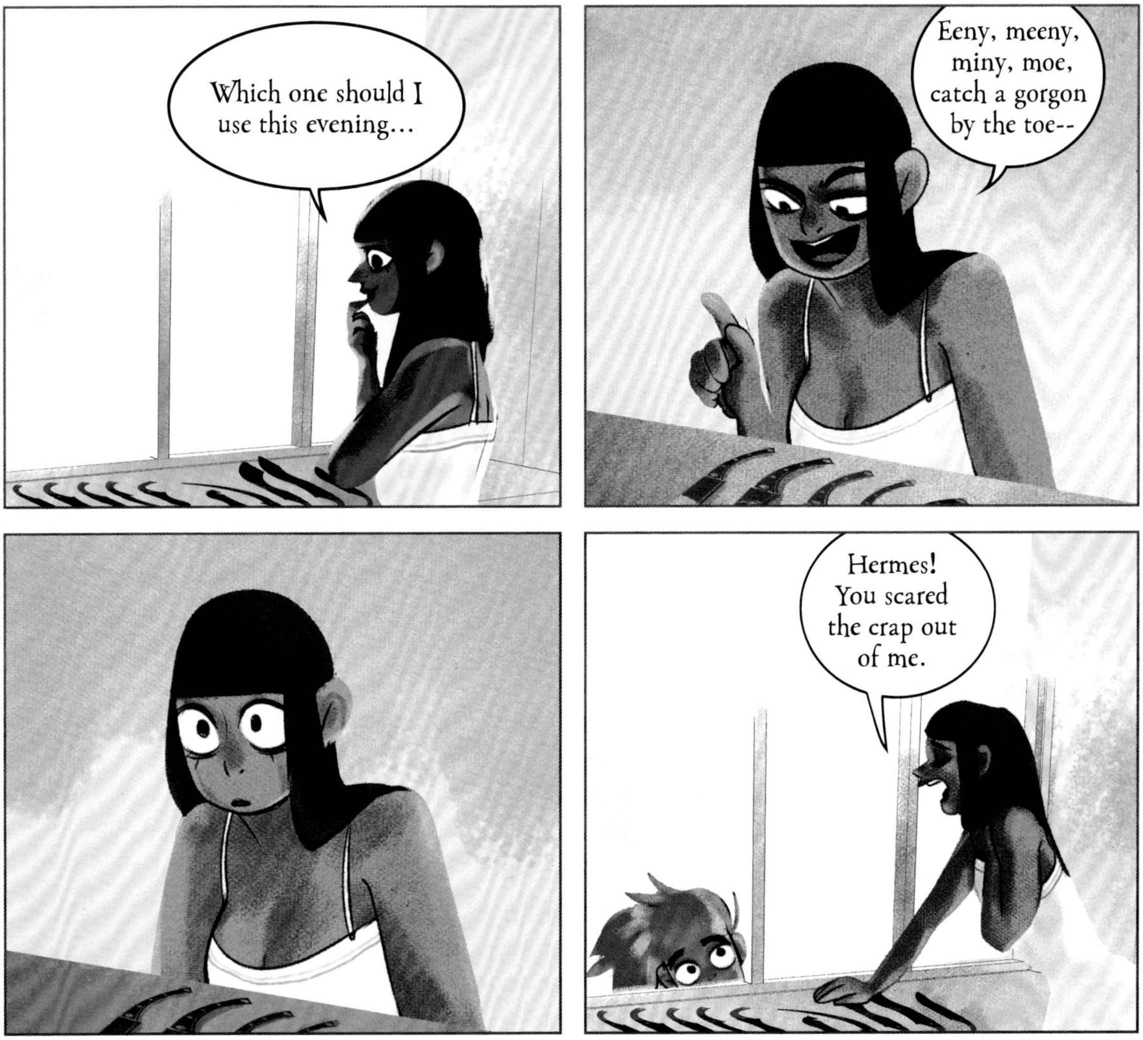
Which one should I use this evening...
Eeny, meeny, miny, moe, catch a gorgon by the toe--
Hermes! You scared the crap out of me.

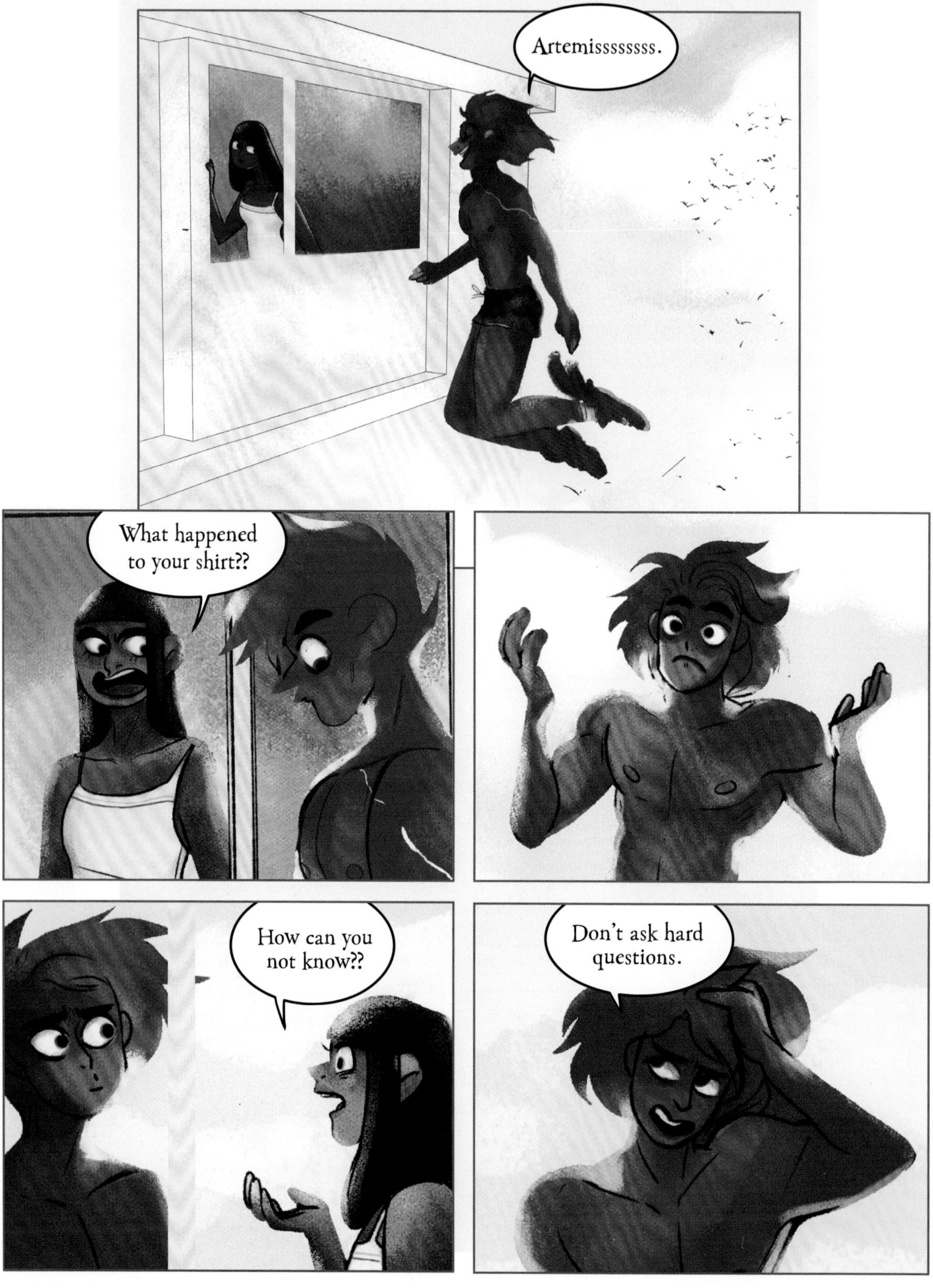
Artemisssssssss.
What happened to your shirt??
How can you not know??
Don't ask hard questions.

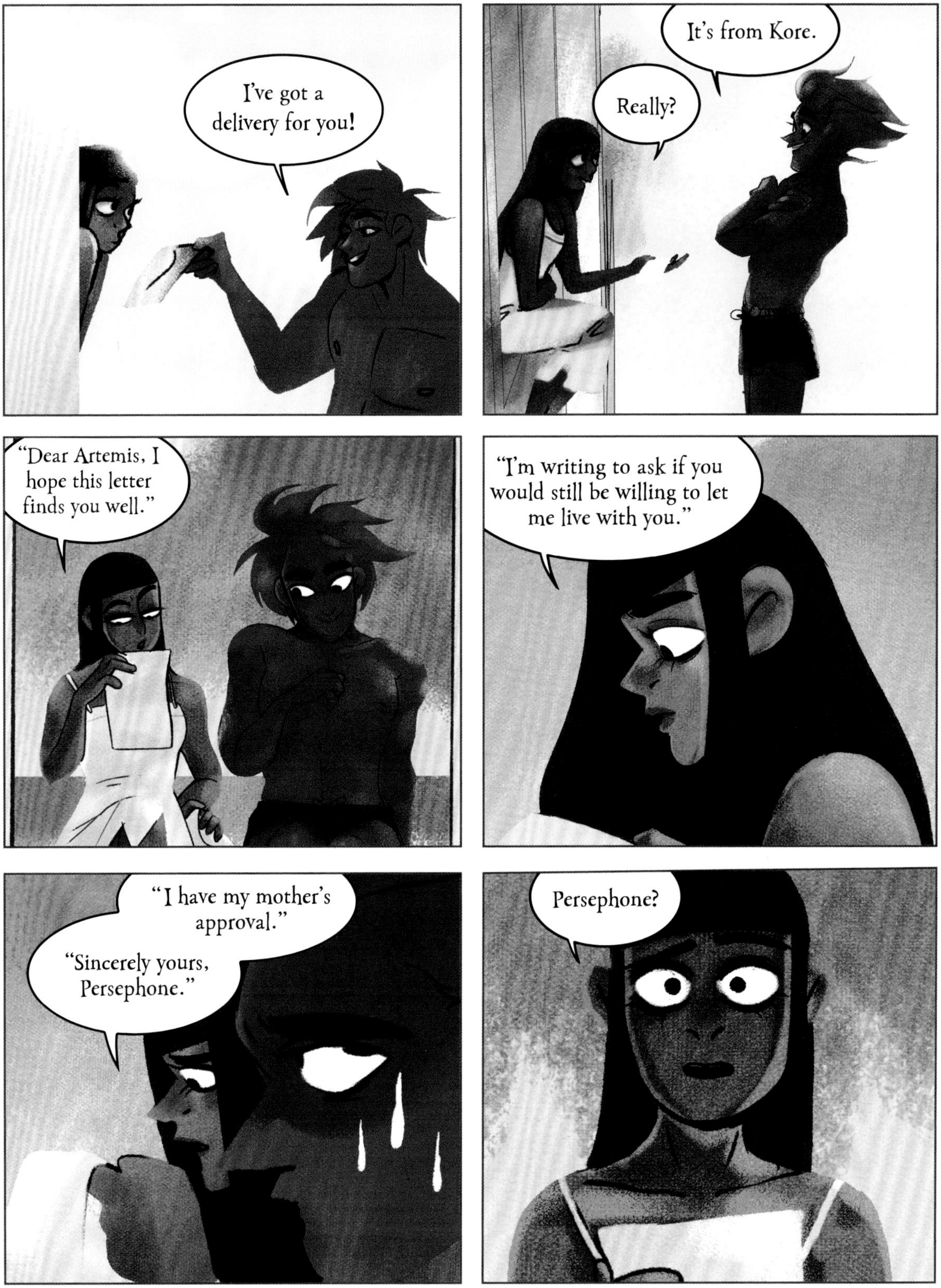
I've got a delivery for you!
It's from Kore.
Really?
"Dear Artemis, I hope this letter finds you well."
"I'm writing to ask if you would still be willing to let me live with you."
"I have my mother's approval."
"Sincerely yours, Persephone."
Persephone?

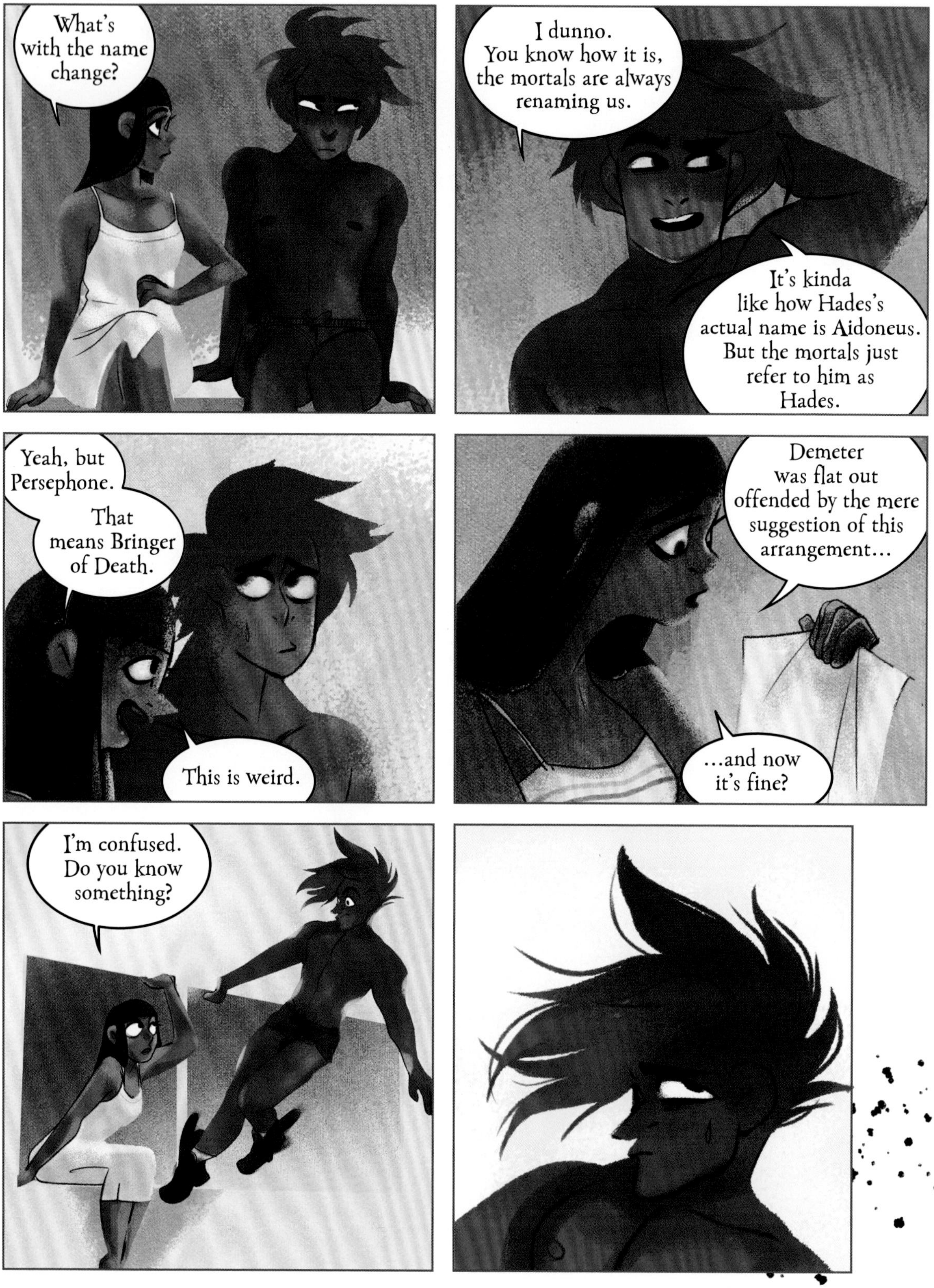
What's with the name change?
I dunno. You know how it is, the mortals are always renaming us.
It's kinda like how Hades's actual name is Aidoneus. But the mortals just refer to him as Hades.
Yeah, but Persephone.
That means Bringer of Death.
This is weird.
Demeter was flat out offended by the mere suggestion of this arrangement...
...and now it's fine?
I'm confused. Do you know something?

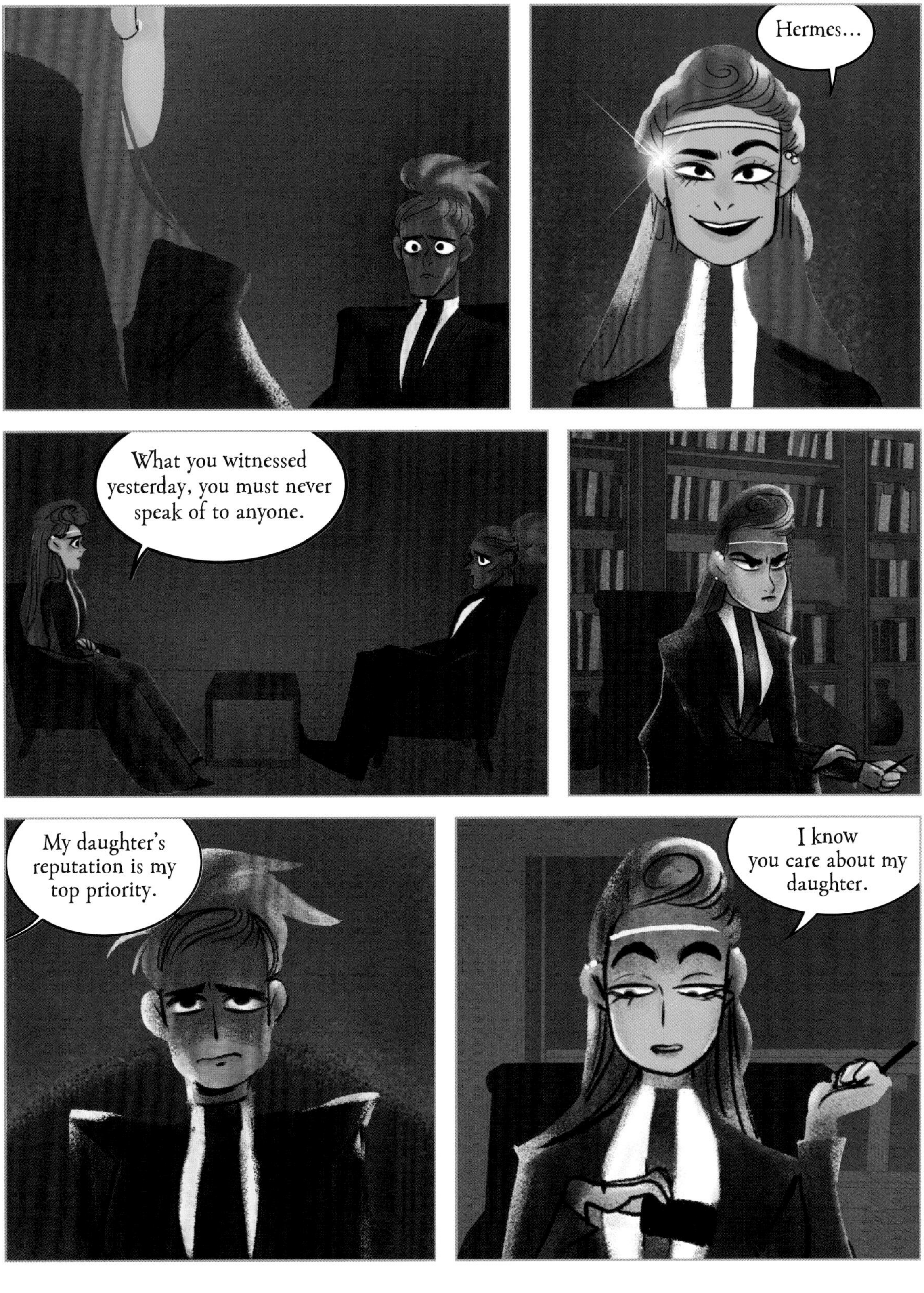
Hermes...
What you witnessed yesterday, you must never speak of to anyone.
My daughter's reputation is my top priority.
I know you care about my daughter.

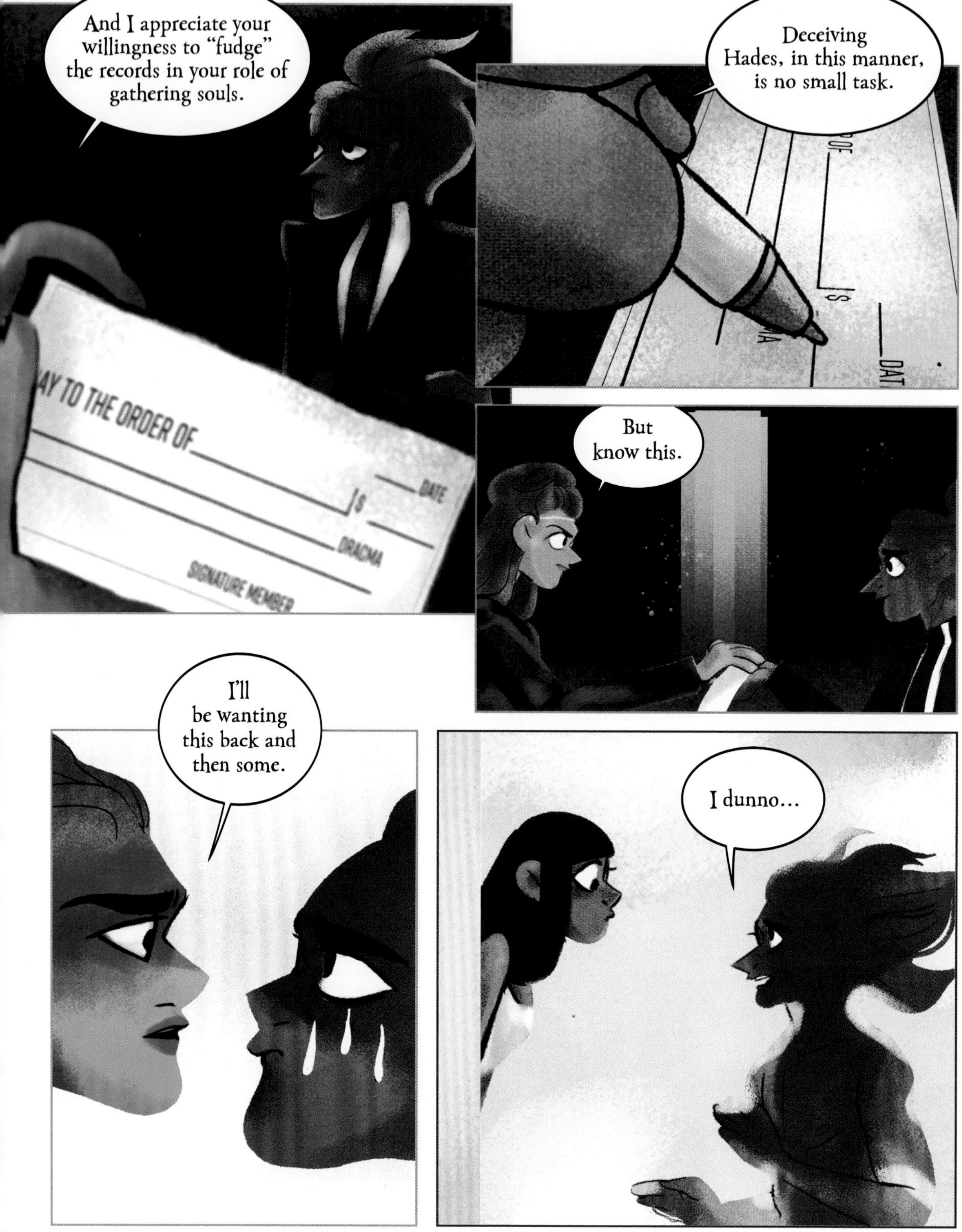
And I appreciate your willingness to "fudge" the records in your role of gathering souls.
PAY TO THE ORDER OF
DATE
$
DRACMA
SIGNATURE MEMBER
Deceiving Hades, in this manner, is no small task.
But know this.
I'll be wanting this back and then some.
I dunno...

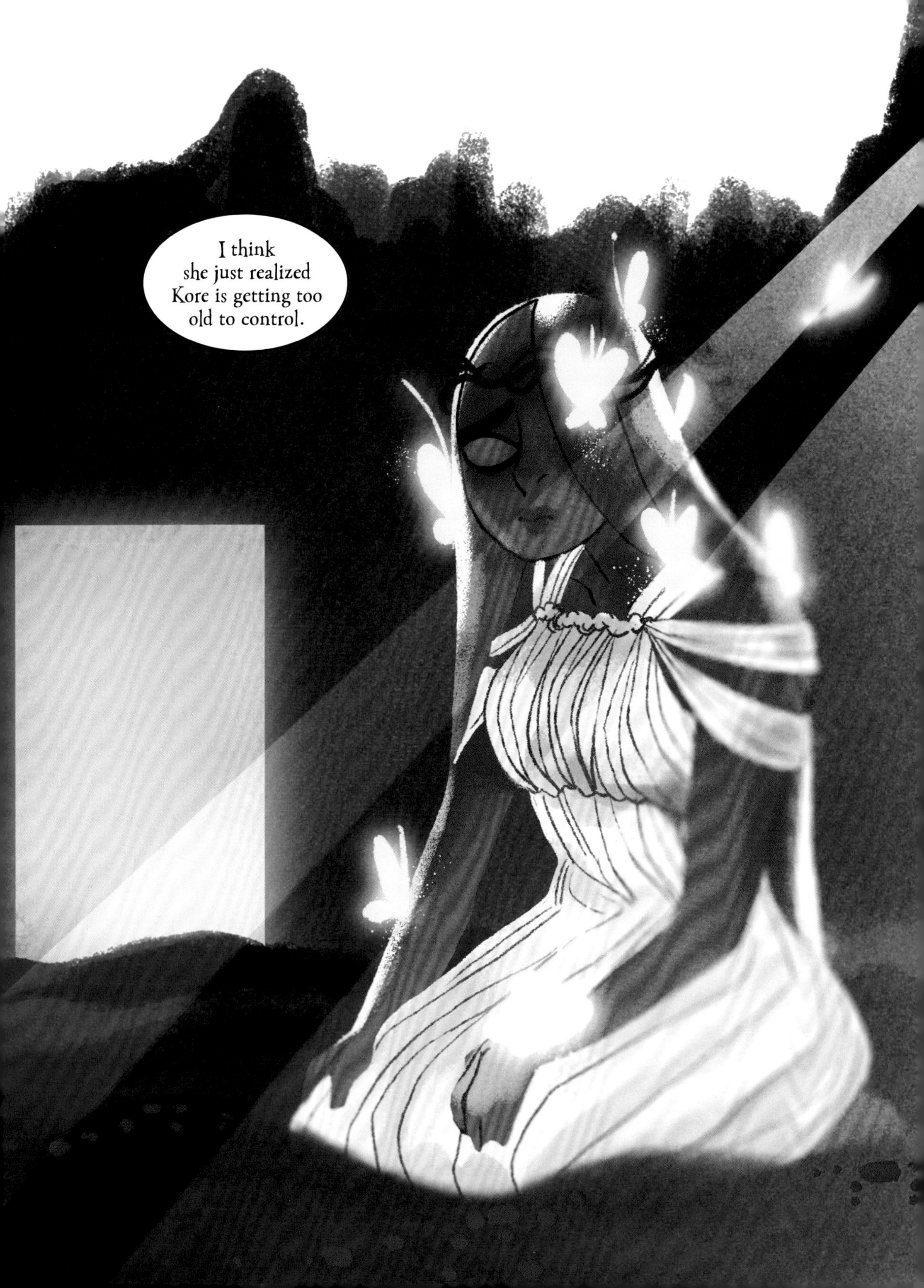
I think she just realized Kore is getting too old to control.

EPISODE 64: DIMPLES

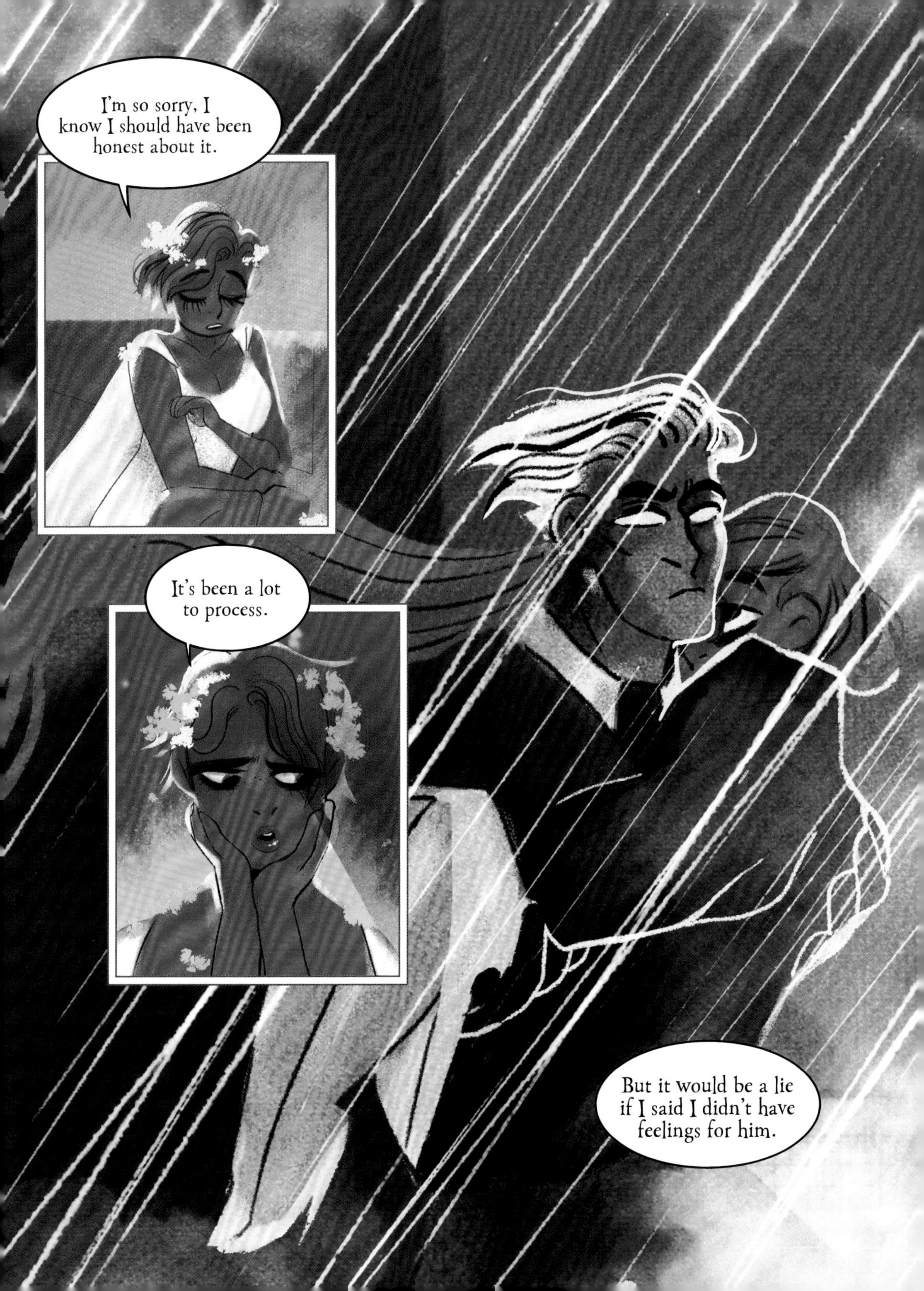
I'm so sorry, I know I should have been honest about it.
It's been a lot to process.
But it would be a lie if I said I didn't have feelings for him.

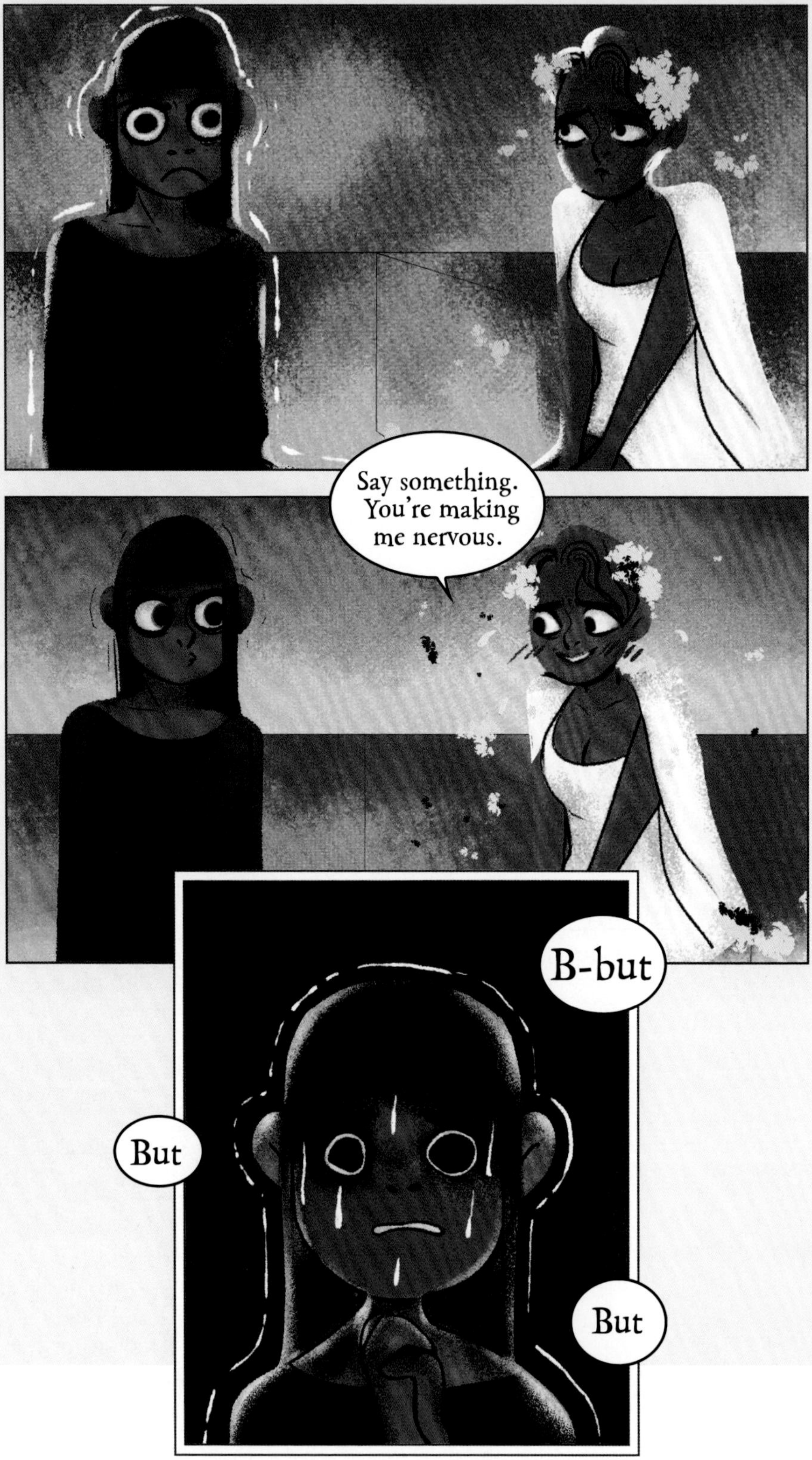
Say something. You're making me nervous.
B-but
But
But

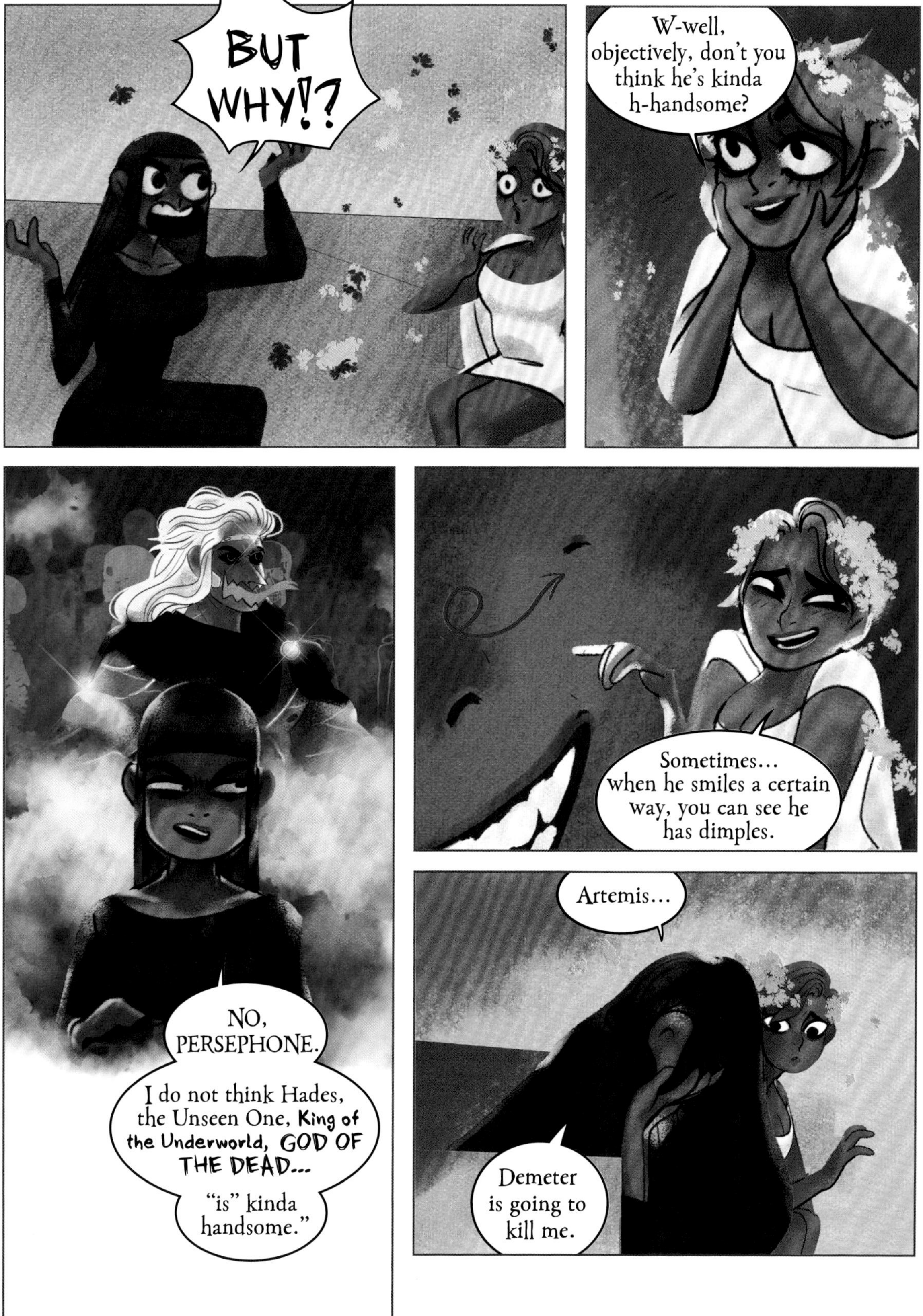

BUT WHY!?
W-well, objectively, don't you think he's kinda h-handsome?
NO, PERSEPHONE.
I do not think Hades, the Unseen One, King of the Underworld, GOD OF THE DEAD...
"is" kinda handsome."
Sometimes... when he smiles a certain way, you can see he has dimples.
Artemis...
Demeter is going to kill me.

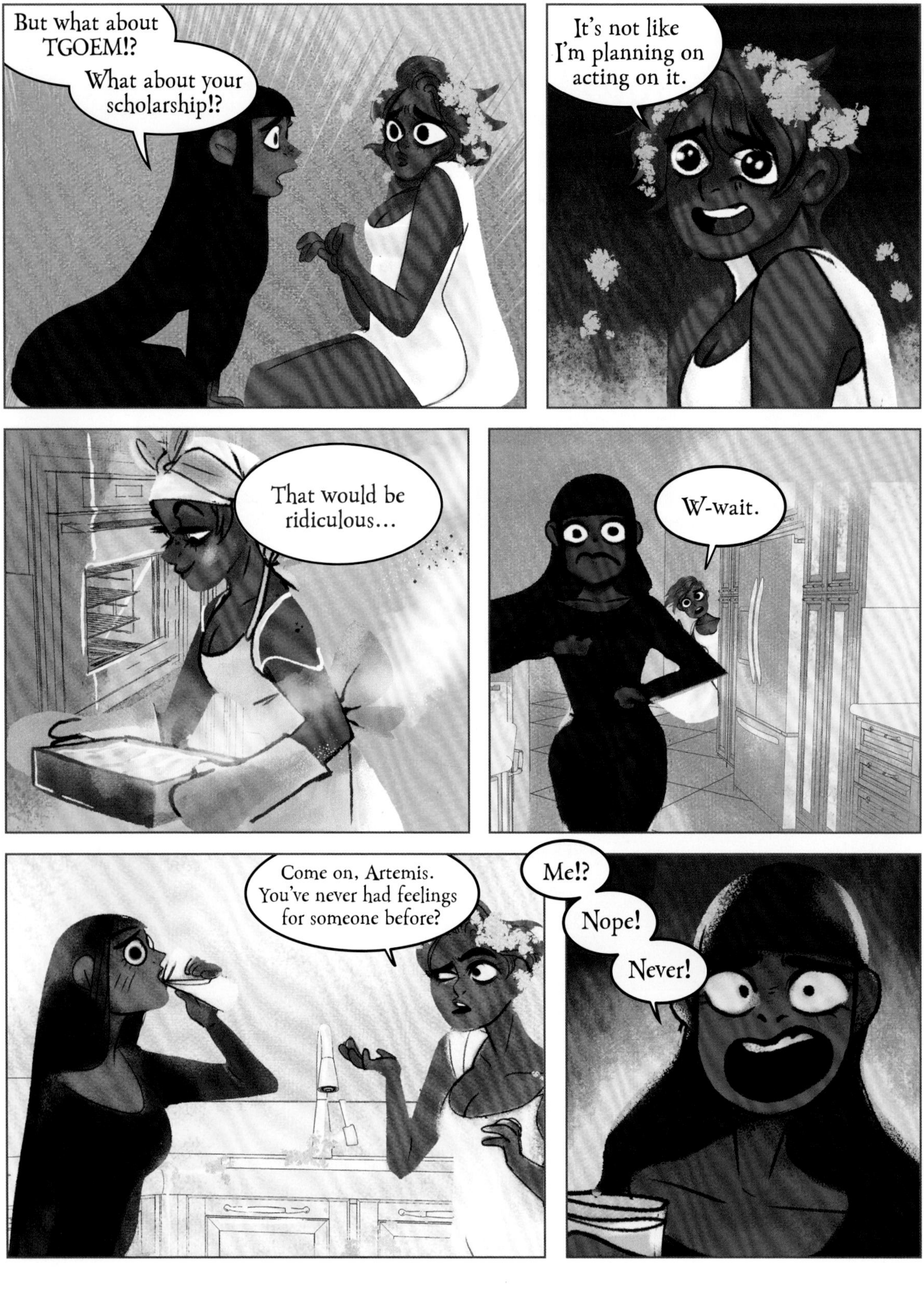
But what about TGOEM!?
What about your scholarship!?
It's not like I'm planning on acting on it.
That would be ridiculous…
W-wait.
Come on, Artemis. You've never had feelings for someone before?
Me!?
Nope!
Never!

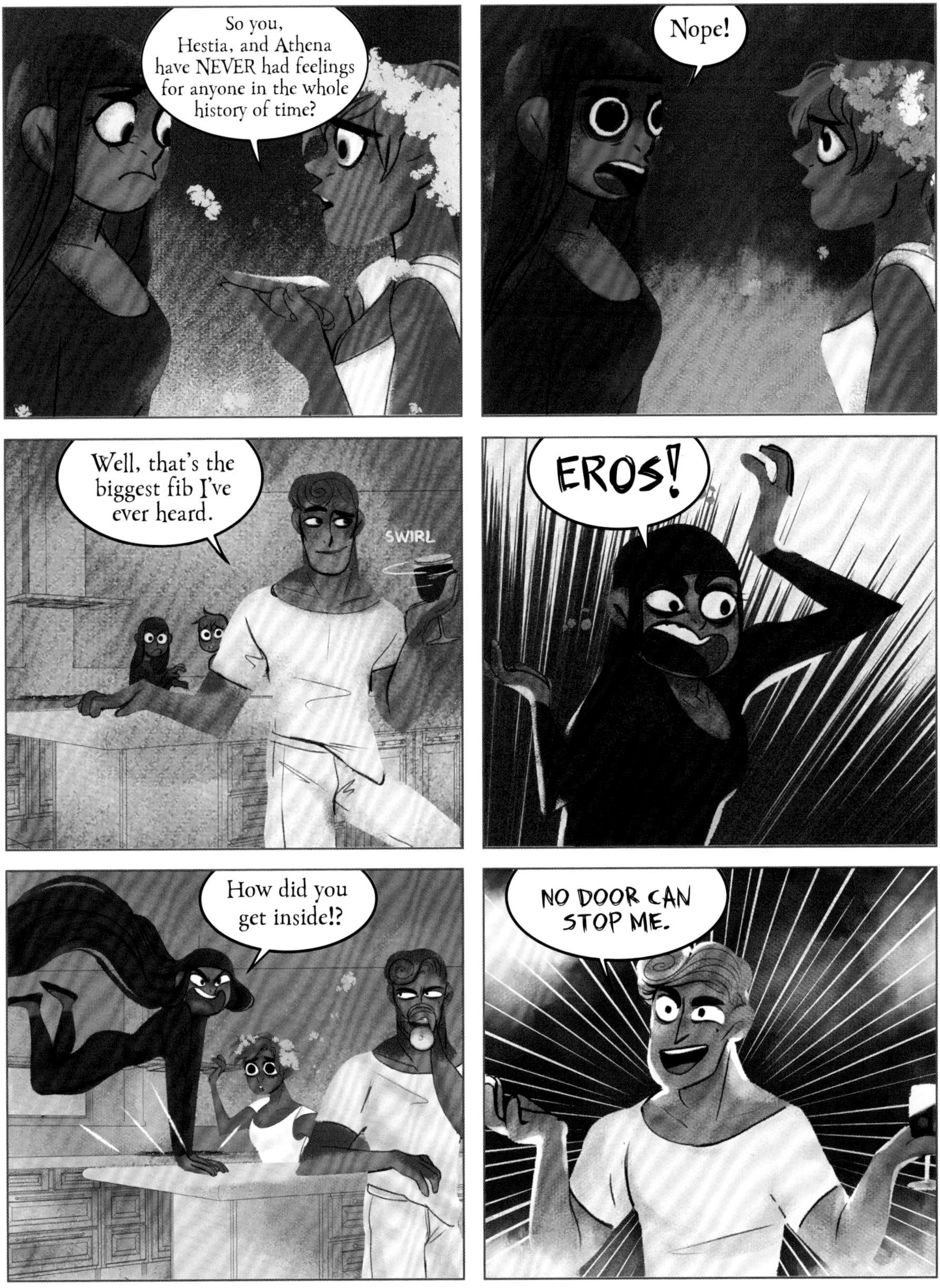
So you, Hestia, and Athena have NEVER had feelings for anyone in the whole history of time?
Nope!
Well, that's the biggest fib I've ever heard.
SWIRL
EROS!
How did you get inside!?
NO DOOR CAN STOP ME.

Okay, key under the doormat.

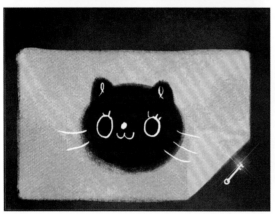

I sensed an admission of a crush, and I came over as fast as I could.

Where are you going?

Someone just admitted they have a crush and I need to get involved.

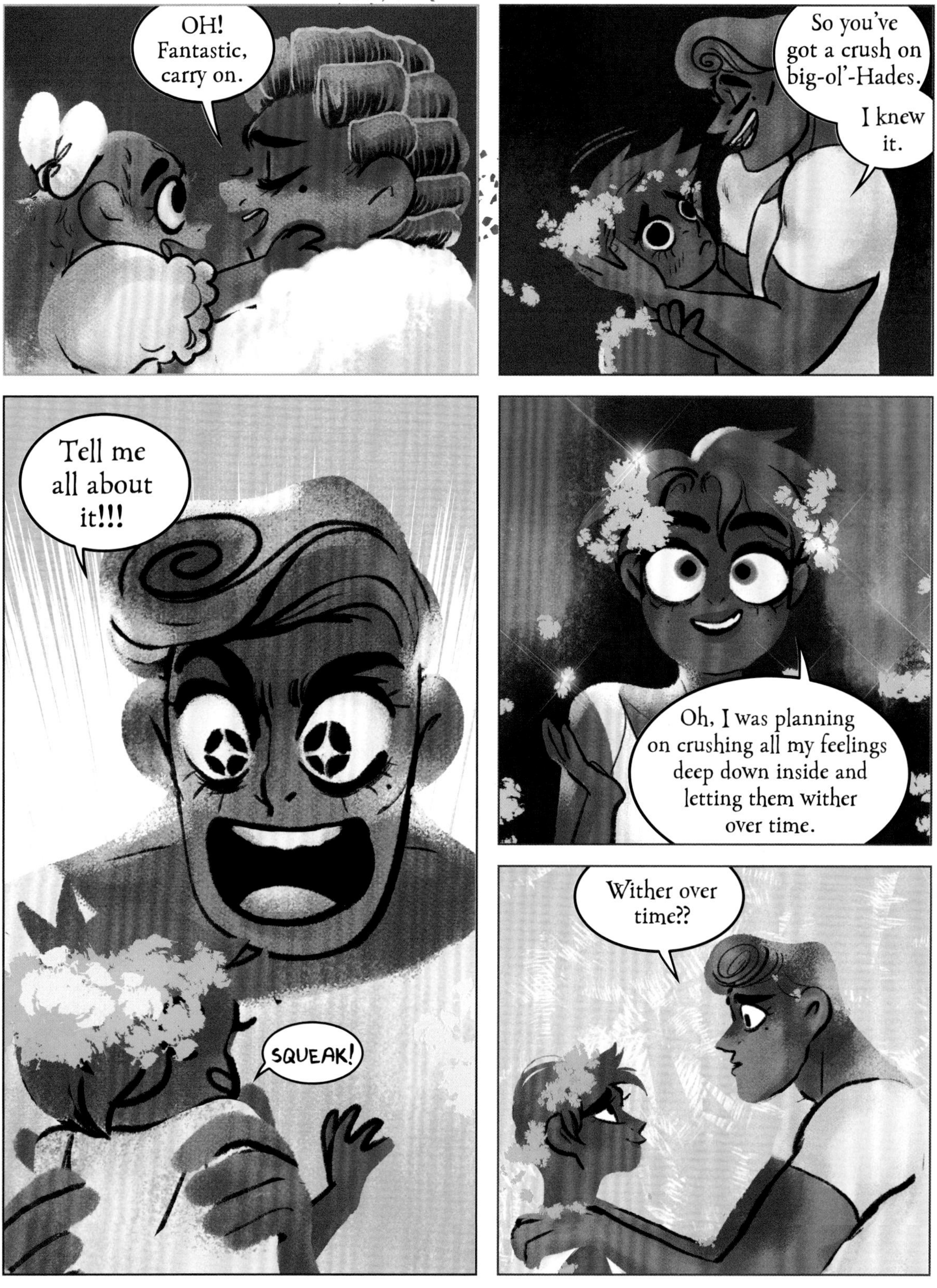
OH! Fantastic, carry on.
So you've got a crush on big-ol'-Hades.
I knew it.
Tell me all about it!!!
SQUEAK!
Oh, I was planning on crushing all my feelings deep down inside and letting them wither over time.
Wither over time??

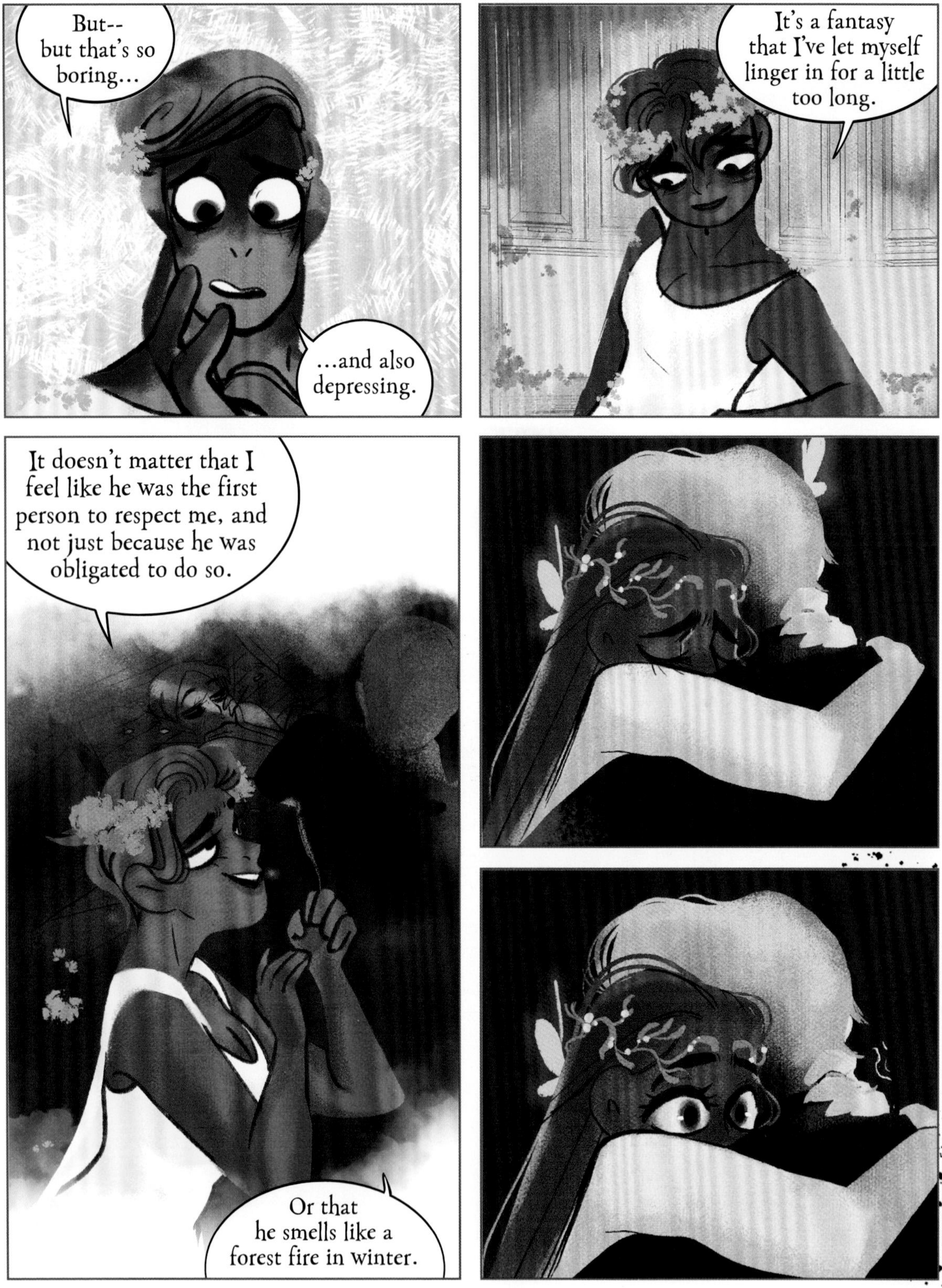
But-- but that's so boring...
...and also depressing.
It's a fantasy that I've let myself linger in for a little too long.
It doesn't matter that I feel like he was the first person to respect me, and not just because he was obligated to do so.
Or that he smells like a forest fire in winter.

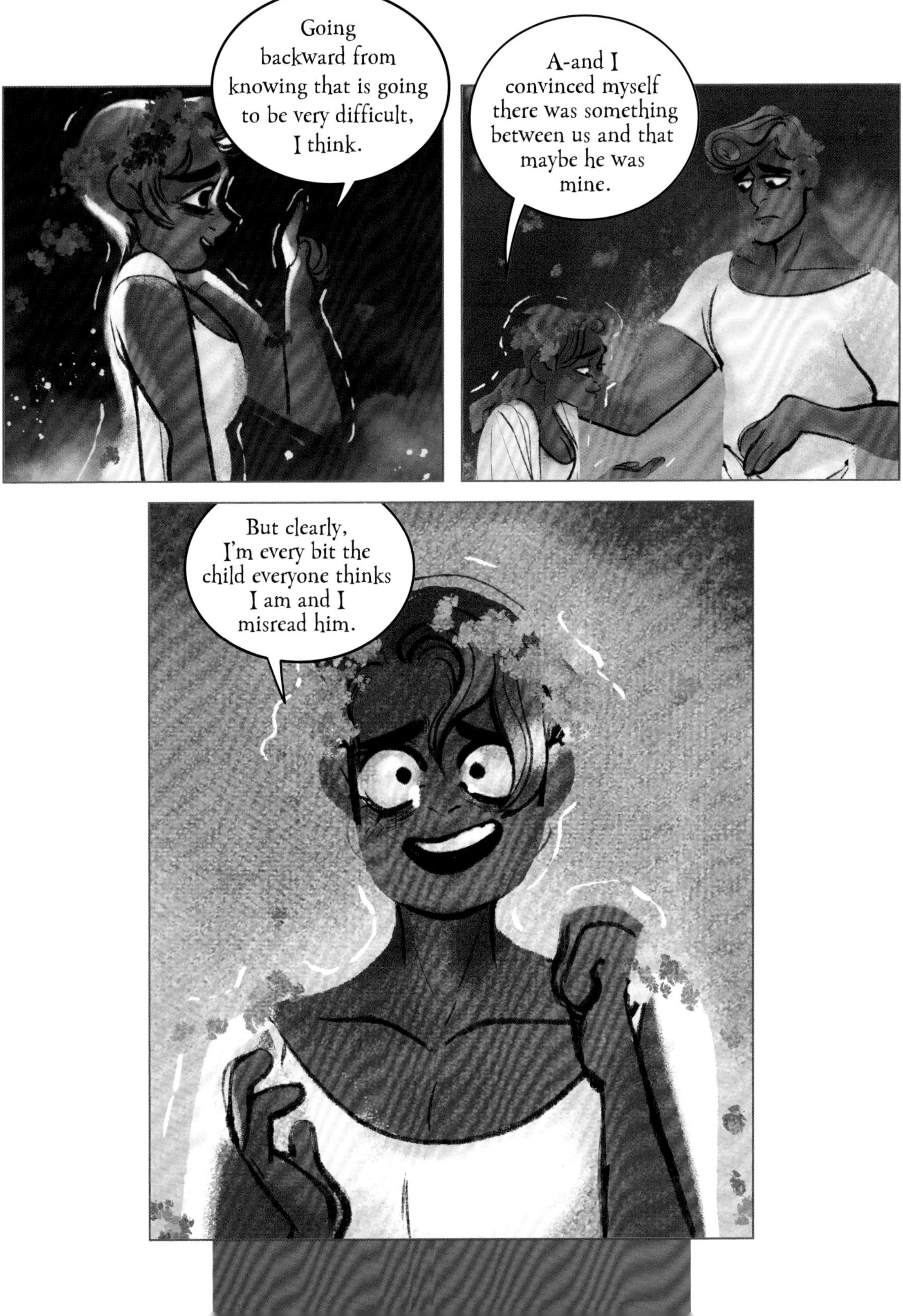
Going backward from knowing that is going to be very difficult, I think.
A-and I convinced myself there was something between us and that maybe he was mine.
But clearly, I'm every bit the child everyone thinks I am and I misread him.

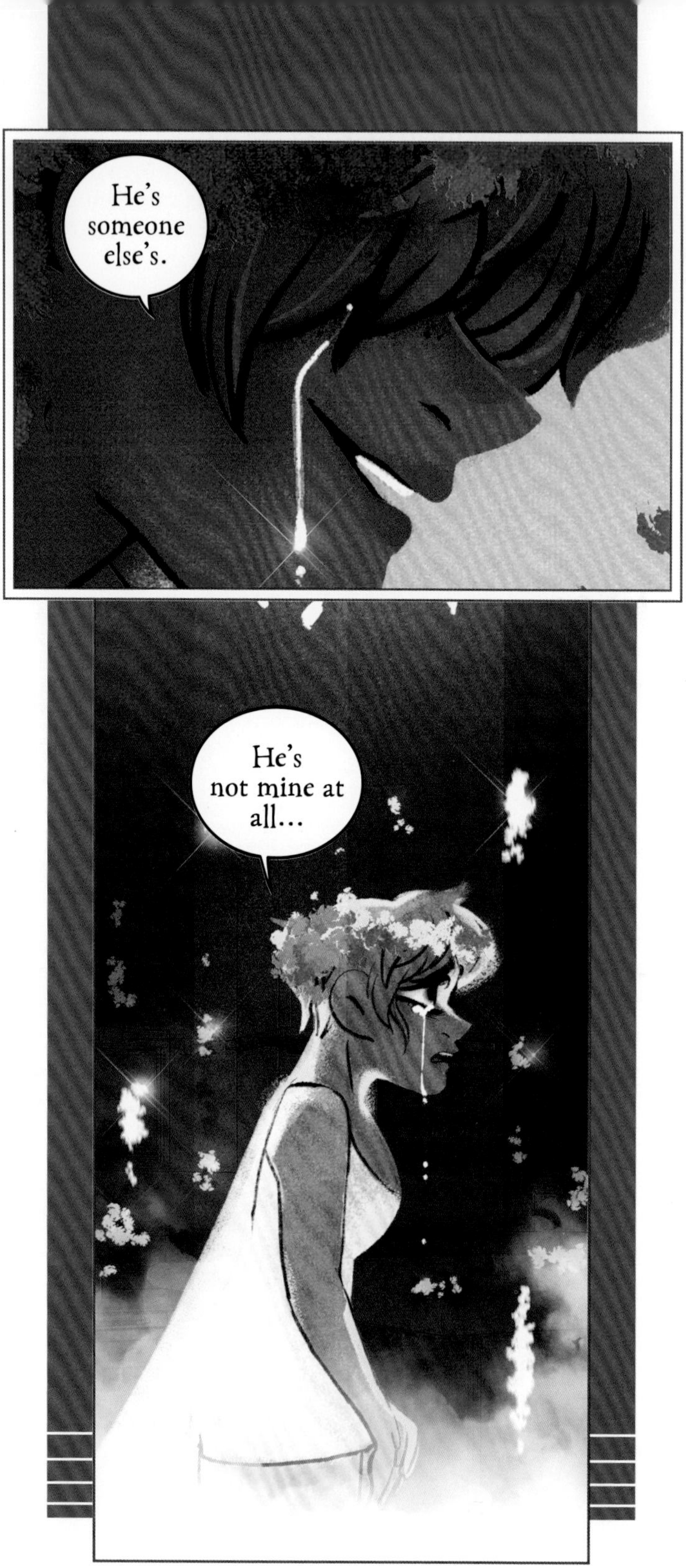
He's someone else's.
He's not mine at all...

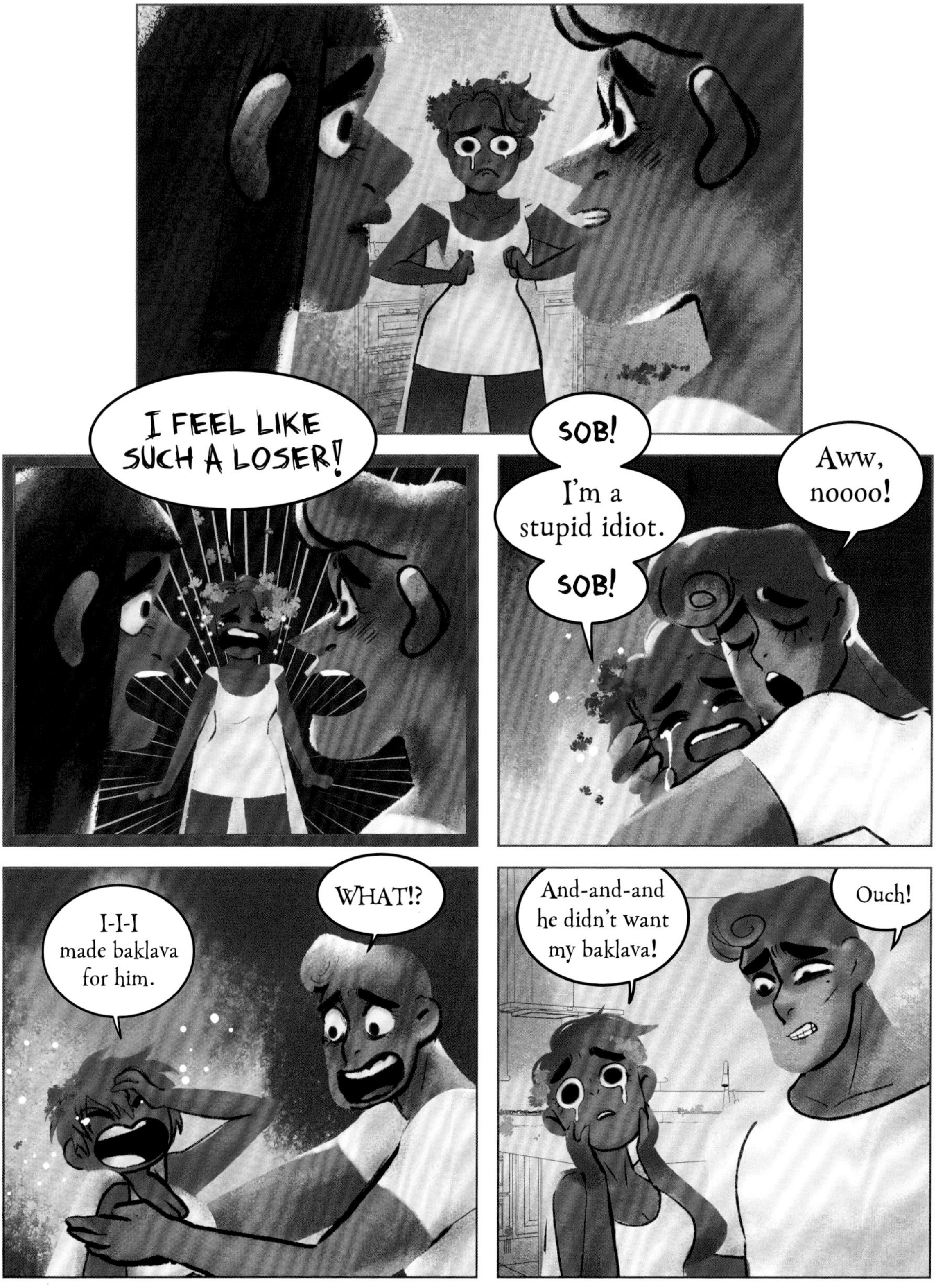
I FEEL LIKE SUCH A LOSER!
SOB!
I'm a stupid idiot.
SOB!
Aww, noooo!
I-I-I made baklava for him.
WHAT!?
And-and-and he didn't want my baklava!
Ouch!

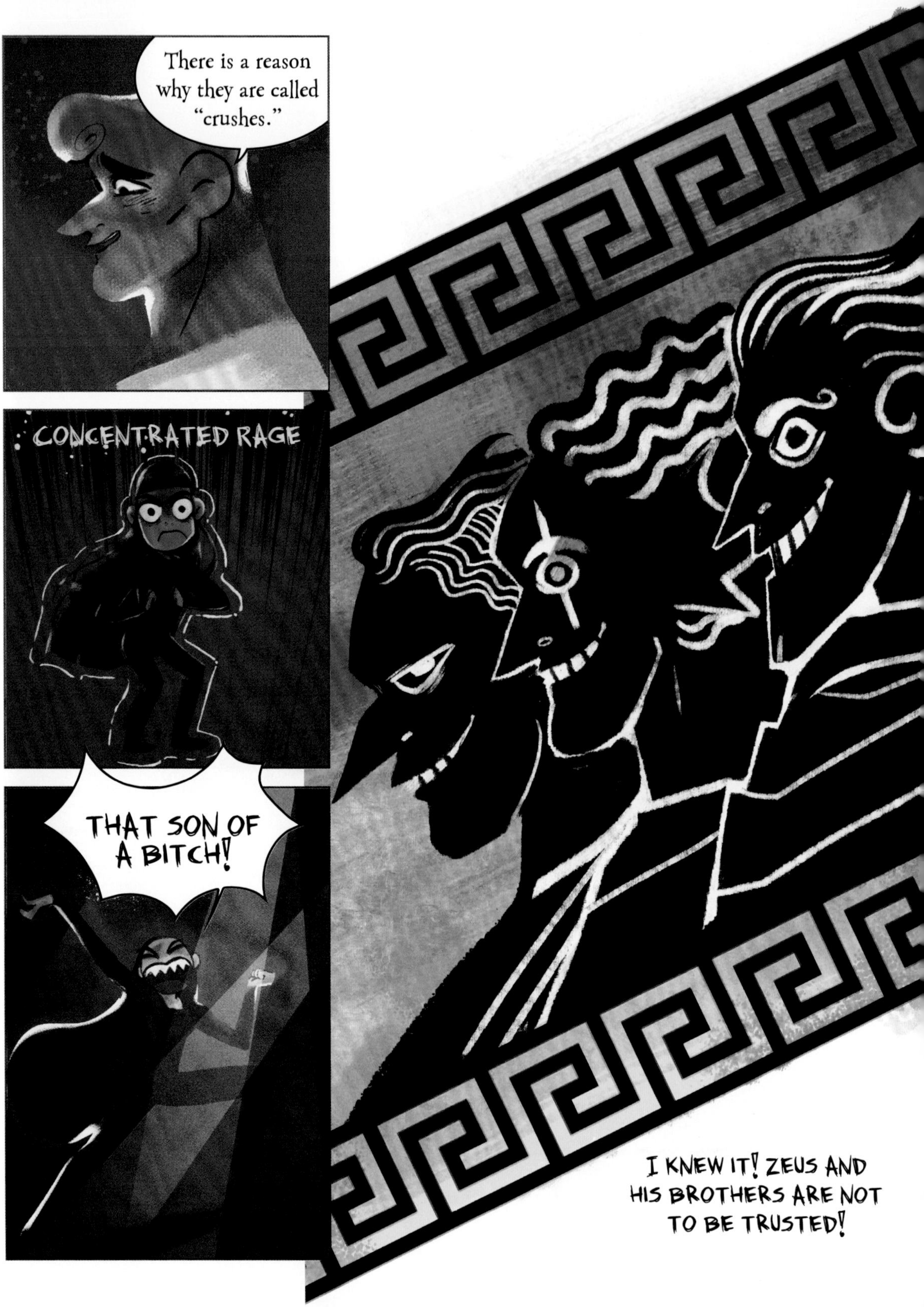
There is a reason why they are called "crushes."
CONCENTRATED RAGE
THAT SON OF A BITCH!
I KNEW IT! ZEUS AND HIS BROTHERS ARE NOT TO BE TRUSTED!

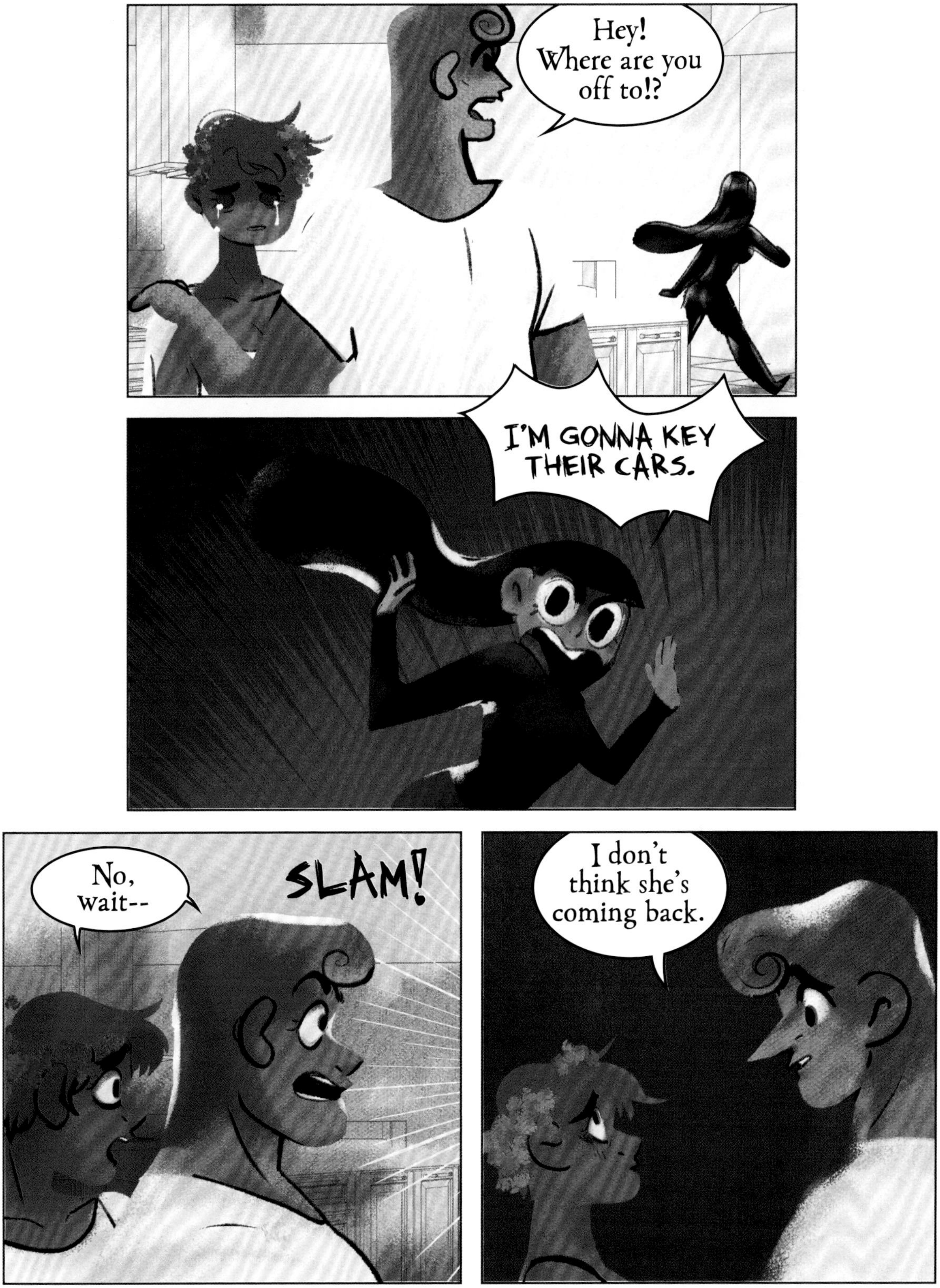
Hey! Where are you off to!?
I'M GONNA KEY THEIR CARS.
No, wait--
SLAM!
I don't think she's coming back.

EPISODE 65: TEA

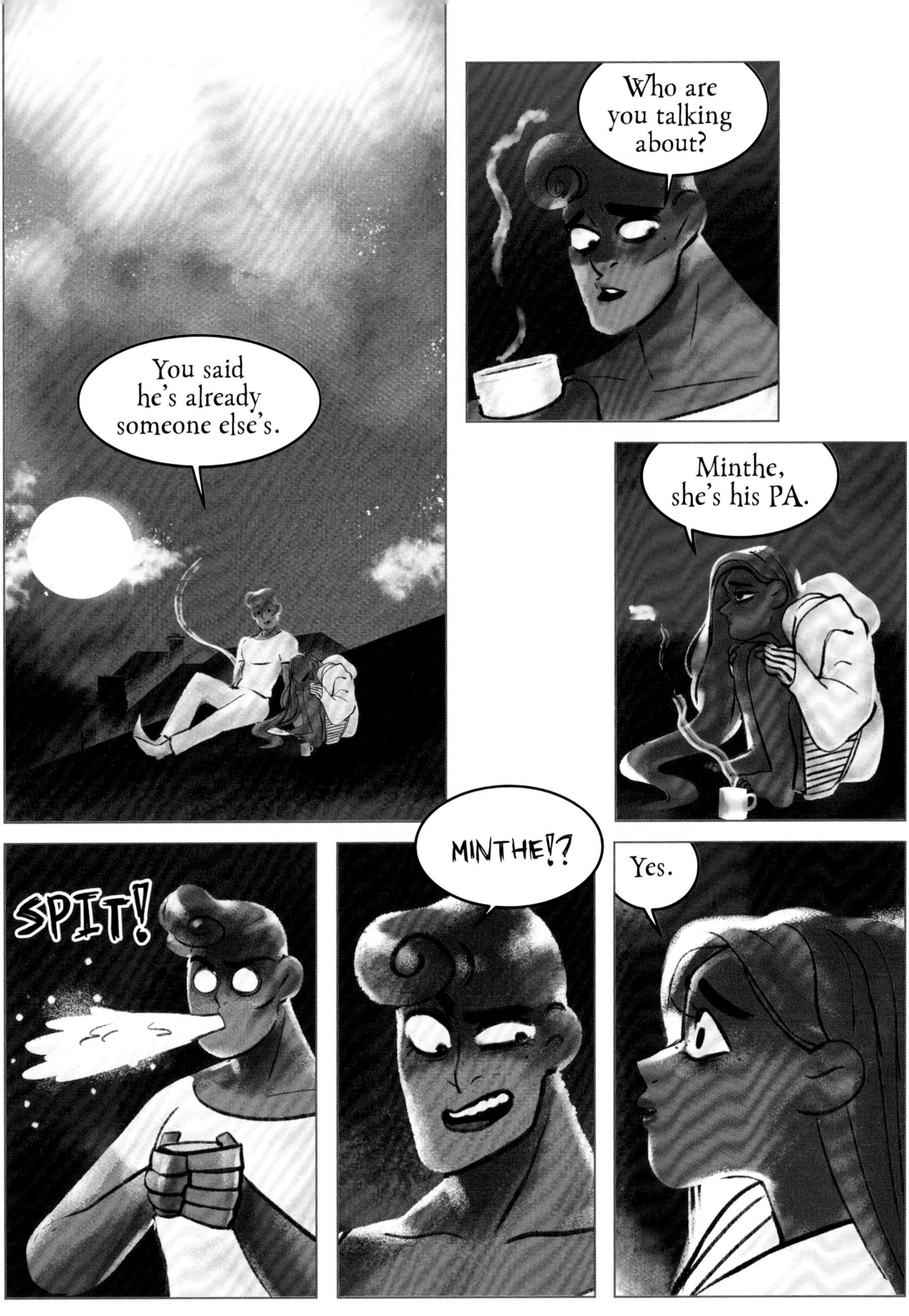
You said he's already someone else's.
Who are you talking about?
Minthe, she's his PA.
SPIT!
MINTHE!?
Yes.

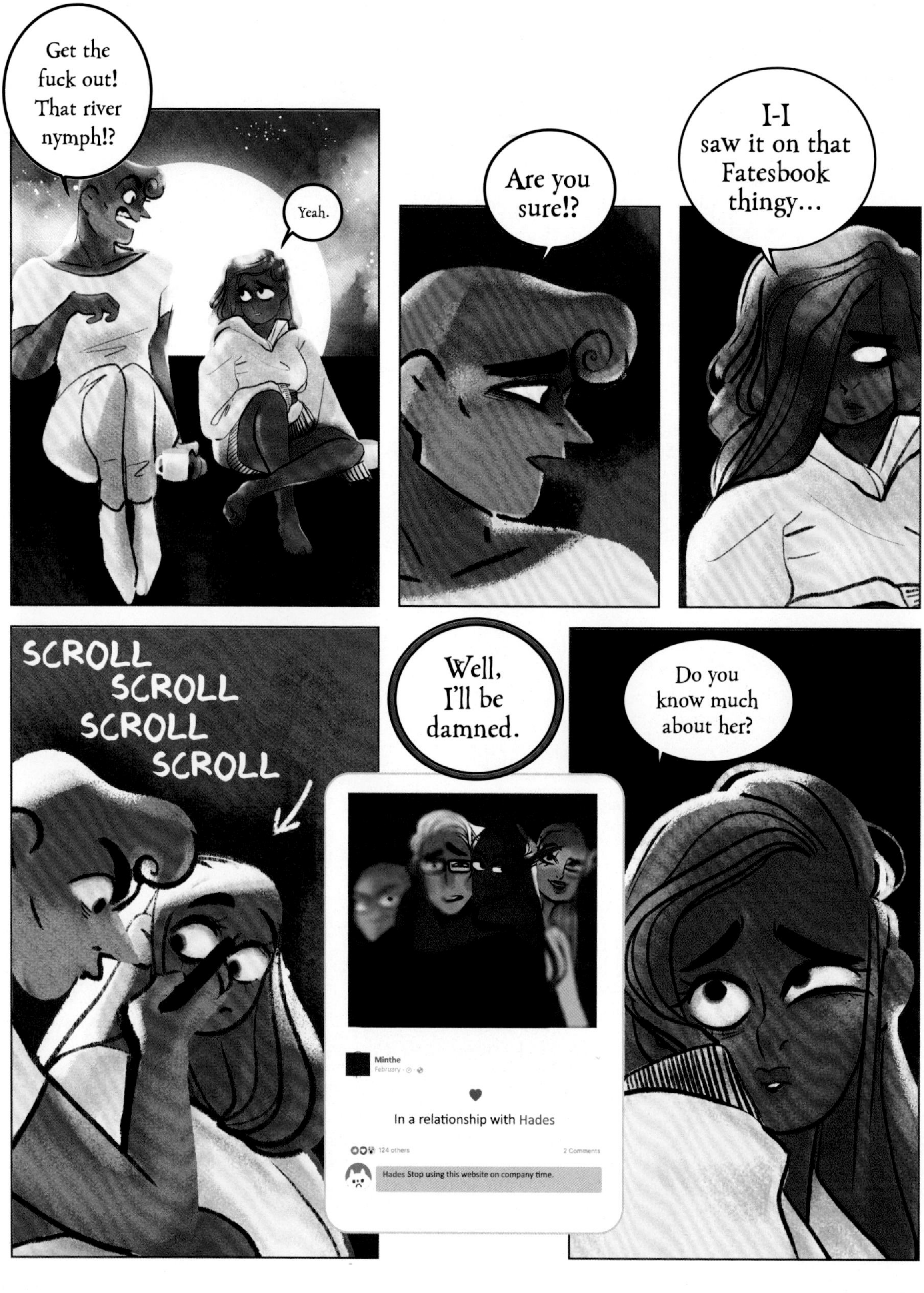
Get the fuck out! That river nymph!?
Yeah.
Are you sure!?
I-I saw it on that Fatesbook thingy...
SCROLL SCROLL SCROLL SCROLL
Well, I'll be damned.
Minthe
February
In a relationship with Hades
124 others
2 Comments
Hades Stop using this website on company time.
Do you know much about her?

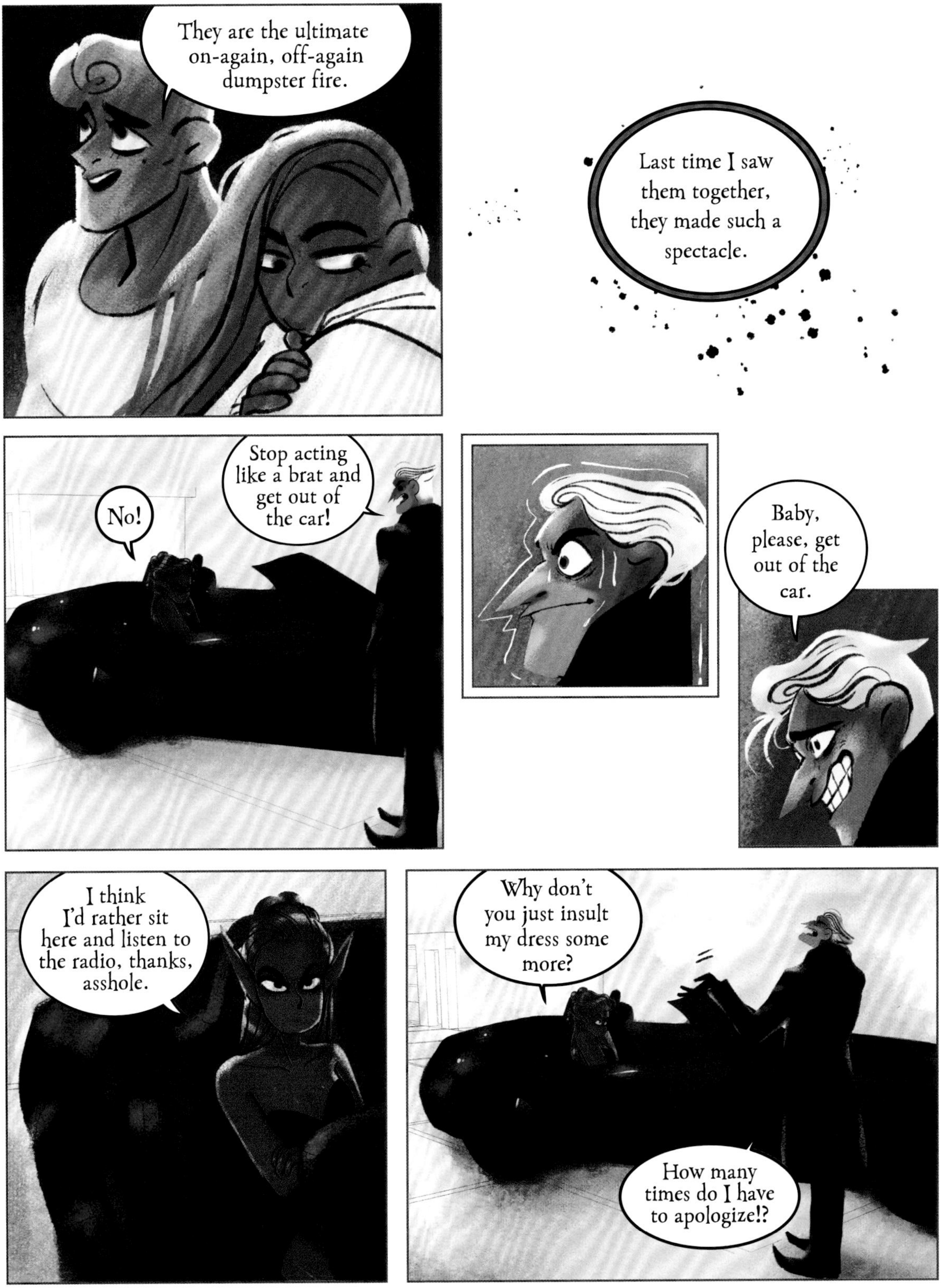
They are the ultimate on-again, off-again dumpster fire.
Last time I saw them together, they made such a spectacle.
Stop acting like a brat and get out of the car!
No!
Baby, please, get out of the car.
I think I'd rather sit here and listen to the radio, thanks, asshole.
Why don't you just insult my dress some more?
How many times do I have to apologize!?

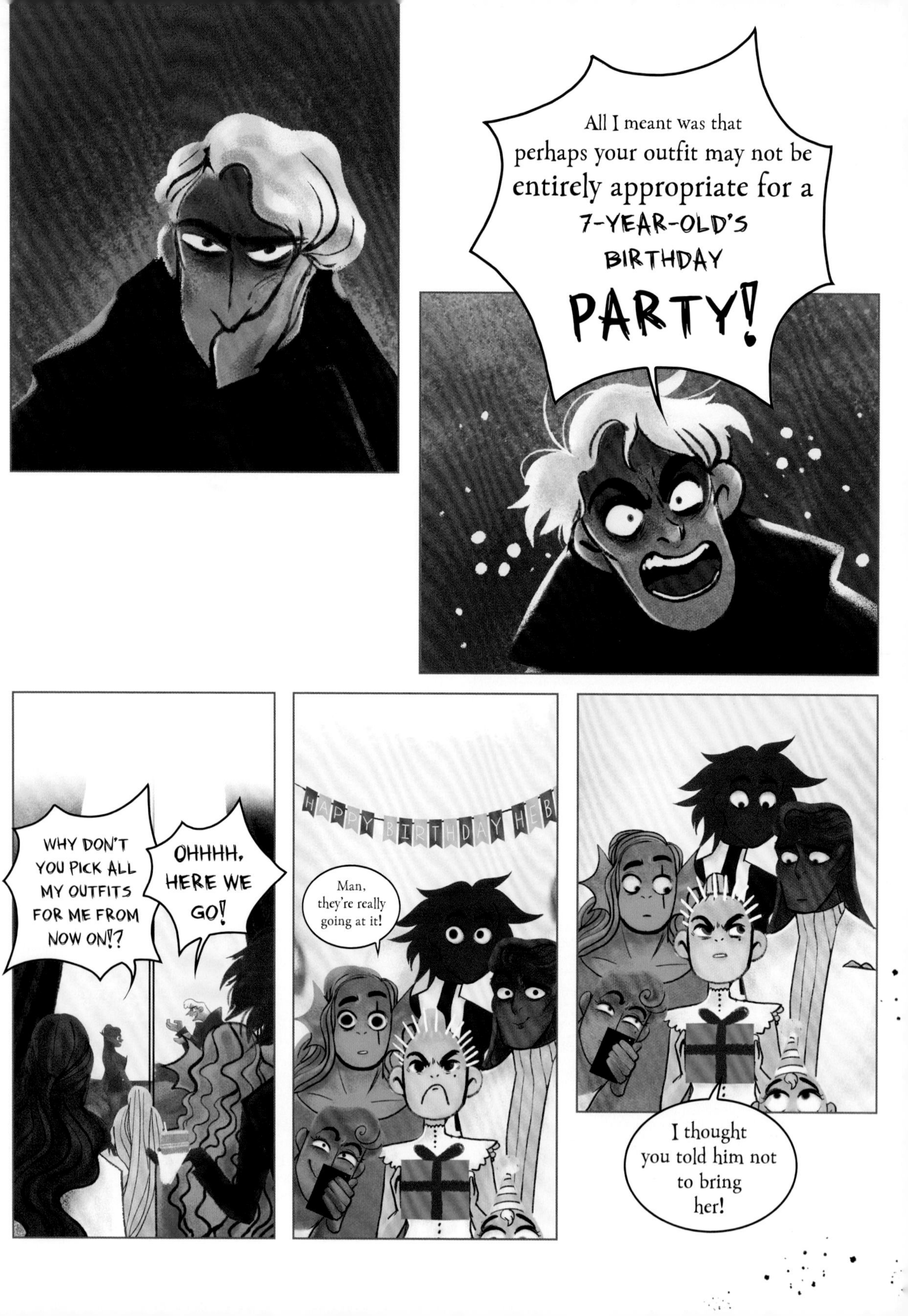
All I meant was that perhaps your outfit may not be entirely appropriate for a 7-YEAR-OLD'S BIRTHDAY PARTY!
WHY DON'T YOU PICK ALL MY OUTFITS FOR ME FROM NOW ON!?
OHHHH, HERE WE GO!
HAPPY BIRTHDAY HEB
Man, they're really going at it!
I thought you told him not to bring her!

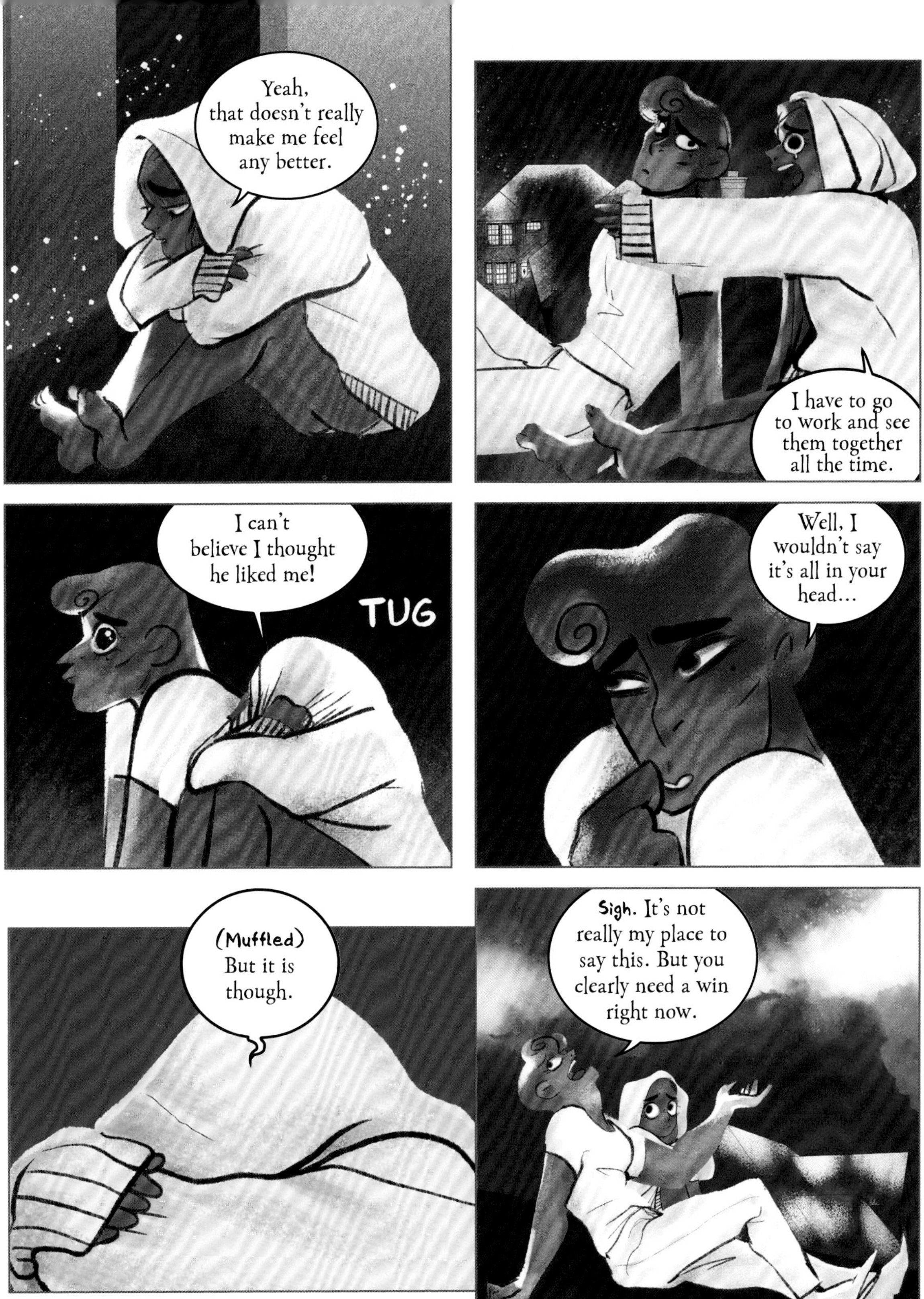
Yeah, that doesn't really make me feel any better.
I have to go to work and see them together all the time.
I can't believe I thought he liked me!
TUG
Well, I wouldn't say it's all in your head...
(Muffled) But it is though.
Sigh. It's not really my place to say this. But you clearly need a win right now.

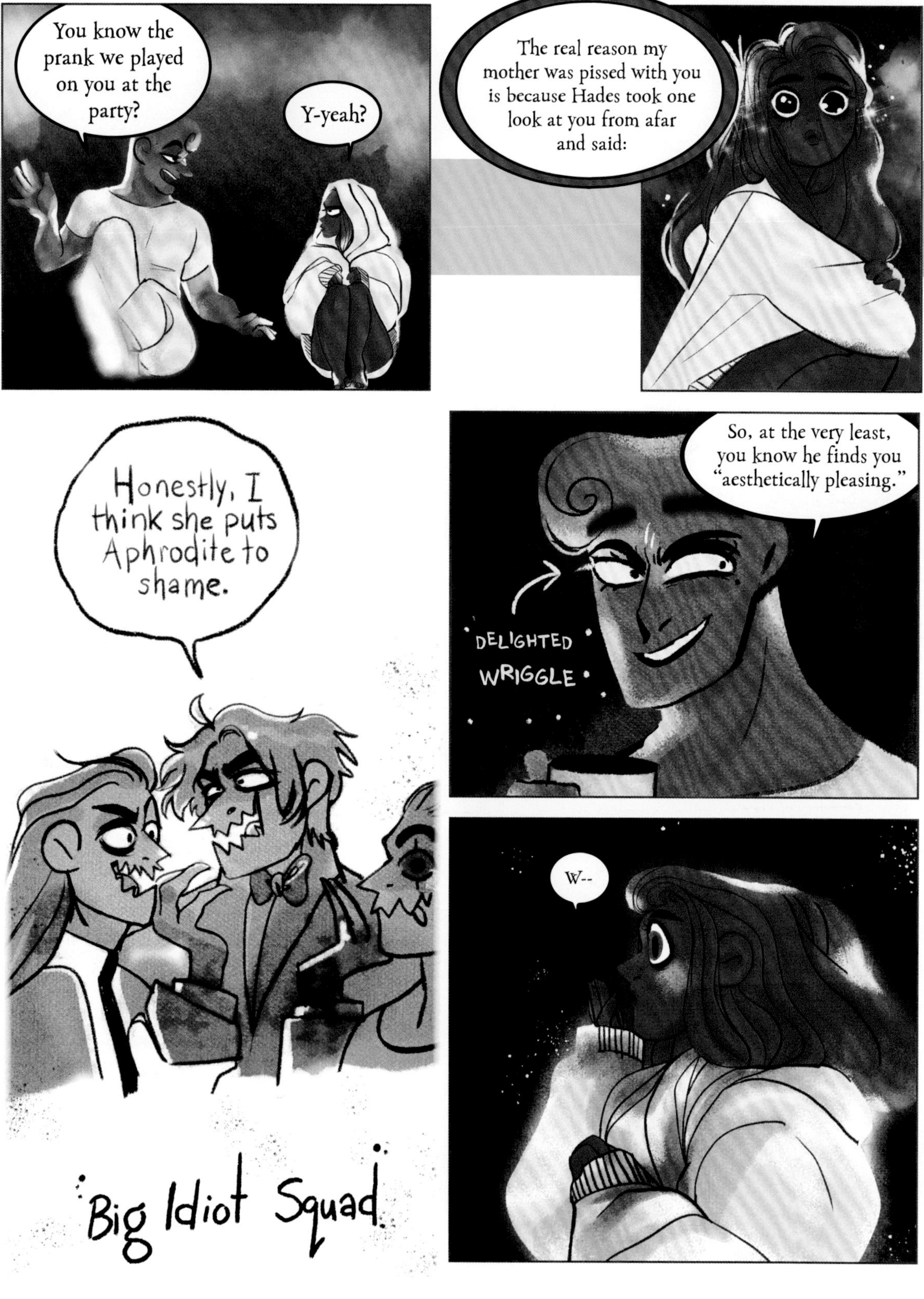
You know the prank we played on you at the party?
Y-yeah?
The real reason my mother was pissed with you is because Hades took one look at you from afar and said:
Honestly, I think she puts Aphrodite to shame.
Big Idiot Squad
So, at the very least, you know he finds you "aesthetically pleasing."
DELIGHTED WRIGGLE
W--

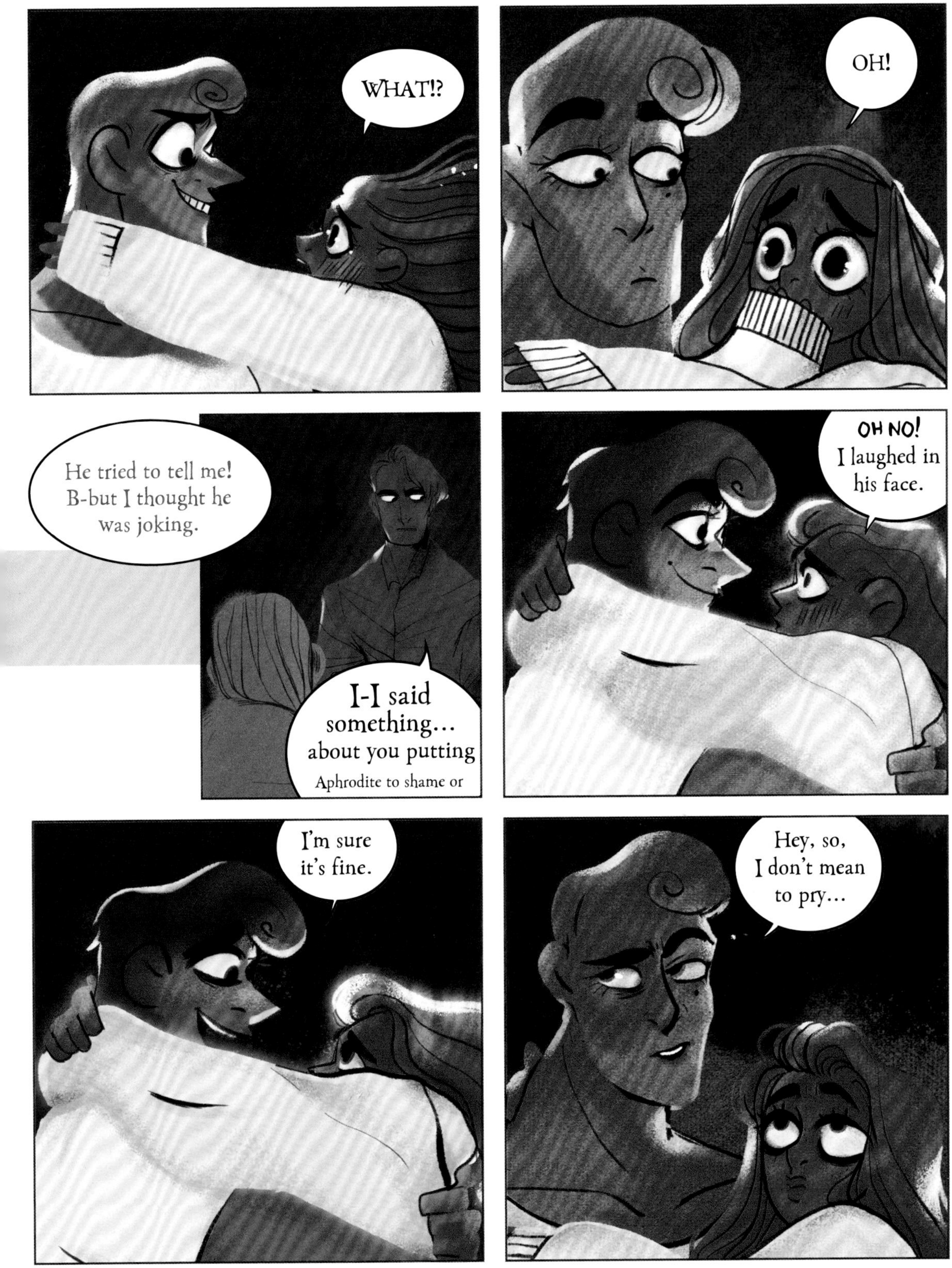
WHAT!?
OH!
He tried to tell me! B-but I thought he was joking.
I-I said something... about you putting Aphrodite to shame or
OH NO! I laughed in his face.
I'm sure it's fine.
Hey, so, I don't mean to pry...

But a prerequisite of being a member of TGOEM is being a virgin.
Last time we talked, you were one.
But you're not anymore.
So what happened?

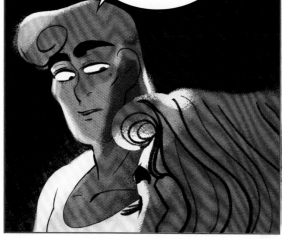

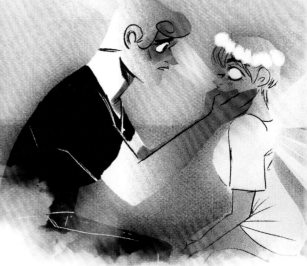

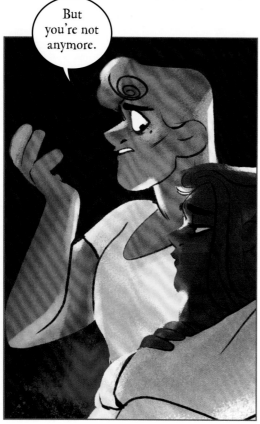

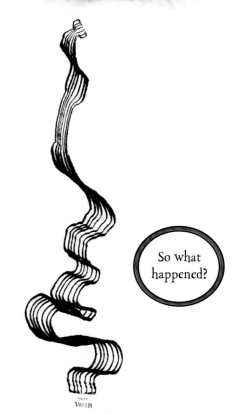

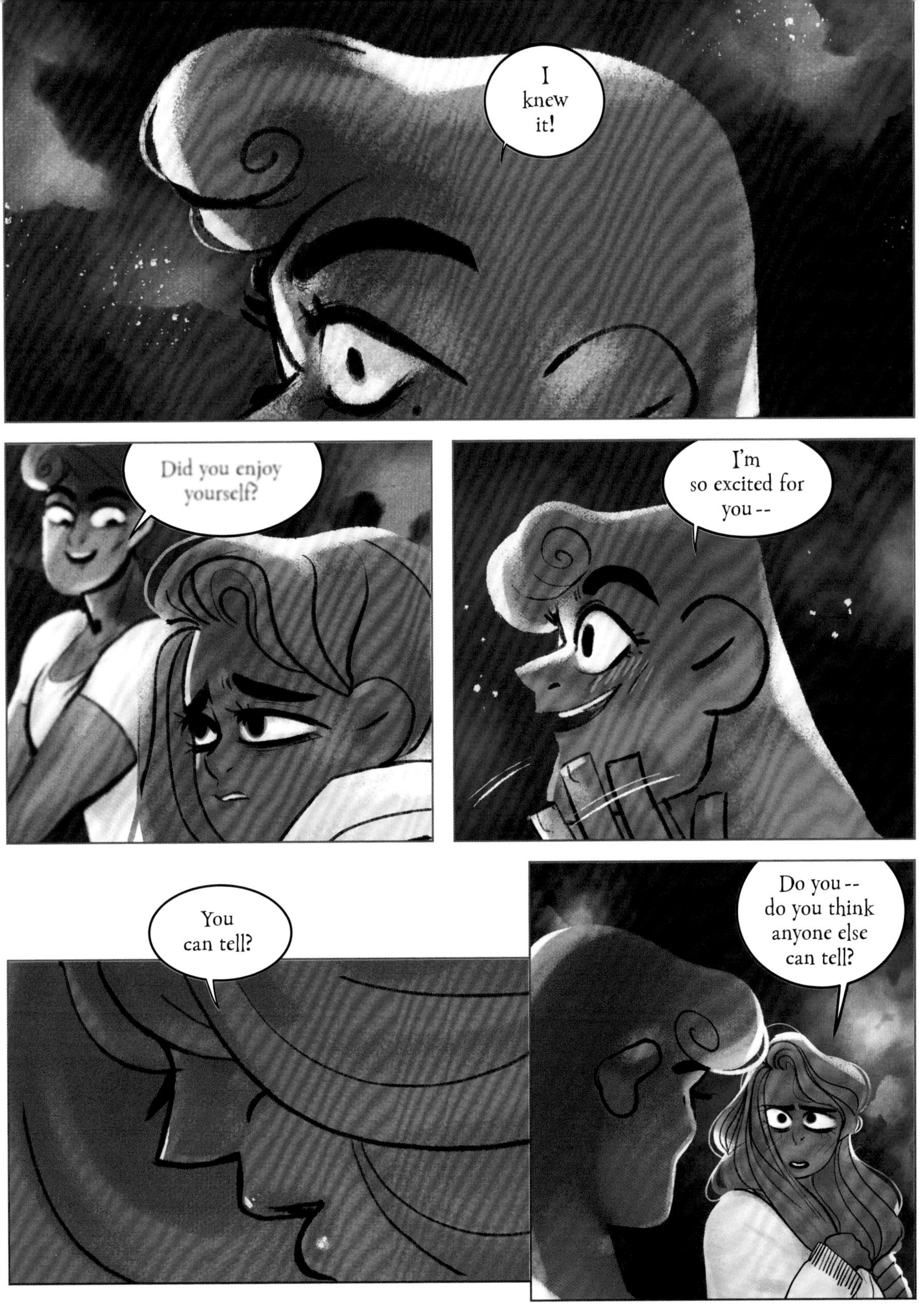
I knew it!
Did you enjoy yourself?
I'm so excited for you --
You can tell?
Do you -- do you think anyone else can tell?

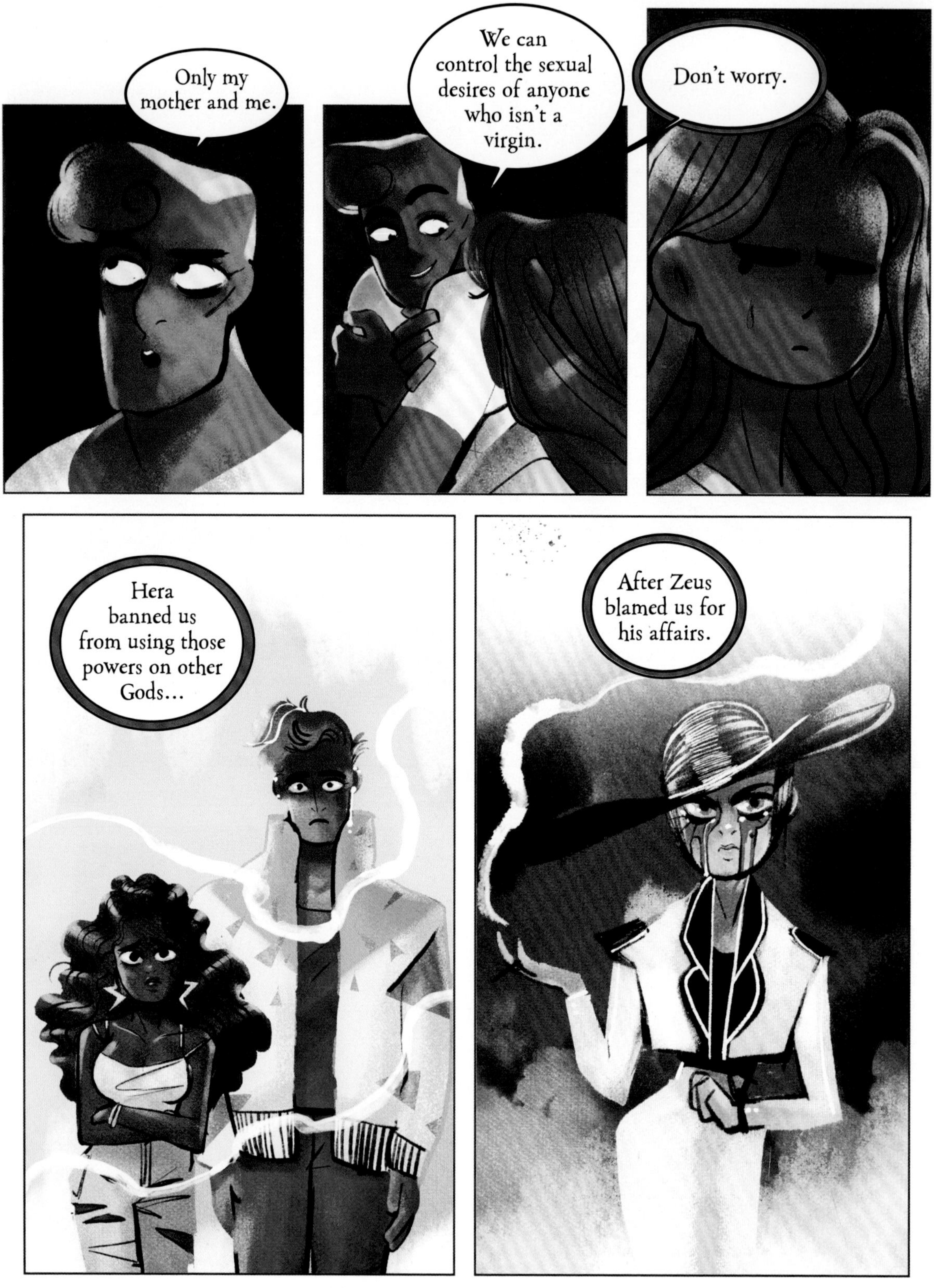
Only my mother and me.
We can control the sexual desires of anyone who isn't a virgin.
Don't worry.
Hera banned us from using those powers on other Gods...
After Zeus blamed us for his affairs.

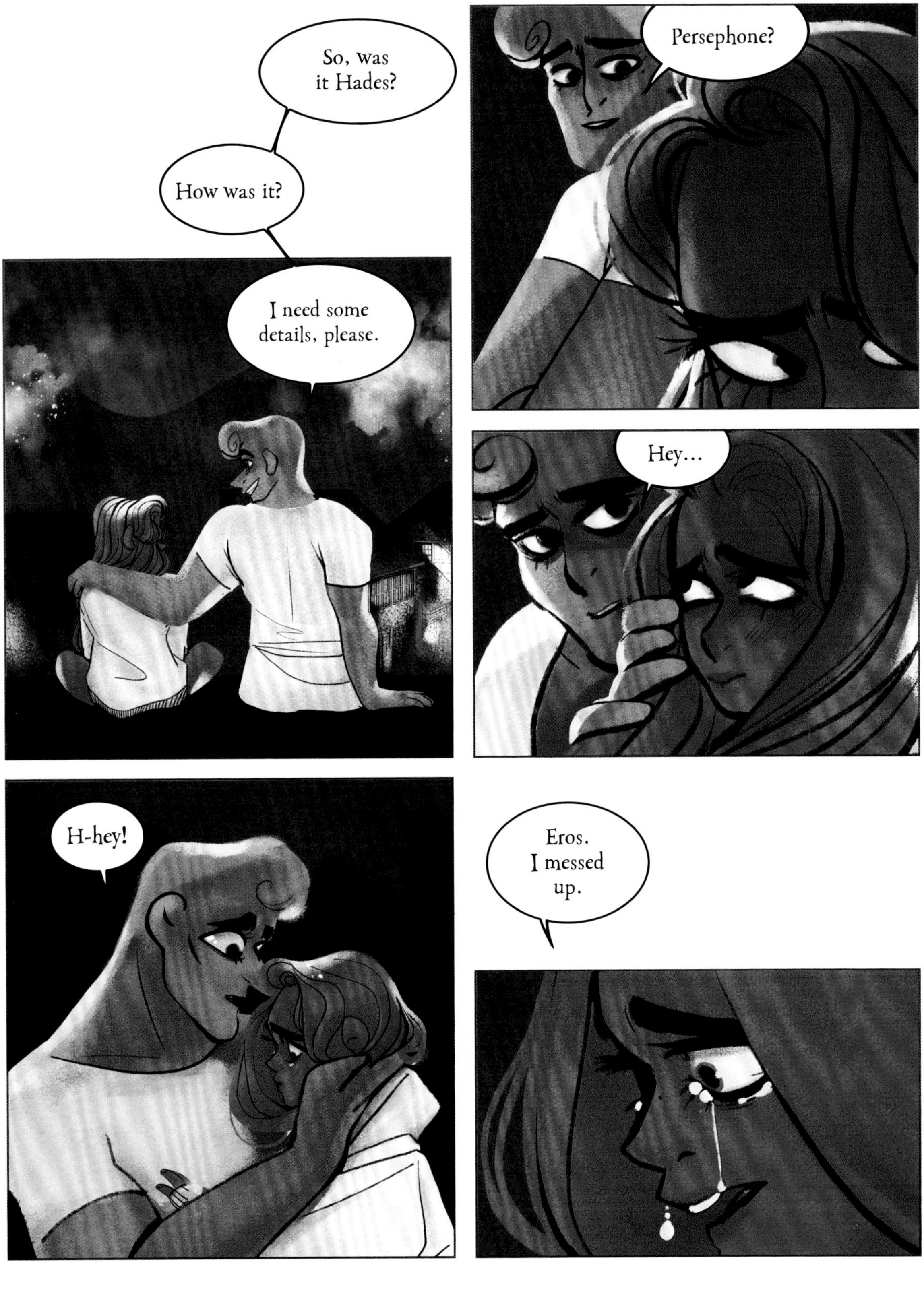
So, was it Hades?
How was it?
I need some details, please.
Persephone?
Hey...
H-hey!
Eros. I messed up.

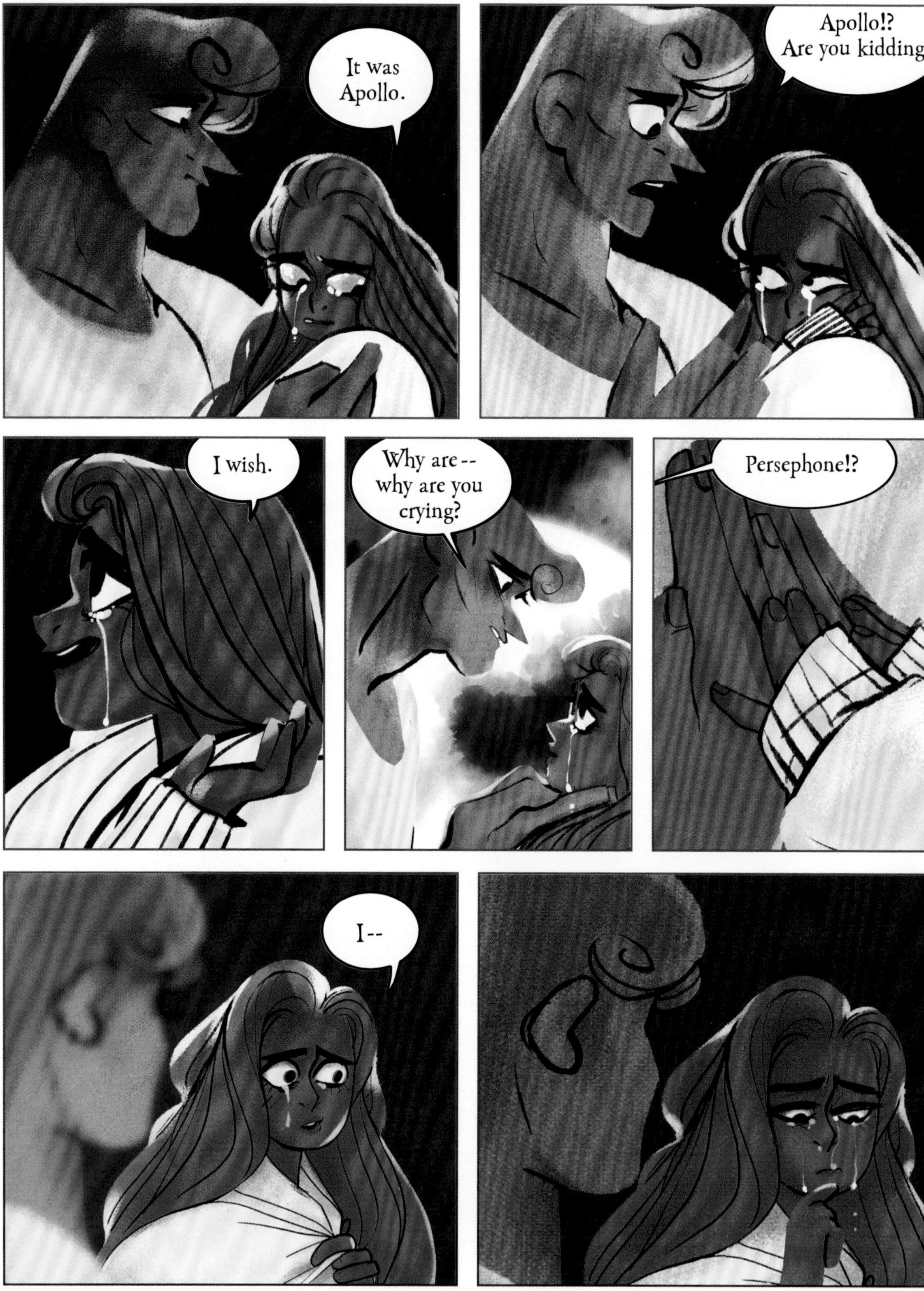

It was Apollo.
Apollo!? Are you kidding?
I wish.
Why are -- why are you crying?
Persephone!?
I--

Just show me, okay?

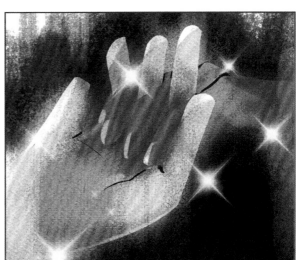

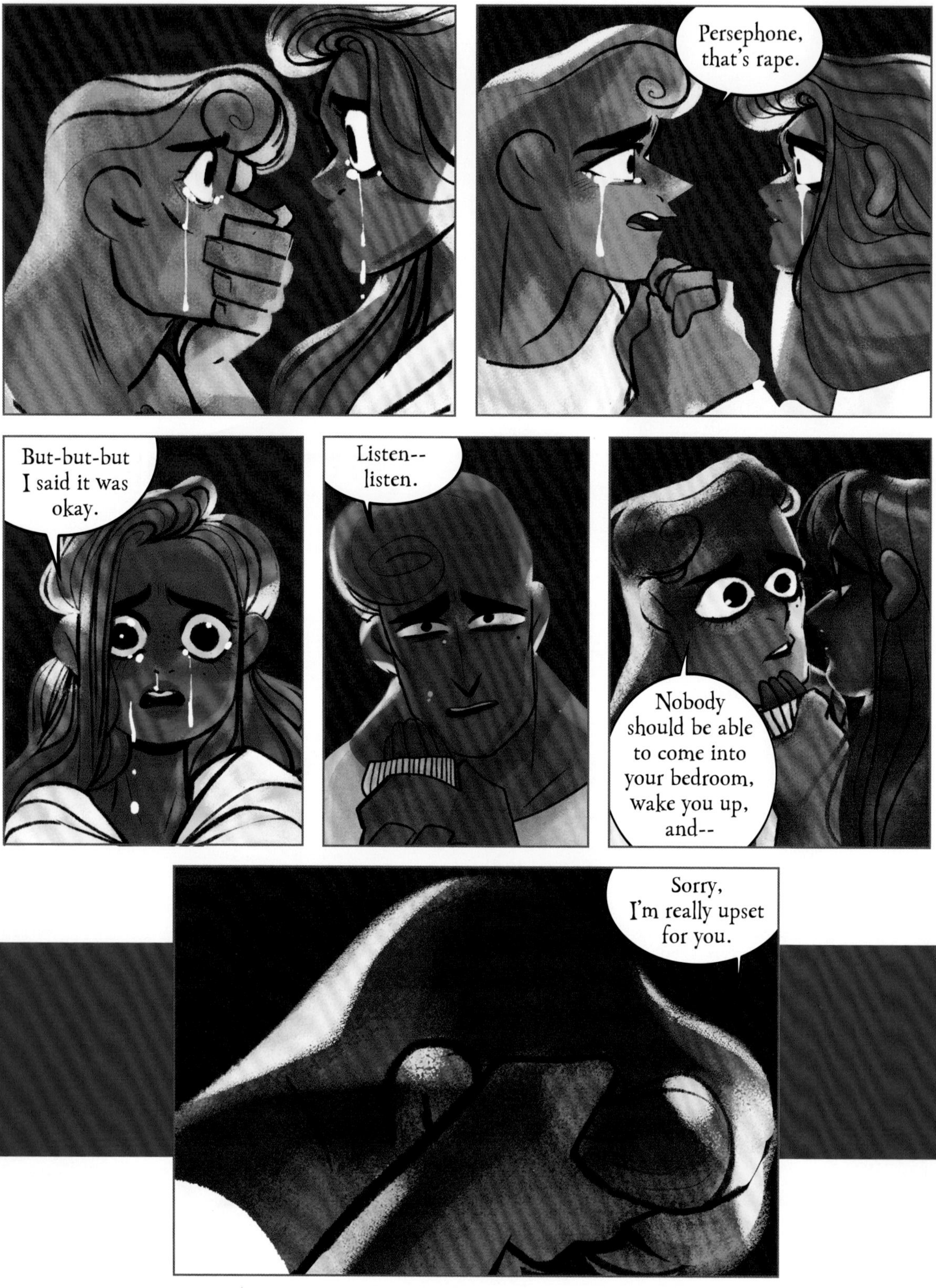
Persephone, that's rape.
But-but-but I said it was okay.
Listen-- listen.
Nobody should be able to come into your bedroom, wake you up, and--
Sorry, I'm really upset for you.

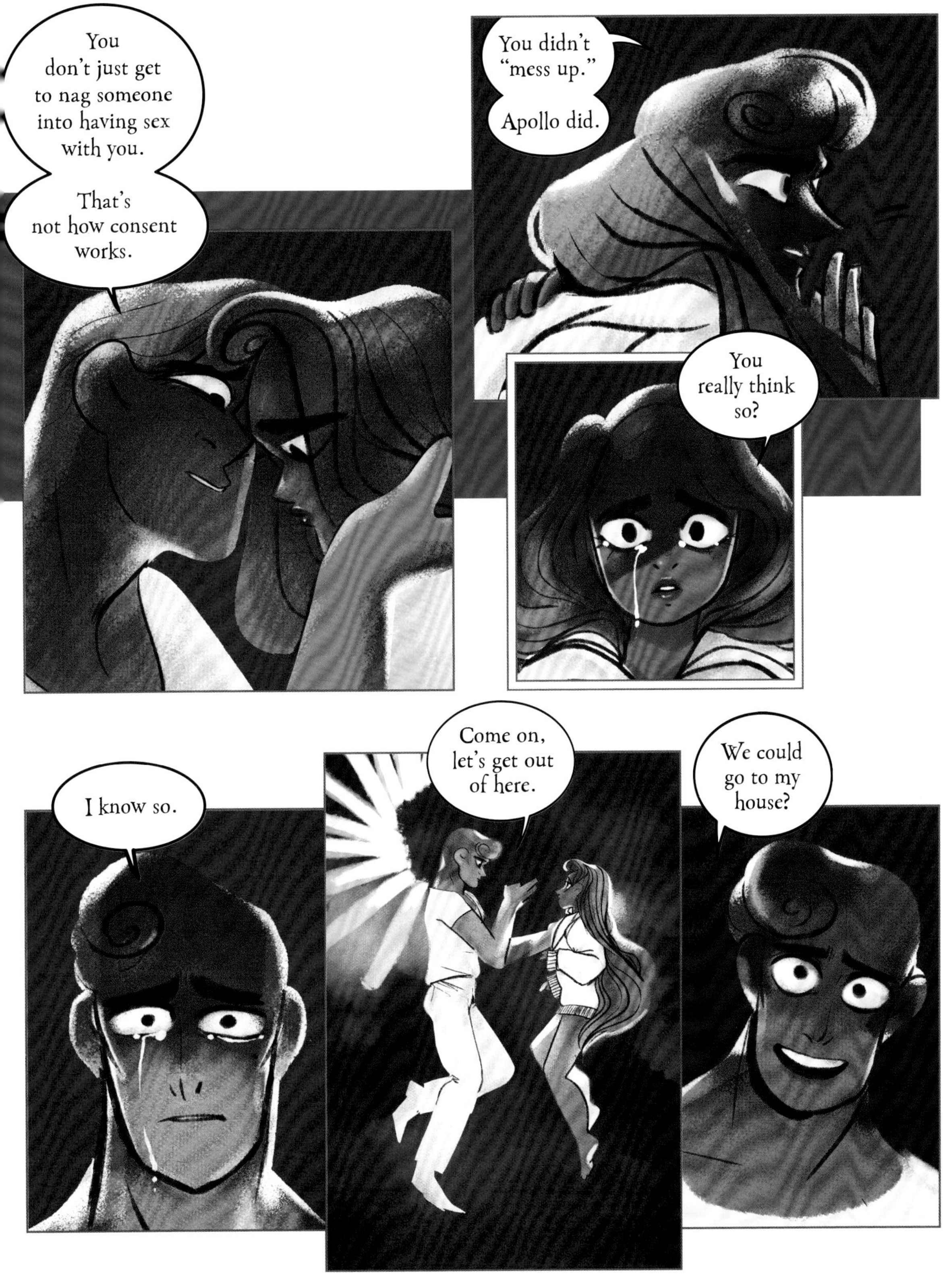
You don't just get to nag someone into having sex with you.
That's not how consent works.
You didn't "mess up."
Apollo did.
You really think so?
I know so.
Come on, let's get out of here.
We could go to my house?

EPISODE 66: HERE

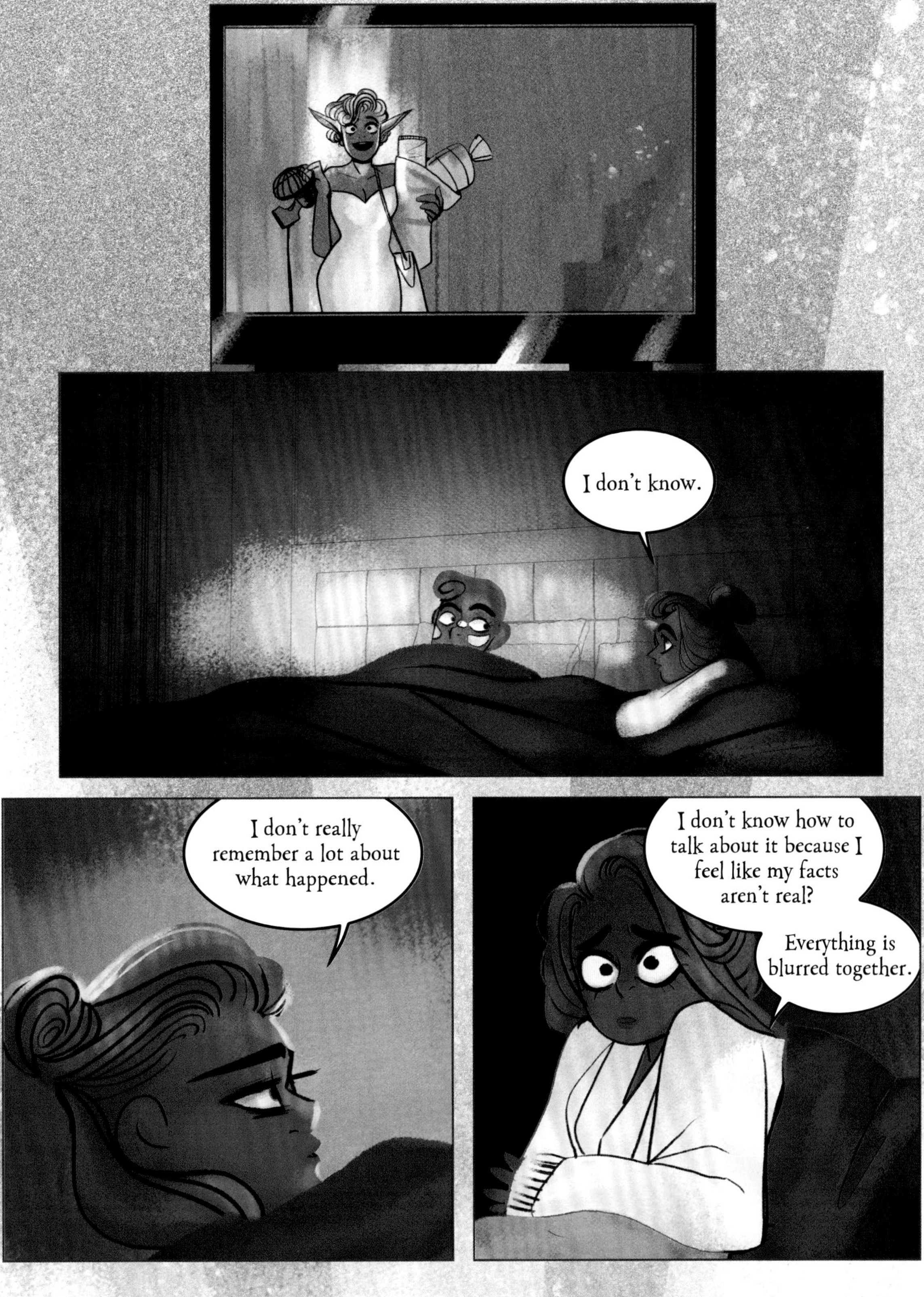
I don't know.
I don't really remember a lot about what happened.
I don't know how to talk about it because I feel like my facts aren't real?
Everything is blurred together.

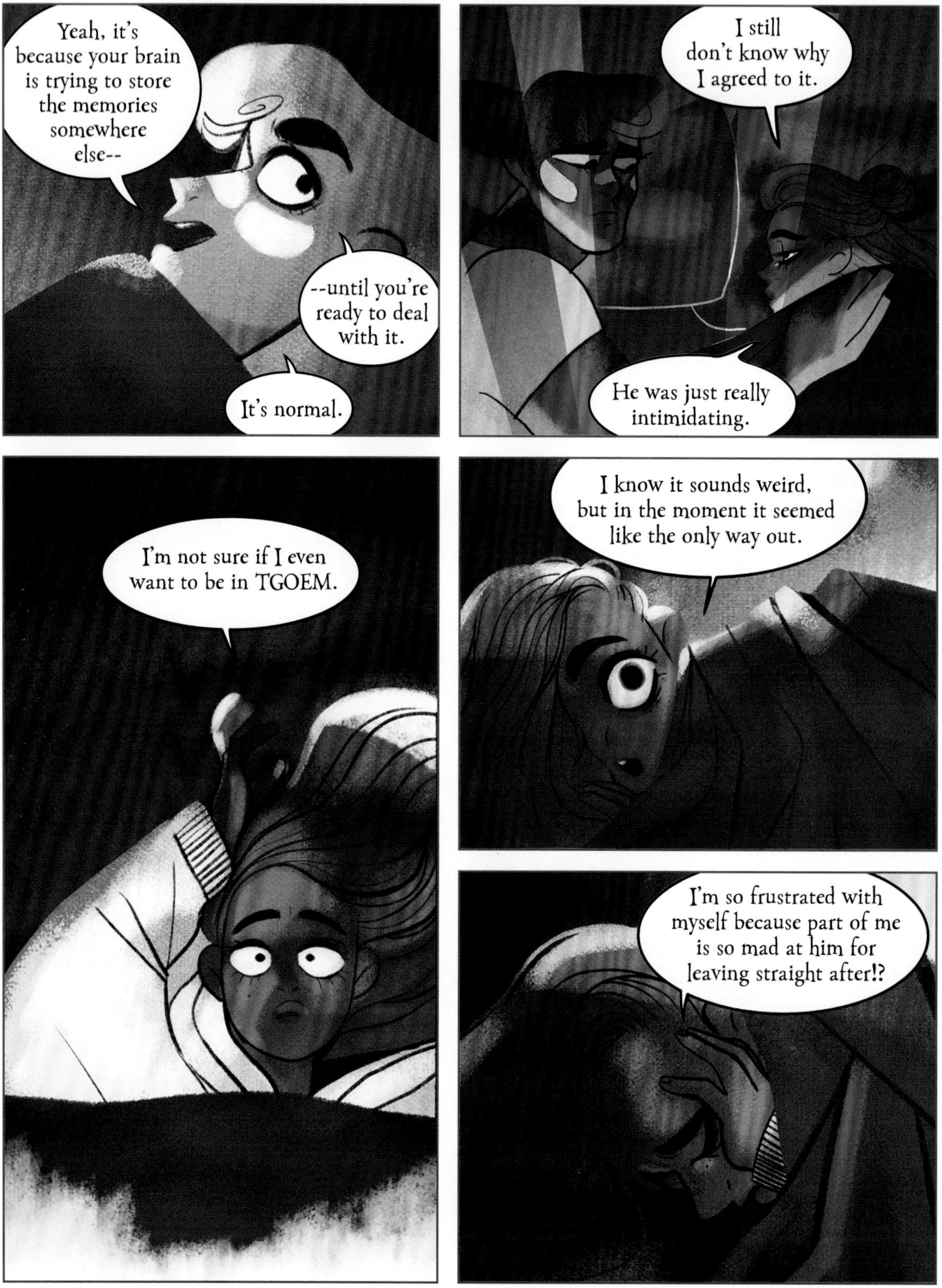

Yeah, it's because your brain is trying to store the memories somewhere else--
--until you're ready to deal with it.
It's normal.
I still don't know why I agreed to it.
He was just really intimidating.
I'm not sure if I even want to be in TGOEM.
I know it sounds weird, but in the moment it seemed like the only way out.
I'm so frustrated with myself because part of me is so mad at him for leaving straight after!?

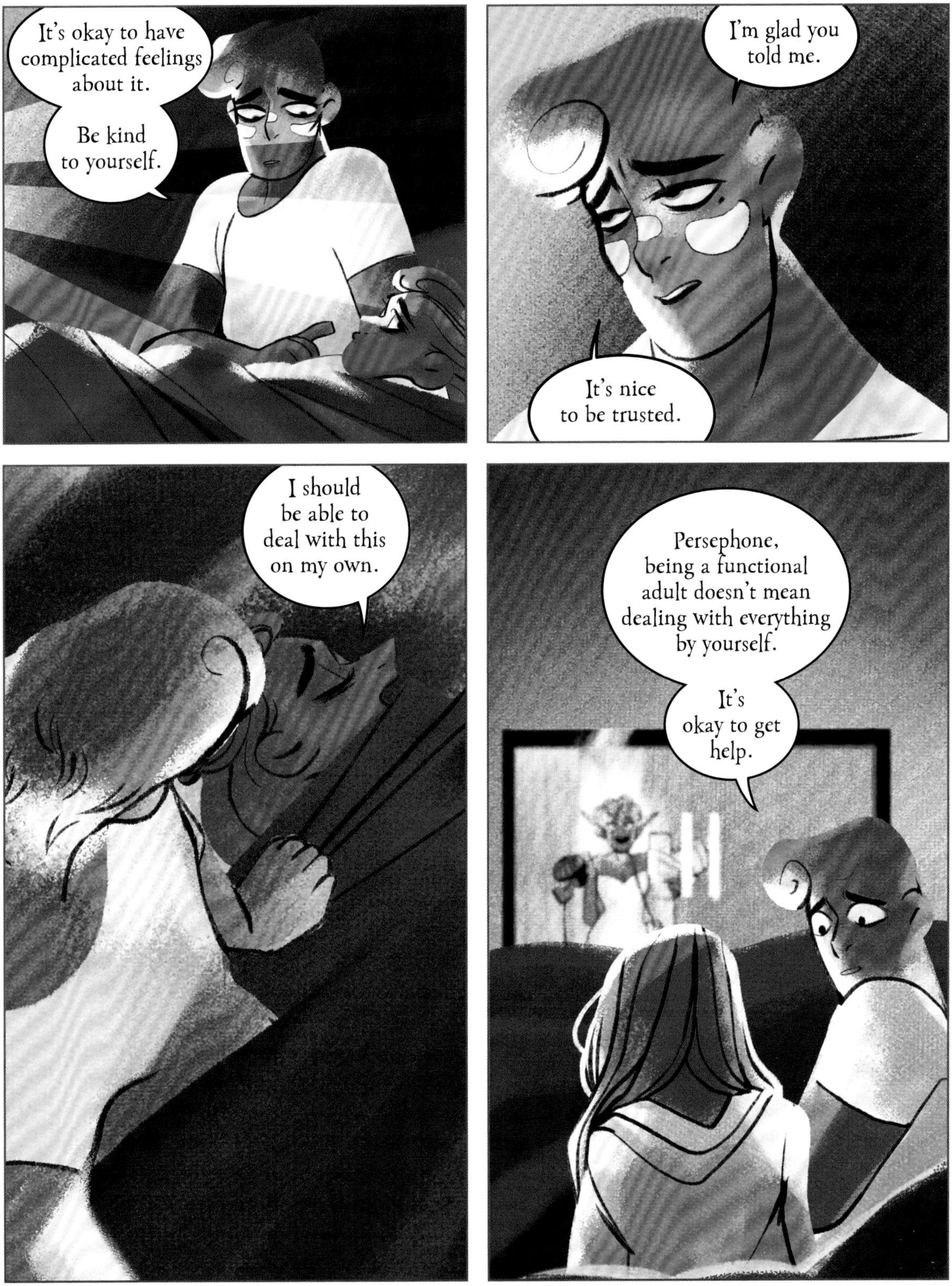
It's okay to have complicated feelings about it.
Be kind to yourself.
I'm glad you told me.
It's nice to be trusted.
I should be able to deal with this on my own.
Persephone, being a functional adult doesn't mean dealing with everything by yourself.
It's okay to get help.

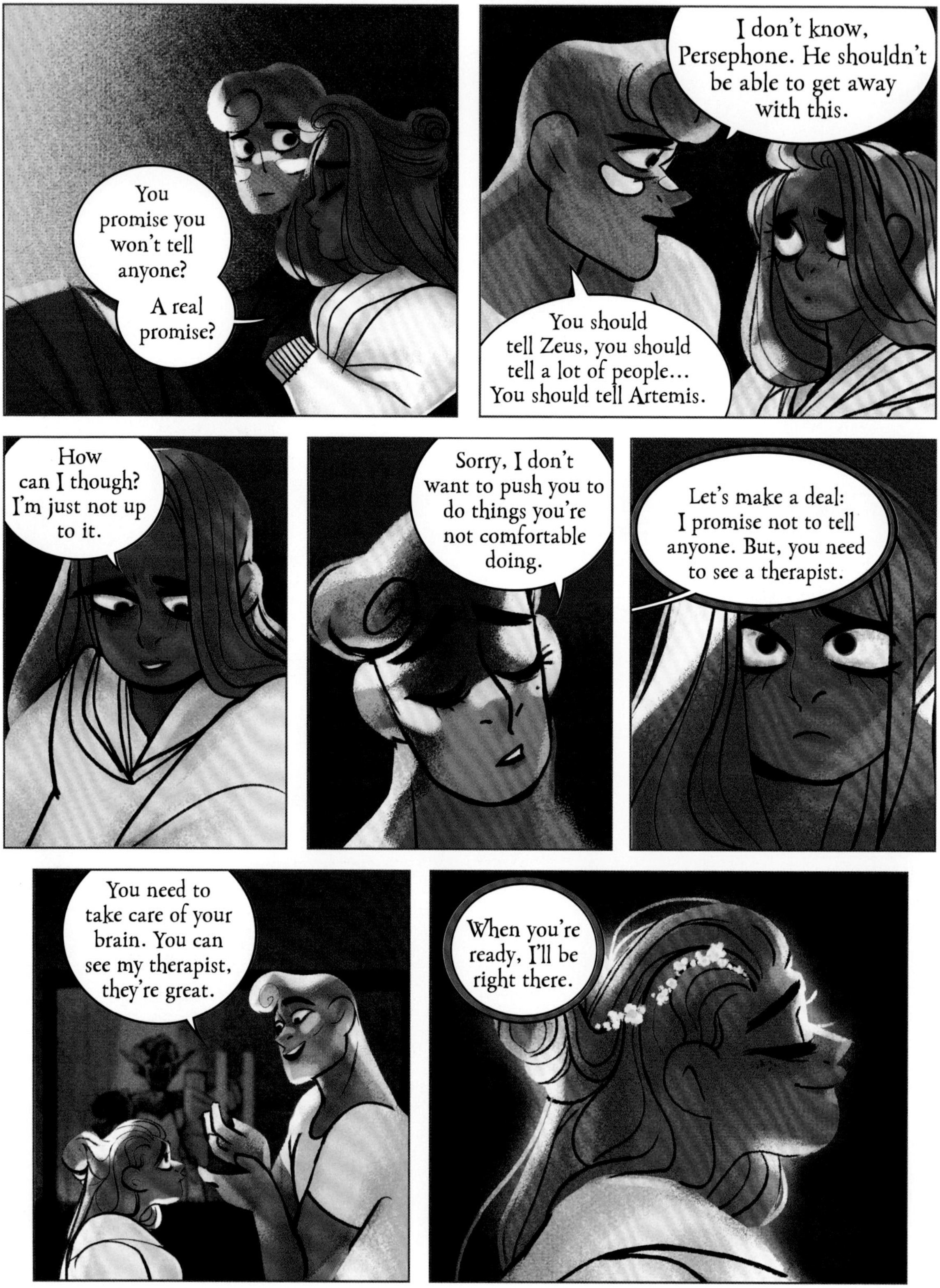
You promise you won't tell anyone?
A real promise?
I don't know, Persephone. He shouldn't be able to get away with this.
You should tell Zeus, you should tell a lot of people... You should tell Artemis.
How can I though? I'm just not up to it.
Sorry, I don't want to push you to do things you're not comfortable doing.
Let's make a deal: I promise not to tell anyone. But, you need to see a therapist.
You need to take care of your brain. You can see my therapist, they're great.
When you're ready, I'll be right there.

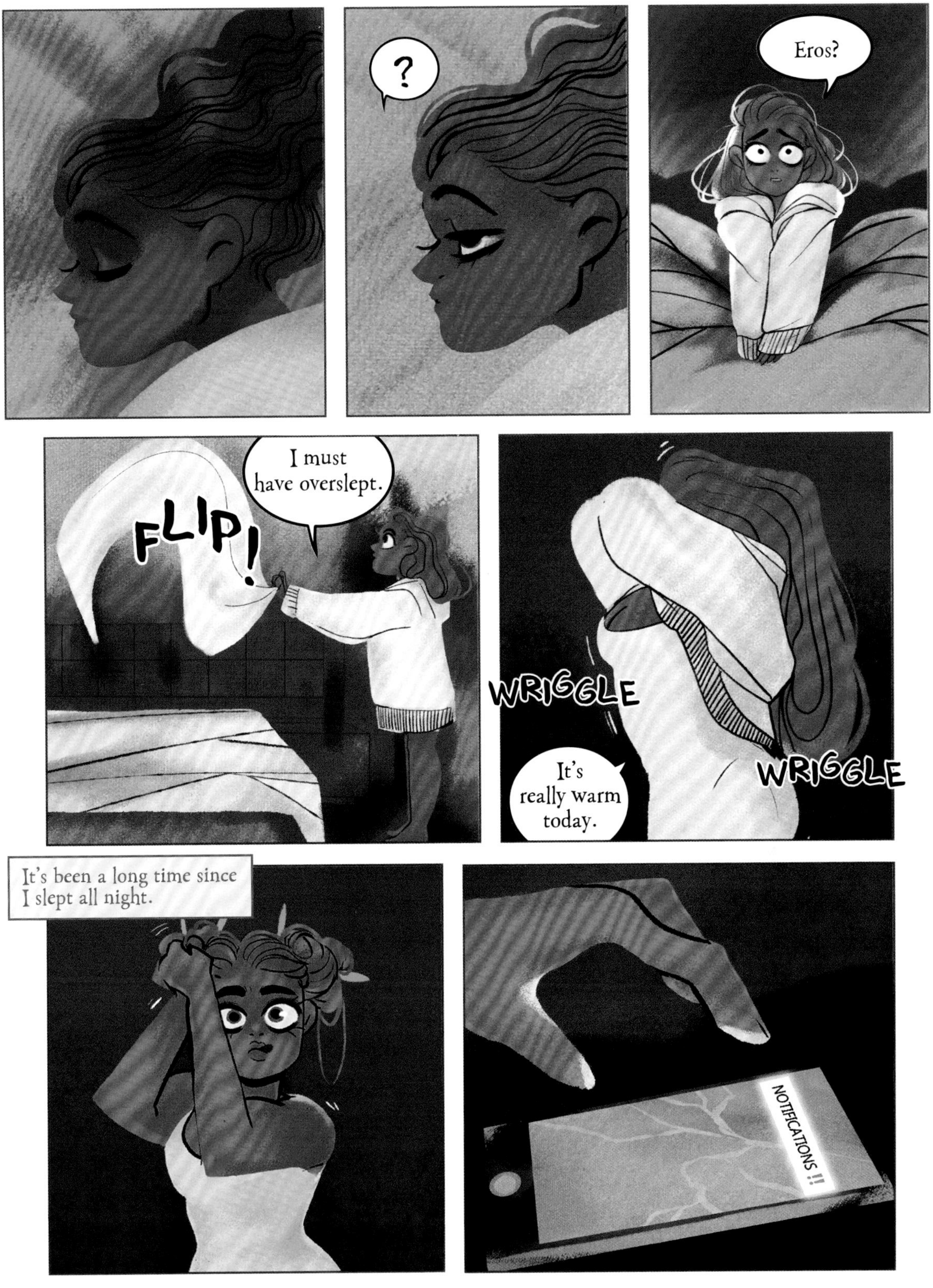
?
Eros?
I must have overslept.
FLIP!
WRIGGLE
WRIGGLE
It's really warm today.
It's been a long time since I slept all night.
NOTIFICATIONS !!

Artemis:

It turns out Poseidon doesn't have a car.
Unrelated, I adopted this wolf.

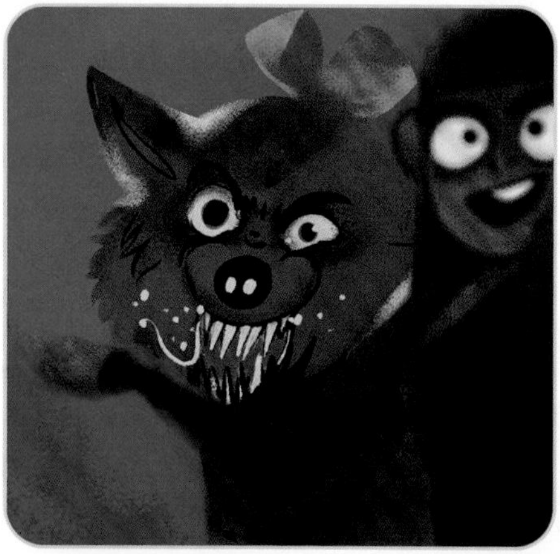

Apollo:

Hey, can we talk soon?

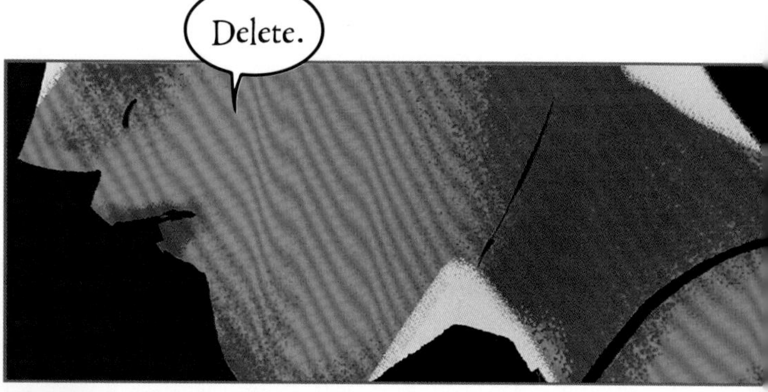
Delete.

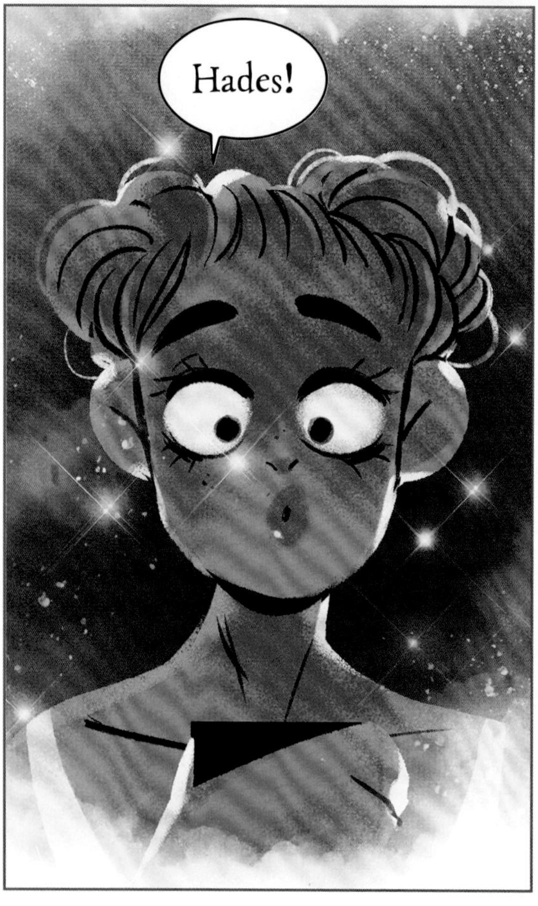
Hades!

The baklava was good. I regret sharing the majority of my portion with Hermes.

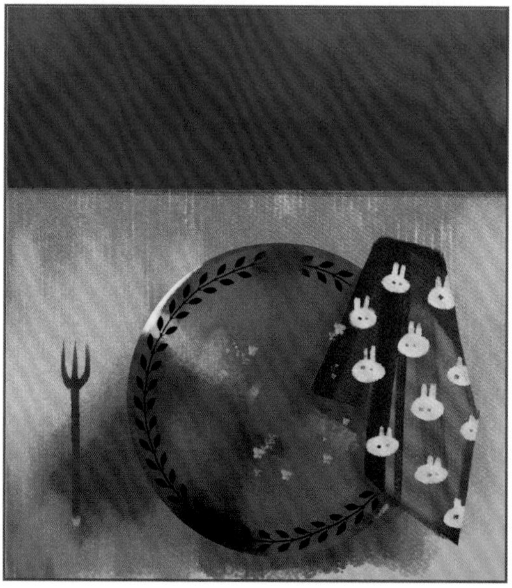

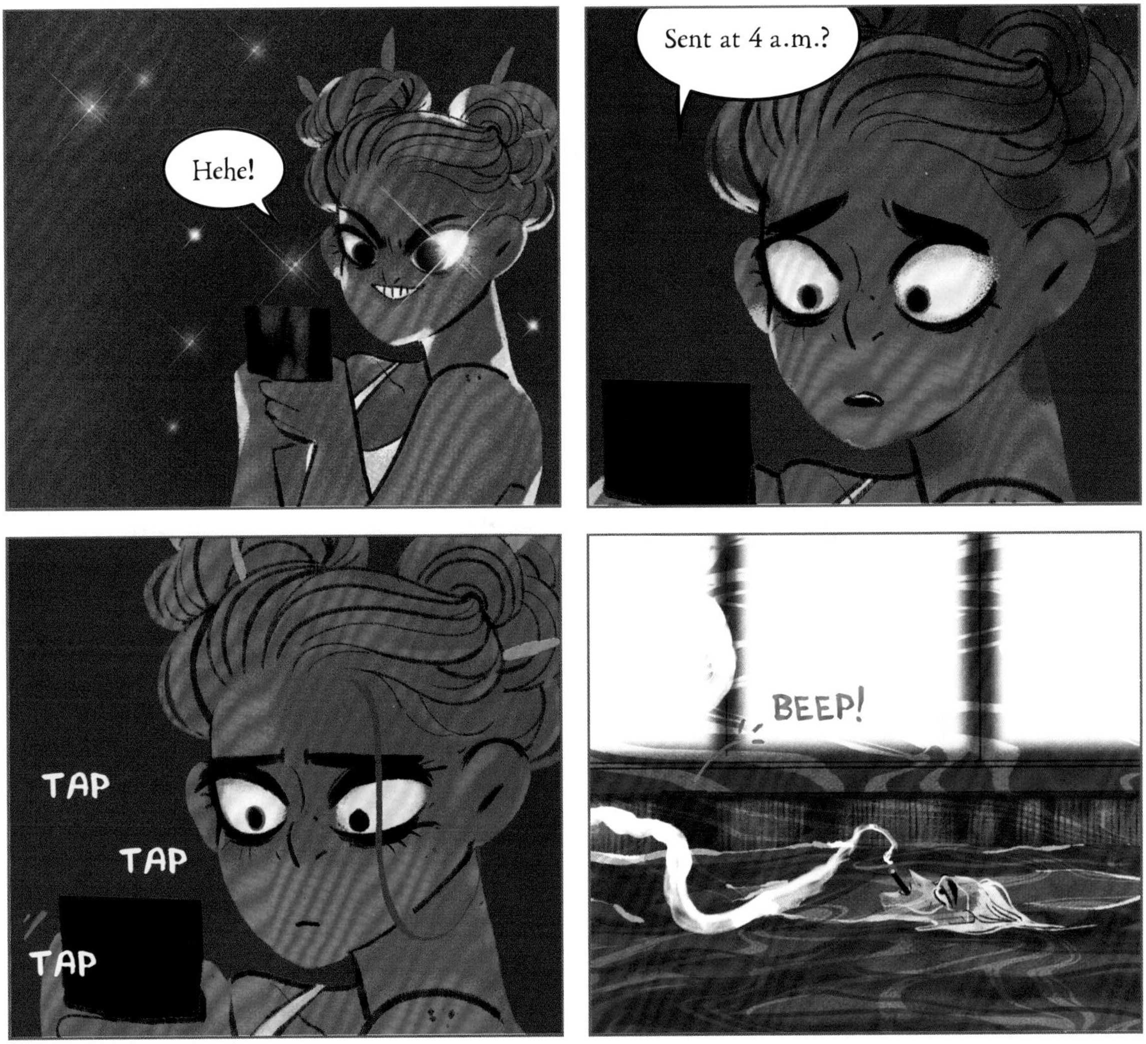
Hehe!
Sent at 4 a.m.?
TAP
TAP
TAP
BEEP!

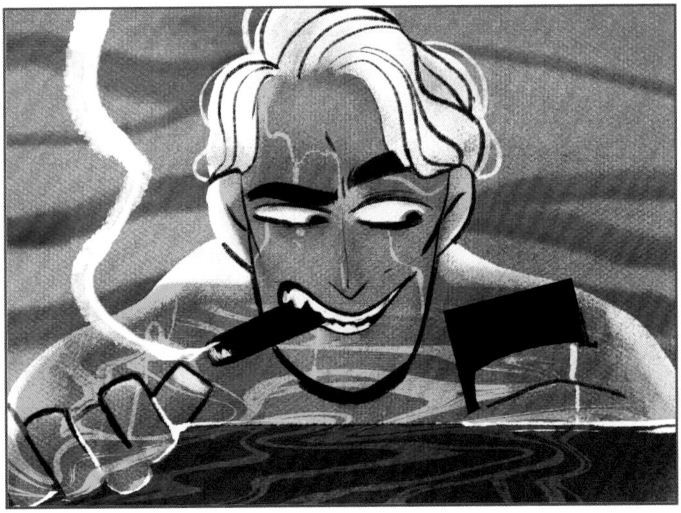

Kore:

If you play your cards right,
I'll make you some more.

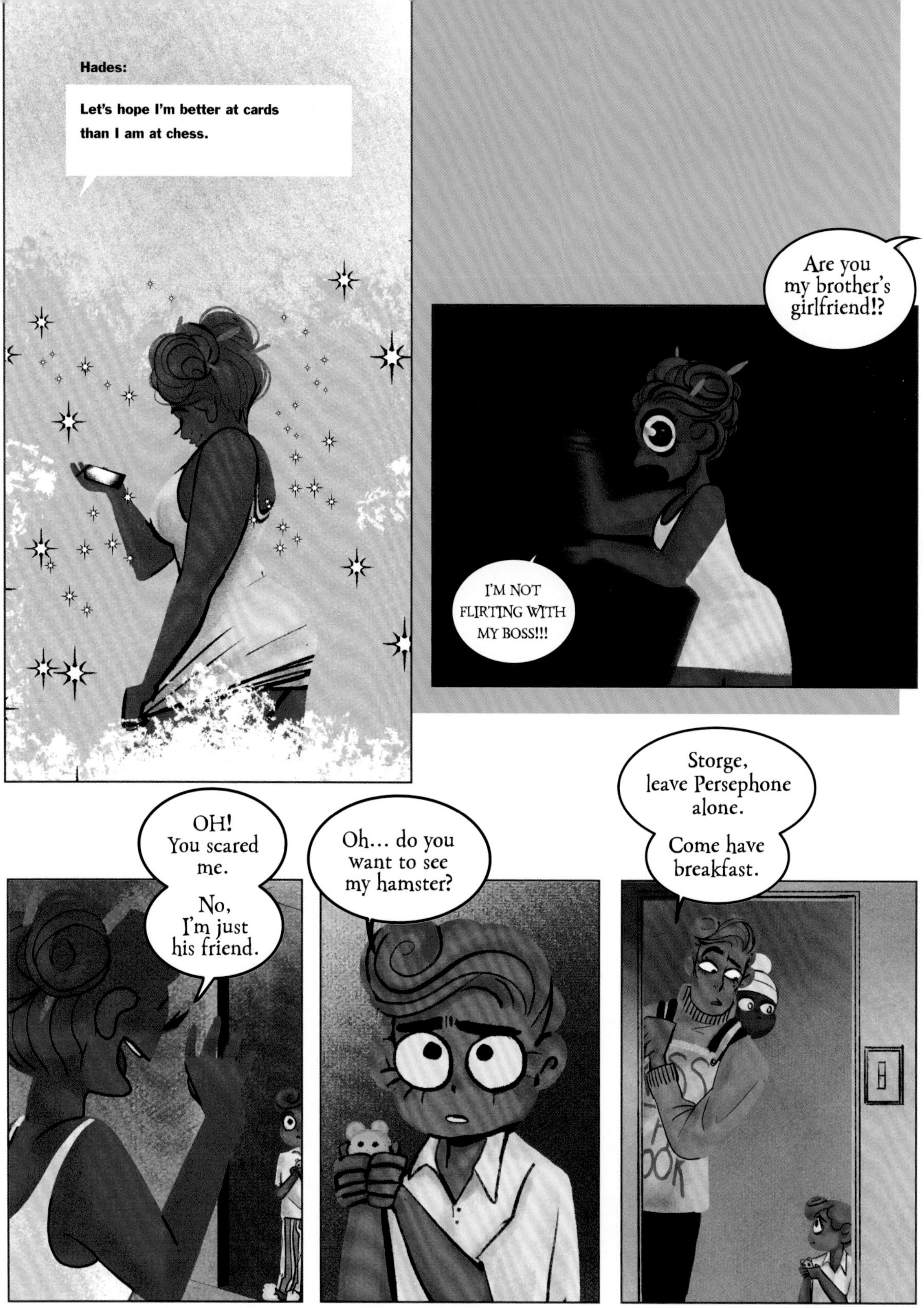
Hades:
Let's hope I'm better at cards than I am at chess.
Are you my brother's girlfriend!?
I'M NOT FLIRTING WITH MY BOSS!!!
OH! You scared me.
No, I'm just his friend.
Oh... do you want to see my hamster?
Storge, leave Persephone alone.
Come have breakfast.

EPISODE 67: SIBLINGS

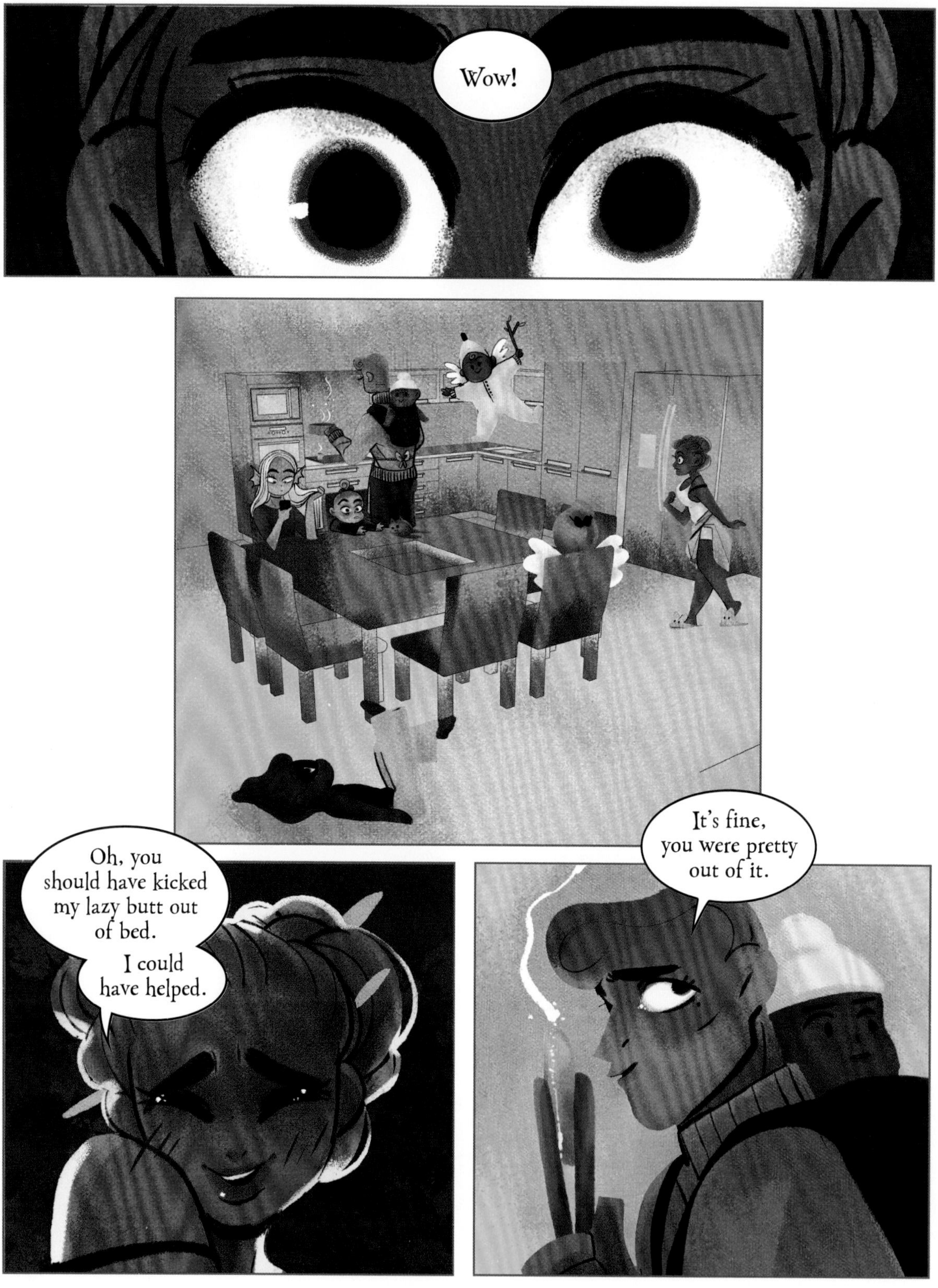
Wow!
Oh, you should have kicked my lazy butt out of bed.
I could have helped.
It's fine, you were pretty out of it.

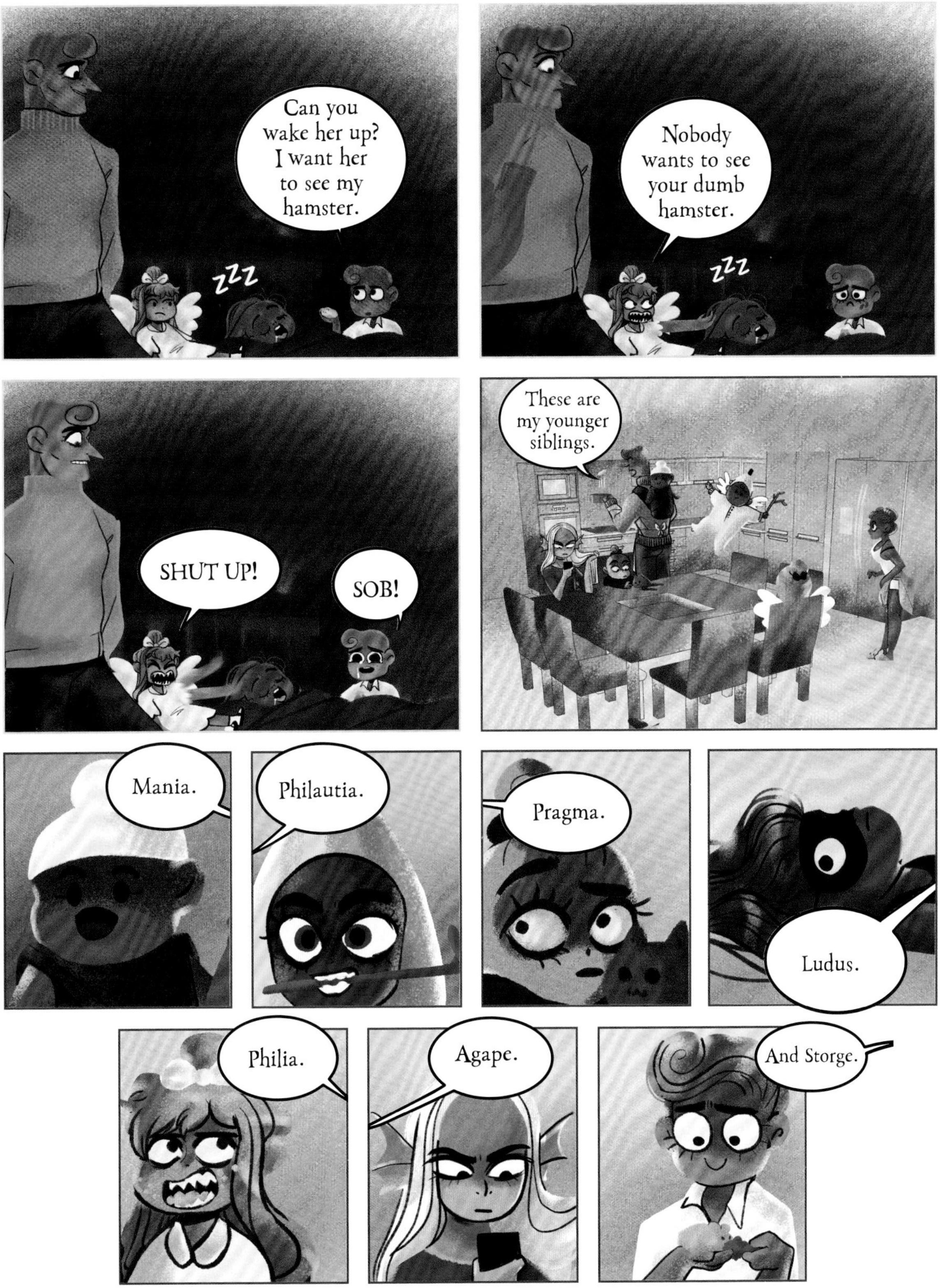
Can you wake her up? I want her to see my hamster.
ZZZ
Nobody wants to see your dumb hamster.
ZZZ
SHUT UP!
SOB!
These are my younger siblings.
Mania.
Philautia.
Pragma.
Ludus.
Philia.
Agape.
And Storge.

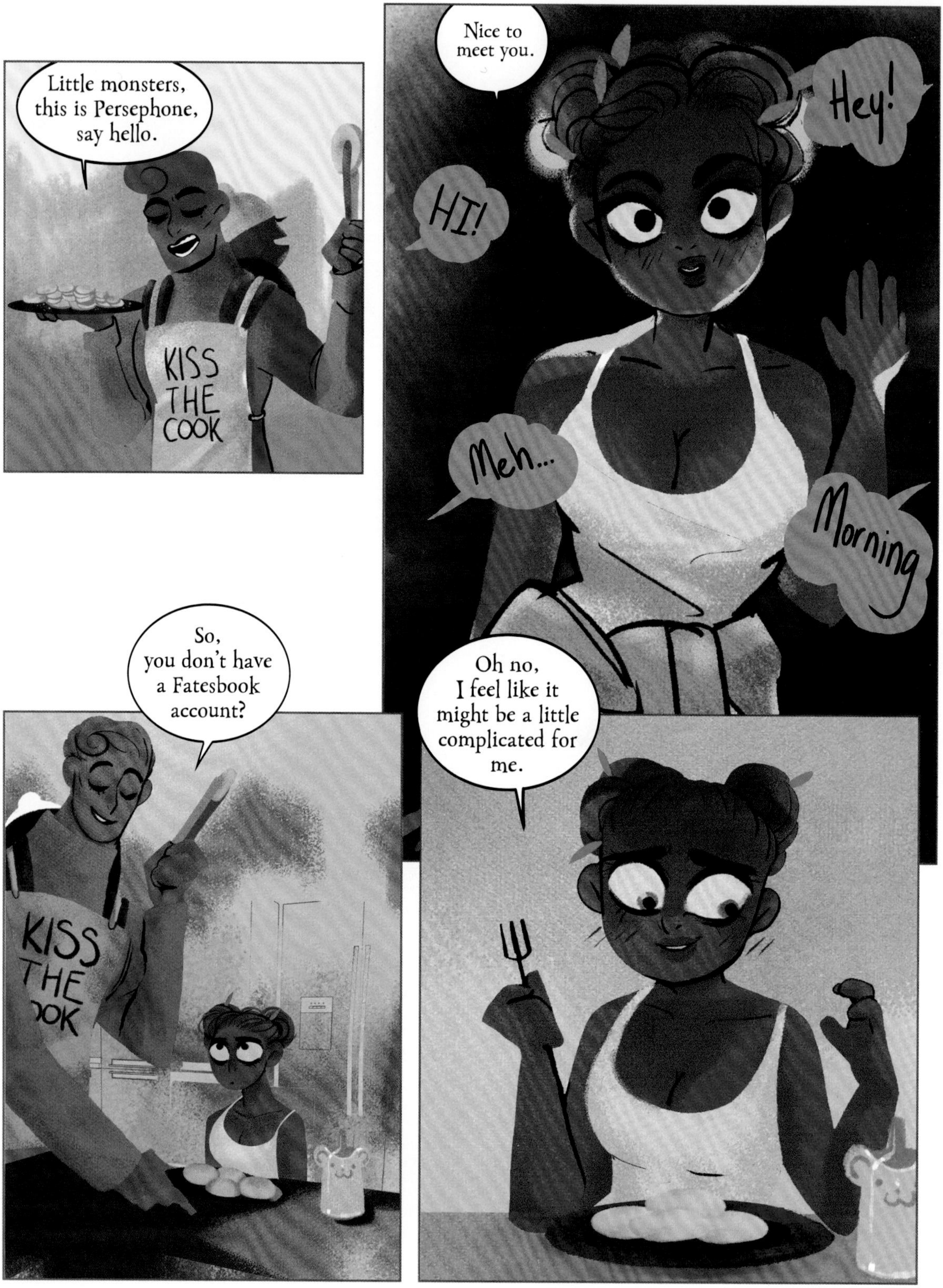
Little monsters, this is Persephone, say hello.
KISS THE COOK
Nice to meet you.
Hey!
HI!
Meh...
Morning
So, you don't have a Fatesbook account?
KISS THE OOK
Oh no, I feel like it might be a little complicated for me.

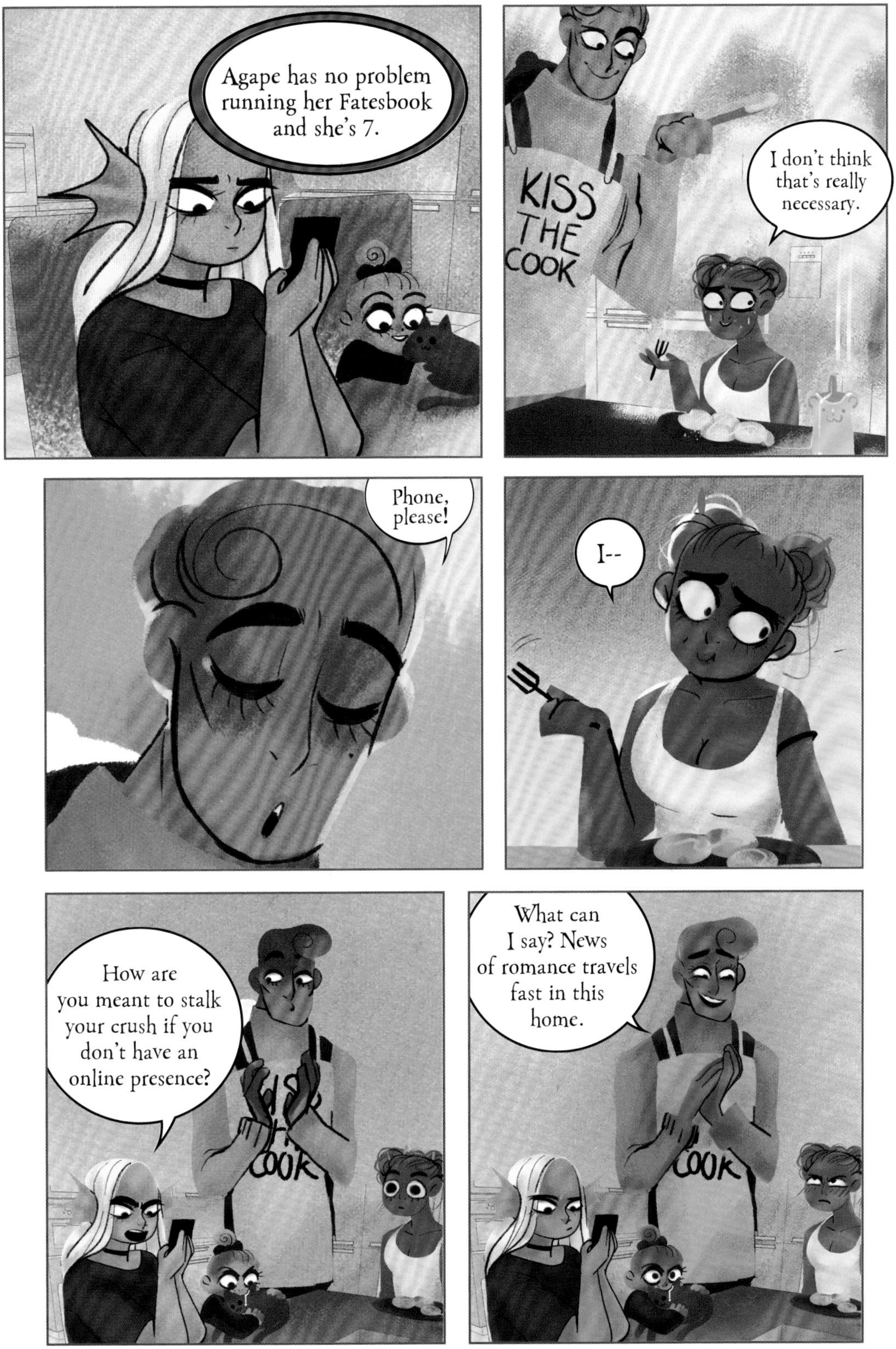
Agape has no problem running her Fatesbook and she's 7.
I don't think that's really necessary.
Phone, please!
I--
How are you meant to stalk your crush if you don't have an online presence?
What can I say? News of romance travels fast in this home.
KISS THE COOK

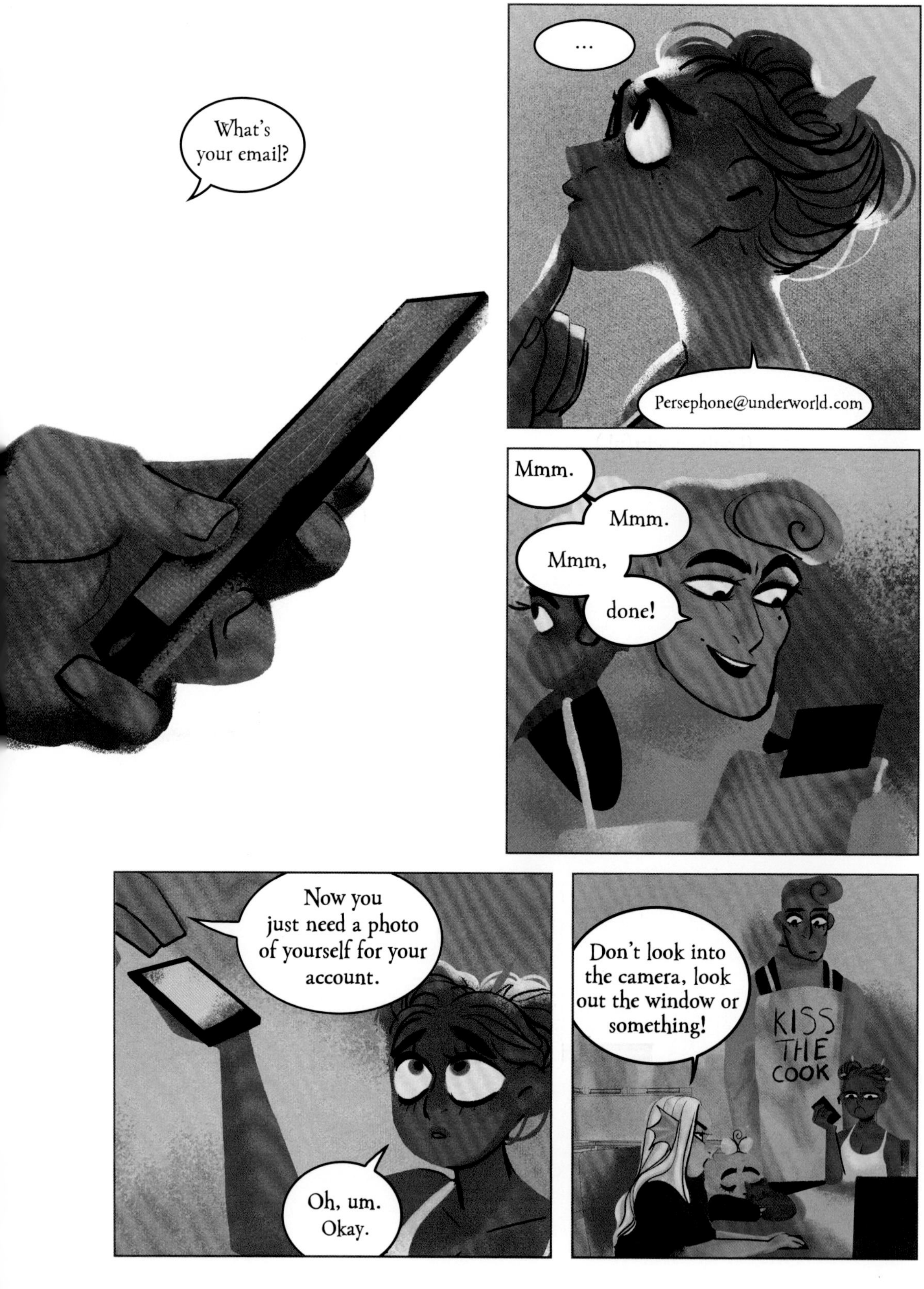
What's your email?
...
Persephone@underworld.com
Mmm.
Mmm.
Mmm,
done!
Now you just need a photo of yourself for your account.
Oh, um. Okay.
Don't look into the camera, look out the window or something!
KISS THE COOK

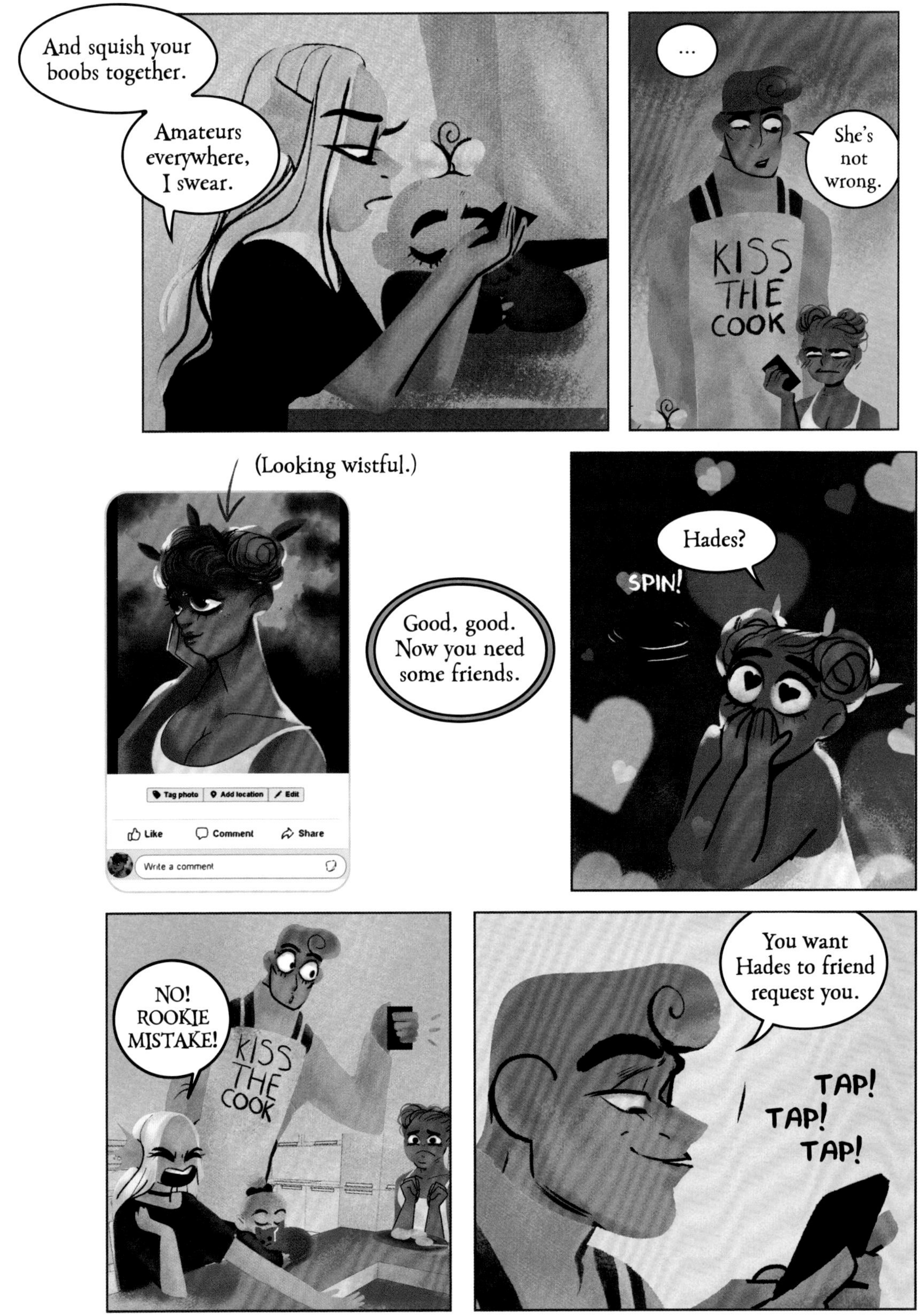
And squish your boobs together.
Amateurs everywhere, I swear.
...
She's not wrong.
(Looking wistful.)
Tag photo
Add location
Edit
Like
Comment
Share
Write a comment
Good, good. Now you need some friends.
Hades?
SPIN!
NO! ROOKIE MISTAKE!
KISS THE COOK
You want Hades to friend request you.
TAP!
TAP!
TAP!

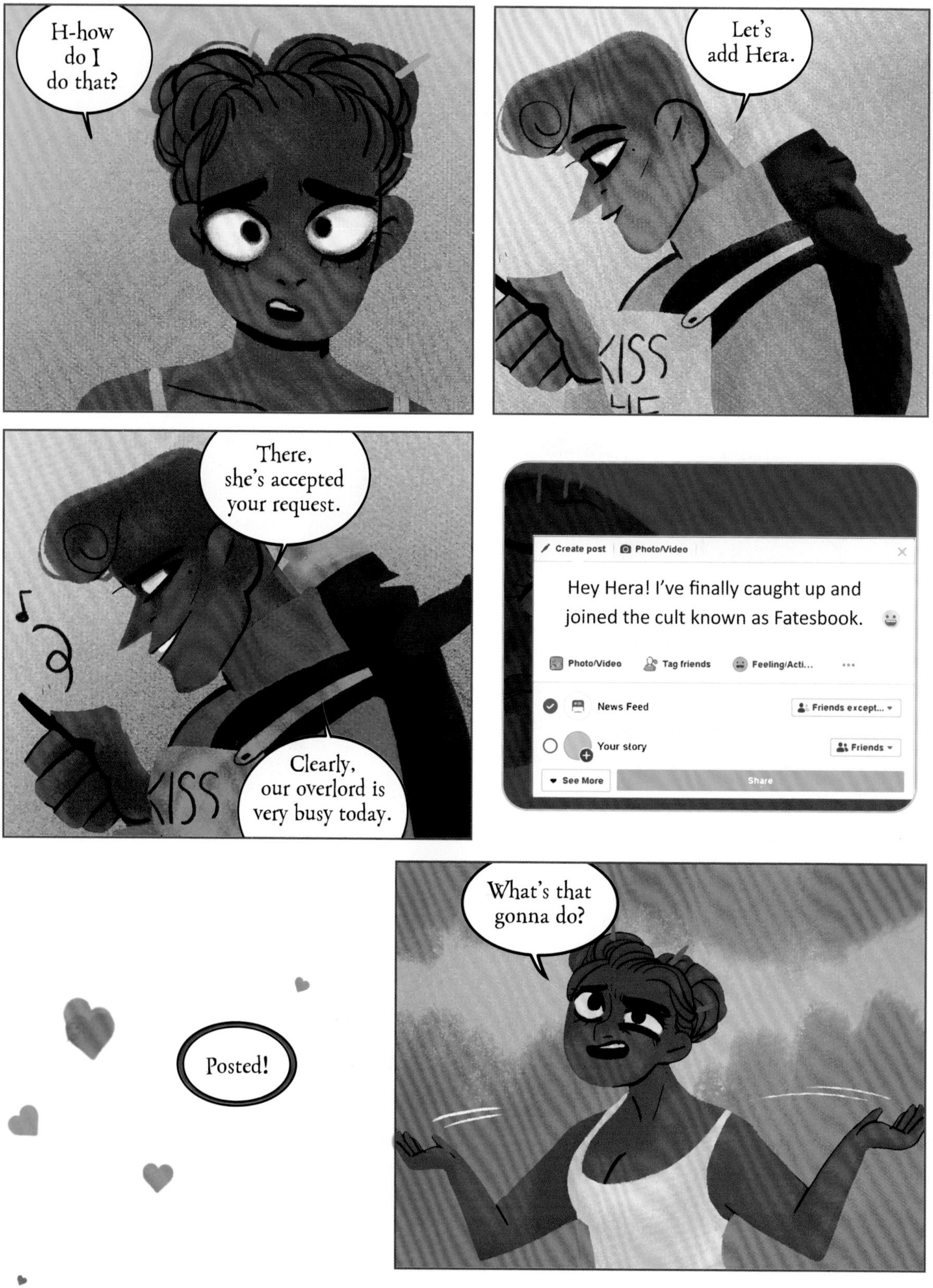
H-how do I do that?
Let's add Hera.
There, she's accepted your request.
Clearly, our overlord is very busy today.
Create post
Photo/Video
Hey Hera! I've finally caught up and joined the cult known as Fatesbook.
Photo/Video
Tag friends
Feeling/Acti...
News Feed
Friends except...
Your story
Friends
See More
Share
Posted!
What's that gonna do?

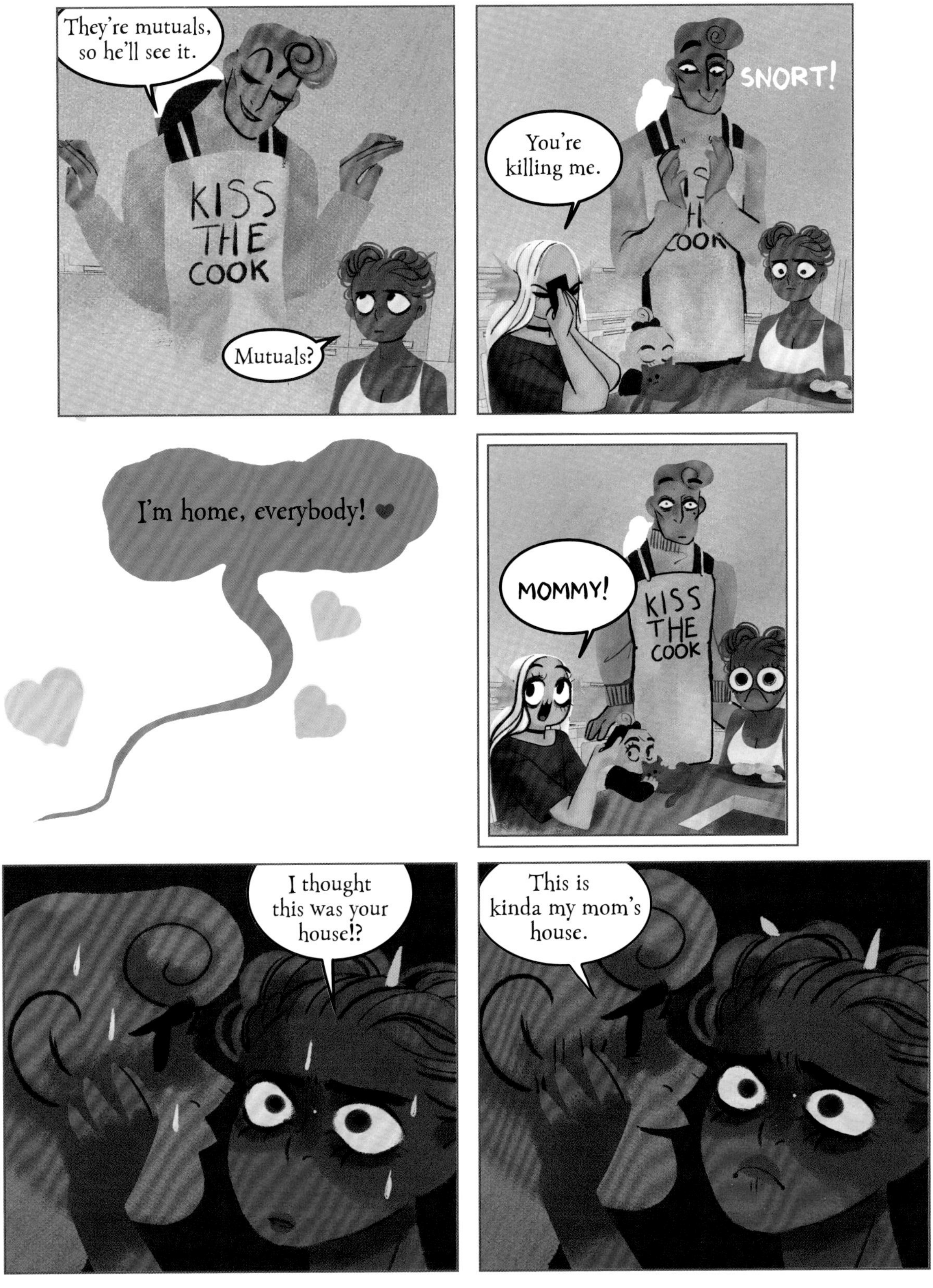
They're mutuals, so he'll see it.
KISS THE COOK
Mutuals?
SNORT!
You're killing me.
I'm home, everybody!
MOMMY!
KISS THE COOK
I thought this was your house!?
This is kinda my mom's house.

EPISODE 68: MA'AM

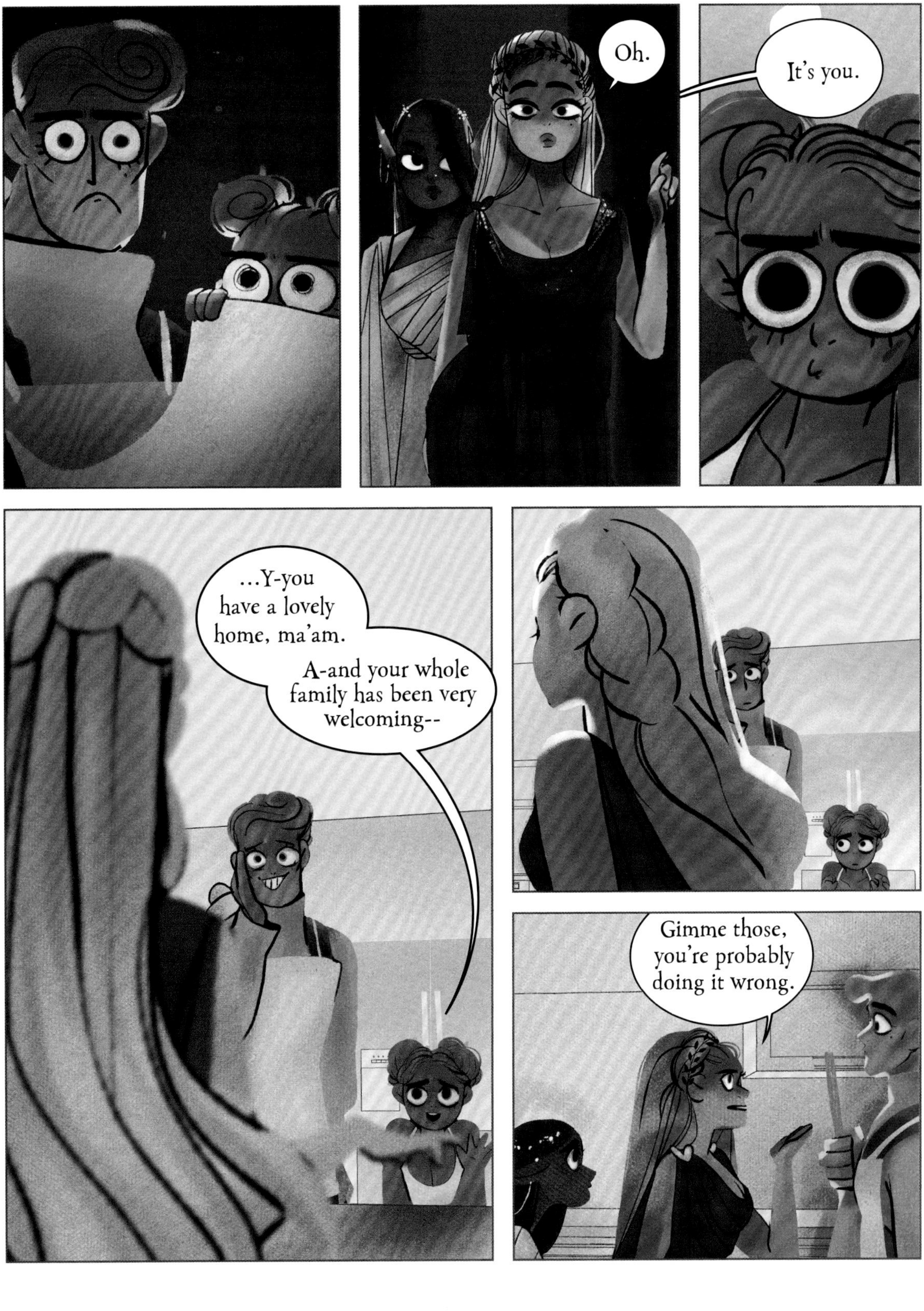
Oh.
It's you.
...Y-you have a lovely home, ma'am.
A-and your whole family has been very welcoming--
Gimme those, you're probably doing it wrong.

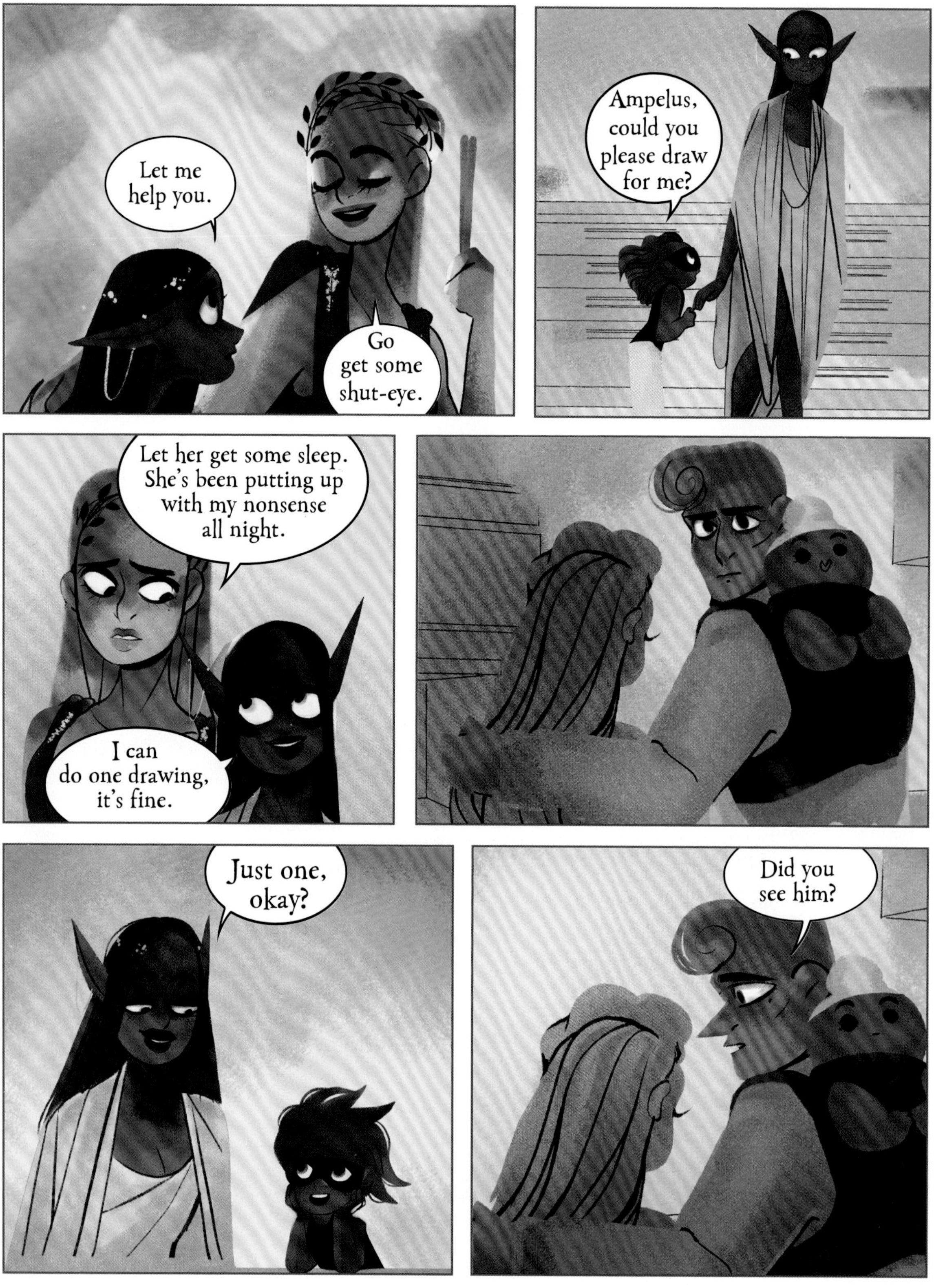
Let me help you.
Go get some shut-eye.
Ampelus, could you please draw for me?
Let her get some sleep. She's been putting up with my nonsense all night.
I can do one drawing, it's fine.
Just one, okay?
Did you see him?

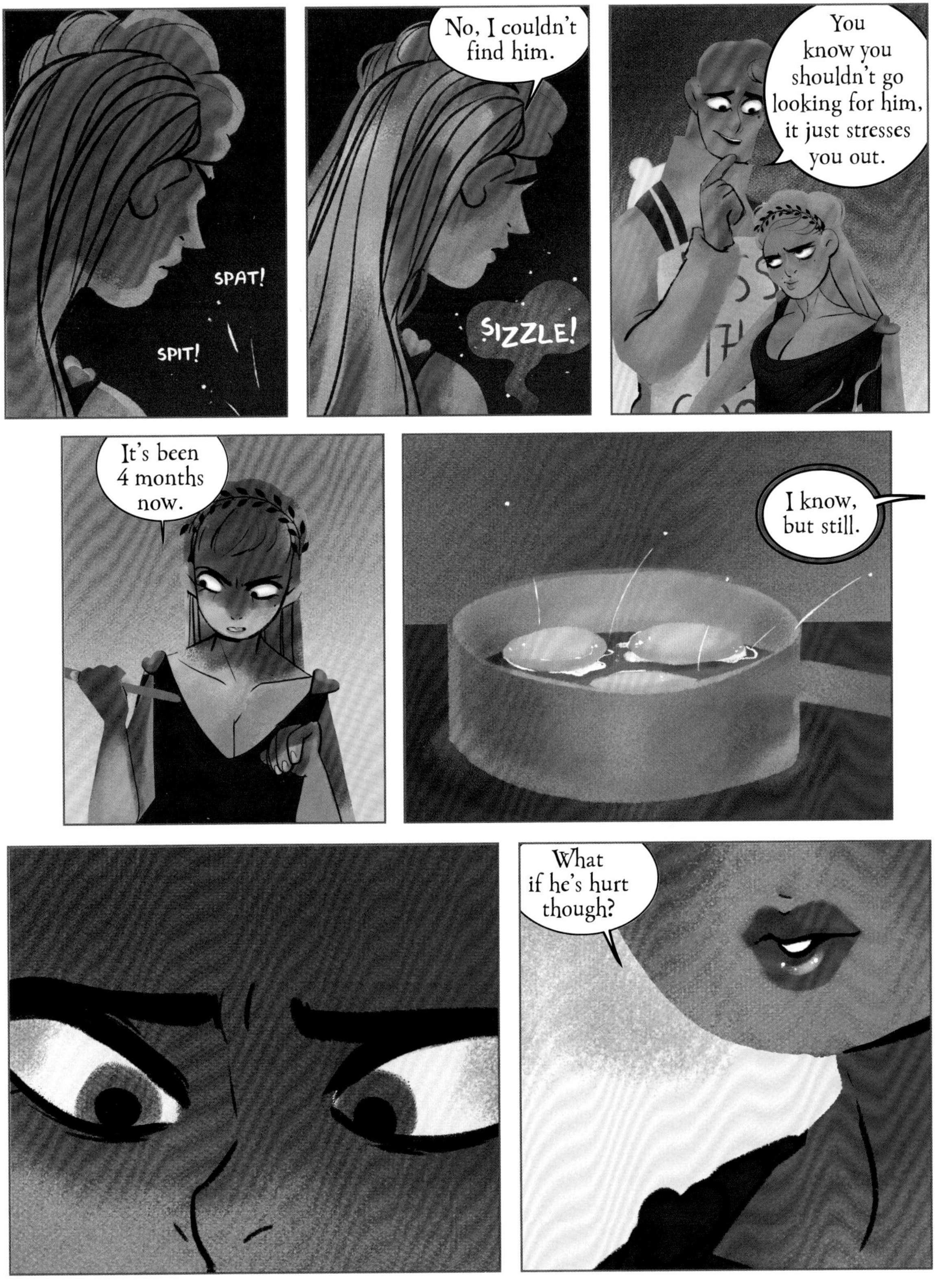
SPAT!
SPIT!
No, I couldn't find him.
SIZZLE!
You know you shouldn't go looking for him, it just stresses you out.
It's been 4 months now.
I know, but still.
What if he's hurt though?

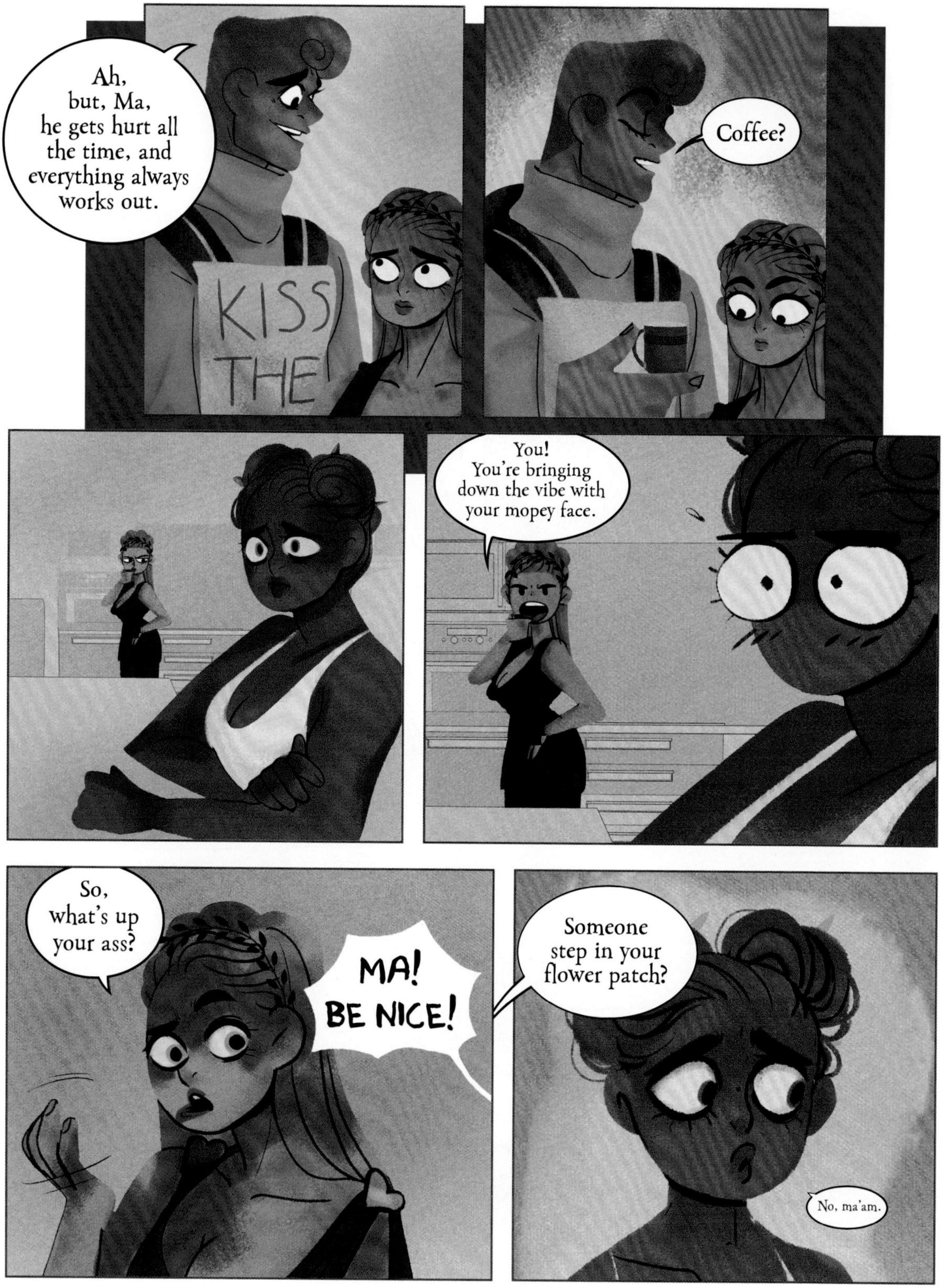

Ah, but, Ma, he gets hurt all the time, and everything always works out.
KISS THE
Coffee?
You! You're bringing down the vibe with your mopey face.
So, what's up your ass?
MA! BE NICE!
Someone step in your flower patch?
No, ma'am.

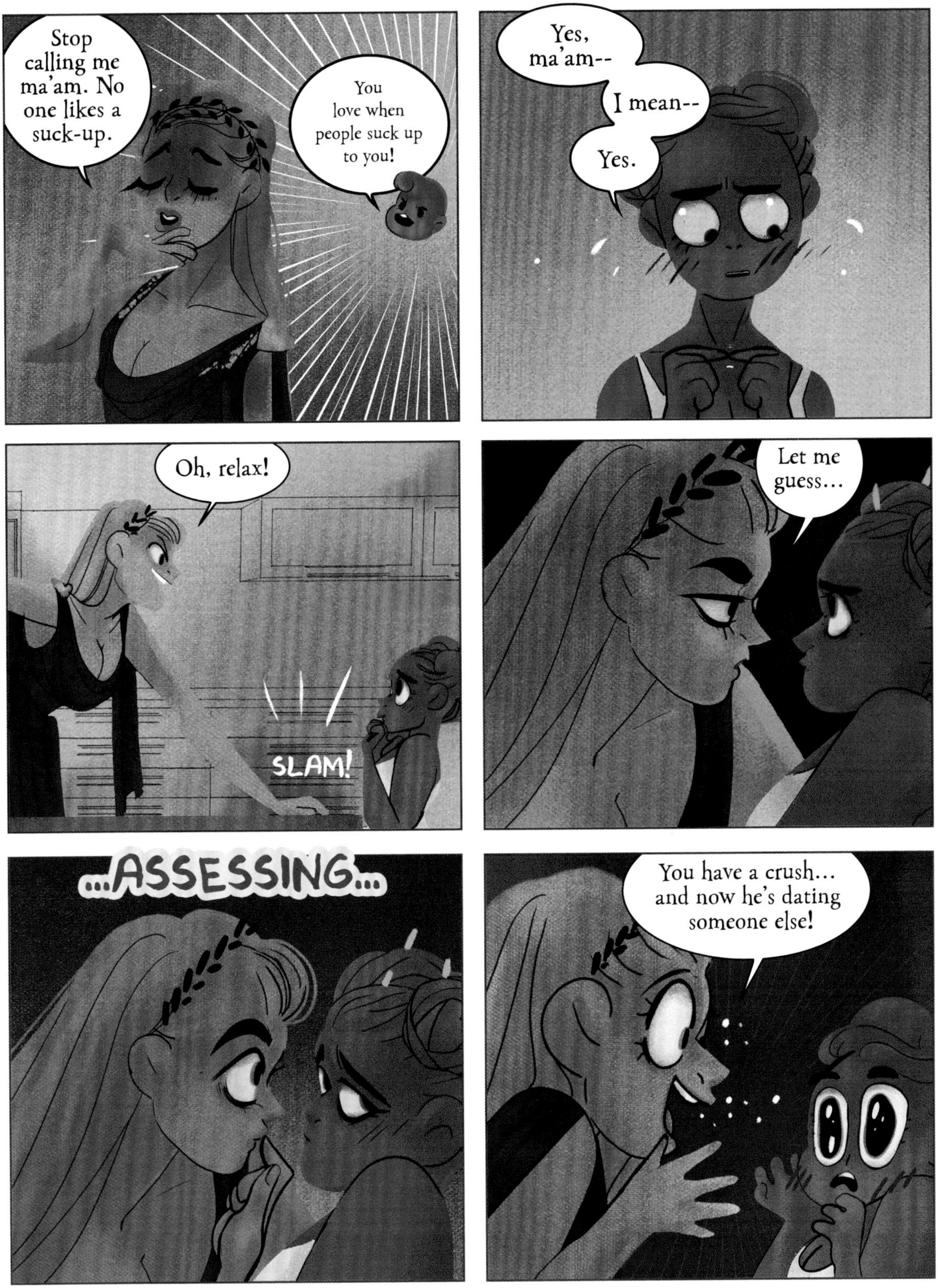
Stop calling me ma'am. No one likes a suck-up.
You love when people suck up to you!
Yes, ma'am--
I mean--
Yes.
Oh, relax!
SLAM!
Let me guess...
...ASSESSING...
You have a crush... and now he's dating someone else!

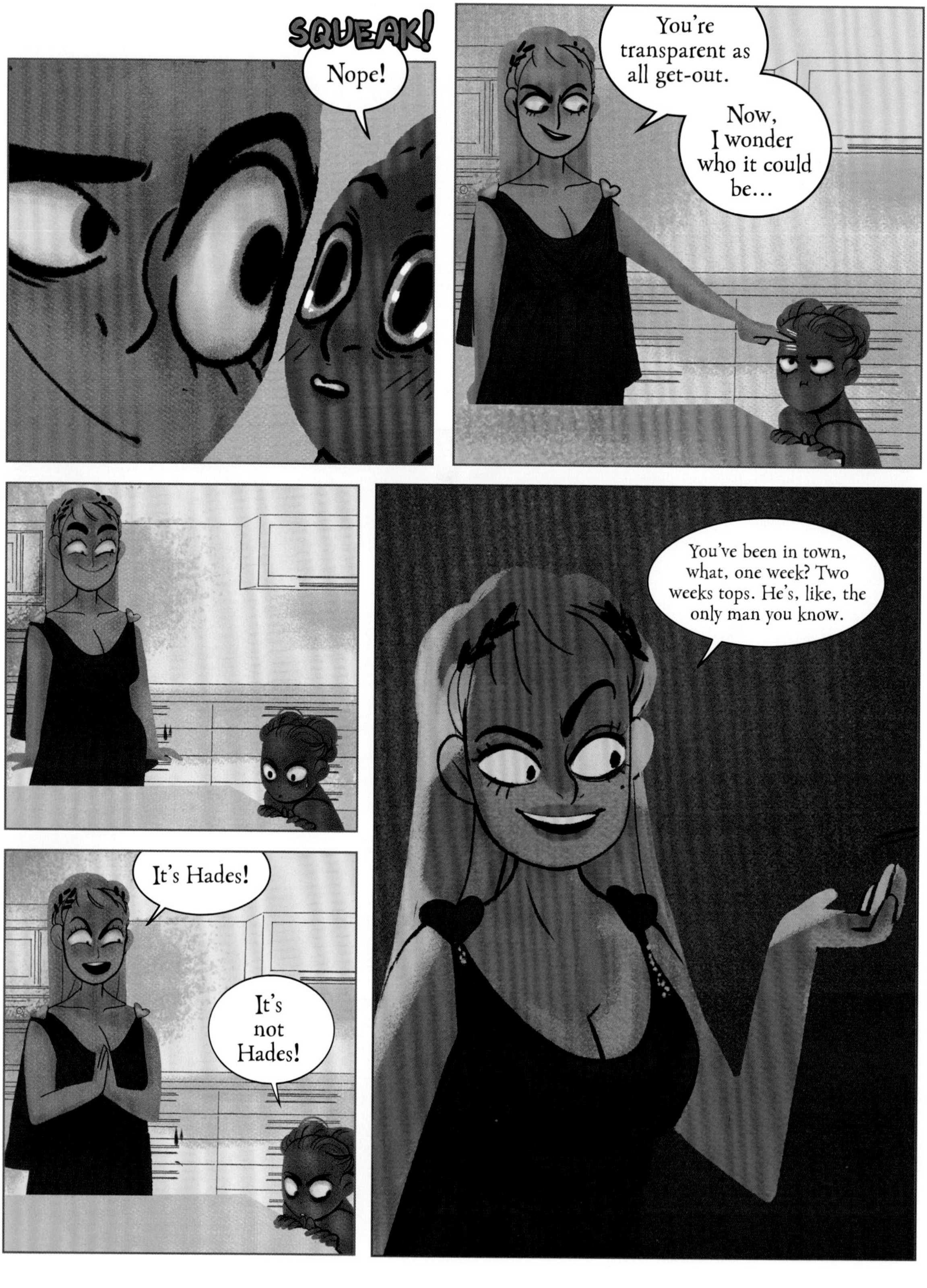
SQUEAK!
Nope!
You're transparent as all get-out.
Now, I wonder who it could be...
You've been in town, what, one week? Two weeks tops. He's, like, the only man you know.
It's Hades!
It's not Hades!

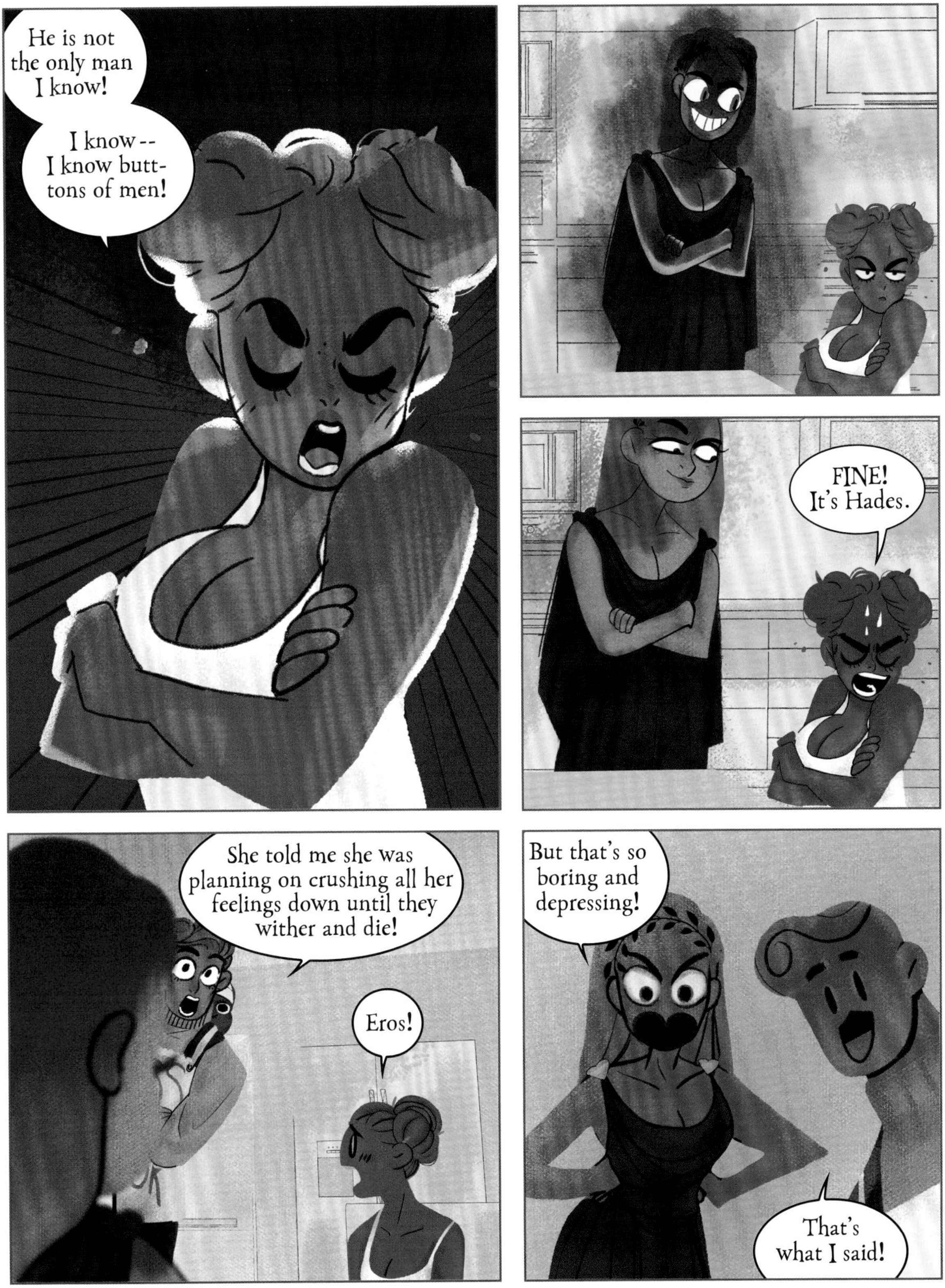
He is not the only man I know!
I know-- I know butt-tons of men!
FINE! It's Hades.
She told me she was planning on crushing all her feelings down until they wither and die!
Eros!
But that's so boring and depressing!
That's what I said!

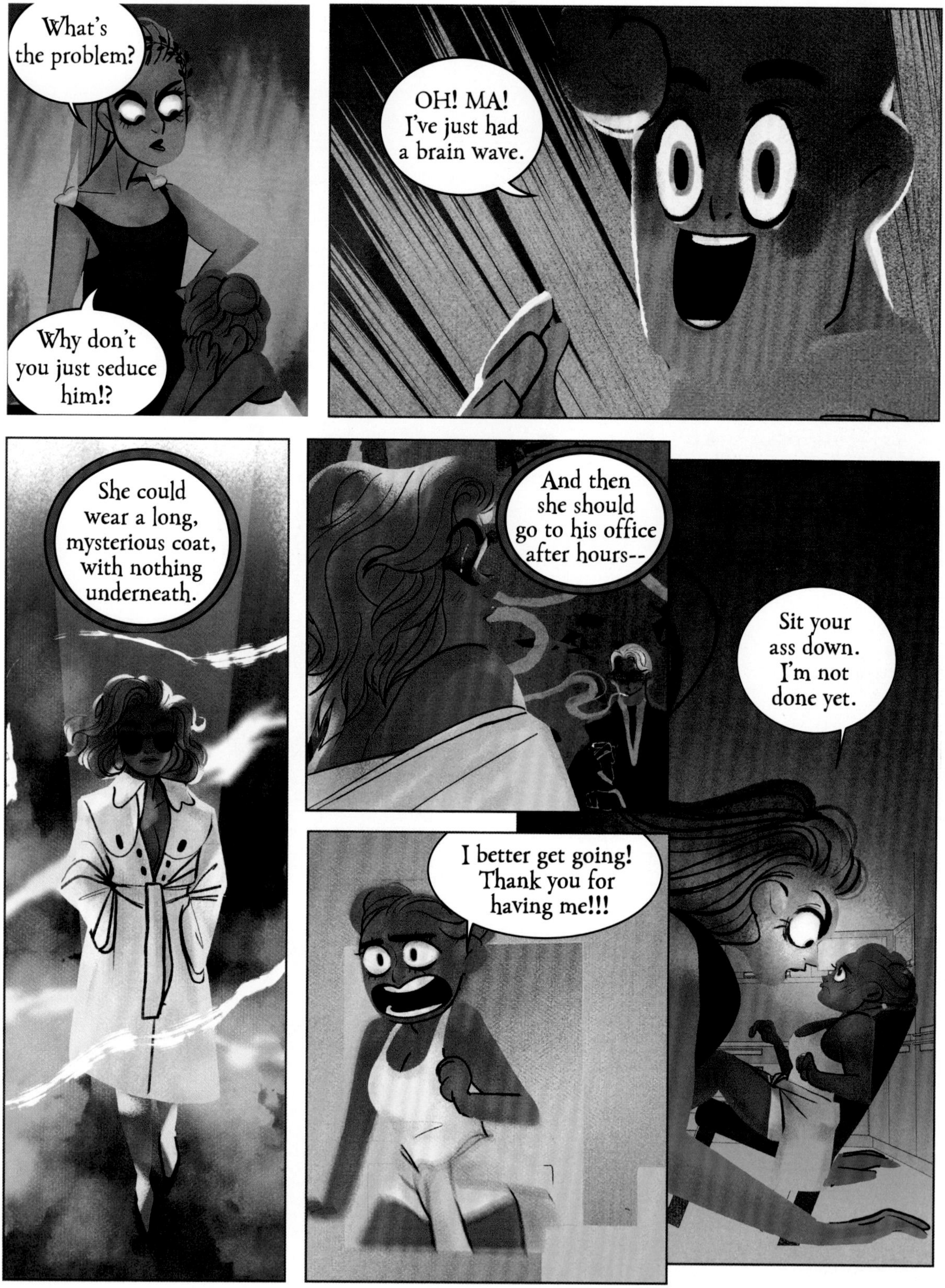
What's the problem?
Why don't you just seduce him!?
OH! MA! I've just had a brain wave.
She could wear a long, mysterious coat, with nothing underneath.
And then she should go to his office after hours--
Sit your ass down. I'm not done yet.
I better get going! Thank you for having me!!!

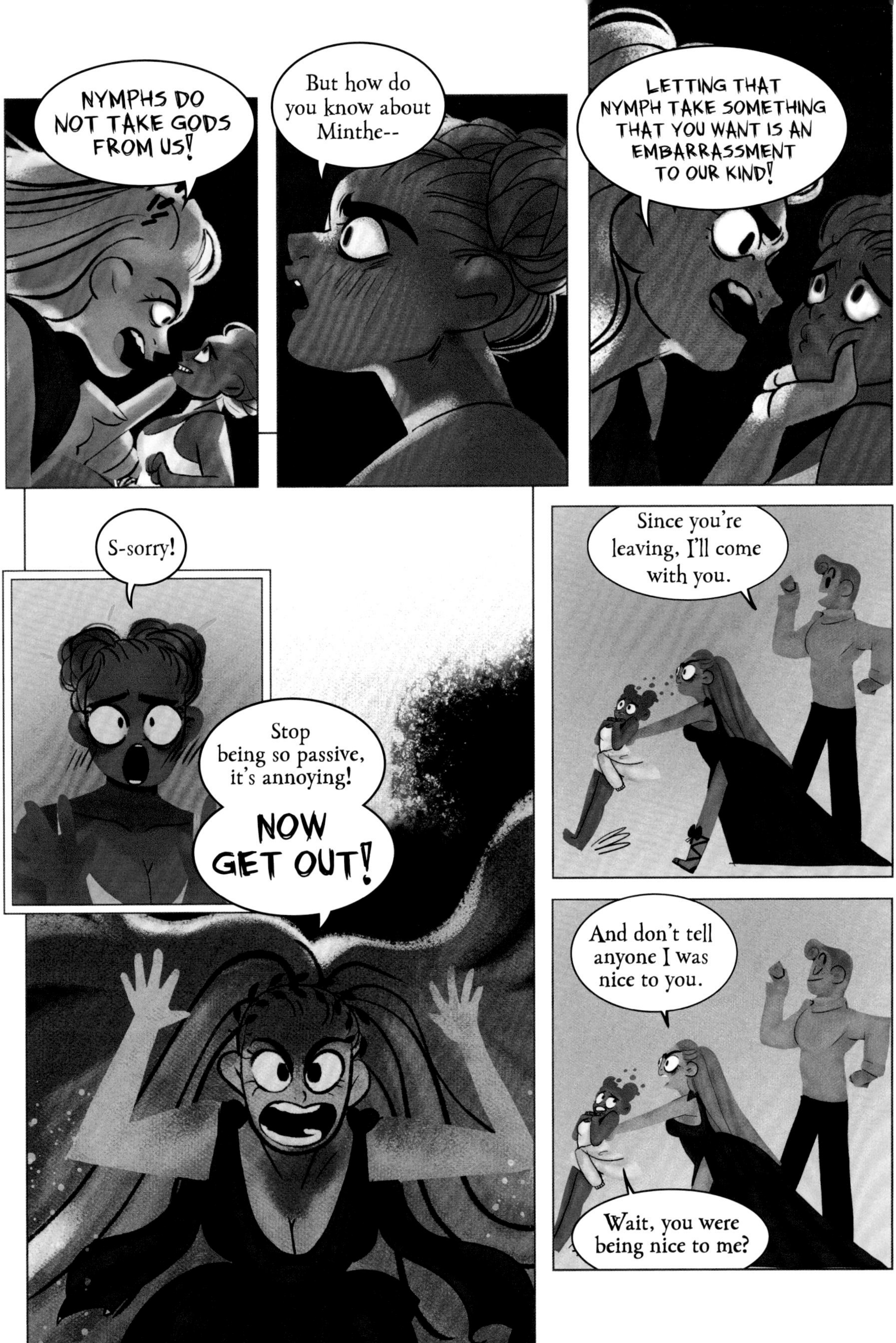
NYMPHS DO NOT TAKE GODS FROM US!
But how do you know about Minthe--
LETTING THAT NYMPH TAKE SOMETHING THAT YOU WANT IS AN EMBARRASSMENT TO OUR KIND!
S-sorry!
Stop being so passive, it's annoying!
NOW GET OUT!
Since you're leaving, I'll come with you.
And don't tell anyone I was nice to you.
Wait, you were being nice to me?

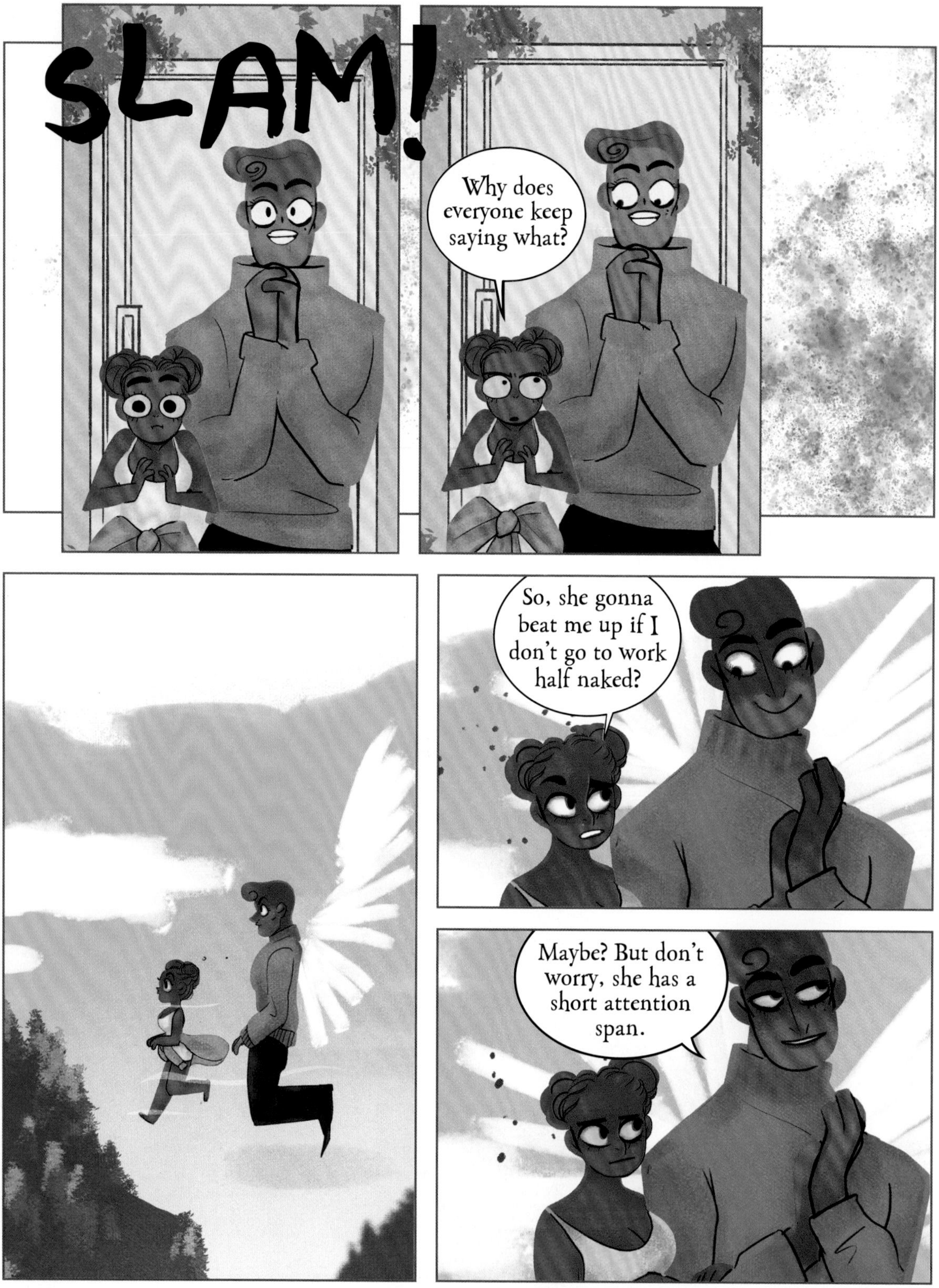
SLAM!
Why does everyone keep saying what?
So, she gonna beat me up if I don't go to work half naked?
Maybe? But don't worry, she has a short attention span.

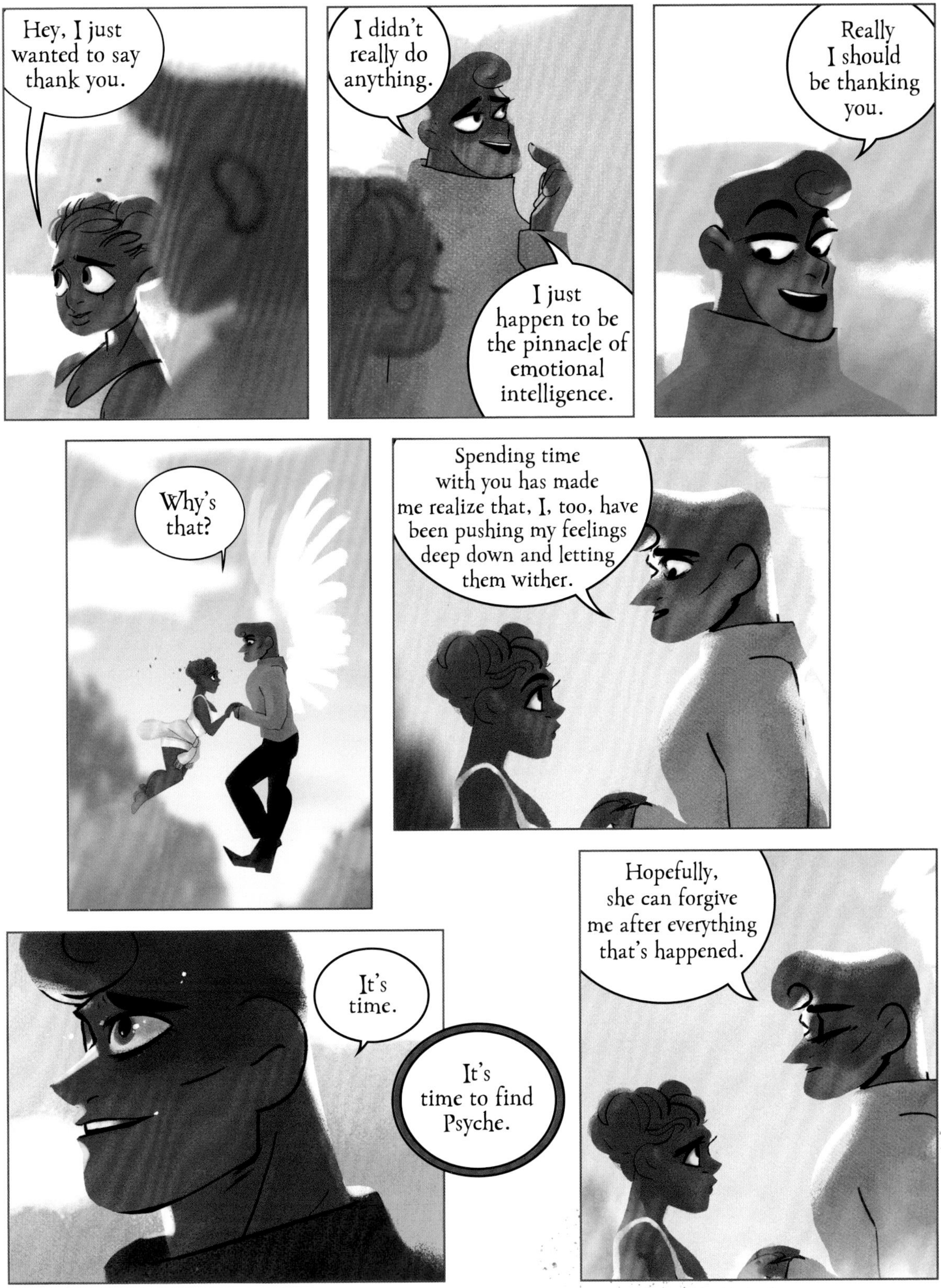
Hey, I just wanted to say thank you.
I didn't really do anything.
I just happen to be the pinnacle of emotional intelligence.
Really I should be thanking you.
Why's that?
Spending time with you has made me realize that, I, too, have been pushing my feelings deep down and letting them wither.
Hopefully, she can forgive me after everything that's happened.
It's time.
It's time to find Psyche.

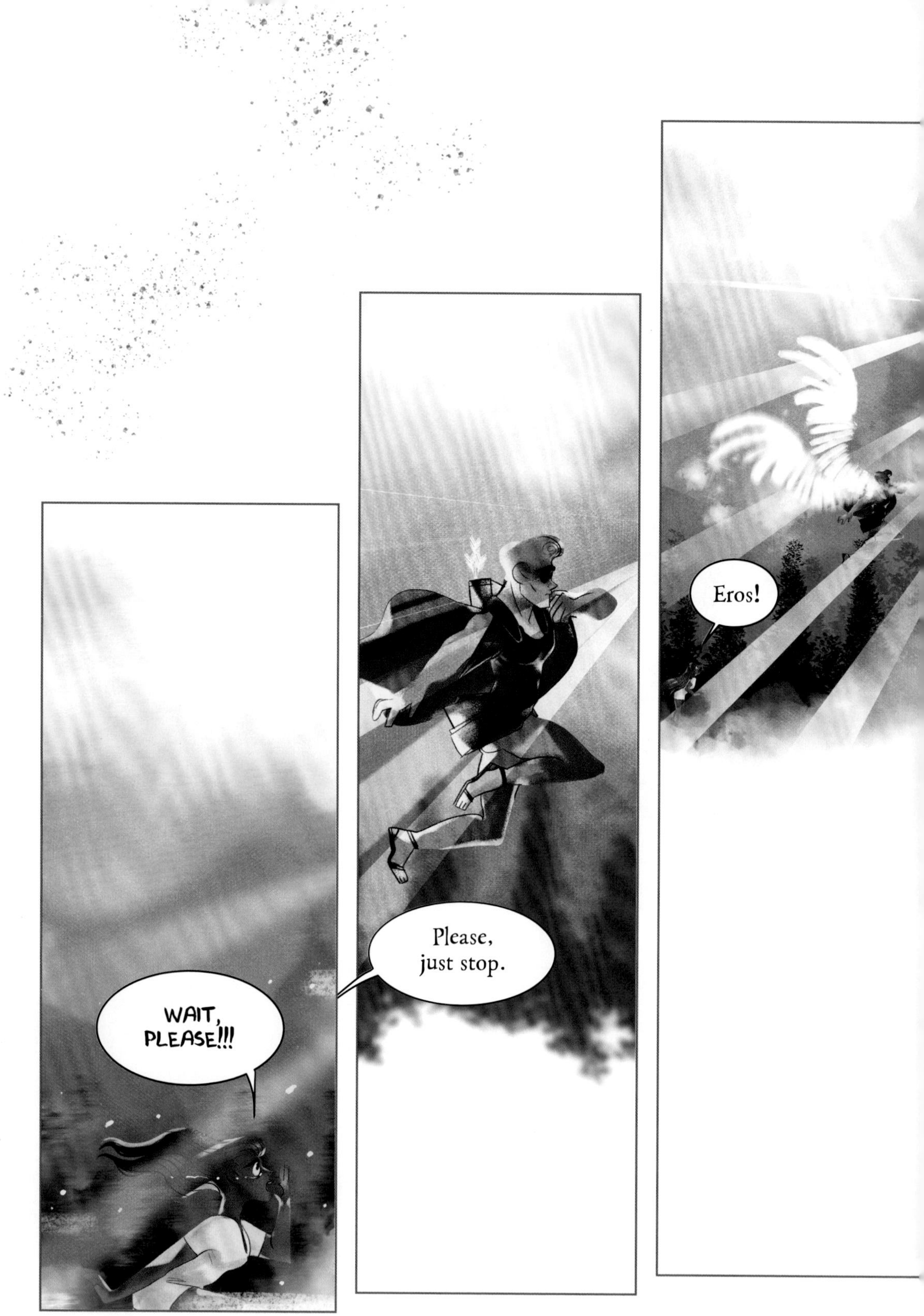
WAIT, PLEASE!!!
Please, just stop.
Eros!

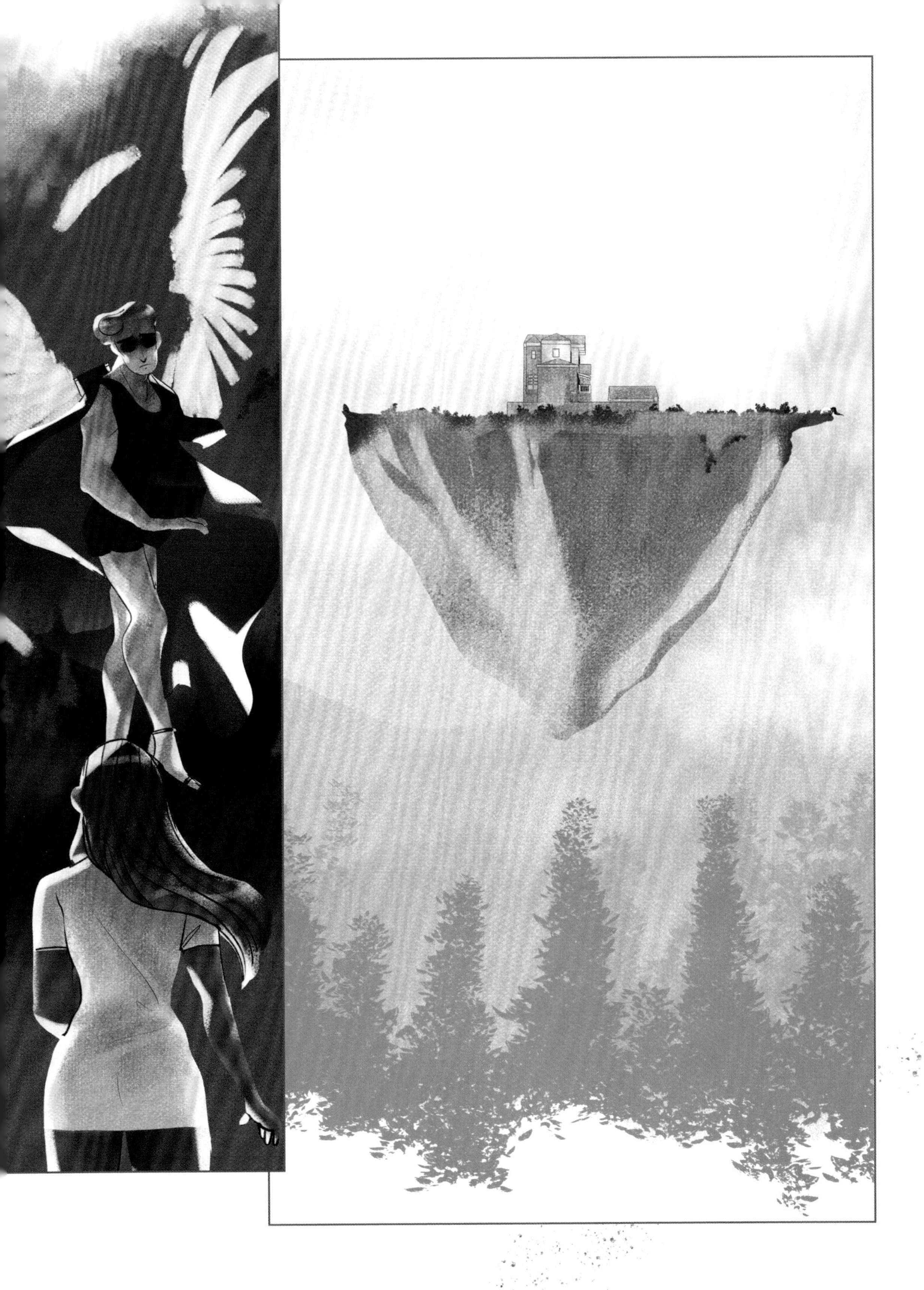

EPISODE 69: GHOSTED

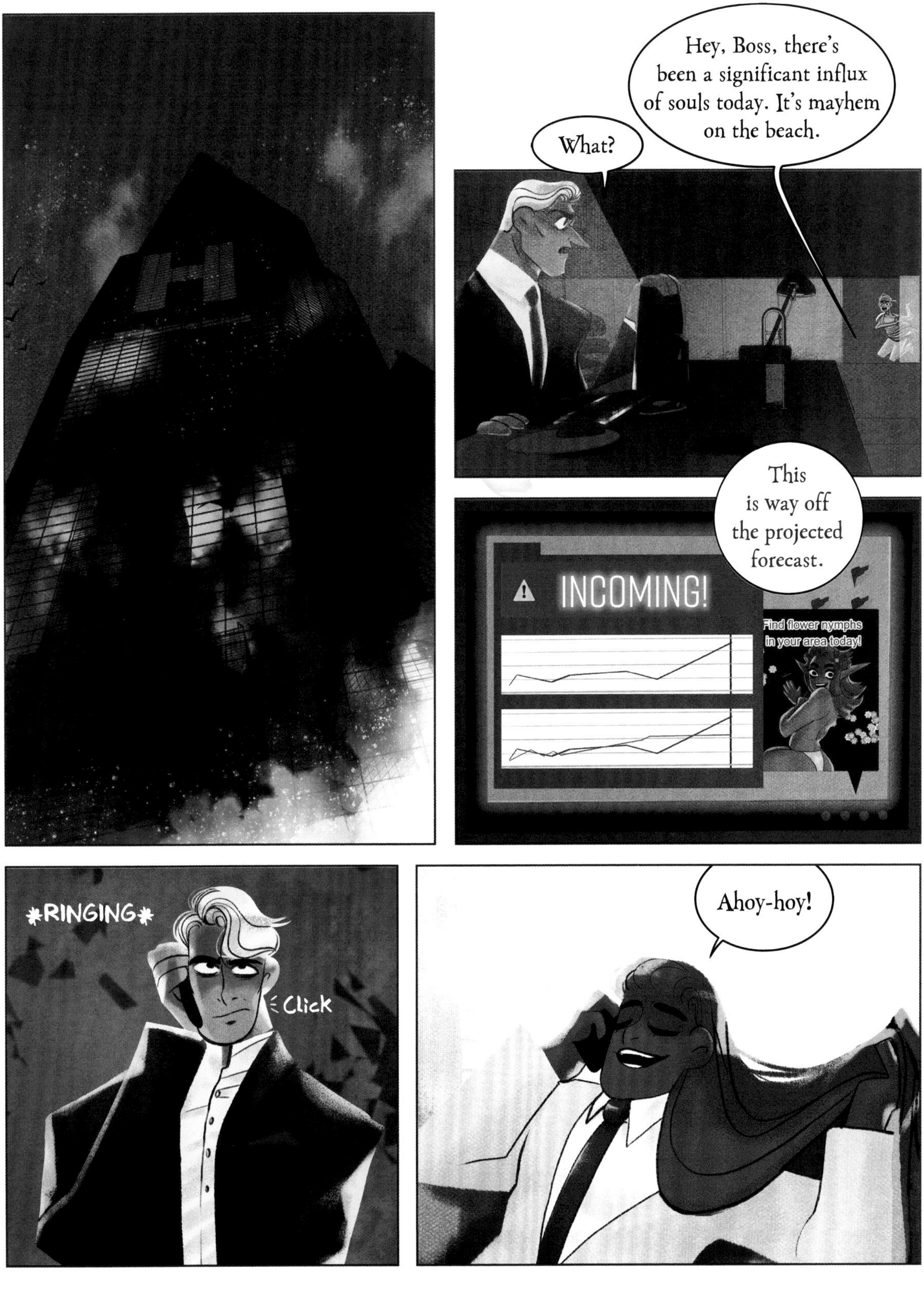

What?
Hey, Boss, there's been a significant influx of souls today. It's mayhem on the beach.
This is way off the projected forecast.
INCOMING!
Find flower nymphs in your area today!
RINGING
Click
Ahoy-hoy!

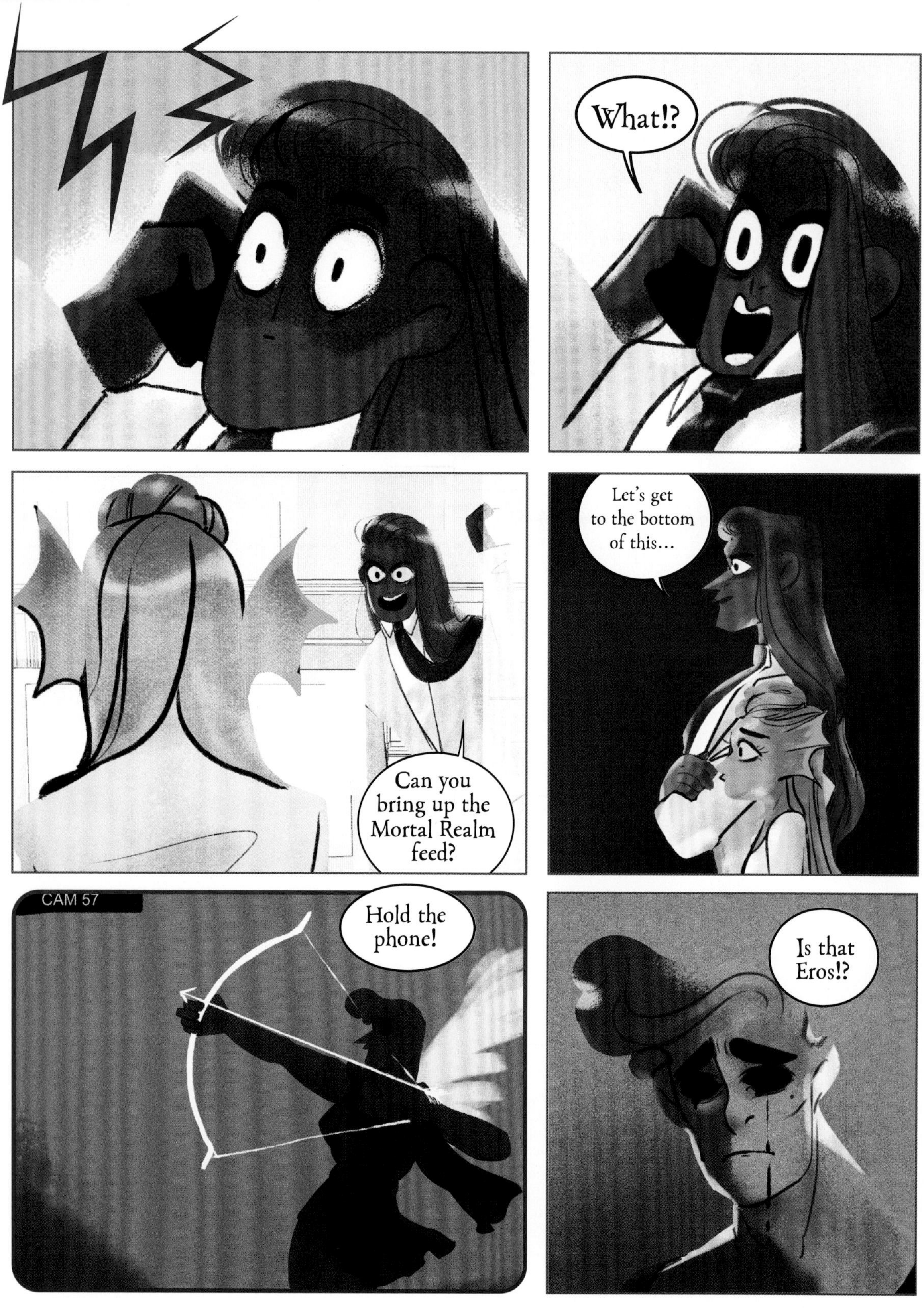
What!?
Can you bring up the Mortal Realm feed?
Let's get to the bottom of this...
CAM 57
Hold the phone!
Is that Eros!?

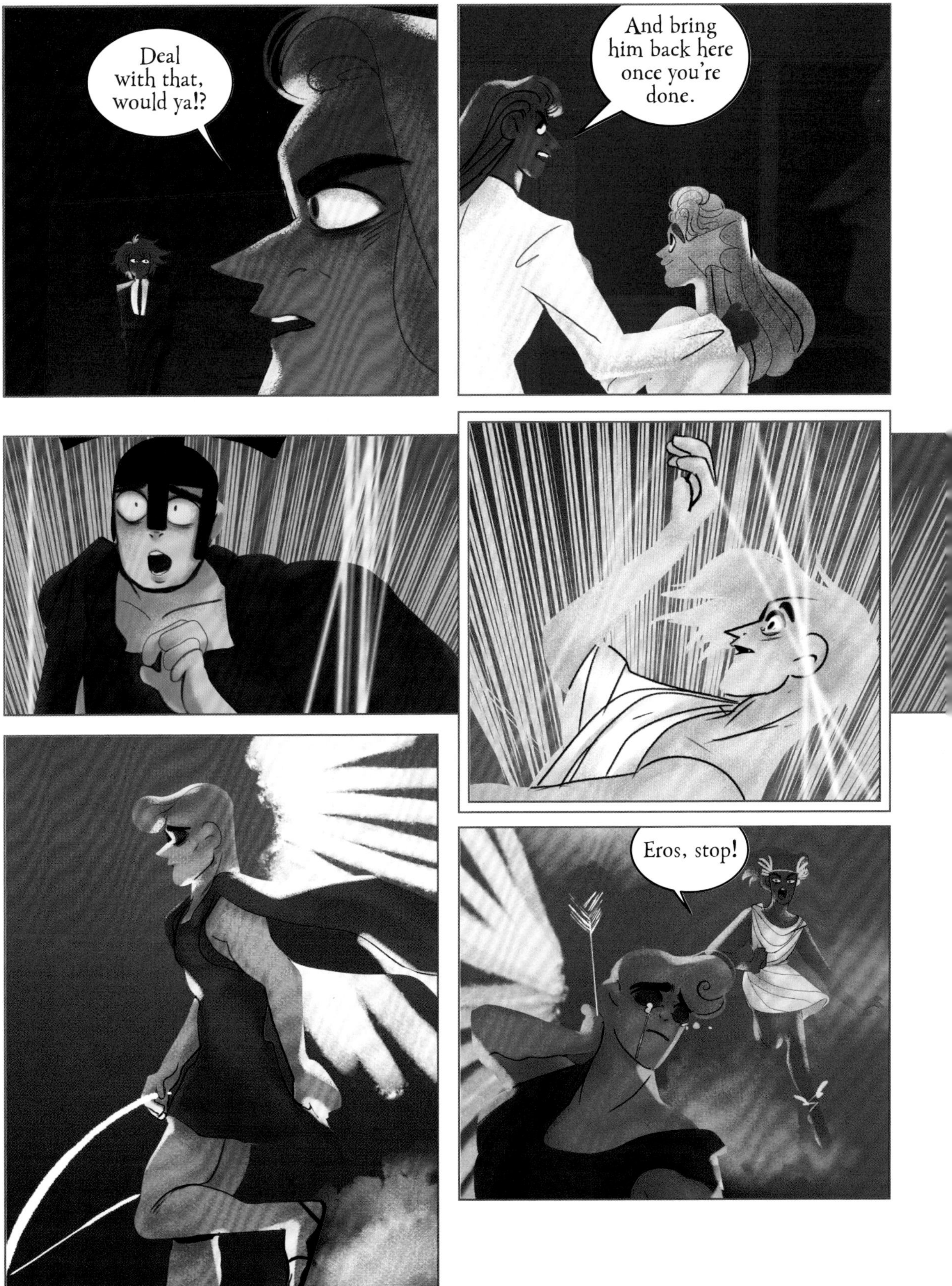
Deal with that, would ya!?
And bring him back here once you're done.
Eros, stop!

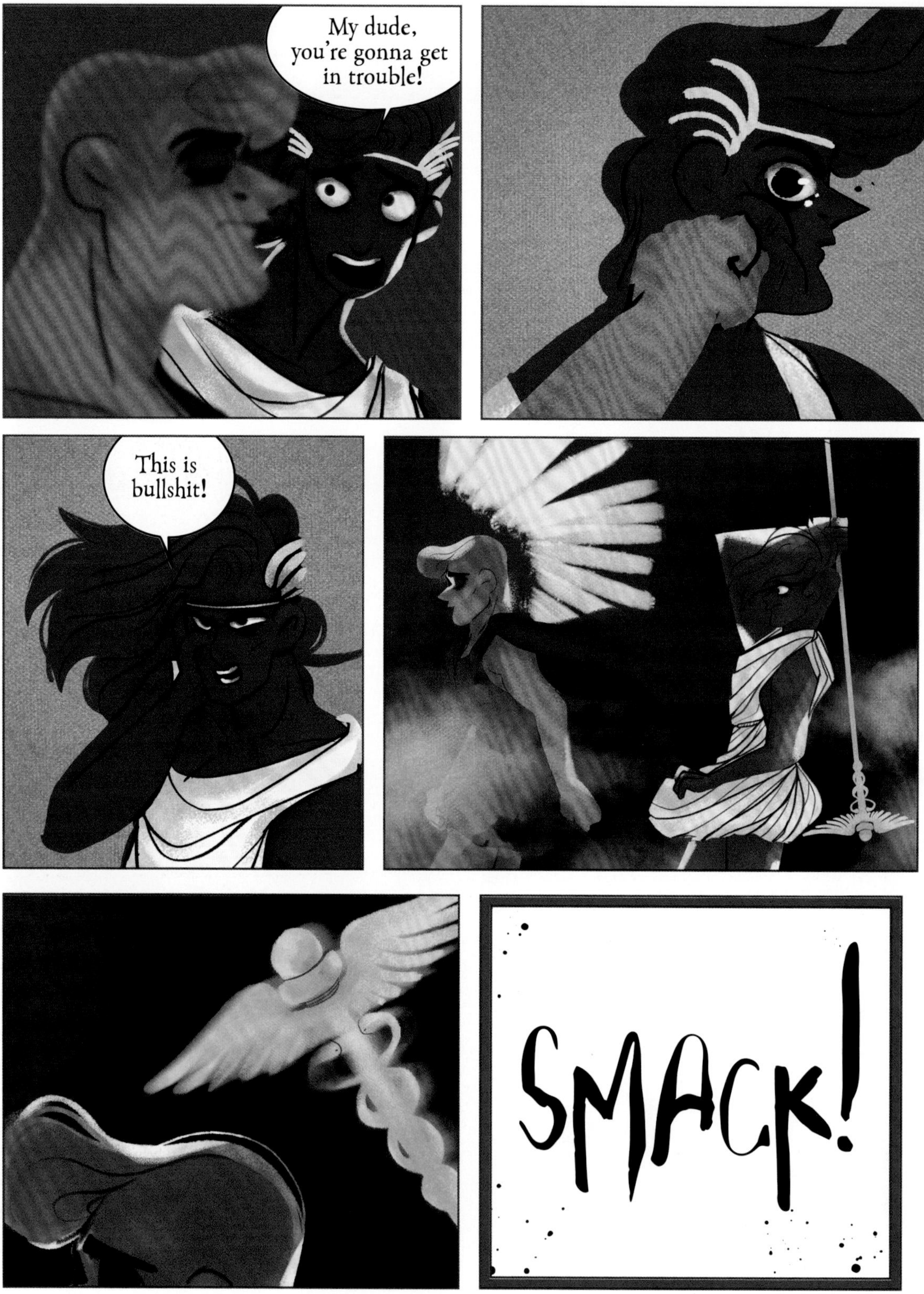
My dude, you're gonna get in trouble!
This is bullshit!
SMACK!

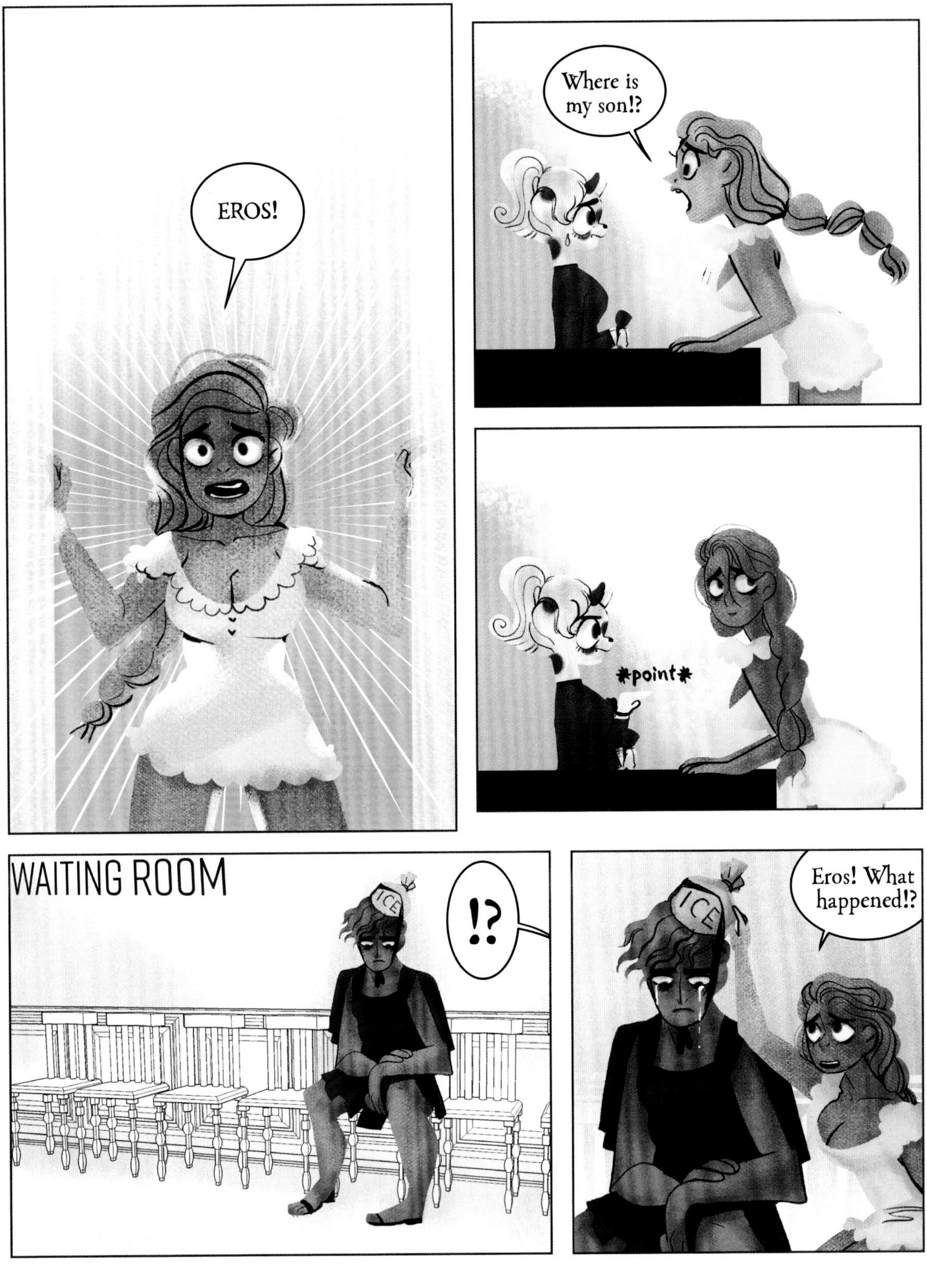
EROS!
Where is my son!?
point
WAITING ROOM
ICE
!?
ICE
Eros! What happened!?

I'm sorry, Ma.

I don't know what came over me.

Zeus is ready to see you now.

THUNDER
(IT'S GOOD)

Would someone please tell me what's going on!?

Well, it would seem Eros has a little bit more of his father's spirit than we thought.

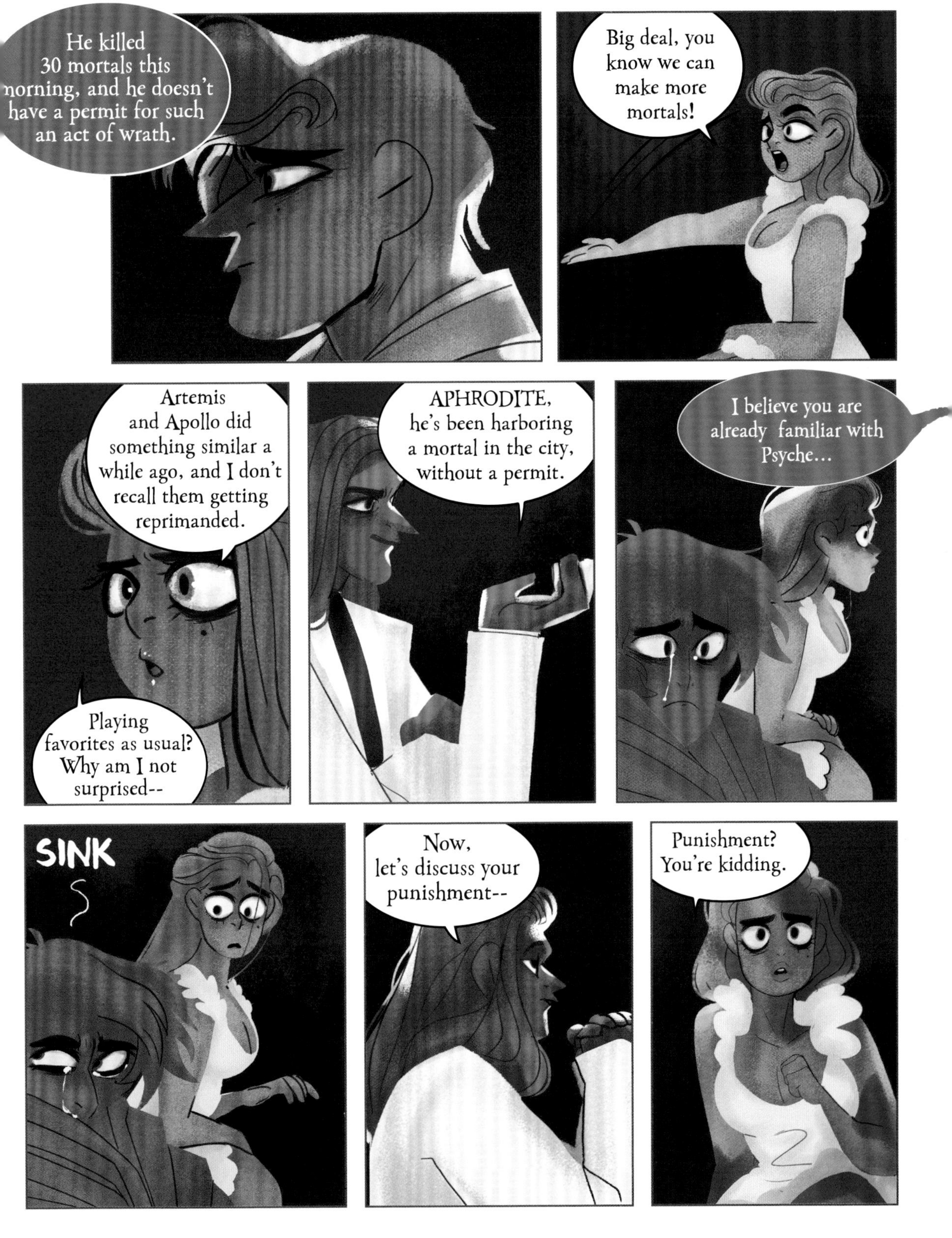
He killed 30 mortals this morning, and he doesn't have a permit for such an act of wrath.
Big deal, you know we can make more mortals!
Artemis and Apollo did something similar a while ago, and I don't recall them getting reprimanded.
Playing favorites as usual? Why am I not surprised--
APHRODITE, he's been harboring a mortal in the city, without a permit.
I believe you are already familiar with Psyche...
SINK
Now, let's discuss your punishment--
Punishment? You're kidding.

Yeah, well, he punched poor Hermes in the face, too.

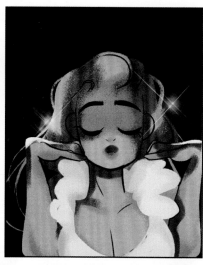

Surely you and I can come to some sort of agreement?

shake shake

I'm sure we could work something out!

THUNDER (IT'S GOOD)

Ma--

Just shut up and go wait out in the car.

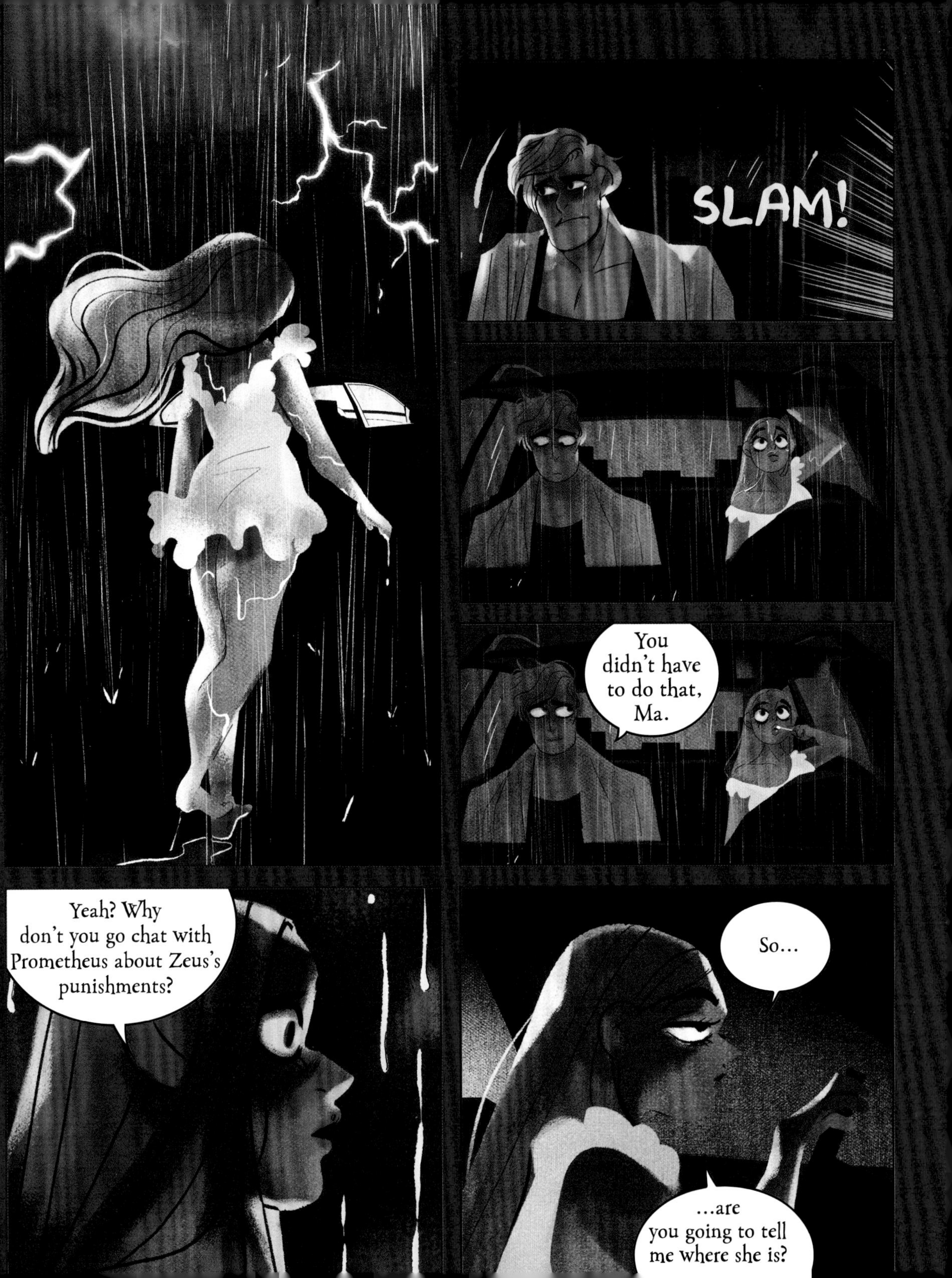
SLAM!
You didn't have to do that, Ma.
Yeah? Why don't you go chat with Prometheus about Zeus's punishments?
So…
…are you going to tell me where she is?

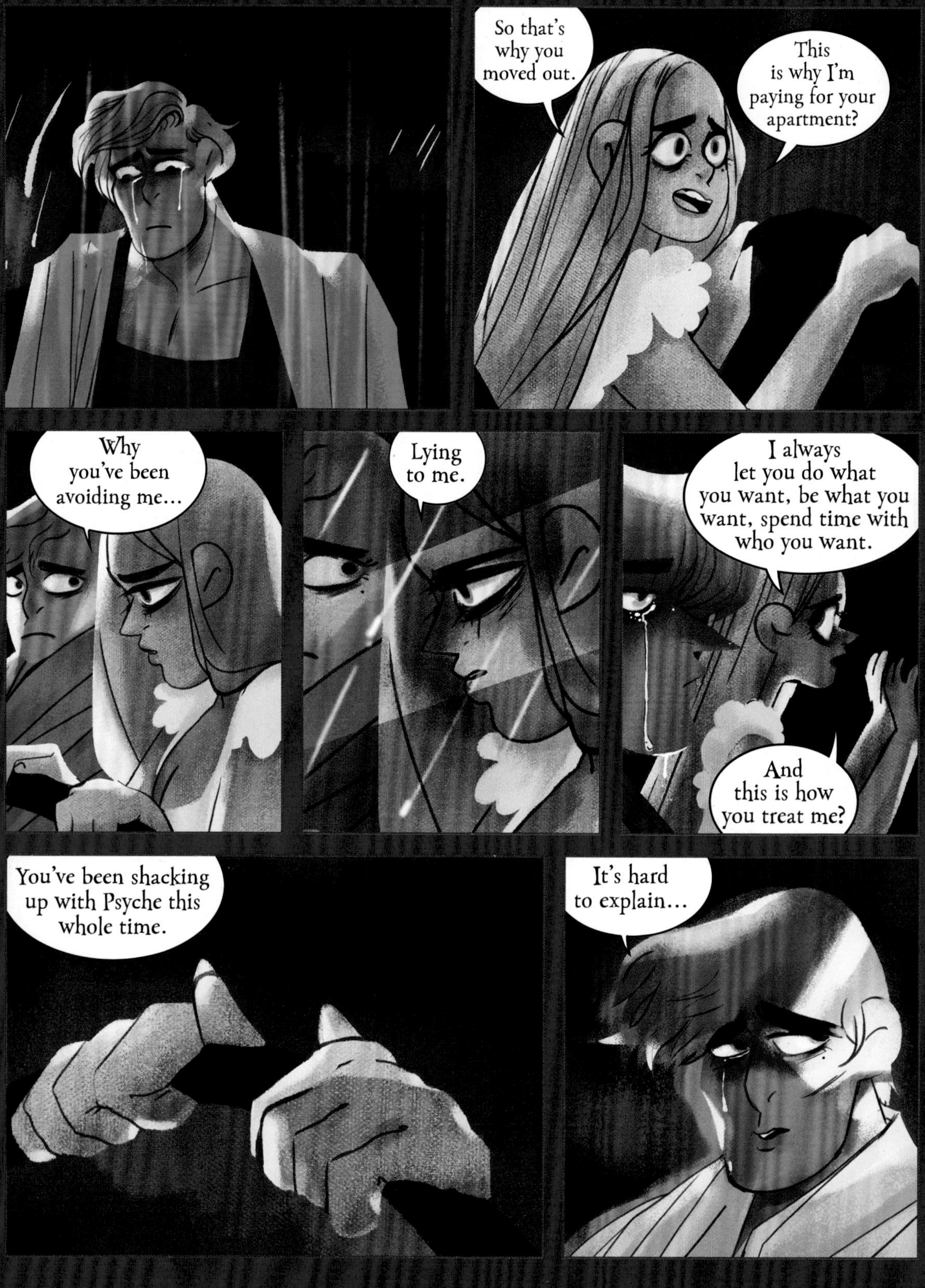
So that's why you moved out.
This is why I'm paying for your apartment?
Why you've been avoiding me...
Lying to me.
I always let you do what you want, be what you want, spend time with who you want.
And this is how you treat me?
You've been shacking up with Psyche this whole time.
It's hard to explain...

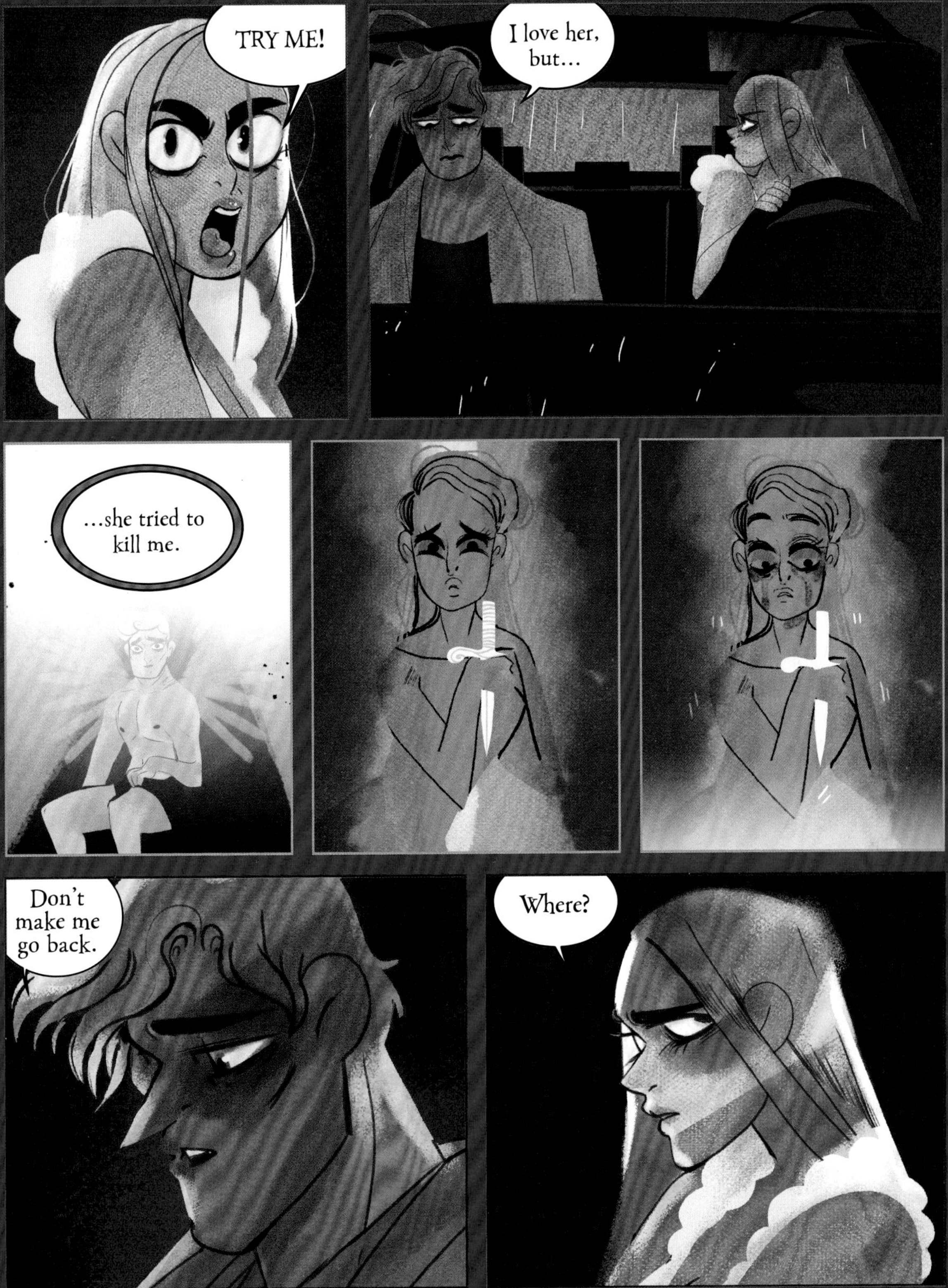
TRY ME!
I love her, but…
…she tried to kill me.
Don't make me go back.
Where?

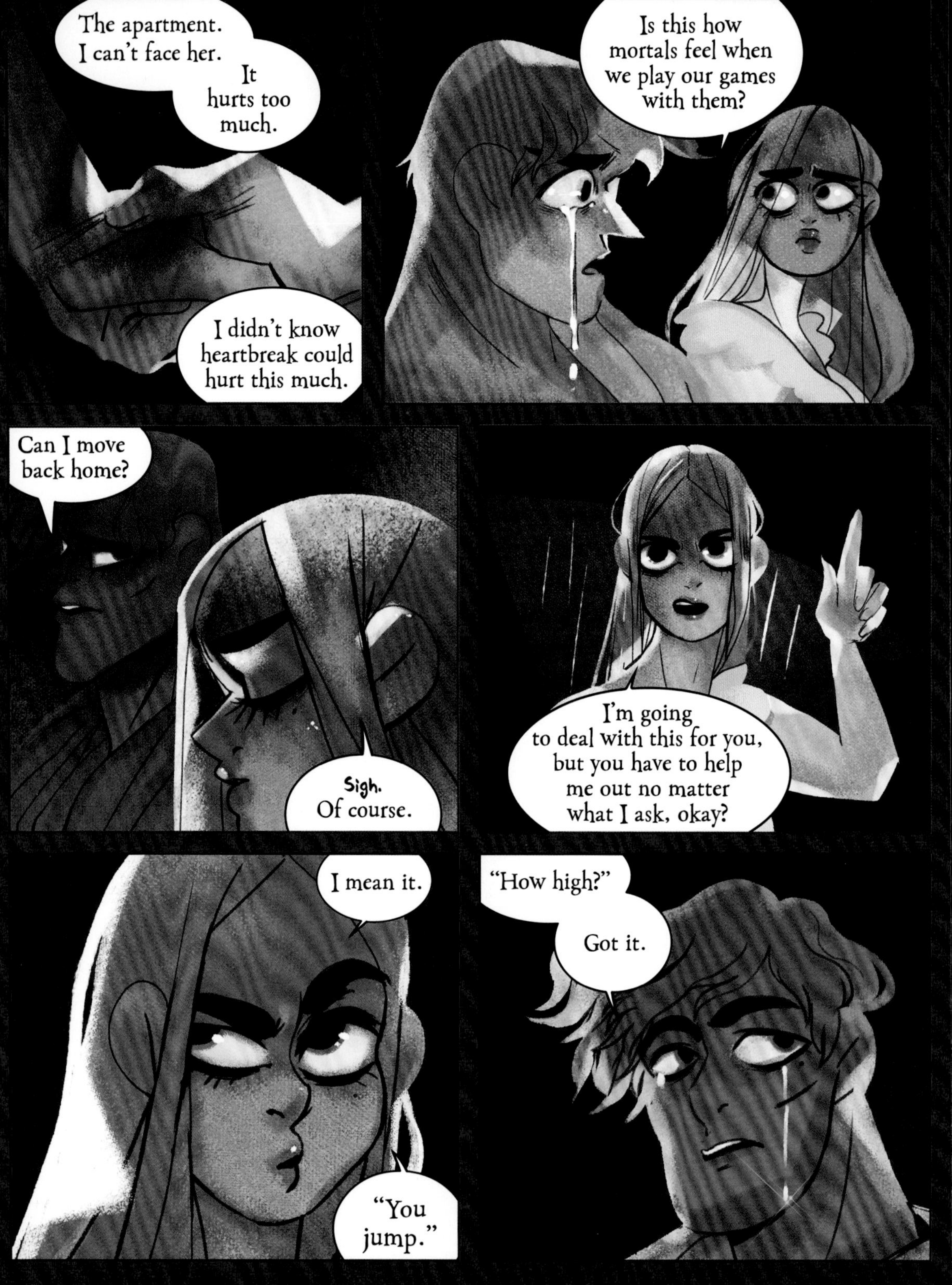
The apartment. I can't face her.
It hurts too much.
I didn't know heartbreak could hurt this much.
Is this how mortals feel when we play our games with them?
Can I move back home?
Sigh.
Of course.
I'm going to deal with this for you, but you have to help me out no matter what I ask, okay?
I mean it.
"You jump."
"How high?"
Got it.

EPISODE 70: MA-IN-LAW

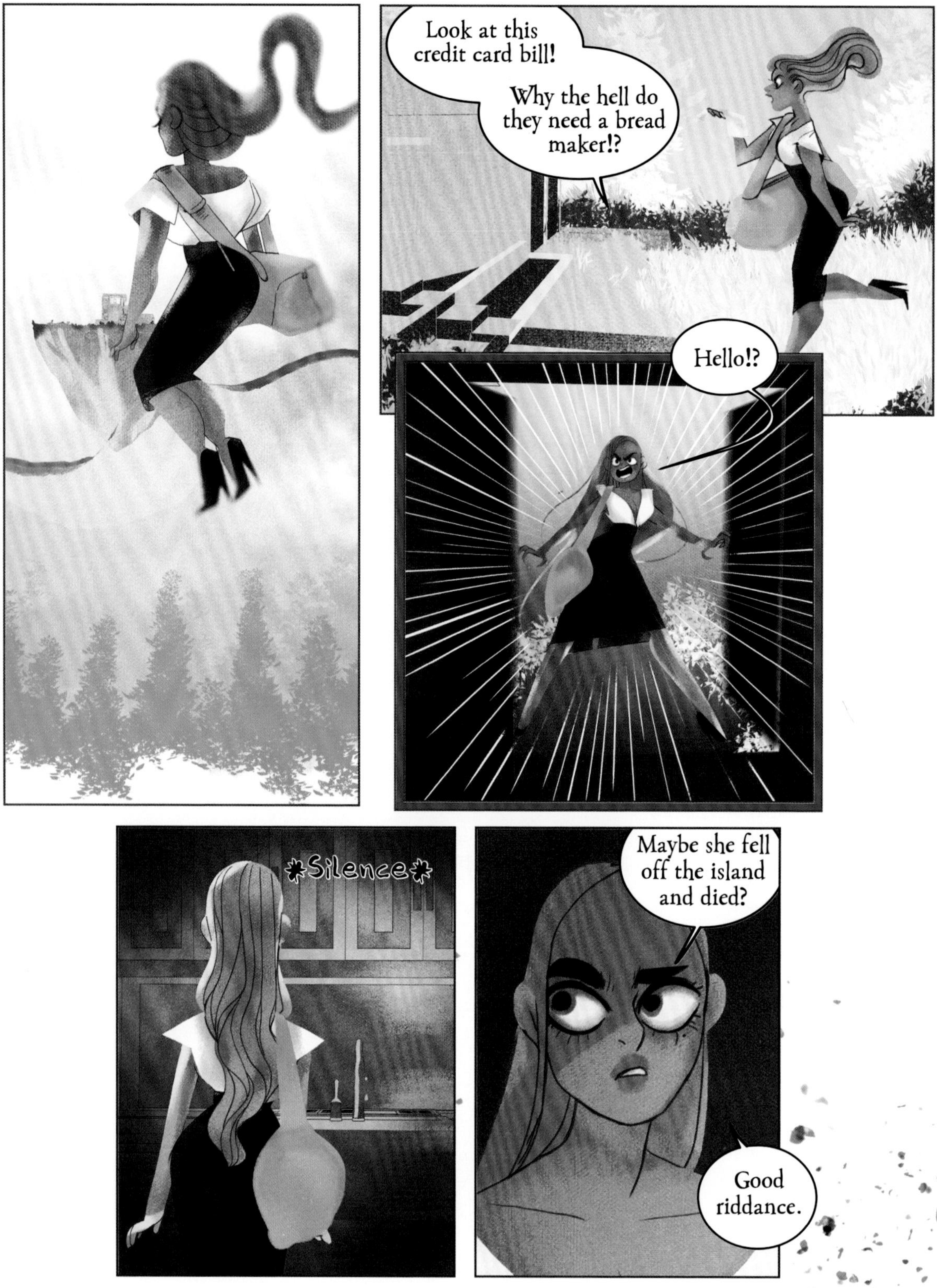
Look at this credit card bill!
Why the hell do they need a bread maker!?
Hello!?
Silence
Maybe she fell off the island and died?
Good riddance.

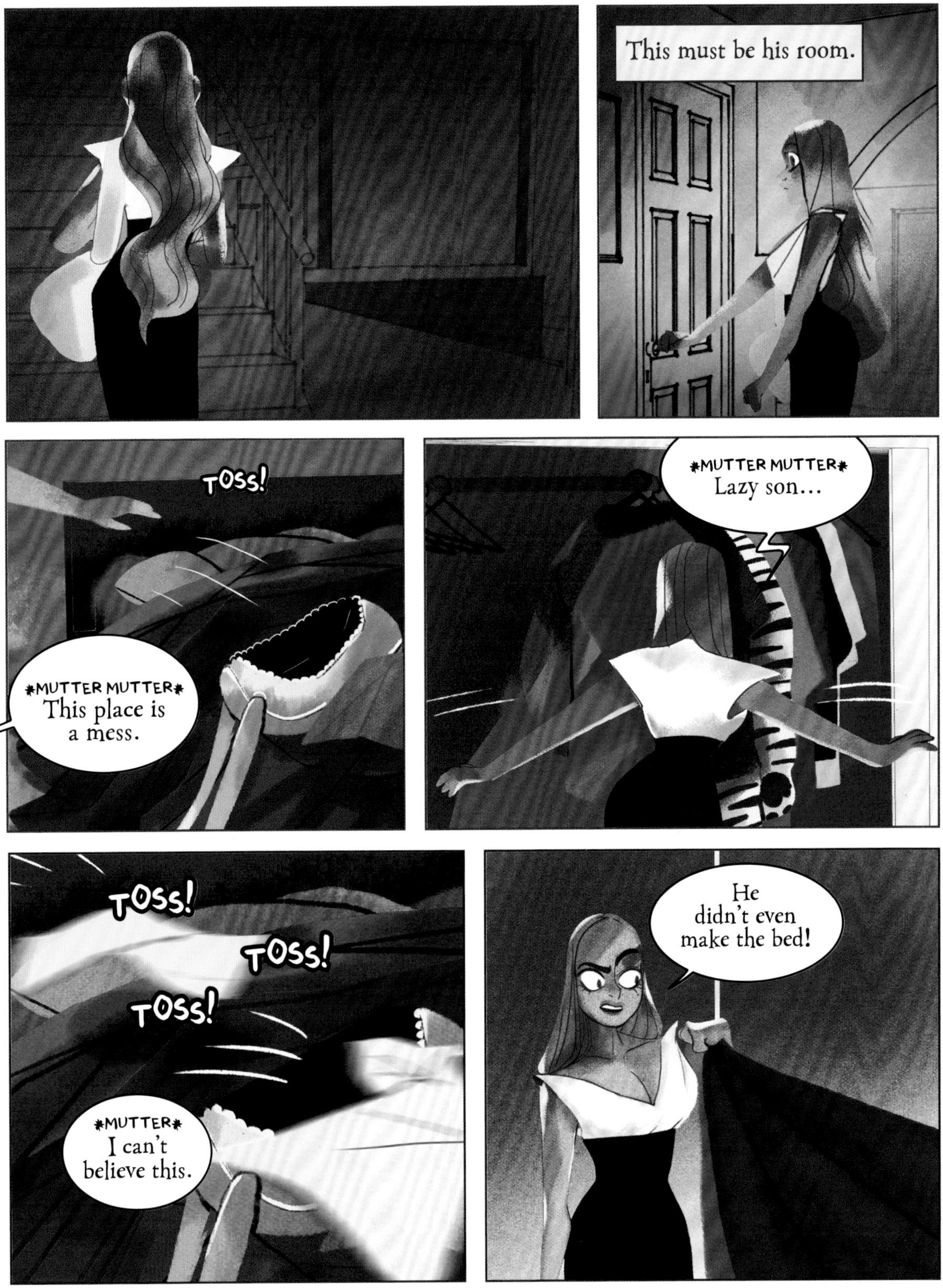
This must be his room.
TOSS!
MUTTER MUTTER This place is a mess.
MUTTER MUTTER Lazy son...
TOSS!
TOSS!
TOSS!
MUTTER I can't believe this.
He didn't even make the bed!

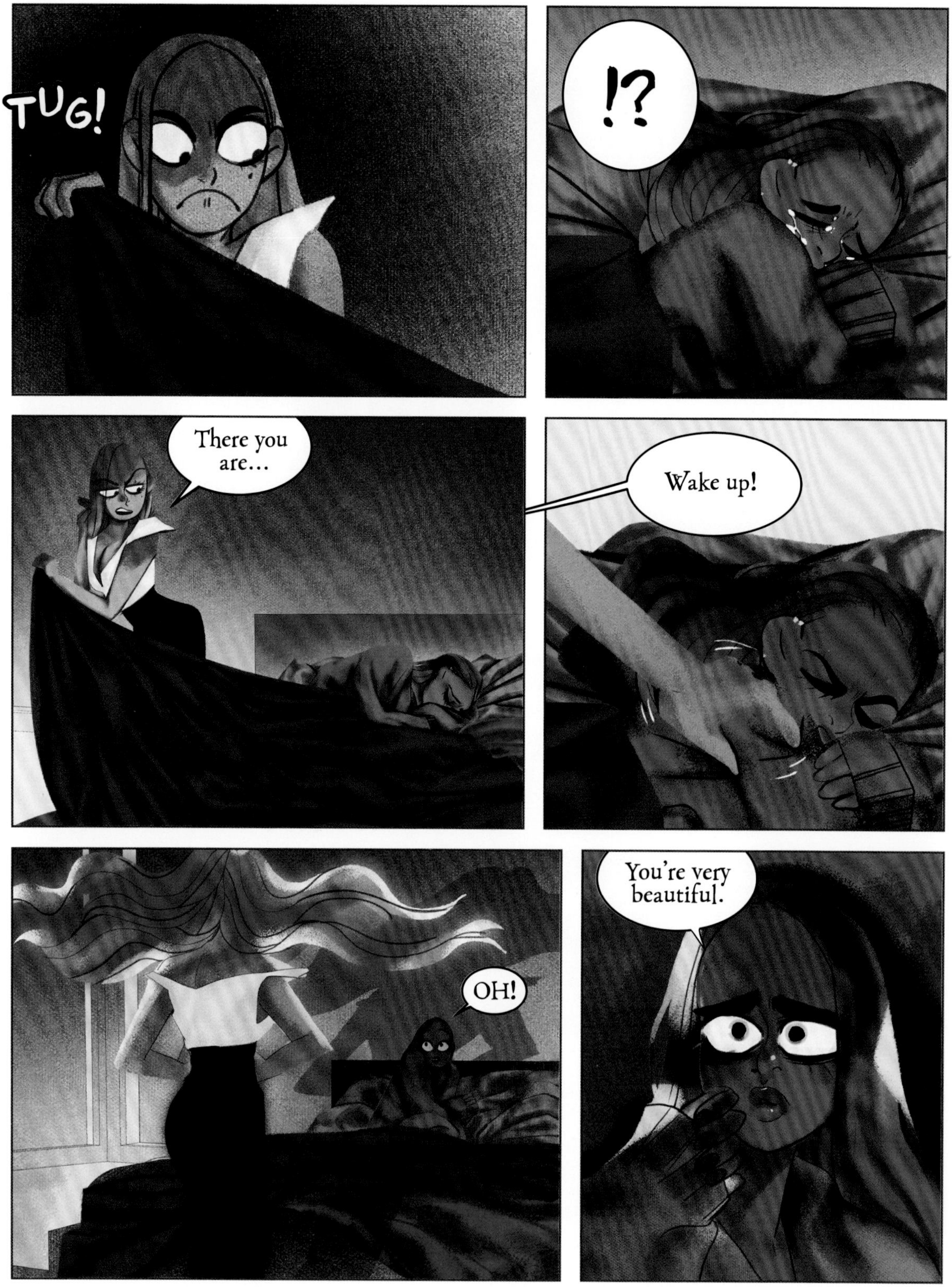
TUG!
!?
There you are...
Wake up!
OH!
You're very beautiful.

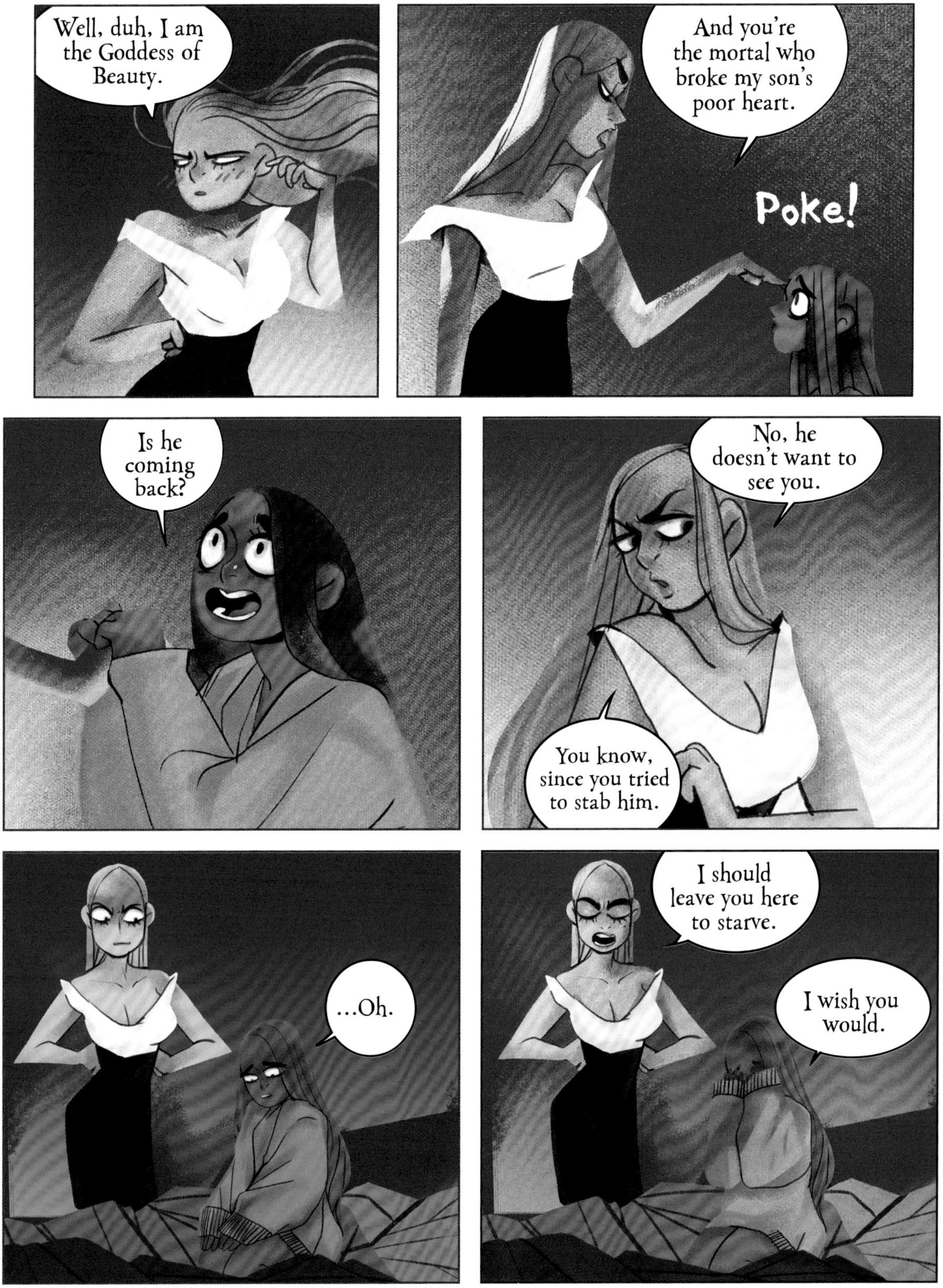
Well, duh, I am the Goddess of Beauty.
And you're the mortal who broke my son's poor heart.
Poke!
Is he coming back?
No, he doesn't want to see you.
You know, since you tried to stab him.
...Oh.
I should leave you here to starve.
I wish you would.

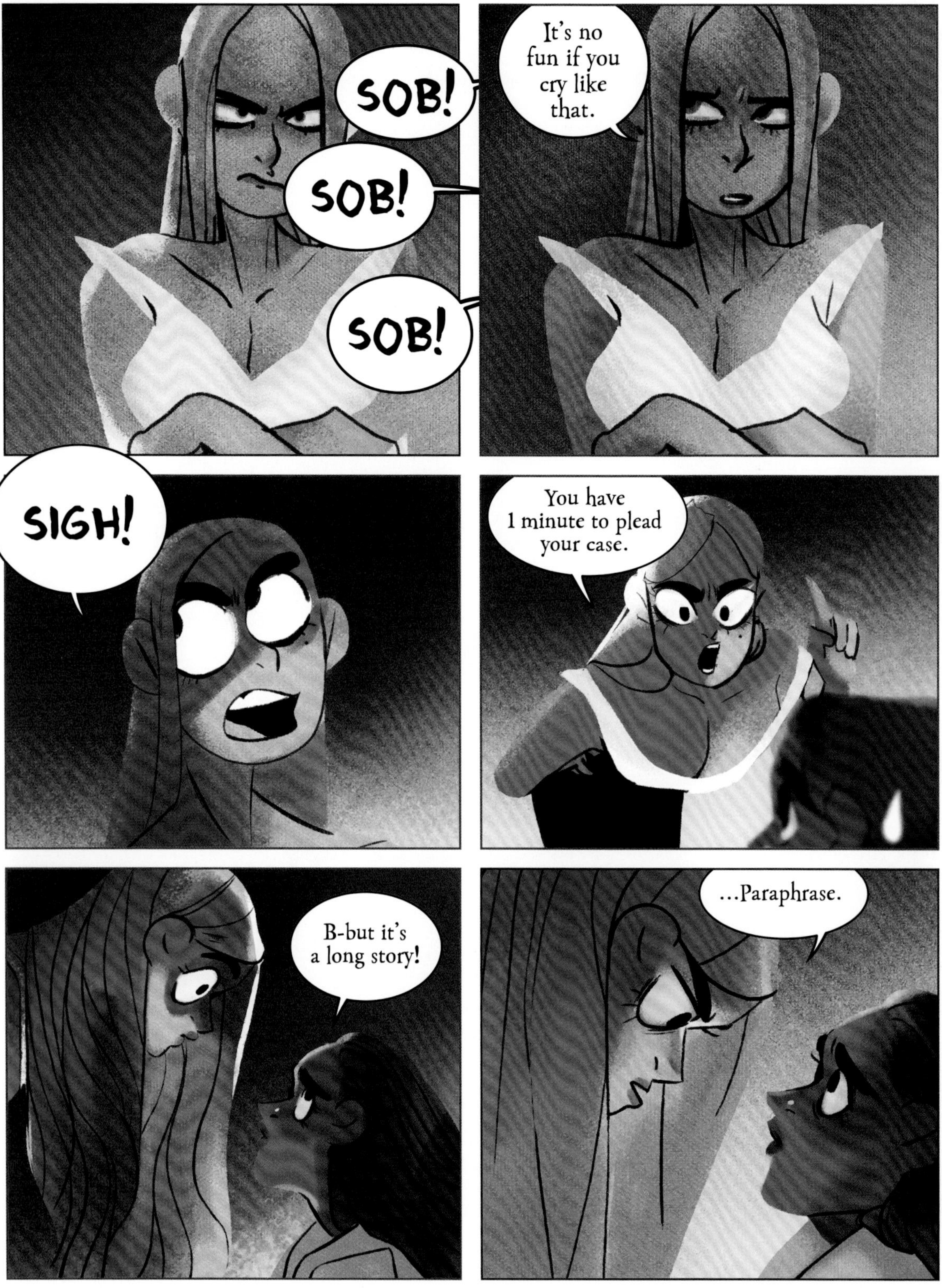
SOB!
SOB!
SOB!
It's no fun if you cry like that.
SIGH!
You have 1 minute to plead your case.
B-but it's a long story!
...Paraphrase.

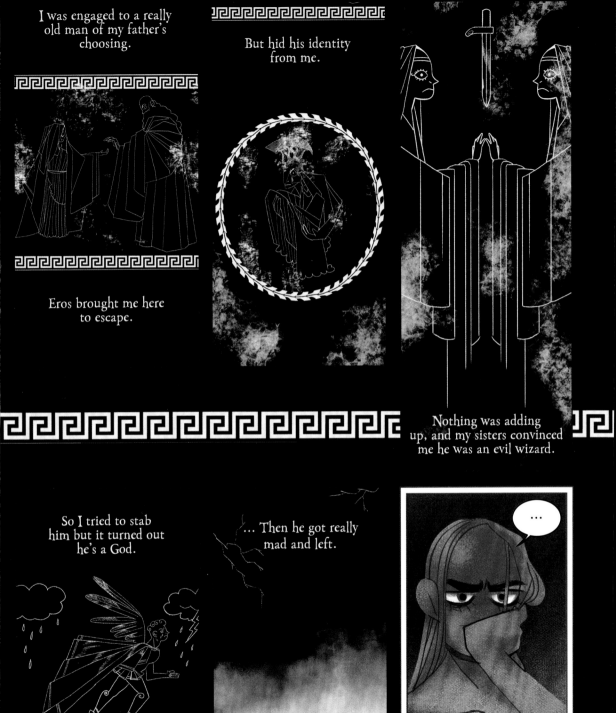

I was engaged to a really old man of my father's choosing.

But hid his identity from me.

Eros brought me here to escape.

Nothing was adding up, and my sisters convinced me he was an evil wizard.

So I tried to stab him but it turned out he's a God.

... Then he got really mad and left.

...

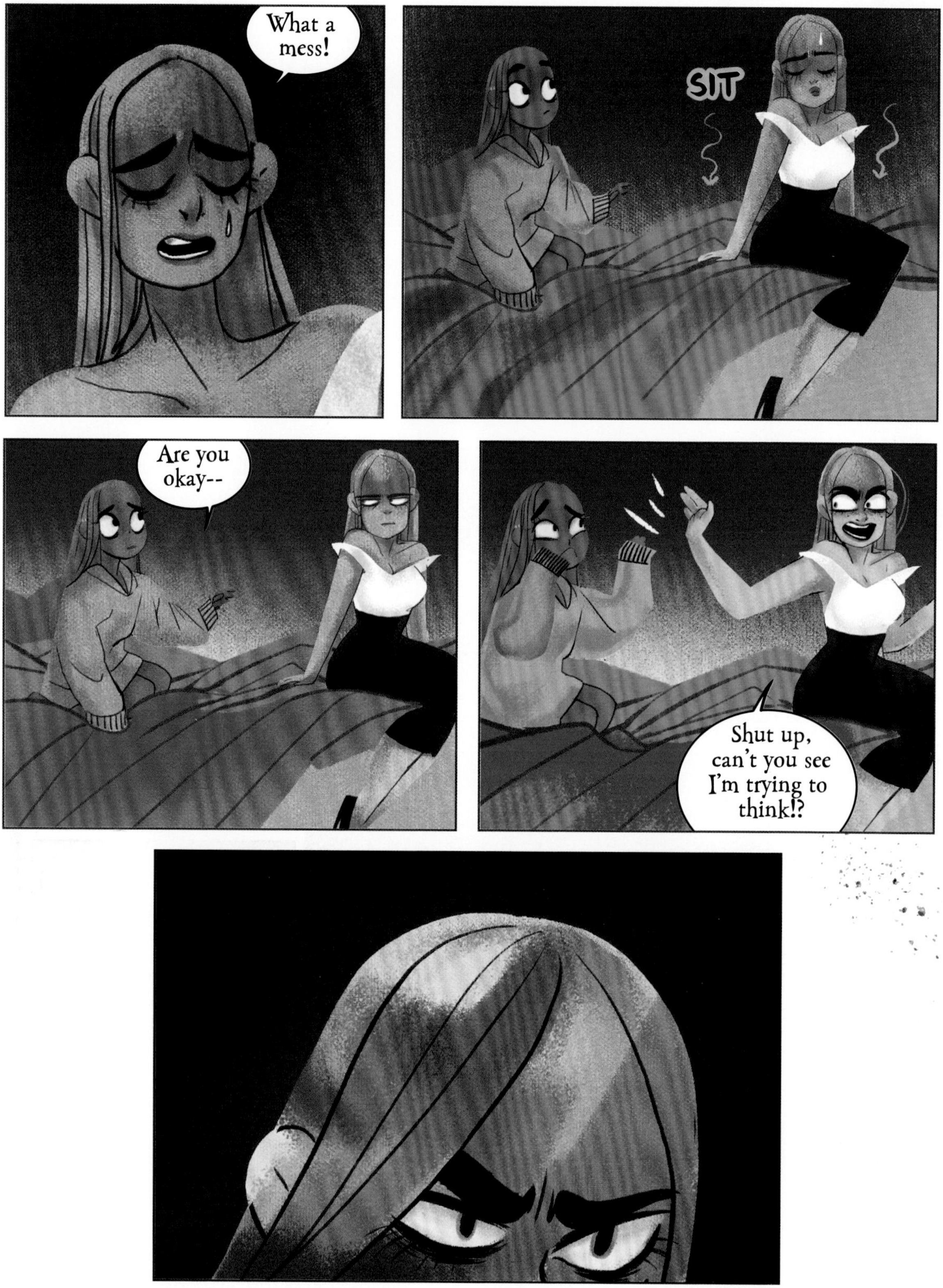
What a mess!
SIT
Are you okay--
Shut up, can't you see I'm trying to think!?

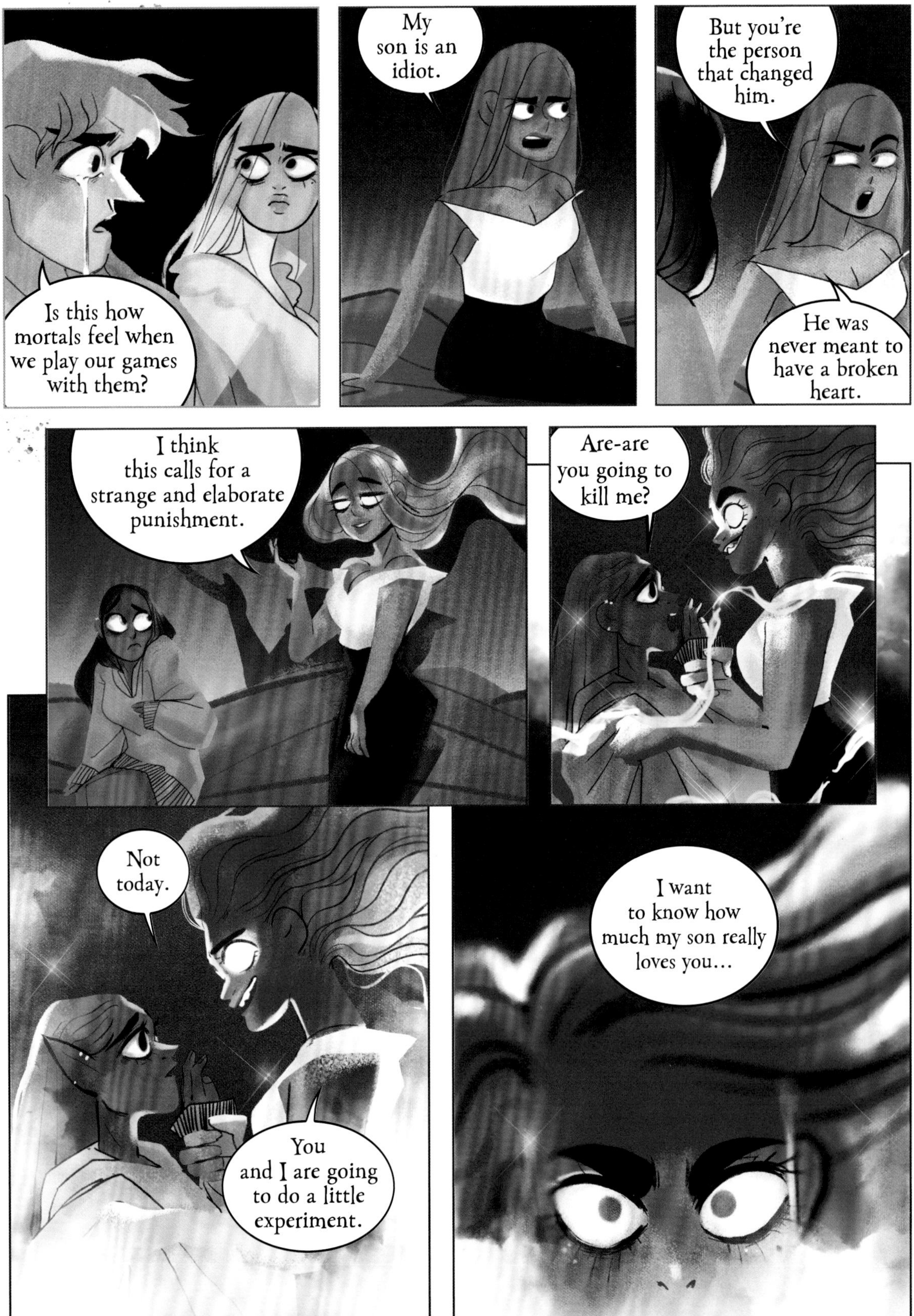
Is this how mortals feel when we play our games with them?
My son is an idiot.
But you're the person that changed him.
He was never meant to have a broken heart.
I think this calls for a strange and elaborate punishment.
Are-are you going to kill me?
Not today.
You and I are going to do a little experiment.
I want to know how much my son really loves you...

PREVIOUSLY ON LORE OLYMPUS

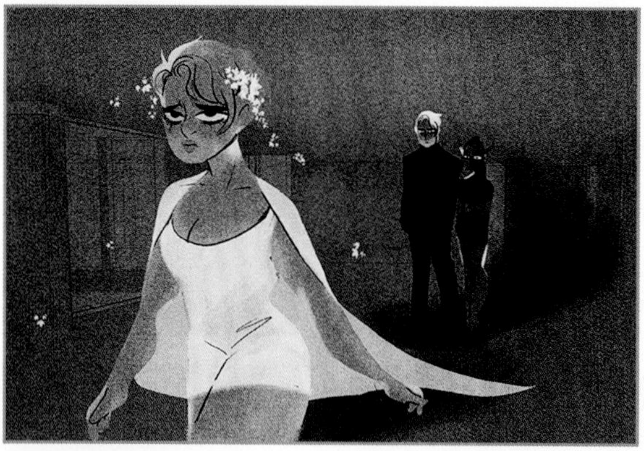

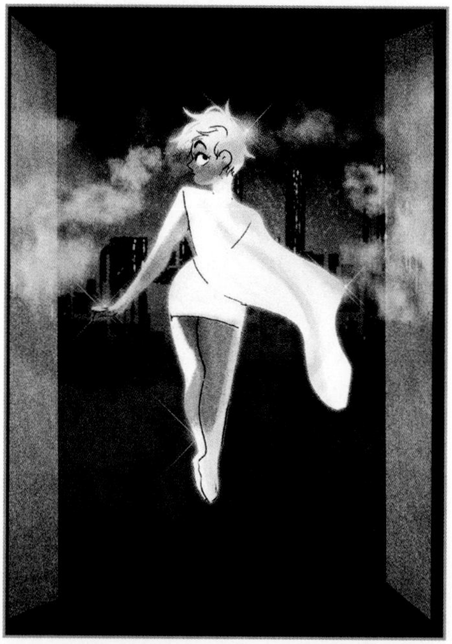

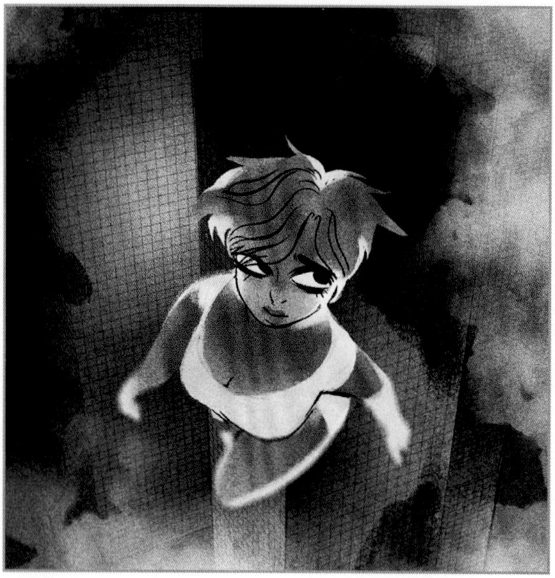

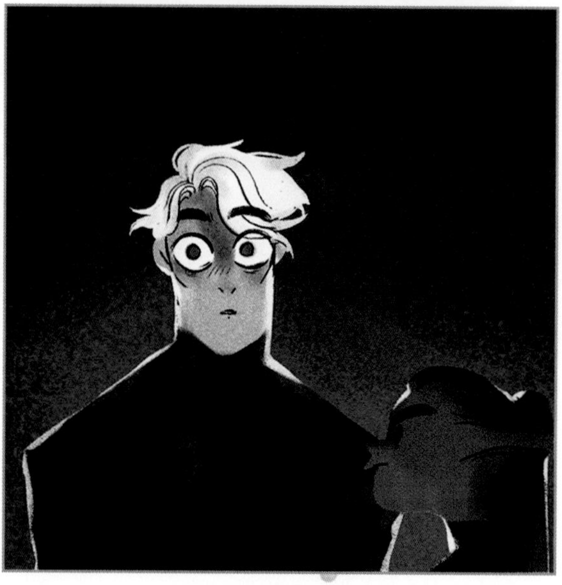

AND NOW...

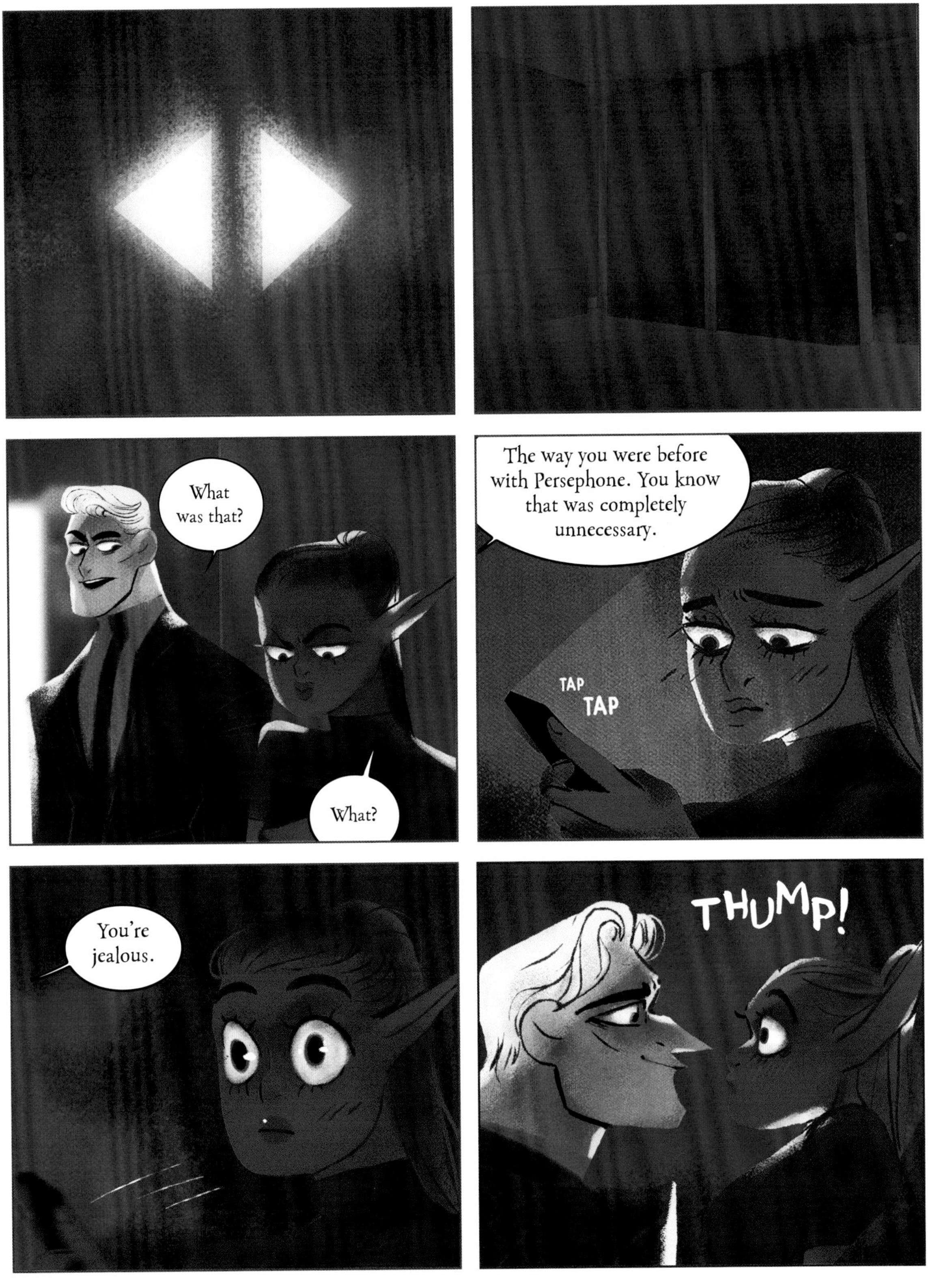
What was that?
What?
The way you were before with Persephone. You know that was completely unnecessary.
TAP TAP
You're jealous.
THUMP!

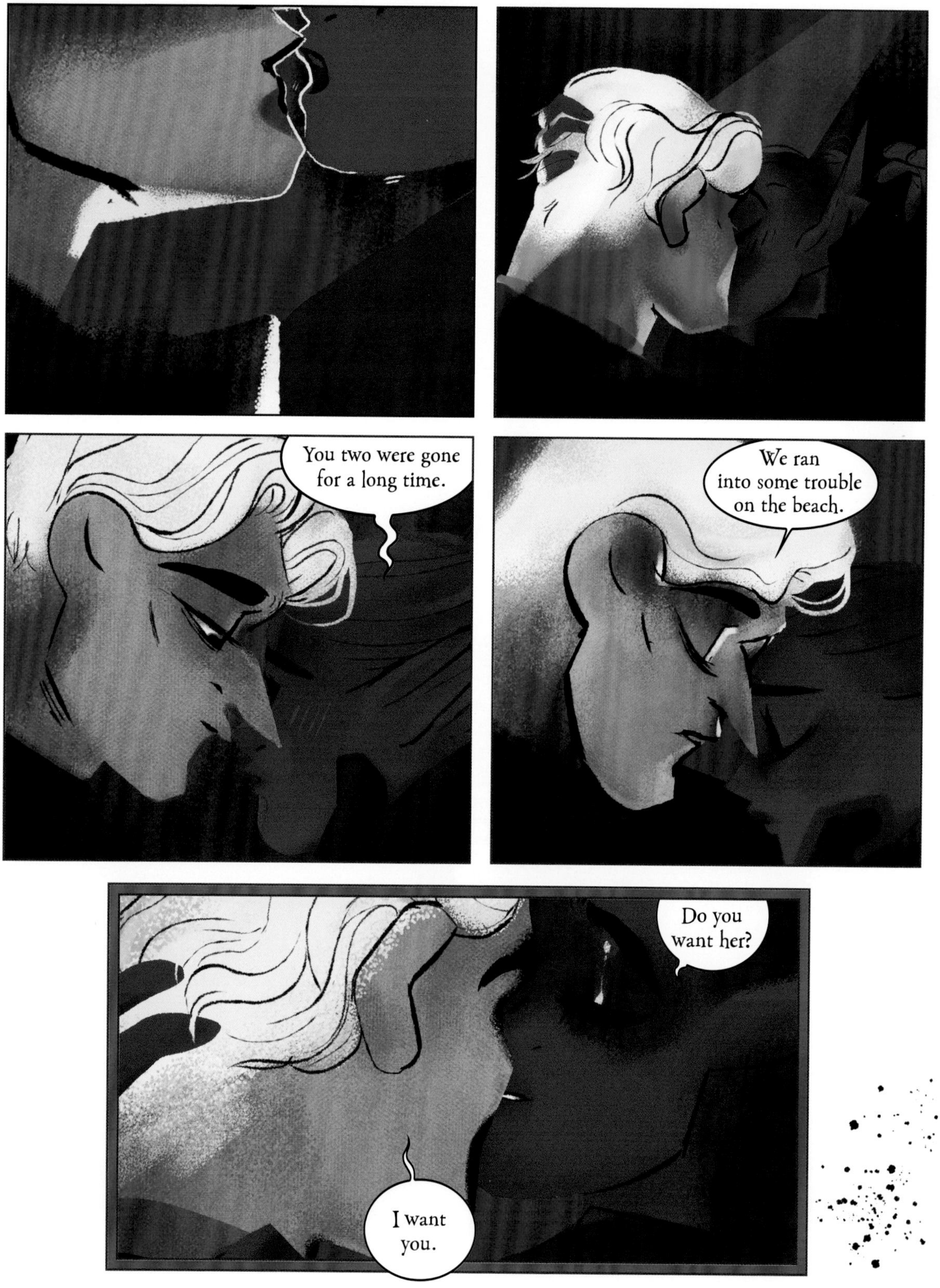
You two were gone for a long time.
We ran into some trouble on the beach.
Do you want her?
I want you.

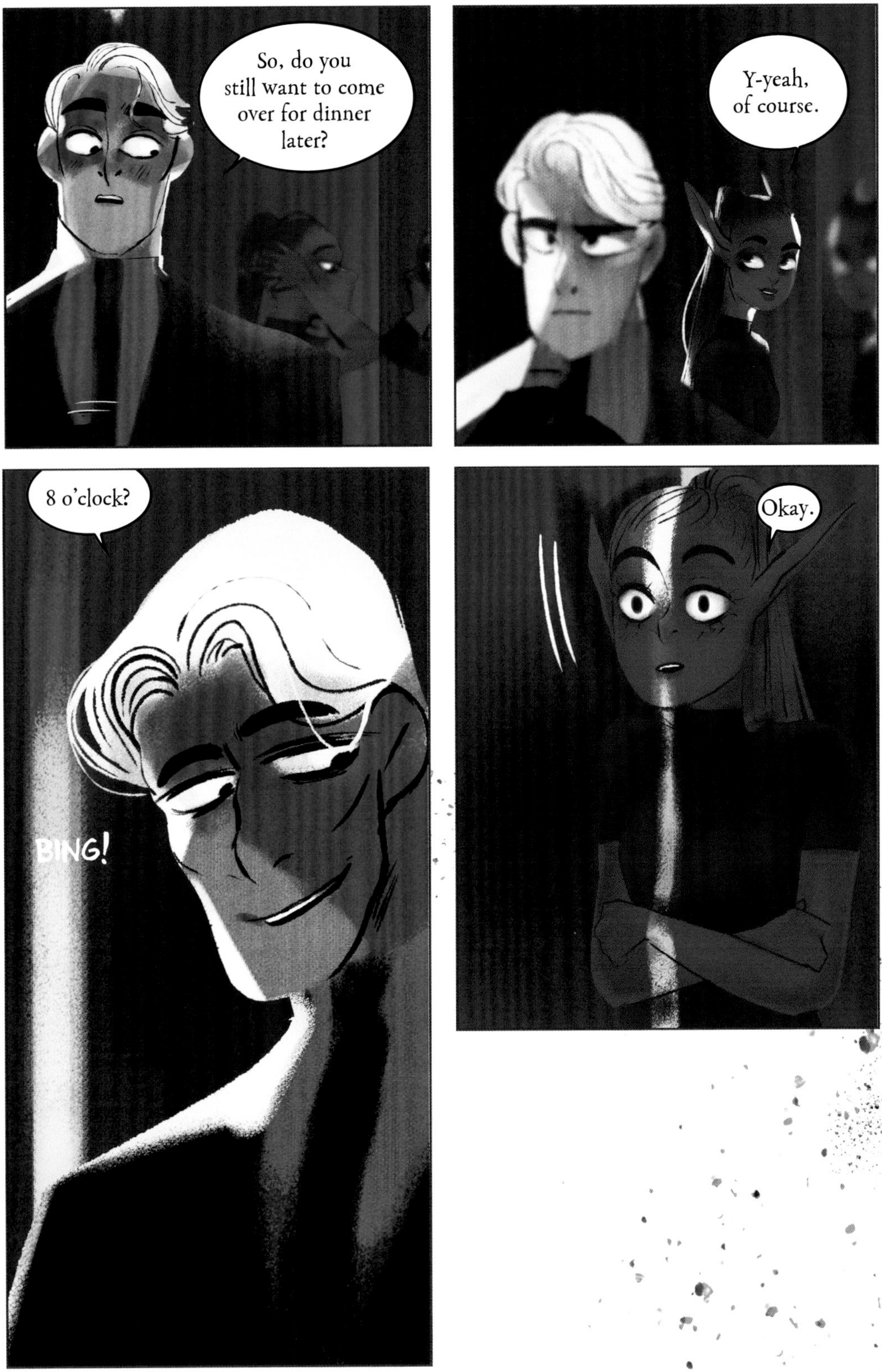
So, do you still want to come over for dinner later?
Y-yeah, of course.
8 o'clock?
BING!
Okay.

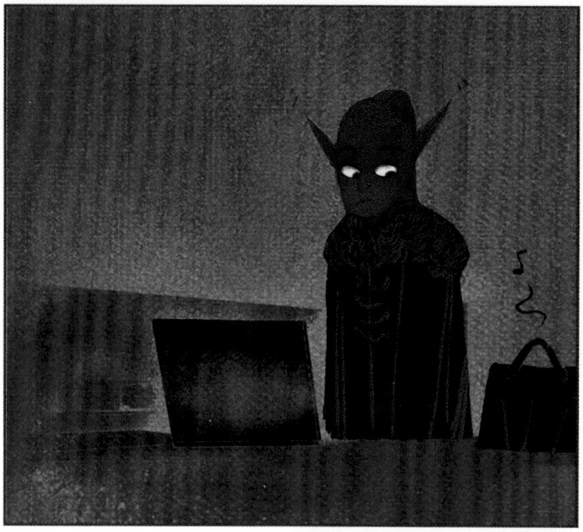

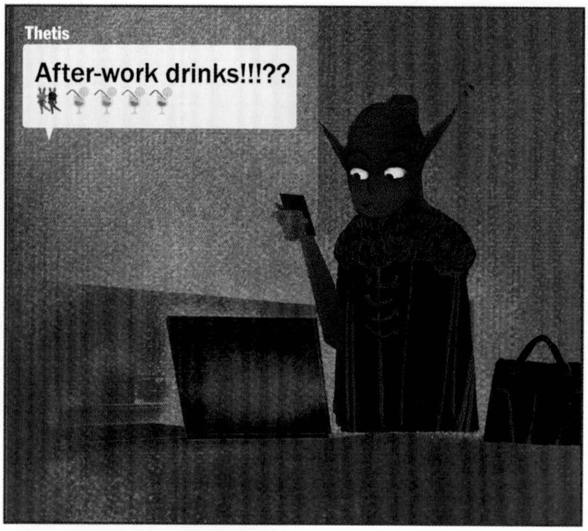
Thetis
After-work drinks!!!??

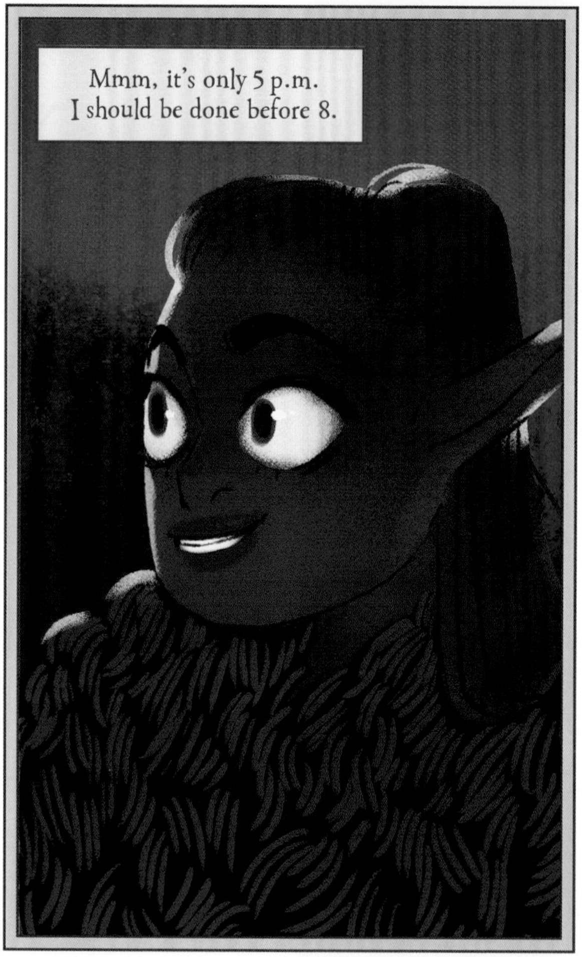
Mmm, it's only 5 p.m.
I should be done before 8.

EPISODE 71: LET DOWN

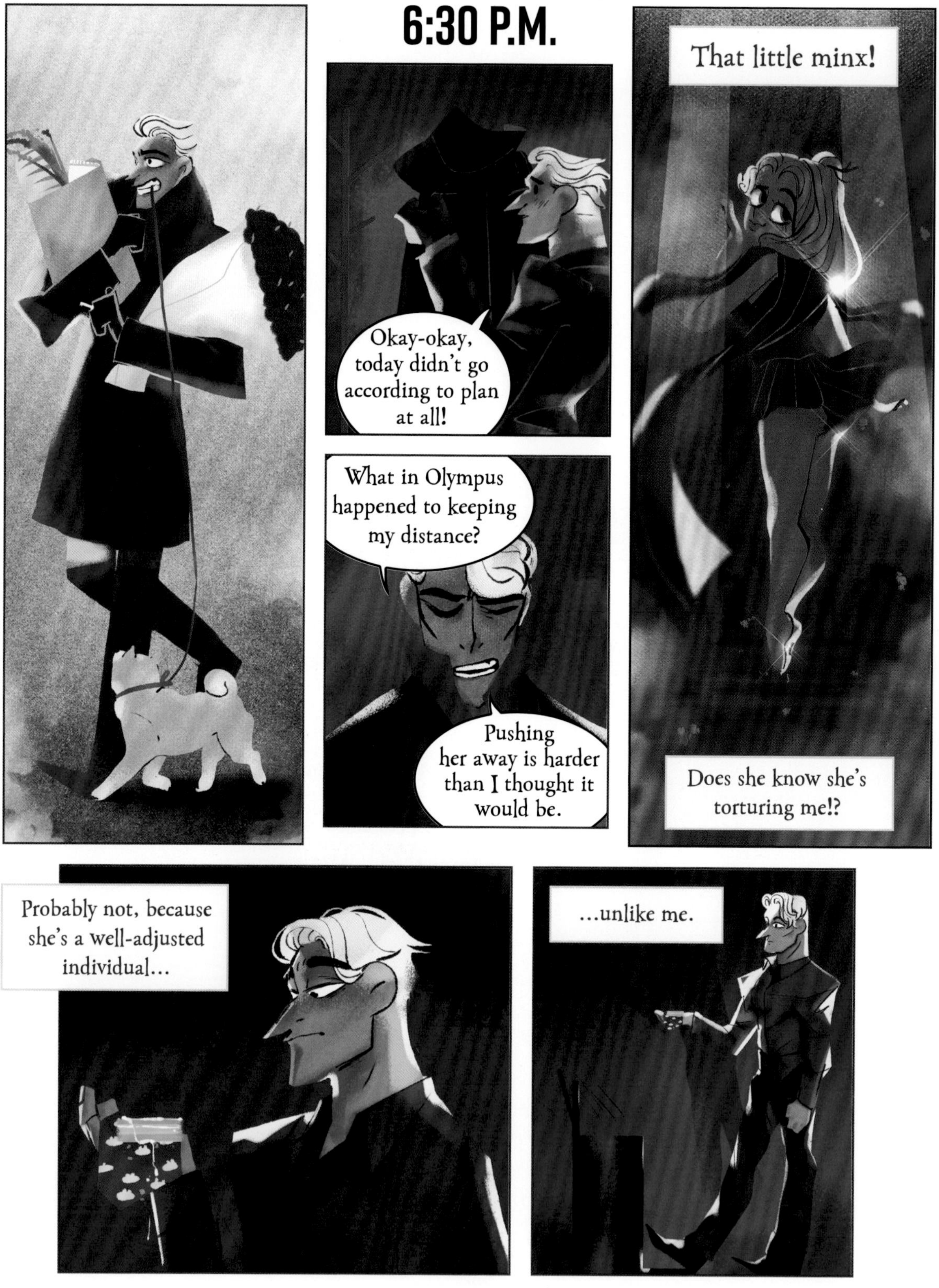
6:30 P.M.
Okay-okay, today didn't go according to plan at all!
What in Olympus happened to keeping my distance?
Pushing her away is harder than I thought it would be.
That little minx!
Does she know she's torturing me!?
Probably not, because she's a well-adjusted individual...
...unlike me.

Nobody's ever made something like this for me before.

It feels wrong to throw it away.

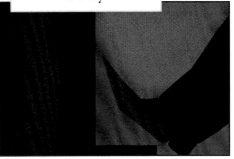

It feels wrong to eat it.

6:50 P.M.

Hey, Tadpole, did you want me to pick you up later?

BARK!

BARK!

Guess I'd better get ready.

BARK!
BARK!
BARK!
BARK!
BARK!
BARK!
BARK!
BARK!
BARK!

WOULD YA GIVE IT A REST? CAN'T I HAVE A MOMENT TO MYSELF?

7:10 P.M

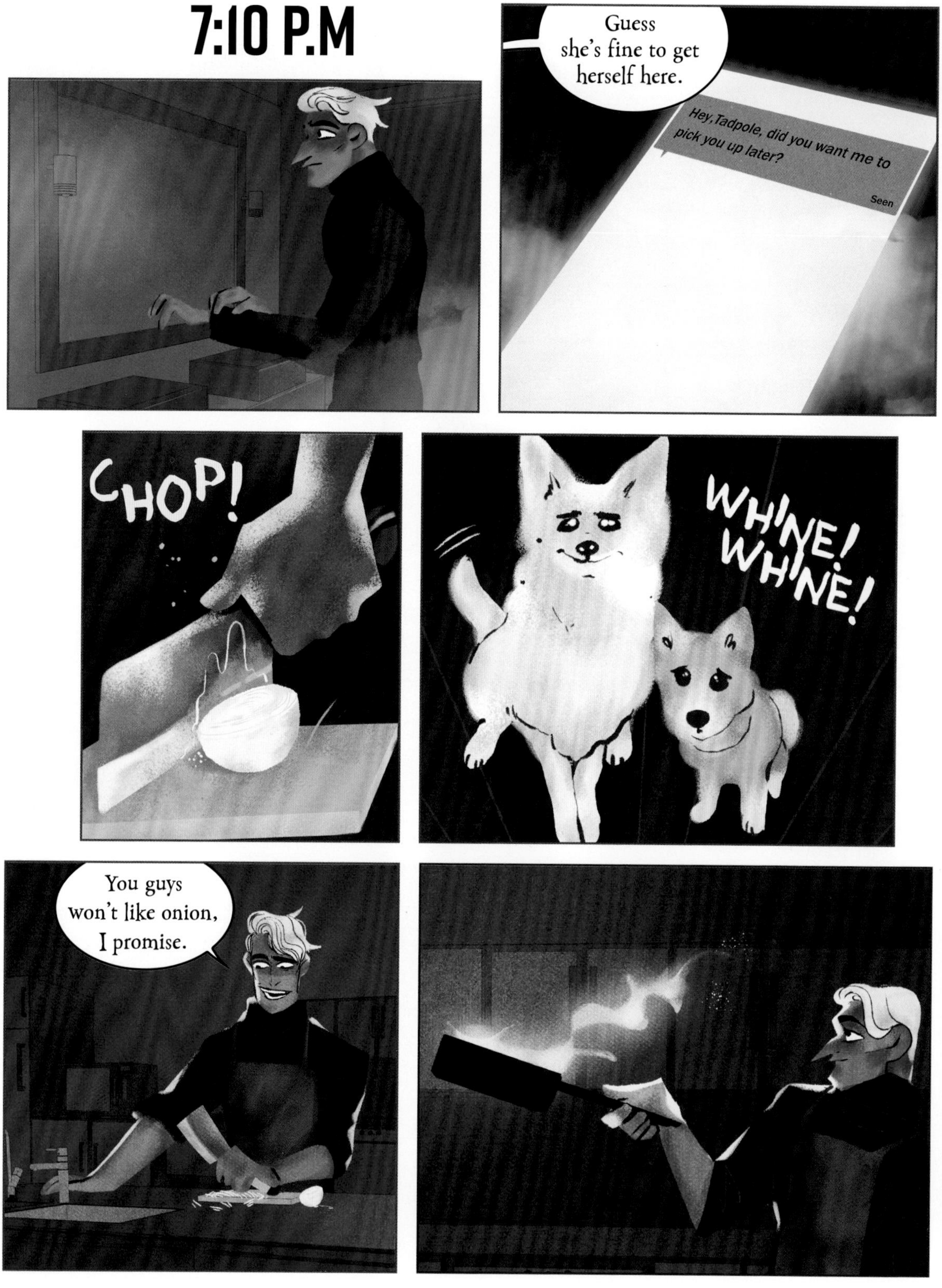
Guess she's fine to get herself here.
Hey,Tadpole, did you want me to pick you up later?
Seen
CHOP!
WHINE! WHINE!
You guys won't like onion, I promise.

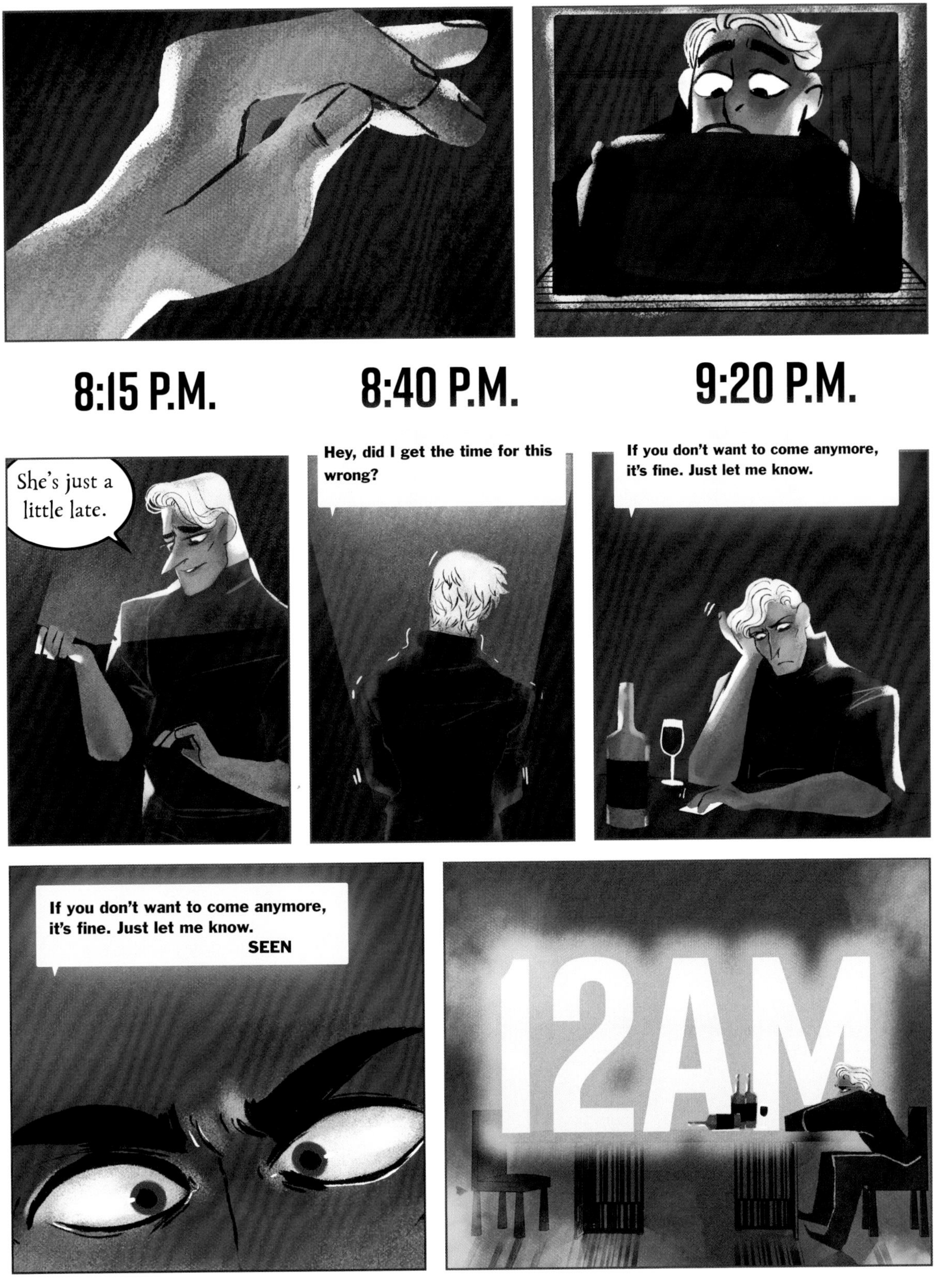
8:15 P.M.
8:40 P.M.
9:20 P.M.
She's just a little late.
Hey, did I get the time for this wrong?
If you don't want to come anymore, it's fine. Just let me know.
If you don't want to come anymore, it's fine. Just let me know.
SEEN
12AM

I've spent entire lifetimes outrunning that deep feeling of loneliness.

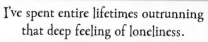

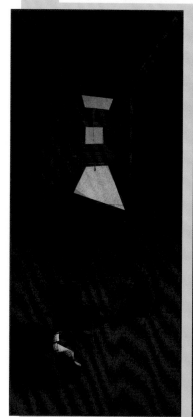

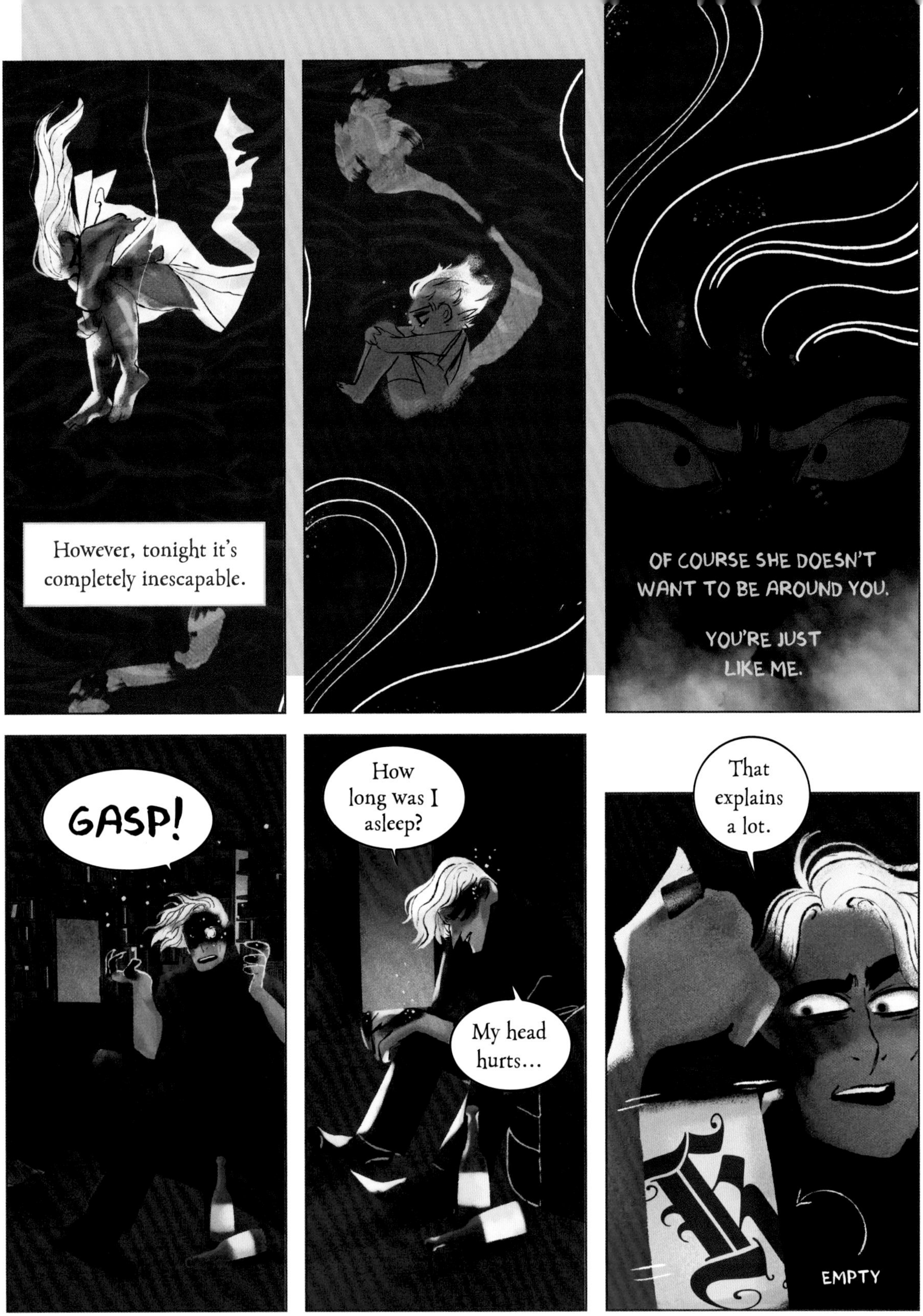

However, tonight it's completely inescapable.
OF COURSE SHE DOESN'T WANT TO BE AROUND YOU.
YOU'RE JUST LIKE ME.
GASP!
How long was I asleep?
My head hurts...
That explains a lot.
EMPTY

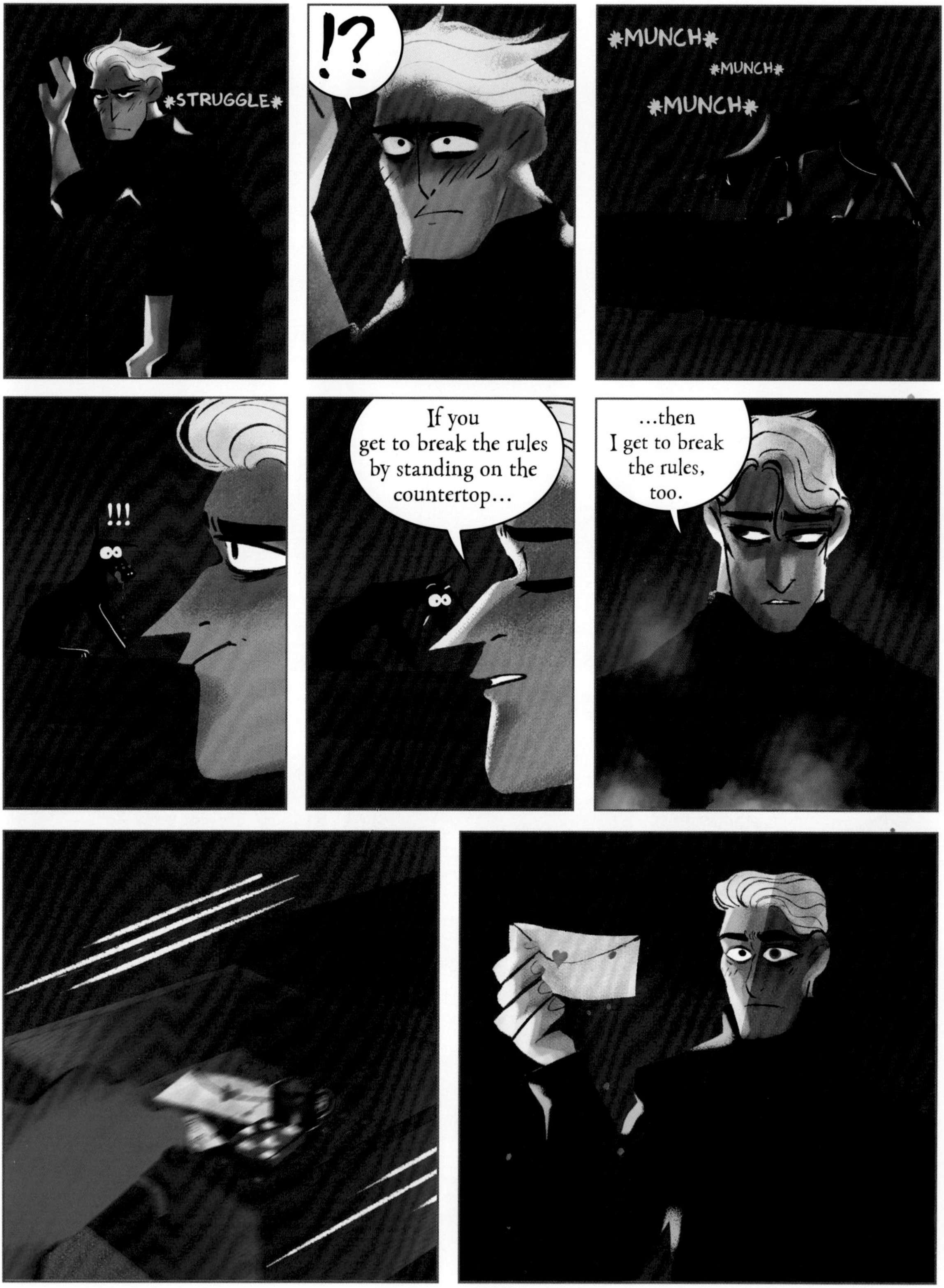
STRUGGLE
!?
MUNCH
MUNCH
MUNCH
!!!
If you get to break the rules by standing on the countertop...
...then I get to break the rules, too.

PREVIOUSLY ON

LORE OLYMPUS

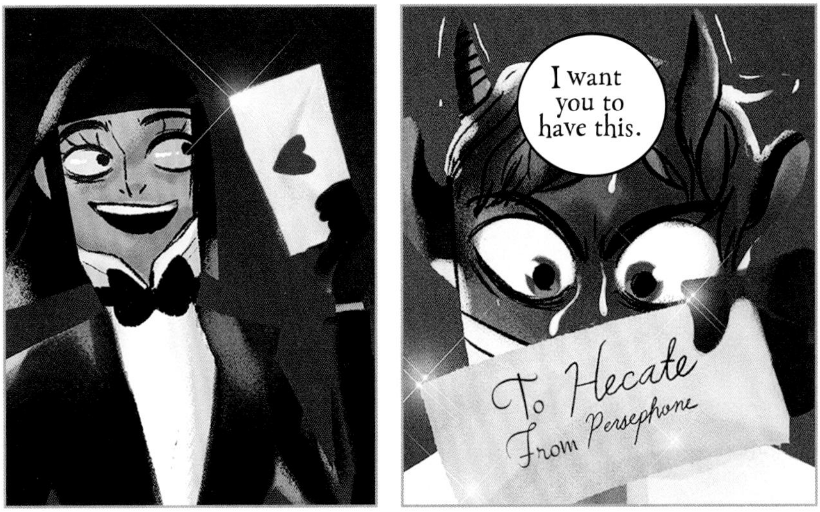
I want you to have this.
To Hecate
From Persephone

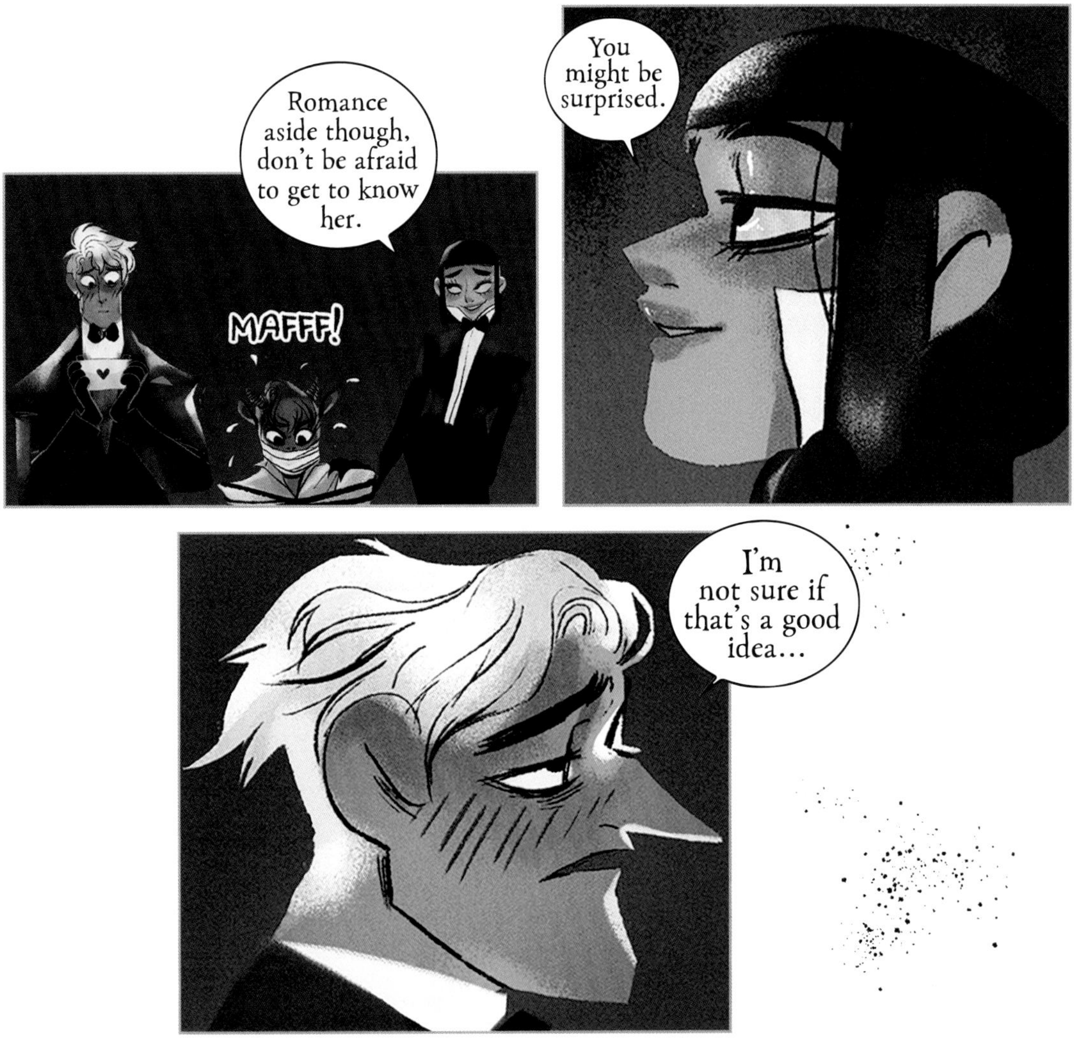
Romance aside though, don't be afraid to get to know her.
MAFFF!
You might be surprised.
I'm not sure if that's a good idea...

I'm going to eat this baklava, and then I'm going to read this letter that isn't addressed to me.

To Hecate
From Persephone

Of course, it's perfectly delicious!

MUNCH Lousy Hermes *MUNCH*

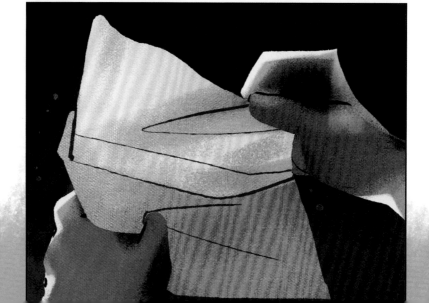

Dear Hecate...

How is everything? I'm sorry you had to cut your visit with us short, I miss your company very much.

I'm so sorry Mother was mad about your surprise guest. She just doesn't want men on the property because of me.

I hope the King of the Underworld didn't have too nasty of a hangover.

WHAT!????

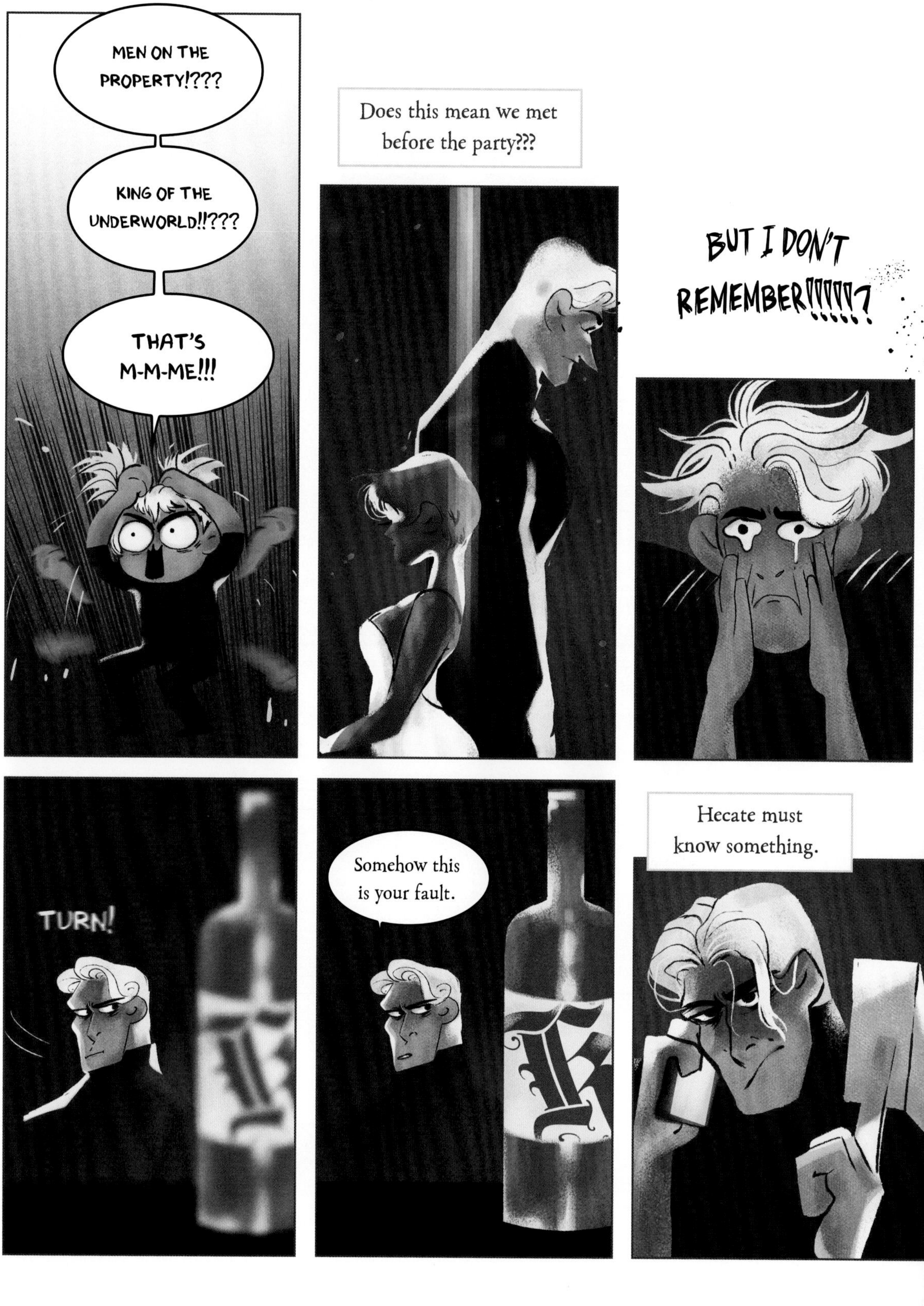
MEN ON THE PROPERTY!???
KING OF THE UNDERWORLD!!???
THAT'S M-M-ME!!!
Does this mean we met before the party???
BUT I DON'T REMEMBER!!!!!?
TURN!
Somehow this is your fault.
Hecate must know something.

EPISODE 72: DEAR HECATE

RING RING!!!
RING RING!!!

HADES
INCOMING

What is
your crisis,
Hades?

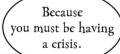

Because
you must be having
a crisis.

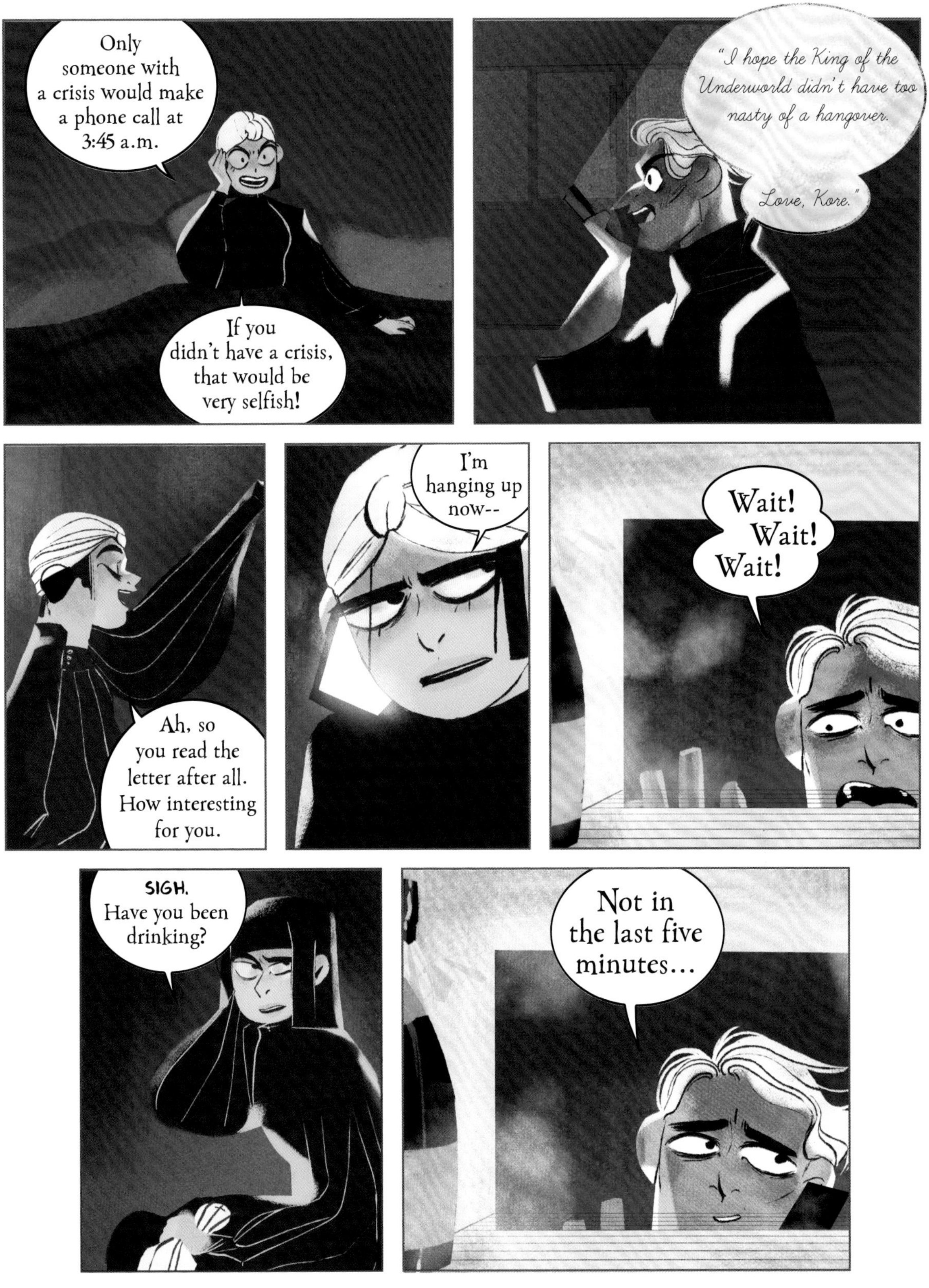
Only someone with a crisis would make a phone call at 3:45 a.m.
If you didn't have a crisis, that would be very selfish!
"I hope the King of the Underworld didn't have too nasty of a hangover.
Love, Kore."
Ah, so you read the letter after all. How interesting for you.
I'm hanging up now--
Wait! Wait! Wait!
SIGH.
Have you been drinking?
Not in the last five minutes...

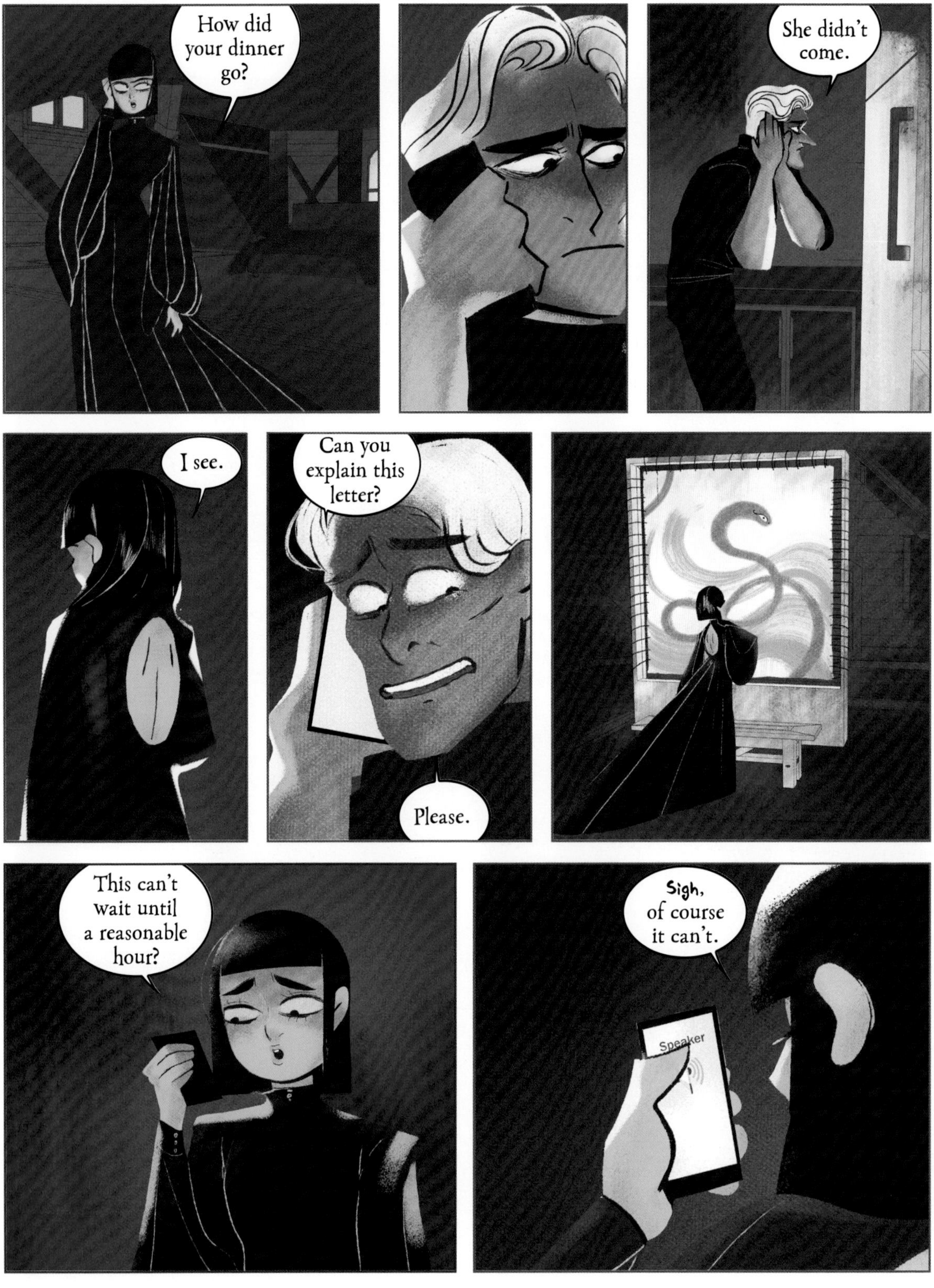
How did your dinner go?
She didn't come.
I see.
Can you explain this letter?
Please.
This can't wait until a reasonable hour?
Speaker
Sigh, of course it can't.

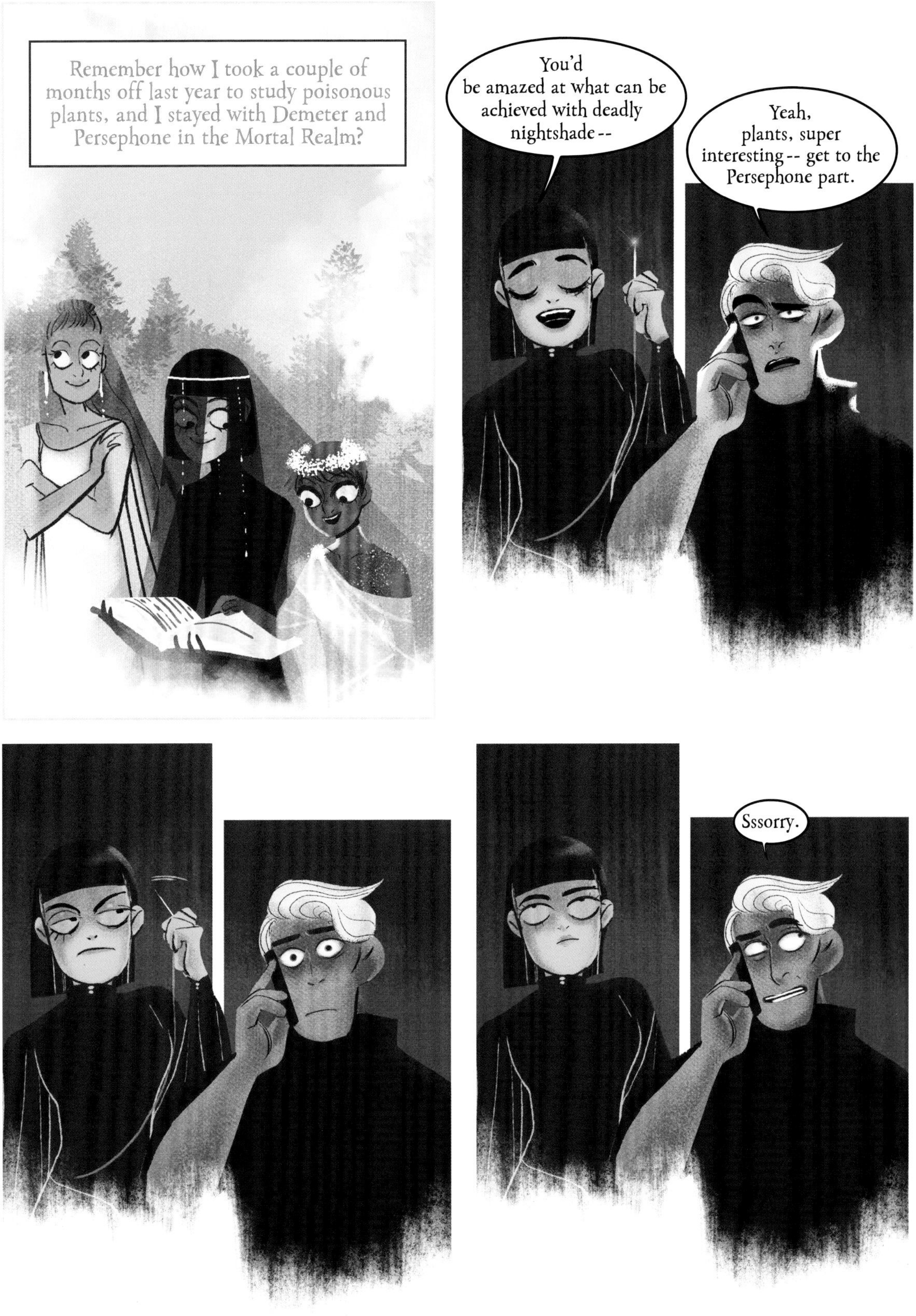
Remember how I took a couple of months off last year to study poisonous plants, and I stayed with Demeter and Persephone in the Mortal Realm?
You'd be amazed at what can be achieved with deadly nightshade --
Yeah, plants, super interesting -- get to the Persephone part.
Sssorry.

One night, you came to visit me out of the blue.

HAHA!

You were... very, very drunk.

Demeter was not happy.

The two of us had to take you back to the Underworld that night.

I don't remember... WHY DIDN'T YOU SAY ANYTHING!?

I didn't want to embarrass you. Your ego is very delicate.

That doesn't explain the Persephone part!

We tried to make sure no one knew you were on the property.

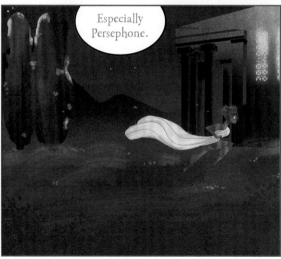

Especially Persephone.

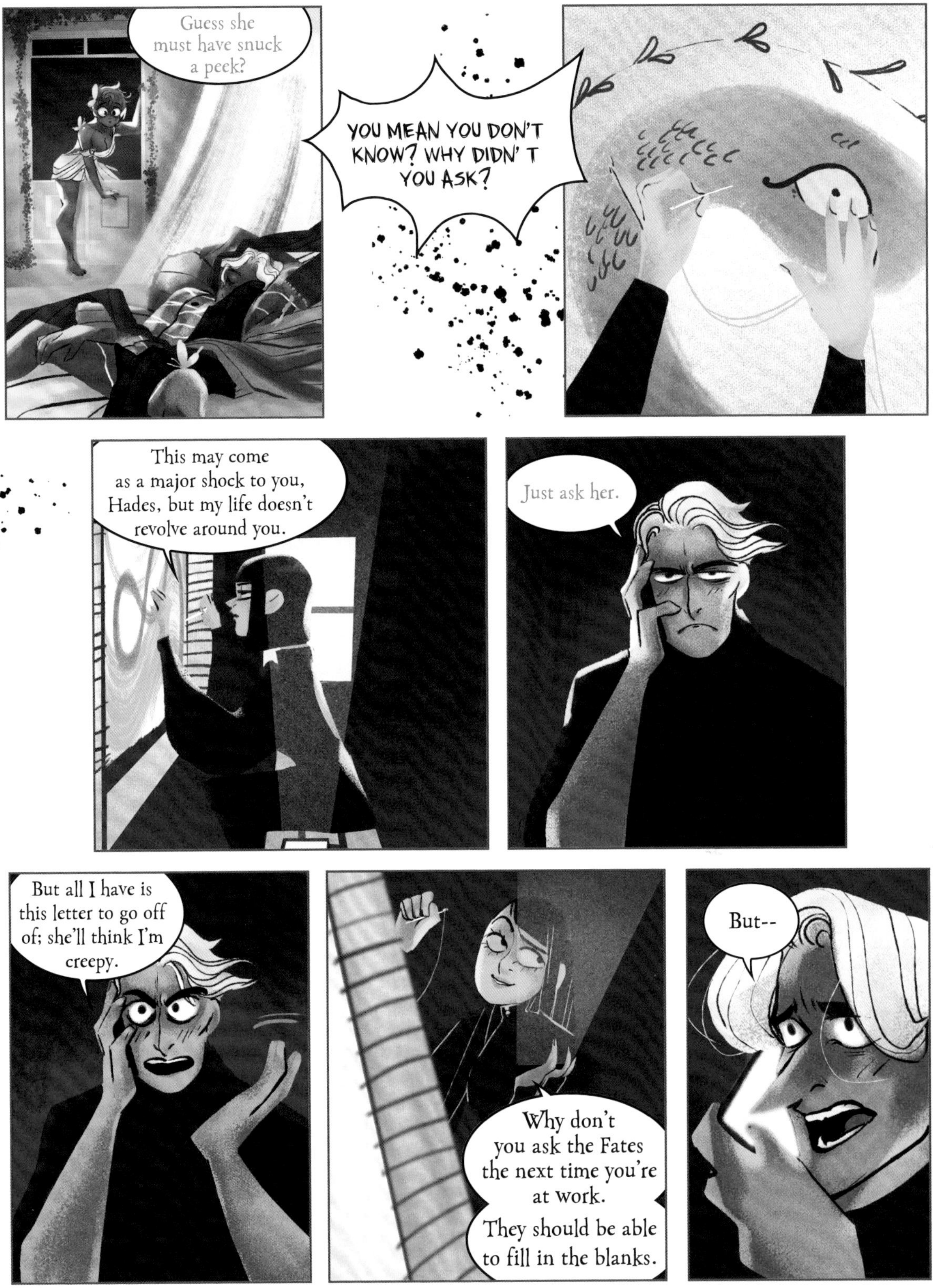
Guess she must have snuck a peek?
YOU MEAN YOU DON'T KNOW? WHY DIDN' T YOU ASK?
This may come as a major shock to you, Hades, but my life doesn't revolve around you.
Just ask her.
But all I have is this letter to go off of; she'll think I'm creepy.
Why don't you ask the Fates the next time you're at work.
They should be able to fill in the blanks.
But--

BYEEE!

SNAP!

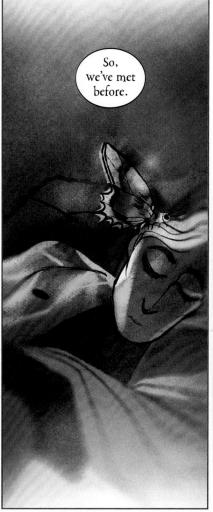

So, we've met before.

Which makes me wonder...

...what else is she hiding?

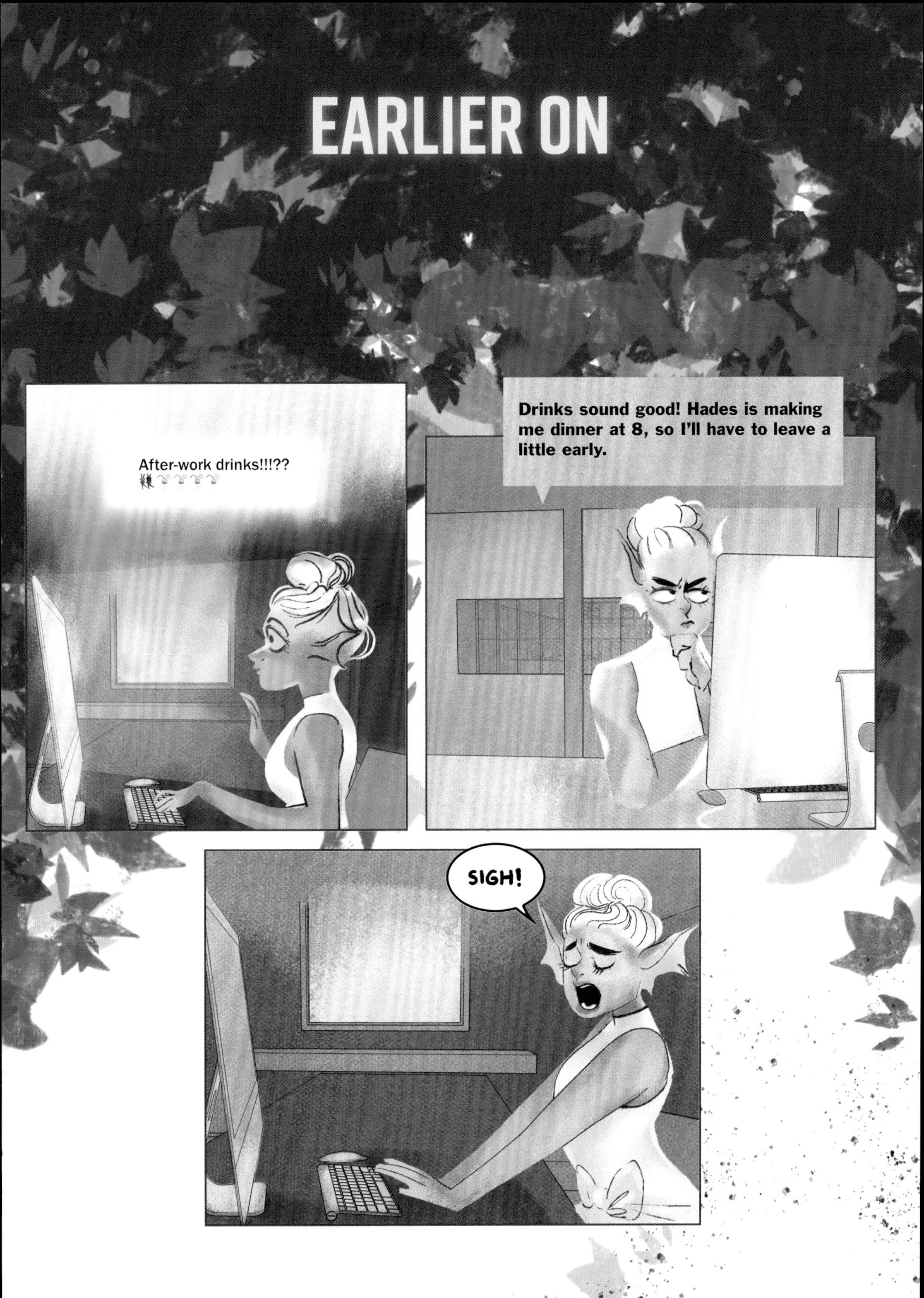
EARLIER ON
After-work drinks!!!??
Drinks sound good! Hades is making me dinner at 8, so I'll have to leave a little early.
SIGH!

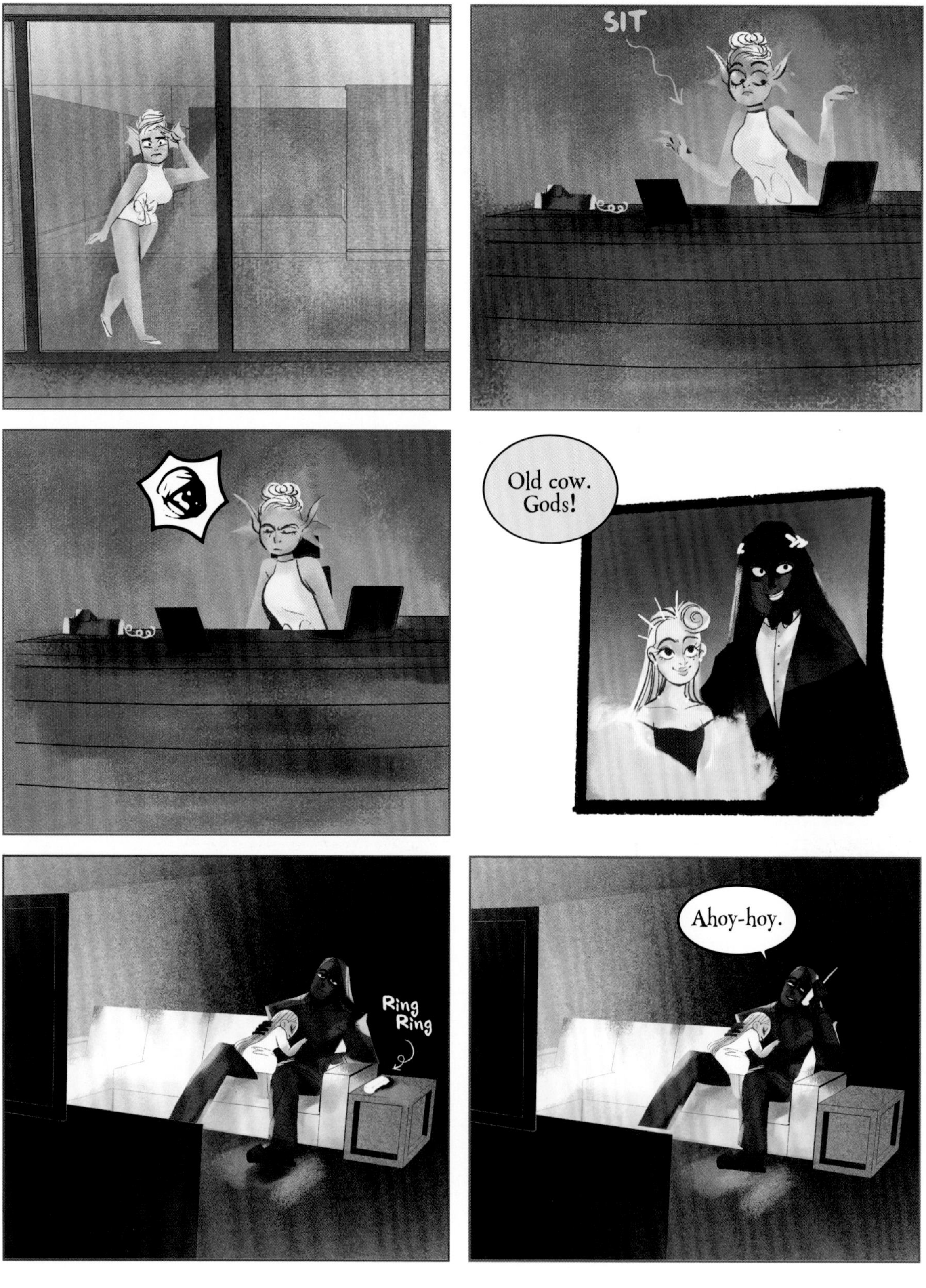
SIT
Old cow.
Gods!
Ring
Ring
Ahoy-hoy.

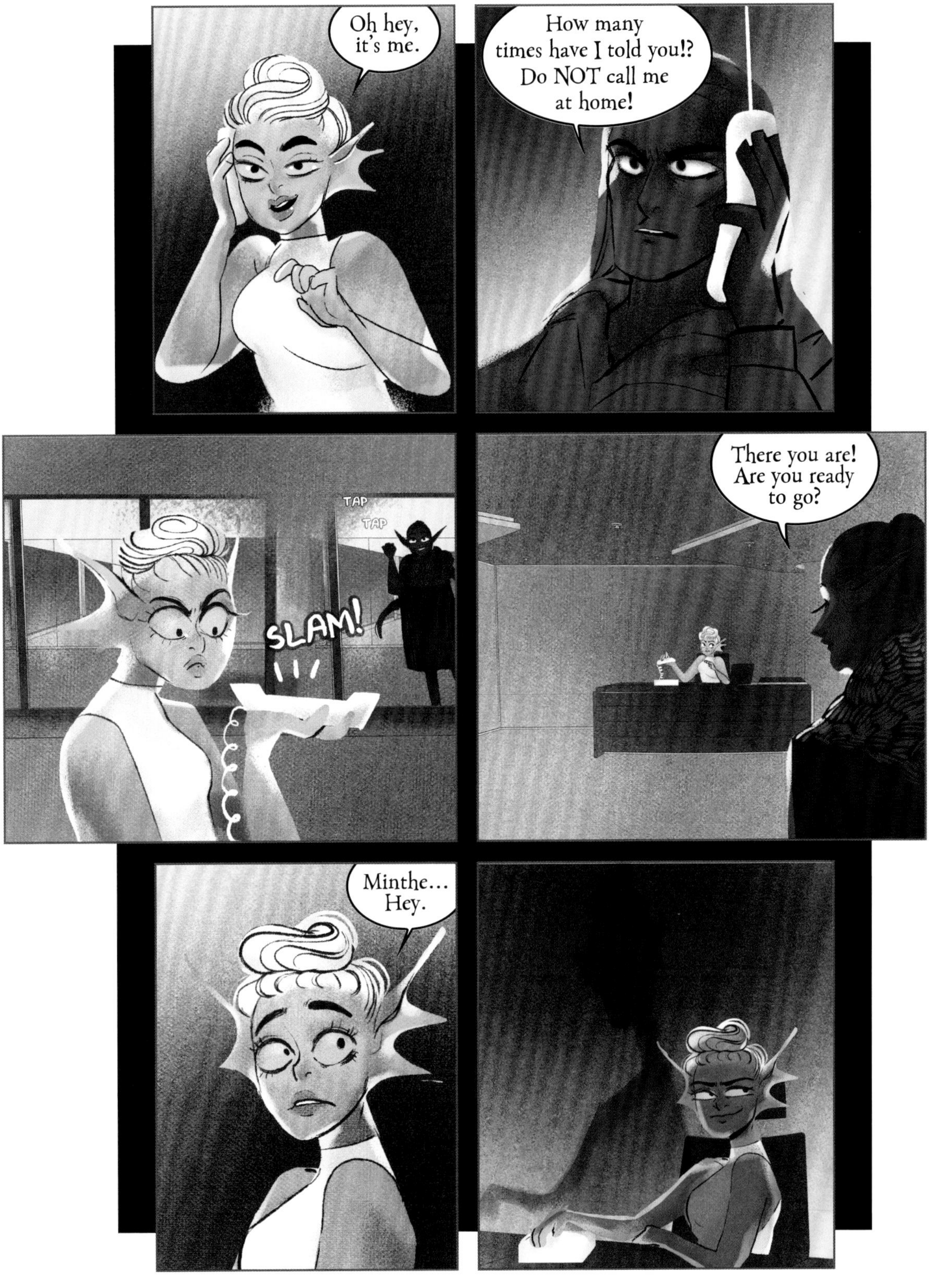
Oh hey, it's me.
How many times have I told you!? Do NOT call me at home!
TAP
TAP
SLAM!
There you are! Are you ready to go?
Minthe... Hey.

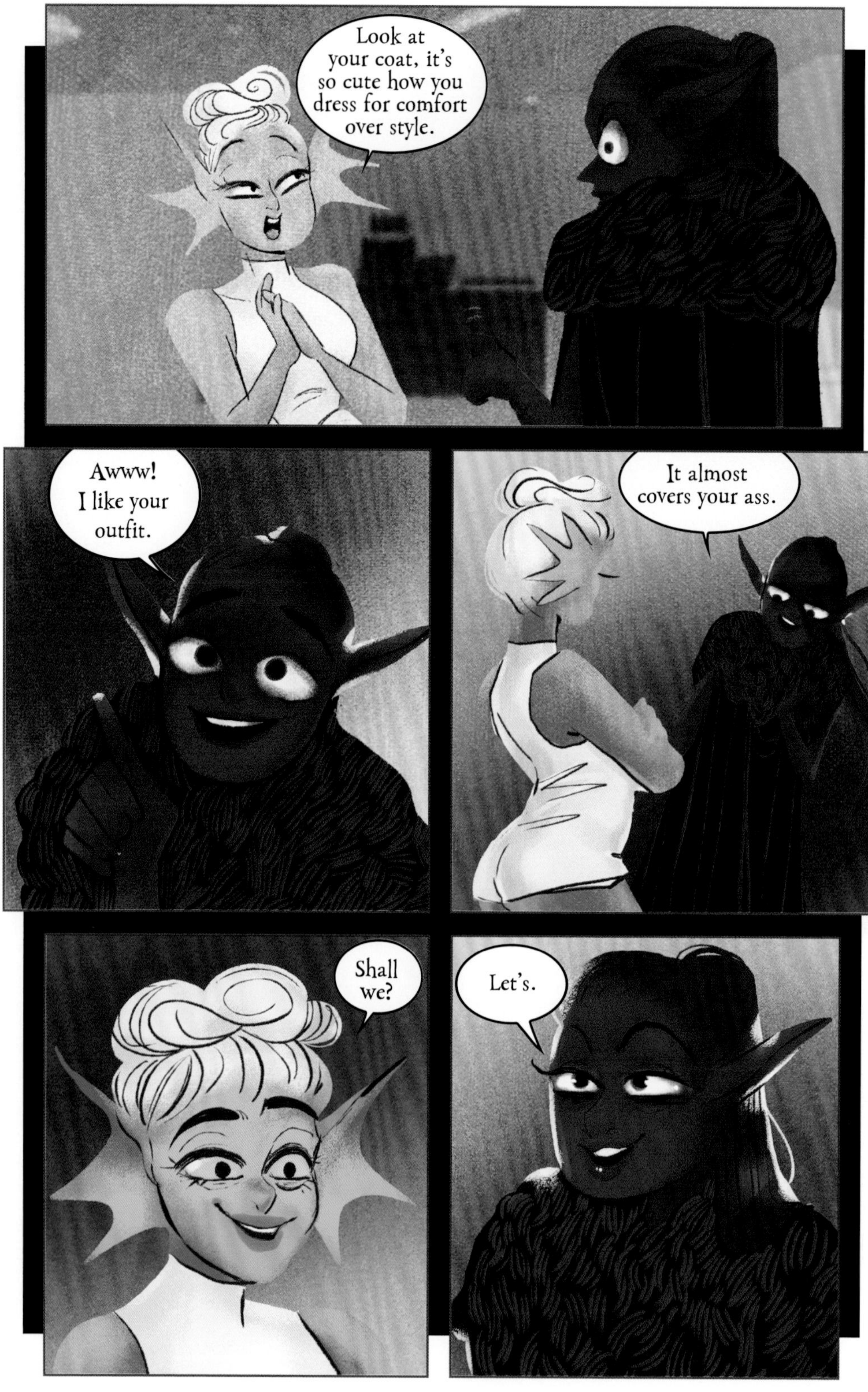
Look at your coat, it's so cute how you dress for comfort over style.
Awww! I like your outfit.
It almost covers your ass.
Shall we?
Let's.

EPISODE 73: BFF

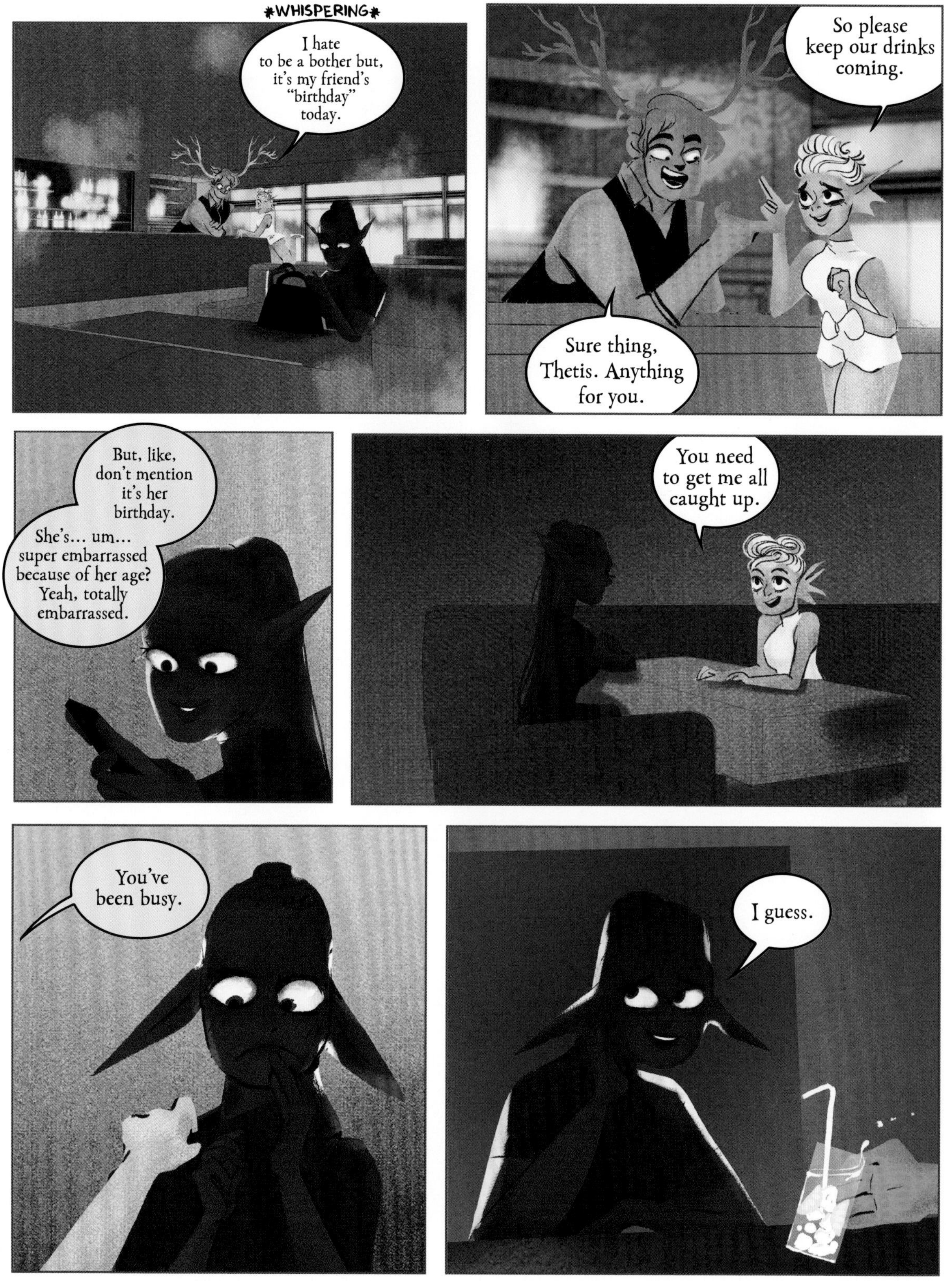
WHISPERING
I hate to be a bother but, it's my friend's "birthday" today.
So please keep our drinks coming.
Sure thing, Thetis. Anything for you.
But, like, don't mention it's her birthday.
She's... um... super embarrassed because of her age? Yeah, totally embarrassed.
You need to get me all caught up.
You've been busy.
I guess.

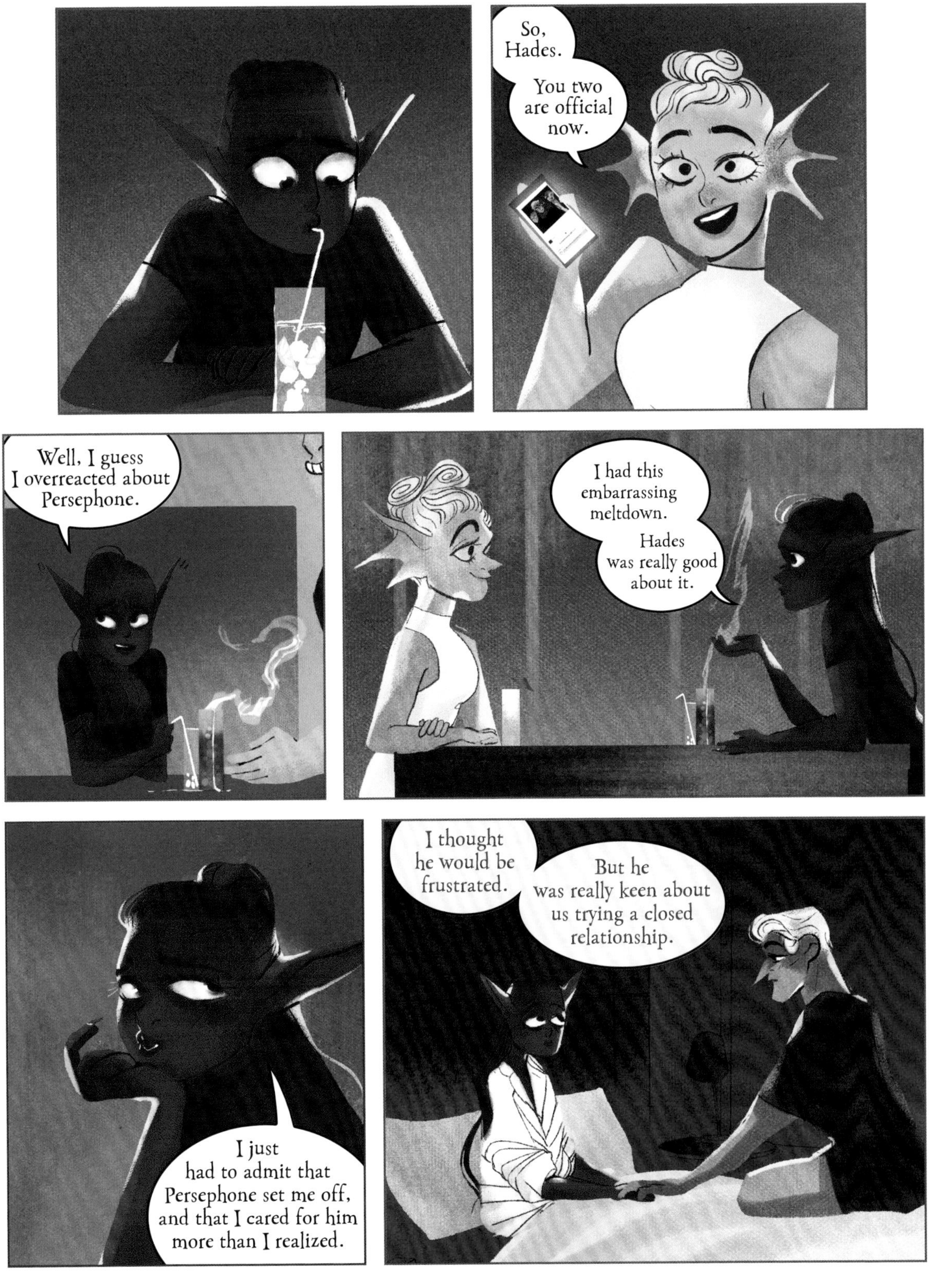
So, Hades.
You two are official now.
Well, I guess I overreacted about Persephone.
I had this embarrassing meltdown.
Hades was really good about it.
I just had to admit that Persephone set me off, and that I cared for him more than I realized.
I thought he would be frustrated.
But he was really keen about us trying a closed relationship.

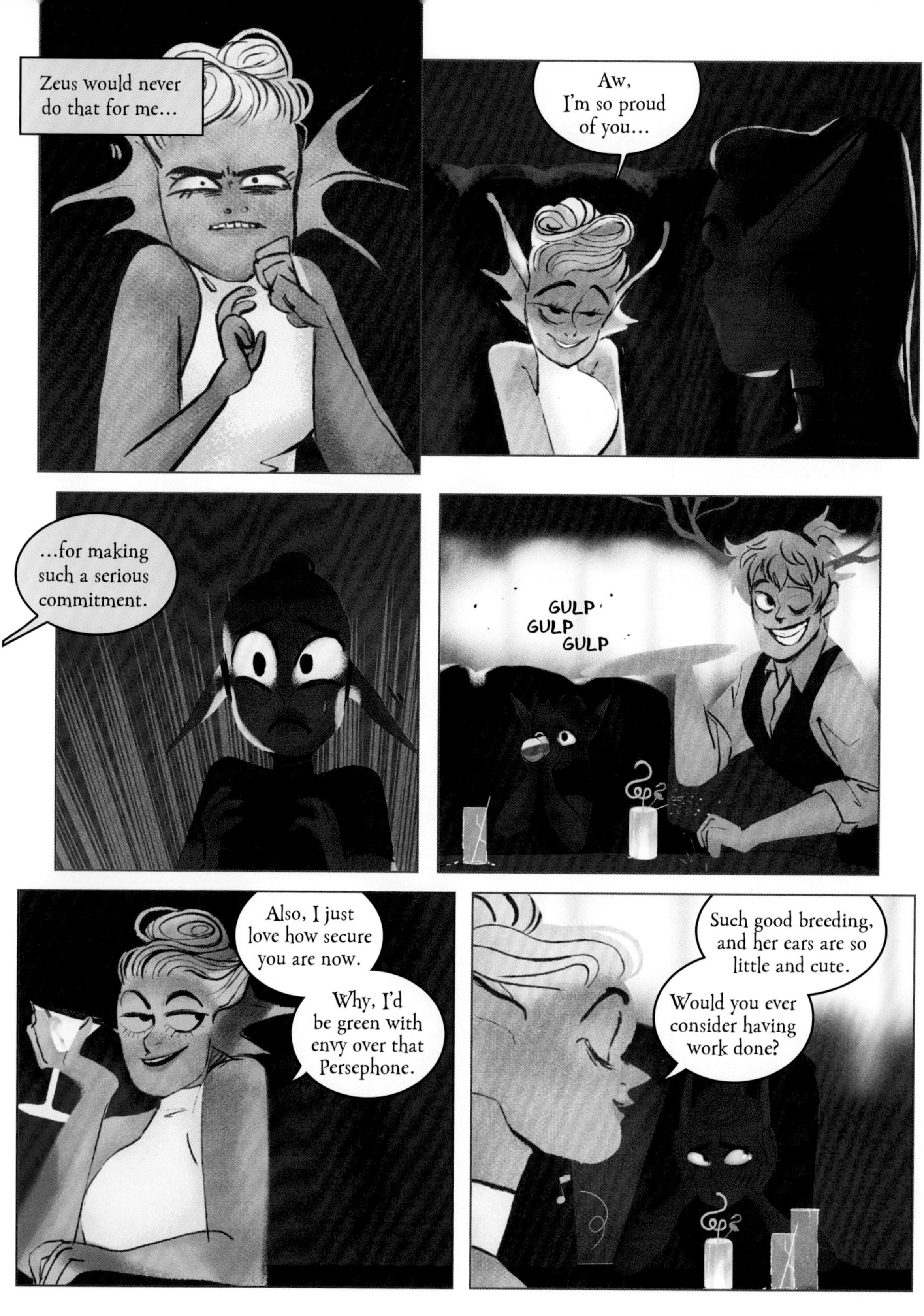
Zeus would never do that for me...
Aw, I'm so proud of you...
...for making such a serious commitment.
GULP GULP GULP
Also, I just love how secure you are now.
Why, I'd be green with envy over that Persephone.
Such good breeding, and her ears are so little and cute.
Would you ever consider having work done?

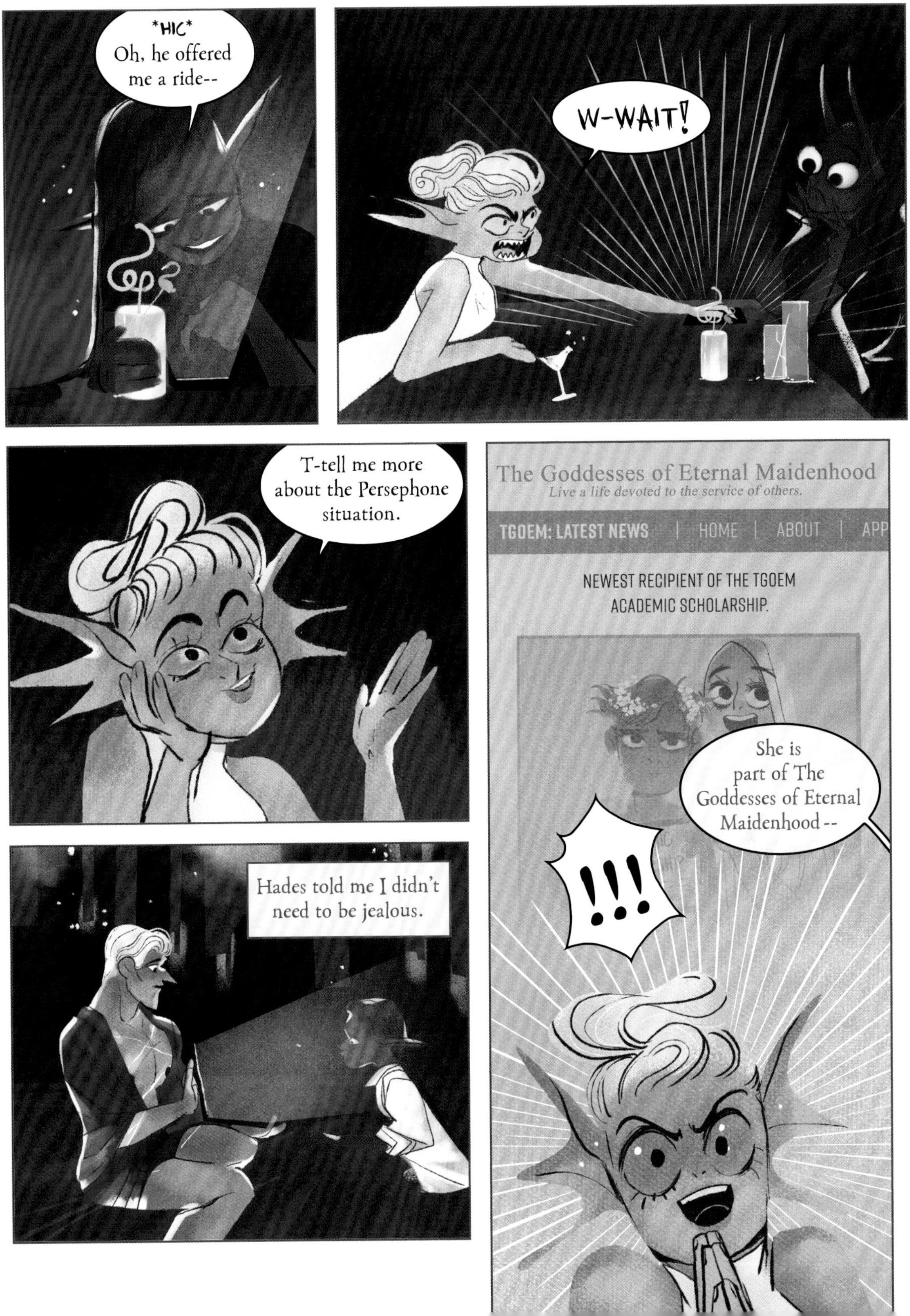
HIC
Oh, he offered me a ride--
W-WAIT!
T-tell me more about the Persephone situation.
Hades told me I didn't need to be jealous.
The Goddesses of Eternal Maidenhood
Live a life devoted to the service of others.
TGOEM: LATEST NEWS | HOME | ABOUT | APP
NEWEST RECIPIENT OF THE TGOEM ACADEMIC SCHOLARSHIP.
She is part of The Goddesses of Eternal Maidenhood --
!!!

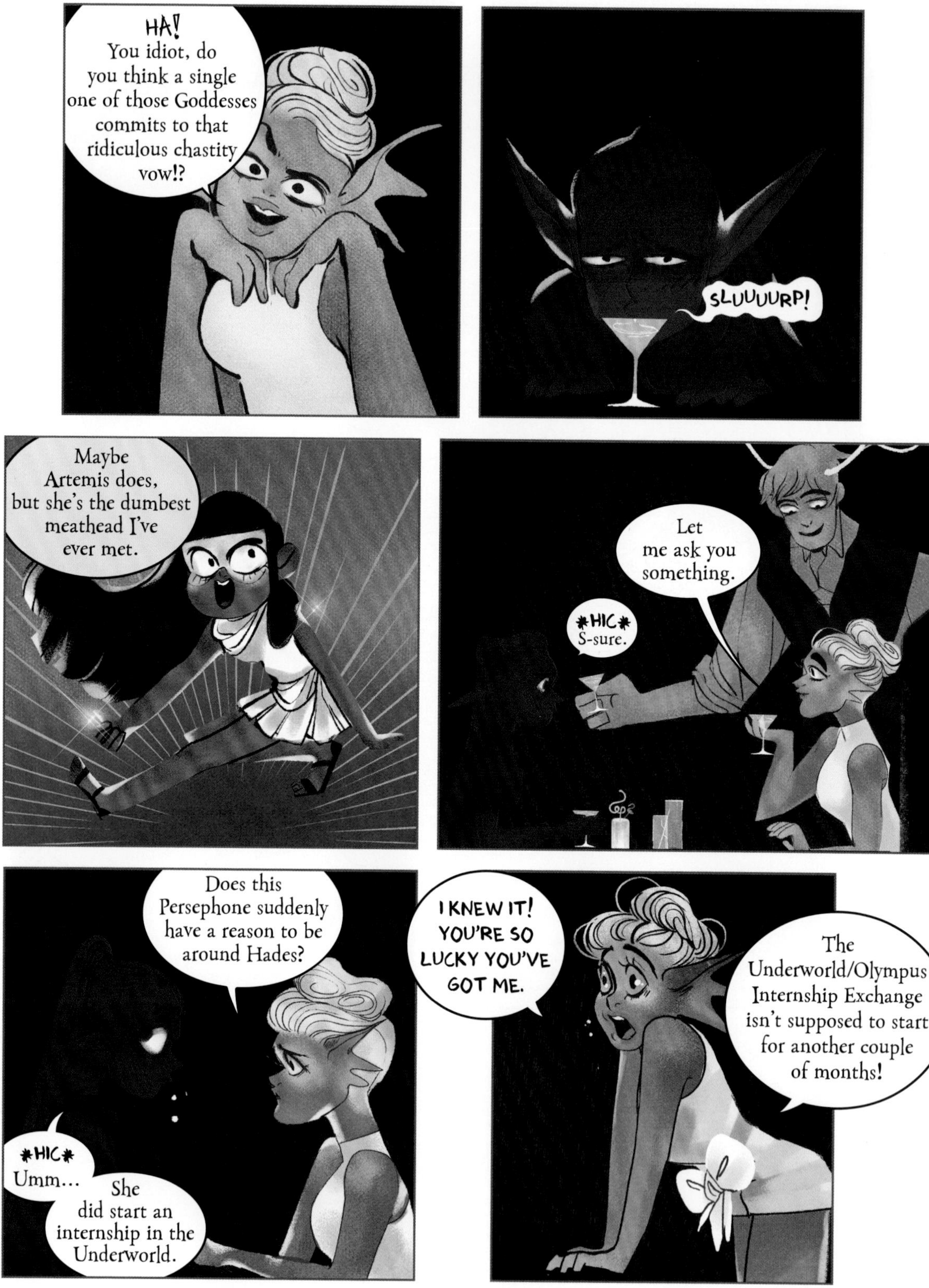
HA! You idiot, do you think a single one of those Goddesses commits to that ridiculous chastity vow!?
SLUUUURP!
Maybe Artemis does, but she's the dumbest meathead I've ever met.
Let me ask you something.
HIC S-sure.
Does this Persephone suddenly have a reason to be around Hades?
HIC Umm...
She did start an internship in the Underworld.
I KNEW IT! YOU'RE SO LUCKY YOU'VE GOT ME.
The Underworld/Olympus Internship Exchange isn't supposed to start for another couple of months!

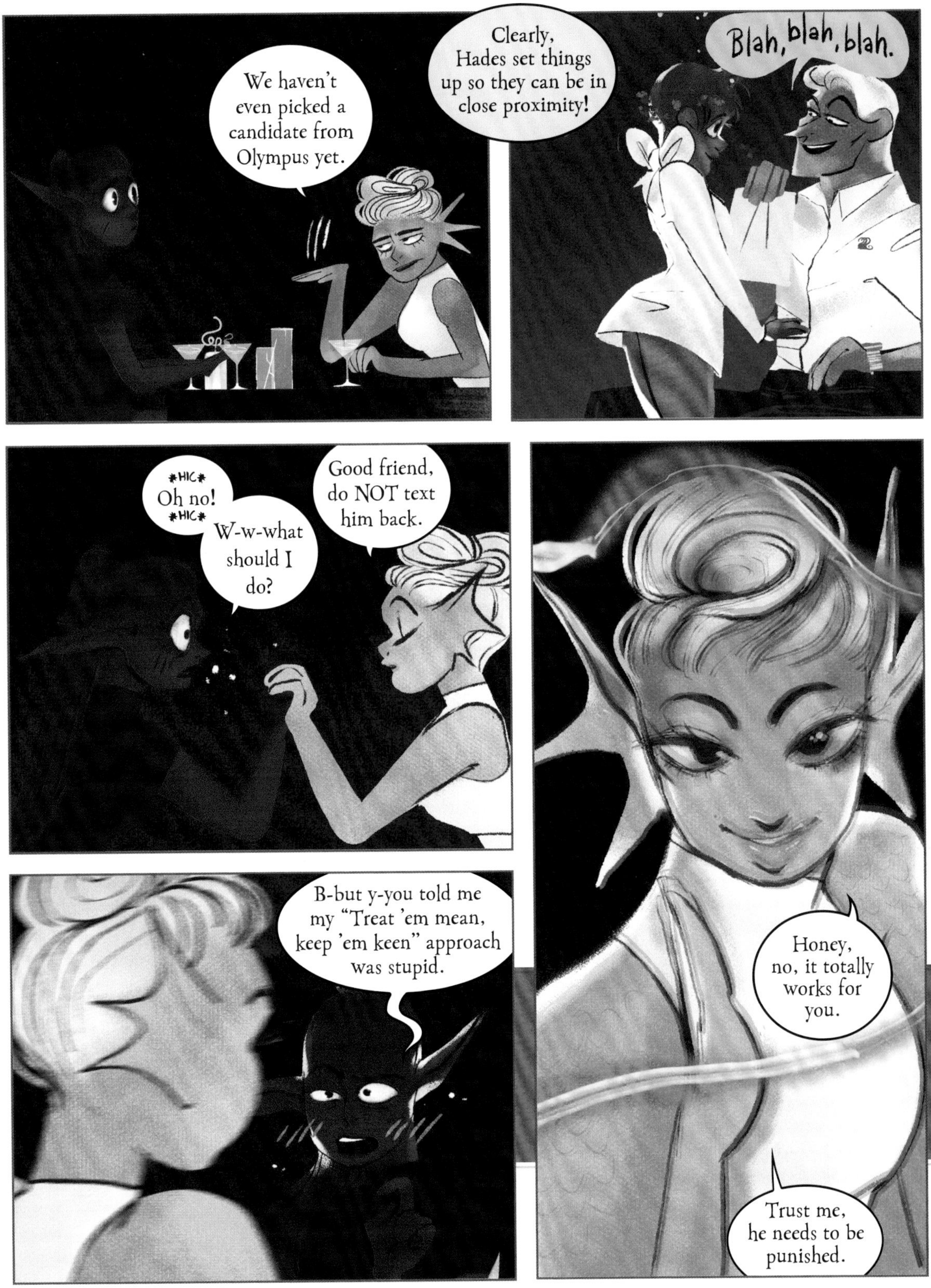
We haven't even picked a candidate from Olympus yet.
Clearly, Hades set things up so they can be in close proximity!
Blah, blah, blah.
HIC Oh no! *HIC*
W-w-what should I do?
Good friend, do NOT text him back.
Honey, no, it totally works for you.
B-but y-you told me my "Treat 'em mean, keep 'em keen" approach was stupid.
Trust me, he needs to be punished.

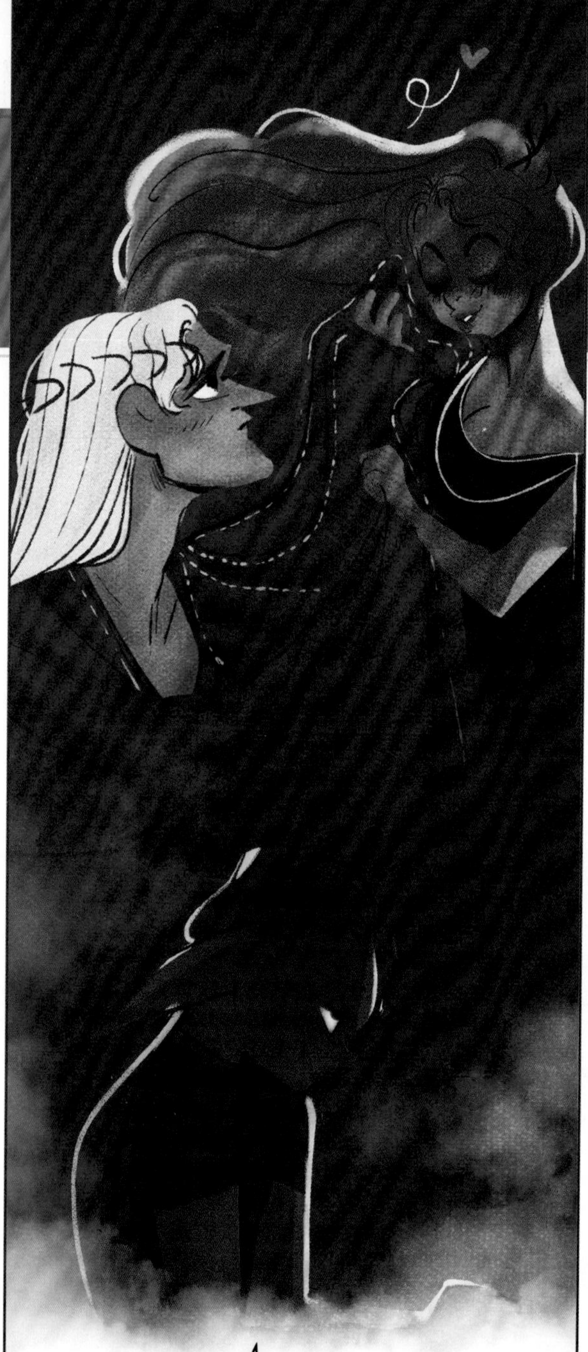
HIC
H-he did spend a lot of t-time with her this afternoon.

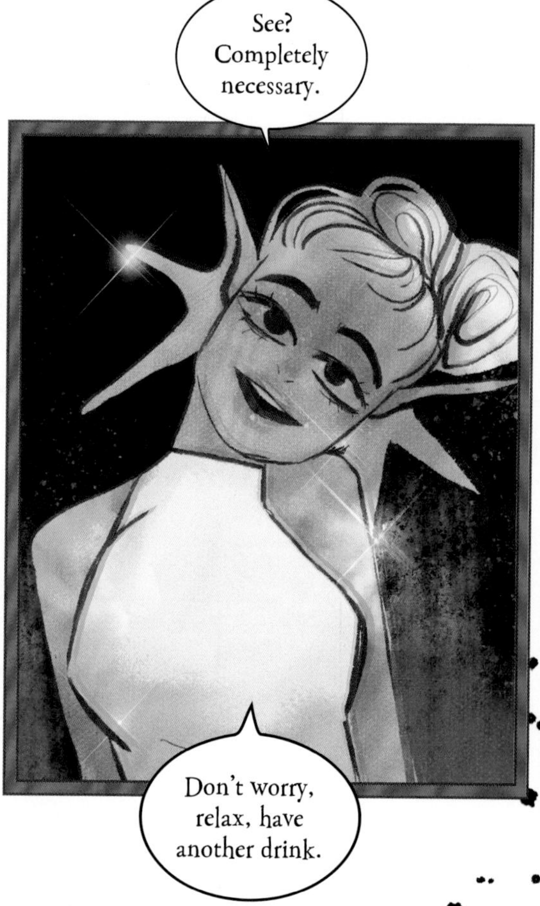
See? Completely necessary.
Don't worry, relax, have another drink.

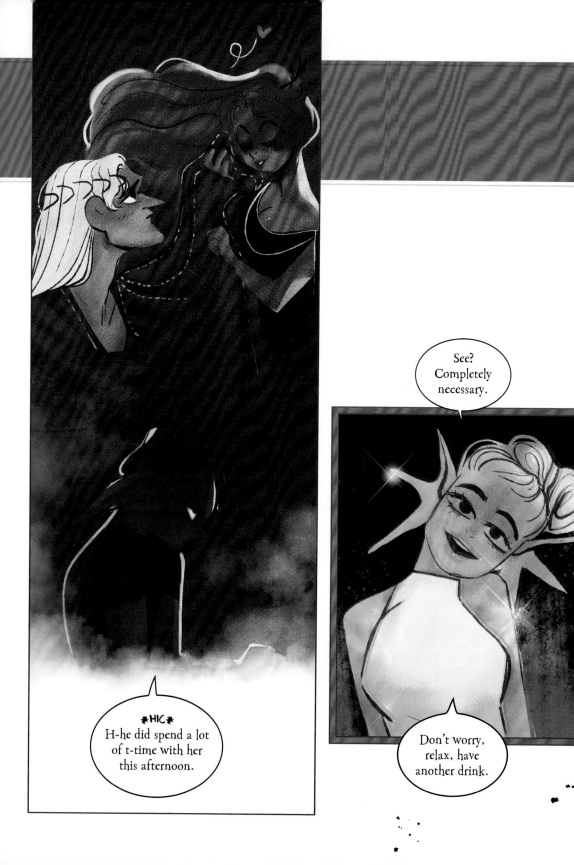

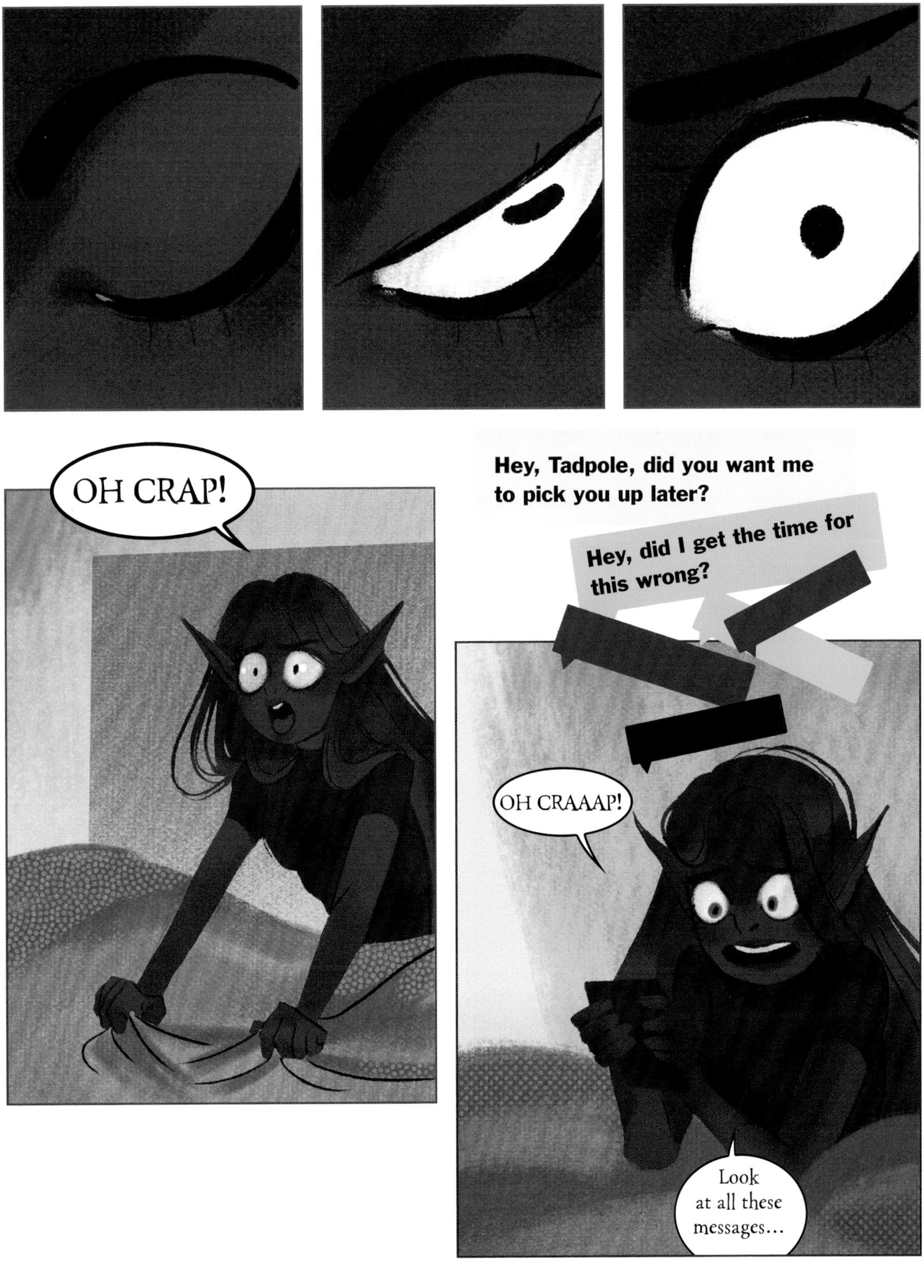
OH CRAP!
Hey, Tadpole, did you want me to pick you up later?
Hey, did I get the time for this wrong?
OH CRAAAP!
Look at all these messages...

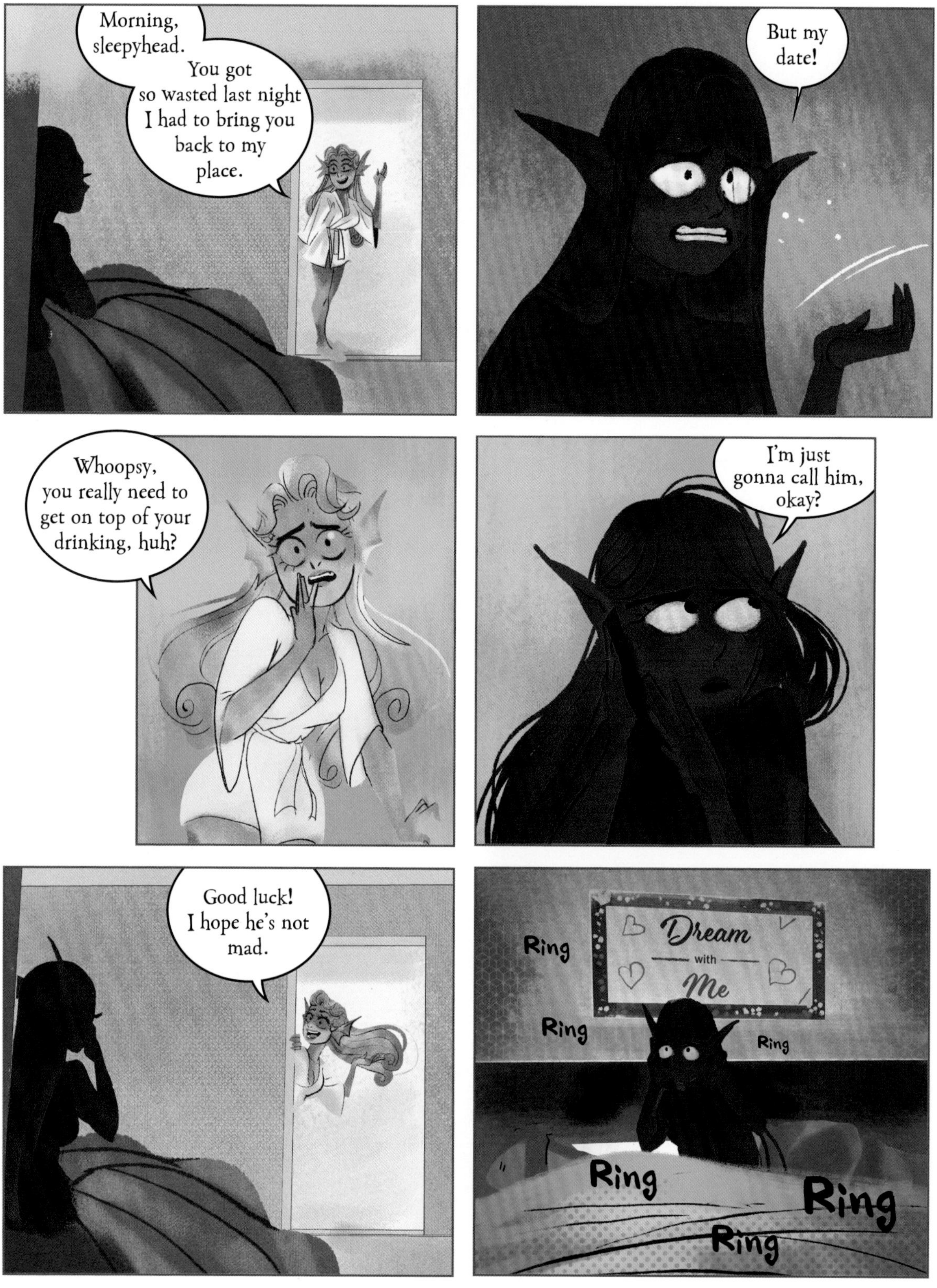

Morning, sleepyhead. You got so wasted last night I had to bring you back to my place.
But my date!
Whoopsy, you really need to get on top of your drinking, huh?
I'm just gonna call him, okay?
Good luck! I hope he's not mad.
Dream with Me
Ring
Ring
Ring
Ring
Ring
Ring

EPISODE 74: I THINK IT SUITS YOU

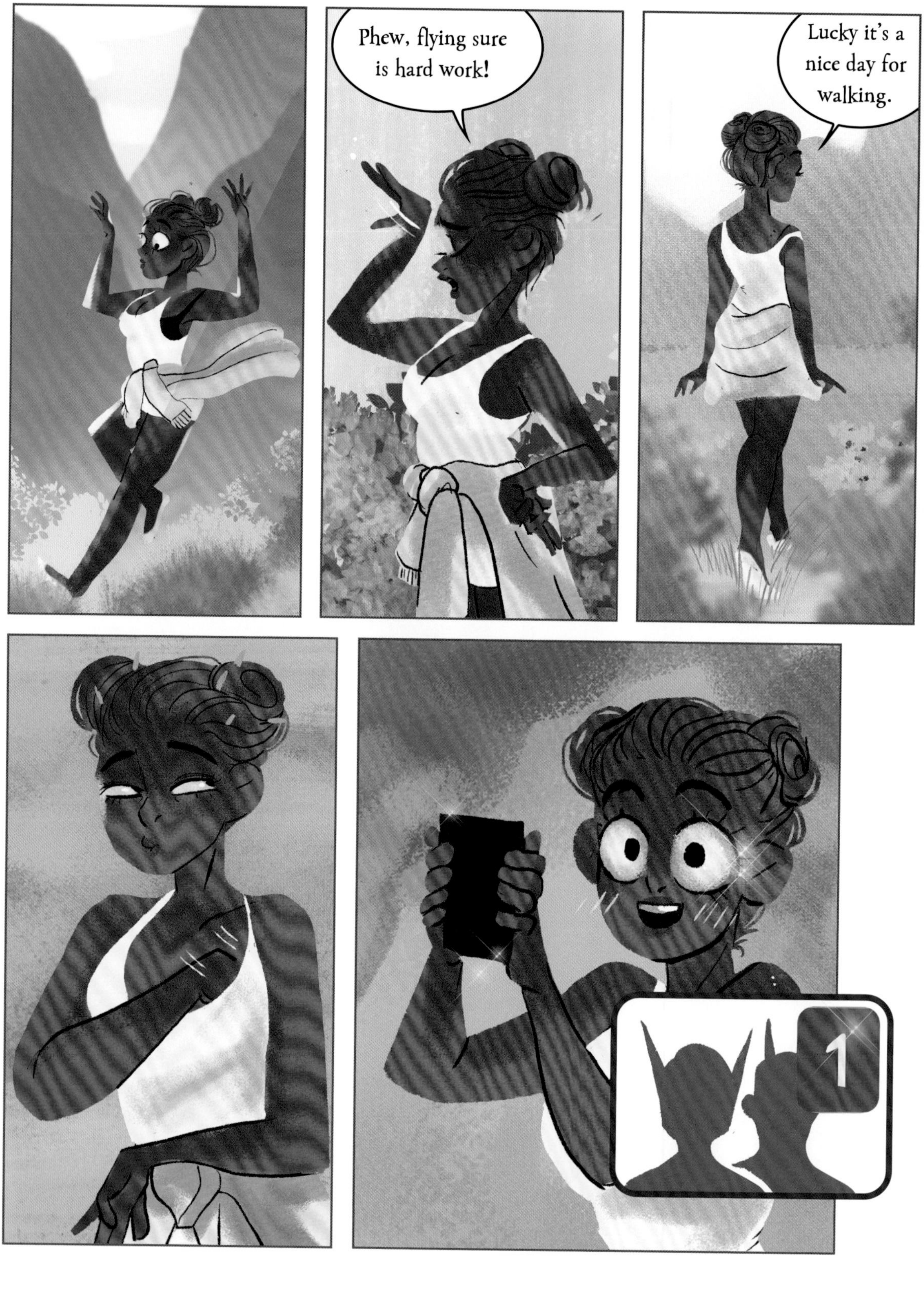

Phew, flying sure is hard work!
Lucky it's a nice day for walking.
1

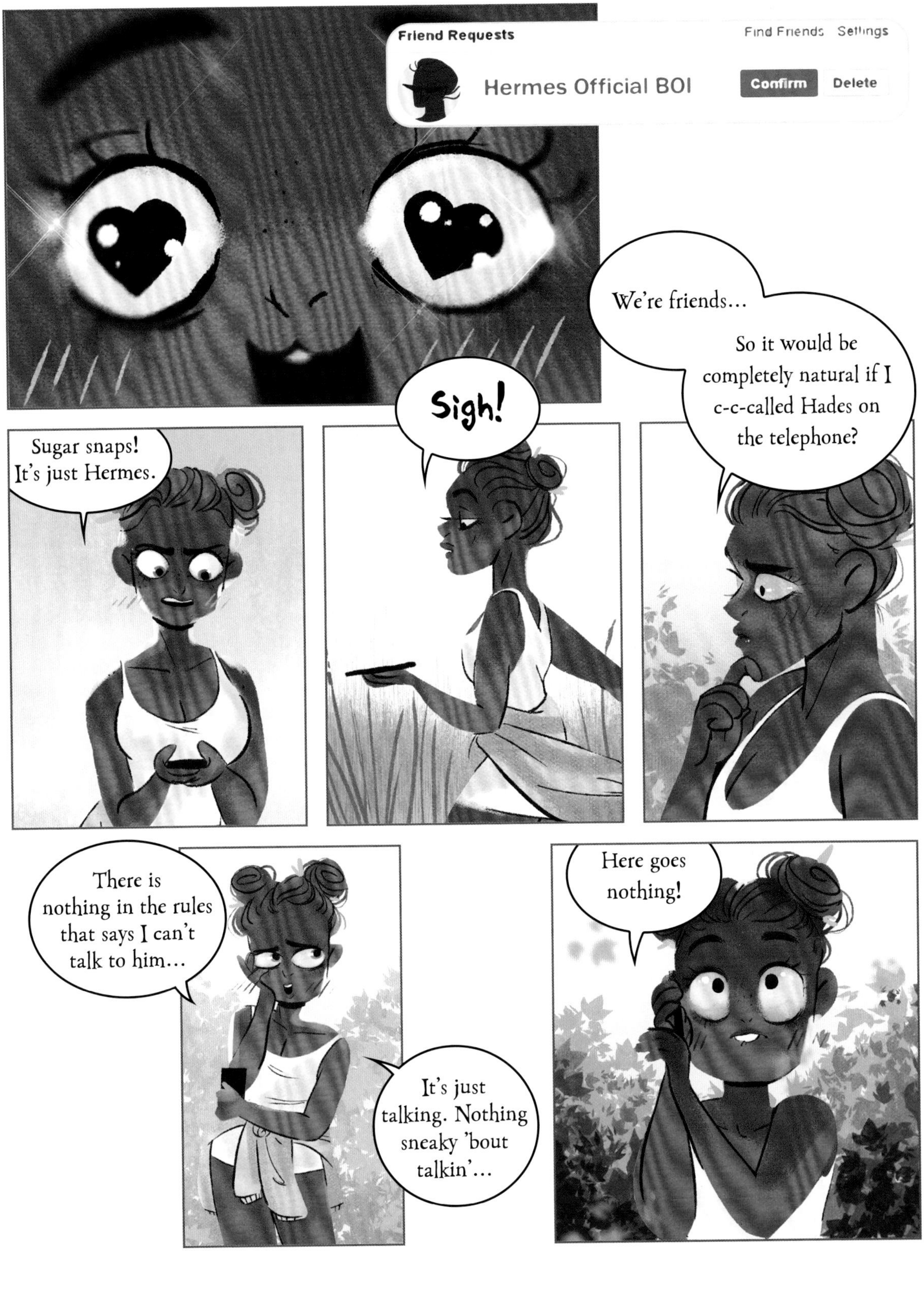

Friend Requests
Find Friends Settings
Hermes Official BOI
Confirm
Delete
We're friends...
So it would be completely natural if I c-c-called Hades on the telephone?
Sugar snaps! It's just Hermes.
Sigh!
There is nothing in the rules that says I can't talk to him...
It's just talking. Nothing sneaky 'bout talkin'...
Here goes nothing!

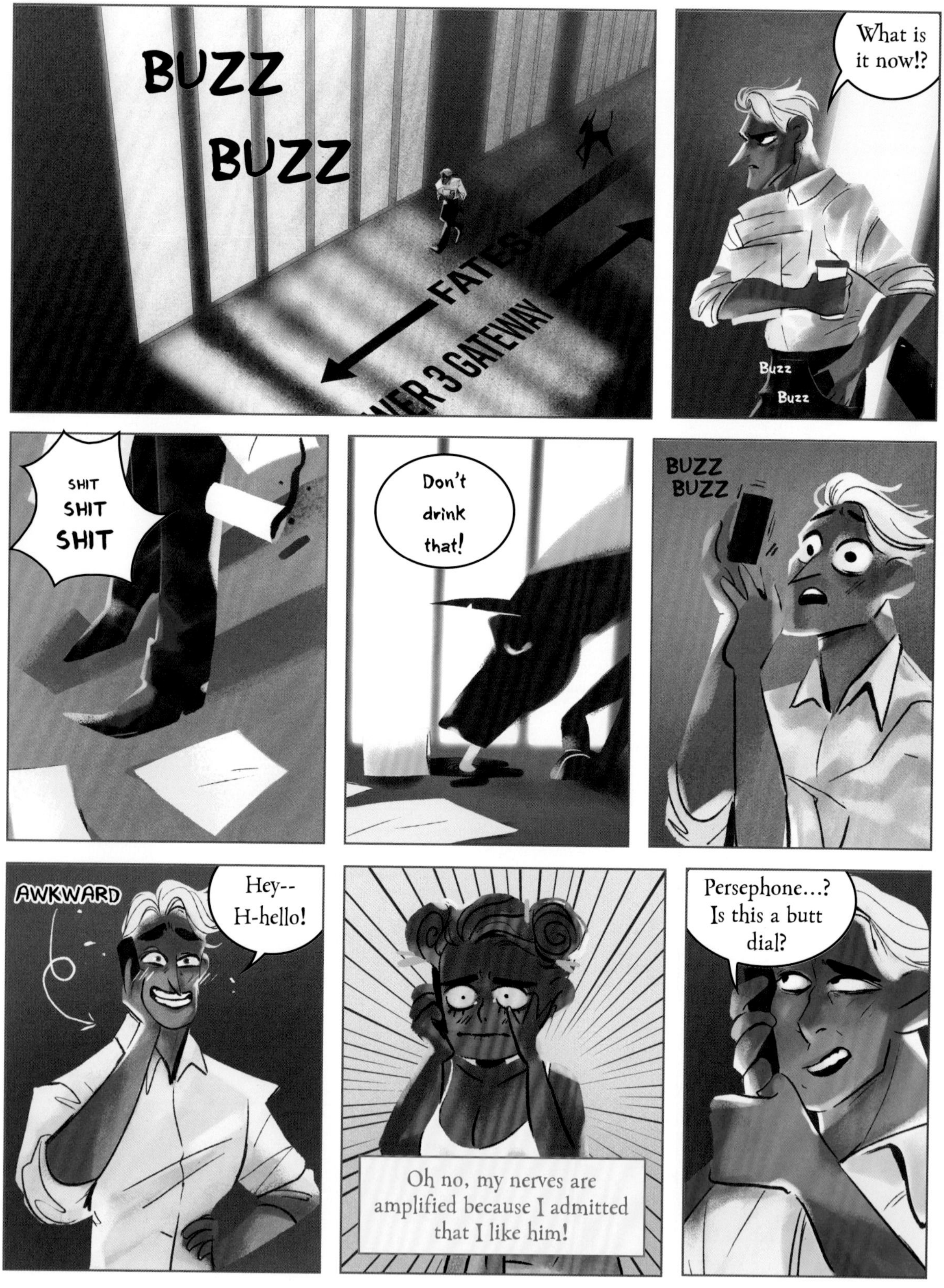
BUZZ
BUZZ
FATES
VER 3 GATEWAY
What is it now!?
Buzz
Buzz
SHIT SHIT SHIT
Don't drink that!
BUZZ BUZZ
AWKWARD
Hey-- H-hello!
Oh no, my nerves are amplified because I admitted that I like him!
Persephone...? Is this a butt dial?

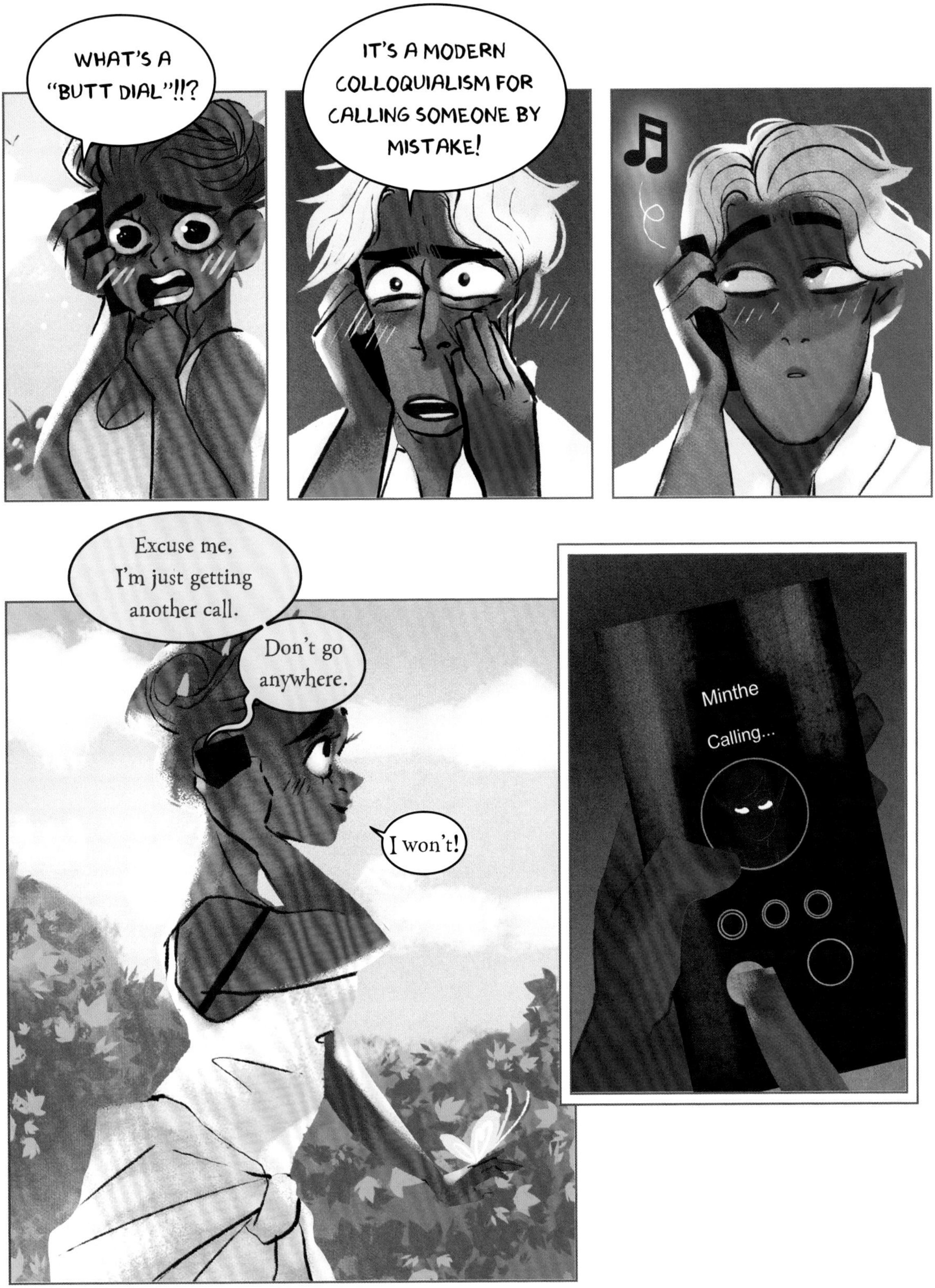
WHAT'S A "BUTT DIAL"!!?
IT'S A MODERN COLLOQUIALISM FOR CALLING SOMEONE BY MISTAKE!
Excuse me, I'm just getting another call.
Don't go anywhere.
I won't!
Minthe
Calling...

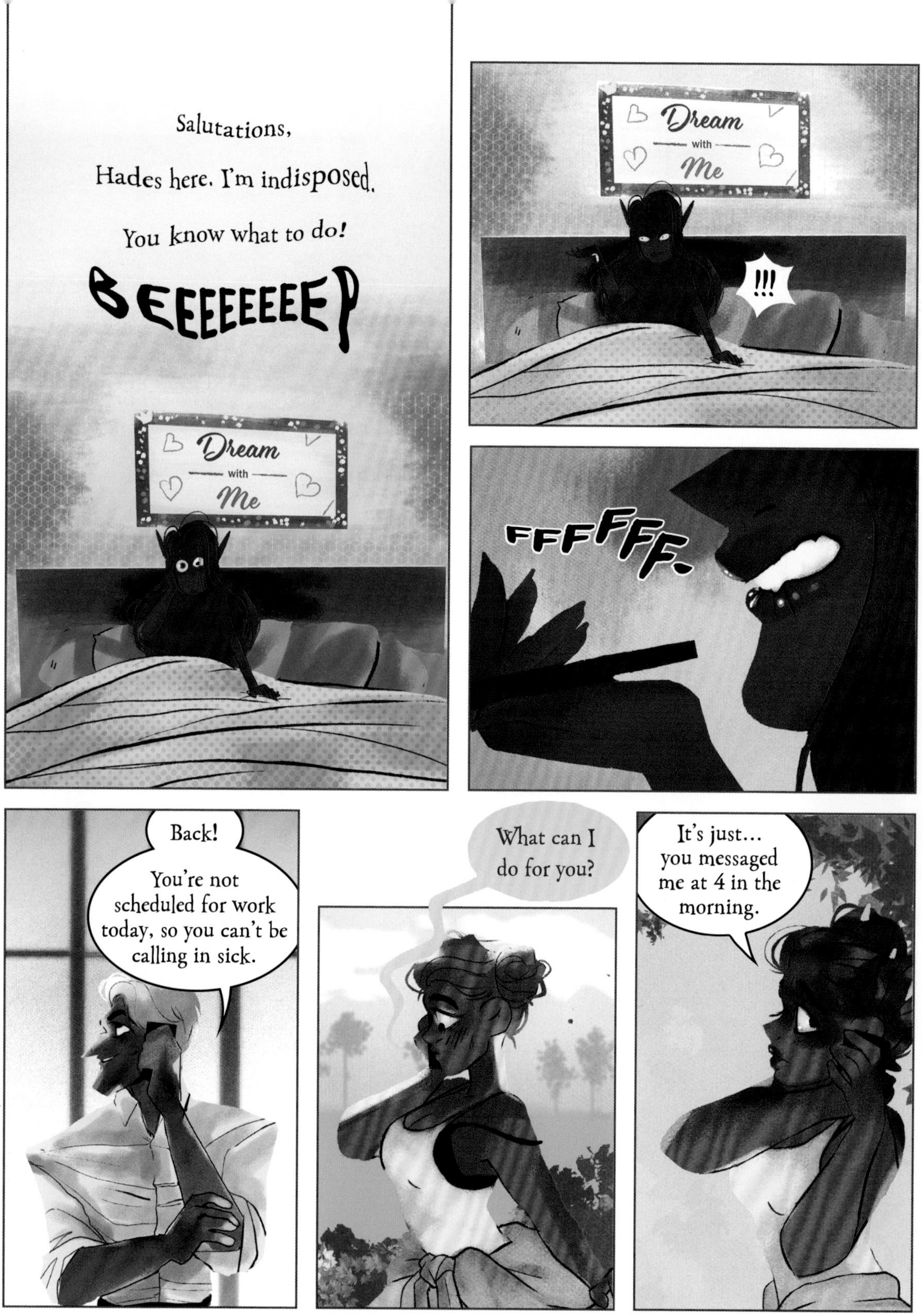
Salutations,
Hades here. I'm indisposed.
You know what to do!
BEEEEEEEP
Dream with Me
Dream with Me
!!!
FFFFFFF-
Back!
You're not scheduled for work today, so you can't be calling in sick.
What can I do for you?
It's just... you messaged me at 4 in the morning.

YOU IDIOT!

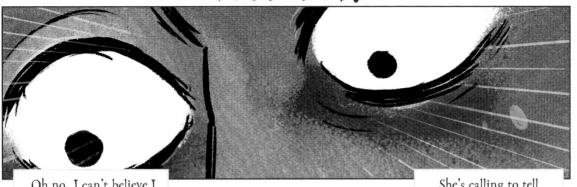

Oh no, I can't believe I didn't consider the time when I messaged her!

She probably thinks I'm a huge loser.

She's calling to tell me she's doesn't want to come here anymore.

Gulp

Maybe Zeus paid her to be nice to me all this time?

Listen, Ko-Persephone, I'm sorry--

Are you all right?

Fizz!

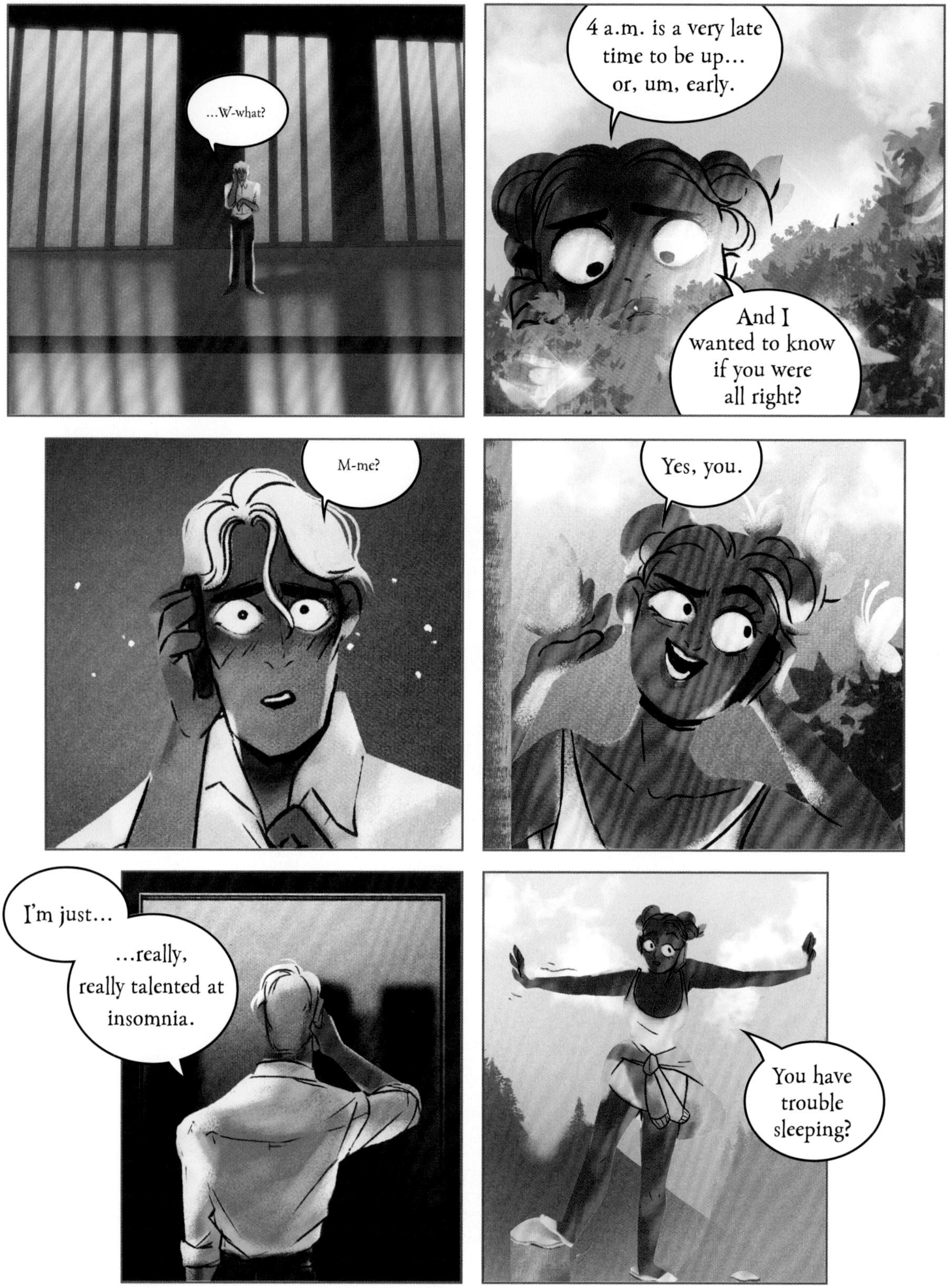
...W-what?
4 a.m. is a very late time to be up... or, um, early.
And I wanted to know if you were all right?
M-me?
Yes, you.
I'm just...
...really, really talented at insomnia.
You have trouble sleeping?

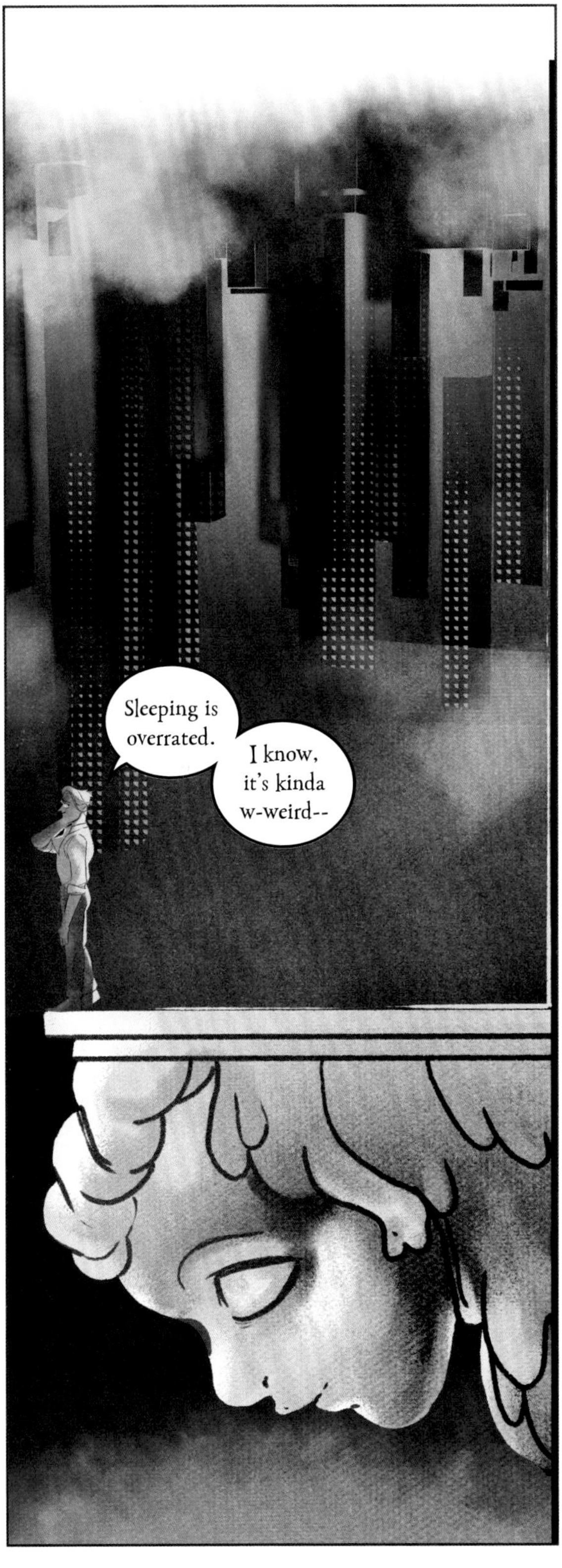
Sleeping is overrated.
I know, it's kinda w-weird--

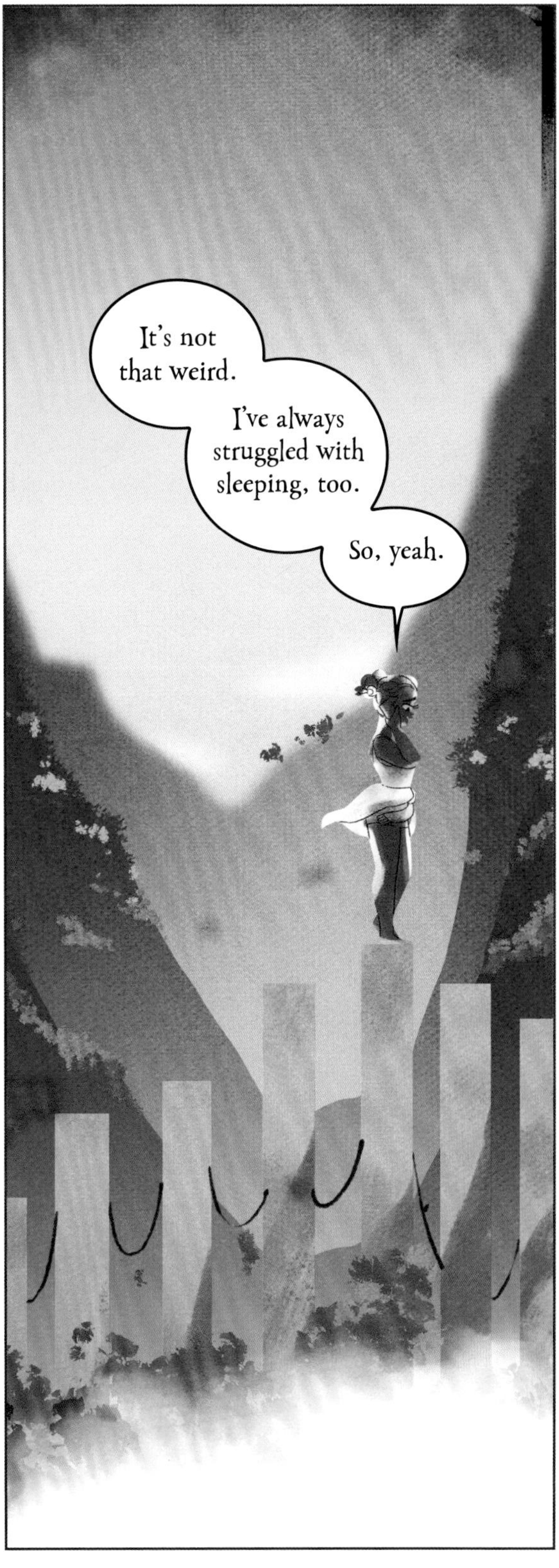
It's not that weird.
I've always struggled with sleeping, too.
So, yeah.

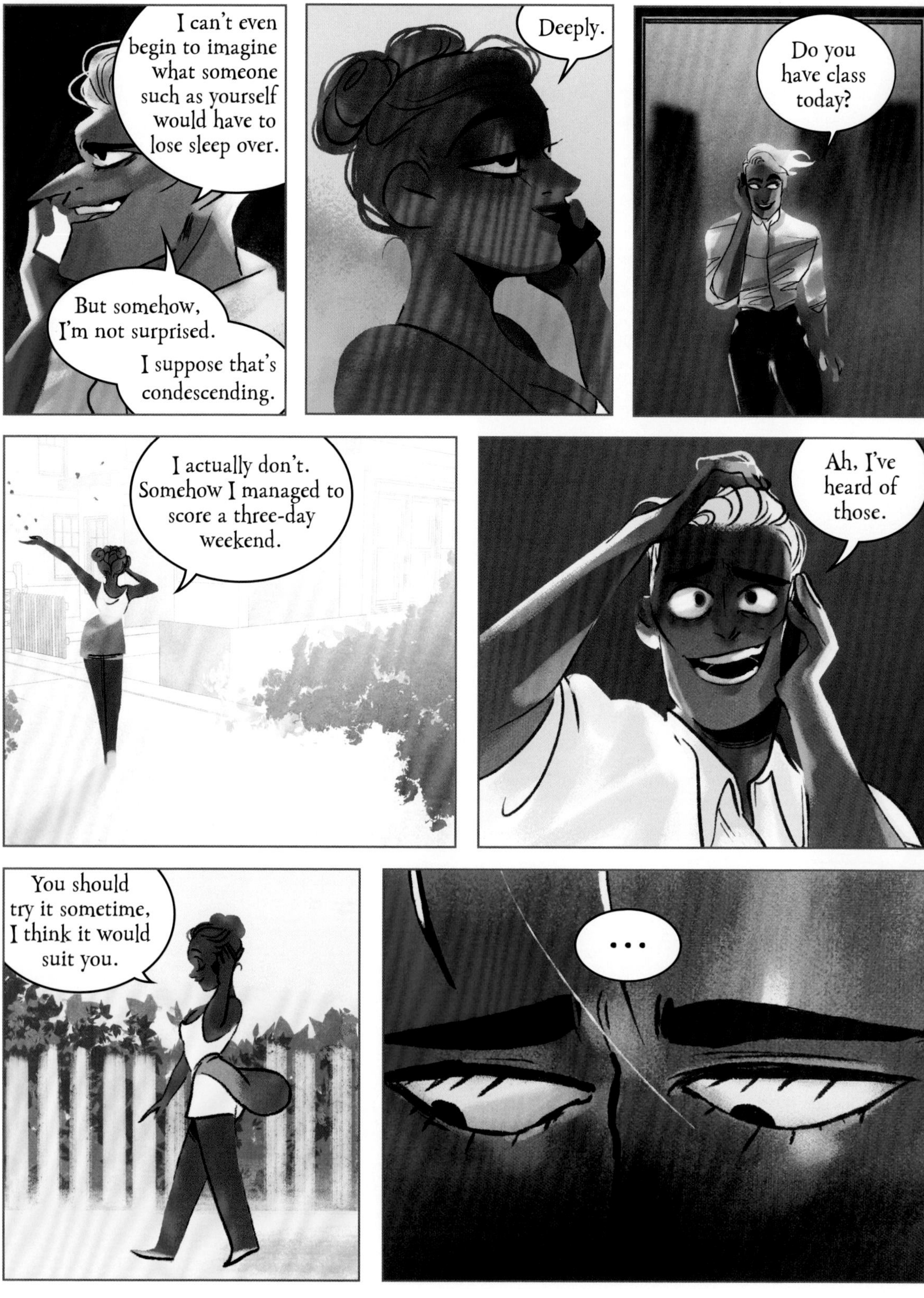
I can't even begin to imagine what someone such as yourself would have to lose sleep over.
But somehow, I'm not surprised.
I suppose that's condescending.
Deeply.
Do you have class today?
I actually don't. Somehow I managed to score a three-day weekend.
Ah, I've heard of those.
You should try it sometime, I think it would suit you.
...

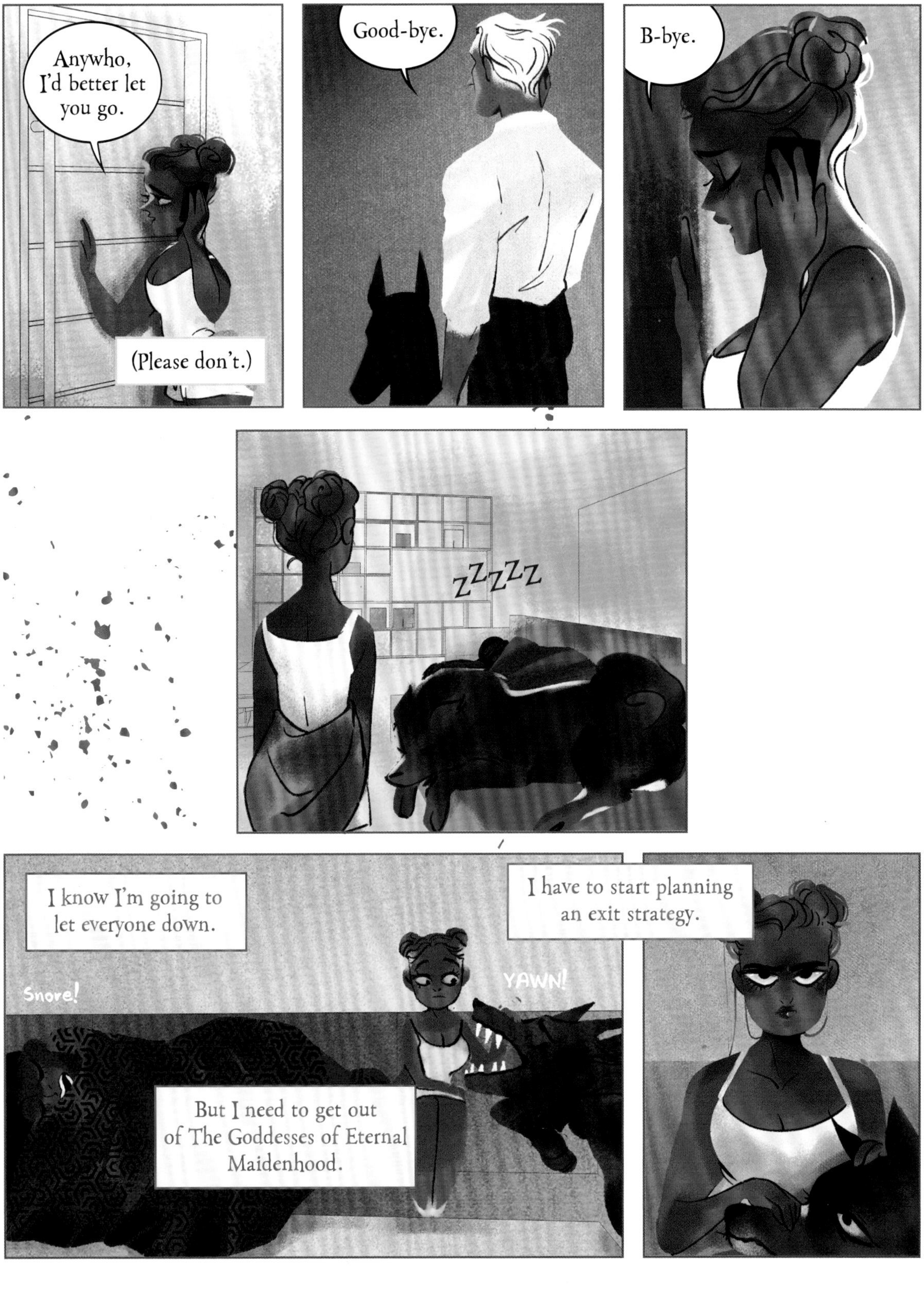
Anywho, I'd better let you go.
(Please don't.)
Good-bye.
B-bye.
ZZZZZ
I know I'm going to let everyone down.
Snore!
YAWN!
But I need to get out of The Goddesses of Eternal Maidenhood.
I have to start planning an exit strategy.

EPISODE 75: FATE

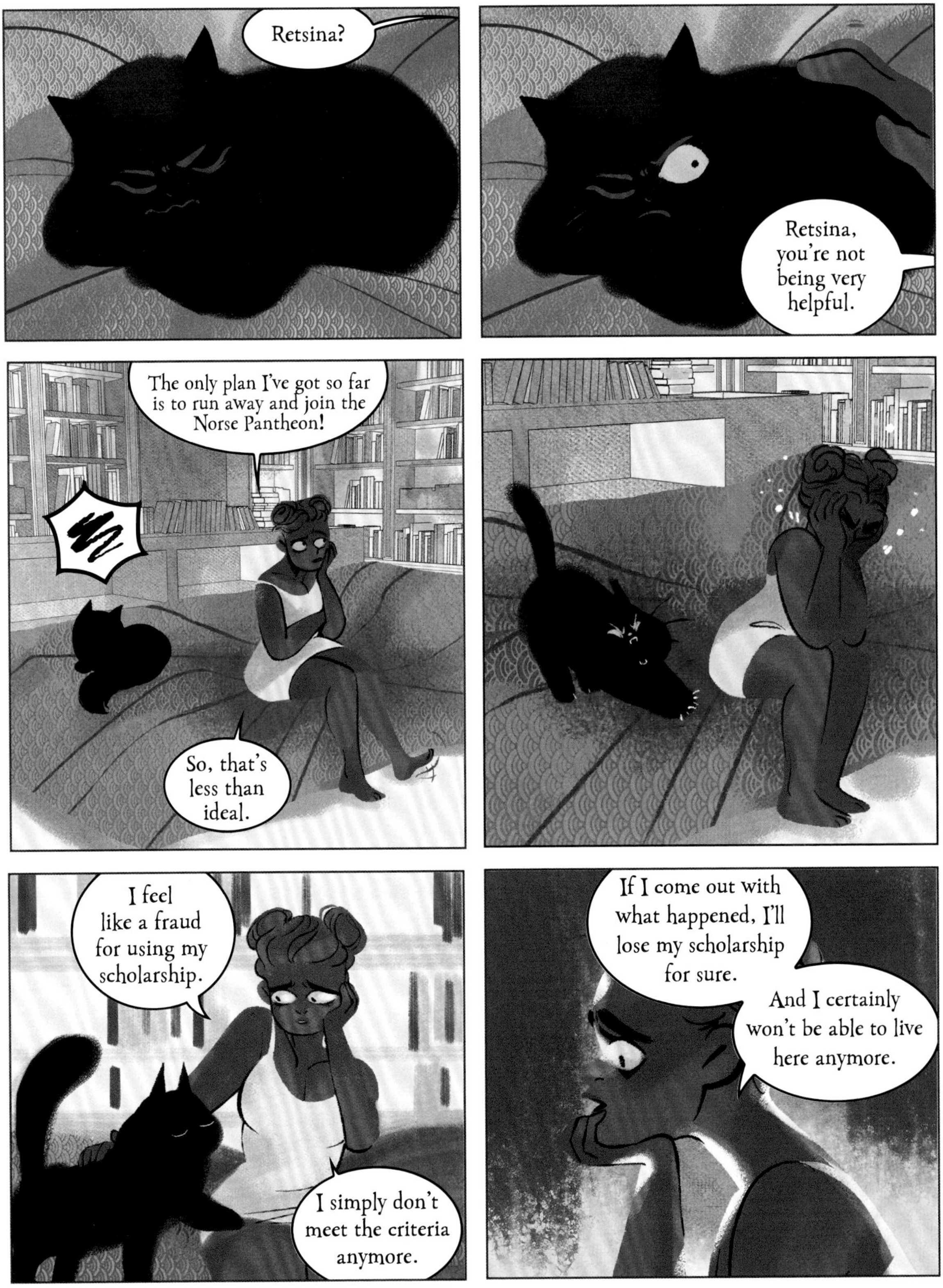
Retsina?
Retsina, you're not being very helpful.
The only plan I've got so far is to run away and join the Norse Pantheon!
So, that's less than ideal.
I feel like a fraud for using my scholarship.
I simply don't meet the criteria anymore.
If I come out with what happened, I'll lose my scholarship for sure.
And I certainly won't be able to live here anymore.

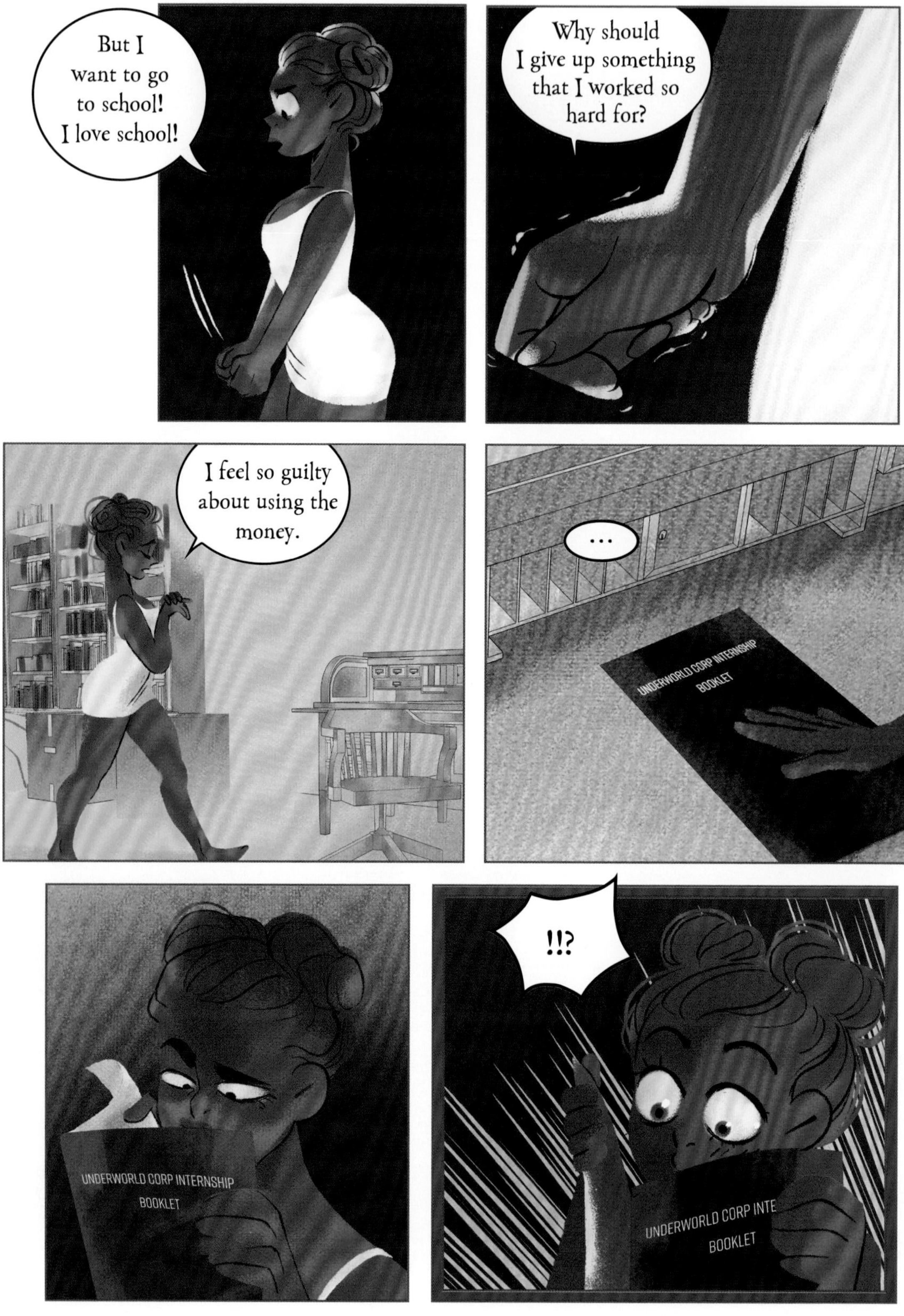
But I want to go to school! I love school!
Why should I give up something that I worked so hard for?
I feel so guilty about using the money.
...
UNDERWORLD CORP INTERNSHIP BOOKLET
UNDERWORLD CORP INTERNSHIP BOOKLET
!!?
UNDERWORLD CORP INTE BOOKLET

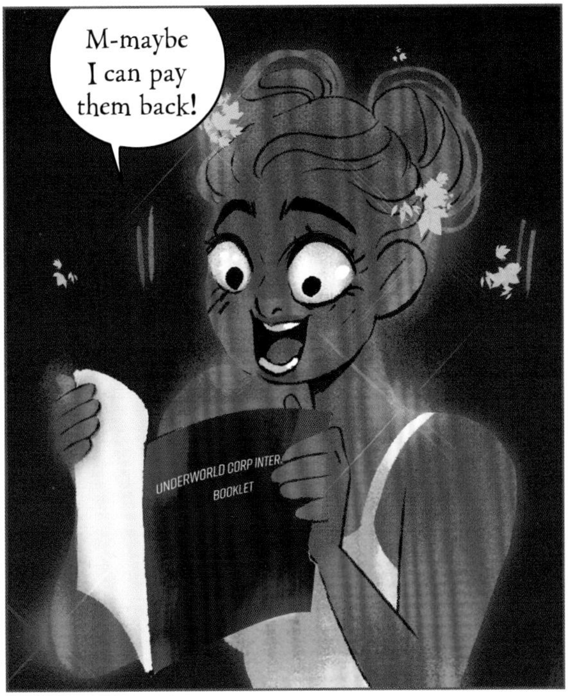
M-maybe I can pay them back!
UNDERWORLD CORP INTER
BOOKLET

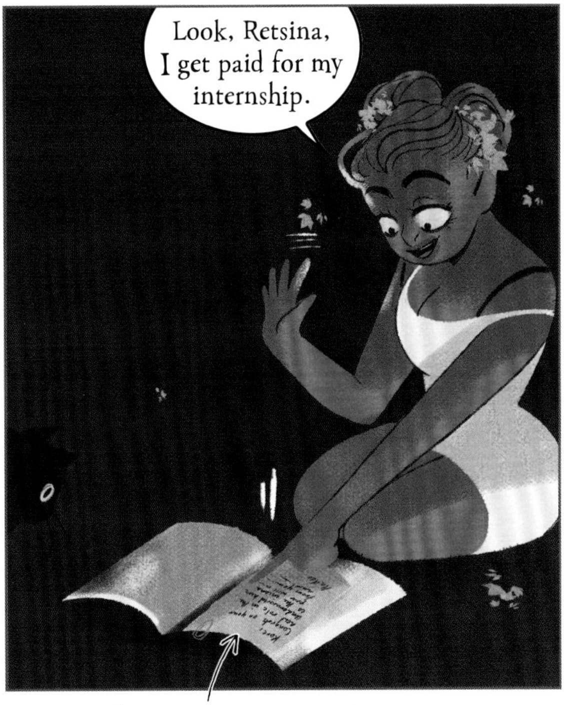
Look, Retsina, I get paid for my internship.

(Clearly added in by Hades.)

YESTERDAY

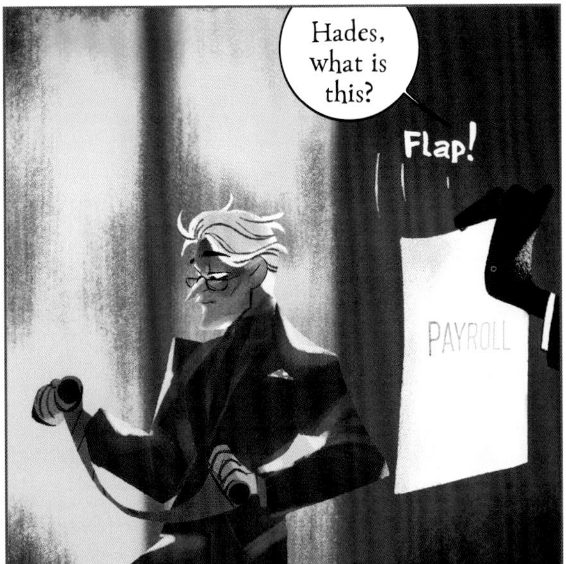
Hades, what is this?
Flap!
PAYROLL

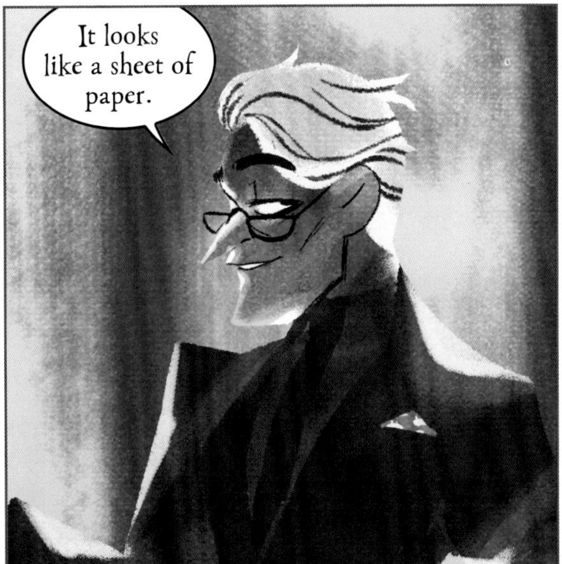
It looks like a sheet of paper.

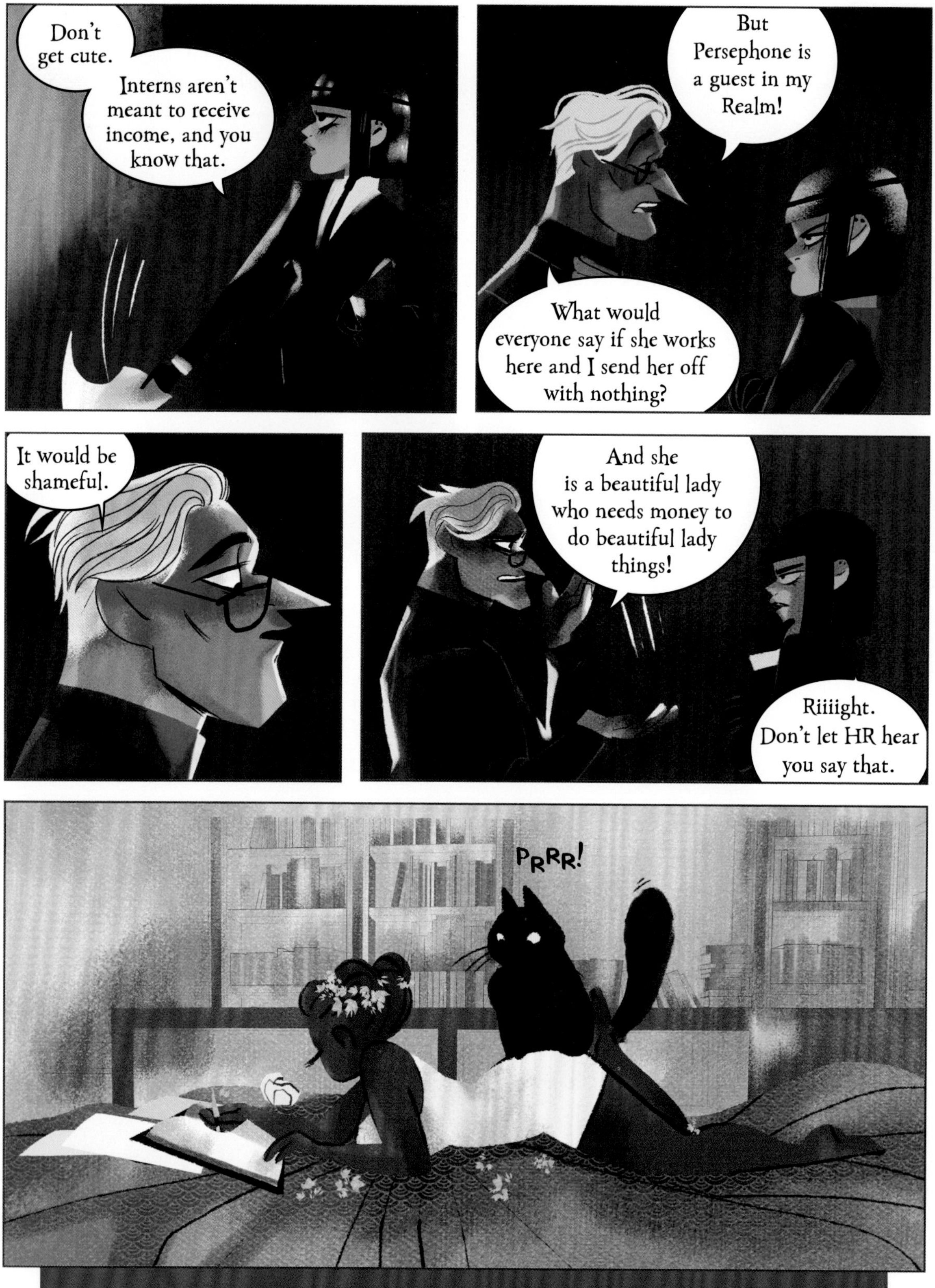
Don't get cute.
Interns aren't meant to receive income, and you know that.
But Persephone is a guest in my Realm!
What would everyone say if she works here and I send her off with nothing?
It would be shameful.
And she is a beautiful lady who needs money to do beautiful lady things!
Riiiight. Don't let HR hear you say that.
PRRR!

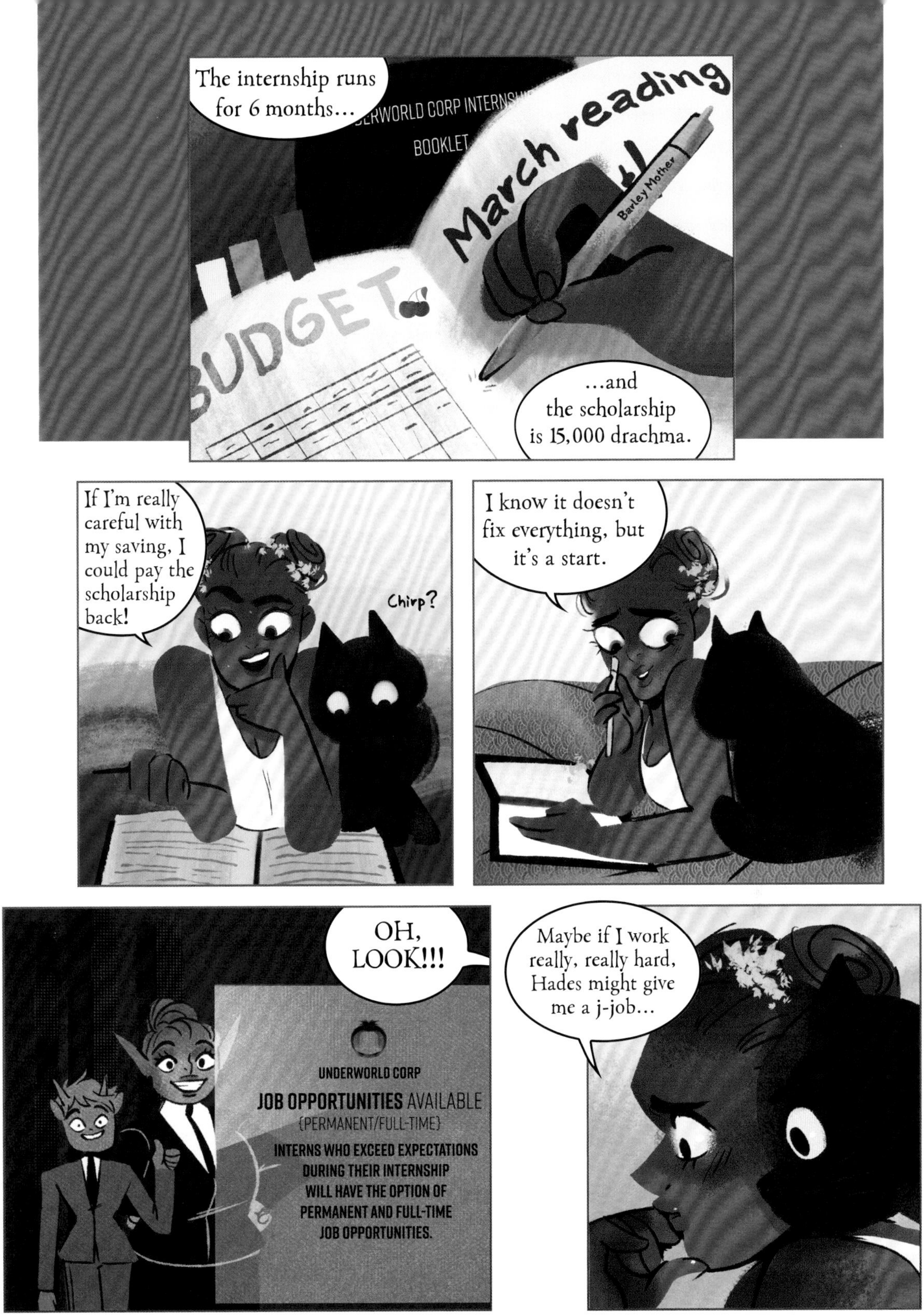

The internship runs for 6 months...
ERWORLD CORP INTERNSH
BOOKLET
March reading
Barley Mother
BUDGET
...and the scholarship is 15,000 drachma.
If I'm really careful with my saving, I could pay the scholarship back!
Chirp?
I know it doesn't fix everything, but it's a start.
OH, LOOK!!!
UNDERWORLD CORP
JOB OPPORTUNITIES AVAILABLE
{PERMANENT/FULL-TIME}
INTERNS WHO EXCEED EXPECTATIONS DURING THEIR INTERNSHIP WILL HAVE THE OPTION OF PERMANENT AND FULL-TIME JOB OPPORTUNITIES.
Maybe if I work really, really hard, Hades might give me a j-job...

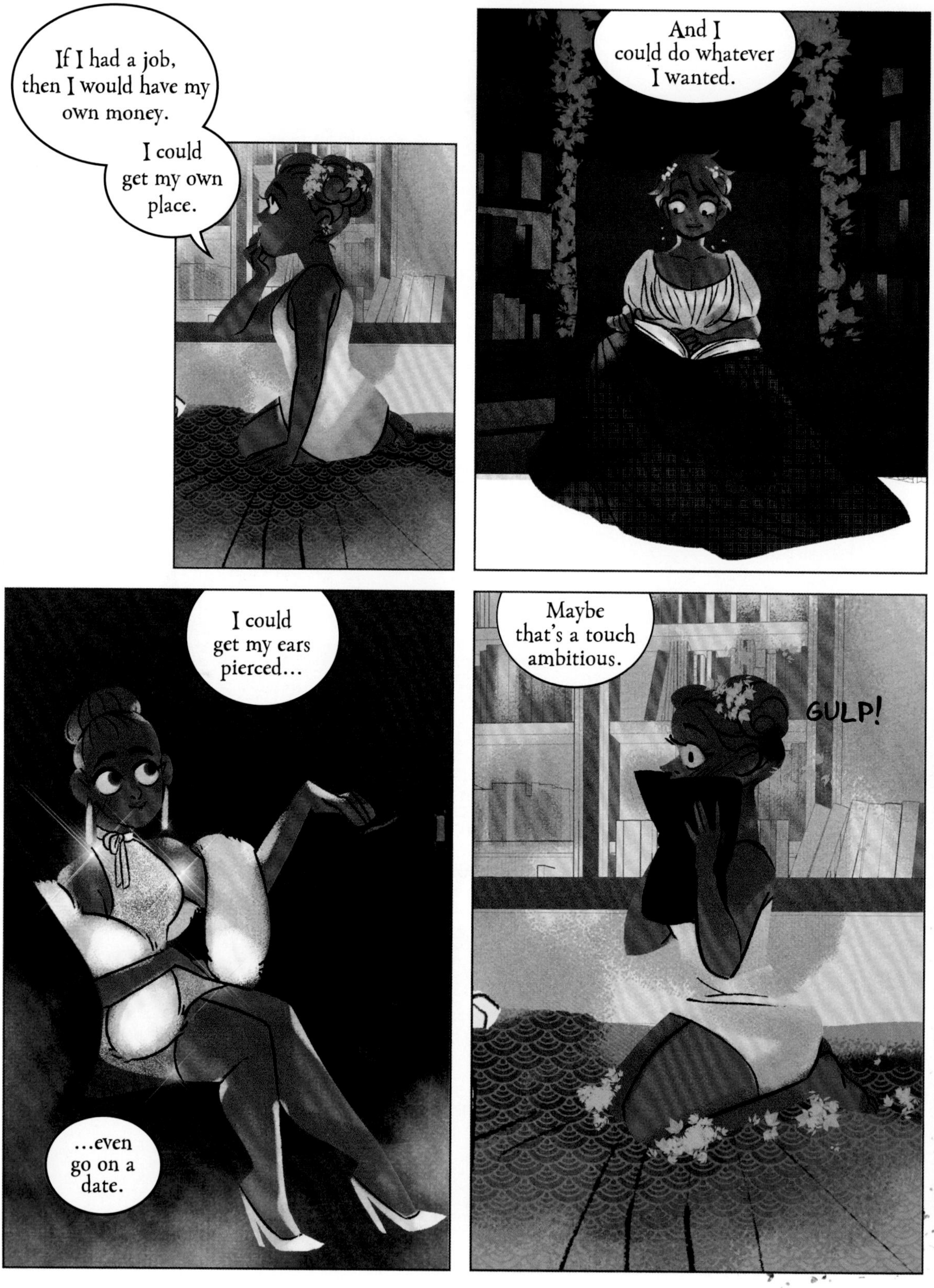
If I had a job, then I would have my own money.
I could get my own place.
And I could do whatever I wanted.
I could get my ears pierced...
...even go on a date.
Maybe that's a touch ambitious.
GULP!

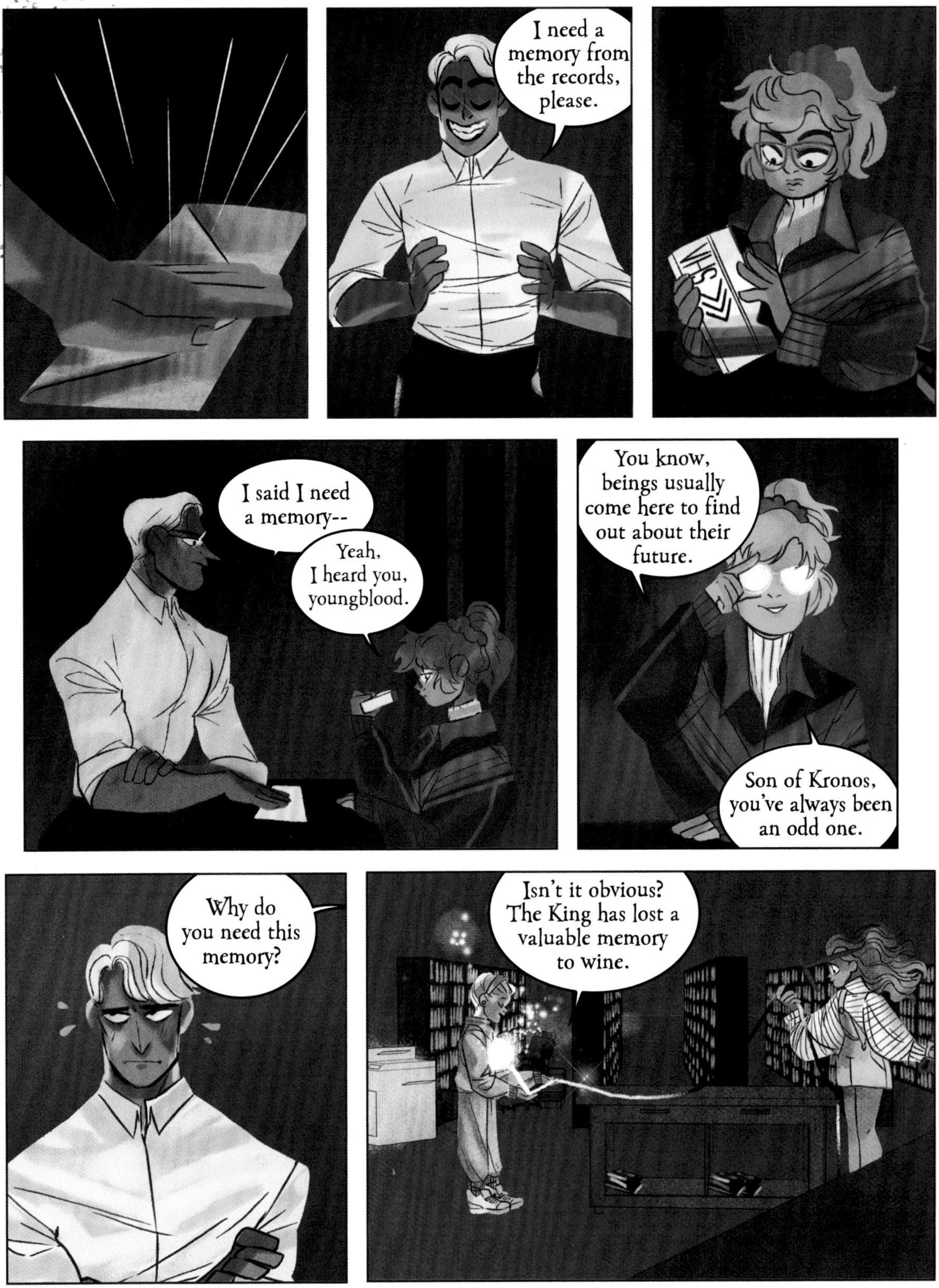
I need a memory from the records, please.
I said I need a memory--
Yeah, I heard you, youngblood.
You know, beings usually come here to find out about their future.
Son of Kronos, you've always been an odd one.
Why do you need this memory?
Isn't it obvious? The King has lost a valuable memory to wine.

And this memory involves a young lady...

HA HA HA! HA HA HA! HA HA! HA HA HA! HA HA!

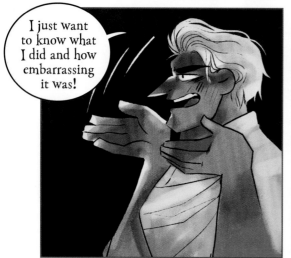

I just want to know what I did and how embarrassing it was!

Do you have the paperwork?

I was kinda hoping you'd do me a solid since I'm a King.

I need signed consent from Kore.

After all, it's her memory, too.

But--

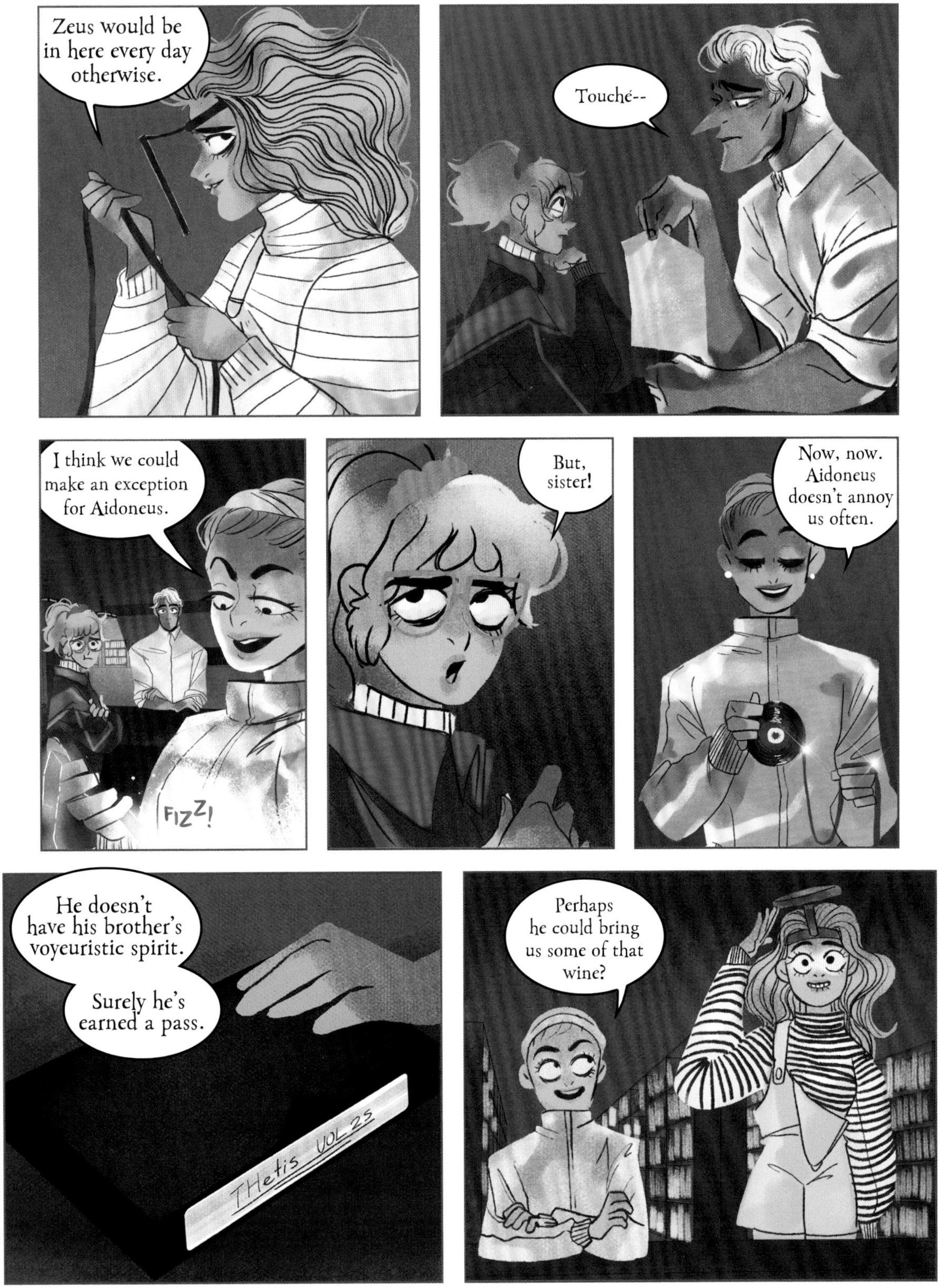

Zeus would be in here every day otherwise.
Touché--
I think we could make an exception for Aidoneus.
FIZZ!
But, sister!
Now, now. Aidoneus doesn't annoy us often.
He doesn't have his brother's voyeuristic spirit.
Surely he's earned a pass.
THetis VOL 25
Perhaps he could bring us some of that wine?

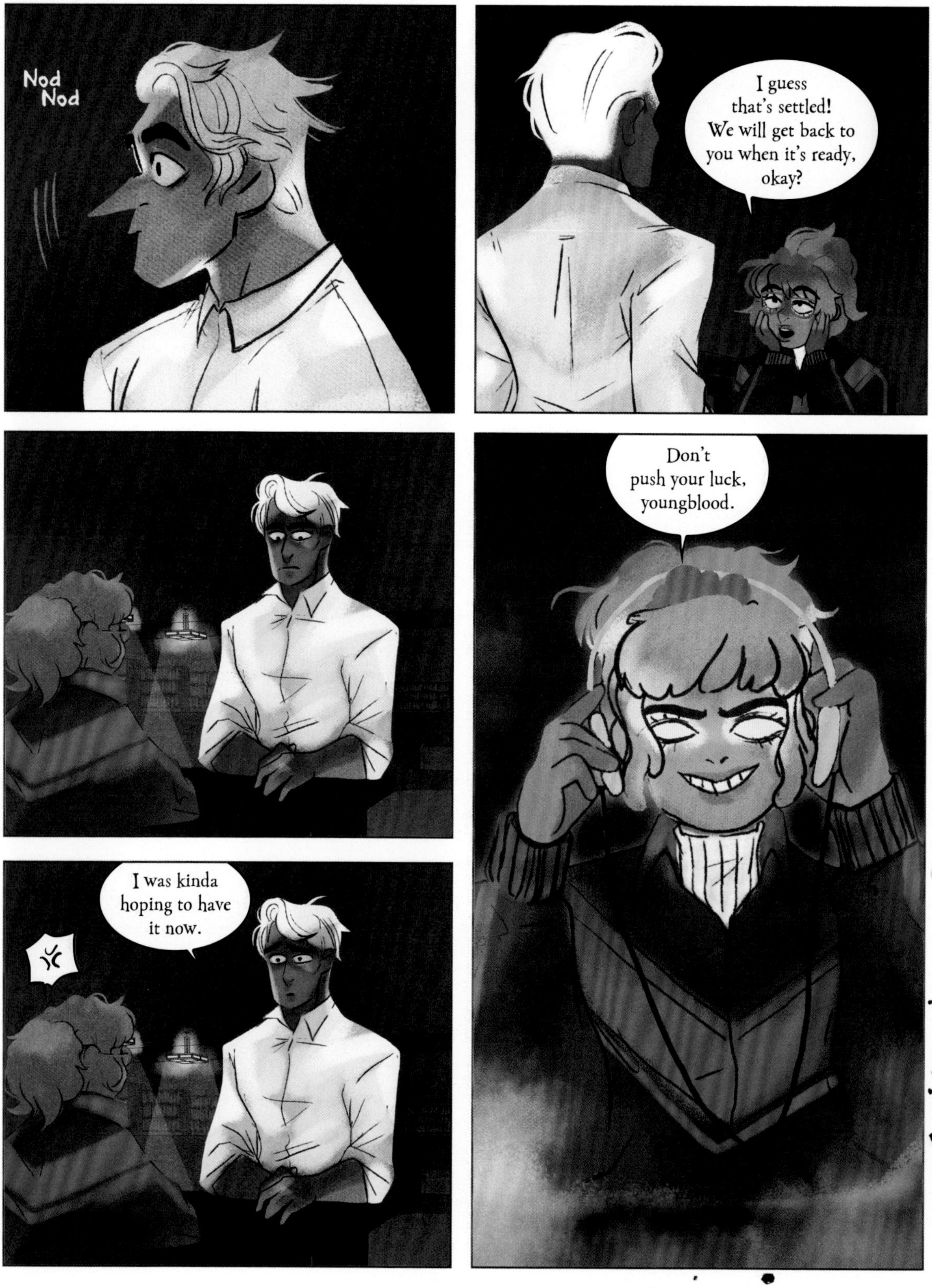
Nod
Nod
I guess that's settled! We will get back to you when it's ready, okay?
I was kinda hoping to have it now.
Don't push your luck, youngblood.

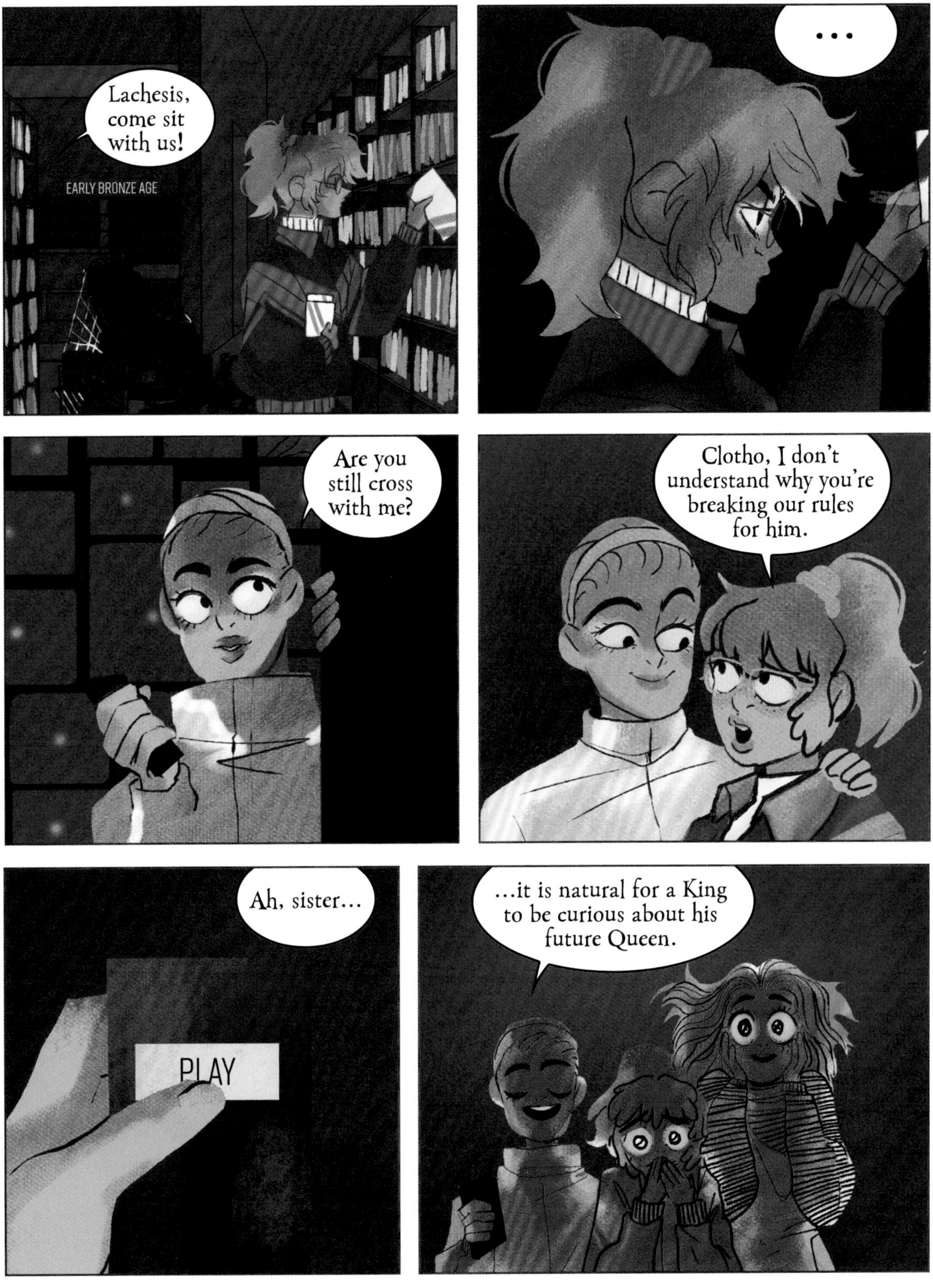
Lachesis, come sit with us!
EARLY BRONZE AGE
...
Are you still cross with me?
Clotho, I don't understand why you're breaking our rules for him.
Ah, sister...
PLAY
...it is natural for a King to be curious about his future Queen.

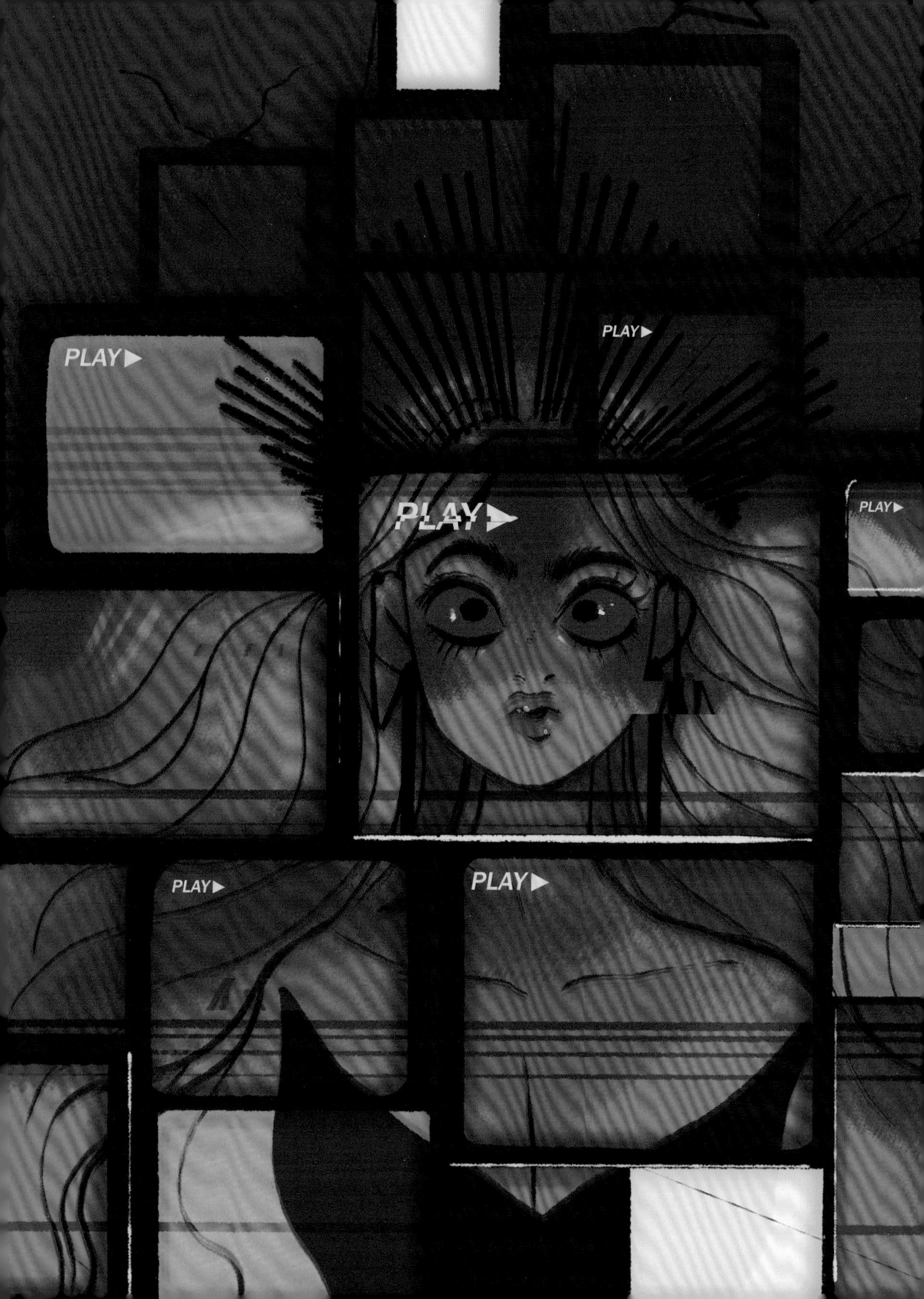
PLAY ▶
PLAY ▶
PLAY ▶
PLAY ▶
PLAY ▶
PLAY ▶

If it were up to me, I would create an endless number of chapters featuring Hades and Persephone aimlessly wandering the streets of the Underworld together.

There are still many elements of the Underworld that I wish I had time to share, but I must balance my desire for worldbuilding with the largely character-driven story.

I hope you enjoy this bonus chapter, in which Hades and Persephone experience some of the everyday nature of the Underworld.

With thanks to:
Johana R. Ahumada, Yulia Garibova (Hita), Jaki Haboon,
Amy Kim, Kristina Ness, Karen Pavon, M. Rawlings, Court Rogers

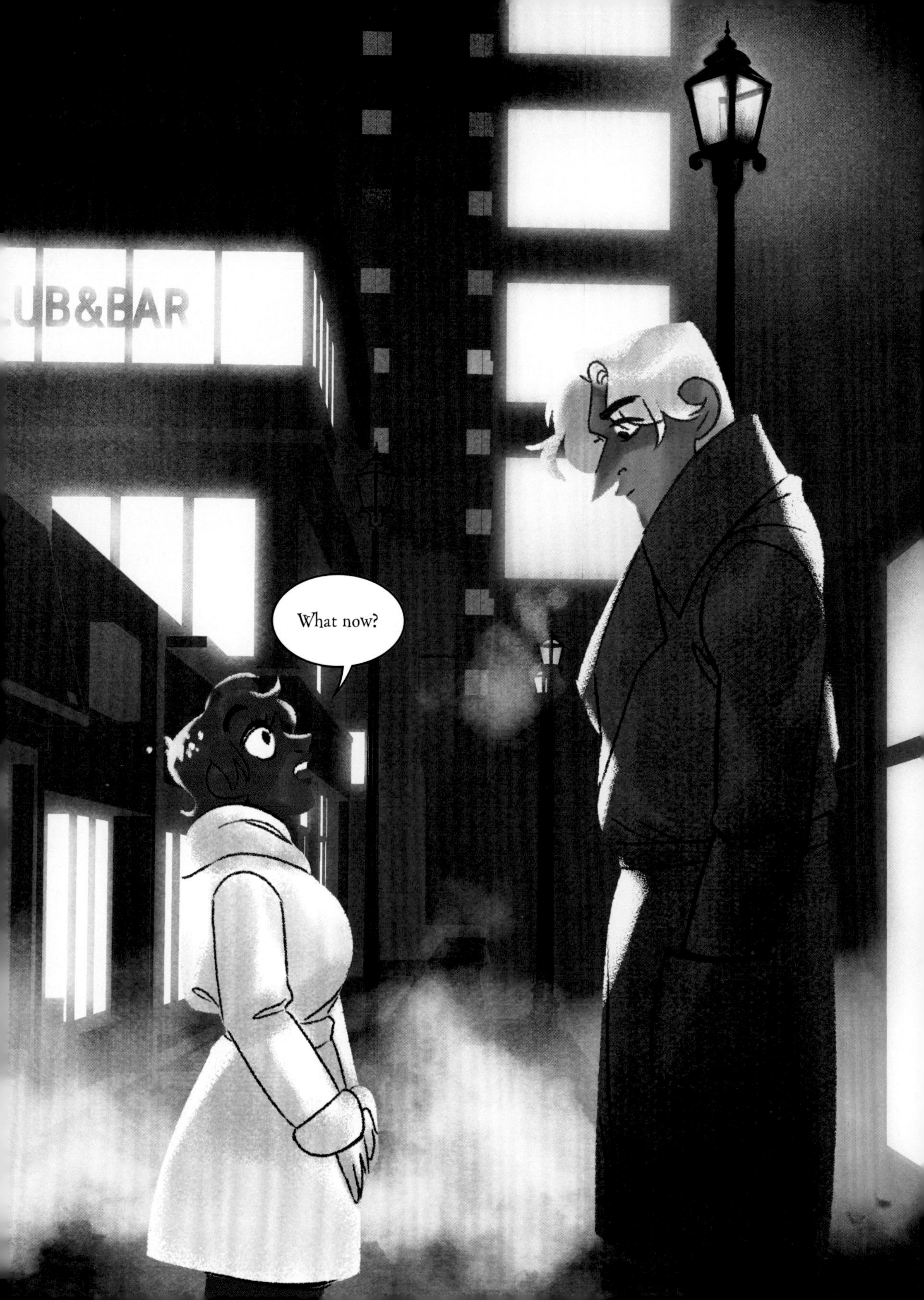
UB&BAR
What now?

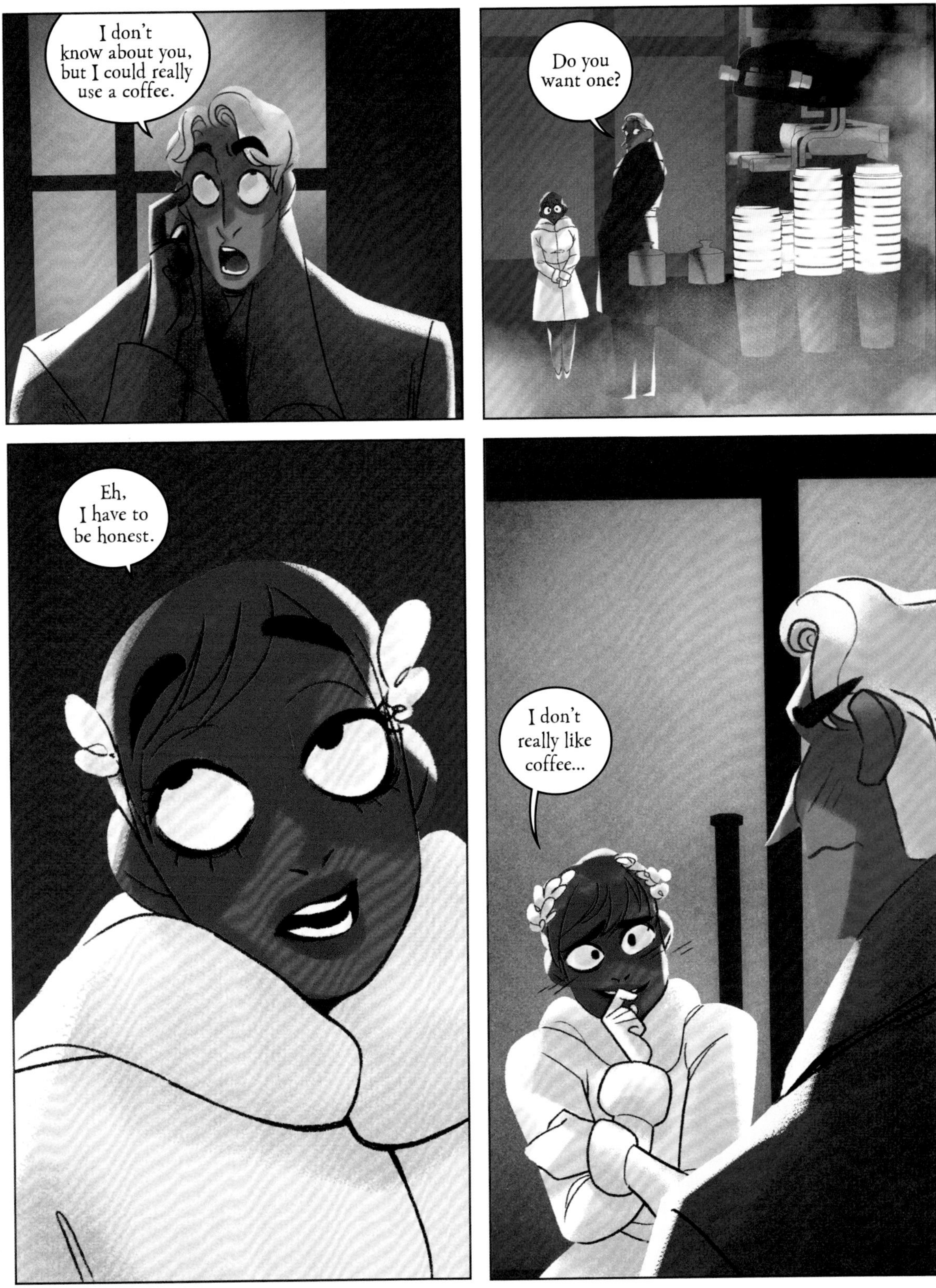
I don't know about you, but I could really use a coffee.
Do you want one?
Eh, I have to be honest.
I don't really like coffee...

Wait...
but you had coffee
at my house.

Well,
yeah, I couldn't
refuse a King's
hospitality.

SIGH

You
don't want
anything?

Chai
latte?

Cold-
pressed
juice?

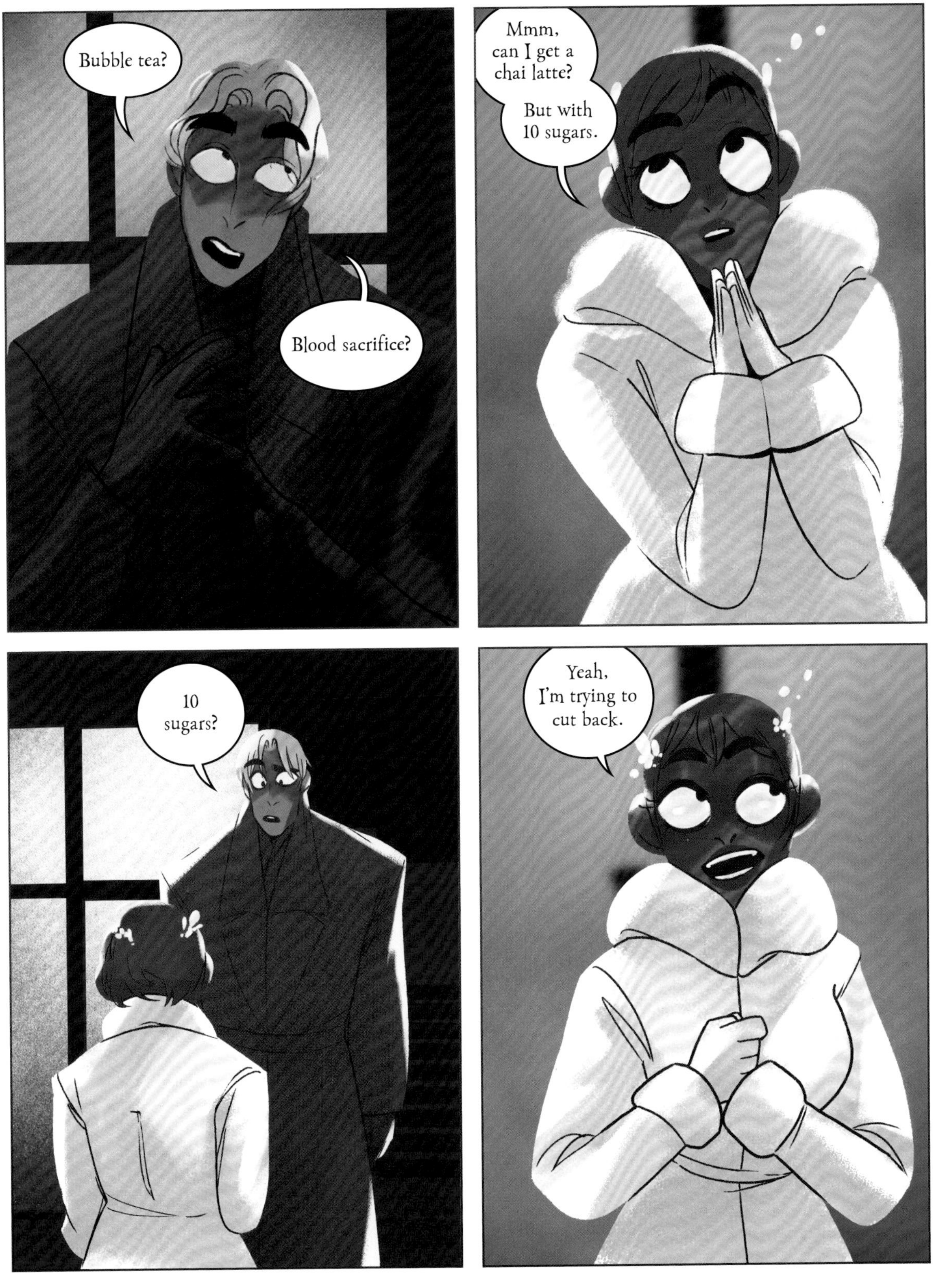
Bubble tea?
Blood sacrifice?
Mmm, can I get a chai latte?
But with 10 sugars.
10 sugars?
Yeah, I'm trying to cut back.

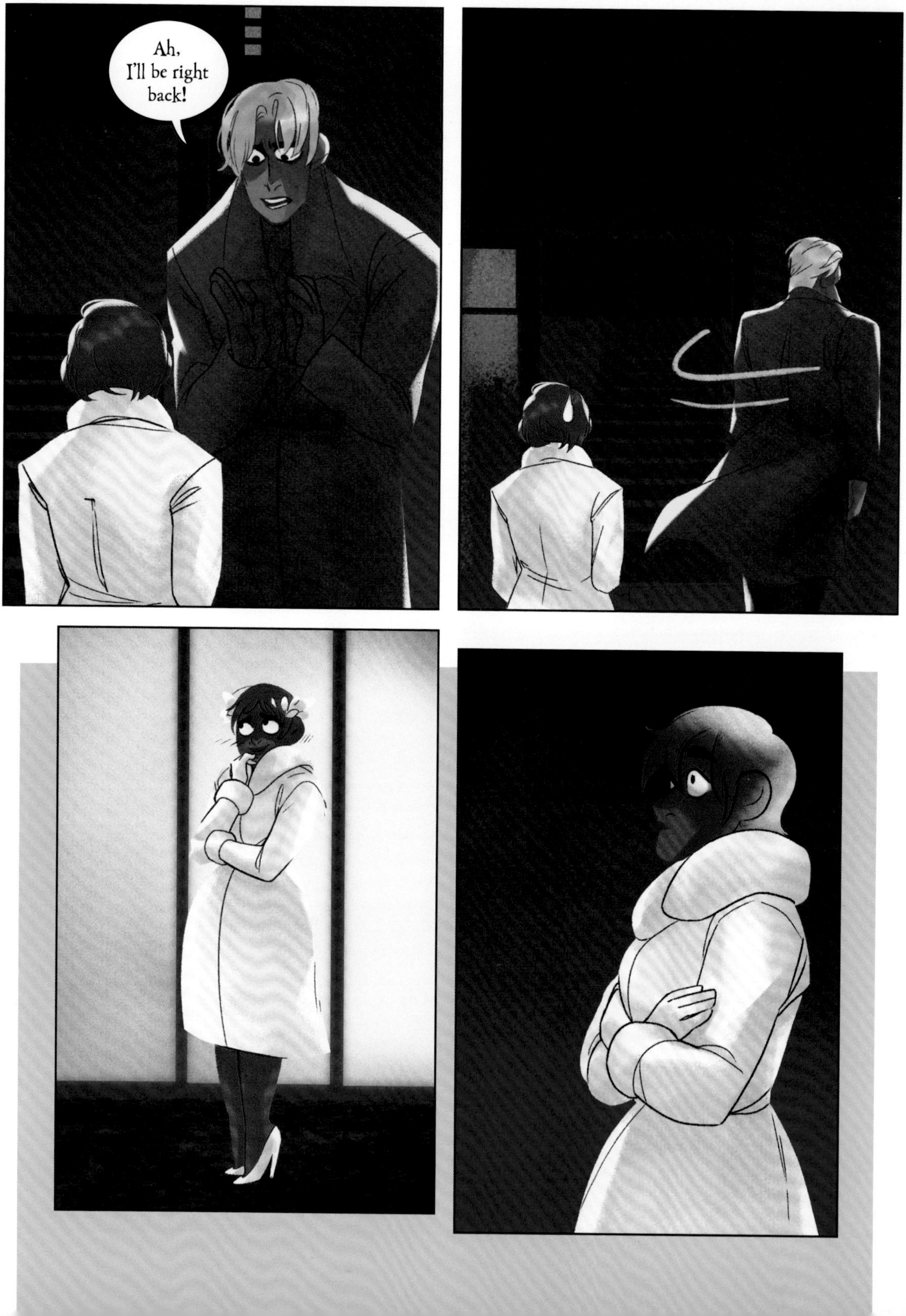
Ah,
I'll be right
back!

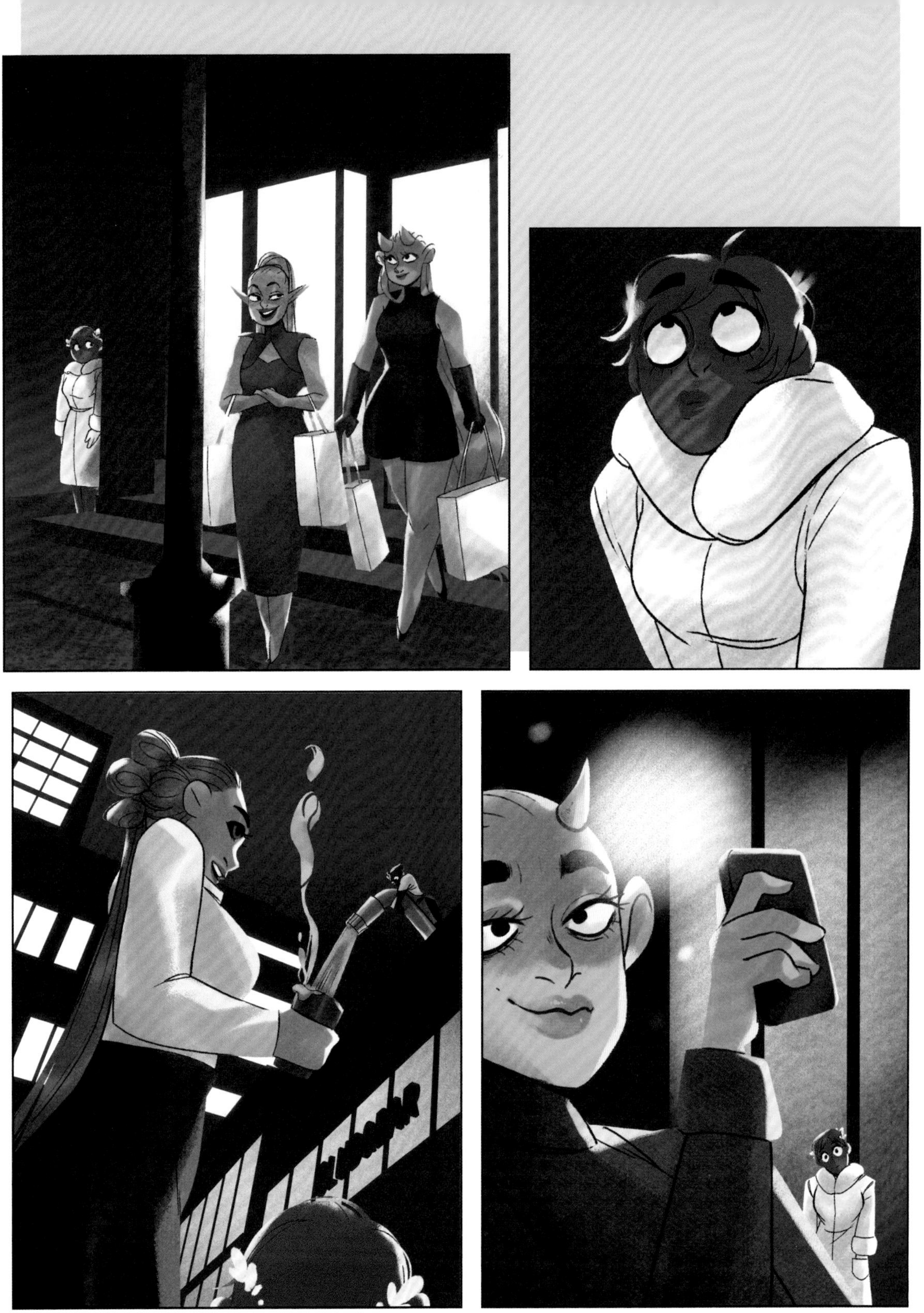

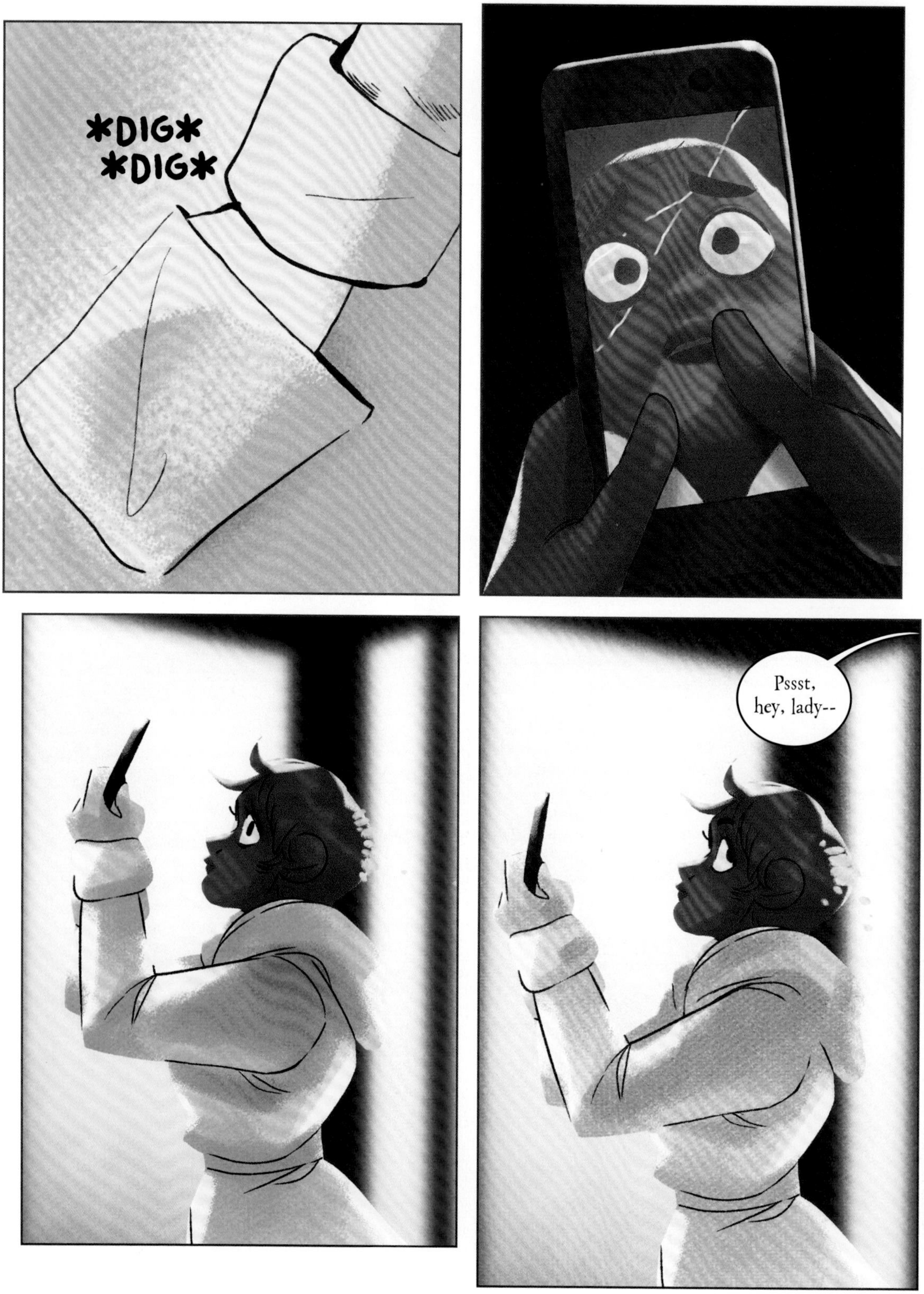
DIG
DIG
Pssst, hey, lady--

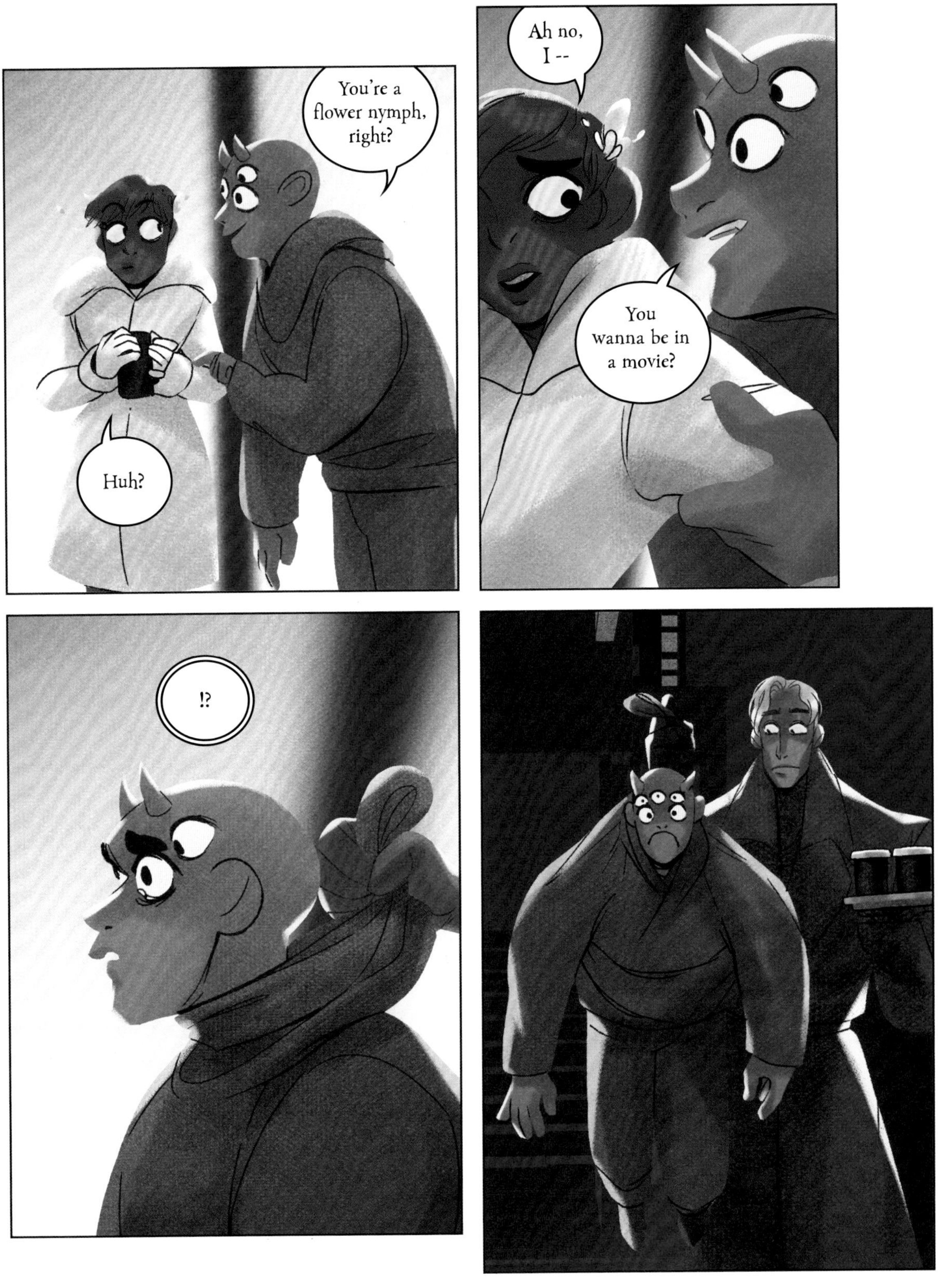
You're a flower nymph, right?
Huh?
Ah no, I --
You wanna be in a movie?
!?

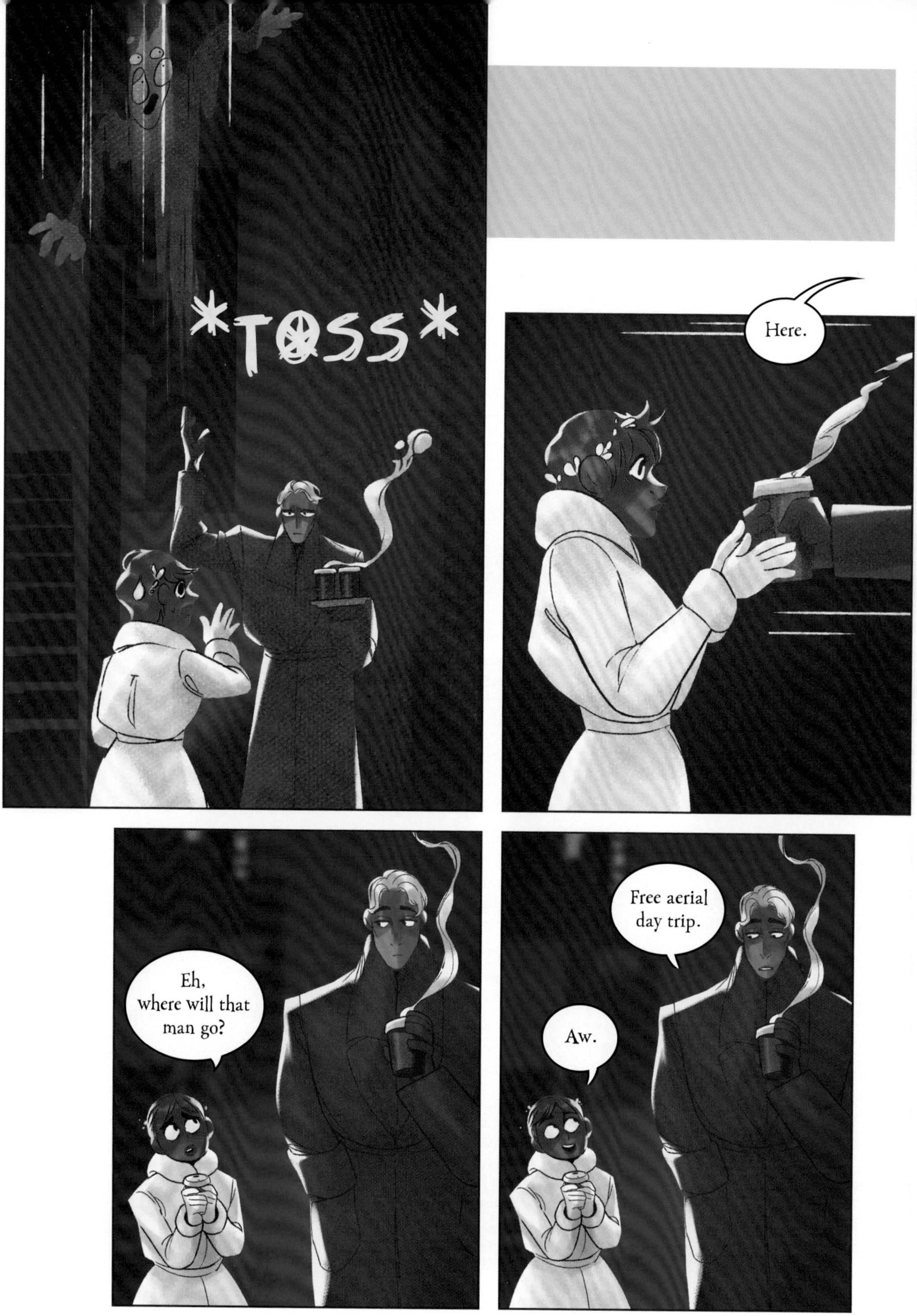
TOSS
Here.
Eh, where will that man go?
Free aerial day trip.
Aw.

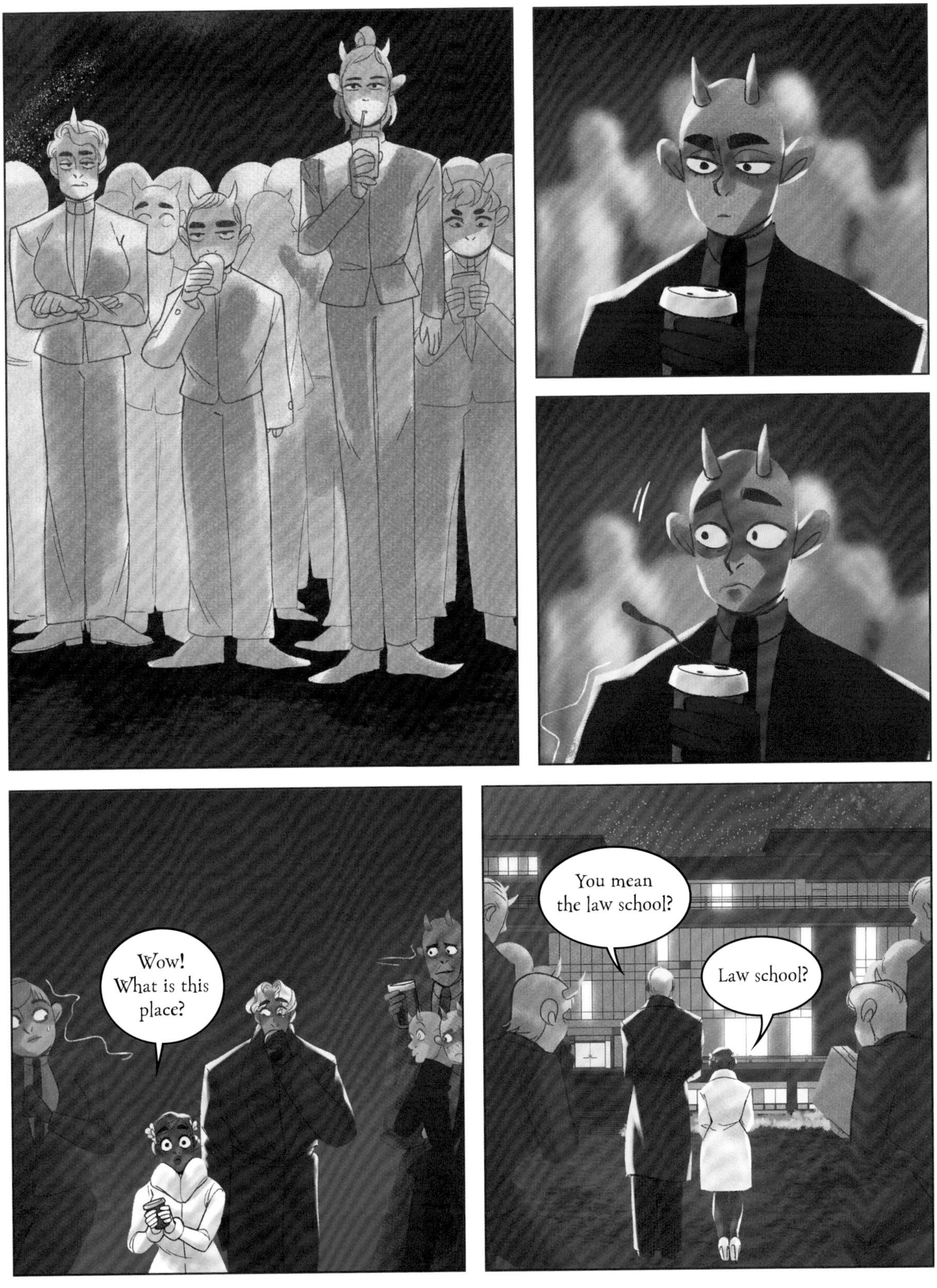
Wow! What is this place?
You mean the law school?
Law school?

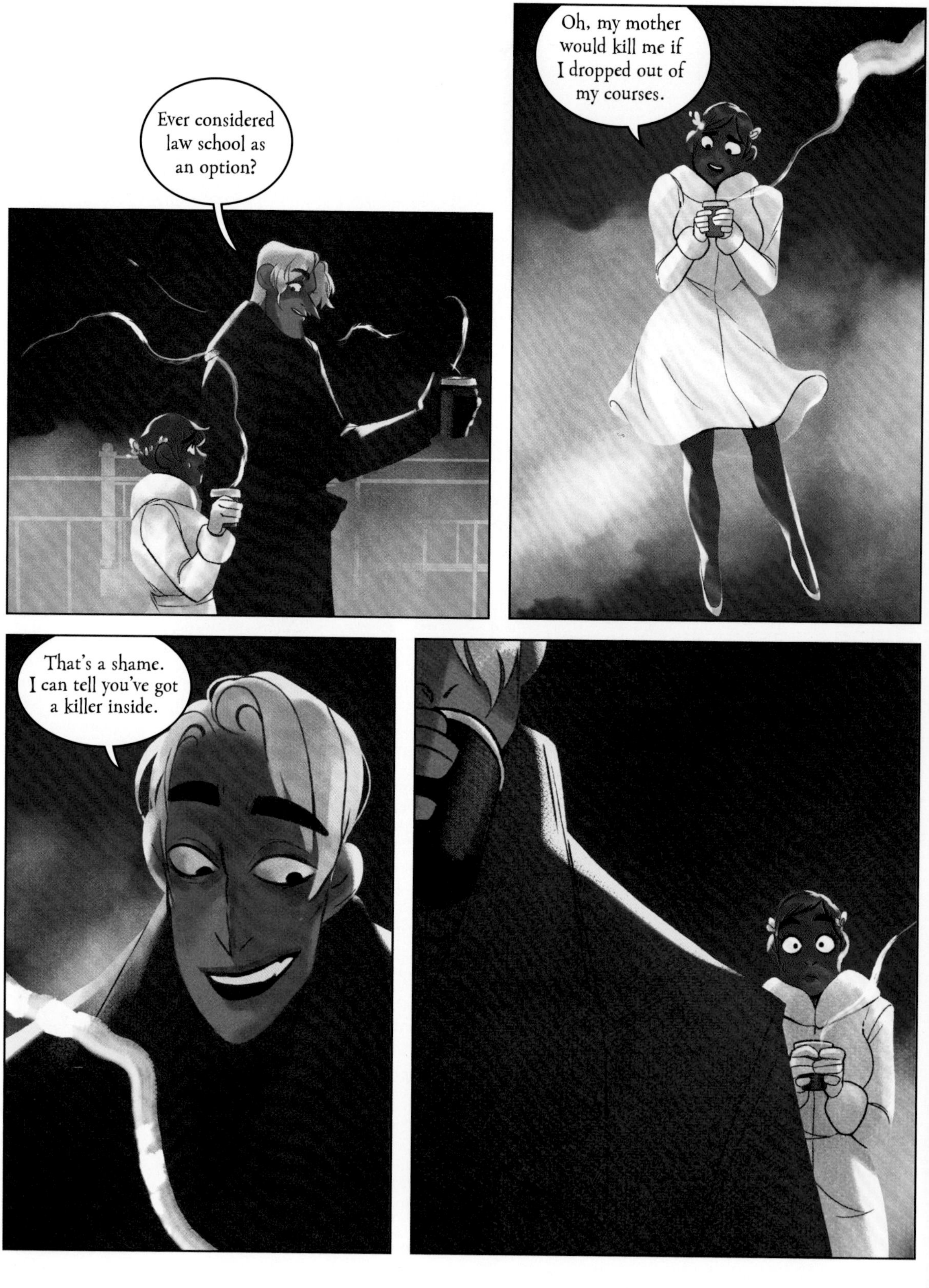
Ever considered law school as an option?
Oh, my mother would kill me if I dropped out of my courses.
That's a shame. I can tell you've got a killer inside.

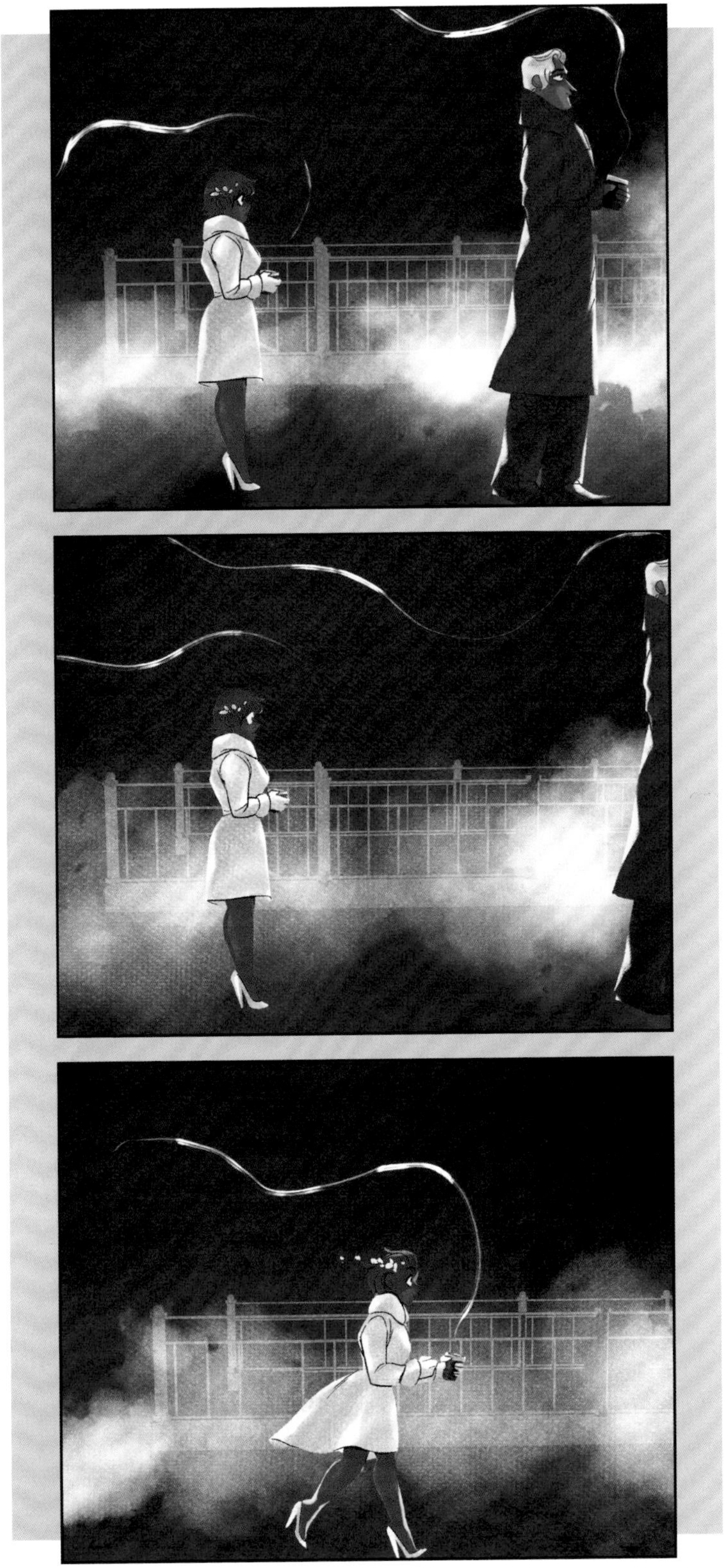

ABOUT THE AUTHOR

RACHEL SMYTHE is the creator of the Eisner-nominated
Lore Olympus, published via WEBTOON.

Twitter: @used_bandaid

Instagram: @usedbandaid

Facebook.com/Usedbandaidillustration

LoreOlympusBooks.com

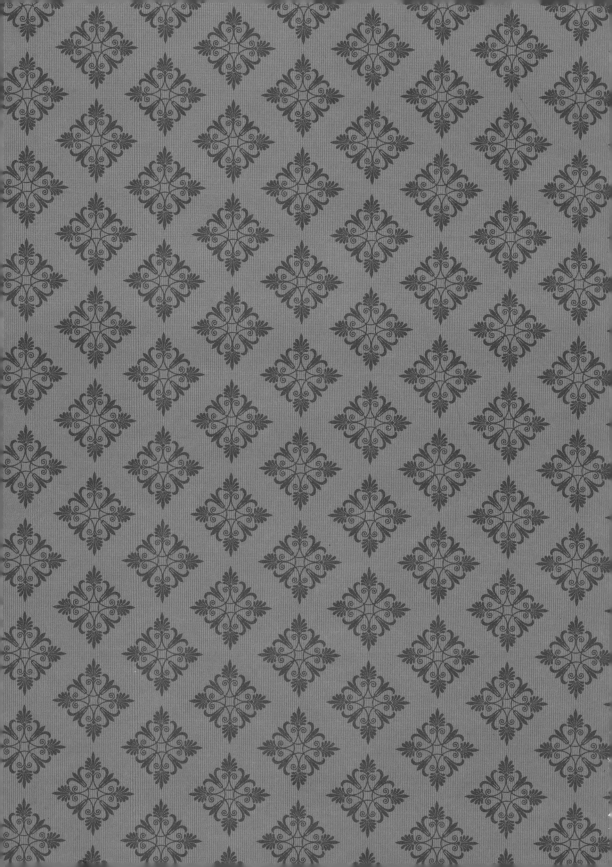

Lore Olympus

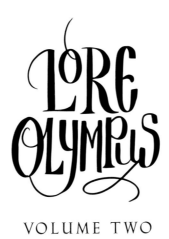

VOLUME TWO

VOLUME TWO

RACHEL SMYTHE

NEW YORK

Published in the United States by Del Rey, an imprint of Random House,
a division of Penguin Random House LLC, New York.

DEL REY and the HOUSE colophon are registered trademarks of Penguin Random House LLC.

Portions of this work originally appeared on Webtoons.com.

LIBRARY OF CONGRESS CATALOGING-IN-PUBLICATION DATA
Names: Smythe, Rachel (Comics artist), author, artist.
Title: Lore Olympus / Rachel Smythe.
Description: First edition. | New York : Del Rey, 2022
Identifiers: LCCN 2021008087 | Hardcover ISBN 9780593160305 (v. 2) |
Trade paperback ISBN 9780593356081 (v. 2)
Subjects: LCSH: Mythology, Greek—Comic books, strips, etc. | Graphic novels.
Classification: LCC PN6727.S54758 L67 2021 | DDC 741.5/973—dc23
LC record available at https://lccn.loc.gov/2021008087

Printed in China

Original WEBTOON editors: Bekah Caden, Annie LaHue
Rachel Smythe art assistants: Johana R. Ahumada, M. Rawlings, Court Rogers
WEBTOON translation: Anastasia Gkortsila
Penguin Random House team: Ted Allen, Erin Korenko, and Sarah Peed

randomhousebooks.com

2 4 6 8 9 7 5 3 1

First Edition

Book design by Edwin Vazquez

To Eunice Yooni Kim,
thank you for noticing me.

CONTENT WARNING
FROM RACHEL SMYTHE

Lore Olympus regularly deals with themes of physical
and mental abuse, sexual trauma, and toxic relationships.

Some of the interactions in this volume may be distressing
for some readers. Please exercise discretion, and seek out
the support of others if you require it.

EPISODE 26

YOU CALLED
YOU ANSWERED

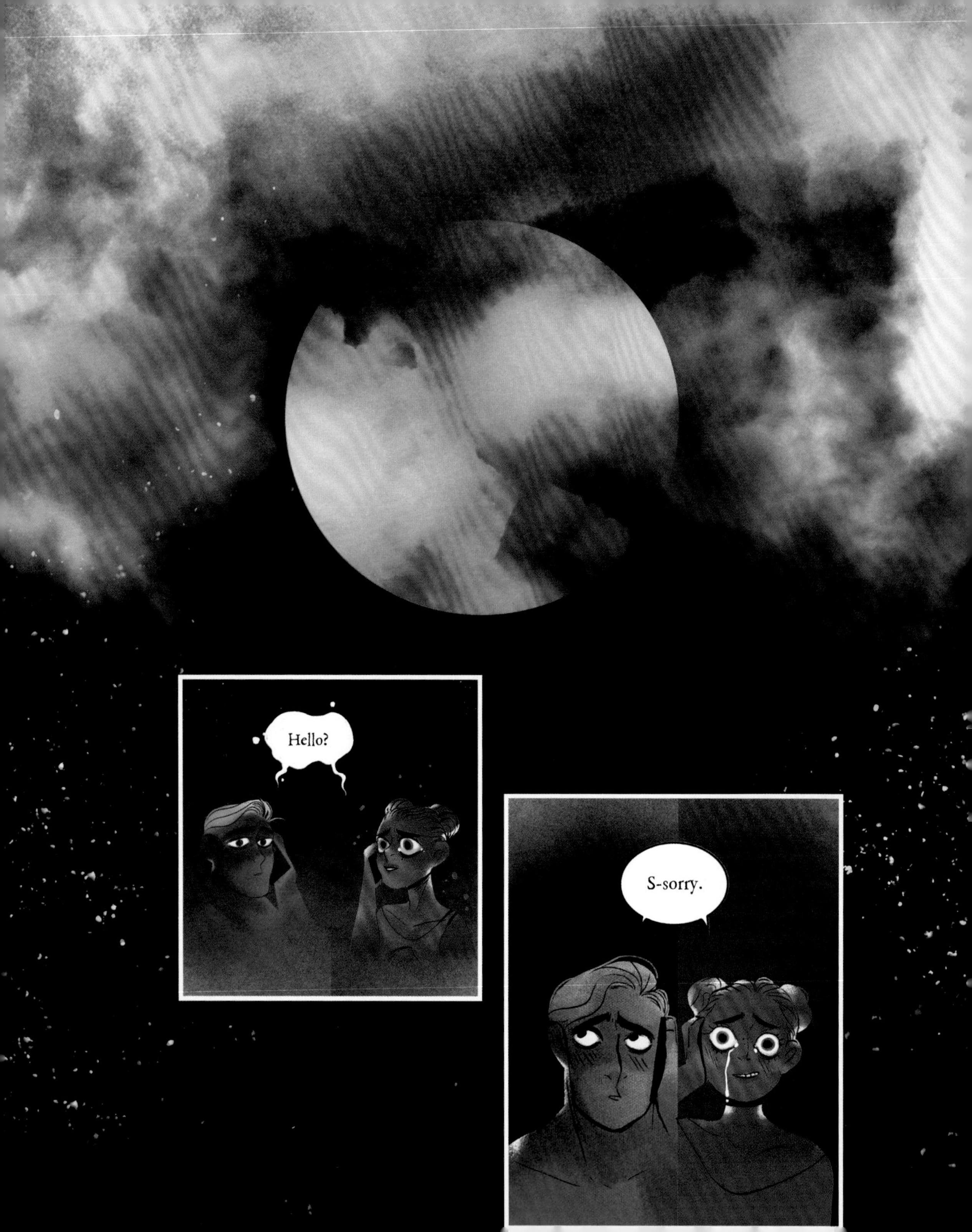
Hello?
S-sorry.

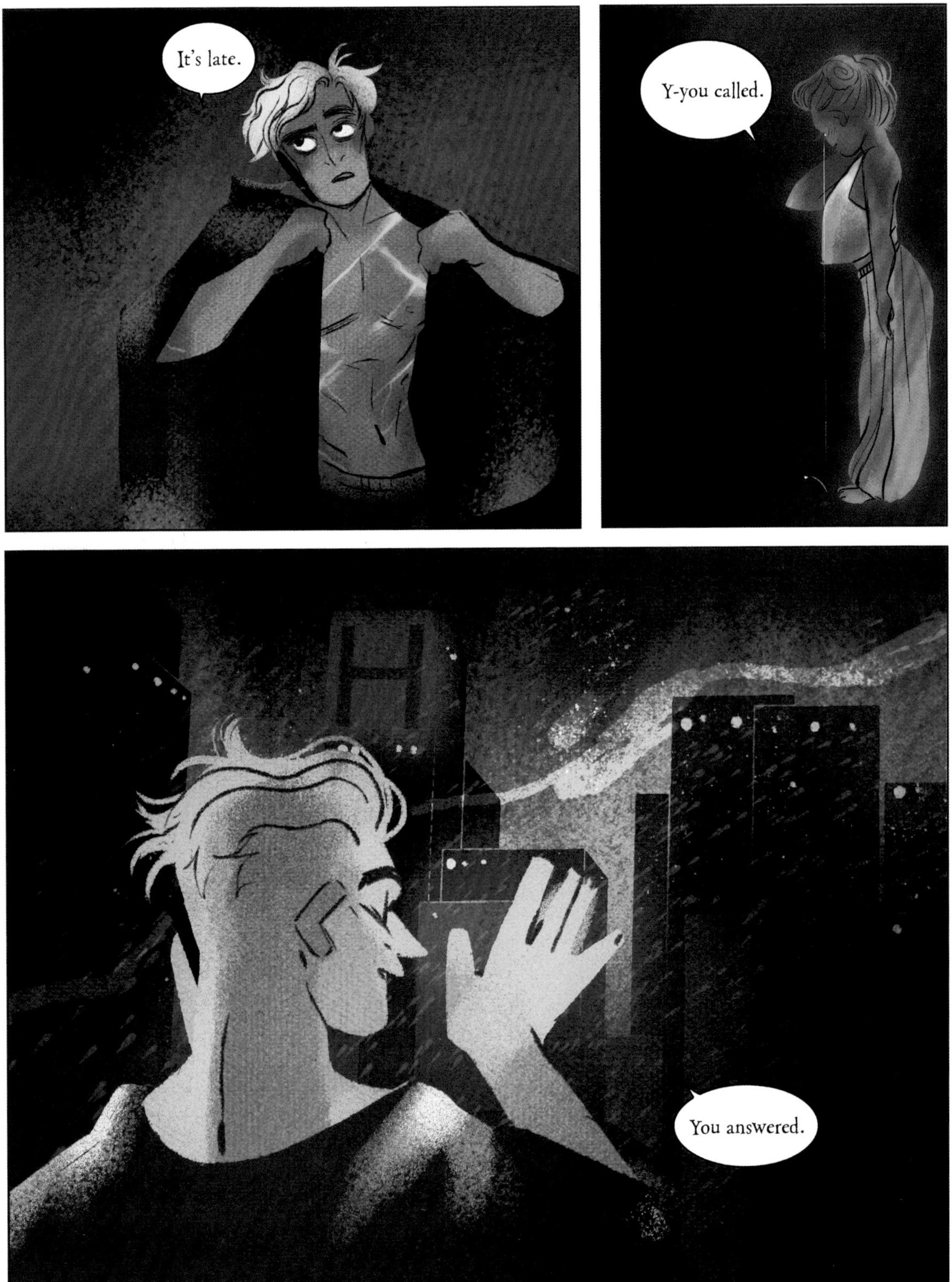
It's late.
Y-you called.
You answered.

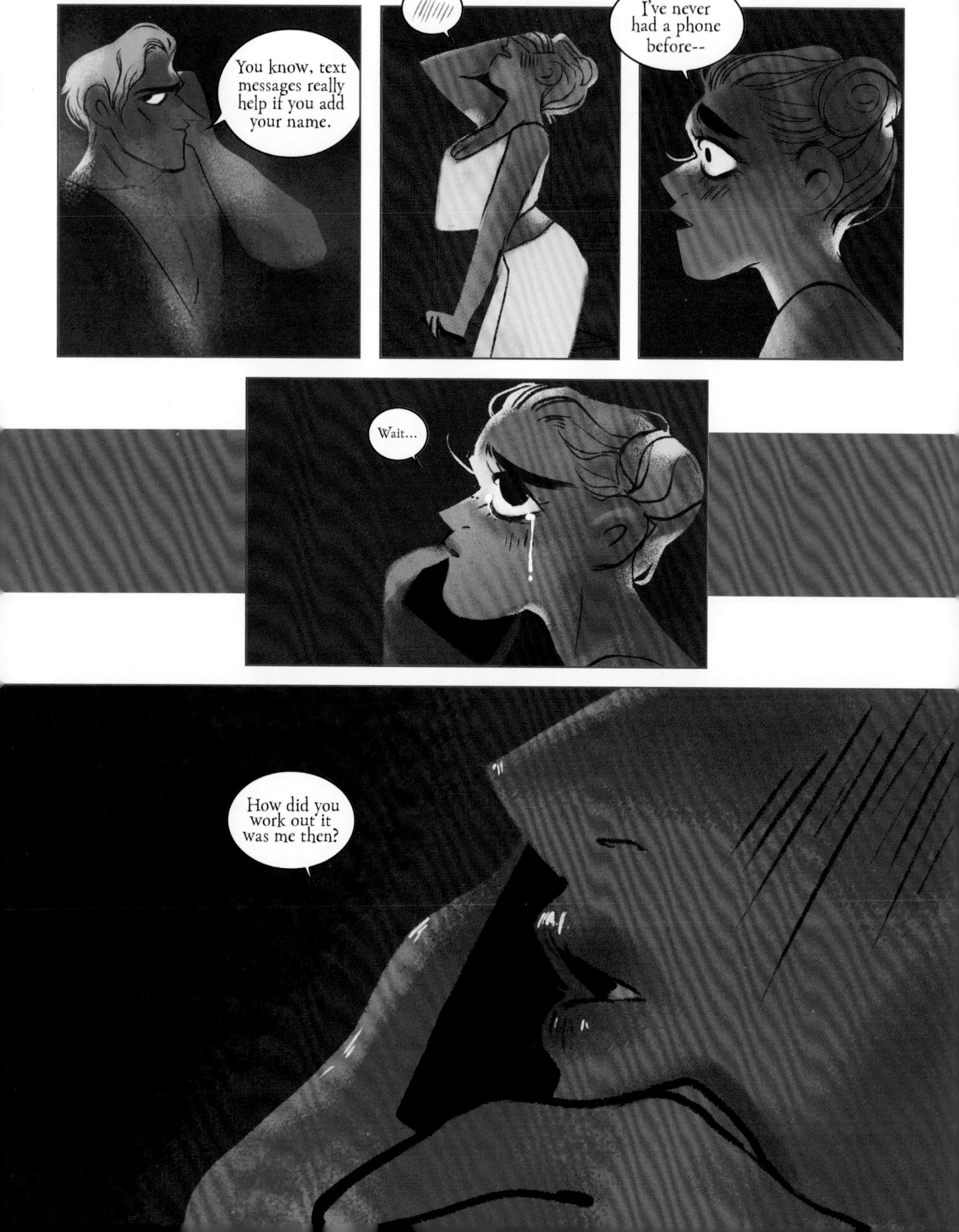
You know, text messages really help if you add your name.
I've never had a phone before--
Wait...
How did you work out it was me then?

I know it's hard to believe...

...but I don't go around gifting fur coats to beautiful women all day long.

Although that sounds like a vast improvement to my current line of work.

You know, you could've just asked.

...

I know.

I'm sorry, Kore.

100 percent.

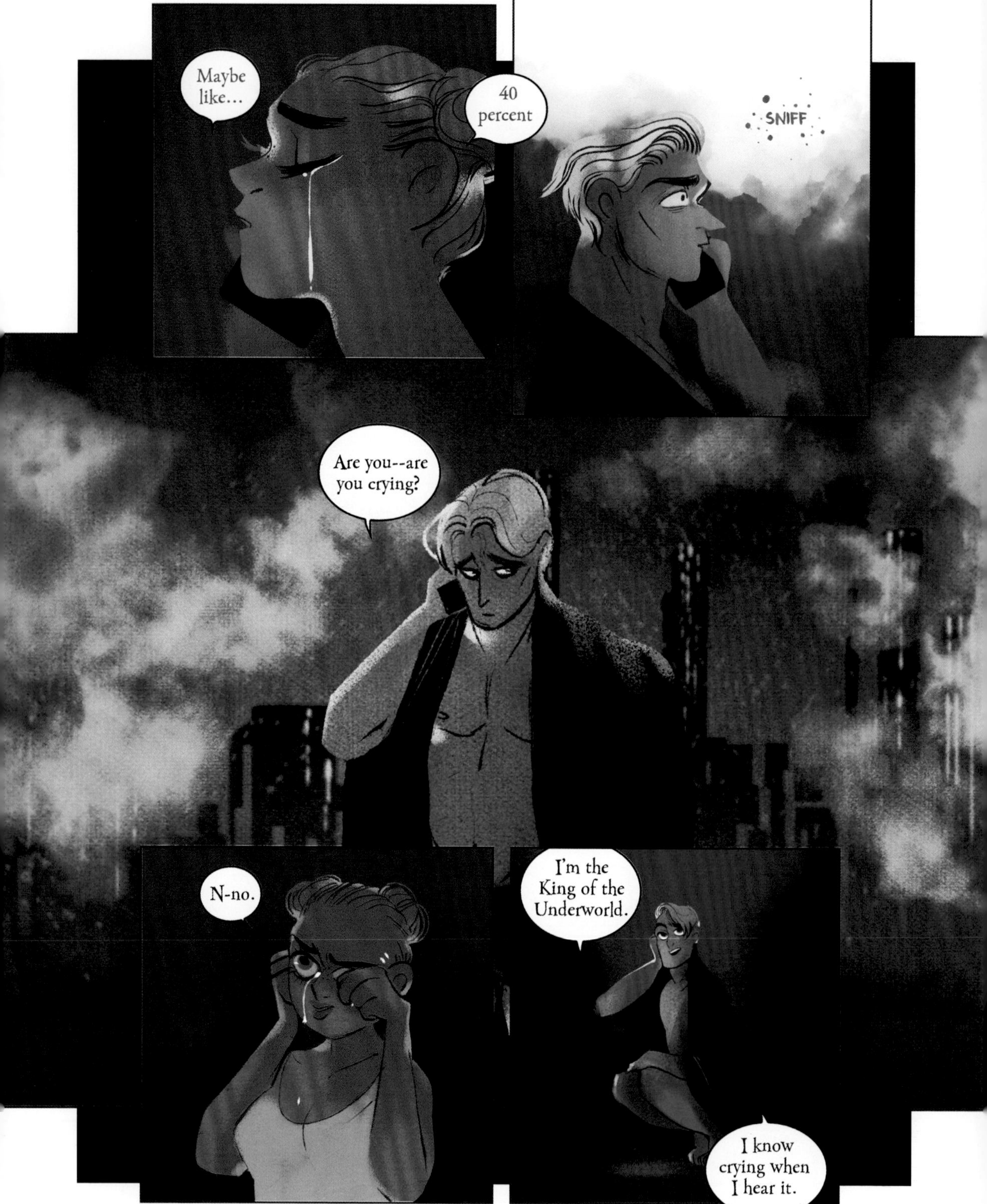
Maybe like…
40 percent
SNIFF
Are you--are you crying?
N-no.
I'm the King of the Underworld.
I know crying when I hear it.

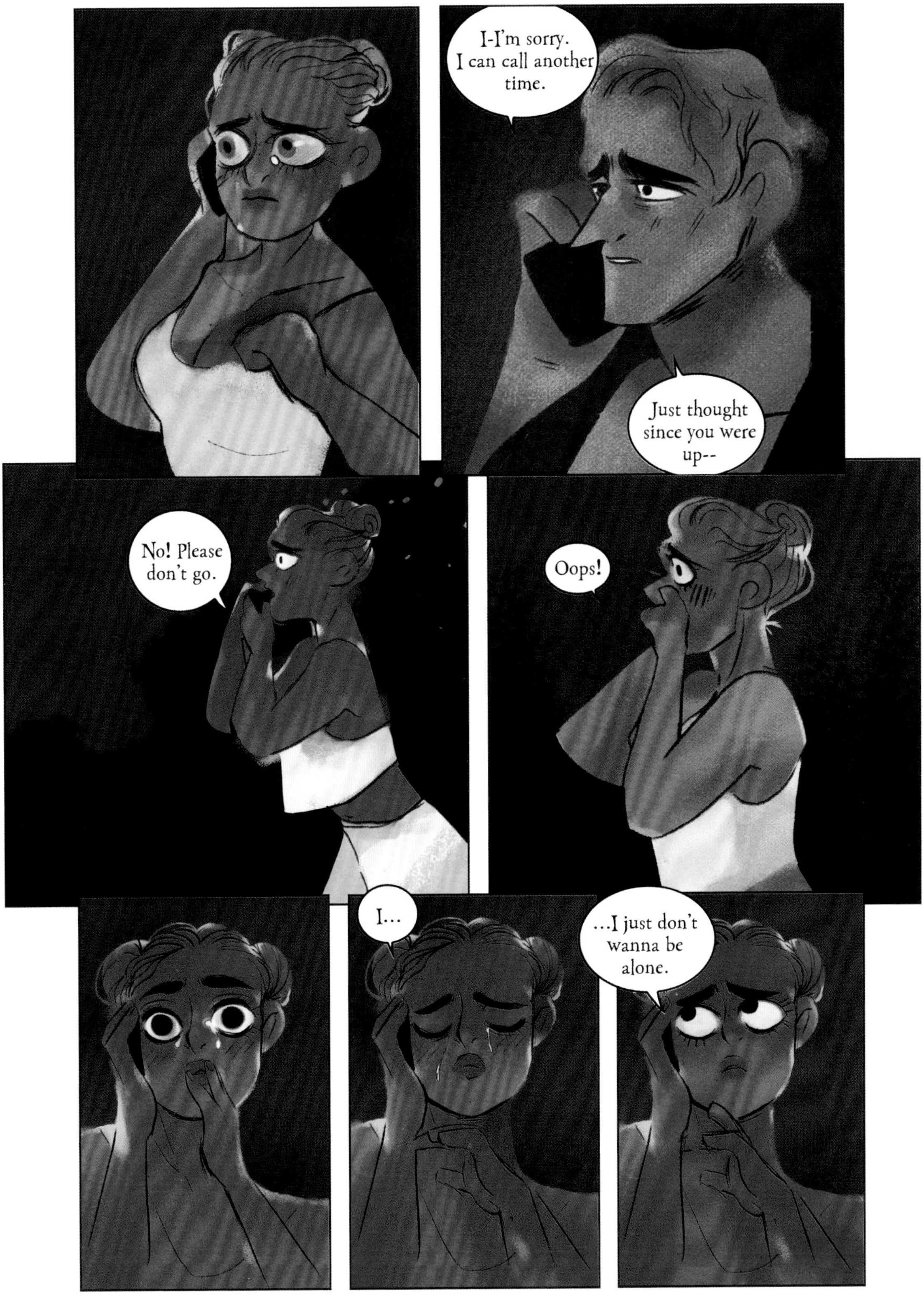
I-I'm sorry.
I can call another time.
Just thought since you were up--
No! Please don't go.
Oops!
I...
...I just don't wanna be alone.

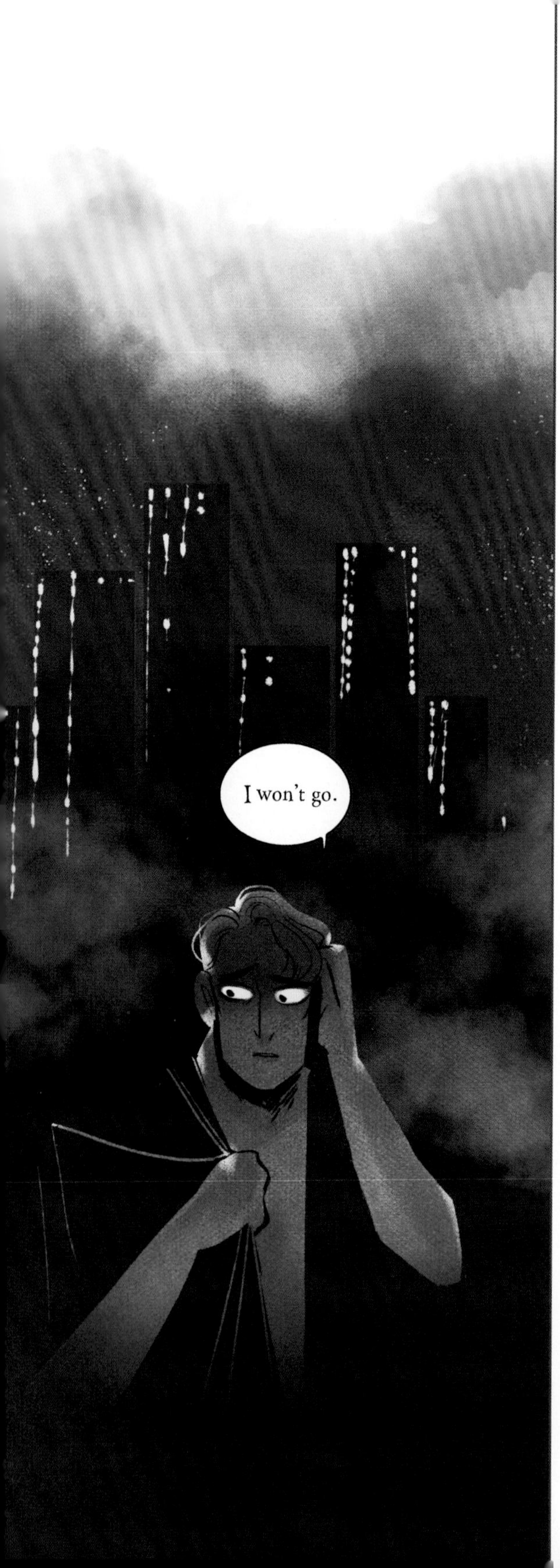
I won't go.

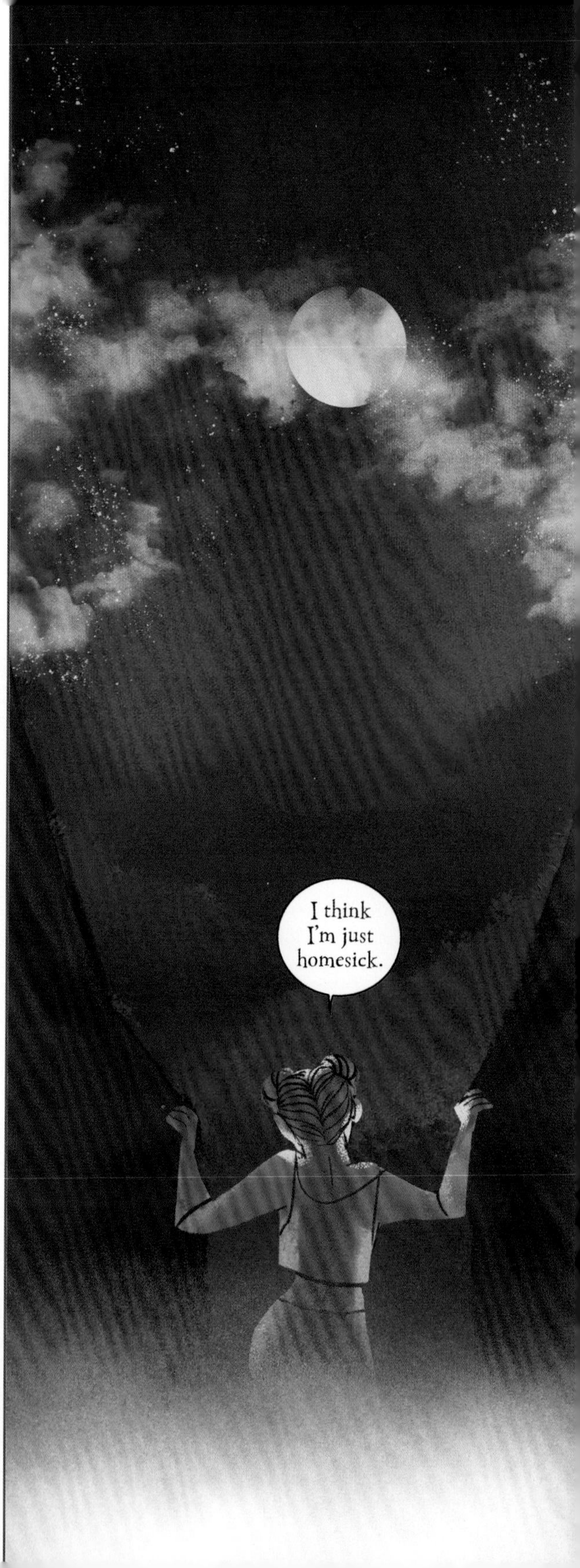
I think I'm just homesick.

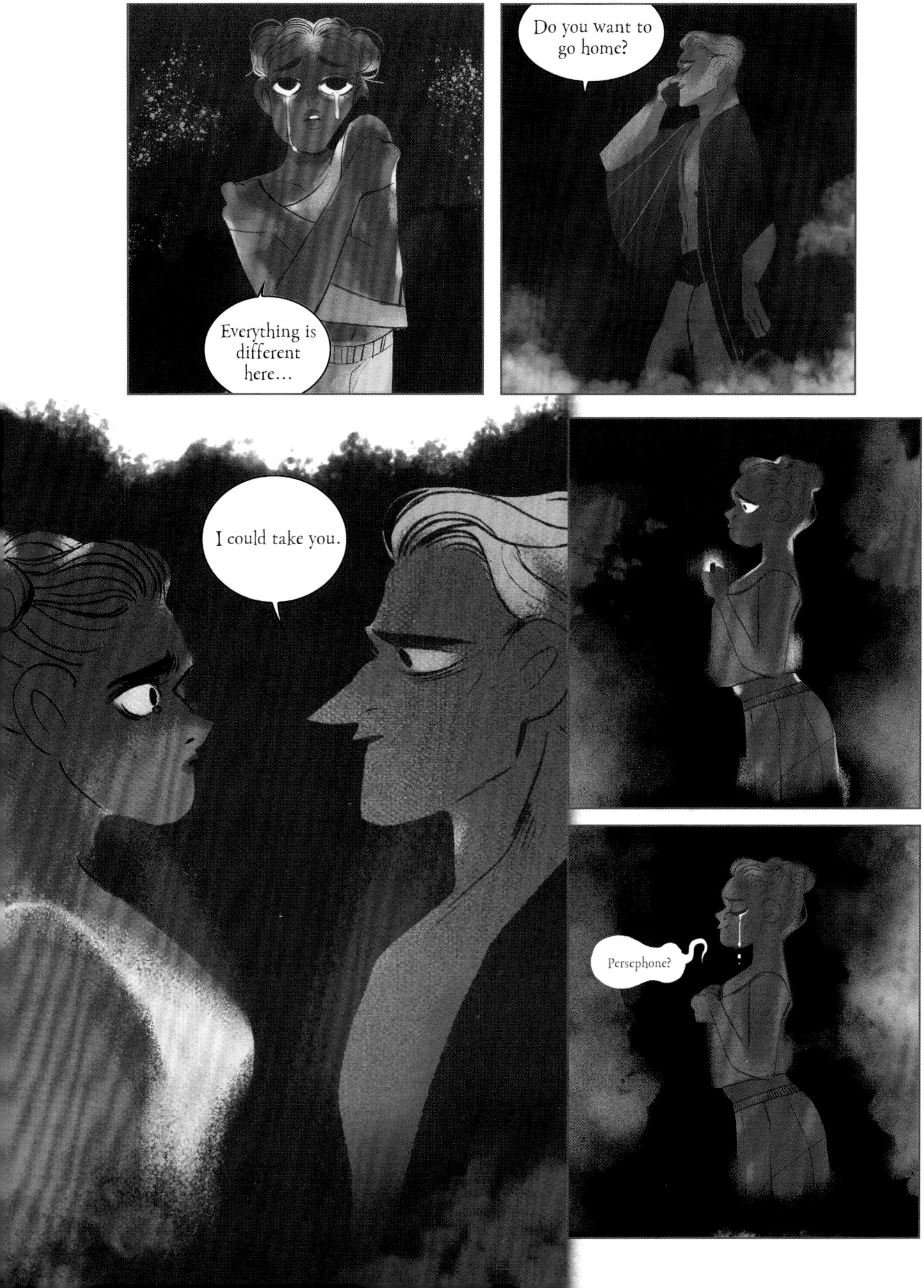
Everything is different here...
Do you want to go home?
I could take you.
Persephone?

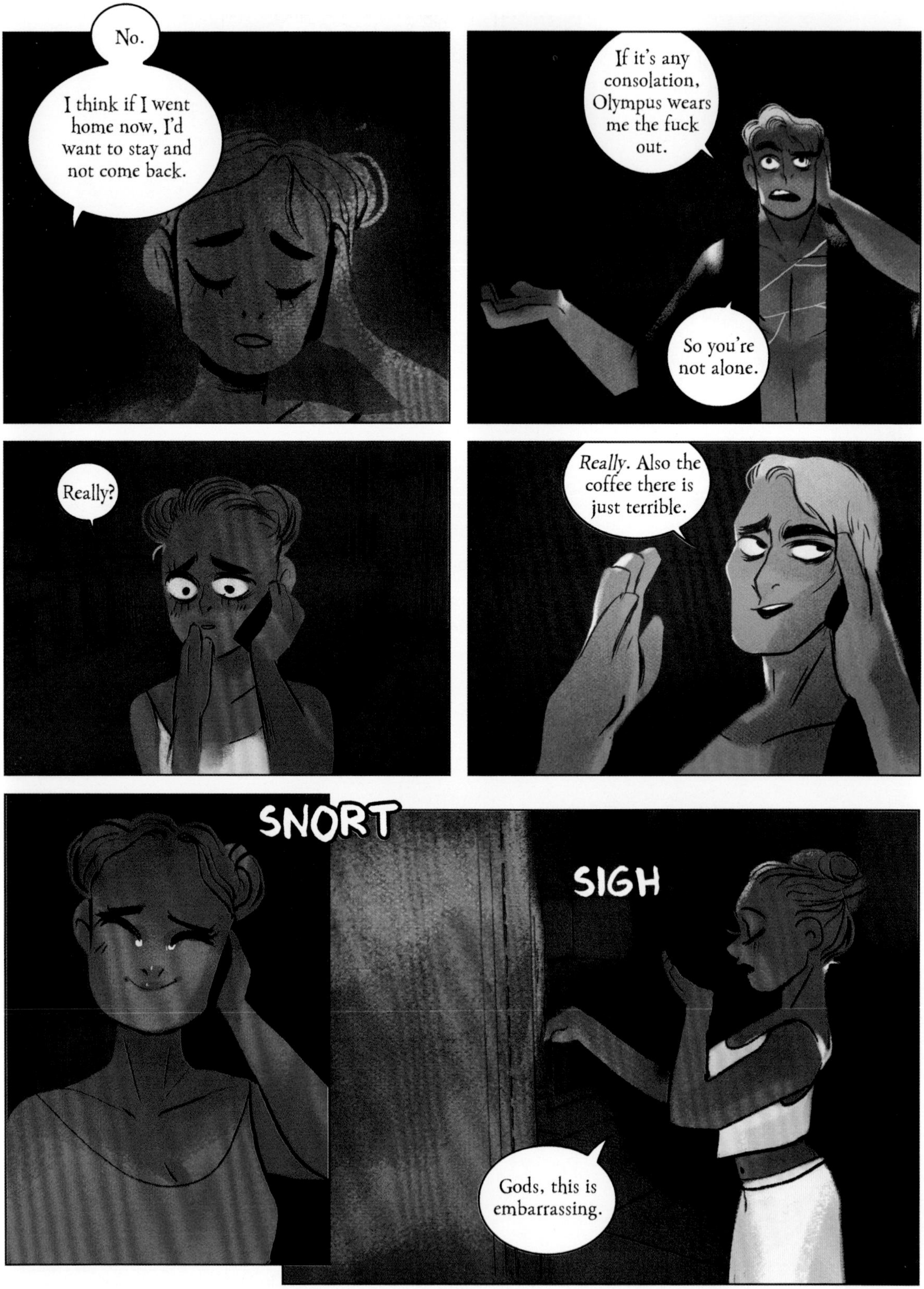
No.
I think if I went home now, I'd want to stay and not come back.
If it's any consolation, Olympus wears me the fuck out.
So you're not alone.
Really?
Really. Also the coffee there is just terrible.
SNORT
SIGH
Gods, this is embarrassing.

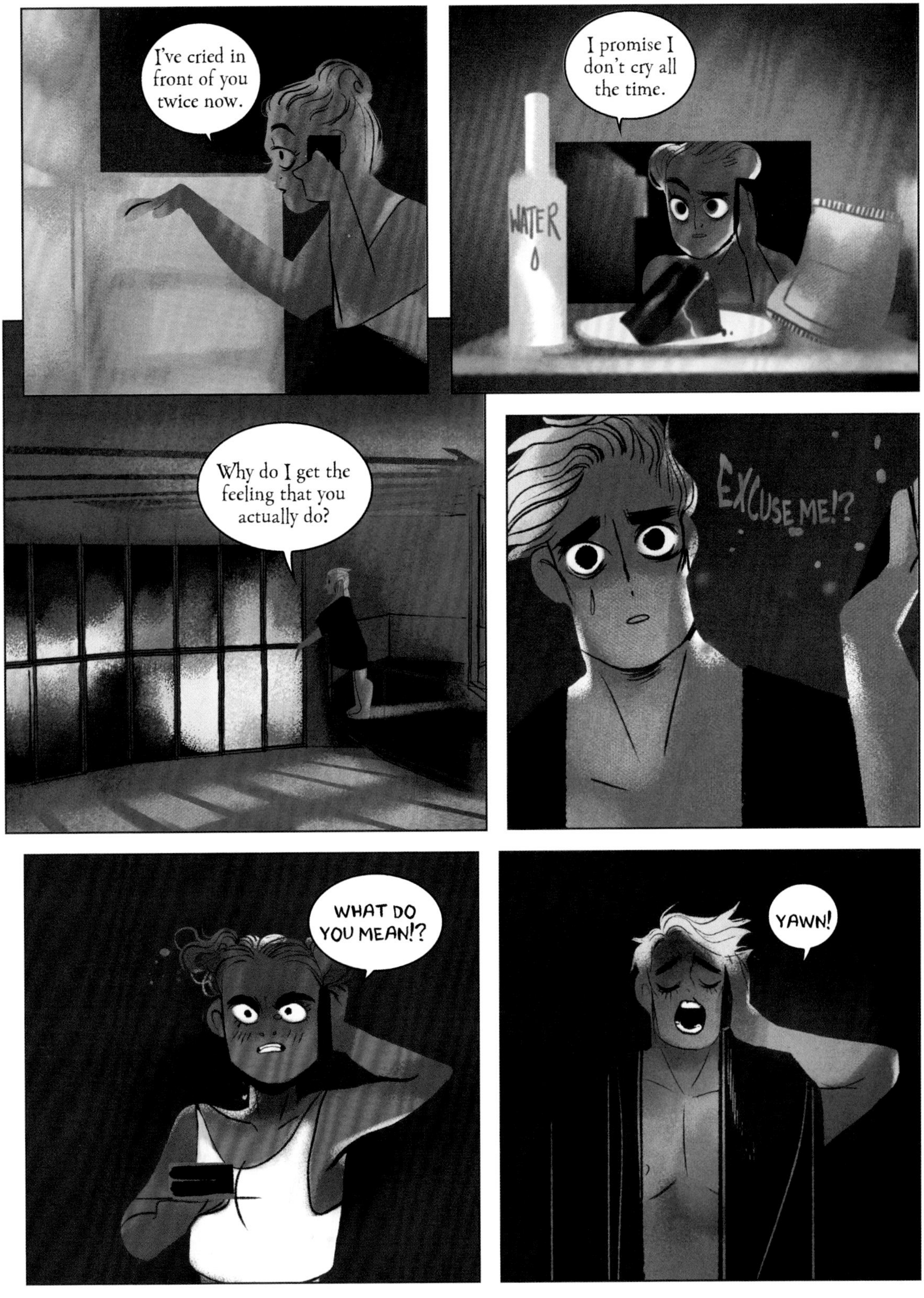
I've cried in front of you twice now.
I promise I don't cry all the time.
WATER
Why do I get the feeling that you actually do?
EXCUSE ME!?
WHAT DO YOU MEAN!?
YAWN!

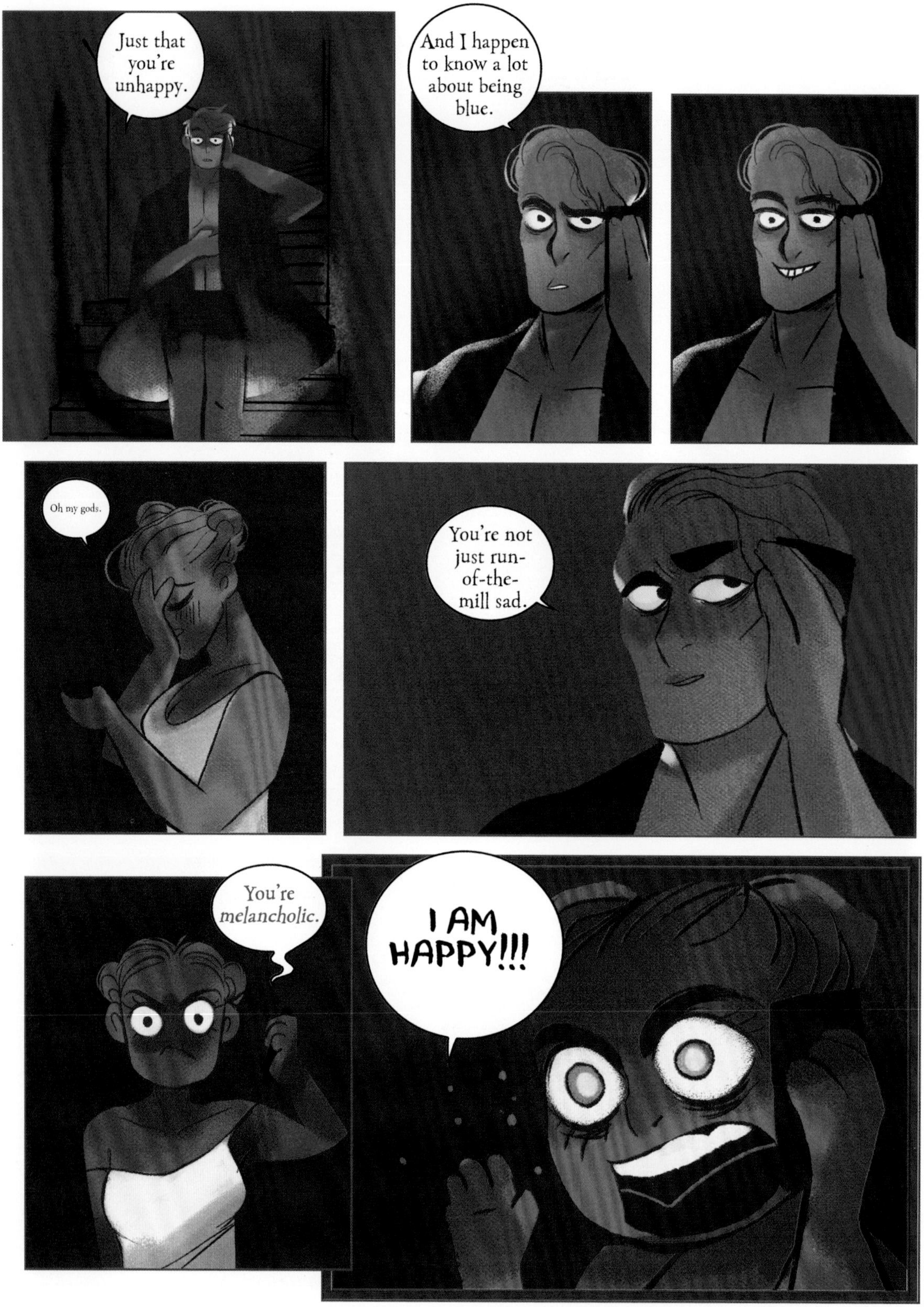

Just that you're unhappy.
And I happen to know a lot about being blue.
Oh my gods.
You're not just run-of-the-mill sad.
You're *melancholic.*
I AM HAPPY!!!

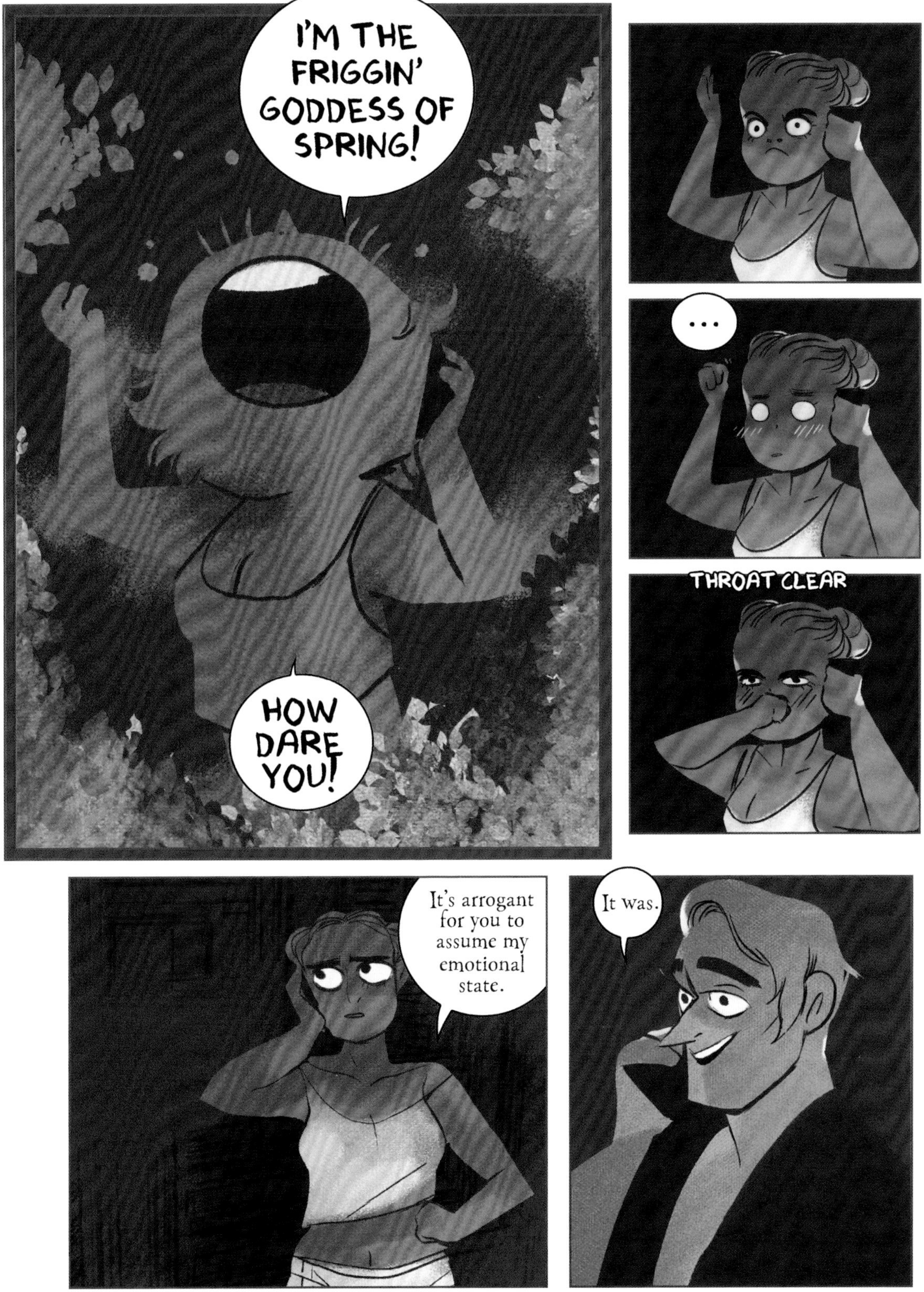
I'M THE FRIGGIN' GODDESS OF SPRING!
HOW DARE YOU!
...
THROAT CLEAR
It's arrogant for you to assume my emotional state.
It was.

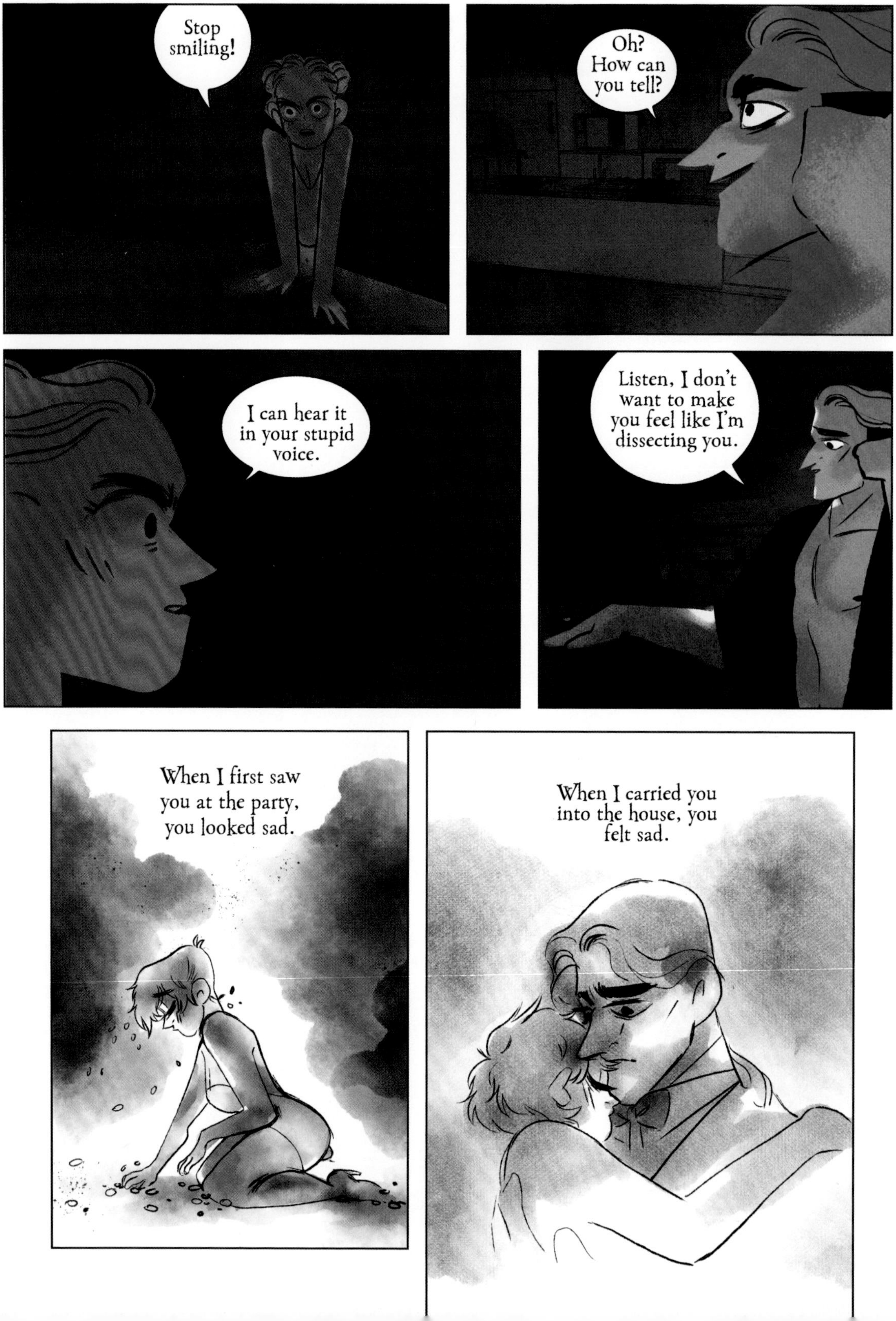
Stop smiling!
Oh? How can you tell?
I can hear it in your stupid voice.
Listen, I don't want to make you feel like I'm dissecting you.
When I first saw you at the party, you looked sad.
When I carried you into the house, you felt sad.

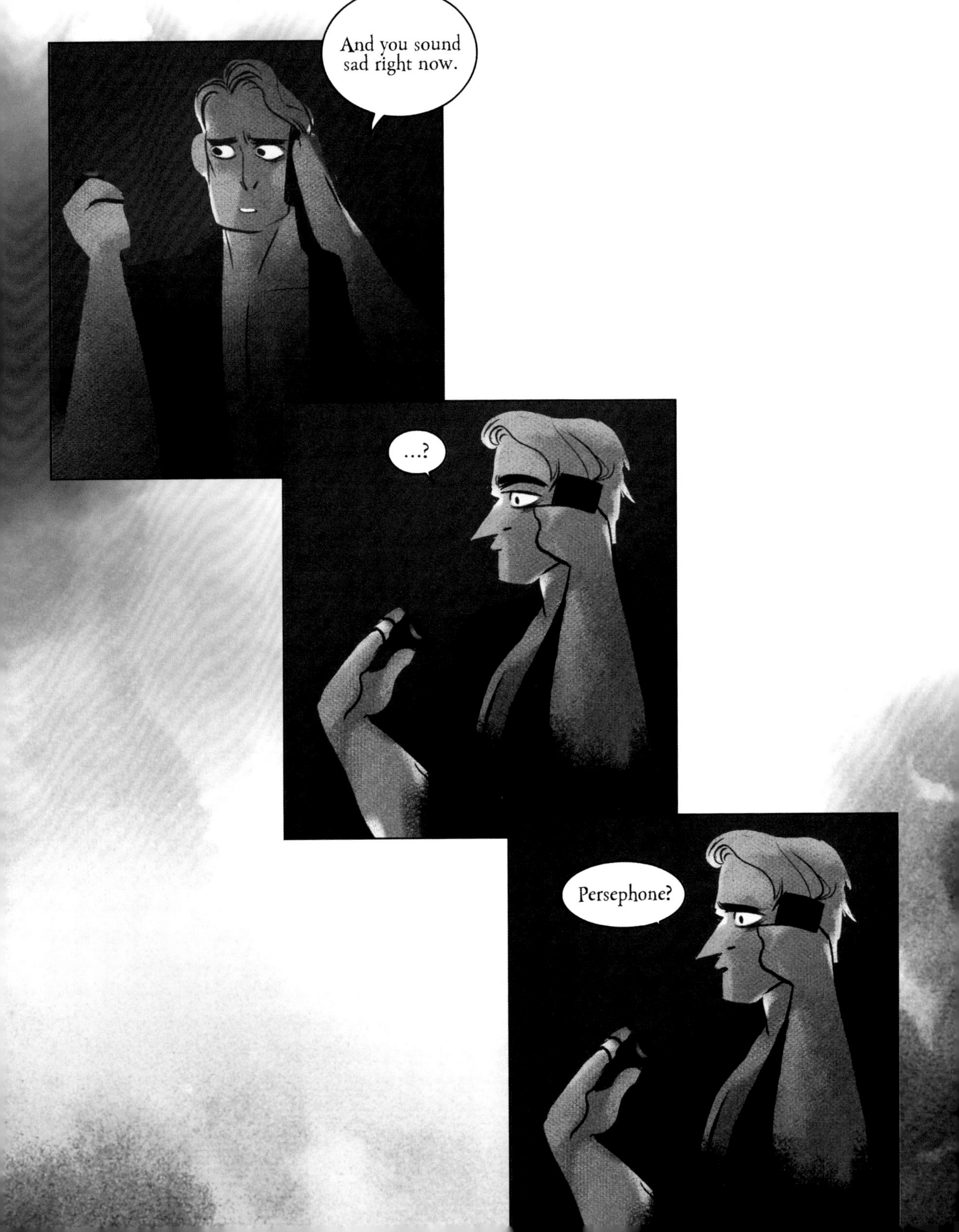
And you sound sad right now.
...?
Persephone?

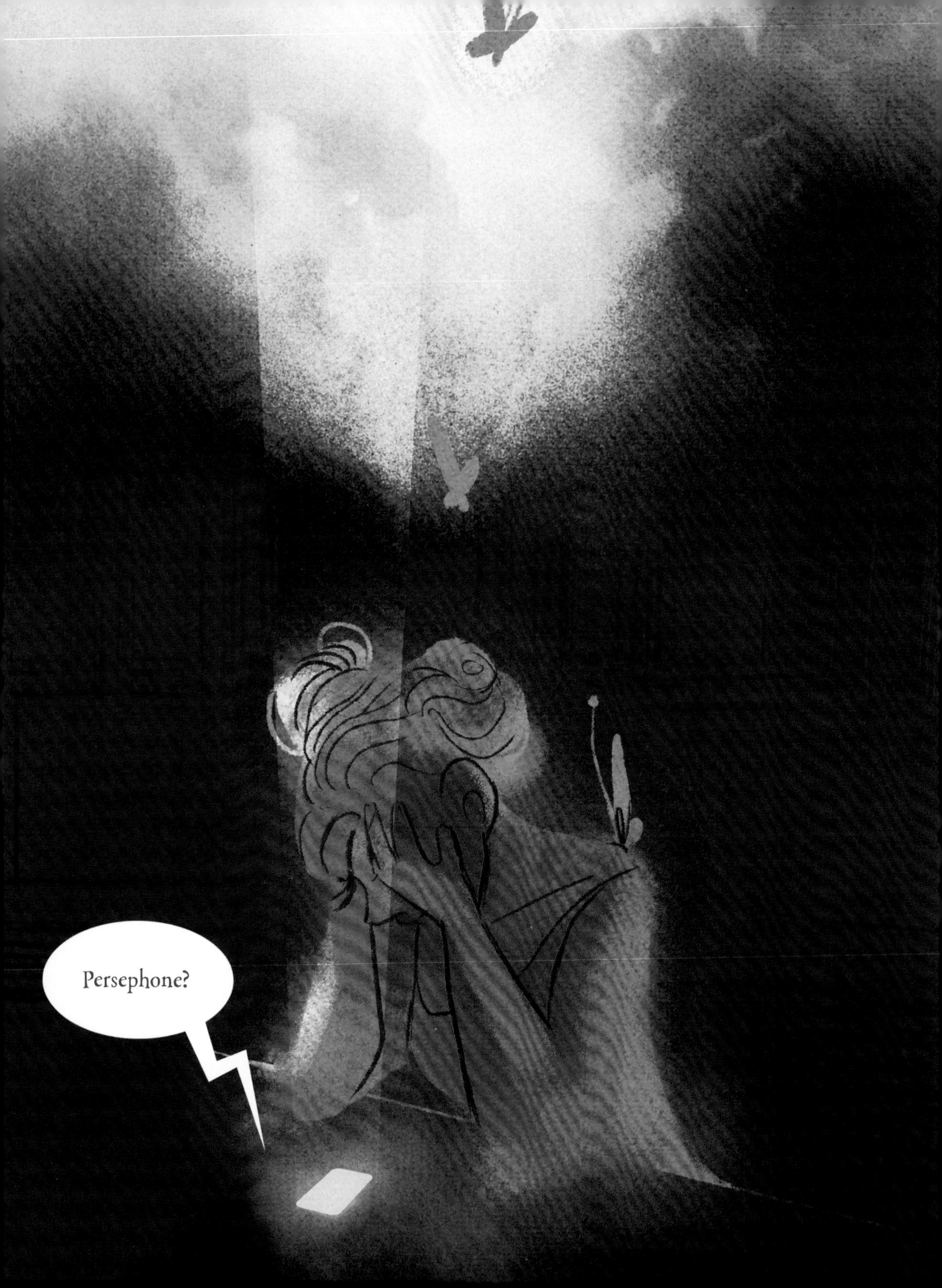
Persephone?

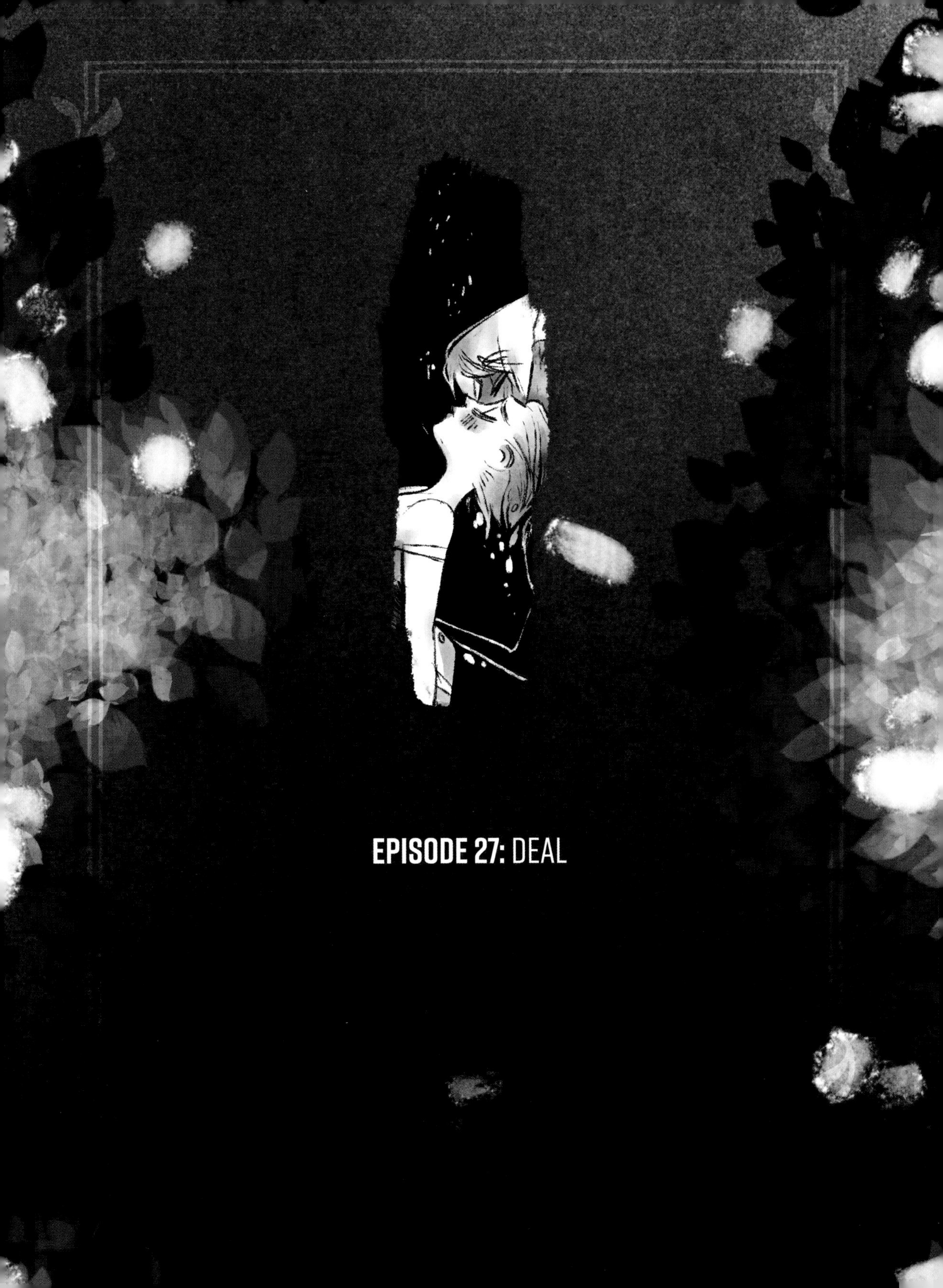
EPISODE 27: DEAL

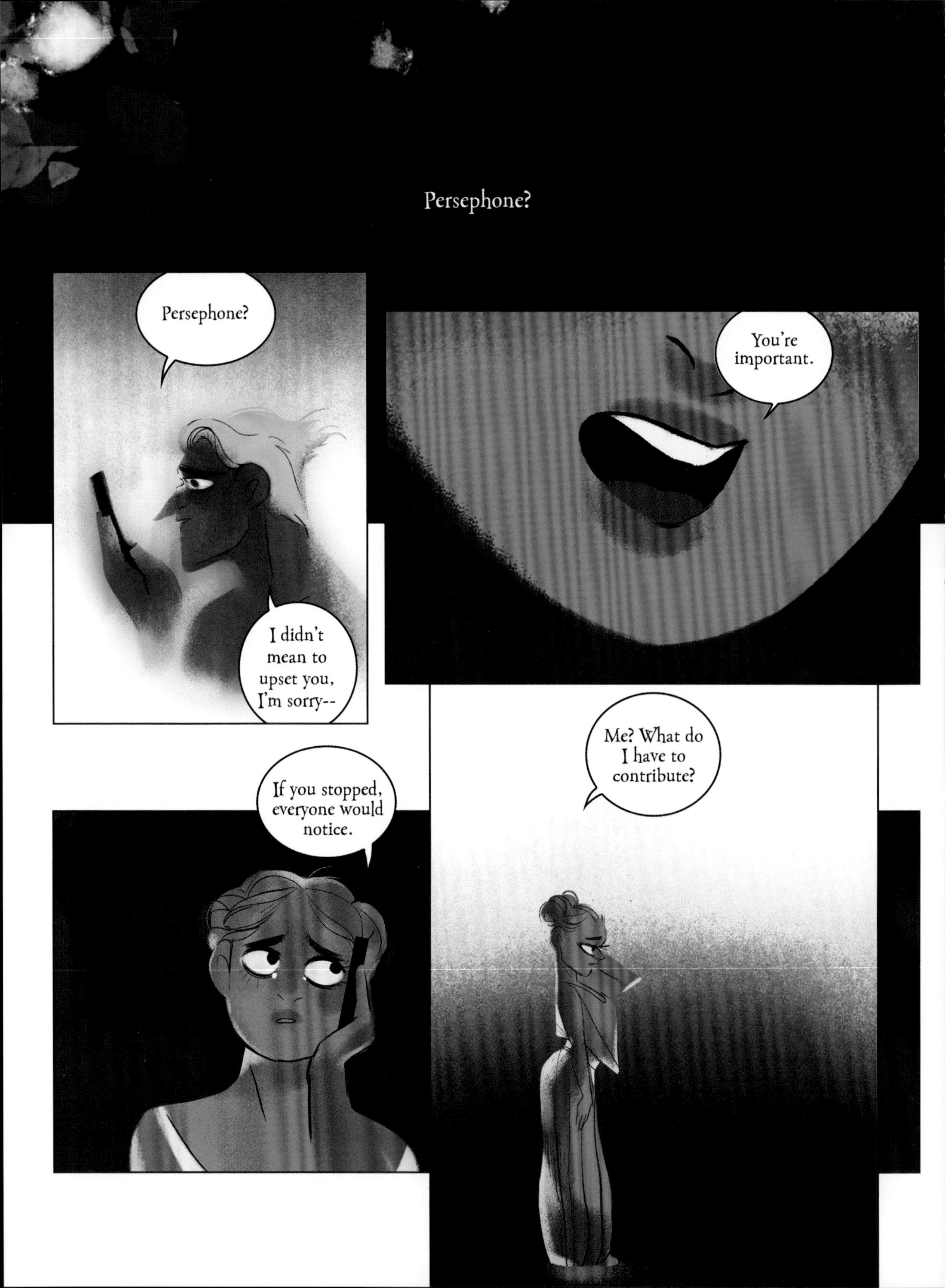
Persephone?
Persephone?
I didn't mean to upset you, I'm sorry--
You're important.
If you stopped, everyone would notice.
Me? What do I have to contribute?

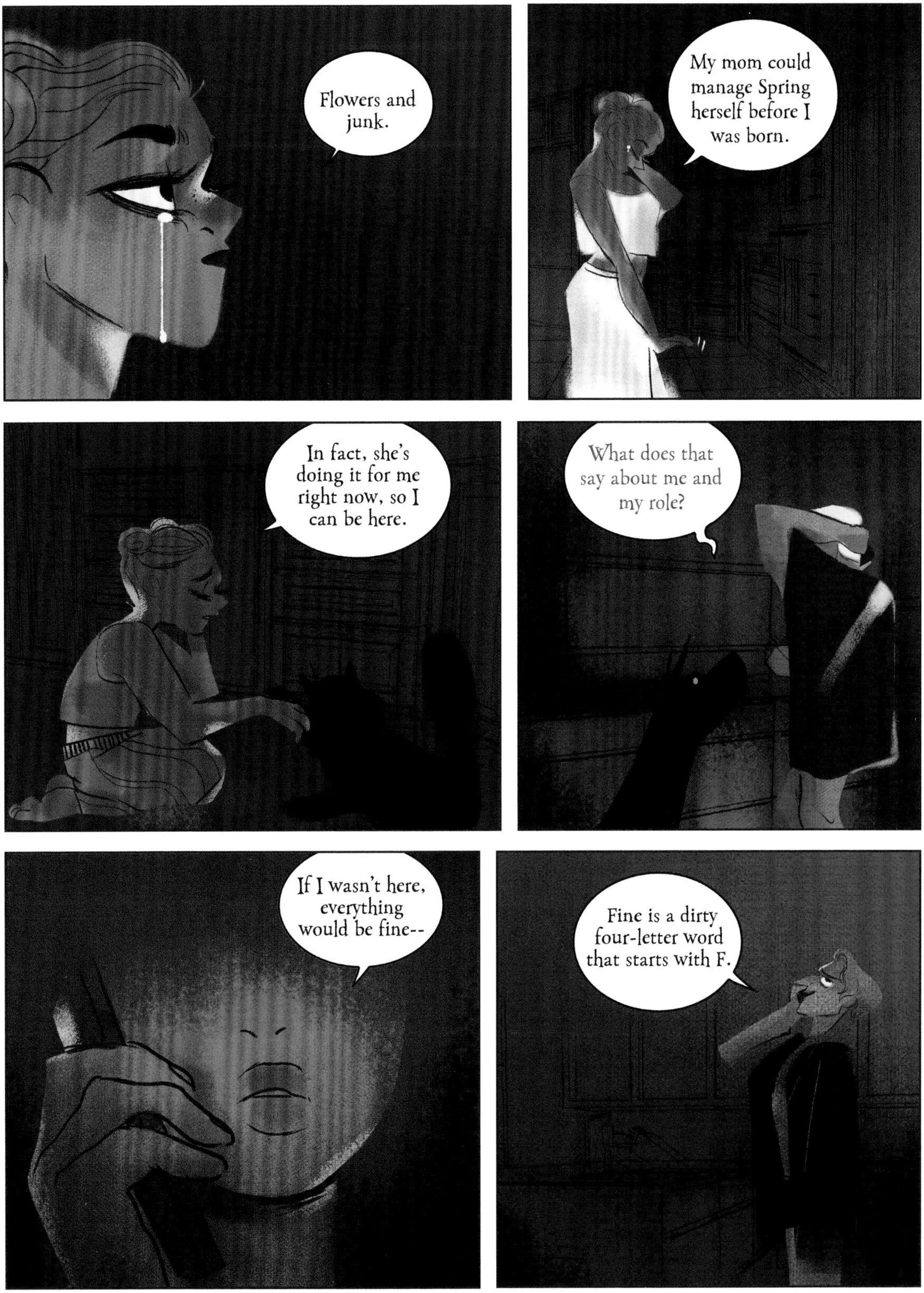
Flowers and junk.
My mom could manage Spring herself before I was born.
In fact, she's doing it for me right now, so I can be here.
What does that say about me and my role?
If I wasn't here, everything would be fine--
Fine is a dirty four-letter word that starts with F.

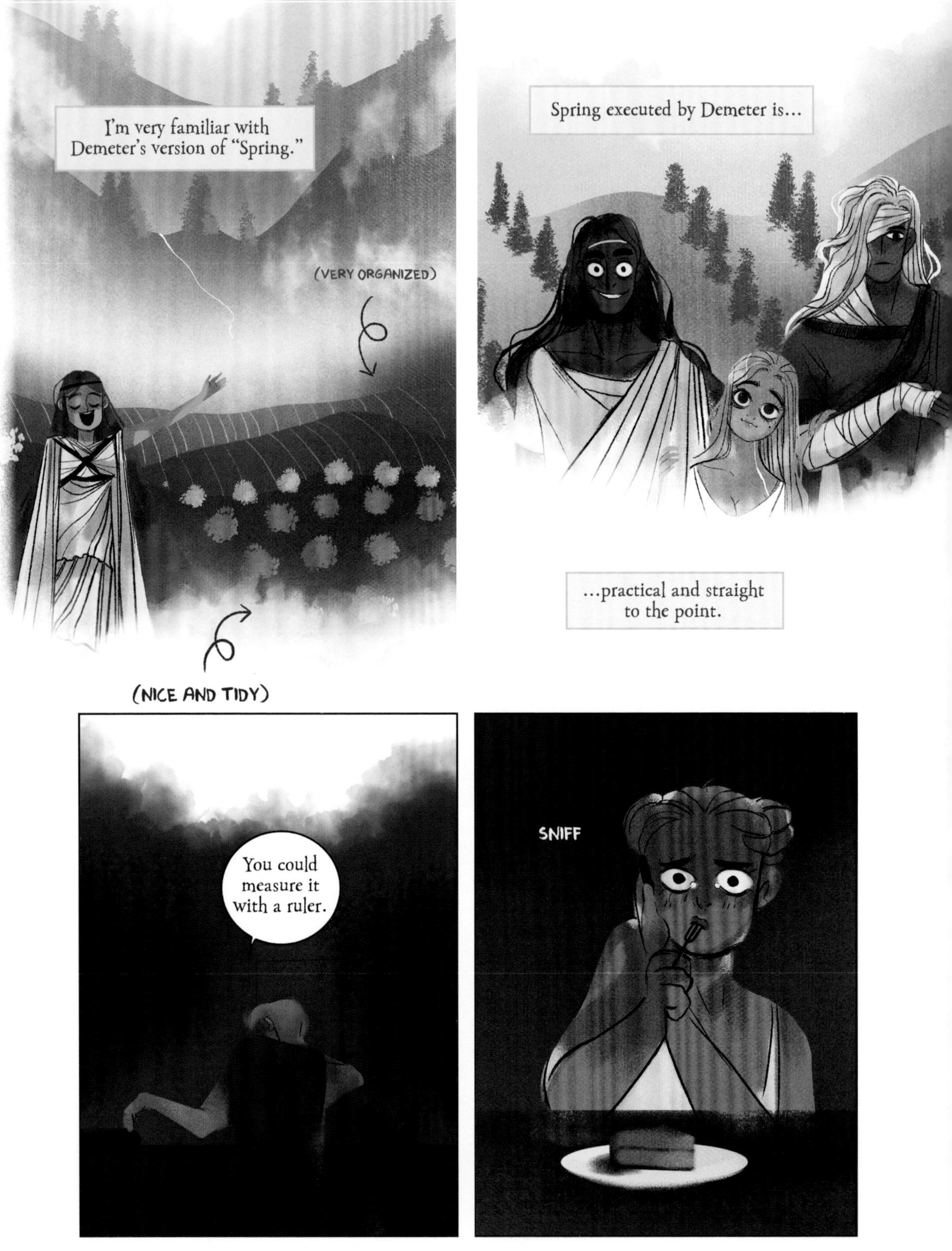
I'm very familiar with Demeter's version of "Spring."
(VERY ORGANIZED)
(NICE AND TIDY)
Spring executed by Demeter is...
...practical and straight to the point.
You could measure it with a ruler.
SNIFF

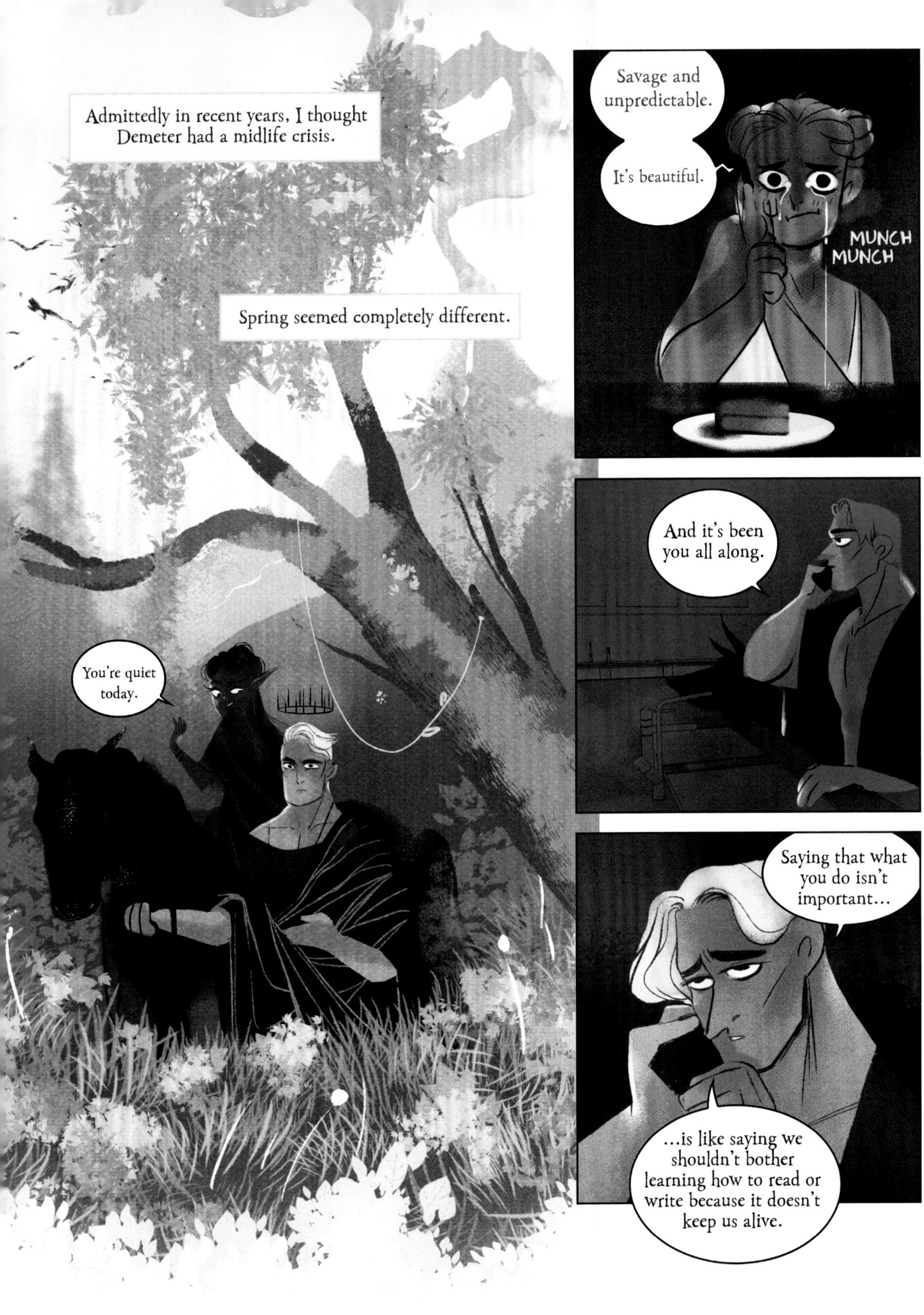
Admittedly in recent years, I thought Demeter had a midlife crisis.
Spring seemed completely different.
You're quiet today.
Savage and unpredictable.
It's beautiful.
MUNCH MUNCH
And it's been you all along.
Saying that what you do isn't important...
...is like saying we shouldn't bother learning how to read or write because it doesn't keep us alive.

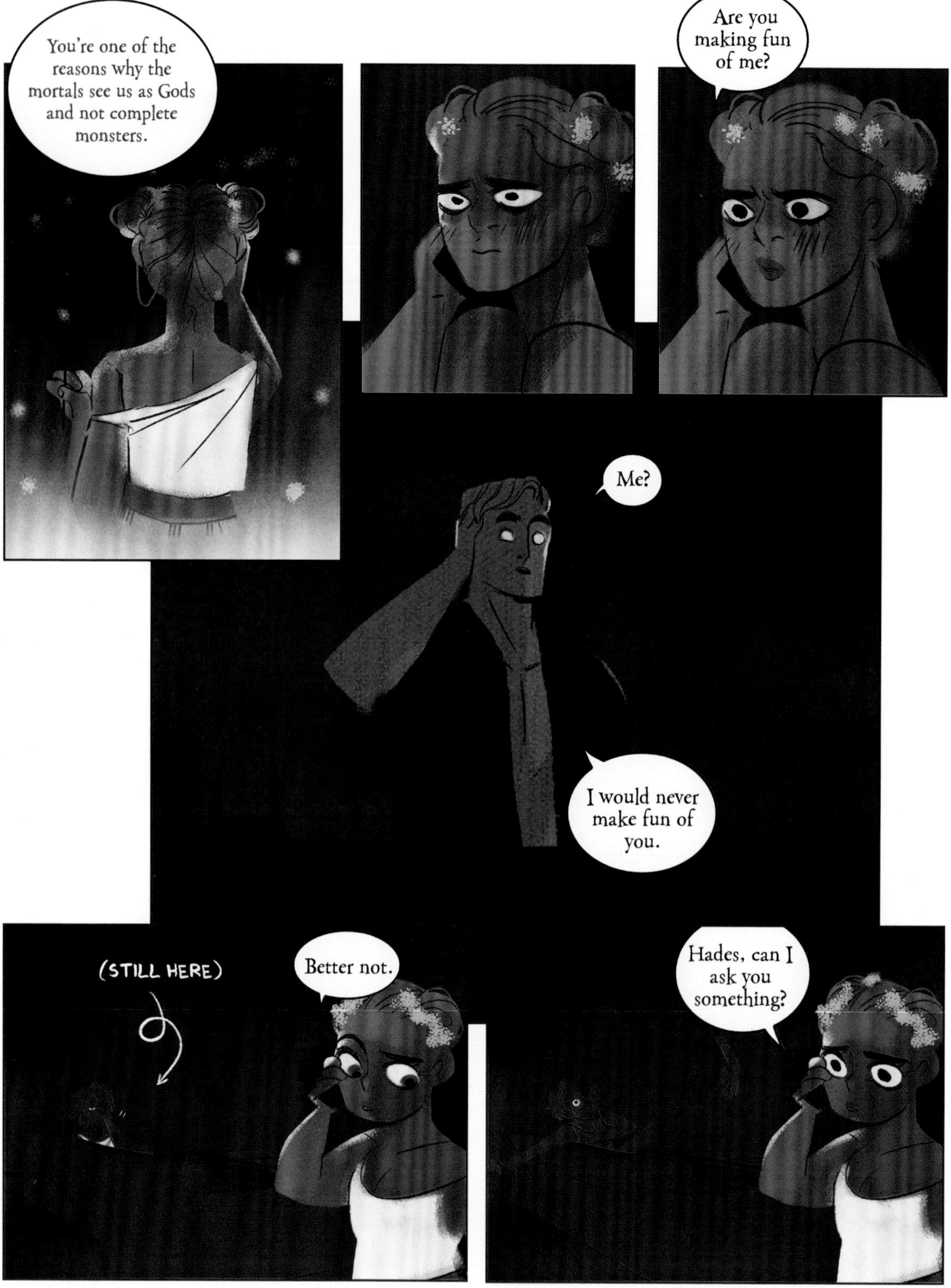
You're one of the reasons why the mortals see us as Gods and not complete monsters.
Are you making fun of me?
Me?
I would never make fun of you.
(STILL HERE)
Better not.
Hades, can I ask you something?

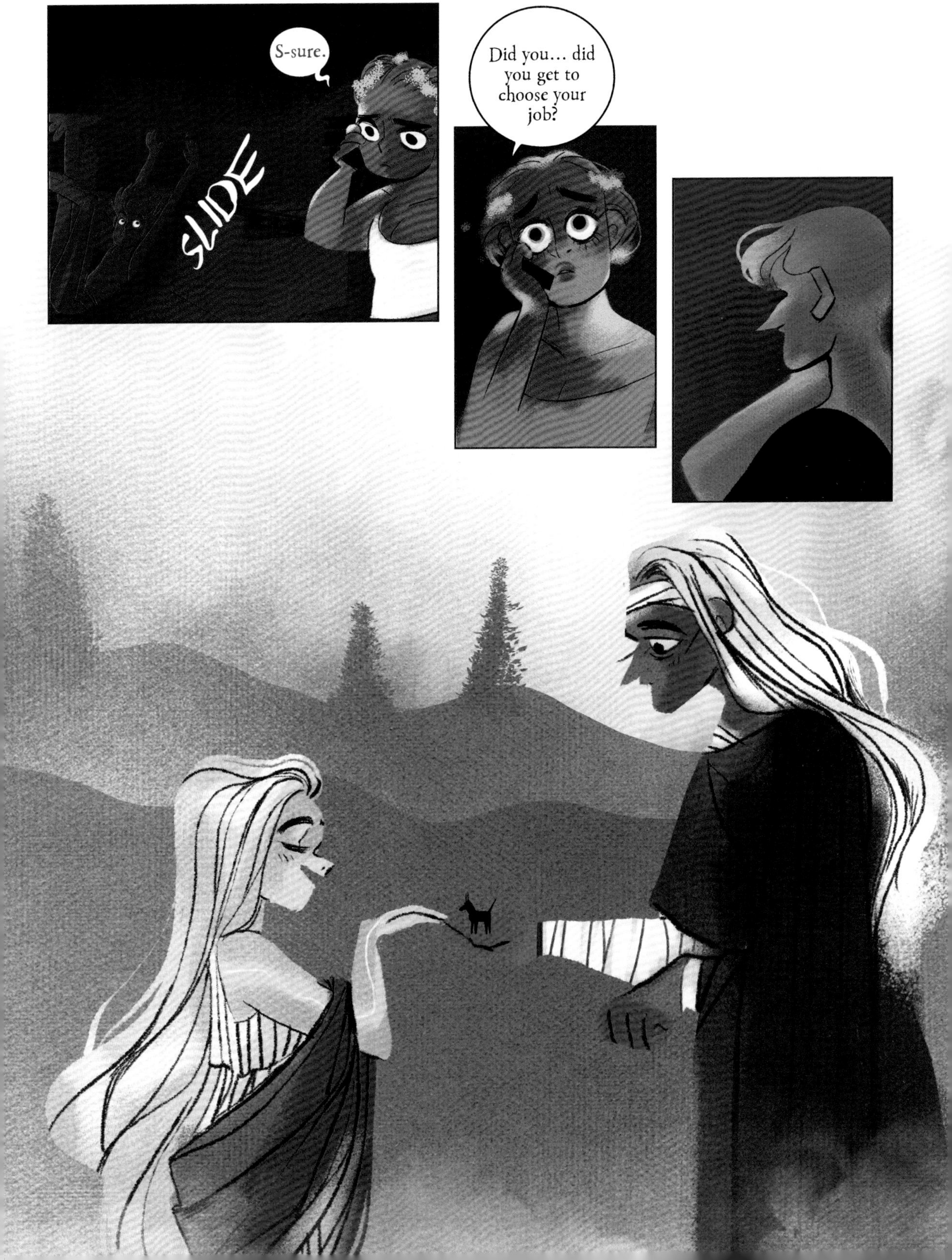

S-sure.
SLIDE
Did you… did you get to choose your job?

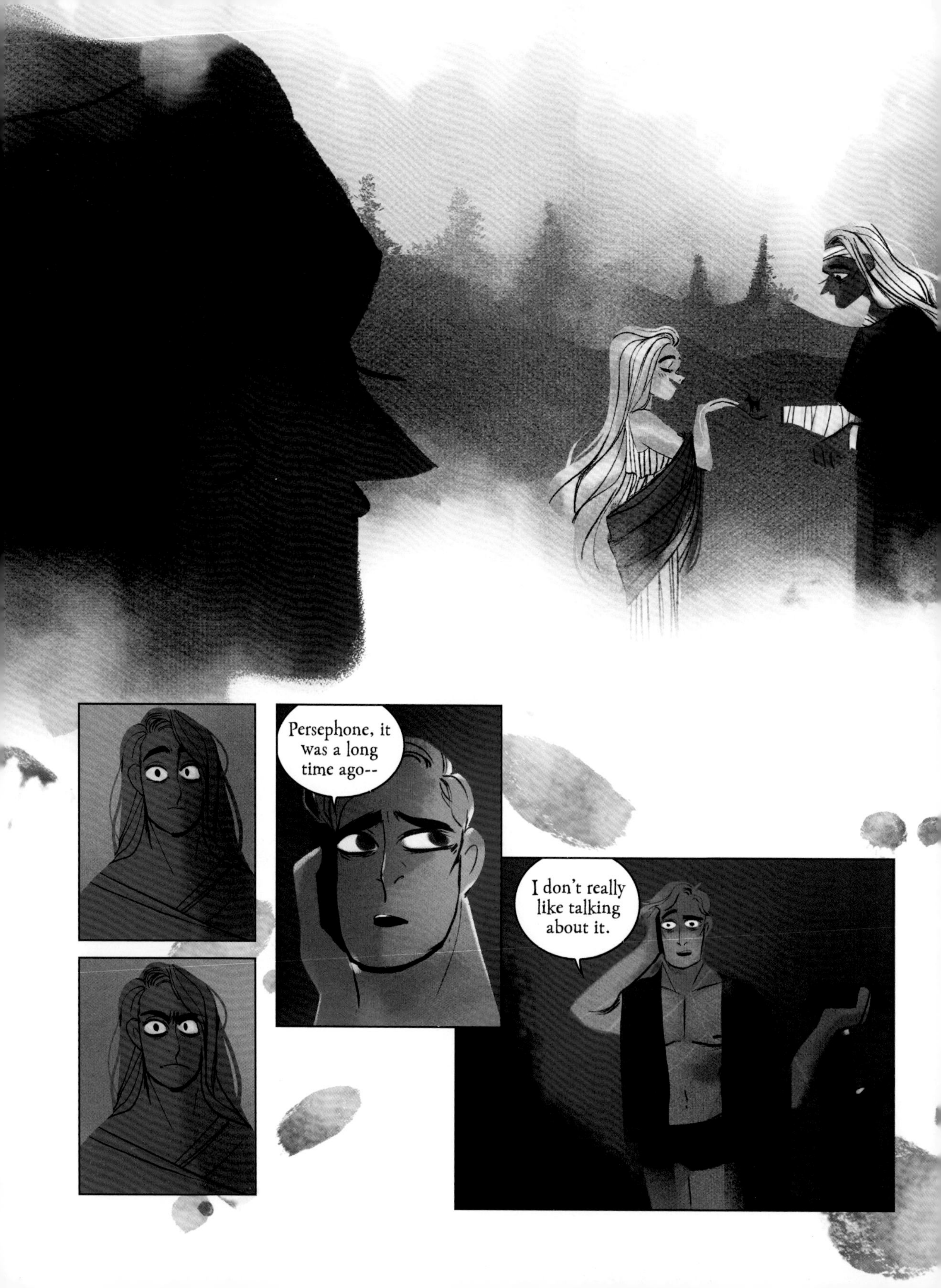
Persephone, it was a long time ago--
I don't really like talking about it.

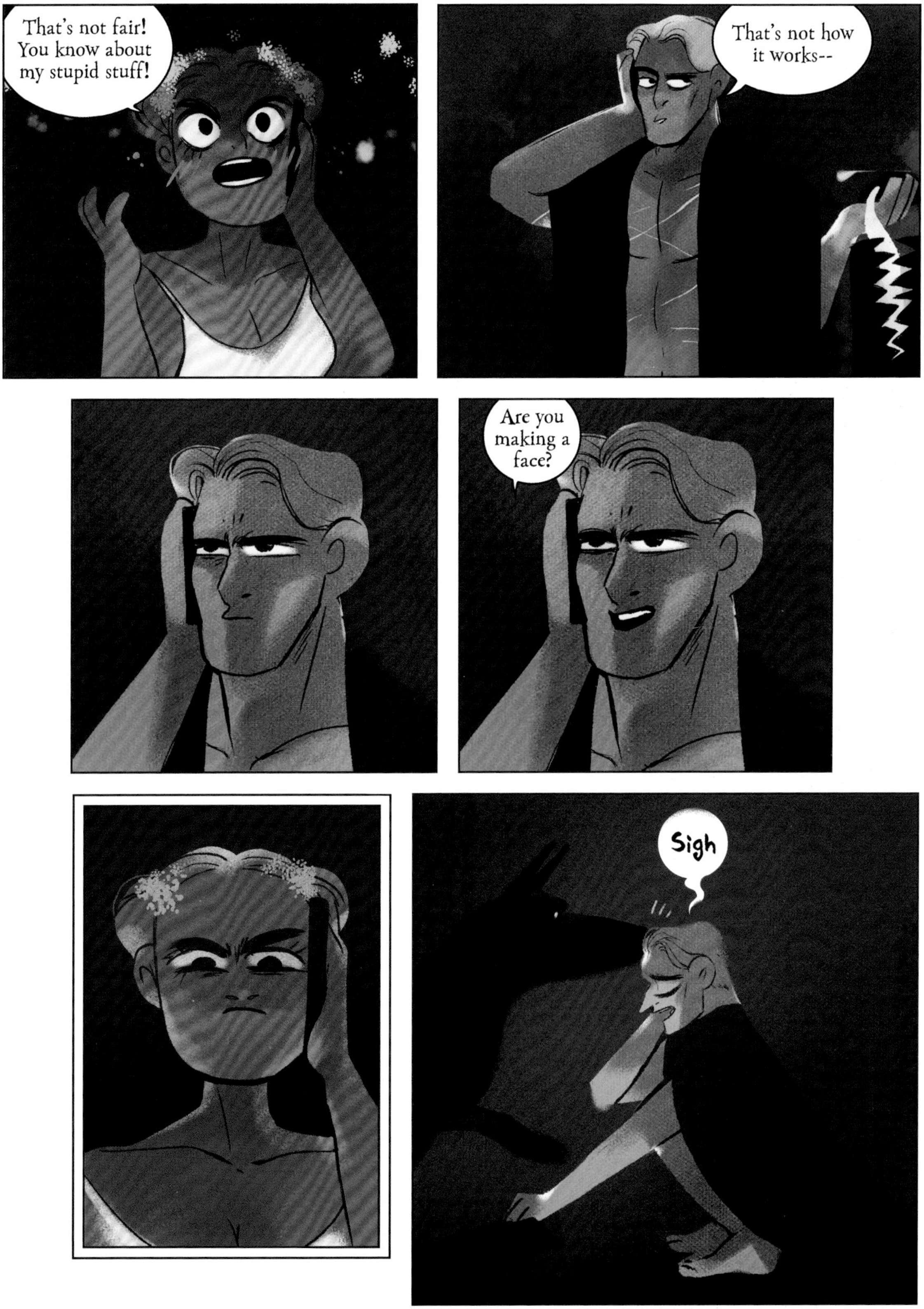
That's not fair! You know about my stupid stuff!
That's not how it works--
Are you making a face?
Sigh

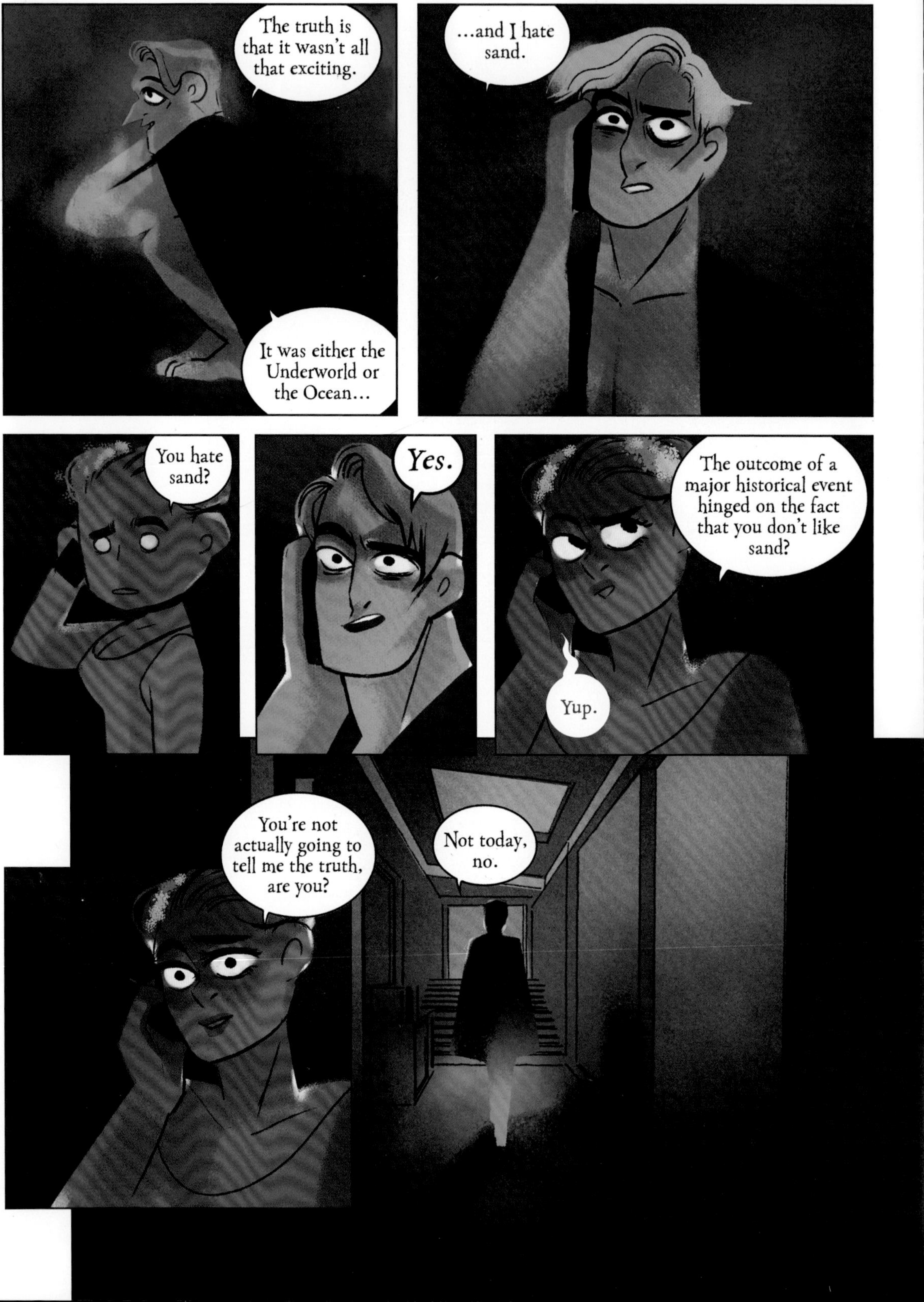
The truth is that it wasn't all that exciting.
It was either the Underworld or the Ocean…
…and I hate sand.
You hate sand?
Yes.
The outcome of a major historical event hinged on the fact that you don't like sand?
Yup.
You're not actually going to tell me the truth, are you?
Not today, no.

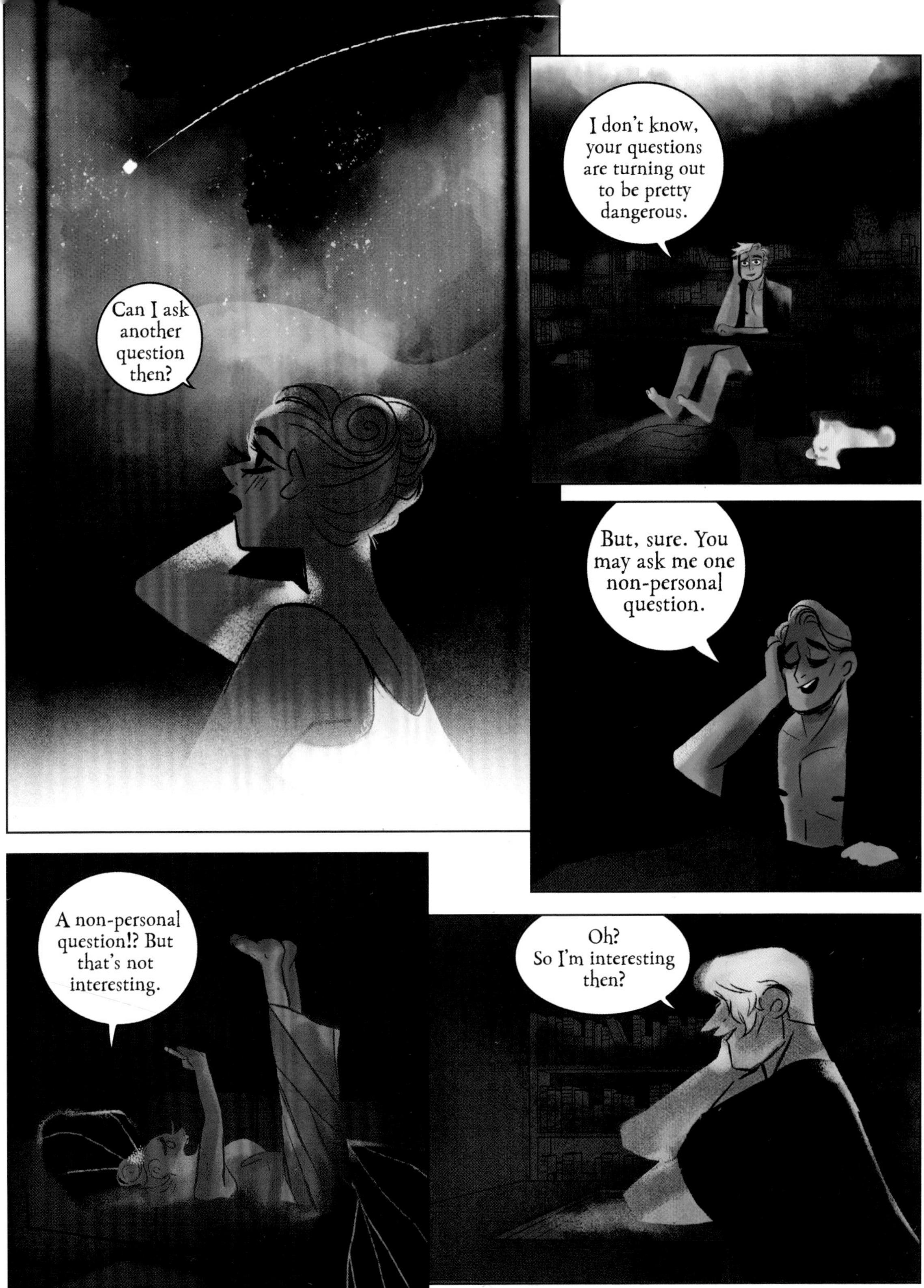
Can I ask another question then?
I don't know, your questions are turning out to be pretty dangerous.
But, sure. You may ask me one non-personal question.
A non-personal question!? But that's not interesting.
Oh? So I'm interesting then?

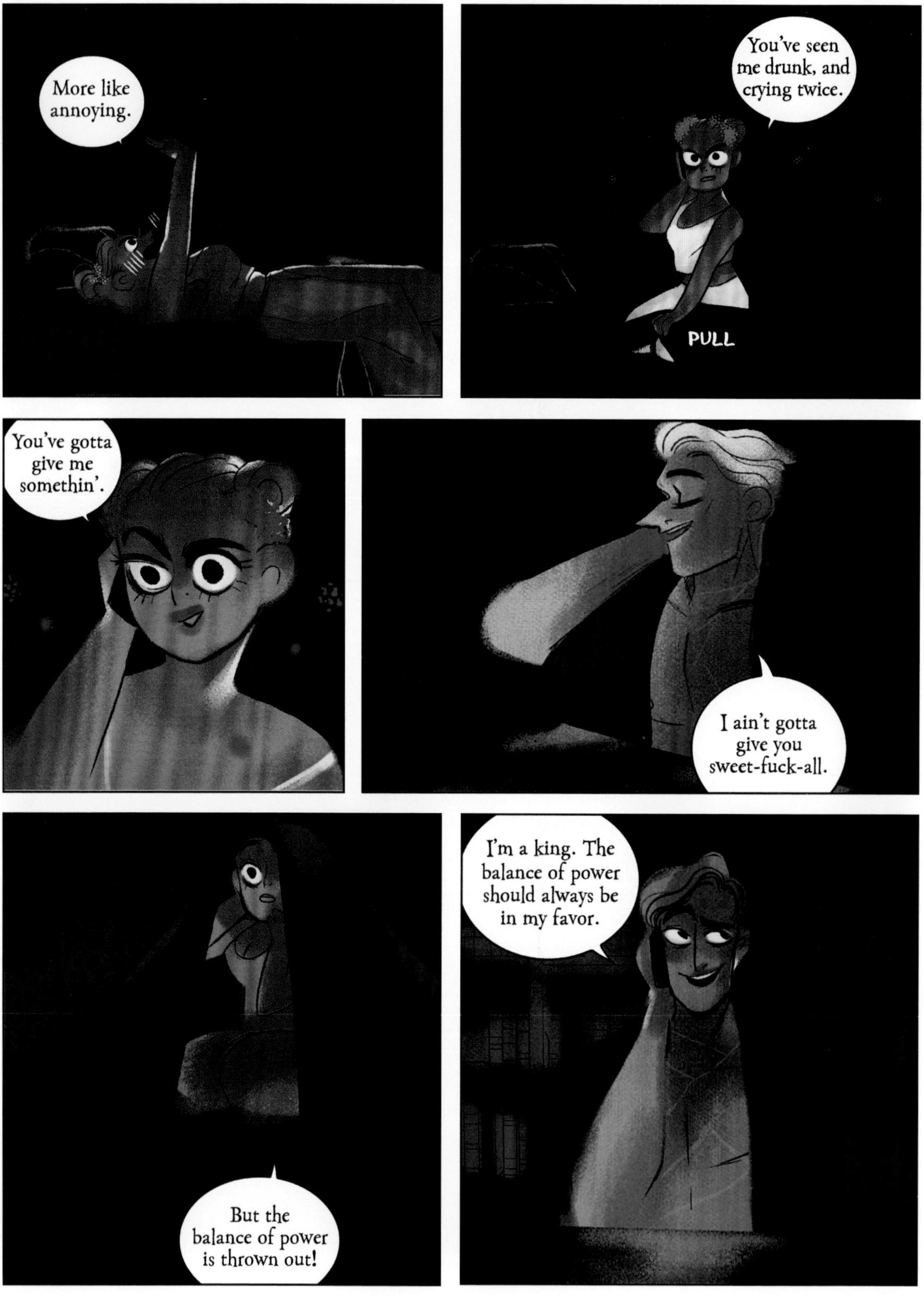
More like annoying.
You've seen me drunk, and crying twice.
PULL
You've gotta give me somethin'.
I ain't gotta give you sweet-fuck-all.
But the balance of power is thrown out!
I'm a king. The balance of power should always be in my favor.

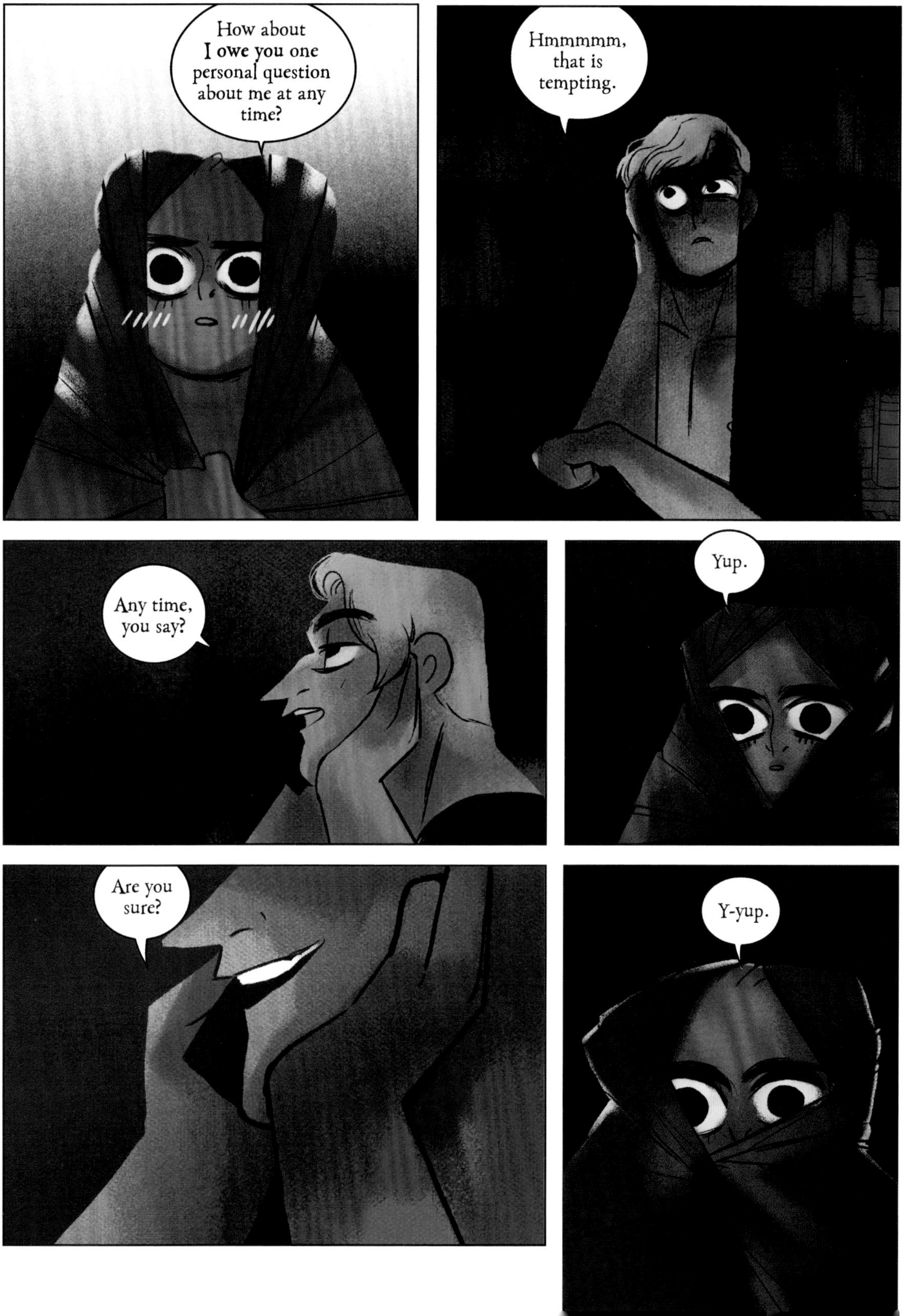
How about **I owe you** one personal question about me at any time?
Hmmmmm, that is tempting.
Any time, you say?
Yup.
Are you sure?
Y-yup.

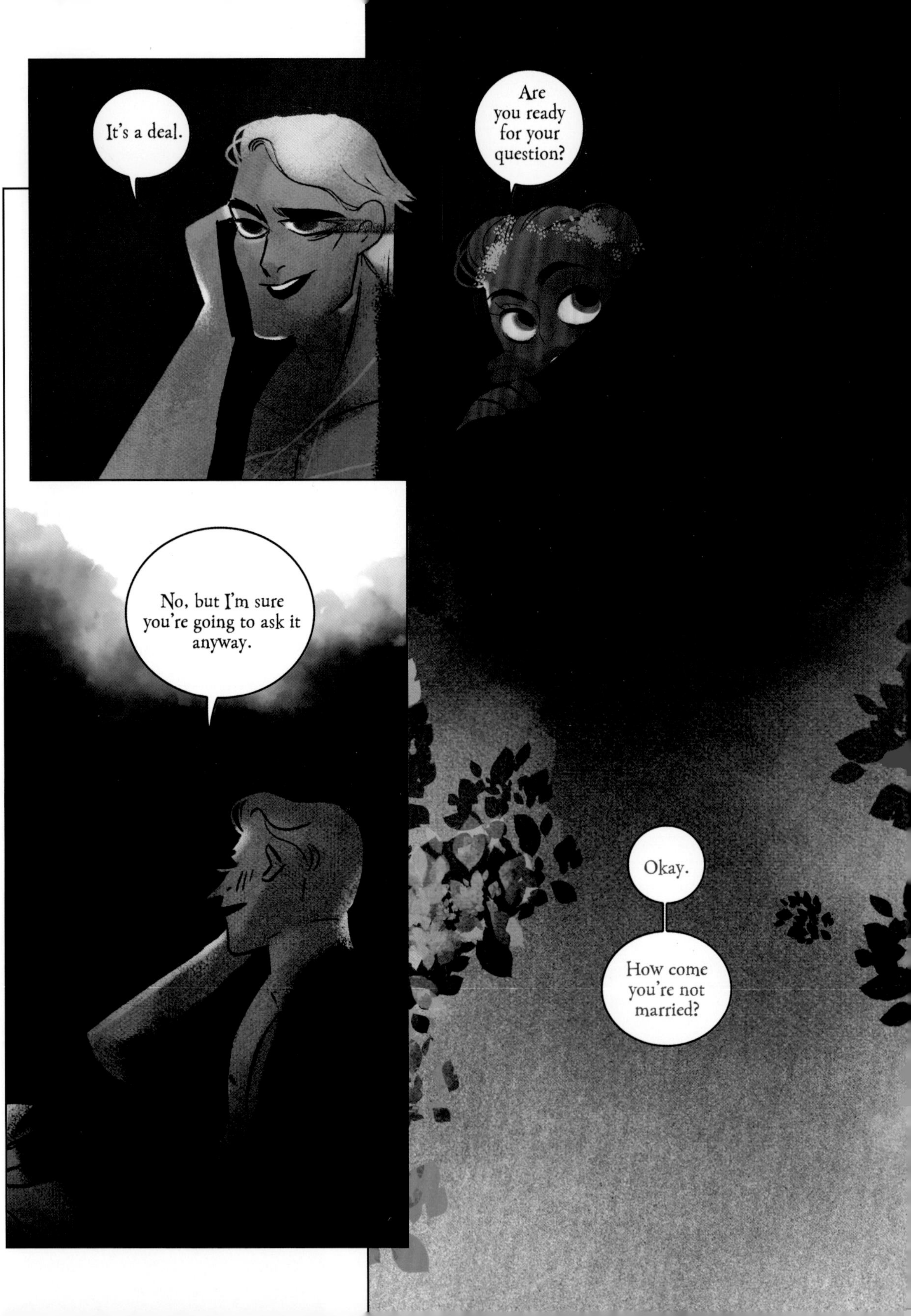
It's a deal.
Are you ready for your question?
No, but I'm sure you're going to ask it anyway.
Okay.
How come you're not married?

EPISODE 28: AWKWARD SILENCE

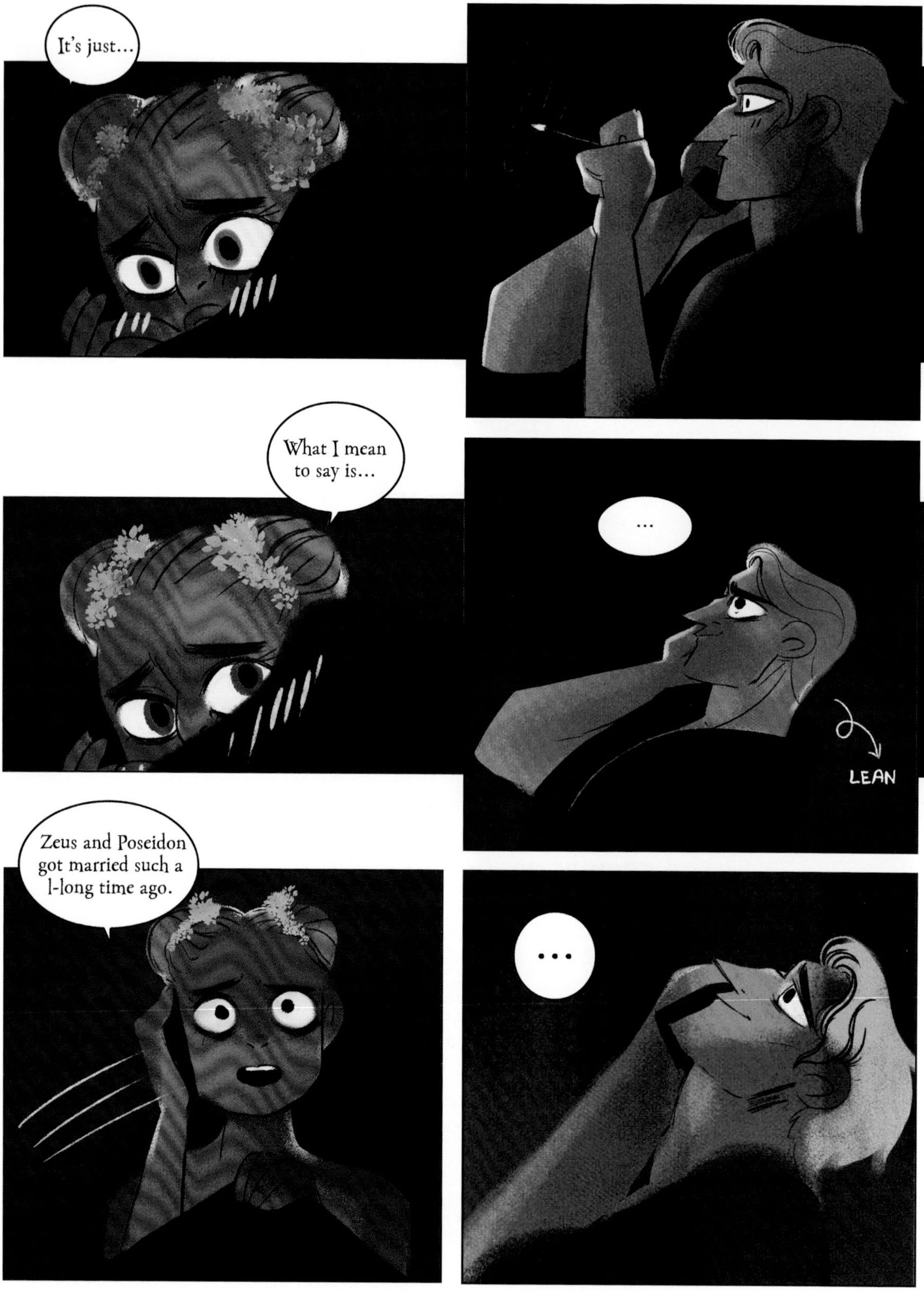
It's just...
What I mean to say is...
...
LEAN
Zeus and Poseidon got married such a l-long time ago.
...

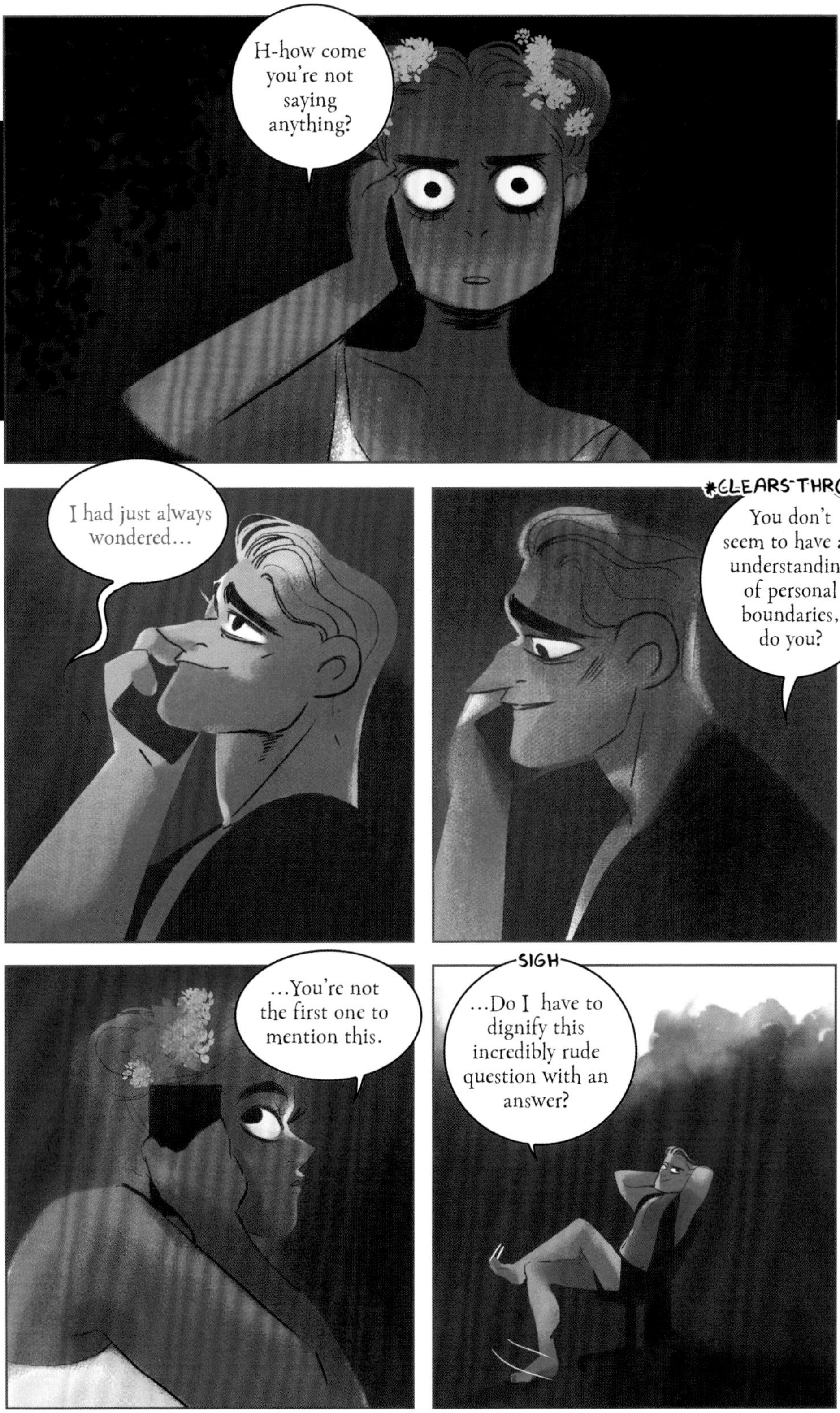
H-how come you're not saying anything?
I had just always wondered...
CLEARS THROAT
You don't seem to have an understanding of personal boundaries, do you?
...You're not the first one to mention this.
SIGH
...Do I have to dignify this incredibly rude question with an answer?

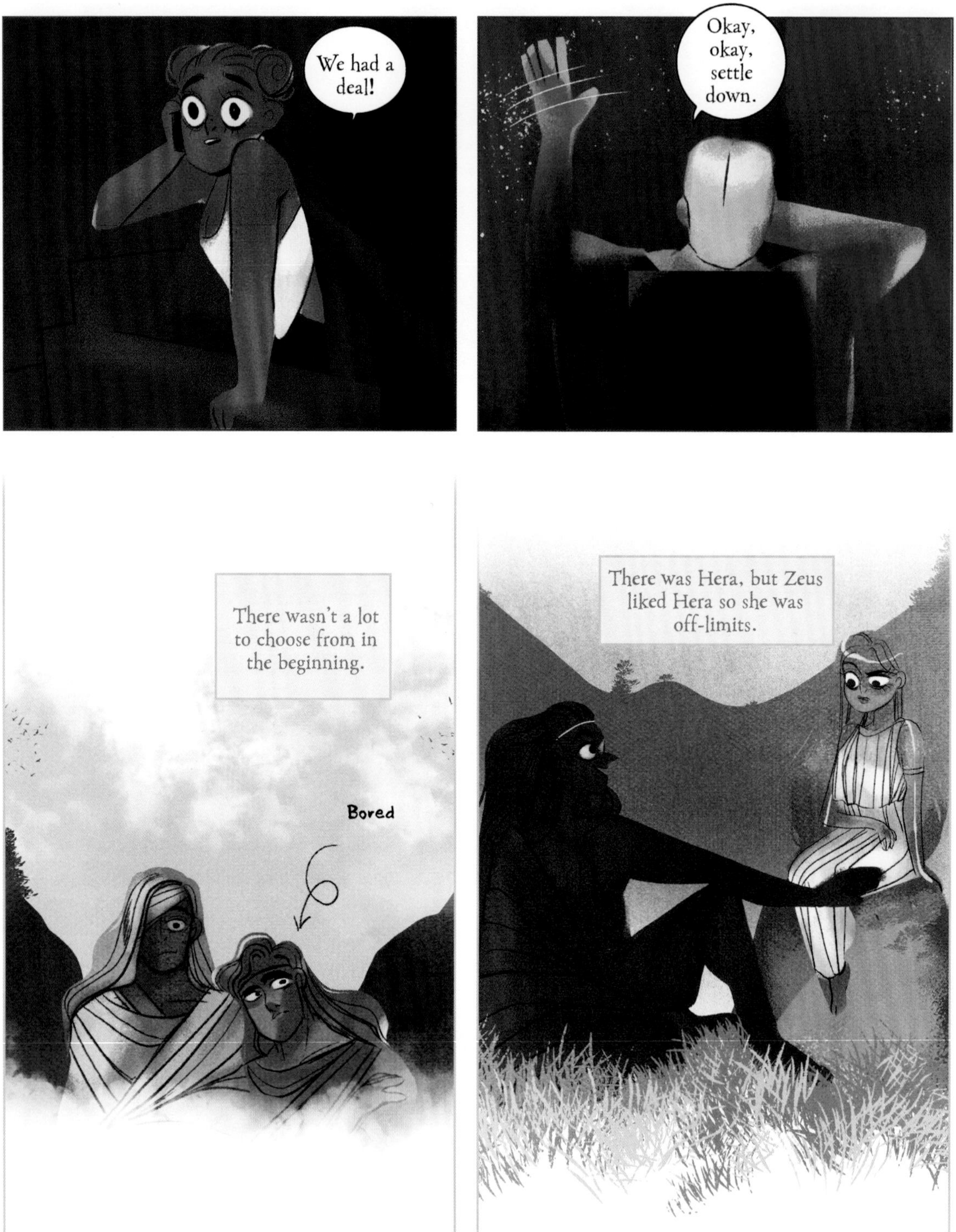
We had a deal!
Okay, okay, settle down.
There wasn't a lot to choose from in the beginning.
Bored
There was Hera, but Zeus liked Hera so she was off-limits.

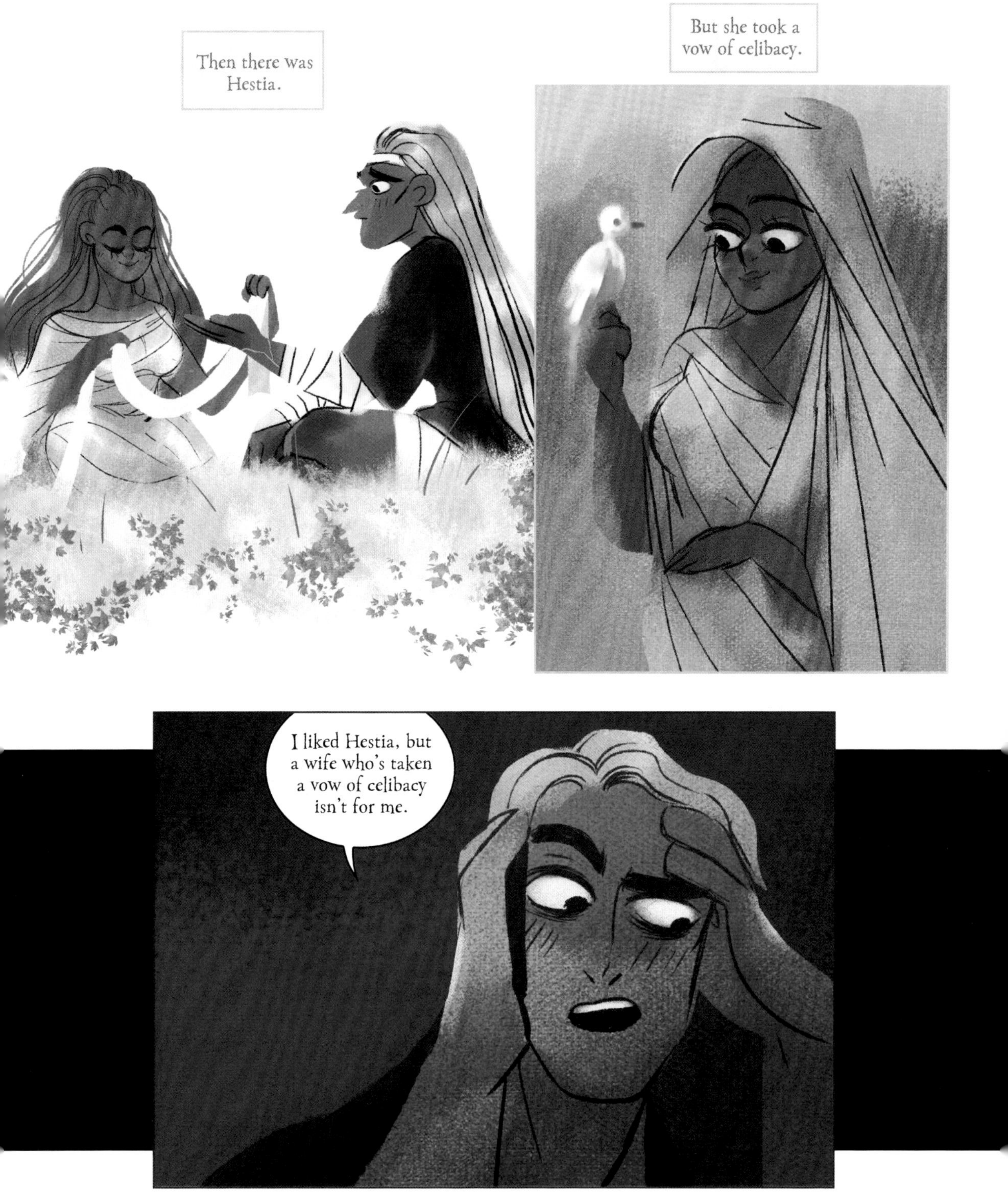
Then there was Hestia.
But she took a vow of celibacy.
I liked Hestia, but a wife who's taken a vow of celibacy isn't for me.

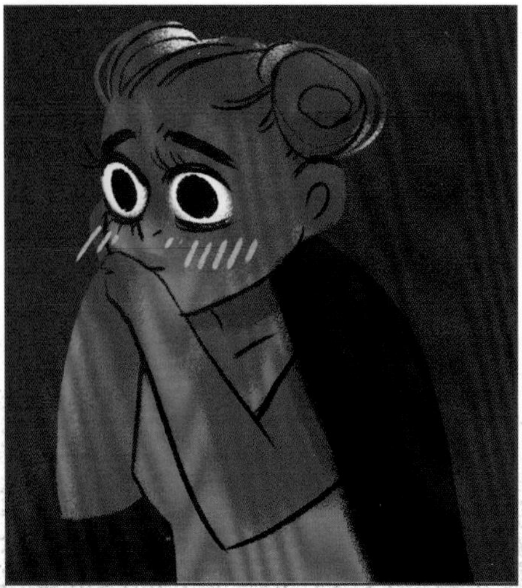

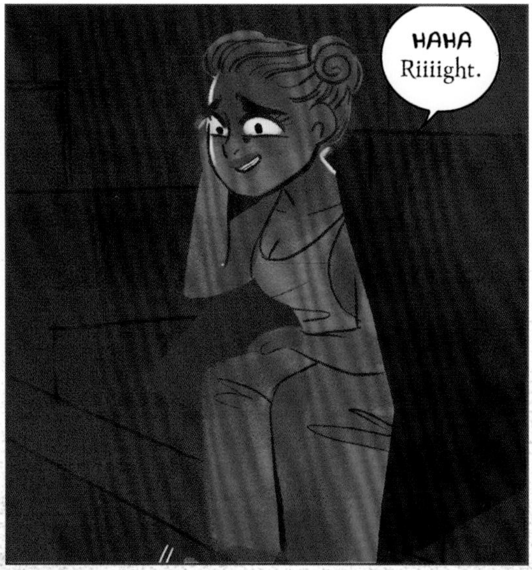
HAHA
Riiiight.

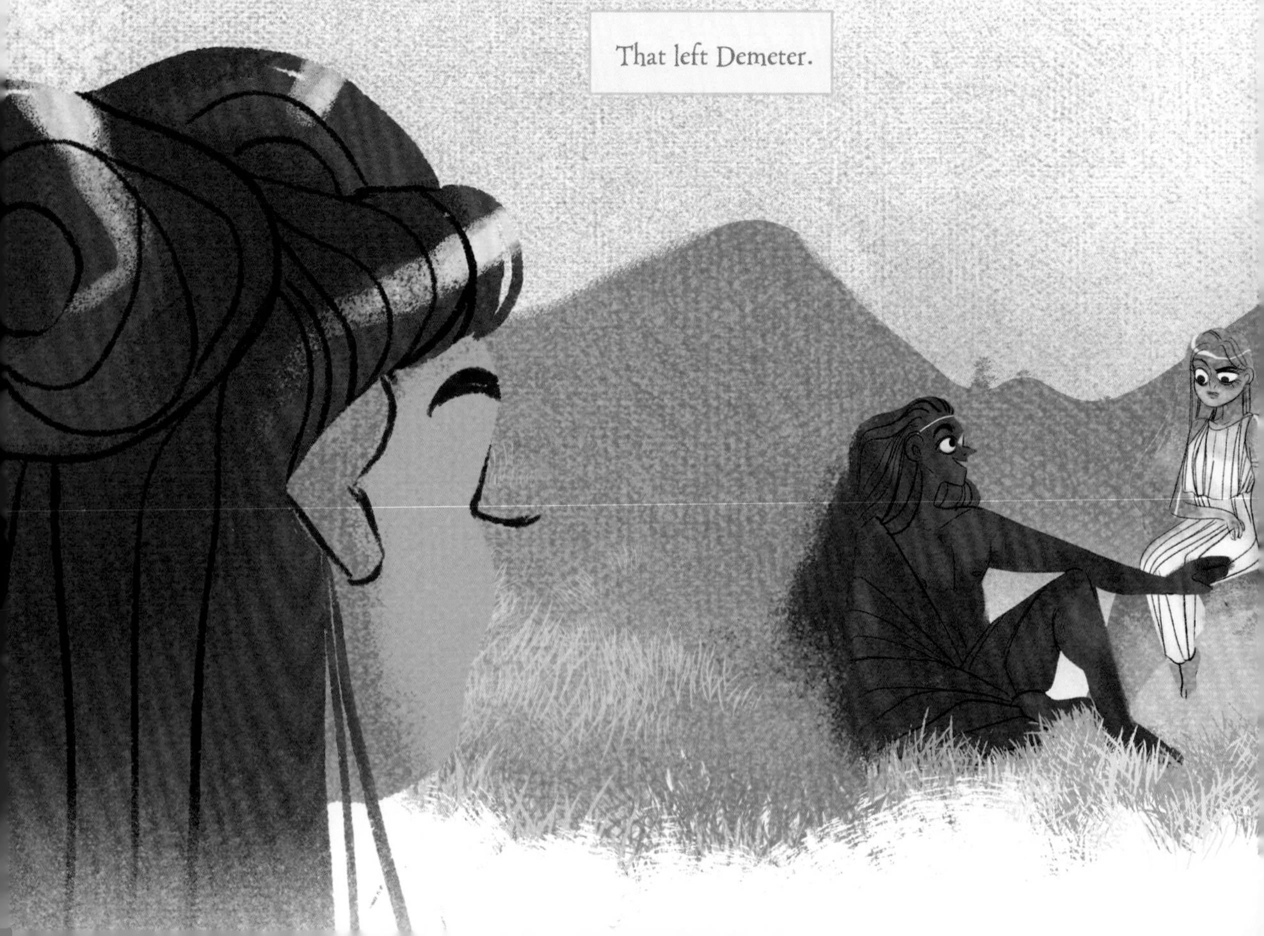
That left Demeter.

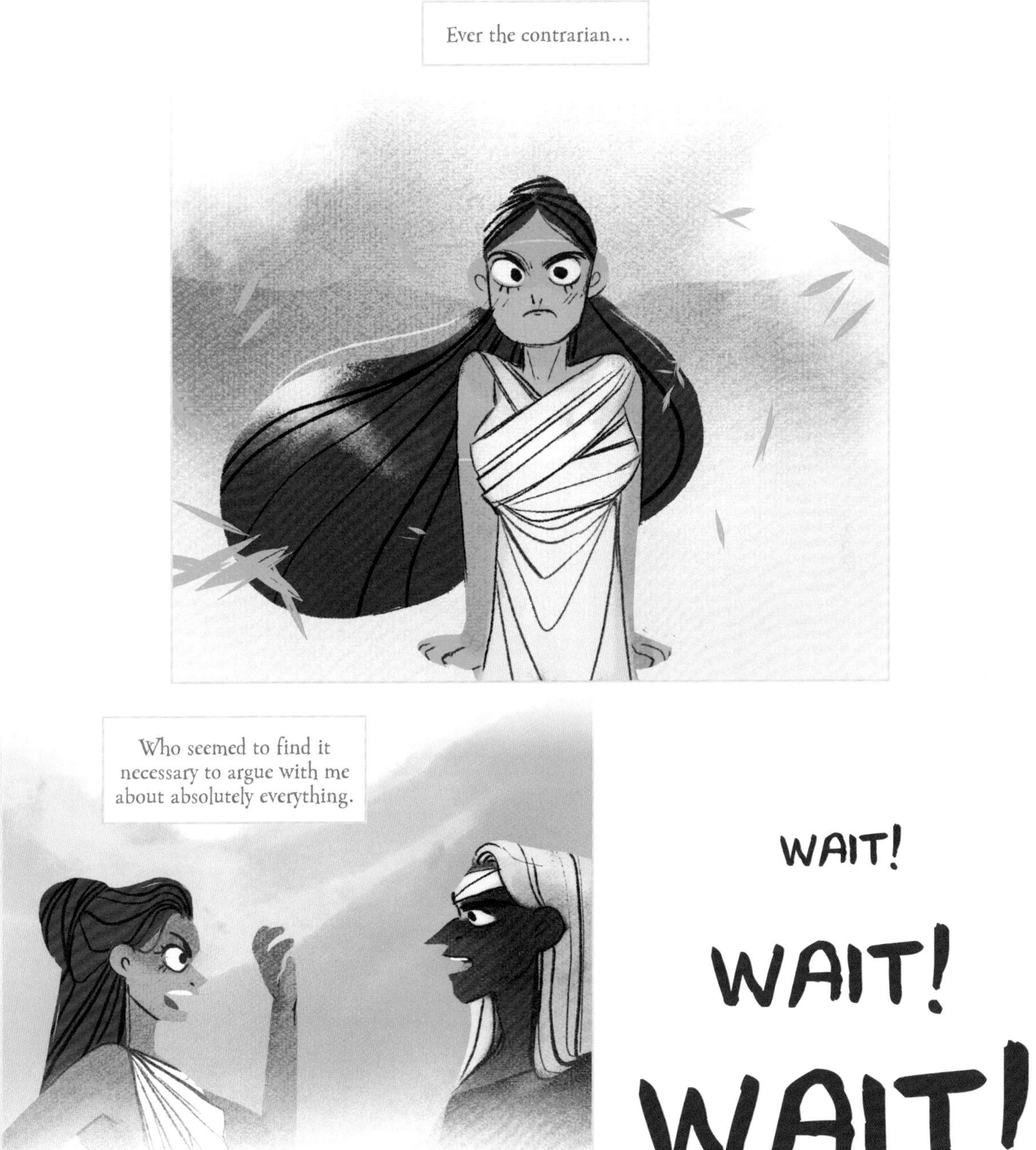
Ever the contrarian...
Who seemed to find it necessary to argue with me about absolutely everything.
WAIT!
WAIT!
WAIT!

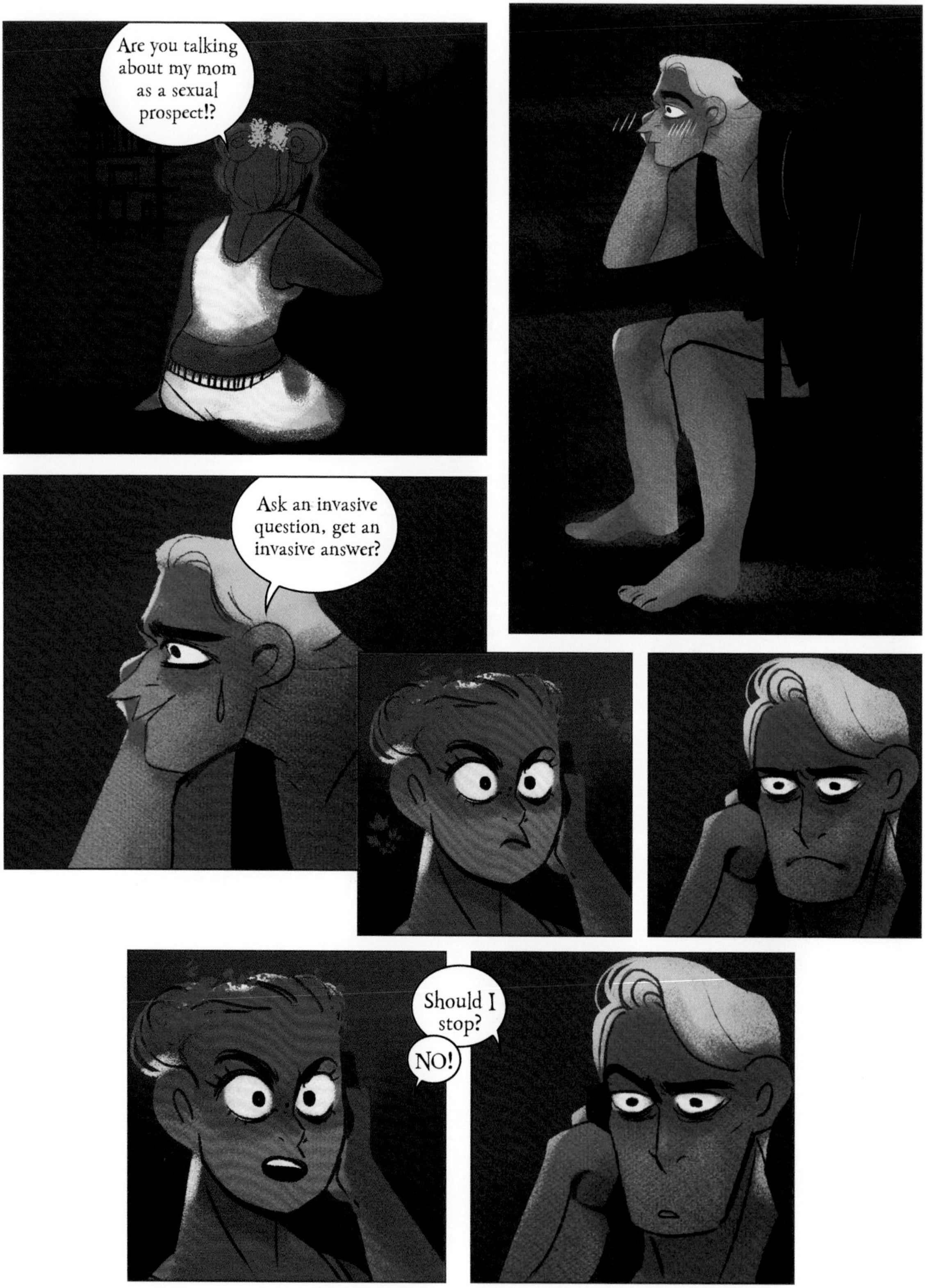
Are you talking about my mom as a sexual prospect!?
Ask an invasive question, get an invasive answer?
Should I stop?
NO!

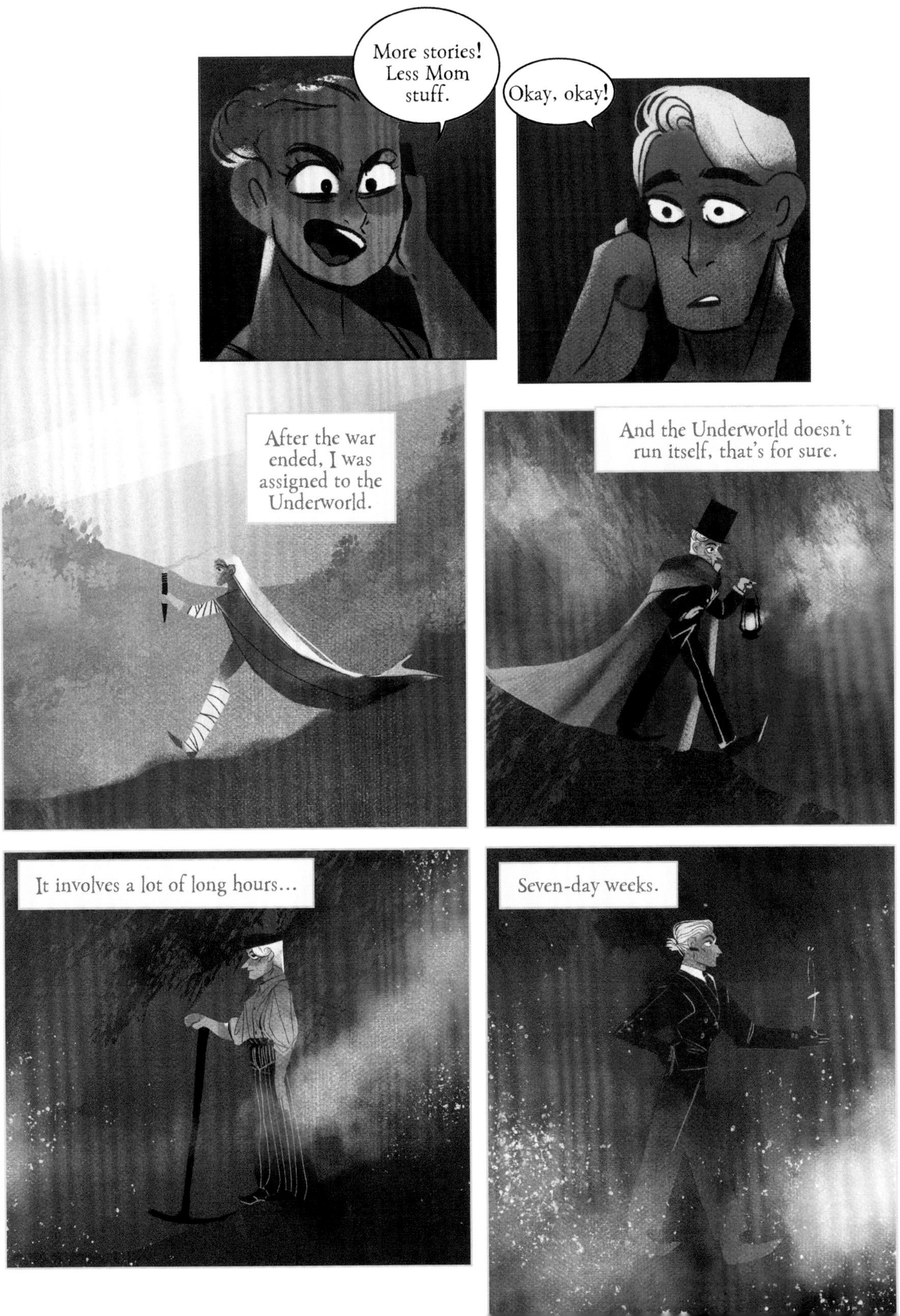
More stories! Less Mom stuff.
Okay, okay!
After the war ended, I was assigned to the Underworld.
And the Underworld doesn't run itself, that's for sure.
It involves a lot of long hours...
Seven-day weeks.

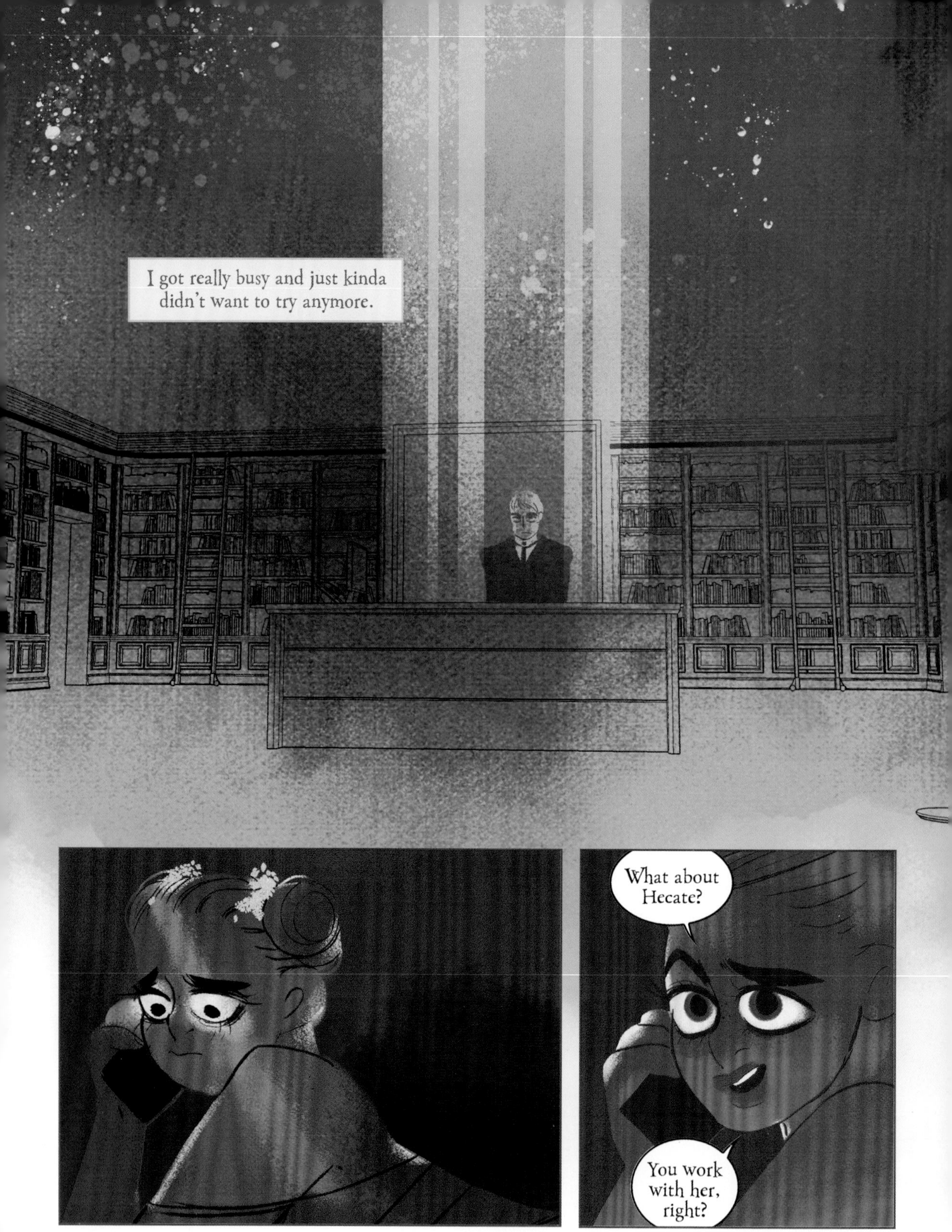
I got really busy and just kinda didn't want to try anymore.
What about Hecate?
You work with her, right?

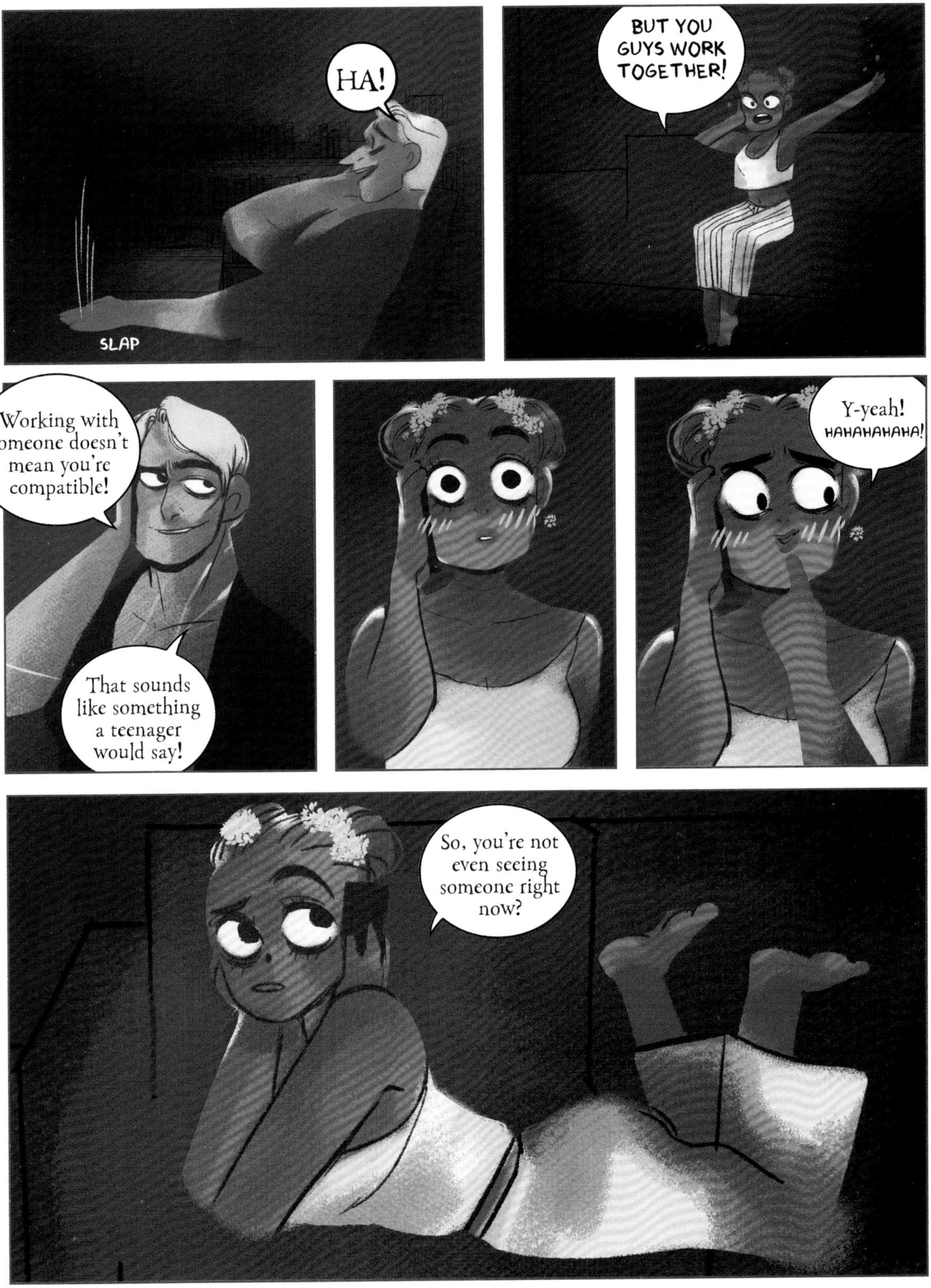
HA!
SLAP
BUT YOU GUYS WORK TOGETHER!
Working with someone doesn't mean you're compatible!
That sounds like something a teenager would say!
Y-yeah! HAHAHAHAHA!
So, you're not even seeing someone right now?

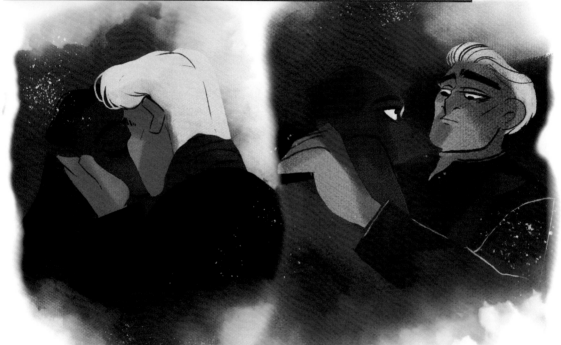

N-no.

You?

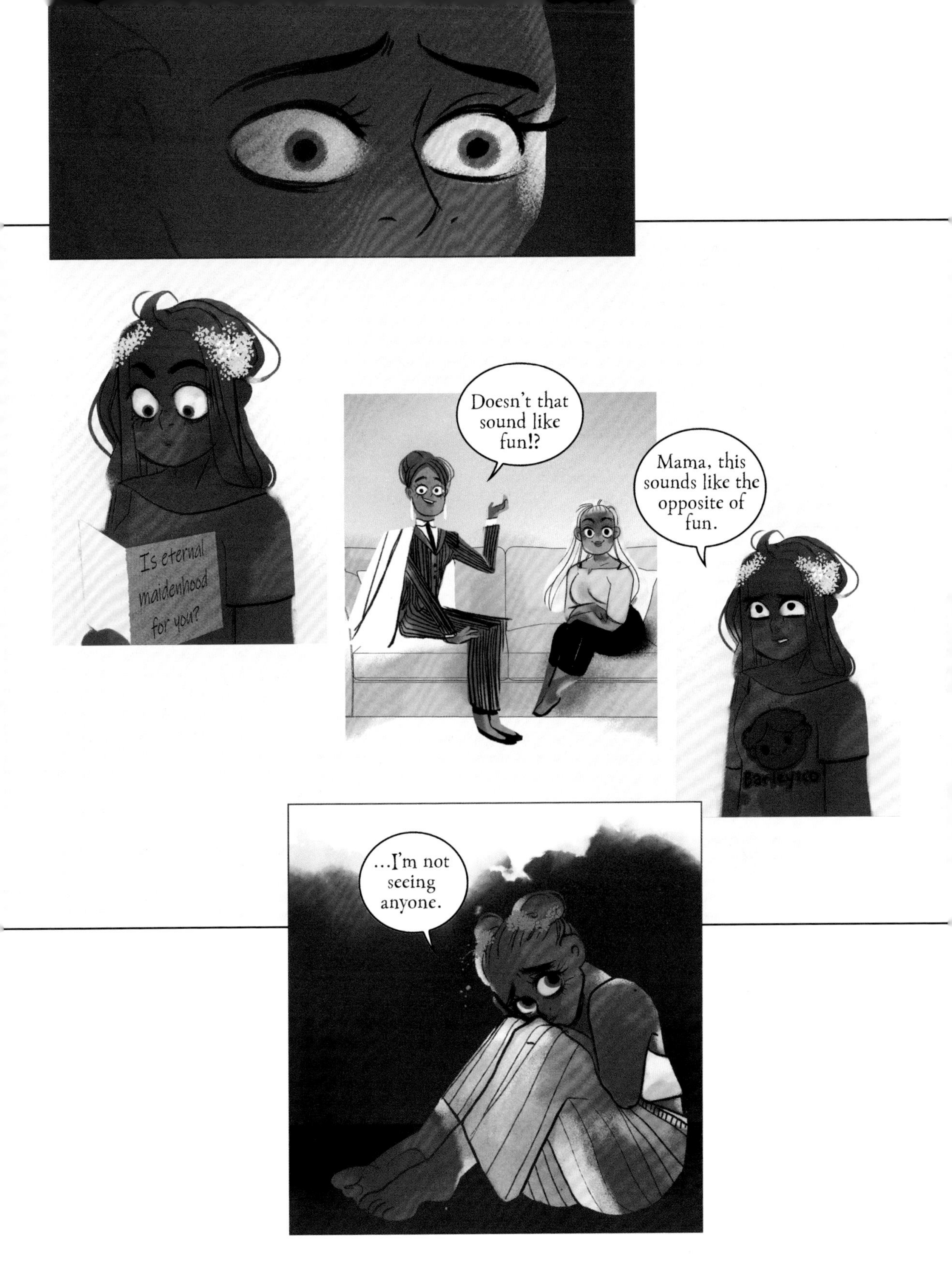
Is eternal maidenhood for you?
Doesn't that sound like fun!?
Mama, this sounds like the opposite of fun.
...I'm not seeing anyone.

RUB RUB
I must be keeping you.
Nah, I'm normally up at this time anyway.
SIGH
Good.
Don't go telling everyone about this.
I've got a reputation to maintain.
I won't, I promise.

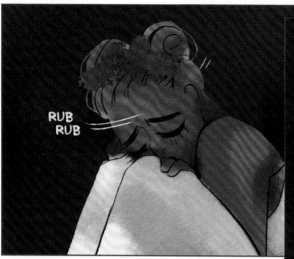

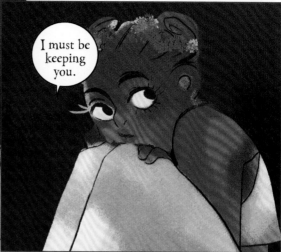

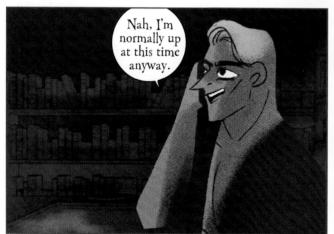

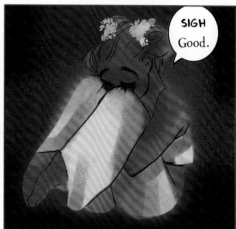

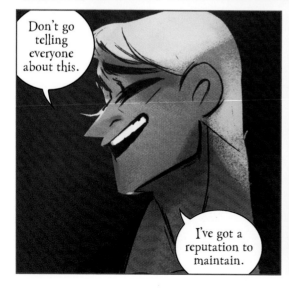

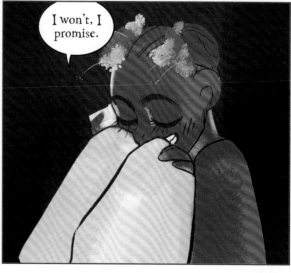

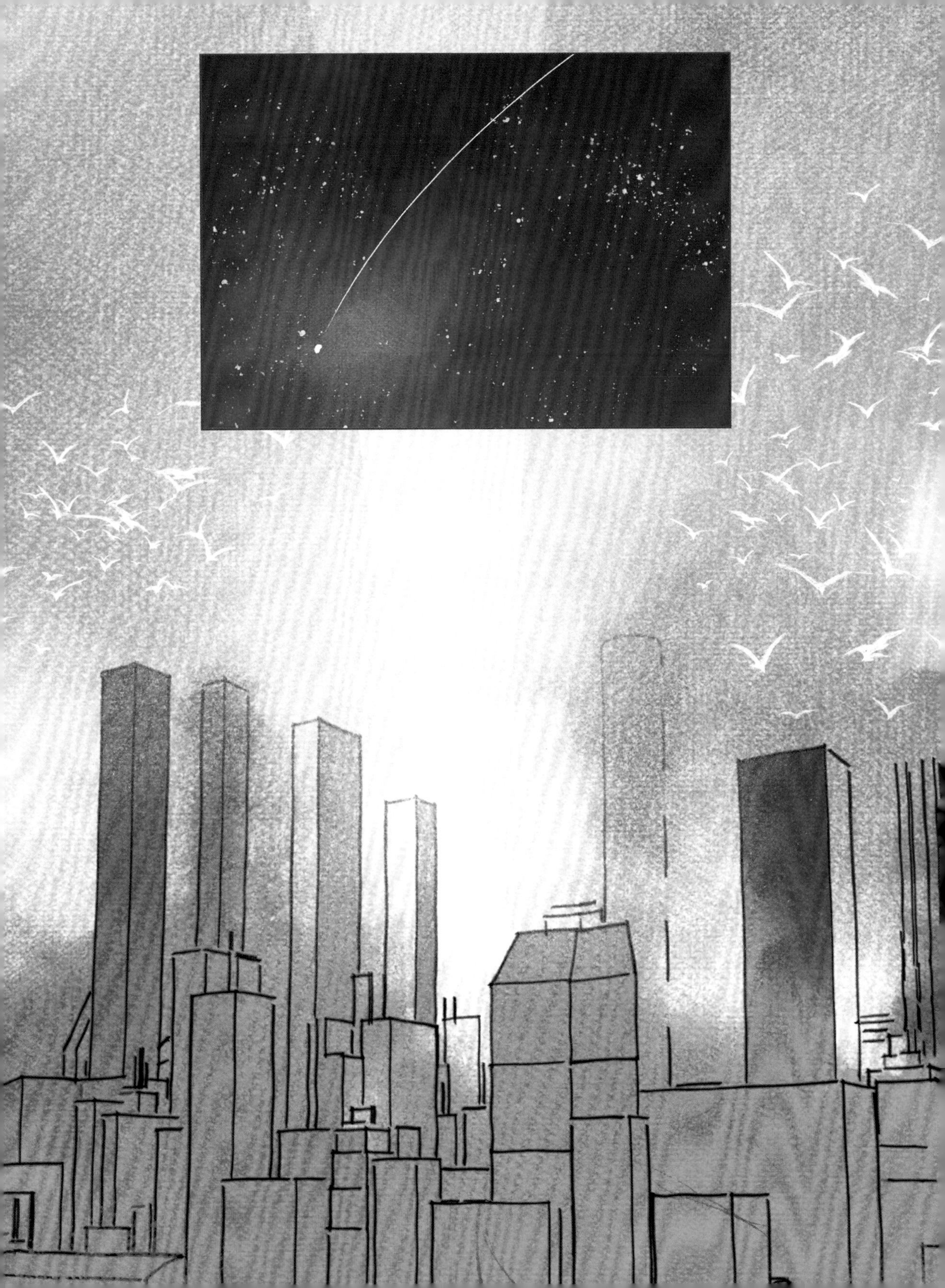

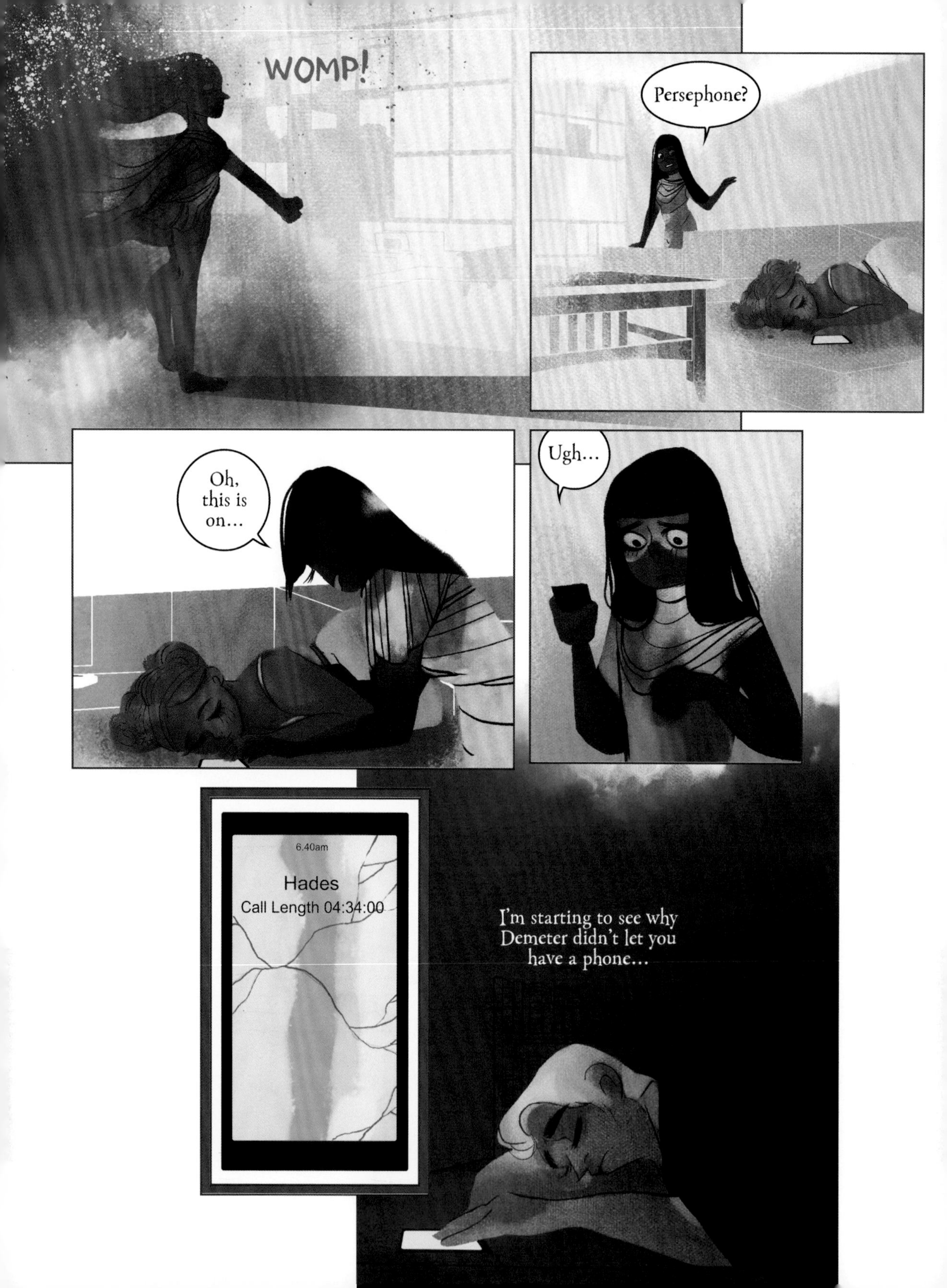
WOMP!
Persephone?
Oh, this is on...
Ugh...
6.40am
Hades
Call Length 04:34:00
I'm starting to see why Demeter didn't let you have a phone...

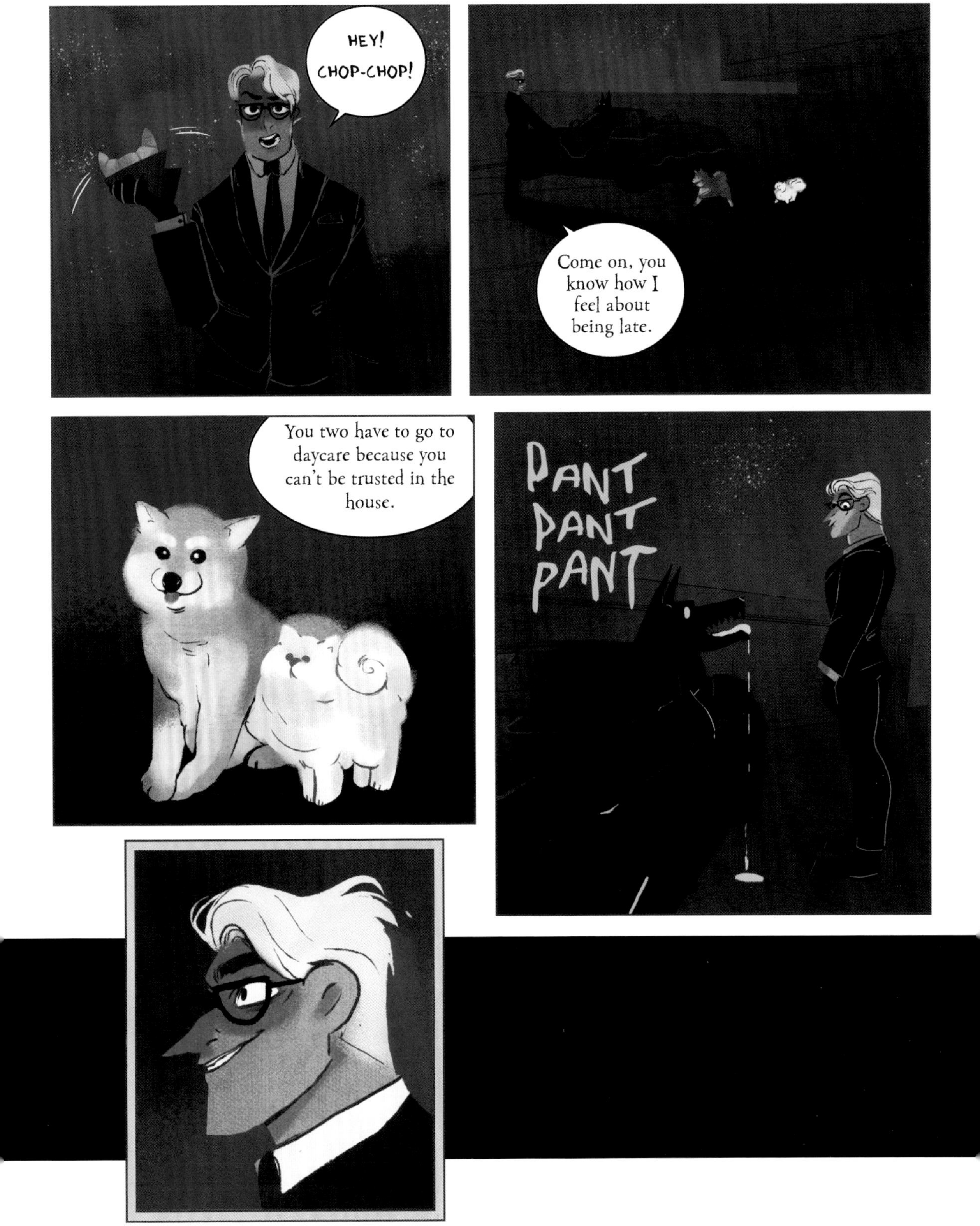
HEY! CHOP-CHOP!
Come on, you know how I feel about being late.
You two have to go to daycare because you can't be trusted in the house.
PANT PANT PANT

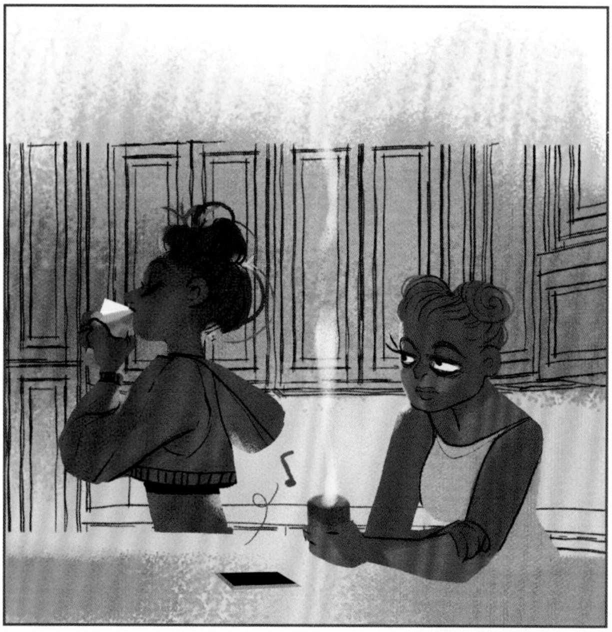
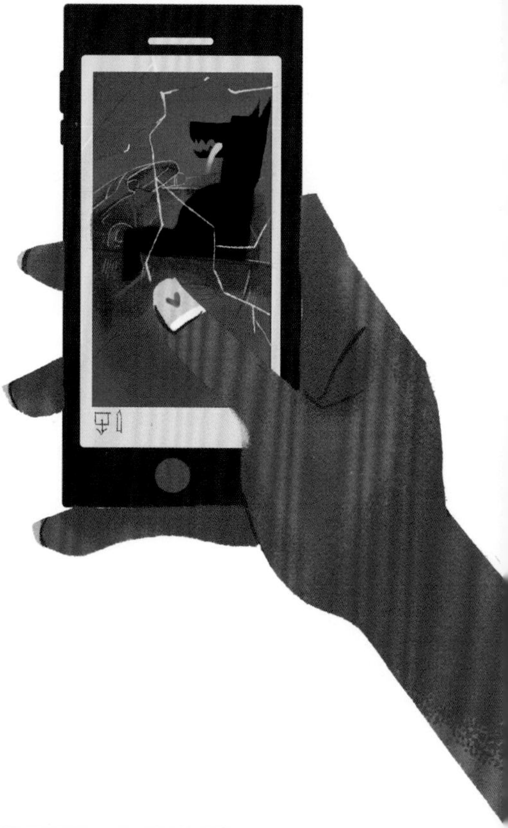
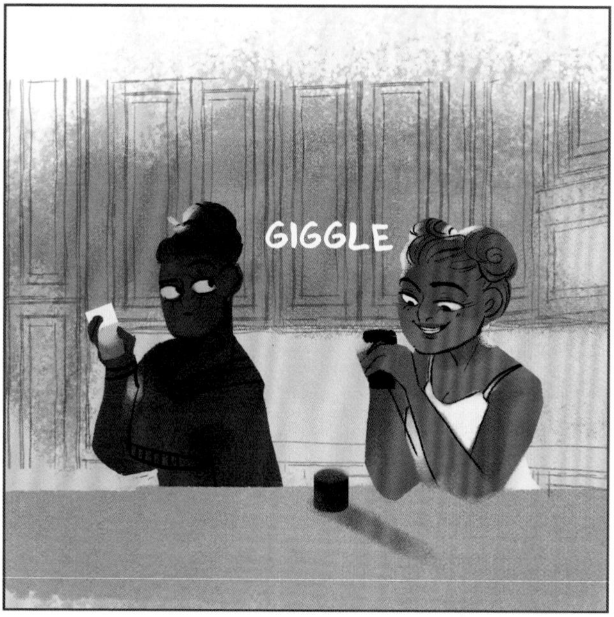
GIGGLE
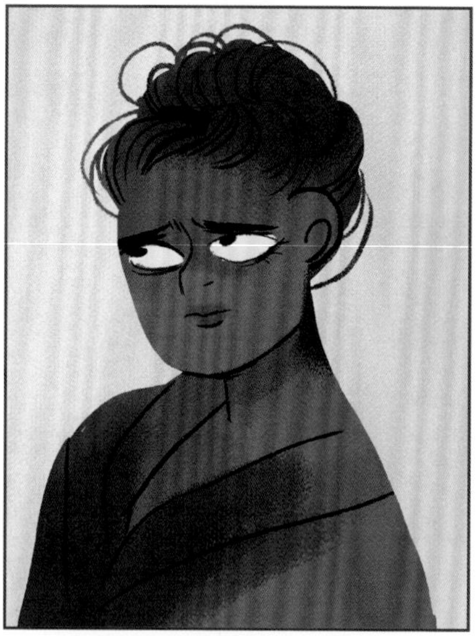

EPISODE 29: THUNDER

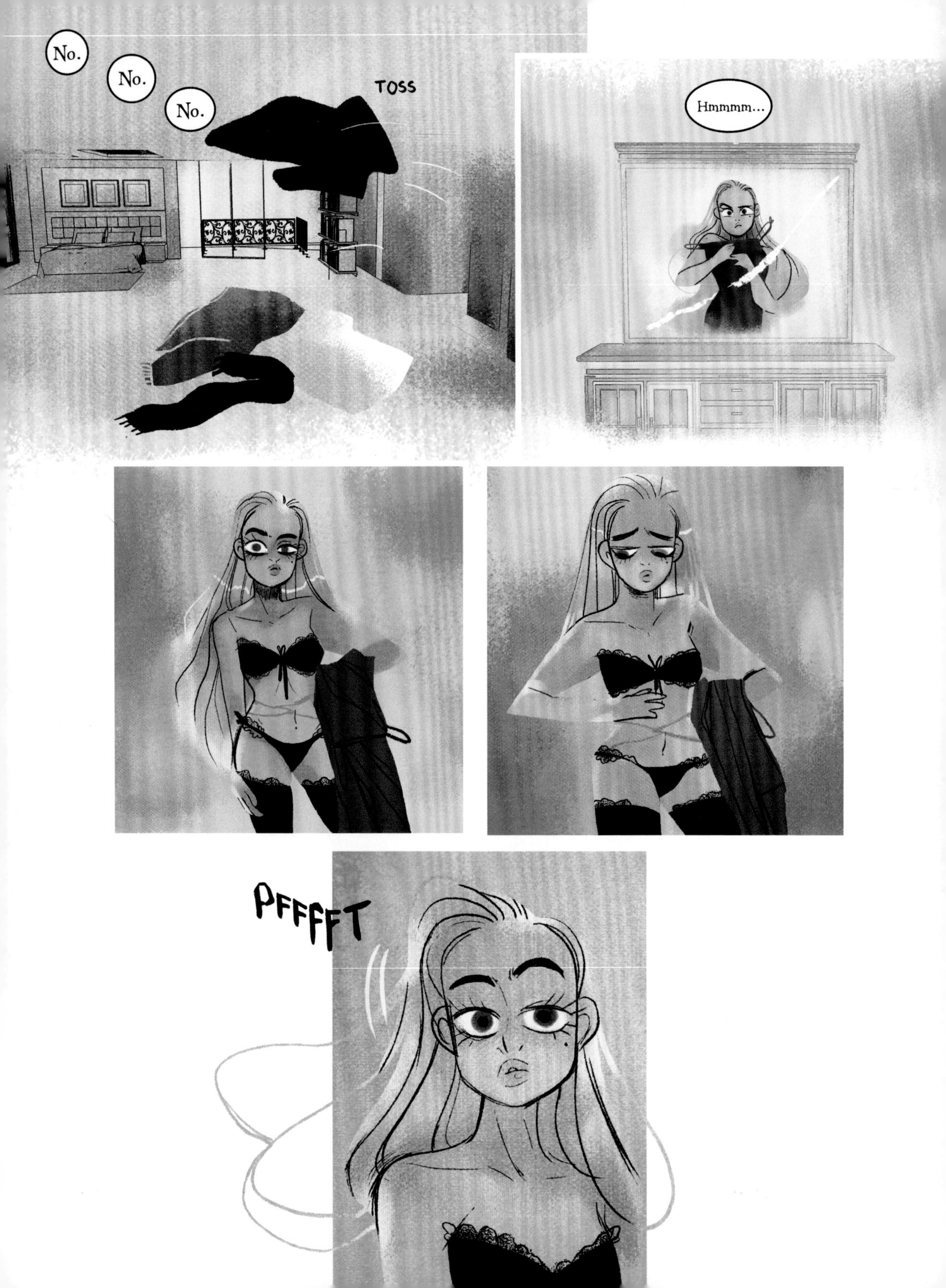
No.
No.
No.
TOSS
Hmmmm...
PFFFFT

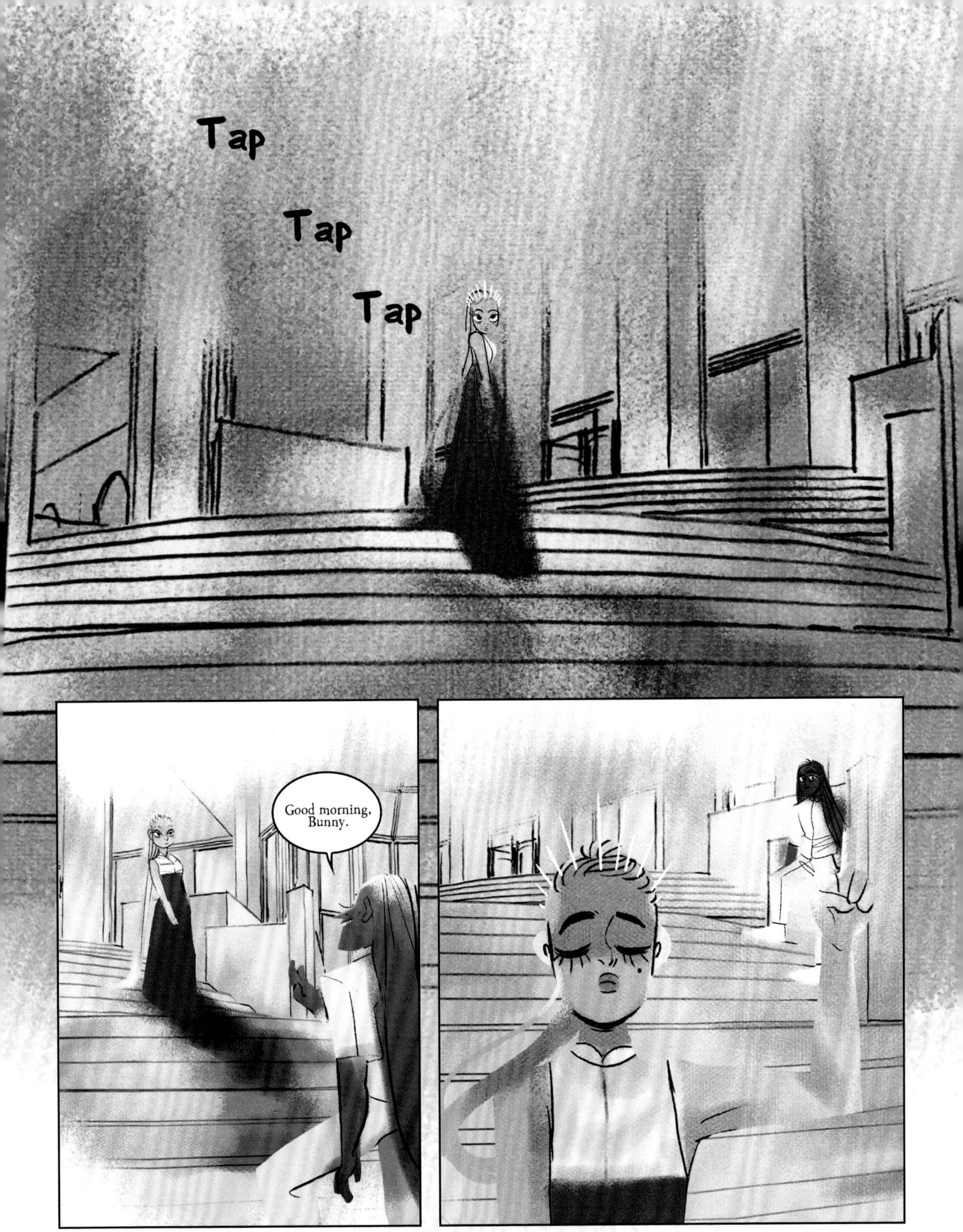
Tap
Tap
Tap
Good morning, Bunny.

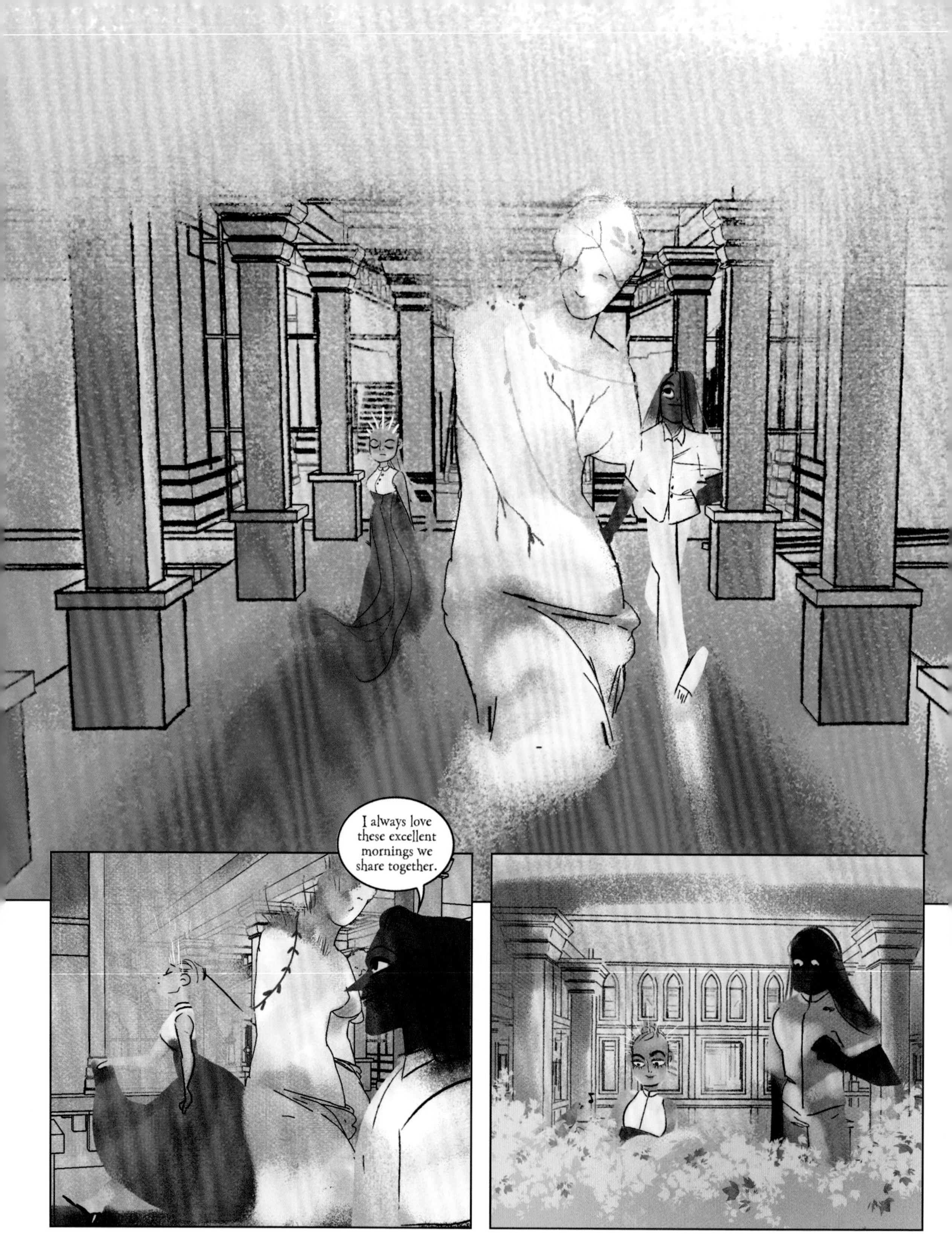
I always love these excellent mornings we share together.

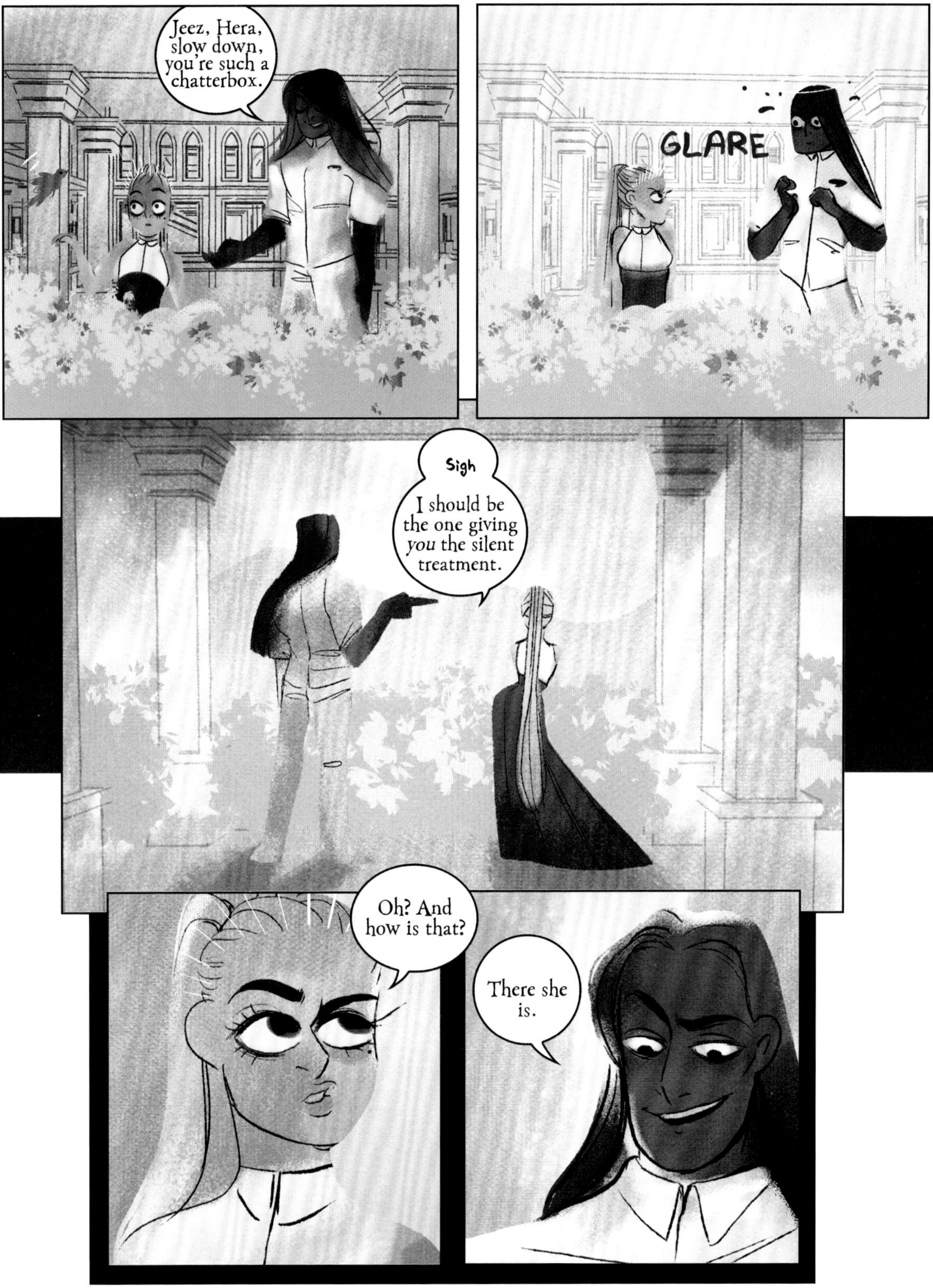

Jeez, Hera, slow down, you're such a chatterbox.
GLARE
Sigh
I should be the one giving *you* the silent treatment.
Oh? And how is that?
There she is.

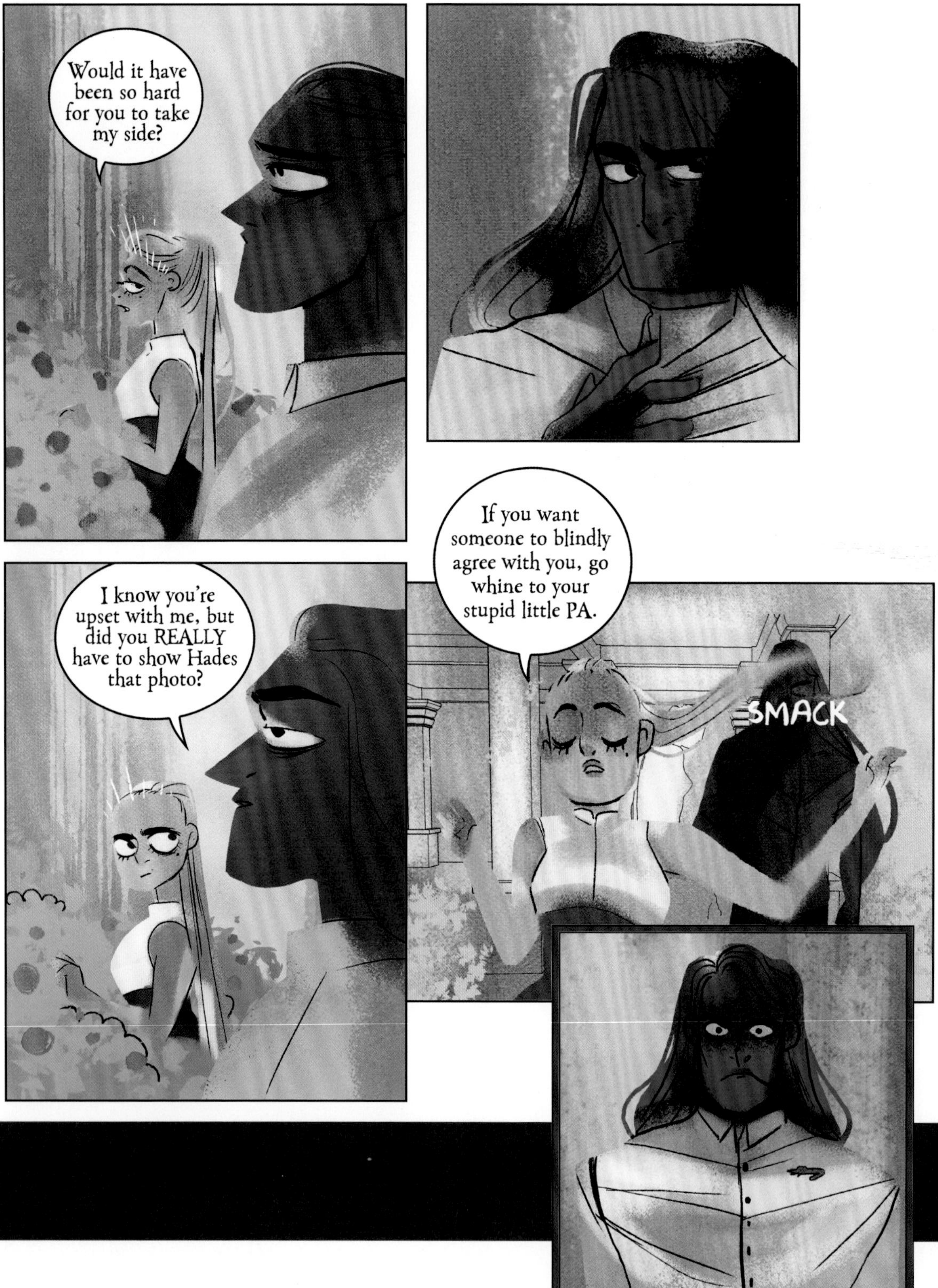
Would it have been so hard for you to take my side?
I know you're upset with me, but did you REALLY have to show Hades that photo?
If you want someone to blindly agree with you, go whine to your stupid little PA.
SMACK

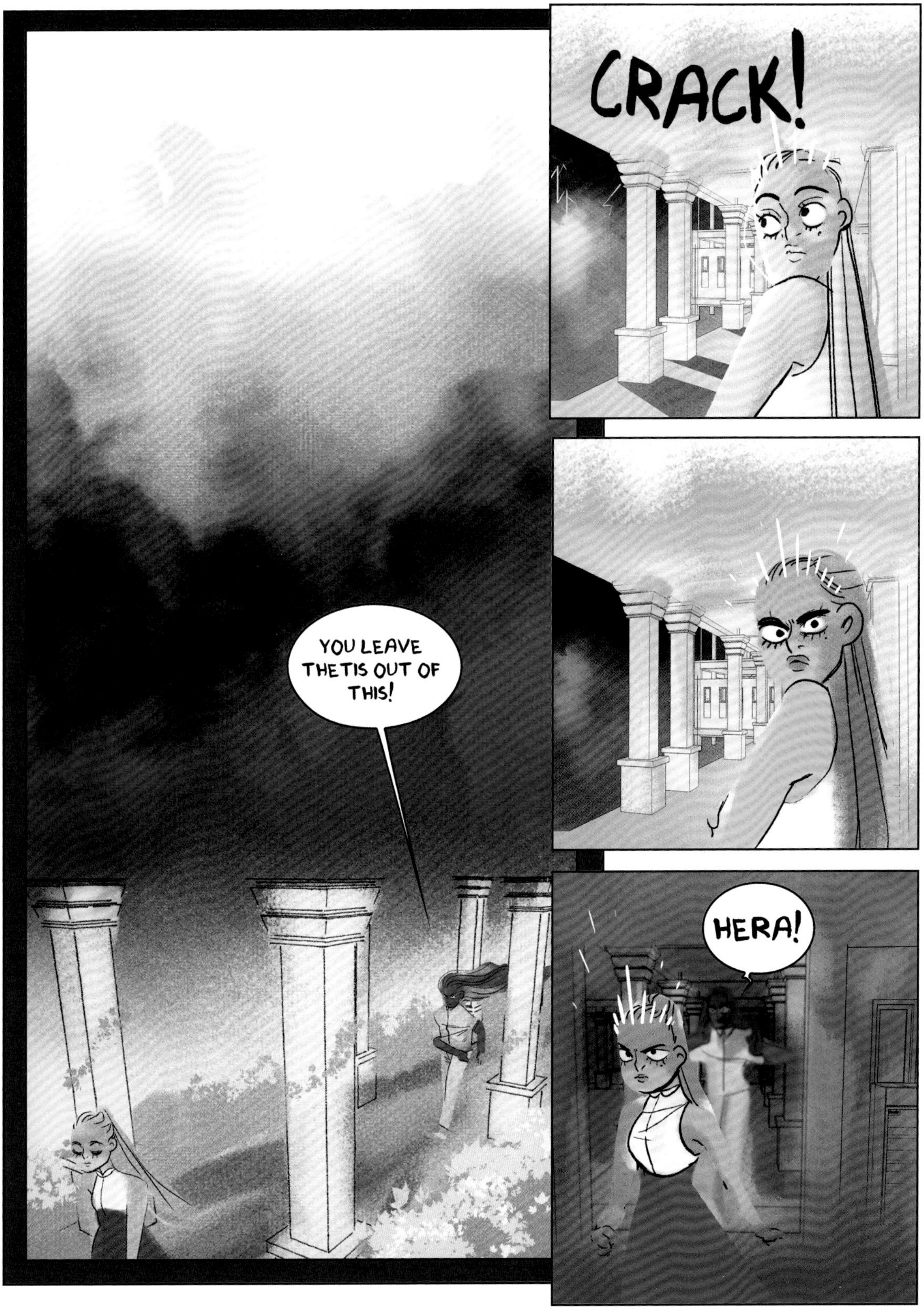
CRACK!
YOU LEAVE THETIS OUT OF THIS!
HERA!

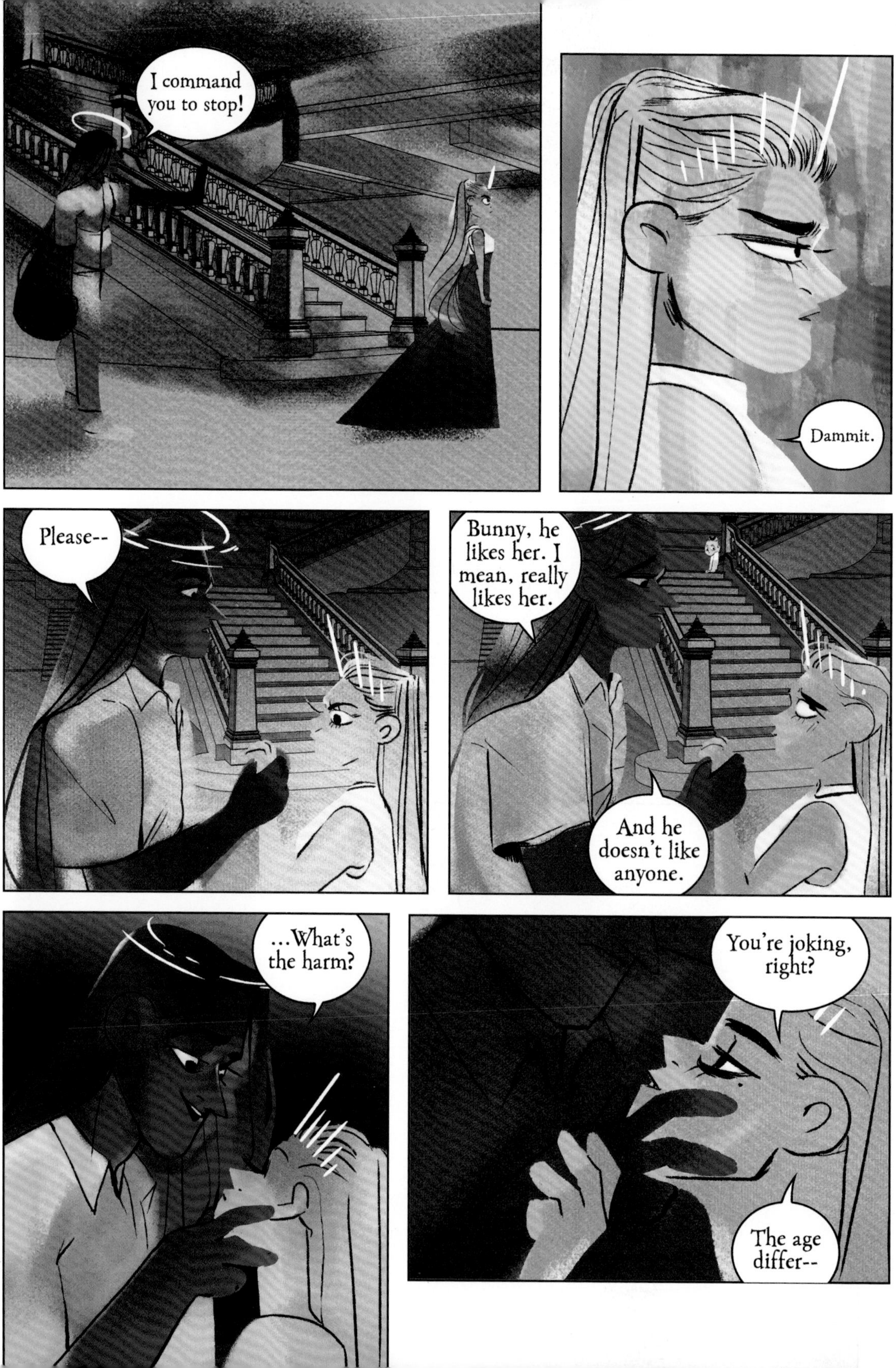
I command you to stop!
Dammit.
Please--
Bunny, he likes her. I mean, really likes her.
And he doesn't like anyone.
...What's the harm?
You're joking, right?
The age differ--

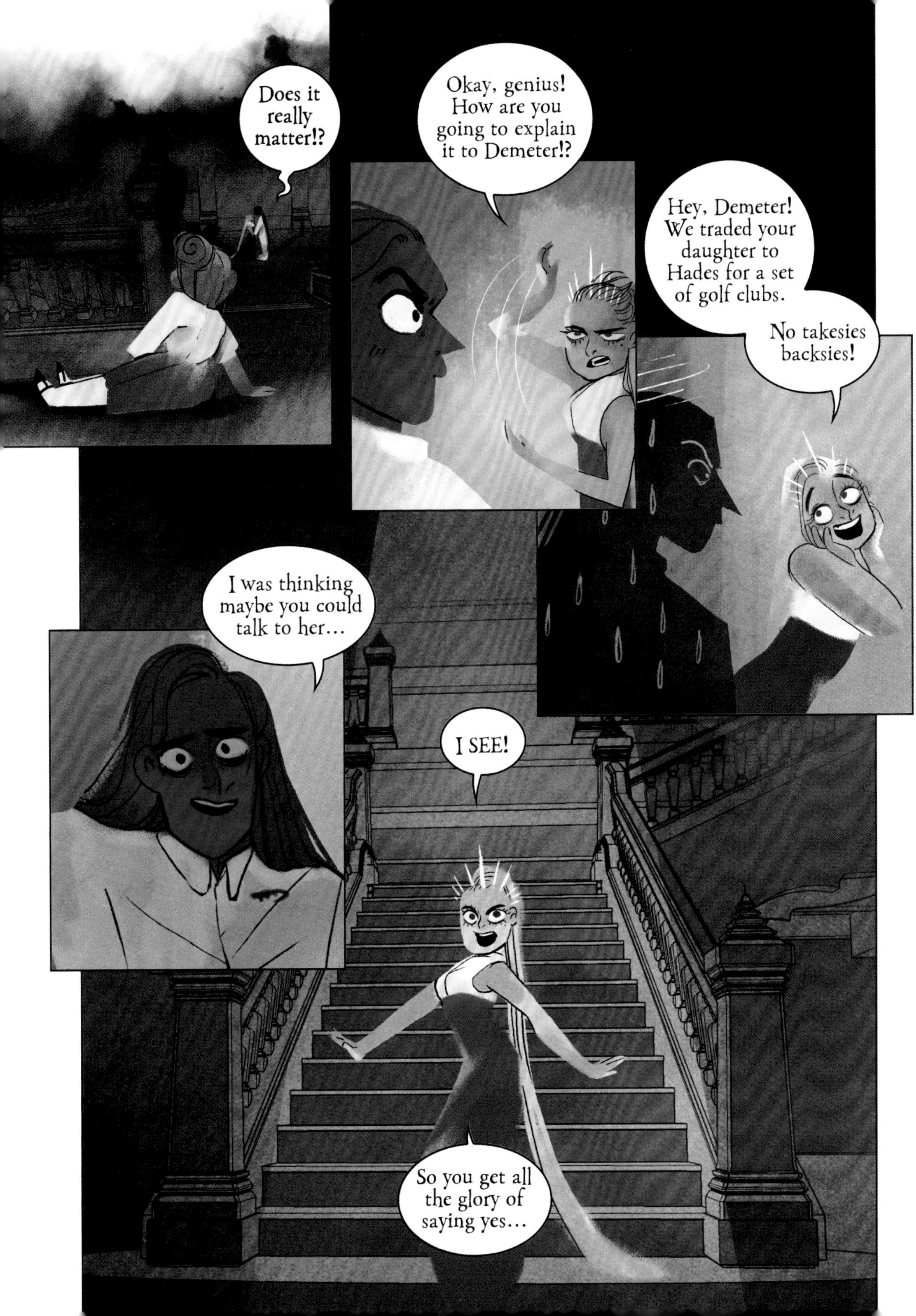
Does it really matter!?
Okay, genius! How are you going to explain it to Demeter!?
Hey, Demeter! We traded your daughter to Hades for a set of golf clubs.
No takesies backsies!
I was thinking maybe you could talk to her...
I SEE!
So you get all the glory of saying yes...

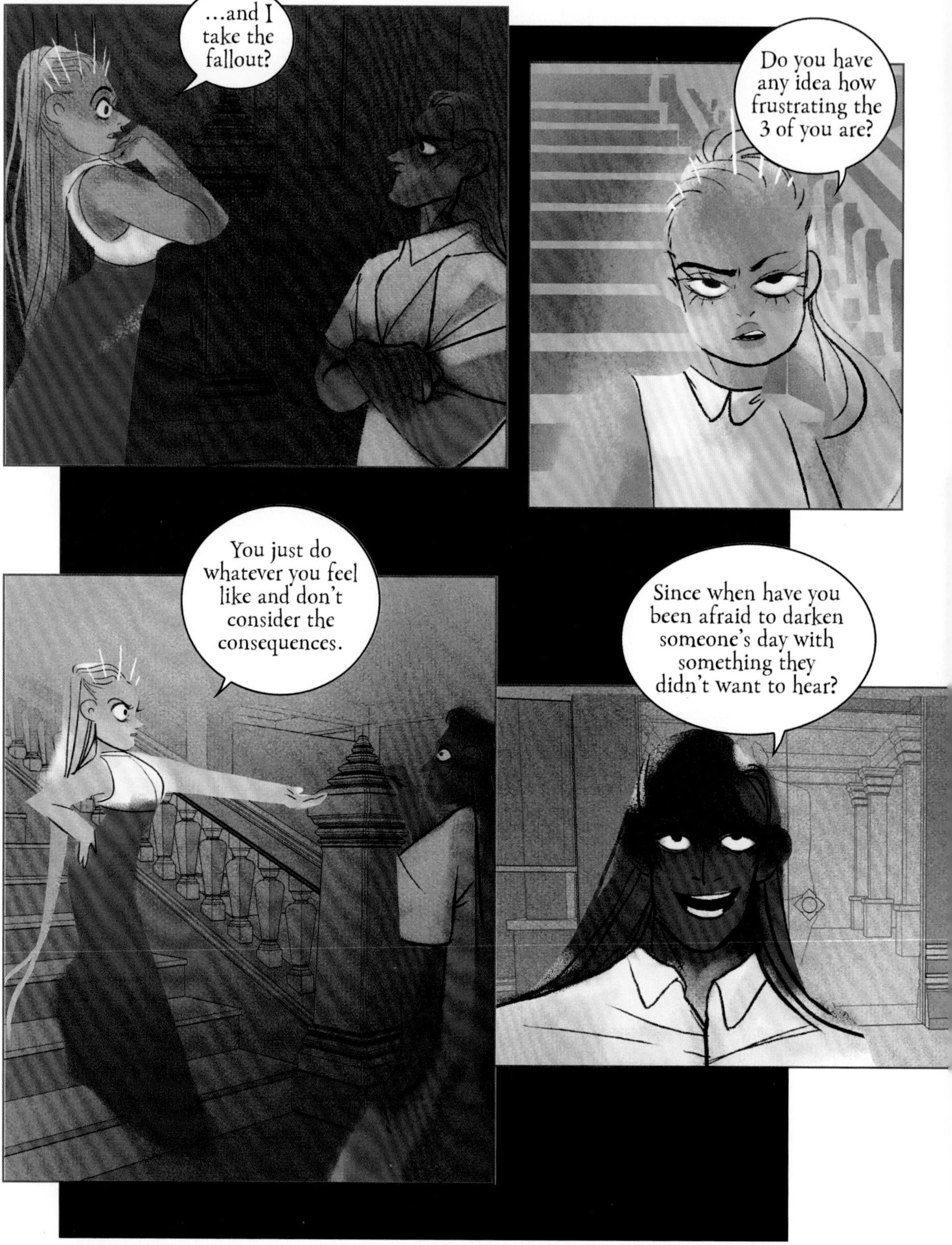
…and I take the fallout?
Do you have any idea how frustrating the 3 of you are?
You just do whatever you feel like and don't consider the consequences.
Since when have you been afraid to darken someone's day with something they didn't want to hear?

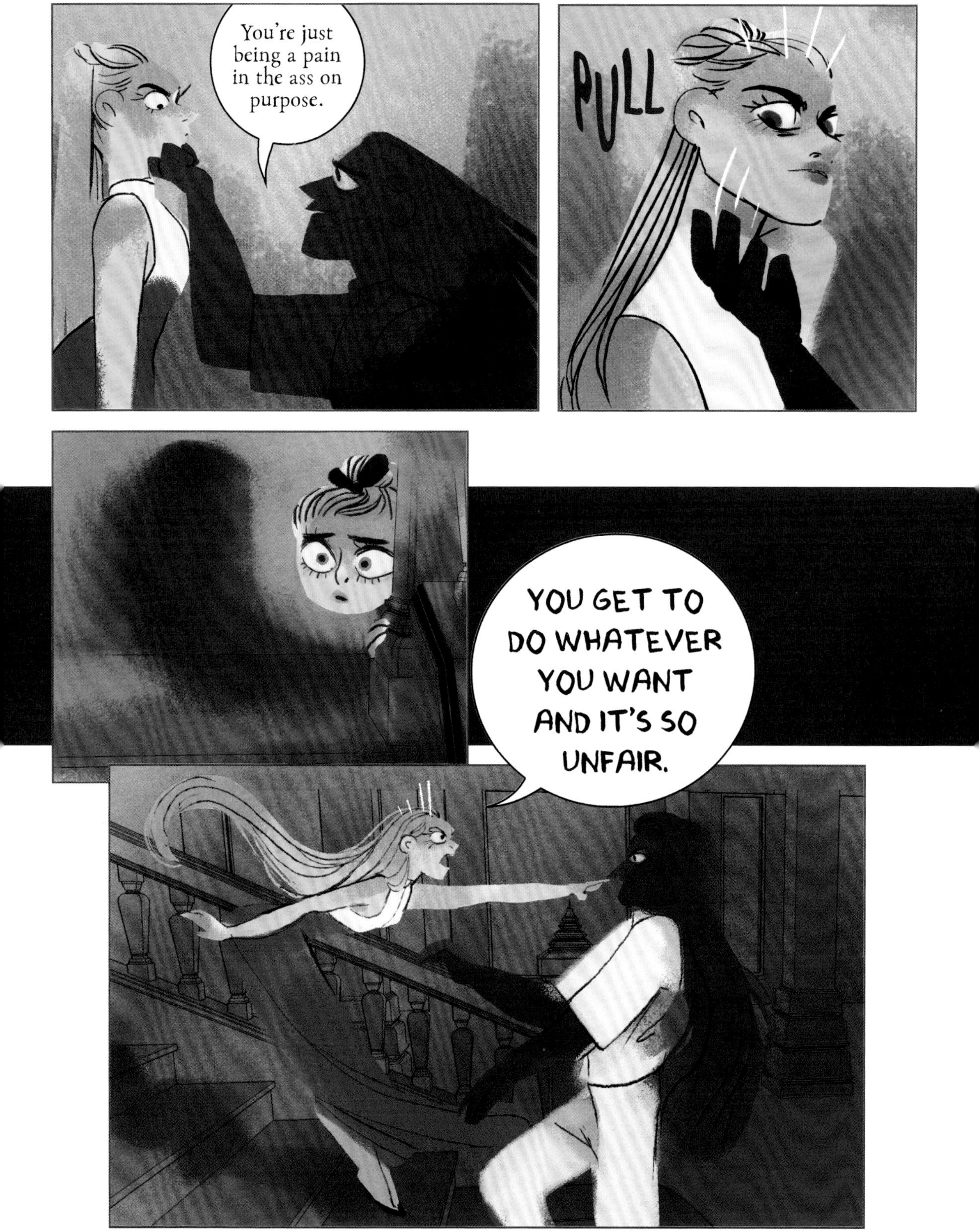
You're just being a pain in the ass on purpose.
PULL
YOU GET TO DO WHATEVER YOU WANT AND IT'S SO UNFAIR.

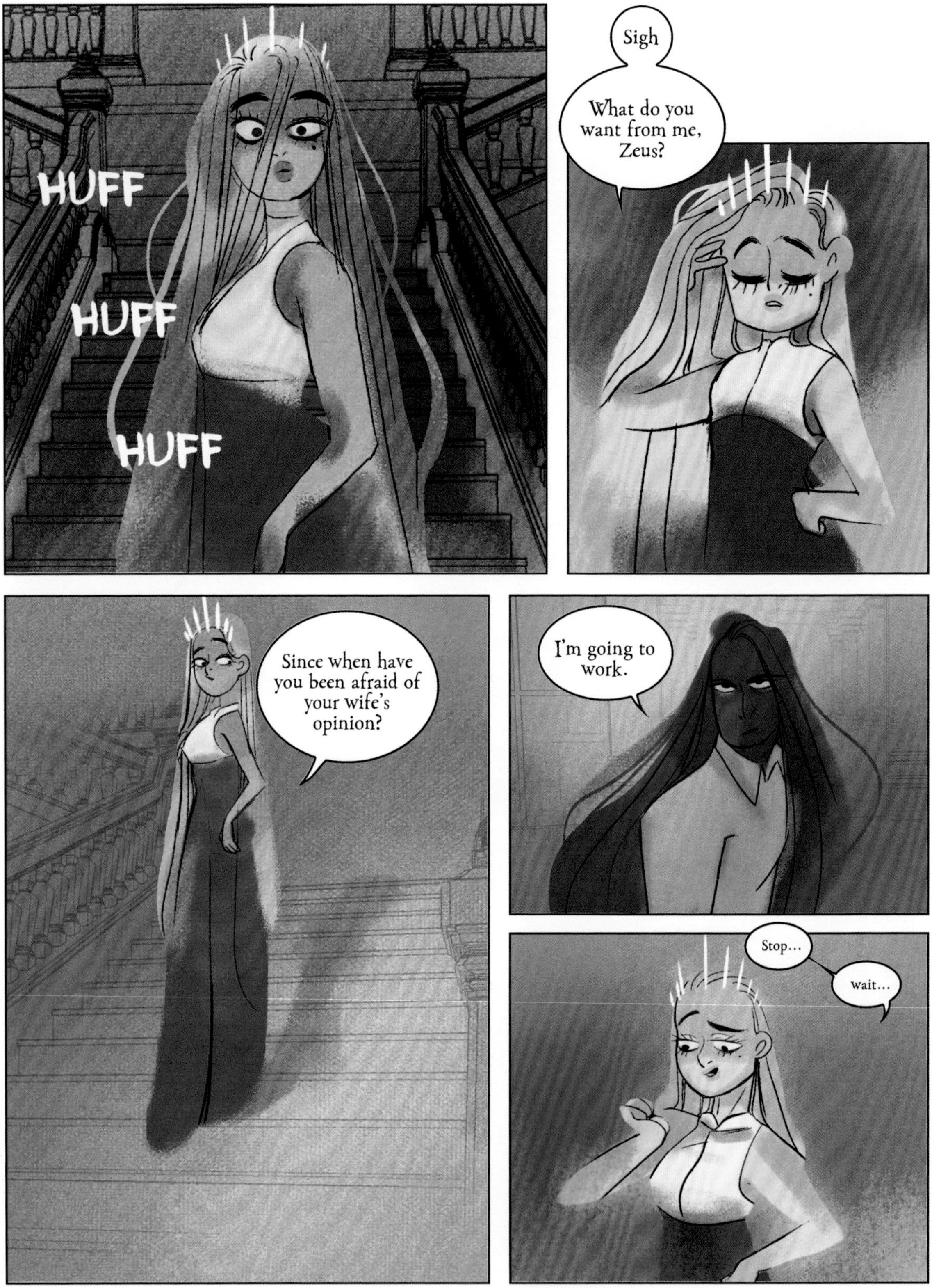
HUFF
HUFF
HUFF
Sigh
What do you want from me, Zeus?
Since when have you been afraid of your wife's opinion?
I'm going to work.
Stop...
wait...

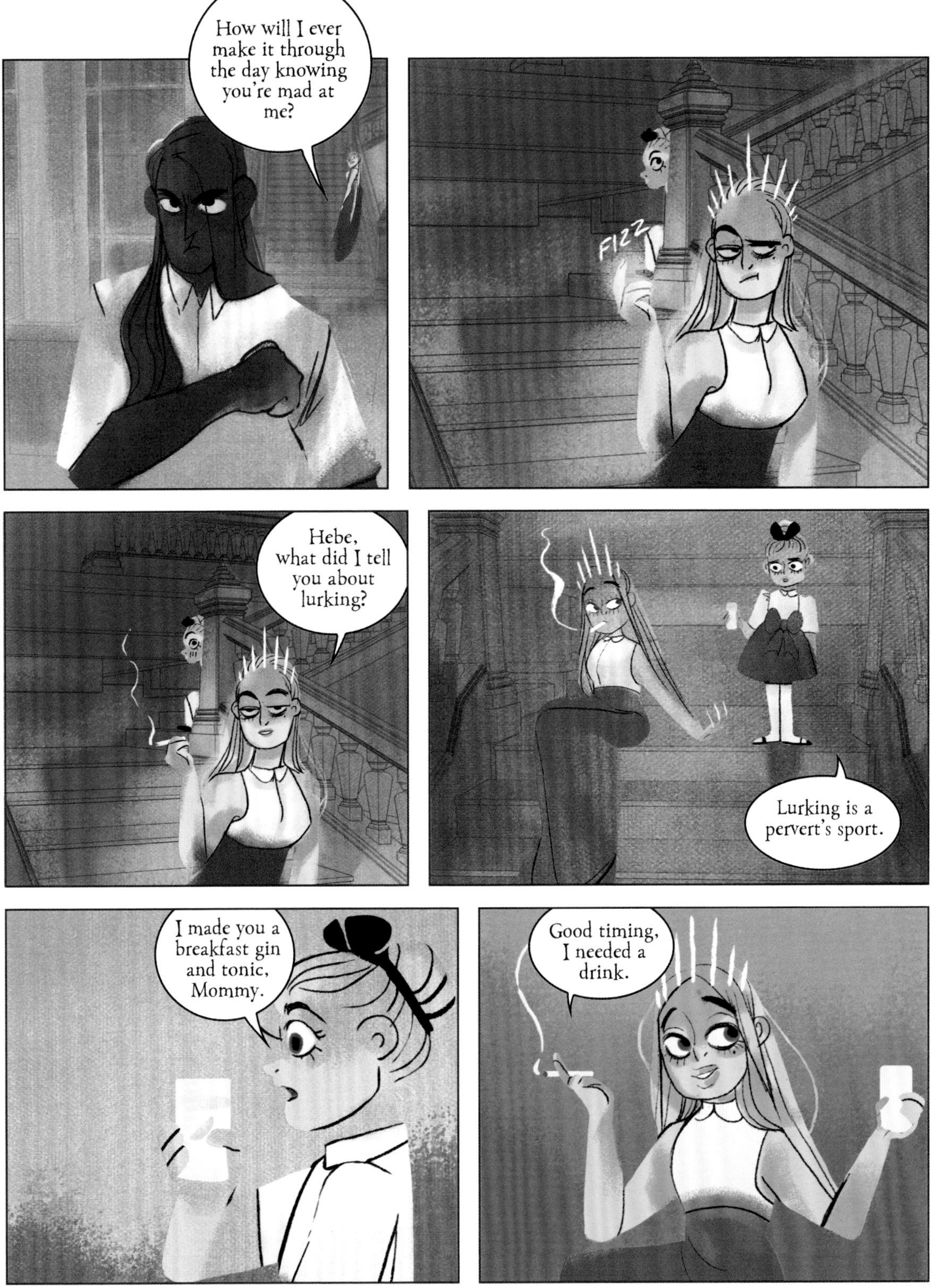
How will I ever make it through the day knowing you're mad at me?
FIZZ
Hebe, what did I tell you about lurking?
Lurking is a pervert's sport.
I made you a breakfast gin and tonic, Mommy.
Good timing, I needed a drink.

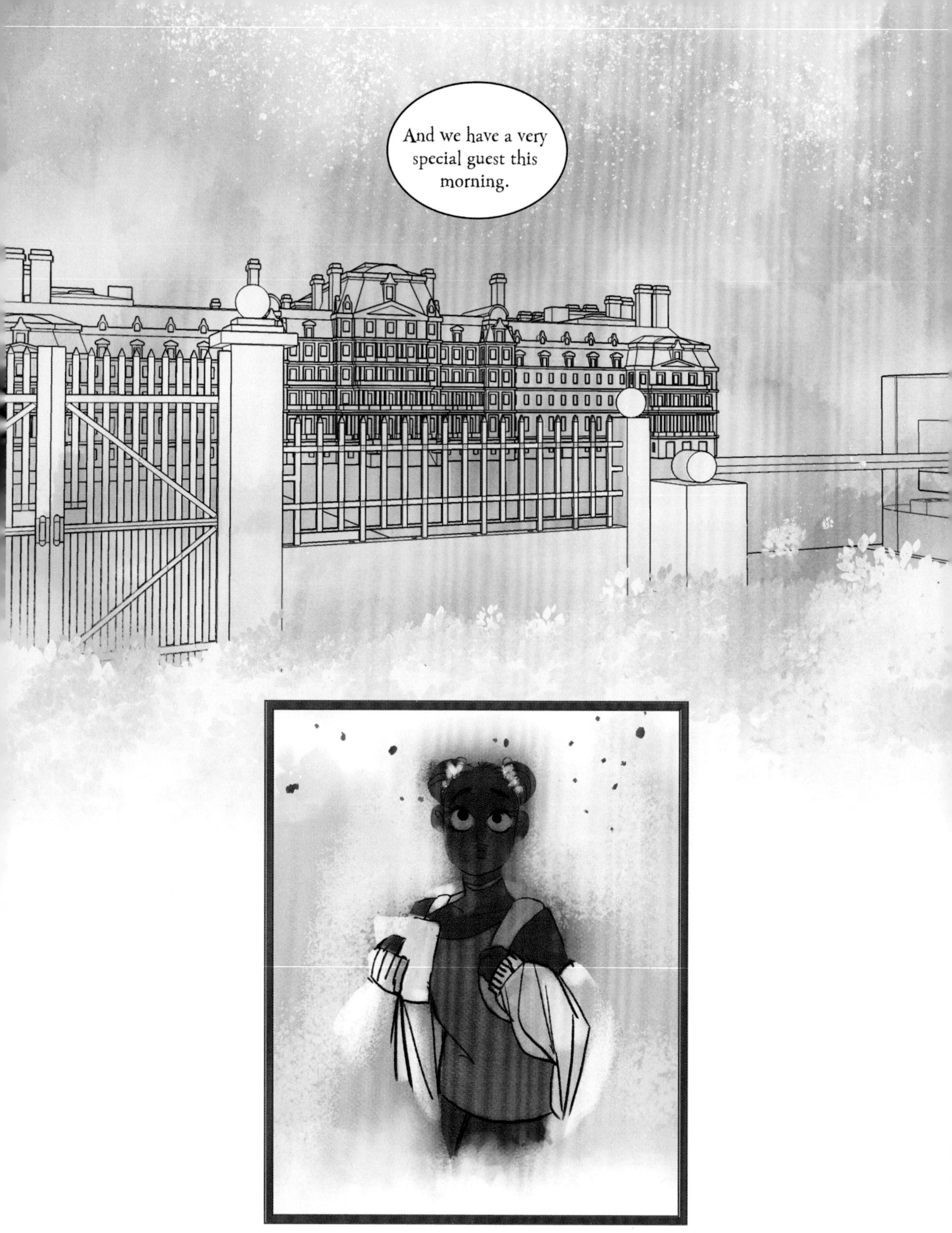
And we have a very special guest this morning.

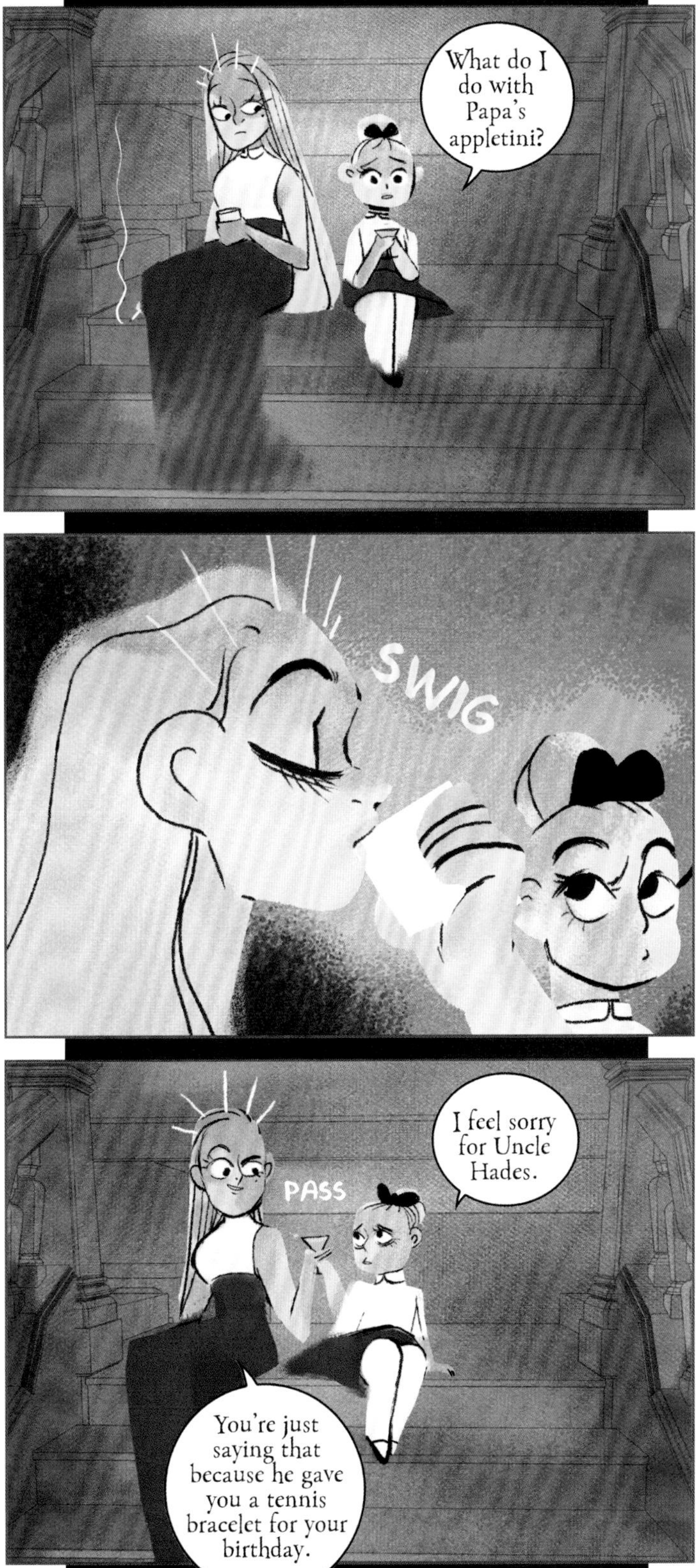
What do I do with Papa's appletini?
SWIG
PASS
I feel sorry for Uncle Hades.
You're just saying that because he gave you a tennis bracelet for your birthday.

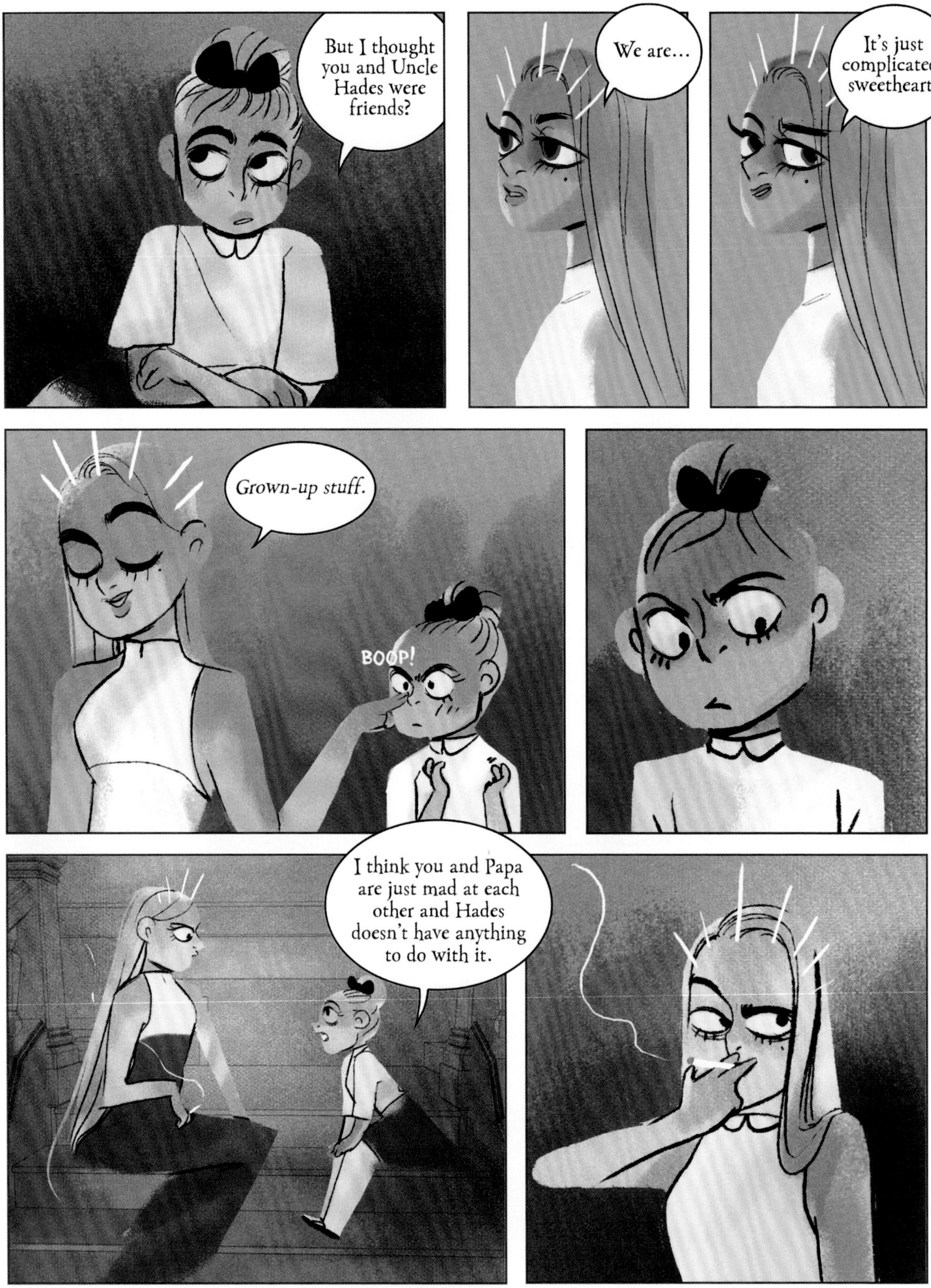

But I thought you and Uncle Hades were friends?
We are...
It's just complicated, sweetheart.
Grown-up stuff.
BOOP!
I think you and Papa are just mad at each other and Hades doesn't have anything to do with it.

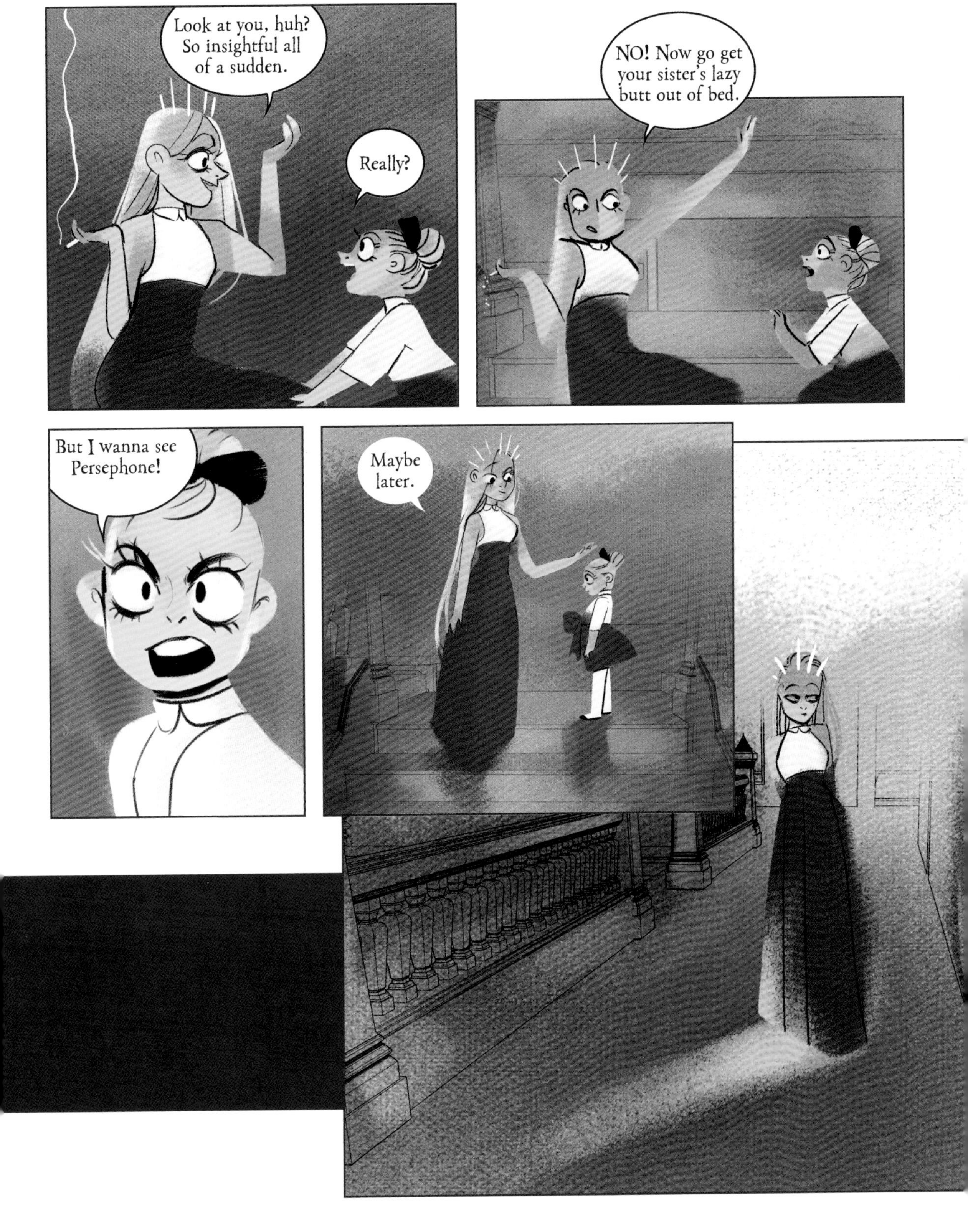
Look at you, huh? So insightful all of a sudden.
Really?
NO! Now go get your sister's lazy butt out of bed.
But I wanna see Persephone!
Maybe later.

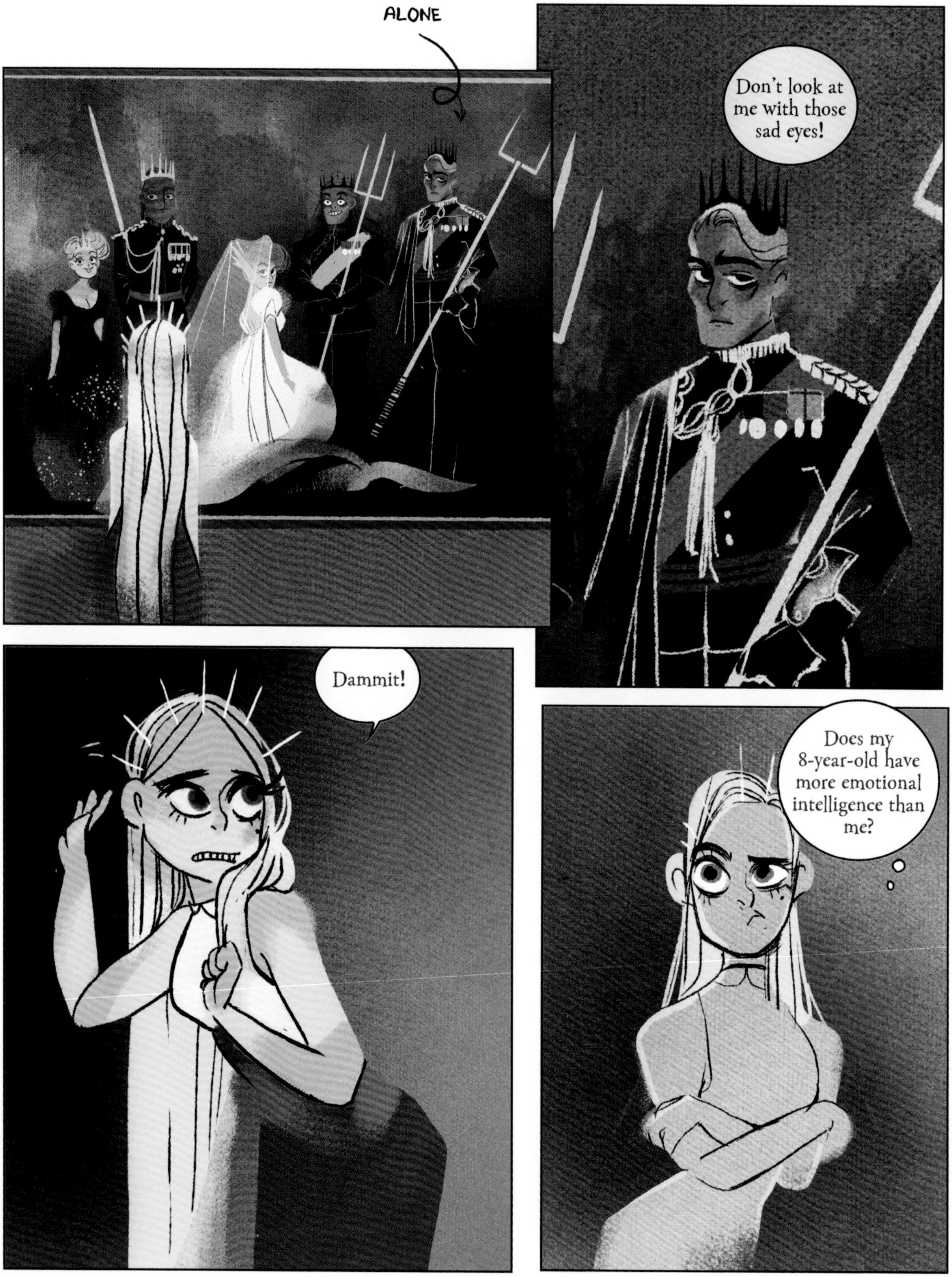
ALONE
Don't look at me with those sad eyes!
Dammit!
Does my 8-year-old have more emotional intelligence than me?

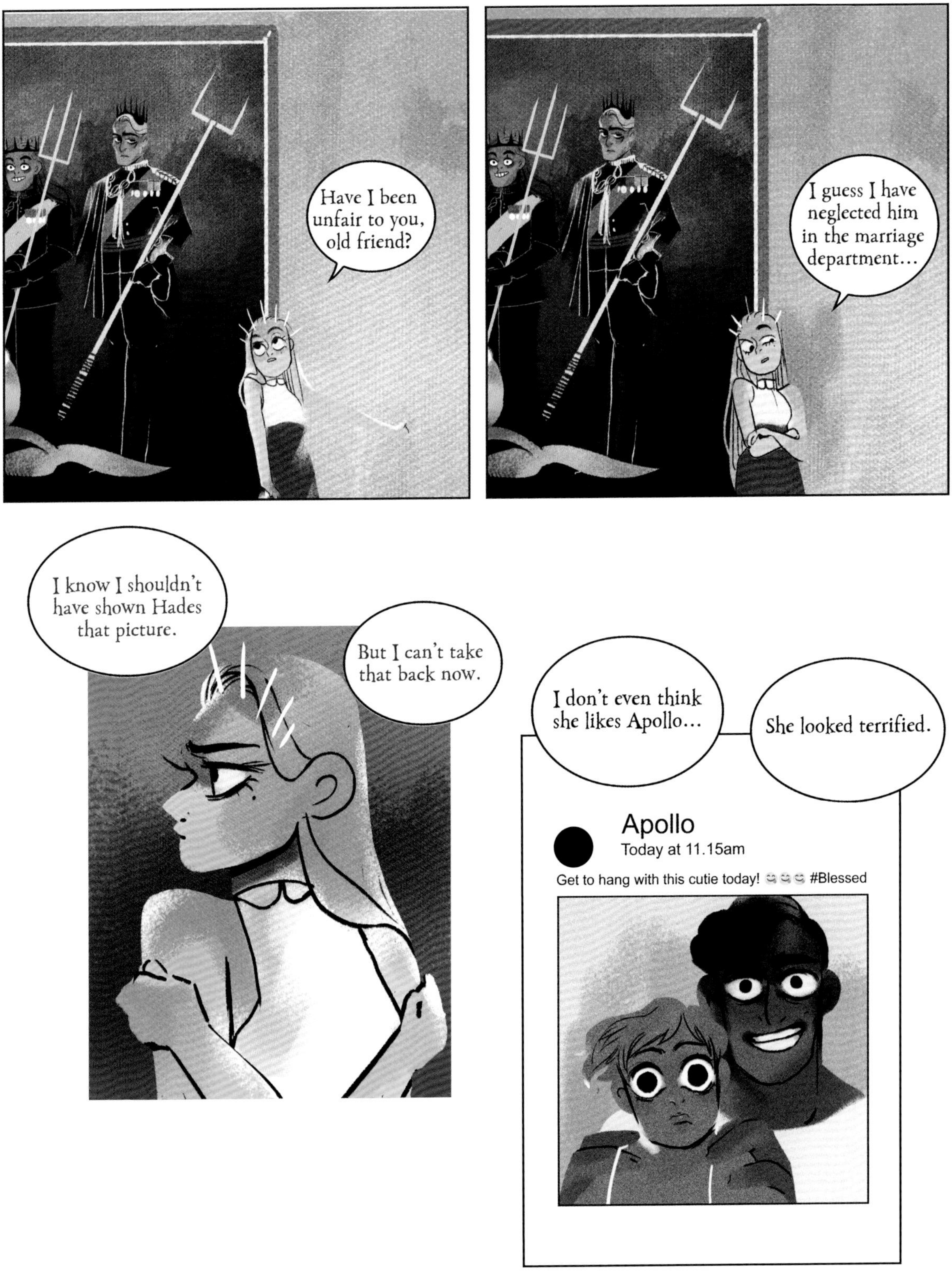
Have I been unfair to you, old friend?
I guess I have neglected him in the marriage department...
I know I shouldn't have shown Hades that picture.
But I can't take that back now.
I don't even think she likes Apollo...
She looked terrified.
Apollo
Today at 11.15am
Get to hang with this cutie today! #Blessed

SILENT PLOTTING

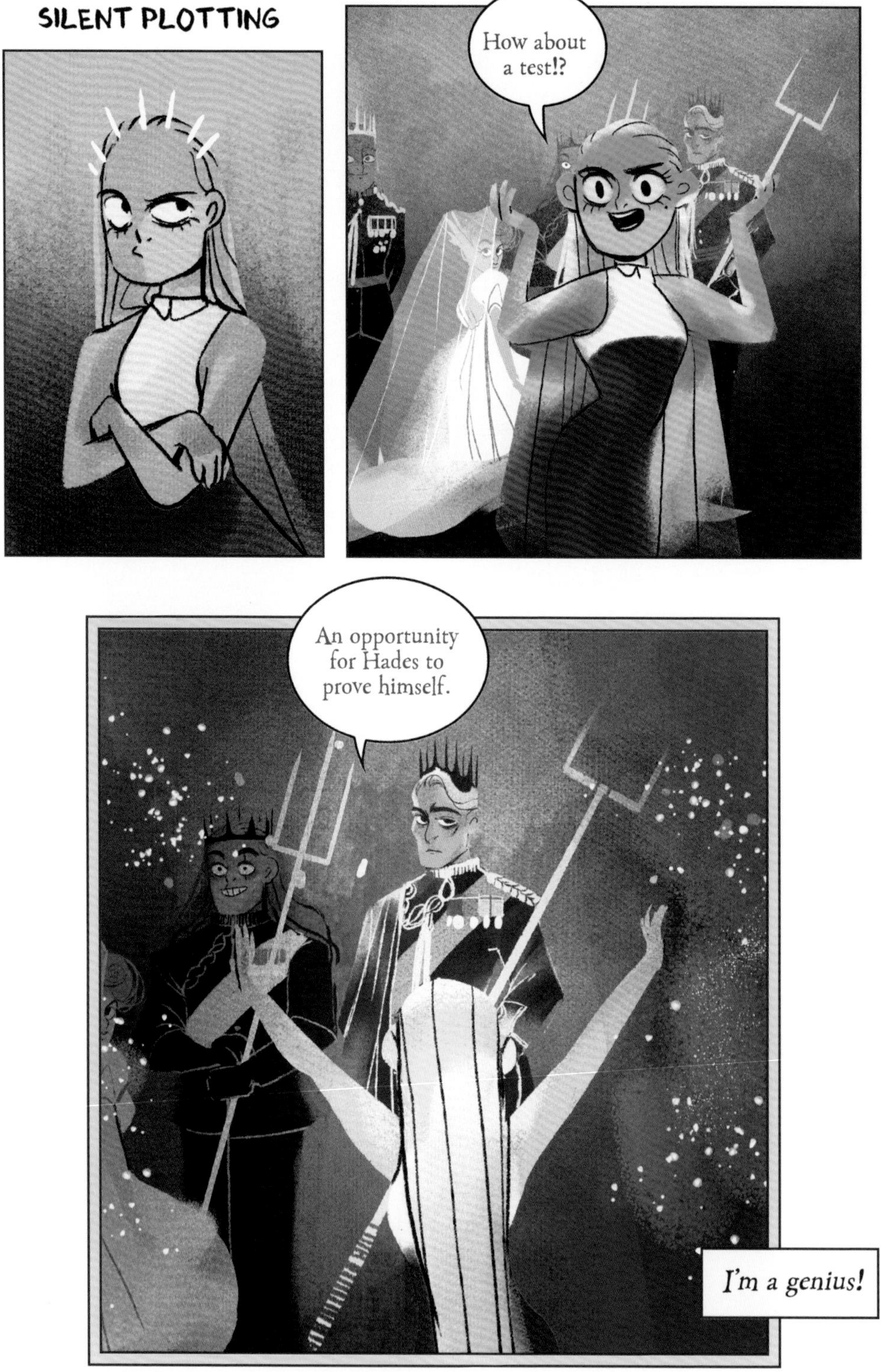
How about a test!?
An opportunity for Hades to prove himself.
I'm a genius!

EPISODE 30: HERA INTERFERES

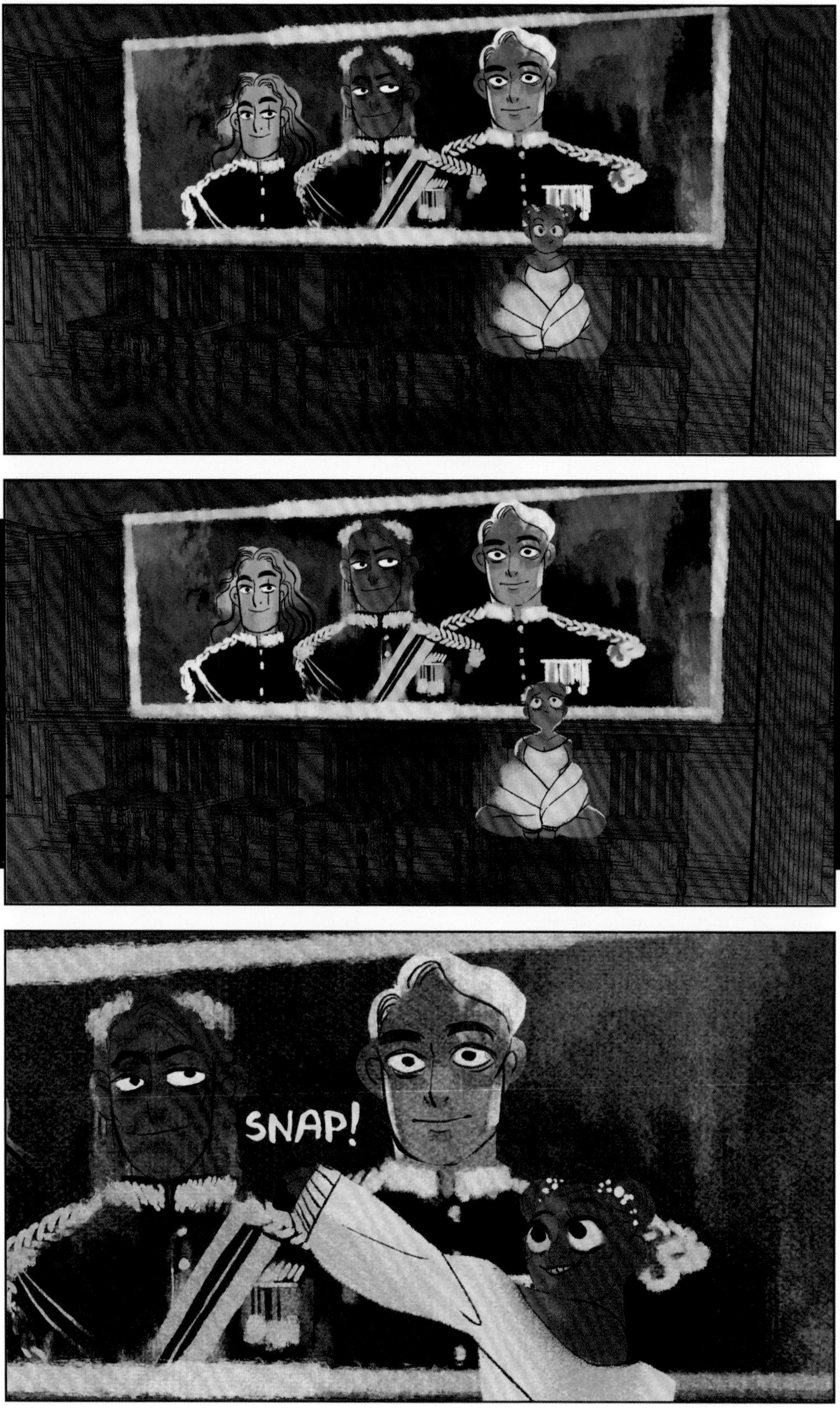
SNAP!

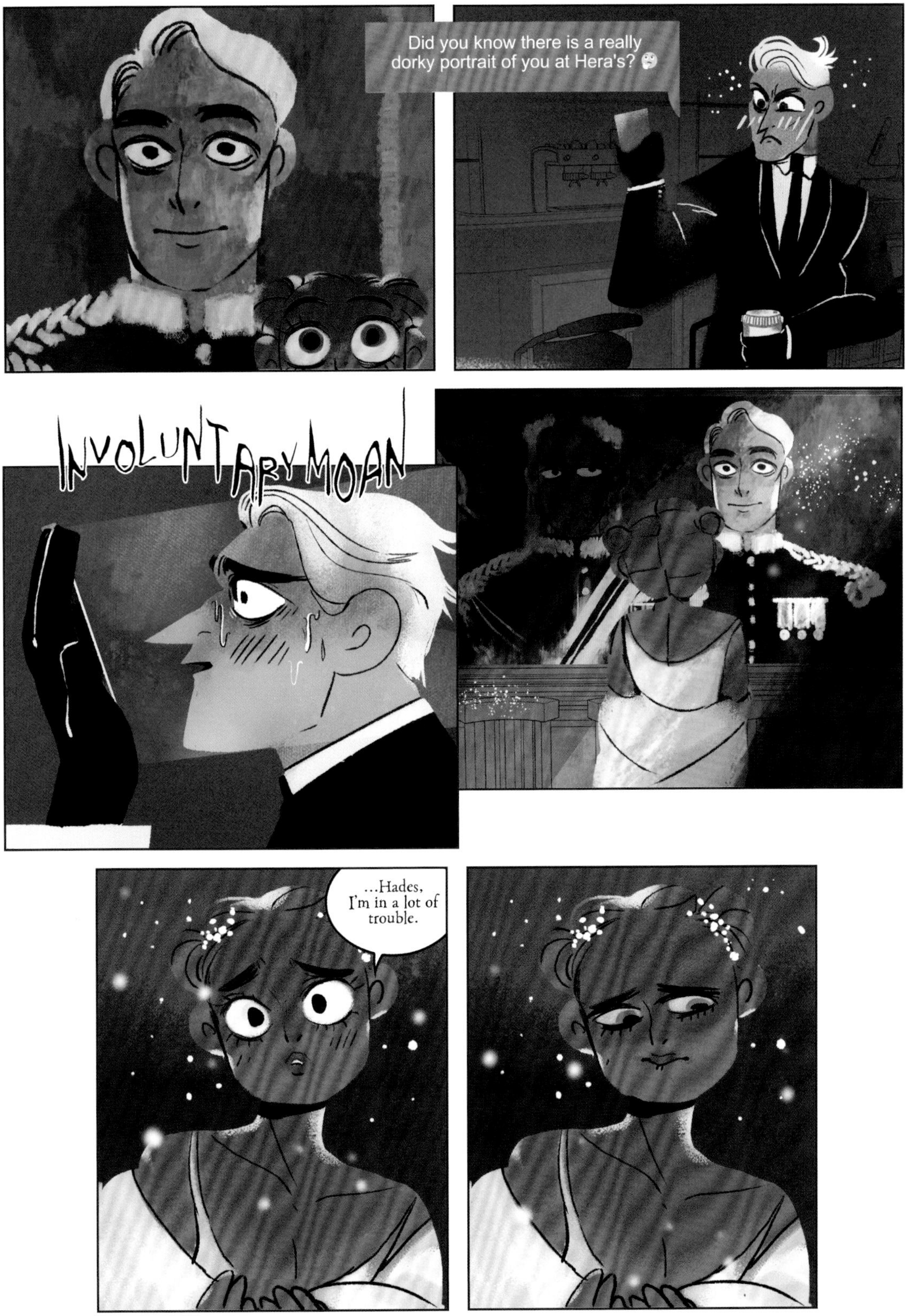
Did you know there is a really dorky portrait of you at Hera's?
INVOLUNTARY MOAN
...Hades, I'm in a lot of trouble.

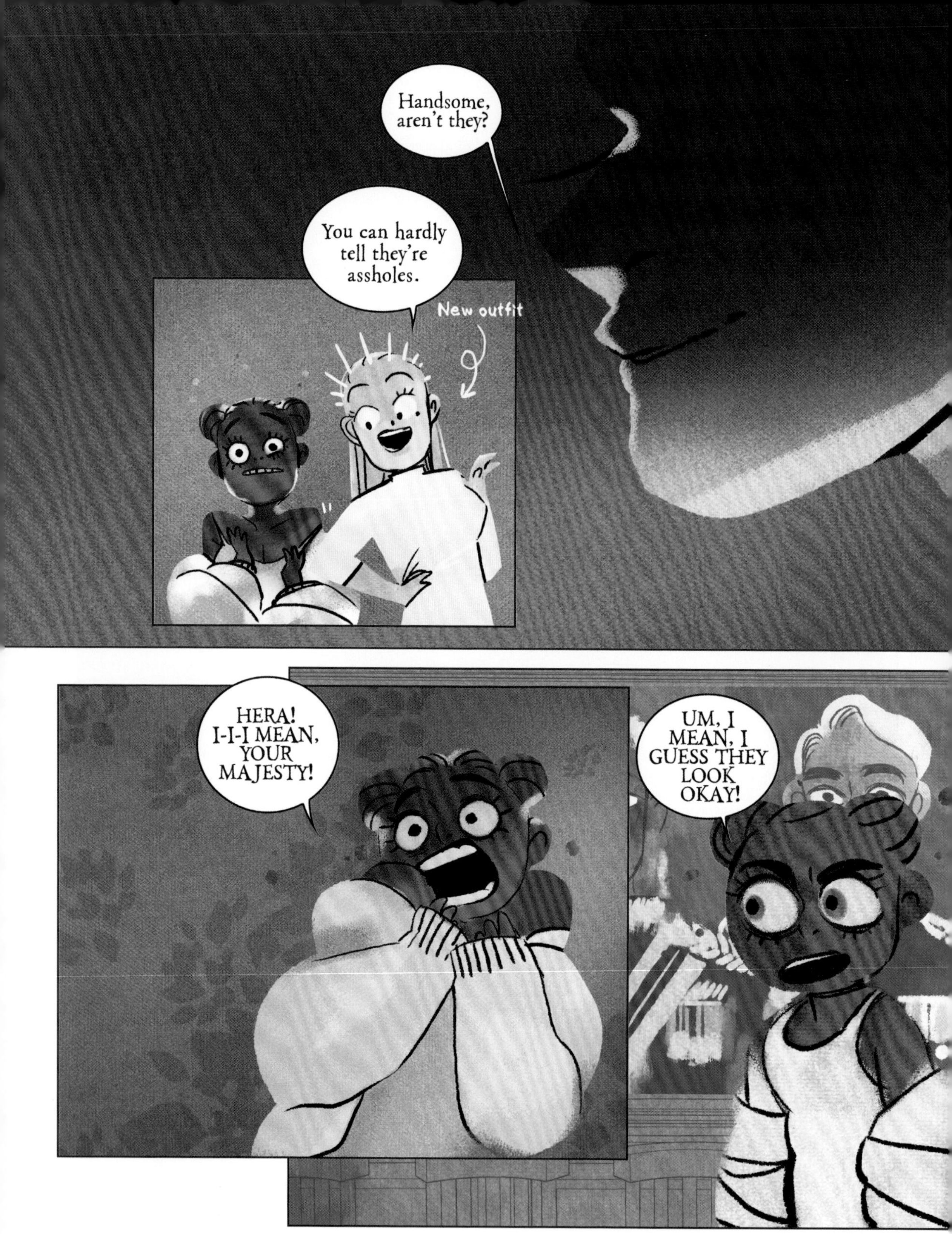
Handsome, aren't they?
You can hardly tell they're assholes.
New outfit
HERA! I-I-I MEAN, YOUR MAJESTY!
UM, I MEAN, I GUESS THEY LOOK OKAY!

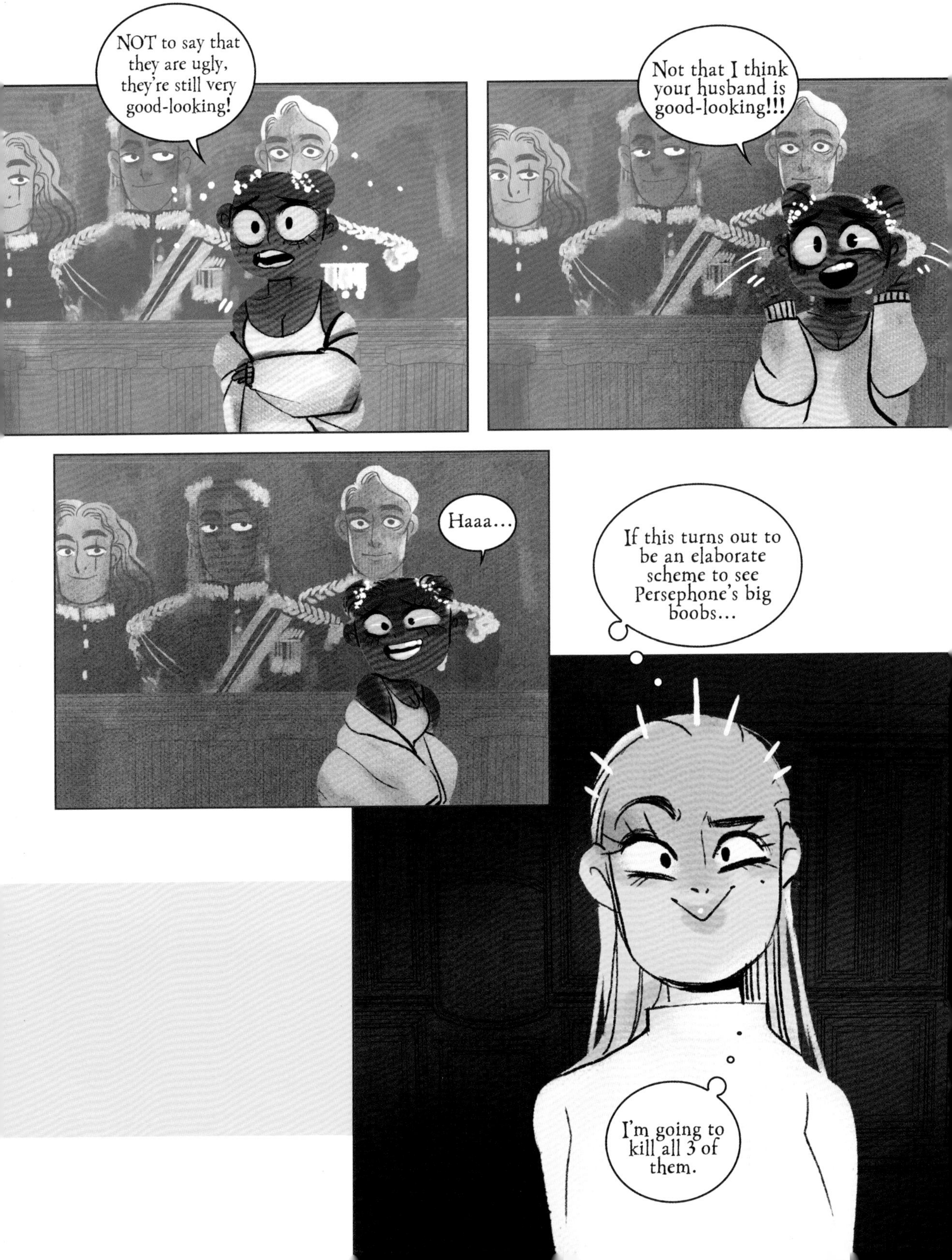
NOT to say that they are ugly, they're still very good-looking!
Not that I think your husband is good-looking!!!
Haaa...
If this turns out to be an elaborate scheme to see Persephone's big boobs...
I'm going to kill all 3 of them.

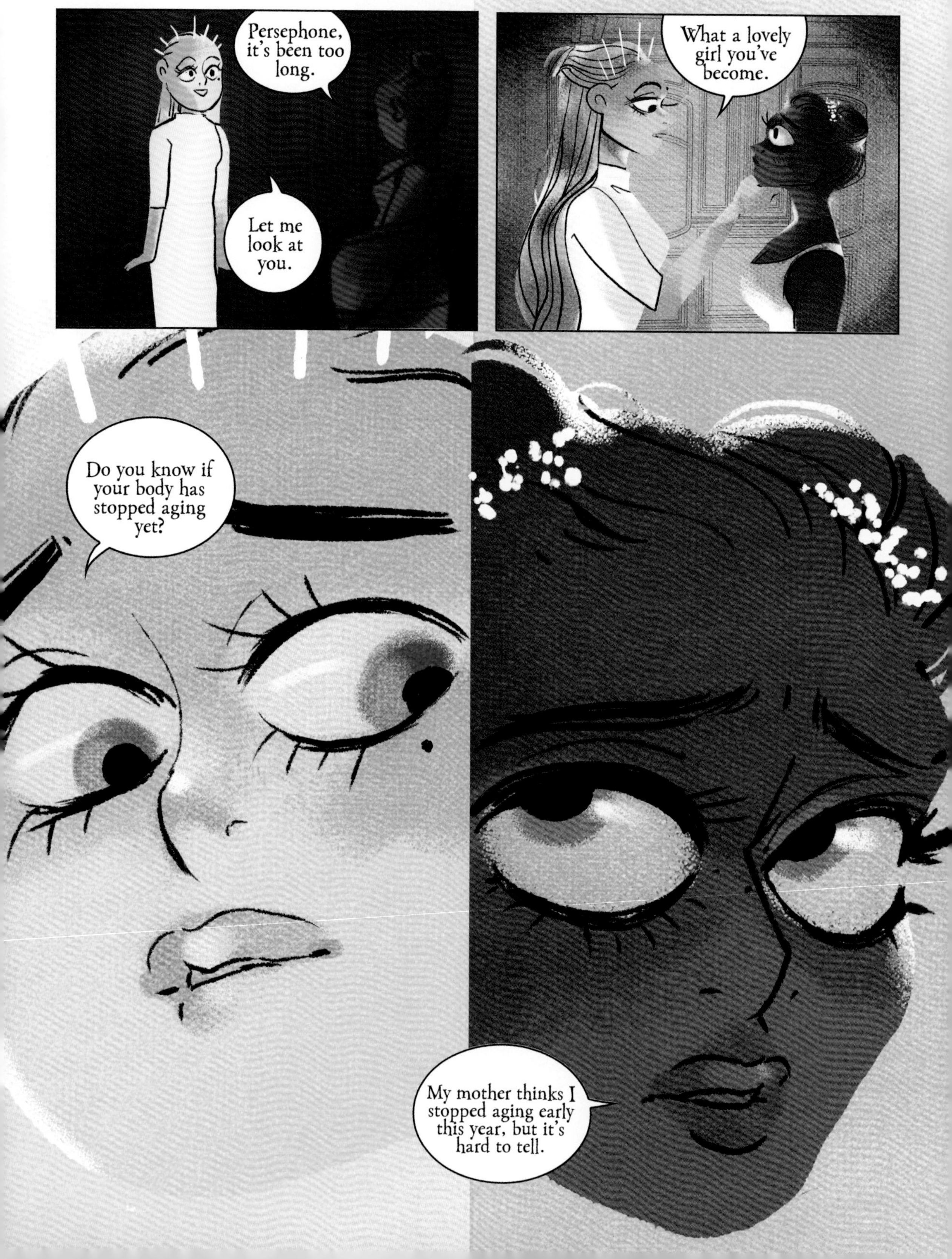
Persephone, it's been too long.
Let me look at you.
What a lovely girl you've become.
Do you know if your body has stopped aging yet?
My mother thinks I stopped aging early this year, but it's hard to tell.

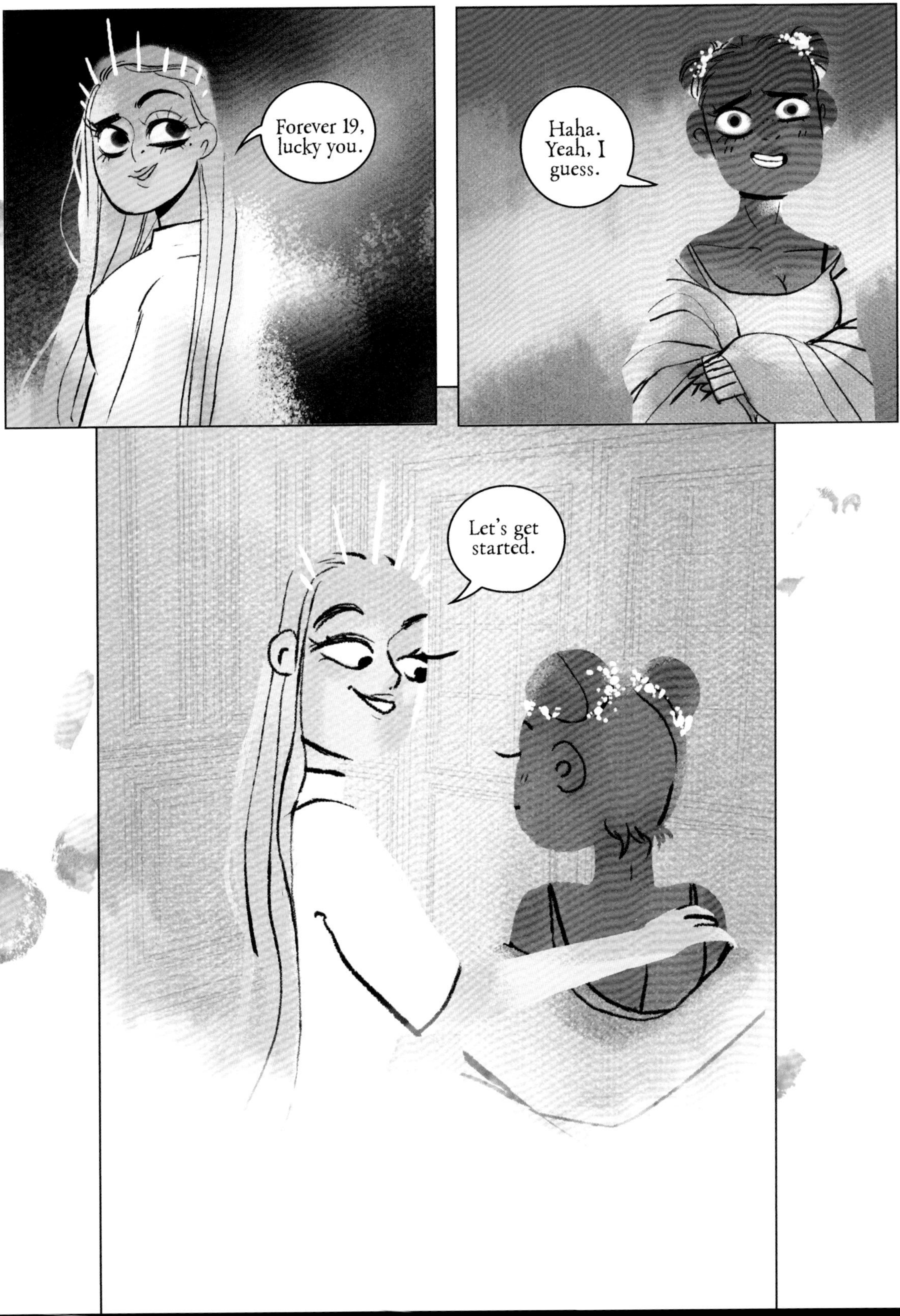
Forever 19,
lucky you.
Haha.
Yeah, I
guess.
Let's get
started.

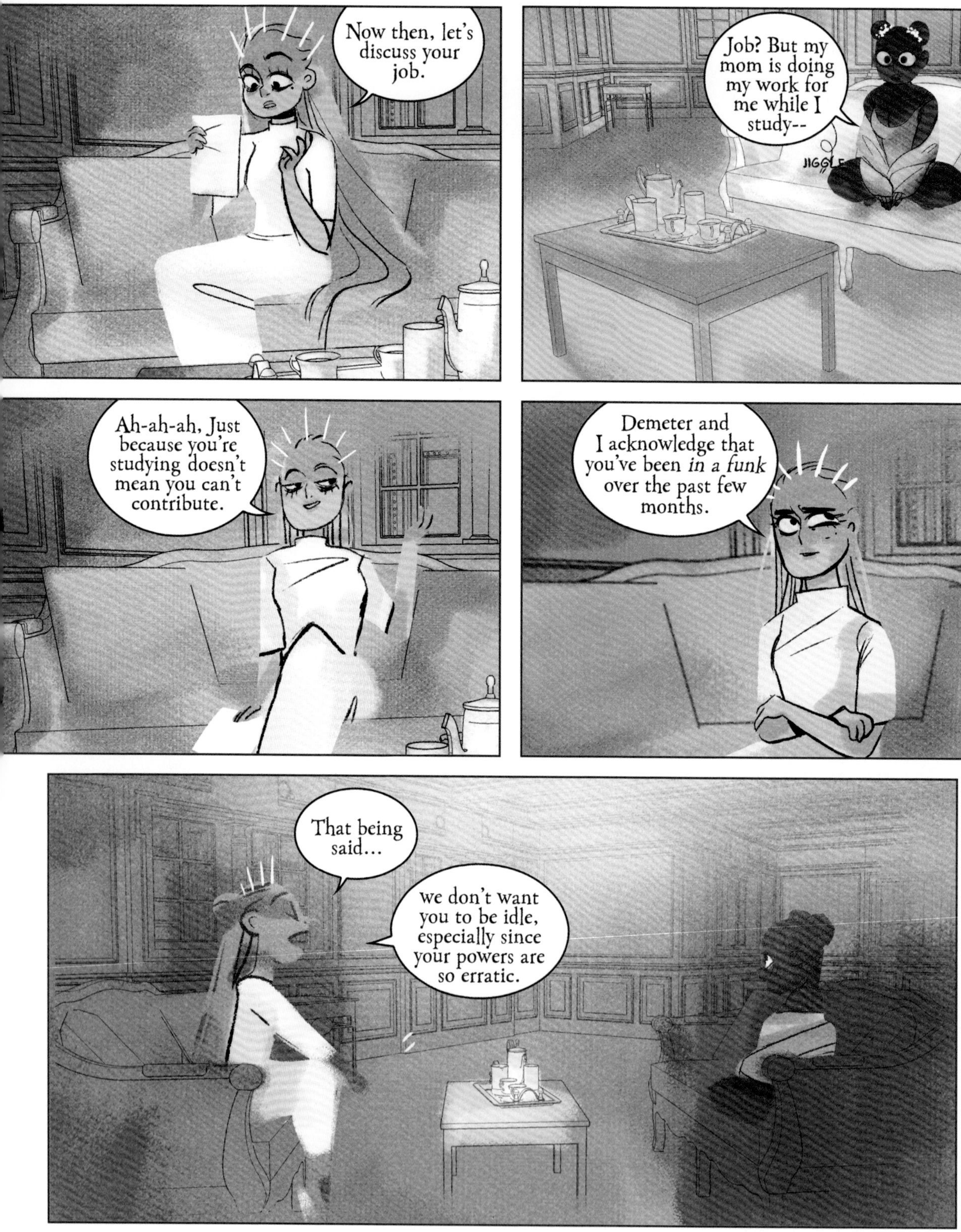
Now then, let's discuss your job.
Job? But my mom is doing my work for me while I study--
JIGGLE
Ah-ah-ah, Just because you're studying doesn't mean you can't contribute.
Demeter and I acknowledge that you've been *in a funk* over the past few months.
That being said...
we don't want you to be idle, especially since your powers are so erratic.

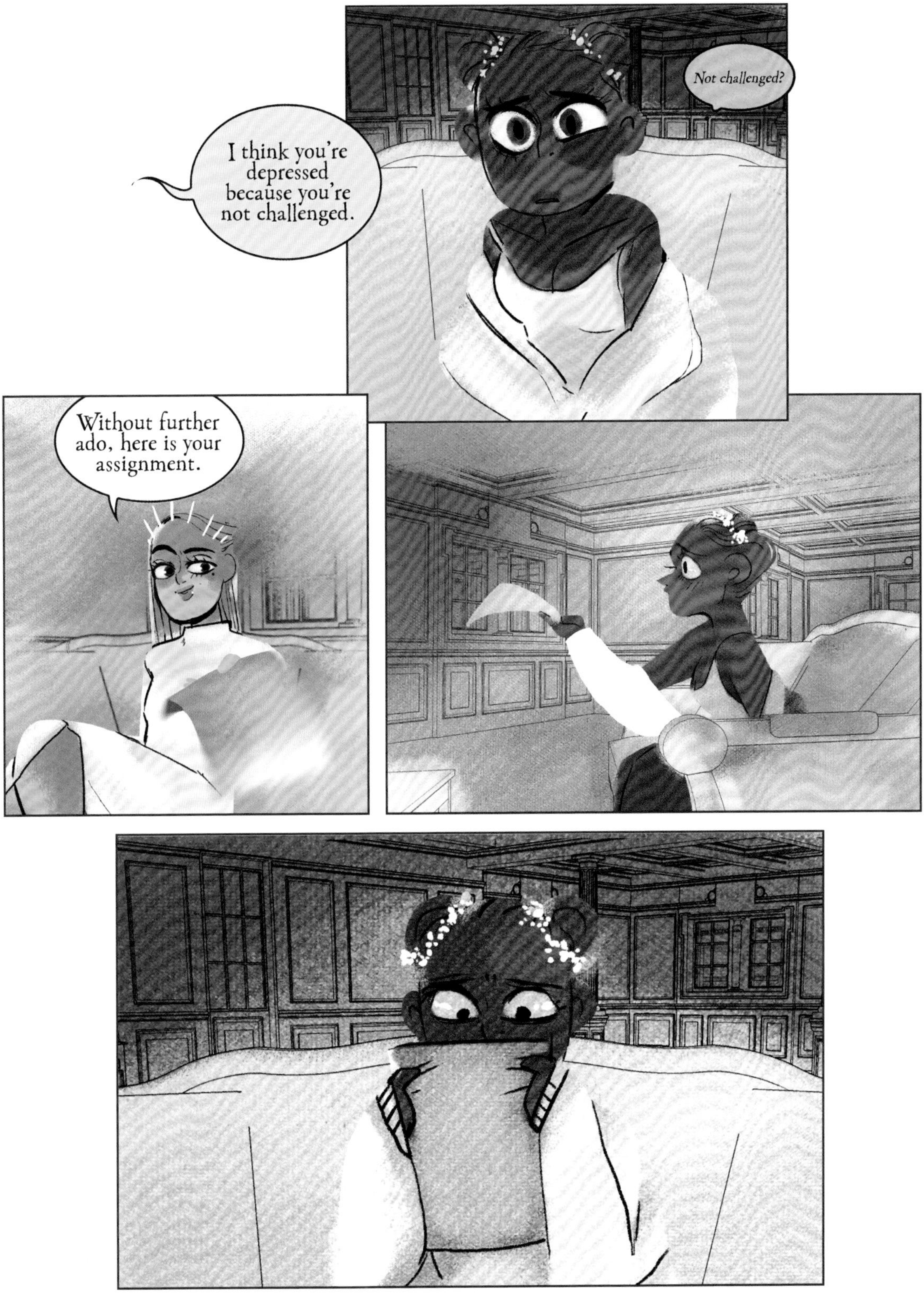
I think you're depressed because you're not challenged.
Not challenged?
Without further ado, here is your assignment.

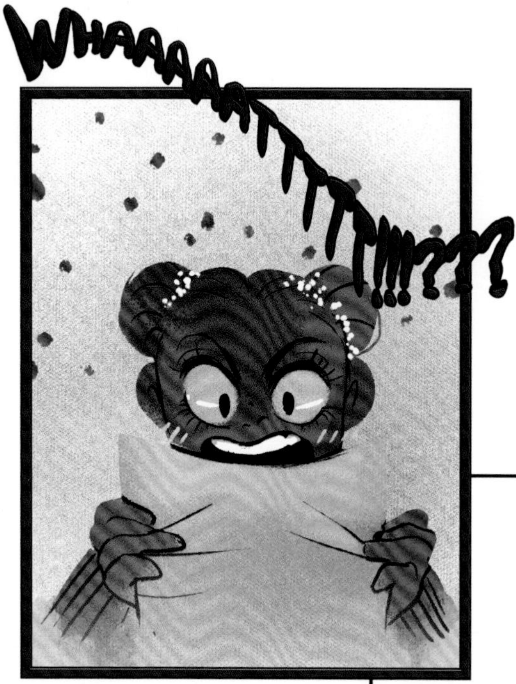
WHAAAAATTTT!!!???

UNDERWORLD CORP

OLYMPUS TO UNDERWORLD INTERN EXCHANGE PROGRAM

APPLICANT: PERSEPHONE (KORE)

REPORT TO: HADES, GOD/KING OF THE DEAD/UNDERWORLD

LOCATION: UNDERWORLD CORP, TOWER I, LV 99

TIME: ASAP

INTERNSHIP ROLE DESCRIPTION : TO BE DISCUSSED

STATUS: APPROVED BY HERA, QUEEN OF THE GODS

PLEASE ATTACH PHOTO ID

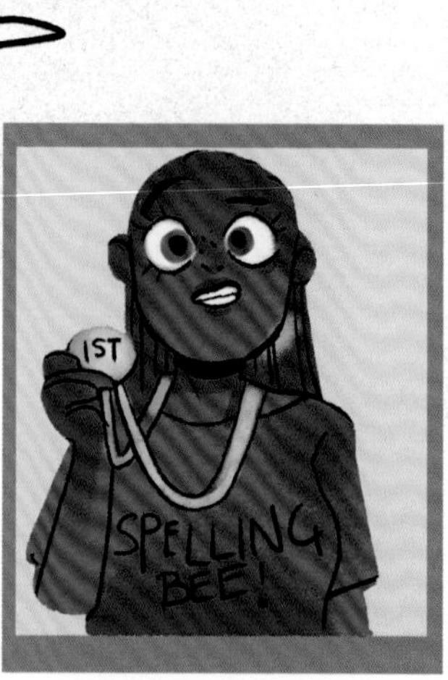
1ST
SPELLING BEE!

Embarrassing old photo.

NO.

NO.

NO.

NO.

Huff

Huff.

Huff

I can't work with Hades.

I told him all that personal stuff about me!

He's gonna be my boss?

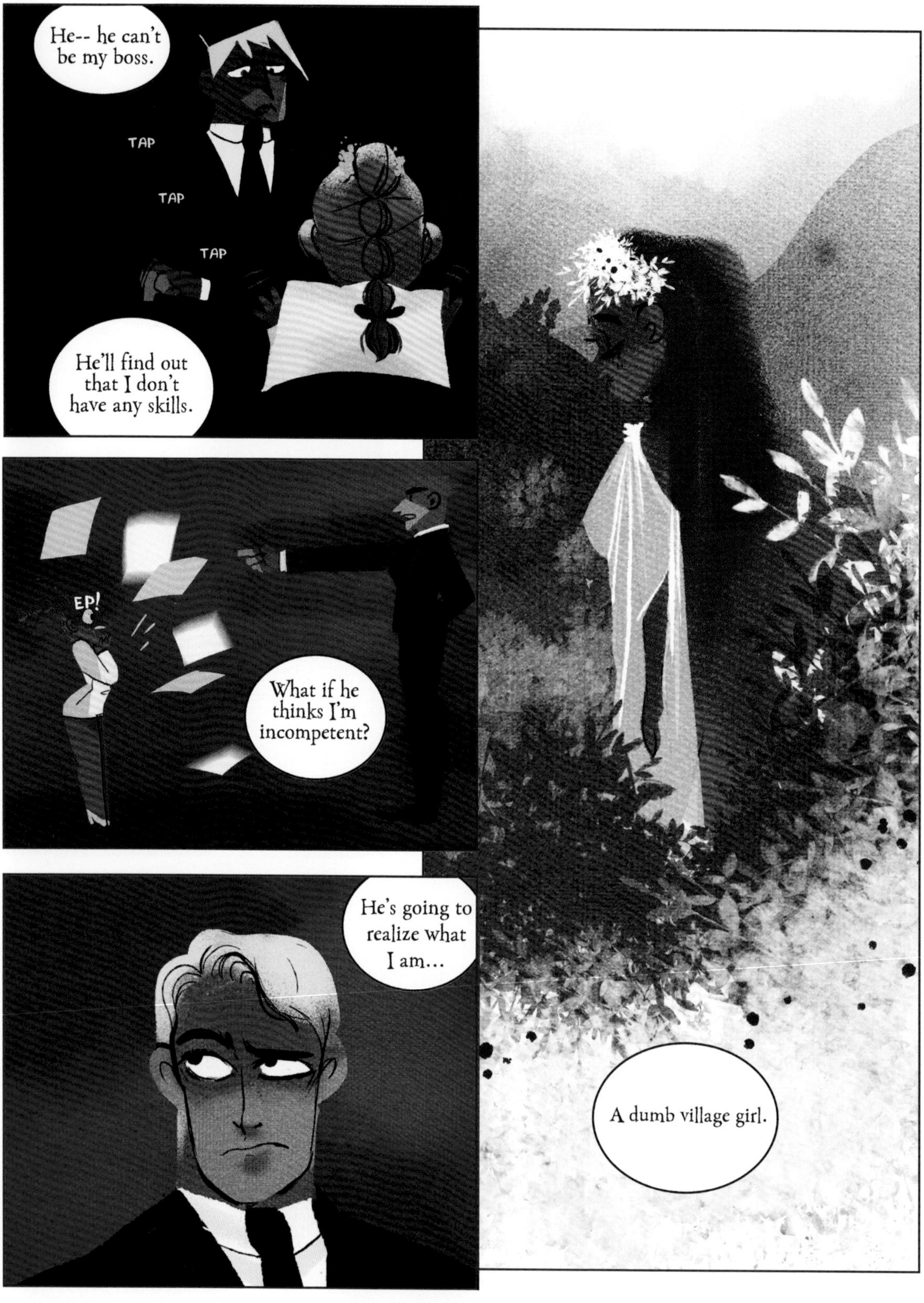
He-- he can't be my boss.
TAP
TAP
TAP
He'll find out that I don't have any skills.
EP!
What if he thinks I'm incompetent?
He's going to realize what I am...
A dumb village girl.

EPISODE 31: A TREAT FOR BEING A FOOL

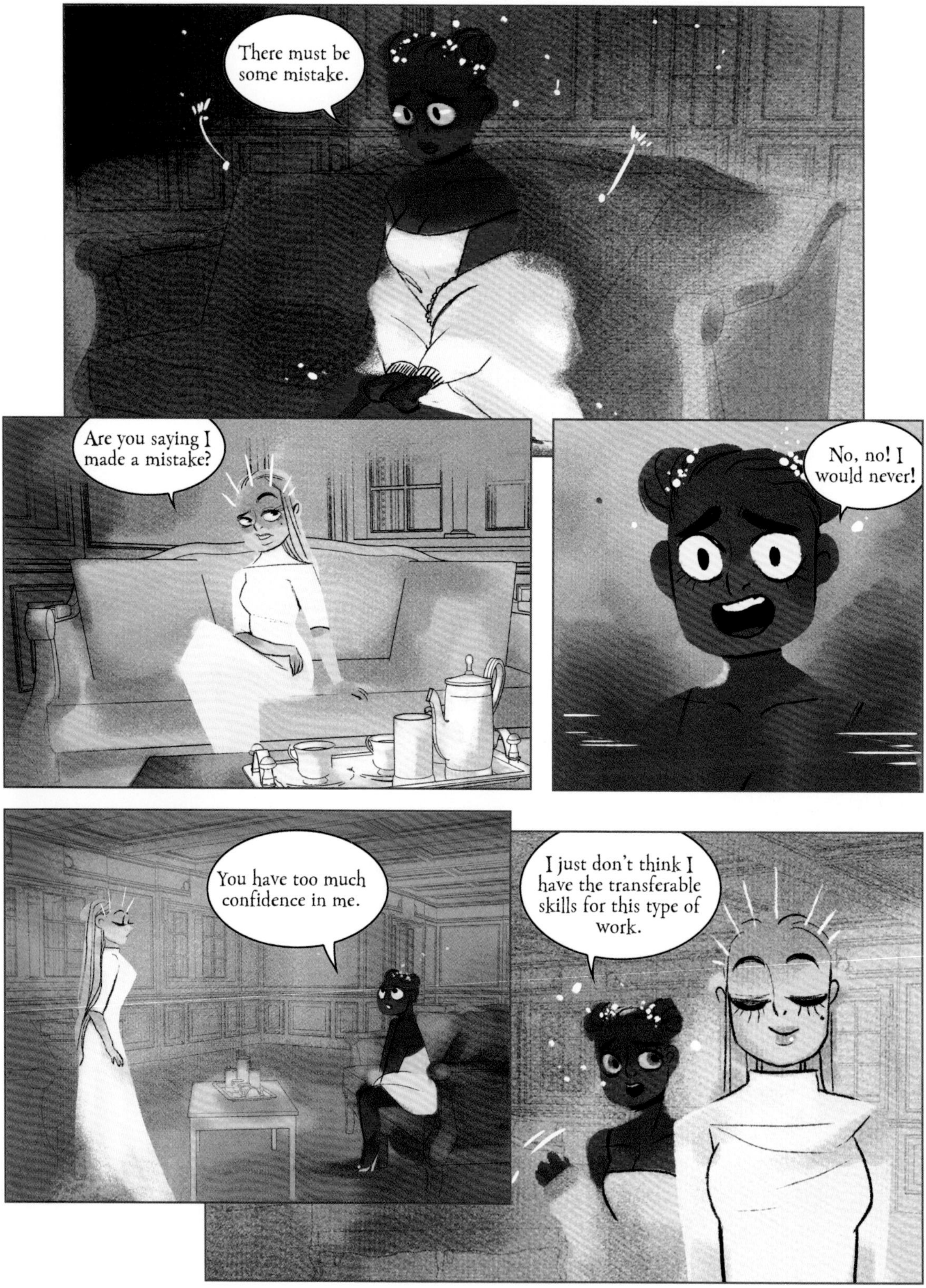
There must be some mistake.
Are you saying I made a mistake?
No, no! I would never!
You have too much confidence in me.
I just don't think I have the transferable skills for this type of work.

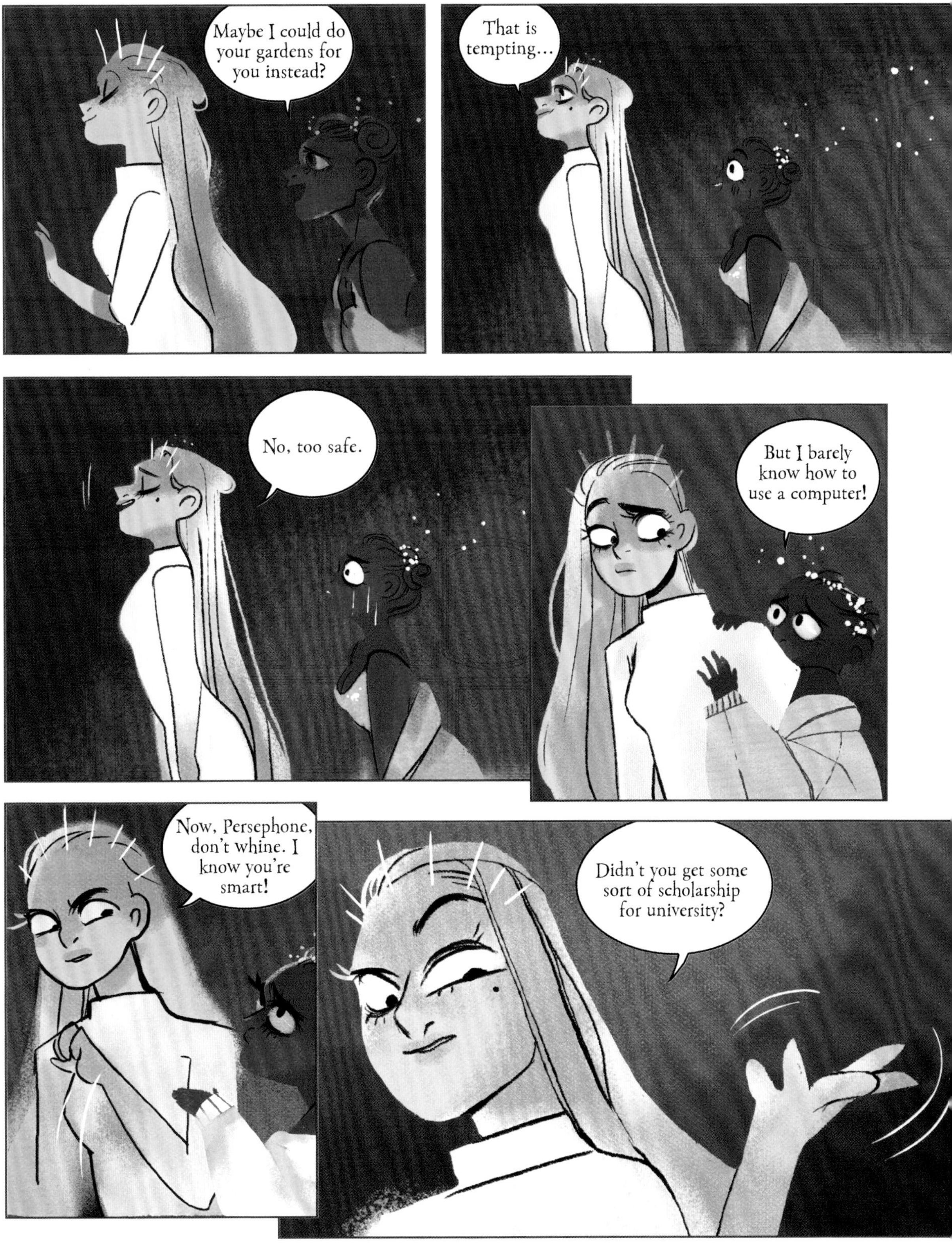

Maybe I could do your gardens for you instead?
That is tempting…
No, too safe.
But I barely know how to use a computer!
Now, Persephone, don't whine. I know you're smart!
Didn't you get some sort of scholarship for university?

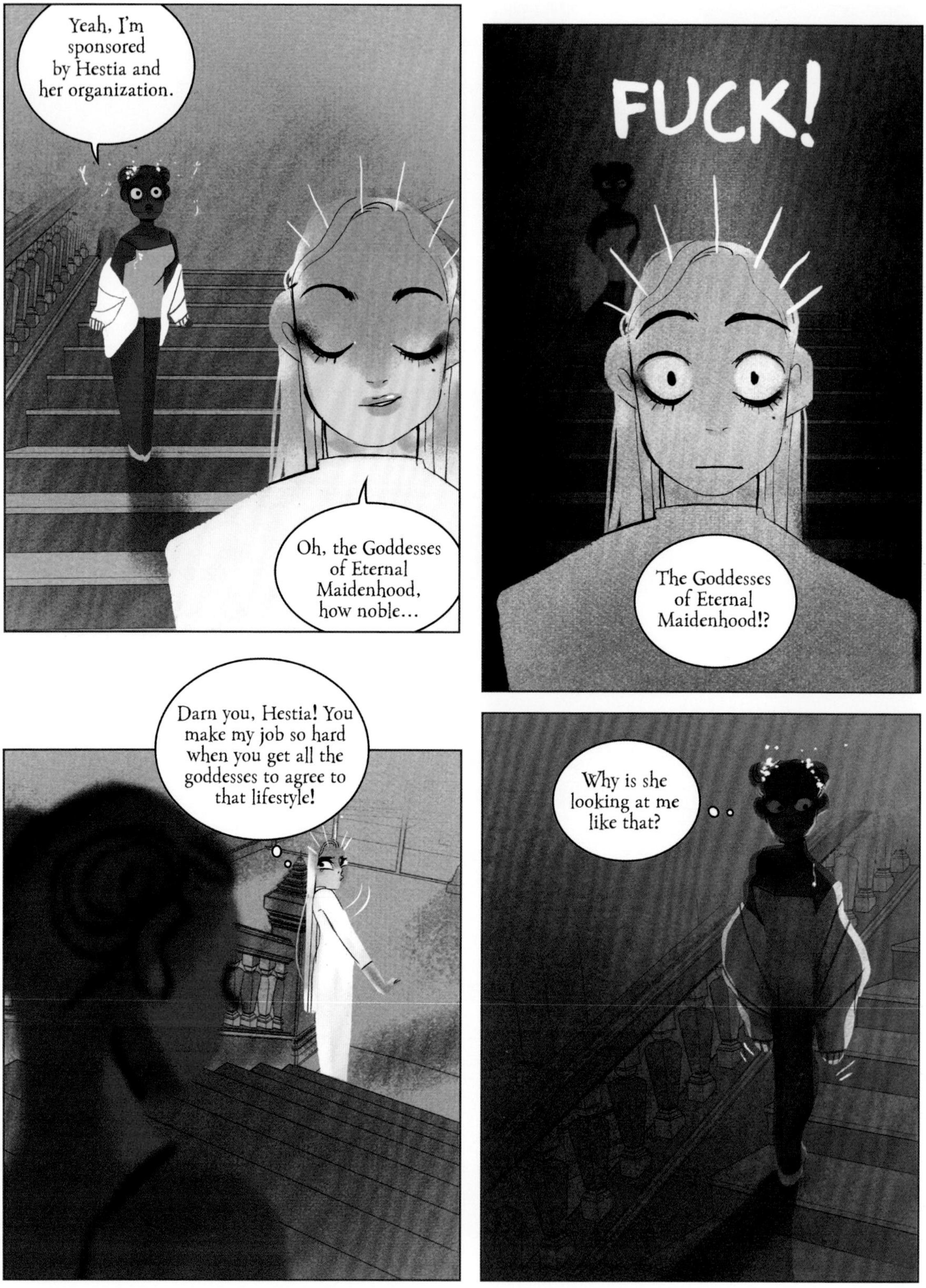
Yeah, I'm sponsored by Hestia and her organization.
Oh, the Goddesses of Eternal Maidenhood, how noble...
FUCK!
The Goddesses of Eternal Maidenhood!?
Darn you, Hestia! You make my job so hard when you get all the goddesses to agree to that lifestyle!
Why is she looking at me like that?

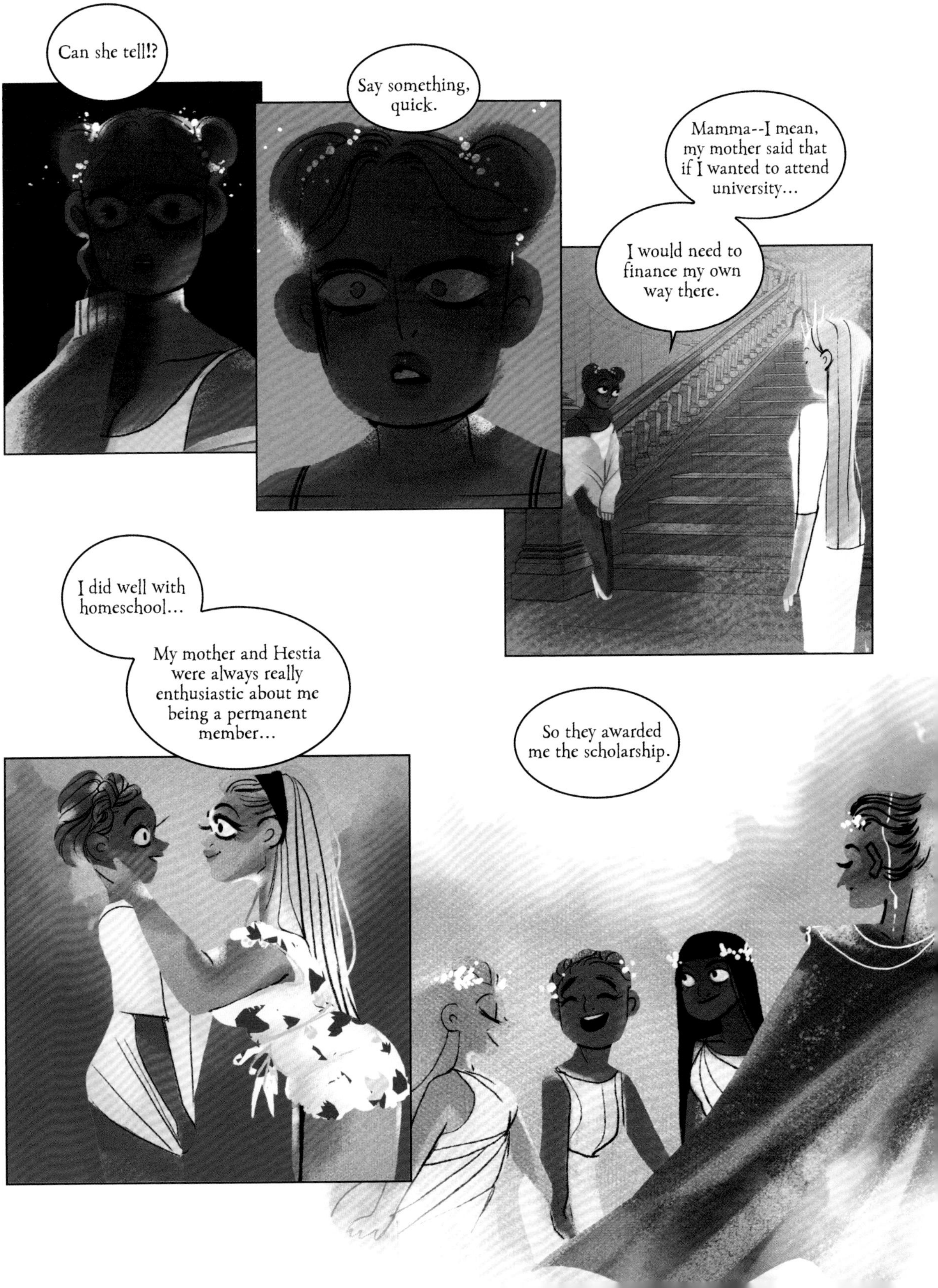
Can she tell!?
Say something, quick.
Mamma--I mean, my mother said that if I wanted to attend university...
I would need to finance my own way there.
I did well with homeschool...
My mother and Hestia were always really enthusiastic about me being a permanent member...
So they awarded me the scholarship.

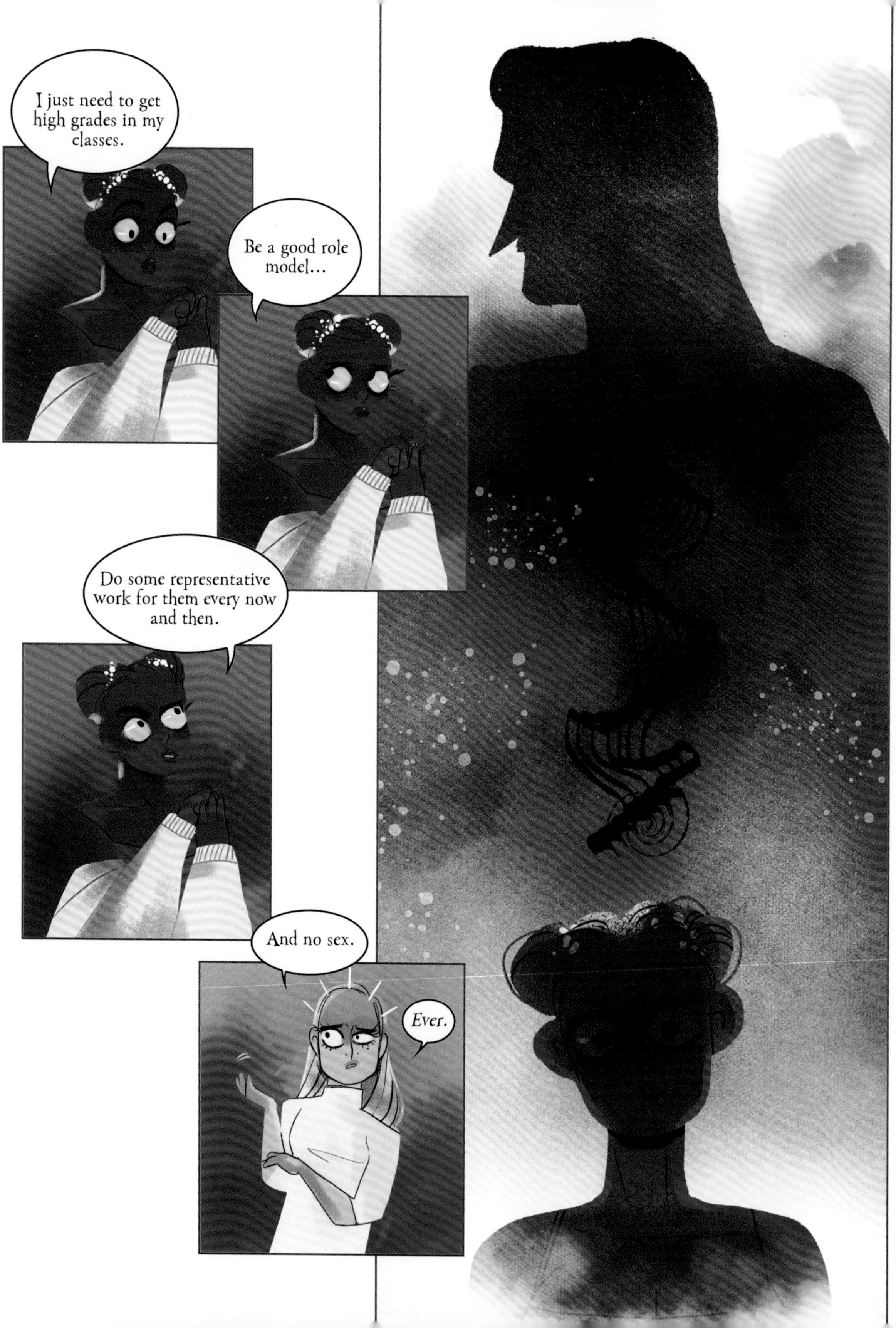
I just need to get high grades in my classes.
Be a good role model...
Do some representative work for them every now and then.
And no sex.
Ever.

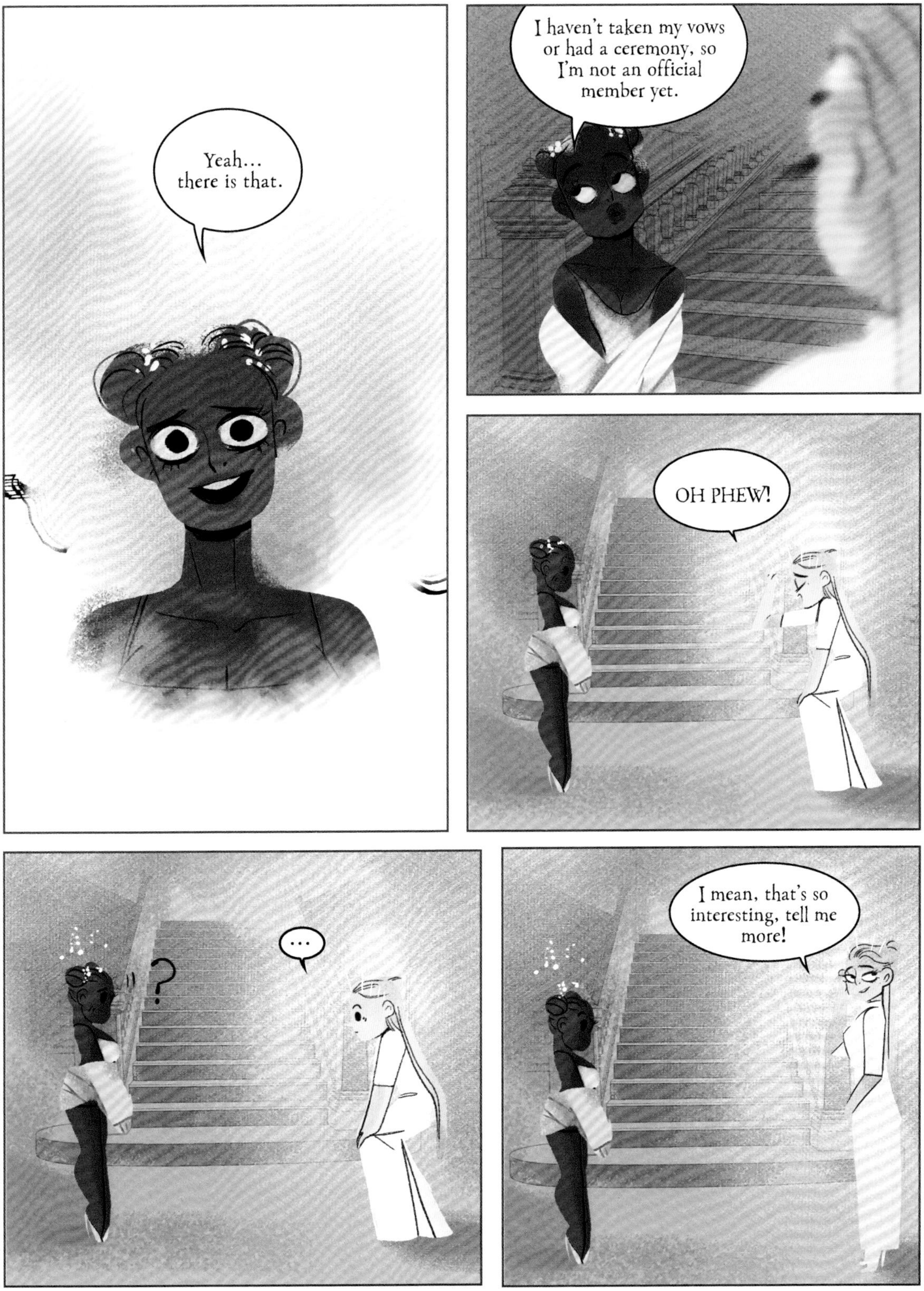
Yeah...
there is that.
I haven't taken my vows
or had a ceremony, so
I'm not an official
member yet.
OH PHEW!
?
...
I mean, that's so
interesting, tell me
more!

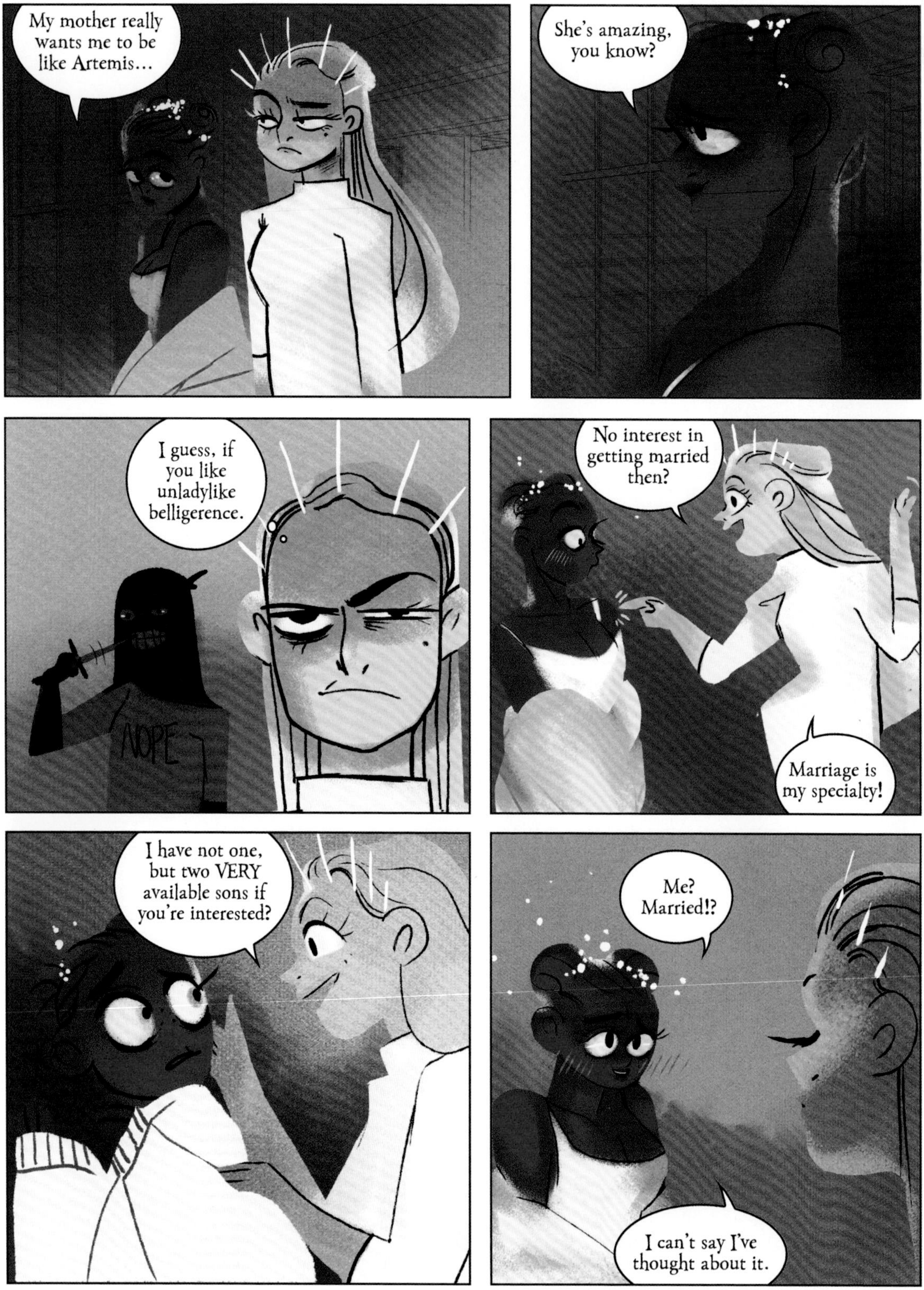
My mother really wants me to be like Artemis...
She's amazing, you know?
I guess, if you like unladylike belligerence.
NOPE
No interest in getting married then?
Marriage is my specialty!
I have not one, but two VERY available sons if you're interested?
Me? Married!?
I can't say I've thought about it.

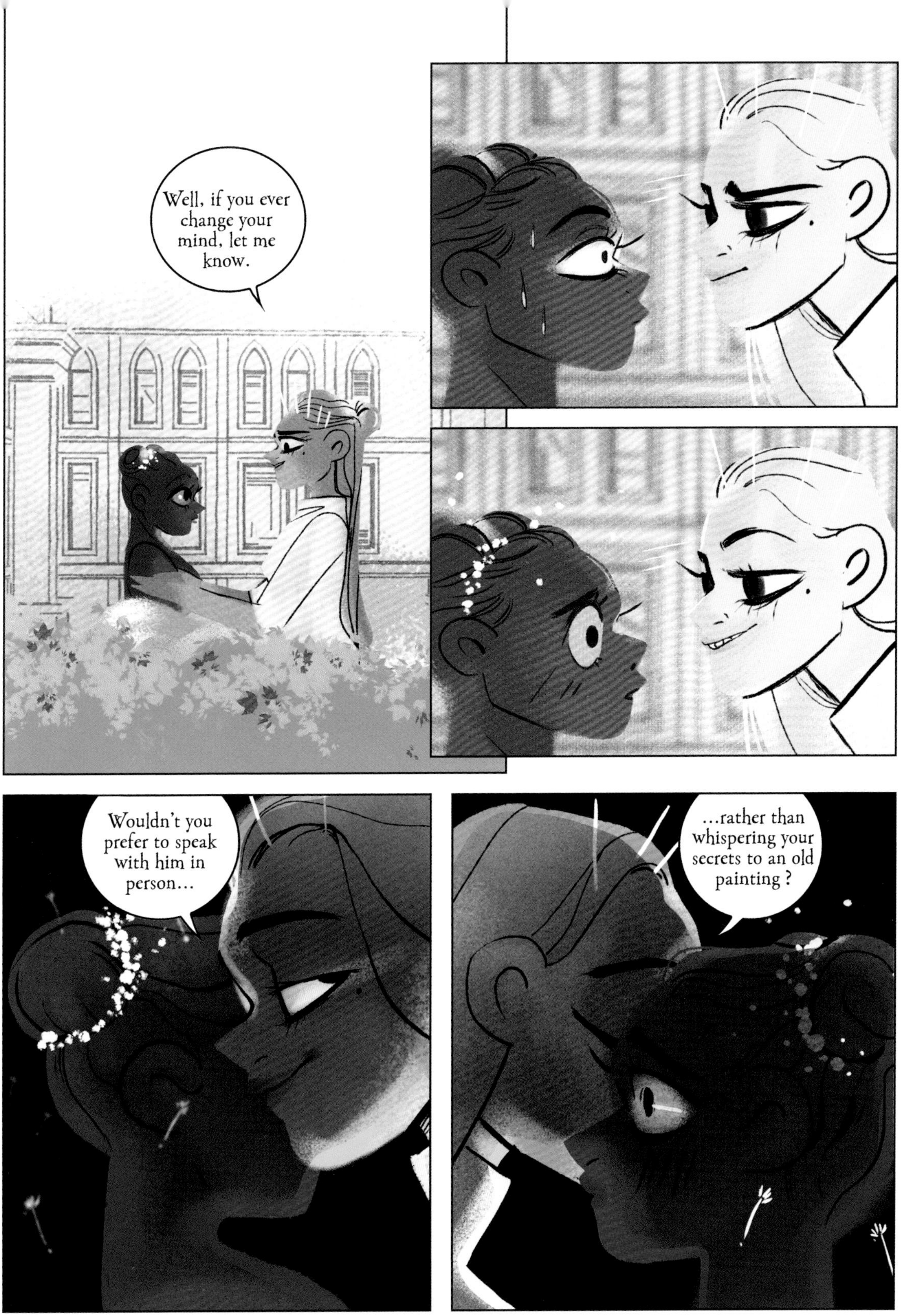
Well, if you ever change your mind, let me know.
Wouldn't you prefer to speak with him in person...
...rather than whispering your secrets to an old painting ?

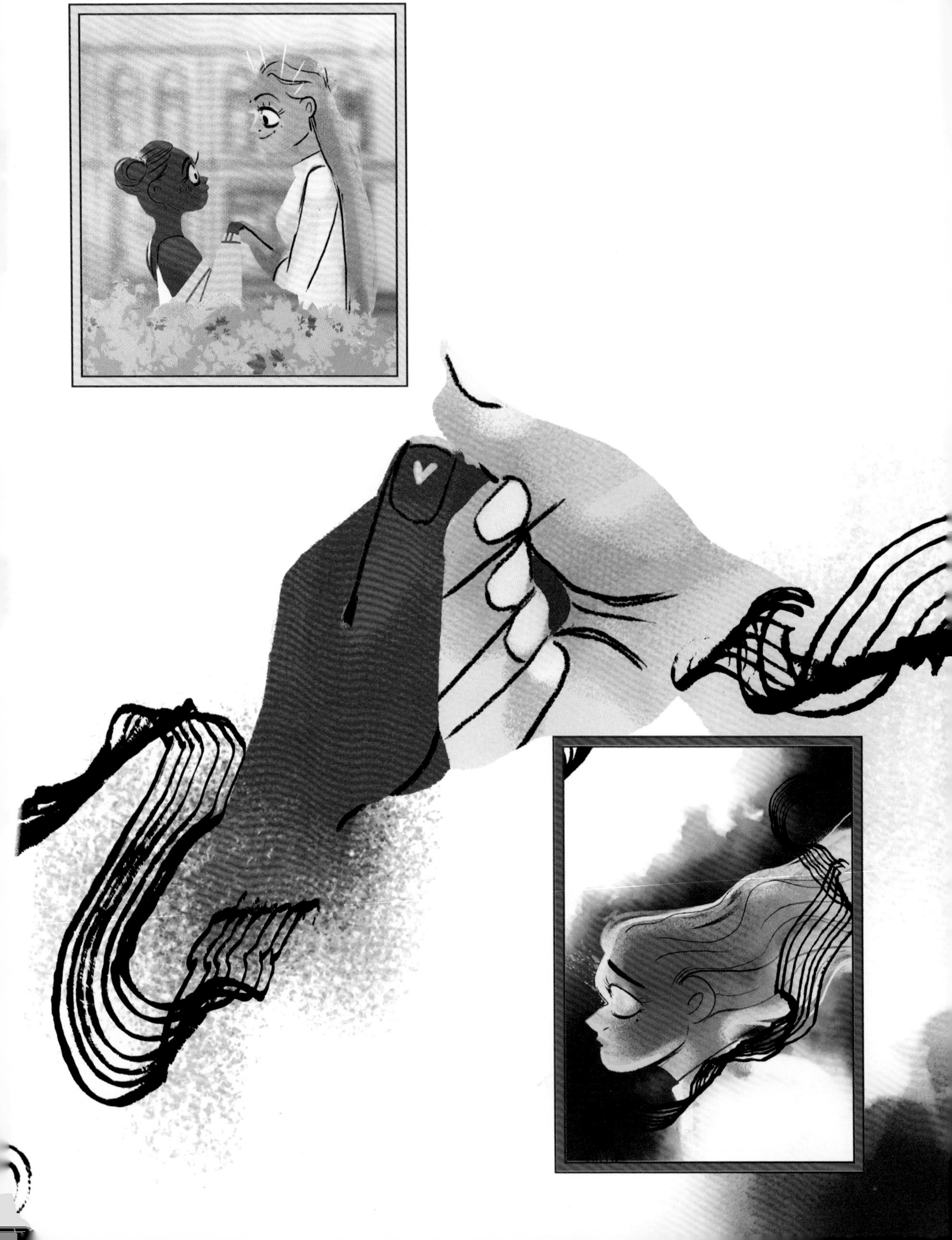

Um, Your Majesty?

Sorry, just lost in thought!

I'd better get going. I've got class.

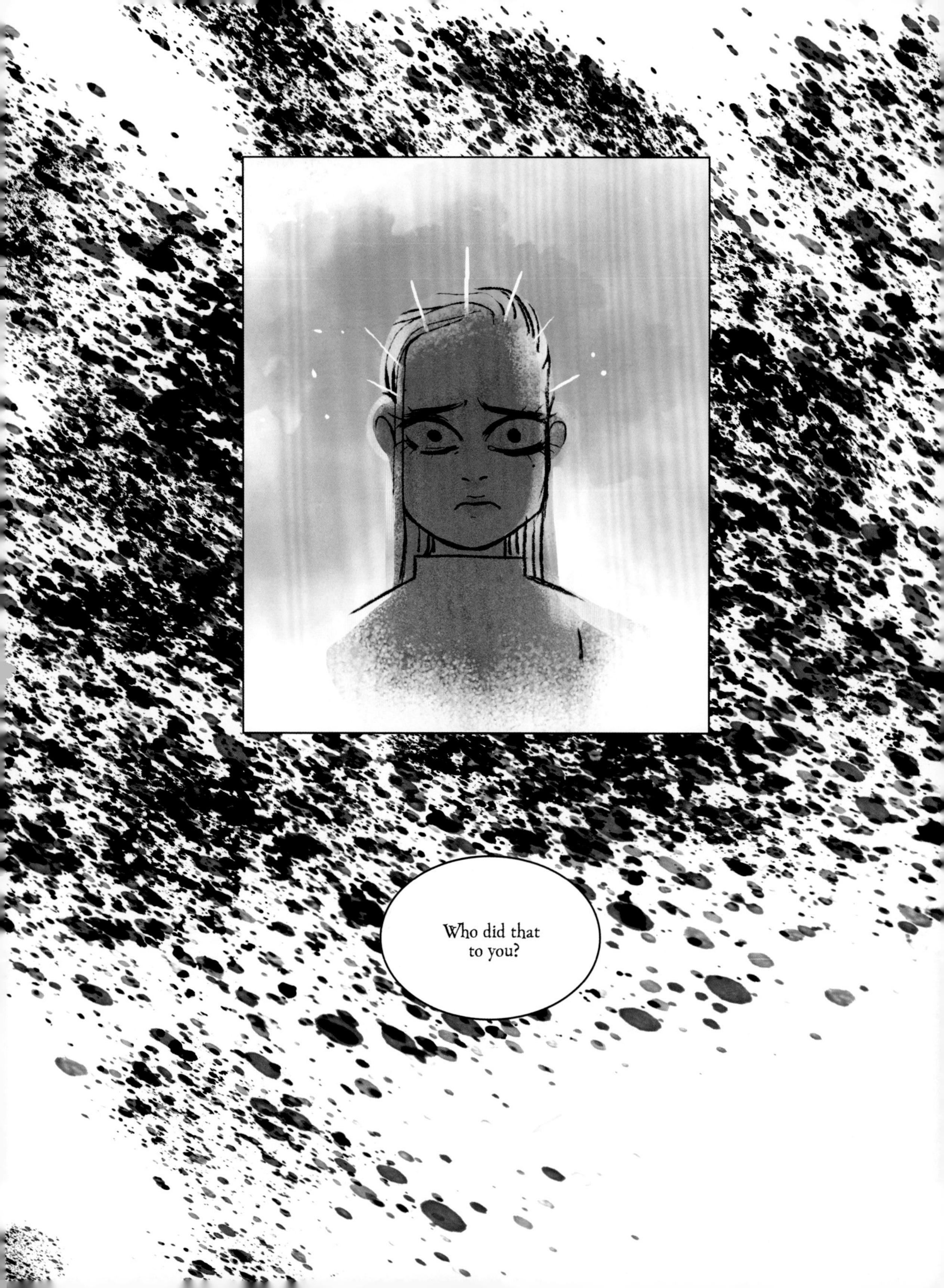
Who did that to you?

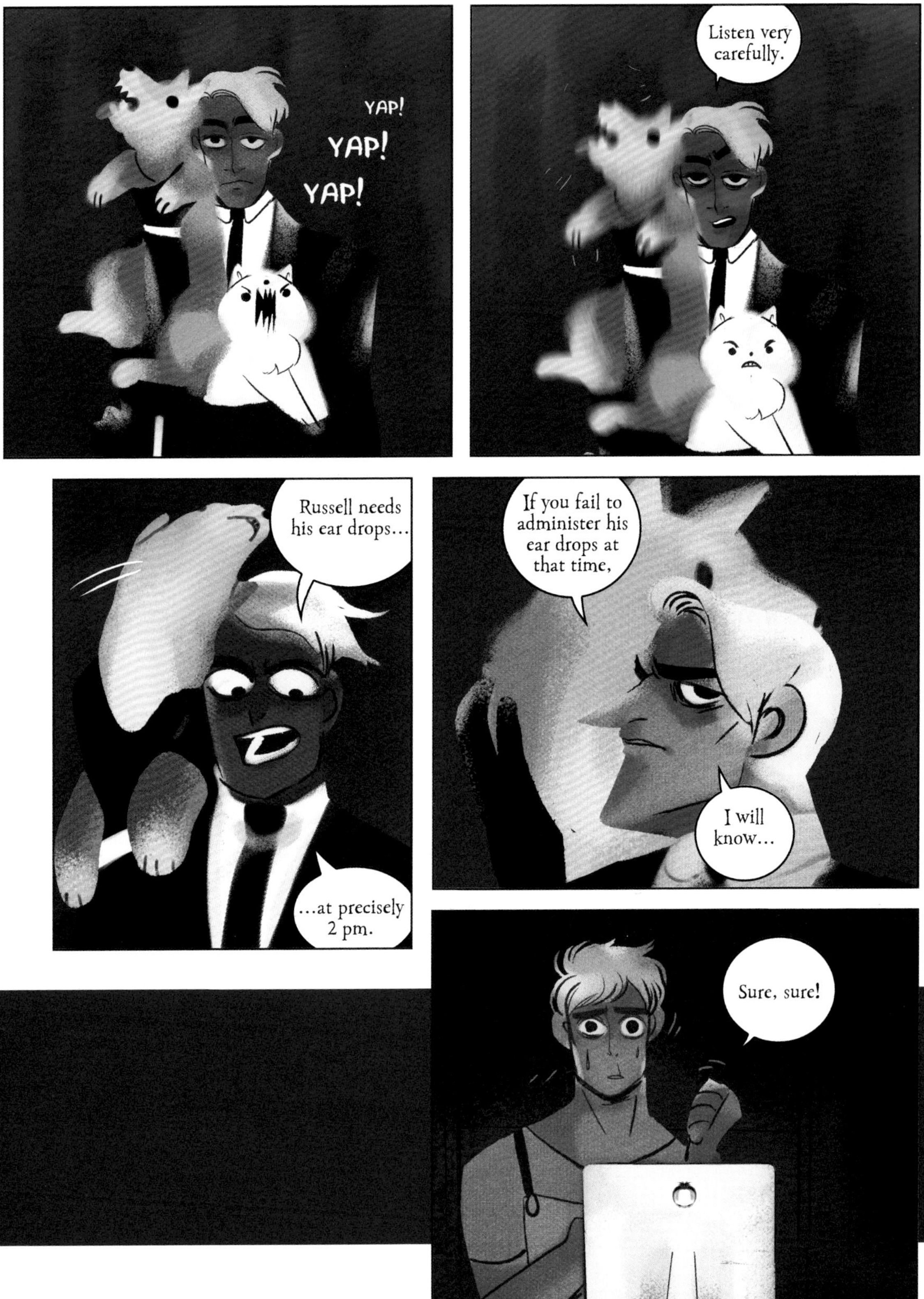
YAP!
YAP!
YAP!
Listen very carefully.
Russell needs his ear drops...
...at precisely 2 pm.
If you fail to administer his ear drops at that time,
I will know...
Sure, sure!

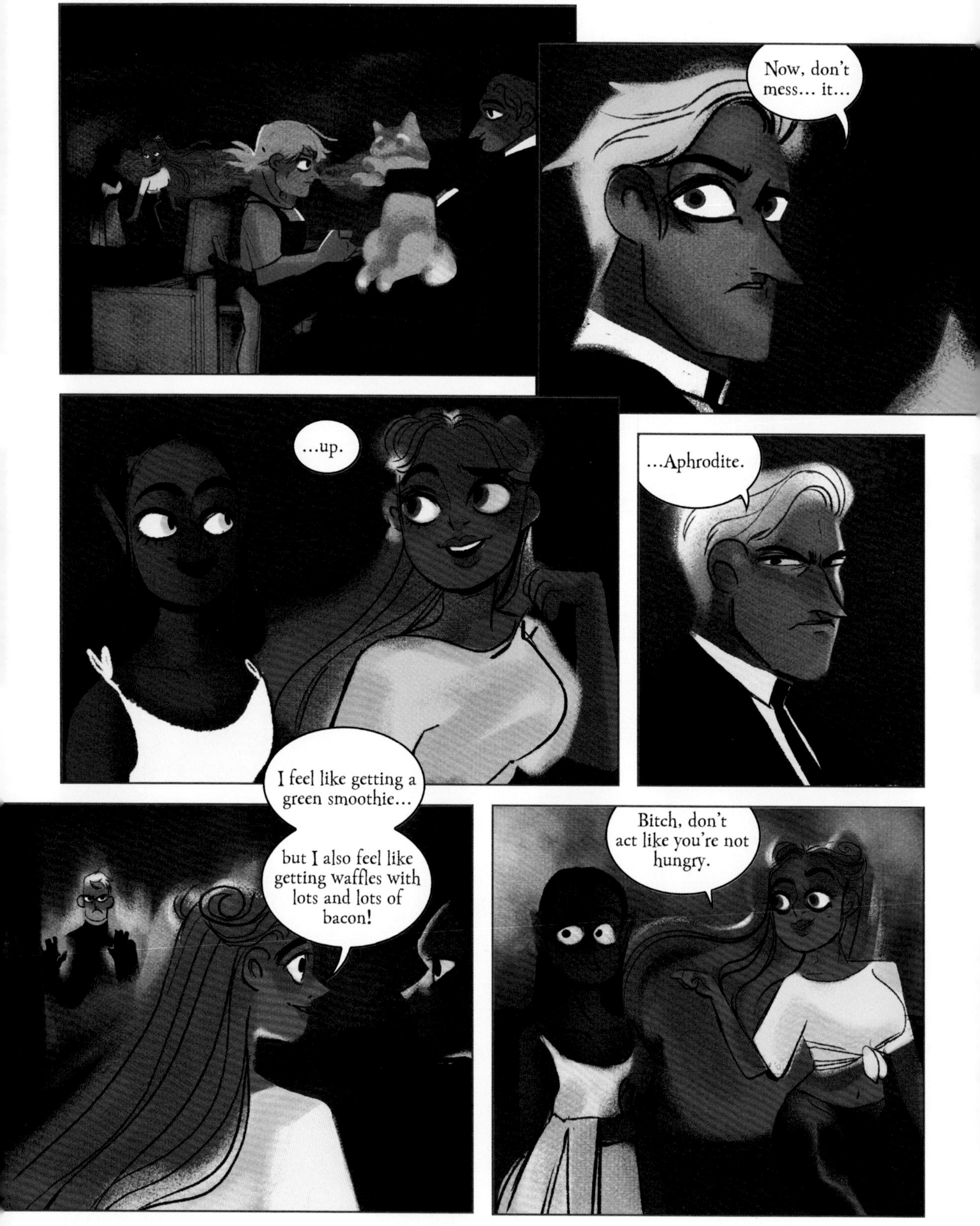
Now, don't mess… it…
…up.
…Aphrodite.
I feel like getting a green smoothie…
but I also feel like getting waffles with lots and lots of bacon!
Bitch, don't act like you're not hungry.

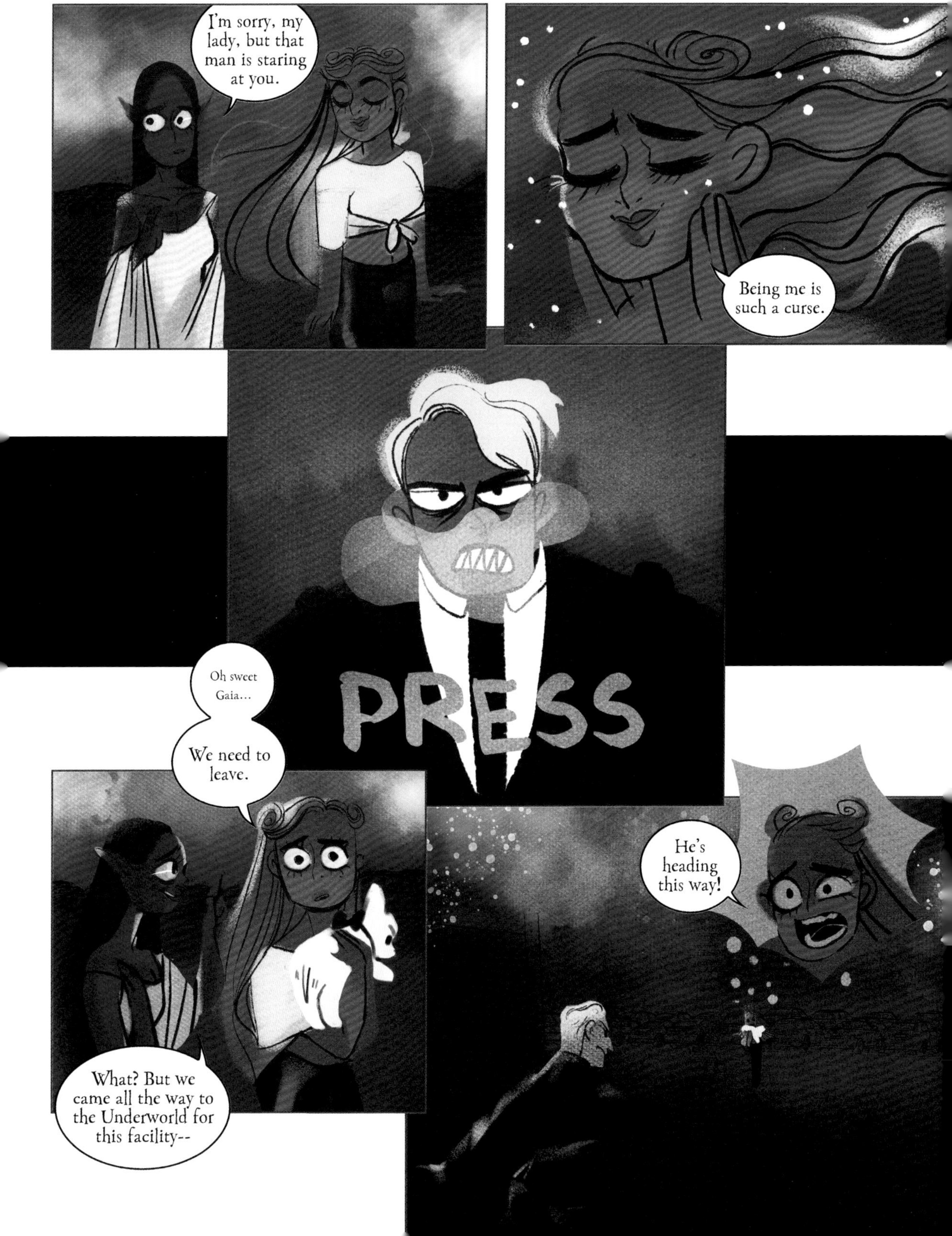
I'm sorry, my lady, but that man is staring at you.
Being me is such a curse.
PRESS
Oh sweet Gaia...
We need to leave.
What? But we came all the way to the Underworld for this facility--
He's heading this way!

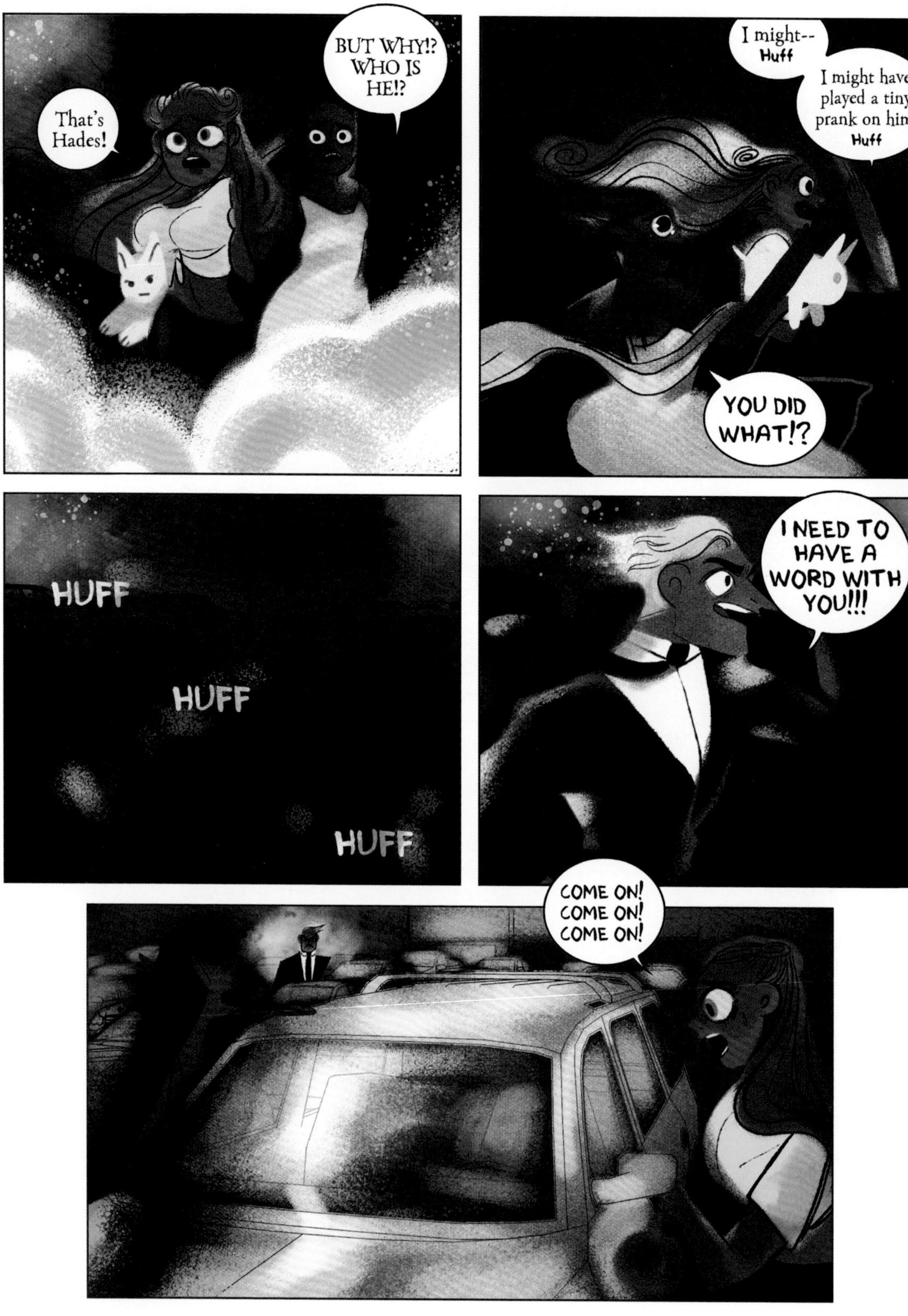
That's Hades!
BUT WHY!? WHO IS HE!?
I might-- Huff
I might have played a tiny prank on him. Huff
YOU DID WHAT!?
HUFF
HUFF
HUFF
I NEED TO HAVE A WORD WITH YOU!!!
COME ON! COME ON! COME ON!

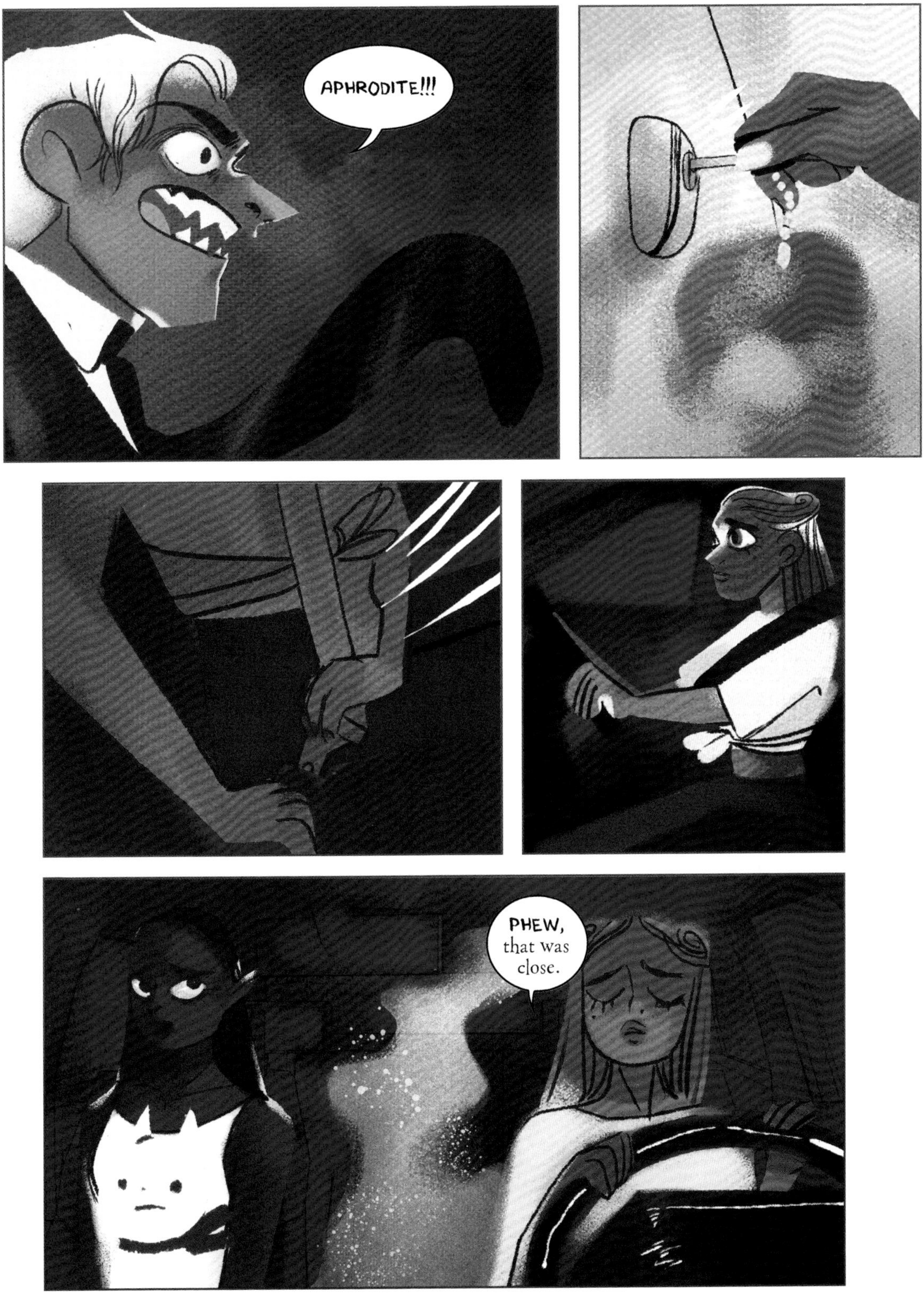
APHRODITE!!!
PHEW, that was close.

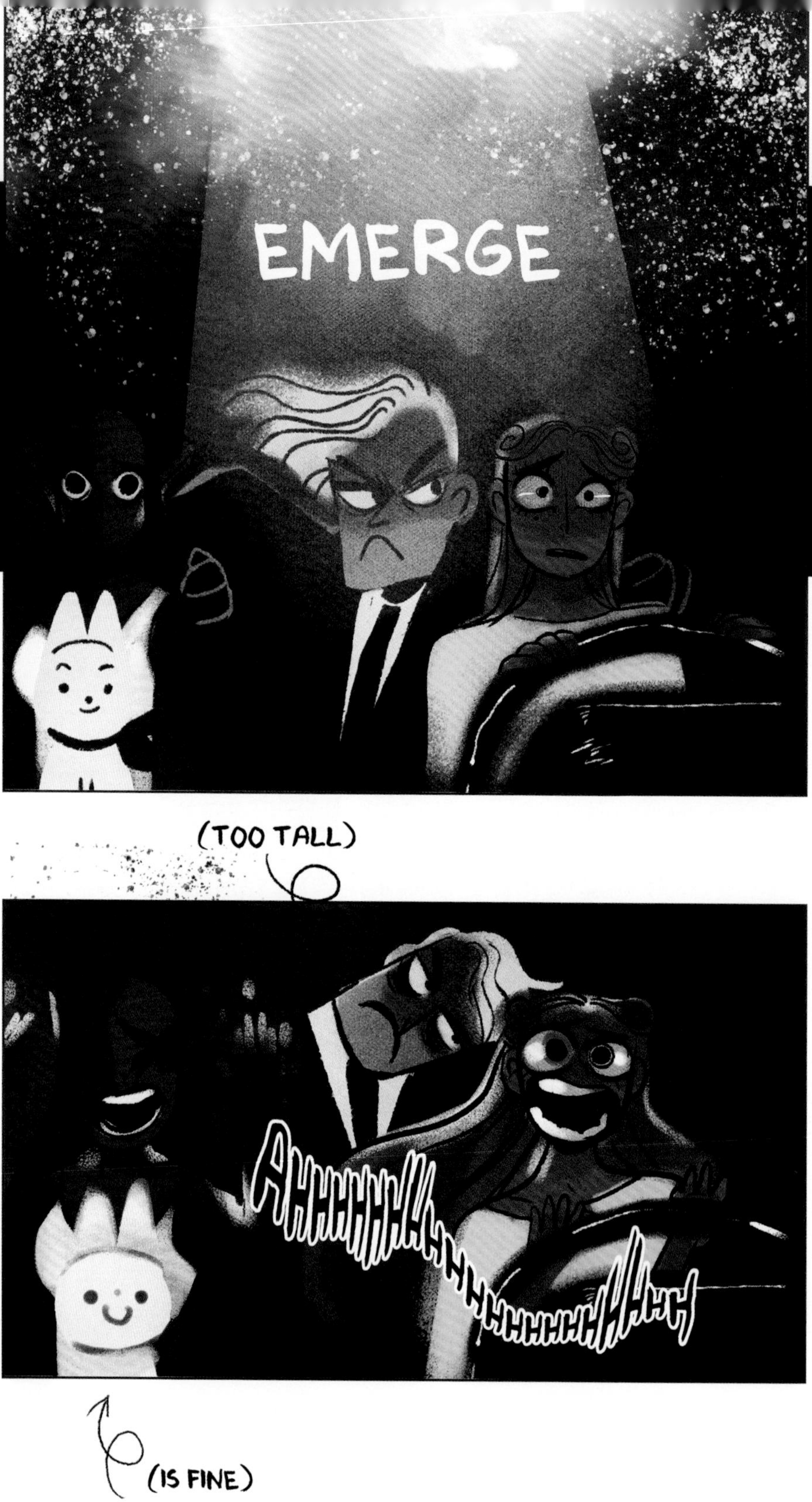
EMERGE
(TOO TALL)
AHHHHHHHHHHHHHHHHHHHHHHHH
(IS FINE)

EPISODE 32: SMALL

AWKWARD SILENCE

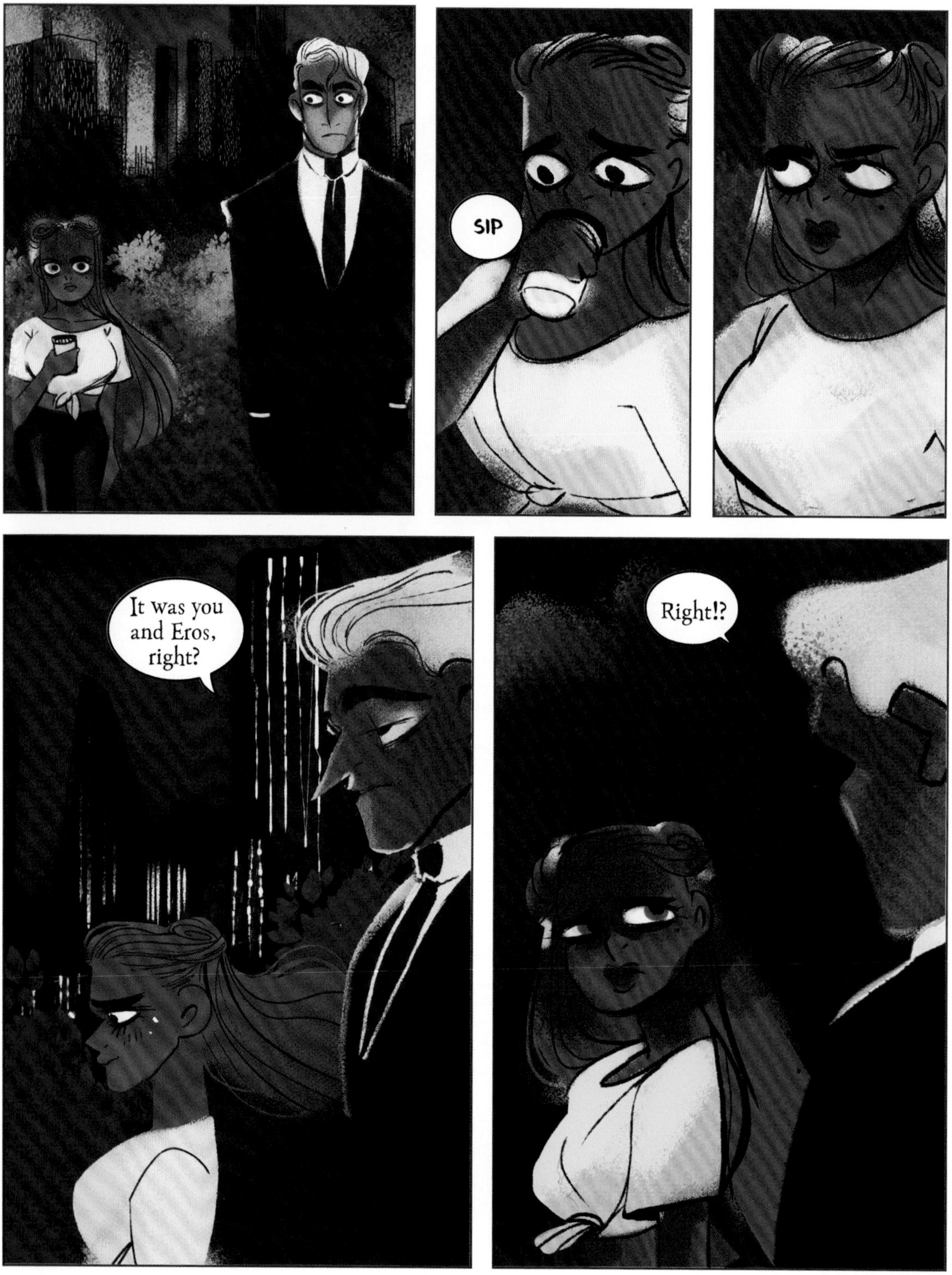
SIP
It was you and Eros, right?
Right!?

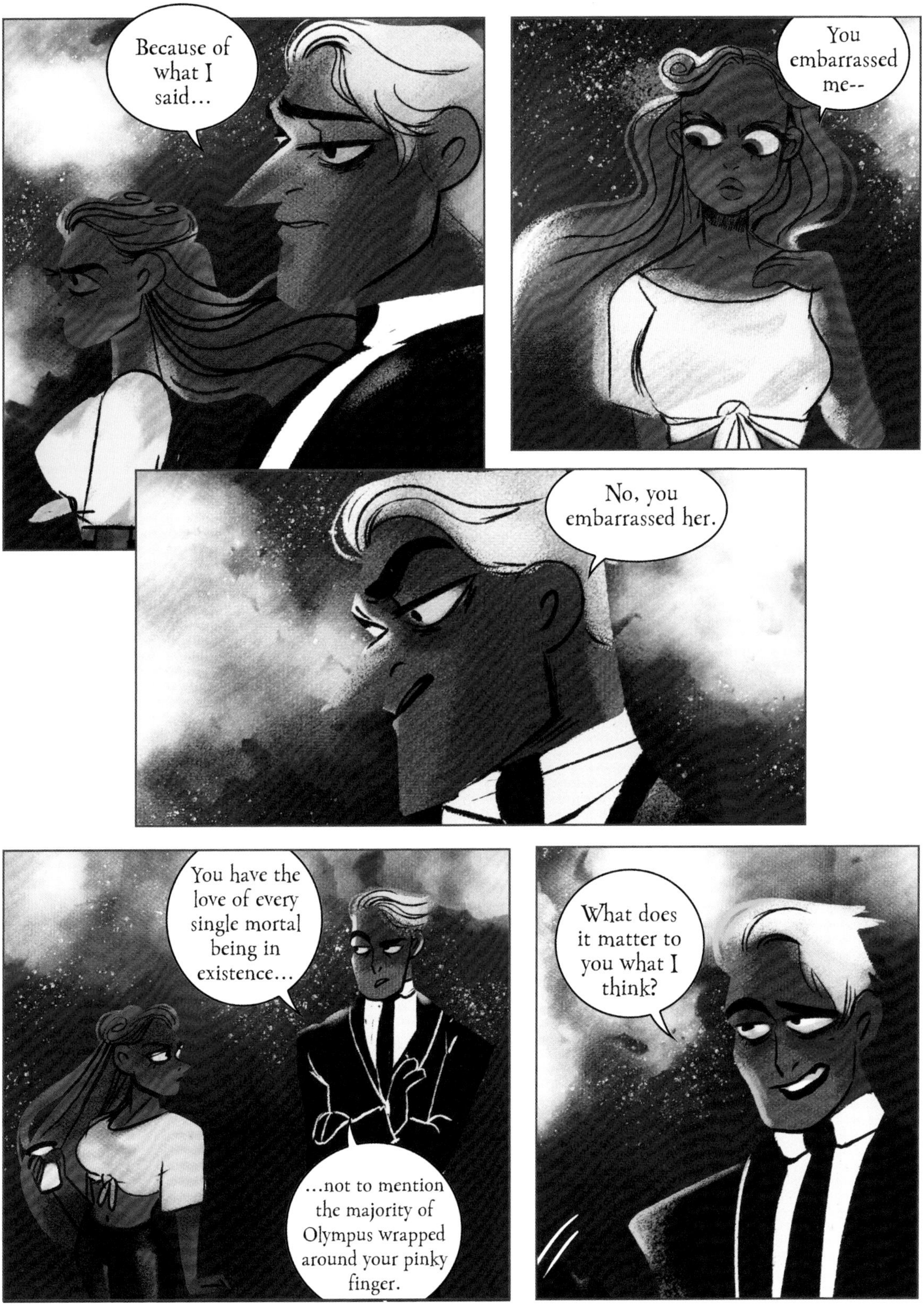
Because of what I said...
You embarrassed me--
No, you embarrassed her.
You have the love of every single mortal being in existence...
...not to mention the majority of Olympus wrapped around your pinky finger.
What does it matter to you what I think?

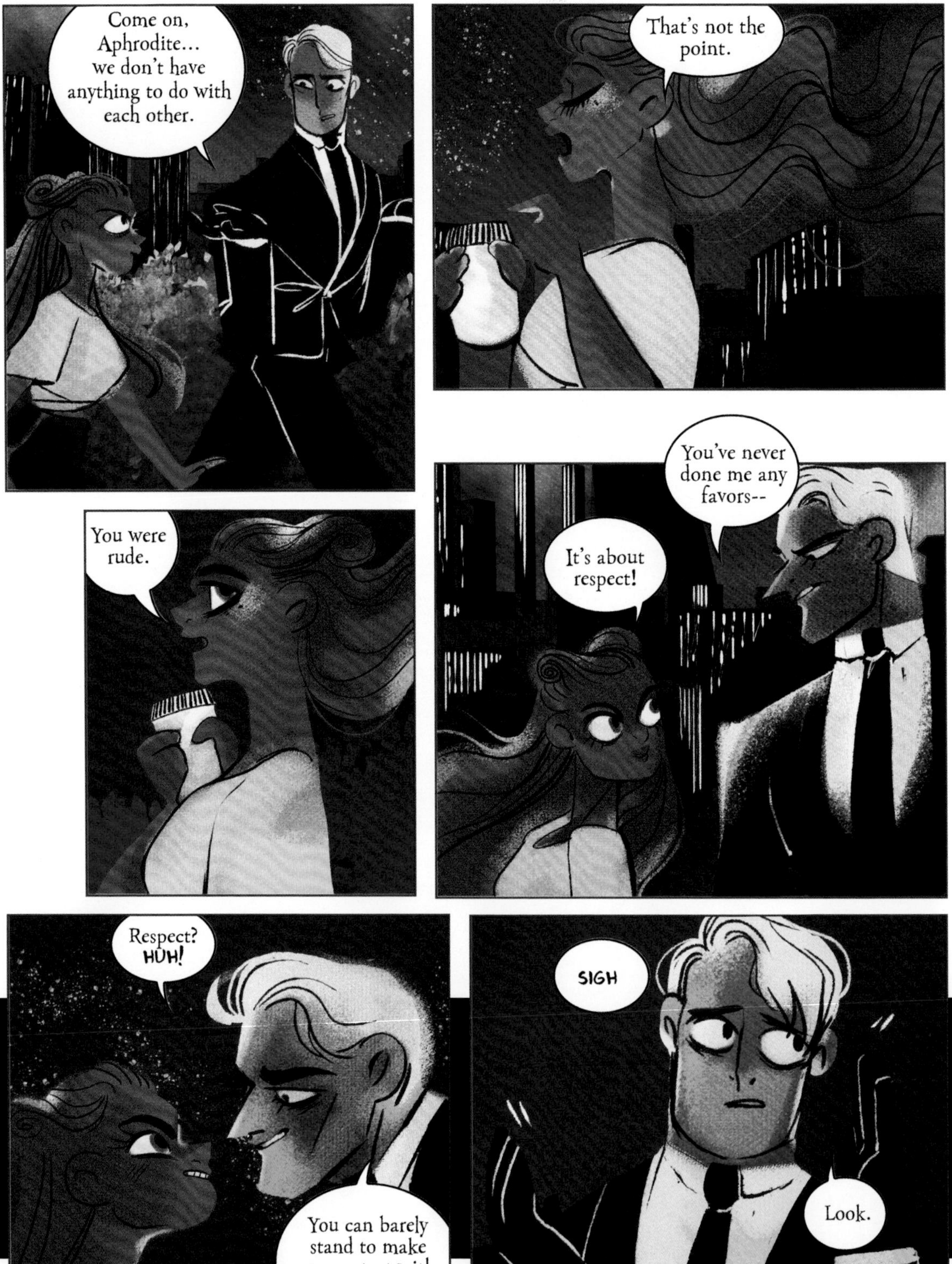
Come on, Aphrodite... we don't have anything to do with each other.
That's not the point.
You were rude.
You've never done me any favors--
It's about respect!
Respect? HUH!
You can barely stand to make eye contact with me half the time.
SIGH
Look.

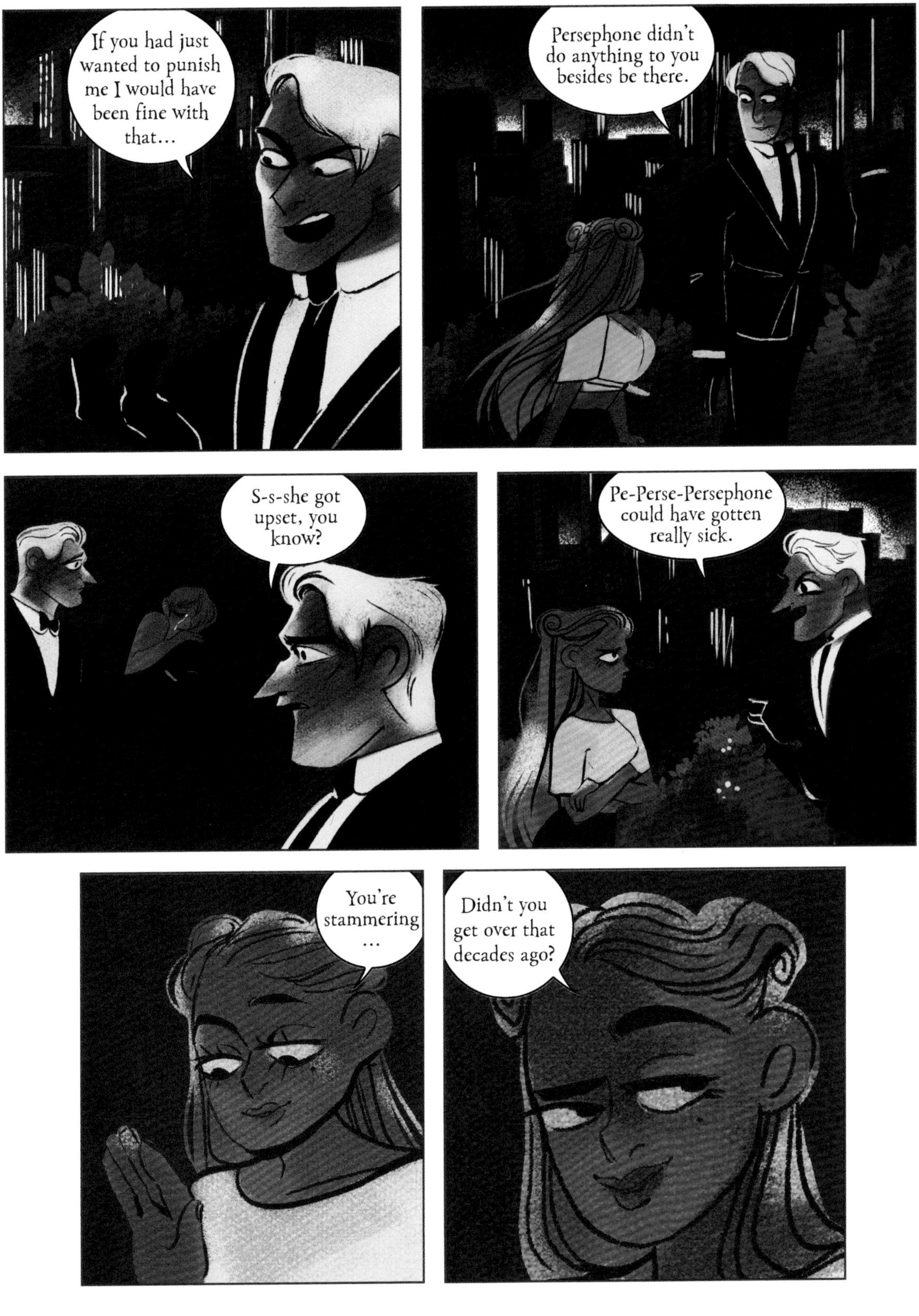

If you had just wanted to punish me I would have been fine with that...
Persephone didn't do anything to you besides be there.
S-s-she got upset, you know?
Pe-Perse-Persephone could have gotten really sick.
You're stammering ...
Didn't you get over that decades ago?

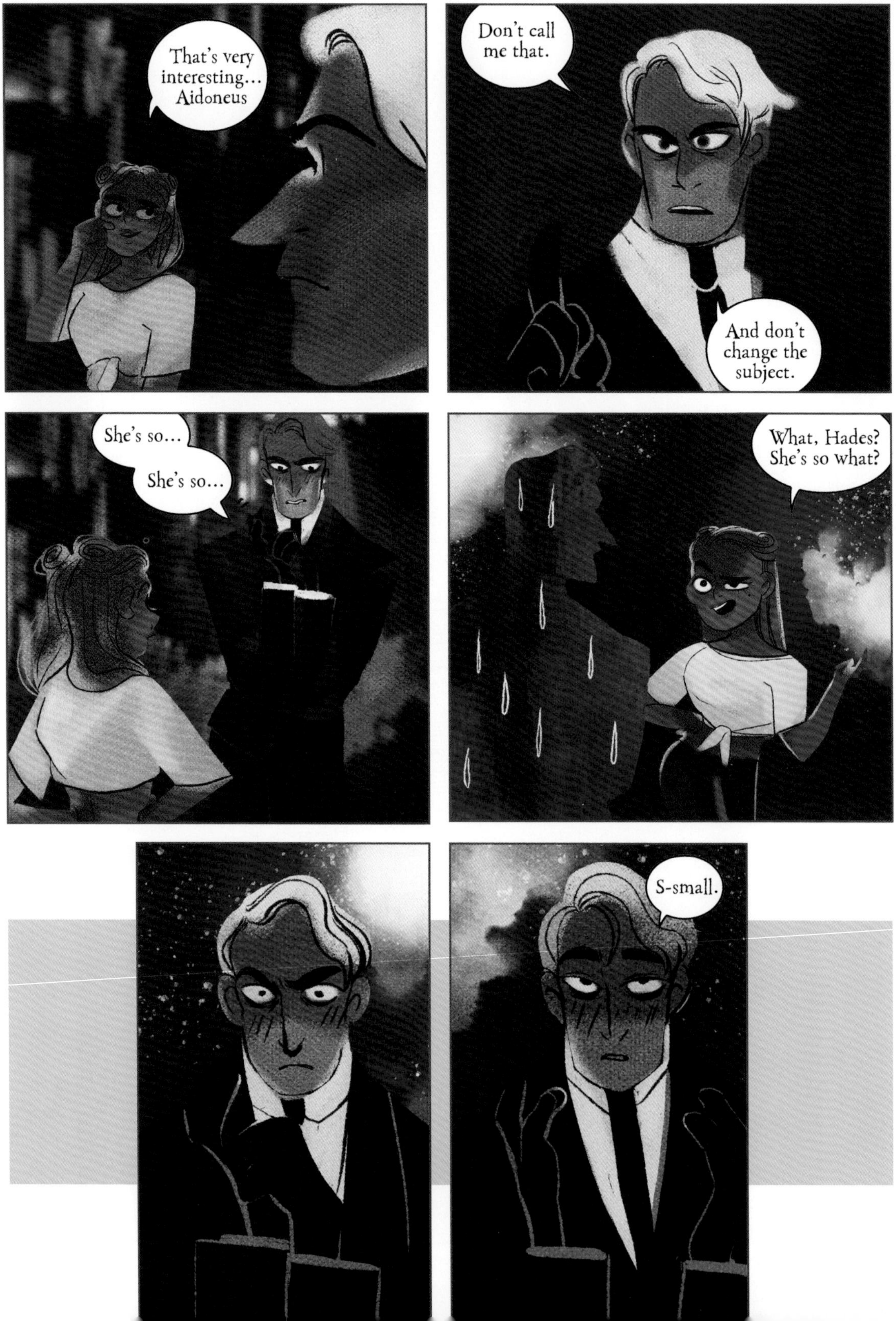
That's very interesting... Aidoneus
Don't call me that.
And don't change the subject.
She's so...
She's so...
What, Hades? She's so what?
S-small.

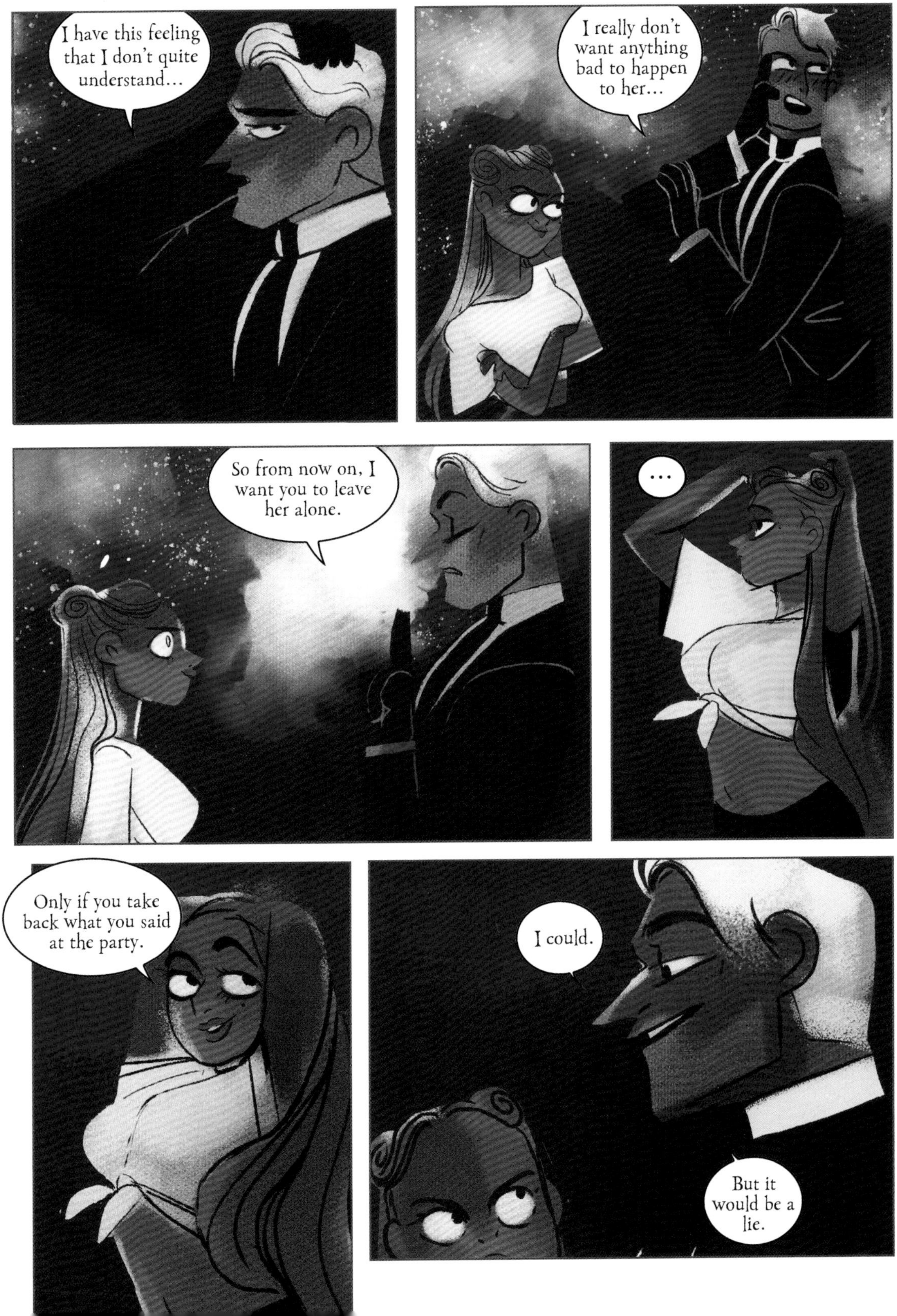
I have this feeling that I don't quite understand...
I really don't want anything bad to happen to her...
So from now on, I want you to leave her alone.
...
Only if you take back what you said at the party.
I could.
But it would be a lie.

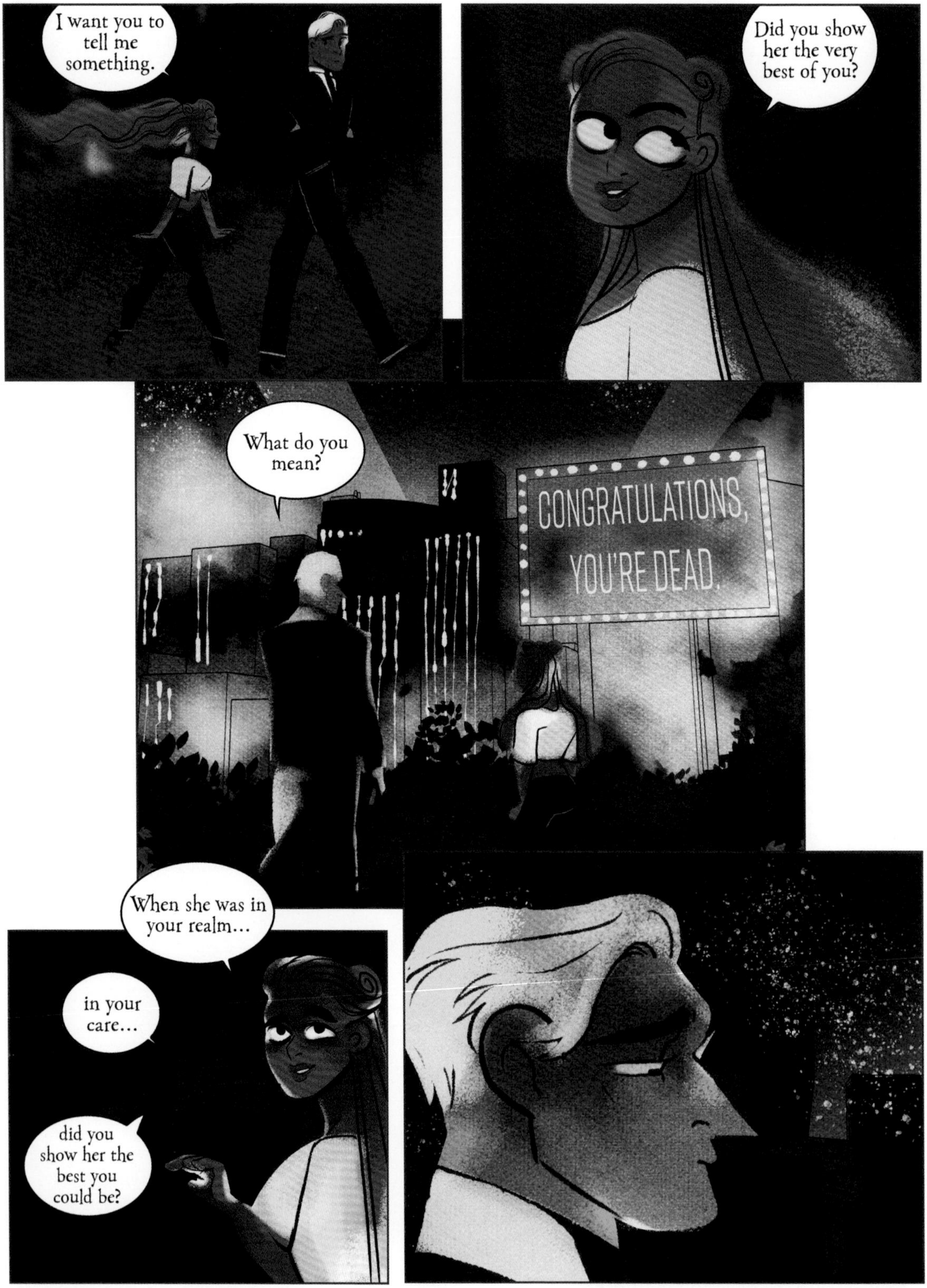
I want you to tell me something.
Did you show her the very best of you?
What do you mean?
CONGRATULATIONS, YOU'RE DEAD.
When she was in your realm...
in your care...
did you show her the best you could be?

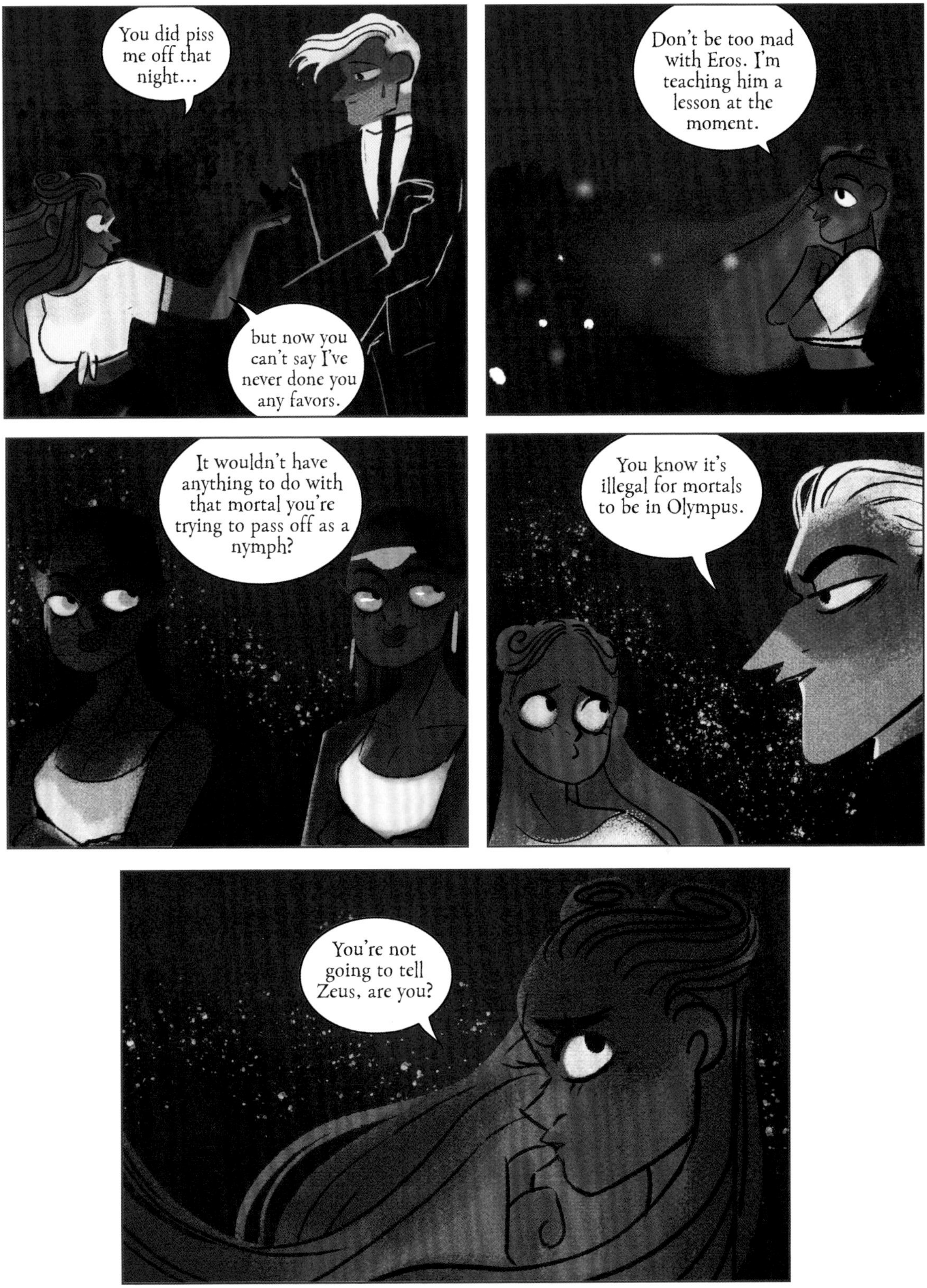
You did piss me off that night...
but now you can't say I've never done you any favors.
Don't be too mad with Eros. I'm teaching him a lesson at the moment.
It wouldn't have anything to do with that mortal you're trying to pass off as a nymph?
You know it's illegal for mortals to be in Olympus.
You're not going to tell Zeus, are you?

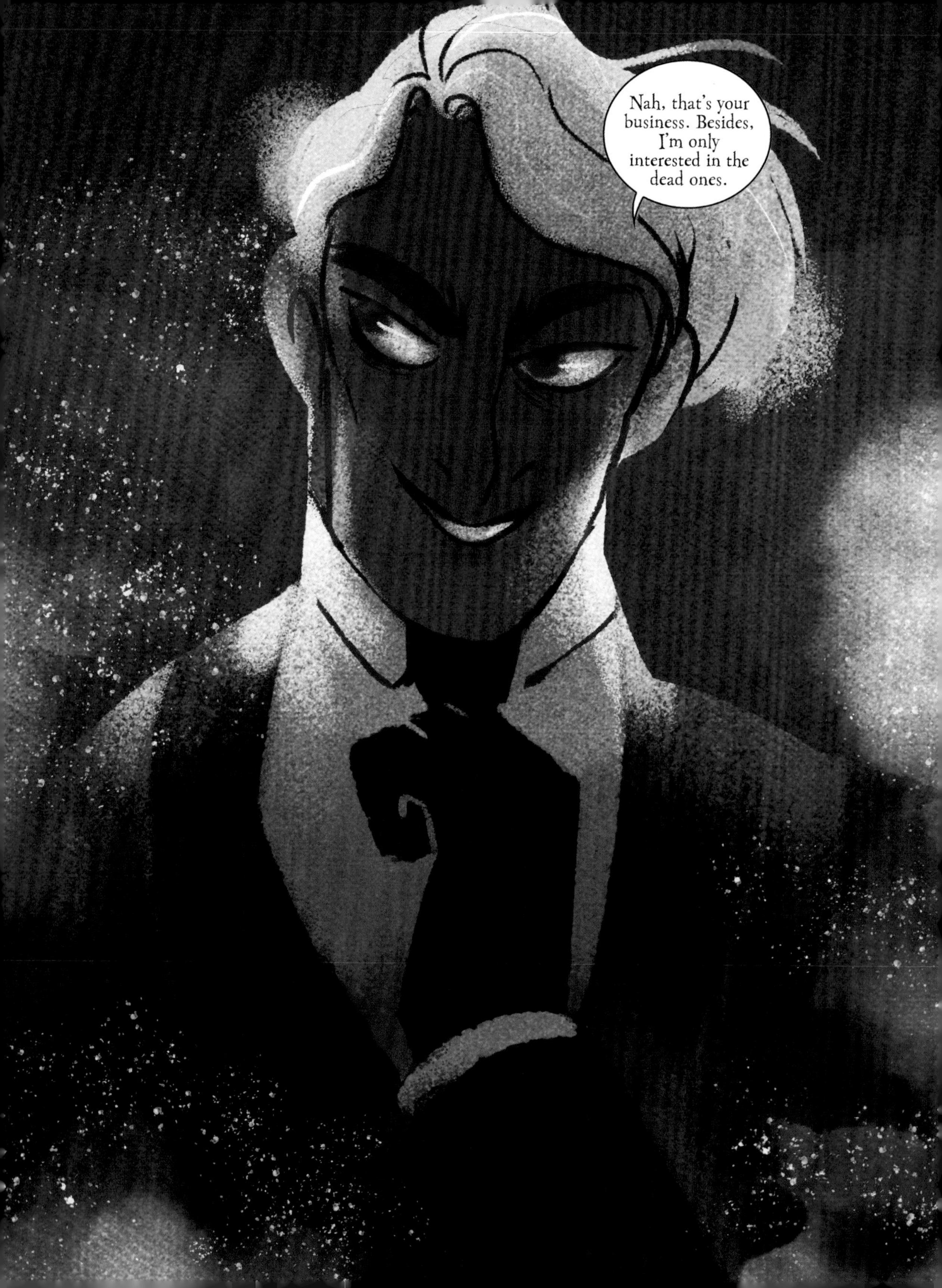
Nah, that's your business. Besides, I'm only interested in the dead ones.

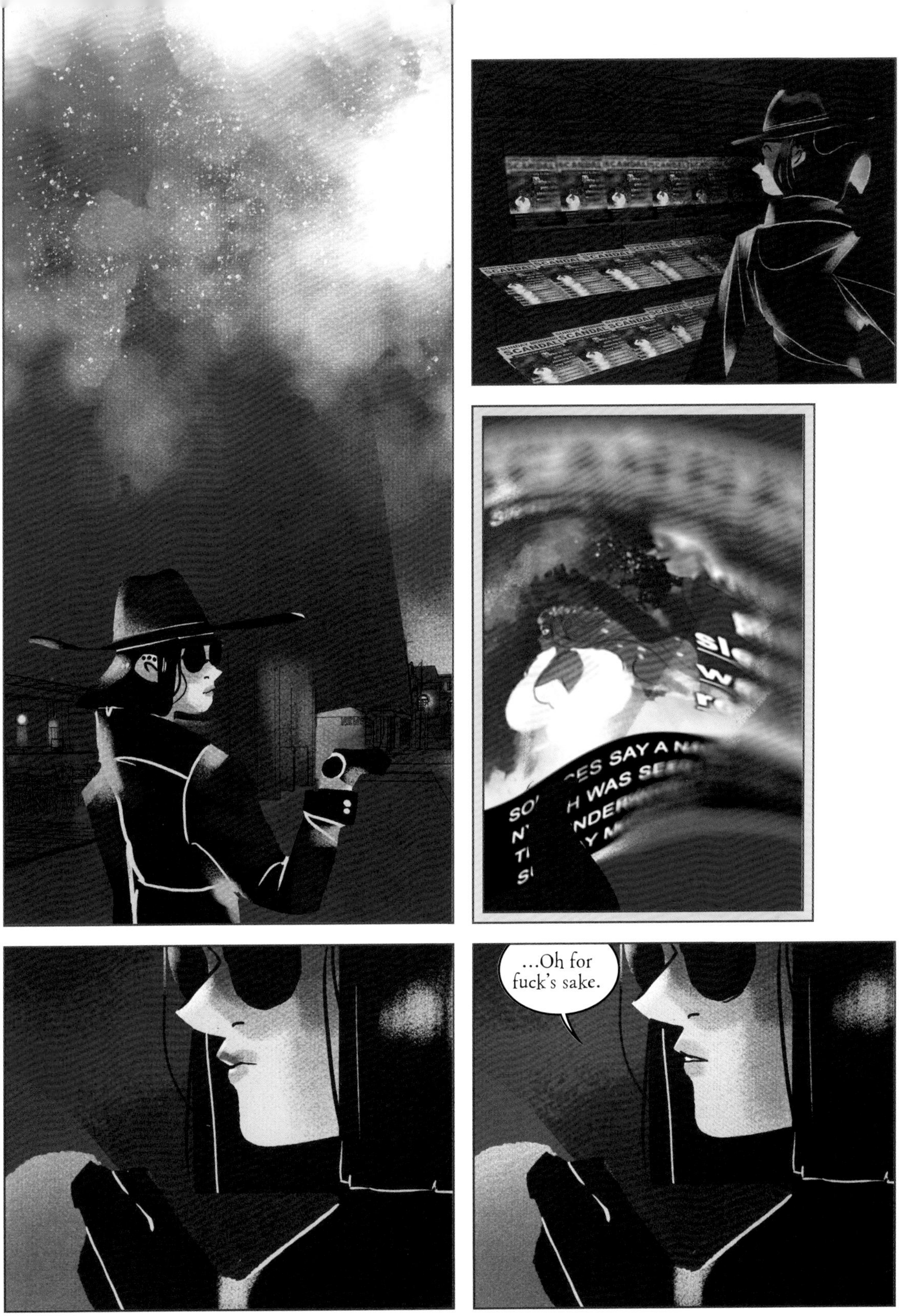
SCANDAL
...Oh for fuck's sake.

EPISODE 33: YOUR ROYAL MAJESTY

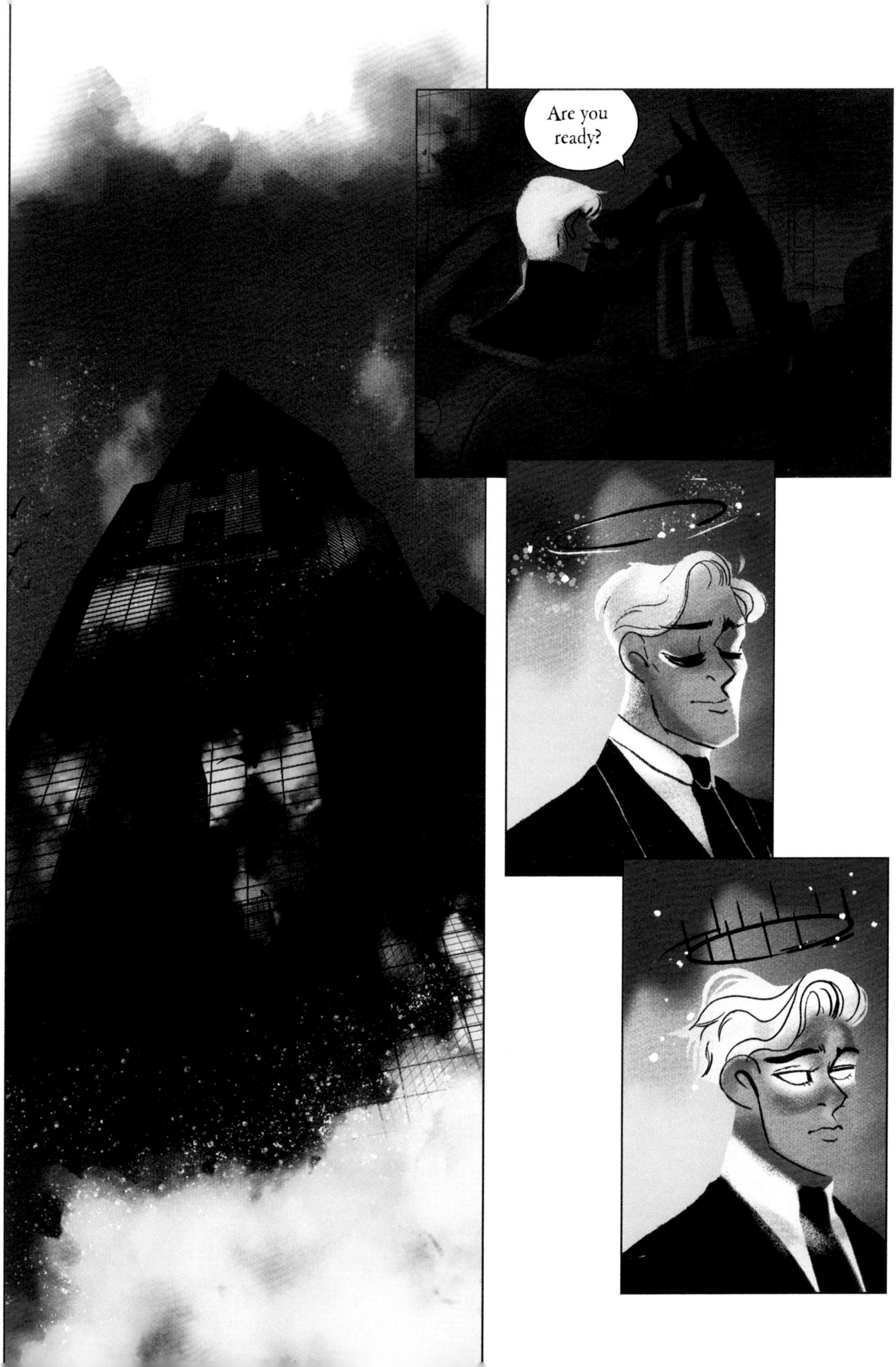
Are you
ready?

♪♪ Another daaaaay ♪♪
♪♪Another doooollar♪♪
UNDERWORLD CORP
UNDERWORLD CORP
UNDERWORLD CORP
NDERWORLD CORP
UNDERWORLD CORP

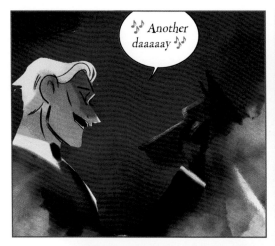

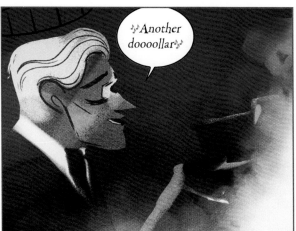

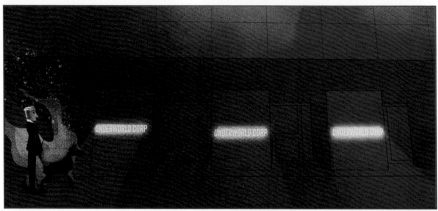

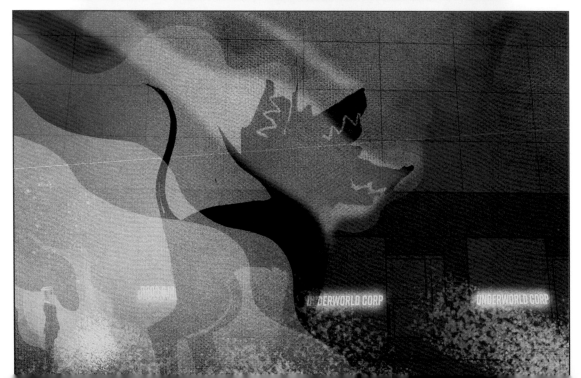

(Self-sufficient.)

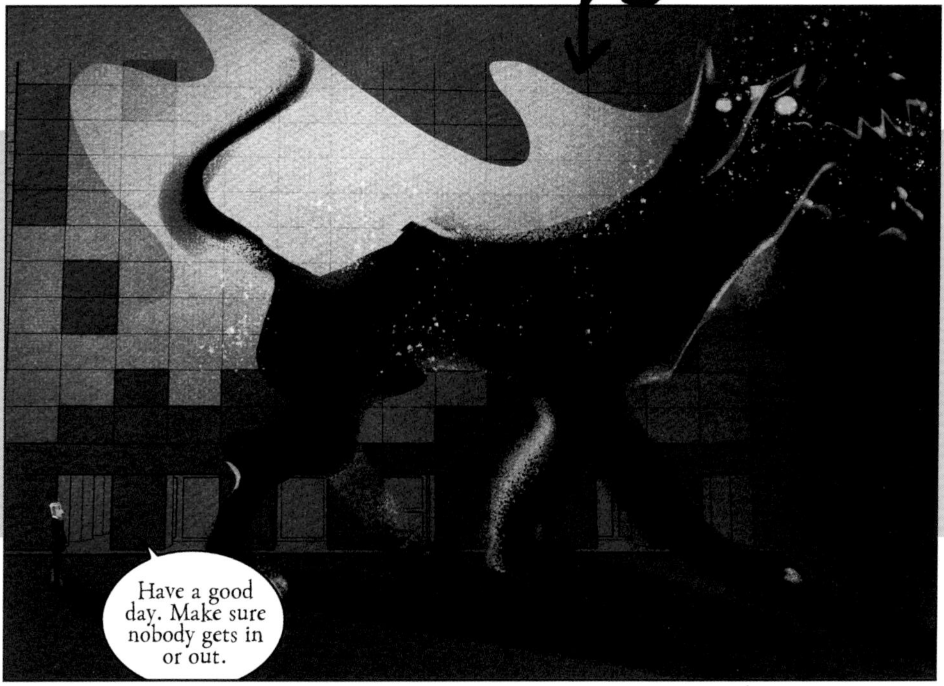
Have a good day. Make sure nobody gets in or out.

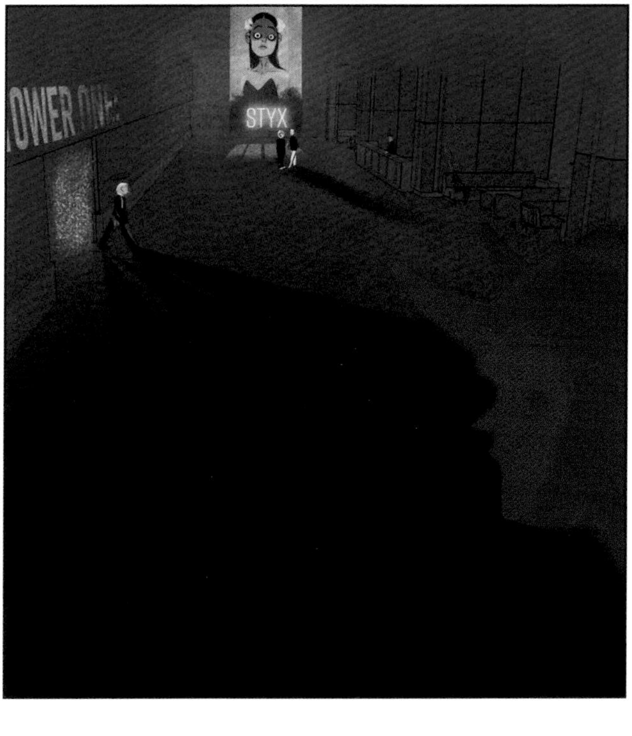
OWER ONE
STYX

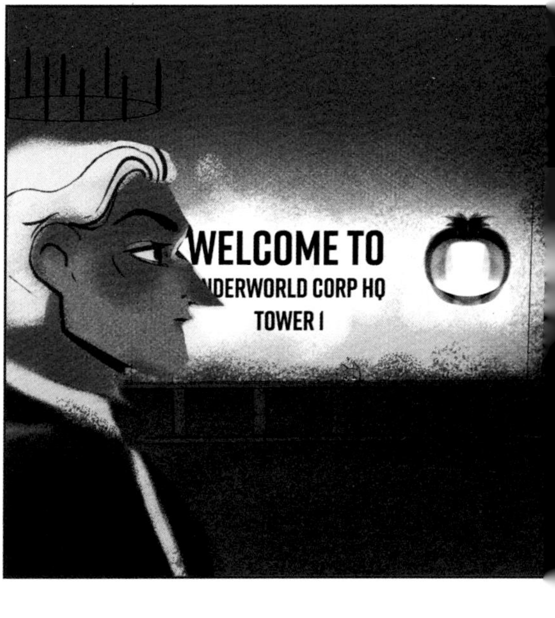
WELCOME TO
IDERWORLD CORP HQ
TOWER 1

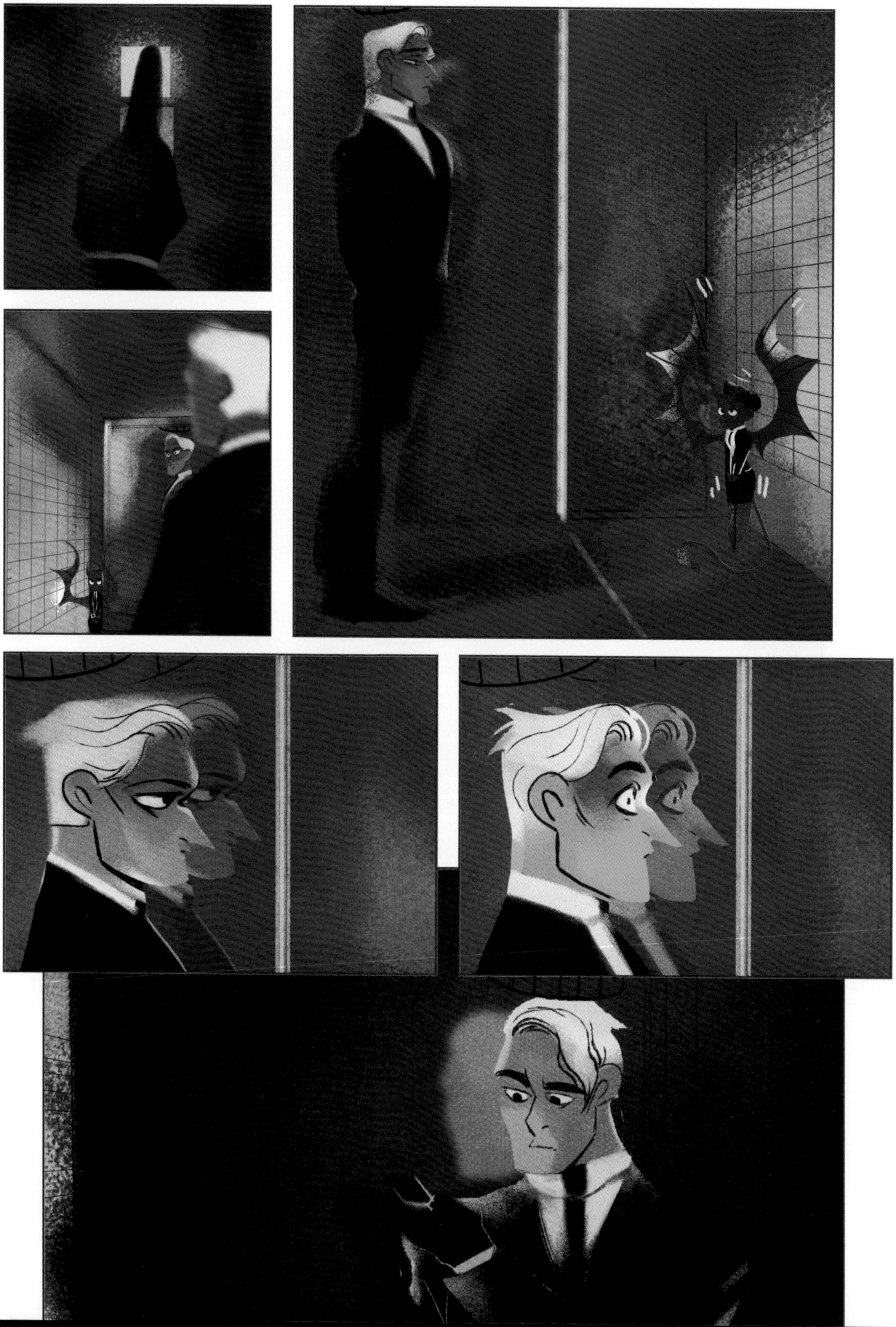

Did you know there is a really dorky portrait of you at Hera's? 🤭

I don't know what to reply.

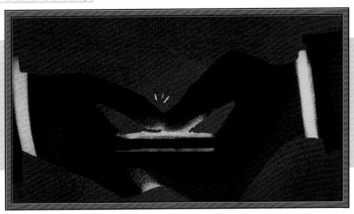

Did you know there is a really dorky portrait of you at Hera's? 🤭

You would make a much better subject for a painting.

Ah! Don't send her that, you idiot.

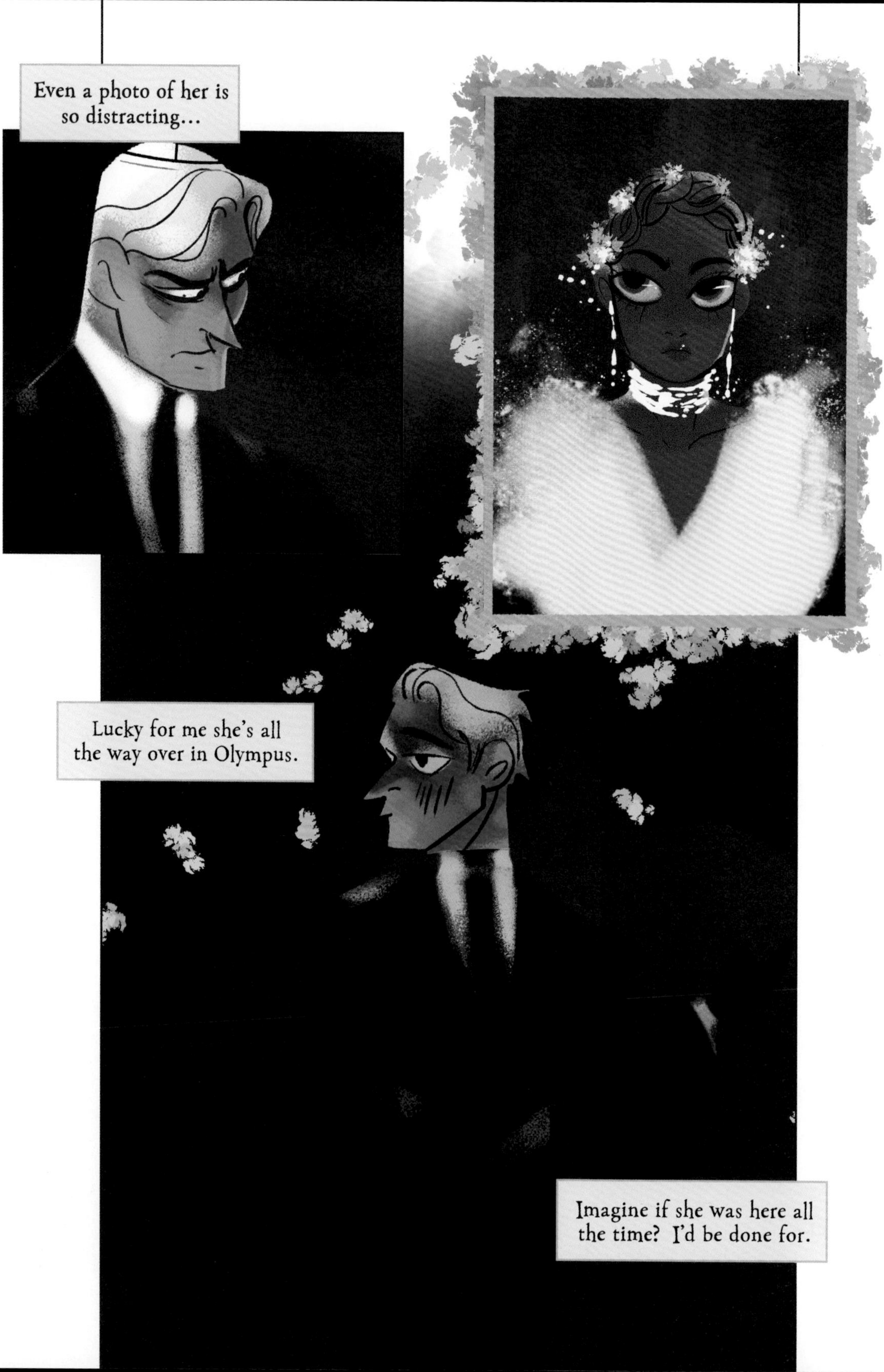
Even a photo of her is so distracting...
Lucky for me she's all the way over in Olympus.
Imagine if she was here all the time? I'd be done for.

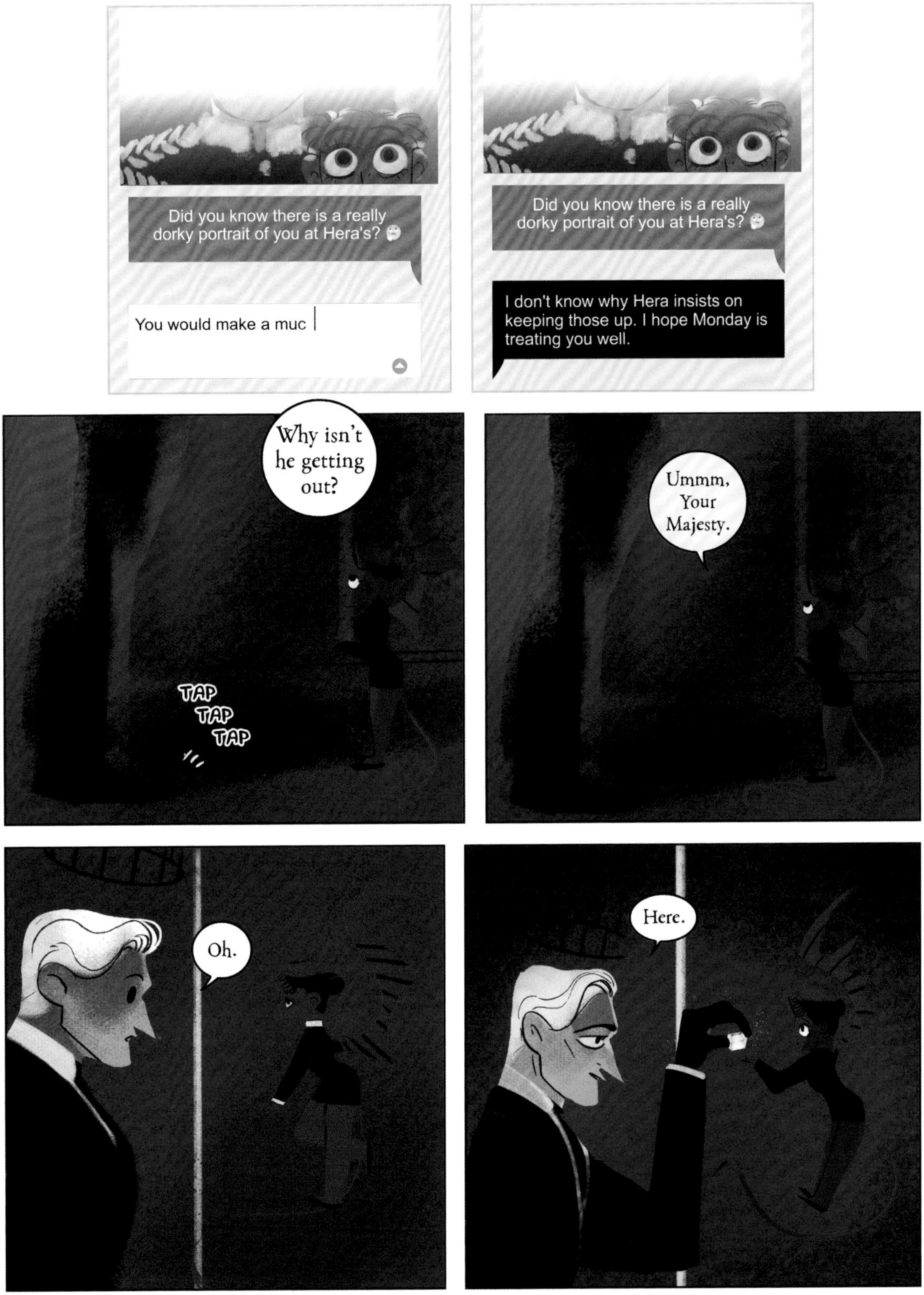
Did you know there is a really dorky portrait of you at Hera's?
You would make a muc
Did you know there is a really dorky portrait of you at Hera's?
I don't know why Hera insists on keeping those up. I hope Monday is treating you well.
Why isn't he getting out?
TAP
TAP
TAP
Ummm, Your Majesty.
Oh.
Here.

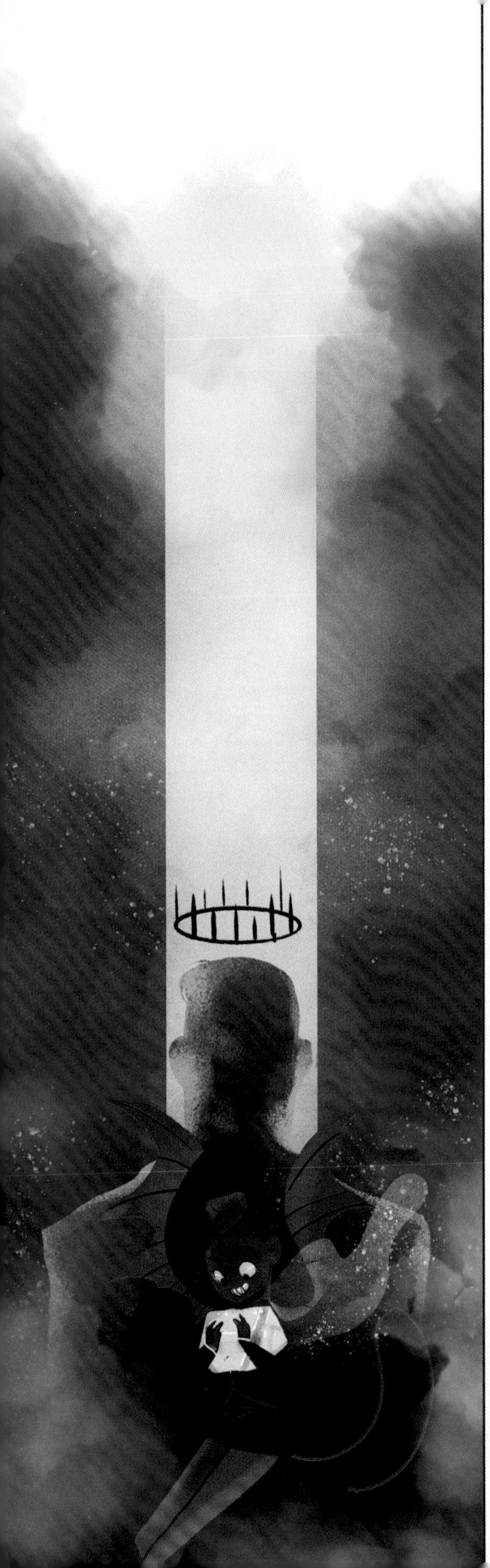
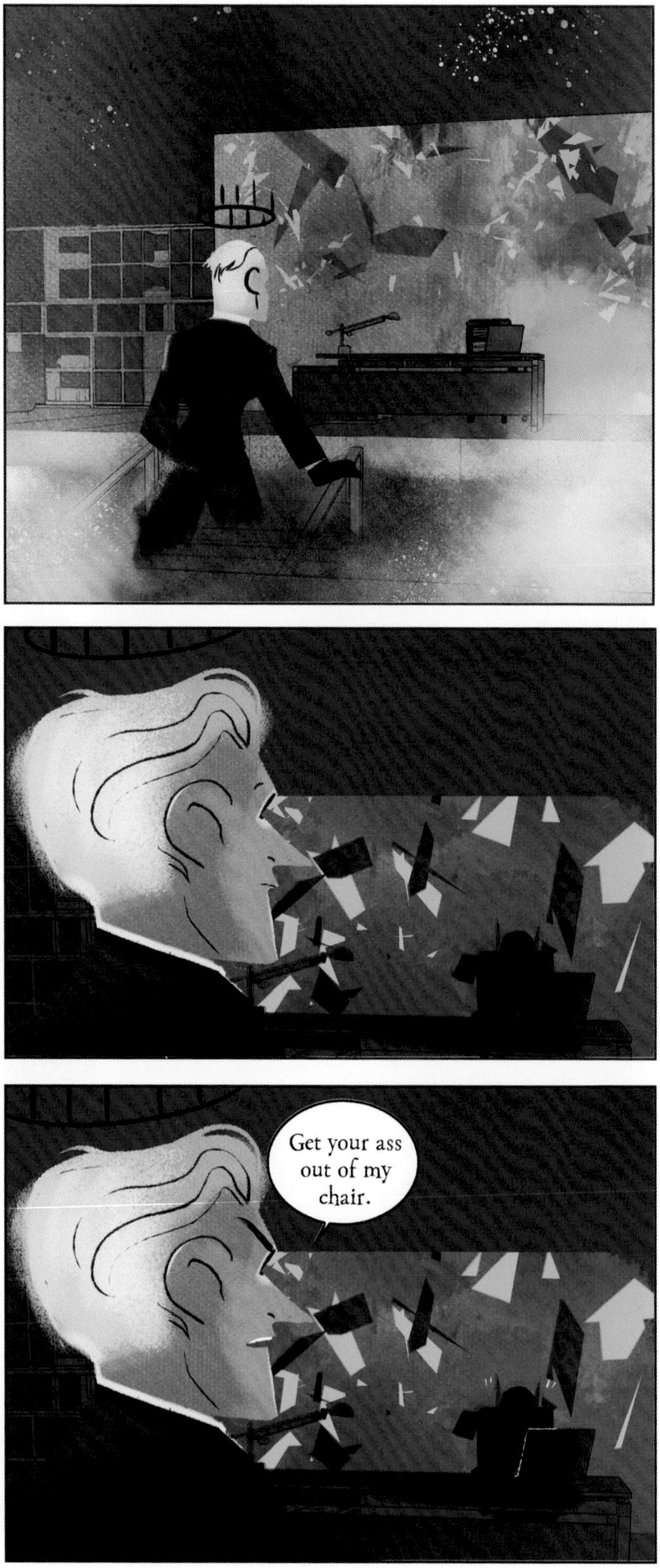
Get your ass out of my chair.

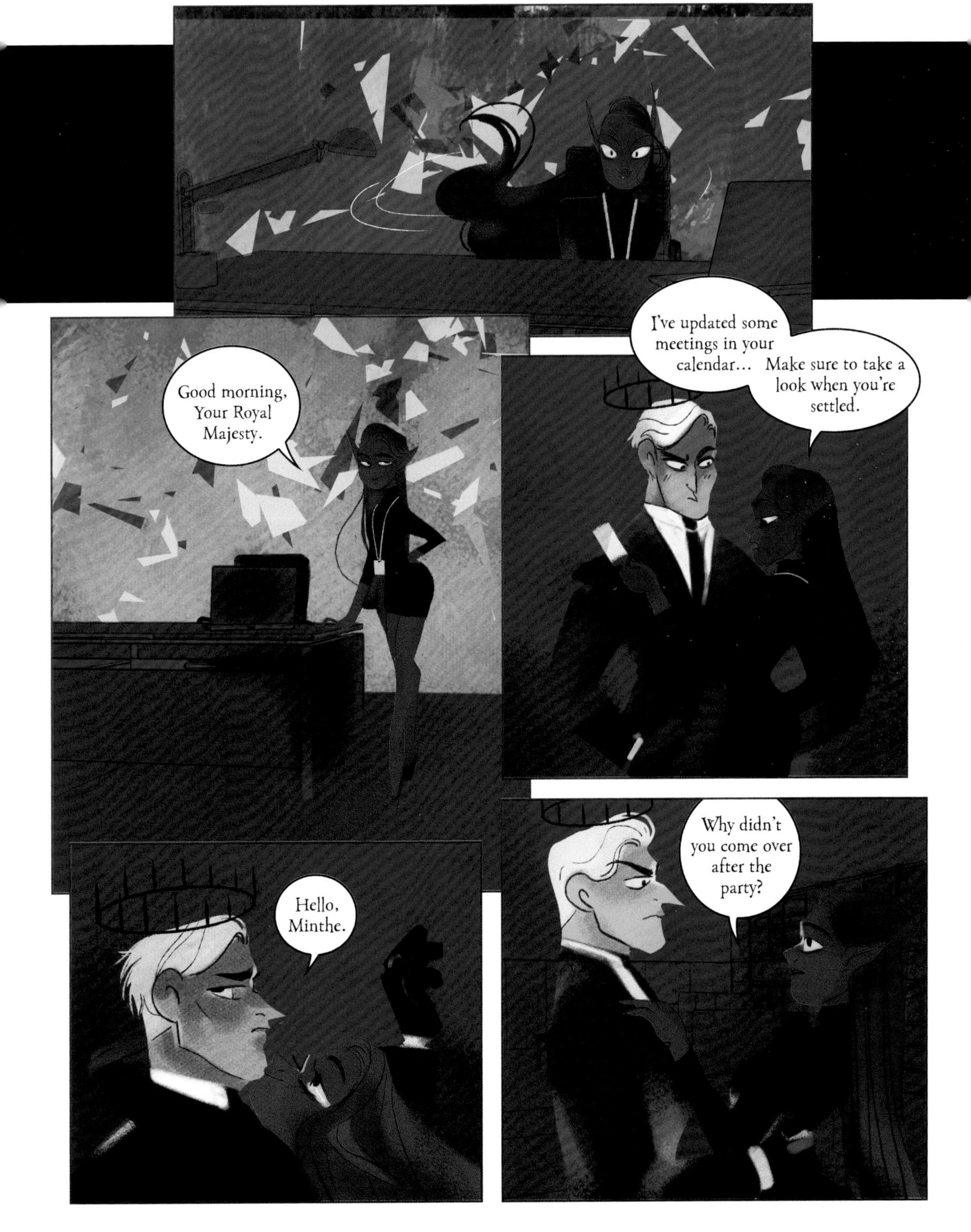
Good morning, Your Royal Majesty.
I've updated some meetings in your calendar…
Make sure to take a look when you're settled.
Hello, Minthe.
Why didn't you come over after the party?

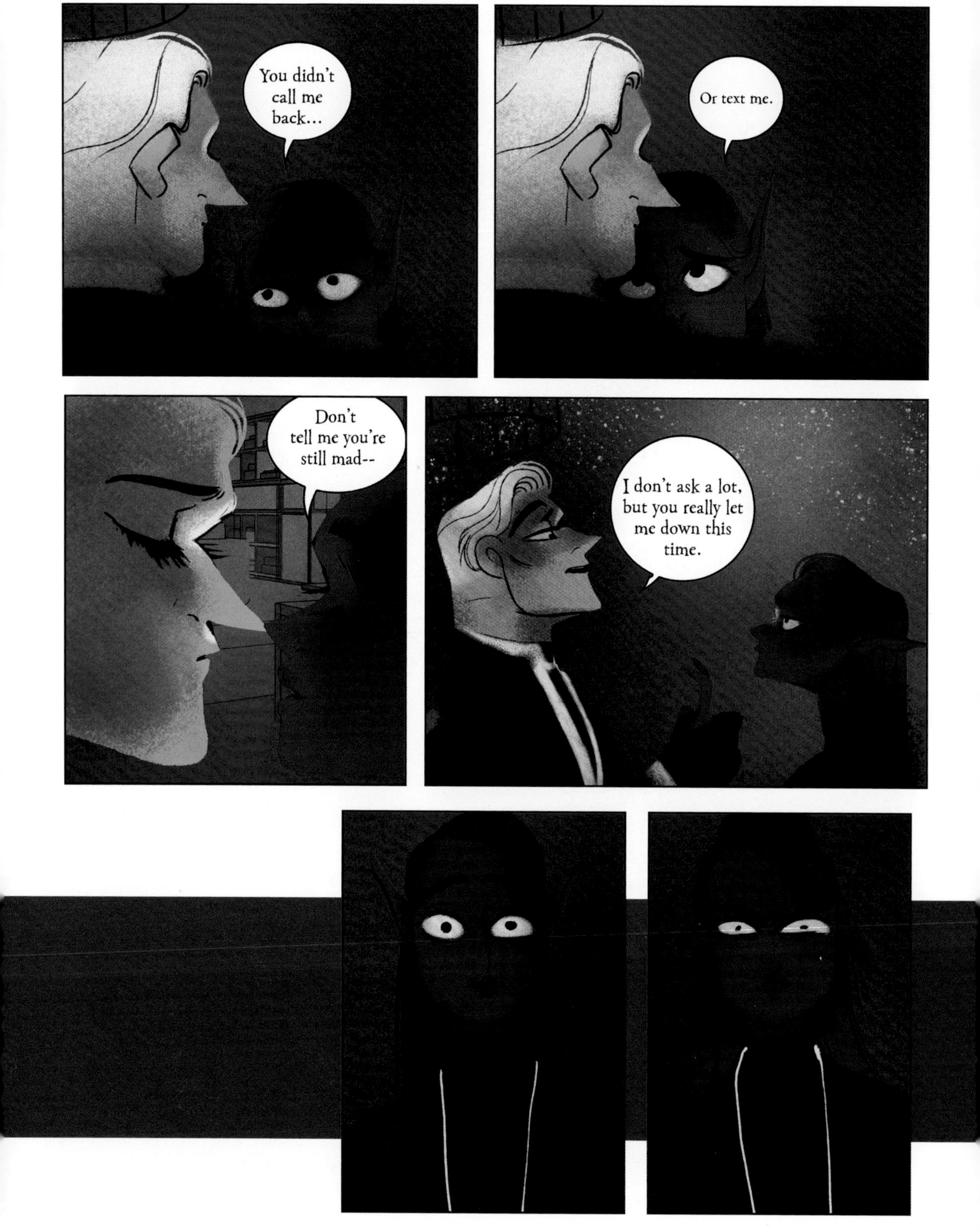
You didn't call me back...
Or text me.
Don't tell me you're still mad--
I don't ask a lot, but you really let me down this time.

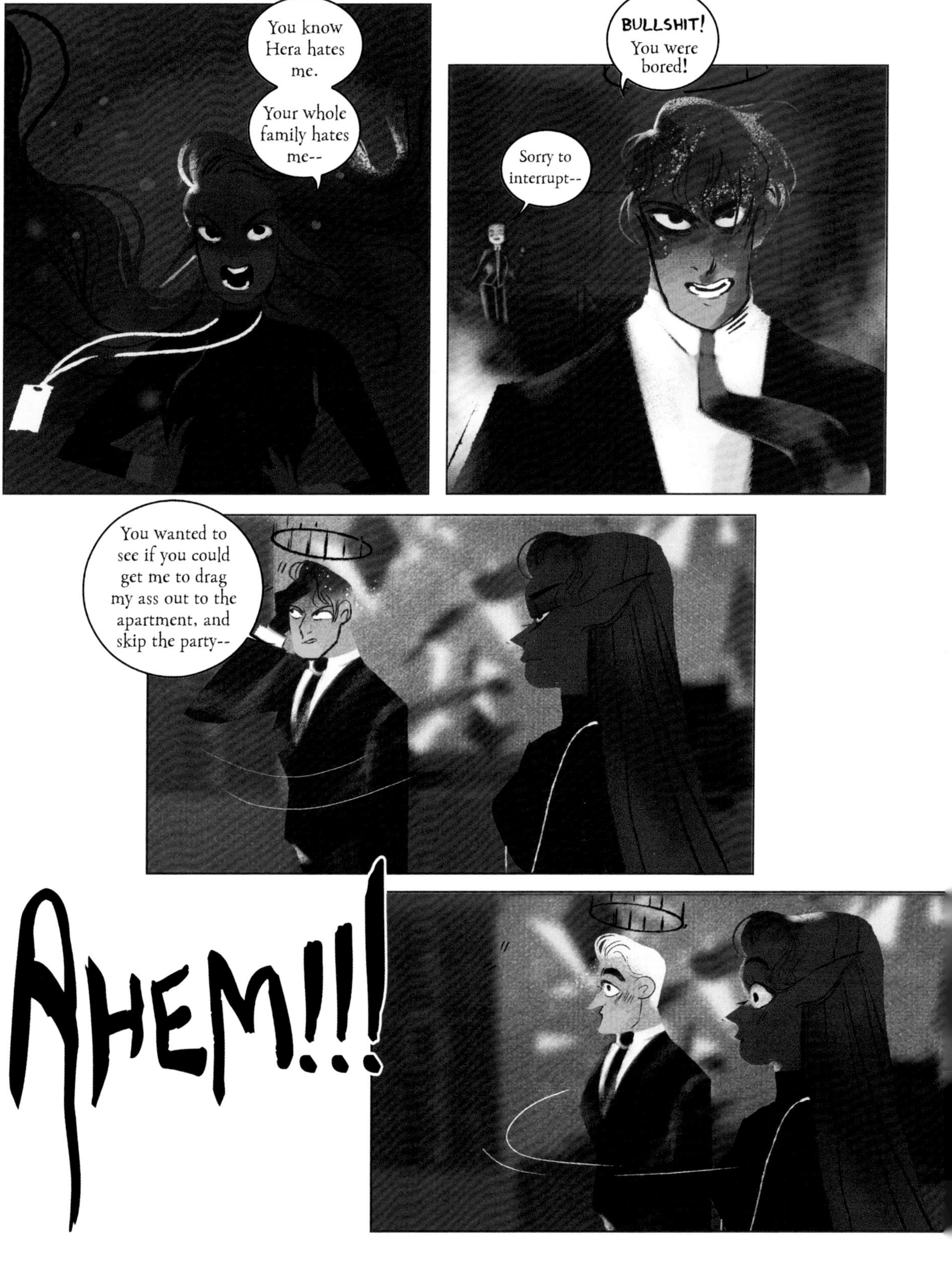
You know Hera hates me.
Your whole family hates me--
BULLSHIT! You were bored!
Sorry to interrupt--
You wanted to see if you could get me to drag my ass out to the apartment, and skip the party--
AHEM!!!

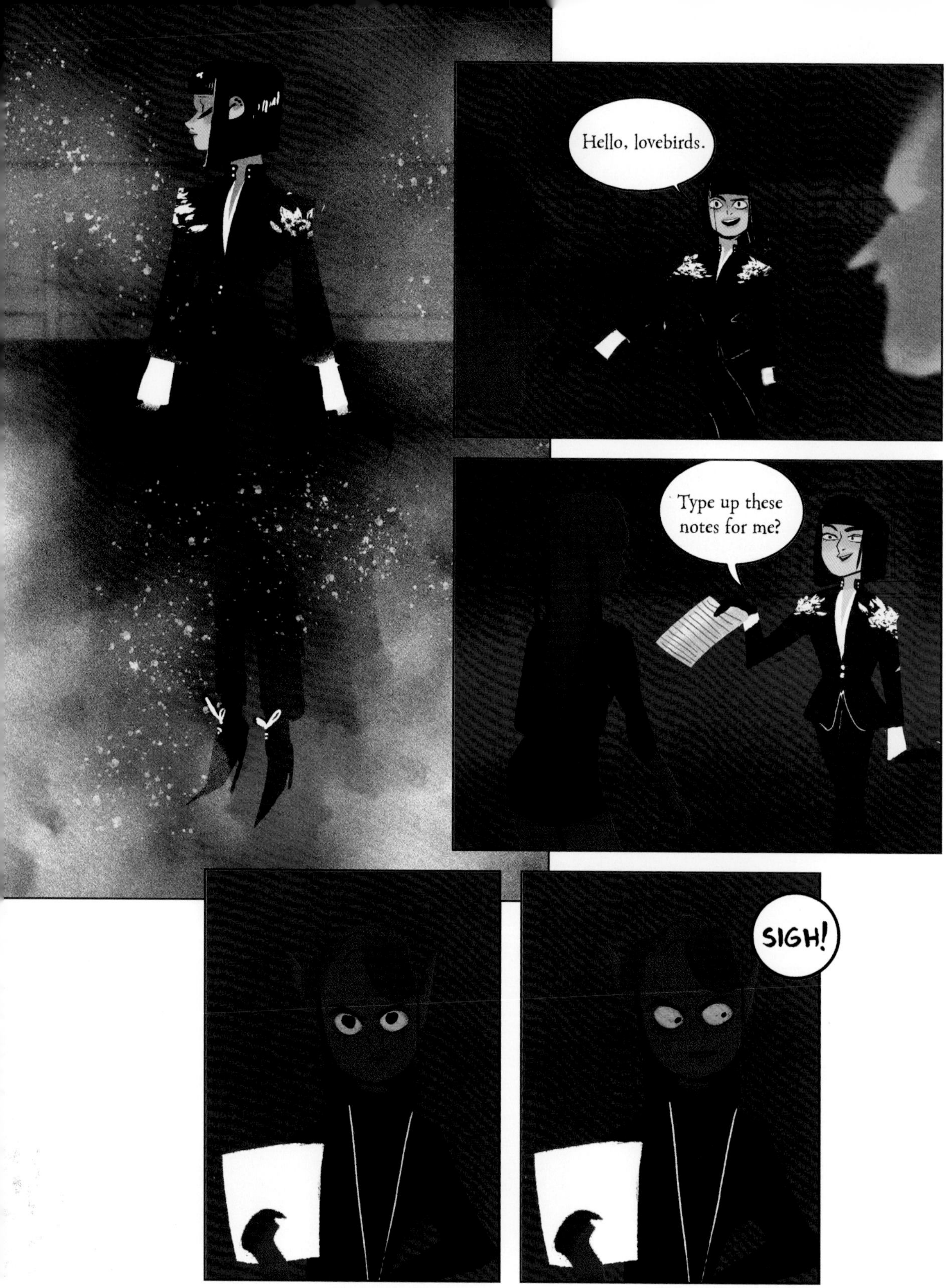
Hello, lovebirds.
Type up these notes for me?
SIGH!

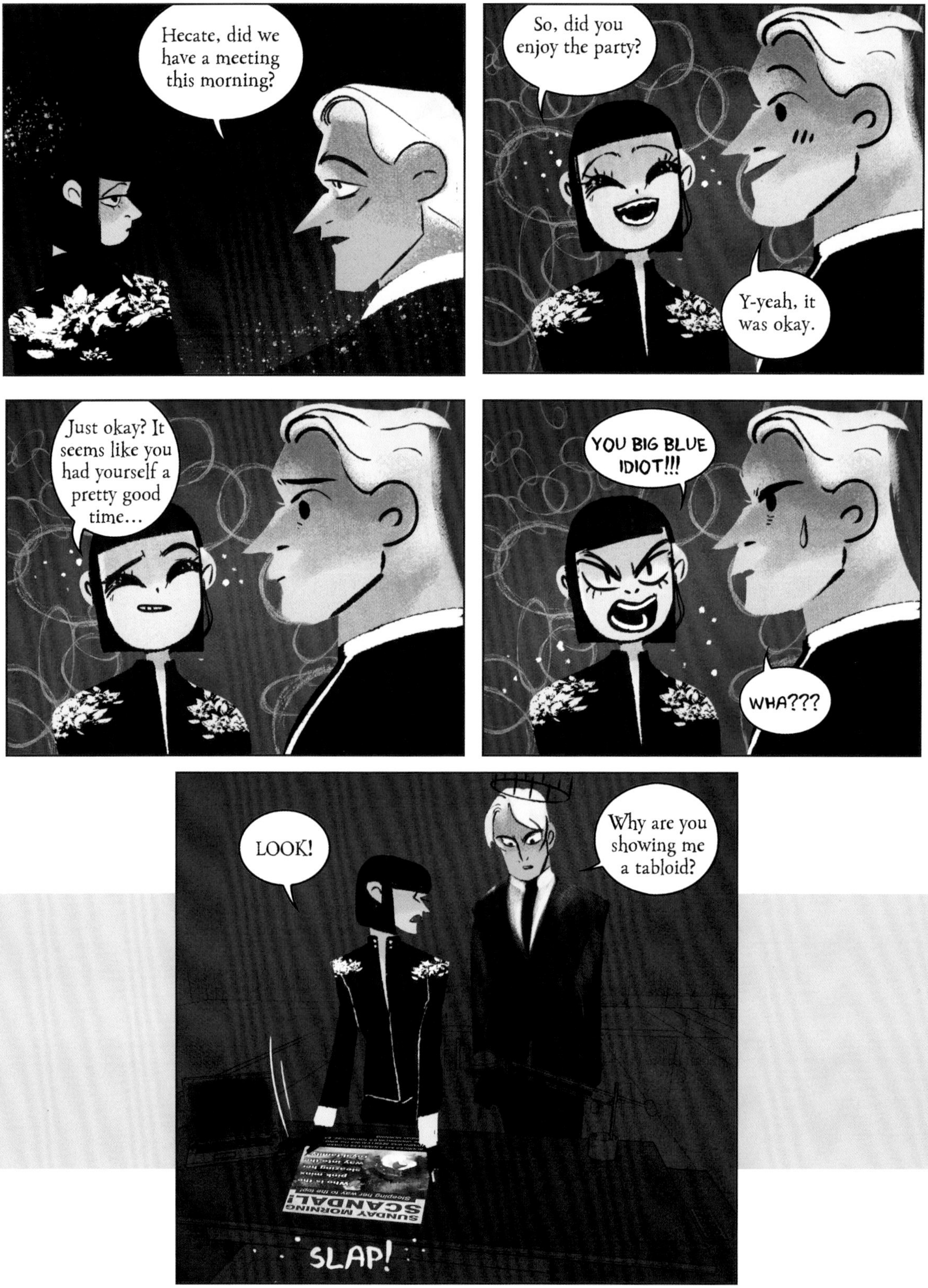
Hecate, did we have a meeting this morning?
So, did you enjoy the party?
Y-yeah, it was okay.
Just okay? It seems like you had yourself a pretty good time...
YOU BIG BLUE IDIOT!!!
WHA???
LOOK!
Why are you showing me a tabloid?
SUNDAY MORNING
SCANDAL!
Sleeping her way to the top!
SLAP!

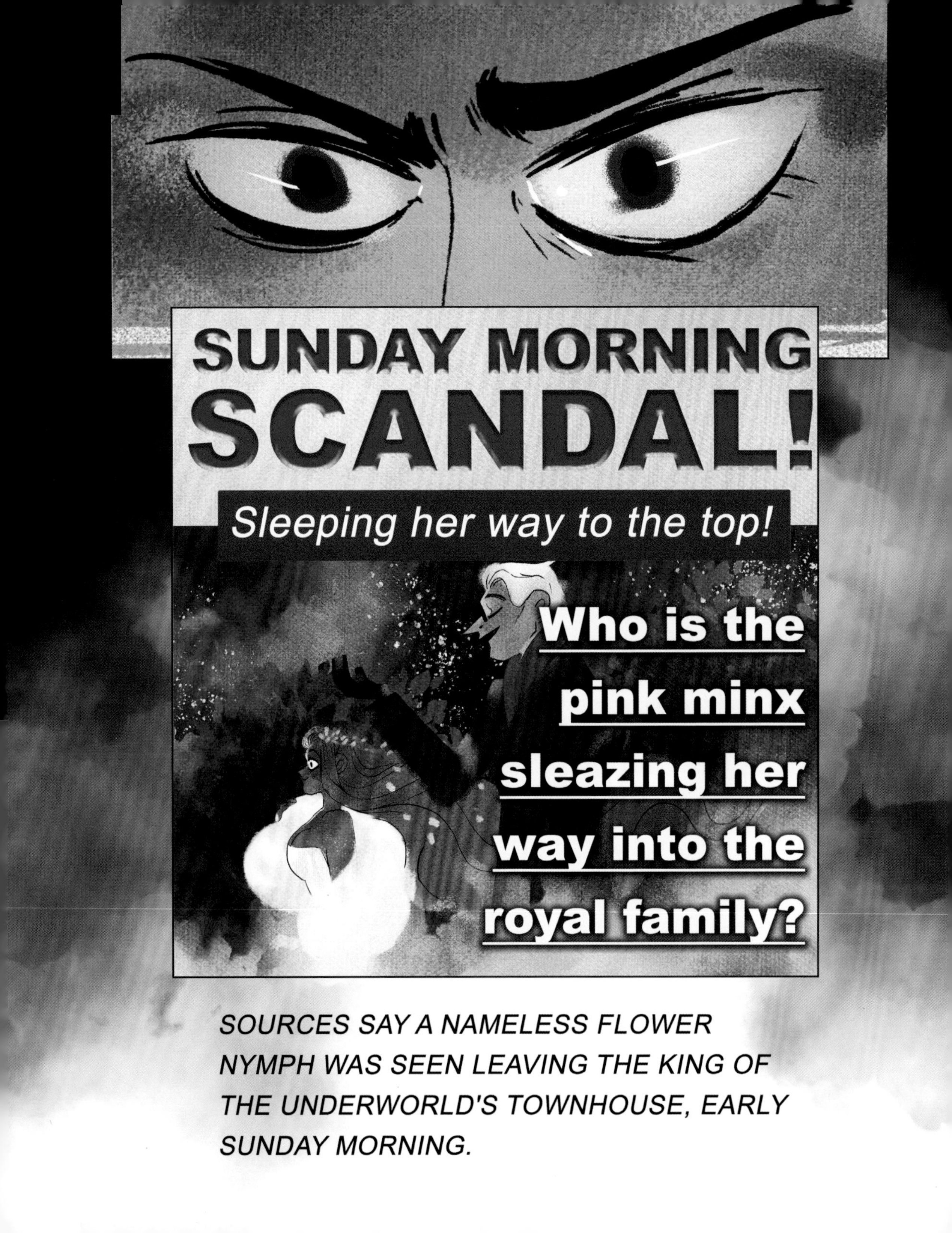
SUNDAY MORNING SCANDAL!
Sleeping her way to the top!
Who is the pink minx sleazing her way into the royal family?
SOURCES SAY A NAMELESS FLOWER NYMPH WAS SEEN LEAVING THE KING OF THE UNDERWORLD'S TOWNHOUSE, EARLY SUNDAY MORNING.

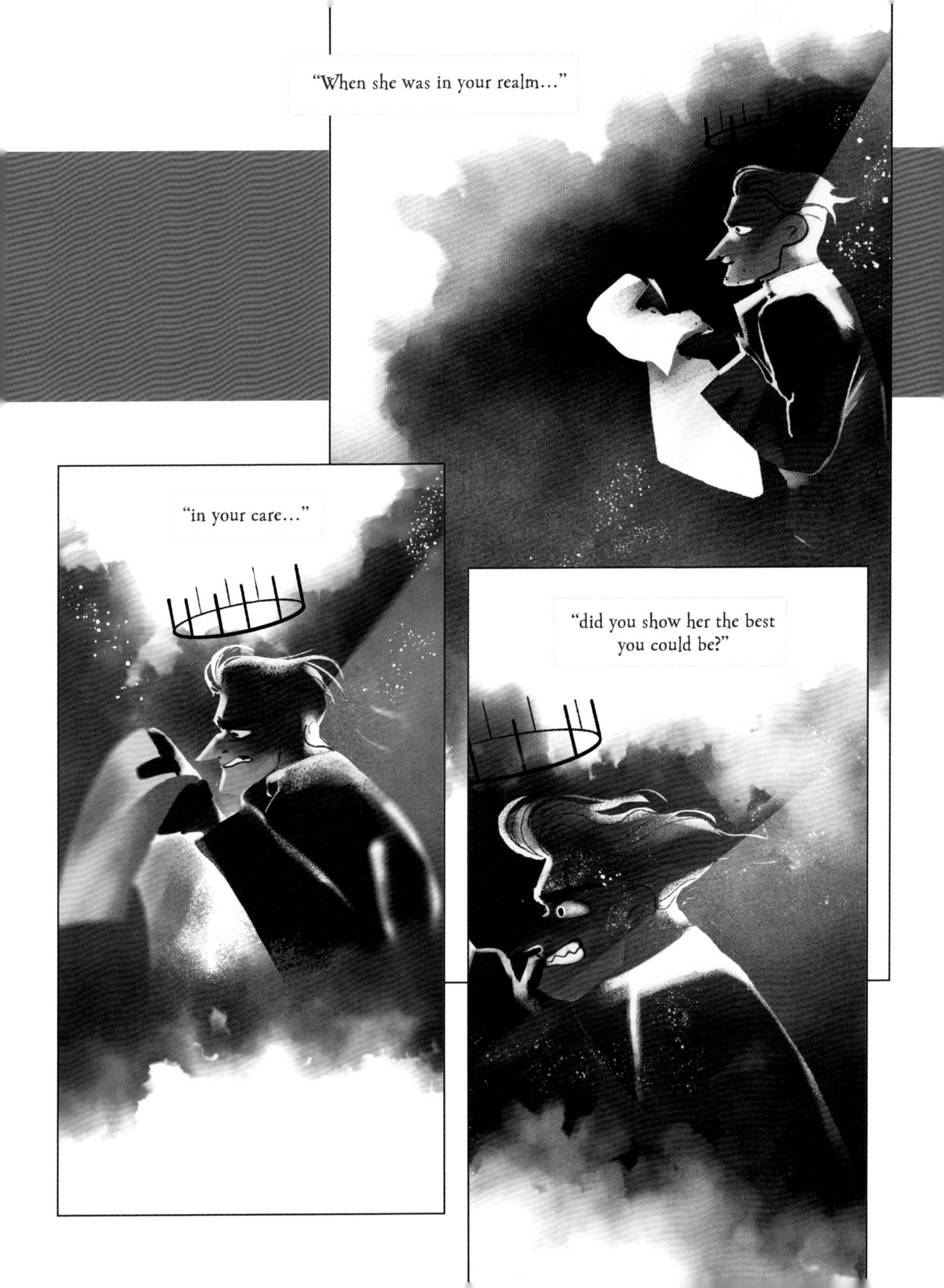
"When she was in your realm..."
"in your care..."
"did you show her the best you could be?"

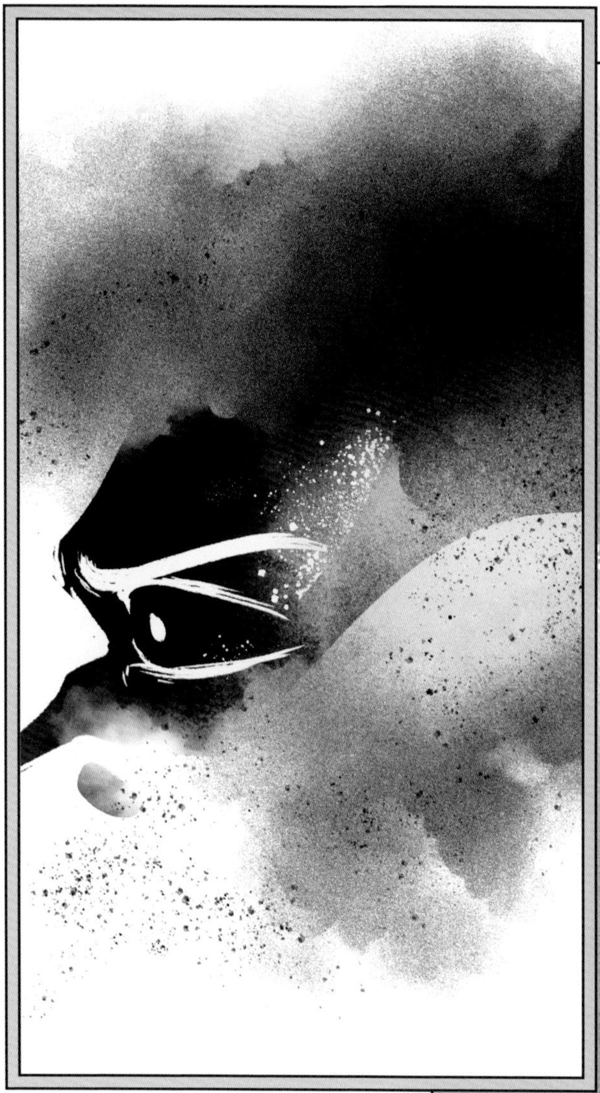
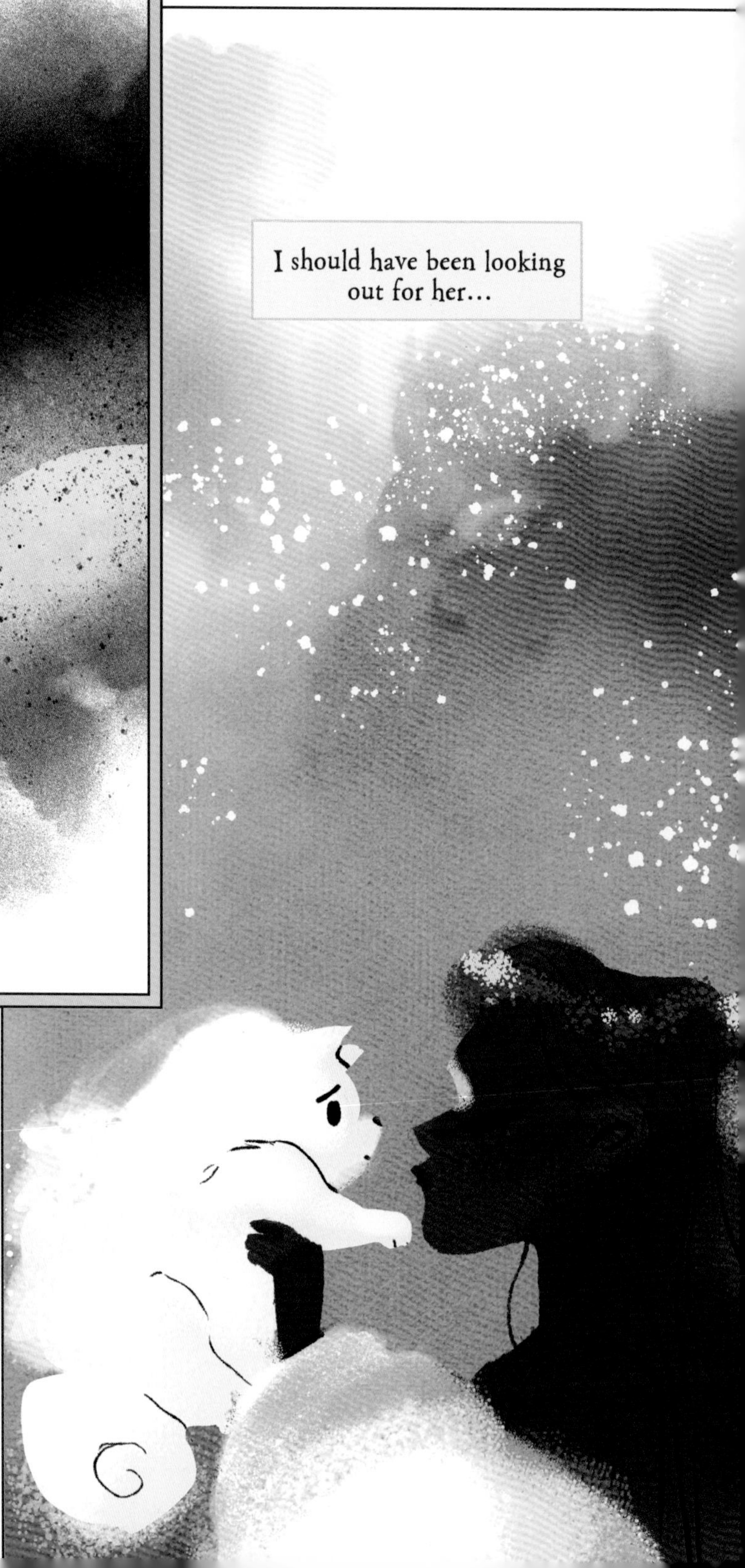
I should have been looking
out for her...

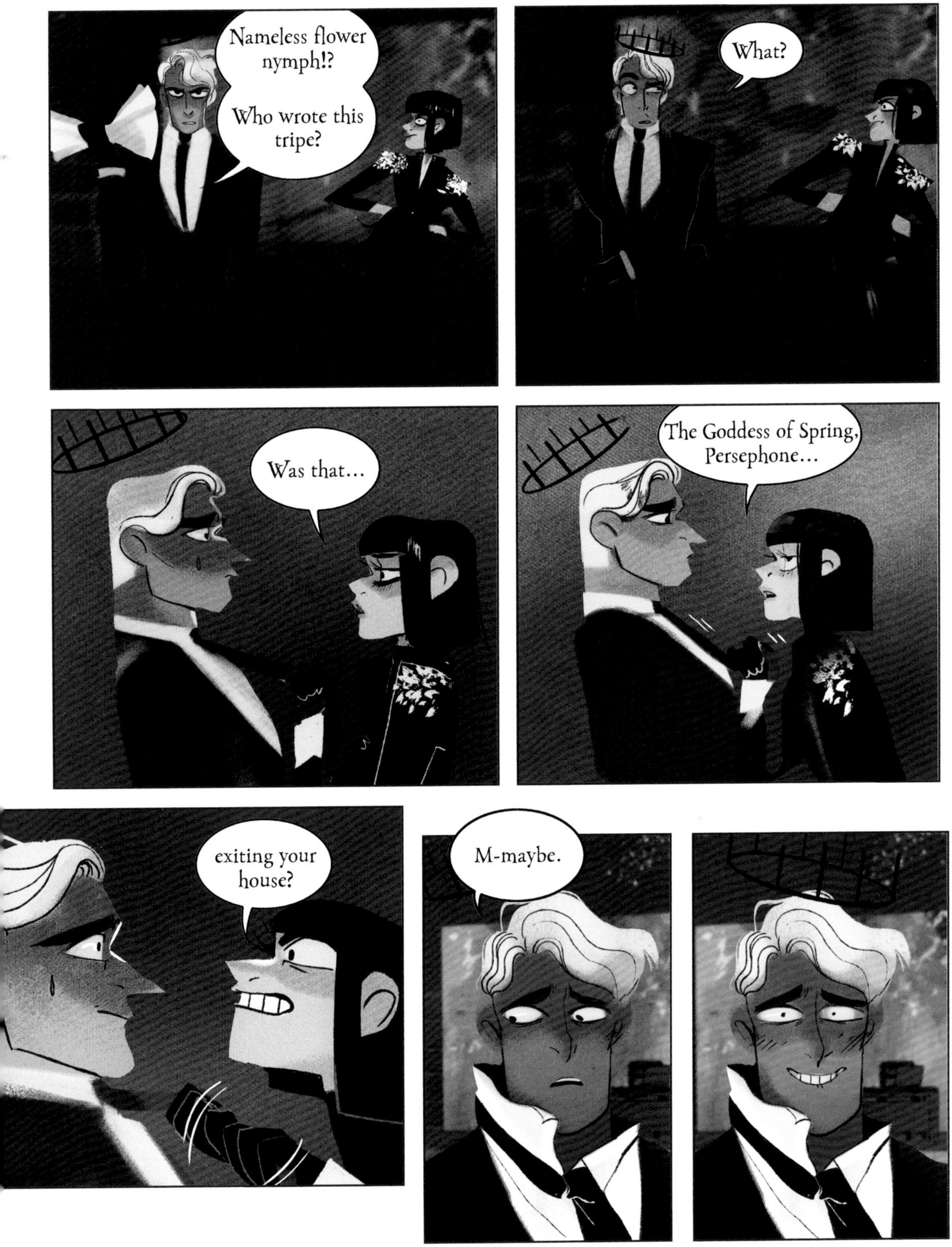

Nameless flower nymph!?
Who wrote this tripe?
What?
Was that...
The Goddess of Spring, Persephone...
exiting your house?
M-maybe.

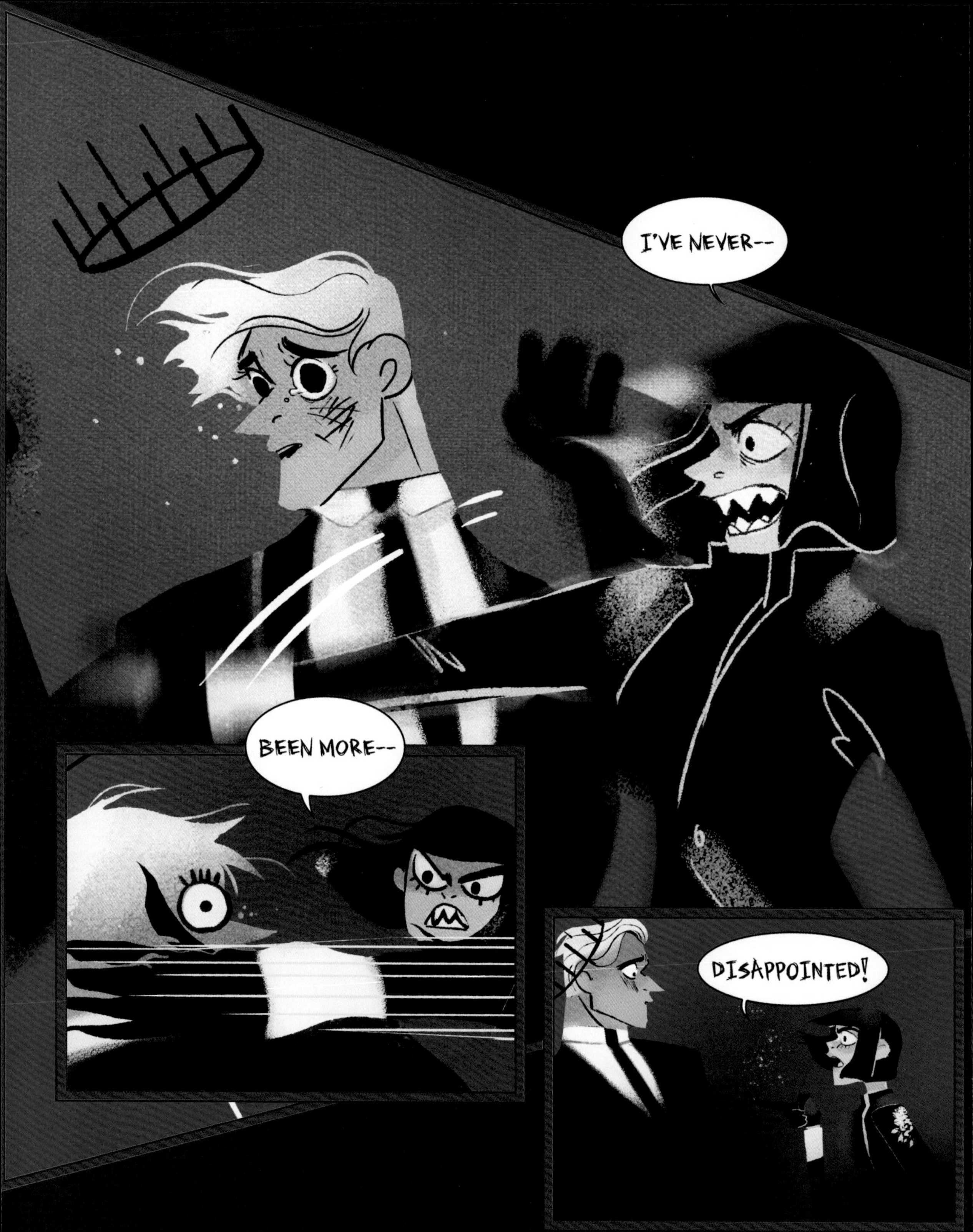
I'VE NEVER--
BEEN MORE--
DISAPPOINTED!

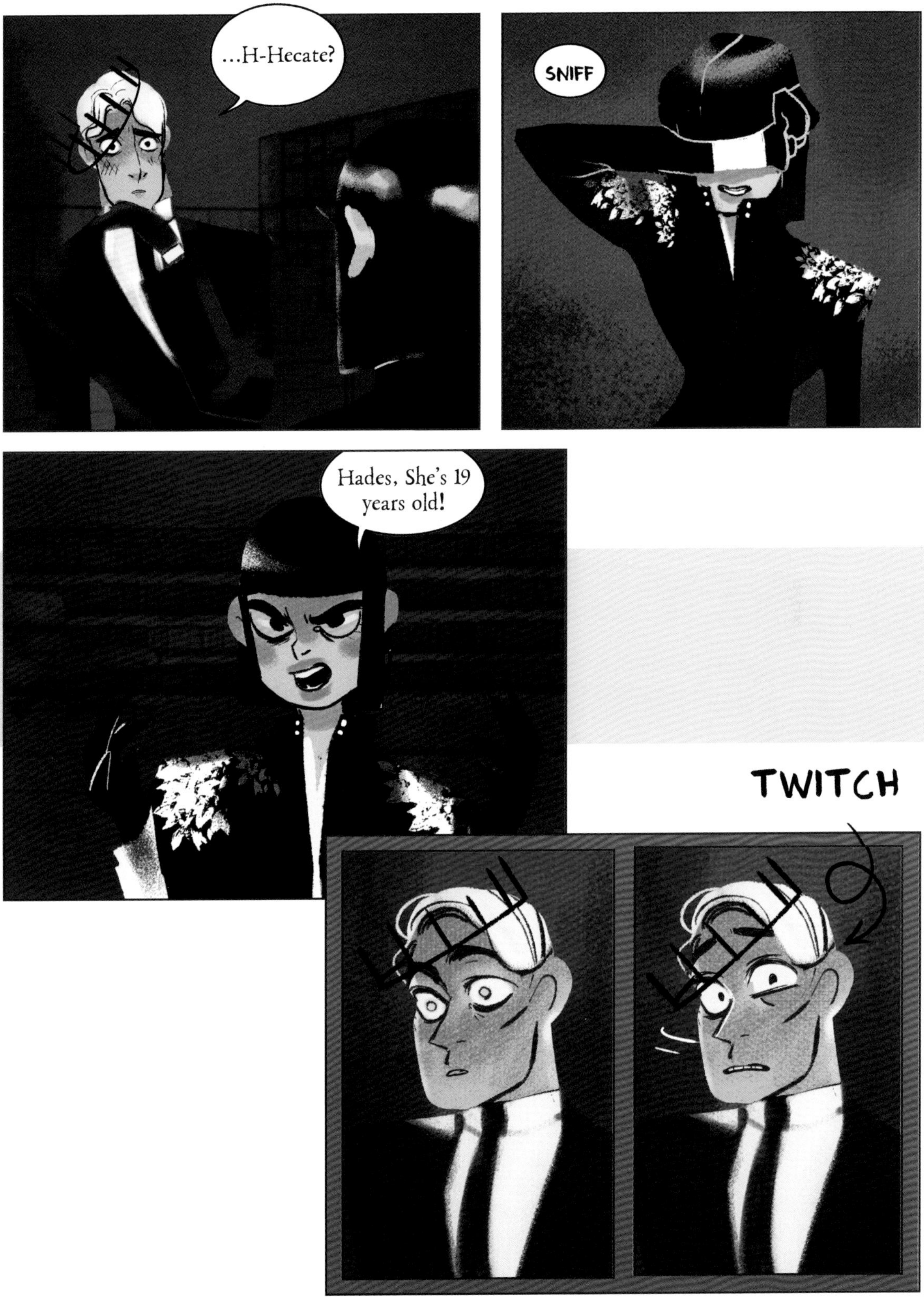
...H-Hecate?
SNIFF
Hades, She's 19 years old!
TWITCH

EPISODE 34: MIND THE GAP

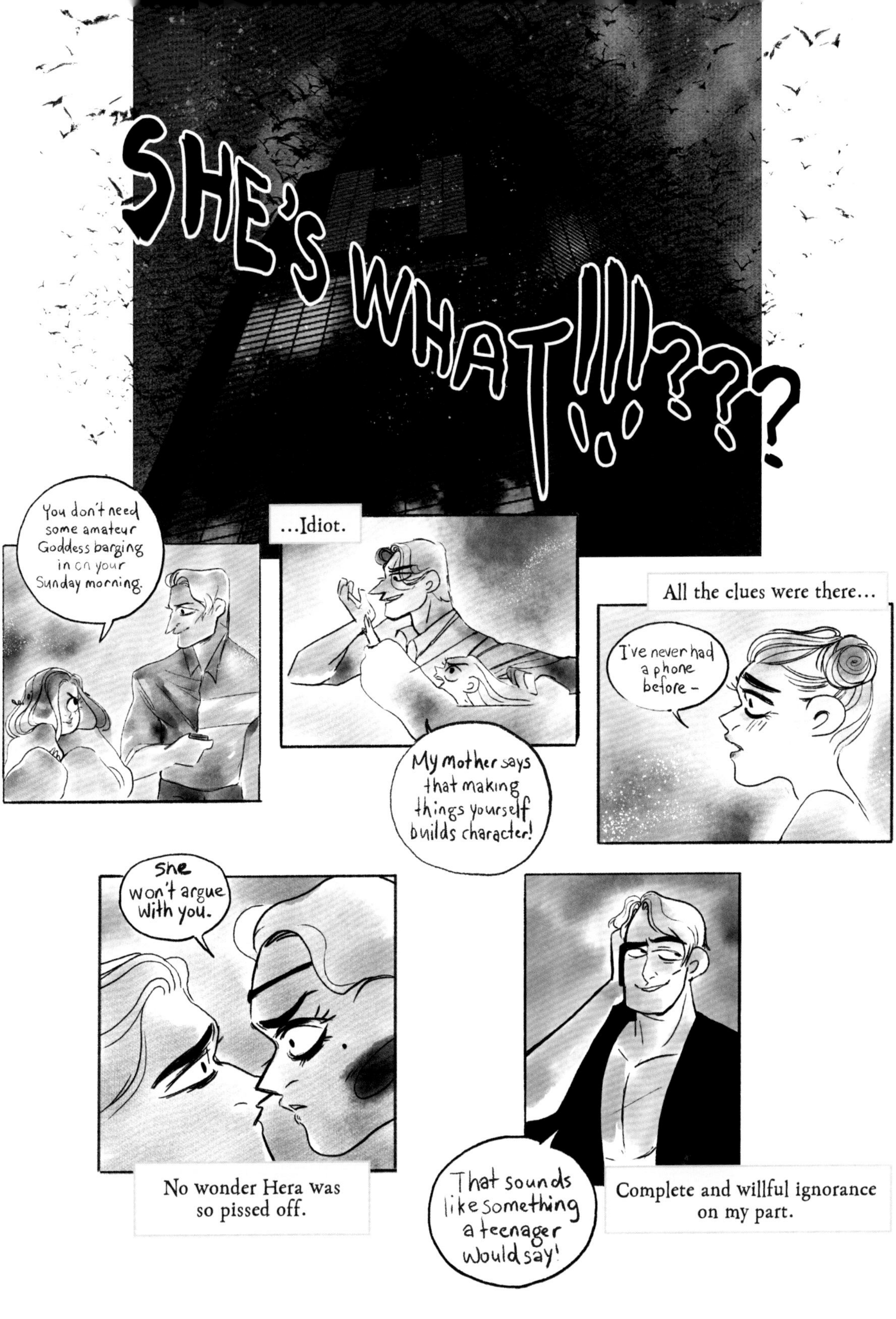
SHE'S WHAT!!!???
You don't need some amateur Goddess barging in on your Sunday morning.
...Idiot.
My mother says that making things yourself builds character!
All the clues were there...
I've never had a phone before -
She won't argue with you.
No wonder Hera was so pissed off.
That sounds like something a teenager would say!
Complete and willful ignorance on my part.

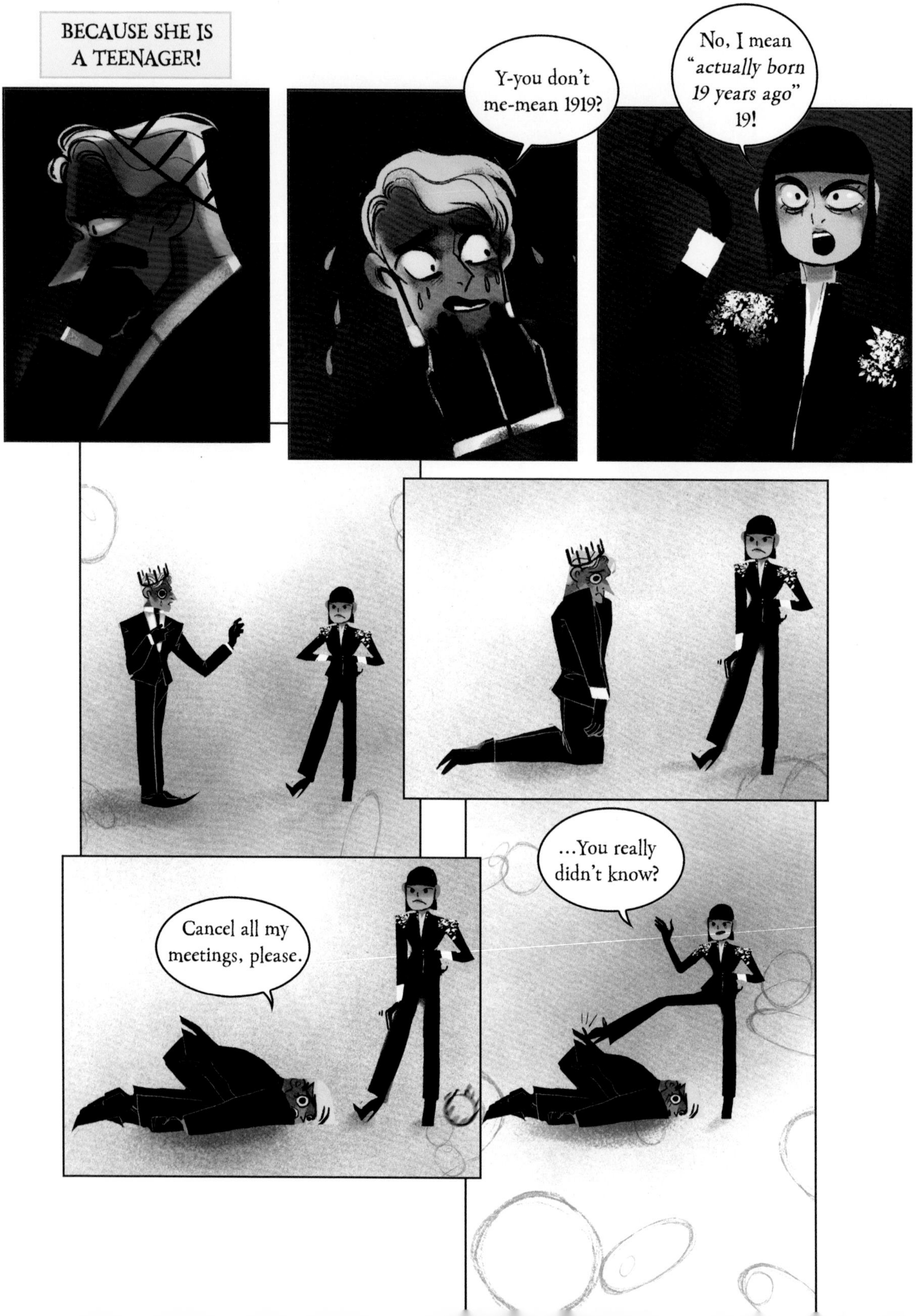
BECAUSE SHE IS A TEENAGER!
Y-you don't me-mean 1919?
No, I mean "*actually born 19 years ago*" 19!
Cancel all my meetings, please.
...You really didn't know?

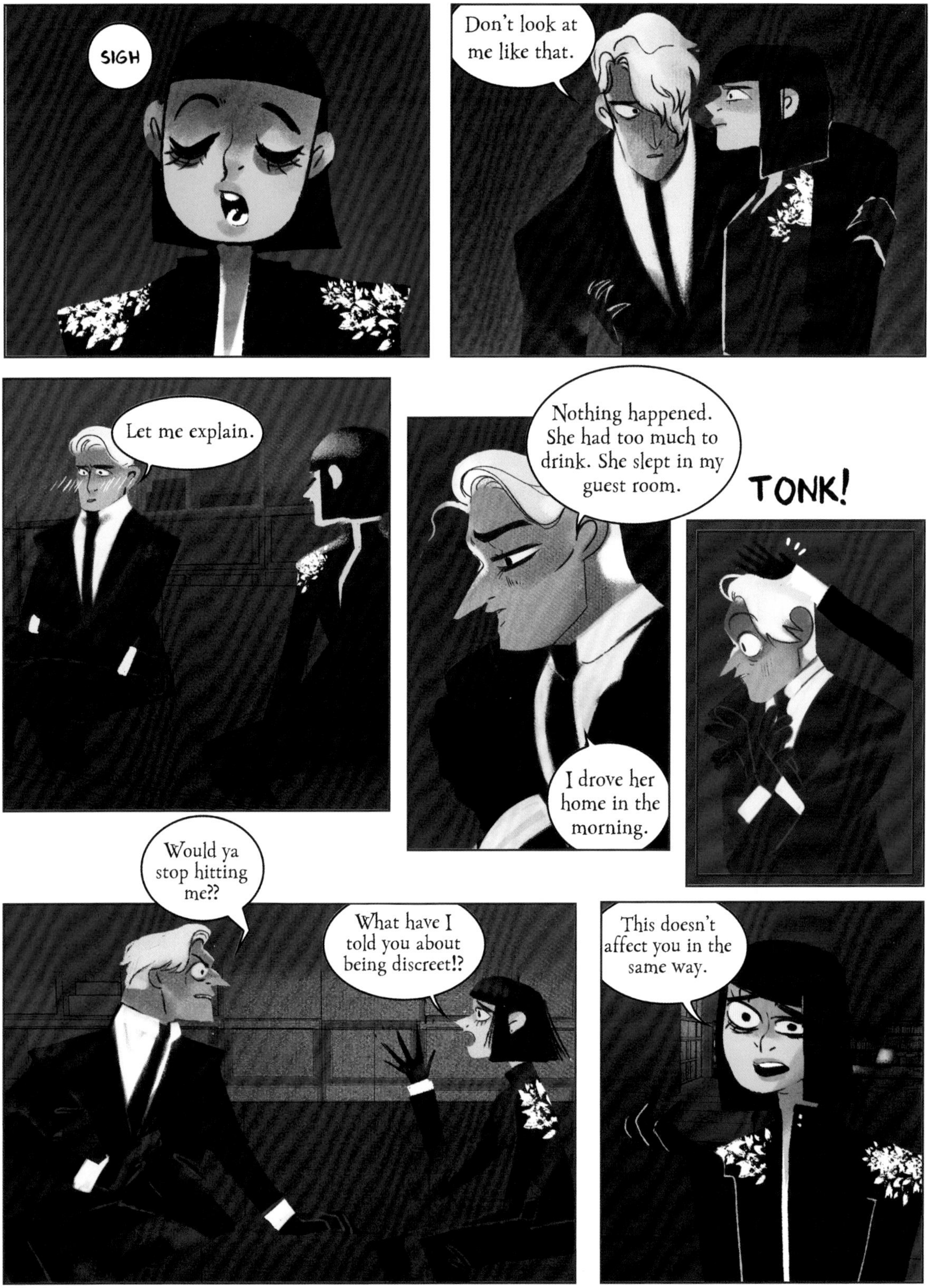
SIGH
Don't look at me like that.
Let me explain.
Nothing happened. She had too much to drink. She slept in my guest room.
I drove her home in the morning.
TONK!
Would ya stop hitting me??
What have I told you about being discreet!?
This doesn't affect you in the same way.

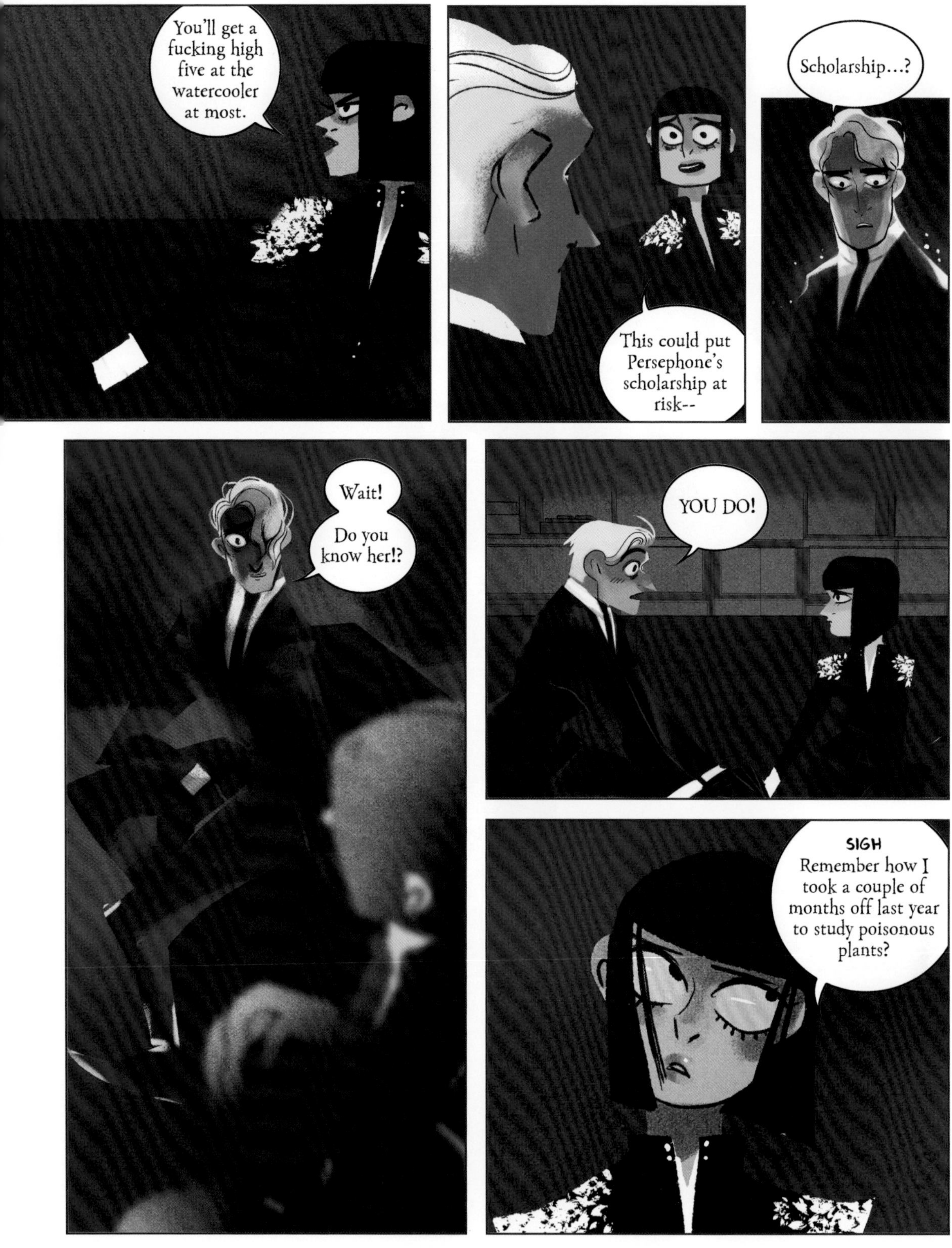

You'll get a fucking high five at the watercooler at most.
This could put Persephone's scholarship at risk--
Scholarship...?
Wait!
Do you know her!?
YOU DO!
SIGH
Remember how I took a couple of months off last year to study poisonous plants?

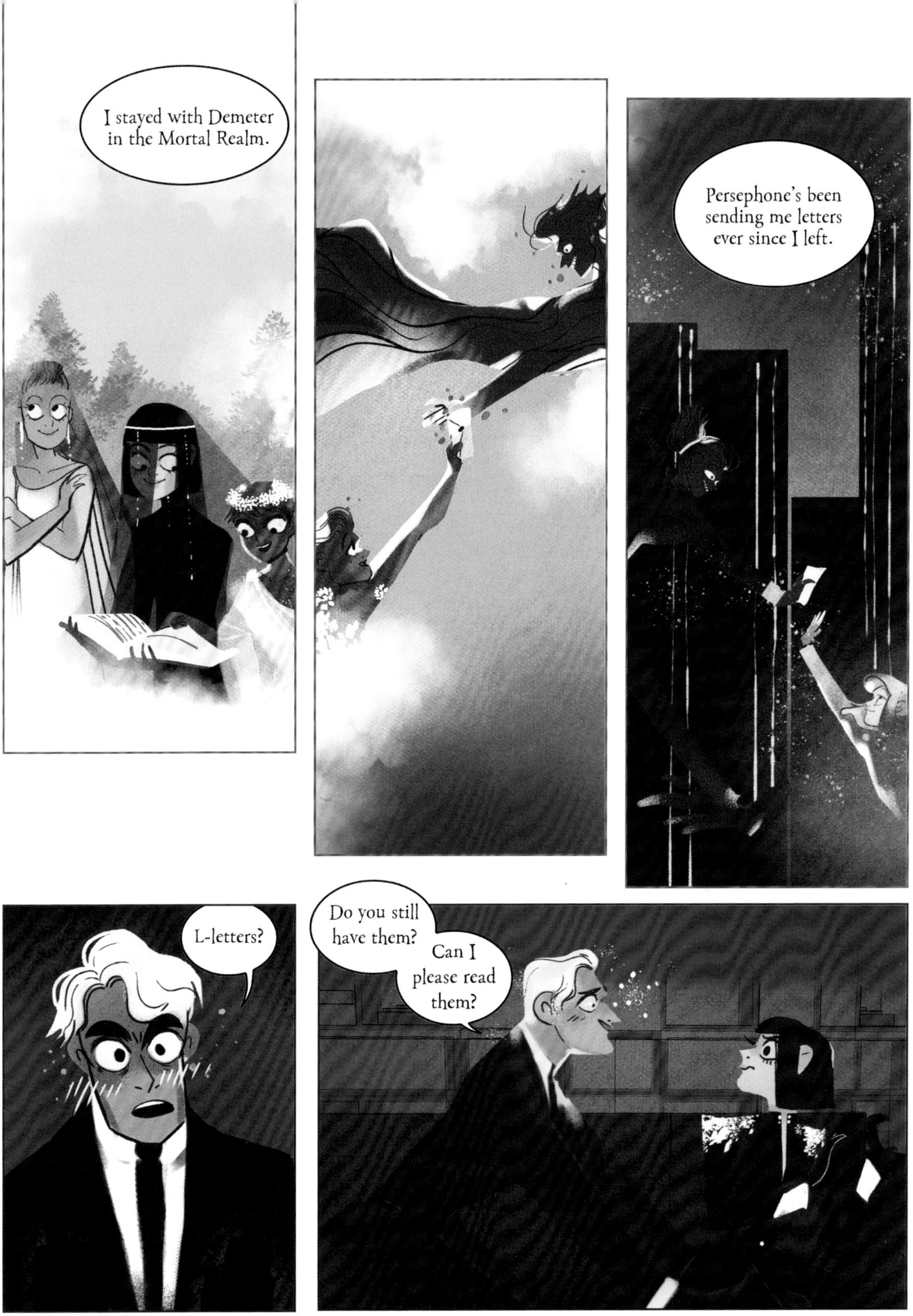
I stayed with Demeter in the Mortal Realm.
Persephone's been sending me letters ever since I left.
L-letters?
Do you still have them?
Can I please read them?

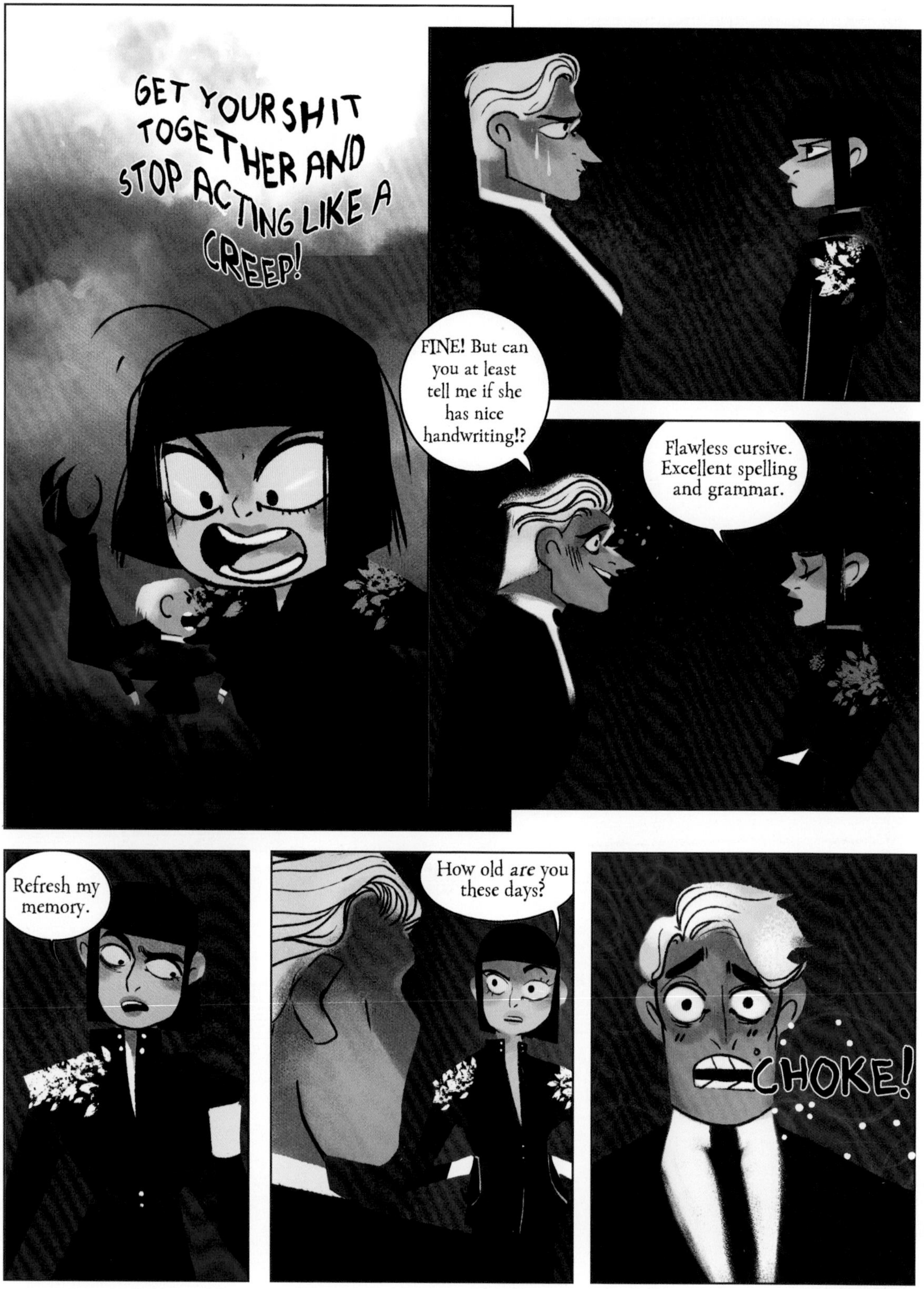
GET YOUR SHIT TOGETHER AND STOP ACTING LIKE A CREEP!
FINE! But can you at least tell me if she has nice handwriting!?
Flawless cursive. Excellent spelling and grammar.
Refresh my memory.
How old *are* you these days?
CHOKE!

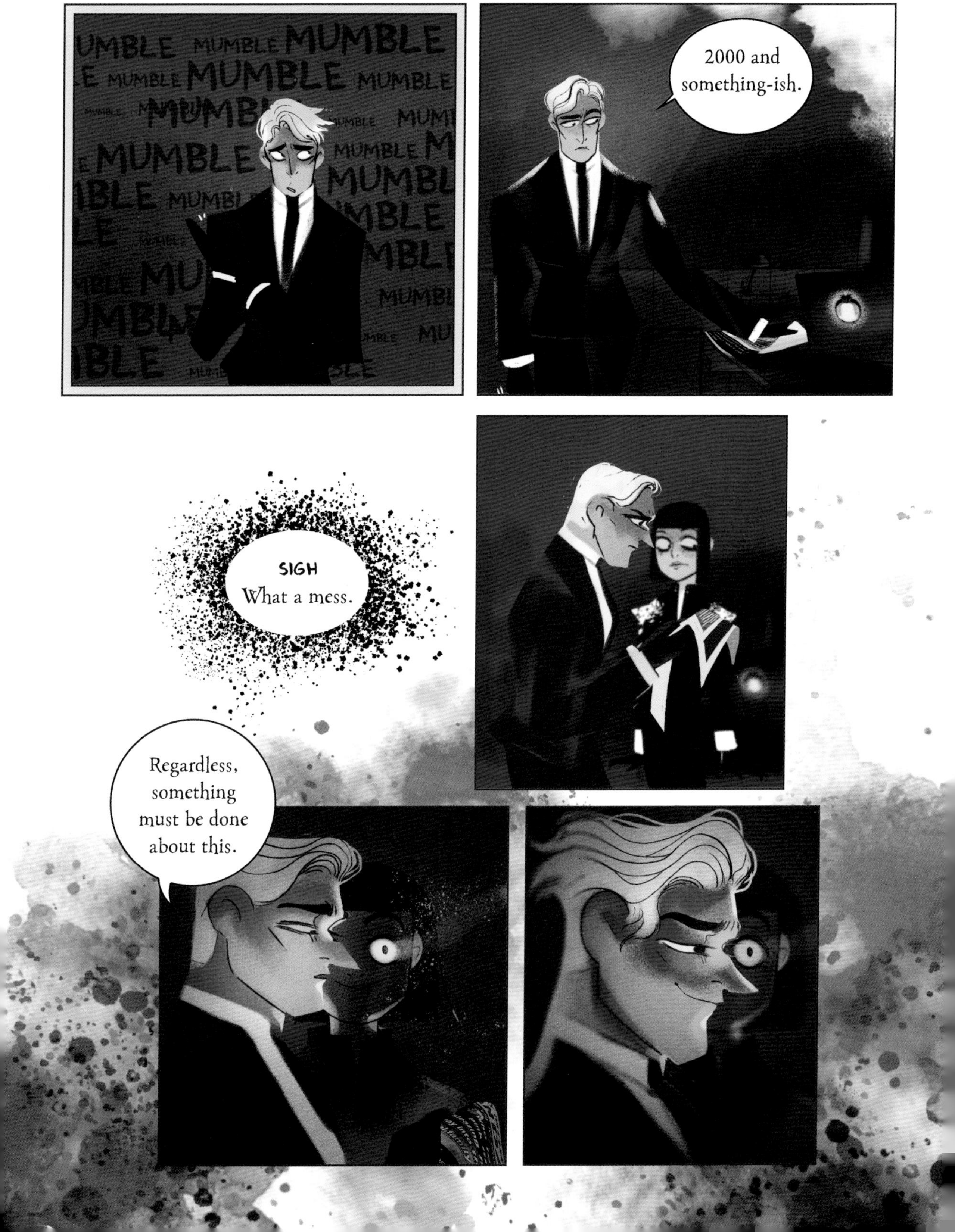
MUMBLE MUMBLE MUMBLE MUMBLE MUMBLE MUMBLE MUMBLE MUMBLE MUMBLE
2000 and something-ish.
SIGH
What a mess.
Regardless, something must be done about this.

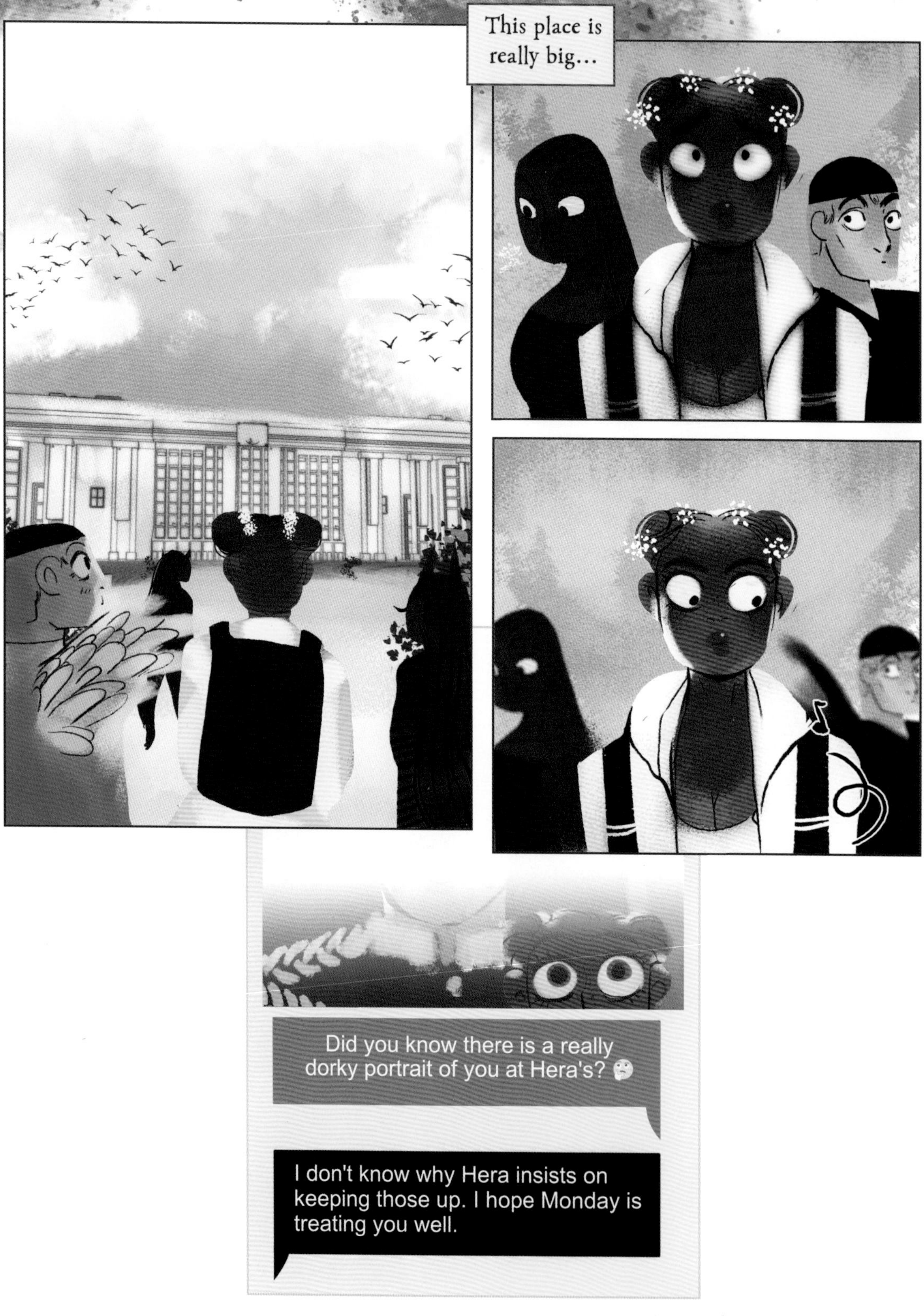
This place is really big...
Did you know there is a really dorky portrait of you at Hera's?
I don't know why Hera insists on keeping those up. I hope Monday is treating you well.

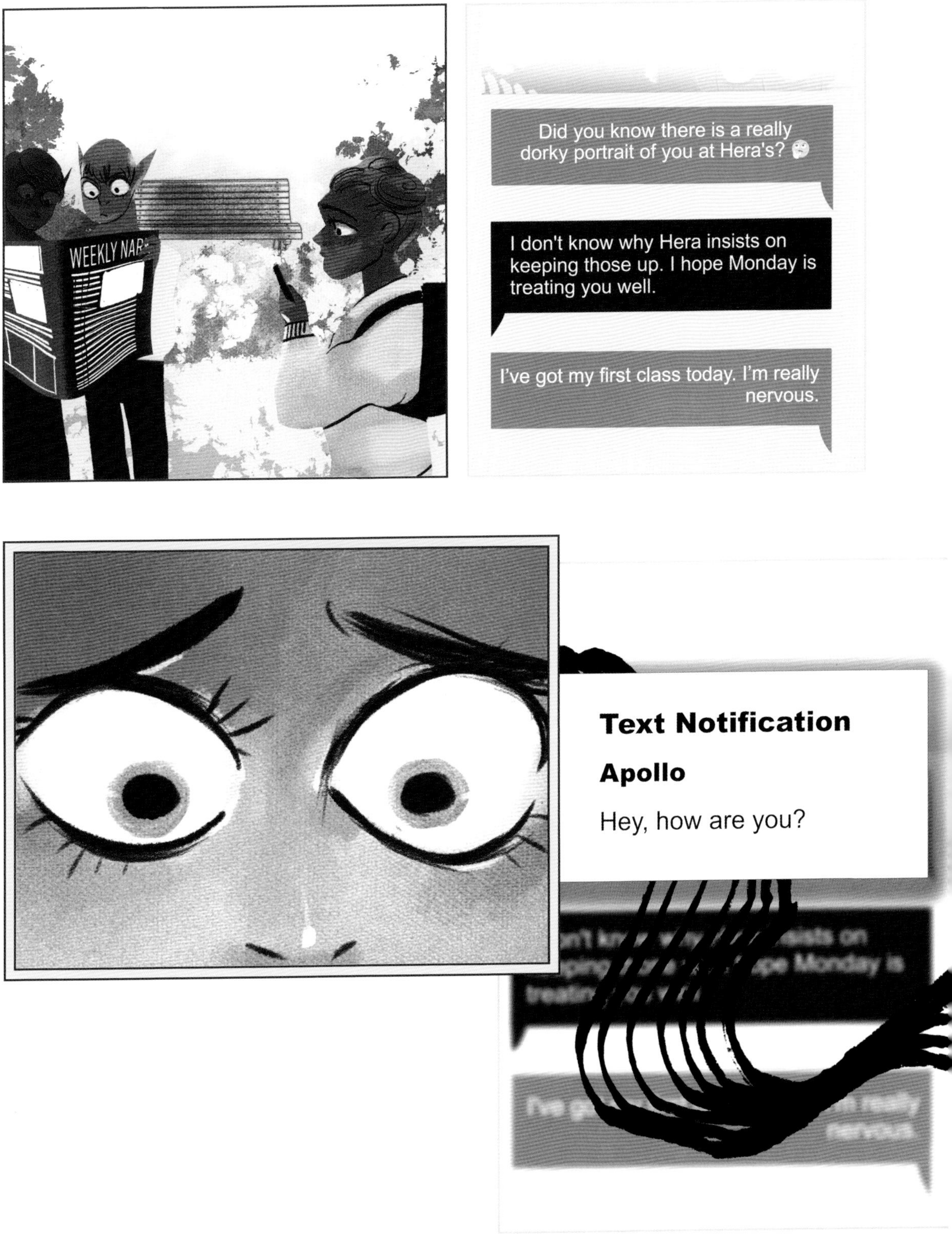
Did you know there is a really dorky portrait of you at Hera's?
I don't know why Hera insists on keeping those up. I hope Monday is treating you well.
I've got my first class today. I'm really nervous.
Text Notification
Apollo
Hey, how are you?

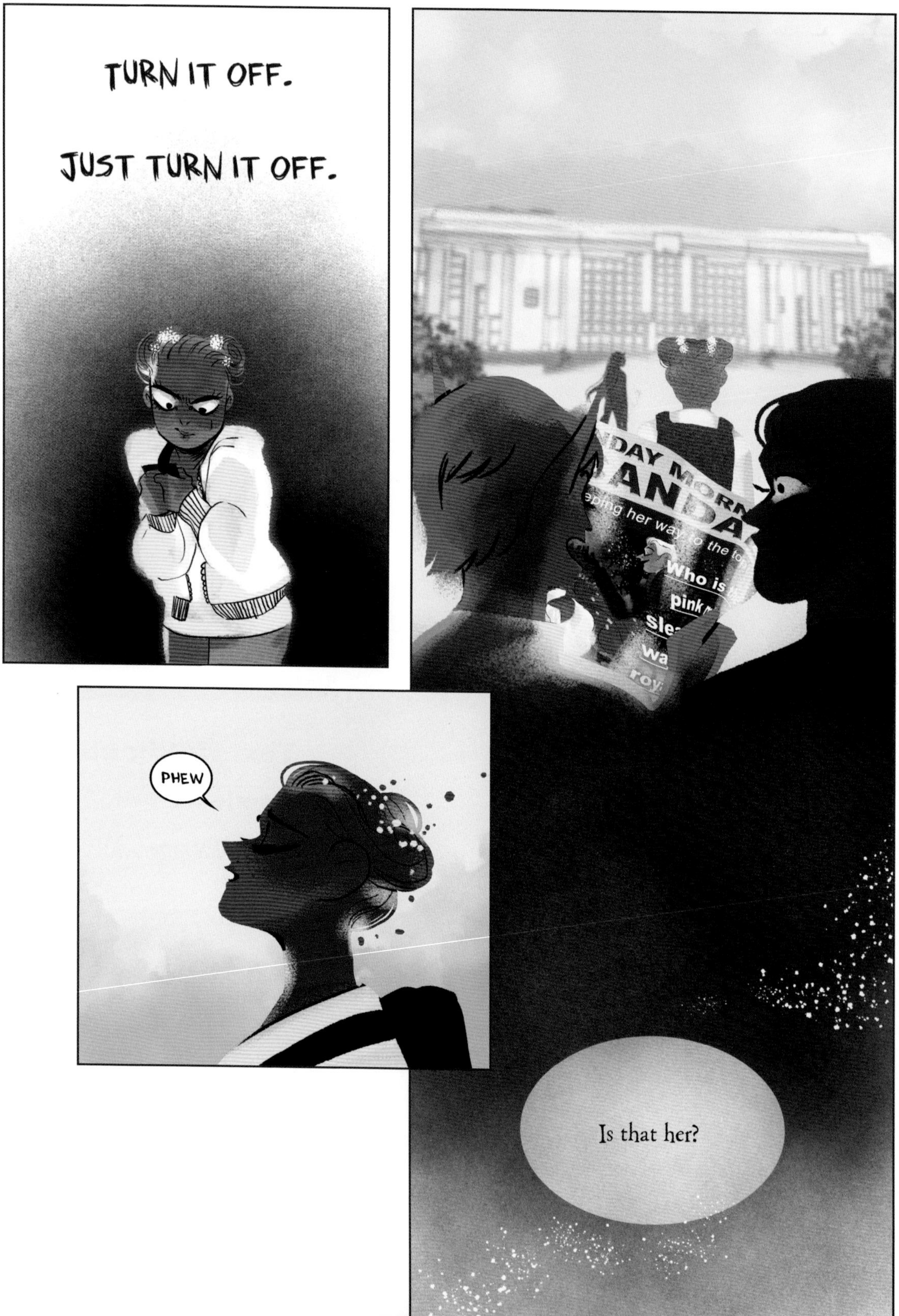
TURN IT OFF.
JUST TURN IT OFF.
PHEW
Is that her?

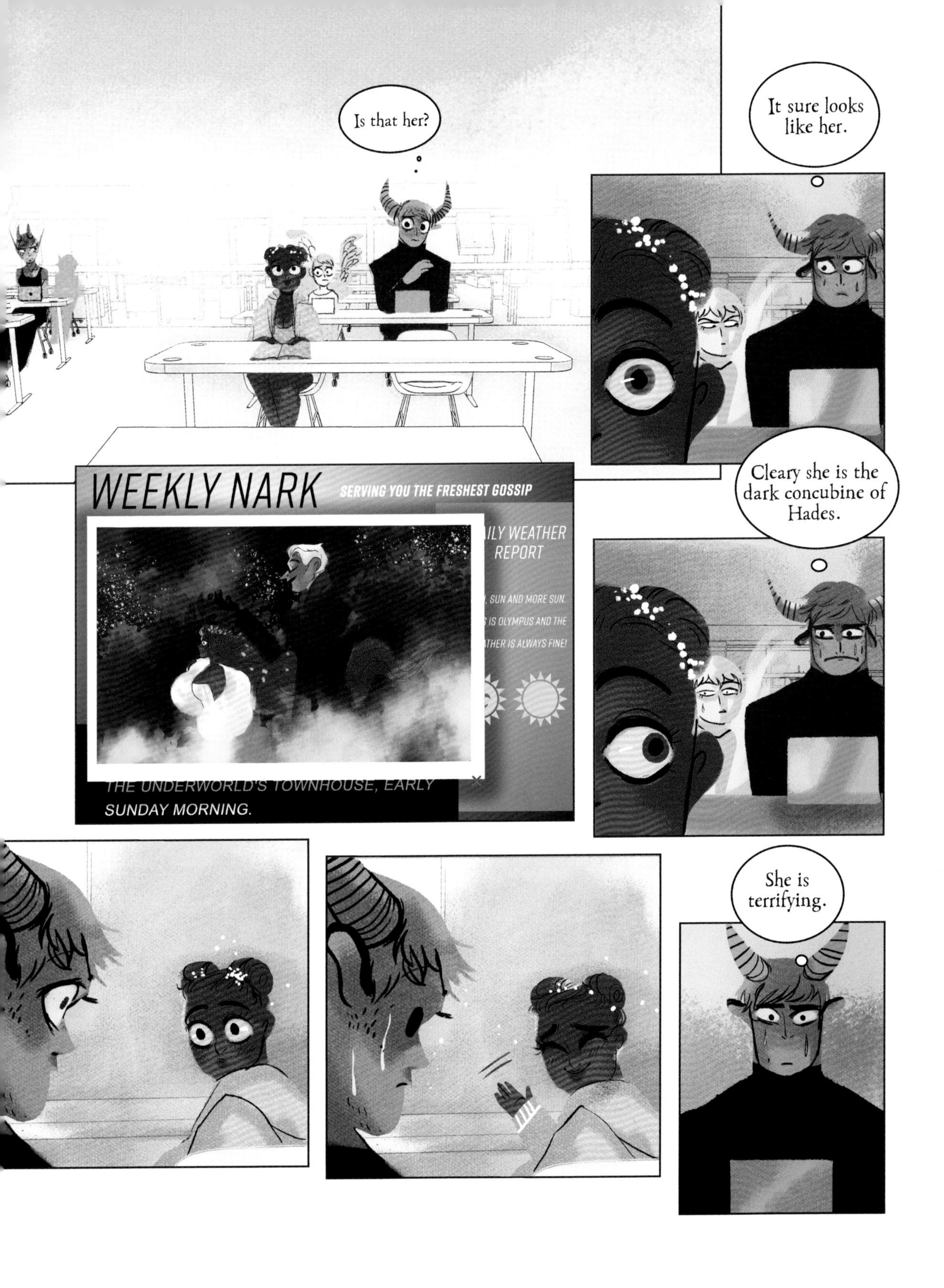
Is that her?
It sure looks like her.
WEEKLY NARK
SERVING YOU THE FRESHEST GOSSIP
REPORT
, SUN AND MORE SUN.
IS OLYMPUS AND THE
ATHER IS ALWAYS FINE!
THE UNDERWORLD'S TOWNHOUSE, EARLY SUNDAY MORNING.
Cleary she is the dark concubine of Hades.
She is terrifying.

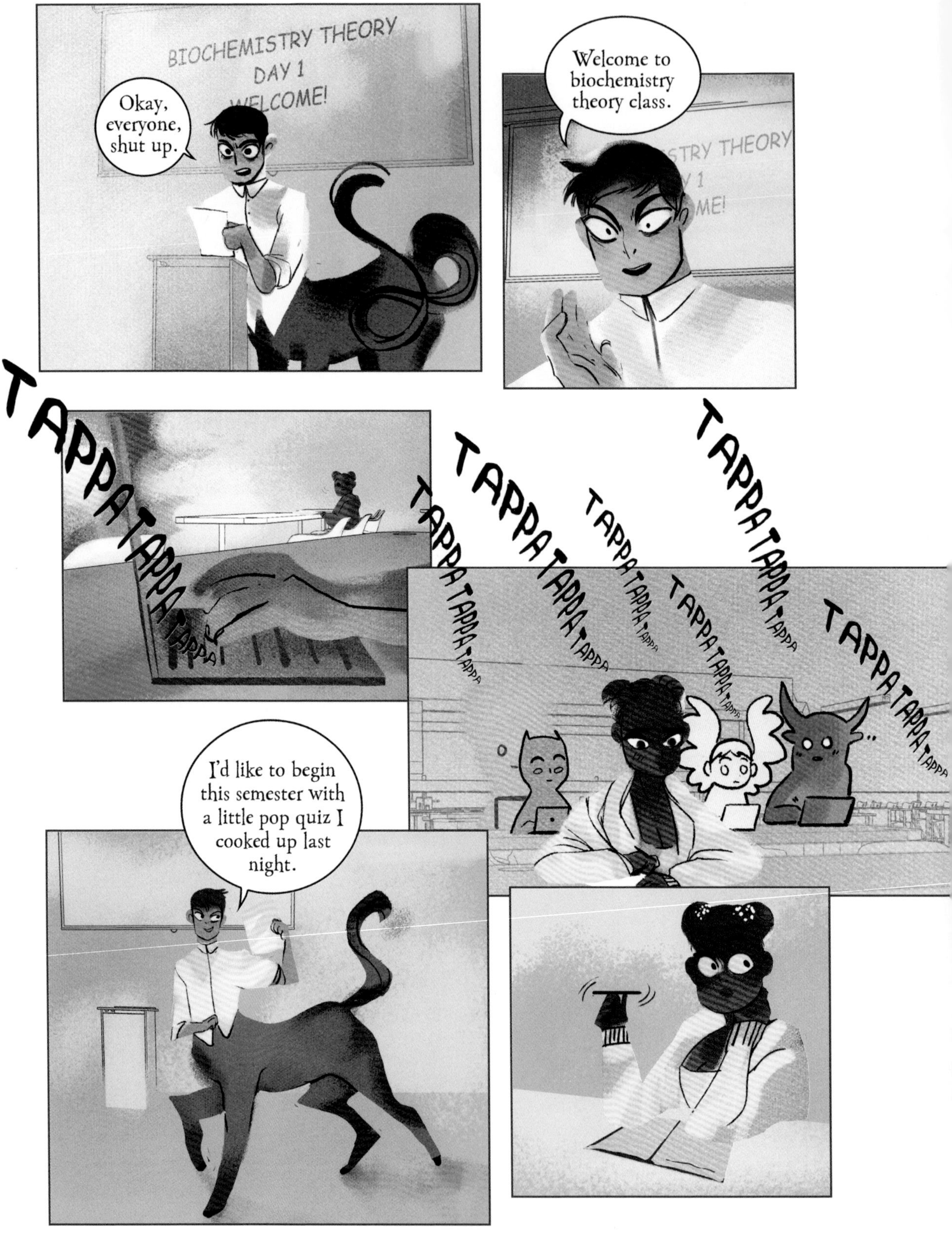
BIOCHEMISTRY THEORY
DAY 1
WELCOME!
Okay, everyone, shut up.
Welcome to biochemistry theory class.
TAPPATAPPATAPPATAPPA
TAPPATAPPATAPPA
TAPPATAPPATAPPA
TAPPATAPPATAPPA
TAPPATAPPATAPPA
TAPPATAPPATAPPA
TAPPATAPPATAPPA
I'd like to begin this semester with a little pop quiz I cooked up last night.

EPISODE 35: THE MEAL TICKET

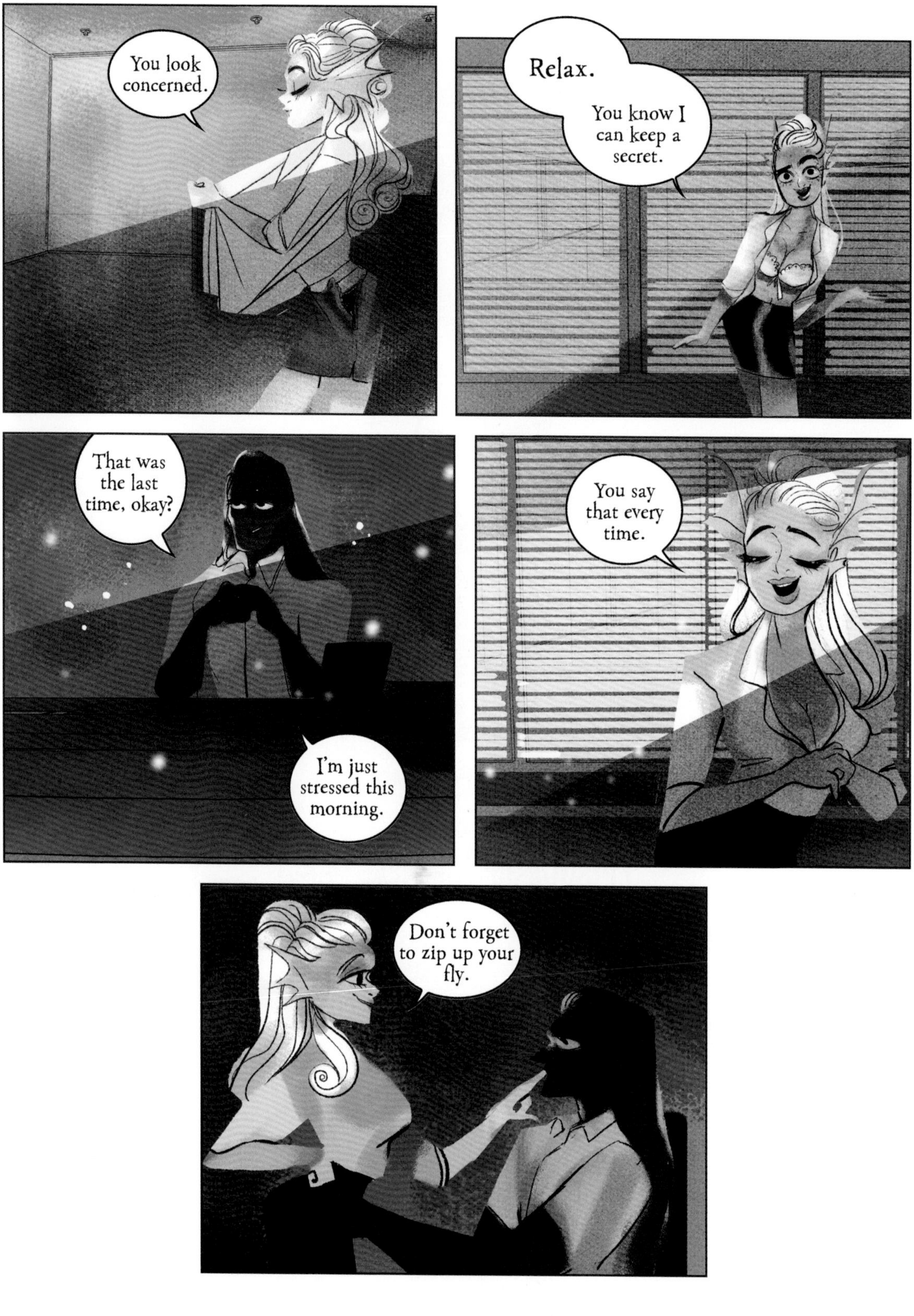
You look concerned.
Relax.
You know I can keep a secret.
That was the last time, okay?
I'm just stressed this morning.
You say that every time.
Don't forget to zip up your fly.

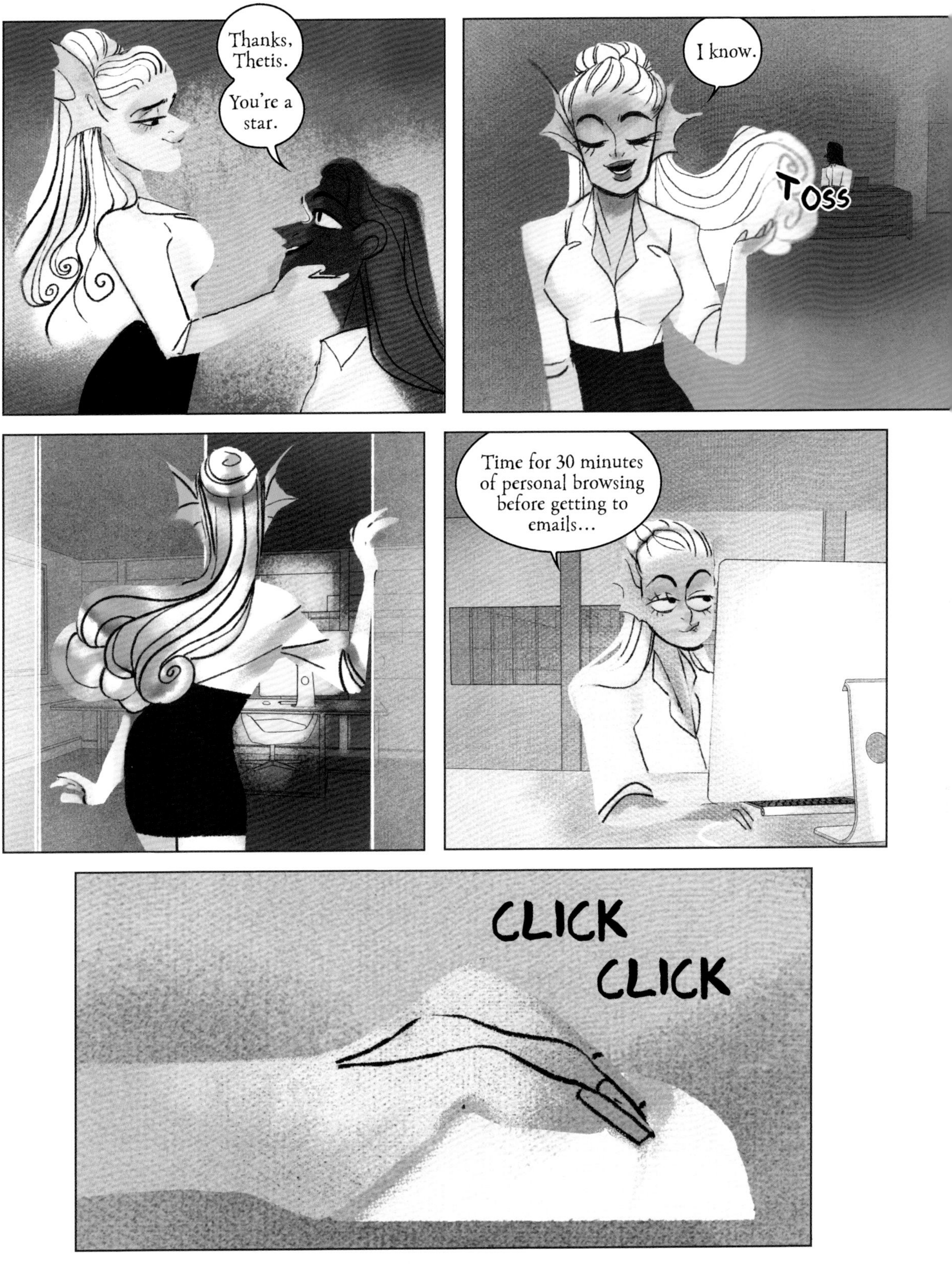
Thanks, Thetis.
You're a star.
I know.
TOSS
Time for 30 minutes of personal browsing before getting to emails...
CLICK
CLICK

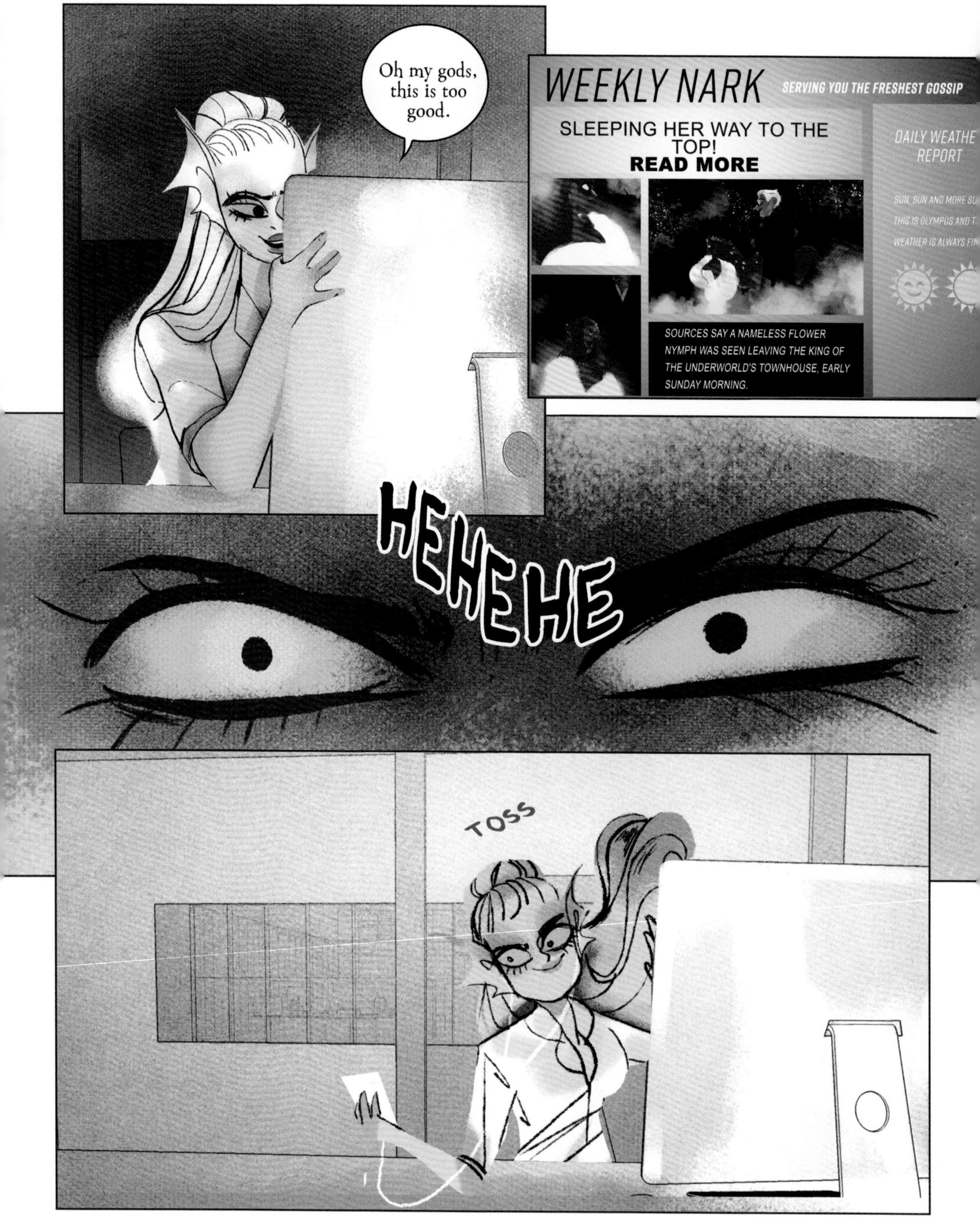
Oh my gods, this is too good.
WEEKLY NARK
SERVING YOU THE FRESHEST GOSSIP
SLEEPING HER WAY TO THE TOP!
READ MORE
DAILY WEATHE
REPORT
SOURCES SAY A NAMELESS FLOWER NYMPH WAS SEEN LEAVING THE KING OF THE UNDERWORLD'S TOWNHOUSE, EARLY SUNDAY MORNING.
HEHEHEHE
TOSS

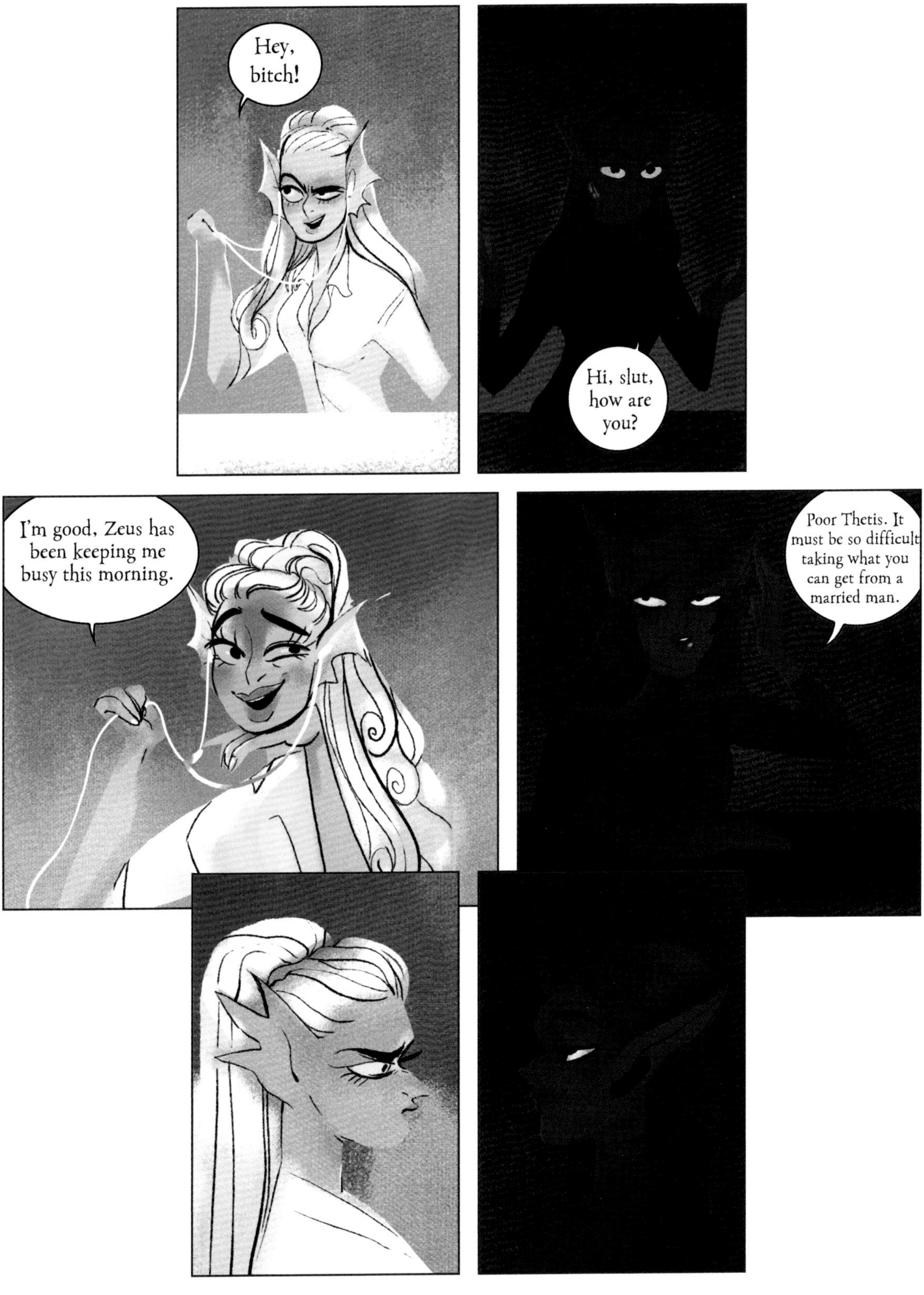
Hey, bitch!
Hi, slut, how are you?
I'm good, Zeus has been keeping me busy this morning.
Poor Thetis. It must be so difficult taking what you can get from a married man.

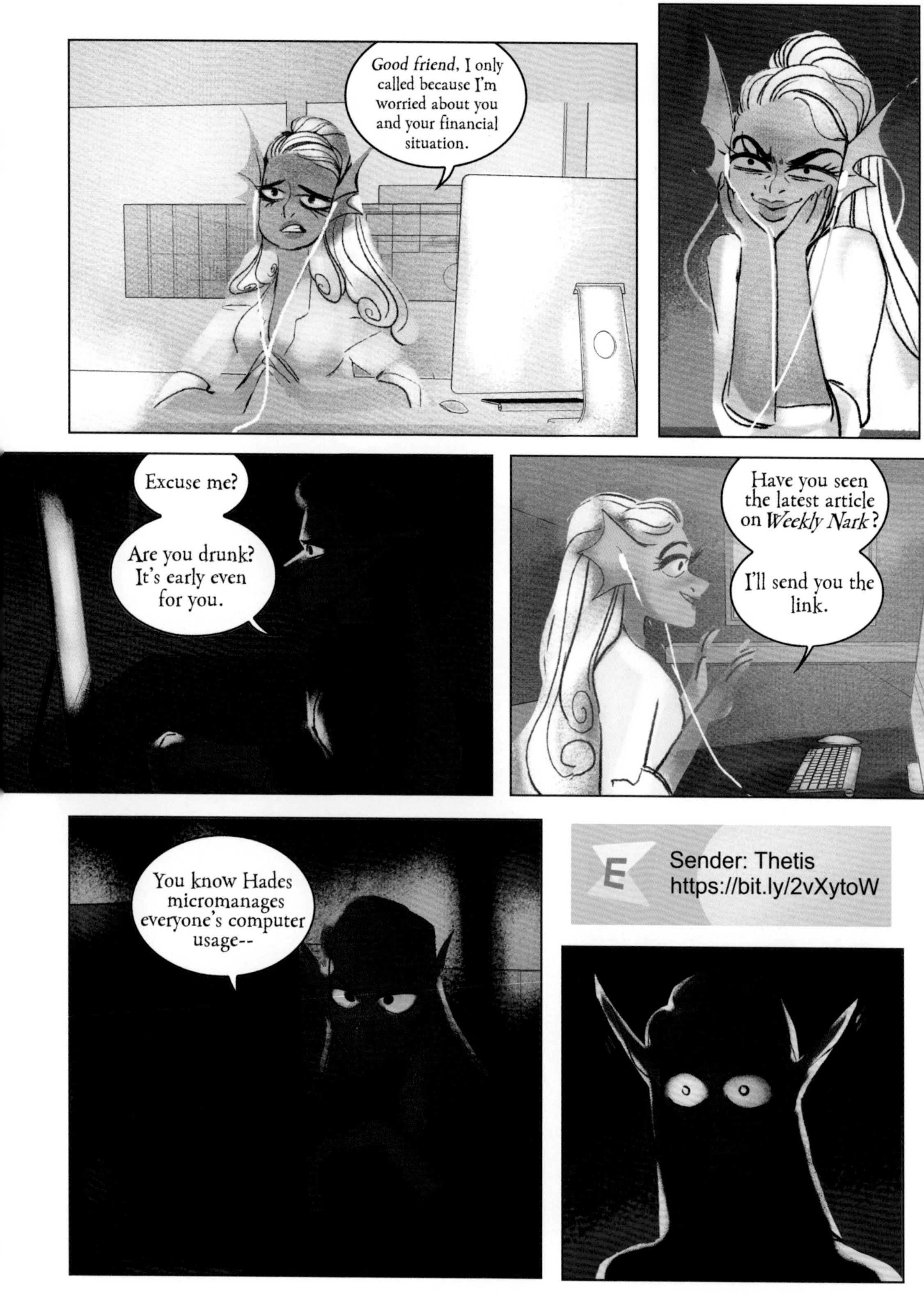
Good friend, I only called because I'm worried about you and your financial situation.
Excuse me?
Are you drunk? It's early even for you.
Have you seen the latest article on Weekly Nark?
I'll send you the link.
You know Hades micromanages everyone's computer usage--
E
Sender: Thetis
https://bit.ly/2vXytoW

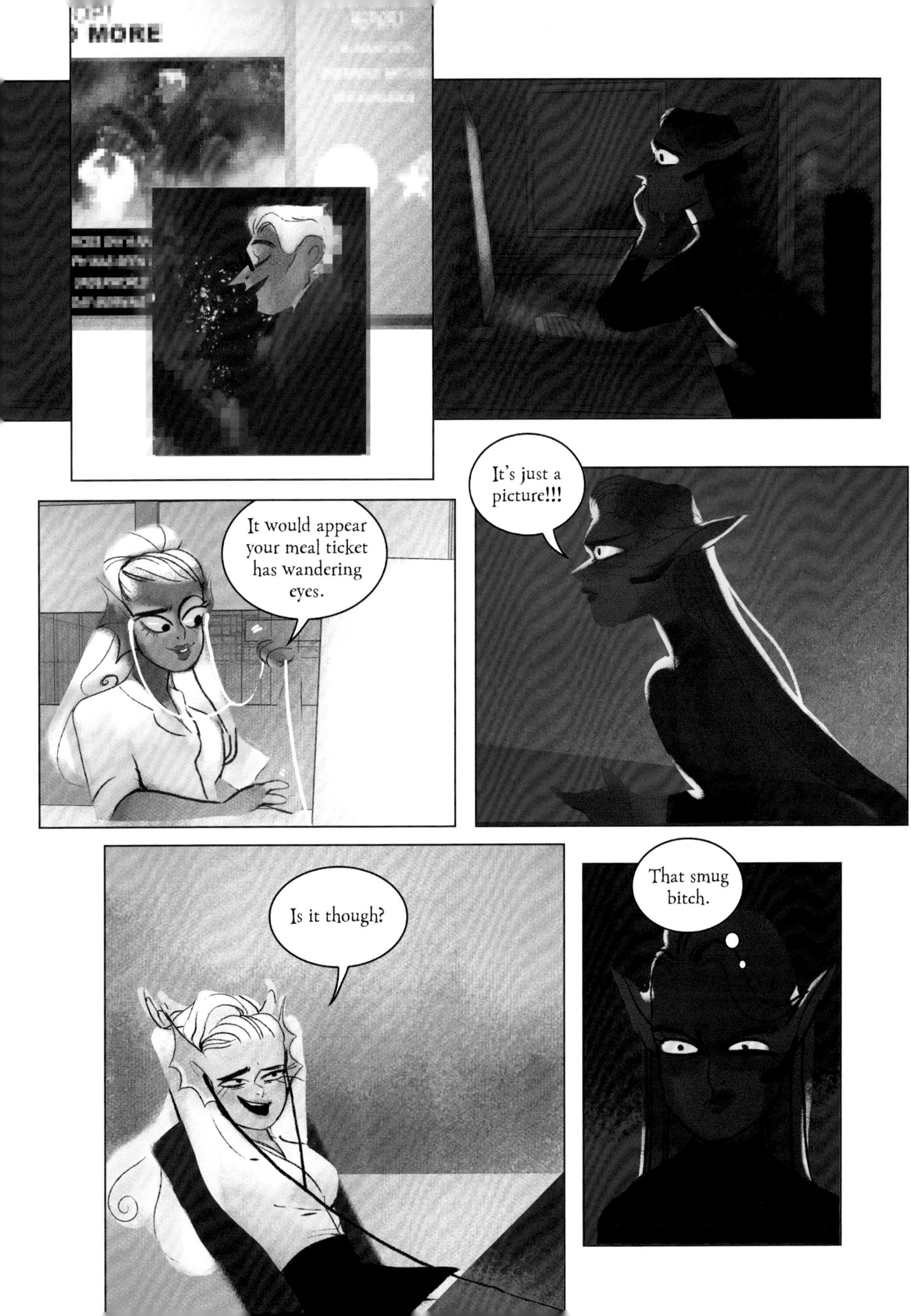
MORE
It would appear your meal ticket has wandering eyes.
It's just a picture!!!
Is it though?
That smug bitch.

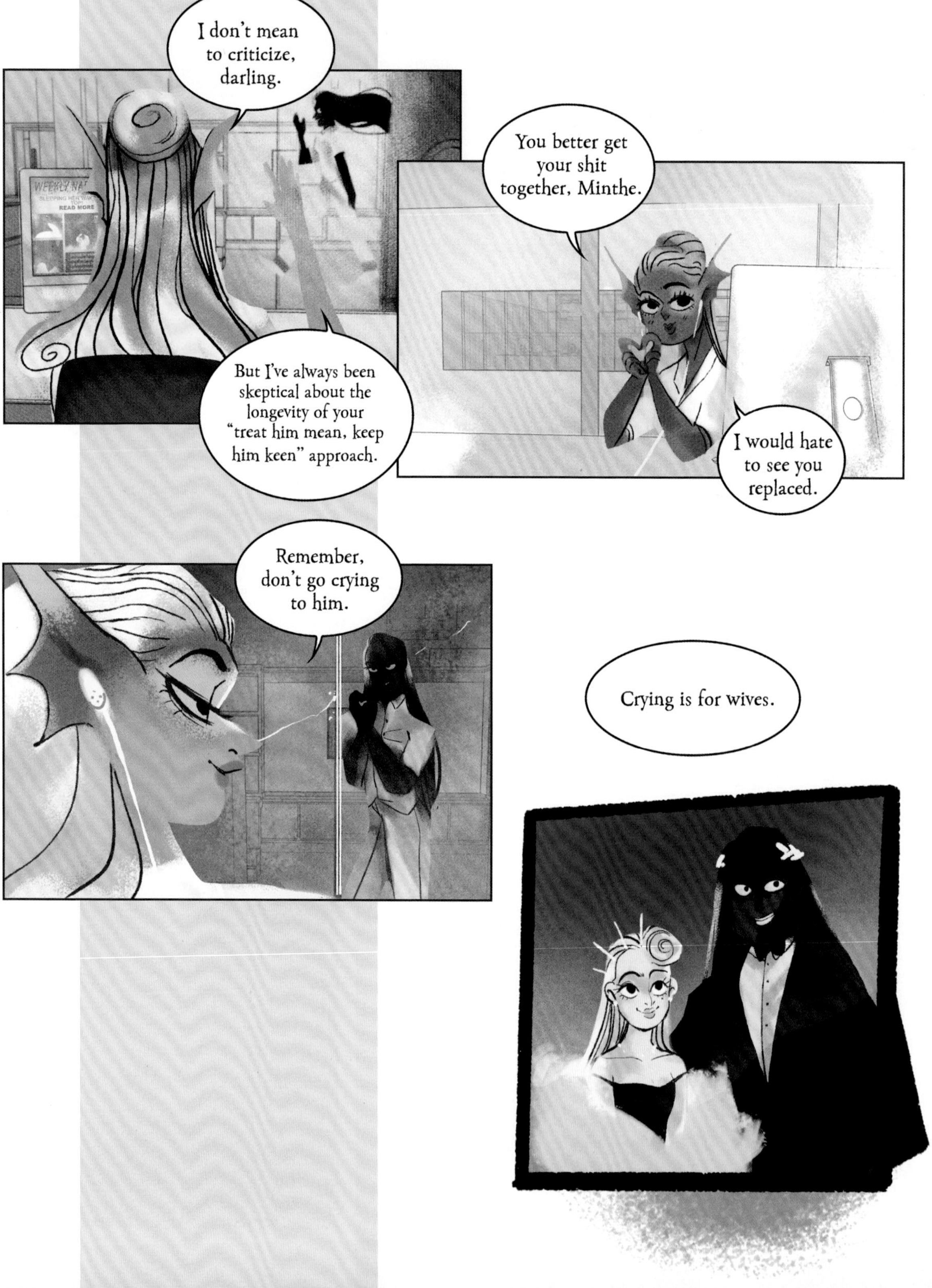
I don't mean to criticize, darling.
But I've always been skeptical about the longevity of your "treat him mean, keep him keen" approach.
READ MORE
You better get your shit together, Minthe.
I would hate to see you replaced.
Remember, don't go crying to him.
Crying is for wives.

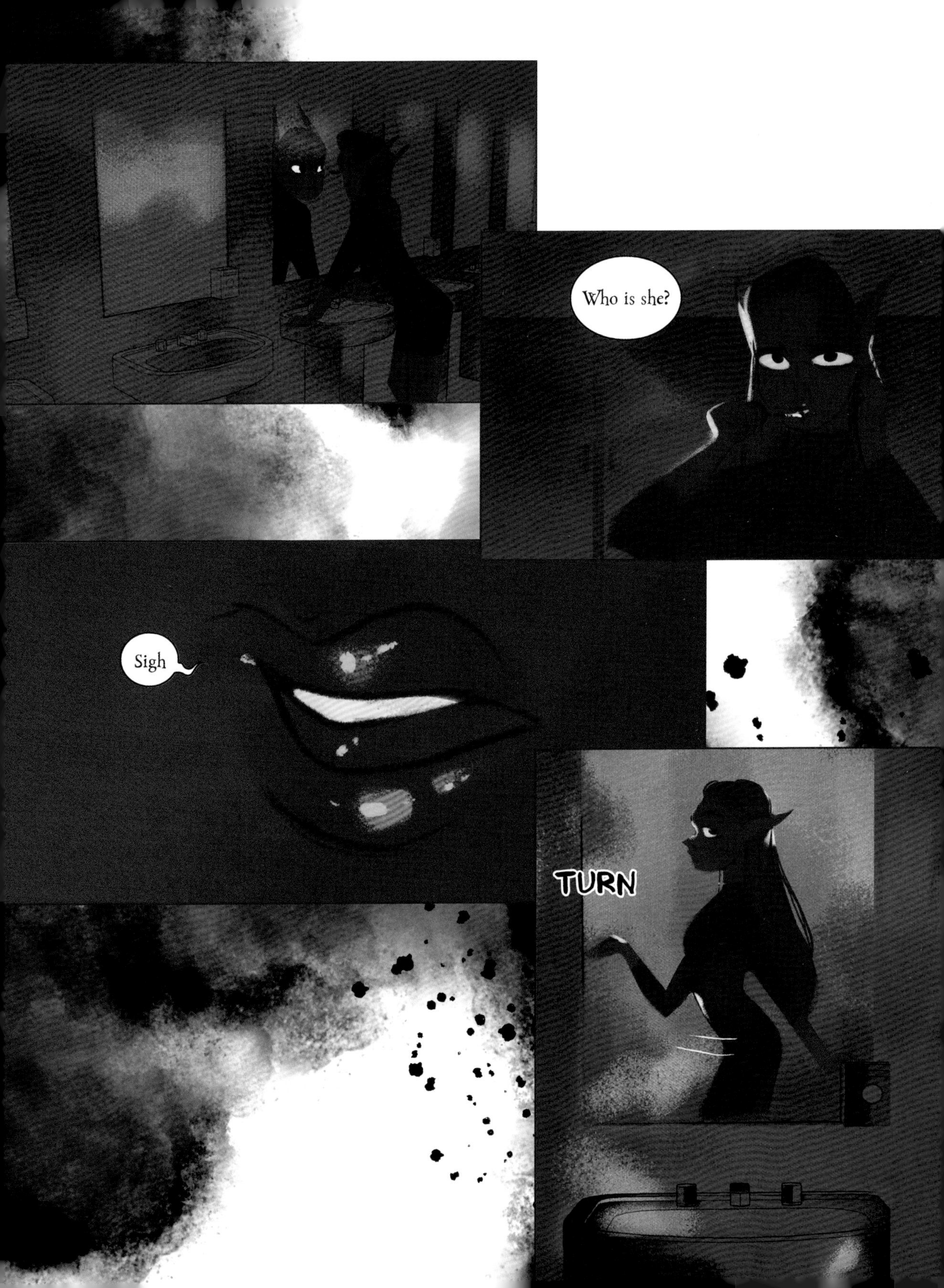
Who is she?
Sigh
TURN

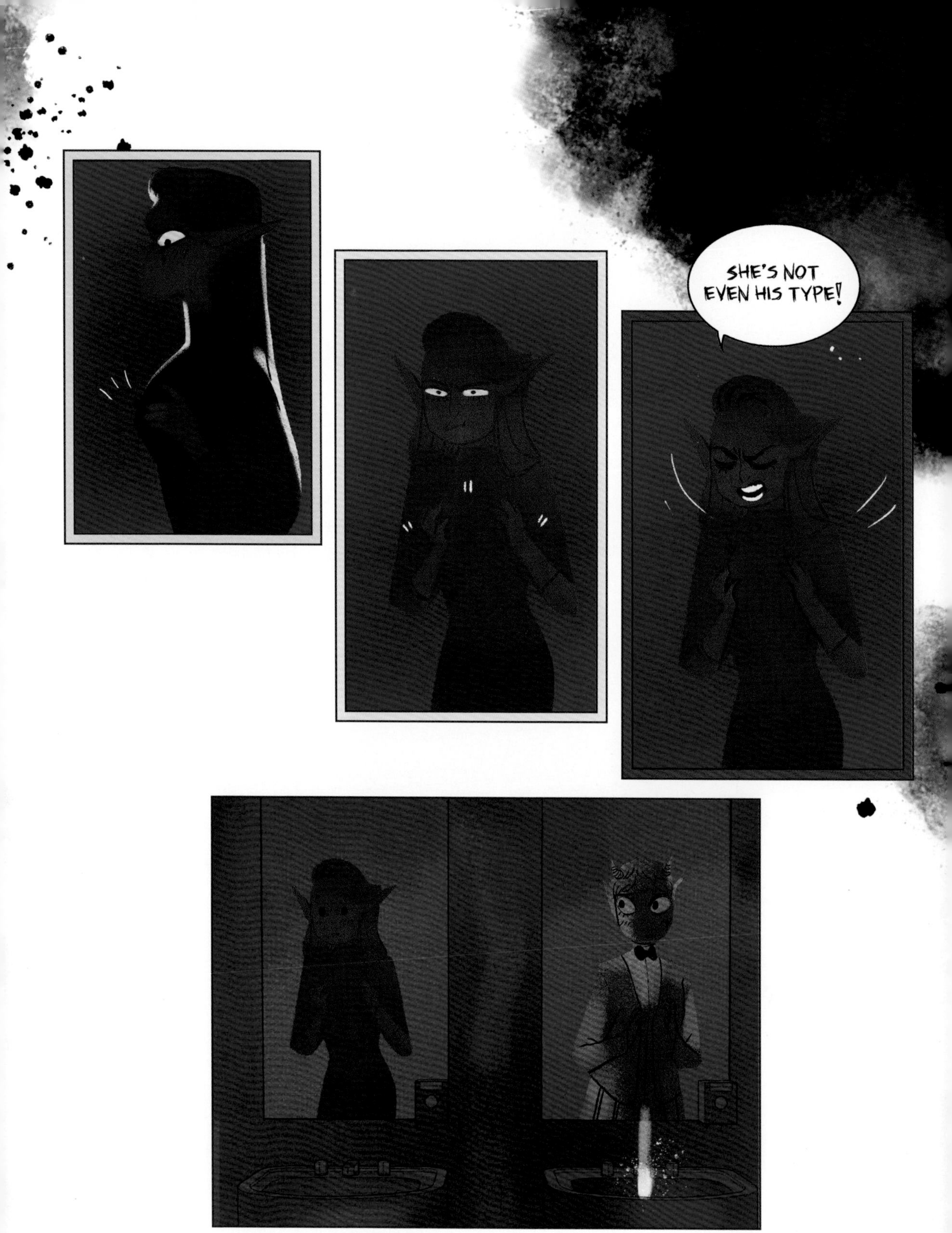
SHE'S NOT EVEN HIS TYPE!

Artemis,
do I start
talking now?

**Yes! It's already
recording.**

*OH! Oops! Hello, Ko-- I mean,
Persephone here! I'm sorry,
I can't take your call right now.*

*Please leave a message
and I'll get back to you
as soon as I can.*

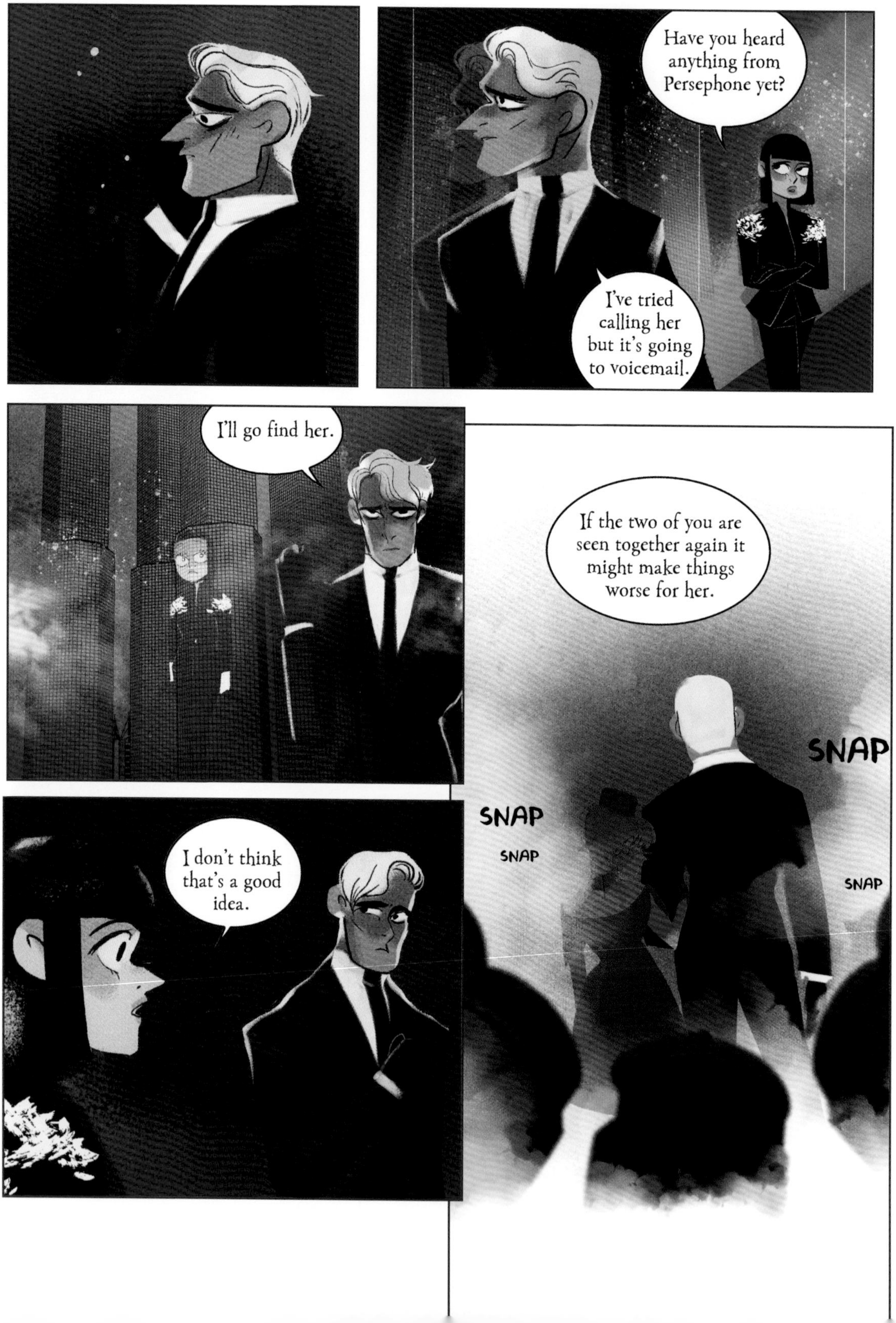
Have you heard anything from Persephone yet?
I've tried calling her but it's going to voicemail.
I'll go find her.
If the two of you are seen together again it might make things worse for her.
I don't think that's a good idea.
SNAP
SNAP
SNAP
SNAP

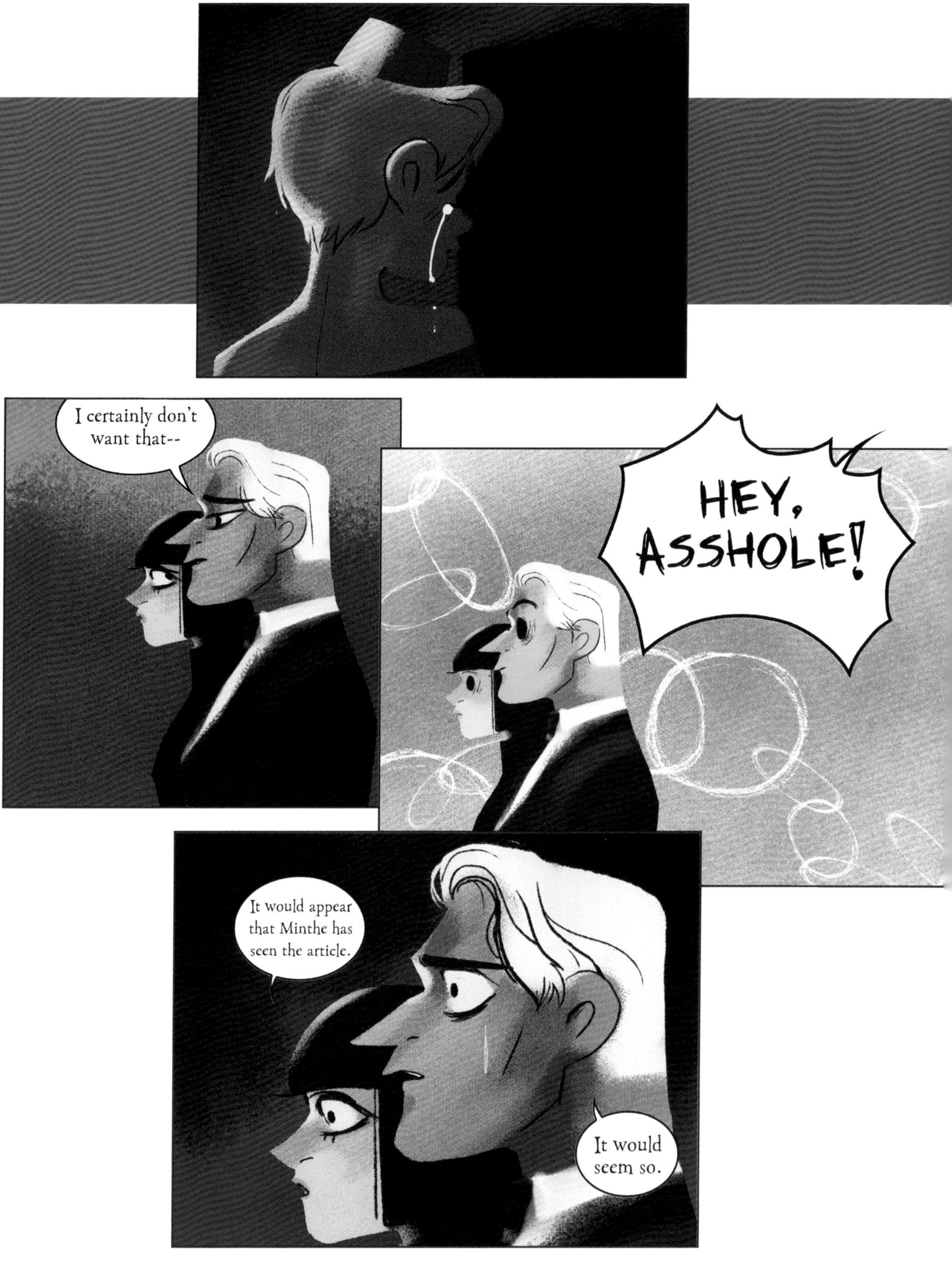
I certainly don't want that--
HEY, ASSHOLE!
It would appear that Minthe has seen the article.
It would seem so.

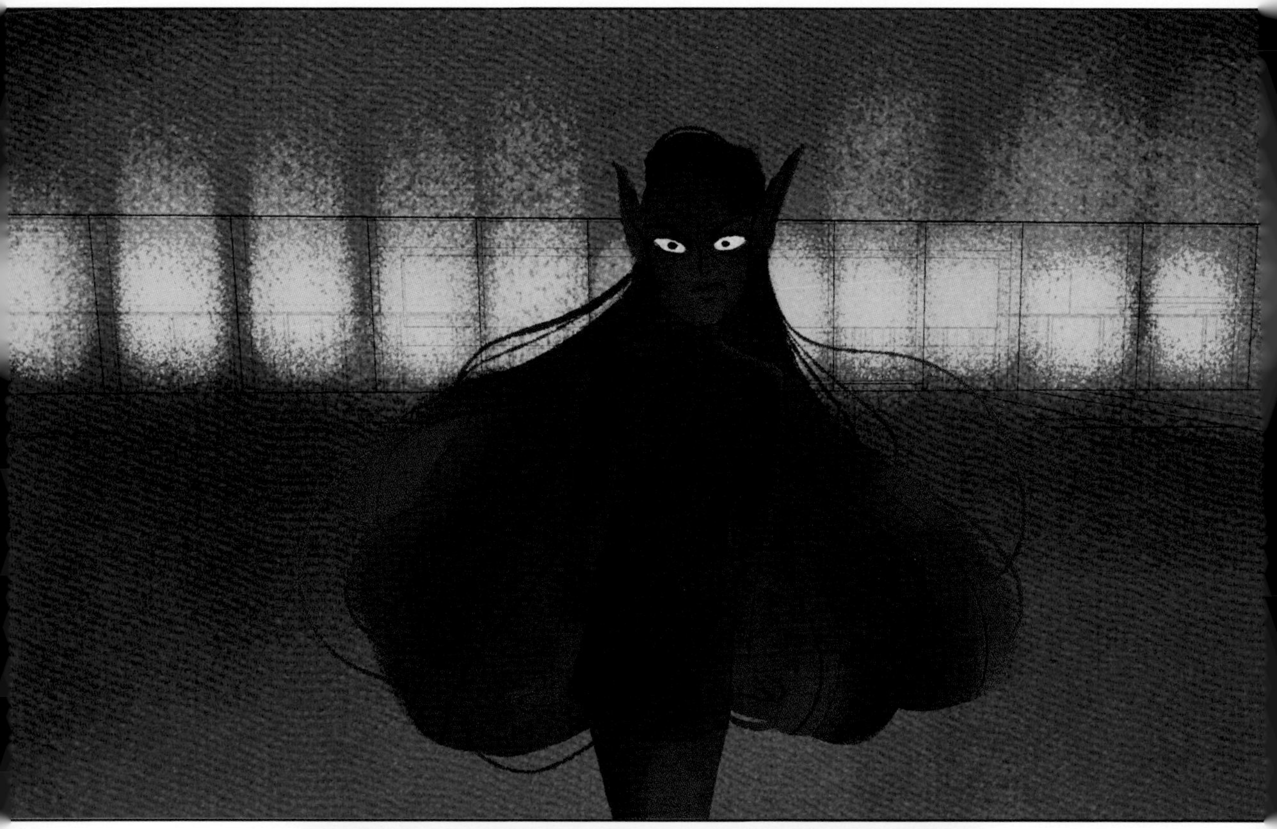

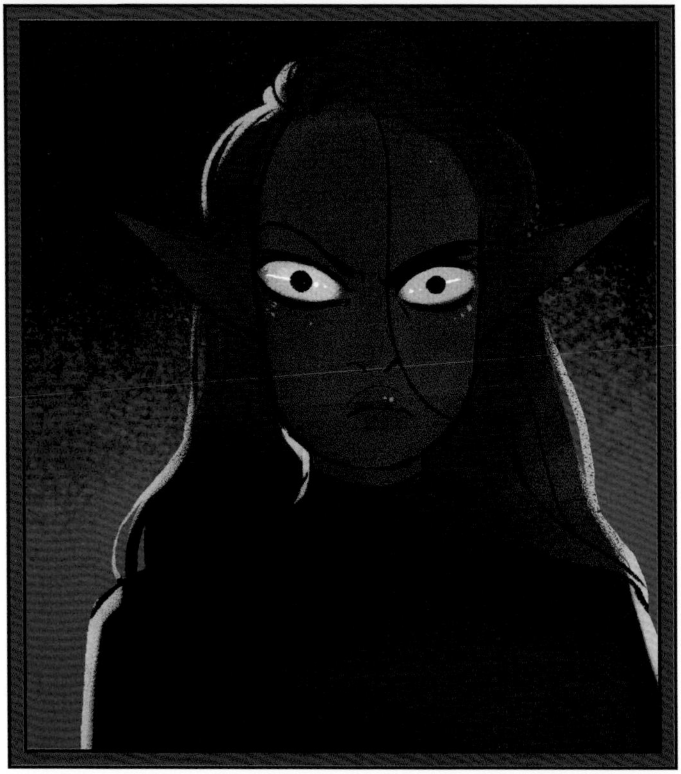

EPISODE 36: SMARTY PANTS

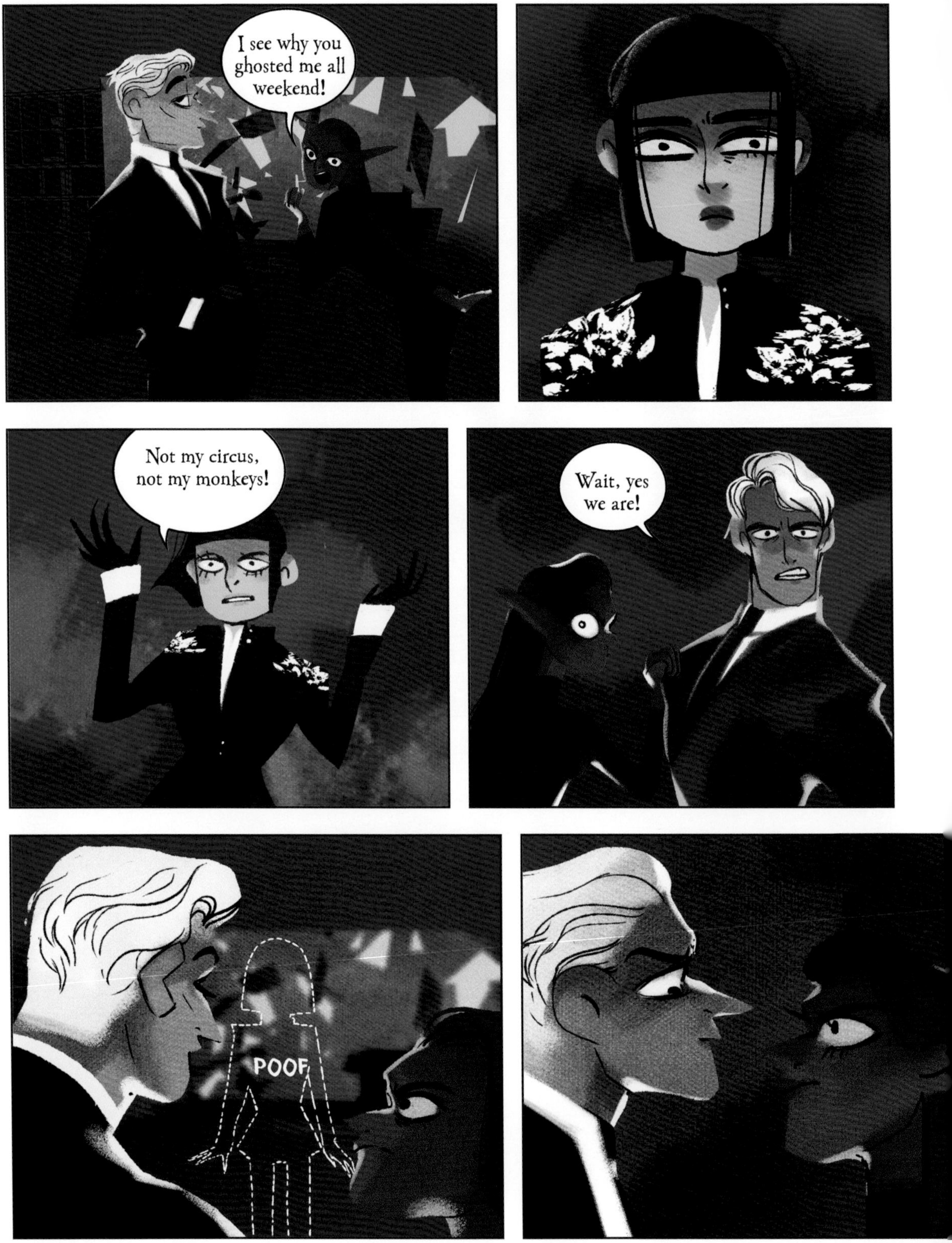
I see why you ghosted me all weekend!
Not my circus, not my monkeys!
Wait, yes we are!
POOF

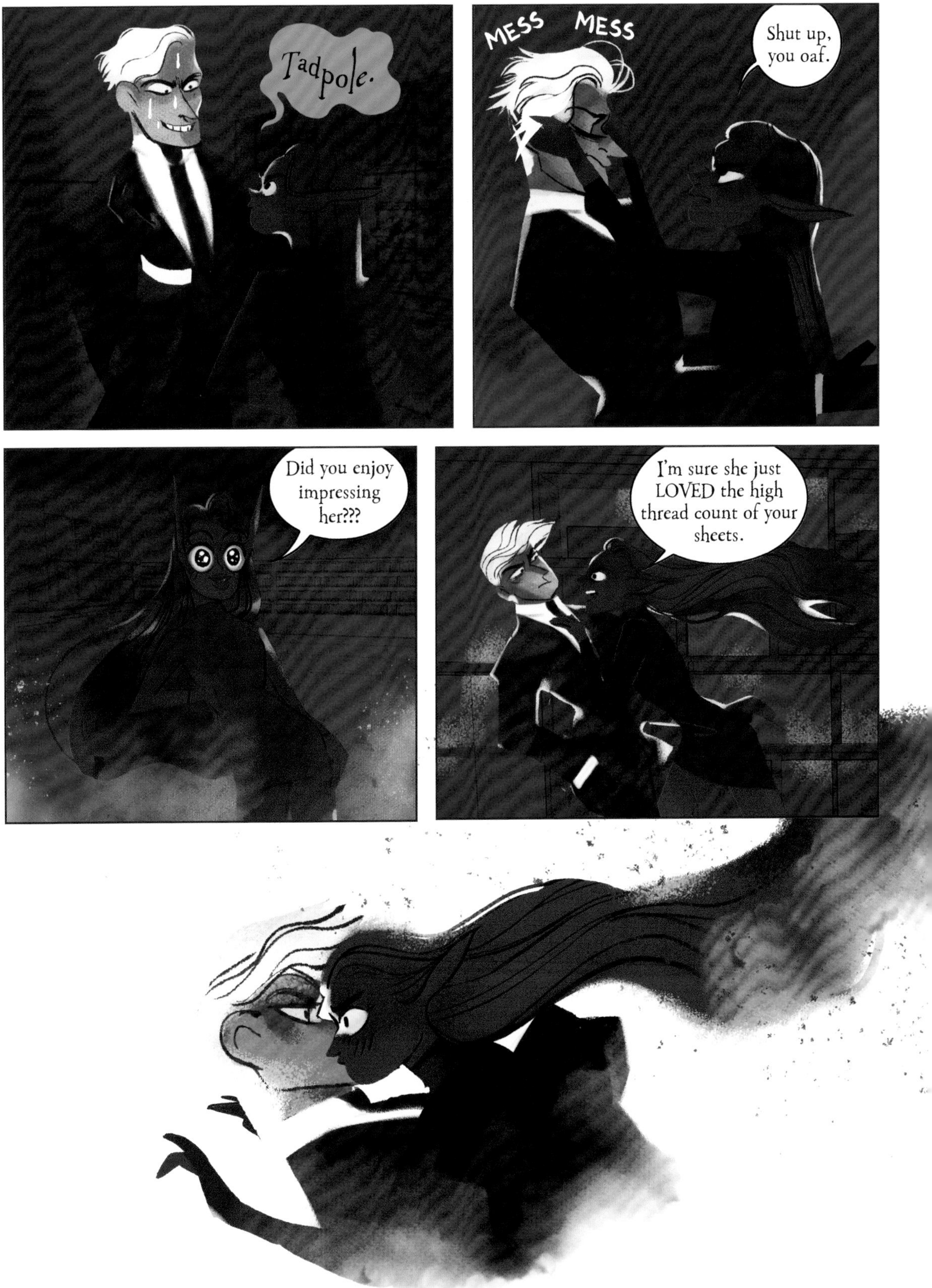
Tadpole.
MESS MESS
Shut up, you oaf.
Did you enjoy impressing her???
I'm sure she just LOVED the high thread count of your sheets.

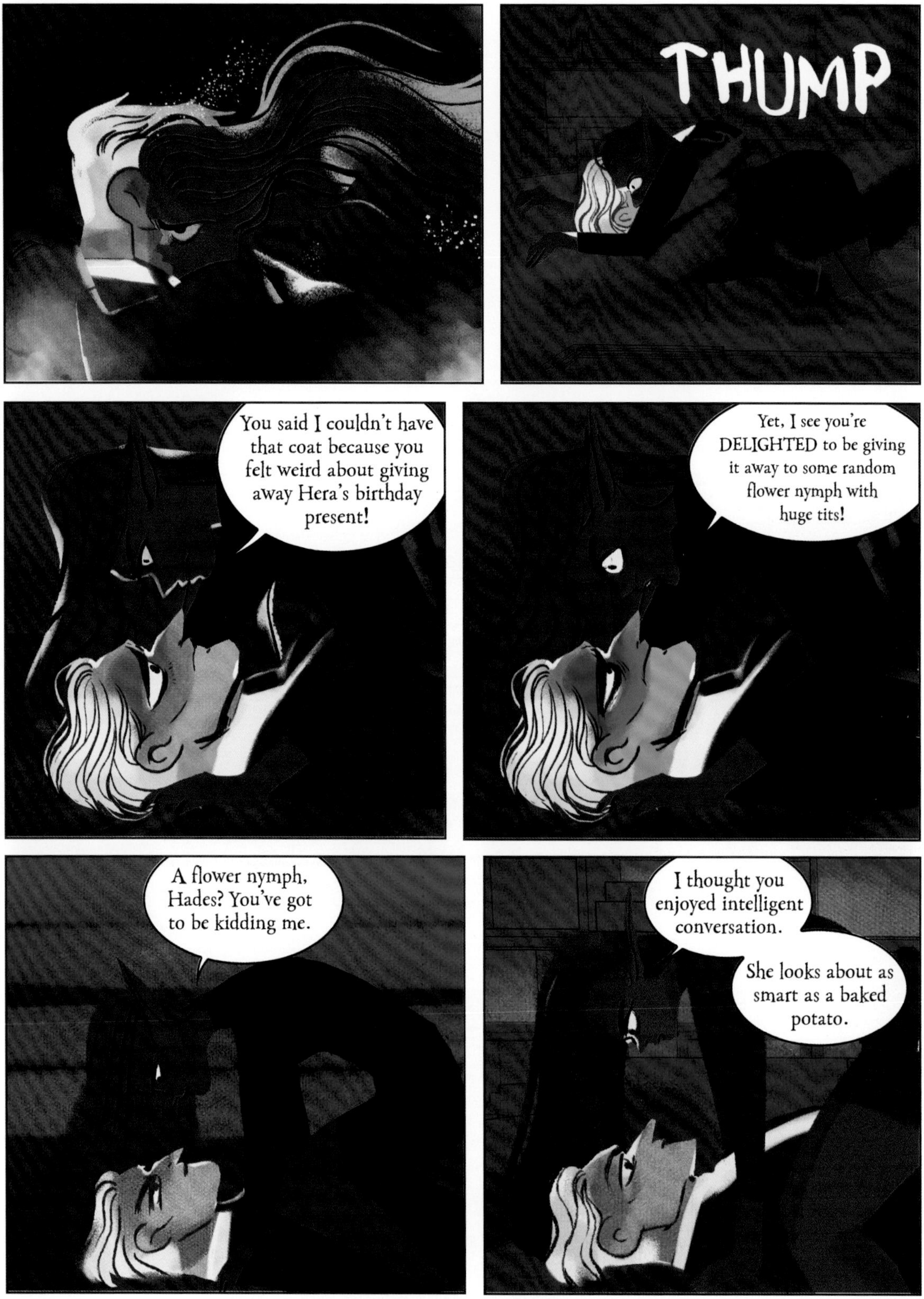
THUMP
You said I couldn't have that coat because you felt weird about giving away Hera's birthday present!
Yet, I see you're DELIGHTED to be giving it away to some random flower nymph with huge tits!
A flower nymph, Hades? You've got to be kidding me.
I thought you enjoyed intelligent conversation.
She looks about as smart as a baked potato.

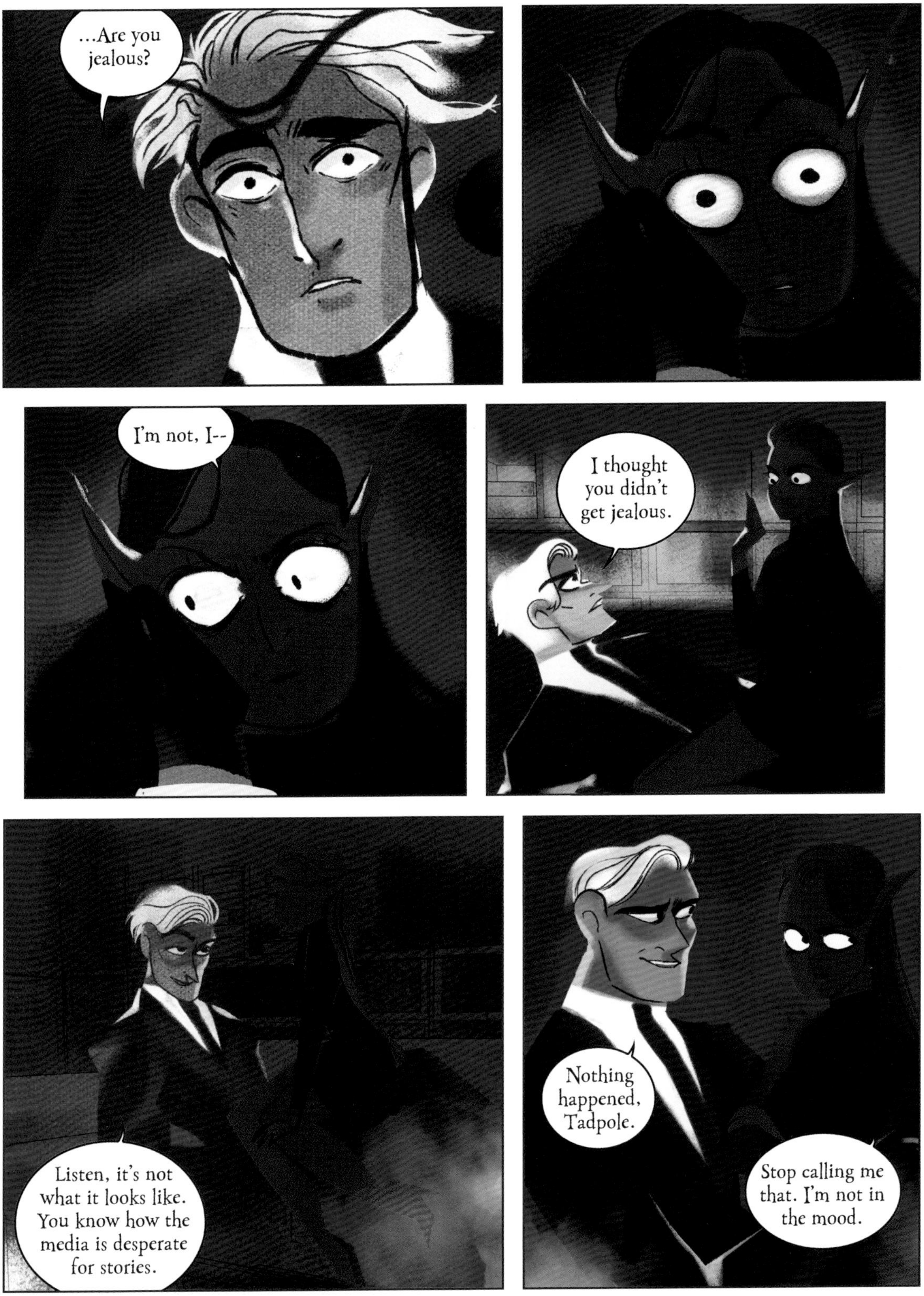
...Are you jealous?
I'm not, I--
I thought you didn't get jealous.
Listen, it's not what it looks like. You know how the media is desperate for stories.
Nothing happened, Tadpole.
Stop calling me that. I'm not in the mood.

She's actually a goddess from the Mortal Realm.

The daughter of an old friend.

...Oh

Minthe.

What happened?

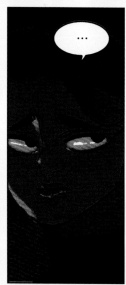

...

Why didn't you come to the party?

I thought we were doing so well.

Speed-grading!

That was so easy.

I don't know why everyone looks so stressed.

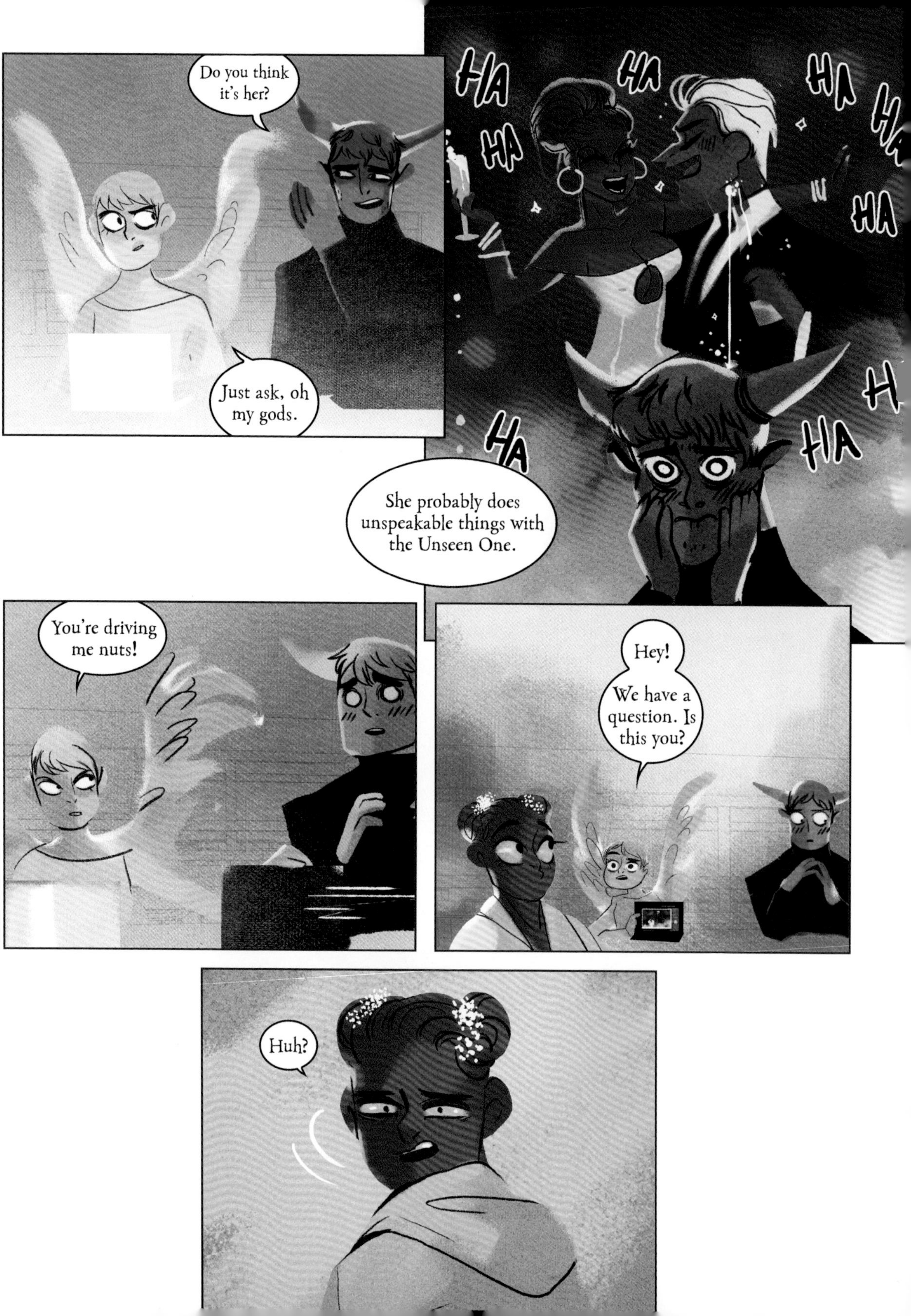
Do you think it's her?
Just ask, oh my gods.
HA HA HA HA HA HA HA HA HA HA
She probably does unspeakable things with the Unseen One.
You're driving me nuts!
Hey!
We have a question. Is this you?
Huh?

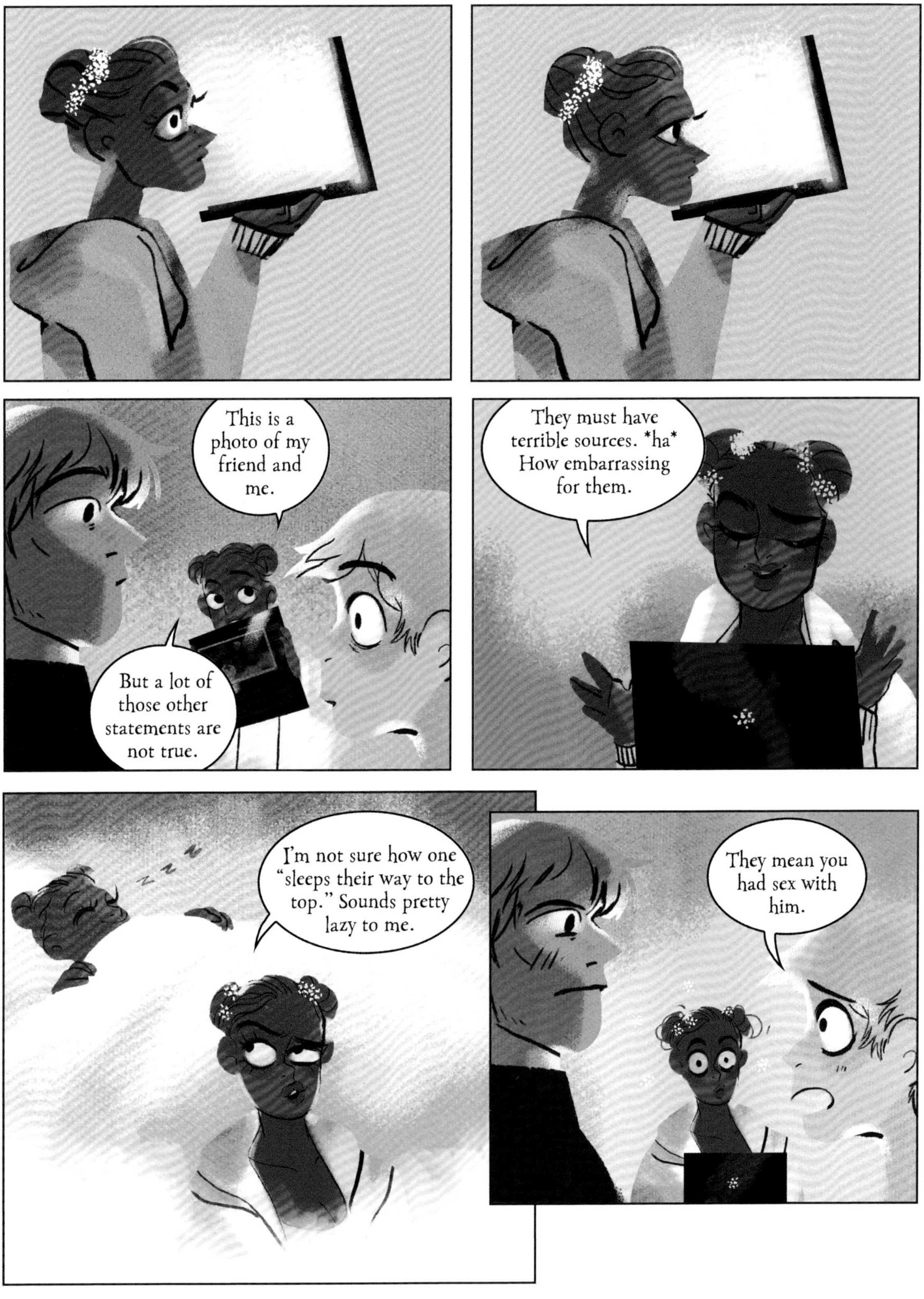
This is a photo of my friend and me.
But a lot of those other statements are not true.
They must have terrible sources. *ha* How embarrassing for them.
z z z
I'm not sure how one "sleeps their way to the top." Sounds pretty lazy to me.
They mean you had sex with him.

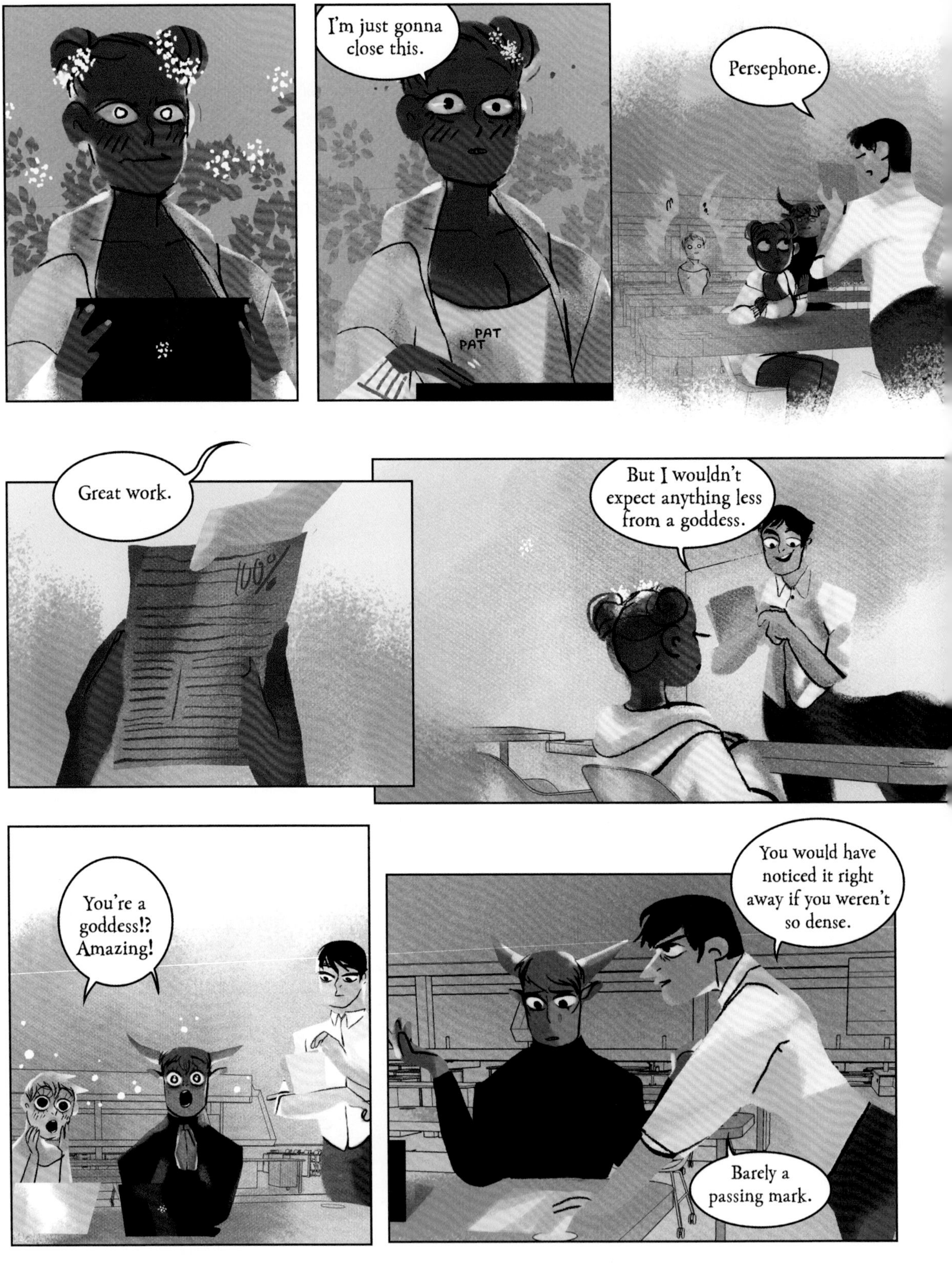

I'm just gonna close this.
PAT
PAT
Persephone.
Great work.
100%
But I wouldn't expect anything less from a goddess.
You're a goddess!? Amazing!
You would have noticed it right away if you weren't so dense.
Barely a passing mark.

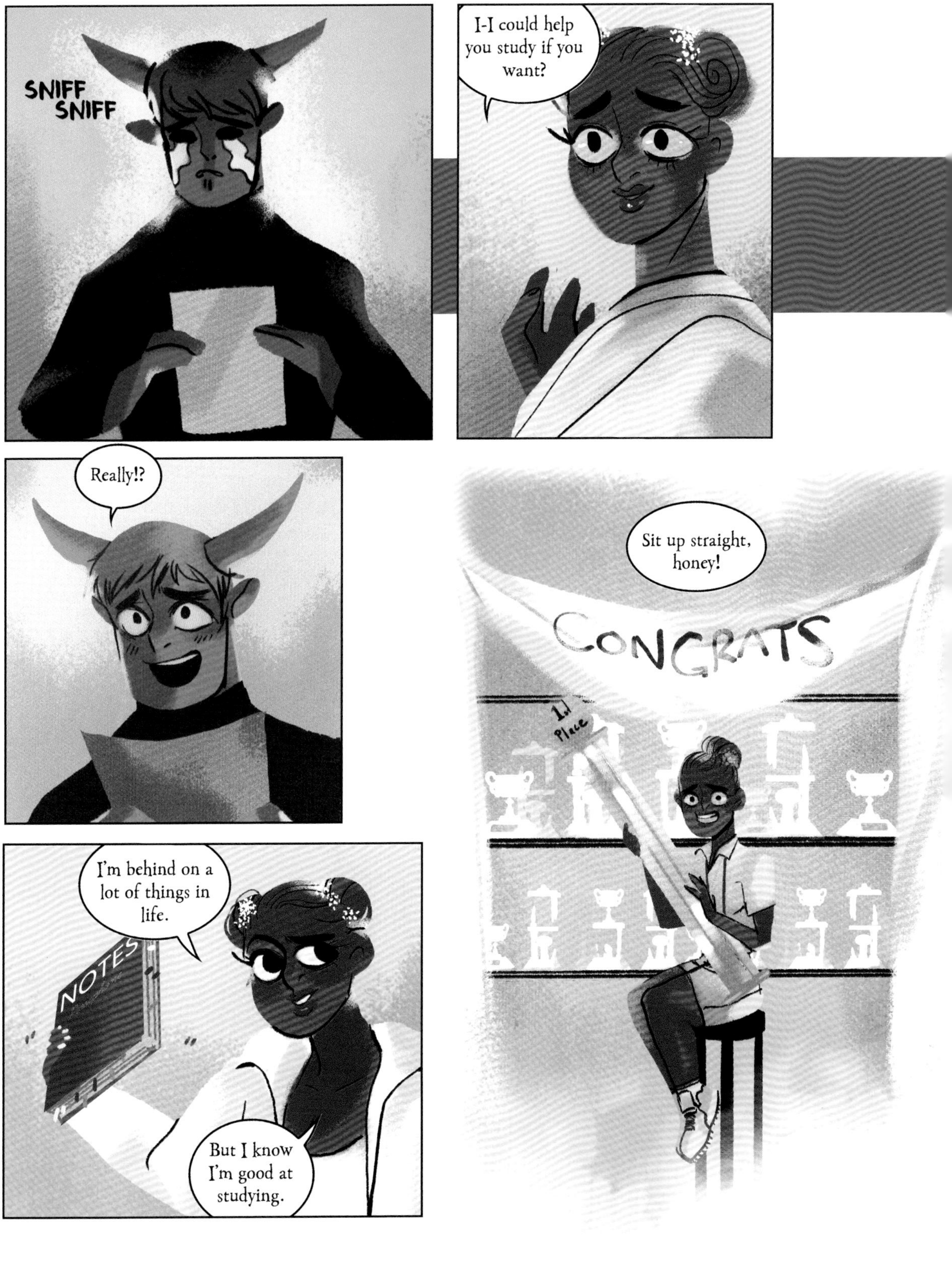

SNIFF SNIFF
I-I could help you study if you want?
Really!?
I'm behind on a lot of things in life.
NOTES
But I know I'm good at studying.
Sit up straight, honey!
CONGRATS
1st Place

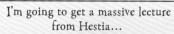
I'm going to get a massive lecture from Hestia...

Phew, that wasn't so bad.

I'm not sure what I'm going to do about that article, though.

GRAB

Hey, Persie.

Surprise! I came to pick you up from class!

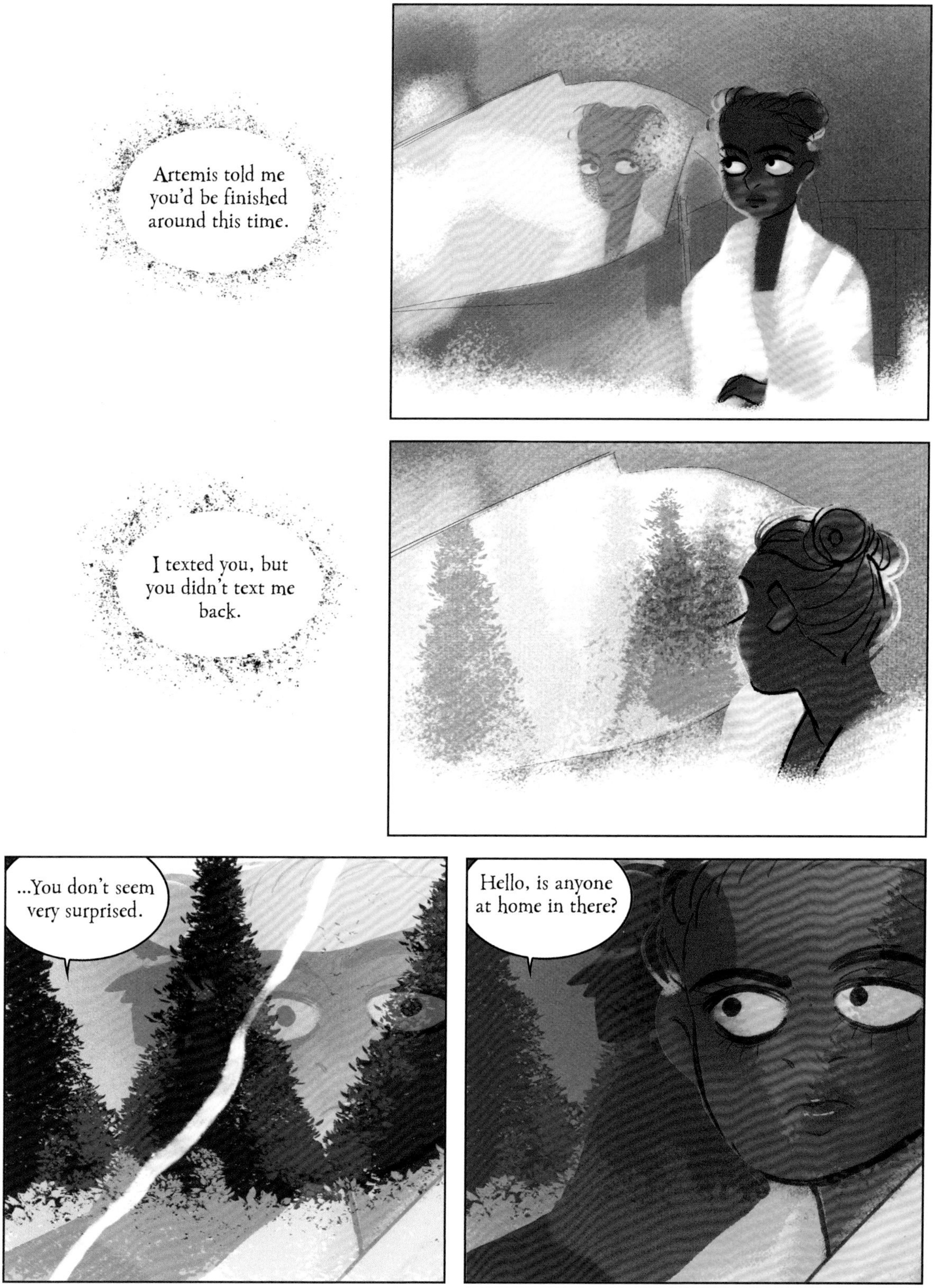
Artemis told me you'd be finished around this time.
I texted you, but you didn't text me back.
...You don't seem very surprised.
Hello, is anyone at home in there?

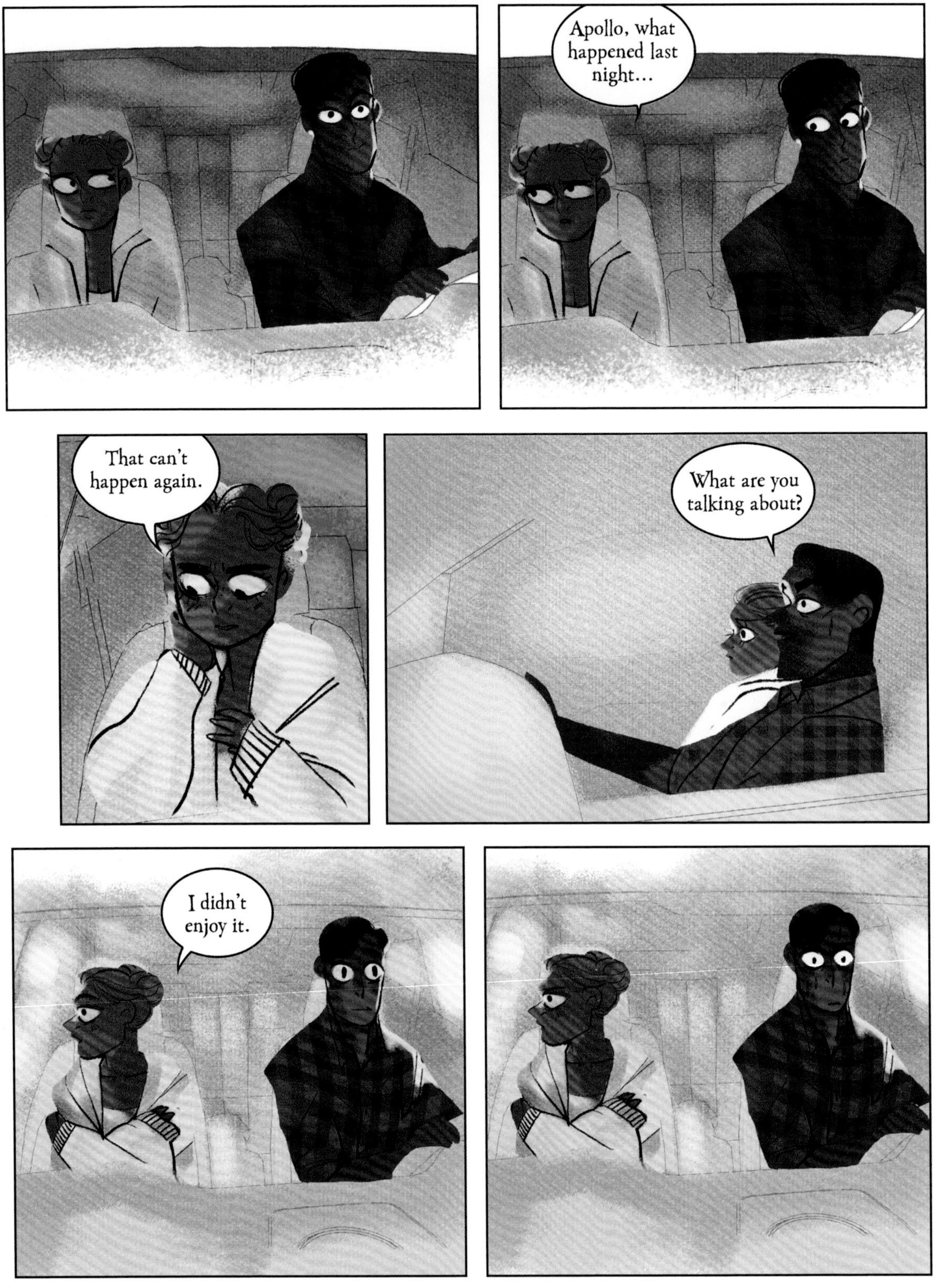
Apollo, what happened last night…
That can't happen again.
What are you talking about?
I didn't enjoy it.

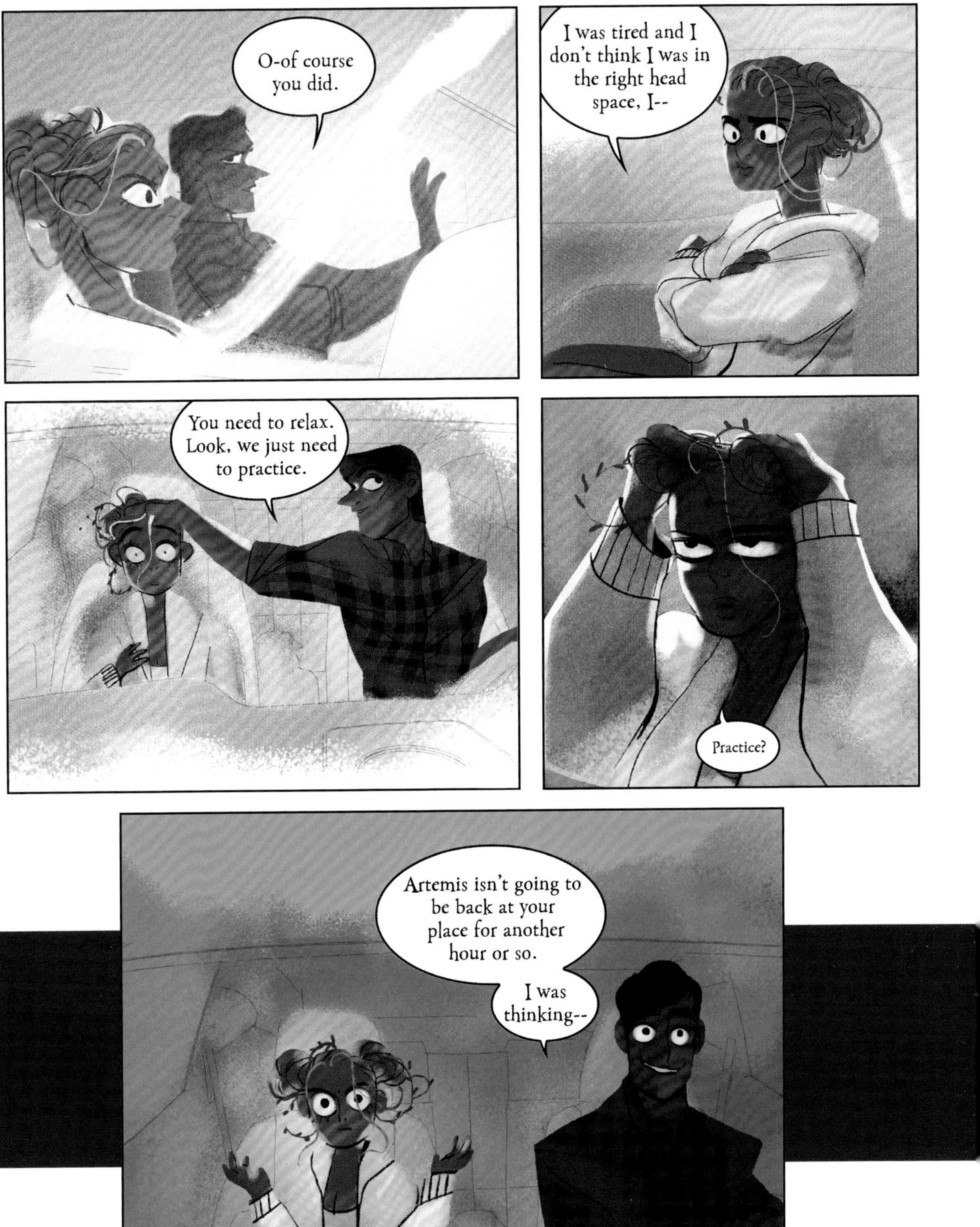
O-of course you did.
I was tired and I don't think I was in the right head space, I--
You need to relax. Look, we just need to practice.
Practice?
Artemis isn't going to be back at your place for another hour or so.
I was thinking--

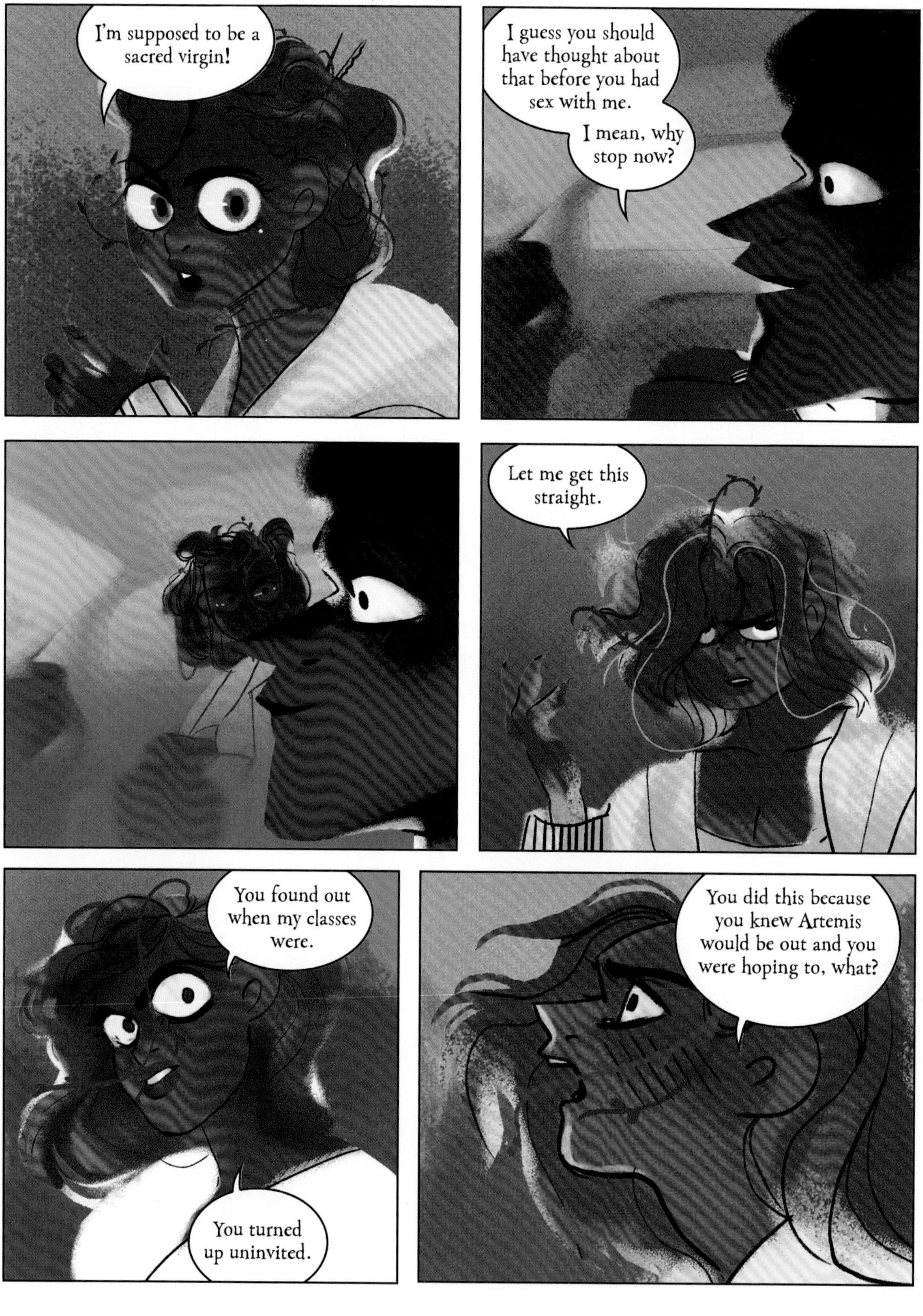
I'm supposed to be a sacred virgin!
I guess you should have thought about that before you had sex with me.
I mean, why stop now?
Let me get this straight.
You found out when my classes were.
You turned up uninvited.
You did this because you knew Artemis would be out and you were hoping to, what?

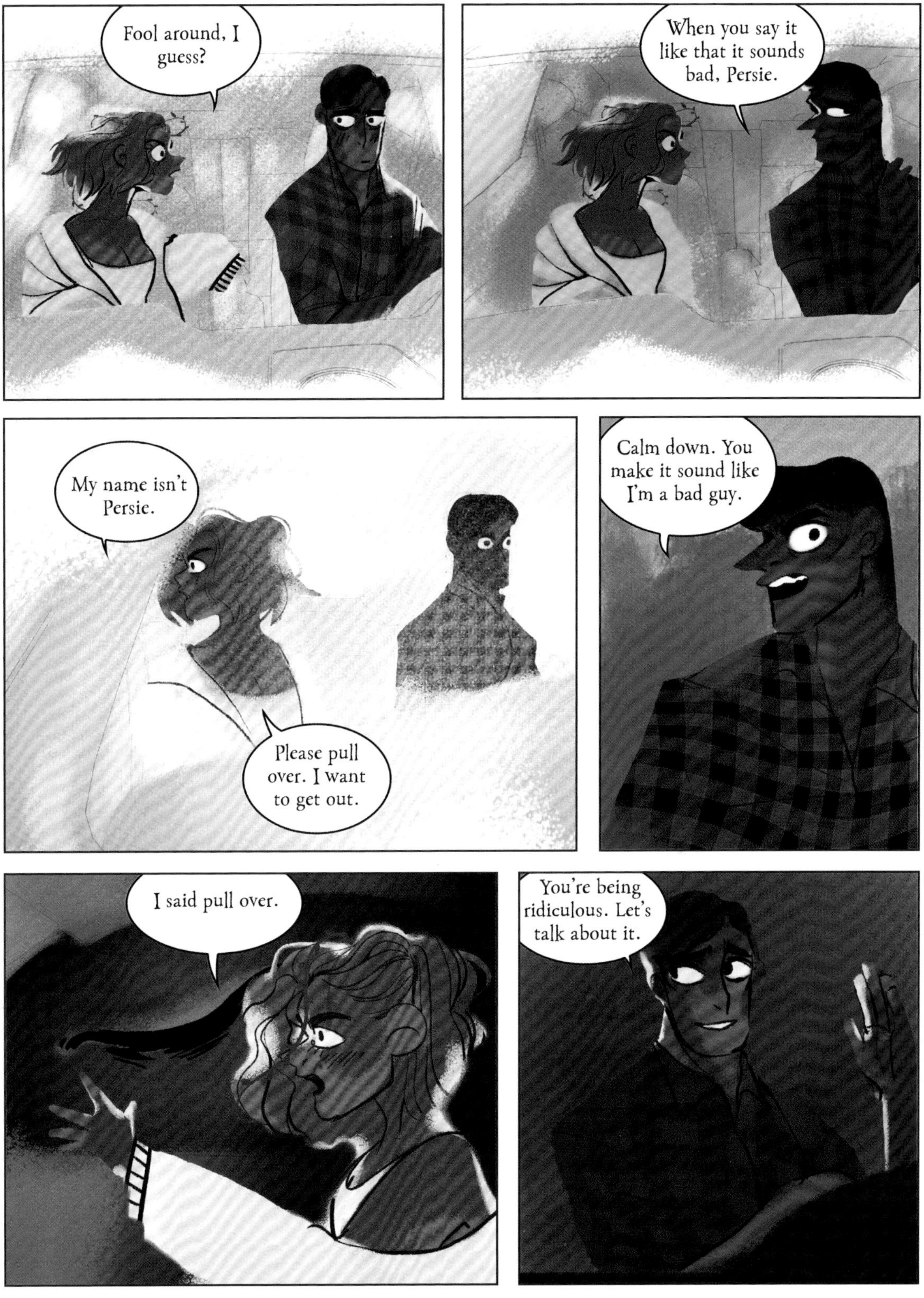
Fool around, I guess?
When you say it like that it sounds bad, Persie.
My name isn't Persie.
Please pull over. I want to get out.
Calm down. You make it sound like I'm a bad guy.
I said pull over.
You're being ridiculous. Let's talk about it.

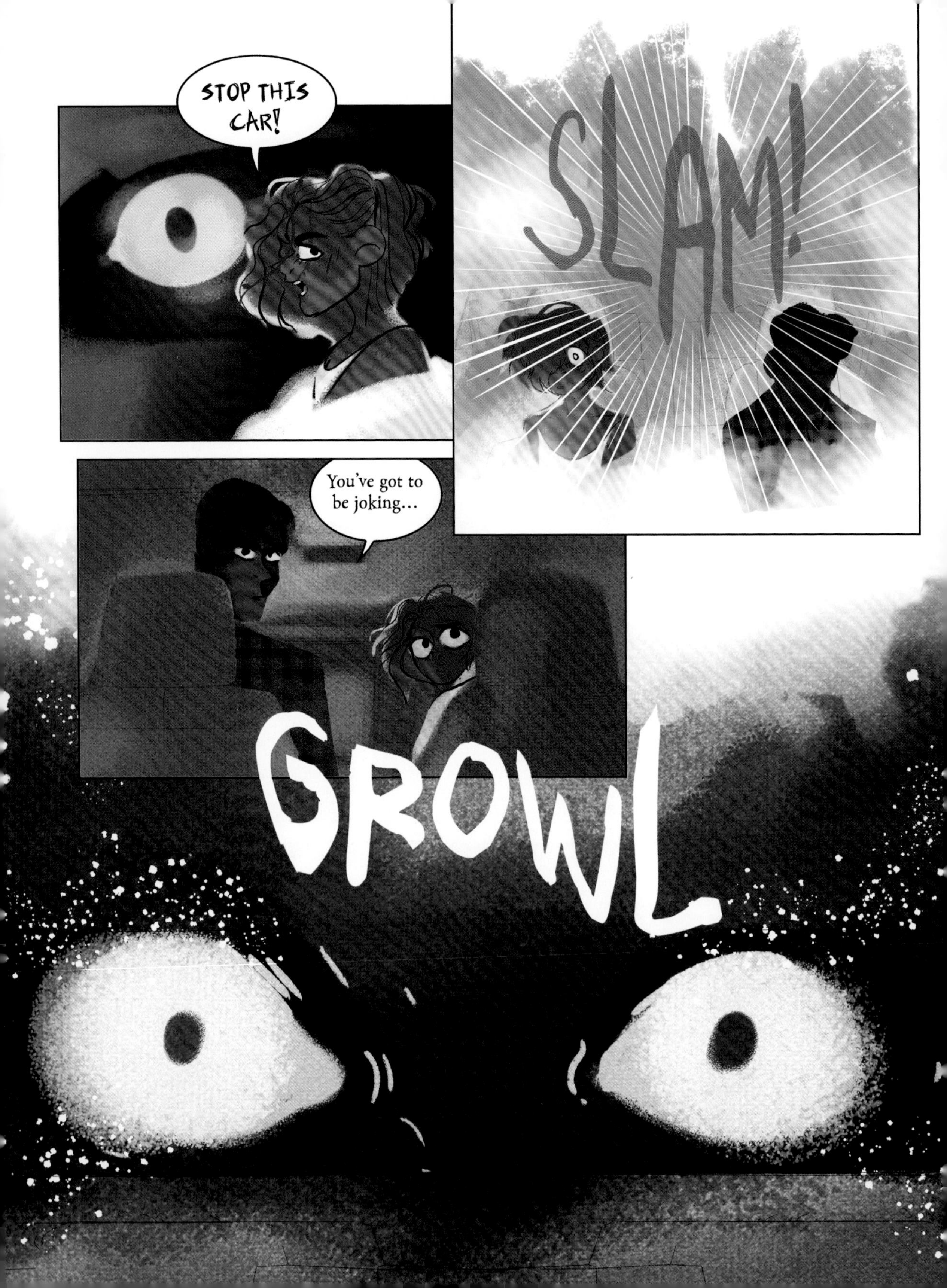
STOP THIS CAR!
SLAM!
You've got to be joking…
GROWL

EPISODE 37: A PRINCE IN DARK VELVET

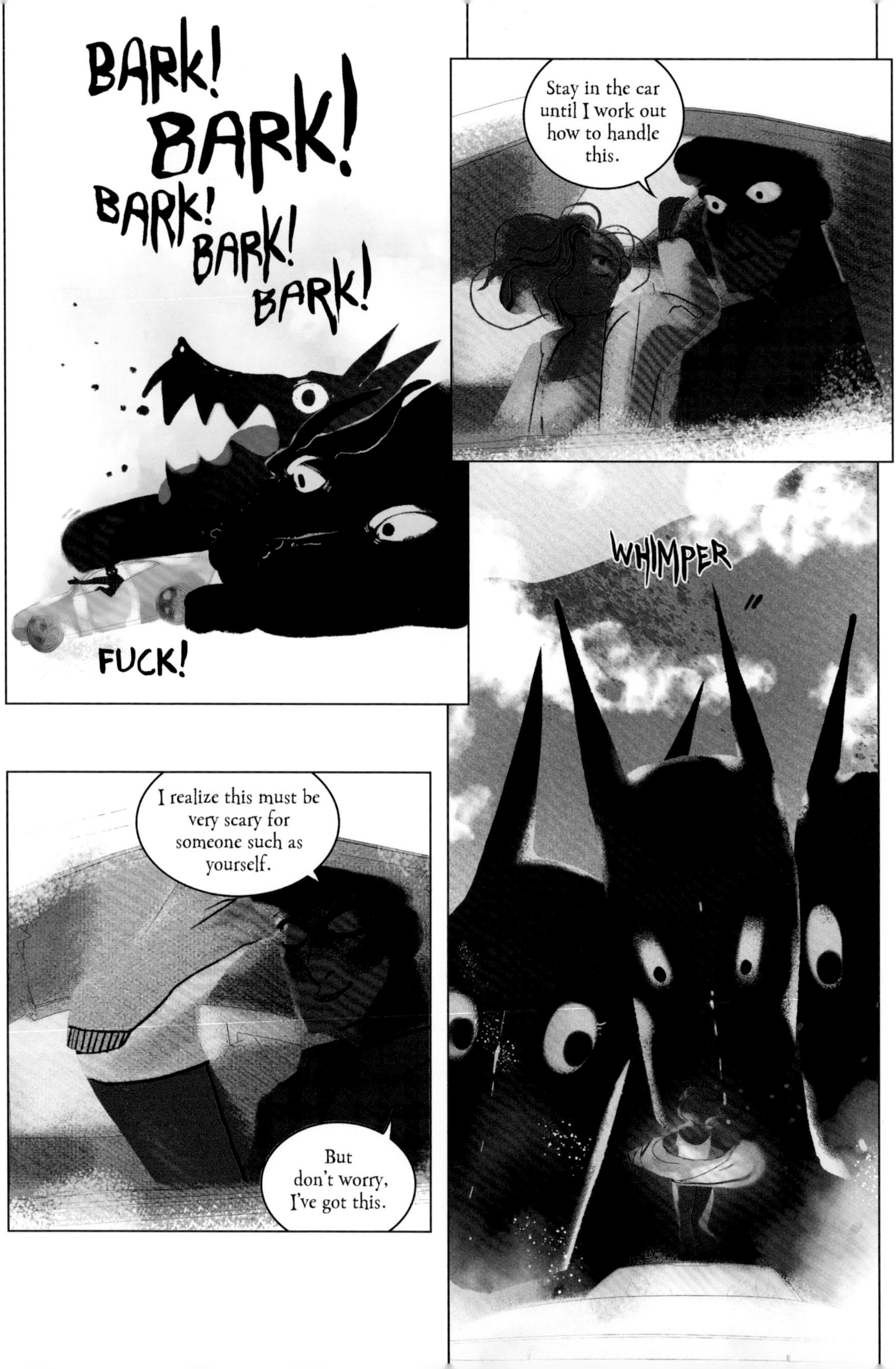

BARK!
BARK!
BARK!
BARK!
BARK!
FUCK!
Stay in the car until I work out how to handle this.
I realize this must be very scary for someone such as yourself.
But don't worry, I've got this.
WHIMPER

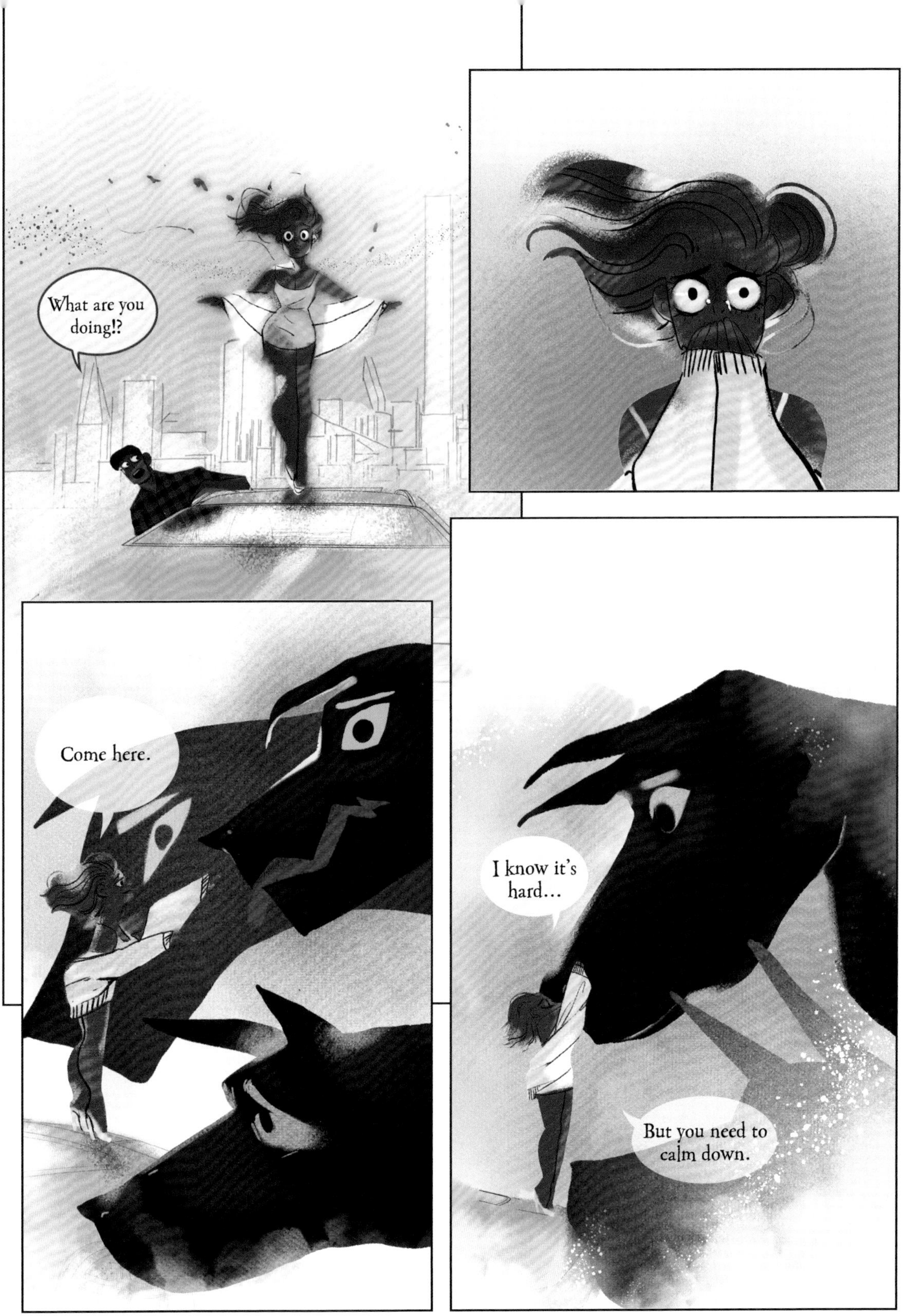
What are you doing!?
Come here.
I know it's hard...
But you need to calm down.

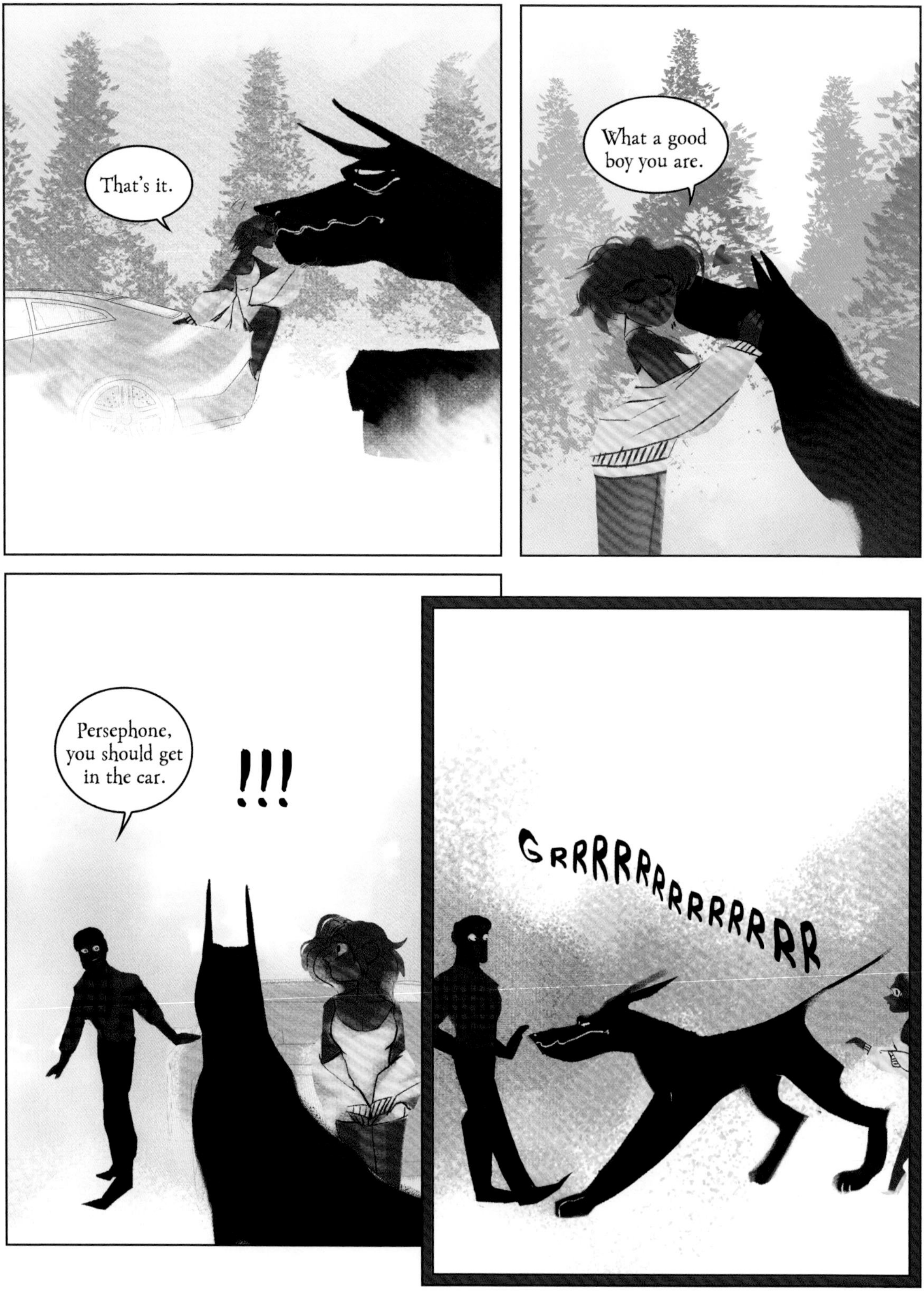

That's it.
What a good boy you are.
Persephone, you should get in the car.
!!!
GRRRRRRRRRRRRRR

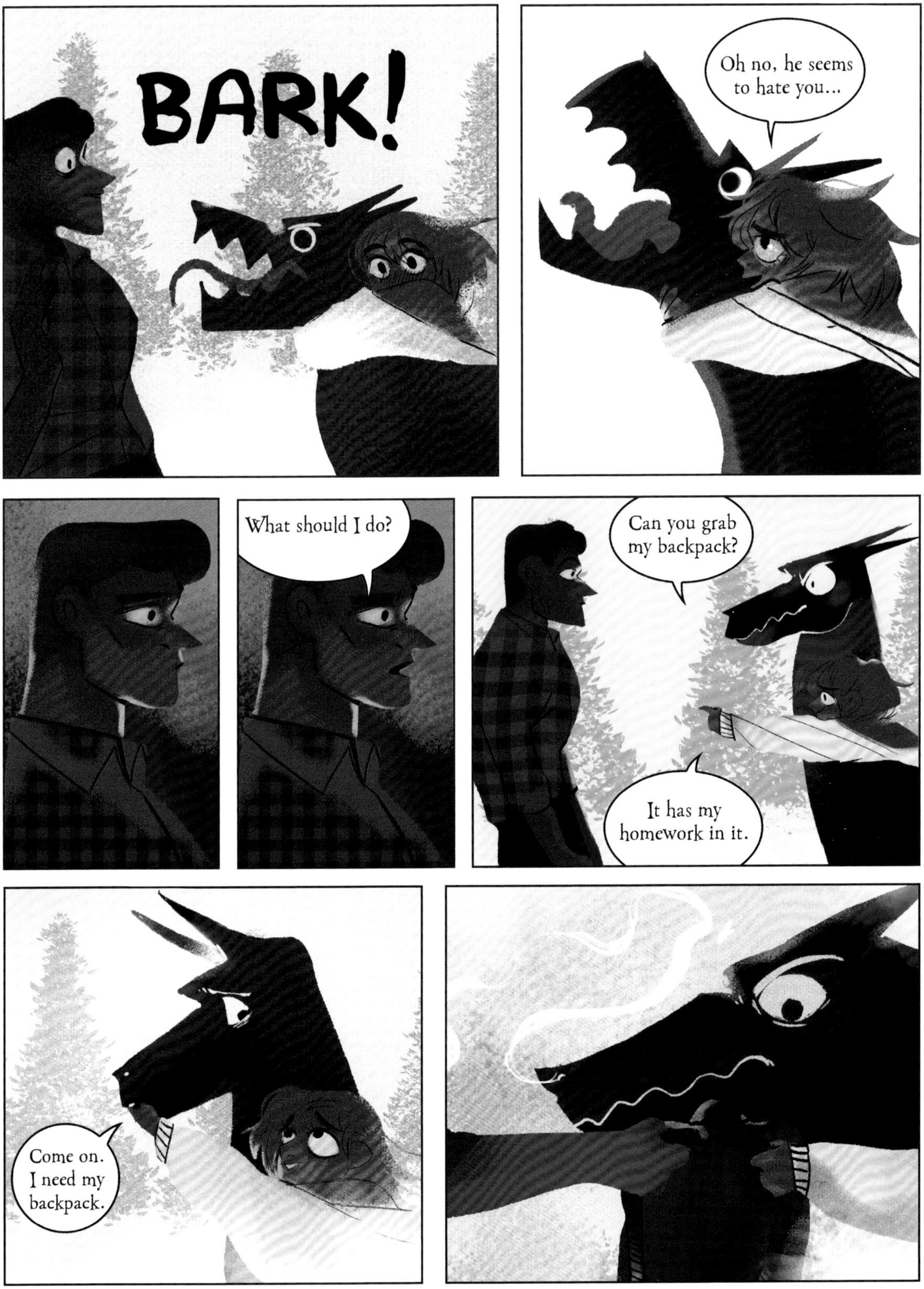
BARK!
Oh no, he seems to hate you...
What should I do?
Can you grab my backpack?
It has my homework in it.
Come on. I need my backpack.

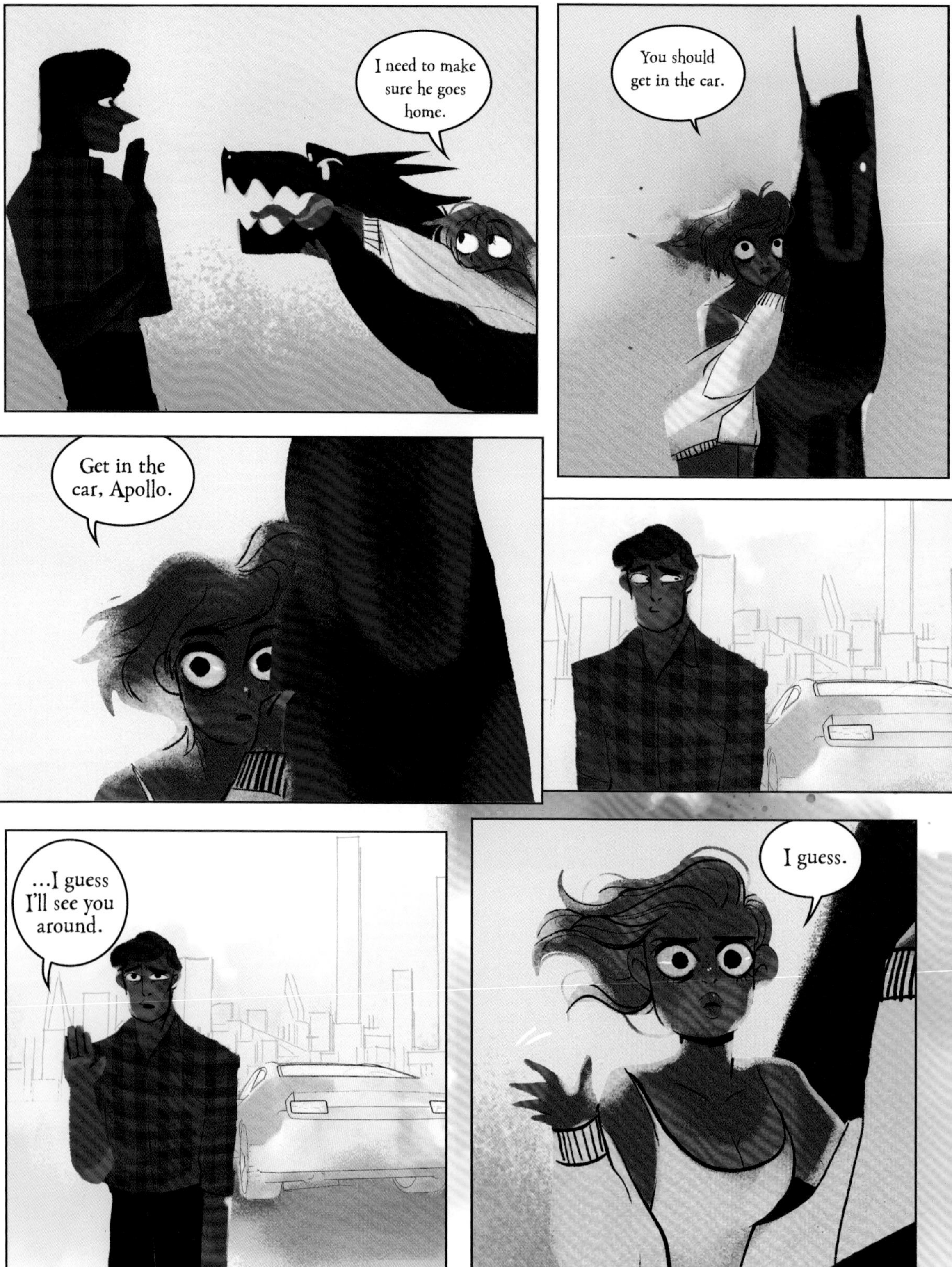
I need to make sure he goes home.
You should get in the car.
Get in the car, Apollo.
...I guess I'll see you around.
I guess.

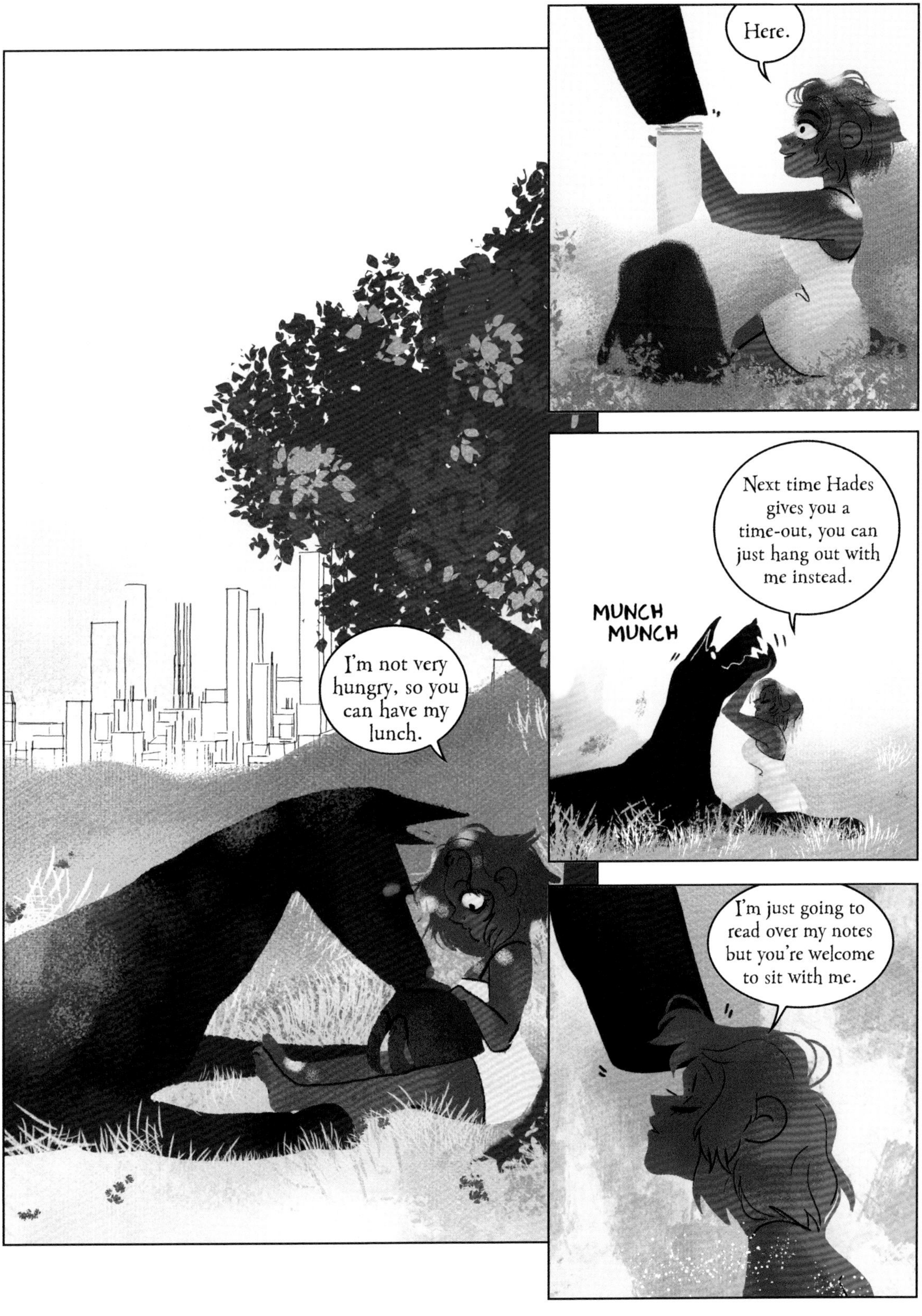
I'm not very hungry, so you can have my lunch.
Here.
Next time Hades gives you a time-out, you can just hang out with me instead.
MUNCH MUNCH
I'm just going to read over my notes but you're welcome to sit with me.

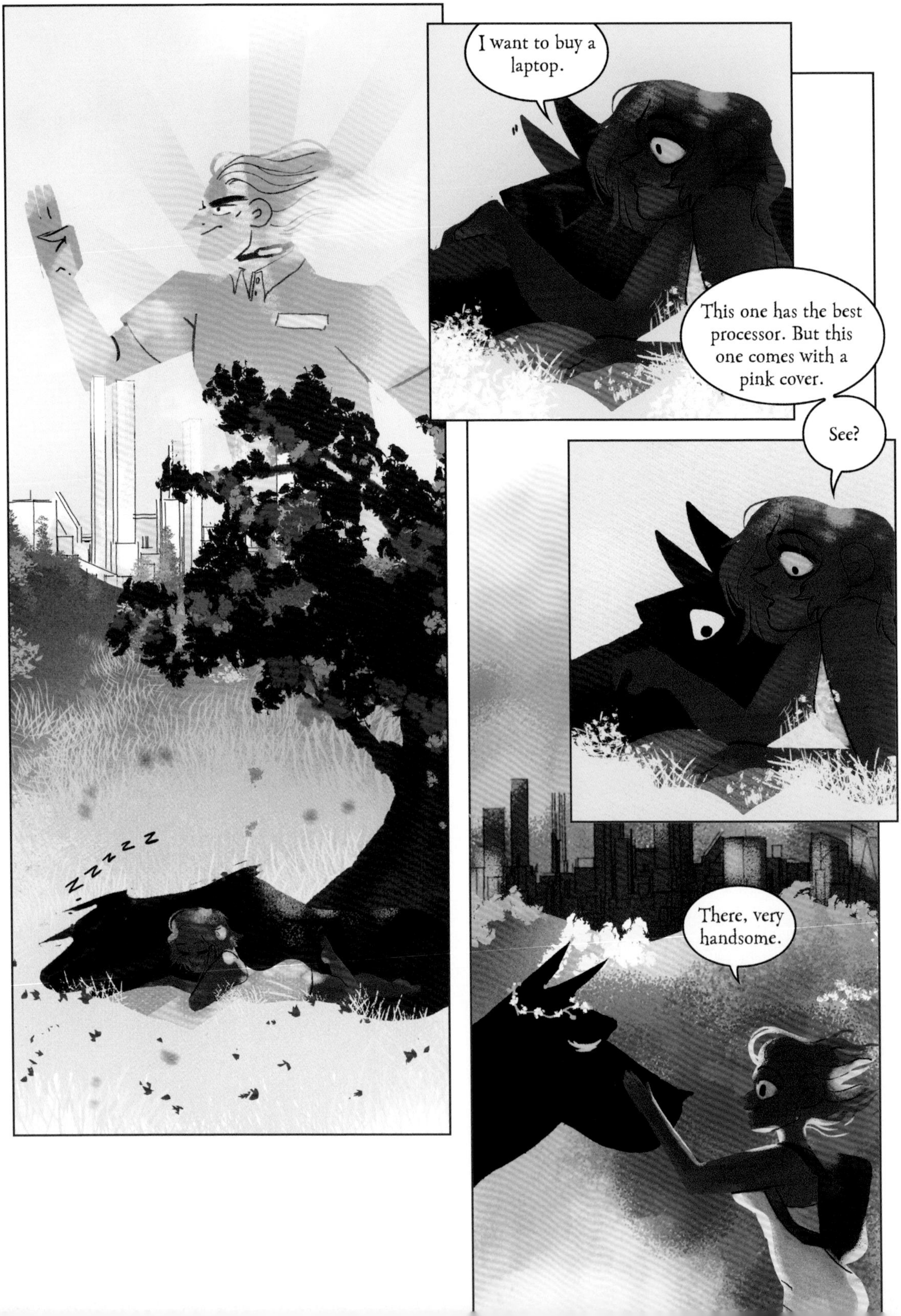
ZZZZZ
I want to buy a laptop.
This one has the best processor. But this one comes with a pink cover.
See?
There, very handsome.

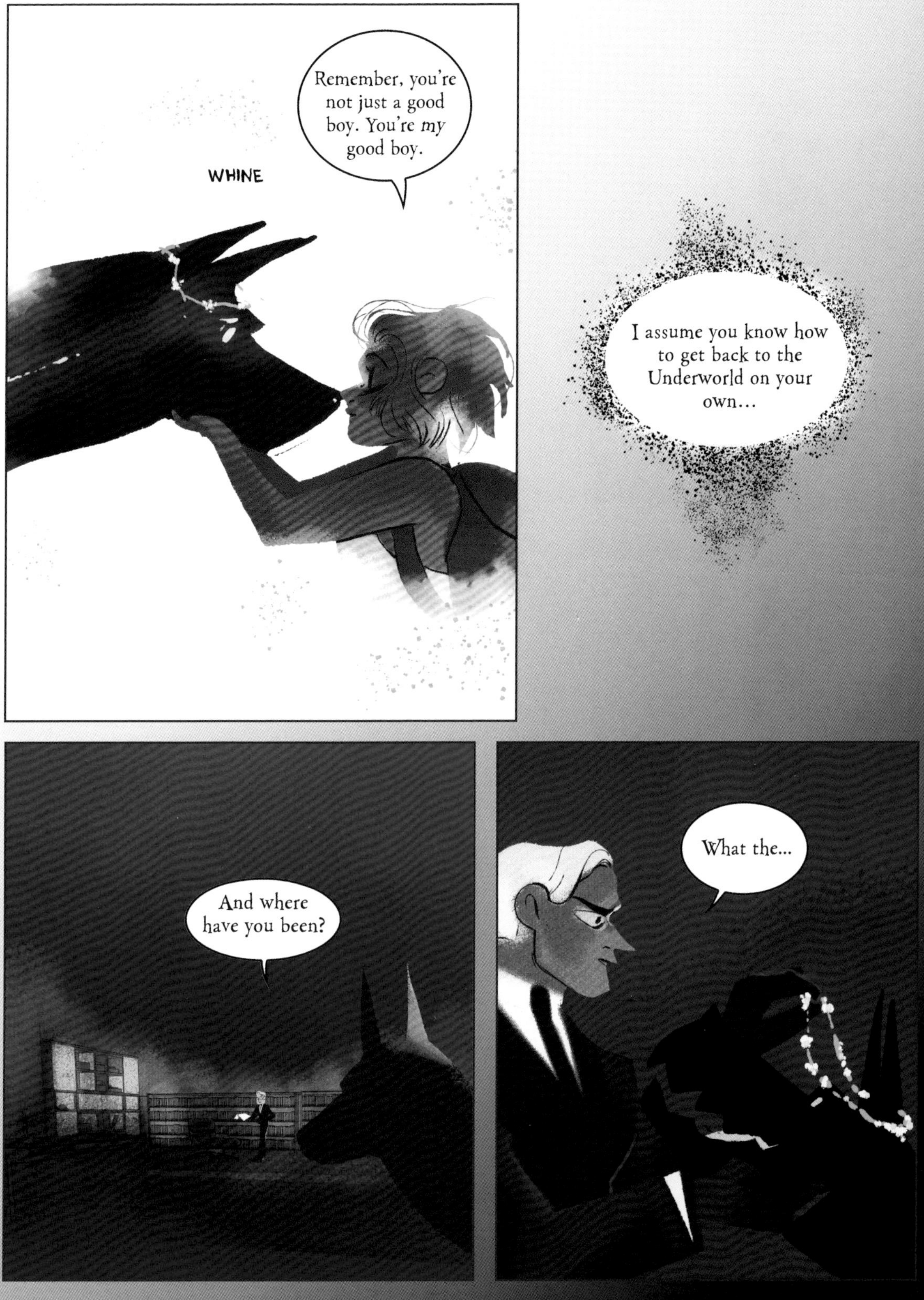

WHINE
Remember, you're not just a good boy. You're *my* good boy.
I assume you know how to get back to the Underworld on your own...
And where have you been?
What the...

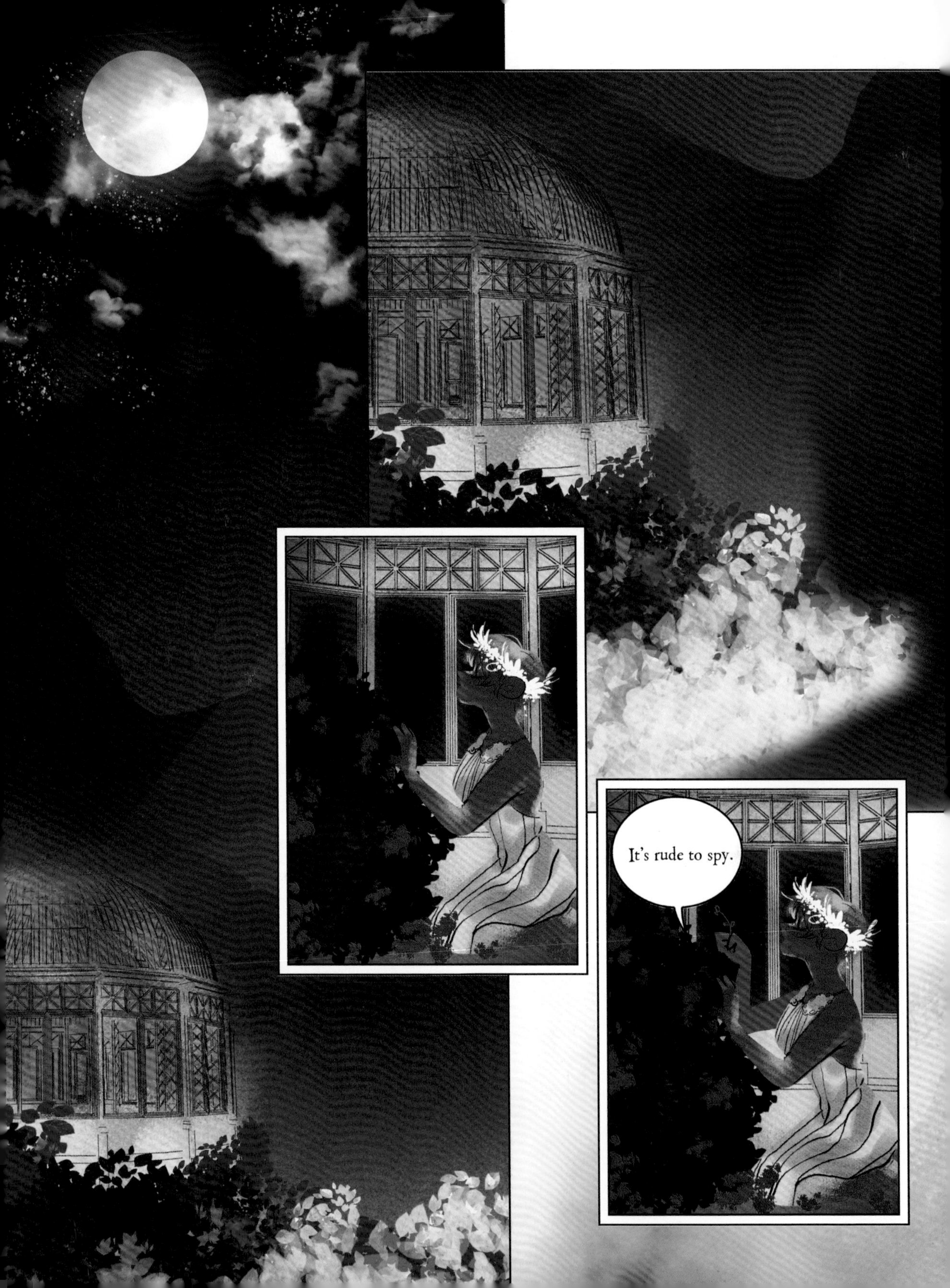
It's rude to spy.

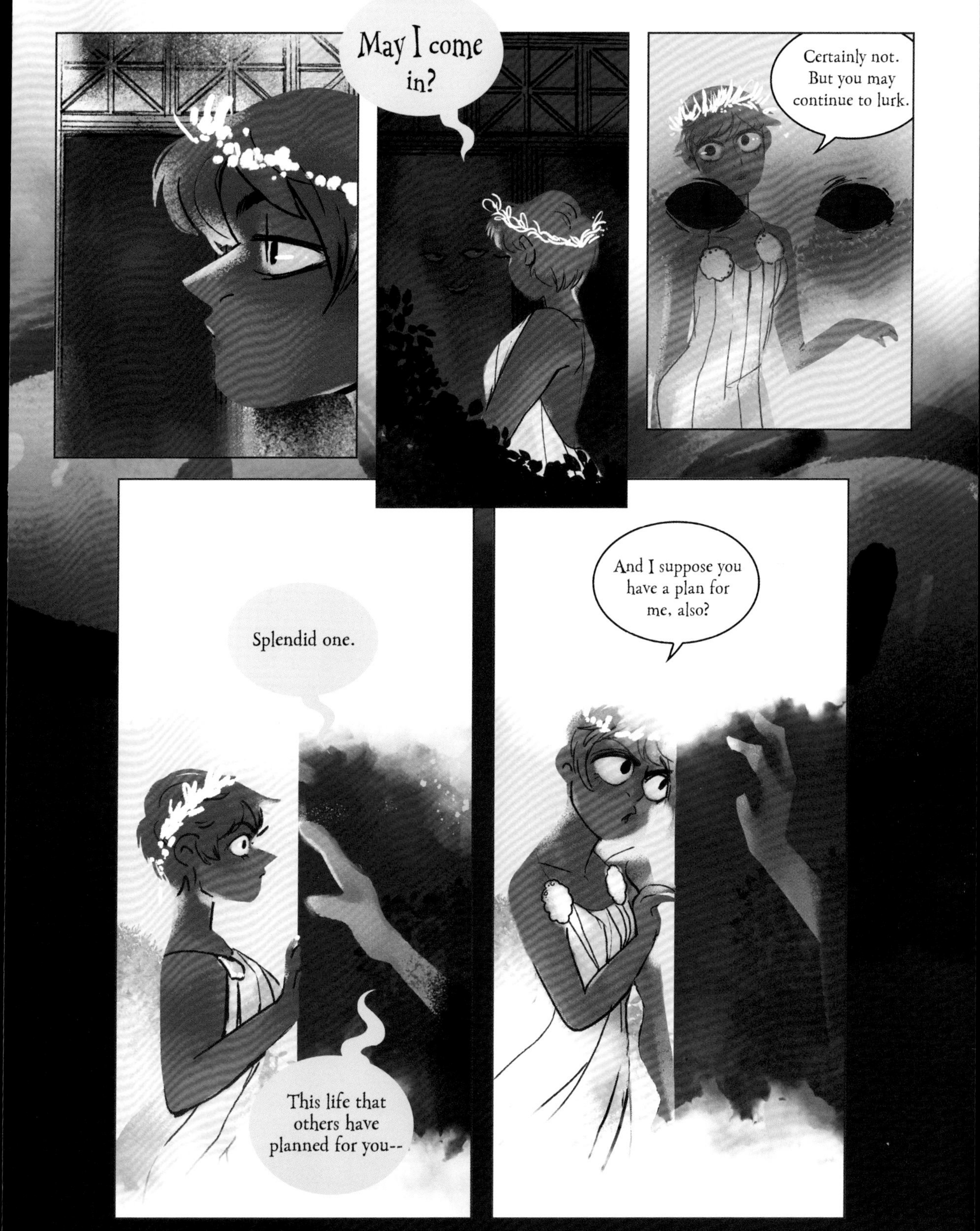
May I come in?
Certainly not. But you may continue to lurk.
Splendid one.
This life that others have planned for you--
And I suppose you have a plan for me, also?

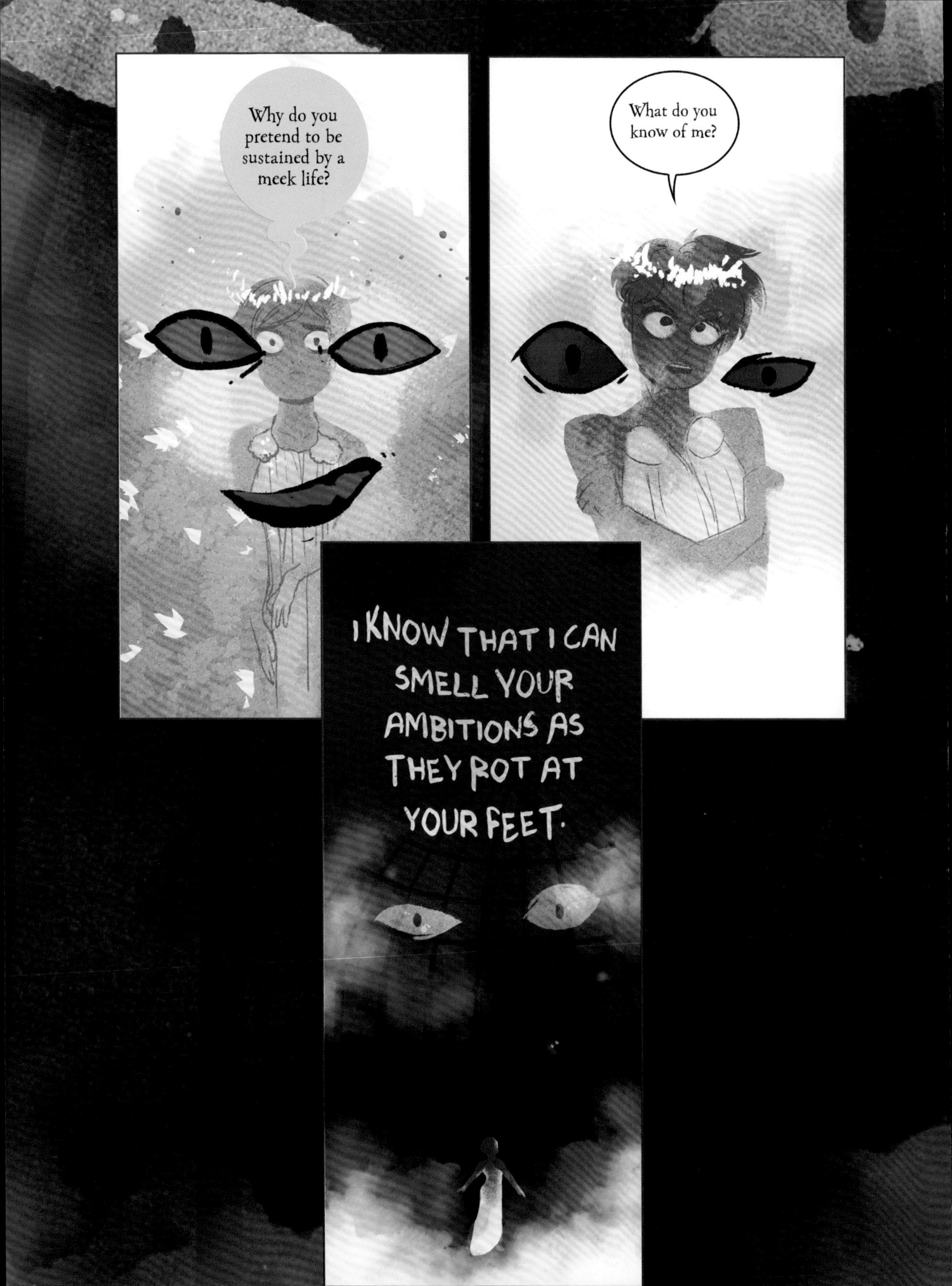
Why do you pretend to be sustained by a meek life?
What do you know of me?
I KNOW THAT I CAN SMELL YOUR AMBITIONS AS THEY ROT AT YOUR FEET.

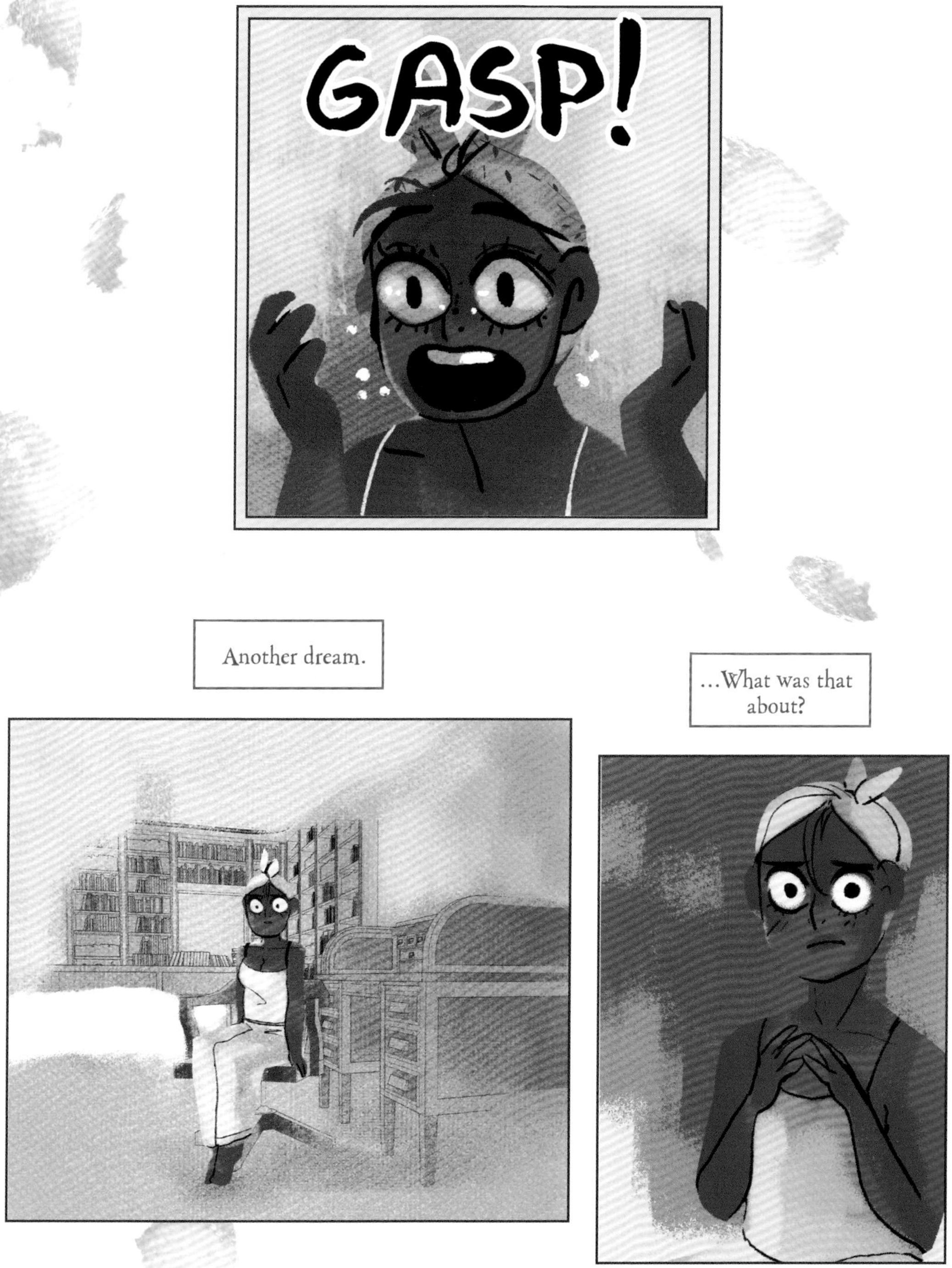
GASP!
Another dream.
...What was that about?

EPISODE 38: MEETING READY

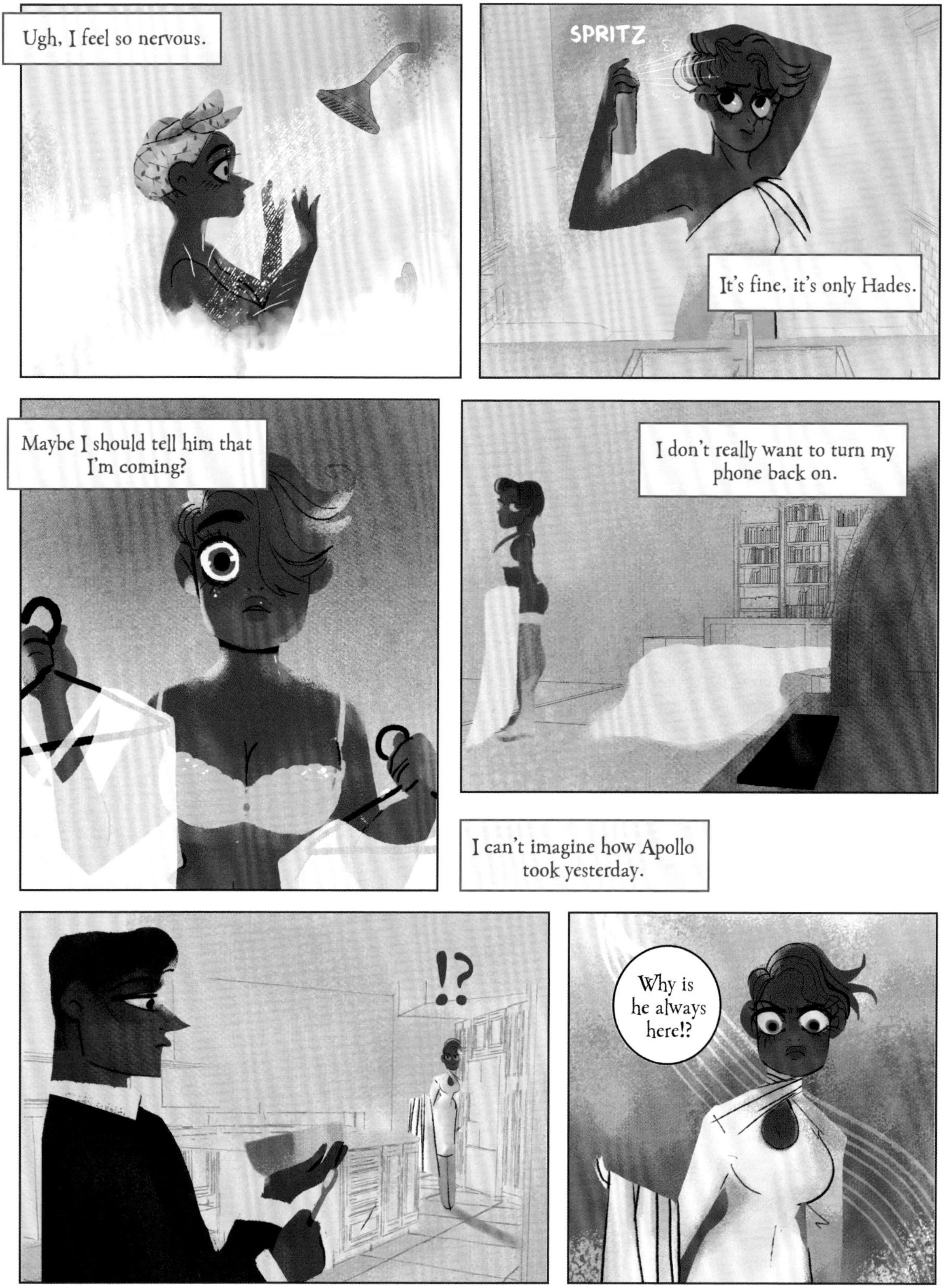
Ugh, I feel so nervous.
SPRITZ
It's fine, it's only Hades.
Maybe I should tell him that I'm coming?
I don't really want to turn my phone back on.
I can't imagine how Apollo took yesterday.
!?
Why is he always here!?

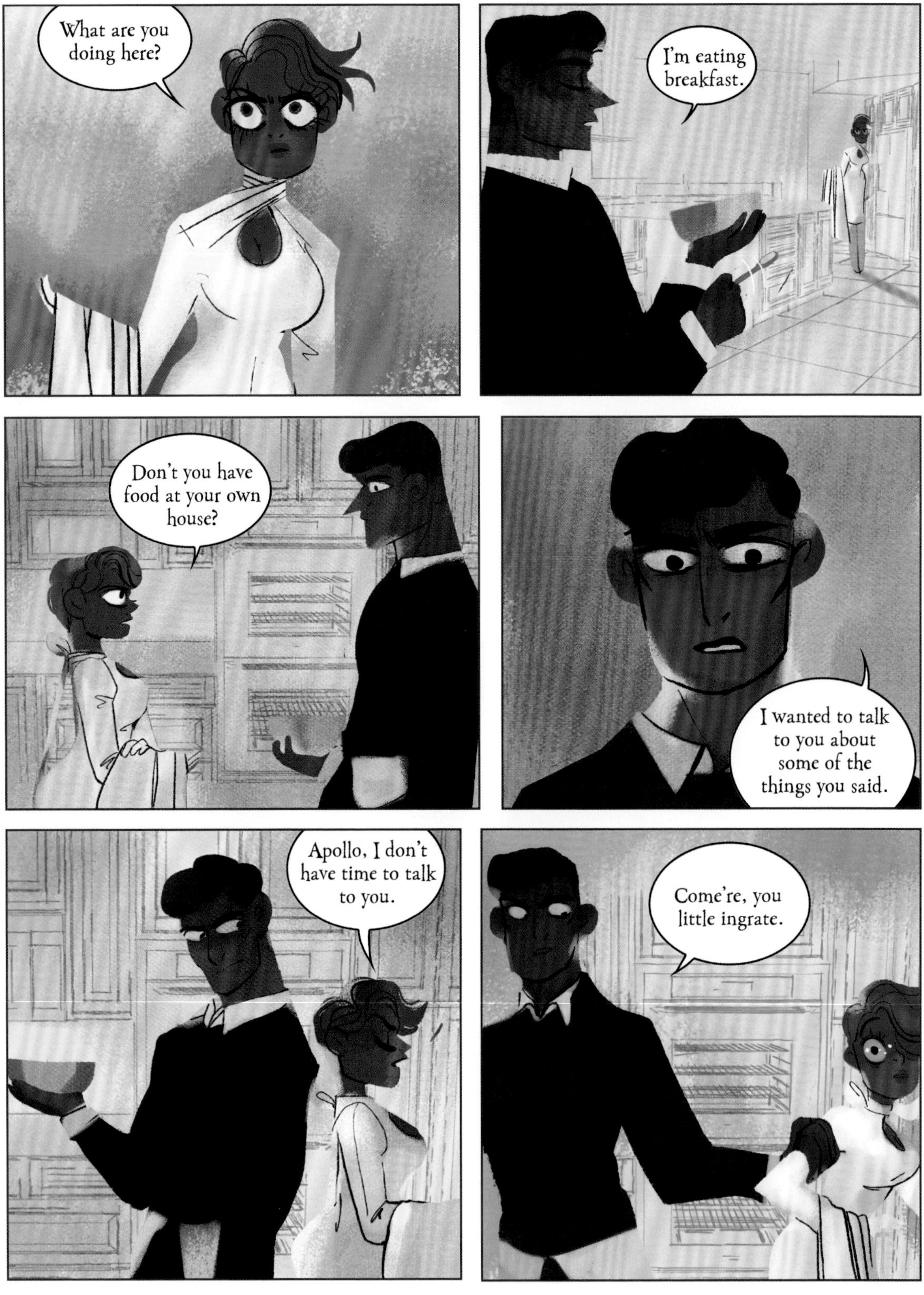
What are you doing here?
I'm eating breakfast.
Don't you have food at your own house?
I wanted to talk to you about some of the things you said.
Apollo, I don't have time to talk to you.
Come're, you little ingrate.

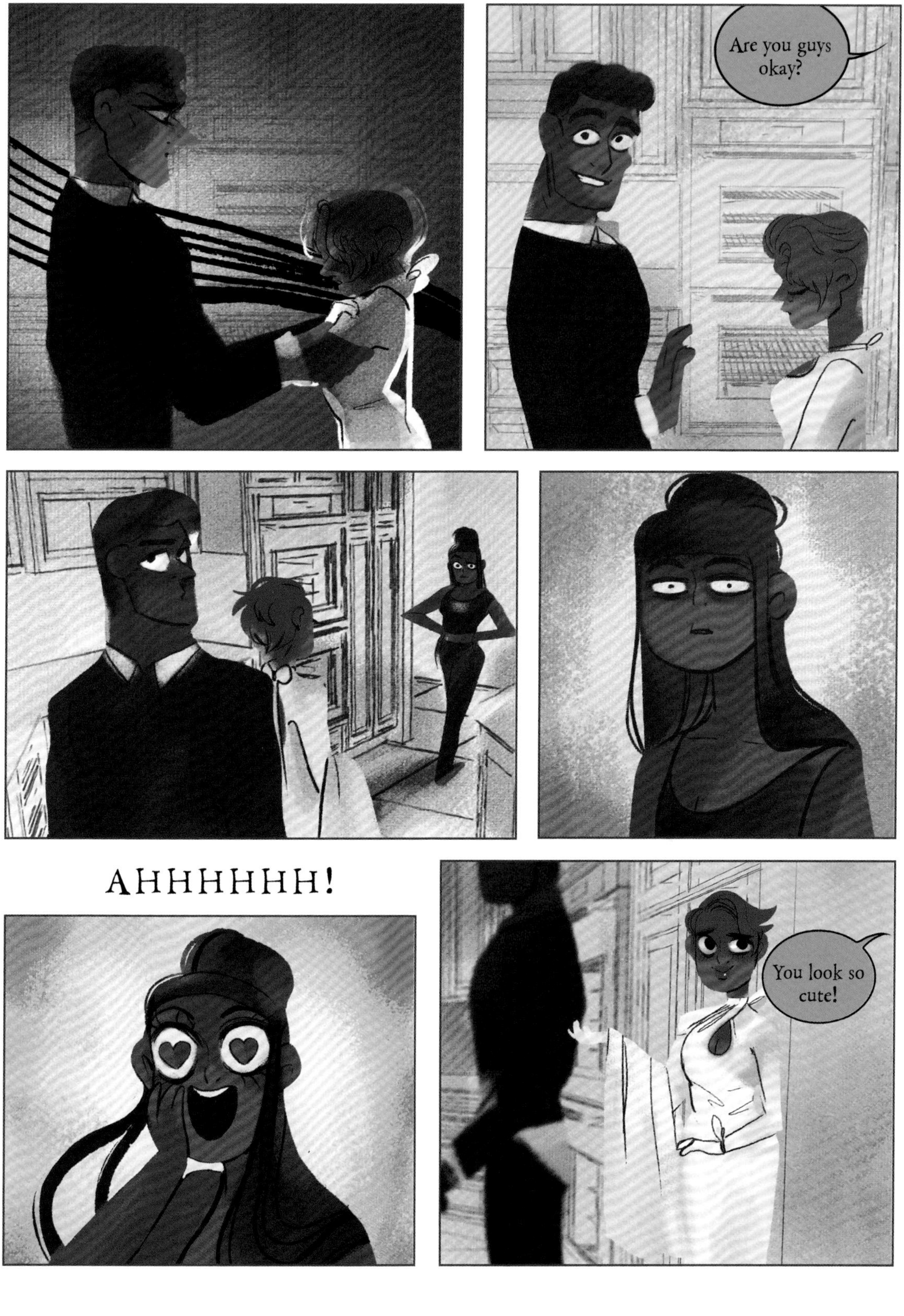
Are you guys okay?
AHHHHHH!
You look so cute!

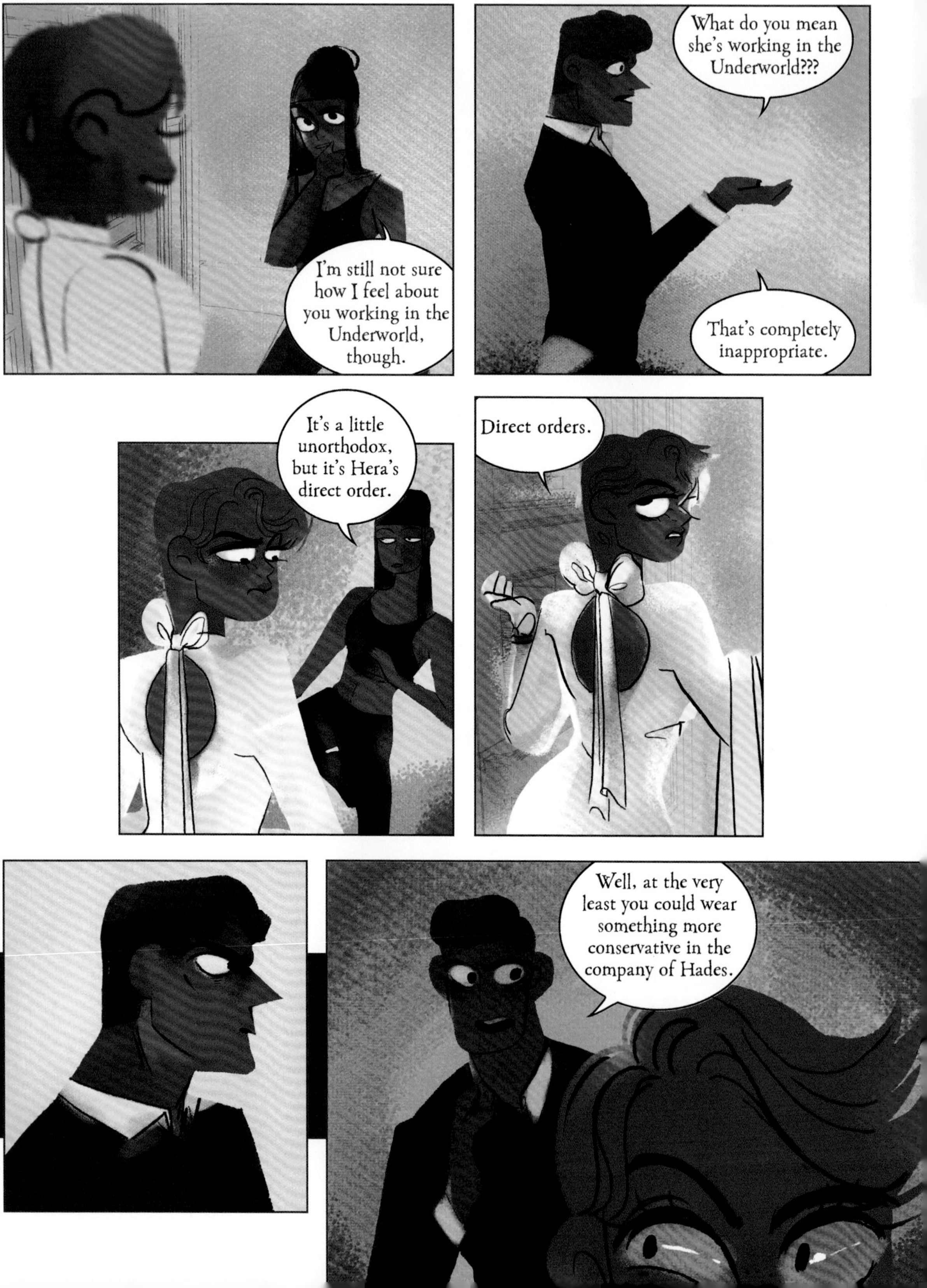
I'm still not sure how I feel about you working in the Underworld, though.
What do you mean she's working in the Underworld???
That's completely inappropriate.
It's a little unorthodox, but it's Hera's direct order.
Direct orders.
Well, at the very least you could wear something more conservative in the company of Hades.

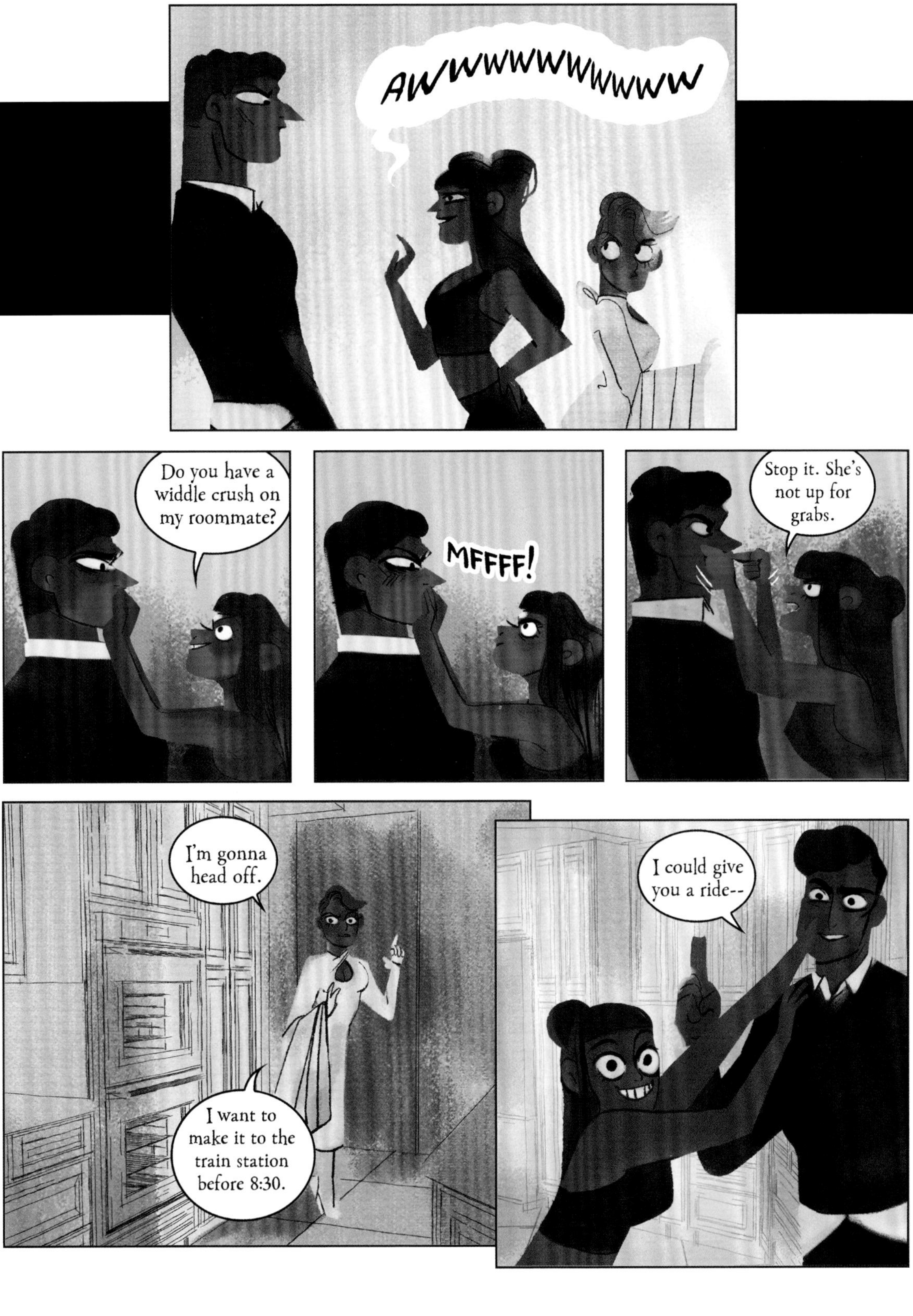
AWWWWWWWWWWW
Do you have a widdle crush on my roommate?
MFFFF!
Stop it. She's not up for grabs.
I'm gonna head off.
I want to make it to the train station before 8:30.
I could give you a ride--

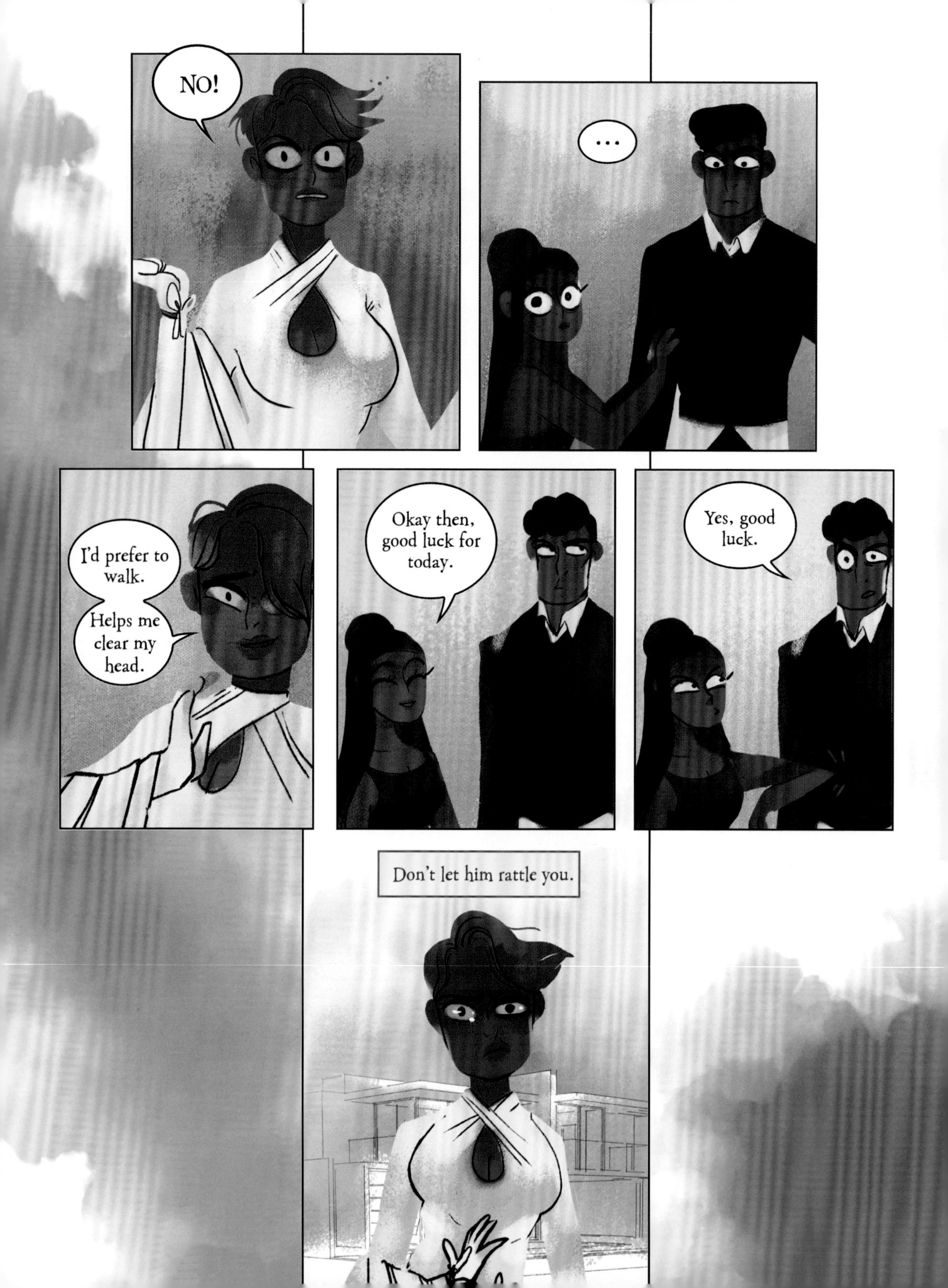
NO!
...
I'd prefer to walk.
Helps me clear my head.
Okay then, good luck for today.
Yes, good luck.
Don't let him rattle you.

Oh my, it's very crowded.

Sorry, princess, but I'm late for my meeting.

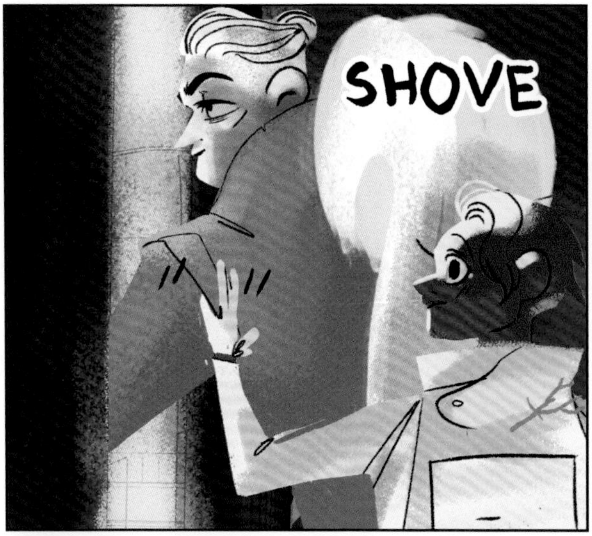
SHOVE

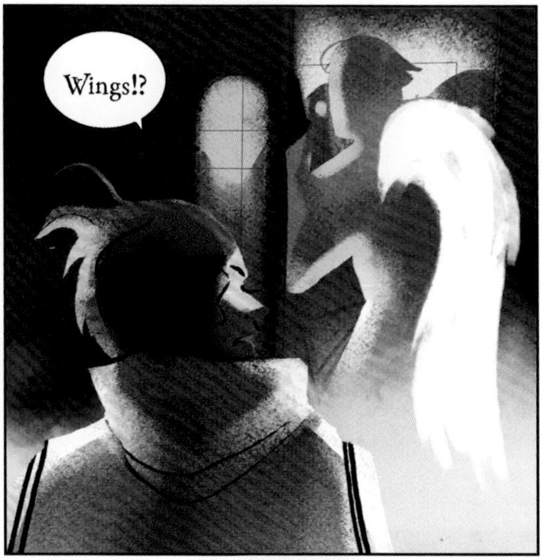
Wings!?

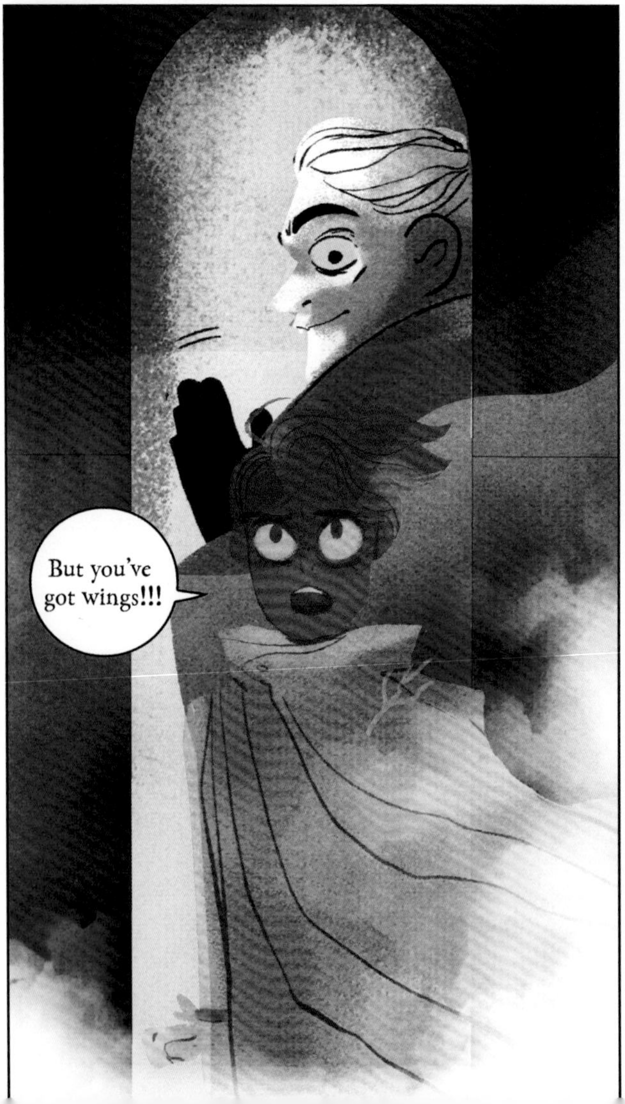
But you've
got wings!!!

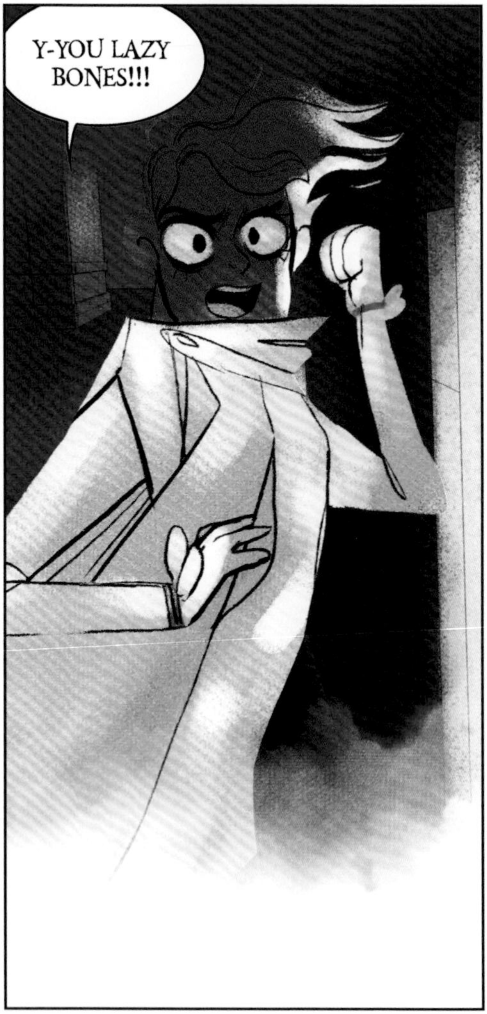
Y-YOU LAZY
BONES!!!

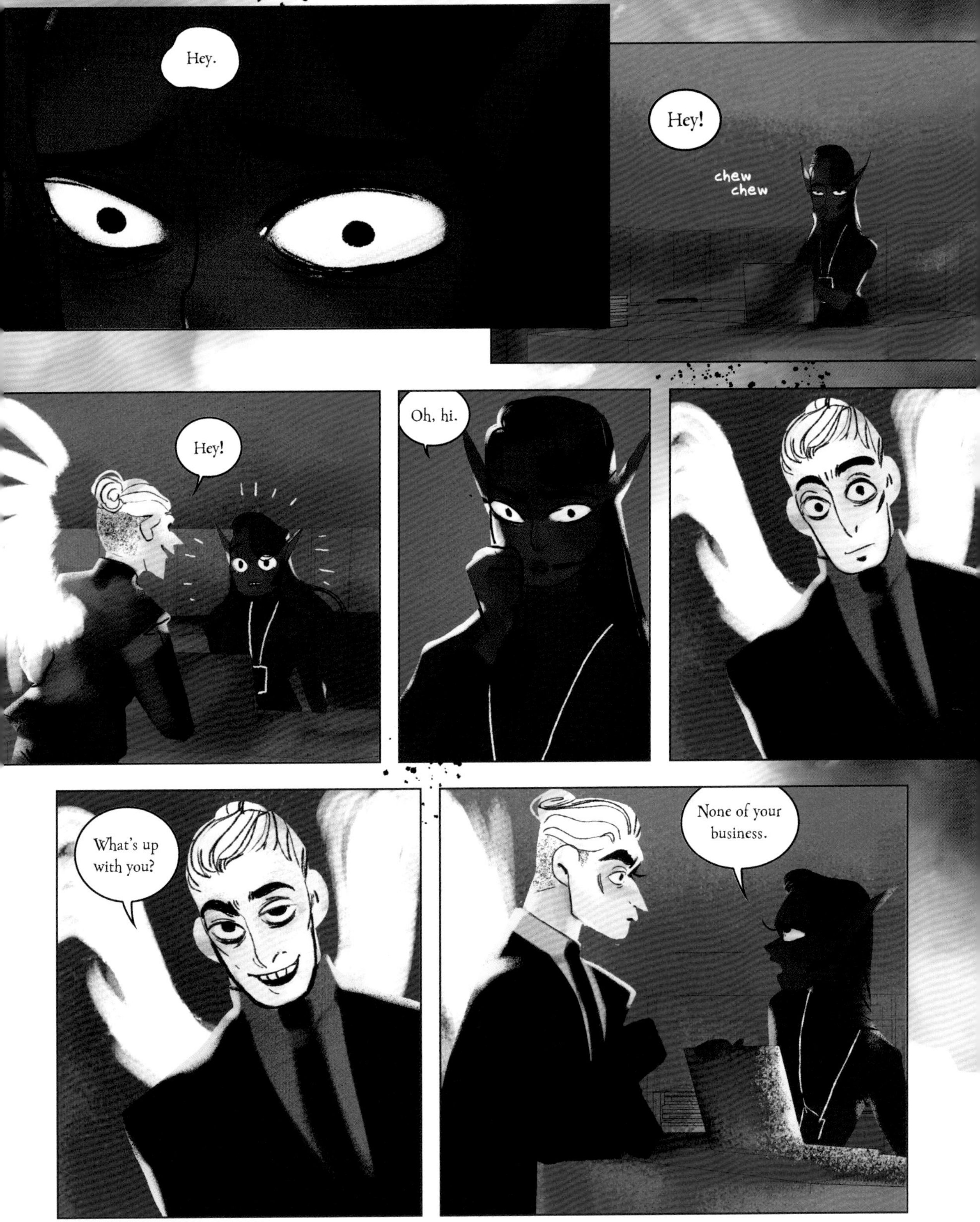
Hey.
Hey!
chew chew
Hey!
Oh, hi.
What's up with you?
None of your business.

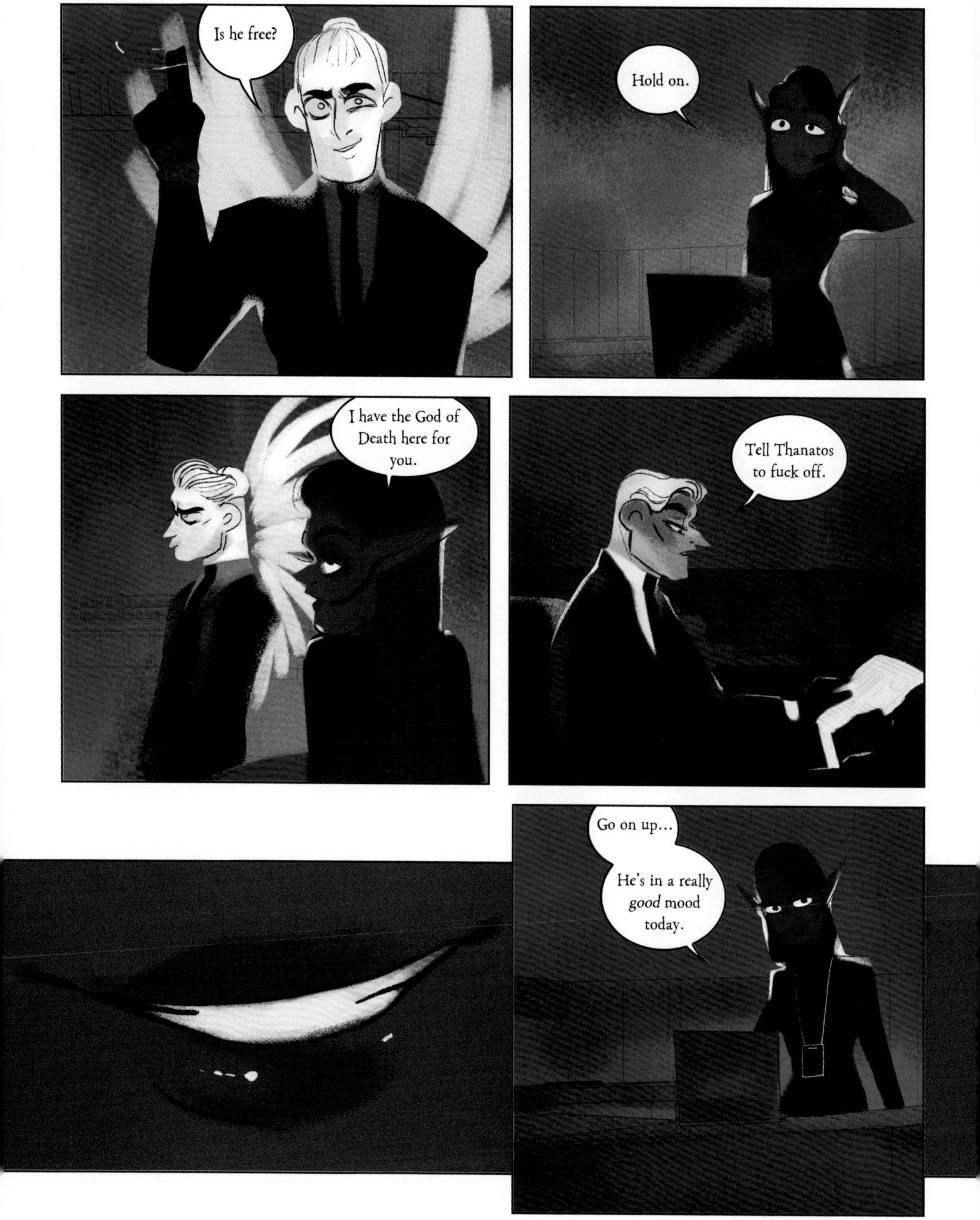
Is he free?
Hold on.
I have the God of Death here for you.
Tell Thanatos to fuck off.
Go on up...
He's in a really *good* mood today.

EPISODE 39: TOWER 4

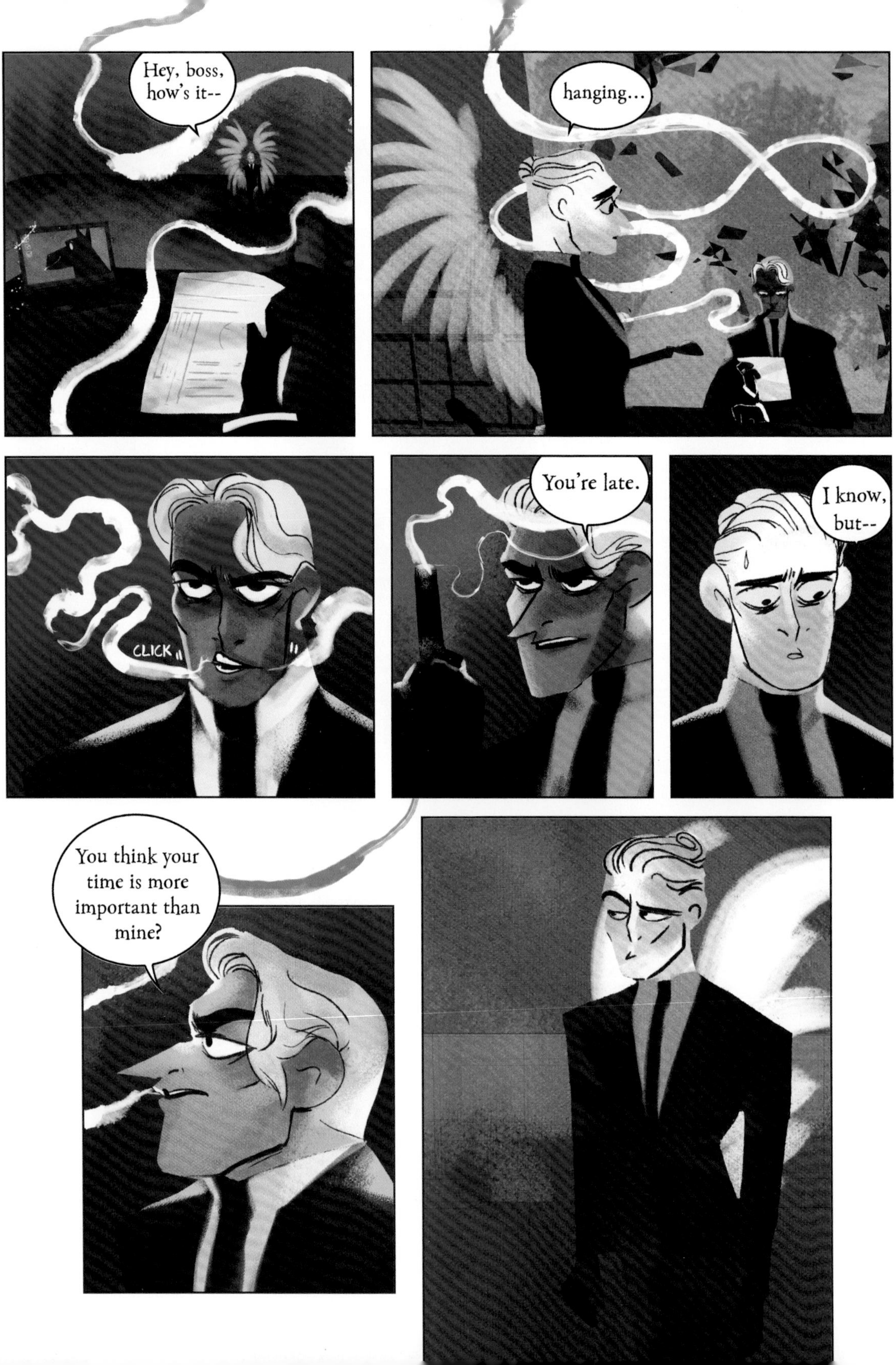
Hey, boss, how's it--
hanging...
CLICK
You're late.
I know, but--
You think your time is more important than mine?

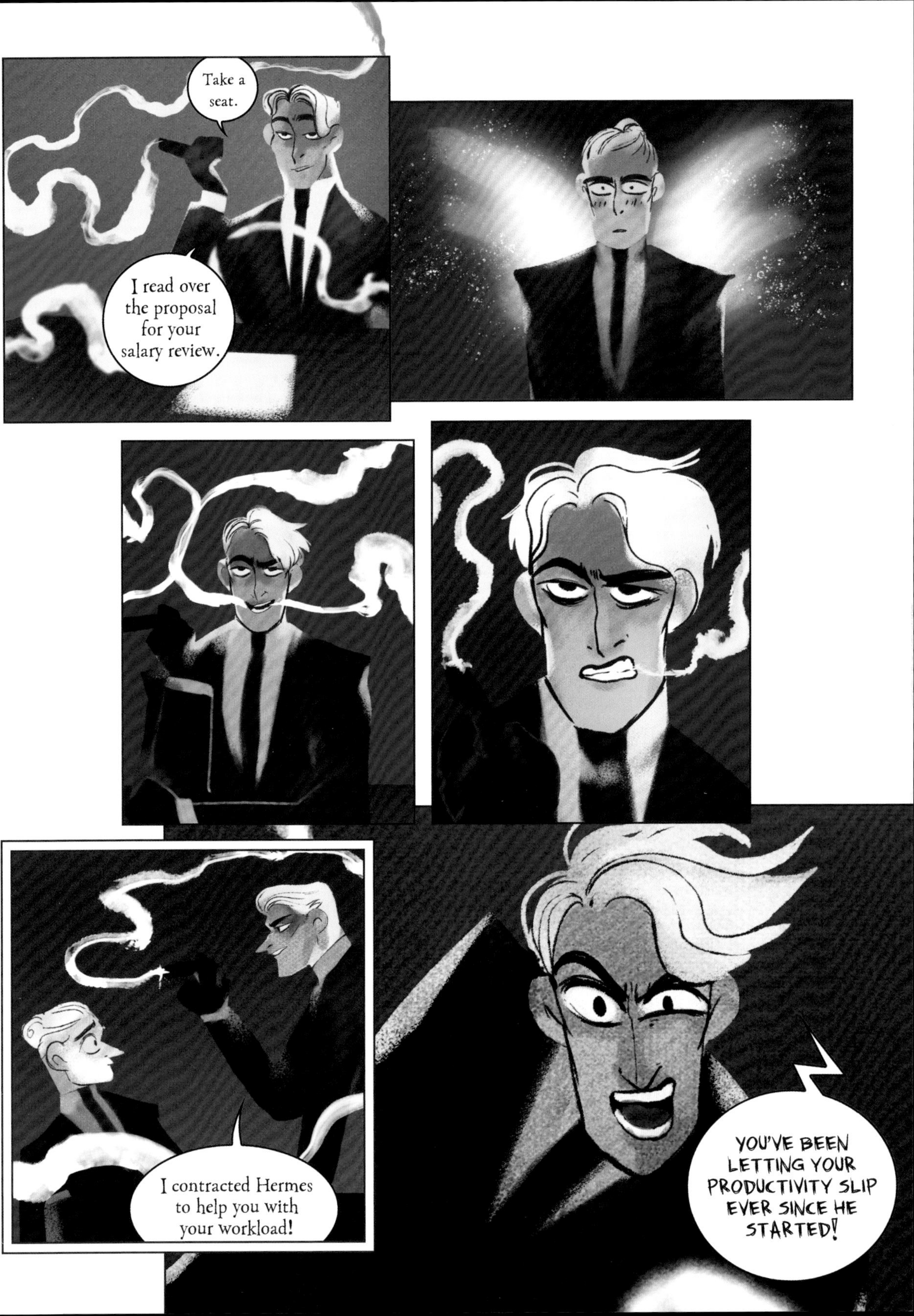
Take a seat.
I read over the proposal for your salary review.
I contracted Hermes to help you with your workload!
YOU'VE BEEN LETTING YOUR PRODUCTIVITY SLIP EVER SINCE HE STARTED!

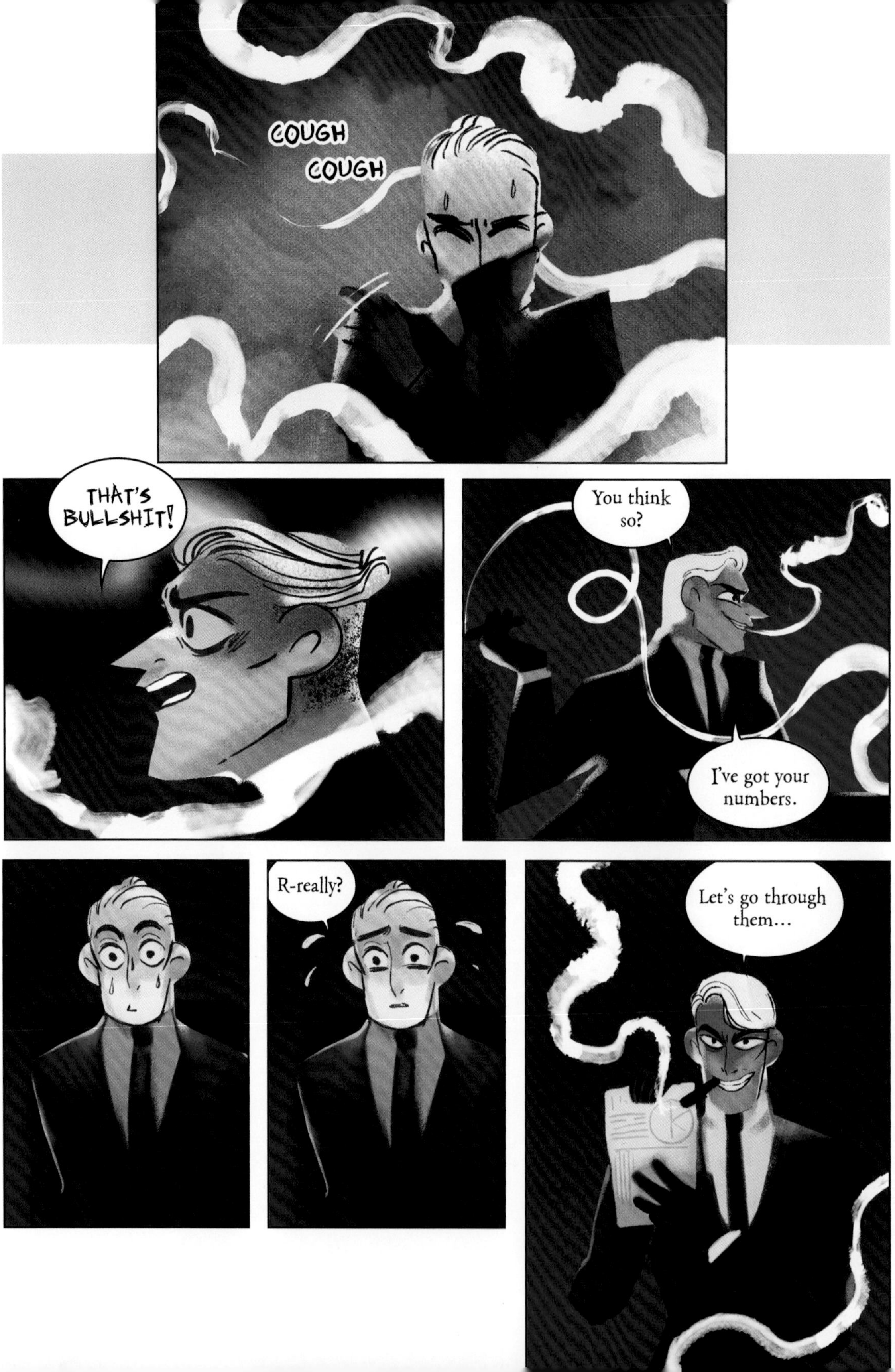
COUGH
COUGH
THAT'S BULLSHIT!
You think so?
I've got your numbers.
R-really?
Let's go through them...

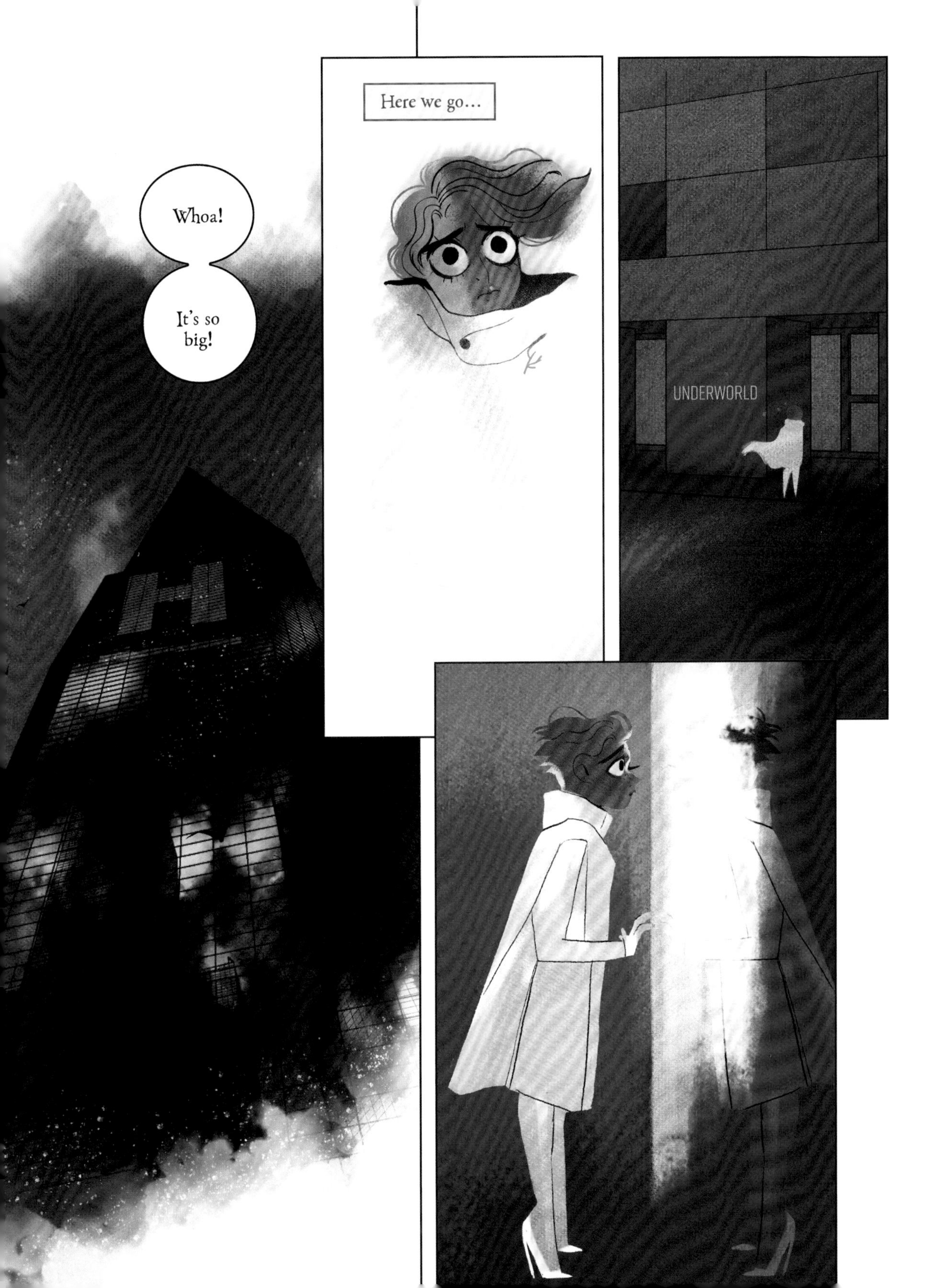
Whoa!
It's so big!
Here we go...
UNDERWORLD

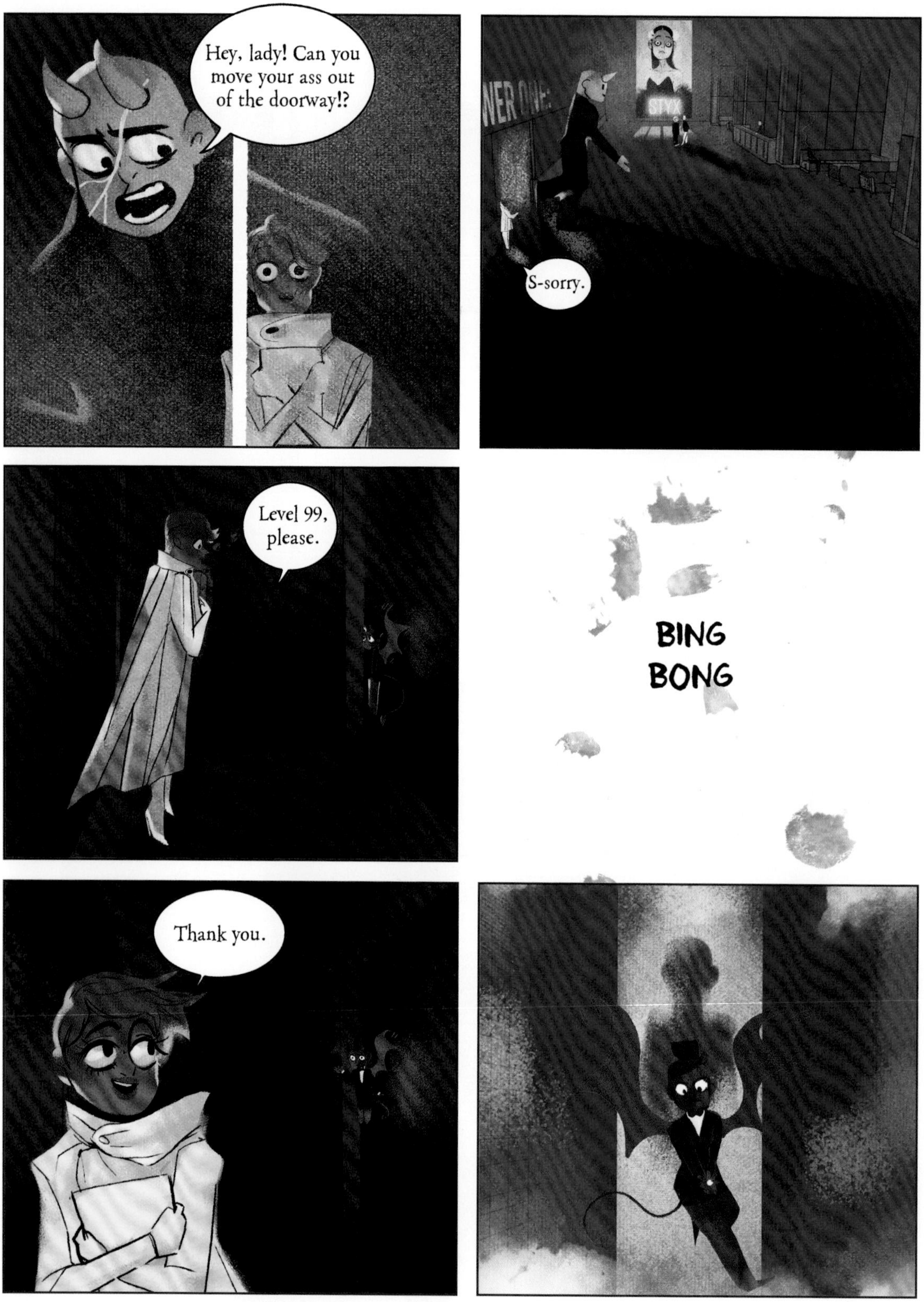
Hey, lady! Can you move your ass out of the doorway!?
STYX
S-sorry.
Level 99, please.
BING
BONG
Thank you.

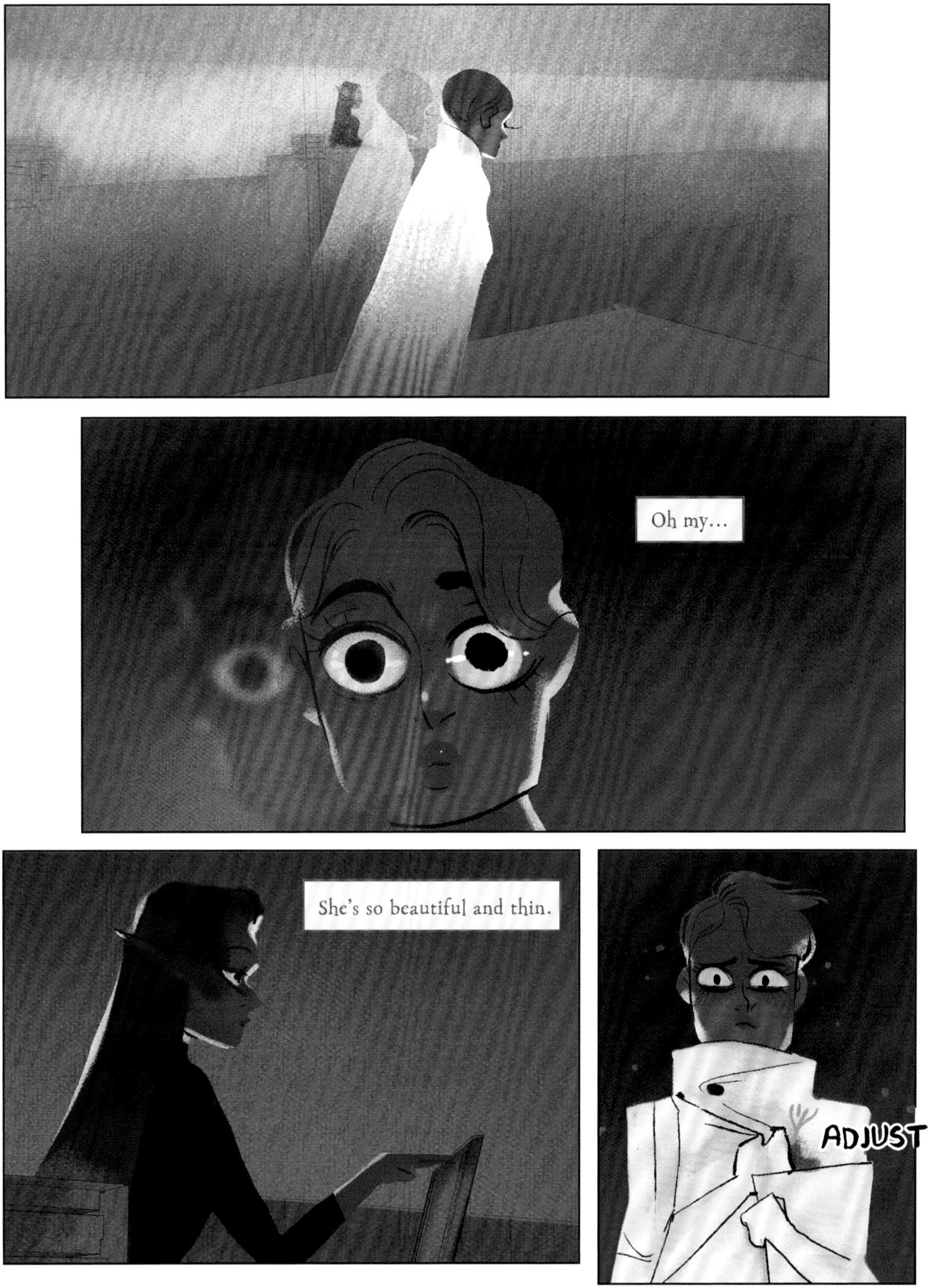

Oh my…
She's so beautiful and thin.
ADJUST

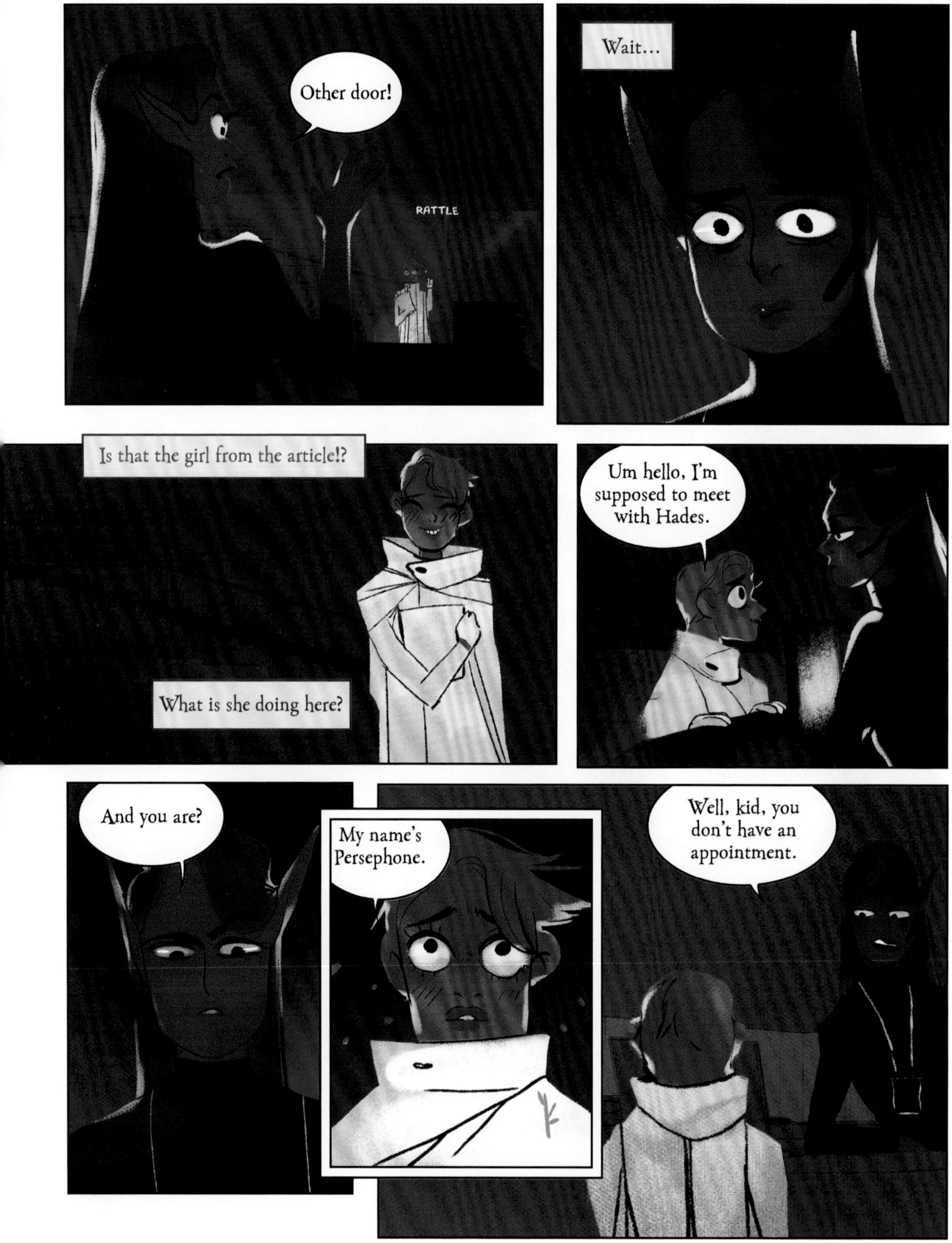
Other door!
RATTLE
Wait...
Is that the girl from the article!?
What is she doing here?
Um hello, I'm supposed to meet with Hades.
And you are?
My name's Persephone.
Well, kid, you don't have an appointment.

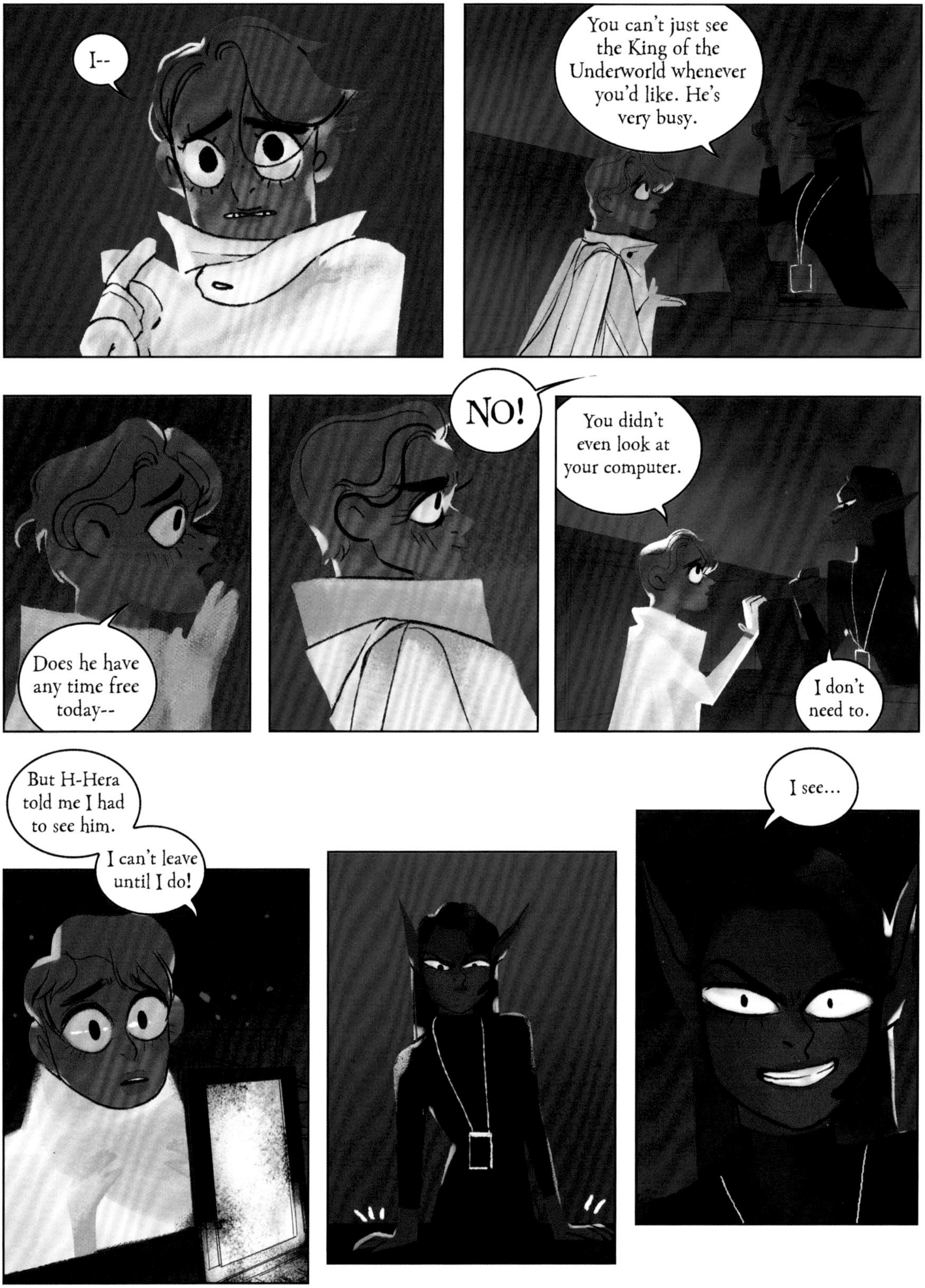
I--
You can't just see the King of the Underworld whenever you'd like. He's very busy.
Does he have any time free today--
NO!
You didn't even look at your computer.
I don't need to.
But H-Hera told me I had to see him.
I can't leave until I do!
I see...

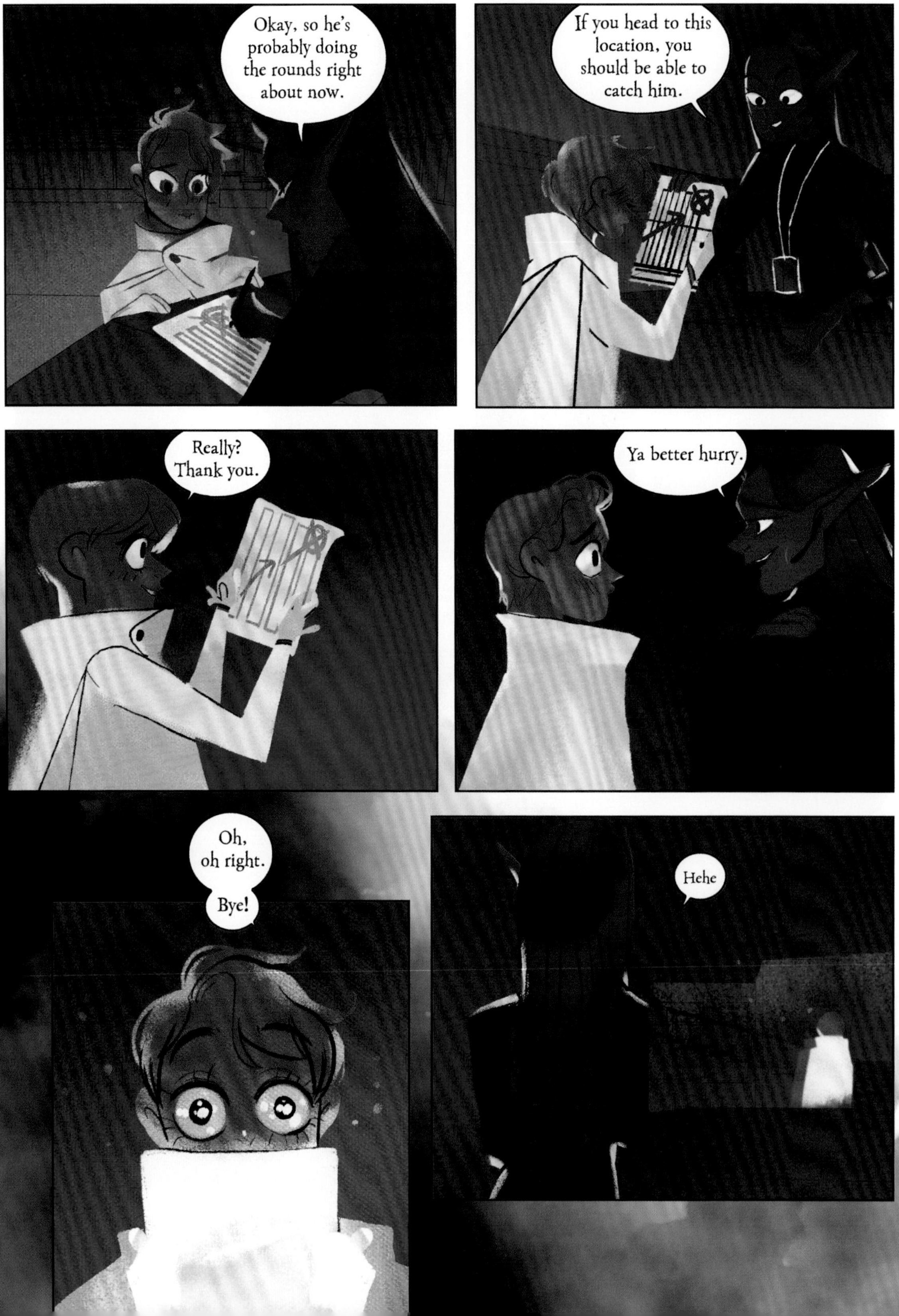
Okay, so he's probably doing the rounds right about now.
If you head to this location, you should be able to catch him.
Really? Thank you.
Ya better hurry.
Oh, oh right.
Bye!
Hehe

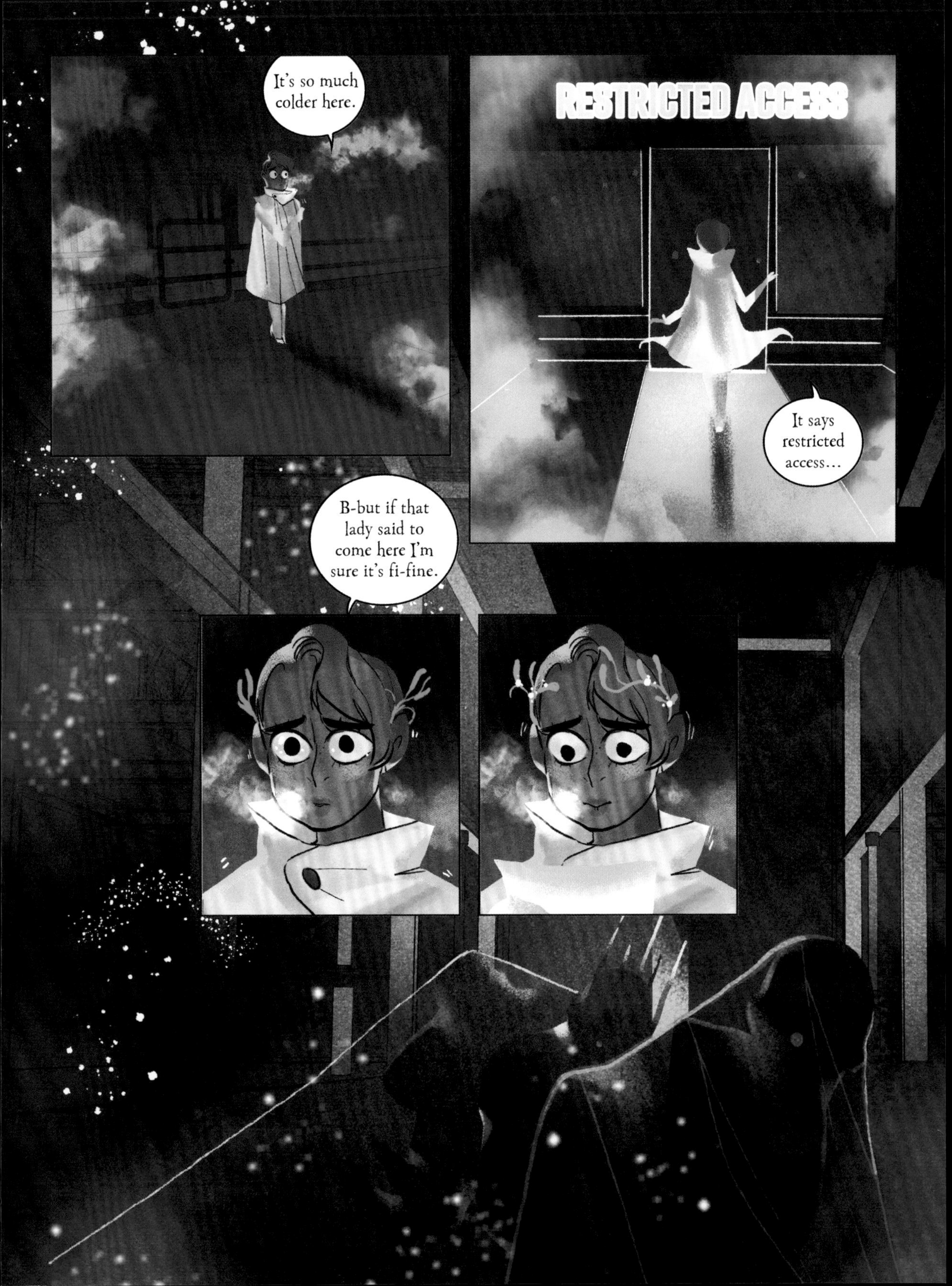
It's so much colder here.
RESTRICTED ACCESS
It says restricted access...
B-but if that lady said to come here I'm sure it's fi-fine.

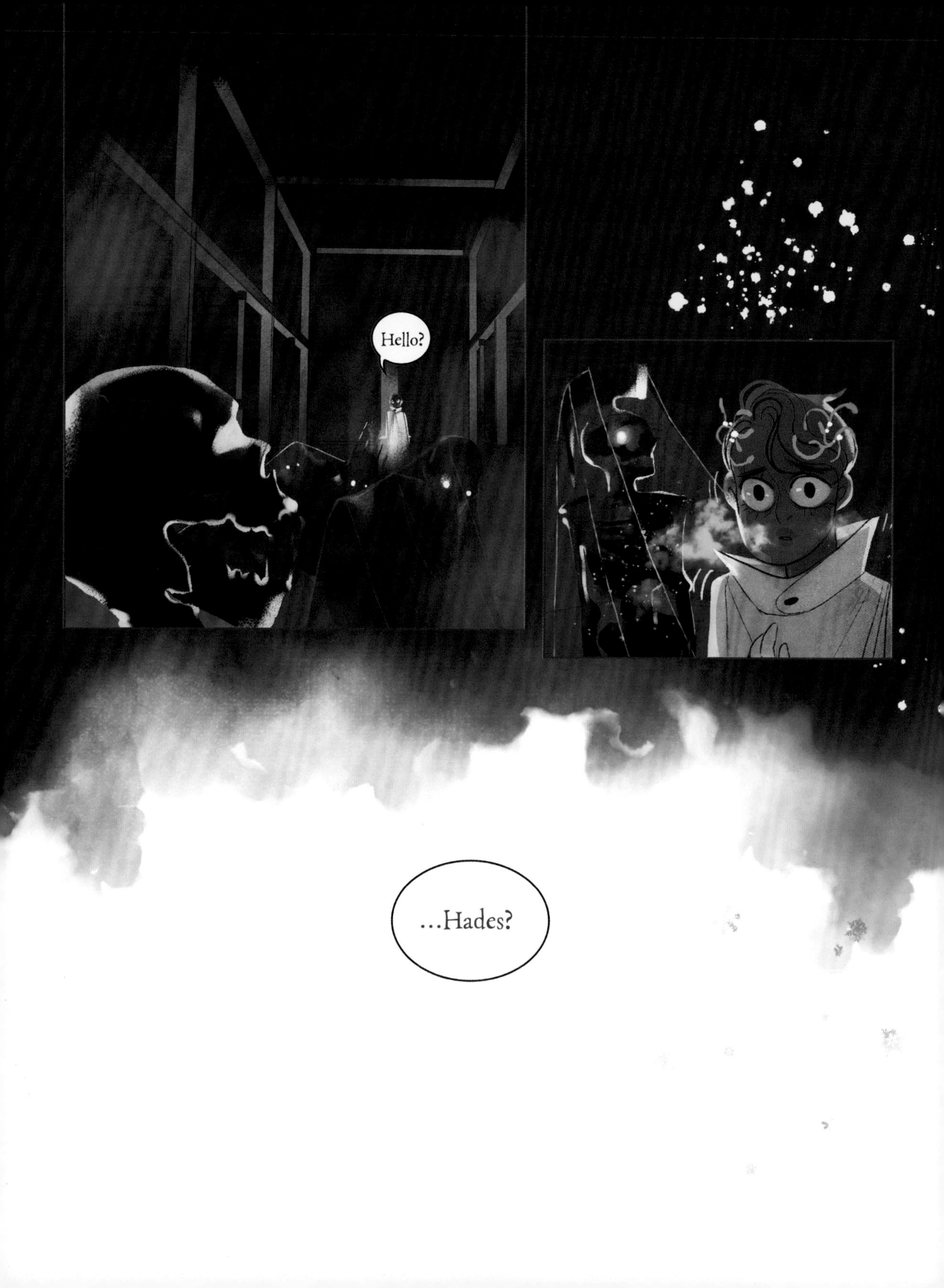
Hello?
...Hades?

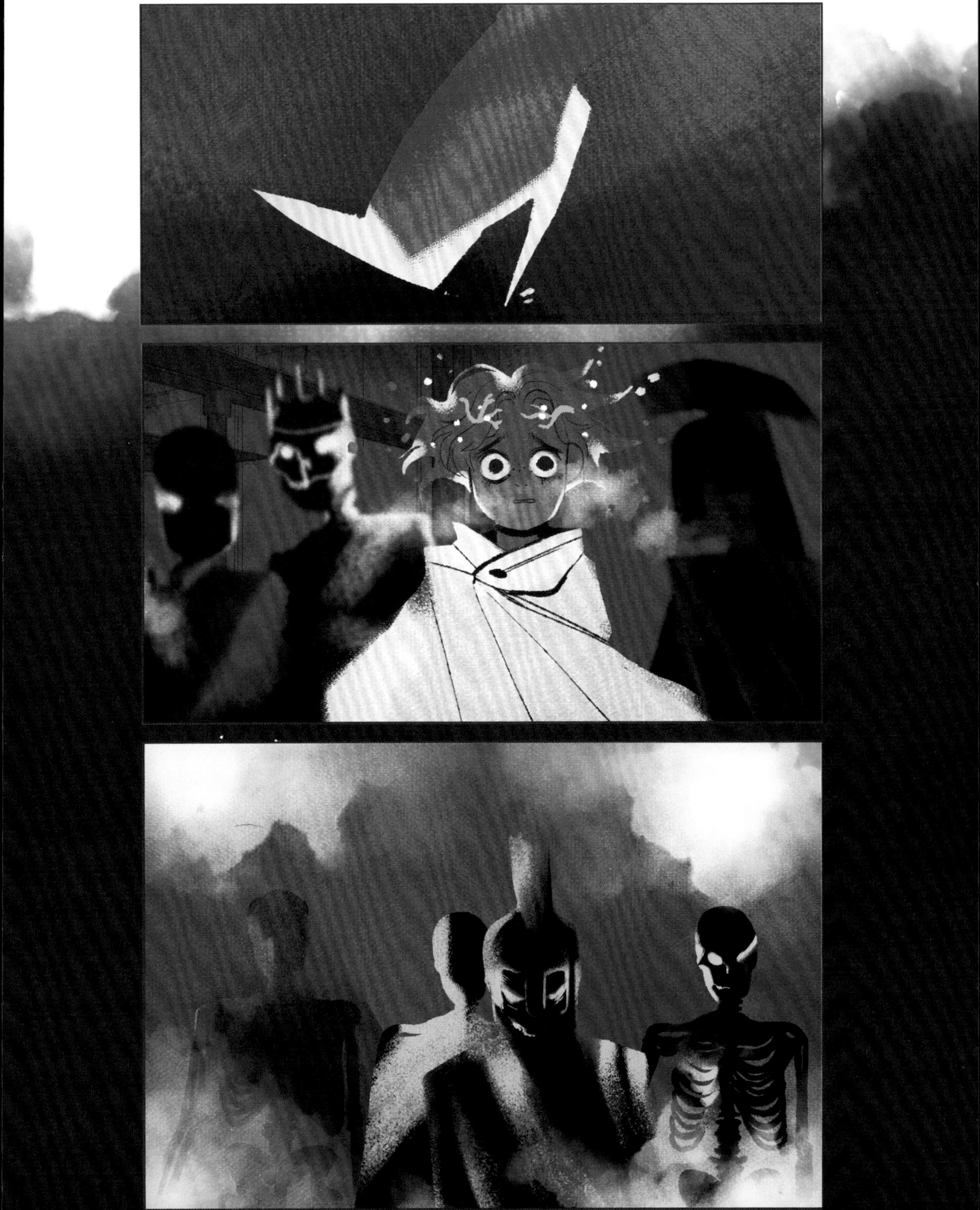

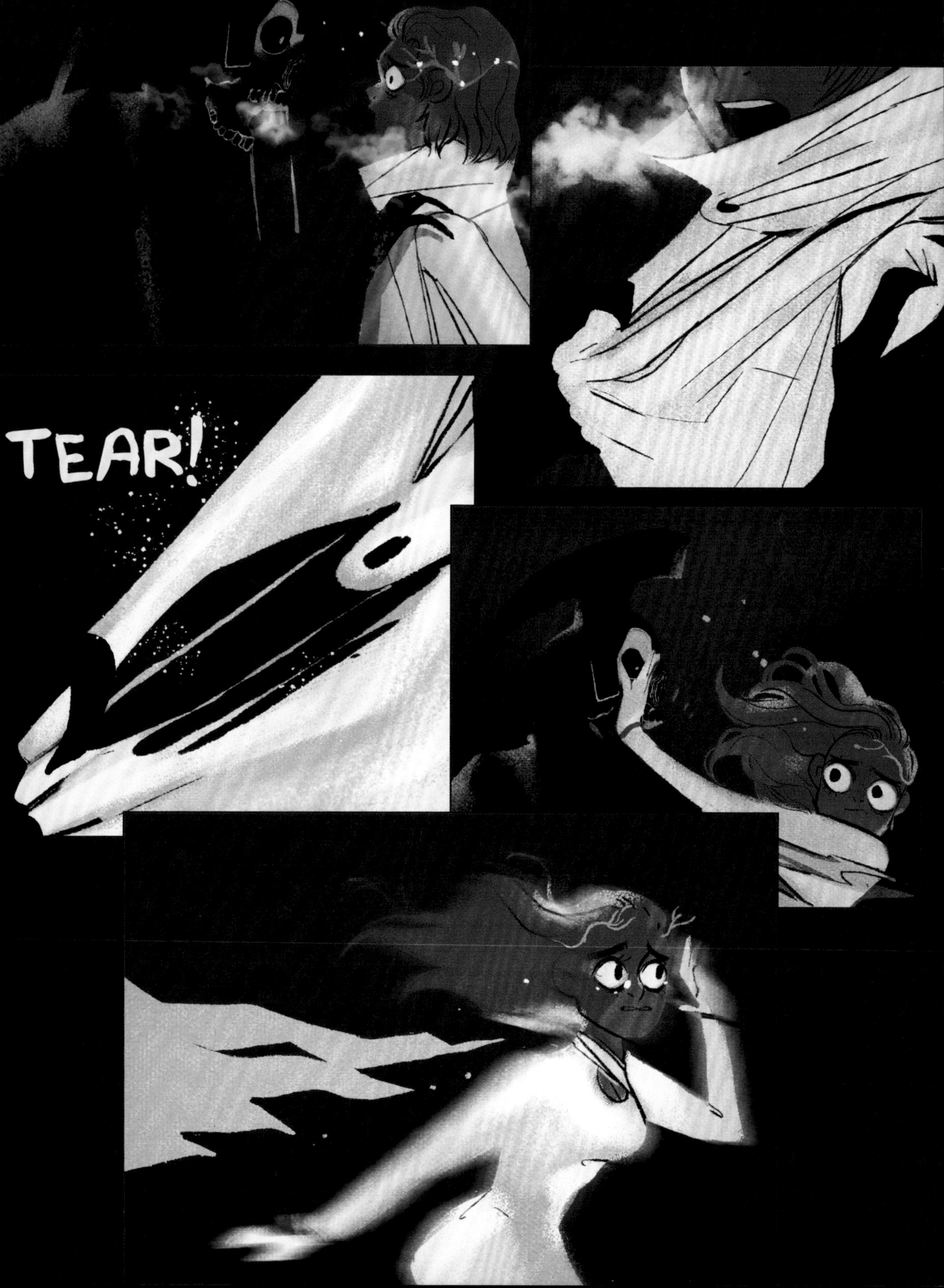
TEAR!

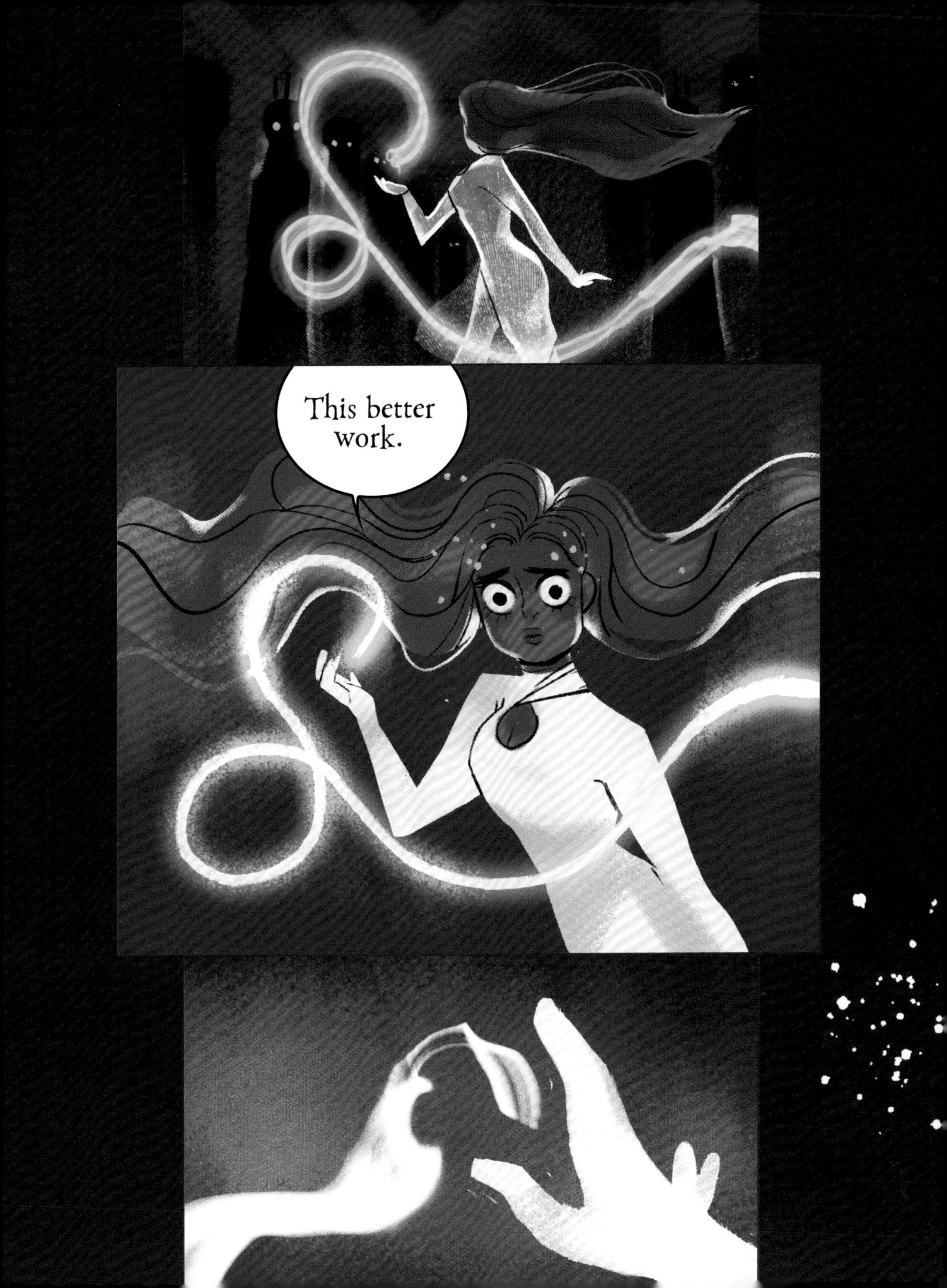
This better work.

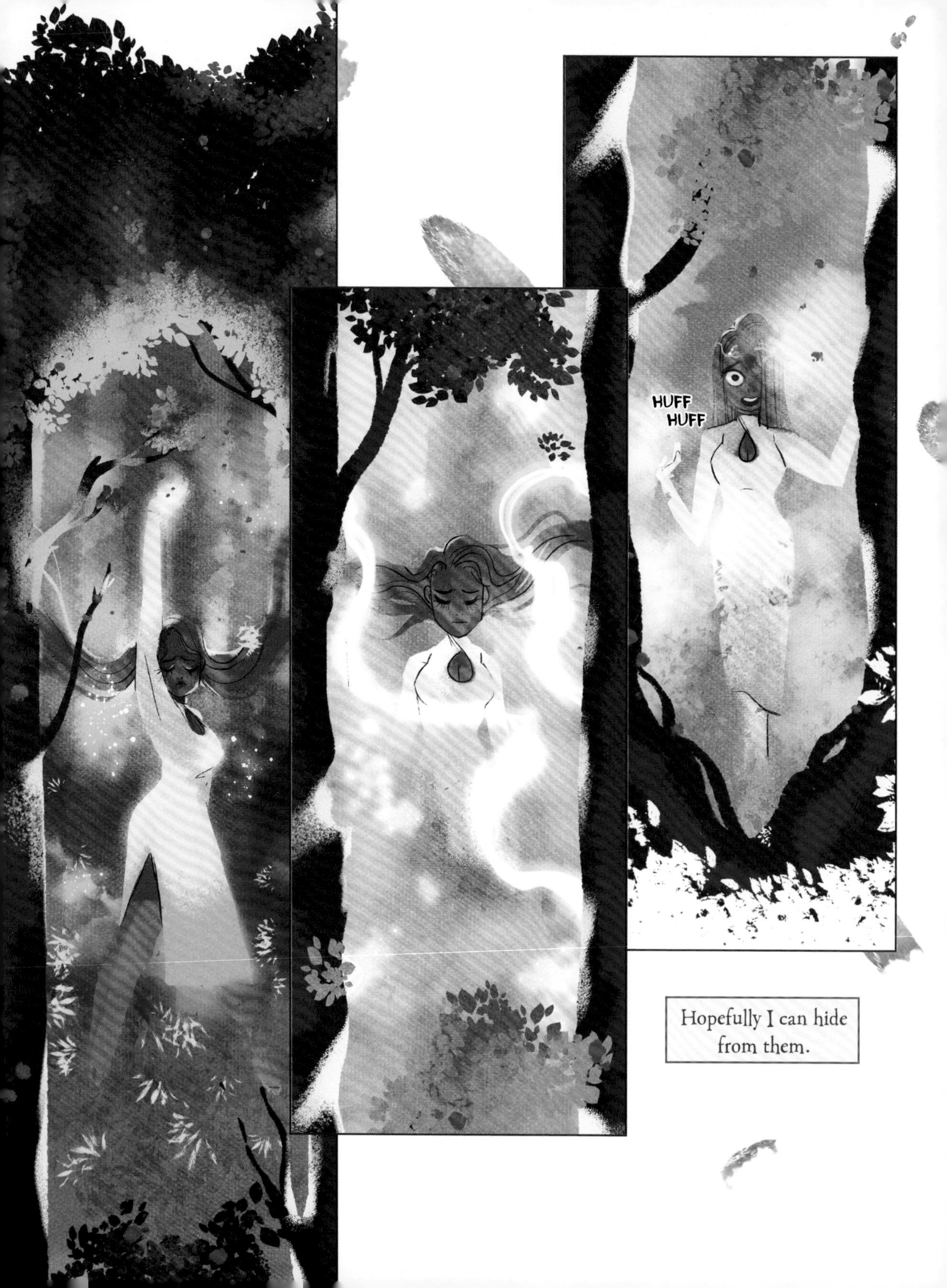
HUFF
HUFF
Hopefully I can hide from them.

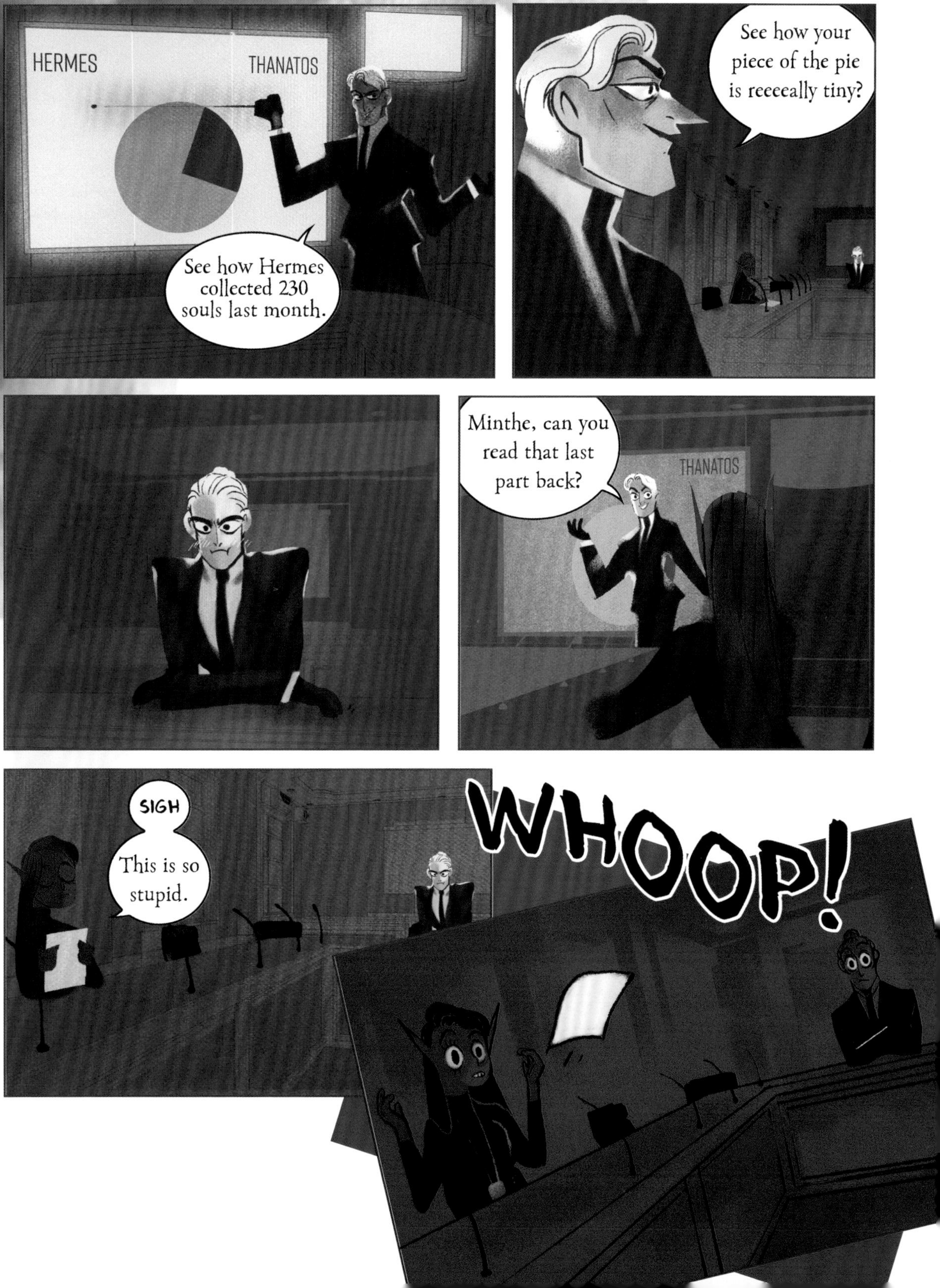
HERMES
THANATOS
See how Hermes collected 230 souls last month.
See how your piece of the pie is reeeeally tiny?
Minthe, can you read that last part back?
THANATOS
SIGH
This is so stupid.
WHOOP!

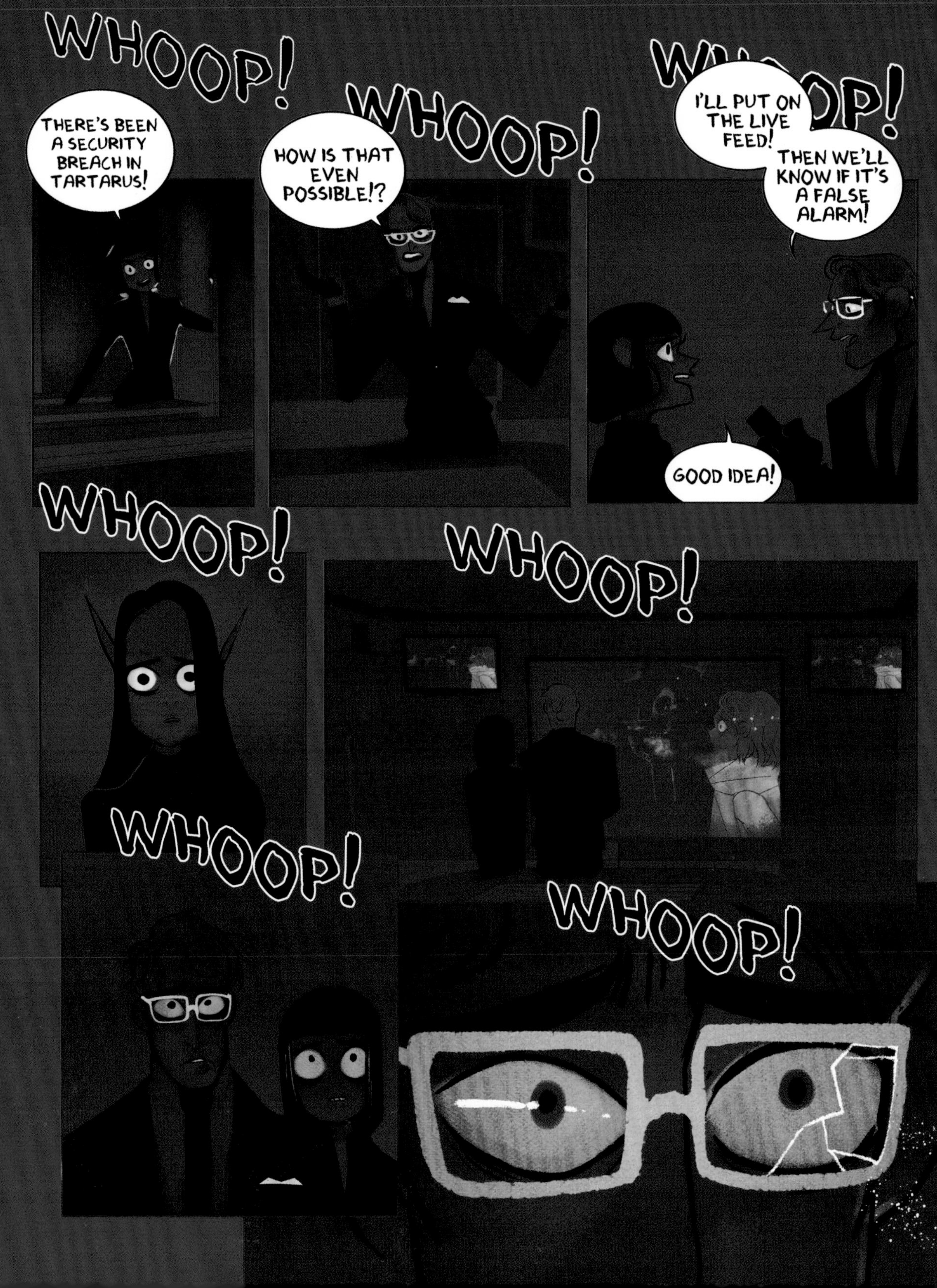
WHOOP!
THERE'S BEEN A SECURITY BREACH IN TARTARUS!
WHOOP!
HOW IS THAT EVEN POSSIBLE!?
WHOOP!
I'LL PUT ON THE LIVE FEED!
THEN WE'LL KNOW IF IT'S A FALSE ALARM!
GOOD IDEA!
WHOOP!
WHOOP!
WHOOP!
WHOOP!

EPISODE 40: HIDE AND SNEAK

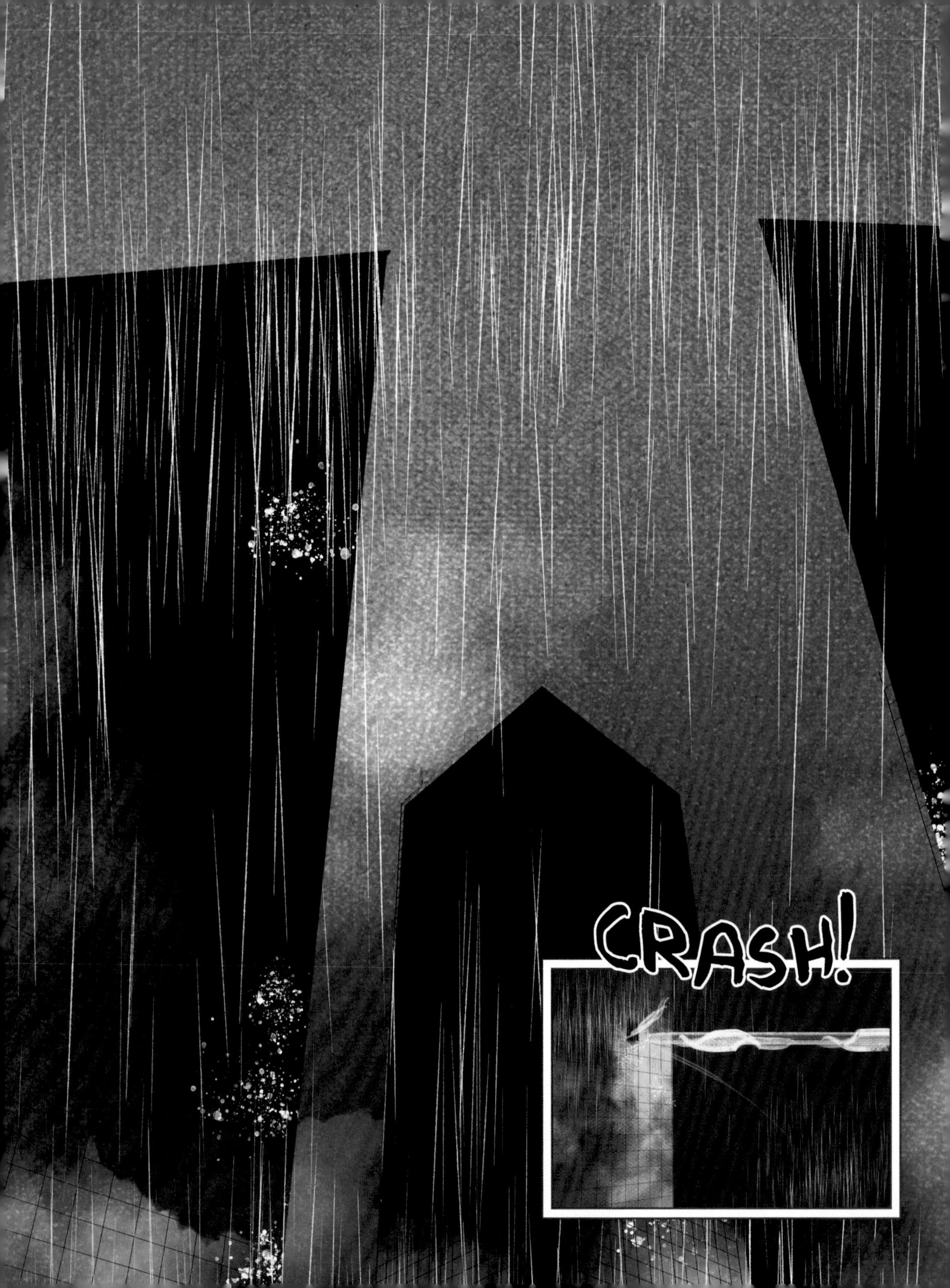
CRASH!

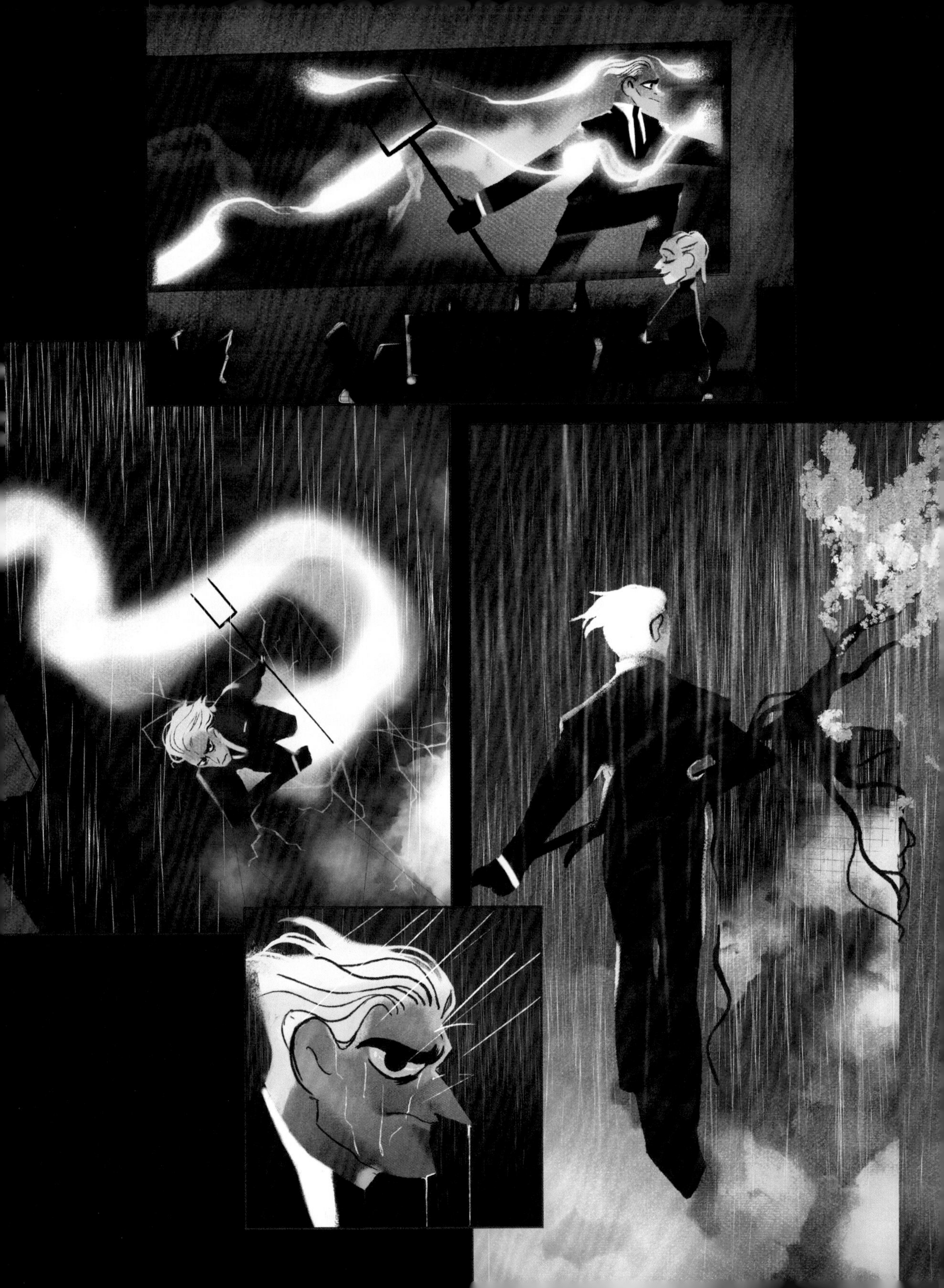

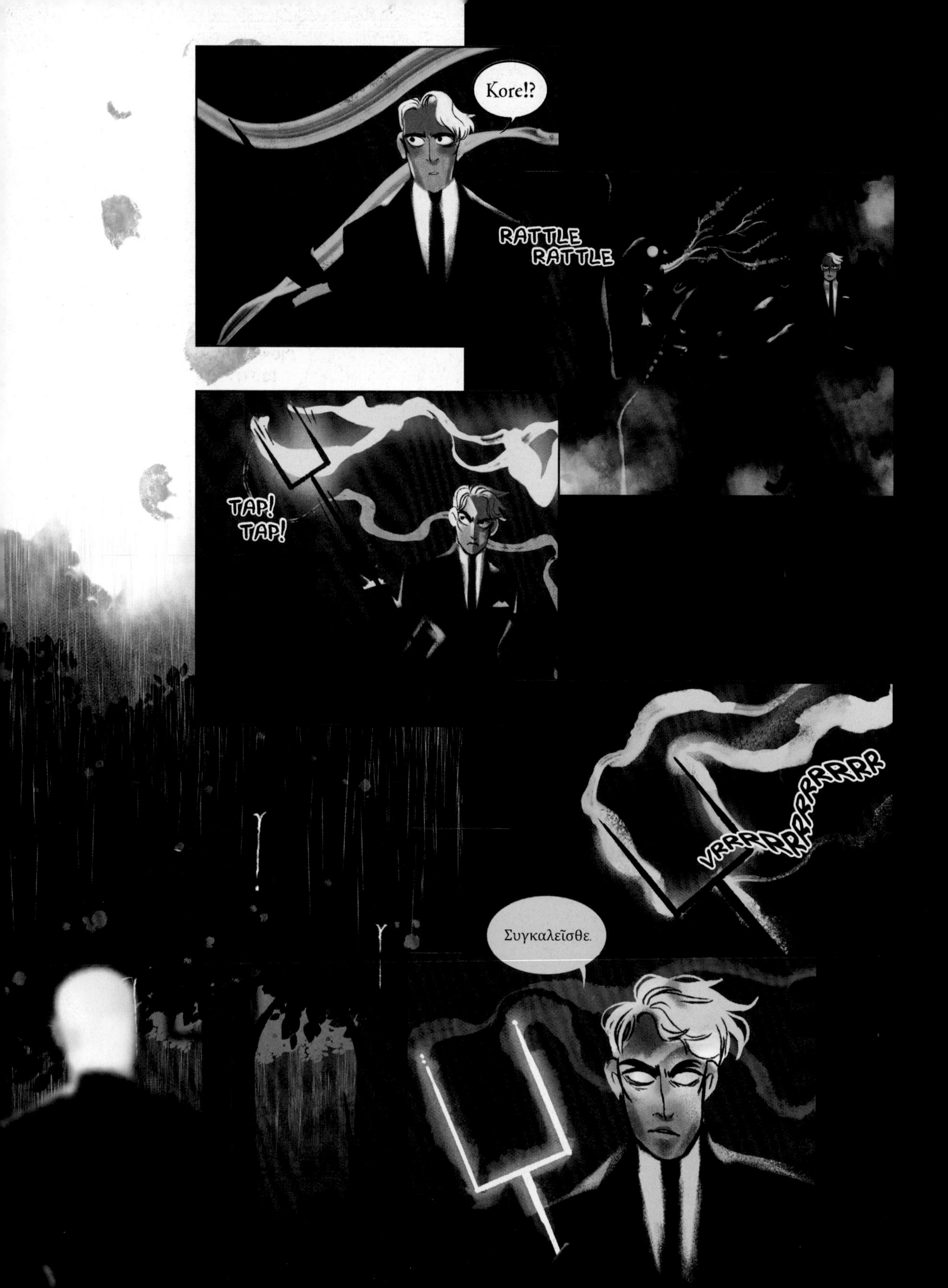
Kore!?
RATTLE
RATTLE
TAP!
TAP!
VRRRRRRRRRRRRR
Συγκαλεῖσθε.

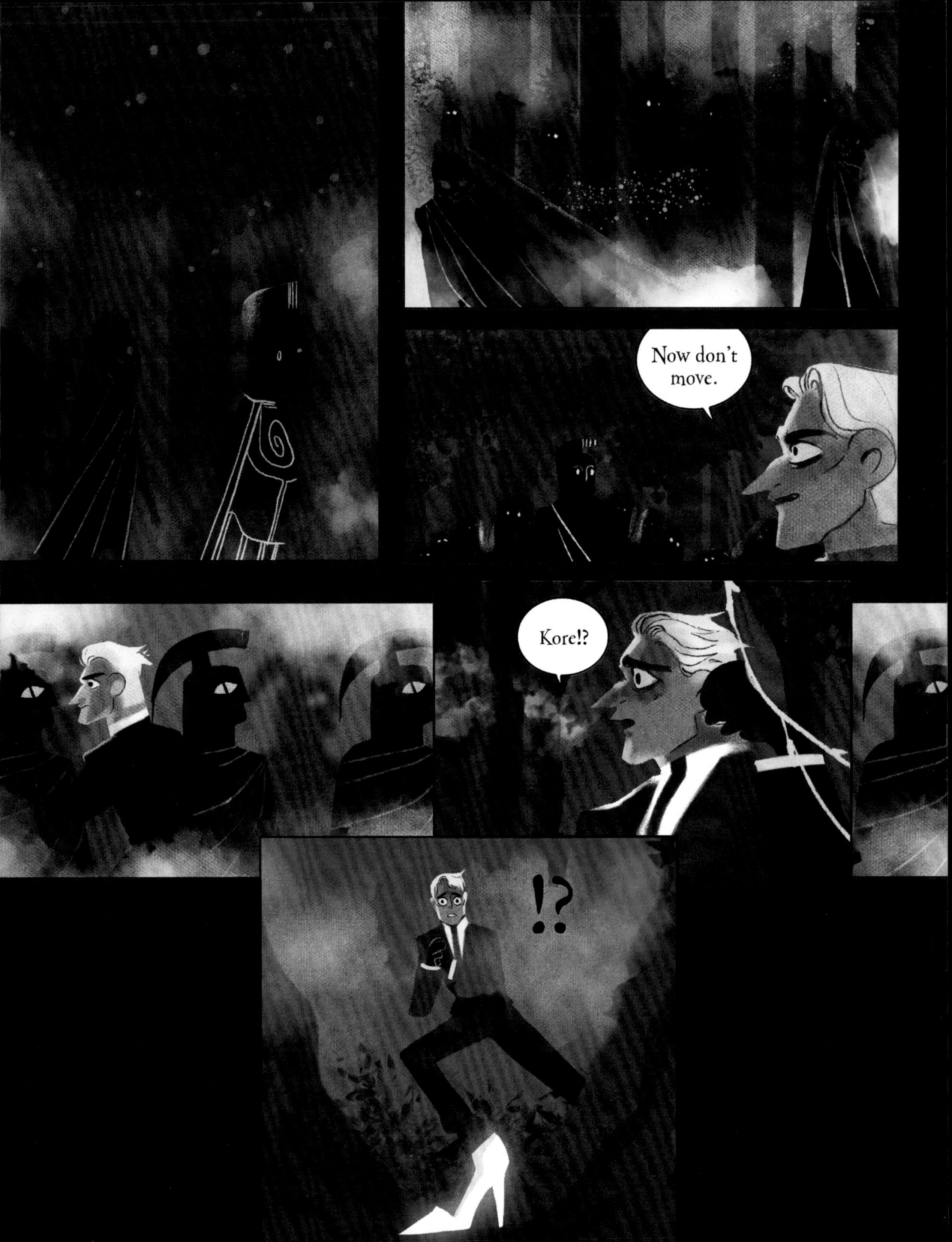
Now don't move.
Kore!?
!?

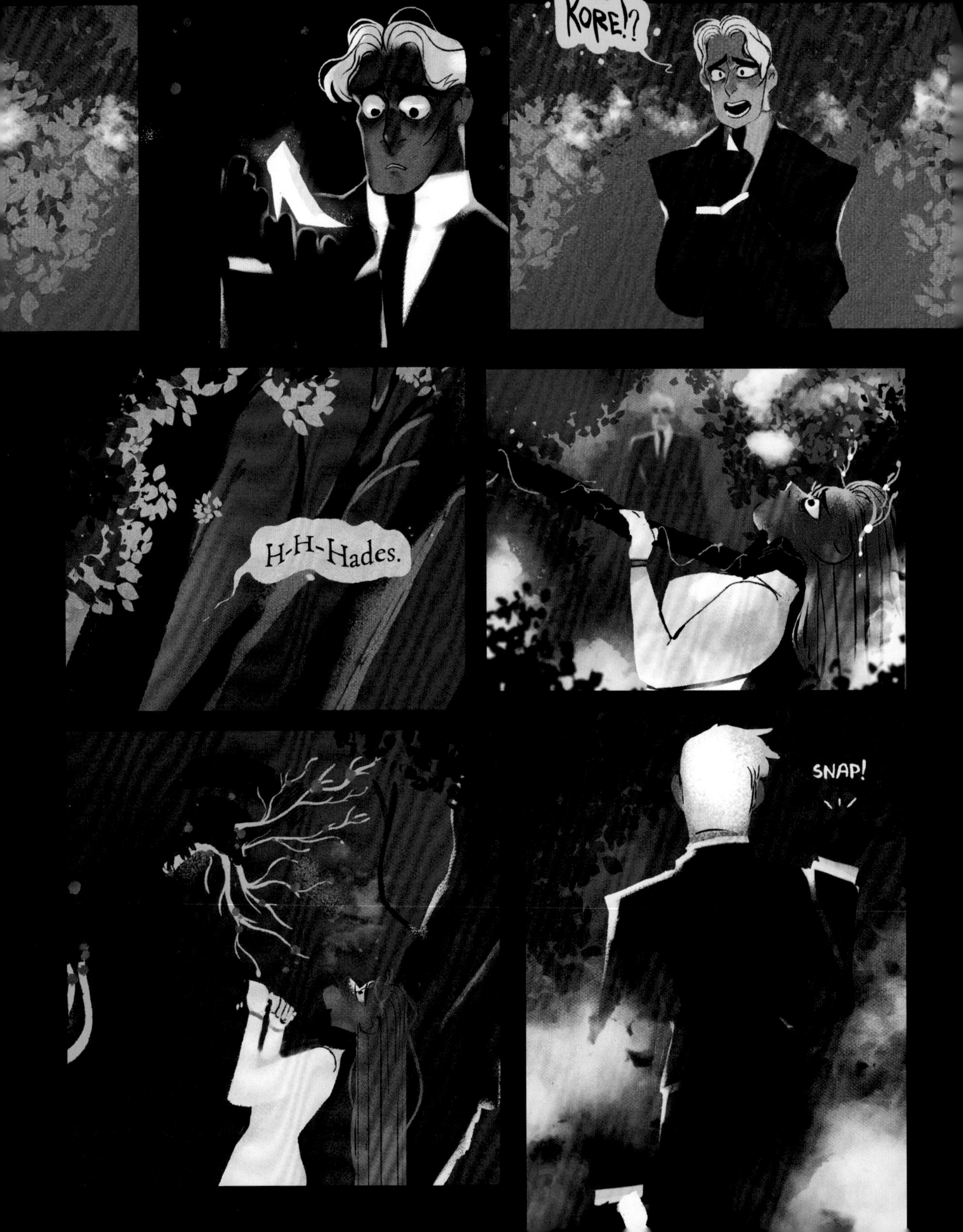
KORE!?
H-H-Hades.
SNAP!

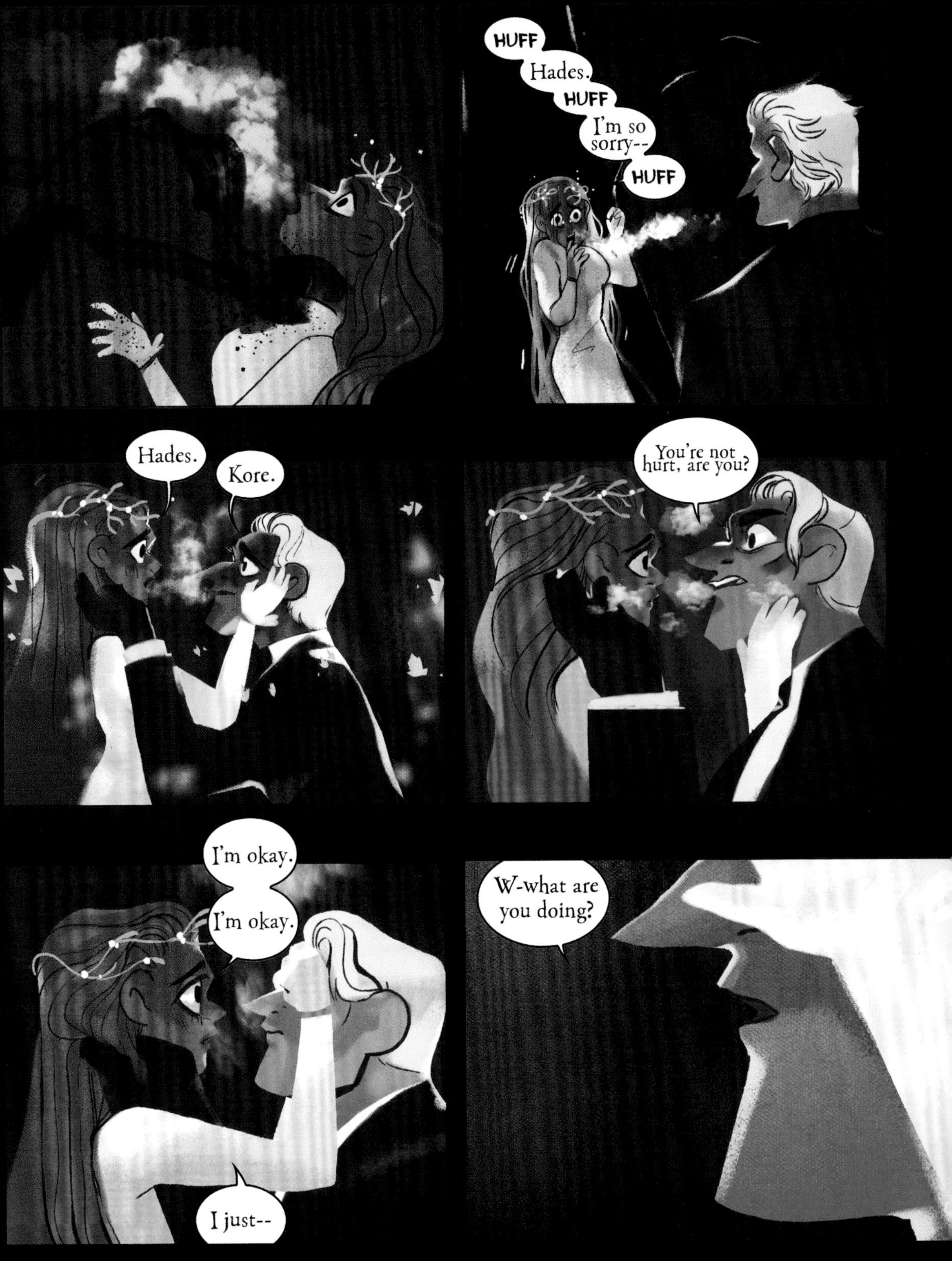
HUFF
Hades.
HUFF
I'm so sorry--
HUFF
Hades.
Kore.
You're not hurt, are you?
I'm okay.
I'm okay.
I just--
W-what are you doing?

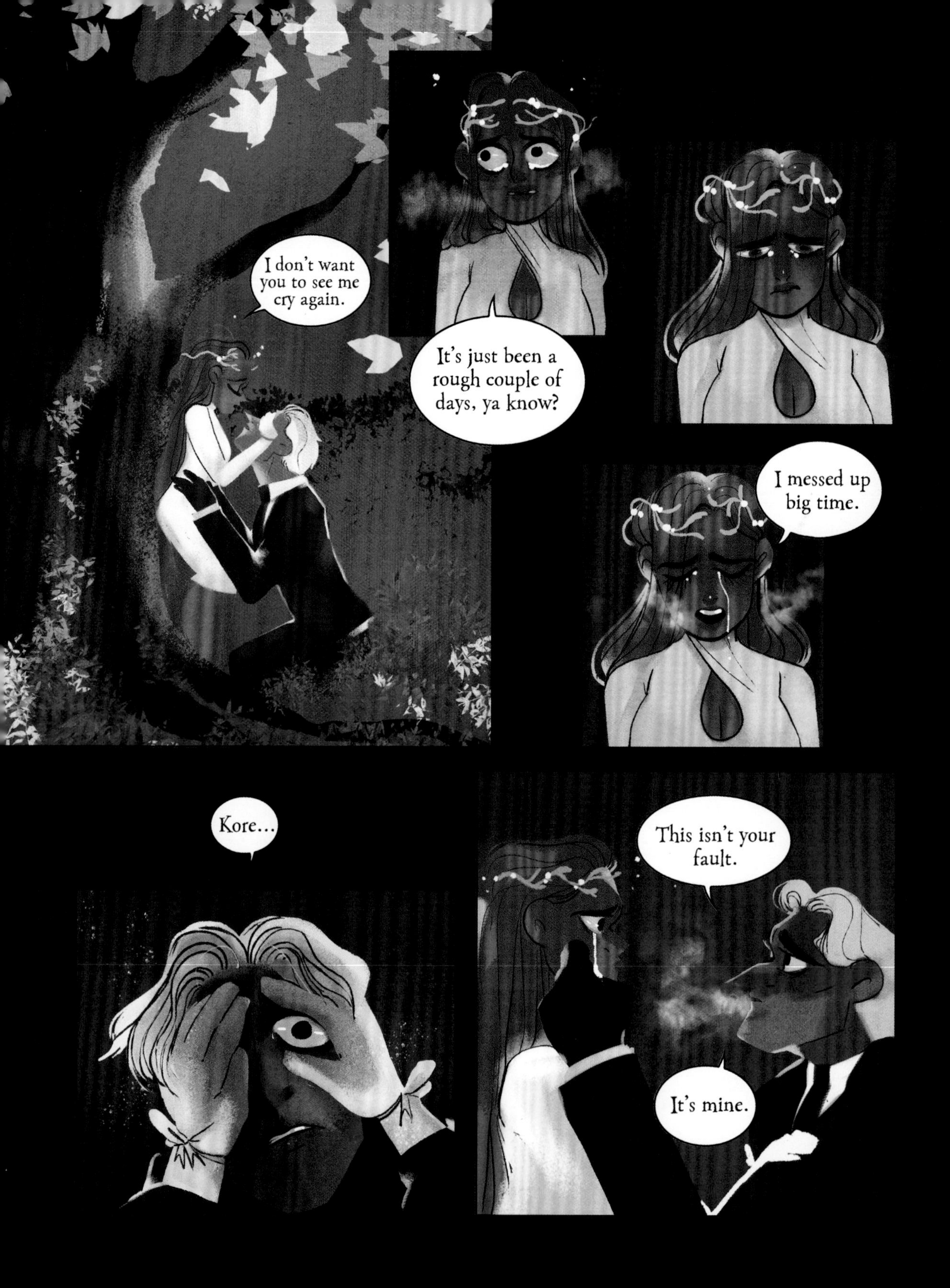
I don't want you to see me cry again.
It's just been a rough couple of days, ya know?
I messed up big time.
Kore...
This isn't your fault.
It's mine.

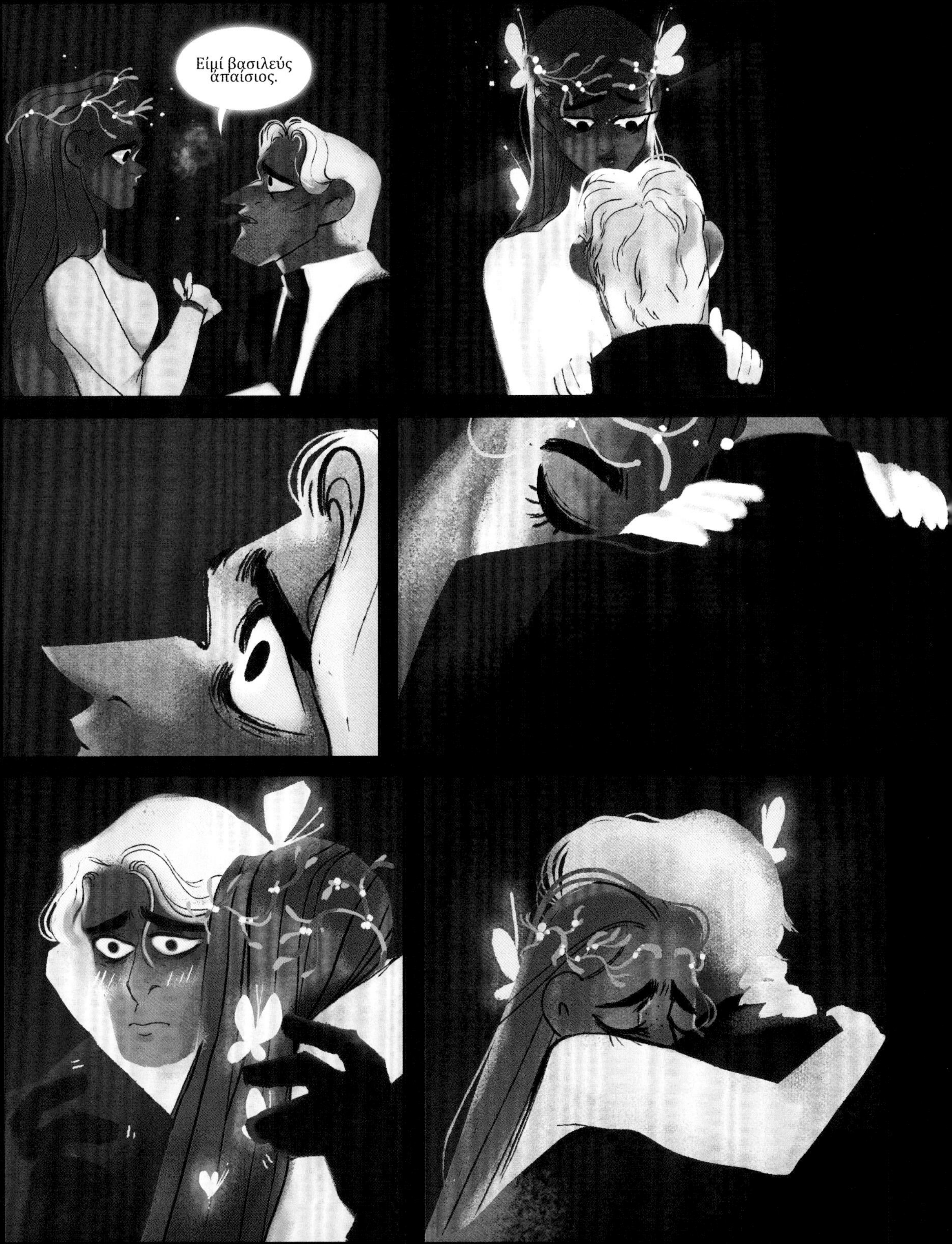
Ειμί βασιλεύς απαίσιος.

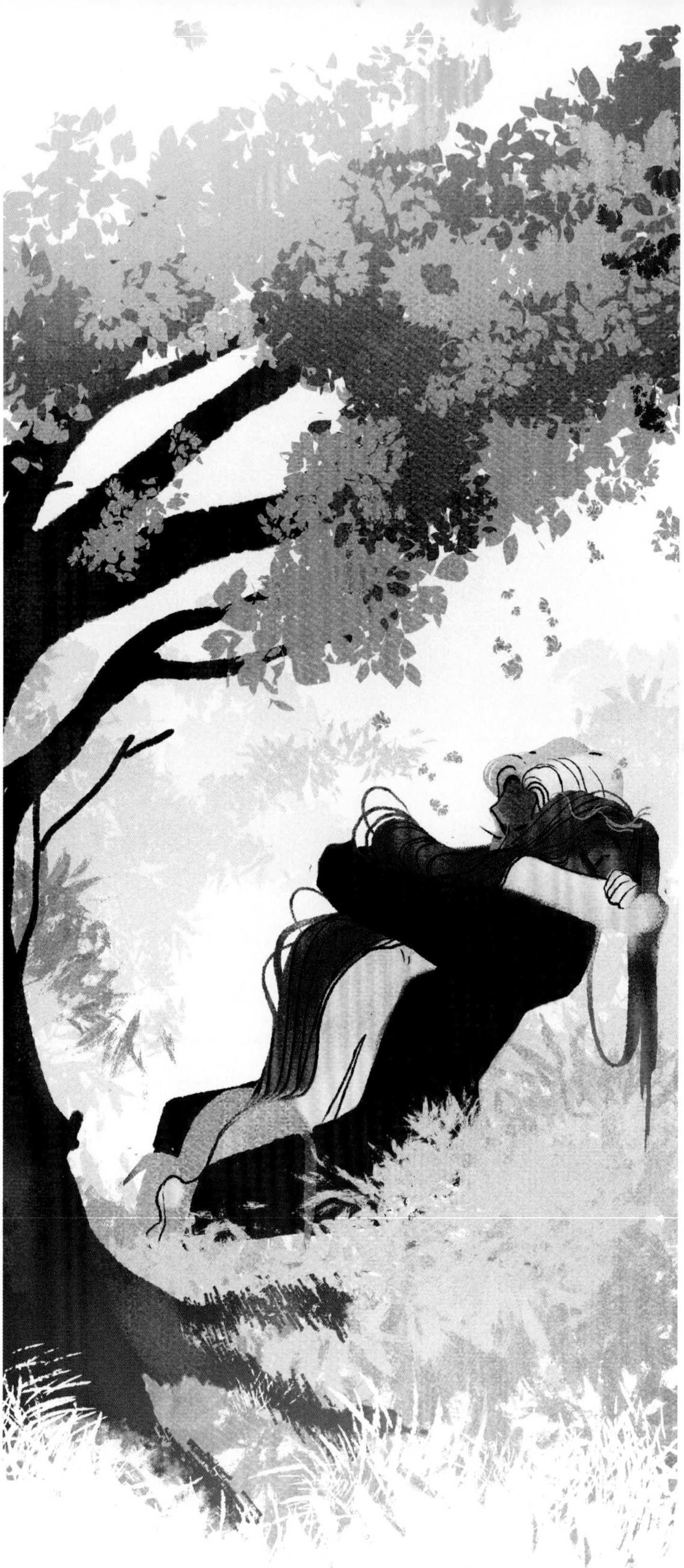

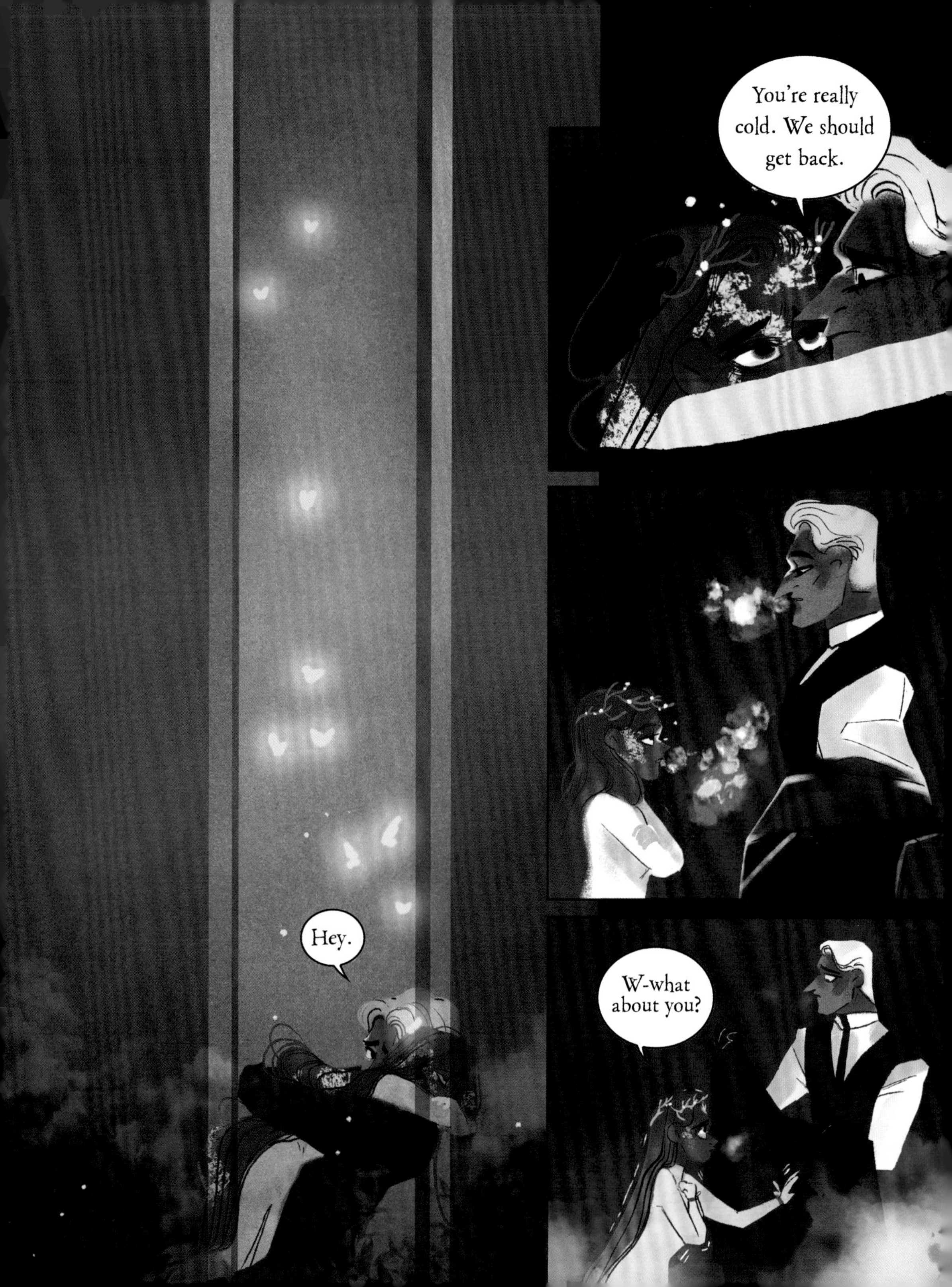
You're really cold. We should get back.
Hey.
W-what about you?

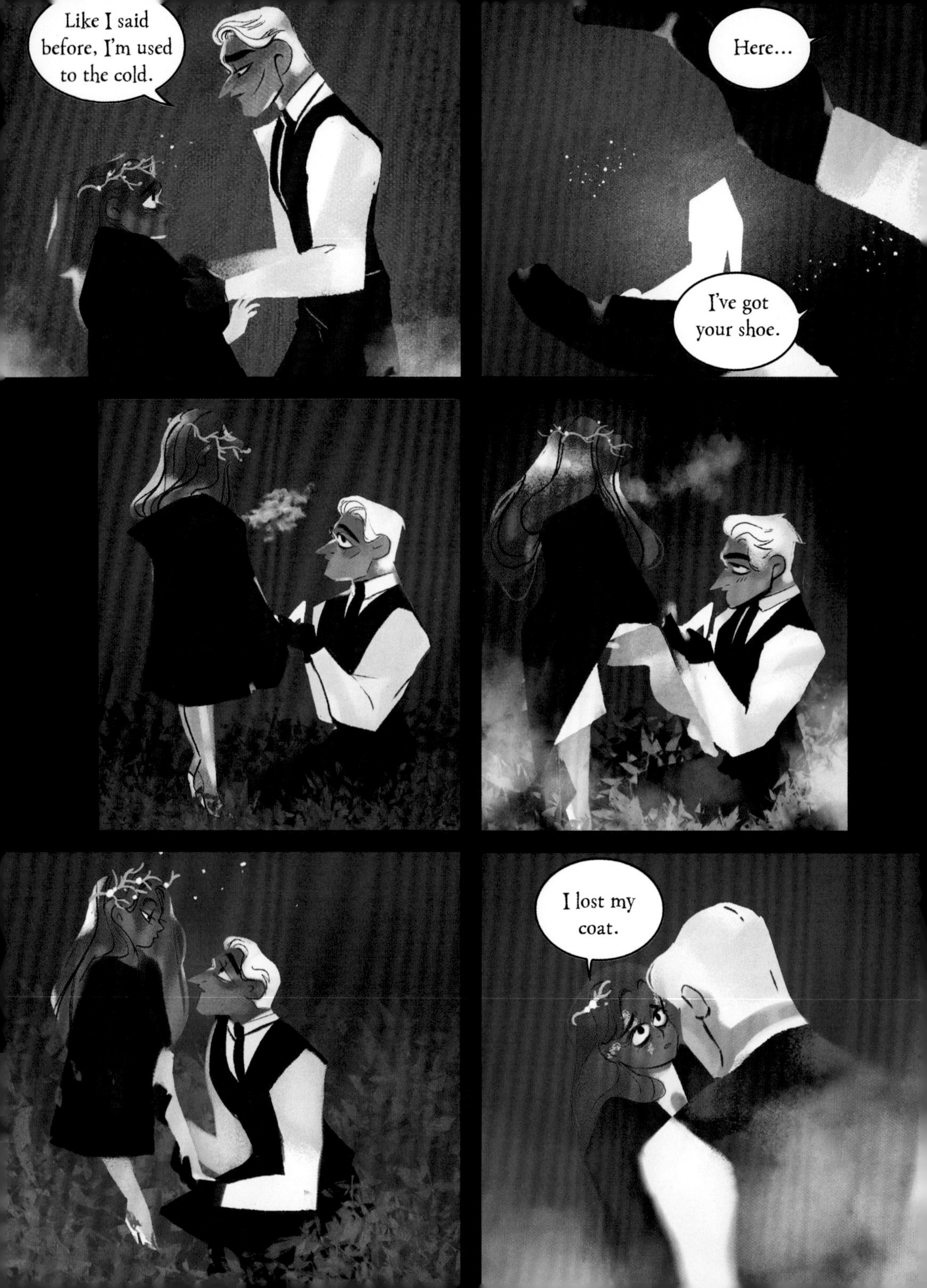
Like I said before, I'm used to the cold.
Here...
I've got your shoe.
I lost my coat.

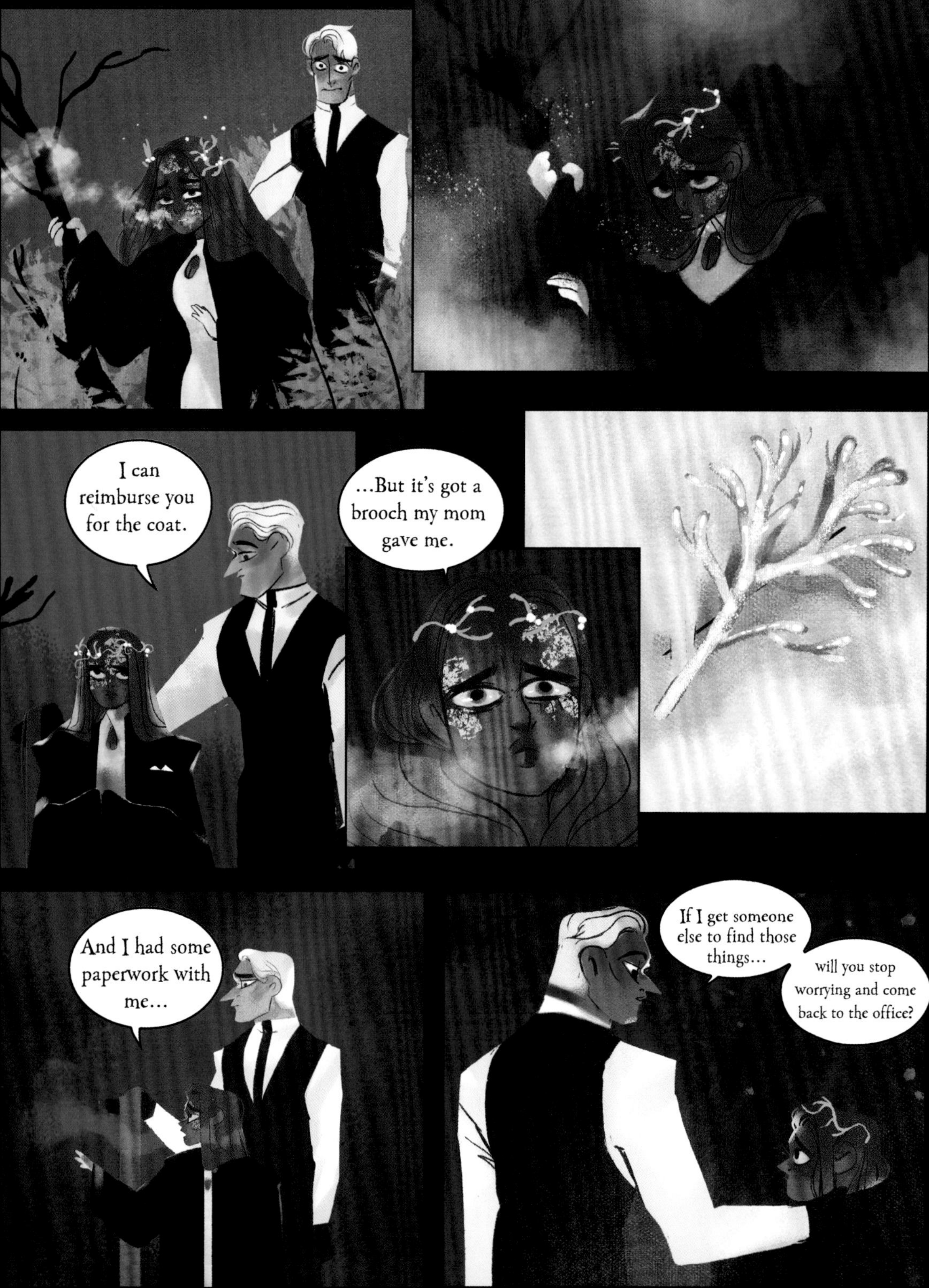
I can reimburse you for the coat.
...But it's got a brooch my mom gave me.
And I had some paperwork with me...
If I get someone else to find those things...
will you stop worrying and come back to the office?

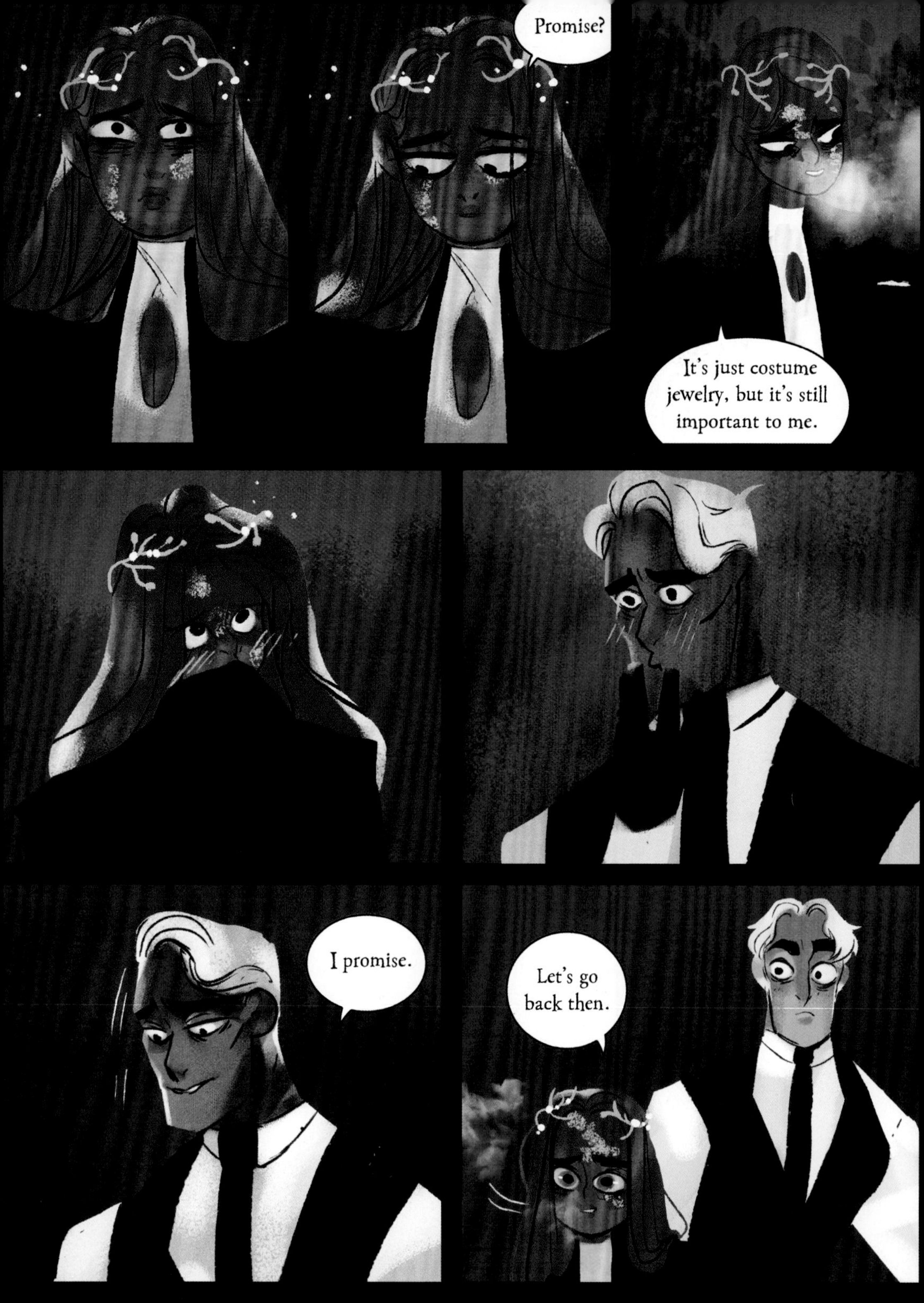
Promise?
It's just costume jewelry, but it's still important to me.
I promise.
Let's go back then.

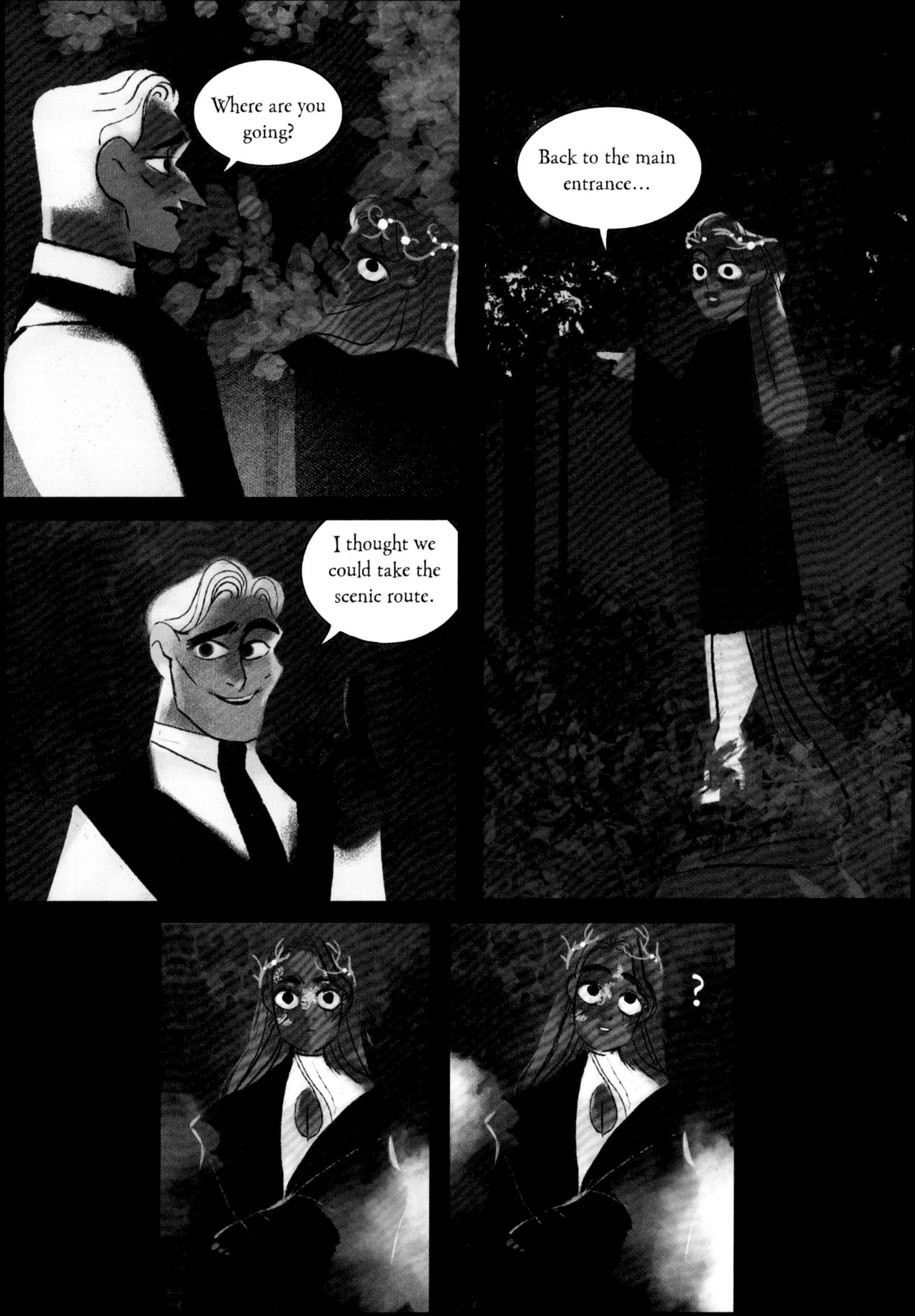
Where are you going?
Back to the main entrance...
I thought we could take the scenic route.
?

EPISODE 41: RETURN OF THE PRINCESS

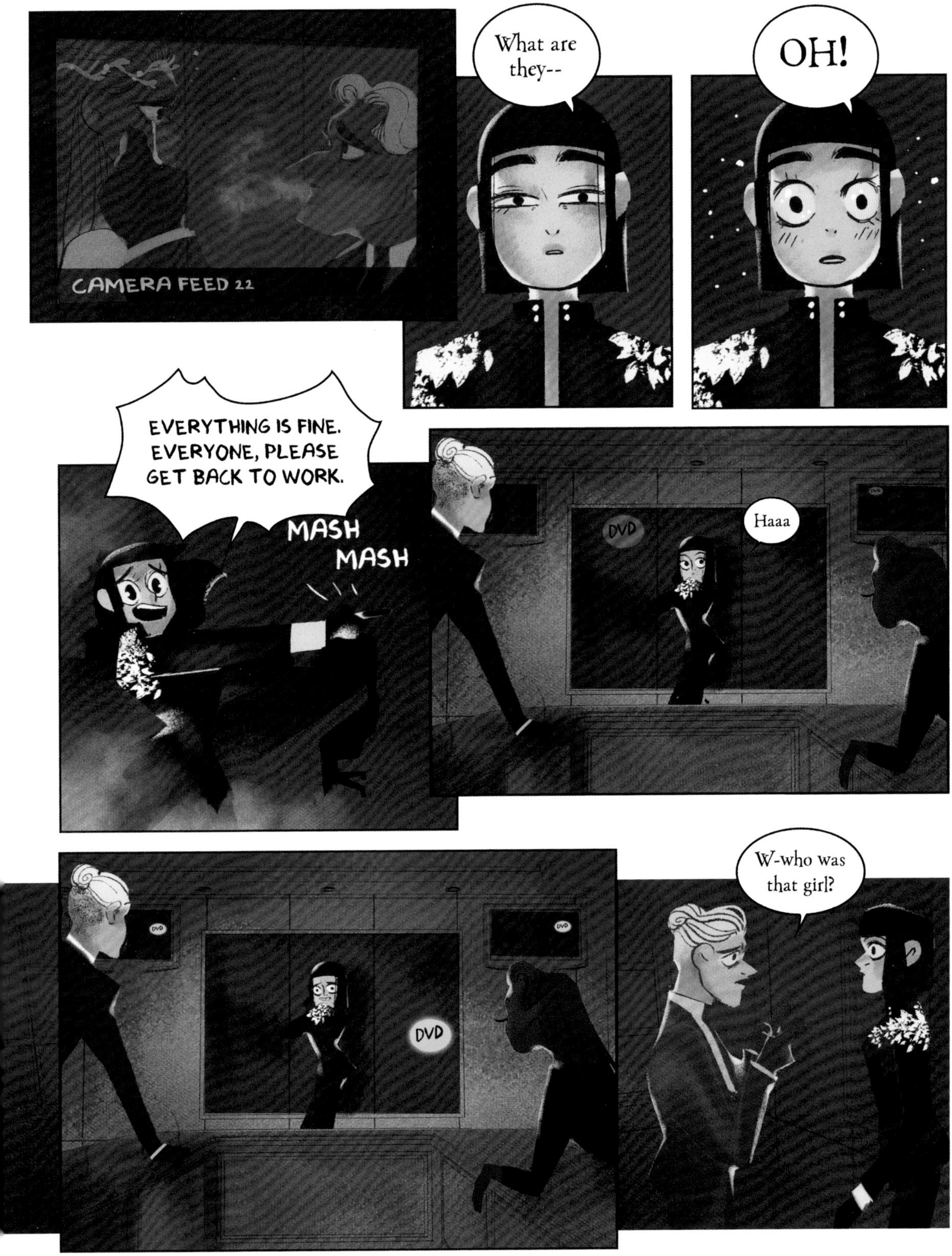
CAMERA FEED 22
What are they--
OH!
EVERYTHING IS FINE. EVERYONE, PLEASE GET BACK TO WORK.
MASH MASH
DVD
Haaa
DVD
DVD
DVD
W-who was that girl?

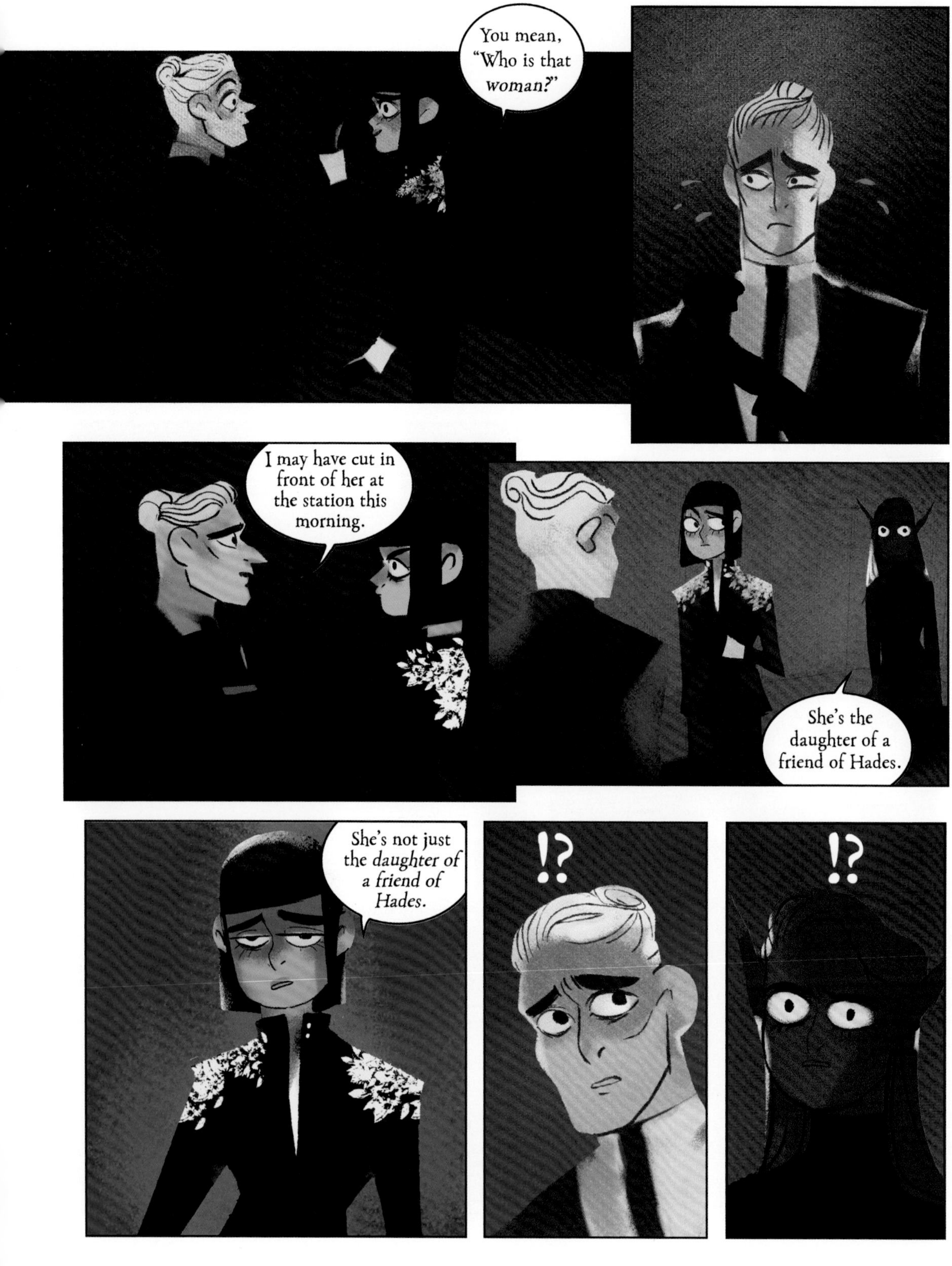
You mean, "Who is that *woman?*"
I may have cut in front of her at the station this morning.
She's the daughter of a friend of Hades.
She's not just the *daughter of a friend of* Hades.
!?
!?

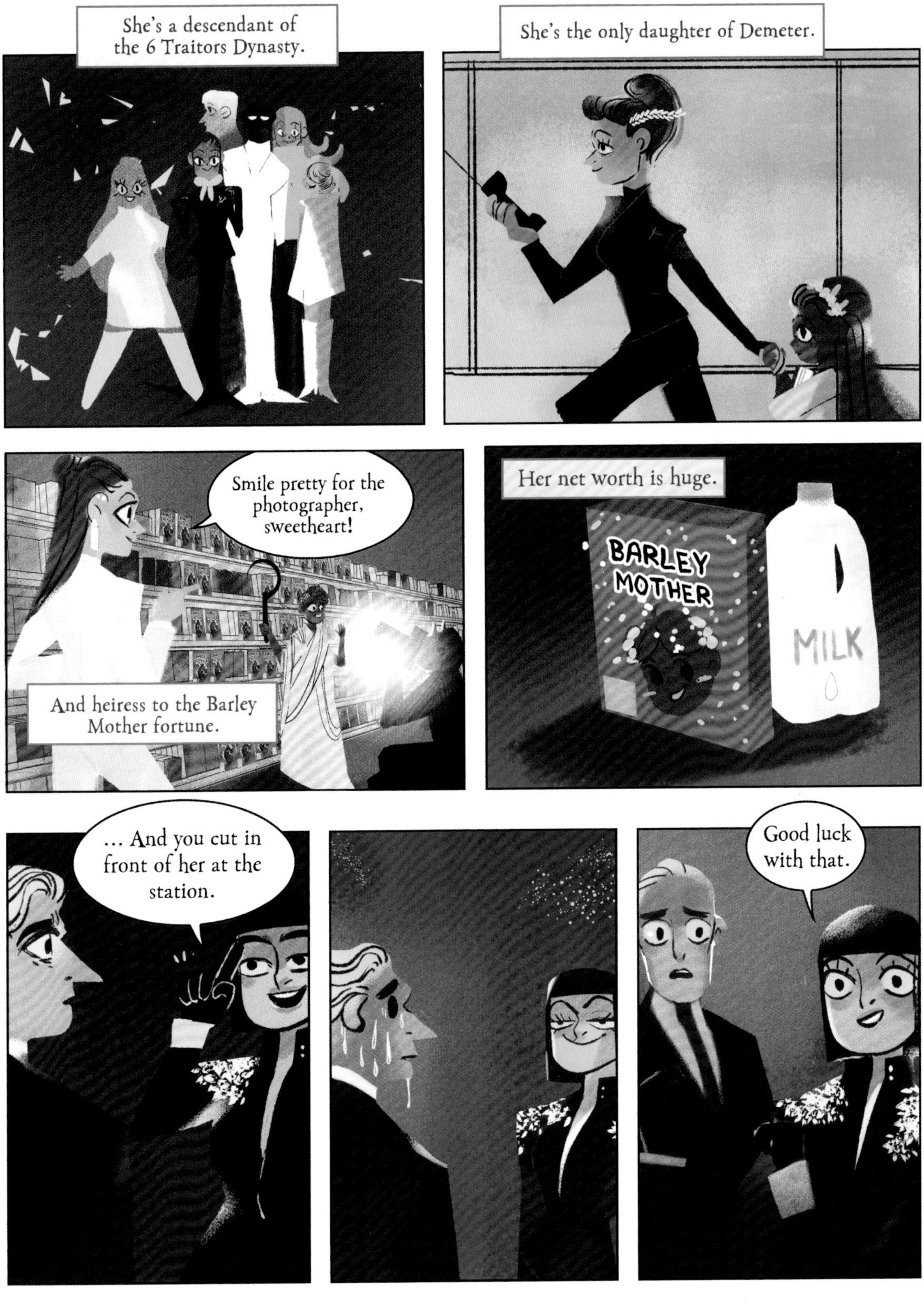
She's a descendant of the 6 Traitors Dynasty.
She's the only daughter of Demeter.
Smile pretty for the photographer, sweetheart!
And heiress to the Barley Mother fortune.
Her net worth is huge.
BARLEY MOTHER
MILK
... And you cut in front of her at the station.
Good luck with that.

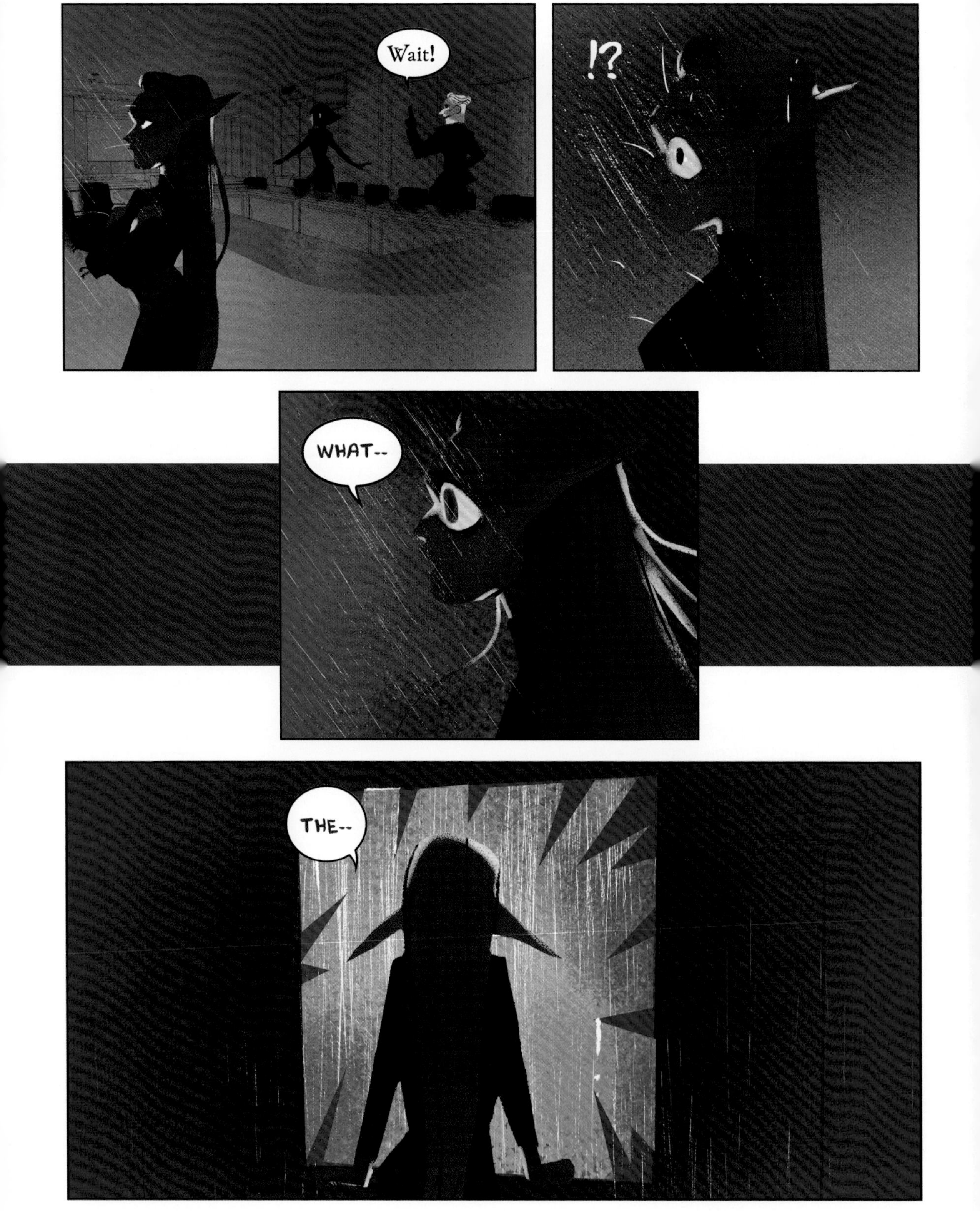
Wait!
!?
WHAT--
THE--

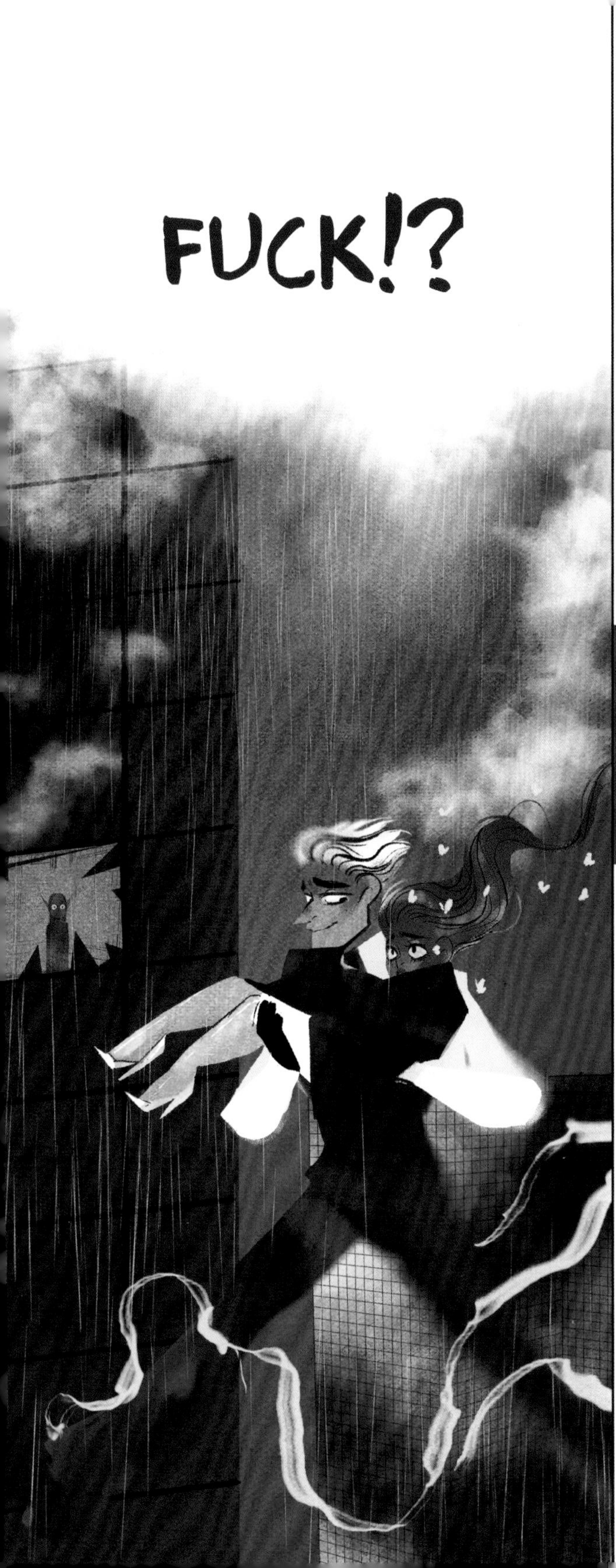
FUCK!?

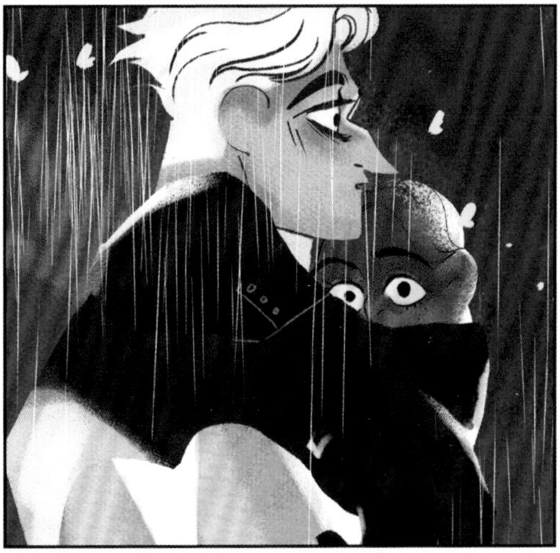

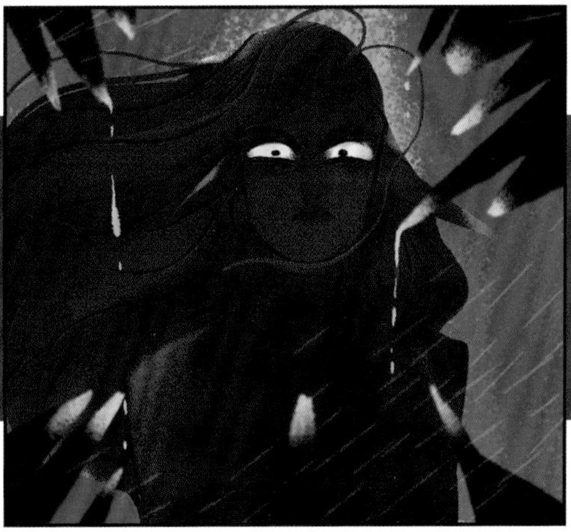

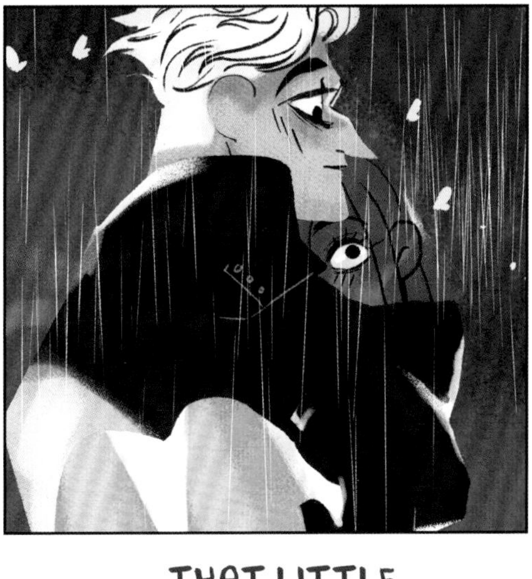
THAT LITTLE
BITCH!

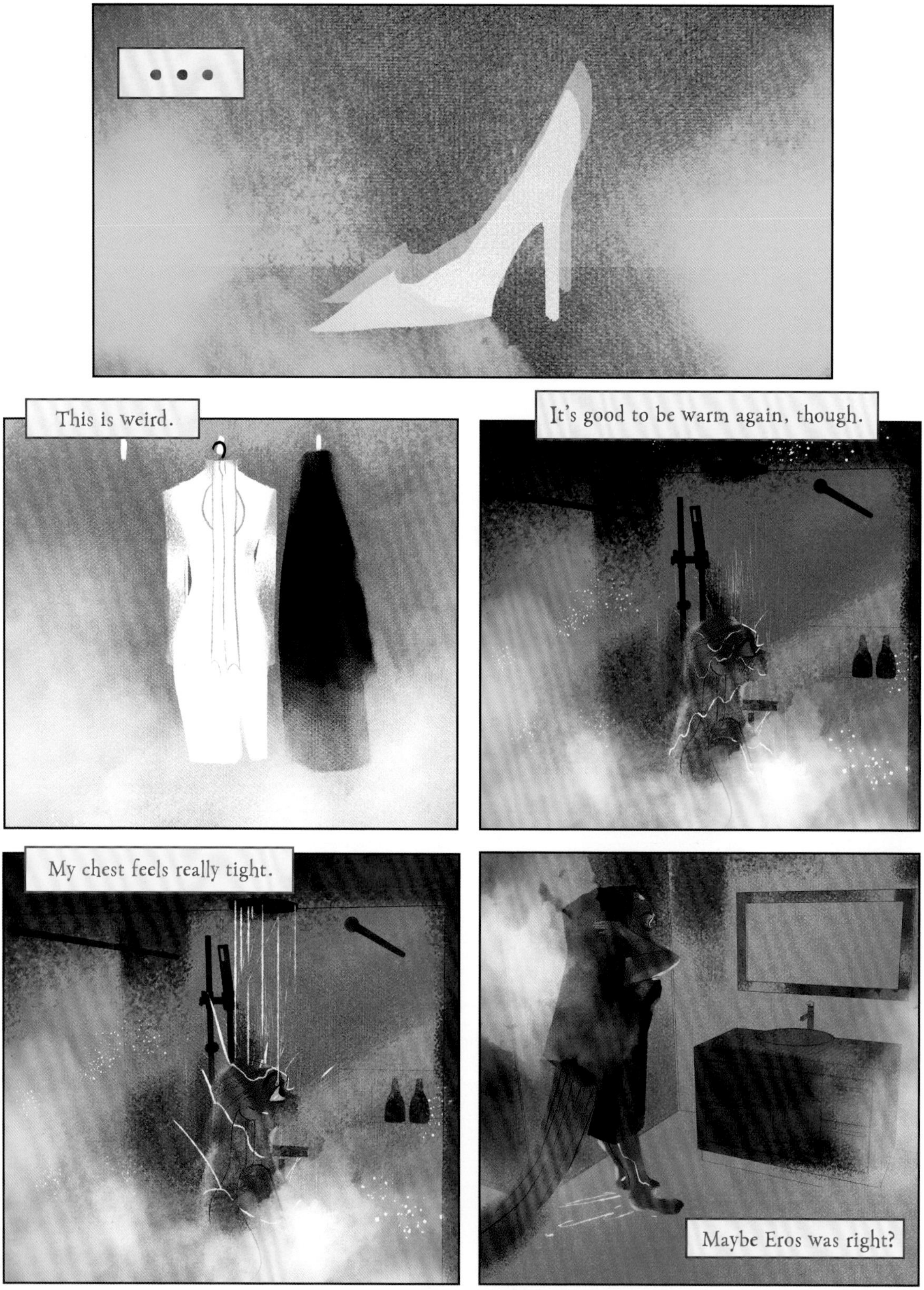
. . .
This is weird.
It's good to be warm again, though.
My chest feels really tight.
Maybe Eros was right?

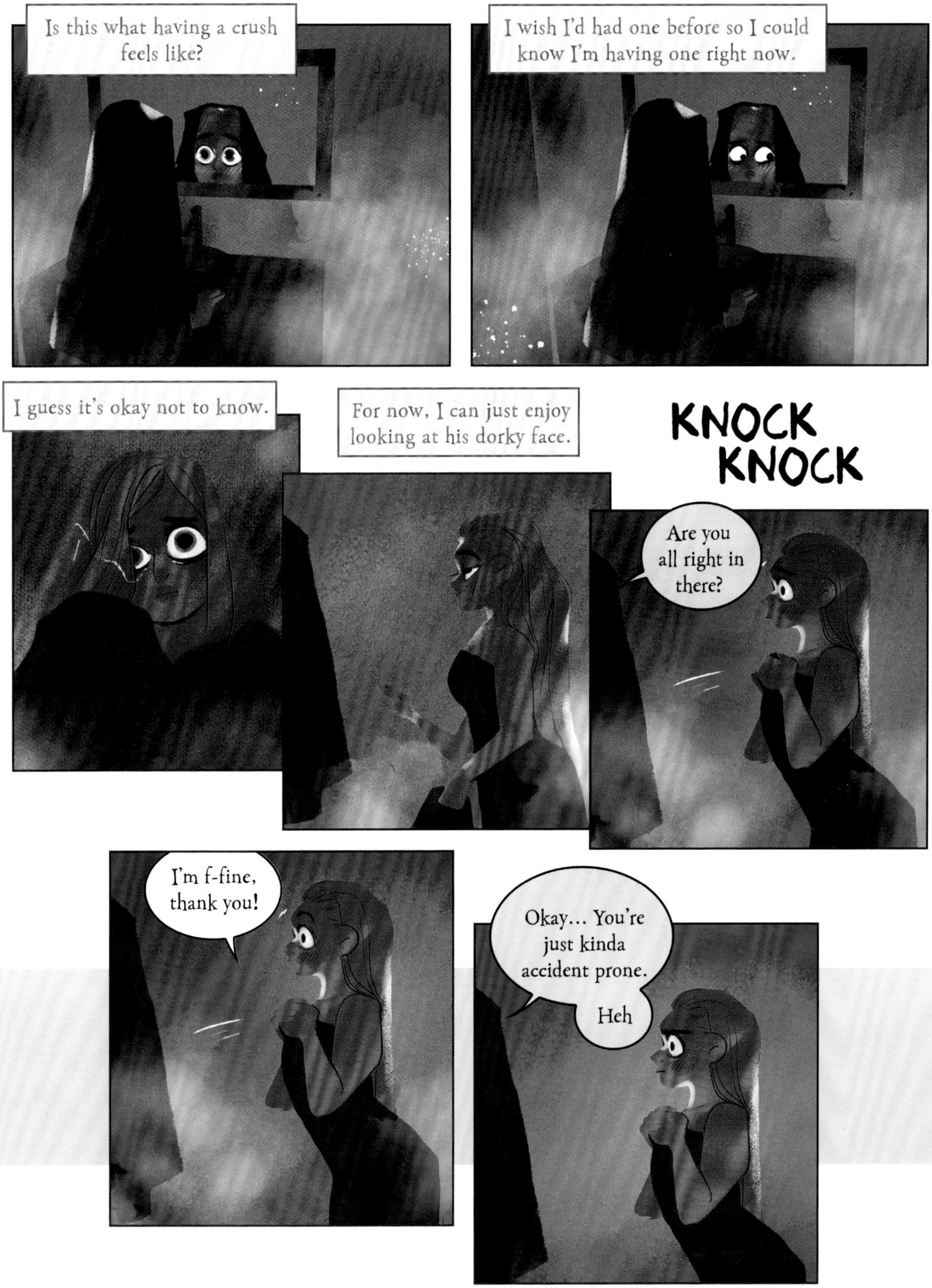

Is this what having a crush feels like?
I wish I'd had one before so I could know I'm having one right now.
I guess it's okay not to know.
For now, I can just enjoy looking at his dorky face.
KNOCK KNOCK
Are you all right in there?
I'm f-fine, thank you!
Okay... You're just kinda accident prone.
Heh

EPISODE 42: THE WAY SHE LOOKED AT ME

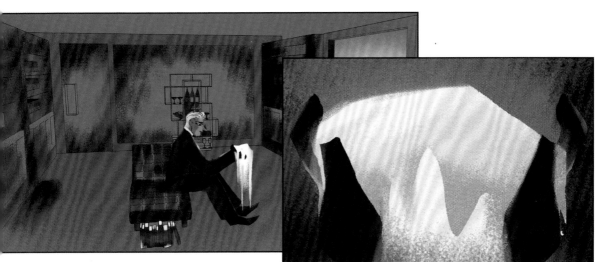

Every time she's around me, she ends up getting hurt.

But, the way she looked at me...

No, don't be an idiot.

Even if there is the smallest chance she does want me...

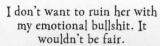

...she's still too young, and I'm still a complete mess.

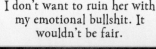

I don't want to ruin her with my emotional bullshit. It wouldn't be fair.

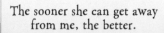

The sooner she can get away from me, the better.

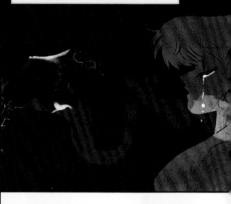

Um, excuse me, don't you have a gateway to guard?

I see I'm old news, huh?

Would you cut that out?

BARK! BARK! BARK! BARK!

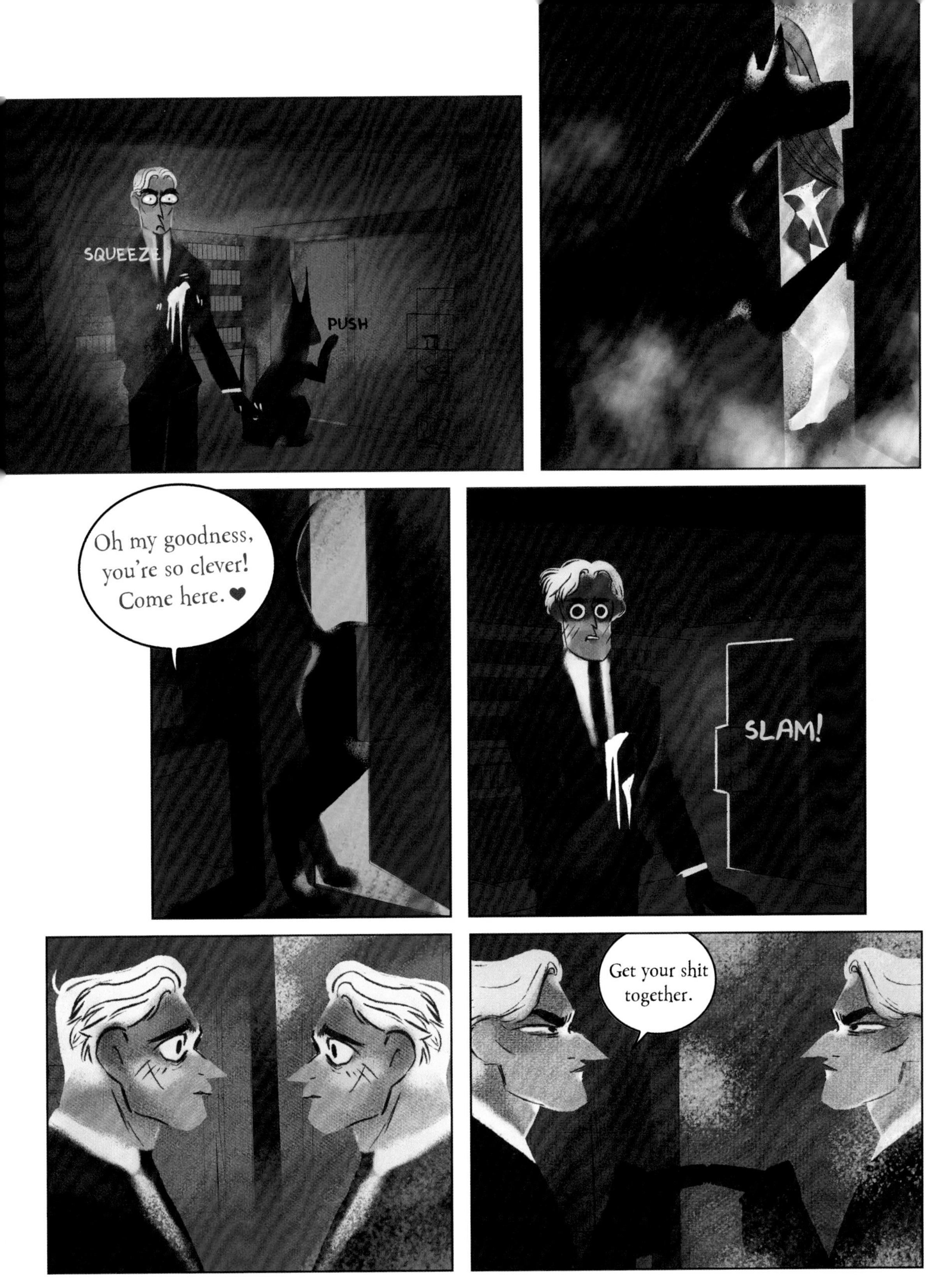
SQUEEZE
PUSH
Oh my goodness, you're so clever! Come here. ❤
SLAM!
Get your shit together.

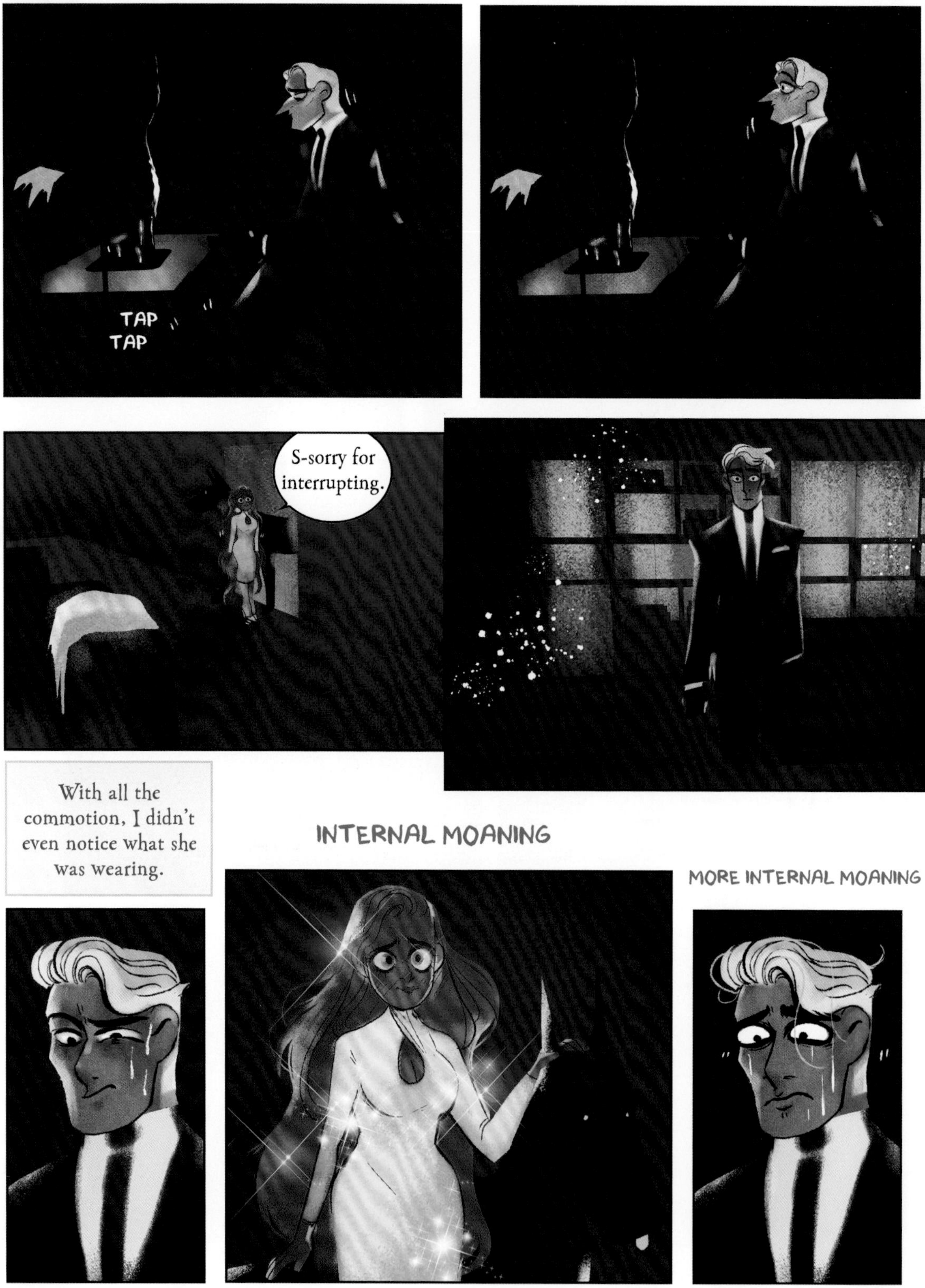
TAP
TAP
S-sorry for interrupting.
With all the commotion, I didn't even notice what she was wearing.
INTERNAL MOANING
MORE INTERNAL MOANING

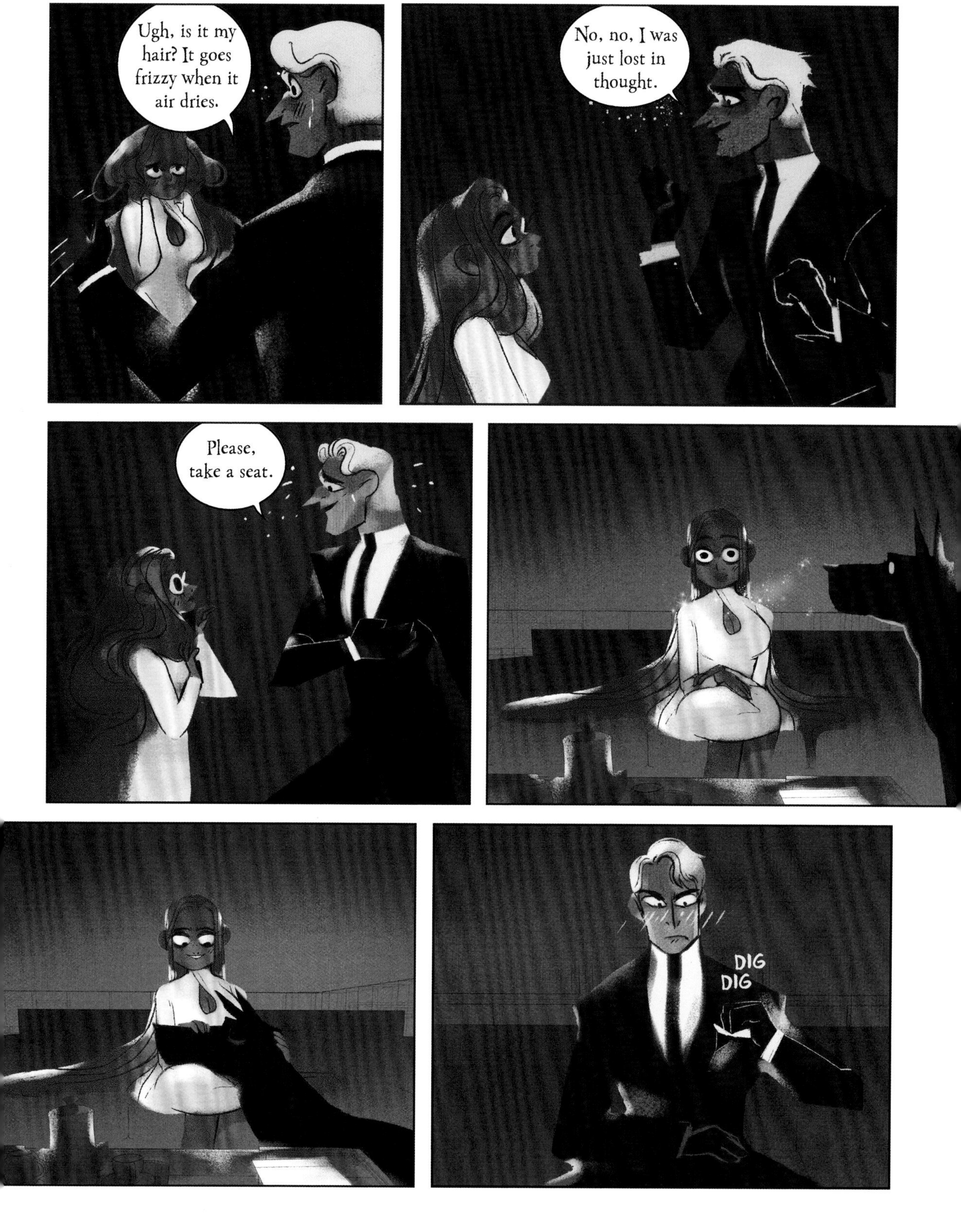
Ugh, is it my hair? It goes frizzy when it air dries.
No, no, I was just lost in thought.
Please, take a seat.
DIG
DIG

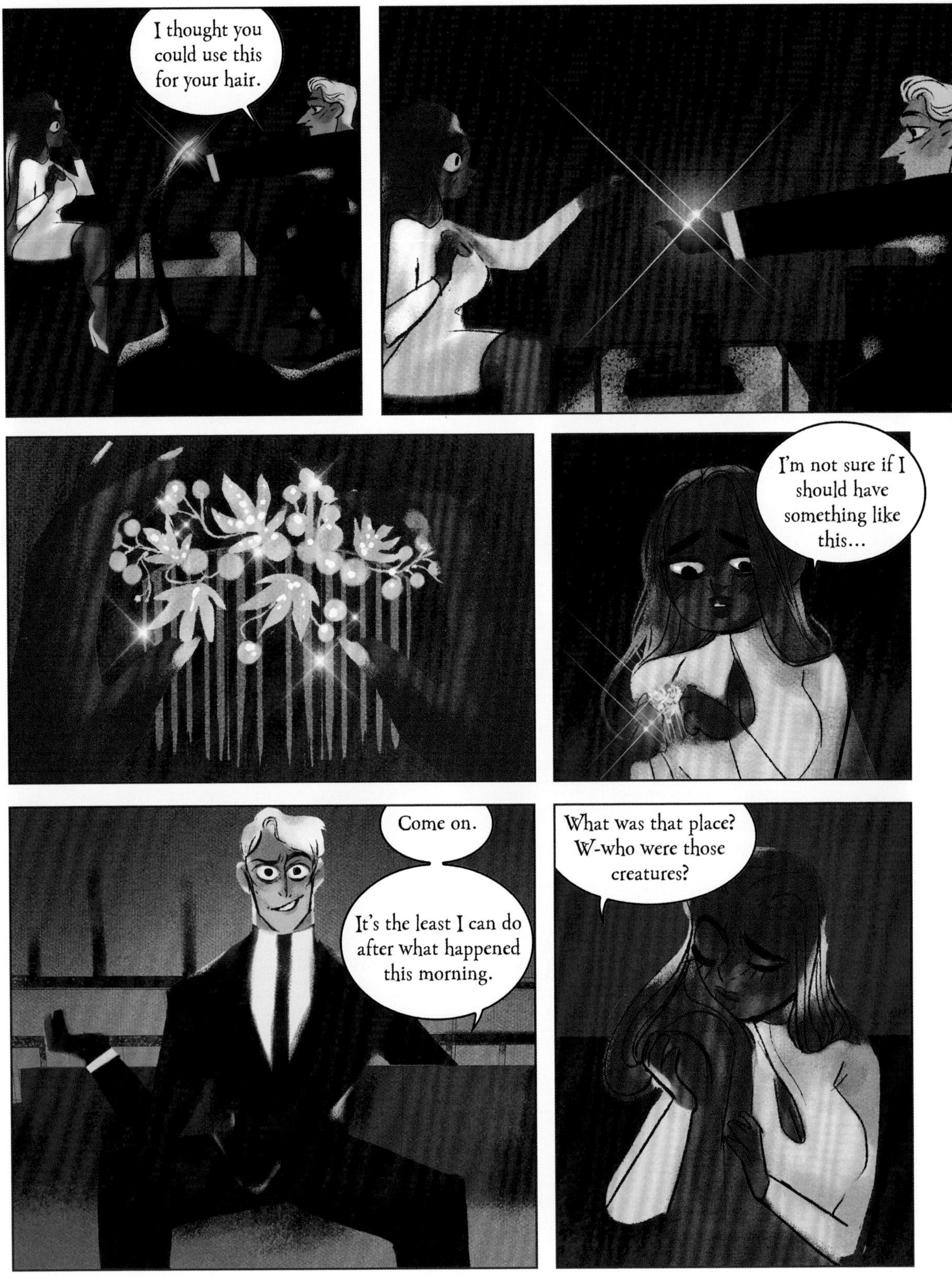
I thought you could use this for your hair.
I'm not sure if I should have something like this...
Come on.
It's the least I can do after what happened this morning.
What was that place? W-who were those creatures?

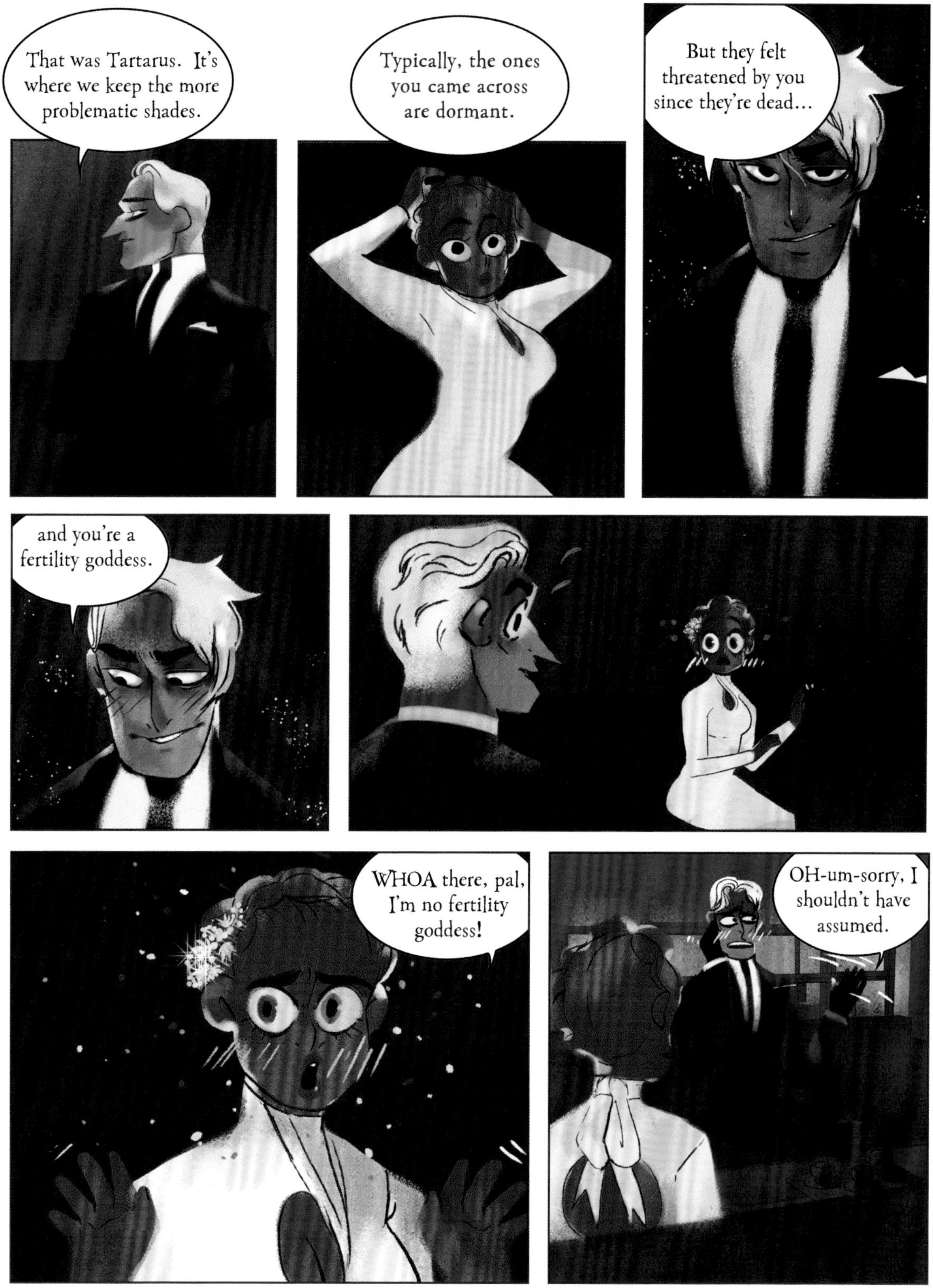
That was Tartarus. It's where we keep the more problematic shades.
Typically, the ones you came across are dormant.
But they felt threatened by you since they're dead...
and you're a fertility goddess.
WHOA there, pal, I'm no fertility goddess!
OH-um-sorry, I shouldn't have assumed.

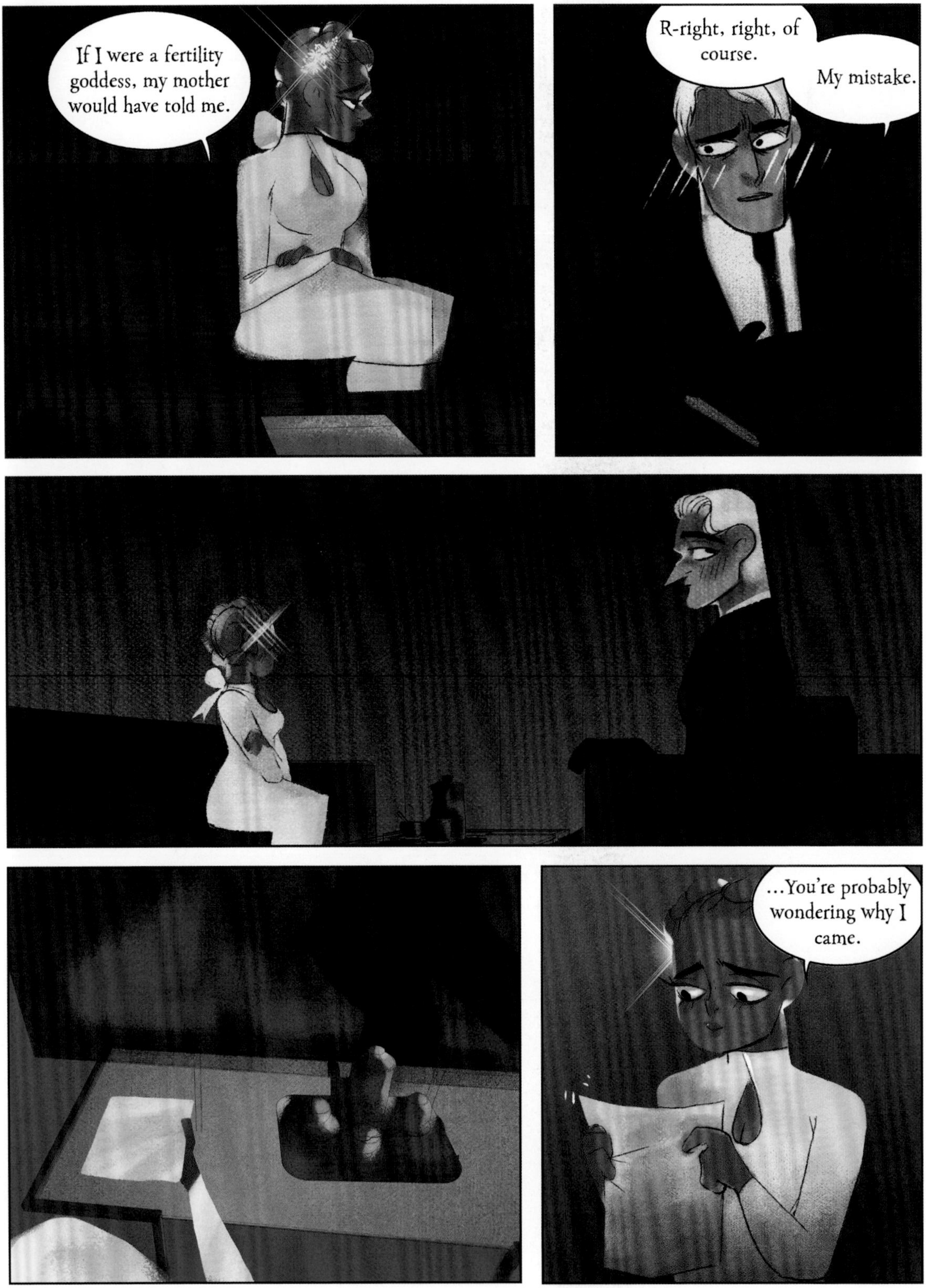
If I were a fertility goddess, my mother would have told me.
R-right, right, of course.
My mistake.
...You're probably wondering why I came.

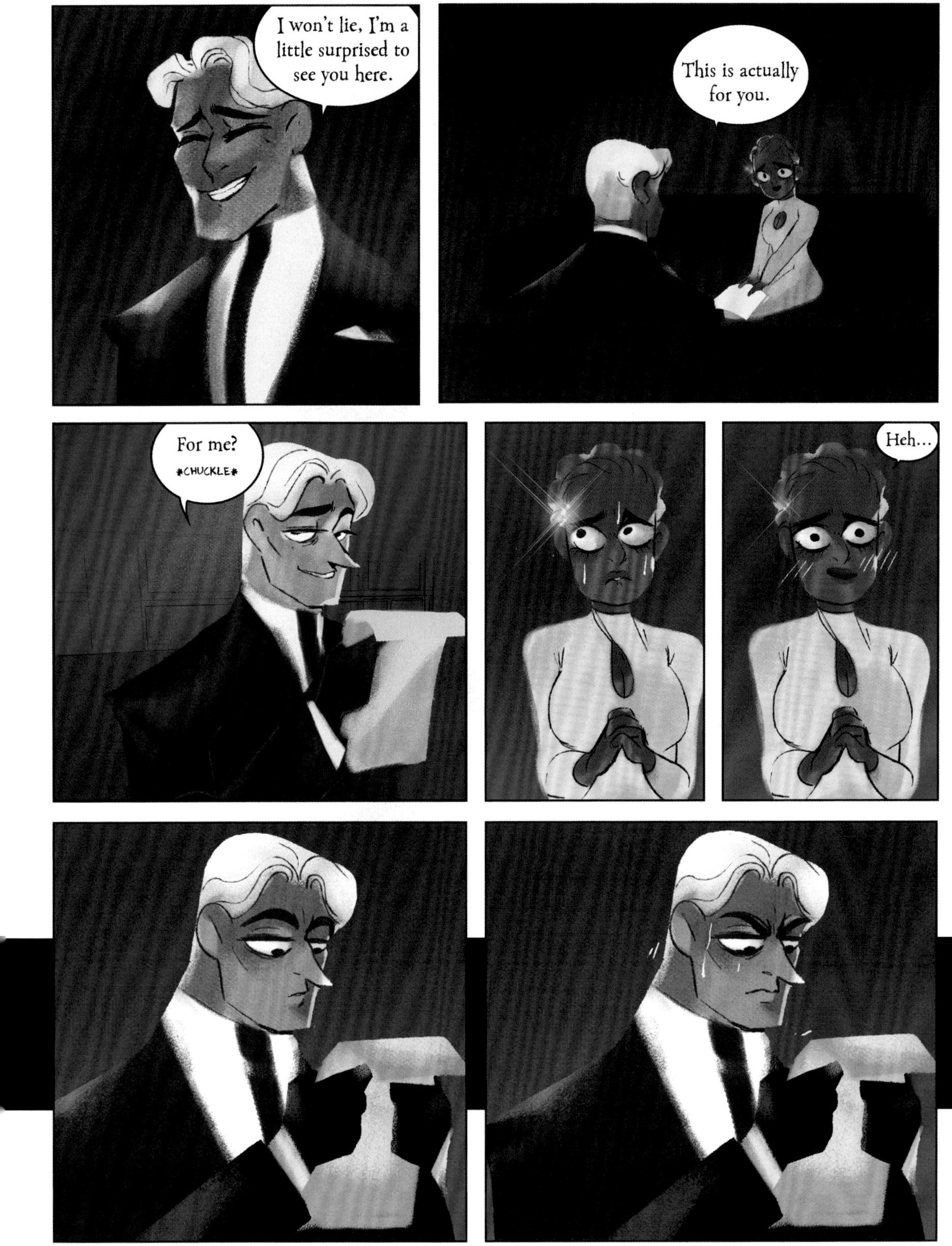
I won't lie, I'm a little surprised to see you here.
This is actually for you.
For me?
#CHUCKLE#
Heh...

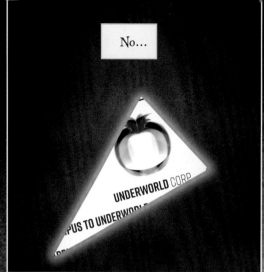

No...
UNDERWORLD CORP
No!
UNDERWORLD CORP
APPLICANT: PERSEPHONE (KORE)
REPORT TO: HADES, GOD/KING OF THE DEAD/UNDERWORLD
LOCATION: UNDERWORLD CORP, TOWER I, LV 99
TIME: ASAP
INTERNSHIP ROLE:
OH N-NO, NO!
1ST
SPELLING BEE
Who is responsible for this!?
STATUS: APPROVED BY HERA, QUEEN OF THE GODS
Hera.
FUCKING HERA!

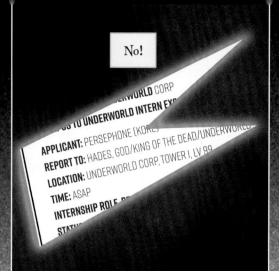

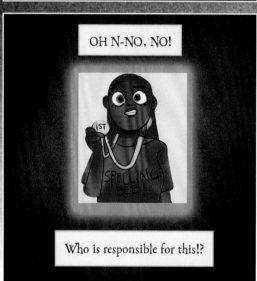

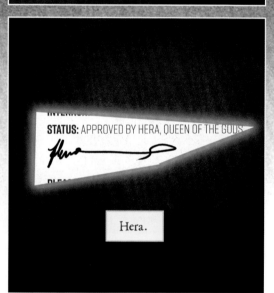

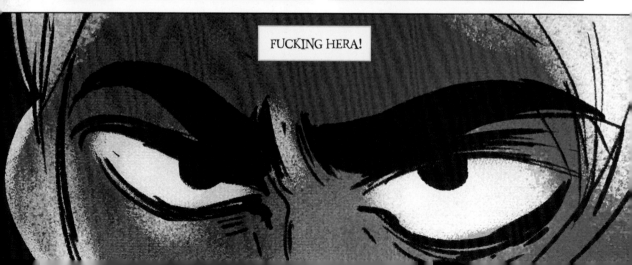

I'm sorry, but this is out of the question.
What!? B-but why?
You were here for all of 2 seconds, and you were nearly strangled.
But that wasn't my fault! I--
I-I-I'll talk to Hera and make new arrangements for you.

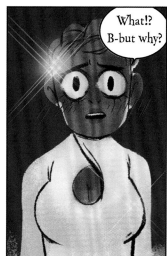

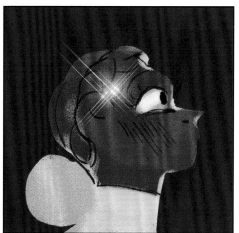

If I can't manage this on my own, what will Hera think of me?

No, but I need *this* job.

Listen, I'll tell Hera you did the internship.

I'll pay you the salary.

And you can just... do something else with your time.

I can't just not do the work.

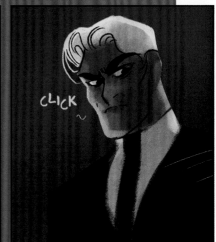

CLICK

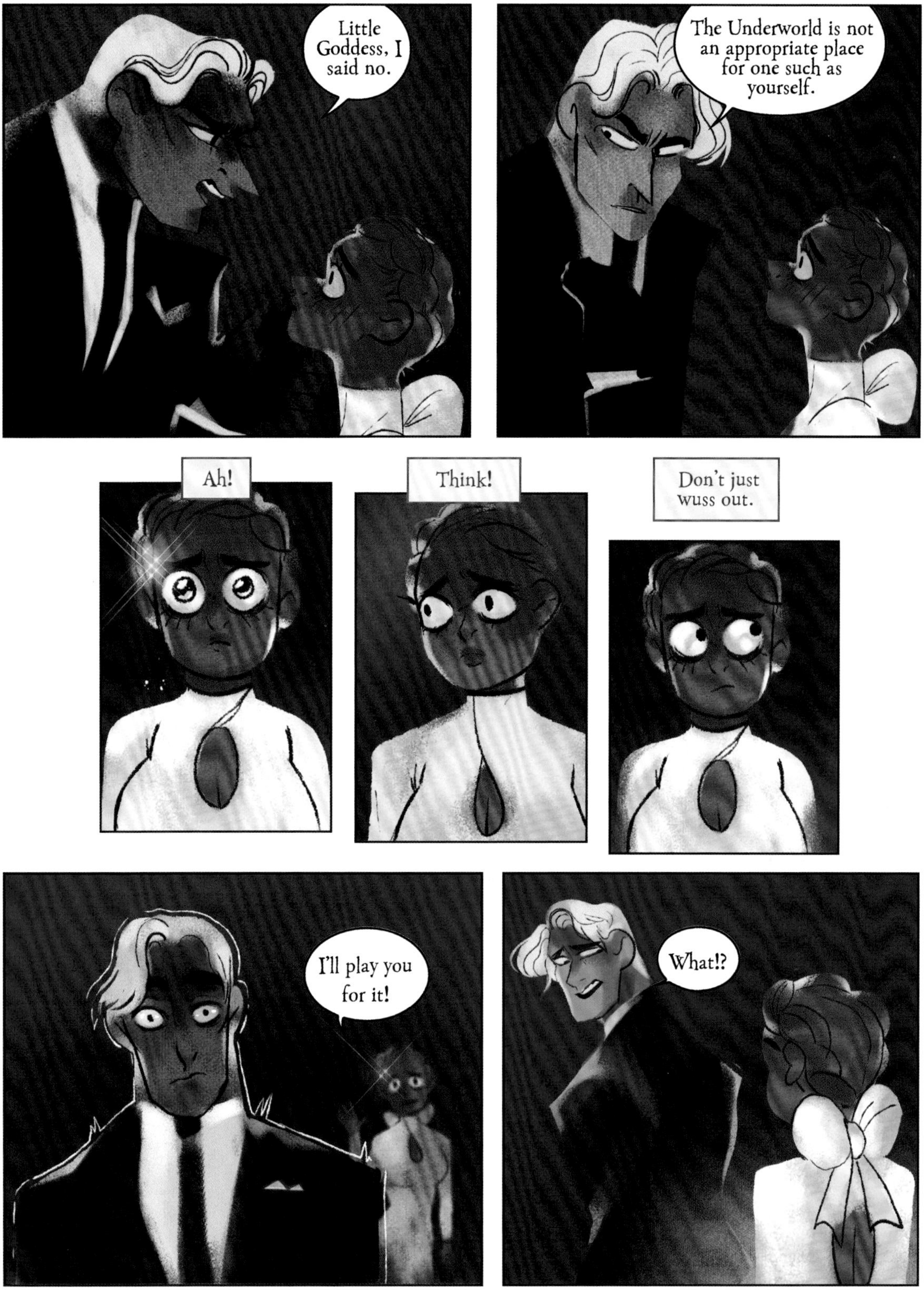

Little Goddess, I said no.
The Underworld is not an appropriate place for one such as yourself.
Ah!
Think!
Don't just wuss out.
I'll play you for it!
What!?

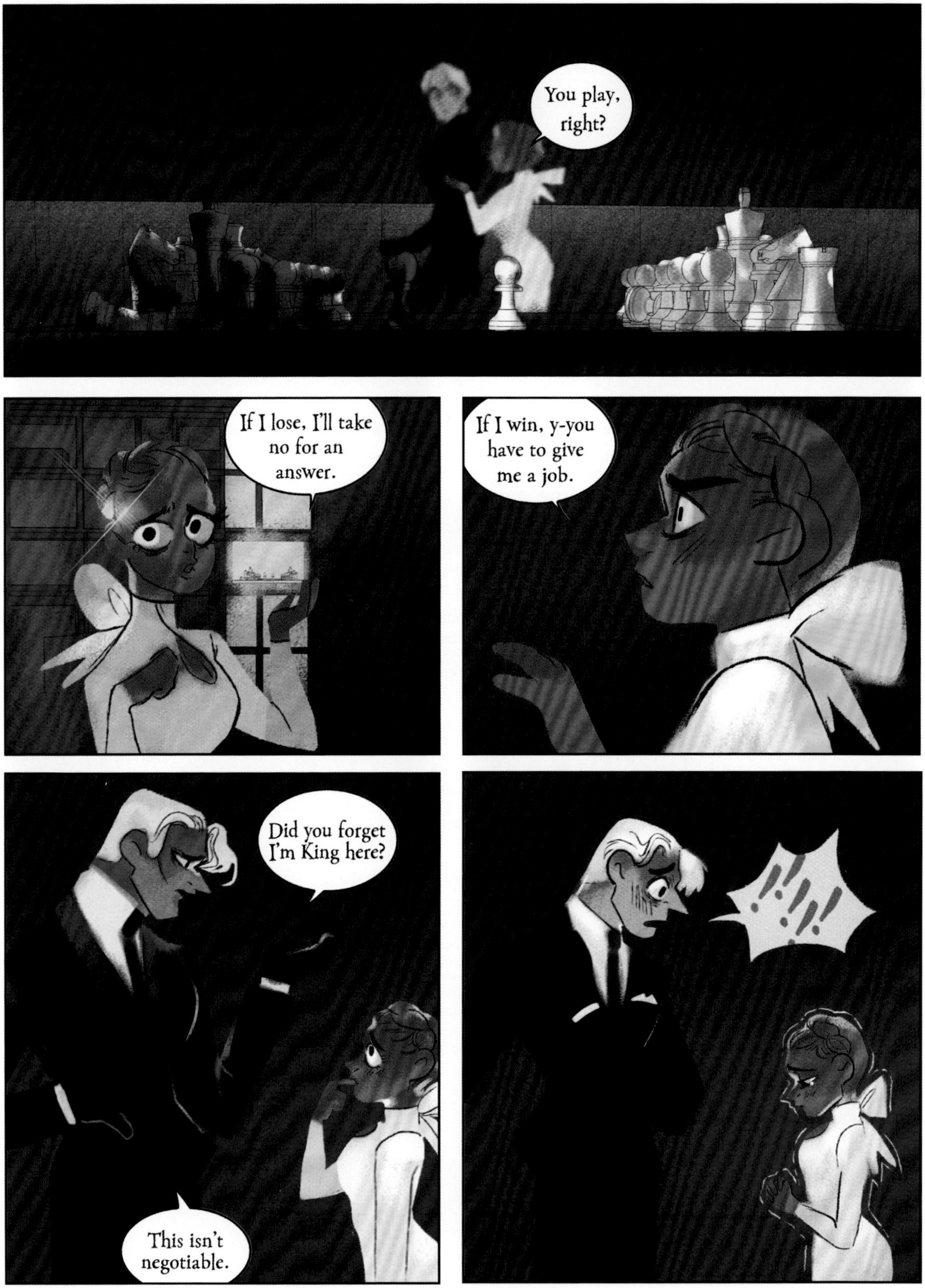
You play, right?
If I lose, I'll take no for an answer.
If I win, y-you have to give me a job.
Did you forget I'm King here?
This isn't negotiable.
!!!!

EPISODE 43: THE WAGER

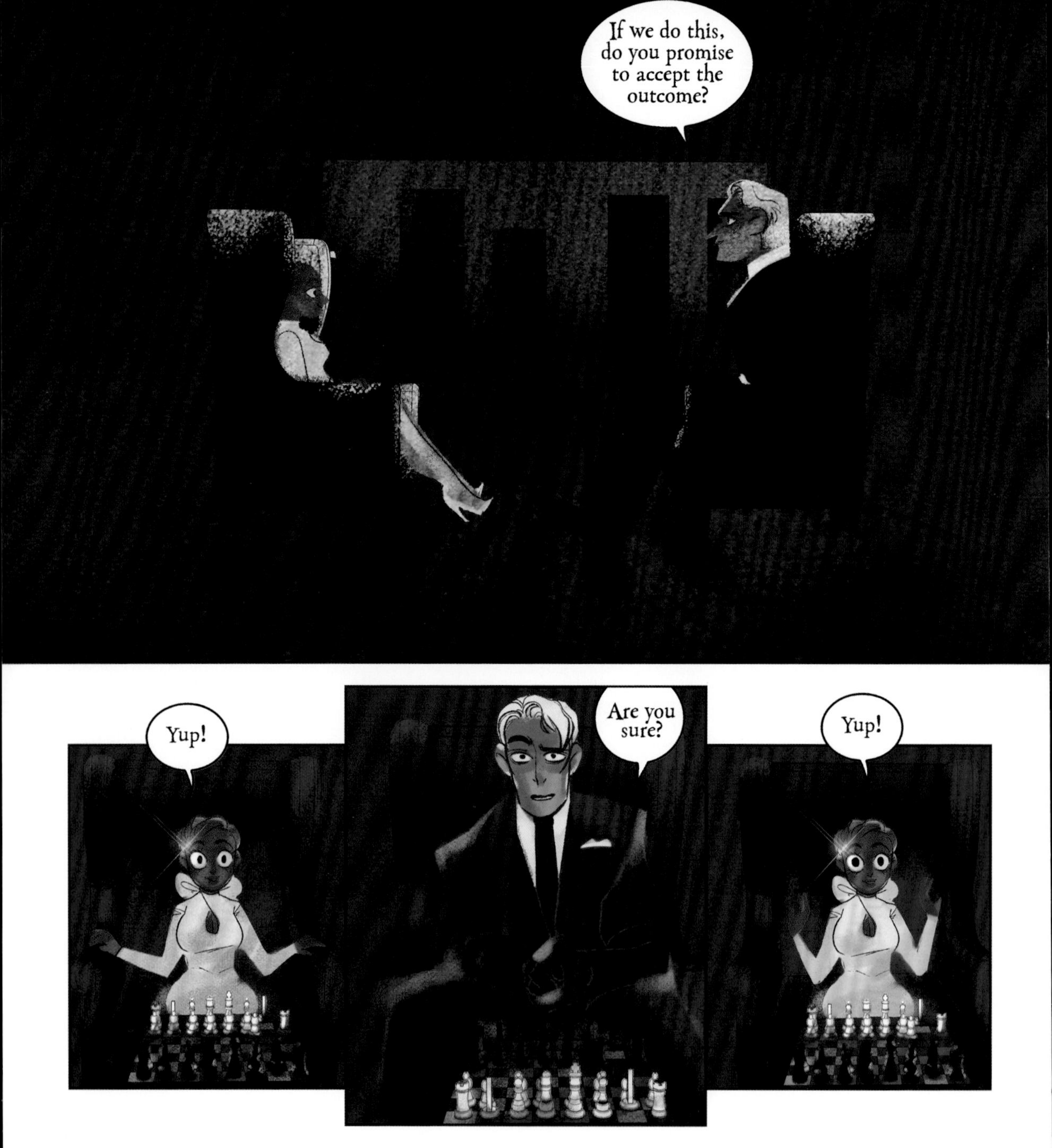
If we do this, do you promise to accept the outcome?
Yup!
Are you sure?
Yup!

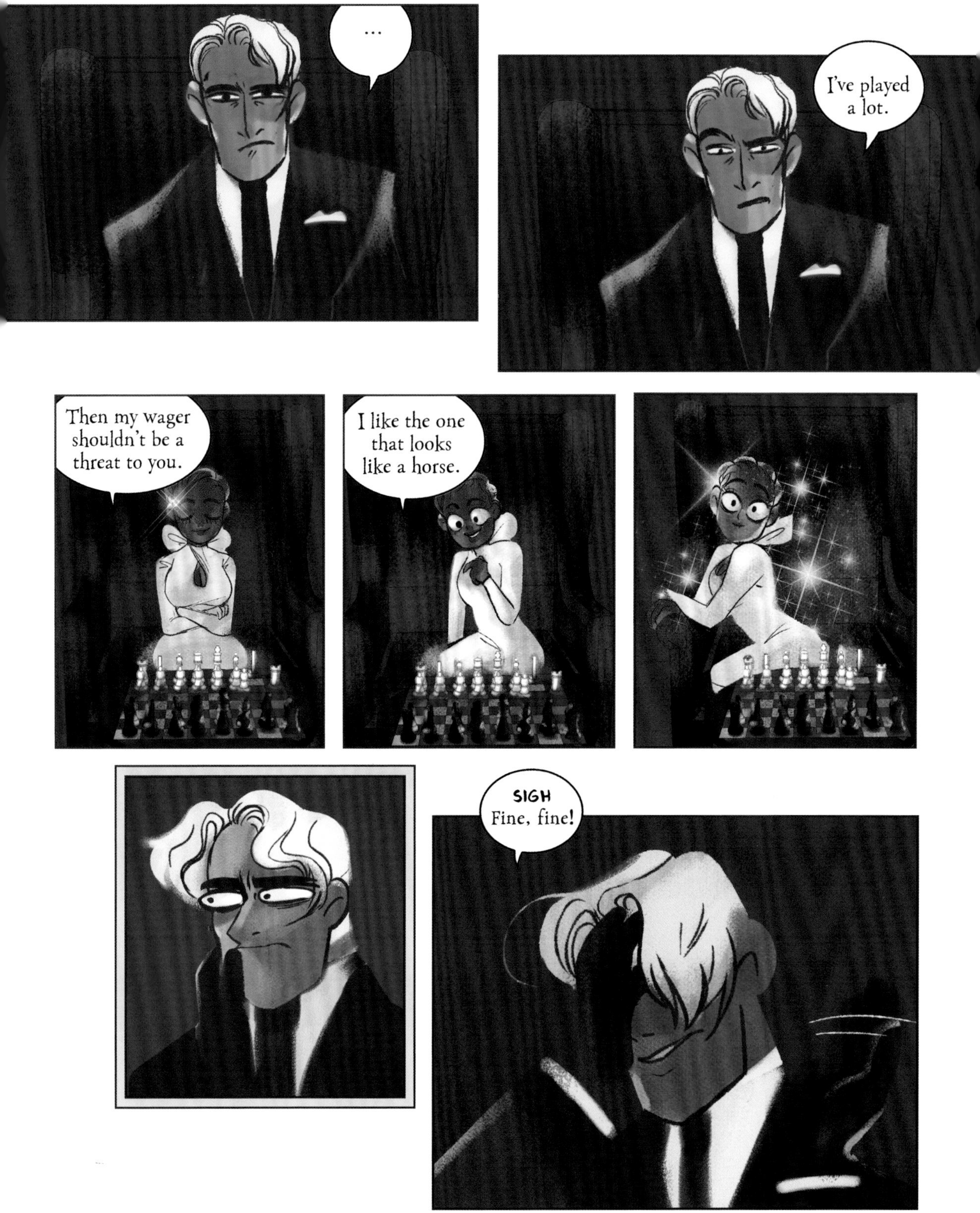
...
I've played a lot.
Then my wager shouldn't be a threat to you.
I like the one that looks like a horse.
SIGH
Fine, fine!

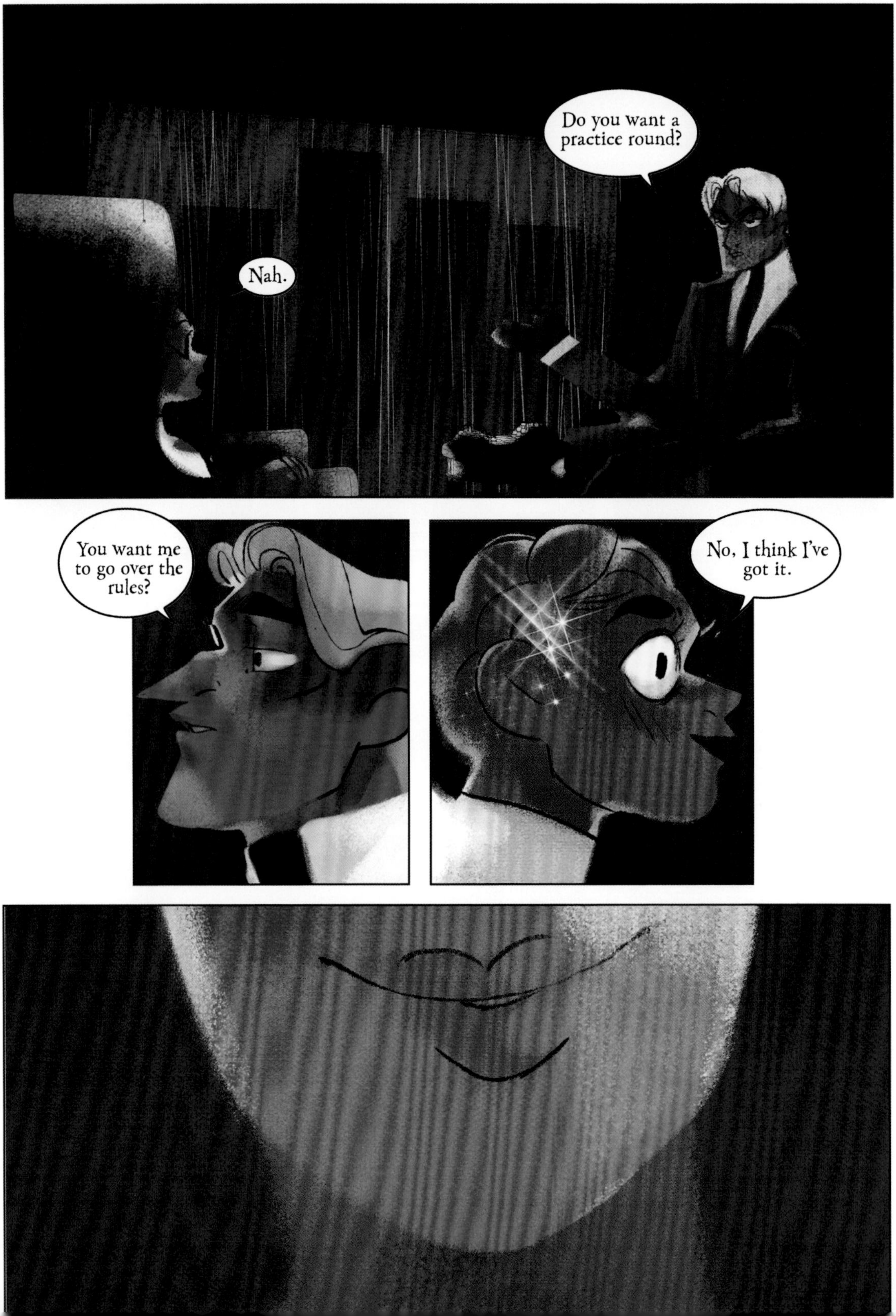
Do you want a practice round?
Nah.
You want me to go over the rules?
No, I think I've got it.

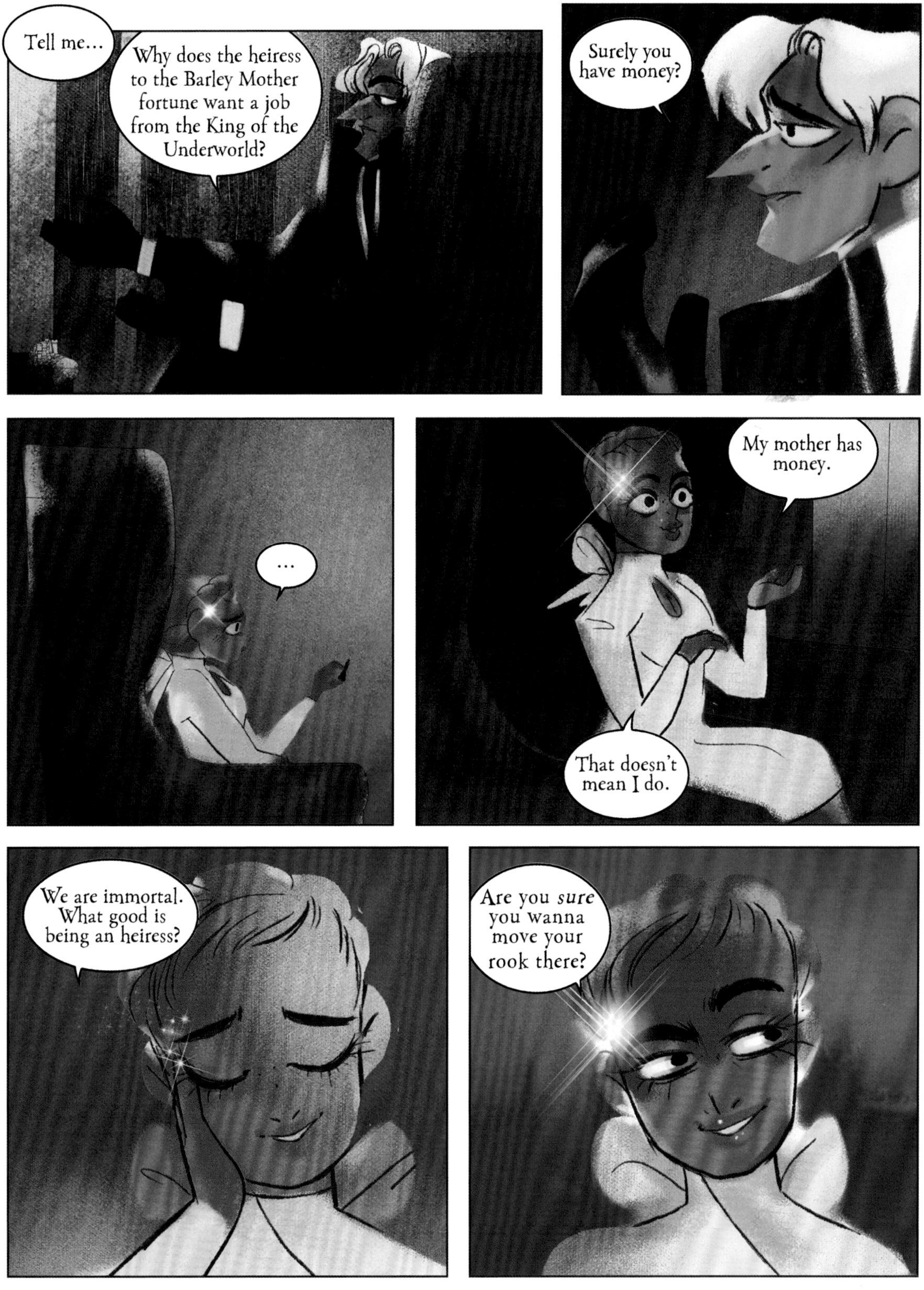
Tell me...
Why does the heiress to the Barley Mother fortune want a job from the King of the Underworld?
Surely you have money?
...
My mother has money.
That doesn't mean I do.
We are immortal. What good is being an heiress?
Are you *sure* you wanna move your rook there?

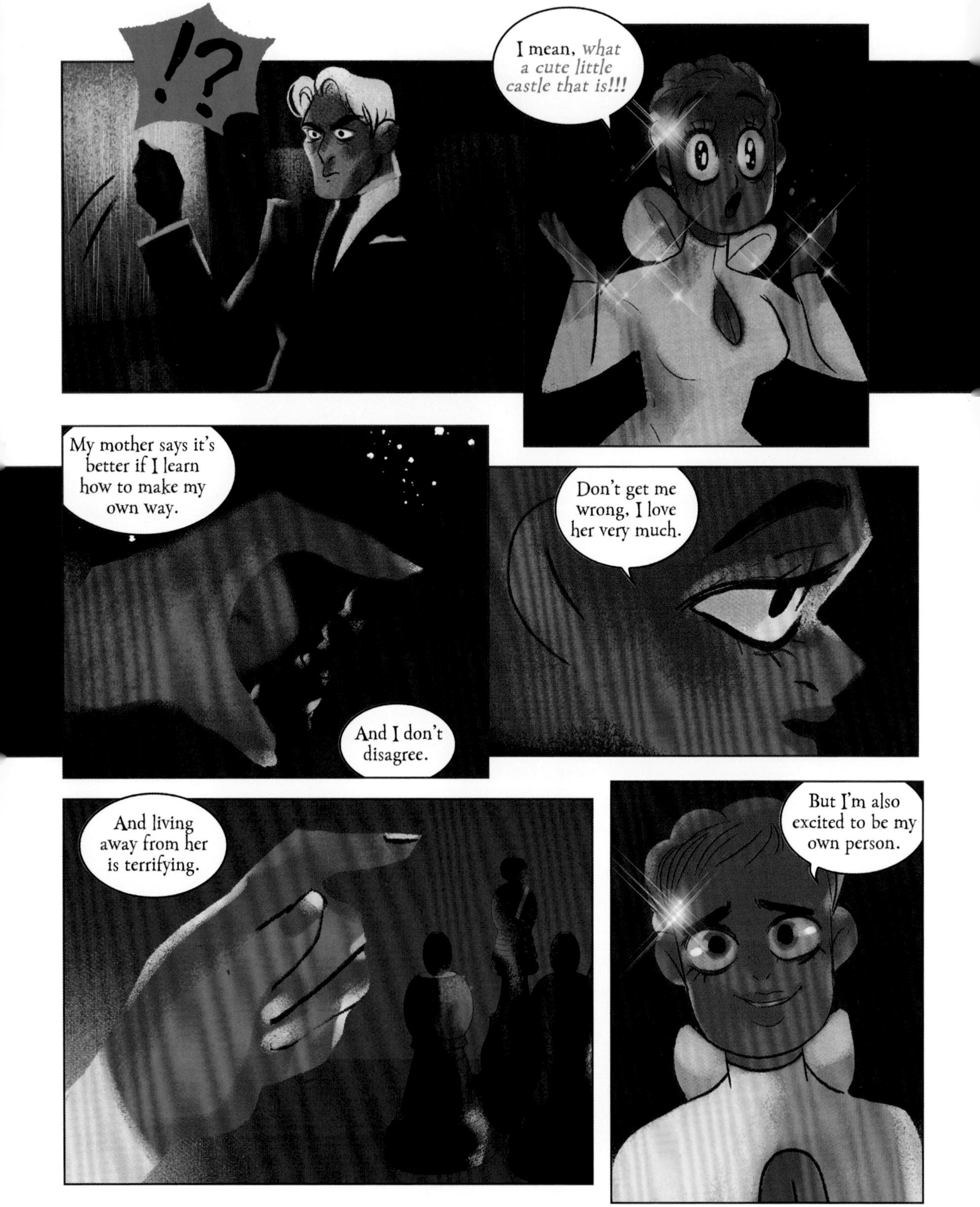
!?
I mean, what a cute little castle that is!!!
My mother says it's better if I learn how to make my own way.
And I don't disagree.
Don't get me wrong, I love her very much.
And living away from her is terrifying.
But I'm also excited to be my own person.

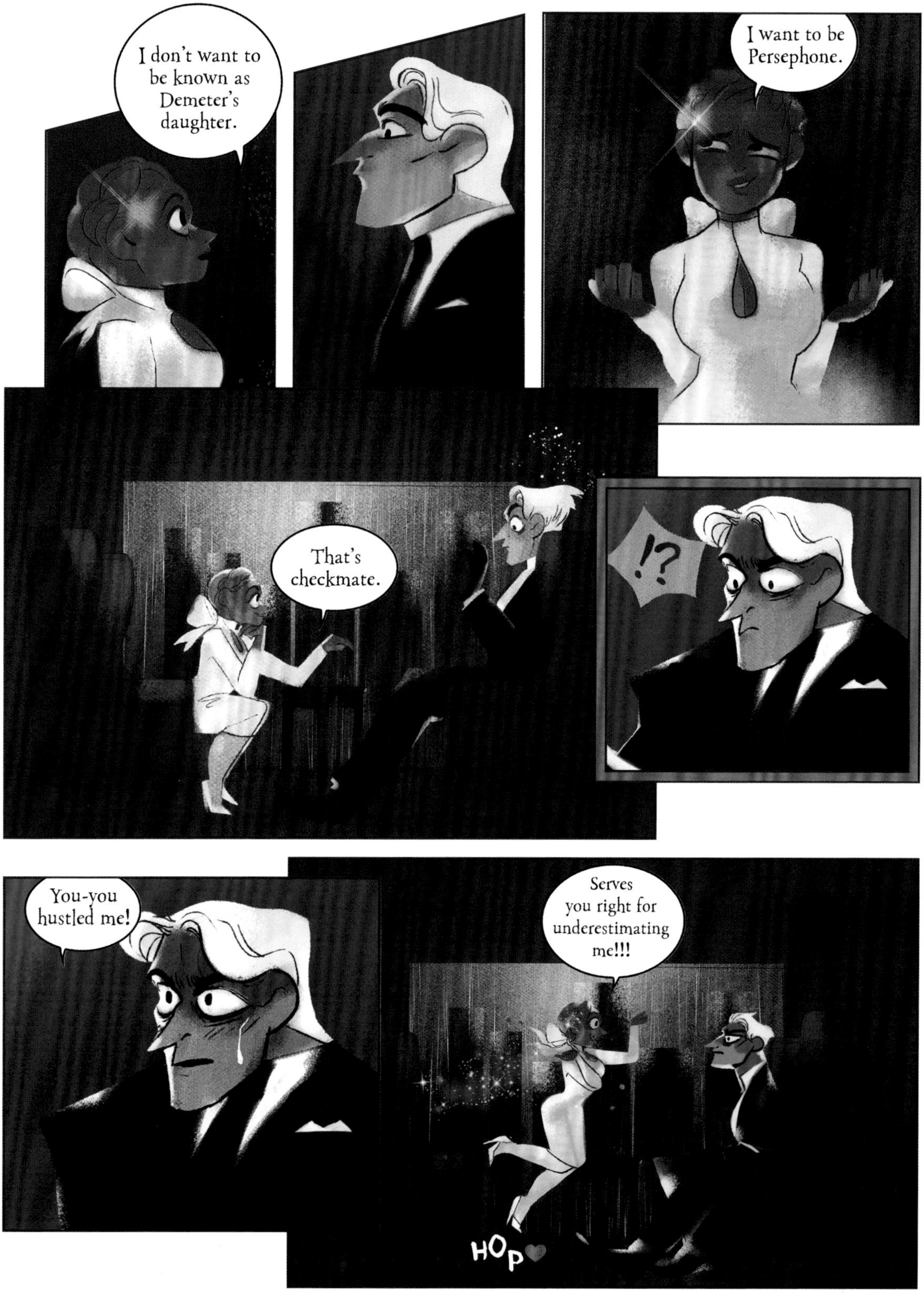
I don't want to be known as Demeter's daughter.
I want to be Persephone.
That's checkmate.
!?
You-you hustled me!
Serves you right for underestimating me!!!
HOP

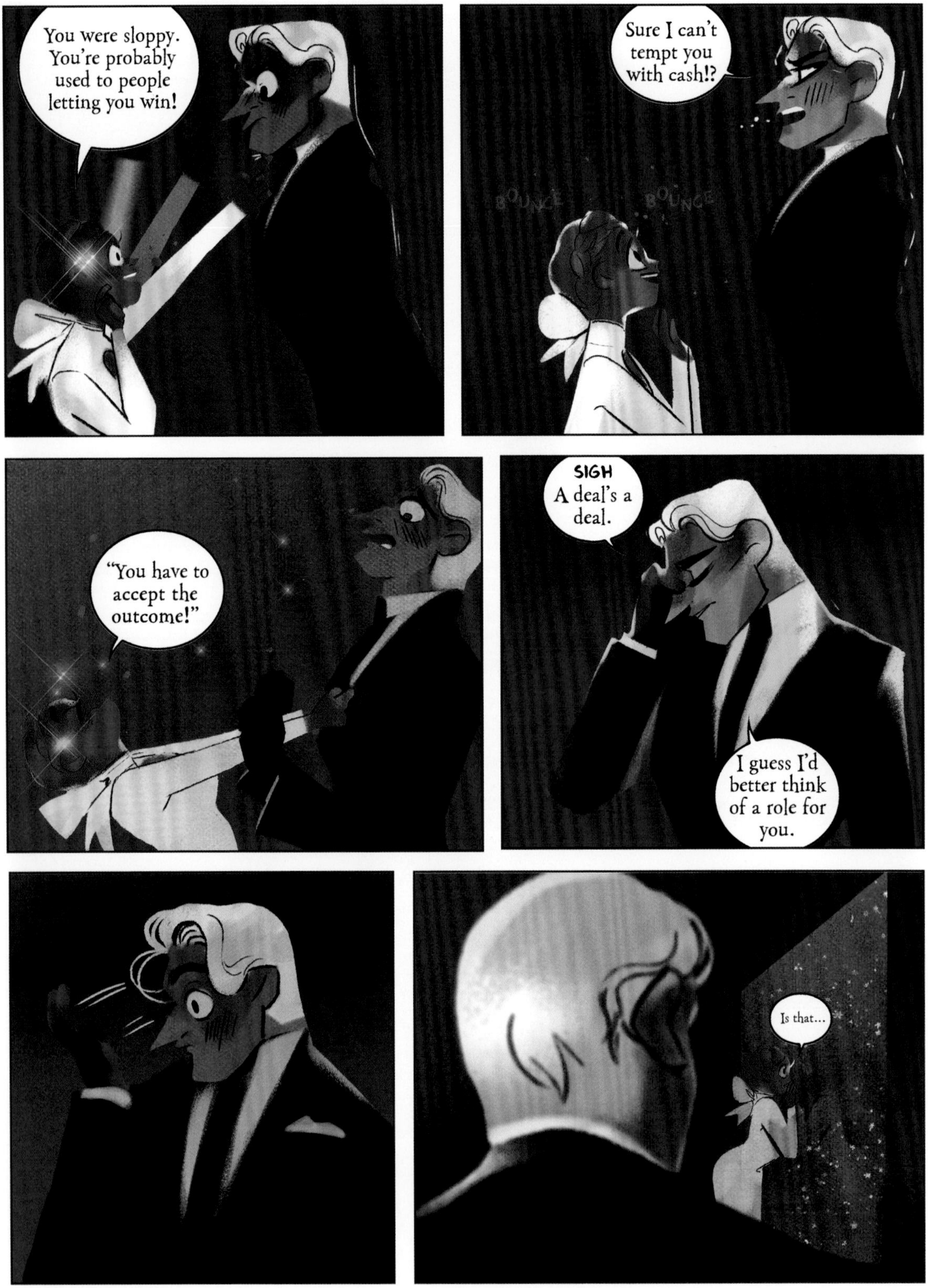
You were sloppy. You're probably used to people letting you win!
Sure I can't tempt you with cash!?
BOUNCE
BOUNCE
"You have to accept the outcome!"
SIGH
A deal's a deal.
I guess I'd better think of a role for you.
Is that...

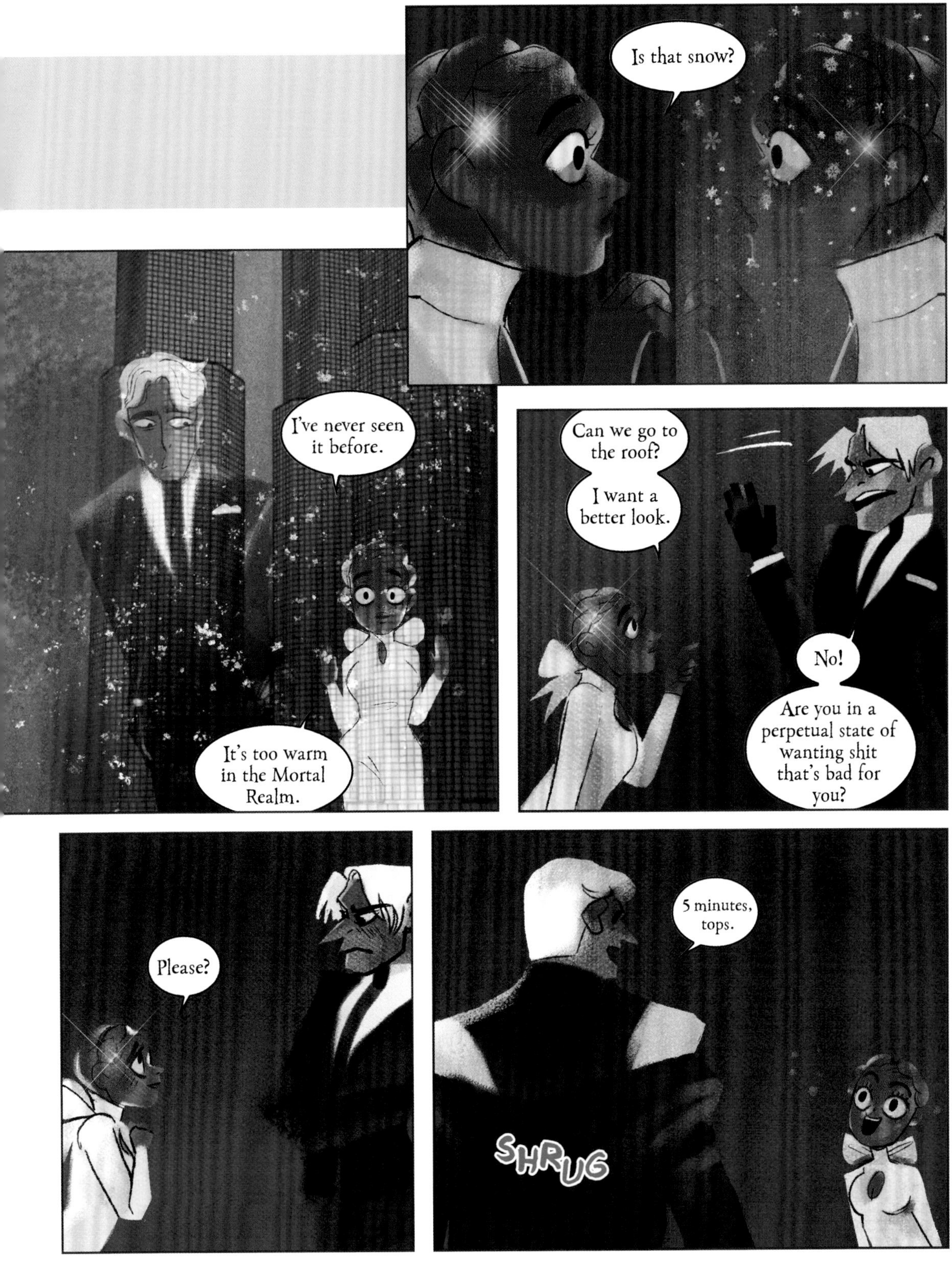

Is that snow?
I've never seen it before.
It's too warm in the Mortal Realm.
Can we go to the roof?
I want a better look.
No!
Are you in a perpetual state of wanting shit that's bad for you?
Please?
5 minutes, tops.
SHRUG

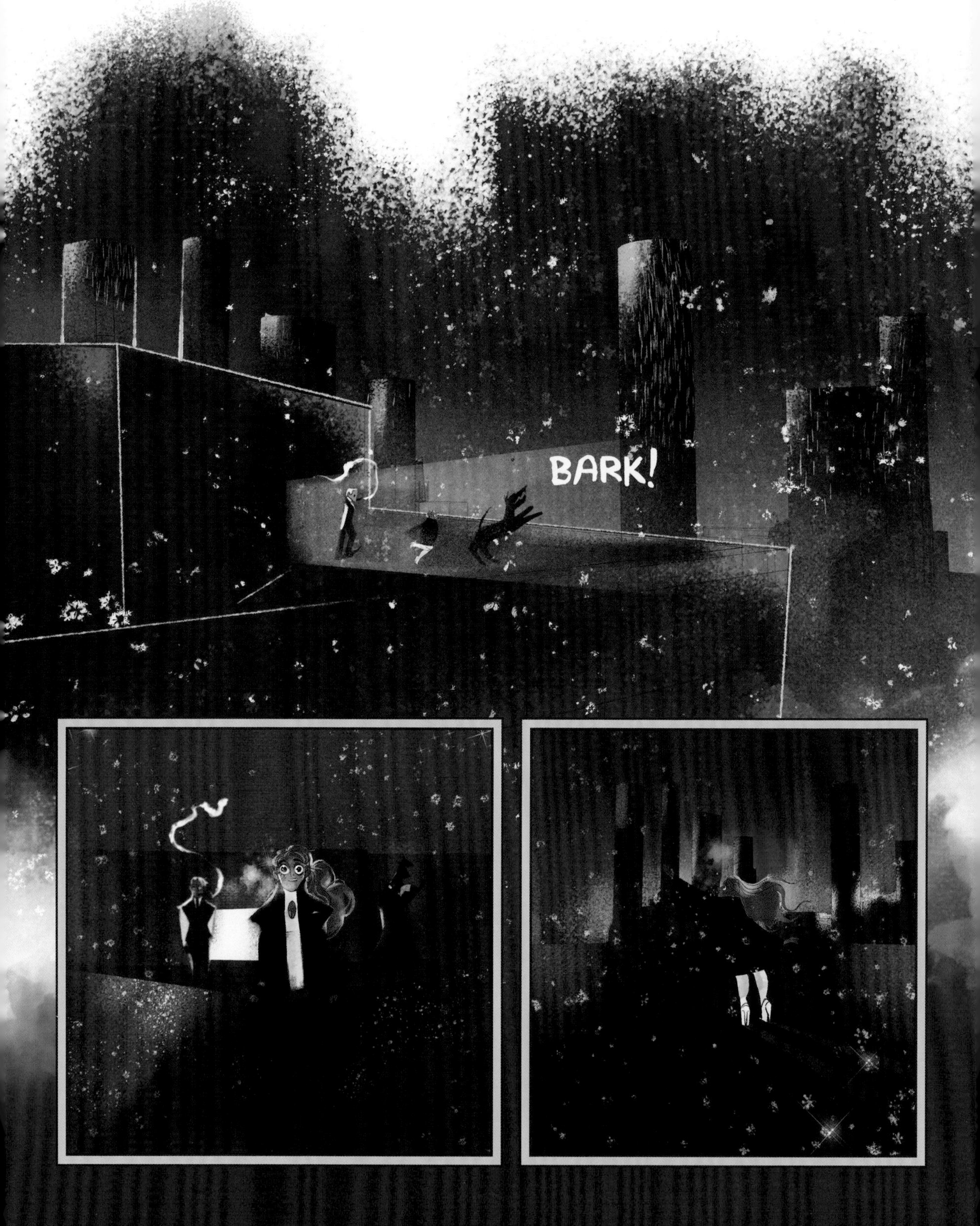
BARK!

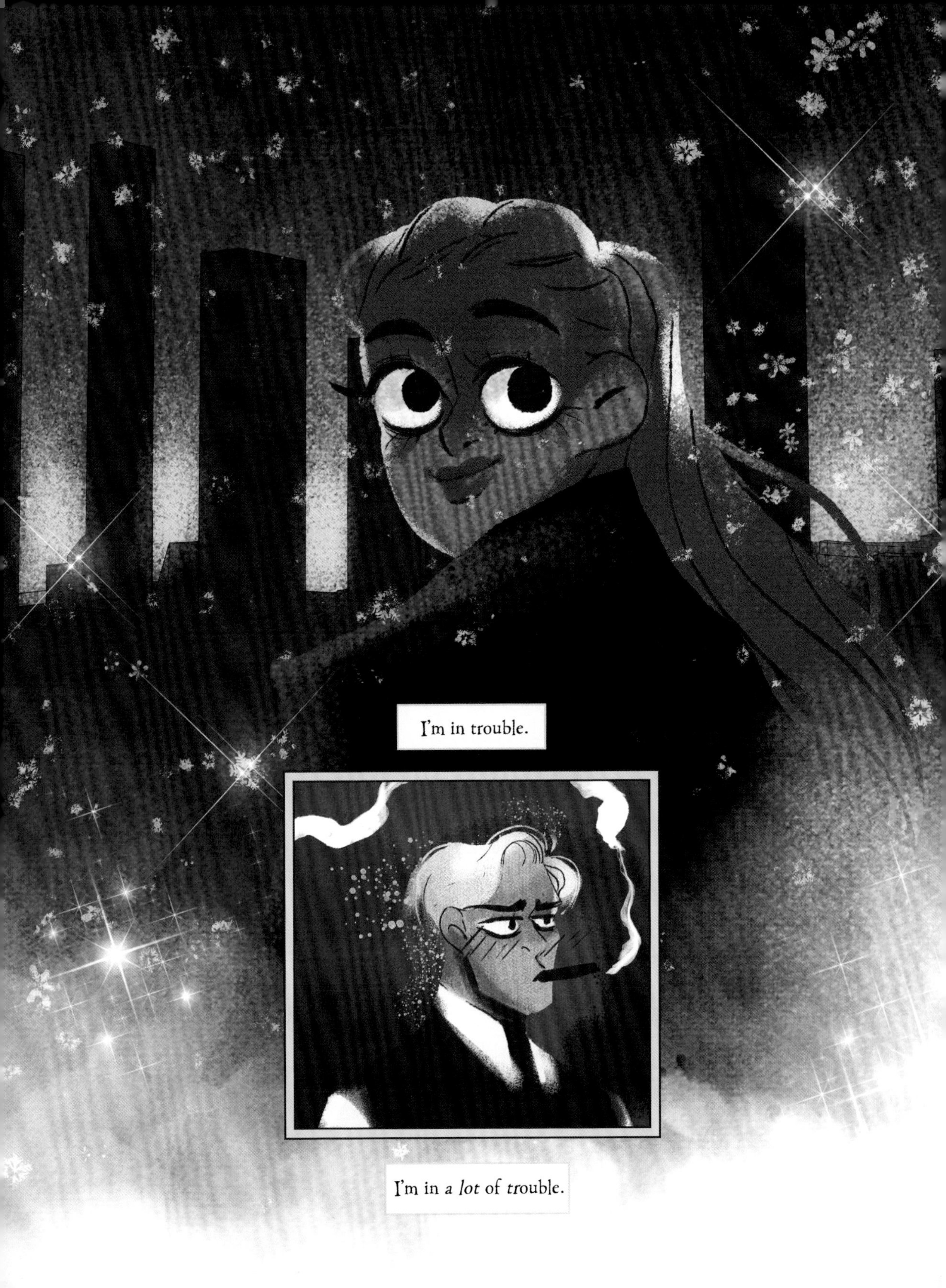
I'm in trouble.
I'm in a *lot* of *trouble.*

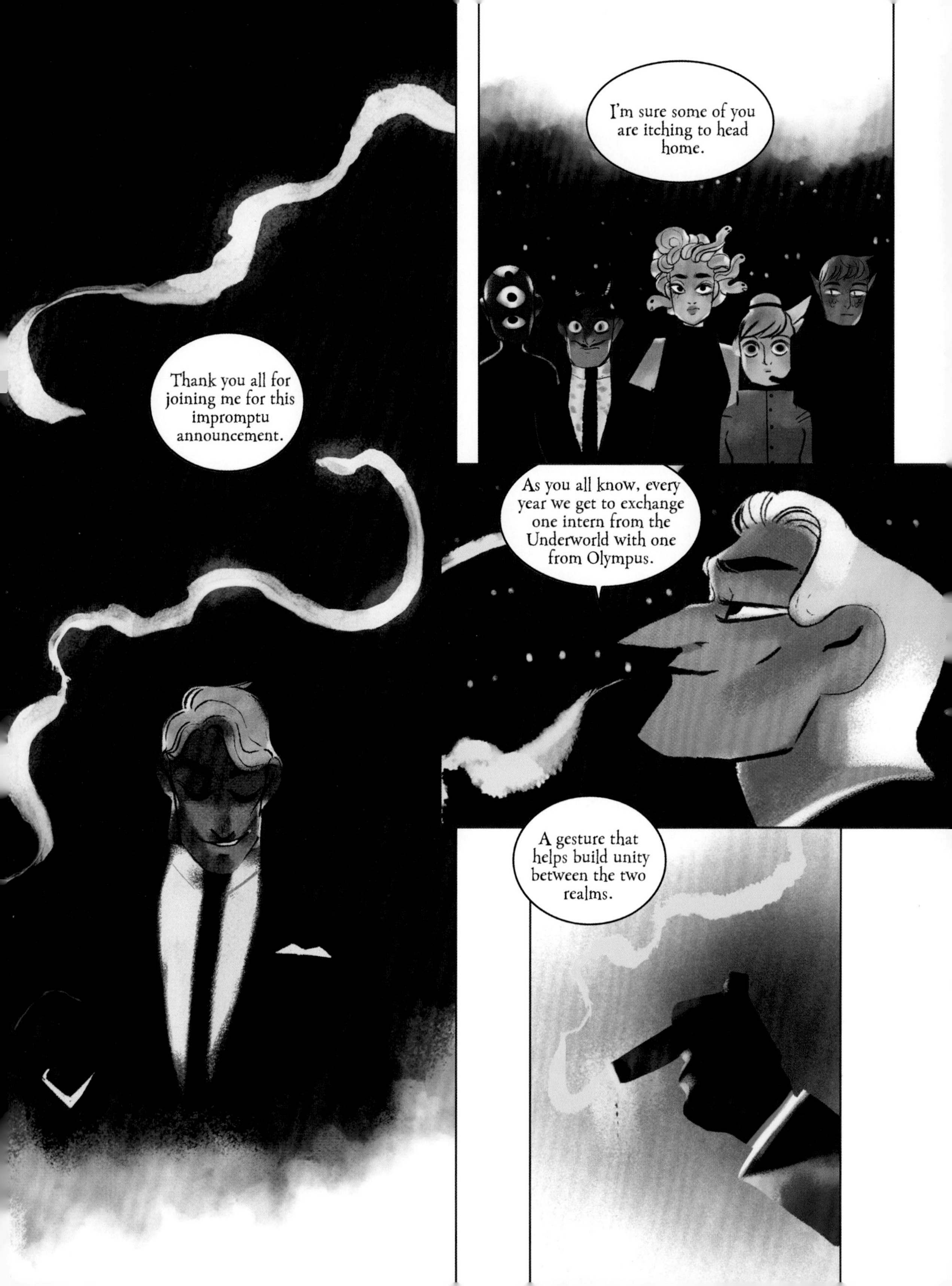
Thank you all for joining me for this impromptu announcement.
I'm sure some of you are itching to head home.
As you all know, every year we get to exchange one intern from the Underworld with one from Olympus.
A gesture that helps build unity between the two realms.

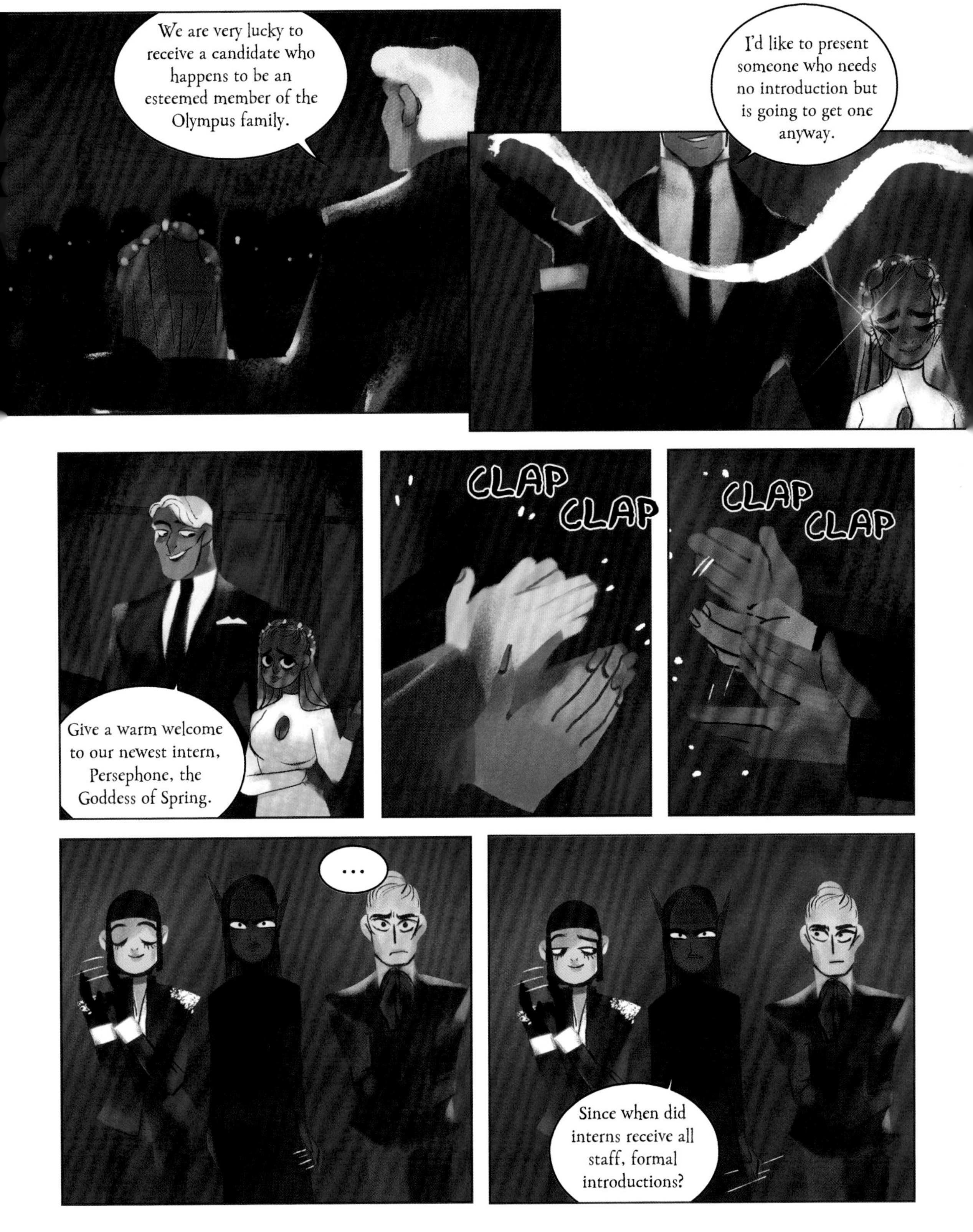
We are very lucky to receive a candidate who happens to be an esteemed member of the Olympus family.
I'd like to present someone who needs no introduction but is going to get one anyway.
Give a warm welcome to our newest intern, Persephone, the Goddess of Spring.
CLAP CLAP
CLAP CLAP
...
Since when did interns receive all staff, formal introductions?

EPISODE 44: SOFT

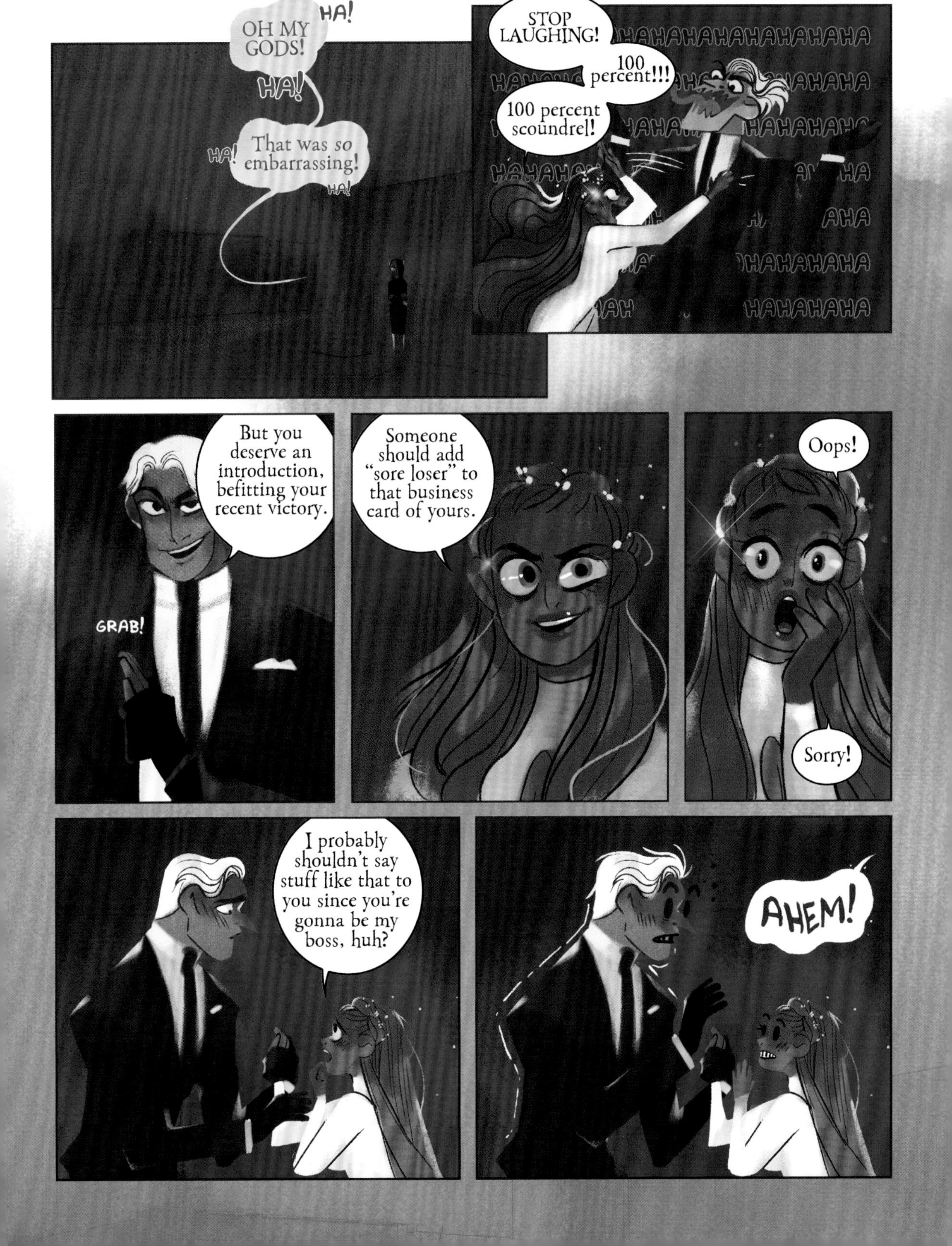
OH MY GODS!
HA!
HA!
That was *so* embarrassing!
HA!
HA!
STOP LAUGHING!
100 percent scoundrel!
100 percent!!!
HAHAHAHAHAHAHAHAHAHA
But you deserve an introduction, befitting your recent victory.
GRAB!
Someone should add "sore loser" to that business card of yours.
Oops!
Sorry!
I probably shouldn't say stuff like that to you since you're gonna be my boss, huh?
AHEM!

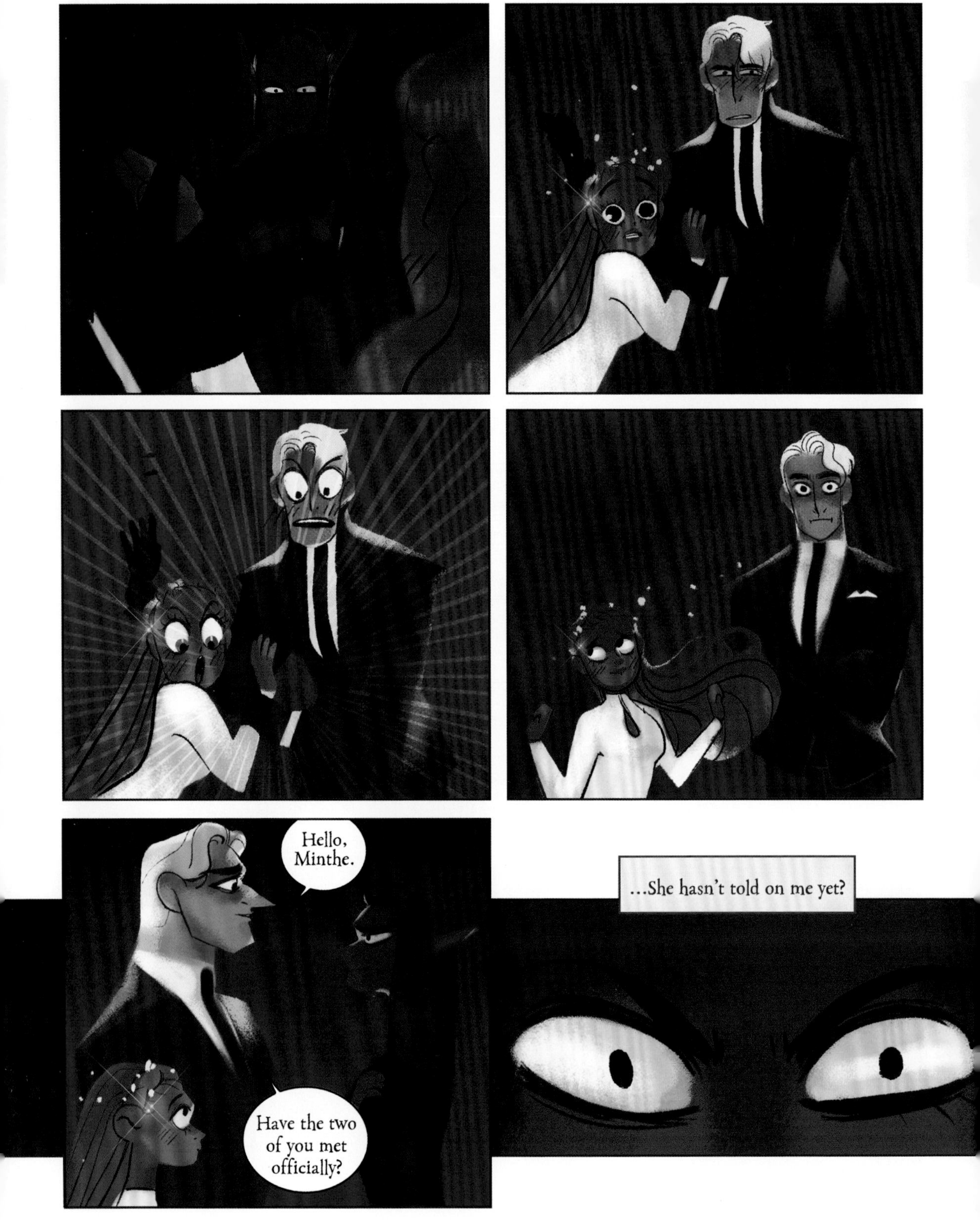
Hello, Minthe.
Have the two of you met officially?
...She hasn't told on me yet?

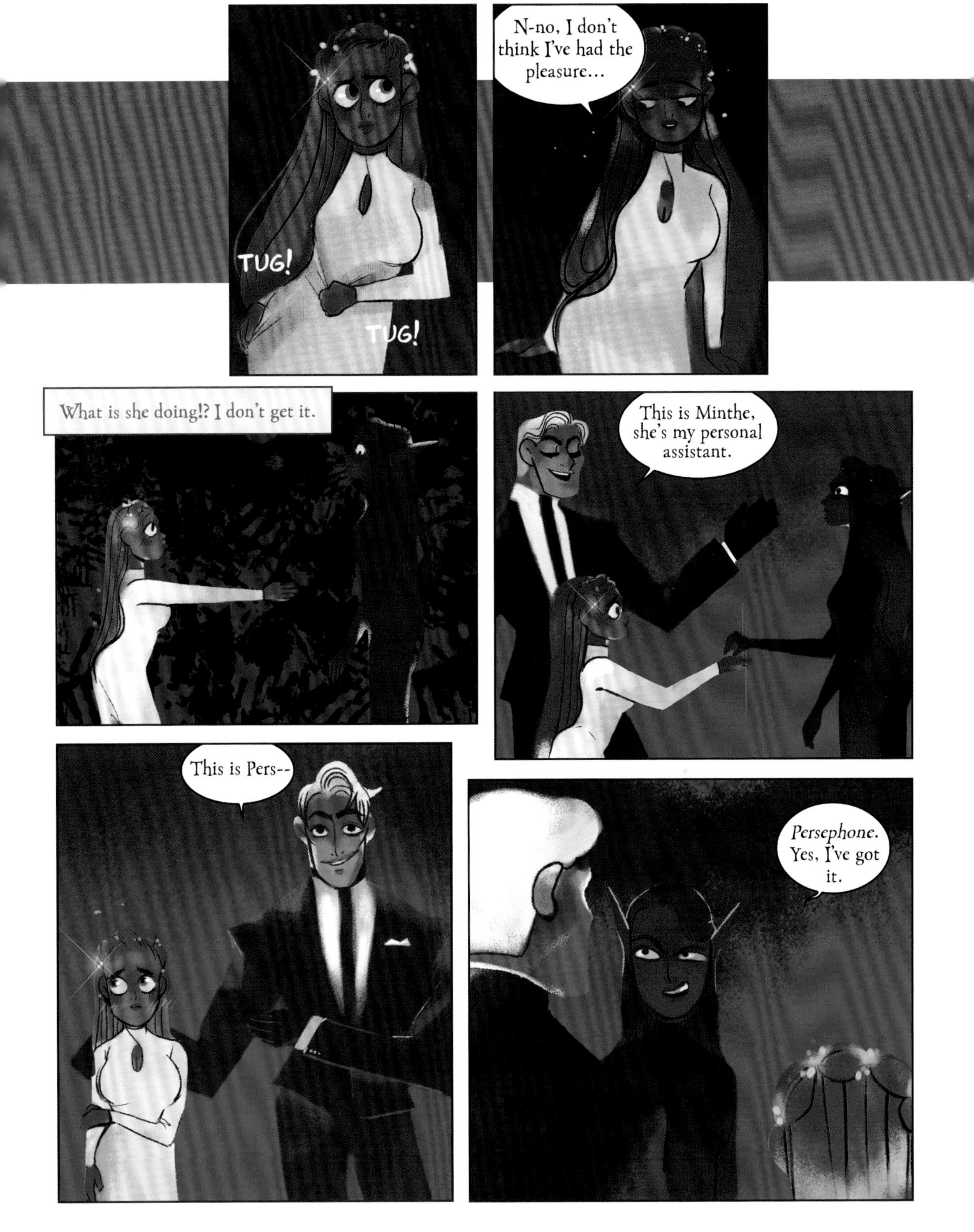
TUG!
TUG!
N-no, I don't think I've had the pleasure...
What is she doing!? I don't get it.
This is Minthe, she's my personal assistant.
This is Pers--
Persephone. Yes, I've got it.

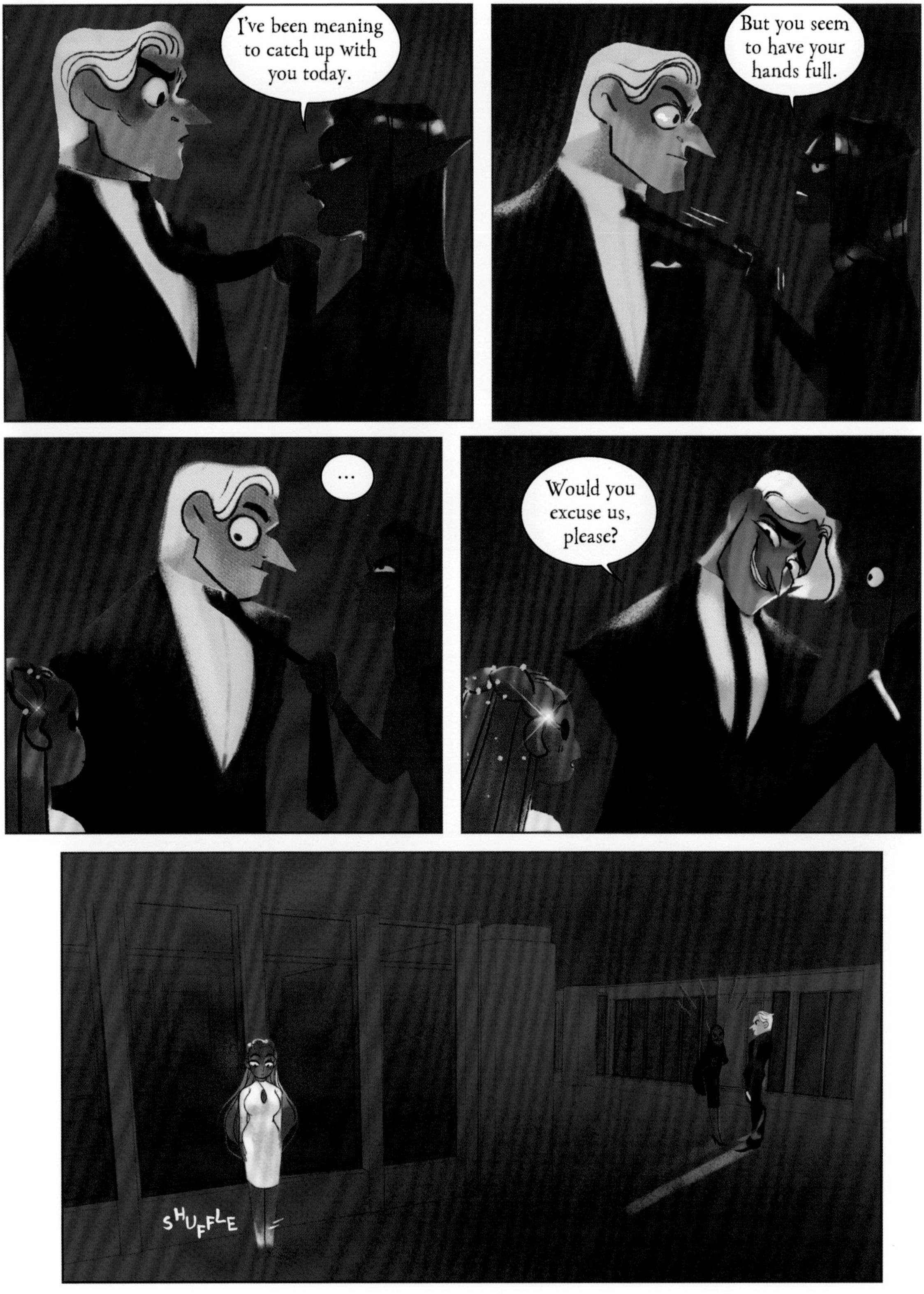
I've been meaning to catch up with you today.
But you seem to have your hands full.
...
Would you excuse us, please?
SHUFFLE

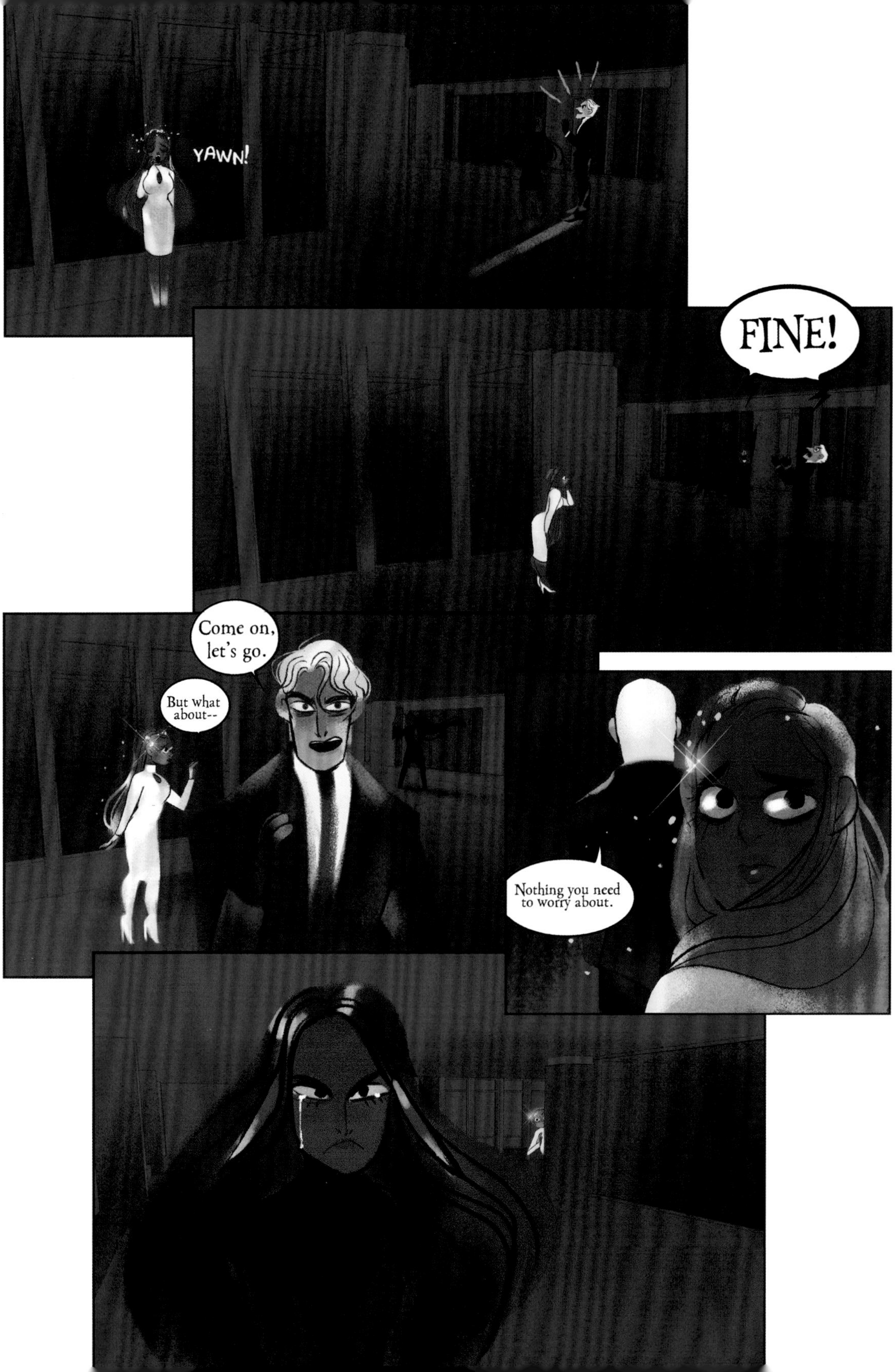

YAWN!
FINE!
Come on, let's go.
But what about--
Nothing you need to worry about.

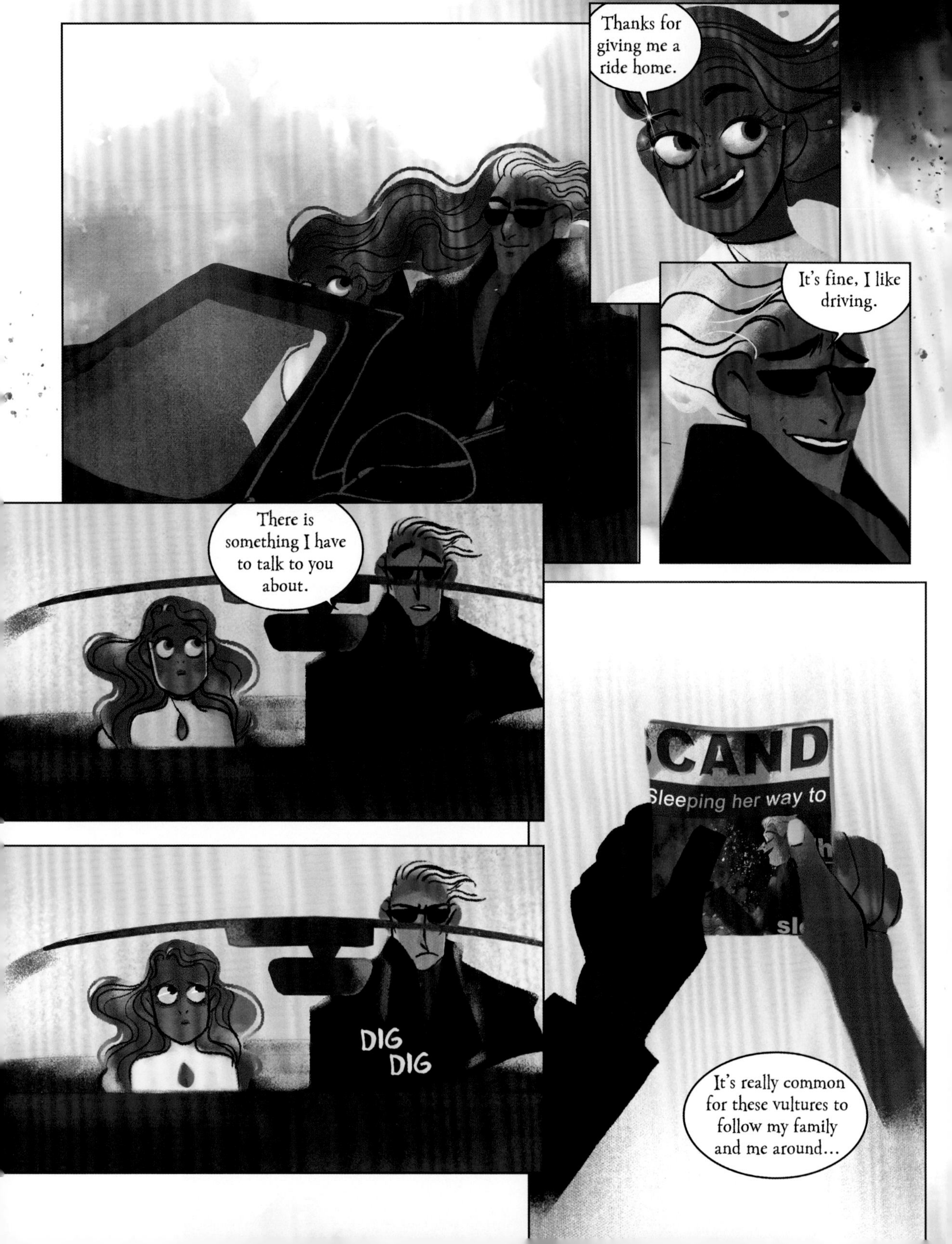
Thanks for giving me a ride home.
It's fine, I like driving.
There is something I have to talk to you about.
SCAND
Sleeping her way to
DIG DIG
It's really common for these vultures to follow my family and me around...

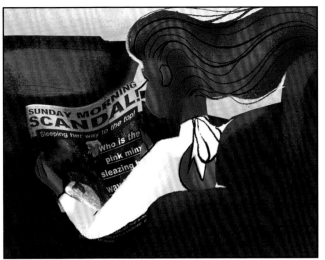

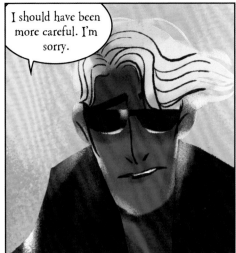

SUNDAY MORNING
SCANDAL!
Sleeping her way to the top!
I should have been more careful. I'm sorry.
…
I must admit I got a kick out of this version of me they've cooked up.
SUNDAY MORNING
SCANDAL
Sleeping her way to the top!
Who is the
pink minx
sleazing her
way into the
royal family?
The real thing is far less interesting…

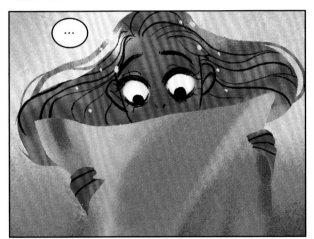

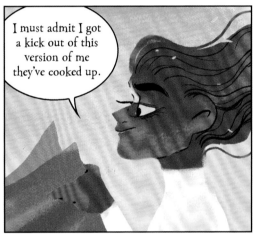

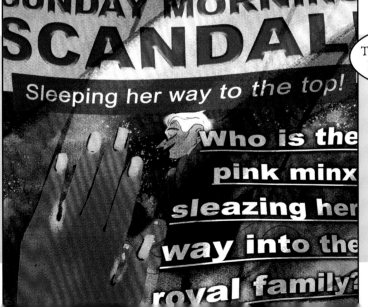

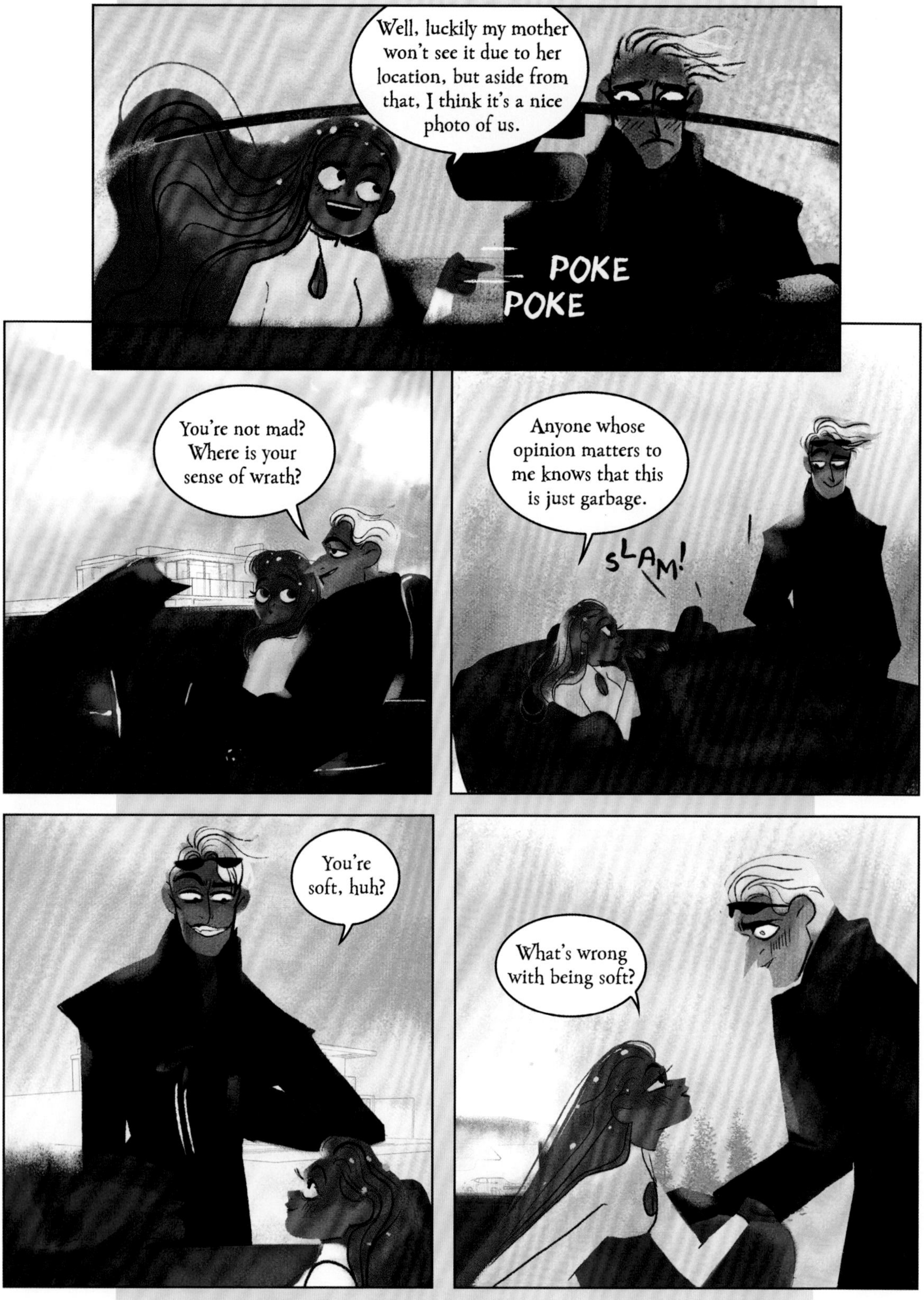
Well, luckily my mother won't see it due to her location, but aside from that, I think it's a nice photo of us.
POKE
POKE
You're not mad? Where is your sense of wrath?
Anyone whose opinion matters to me knows that this is just garbage.
SLAM!
You're soft, huh?
What's wrong with being soft?

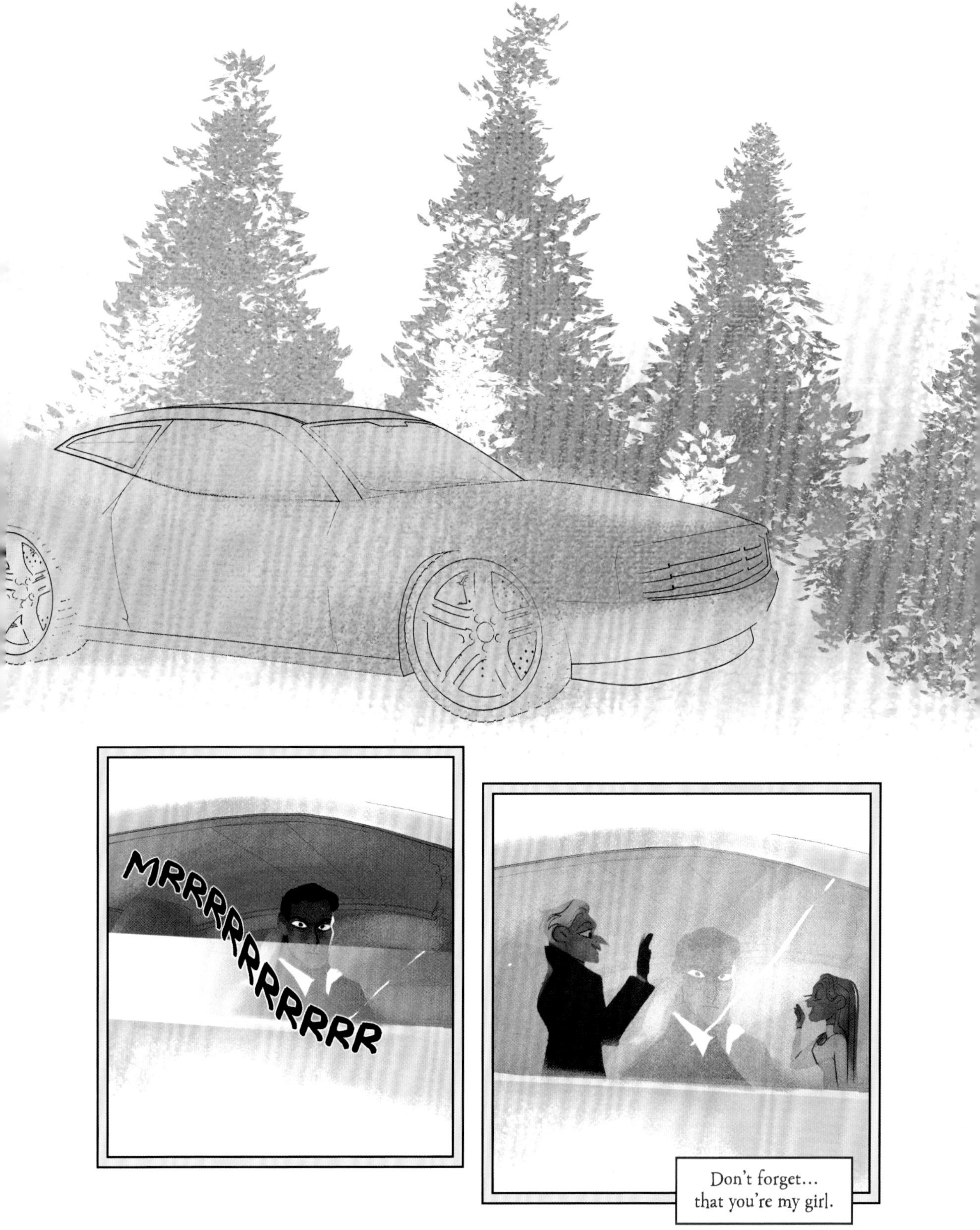
MRRRRRRRRRRRRR
Don't forget...
that you're my girl.

EPISODE 45: CRUSHED

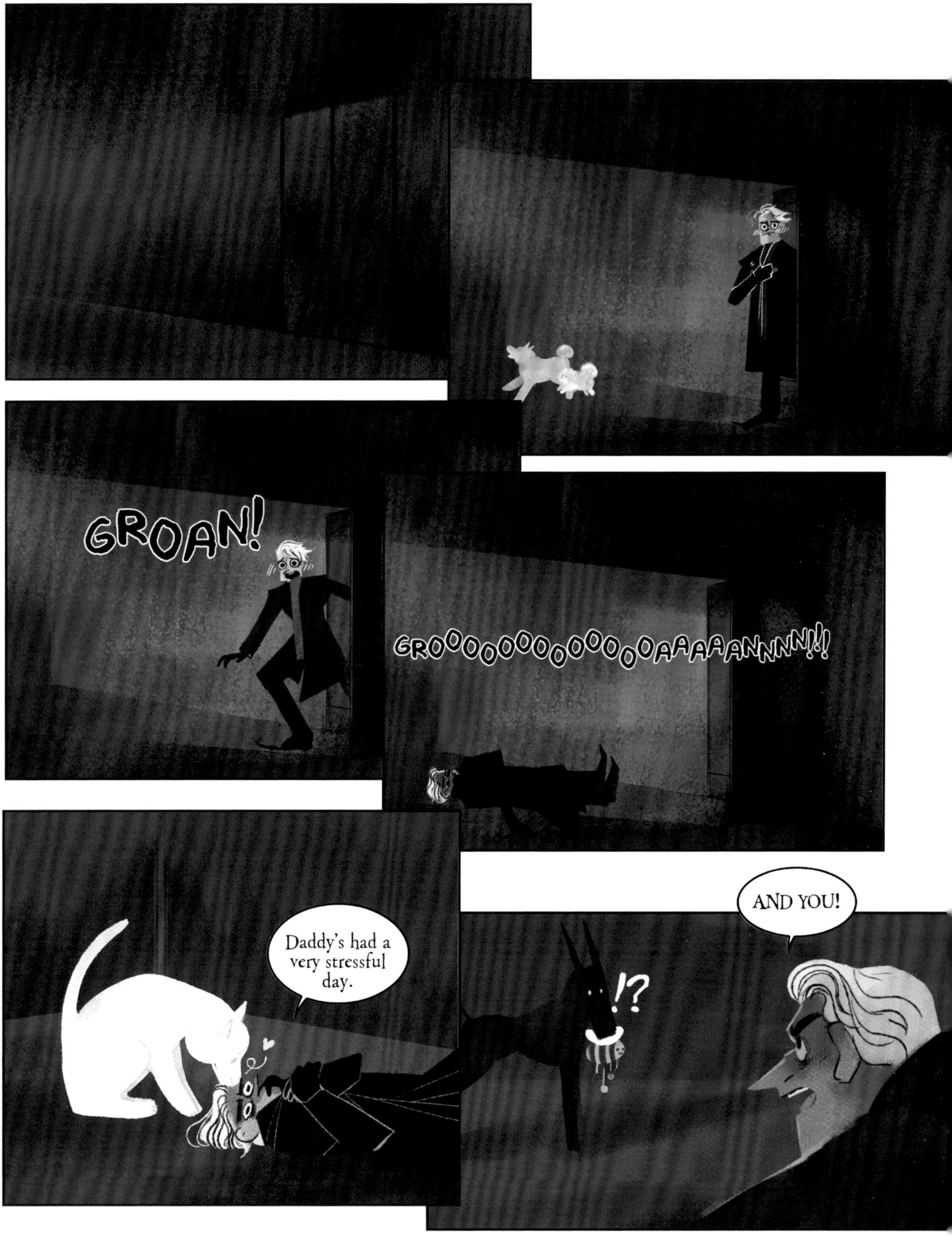
GROAN!
GROOOOOOOOOOOOOOAAAAANNNN!!!
Daddy's had a very stressful day.
AND YOU!
!?

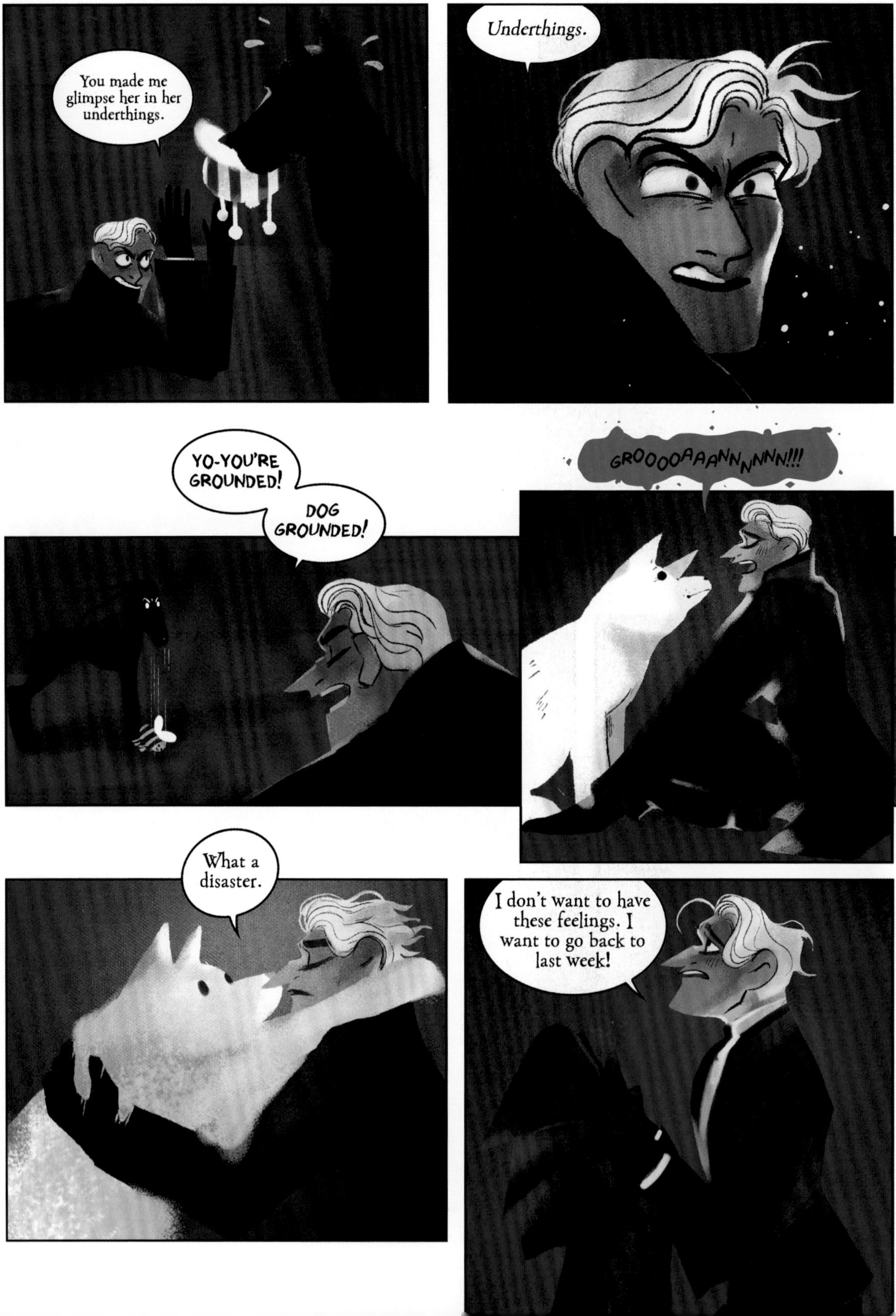
You made me glimpse her in her underthings.
Underthings.
YO-YOU'RE GROUNDED!
DOG GROUNDED!
GROOOOAAANNNNNN!!!
What a disaster.
I don't want to have these feelings. I want to go back to last week!

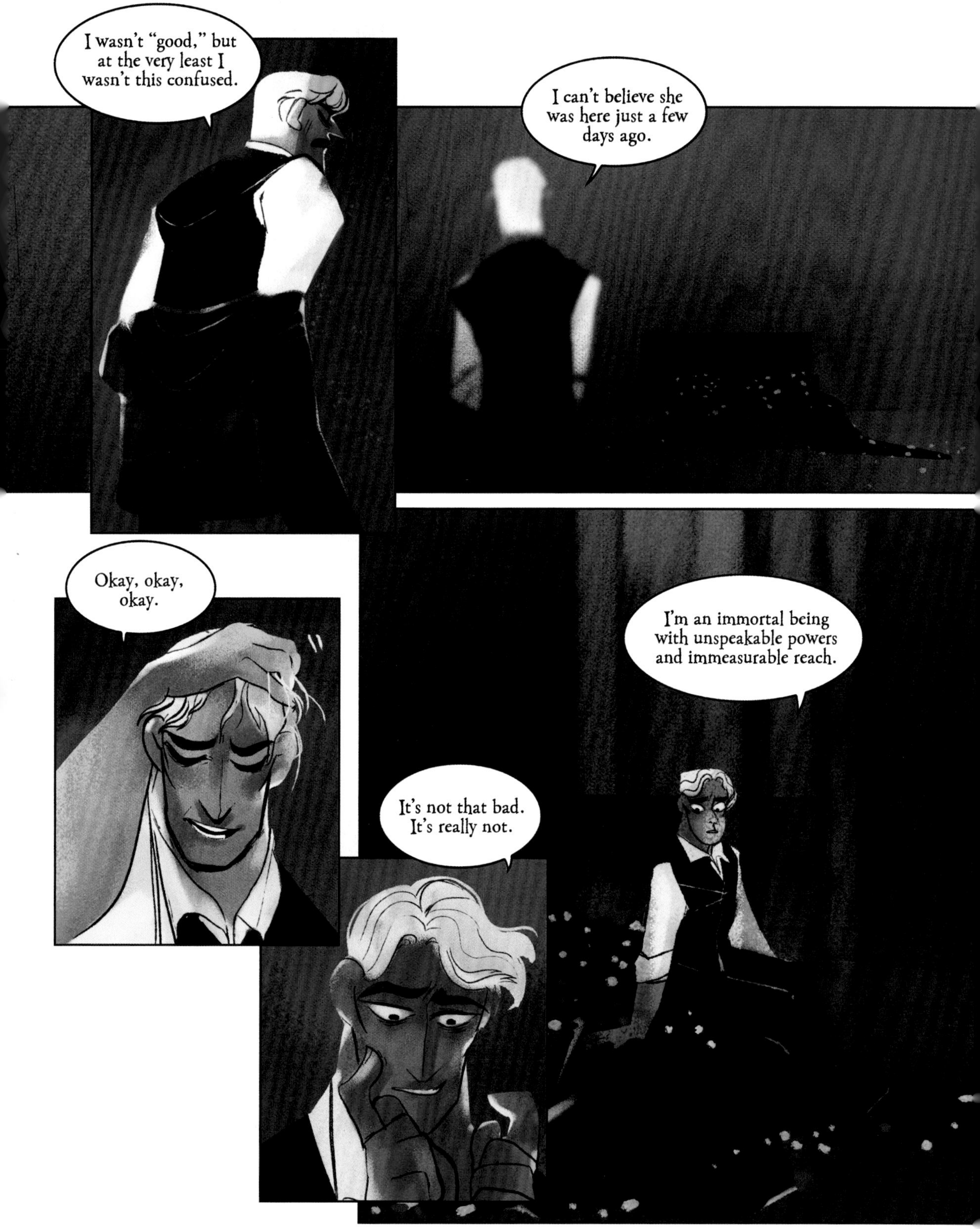

I wasn't "good," but at the very least I wasn't this confused.
I can't believe she was here just a few days ago.
Okay, okay, okay.
I'm an immortal being with unspeakable powers and immeasurable reach.
It's not that bad. It's really not.

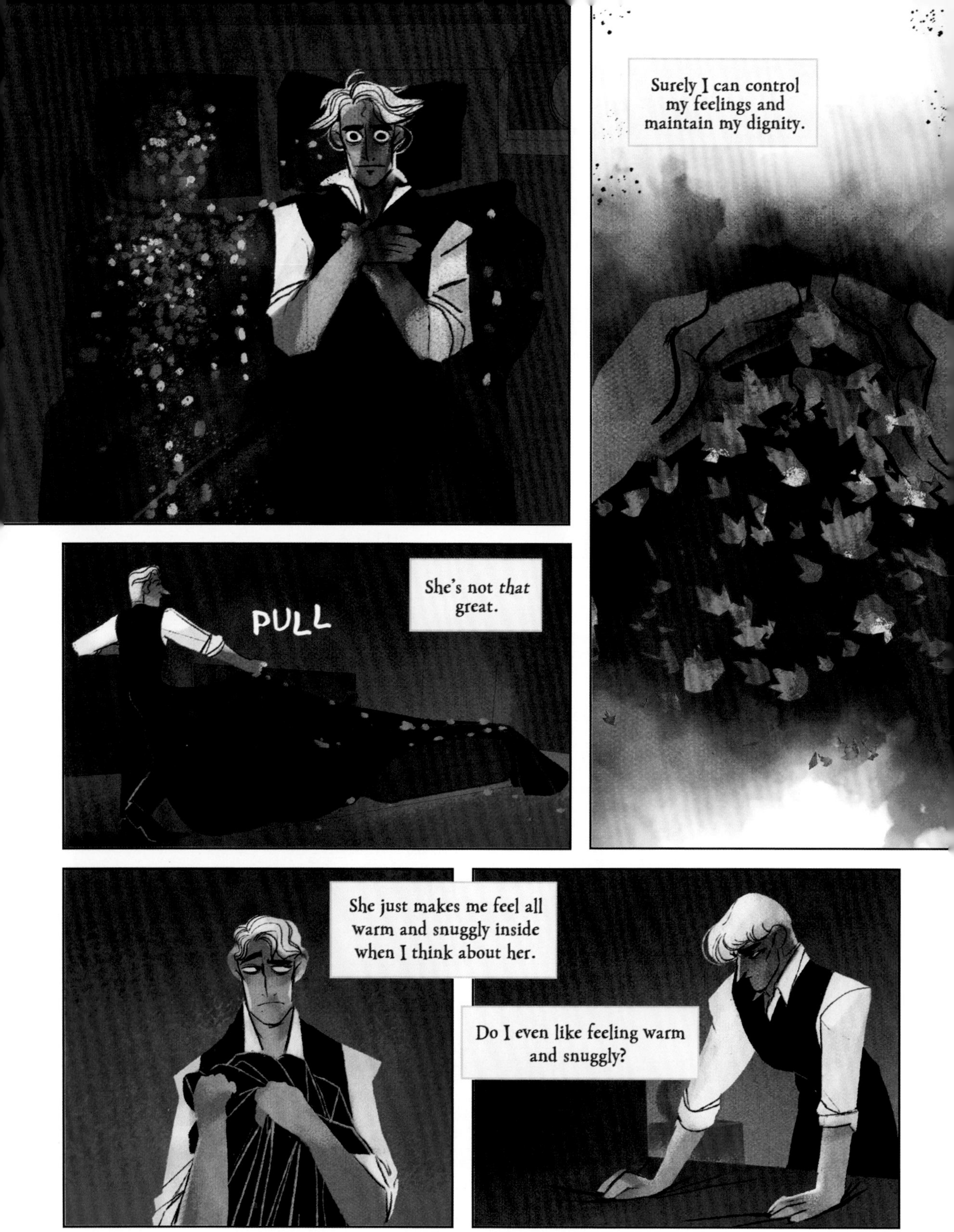
Surely I can control my feelings and maintain my dignity.
PULL
She's not *that* great.
She just makes me feel all warm and snuggly inside when I think about her.
Do I even like feeling warm and snuggly?

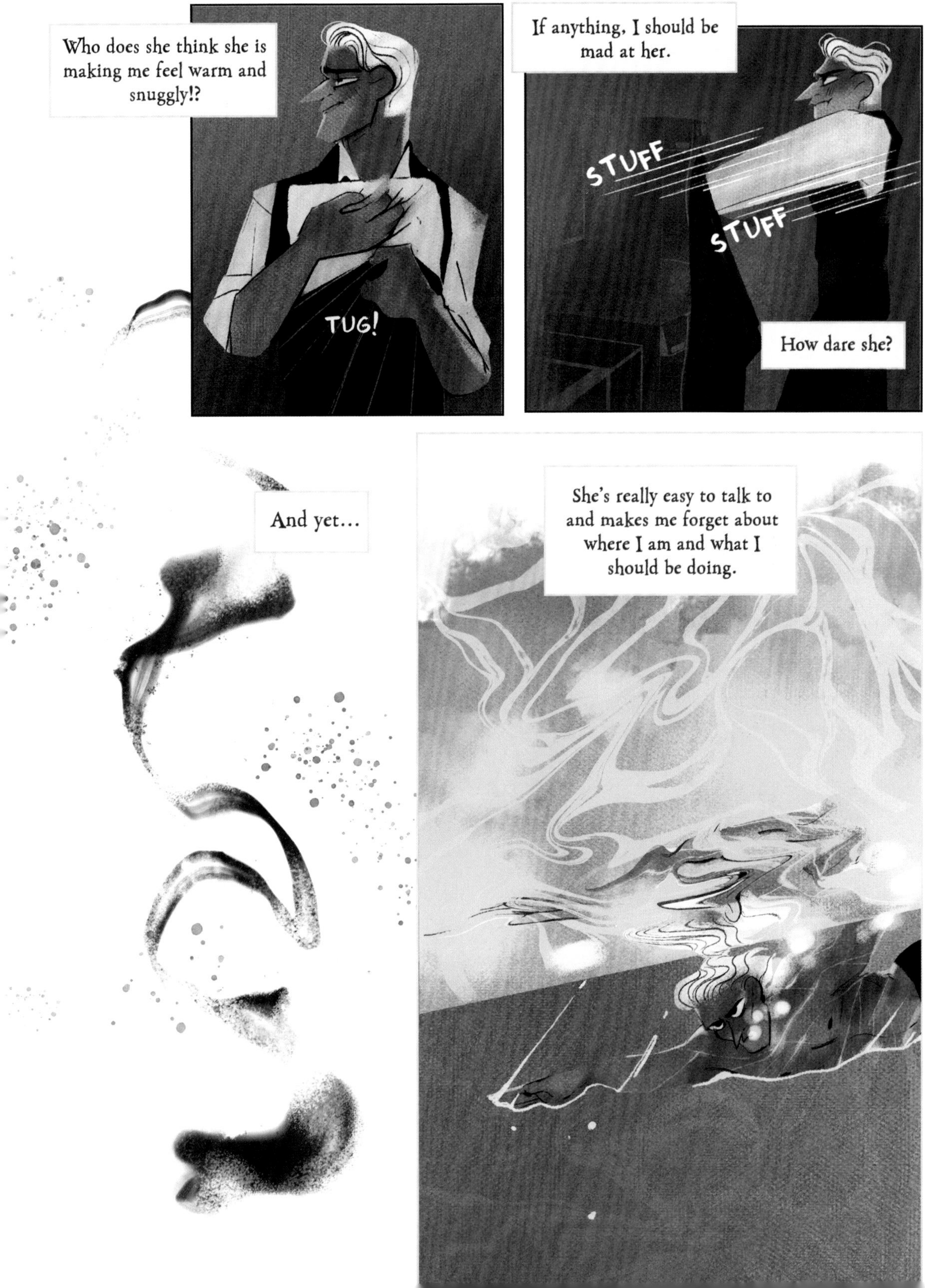
Who does she think she is making me feel warm and snuggly!?
TUG!
If anything, I should be mad at her.
STUFF
STUFF
How dare she?
And yet…
She's really easy to talk to and makes me forget about where I am and what I should be doing.

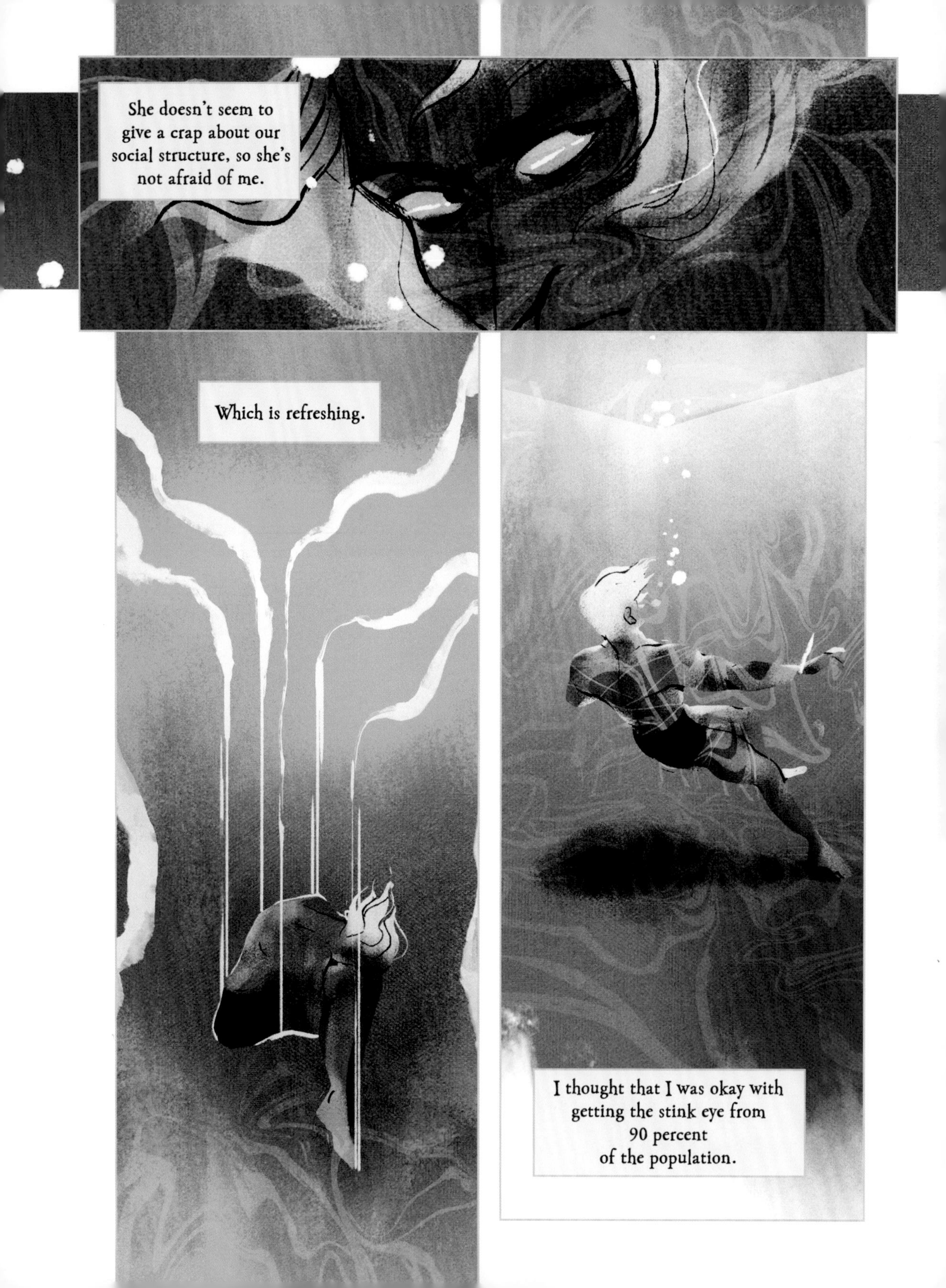

She doesn't seem to give a crap about our social structure, so she's not afraid of me.
Which is refreshing.
I thought that I was okay with getting the stink eye from 90 percent of the population.

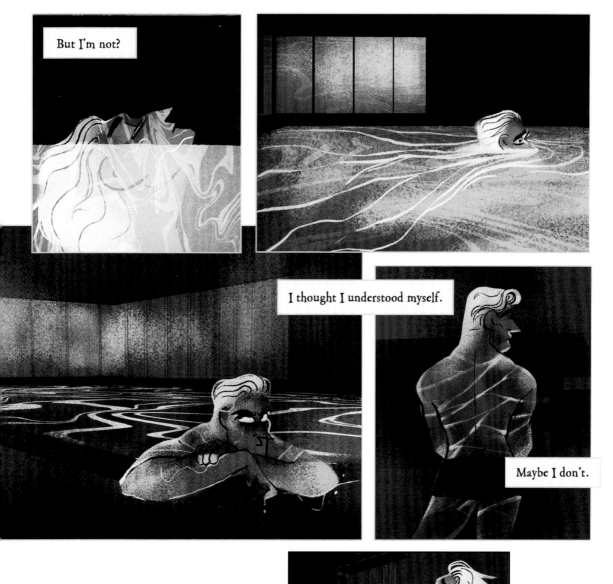

But I'm not?

I thought I understood myself.

Maybe I don't.

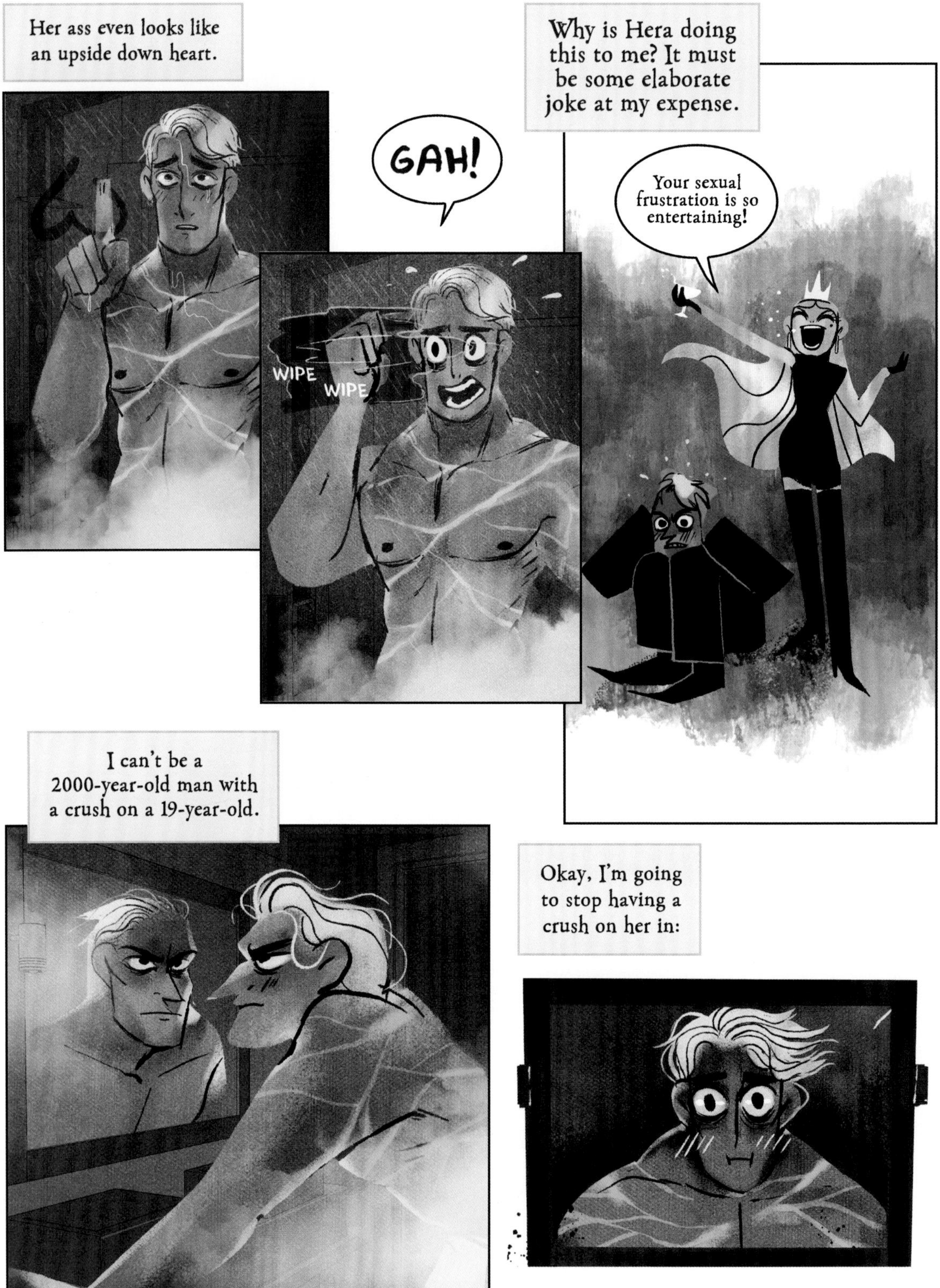
Her ass even looks like an upside down heart.
GAH!
WIPE
WIPE
Why is Hera doing this to me? It must be some elaborate joke at my expense.
Your sexual frustration is so entertaining!
I can't be a 2000-year-old man with a crush on a 19-year-old.
Okay, I'm going to stop having a crush on her in:

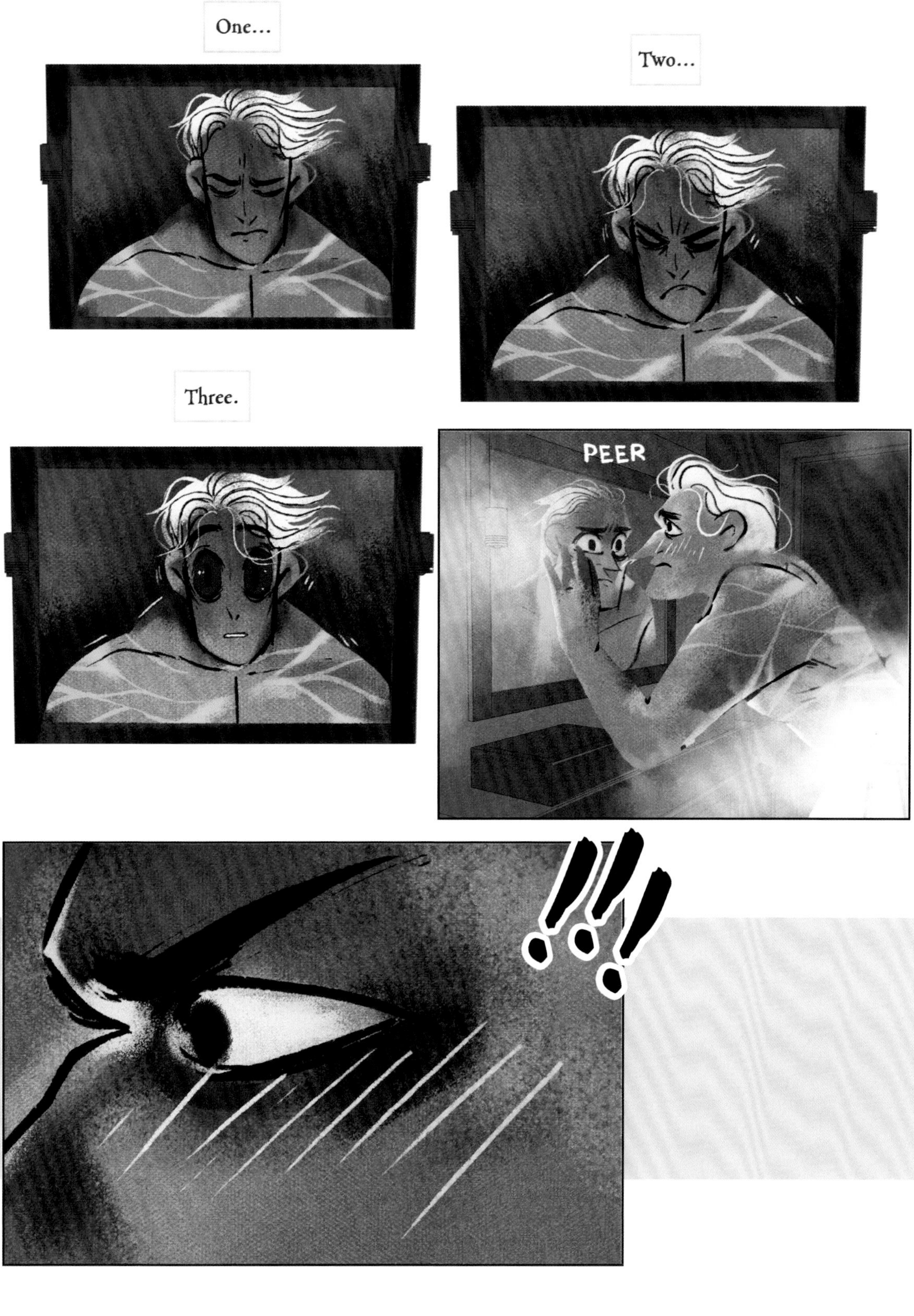
One...
Two...
Three.
PEER
!!!

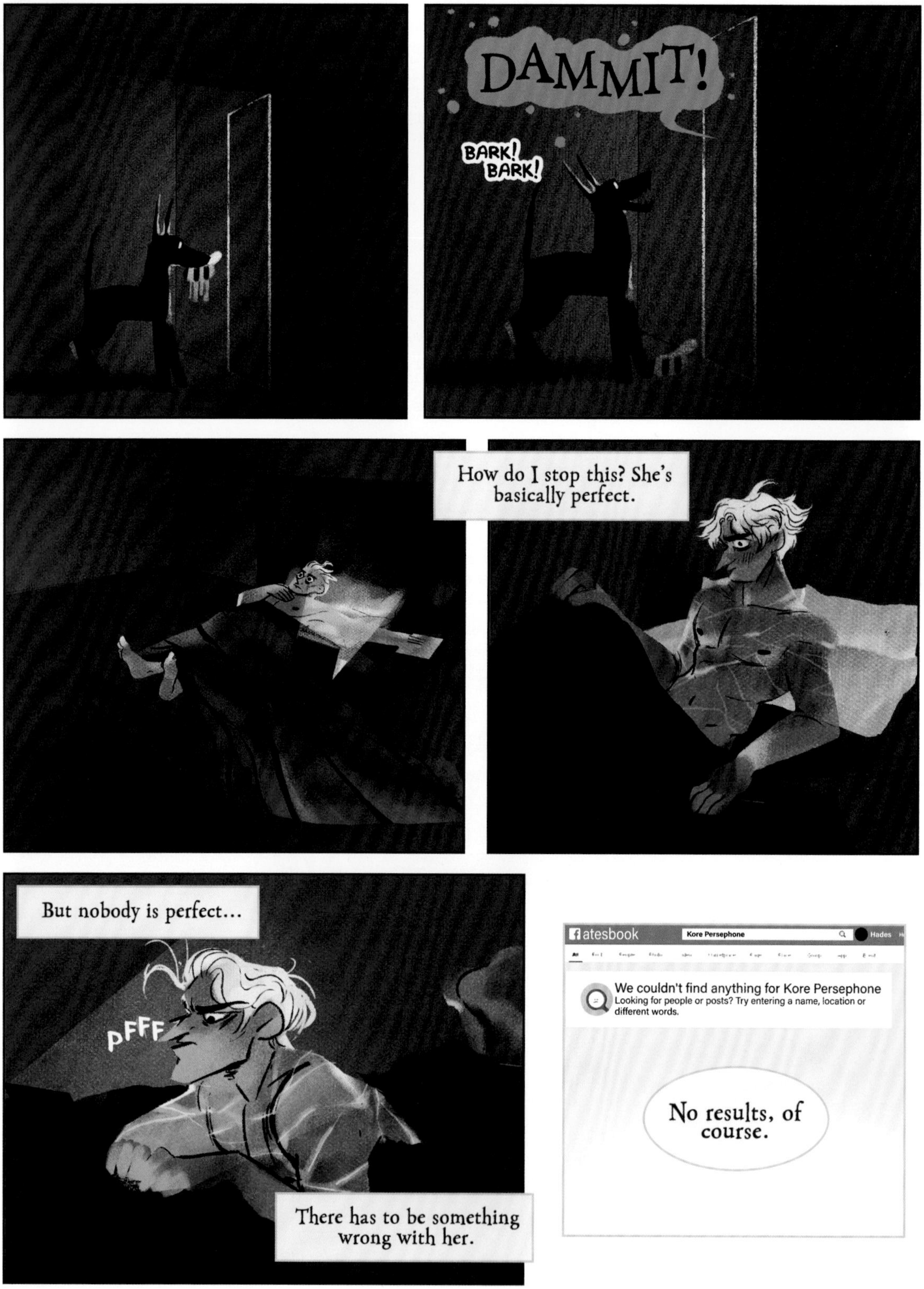
DAMMIT!
BARK! BARK!
How do I stop this? She's basically perfect.
But nobody is perfect...
PFFF
There has to be something wrong with her.
atesbook
Kore Persephone
Hades
We couldn't find anything for Kore Persephone
Looking for people or posts? Try entering a name, location or different words.
No results, of course.

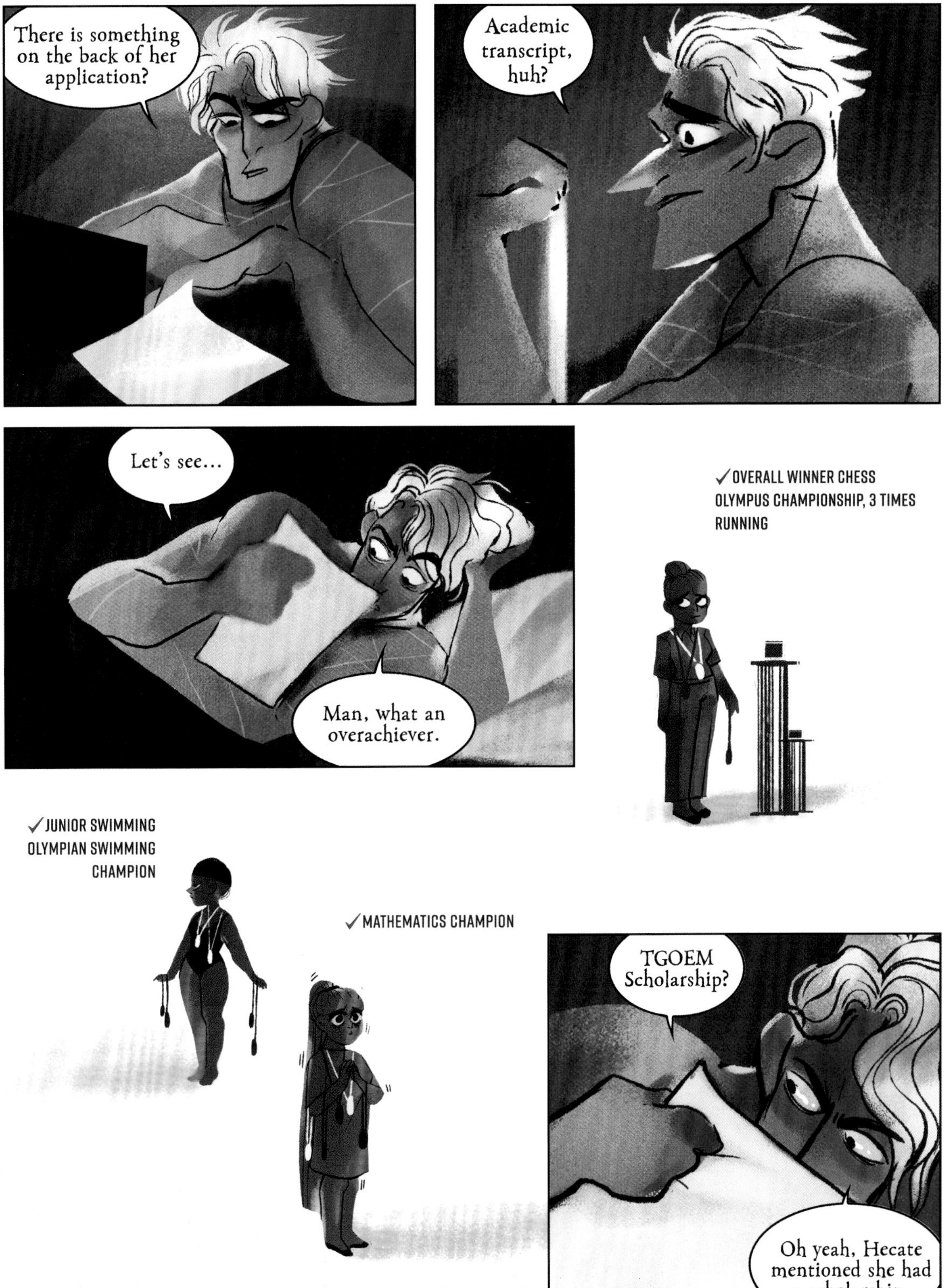
There is something on the back of her application?
Academic transcript, huh?
Let's see...
Man, what an overachiever.
✓OVERALL WINNER CHESS OLYMPUS CHAMPIONSHIP, 3 TIMES RUNNING
✓JUNIOR SWIMMING OLYMPIAN SWIMMING CHAMPION
✓MATHEMATICS CHAMPION
TGOEM Scholarship?
Oh yeah, Hecate mentioned she had a scholarship.

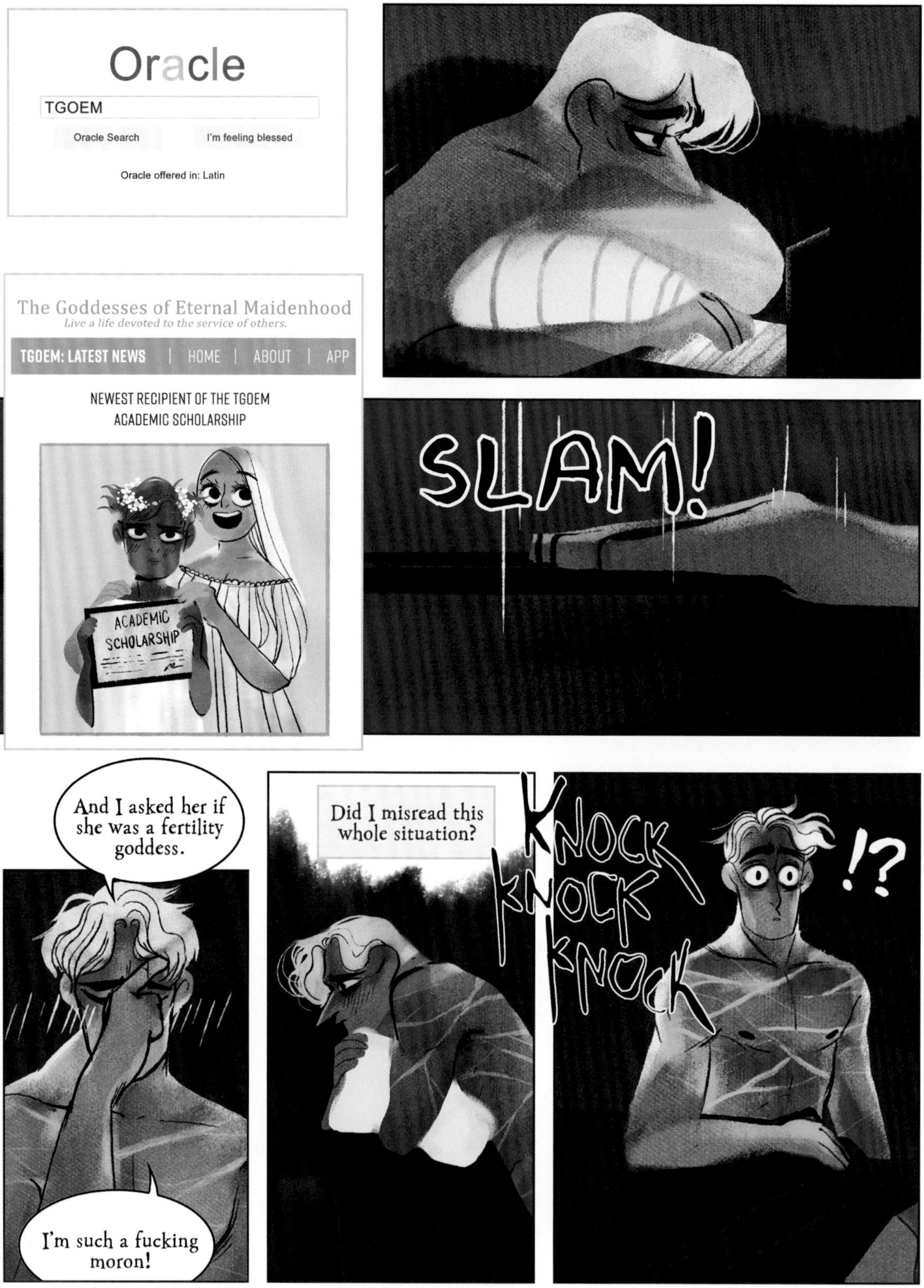
Oracle
TGOEM
Oracle Search
I'm feeling blessed
Oracle offered in: Latin
The Goddesses of Eternal Maidenhood
Live a life devoted to the service of others.
TGOEM: LATEST NEWS | HOME | ABOUT | APP
NEWEST RECIPIENT OF THE TGOEM ACADEMIC SCHOLARSHIP
ACADEMIC SCHOLARSHIP
SLAM!
And I asked her if she was a fertility goddess.
I'm such a fucking moron!
Did I misread this whole situation?
KNOCK KNOCK KNOCK
!?

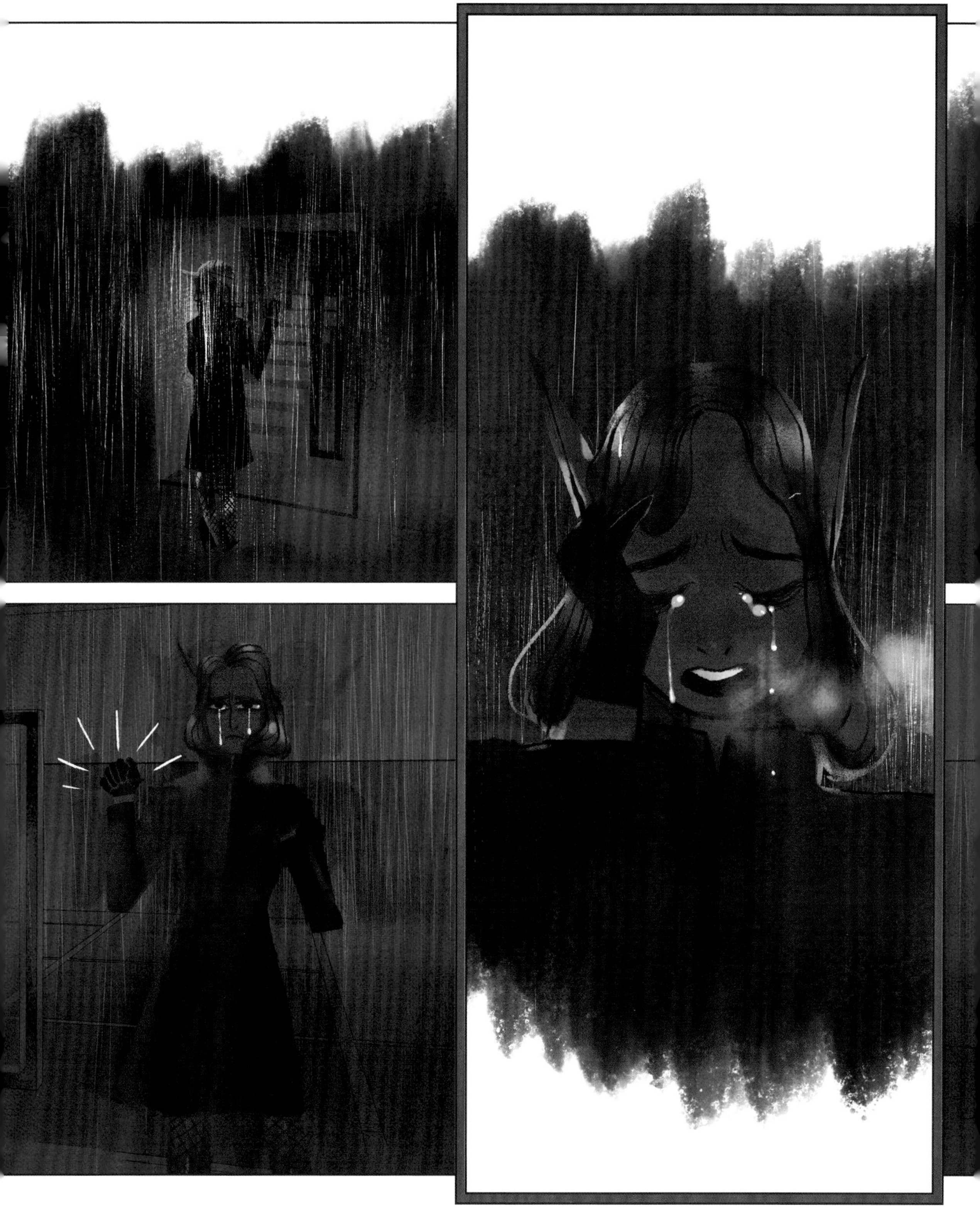

4 DAYS AGO!
(THE DAY OF THE PARTY)

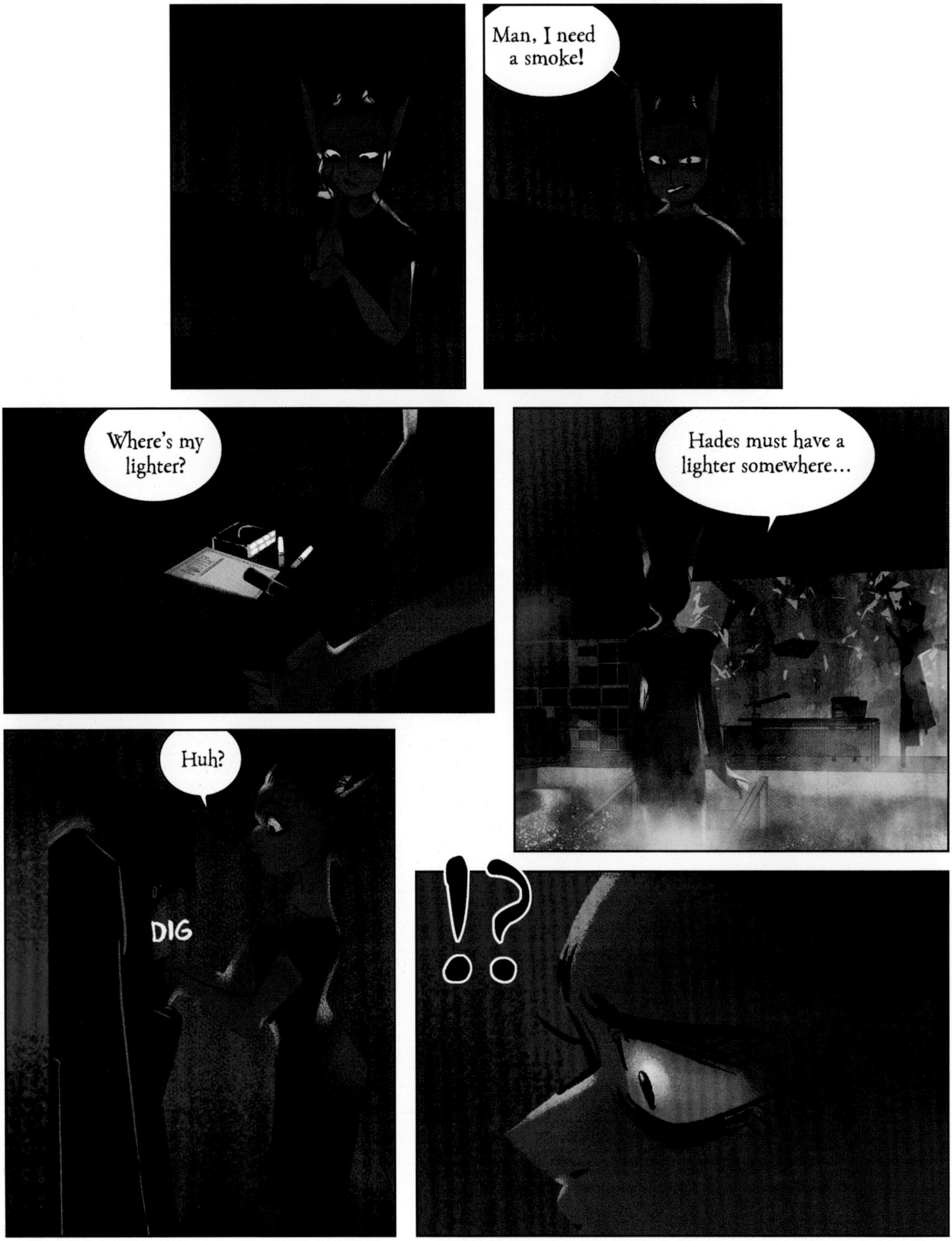

Man, I need a smoke!
Where's my lighter?
Hades must have a lighter somewhere...
Huh?
DIG
!?

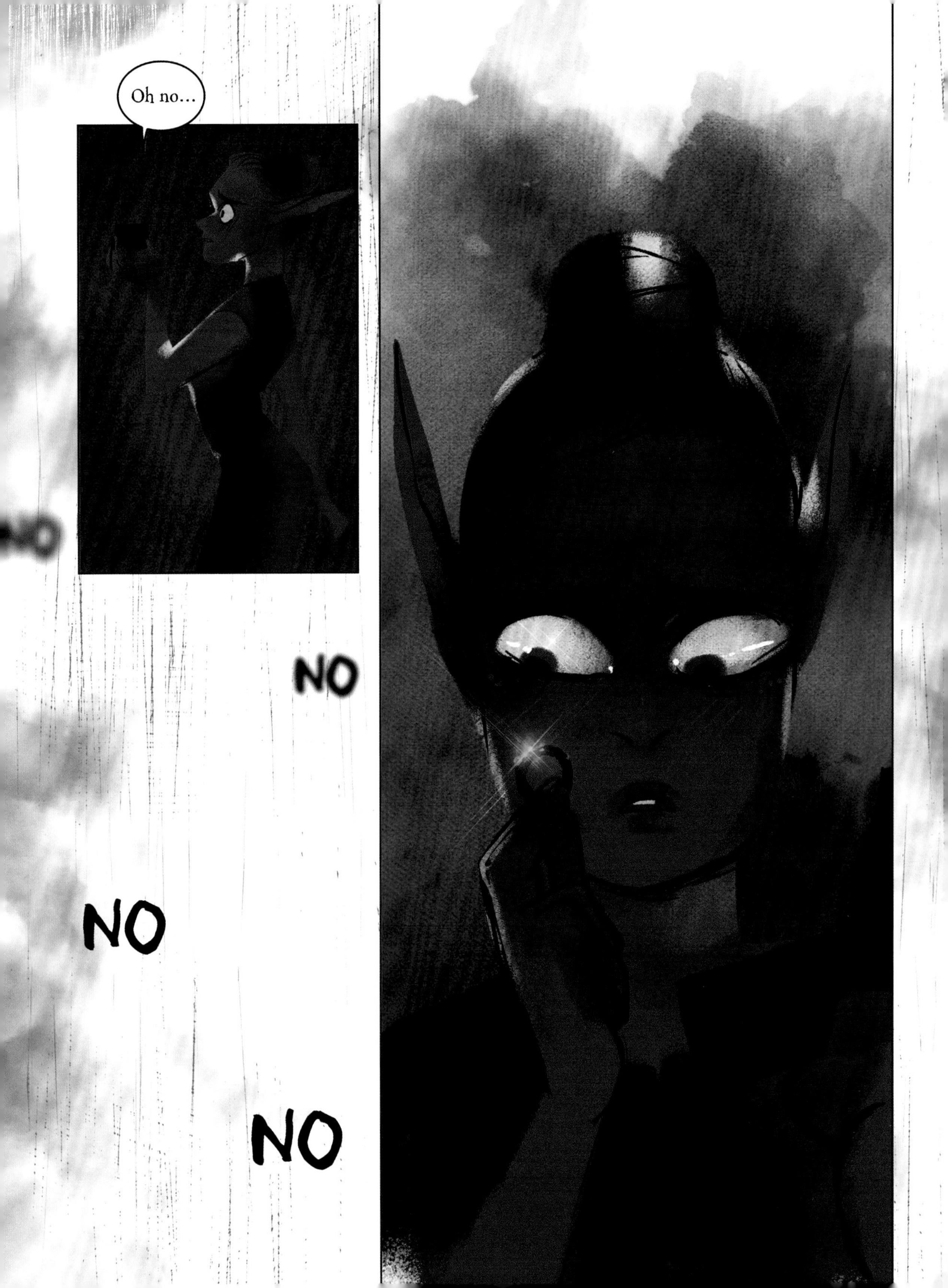
Oh no…
NO
NO
NO

EPISODE 46: RED RAW

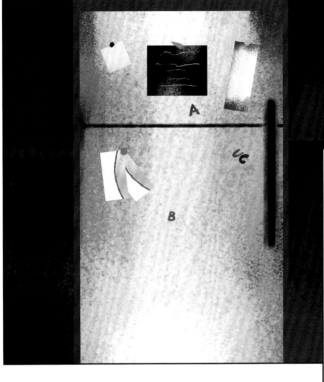

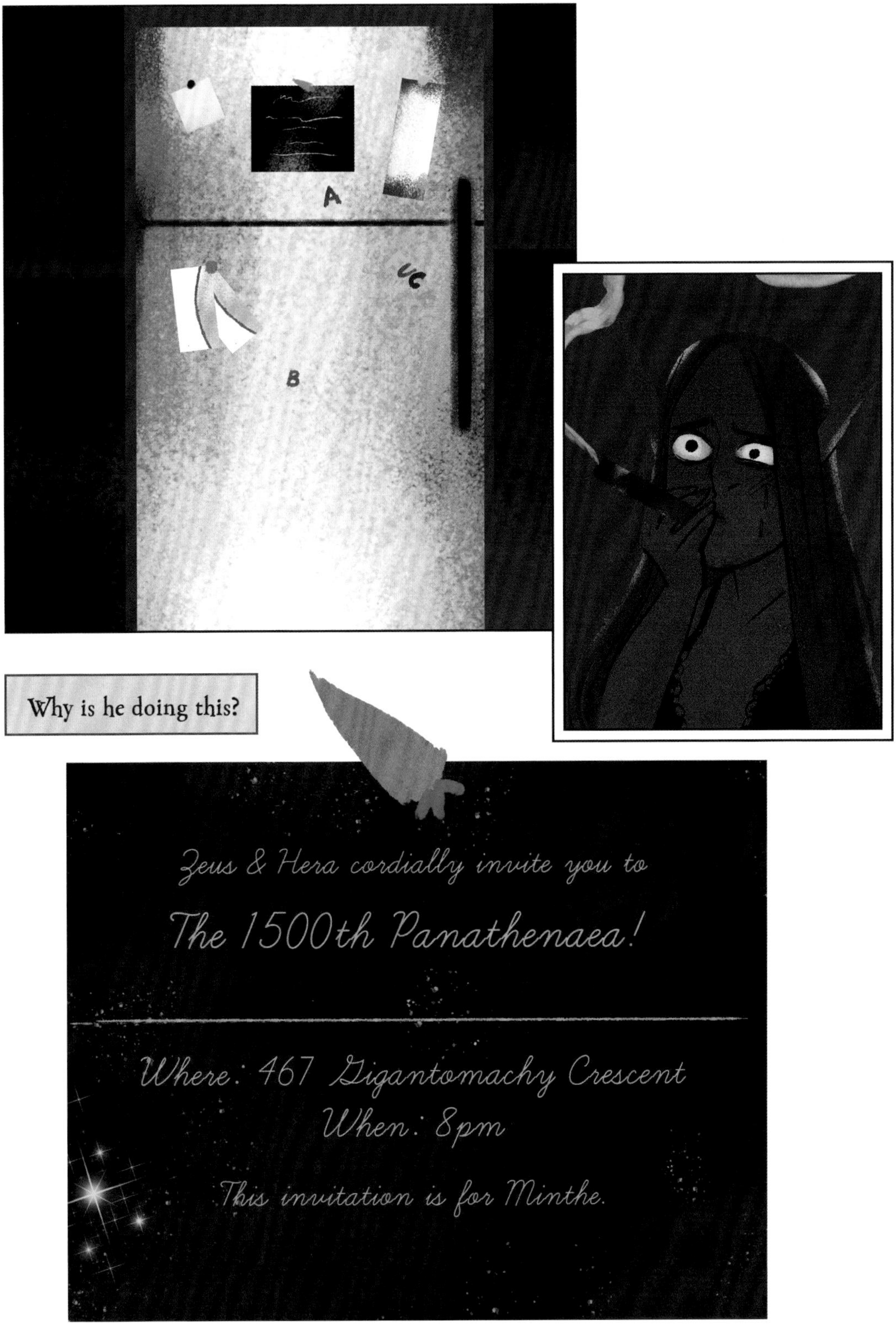

Why is he doing this?

Zeus & Hera cordially invite you to

The 1500th Panathenaea!

Where: 467 Gigantomachy Crescent
When: 8pm

This invitation is for Minthe.

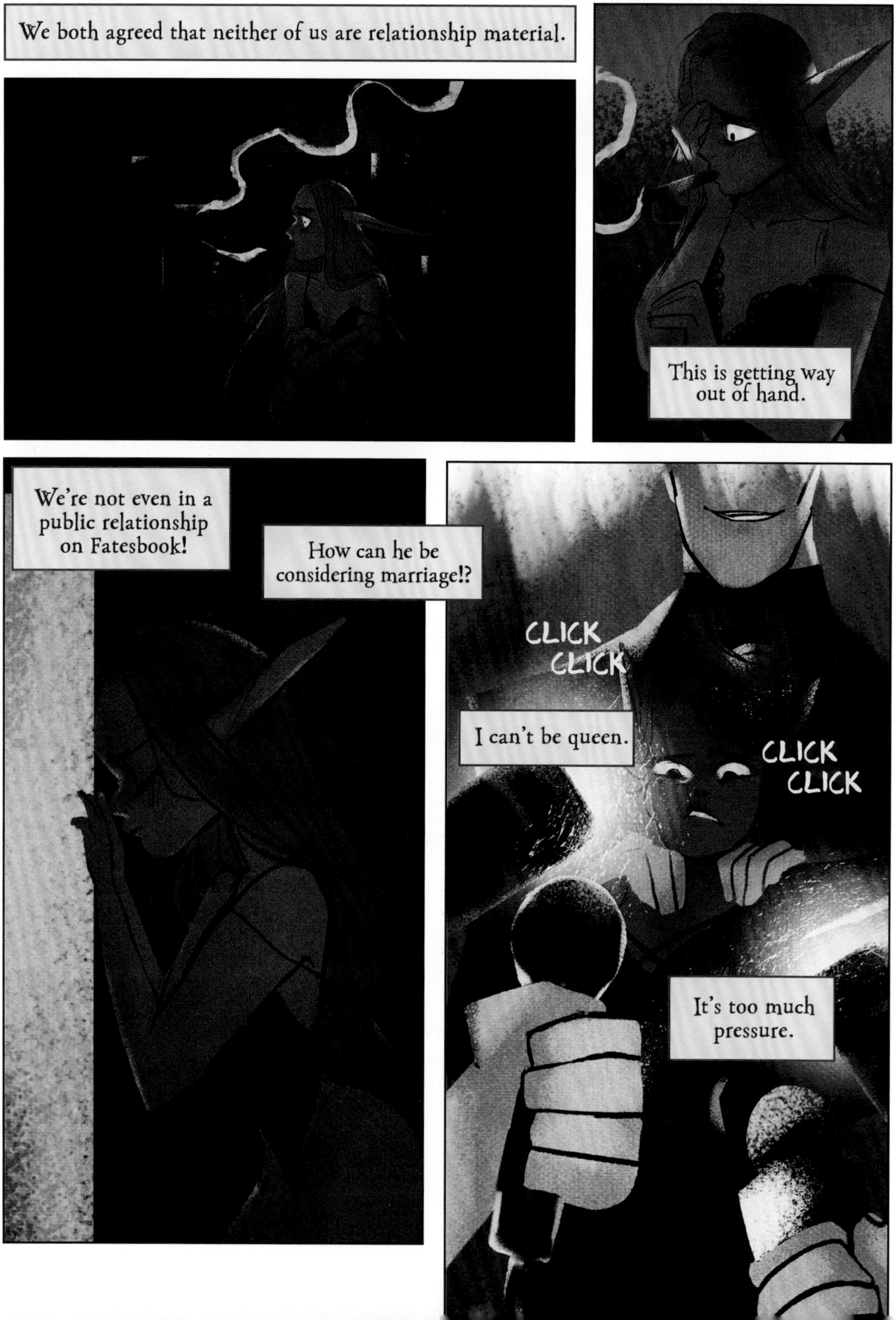
We both agreed that neither of us are relationship material.
This is getting way out of hand.
We're not even in a public relationship on Fatesbook!
How can he be considering marriage!?
CLICK CLICK
I can't be queen.
CLICK CLICK
It's too much pressure.

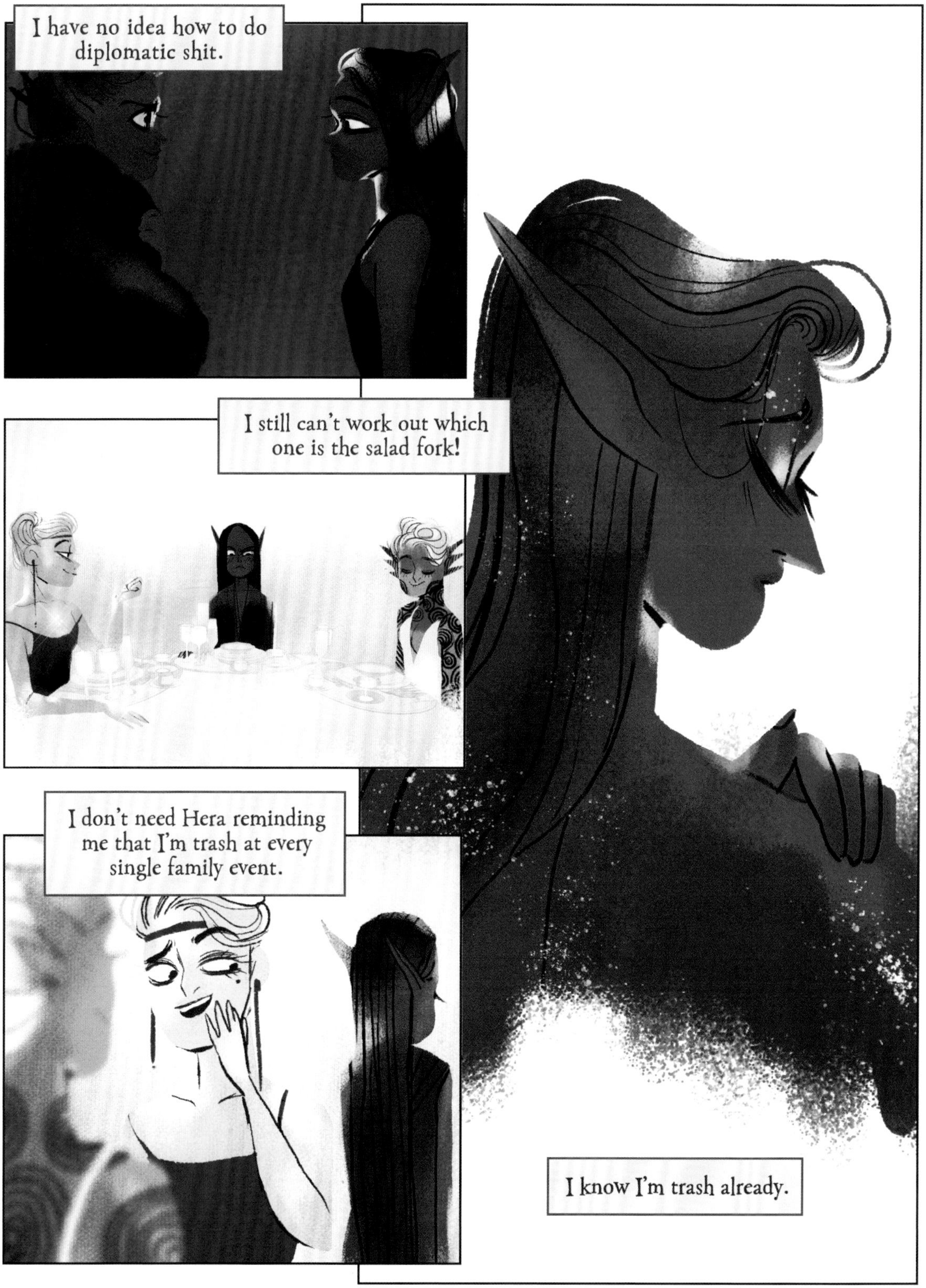
I have no idea how to do diplomatic shit.
I still can't work out which one is the salad fork!
I don't need Hera reminding me that I'm trash at every single family event.
I know I'm trash already.

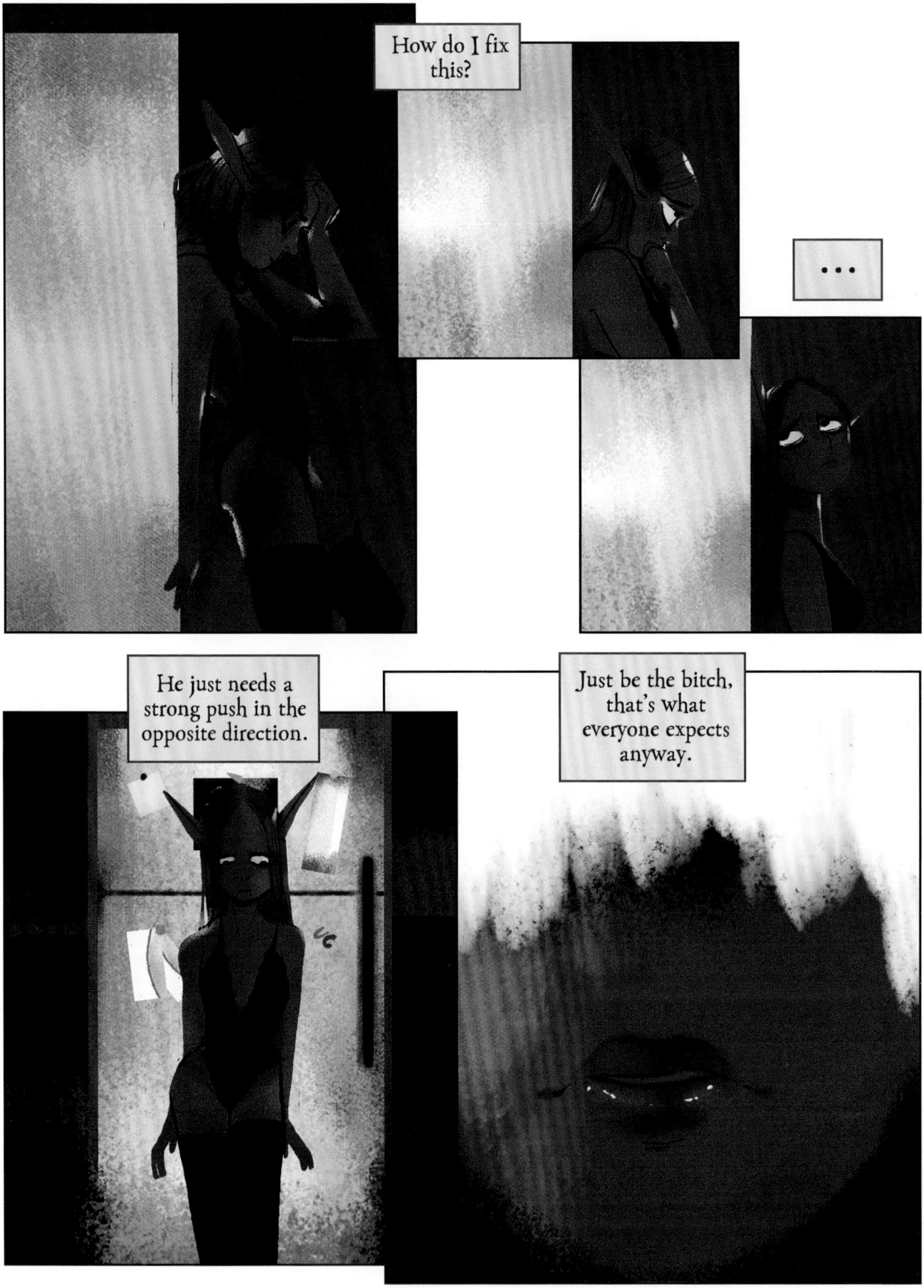
How do I fix this?
...
He just needs a strong push in the opposite direction.
Just be the bitch, that's what everyone expects anyway.

PRESENT DAY

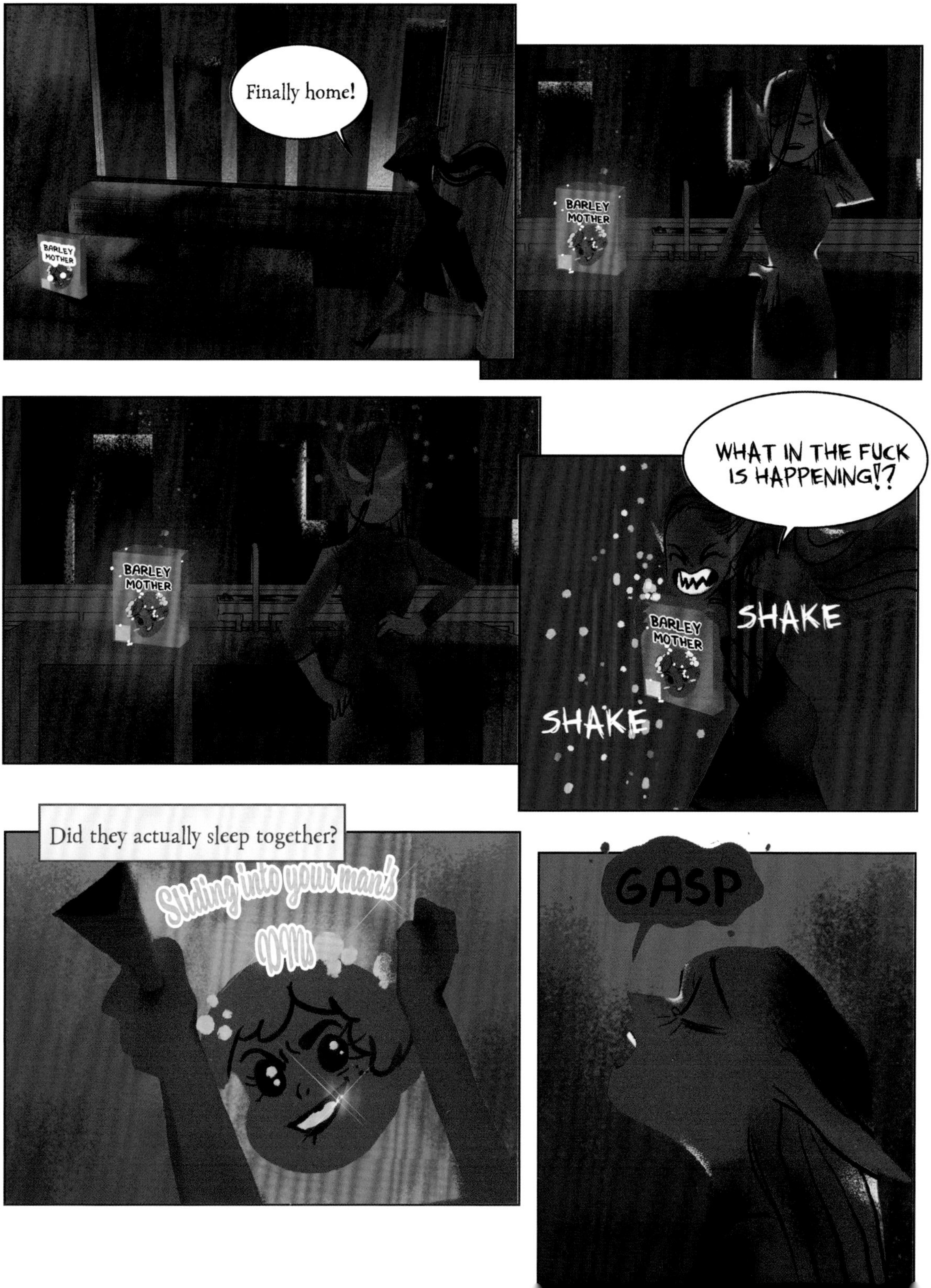
Finally home!
BARLEY MOTHER
BARLEY MOTHER
BARLEY MOTHER
WHAT IN THE FUCK IS HAPPENING!?
BARLEY MOTHER
SHAKE
SHAKE
Did they actually sleep together?
Sliding into your man's DMs
GASP

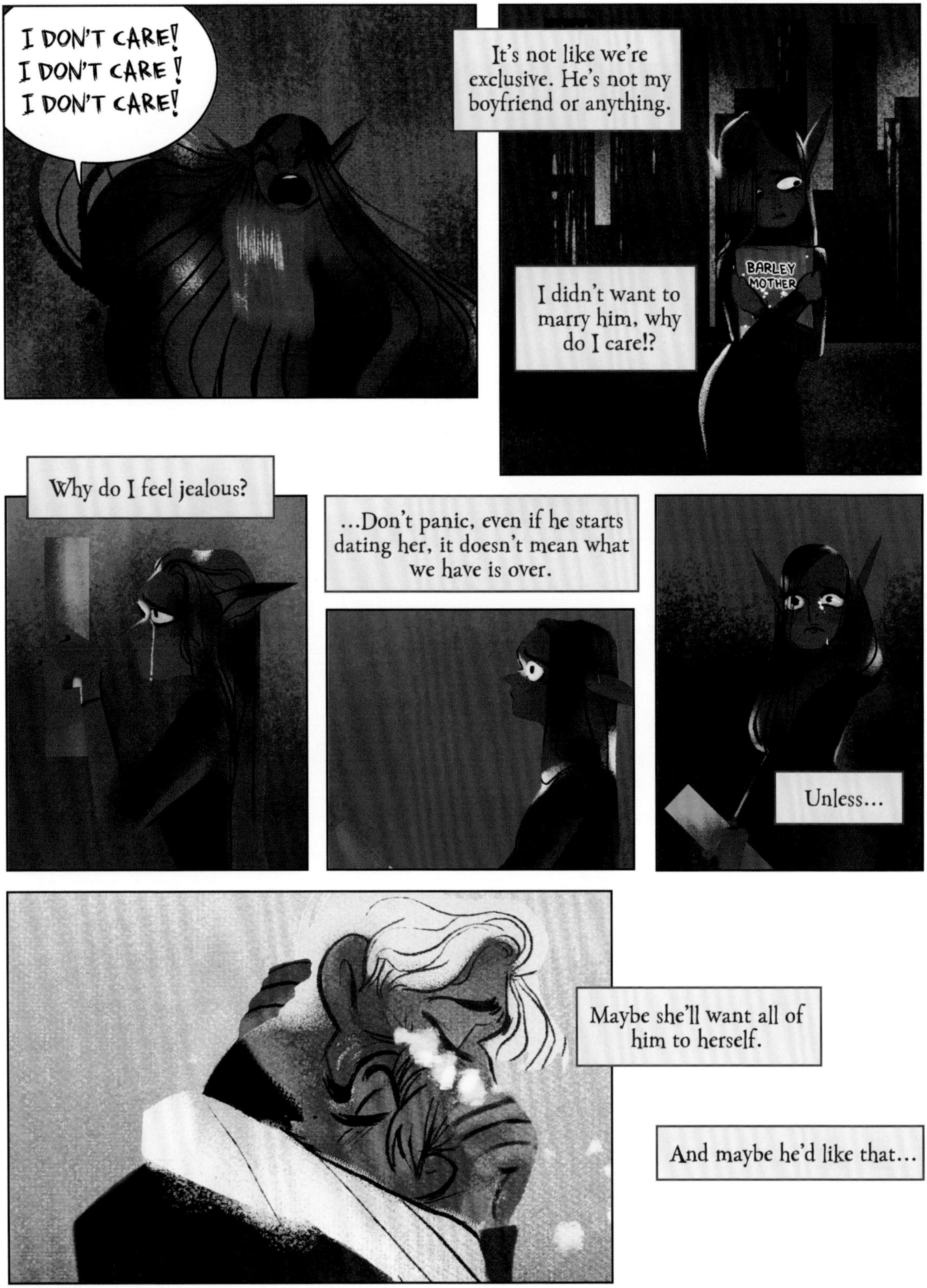
I DON'T CARE! I DON'T CARE! I DON'T CARE!
It's not like we're exclusive. He's not my boyfriend or anything.
BARLEY MOTHER
I didn't want to marry him, why do I care!?
Why do I feel jealous?
...Don't panic, even if he starts dating her, it doesn't mean what we have is over.
Unless...
Maybe she'll want all of him to herself.
And maybe he'd like that...

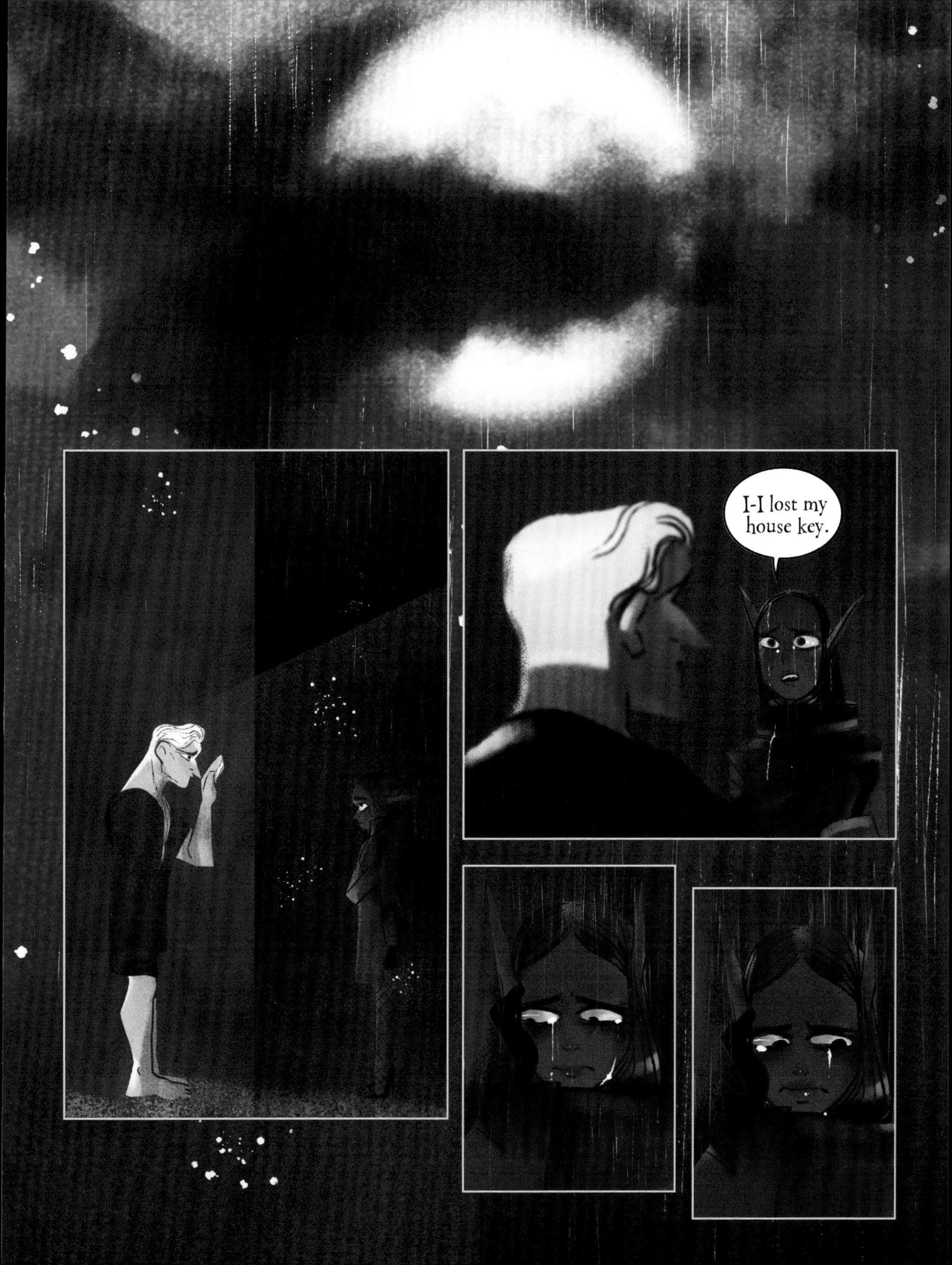
I-I lost my house key.

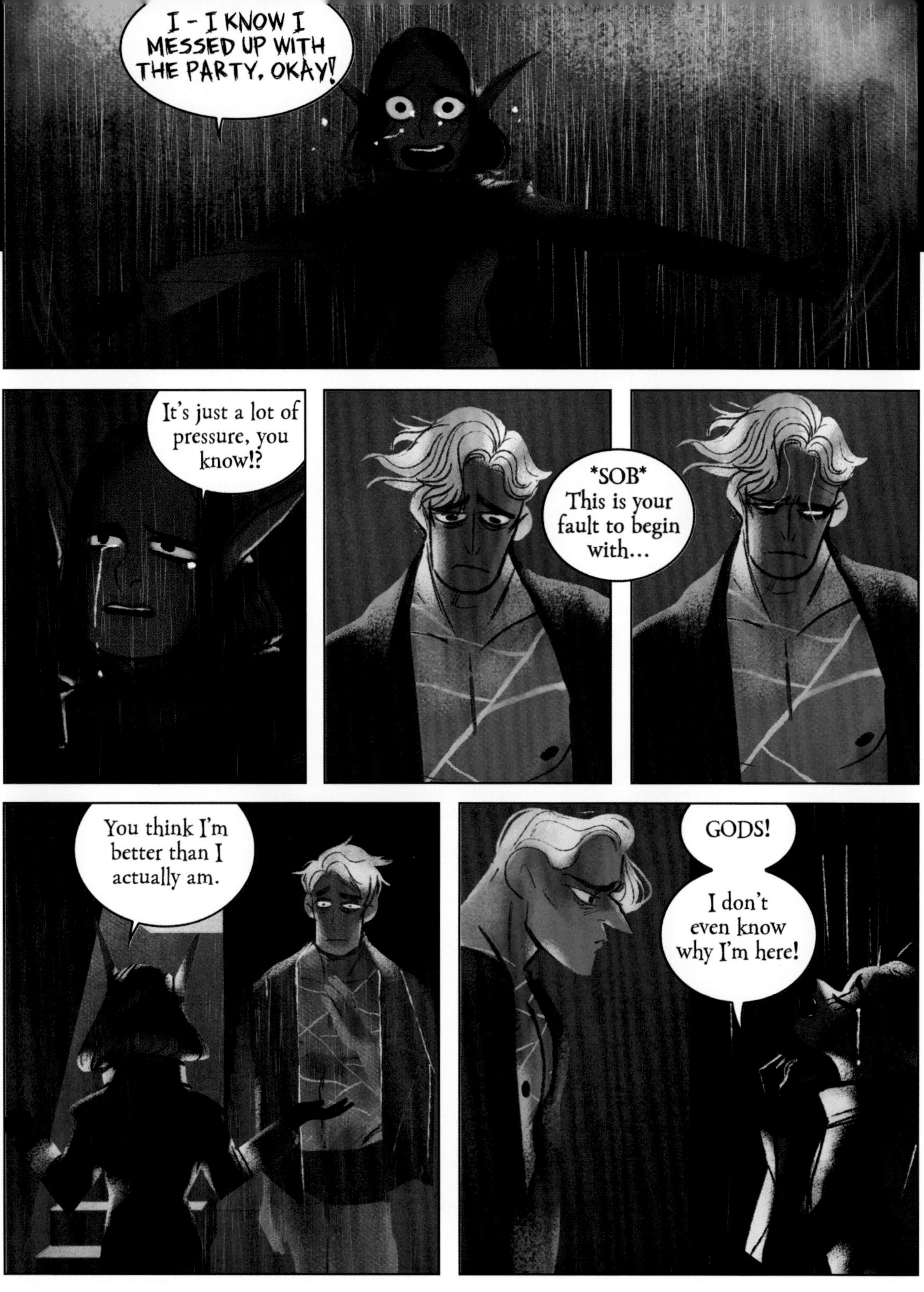
I - I KNOW I MESSED UP WITH THE PARTY, OKAY!
It's just a lot of pressure, you know!?
SOB This is your fault to begin with...
You think I'm better than I actually am.
GODS!
I don't even know why I'm here!

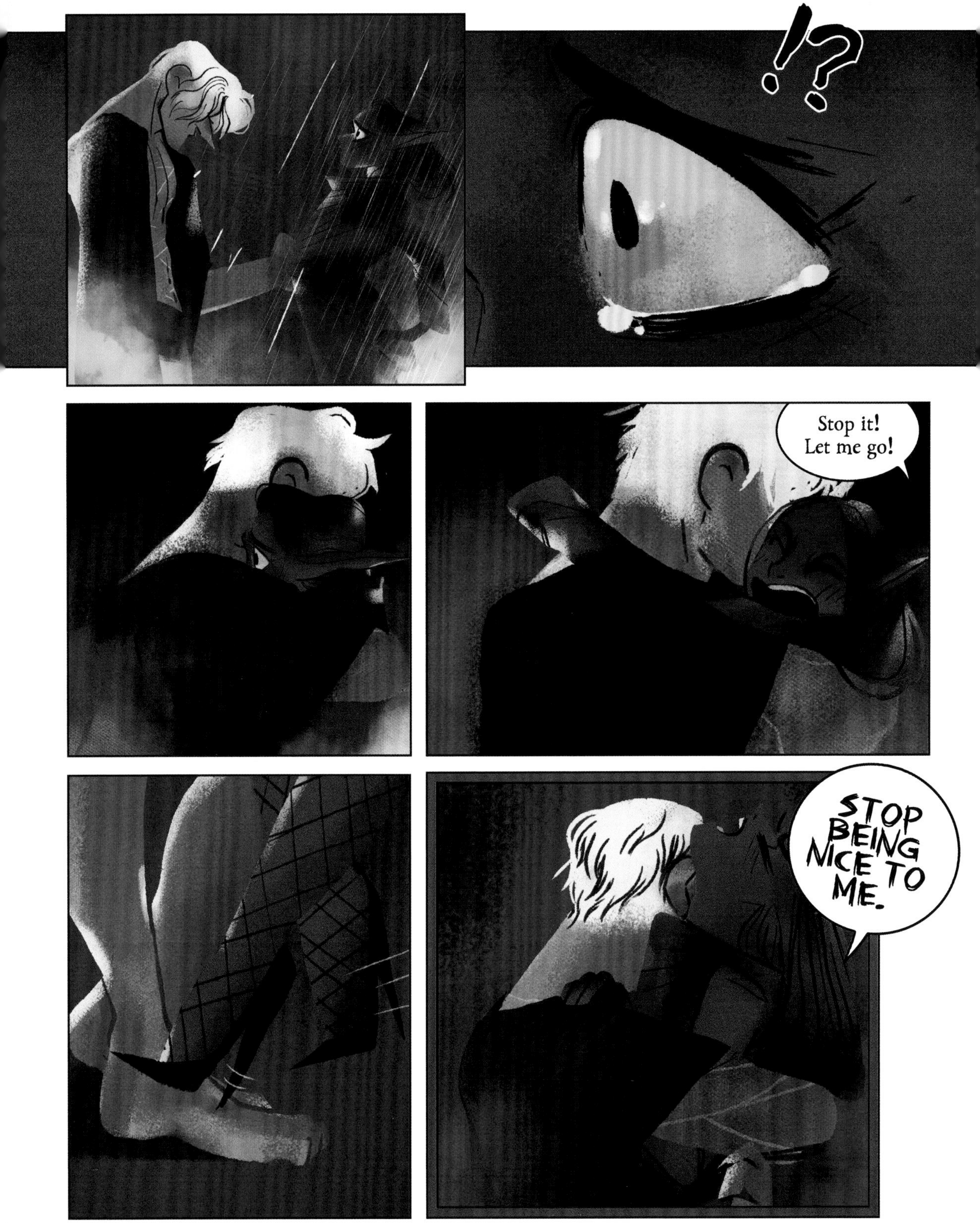
!?
Stop it! Let me go!
STOP BEING NICE TO ME.

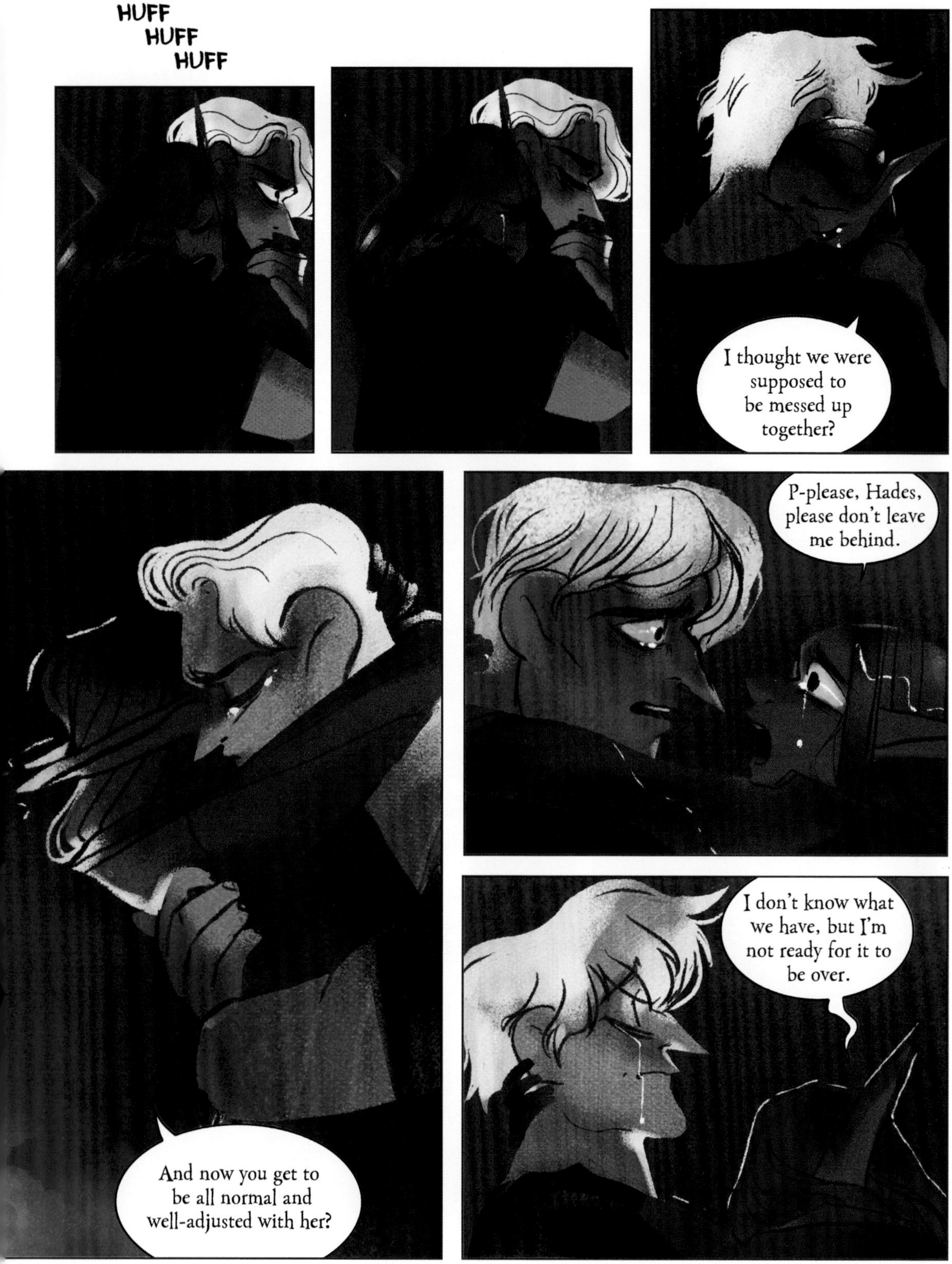
HUFF HUFF HUFF
I thought we were supposed to be messed up together?
And now you get to be all normal and well-adjusted with her?
P-please, Hades, please don't leave me behind.
I don't know what we have, but I'm not ready for it to be over.

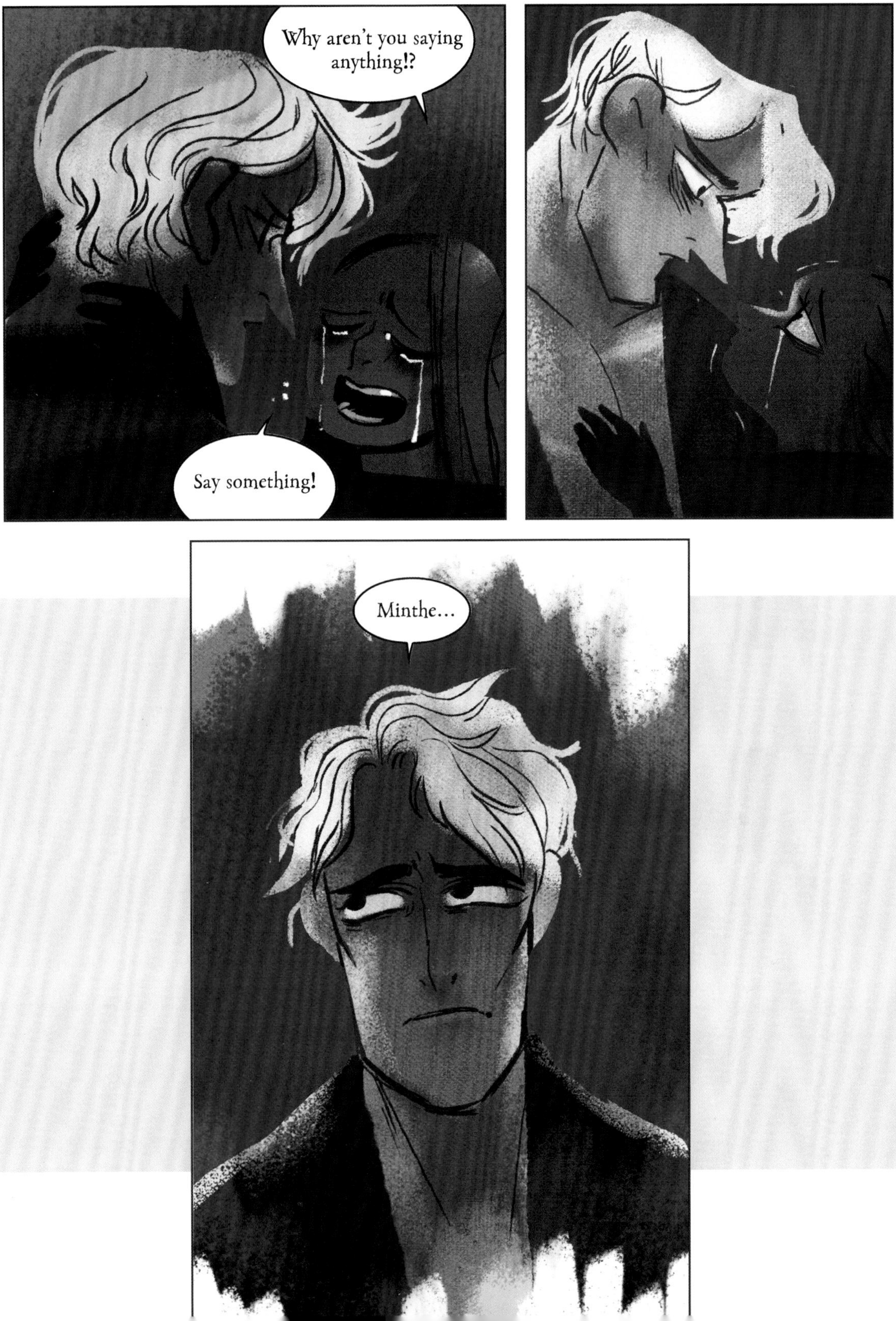

Why aren't you saying anything!?
Say something!
Minthe...

EPISODE 47: NEEDED

Dear Persephone,

My therapist assigned me the exercise of writing letters of what I would hypothetically tell others about what I'm feeling.

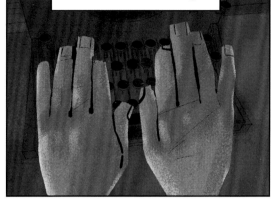

Apparently doing this will help me "UNPACK MY EMOTIONS AND GAIN A GREATER UNDERSTANDING OF MYSELF."

Gods, why do I pay that hack?

Luckily I never have to show anybody these letters so I guess it doesn't hurt to try.

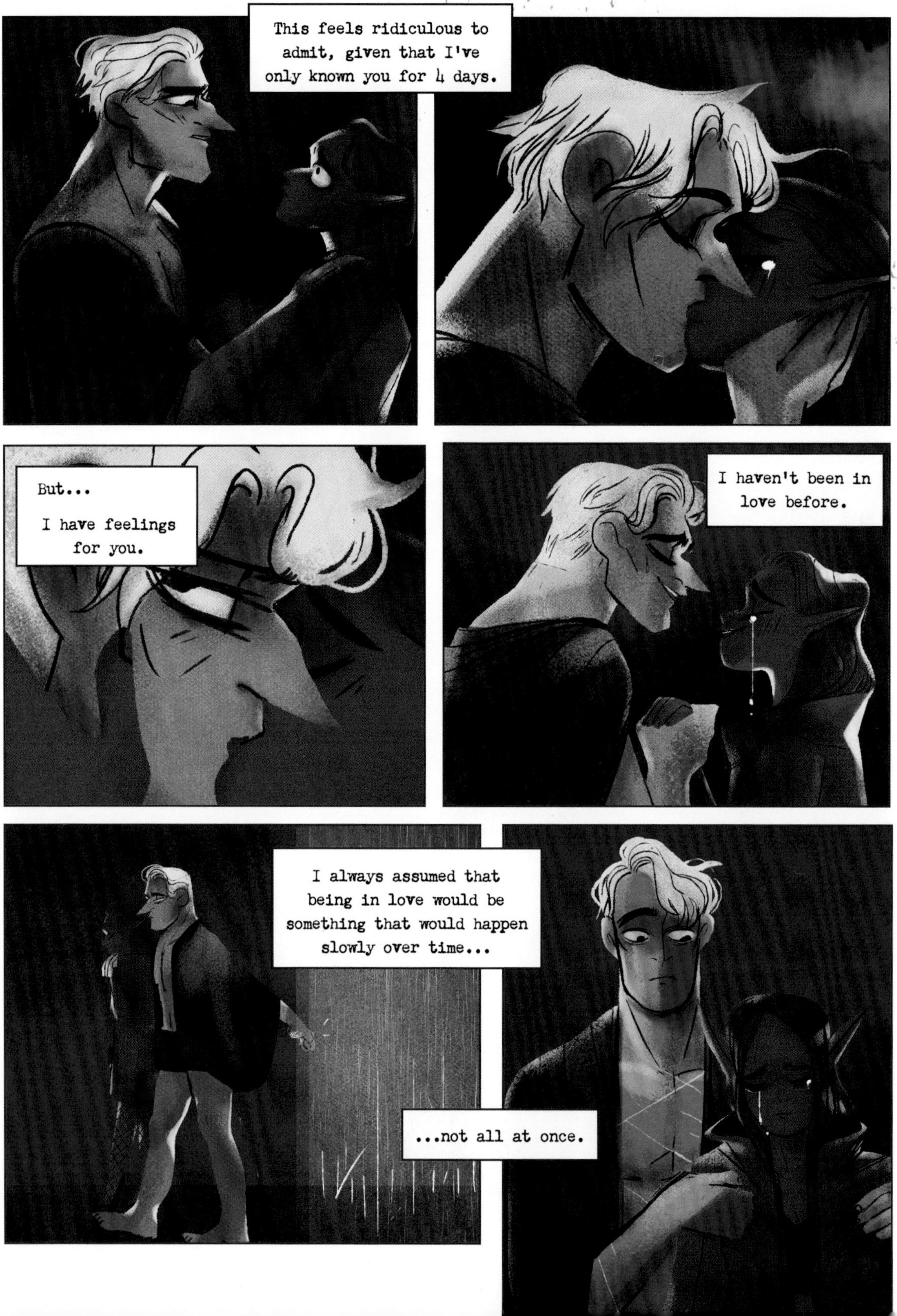
This feels ridiculous to admit, given that I've only known you for 4 days.
But...
I have feelings for you.
I haven't been in love before.
I always assumed that being in love would be something that would happen slowly over time...
...not all at once.

The thing is,
I don't really know you.

I don't know what your
favorite food is or the top
ten things you hate.

I don't know if you're a
morning person or if you like
sleeping in for hours...

Love isn't something I know
a lot about...

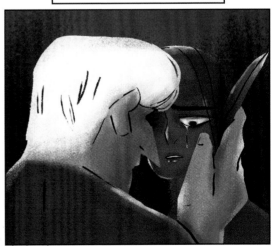

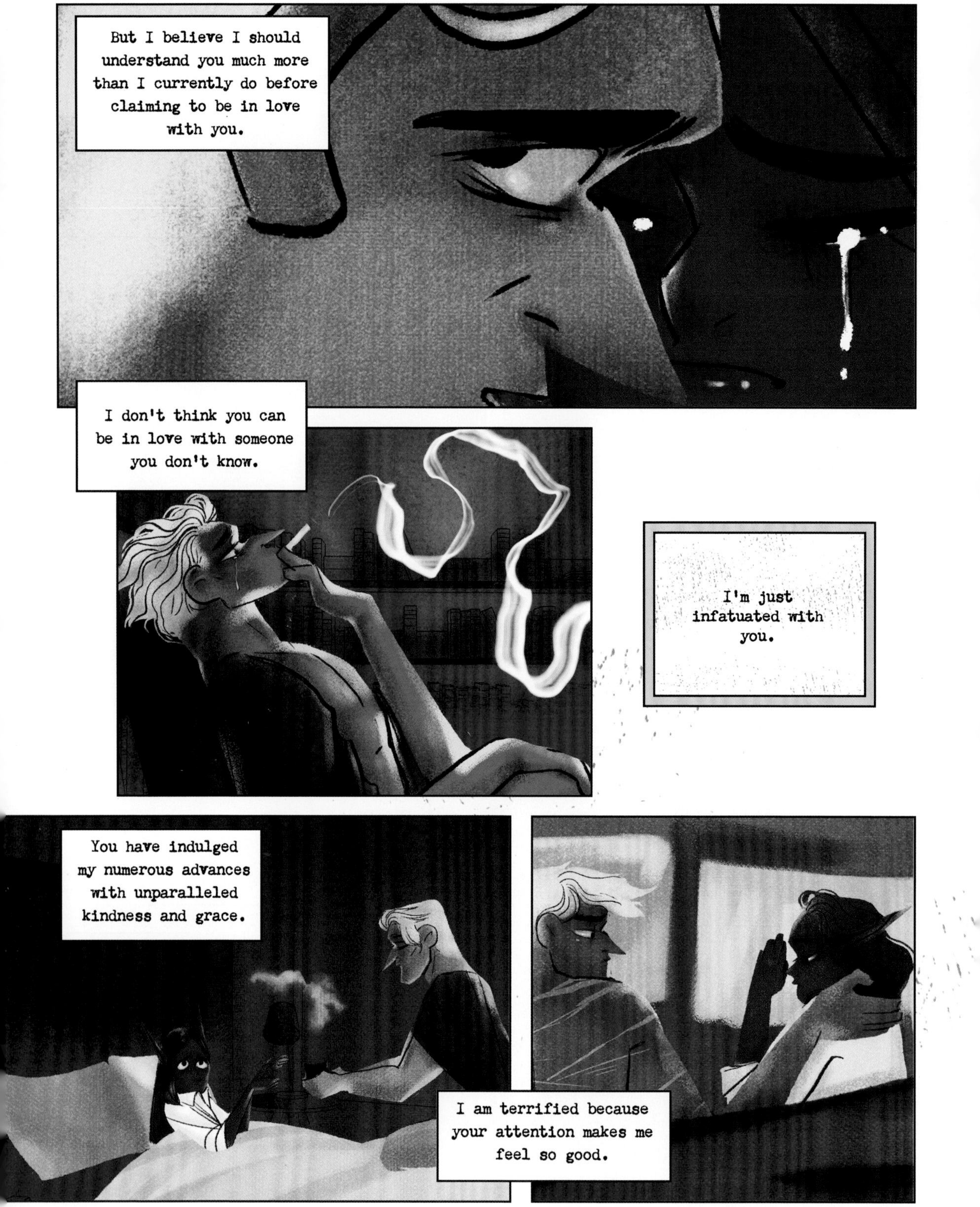

But I believe I should understand you much more than I currently do before claiming to be in love with you.
I don't think you can be in love with someone you don't know.
I'm just infatuated with you.
You have indulged my numerous advances with unparalleled kindness and grace.
I am terrified because your attention makes me feel so good.

The concept of not being able to feel that way again is devastating.

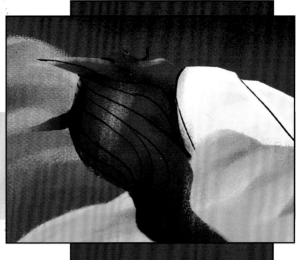

I have a lot of shame in regard to feeling like this about you.

That's a lot to put on someone who is so young.

It goes without saying, I have a lot of baggage.

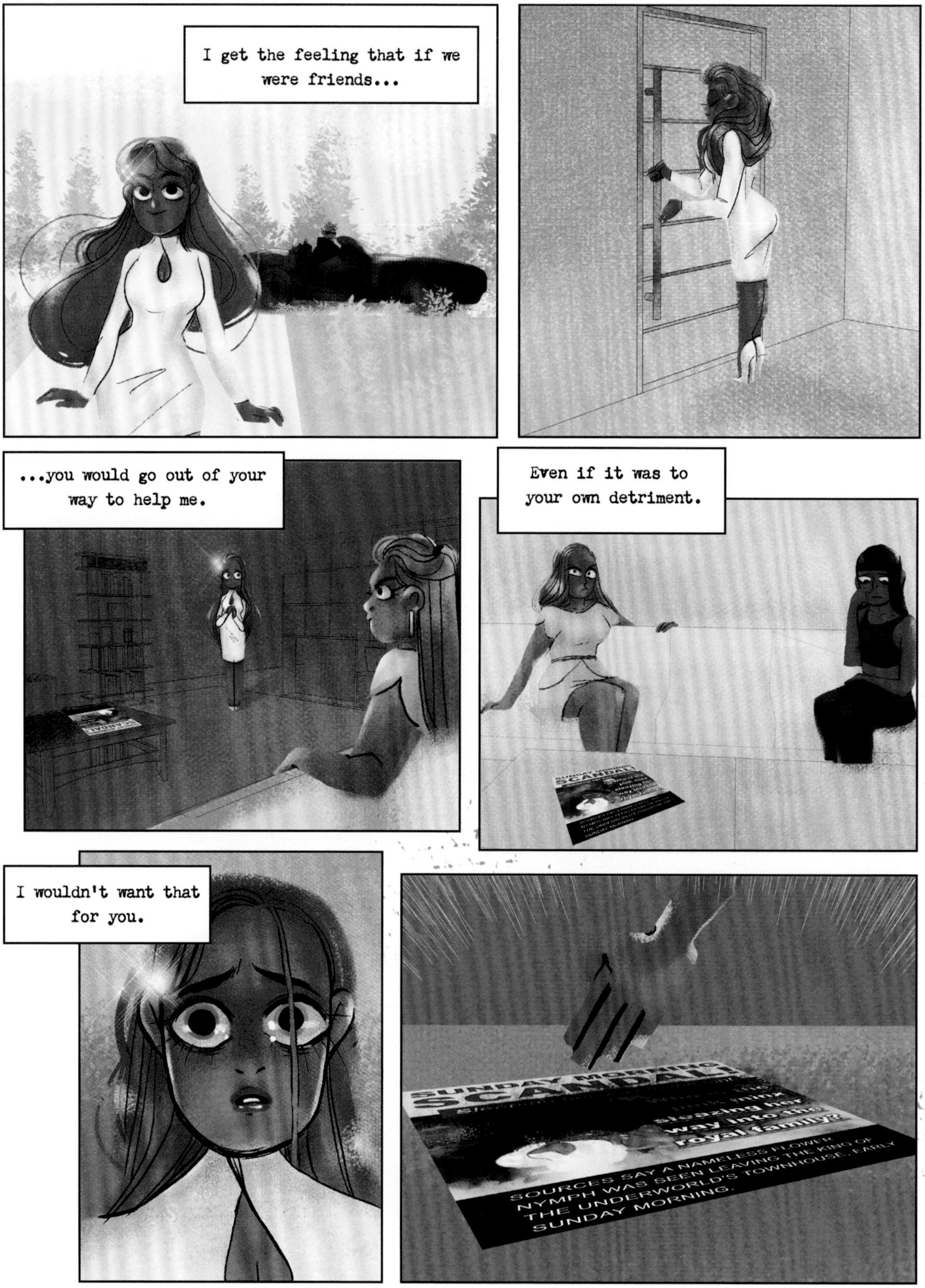
I get the feeling that if we were friends...
...you would go out of your way to help me.
Even if it was to your own detriment.
I wouldn't want that for you.
SUNDAY MORNING SCANDAL!
sleazing her way into the royal family?
SOURCES SAY A NAMELESS FLOWER NYMPH WAS SEEN LEAVING THE KING OF THE UNDERWORLD'S TOWNHOUSE, EARLY SUNDAY MORNING.

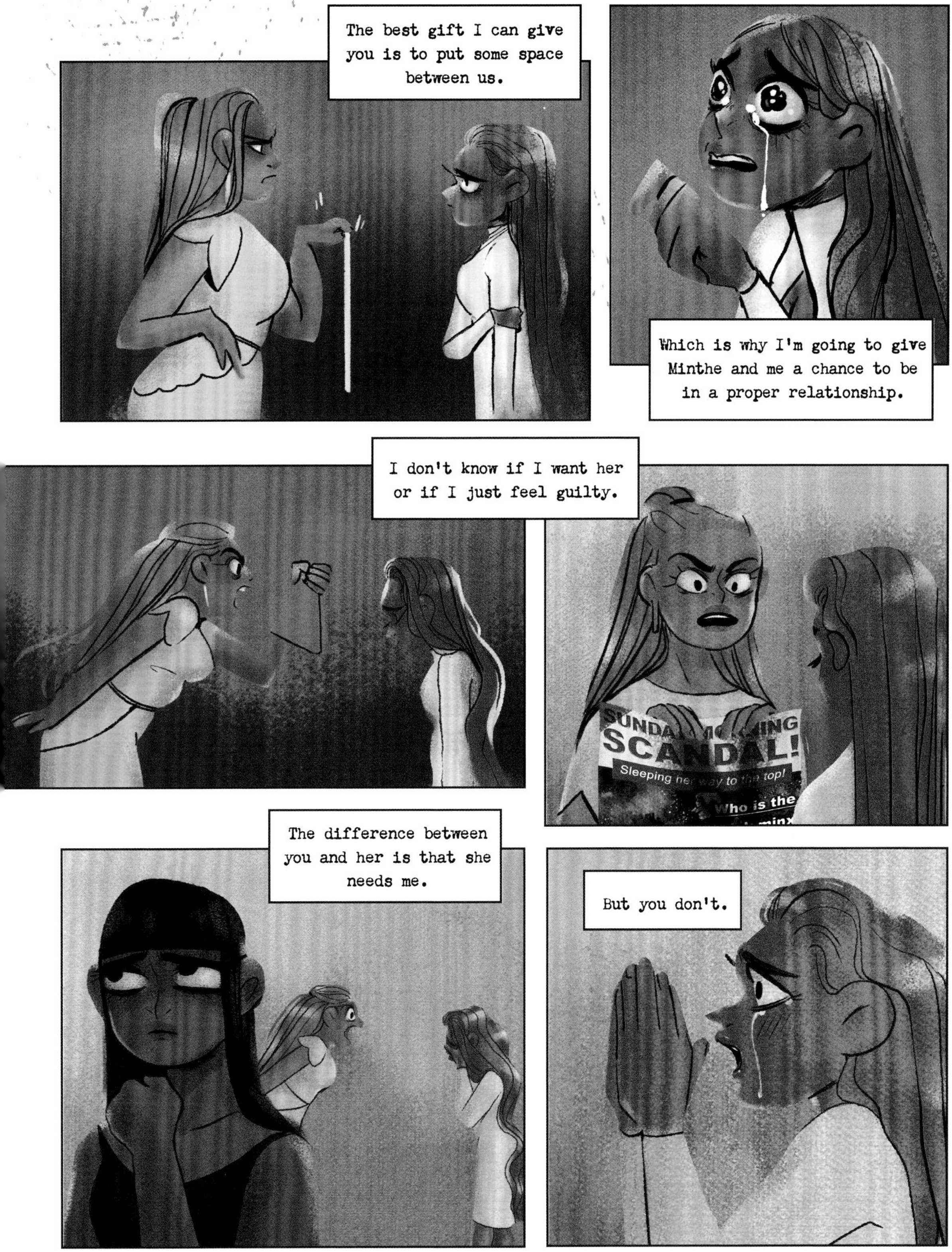
The best gift I can give you is to put some space between us.
Which is why I'm going to give Minthe and me a chance to be in a proper relationship.
I don't know if I want her or if I just feel guilty.
The difference between you and her is that she needs me.
But you don't.

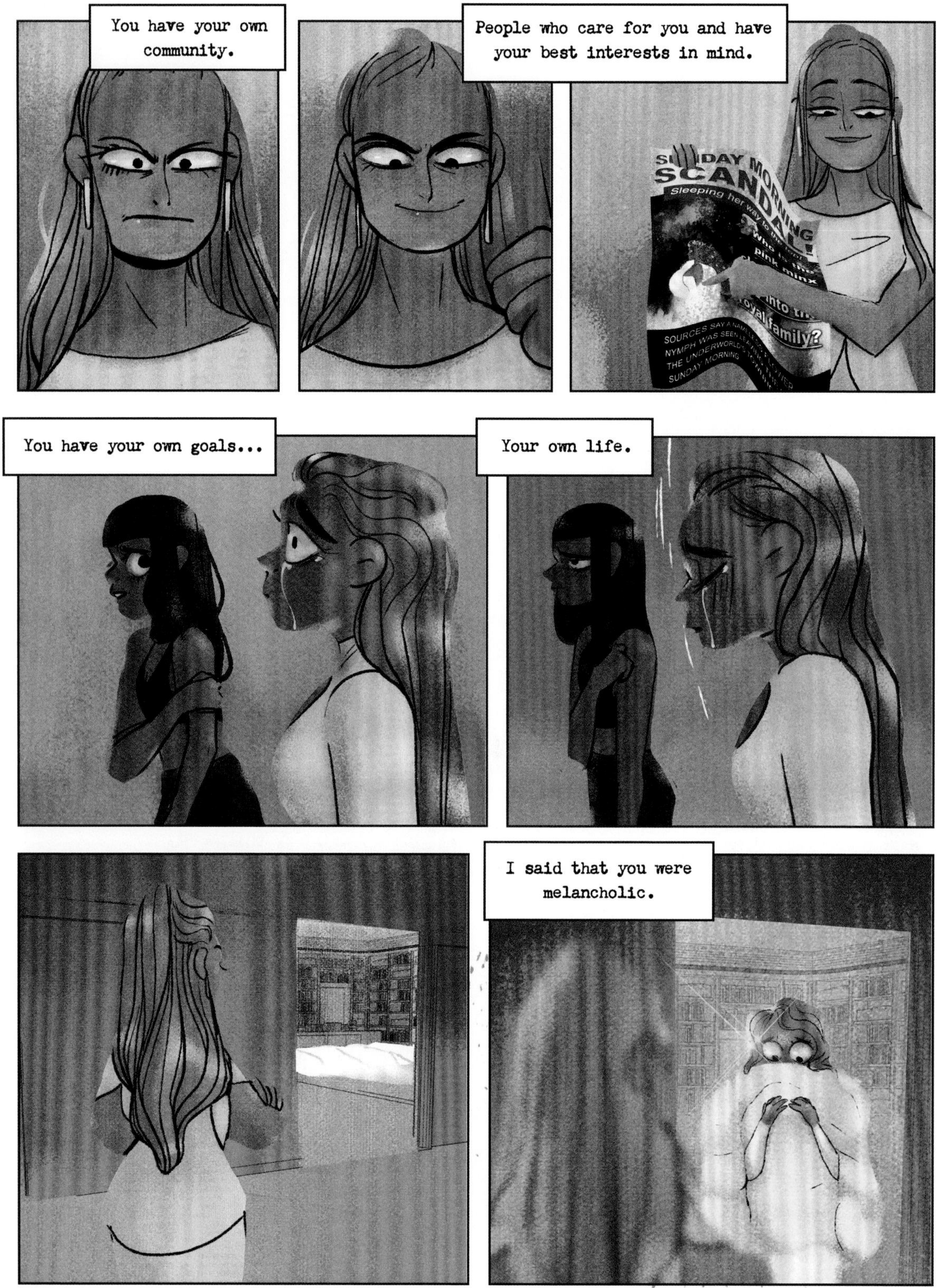
You have your own community.
People who care for you and have your best interests in mind.
SCANDAL
pink minx
royal family?
You have your own goals...
Your own life.
I said that you were melancholic.

This is still the case, but I can tell that you're tough as well.

If you're the daughter of Demeter, you'll be tough.

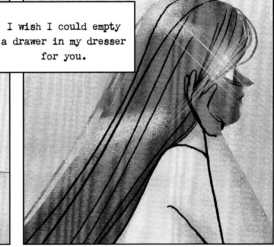

I wish I could empty a drawer in my dresser for you.

Or buy you a toothbrush to keep in my bathroom.

The truth is, every time we have something to do with each other...

it ends up hurting you.

Ultimately, you're better off if I limit my contact with you.

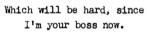

Which will be hard, since I'm your boss now.

But I'll try my best to keep you safe in my own way.

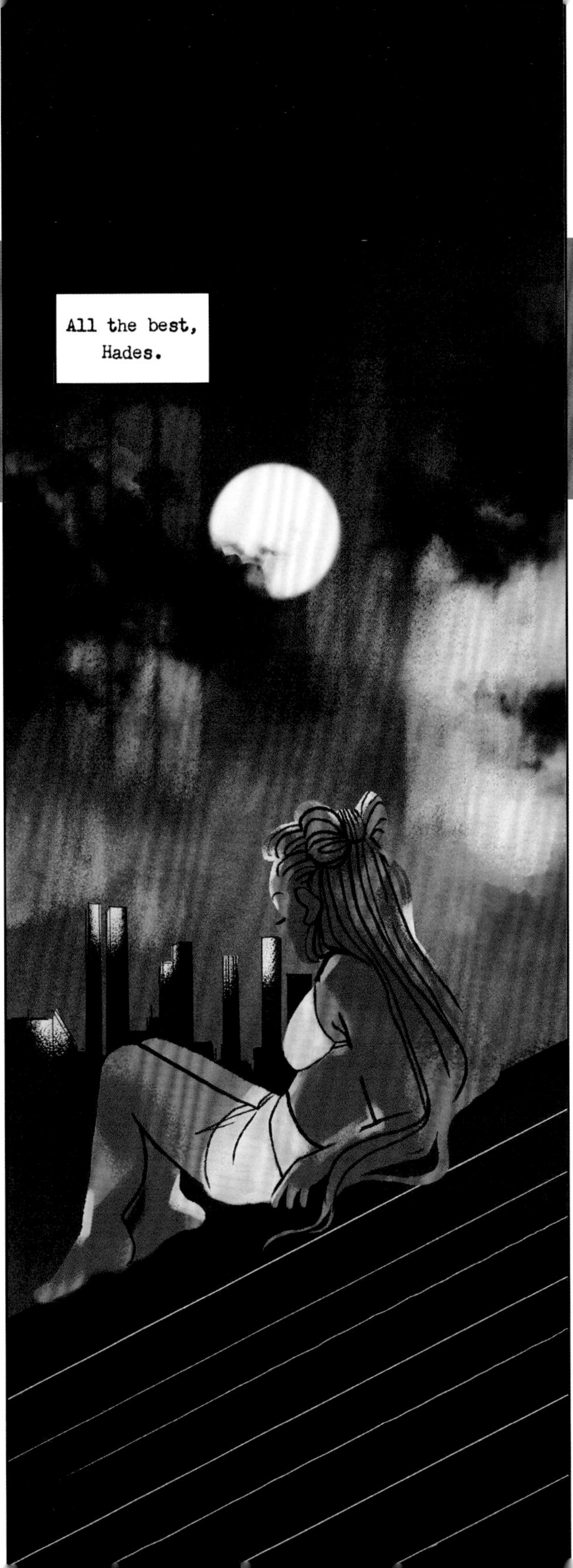
All the best,
Hades.

PS: How does a goddess go from being called Kore to Persephone?

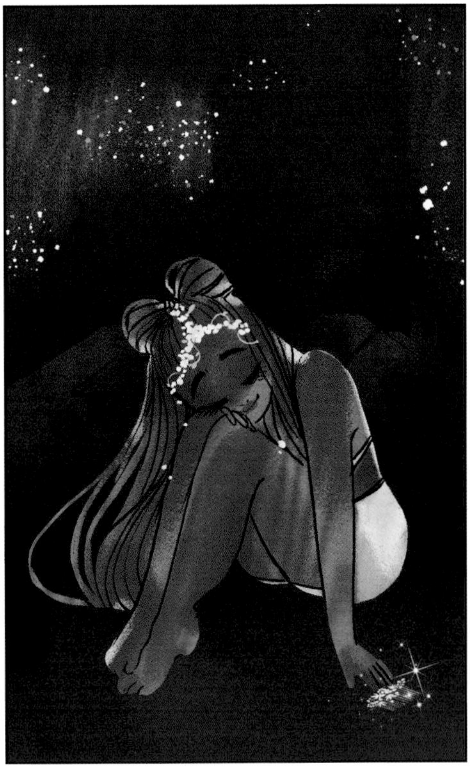

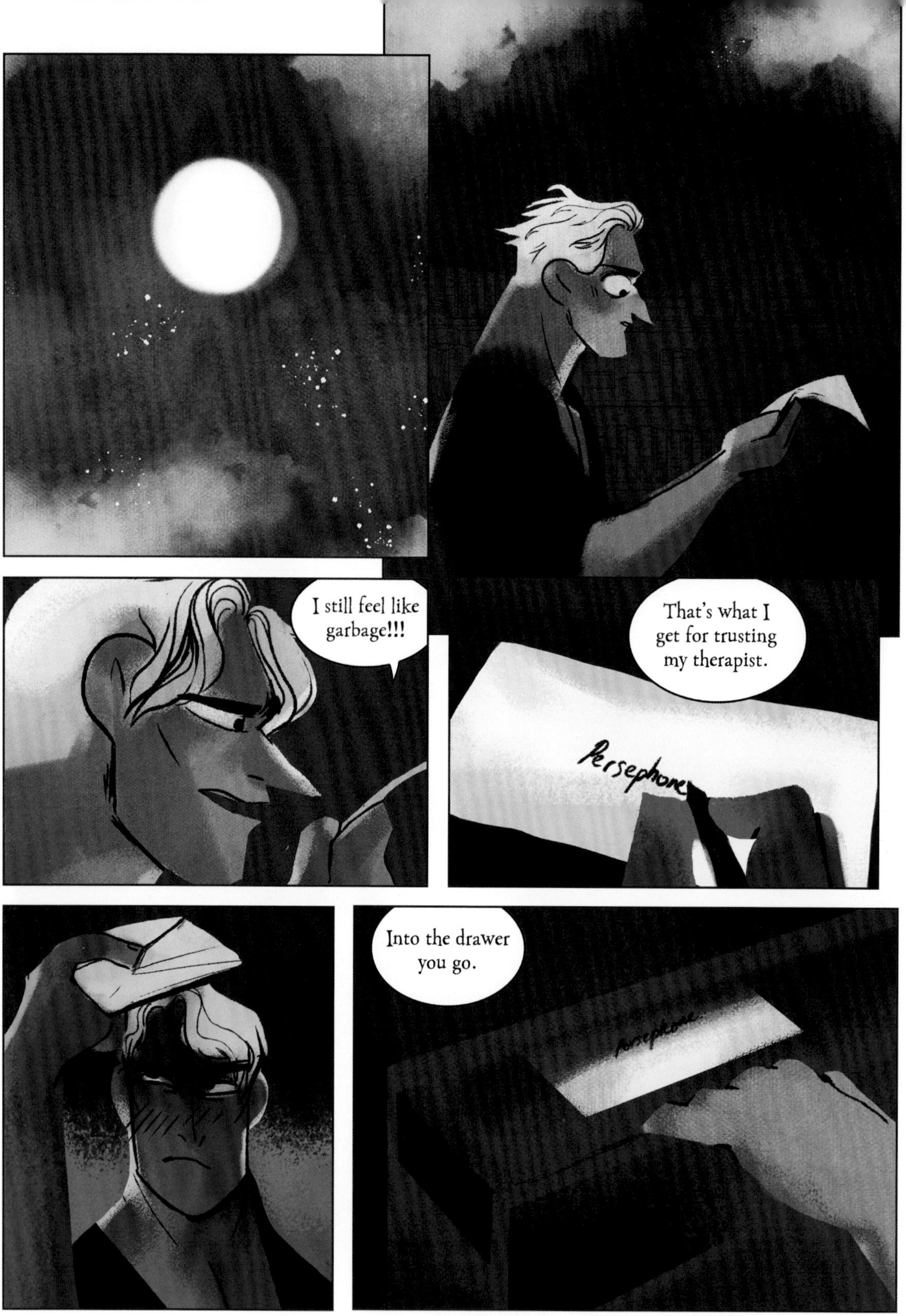
I still feel like garbage!!!
That's what I get for trusting my therapist.
Persephone
Into the drawer you go.
Persephone

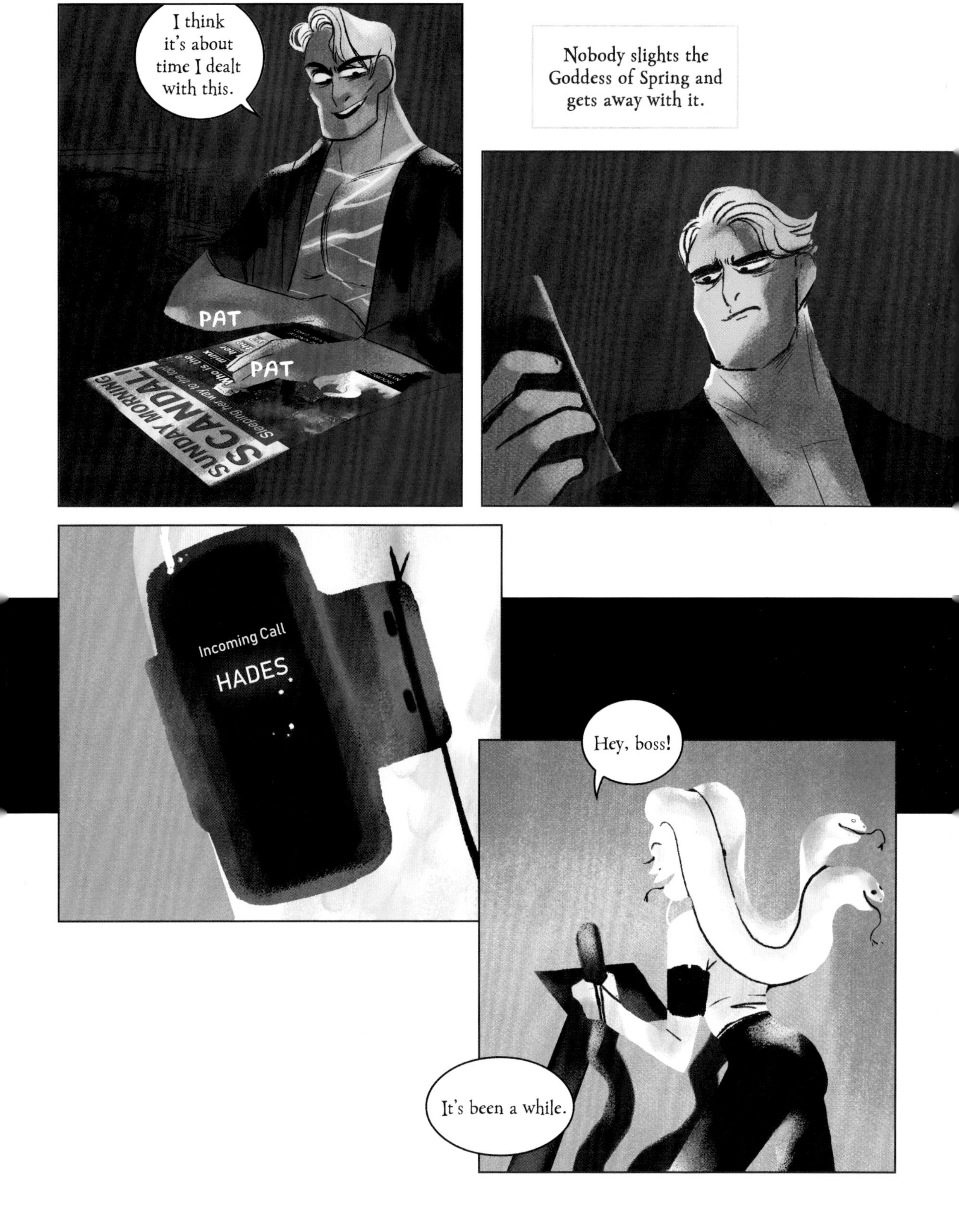
I think it's about time I dealt with this.
PAT
PAT
SUNDAY MORNING
SCANDAL!!
Sleeping her way to the top
Who is the
Nobody slights the Goddess of Spring and gets away with it.
Incoming Call
HADES
Hey, boss!
It's been a while.

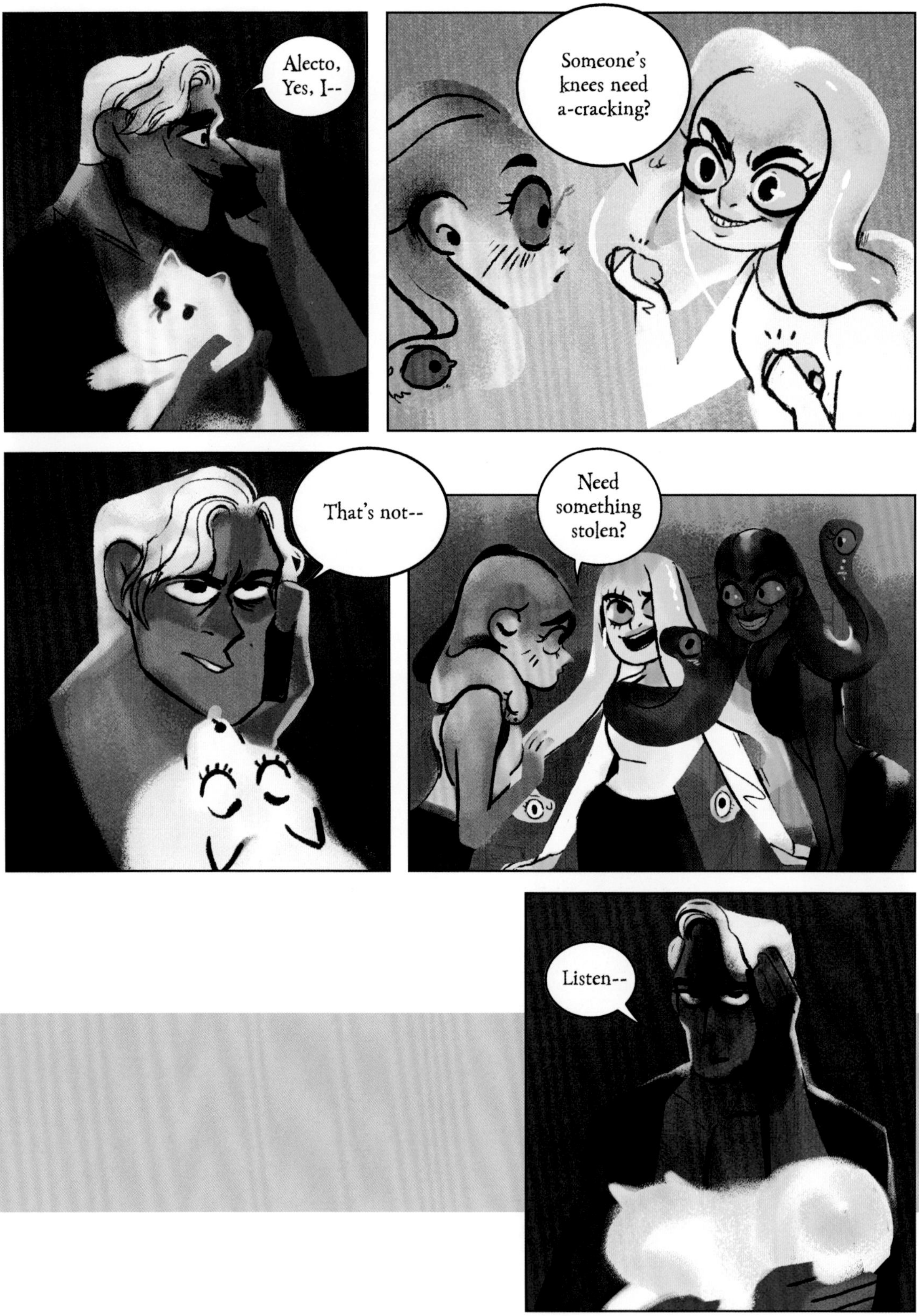
Alecto, Yes, I--
Someone's knees need a-cracking?
That's not--
Need something stolen?
Listen--

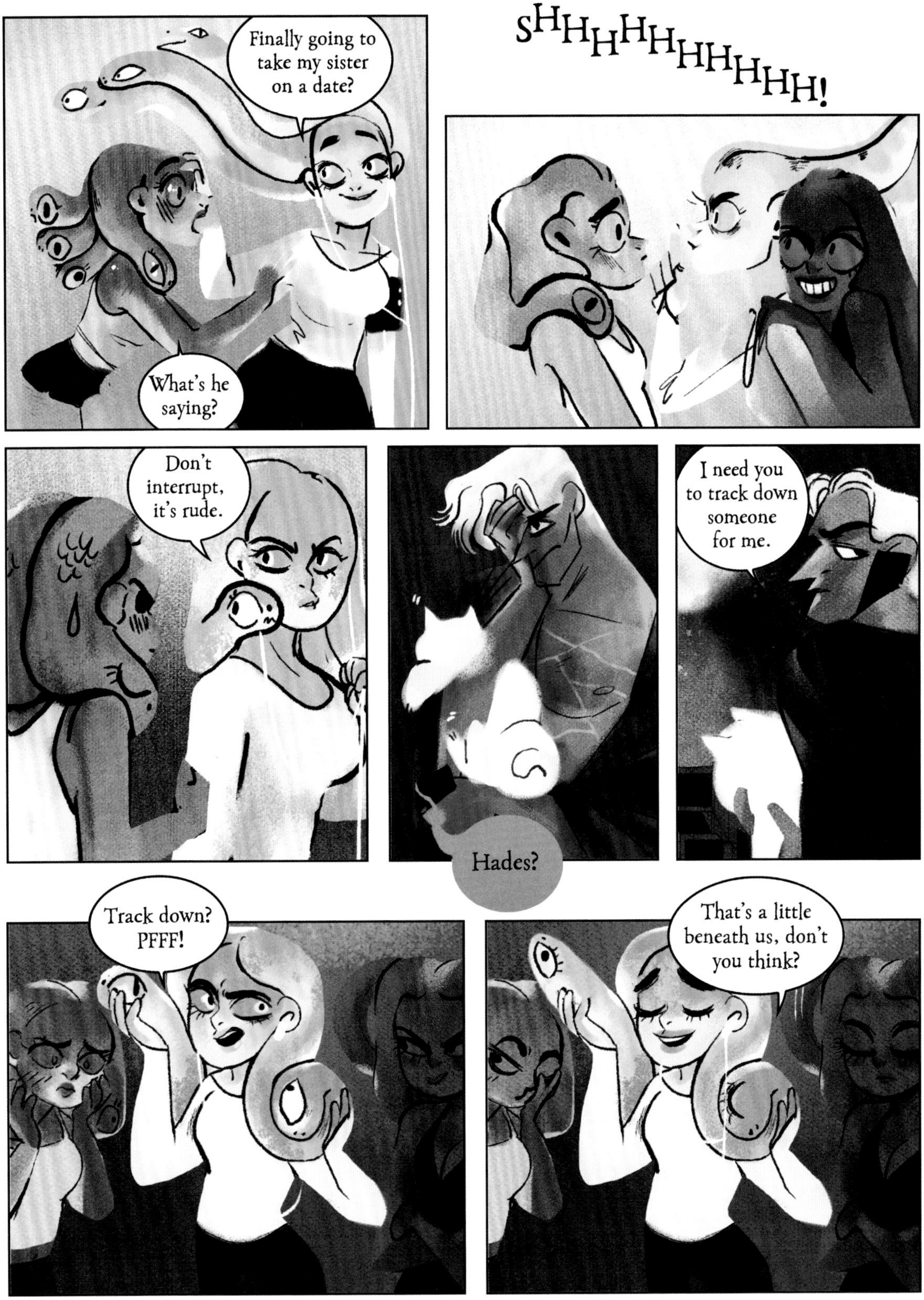
Finally going to take my sister on a date?
What's he saying?
SHHHHHHHHHHH!
Don't interrupt, it's rude.
Hades?
I need you to track down someone for me.
Track down? PFFF!
That's a little beneath us, don't you think?

2 WEEKS AGO.

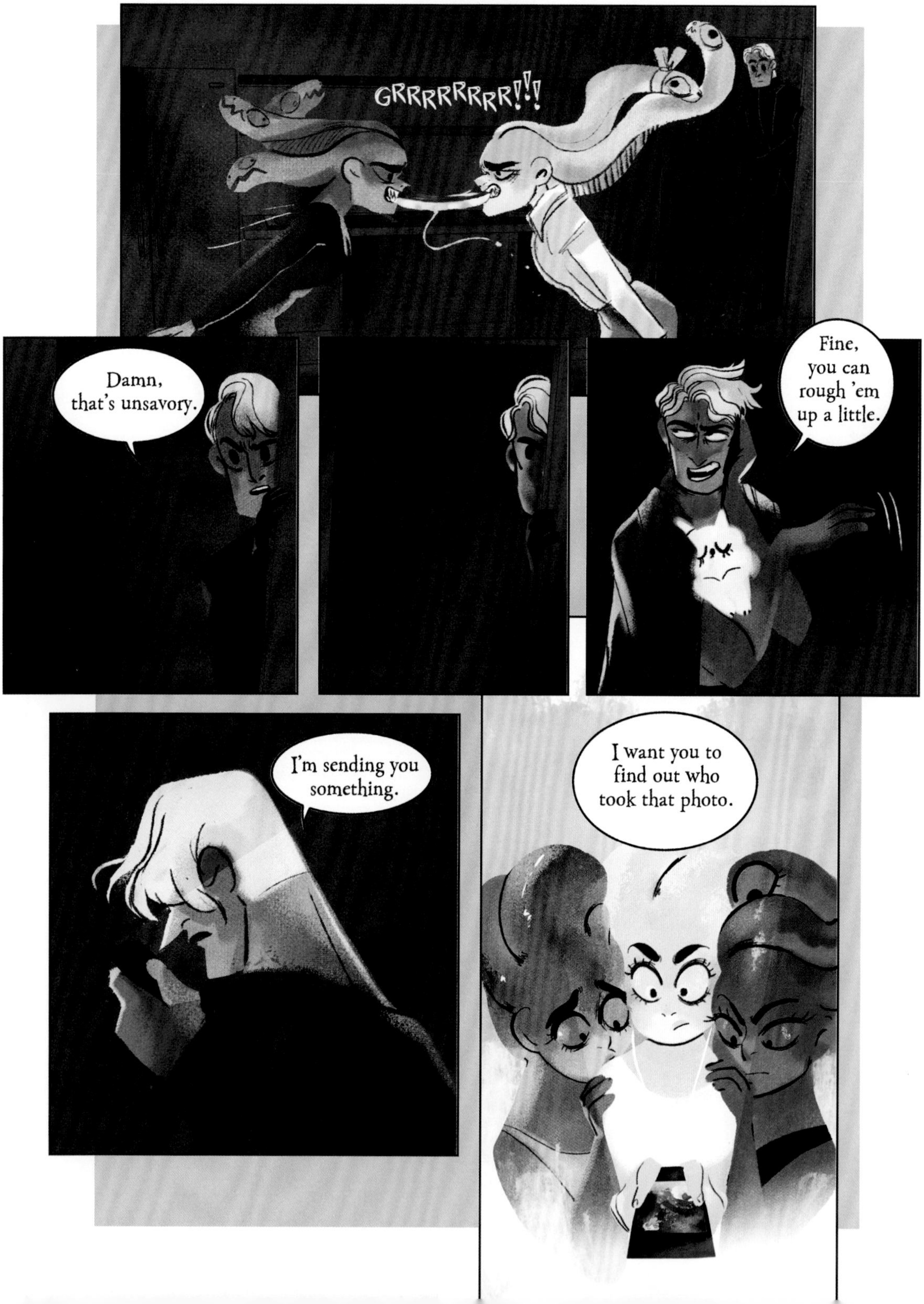
GRRRRRRRR!!!
Damn, that's unsavory.
Fine, you can rough 'em up a little.
I'm sending you something.
I want you to find out who took that photo.

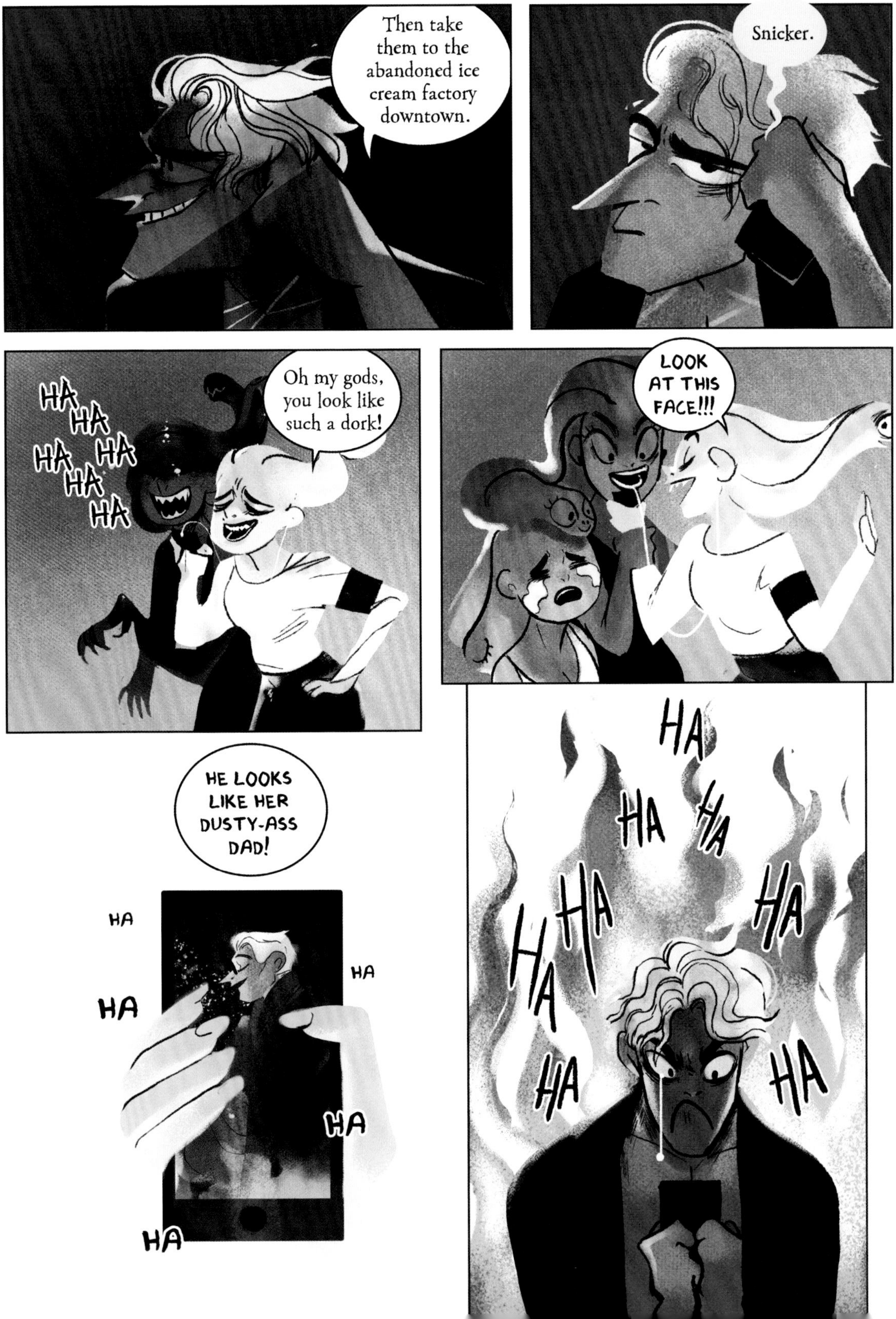
Then take them to the abandoned ice cream factory downtown.
Snicker.
HA HA HA HA HA HA
Oh my gods, you look like such a dork!
LOOK AT THIS FACE!!!
HE LOOKS LIKE HER DUSTY-ASS DAD!
HA
HA
HA
HA
HA
HA HA HA HA HA HA HA HA

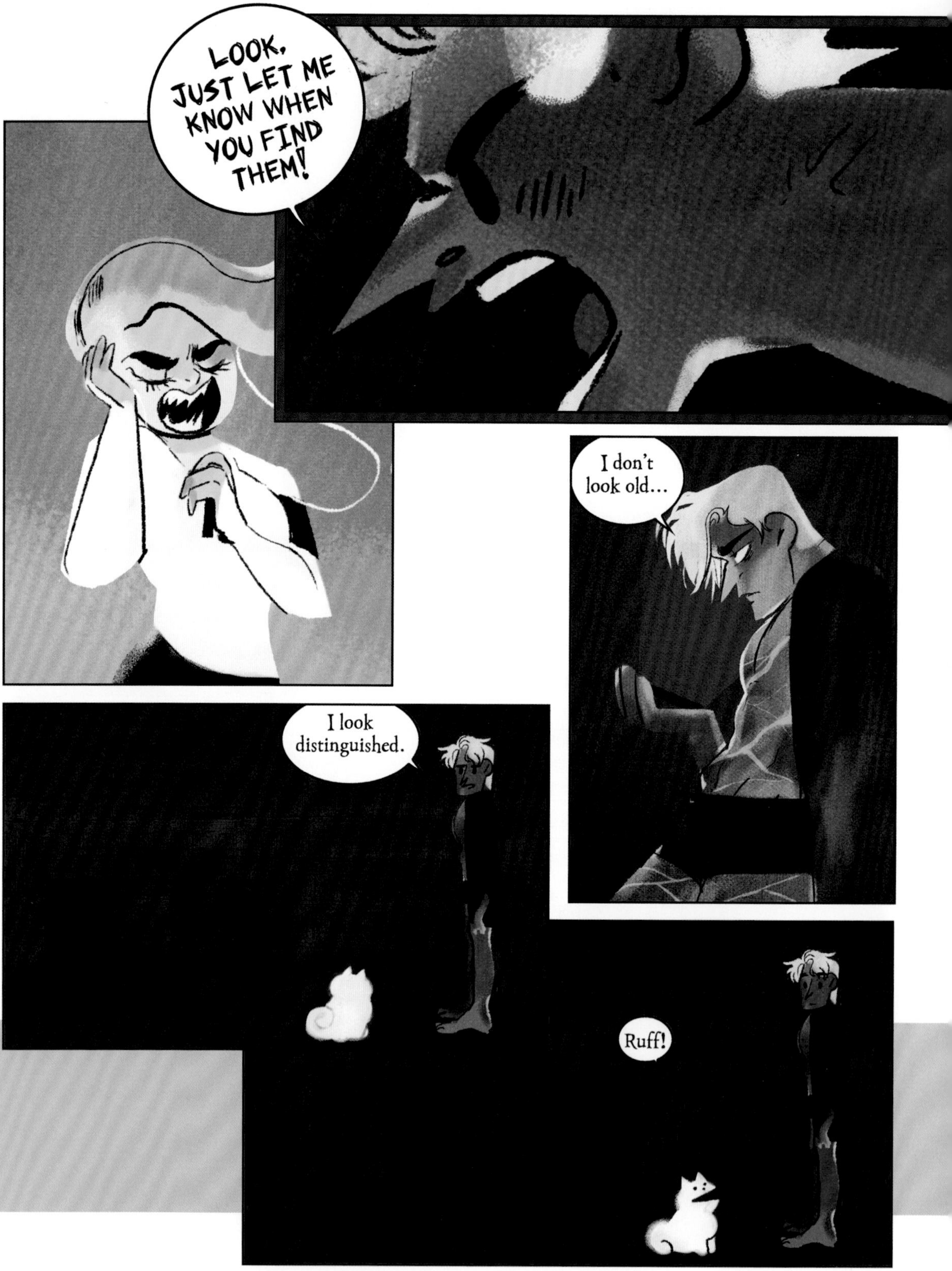
LOOK, JUST LET ME KNOW WHEN YOU FIND THEM!
I don't look old...
I look distinguished.
Ruff!

EPISODE 48: SISSSS

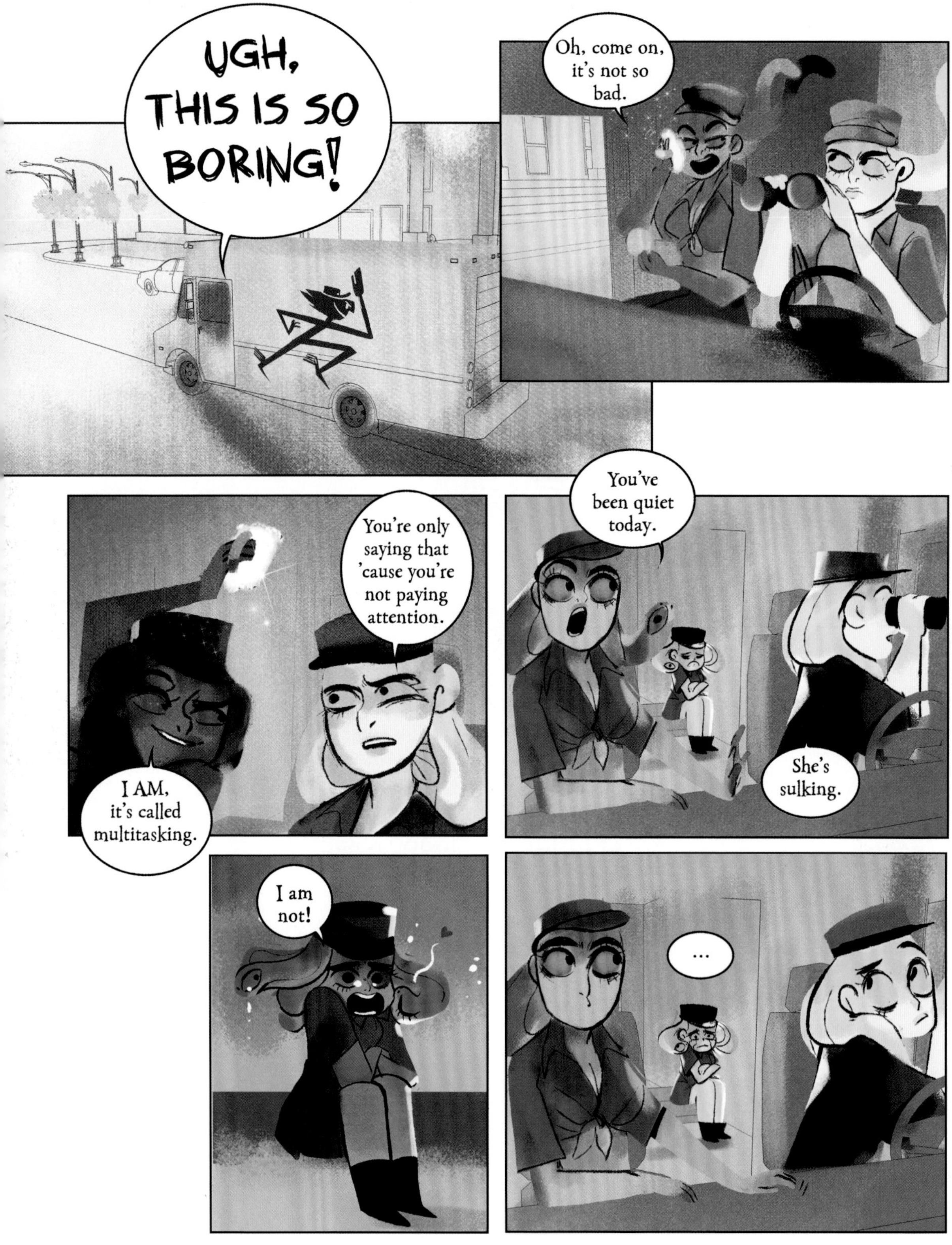
UGH, THIS IS SO BORING!
Oh, come on, it's not so bad.
You're only saying that 'cause you're not paying attention.
I AM, it's called multitasking.
You've been quiet today.
She's sulking.
I am not!
...

SOB!

IT SHOULD HAVE BEEN ME!

Sleeping her way to the top

Who is tl

~~lilac~~ **min**

sleazing h

way into tl

royal family

I HAVE PROOF! FACTS! DOC-U-MEN-TA-TION!

You need to stop it with that book!

You just have it on you!?

HADES

I'm sorry, but I just don't think Hades is into you.

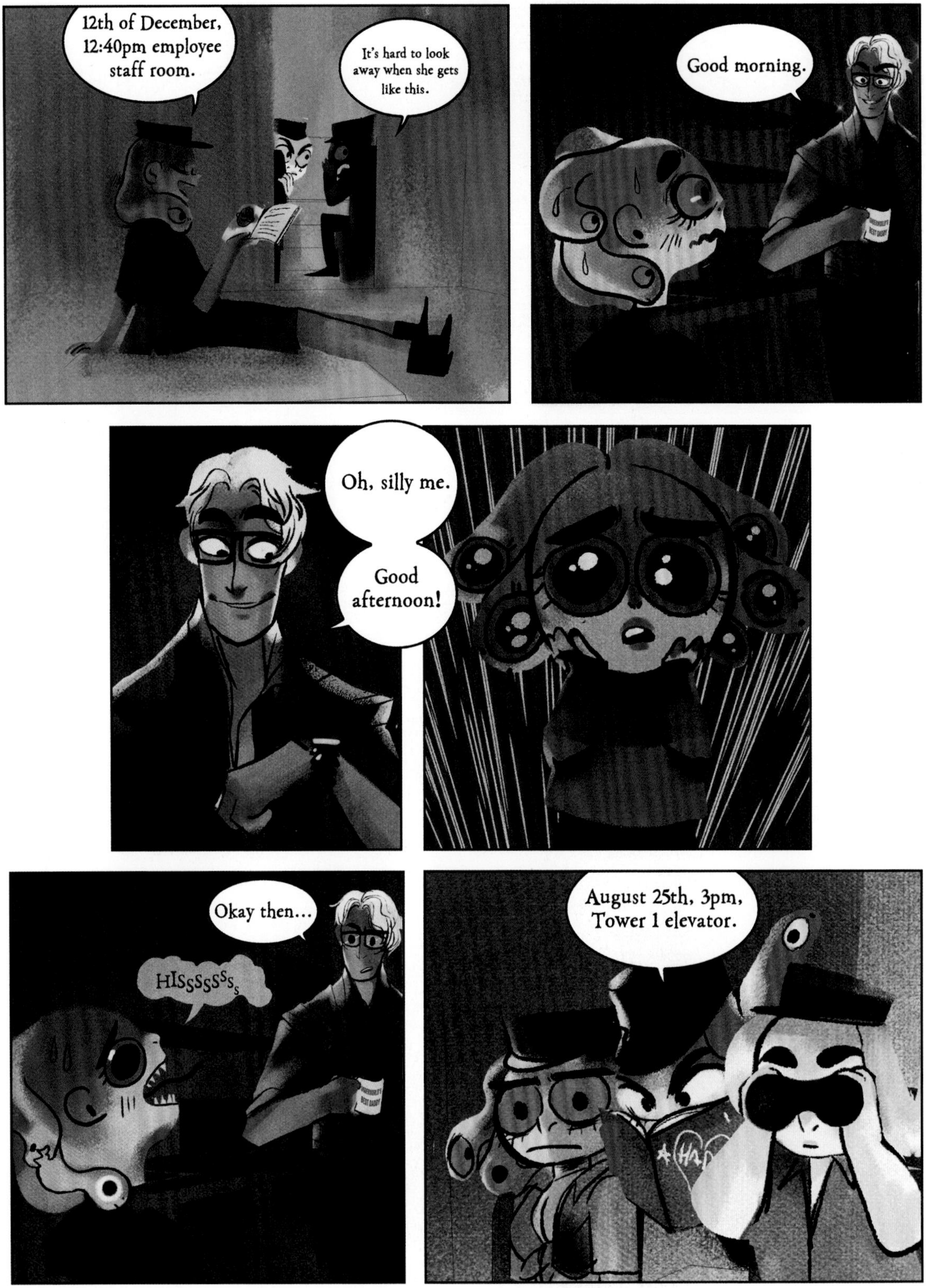
12th of December, 12:40pm employee staff room.
It's hard to look away when she gets like this.
Good morning.
Oh, silly me.
Good afternoon!
Okay then...
HISSSSSSS
August 25th, 3pm, Tower 1 elevator.

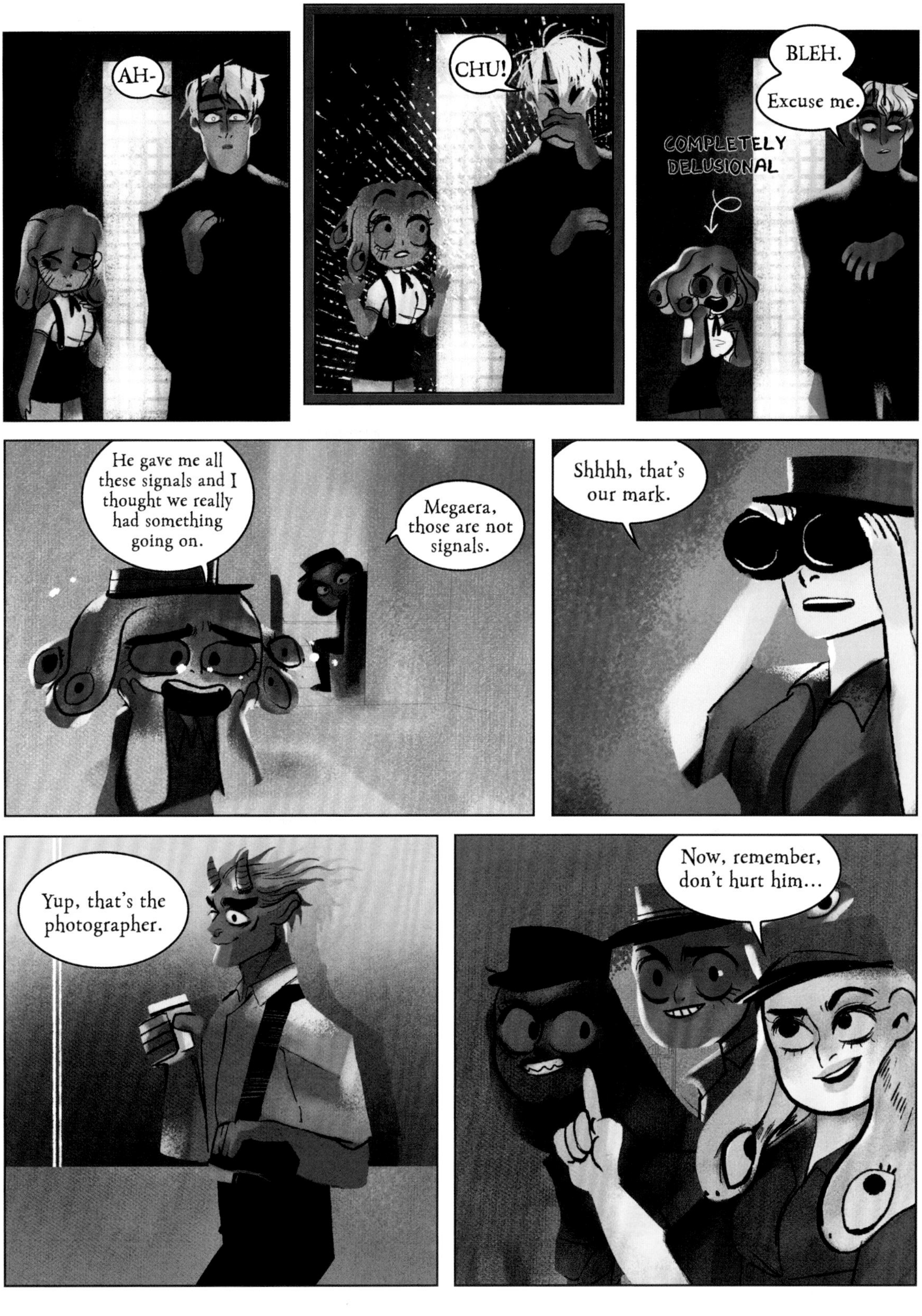
AH-
CHU!
BLEH.
Excuse me.
COMPLETELY DELUSIONAL
He gave me all these signals and I thought we really had something going on.
Megaera, those are not signals.
Shhhh, that's our mark.
Yup, that's the photographer.
Now, remember, don't hurt him...

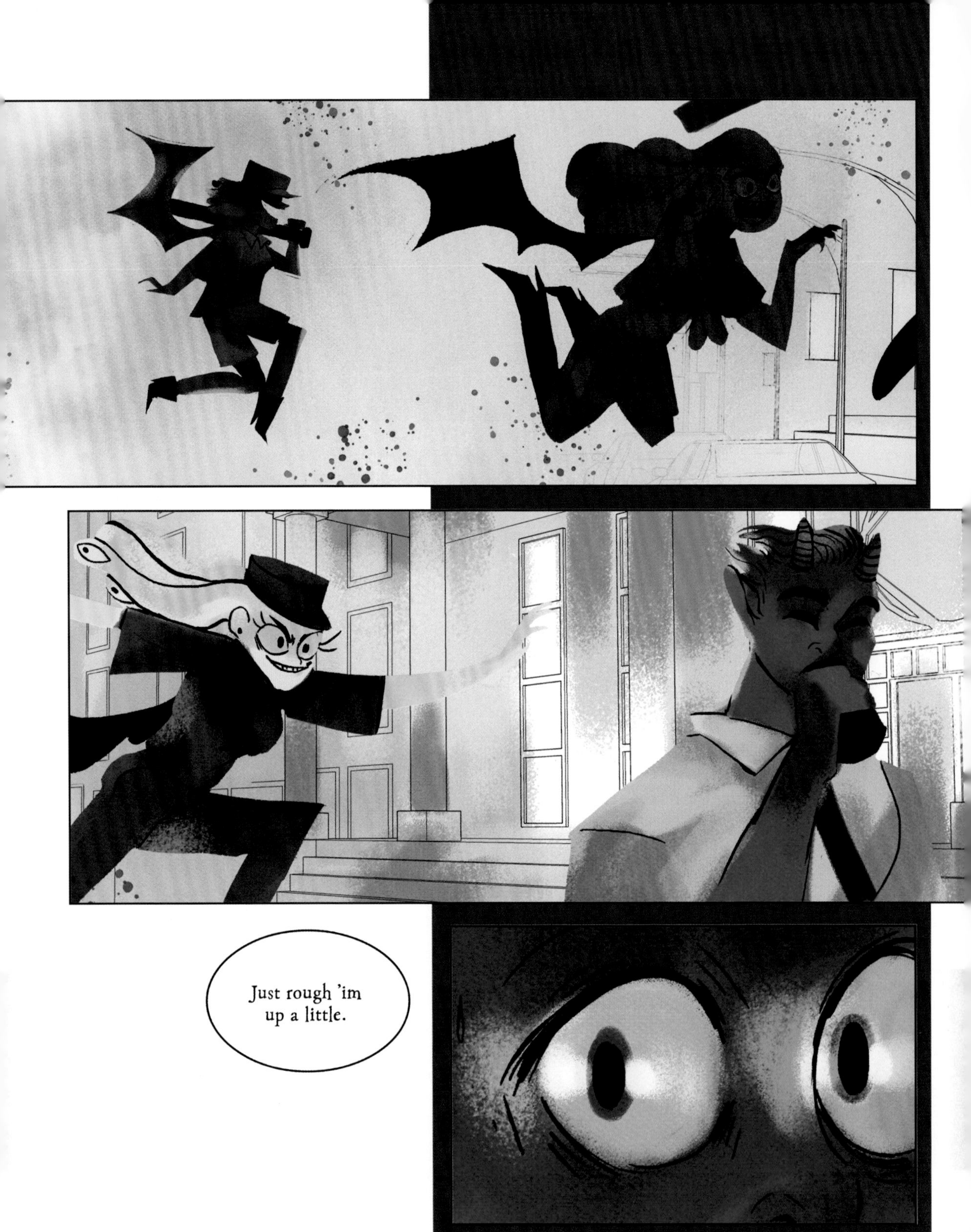
Just rough 'im up a little.

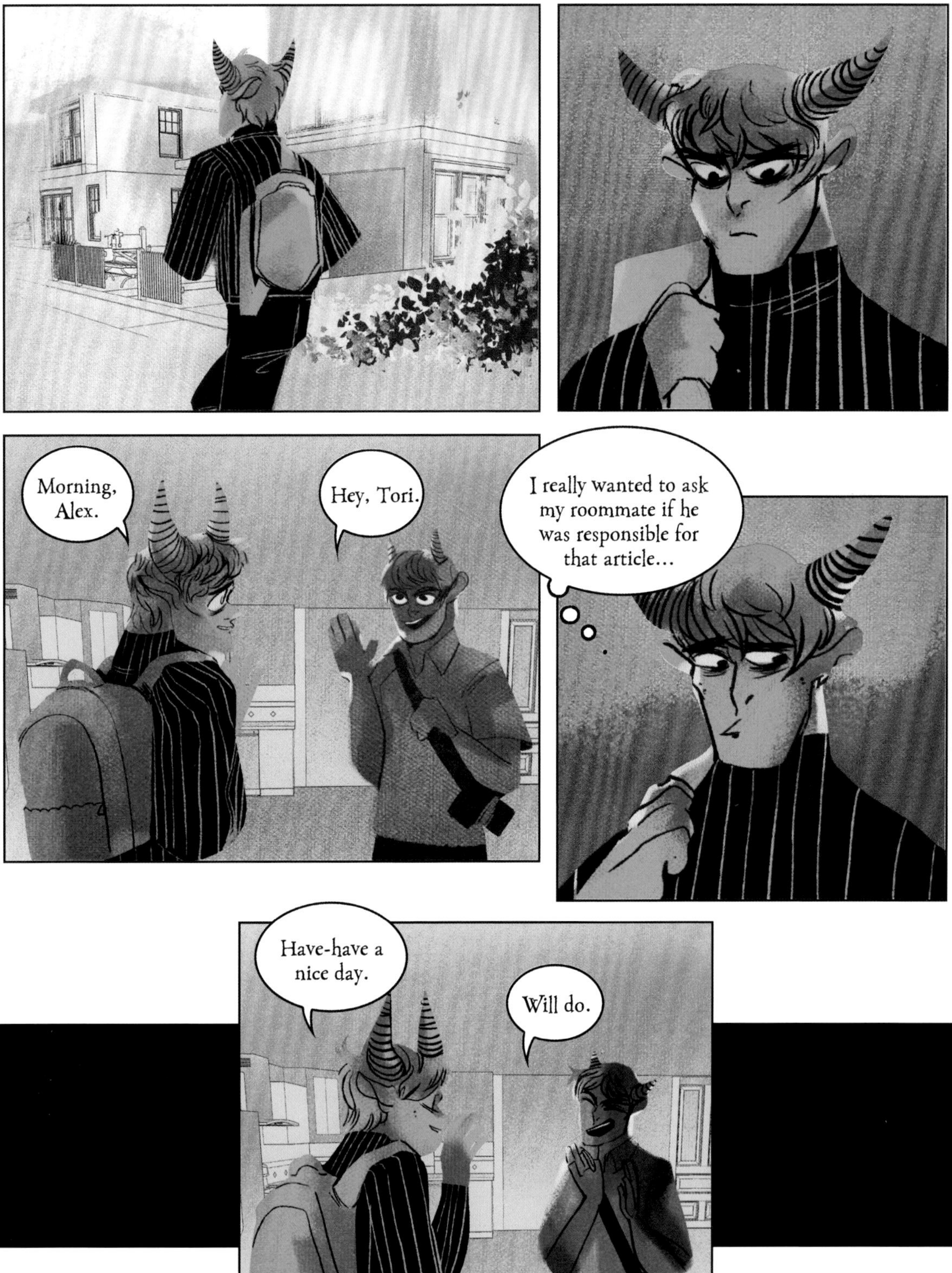
Morning, Alex.
Hey, Tori.
I really wanted to ask my roommate if he was responsible for that article...
Have-have a nice day.
Will do.

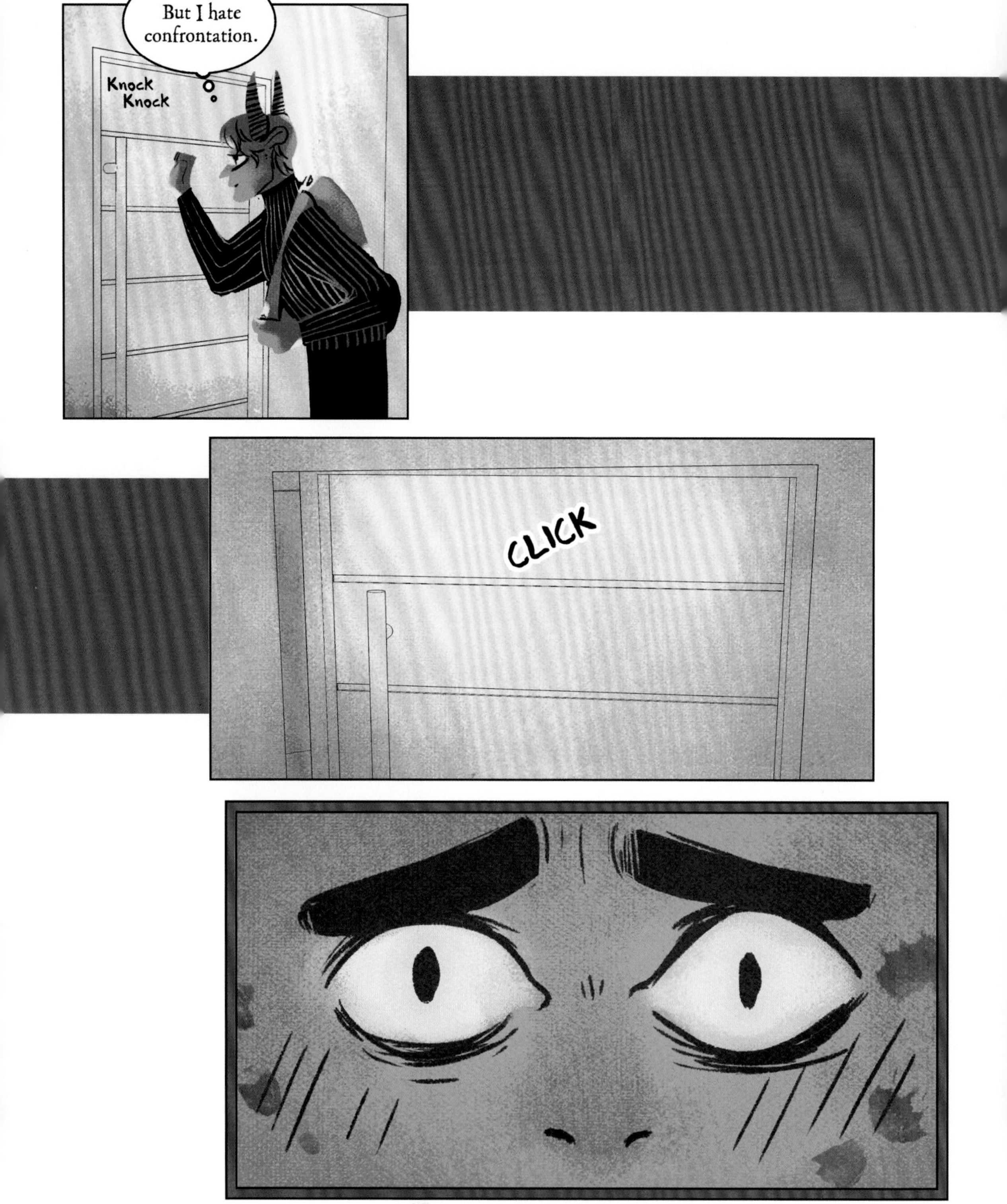
But I hate confrontation.
Knock Knock
CLICK

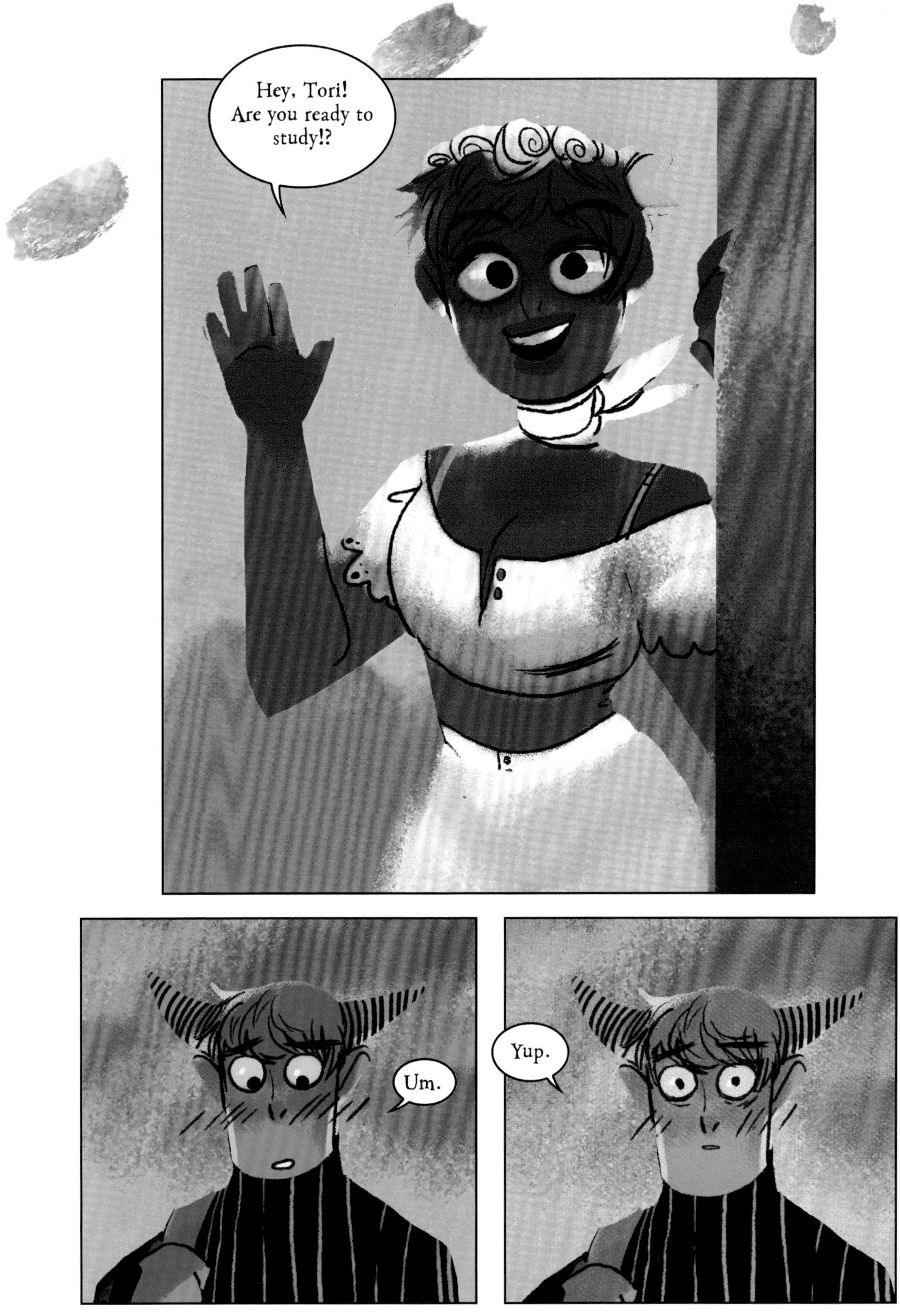
Hey, Tori!
Are you ready to
study!?
Um.
Yup.

EPISODE 49: EYE FOR AN EYE

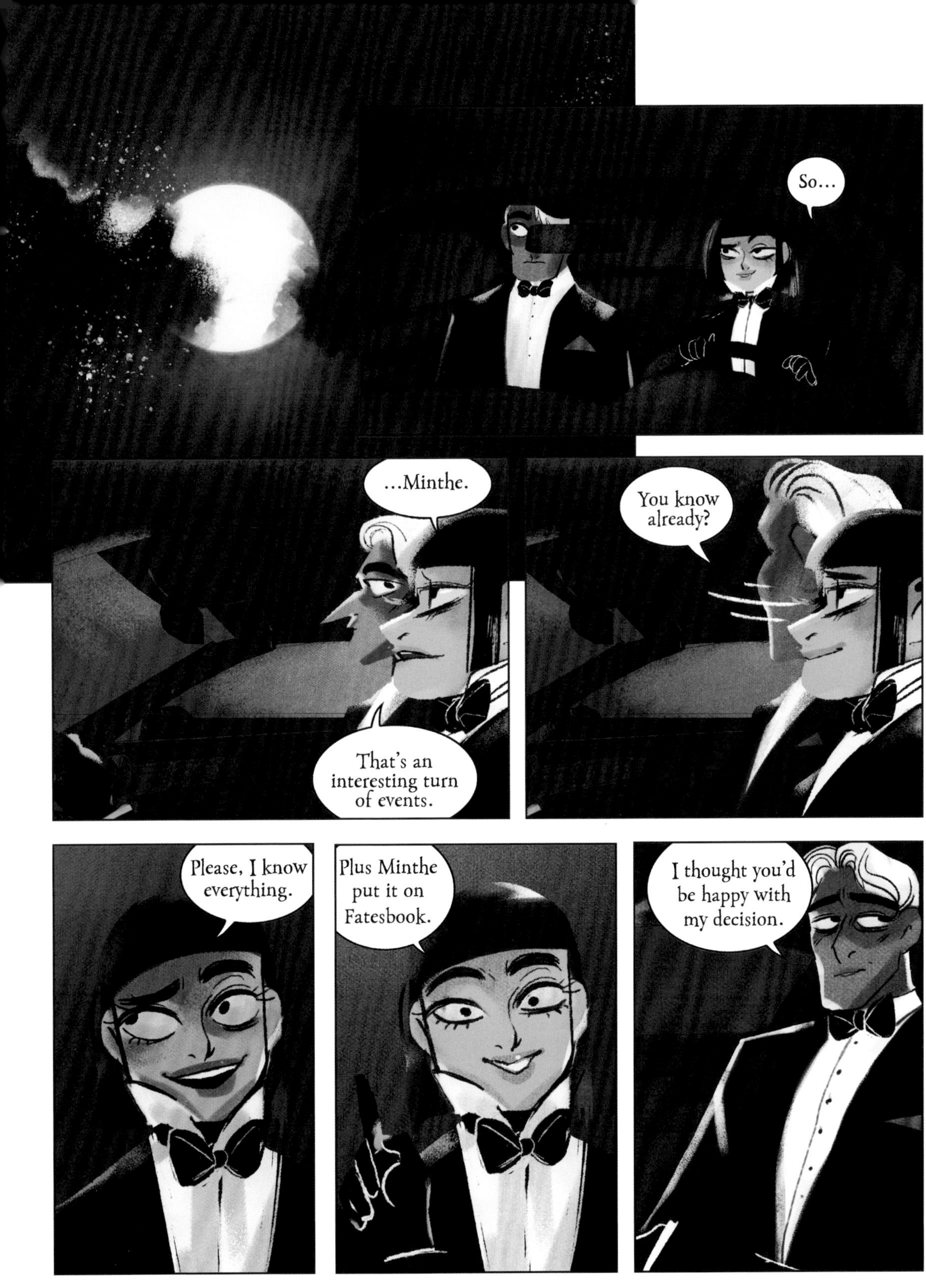
So...
...Minthe.
That's an interesting turn of events.
You know already?
Please, I know everything.
Plus Minthe put it on Fatesbook.
I thought you'd be happy with my decision.

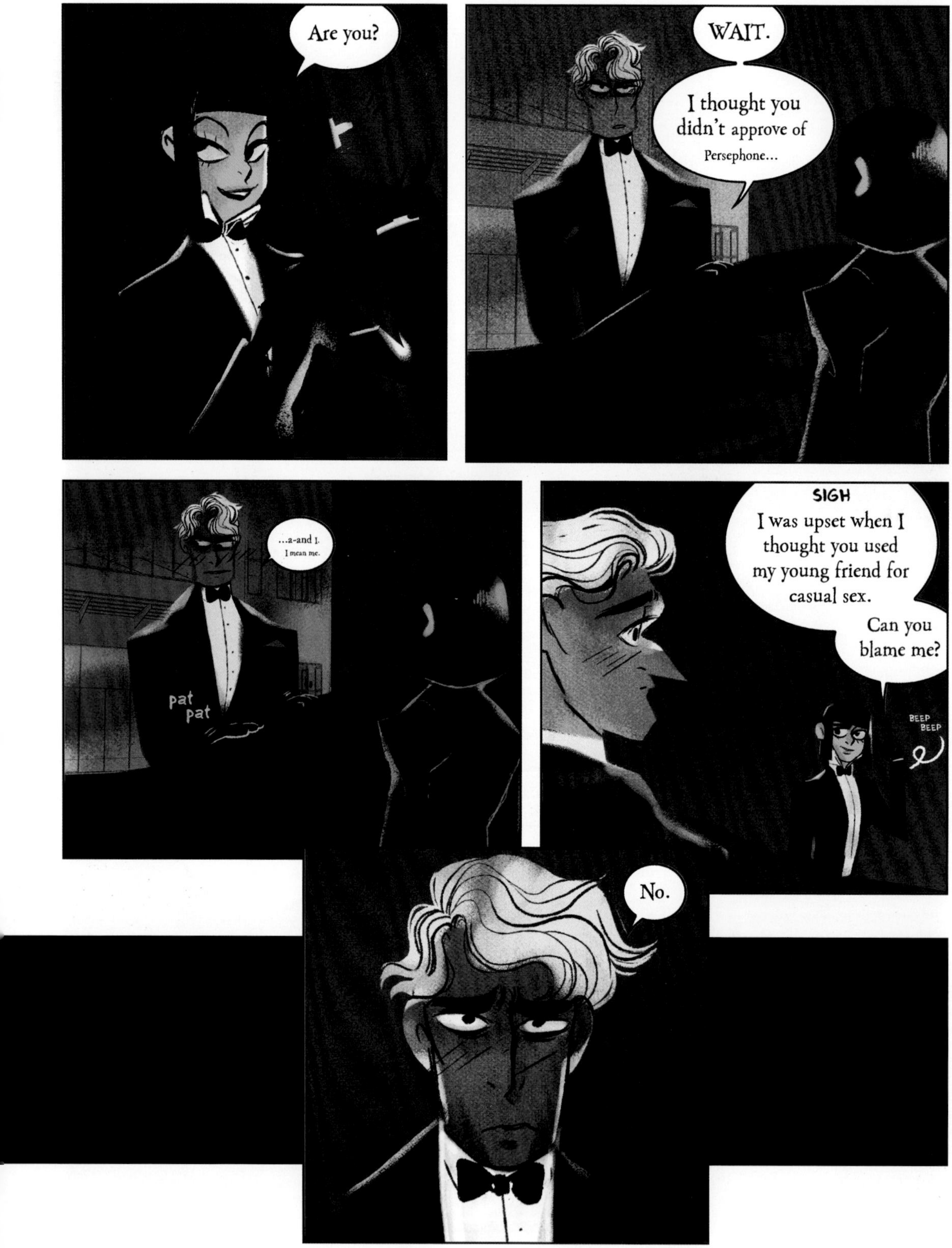
Are you?
WAIT.
I thought you didn't approve of Persephone...
...a-and I. I mean me.
pat pat
SIGH
I was upset when I thought you used my young friend for casual sex.
Can you blame me?
BEEP BEEP
No.

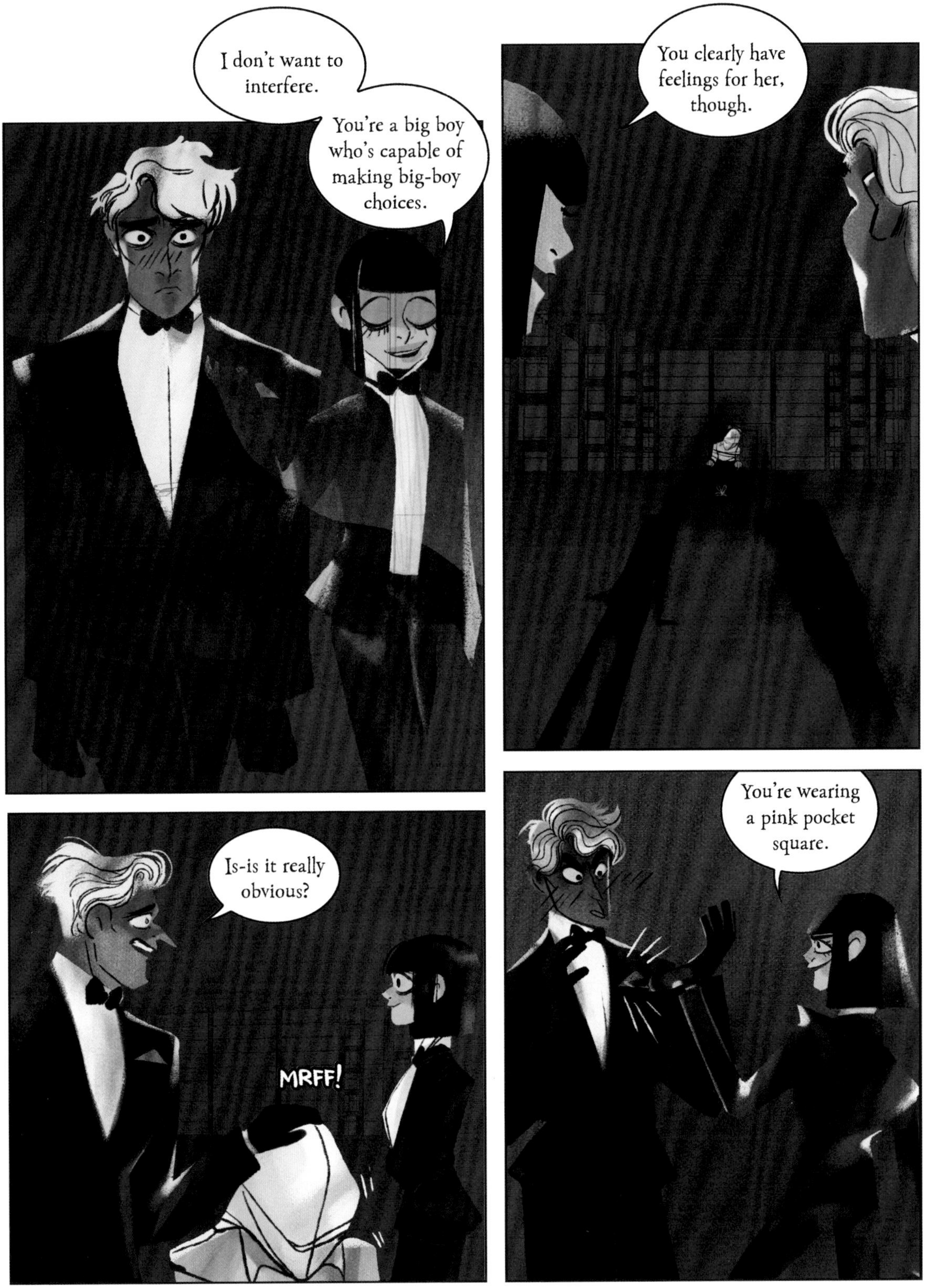
I don't want to interfere.
You're a big boy who's capable of making big-boy choices.
You clearly have feelings for her, though.
Is-is it really obvious?
MRFF!
You're wearing a pink pocket square.

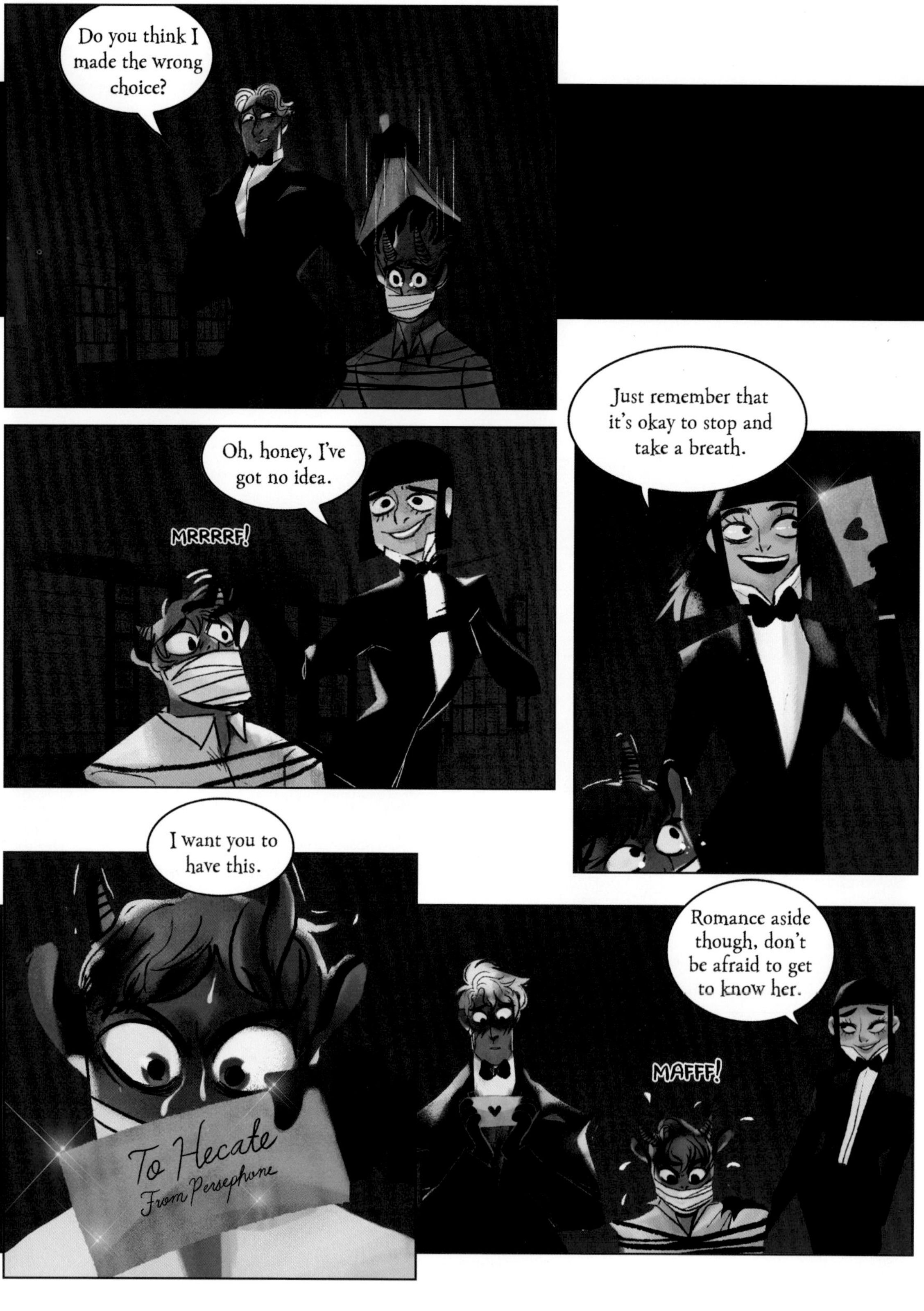
Do you think I made the wrong choice?
Oh, honey, I've got no idea.
MRRRRF!
Just remember that it's okay to stop and take a breath.
I want you to have this.
To Hecate
From Persephone
Romance aside though, don't be afraid to get to know her.
MAFFF!

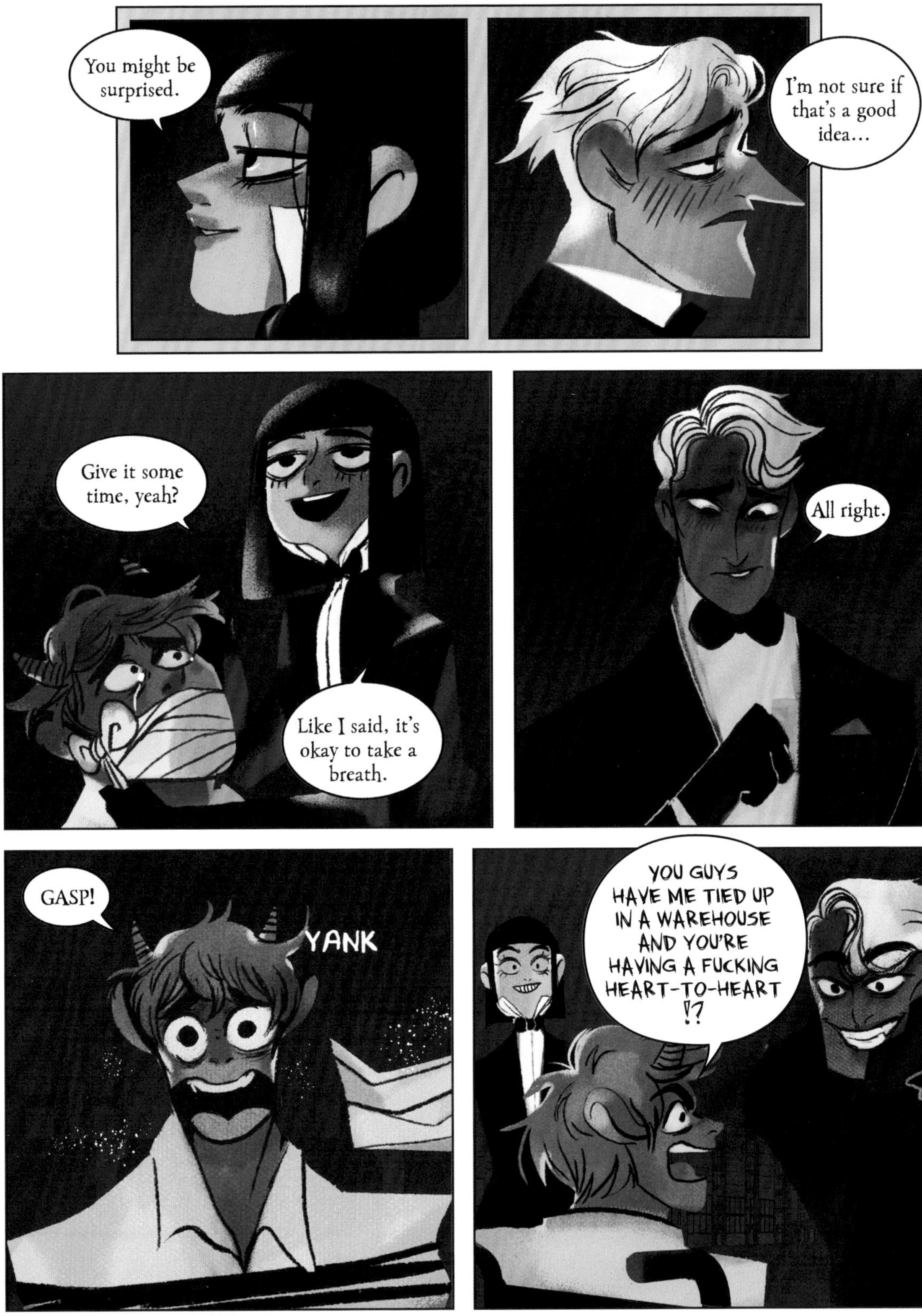
You might be surprised.
I'm not sure if that's a good idea...
Give it some time, yeah?
Like I said, it's okay to take a breath.
All right.
GASP!
YANK
YOU GUYS HAVE ME TIED UP IN A WAREHOUSE AND YOU'RE HAVING A FUCKING HEART-TO-HEART !?

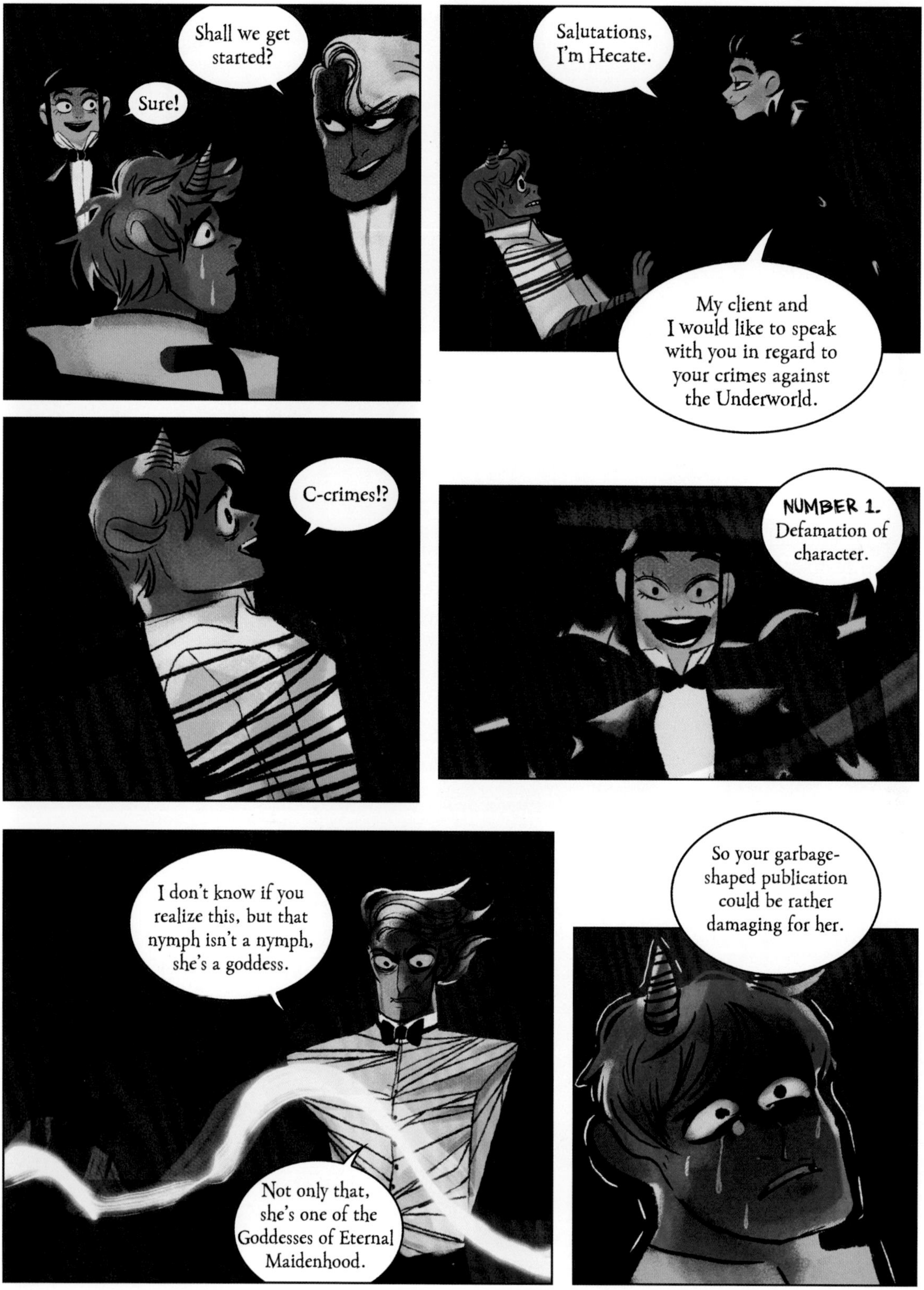
Shall we get started?
Sure!
Salutations, I'm Hecate.
My client and I would like to speak with you in regard to your crimes against the Underworld.
C-crimes!?
NUMBER 1. Defamation of character.
I don't know if you realize this, but that nymph isn't a nymph, she's a goddess.
Not only that, she's one of the Goddesses of Eternal Maidenhood.
So your garbage-shaped publication could be rather damaging for her.

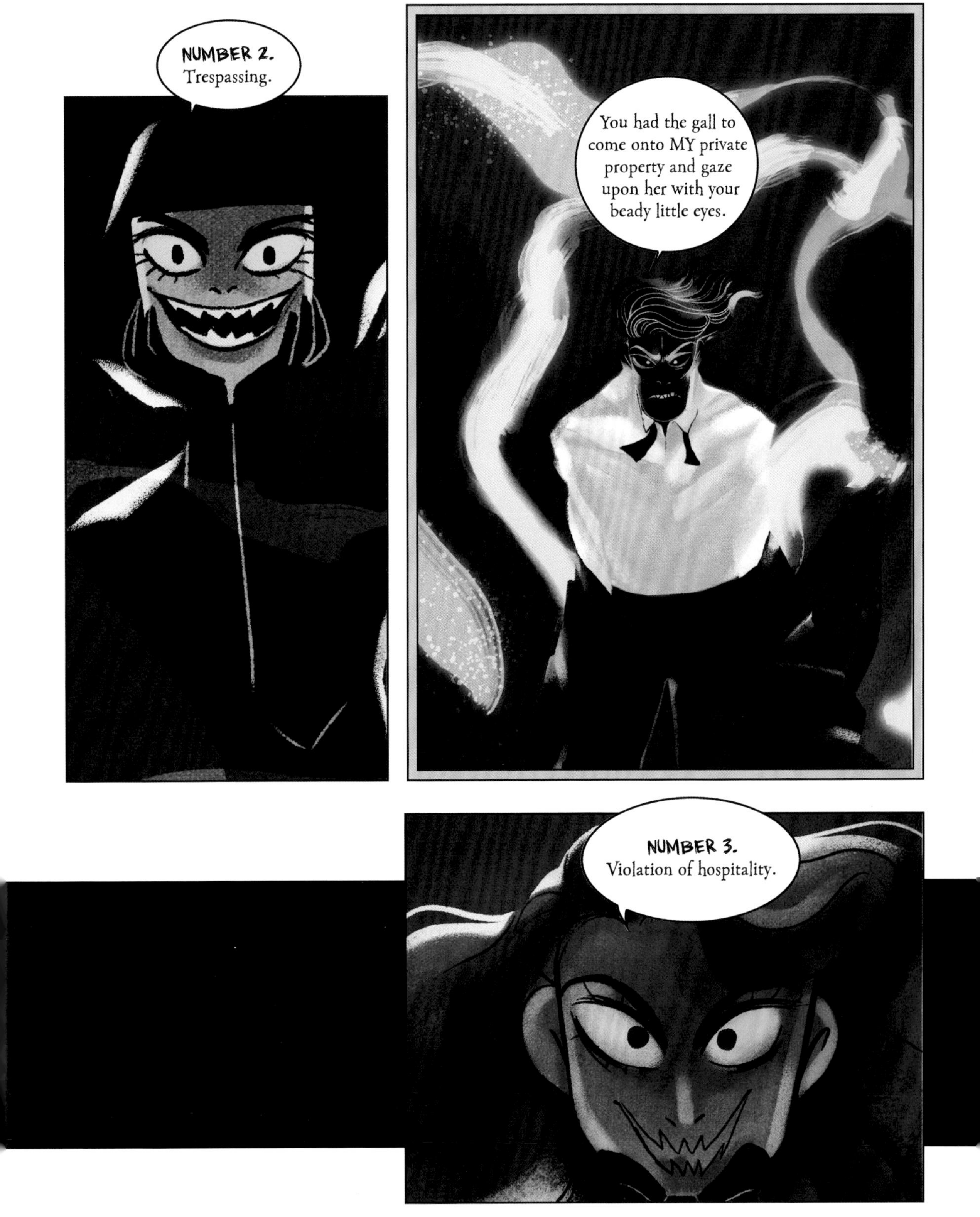
NUMBER 2.
Trespassing.
You had the gall to come onto MY private property and gaze upon her with your beady little eyes.
NUMBER 3.
Violation of hospitality.

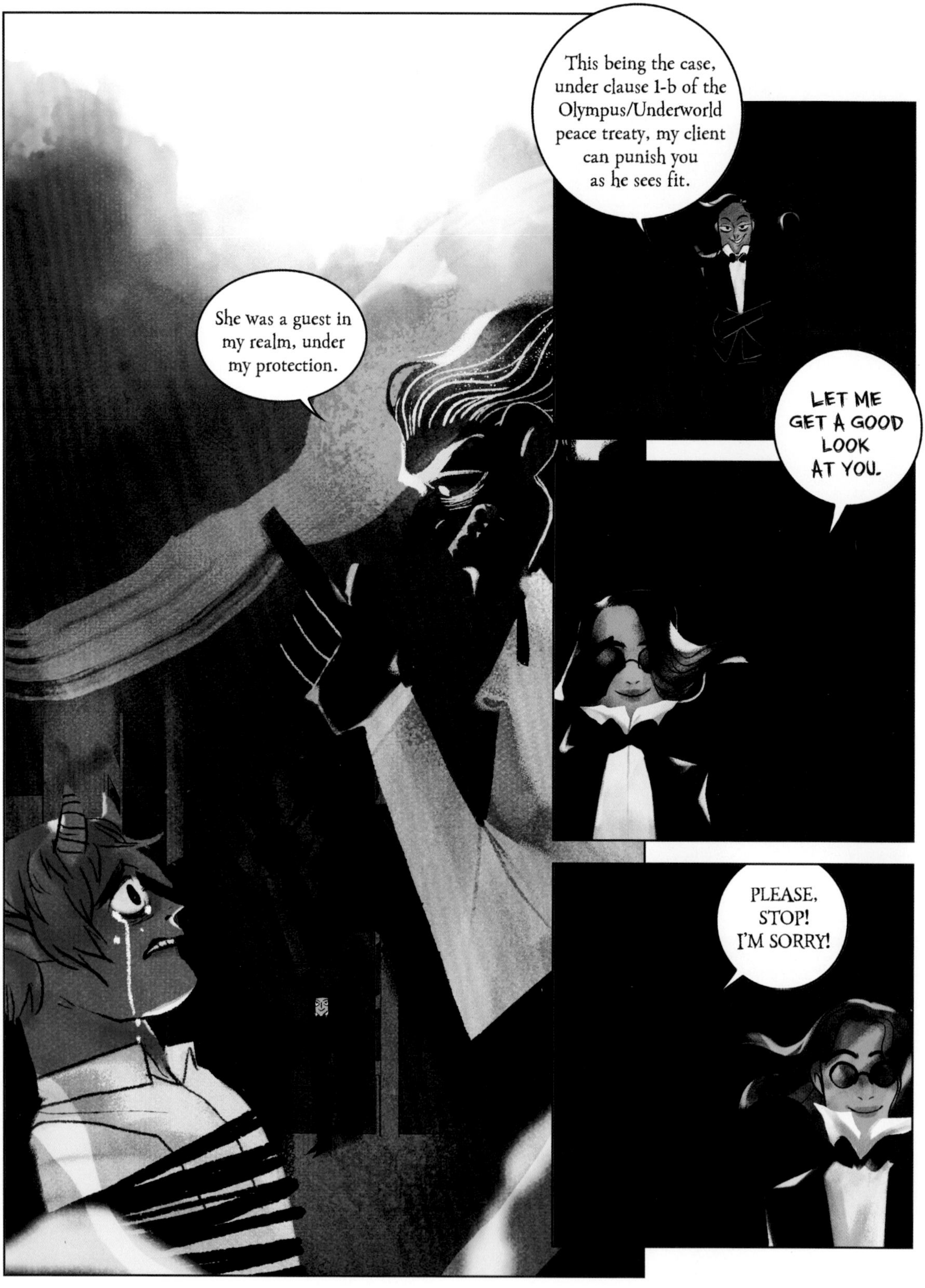
She was a guest in my realm, under my protection.
This being the case, under clause 1-b of the Olympus/Underworld peace treaty, my client can punish you as he sees fit.
LET ME GET A GOOD LOOK AT YOU.
PLEASE, STOP! I'M SORRY!

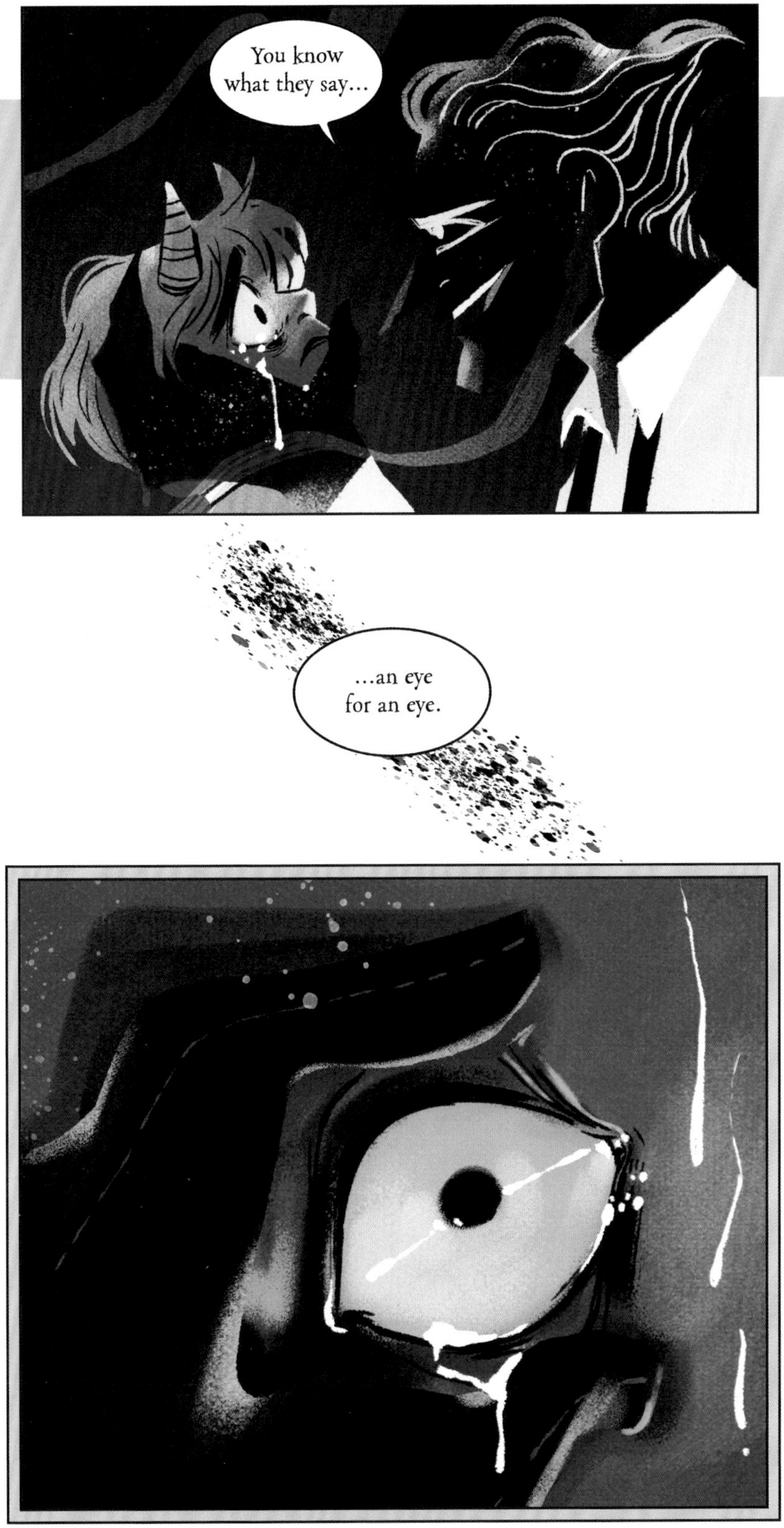
You know what they say...
...an eye for an eye.

This chapter takes place before Persephone's coat was confiscated by Hestia.

I was initially planning to include this, but I was unable to structure in the concept at the time. In some ways I think that contextualizing Hestia's seemingly cruel behavior takes away from the emotional impact of episode 47, "Needed," which to this day, is one of my favorite pieces of work.

With all that being said, part of me still really wants the readers of *Lore Olympus* to know this missing part of the story.

Edited by Kathleen Wisneski
Art Assistants Jaki Haboon & Amy Kim

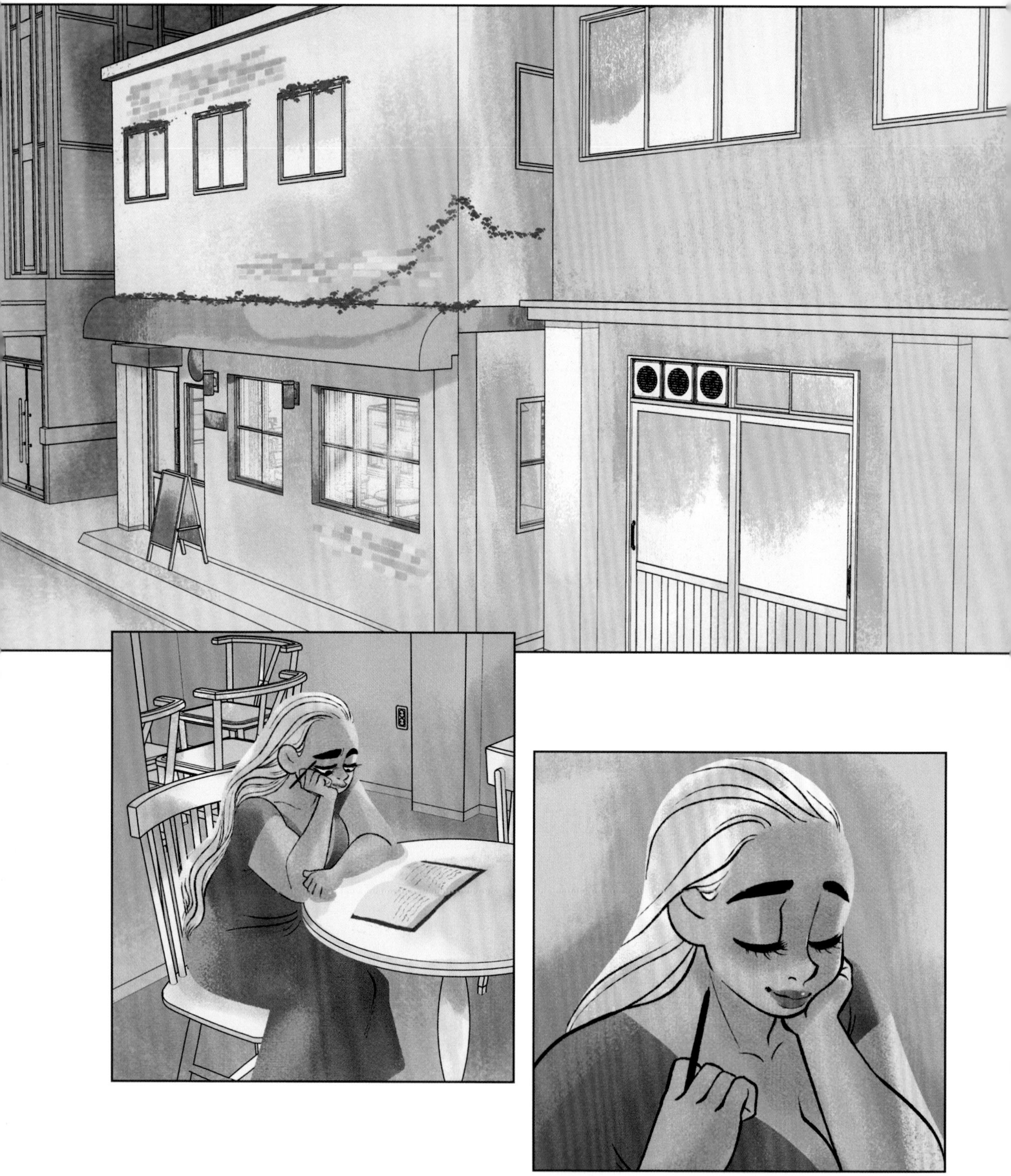

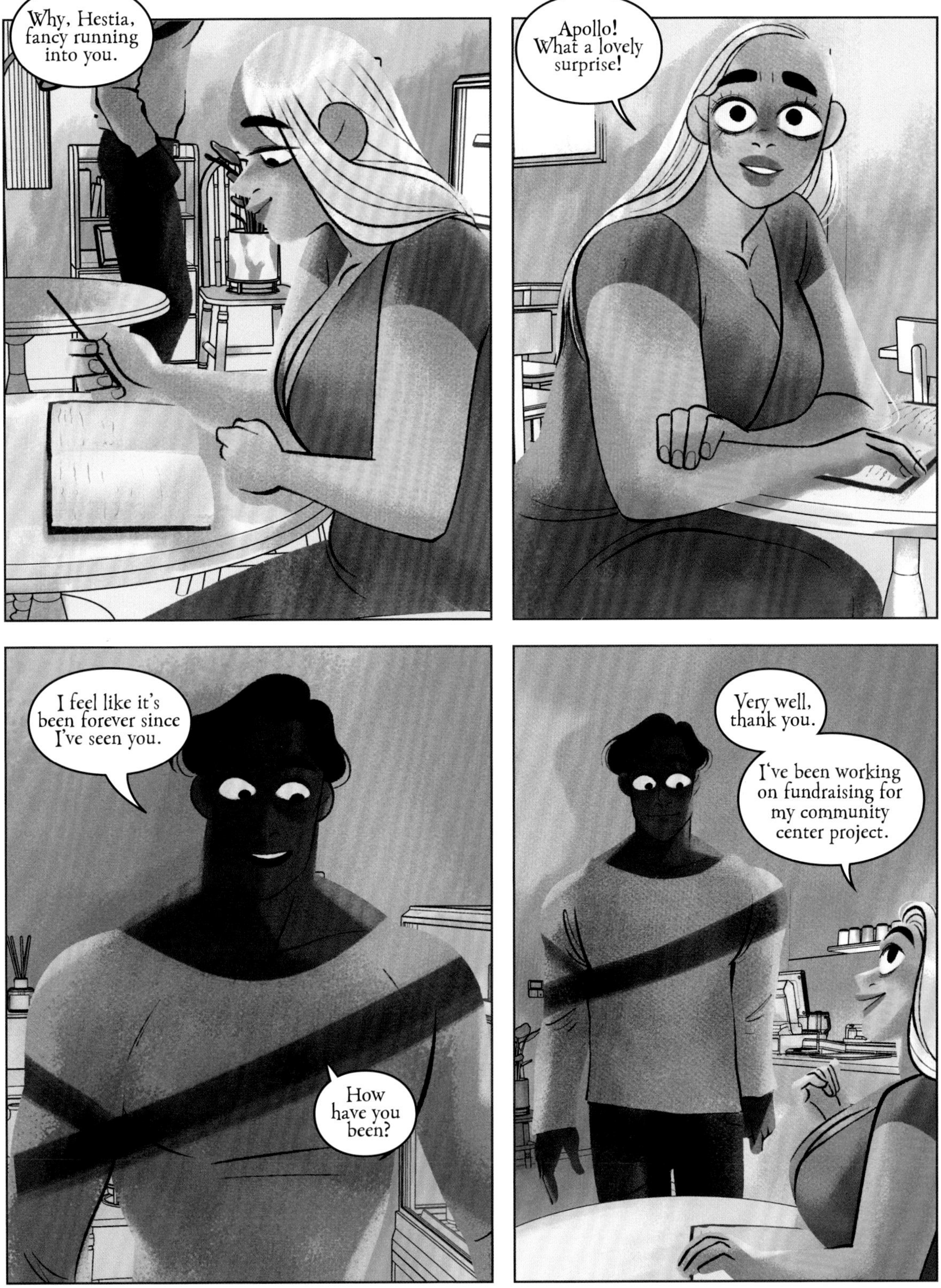
Why, Hestia, fancy running into you.
Apollo! What a lovely surprise!
I feel like it's been forever since I've seen you.
How have you been?
Very well, thank you.
I've been working on fundraising for my community center project.

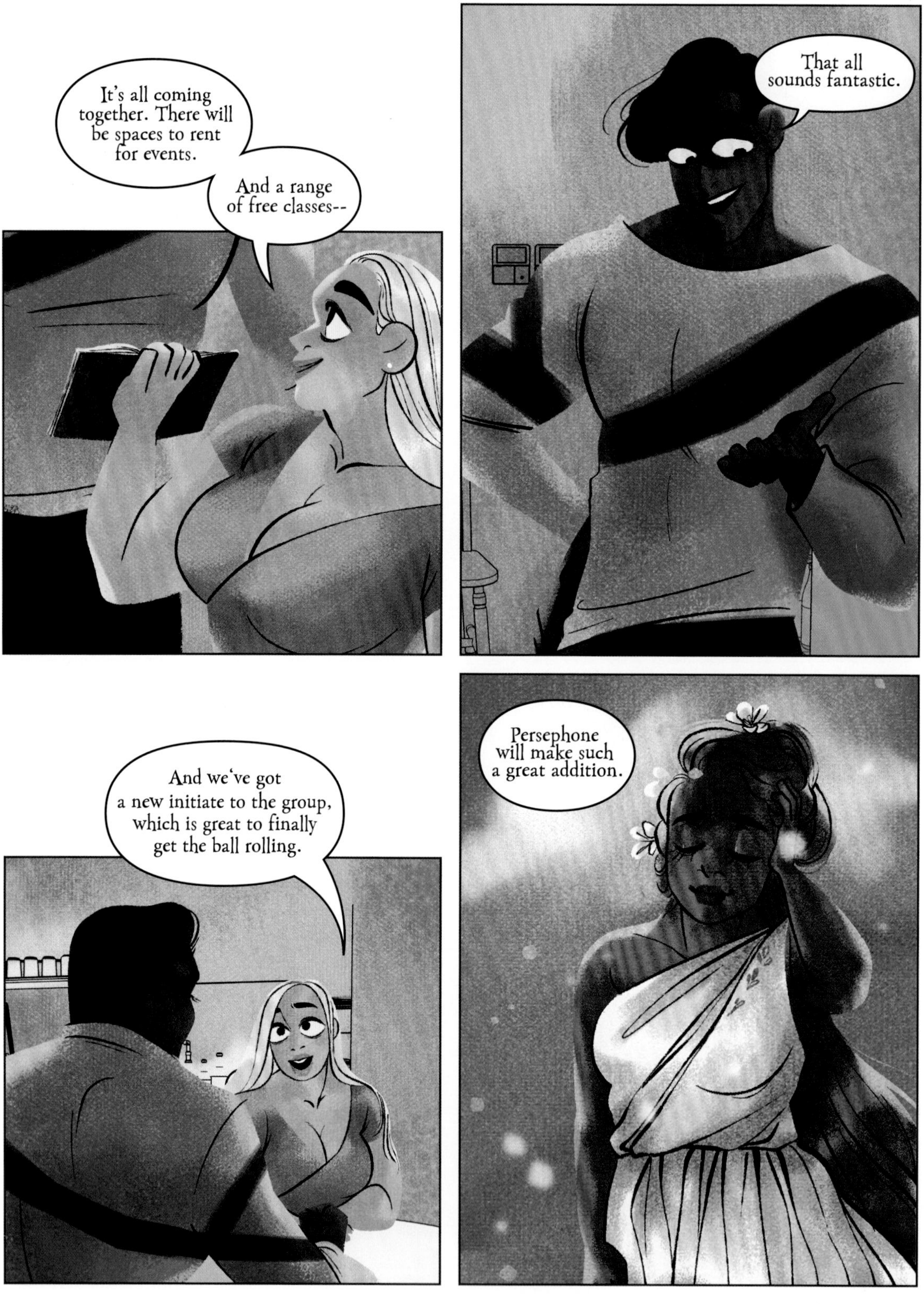
It's all coming together. There will be spaces to rent for events.
And a range of free classes--
That all sounds fantastic.
And we've got a new initiate to the group, which is great to finally get the ball rolling.
Persephone will make such a great addition.

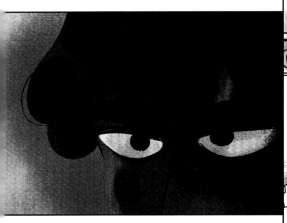

Persephone, you say?

Yeah.

...What is it?

Well, gosh, Hestia, I don't know if it's my place to say.

Well, now you have to tell me!

It's just that...

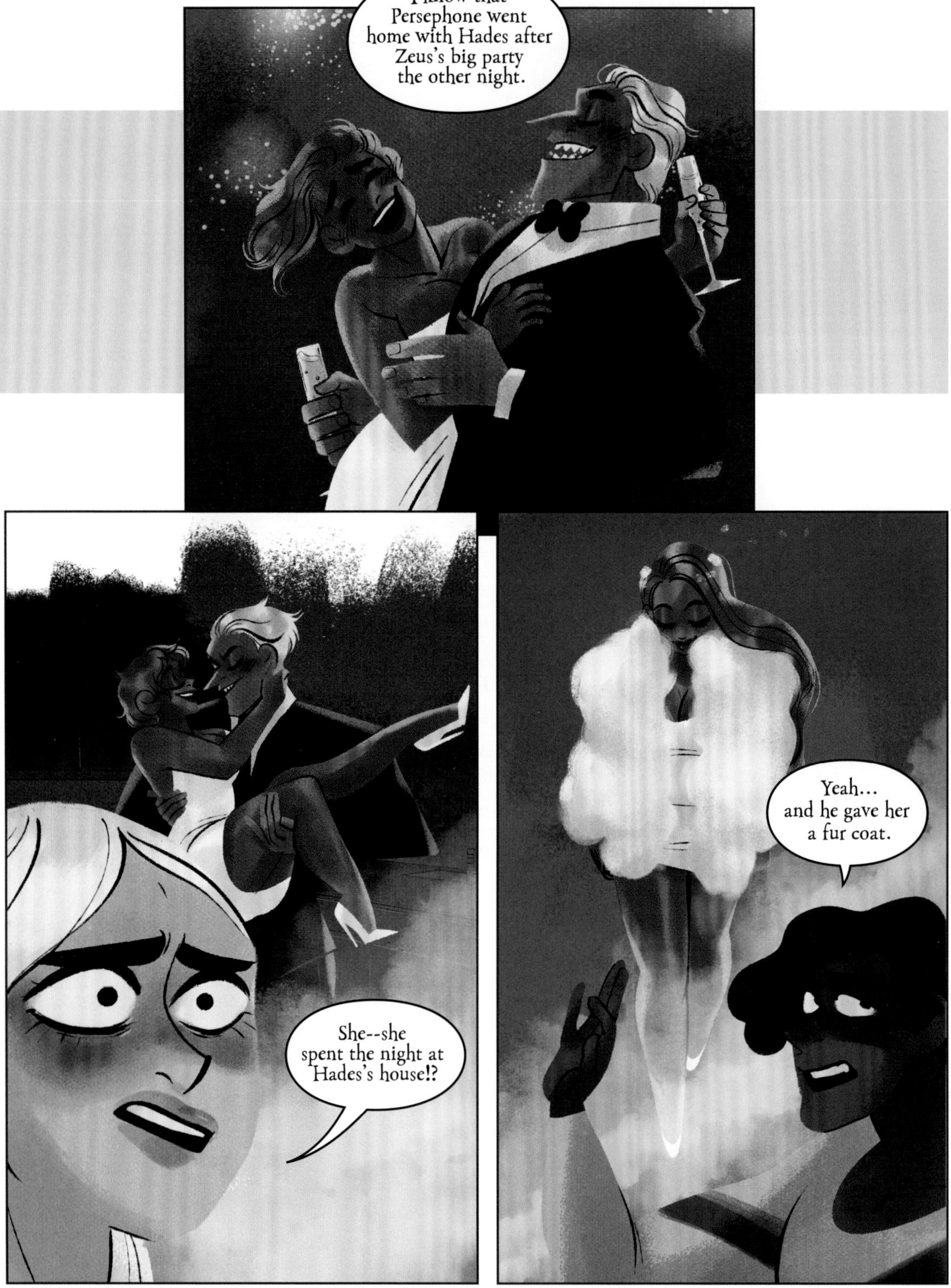
I know that Persephone went home with Hades after Zeus's big party the other night.
She--she spent the night at Hades's house!?
Yeah... and he gave her a fur coat.

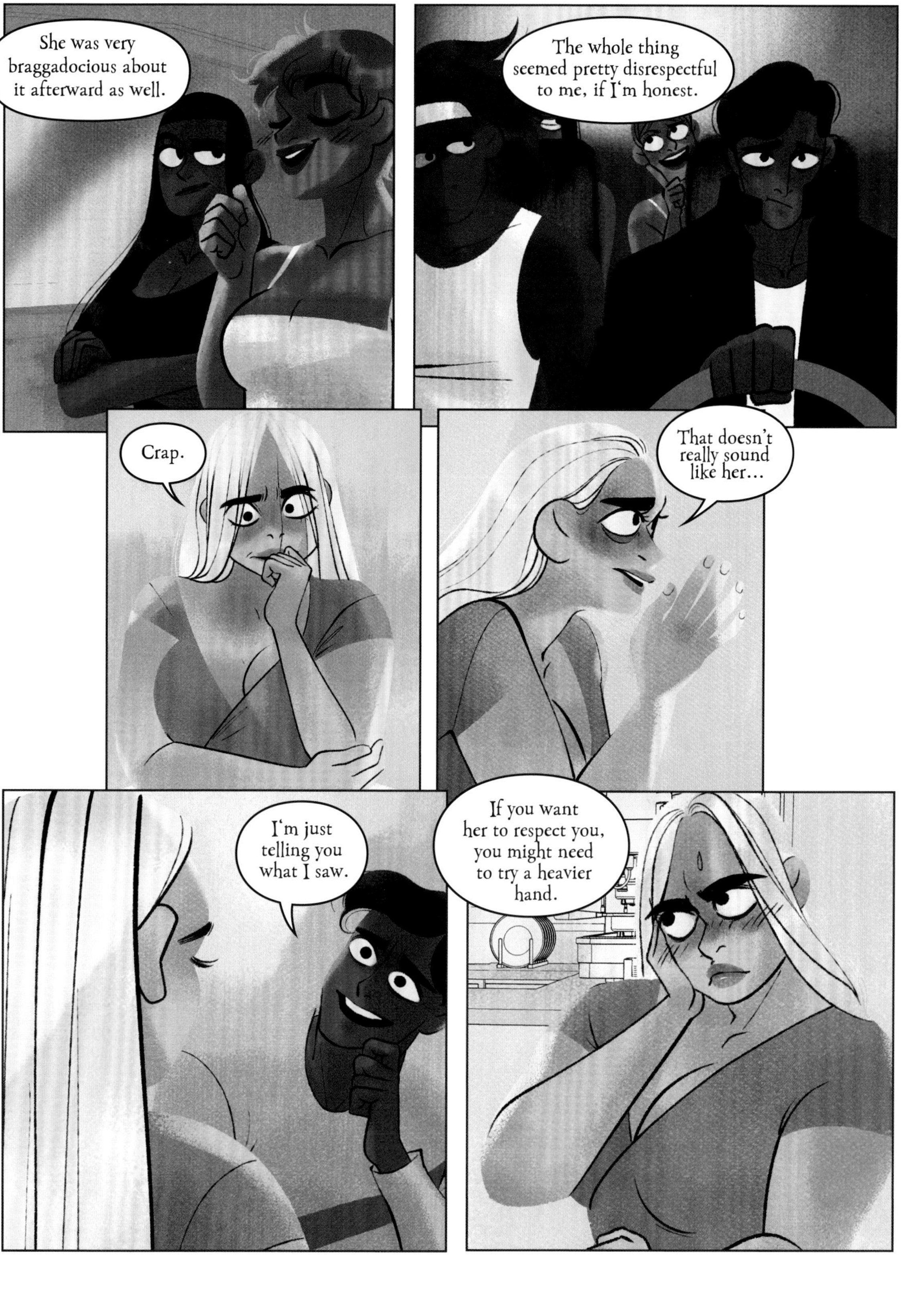
She was very braggadocious about it afterward as well.
The whole thing seemed pretty disrespectful to me, if I'm honest.
Crap.
That doesn't really sound like her...
I'm just telling you what I saw.
If you want her to respect you, you might need to try a heavier hand.

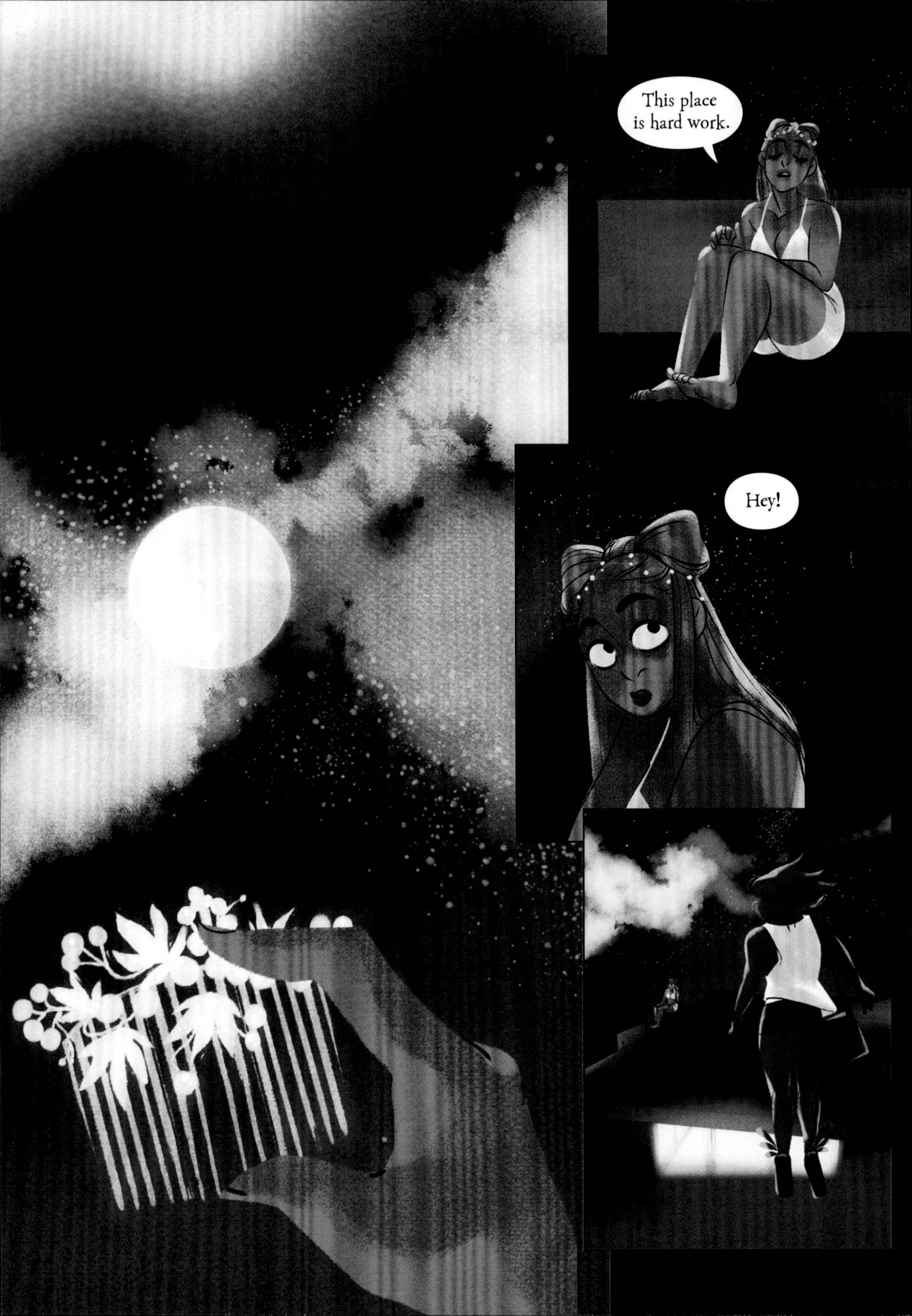
This place is hard work.
Hey!

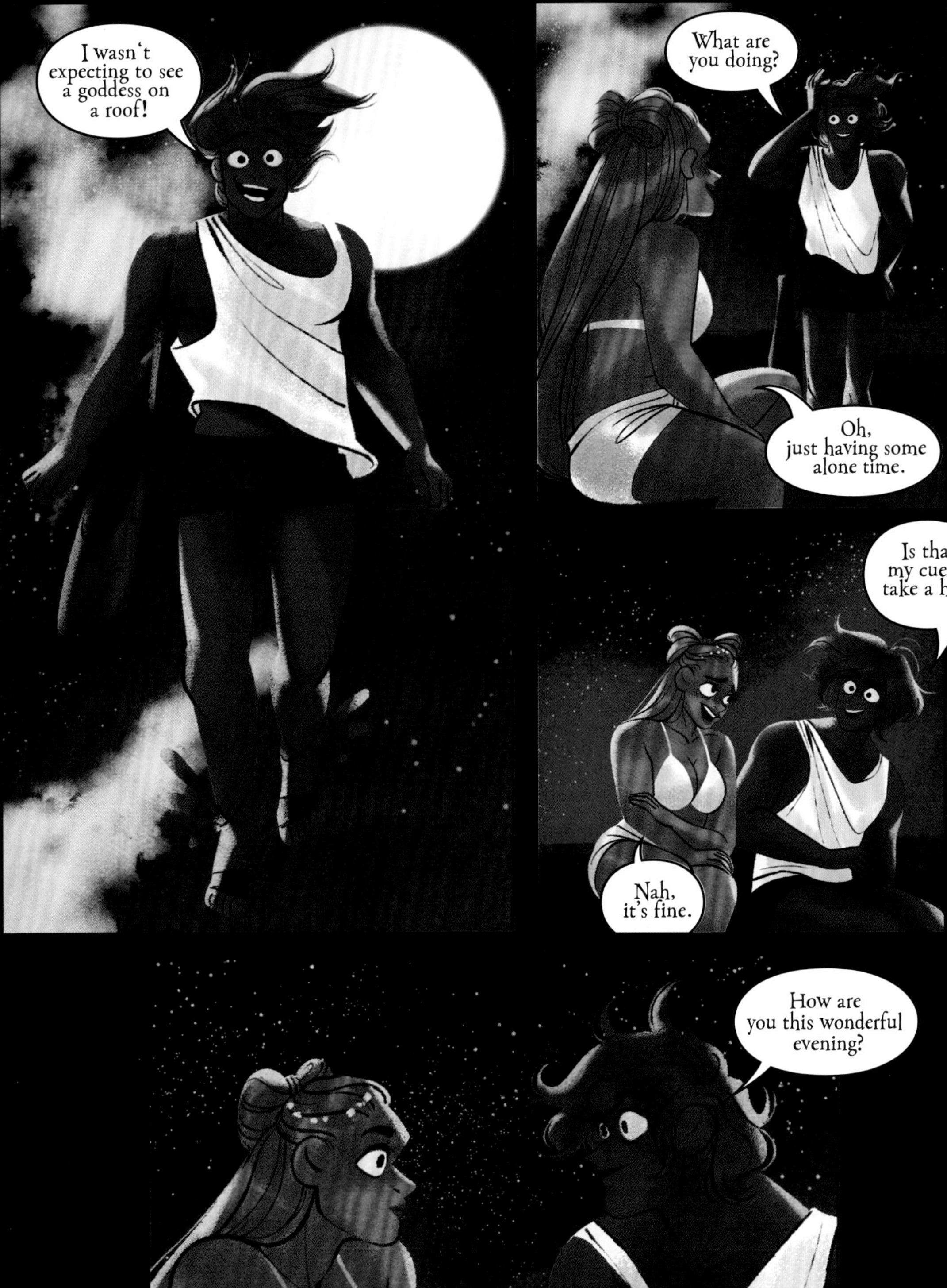
I wasn't expecting to see a goddess on a roof!
What are you doing?
Oh, just having some alone time.
Is that my cue to take a hike?
Nah, it's fine.
How are you this wonderful evening?

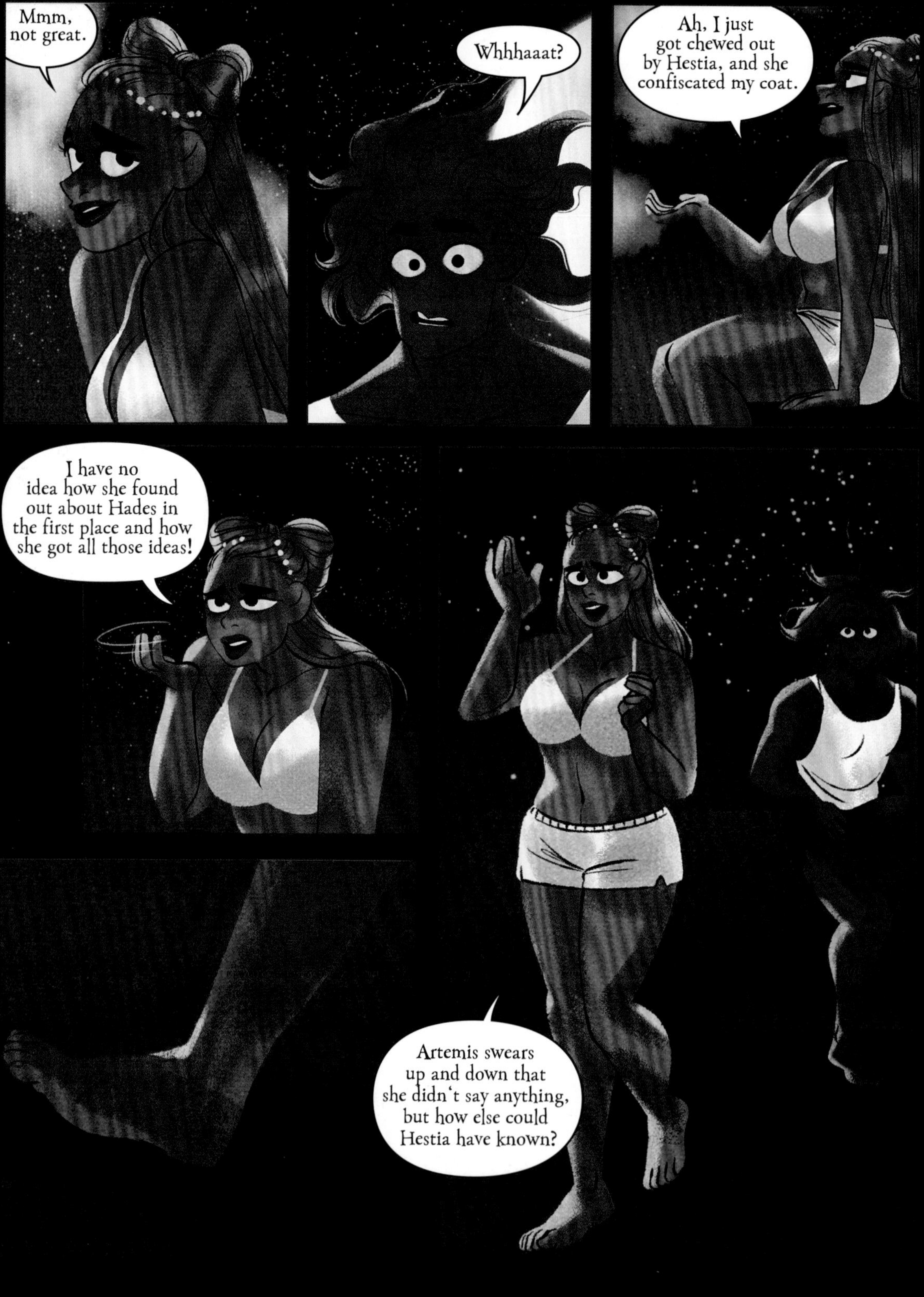
Mmm, not great.
Whhhaaat?
Ah, I just got chewed out by Hestia, and she confiscated my coat.
I have no idea how she found out about Hades in the first place and how she got all those ideas!
Artemis swears up and down that she didn't say anything, but how else could Hestia have known?

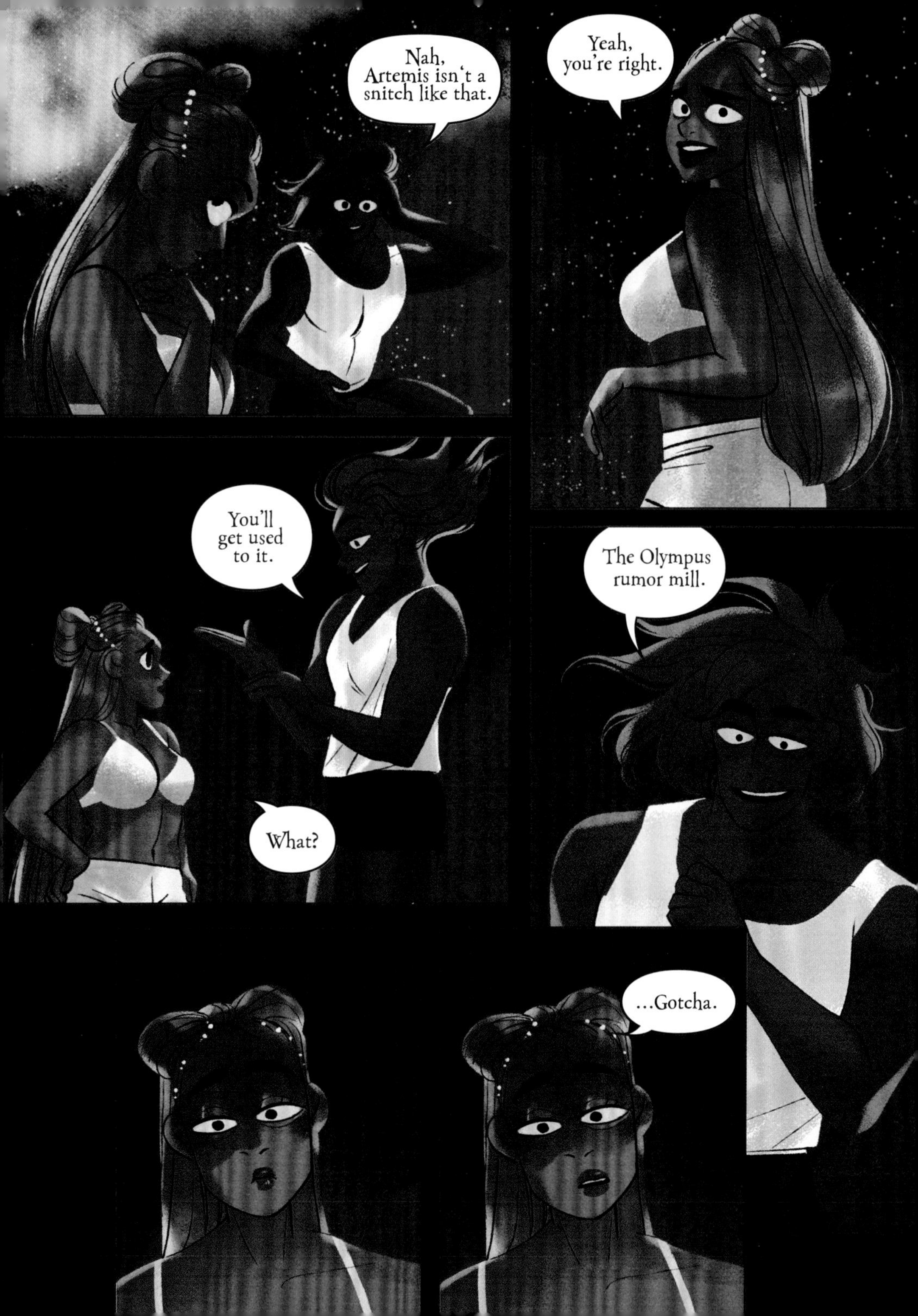
Nah, Artemis isn't a snitch like that.
Yeah, you're right.
You'll get used to it.
What?
The Olympus rumor mill.
...Gotcha.

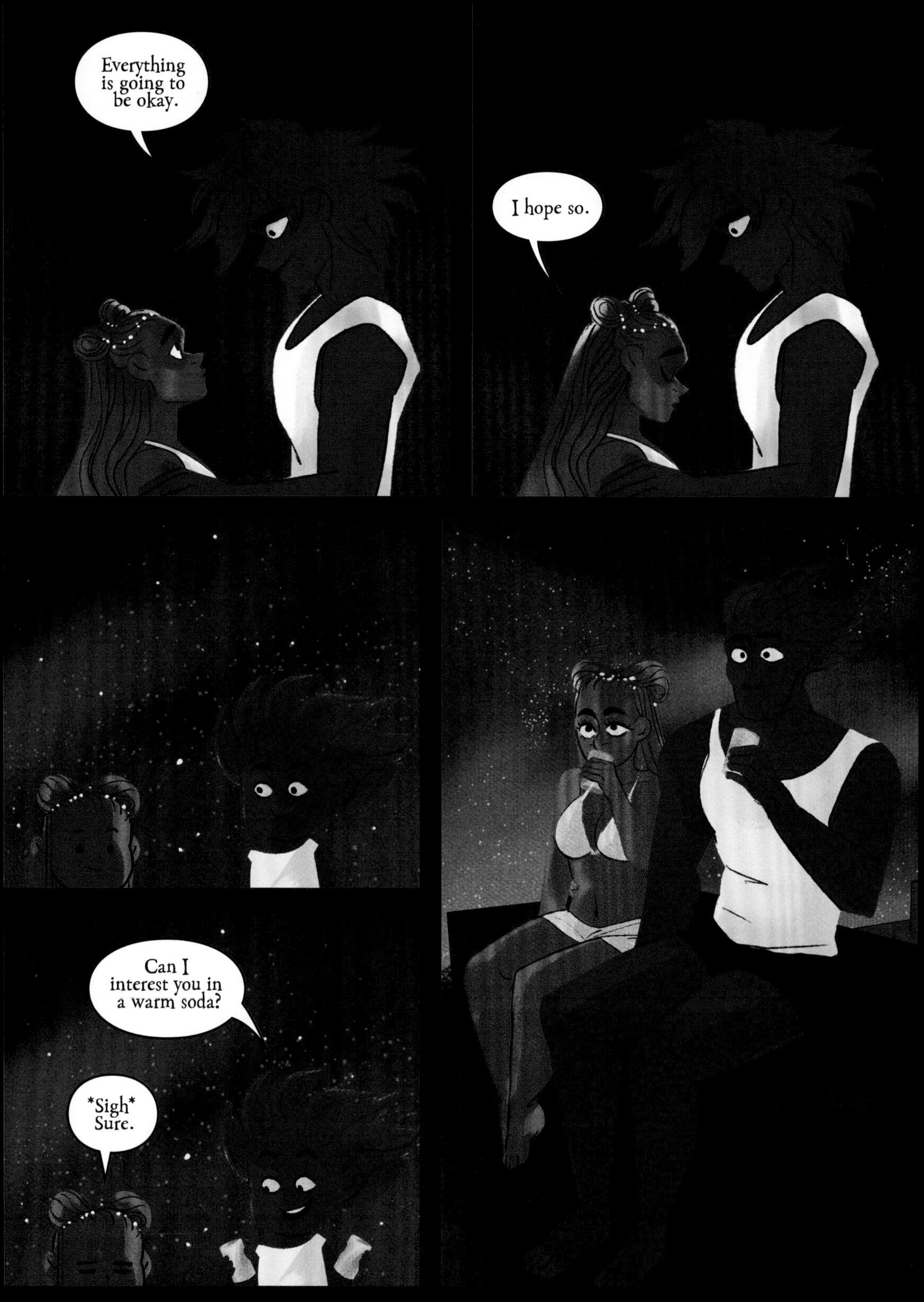
Everything is going to be okay.
I hope so.
Can I interest you in a warm soda?
Sigh Sure.

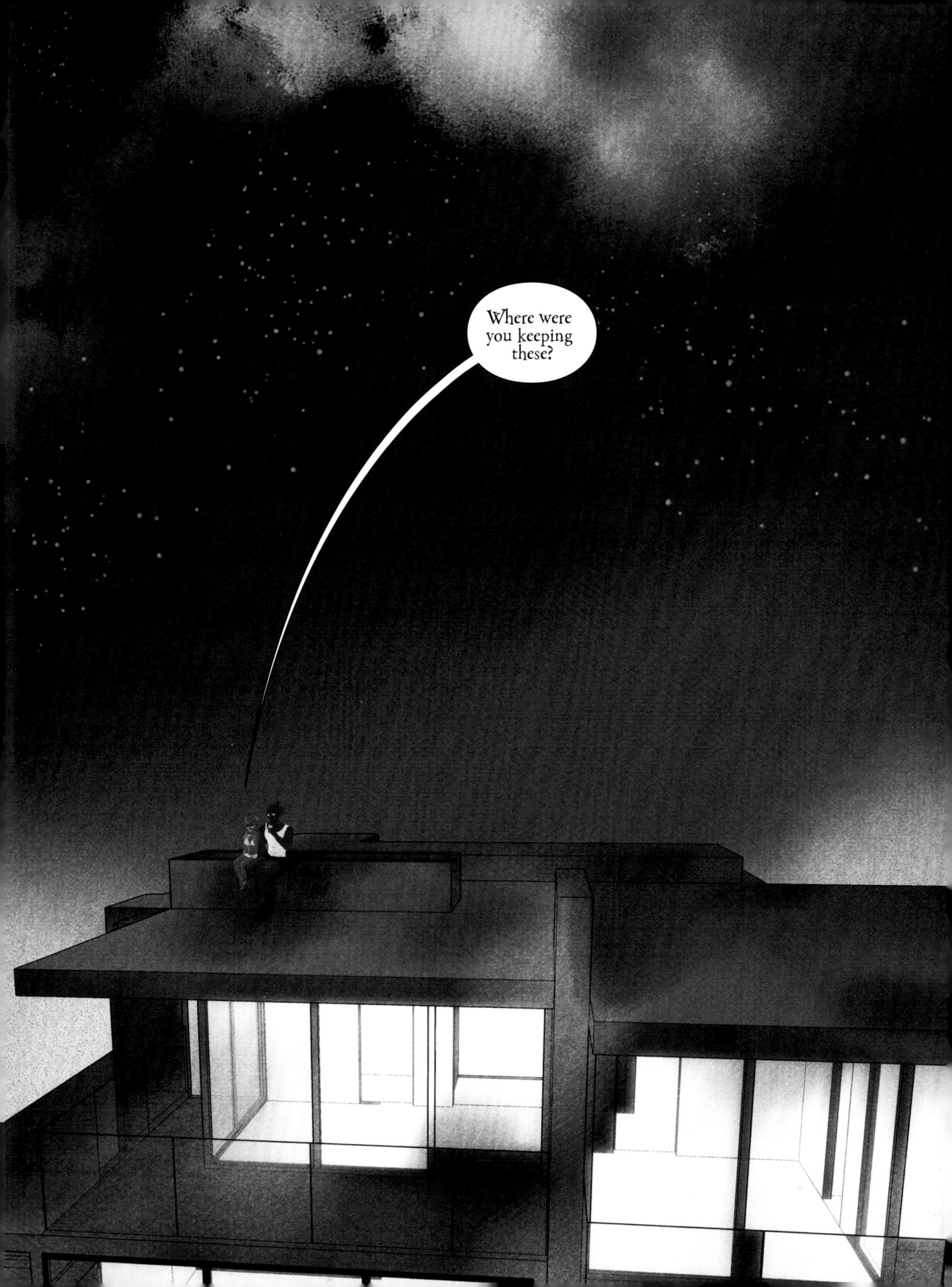
Where were you keeping these?

ABOUT THE AUTHOR

RACHEL SMYTHE is the creator of the Eisner-nominated *Lore Olympus*, published via WEBTOON.

Twitter: @used_bandaid

Instagram: @usedbandaid

Facebook.com/Usedbandaidillustration

LoreOlympusBooks.com

LORE
OLYMPUS

VOLUME ONE

RACHEL SMYTHE

NEW YORK

Published in the United States by Del Rey, an imprint of Random House,
a division of Penguin Random House LLC, New York.

DEL REY and the HOUSE colophon are registered trademarks of
Penguin Random House LLC.

Portions of this work originally appeared on webtoons.com.

LIBRARY OF CONGRESS CATALOGING-IN-PUBLICATION DATA
Names: Smythe, Rachel (Comics artist), author, artist.
Title: Lore Olympus / Rachel Smythe.
Description: First edition. | New York : Del Rey, 2021
Identifiers: LCCN 2021008087 | Hardcover ISBN 9780593160299 (v. 1) |
Trade paperback ISBN 9780593356074 (v. 1) |
Barnes & Noble edition ISBN 9780593359358 (v. 1) |
Subjects: LCSH: Mythology, Greek—Comic books, strips, etc. |
Graphic novels.
Classification: LCC PN6727.S54758 L67 2021 | DDC 741.5/973—dc23
LC record available at https://lccn.loc.gov/2021008087

Printed in China

randomhousebooks.com

6 8 9 7 5

Book design by Edwin Vazquez

To my family, friends, and fans.

CONTENT WARNING
FROM RACHEL SMYTHE

Lore Olympus regularly deals with themes of physical and mental abuse, sexual trauma, and toxic relationships.

Some of the interactions in this volume may be distressing for some readers. Please exercise discretion, and seek out the support of others if you require it.

"WHILE YOU ARE HERE, YOU SHALL RULE ALL THAT LIVES AND MOVES AND SHALL HAVE THE GREATEST RIGHTS AMONG THE DEATHLESS GODS : THOSE WHO DEFRAUD YOU AND DO NOT APPEASE YOUR POWER WITH OFFERINGS, REVERENTLY PERFORMING RITES AND PAYING FIT GIFTS, SHALL BE PUNISHED FOR EVERMORE."

— HADES TO PERSEPHONE

HESIOD, THE HOMERIC HYMNS, AND HOMERICA
BY HESIOD; HOMER; EVELYN-WHITE, HUGH G.
(HUGH GERARD), D. 1924

EPISODE 01: STAG, YOU'RE IT

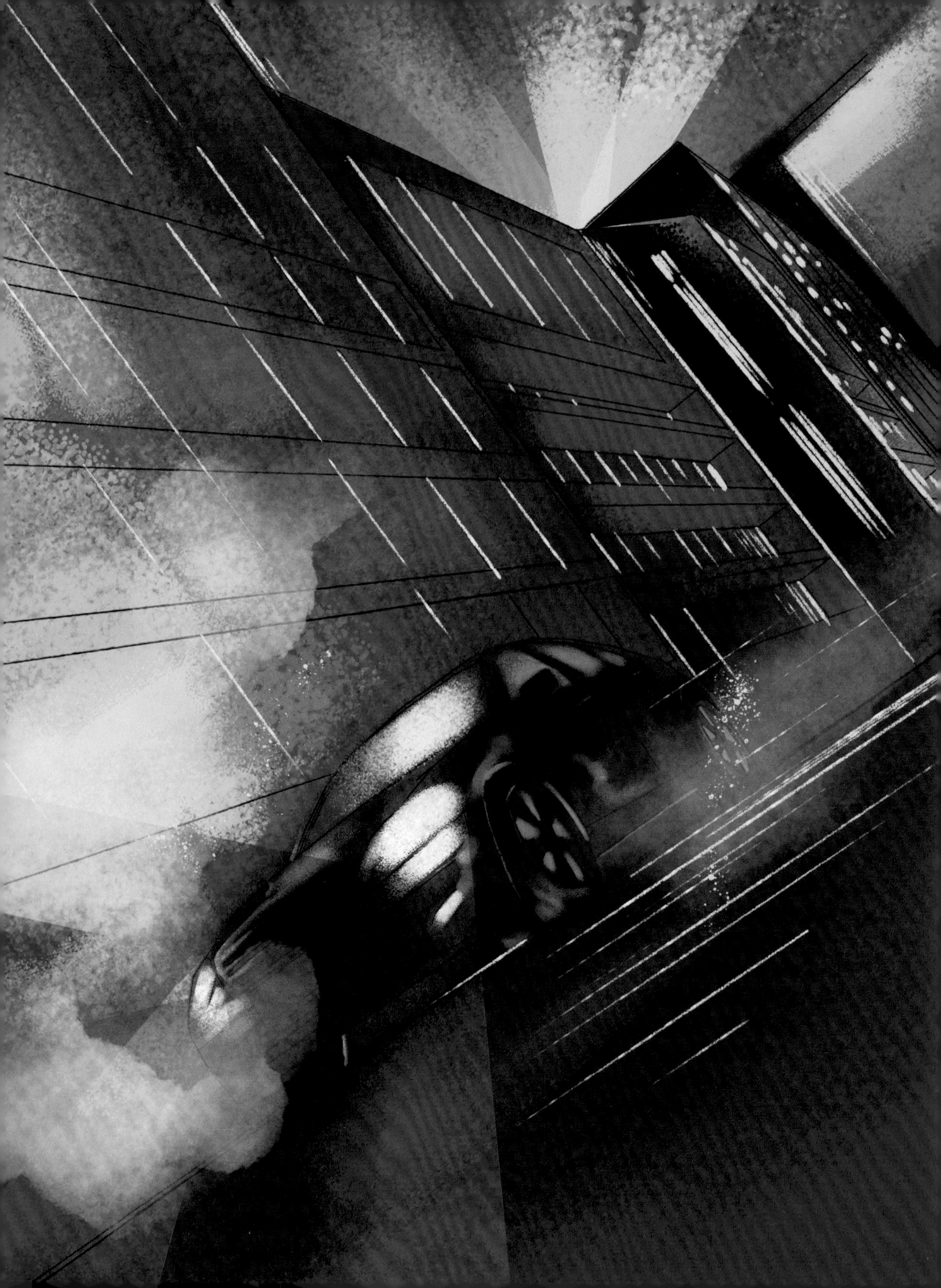

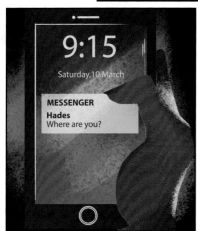

9:15

Saturday, 10 March

MESSENGER
Hades
Where are you?

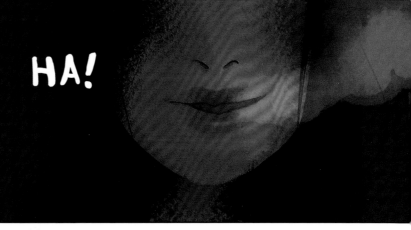

HA!

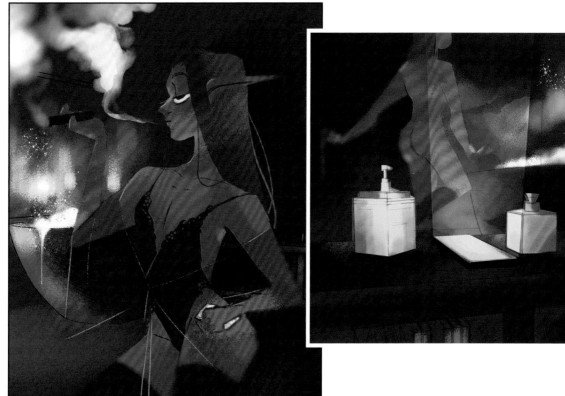

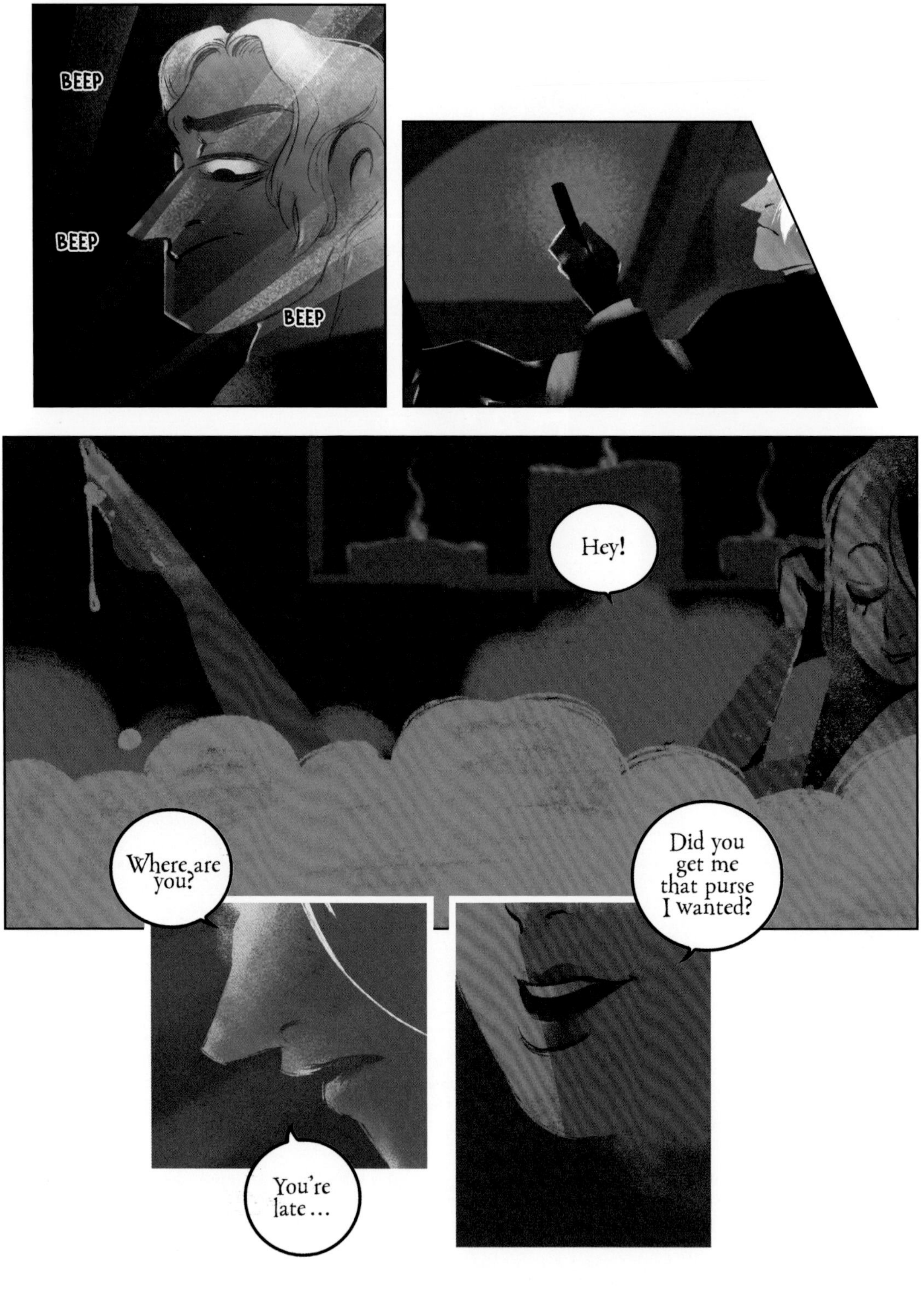
BEEP
BEEP
BEEP
Hey!
Where are you?
Did you get me that purse I wanted?
You're late...

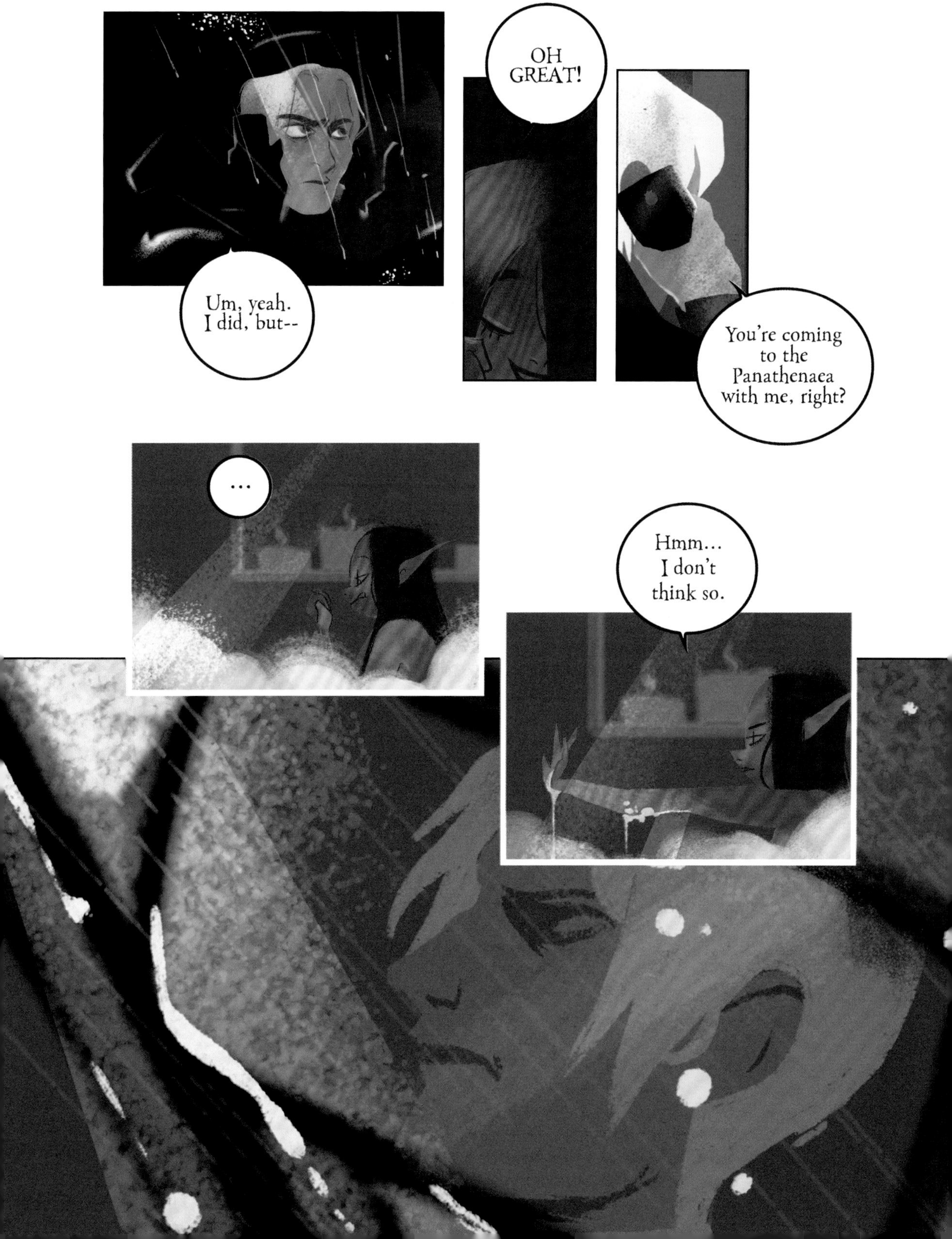
Um, yeah. I did, but--
OH GREAT!
You're coming to the Panathenaea with me, right?
...
Hmm... I don't think so.

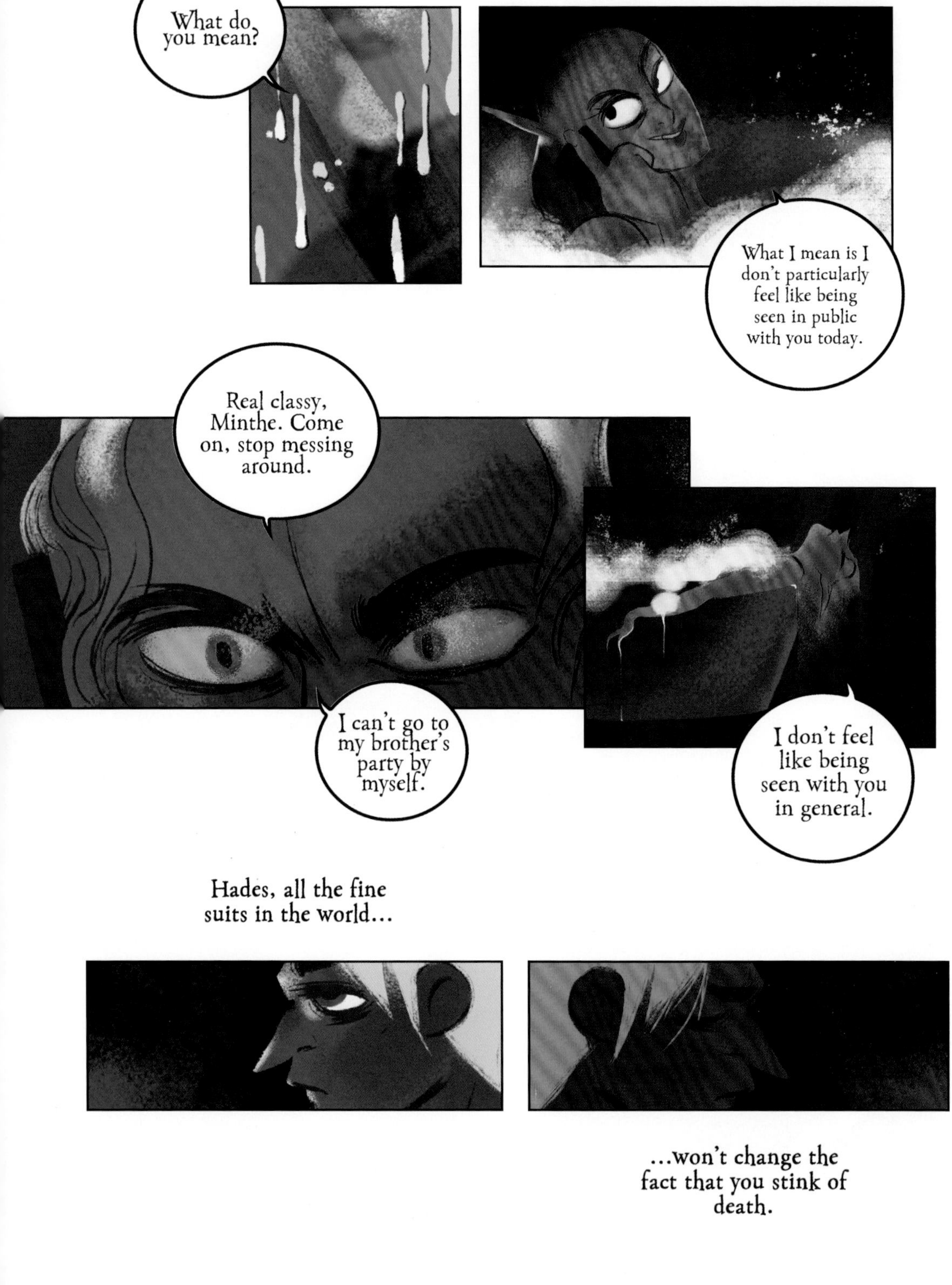
What do you mean?
What I mean is I don't particularly feel like being seen in public with you today.
Real classy, Minthe. Come on, stop messing around.
I can't go to my brother's party by myself.
I don't feel like being seen with you in general.
Hades, all the fine suits in the world...
...won't change the fact that you stink of death.

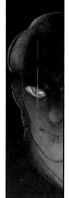
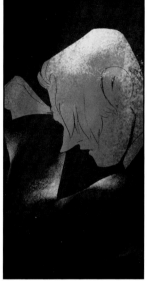

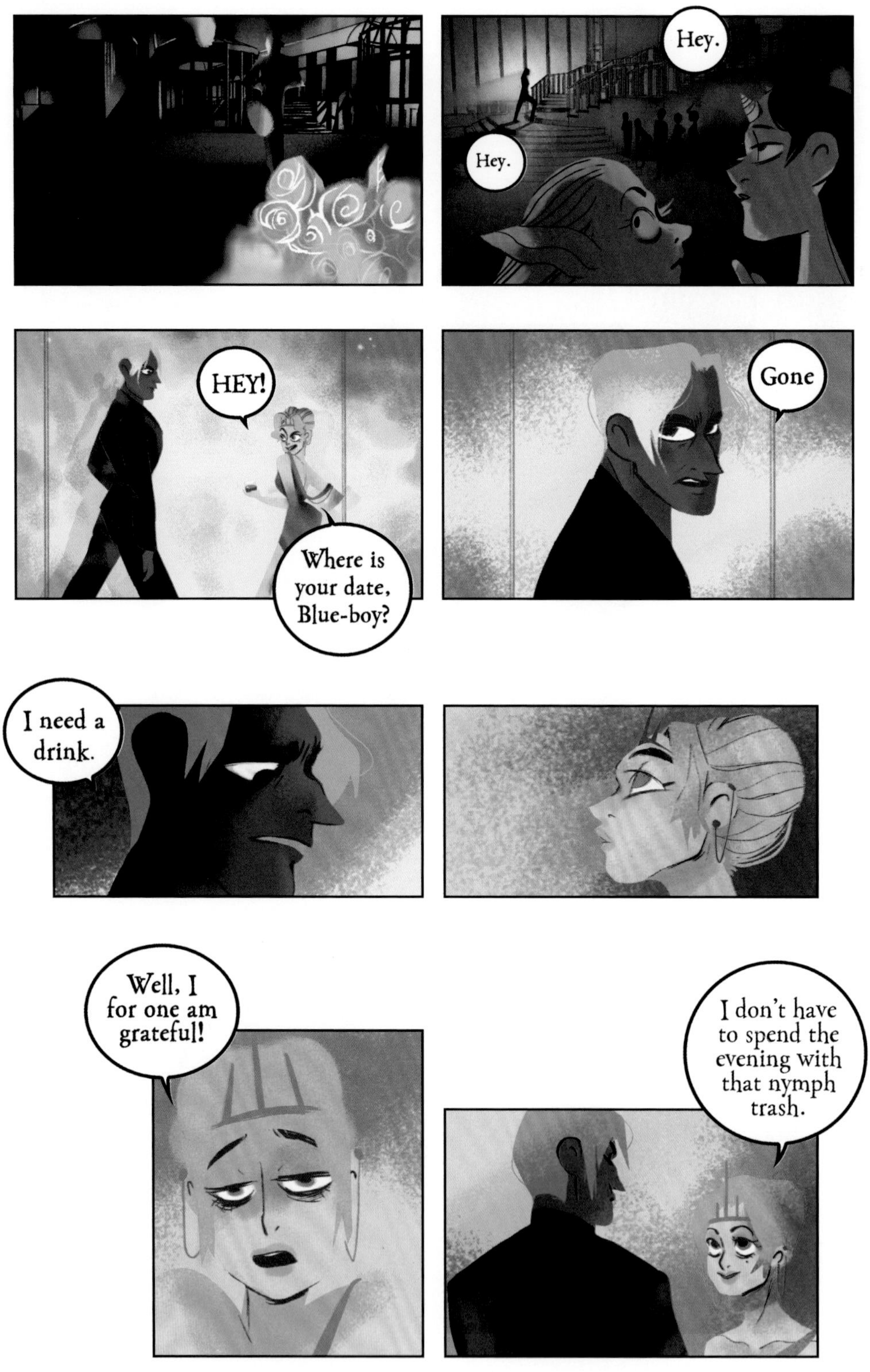
Hey.
Hey.
HEY!
Where is your date, Blue-boy?
Gone
I need a drink.
Well, I for one am grateful!
I don't have to spend the evening with that nymph trash.

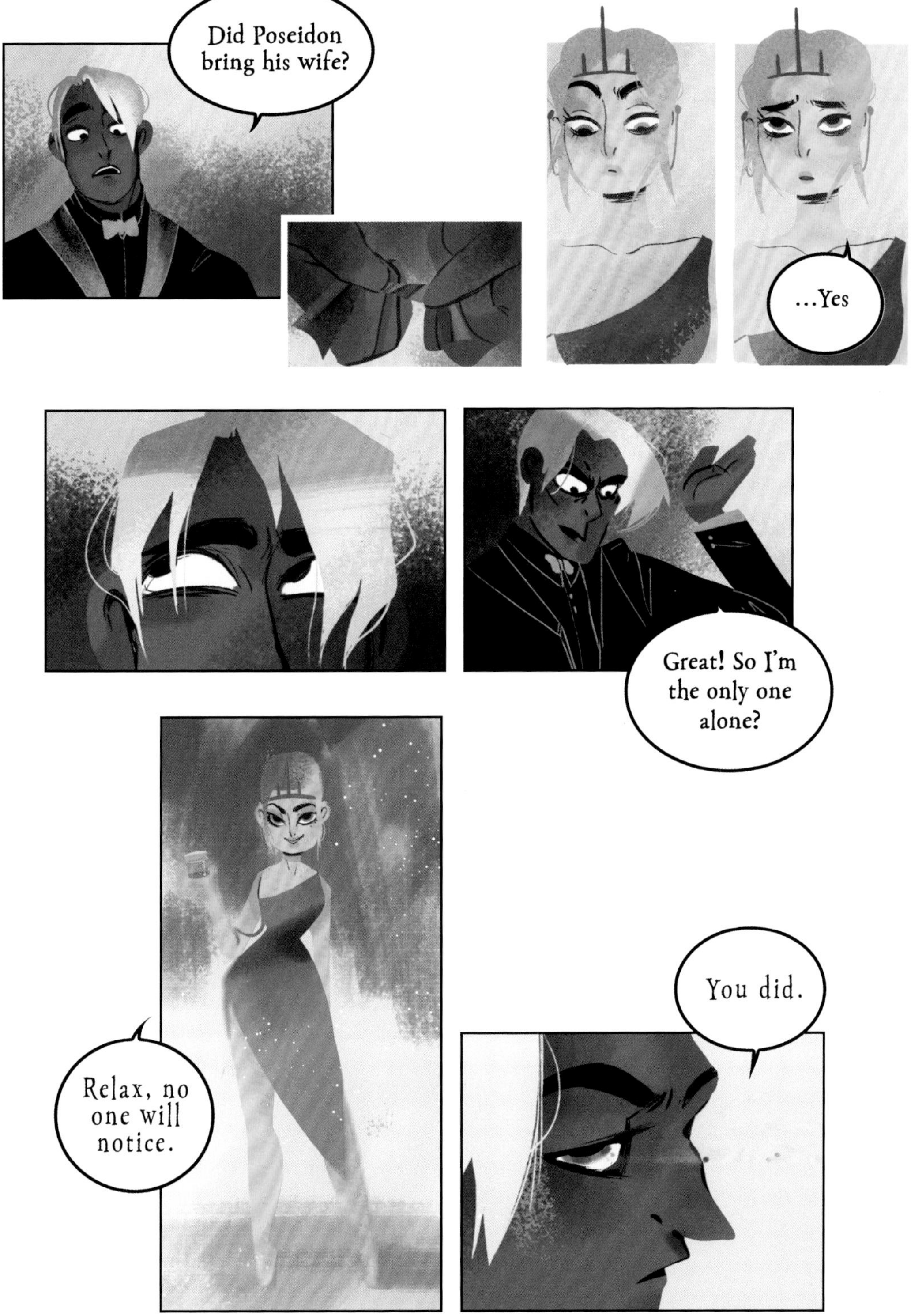
Did Poseidon bring his wife?
...Yes
Great! So I'm the only one alone?
Relax, no one will notice.
You did.

HERA!
Hera, I've been looking for you everywhere!
You look so beautiful tonight!
Oh stop, you're embarrassing me!

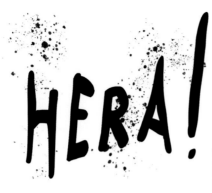

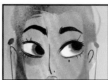

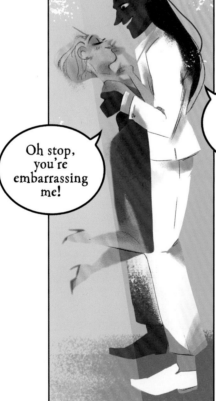

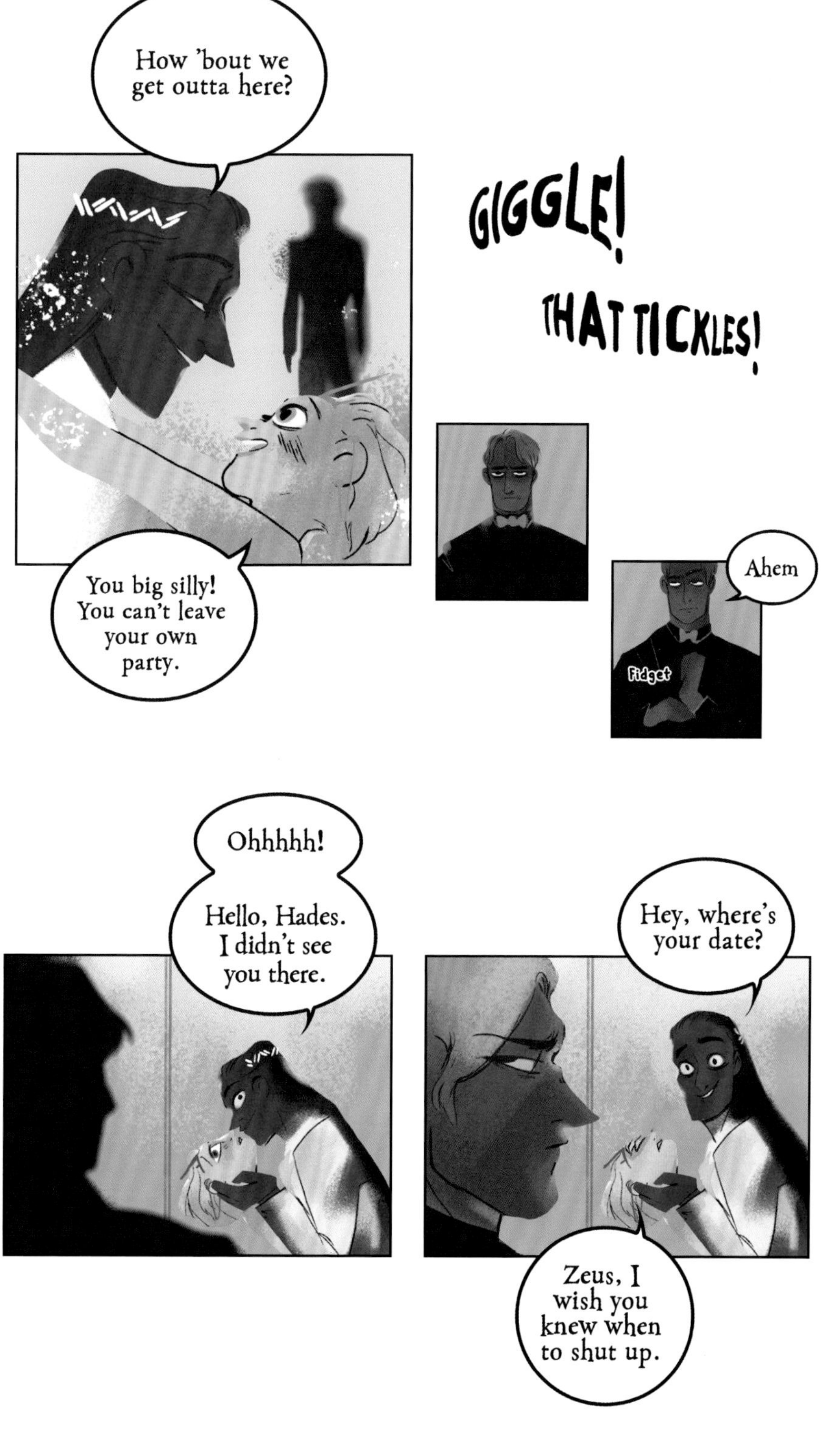
How 'bout we get outta here?
You big silly! You can't leave your own party.
GIGGLE!
THAT TICKLES!
Ahem
Fidget
Ohhhhh!
Hello, Hades. I didn't see you there.
Hey, where's your date?
Zeus, I wish you knew when to shut up.

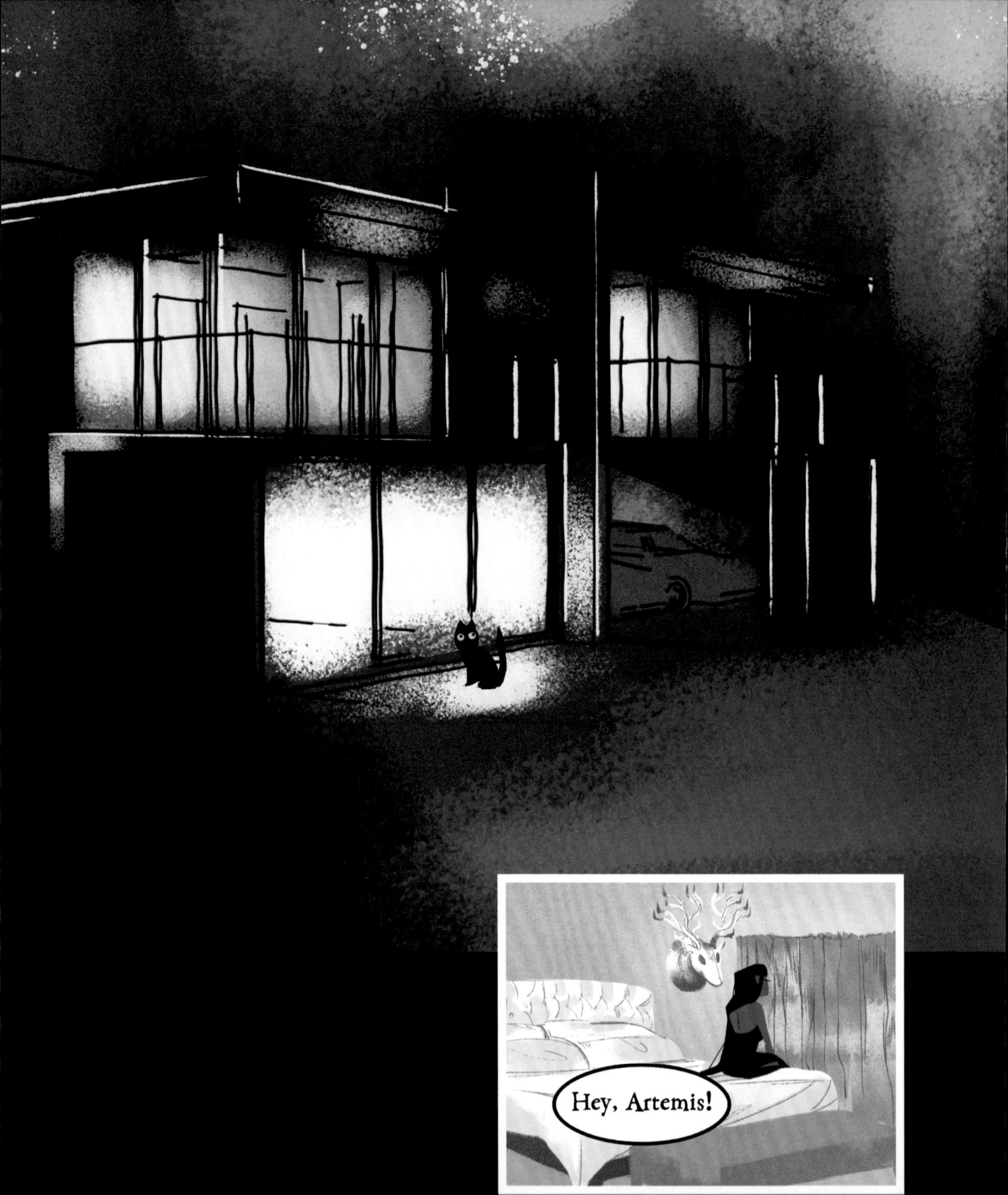
Hey, Artemis!

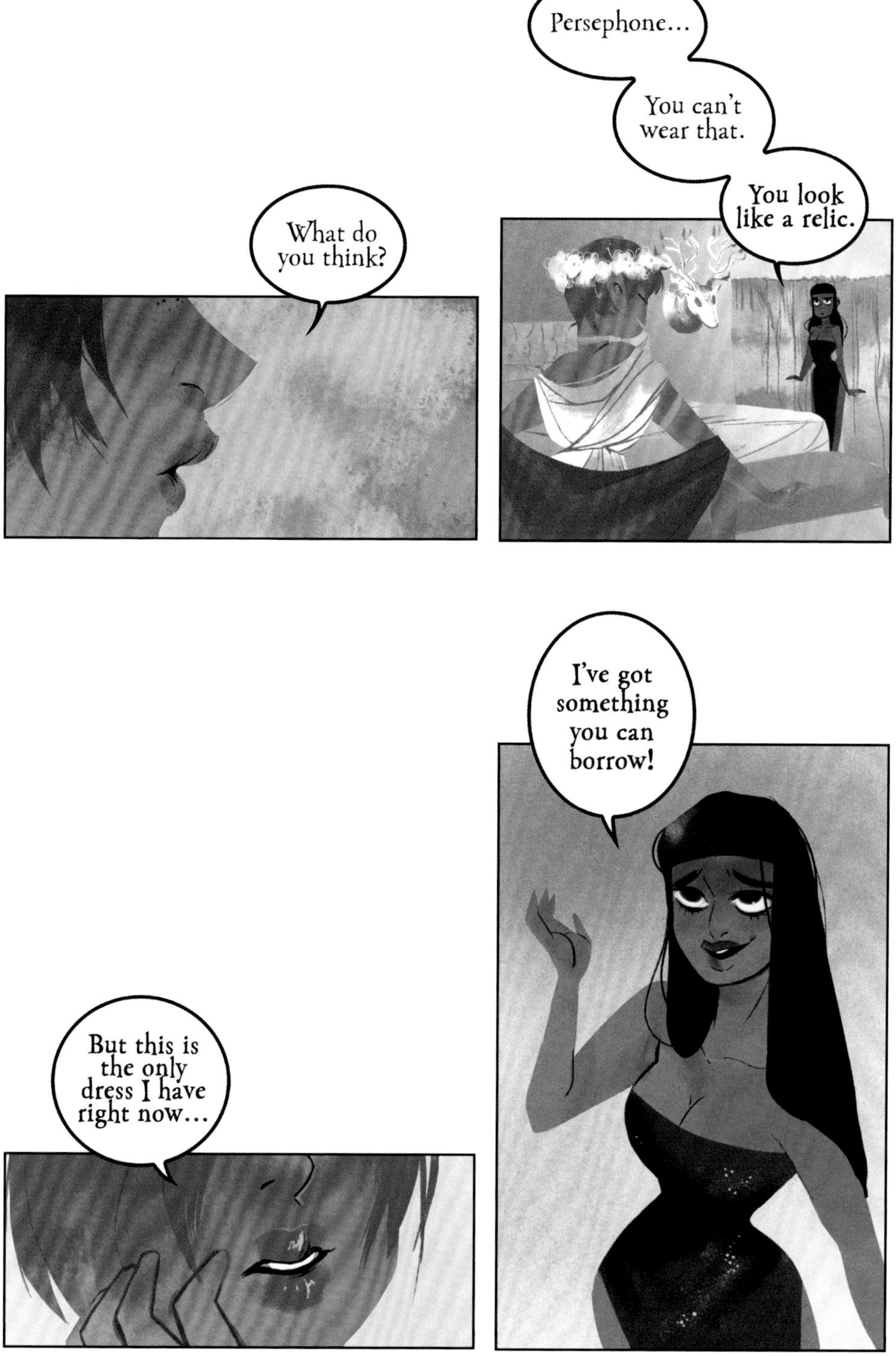
What do you think?
Persephone...
You can't wear that.
You look like a relic.
But this is the only dress I have right now...
I've got something you can borrow!

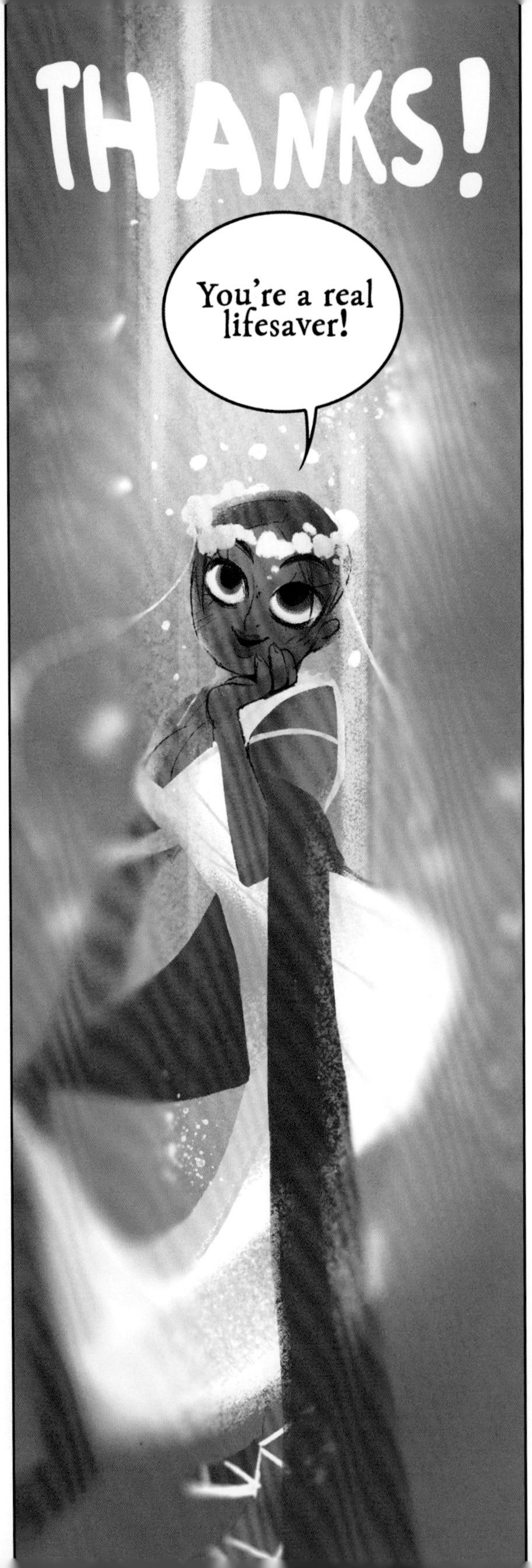
THANKS!
You're a real lifesaver!

EPISODE 02: WHO IS SHE? (PART I)

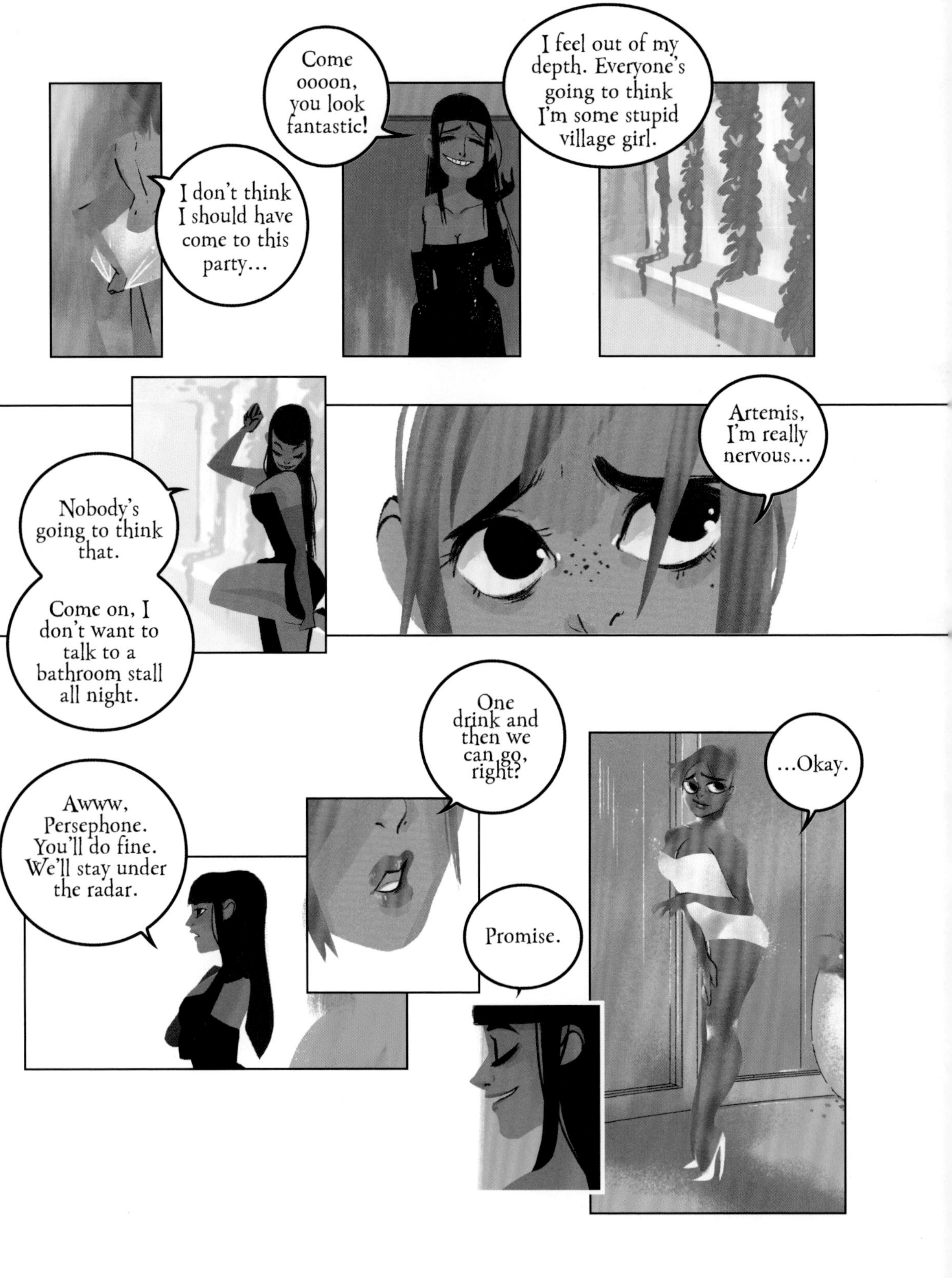

I don't think I should have come to this party...
Come oooon, you look fantastic!
I feel out of my depth. Everyone's going to think I'm some stupid village girl.
Artemis, I'm really nervous...
Nobody's going to think that.
Come on, I don't want to talk to a bathroom stall all night.
Awww, Persephone. You'll do fine. We'll stay under the radar.
One drink and then we can go, right?
Promise.
...Okay.

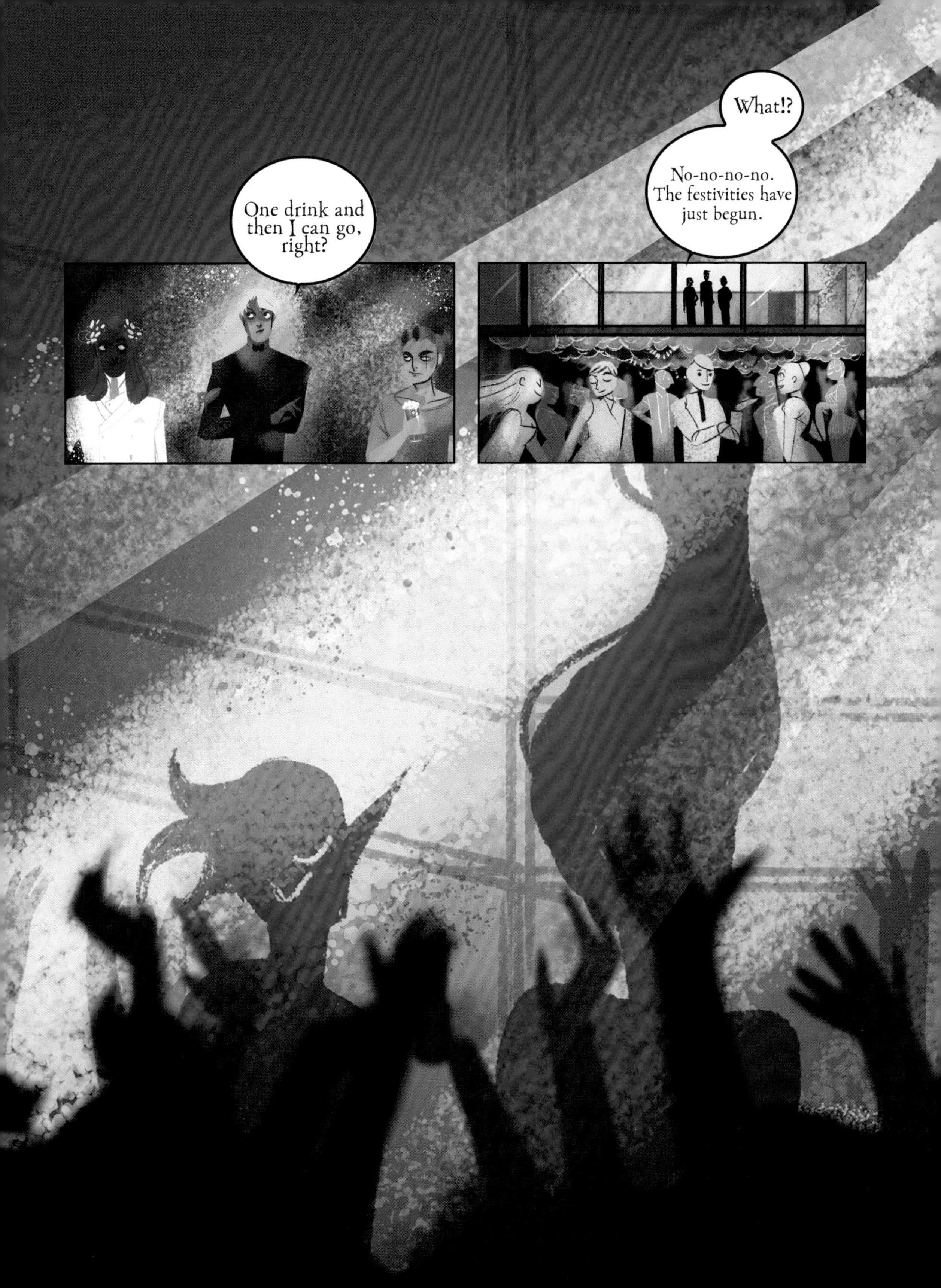
One drink and then I can go, right?
What!?
No-no-no-no. The festivities have just begun.

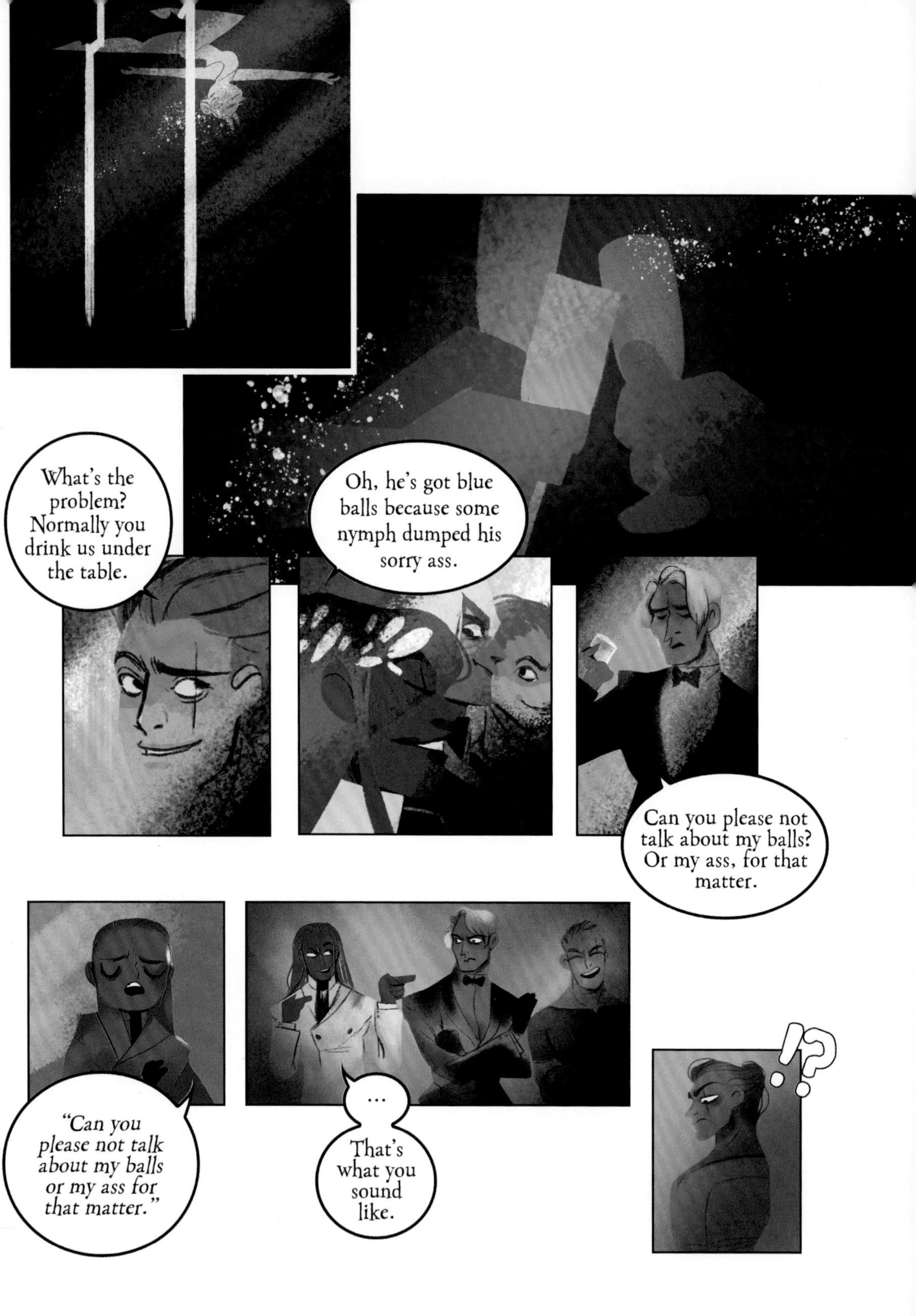

What's the problem? Normally you drink us under the table.
Oh, he's got blue balls because some nymph dumped his sorry ass.
Can you please not talk about my balls? Or my ass, for that matter.
"Can you please not talk about my balls or my ass for that matter."
...
That's what you sound like.
!?

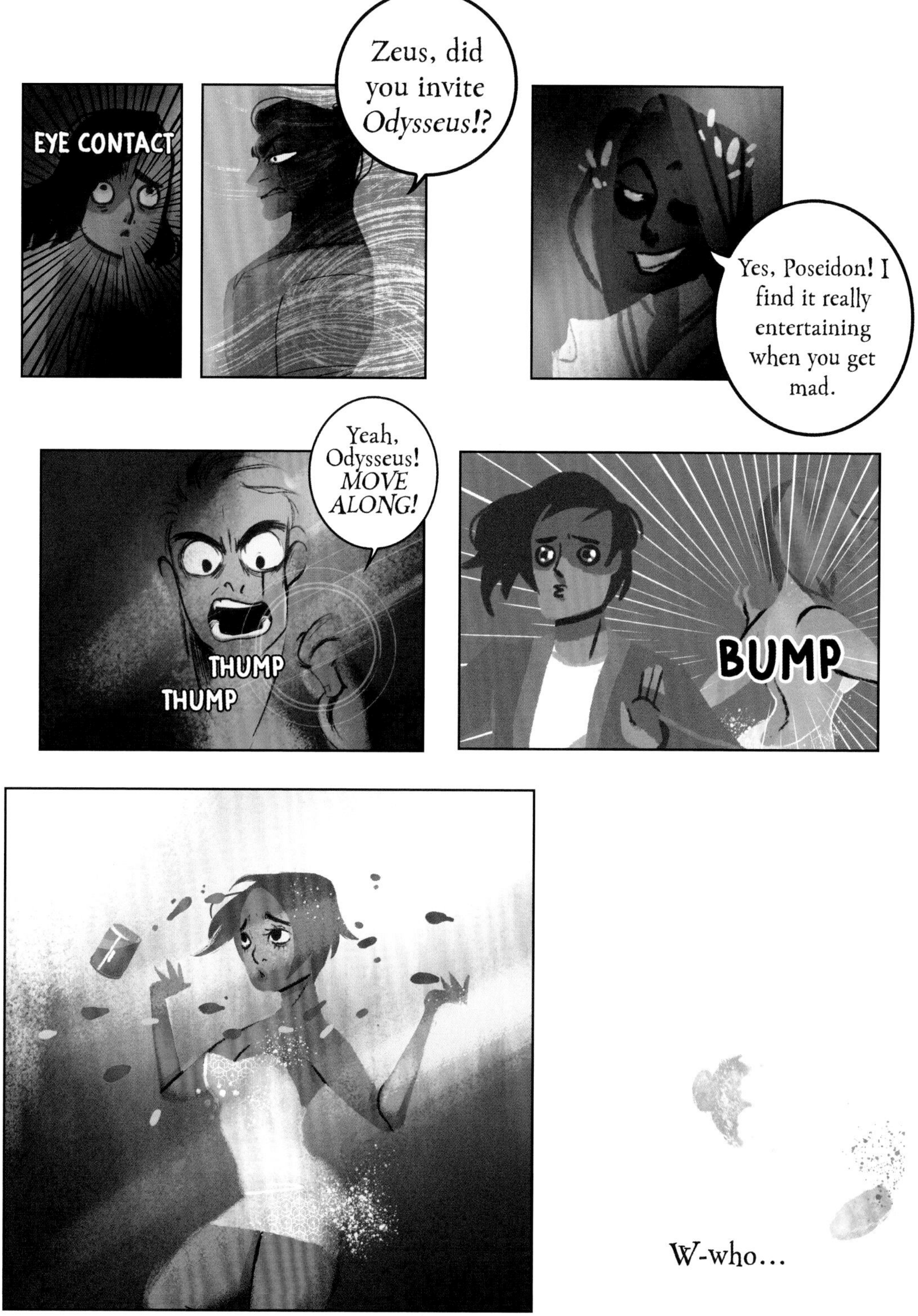
EYE CONTACT
Zeus, did you invite Odysseus!?
Yes, Poseidon! I find it really entertaining when you get mad.
Yeah, Odysseus! MOVE ALONG!
THUMP
THUMP
BUMP
W-who...

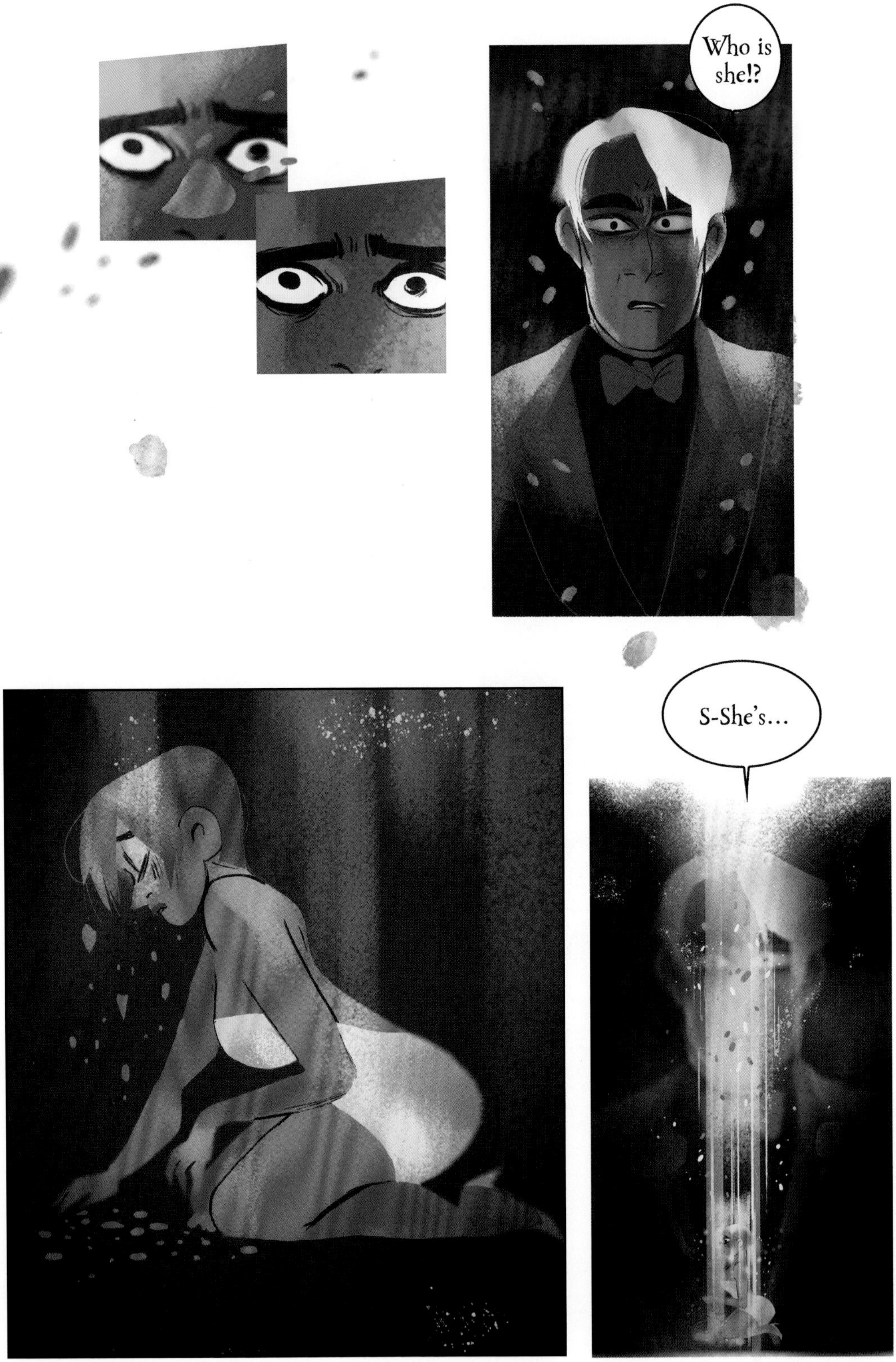
Who is she!?
S-She's...

She's
beautiful.

EPISODE 03: WHO IS SHE? (PART 2)

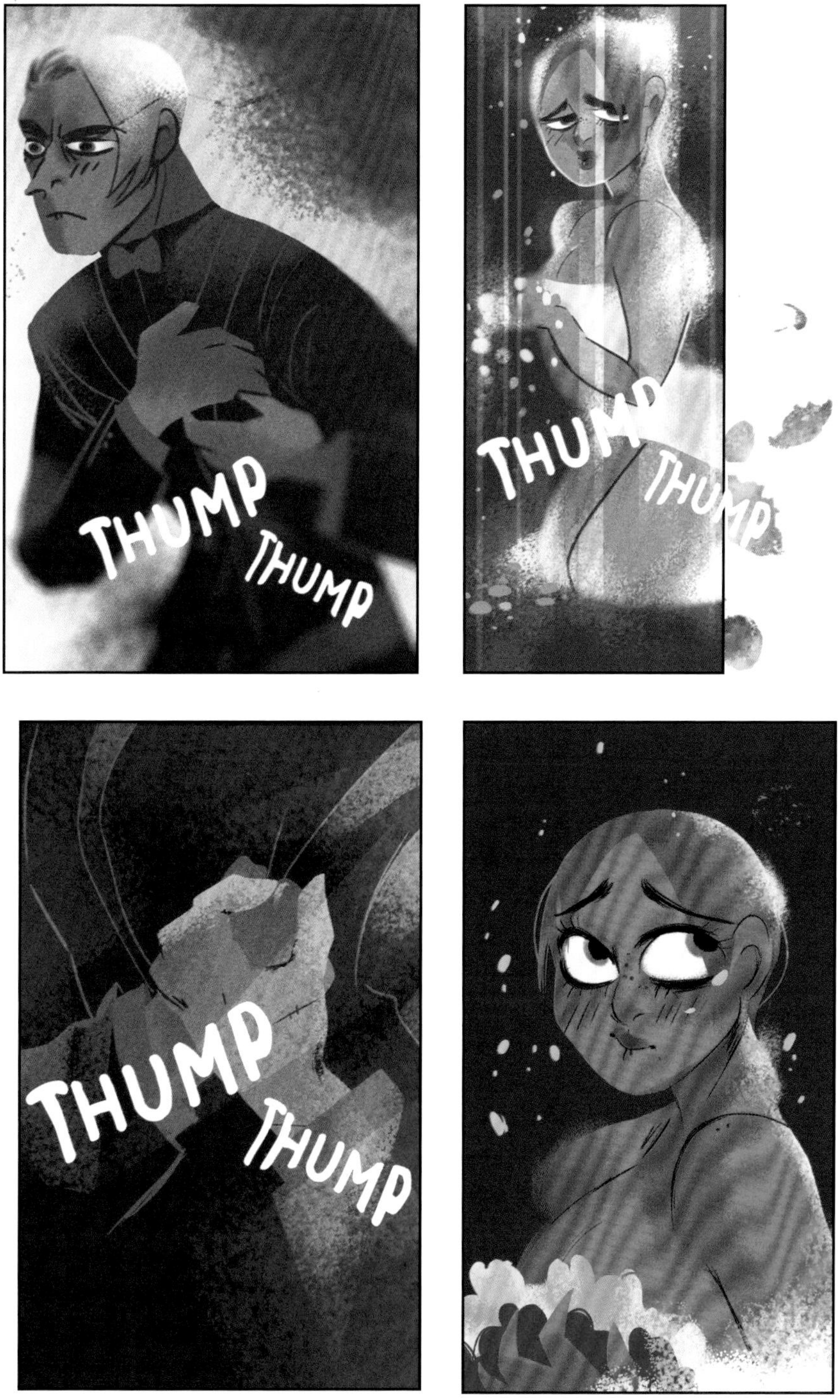
THUMP
THUMP
THUMP
THUMP
THUMP
THUMP
THUMP
THUMP

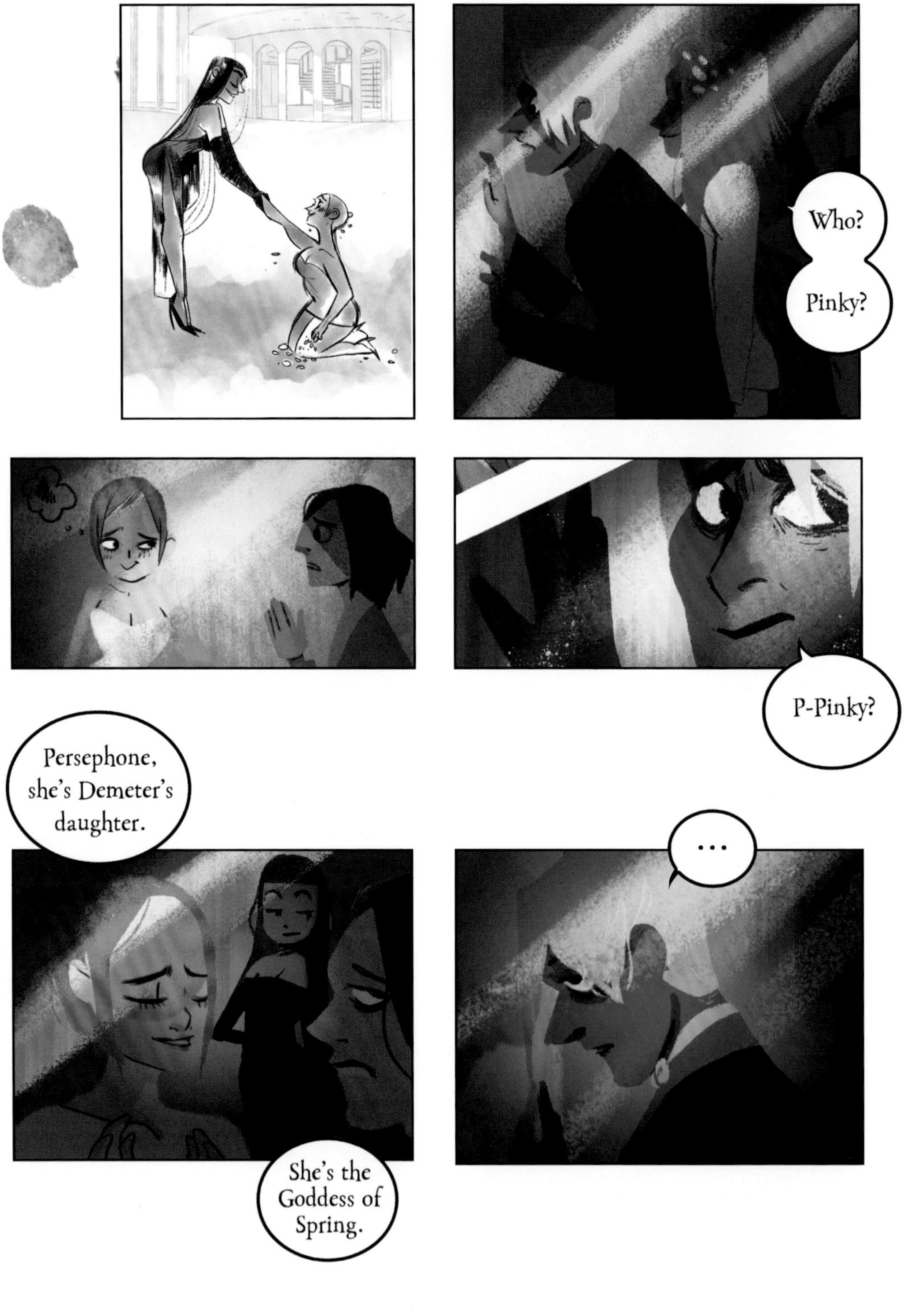
Who?
Pinky?
P-Pinky?
Persephone, she's Demeter's daughter.
...
She's the Goddess of Spring.

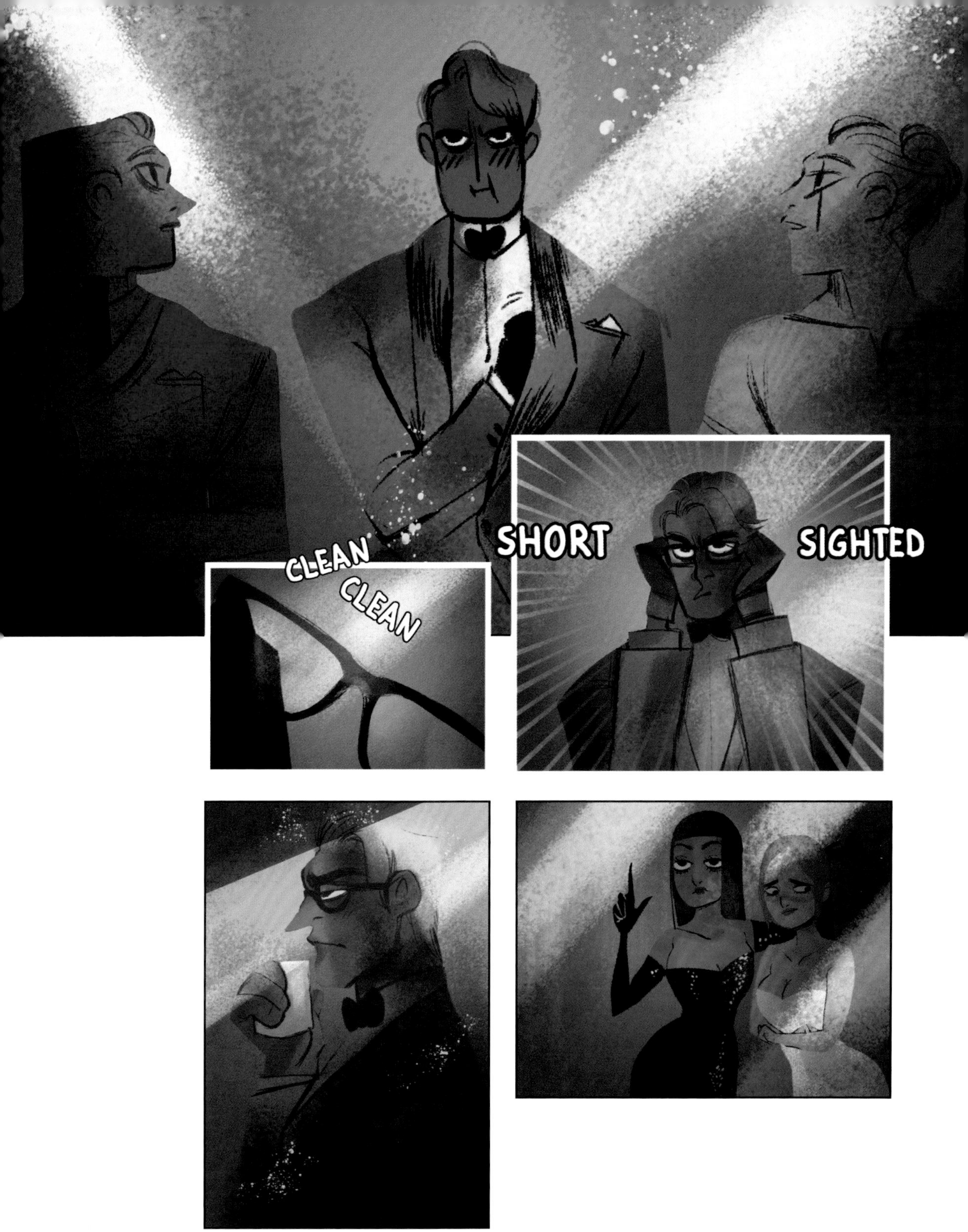
CLEAN
CLEAN
SHORT
SIGHTED

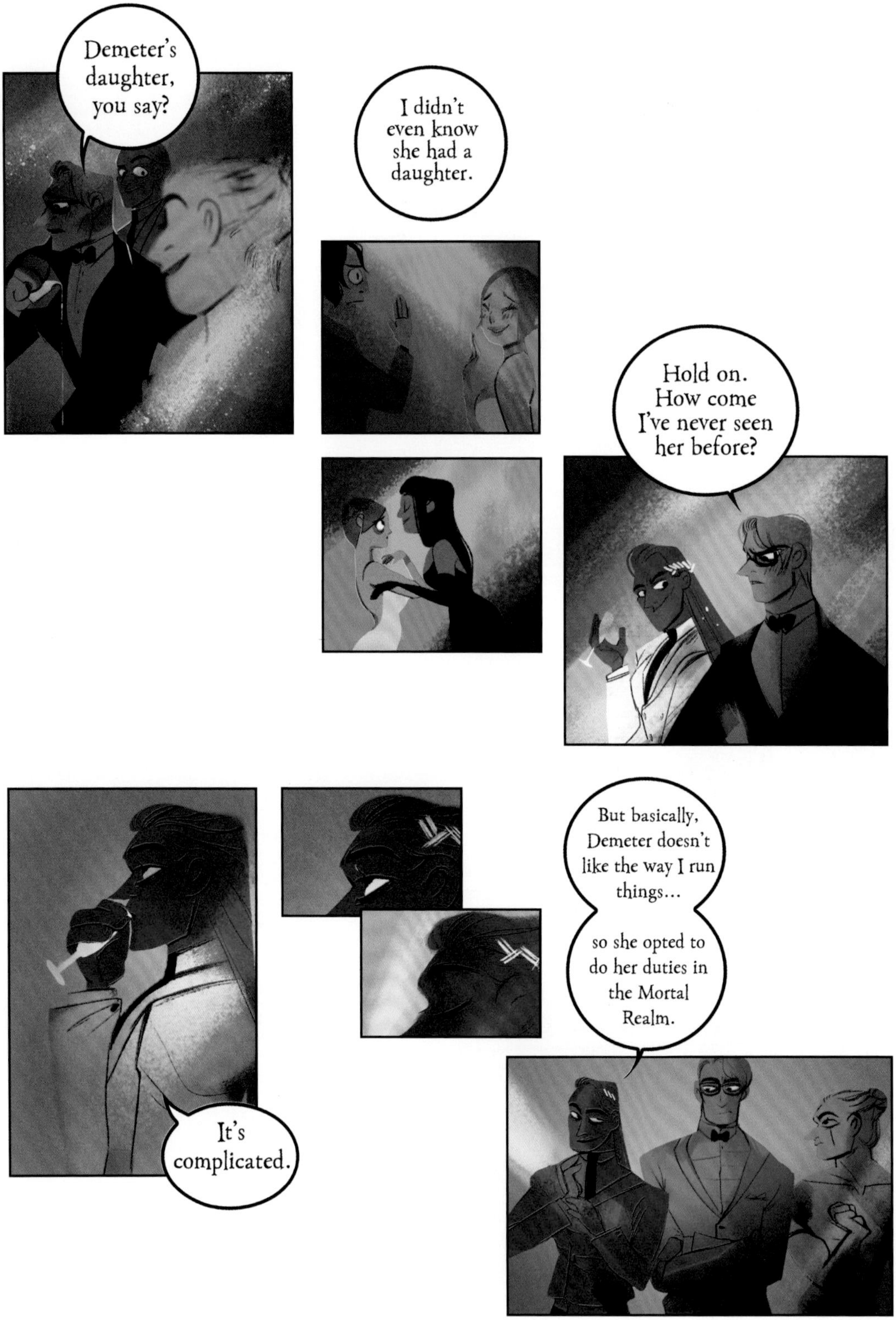
Demeter's daughter, you say?
I didn't even know she had a daughter.
Hold on. How come I've never seen her before?
It's complicated.
But basically, Demeter doesn't like the way I run things...
so she opted to do her duties in the Mortal Realm.

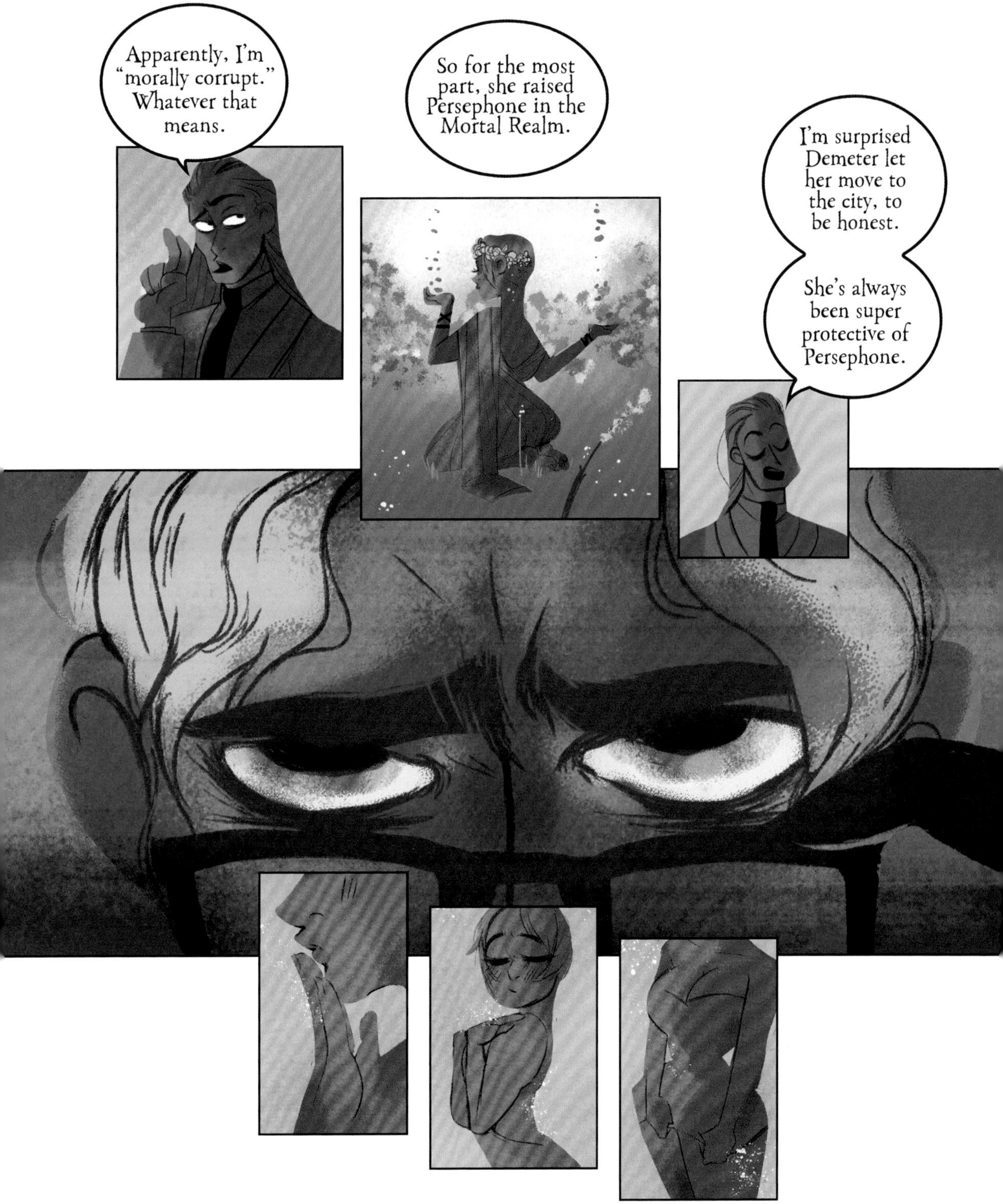
Apparently, I'm "morally corrupt." Whatever that means.
So for the most part, she raised Persephone in the Mortal Realm.
I'm surprised Demeter let her move to the city, to be honest.
She's always been super protective of Persephone.

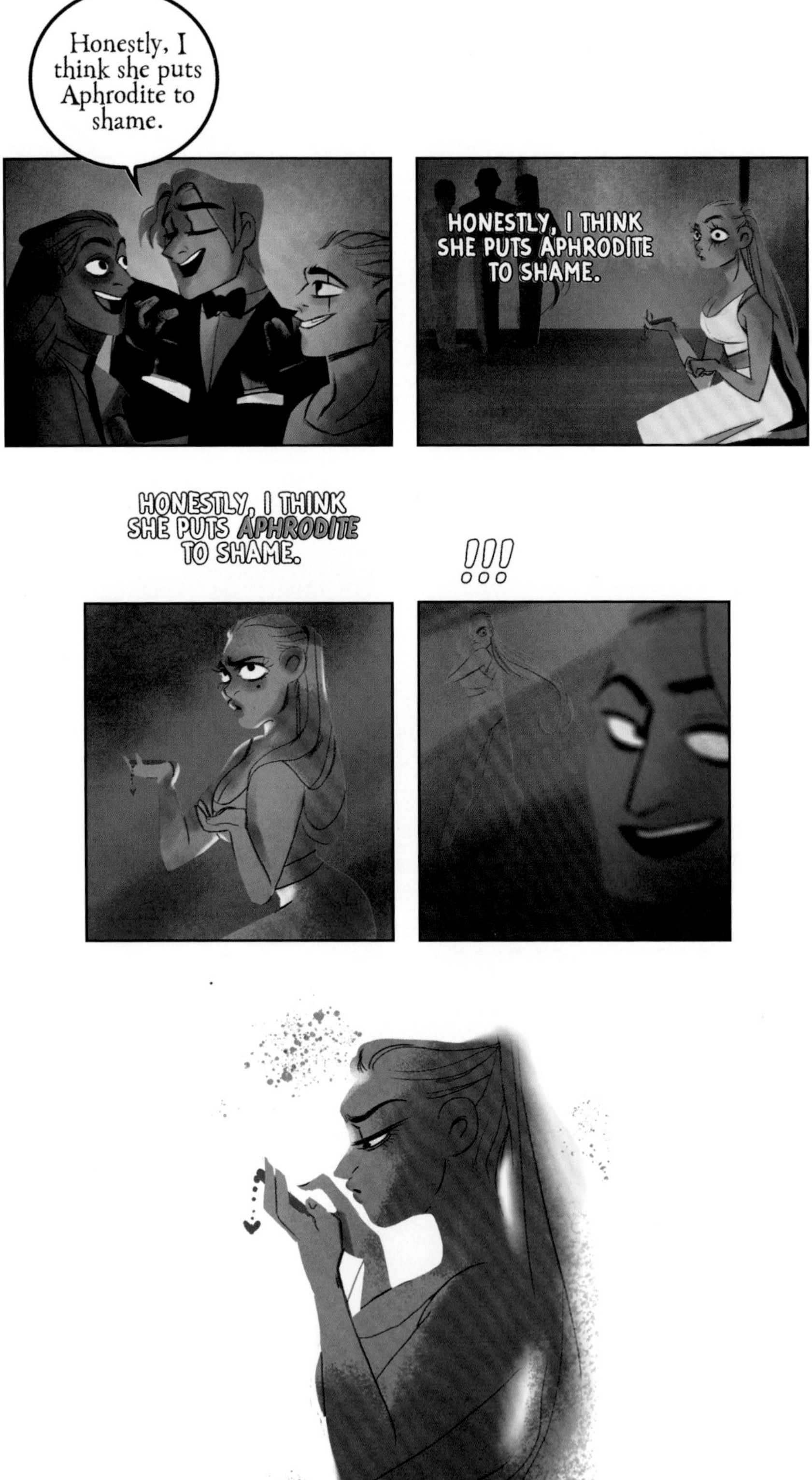
Honestly, I think she puts Aphrodite to shame.
HONESTLY, I THINK SHE PUTS APHRODITE TO SHAME.
HONESTLY, I THINK SHE PUTS APHRODITE TO SHAME.
!!!

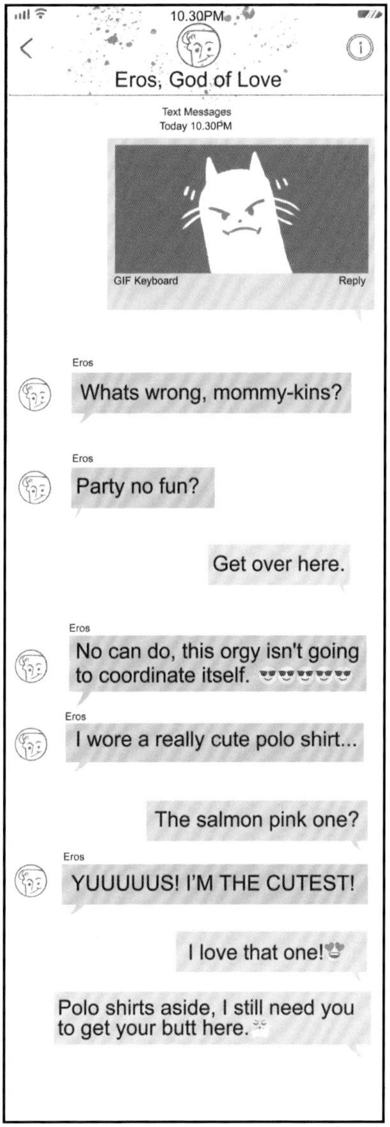
10.30PM
Eros, God of Love
Text Messages
Today 10.30PM
GIF Keyboard
Reply
Eros
Whats wrong, mommy-kins?
Eros
Party no fun?
Get over here.
Eros
No can do, this orgy isn't going to coordinate itself. 😎😎😎😎😎
Eros
I wore a really cute polo shirt...
The salmon pink one?
Eros
YUUUUUS! I'M THE CUTEST!
I love that one!😍
Polo shirts aside, I still need you to get your butt here.😤

EPISODE 04: WHO IS SHE? (PART 3)

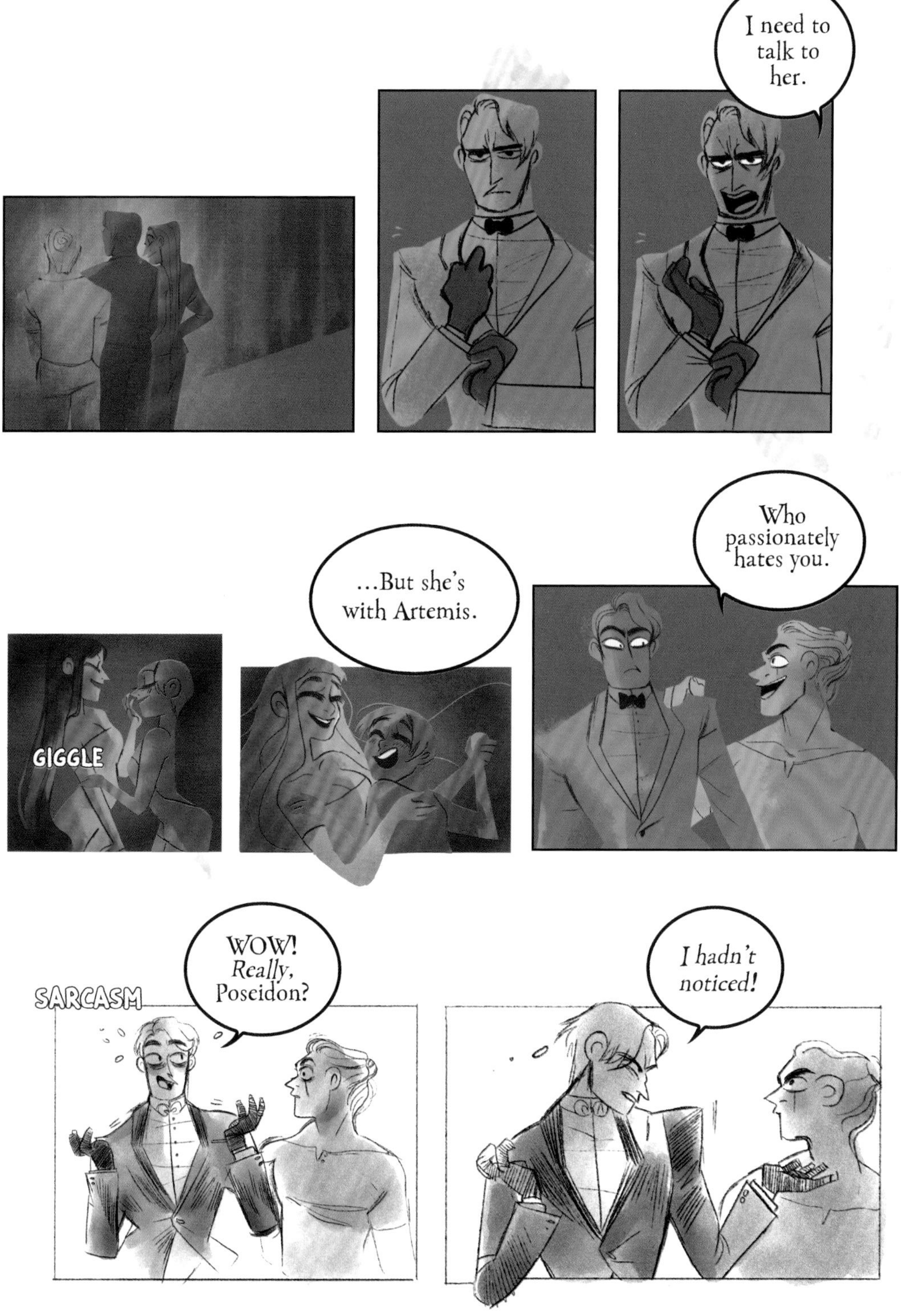
I need to talk to her.
...But she's with Artemis.
GIGGLE
Who passionately hates you.
SARCASM
WOW! *Really,* Poseidon?
I hadn't noticed!

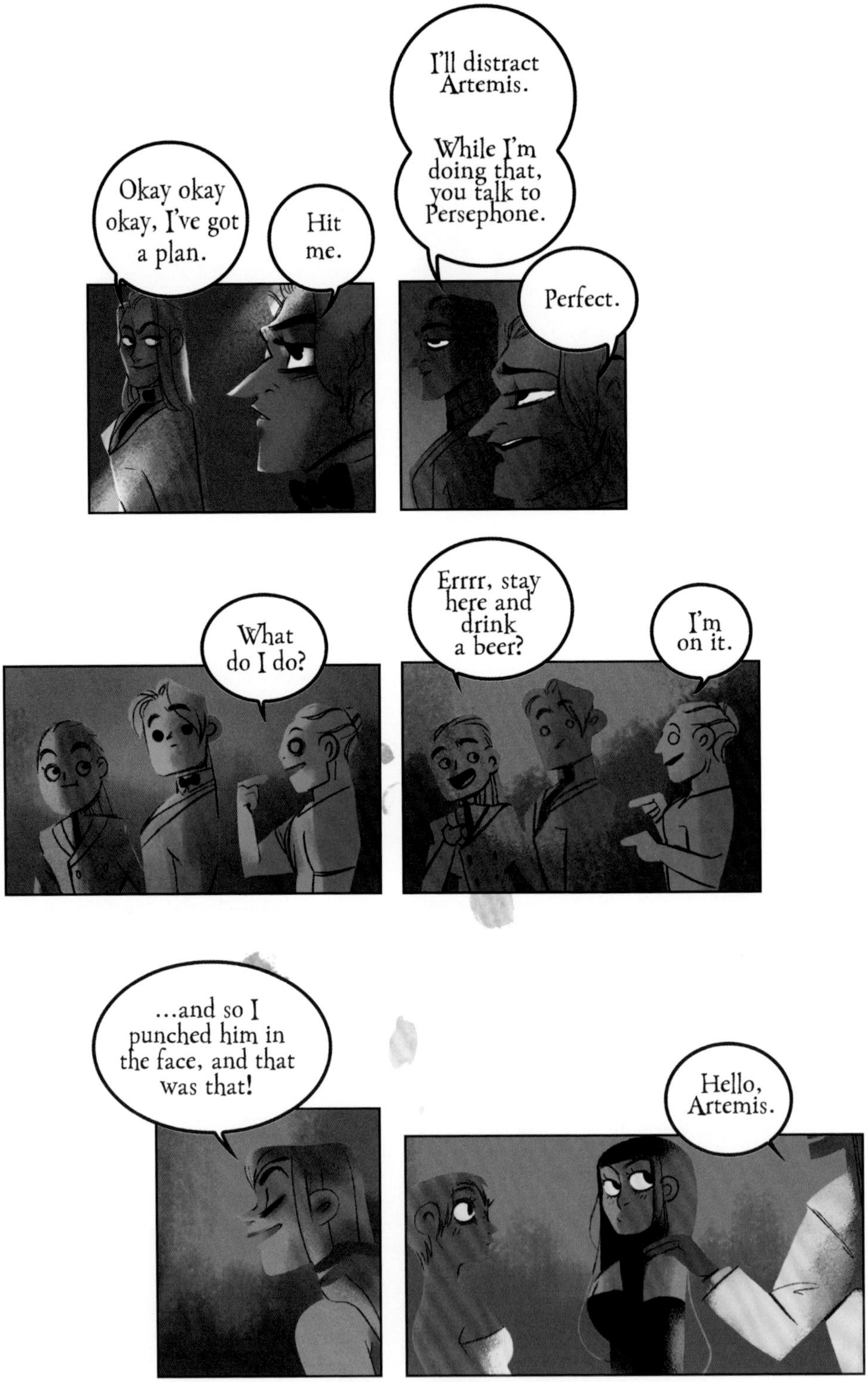
Okay okay okay, I've got a plan.
Hit me.
I'll distract Artemis.
While I'm doing that, you talk to Persephone.
Perfect.
What do I do?
Errrr, stay here and drink a beer?
I'm on it.
...and so I punched him in the face, and that was that!
Hello, Artemis.

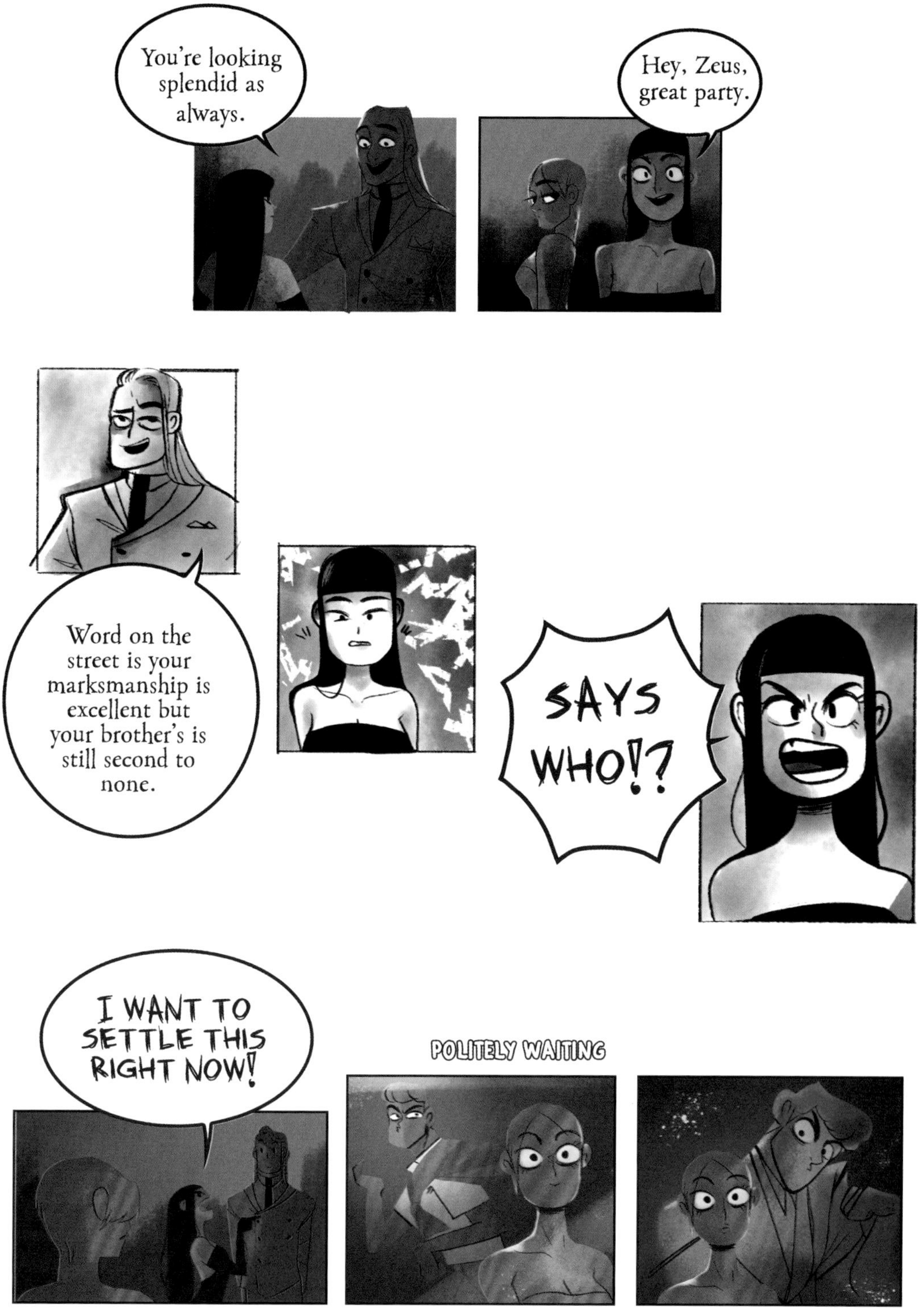
You're looking splendid as always.
Hey, Zeus, great party.
Word on the street is your marksmanship is excellent but your brother's is still second to none.
SAYS WHO!?
I WANT TO SETTLE THIS RIGHT NOW!
POLITELY WAITING

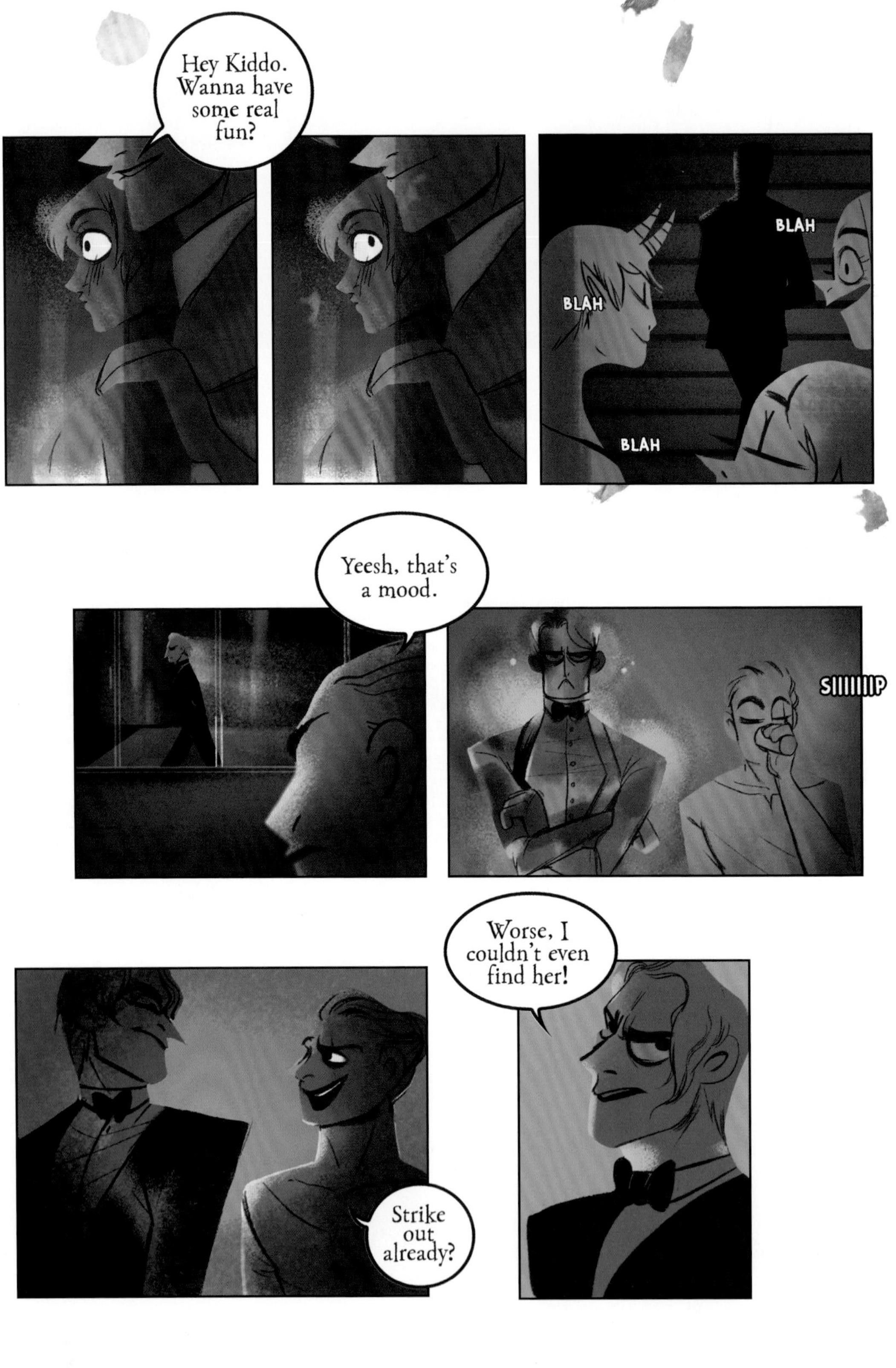

Hey Kiddo. Wanna have some real fun?
BLAH
BLAH
BLAH
Yeesh, that's a mood.
SIIIIIIP
Strike out already?
Worse, I couldn't even find her!

It's as if she vanished into thin air!

Where did Artemis go?

I guess I don't want to be clingy...

Another drink?

I feel...

I feel awful

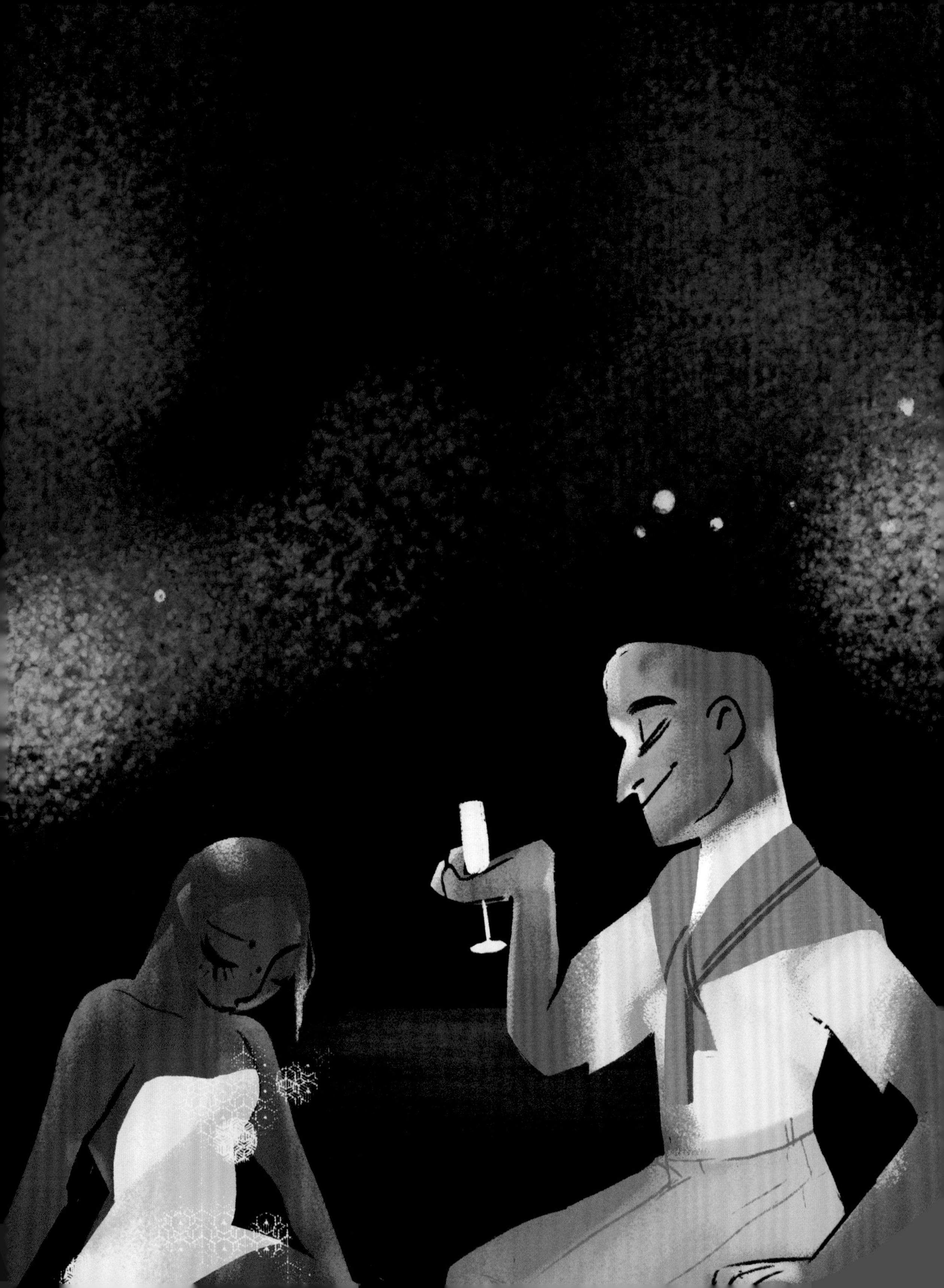

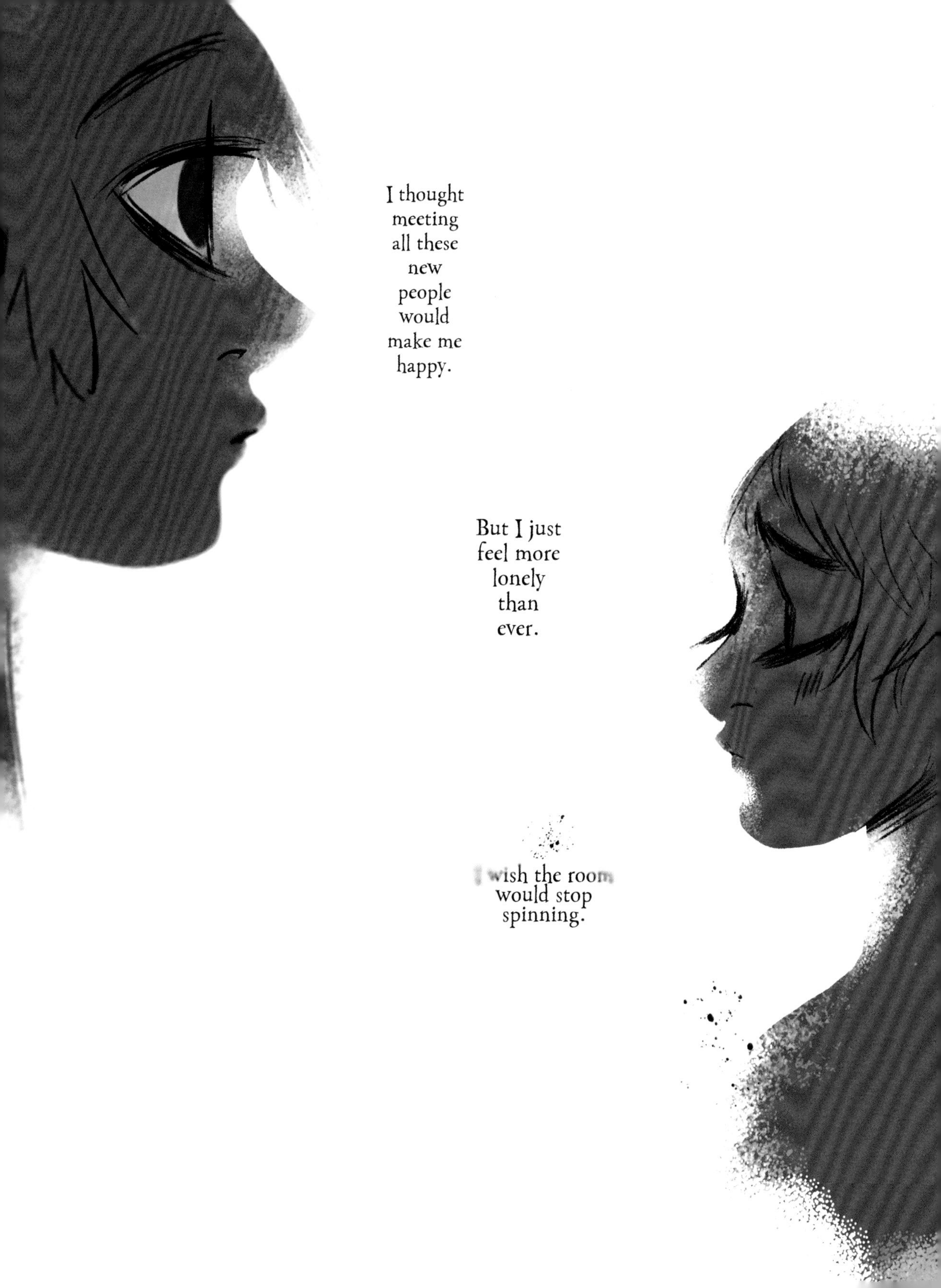
I thought meeting all these new people would make me happy.
But I just feel more lonely than ever.
I wish the room would stop spinning.

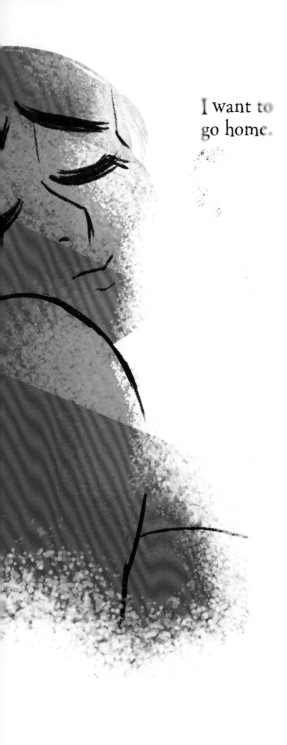

I want to
go home.

I'm very
sorry about
all of this.

But as far as I'm
concerned...

...Aphrodite's word is law.

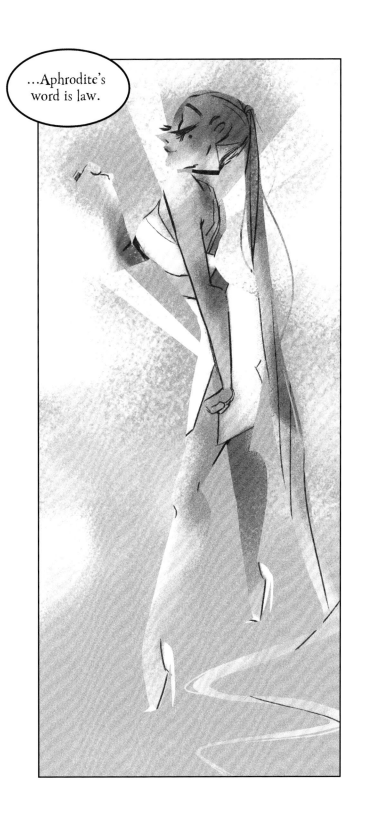

EPISODE 05: SWEET REVENGE

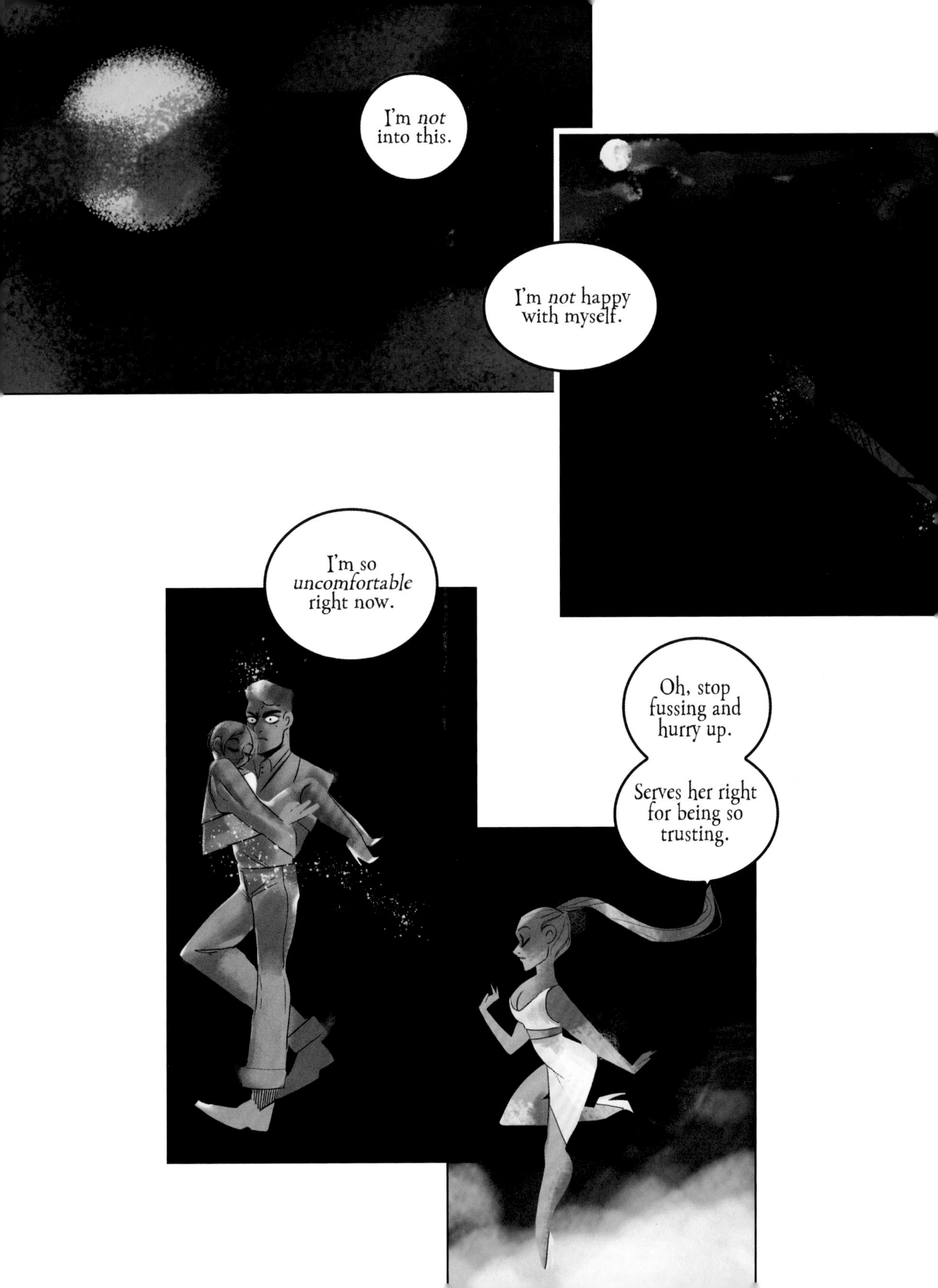

I'm *not* into this.
I'm *not* happy with myself.
I'm so *uncomfortable* right now.
Oh, stop fussing and hurry up.
Serves her right for being so trusting.

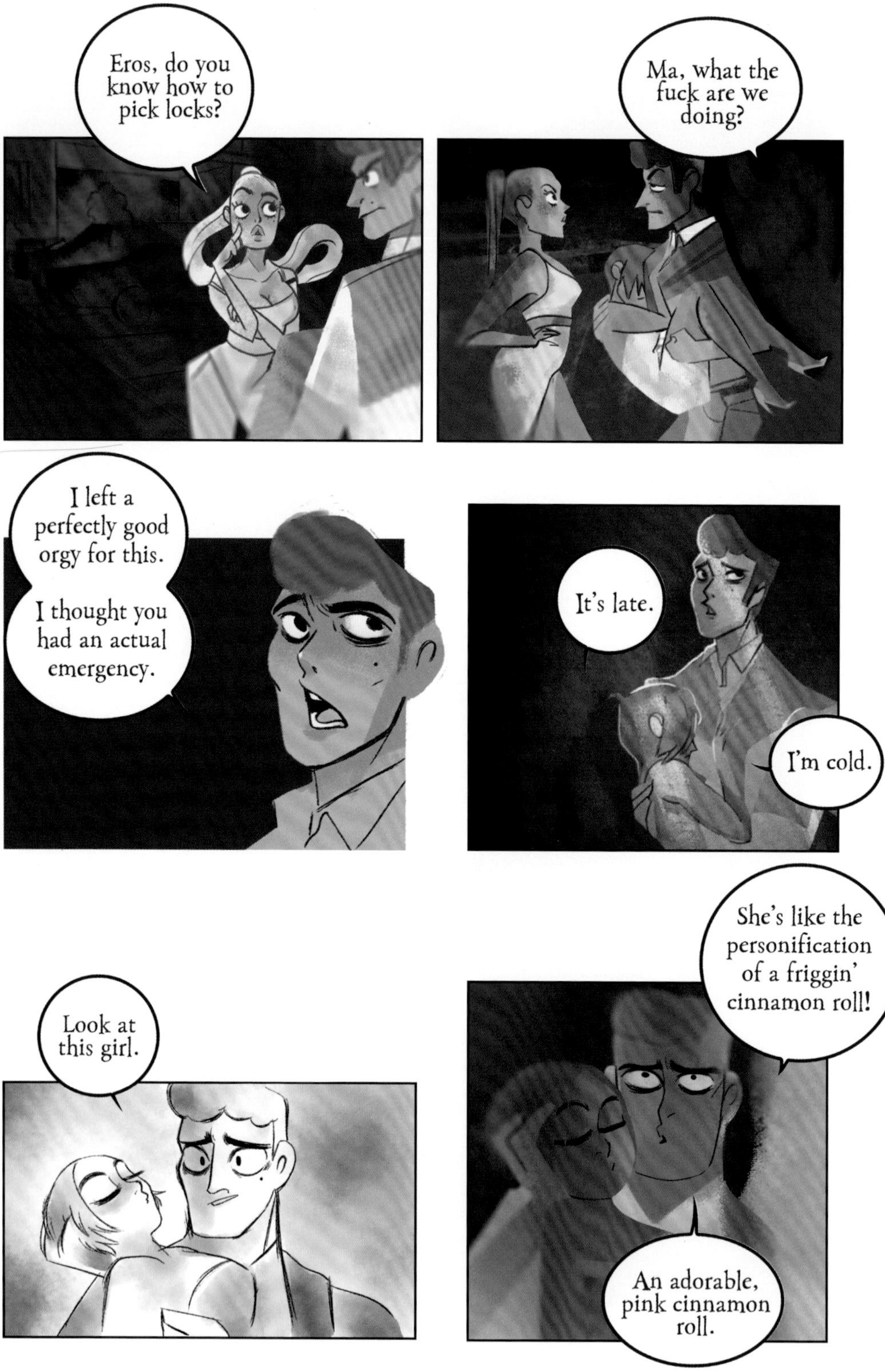
Eros, do you know how to pick locks?
Ma, what the fuck are we doing?
I left a perfectly good orgy for this.
I thought you had an actual emergency.
It's late.
I'm cold.
Look at this girl.
She's like the personification of a friggin' cinnamon roll!
An adorable, pink cinnamon roll.

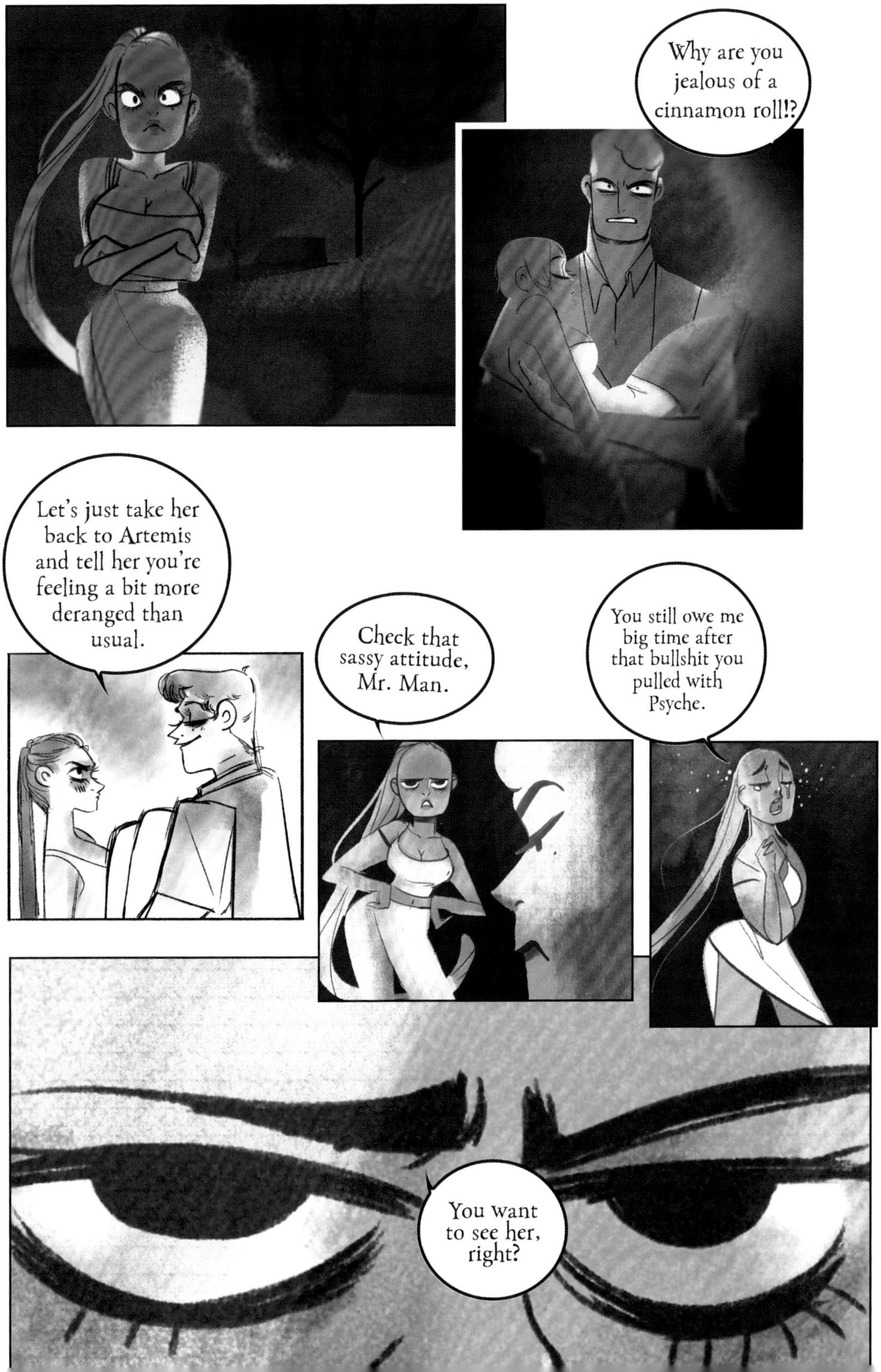
Why are you jealous of a cinnamon roll!?
Let's just take her back to Artemis and tell her you're feeling a bit more deranged than usual.
Check that sassy attitude, Mr. Man.
You still owe me big time after that bullshit you pulled with Psyche.
You want to see her, right?

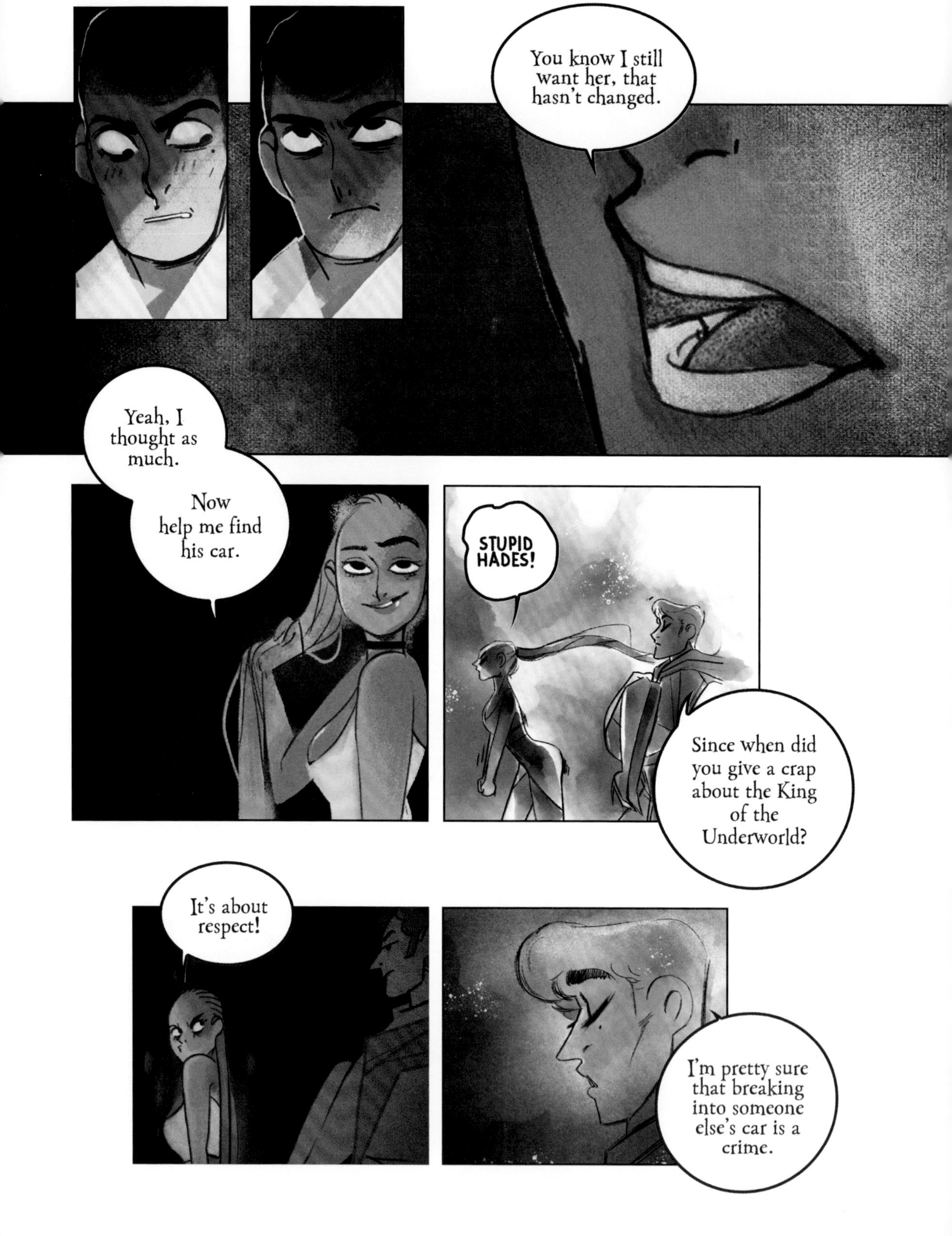
You know I still want her, that hasn't changed.
Yeah, I thought as much.
Now help me find his car.
STUPID HADES!
Since when did you give a crap about the King of the Underworld?
It's about respect!
I'm pretty sure that breaking into someone else's car is a crime.

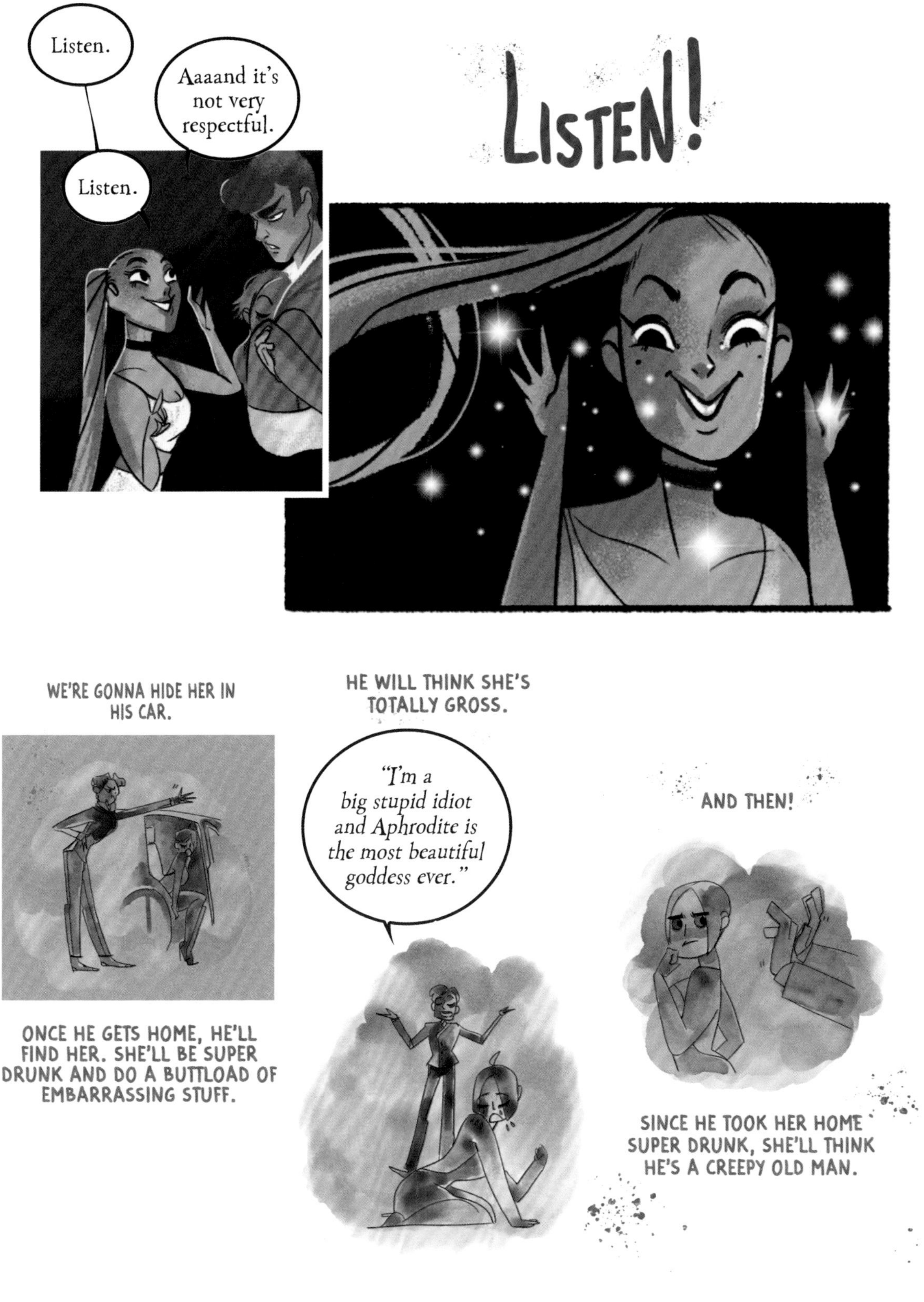
Listen.
Aaaand it's not very respectful.
Listen.
LISTEN!
WE'RE GONNA HIDE HER IN HIS CAR.
ONCE HE GETS HOME, HE'LL FIND HER. SHE'LL BE SUPER DRUNK AND DO A BUTTLOAD OF EMBARRASSING STUFF.
HE WILL THINK SHE'S TOTALLY GROSS.
"I'm a big stupid idiot and Aphrodite is the most beautiful goddess ever."
AND THEN!
SINCE HE TOOK HER HOME SUPER DRUNK, SHE'LL THINK HE'S A CREEPY OLD MAN.

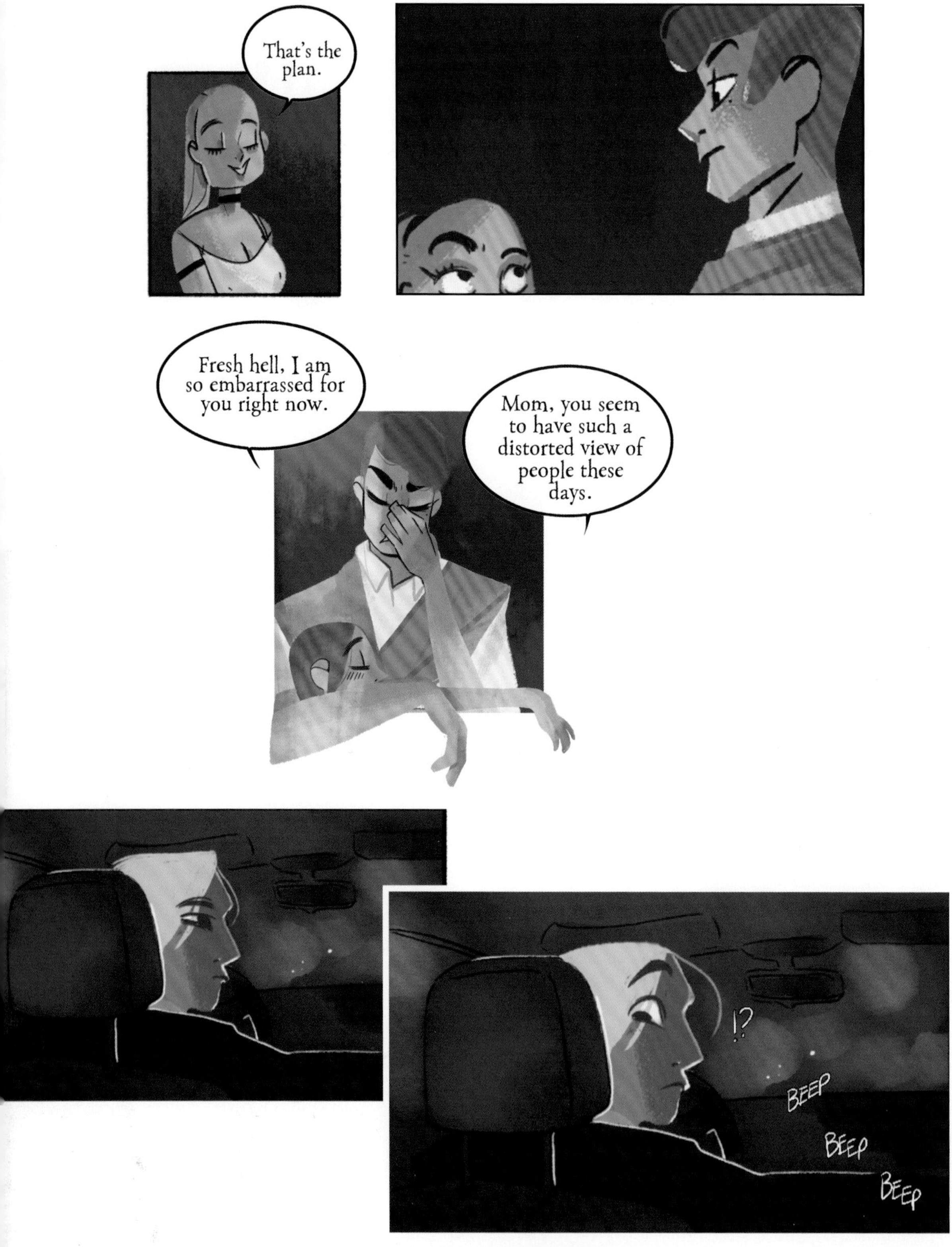
That's the plan.
Fresh hell, I am so embarrassed for you right now.
Mom, you seem to have such a distorted view of people these days.
!?
BEEP
BEEP
BEEP

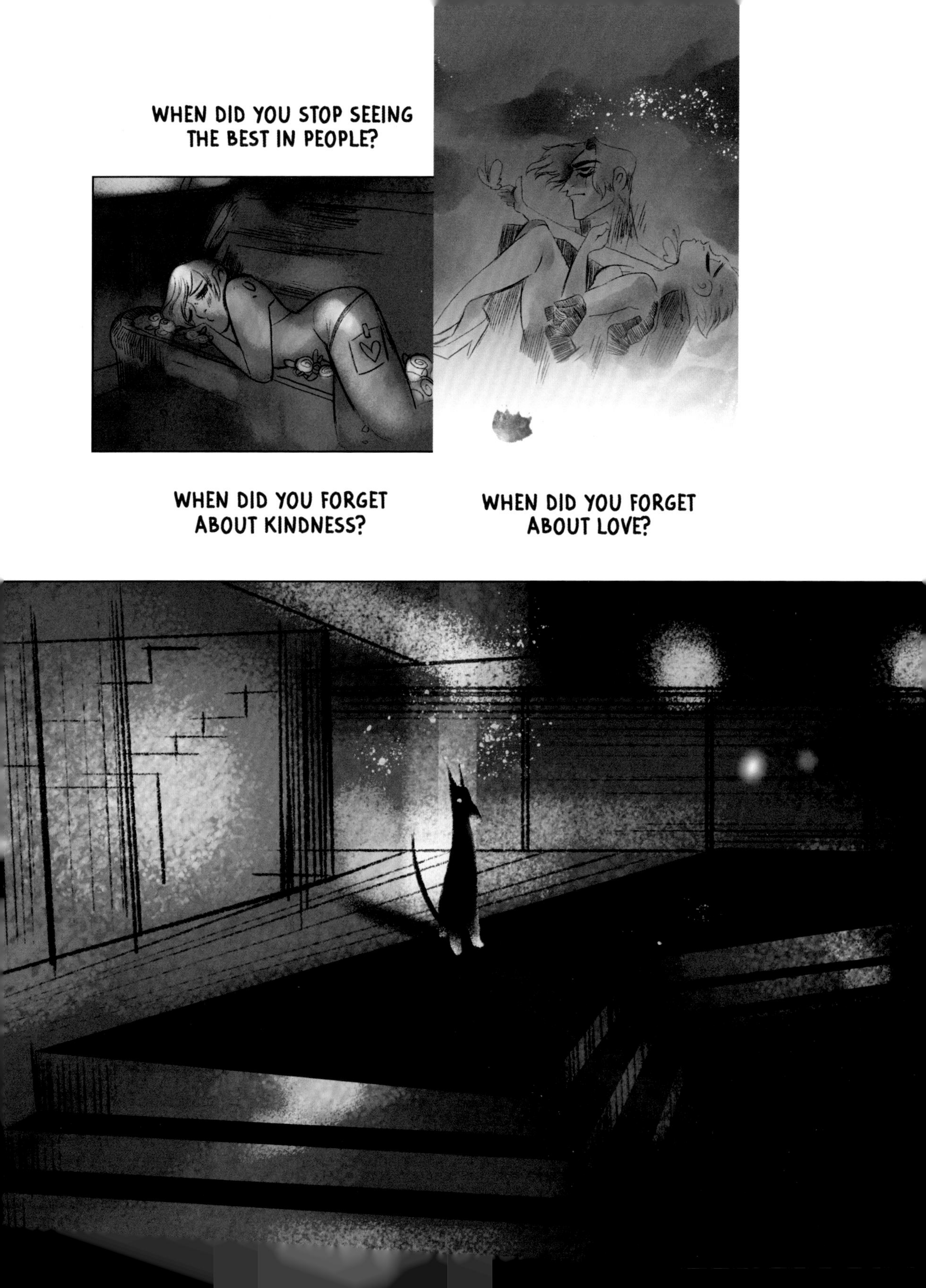
WHEN DID YOU STOP SEEING THE BEST IN PEOPLE?
WHEN DID YOU FORGET ABOUT KINDNESS?
WHEN DID YOU FORGET ABOUT LOVE?

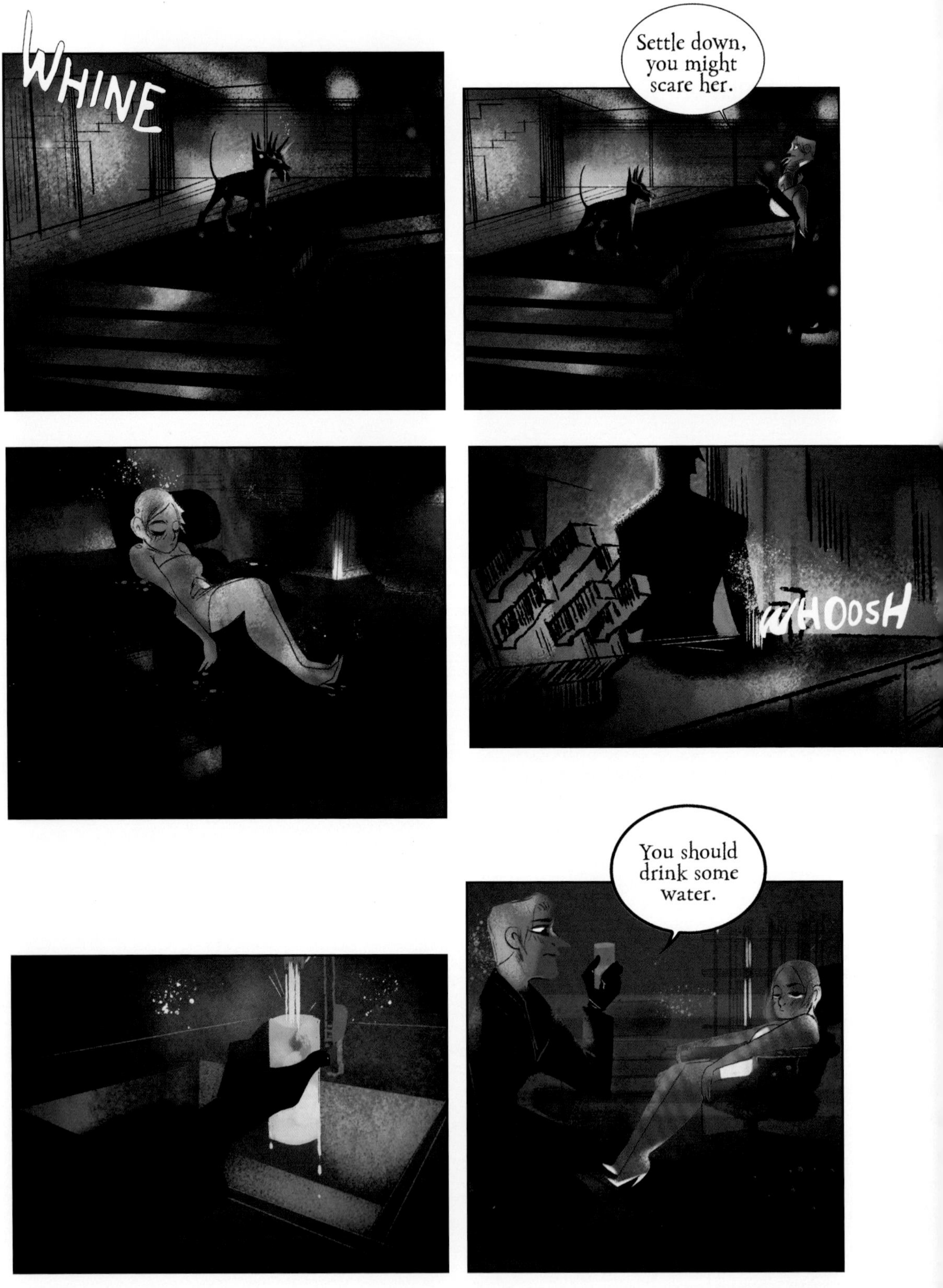
WHINE
Settle down, you might scare her.
WHOOSH
You should drink some water.

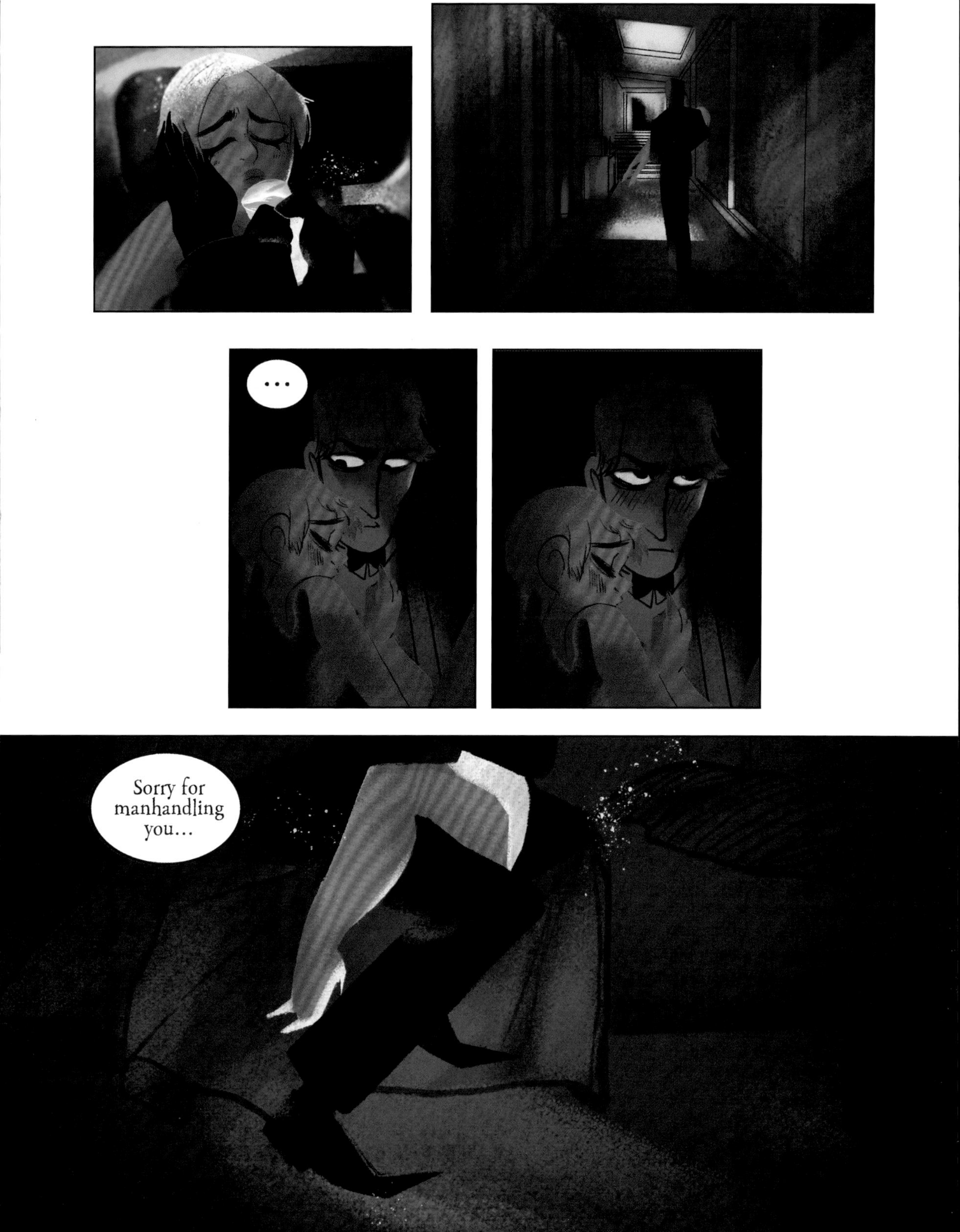
...
Sorry for manhandling you...

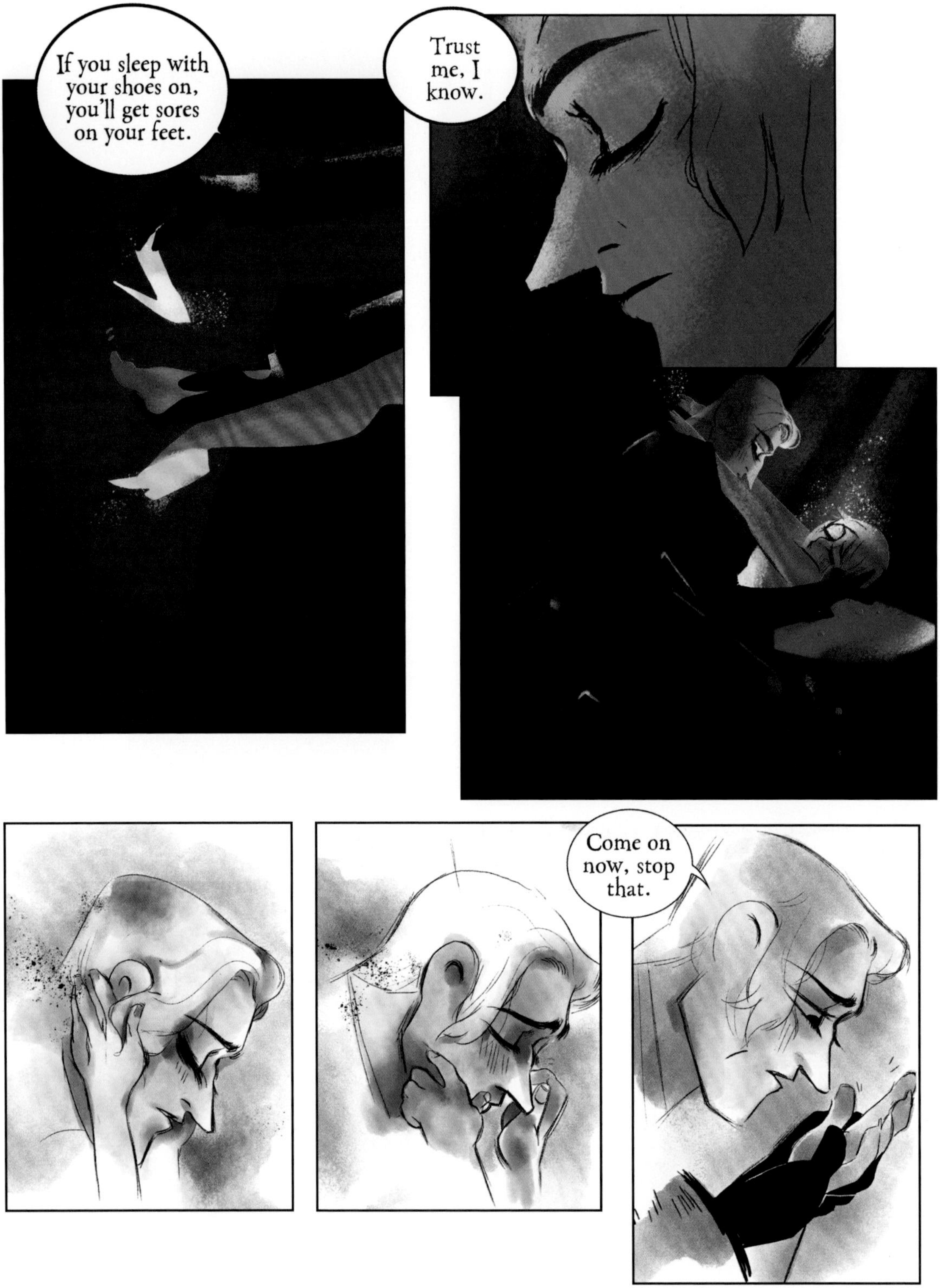

If you sleep with your shoes on, you'll get sores on your feet.
Trust me, I know.
Come on now, stop that.

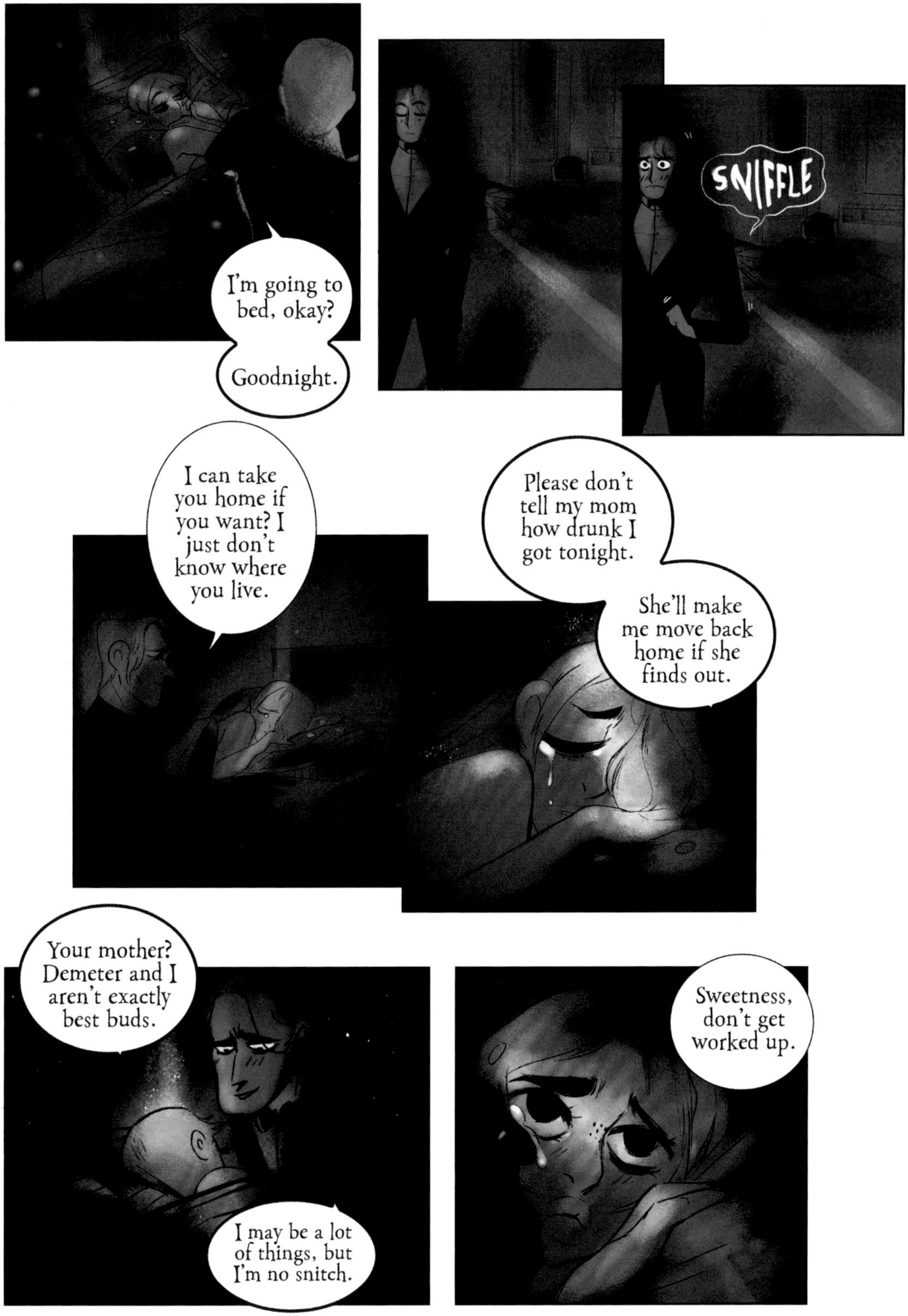
I'm going to bed, okay?
Goodnight.
SNIFFLE
I can take you home if you want? I just don't know where you live.
Please don't tell my mom how drunk I got tonight.
She'll make me move back home if she finds out.
Your mother? Demeter and I aren't exactly best buds.
I may be a lot of things, but I'm no snitch.
Sweetness, don't get worked up.

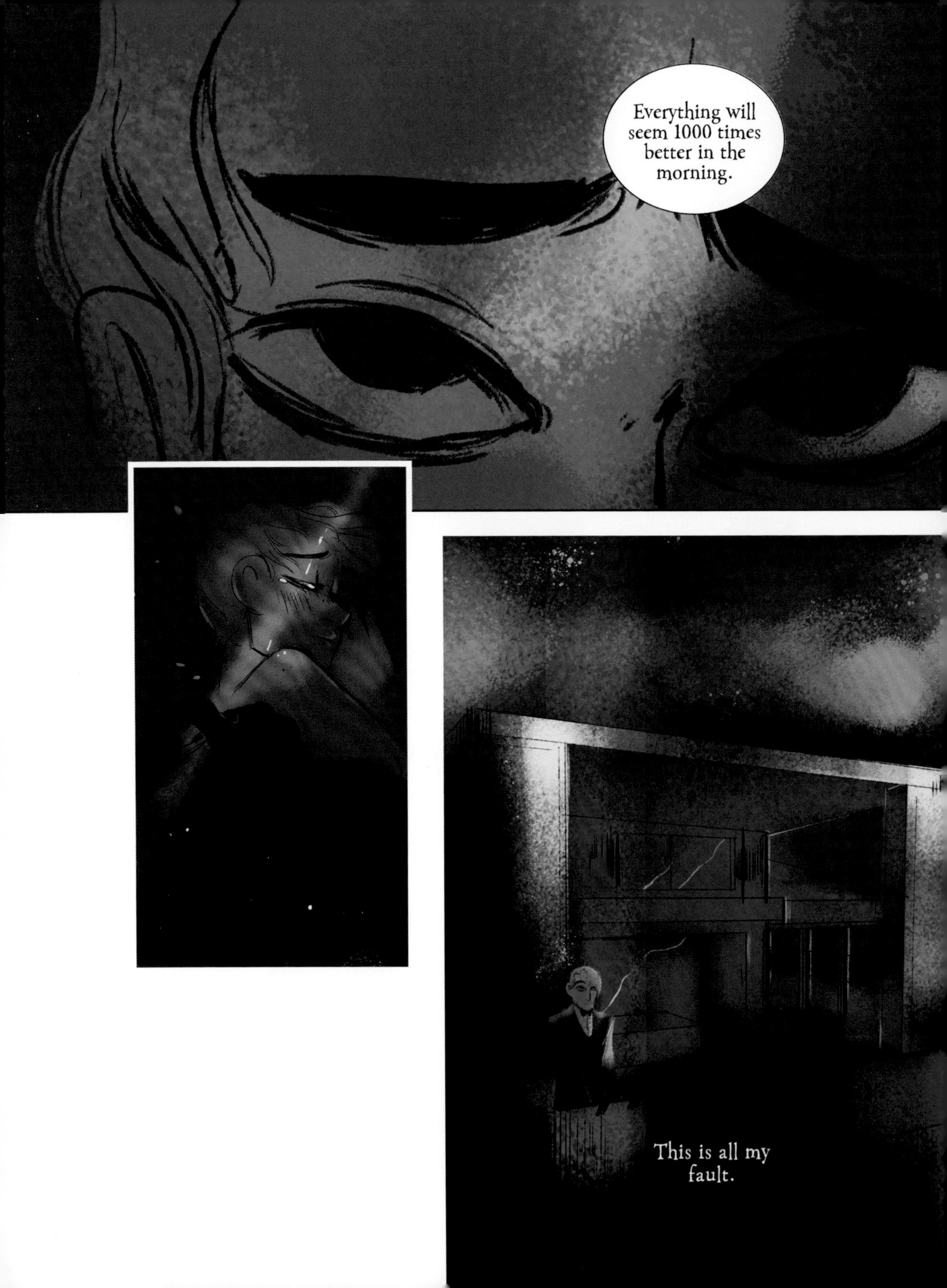
Everything will seem 1000 times better in the morning.
This is all my fault.

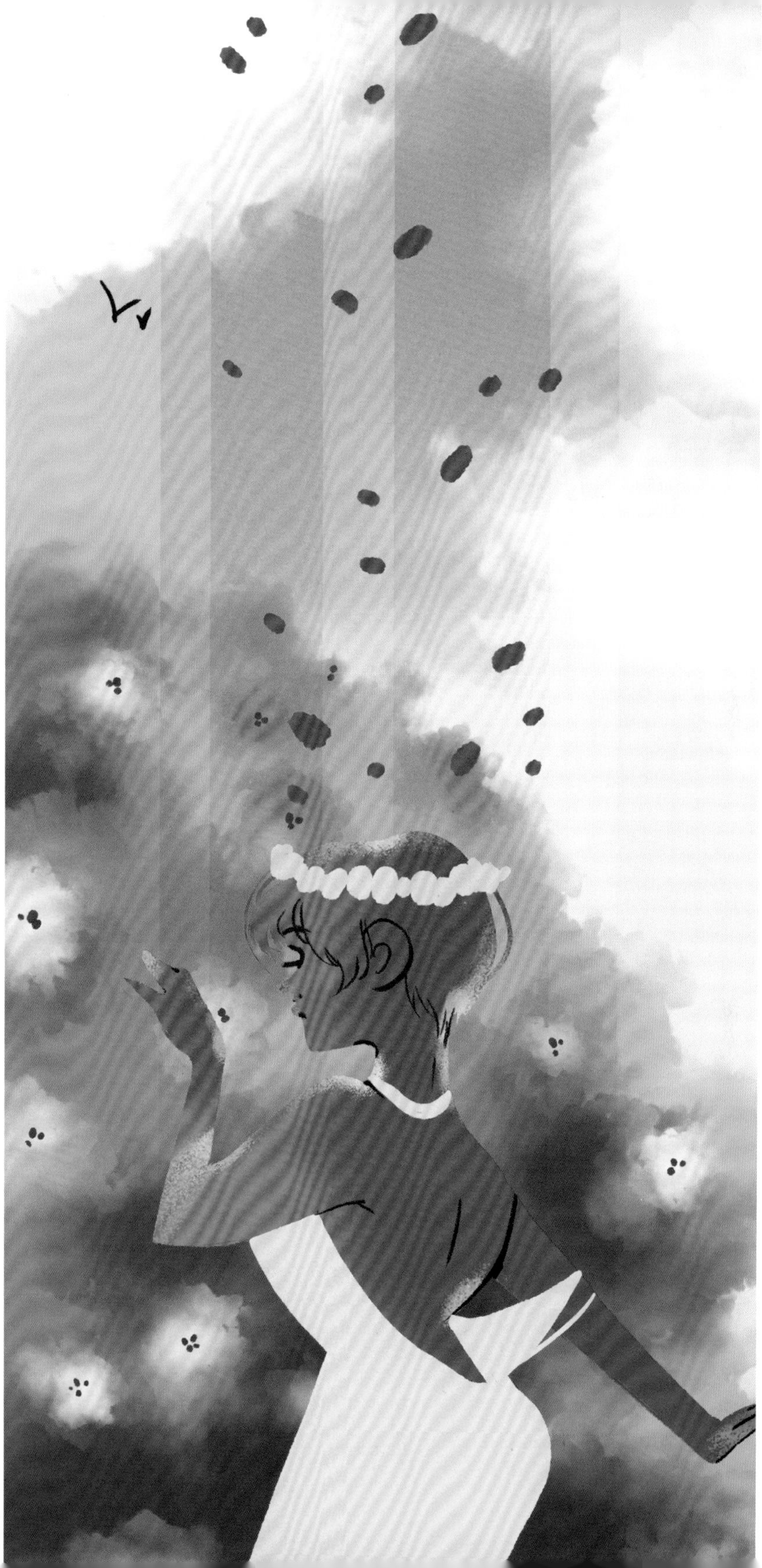

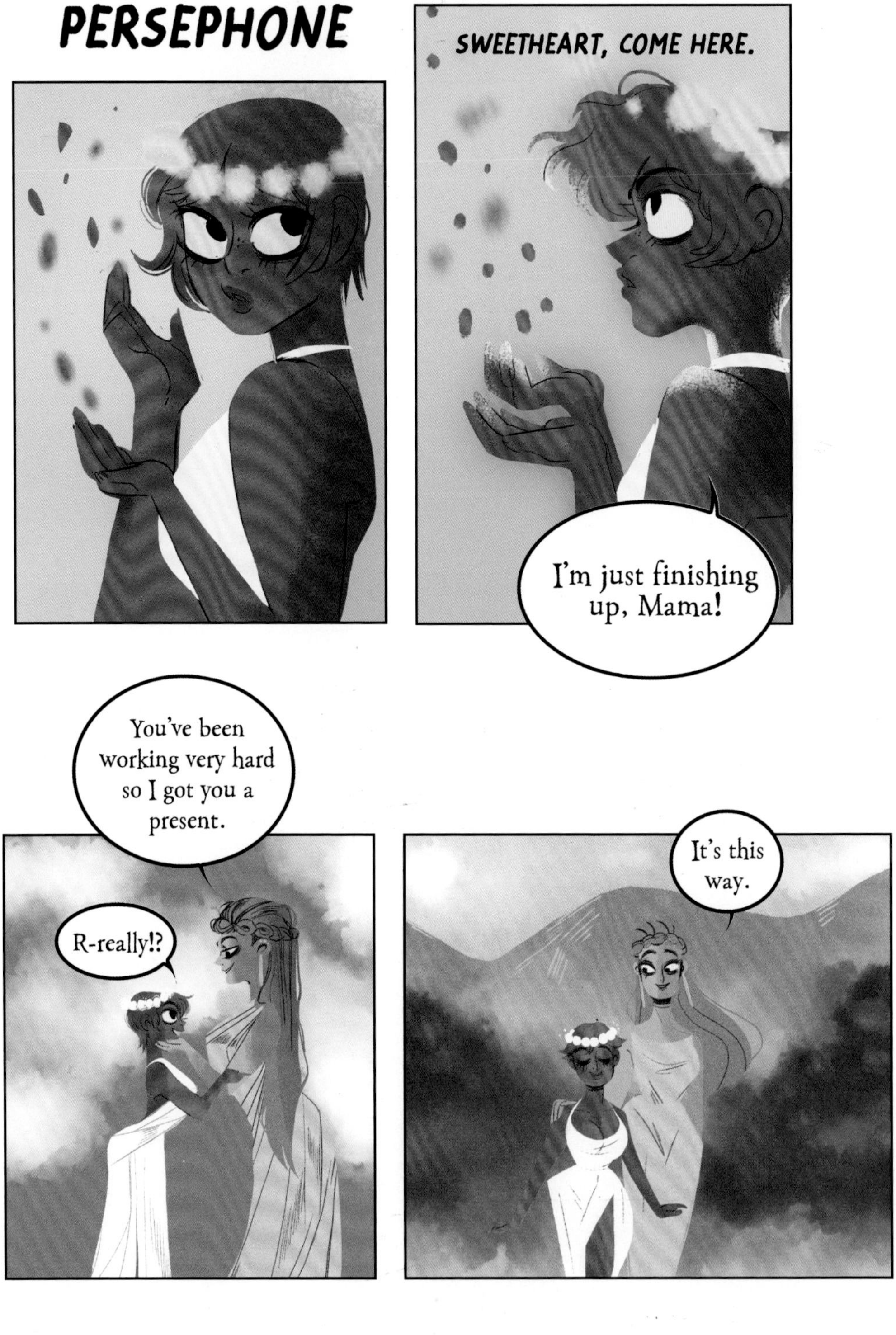
PERSEPHONE
SWEETHEART, COME HERE.
I'm just finishing up, Mama!
You've been working very hard so I got you a present.
R-really!?
It's this way.

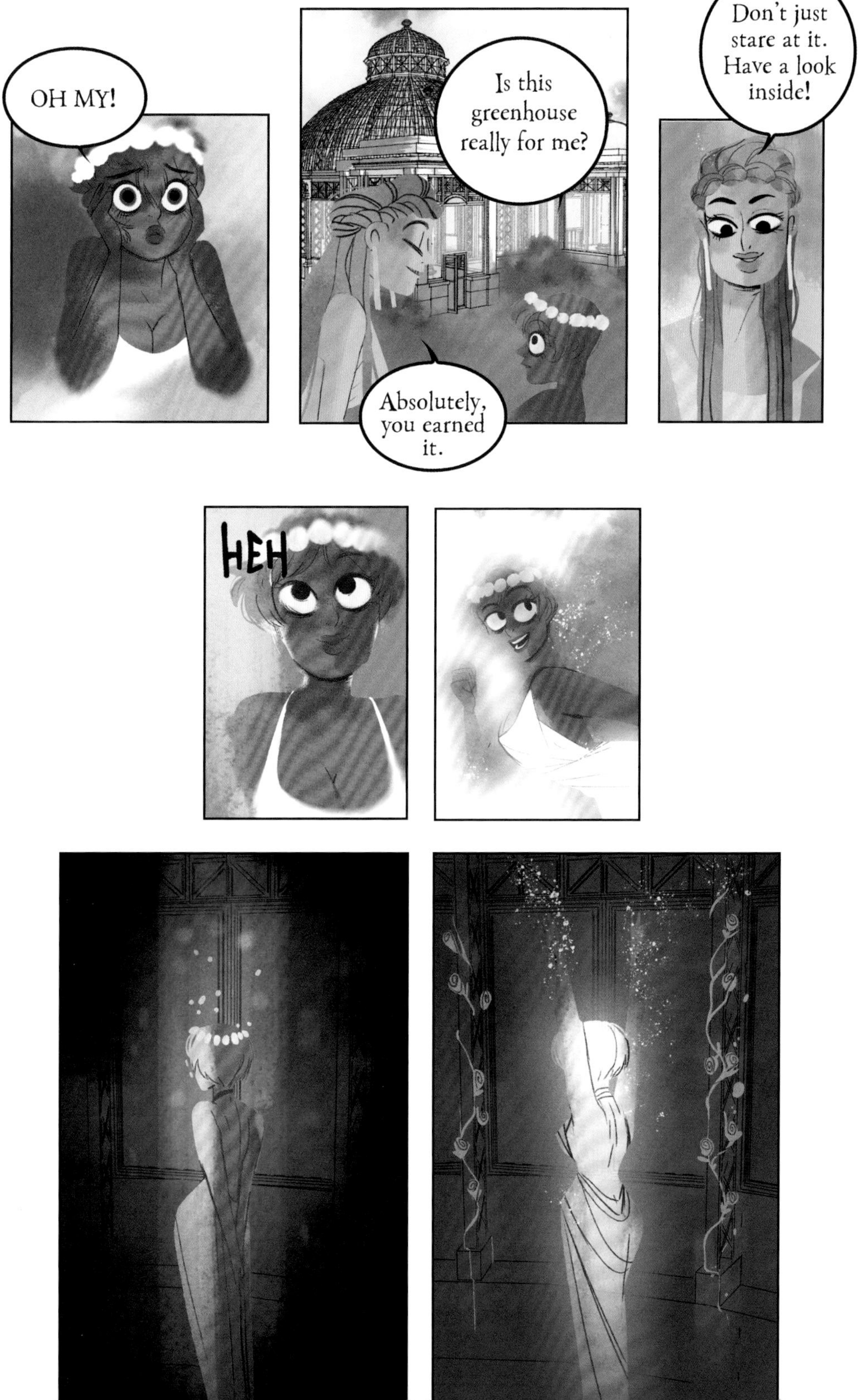
OH MY!
Is this greenhouse really for me?
Absolutely, you earned it.
Don't just stare at it. Have a look inside!
HEH

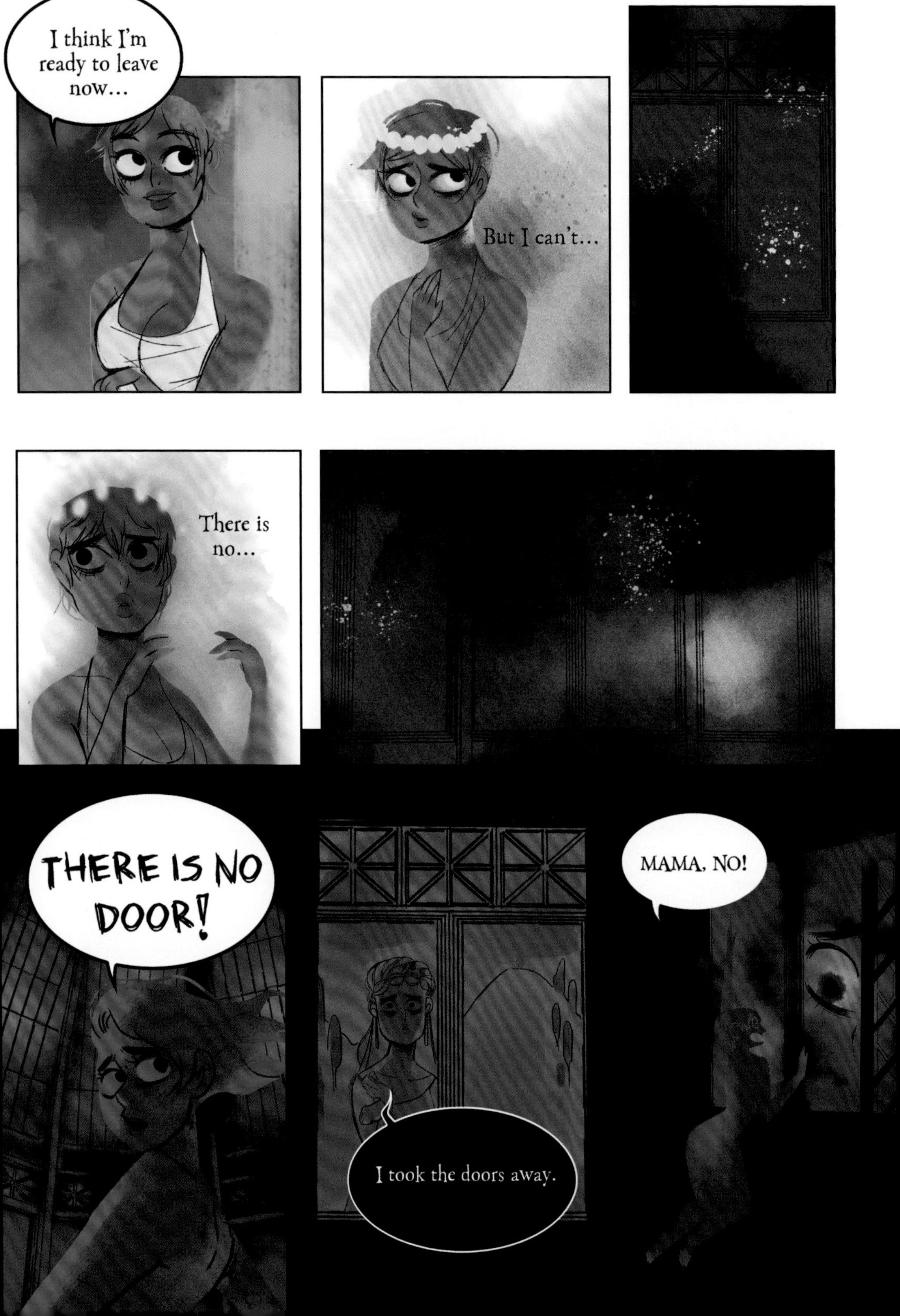
I think I'm ready to leave now...
But I can't...
There is no...
THERE IS NO DOOR!
I took the doors away.
MAMA, NO!

> You don't have to do this.

> Persephone, I know this may seem cruel, but it's for the best.

> Don't make me stay in here, I promise to be good!

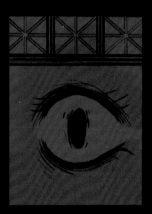

When you're in here...

...no one can hurt you.

NO ONE!

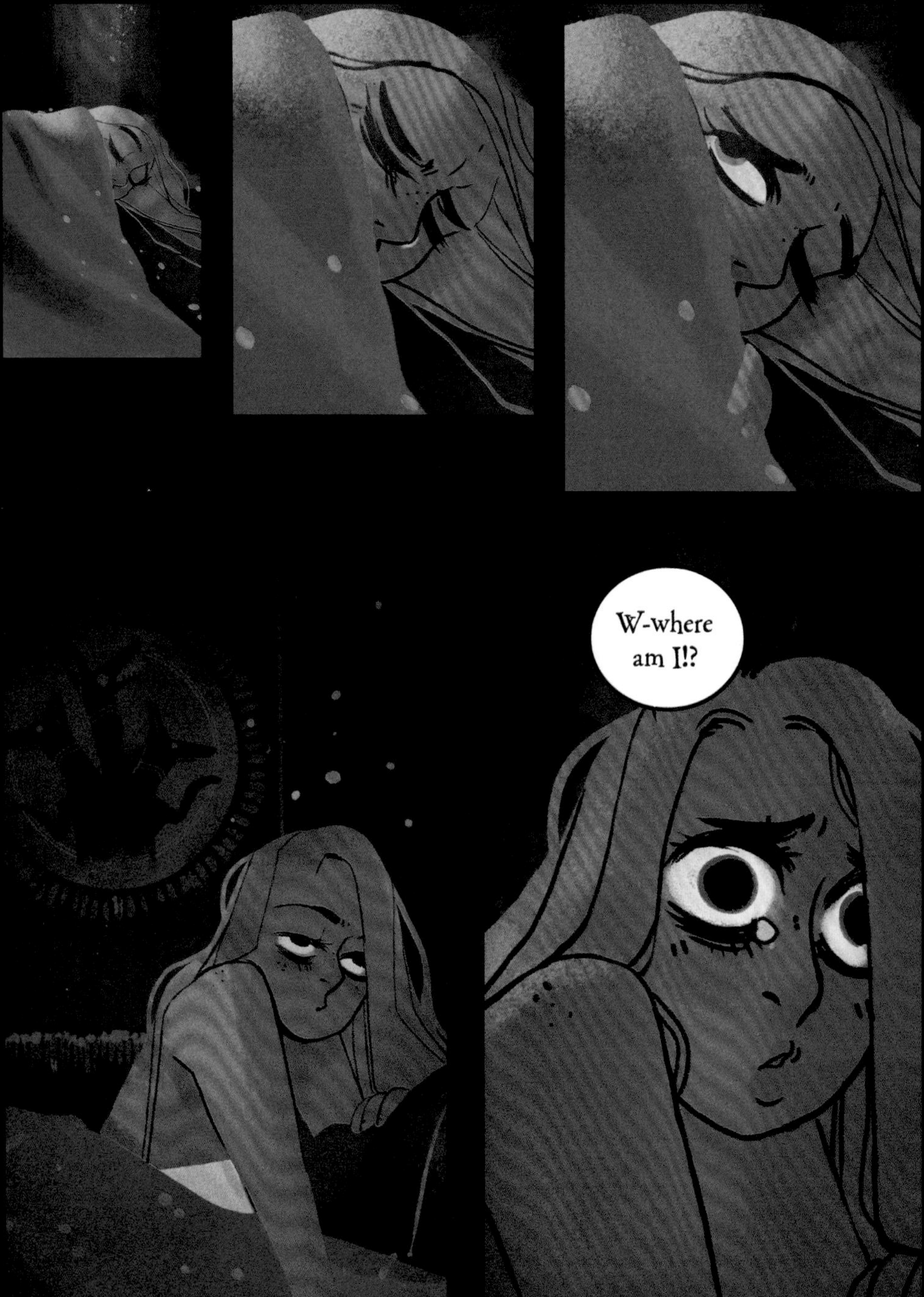
W-where am I!?

EPISODE 06: THE GREENHOUSE

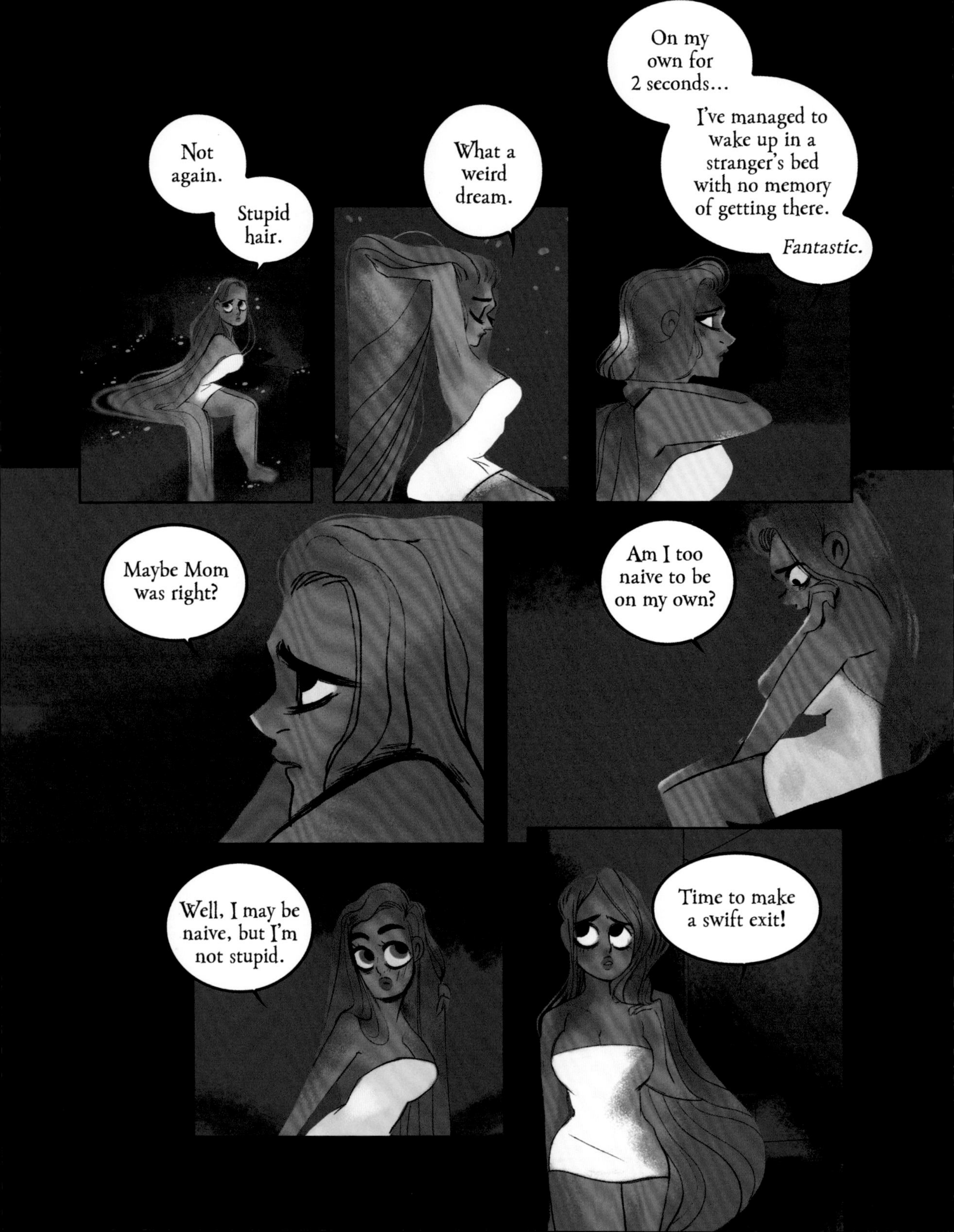
Not again.
Stupid hair.
What a weird dream.
On my own for 2 seconds...
I've managed to wake up in a stranger's bed with no memory of getting there.
Fantastic.
Maybe Mom was right?
Am I too naive to be on my own?
Well, I may be naive, but I'm not stupid.
Time to make a swift exit!

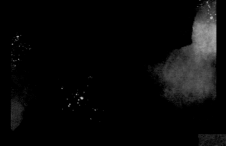

Persephone, you've
really outdone
yourself this time...

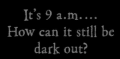

No way...

It's 9 a.m....
How can it still be
dark out?

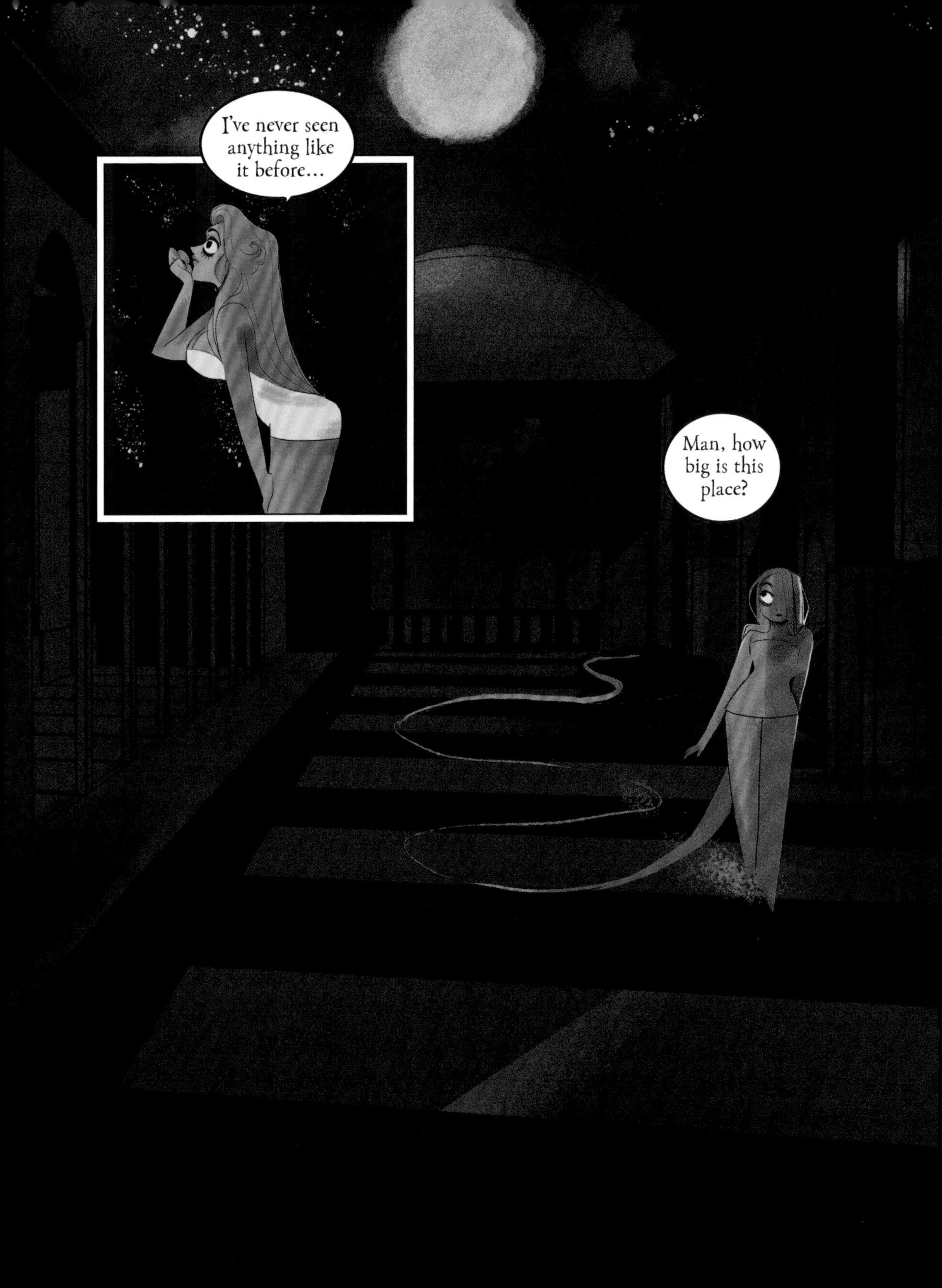
I've never seen anything like it before...
Man, how big is this place?

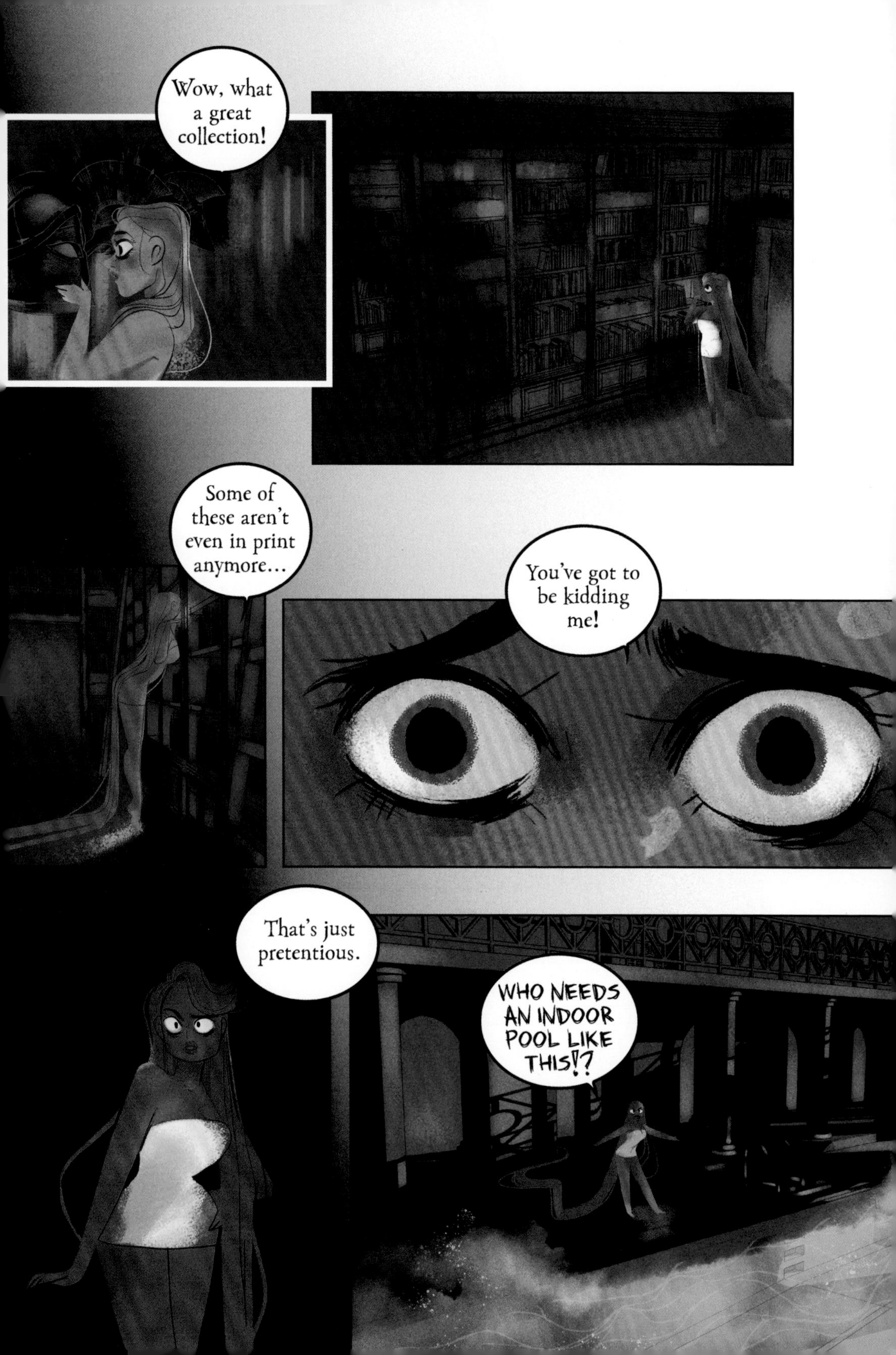
Wow, what a great collection!
Some of these aren't even in print anymore...
You've got to be kidding me!
That's just pretentious.
WHO NEEDS AN INDOOR POOL LIKE THIS!?

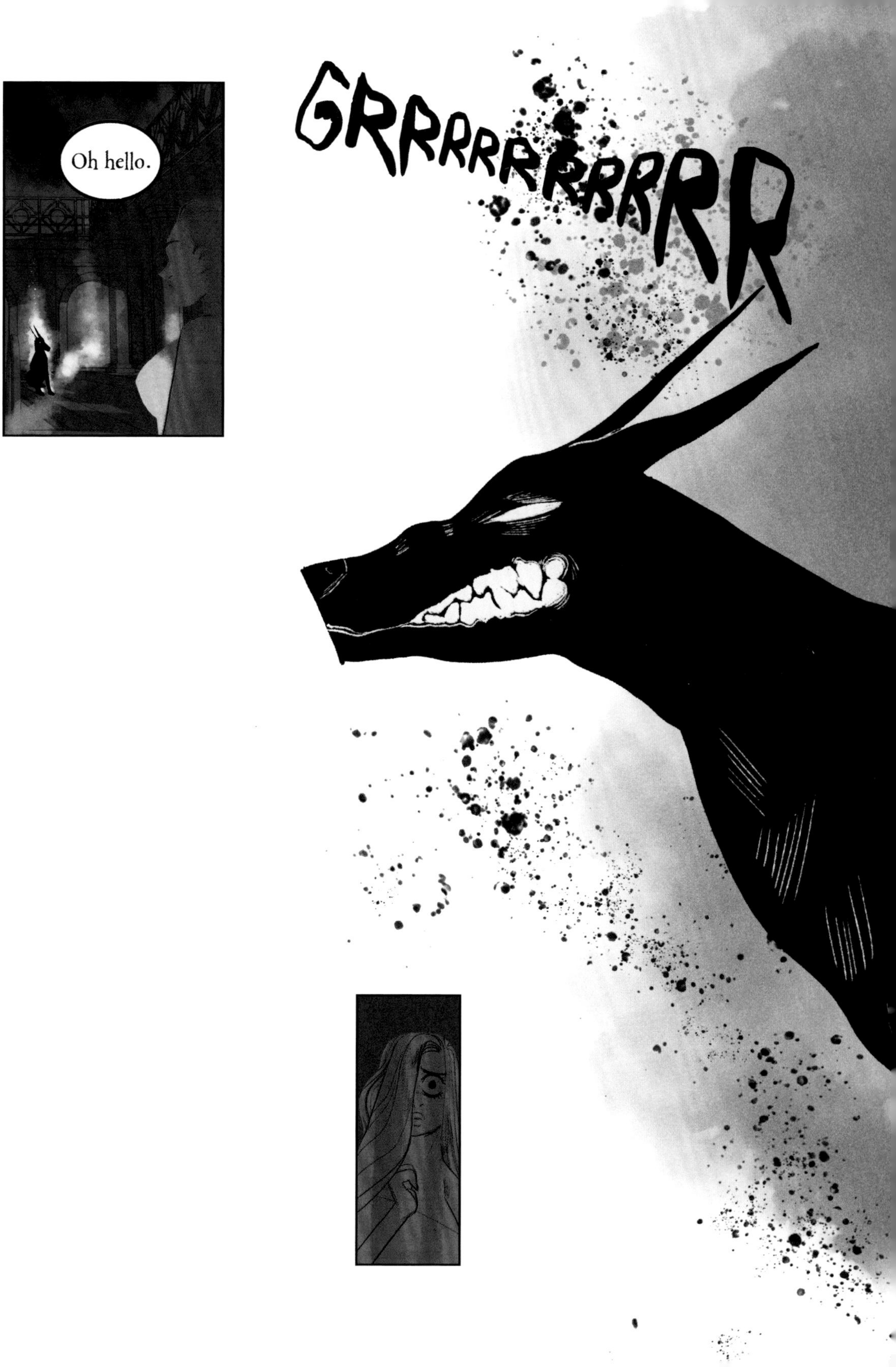
Oh hello.
GRRRRRRRRRR

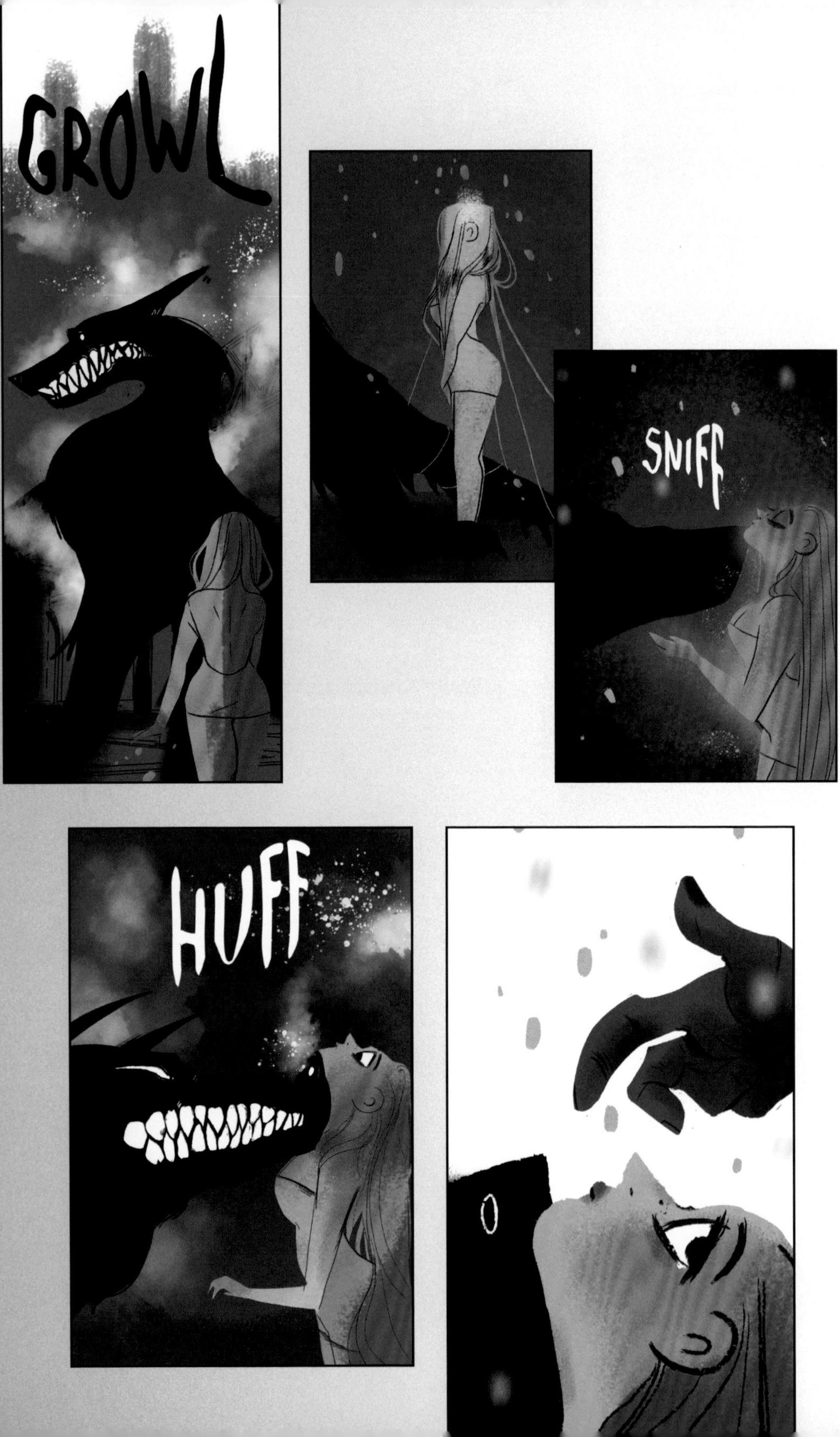
GROWL
SNIFF
HUFF

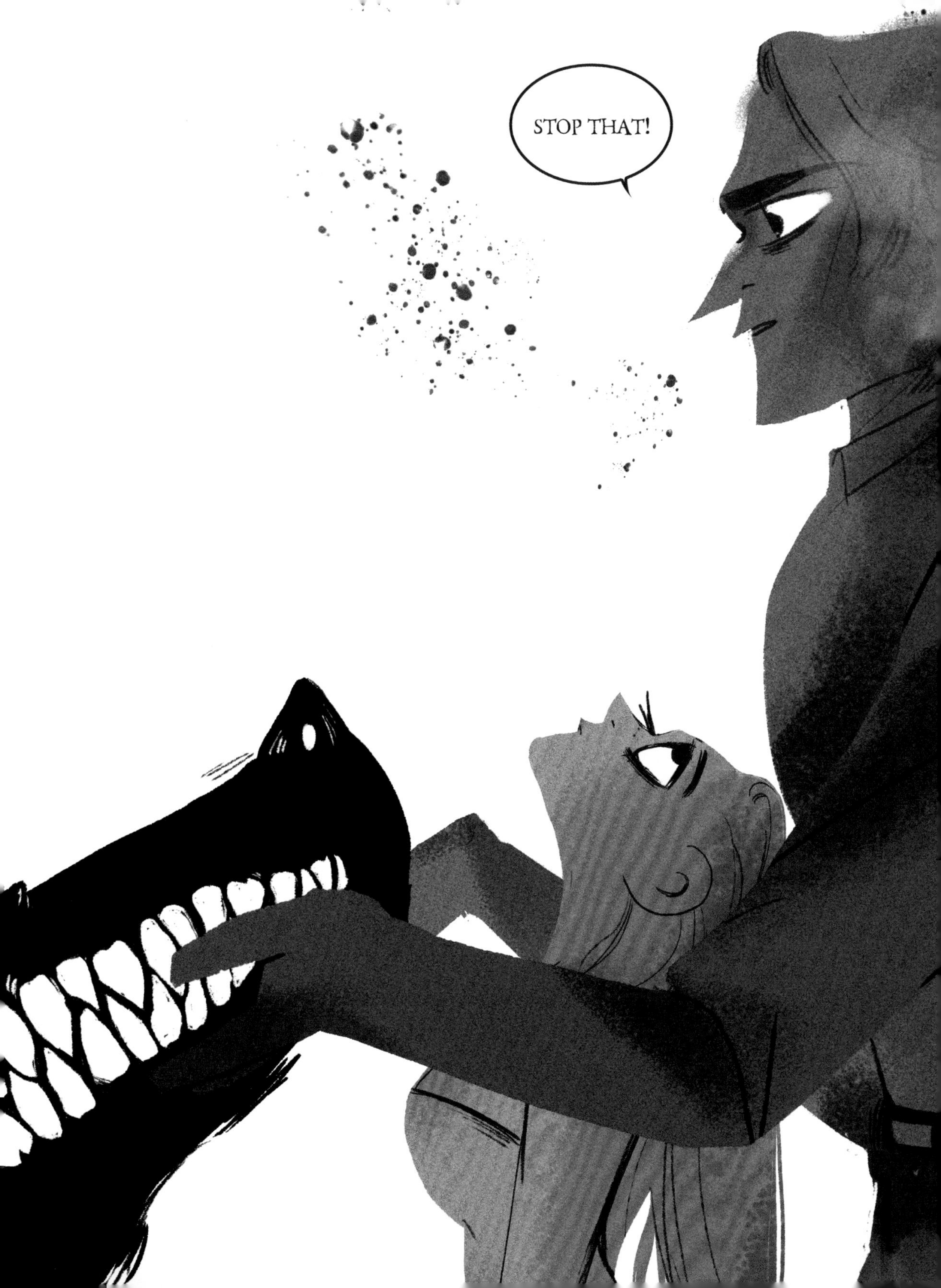
STOP THAT!

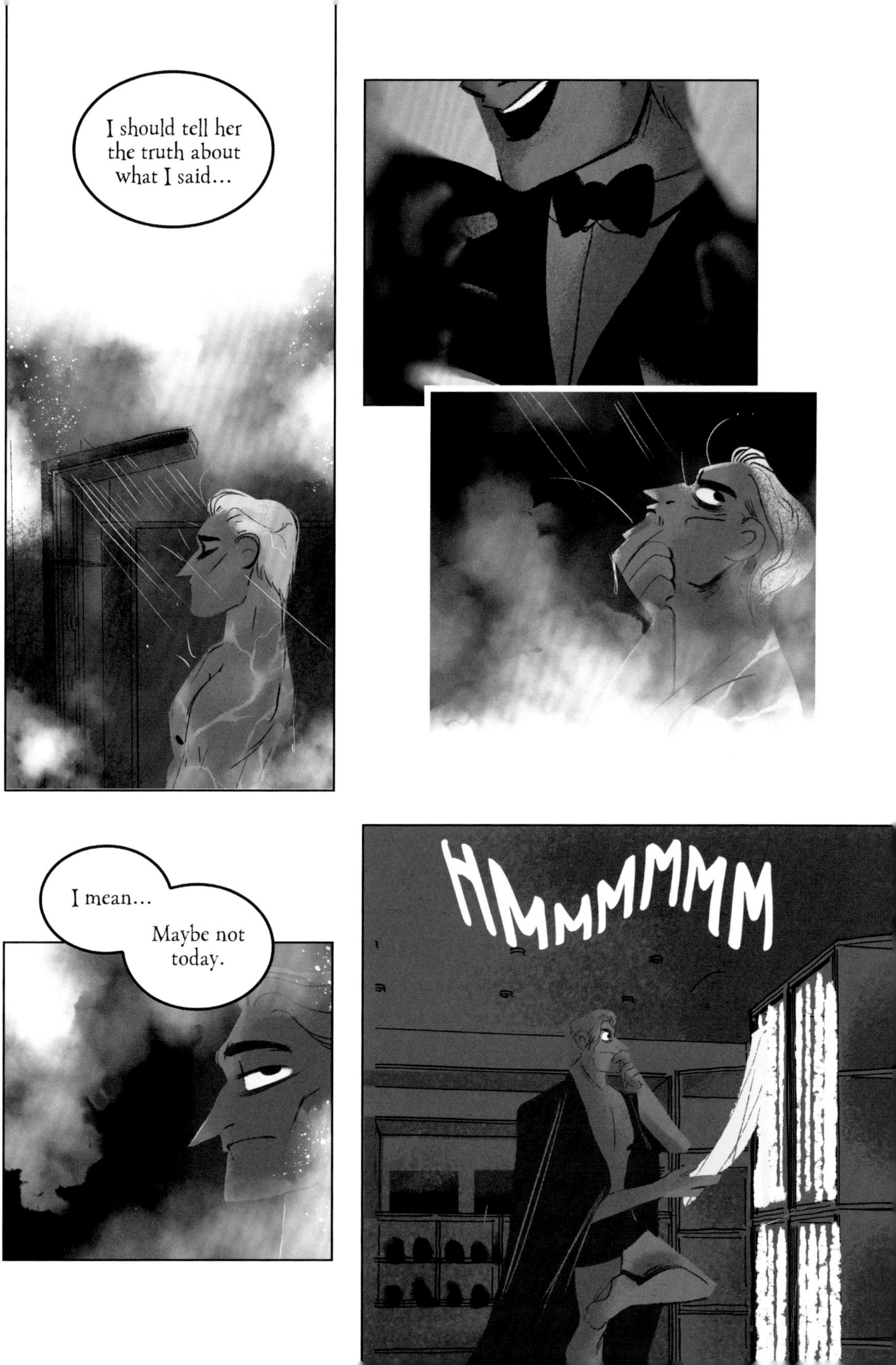
I should tell her the truth about what I said...
I mean...
Maybe not today.
HMMMMMM

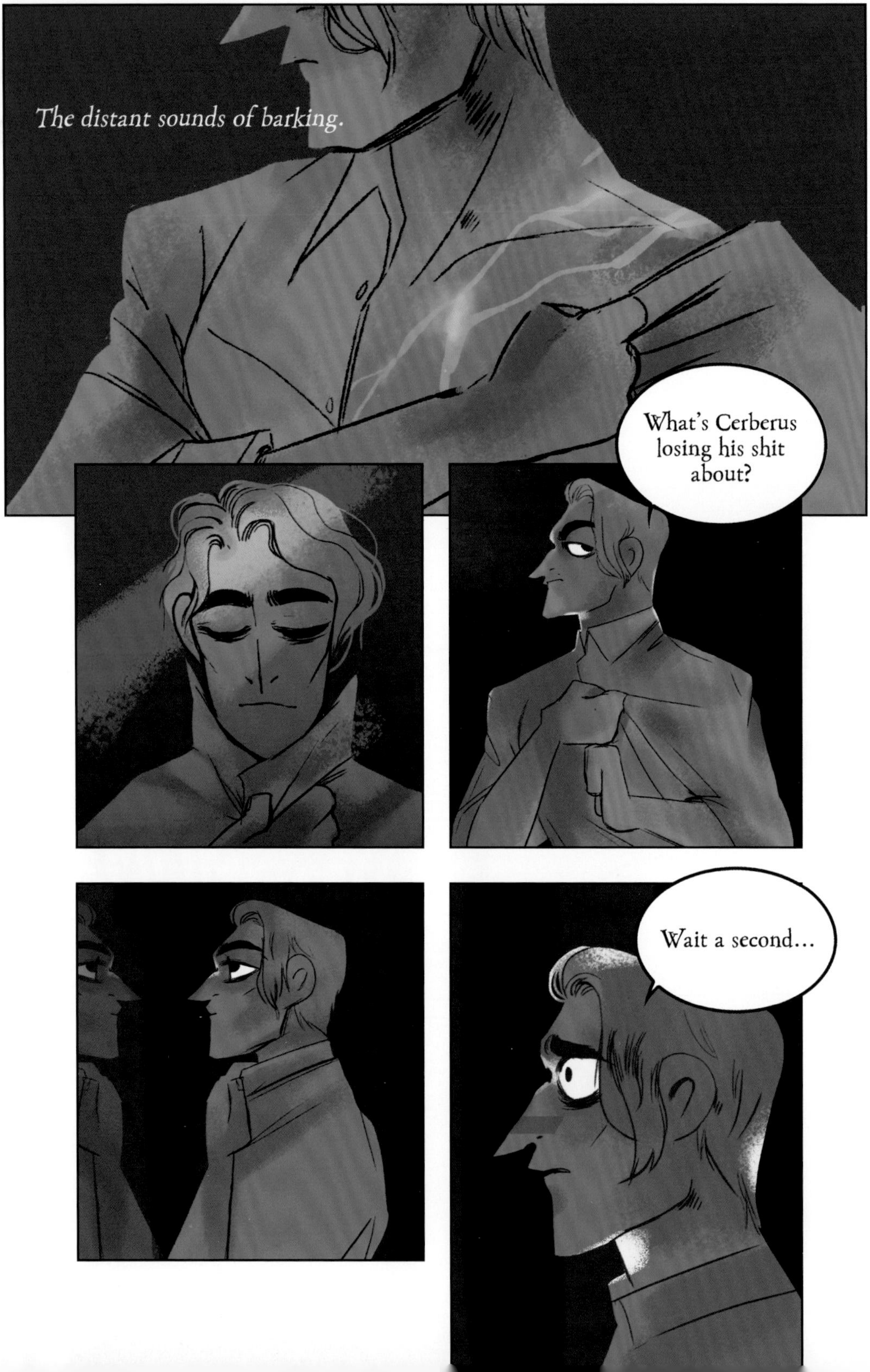
The distant sounds of barking.
What's Cerberus losing his shit about?
Wait a second...

EPISODE 07: A VERY GOOD BOY

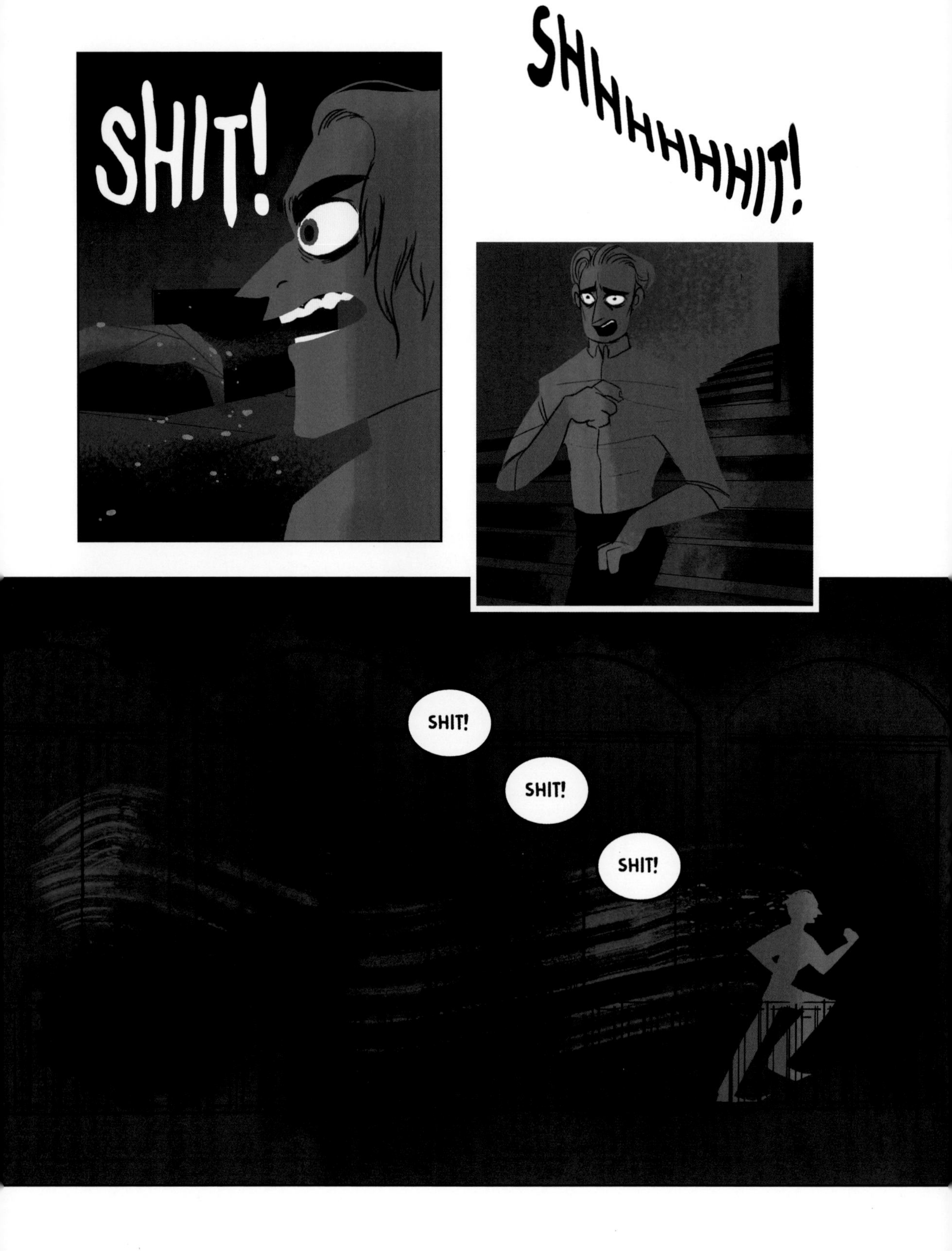

SHIT!
SHHHHHHHIT!
SHIT!
SHIT!
SHIT!

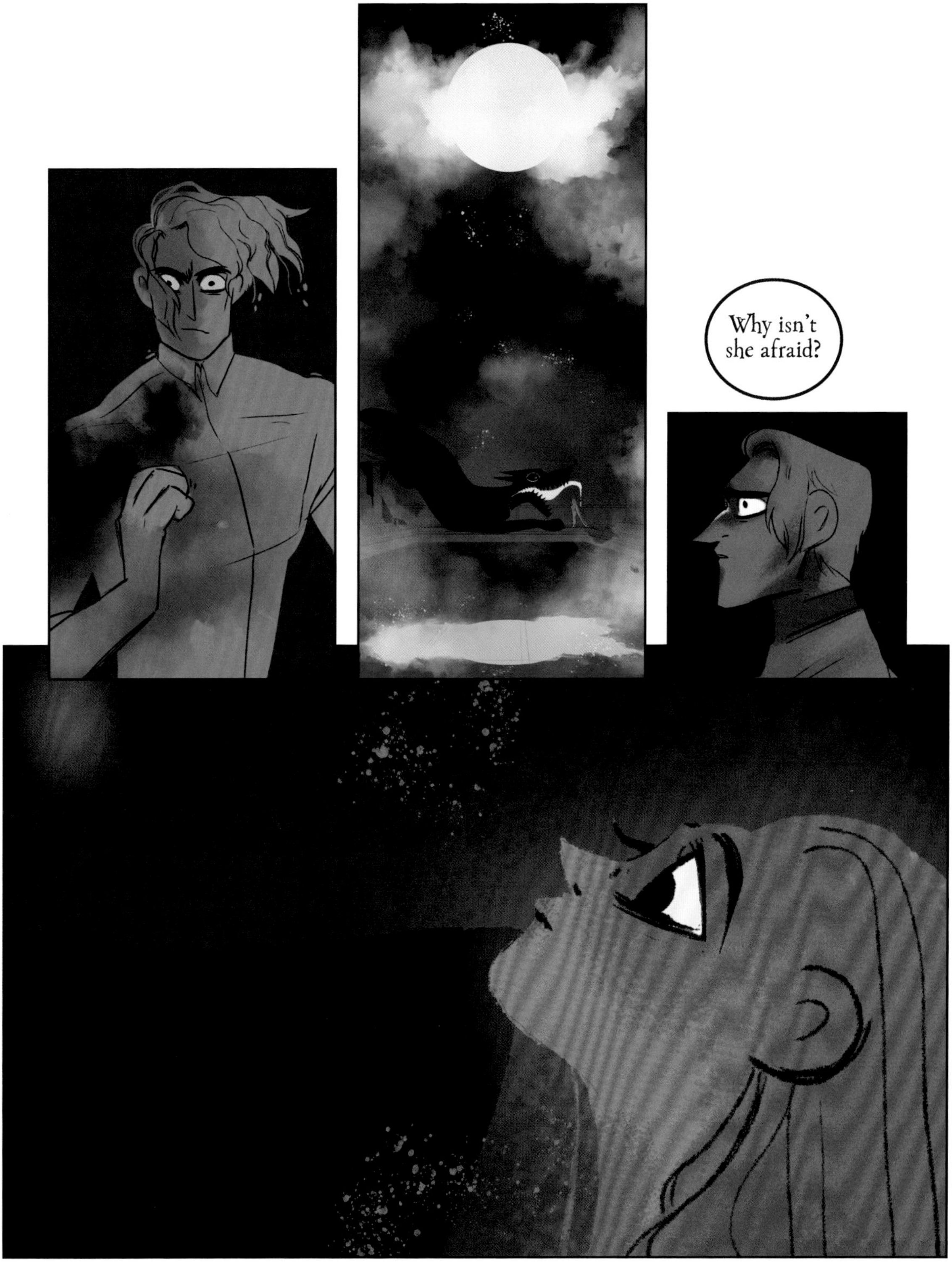
Why isn't she afraid?

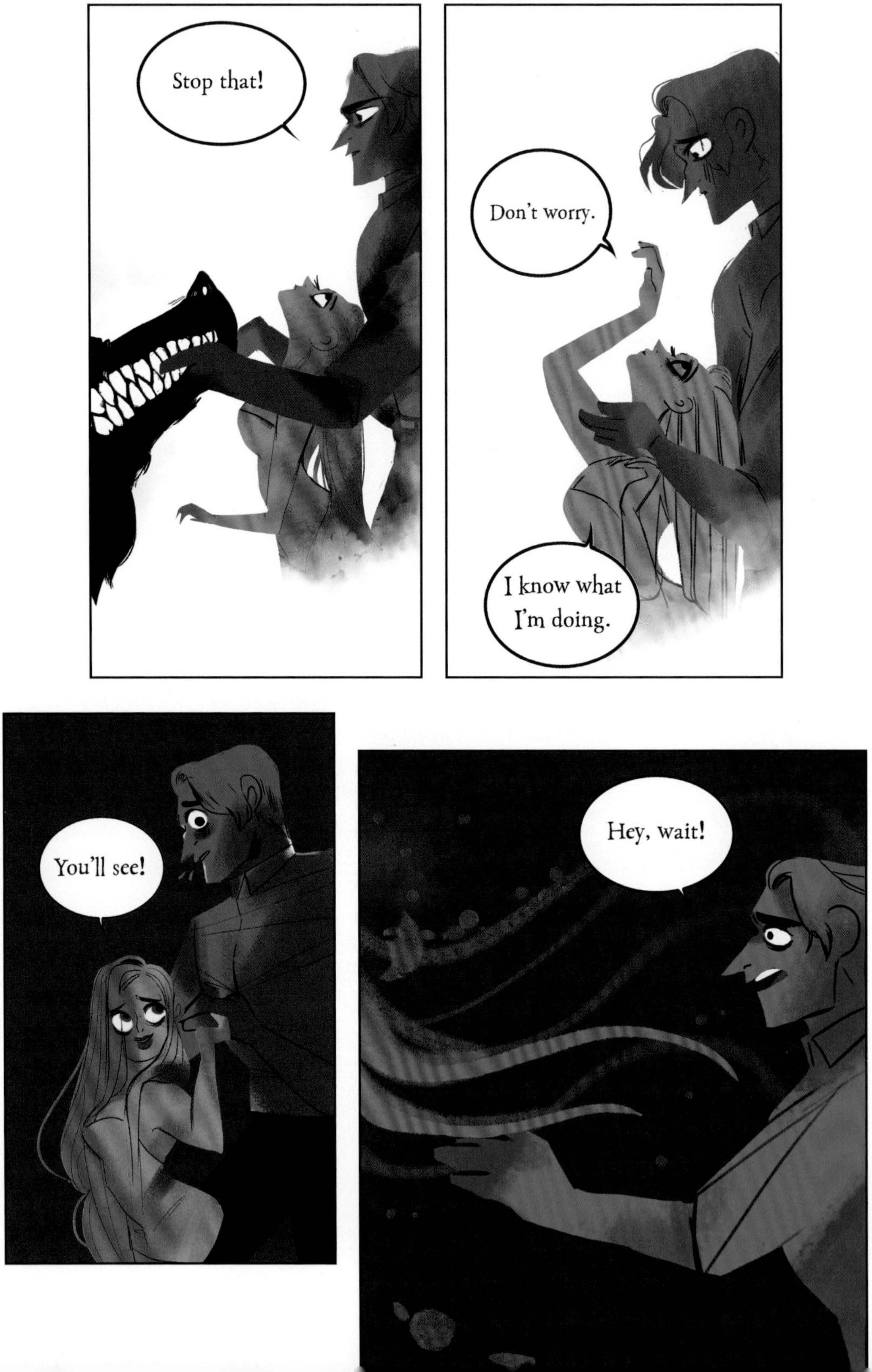
Stop that!
Don't worry.
I know what I'm doing.
You'll see!
Hey, wait!

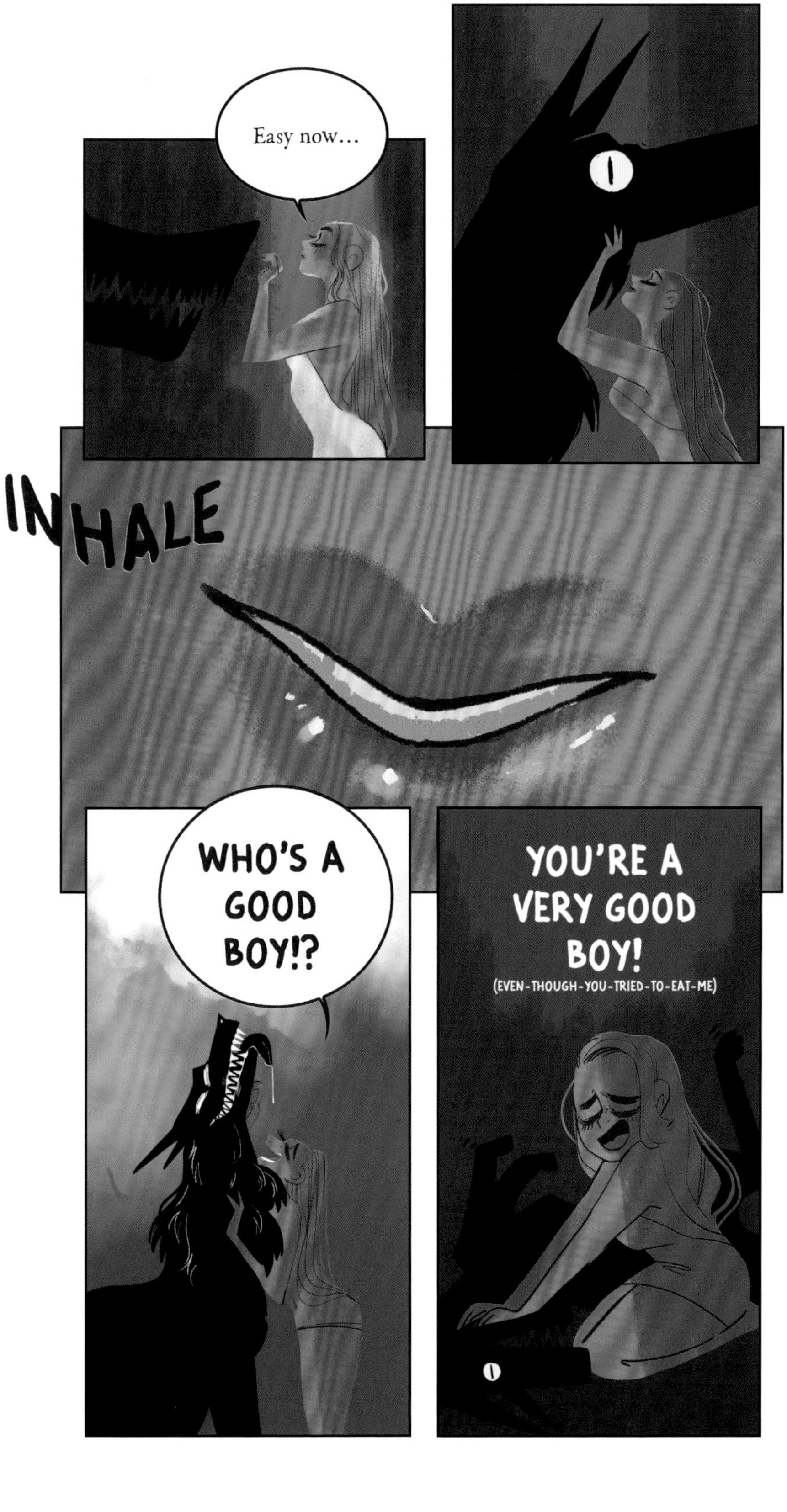
Easy now…
INHALE
WHO'S A GOOD BOY!?
YOU'RE A VERY GOOD BOY!
(EVEN-THOUGH-YOU-TRIED-TO-EAT-ME)

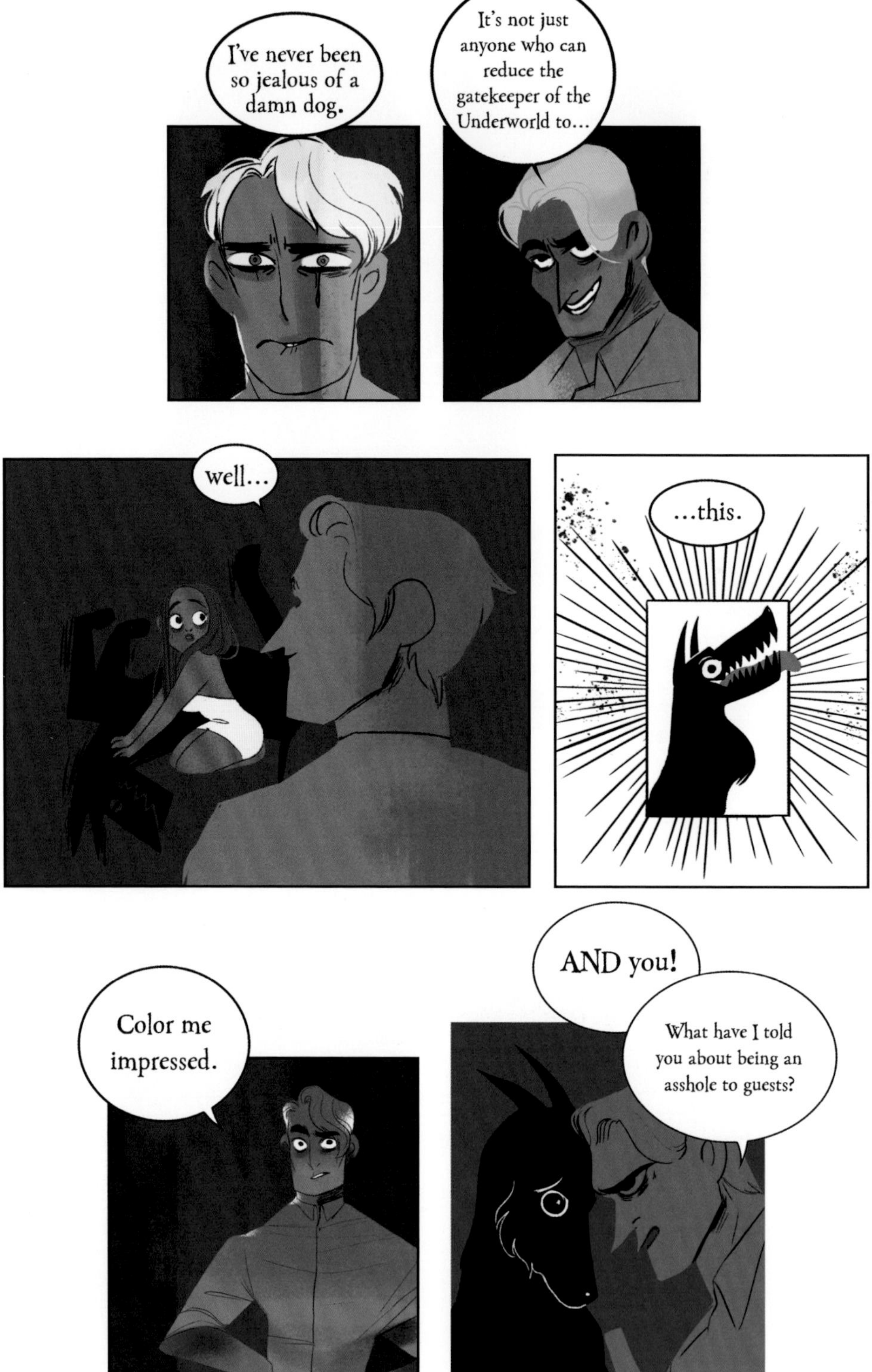
I've never been so jealous of a damn dog.
It's not just anyone who can reduce the gatekeeper of the Underworld to...
well...
...this.
Color me impressed.
AND you!
What have I told you about being an asshole to guests?

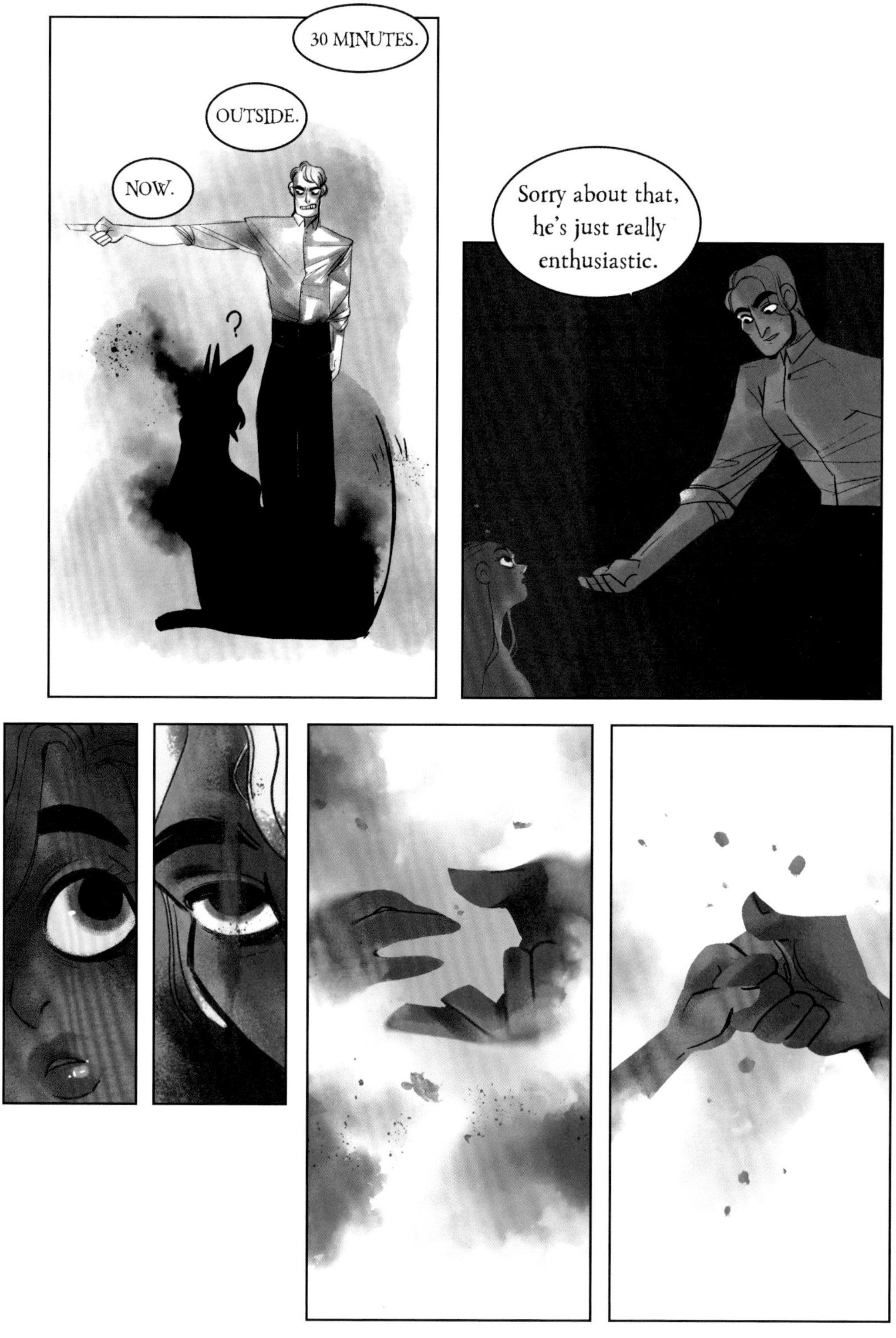
NOW.
OUTSIDE.
30 MINUTES.
?
Sorry about that, he's just really enthusiastic.

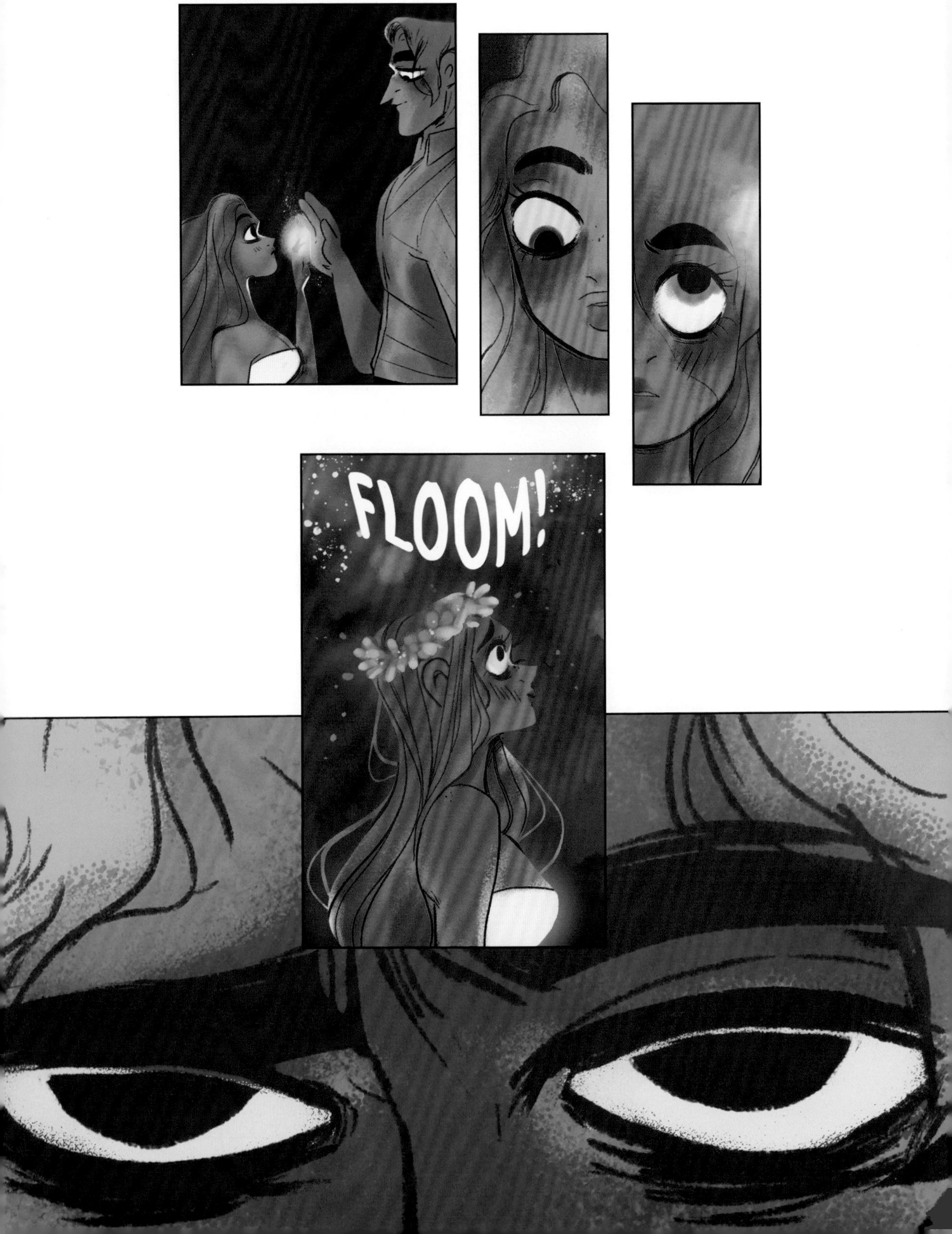
FLOOM!

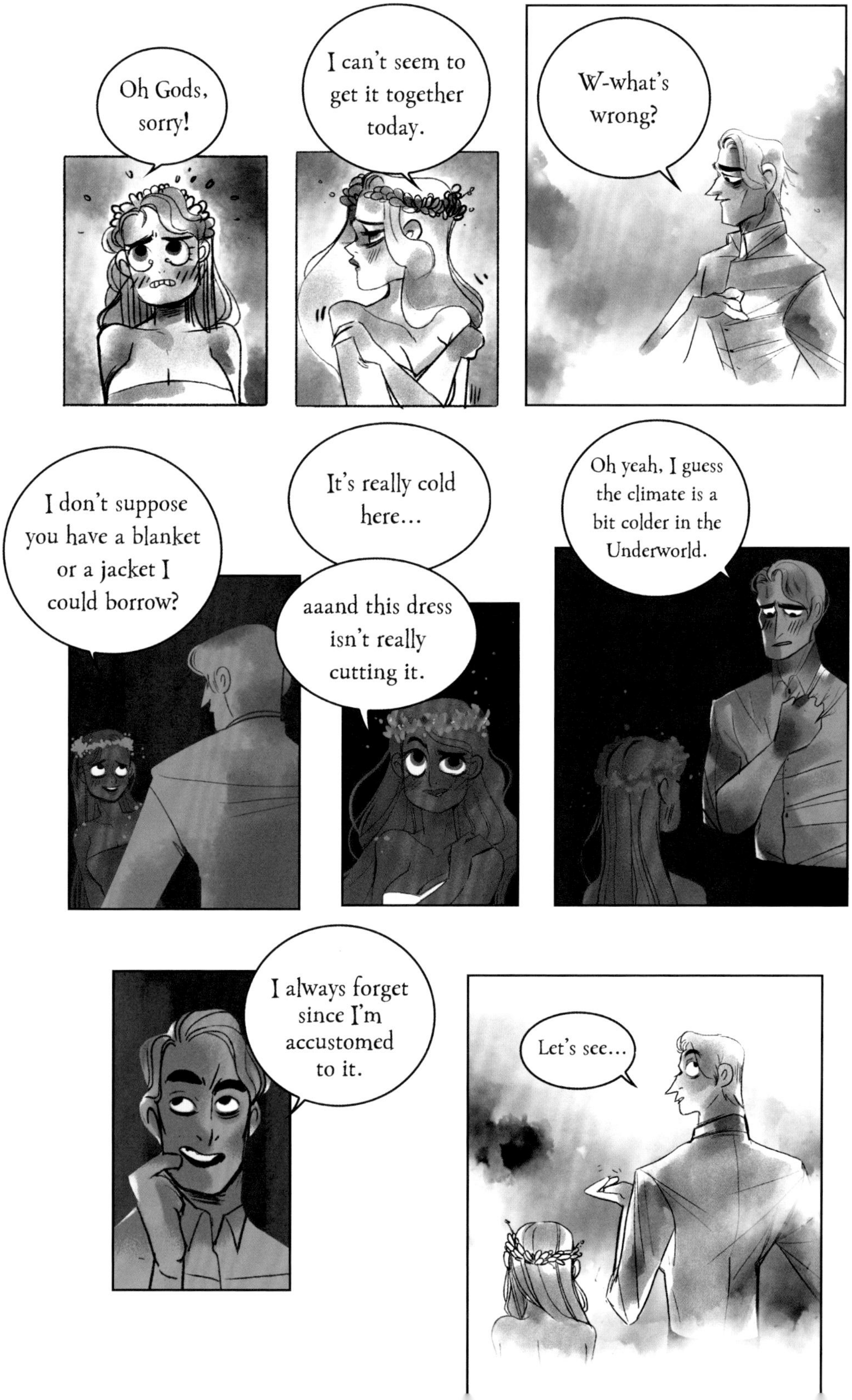
Oh Gods, sorry!
I can't seem to get it together today.
W-what's wrong?
I don't suppose you have a blanket or a jacket I could borrow?
It's really cold here...
aaand this dress isn't really cutting it.
Oh yeah, I guess the climate is a bit colder in the Underworld.
I always forget since I'm accustomed to it.
Let's see...

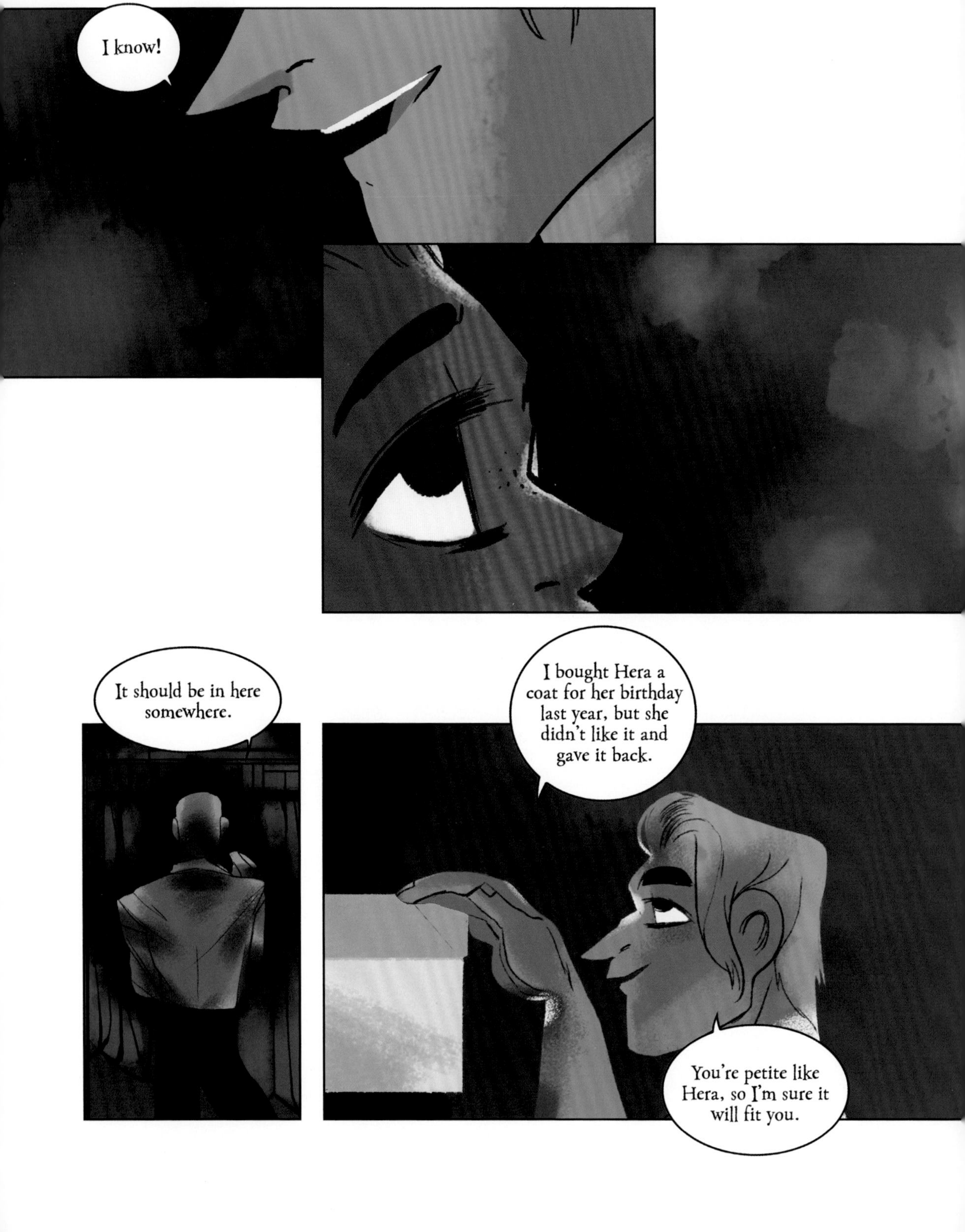
I know!
It should be in here somewhere.
I bought Hera a coat for her birthday last year, but she didn't like it and gave it back.
You're petite like Hera, so I'm sure it will fit you.

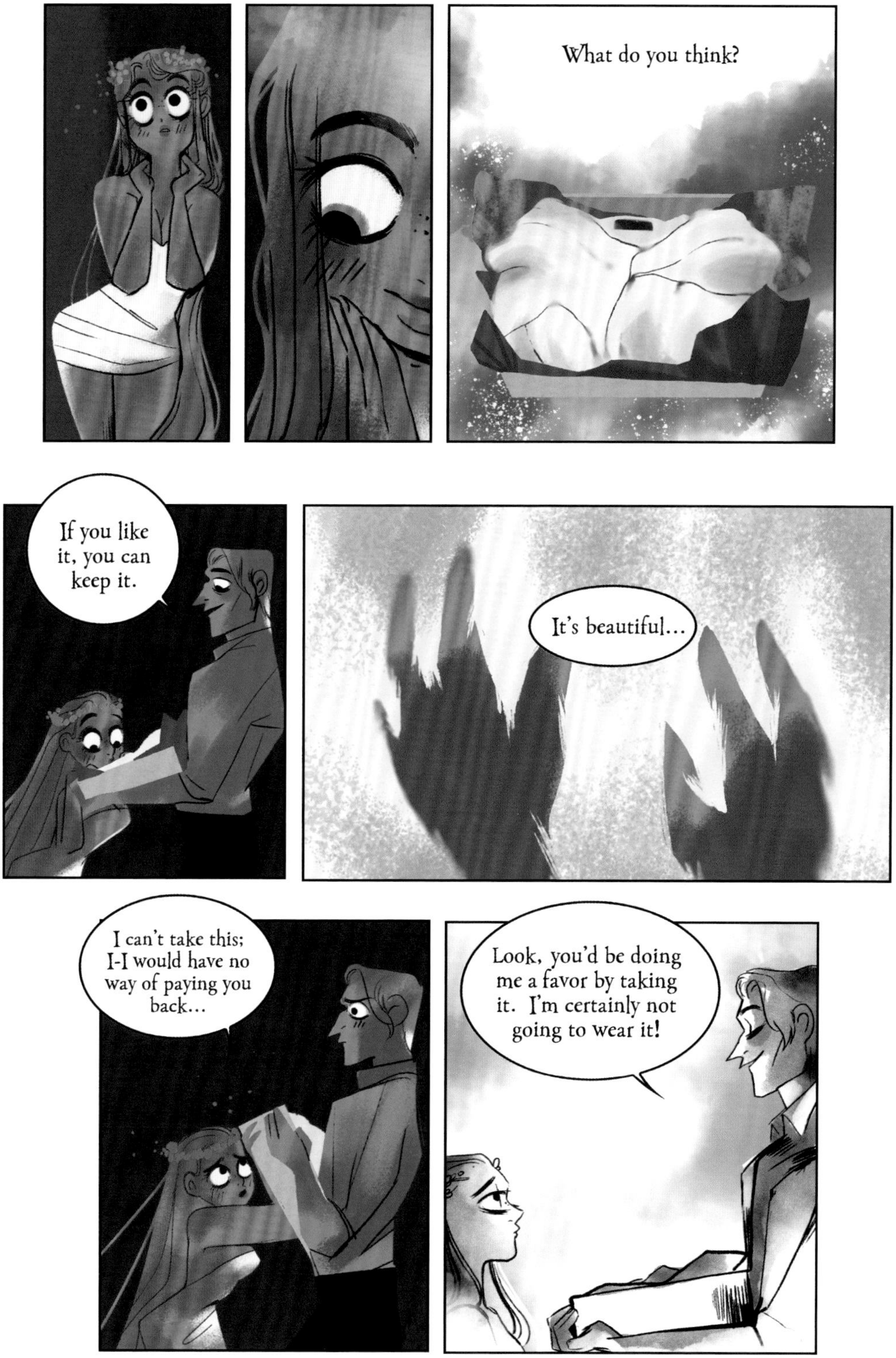
What do you think?
If you like it, you can keep it.
It's beautiful...
I can't take this; I-I would have no way of paying you back...
Look, you'd be doing me a favor by taking it. I'm certainly not going to wear it!

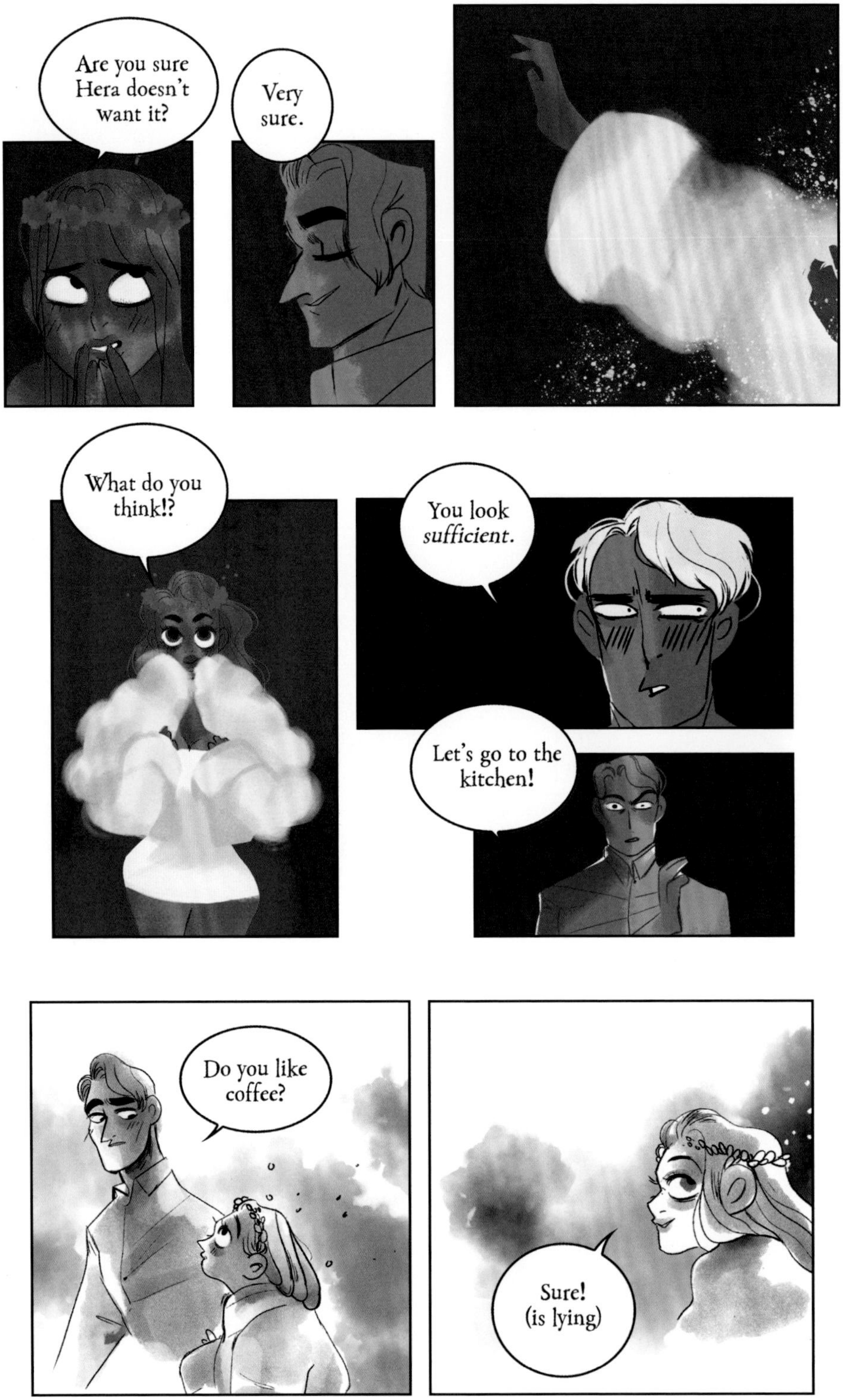
Are you sure Hera doesn't want it?
Very sure.
What do you think!?
You look *sufficient.*
Let's go to the kitchen!
Do you like coffee?
Sure! (is lying)

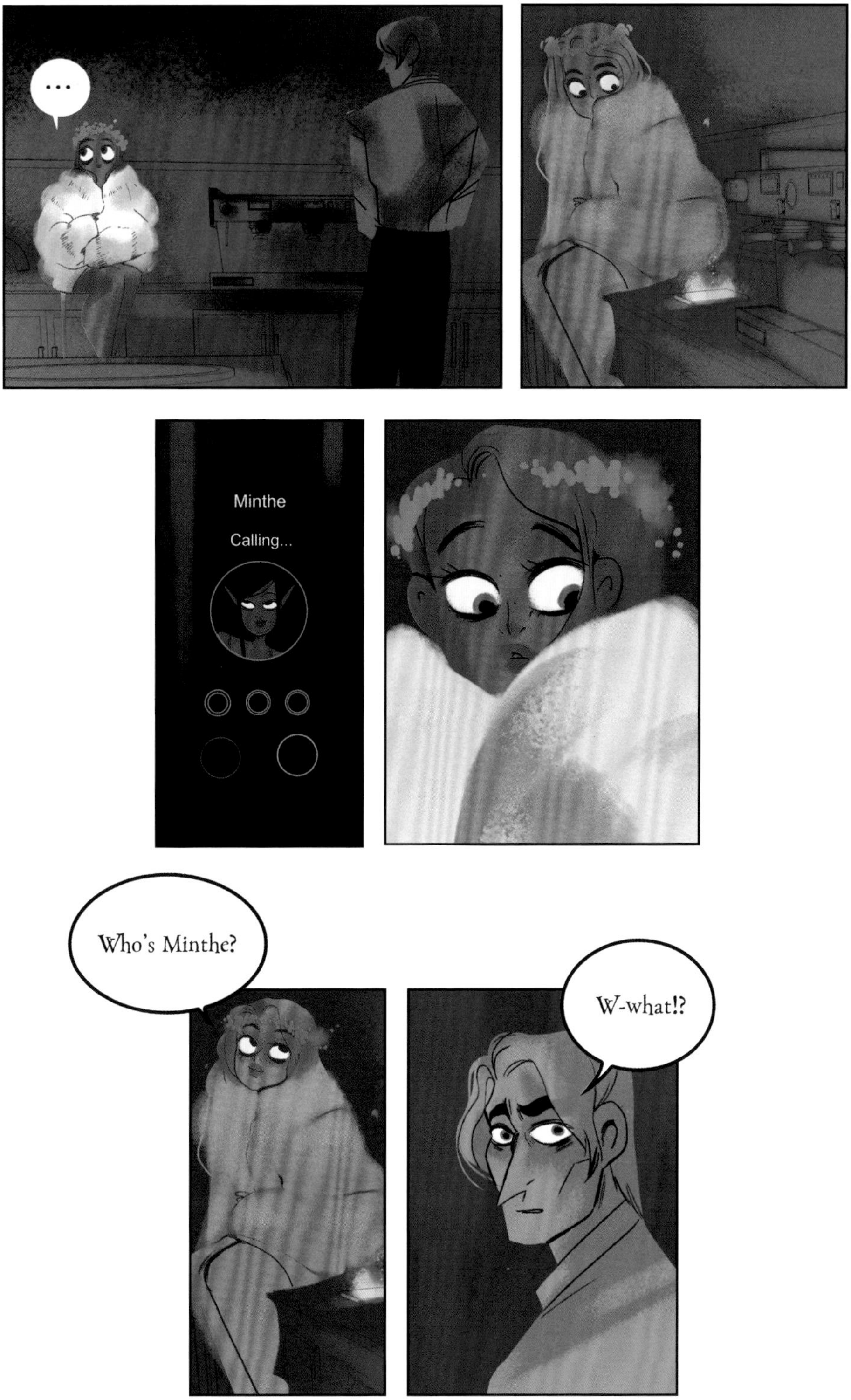
...
Minthe
Calling...
Who's Minthe?
W-what!?

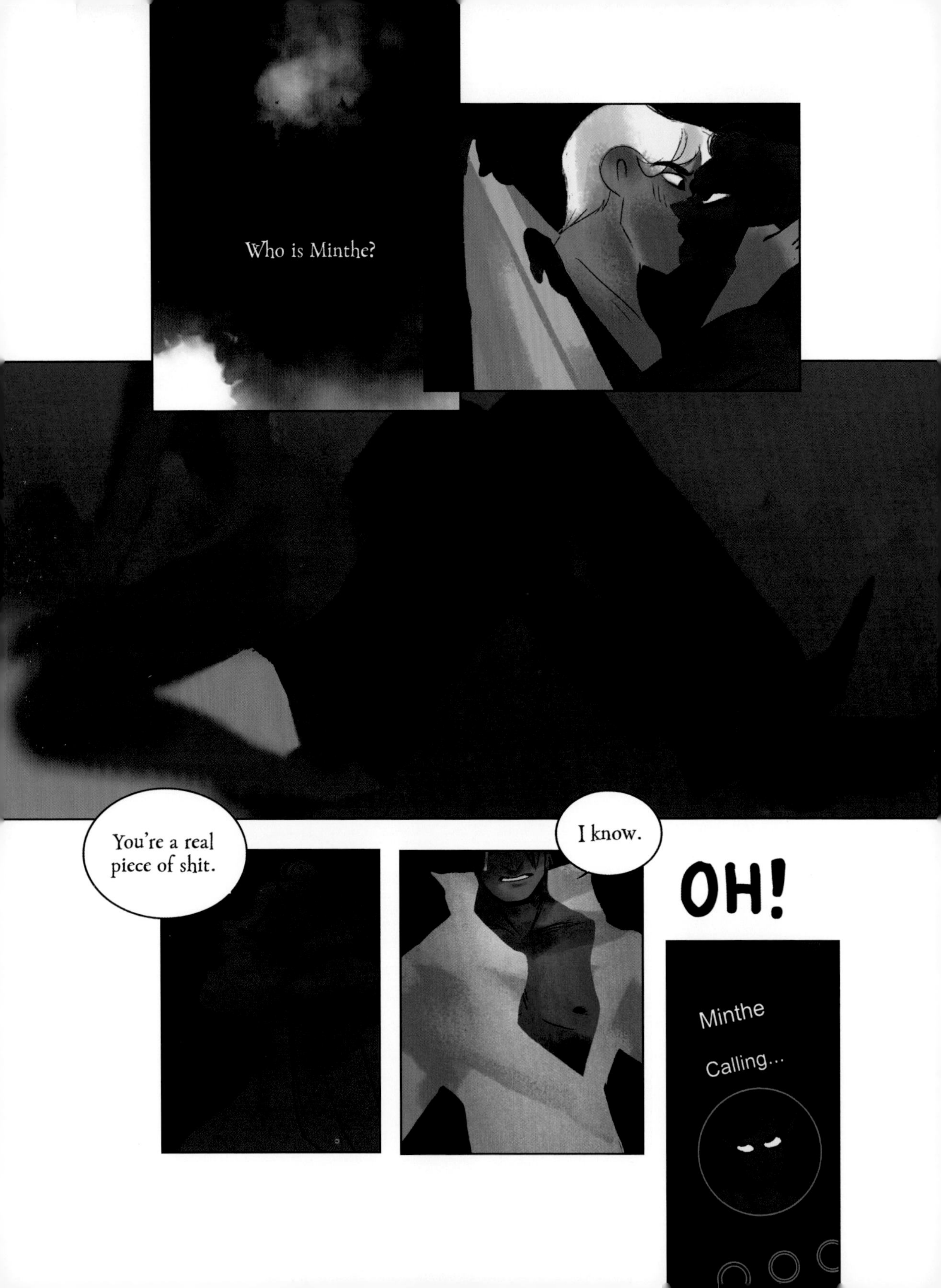
Who is Minthe?
You're a real piece of shit.
I know.
OH!
Minthe
Calling...

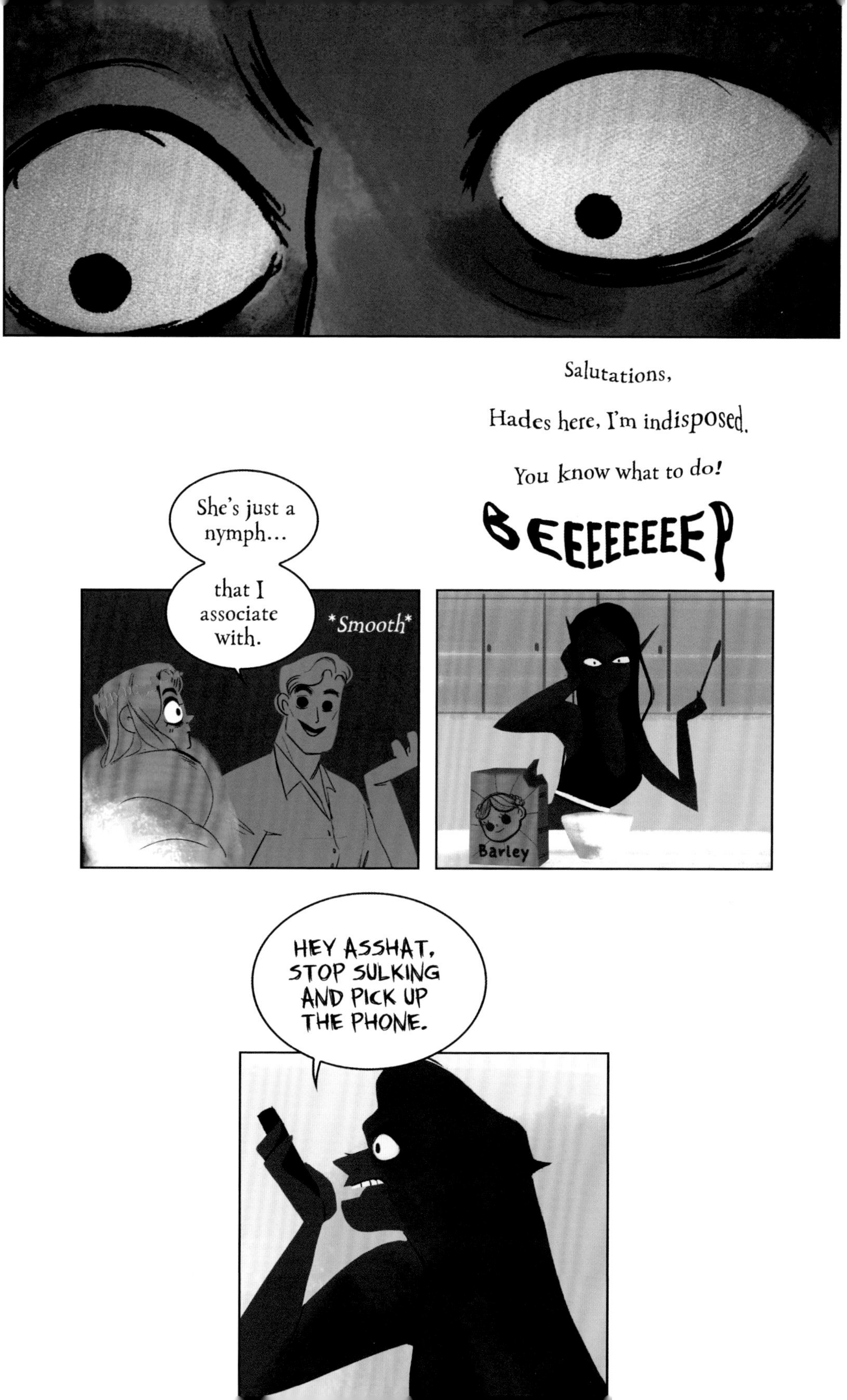
Salutations,
Hades here, I'm indisposed.
You know what to do!
BEEEEEEEP
She's just a nymph...
that I associate with.
Smooth
Barley
HEY ASSHAT, STOP SULKING AND PICK UP THE PHONE.

EPISODE 08: HANDFUL

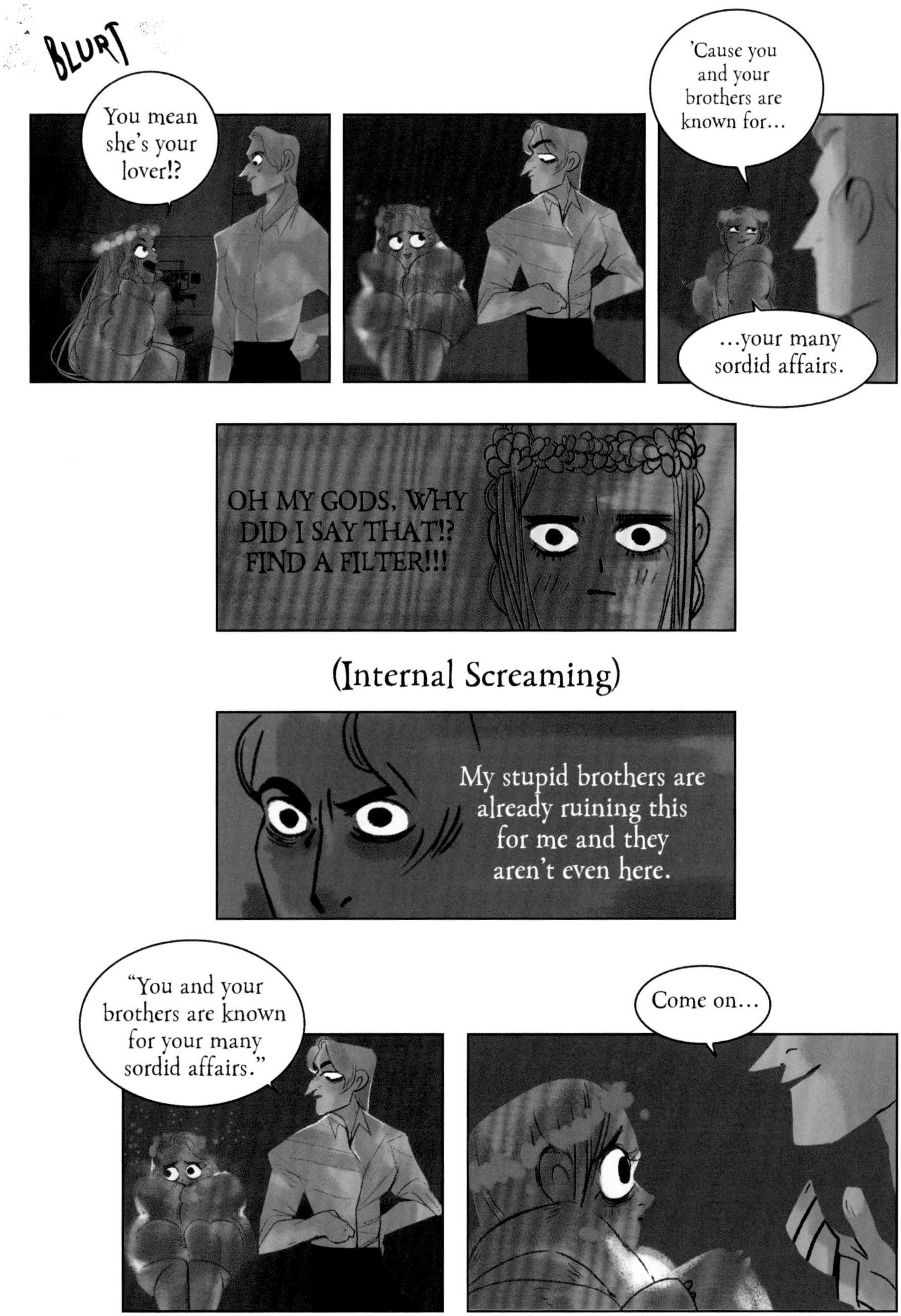
BLURT
You mean she's your lover!?
'Cause you and your brothers are known for...
...your many sordid affairs.
OH MY GODS, WHY DID I SAY THAT!? FIND A FILTER!!!
(Internal Screaming)
My stupid brothers are already ruining this for me and they aren't even here.
"You and your brothers are known for your many sordid affairs."
Come on...

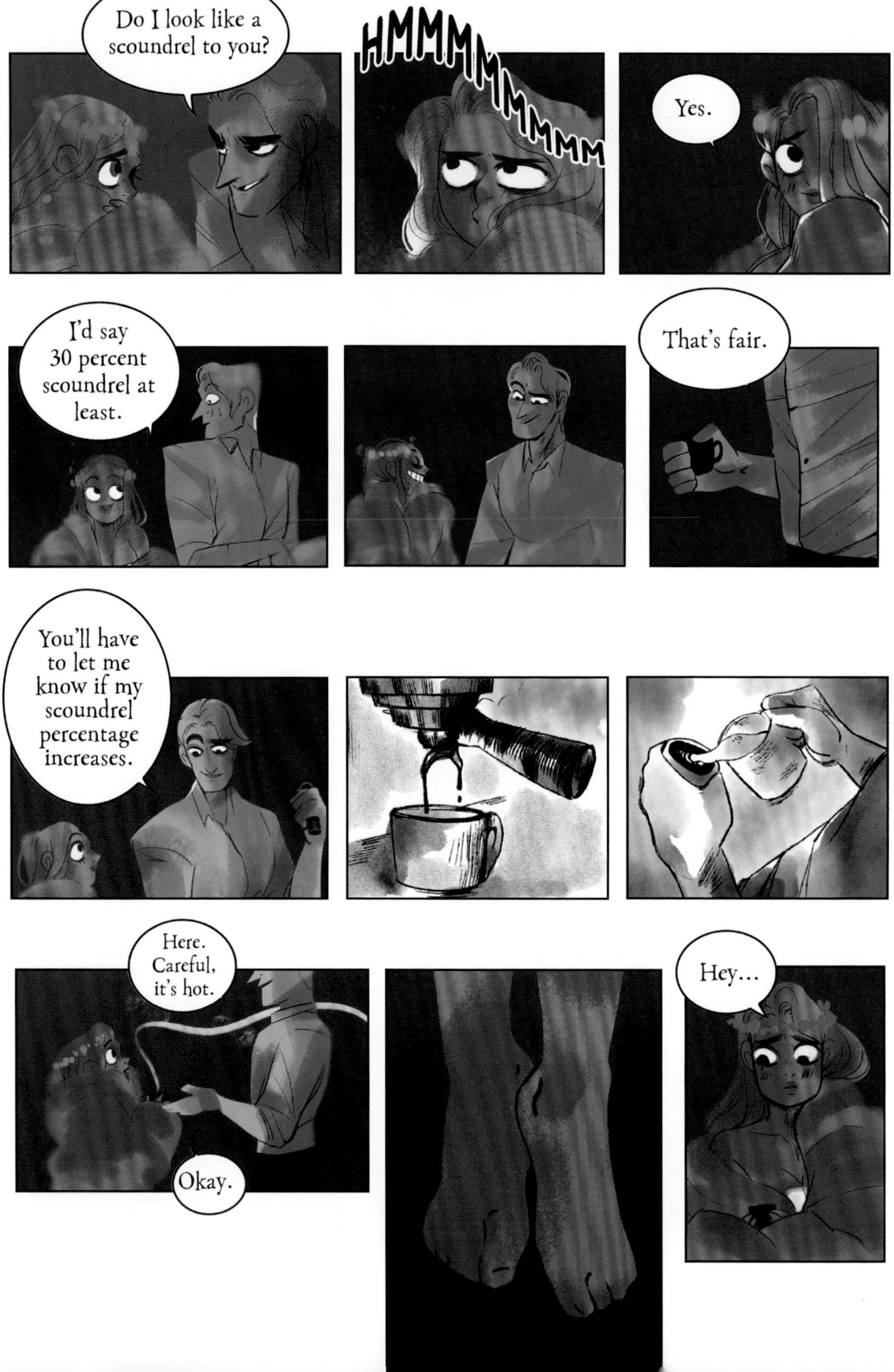
Do I look like a scoundrel to you?
HMMMMMMMMMM
Yes.
I'd say 30 percent scoundrel at least.
That's fair.
You'll have to let me know if my scoundrel percentage increases.
Here. Careful, it's hot.
Okay.
Hey…

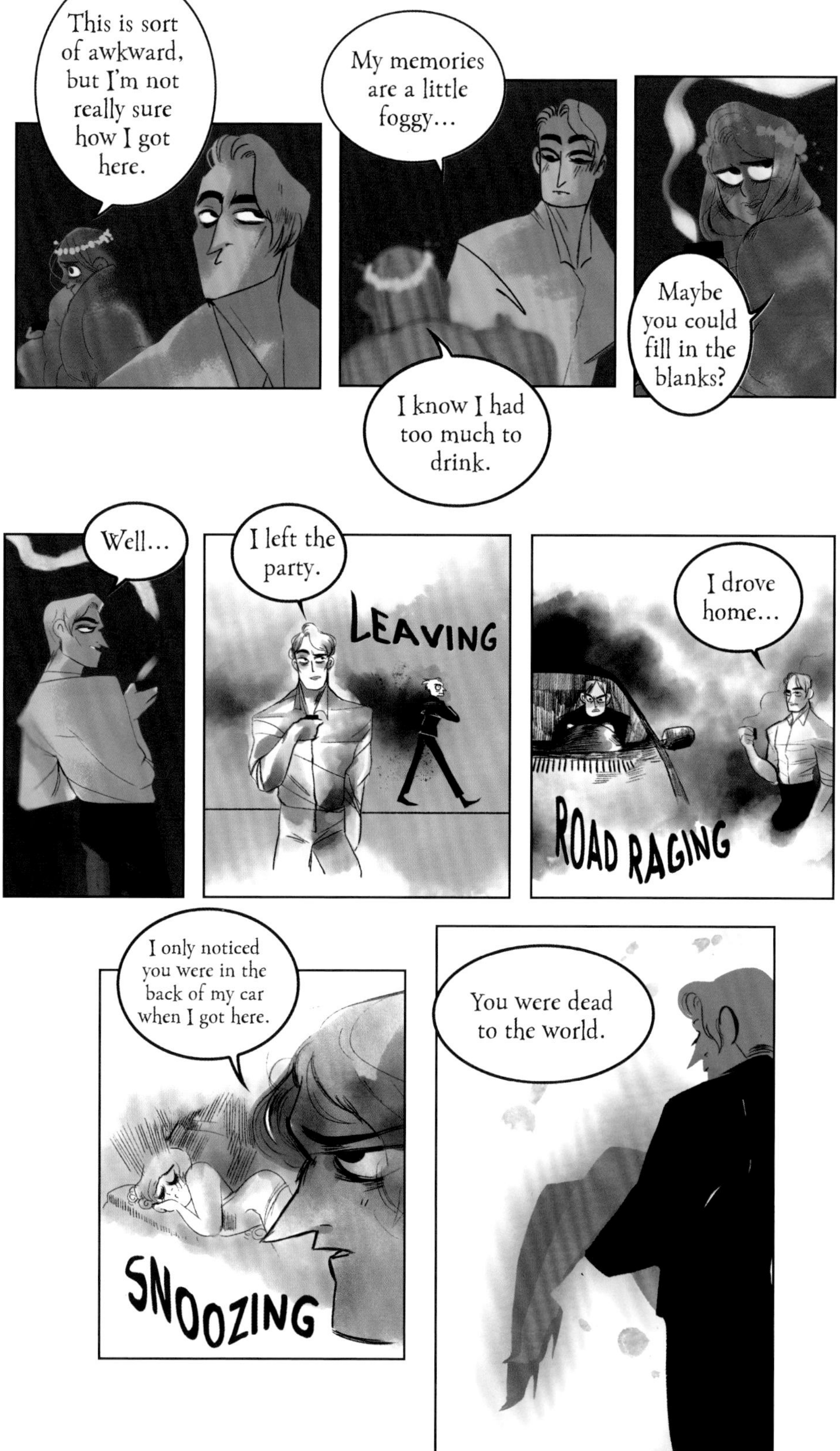
This is sort of awkward, but I'm not really sure how I got here.
My memories are a little foggy...
I know I had too much to drink.
Maybe you could fill in the blanks?
Well...
I left the party.
LEAVING
I drove home...
ROAD RAGING
I only noticed you were in the back of my car when I got here.
SNOOZING
You were dead to the world.

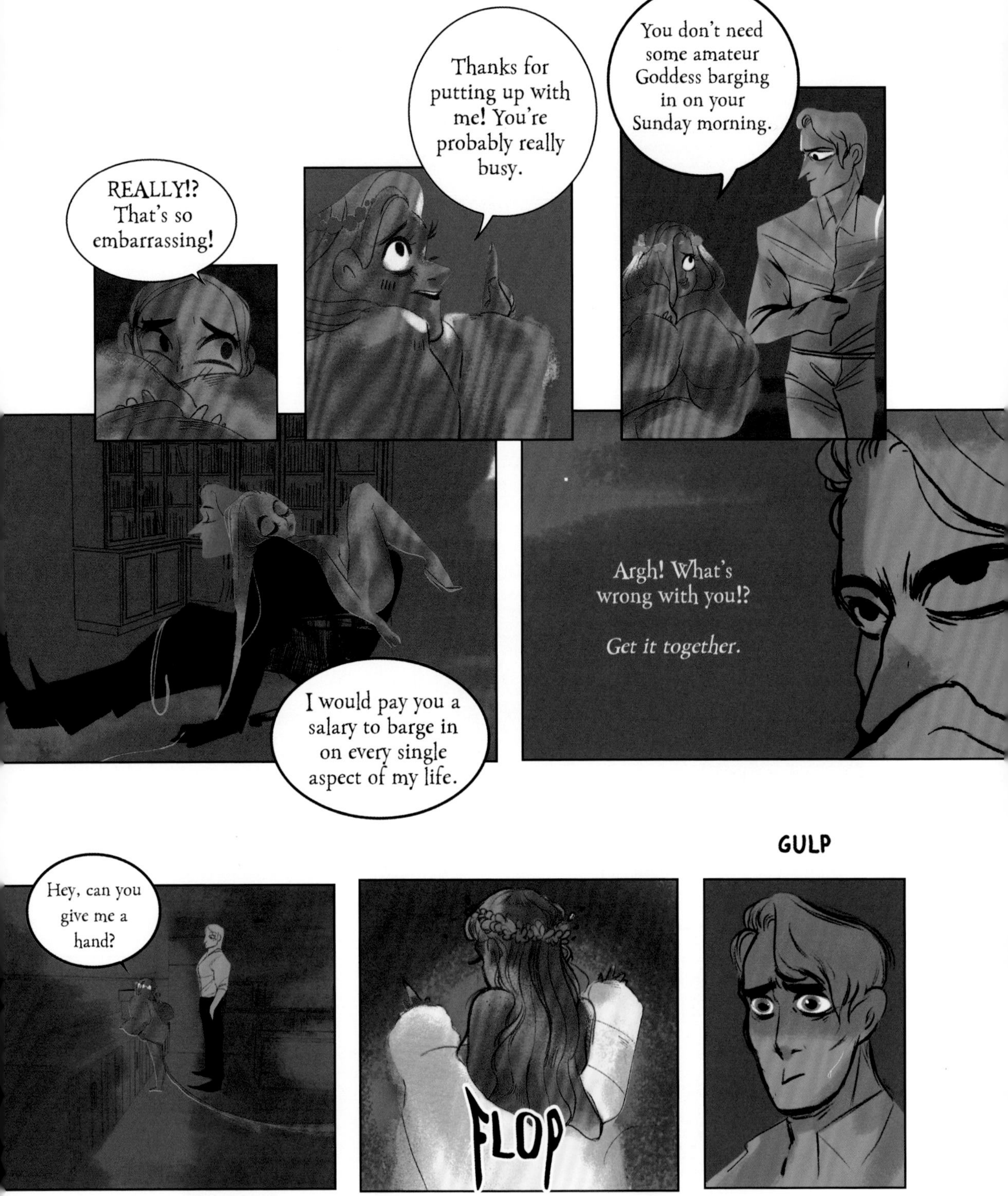
REALLY!? That's so embarrassing!
Thanks for putting up with me! You're probably really busy.
You don't need some amateur Goddess barging in on your Sunday morning.
I would pay you a salary to barge in on every single aspect of my life.
Argh! What's wrong with you!?
Get it together.
Hey, can you give me a hand?
FLOP
GULP

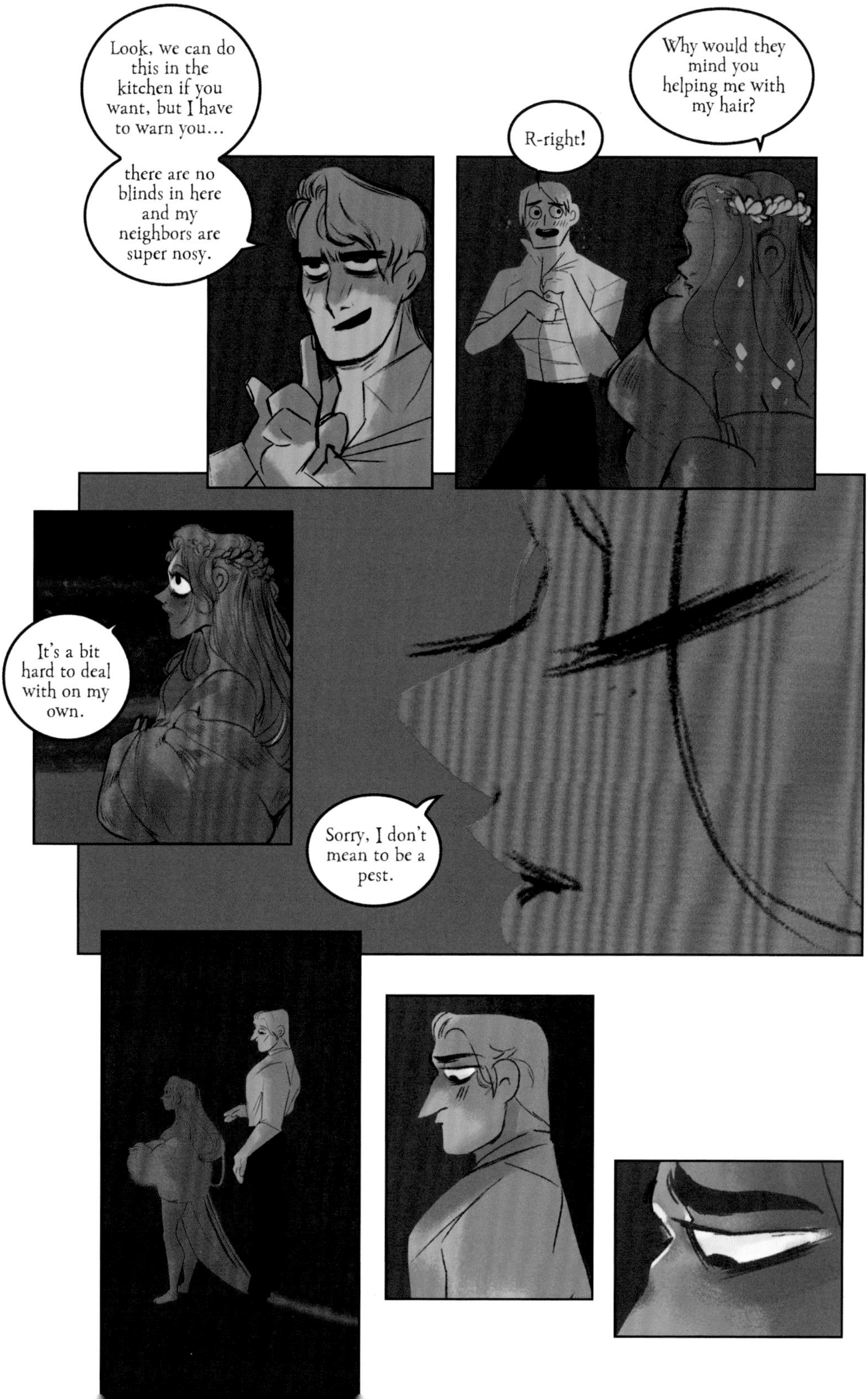
Look, we can do this in the kitchen if you want, but I have to warn you...
there are no blinds in here and my neighbors are super nosy.
Why would they mind you helping me with my hair?
R-right!
It's a bit hard to deal with on my own.
Sorry, I don't mean to be a pest.

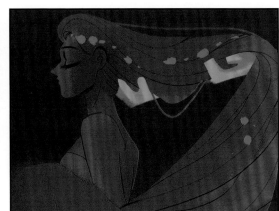

I've got a question...

Stab in the dark, is it about my "silky flowing goddess hair"?

It is.

...

What made you lose control?

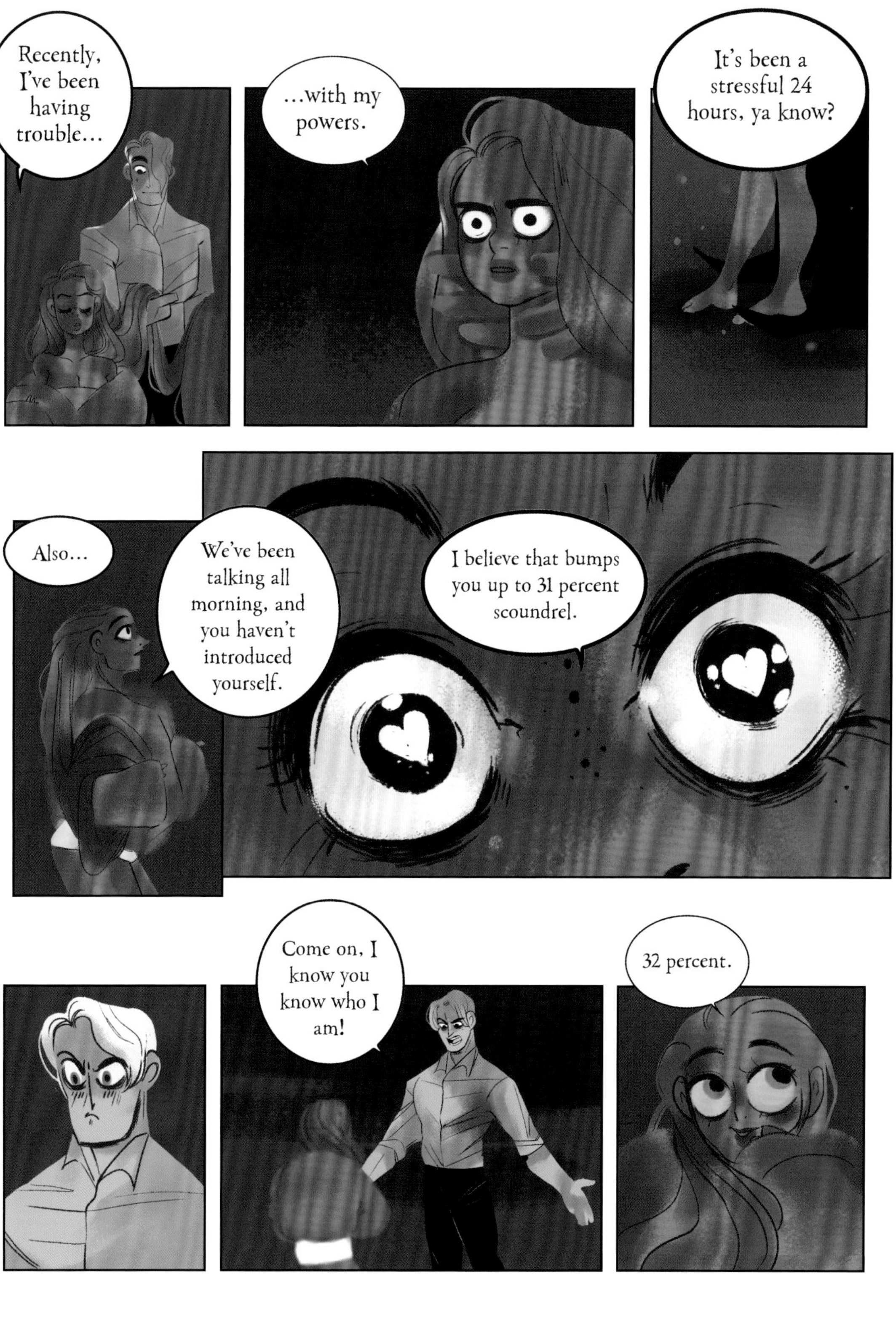
Recently, I've been having trouble...
...with my powers.
It's been a stressful 24 hours, ya know?
Also...
We've been talking all morning, and you haven't introduced yourself.
I believe that bumps you up to 31 percent scoundrel.
Come on, I know you know who I am!
32 percent.

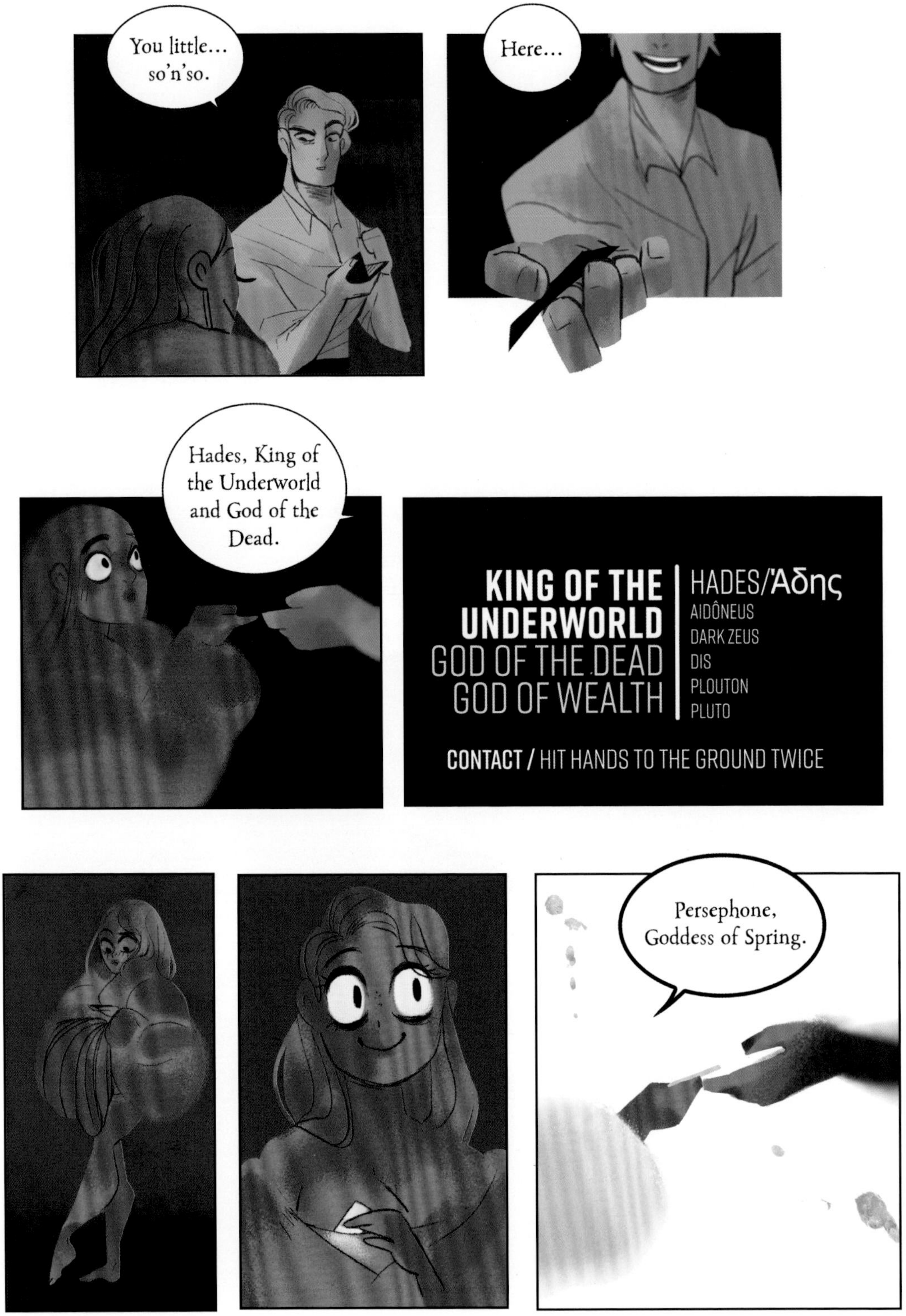
You little... so'n'so.
Here...
Hades, King of the Underworld and God of the Dead.
KING OF THE UNDERWORLD
GOD OF THE DEAD
GOD OF WEALTH
HADES/Ἅδης
AIDÔNEUS
DARK ZEUS
DIS
PLOUTON
PLUTO
CONTACT / HIT HANDS TO THE GROUND TWICE
Persephone, Goddess of Spring.

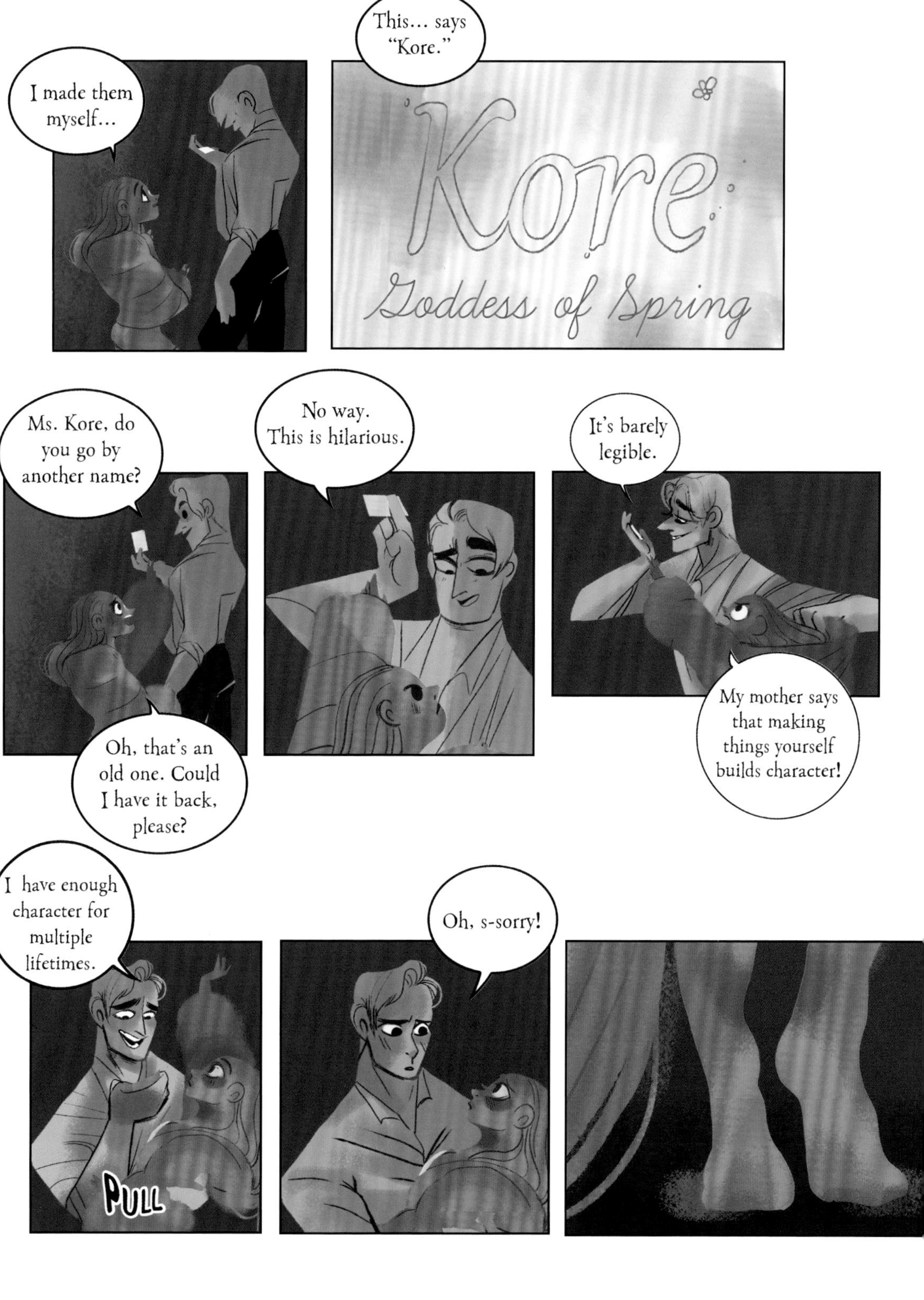
I made them myself...
This... says "Kore."
Kore
Goddess of Spring
Ms. Kore, do you go by another name?
Oh, that's an old one. Could I have it back, please?
No way. This is hilarious.
It's barely legible.
My mother says that making things yourself builds character!
I have enough character for multiple lifetimes.
PULL
Oh, s-sorry!

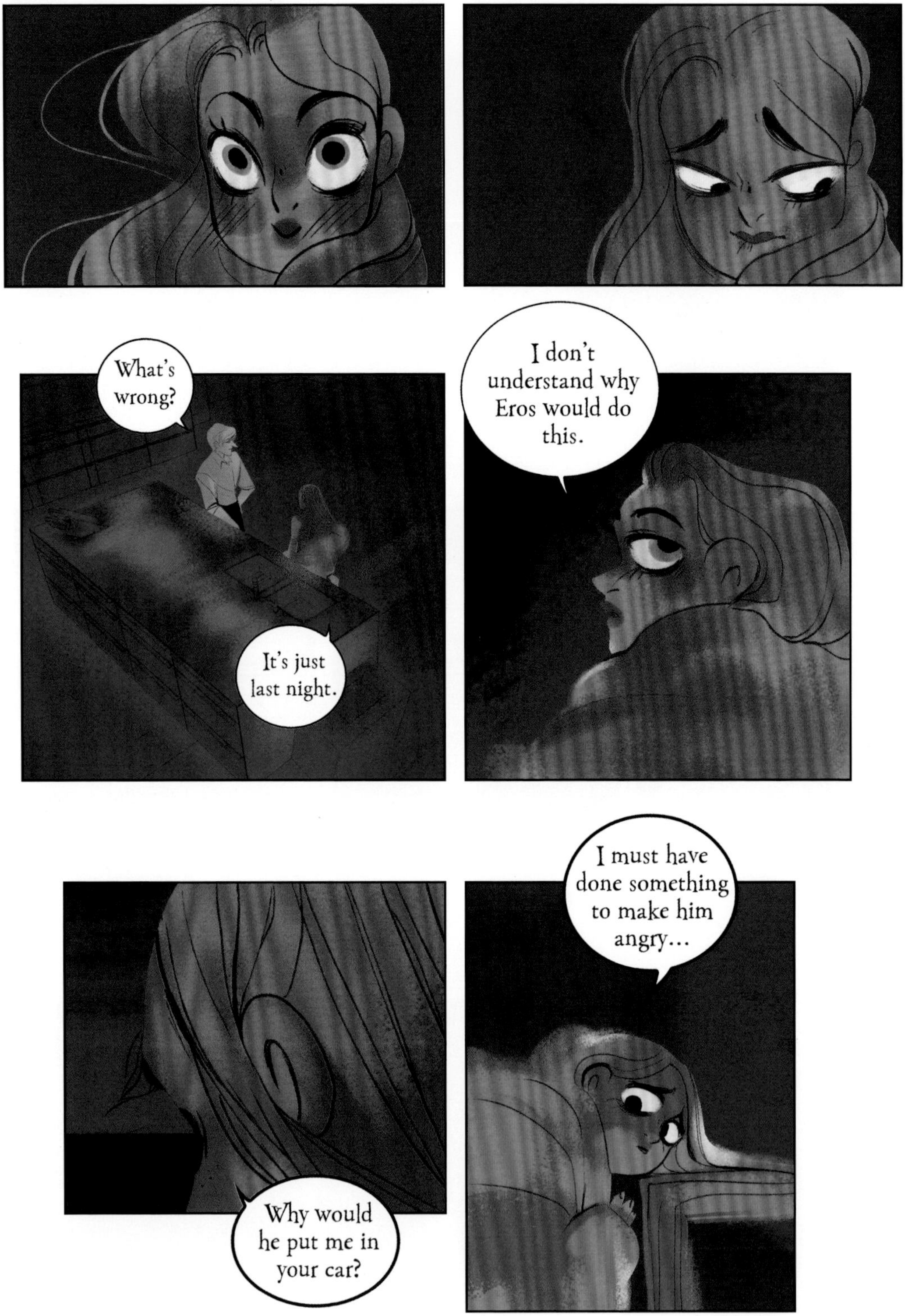
What's wrong?
It's just last night.
I don't understand why Eros would do this.
Why would he put me in your car?
I must have done something to make him angry…

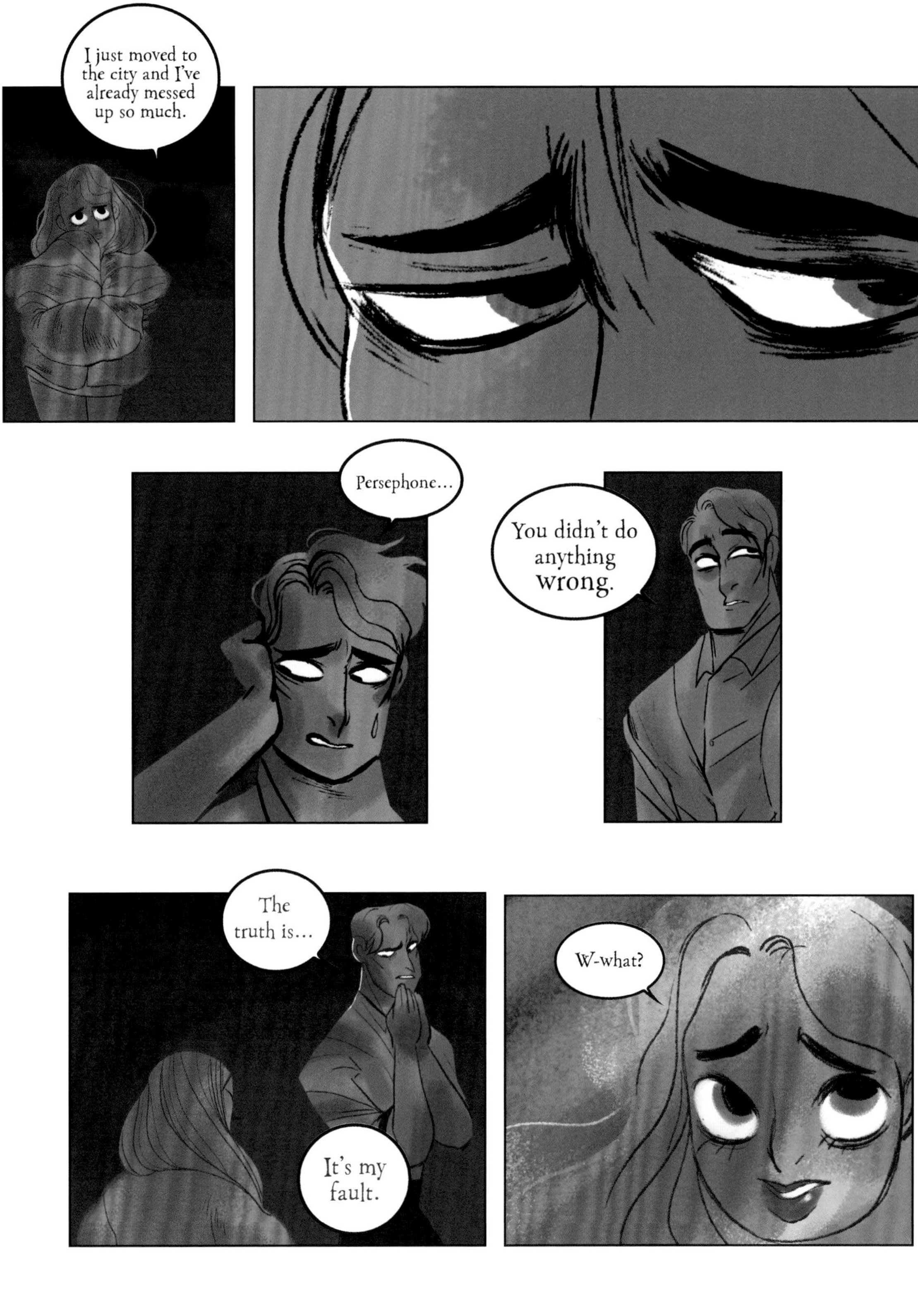
I just moved to the city and I've already messed up so much.
Persephone...
You didn't do anything wrong.
The truth is...
It's my fault.
W-what?

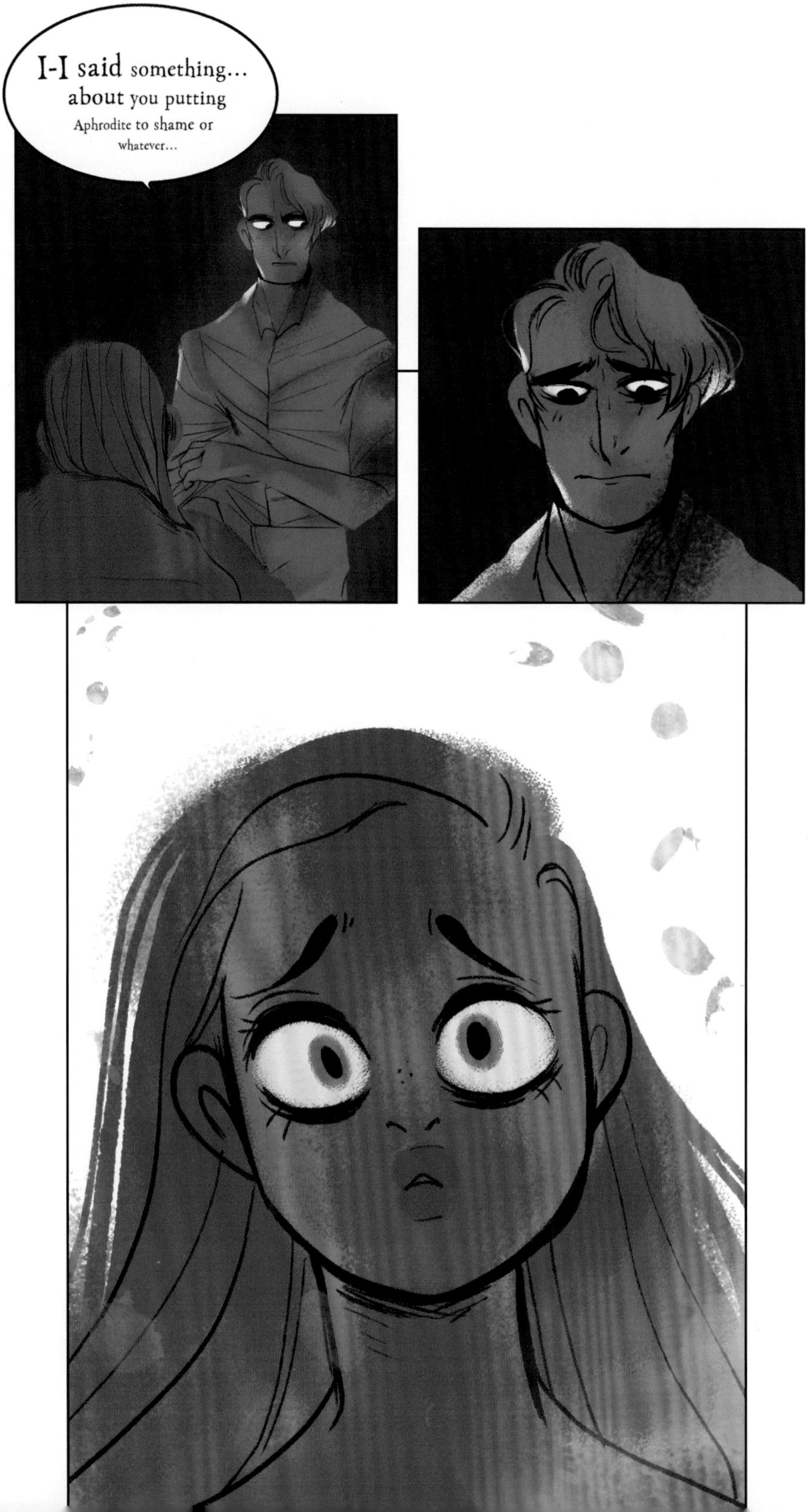
I-I said something... about you putting Aphrodite to shame or whatever...

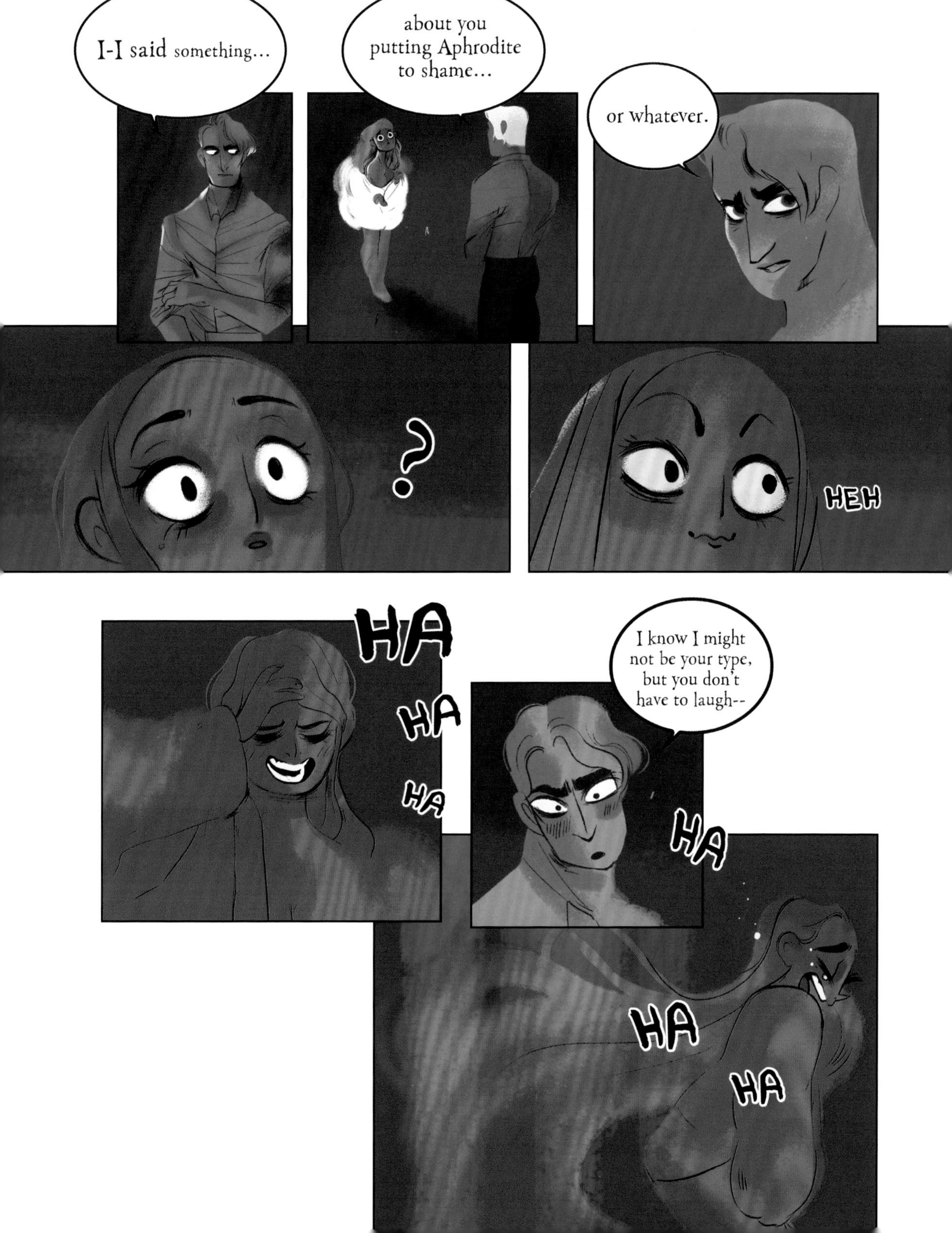
I-I said something...
about you putting Aphrodite to shame...
or whatever.
?
HEH
HA
HA
HA
I know I might not be your type, but you don't have to laugh--
HA
HA
HA

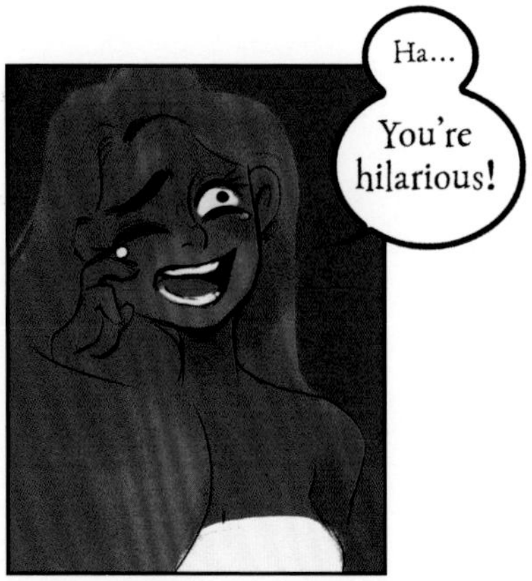
Ha...
You're hilarious!

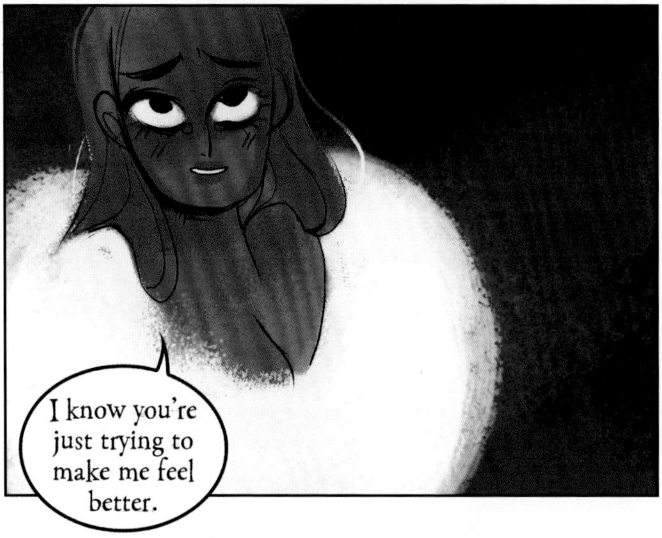
I know you're just trying to make me feel better.

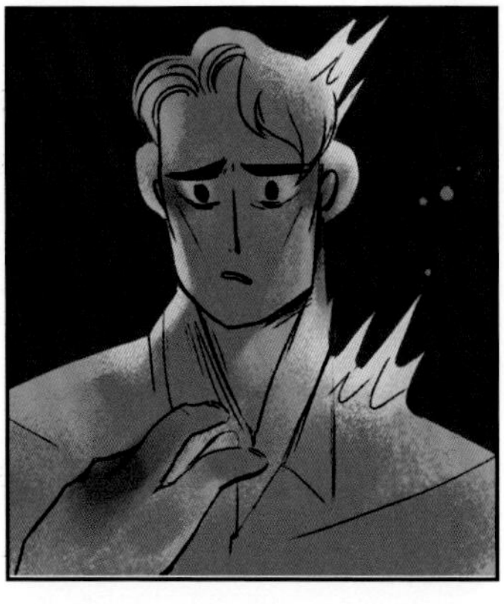

EPISODE 09: GONE TO THE DOGS

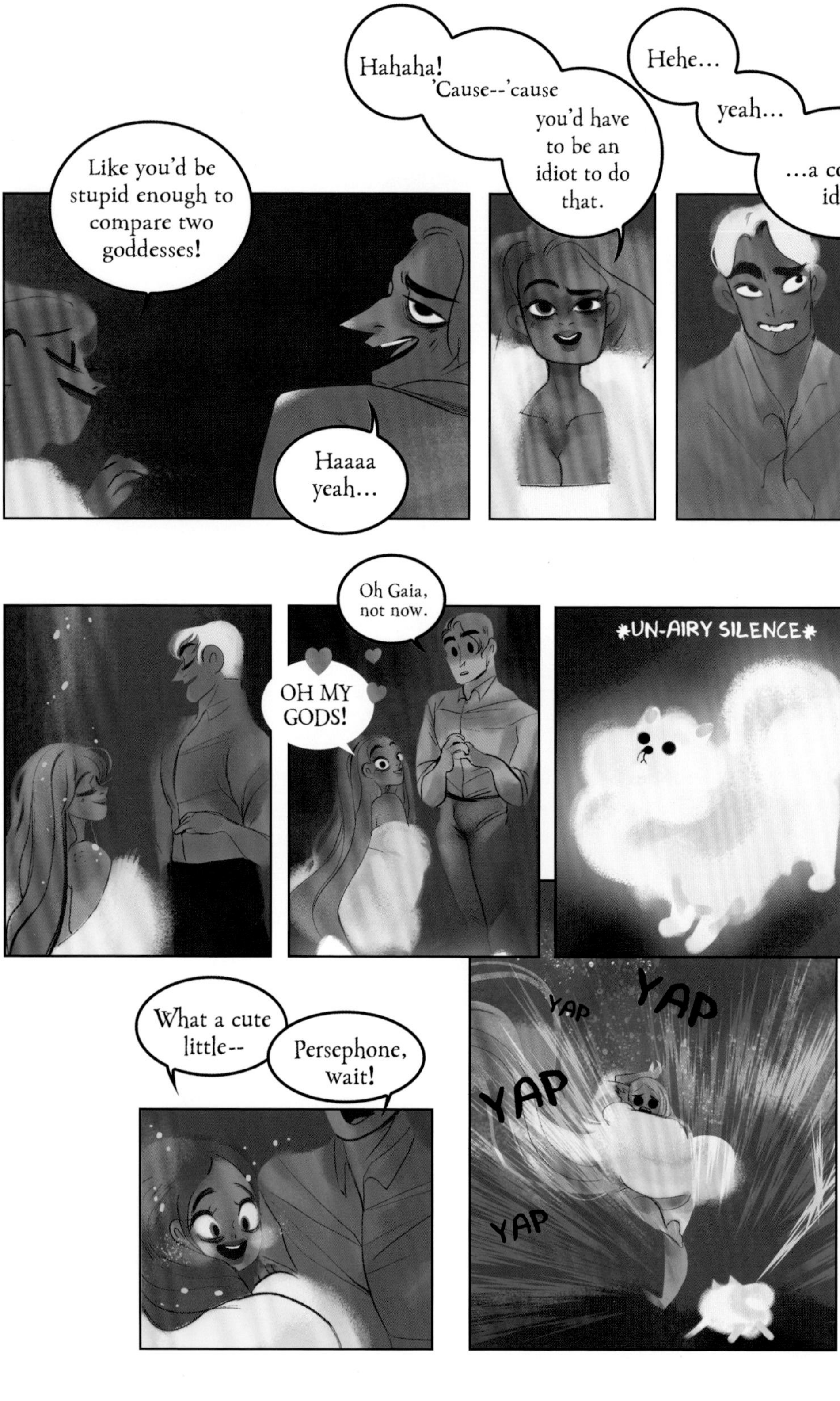
Like you'd be stupid enough to compare two goddesses!
Haaaa yeah...
Hahaha! 'Cause--'cause you'd have to be an idiot to do that.
Hehe... yeah... ...a complete idiot.
Oh Gaia, not now.
OH MY GODS!
UN-AIRY SILENCE
What a cute little--
Persephone, wait!
YAP
YAP
YAP
YAP

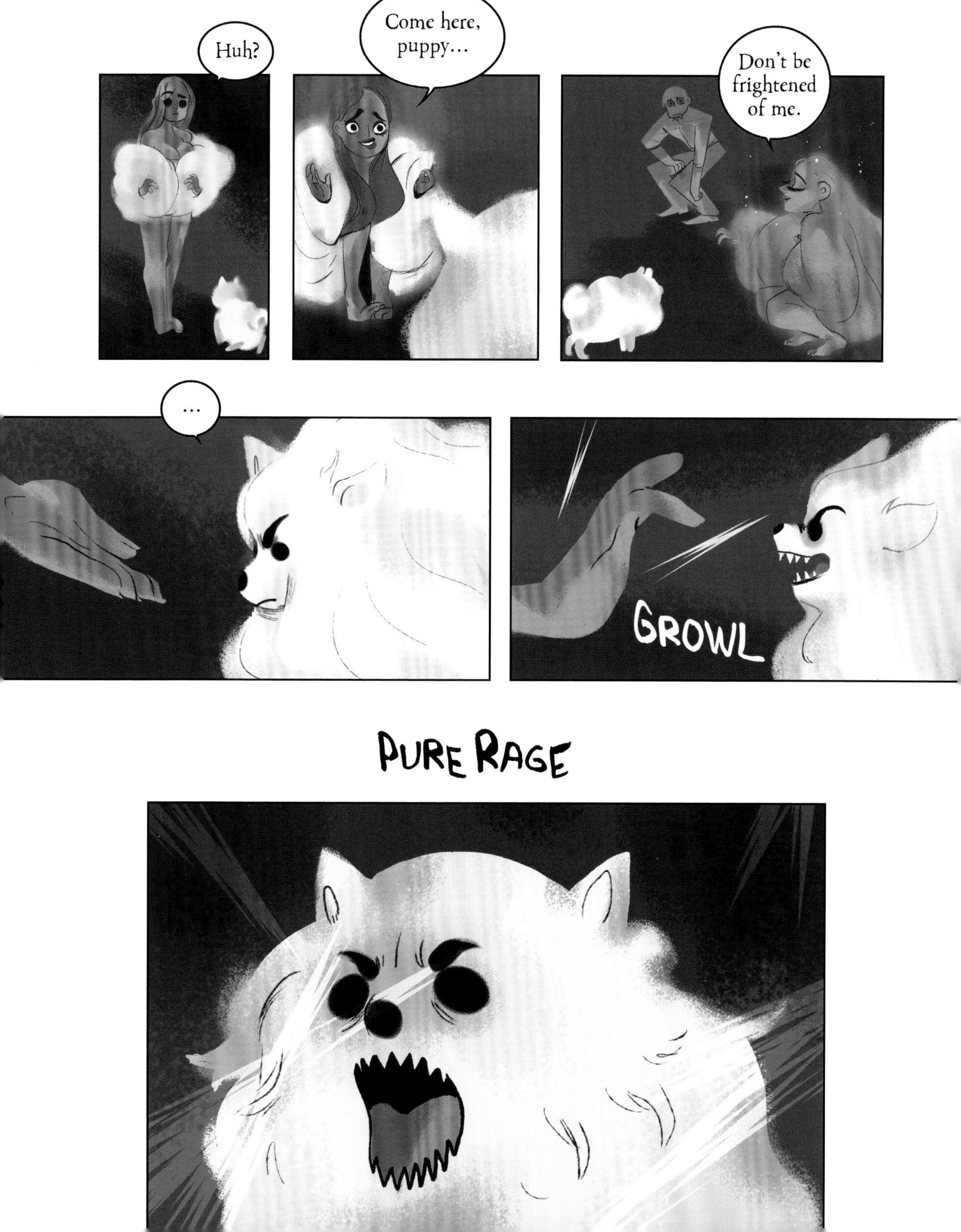
Huh?
Come here, puppy...
Don't be frightened of me.
...
GROWL
PURE RAGE

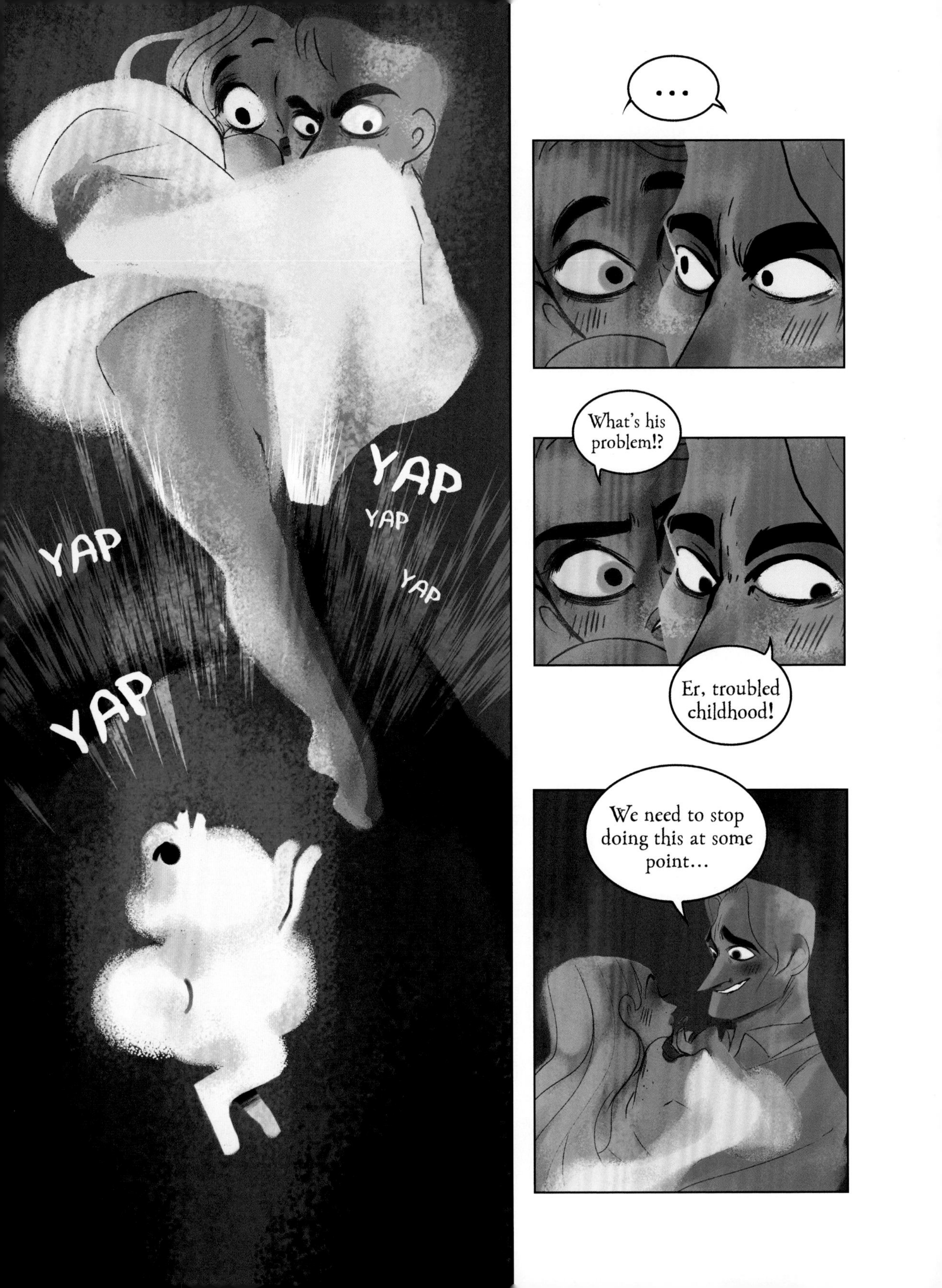
YAP
YAP
YAP
YAP
YAP
...
What's his problem!?
Er, troubled childhood!
We need to stop doing this at some point...

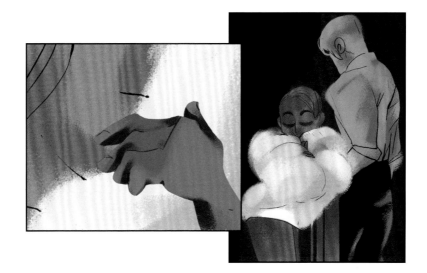

How many dogs do you have?

7, but it might be 6 soon...

Well?

Aren't you going to tell me their names?

Let's see...

CORDON BLEU
(WHO YOU JUST MET)

MUSHROOM

RUSSELL

J.P.

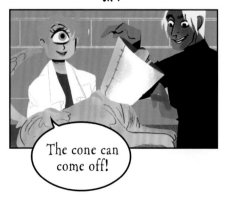

The cone can come off!

FUDGE
Let them unionize, see if I care.
BIG JOHN
...AND FINALLY CERBERUS
His coat is SO shiny, what do you feed him?
The souls of murderers and sometimes egg whites.
So do you--
BRRRRRRR BRRRRRRR
Zeus
Calling...
Sorry, I have to take this. It's my brother.
(loud whispering)
What!? I'M BUSY!

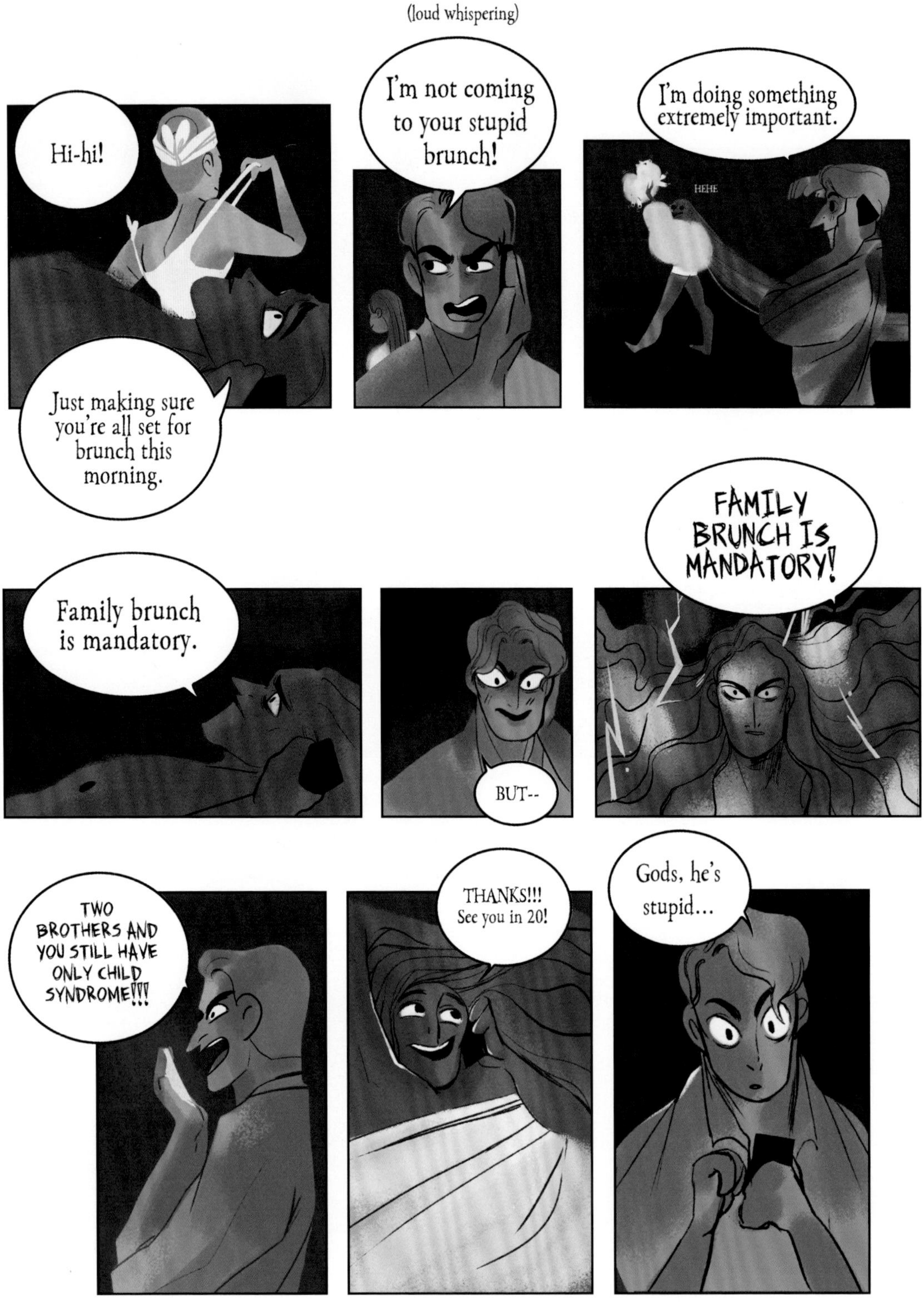
(loud whispering)
Hi-hi!
Just making sure you're all set for brunch this morning.
I'm not coming to your stupid brunch!
I'm doing something extremely important.
HEHE
Family brunch is mandatory.
BUT--
FAMILY BRUNCH IS MANDATORY!
TWO BROTHERS AND YOU STILL HAVE ONLY CHILD SYNDROME!!!
THANKS!!! See you in 20!
Gods, he's stupid...

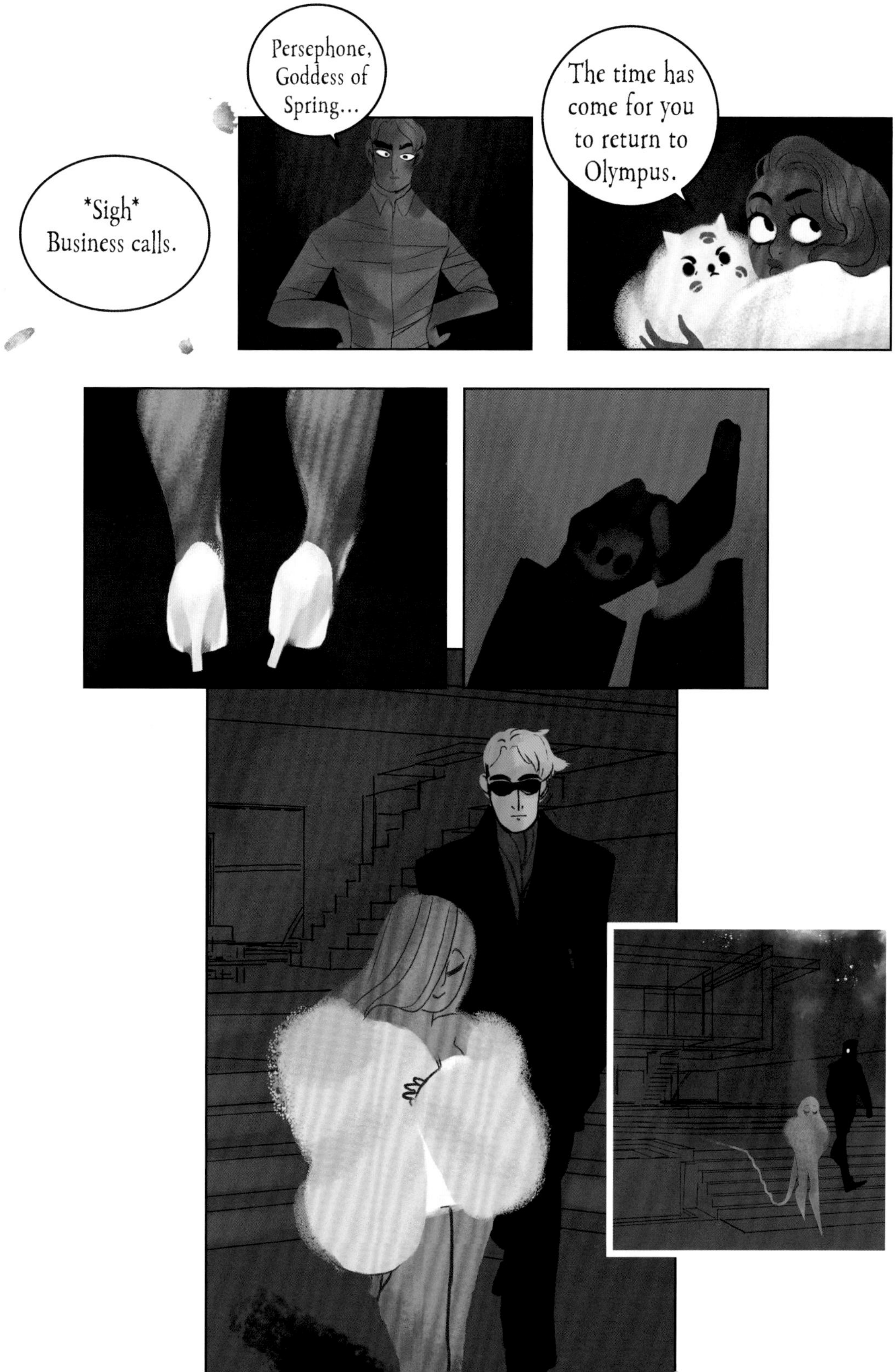
Sigh Business calls.
Persephone, Goddess of Spring...
The time has come for you to return to Olympus.

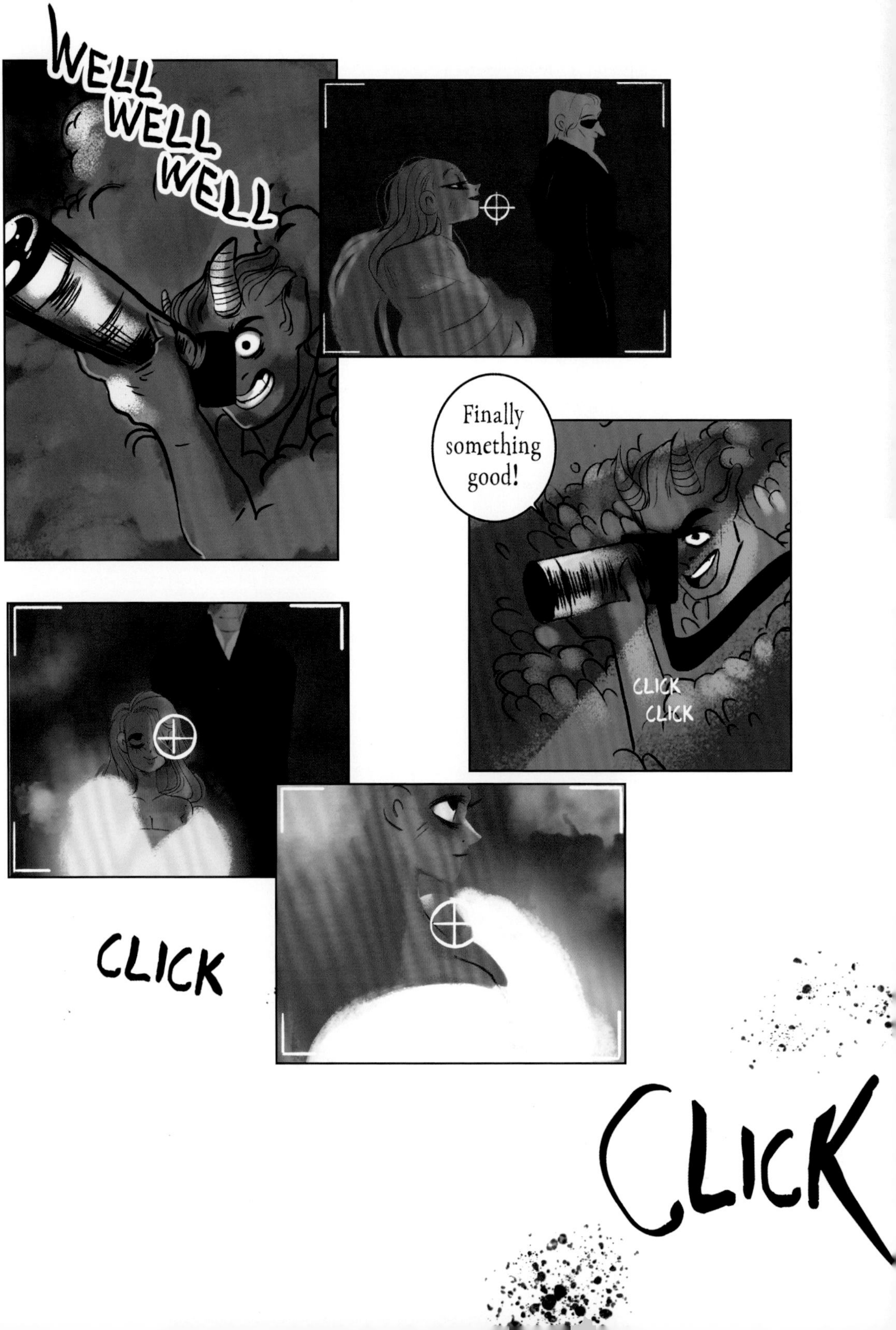
WELL WELL WELL
Finally something good!
CLICK CLICK
CLICK
CLICK

WHAAAAAAAAT!?

That's a lot of cars!

Do you own enough cars?

I'm not sure.

Do you want to walk back to Olympus?

'Cause that's what it sounds like.

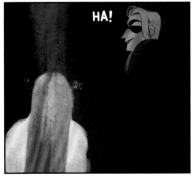

HA!

CAN I DRIVE?

!?

DELIGHTED WRIGGLE

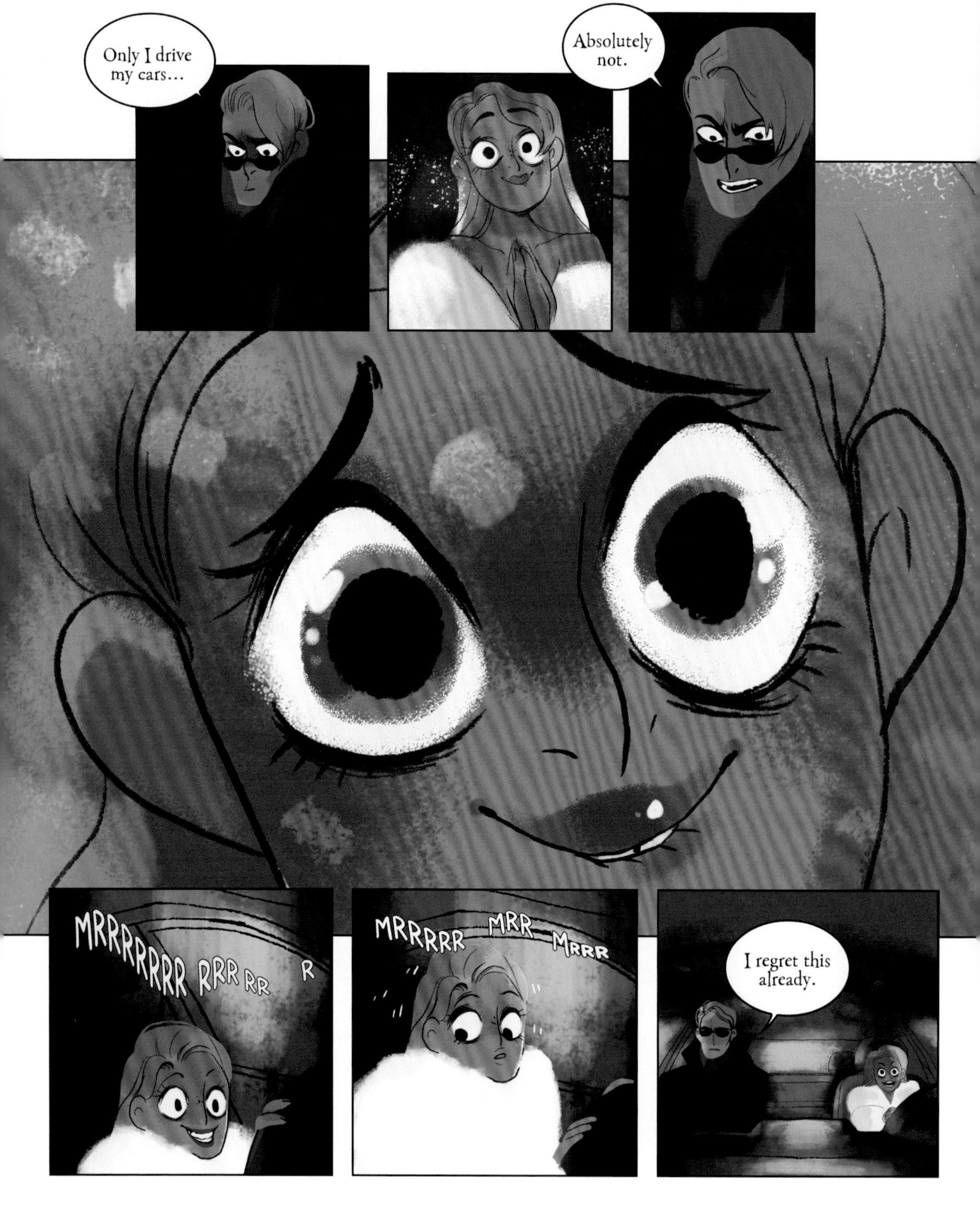
Only I drive my cars…
Absolutely not.
MRRRRRRRR RRR RR R
MRRRRR MRR MRRR
I regret this already.

EPISODE 10: DISEMBARK

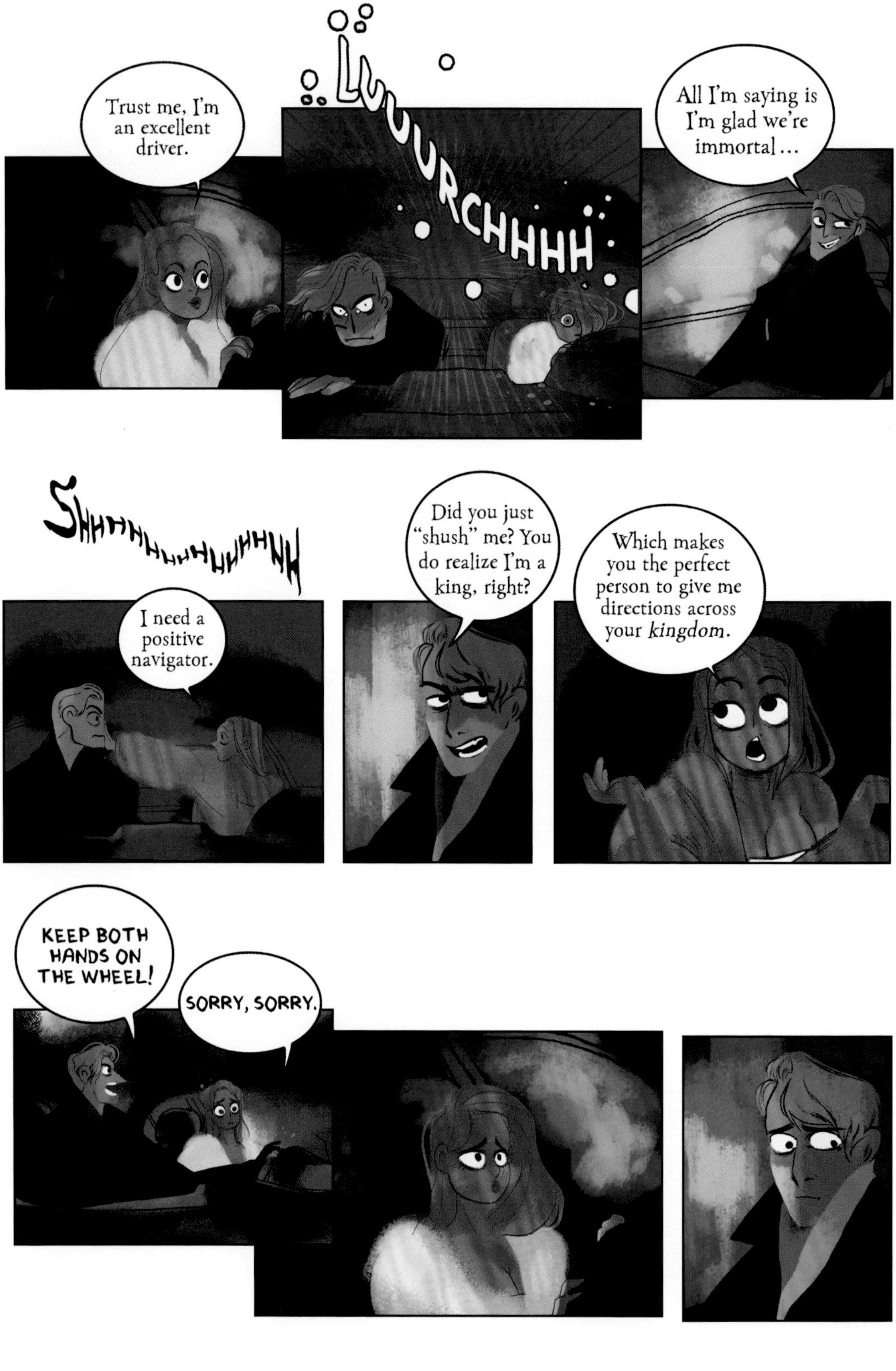
Trust me, I'm an excellent driver.
LUUUURCHHHH
All I'm saying is I'm glad we're immortal...
SHHHHHHHHHHHHNK
I need a positive navigator.
Did you just "shush" me? You do realize I'm a king, right?
Which makes you the perfect person to give me directions across your *kingdom*.
KEEP BOTH HANDS ON THE WHEEL!
SORRY, SORRY.

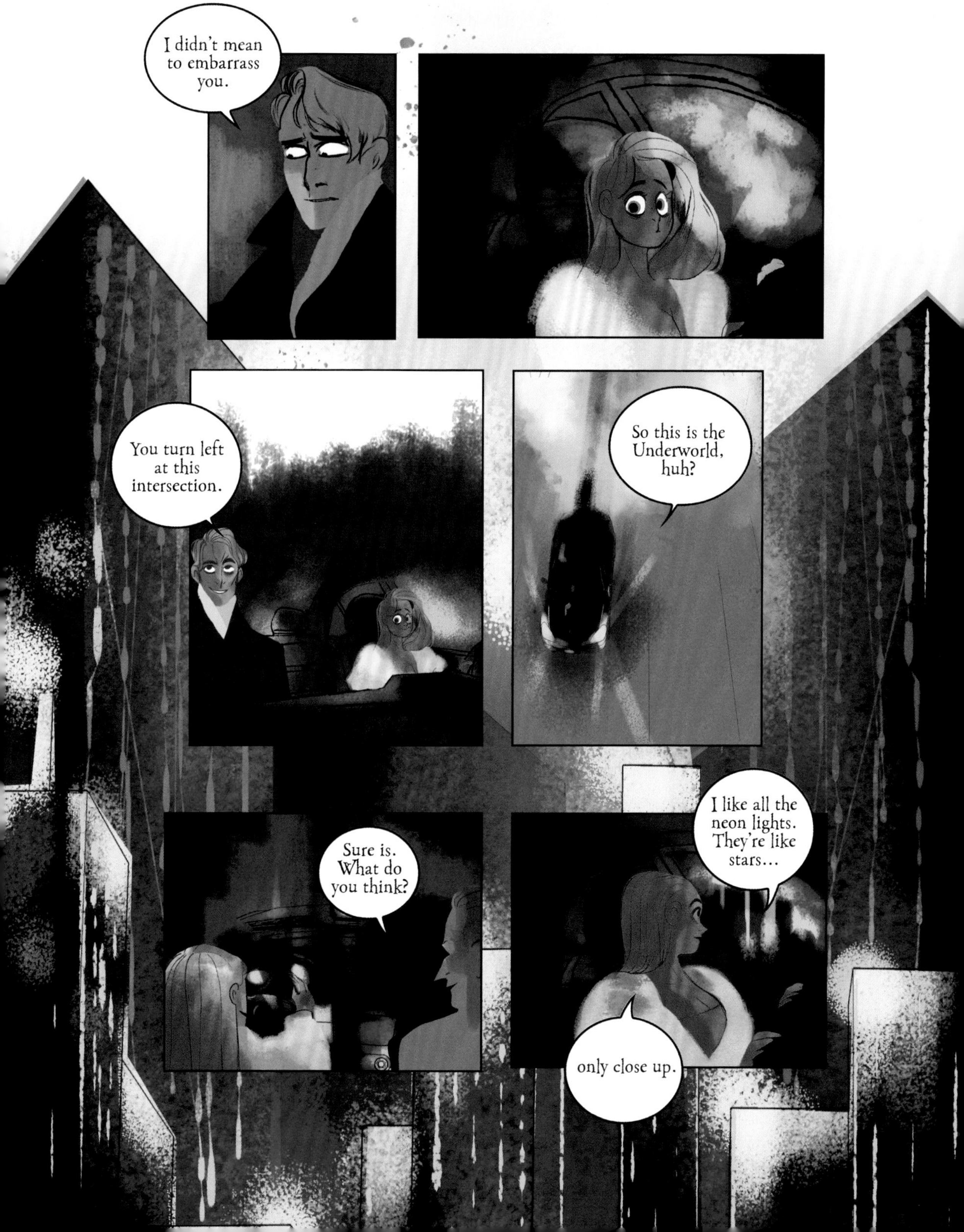
I didn't mean to embarrass you.
You turn left at this intersection.
So this is the Underworld, huh?
Sure is. What do you think?
I like all the neon lights. They're like stars…
only close up.

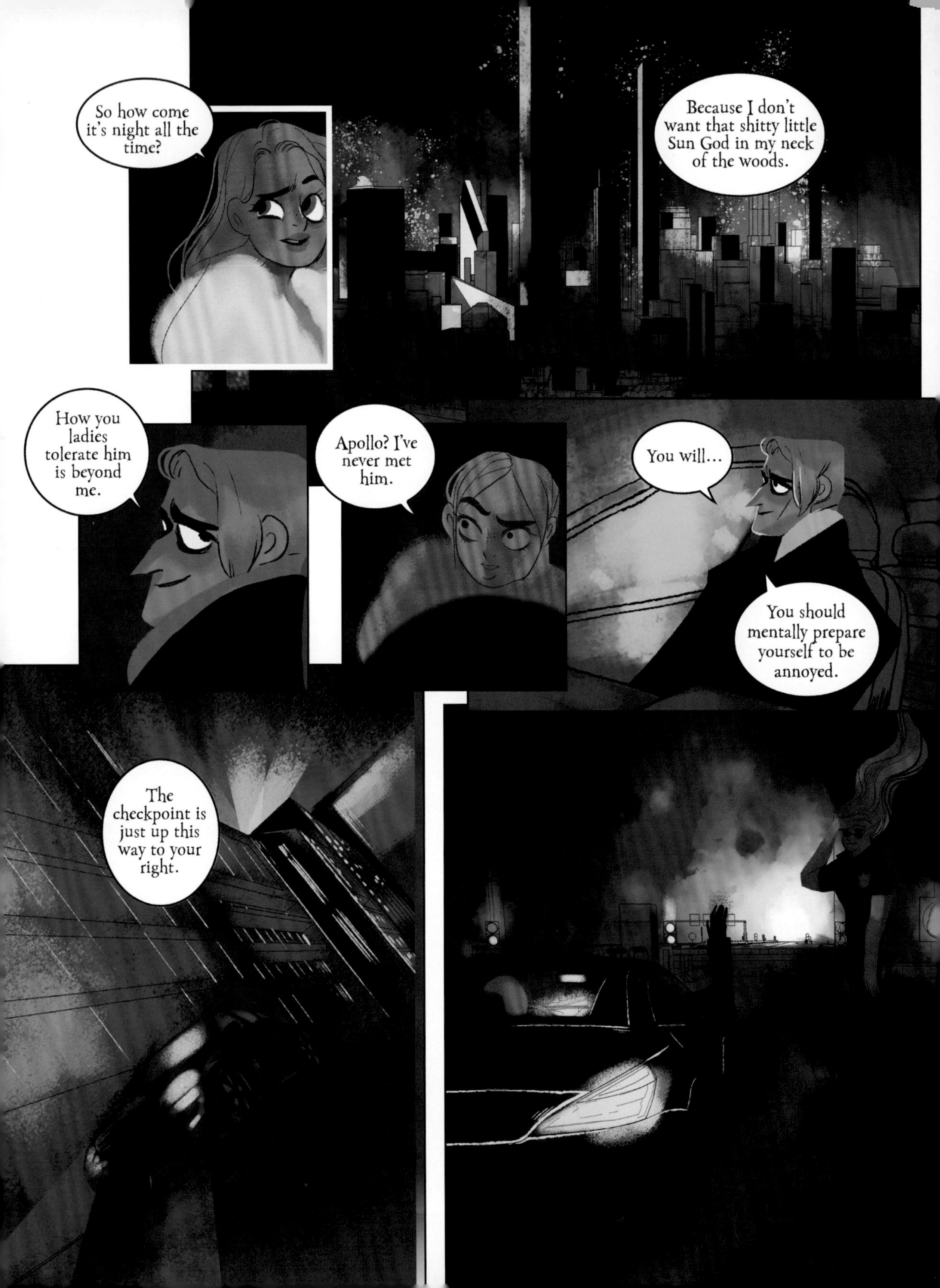
So how come it's night all the time?
Because I don't want that shitty little Sun God in my neck of the woods.
How you ladies tolerate him is beyond me.
Apollo? I've never met him.
You will...
You should mentally prepare yourself to be annoyed.
The checkpoint is just up this way to your right.

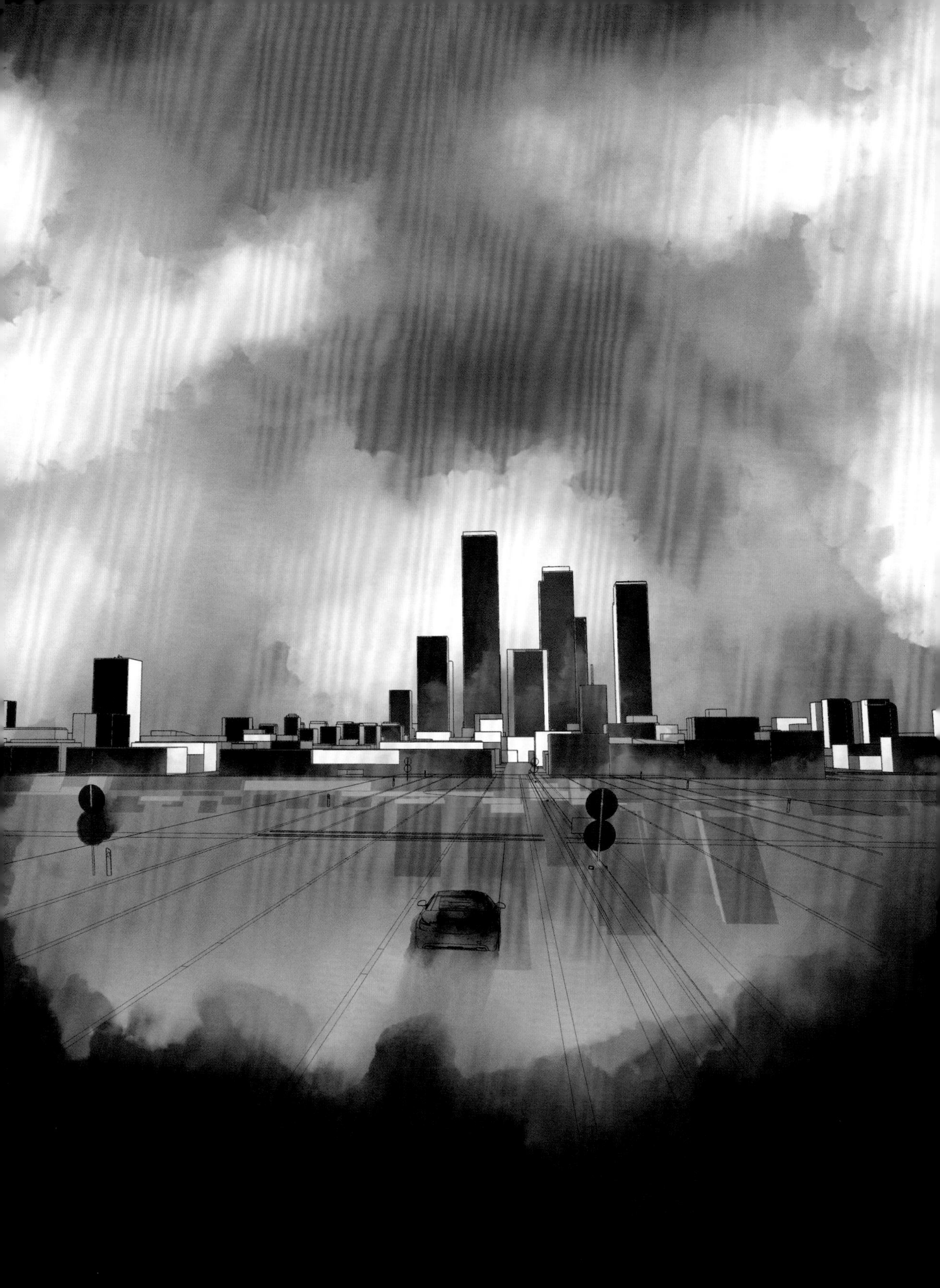

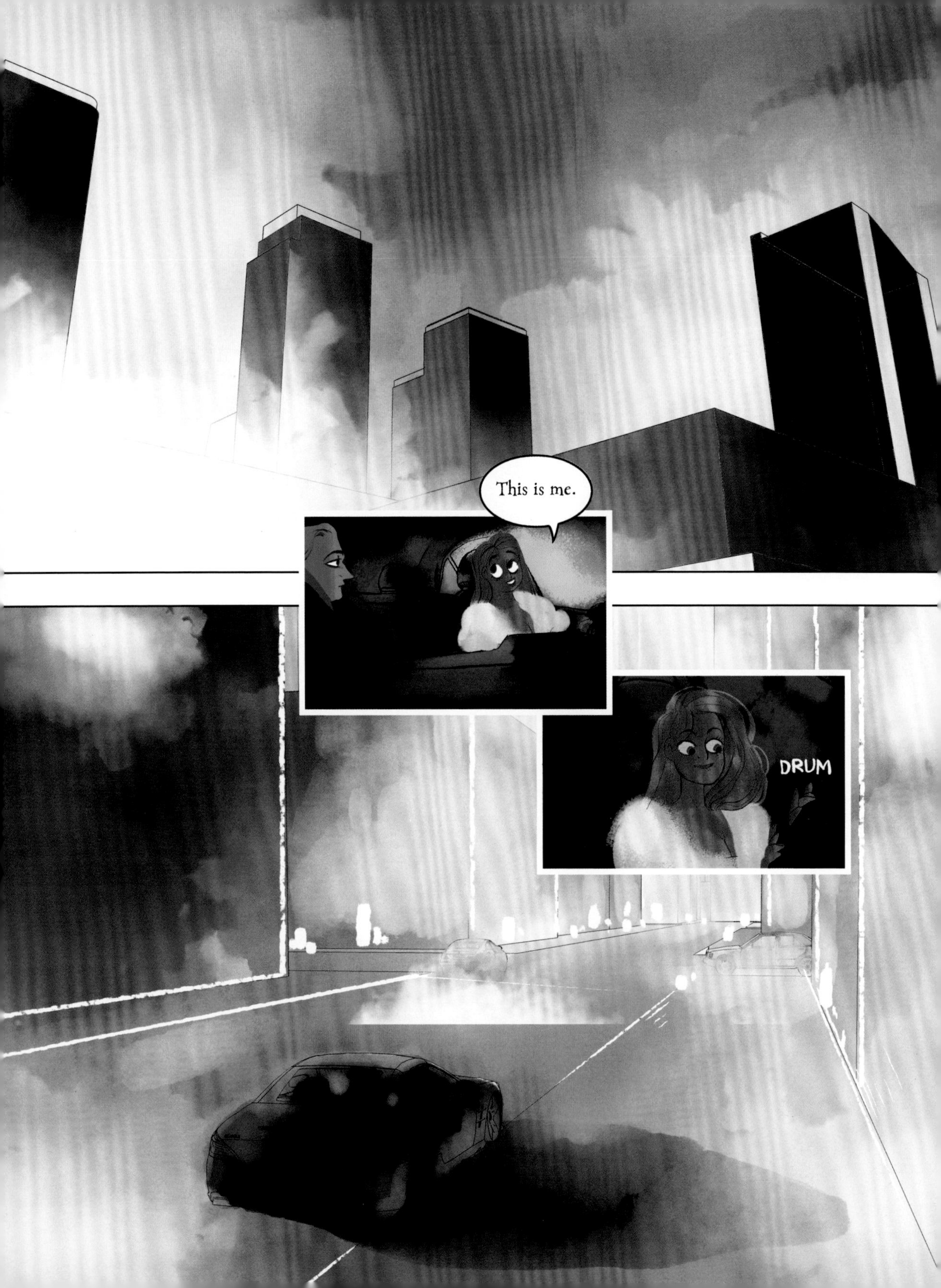
This is me.
DRUM

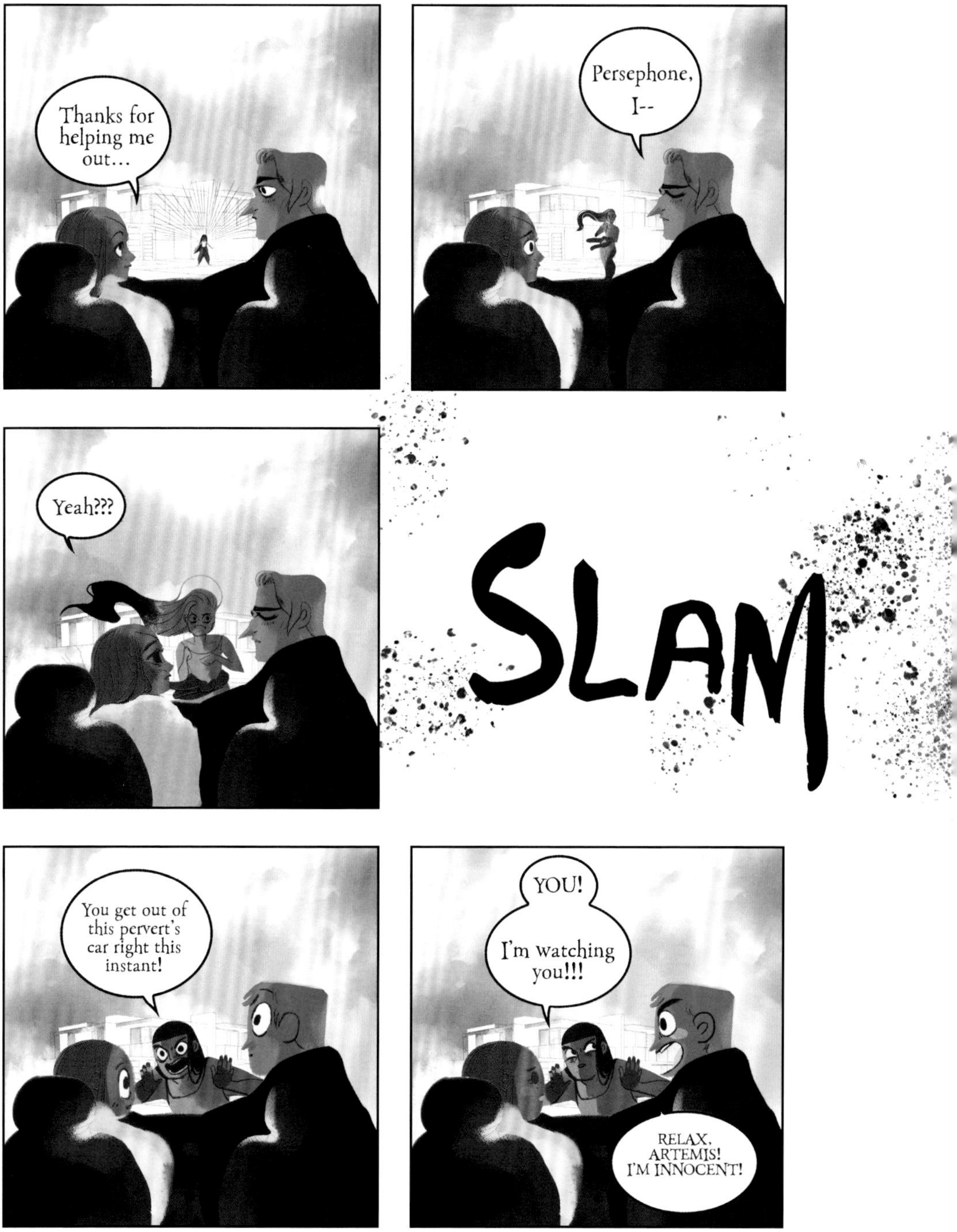
Thanks for helping me out...
Persephone, I--
Yeah???
SLAM
You get out of this pervert's car right this instant!
YOU!
I'm watching you!!!
RELAX, ARTEMIS! I'M INNOCENT!

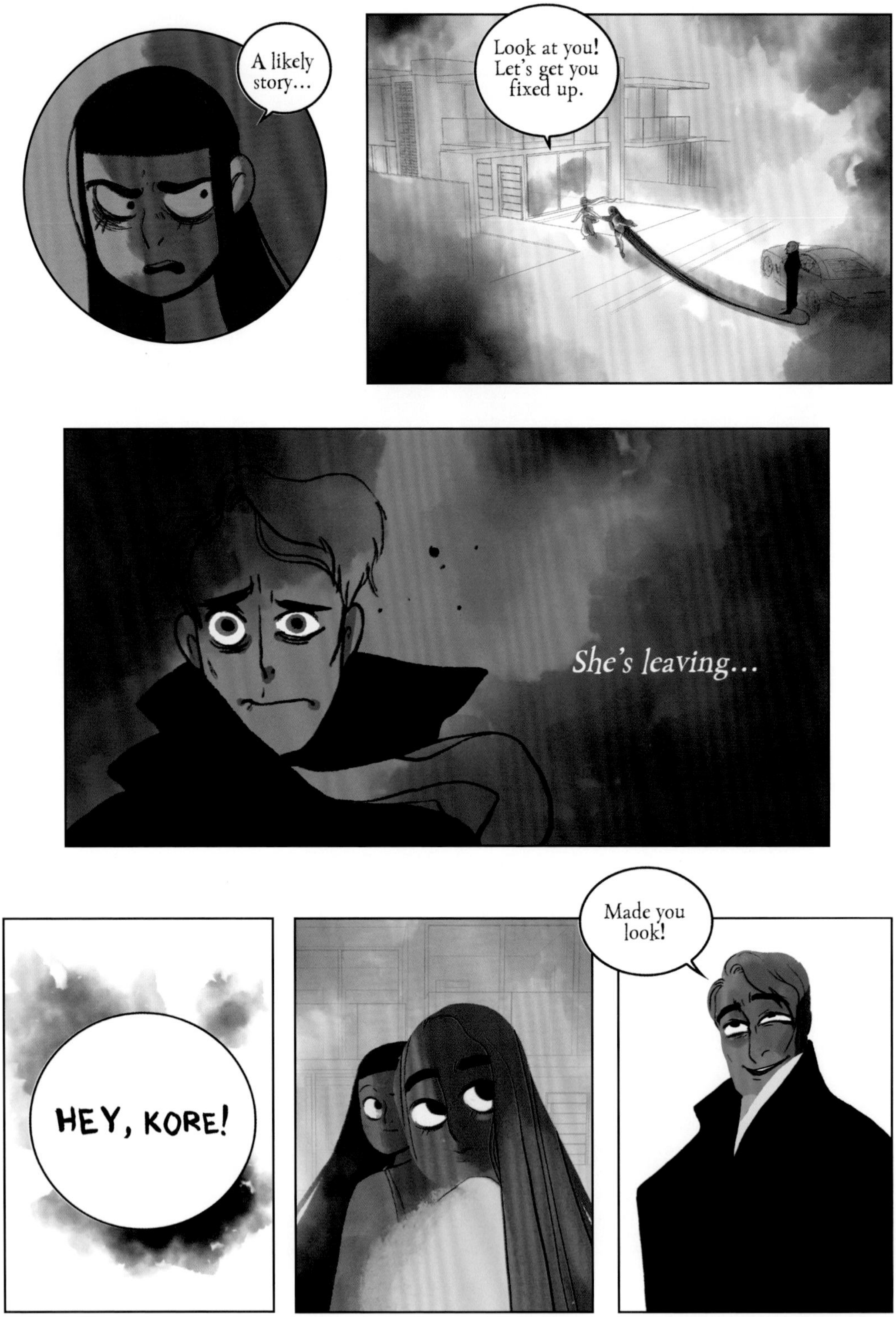
A likely story…
Look at you! Let's get you fixed up.
She's leaving…
HEY, KORE!
Made you look!

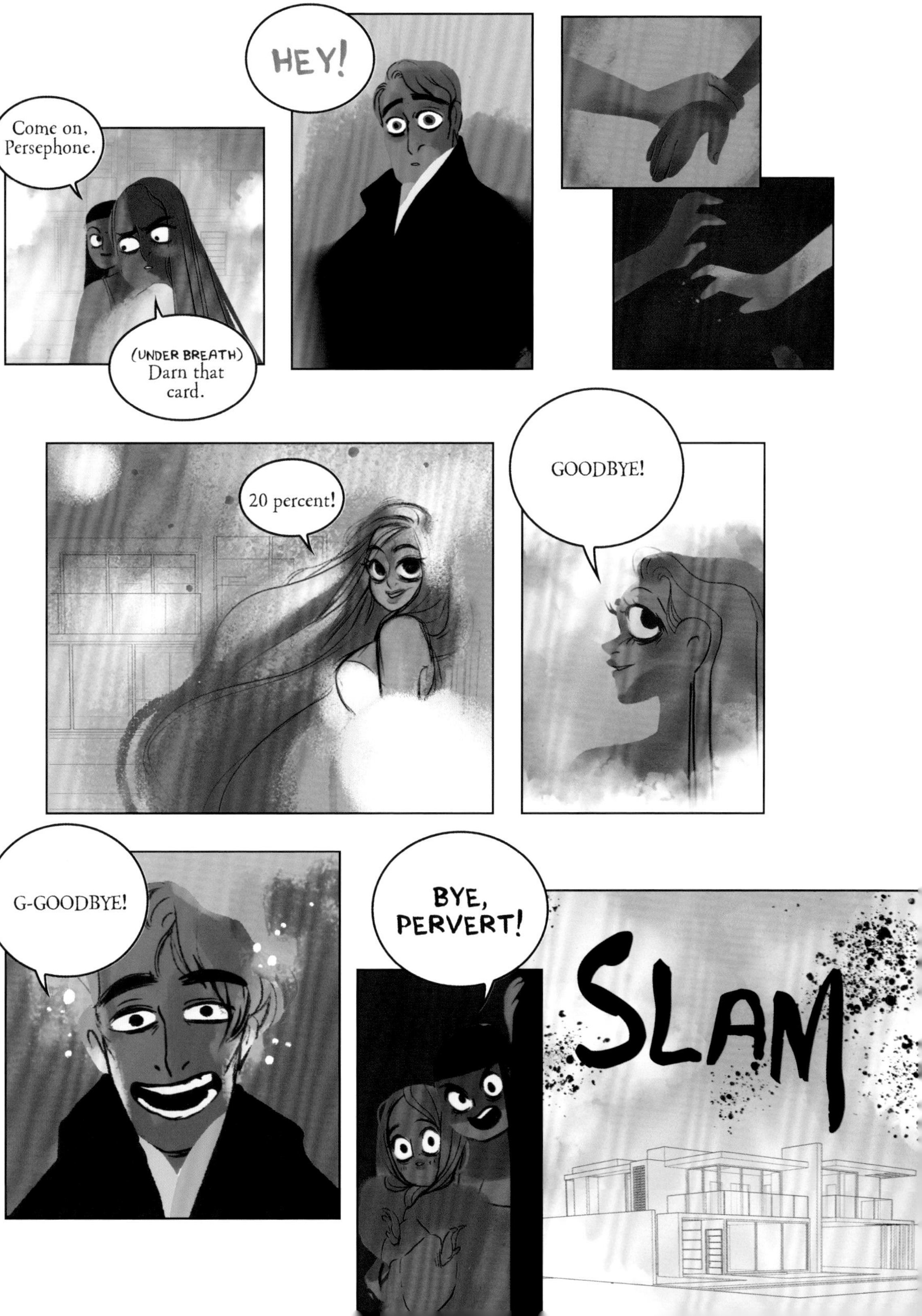
Come on, Persephone.
(UNDER BREATH) Darn that card.
HEY!
20 percent!
GOODBYE!
G-GOODBYE!
BYE, PERVERT!
SLAM

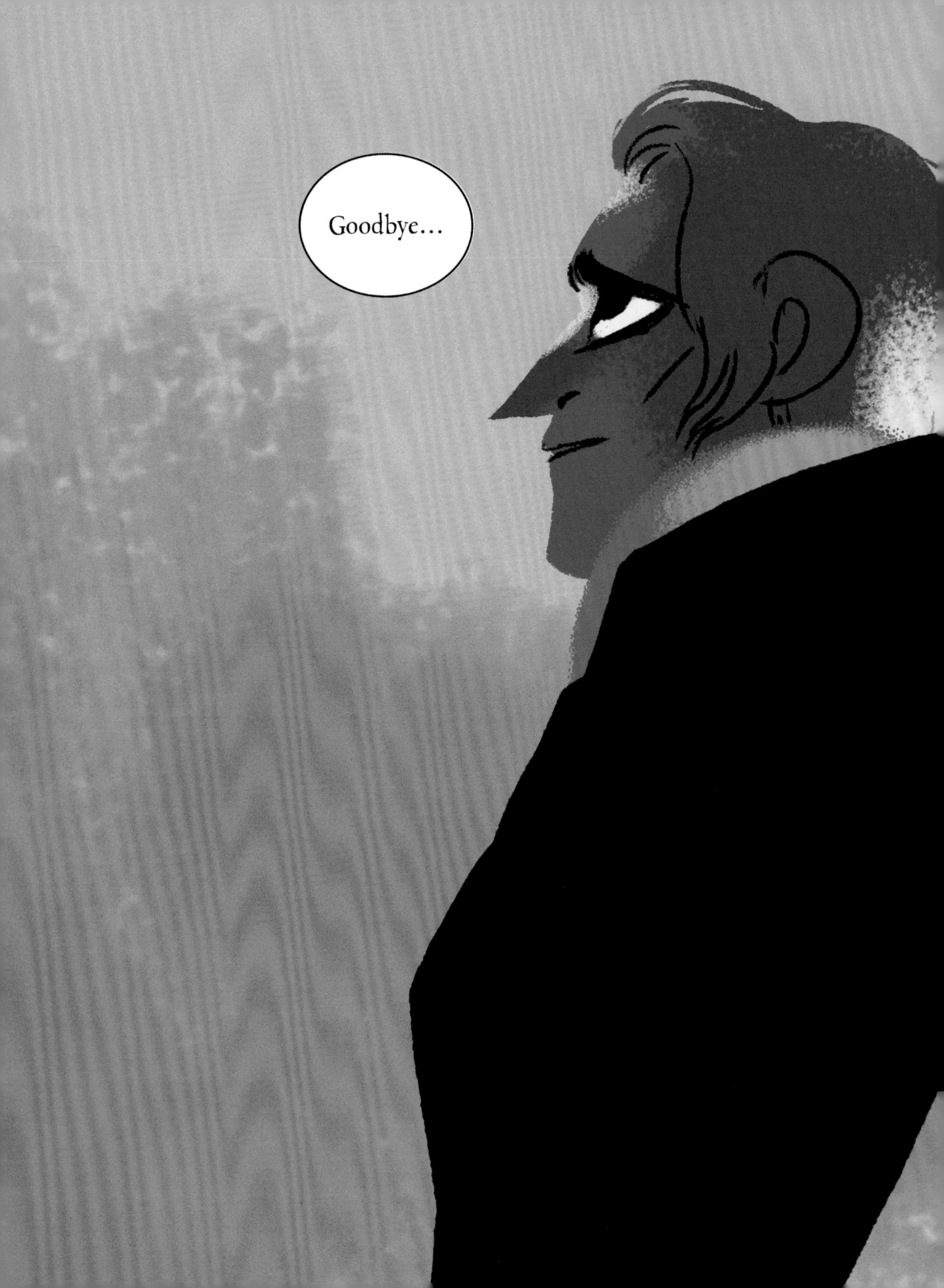
Goodbye…

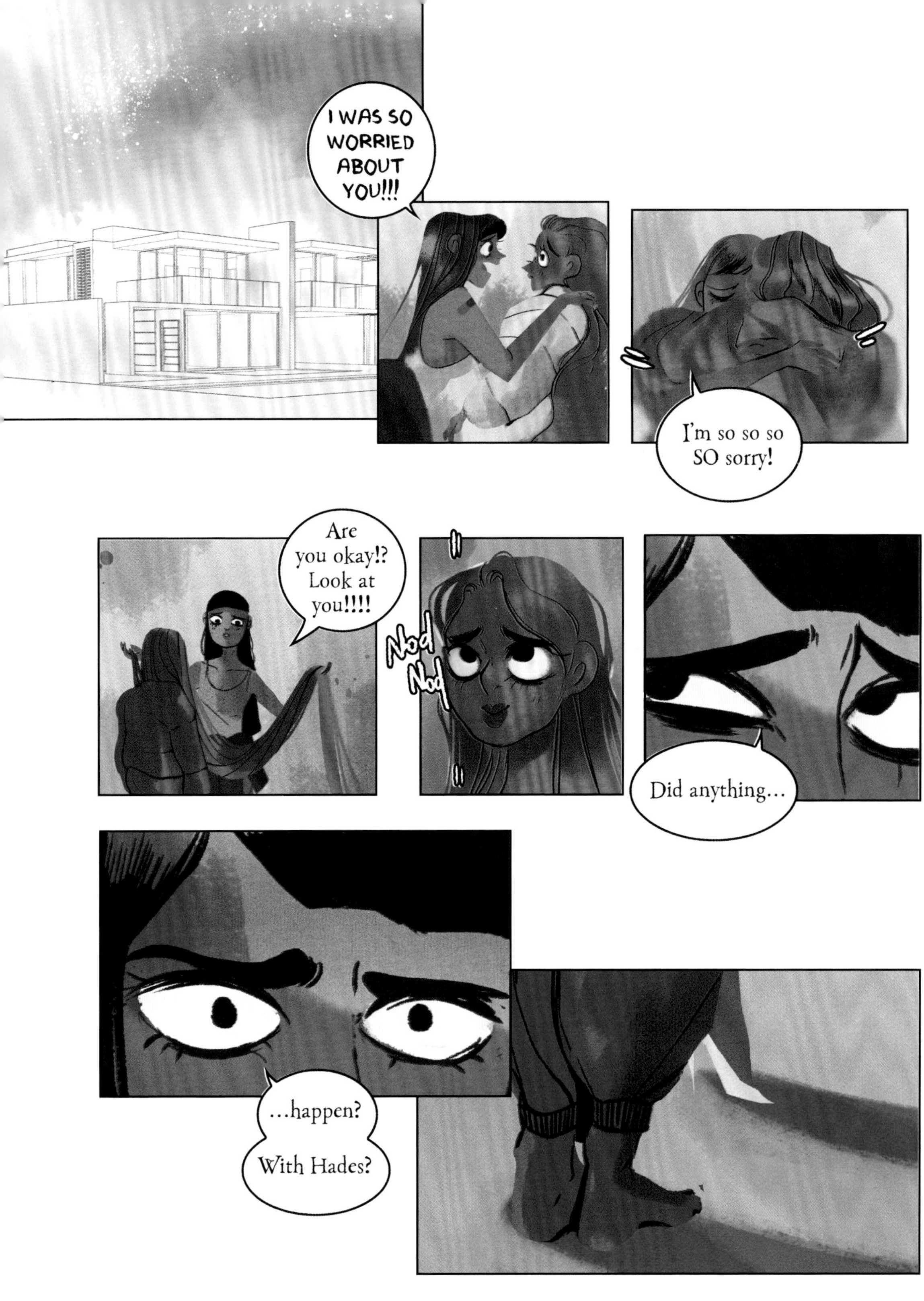
I WAS SO WORRIED ABOUT YOU!!!
I'm so so so SO sorry!
Are you okay!? Look at you!!!!
Nod Nod
Did anything...
...happen?
With Hades?

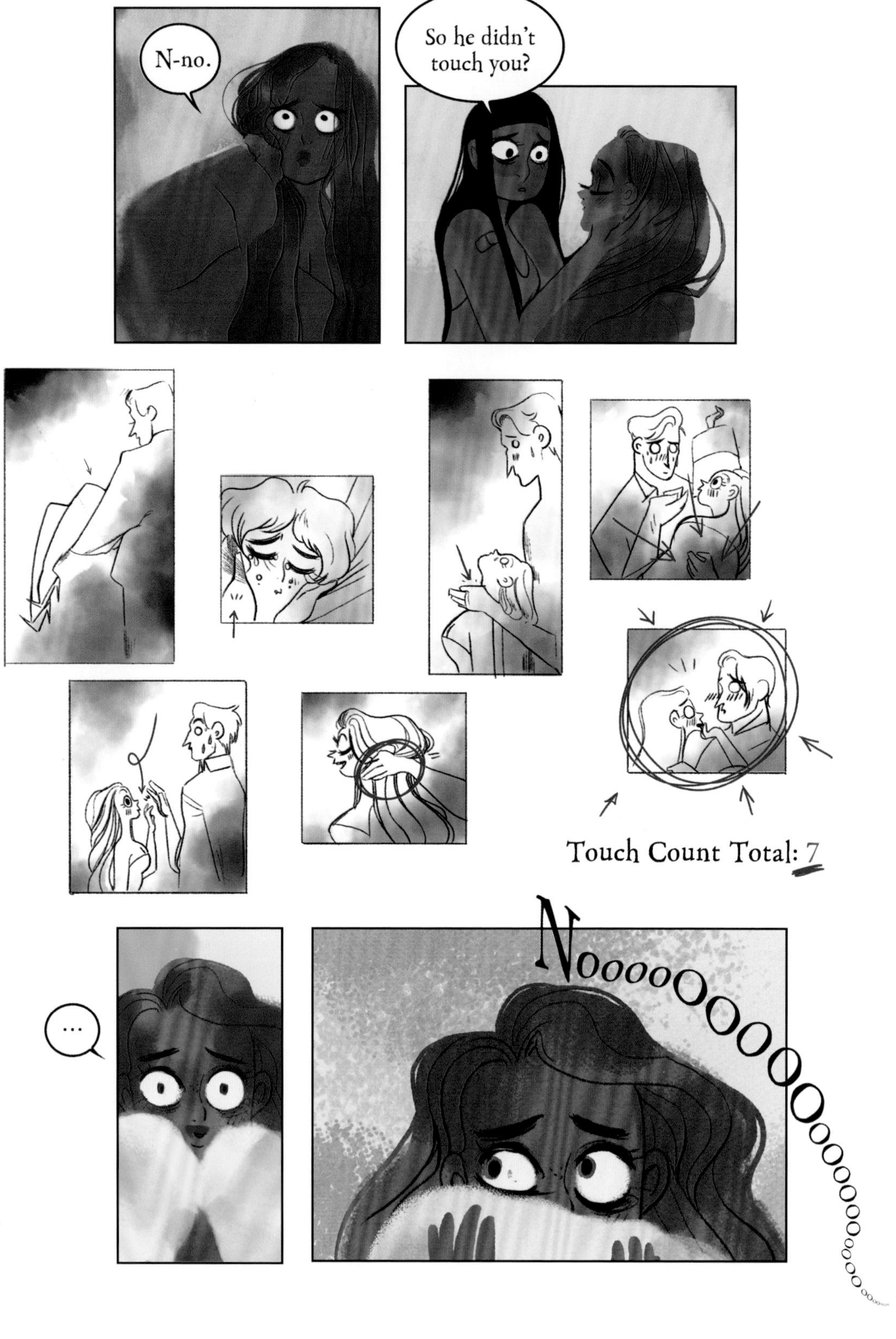
N-no.
So he didn't touch you?
Touch Count Total: 7
...
NoooooOOOOOOooooooooooooooooo

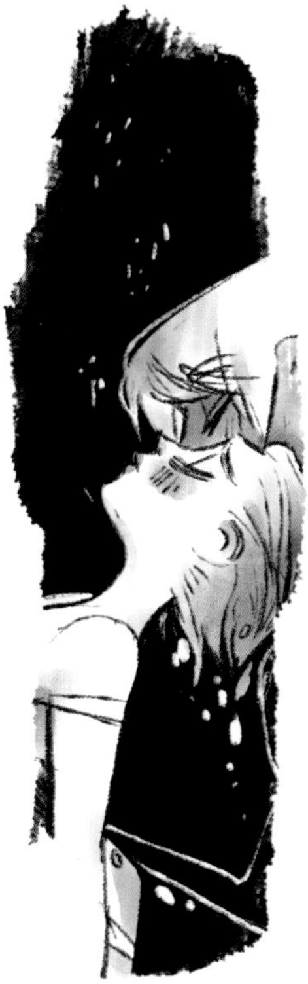

EPISODE II: UNSUPERVISED

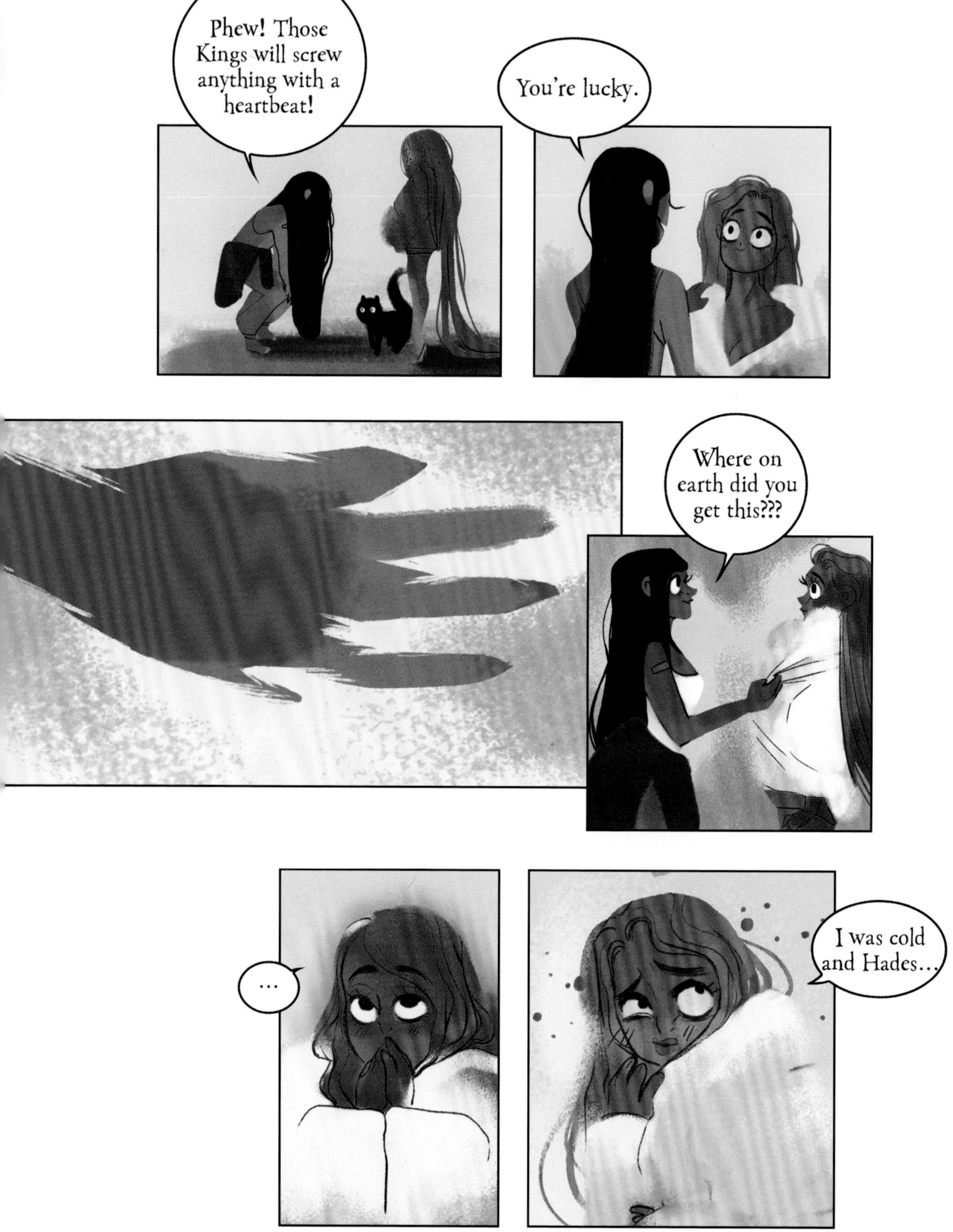
Phew! Those Kings will screw anything with a heartbeat!
You're lucky.
Where on earth did you get this???
...
I was cold and Hades...

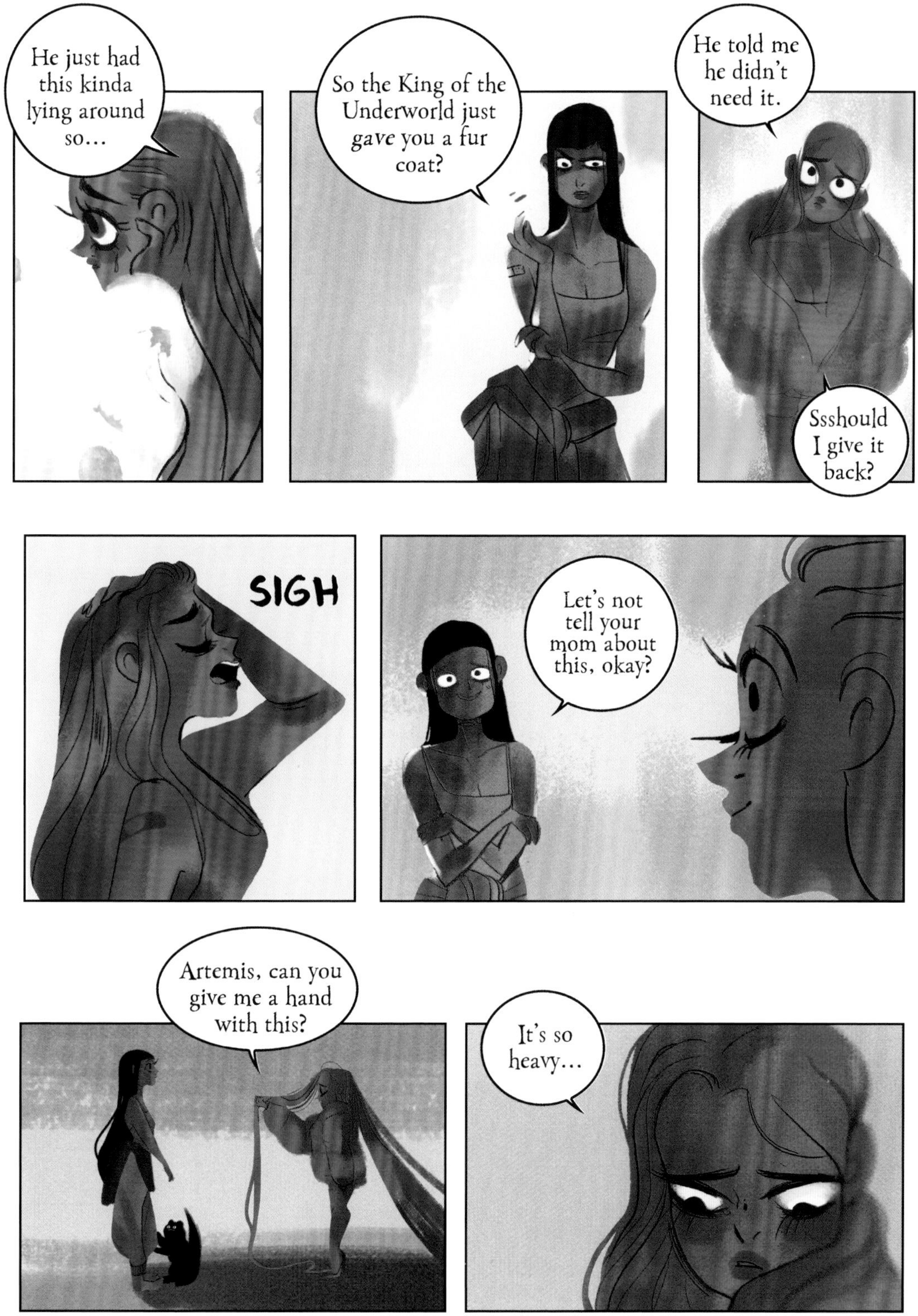
He just had this kinda lying around so...
So the King of the Underworld just *gave* you a fur coat?
He told me he didn't need it.
Ssshould I give it back?
SIGH
Let's not tell your mom about this, okay?
Artemis, can you give me a hand with this?
It's so heavy...

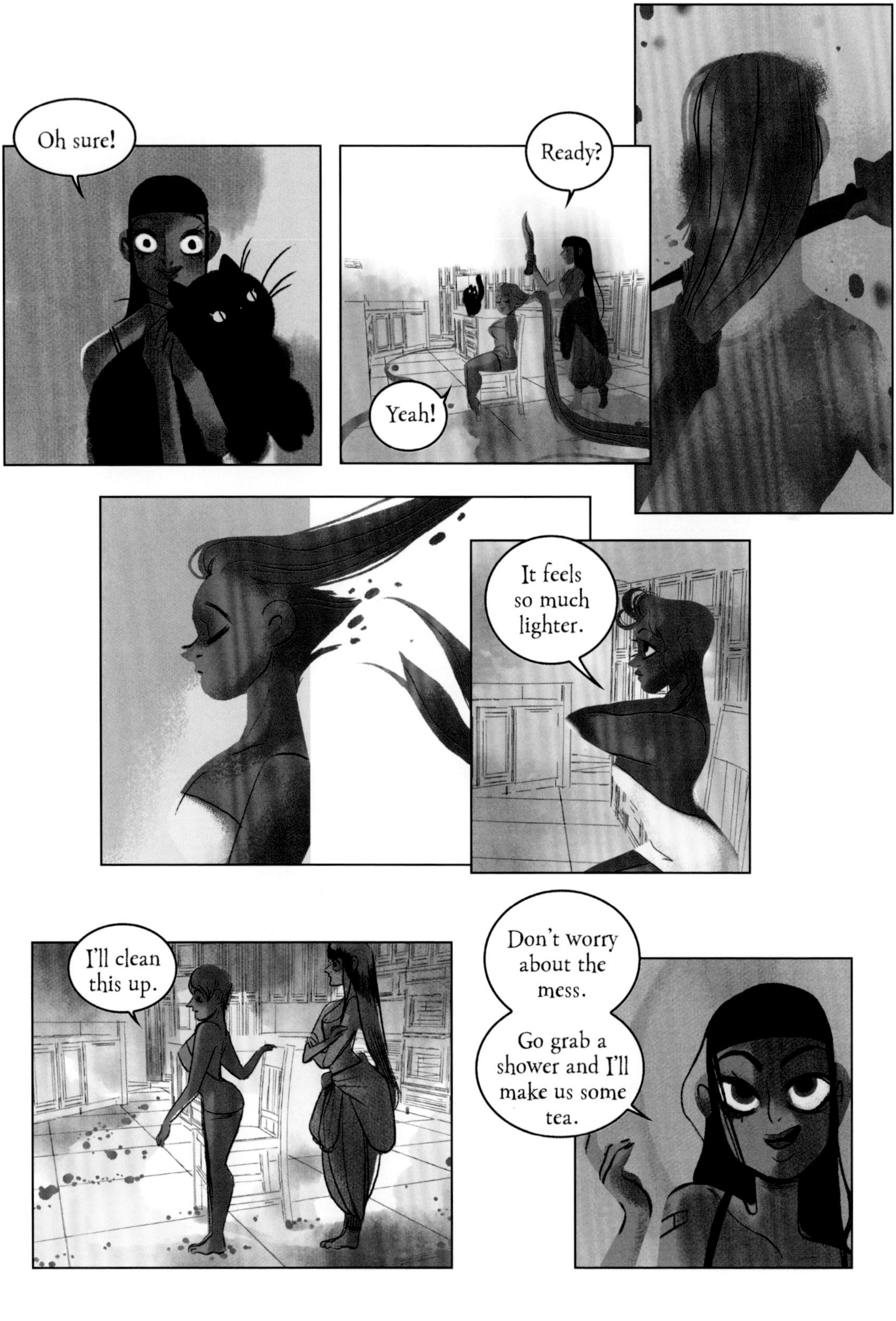
Oh sure!
Ready?
Yeah!
It feels so much lighter.
I'll clean this up.
Don't worry about the mess.
Go grab a shower and I'll make us some tea.

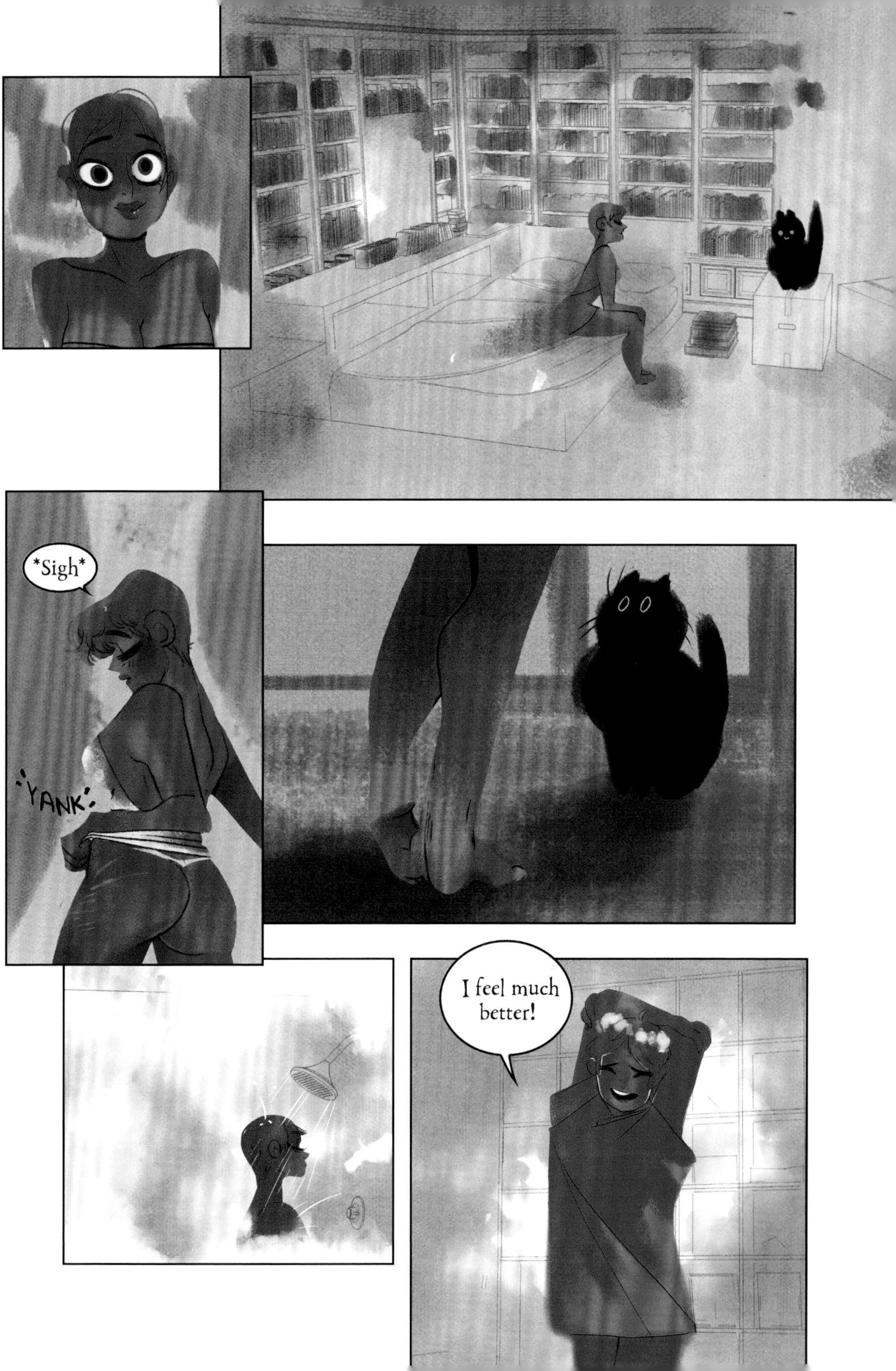
Sigh
YANK
I feel much better!

I've been thinking...

I know your mother said you're not allowed to have a phone.

But if you had one then you could message me if you needed help.

I thought you could have my old one...

I know it's an older model with a cracked screen--

You're giving this to me?

Y-yeah. Sorry, I know it's not--

IT'S ABSOLUTELY PERFECT!!!

THANK YOU!!!

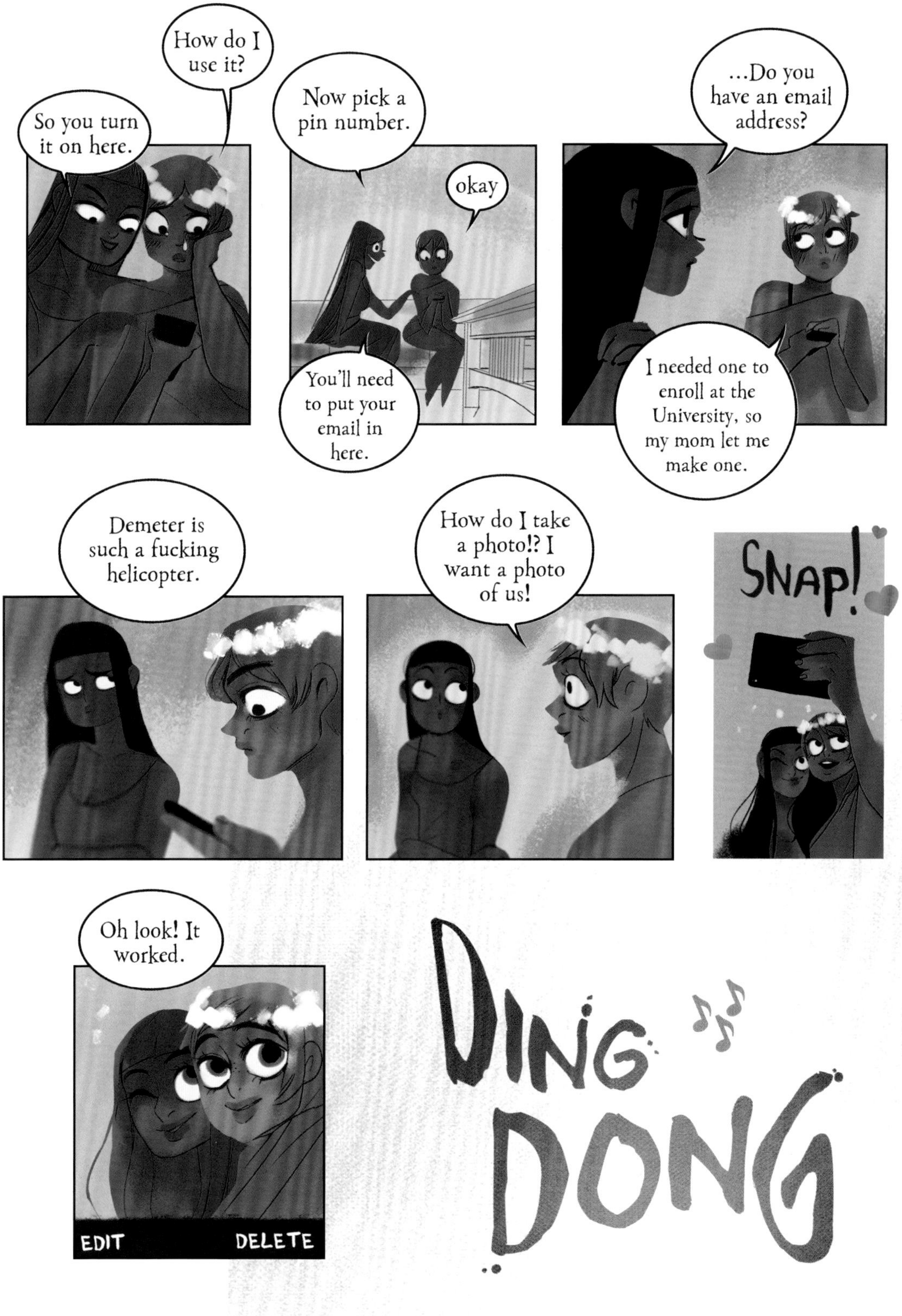
So you turn it on here.
How do I use it?
Now pick a pin number.
okay
You'll need to put your email in here.
...Do you have an email address?
I needed one to enroll at the University, so my mom let me make one.
Demeter is such a fucking helicopter.
How do I take a photo!? I want a photo of us!
SNAP!
Oh look! It worked.
EDIT
DELETE
DING
DONG

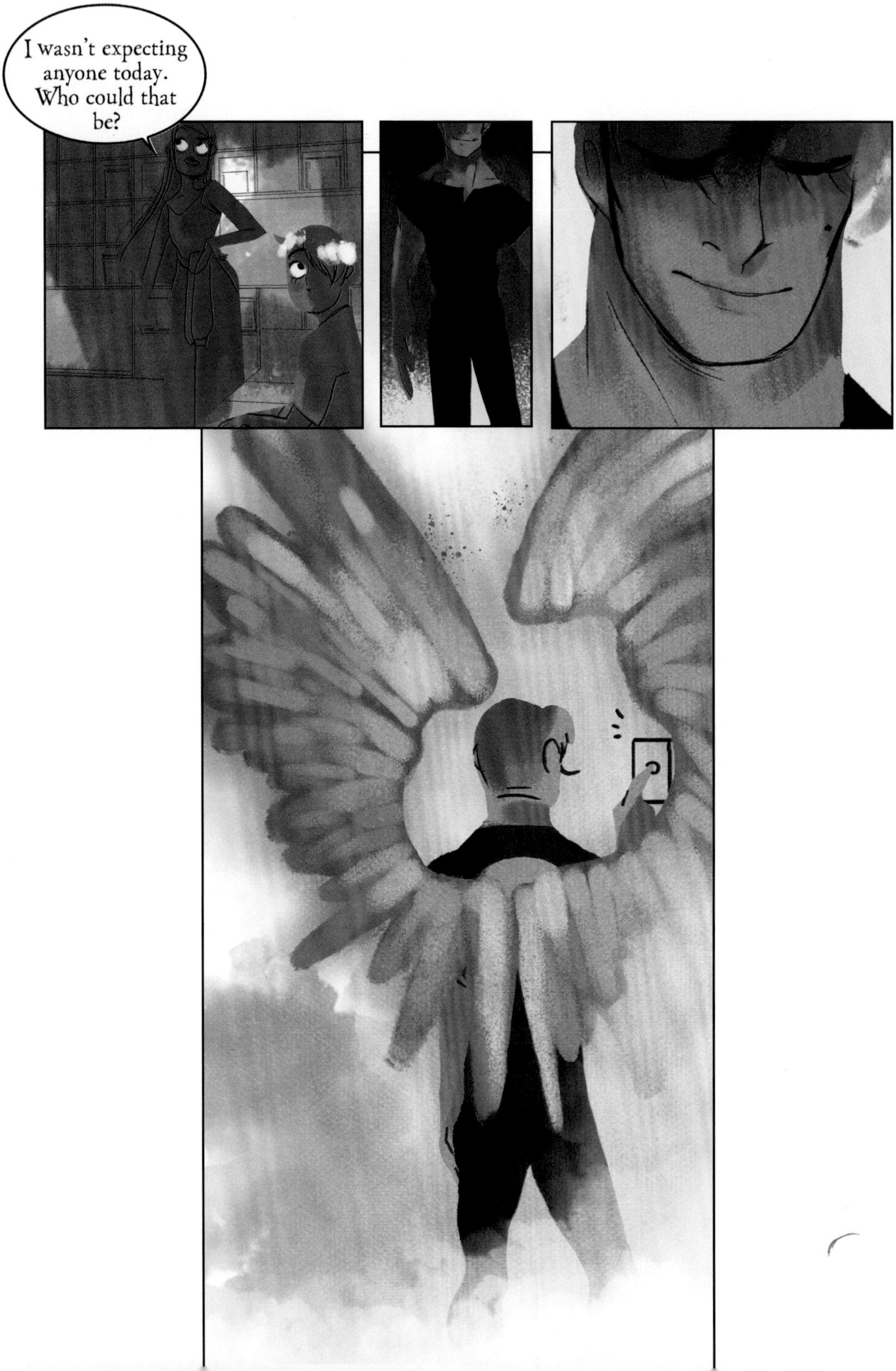
I wasn't expecting anyone today. Who could that be?

Okay…

Turning my life around.

Self-improvement is happening…

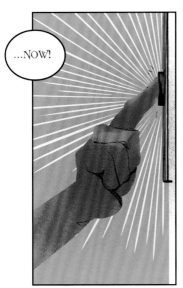

…NOW!

THUMP

THUMP

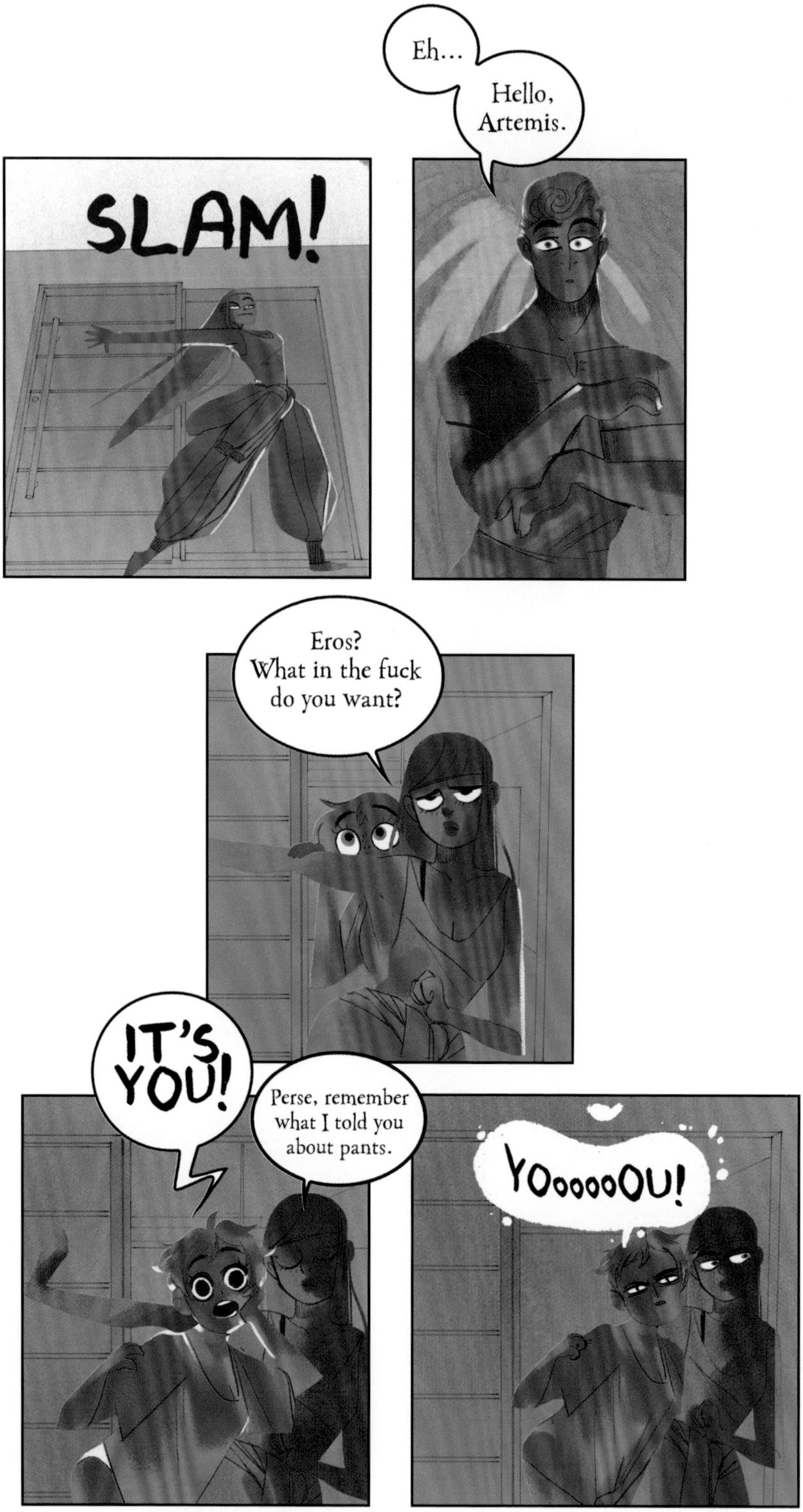
SLAM!
Eh...
Hello, Artemis.
Eros? What in the fuck do you want?
IT'S YOU!
Perse, remember what I told you about pants.
YOooooOU!

EPISODE 12: *Rose-Colored Boy* ♡
xox

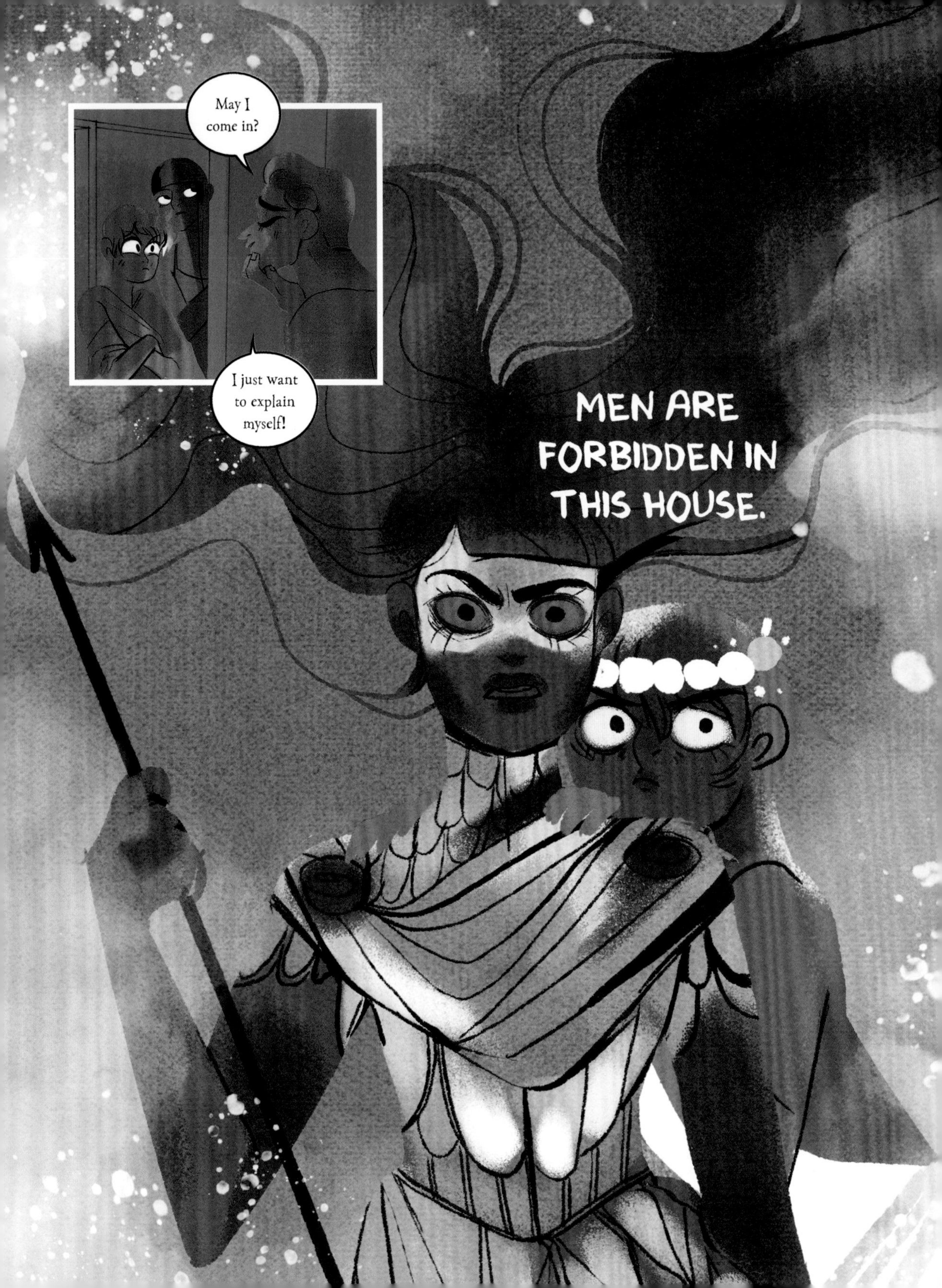
May I come in?
I just want to explain myself!
MEN ARE FORBIDDEN IN THIS HOUSE.

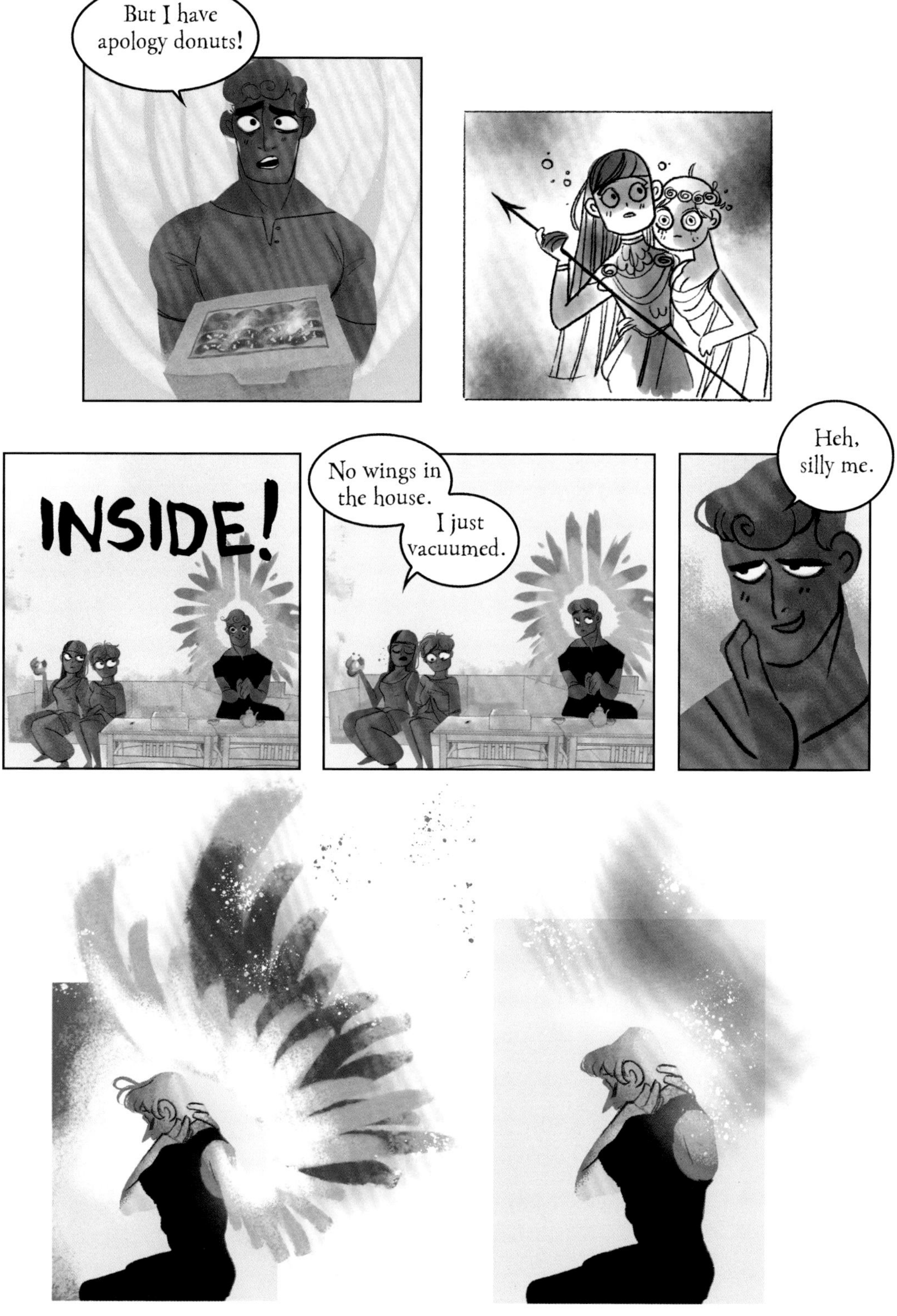
But I have apology donuts!
INSIDE!
No wings in the house.
I just vacuumed.
Heh, silly me.

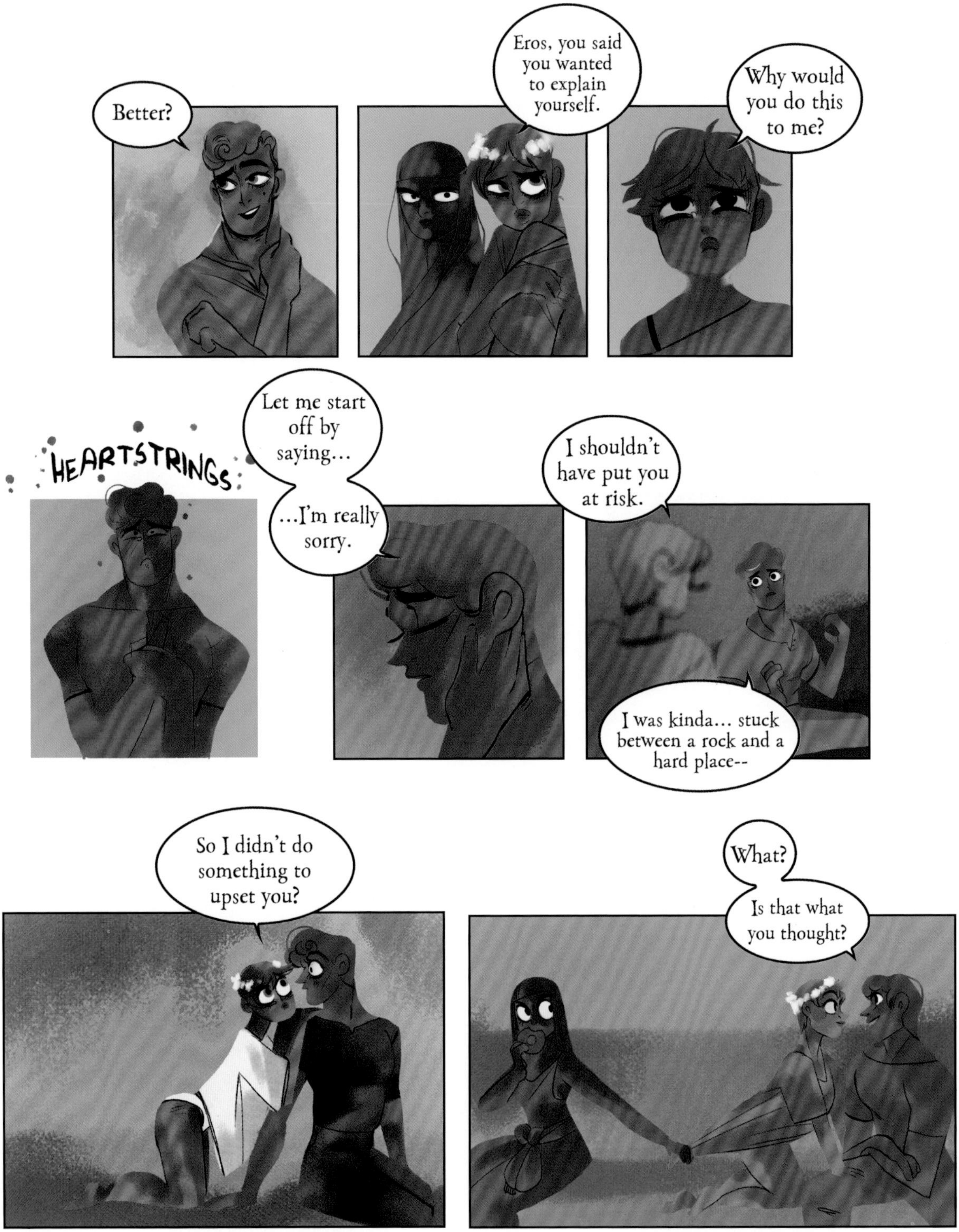
Better?
Eros, you said you wanted to explain yourself.
Why would you do this to me?
HEARTSTRINGS
Let me start off by saying...
...I'm really sorry.
I shouldn't have put you at risk.
I was kinda... stuck between a rock and a hard place--
So I didn't do something to upset you?
What?
Is that what you thought?

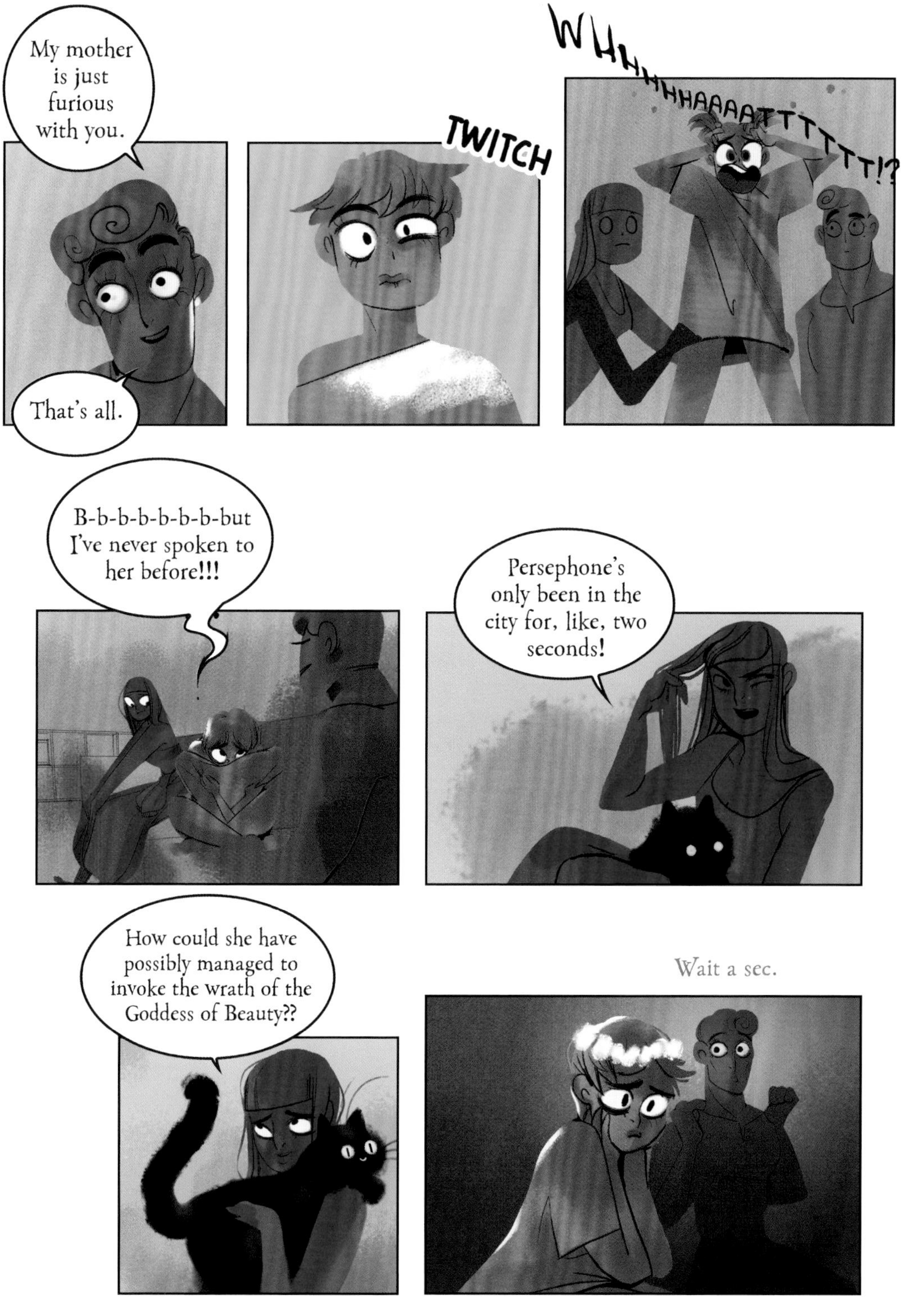
My mother is just furious with you.
That's all.
TWITCH
WHHHHHHAAAATTTTTTT!?
B-b-b-b-b-b-b-but I've never spoken to her before!!!
Persephone's only been in the city for, like, two seconds!
How could she have possibly managed to invoke the wrath of the Goddess of Beauty??
Wait a sec.

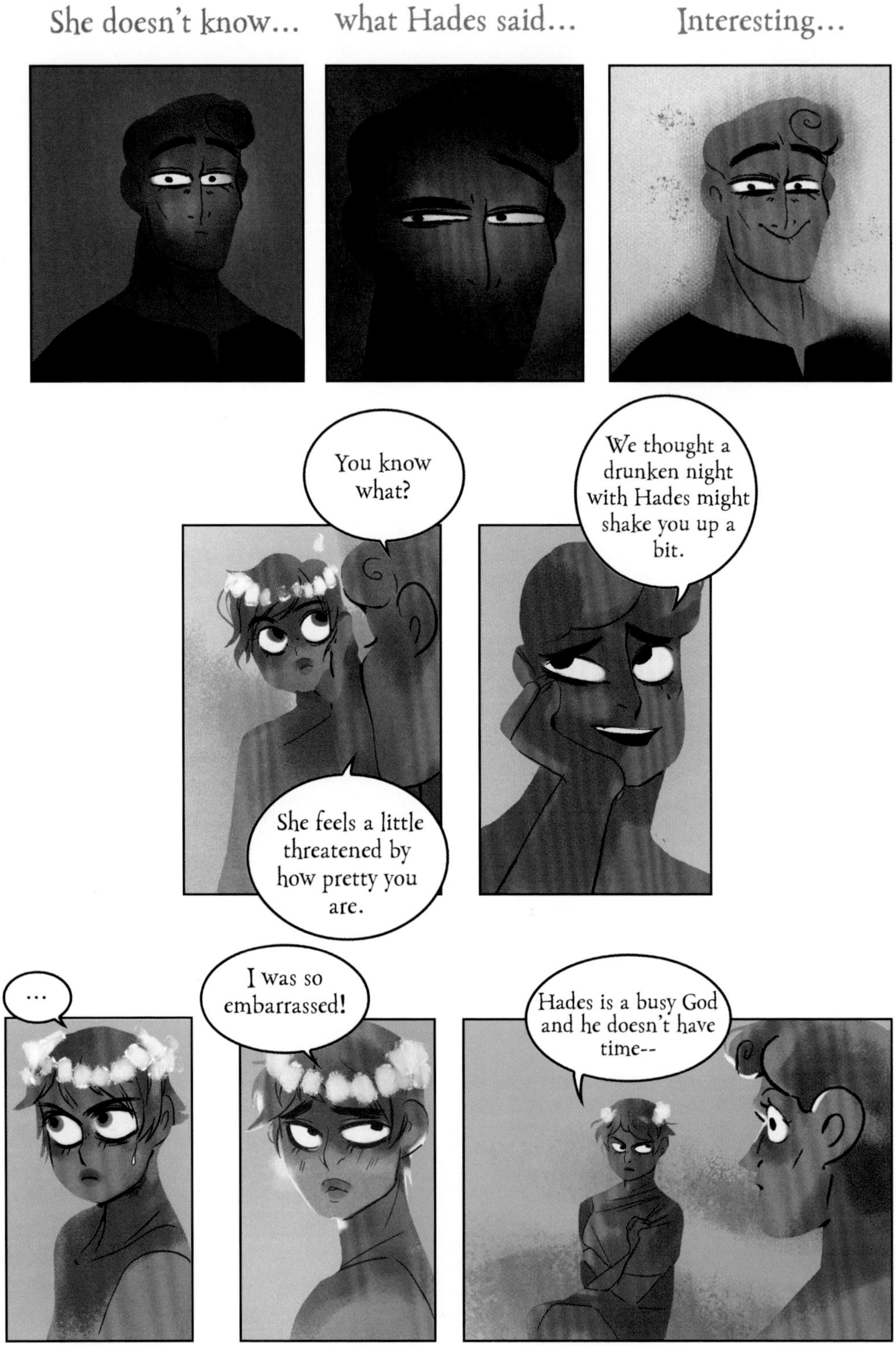
She doesn't know...
what Hades said...
Interesting...
You know what?
We thought a drunken night with Hades might shake you up a bit.
She feels a little threatened by how pretty you are.
...
I was so embarrassed!
Hades is a busy God and he doesn't have time--

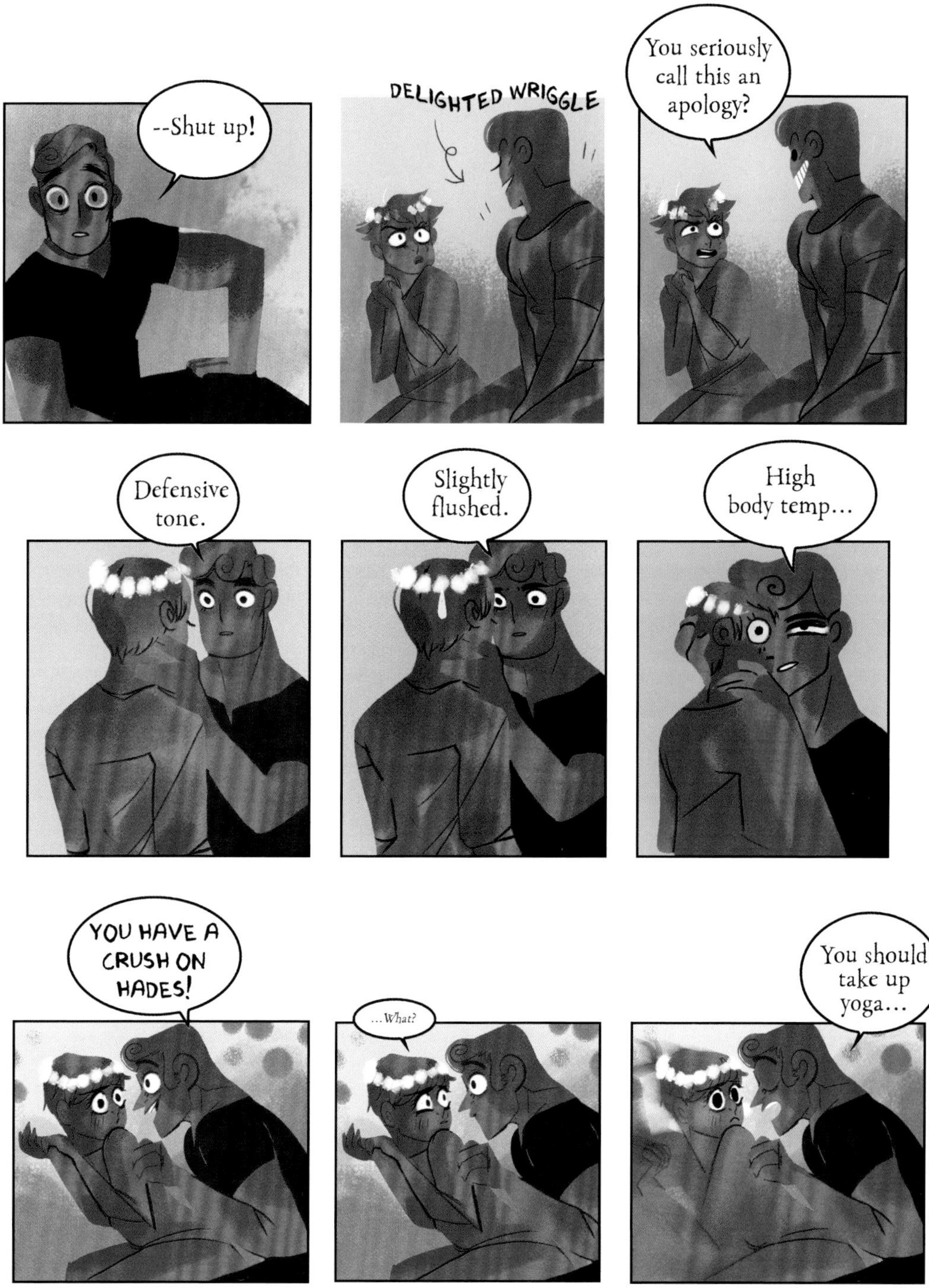
--Shut up!
DELIGHTED WRIGGLE
You seriously call this an apology?
Defensive tone.
Slightly flushed.
High body temp...
YOU HAVE A CRUSH ON HADES!
...What?
You should take up yoga...

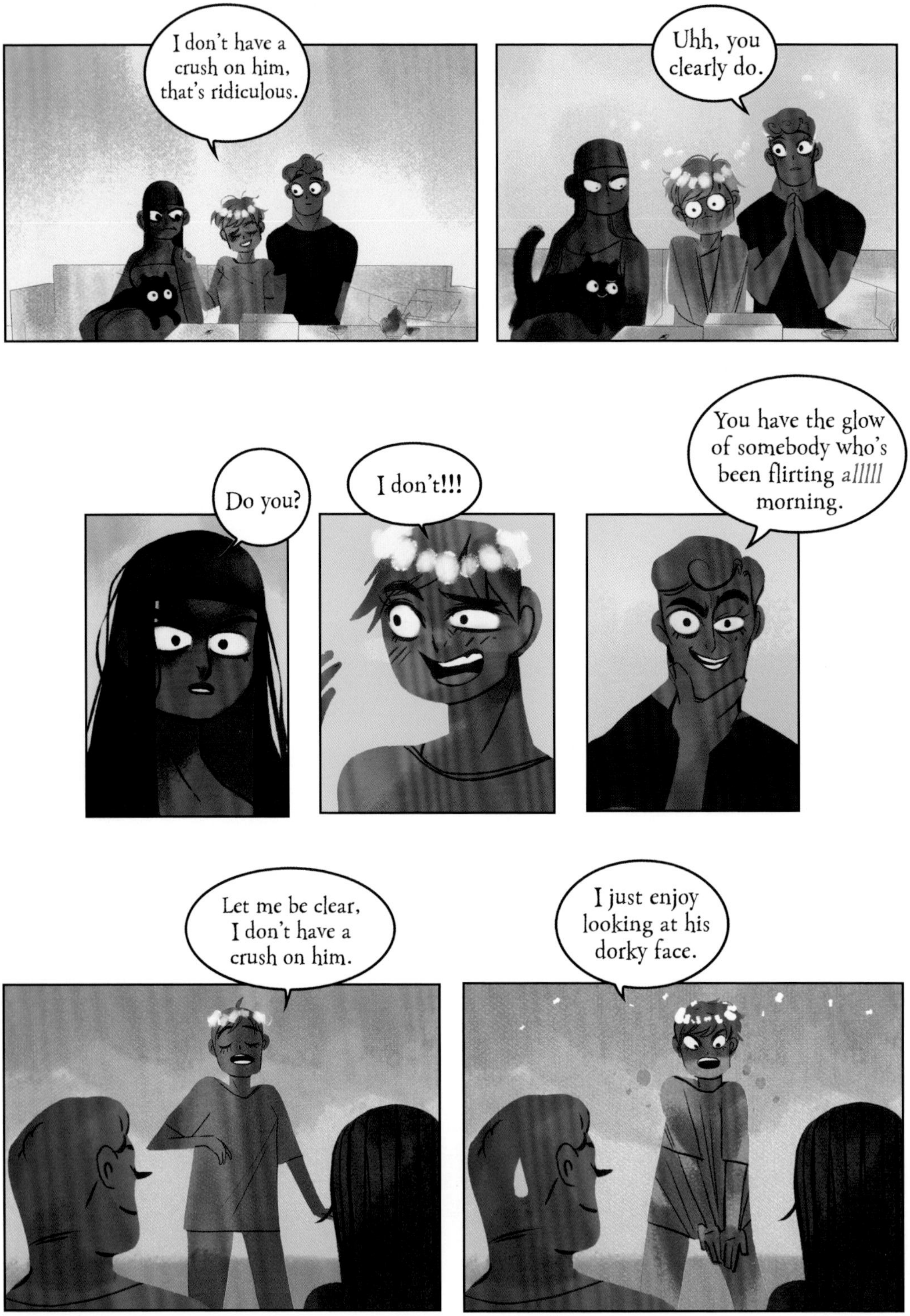
I don't have a crush on him, that's ridiculous.
Uhh, you clearly do.
Do you?
I don't!!!
You have the glow of somebody who's been flirting *alllll* morning.
Let me be clear, I don't have a crush on him.
I just enjoy looking at his dorky face.

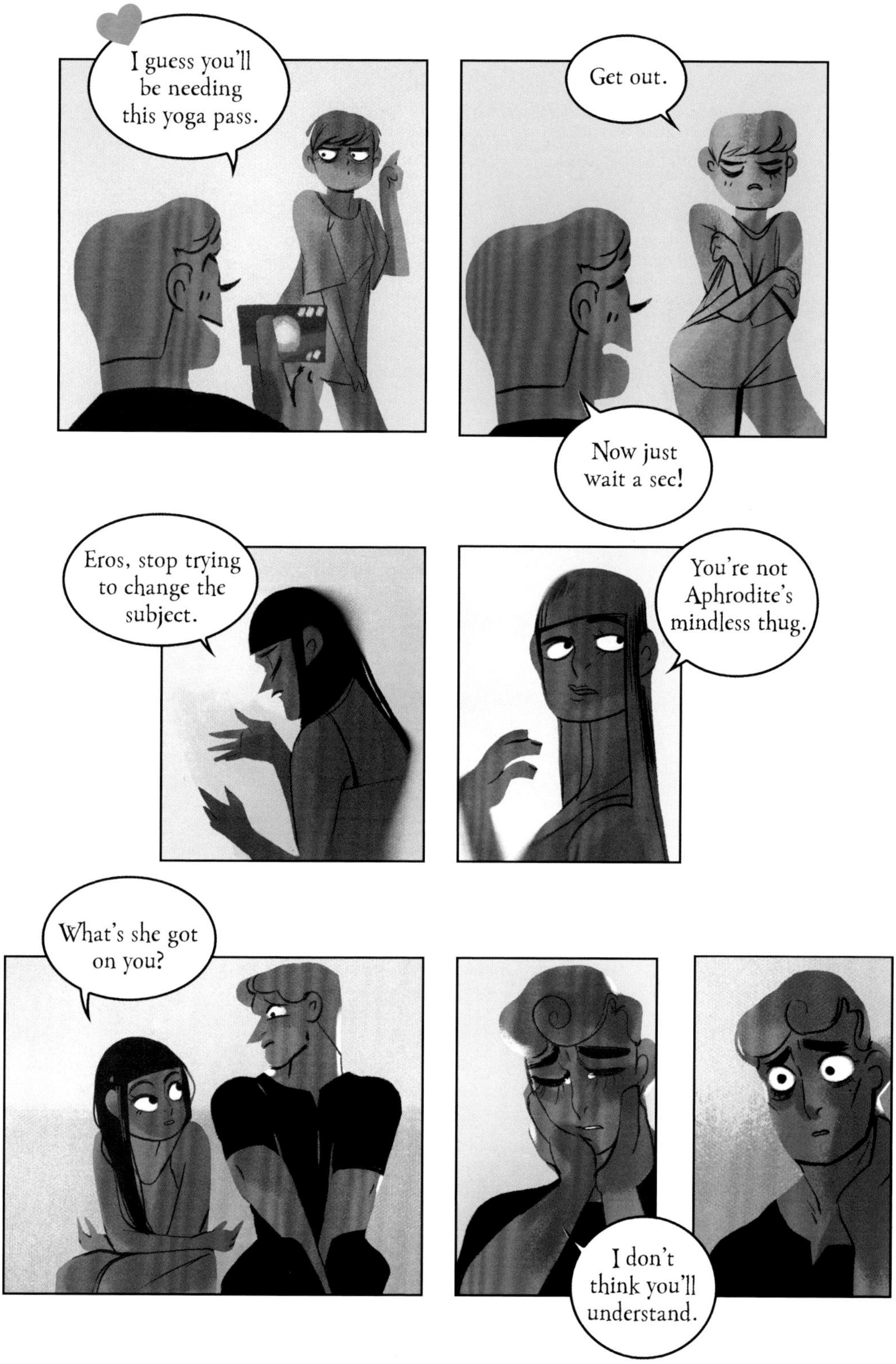
I guess you'll be needing this yoga pass.
Get out.
Now just wait a sec!
Eros, stop trying to change the subject.
You're not Aphrodite's mindless thug.
What's she got on you?
I don't think you'll understand.

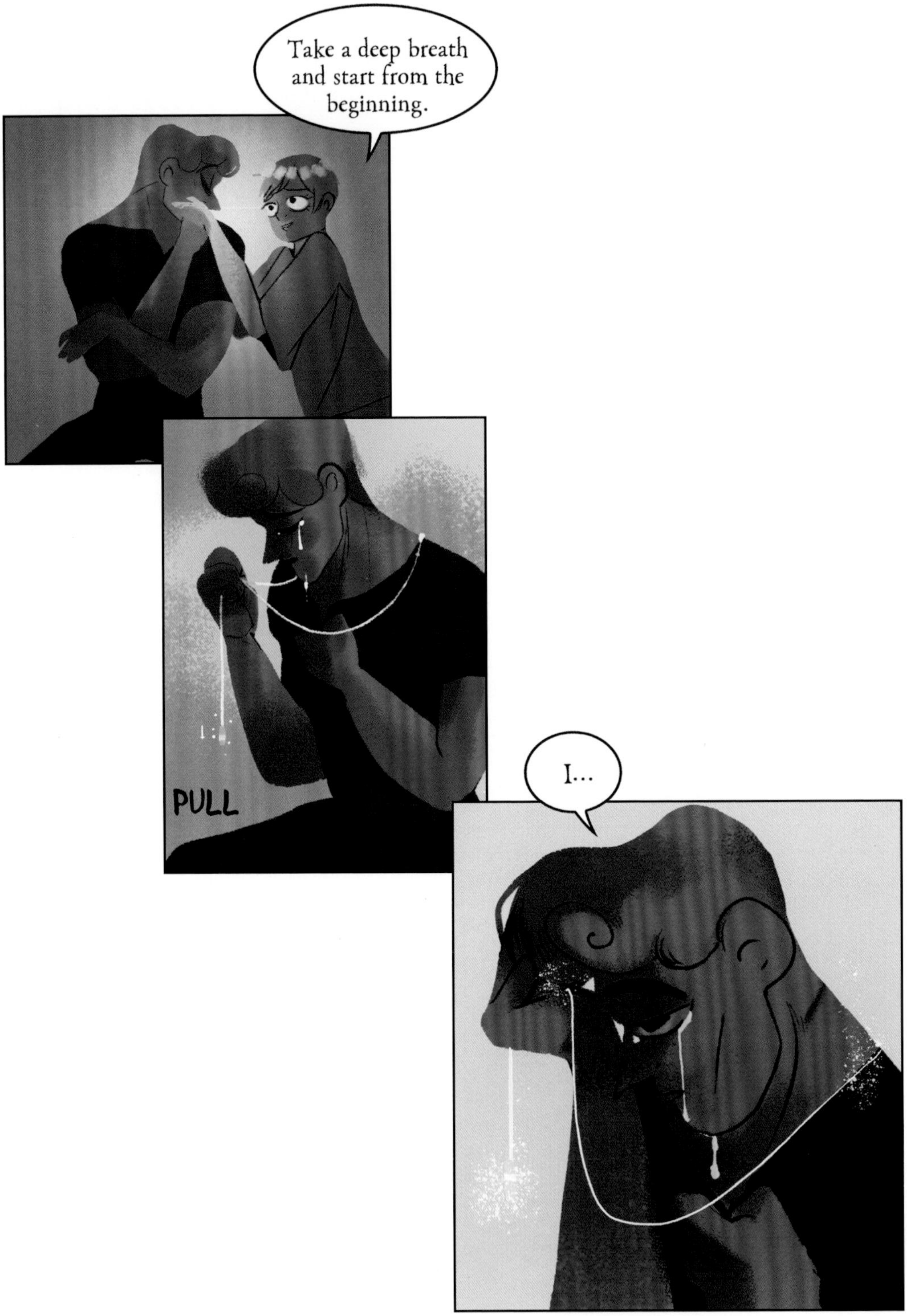
Take a deep breath and start from the beginning.
PULL
I...

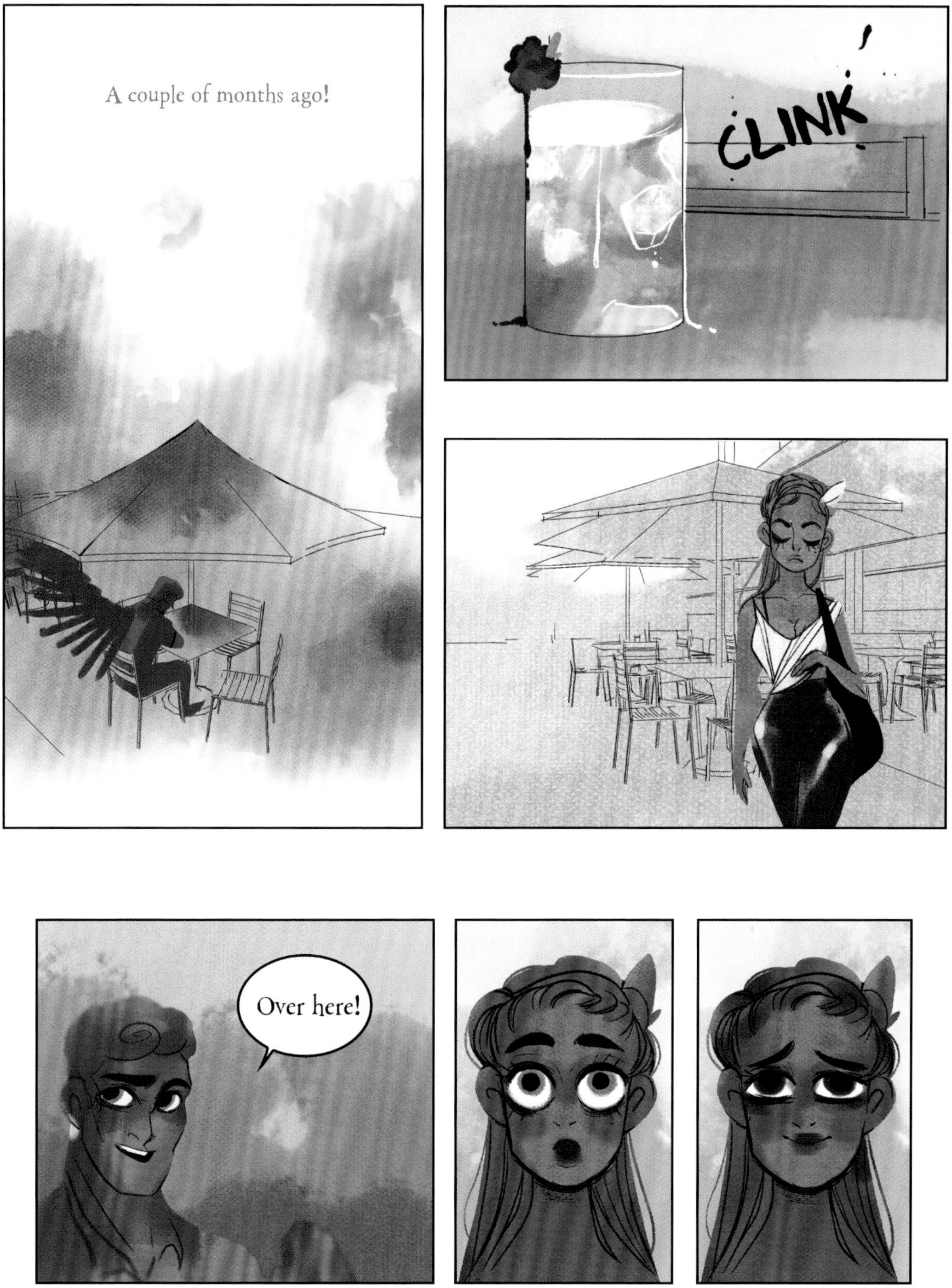
A couple of months ago!
CLINK
Over here!

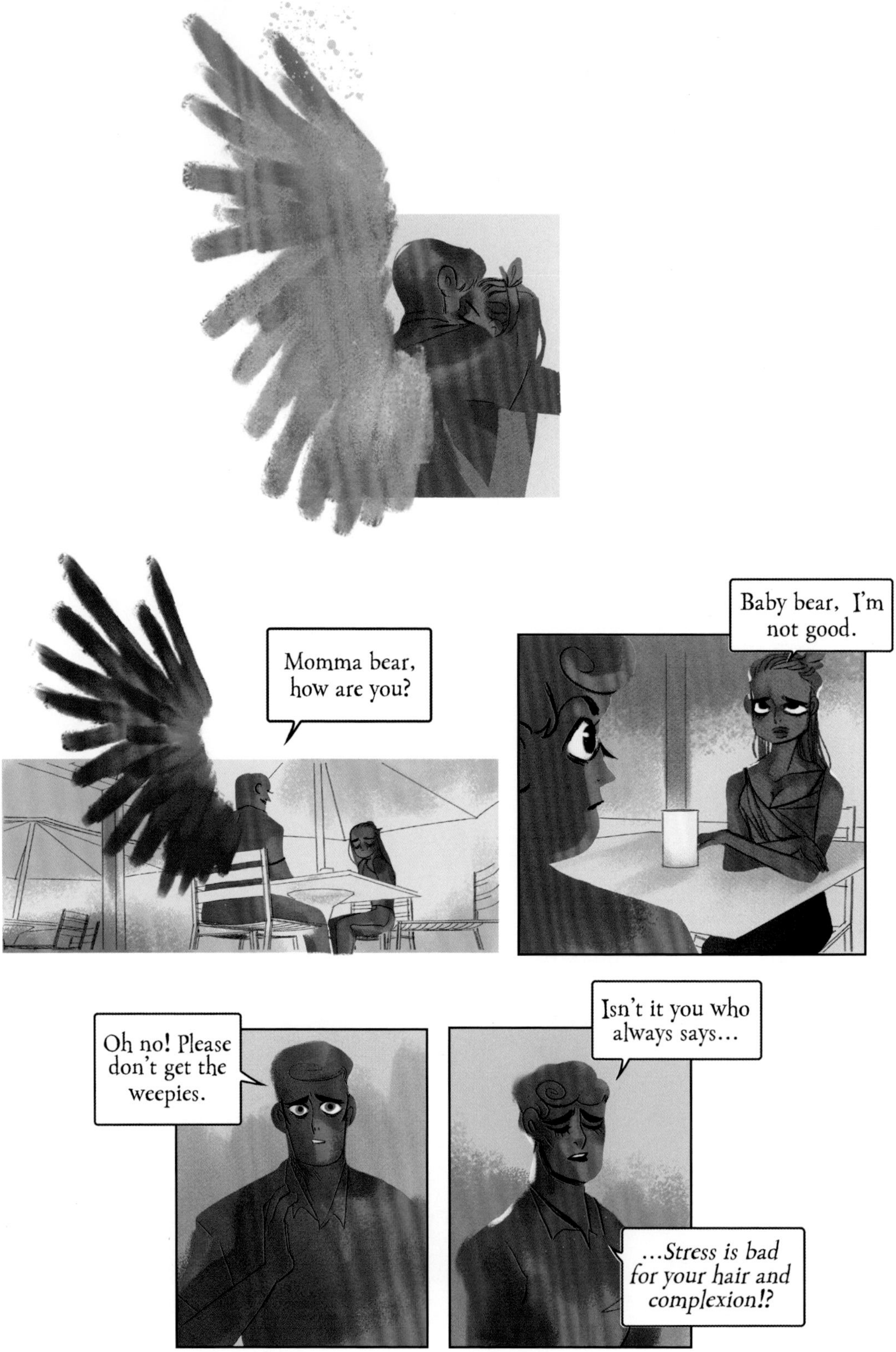

Momma bear, how are you?
Baby bear, I'm not good.
Oh no! Please don't get the weepies.
Isn't it you who always says...
...Stress is bad for your hair and complexion!?

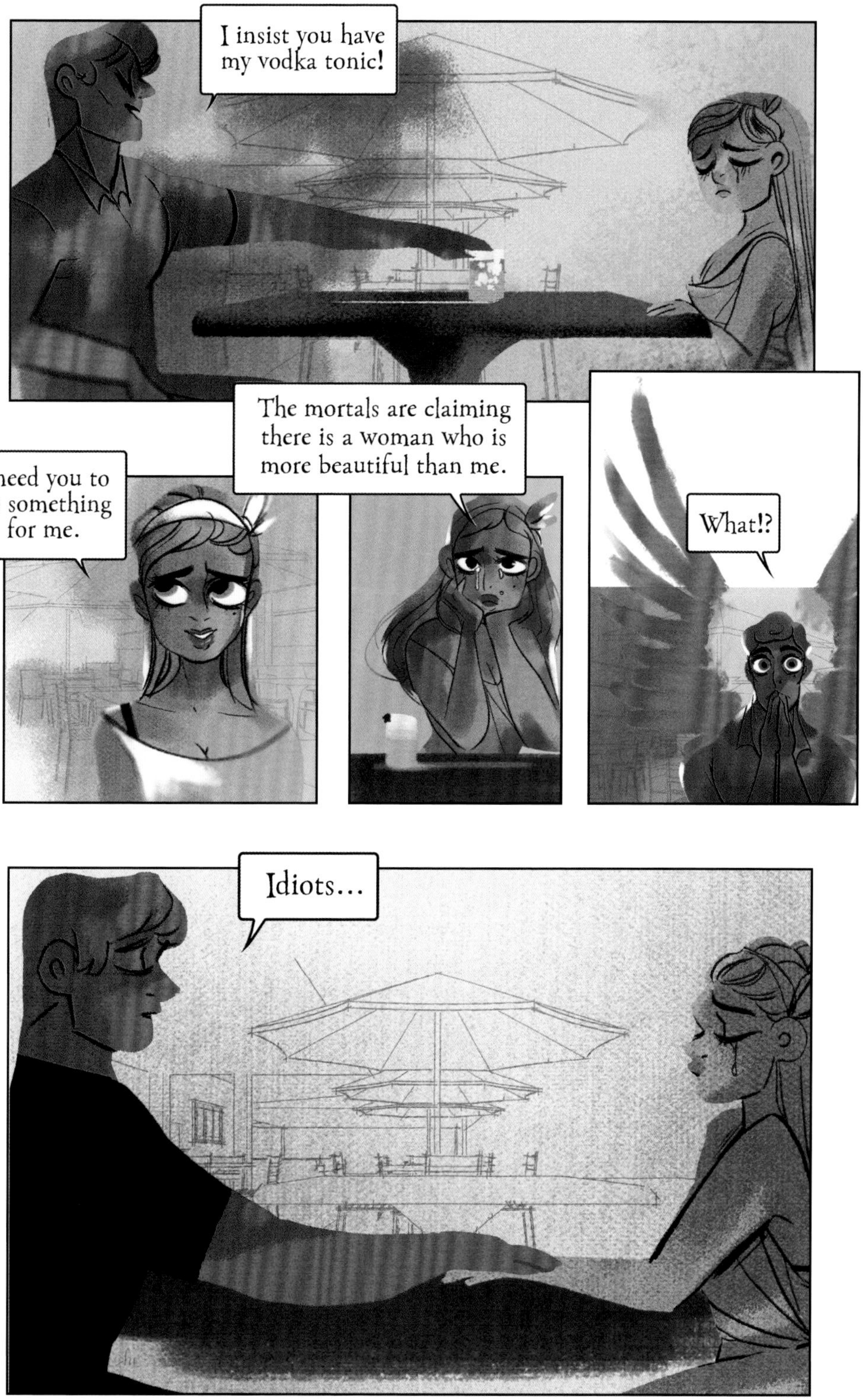
I insist you have my vodka tonic!
I need you to do something for me.
The mortals are claiming there is a woman who is more beautiful than me.
What!?
Idiots...

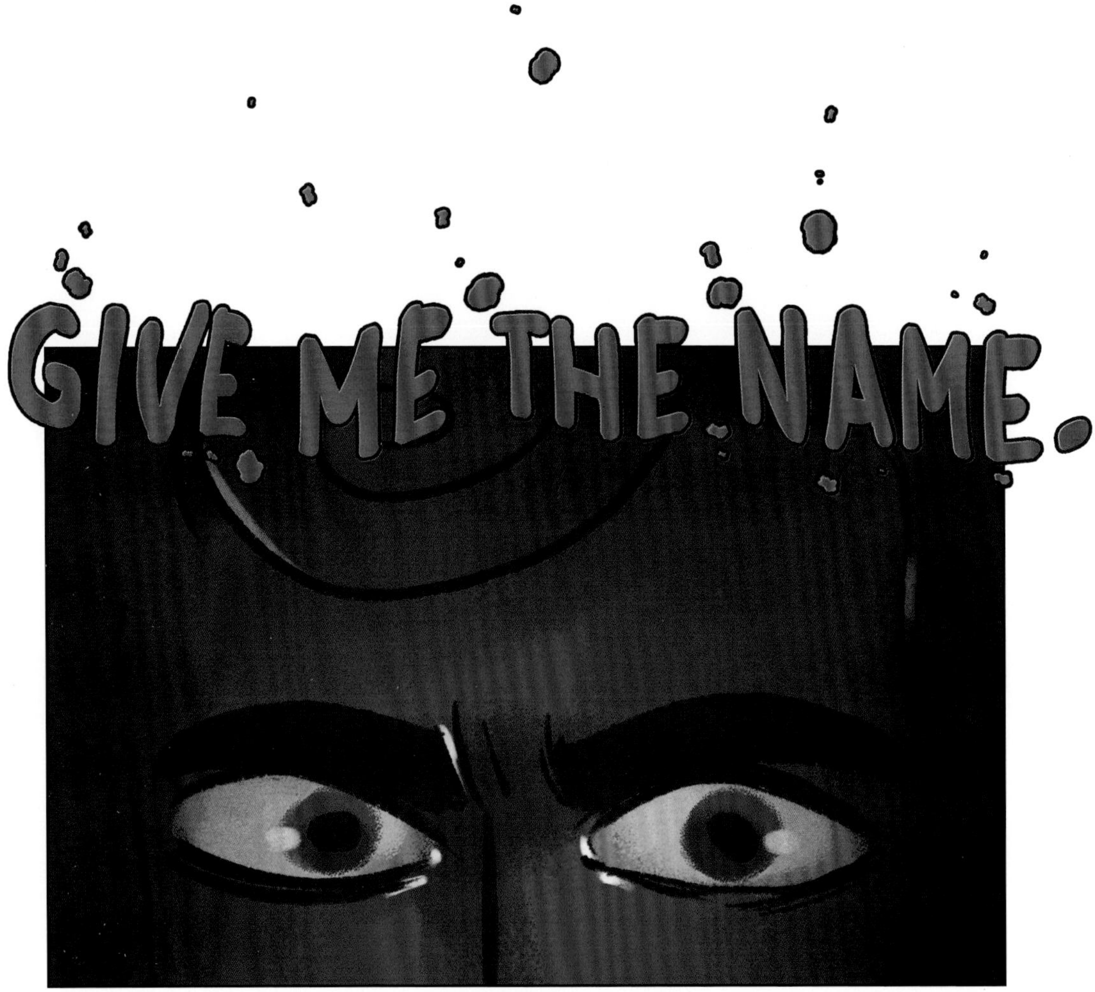
GIVE ME THE NAME.

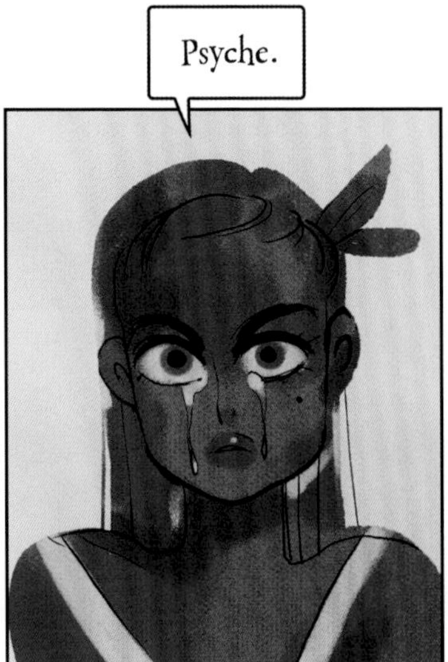
Psyche.

EPISODE 13: MAMA'S BOY

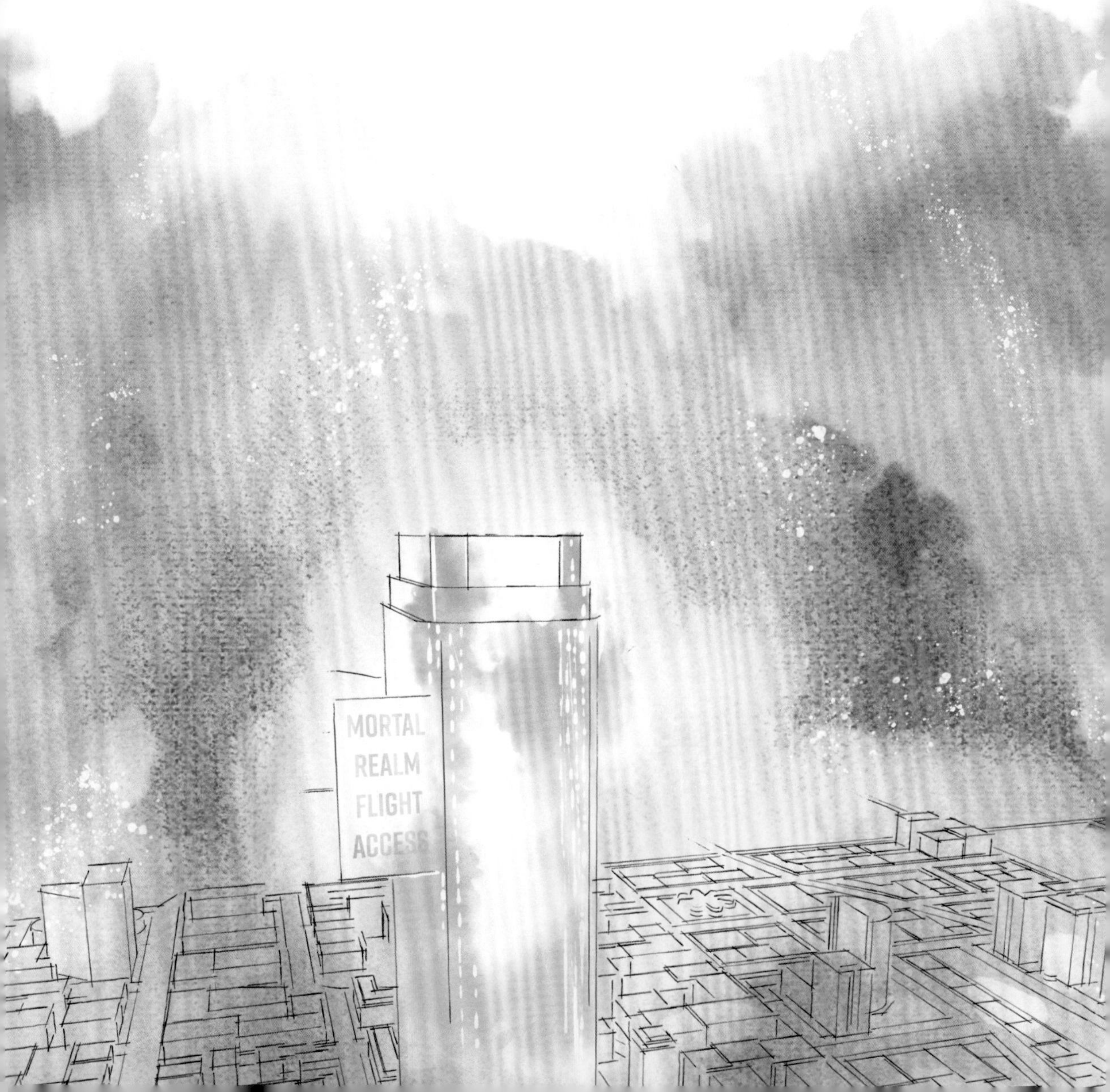
MORTAL
REALM
FLIGHT
ACCESS

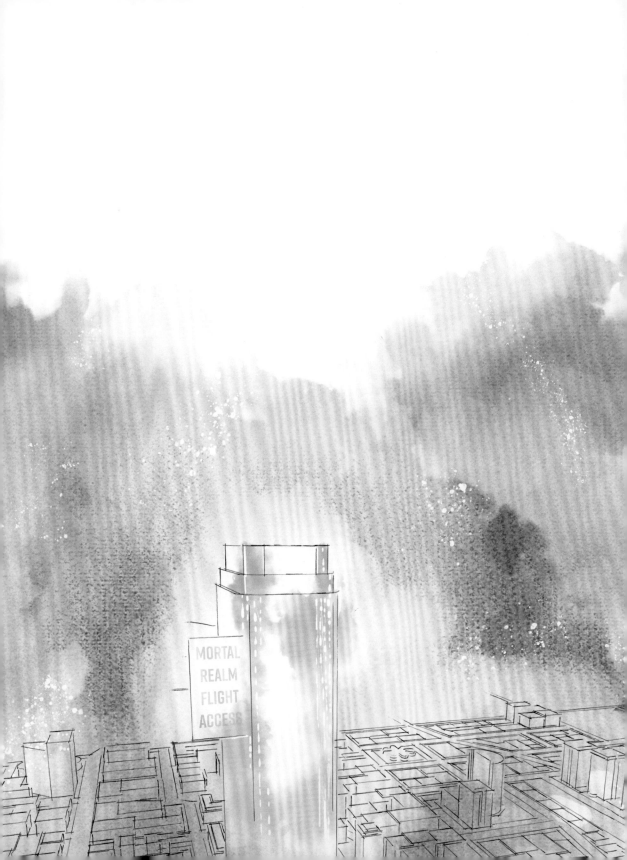

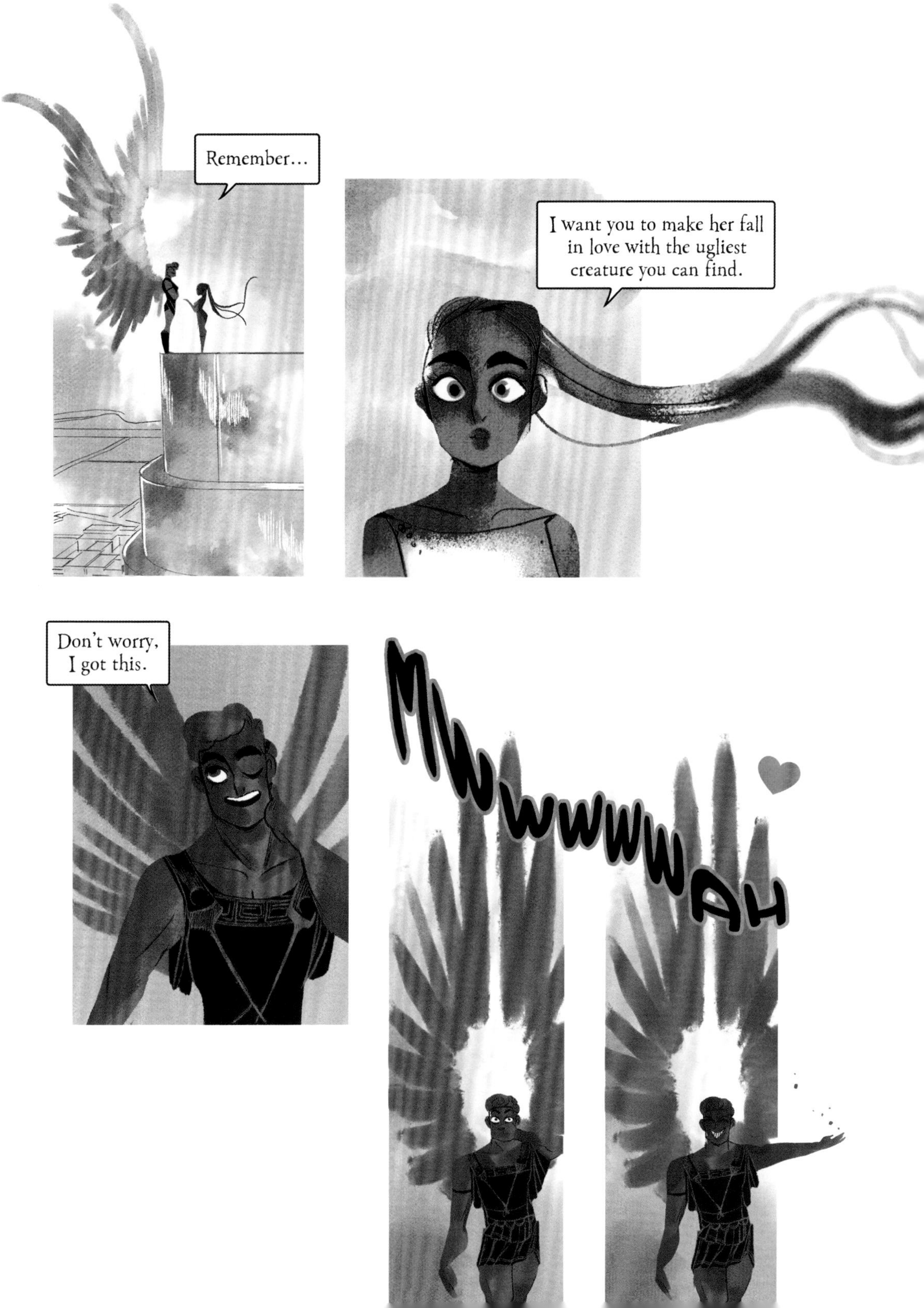
Remember…
I want you to make her fall in love with the ugliest creature you can find.
Don't worry, I got this.
MWWWWWWAH

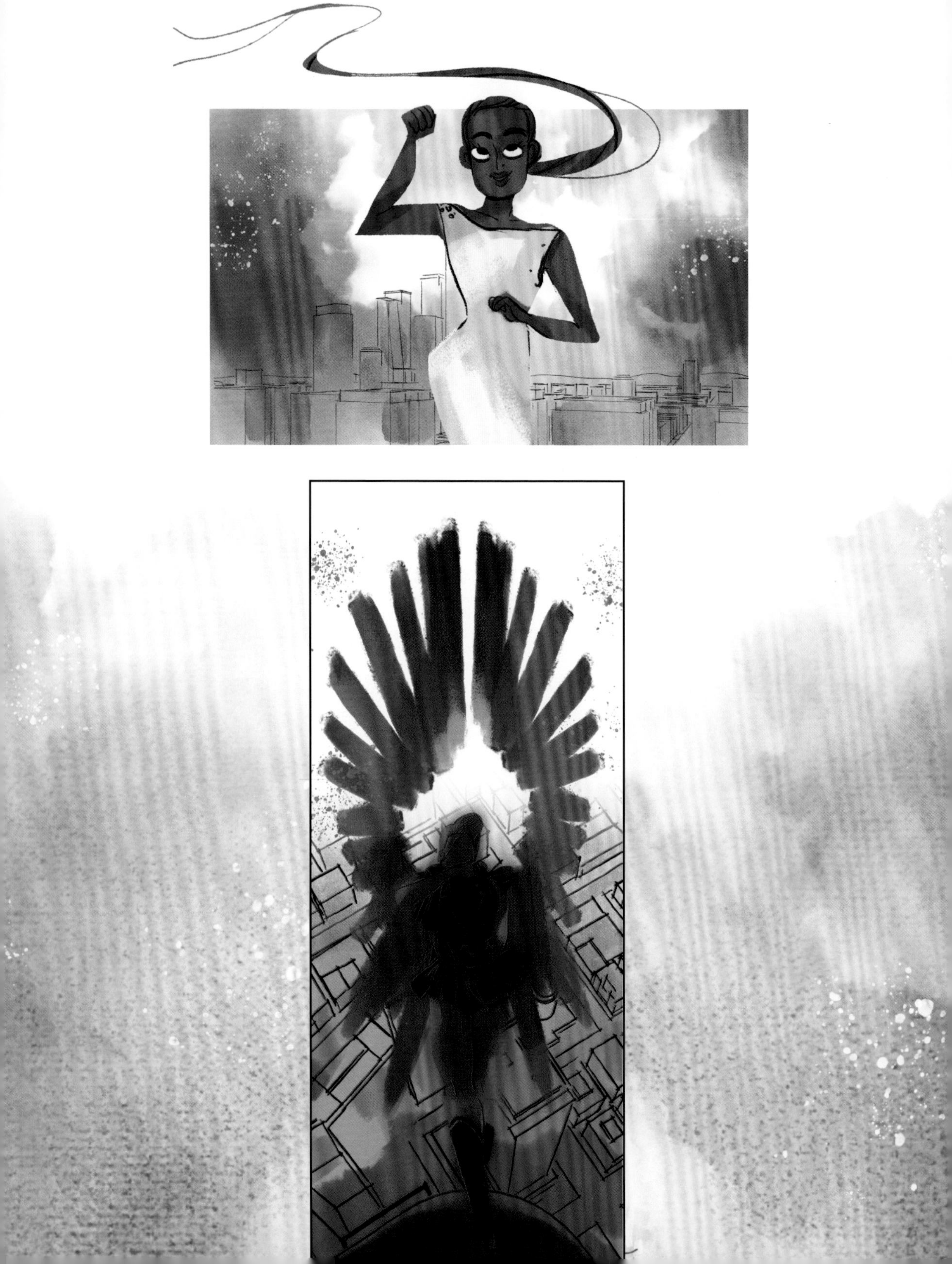

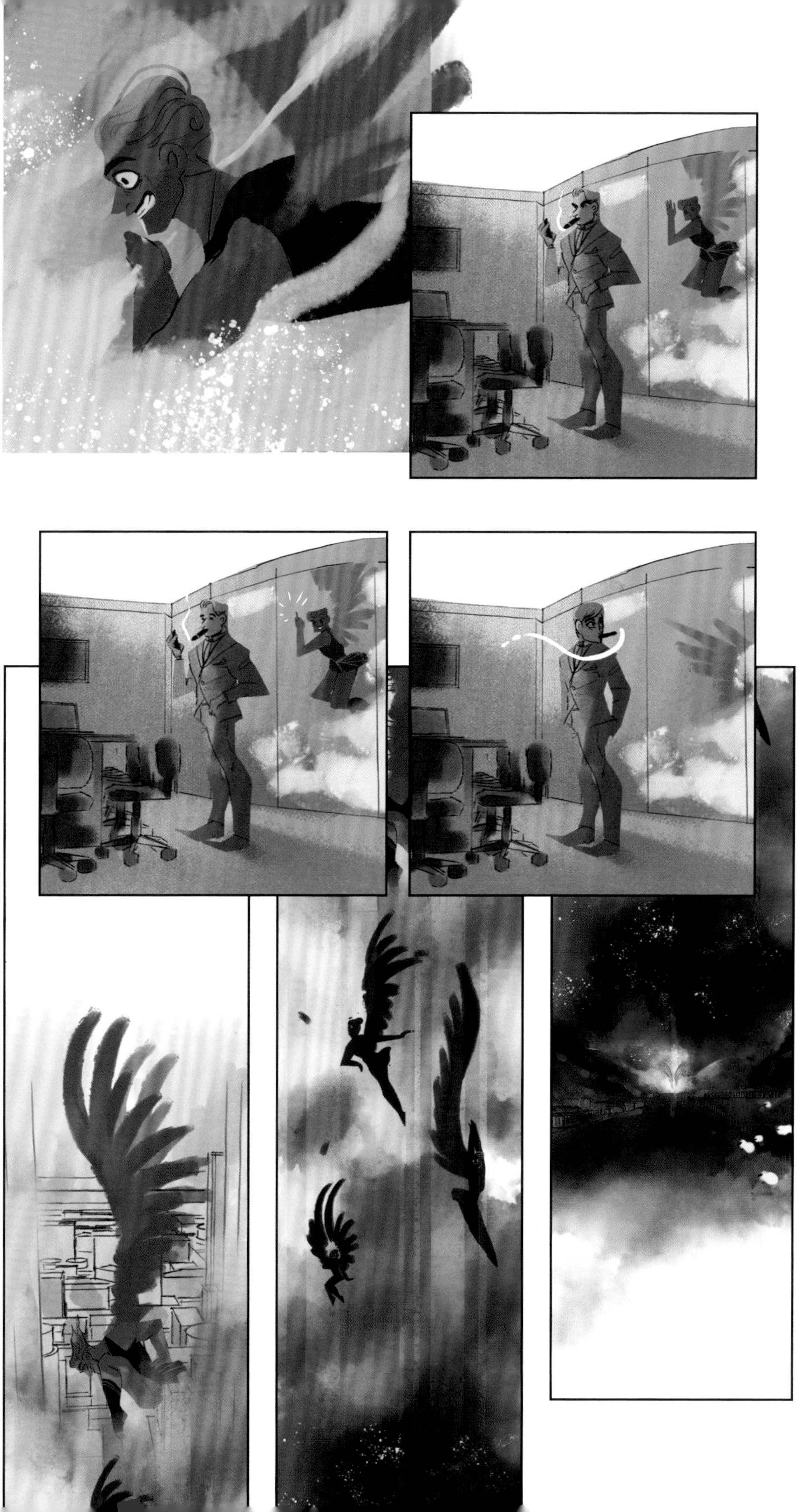

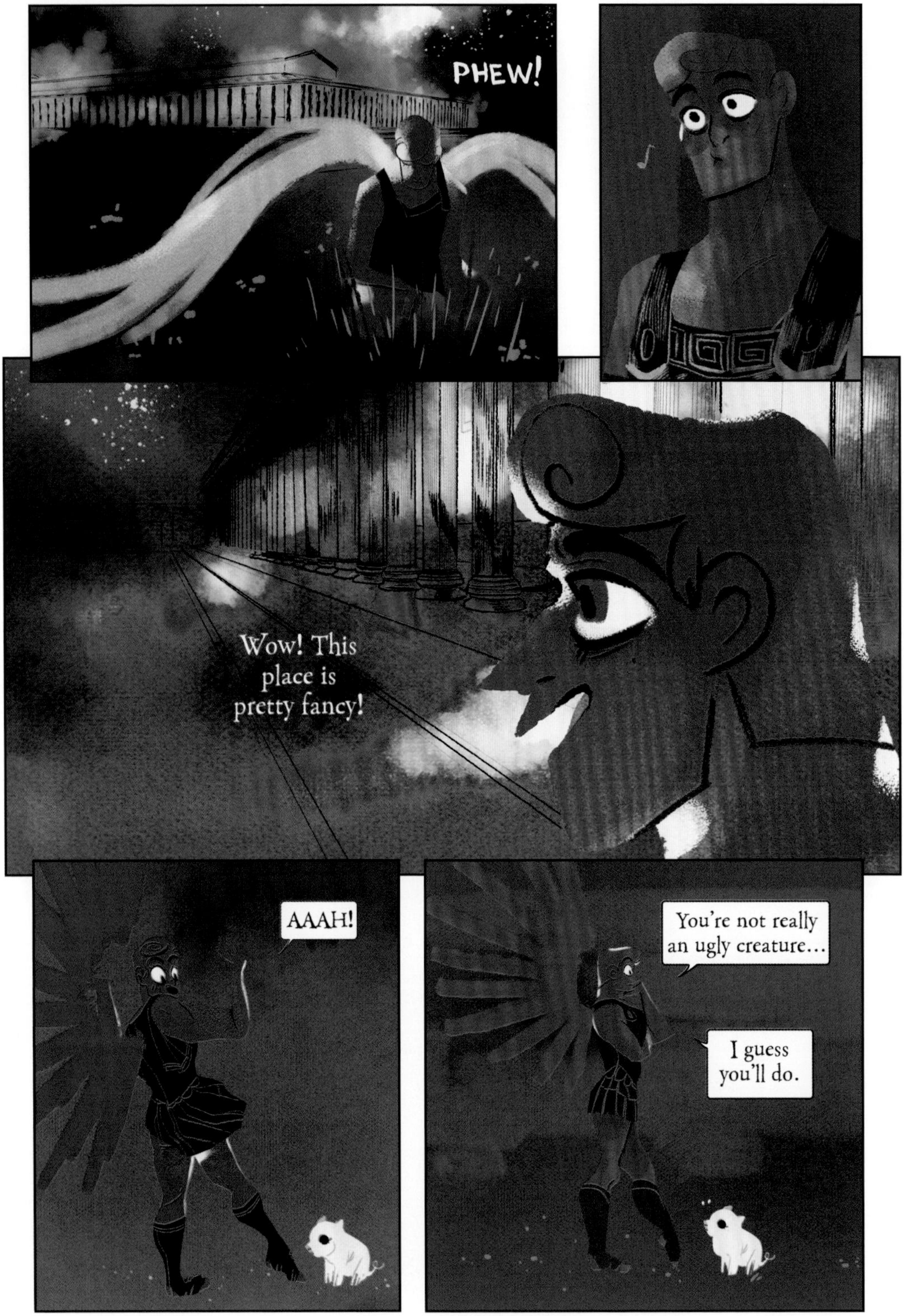
PHEW!
Wow! This place is pretty fancy!
AAAH!
You're not really an ugly creature...
I guess you'll do.

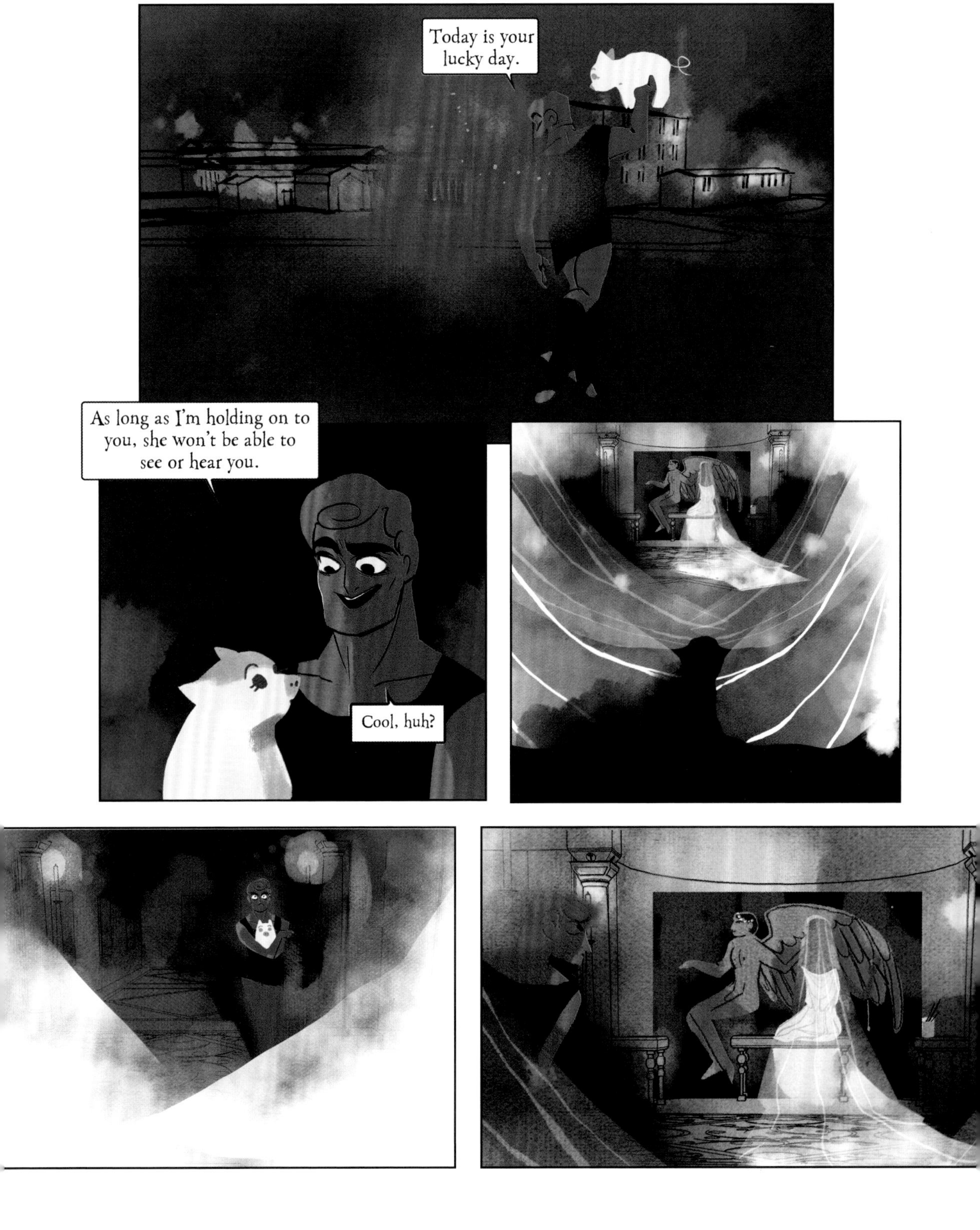
Today is your lucky day.
As long as I'm holding on to you, she won't be able to see or hear you.
Cool, huh?

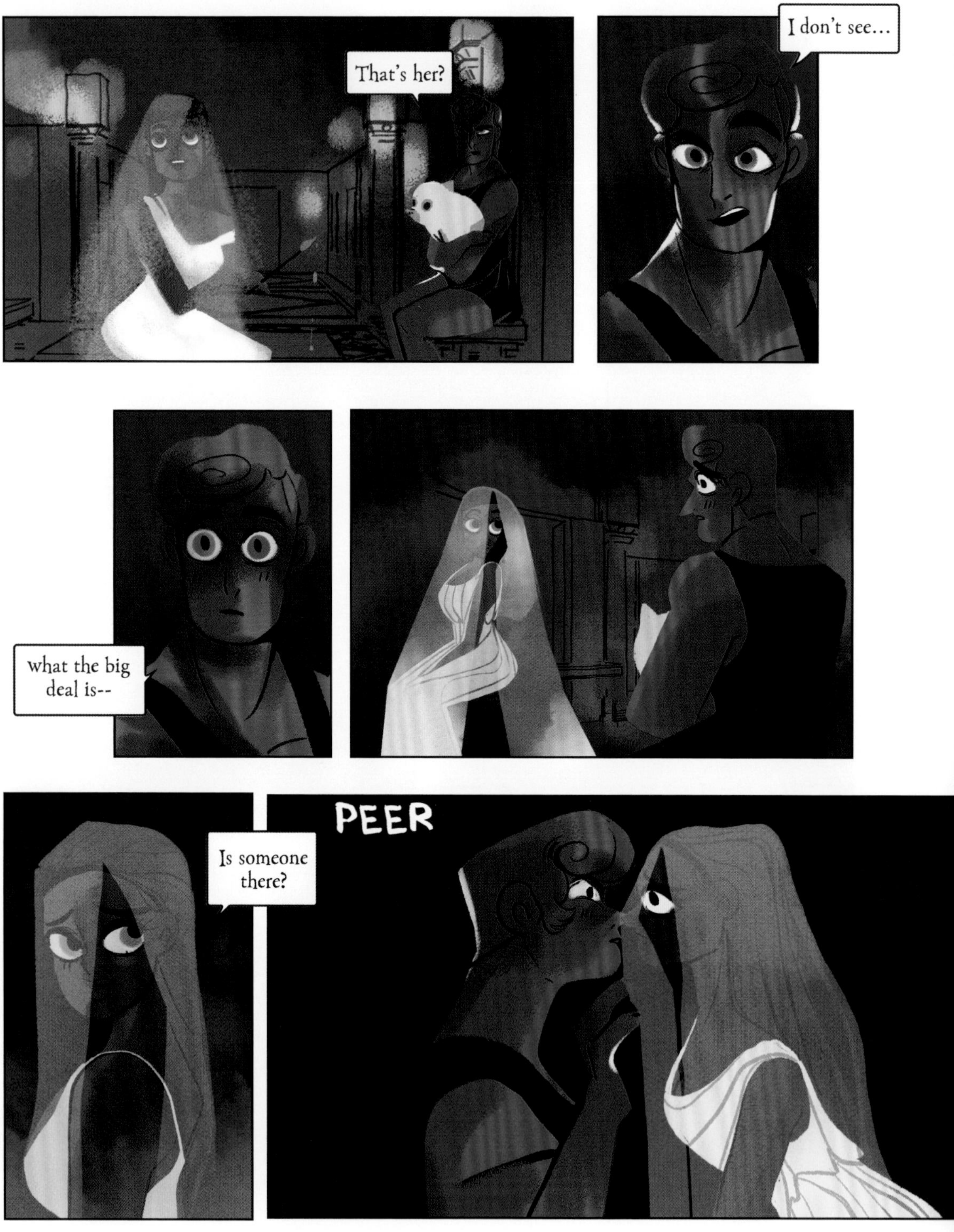
That's her?
I don't see...
what the big deal is--
Is someone there?
PEER

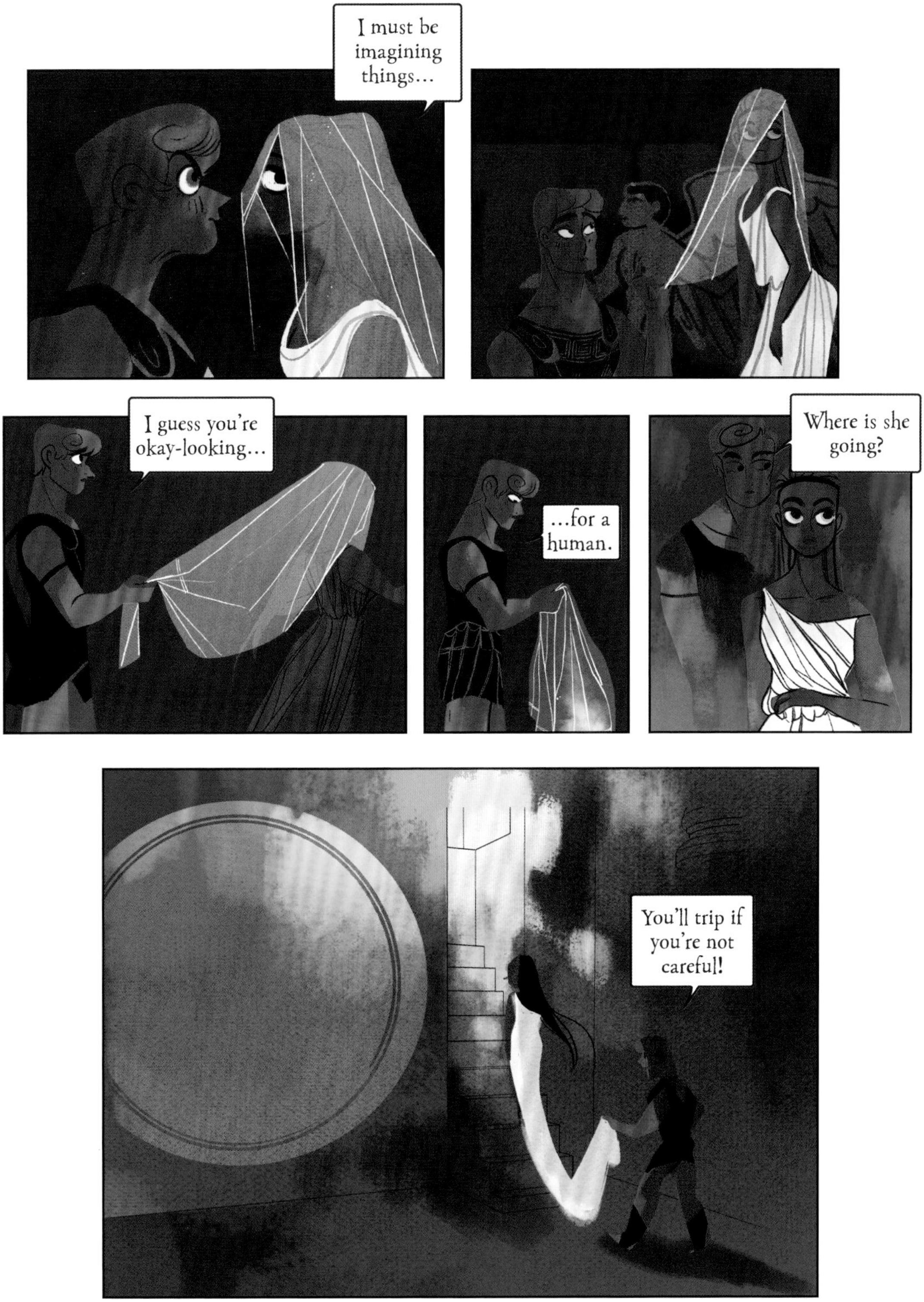
I must be imagining things...
I guess you're okay-looking...
...for a human.
Where is she going?
You'll trip if you're not careful!

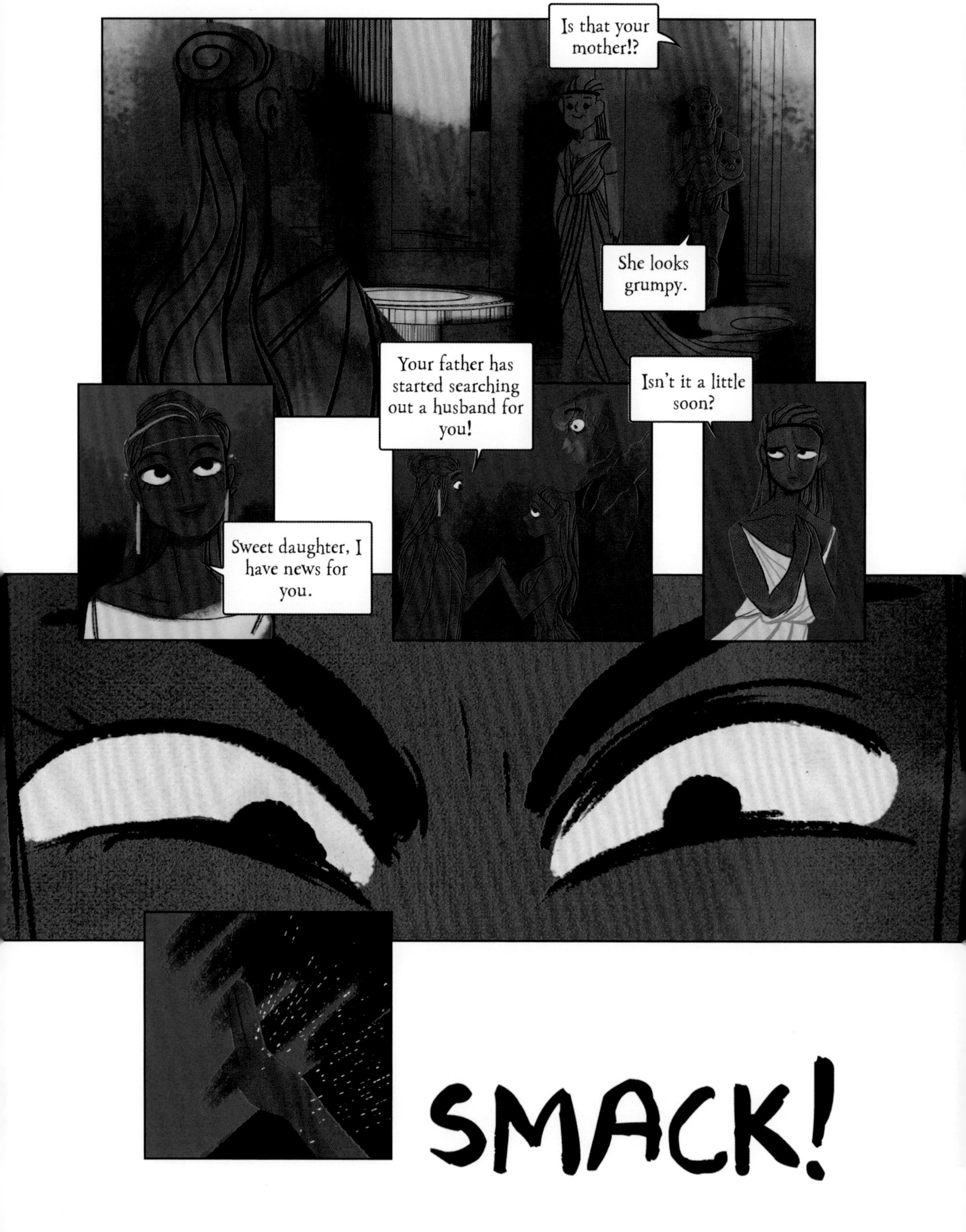
Is that your mother!?
She looks grumpy.
Sweet daughter, I have news for you.
Your father has started searching out a husband for you!
Isn't it a little soon?
SMACK!

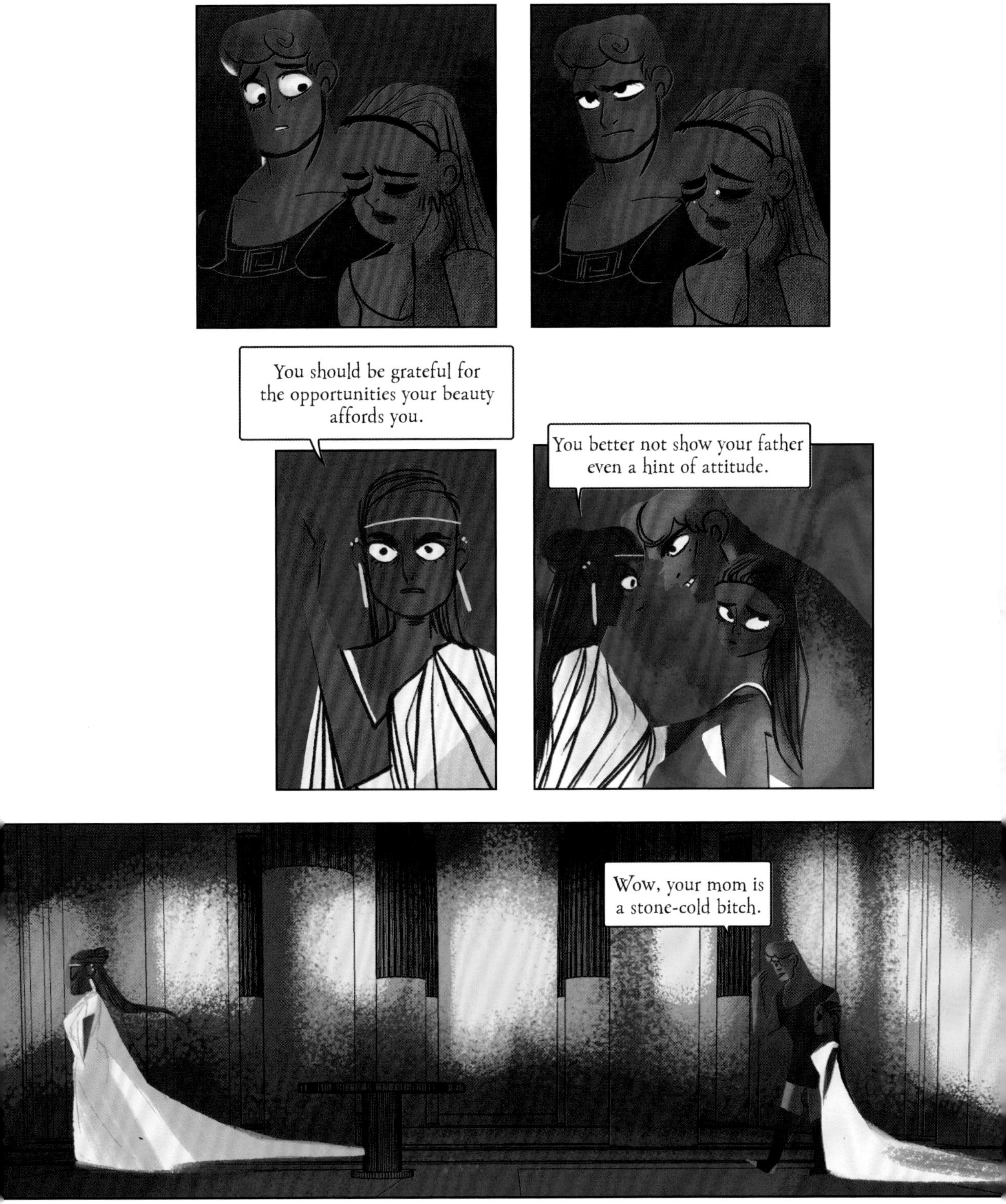

You should be grateful for the opportunities your beauty affords you.
You better not show your father even a hint of attitude.
Wow, your mom is a stone-cold bitch.

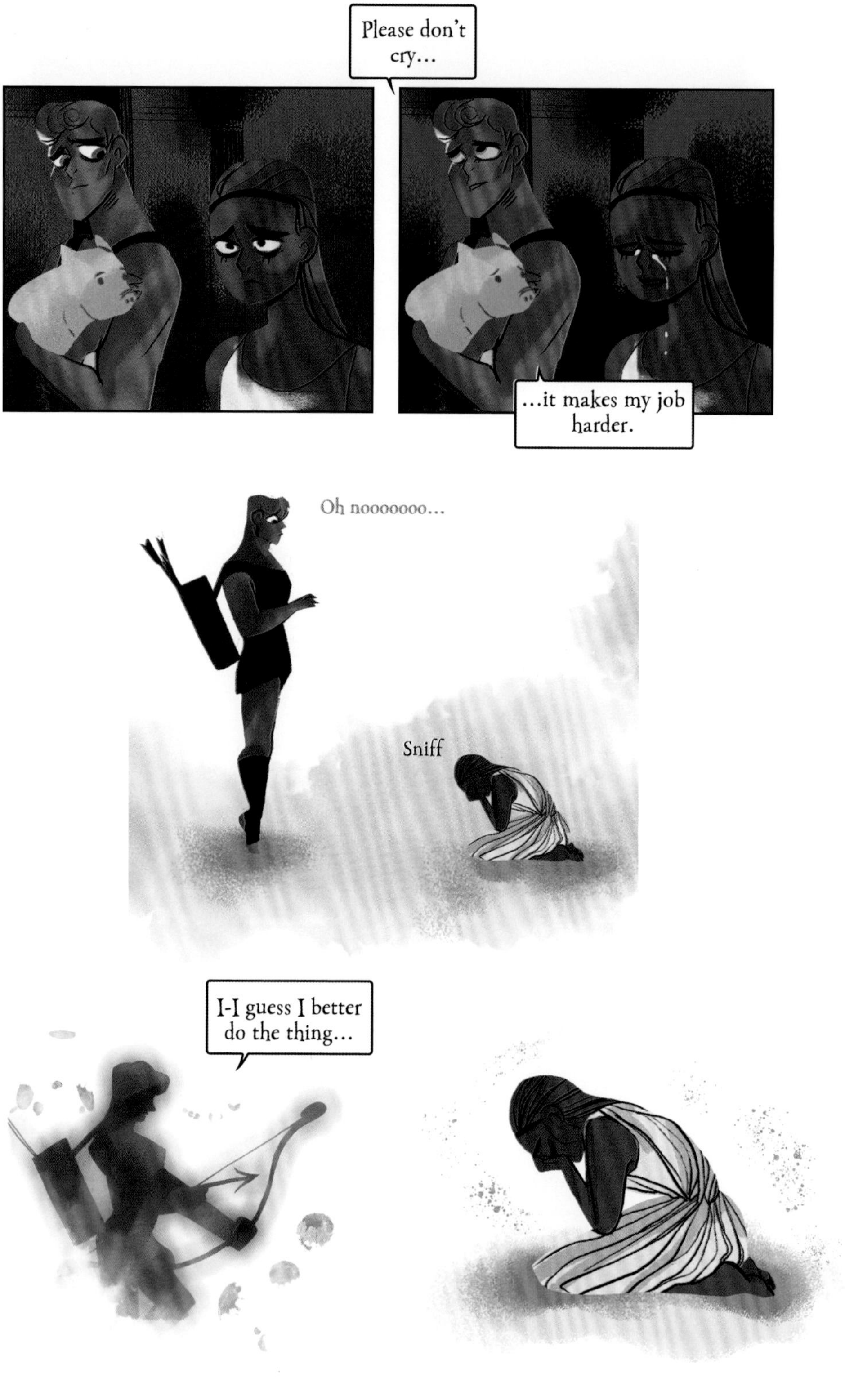

Please don't cry...
...it makes my job harder.
Oh noooooooo...
Sniff
I-I guess I better do the thing...

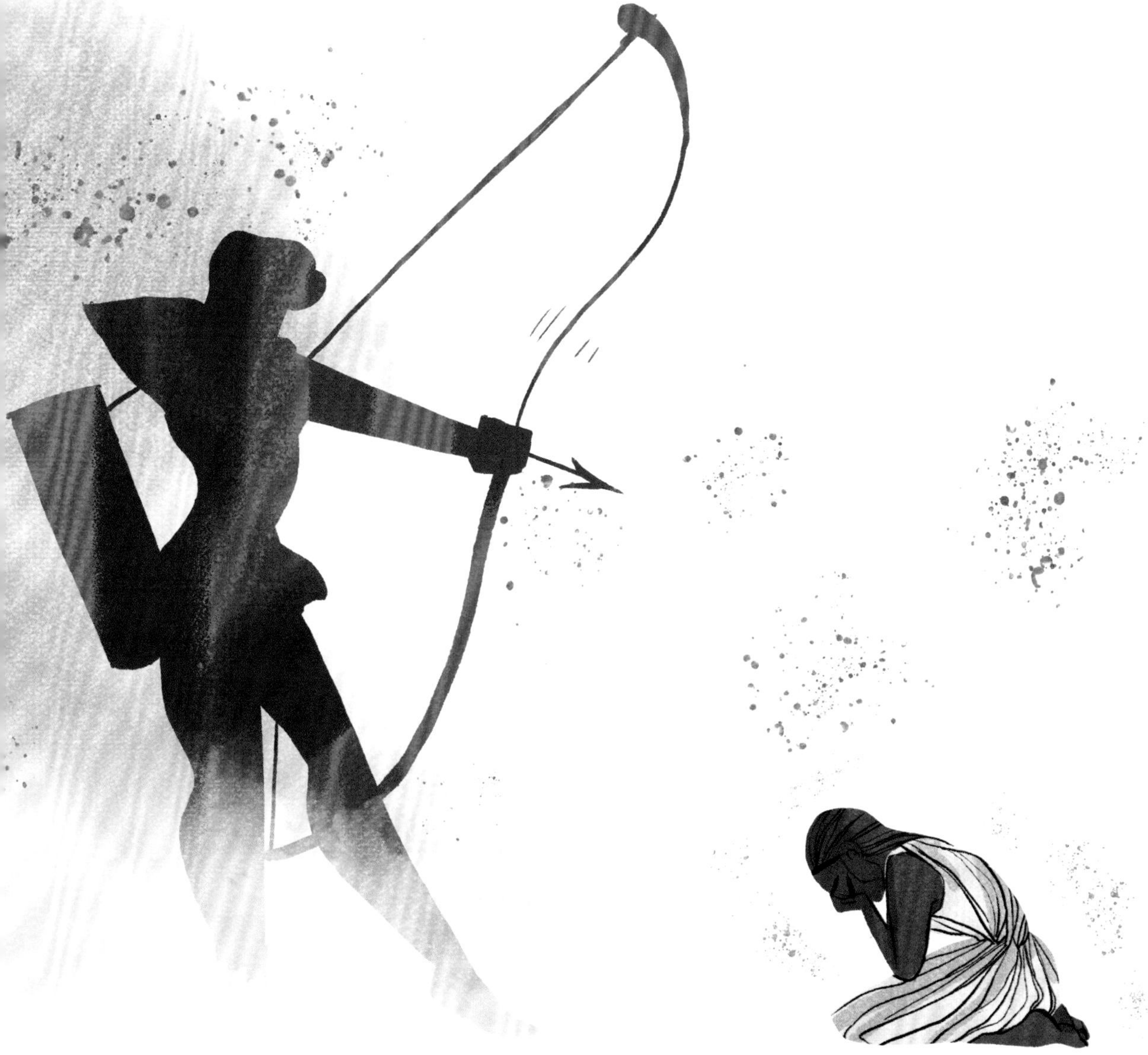
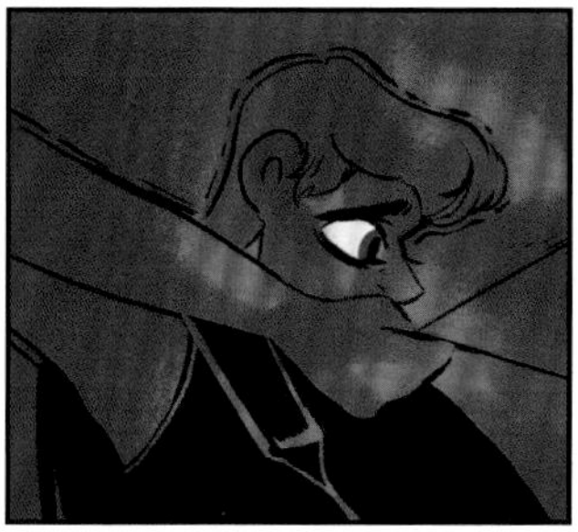

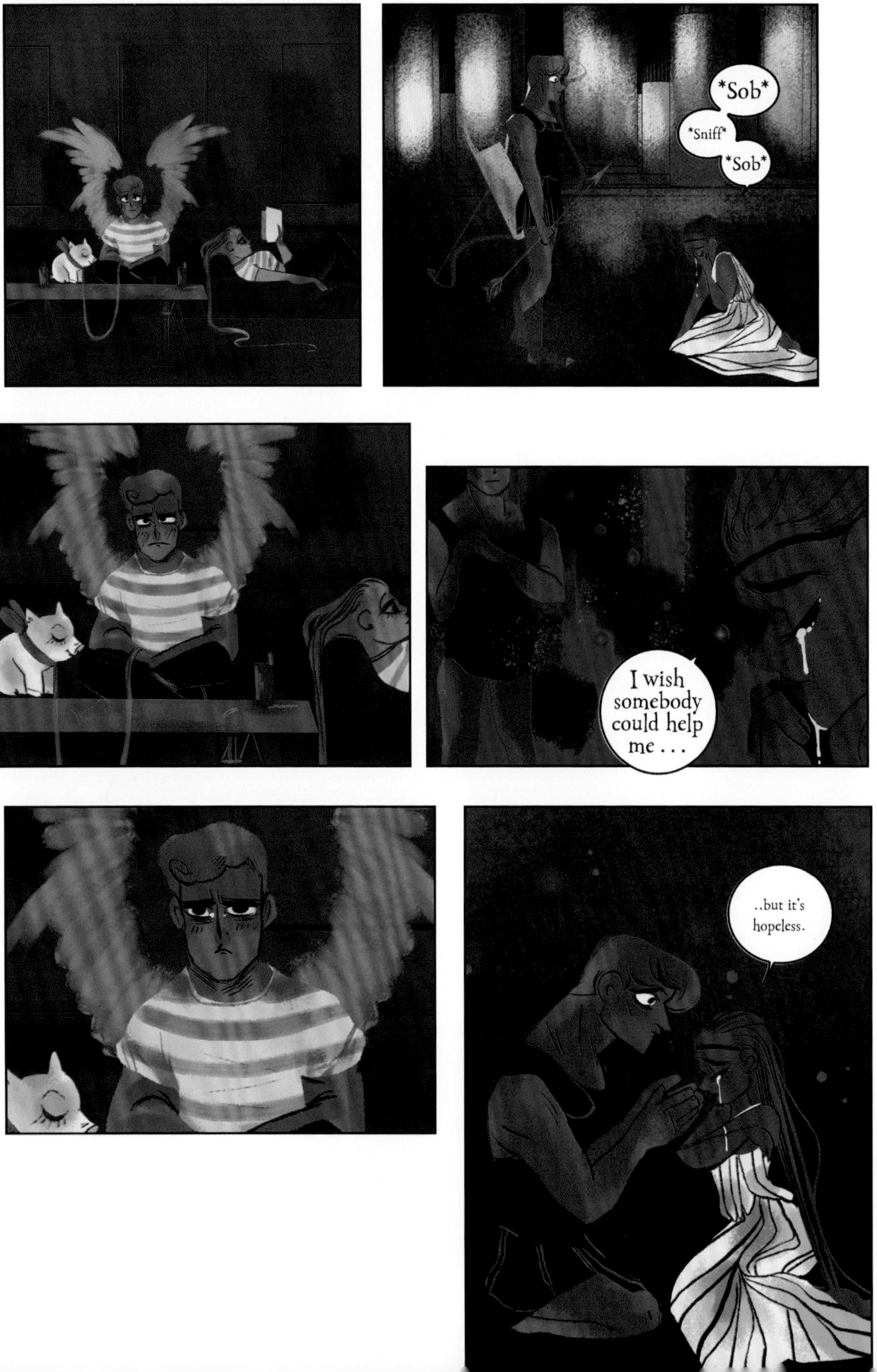
Sob
Sniff
Sob
I wish somebody could help me . . .
..but it's hopeless.

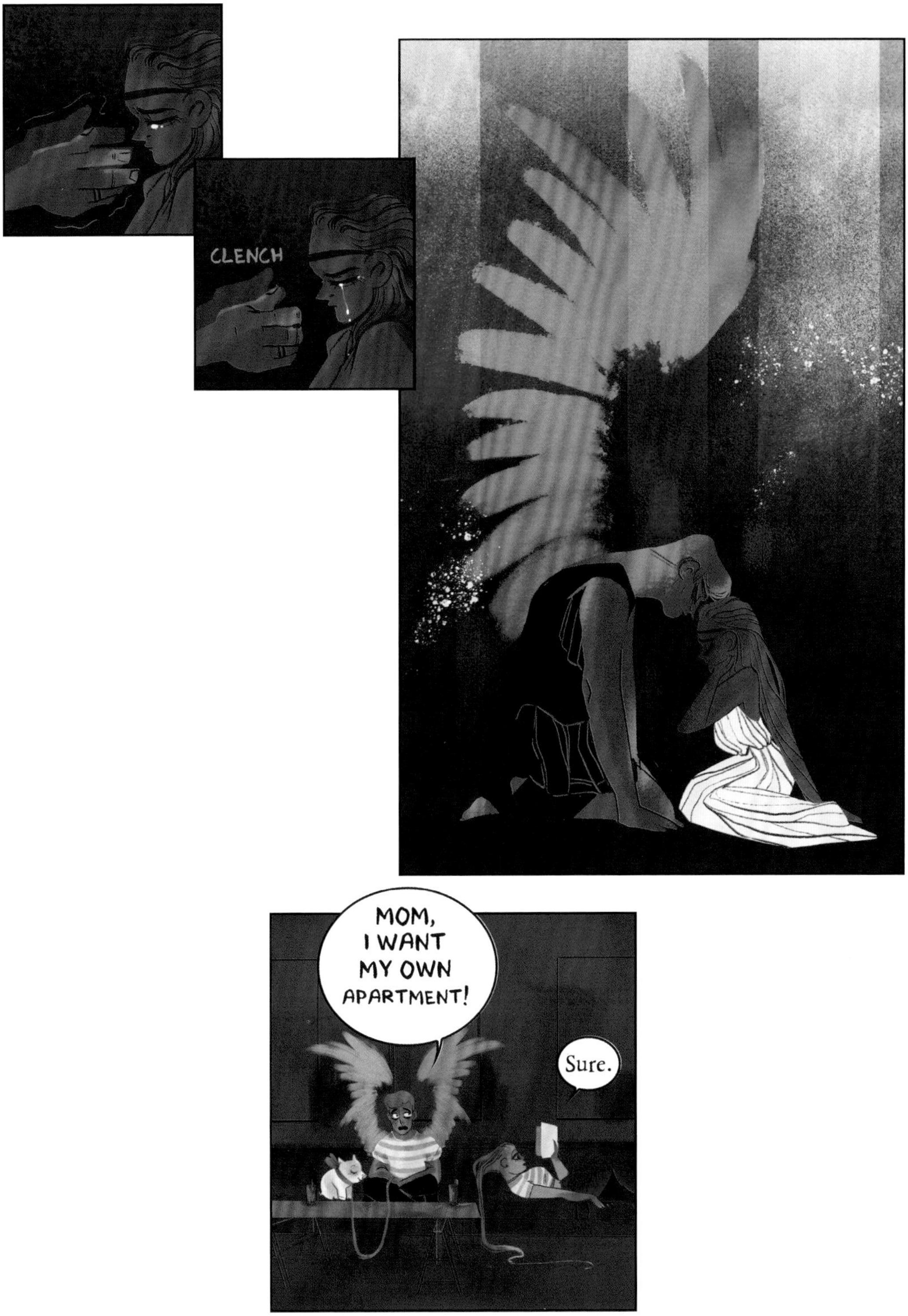
CLENCH
MOM, I WANT MY OWN APARTMENT!
Sure.

EPISODE 14: MONSTER BOY

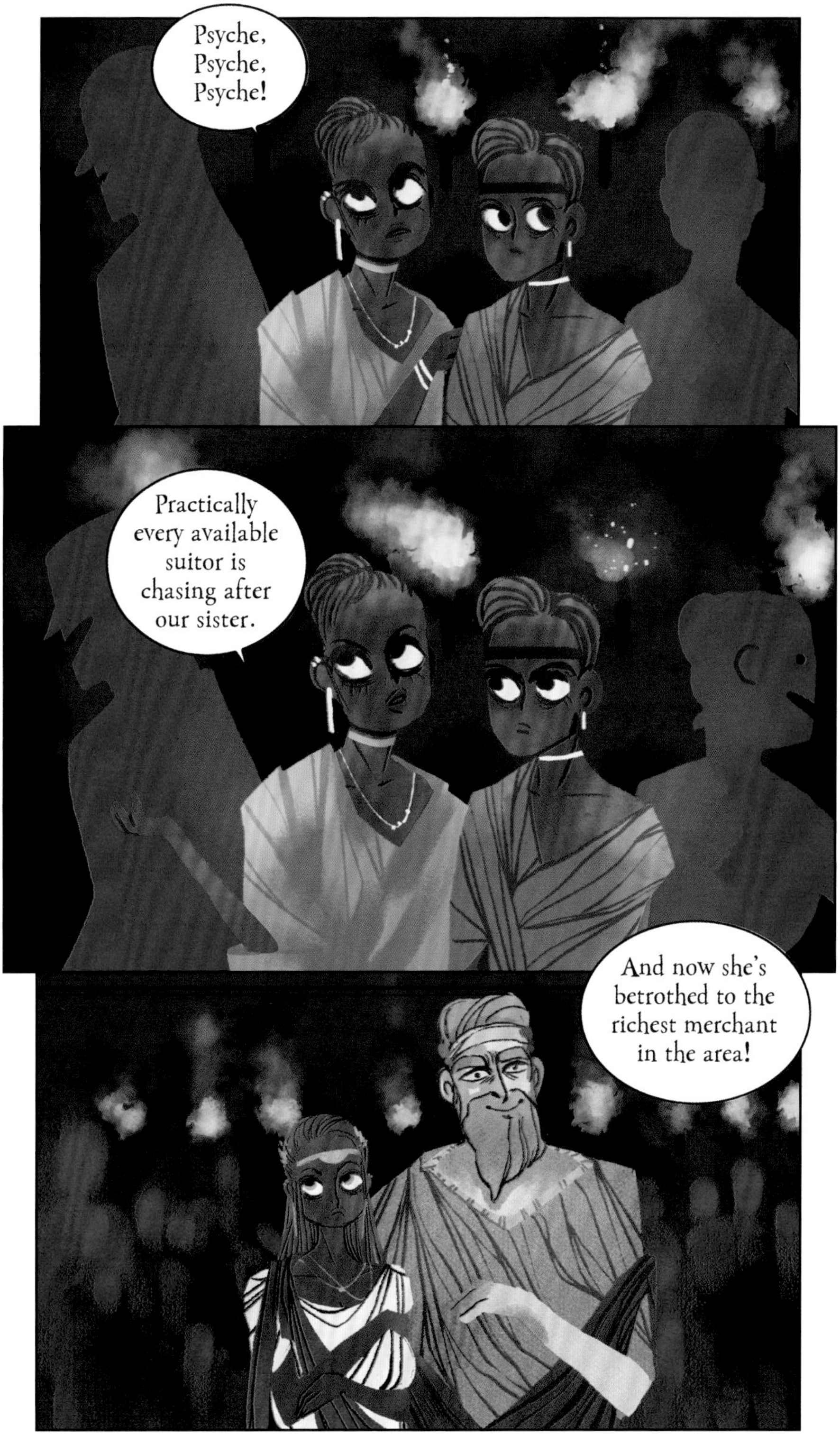
Psyche, Psyche, Psyche!
Practically every available suitor is chasing after our sister.
And now she's betrothed to the richest merchant in the area!

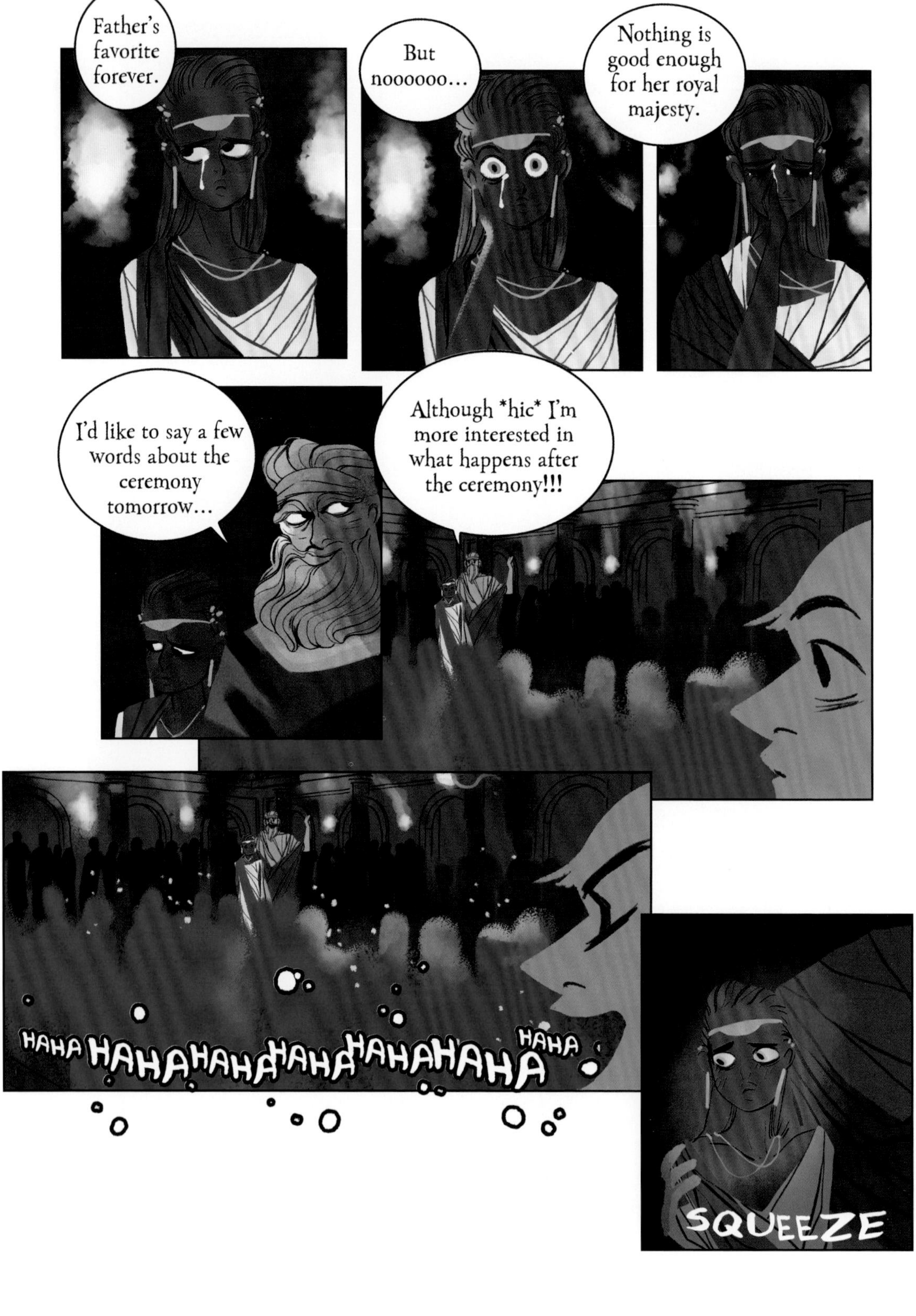
Father's favorite forever.
But noooooo...
Nothing is good enough for her royal majesty.
I'd like to say a few words about the ceremony tomorrow...
Although *hic* I'm more interested in what happens after the ceremony!!!
HAHA HAHAHAHAHAHAHAHAHAHA HAHA
SQUEEZE

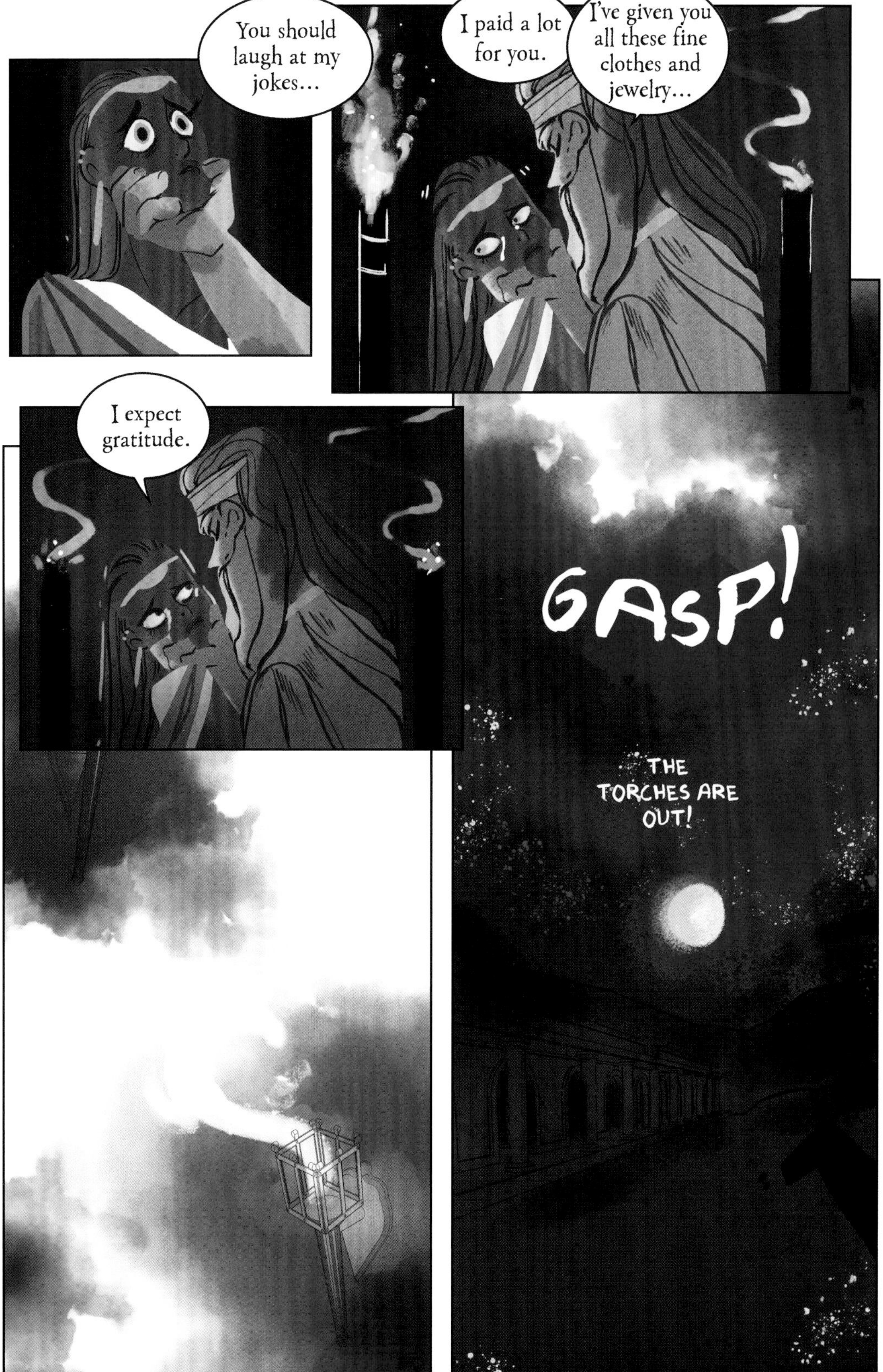
You should laugh at my jokes...
I paid a lot for you.
I've given you all these fine clothes and jewelry...
I expect gratitude.
GASP!
THE TORCHES ARE OUT!

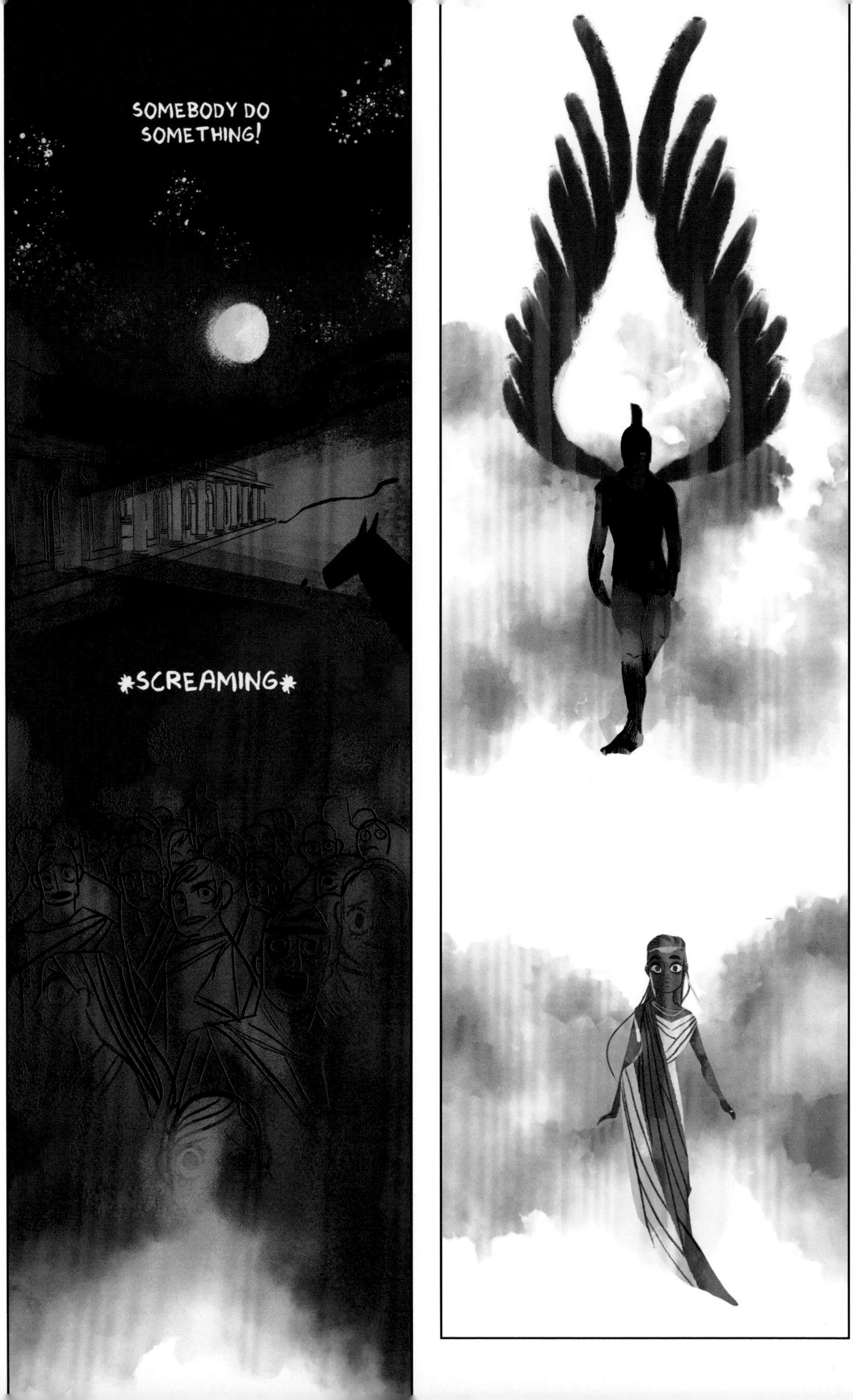
SOMEBODY DO SOMETHING!
SCREAMING

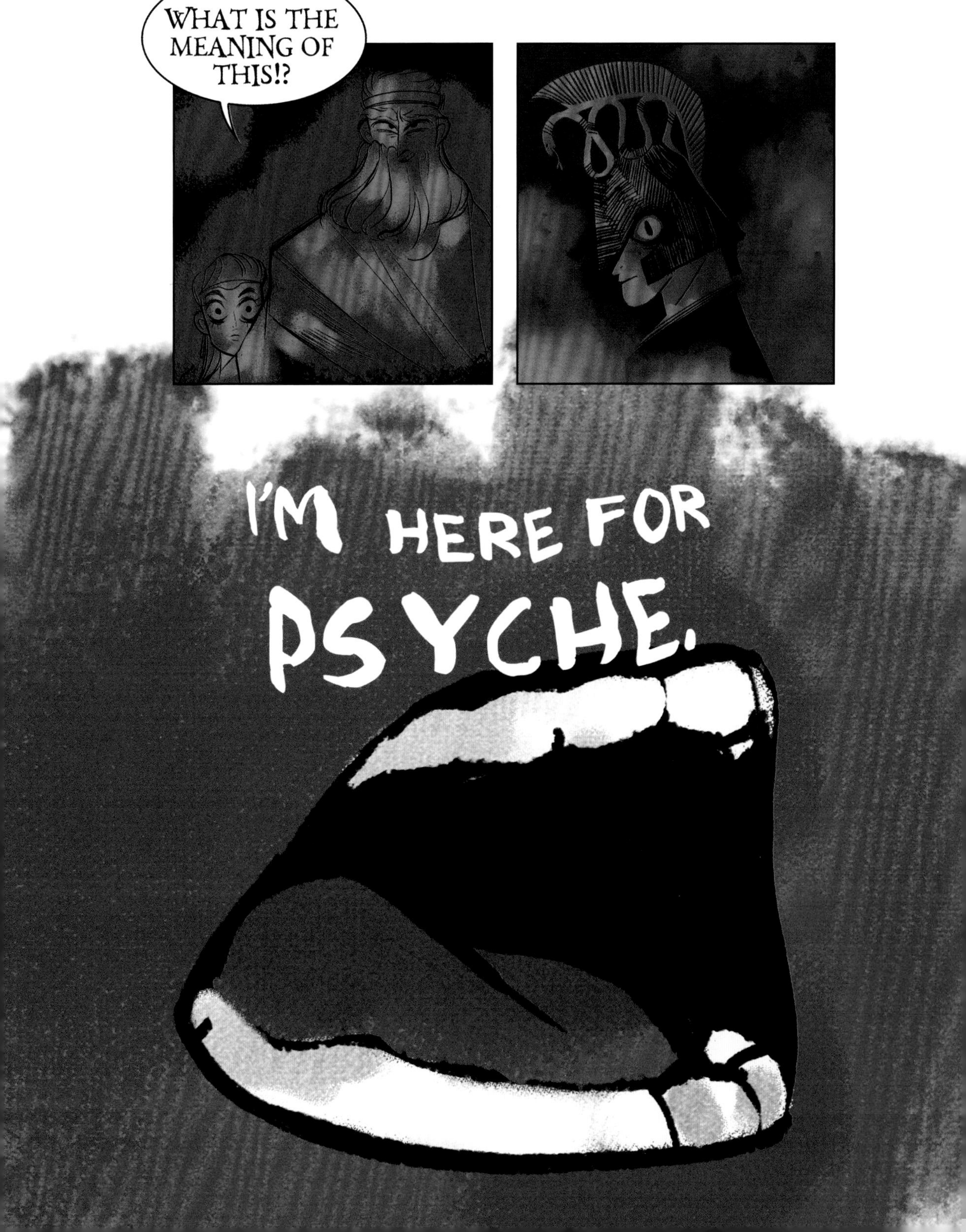
WHAT IS THE MEANING OF THIS!?
I'M HERE FOR PSYCHE.

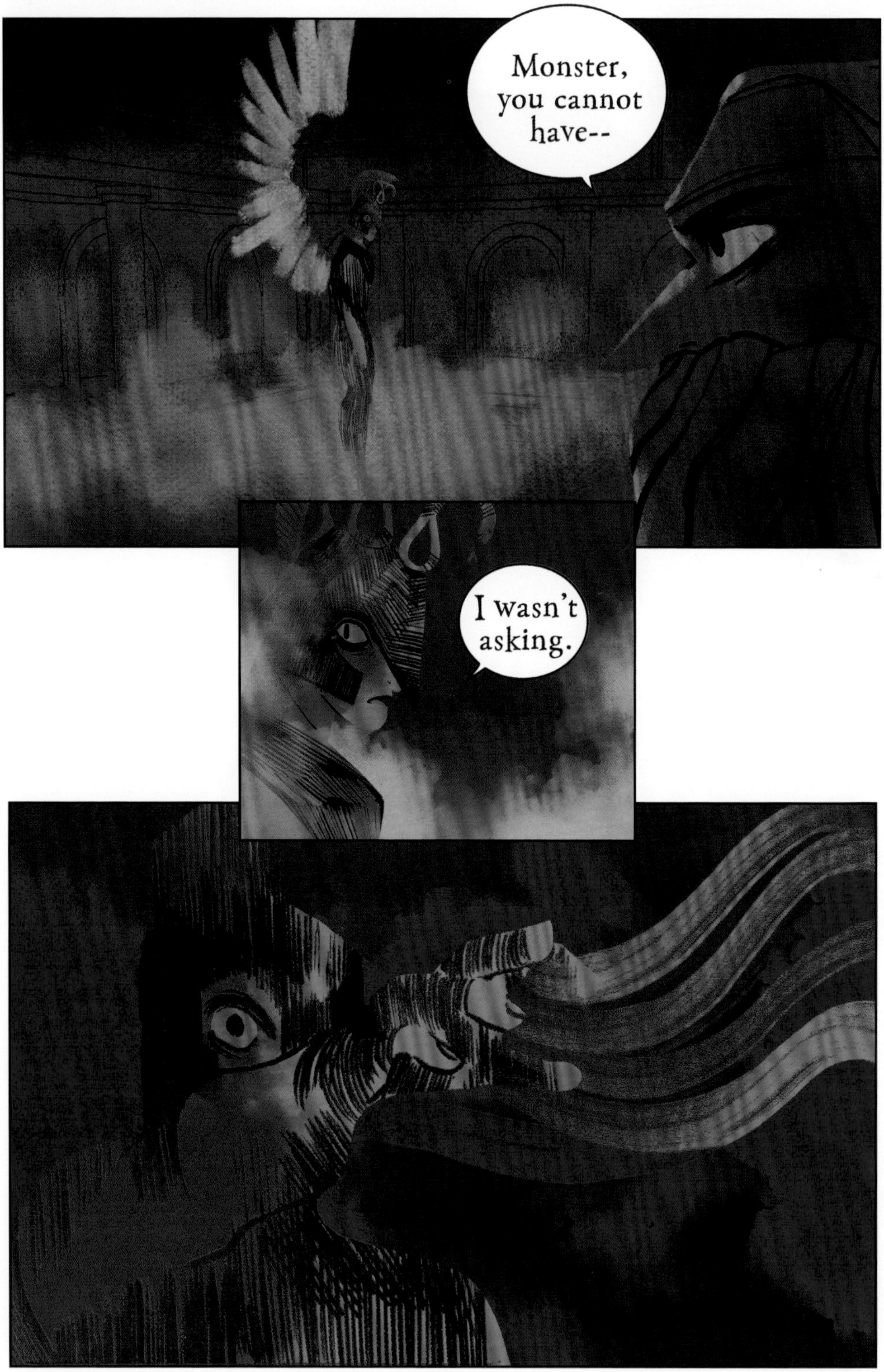
Monster, you cannot have--
I wasn't asking.

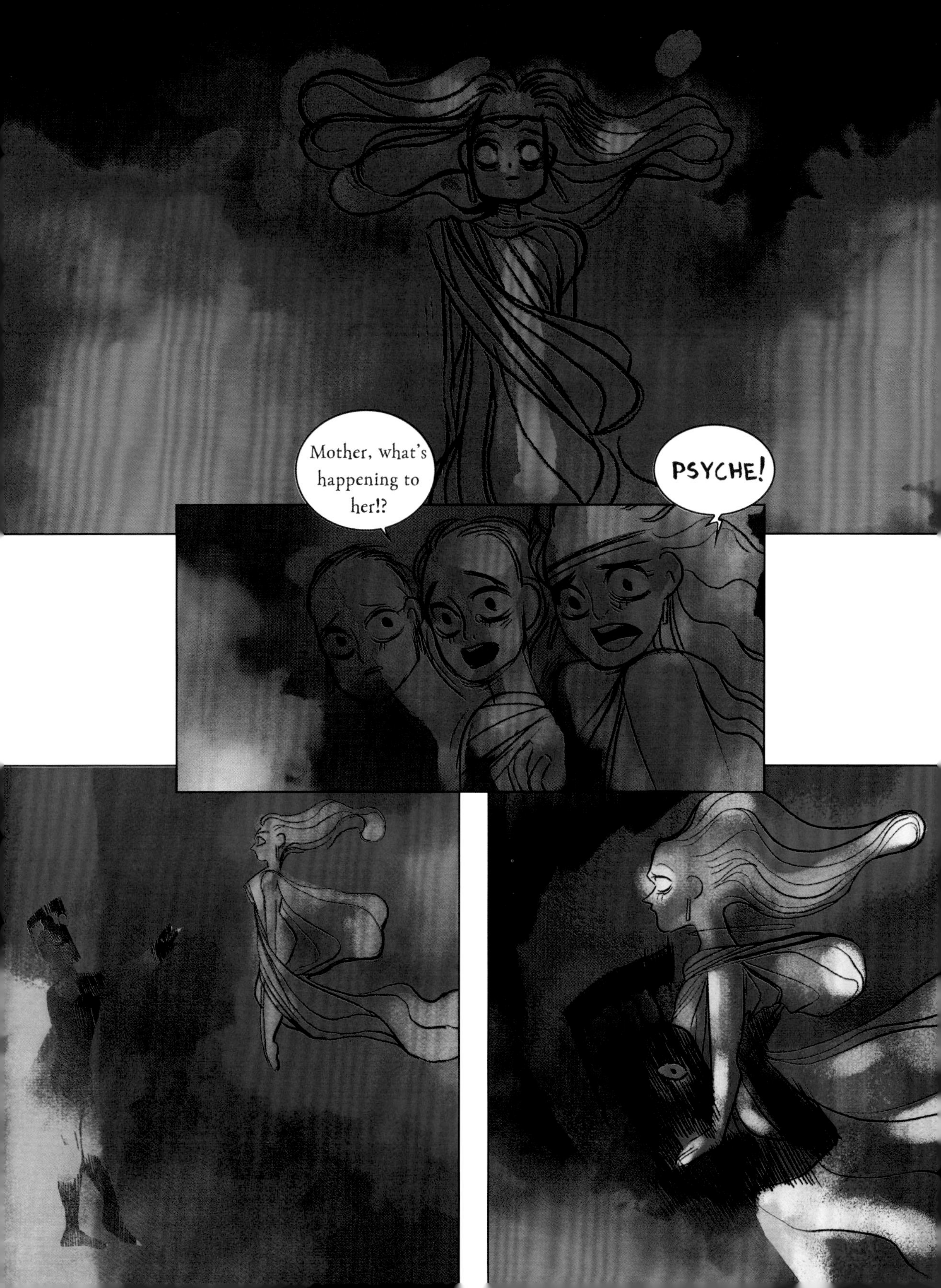
Mother, what's happening to her!?
PSYCHE!

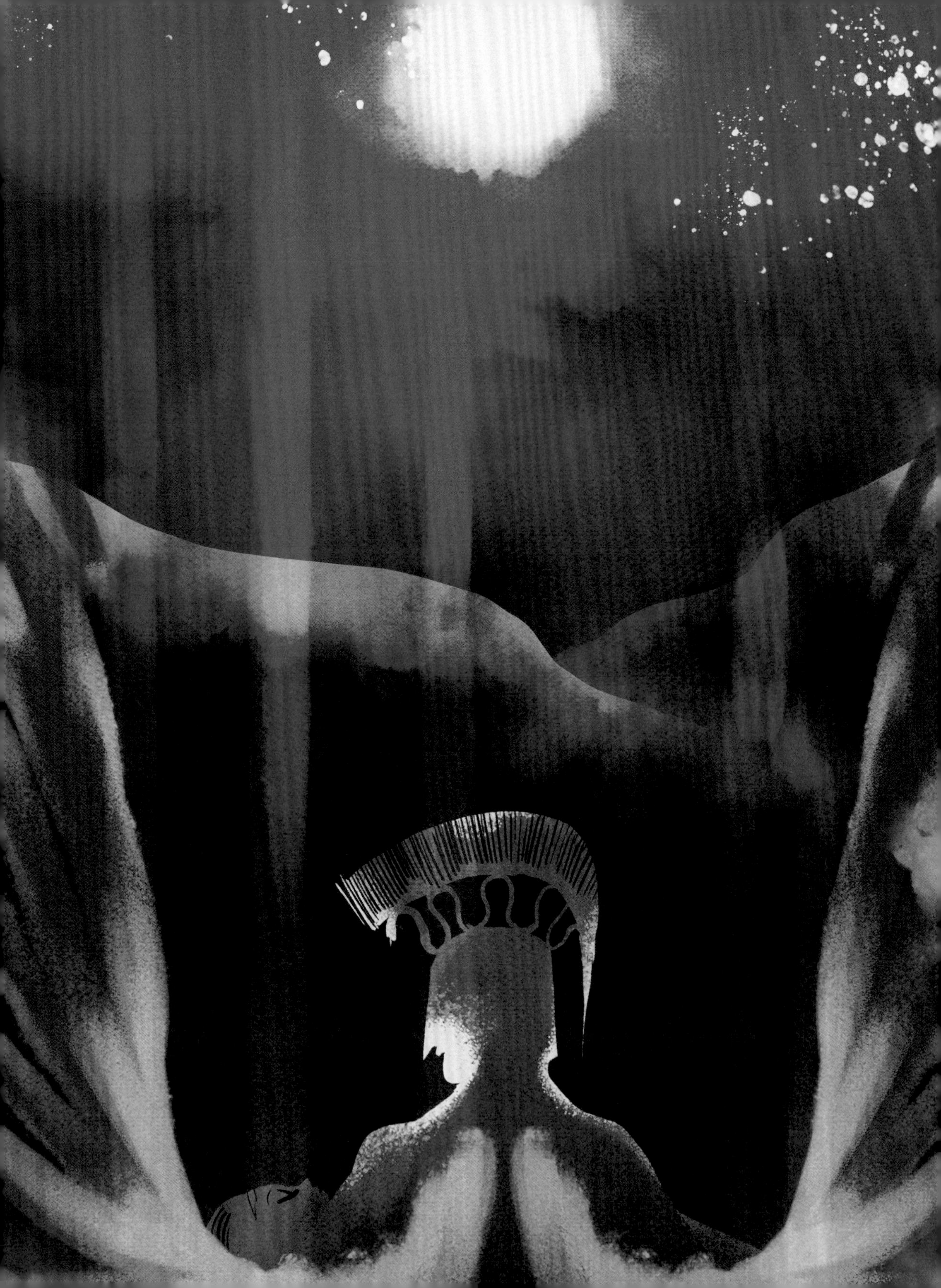

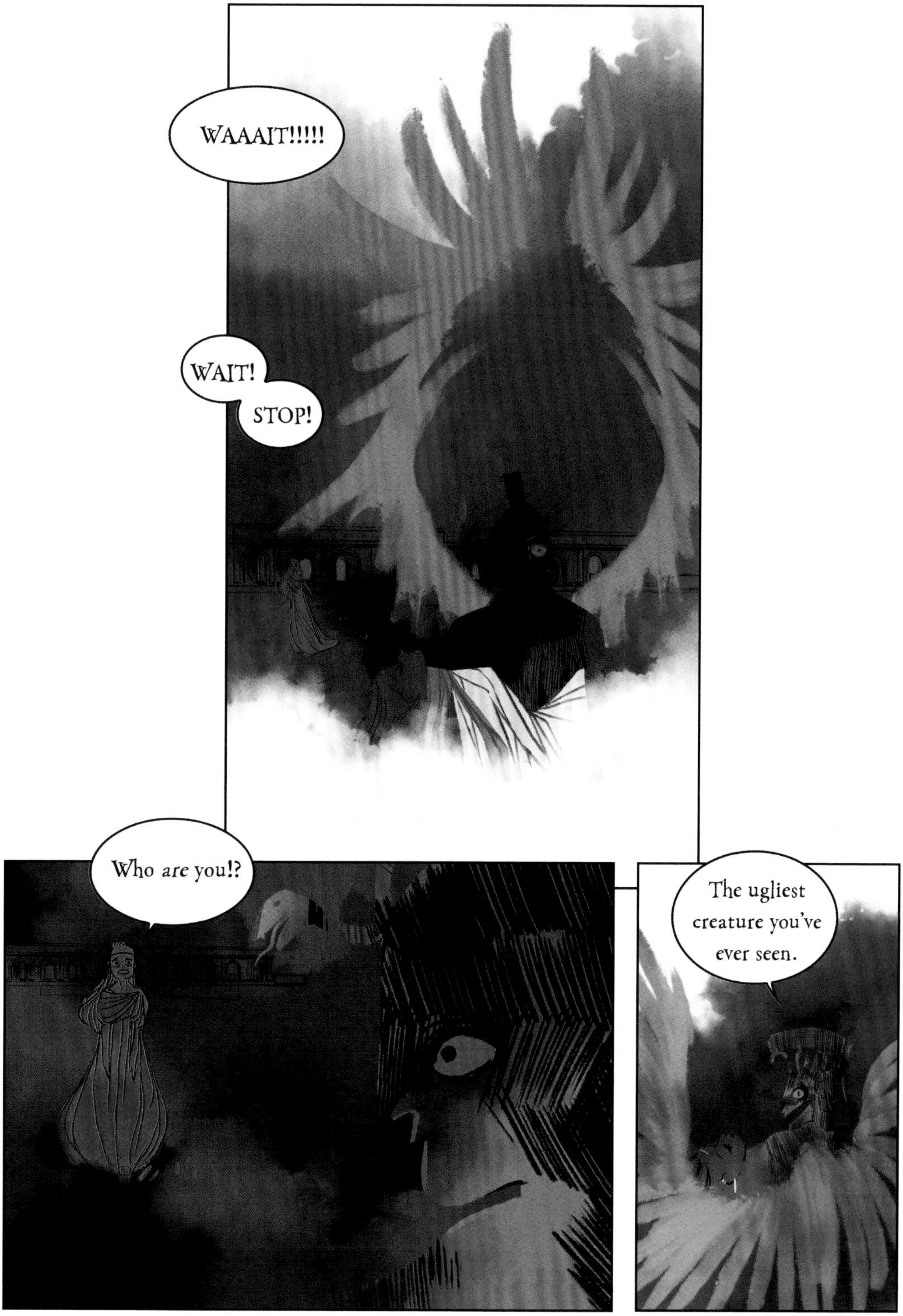
WAAAIT!!!!!
WAIT!
STOP!
Who are you!?
The ugliest creature you've ever seen.

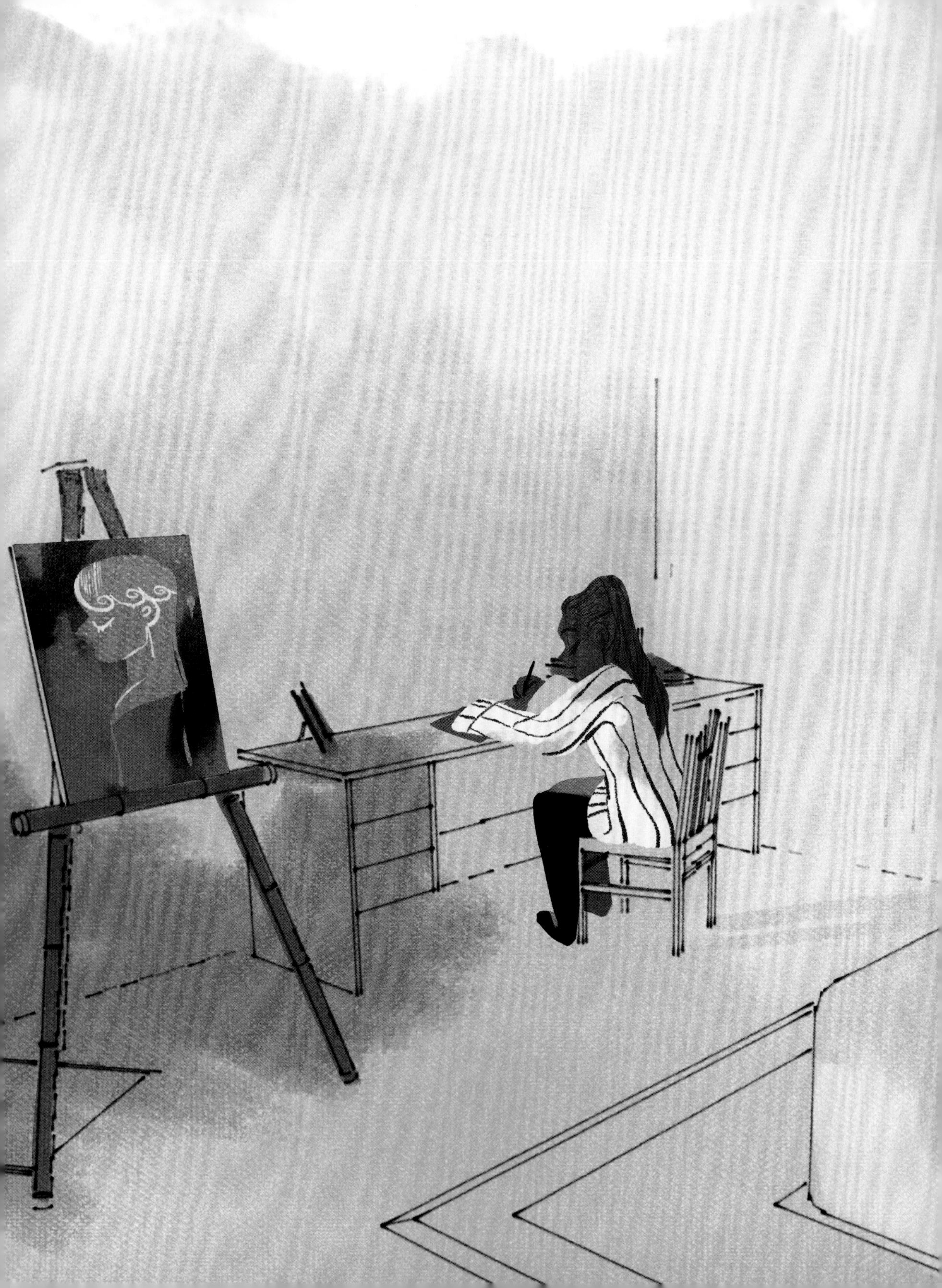

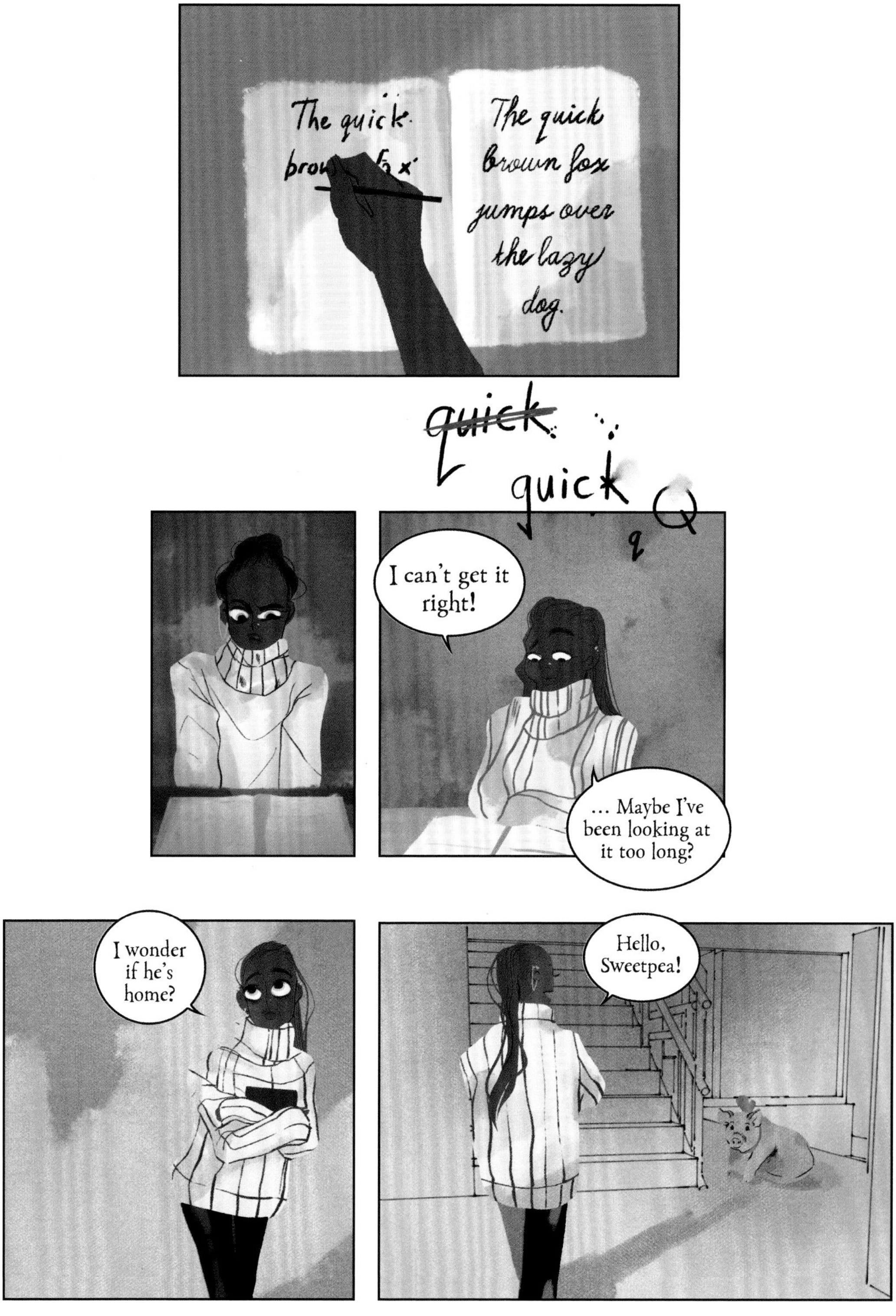
The quick brown fox jumps over the lazy dog.
quick
quick
I can't get it right!
... Maybe I've been looking at it too long?
I wonder if he's home?
Hello, Sweetpea!

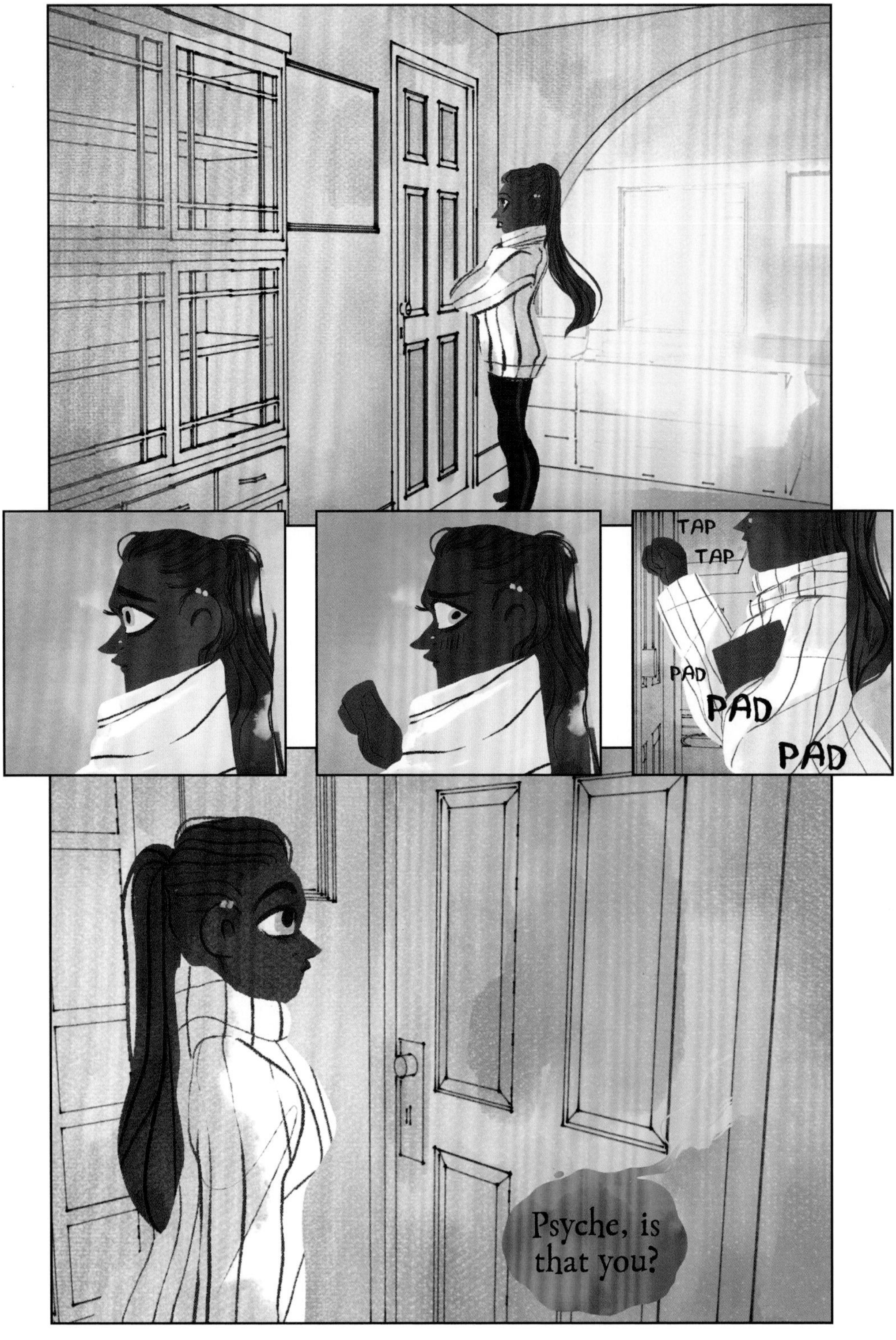
TAP
TAP
PAD
PAD
PAD
Psyche, is that you?

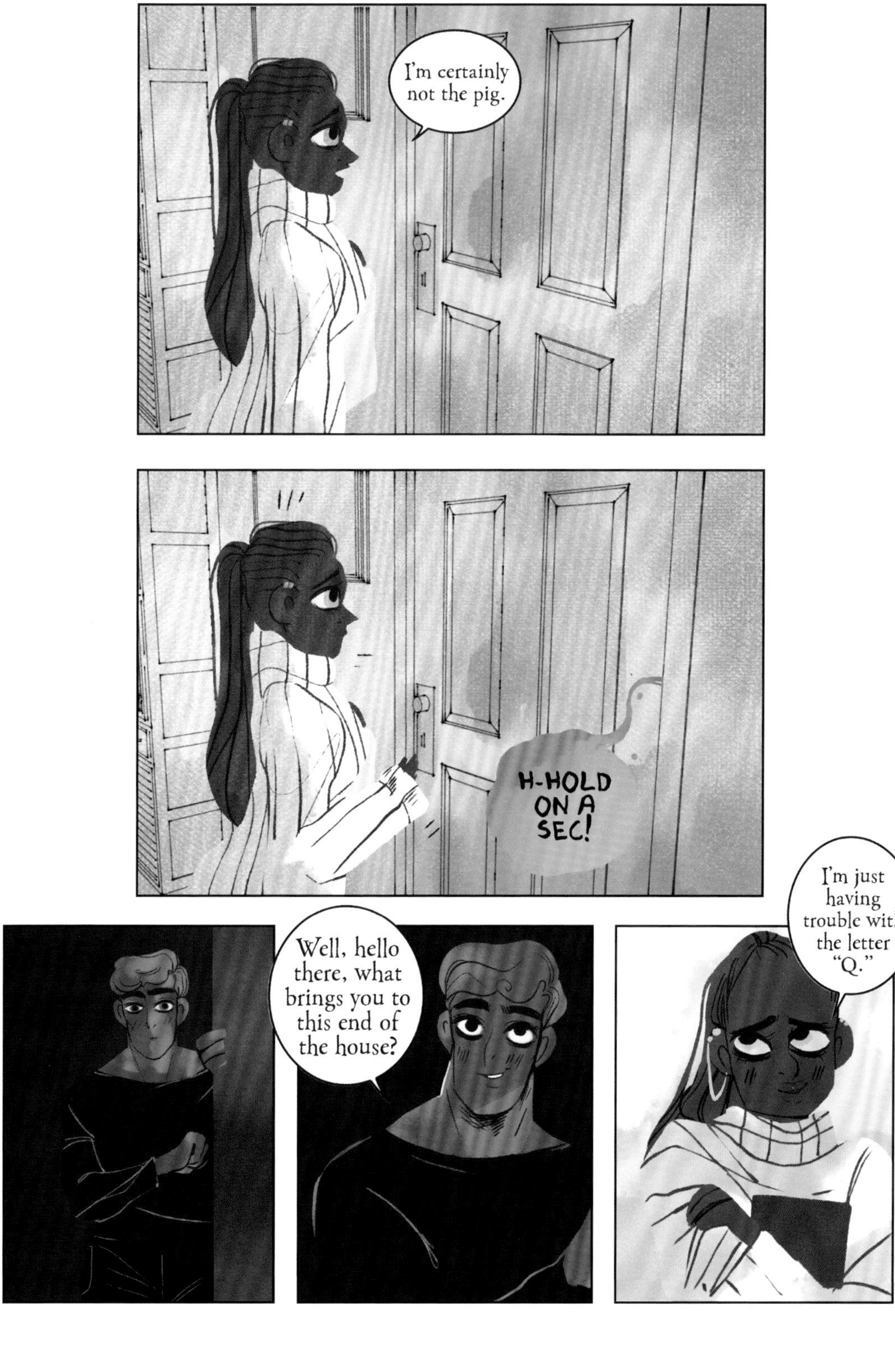
I'm certainly not the pig.
H-HOLD ON A SEC!
Well, hello there, what brings you to this end of the house?
I'm just having trouble with the letter "Q."

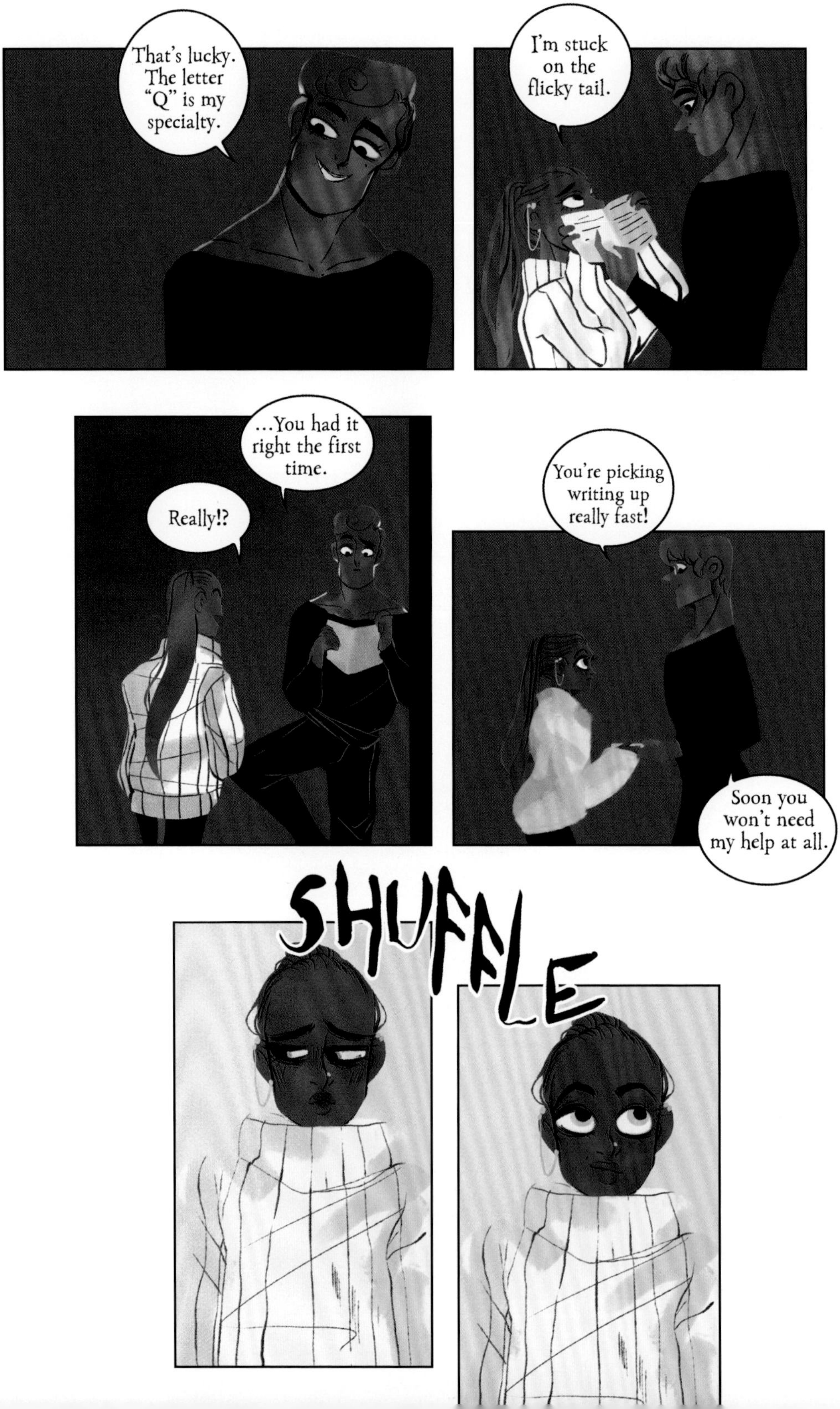
That's lucky. The letter "Q" is my specialty.
I'm stuck on the flicky tail.
...You had it right the first time.
Really!?
You're picking writing up really fast!
Soon you won't need my help at all.
SHUFFLE

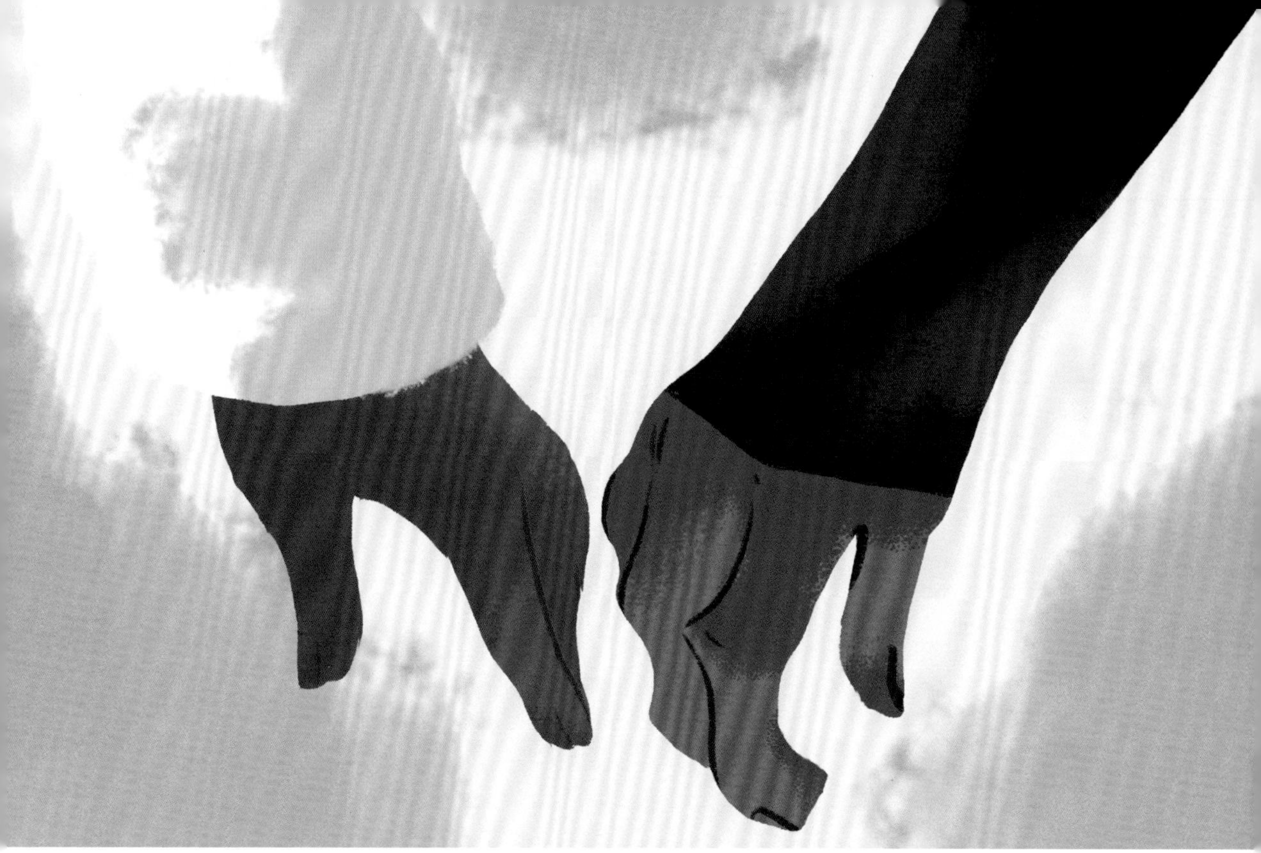
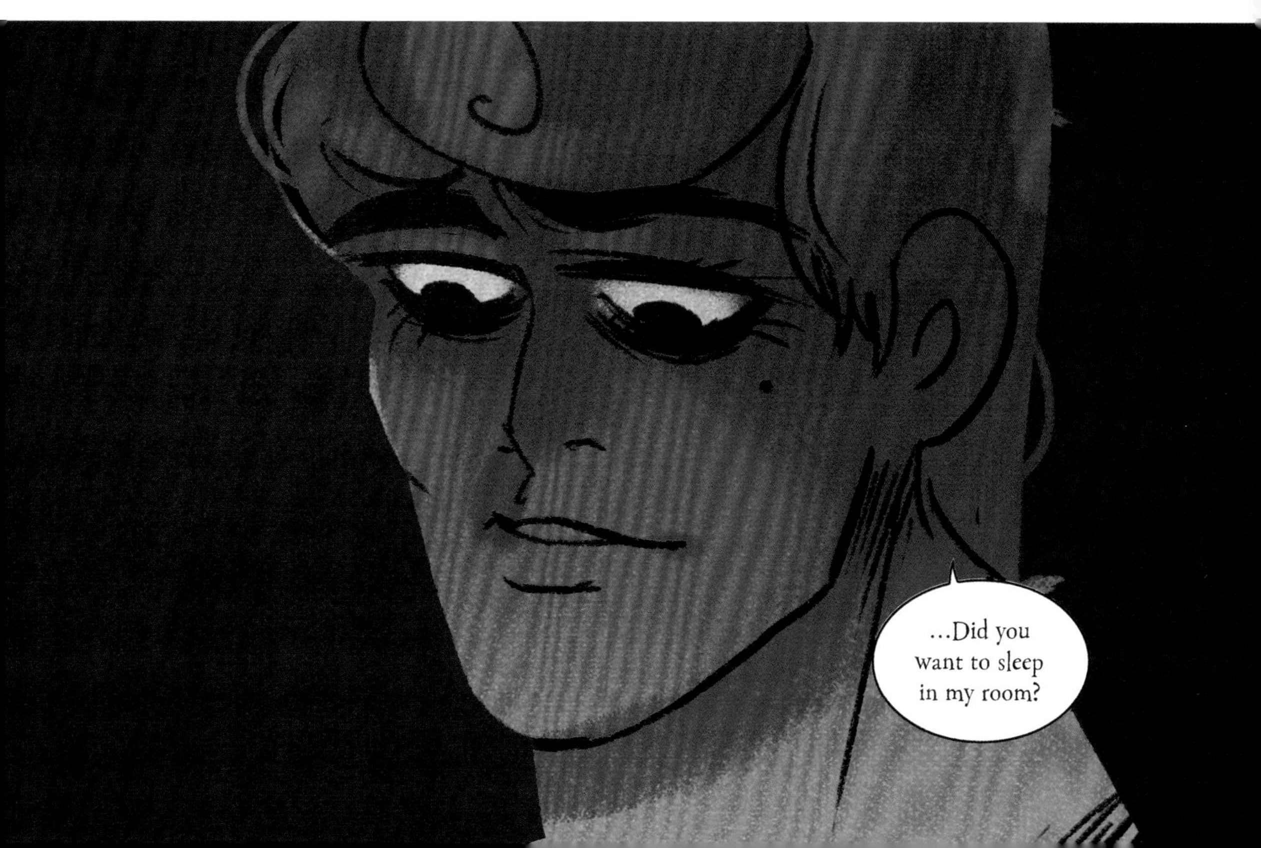
...Did you
want to sleep
in my room?

EPISODE 15: LOVER BOY

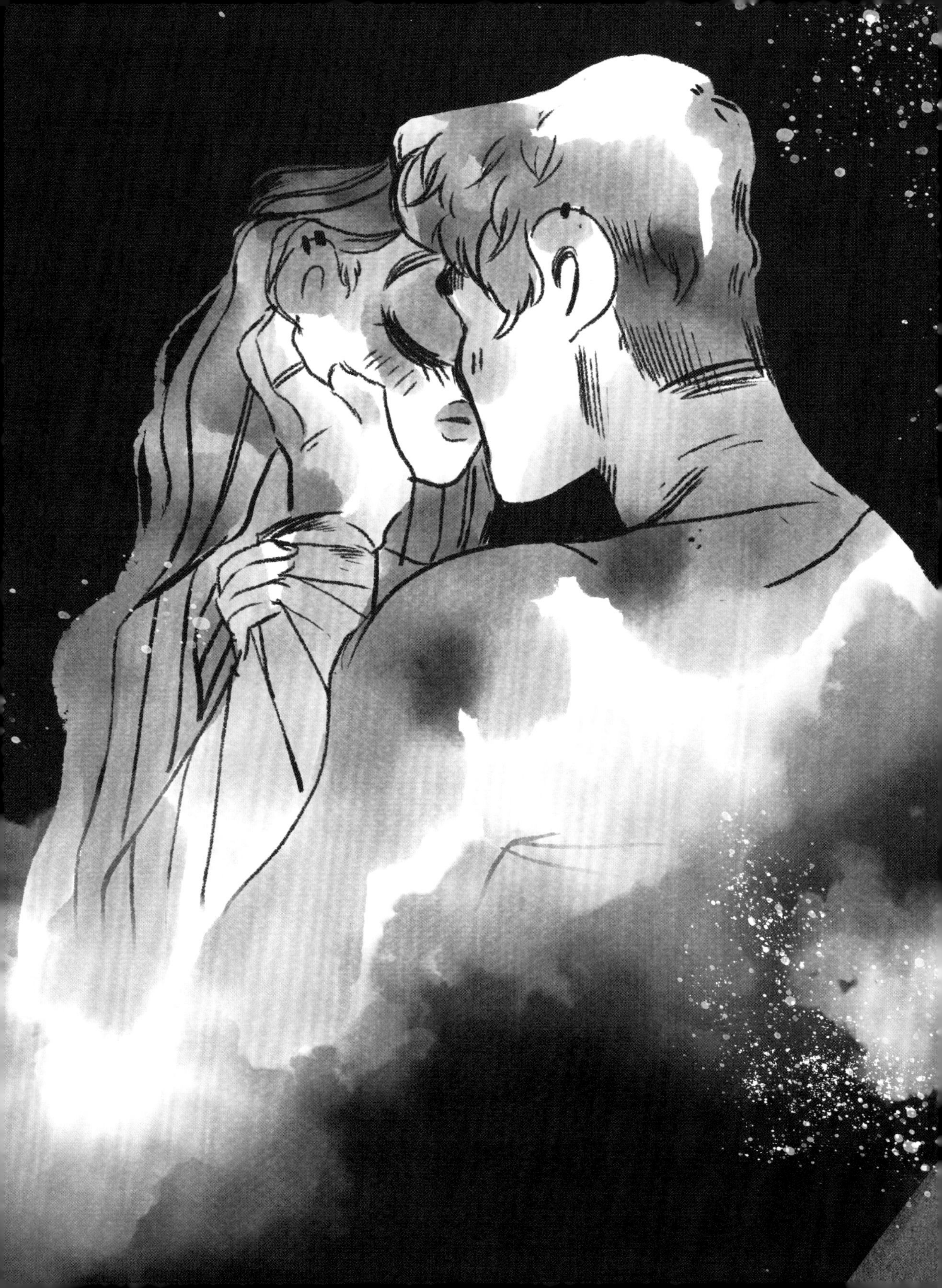

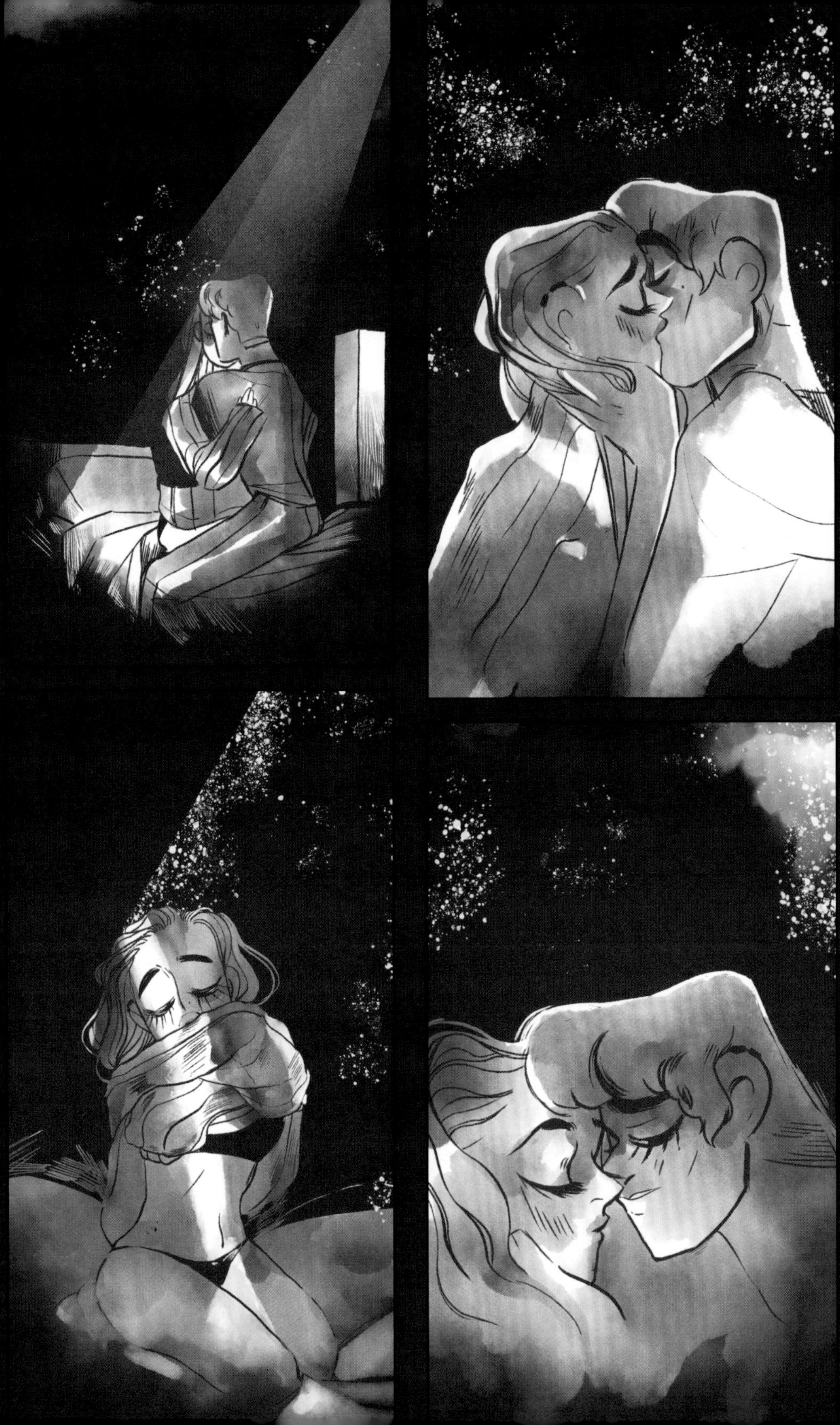

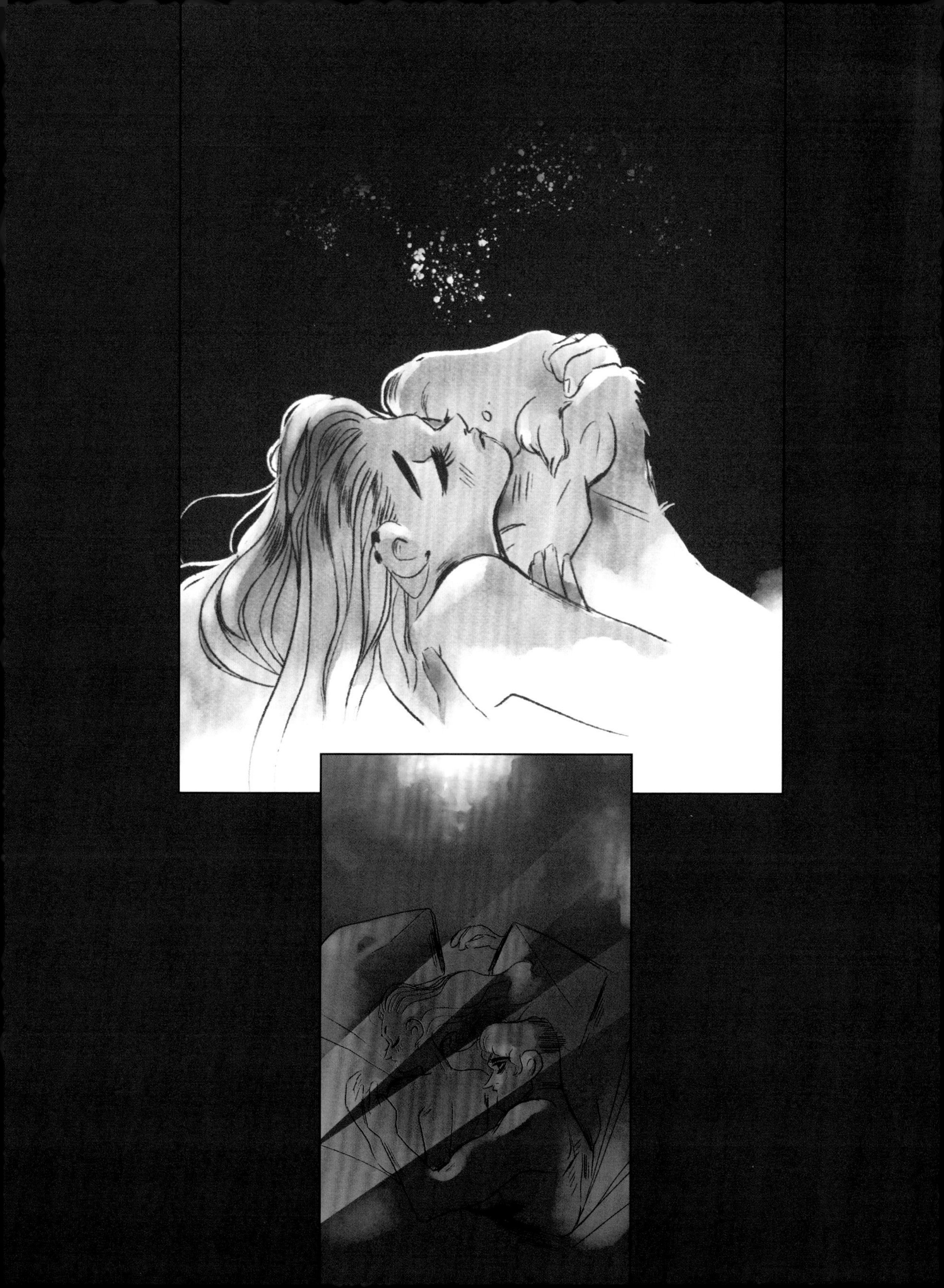

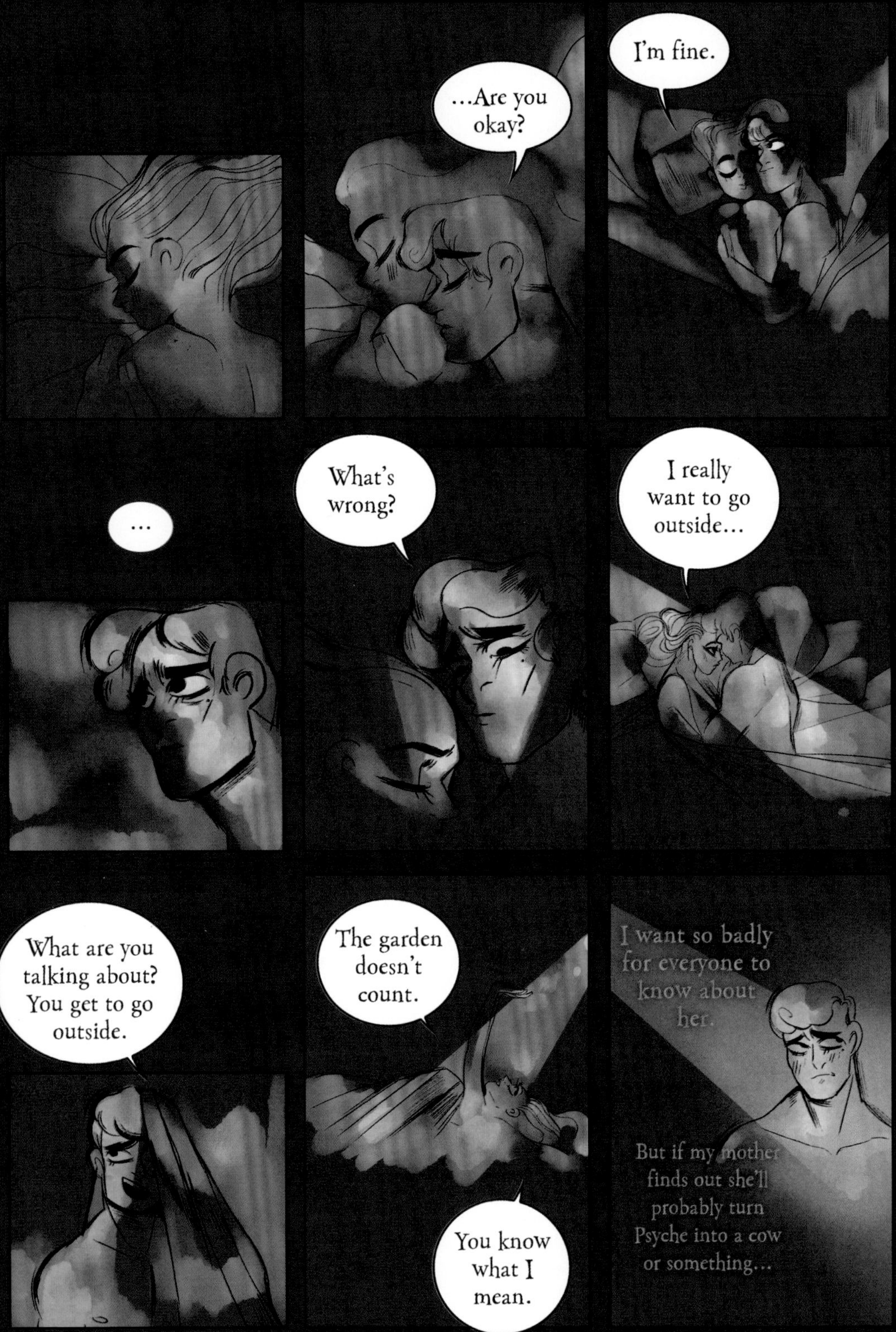
...Are you okay?
I'm fine.
...
What's wrong?
I really want to go outside...
What are you talking about? You get to go outside.
The garden doesn't count.
You know what I mean.
I want so badly for everyone to know about her.
But if my mother finds out she'll probably turn Psyche into a cow or something...

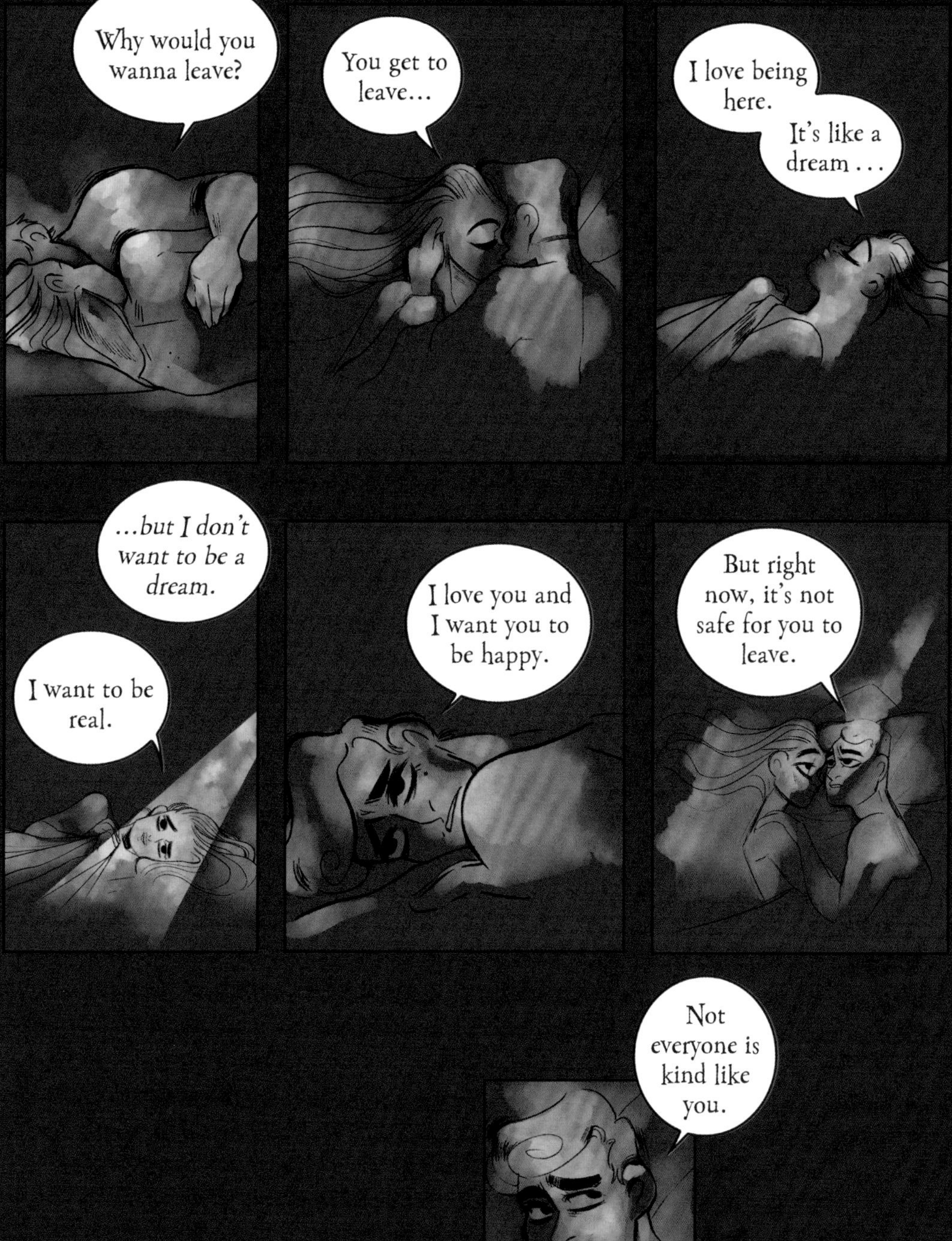
Why would you wanna leave?
You get to leave...
I love being here.
It's like a dream . . .
...but I don't want to be a dream.
I want to be real.
I love you and I want you to be happy.
But right now, it's not safe for you to leave.
Not everyone is kind like you.

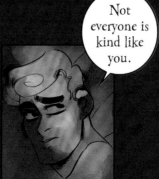

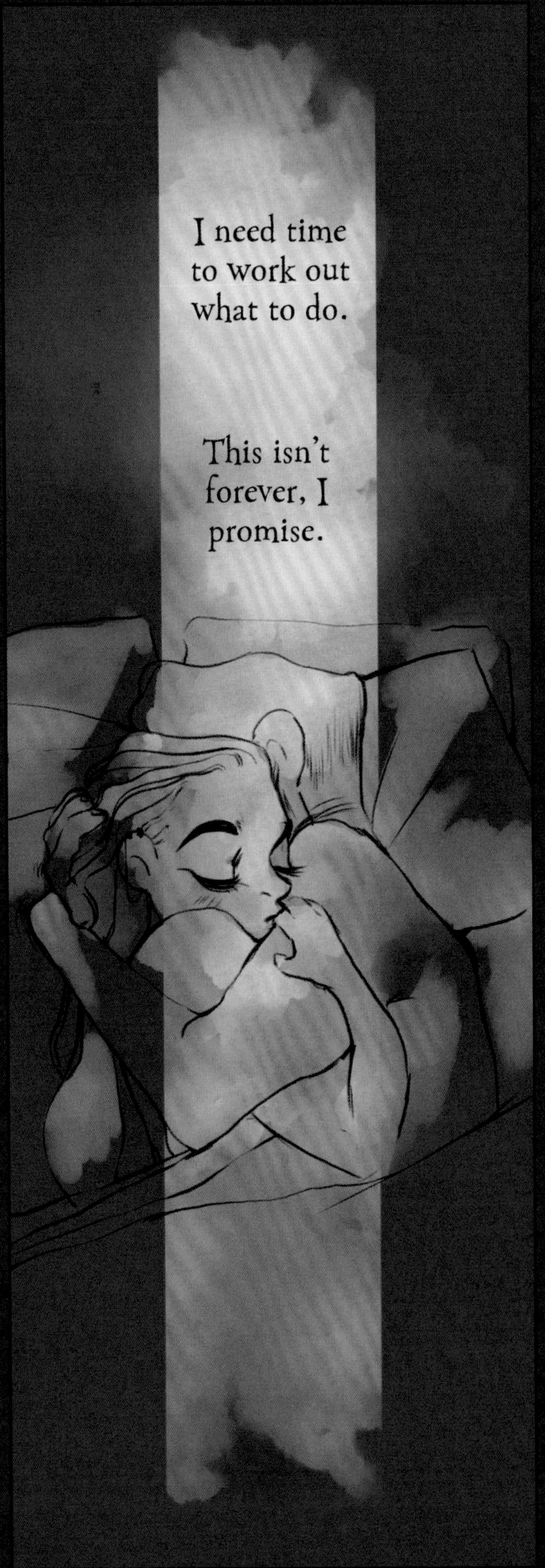
I need time to work out what to do.
This isn't forever, I promise.

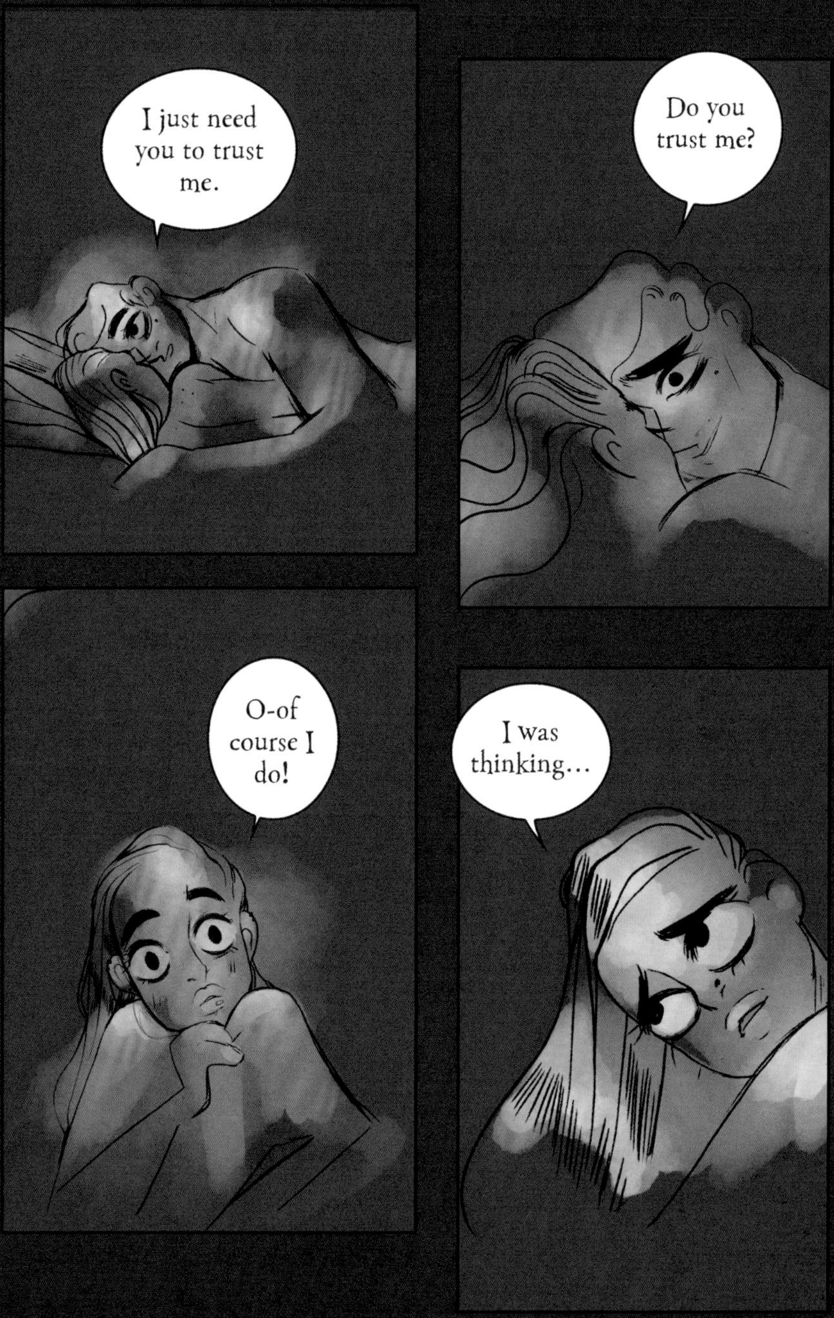
I just need you to trust me.
Do you trust me?
O-of course I do!
I was thinking…

Maybe I could have some visitors...

I can't keep saying no to her.

S-sure.

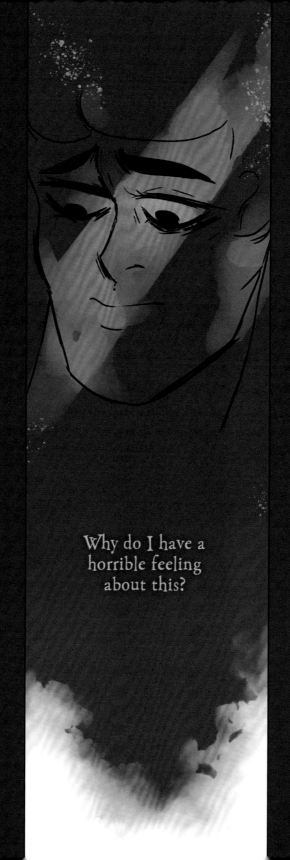

Why do I have a
horrible feeling
about this?

EPISODE 16: STUPID BOY

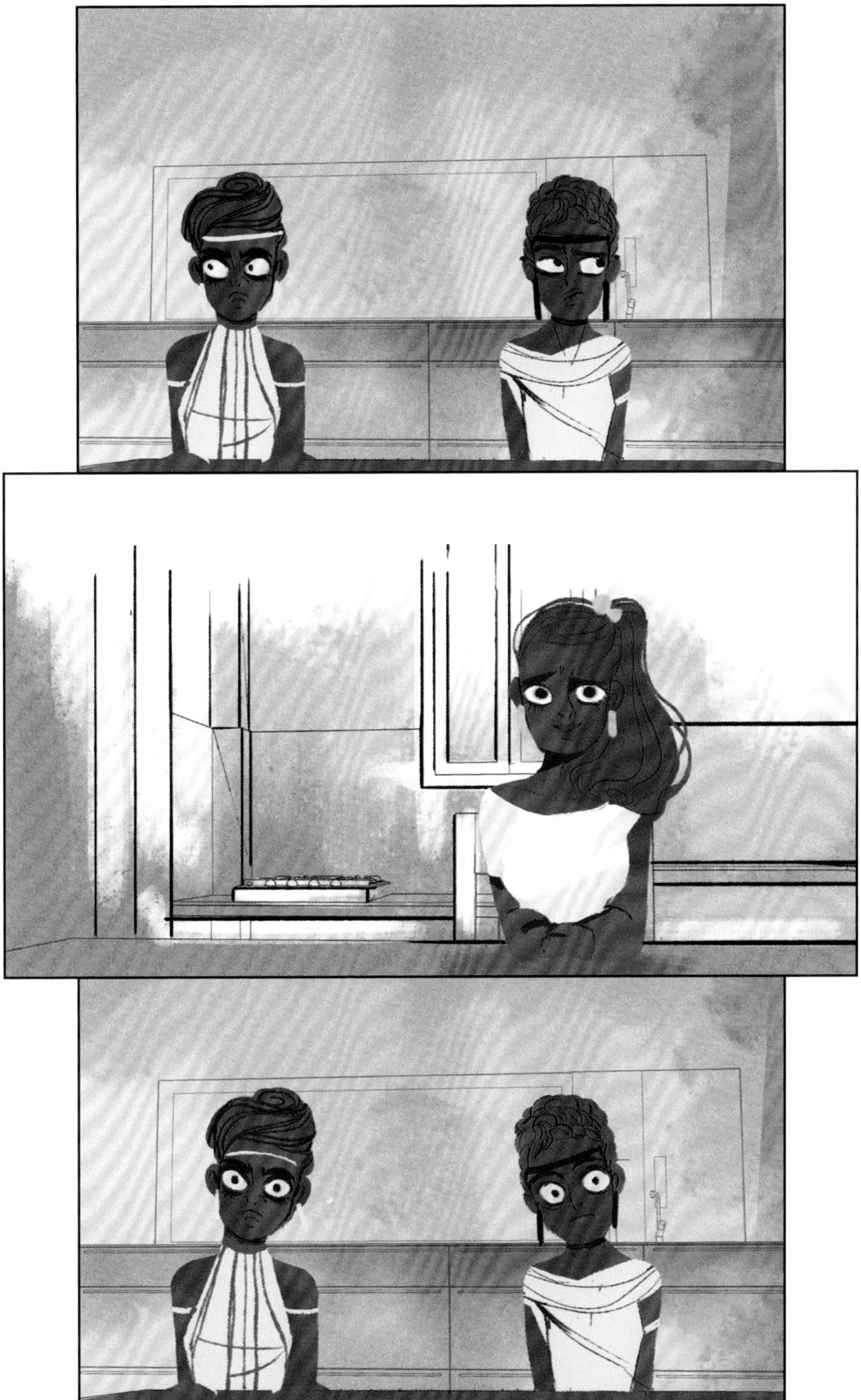

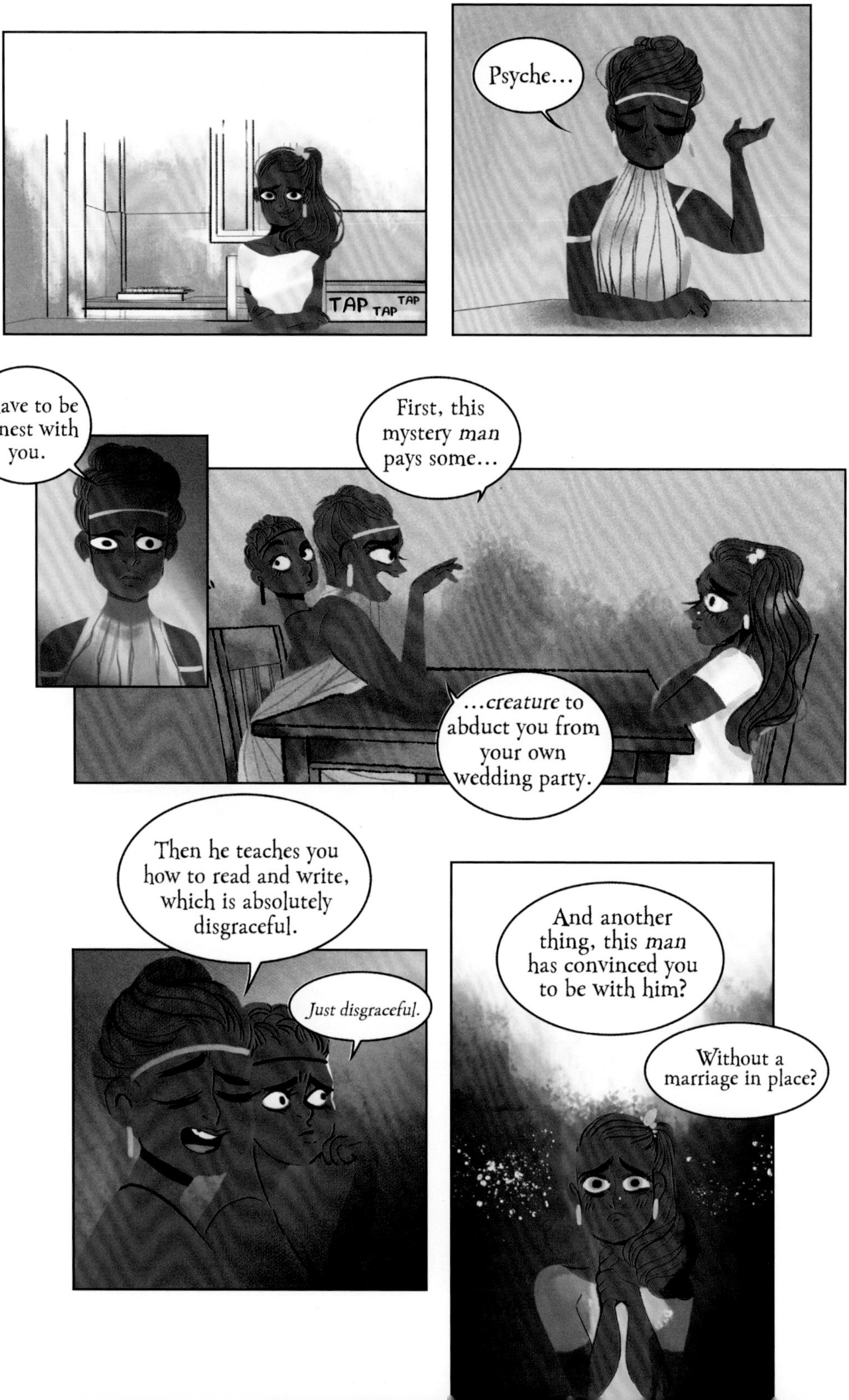
TAP TAP TAP
Psyche...
I have to be honest with you.
First, this mystery *man* pays some...
...*creature* to abduct you from your own wedding party.
Then he teaches you how to read and write, which is absolutely disgraceful.
Just disgraceful.
And another thing, this *man* has convinced you to be with him?
Without a marriage in place?

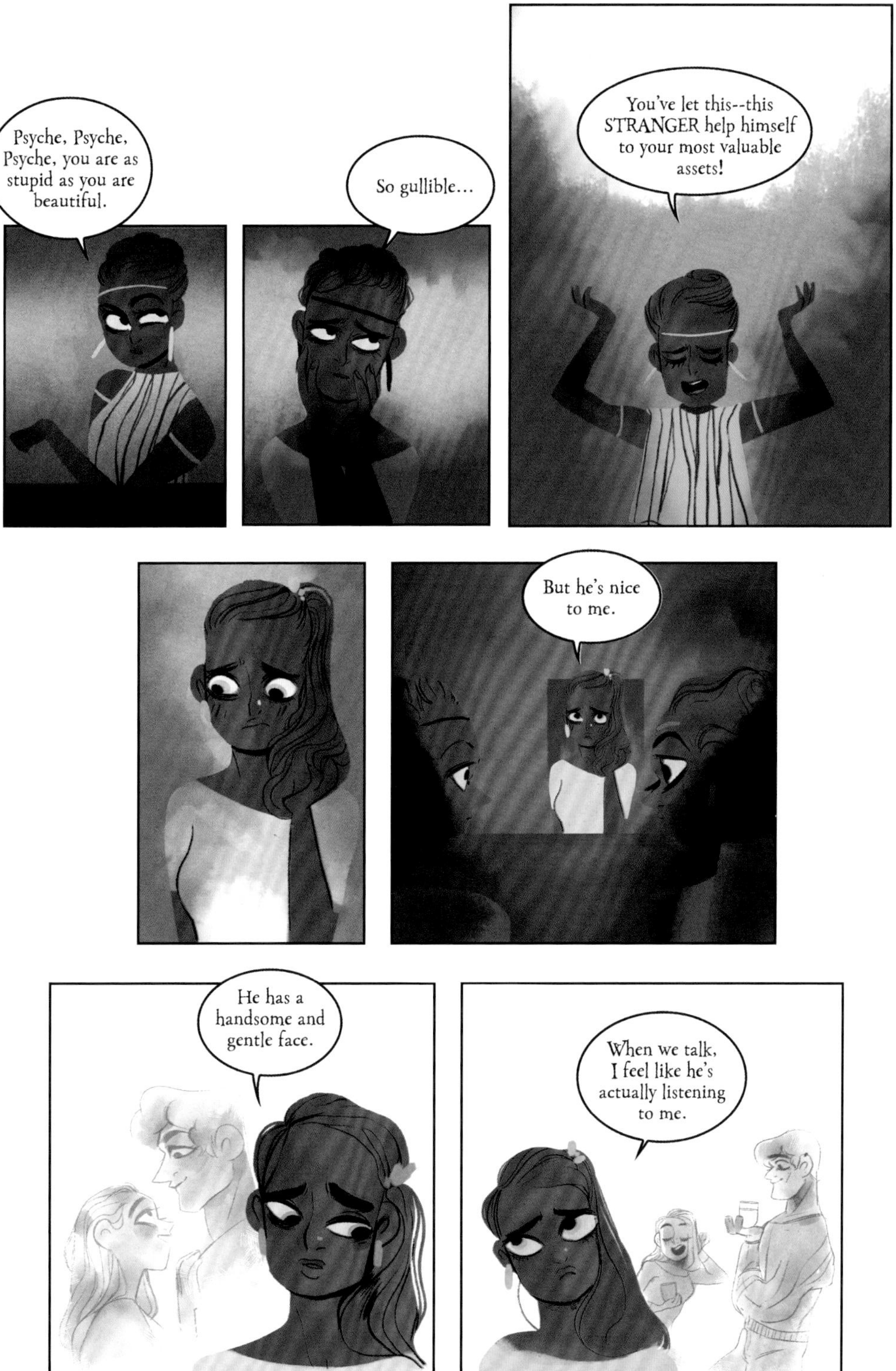
Psyche, Psyche, Psyche, you are as stupid as you are beautiful.
So gullible...
You've let this--this STRANGER help himself to your most valuable assets!
But he's nice to me.
He has a handsome and gentle face.
When we talk, I feel like he's actually listening to me.

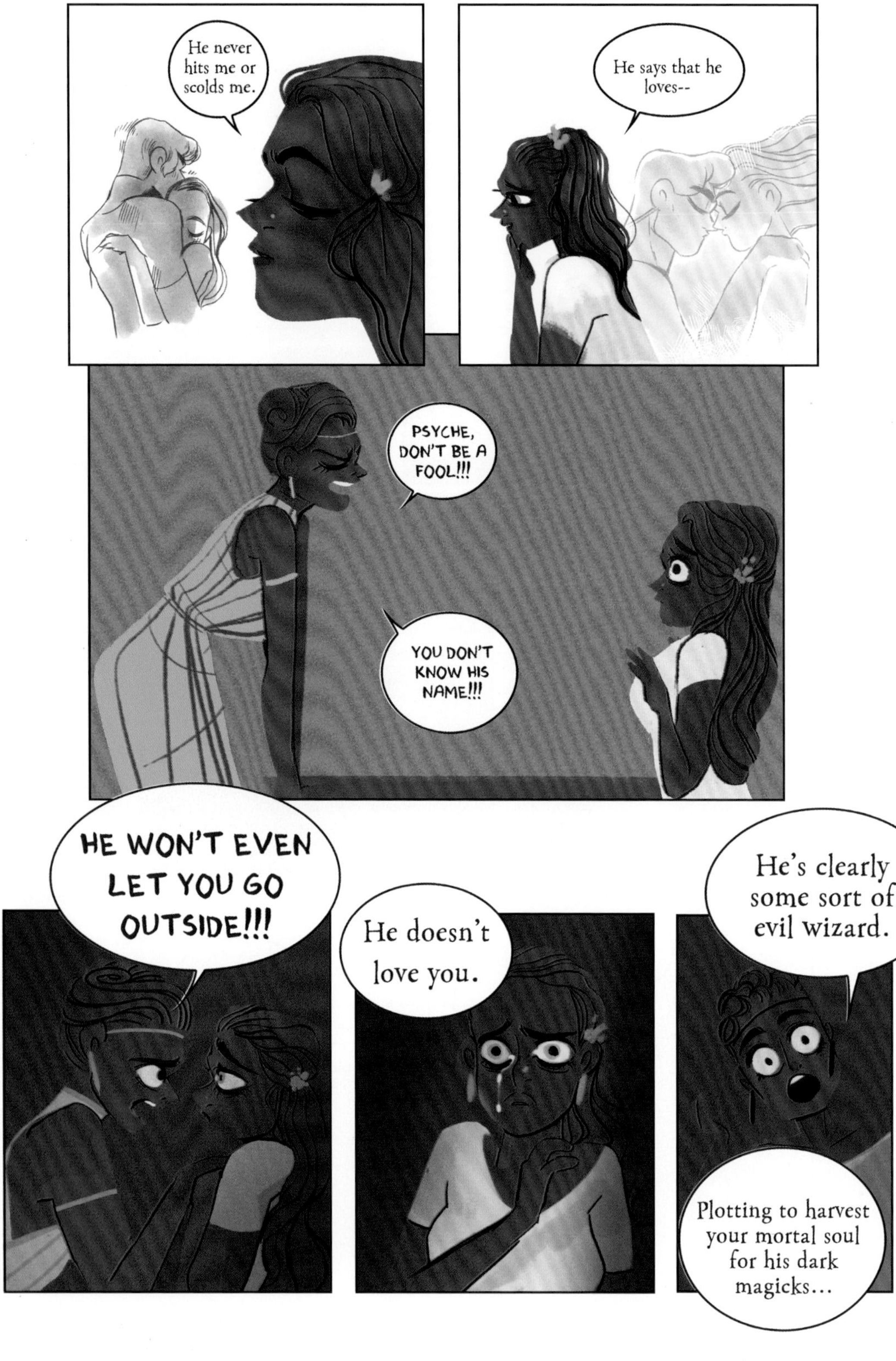
He never hits me or scolds me.
He says that he loves--
PSYCHE, DON'T BE A FOOL!!!
YOU DON'T KNOW HIS NAME!!!
HE WON'T EVEN LET YOU GO OUTSIDE!!!
He doesn't love you.
He's clearly some sort of evil wizard.
Plotting to harvest your mortal soul for his dark magicks...

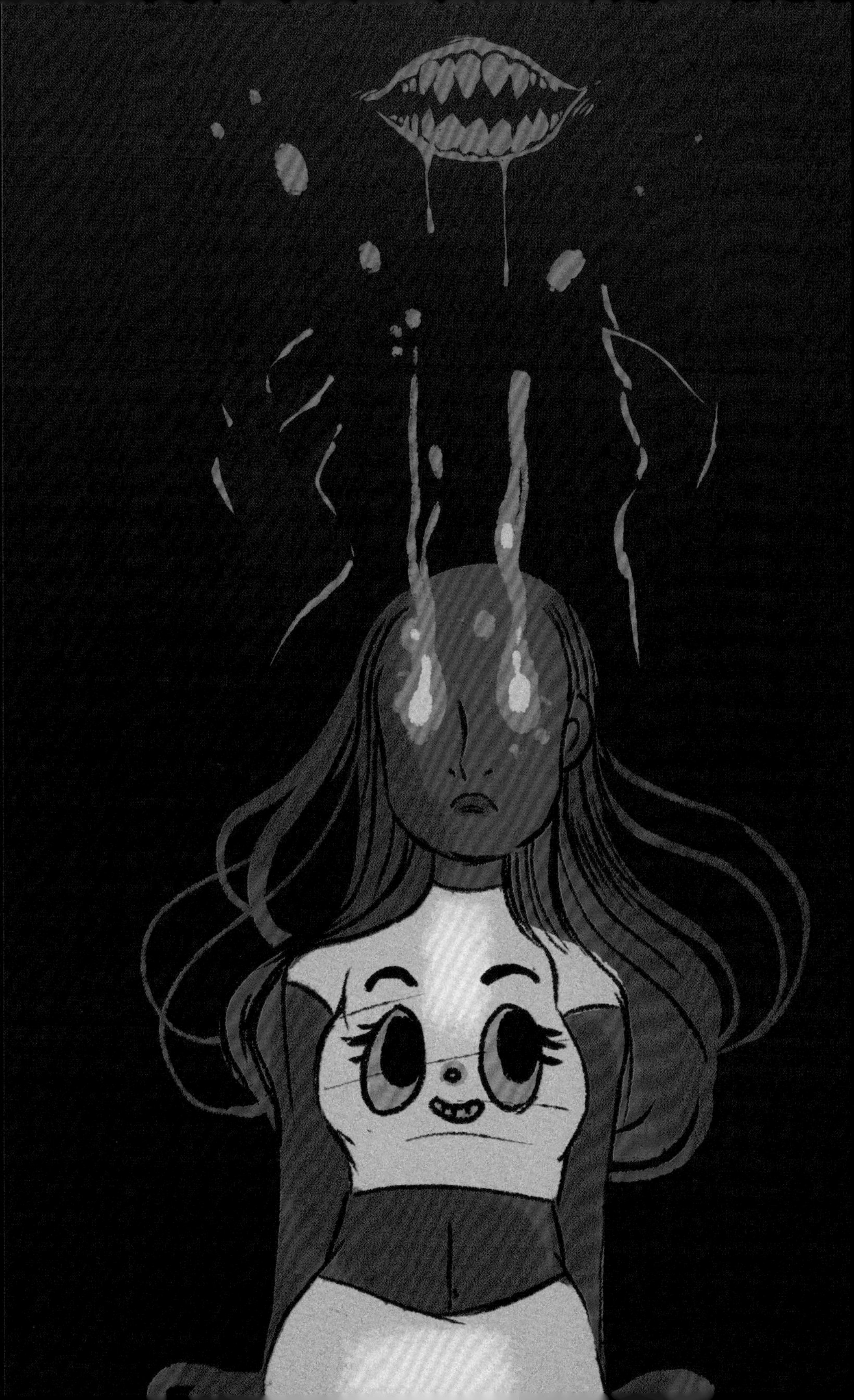

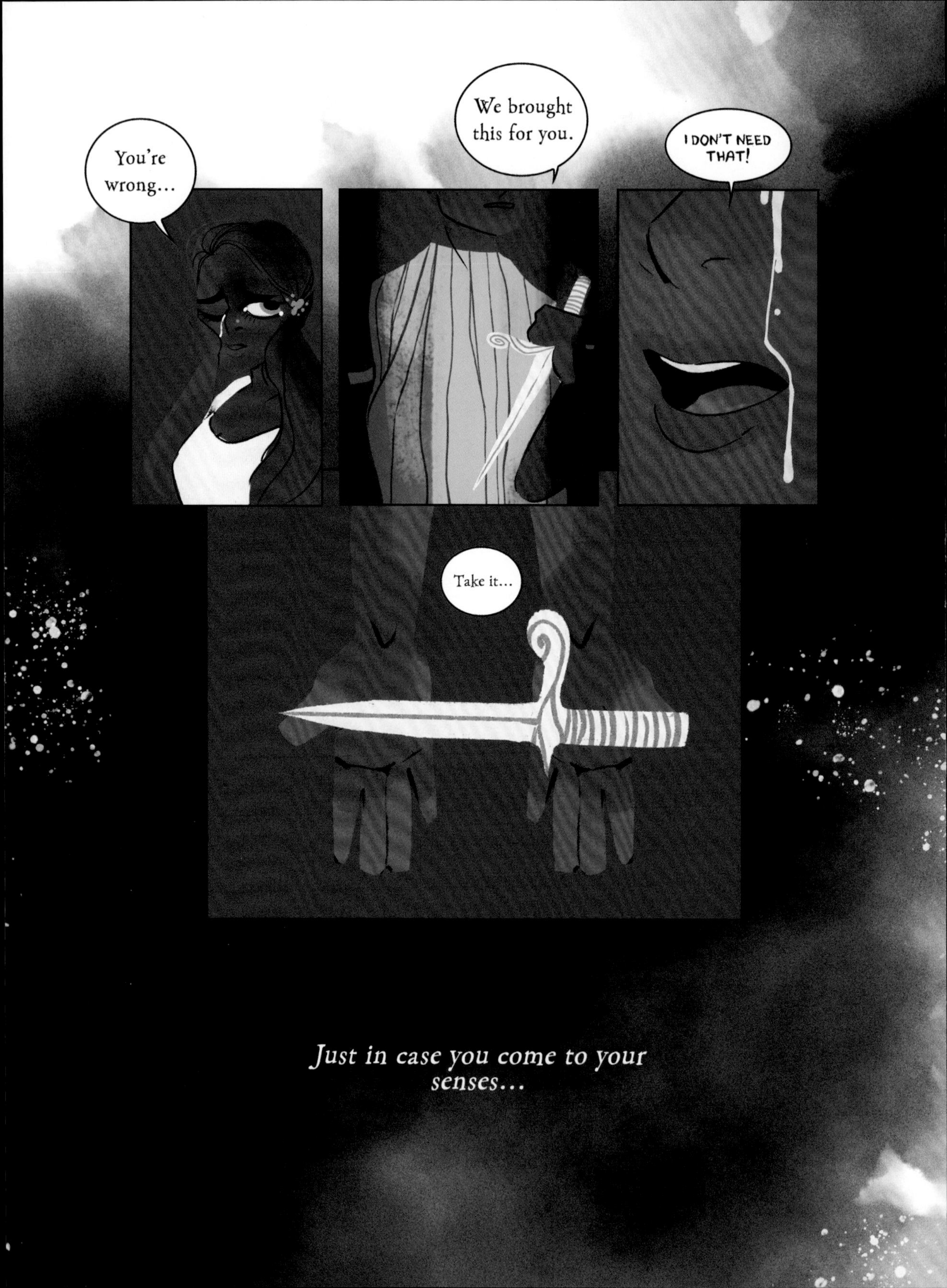
You're wrong...
We brought this for you.
I DON'T NEED THAT!
Take it...
Just in case you come to your senses...

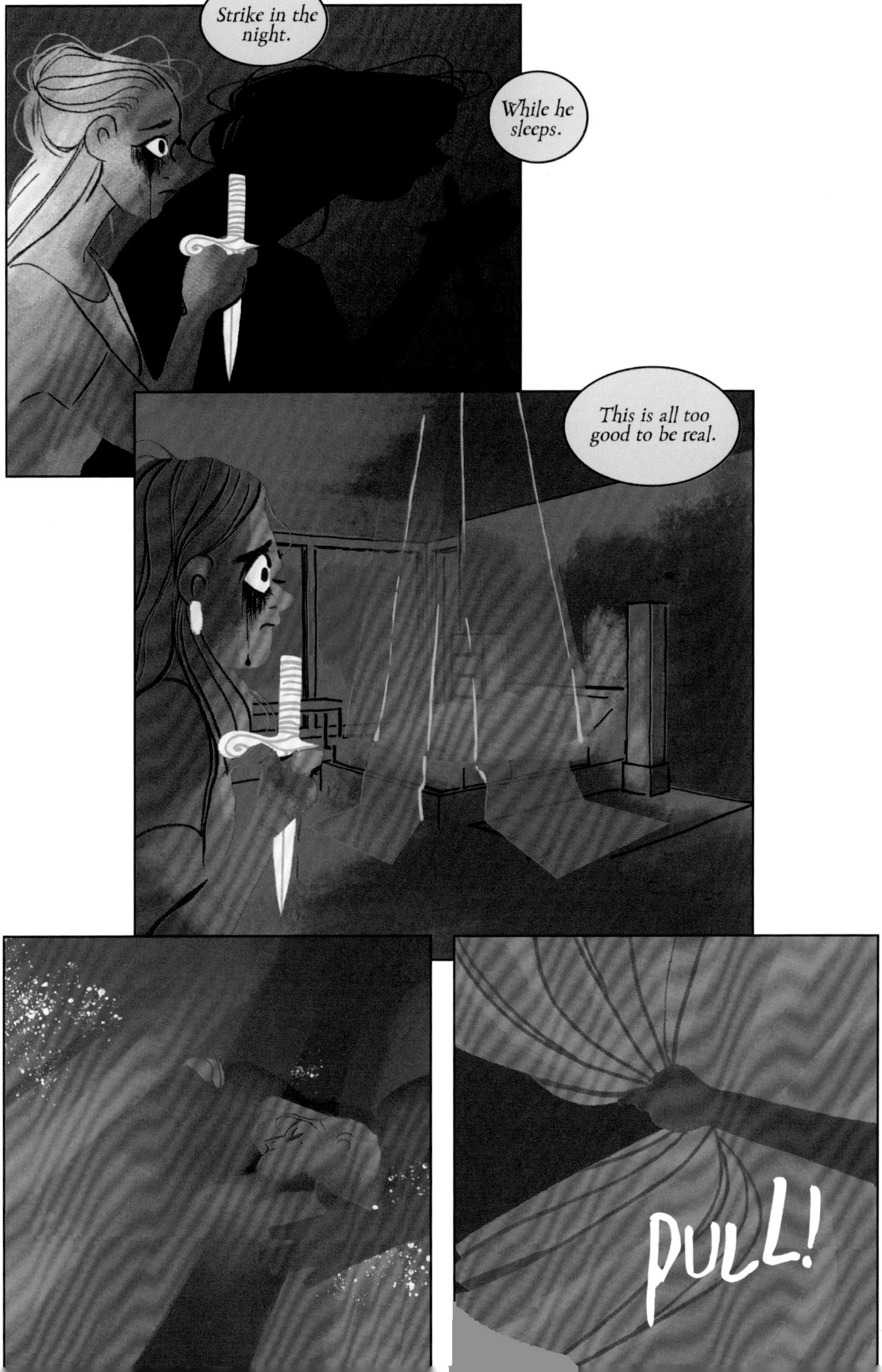
Strike in the night.
While he sleeps.
This is all too good to be real.
PULL!

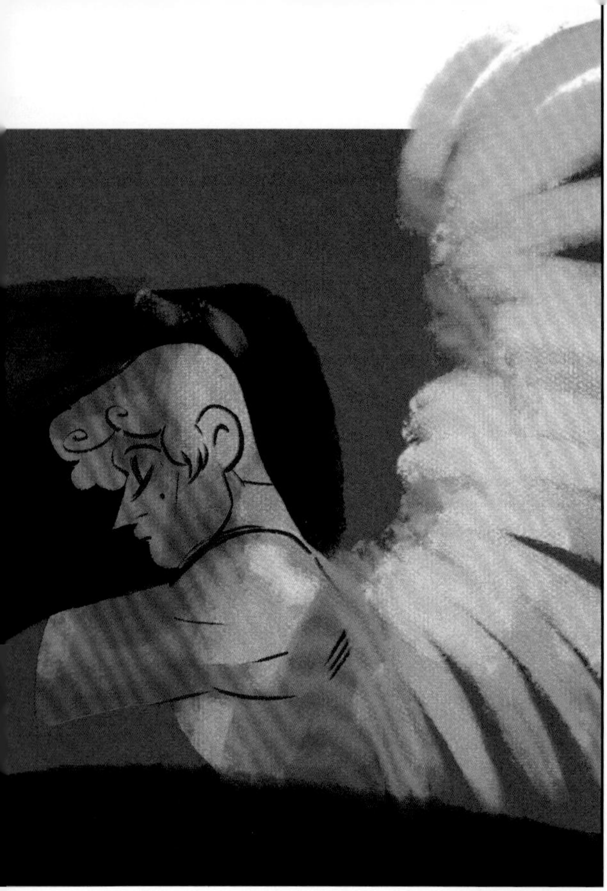

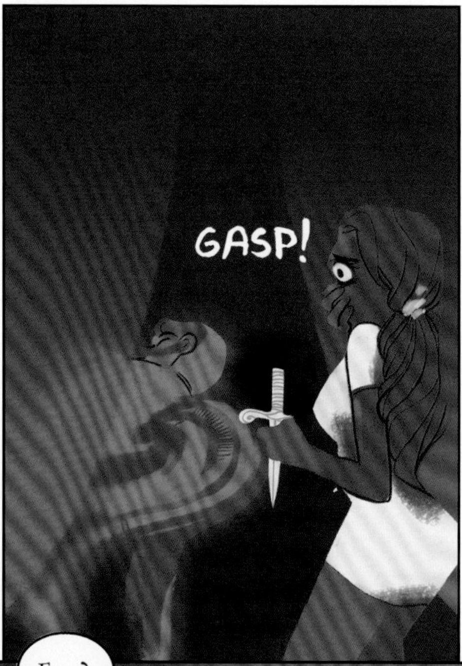
GASP!

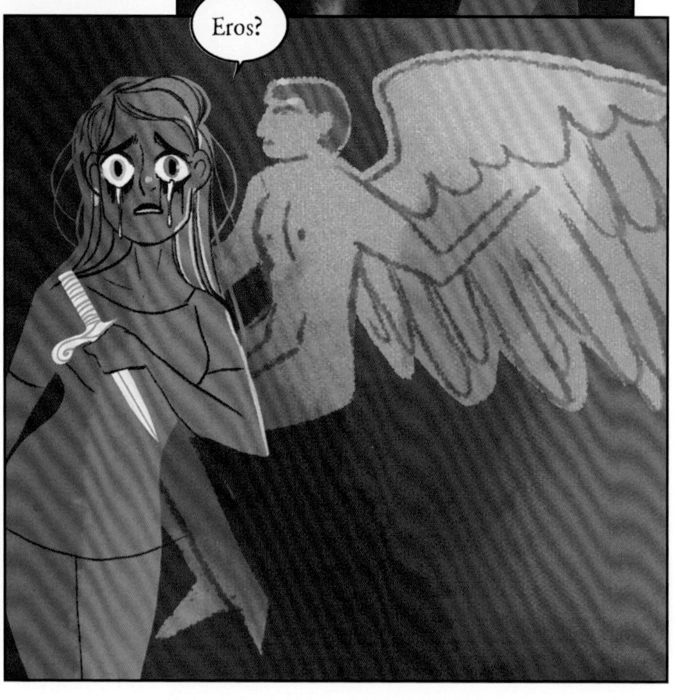
Eros?

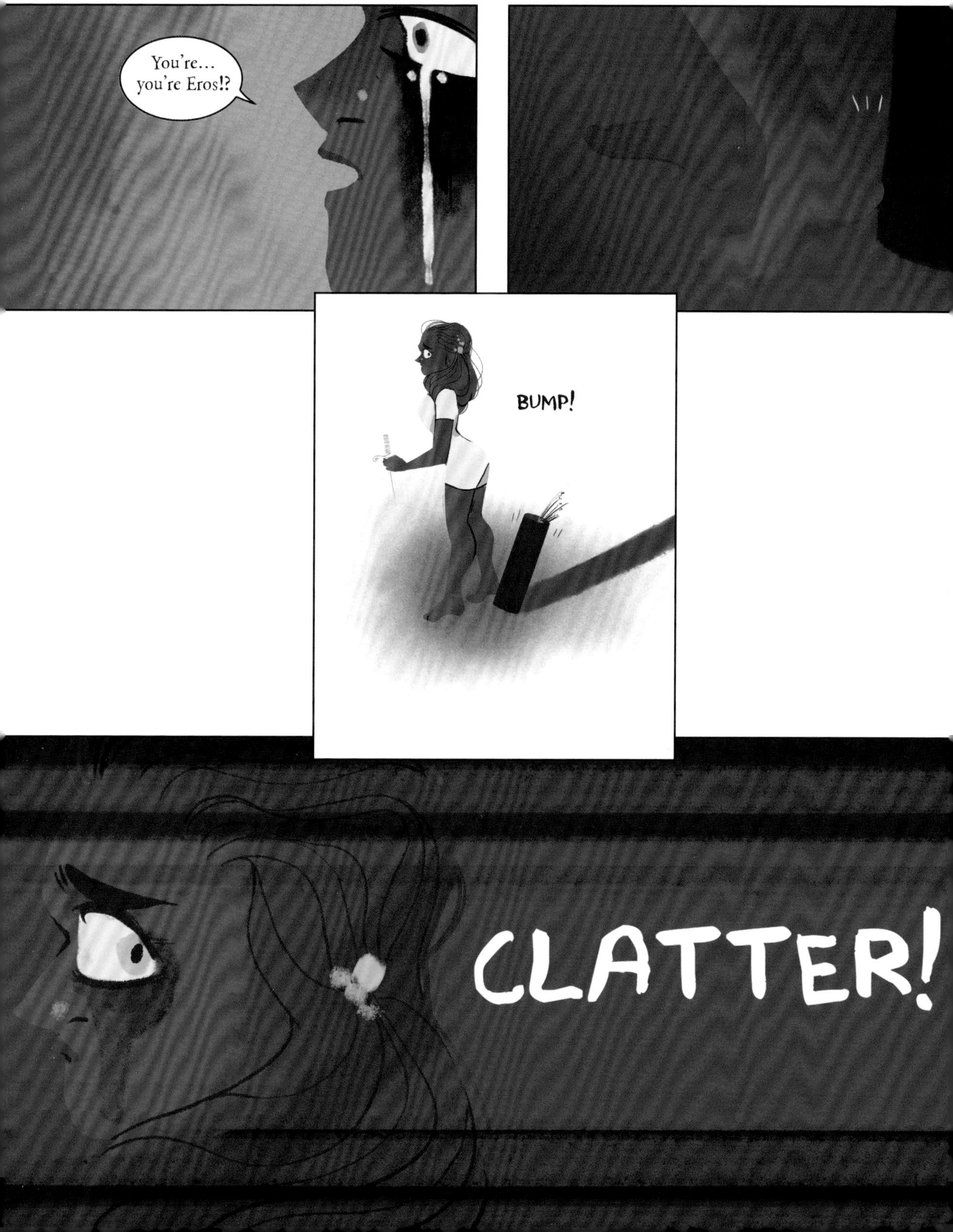
You're…
you're Eros!?
BUMP!
CLATTER!

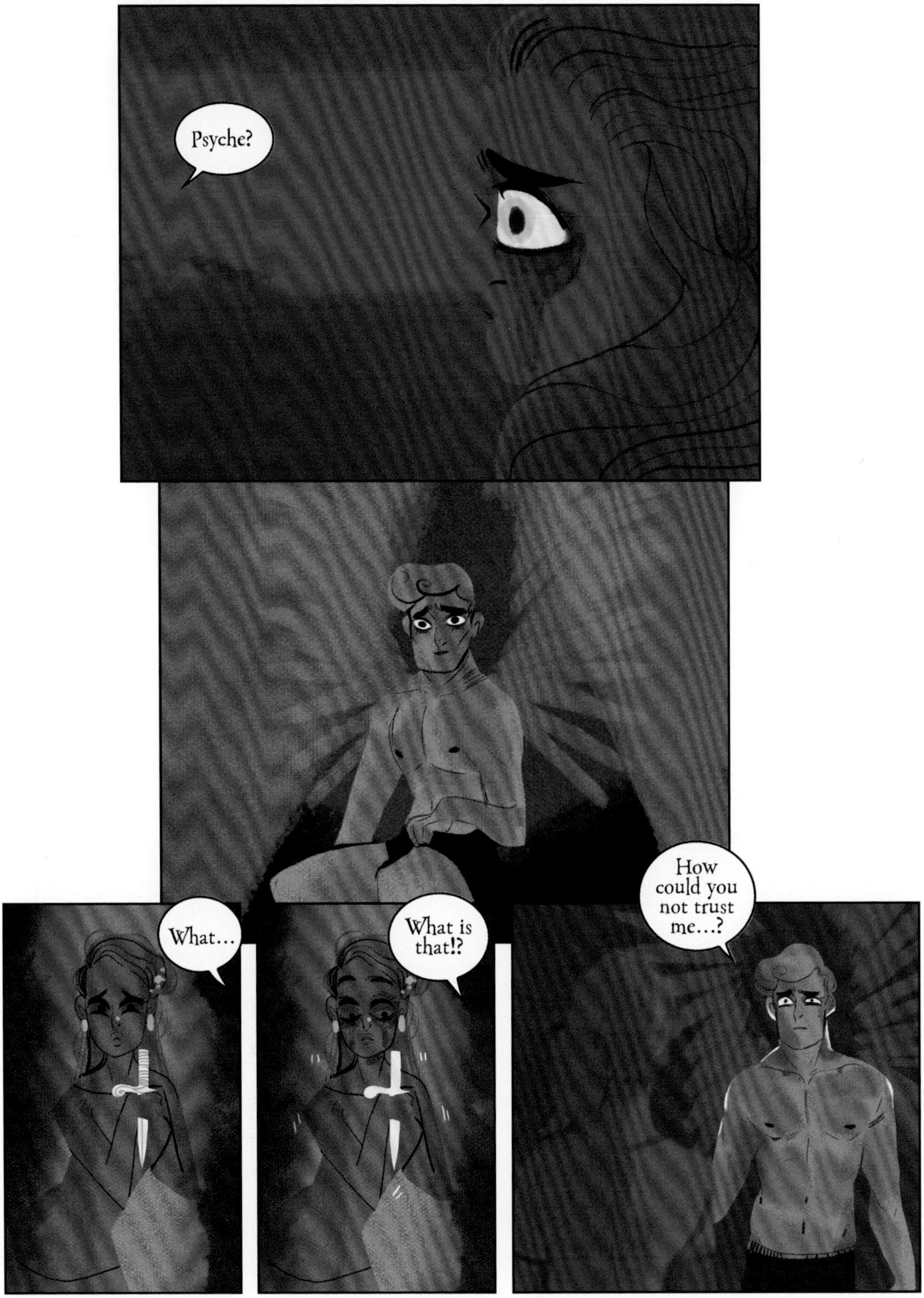
Psyche?
What…
What is that!?
How could you not trust me…?

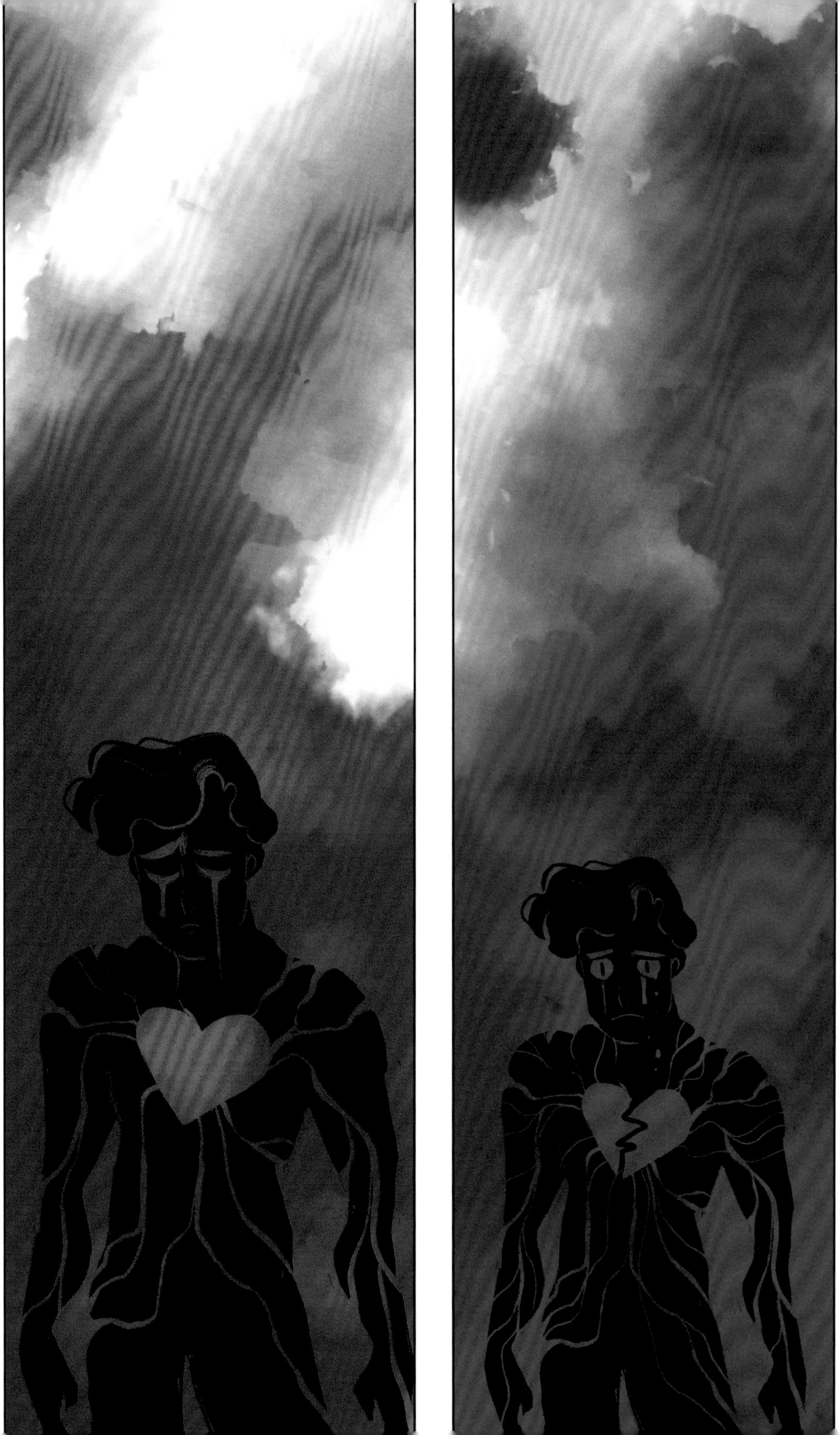

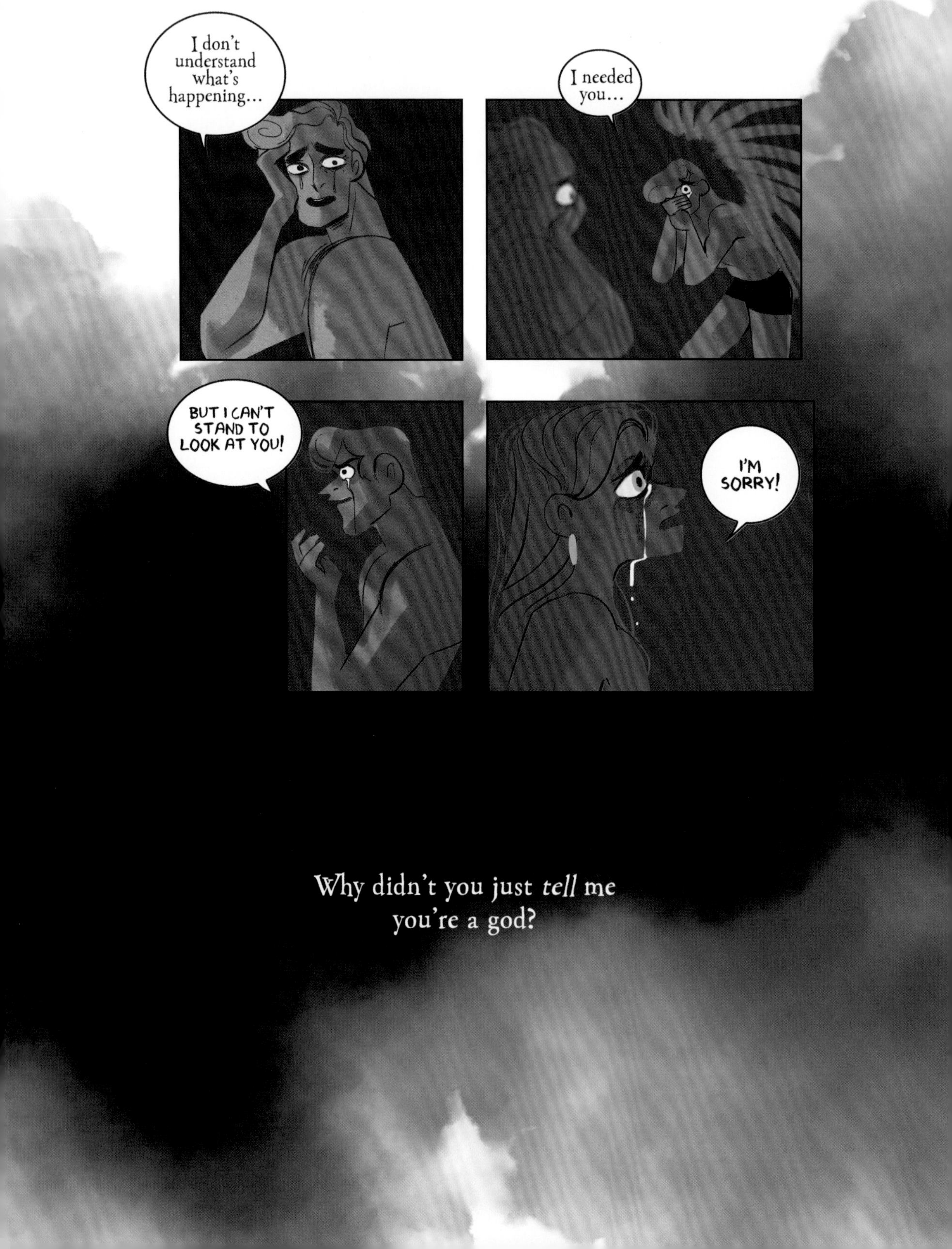
I don't understand what's happening...
I needed you...
BUT I CAN'T STAND TO LOOK AT YOU!
I'M SORRY!

Why didn't you just *tell* me
you're a god?

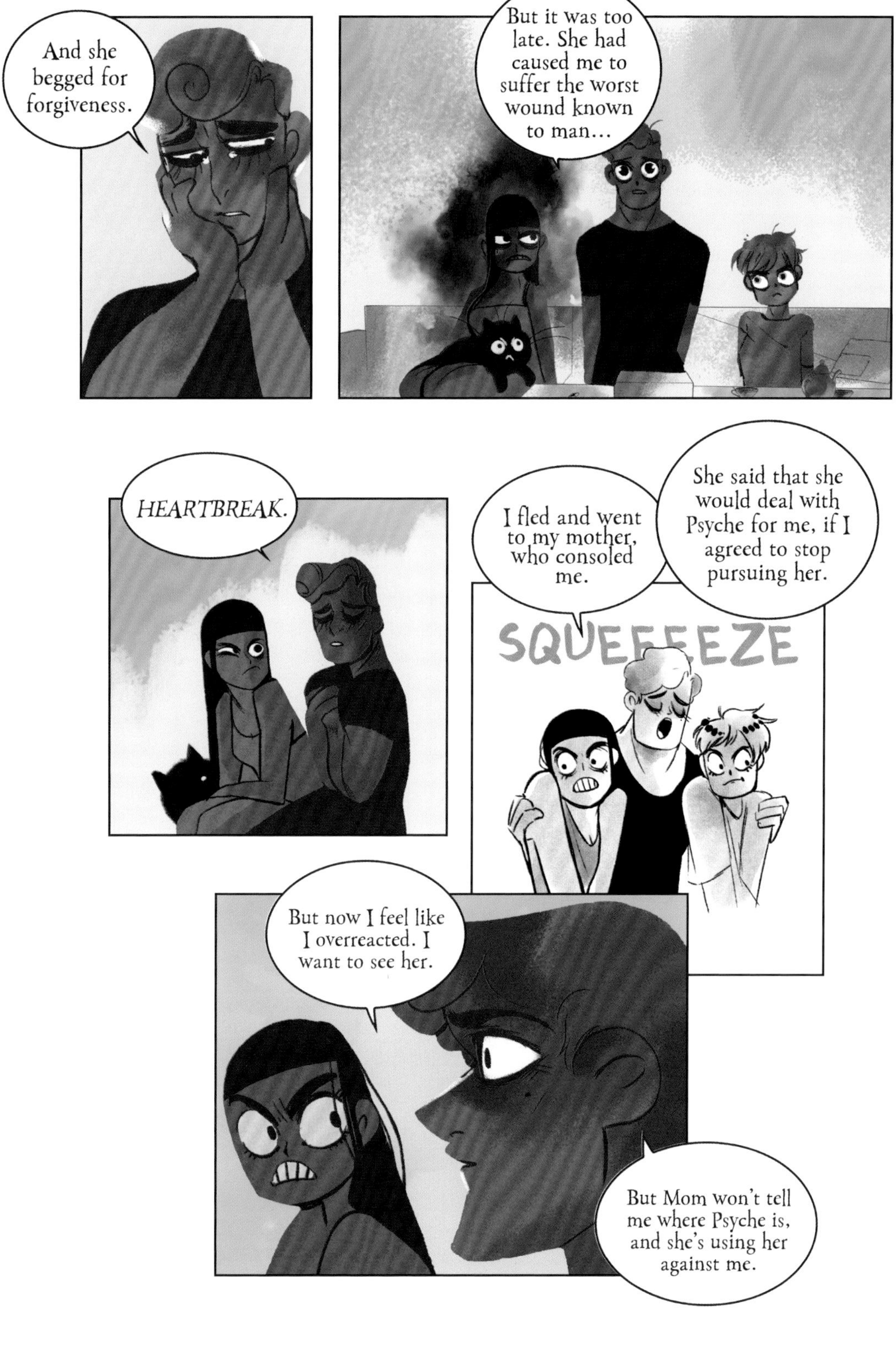

And she begged for forgiveness.
But it was too late. She had caused me to suffer the worst wound known to man…
HEARTBREAK.
I fled and went to my mother, who consoled me.
She said that she would deal with Psyche for me, if I agreed to stop pursuing her.
SQUEEEEZE
But now I feel like I overreacted. I want to see her.
But Mom won't tell me where Psyche is, and she's using her against me.

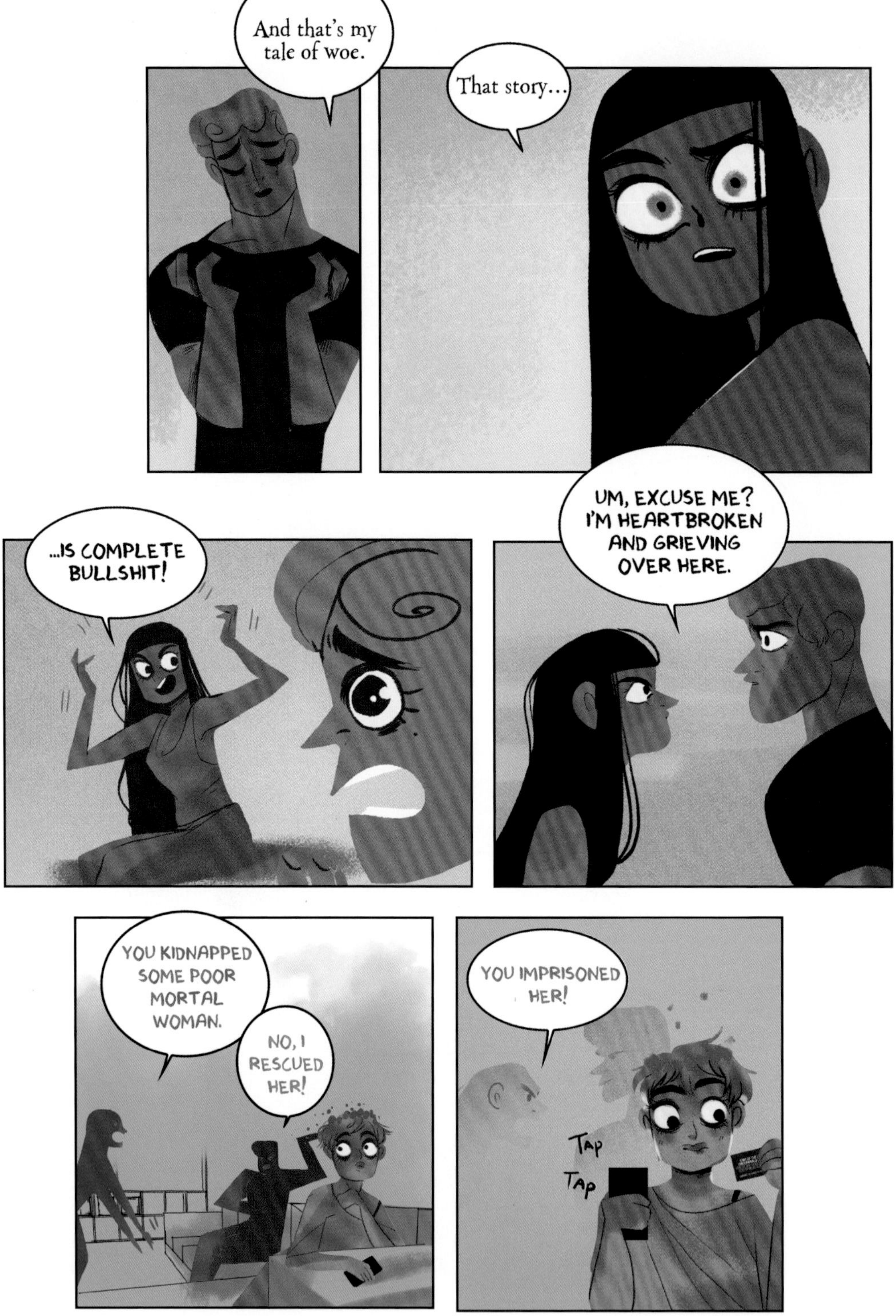
And that's my tale of woe.
That story...
...IS COMPLETE BULLSHIT!
UM, EXCUSE ME? I'M HEARTBROKEN AND GRIEVING OVER HERE.
YOU KIDNAPPED SOME POOR MORTAL WOMAN.
NO, I RESCUED HER!
YOU IMPRISONED HER!
TAP
TAP

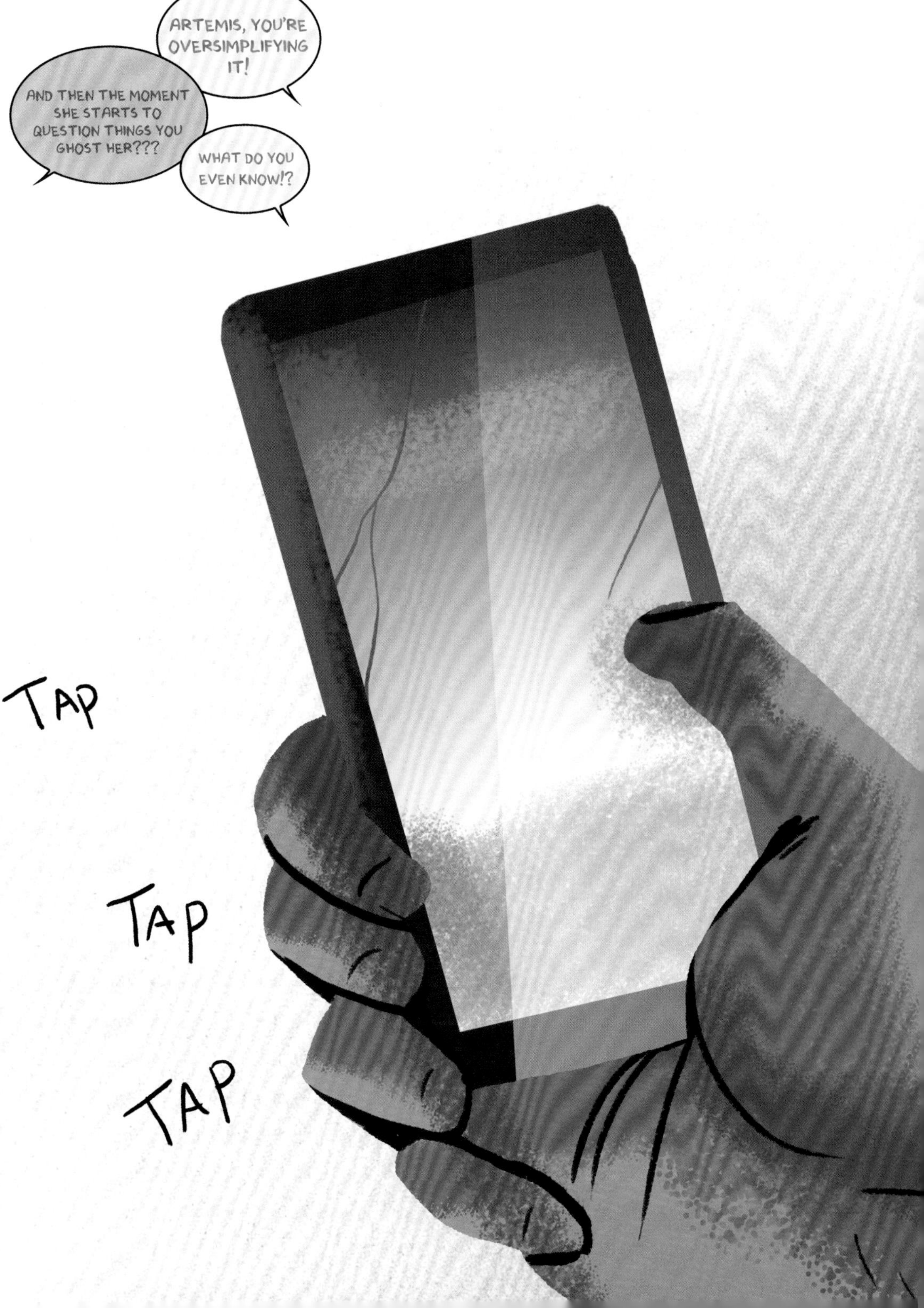
ARTEMIS, YOU'RE OVERSIMPLIFYING IT!
AND THEN THE MOMENT SHE STARTS TO QUESTION THINGS YOU GHOST HER???
WHAT DO YOU EVEN KNOW!?
TAP
TAP
TAP

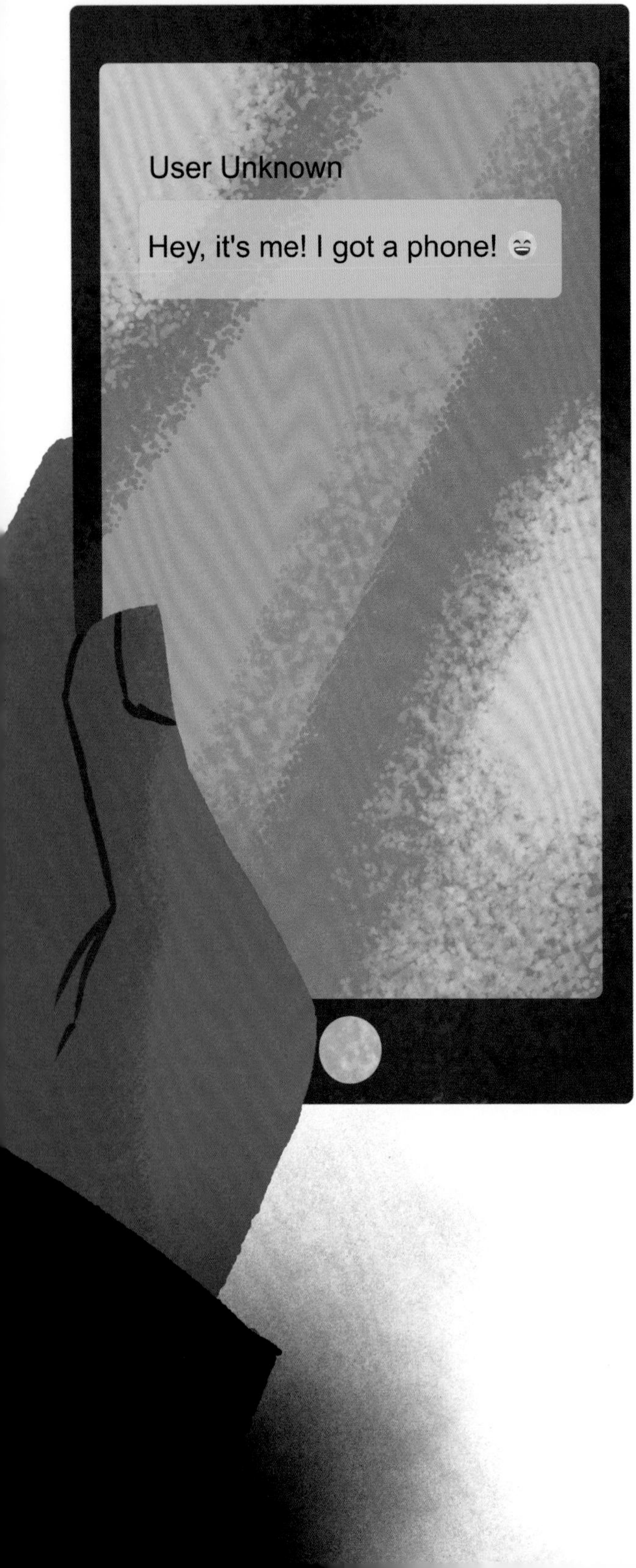
User Unknown
Hey, it's me! I got a phone! 😁

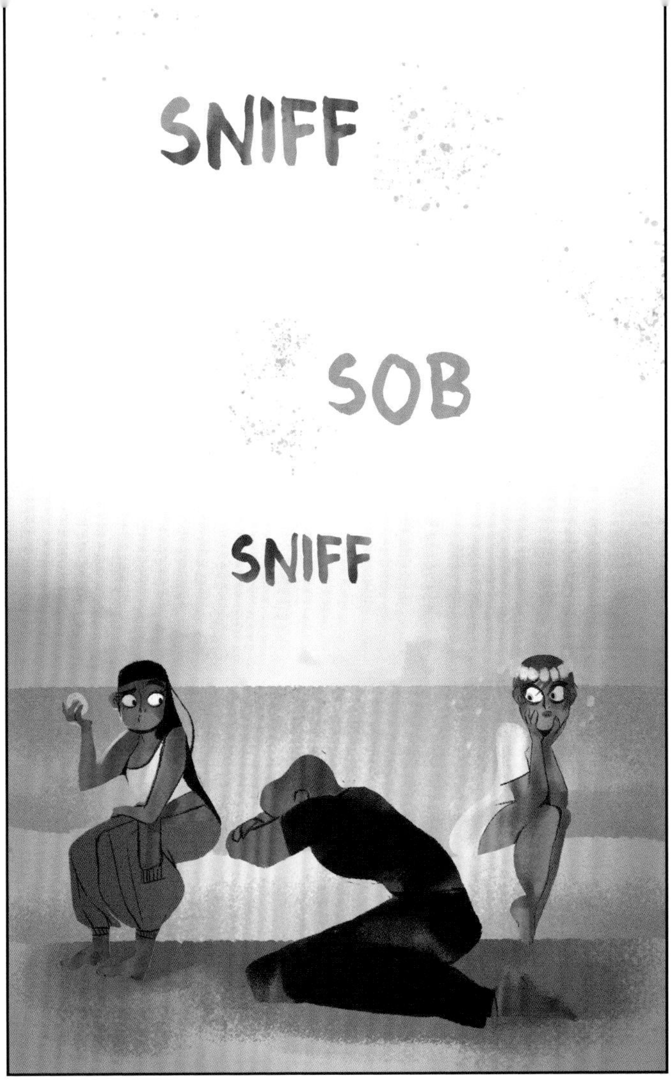
SNIFF
SOB
SNIFF

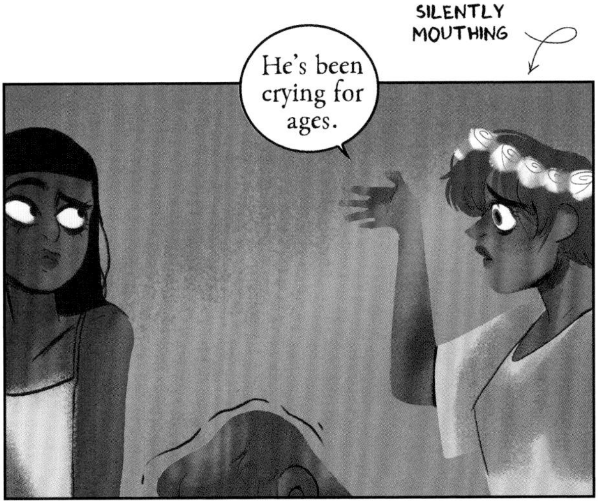
He's been crying for ages.
SILENTLY MOUTHING

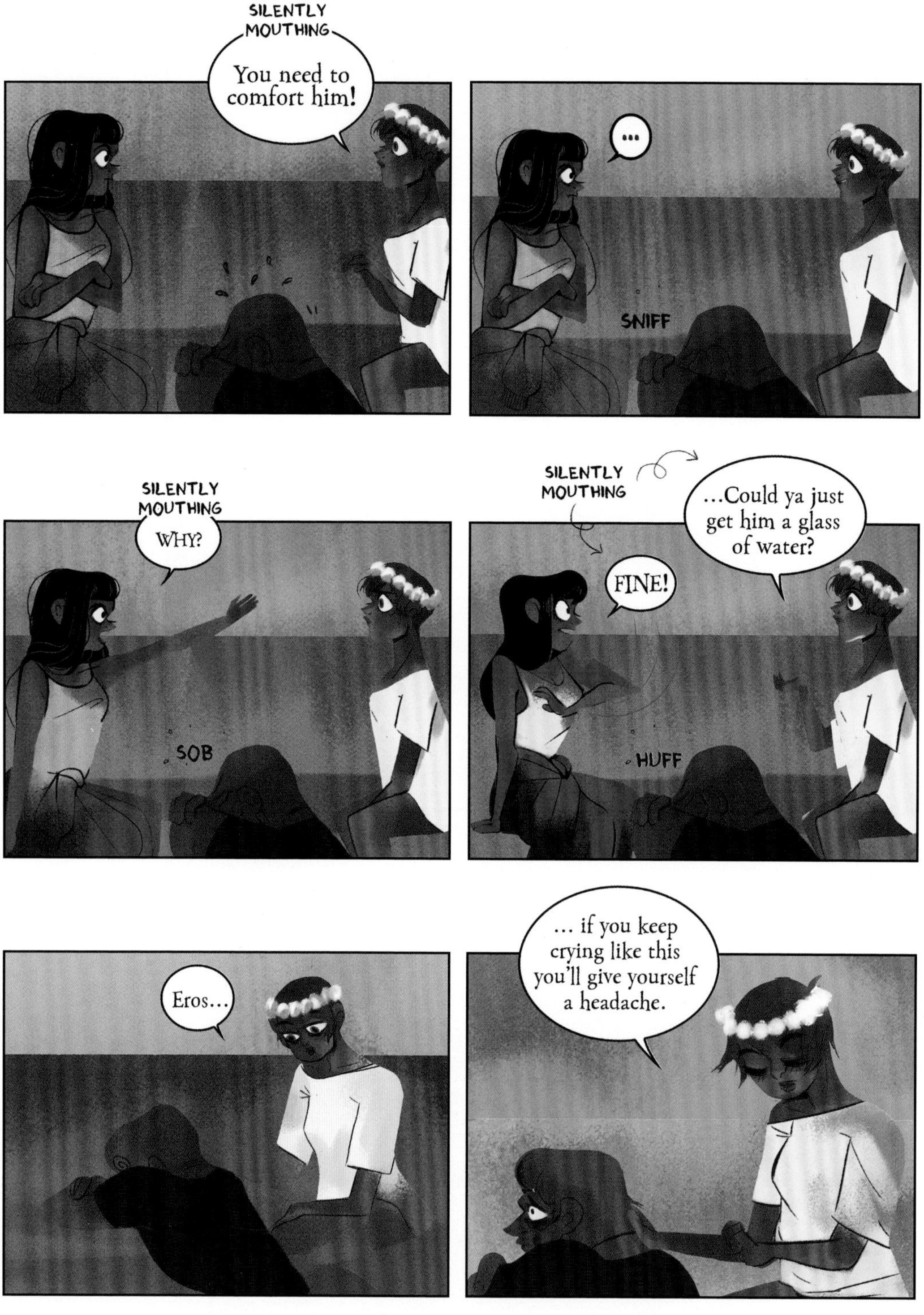
SILENTLY MOUTHING
You need to comfort him!
...
SNIFF
SILENTLY MOUTHING
WHY?
SOB
SILENTLY MOUTHING
...Could ya just get him a glass of water?
FINE!
HUFF
Eros...
... if you keep crying like this you'll give yourself a headache.

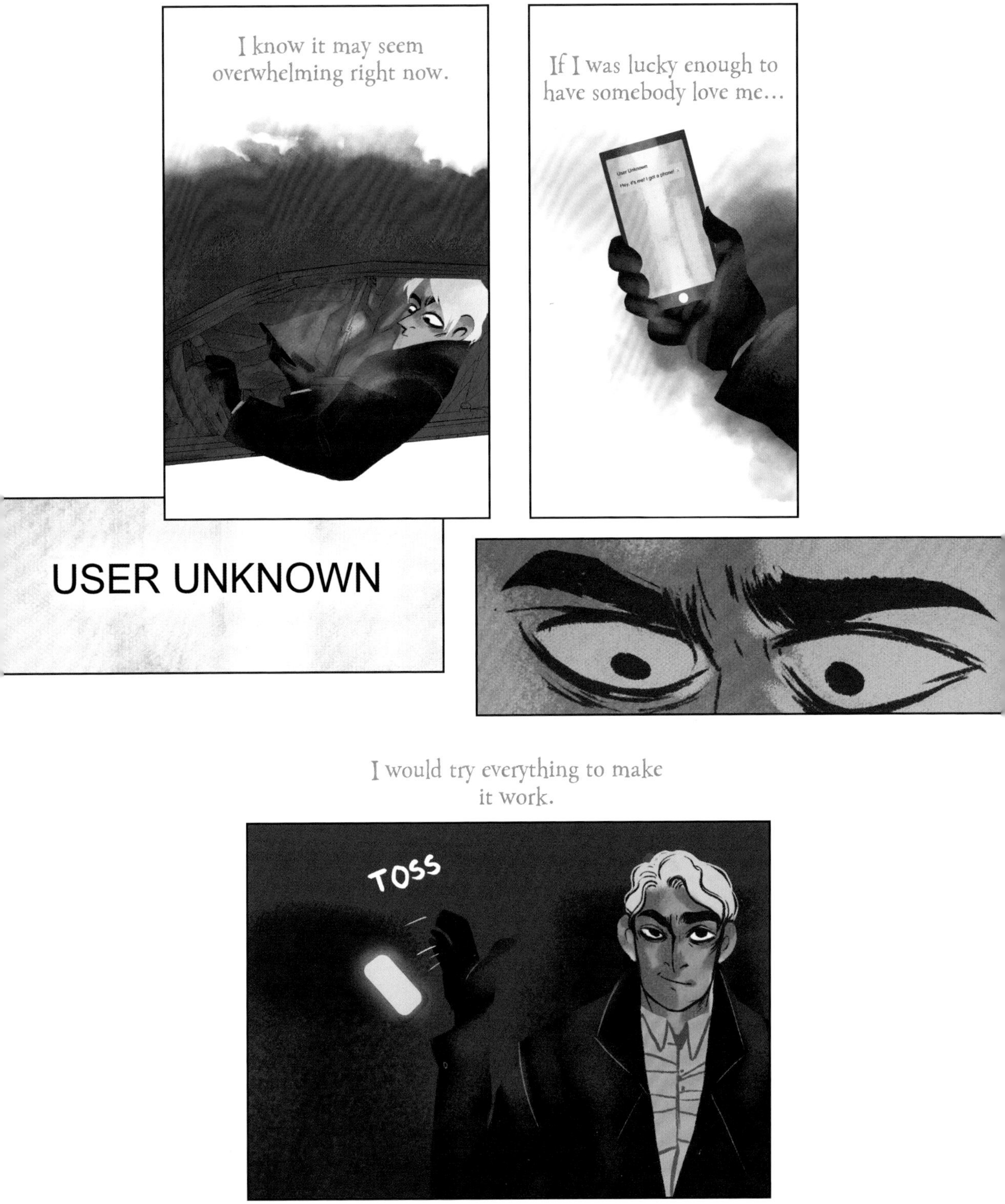
I know it may seem overwhelming right now.
If I was lucky enough to have somebody love me...
USER UNKNOWN
I would try everything to make it work.
TOSS

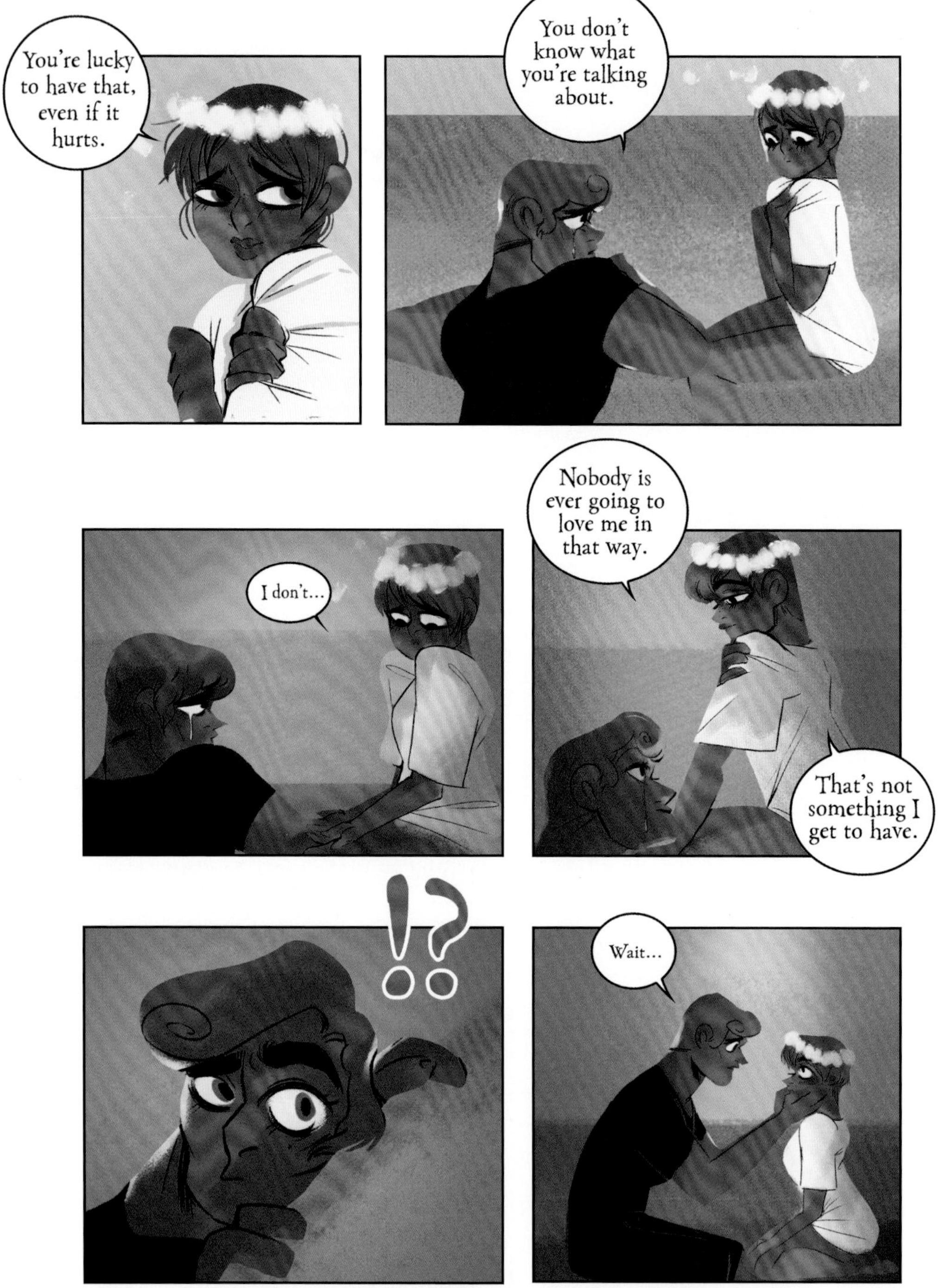
You're lucky to have that, even if it hurts.
You don't know what you're talking about.
I don't...
Nobody is ever going to love me in that way.
That's not something I get to have.
!?
Wait...

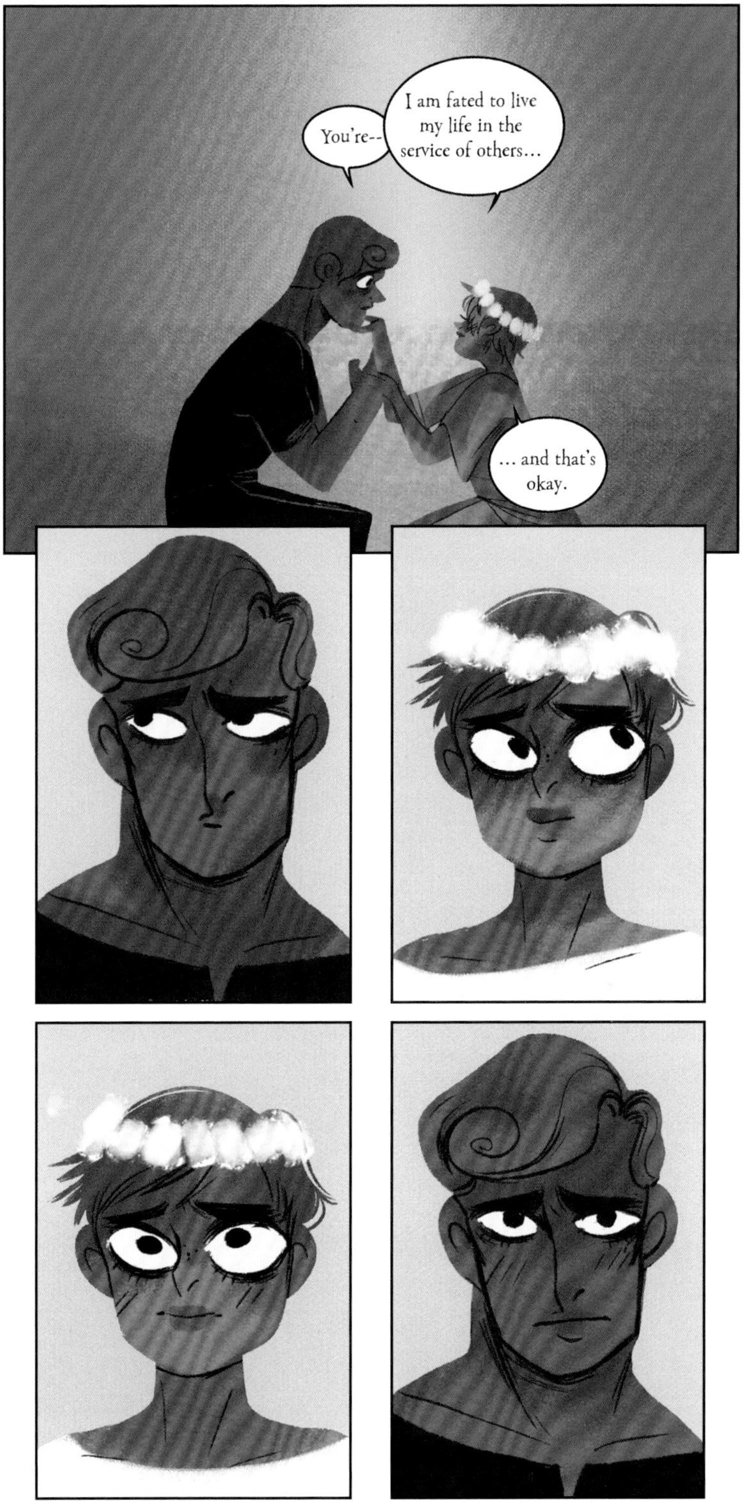
You're--
I am fated to live my life in the service of others...
... and that's okay.

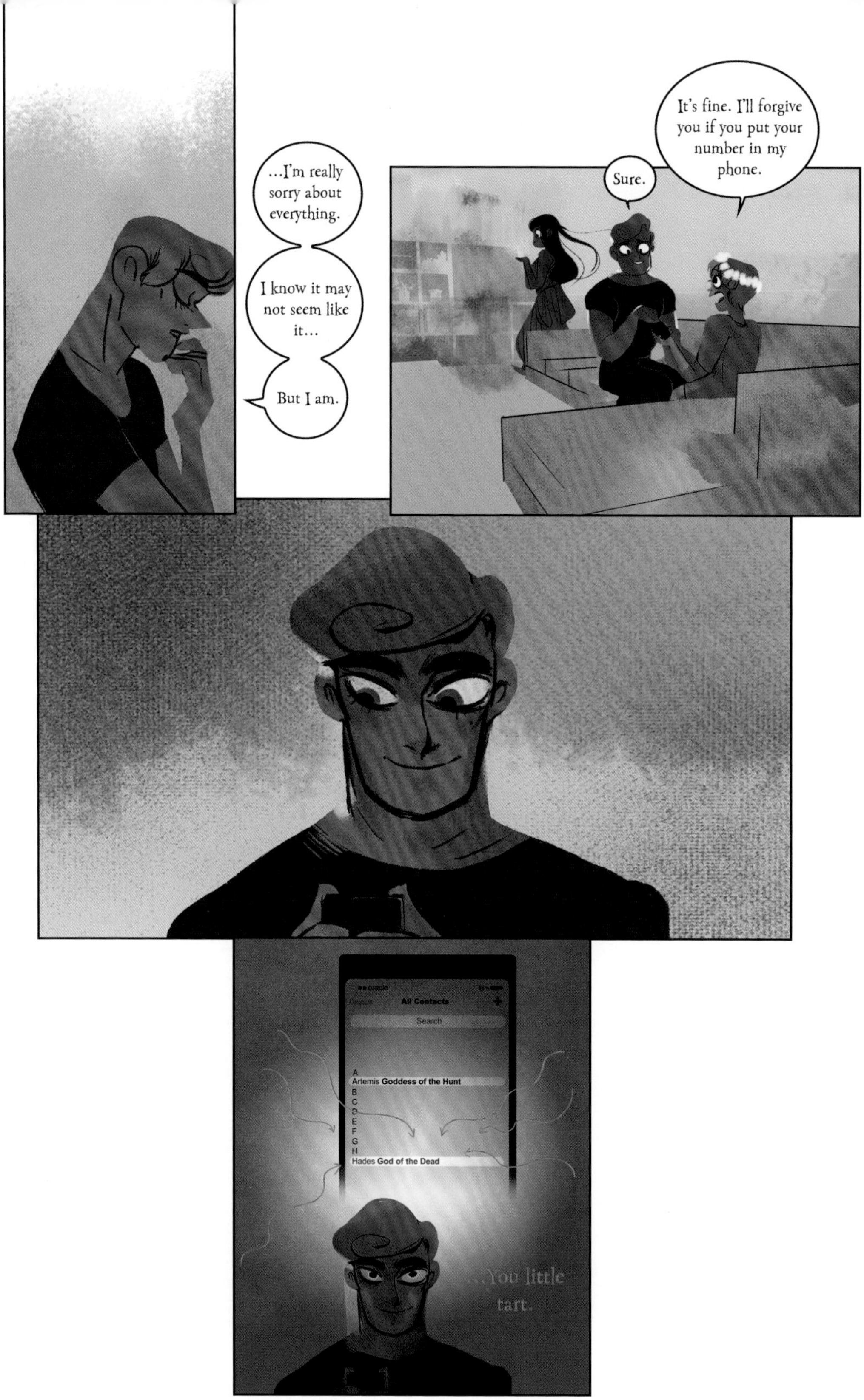
...I'm really sorry about everything.
I know it may not seem like it...
But I am.
Sure.
It's fine. I'll forgive you if you put your number in my phone.
All Contacts
Search
A
Artemis Goddess of the Hunt
B
C
D
E
F
G
H
Hades God of the Dead
...You little tart.

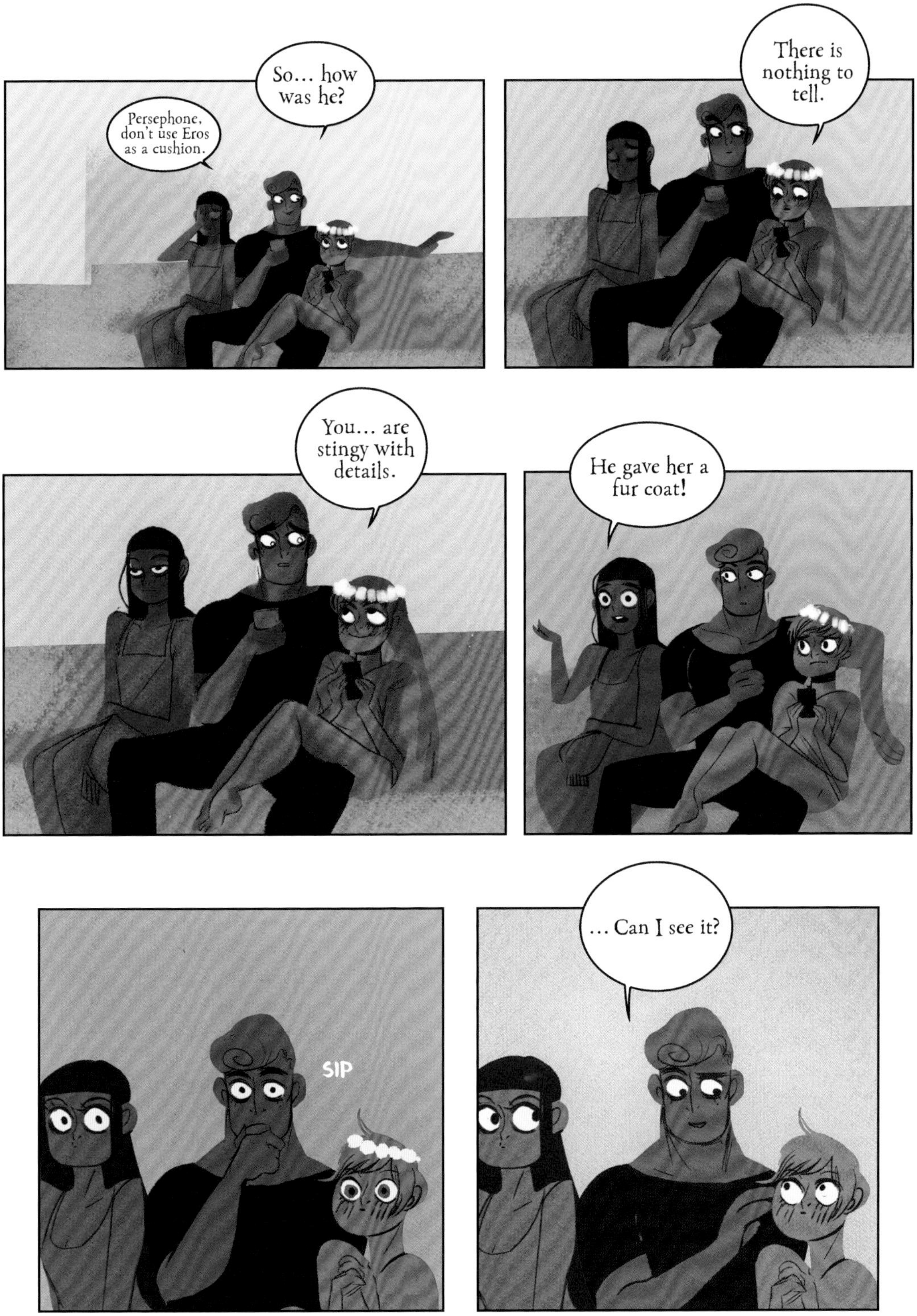
So… how was he?
Persephone, don't use Eros as a cushion.
There is nothing to tell.
You… are stingy with details.
He gave her a fur coat!
SIP
… Can I see it?

OH MY GODS!

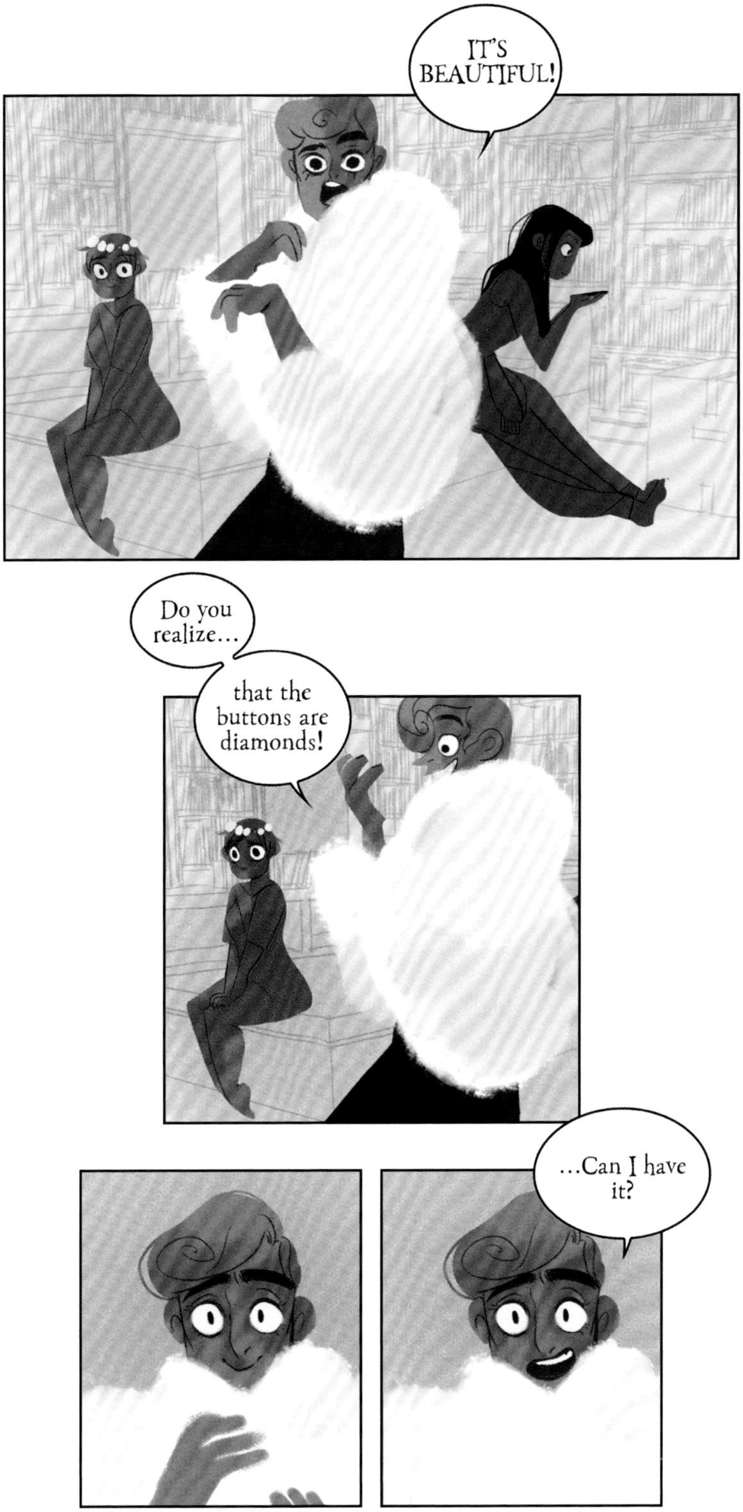
IT'S BEAUTIFUL!
Do you realize...
that the buttons are diamonds!
...Can I have it?

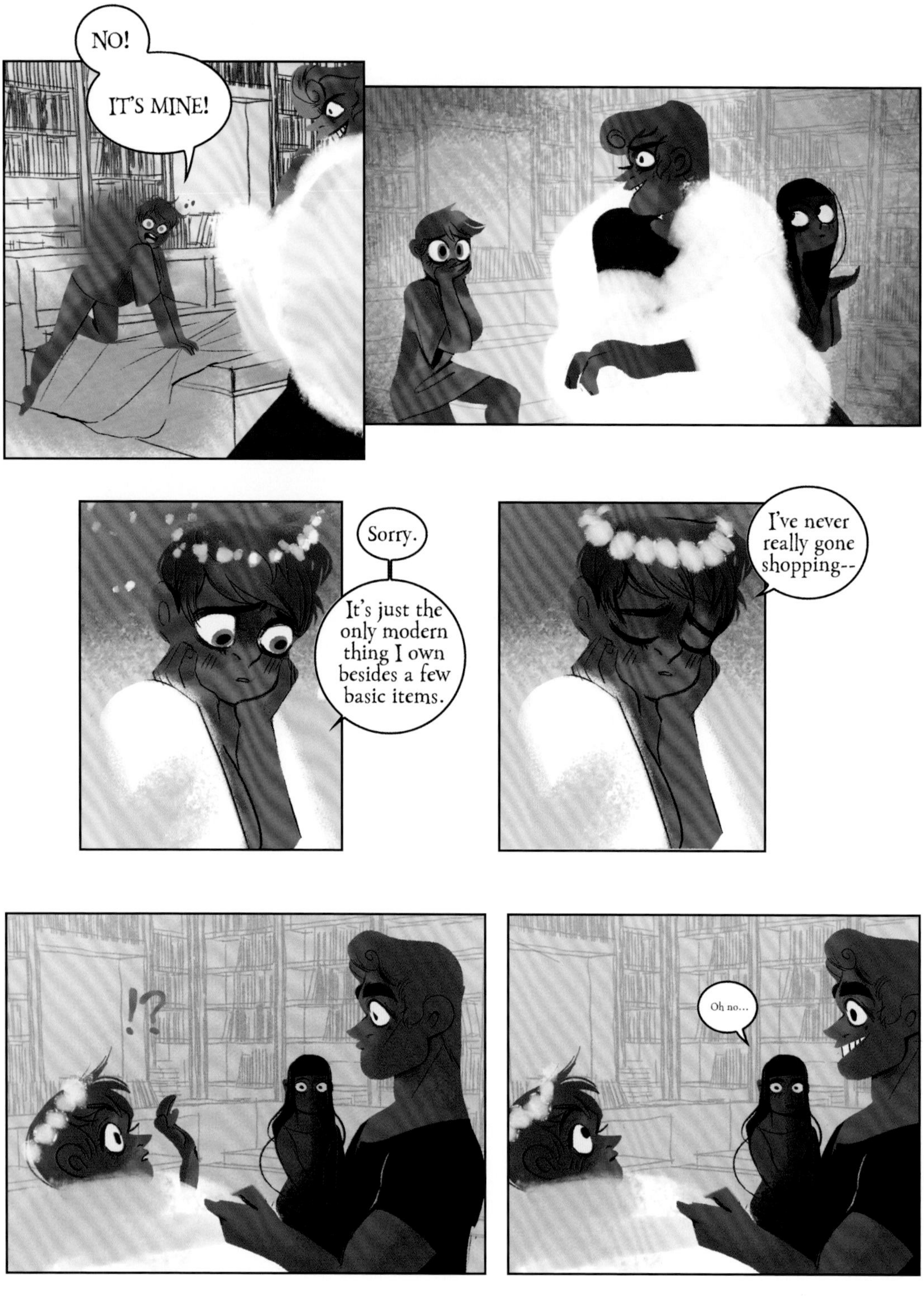
NO!
IT'S MINE!
Sorry.
It's just the only modern thing I own besides a few basic items.
I've never really gone shopping--
!?
Oh no...

EPISODE 17: GET IN

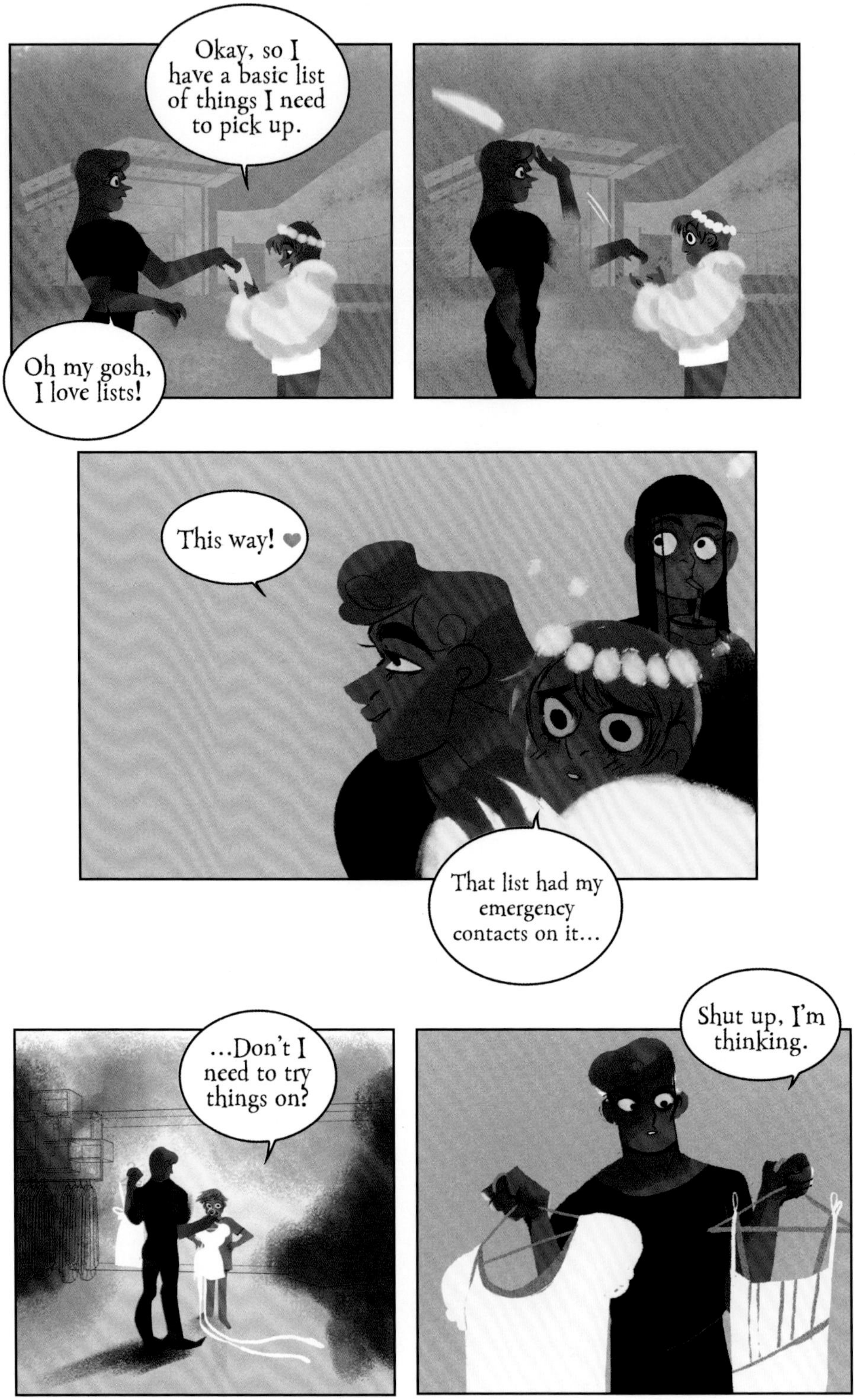
Okay, so I have a basic list of things I need to pick up.
Oh my gosh, I love lists!
This way! ❤
That list had my emergency contacts on it...
...Don't I need to try things on?
Shut up, I'm thinking.

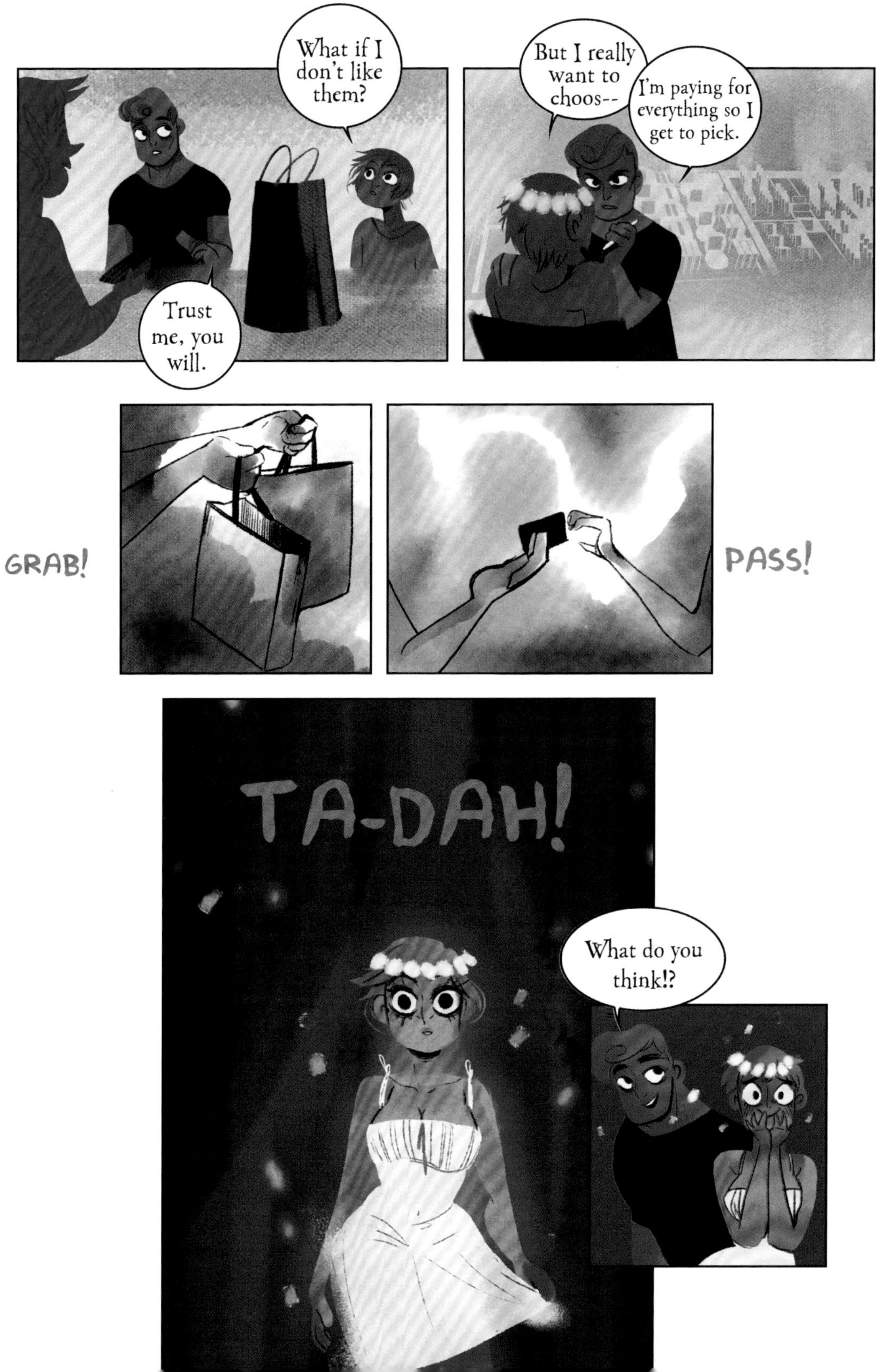
What if I don't like them?
Trust me, you will.
But I really want to choos--
I'm paying for everything so I get to pick.
GRAB!
PASS!
TA-DAH!
What do you think!?

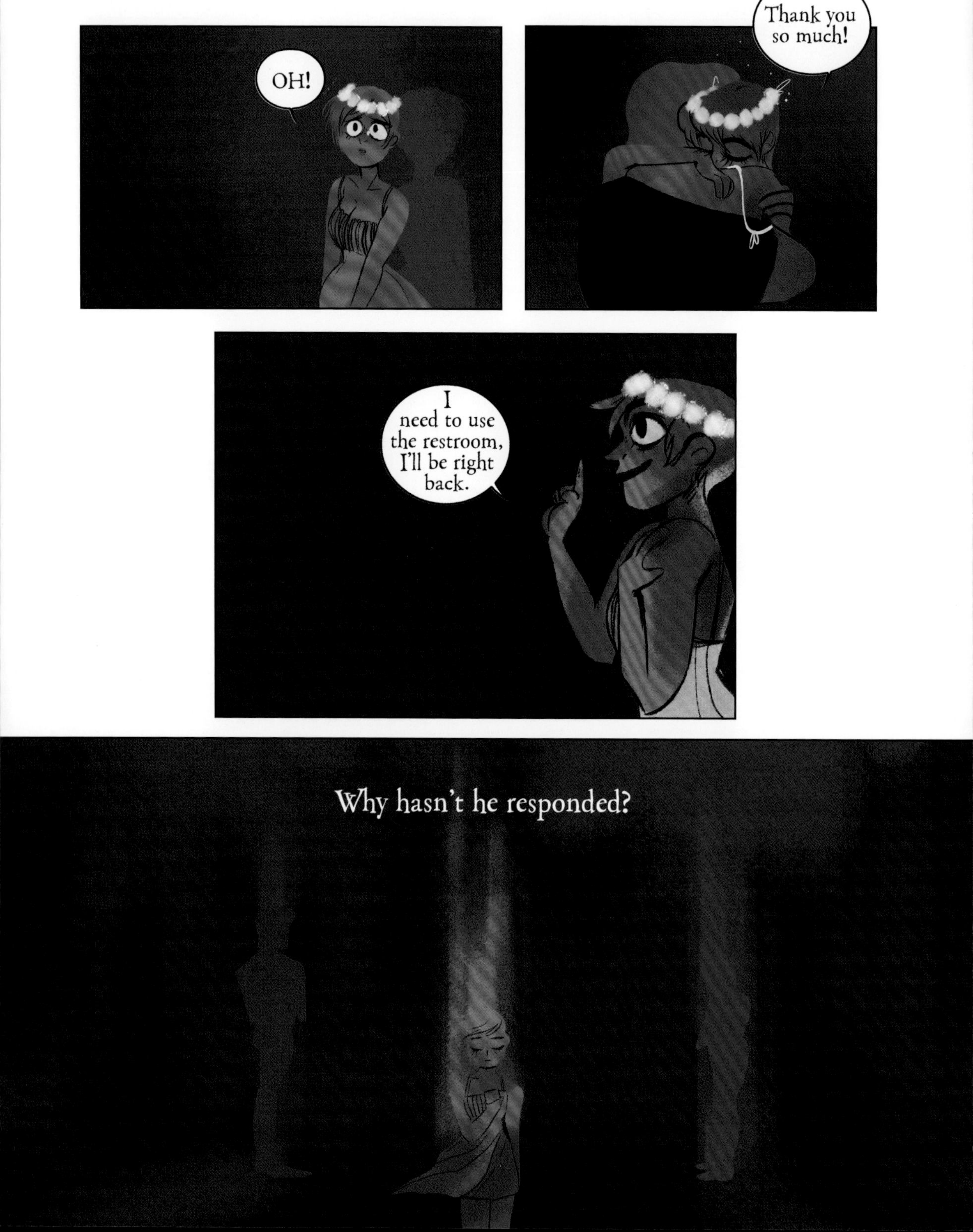
OH!
Thank you so much!
I need to use the restroom, I'll be right back.
Why hasn't he responded?

MENSWEAR

Did I write the number wrong?

Was he just humoring me?

Maybe he doesn't want
to be my friend?

What am I even trying
to achieve anyway?

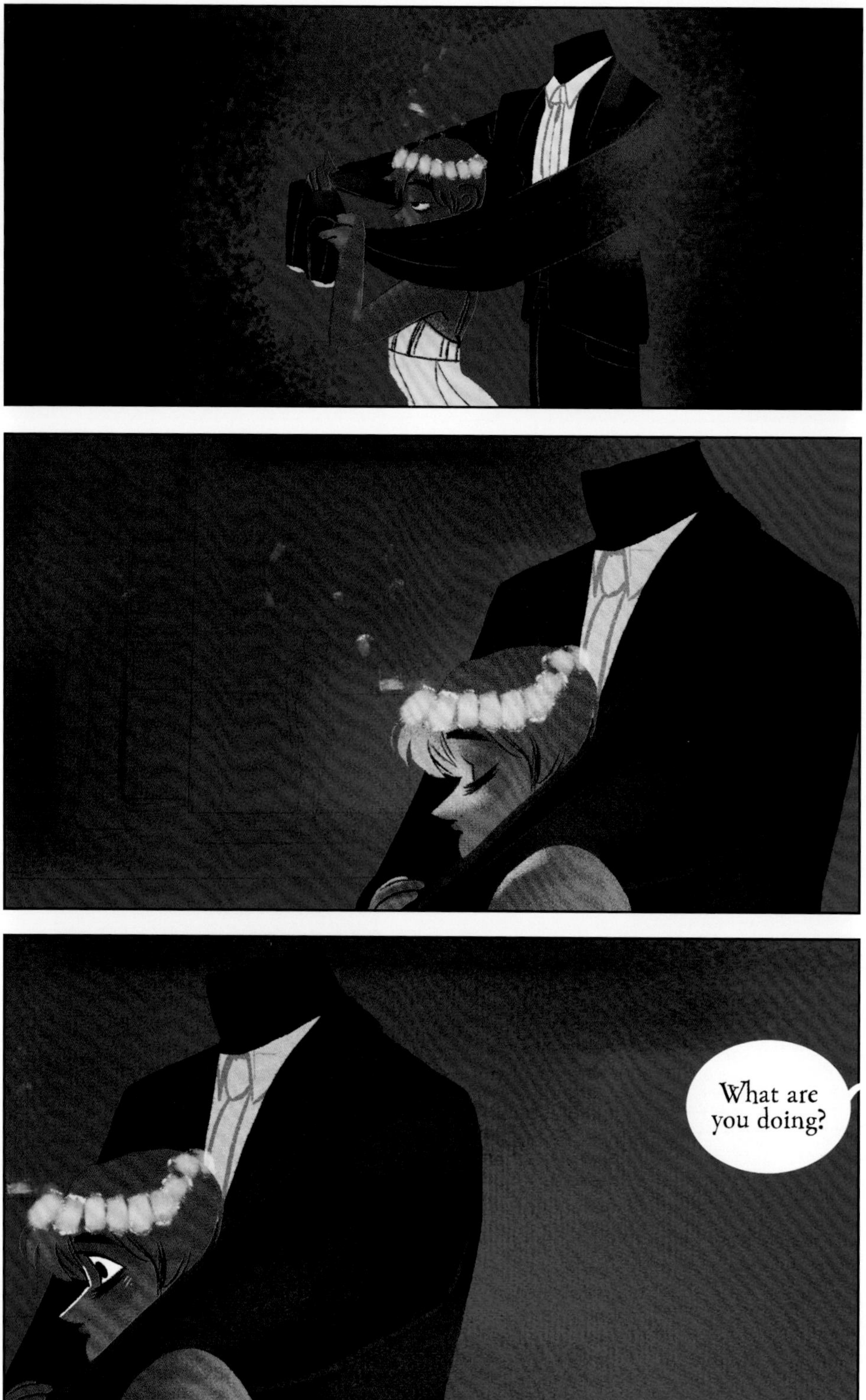
What are you doing?

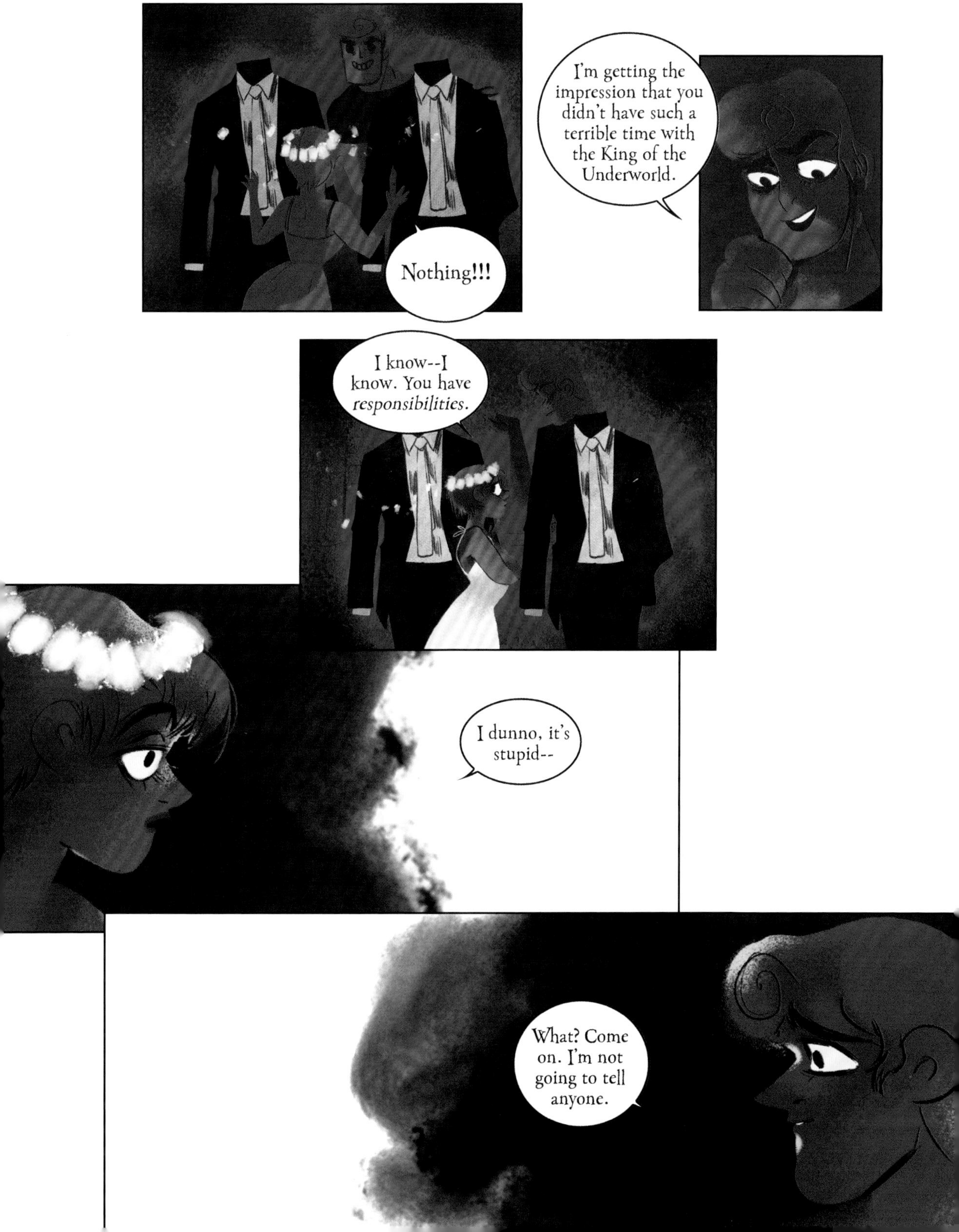
I'm getting the impression that you didn't have such a terrible time with the King of the Underworld.
Nothing!!!
I know--I know. You have *responsibilities*.
I dunno, it's stupid--
What? Come on. I'm not going to tell anyone.

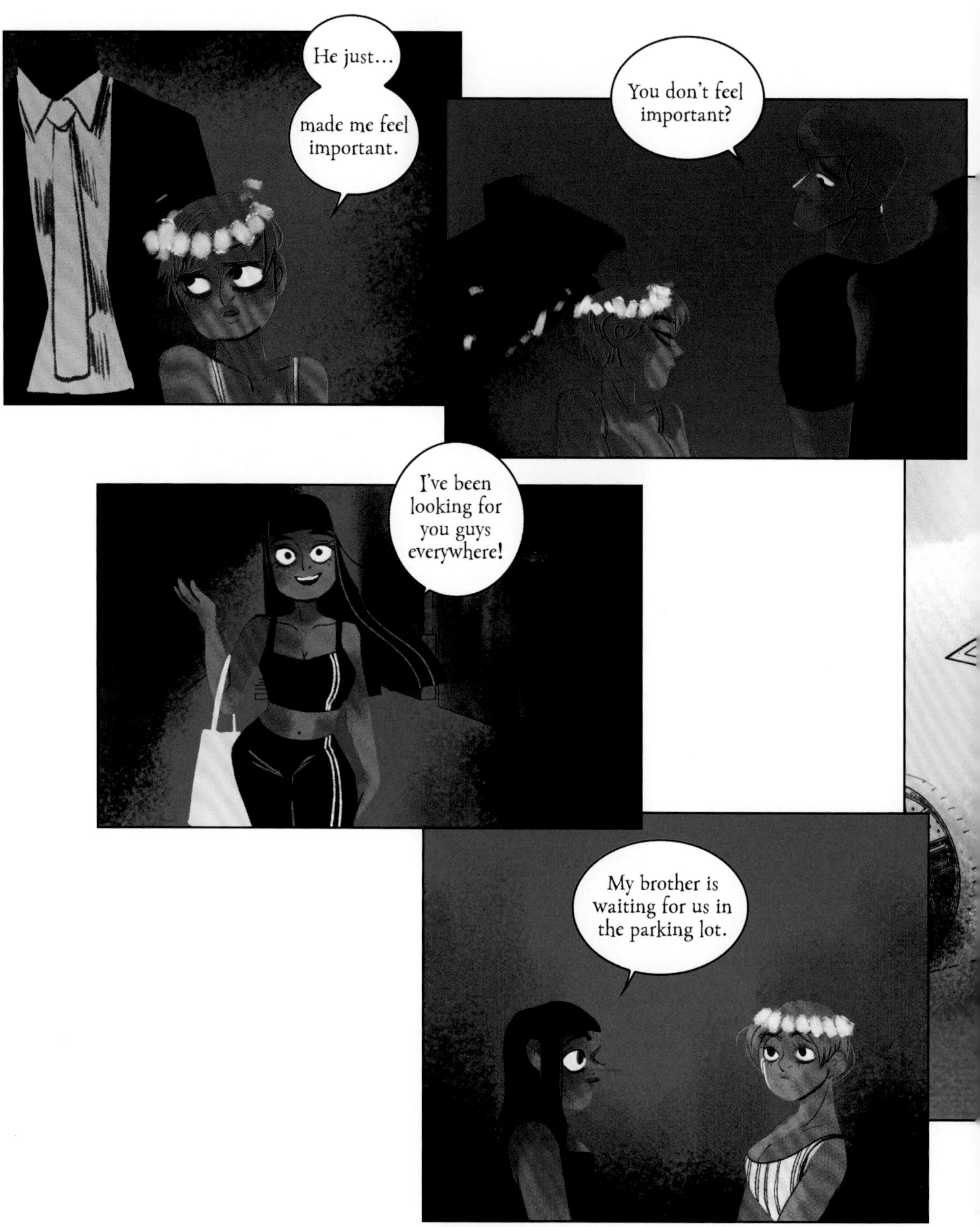
He just…
made me feel important.
You don't feel important?
I've been looking for you guys everywhere!
My brother is waiting for us in the parking lot.

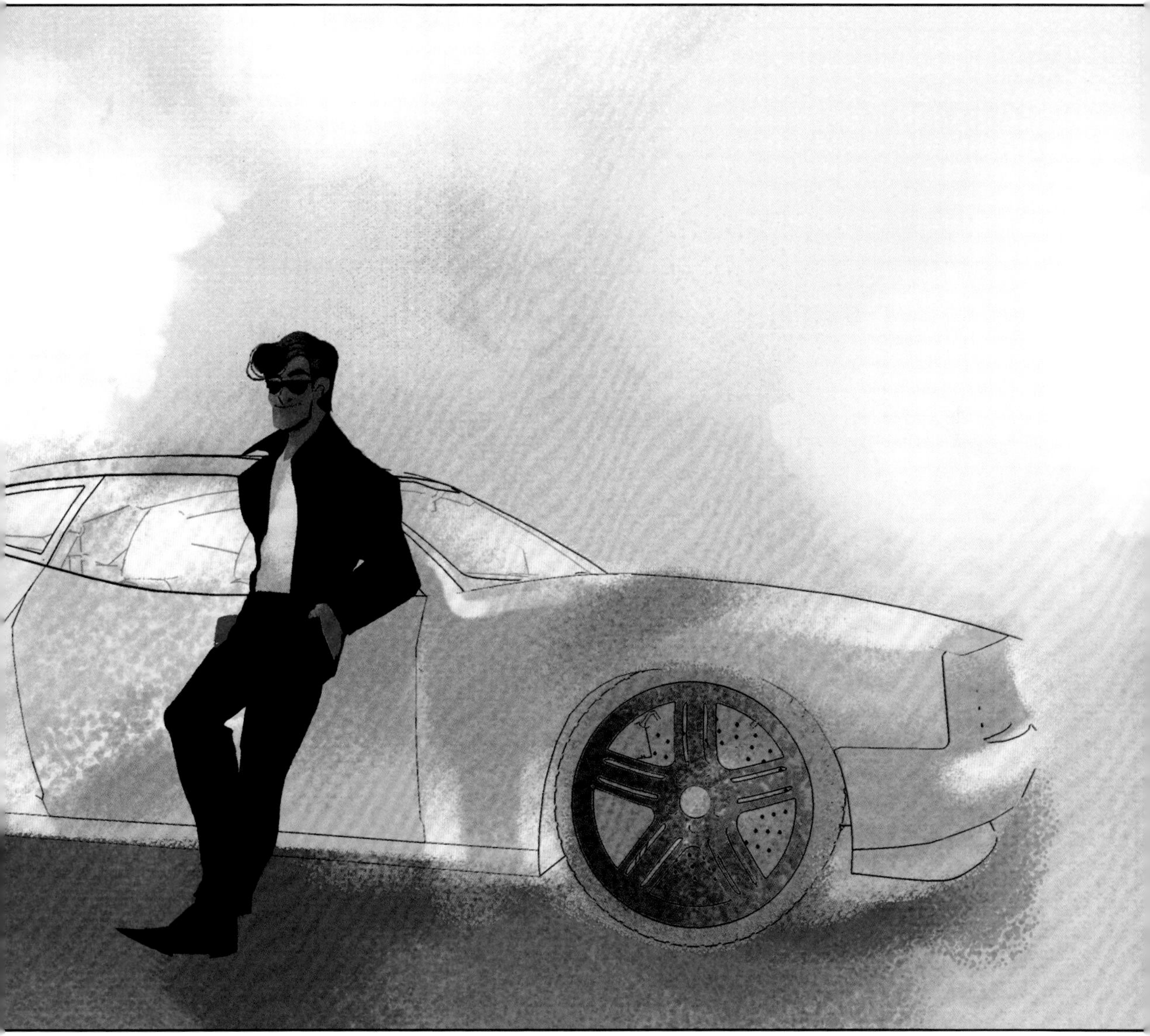

He's coming over for dinner.

You'll get a chance to meet him.

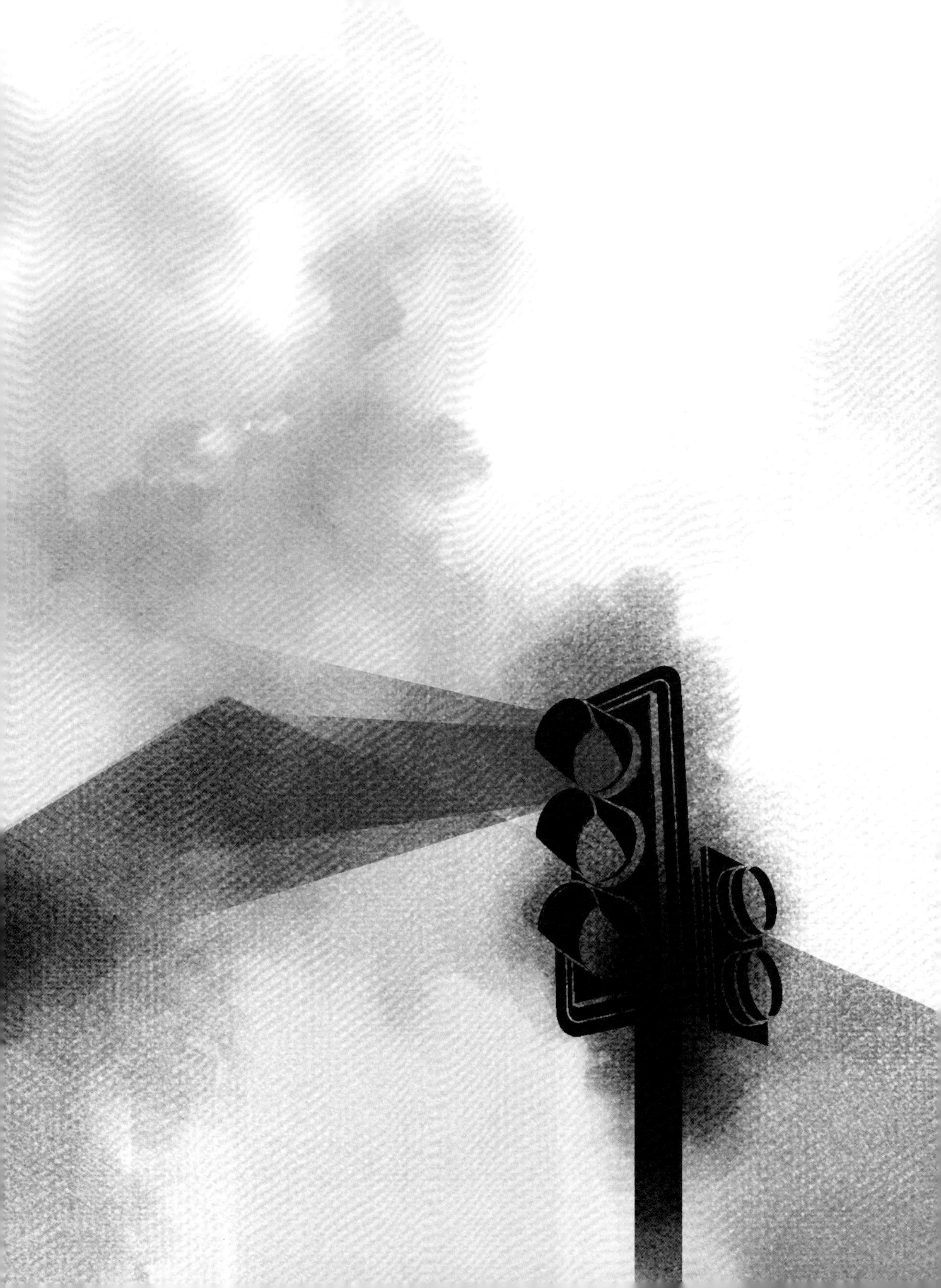

YOU HAVE FOUR VOICE MESSAGES.

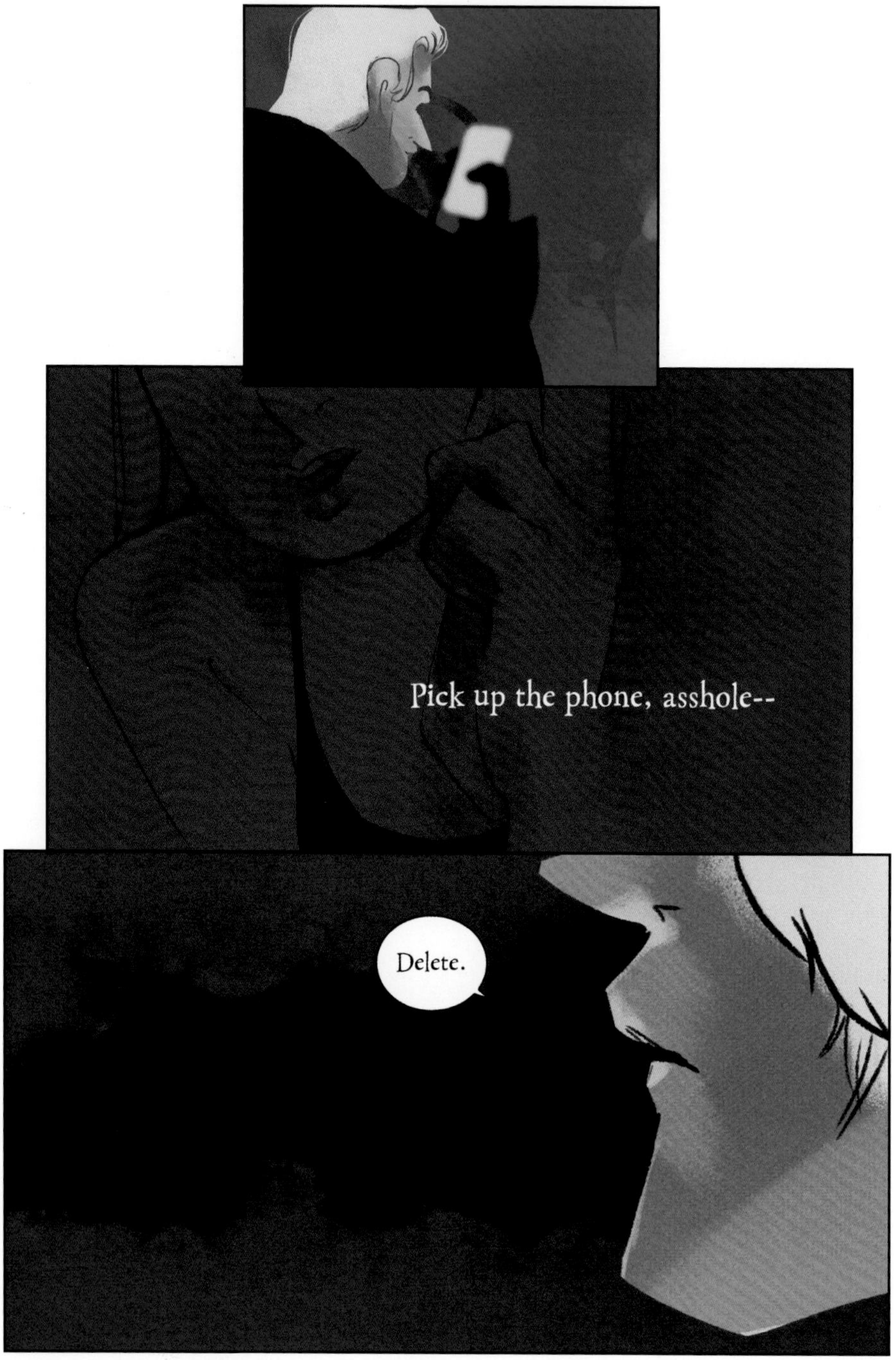
Pick up the phone, asshole--
Delete.

I thought you were going to come
over after the party--

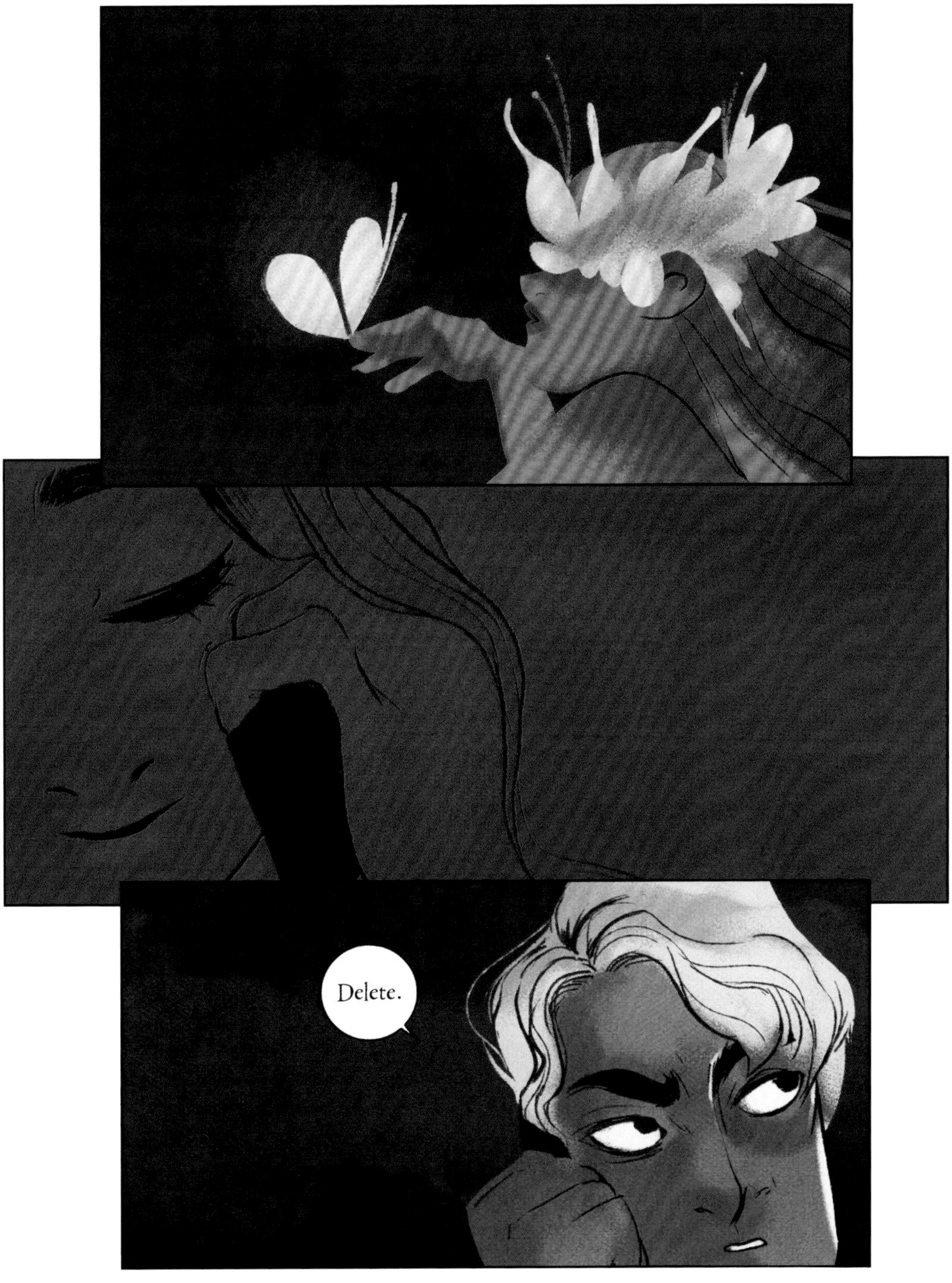
Delete.

What!? Huh!? You're just
going to sulk!?

Delete.

Come onnnnn, I'm sorry.

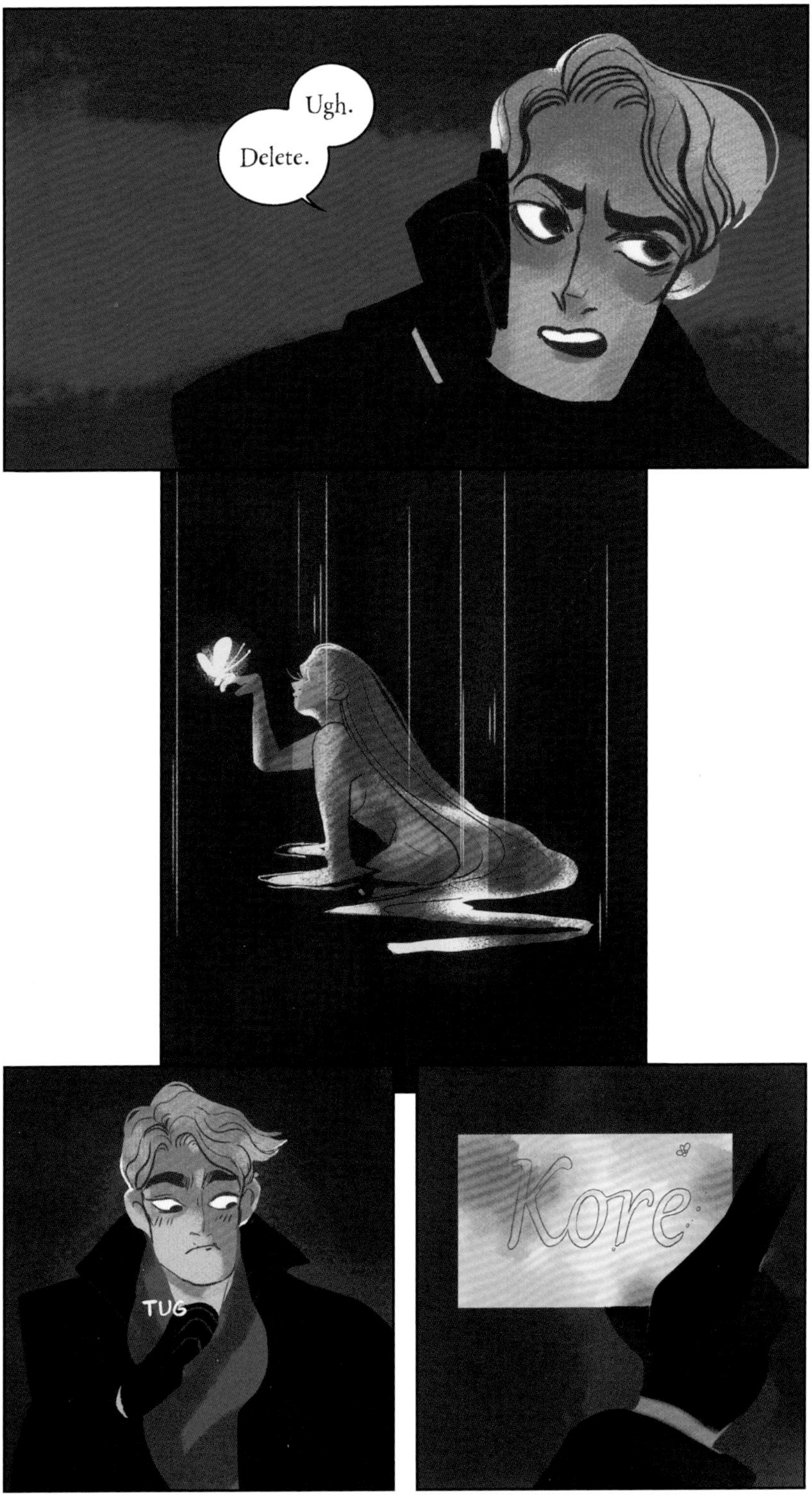
Ugh.
Delete.
TUG
Kore

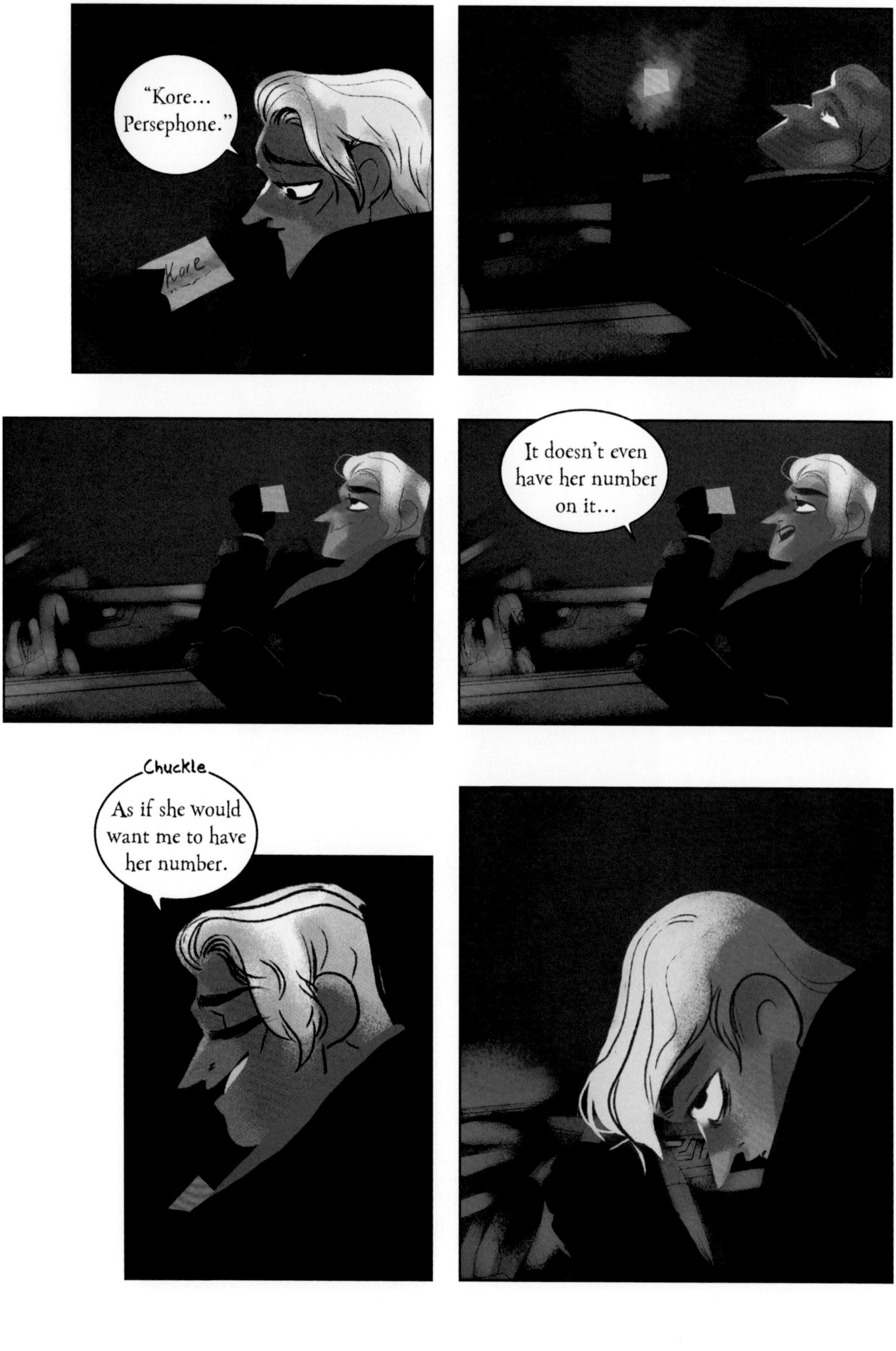
"Kore... Persephone."
Kore
It doesn't even have her number on it...
Chuckle
As if she would want me to have her number.

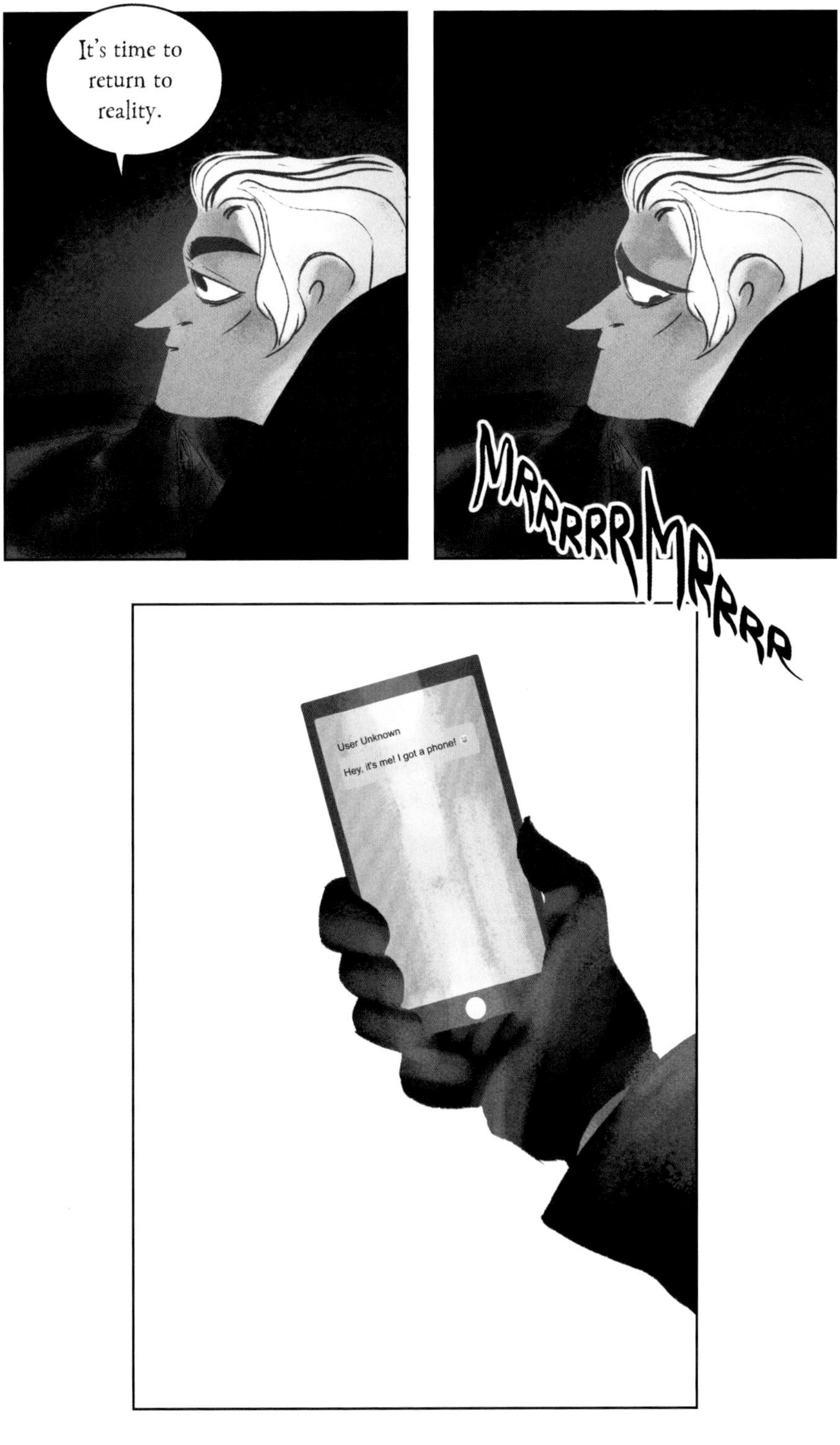
It's time to return to reality.
MRRRRR MRRRRR
User Unknown
Hey, it's me! I got a phone!

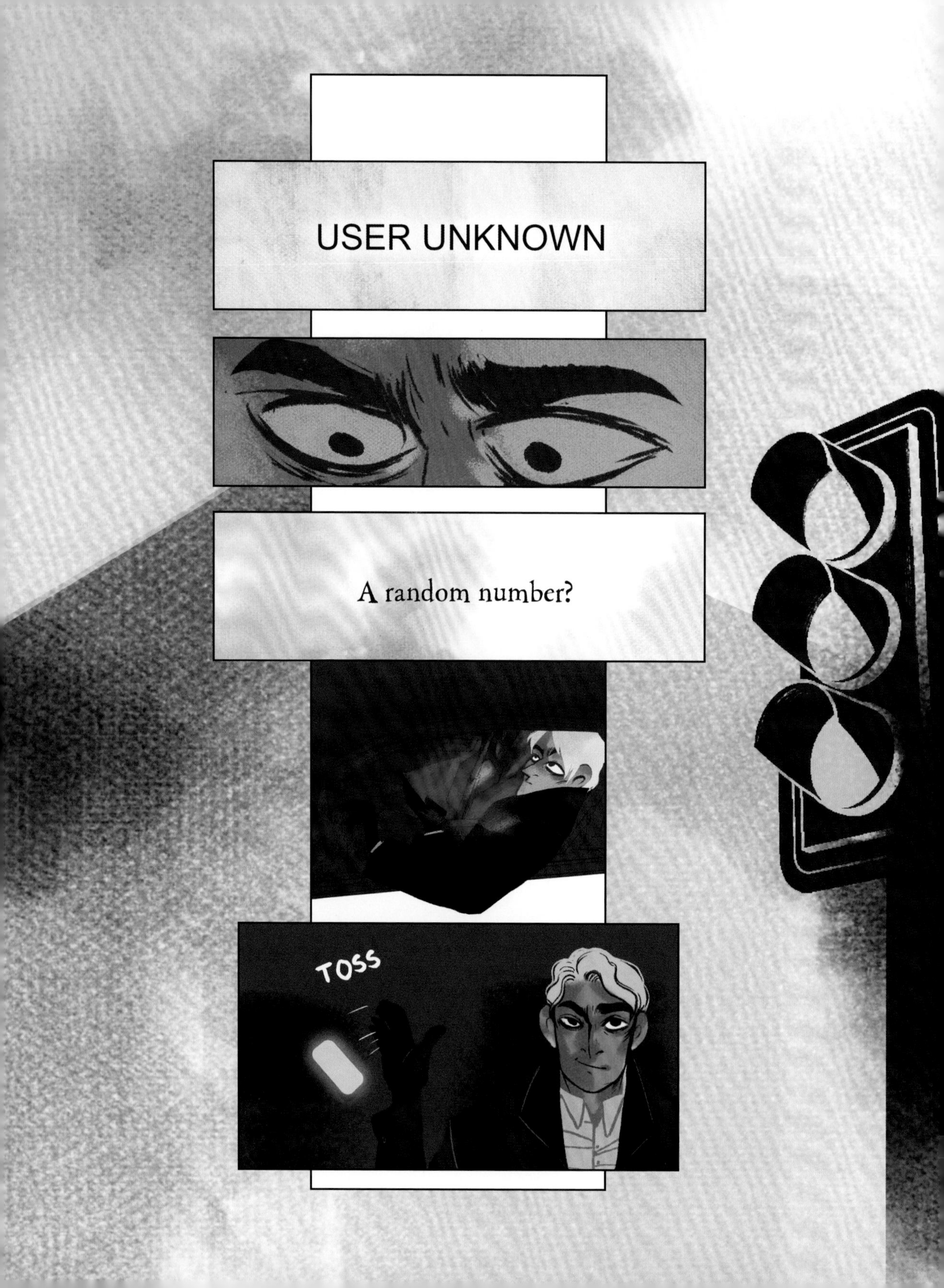
USER UNKNOWN
A random number?
TOSS

EPISODE 18: FOREST FOR THE TREES

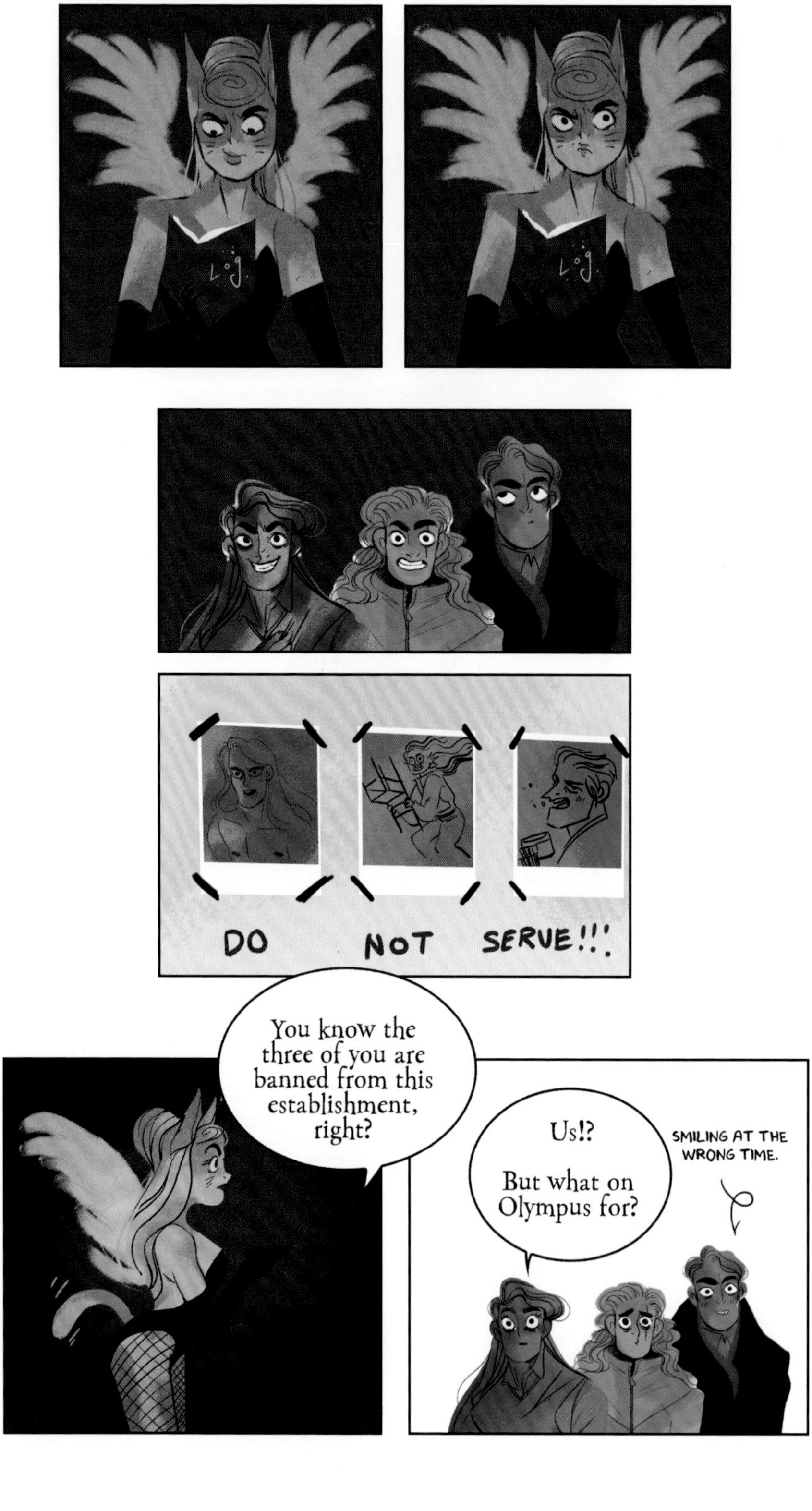
L.o.g.
DO NOT SERVE!!!
You know the three of you are banned from this establishment, right?
Us!? But what on Olympus for?
SMILING AT THE WRONG TIME.

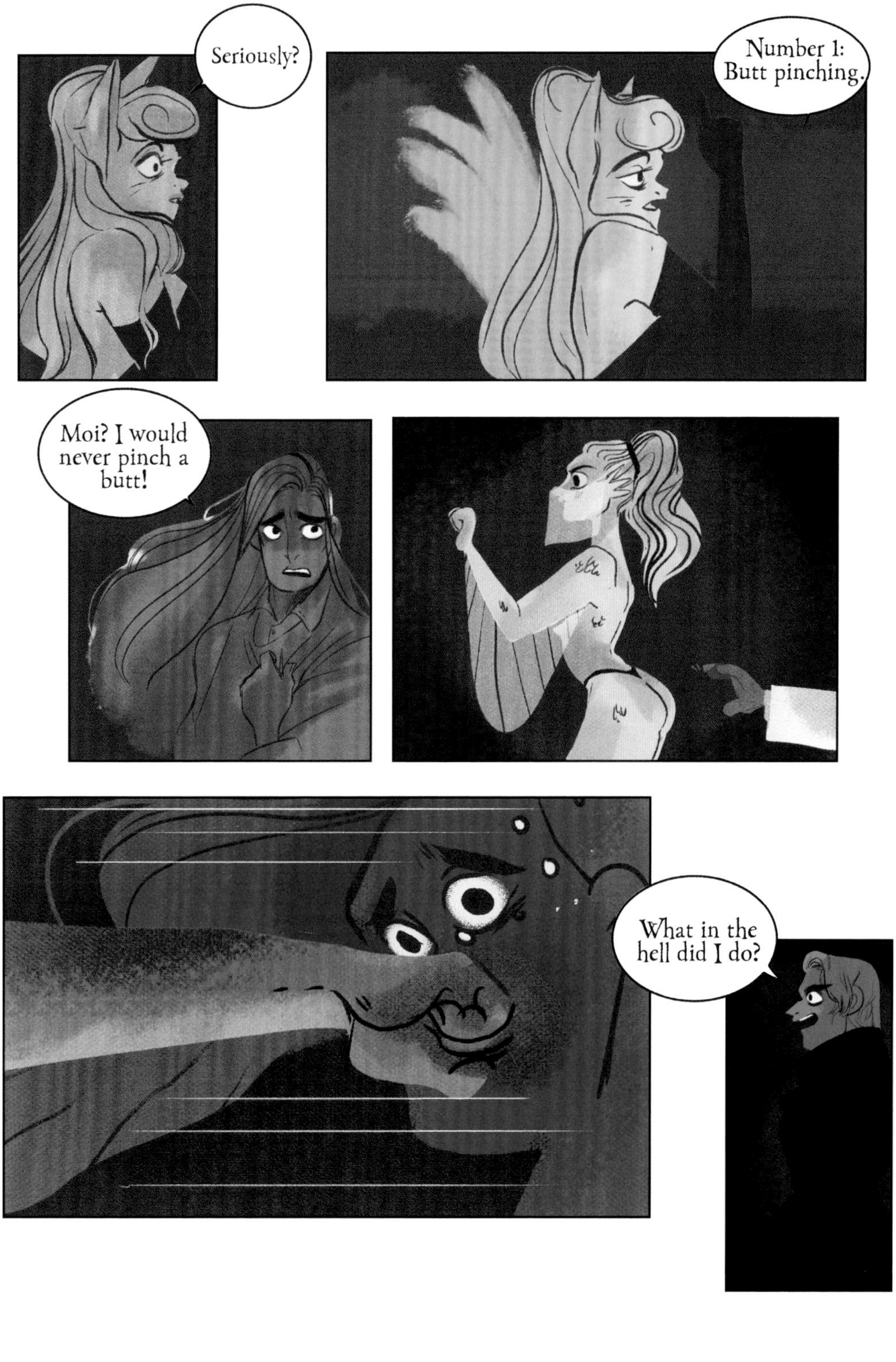
Seriously?
Number 1: Butt pinching.
Moi? I would never pinch a butt!
What in the hell did I do?

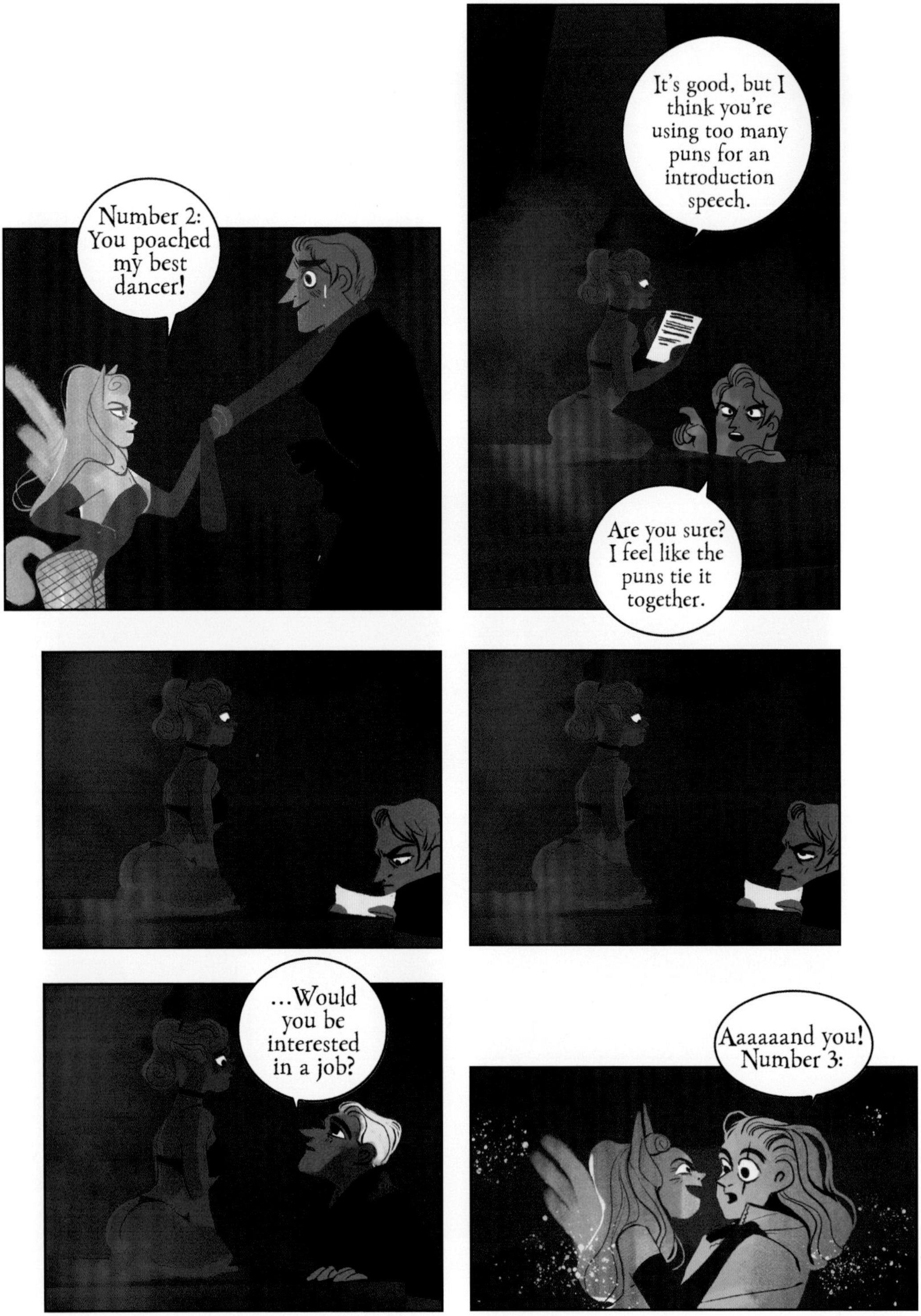
Number 2: You poached my best dancer!
It's good, but I think you're using too many puns for an introduction speech.
Are you sure? I feel like the puns tie it together.
...Would you be interested in a job?
Aaaaaand you! Number 3:

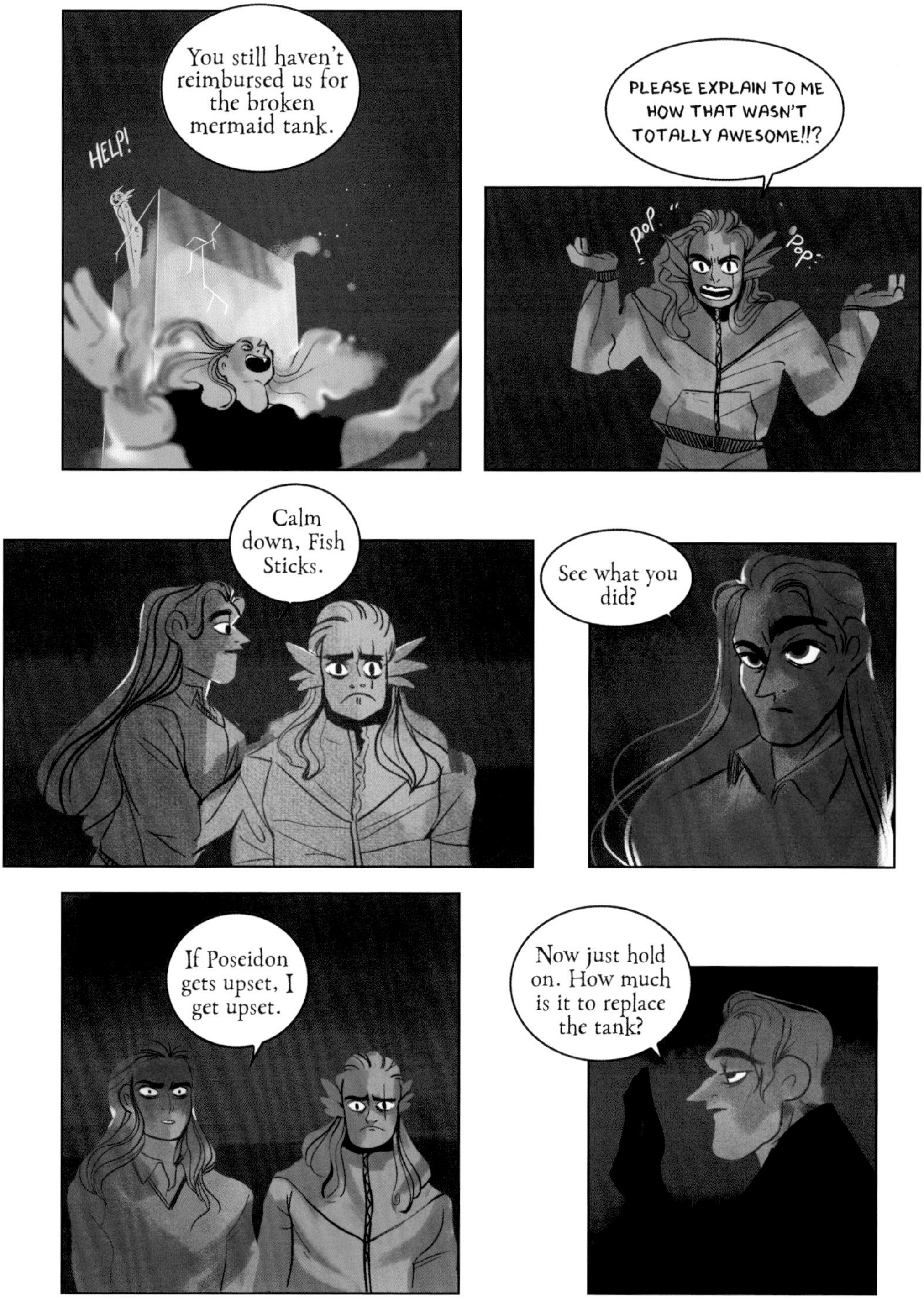
You still haven't reimbursed us for the broken mermaid tank.
HELP!
PLEASE EXPLAIN TO ME HOW THAT WASN'T TOTALLY AWESOME!!?
POP.
POP.
Calm down, Fish Sticks.
See what you did?
If Poseidon gets upset, I get upset.
Now just hold on. How much is it to replace the tank?

MMM...
2000 drachmas!
Do you take diamonds?

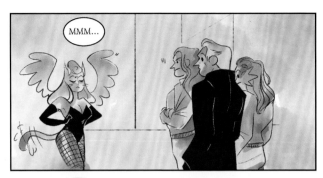

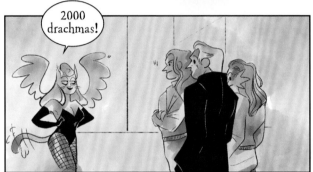

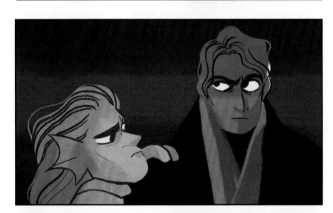

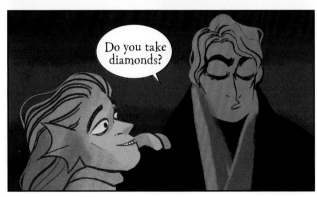

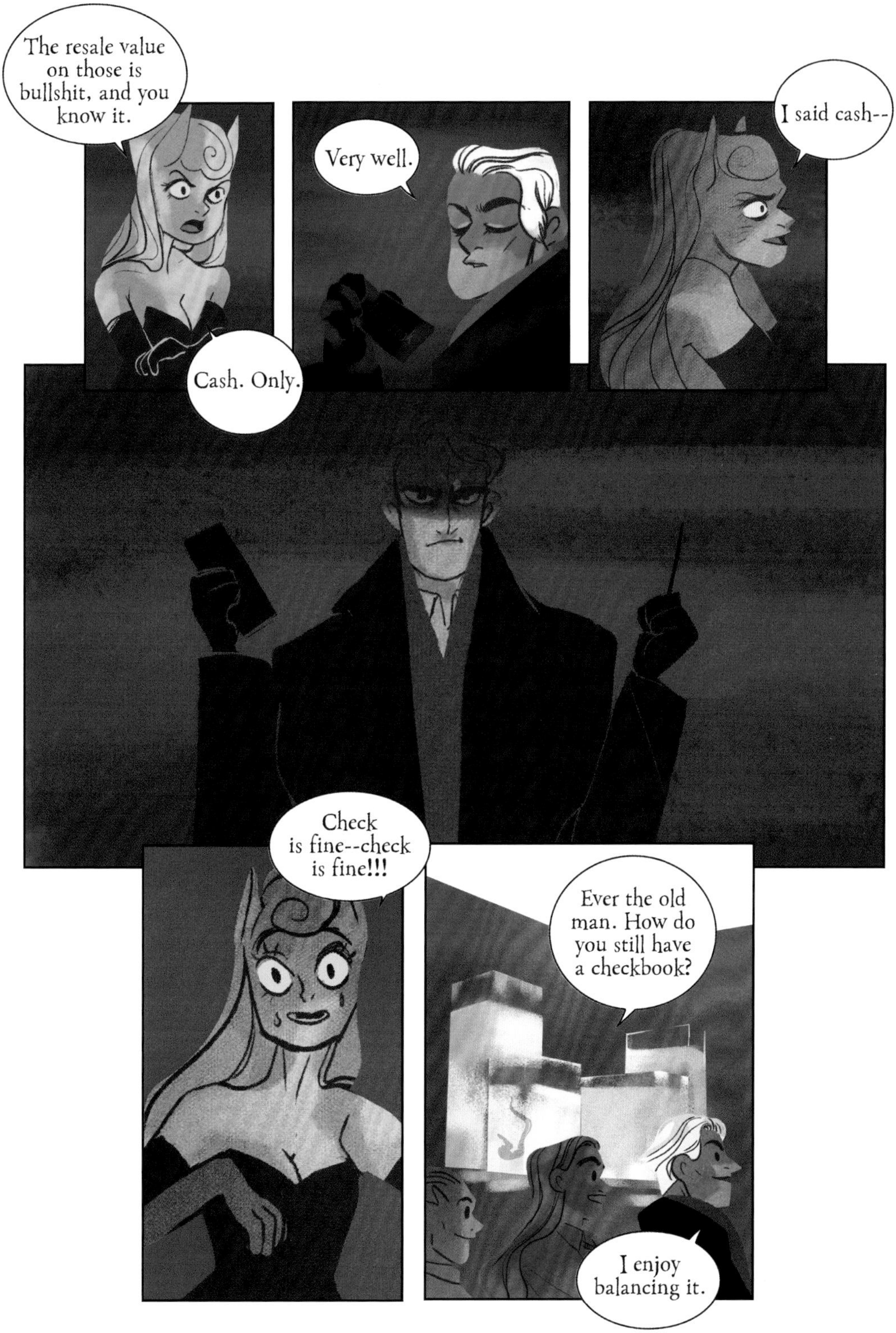
The resale value on those is bullshit, and you know it.
Cash. Only.
Very well.
I said cash--
Check is fine--check is fine!!!
Ever the old man. How do you still have a checkbook?
I enjoy balancing it.

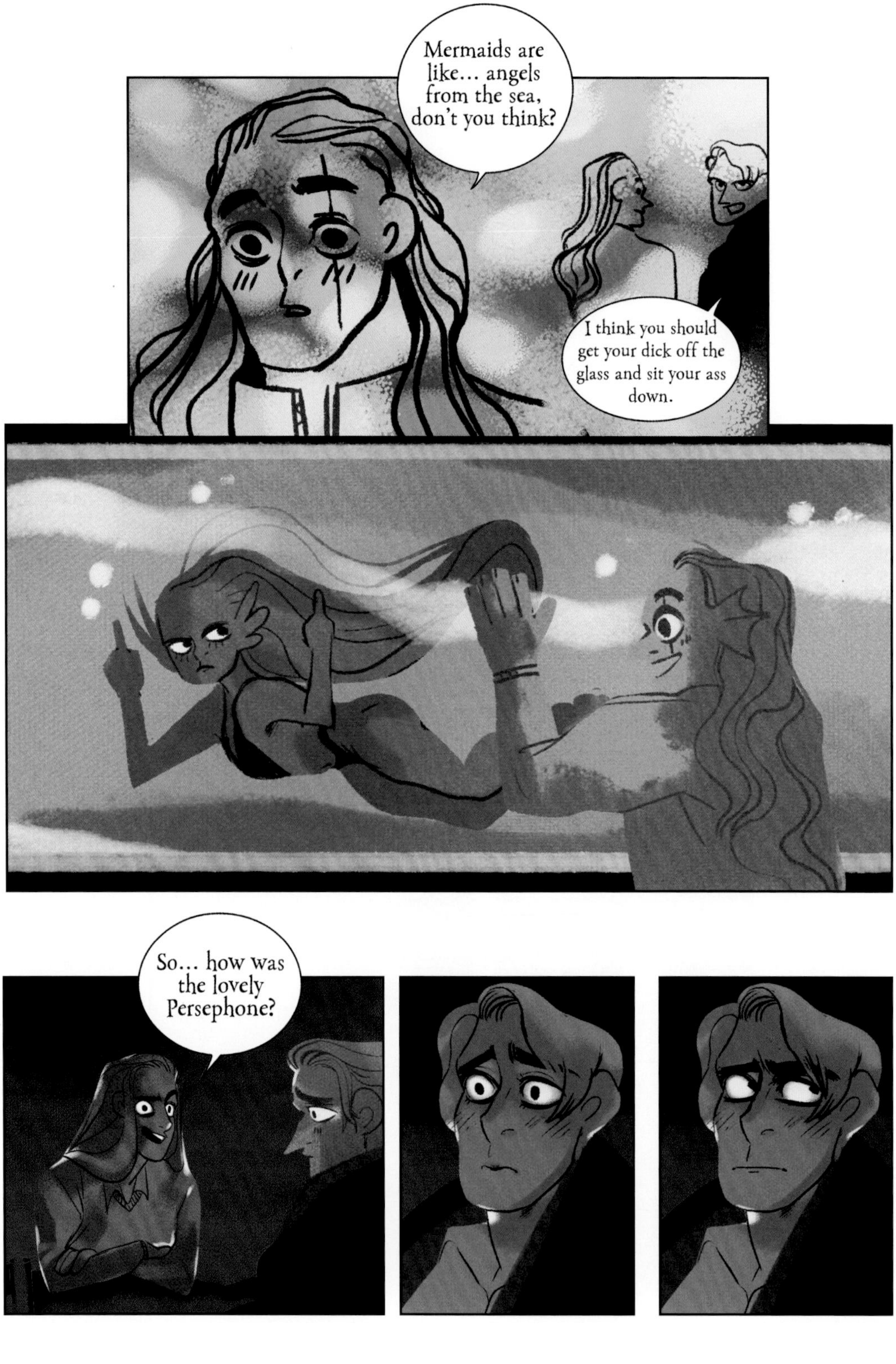
Mermaids are like… angels from the sea, don't you think?
I think you should get your dick off the glass and sit your ass down.
So… how was the lovely Persephone?

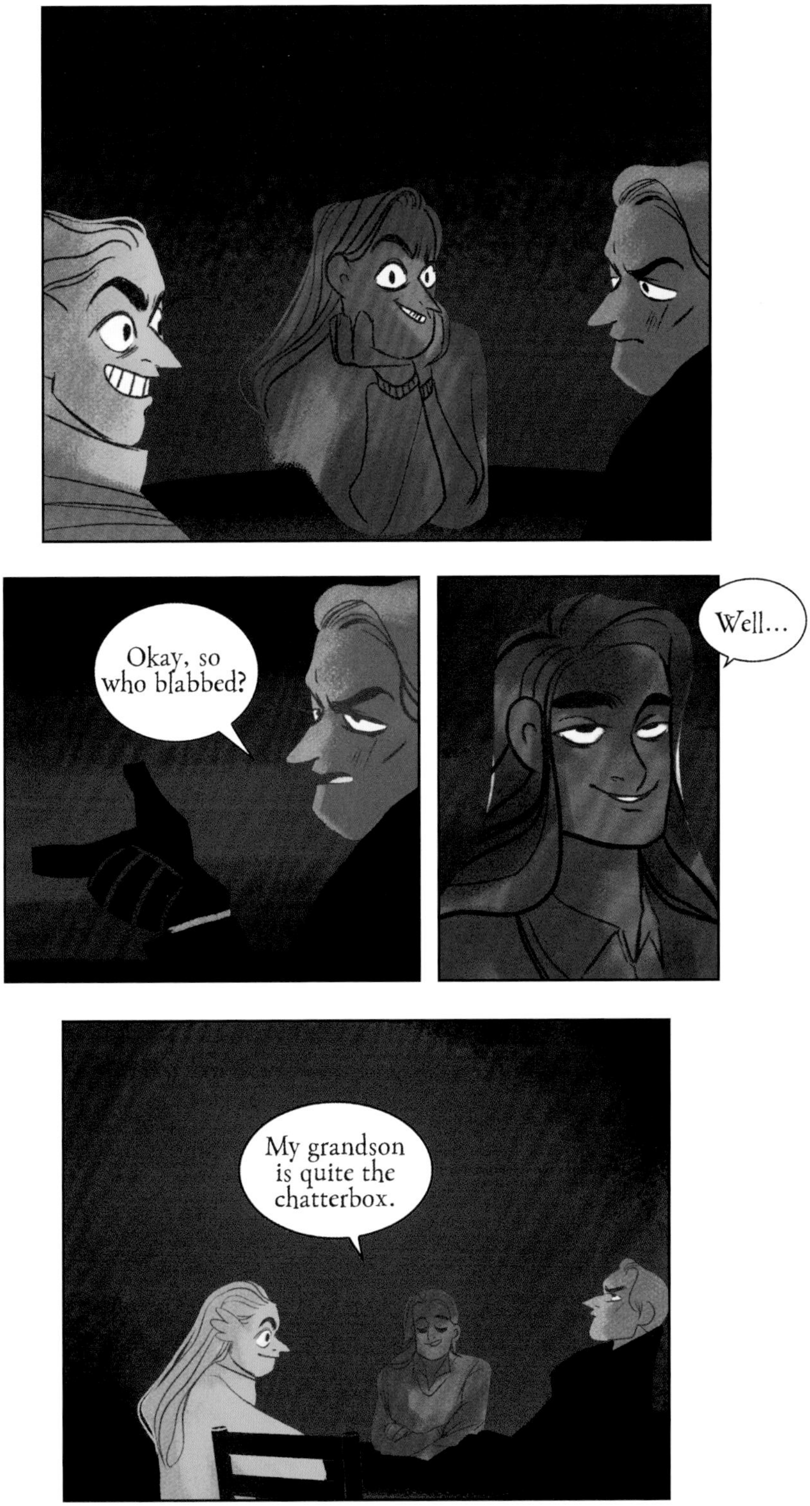
Okay, so who blabbed?
Well...
My grandson is quite the chatterbox.

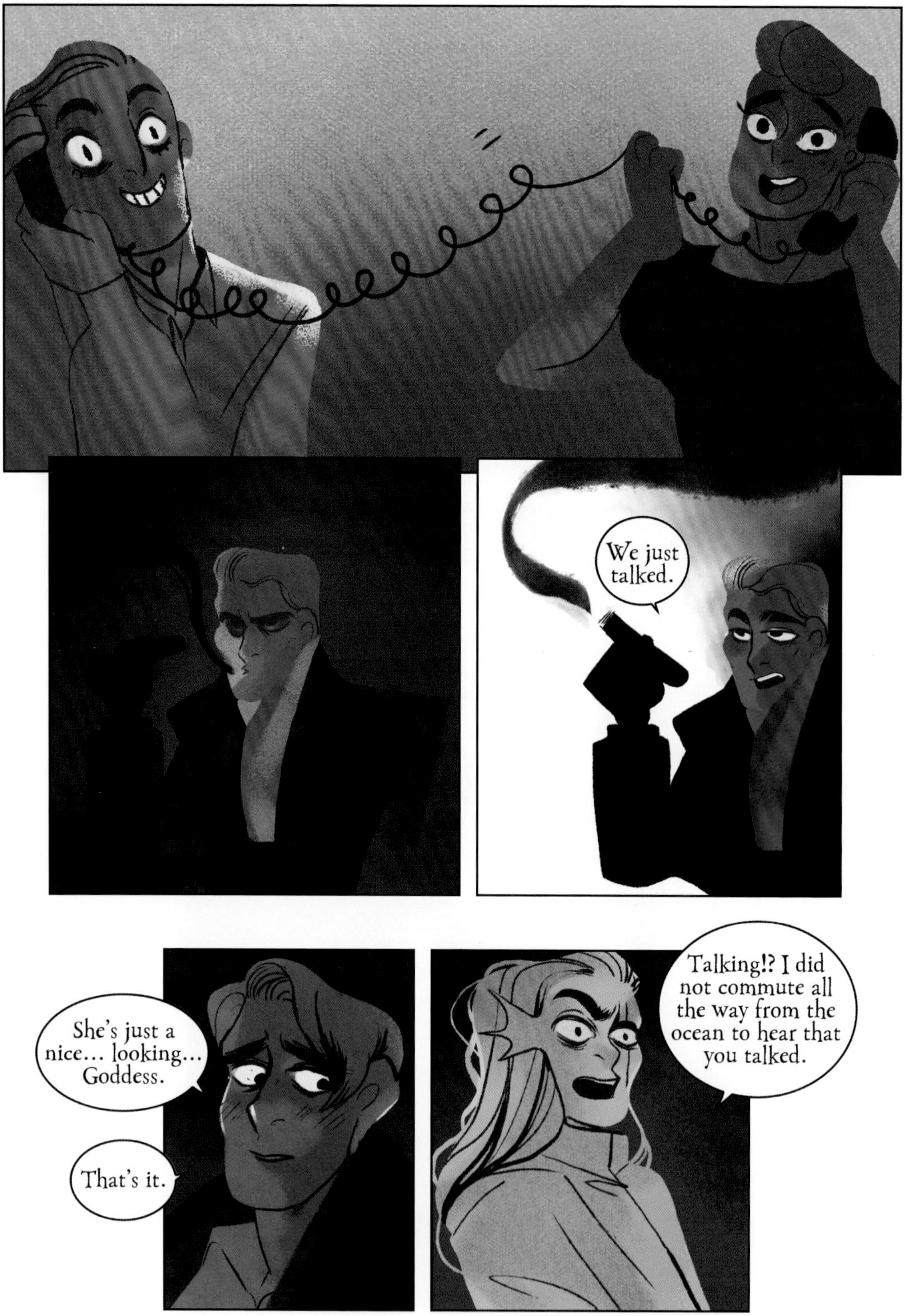
We just talked.
She's just a nice... looking... Goddess.
That's it.
Talking!? I did not commute all the way from the ocean to hear that you talked.

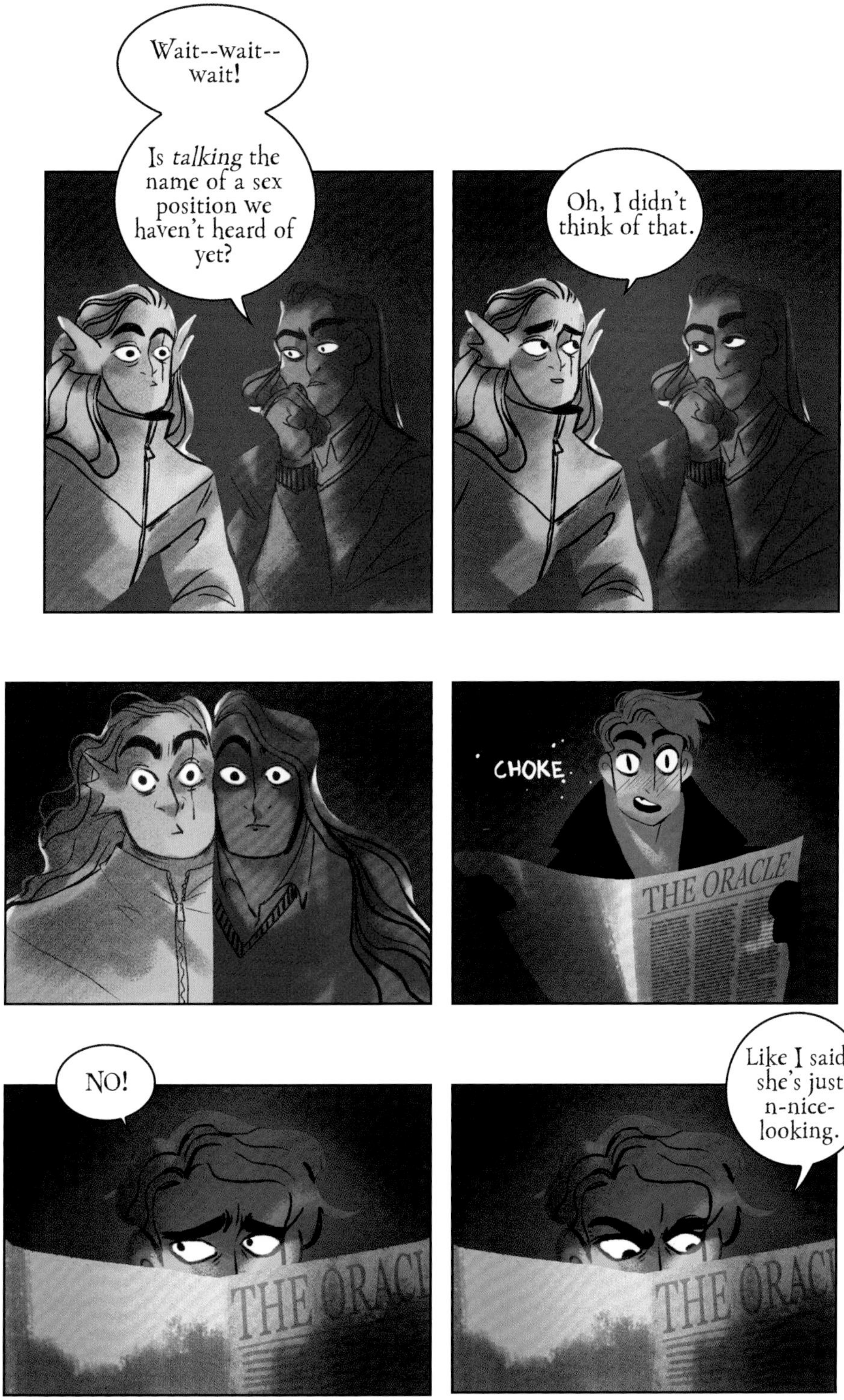

Wait--wait--wait!
Is *talking* the name of a sex position we haven't heard of yet?
Oh, I didn't think of that.
CHOKE.
THE ORACLE
NO!
Like I said, she's just n-nice-looking.

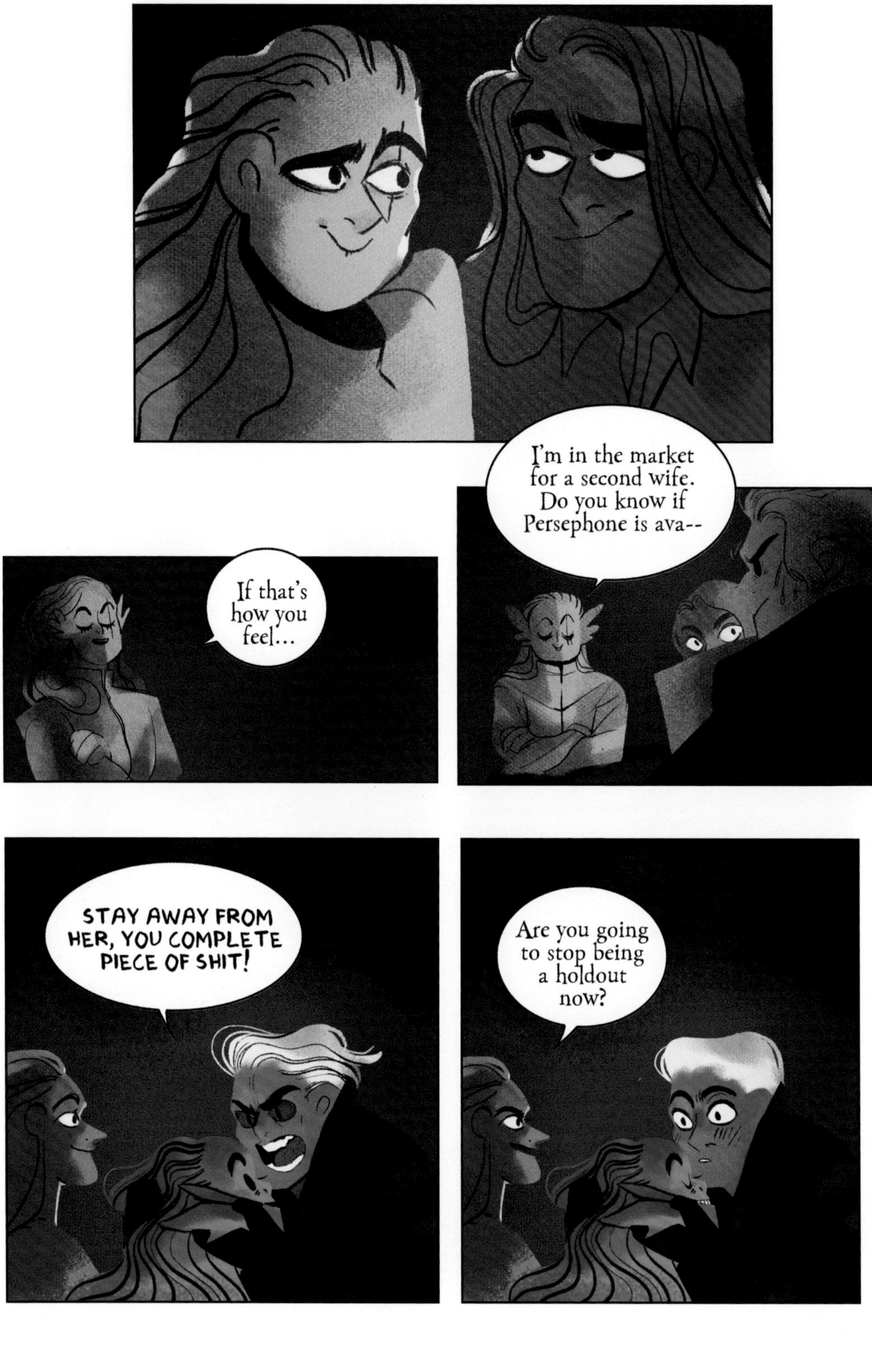
If that's how you feel...
I'm in the market for a second wife. Do you know if Persephone is ava--
STAY AWAY FROM HER, YOU COMPLETE PIECE OF SHIT!
Are you going to stop being a holdout now?

EPISODE 19: A FIFTH OF GIN

S-sorry, buddy.

Yeah--um--sorry.

PAT PAT

Fine...

I can't...

HESITATE

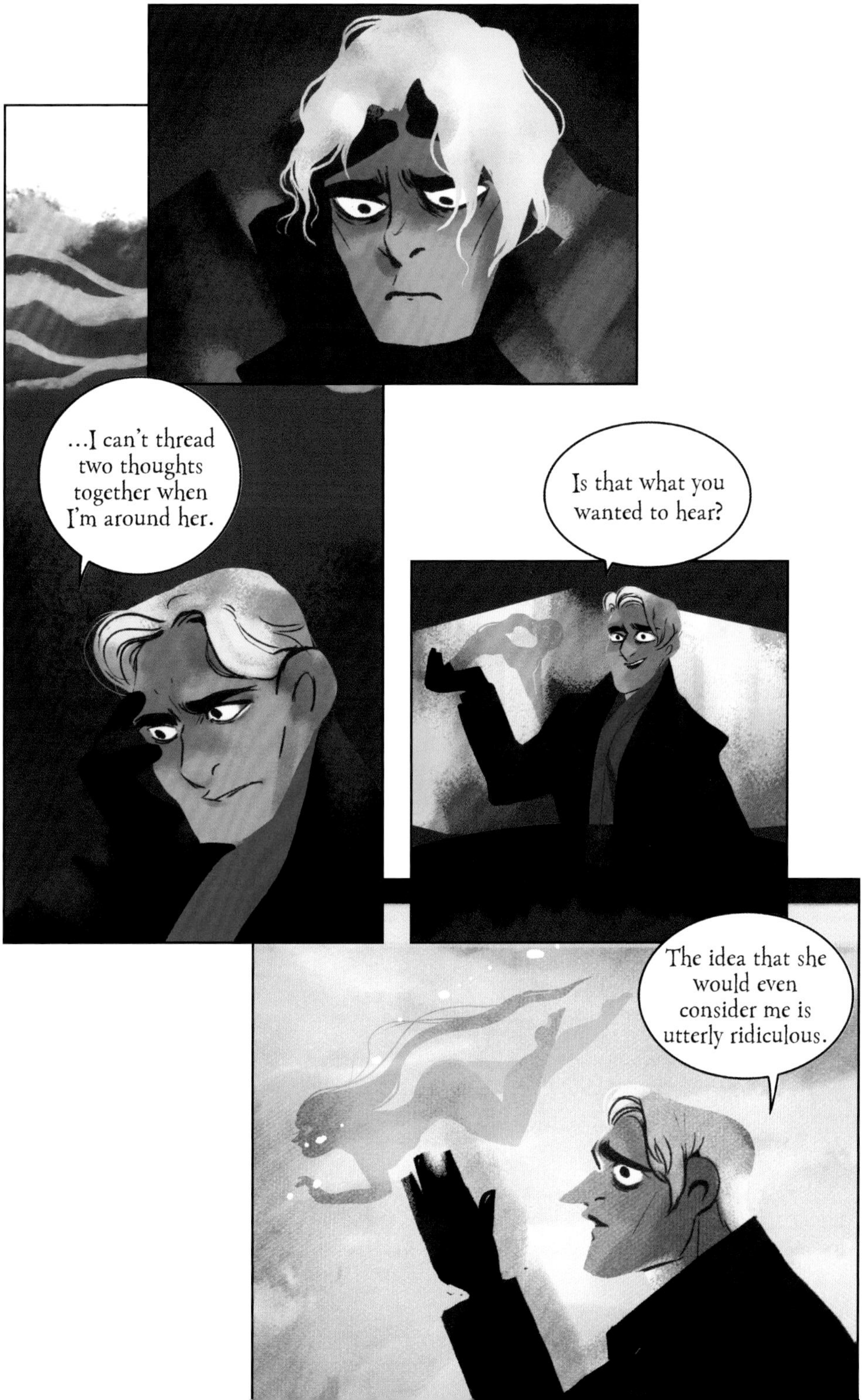
...I can't thread two thoughts together when I'm around her.
Is that what you wanted to hear?
The idea that she would even consider me is utterly ridiculous.

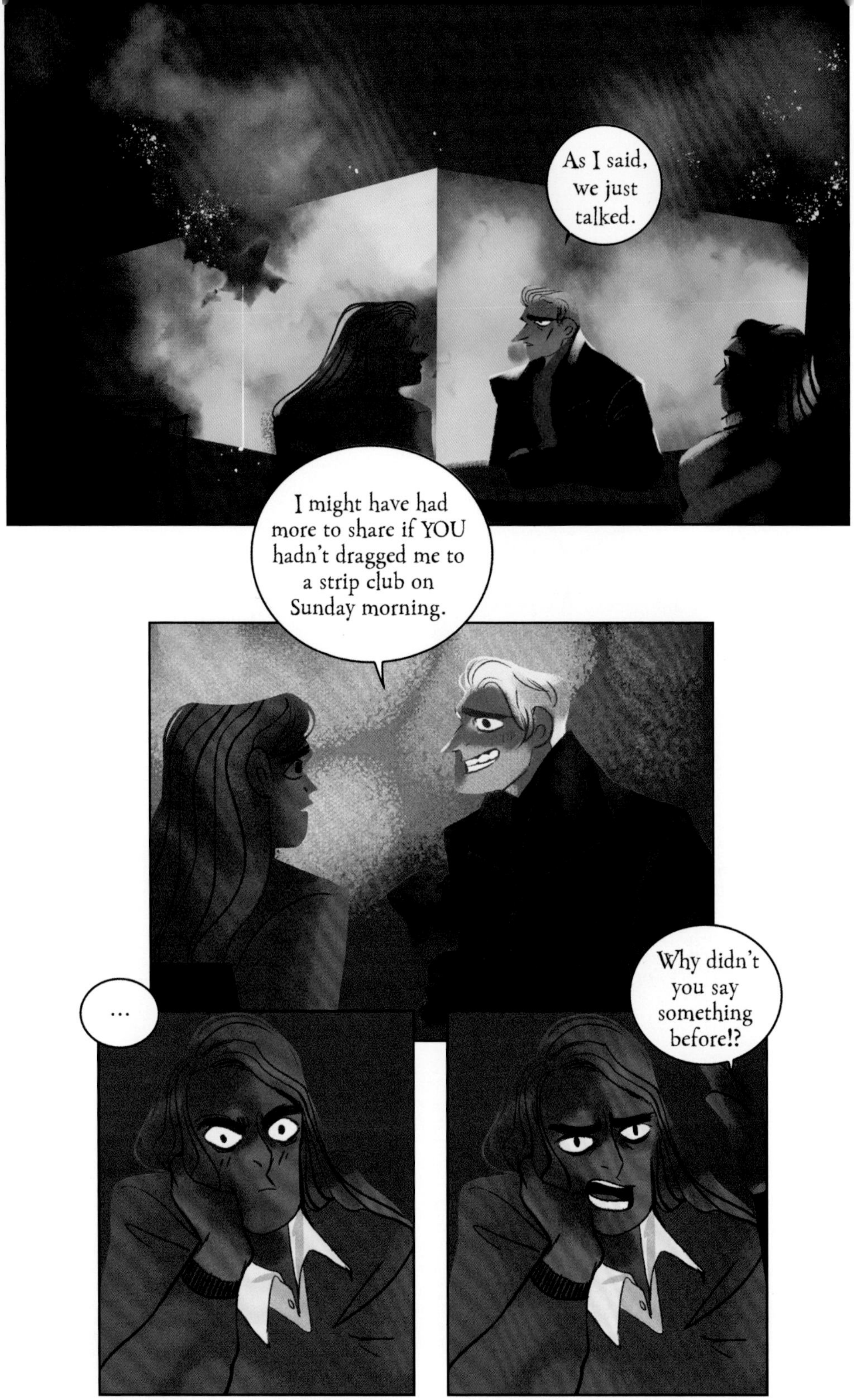

As I said, we just talked.
I might have had more to share if YOU hadn't dragged me to a strip club on Sunday morning.
...
Why didn't you say something before!?

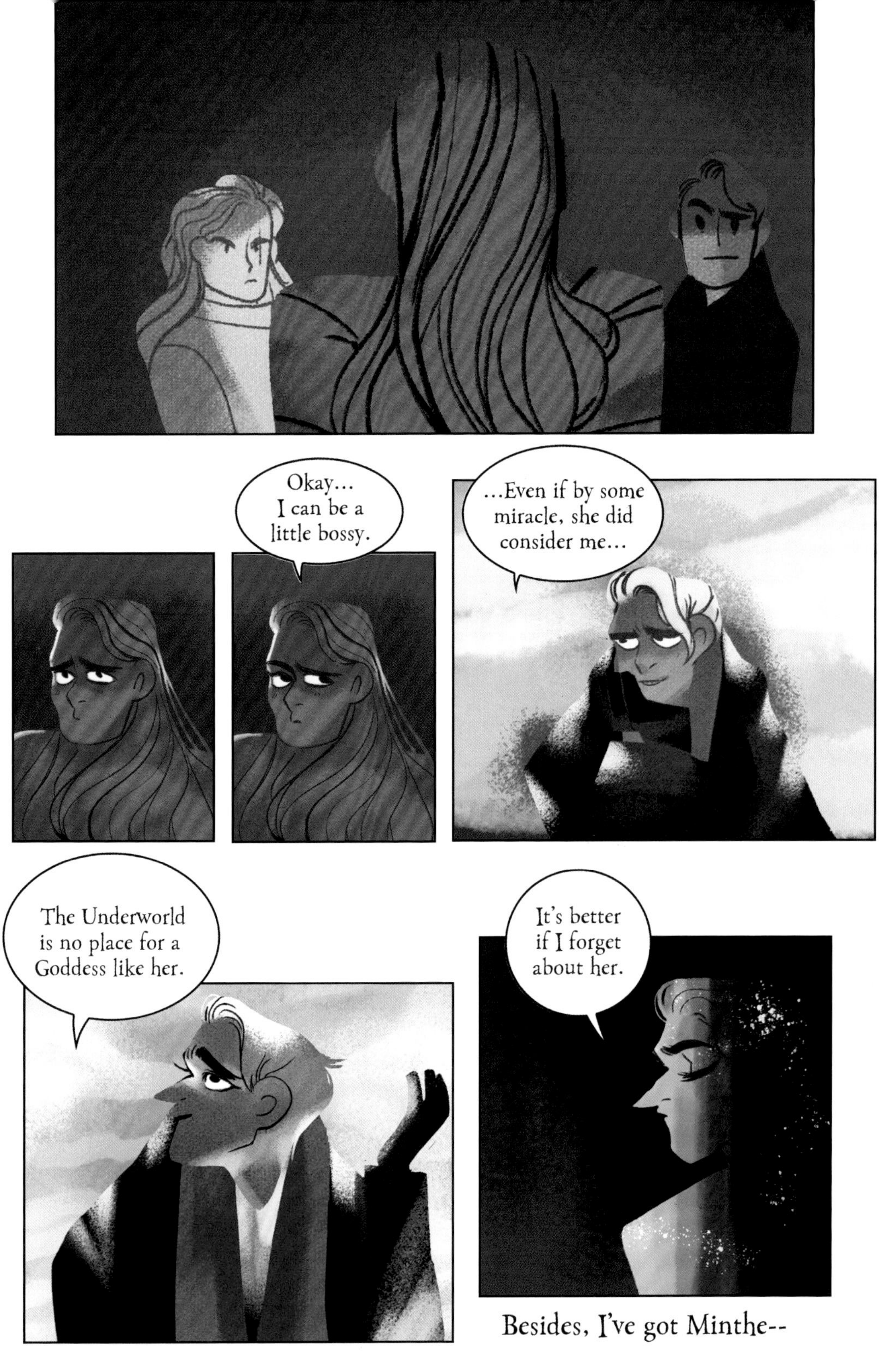
Okay...
I can be a
little bossy.
...Even if by some
miracle, she did
consider me...
The Underworld
is no place for a
Goddess like her.
It's better
if I forget
about her.
Besides, I've got Minthe--

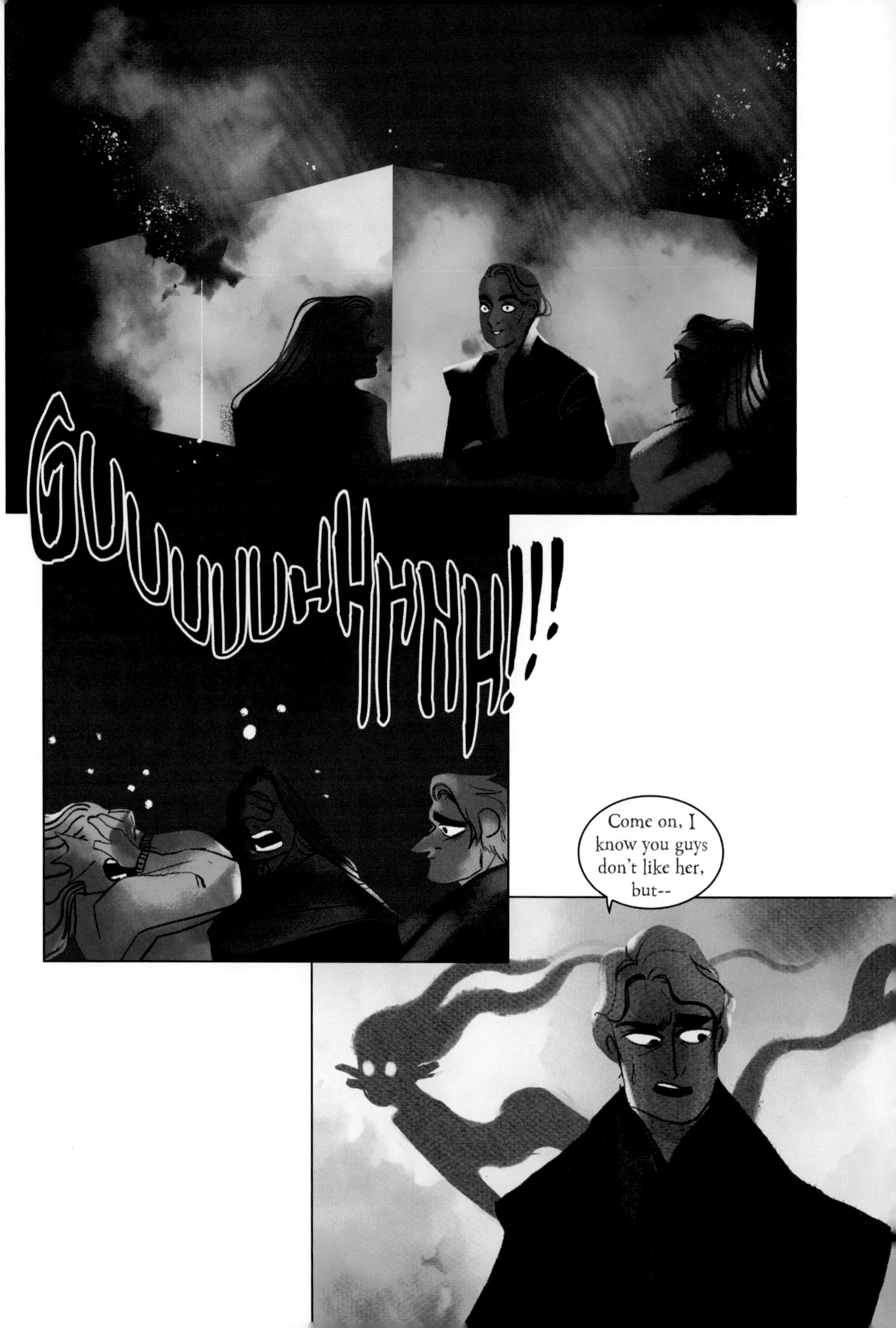
GUUUUUHHHH!!!
Come on, I know you guys don't like her, but--

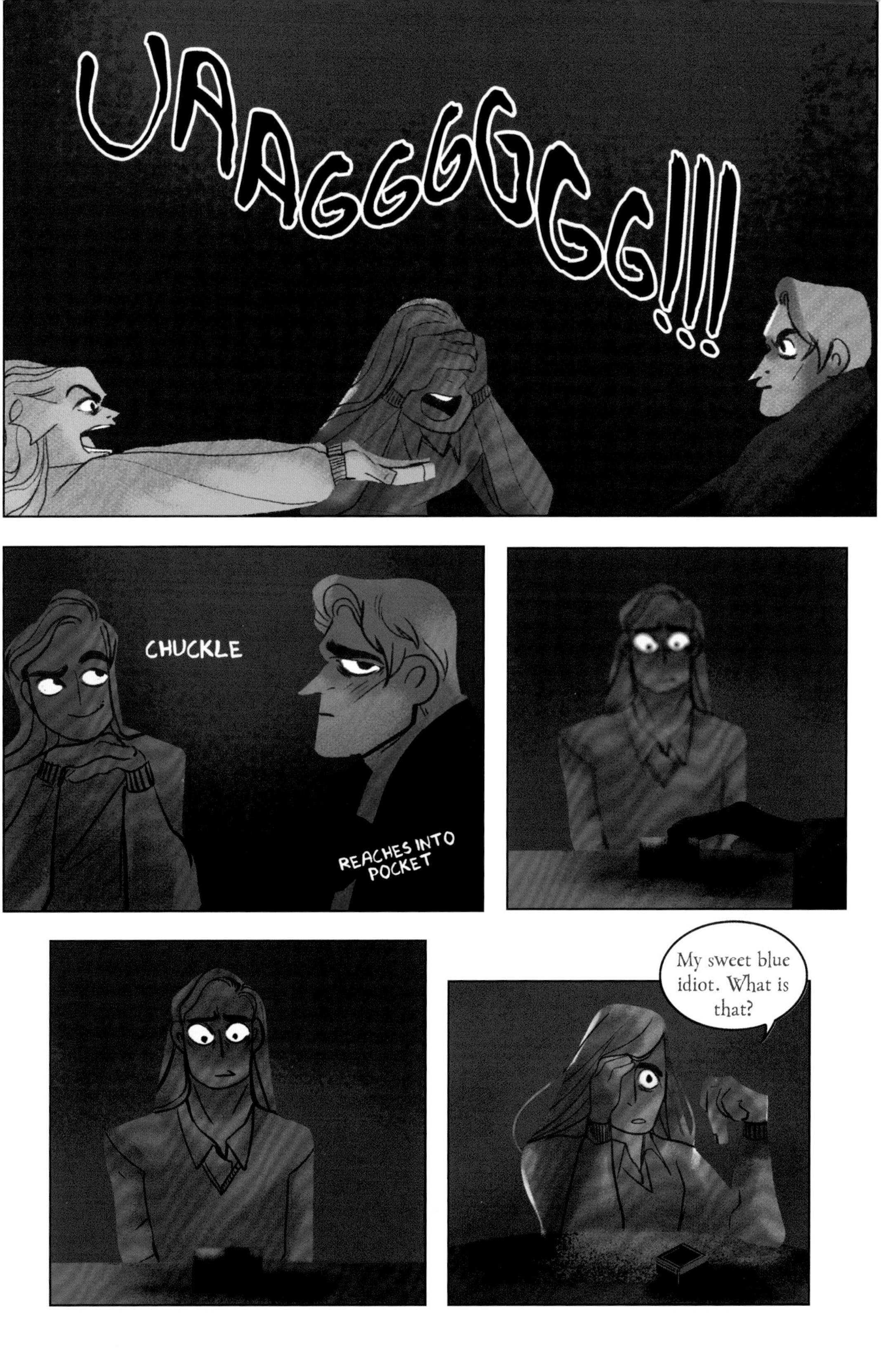
UAAGGGGGG!!!
CHUCKLE
REACHES INTO POCKET
My sweet blue idiot. What is that?

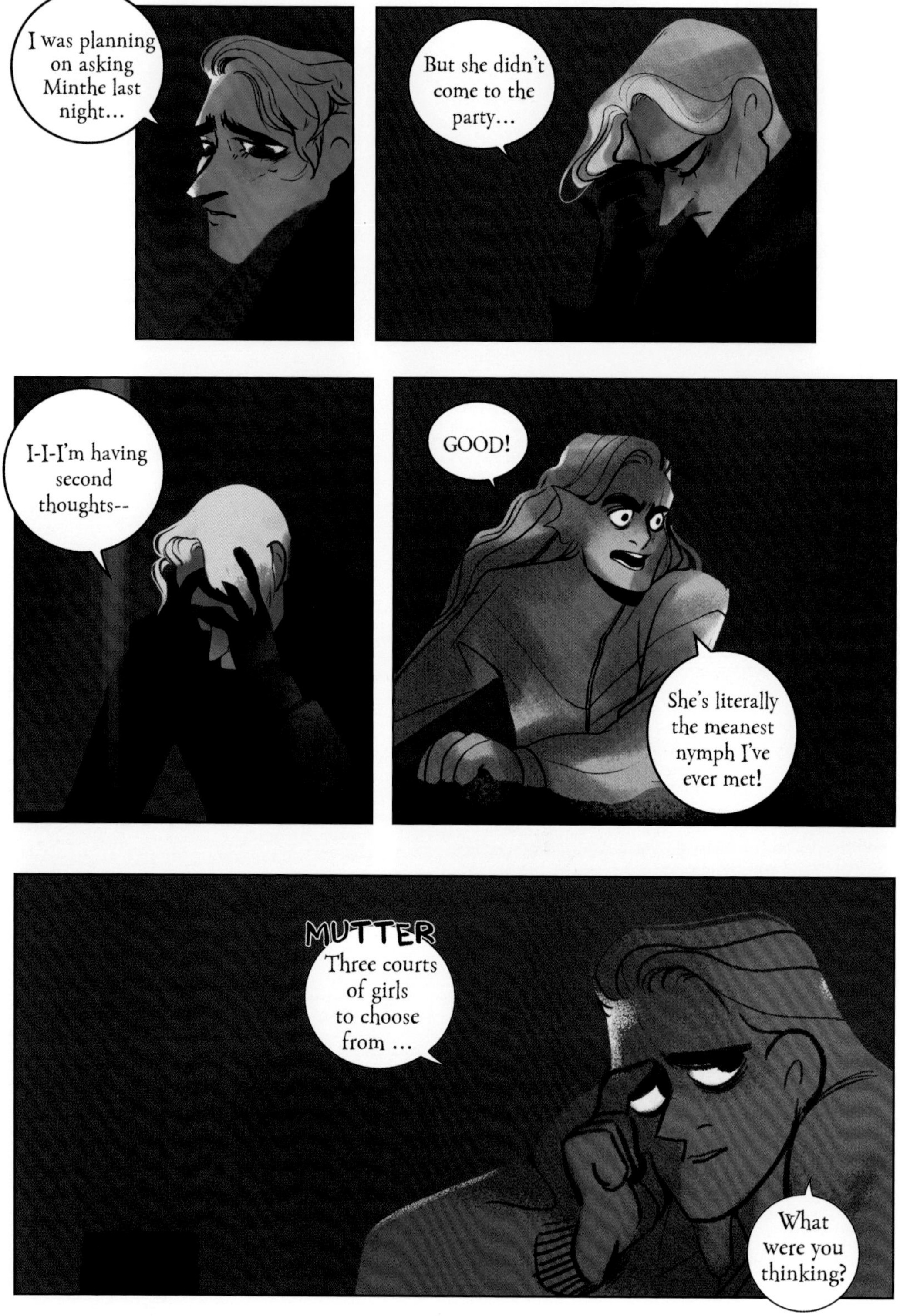
I was planning on asking Minthe last night...
But she didn't come to the party...
I-I-I'm having second thoughts--
GOOD!
She's literally the meanest nymph I've ever met!
MUTTER
Three courts of girls to choose from ...
What were you thinking?

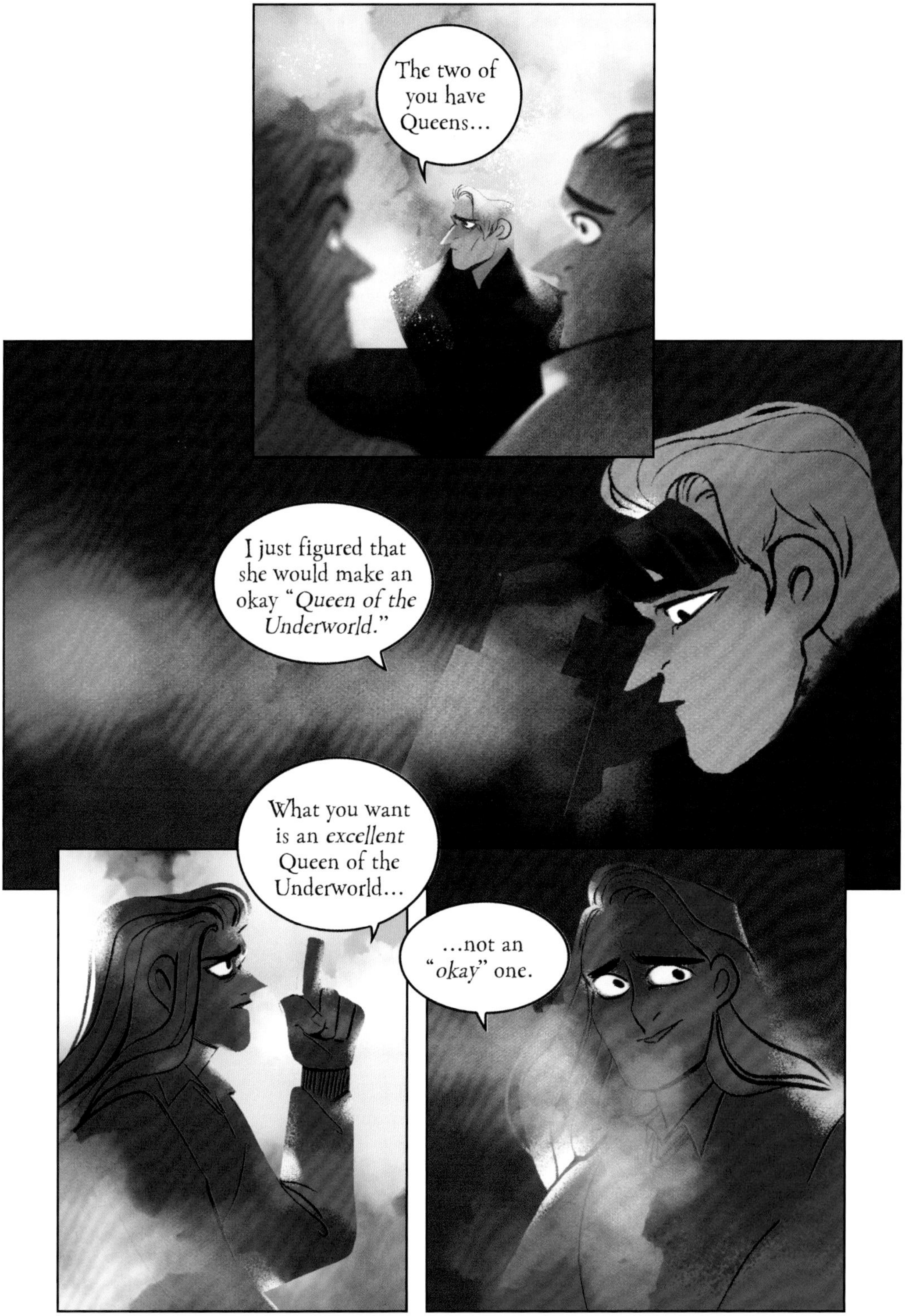
The two of you have Queens...
I just figured that she would make an okay "*Queen of the Underworld*."
What you want is an *excellent* Queen of the Underworld...
...not an "*okay*" one.

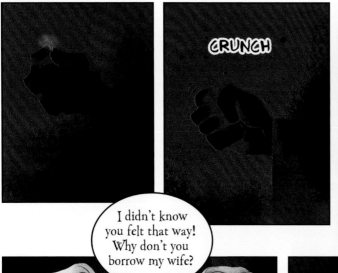

CRUNCH

I didn't know you felt that way! Why don't you borrow my wife?

No--no! It's fine.

But that Persephone, huh?

She's nice, right?

TUCK

She possesses a melancholic quality that I can't quite put my finger on.

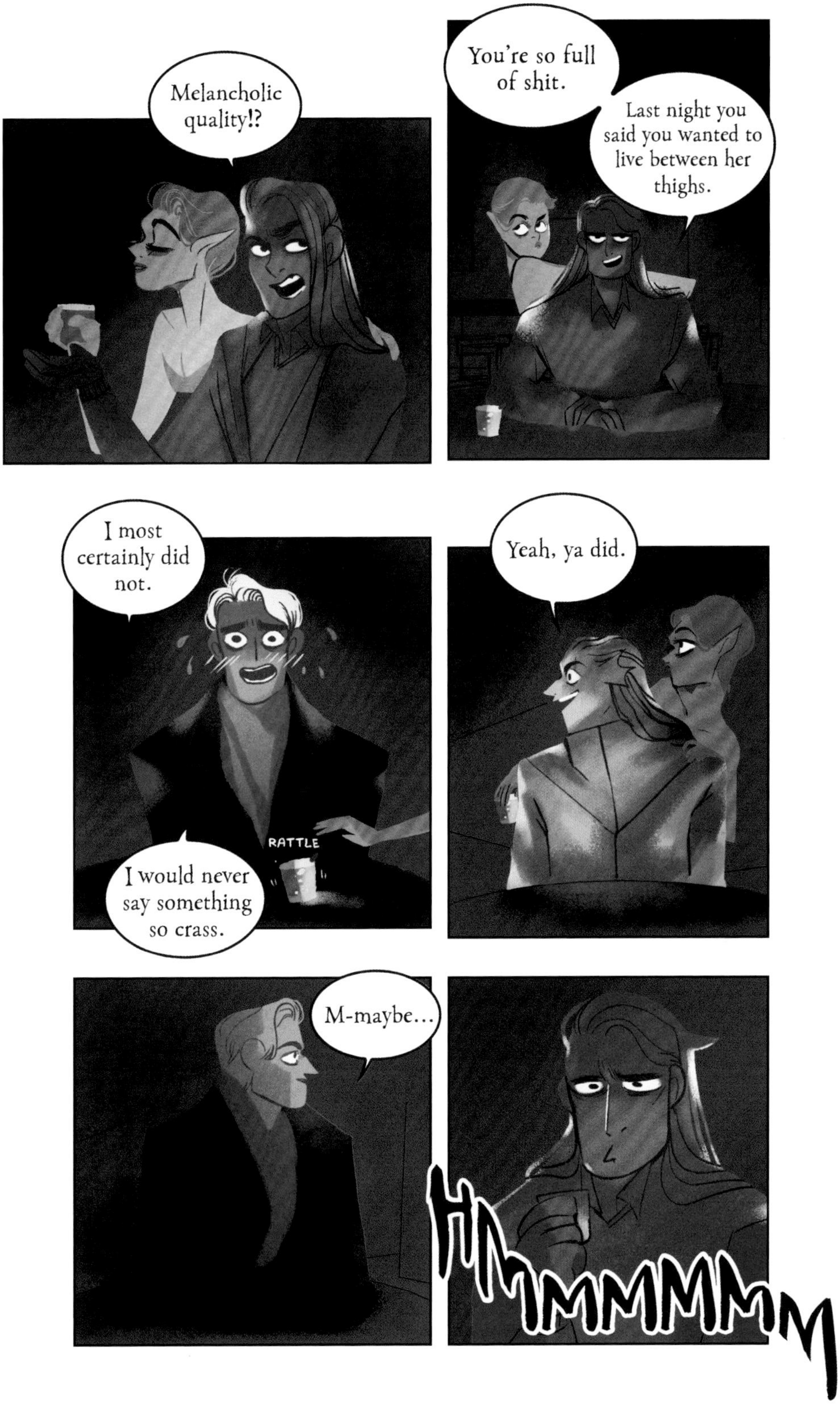
Melancholic quality!?
You're so full of shit.
Last night you said you wanted to live between her thighs.
I most certainly did not.
RATTLE
I would never say something so crass.
Yeah, ya did.
M-maybe...
HMMMMMMM

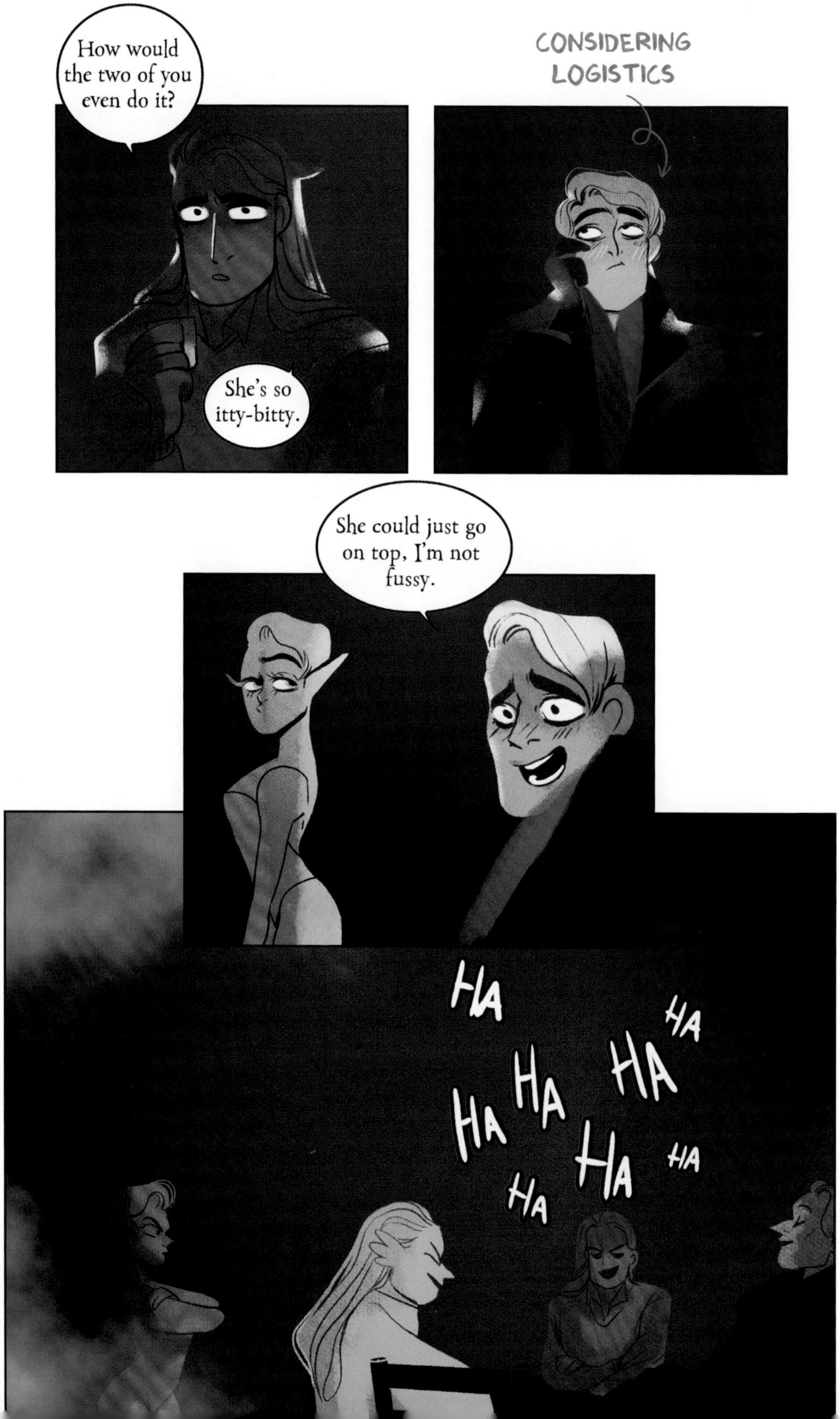
How would the two of you even do it?
She's so itty-bitty.
CONSIDERING LOGISTICS
She could just go on top, I'm not fussy.
HA HA HA HA HA HA HA HA HA

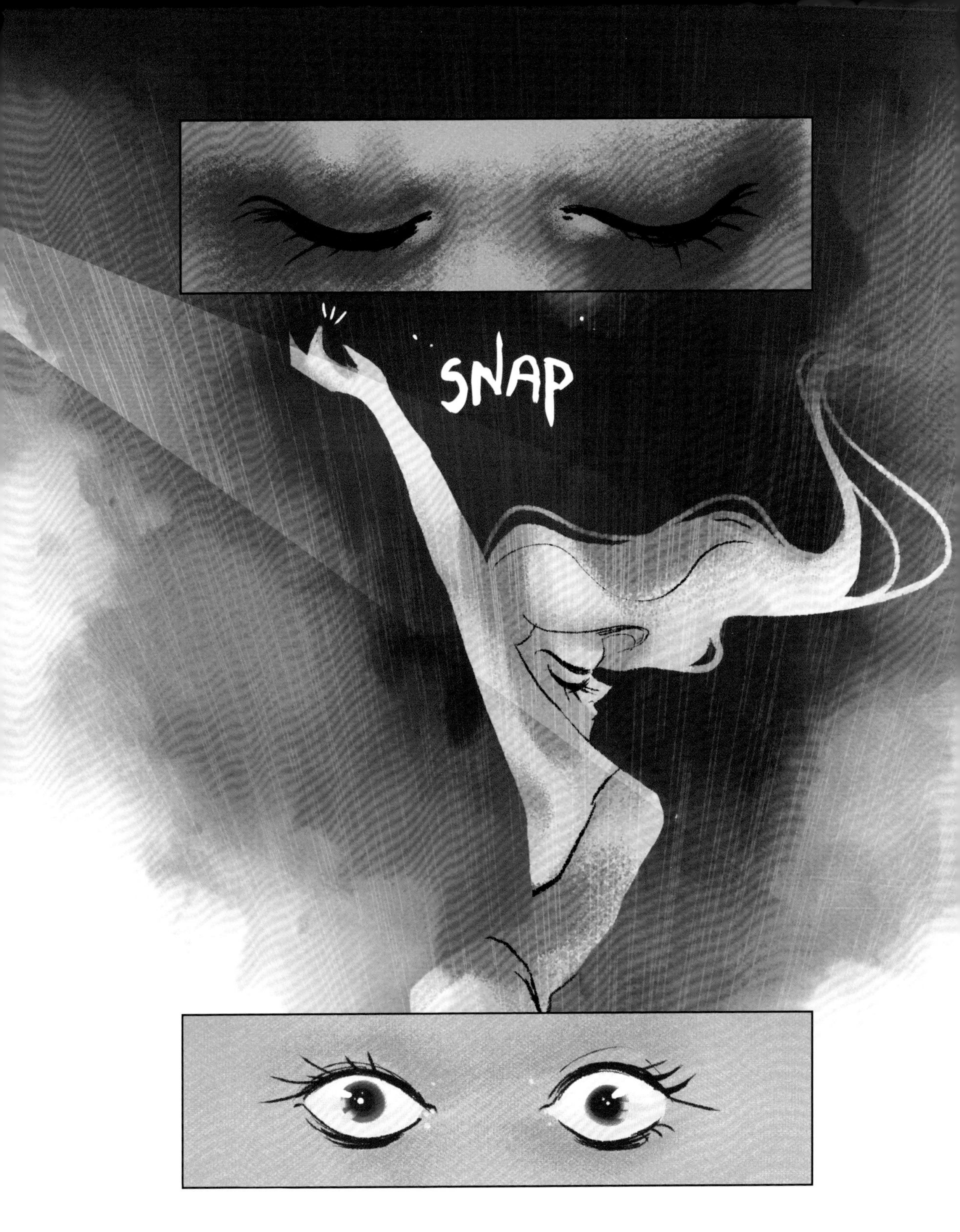
SNAP

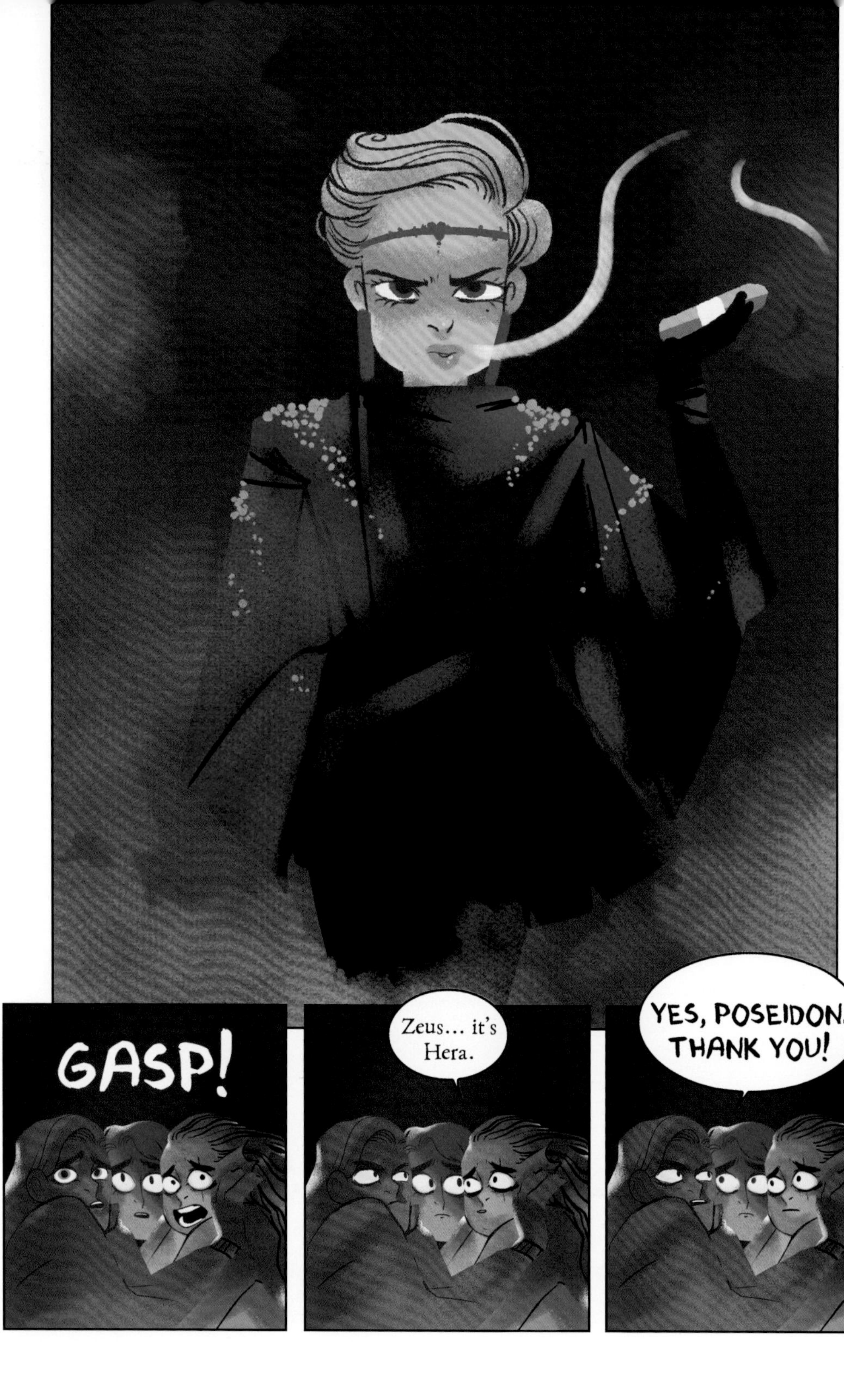
GASP!
Zeus... it's Hera.
YES, POSEIDON. THANK YOU!

Some time ago!

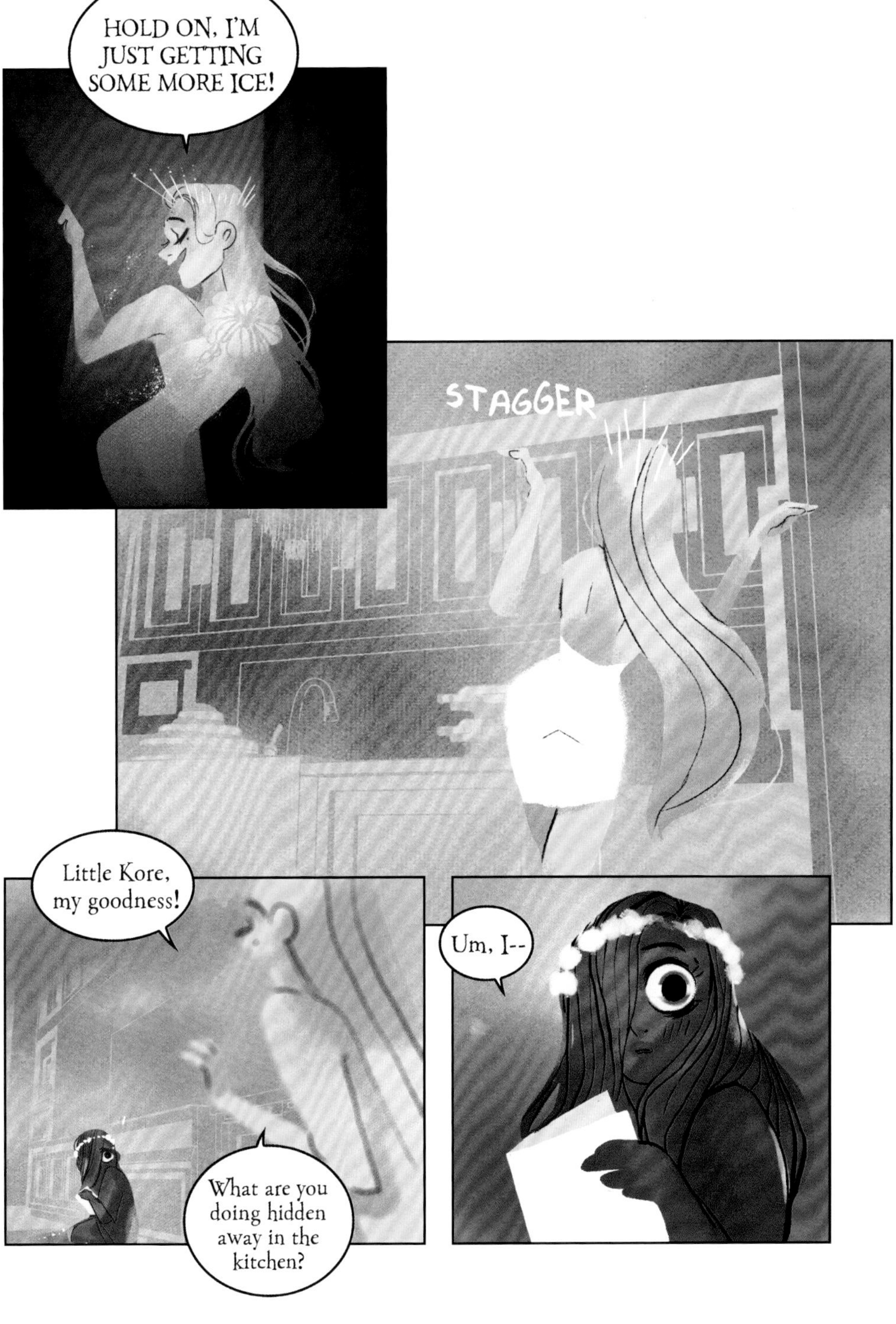
HOLD ON, I'M JUST GETTING SOME MORE ICE!
STAGGER
Little Kore, my goodness!
What are you doing hidden away in the kitchen?
Um, I--

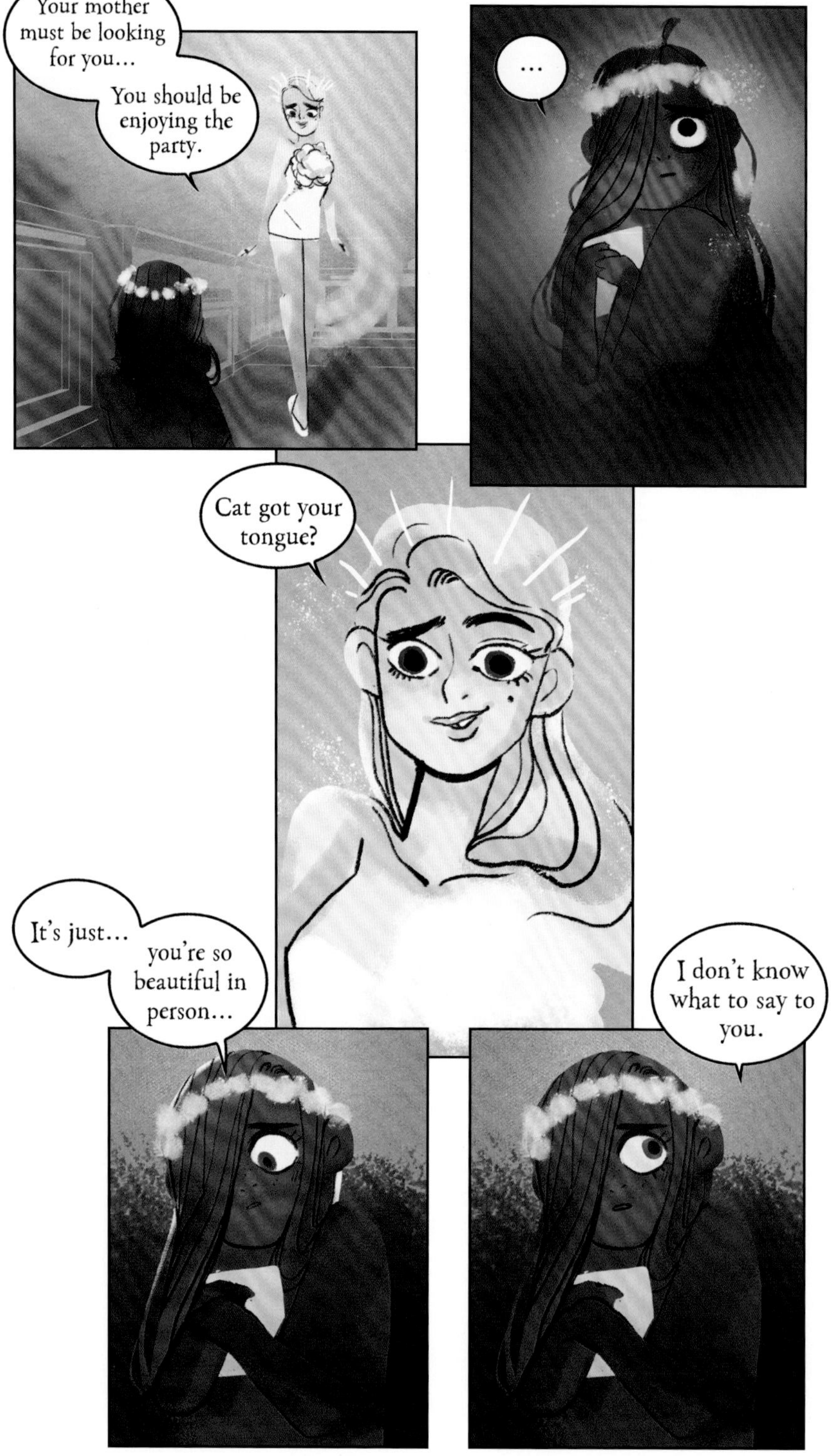
Your mother must be looking for you...
You should be enjoying the party.
...
Cat got your tongue?
It's just...
you're so beautiful in person...
I don't know what to say to you.

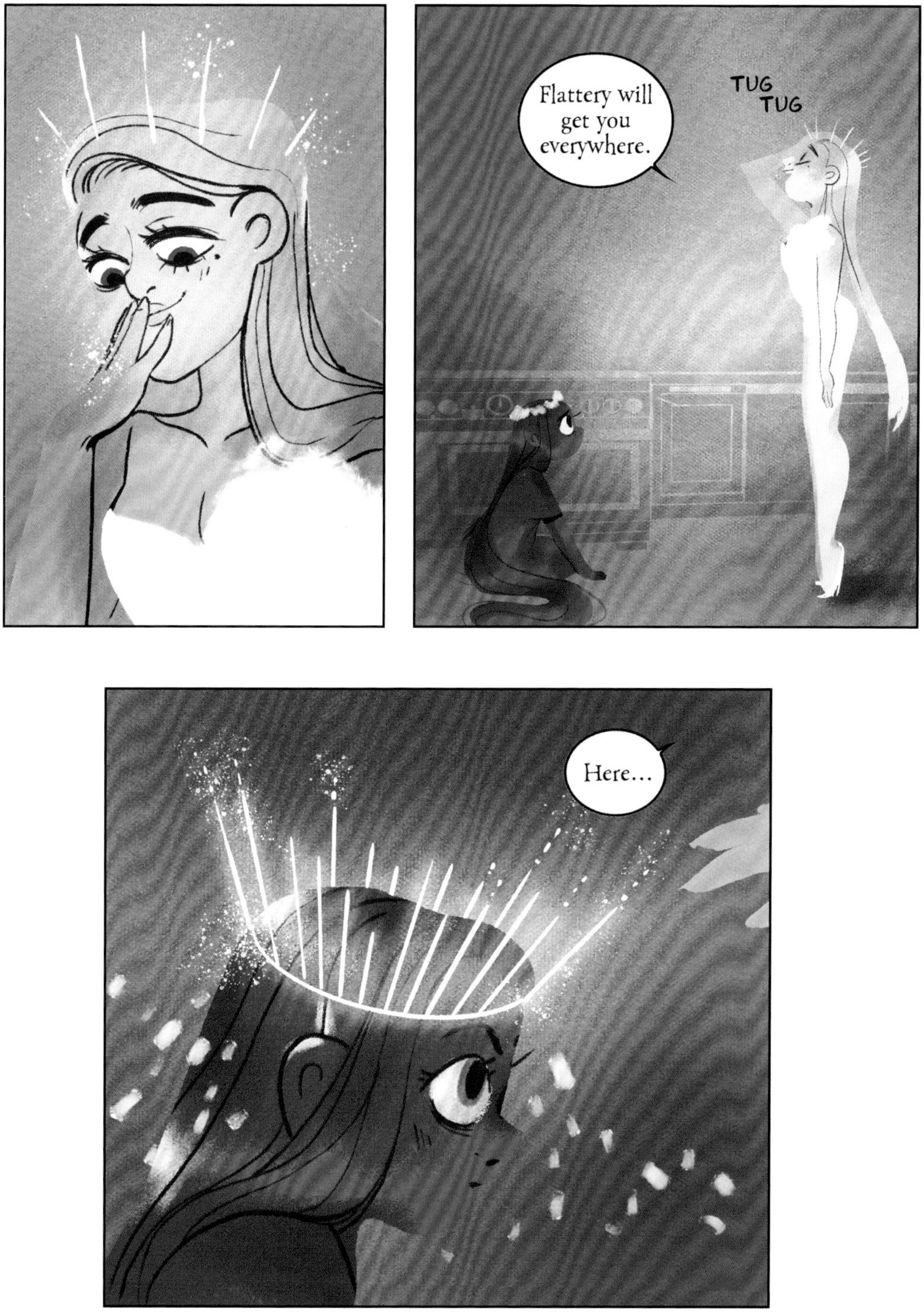
Flattery will get you everywhere.
TUG TUG
Here...

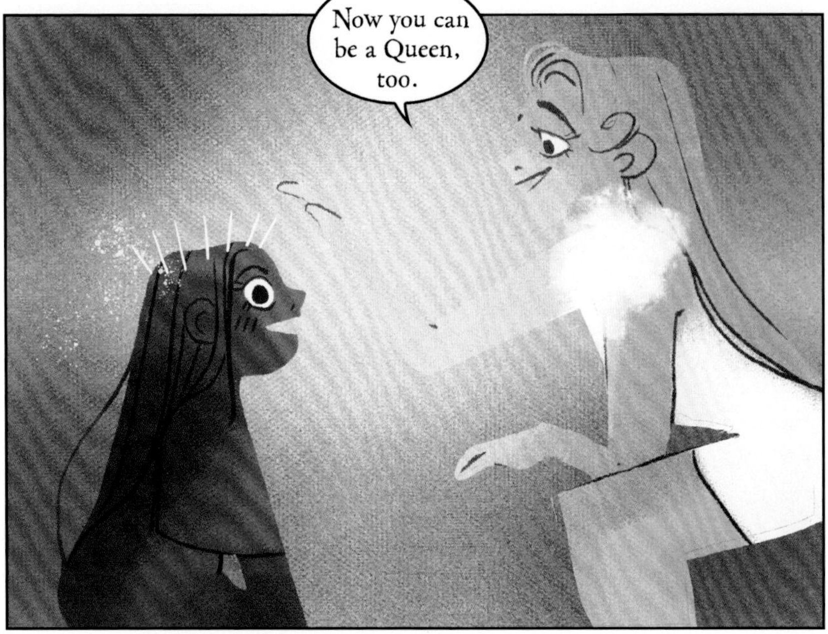
Now you can be a Queen, too.

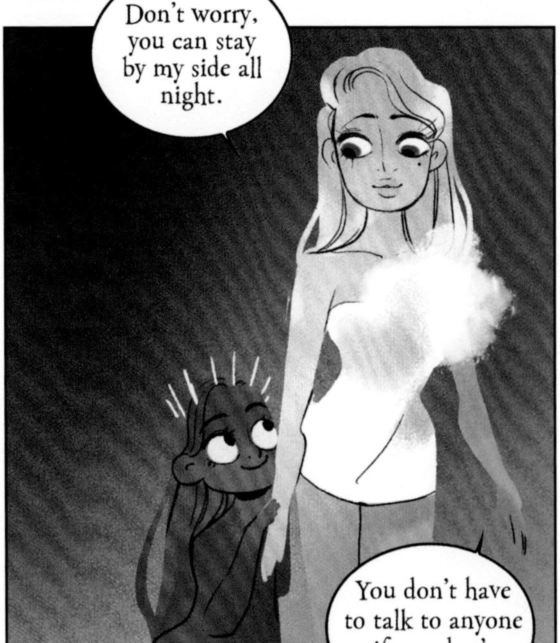
Don't worry, you can stay by my side all night.
You don't have to talk to anyone if you don't want to.

EPISODE 20: TREAT

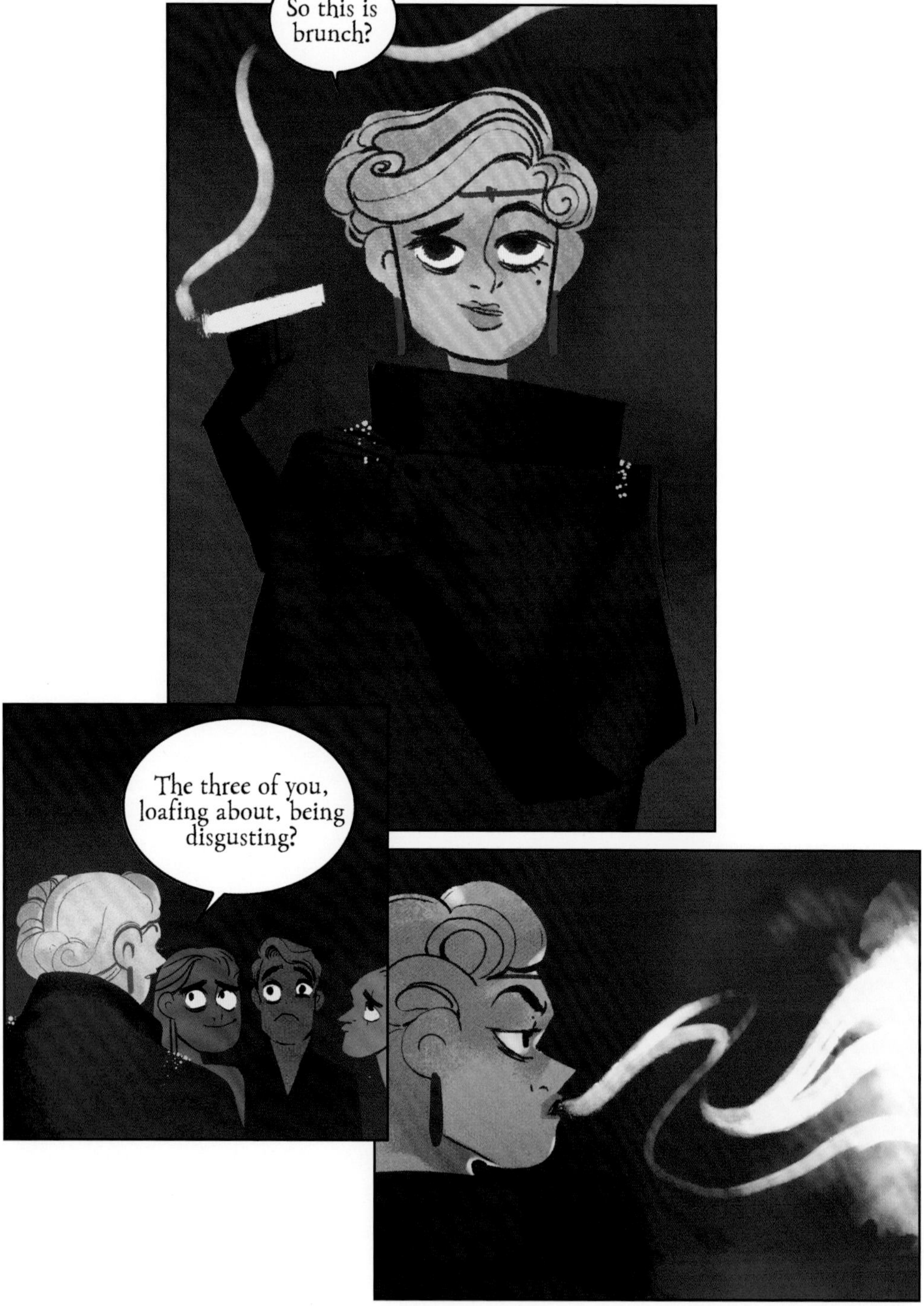
So this is brunch?
The three of you, loafing about, being disgusting?

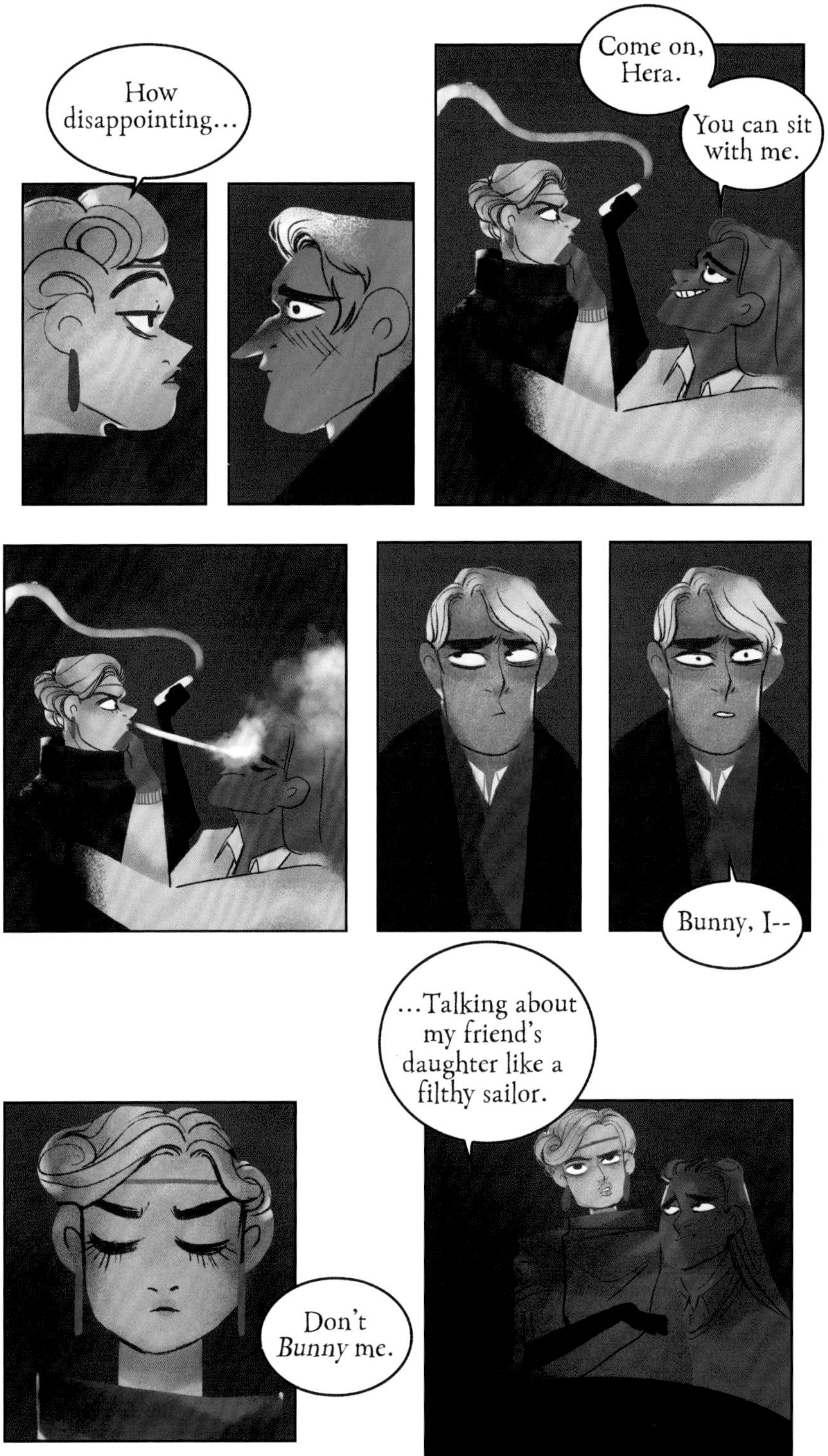
How disappointing...
Come on, Hera.
You can sit with me.
Bunny, I--
...Talking about my friend's daughter like a filthy sailor.
Don't *Bunny* me.

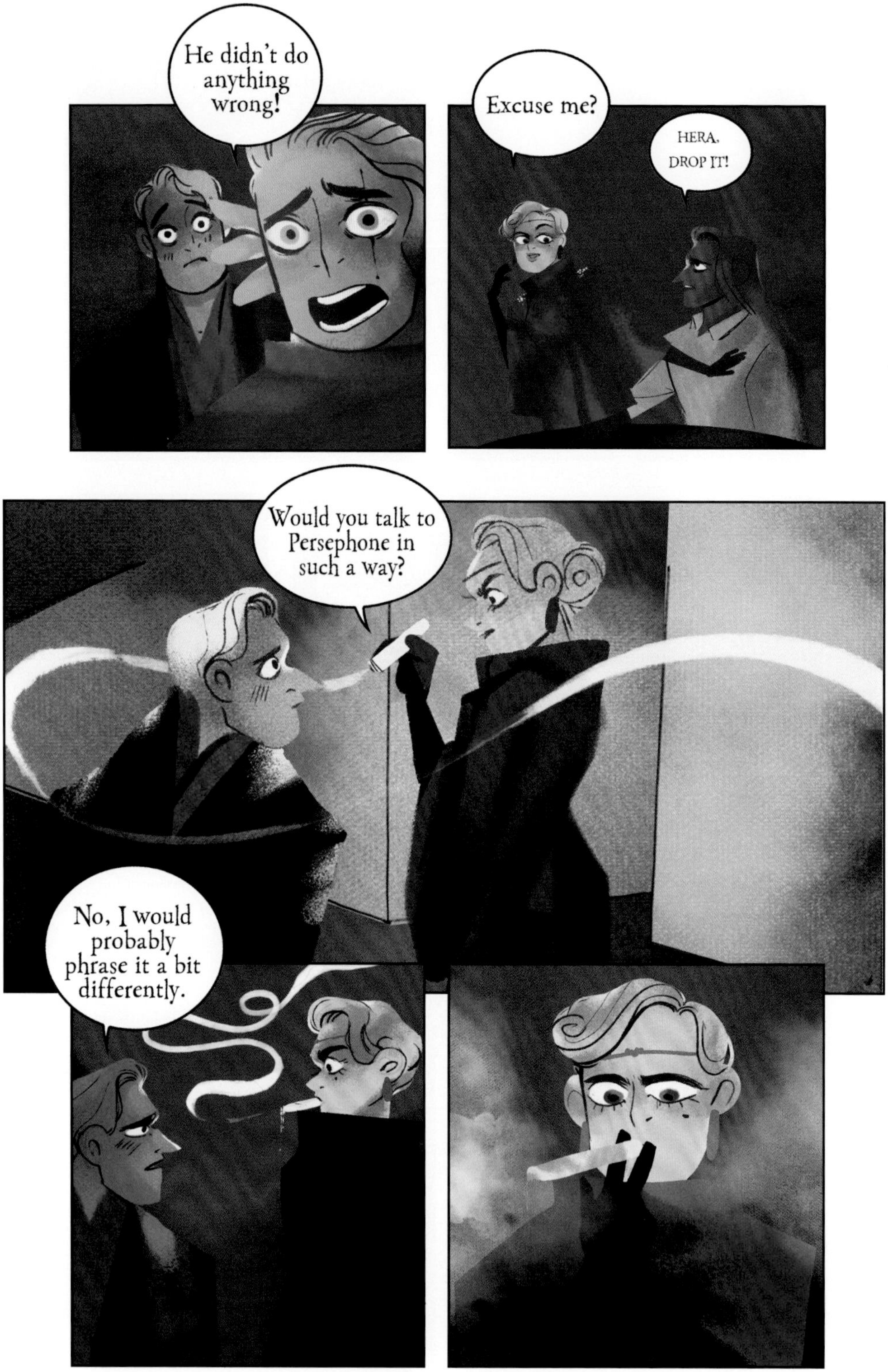
He didn't do anything wrong!
Excuse me?
HERA, DROP IT!
Would you talk to Persephone in such a way?
No, I would probably phrase it a bit differently.

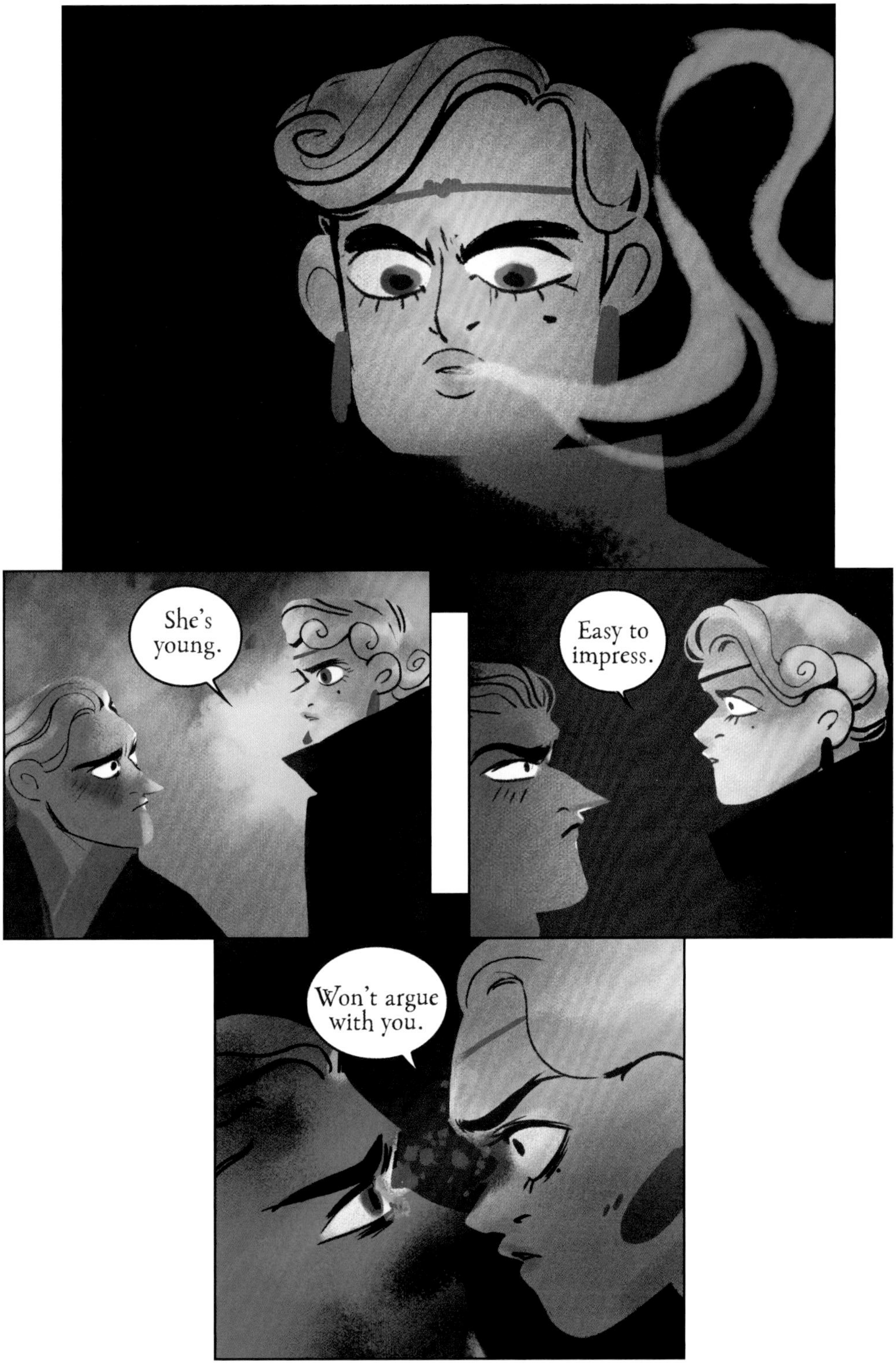
She's young.
Easy to impress.
Won't argue with you.

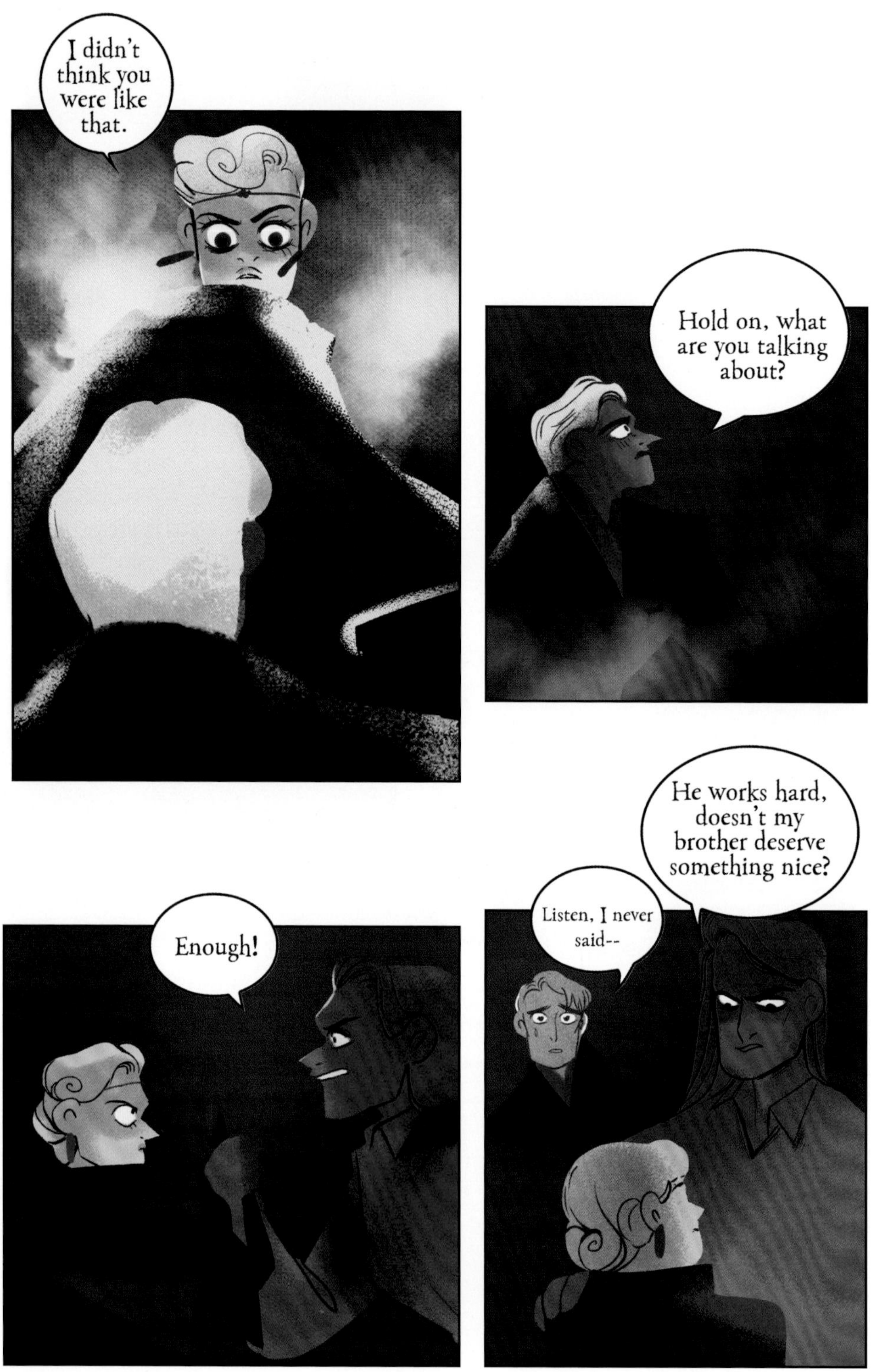
I didn't think you were like that.
Hold on, what are you talking about?
Enough!
He works hard, doesn't my brother deserve something nice?
Listen, I never said--

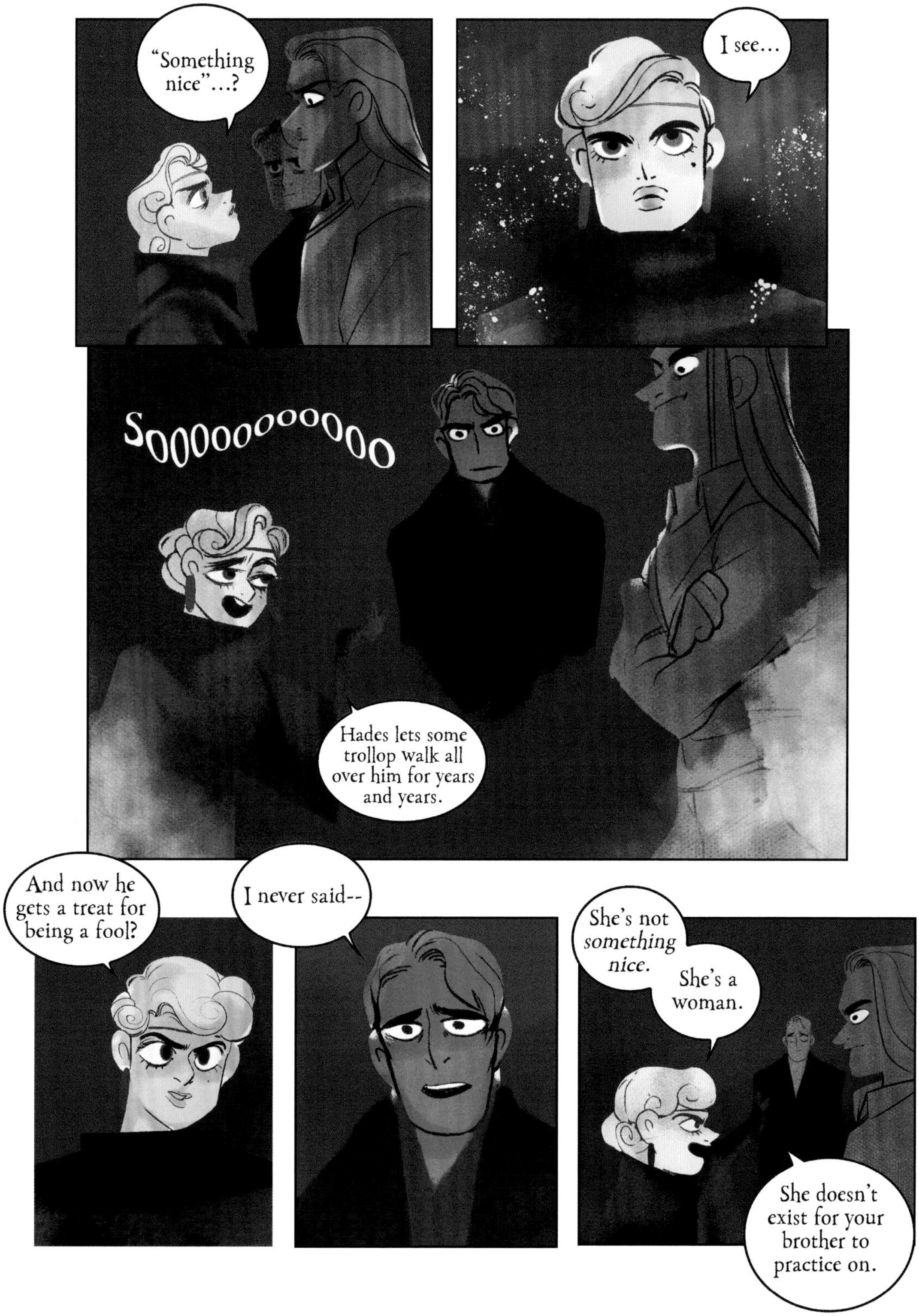
"Something nice"...?
I see...
SOOOOOOOOOOO
Hades lets some trollop walk all over him for years and years.
And now he gets a treat for being a fool?
I never said--
She's not *something nice.*
She's a woman.
She doesn't exist for your brother to practice on.

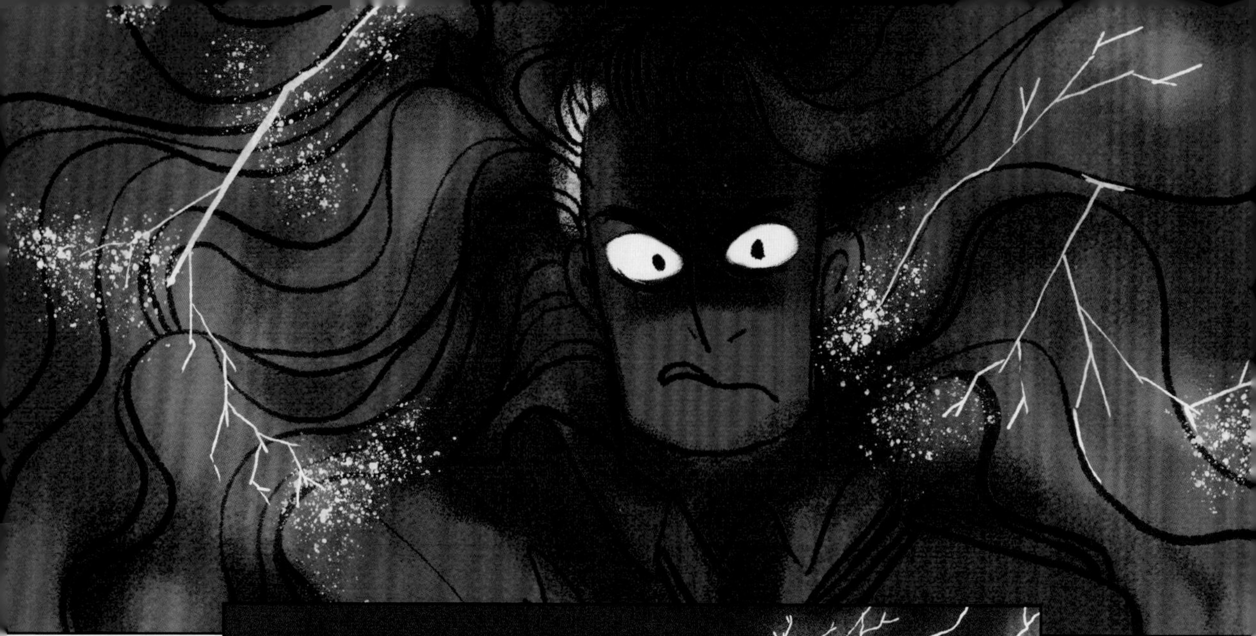

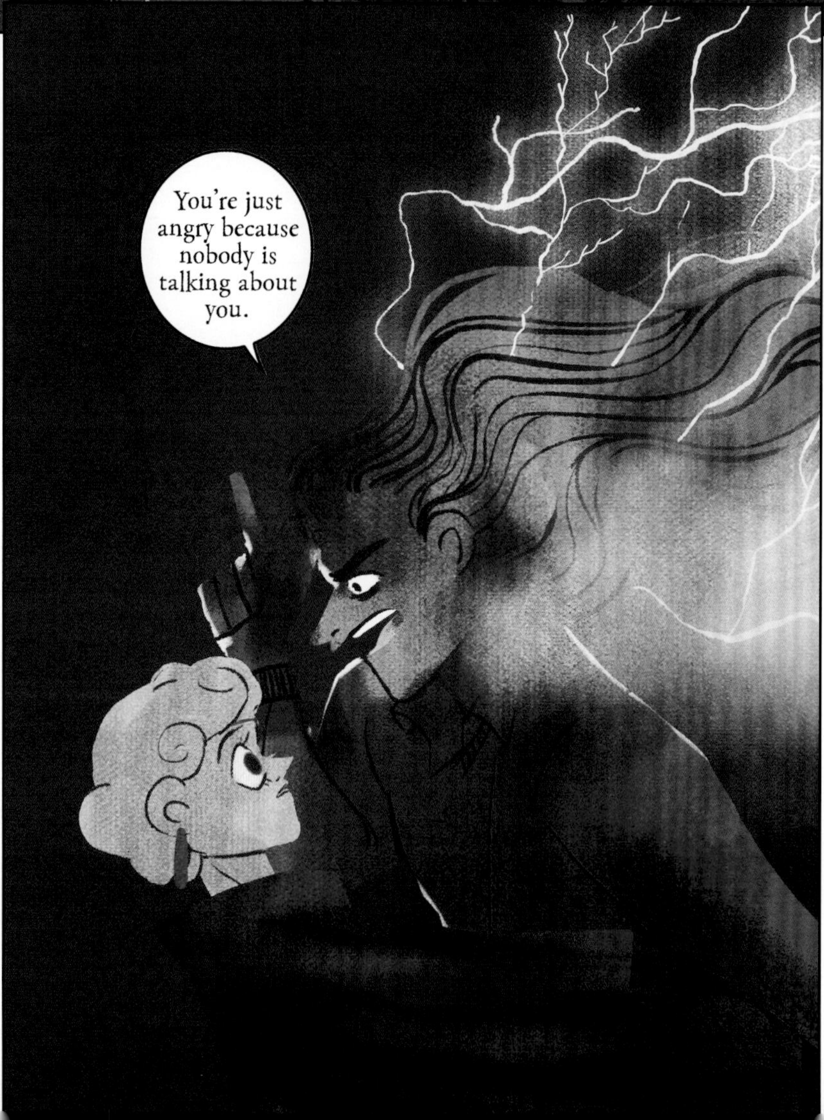
You're just angry because nobody is talking about you.

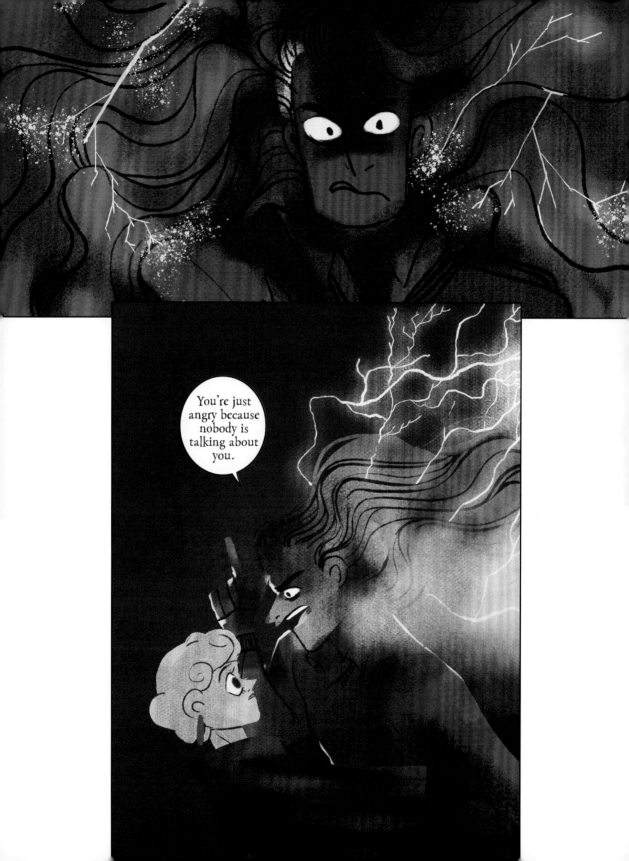

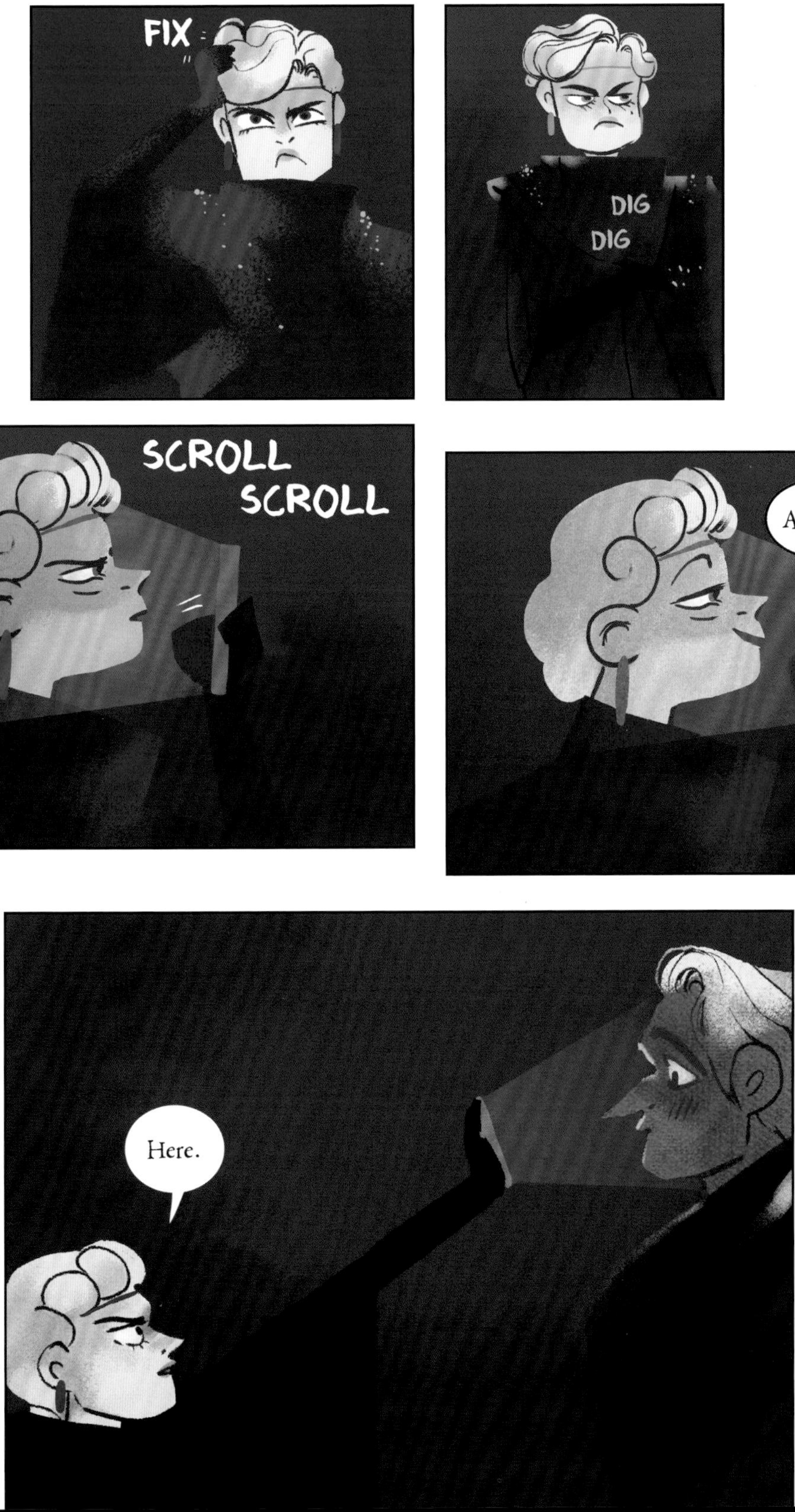

FIX
DIG
DIG
SCROLL
SCROLL
Ah ha!
Here.

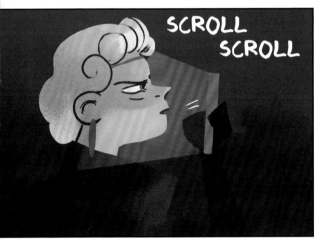

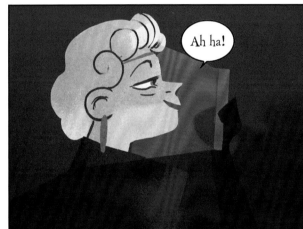

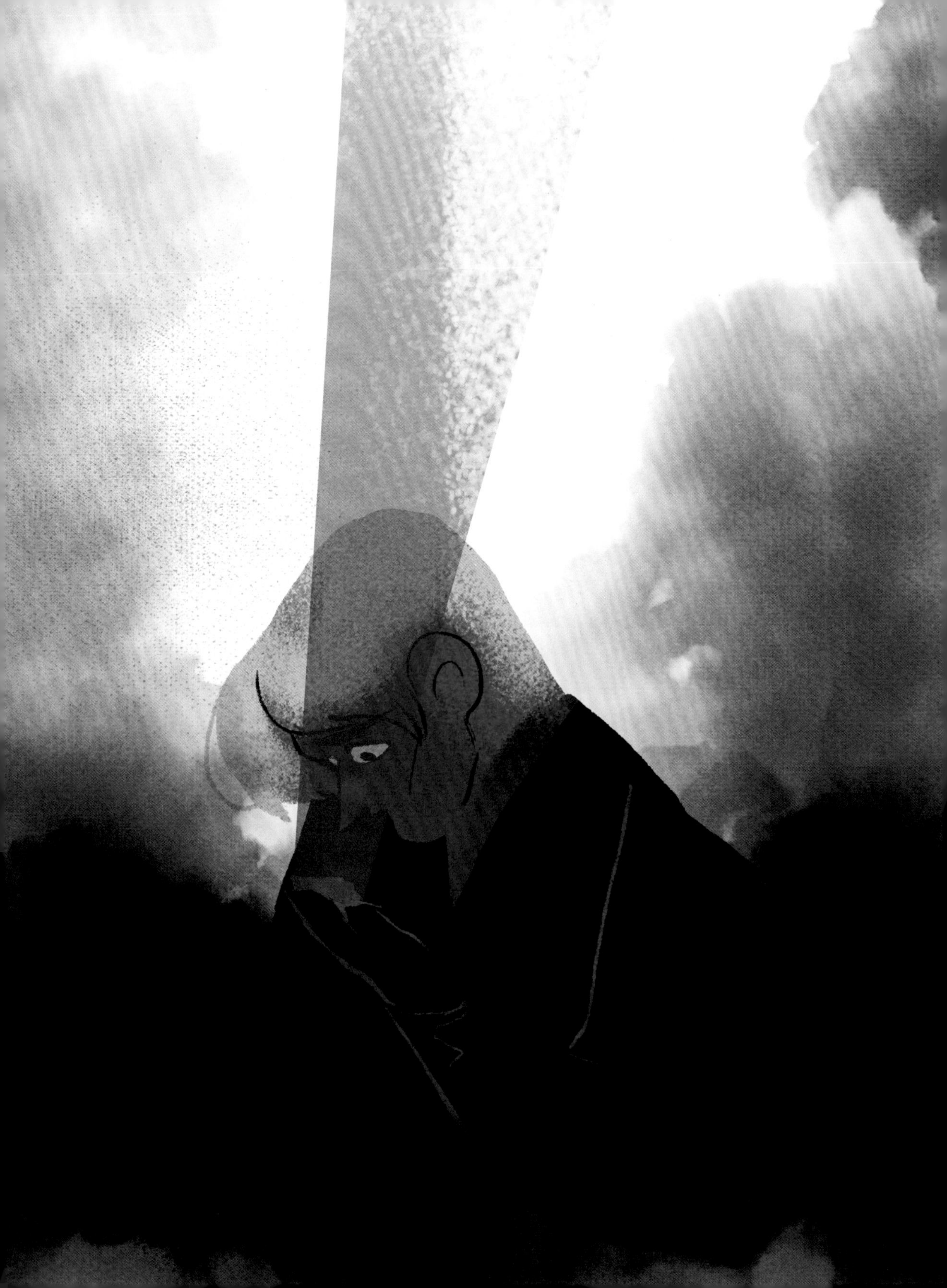

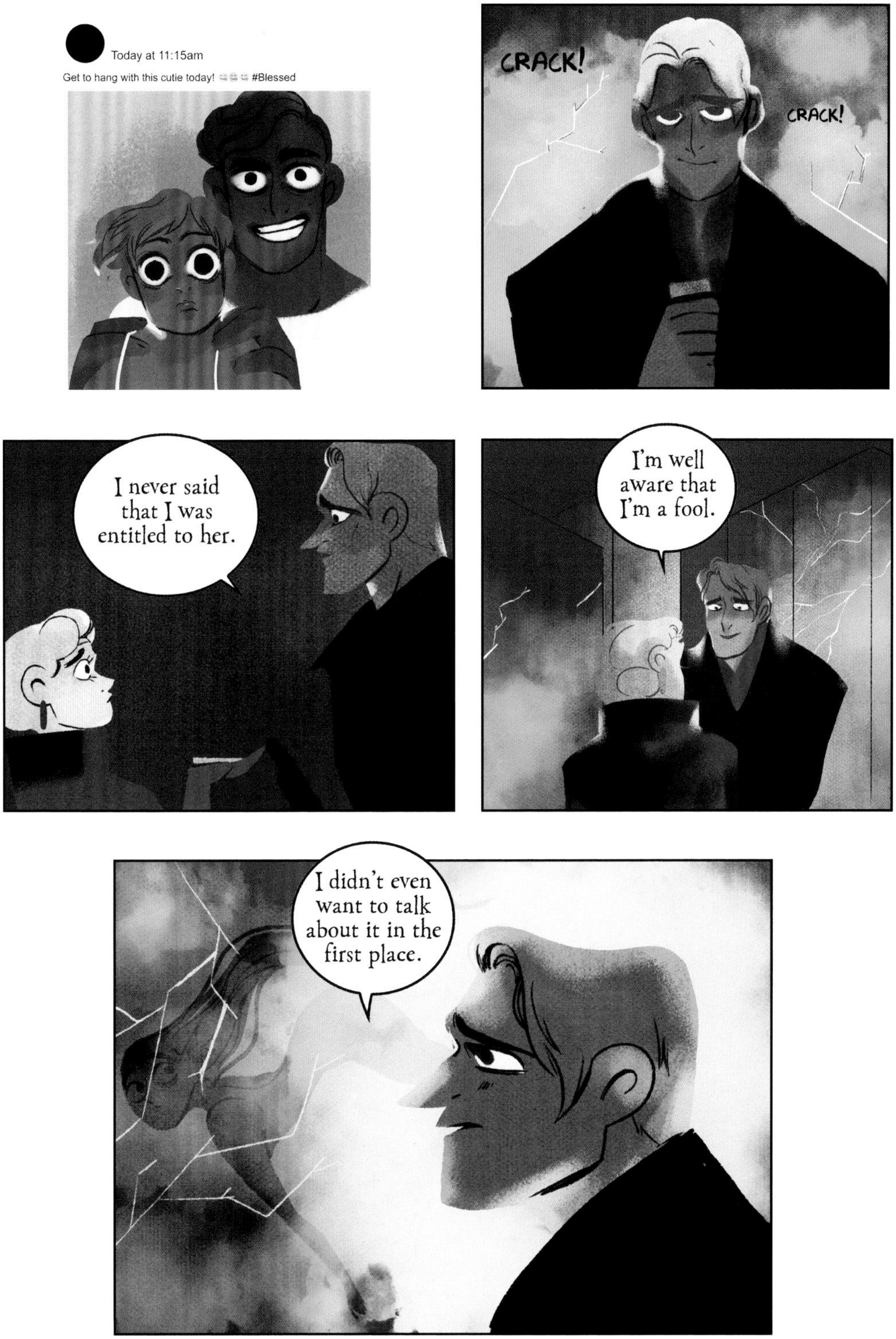
Today at 11:15am
Get to hang with this cutie today! #Blessed
CRACK!
CRACK!
I never said that I was entitled to her.
I'm well aware that I'm a fool.
I didn't even want to talk about it in the first place.

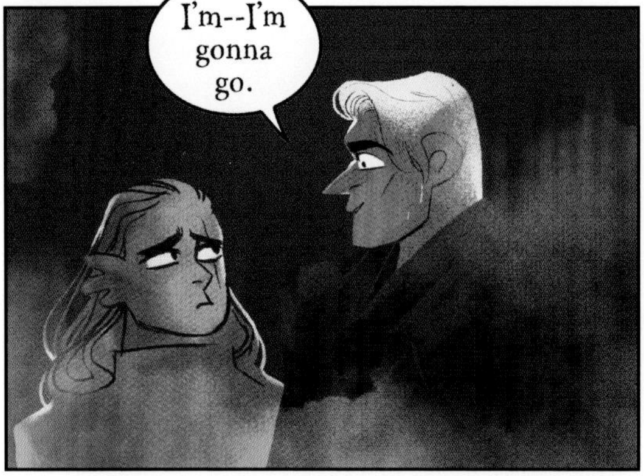
I'm--I'm gonna go.

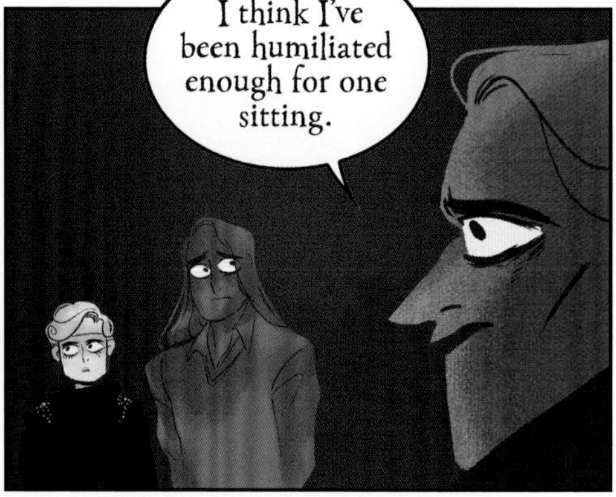
I think I've been humiliated enough for one sitting.

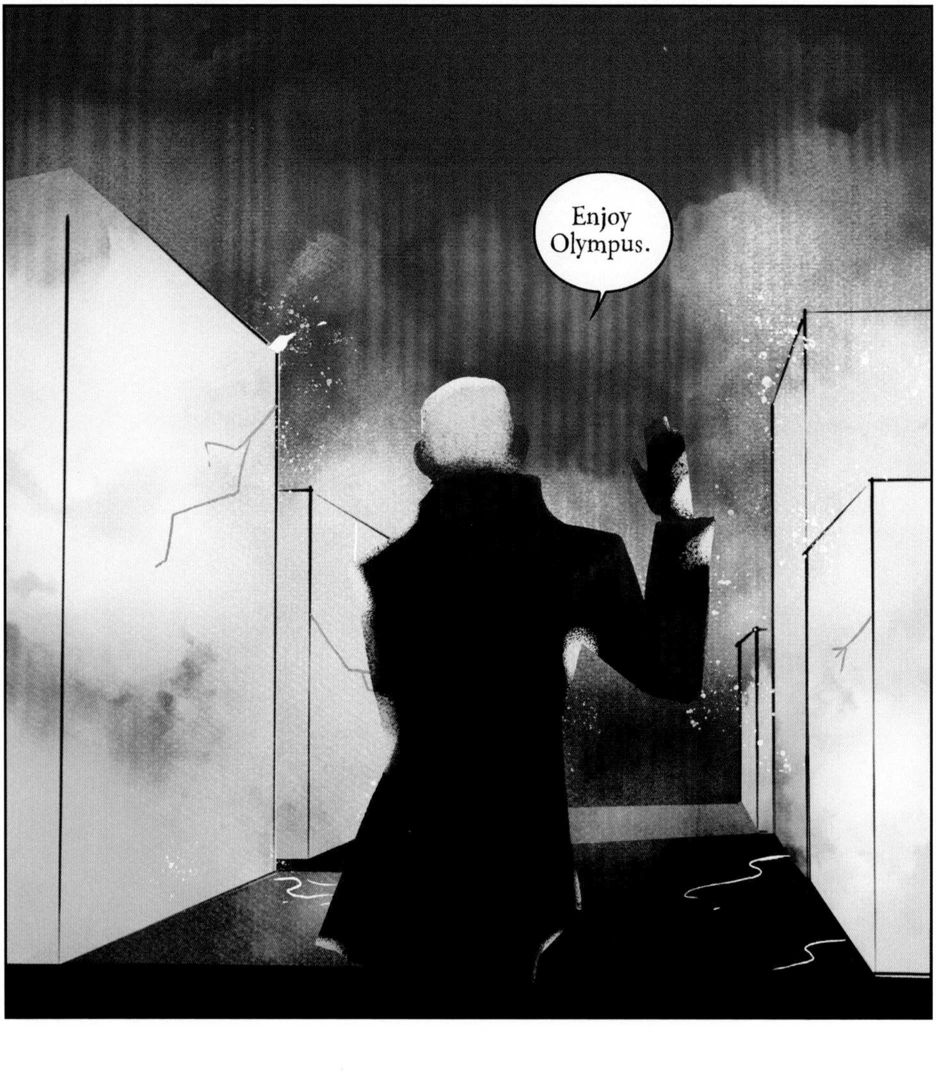
Enjoy Olympus.

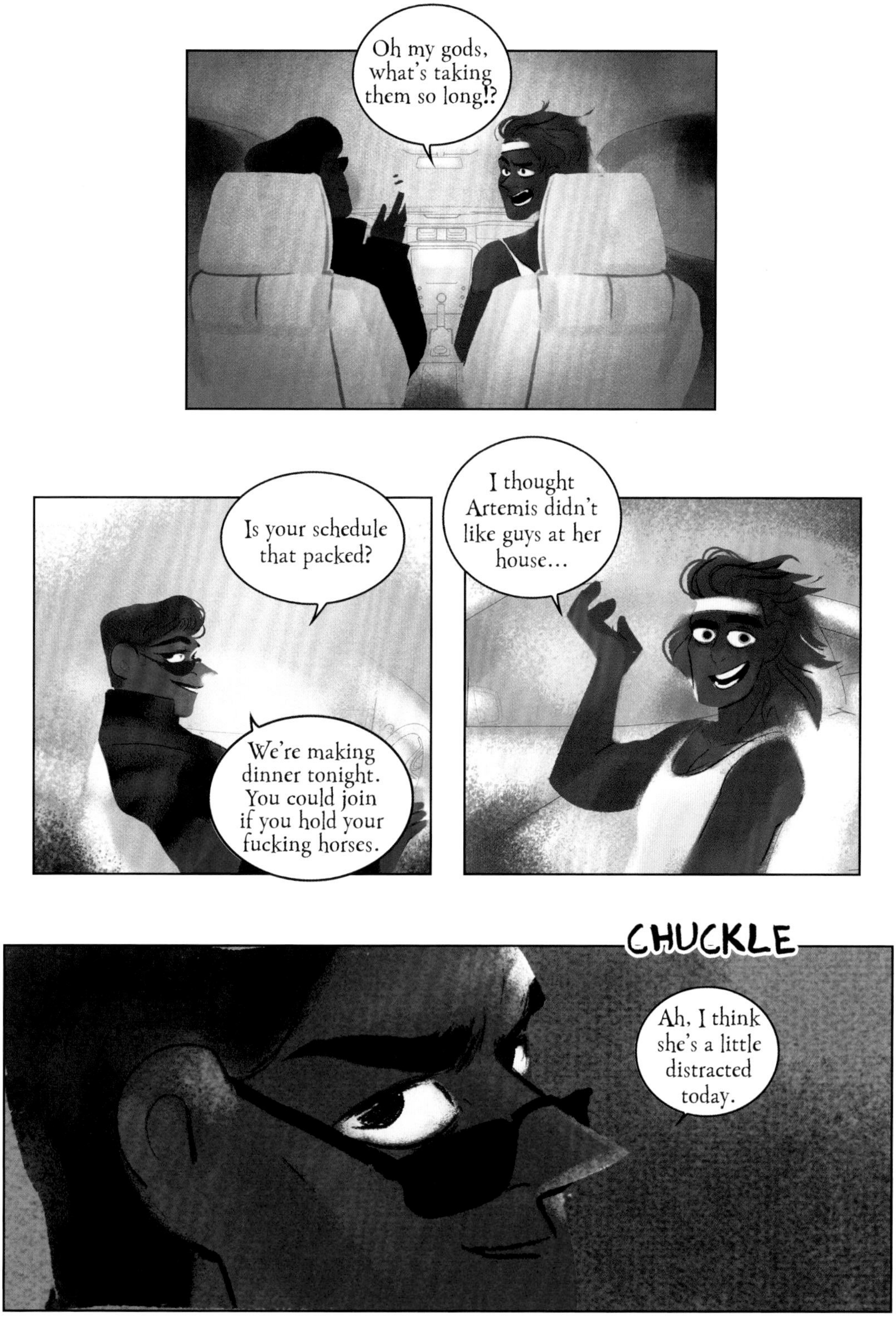

Oh my gods, what's taking them so long!?
Is your schedule that packed?
We're making dinner tonight. You could join if you hold your fucking horses.
I thought Artemis didn't like guys at her house...
CHUCKLE
Ah, I think she's a little distracted today.

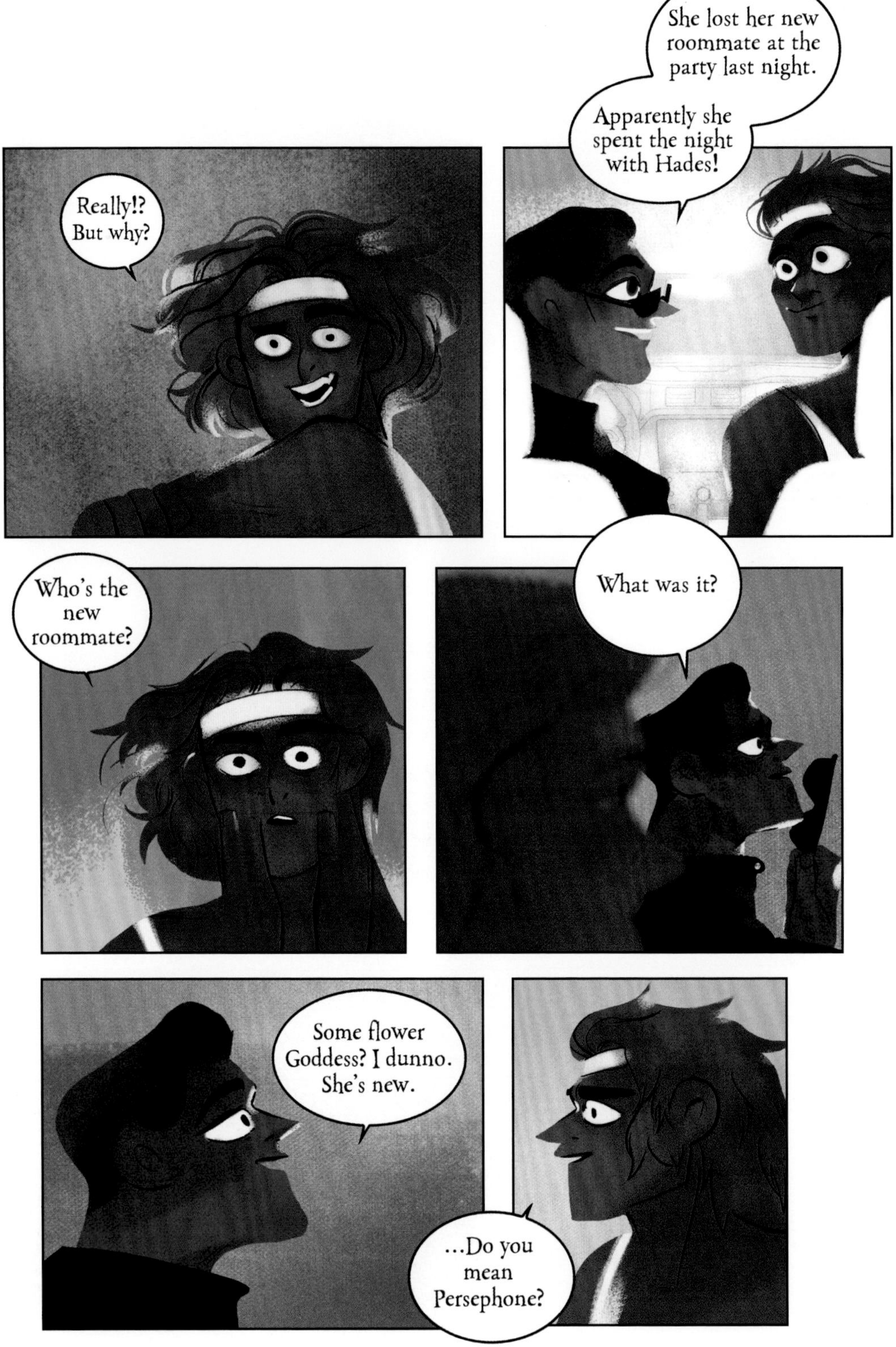
Really!? But why?
She lost her new roommate at the party last night.
Apparently she spent the night with Hades!
Who's the new roommate?
What was it?
Some flower Goddess? I dunno. She's new.
...Do you mean Persephone?

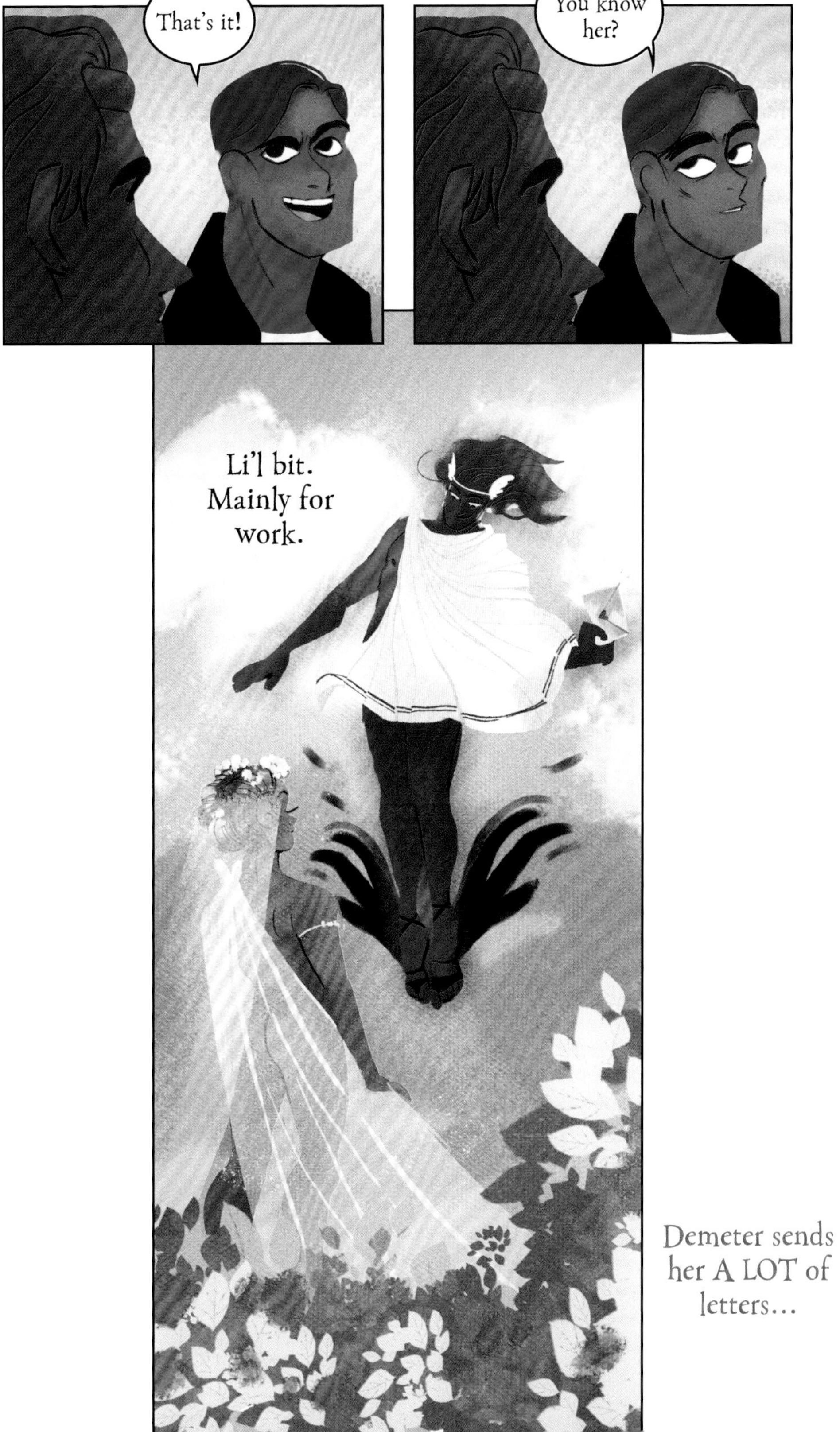
That's it!
You know her?
Li'l bit. Mainly for work.
Demeter sends her A LOT of letters...

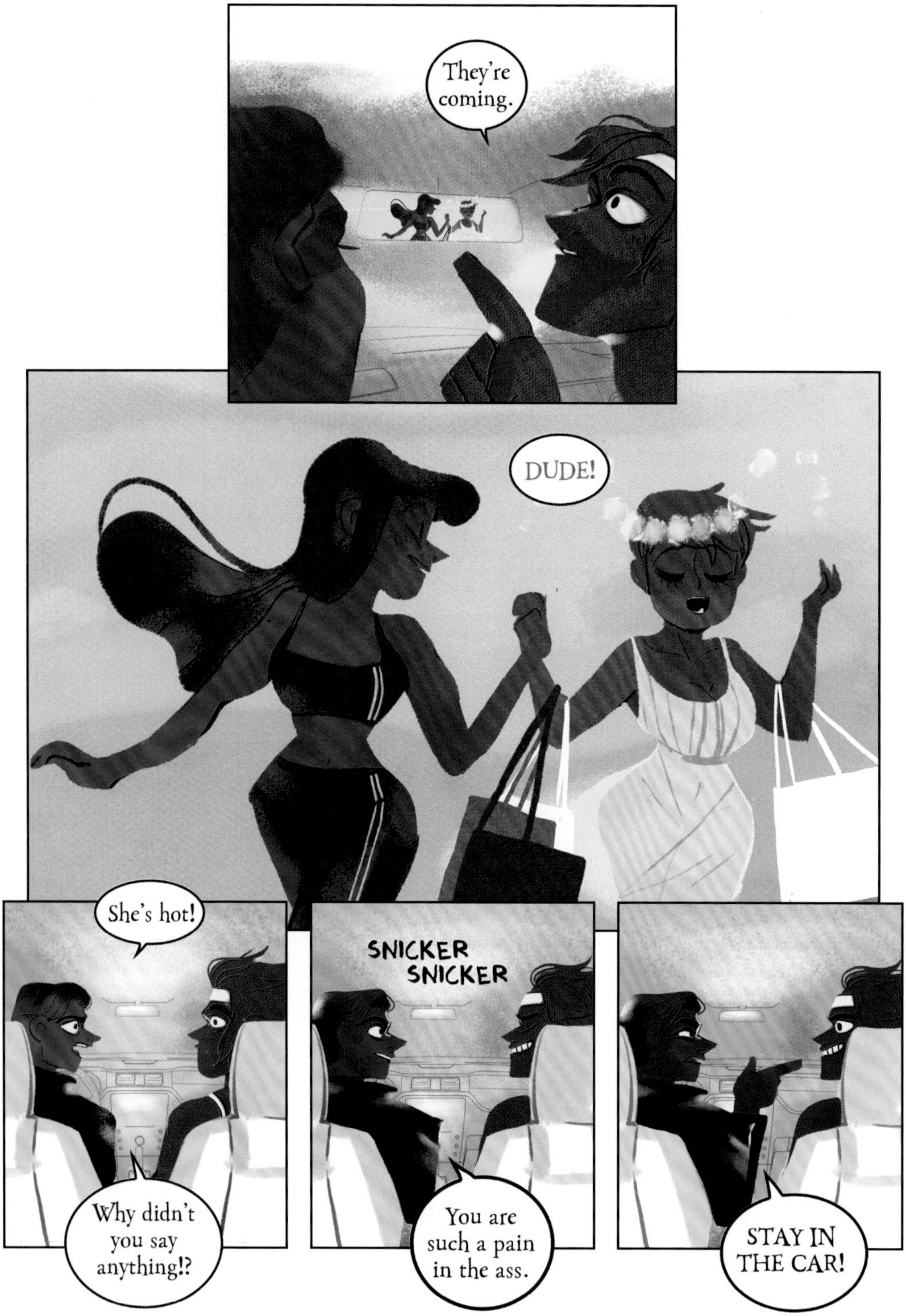
They're coming.
DUDE!
She's hot!
Why didn't you say anything!?
SNICKER SNICKER
You are such a pain in the ass.
STAY IN THE CAR!

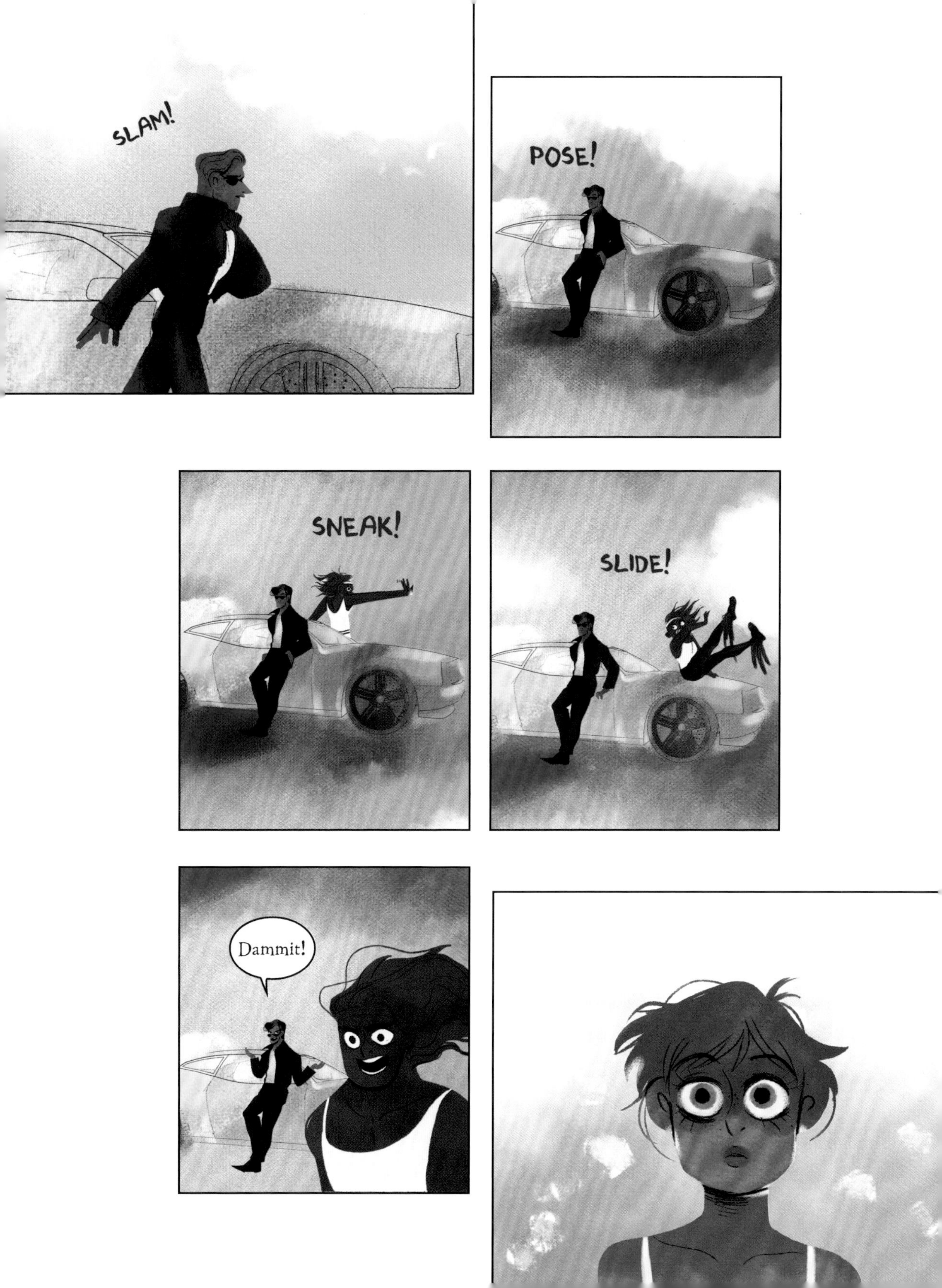
SLAM!
POSE!
SNEAK!
SLIDE!
Dammit!

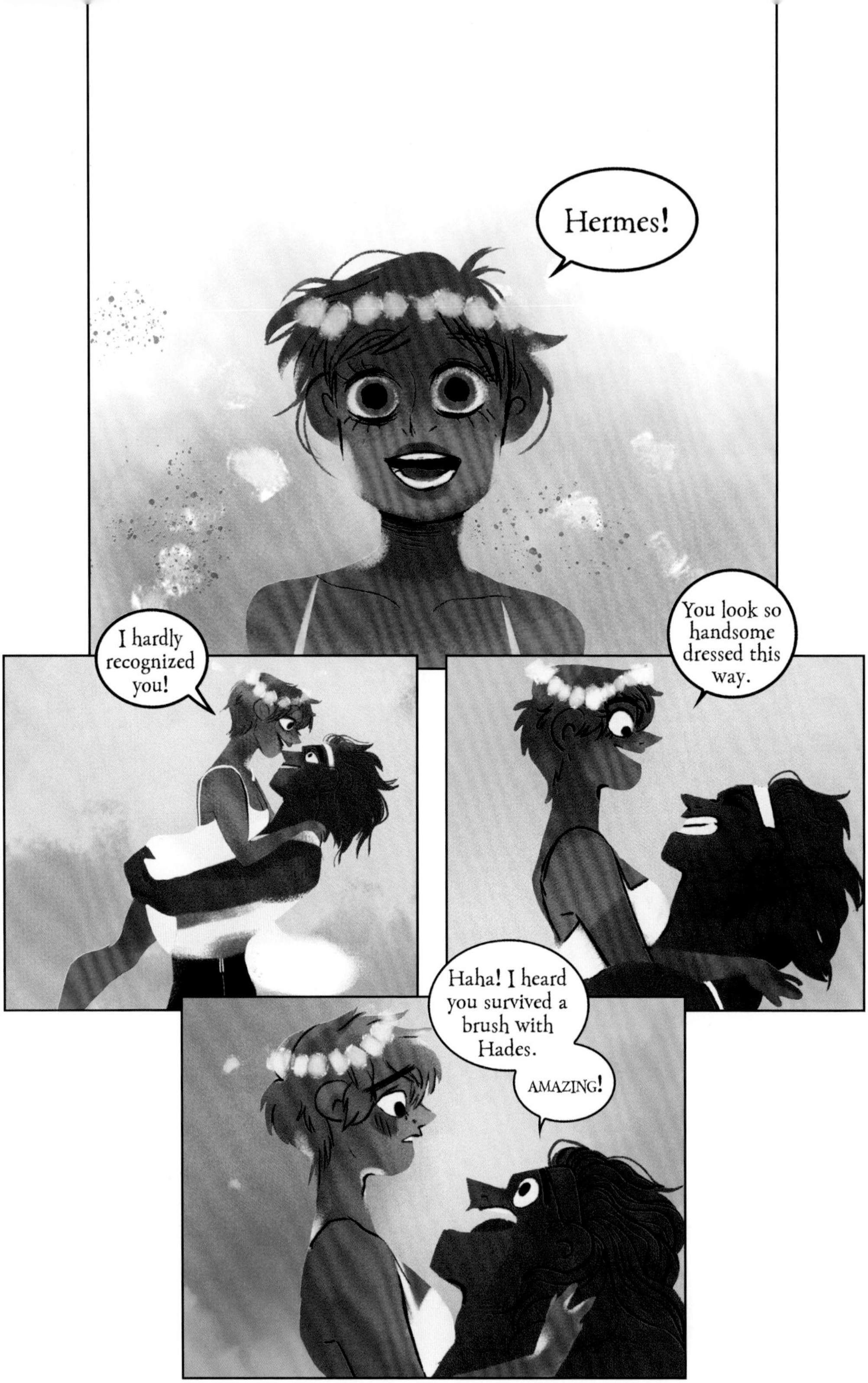
Hermes!
I hardly recognized you!
You look so handsome dressed this way.
Haha! I heard you survived a brush with Hades.
AMAZING!

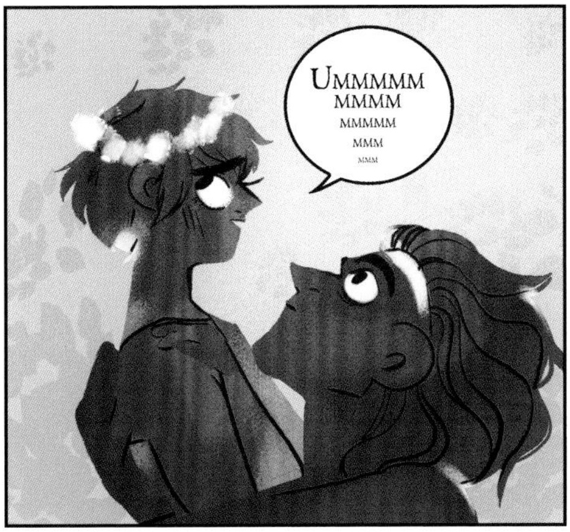
UMMMMM MMMM MMMMM MMM MMM

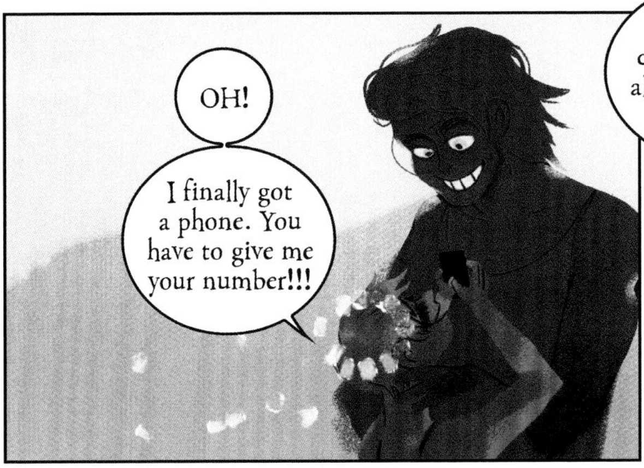
OH!
I finally got a phone. You have to give me your number!!!

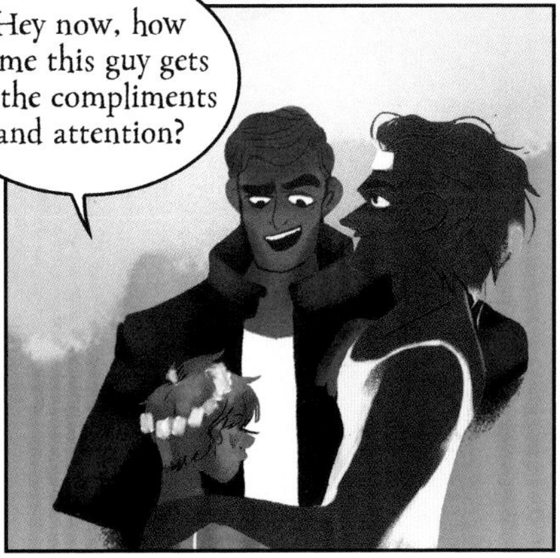
Hey now, how come this guy gets all the compliments and attention?

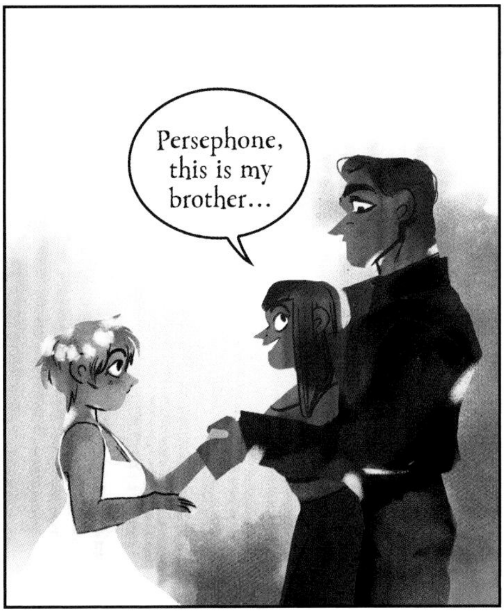
Persephone, this is my brother...

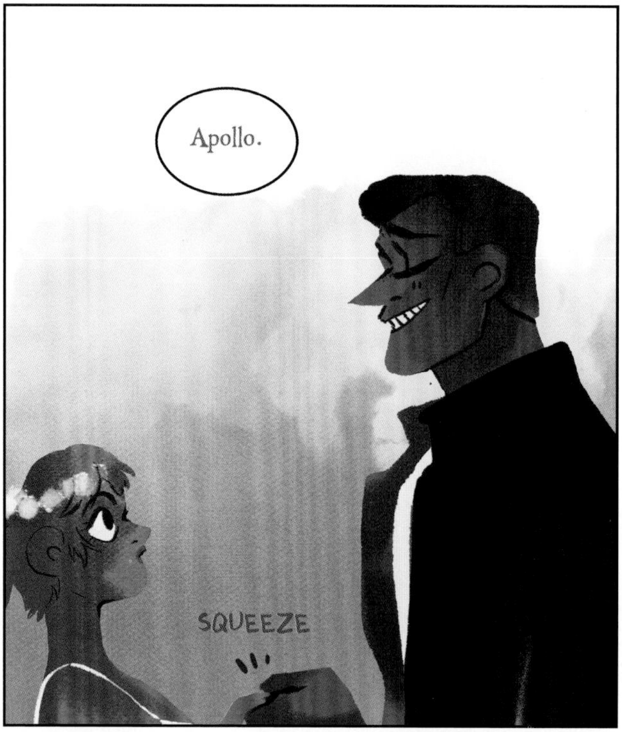
Apollo.
SQUEEZE

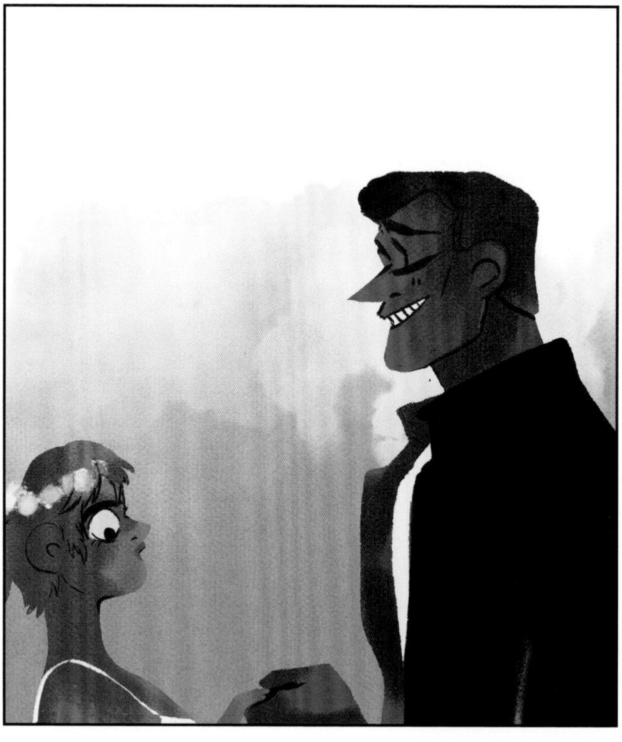

EPISODE 21: THANKS BUT NAH

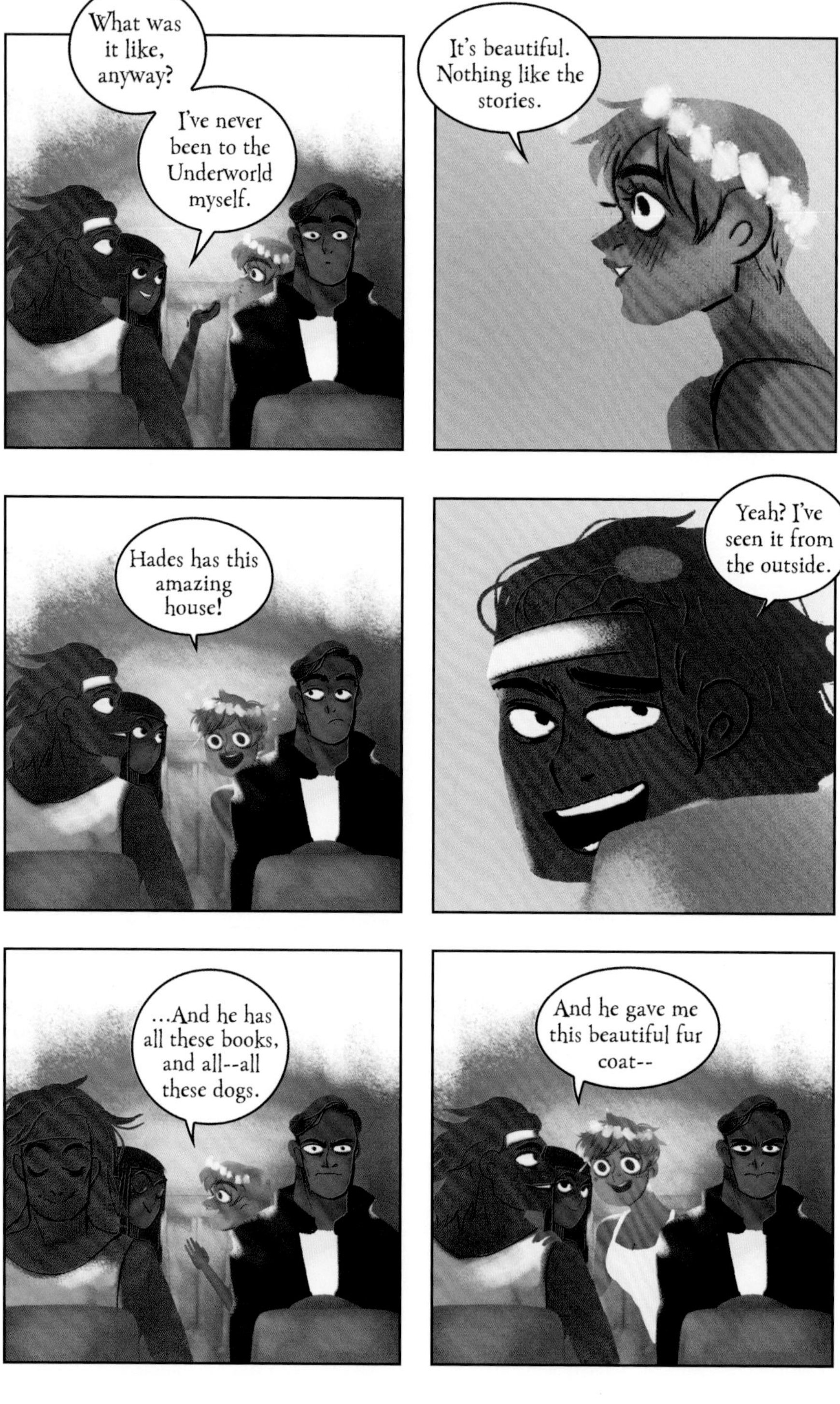
What was it like, anyway?
I've never been to the Underworld myself.
It's beautiful. Nothing like the stories.
Hades has this amazing house!
Yeah? I've seen it from the outside.
...And he has all these books, and all--all these dogs.
And he gave me this beautiful fur coat--

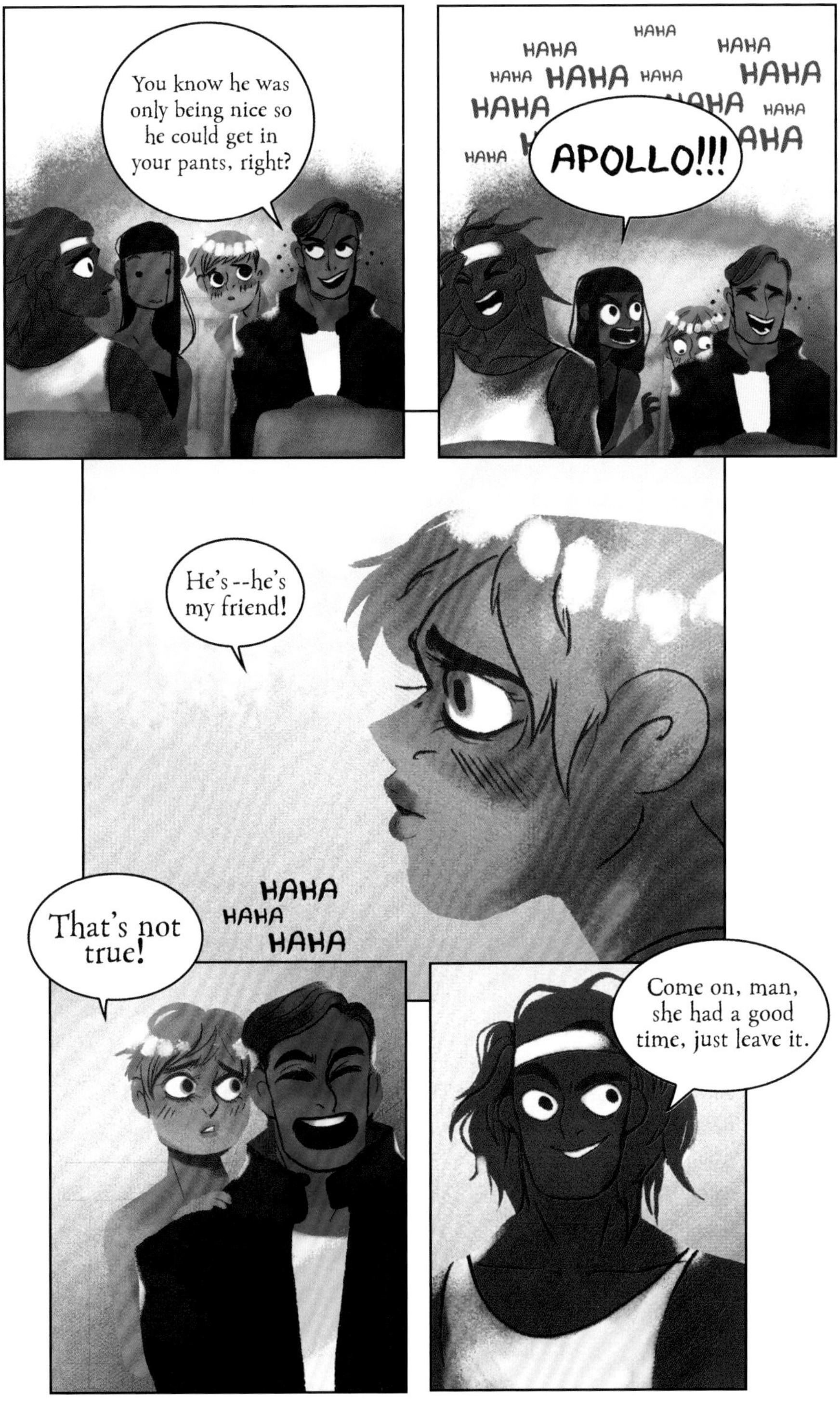
You know he was only being nice so he could get in your pants, right?
HAHA HAHA HAHA HAHA HAHA HAHA HAHA HAHA
APOLLO!!!
He's--he's my friend!
HAHA HAHA HAHA
That's not true!
Come on, man, she had a good time, just leave it.

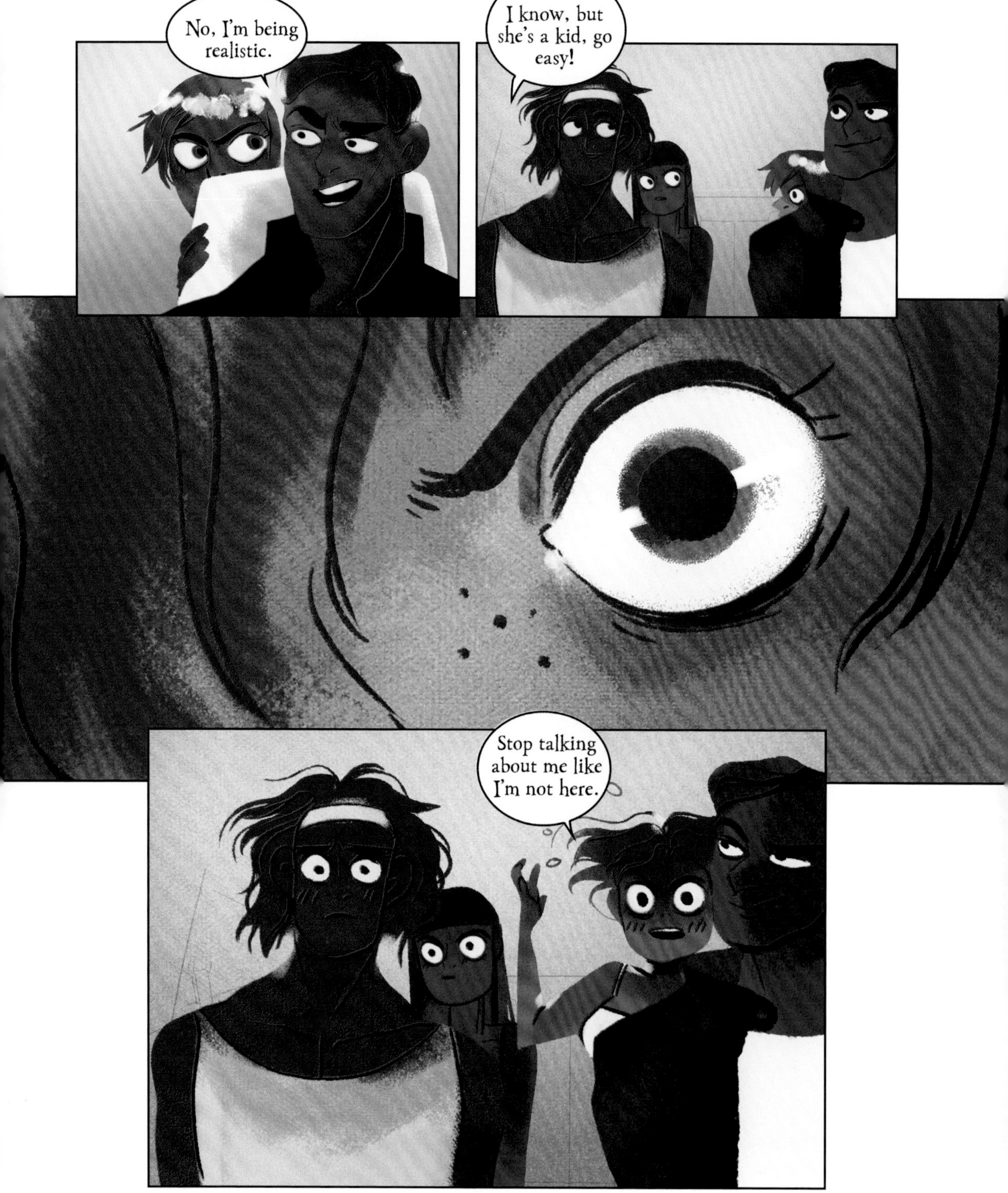
No, I'm being realistic.
I know, but she's a kid, go easy!
Stop talking about me like I'm not here.

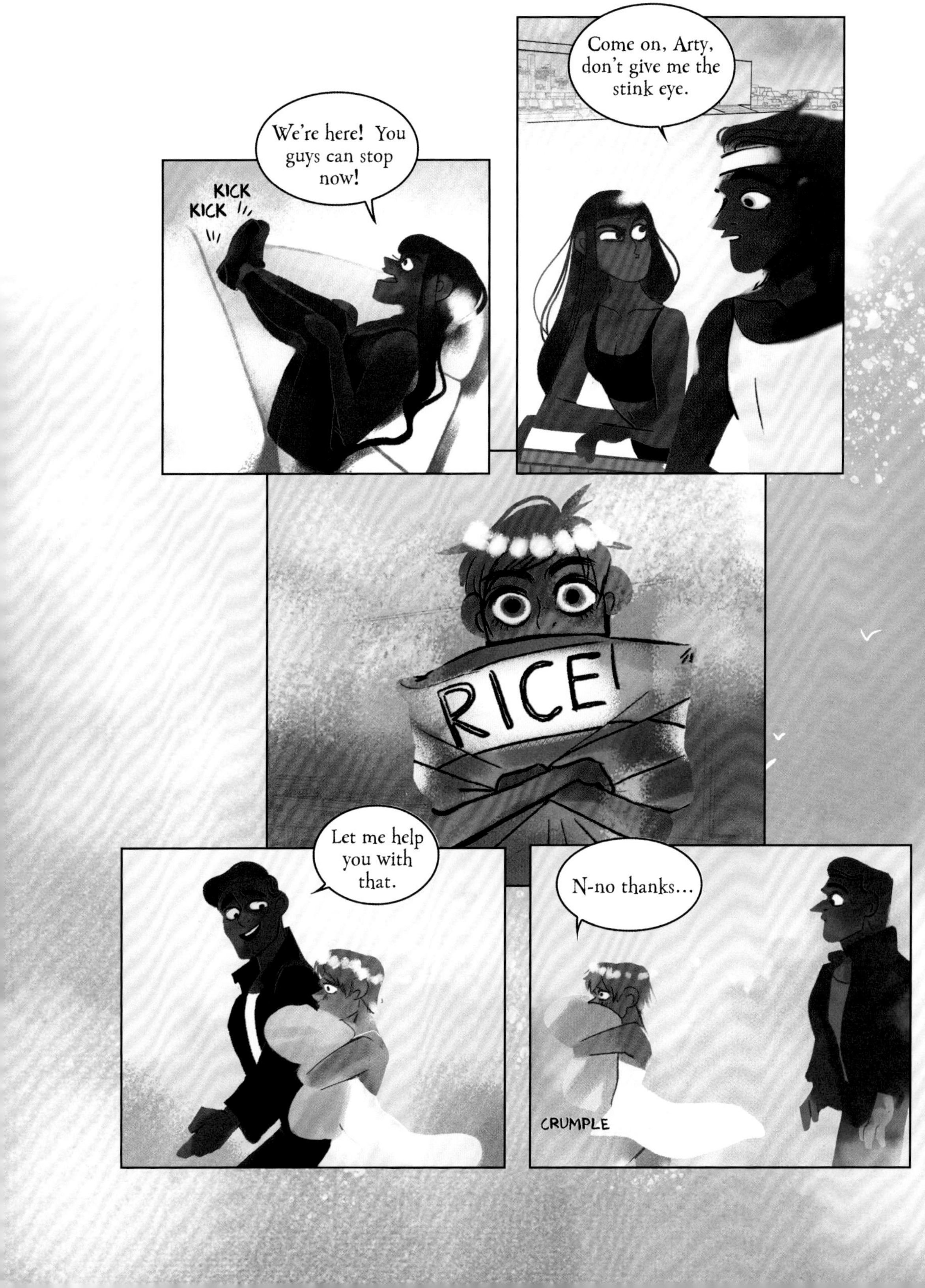
We're here! You guys can stop now!
KICK
KICK
Come on, Arty, don't give me the stink eye.
RICE!
Let me help you with that.
N-no thanks...
CRUMPLE

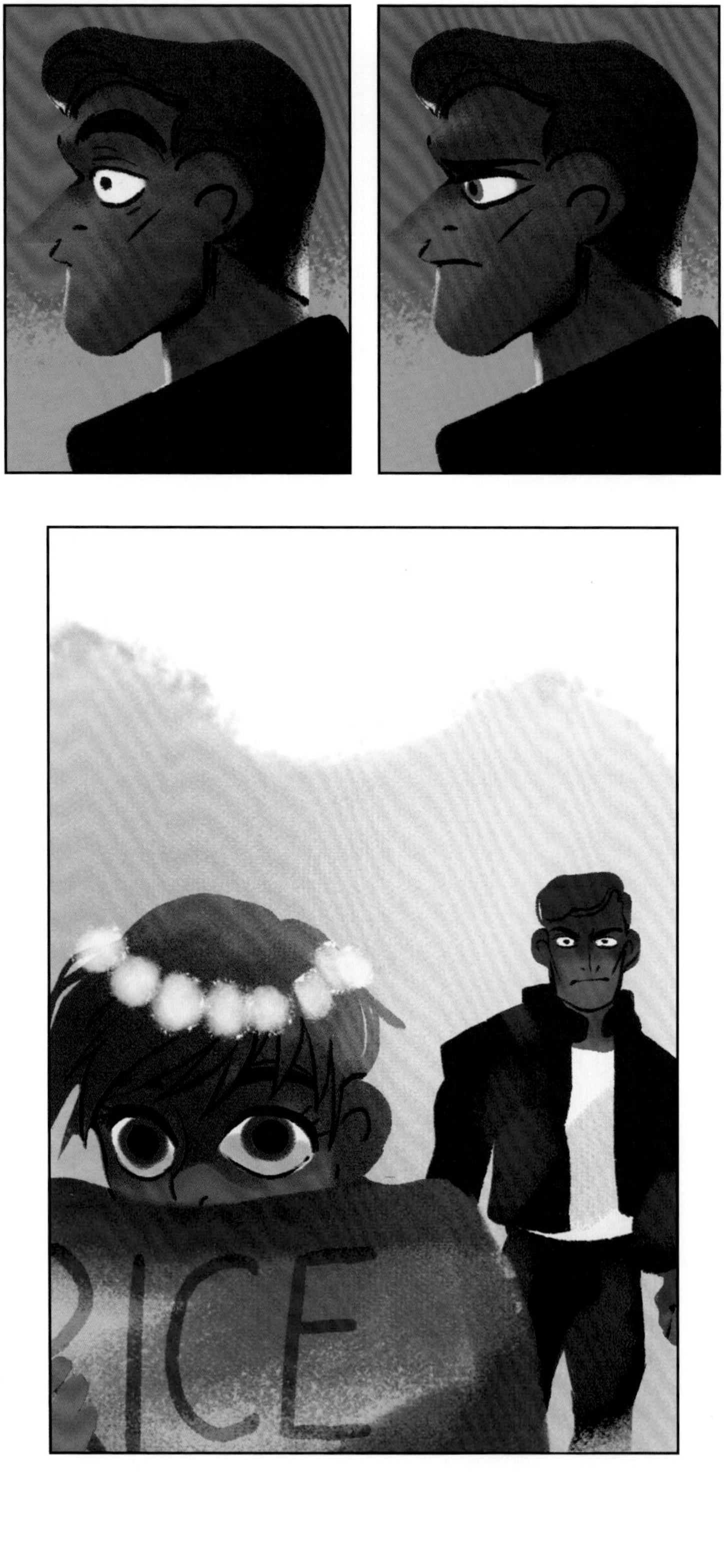
ICE

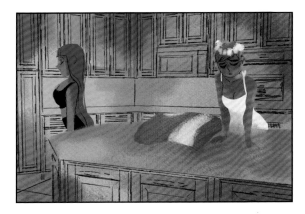

I thought we didn't allow men in the house?

Persephone, he's my brother. Come on?

Sigh, sorry. I think I'm just a little overtired from last night.

I'm sorry he's being weird.

He's just trying to look out for you in his own way.

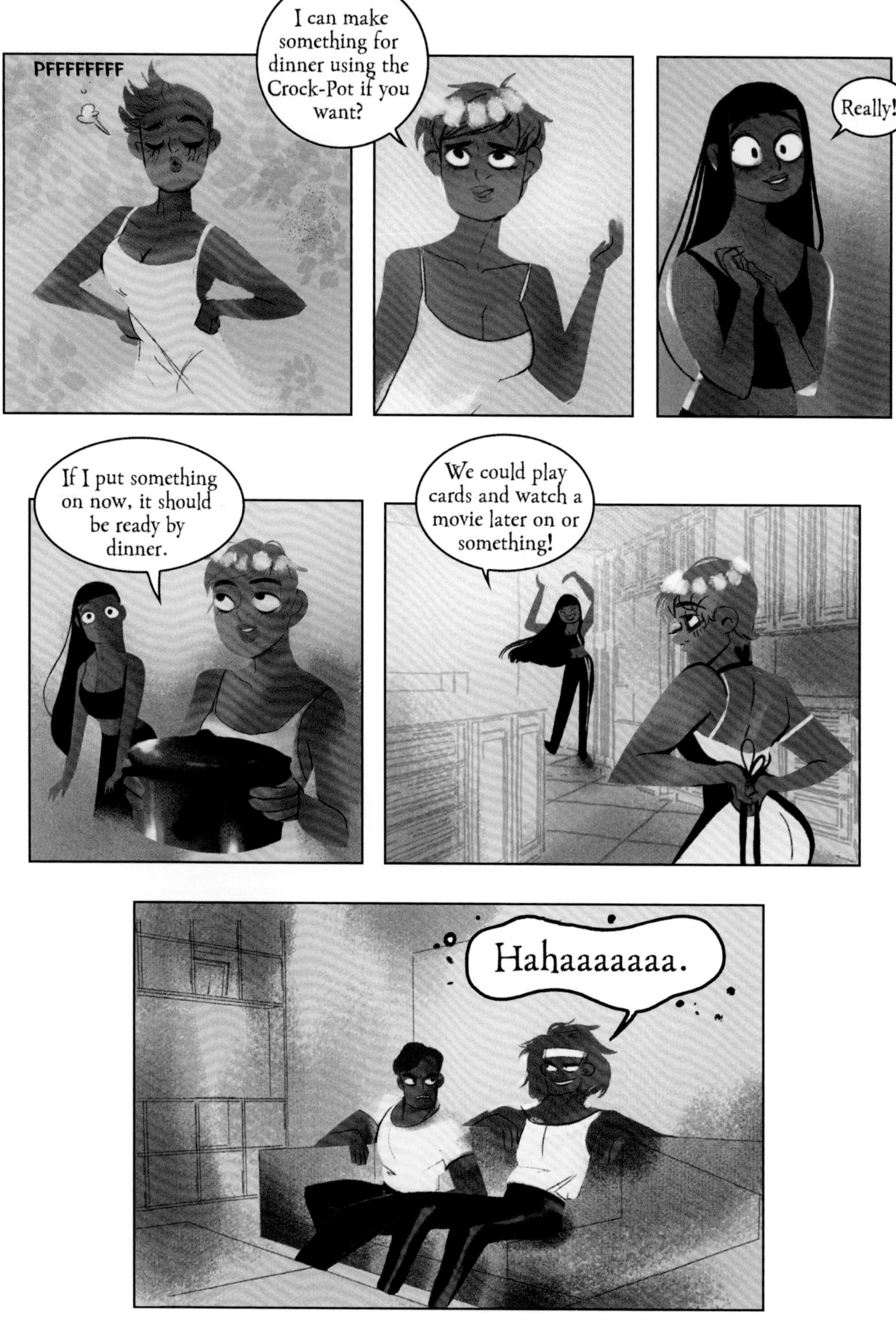
PFFFFFFFF
I can make something for dinner using the Crock-Pot if you want?
Really!?
If I put something on now, it should be ready by dinner.
We could play cards and watch a movie later on or something!
Hahaaaaaaa.

She can't stand you. I've never seen her so worked up.
What kind of an outfit is that?
I can see your damned belly button.
Maybe you should cover up.

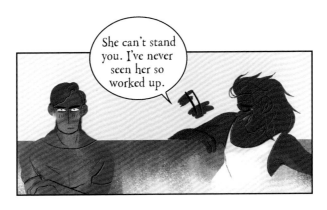

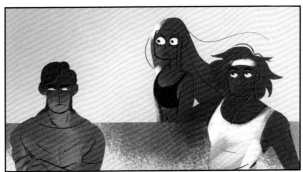

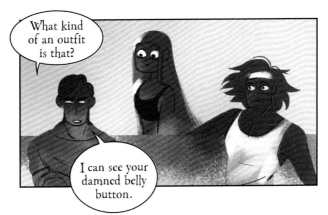

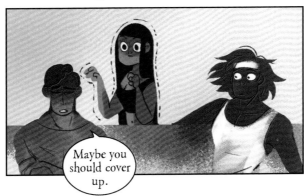

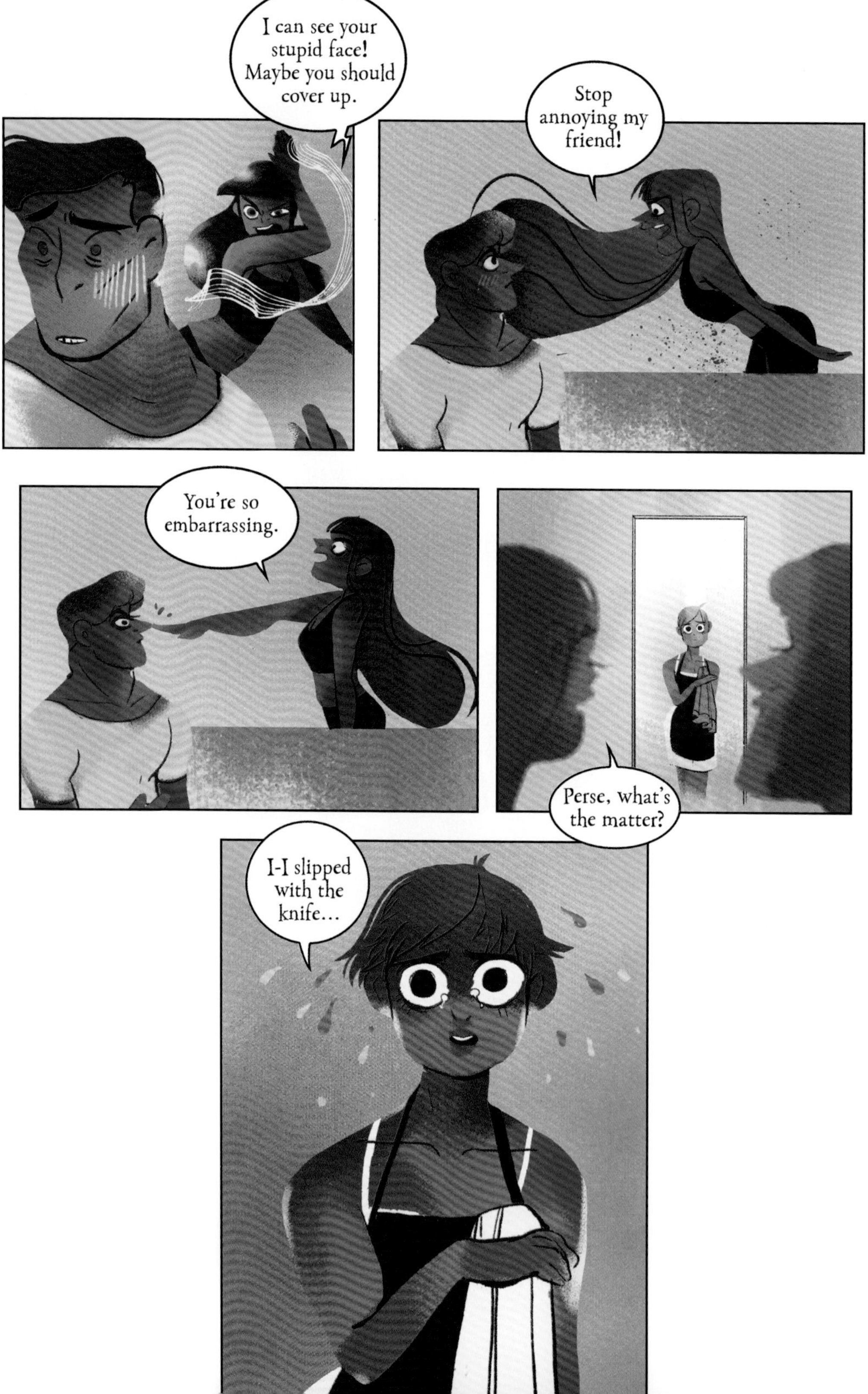
I can see your stupid face! Maybe you should cover up.
Stop annoying my friend!
You're so embarrassing.
Perse, what's the matter?
I-I slipped with the knife...

EPISODE 22: A WOLF IN THE HENHOUSE (PART I)

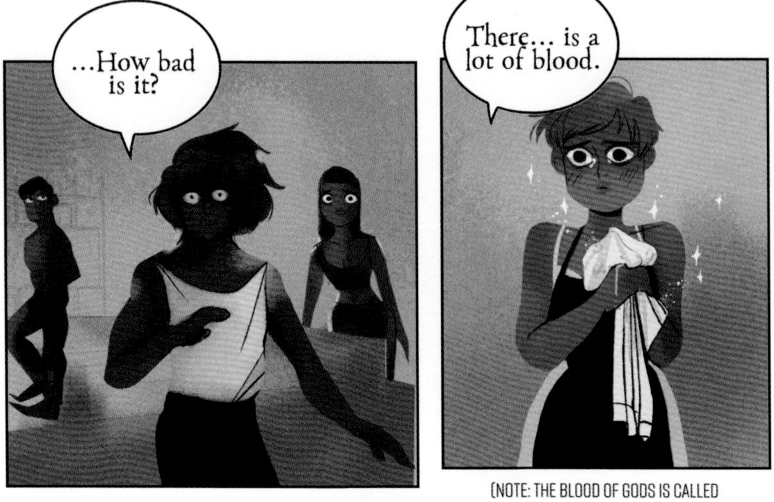
...How bad is it?
There... is a lot of blood.

(NOTE: THE BLOOD OF GODS IS CALLED **ICHOR** AND IS A GOLDEN COLOR)

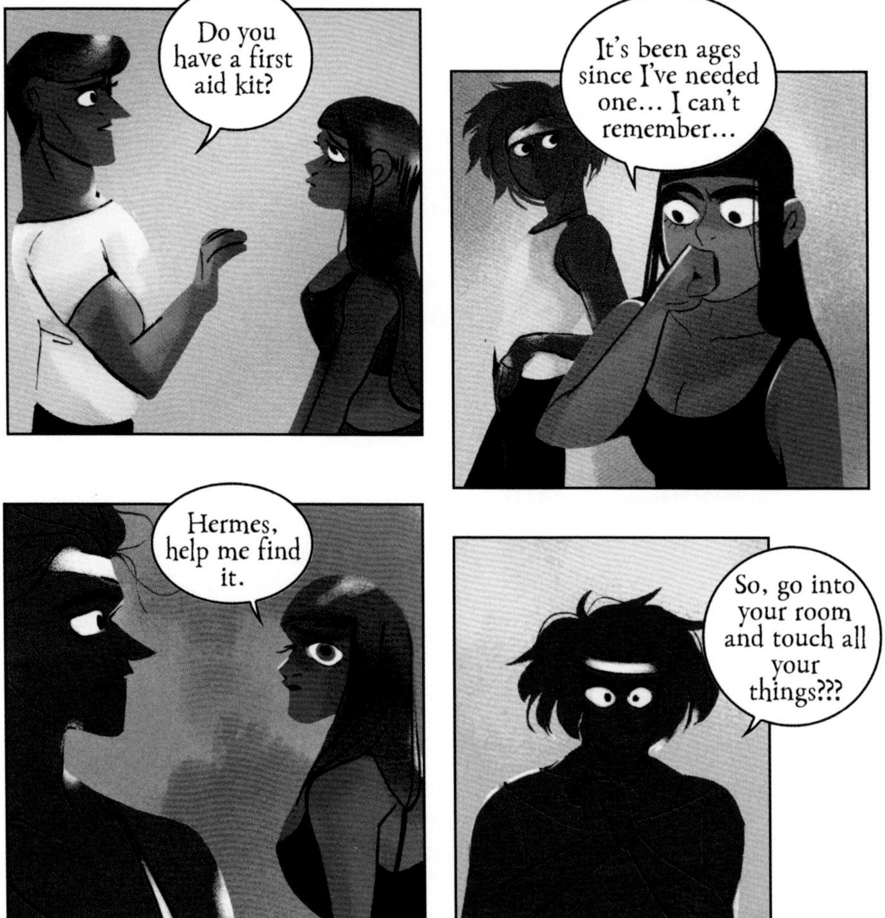
Do you have a first aid kit?
It's been ages since I've needed one... I can't remember...
Hermes, help me find it.
So, go into your room and touch all your things???

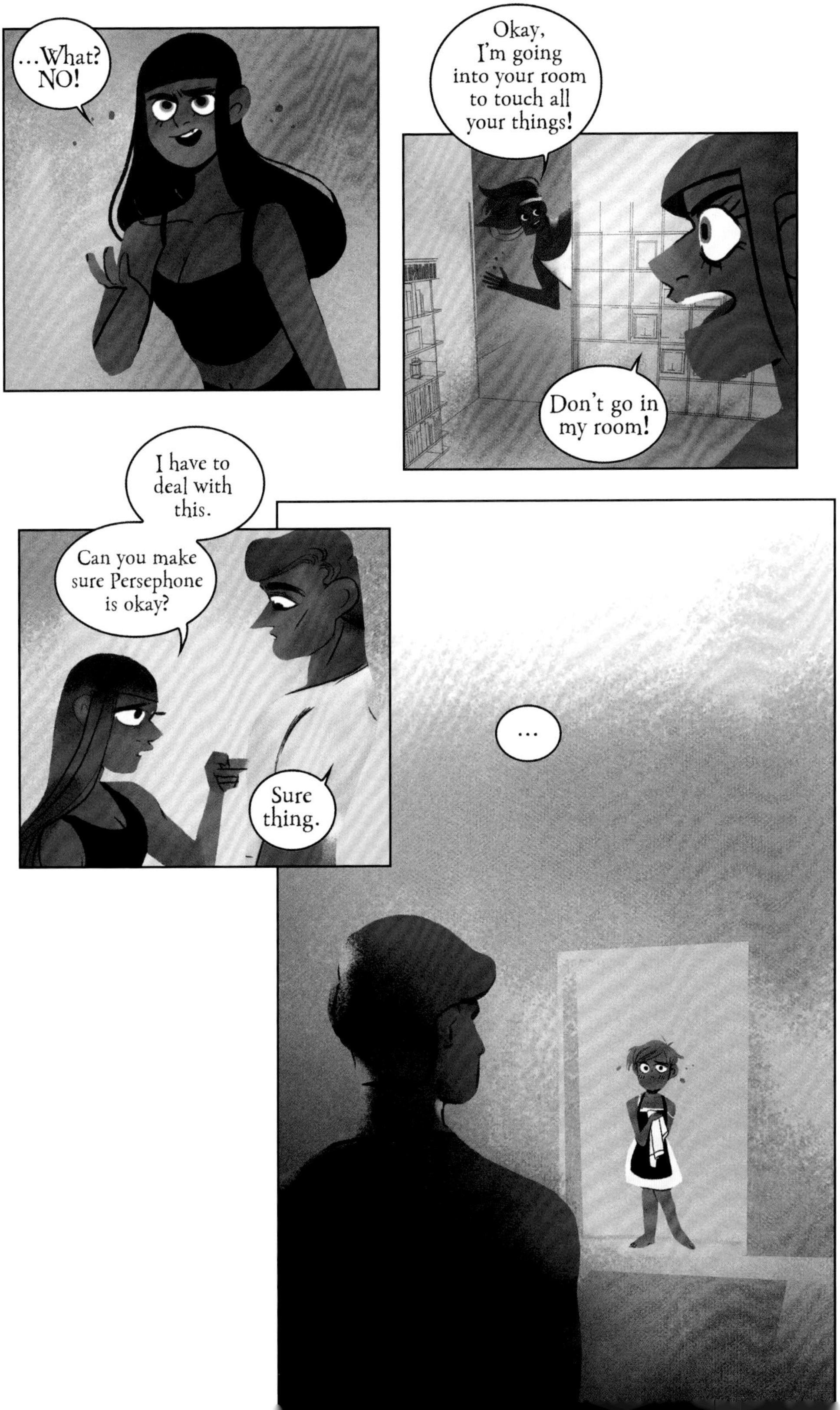

...What? NO!
Okay, I'm going into your room to touch all your things!
Don't go in my room!
I have to deal with this.
Can you make sure Persephone is okay?
Sure thing.
...

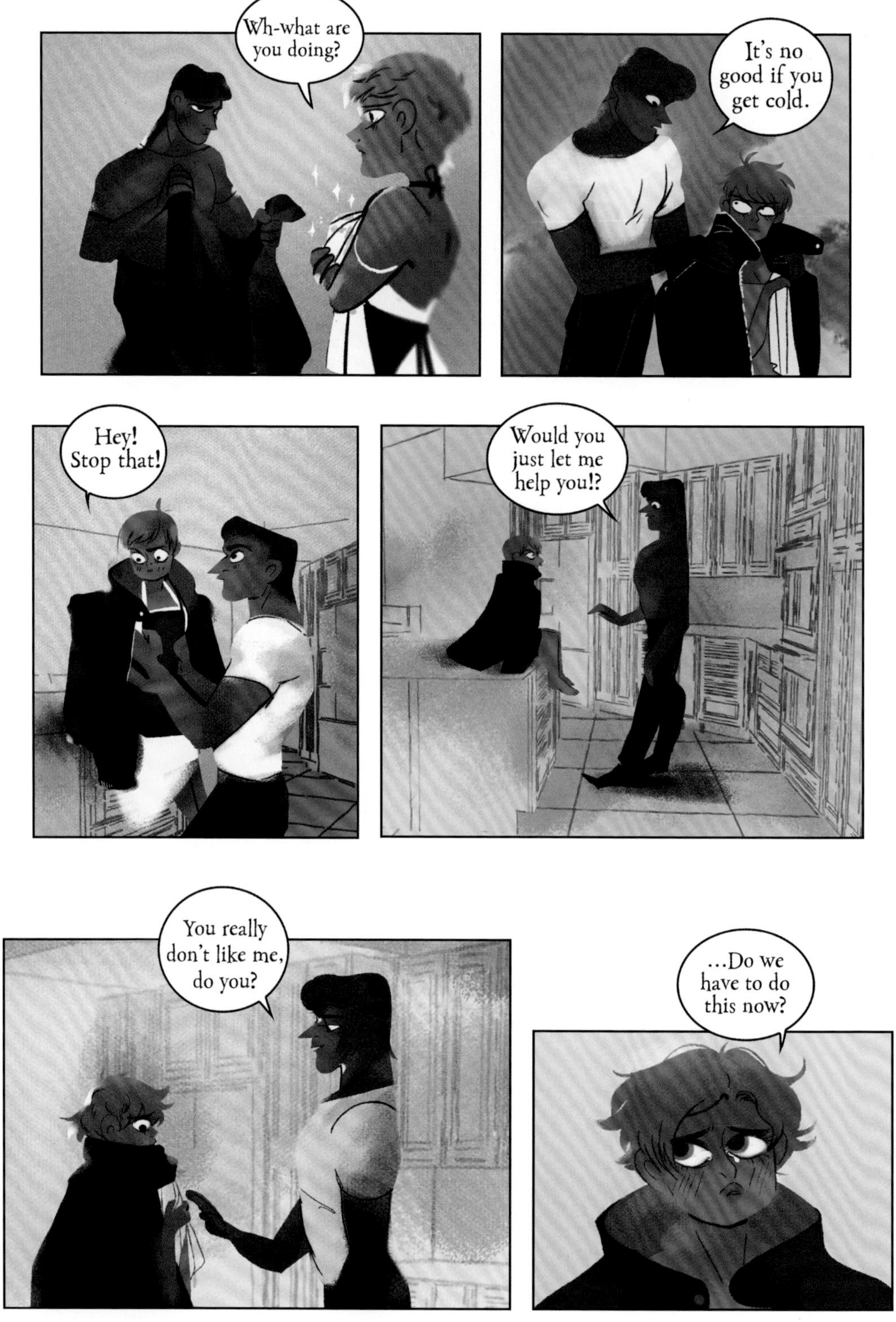
Wh-what are you doing?
It's no good if you get cold.
Hey! Stop that!
Would you just let me help you!?
You really don't like me, do you?
...Do we have to do this now?

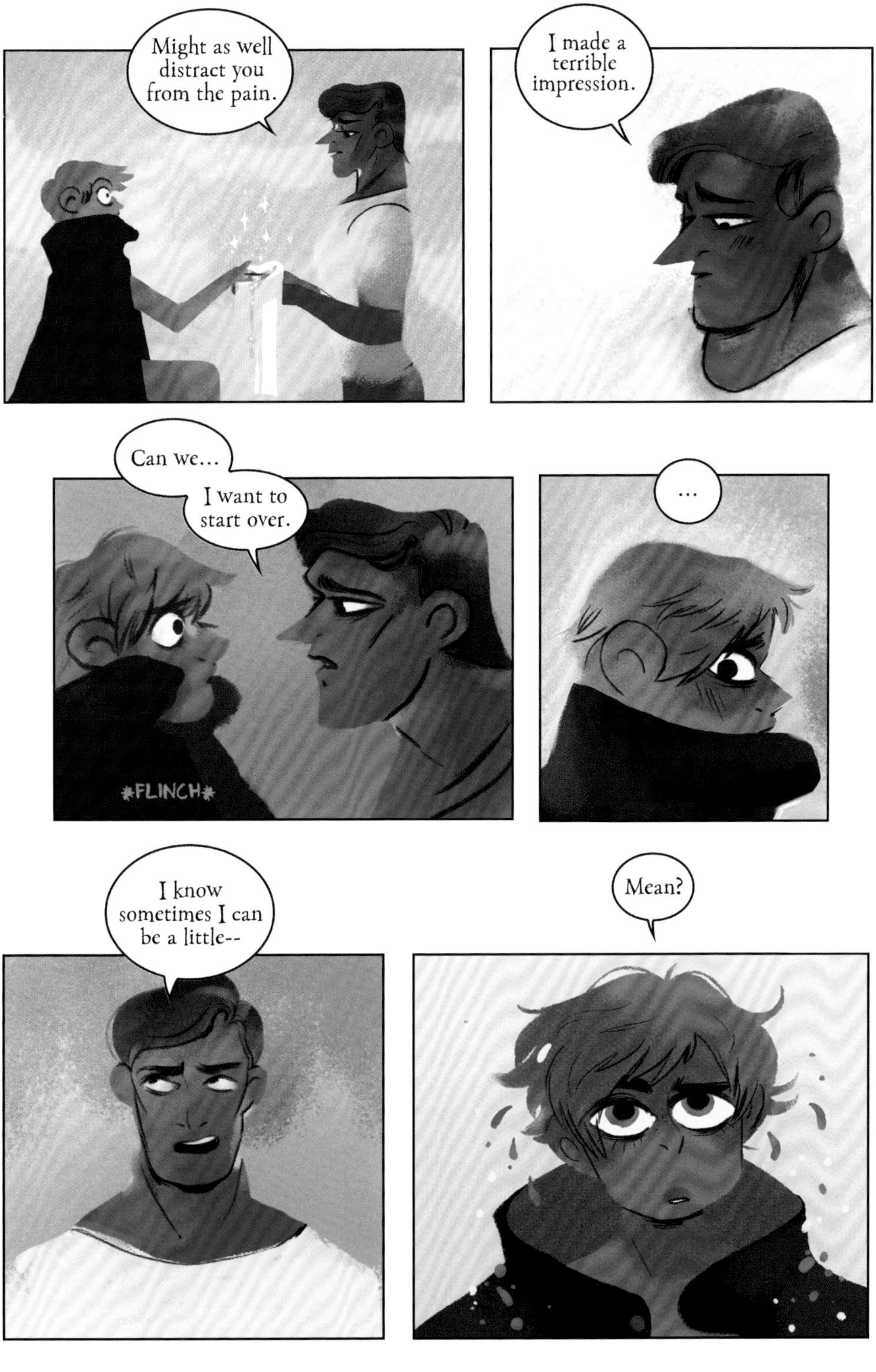
Might as well distract you from the pain.
I made a terrible impression.
Can we...
I want to start over.
FLINCH
...
I know sometimes I can be a little--
Mean?

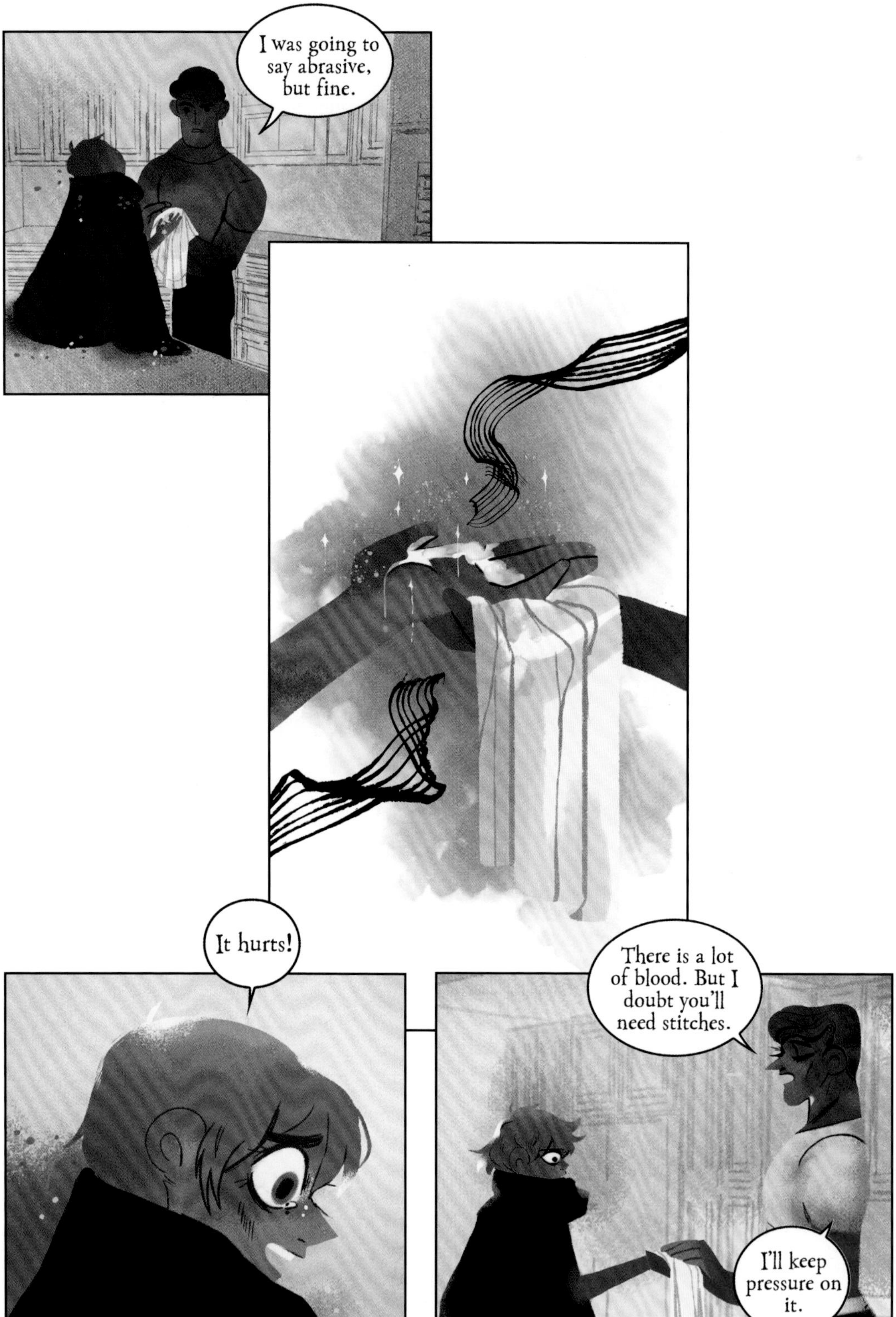
I was going to say abrasive, but fine.
It hurts!
There is a lot of blood. But I doubt you'll need stitches.
I'll keep pressure on it.

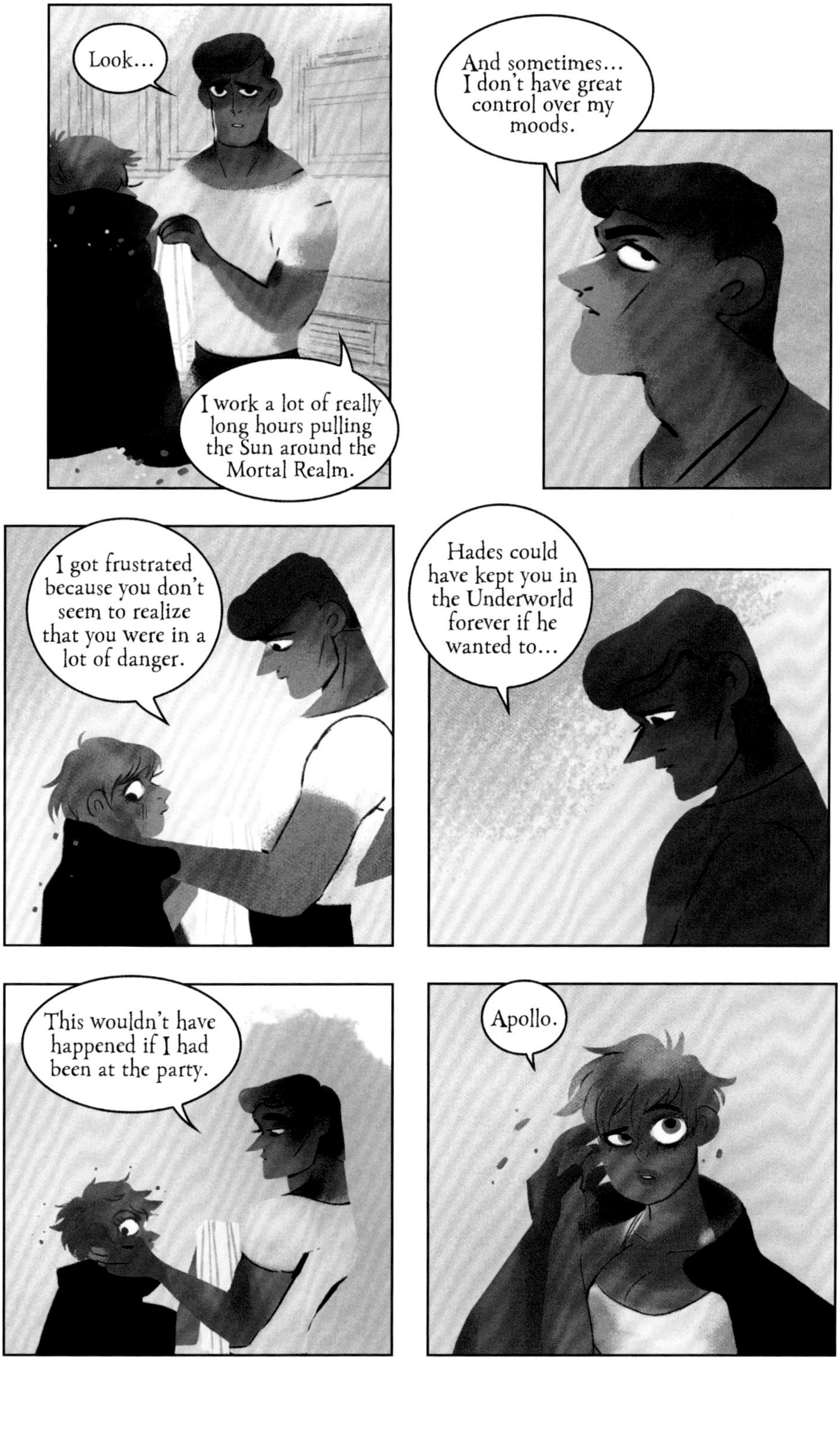
Look...
I work a lot of really long hours pulling the Sun around the Mortal Realm.
And sometimes... I don't have great control over my moods.
I got frustrated because you don't seem to realize that you were in a lot of danger.
Hades could have kept you in the Underworld forever if he wanted to...
This wouldn't have happened if I had been at the party.
Apollo.

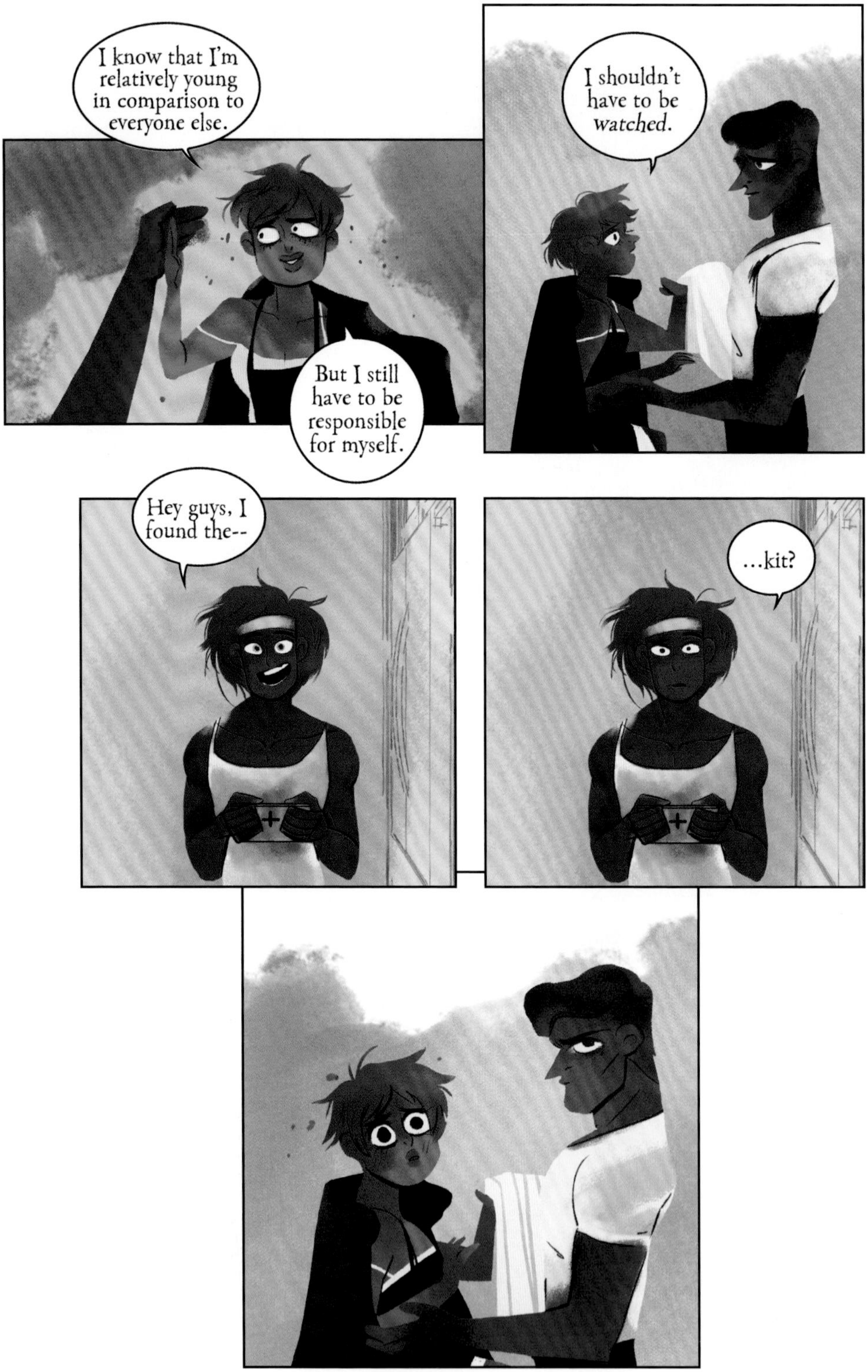

I know that I'm relatively young in comparison to everyone else.
But I still have to be responsible for myself.
I shouldn't have to be *watched*.
Hey guys, I found the--
...kit?

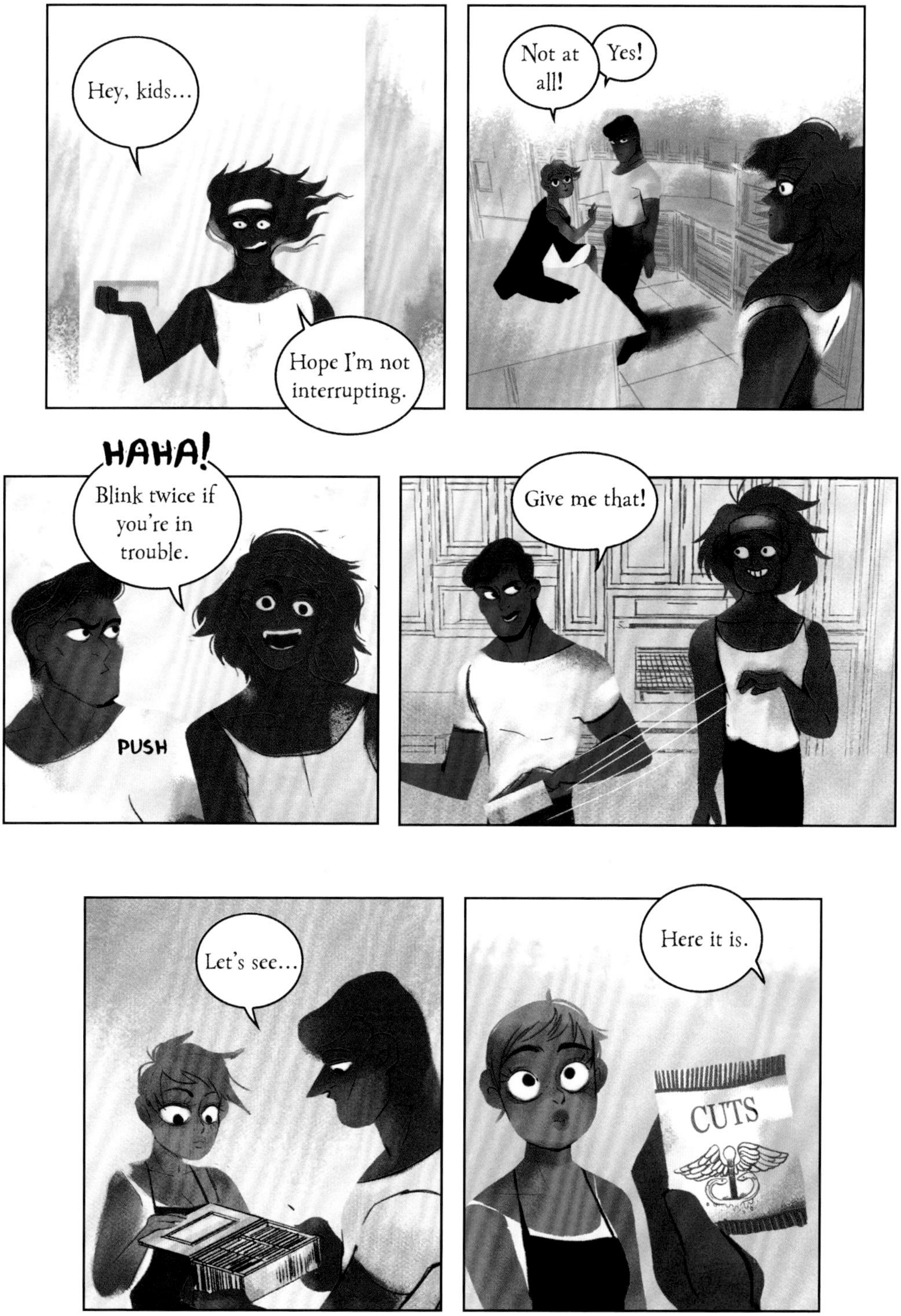
Hey, kids...
Hope I'm not interrupting.
Not at all!
Yes!
HAHA!
Blink twice if you're in trouble.
PUSH
Give me that!
Let's see...
Here it is.
CUTS

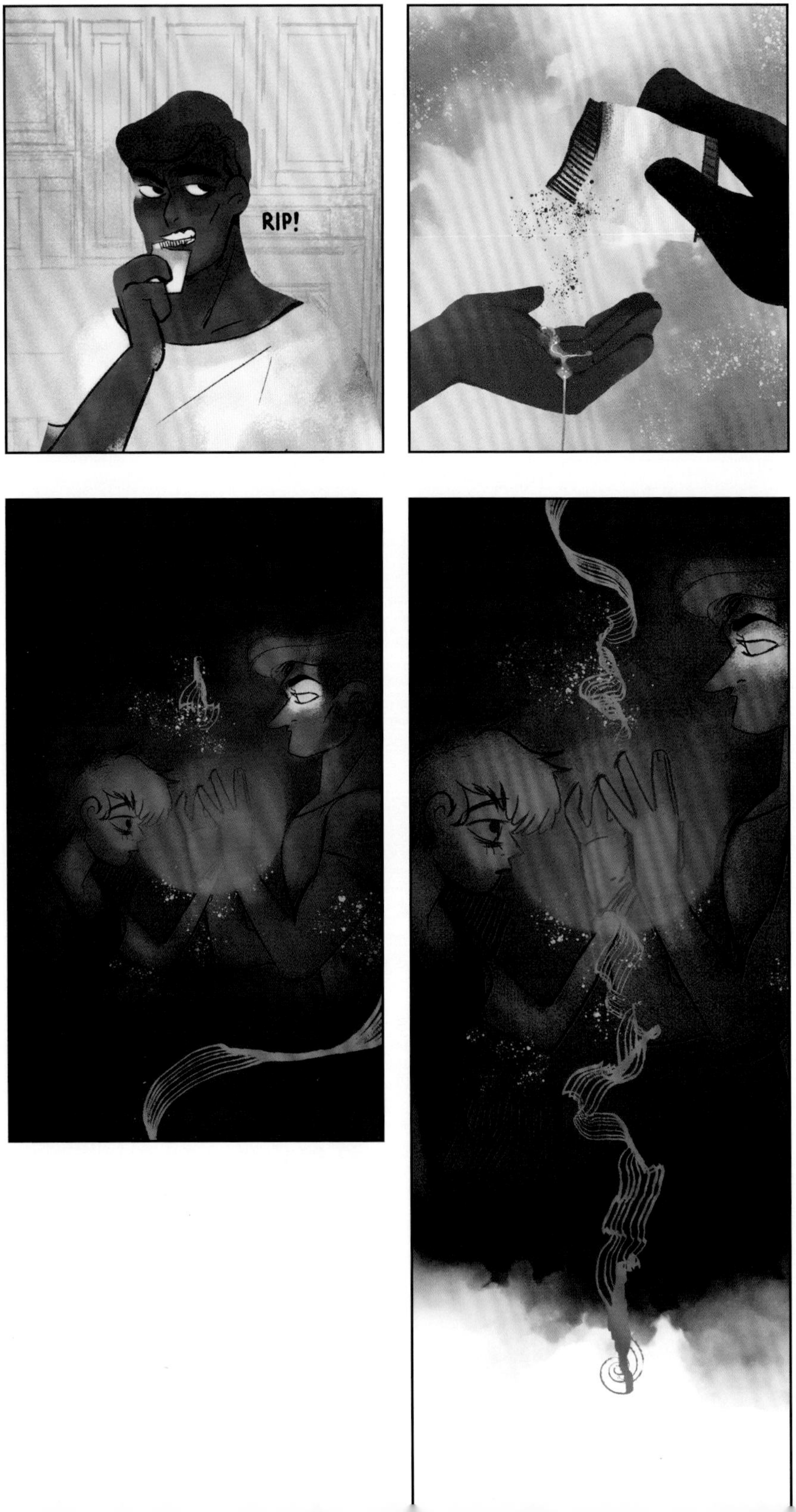
RIP!

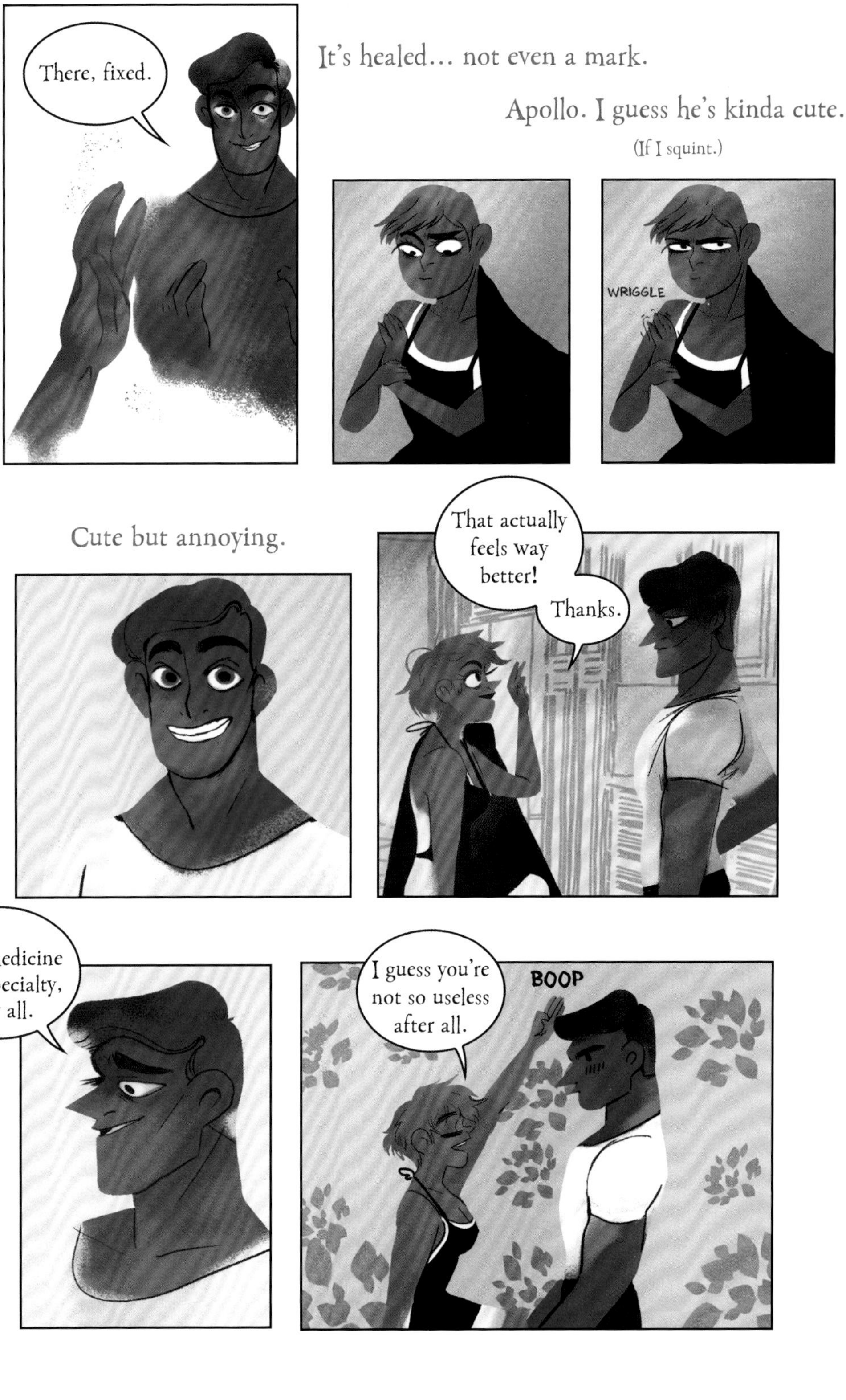

There, fixed.
It's healed... not even a mark.
Apollo. I guess he's kinda cute.
(If I squint.)
WRIGGLE
Cute but annoying.
That actually feels way better!
Thanks.
Well, medicine is my specialty, after all.
I guess you're not so useless after all.
BOOP

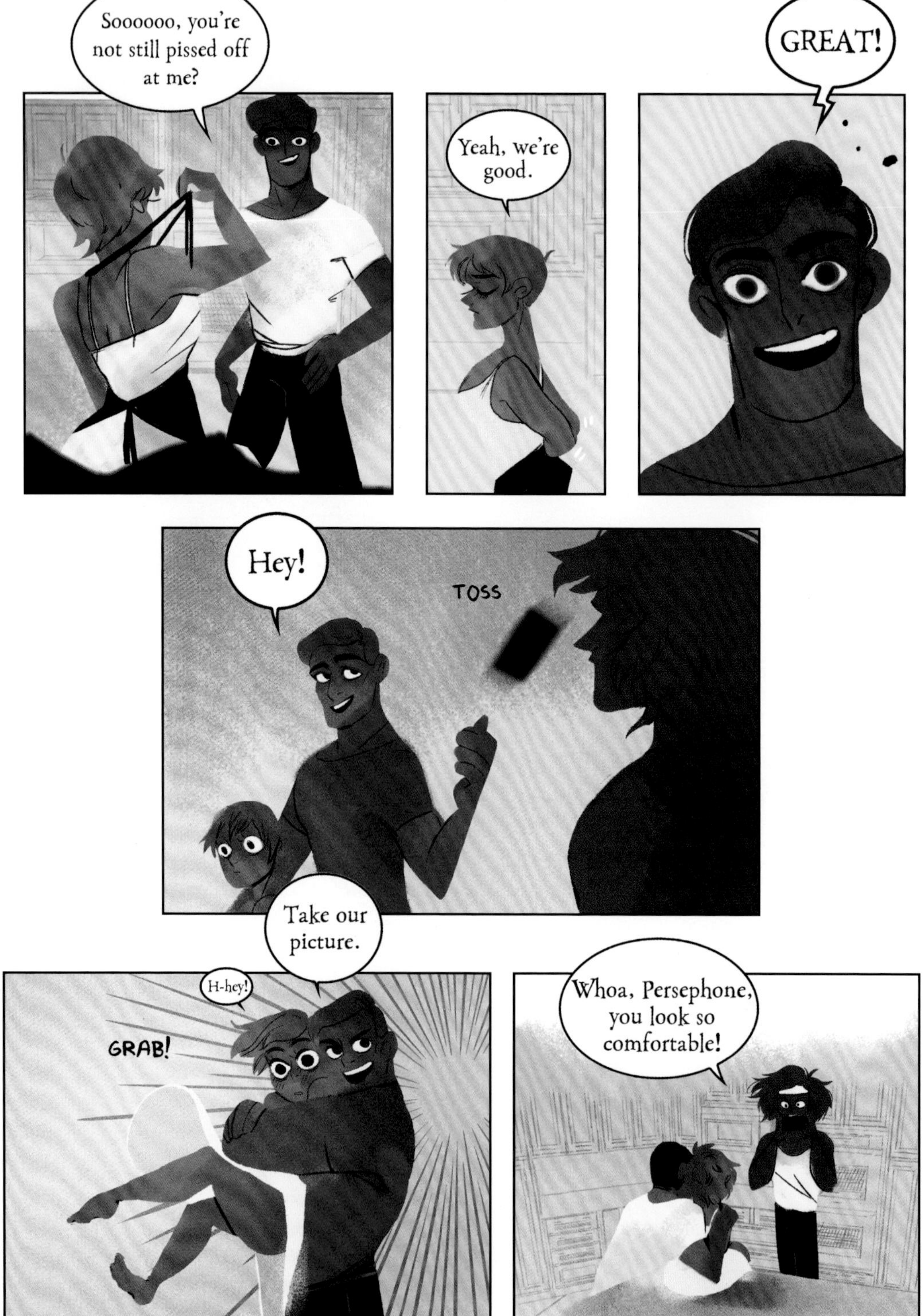
Soooooo, you're not still pissed off at me?
Yeah, we're good.
GREAT!
Hey!
TOSS
Take our picture.
H-hey!
GRAB!
Whoa, Persephone, you look so comfortable!

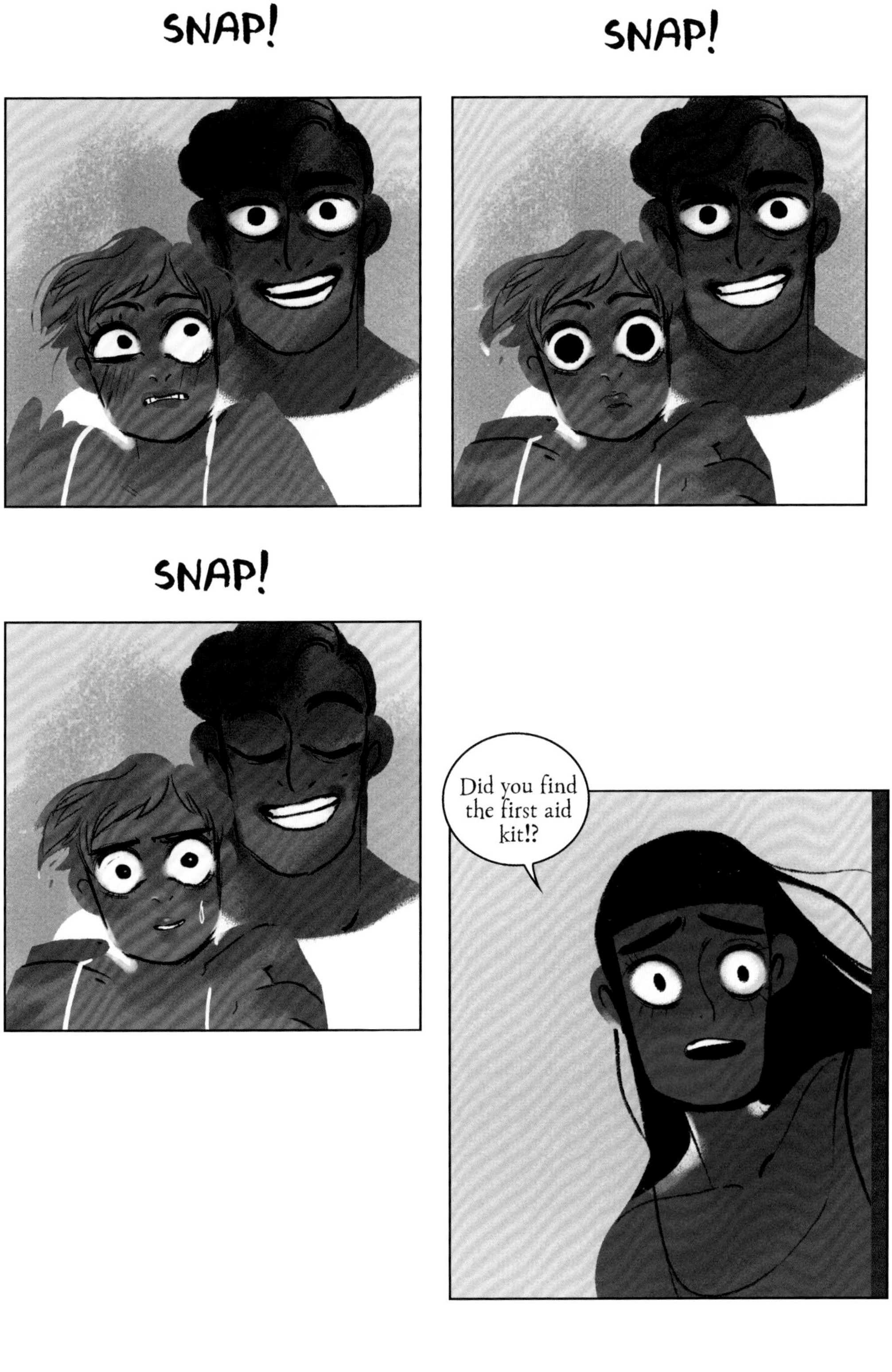
SNAP!
SNAP!
SNAP!
Did you find the first aid kit!?

FIXED!

EPISODE 23: A WOLF IN THE HENHOUSE (PART 2)

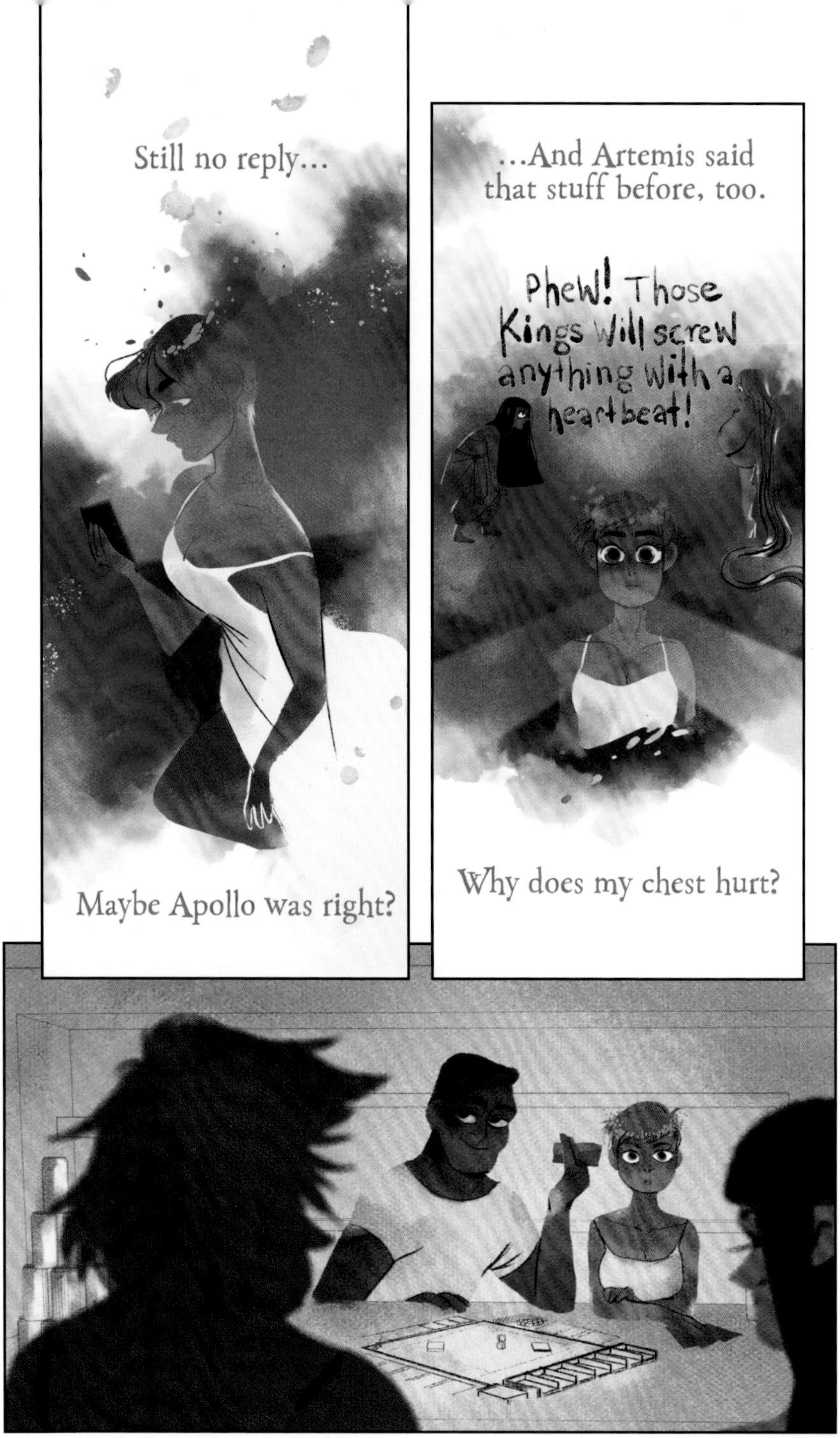
Still no reply...
Maybe Apollo was right?
...And Artemis said that stuff before, too.
Phew! Those Kings will screw anything with a heartbeat!
Why does my chest hurt?

Do they have a point?

All I ever hear about
are Zeus's and Poseidon's escapades.

Is Hades the same?

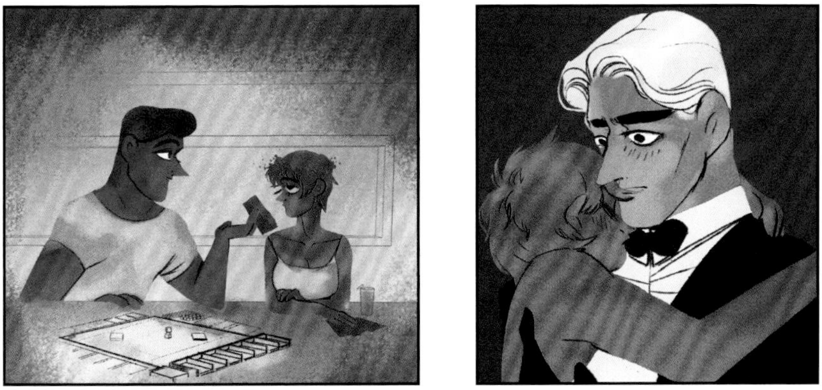

He didn't seem that way.

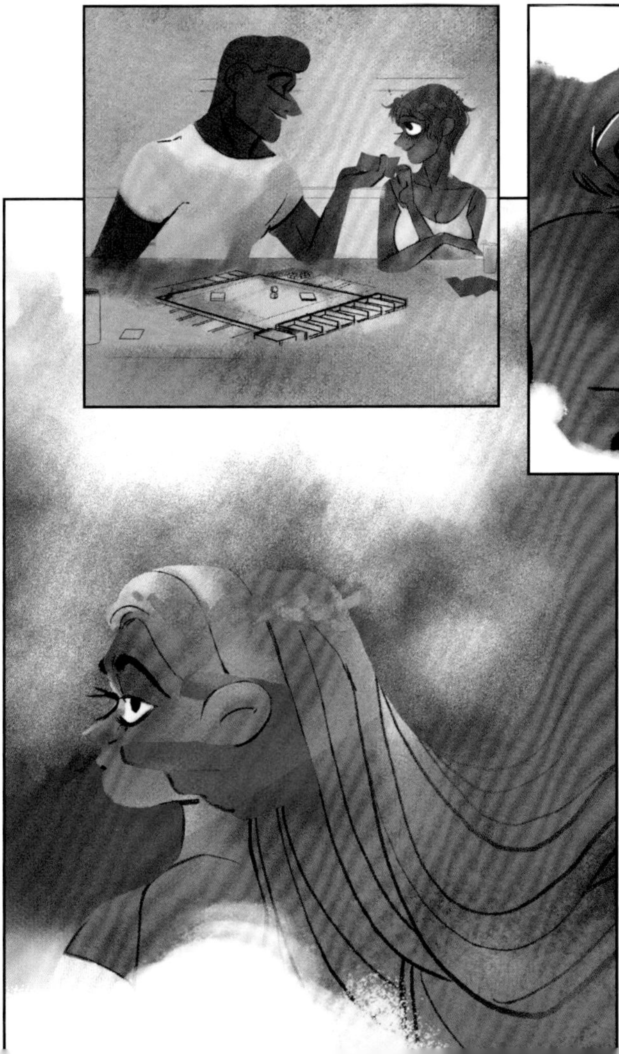

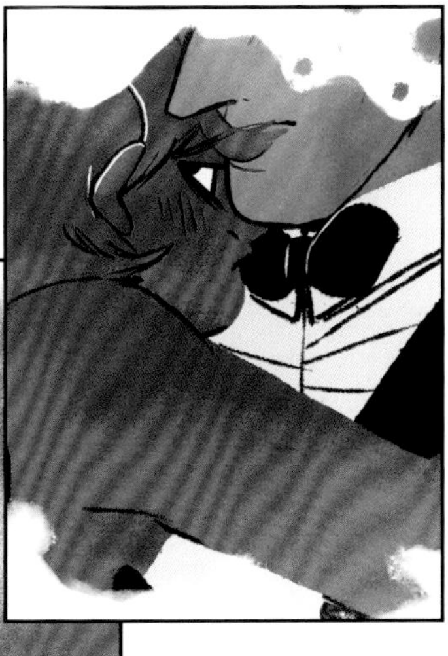

I'd be lying if I said I didn't find
the attention exciting.

I like the way I feel when he looks at me.

So unrealistic!

zzzz

GULP

I shouldn't be thinking about this sort of stuff in the first place.

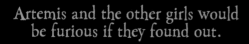

Artemis and the other girls would be furious if they found out.

It was so refreshing not to be treated like a child for once.

Why would he be interested in knowing me?

Just a minor goddess with a role of little to no impact.

YAWN

Everything is set out already...
for the rest of eternity.

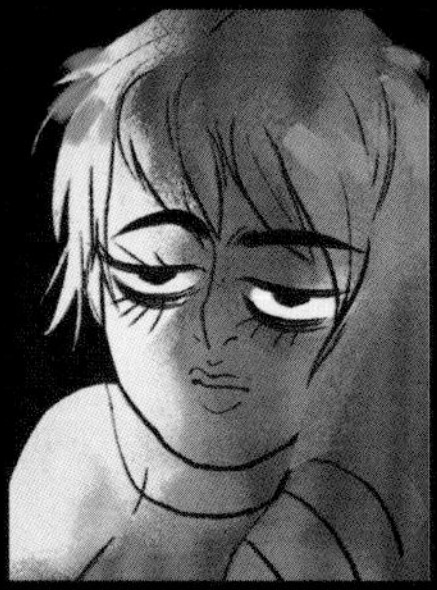

At least I can pick my own bedtime.

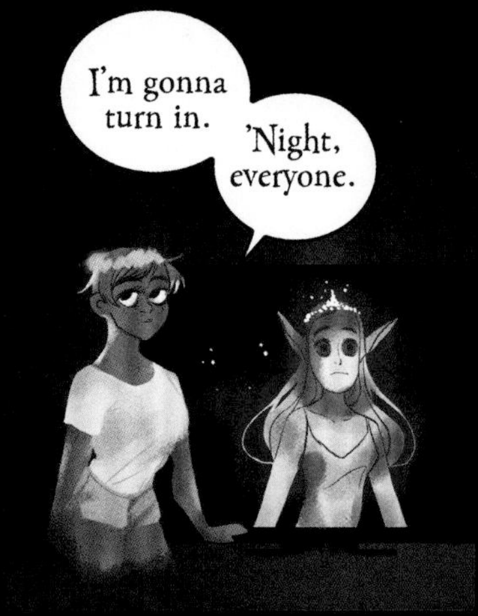
I'm gonna turn in.
'Night, everyone.

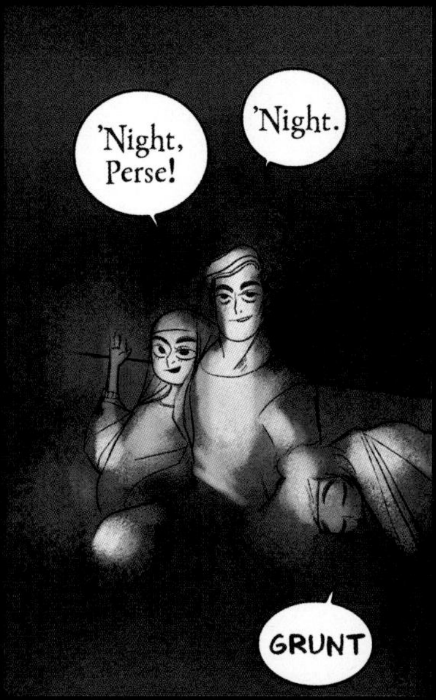
'Night, Perse!
'Night.
GRUNT

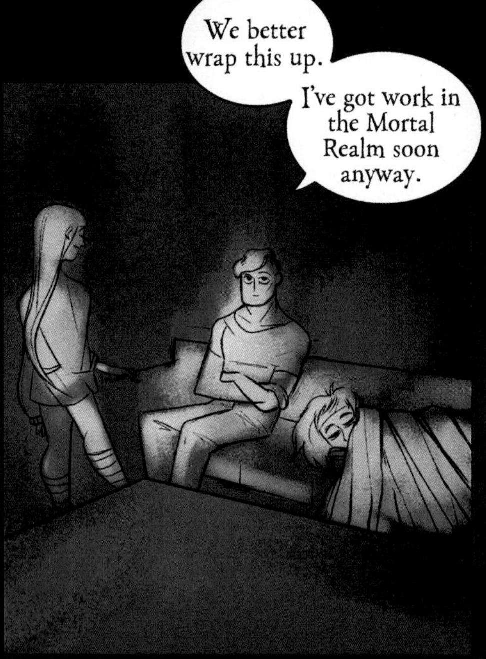
We better wrap this up.
I've got work in the Mortal Realm soon anyway.

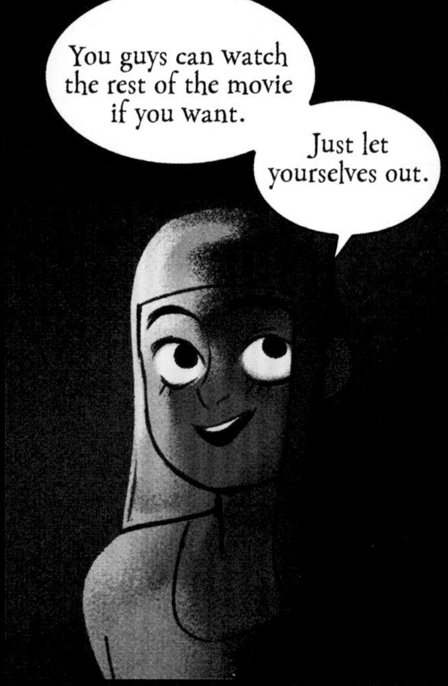
You guys can watch the rest of the movie if you want.
Just let yourselves out.

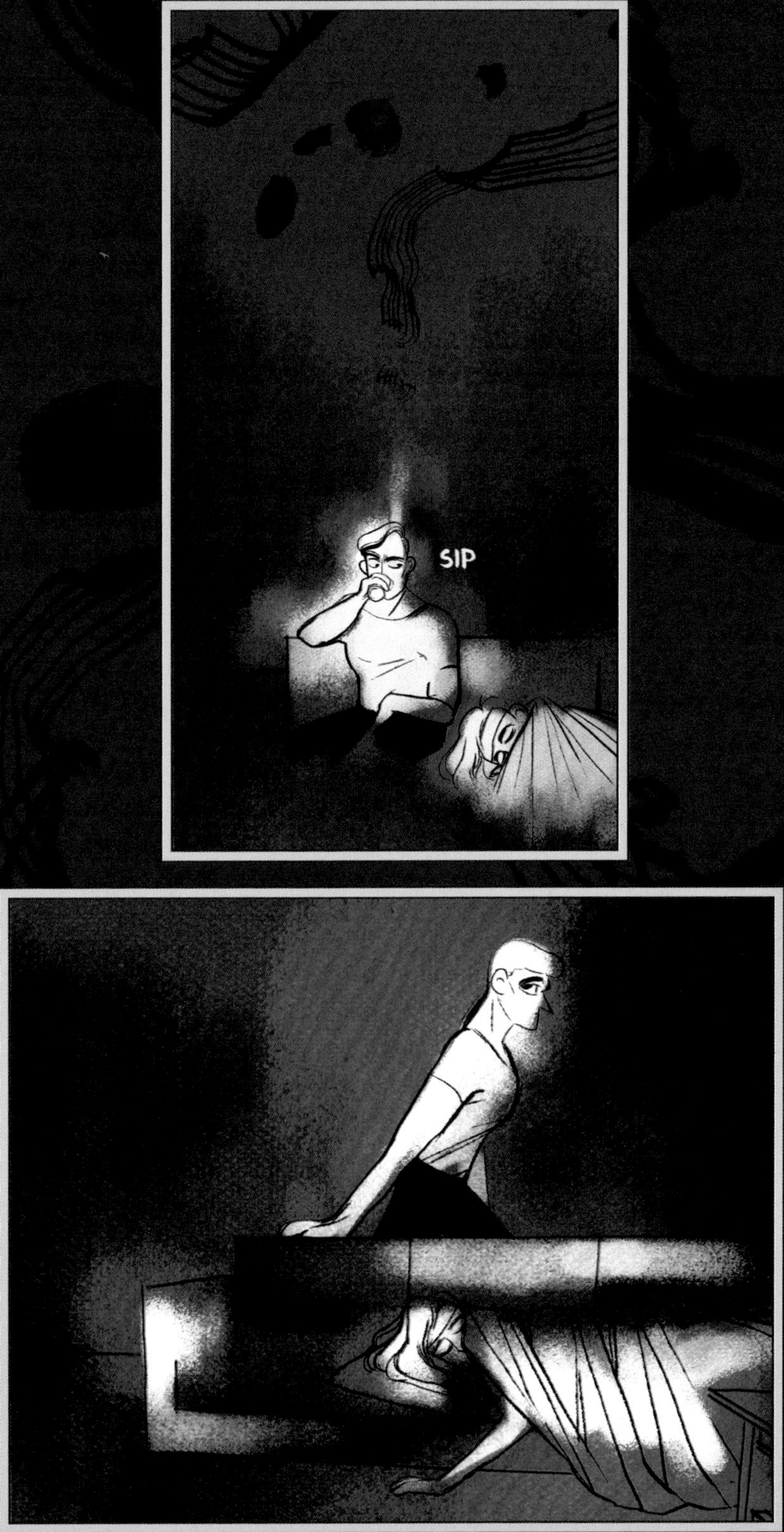
SIP

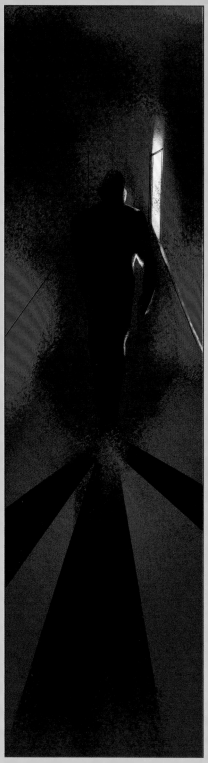

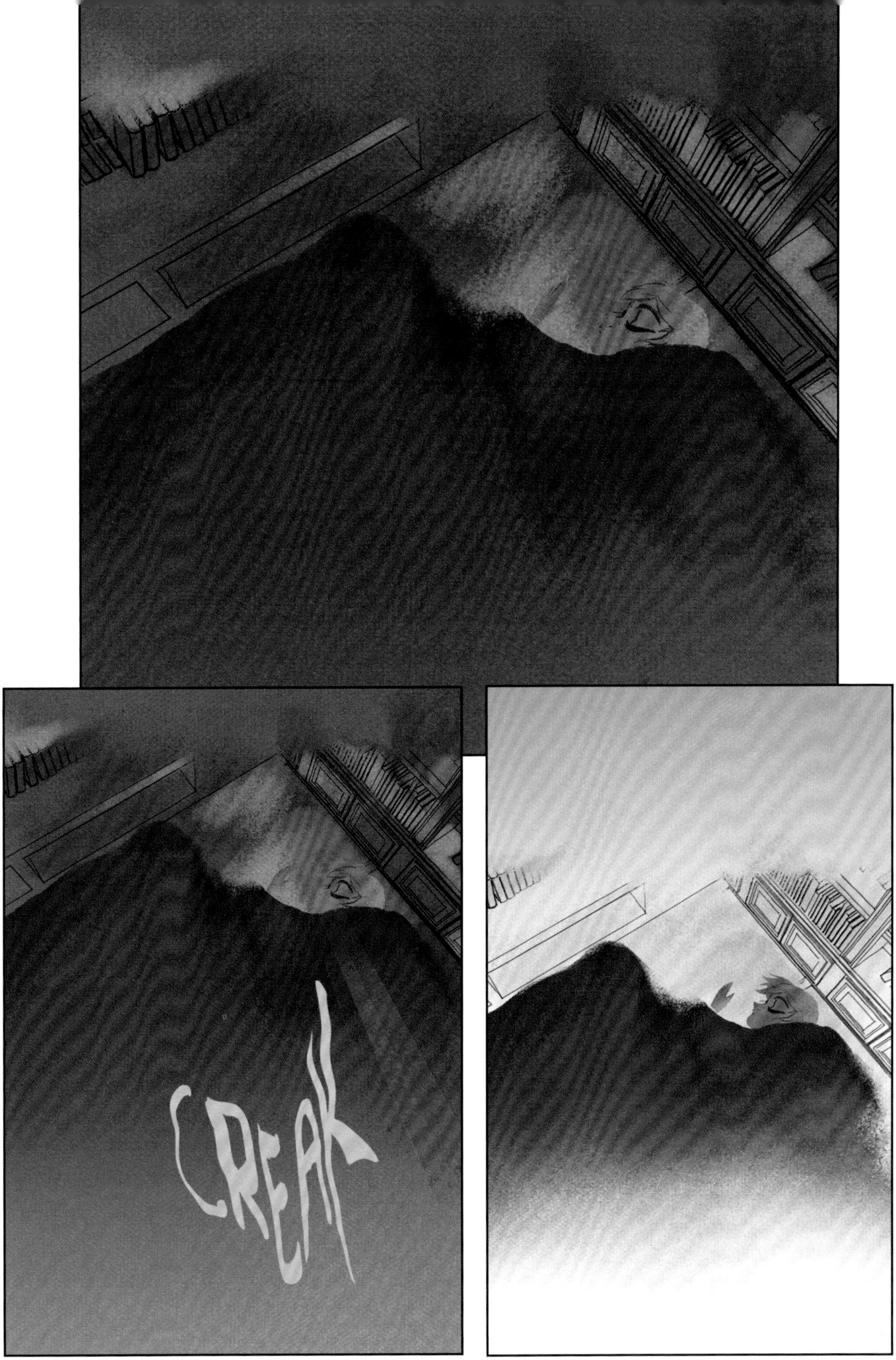
CREAK

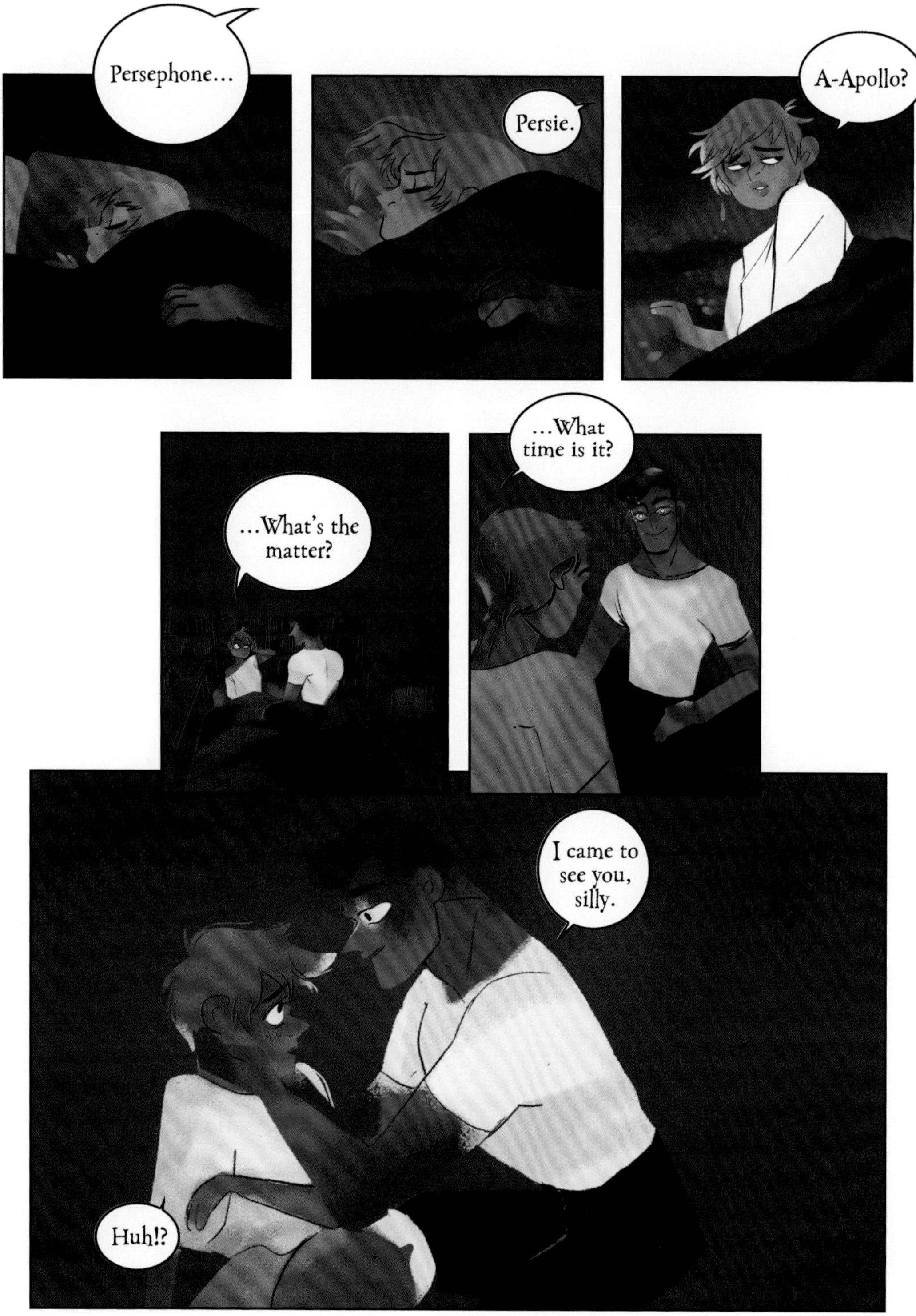
Persephone...
Persie.
A-Apollo?
...What's the matter?
...What time is it?
I came to see you, silly.
Huh!?

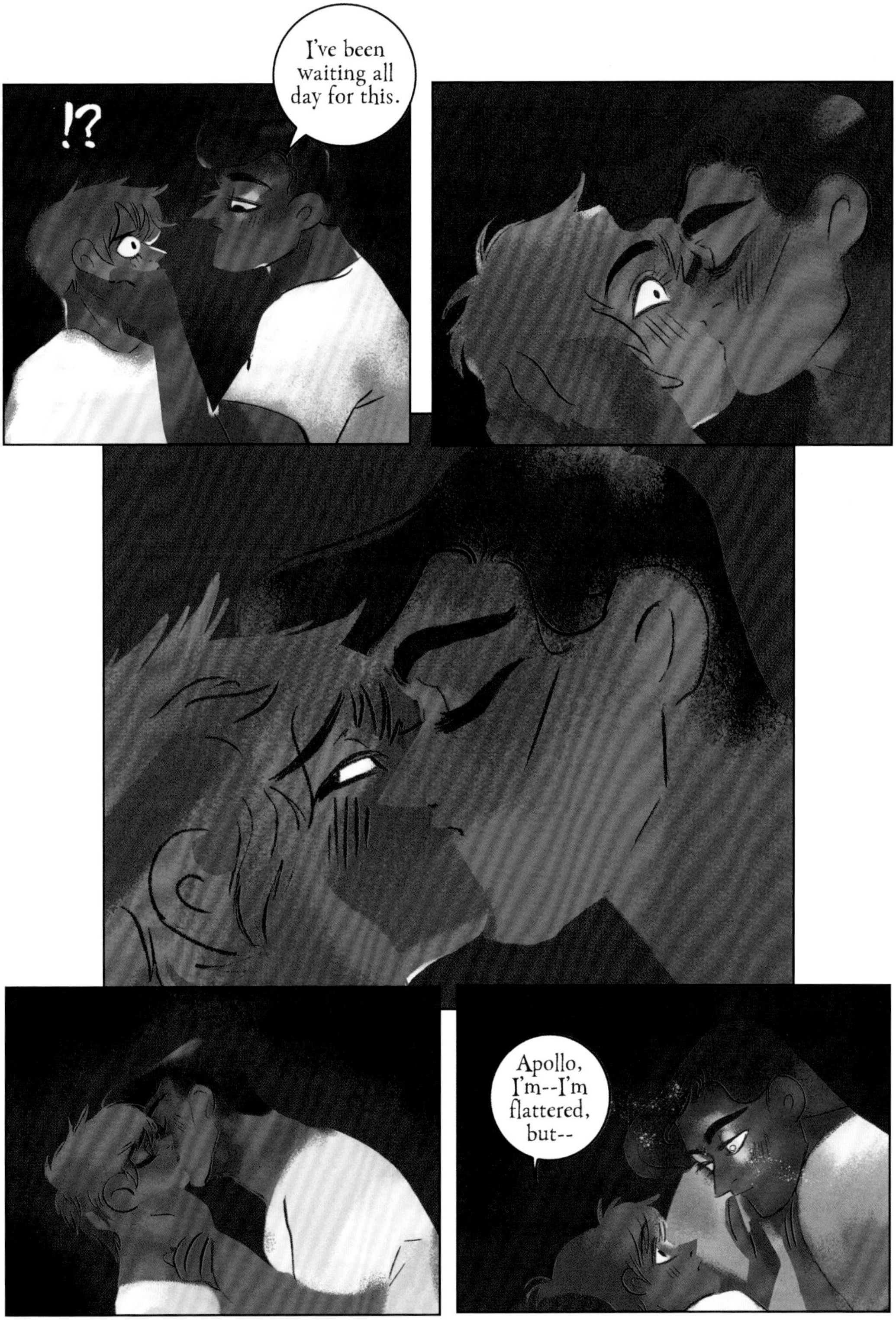
!?
I've been waiting all day for this.
Apollo, I'm--I'm flattered, but--

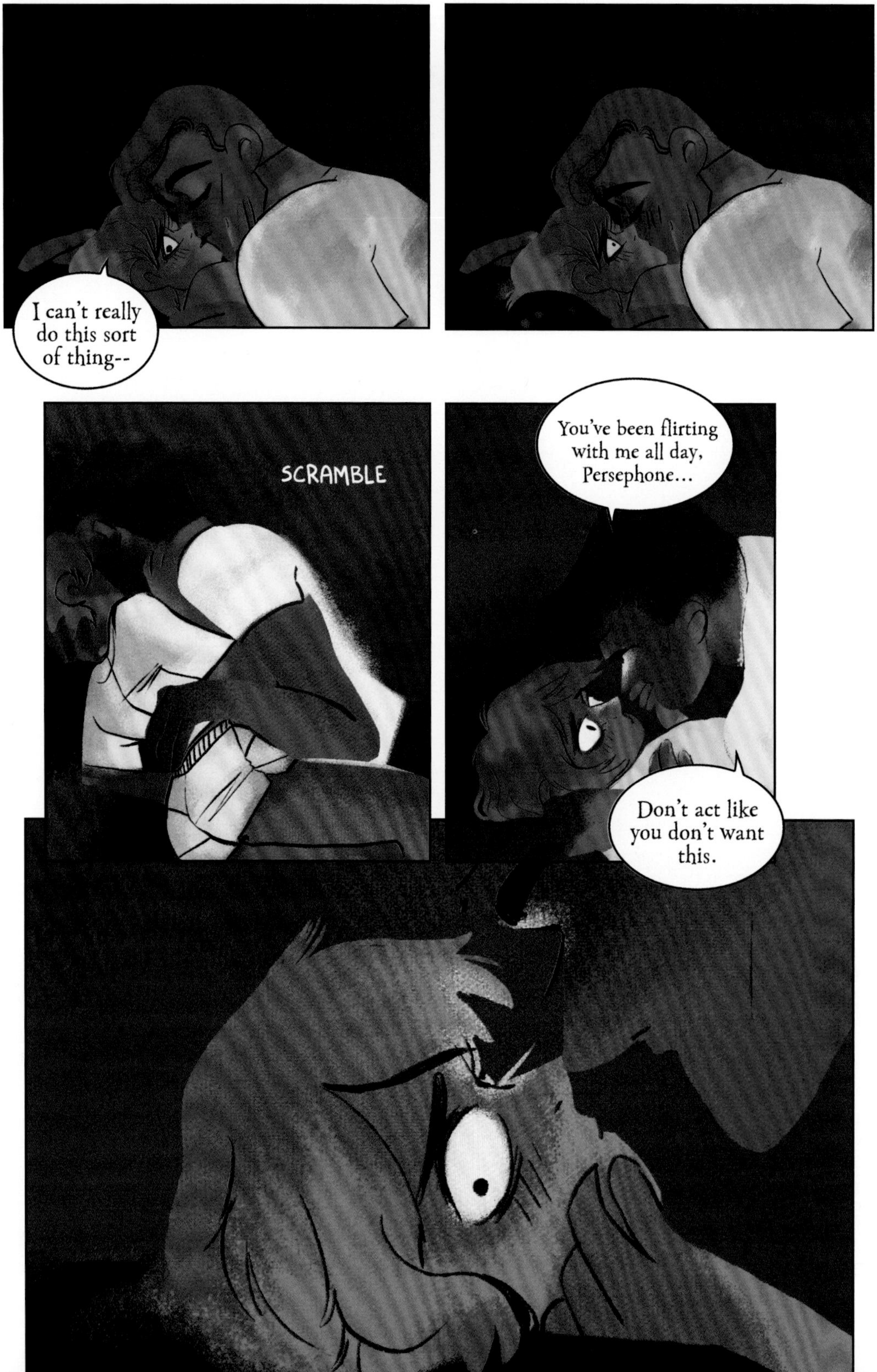
I can't really do this sort of thing--
SCRAMBLE
You've been flirting with me all day, Persephone...
Don't act like you don't want this.

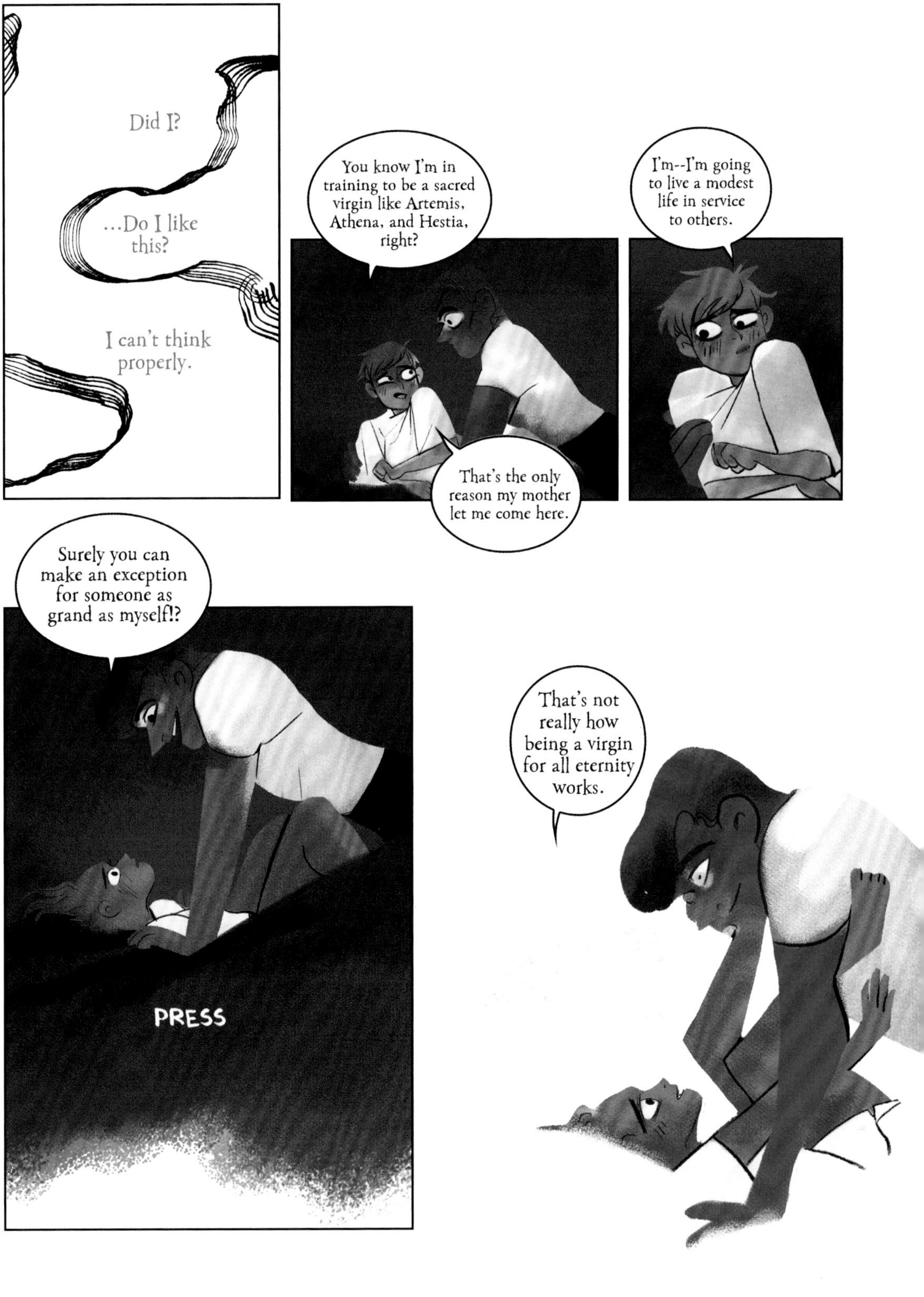
Did I?
...Do I like this?
I can't think properly.
You know I'm in training to be a sacred virgin like Artemis, Athena, and Hestia, right?
That's the only reason my mother let me come here.
I'm--I'm going to live a modest life in service to others.
Surely you can make an exception for someone as grand as myself!?
PRESS
That's not really how being a virgin for all eternity works.

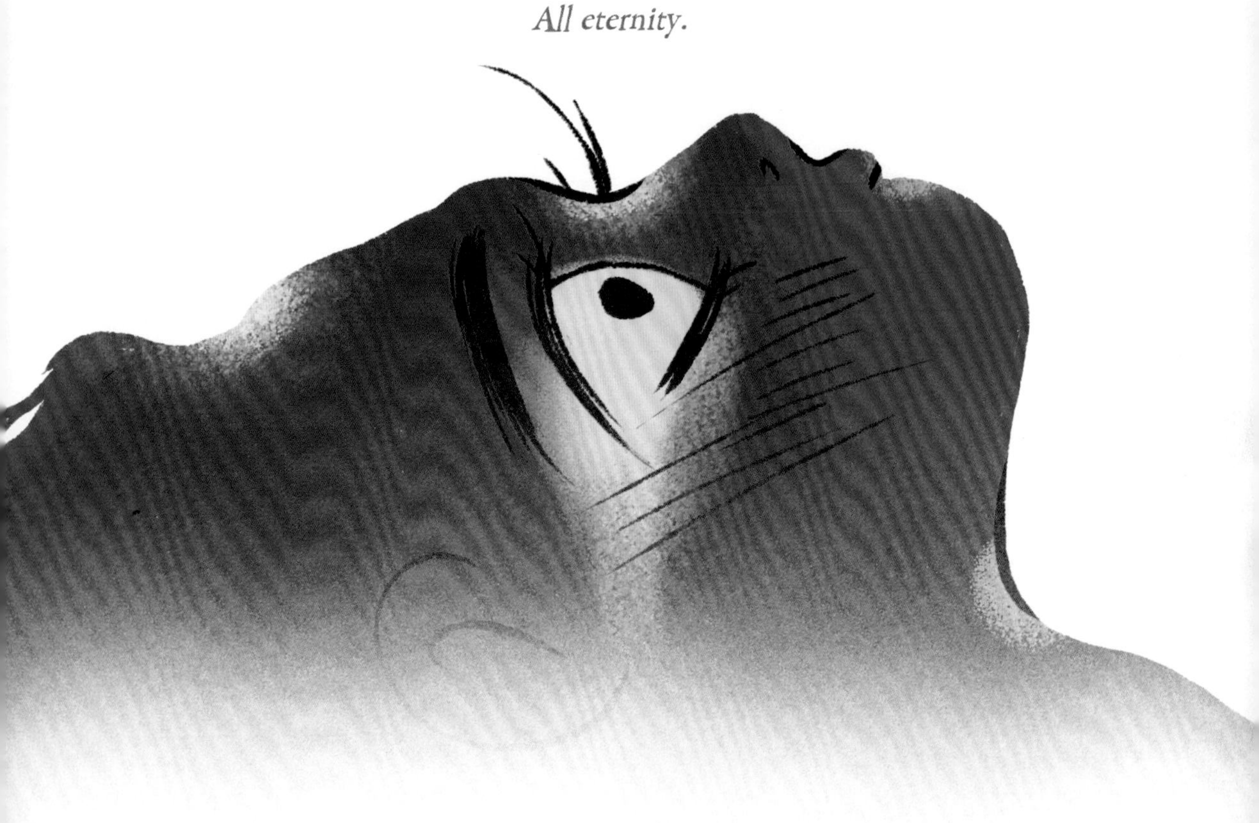
All eternity.

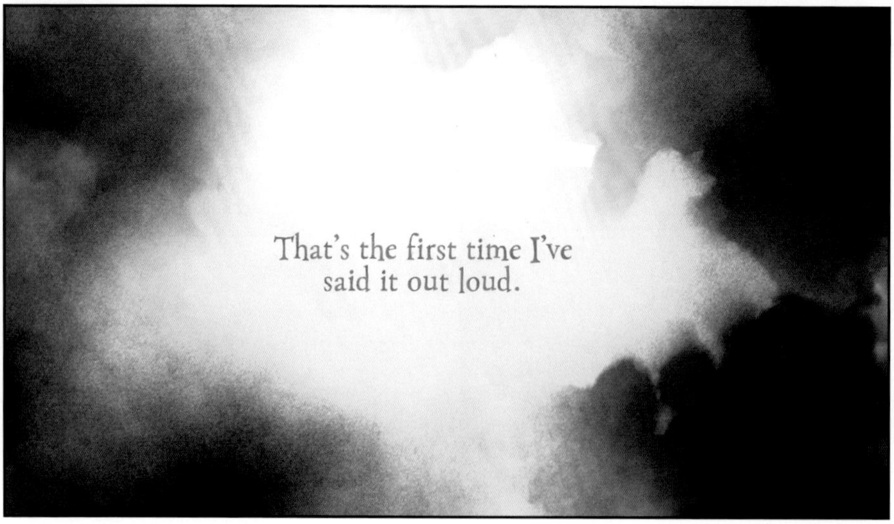
That's the first time I've said it out loud.

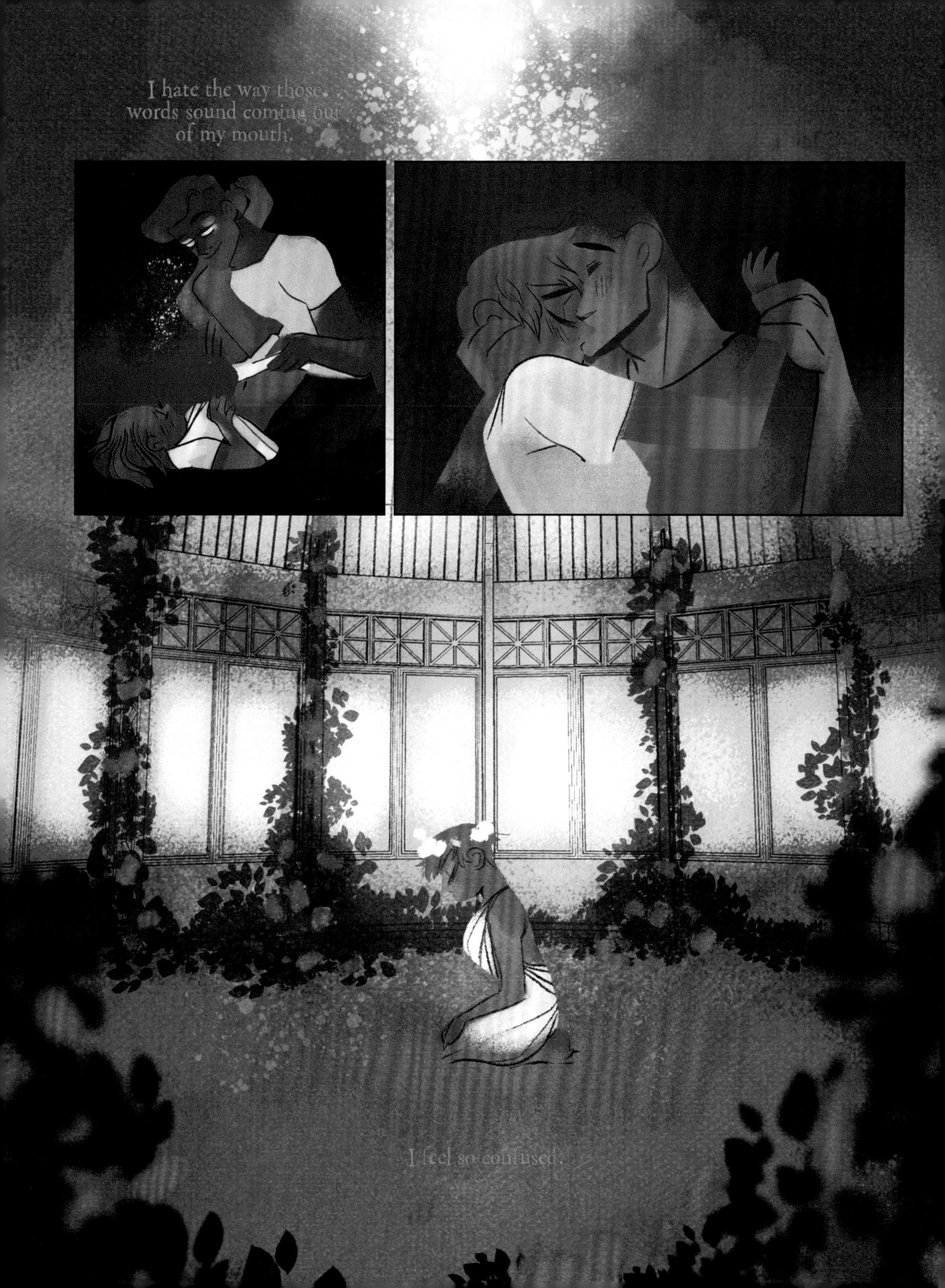
I hate the way those words sound coming out of my mouth.
I feel so confused.

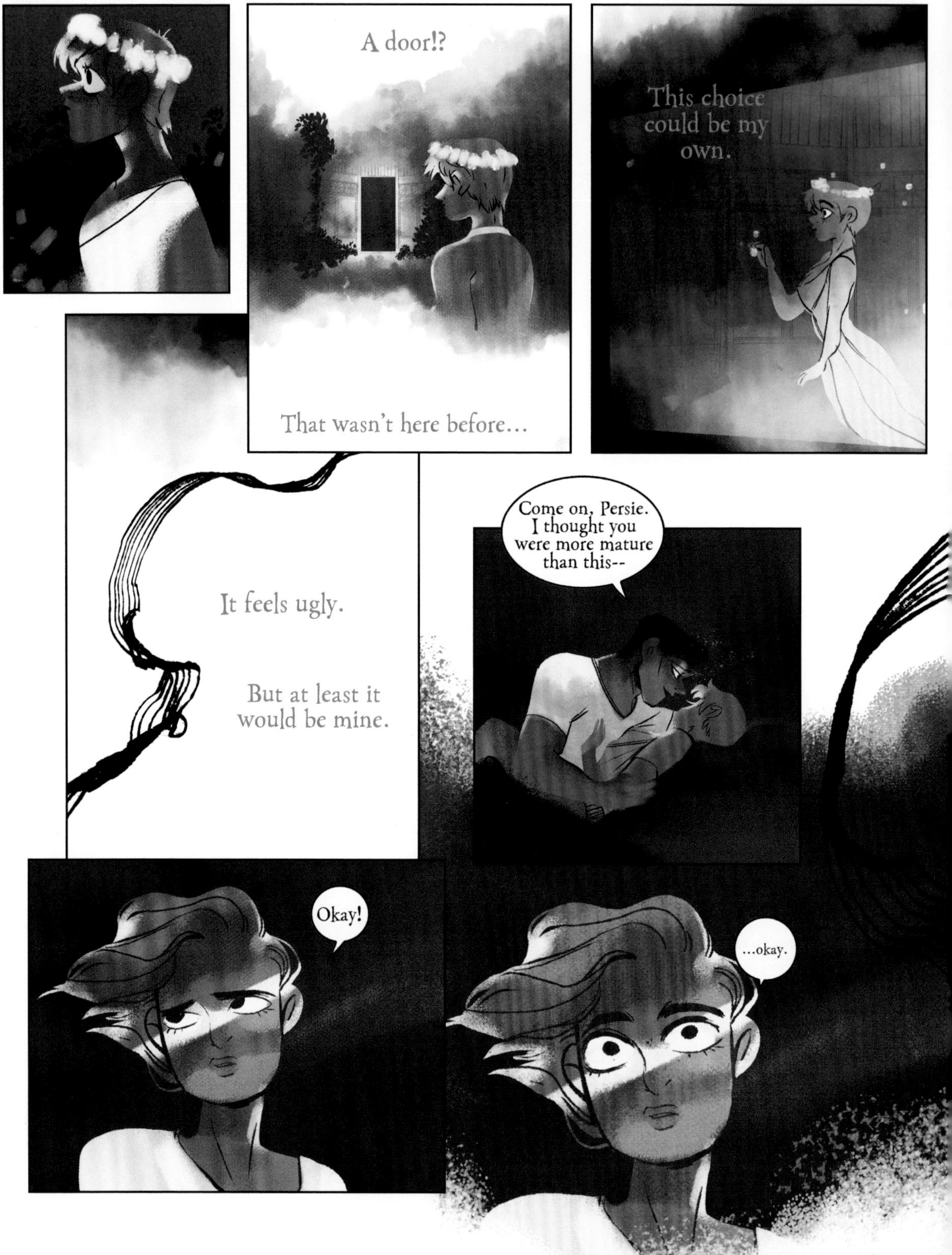

A door!?
That wasn't here before...
This choice could be my own.
It feels ugly.
But at least it would be mine.
Come on, Persie. I thought you were more mature than this--
Okay!
...okay.

EPISODE 24: A WOLF IN THE HENHOUSE (PART 3)

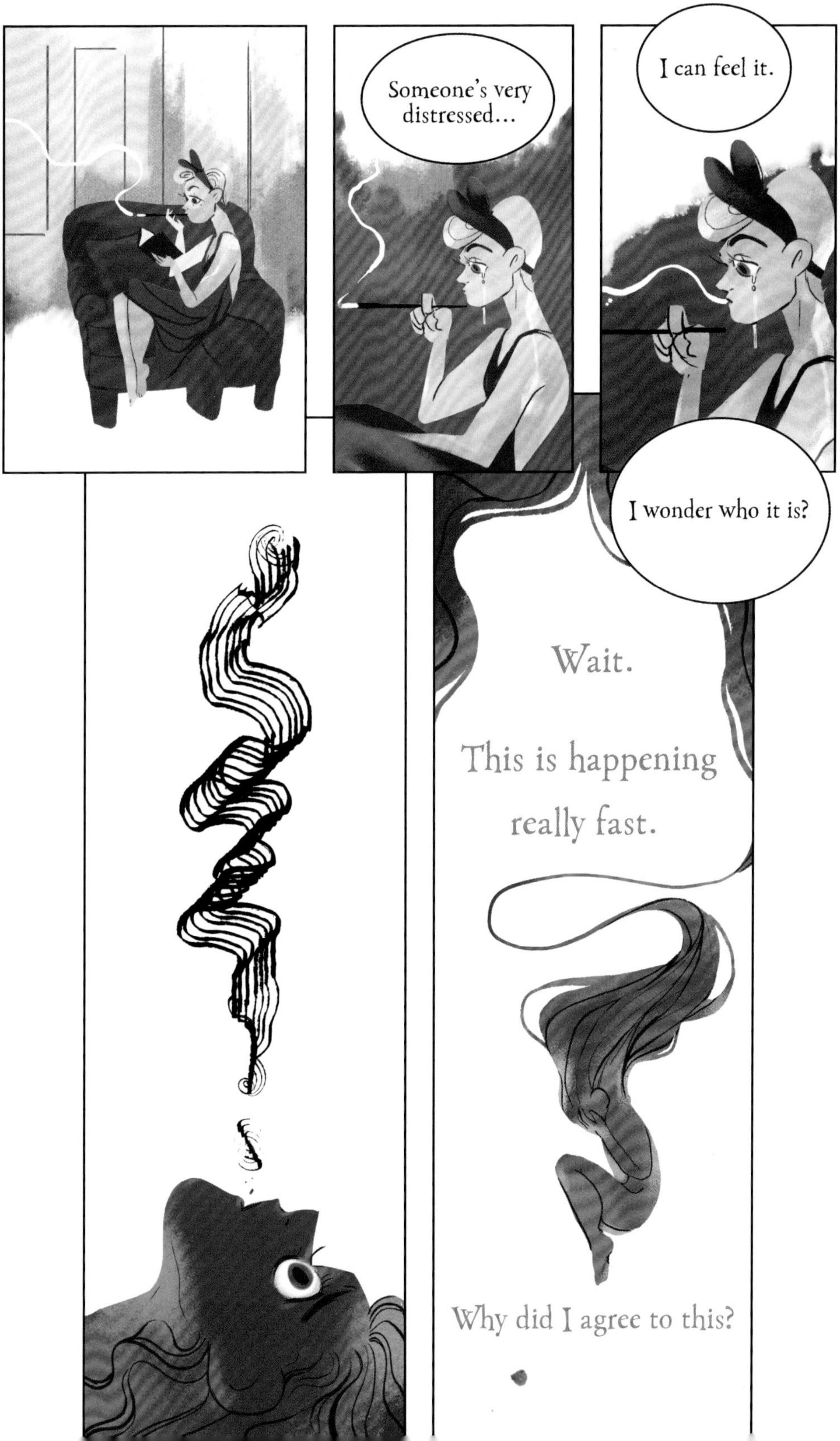
Someone's very distressed...
I can feel it.
I wonder who it is?
Wait.
This is happening really fast.
Why did I agree to this?

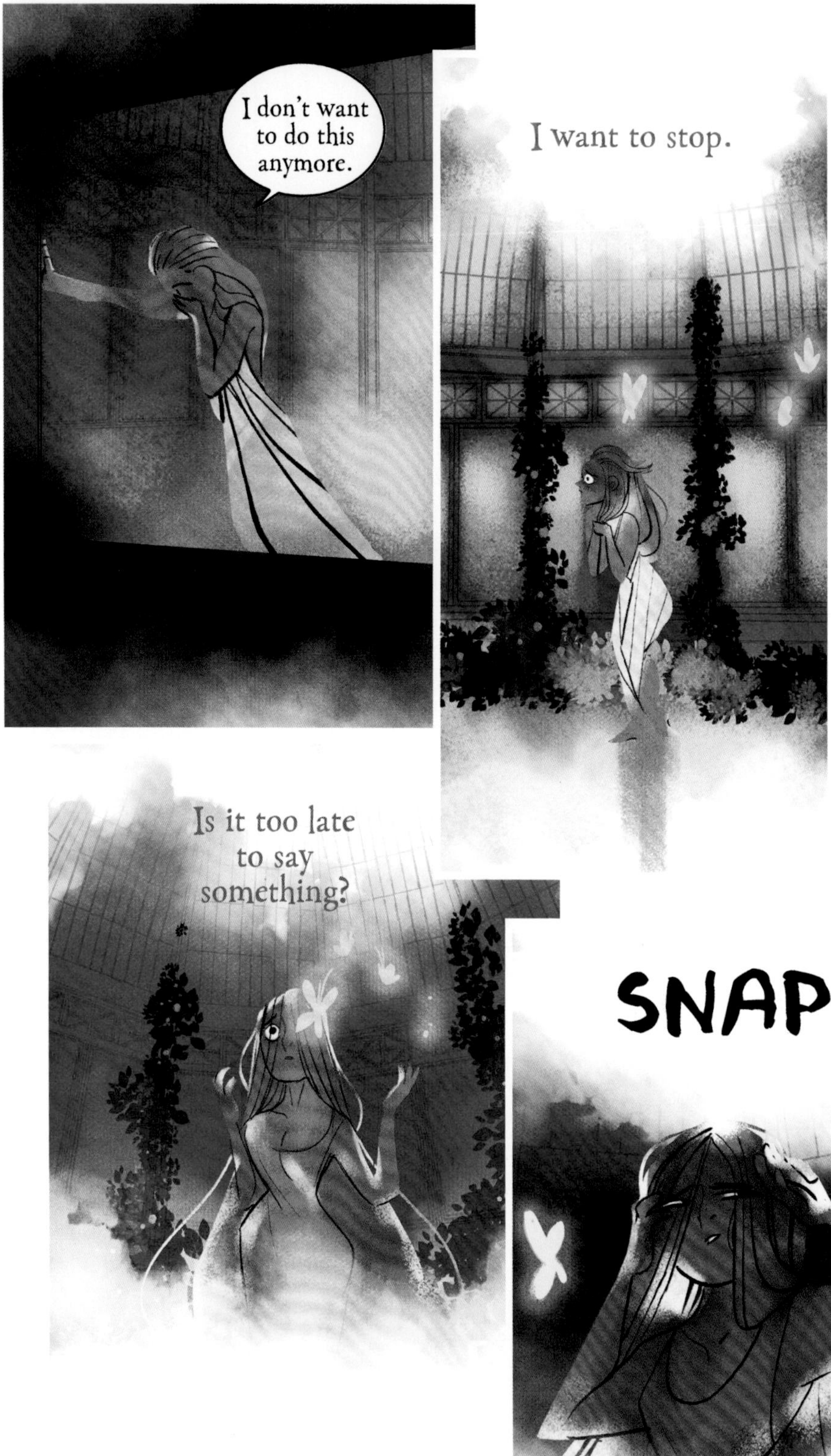

I don't want to do this anymore.
I want to stop.
Is it too late to say something?
SNAP

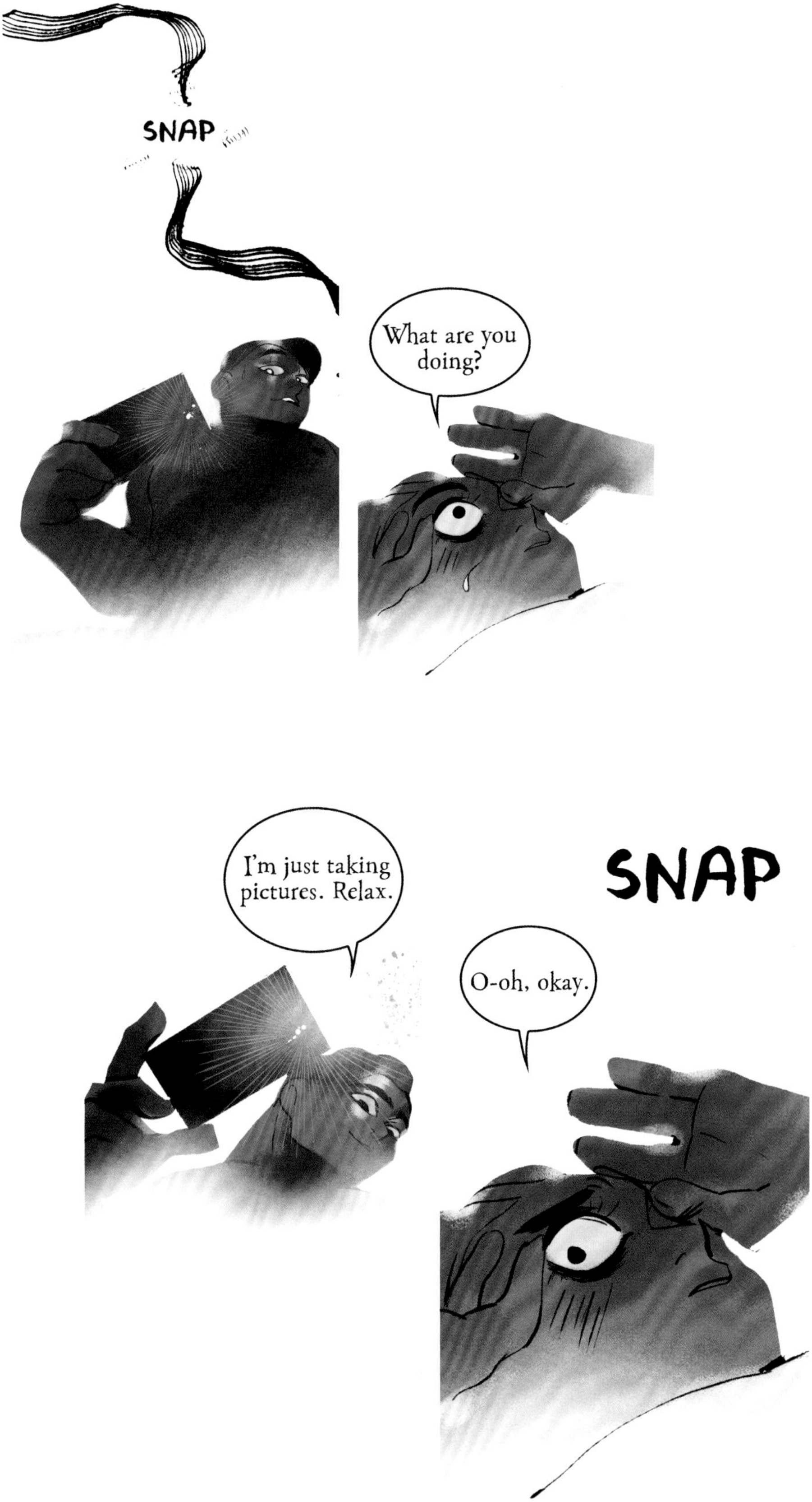
SNAP
What are you doing?
I'm just taking pictures. Relax.
SNAP
O-oh, okay.

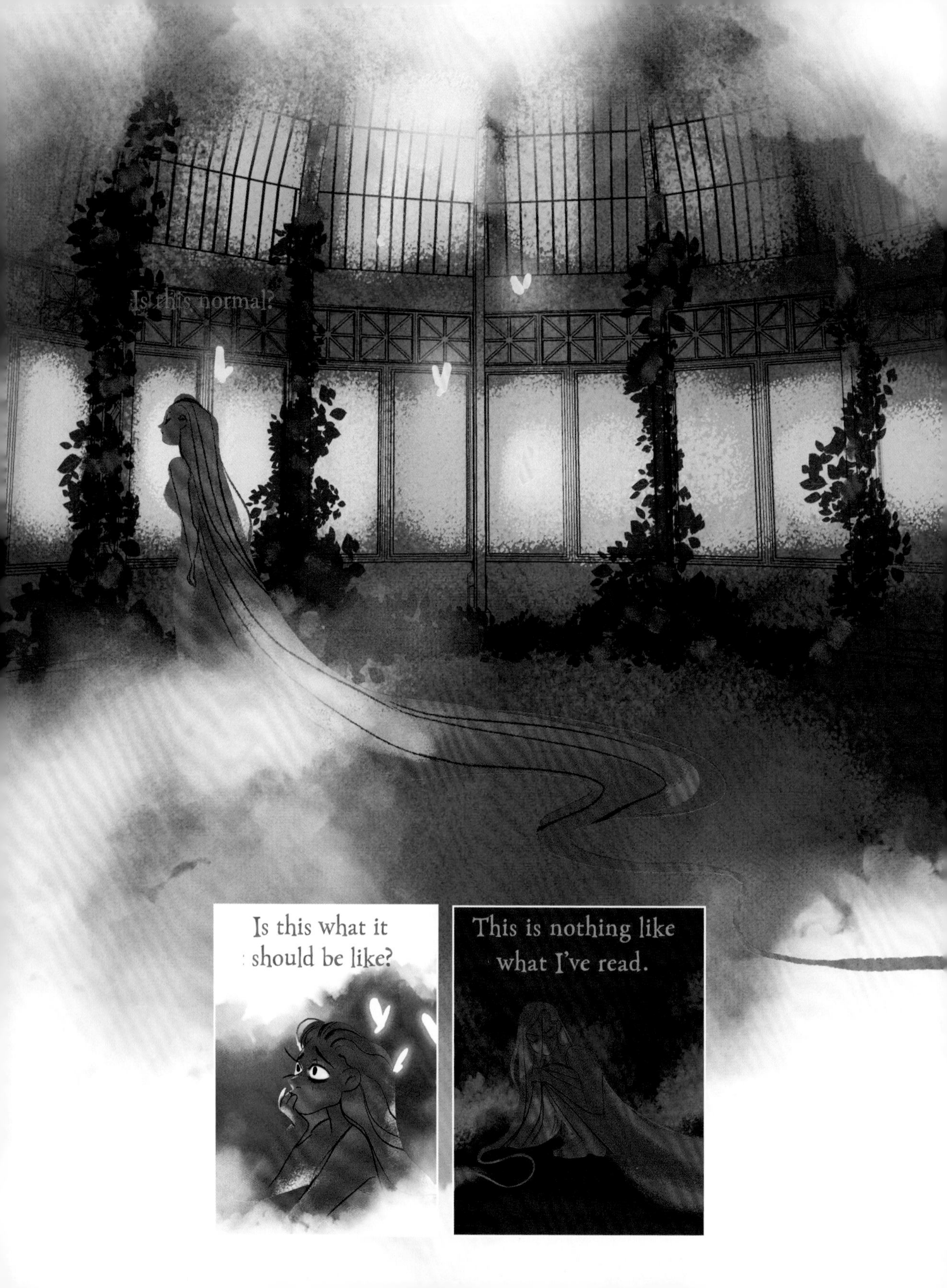
Is this normal?
Is this what it should be like?
This is nothing like what I've read.

I don't see what all
the fuss is about...

I'm going to stay here where it's
safe until he's finished.

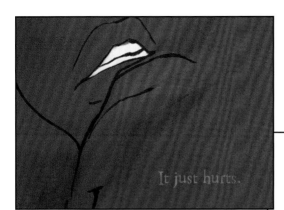

It just hurts.

Don't let him see
you cry.

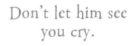

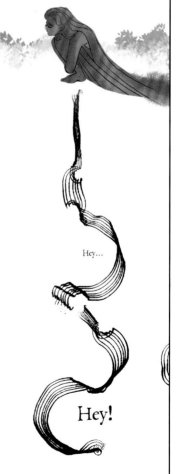

Hey...

Hey!

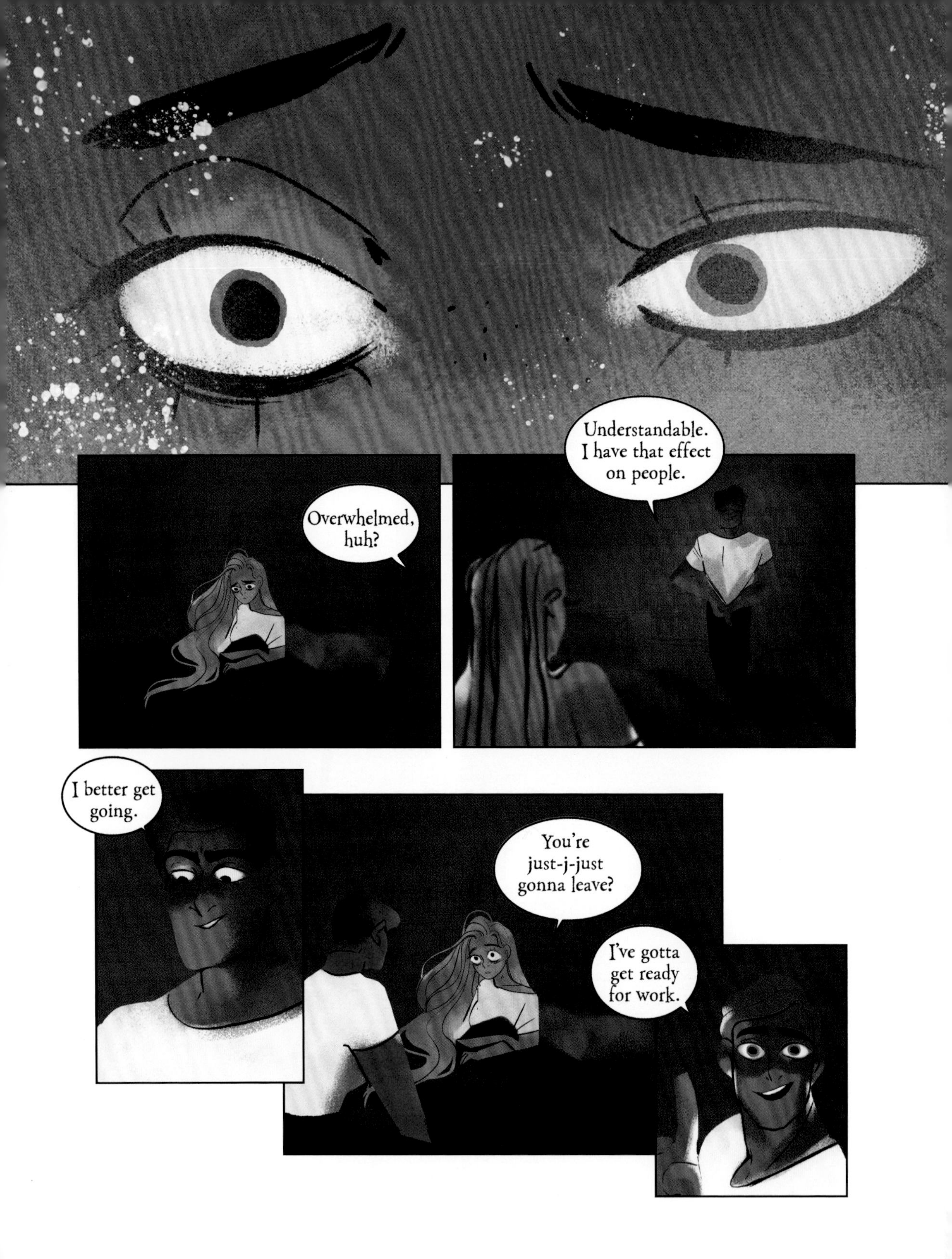
Overwhelmed, huh?
Understandable. I have that effect on people.
I better get going.
You're just-j-just gonna leave?
I've gotta get ready for work.

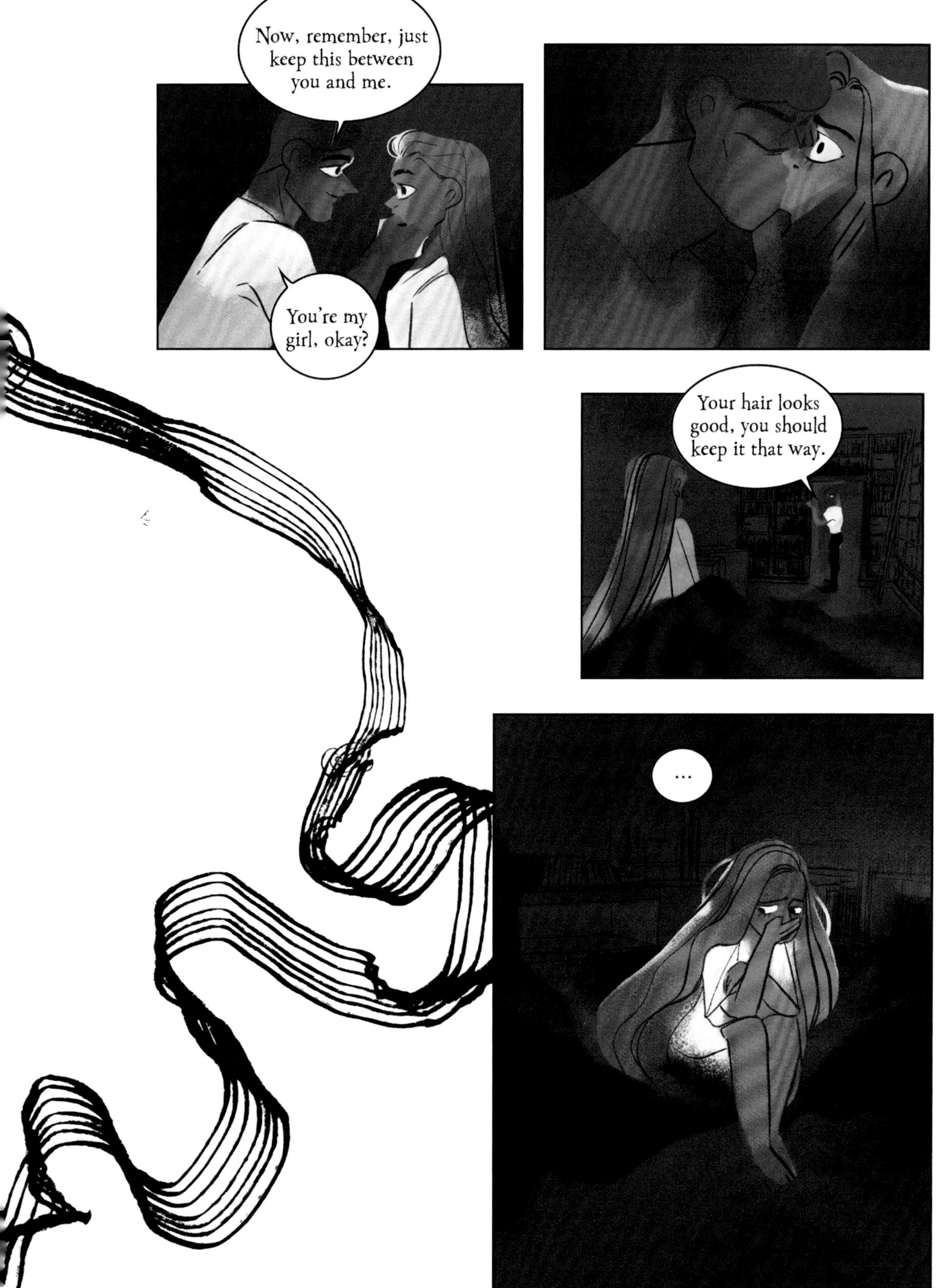
Now, remember, just keep this between you and me.
You're my girl, okay?
Your hair looks good, you should keep it that way.
...

SNIP
SNIP
I still look the same.

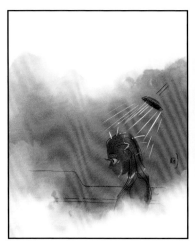

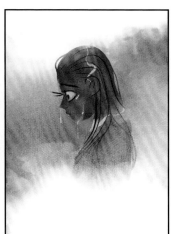

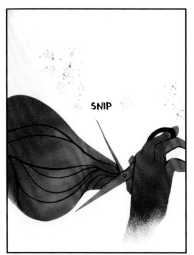

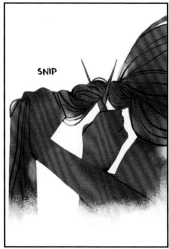

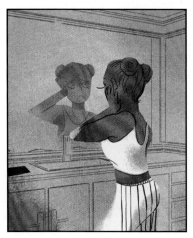

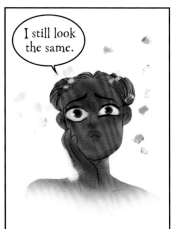

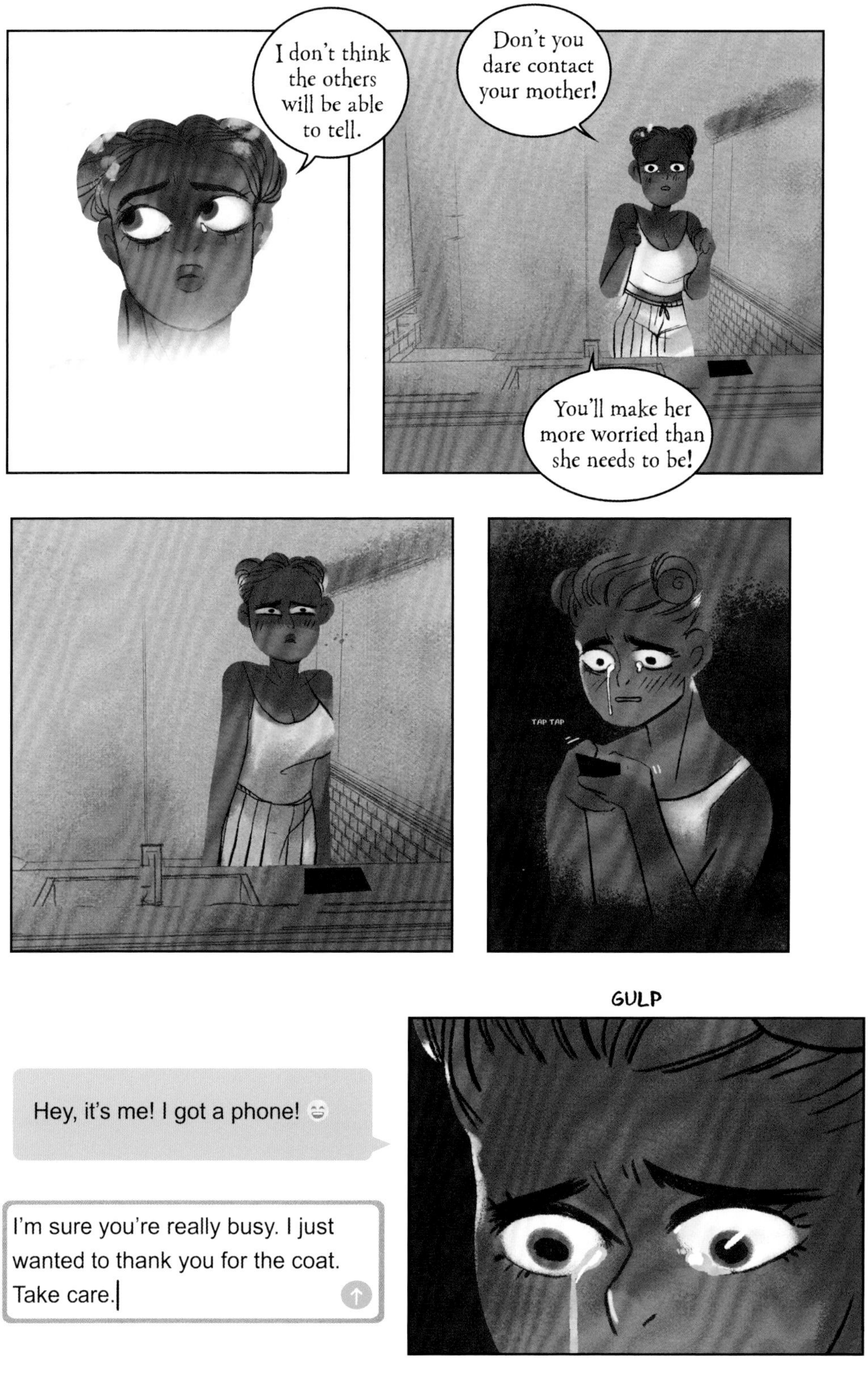
I don't think the others will be able to tell.
Don't you dare contact your mother!
You'll make her more worried than she needs to be!
TAP TAP
GULP
Hey, it's me! I got a phone!
I'm sure you're really busy. I just wanted to thank you for the coat. Take care.

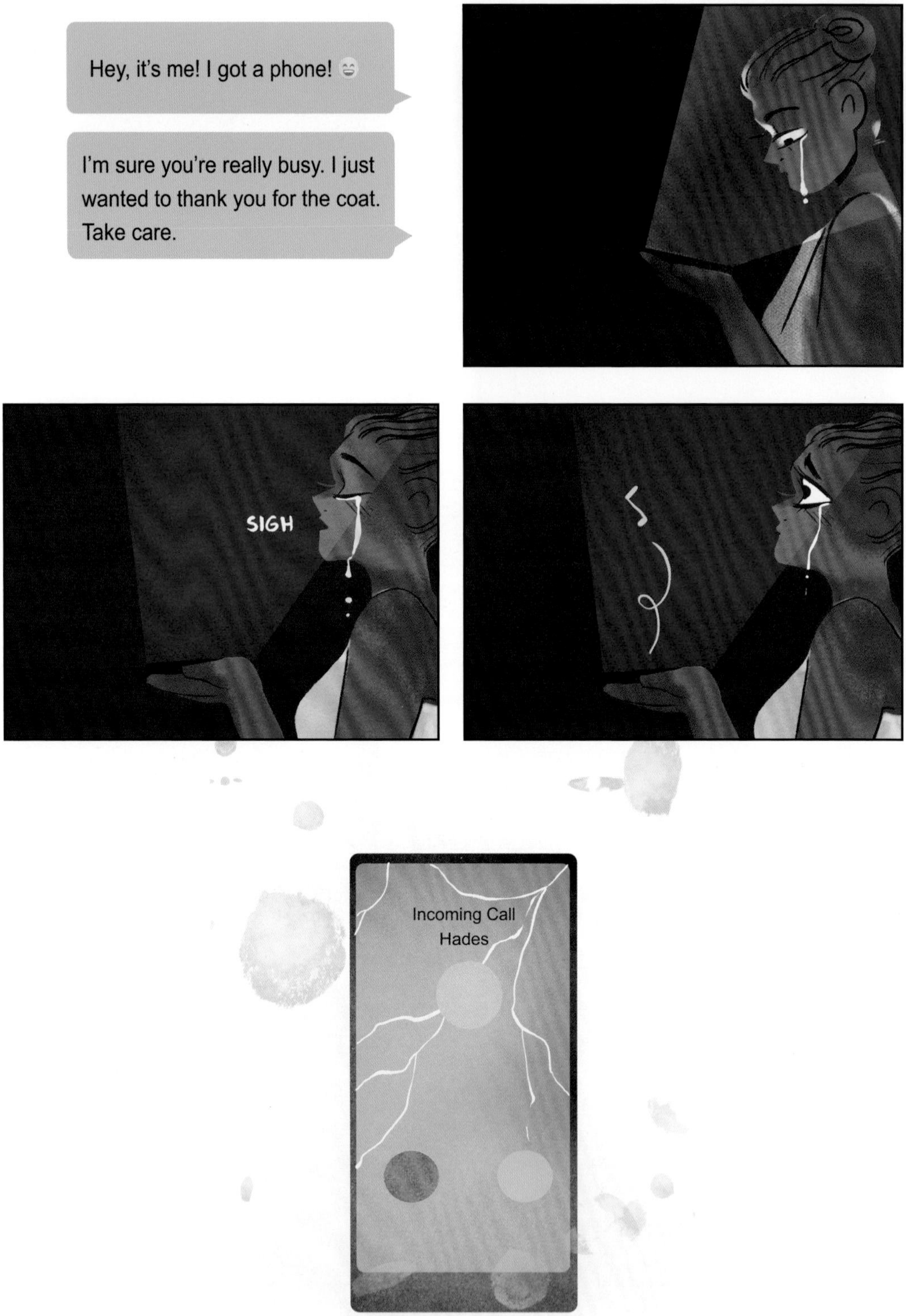
Hey, it's me! I got a phone!
I'm sure you're really busy. I just wanted to thank you for the coat. Take care.
SIGH
Incoming Call
Hades

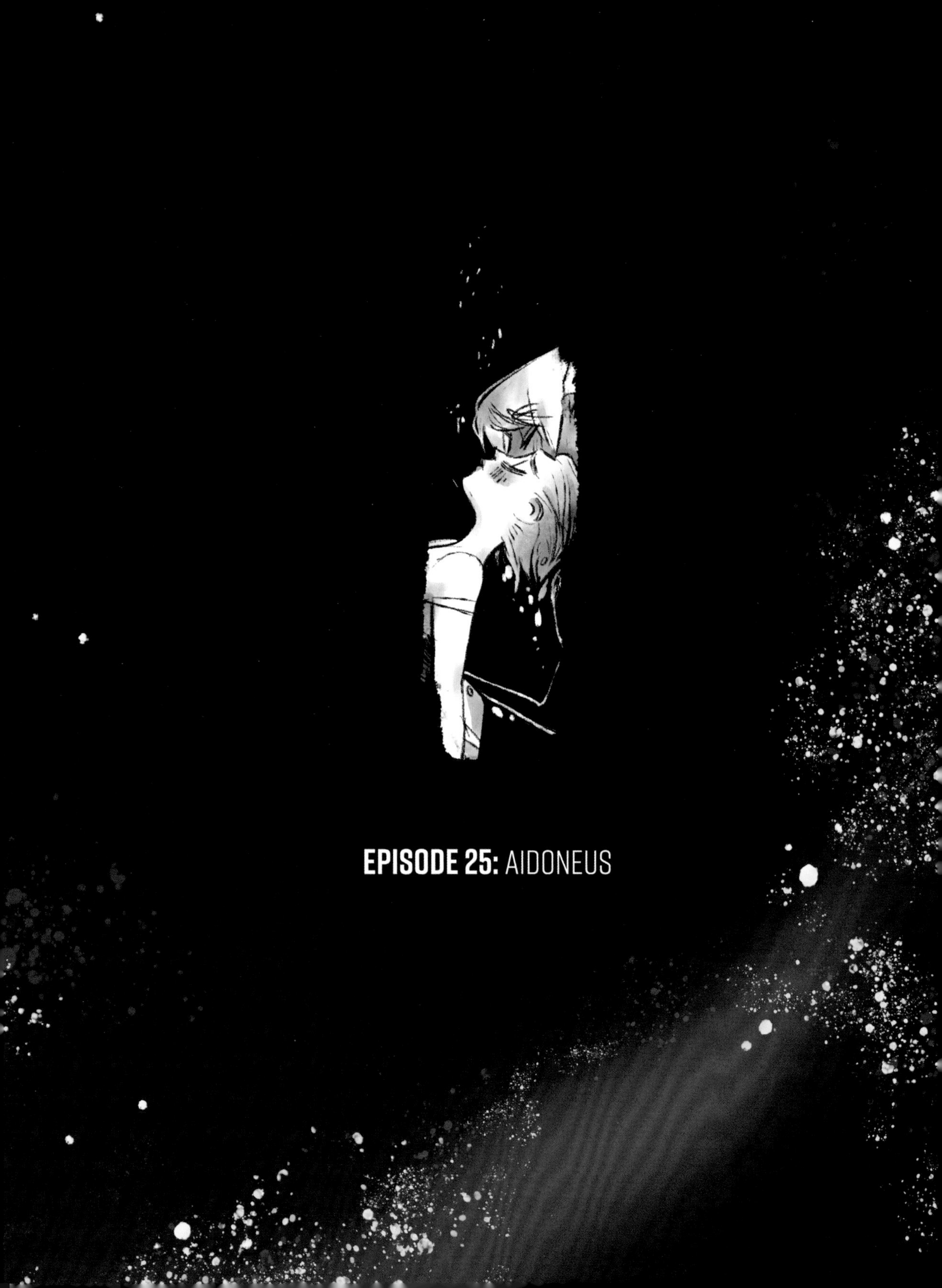

EPISODE 25: AIDONEUS

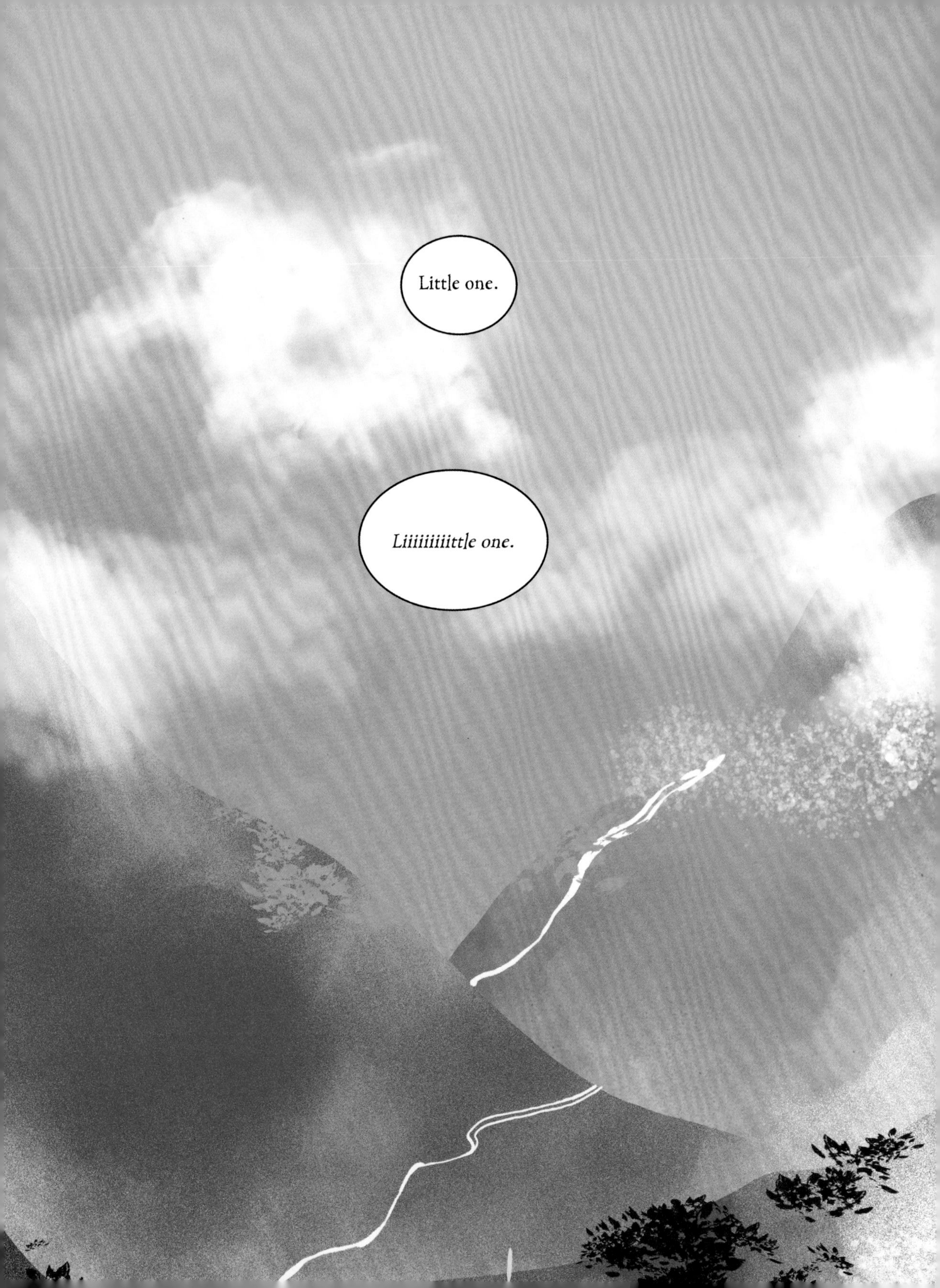
Little one.
Liiiiiiiiittle one.

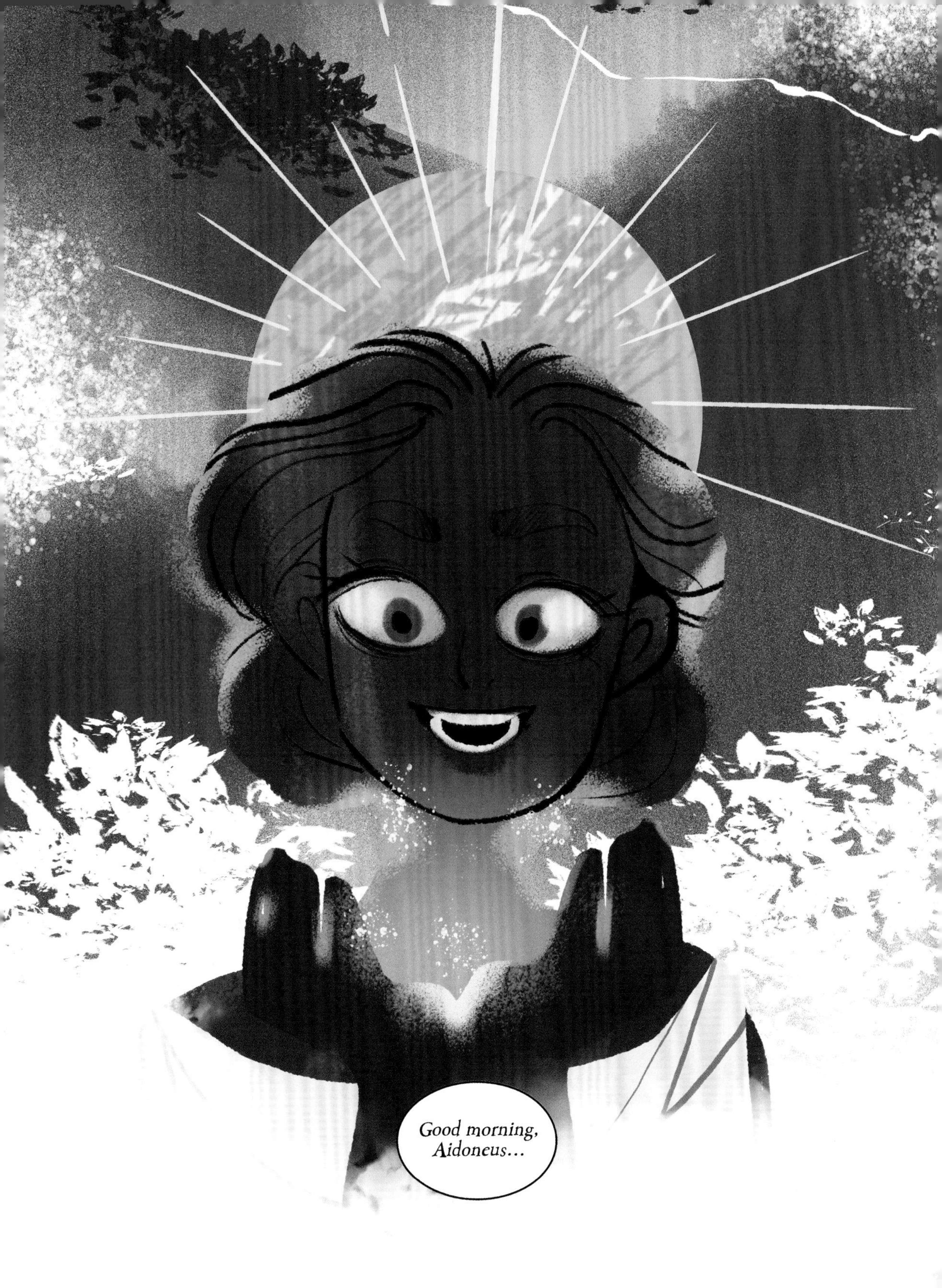
Good morning, Aidoneus...

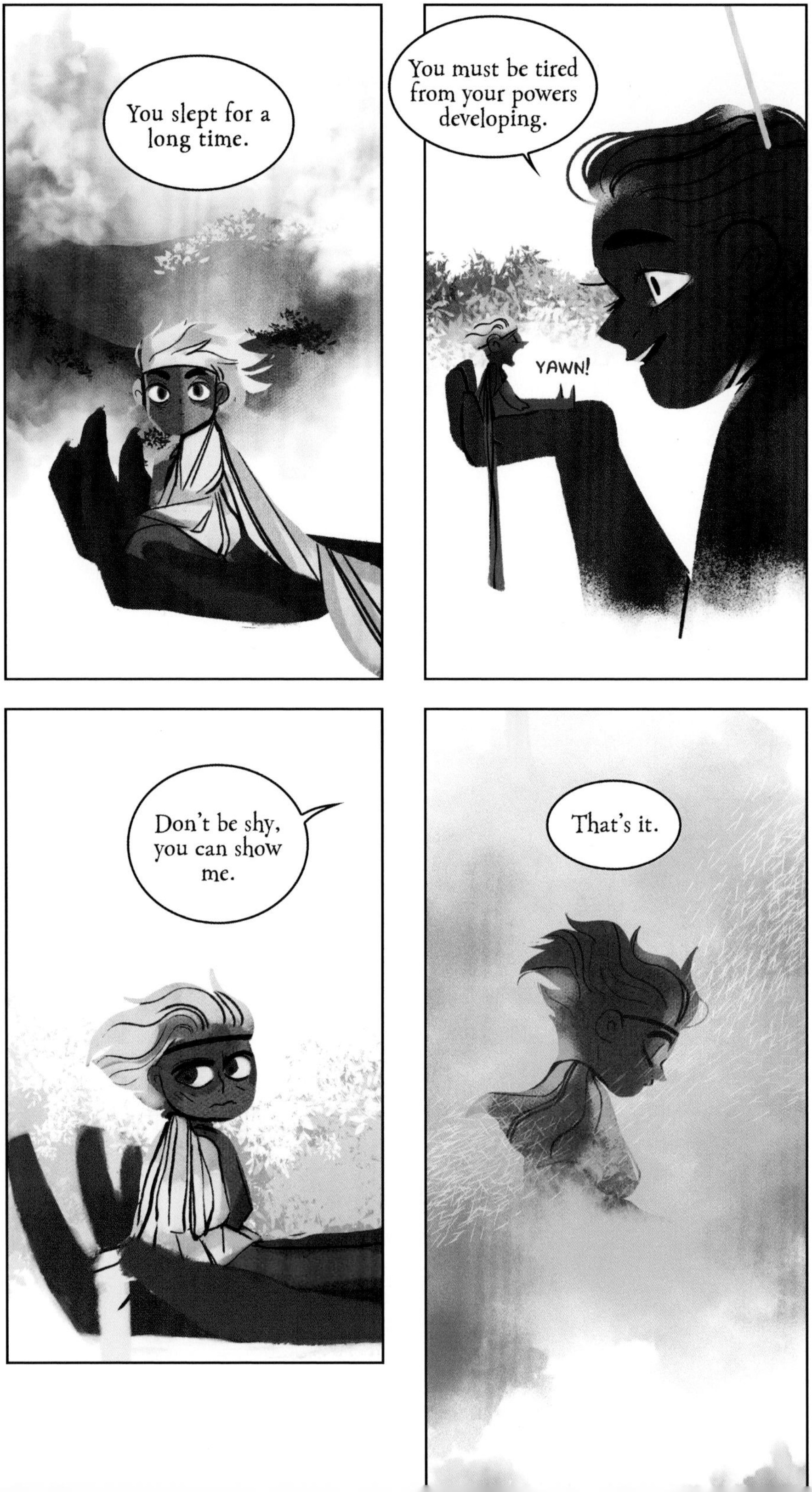
You slept for a long time.
You must be tired from your powers developing.
YAWN!
Don't be shy, you can show me.
That's it.

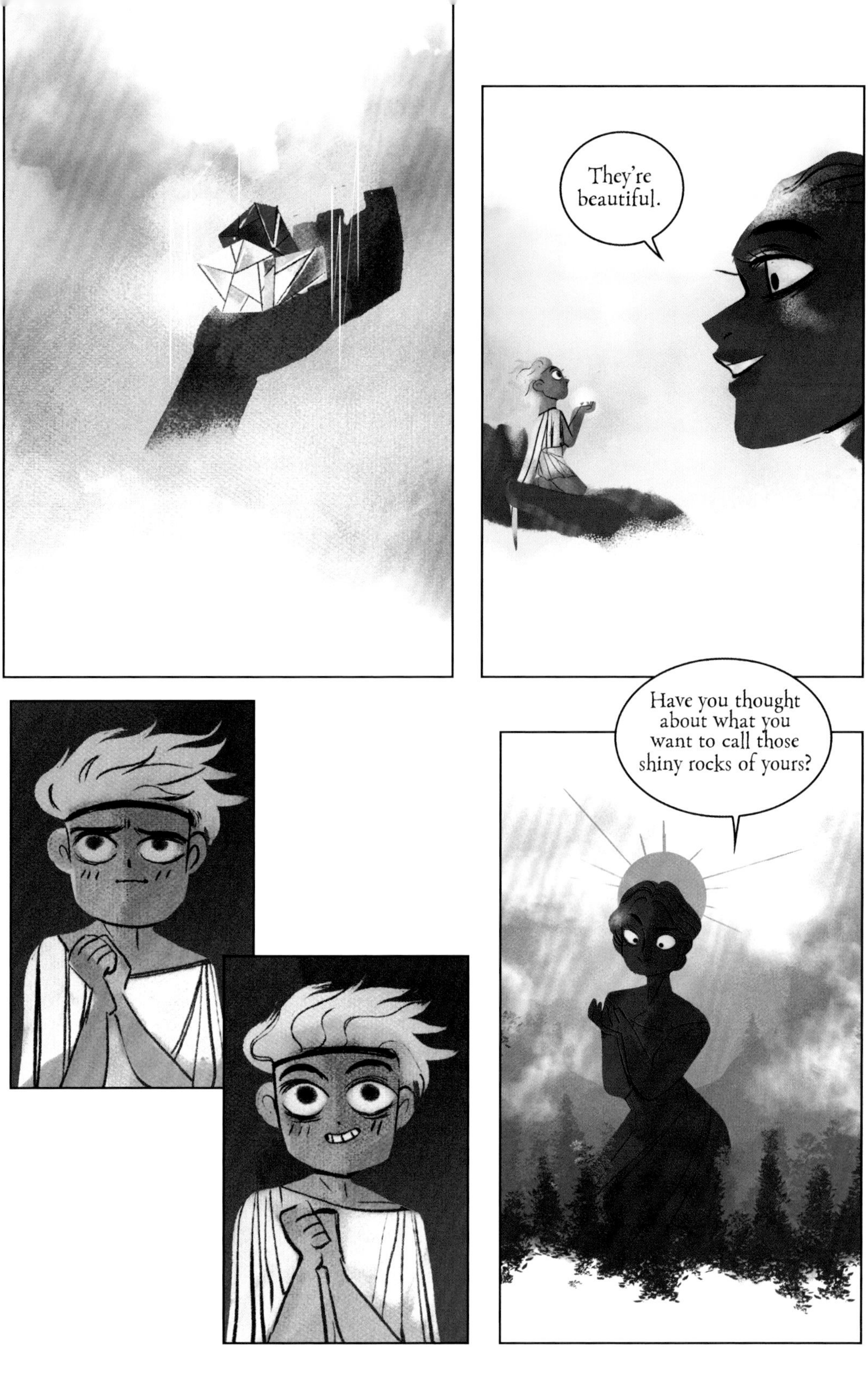
They're beautiful.
Have you thought about what you want to call those shiny rocks of yours?

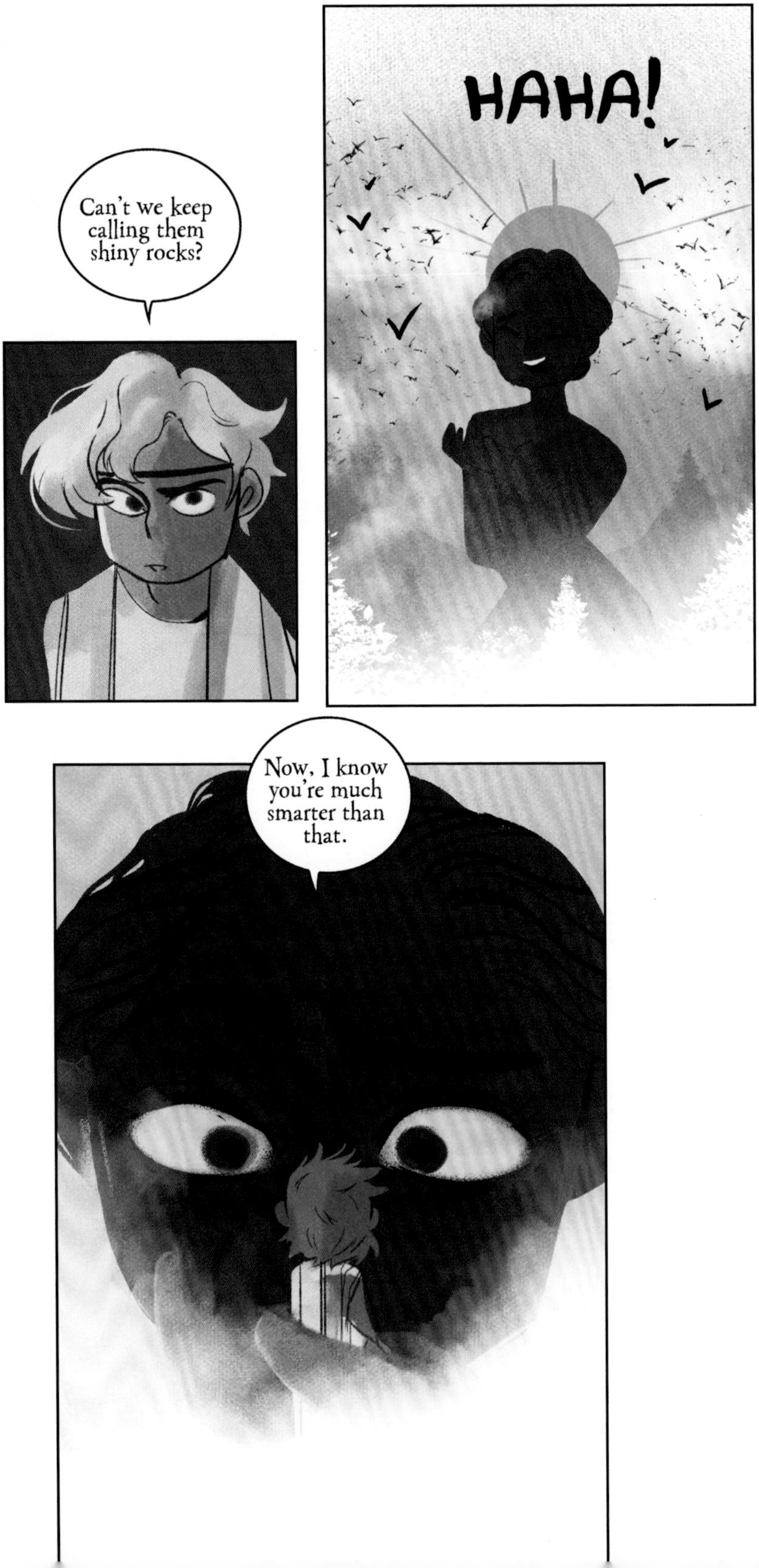
Can't we keep calling them shiny rocks?
HAHA!
Now, I know you're much smarter than that.

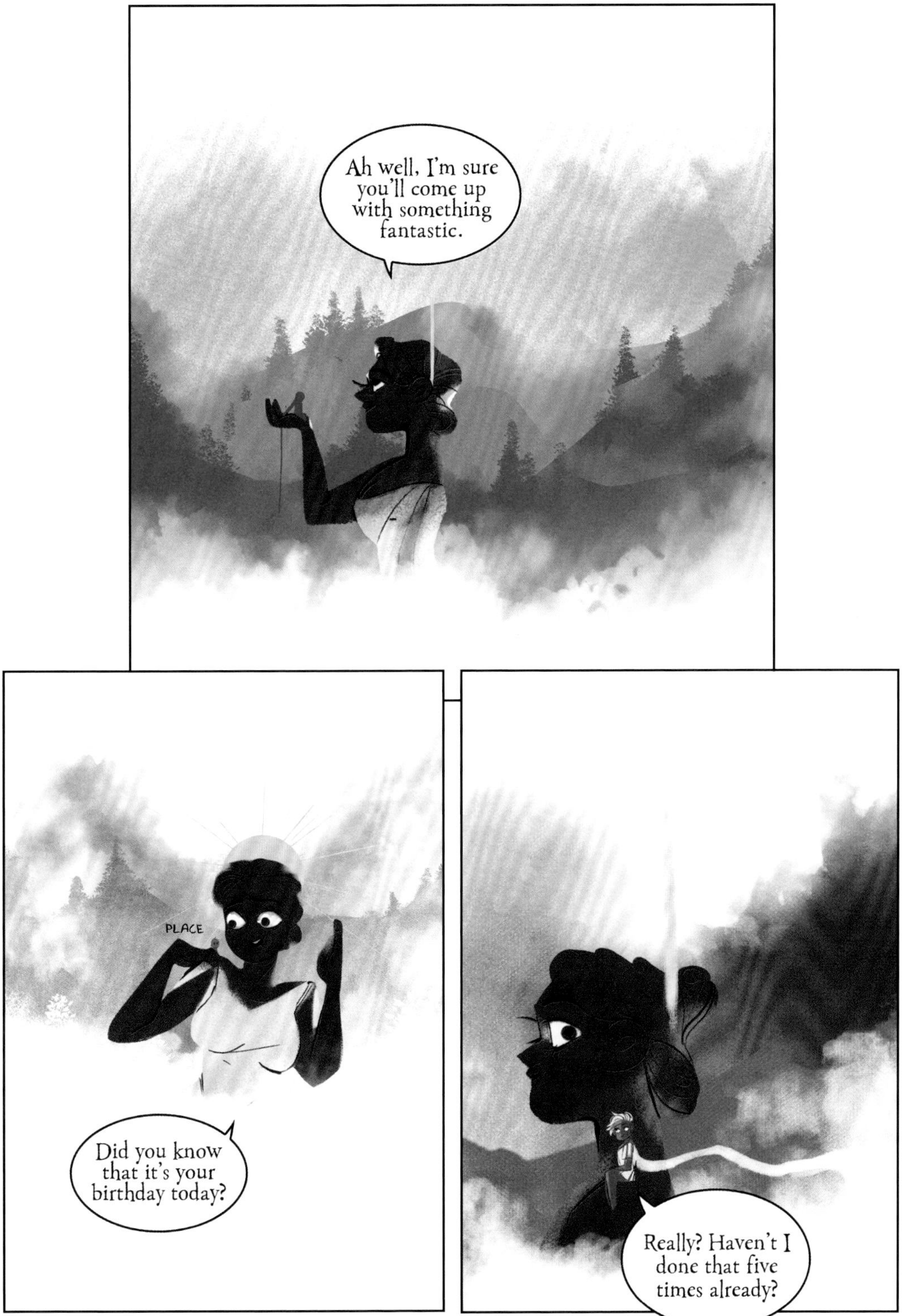
Ah well, I'm sure you'll come up with something fantastic.
PLACE
Did you know that it's your birthday today?
Really? Haven't I done that five times already?

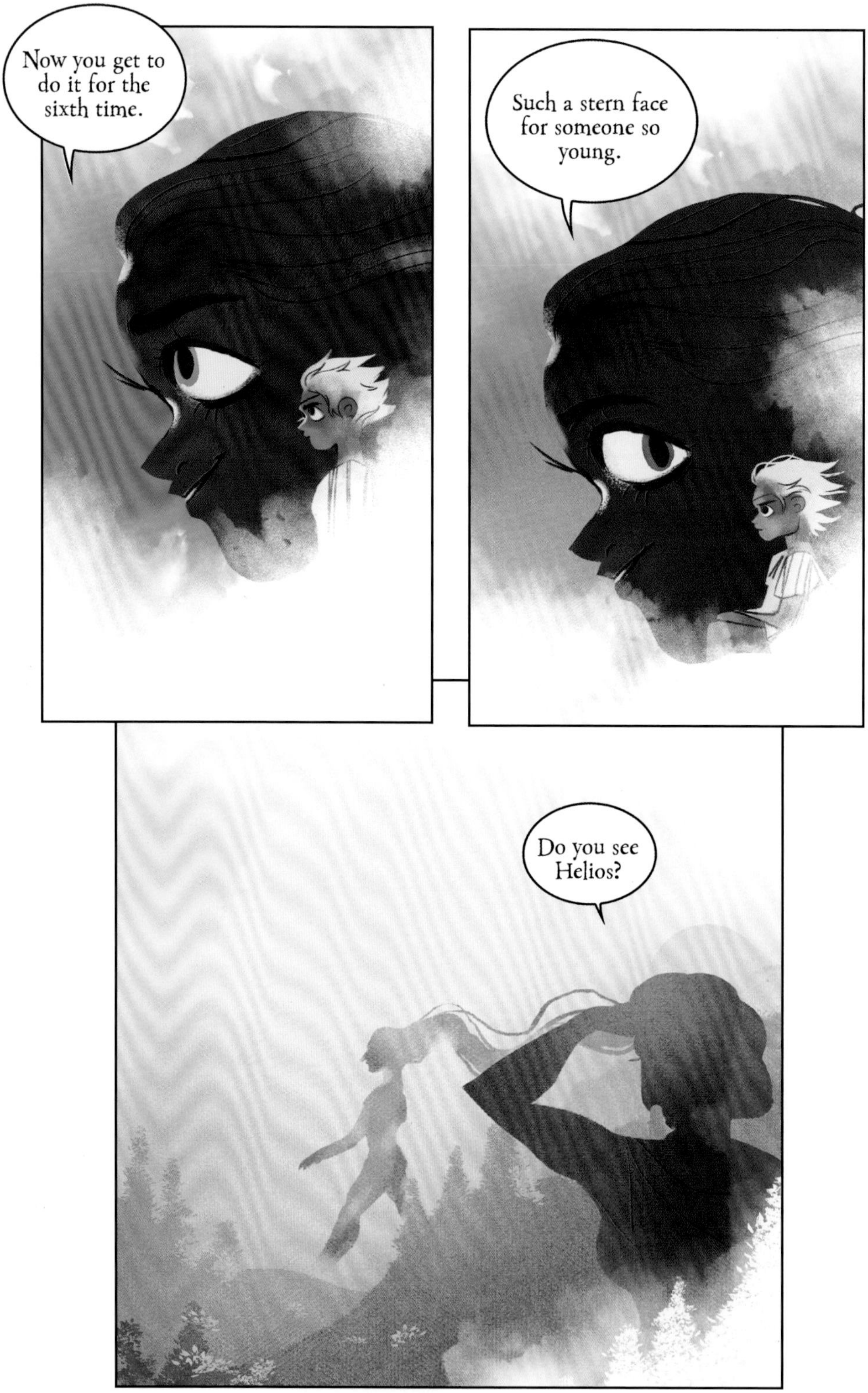

Now you get to do it for the sixth time.
Such a stern face for someone so young.
Do you see Helios?

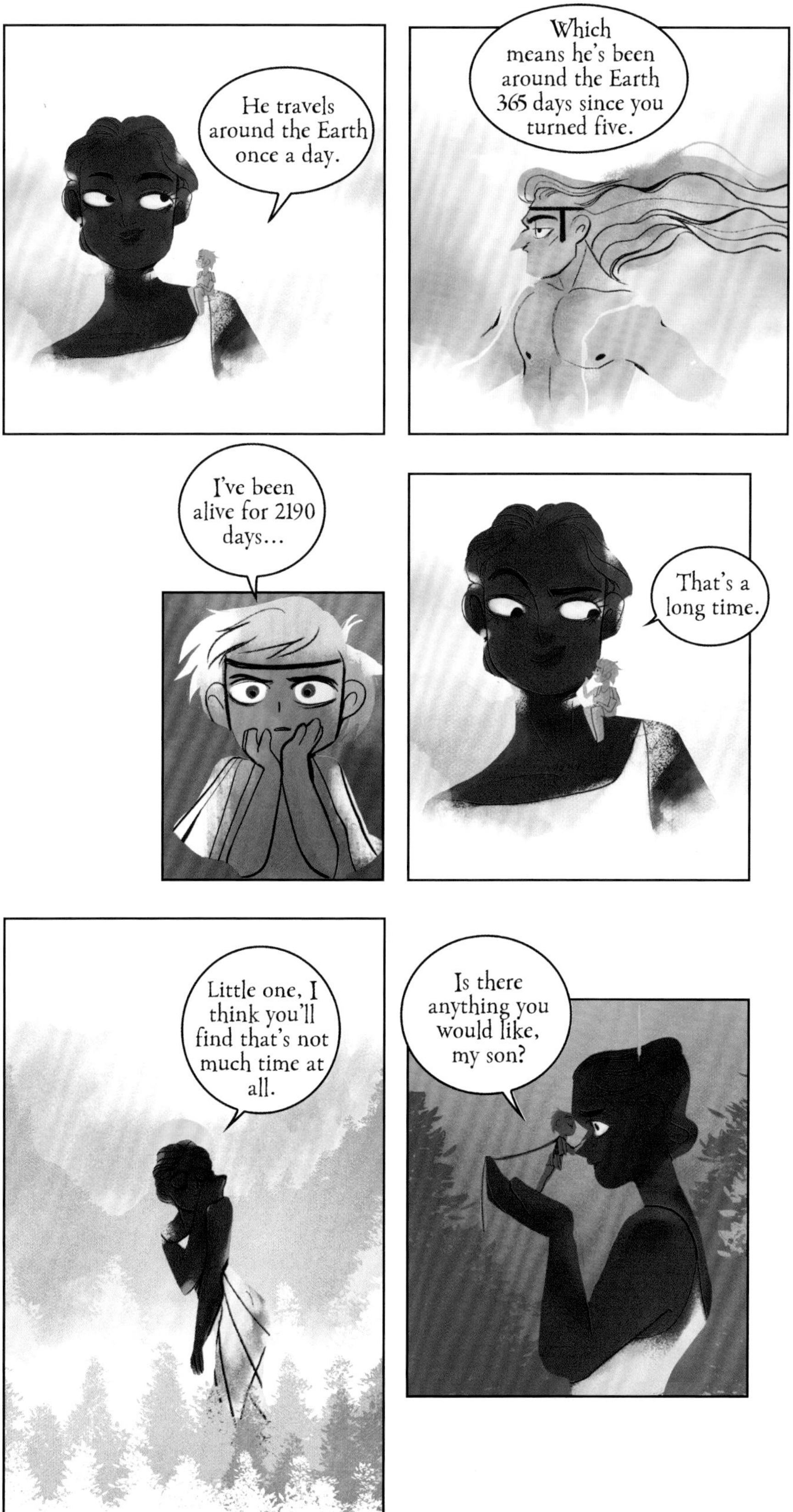

He travels around the Earth once a day.
Which means he's been around the Earth 365 days since you turned five.
I've been alive for 2190 days...
That's a long time.
Little one, I think you'll find that's not much time at all.
Is there anything you would like, my son?

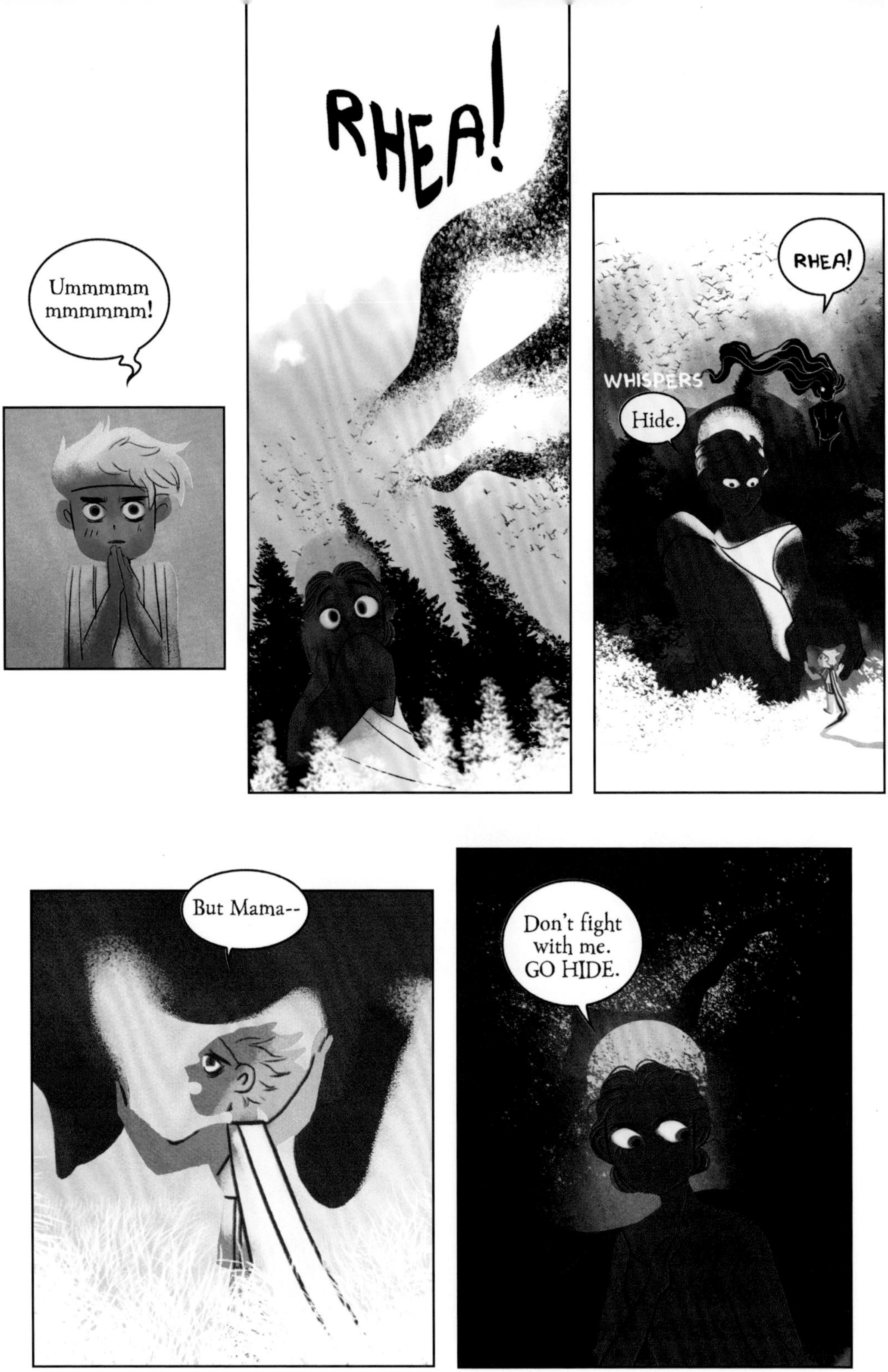

Ummmmm mmmmmm!
RHEA!
RHEA!
WHISPERS
Hide.
But Mama--
Don't fight with me. GO HIDE.

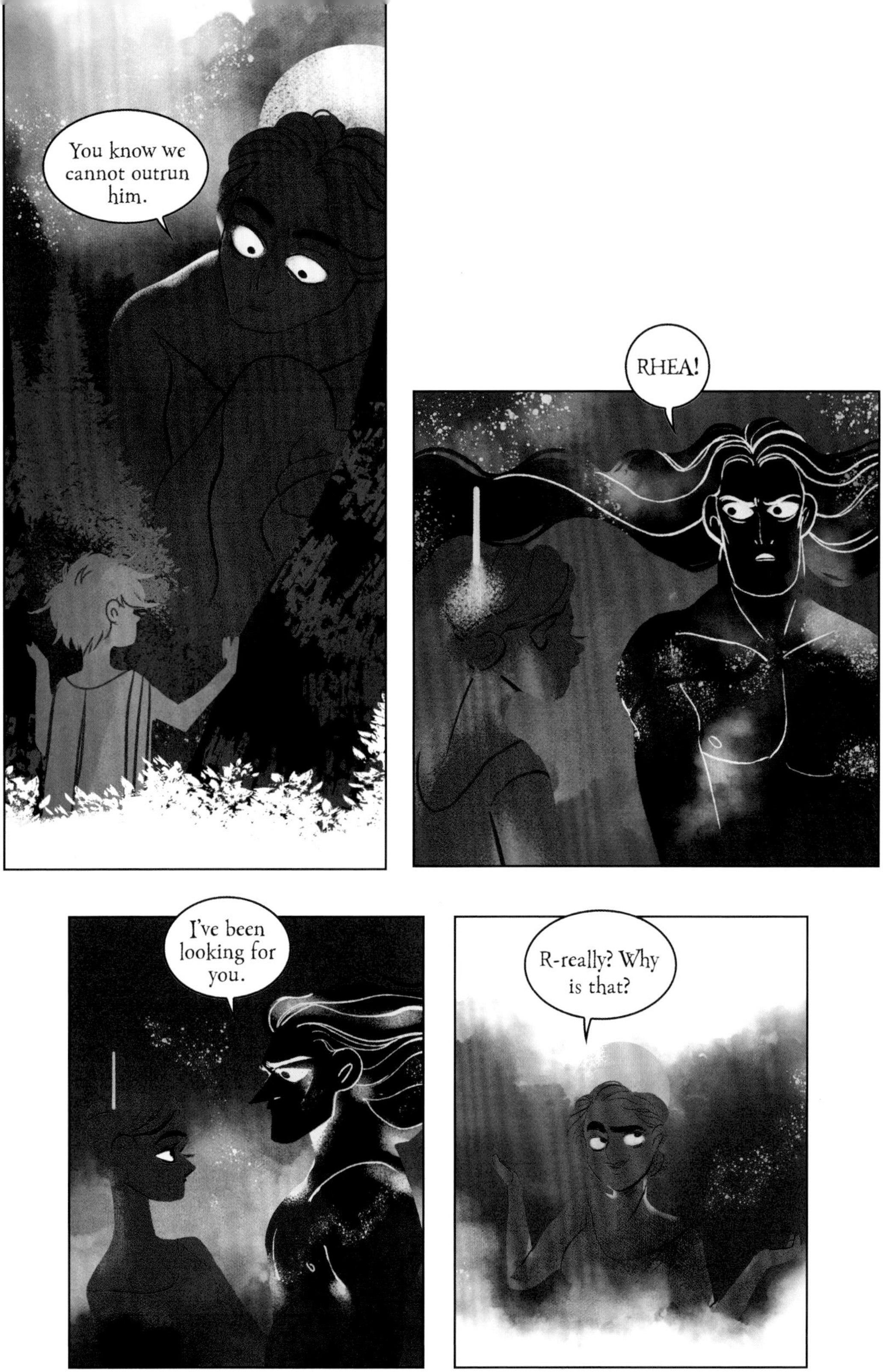
You know we cannot outrun him.
RHEA!
I've been looking for you.
R-really? Why is that?

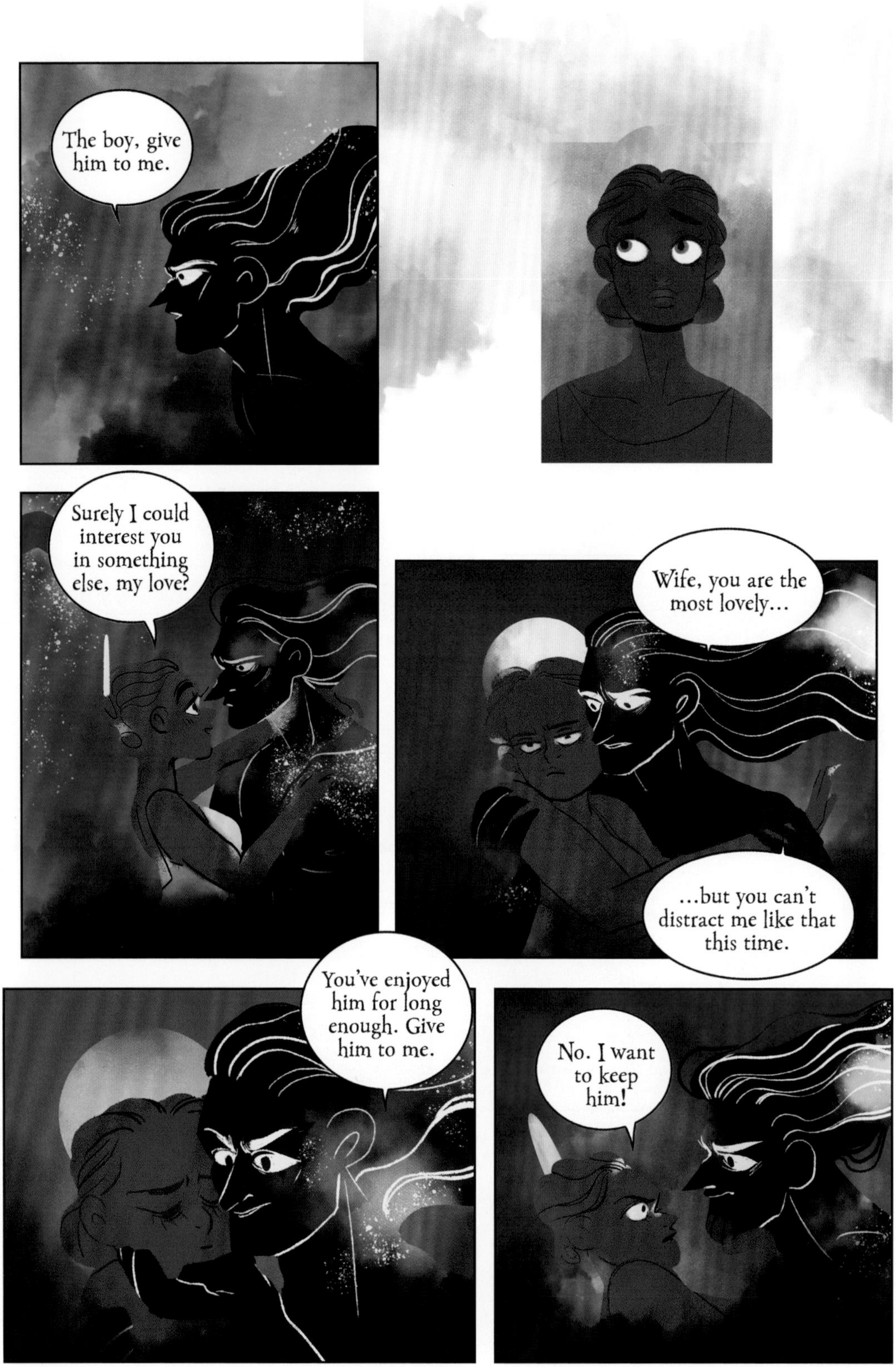
The boy, give him to me.
Surely I could interest you in something else, my love?
Wife, you are the most lovely...
...but you can't distract me like that this time.
You've enjoyed him for long enough. Give him to me.
No. I want to keep him!

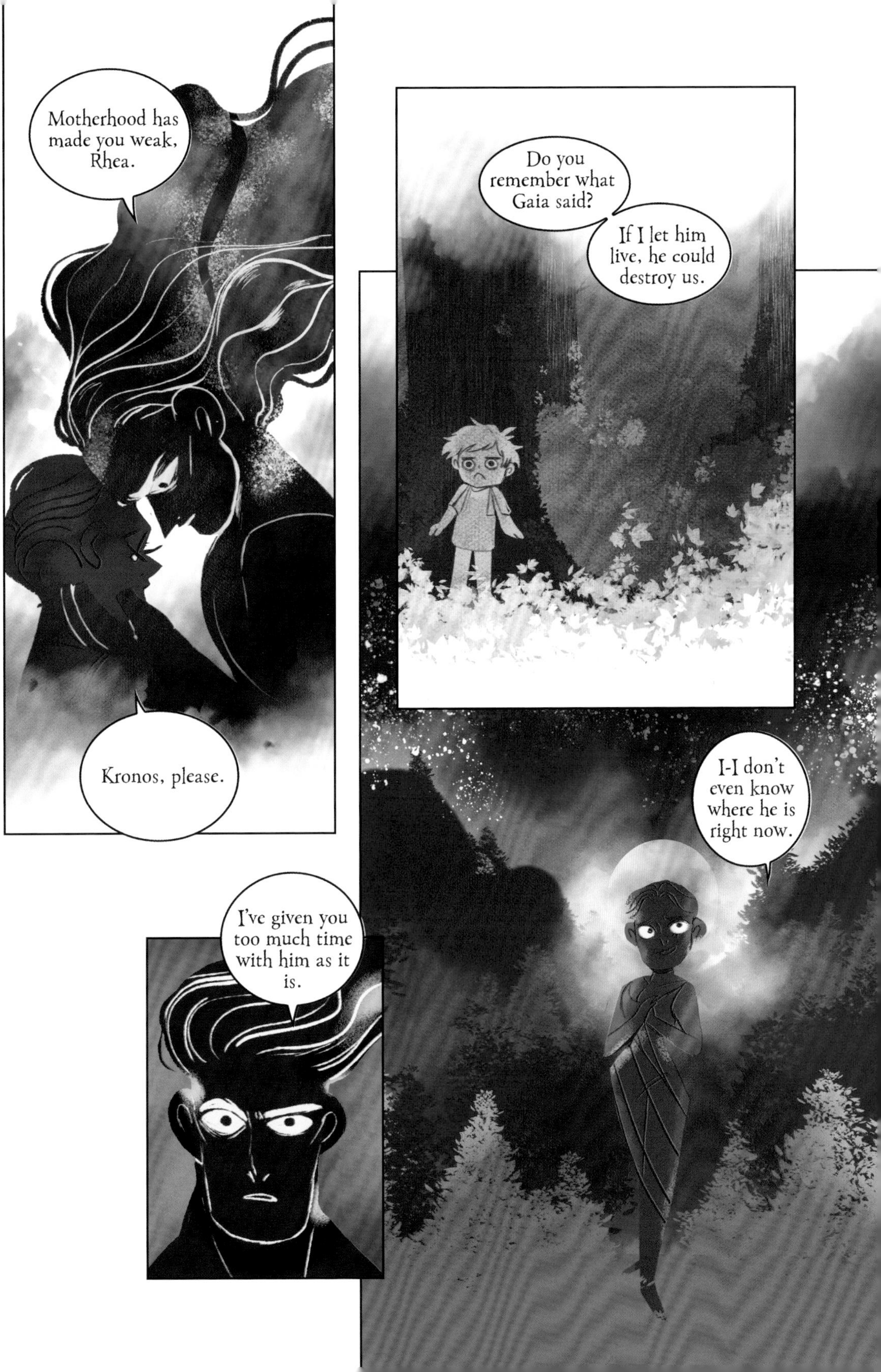

Motherhood has made you weak, Rhea.
Kronos, please.
Do you remember what Gaia said?
If I let him live, he could destroy us.
I-I don't even know where he is right now.
I've given you too much time with him as it is.

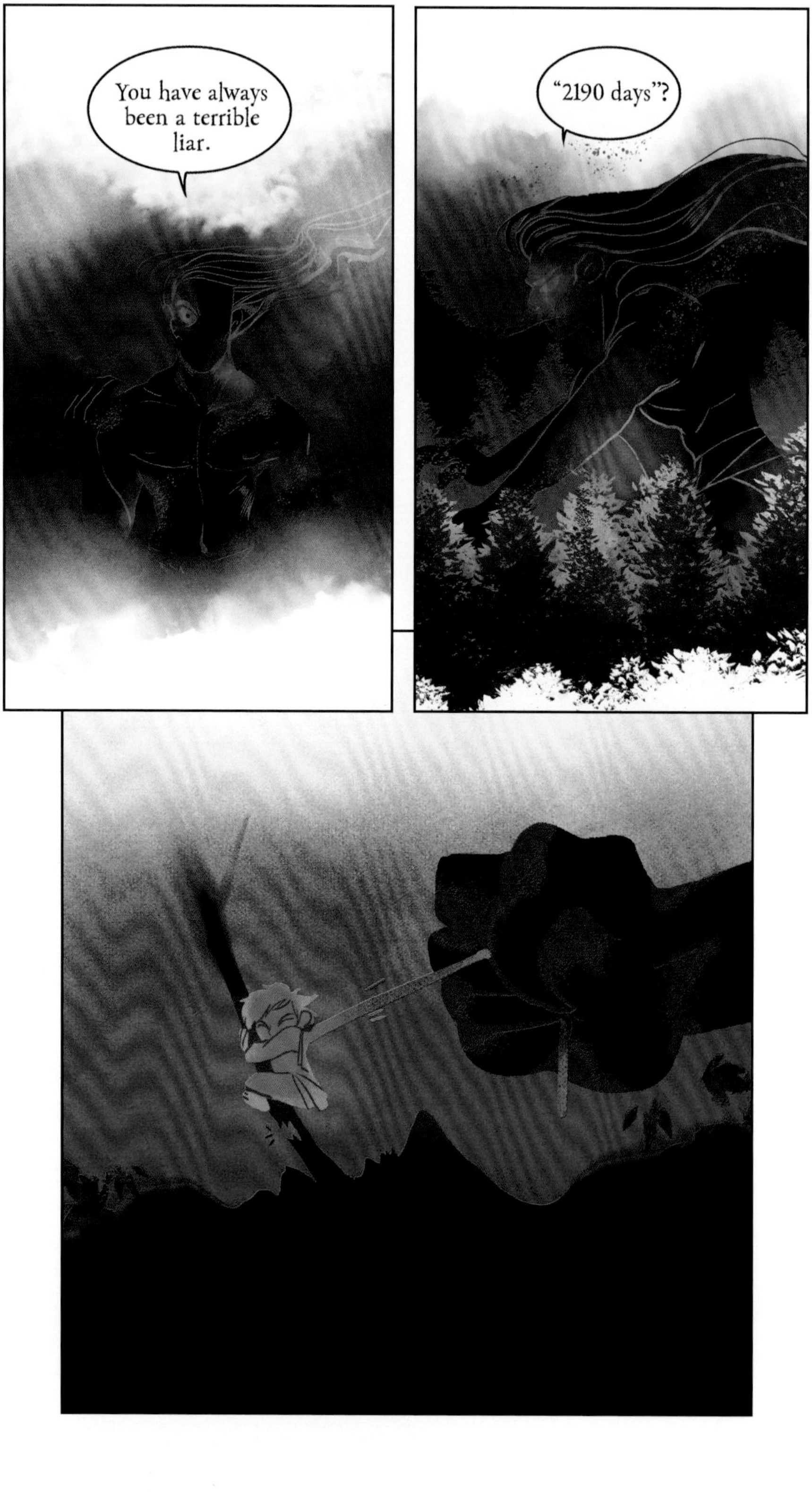
You have always been a terrible liar.
"2190 days"?

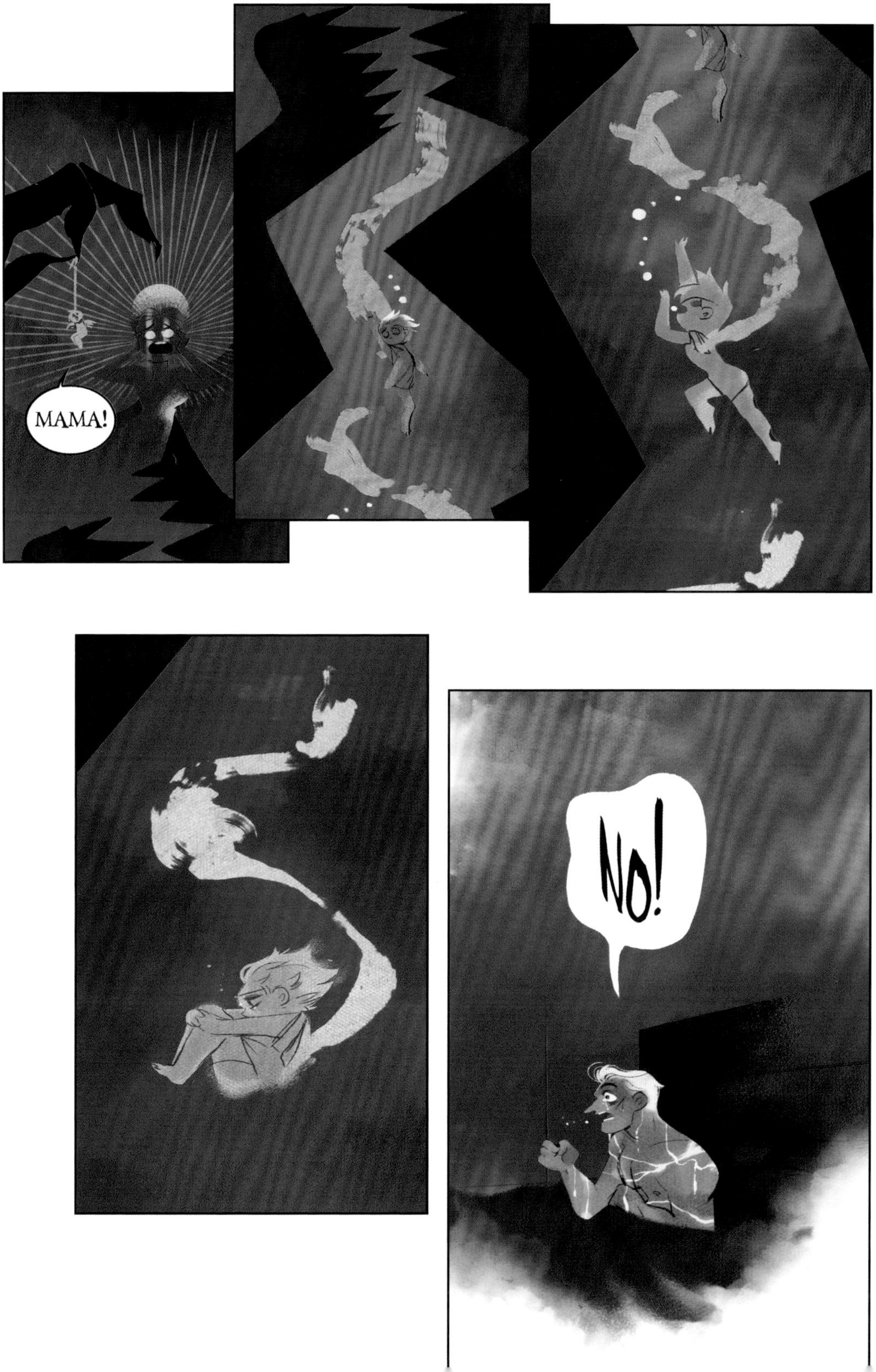
MAMA!
NO!

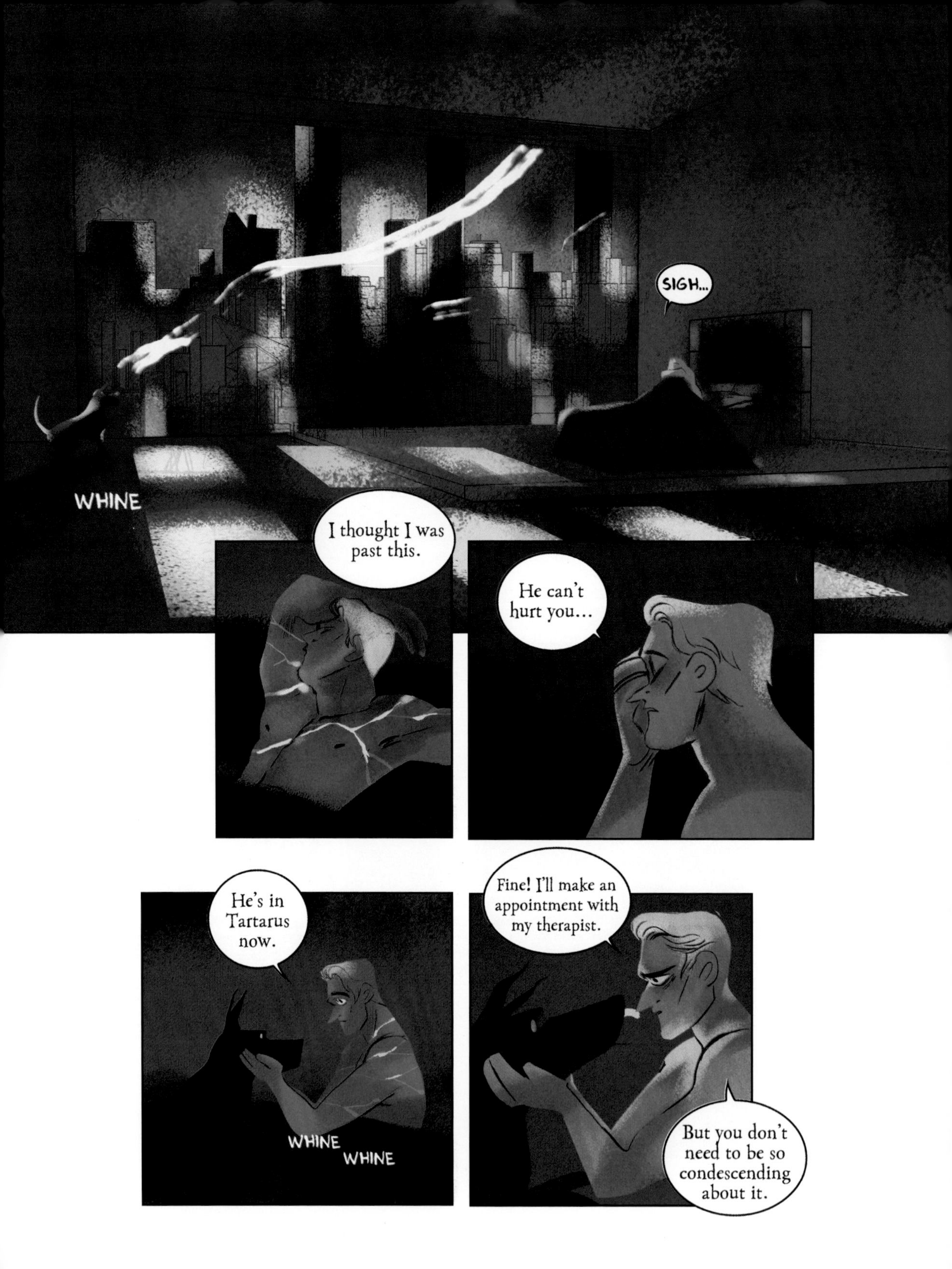
SIGH...
WHINE
I thought I was past this.
He can't hurt you...
He's in Tartarus now.
WHINE
WHINE
Fine! I'll make an appointment with my therapist.
But you don't need to be so condescending about it.

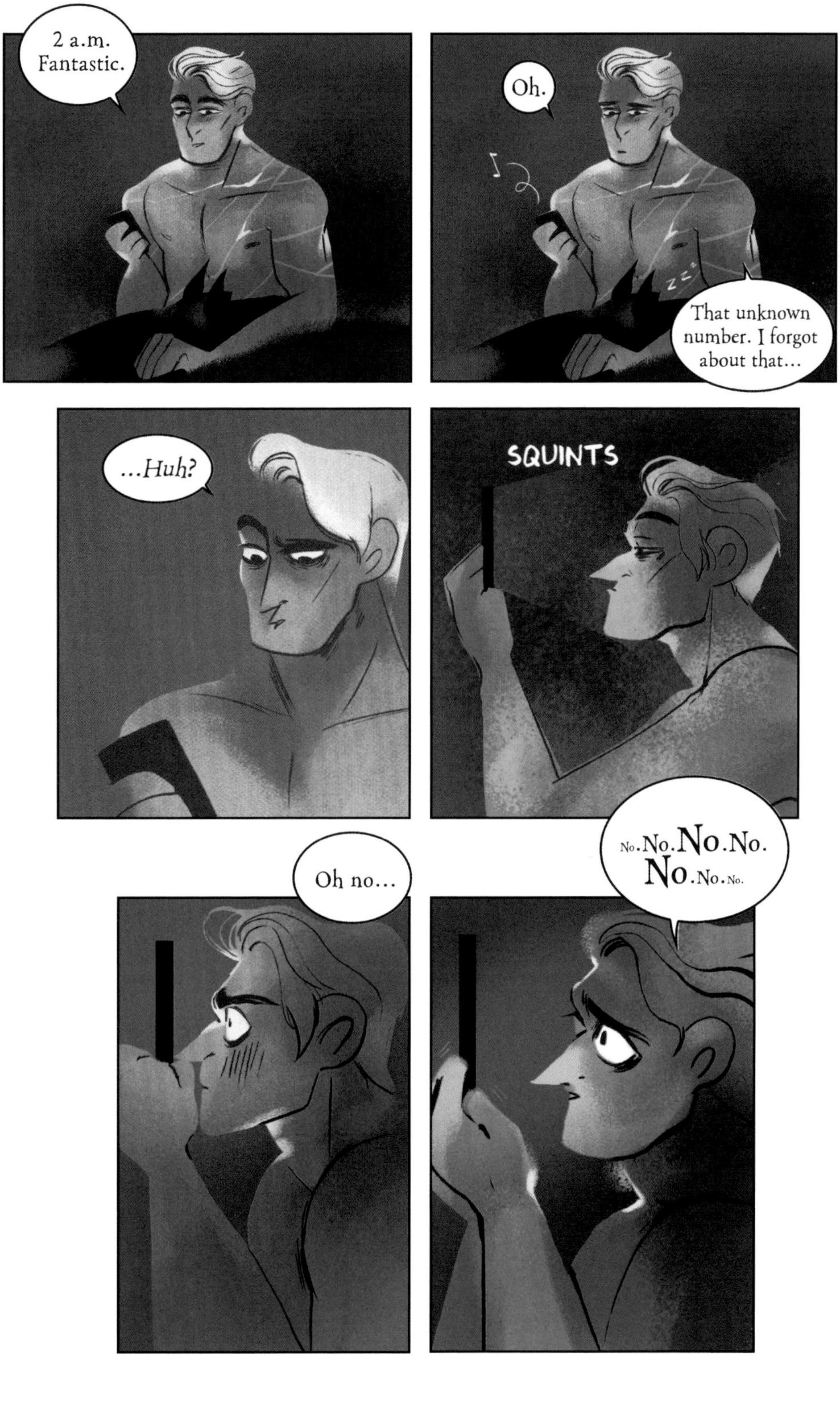

2 a.m. Fantastic.
Oh.
That unknown number. I forgot about that...
...Huh?
SQUINTS
Oh no...
No.No.No.No.
No.No.No.

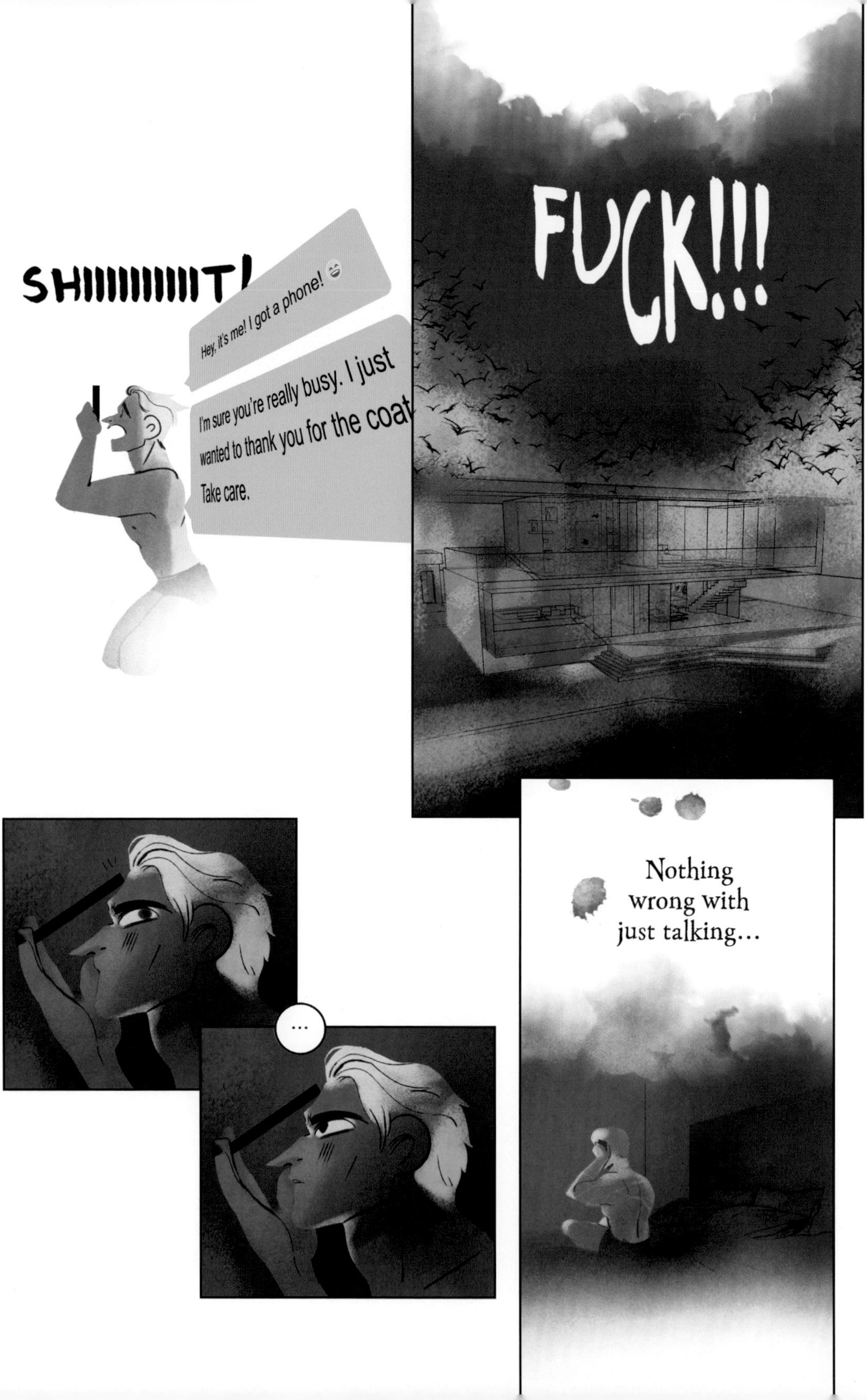
SHIIIIIIIIIT!
Hey, it's me! I got a phone! 😄
I'm sure you're really busy. I just wanted to thank you for the coat.
Take care.
FUCK!!!
...
Nothing wrong with just talking...

I originally wrote this chapter to be episode 10 of *Lore Olympus*. However, after a discussion with my editor at the time we decided that the first Hera-focused chapter shouldn't be about Hades (which is fair). The spot was filled with an episode where Persephone and Hades go for a drive, which suited the narrative better at that time and meant that Hera wasn't defined by her relationship with Hades.

Ultimately, the chapter I had written for Hera didn't fit naturally into the flow of the story and ended up in the story-beat graveyard.

With this publication, I'm glad to have the opportunity to share this moment.

Art assistants: Kristina Ness & Amy Kim

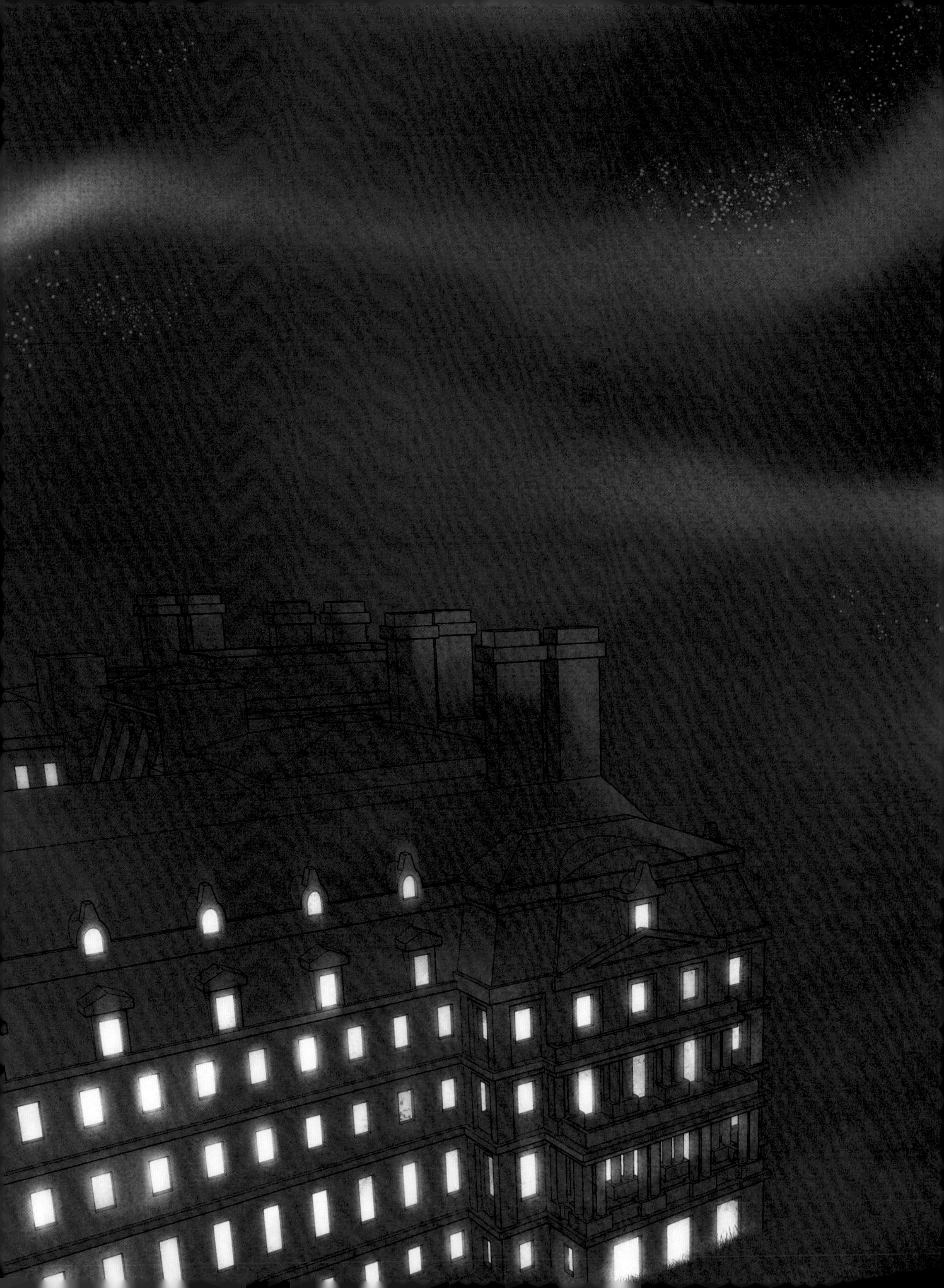

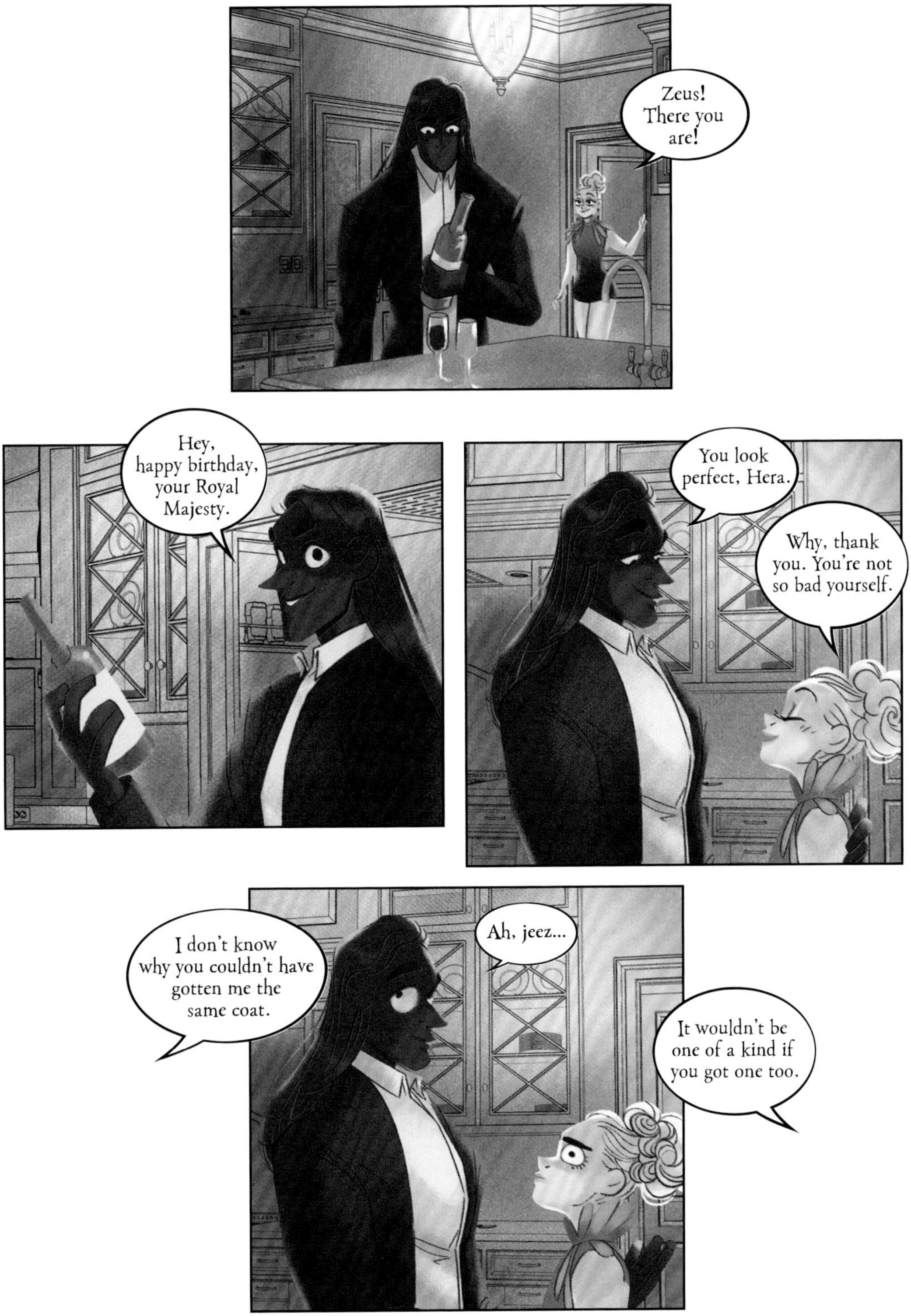
Zeus! There you are!
Hey, happy birthday, your Royal Majesty.
You look perfect, Hera.
Why, thank you. You're not so bad yourself.
I don't know why you couldn't have gotten me the same coat.
Ah, jeez...
It wouldn't be one of a kind if you got one too.

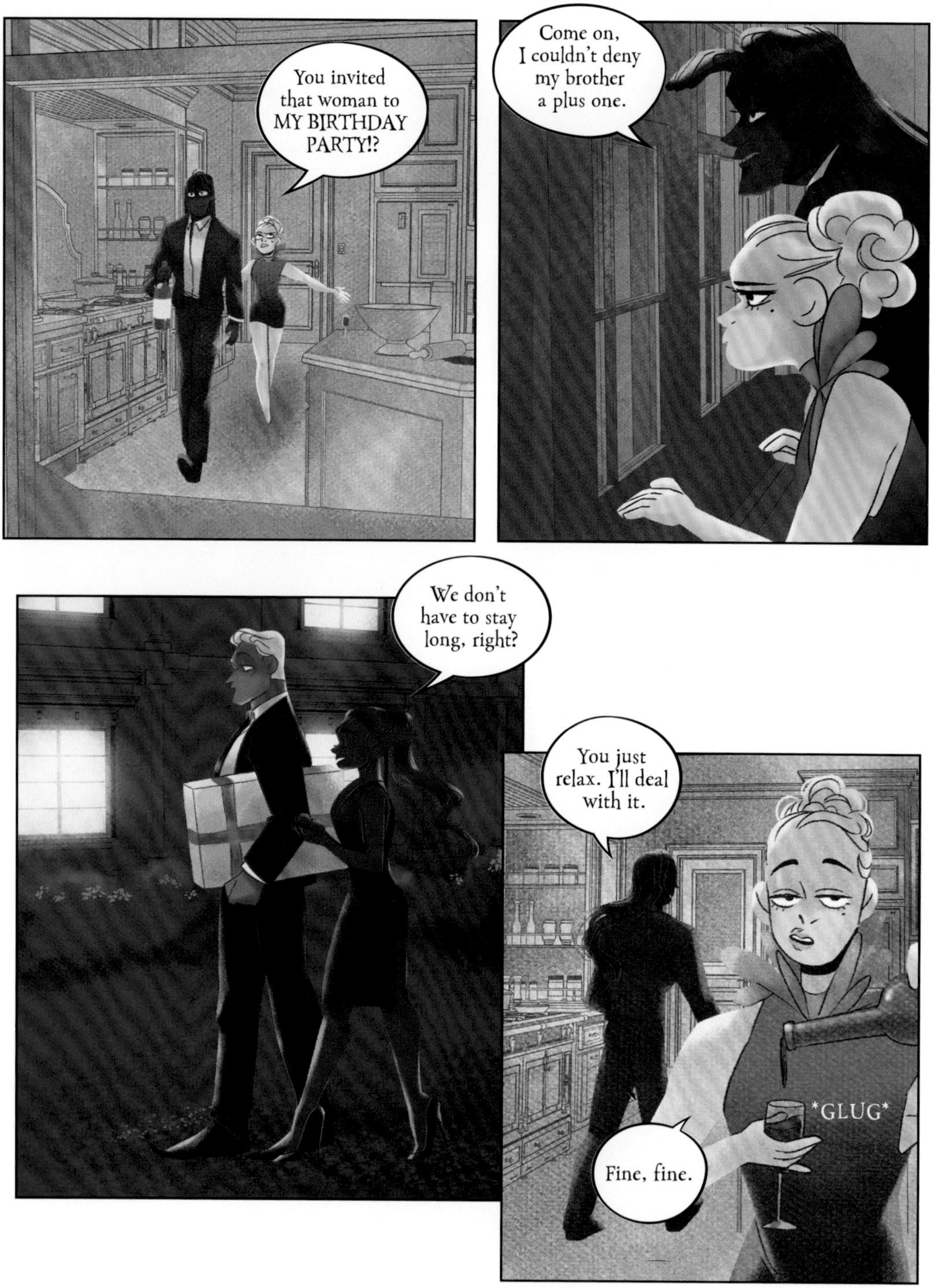
You invited that woman to MY BIRTHDAY PARTY!?
Come on, I couldn't deny my brother a plus one.
We don't have to stay long, right?
You just relax. I'll deal with it.
GLUG
Fine, fine.

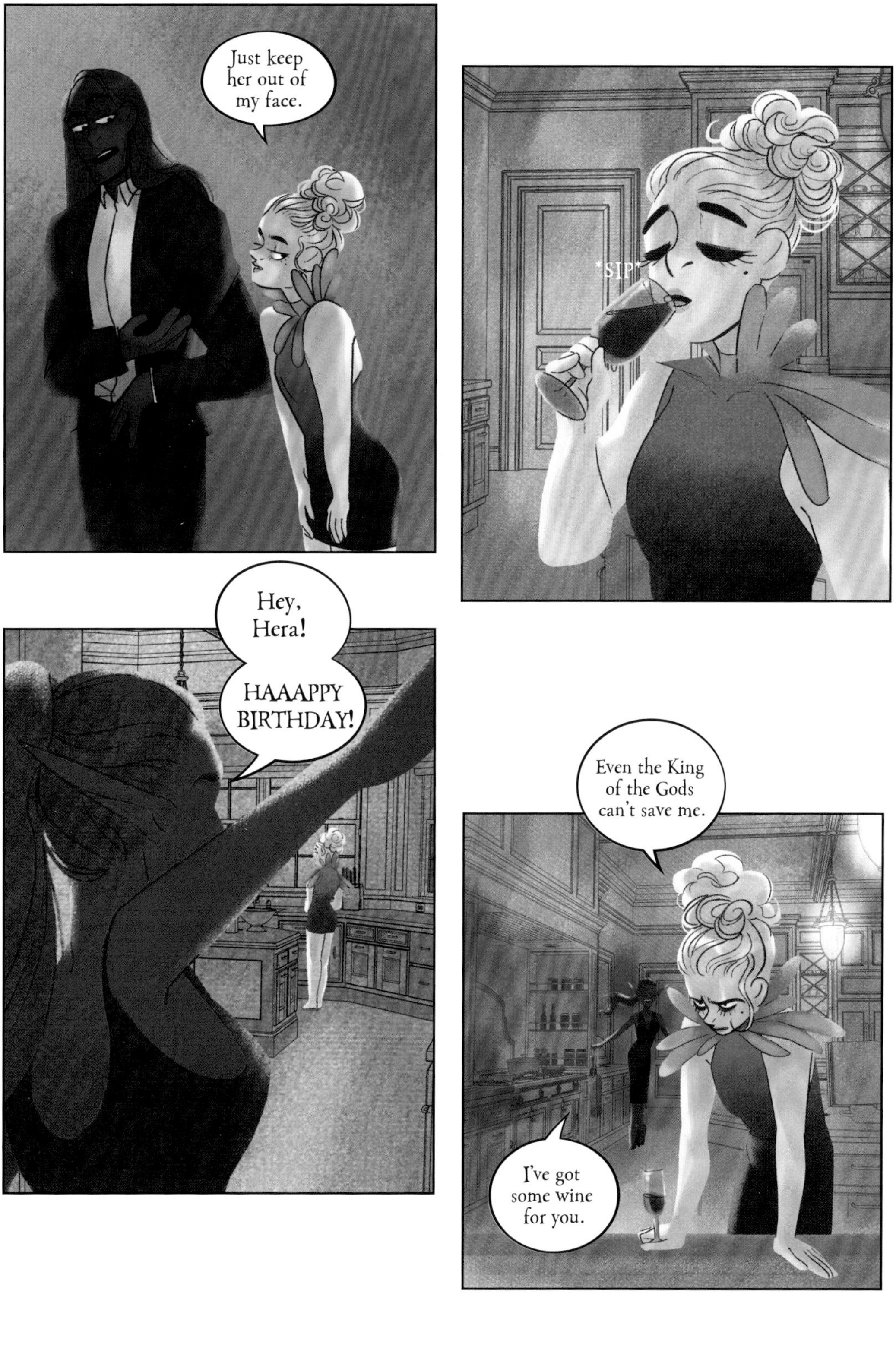
Just keep her out of my face.
SIP
Hey, Hera!
HAAAPPY BIRTHDAY!
Even the King of the Gods can't save me.
I've got some wine for you.

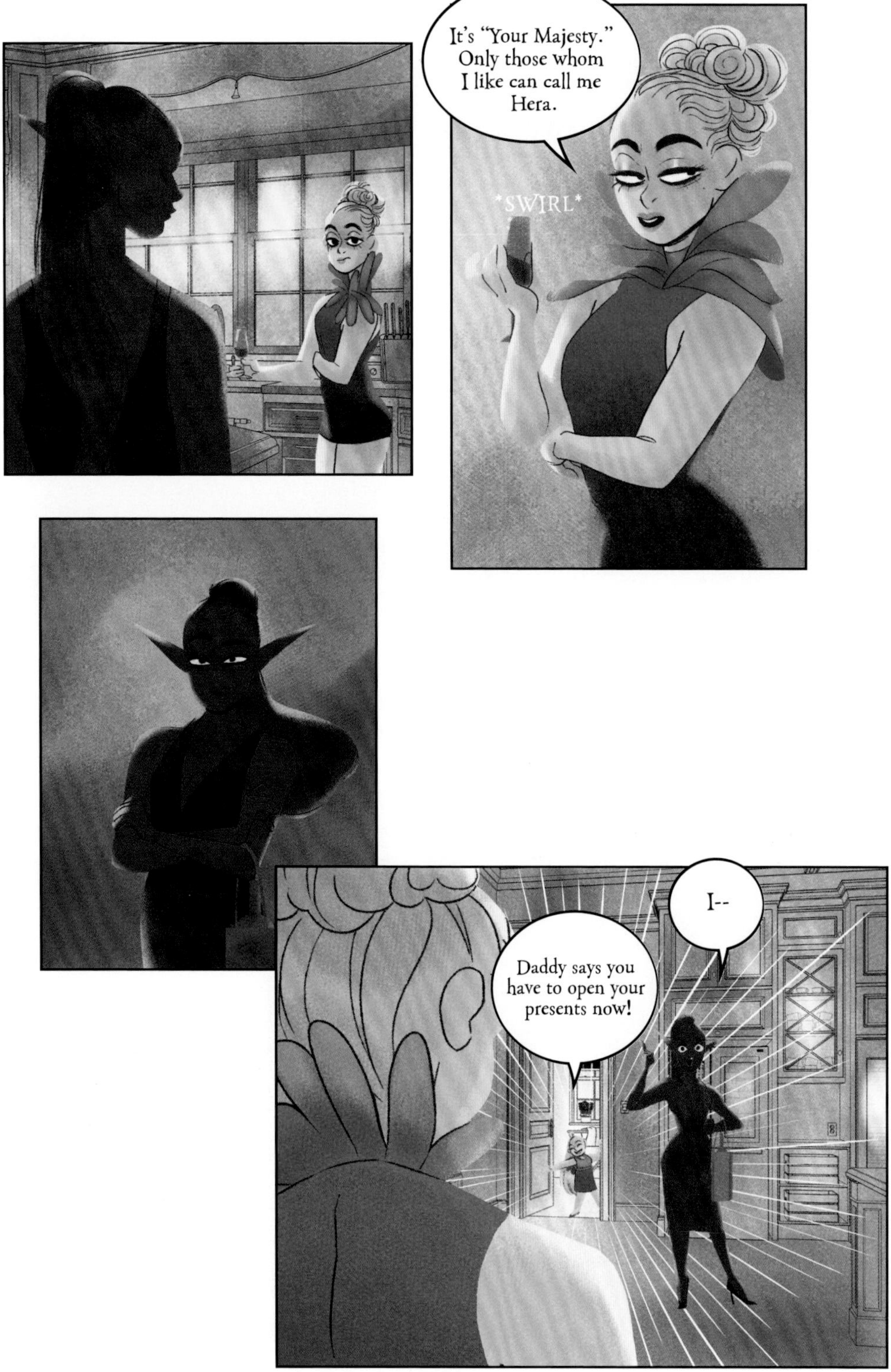
It's "Your Majesty." Only those whom I like can call me Hera.
SWIRL
I--
Daddy says you have to open your presents now!

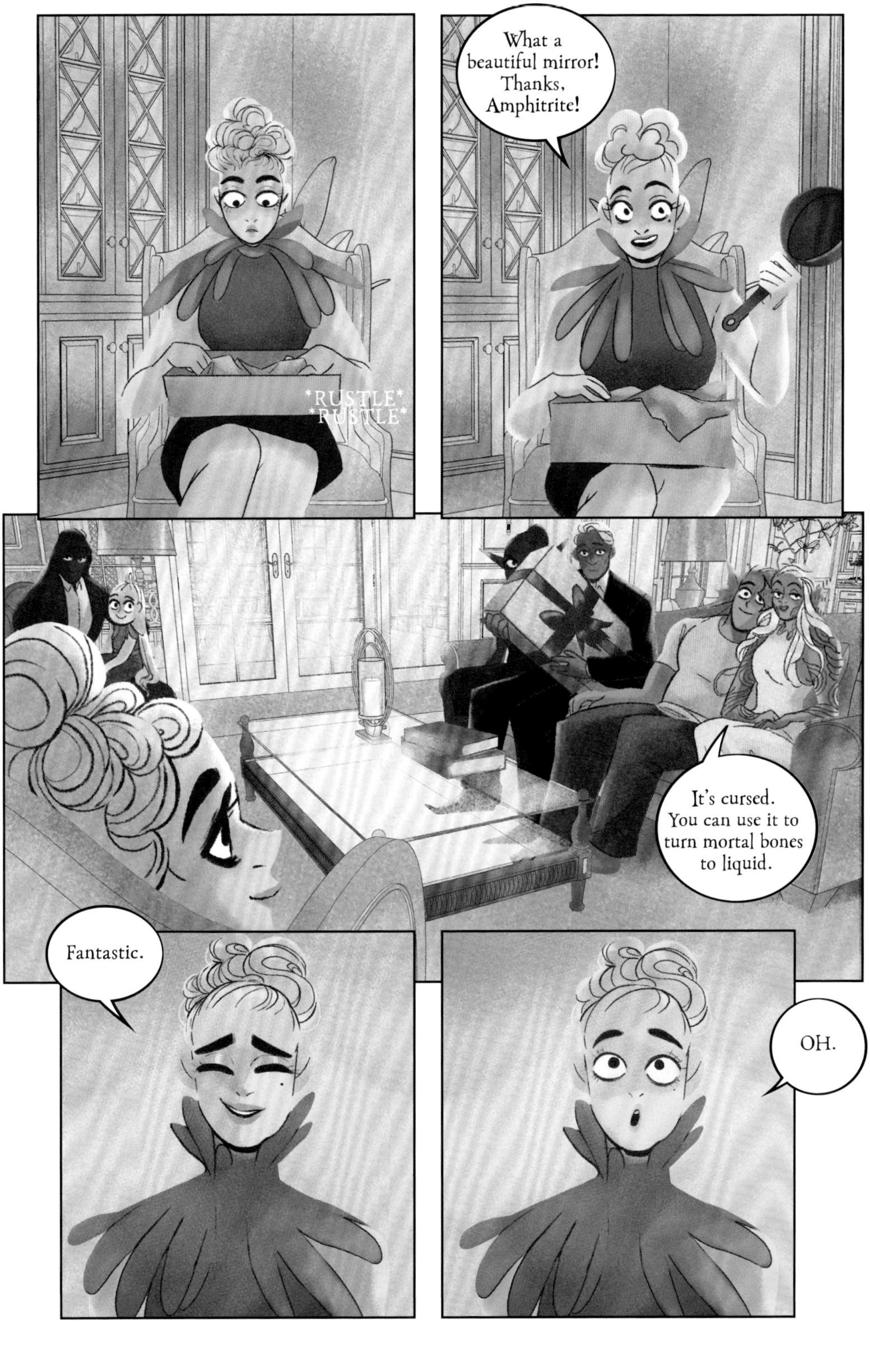
RUSTLE
RUSTLE
What a beautiful mirror! Thanks, Amphitrite!
It's cursed. You can use it to turn mortal bones to liquid.
Fantastic.
OH.

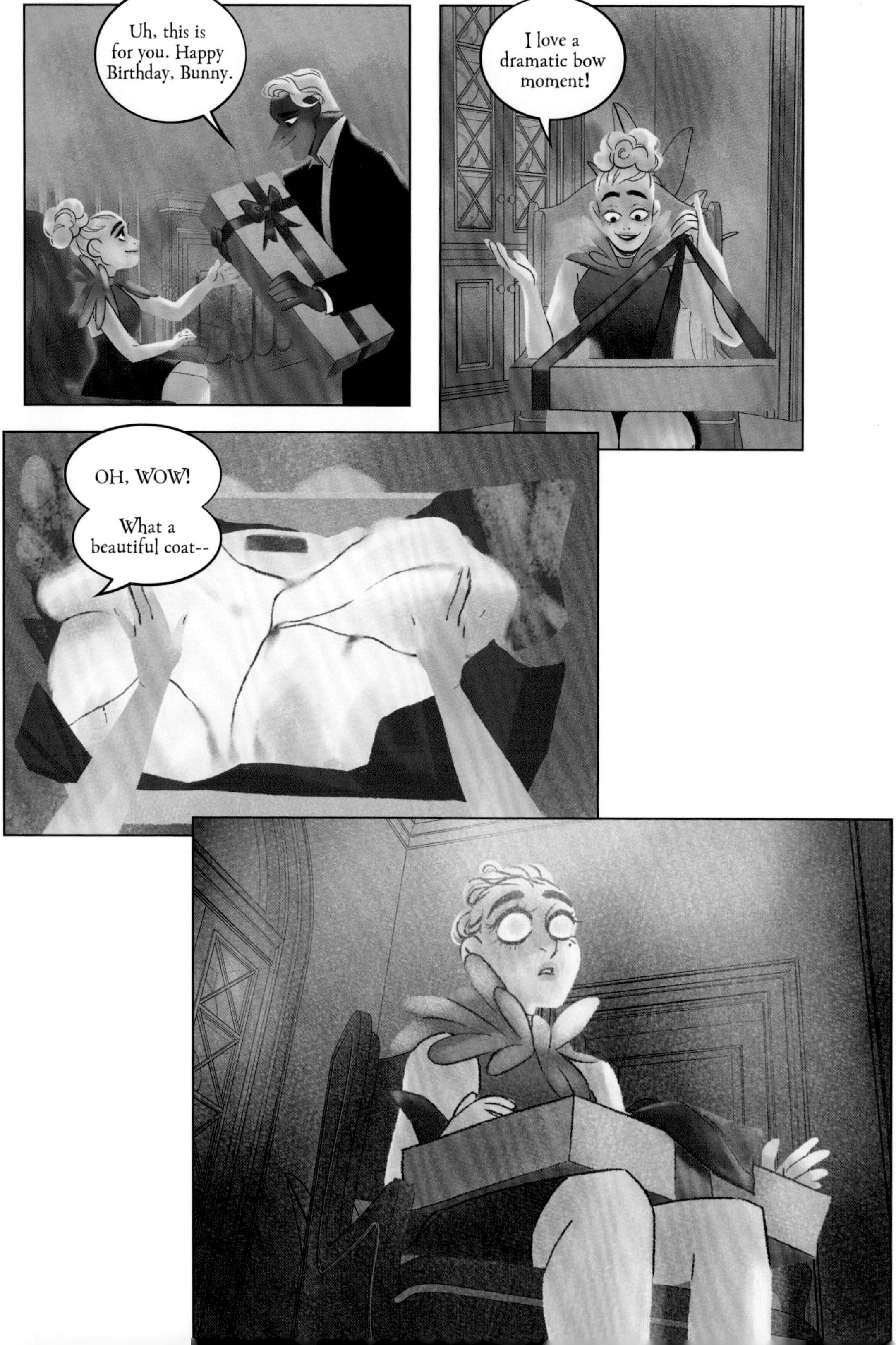

Uh, this is for you. Happy Birthday, Bunny.
I love a dramatic bow moment!
OH, WOW!
What a beautiful coat--

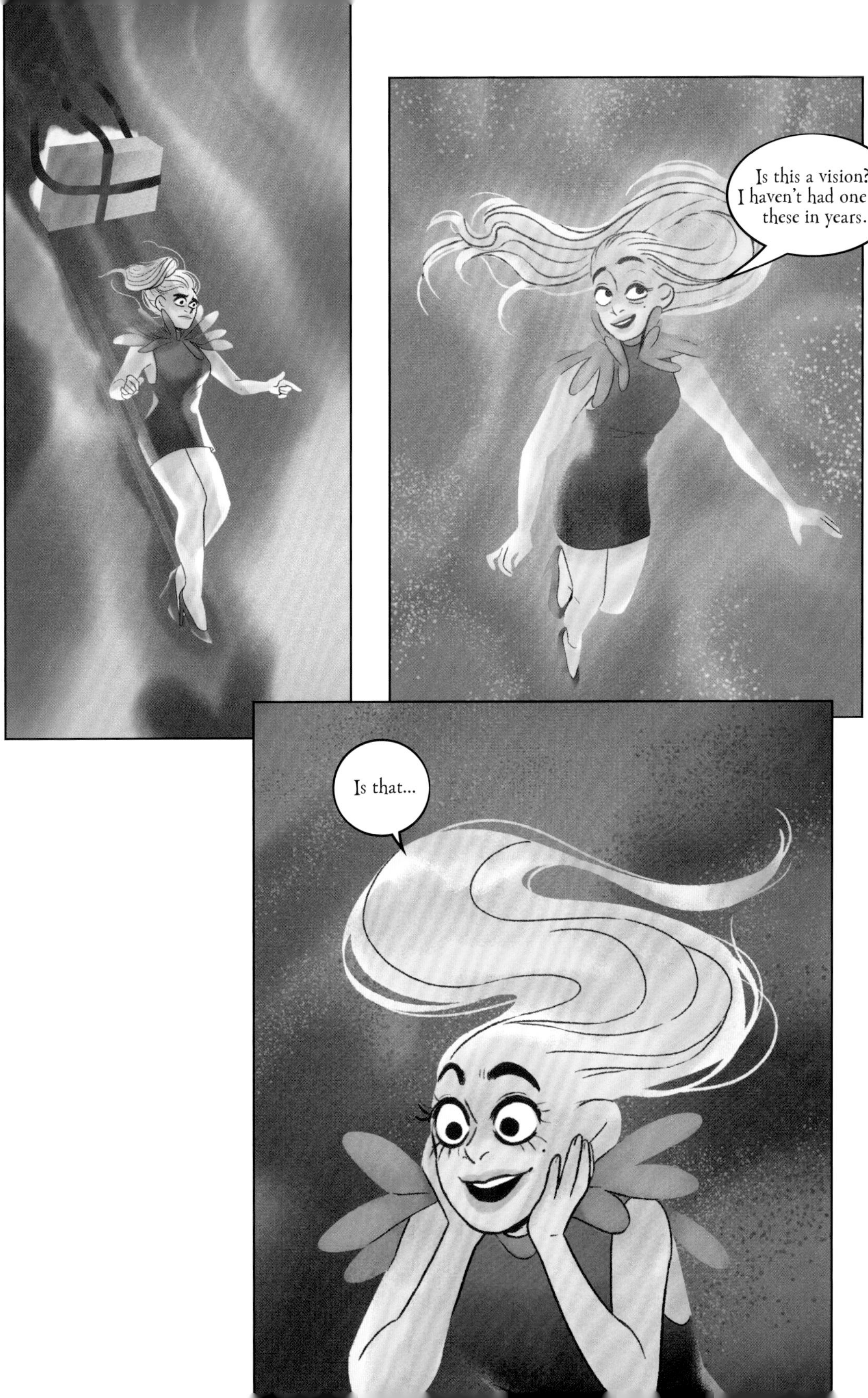
Is this a vision? I haven't had one of these in years.
Is that...

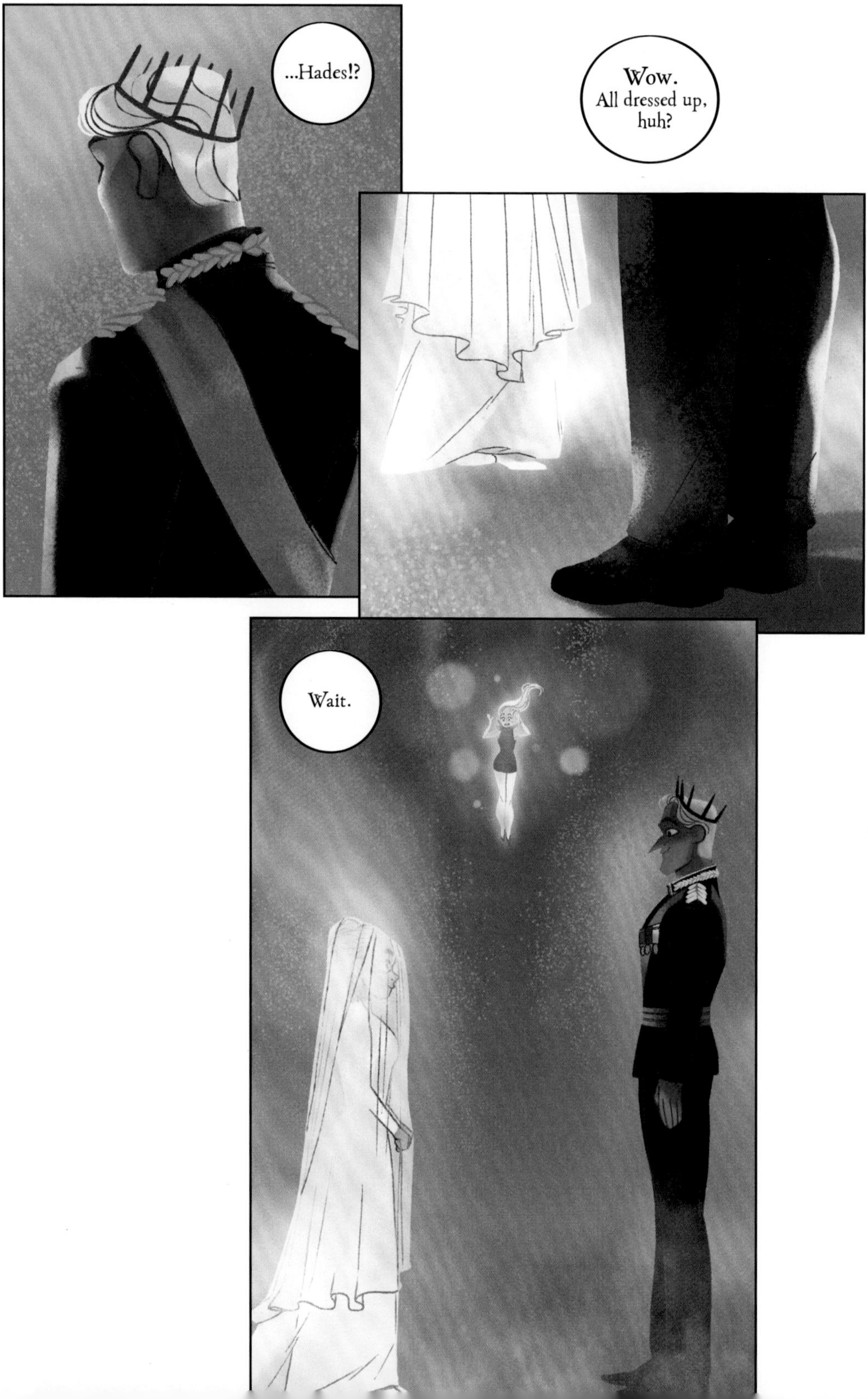
...Hades!?
Wow.
All dressed up,
huh?
Wait.

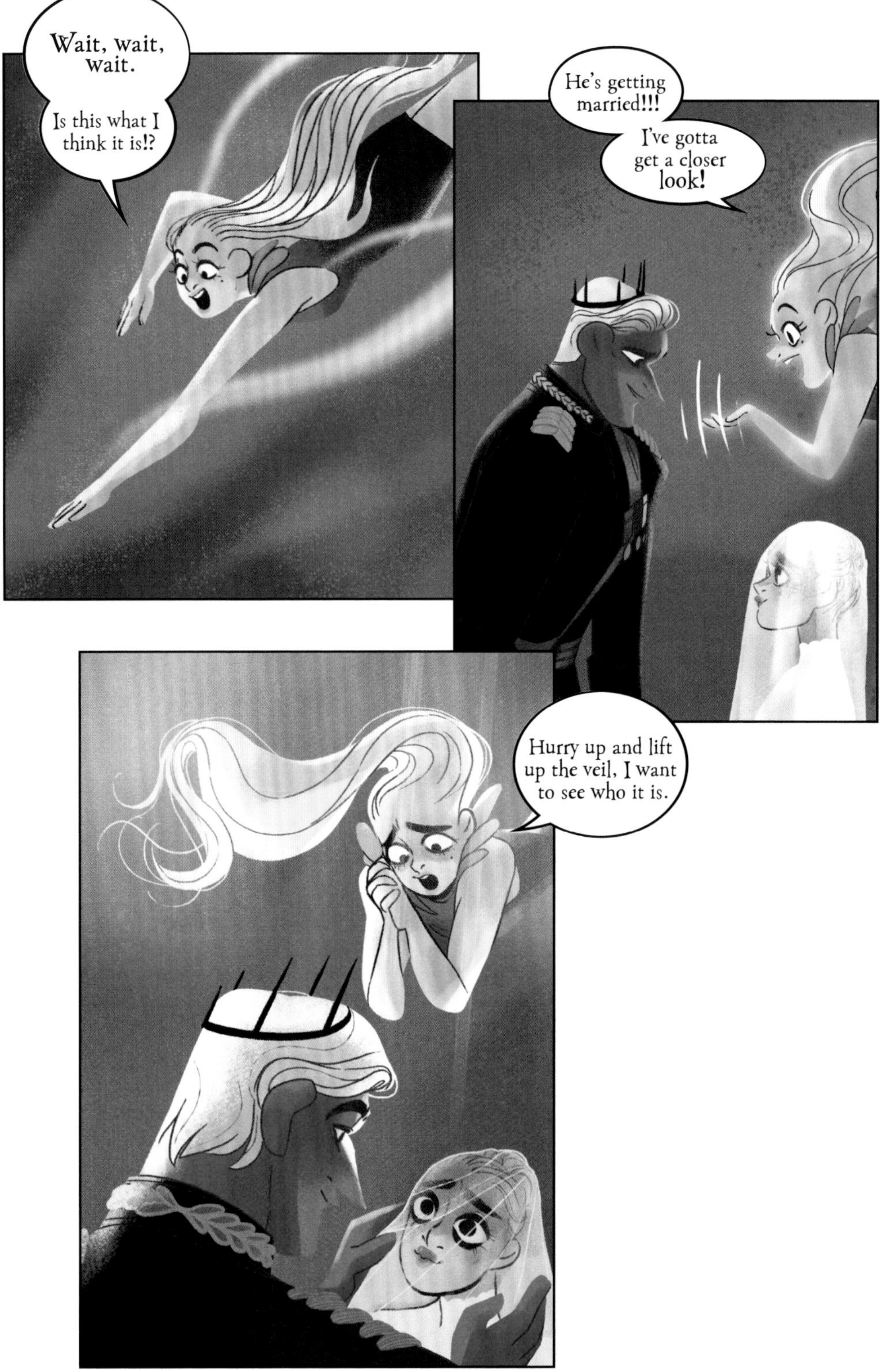
Wait, wait, wait.
Is this what I think it is!?
He's getting married!!!
I've gotta get a closer look!
Hurry up and lift up the veil, I want to see who it is.

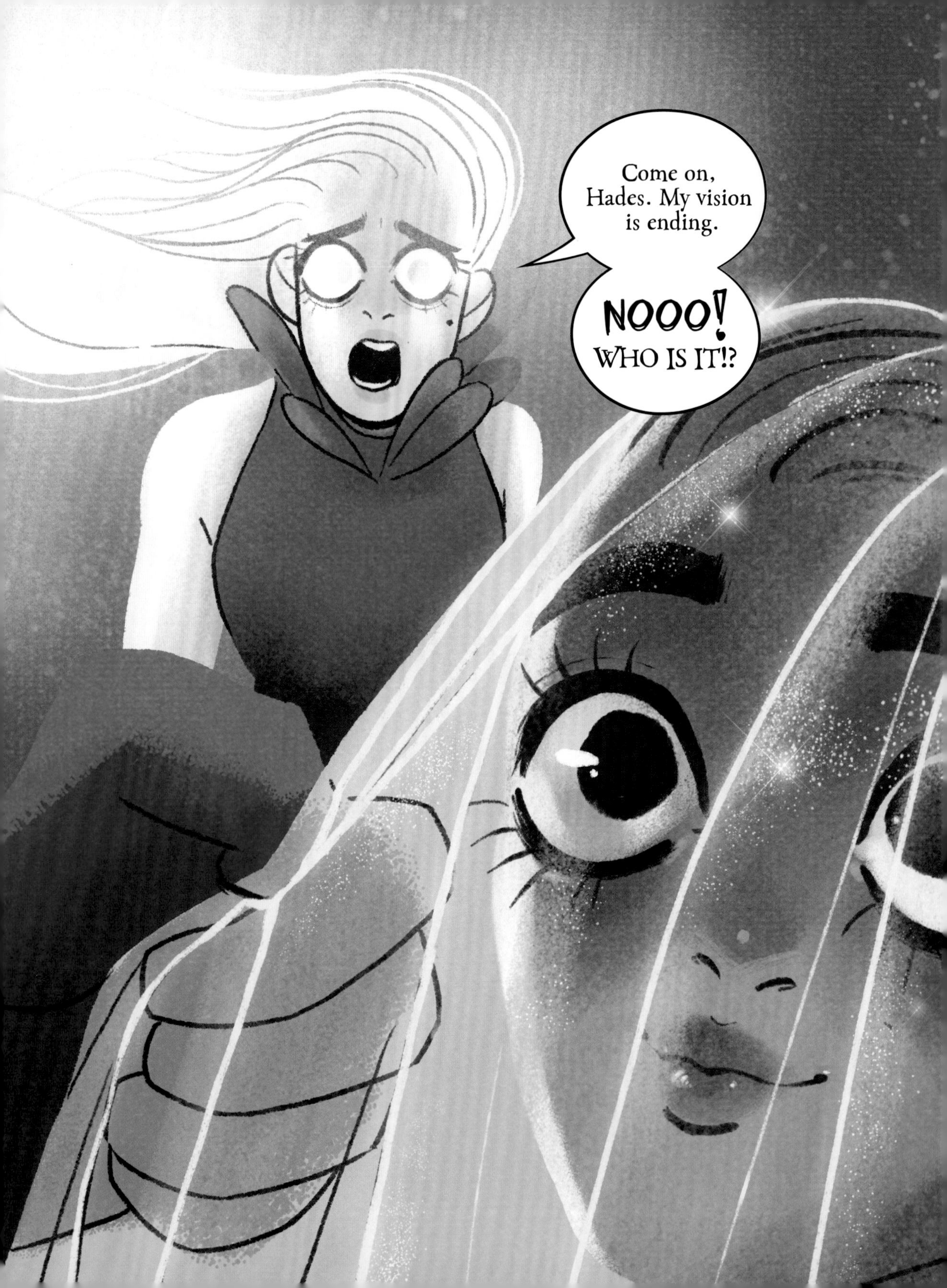
Come on, Hades. My vision is ending.
NOOO! WHO IS IT!?

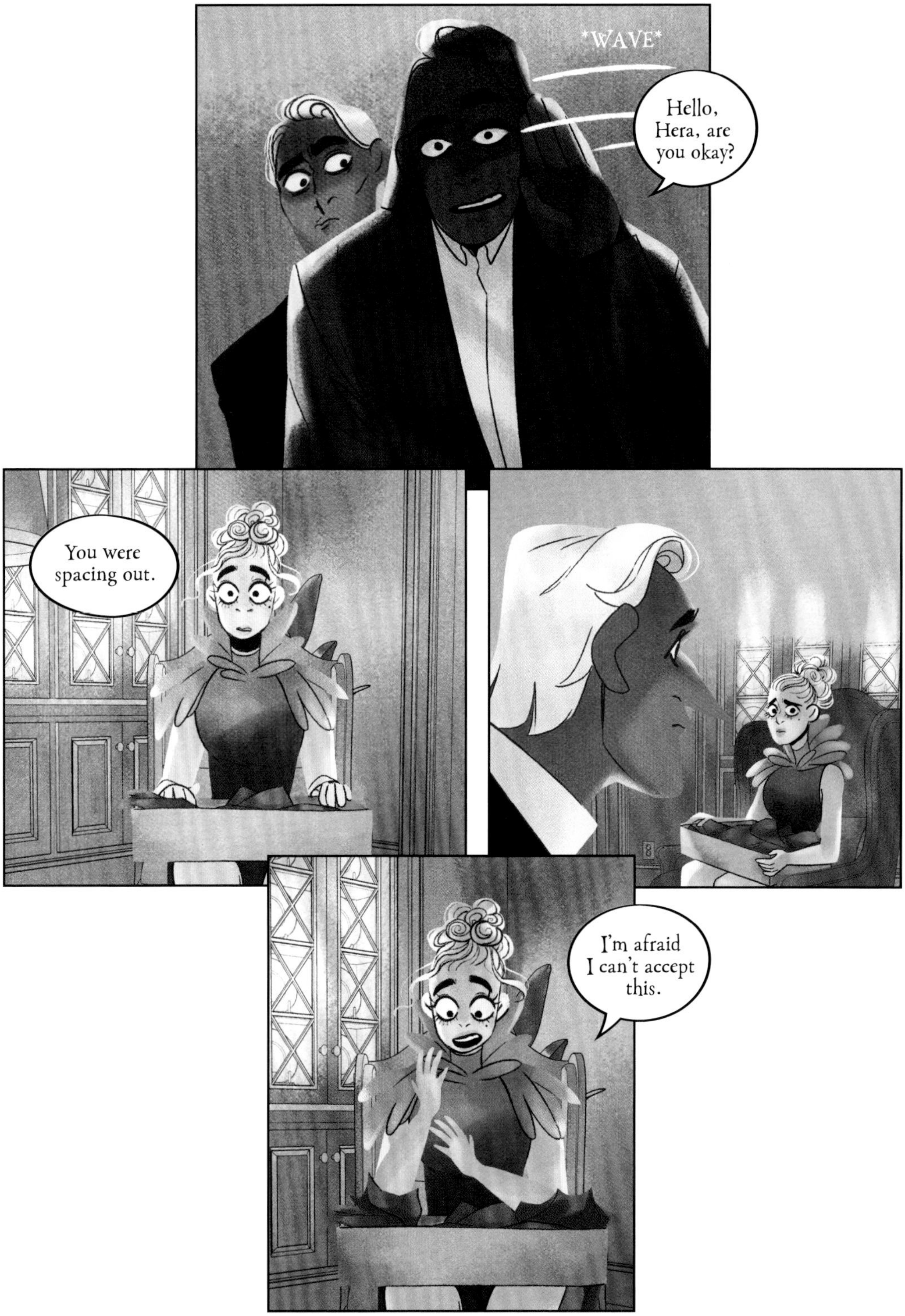
WAVE
Hello, Hera, are you okay?
You were spacing out.
I'm afraid I can't accept this.

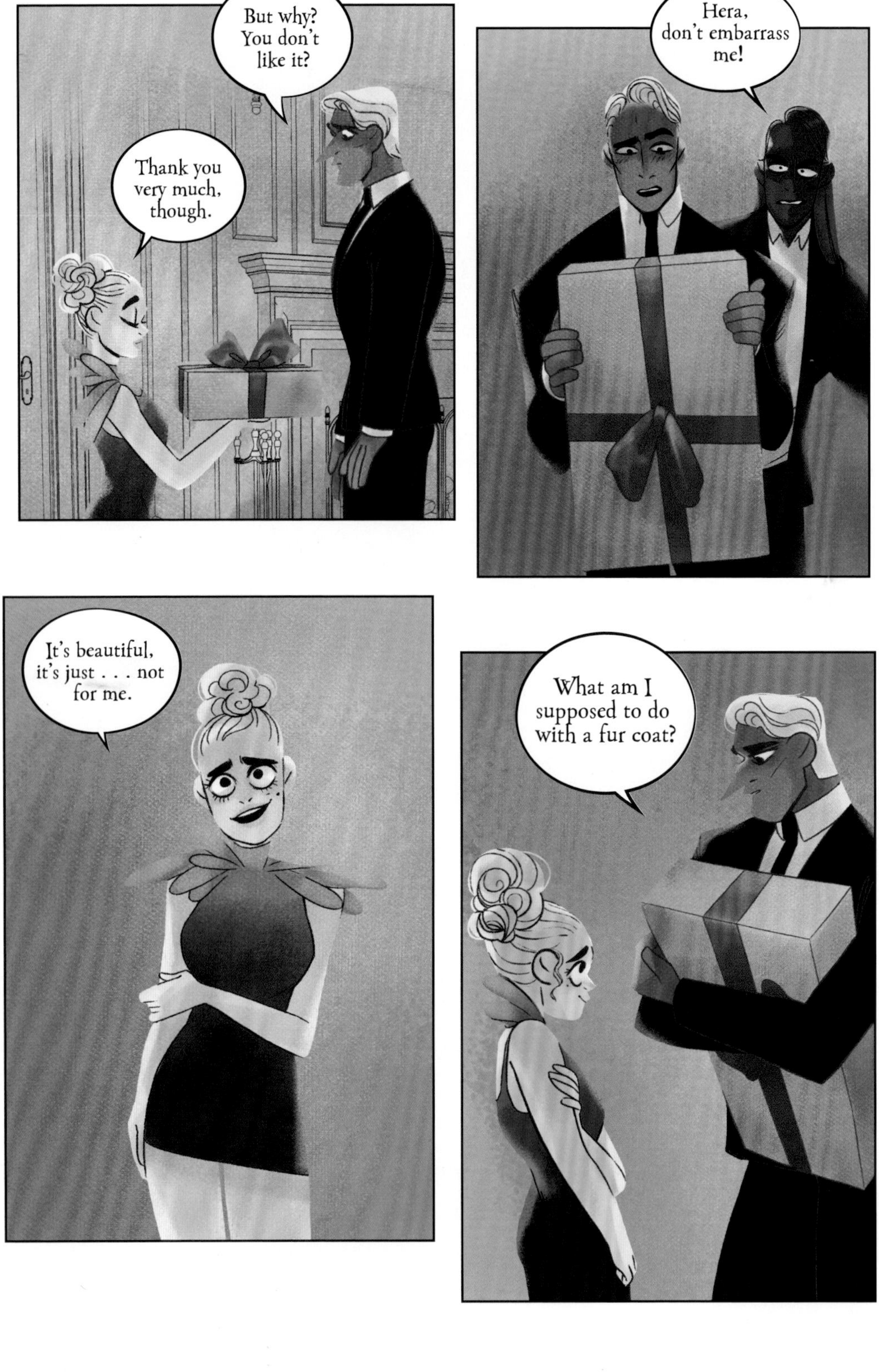
But why? You don't like it?
Thank you very much, though.
Hera, don't embarrass me!
It's beautiful, it's just . . . not for me.
What am I supposed to do with a fur coat?

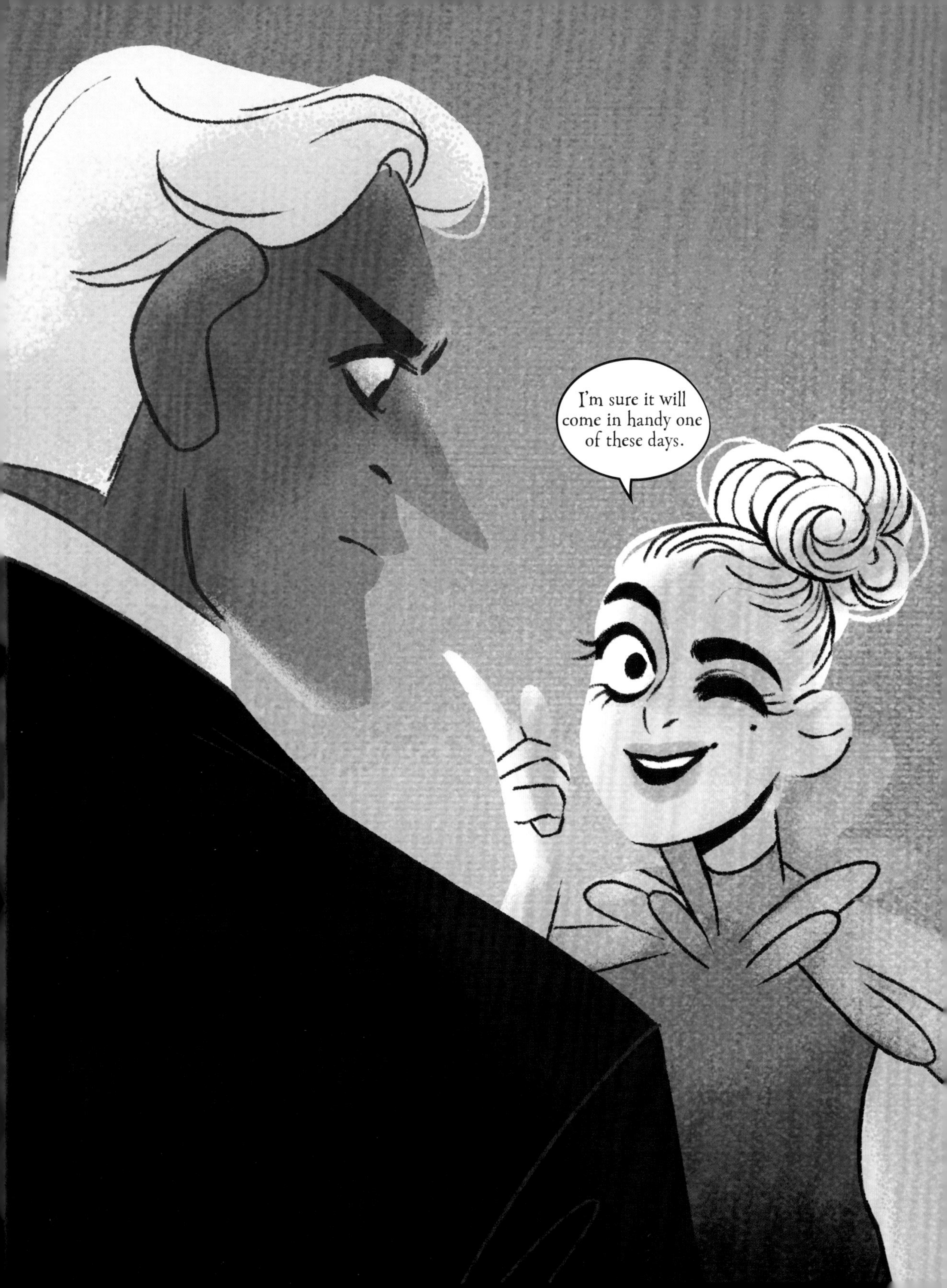
I'm sure it will come in handy one of these days.

ABOUT THE AUTHOR

RACHEL SMYTHE is the creator of the Eisner-nominated *Lore Olympus*, published via WEBTOON.

Twitter: @used_bandaid

Instagram: @usedbandaid

Facebook.com/Usedbandaidillustration

LoreOlympusBooks.com